CW01262294

NO TOMORROW

The Complete Series

By

BK Boes

Mike Kraus

MUONIC PRESS

www.muonic.com

* * *

www.bkboes.com

facebook.com/bkboes

twitter.com/bkboes

instagram.com/bkboes

* * *

www.MikeKrausBooks.com

hello@mikeKrausBooks.com

www.facebook.com/MikeKrausBooks

Want More Awesome Books?

Find more fantastic tales right here, at books.to/readmorepa.

***

If you're new to reading Mike Kraus, consider visiting his website and signing up for his free newsletter. You'll receive several free books and a sample of his audiobooks, too, just for signing up, you can unsubscribe at any time and you will receive absolutely *no* spam.

***

You can also stay updated on B.K.'s books by signing up for her newsletter (books.to/kpcky).

Decimation

No Tomorrow Book 1

Chapter 1

Alexander Roman

Alexander Roman gripped the cold, hard edge of his seat with sweaty hands as the glass death-box shuddered to a stop five-hundred-and-sixty-feet above ground. He resisted the urge to snatch his son, Oliver, away from the glass as the ten-year-old pressed his forehead against the window of the world's tallest Ferris Wheel. Oliver was currently trying to identify every booth, ride, and exhibit they'd seen so far at the 2035 St. Louis World's Fair, his observation hampered by the sun's recent descent below the horizon. He had insisted on taking up the entire bench opposite the one his parents occupied so he could slide from one side to the other at a whim.

Alex, on the other hand, had broken out in a cold sweat one fourth of the way up, and his entire body ached from the tension of constricted muscles as his attempts to relax failed repeatedly. His wife, Naomi, had sympathetically patted his knee more than once, but at the moment, she was engaged in looking out the window with their son. The highest point of the Ferris Wheel was, according to her, the best part.

Human beings were not meant to be this far from solid ground. Alex kept the thought to himself; if he were to speak, he had no doubt his voice would tremble, and his wife and son clearly disagreed.

Oliver was still captivated by the scene all around them. Despite having been on the ride for an hour, he was wide-eyed and alert. The sounds of the fair were muffled, but the excitement of the event was telegraphed to their glass pod via a technicolor rainbow of lights made brighter by the dark of night. The aroma of fresh popcorn, funnel cakes, and a variety of savory meats reached them even at their current height.

A deep, amplified voice, no more than a mumble from where he sat, resounded across the fairgrounds as a new presentation began at one of the stages at the north end of the fair. Alex chanced a glance in that direction, wishing he were there instead of sitting in the glass pod. But he owed a family day to Naomi and Oliver; they'd had to go it alone the last two days as he'd participated in all-day question-and-answer sessions at the CDC booth representing disease detectives on a reoccurring panel. His obligation there was finally done, and he'd promised his wife and son a vacation day — whatever they wanted to do. He had not anticipated fighting to keep his dinner down as he trembled hundreds of feet in the air. The glance northward drew his attention to the nearby Wind Breaker, a terrifying ride that lifted rows of swings three hundred feet in the air only to spin them at forty miles an hour.

At least I'm not on that. Alex swallowed rising bile at just the thought of it; the nausea stuck with him, though, even as he turned away from the Wind Breaker and tried to get the image of flying through the air, secured only by cords attached to a bucket seat, out of his head.

The Ferris Wheel lurched forward once again, and Oliver laughed. Alex feigned a smile as he bit the inside of his cheek so hard he tasted blood. If he'd known how long the ride would drag on, he would have tried harder to get out of it. Another fifteen minutes of starts and stops brought them a little closer to the ground, and just as Oliver was finally losing interest, fireworks burst into the night sky, causing him to gasp with delight.

"Look, Dad! Are those airplanes?" Oliver pointed as two small planes circled each other, fireworks shooting off the perimeter of their wings. A colorful backdrop of chrysanthemum and willow fireworks made for quite the show.

Even Alex had to admit the sight was impressive. "Yeah, I think so, bud."

Naomi sat back and watched with a genuine grin. "It's gorgeous, isn't it, Ollie?" She looked over at Alex. "I kind of wish we were still at the top."

"We can see it fine from right here," Alex said as he let the fireworks distract him. Just as Alex found himself fully immersed in the sight of the unique fireworks show, a scream pierced the faint cacophony of the crowd below.

No… not just one scream. Alex squinted at the crowd which was illuminated by flashing lights of every color. A circle had formed around one individual who had fallen to their knees, but no one was even attempting to help. Instead, a few fled, breaking into a run, knocking down anyone who got in their way. A ripple in the crowd closer to the Ferris Wheel caught Alex's eye as a second circle formed around another person on the ground who seemed to be having a seizure.

What the heck is going on? And then, Alex froze as the thrilled screaming of those on the Wind Breaker turned to cries of pain and terror. He turned his head slowly toward the tower, unsure if he wanted to see but unable to stop himself from looking.

The arms of the Wind Breaker spun in the near distance like a giant ceiling fan. Alex followed the line of the cords until his eyes settled on the people strapped into the bucket seats. It took a moment to focus on their faces as they swung by. A woman screaming in pain as she pressed her palms against her eyes was quickly followed by a young man, his legs and arms red and blotchy, vomiting blood. The blood spewed out of his mouth and streamed around the seat to splatter the person in the next swing, who was too busy clawing at welts to even notice. At the sight of a fourth person — a balding man whose eyes bulged out of their sockets, whose mouth stretched wide in a scream as blood seeped from his nose, his mouth, and his ears — Alex shouted and jumped back in his seat.

"Alex, what is wrong with you?" Naomi asked as he collided with her, pushing her against her side of the pod.

"Something's wrong," Alex said. "Something is really, really wrong." He pulled out his phone and started to dial his boss at the CDC.

Oliver slid across his bench toward the sight of the Wind Breaker. "What's going on over there? The people sound… weird."

Alex's parental instincts kicked in. He dropped his phone and leaned forward to bat Oliver away from the window. "No! Don't look, Oliver. Just… look at the fireworks." He must have sounded as desperate as he felt because Naomi transferred to Oliver's bench, putting her body between their son and the Wind Breaker.

"It's okay, Ollie," she said, wrapping her arm around their son. "Listen to your father." As Oliver turned his attention back to the fireworks, she turned to look at the Wind Breaker for herself. Naomi's brow furrowed in confusion before her hand flew to cover her mouth and she turned quickly away, her body rigid.

Alex reached for his phone on the metallic floor, the chaos below visible through the lower glass panes of the pod. Fairgoers dropped to the ground as those still standing gave in to panic, rushing every which way, mowing over each other in the process.

"Alex?" Naomi asked, her voice too high pitched. "Shouldn't we be moving by now?"

Fresh fear blossomed in the pit of Alex's stomach. "Where are the binoculars?"

Naomi's reply was more of a squeak. "In my purse."

He retrieved the little set of binoculars they'd brought with them for viewing the acrobats from their cheap, back row seats. Alex turned around on the bench and sat on his knees so he could look out the back of the pod. His head swam and his stomach knotted as he looked down toward the control booth of the Ferris Wheel. They were still *so* far up. Alex gripped the back of the bench and willed himself to stay steady as he brought the binoculars to his eyes.

The windows of the control booth were coated in blood. A teenager in a World's Fair staff uniform lay on the ground, his head and torso sticking out of the narrow doorway. His eyes bulged, his skin raged with welts and blotches, and his body exhibited distortions due to severe swelling.

Alex swallowed hard and gripped the back of the bench harder. *He's dead. How are we going to get down from here?*

Heart thundering in his chest, head pounding, body so stiff he wasn't sure he *could* move, Alex closed his eyes, willing himself to stay calm and clear-headed. The last thing his family needed was for him to freak out or shut down. The moment brought him back to another disaster, a time before Naomi, when he'd frozen solid and stopped up his ears in the midst of smoke and searing heat and the cries of a familiar voice.

"Mom, what's the plane doing?"

Alex's eyes snapped open at the sound of his son's voice. He looked toward the fireworks show and put one hand on the glass of the pod, blinking rapidly, hoping that what he was seeing would somehow change. One of the planes had broken off from the show, flying lower and lower, bouncing up and down as it headed straight for the Ferris Wheel. Its shadow fell over the still-flashing, bright lights of the booths and rides just beneath it. The crowd on the ground directly below the path of the plane had, moments earlier, seemed like a rapid, churning river, but at the sight above them, the rushing crowd burst into perpendicular aisles as if a dam had broken, chaos spilling further east and west.

Naomi came up beside him, her breathing now quick and shallow. "Alex… what do we do?"

"Maybe it will turn before it hits…" Alex trailed off. If it didn't hit the Ferris Wheel, it would hit something.

Fireworks still streamed from the plane's wings as it skated over the tops of booths, setting the World's Fair on fire and adding to the pandemonium on the ground. The blood drained from Alex's face as the number of bodies left behind by the turbulent crowd increased in their wake as the trampled and maimed joined the dead.

"Mom? Dad?" It was clear from his tone that Oliver finally understood they were in real trouble; there was no protecting him from it, though hiding the tragedy unfolding before them had been a futile thought from the start.

Naomi sat beside Oliver and held him close. "It's going to be okay, Ollie," she said. "You are ours, and you are loved." Tears welled up in her eyes and rolled down her cheeks as she repeated their routine bedtime mantra that had originated on Oliver's first night as a newborn.

The plane bounced one more time, veering just slightly, before it hit the other side of the Ferris Wheel. The structure ripped apart as the plane took a chunk out of one side, bringing more metal and glass and bodies with it as it collided with the ground and exploded. Fireworks shot in every direction as it carved a flaming path through booths, food trucks, and smaller rides before smashing into the side of a pole barn.

As the plane hit, Alex was thrown against the window of the pod and fell to the metal floor, fully expecting his life to end then and there. The impact sent shock waves throughout the metal of the Ferris Wheel, and a violent tremor threatened to consume Alex as it erupted throughout his body. He had a moment to wonder if their half of the Ferris Wheel might stay standing before a deafening groan of metal ruptured the air.

Bones resisting movement and muscles screaming for him to be still, Alex forced his body to move. He pushed himself to his knees and turned toward his family. Oliver clung to Naomi, sobbing into her chest. She'd hit her head, and blood seeped from a cut on her forehead. She shushed Oliver gently even as her own tears flowed unchecked. She looked at Alex and mouthed the words, "I love you."

Alex wrapped his arms around his wife and his son and held them close. "You are both mine," he said, his voice breaking. "And you are both loved so, so much." He was able to savor one more second before what remained of the Ferris Wheel tipped and plummeted toward the ground.

Chapter 2

Zara Williams

1 Hour Earlier

Zara Williams secured her thick curls with a feathery, pink scrunchy and raised her weapon. The artificial light inside the pole barn shone dully in the bit of the solid steel axe head. The bevel was a little thicker than she was used to, but the weight of the axe felt right in her hand. Zara breathed steadily, tuning out the chatter of the dozens of onlookers behind her. The red circle in the center of the target became her focus as she stepped forward and threw the axe in one fluid motion. The axe left her hand and hurtled toward the target twelve feet away, rotating once midway, before sticking into the center with a satisfying *thwack*. She glanced at her competitor's target. He had missed the center by centimeters.

"Yes!" Lizzy Peters, Zara's best friend, squealed and skipped up behind her and threw her arms around Zara's neck from behind, nearly knocking her over.

Zara laughed as she wriggled out of her friend's grasp. "Calm down, Liz. It's just a game." She nodded at her competition. "Good throw, man."

"Thanks," he said as he slipped on his leather jacket and winked at Lizzy. He ran a hand through his dark, wavy hair and nodded their way. "You ladies up for some funnel cake?" He let his eyes run up and down them both, but he lingered on Lizzy.

Zara rolled her eyes. Guys always acted like that around Lizzy. Her best friend tipped her cowboy hat – the final touch to her World's Fair ensemble of designer ripped jeans, a plaid button-up shirt, and five-hundred-dollar snakeskin boots – and returned the wink.

Well, that certainly doesn't help. Zara elbowed Lizzy, ignored her pouting frown, and pulled her toward the exit.

"Sorry, we've got places to be," Zara said over her shoulder.

"What are you doing?" Lizzy asked as she tried to flash a smile through the crowd at the young man. "Aren't you going to get your prize bear?"

"We don't know him, Liz. He could be crazy. And I don't need a stuffed bear." Zara continued to weave through the crowd, leaving the axe throwing cages and the stranger behind.

"Don't be ridiculous, Zee. He's just a boy looking to buy some funnel cake for some pretty girls." Lizzy yanked her arm from Zara's grasp and stopped to smooth the front of her shirt.

Zara levelled a stare at Lizzy. "Or he's a serial killer."

It was Lizzy's turn to roll her eyes. "Oh, come on, Zara. He seemed nice to me."

"Like that guy at Jason's party last month?" Zara crossed her arms.

Lizzy's cheeks turned bright red. "How was I supposed to know he was dealing?"

"He was sketchy as hell, that's how." Zara nodded down the row of food trucks. "If you want funnel cake, let's get funnel cake, okay?"

Zara breathed a sigh of relief as her friend relented and walked with her toward the food trucks. Lizzy always seemed to find a way to get them into trouble, and Zara was determined that this adventure to the World's Fair would be different. She deserved some fun after she'd busted her butt all senior year to ensure she not only kept her scholarship to her prestigious prep school but also qualified to apply for more scholarships so she could go to Yale. She was going to be somebody, and she didn't have Lizzy's luck of being born with a silver spoon in her mouth. Zara had to get there all on her own – financially speaking, anyway. She'd take her dad with his support, integrity, and kindness over Lizzy's father with all his money and connections any day of the week. Besides, it was her fault her family was in dire financial straits. It was only right that she did everything she could to balance the scales.

They grabbed a funnel cake to share and started walking north. The World's Fair had everything from carnival rides to international foods to entertainment acts, but what most people considered the most important part was the Worldwide Innovations Exposition. That's where Lizzy was supposed to be at 9 p.m. sharp so Mr. Peters could showcase his daughter in the background as he spouted how important family was to his company, Vanguard. That was also the section of the fair that Zara found most fascinating, where the inventions of the world's brightest minds would be on display for everyone to see, no matter their social standing or lack thereof.

But halfway to their destination, Lizzy took a sharp turn down a row of booths belonging to various charities and activist groups. Zara groaned. Twilight was upon them, and she'd wanted to at least see a few of the innovation exhibits before suffering through Mr. Peters's speech. The row they'd turned into had mostly softer, white lights switching on, but ahead and behind, lights of all colors began to shine and illuminate the fair in a wash of reds, yellows, greens, and blues.

"What are you doing?" Zara asked as she caught up with Lizzy, trudging up the incline of the makeshift grassy road created by the line of booths on either side.

Lizzy shrugged and threw Zara a wide-eyed, innocent look. "I thought you might want to see Jordan one more time before we have to go home."

"We saw my brother already," Zara said quickening her step and cutting Lizzy off. She pointed north. "We need to get closer to where your dad is giving his speech."

"We have plenty of time." Lizzy side-stepped her and continued walking.

Zara sighed and looked up at the darkening sky. "You just want to see Jordan because you think he's cooler than he actually is, and you've got a crush on him, which isn't cool with me, by the way." She didn't want to bring this up again, but the fact that her best friend was interested in her older brother made her cringe. Jordan wasn't a bad guy, but he was reckless. Not to mention the fact that he had gotten himself involved with the crazies at the Green Earth Futurists, which was why he was at the fair to begin with. He'd agreed to man the booth and hand out pamphlets or whatever; the fair was only a few hours from The University of Missouri where Jordan currently resided, and apparently the GEF *needed* him there.

"I won't date him until you give your blessing, Zee, but the heart wants what the heart wants." Lizzy patted her chest and smiled sweetly.

"I thought your heart wanted Mr. Fonzie-wanna-be back at the axe throwing barn." Zara arched an eyebrow.

"You've *got* to stop watching all those old movies." Lizzy shook her head and rested an elbow on Zara's shoulder as they meandered toward the GEF booth.

"Um, *Happy Days* was a national treasure, Liz, and it was a television show, not a movie."

"Well, excuse me," Lizzy said, "but I believe you've just proven my point."

Zara stopped in front of the GEF booth at the top of the hill as Lizzy slid behind the table and gave one of the women in the back of the booth a hug. They started chatting, but Zara stayed where she was. It had surprised her that morning when they'd first visited her brother to find that Lizzy knew by name most of the GEF booth workers, and they knew her, too. The girls had been best friends for three years, and they told each other a lot, but apparently, they weren't as open with each other as Zara had believed. It irked her that she didn't know that Lizzy had not only become a member of the Green Earth Futurists but had been joining their worldwide online meetings for a full year.

Maybe she really does like Jordan if she was willing to join their nutso meetings. Zara chewed on her lower lip. She wanted Lizzy to be happy, but why did she have to be interested in Jordan? She could bat her eyes at some country club pretty boy and have a brand-new boyfriend with a Porsche within the week if she wanted to; she'd done it before, actually.

"Hey, Zara." Adam, one of Jordan's buddies, nodded at her as he straightened up the brochures on the table. One of them had the word "Vanguard" in bold, red letters stamped across Lizzy's father's face. Below the unflattering picture, it read: "Walter Peters is no saint."

Zara chuckled. "Where did you guys get this picture of Mr. Peters?" she asked as she picked up a brochure. The normally stoic and perfectly-put-together CEO glared at the camera, his face screwed up into an ugly scowl.

Adam pointed behind him. "Lizzy sent it to us," he said. "Snapped it on her phone." The twenty-something-year-old activist must have been working all day; his skin was red and blotchy, and he looked exhausted.

"Well, I hope he never sees it, or she's in big trouble." Zara put it back. "Actually, he'll probably blame me, just like he'll blame me if she's not at stage two by nine o'clock."

She stood on tiptoes and looked around Adam to where the woman was giving Lizzy something that looked like a business card. Her friend gave the woman another hug before rejoining Zara outside the booth.

"I've got something to show you later," Lizzy said indicating the card in her hand. "You're going to love it. Pam just gave me the password to a shared folder in the GEF private forum. Only a handful of people have access, but Jordan wanted me to be one of the first to see his video."

"What video?" Zara asked. "And you're on their private forum? Since when?"

Lizzy shrugged. "Since… I don't know. It's been a while." She shoved the card into her pocket.

"Where is Jordan anyway?" Zara asked, looking between Lizzy and Adam.

"Some top-secret mission," Adam said. "He's, like, going to be a hero."

Zara burst into laughter, expecting Lizzy or Adam or… someone… to join her. But his offended expression and Lizzy's grimace told her that Adam wasn't trying to be funny. She coughed and reined in her laughter.

"You know," Lizzy said, "maybe Jordan *is* as cool as I think he is, and maybe you're the one who doesn't see his potential."

Adam put his hands flat on the table in front of him. "I'm not feeling so great," he said. A raging red welt the size of a half-dollar was swelling up on his arm, blue veins popping against his skin, snaking up toward his shoulder and down toward his hand. He pressed his fingers against his eyes and groaned. Blood started dripping from his nose, and then he doubled over, one arm against his stomach.

"Hey, man, maybe you should sit d—" Zara was cut off by a horrendous crash that made her instinctively duck and cover her head. "What was that?"

She turned to witness the disaster unfold about half a mile from the GEF booth where they had a clear line of sight atop a small hill. A plane with fireworks shooting off its wings was tearing into the Ferris Wheel, leaving a long trail of burning booths on the ground behind it. The plane barely snagged on the metal frame, its speed enabling it to rip steel beams and glass pods free of their structure, flinging debris across the fairgrounds. The sound of screeching metal cut the night air, and Zara covered her ears. When the plane hit the ground, the earth quaked beneath her feet and Zara reached out for Lizzy. They kept each other from toppling to the ground. An explosion rocked the fairgrounds again, and fireworks shot into the air where the plane was now merely a ball of fire where the pole barn had been.

Zara shouted and pulled Lizzy to the ground as a contorted, flaming chunk of metal flew from the wreckage and crushed a booth only a few yards away. Heat washed over her as she clung to her best friend. Debris battered them both, and Zara curled herself into a ball around Lizzy's head, covering her own head with her arms. Searing pain cut across Zara's arm, her side, her hip, her thigh. She squeezed her eyes shut until Lizzy dislodged herself and sat up. Zara opened her eyes to stinging smoke and had to blink away tears before she could see anything at all.

"Zee, we have to get out of here," Lizzy said, sobbing between words. Lizzy's perfect clothes were covered in soot, her cowboy hat was gone, and small, bloody cuts littered her face, neck, and arms. She grabbed hold of Zara's arm and pulled.

"Ouch!" Zara wrenched her arm away to find she wasn't in any better shape. Her arm was smeared with blood where Lizzy had grabbed broken and bleeding skin.

"Oh my—" Lizzy's words cut off as her hand flew to her mouth. Her eyes were wide as saucers as she stared beyond Zara.

Zara struggled to sit up, but she did it, gritting her teeth. Her entire left side looked like it had been dragged across asphalt. Every little cut — there must have been dozens of tiny gashes and scrapes — stung in its own right; Zara had to bite her tongue to keep from crying out in pain as she moved. But, when she followed Lizzy's gaze, the cry escaped her lips despite her efforts as she scrambled away from the table behind them.

Adam lay draped over the table, but whatever had happened to him had not been caused by the crash. Zara's eyes were drawn first to the way his red, bloodshot eyes bulged out of his head. She slowly stood up, wincing at the pain, and took one step toward him before freezing. Small, bloody chunks were scattered across the brochures, fanning out from his wide-open mouth. His body twitched and his lips parted.

"Help... me..." The words wheezed out of him, blood sputtering onto the table with each word. Then he went completely still.

"He's... dead." Zara whispered the words, barely believing them.

Lizzy stood next to Zara, tears streaming down her cheeks. "What do we do?" she asked, panic overwhelming her as she wrung her hands. Her eyes darted from Adam to the wreckage and back again. Other people were beginning to get up around them, and some of them were staggering away from the spreading fire.

"Get out of here, like you said," Zara said, her mind beginning to clear as shock was replaced with a rush of adrenaline.

"What about Pam?" Lizzy rushed toward the side of the booth but stopped short before entering the space.

Zara followed. Pam lay on the ground, a piece of metal jutting from her chest, her eyes lifeless. "We can't do anything for either of them," Zara said as she put a gentle hand on Lizzy's shoulder. "We need to find your father, okay? He'll know what to do." She coughed; the smoke was getting thicker as the fire spread along the line of booths on the other side of the grassy pathway.

Lizzy nodded and silently turned away from the woman she'd been hugging just moments before, and Zara took her hand. They darted behind the GEF booth into the next row and started to jog north, cutting through the narrow spaces between booths. The joyous sounds of the World's Fair had become sounds of panic, desperation, and fear. People ran in every direction, many of them calling out for loved ones.

Sections of the fair had been plunged into complete darkness, and where there were no lights, the moonlight wasn't enough to see more than shadows in the near distance. But wherever there was light, the girls were exposed to horror after horror. Zara expected there to be less bodies littering the ground the farther they got from the wreckage, but even where there was no fire and no debris, there was still the dead. The same scenes played out over and over as they ran row to row toward the stages. People rocked and moaned in grief over bodies of friends and family. Figures fleeing the catastrophe fell to their knees, screaming in pain, their hands covering their temples or their eyes or their stomachs as they vomited blood. Mothers and fathers ran past with children either clinging to them or hanging limply in their arms. It was a never-ending nightmare.

When they broke through the last row of booths and Stage 2 came into view, Zara stopped short and gasped. Her stomach sank, and she looked at Lizzy, who simply stared ahead, her face ashen. A sea of bodies tangled with overturned folding chairs lay before a crushed platform consumed with flames; a twisted, mangled pod from the Ferris Wheel had landed center stage, and the stage trusses and scaffolding had collapsed inward, creating a sort of triangle around the once spherical pod.

"I have to find my dad." Lizzy bolted forward before Zara could stop her, screaming for her father to answer her calls.

Damn it, Liz. Zara hesitated only a moment before sprinting after Lizzy toward the fiery devastation.

Chapter 3

Alexander Roman

A low, terrifying groan of metal tore through the air, vibrating Alex's entire body and startling him awake. The first moments of consciousness were filled with confusion. It was dark and hot, and Alex's legs and arms dangled loosely. His bare stomach lay flat against a hard, gritty surface. His shirt had bunched up under his armpits, and he lifted one hand up to pull it down. The movement sent him teetering.

He was folded over a metal beam like clothes hung on a wire, hundreds of feet in the air. Scrambling to find equilibrium while his head swam, Alex clung to the rusty metal that was his only source of stability. A tower, beams set in squares, surrounded him and descended to the ground below. More carefully this time, Alex climbed onto the horizontal beam he'd been slung over, dragged his body to the nearest vertical beam, sat up, and wrapped his arms around it as he willed the world to stop spinning.

Shortly after he'd found some semblance of safety, the memory of what had happened rushed over him like a tidal wave, stealing his breath away and numbing him to the core. The dropping bodies on the ground far below. The fireworks plane bobbing in the air, setting everything on fire before it hit the Ferris Wheel. The scent of lavender, of Naomi. The soft caress of Oliver's hair on Alex's cheek. An unsettling, weightless feeling as what remained of the Ferris Wheel tipped. The last memory he had was of glass shattering and something ripping through the pod, tearing Alex from his family. The all-encompassing crash threw Alex out of the pod. He had hit his head against the pod's frame, and the last thing he'd heard was his wife's scream.

"Naomi!" Alex yelled as loudly as he could. "Oliver, where are you?" His lungs and throat burned. The smoke rising from the booths below wasn't thick, but he had no idea how long he'd been breathing it in.

The fires below and the lights still shining in the near distance only illuminated the destruction on the ground. The crowd had dispersed completely from the area, leaving behind the dead and dying. A woman slowly dragged herself away from the fires and smoke, rolling away from the dead and continuing on her way one inch at a time. Down another aisle, a man with tattered clothes staggered from body to body, moving some to get a look at their faces.

However, the glow of the flickering flames fell short of his current height. Alex blinked and squinted in the dim light of the moon as his eyes adjusted, focusing first on the beams directly around him. But he couldn't see anyone else hanging on to the tower. When he swung his head down and just ahead, still searching, bile rose at the sight just four or five yards below. The moonlight glistened against the whites of a woman's bulging eyes as she stared up, her gaze vacant. Her face was streaked with blood, her mouth hung open, and her arms and legs dangled lifelessly from her bucket seat.

The Wind Breaker… Alex's fingers curled around the rough, cool-to-the-touch metal, and he shuddered despite the warmth of the summer night. He'd been flung from the Ferris Wheel pod onto the center tower of that terrible ride.

But… the bucket seats were far from the center. He looked back down at the dead woman. She shouldn't be butted up against the tower. That's when he picked out the cables in the darkness. They extended from the seat upward, and when he followed the line to its end, he gasped. The frame of a pod had been strung along an arm of the Wind Breaker, threading the cable and pinning the bucket seat below to the tower. Hope blossomed at the sight of the pod. It was a little crumpled and the glass had been blown out, leaving only the frame, but it was there.

"Naomi, are you up there?" Alex shouted again. "Oliver, answer me!" He closed his eyes and listened, holding his breath. A small cough sounded from above, and the frame of the pod creaked in protest as it moved slightly. That cough could have been angels singing. "Don't move!" he said as loudly as he could. "I'm coming!"

Alex pulled himself to a standing position on the beam under him, keeping a tight grip on the sides of the vertical beam as he searched for a way up to the pod. His heart leapt at the sight of rungs on the inside of the tower one beam over. They ascended all the way up.

Now all I have to do is get around this beam. Alex swallowed hard. The H-profile of the beams and the huge bolts running along their centers provided some hand and footholds, but Alex was no climber.

"Dad? Where are you?"

Oliver's voice put fire in Alex's veins. "I'm here, Oliver! Don't move, bud, okay?" Alex reached for the other side of the beam and stepped carefully into the nook of the H-profile. He did his best not to think about the drop to the ground as he swung himself to the other side and turned to press his back against the vertical beam and clutch the sides of it behind him.

He took a small step, loosening his grip, and at that moment the wind whipped through the frame of the tower. He jumped back, flattening himself against the beam. The gust of air roared in his ears and tugged at his clothes, threatening to push him off the edge. But as it died down, it was a dull metallic clangor that stopped Alex's heart. All that was left of the pod was the flooring, seats, and two circular frames; one of the metal circles snapped, the top springing away from the arm of the Wind Breaker, sending the pod rocking precariously.

"Dad!" Oliver shrieked, panic infusing his voice.

Alex took a breath and bolted across the horizontal beam, hands trembling as he took hold of the vertical beam with rungs going up the length of the inside of the tower. He took hold of a rung and positioned himself on the ladder. The smoke, the feel of the rungs in his hands, the way his body trembled — it all echoed his greatest regret.

But I ran away then. I'm not running now. He leaned his head forward, resting it on a rung. Every breath seemed a little harder, a little less efficient. Waves of nausea left him dizzy as his heartbeat thrummed loudly in his ears. His body ached all over. A thousand questions ran through his mind, not the least of which was if his family would survive even if he was able to get them all to the ground. *I have to try. I won't run. Not this time.*

It took everything he had to reach up for the next rung, and then the next. Finally, he reached the pod. He stepped off the ladder onto a beam that was nearly even with the dented metal floor of the pod. And Oliver was there, eyes closed, leaning against Naomi, one hand clinging to the back of the bench and the other wrapped around his mother.

"Oliver." His son's name came out with a sigh of relief.

Oliver opened his eyes and sat up. "Dad!" His body shifted as if to jump up, but he paused almost immediately, eyes wide as the frame of the pod shifted again.

Alex held up his hands. "Don't move, bud. Not yet. I'll get you out of there." He frowned and looked at Naomi, who slowly blinked in his direction. She didn't move. "Naomi?" he asked. "You okay?"

She smiled, her head still resting on the frame behind her, but then she coughed violently, blood spurting from her mouth. Alex reached out a hand to steady himself on the beam next to him. Oliver slowly moved just a little closer to him at the sound of his mother's coughing, and he revealed the answer to Alex's question. Naomi was *not* okay. The back of the bench had been mangled and torn apart, and a jagged piece of it jutted forward, stabbing into his wife's side. She wasn't leaning; she was pinned.

"No." It was the only word Alex could find.

"She's going to be okay, right, dad?" Oliver asked.

Alex blinked several times, trying to register his son's question as he met Naomi's eyes with his own.

"Dad?" Oliver asked again. "She's going to be okay, right?"

Naomi managed a slight nod at their son. "Ollie," she said, rasping out his name.

Oliver turned to his mother, but she wasn't talking to him. Alex nodded. "Alright, Naomi. I'll get Oliver out of there, but then we're getting you, too, okay?"

She smiled again, sadly. She reached out her hand toward Oliver, but it dropped back into her lap. Oliver took it and held it, rolling his shoulder forward and wiping his eyes on his shirtsleeve.

"Dad will get you out, like he said." Oliver squeezed his mother's hand. "I love you, mom."

"Love… I love… you…"

"I know, mom," Oliver said. "I know you love me, okay?" He turned to Alex. "What do I do?" His voice cracked, and his face scrunched up like he was trying to keep from crying.

Alex tore his eyes from his wife and focused on his son. *Be strong. You didn't run. It's going to be okay.*

"You're going to be brave," Alex said. "I'm going to reach out my hand, and you're going to slowly move toward me." Alex stepped one foot to the edge of the horizontal beam, held onto the vertical beam with his left hand, and reached out toward Oliver with his right. "Come on," he said. "I'm going to get you over here, with me, and then you're going to hold on to this beam. Then, I'm going to get your mom, and we're all going to climb this ladder to the ground."

Oliver slid cautiously away from Naomi. Halfway across the bench, the metal frame moaned. Oliver froze and grabbed the back of the bench as the fragile construct shuddered. Alex's breath caught in his throat as he looked up at where part of the frame had broken before.

It's not going to hold, not for much longer. Alex snapped his attention back to his son.

"It's okay, bud. Just… keep coming. Slowly." Alex reached as far as he could across the gap between the tower and the floor of the pod. It was only a few feet, but it was enough for Oliver to slip through. He pushed that mental image aside, refusing to entertain it, and firmly opened his hand, stretching toward his son.

Oliver stood tentatively, flinching at the creaking of the metal beneath his feet. He reached out his hand, and Alex took hold of his forearm.

"Son, listen to me," he said. "I'm going to count to three, and you're going to carefully make a *big* step onto this beam, okay? I'm going to help you. Are you ready?"

Oliver looked back at his mother, and Naomi offered a weak nod. Alex braced himself, took a deep breath, and counted to three. As Oliver stepped off the frame and onto the beam, the frame snapped and tilted. Naomi screamed as she fell to the floor of the pod and the metal was ripped from her side. The frame hung on the arm of the Wind Breaker like a buckling half-moon, and Naomi sat propped against the bench opposite the one she'd previously been sitting on. She was nearly parallel with the ground. Blood gushed from the wound in her side. The frame swung slightly but held.

Alex pushed Oliver back against the vertical beam, one arm on each side of his son. "Stay here," he said. "Do. Not. Move. Got it?" Alex asked.

Oliver looked toward his mother. "But—"

"I can't get her if I have to worry about you moving, okay?" Alex put a hand on Oliver's shoulder. "You've got to look away, no matter what. If something happens…" Alex took a shaky breath. "If something happens, you've got to promise me you'll climb down this ladder and make it to the ground safely."

Tears streamed down Oliver's face. "But, Dad—"

"Promise, and I'll go get your mom."

"I promise."

"Don't look."

Oliver faced the beam, held onto it tightly, and stayed put. Alex turned toward the suspended pod to assess the situation. Naomi was sobbing weakly, holding her side. The frame had stopped swinging, but Alex couldn't see a way to get to Naomi.

"Hon," Alex called. "I know it hurts. I know you're scared, but please… you've got to come to me."

"Alex, I can't." Naomi coughed up more blood. She was covered by it. And she looked so feeble. Her hand kept falling away from her side, and her head kept drooping forward.

Alex raised his hands to his head, panic creeping into every pore. "Yes, you can. You *have* to." He carefully knelt on the three-foot wide beam, still looking for a way to grab hold of her.

"If you… try…" Naomi swallowed hard as tears made paths down her blood-caked cheeks. "… you'll die. Who would take care… of Ollie?" She looked at him and scooted backward just an inch. The frame rocked. "I love… you both." She licked her lips and sucked in a deep breath.

"Naomi, don't." Alex froze, his stomach dropping. He lay flat on the beam and scooted to the edge. If he could just grasp her foot…

"Take care of Ollie." She grunted as she bent her knees, and the frame rocked again.

"Naomi, come back this way." Alex reached out for her.

"I'm… already… dead." She leaned back, kicked against the frame with the last of her energy, and pushed herself over the edge. The frame of the pod swung one more time and then plummeted to the ground after her.

Alex stared at the spot where she'd just been, where she wasn't anymore, as pure agony filled him to bursting. Every nerve fired as his brain tried to process what had happened. Pinpricks of pain cascaded from his head to his toes and back again, and yet somehow his body was numb. A guttural, inhuman sound ripped from Alex's throat and echoed into the night. He pressed his forehead against the rough surface of the beam and screamed again.

Take care of Ollie. Naomi's voice broke through his grief.

Alex's breaths came too quickly, and he closed his eyes, willing himself to gain control. His body shivered violently, and though every movement was like pushing through mud, he looked up. Oliver sat with his back to the vertical beam, staring at Alex with a shellshocked expression.

Take care of Ollie.

Alex fought to calm himself, fought to push aside his grief. He fought for Naomi. For Oliver. He forced himself to embrace the numbness, let it spread throughout his body, deaden his emotions. It was easier than he thought it would be. When he finally stopped shaking, he got to his hands and knees, then crawled forward.

He wanted to say he was sorry, to offer some comfort, but he couldn't, not yet. Providing comfort would mean acknowledging that Naomi was gone, and he had to push that aside until they were on the ground. Instead, he steadied his voice and said, "Oliver, we're going to climb down the ladder, now, okay?"

Oliver pulled his knees to his chest. He was crying rivers, but he made no sound. Alex stood up and leaned over his son, putting one hand on the beam. He held out his other hand.

"Take my hand. I'll carry you down," Alex said. When Oliver didn't move, Alex said more sternly, "Oliver, we have to go right now."

Oliver took his hand without looking at him, and Alex hauled him to his feet. Alex stepped halfway onto the ladder and instructed his son to wrap his arms around Alex's neck and his legs around Alex's middle. Alex didn't have to tell him to hang on tight; his son clung to him like glue. It had been a while since he'd picked up his son, but the kid was small for his age and wiry. His thin body was a little awkward between Alex and the rungs of the ladder, but the weight was manageable. Wind whistled through the tower of the Wind Breaker and whipped away the last of Alex's tears from his eyes. He took hold of the next rung, unfurled his other hand, and took another step down toward a world in distress, a world of chaos, a world without Naomi.

He was still a hundred feet in the air, every muscle exhausted, when it began to drizzle and the rungs became slick enough for his foot to slip.

Chapter 4

Timothy Peters

Timothy Peters stared at the newest family portrait in his mother's hallway and tried to tell himself it didn't matter that he and his wife, Heather, weren't in it. His father stood tall and proud, clean shaven, his silver-gray hair and green eyes lending credibility to his distinguished persona. Beside him, Timothy's mom, Dana, beamed, her hands resting on Lizzy's shoulders. Lizzy and the youngest Peters, George, were perched on white stools in front of their parents. They were all dressed in their Sunday best, and the photo made them look so… happy.

But Timothy knew better. He'd spent most of his life living with Walter Peters; no one could *actually* be happy under his roof. Lizzy understood why Timothy had cut ties with their father. George, only twelve, was beginning to see it, too. Granted, their mother was in denial, but she had been for a long time. How else was she supposed to survive?

"Hey, Tim, you coming?" George's head popped around the corner. "I think Heather could use some back up. She's doing that thing where her lips get real thin, and she looks like she has to fart, but really, she's just mad."

Timothy chuckled. "Don't *ever* let Heather hear you say that," he said as he left the hallway of portraits and rounded the corner with George.

"But it's true, right?" George asked.

"Yeah, that's pretty much exactly what she looks like when she's about to blow a gasket, but avoiding descriptions like that will keep you out of a lot of trouble." Timothy ruffled George's hair. "One day when you have a girlfriend, you'll understand."

"Gross." George's face screwed up like he'd just eaten something sour.

Timothy led the way down the stairs and into the open concept living area. His entire apartment could fit in that one room of his father's house, and he preferred the cozy feel of his adult home to the cold, meticulous décor of his childhood one. The hallway upstairs and the game room were Timothy's favorite spots; they had a touch of his mother's tastes. But downstairs, his father had always hired decorators to create magazine-ready spaces for the perusal of high-profile guests. His mom couldn't even pick out her own salt and pepper shakers.

"I know you like these, Dana, but wouldn't you rather have the best?" Walter had said when she'd come home with ceramic shakers in the shape of Mr. and Mrs. Claus. She'd only wanted to use them for the Christmas season. "This is a busy time for me, sweetheart." He held up his large, wooden salt and pepper grinders. "Those won't work for the pink Himalayan salt we buy."

Timothy had been fourteen then; it was the first time he realized that his mother almost never got anything she wanted, not really. She'd packed away Mr. and Mrs. Claus, and they only came out at Christmas. His mother put them on a side table in the game room next to the little tree she decorated herself with ornaments from her childhood. Every year, she told the story of how silly she'd been, how she hadn't considered the Himalayan salt, and how nice it was that the shakers could be used as decoration in the game room.

"And how are the two most important ladies in my life?" Timothy asked with gusto as he approached the oversized kitchen. His mother and his wife had set out three wine glasses, and his mother was uncorking a bottle of merlot.

Heather flashed him a grin that bordered more on clenched teeth. "Dana has been telling me all about how much better my pie would have been if I'd used your granny's recipe for the crust."

"And the filling," Dana said, patting Heather on the shoulder. "Next time, I can just make the pie. You can bring the salad, sweetie."

Ouch. George was right.

"Mom," Timothy said, keeping his voice light. "You can't really compare Granny's apple pie to Heather's peach. They're apples and oranges. I absolutely love Heather's pie."

"That's a lot of fruit," George said, hopping up onto one of the bar chairs at the island. He sat back, smiled, and popped a candy from a trail mix bowl into his mouth. "Personally, my favorite is cherry pie. Sweet and tart."

"Well, maybe next time, I can try a cherry pie, then," Heather said.

"Or, better yet," his mother said as she poured herself a few ounces of wine, "you can come over early, and I can teach you how to make granny's crust. You're going to need it to pass down to my grandbabies." She offered the wine bottle to Heather.

Oh boy. Timothy grimaced as Heather grabbed the bottle and filled the glass to a little over halfway. She set the bottle on the counter hard enough to startle his mother.

"I'm going to be on the couch, watching the news." Heather raised her glass and sipped it as she walked to the other side of the room. As she passed Timothy, she stopped and whispered in his ear. "As soon as I'm finished with this merlot, which is the best thing about tonight, I'll be ready to go whenever you are."

Timothy nodded and kissed her forehead. He spoke quietly. "She doesn't mean to be pushy."

"Mmm-hmm." Heather quirked an eyebrow and took a drink.

He watched her back as she retreated to the couch and flipped on the massive television. She kept it on mute as she flipped through the channels. Timothy turned back to his mom and gave her a chastising look.

"What? I was only trying to help." She set down her wine glass, her lips pouty. "Is it too much for me to ask for you to give me grandbabies?"

Timothy walked over to his mom, wrapped his arms around her, and rested his chin on her head. "Yes, mom. It is absolutely too much to ask. Especially when you know how long we've *tried.*"

She pulled away and swatted at him, frowning. "Well, it's not too much to ask that she learn granny's recipe. I hardly ever see you anymore."

"That's not our fault," Timothy said, his own defenses going up.

"I know it's not *all* your fault, Timmy," Dana said. "But I do miss you. The only time I see you these days is when your father is away on business, and I'm too sick to go."

You mean you pretend to be too sick to go. He didn't say that out loud, though. Her frail health was part of her coping mechanism. At least, that's the conclusion he'd come to over the years. Her undiagnosable illness only seemed to spring up at the most convenient times.

"I just don't understand why Heather doesn't like me." Dana sipped her wine and eyed Heather's back from across the room.

"Mom, she does like you," Timothy said, stretching the truth a little. "Maybe if you gave her some credit for what she *does* do—"

"Hey, um, babe?" Heather's worried voice cut Timothy off. "I think this is about the World's Fair." She stood up and switched on the sound. "You need to come look at this."

A woman looked straight at the camera, gesturing reservedly with her hands as she spoke. "Hello, Boston, I'm Lisa Wyckoff here with my co-host, Dan Locke at News 9. If you're tuning in now, there are unconfirmed reports of a terrible accident at the 2035 World's Fair in St. Louis, Missouri. We have lost contact with our team on the ground who had been there to cover the World's Fair Innovations Exposition."

Her co-host frowned, his hands flat on the desk, as he seemed to be listening to something in his earpiece. "What we do have is video footage that was transmitted to us before we lost contact. We must warn you that the images you're about to see are alarming."

"George… maybe you should go to your room," Dana set her wine glass down and stepped to the end of the island, not taking her eyes of the screen across the room.

"No way, Mom." George hopped down off the stool and came to stand beside Dana. Instead of telling him to go again, she put an arm around his shoulder.

Timothy slowly walked across the room, engrossed as every second added weight to the rock in his stomach. At first, the camera showed a young man, a news reporter, with a stage and crowd at his back, the twilight sky washed out by artificial lighting. He had a small lapel mike clipped to his tie. Bright eyed and energetic, he was in the midst of listing the top innovations to be unveiled at the exposition side of the World's Fair.

"And the runner-up for the innovation to beat is—" he stopped and froze, as if the footage had been paused, except for his eyes which got significantly wider. He suddenly gestured wildly at the person behind the camera. "Turn the camera, Janet. There! The plane… there's something wrong with the pilot!"

The camera swung in the opposite direction, spanning over the fairgrounds, from the area designated for the Innovations Exposition to the family-friendly, traditional-fair-on-steroids behind them. The camera zoomed in, and Timothy gasped as the plane, wings nearly perpendicular to the ground hit the Ferris Wheel. An explosion sounded, and the camera rocked as debris flew hundreds of feet into the air. A chunk of metal landed just yards away, the reporter yelped, and the video cut.

"You don't think Lizzy would have been on the Ferris Wheel?" George asked.

Dana's hand flew to her mouth as she breathed in sharply, and then she frantically patted her pockets. "Where is my phone? I've got to call your father or Lizzy." Her pockets came up empty, and she glanced around the room.

"More breaking news." Dan Locke's voice froze Dana in place as everyone's attention was returned to the television. "We have cell phone footage that was sent by our reporter, Willis Young, who you just saw report on the Ferris Wheel. It appears he was able to send it before we lost contact."

"We are being told that the video is more graphic than the footage of the plane hitting the Ferris Wheel," Lisa Wycoff said. "We advise children be removed from the room."

"George…" Dana said uncertainly.

"Mom, I want to know what's happening. I'm not a child. I'm almost thirteen!" George walked over to the couches and sat down, curling up with his knees to his chest. "I'm staying."

Dana looked at Timothy with pleading in her eyes, but he didn't have time to do anything about his younger brother before the cell phone footage came on screen. The same reporter came on screen, his hair a mess, soot on his face, and his tie askew. He was breathing heavily, and the camera and light on his phone made for eerie, pale lighting in the dark.

"Janet's dead," he said, his eyes darting from side to side as he stumbled forward, the camera bouncing in his hand. "About fifteen minutes after the explosion, she just… I don't know, got sick?" He ran his fingers through his hair, stopped, and shook his head. "I'm not sure what happened, but she's not the only one. When she died, we were trying to get closer to the wreckage, and I'm in the thick of it, now." He put his head down, revealing a bleeding cut on the top of his head, and coughed violently. When he looked back up, he blinked several times before continuing. "There's a thin layer of smoke here," he said. "I don't think I can get closer. I'm going to show you the devastation now, but it's pretty bad, so… I don't know if you can put it on, but someone needs to see this." His finger came into view, he pressed the screen, and the camera flipped.

Everyone in the living room gasped at the same time, except for George, who shouted and threw his hands over his eyes. Dana rushed forward and put her body between George and the screen, but she looked over her shoulder. Timothy couldn't look away, either. A glow of white light from the camera illuminated the haze, and through it, the shapes of dozens of dead bodies could be seen. Mr. Young moved his phone closer to reveal an old man, face and shirt smeared with blood, one eye bulging and the other hanging completely out of his skull by the optic nerve. A welt the size of Timothy's palm was on his neck, and it was split open and oozing.

"What happened to him?" Heather whispered. She too, had curled her knees to her chest. Timothy took slow, shuffling steps forward and put his hands on the back of the couch. Heather reached over her shoulder, and he took her hand.

The camera flipped back to Mr. Young's face. "This isn't from the accident. This didn't happen because he was thrown or because of fire or anything like that. That's how Janet died." He sucked in a breath as his voice cracked on the name of his camerawoman. He looked away and let his hand fall, and the screen cut back to the news anchors.

Ms. Wycoff had her hands flat against her stomach, and Mr. Locke stared blankly ahead before he cleared his throat. "This… this is the first time my co-host and I have seen…" He trailed off, and then both news anchors frowned and put a hand on their ear. The blood drained completely from their faces.

"We have reports coming in from a hospital charity event at the Franklin Park Zoo here in Boston." She pressed her lips together and grasped the lapels of her suit too tightly. "There are people at the event exhibiting the same symptoms as what Mr. Young described just moments ago at the World's Fair."

Timothy rounded the couch and sunk next to Heather. He glanced at his mother who still shielded George as she tried to see the screen out of the corner of her eye. On screen, Mr. Locke stared ahead, shellshocked. With visible effort, Ms. Wycoff unfurled her fingers and lay her hands flat on the news desk before looking directly into the camera.

The tremble in her voice was barely detectable as she straightened her shoulders and a mask of professionalism slid over her own stunned expression. "It seems that whatever is happening at the World's Fair is also happening here in Boston. News 9 has not received confirmation on the source of the illness, but early reports suggest that this is a coordinated terrorist attack. Whatever is going on out there, we urge you to stay inside, Boston. This is going to be a long night."

Chapter 5

Zara Williams

A wave of heat accosted Zara as she charged haphazardly after Lizzy toward the flaming wreckage. She kept her eyes on her best friend's back — shirt riddled with holes and dotted with blood — as they skirted the edges of the mass of folding chairs and bodies. Embers floated on the air, bright specks in the night. The smoke from the stage fire joined the other fires springing up throughout the World's Fair to block out the stars and most of the moonlight.

"Liz, wait!" Zara shouted. Her entire left side looked like Liz's back, maybe worse, but whereas she limped forward, her friend hadn't slowed down one bit.

Liz didn't stop and within seconds, she was swallowed by the hazy, smokey night. At the same time that she lost sight of Liz, Zara's foot caught, and she fell to the ground. She rotated her body so that her right side took the brunt of the impact. Zara rolled onto her back, wincing as her body came to a stop.

Part of her wanted to stay put. The ground beneath her was almost comforting. If she lay completely still, the cuts, bruises, aches, and pains all over her body weren't quite as bad. She closed her eyes and let her fingers spread out. Blades of grass tickled her palm. The dirt was soft, just a little damp. She dug into it and pressed a handful into her palm. It reminded her of sugar cookie dough, and that reminded her of her mother.

Hot tears sprung into Zara's eyes at the thought of family. *I just want to go home…*

"Zee? Oh, God, don't let her be dead." Lizzy's voice broke as a *thud* beside Zara's head made her open her eyes.

Liz knelt over her, eyes closed, mumbling repeatedly the same prayer. Zara blinked away the moisture in her eyes. "I thought you didn't believe in God."

"Zee!" Liz flung herself over Zara, hugging her tight.

Zara wheezed. "I'm not dead, but you're going to kill me if you keep squeezing like that."

"Sorry," Lizzy pulled back, wincing. "What happened? Why are you on the ground?"

Zara sat up. "I tripped."

"And you, what? Decided to take a nap?" Lizzy asked, her voice high pitched.

Zara quirked an eyebrow at Lizzy. "That's more in character for me than you praying."

Lizzy groaned. "Is that actually important right now?"

"Probably."

"You're so weird, Zee."

"You love that about me." Zara struggled to her feet. "Come on," she said, holding out her right hand and helping Lizzy up. "Let's find your dad. If we find him, he can help find Jordan."

Lizzy put a hand on Zara's shoulder. "Jordan was supposed to be near the outskirts of the fair shooting a video or something. I'm sure he's okay."

"I'm just worried about him." Zara smiled half-heartedly and added, "Even if he is a blockhead."

"He loves you, too," Lizzy said.

Tears sprung up despite Zara's efforts to hold them at bay, and she wiped them away with her sleeve. Her brother had given their family no end of trouble in his twenty-three years. But that was partly Zara's fault, too, just like everything else. The first time he'd stolen something, it had been the misguided attempt of a twelve-year-old to help his family during a financial crisis, a crisis she'd caused. She hadn't been close to Jordan for a long time, but she'd always thought of it as a temporary hiccup. After the events of the day, she wanted to fix that.

Zara and Lizzy walked together toward the side of what remained of the stage and stopped, huddling close together. They couldn't get much closer to the stage for the heat of the flames. The Ferris Wheel pod had smashed through the trusses and scaffolding so that the sides of the structure buckled inward. Fire licked at the broken floor, the speakers, and a giant, crumpled curtain.

"It wasn't nine yet. Dad shouldn't have been on stage, right?" Lizzy stared at the rubble and folded her arms against her stomach.

Zara chewed on her lower lip. "Maybe we should check around the back?"

Lizzy nodded and coughed, waving away the smoke.

"Cover your face with your shirt," Zara said as she pulled her t-shirt over her nose. "We need to hurry and try to get out of this smoke."

Lizzy buttoned the top two buttons on her shirt and followed suit, covering half her face. Zara followed her as they rounded the debris to the back. They were met with a web of broken light trusses that extended fifty feet from the stage. The light from the flames on the stage danced over the wreckage and reflected off the steel nearby, but they could barely see any details past ten feet or so from the fire.

"Maybe call your dad," Zara said as she pulled out her phone and turned on the flashlight. "If he's under there, maybe we'll hear it ring." She walked away from the stage and shone the light through the steel lattice trusses, sweeping over the area inch by inch.

"He keeps his phone on silent," Lizzy said, but she pulled out her phone anyway and dialed.

The hazy air near the back of the mess was illuminated just slightly, just for a moment, a little halo of light in the dark. "There! Is that his phone?" Zara ran over clear ground to get closer to where the light had been, and Lizzy followed.

"Do you see anything?" Lizzy asked as she dialed again.

This time they were closer, and they spotted the phone just a few yards into the wreckage. It rested in a limp hand.

"Dad!" Lizzy climbed into the steel obstacle course and headed toward the phone. "Dad, can you hear me?"

"Mr. Peters!" Zara shouted as she tentatively worked her way over the first barrier of a two-foot-wide lattice truss.
Lizzy got there a lot faster. She bent down and stuck her hand between the steel latticework. "Dad, wake up."
As Zara came closer, Lizzy's pleas became more frantic. She pushed on Mr. Peters's shoulder awkwardly, her arm strung through the truss.
"Be careful, Liz." Zara stepped up to Lizzy.
"He won't wake up, but he's warm. That's good, right? I mean, if he were dead, he'd be cold?" Lizzy reached further with her fingertips and tugged on her father's ear lobe. "Wake. Up!"
Zara winced as Mr. Peters's head lolled to the side and Lizzy attacked the other ear. "I don't think—"
"Dad!" Lizzy shouted and patted his cheek with more force than Zara would have.
Mr. Peters woke with a gasp. His whole body jerked, and Zara was glad to see that his limbs weren't pinned down. He was just trapped in a heavy steel cage. There were gaps in several places, but she wasn't sure they were large enough for him to wiggle through.
"Elizabeth? What… what happened? Are you okay?" Mr. Peters whipped his head from side to side as his hands brushed the steel lattices all around him. There was just enough of a cavity for him to pull one of his legs up to his chest.
"I'm not the one we need to worry about right now," Lizzy said. "Are you hurt?"
"My head hurts a little, and—" He winced as he moved his other leg. "Something's wrong with my right leg. I don't think it's broken. Could be a fracture." He looked back up at Lizzy. "What about you?"
"I'm a little banged up, but I'm fine."
Mr. Peters glanced at Zara but only frowned. He went back to examining the steel frame of his makeshift cage.
"I'm fine, too, thanks," Zara said. "Except for all this." She gestured from her scratched up left cheek and ear to the bruises and scrapes on her arm and leg to the gashes above her ankle.
"You look like you'll live," Mr. Peters said. "Maybe, for once, you could make yourself useful instead of complaining."
They had never gotten along, but Zara had been willing to push that aside. It appeared Mr. Peters's disdain for her knew no bounds. She narrowed her eyes but bit her tongue.
"Give it a rest, Dad," Lizzy said. Her angry whisper carried farther than she thought it did, which was also par for the course.
Zara's cheeks flushed hot as she moved away to let them argue about her, again. After the day she'd had, she really didn't feel like listening to Mr. Peters's opinions of her and her family. It didn't matter to him that her mom had always stayed home with her kids, just like his wife, or that her father was a police officer, a profession he claimed to respect. Where they lived and who they were meant they didn't belong in the same circles as he did. And that much was true. Zara knew it just as much as he did. If it weren't for Lizzy's mom, Dana, Zara wasn't sure she and Lizzy would have much of a friendship.
Thinking of her family, she dialed home while she meandered farther from Lizzy and her father. She held her breath as the phone rang, but no one picked up. She frowned at her phone as her mom's voicemail message sounded.
All of this must not be on the news yet.
Her parents would have called by now if they'd known what was happening. She shrugged, trying not to overreact, and switched on the flashlight on her phone again as she started searching for something to help them get Mr. Peters out of his predicament. He was an ass, but he was Lizzy's dad. And that counted for something.
There. That should do it. Zara spotted the outline of a road sign beyond the rubble. *If that's a metal pole, we're set.* She turned and quickly hobbled back to where Lizzy and her father were. Lizzy was pinching the bridge of her nose, her head down as Mr. Peters used his I-know-what's-best-for-you voice. She never managed to stay in a fight with her father for very long. Eventually, she just shut down.
"She's a freeloader," Mr. Peters said. "And her brother. Don't even get me started—"
"Hey!" Zara shouted, interrupting him before he could say enough to make her shut her mouth and leave him to rot. She was the only person who was allowed to point out Jordan's faults. "This freeloader just figured out how to get you out of there."
Lizzy stood up abruptly, crossed her arms, and turned away from her father to follow Zara. "We'll be back, Dad. Don't go anywhere."
"Very funny." Mr. Peters sighed and rubbed his temples.
After a few minutes of climbing over obstacles in silence, Lizzy cleared her throat. "So, my dad's just being my dad. He's wrong about you. You're smart, and you work harder than anyone I know."
Zara didn't try to hide the annoyance in her tone. "It would have been nice for you to, I don't know, say that to *him*." She threw a pointed look Lizzy's way as she cleared another truss.
"It's over faster if I just shut up and take it," Lizzy said. "No one cares what he thinks."
"I care!" Zara said louder than she intended, blurting out the words and immediately wishing she could take them back.
"What? Why?" Lizzy asked.
"Because, Liz." Zara sighed. "Everyone *else* listens to your father. He's, like, the big cheese, you know?"
Lizzy's laugh quickly turned to a cough. When she caught her breath, she shook her head. "The big cheese? Really?"
"It's not funny." Zara cleared the last of the trusses and trudged toward the sign. "You don't get it because you've always been at the top of the food chain. People look at you and assume the best. They look at me and assume the worst."
"That's not true," Lizzy said. "And if it were, you prove them wrong every day. You're the biggest overachiever I've ever met."
Zara stopped in her tracks and threw up her hands. "Do you think I *like* having to prove myself every day?"
Lizzy sighed in frustration. "What do you want from me, Zee? You don't have to prove anything to me, okay? That's all I can give you right now."
Zara inhaled deeply, and her shoulders sagged. She was *so* tired. "I know, and… I'm sorry. Your dad just gets under my skin. It's been a long day."
"That would be the biggest understatement of the year," Lizzy said.
"Well, you did say I was only 'smart.'"
"Brilliant, then?"

"That's better." Zara lifted her chin and smiled, and they both giggled. It felt good to laugh, to just be normal for a minute.
"Hug it out?" Lizzy held open her arms.
"Considering your back and my… everything, maybe we can settle for a hand squeeze?" Zara held out her hand, and Lizzy squeezed it tight. "Alright," Zara said as she started moving again toward their destination, "let's go dig up this sign and use the metal pole as a lever to get your dad out."
"What are we going to dig it out with?" Lizzy asked.
Zara held up her right hand. "We're going to get our hands dirty, princess. The ground is soft, and if it's only buried a few feet, with the two of us digging, it shouldn't take too long."
"What about your left arm?" Lizzy asked.
"Okay, with one and a half of us digging," Zara said, "it shouldn't take too long."
Lizzy frowned at her manicure and pursed her lips before feebly letting her hands fall to her side. When they got to the sign, Zara examined the pole. There was no concrete anywhere in sight, but the ground was a bit rocky from the nearby gravel road. Zara dropped to her knees and began to dig, one handful at a time, and Lizzy joined her. She worked methodically, giving in to the monotony, letting it numb her mind. The last thing she wanted to do right now was think. They were a couple feet down and twenty minutes into the task when Lizzy broke the silence.
"This used to be farmland," Lizzy said, gesturing behind them where the fair spread out for over a mile. In front of them, on the other side of the gravel road, there was a small, paved parking lot. Mr. Peters's six-person limousine, along with two more limousines and a few Teslas and BMWs, was parked there. Beyond the lot, a fence extended in either direction, separating the fairgrounds from cornfields. "The GEF had a pamphlet," Lizzy continued, "on how the World's Fair cheated the farmers. I think they had a protest about it and everything."
"They set up a booth at a fair they protested?" Zara rolled her eyes. "That sounds just like them." She put her fingers against the pole, dug her hand into the dirt, and used her hand and arm to scoop more dirt up and out of the hole.
"They're just trying to do some good in the world. You're too hard on them." Lizzy removed her own layer of earth and rubbed her hands together before going in for more.
Jordan's face flashed in Zara's mind's eye, and she relented. "Yeah, maybe I am."
Lizzy smiled in response, but then she held out one hand, palm up. "Is that rain?" she asked, looking up at the sky.
"That's just what we need." Zara frowned at the ensuing drizzle. "There shouldn't be too much left before we reach the bottom." She stood and grabbed hold of the pole, which was already leaning a bit, and pulled. It budged a little, so she continued to push and pull, loosening it until she could pull it out. With her final tug, she fell and landed on the ground with a thud.
"Yes!" Lizzy pumped her fist in the air. "We did it!" She hopped over to Zara and took the pole.
Zara grimaced as she stood and rubbed her back. "I'm going to need to cash in on that spa day you're always offering when we get home." Zara rolled her shoulders and stretched her neck back and forth.
The drizzle did little to clear the smokey air, but the fire on the stage was turning to more of a smolder as they climbed back through the trusses. Zara hoped a little rain would do something to control the fires throughout the fairgrounds.
"It's about time," Mr. Peters said. He frowned through the latticework. "Is that a stop sign?"
"It's a lever," Zara said. She pointed to the larger end of one of the gaps and then to the broken truss on top of the pile surrounding him. "We're going to lift this beam-thing using this pole as a lever, and you're going to climb out."
Mr. Peters smirked. "That's not going to work."
"Well, we're going to try. If we can open that gap just a few inches, you should be able to crawl out. Can you move?" Zara asked. "Is your leg too bad for you to get out?"
"I can crawl out if you can manage to make the gap bigger, but what if you collapse all of this on top of me? What if you two aren't strong enough? What if I'm halfway through the gap and the pole snaps?" Mr. Peters crossed his arms and raised his eyebrows. Zara hated how much he reminded her of Lizzy in that moment.
"What if we just leave you here forever?" Zara asked as she wedged the pole into the corner of the gap where it was smallest.
"We should try, Dad," Lizzy said. "It's starting to rain, and something isn't right about what's happened. I think the people are sick."
"Sick? Is there something else going on?" Mr. Peters asked, his eyes wide. "I thought the plane just crashed into the Ferris Wheel."
"It did," Zara said, "but people are dying from something else. I don't know, it's like… their eyes pop out of their heads, there's a ton of blood, and—"
"Welts?" Mr. Peters asked, his tone trepidatious.
"Yes," Zara said, frowning at the way Mr. Peters's face blanched. "Do you know what's going on?"
"What?" Mr. Peters genuinely didn't seem to have heard her.
"Dad," Lizzy said, "do you know what's happening?"
"Um, no… of course not," he said, pointing toward the gap. "But you girls are right. We need to get out of here. Let's try the lever idea."
Zara narrowed her eyes, her grip loosening on the pole. "Mr. Peters, if you know—"
"I just remembered seeing someone with welts before the stage lighting fell on top of me," Mr. Peters said abruptly and with not a small amount of exasperation. "Now, let's get out of here before the smoke clears."
Before the smoke clears? Zara took one hand off the pole and stared at Lizzy's father, who avoided eye contact with her as if she were Medusa.
"Zee?" Lizzy grabbed the pole. "Are we going to do this or not? The rain's picking up."
Zara blinked a few times and looked at Lizzy. "Right," she said. "You ready, Mr. Peters?"
He cleared his throat. "Just hurry up," he said.
"Why is he so anxious to try this now?" Zara whispered to Lizzy, leaning close.

Lizzy shrugged. "He wants to get out of there. He's just too prideful to admit you had a good idea." She began to put her weight on the pole. "Come on, Zee."

Zara shook her head and gripped the pole, not sure she believed that was all there was to Mr. Peters's sudden change of heart. Still, Lizzy was right. They needed to get him out. They both put all their weight on the far end of the pole, Lizzy going so far as to lay across the back of the stop sign as Zara pushed it down with all the strength she could muster with her injuries. The metal truss creaked and groaned as it raised a few inches. Mr. Peters squeezed through the gap, favoring his right leg and using mostly his upper body strength to get out. His foot barely cleared the gap when the pole bent suddenly, and the truss crashed downward. The cavity of free space once occupied by Mr. Peters was gone.

"Well, that was close," Zara said.

"Too close. You're lucky it worked," Mr. Peters said. He ran his fingers through his hair and breathed in deeply, exhaling slowly.

"Gosh, Dad. You could say 'thank you' every once in a while. If it weren't for Zee—"

A groan from a few yards away caught the attention of all three of them. Zara turned to see a shadowy figure staggering in the dark just beyond the wreckage.

The figure called out, voice wet and gurgling. "Hello? Please, help."

Mr. Peters took a faltering step forward, grabbed Lizzy's upper arm, and pulled her behind him. He had to hop on his left leg to maintain balance with the motion.

"Mr. Peters, it's okay. They just need help," Zara said, looking over her shoulder at her best friend's father. But then she did a double-take and scrambled away.

Mr. Peters's eyes were crazed with fear, and he had a pistol pointed straight at her.

Chapter 6

Alexander Roman

For a terrifying moment, the grip of one hand was the only thing standing between Alex and a plummet to his death and the death of his son. The rain had made the rungs dangerous, and when his foot had slipped, one of Alex's hands had lost hold. He hung with Oliver's back to the elements as his arms and legs were wrapped around Alex's body. Alex's arm twisted painfully as he willed himself not to let go. But Oliver — the weight of him, the way he clung so tightly, his breath on Alex's neck, the sound of his whimpering — infused Alex with the will to survive. And Naomi's words kept repeating in his head.

Take care of Ollie.

Alex shouted in pain as he swung his body around, once more placing Oliver between himself and the ladder, and took hold of a rung with both hands. When his feet finally found a rung, Alex held fast, not daring to move as the rain splattered his face, soaked into his clothes, and slickened the ladder. He fought to steady his breathing as his body shook violently. Every beat of his heart was like an explosion against his ribcage, and the pulsing in his head made it hard to think. Oliver cried softly into his neck, and his chin dug into Alex's collarbone. He, too, trembled.

Don't give up. One step at a time. Take care of Ollie.

He pried his hands from the wet, metal rung and descended one step closer to the ground. And then he did it again. And again. Each time, his breath hitched, and he had to force himself to return to breathing more normally as he regained control over the way his body shivered.

When the toe of his shoe hit solid ground, it startled Alex. He had gotten used to the perilous downward rhythm. All thought, all semblance of himself, had vanished into the terrible monotony. There had only been rain, and metal rungs, and the threat of plunging to his death, to Oliver's death. Solid ground almost felt wrong, as if it didn't *belong* in his world anymore. Frozen with one toe on concrete, one foot on a rung, two hands still clinging just above his head, Alex squeezed his eyes shut and then pressed his weight onto the ground.

"We did it," he whispered as he slowly put his other foot down, as he peeled his hands away from the rungs and stood. "Oliver, we... we're okay." He laughed and shouted and threw his hands in the air. He hugged his son and bounced on the balls of his feet. "We're okay!" He shouted to the world, but then, his smile faded. Naomi wasn't okay. Naomi was dead. *I can't leave her here... I have to find her.*

Oliver hadn't let go. He hadn't loosened his death grip on Alex even a little. Gently, Alex got to his knees and then sat on the ground and held Oliver. And then he broke down, sobbing until his throat was raw. The smoke in the air had gotten thicker as they'd gotten lower, but he'd been so focused on survival, he'd barely noticed. He coughed and sputtered as he took great, gulping breaths. Light rain mixed with his tears and dripped off his chin. When he collapsed onto his back, Oliver finally let go of him, and Alex rolled onto his side, squeezing his eyes shut as he tried to get himself under control.

A small brush of human touch on his cheek made Alex open his eyes. Oliver lay beside him, facing him. He was soaked, his eyes were bloodshot, his nose raw, and he shivered, but he still tried to wipe Alex's tears away.

"I'm sorry, bud," Alex said. His voice shook, but he was all out of tears. "I'm so sorry."

Oliver just stood up and held out a hand. A calm came over Alex, a determination that was different than the frantic, desperate determination he had felt before. His head cleared as he took in his ten-year-old son who was clearly trying to be strong.

No... I have to be strong for Oliver, not the other way around. With that thought on repeat, Alex took Oliver's hand and got up.

"You ready to get out of this... cage?" Alex asked.

Oliver nodded, so Alex surveyed the chain-link fence meant to keep fairgoers away from the base of the Windbreaker, looking for the gate but seeing none. It wasn't much of a plan, but it was a first step. He led Oliver to the fence, groaning at the thought of climbing it. It was about three heads taller than he was, and while he could hoist Oliver over, he wasn't sure Oliver could climb down the other side. And if he could climb down, the next problem would be how Alex would manage to jump the fence himself.

I guess there's nothing to do but try.

"Alright, Oliver. We're going to—" He looked down to where his son had been, but Oliver wasn't there. And he wasn't behind Alex, either. "Oliver!" he shouted, panic seizing his chest. He looked through the dark, hazy night, a gate swung outward catching his eye. *How did I miss that?* He shouted his son's name again and ran to the gate.

When he spotted Oliver's outline in the smog in between two hunks of debris from the Ferris Wheel, he breathed a sigh of relief and jogged to him, getting down on one knee and wrapping his arms around Oliver. "You can't do that, Oliver. You have to stay with me, do you understand?" Alex looked up at his son, but Oliver just stared straight ahead. "What are you looking at?"

When he turned to follow his son's line of sight, Alex slowly stood as he tried to process the scene before him. Alex counted five dead bodies, and those were the ones he could see in the gloomy night. He thought back to before the plane had hit, when he'd seen some sort of sickness popping up among fairgoers.

"Stay here," Alex said as he stepped toward the nearest body, his CDC training taking over. He squatted at a safe distance and squinted, trying to see any clues as to how the person died. His eyes landed on a piece of metal sticking out of the side opposite him.

Okay, that'll do it. He moved on to the next body, a woman with eyes popping out of her head. She was covered in blood, but besides her eyes he couldn't see any injuries besides the welt on her arm. Her limbs were swollen, too. *Almost like an allergic reaction... except it's widespread.* The memory of people falling to the ground as others backed away from them in circles made Alex frown. *If it were an airborne biological weapon, it would have struck everyone in a specified circumference, not one or two at a time.*

He glanced at a third body which had the same symptoms as the second. A disease or a reaction to an agent, be it foreign or environmental, seemed to be the origin of the destruction around him. He suspected the pilot of the erratic plane had been affected. Whatever happened didn't make sense to him, not yet.

Oliver moved, and Alex immediately took notice.

"Oliver, stop!" he shouted as his son bent down and grabbed something from under the debris. "Don't touch that!" He rushed to his son and reached for the object, but Oliver curled around it, protecting it with his body.

"We don't know what's going on here," Alex said, trying to keep calm. "You shouldn't touch anything."

Oliver clutched the thing tighter.

"Will you at least show me what it is?" Alex held up his hands and backed away, fully intending on snatching it out of Oliver's hands and throwing it as far from them as possible if he got the chance.

Slowly, Oliver turned back toward Alex and opened his hands. Alex swallowed a lump in his throat. It was Naomi's macrame purse; she'd made it herself. The handle had been torn loose and had begun to unravel. Alex took a step forward, and he noticed the scent of lavender. It was so strong, the glass vial she'd kept her essential oils in must have broken and saturated the bag. The debris had sheltered it from the rain.

"Okay." Alex nodded. "You can keep it." Alex took his son gently by the shoulder. "I need you to come with me, but… you can't leave my side and you can't touch anything else, okay?"

Oliver nodded and hugged the bag to his chest.

Alex chose a different direction, exploring a new area of the devastation to look for Naomi's body. He walked slowly, searching for her in the flickering, dim light of fires. He listened, too, for the sound of emergency responders. It had been more than an hour since people started dying and the plane had crashed. *Why aren't they here, looking for survivors?* There were no sirens, no voices, no evidence of life. *What if the fairgrounds are cordoned? Or this… this* thing *has spread into the city? What if help isn't coming?*

He buried all the *what ifs* as he picked his way through the fallen bodies and kept guiding Oliver. Alex had to keep his son at a safe distance from the dead, but he got as close as he could, trying to make out details — the color of their skin or hair or clothing. And then he froze as familiarity, usually so warm and comforting, seized his chest and stole his breath. Oliver wrenched free from Alex's hand and rushed to Naomi's body, falling to her side and Alex fell to the wet grass, too.

"Move, Naomi. Blink. Something," Alex whispered, pleading. It didn't matter that her half-closed eyes stared blankly at nothing or that her limbs were splayed at impossible angles. The white of bone poked out of her forearm and shin. When Oliver threw his arms around her, her head lolled to the side, and Alex gasped as the movement exposed a cracked skull.

To be so broken and empty that he was past the point of weeping was not completely foreign to Alex, but he hadn't been prepared to endure it again. He'd thought when he was old and gray, *maybe* if Naomi died first… but he'd imagined this pain would come after decades of life together. He lightly rested his hand on Oliver's back.

Alex waited for someone to come. No one did, and after sitting numbly in his wet clothes for what seemed like forever, the only sound the crying of his son, he lifted his hand. *If this is widespread, it could be hours… days even before someone comes.* He pulled his wallet out of his pocket and slipped out a business card, sliding it into Naomi's shirt pocket and hoping it was enough for her body to be identified later.

"Oliver?" Alex tried to pry Oliver away from Naomi's body. "I… need you to look at me." He had to use carefully measured pressure to get him to let go of his mother, and when Oliver did let go, he buried his head in Alex's chest and held on tight. "She's gone," Alex said, "and I don't think anyone's coming to help us." His chest felt as though it were rending in two as sharp pain lanced through him. "We… we have to go."

Oliver pushed away from him, shaking his head and reaching again for Naomi's body. Alex wrapped his arms around Oliver, refusing to let him go. "We can't stay," he said. "I don't think it's safe." Oliver struggled against Alex's hold for a few minutes longer before slumping against him. "Mom loved you so much, bud. She would want you to be safe, okay? Can you do that for her? Can you come with me to somewhere safe?" Oliver didn't speak, but he also didn't resist as Alex got to his feet and pulled Oliver up, too.

Leaving Naomi there, prodding his son to walk away from her, was one of the hardest things Alex had ever had to do. He led Oliver through the maze of debris and dead bodies, trying to remember where the fairground exit was located. The World's Fair was huge; they had at least a few miles to walk, both of them exhausted. Alex trudged forward, and with every step, his spirit was crushed a little more by the weight of the silence.

The sound of a knocking engine was like a long drink after days of thirst. Beams from headlights pierced the murky night, and a small food truck ambled through the wreckage, driving west as he faced north. The signage on the side read in bubbly, pink lettering: Minnie's Muffins and More. It was going slow, weaving around bodies where it could, running over limbs like speed bumps where it couldn't avoid bodies completely.

"Hey!" Alex waved his arms, but the driver either didn't see him or chose not to stop. He grabbed Oliver's hand. "We're going to catch up to that truck, bud, okay? We're going to see some more things I wish you didn't have to see, but then we're going to get out of here."

They didn't have to go very fast to catch the truck, which was good because Alex's path forward zigzagged and doubled back to avoid the bodies that looked diseased. Oliver trotted along beside him, still not speaking, still clutching the macrame purse to his chest. They rounded a corner into another destroyed thoroughfare that had been filled with happy families and friends only hours ago. The taillights of the truck crawled away from them, lurching right and left, one side or the other rising and falling gradually over bodies.

"Hey! Stop!" He shouted, waving his arm and trying to position himself where he could be seen in the side-view mirror. "Wait!"

The truck halted when he was only a few feet away. He lifted Oliver over a body directly in front of them — this one's head had been bashed in — and came up to the driver's window. He was greeted by a freckled, round-faced woman with long, curly white hair, half put up into a barrette at the back of her head. She looked at Alex through the window, and he could see the battle in her eyes: would she talk to him or just keep going and try to ignore him? She looked from her hands on the steering wheel, down at Alex, and then back at her hands.

"Ma'am? Please…" Alex began to talk, but she wouldn't look at him. Not until Oliver stepped up on the foot rail, knocked on the window, and smiled at her. Her hands fell from the steering wheel, and she leaned her forehead against it for a moment, her body sagging. Then, she sat up and cracked the window.

"You sick?" she asked with a southern twang.

"No, ma'am." Alex said. "We're not sick." *I hope.*

"Y'all look like ten miles of bad road," she said.

Alex frowned and looked down at himself. "I suppose I do," he agreed. "We just need to get to the east parking lot—"

"Nope. Just been there. It's just one big pile-up at this point. You ain't gettin' out that way." She sighed. "You live near here?"

Alex shook his head. "No, but our motel isn't far."

"All right. Here's the rules. You listenin'?" She raised her eyebrows, and Alex nodded. "I let you in my food truck, you stay at the back. I see a welt or bug eyes or anything like that, you're out. Otherwise, I'll get you to the motel. Deal?"

Relief welled up in Alex. "Yes, thank you. You have no idea how much we would appreciate that."

"I'll open the back door." She put the truck in park and got up out of her seat, disappearing into the back.

Alex lifted Oliver back over the dead body and walked him to the back of the truck. The sound of a sliding metal bolt was followed by a creak as the door swung outward.

The woman tsked. "You two are a sight," she said. "C'mon." She waved them in and stepped backward as Alex and Oliver climbed inside. "Shut and bolt the door," she said, and when it was done, she shook her head, mumbled, opened a drawer, and pulled out a bunch of hand towels. "I swear, I've seen fish drier than you two."

Alex took the towels when she held them out. "Thank you, ma'am." He set to drying Oliver's hair first.

She put her hands on her hips. "No more of that 'ma'am' stuff. I'm not my momma. You can call me Minnie." She tsked one more time before turning back toward the front. "And y'all better sit down on the floor," she said over her shoulder. "It's going to be a long, bumpy ride."

Chapter 7

Zara Williams

As Mr. Peters held the pistol steady, he set his jaw, and the fear in his eyes melted away into cold resolve.
"Whoa, Mr. Peters." Zara held up her hands. "What are you doing?"
"Get out of the way," he said. "Whoever that is can't be allowed near us."
"Dad, put the gun away." Lizzy's voice shook. She was pinned between her father and the debris at her back.
"They're just hurt," Zara said. "They need our help. We haven't heard *one* siren since all of this started. If we don't help people, who will?"
Mr. Peters raised his voice. "I said, get out of the way!"
Zara jumped at his volume, her heart in her throat as she sidestepped and tripped, falling over a truss into the muddy grass. She cried out as pain lanced up and down her body upon impact. Every muscle had been exhausted, and Zara wasn't sure how much more she could take. Her breathing came fast and hard and her head swam as she tried to refocus.
"Zara!" Lizzy shouted and ducked under her father's arm, scrambling over the truss to kneel beside her. Lizzy glared at her father. "Put the gun away, Dad!" This time, she said it forcefully.
Mr. Peters lowered the pistol just slightly until a hacking, wet cough came from the approaching figure. In an instant, he raised it once more, pointing it toward the stranger.
"We don't even know who it is!" Zara pulled out her phone once more and switched on the flashlight, shining it into the dark, hoping the sight of an actual human being would make Mr. Peters put his pistol away.
He wouldn't actually shoot someone. He's just scared.
The beam of light revealed a woman, her t-shirt covered in blood. She coughed again, and more blood dribbled out of her mouth. The woman shielded her eyes from the light too quickly for Zara to see her face, but when she raised her hand, the light shone dully off a large welt, skin taut and smooth and raging red around a white center.
A crack split the air and echoed into the night. Dark, fresh blood bloomed from the woman's chest, and she dropped her arm. Her face was swollen, and her eyes protruded. When she collapsed, the hard, wet thud made Zara's stomach flip-flop. The only sound afterward was the pinging of rain on steel. Zara looked back at Mr. Peters, who lowered the gun and holstered it behind his back under his blazer. He didn't look shocked or upset; he looked… assured. Relieved even.
"What. Did. You. Do?" Lizzy's voice broke the silence.
"What I had to." Mr. Peters hobbled forward as he favored his right leg. He sat on a truss, swung his legs over, and moved on to the next obstacle until he cleared the fallen framework for the stage lighting. He sat on a truss and shone his own phone's light on the body of the woman he'd just killed, studying her.
"Liz, we need to find my brother and get out of here," Zara said in a whisper, her mind thawing from the shock of seeing her best friend's father shoot a woman in the chest.
Lizzy shook her head, stumbling over her words. "He… his finger must have slipped. He didn't mean it."
"He didn't mean it? Are you serious?" Zara put her hands on Lizzy's shoulders. "Look at me, Liz. Your dad just shot a woman. Killed her. She's dead."
"She would have died anyway," Mr. Peters said.
His voice startled Zara. She whipped her head to look at where he stood. "You don't know that," she said.
"I do know that." He pointed at the dead woman. "Have you seen anyone so far who looked like that and didn't die?"
"No, but—"
"And you said there were several people dying of this same disease, which means it's contagious," Mr. Peters said.
"Yes," Zara said. "I mean, maybe. We don't know if it's con—"
"We need to get to the limo and leave." Mr. Peters looked at Lizzy. "Let's go, Elizabeth. Right now."
Zara growled in frustration at the second time he didn't let her finish her thought. "What you did was wrong."
"That depends on who you ask." Mr. Peters raised his eyebrows. "Elizabeth, we're leaving."
Lizzy stood up, eyes welling with tears as she looked at Zara. "We have to go, Zee. We can't stay here." She held out a hand. "Come on."
Zara bit her lip and looked down at the ground. There was no way she'd be able to find Jordan on her own. And I can tell my dad about what Mr. Peters did. He'll know what to do. Doesn't he always say the system works?
She took Lizzy's hand and got to her feet. "Fine. Let's go."
Lizzy let her dad lean on her while they walked to the small lot nearby where the limousine was parked. It had been created and reserved for speakers like Mr. Peters so they wouldn't have to walk a long way to the stages at the Innovations Exposition.
Zara limped along, willing her body to keep taking one step after another. She dialed her mother again and again, but she got nothing but voicemail. She dialed her father to the same affect. And Jordan. No one was picking up. *That's strange…*
They soon passed the hole she and Lizzy had dug, where the stop sign had been, and as they crossed the lot, Mr. Peters dug a key fob out of his pocket and unlocked the door. When they got to the limo, Mr. Peters had Lizzy climb inside first and shut the door behind her. She tried to open the door again, but he held up a finger and told her to go make herself comfortable.
Then he looked at Zara. "How are you feeling?" he asked. "Any headaches? Nausea?" He reached out to touch Zara's forehead.

"Of course my head is pounding." She jerked away and swatted at his hand. "Isn't yours? And nausea? How could I not be sick after watching you murder someone right in front of me?"

"I ended her suffering," Mr. Peters said, but he was narrowing his eyes at her as if weighing something important. "Have you had any nose bleeds? Blood from your ears? Gums?"

"No," Zara said. "But what if I did? Would you shoot me, too?"

"You can get in the limo, but I want you up front, driving, with the partition between you and us." Mr. Peters pointed at the front of the limo.

It didn't escape her attention that he hadn't answered her question, but his instructions made her drop her jaw. "You want *me* to drive your limo?"

"It's a rental." Mr. Peters nodded toward the front of the car. "You can stay here, but I have the feeling things won't go well for you if you do. The smoke…" He trailed off, looked away, and then met Zara's eyes again. "If I were you, I'd take this opportunity to get out of here. We need to get to the private airport."

"What about the actual limo driver?" Zara asked.

"We're leaving without him." Mr. Peters nodded toward the front of the limo. "Get in, or I will, and we will leave you here."

"What about my brother? Lizzy and I thought once we found you—"

Mr. Peters's sharp laugh caught Zara off guard. He shook his head. "Stupid girl. You're already dragging us down. I'm getting my daughter out of here. Your brother is a big boy, but if you want to go after him and get yourself killed, go ahead. I won't stop you. You're not doing it with me, and you're certainly not doing it with my daughter."

Zara's throat ran dry. She looked back at the fair in the distance. She had no idea where Jordan was, no way to find him, and what if the illness *was* contagious?

"I don't have all night, and frankly, neither do you," Mr. Peters said. "Are you getting in?"

"There will be some kind of emergency response, right?" Zara asked. "I mean, someone will find him if he's hurt…"

Mr. Peters sighed. "You've got five seconds to get in before I do, and once I'm in the driver's seat, you're staying here."

"Lizzy would jump out of that limo before leaving me here," Zara said.

Mr. Peters blinked at that, and his lips pressed together tightly before he spoke. "Then you would be responsible for her death. Because if we stay here, we die."

That statement was like a punch to the gut, but Zara did her best to not show it. "If I drive, I'm driving slow, and I'm keeping my eyes out for Jordan. He was supposed to be on the outskirts of the fair somewhere, shooting some stupid video. If we see him, I stop."

"He stays in front with you," Mr. Peters said.

"Deal." Zara had never hated Mr. Peters more than at that moment, but that was the farthest she felt she could push him. It was her only chance of helping her brother, albeit a slim one. She limped toward the front seat and opened the door. "Keys?" she asked.

"It's a push button." He held up the key fob. "As long as I've got this in range, it will start. You don't need the fob."

She nodded. Mr. Peters got into the car, and Zara slid into the driver's seat. The partition cracked an inch.

"I want to talk to her, Dad!" Lizzy said. "I can't believe you're making her drive. She's never driven a limo!"

"I need to call your mother, Elizabeth. I don't have time for this. Roll up the partition."

Zara looked over her shoulder as the partition shuddered up and down, and she rolled her eyes. "Liz, stop, okay? Mr. Peters, just let me tell Dana to tell my parents I'm okay. Leave the partition down a crack, and you can roll it up again once the call is over."

"No, we can tell my wife that without you listening in or breathing your germs back here." The limo rocked as Mr. Peters and Lizzy continued to fight over the partition.

"Dad, stop being a germophobe. I've been with Zara all night. Whatever she's got, I've got, if we've got anything at all." Lizzy grunted, and Mr. Peters shouted in pain.

"You bit my hand!" Mr. Peters shouted, sounding shocked.

"You put your hand on my face!" Lizzy said. "Just let the partition down!"

Zara couldn't help but laugh. *Wish I could have seen that.*

"Fine, but you're walking on thin ice, Ms. Williams," Mr. Peters said as the partition rolled all the way down. "If Elizabeth wasn't right about the fact she probably has the illness if you do…"

The ringing of a phone sounded over the speakers in the back of the limo. Zara winced as she sat on her knees, looking through the partition so she could see Lizzy and her father. Lizzy shrugged as she held up her phone, which was dialing her mother, and Mr. Peters held onto the edge of his seat like he wanted to rip the stuffing right out of it.

"When she picks up, I talk, not you—" He pointed at Lizzy and then jabbed his finger at Zara. "—and certainly not you. I need to talk to your mother. I don't know how long cell towers will be active."

Zara frowned. "Cell towers? But why would—"

"Shut it, or I confiscate both your phones." Mr. Peters held up a hand, and he looked like he was at the end of his rope.

Zara and Lizzy both nodded, but Zara had a growing knot in her stomach. When Dana's voice sounded through the speakers, the knot tightened.

"Hello? Walt?" Dana didn't sound only worried for them, which Zara expected; she sounded frightened out of her mind.

"We're okay," Mr. Peters said. "Lizzy and I are okay."

"And me, too, Mrs. Peters," Zara called, not holding her breath that Mr. Peters would include her.

"Hey, Mom." Lizzy's chin quivered as she sagged into her seat, looking utterly exhausted. "We made it to the limo, but it was the worst day of my life."

"Oh, sweetie—" Dana started, but then her husband cut her off.

"I said I would do the talking," Mr. Peters said sharply. "Dana, are you listening to me? Have you been watching the news? I need you to tell me what's going on, what they know."

Zara scoffed. That's his first question. Really?

"Walt, they're saying it's some kind of terrorist attack," Dana said. "They've shown the most awful images on the television, the way people are dying…"

Dana kept talking, but Zara stared at Mr. Peters. He let out a long, slow breath, puffed out his cheeks and *relaxed.* He seemed relieved at the news, if only for a moment. He rolled his shoulders, rested his elbow on his knee while he rested his injured leg on the long seat beside him, clasped his hands, and listened as his wife described what she'd seen on the news. He was used to high stakes and thrived on pressure in the business world. She'd seen him shake hands with the President of the United States on television, read stories of his iconic business deals, and had only seen him afraid once, the moment before he shot that woman. He was one of those alpha males, the kind that always found a way to get what he wanted. Once she and Lizzy had been shortchanged a small fry, and Mr. Peters had gotten the fast-food restaurant to throw in two large fries for free by the time he was done with them.

But his reaction to what was happening… it just didn't sit right with Zara. *Would any reaction from him sit right with me, though?* She shook her head. *Probably not. He's a soulless tyrant.*

Dana's words pulled Zara's attention away from Mr. Peters. "… and they say there's some event here in Boston where people are dying in the same way, and—"

"Stop," Mr. Peters sat up, back poker straight. "It's in Boston? That's impossible. You must have heard wrong."

"No, that's what the news said."

The knot in Zara's stomach twisted. *It's in Boston? What does that mean?*

She pulled out her phone and dialed home again, willing someone to pick up.

"Put Timothy on," Mr. Peters said. Zara knew that any time Mr. Peters was out of town, Timothy and his wife came to visit Dana, but she didn't know Mr. Peters knew that. She didn't have enough energy to care, though, not when her phone call ended again with voicemail.

"I don't know what you mean," Dana finally said.

"Yes, you do." Mr. Peters sighed, and Zara thought she detected something kind in his voice. "It's okay, Dana. I've known for a long time. He's our son, and despite what everyone thinks, I've never hated him. Just put him on. I need to talk to him."

How can it be in Boston? The thought kept swirling in Zara's head as she cycled through family phone numbers. Her mother, father, aunt, uncle, cousin… all voicemail. *What the hell does that mean?* She half listened to the conversation as hot tears welled up and spilled over. It was too much. The nightmare was supposed to be almost over, not just beginning.

"Okay, you're on speaker phone," Dana said.

"Timothy?" Mr. Peters asked.

"Hello, Walter." Timothy's voice was hard and frigid.

Mr. Peters pursed his lips at the use of his first name but didn't address it. "We don't have time for whatever this is between us, son. We need to protect the family, do you understand?"

Another pause. "Go on," Timothy said. "I wouldn't let my emotions get in the way of doing what's right."

Tears burned Zara's eyes. "Someone needs to check on my family," she said loudly enough for Timothy to hear, not caring that she was interrupting. "No one is picking up their phone."

Timothy had always been kind, and Zara felt the beginnings of relief when he started to speak. "Sure, Zara," he said. "I can—"

"No!" Mr. Peters practically roared. He slapped his palm on the mini bar, his voice filling the limo with frustrated anger. "Timothy, you will not leave the house, do you hear me?"

"What? Walter, the incident is nowhere near us, and it's not that close to Zara's house, either."

Zara nodded furiously. "Thank you, Timothy. I—"

"Timothy," Mr. Peters cut her off, and his tone was dead serious. He stared daggers at her as he spoke. "You are going to lock down the house and shut and lock all the windows. Then, you're going to get your mother, your brother, and your wife, and you're going to go to the basement safe room, and you're going to stay there until at least 10 a.m."

"Walt," Dana broke in, "surely we can check on the Williams family."

"Dad," Lizzy said, "if they're not answering their phones, we need to make sure they know Zara is okay."

"We need to make sure *they* are okay," Zara said, pleading.

"Dana, Timothy, I'm begging you to listen to me," Mr. Peters said. "Lock up the house. Go to the safe room. We don't know how dangerous it is out there. If this is a terrorist attack in two places a thousand miles apart, we have no idea what could be coming."

Zara held her breath during another pause, and her heart sank as Timothy spoke again.

"Fine, Walter. You win." Timothy sounded resigned. "Zara, I'm sorry. We will check on your family tomorrow. I promise."

"No, Timothy, please—" Zara was cut off by Mr. Peters as he tersely said goodbye, hung up the phone, and handed it back to Lizzy.

"Let's get to the airport," he said.

"You cold hearted bastard," Zara said. "What about my family?"

"You said you wanted to keep an eye out for your brother, didn't you?" Mr. Walters reached for a mini bottle of spiced rum and twisted off the cap. "If you go west, we'll just pop right out onto the highway. I tell you what," he said. "Why don't you go east? Take the long outer road around the fairgrounds. Maybe you'll find Jordan." He took a drink. "Or," he said, "you can get out of my limo. I'll knock Lizzy out myself to keep her from following you, and you'll die here without ever finding out about your family."

Lizzy's eyes went wide, and her jaw dropped as she stared at her father. "You don't mean that," she said.

Zara believed every word. As she carefully twisted around in her seat and settled facing the windshield, angry tears streamed down her cheeks. She pushed the limo's ignition button, and the engine roared to life. He'd thrown her a bone like she was a stray dog, and though she'd never in her life felt such disdain for another human being, she shut her mouth and took it.

Chapter 8

Alexander Roman

Alex studied his son, searching for any signs that he might be ill. Oliver still hadn't said a word, not since he'd promised to stay put, not since his mother plunged to her death. Oliver's body caved in on itself like a withering flower as he, still clutching the macrame purse, rested on Alex's lap. Careful to keep his touch gentle and calm, Alex surveyed Oliver's skin for welts among the bruises and scrapes. He couldn't find anything abnormal, but he also couldn't stop checking and re-checking every few minutes.

The cold, hard metallic floor was strangely reassuring. It was solid and dry, if a bit sticky, and it was a bridge of sorts to somewhere safer. Or at least that's what Alex had hoped. Once Minnie reached the onramp to the highway, Alex had expected less destruction and more traffic. He'd gotten the traffic portion right.

The food truck crept forward on the highway in a long line of traffic snaking through pileups and parked vehicles. The motel was normally a thirty-minute drive from the fairgrounds, but it had taken them thirty minutes just to inch forward the last mile.

"Y'all alright back there?" Minnie asked as the food truck lurched forward only to stop again.

"We're fine, thank you," Alex said. Oliver, who had fallen asleep, didn't so much as stir at the sound of his voice. He'd always been a heavy sleeper, and Alex was grateful his son was managing to get some rest.

"Fine, fine? As in, no-bug-eyes fine?" Minnie looked over her shoulder. Lights from vehicles around them shone into the cab, and Alex could see her squinting skeptically.

"No bug eyes back here," Alex said. "I swear. I would never knowingly spread a disease."

"Well, 'course everybody's gonna say that," Minnie said.

"I work for the Center for Disease Control. It's literally my job to hinder the spread of disease. Does that make you feel any better?" Alex asked as he leaned his head against the back of the truck and shifted Oliver's weight to prevent his foot from falling asleep.

"Well, I'll be," she said. "I 'spose that does make me feel better." Minnie turned her attention back to the road and inched forward again. "You say the motel is just off Exit 9?"

"Yes, ma'am," Alex said.

"Young man, it's Minnie, and I mean it. Min-nie," she said, enunciating the syllables in her name.

"Sorry, Minnie."

"Whatcha gonna do when you get to the motel?" Minnie asked.

Alex sighed. "I don't know, exactly. First thing's first, though. I'm going to sleep. Our motel isn't fancy, but there's a bed."

"Don't underestimate the power of simple things, I like to say." Minnie switched lanes abruptly, jostling Alex and Oliver.

Alex grunted as he struggled to ensure Oliver didn't fall out of his lap, and he winced at the effort. He was pretty sure he had at least one cracked rib, and he'd torn a muscle in his arm, probably when he'd slipped on the ladder of the Wind Breaker. He was covered in lacerations, bruises, and aches and pains from head to toe. When the adrenaline had begun to fade, many of the injuries had become much more apparent. Part of him wondered if he would be able to manage moving again now that he'd sat down and let his body rest.

"Sorry about that," Minnie said as she switched lanes again. "Just fixin' to get off the highway."

"We're fine," Alex repeated, pushing through the throbbing pain building in his chest. "Thank you for doing this."

"I guess I'm just a marshmallow at h—Dagnabbit!" She shouted and slammed on the breaks, making Alex slide forward an inch or two. She looked over her shoulder. "Sorry 'bout that. These city drivers..." She shrugged.

"My wife hates traffic," Alex said, smiling. "This morning she—" He stopped, and the rest of the words wouldn't come. He looked down at Oliver, and his heart ached. "She *hated* traffic," he amended.

"Oh, my... you poor thing." Minnie's expression turned to one of pity before she turned back toward the road and moved the truck forward.

The rest of the agonizingly slow journey to the motel was driven in silence. When Minnie finally turned into the lot, she breathed a curse under her breath.

"What is it?" Alex asked.

"This place looks like a bear poked a hornet's nest." She put the truck in park. "You might wanna take a look before you make any decisions on where I drop y'all off."

Alex slid Oliver off his lap gently and placed a few spare hand towels under his head as a makeshift pillow. Using the counter to help him stand, Alex got to his feet and limped to the front of the truck to look out the front window. The U-shaped motel consisted of three stories of rooms facing a parking lot. To the left, a small diner and a front office were located on the bottom floor. It had been a well-reviewed, affordable option. When the Roman family had arrived two days ago, they'd found most of the hotel guests to be in town for the World's Fair. As Alex looked through the windshield of Minnie's food truck, he wished they'd chosen the country cabin another twenty minutes south.

But no... I wanted to save money. He shook his head. You were right, Naomi. The extra thirty dollars a night would have been worth it.

"Well," Alex said, "that's not good." At least six bodies lay on the ground. A woman darted across the lot, frantically hopped in her car, and sped away. Someone burst out of a second story room, their hands pressing against their eyes. They screamed in pain, twisting as they ran, as if they were trying to flee the pain. They hit the railing and catapulted themselves over it, landing on top of a car with sickening *crunch.*

Minnie looked up at Alex, eyes wide. "How are these poor souls afflicted with the same thing that killed all those people at the World's Fair? I thought… I mean, if it was a terrorist attack, wouldn't it just be there, at the fair, and that's it?"

"These people were probably at the fair recently," Alex said. "They must have left before all hell broke loose and died here instead."

"And the dead on the highway, in the parked cars and pileups?" Minnie asked. "They're from the fair, too?"

Alex nodded. "Makes sense. Hotels and motels booked up for miles for the World's Fair. We booked this motel two months ago, and it was the closest affordable option. So, my guess is that there was an attack of some sort, maybe powder that dusted the area or… I don't know… something that wouldn't affect everyone, at least not everyone all at once. Anyone at the fair could have been exposed, and then when people started getting sick, that's when the domino effect happened. The pilot, the Ferris Wheel, the panic…"

"But why wouldn't that guy have died hours ago?" Minnie pointed toward where the man had fallen over the balcony.

Alex shrugged. "Whatever it is, it could affect some faster than others. But it is fast-acting, so I'd assume we'll stop seeing an onset of symptoms by morning. Or…" Alex trailed off, not wanting to go down the road his mind was heading.

"Or what?" Minnie asked.

Alex swallowed hard, wishing he'd kept his mouth shut. "Or, it's contagious. If it's a disease, and it's contagious… well, I'm not sure I want to think about that."

Minnie shuddered. "Alright, so what's your plan? You ain't takin' that precious baby in there, are ya?"

Alex looked over his shoulder to where Oliver slept. "I don't know where else to go, and I've got my CDC go-bag in there." He was lucky he'd brought it for props during the question-and-answer panel; the supplies inside would give him an advantage.

"Well…" Minnie looked at Oliver, too, then she squared her shoulders and set her jaw and looked straight at Alex. "You can come with me. I've got a spare room, and I live an hour south. It'll be safe there."

"Minnie, you brought us this far. I can't ask you to do anything more," Alex said. "Our motel room should be safe enough if I lock the door and keep us inside. I'll call my boss, and he'll give me further instructions."

Minnie narrowed her eyes. "Young man, you're bringin' that angel out to my house where it's safe, and I don't want to hear another word about it. I'm not goin' to my grave knowin' I left you at this hell hole. Now, use the sense God gave ya, nod your head, and say 'Yes, ma'am.'"

Alex blinked and smiled, shaking his head. "I thought you didn't want me to call you 'ma'am.'"

Minnie smirked. "When I sound like my momma, I 'spose I don't mind it. But only when I say so, got it?"

"Yes, ma'am," Alex said. "And thank you, Minnie." He glanced back at the motel. "I do need to get my bag, though. It's got a satellite phone in it and a few supplies that could be useful if this thing gets worse."

"Well, get on with it, then," Minnie said, waving him off. "I'll look after your boy."

"Oliver." Alex said.

Minnie grinned. "That's a right good name," she said.

"I don't know if I can leave him with you," Alex said. He meant no offense, but he had only met the woman a few hours ago.

"I understand," she said. "How 'bout this." She turned off the truck and handed him the keys. "You take my keys. I'm puttin' my life in your hands. You don't come back with those keys, I'm in trouble."

Alex took the keys and rolled them over in his hands. "Who's Lauren?" he asked, running his thumb over a name on a keychain.

"My baby girl," Minnie said. "She's grown now, but… they're always your baby, no matter how old they get."

"Yeah, I guess they are." Alex nodded and pocketed the keys. Knowing that Minnie was a parent somehow helped make the decision easier. Alex grabbed a hand towel to cover his mouth and nose; it wouldn't filter out all the contaminants, but it was better than nothing. He pulled out his wallet and slipped out the plastic card that opened their motel room door. "Okay, I'll go as fast as I can. I'll be right back."

Alex opened the door to the food truck and stepped off into the parking lot. He took a deep breath, slowly so as to not cause too much pain, and he closed the door behind him and faced the motel. Their room was on the second floor, in the middle of two staircases. He moved forward awkwardly, his muscles stiff. He couldn't even favor one side of his body over the other; everything hurt. But he needed that go-bag. His boss would know more about what was happening than the news would let on, and the CDC might be able to help him when it came to retrieving Naomi's body. He couldn't imagine going home to Atlanta without her, even if it meant going home with her ashes.

So, Alex hobbled forward, steering clear of the bodies. He got to the nearest stairway and eyed the stairs with disdain. Every step was a challenge, and he clung to the handrail as his body screamed at him to stop. He finally reached the top of the stairs only to find a woman propped up against the railing, blood seeping from her nose, her mouth, and her ears. Her breathing was labored, and she had a welt on her thigh below the hem of her shorts. She looked up at him, pleading in her eyes, but she didn't speak. Her eyes only bulged slightly, something Alex noted. Most of the dead he'd seen who'd obviously been infected had eyes practically falling out of their heads. He stayed at a safe distance but couldn't just ignore her. "You were at the fair?" Alex asked.

She nodded slowly.

"Are you alone?"

She shook her head and pointed across the walkway to an open motel room door. Alex peeked inside but turned away quickly. A teenage girl lay on the bed, dead, exhibiting the same symptoms he'd seen all night.

Alex turned back to the woman. "Did you eat anything strange?"

She shook her head again and grunted, pointing back into the room. Then, she coughed, and blood spurted out of her mouth. "Alyssa," she said, the syllables stretched and strained between gurgling noises. "Help… her." Her chest heaved, and she arched her back. She convulsed, and tears marked fresh paths down her bloodied cheeks.

"I'll help her," Alex said, unable to tell the woman that the girl, who was likely her daughter, was already dead. He wanted to reach out and touch her hand, give her comfort, but he couldn't risk it. Instead, he told her what he thought she needed to hear. "It's okay. Alyssa is not alone."

Alex stayed a moment more while the woman's convulsions continued, while she tried to thank him with her dying breaths. Once she was gone, he moved on. It felt wrong to leave her there, but everything about what had happened was wrong. He got to their room, slid the card in the slot, and opened the door. He shut it again behind him, not keen on the idea of someone sick coming inside while he gathered whatever he could carry.

He first went to the closet and grabbed his CDC go-bag from where he'd stashed it on the upper shelf. Then, he went to their luggage and chose the backpack Oliver had brought his toys in. He dumped it out on the bed. There was a tablet Oliver used mostly for games, a few notebooks, coloring pencils, and some flash cards Naomi had insisted on bringing so he could brush up on multiplication facts. Alex sifted through all of that for Mr. Brownie, the small bear Oliver had had since he was an infant. He stuck that back in the backpack and moved on to pack a couple changes of clothes for both him and Oliver. A few toiletries were added to the bag, and then Alex saw Naomi's daily journal. He packed that, too, and then carefully threaded his arms through the straps of the backpack. The go-bag had a long strap he put over his head and wore across his chest, the bag hanging at his hip. For a moment, he contemplated taking some more of Naomi's things, but there was nothing left there that truly meant something. He looked down at his wedding ring, banished the tears that threatened to surface, and headed back toward the food truck.

When he finally got to the food truck, Minnie unlocked the door and put her hands on her hips. "Took your sweet time, did ya?" she asked.

"Sorry," Alex said as he climbed back into the truck and set his bags on the floor. He glanced at where Oliver still slept soundly. "Everything okay here?"

"Of course it is." Minnie held out her hand. "Let's get out of here, though."

Alex dug out the keys and handed them to her. "I'm going to call my boss at the CDC, see if he knows anything."

Minnie nodded. "I'm gonna take the back way out, avoid the big highways and whatnot. Might take a mite longer, but I think we've got less chance of gettin' stuck."

"If you say so," Alex said. "You know this area better than I do, so whatever you think is best." He dragged his go-bag to the back of the truck and eased himself onto the floor, grimacing as he went. He leaned against a steel cabinet, Oliver laying by his outstretched legs, and dug out his work phone. If things got worse, he'd need the satellite phone to communicate with Atlanta, but he hoped the phone lines were still functioning. He was relieved when his call went through and his boss, Dr. Jonah Newton, answered.

"Alex, is that you?" Jonah answered the phone with urgency in his voice, and a little bit of shock.

"Yes, it's me." Alex let his chin fall to his chest, and he closed his eyes. "And yes, I was at the World's Fair. Naomi…" Alex swallowed hard. "Naomi didn't make it."

"I'm sorry to hear that," Jonah said. "And your son?"

"He's okay, at least physically." Alex reached out and softly brushed the hair from Oliver's face. "Jonah, I need a favor. Naomi's body… I don't want to leave for Atlanta until she's found, until I can bring her home and give her a proper burial."

"Alex, I'm not sure we can help you with that right now," Jonah said. "We might need you on the job."

"What? Didn't you hear me? I just lost my wife. I'm in no condition to work right now."

Jonah didn't answer right away. After a pause, he said, "Alex, do you know what's going on?"

"Yeah, there was some kind of terrorist attack, or maybe some environmental anomaly. Has anyone taken credit?" Alex asked.

"It's more than that, and if it is a terrorist attack, it went really wrong. Whatever happened in St. Louis didn't just happen in St. Louis," Jonah said.

"You mean other cities were hit?" Alex asked.

"Yes, Alex."

The next words that came out of Jonah's mouth chilled Alex to the bone.

"This is bigger than you, and it's bigger than me. Whatever this is, we're getting reports of similar incidents worldwide. I don't think this thing is anywhere close to being over, Alex. This is just the beginning."

Chapter 9

Zara Williams

The World's Fair was supposed to symbolize a bright future, so it seemed fitting that as the world fell apart, the fair lay in ashes and destruction. If the sickness that hit the World's Fair hit Boston, Zara could only imagine the chaos unfolding in her hometown. And if it was in Boston, where else had the illness reared its ugly head?

The long, eastbound outer road of the fairgrounds kept them distanced from the fair itself. A few wanderers staggered across their path, trying to wave them down, but Mr. Peters wouldn't let Zara stop for any of them. Once it was clear that the person was *not* Jordan, she had little choice but to comply and keep driving. When they came upon the gate to a back road that led away from the fair, Zara's heart sank. She slowed the vehicle to a stop and gripped the steering wheel, knuckles turning white.

"Keep moving," Mr. Peters said.

"Dad, maybe we should drive through one more time?" Lizzy asked.

Her best friend couldn't see Zara's sad smile as she took one last look out of the windows, hoping against all reason that she'd spot Jordan in the dark.

"Our priority needs to be getting to safety," Mr. Peters said. "If the authorities come while we are still here, there will be no getting out."

"Dramatic much?" Lizzy asked. "They can't keep us against our will."

Mr. Peters scoffed. "They wouldn't hesitate. Not after they see what's happened here. They'll want us quarantined, and they'll want to control the information. That means no phones, no hearing about family back in Boston. At least not for a while."

"How do you know that?" Lizzy asked.

"Because the authorities aren't stupid, and because I've seen government contingency plans for a fast-acting contagion. Once they put the puzzle pieces together, that is," Mr. Peters said. "Not to mention that the longer we're here, the more probable it is that we get sick and die."

Zara watched Mr. Peters in the rearview mirror. "You seem to know a lot about this, Mr. Peters. Like, you know a weird amount of information."

Mr. Peters shifted his weight. "I have connections you wouldn't understand, Ms. Williams. Vanguard is in the play pen with governments, and sometimes our projects require us to have a 'weird amount' of knowledge about things."

"If they want us quarantined, shouldn't we stay and let them quarantine us?" Lizzy asked.

"Liz is right," Zara said. "Isn't that the right thing to do?"

Mr. Peters pressed his lips together, and his jaw worked back and forth just slightly as if he were grinding his teeth. Lizzy looked from her father to the rearview mirror, where Zara could see her, and she could see Zara. Circles had formed under Lizzy's eyes. She sagged in her seat, and her chin quivered.

"Ms. Williams." Mr. Peters nearly spat her name. "My weird amount of knowledge means I know things you don't. I'm an adult. You're practically a child. I'm the CEO of a world-renowned company, and you're a seventeen-year-old girl from Mattapan, of all places. I graduated from Harvard. You haven't even graduated high school." His next words were accompanied by an icy tone. "Stay here if you want to do the so-called right thing. Get out, now, and go find your delinquent brother. I have been patient and generous with you because you're my daughter's friend, but I'm about to lose all patience."

Zara blinked at his assertion that he'd been patient and generous, but she swallowed her retort. He was right. She was nobody, and she hadn't lived long enough to change that yet. And his certainty that anyone who stayed behind would die... it unsettled Zara. She pulled out her phone and dialed Jordan one more time.

As voicemail picked up, Mr. Peters said, "Well? Are we going with you or without you?"

"Dad," Lizzy's voice cracked, and tears welled in her eyes. "We can't leave her. We *can't*."

"It's okay, Liz," Zara said as she ended the call and glowered at Mr. Peters through the rearview mirror.

Does he always get what he wants? Part of her wanted to buck against him just for the sake of messing with his sense of normality. But another part of her wanted to be safe. And her parents' faces kept popping up in her head. If Jordan was already dead, if she stayed and died, too... what would that do to them?

Zara stepped on the gas, easing out of the back entrance to the fairgrounds. She wanted to scream at the smug look on Mr. Peters's face the second she gave in, but she held her tongue as they drove past the barrier gate arm that had been smashed through by someone else. She took a deep breath as the road transitioned from gravel to smooth pavement, but when she turned right, her headlights revealed a blocked road. A four-door truck and trailer were turned over, the trailer tipped against a smaller car. A body lay in front of the wreckage, but whoever it was looked dead already.

"This is the way to the highway," Zara said. "Now what?"

"Turn around. We can get to the highway another way." Mr. Peters directed her to what seemed to be just a country road stretching into cornfields, but according to him, it would take them in the right direction. There were a few cars in the ditches on either side, but it was clear otherwise. It took them ten minutes to reach an overpass, and when they did, Zara gasped.

"Um, Mr. Peters... are you sure we should get on the highway?" she asked as she slowed to a stop.

Mr. Peters and Lizzy both looked out of their windows, but Zara had the best view. She could only see the top half of the vehicles above, some parked, others slowly moving forward. One car was on fire in the center of the overpass. Horns blared, echoing through the night.

"We need to get to the airport," Mr. Peters said.

"Maybe we should just drive out of the city and get a plane somewhere else," Zara said.

"Yeah, Dad. This whole area is a disaster." Lizzy stared out of her window as she spoke, never taking her eyes off the overpass.

"I can't believe I'm arguing with teenagers right now." Mr. Peters pinched the bridge of his nose. "If I say the airport is where we need to go, the airport is where we need to go." He raised his voice, his hand dropping, his face scrunching up with anger. "This area *is* a disaster. Soon the entire *city* will be a disaster. We'll need to get out of here tomorrow before they start grounding flights. I give it forty-eight hours max before that happens all across the damn country."

He was roaring, and Lizzy stared at him horrified as she cowered in her seat. Zara put the limo in park and crossed her arms as Mr. Peters railed on. She'd never heard him shout before that night; he'd always seemed so put together, even when he was angry. She'd seen his face contort, seen him set his jaw, grind his teeth, and speak with a dead serious tone, but this… this was too much.

"I'm *not* getting stuck in fly-over country while the world goes to hell in a hand basket, do you girls understand me? We need to get back to Boston, and we need to get back to Boston now. I can still—" He cut himself off, clamping his mouth shut and running his fingers through his hair. He closed his eyes and breathed slowly in and out. Then, he rolled his shoulders, opened his eyes, and a calmer Mr. Peters emerged. "I can still do something about this, if I can get back to my team, if we can study this illness. I can help."

Zara raised an eyebrow. "I've never heard you say anything about helping anyone. Ever."

"I'm not a monster," Mr. Peters said, but when his eyes met Zara's glare in the rearview mirror, he added, "I also didn't say I'd help for free."

Zara shook her head and bit the inside of her cheek. That sounds about right. Using a national tragedy as a way to fatten his pocketbook.

"Is that why you made me leave Jordan?" It was Zara's turn to shout. "So you can get back to Boston, create some antidote or vaccine or whatever, and make bank?"

"I didn't make you do anything. I gave you a choice, sweetheart." Mr. Peters sneered, and his words pierced Zara's heart. "But, no. That's not the only reason I wanted to get out of there, why I want to get back to Boston. Everything I said about this thing being deadly, about getting stuck here if we don't get out by tomorrow… it's all true."

Lizzy was still staring wide-eyed at her father, seemingly unable to speak. Tears ran down her cheeks, though she made no sound. Zara didn't know what to think; she wasn't sure her brain was capable of processing everything that had happened, everything Mr. Peters had said. So, she relented, again.

"Fine." Zara stopped fighting; she just couldn't do it anymore. "What do I do, now, though?" She peered into the dark. "I'm not even sure there's an on-ramp here, but that road turns toward the city. Should I follow the highway that way until it looks like we can get on?"

Mr. Peters cocked his head. "Well, look who has a brain." He waved dismissively. "Follow the road, as you said, but turn on the GPS. It might have an alternate route that doesn't require much highway at all." He glanced at his daughter. "And stop looking at me like that, Elizabeth." He leaned against the head rest and closed his eyes.

Lizzy looked away, brought her knees to her chest, and buried her head in her arms. Zara was too tired to offer any comfort, so she pushed the button to turn on the GPS screen, punched in the airport, and studied the routes. Mr. Peters was right; there was a way that only required a couple miles on a major highway. She drove in the dark down country roads until she was driving through neighborhoods, following the highway's trajectory.

When Mr. Peters called the pilot, Zara didn't so much as glance in the rearview mirror, but she listened.

"I want to see you at the airport, Mr. Ludlow, but don't leave the hotel until 10 a.m., and do *not* go anywhere between now and then." Mr. Peters spoke with cold, deliberate words that left no room for interpretation. He was giving orders, not suggestions. "Don't talk to anyone whose been at the World's Fair." Mr. Peters paused. "No, it's worse than whatever they've said on the news. I'm telling you now, if I find out that you didn't follow my instructions to the letter, I'll never use your services again. I don't care how long you've been with the family." He hung up abruptly, and only then did Zara try to get a glimpse of him.

For just one second, his macho certainty dissolved as he ran his hands over his face. He allowed himself to grimace in pain as he checked on his leg, and Zara realized he must have been as exhausted and as sore as she was. He just knew how to hide it. And to be honest, Zara wished she could conceal her own emotions and pains half as well as he did.

After a while, Lizzy's soft snoring drew Zara's attention. She sighed and tried not to think about how badly she wanted to drift off. When the time came to get off the side roads, the stretch of highway looked mostly normal besides a few more cars than usual pulled onto the shoulder. She carefully merged into traffic and looked back at Mr. Peters.

"Almost there," she said.

"I prefer the silence," Mr. Peters said.

"Well, I'm about to fall asleep, so if we could talk about something, that would be great," Zara said. "Preferably something that doesn't make me want to punch you in the face."

Mr. Peters chuckled. "Well, if you did, it wouldn't be the first time I'd been punched." He sighed. "You know, we do have something in common."

Zara laughed. "Yeah, right. We both breathe?"

"We both care about Elizabeth."

Zara looked in the rearview as Mr. Peters glanced at Lizzy, who was fast asleep. "Yeah," she said. "She's pretty great, despite you, I might add."

He shrugged. "I wouldn't argue with you on that point. She's more like her mother than she is like me, and I'm glad. Maybe that means she can find some kind of happiness." He glanced out the window. "It's frightening how normal everything looks here."

Zara frowned. "Isn't that a good thing?"

"It's just… they don't know what's coming." Mr. Peters's voice was haunting and quiet.

"And you're so sure? Maybe everything will be okay. I mean, maybe it's not contagious, or maybe they'll get it under control." Zara shrugged and pulled off the exit.

Another twenty minutes, and she was driving around the huge, public airport around to the back where the smaller, private airport was located. She parked and breathed a sigh of relief.

"We're here," she said as she unbuckled her seatbelt, wincing as she stretched. Her left side was stiff, and as she moved, some of the lacerations stung as the little wounds broke open again. "I bet they've got some first aid stuff in there." She nodded toward the small, private lounge and reached for the door handle.

"Wait!" Mr. Peters shouted, but it was a frightened shout. "We need to stay inside the limo tonight, and for once, don't argue. Important people were at the fair, people who would come here to fly out. If even one person goes in for the night, if it is contagious like I think it is, it could be dangerous to stay the whole night in the lounge."

"Okay," Zara said.

"Okay? That's it?" Mr. Peters asked.

"Yeah. But can I at least come back there and sleep on the empty seat?" Zara's seat wouldn't lean back at all.

"Can you crawl through to the back? I'm… concerned about going outside right now."

"Weird knowledge?" Zara asked.

"Yes, Ms. Williams. Weird knowledge." Mr. Peters smiled and shook his head.

Zara turned around, slowly, and carefully climbed through the open partition. "You're lucky I'm too tired to argue with you right now." The empty seat was directly behind, and she was able to just plop into it onto her right side. She groaned at the movement and the pain that accompanied it.

"You know I'd just lock you out if you'd tried to come in another way," Mr. Peters said as he brought the key fob out of his pocket and hit the lock button.

"Yeah, I know," Zara said.

He crossed his arms and closed his eyes. "Once you understand me, Ms. Williams, things will go a lot smoother."

"You mean once I fall in line?"

He nodded. "Precisely."

Zara pursed her lips. *Good luck with that,* she thought as she gave her body permission to shut down and rest. It only took seconds for sleep to claim her. And it seemed only a blink of the eye before she woke to a new day as something crashed into the side of the limousine.

Chapter 10

Timothy Peters

The first time Timothy had heard his father's voice in over two years was the first time he had ever heard his father speak with an undercurrent of pure panic. Walter Peters *never* lost his cool. Someone who didn't know him might not have detected the panic; they might have thought of it as anger or frustration, but Timothy knew the sound of his father's anger. What he heard the night before was something different. If it hadn't been for that panic, Timothy might have gone ahead and checked on the Williams family. Part of him regretted giving in on that point, but…

He wouldn't have sounded like that, wouldn't have had such specific instructions, if it wasn't important we stay here.

Timothy justified his actions for the hundredth time as he lay on the pull-out couch next to Heather in the safe room.

Safe room… ha! More like a whole bunker. An apartment, even.

The accommodations were enclosed with four-foot, reinforced concrete walls and lay a level deeper than the actual basement, buried far beneath the back yard. There were two sets of doors. A thick, steel door opened into the basement, and beside it was an intercom system. A set of concrete stairs led to the second door, this one twice as thick. The project had become important to Walter after his company, Vanguard, expanded and began landing government contracts. Some secretive construction company had come to the house under the guise of remodeling their basement, and Timothy had had plenty of opportunity to roll his eyes at his father's name dropping when comparing his safe room to that of certain high-profile CEO's and politicians. Timothy had always assumed it was an in-vogue paranoia his father had grabbed hold of because it made him feel elite and untouchable.

Or maybe he knew something like this could happen, even back then.

He almost laughed out loud at that thought. When Vanguard was still a small, visionary company, Timothy had actually been proud of his father. He'd thought Walter Peters would change the world for the better. Vanguard's first step to becoming a worldwide research and development company had been acquiring New Horizons Labs. New strains of malaria, dengue, and the Zika virus had just started causing problems on an international level, even in first-world countries, and New Horizons had been tasked with doing something about it. But Timothy's pride slowly turned to utter revulsion over the following years. As the world lauded Vanguard's humanitarian research, Timothy's father used that as a distraction to conceal the increasing number of projects involving weapons development. Suddenly, Timothy found himself not the son of an altruistic innovator but rather the son of a greedy opportunist responsible for the development of more precise and efficient options for warfare.

Of course, his father played it off as patriotism, keeping the United States up-to-date and ahead of the curve. The last decade had seen increasing tensions with portions of Asia and the Middle East where much of the world's power had accumulated over the last decade; experts warned those tensions could lead to a third world war. And Walter Peters was always ready with his favorite maxim, "If we didn't develop it, some other company would have."

Timothy sighed and rolled over to reach for the side table where his cell phone was charging. He pressed a button to reveal the time. It was already seven in the morning, though staying up so late the night before and the absolute darkness of the underground bunker made it seem a lot earlier. Heather still slept soundly, and Timothy had heard no sounds of stirring from the adjacent rooms where his mother and little brother rested.

But he couldn't sleep anymore. He silently crept out of bed, slipped his phone into his pocket, opened the side table drawer, and took out a flashlight. The beam of light pierced the darkness, revealing a slice of the kitchen area. Everything was all sharp lines, shiny steel, and polished wood from the counters and cabinets to the faucet and sink to the table and chairs. A small hallway separated the kitchen from two doors on the left — the bedrooms — and ended at another door that led into the storage area.

Timothy grabbed the small radio on the kitchen counter as he walked into the room beyond the kitchen. Rows of shelves housing canned goods, MREs, toiletries, and other supplies greeted him, and he found a step stool against a wall he could sit on. He switched on the radio.

"It's not good folks," the man on the other side said. "Boston's a mess. Don't go out, and don't go anywhere near the zoo where we saw the outbreak begin. While many of the roads in the city are blocked, the highways are still mostly clear, so get out while you can, if you can. Reports say that the insanity is currently contained to Boston proper, but I say in the next couple days we're gonna see it creep into the metropolitan area and beyond."

Great… Mattapan is less than ten minutes from the zoo. Timothy leaned his head back against the wall. He'd promised Zara, and the Williams had been good to the Peters children over the years. When they'd discovered that Timothy had left home on bad terms and Lizzy had no way of really seeing him, they'd invited him over for dinner when Lizzy had been staying the night. Timothy had connected more with Zara's parents in one night than he'd ever connected with his father. It had become a regular way for Timothy, and later Timothy and Heather, to spend time with Lizzy without dealing with any drama at the Peters home in Wellesley.

He changed the radio station again and again, hoping to discover some good news, but it didn't seem there was much good news to be had. So, he switched off the radio and grabbed some dried fruit, munching on it while thinking about the best way to get to Zara's house.

The way through Milton into the city should be mostly clear if the highways are okay. I could park in one of those commuter lots, walk the last mile or two to Zara's house.

"Tim?" Heather's voice sounded as the door to the storage room opened and light flooded in. "Your mom and George are up. What are you doing in here?"

"Thinking about how to get to the Williams house," Timothy said as he stood up, zipped the bag of dried fruit closed, and walked toward the door. When he came around the aisle of packed shelves, Heather was waiting by the door.

She stood on tiptoes, wrapped her arms around Timothy, and kissed his cheek. "How long do you think we're going to be staying here?" she asked.

"I can't imagine we'll need to stay in this bunker for much longer," Timothy said.

"No, I mean here, as in Wellesley with your mother," Heather said.

"Well, the radio made the city sound like a nightmare." Timothy brushed a strand of hair from Heather's face. "There's enough food here," he said nodding to the storage room. "I might ask if Zara's parents want to come here and ride this out."

"Ride it out?" Heather frowned. "You think we'll be here a few days?"

Timothy shrugged. "Maybe a few weeks."

She groaned. "Tim, I love you, and I love your mom, but… a few weeks? Here? What about when your dad comes back?"

"When my dad comes back, we can see if we can stay with your Aunt Jill. With the looting and sickness the radio was talking about, we should give it time before going back to the apartment." Timothy's stomach knotted at the thought of seeing his father, but he wouldn't leave his mom and brother on their own.

"You sure you want to invite the Williams out?" Heather asked. "I mean, it's a nice thought, but these supplies aren't ours. And your dad isn't a fan of the Williams… or of sharing, actually."

Timothy chuckled. "All the more reason," he said. "But we'll get them out of here before my dad comes back. I wouldn't want to subject them to a Walter Peters stare down."

Heather let her arms fall from Timothy's shoulders. "Are you sure it's safe to go into Boston at all? I mean, I love the Williams, too, but if it's dangerous…" She trailed off, not finishing the thought.

"Babe, they're like family, and we're better than that, okay? If we can't reach them by phone, I need to at least stop by and make sure everybody is hunkered down and safe." Timothy reached out and squeezed Heather's hand. "I'll be careful. I promise."

"No stopping and helping random people," Heather said. "And you should wear some of that protective gear." She pointed behind Timothy.

He turned around to see boxes of N95 masks, disposable gloves, and some first aid supplies. He hadn't noticed them when he'd entered the room with just a flashlight. He walked over and picked up a box of masks. "I guess it couldn't hurt," he said. Then he looked to the right and raised his eyebrows. "What do we have here?"

Heather followed him down that last aisle as they approached a set of shelves without the typical supplies. There were no boxes or food or clothes. Instead, the last shelves had plexiglass doors protecting guns, tasers, ammo, and a variety of knives.

"What is all this? I can't believe your father would leave this stuff in full view where George could stumble across it." Heather's face flushed red. She pulled on the handle and breathed out a long slow breath when her tug didn't open it. "At least it's locked."

Timothy shrugged. "I mean, it's kinda cool. I might take one with me, you know… just in case. It's been a while since I've been to the range, but my license is still good."

She smacked his arm. "Kind of cool? Are you crazy? No one needs this many guns."

"Heather, *we* have a gun." Timothy started looking around for the key to the cabinet.

"We have *a* gun. Not twelve, and not guns like *that*." She pointed to one of three semi-automatic rifles hanging at the back of the top shelf. "Is that even legal?"

"So, I won't take one of those," Timothy said. "But the radio talked about gunshots being reported across the city."

"How about a taser for Plan A and a handgun for Plan B, emergencies only," Heather said.

"Sounds good to me, if I can find the keys to the cabinet."

"Were you kids going to ask me about this?" Dana's voice made both Timothy and Heather jump.

"I didn't hear you come in," Timothy said.

"Did you know Walter had all these weapons down here?" Heather asked.

Dana smiled and walked down the aisle, turning to stand in front of the cabinet. "That one," she pointed to a row of handguns with ornate handles and zeroed in on a small, pink revolver, "is my favorite. I have two. One I keep in my purse, which has a holster built into it, and one I keep here."

"Mom!" Timothy blinked several times. "I didn't know you carried."

"Your father taught me to shoot on our very first date." Dana sighed and the nostalgia in her eyes faded. "But that's neither here nor there." She put her hand on the handle of the door to the cabinet and pressed her thumb into a little square. "There you go," she said as she opened it. "Only your father and I have access via the fingerprint scanner." She stepped back and patted Timothy's shoulder. "And I like Heather's idea, Timmy. These tasers pack a punch."

"Thanks, Dana," Heather said, a little surprise in her voice.

"Yeah, thanks, Mom." Timothy kissed his mom on the forehead and turned back to the cabinet.

"Do you need help with breakfast?" Heather asked. "I make a mean omelet."

Dana laughed. "Oh, Heather, you're so funny." She patted Heather's shoulder and walked away. "Don't forget to shut the cabinet when you're done," she called over her shoulder as she left the storage room.

Timothy grimaced at Heather's flat expression. "She said she liked your taser idea," he said.

Heather crossed her arms. "I *do* make good omelets." When Timothy didn't say anything, she kicked his shin. "Right?" she said forcefully.

Timothy cleared his throat. "Right," he said, pushing away the image of chewy, hard cheese from the last time Heather had made him breakfast. "Really good omelets."

She eyed him sideways before leaving him to finish up. He grabbed the appropriate holsters, weapons, and ammo, opting to leave the gun unloaded until he reached the city. He hoped he wouldn't have to use it at all. Shooting at people was a lot different than shooting at targets. Timothy closed the cabinet door until it clicked, tugging on it to ensure it was locked again.

On the opposite side of the aisle lay a stack of flat backpacks, and he grabbed one of the smaller ones, filling it with a few bottled waters, granola bars, and an MRE. *Better safe than sorry,* he thought. He planned to be back to the Peters home in Wellesley by late afternoon, but he would need to eat, and it was unlikely he'd be able to get a cheeseburger through the drive-thru.

He left the storage room, turned off the lights to the bunker, and joined his family back upstairs. His father had said not to go outside until ten or so, but he hadn't said they needed to stay in the bunker all day. As he took his seat next to Heather on an island bar stool, everything seemed normal besides the undercurrent of worry they all felt about Lizzy and his dad. They ate breakfast, laughed at George's antics, and Timothy played referee every once in a while between his mother and his wife. George even flipped on the television to watch his favorite cartoon when breakfast was done.

"Shouldn't we put the news on?" Heather asked.

"No sense in watching the news 24/7," Dana said. "We can let him have an hour of just being a kid."

Heather looked dubious, but Timothy hugged her tight. "Mom's right, babe. Just try to relax today, okay? Before you know it, things will be back under control, and we'll all be back to complaining about Monday mornings at the office."

"I'm sure you're right," Heather said, "but I can't shake this feeling like things are going to get worse."

"Maybe it will," Timothy said. "But then they'll get better, like they always do. The authorities will do their jobs, the government will roll out a solution, and people will settle."

Heather nodded, but she didn't look convinced as she joined George on the couch. Timothy tried calling the Williams again, but he got no answer. The call went straight to voicemail. Still, the birds were chirping, the sun was shining, and Timothy felt a little silly as he strapped on the ankle gun holster he'd picked out and clipped the taser holster to his belt. It had gotten bad in the city, sure, but these things straightened themselves out.

It'll be okay in a few days, maybe a few weeks.

As Timothy pulled out of the driveway and began driving down the well-manicured streets of his parent's gated community, the reports he'd heard on the radio seemed blown out of proportion. It was true that he was thirty minutes outside of Boston proper, but the way his father had talked, part of him had expected to see chaos even there. Instead, he waved to Mr. Johnson who was grabbing his mail.

"This sickness is spreading fast, people," the radio broadcaster had said. "And the craziness is spreading even faster."

Just like the media to make things seem worse than they are. Timothy scoffed and shook his head. Should have known.

The back way to Mattapan down Highway 135 was par-for-the-course until Timothy reached I-95 where signs of mass panic became more evident. He started to see cars in ditches, and where I-95 branched off and headed away from Boston, traffic was bumper to bumper. There were less cars than usual headed in the same direction as Timothy. When he turned north onto Washington Street on the final stretch toward Mattapan, southbound traffic was crawling by, drivers honking and shouting out their windows. Cars were full of suitcases and children and family pets.

When he drove by the new grocery store where Washington Street became Canton Avenue, a rock started to form in Timothy's stomach. The parking lot was full, and as he drove by, he could see a line out the front door. People were fighting each other trying to get in. An old woman charged out of the store with her grocery cart full of bags, and a teenager tried to shove her out of the way so he could take her cart. She wacked him across the face with her cane, and he flailed backwards, holding his eye. Another man, older and stocky, stepped between the woman and the would-be thief, seeming to give the youth a good talking to as the lady made her escape.

The commuter lot down the road wasn't much better. He pulled in but ended up driving straight through as he noted a car being broken into in broad daylight. He had to skirt around a car parked halfway on the road, halfway in the grass as he continued, and soon all semblance of normal traffic movement was abandoned. Vehicles traveling in the opposite direction wove into Timothy's lane several times as they averted abandoned accident scenes. It was becoming harder and harder to make progress toward Mattapan.

Ahead, Timothy noticed a church with a mostly empty lot. He pulled in and spotted a pathway in the trees at the back of the lot. He cringed as he squeezed his car between trees and parked in front of a small fountain with a statue of a woman kneeling in prayer. He maneuvered into a spot behind the trees so his car couldn't be seen easily from the lot. Timothy accidentally knocked over a few potted plants and his car wheels tore up the flower garden. The sign in front of the fountain read: In Memory of Mrs. Dorothy Redding.

"Sorry, Dorothy," Timothy said as he got out of his car and put on his backpack. "I'll make sure this is all fixed. I'll even come and replant the flowers myself. But the radio was right. Things look crazy out here, and I—" He cut himself off and cocked his head. "And I'm talking to a statue." Timothy shook his head, walked out of the little memorial into the parking lot, and headed north on foot.

He still had more than a mile to go before reaching Zara's home. A few blocks north, the street became impassible by vehicle; he was grateful he'd pulled off when he did and that his car was hidden from plain sight. The longer he walked, the more broken-out windows he saw in both cars and houses. Every so often, someone would dart across the street, slipping between crashed vehicles or sliding over the hoods when there was no other way through. A young woman ahead, a child's hand in each of her own, was making her way south when she saw Timothy coming. She hastily grabbed the smaller child and crossed the street through the obstacle course of vehicles. Timothy stopped and watched her flee from him, sad that an innocent woman would see him as a threat. That's when he noticed not all the cars in the street were empty.

His hand flew to his mouth at the sight of a man sitting in the driver's seat of a car at the center of a pileup, his head leaning back, eyes popping, mouth hanging open, blood everywhere — crusted, thick, and red on his face, on his clothes, on the steering wheel, and splattered on the windshield. Timothy couldn't help but stare. Seeing it made it real, made his heart thump hard in his chest and his mouth run dry. He pulled his backpack around to his front and fumbled to find the N95 mask he'd brought, berating himself for not putting it on the second he stepped out of the car. Just as his hand closed around the mask and he began to fit it to his face, a series of loud, terse *pops* echoed over the city nearby.

Gunshots. As men with guns scrambled into the intersection just ahead, Timothy ducked and ran to a small brick wall that lined the property of the house directly next to him. He jumped over the wall and sat hard on the ground, leaning back against the brick, breathing heavily.

He barely had time to see the sun glint off the stainless steel before a knife was at his throat and a hand clasped over his mouth.

Chapter 11

Zara Williams

Zara wasn't afforded that blissful moment between the dreamworld and reality, that moment amid tragedy wherein one can hold on to normalcy, wherein the mind keeps the terrible at bay for just a second. Instead, she was ripped from her fitful sleep by the sound of screeching tires and crunching metal. She was thrown from the seat on which she'd curled up the night before. Her body rotated midair, and her back slammed against the hard edge of the mini bar. The vehicle spun as her head struck the floorboard, and Lizzy yelped.

The vehicle came to a stop, and Zara cautiously climbed back onto the seat. The back window had shattered over Lizzy, who had also been thrown to the floorboards at the other end of the small limo. Her friend shielded her head with raised arms, laying awkwardly on her back with her legs still in the seat.

"Liz, you okay?" Zara asked, crawling from the seat behind the partition to the one across from the mini bar where Mr. Peters had been when Zara had fallen asleep. He wasn't in the limo. *After how crazy he was about being outside last night? What the heck is wrong with him?*

Lizzy pulled her legs down, turned, and sat on her knees. She held up trembling hands. "I… I think I'm okay. What happened? Where's my dad?"

"I don't know." Zara frowned as she looked out the side window. A small car had smashed into the back tire, which had sent both vehicles spinning. The little, white Honda's hood was buckled. She couldn't see how badly the limo was damaged beyond the broken back window.

"Elizabeth!" Mr. Peters's voice came from outside, and Zara looked up through the window to see him drop a first aid kit on the ground as he bolted toward them. He yanked open the passenger door, sticking his head inside. "Elizabeth, are you hurt?"

"I…" Lizzy looked down at her body and then rubbed her neck. "I don't think so. Not worse than I already was, anyway."

Zara sat back against the seat, relieved, though her head stung badly. She put one hand to her head and winced as she touched warm, thick liquid. She groaned as a sharp stinging pain radiated from the cut.

"Zee, your head!" Lizzy looked from Zara to her father. "She's bleeding, Dad."

"Let me see it," Mr. Peters said, and Zara turned her head. "Did you pass out when you hit your head?"

"No," Zara shook her head. Blood seeped from her hairline past her temple and dripped off her jaw. "Headwounds bleed a lot," she said. "I think it's okay." She was a little nauseous, and she was sore from head to toe, but she wasn't dizzy and she hadn't blacked out.

"None of this is okay!" Lizzy cried as she grabbed napkins from the mini bar and handed them to Zara. She brushed glass pebbles from her clothing as she spoke with increasing volume. "Can anything else go wrong? Is it ever going to end?" Her whole body sagged. "I just want to go home!"

"Keep it together, Elizabeth," Mr. Peters said. He turned to Zara. "Watch her?"

Zara did a double take, but she nodded. Mr. Peters closed the door and paced parallel to the smaller vehicle, never taking his eyes off the unconscious driver. He seemed to be considering his next steps.

"What does he mean by that?" Lizzy asked between gulps of air as tears streamed down her face.

Zara pressed the napkins against the cut on her forehead. From the feel of it, she could tell it wasn't too big or too deep, which was a relief. "I don't know. He's worried about you."

"I can take care of myself." Lizzy grabbed another napkin and blew her nose. Her stomach growled audibly, and she began to cry again.

Zara grabbed a granola bar from the array of snacks stored in the mini bar. "Here," she said, but Lizzy just kept crying. Zara unwrapped the granola bar and offered it to her again. "Eat something, Liz. It will make you feel better.

Liz took a few deep, calming breaths, and grabbed another napkin, blowing her nose and dabbing her cheeks. She took the granola bar and nibbled at it, calming a little as she chewed. The next bite severed the snack in two. She looked out the window, her cheeks bulging like a chipmunk's, and said, "What's he doing now?"

Zara shrugged and watched as Mr. Peters stopped his pacing. The driver had stirred and begun to mumble. Lizzy's father marched over to the vehicle.

"That's Mr. Ludlow, isn't it?" Zara asked. "The pilot?"

Lizzy squinted at the car. "Yeah, I think so."

Mr. Peters started shouting, and Lizzy rolled her eyes. "Well, at least Mr. Ludlow can take us home now."

Zara couldn't make out what Mr. Ludlow was saying; his words were more mumbles. *He's probably dazed from the crash.*

"I wish your dad wouldn't yell at him like that," Zara said. "What's his problem?"

Lizzy swallowed the last of the granola bar and shrugged. "I don't know." Lizzy's tired eyes went wide as if she remembered something. "I was thinking last night…" She pulled out her phone. "You know that video I was telling you about?"

"I don't want to watch some stupid GEF video right now, Liz." Zara dabbed some more blood away from her forehead and got a new wad of napkins.

"No, I mean… Jordan was supposed to be in it. And now that I have access to the forum," she dug out the piece of paper Pam – the woman at the booth – had given her the night before, "maybe there's something on there about Jordan. Or maybe he posted recently."

Zara scooted closer. "Why didn't you say something last night?"

Lizzy tapped away on her phone. "I had a dream last night about Jordan contacting me through the forum and he—"

"Stop." Zara held up a hand. "Is this about to get gross? Like, if Jordan expressed his love to you in your dream, we can skip over that part."

"Right." Lizzy cleared her throat. "Well, the point is, the dream made me think of looking here." She tapped her finger a final time on the screen and then smiled. "I'm downloading the video. Let's see if there's anything on the forum." She held the phone so they could both see.

"What are all these funky names?" Zara asked. "Aquaman, Poison Ivy…Captain Planet? Really? Like Captain Planet and the Planeteers?"

"Wait, these are names of real characters?" Lizzy wrinkled her nose. "I thought they were just cute environmentalist nicknames."

"They're from old television series, movies, comics… Poison Ivy is a Batman character."

"Oh," Lizzy said, frowning. "That's less cute. More geeky."

Zara threw Lizzy a flat stare. "You know I collect movies from the superhero craze of the 10's and 20's?"

"Sorry. How about geeky-chic?" Lizzy asked.

Zara rolled her eyes but couldn't help a small smile. "I guess I'll take it," she said. "My whole family loves that stuff. My grandpa and my dad used to stream Captain Planet and the Planeteers with Jordan when he was little, but I hardly ever joined in. That's from, like, the 90s or something." She paused, putting two and two together. "Wait, is Captain Planet what Jordan uses?"

Lizzy nodded. "I think so. That was his username when we'd have those virtual meetings." She looked at the screen. "The last post from him is from yesterday afternoon." She scrolled up. "This thread looks interesting. It's titled: Leaking to the Press." She tapped on it, and the thread expanded.

Zara scanned the conversation, paying attention only to the usernames. "I don't see Captain Planet anywhere."

"Yeah, but listen to this," Lizzy read. "Aquaman says, 'This is huge. I can't believe the government went this far.' And Poison Ivy says, 'I can believe it.' Then he says, 'I'm getting that video of CP to the press.'"

Zara's heart leapt into her throat. "CP is Jordan. Is the video ready?"

"Let me check." But as Lizzy closed her browser and went to her downloads, the screen went black.

"What happened?" Zara asked.

"My phone died." Lizzy plopped her phone down onto the seat next to her. "And my phone charger is still at the hotel."

Zara let out a frustrated groan. "Can't we catch a break?"

Mr. Peters shouted again, drawing Zara's attention. "Don't get out of the car, Bart," he said.

This time he was loud enough for Zara to make out every word. She opened the car door and peered out to get a better view, listening carefully and shushing Lizzy when she asked what Zara was doing.

"I need help." The pilot's slurred speech was wet, and there was a clear exhaustion behind the words.

Zara climbed out of the car and stood next to the limo, gesturing for Lizzy to join her. She was sore all over, and she grimaced at the movement. But, she intentionally held back any sound of discomfort. The pilot opened his own car door and put one foot outside.

Lizzy's hand flew to her mouth as she came to stand beside Zara.

"He doesn't look so great," Zara whispered.

"Is he sick, or is he just hurt from the accident?" Lizzy asked, taking a step forward.

Zara put a hand on Lizzy's arm to stop her. "I don't know. I can't tell."

"Walter… help." He coughed, and Zara gasped as blood spewed from his mouth.

Mr. Peters's fists clenched and unclenched at his sides. He sounded as haggard as Zara looked. "Don't move another inch, Bart. I told you not to go out, not to talk to anyone from the fair, damn it." He was shouting, but he didn't sound angry. He sounded… despondent.

The pilot leaned forward and screamed, pressing his hands to his eyes. "I'm sorry, Walter. Please…" He coughed again. "Help me, please!"

Mr. Peters took a step forward, hesitated and rocked back and forth on his heels, and then let out a guttural roar as he charged forward. He took hold of the door and slammed it, hard, against the already weak pilot.

"Damn you, Bart," Mr. Peters yelled, each word punctuated with another slam of the car door. "I told you!"

Lizzy screamed for her father to stop and rushed forward.

"Liz, no!" Zara lurched forward as quickly as her tender body would allow, only fast enough to catch Lizzy's belt loop. She tugged hard and sent them both stumbling backwards.

Mr. Peters threw all his weight against the door for one last blow. Mr. Ludlow fell to the ground limply, his eyes closed but his face swollen. Lizzy staggered after just having gained her footing and fell to the ground, vomiting the contents of her stomach and then dry heaving. Zara couldn't take her eyes off of Mr. Peters as he leaned against the limo's trunk. He roared again and began beating the limo with his fist.

Time crawled as all sound was replaced with a loud ringing, as Zara's head pounded, as her body went numb. Like a video on repeat, she saw blood blooming from the woman's chest at the fair, saw the car door slamming again and again. That's all that existed. Mr. Peters with blood on his hands.

He finally stopped hitting the limo and slumped to the ground, turning to lean against the tire. Zara didn't move. She was stuck with a murderer. Two people in two days, dead at the hands of Walter Peters. One of them was someone Mr. Peters had known for years.

Why isn't anyone coming to help? She glanced at the lounge across the parking lot. *Didn't anyone hear?* She wanted to run, but her body wasn't responding.

Mr. Peters looked at Zara, exhaustion painted on his face, then he looked at Lizzy, and Zara followed his gaze when a flash of remorse crossed his face. Lizzy lay crying on the asphalt, curled into a ball. Zara took a step back and sucked in a breath. She hadn't noticed.

"Elizabeth…" Mr. Peters said her name softly. He got on all fours and crawled over to her. "I had to do it," he said. "Mr. Ludlow was infected. I had to do it to keep you safe." He put a gentle hand on his daughter's calf. "He was going to die. I couldn't let him get any closer to you or Zara or anyone."

"You could have left him alone," Zara said, her voice cracking. Her body finally worked as she spun around and took a step toward the lounge.

"No one is in there, Ms. Williams," Mr. Peters called. "They're all dead. Five of them. Three attendants and two guests. I went inside, got the first aid kit, and got out. Don't go inside. Please, I don't want to leave you, or…" He glanced at Mr. Ludlow. "Please, Ms. Williams." He scooted up closer to Lizzy's head and brushed her hair from her face.

Zara paused as her heart skipped a beat. He would kill me if I showed signs that I was sick. He doesn't want to, but he would. I have to get away from him. She swallowed hard. I have to get Liz away from him.

But she couldn't do that. Not yet. Not if the people in the lounge really were dead. She walked over to where Mr. Peters had dropped the first aid kit and began putting the supplies back into the white box that had broken open. When she finished, she walked over to the window and looked inside. A woman in uniform lay face down on a coffee table next to a man halfway falling out of a chair, bloody and eyes bulging. Zara looked away and hugged the first aid kit to her chest.

If we can just get home to Boston, if I can get home to Dad… he can help me. He can help lock up Mr. Peters for the lunatic murderer that he is.

It was the last thing that she wanted to do, but Zara returned to Mr. Peters. She sat down next to Liz and took her hand.

I have to get home, but… She couldn't help but stare at the dead pilot.

"How are we going to get home?" Zara asked.

Mr. Peters shook his head, his voice hoarse, a note of desperation lacing his words. "I don't know. Damn it, I don't know."

Chapter 12

Alexander Roman

A comforting weight pressed against Alex and gently tugged him from sleep. The mattress beneath and the layers of blankets cradled him, creating a nice, warm cocoon. He didn't want to move, didn't want to wake, didn't want to think. Until that weight shifted again, and he heard a strange sniffing noise. Alex's eyes popped open, and he found himself staring straight into the chocolate brown eyes of a dog he'd never seen before. A hot, sandpaper-ish tongue rolled out of the dog's mouth and roughly lapped at Alex's cheek.

He shouted and flailed his arms, successfully batting away the dog as he tumbled out of the bed onto the floor, still tangled in the sheets and blankets. He sat up, holding his ribs, and used the blankets to dry his cheek. A goofy, pure laugh sounded from the bed, and Alex looked at Oliver who now lay on his stomach facing Alex, a pillow stuffed under his chin. His laugh made Alex chuckle, and soon they were laughing together.

Though it felt good to laugh, Alex had to rein it in a little; his ribs were still sore. The discomfort there, and the pain from his other minor injuries brought back an onslaught of memories from the day before. His laughter faded, and so did Oliver's.

"Did you sleep okay, bud?" Alex asked, carefully tucking away thoughts of Naomi. Thinking too much of her would destroy him, keep him from doing the one thing she had asked him to do.

Take care of Oliver. He has to come before everything else. Even grief.

Oliver shrugged and sat up, patting the bed so that the dog jumped up and lay in front of him. Oliver leaned forward and rested his head on the honey-colored dog, wrapping his arms around the animal's neck.

"Samson?" Minnie stuck her head around the open door. "Are you causin' a ruckus?" She put her hands on her hips. "I'm sorry about him," she said. "Did he wake you?"

"You could say that," Alex said as he got to his feet.

"He's harmless," Minnie said. "Wouldn't hurt a fly, but he also don't know when to let up and leave you be."

Alex glanced at where the dog allowed his son to cuddle up to him. "Samson, is it?"

The dog lifted his snout off the bed and cocked his head in response. Oliver burrowed into the dog's side, and Samson sniffed at Oliver's ear, giving him a few friendly dog kisses. Oliver smiled, and that was enough for Alex to decide he liked Samson.

"No, I don't think Samson is causing us any trouble at all," Alex said.

Minnie smiled and let her arms fall back to her sides. "Well, the morning *is* gettin' along. You got a hankerin' for some biscuits and gravy? It won't take long to heat. Made 'em fresh this morning."

Alex put a hand to his stomach. "I am pretty hungry. Oliver?" When Oliver didn't move, Alex came to sit next to him on the bed. "Hey, bud. Biscuits and gravy sound pretty delicious right about now. What do you say?"

Oliver shook his head.

"It wouldn't be nothin' to whip up some chocolate chip pancakes," Minnie offered.

Oliver's head snapped up, and he let go of Samson. He hopped off the bed and walked toward Minnie. Samson stayed on Oliver's heels, his head always an inch or two from Oliver's hand.

"Well, I guess that's our answer," Alex said, following Oliver and Minnie out of the bedroom.

Oliver stopped at the bathroom across the hall, took one step inside, but looked over his shoulder at Alex, suddenly fearful.

"I'll be right here," Alex said. "I promise, okay?"

Oliver nodded slowly and shut the door. Alex sighed and ran his fingers through his hair as Samson sat on his haunches, staring at the closed door.

"I wish he would say something," Alex whispered.

"He will," Minnie said softly. "Just give it time."

"Thanks again for helping us," Alex said. "I don't know what we would have done if you hadn't come along."

Minnie waved him off and blushed. "Well, it was the right thing to do, I 'spose. That's it. Just the right thing to do."

"Not everyone would have done the right thing," Alex said.

"Well, I'm not sure I would have neither," she said, "but that boy of yours… I couldn't leave him." She teared up a bit. "Anyway, I've got biscuits to heat and pancakes to make. The kitchen's through the living room, straight back and to the right." She turned and left Alex in the hall.

Alex was about to knock on the door when Oliver opened it and came out. "Did you wash your hands?"

Oliver nodded and held up his fingers, wiggling them in the air. Then he took Alex's hand, and they walked through the unfamiliar house together with Minnie's dog close behind. There were several pictures of what Alex assumed had to be Minnie's daughter, Lauren, in the hall, but they stopped with a high school graduation picture.

At the end of the hall, there was a traditional wooden front door with a diamond-shaped window, and to the right, there was a small living room only big enough for a couch, a coffee table, and a television. A rectangular doorway interrupted the wall at the far end of the living room on the right, as Minnie had said. The scent of baking biscuits, coffee, and bacon wafted through the air.

They rounded the couch to get to the kitchen. The laminate flooring was a bit yellowed and a few of the cabinet doors a bit crooked, but it had a country-home feel. Rooster-themed hand towels hung from a bar screwed into a red-and-white checkered backsplash. At one end of the counter, six old-fashioned cookbooks sat between rooster-shaped bookends. They sat at a small, round wooden table, and before Alex could say a word, Minnie plopped down a plate of biscuits and gravy in front of him and a glass of orange juice for them both.

"Pancakes'll be up in a minute," Minnie said, winking at Oliver as she set a plate of bacon in the middle of the table.

Alex caught the time on the microwave clock and gaped. "Eleven o'clock? I didn't realize it was so late." He sighed. "We don't want to overstay our welcome," he said. "As soon as breakfast is ready—"

"You'll eat," Minnie said, "and then you'll take your time, do whatever you need to do, and let me show you some southern hospitality."

"Well," Alex looked at Oliver, who snuck a piece of bacon to Samson, "if you wouldn't mind, there's one thing I need to do before heading back to Atlanta." He cut into his biscuit, but suddenly he wasn't so hungry.

I need to claim Naomi's body…

He didn't know how long it would take for the bodies to be identified, and he didn't plan to stay with Minnie if it was going to take several days or weeks. He'd have to find a hotel somewhere safe. He thought about the motel and shuddered. Alex turned in his chair and glanced at the television, then back at Oliver. He wanted to check the news, to see if there were any updates on the situation over at the fair, but he didn't want Oliver to see, didn't want him to be reminded of what had happened. The memories were hard enough. Alex wasn't even sure he could handle images of the destruction.

"I got headphones and a radio," Minnie said as she placed hot pancakes in front of Oliver. She raised her eyebrows knowingly.

Alex sagged in relief. "That would be wonderful, thanks."

She left the room and returned with a bright red radio and cheap, black headphones. "It's already tuned to the right station," she said. "I checked this mornin' when you were sleepin'. I didn't want to wake you."

The material stretched over the speakers' cushions was old and scratchy, but when Alex flipped the radio on, they worked just fine. He carefully watched Oliver as the broadcaster expounded on what Alex knew.

"Paris, London, Johannesburg, Rio de Janeiro… confirmed reports have come out of these cities across the world that mirror what happened last night in San Francisco, St. Louis, and Boston. Rumor has it that Beijing is holding back information, but if video clips leaked on the Internet are to be believed, Asia has not been spared."

Alex pushed his food around on his plate as he listened. *What the heck is going on?*

Oliver was shoveling chocolate chip pancakes into his mouth but paused and frowned at Alex and his plate. Alex took a bite, rolling the buttery biscuit and creamy, spicy gravy in his mouth, and Oliver returned to his own food. It was hard to swallow; it should have been satisfying and comforting. Instead, he could have been eating dirt for all the enjoyment he got out of it. As he listened, as the absence of his wife pressed in all around him, Alex didn't *want* to feel anything — joy or grief. Joy felt almost wrong, and grief would cripple him. Numb acceptance and feigned stability were the best he could do for Oliver.

"Authorities here in the States are requesting that citizens keep their distance from ground zero in the three affected cities. Remain calm and go about your business. We have no reason to believe more attacks are on the horizon."

A terrorist attack… it just doesn't sit right. Alex went over the facts of the incident as he'd witnessed it, taking into account that he didn't have all the information. *Nothing really makes sense, though.* He shook his head. He couldn't focus on that, on what he'd been trained to do, not until he'd brought Naomi home. Not until he and Oliver had a chance to grieve in peace. *If the CDC is too busy to help, I'll have to figure this out on my own.*

He sighed and slid the headphones off, switching the radio off as well. "Minnie, I need to head to the local police department to try to get some information."

"Oliver can stay here, if you want." Minnie smiled. "Samson would love to have someone to play with."

Oliver nearly choked on his food and dropped his fork with a loud clatter. He shook his head furiously, tears welling up in his eyes. He rounded the table and threw his arms around Alex's neck, squeezing tightly.

"Hey," Alex said softly. "It's okay. You can come with me."

"You want me to come, too? I can help," Minnie said, looking with pity on them both.

She'd already done so much, but Alex honestly wasn't sure he could do what he needed to do without her. "That would be great," he said gratefully. "Are you sure you don't have things to do? I'm sure you've got a life to get back to."

Minnie chuckled. "I take my food truck around to events and whatnot, but that's just a little extra on top of my retirement. There was a day when I was busier than a moth in a mitten, but these days…" She shook her head. "I'm mostly just bored out of my mind."

"What about Lauren?" Alex asked. "Do you need to check on her? Does she live around here?"

Minnie stiffened just a little, and while she smiled, something in her eyes remained guarded. "Lauren lives in Nashville," she said. "Far enough from all that's happened, I think. I can't get hold of her, but, well, that's nothin' new." Her smile faltered on those last words, and she turned quickly away. "Y'all get ready to go, and I'll clean up."

Alex nodded. "Okay, bud. Let's get dressed and get your shoes on."

They went back to the bedroom, and once Oliver was dressed, he pulled Naomi's macrame purse from under his pillow. He sat on the bed and put his nose to the purse, breathing deeply. It smelled like her; Alex could detect the lavender as he sat next to his son.

"Do you want me to fix the strap?" Alex asked. The strap had unraveled where it had previously been secured to a brass ring. Oliver handed it over, and Alex strung the end of the strap through the ring and tied a knot. "This isn't perfect, but it should hold until we can get it fixed by someone who knows what they're doing."

Oliver nodded and hastily took it back. He unbuttoned the flap and lifted it, peering inside. He pulled out some lip balm and a small bottle of lotion, then Oliver sighed, staring at the inside of the bag. The spray bottle of natural lavender oil and coconut oil had broken, and Alex had disposed of the glass the night before. But those three things — lip balm, lotion, and lavender — had been part of Naomi's morning routine. She'd included Oliver in that routine every morning since he was three years old, when he'd thought those things were special grown-up items and using them proved he was grown-up, too. Eventually, he'd just come to enjoy it.

"Maybe we can find some lavender oil when we're out today, bud." Alex put a hand on his son's shoulder, smiling sadly at the memories cropping up in his mind. Naomi had loved her oil concoctions, and lavender had been her favorite for many reasons. Besides helping with her and Oliver's mild eczema, the oil was supposed to be a natural way to calm nerves, soothe minor cuts and burns, and even repel all sorts of insects. She'd never left home without it.

Oliver nodded, used the lip balm and lotion, and slung the macrame purse across his body so that it hung shoulder to hip. He still put one protective hand on it, though, as they walked out of the bedroom. Samson was waiting for them in the hall and led them to the front door where Minnie was slipping on some sandals.

"Y'all mind if Samson comes along?" Minnie asked. "He's used to hoppin' in the backseat and stickin' his head out the window. Comes with me most everywhere here in town."

Oliver grinned and scratched behind Samson's ear.

"Of course we don't mind," Alex said as he patted the dog's back. It seemed Samson was good for Oliver, like the animal was watching out for his son and knew that he needed a little extra love.

Minnie's house sat on a bit of property on the edge of town. A long, gravel driveway snaked through the trees and ended in a large, circular patch in front of the house and a small pole barn. Alex noted several dirt trails starting at the tree line and a wooden foot bridge over a creek just a few yards into the woods. The blue summer sky held fluffy white clouds which were moved along by a warm breeze that rustled the treetops. The air was fresh and woodsy, with hints of pine and sweeter scents from the flower bed that lined the front porch of the one-story, yellow house.

"This is a nice place," Alex said. "I didn't really get the chance to see it last night." He looked around. "Where's the food truck?"

Minnie cleared her throat. "Well, I put it behind the barn for now. It needs… a good washin'." Her expression soured. "You don't wanna see the bits stuck in the undercarriage and grill." She nodded at Oliver. "And I'm assumin' you don't want him seein' it neither."

Alex stared wide-eyed at Minnie as she passed him, approaching a rusty, red truck. Bile rose in his throat as he thought of how many bodies Minnie had been forced to drive over.

"But," Minnie said, "there ain't nothin' wrong with my trusty Ford." She patted the hood and opened the driver's side door, the creaking metal like nails on a chalkboard.

"Will we all fit in there?" Alex asked, noting the single bench seat and glancing at Samson. The dog wasn't the biggest one he'd ever seen, but he definitely wasn't small.

"Sure," Minnie said. "There's two little seats in the back. Samson'll fit back there, and Oliver can ride up front in the middle." She pulled a lever and the front seat tilted forward, revealing two seats facing each other on either end of the cab behind the front bench.

Alex shrugged. "Sounds good, I guess."

They hopped in after Samson made himself at home in the back, and Minnie rolled down the windows after asking if they would mind. The fifteen-minute drive into town was short, which was good because Samson kept coming up behind Alex, sticking his head out the window, and letting his tongue hang out. It would have been cute if not for the occasional bit of slobber flying at Alex when Samson shook his head. They passed fields of corn and soybeans and a few other homes, but not much else until they entered the small town of Red Bud. The sign read: Population 3,423.

"Do you think the police here will know anything about the World's Fair?" Alex asked, suddenly a bit concerned that they would need to travel outside of Minnie's small hometown to get any real information.

"We're really just a stone's throw away from the city," Minnie said. "My guess is that they've already sent out some first responders to pitch in like they did when that tornado hit the downtown area a few years back. I bet they know somethin' or, at least, know who does."

I guess it couldn't hurt to ask. Alex thought as he watched the small businesses and quaint neighborhood go by outside.

"Oh, fiddlesticks," Minnie said as they passed a house-turned-veterinarian-office. "I didn't bring my checkbook. I 'bout forgot about Harvey. I'll have to come back out later and get 'im."

Alex was about to ask if Harvey was another dog when some commotion broke out at a dollar store a block down the street. Some people scattered from the small parking lot, and Minnie had to slam on her brakes as a man rushed into the street carrying bags of canned goods. A police car's lights turned on down the street, and it drove up to the lot as the remaining crowd around the entrance to the store began to turn into more of a mob, shoving each other and shouting. Several had packs of toilet paper under each arm, and they seemed to be drawing the most ire from the rest.

"Dagnabbit, Larry!" Minnie shouted out the window at the man who had cut her off. She sighed in frustration and mumbled, "That man ain't got the sense God gave a goose."

Samson barked at the disturbance in the lot as the policeman jumped out of his patrol car and approached the crowd, shouting at people by name. It seemed everyone knew everyone in Red Bud. Alex grimaced as a man with toilet paper under his arms dropped one of them to throw a punch at the officer who easily sidestepped the attempt. A woman snatched the dropped package and ran in the other direction.

"Come back here, Jane!" the man shouted as the policeman began to cuff his hands behind his back. "I paid good money for that!"

"Maybe we should get out of here," Alex said as Oliver stared open-mouthed at the small-town brawl. Another man who looked like a slightly younger version of the one in cuffs stalked up to the officer and began to shout.

Samson's paw pressed on Alex's shoulder as he stuck half his body outside and barked again, this time louder, and then launched himself out of the truck, hitting the pavement and bolting toward the fray.

"Samson!" Minnie shouted. She jerked the truck into the lot and parked, opening her door to go after her dog.

Alex debated whether to get involved as he watched Samson stand his ground beside the one police officer facing off against an angry crowd of twenty-five or thirty townsfolk. Minnie shuffled across the lot after him. Alex had just decided it was best for him to stay in the truck with Oliver when the driver's side door creaked open and slammed shut. Alex looked over to find his son no longer sat beside him and was running toward the fight.

Chapter 13

Timothy Peters

Cold steel bit into the skin at Timothy's throat, and a drop of blood slowly trickled down his neck. He was hot and sweaty in the sweltering summer sun, and as the breeze blew softly, the line of blood chilled. He dared not move, brick at his back, his assailant so close that Timothy could smell garlic on his breath.

"Who're you?" the man asked. "Are you with the Irish? CON?"

"The gangs?" Timothy's voice croaked. One hand was tangled in the strap of his backpack, and the other was pinned down by the stranger. That made his taser and gun unreachable.

"Yeah, the gangs, ya idiot," the man said, his Bostonian accent thick. "I know there's two or three of 'em fightin' over who gets to off me, and I don't plan on giving any of ya the opportunity."

"None of them," Timothy said. "I swear."

The man sniffed. "Prove it."

Timothy's mind raced. How do I prove I'm not in a gang?

"I said, prove it." He pressed the knife harder, and it broke skin again, stinging as another drop of blood oozed down Timothy's neck.

"I came here from Wellesley," Timothy said, frantic. "I'm just here to check on friends."

"Wellesley, eh?" The knife let up a little, and then the stranger dropped his arm and chuckled. "Bunch o' wusses out there," he said. "Ain't nobody from 'round here gonna say they's from Wellesley."

Air rushed out of Timothy's lungs in relief, and he looked over at the stranger. A short, stocky man sat beside him, halfway sandwiched between a bush and the brick wall. He looked to be in his late thirties, but his hairline was already receding, and his left cheek was marked with a long, thin scar. The hand with the knife rested on his bent knee, but he held his other arm close to his body. Timothy didn't know what to do as the stranger breathed heavily beside him, knife still too close for comfort.

"Are you… okay?" Timothy asked, hoping that showing some concern would play in his favor.

"Yeah," the man said. "Bullet grazed my arm and I'm a dead man walkin', but I'm fine." He looked at Timothy. "Name's Frank. Frank Russo."

"I'm Timothy," he said.

"Where ya from?" Frank asked, shifting slightly so Timothy had a better view of the arm he favored. A piece of cloth was haphazardly tied around his bicep. It was soaked through with blood, and the skin all around it was smeared red. Fat drops of blood rolled down to his elbow, slowly dripping onto the ground.

Timothy frowned. "I live in South Boston."

"Southie, eh?" Frank narrowed his eyes. "Thought you said you came from Wellesley?"

"I did," Timothy said, a little perplexed by Frank's line of questioning. "From my parents' house."

"Yeah, well, I asked where ya *from*? Not where d'ya live? You, my friend, ain't from 'round here, not even from Wellesley, I can tell ya that."

"I'm originally from Washington," Timothy said, not sure why that would matter. He always thought of himself as a Bostonian; he'd lived there since he was eight.

"So what? Grew up in Wellesley then spread your wings in Southie?" Frank gestured with his knife as he spoke. "How's a rich kid like you got friends here?"

"I'm not rich," Timothy said.

Frank quirked an eyebrow. "That watch is top o' the line, and those shoes?" He scoffed. "Put that together with Wellesley and the way ya carry yourself, all high and mighty… it don't take a genius to figure out you's rich."

Timothy looked down at his wrist. He hadn't even thought about taking off his watch. He'd worn it every day since he was fifteen. It had been a coming-of-age present from his parents. And he'd worn his least favorite designer sneakers. They weren't even new.

"Well, I'm not rich," he said. "My parents might be, but I'm just a normal guy."

"Normal… yeah, right." He shook his head. "So, I'll ask again. How's a rich kid like you got friends here?"

"I just do," Timothy said. "And I need to check on them, so if you'll excuse me—"

"Nah," Frank said, suddenly straddling Timothy with the knife back at his throat.

Timothy clamped his mouth shut, his heartbeat picking up speed as he jerked his head back. Too close to the wall, his head hit brick. He could only shy away so far with the man pinning him down. *The taser!* He started to reach for it.

"Don't think I ain't seen that taser," Frank said, wincing as he used his injured arm to grab at the weapon and toss it into the bush before Timothy could stop him. "Listen to me, kid. I need help, and you're gonna give it. I need a safe place to crash. How far are your friends?"

A sinking feeling settled in Timothy; the taser was buried in foliage. The gun was out of reach. A desperate, injured, and possibly insane man had a knife to his throat. Frank's strength outmatched Timothy's, even with the flesh wound.

Mr. Williams is a cop… he can deal with this guy better than I can. Timothy swallowed hard, imagining the blade of the knife ripping open his neck. All he wanted was to make it back to Heather. He could use the gun to help Mr. Williams once Frank was no longer focused on him.

"They're not far," Timothy said, his voice cracking, "but I can't help you if you hurt me."

"Fair 'nough," Frank said, raising up on his haunches to peek over the brick wall. "The way looks clear. We should get goin'."

Sweat stung his eyes, but he dared not move. He was on the verge of giving Frank what he wanted. "You won't hurt them?"

"Cross my heart," Frank said. "I just need a place to hide." He stood up and pointed at Timothy with the blade. "But you cross me, and I'll slit your throat. Got it?"

Timothy swallowed hard. "Got it," he said.

With Frank's knife at the ready, they both hopped over the brick wall after Timothy slung his backpack over his shoulders. Timothy noted the N95 mask he'd dropped and pointed to it and then to the dead man in the car. "I think we should wear masks, just in case. If you pick up that one—"

"Ain't got time for that." Frank nudged Timothy with the sharp point of the knife.

He flinched away from the blade and began walking, leaving the mask on the ground. Frank stayed only a step or two behind, knife held out before him. They had to skirt around a minivan that had crashed into a fence and blocked the sidewalk. A bloody handprint was on the outside of the passenger window, and the side door had been slid open and left. An empty car seat was in the bucket seats in the middle of the vehicle. Timothy was careful not to step on the drops of blood leading away from the van, but as they came around the back end, he jumped backward into Frank and turned away, steadying himself on the hood of a car. A young woman lay dead, curled around a baby-blue bundle in her arms. Her hair, matted with blood, covered her face, and her arms and legs were swollen and red.

Frank didn't look away. He didn't flinch. Timothy watched Frank's back incredulously as the man stepped closer, bending over the bodies and inspecting them.

"Damn shame," Frank said, shaking his head, his eyes glistening. He looked genuinely saddened, though it was obvious he'd seen similar gore before. He stood up, knife at his side. "What the hell is goin' on?" he mumbled. Just as Timothy recovered enough from shock to be able to move, Frank nodded at him to keep going. "C'mon, Southie," he said. "Let's get outta here."

Timothy made a point not to look as he passed by the mother and child. "Do you know anything?" he asked. "About what's going on?"

"Nah," Frank said. "Wish I did, though. Why? Do you know?"

Timothy shook his head. "No, but..." *But I think my dad knows something.*

"But what?"

"Nothing." Timothy kept walking. A man like Frank might do something sinister with the information that Walter Peters knew something about what was going on.

Information is power. Walter Peters's voice sounded in Timothy's head. And when you've got information, when you've got power, you've got to be careful with it. Share it with the wrong person, and you'll end up with a knife in your back. Timothy glanced just behind him at Frank and his blade. Literally.

They approached the intersection where the men had been shooting at each other. One of them had taken a bullet to the head and lay in a pool of his own blood between vehicles. Frank spit at his feet. Timothy raised an eyebrow. The same man who'd teared up at the sight of the dead mother showed no reverence for this dead man.

Frank shrugged. "That's Lawrence," he said. "Piece o' work, that one. He chased me all over The Bury this morning, him and his Irish posse." He chuckled, speaking as if telling a funny story from a family get together. "If it weren't for CON, I'd be dead already. Ya see, the Irish want me dead, no question. The ConMen want me dead, too, but they still think they can get somethin' out of me before they off me."

Timothy cleared his throat. "Why is that funny?" His voice sounded small even to him.

Frank threw back his head and laughed harder. "Because, Southie, I'm still livin', ain't I? Frank Russo's like a roach. Can't get rid o' me." He brandished his knife again, but only half-heartedly and with an almost friendly smile. "Now, let's keep at it. Go on."

Timothy tried to keep his expression neutral, but he was getting more concerned about Frank Russo's stability. He couldn't pin the man down. Was he a complete psycho or just a run-of-the-mill criminal? At times, Timothy almost *liked* the man. Until he did something despicable or terrifying. Either way, he continued leading Frank toward the Williams' house.

Every once in a while, Timothy would notice a curtain pull closed or a hole in someone's blinds as they separated two slats just enough to see outside. At one point, his heart leapt at the sight of an ambulance down a side street – maybe they could help him! – only to have his hope crushed by the sight of two uniformed bodies lying on someone's front lawn. Mattapan looked like a war zone, mostly abandoned except for those who stayed behind to hide.

"I don't even know if the Williams will be home," Timothy said as he walked, thinking out loud.

"Whatcha mean?" Frank asked.

"They're smart enough to get out early, but... they weren't answering their phones. When I set out to check on them this morning, I had no idea how bad it was here. I hope they made it out." Timothy felt a growing dread.

"Well, if they ain't home, I'm sure they wouldn't mind sharin' with a friend." Frank shrugged. "If they left, it's not like they'd be comin' back anytime soon. Besides, in situations like these, what you leave behind is fair game for the rest."

Timothy scoffed. "Of course someone like you would say that."

"You don't know nothin' about Frank Russo." The man sniffed and jutted out his chin. "I ain't a bad guy. I done as best I could with the hand that was dealt me. But I ain't never struck a woman or a kid, and I *always* tip the ladies. And I ain't never shot no one in the back."

Such high standards, Timothy thought, though he kept the thought to himself as they made their final turn down the short street the Williams lived on.

Richmere Road was a small one-way street that connected two larger thoroughfares. It had a deserted feel to it as they walked past the initial pile up of vehicles where Richmere poured out onto a main road. Every house had on-street parking available, and there were usually cars lining either side. But most parking spots were empty. Windows were broken out of several homes, and they passed a car sticking out of someone's living room. Timothy found himself holding his breath as he began to recognize houses, began to see homes of people he'd met.

Seeing the Williams' street in disarray was harder than seeing the rest of Mattapan. It seemed Mr. and Mrs. Williams always had a neighbor stopping by, and Timothy had enjoyed getting to know more than a few of them. The Williams' barbeques were a Richmere summer tradition. Neighbors in Wellesley, at least where his parents lived, waved at each other and were generally friendly, but they weren't *friends*. Not really. Even his mother's speed walking group was more about competition and neighborhood politics than it was about friendships. It had been different here, more like extended family.

When the pastel green siding and small brick porch of the Williams' home came into view, Timothy let himself take a deep breath.

"That's my friends' house," he said. "And that's their car." He pointed to a black Nissan.

"Hope they look better than that guy," Frank said, nodding at the house on the other side of the street.

Timothy reluctantly turned his head. Mr. Jackson, a friendly older gentleman who traded minor home repairs for turkey dinners and cherry pies, lay face down, half of his body still inside his small, covered porch, the other half draped over concrete stairs. A summer breeze gently pushed the white aluminum door, and it softly pinged against the iron railing before closing on Mr. Jackson's hip.

He took one step forward, but Frank stopped him. "Don't forget about your friends, kid." He gestured with his knife toward the Williams' house.

"Oh, God, let them be alive." Timothy breathed the prayer before he turned around and shouted, "Mr. Williams?" He bolted through the chain-link fence's open gate up to the door and knocked. "Hello?"

"Kid, not so loud," Frank whispered harshly. "Last thing we need is attention."

Timothy knocked again and looked through the circular window. "Mr. Williams, it's Timothy!" He searched for any signs of Zara's family.

"They have to be here," Timothy said. "Their car is here. They only have the one." His heartbeat quickened as he looked back at Mr. Jackson's dead body. Palms sweaty, the summer heat suddenly heavy and hard to breathe, Timothy pushed past Frank and rounded the house to the door on the side. He took the steps up to the little landing two at a time and was about to pound on the door again when he froze.

Green grass almost concealed the hand, barely sticking out past the corner of the house in the back yard. Timothy's eyes grew wide, and he stepped to the iron railing, gripping it tightly as he looked at that hand. It was swollen and stretched, the fingers bent at odd angles, the skin taught where it should have been wrinkled. A silver bracelet Timothy recognized caught the sunlight, sparkling though it was embedded in an enlarged wrist. Mrs. Williams always wore that bracelet. Zara had given it to her last Christmas.

"No." Timothy exhaled the word as his knuckles turned white, as a nick in the iron work cut into his palm, as he pled for a miracle all in one, long breath.

Limbs wooden, tears blurring his vision, Timothy rushed to the back of the house. He came upon Mrs. Williams first, and the sight of her knocked the wind out of him.

Her kind smile, the warmth in her eyes, the way she would greet newcomers with a hug… her lively, vibrant, motherly self was gone. Timothy couldn't coalesce the Mrs. Williams he knew with the dead body before him. It was like looking at a grotesque, distorted Picasso.

And the horror didn't end with Mrs. Williams. Zara's father sat against the back of the house, both eyes hanging like gruesome ornaments from their sockets. Another dead body sat precariously in a chair at a small, round outdoor table.

Zara's Aunt Rachel…

Four plates of eggs and bacon were at the table, and Timothy's stomach lurched. His eyes scanned the yard, looking for a smaller body. Zara's aunt had an adopted daughter, five or six years of age. Annika had been a light in the Williams' house since she'd joined the family four years ago. Timothy and Heather had only been around the girl a handful of times, but her proud aunt and uncle always had a story about their beloved niece.

The creak of a door opening made Timothy snap his head back to the side of the house. Frank was entering the Williams' home. He'd almost forgotten about Frank, but the sight of him waltzing into the house while its occupants lay dead in the yard made Timothy's blood boil. He strode back to the side door, up the steps, and flung open the door. The tiny kitchen to the left was empty. Frank was to the right, standing in front of a side table placed in front of a window.

"What do you think you're doing?" Timothy shouted. "Didn't you see—"

"The dead people out back? Yeah," Frank said, his voice calm but his tone serious. There was a large family photo centered on the thin table, and as Timothy stepped closer, a lump formed in his throat. "I'm guessin' you thought that guy would be alive." Frank pointed with his knife to Mr. Williams who was dressed in his police uniform in the photo.

Timothy held up his hands, palms outward. "Frank—"

"Save it, Southie," Frank said, gripping the knife in a firm hand. "I told ya, cross me, and I slit your throat." He lurched forward, blade first.

Chapter 14

Zara Williams

It had taken Mr. Peters longer to recover from murdering Mr. Ludlow than Zara had expected. He'd stayed by Lizzy's side, stroking her hair, for half an hour. Zara had even seen a few tears, but slowly he'd regained his composure. And once he had, he'd had them walk to the opposite end of the lot. He said he wanted them far away from the dead, that they had to get out of the city. But the limo's back end was wrecked, and they wouldn't be driving it far any time soon. He said he needed to think, alone and in silence. As he sequestered himself under the shade of a small tree planted in mulch, Zara sat with Lizzy on a curb several yards away.

A scorching sun beat down on her relentlessly, and a film of sweat covered Zara's body as her mind raced. She had a thousand questions and no answers. Was her family in Boston safe? What about Jordan? What was killing people, and what did Mr. Peters know about it? He was holding back information; she could tell at least that much. And he was losing his mind. Zara shuddered. She'd seen so many violent deaths over the last day, and two of them were at the hands of the usually calm, cool, and collected CEO.

"Liz, we can't stay here," Zara said quietly. Her best friend had barely spoken since she'd broken down earlier. She looked exhausted, her body drooping as if barely keeping upright.

"I know. Dad's working on it." Lizzy closed her eyes and lay back on the mulch behind them, her legs stretched over asphalt.

"No, I mean…" She lowered her voice even more. "I mean we can't stay with your dad."

"Now *you're* sounding insane." Lizzy opened her eyes and raised her eyebrows. "Where would we go? How would we make it out there, in a city that's falling apart, without my dad? He's kept us alive."

"He's killed two people. I thought, at first, maybe we should go with him until we got to Boston, but after thinking about it, I've changed my mind. We have to go to the police and—"

"Stop it, Zee." Lizzy sat up. "You're talking about my *dad*, okay? Those people he killed, they were going to die anyway. You heard what he said. They would have infected us."

"Liz, come on," Zara said. "That's not an excuse. That woman at the fair, Mr. Ludlow… they were slow. We could have gotten away from them."

"It doesn't matter," Lizzy said. "They were dying, and my dad thinks they could be spreading the disease. If that's true, even if we got away, what about the next person?"

"I can't believe you're defending what he did." Frustration mounted inside Zara's chest, and heat rushed into her cheeks.

"Well, I can't believe you want to turn my dad in to the police."

Zara stood up abruptly and turned her back on Lizzy. She exhaled sharply through her nose and bit her tongue to keep from shouting. Every nerve in her body was on fire, screaming at her to run before Mr. Peters killed her just for sneezing. She glanced at Lizzy's dad, who hadn't so much as looked their way. He sat knees to chest, arms hugging his legs, head resting on one knee. When he'd first started his thinking session, he'd paced. Then, he'd stood still, and finally he'd sat under the tree. He'd barely moved a muscle since.

"And what about me?" Zara asked, turning back toward Lizzy and crouching in front of her.

Lizzy sat up and met Zara's eyes with a stubborn glare. "What about you? He was protecting you, too, you know."

"No, Liz. He was protecting you and you alone. He doesn't care about me. He doesn't even like me. What happens if I get sick?" Zara jabbed her finger at Lizzy. "Are you going to let him shoot me? Run me over with a car? Push me off a cliff? Because if you get sick, I can see him moving heaven and earth to try to save you, but me? If I get sick, whatever method of getting rid me is closest, that's the way I'm going to die."

Lizzy's mouth fell open, her eyes wide. "Zee, my dad wouldn't hurt you. There's no way. And besides, he'll keep you from getting sick in the first place."

Zara shook her head. "I know you don't want to believe he would hurt me, but I *do* believe it. And I think we need to go to the police."

"Please, Zee," Lizzy reached out and took both of Zara's hands in hers. "Please, don't. Okay? We don't know how bad this is going to get. We *need* him. He knows things. He's got connections. He'll be able to get us home. And besides, you heard what he said at the fair. The authorities aren't going to listen to you. They'll hear you were at the World's Fair, and then they'll quarantine you. They'll be afraid of you, too afraid to listen."

That gave Zara pause, but she shook off her uncertainty. "We don't even know if your dad was telling the truth about that. He says he's seen government contingency plans, but come on, Liz. We're not a threat. We're not sick. They're not going to hurt us."

"No, and I mean it." Lizzy crossed arms and set her jaw. She looked a lot like her father when she did that.

Zara sat back on the curb next to her best friend and sighed. "Fine," she said before plopping back onto the mulch to stare up at the sky. She hadn't changed her mind, but Lizzy wasn't going to agree with her. Not now, not ever, not about this.

So, Zara decided to take a page from Mr. Peters's book. She began to think through her options. She'd heard once that the first three or four ideas one came up with were just warm-ups, remnants of ideas heard before or mediocre options borne from paths of least resistance. So, she sifted through the possibilities, discarding a few before she realized her mistake.

If I'm going to get both me and Liz to safety, away from Mr. Peters, I have to lie to her.

"I think I just need to *do* something to prove myself to your dad," Zara said. "Like it or not, he's been letting me tag along because of you, not because he wants to help me." She swallowed hard and pushed the lie between her teeth. "If I can do something that shows my value, I'll feel less expendable around him. He's a businessman, right? He's invested in you, and now I need him to invest in me."

Lizzy squinted at Zara. "You're my friend, Zee. That's enough for him to care about you."

"It's not," Zara said, "and you know it." Her mouth was running dry. She licked her lips and continued. "What if something happened to you? Do you think he'd still protect me? Be honest."

Lizzy grimaced and averted her eyes. Finally, she sighed. "You're right," she said. "I love my dad, but he's kind of emotionally stunted."

"So, what if we walk to the main terminal and get some supplies?" Zara asked. "We can show him I can be useful, you know?"

"I guess we could ask my dad if he thinks that's a good idea," Lizzy said as she glanced at her father. "But we'd have to wake him up. He's been sleeping for, like, twenty minutes."

Zara looked at Mr. Peters. "Are you sure?" If he *was* asleep, it would be the first bit of luck she'd had in a while.

"Pretty sure," she said, then she shouted, "Hey, Dad!"

Zara slapped Lizzy's arm. "What are you doing?" she hissed, though Mr. Peters didn't move a muscle. She reined in her panic and made her next words calmer. "Don't wake him up. We should let him sleep. I mean, you're right. He's spent all his energy protecting us. Now, maybe we should spend some energy doing something for him."

Lizzy cocked her head and scrunched her nose, but she finally nodded. "I have my credit card. We could get some real food and a change of clothes for all of us."

"Exactly. And we can check on the state of things." Zara stood up. "Your dad loves information, right? I bet we can get a lot of information at the main terminal."

"Save him a trip," Lizzy said, nodding.

"If he didn't sleep last night, he could be asleep for hours, right? He's in the shade, he looks comfortable. I bet we can be back before he even wakes up," Zara said.

"Okay, I'm in." Lizzy popped up with a renewed energy and headed toward the limo. "Let me get one of those sticky notes and leave a message for my dad. He'll want to know where we went if he does wake up."

Damn it, I don't want him coming after us. But Zara couldn't think of an excuse to *not* leave a note.

Lizzy opened the limo door and climbed inside, leaving the door open. Zara tapped her fingers on her thigh as she tried not to look at Mr. Ludlow's swollen body. Instead, she leaned into the limo, a wave of heat hitting her face as she ducked inside, and watched Lizzy scrawl a note on a sticky note in the shape of a heart. The pad of notes and little pencils had been positioned on the mini bar behind the snacks and water bottles, along with a few packages of tissues and wet wipes.

"Where are you going to leave the note?" Zara asked.

"I thought maybe we could stick it to the tree," Lizzy said.

"That's no good," Zara said. "It would blow away. Even if it didn't, you'd wake your dad by getting so close."

"Yeah… what do you think?" Lizzy asked as she finished up.

"I bet he'll look in the limo if we leave the door open. We could stick it to the window above the mini bar, right in plain sight." Zara pointed to the tinted window, and Lizzy stuck the note in the middle of it.

"Let's get going," Lizzy said. "We need to be back ASAP." She climbed back out of the limo.

"I'm going to grab some of those waters," Zara said as she put one foot inside the limo. She turned to Lizzy, acting surprised as she patted her pocket. "Damn it! I think I left my phone over in the mulch. Can you go get it while I grab us some water and a snack?"

"Sure! I'm craving some chocolate," Lizzy said before she turned away toward where they'd been sitting.

Zara grabbed a chocolate chip cookie for them both and a couple of waters, but before she climbed out, she grabbed the note, crumpled it, and tossed it in the little trash can next to the snacks. Then, she got out and met Lizzy over by the mulch, pulling out her phone.

"It was in my other pocket," Zara said. "I know our phones are dead, but it just feels weird to be without it."

"I know," Lizzy said in an exaggerated tone. Then her eyes brightened. "Hey, they usually have those charging stations inside airports. I bet we could charge our phones."

"One look at our charged phones, a cheeseburger, and a fresh t-shirt, and your dad is going to love me for life." Zara tried to sound lighthearted as she ignored the way her stomach churned. She hated lying.

They left the private airport on foot, cutting across a few more parking lots to get to the road that connected back to the main terminal. The path they took skirted lands owned by the airports. The private terminal at the back of the huge property had seemed almost secluded despite being in the middle of the city. As they neared the main terminal, however, Zara picked out disturbing sounds from the city she hadn't noticed before. A fence separated airport land from the city, so she couldn't see anything. But the city was louder. There was more shouting, more honking. Every so often she heard a crash of metal, as if there were car accidents and pileups happening at regular intervals.

"It doesn't sound good out there," Zara said, hugging her middle.

"Are those gunshots?" Lizzy asked as a *pop, pop, pop* rose over the din.

"I think so, but they're not close." Zara bit her lower lip.

"Do you think the main airport is safe?" Lizzy asked. "I mean, don't you think people will be trying to get out of town?"

"I'm sure there are police all over the airport situation," Zara said. "But flights have been shut down all day. We haven't seen one plane leaving, just those two that landed. I'm sure word has gotten out that flights are all delayed."

"Wouldn't that just make people mad?" Lizzy asked.

"Maybe." Zara shrugged. "If it's bad, we can just go back."

There was no parking at the main terminal, only lanes meant for taxis and buses. Passengers with vehicles normally had to shuttle in and out from parking garages. But when they turned the corner and the front of the terminal came into view, Zara stopped short. Vehicles of all sorts filled every drop off and pickup lane, some of them parked on sidewalks. None of the vehicles were moving. Smoke rose from the hoods of several separate accidents. The lights of ambulances and police cars took up one lane that looked like it had been cleared by force, with cars pushed over onto sidewalks and into other lanes.

A haphazard, one-vehicle-wide pathway was being cleared with tow trucks that looked like they had been working their way into the fray for some time. Blocky, black trucks, intimidating and meant to carry at least fifteen passengers, idled in front of the ambulances. Dozens of red and blue lights flashed in the distance. And there were people *everywhere.*

"Maybe we should go back." Lizzy frowned and rubbed the back of her neck, her expression uncertain. "That looks like a hot mess."

Panic welled up in Zara's chest as Lizzy began to turn around. "There are still people down there," she said. "People with information. Even if we can't get supplies, we could still ask questions."

Lizzy didn't look entirely convinced. "I don't know, Zee."

"Let's just get closer, listen in on what people are saying. We can turn back at any time." Zara hooked her arm through Lizzy's and pulled her toward the jumble of vehicles and people.

Lizzy groaned as she allowed herself to be tugged along. "If I see anyone with eyes popping out of their heads, I'm out, Zee."

"That's fair," Zara said. "Keep your eyes peeled." She widened her eyes and made circles around them with her fingers.

"Is that a joke?" Lizzy asked.

Zara shrugged. "Too soon?"

"Yes, Zee. Like, way too soon." Lizzy rolled her eyes.

"Sorry." Zara cringed, but she didn't have time to say much else before they were stepping into the chaos.

Men and women in uniform blocked every door to get inside the terminal, and each of them wore heavy duty gas masks. The medical personnel in scrubs interspersed along the line of police officers were only slightly less intimidating in their gloves, face shields, surgical masks, and goggles. There were lines on either side of the glass doors, some going in and some going out. Every person talked to an officer before being allowed to move forward.

"Let's try to get inside," Zara said. And when we get to the police, I'll tell them everything, and we'll be safe. Maybe they can get a hold of the Boston PD to tell my dad where I am.

"Are you sure?" Lizzy asked. "I know your dad is an officer, Zee, but these guys don't look friendly."

"They're just doing their jobs." Zara pulled Lizzy into a line. "They look scary because of their gear, but they're people just like you and me."

"If you say so…" Lizzy trailed off as she looked ahead.

About twenty people stood between Zara and Lizzy and the end to the nightmare. Or at least, it would be the end of this *part* of it. It was obvious that whatever was happening wasn't going to end when they got home, but Zara would be *home* with people she could trust. She'd learned long ago that she could get through anything with her mom and dad by her side. For years as a child, she'd been in and out of hospitals, battling illness, and she'd won. They would win this, too.

She pictured her father working overtime like these men and women, keeping Boston safe, worrying about her and Jordan. He had always fought for what was right. He wouldn't stand by idly while his fellow officers kept Boston under control. Her father would fight through his worry and fear and he would get the job done.

Zara found comfort in her confidence that her dad would understand why she'd had to lie to get Lizzy away from Mr. Peters. She had to keep reminding herself of that as the line crept forward, as she got closer to the moment when she would betray Lizzy's trust. Zara went over what she would say and how she would say it, trying out different options. It had to be urgent, but she didn't want to induce panic.

I'll lead with the fact that we're not sick. No symptoms. She chewed on her lower lip and took another step forward. No… I'll lead with who my dad is. Hi, I'm Zara Williams. My dad is Officer John Williams of the Boston PD, shield number—

"Dad!" Lizzy said, her voice surprised as she shouted and waved. "Zara, he found my note." She frowned. "How did he get here so fast? He must have woken up just a few minutes after we left."

"No…" It was all Zara could say as a weight settled into her chest and a sour taste formed in her mouth. She began to tremble.

"He doesn't look happy." Lizzy grimaced. She looked at Zara and put a hand on her shoulder. "Hey, it's okay. He will understand after we explain it in more detail."

"No." Zara said it again, this time more forcefully.

"Yes, he will," Lizzy said, her tone comforting. "Really, Zee. You look scared out of your mind. It's going to be fine."

"No!" Zara shouted this time and turned toward the officer who was still six people ahead. She grabbed Lizzy's hand and pulled, hard, shoving her way past the people in line to the front.

"What are you doing?" Lizzy jerked her hand away.

"Liz, come with me," Zara said, frantic.

Lizzy put her hand on her hip. "You're so dramatic. I'm going to go talk to him." She turned on her heel and started making her way toward her father.

"Damn it!" Zara shouted, not caring if she sounded crazy.

"What's going on?" A stern voice behind her made Zara turn back toward the glass doors.

"Officer, you have to help me," she said, tears welling up in her eyes.

The officer's eyes widened as he took in her frazzled, dirty appearance. "Were you at the World's Fair, miss?" His question had a hint of fear in it, and those around her who were close enough to hear his question jerked their heads to look at her. It seemed everyone nearby was waiting on her response.

Zara took a step back. "Yes, but—"

The crowd around her scrambled away, all except the officer.

"We've got one!" he shouted as he grabbed hold of Zara's arm.

"Hey! Let me go," she said. "I didn't do anything."

"Sorry, miss. You're going to have to come with me." The officer pushed her toward the large, black trucks. The way before him quickly cleared as he shouted, "Coming through! We've got one here!"

"Stop!" Zara shouted. She looked desperately for a friendly face in the crowd. "Someone help!" Most turned away at her pleas. "I'm not sick, I swear!"

"You look feverish to me." The officer said as he resisted her attempts to pull away from him.

"It's ninety-five degrees out here!" Zara struggled, but it was no use.

He half pushed, half pulled her to the truck, and another officer opened up the back. When the door swung open, pure terror filled Zara's entire body. Six individuals were in the back of the truck. They had on surgical masks, but their eyes were bloodshot. Three held their heads in their hands, rocking back and forth, moaning. All of them looked weak, barely able to move.

Zara screamed. "You can't put me in there!"

"We're going to have to drug this one, too," the officer said.

His hands dug into her arm as he held it out and a person in scrubs stepped around the truck, preparing a syringe. No matter how hard she pulled, she wasn't strong to break his hold. Tears blurred her vision, and she sobbed in despair as the needle pierced her skin.

Chapter 15

Timothy Peters

Timothy barely had time to dodge as Frank thrust the sharp blade right where his torso had been. Frank stumbled past Timothy, cutting nothing but air, catching his balance far too quickly. His arm swung in a wide arc, and Timothy ducked, his heart racing.
"Frank, stop!" Timothy scrambled back, running into the dining table and knocking a chair to the ground. It clattered on the floor behind him, and Timothy tripped, falling and skidding across the hardwood and into the wall. Hands trembling, he reached for his ankle holster.
"Thought you could pull the wool over my eyes, eh, Southie," Frank said, his expression dark as he stalked forward. "Thought one o' the Boys would back ya up? Thought old Frank was too stupid to figure it out?" He kicked the chair out of his way.
Timothy scooted back against the wall, fighting the illogical urge to curl into a ball as he fumbled to release the gun from the ankle holster. "No, Frank... you've got to listen to me," he said. "I was on my way here before I met you. You *made* me bring you here."
Frank narrowed his eyes. "Ya coulda told me your friend was a cop."
"I thought you were in trouble, that Mr. Williams could help." Timothy lied, hoping that his very real panic covered over his deceit. "How was I supposed to know you would want to stay away from the police?" He finally jerked the gun free, but before he could bring it up to aim it, Frank kicked it out of his hand. It sailed through the air and into the living room, clacking against the floor as it slid under the couch.
Frank threw his head back and laughed, but when he snapped his head back down, his eyes were wide with fury. "You really do think I'm stupid!" He looked at his knife, tilting it so that the sunlight coming through the window shone off the steel. "Maybe slittin' your throat is too good for you. Maybe," he said slowly, "I oughtta tie you down and skin your sorry ass."
Timothy's stomach lurched, and he heaved, which only seemed to amuse Frank more. "Frank," Timothy said, catching his breath, "I'm sorry. I should have mentioned that Mr. Williams was a cop. That's on me. But you can't seriously be considering murder? I thought you were a decent guy. You've never harmed a woman or a child, remember?"
"You ain't no woman, and you ain't no child." Frank stepped closer. "You're a liar, and I gave you fair warning. You crossed me, Southie."
Timothy kicked hard when Frank took his next step, and his heel connected with the side of Frank's kneecap. Frank lost his balance this time and went down on one knee with a grunt. Timothy struck, his fist colliding with Frank's jaw. Timothy clambered for the knife, trying to take advantage of the flesh wound on Frank's arm by digging his fingers into it. He gained the advantage, but not for long. One second he was grasping Frank's wrist, banging his hand on the floor to try to dislodge the knife, and the next, Frank had jammed a knee into Timothy's stomach, winding him, throwing him on his back. Once more, Timothy found himself with Frank's knife to his throat.
"You can join your friends in hell, Southie," Frank said, and the knife began to cut.
"Tim?" A small, quivering voice hammered through the air and seemed to hit both Timothy and Frank at the same time.
The knife let up, and Timothy's hand shot to the laceration as he looked up to find Zara's cousin, Annika, standing where the hallway met the open dining room and living room. She wore a floor-length, pink nightgown, frills at the hems, dotted with butterflies. Annika looked wide-eyed, horrified, at the two men.
"Hey, sweetheart," Frank said, putting the knife behind his back, standing up quickly. He suddenly had a smile on his face, and his voice was gentle and kind. "We were just playin' around, wrestlin' like boys do, you know? Ain't that right?" He looked down at Timothy.
"Um, yeah, that's right," Timothy said. He sat up, but the room swayed a little. Blood was seeping from the cut, and his head was pounding.
"You're bleeding!" Annika said, tears welling up in her eyes.
"Uh... you got any Band-Aids, sweetheart?" Frank asked.
She nodded. "In the bathroom."
"Why don't you go get some." He smiled again, and Annika scurried back down the hallway. He turned a scowl on Timothy as he put away the knife in a sheath on his belt. "You're a lucky man, Southie. I ain't killin' ya in front of a kid. Wouldn't be right." He stomped over to the kitchen, ripped some paper towels from a roll, and came back to kneel in front of him. He tossed the wad of paper towels at Timothy and gestured to the cut. "Ya got a little somethin' right there," he said sarcastically.
"You're not going to kill me?" Timothy asked as he pressed the paper towels against the wound, the spinning room stabilizing around him.
"You complainin'?" he asked, voice rising.
"No," Timothy shook his head, the motion making him nauseous. He swallowed bile, and closed his eyes, trying to gather himself together.
"I don't hurt kids," Frank said. "Killin' you would be hurtin' her. I ain't takin' her with me, and all her kin is dead. You *are* takin' her with you, right?"
"Yes," Timothy said. "Absolutely."
Frank ground his teeth. "You really know how to work a guy up," he said. He stood and shook out his arms. Then, he began to count to ten over and over again in a whispering voice.

Annika reappeared with a box of Band-Aids, and her face scrunched up in confusion. "What are you doing?" she asked.
Frank stopped counting and spun to face her. He looked almost embarrassed. "My therapist told me countin' to ten would help when I'm feelin'…" He looked at Timothy. "… upset."
Annika walked lightly over to where Timothy was and handed him the box. "My mom tells me to do the same thing," she said. "Where is my mom?" she asked. "Do you know? I've been by myself all day."
Timothy blinked. "You… haven't been outside?"
"I'm not allowed outside without permission, silly." Annika shook her head and gestured with one finger as she spoke, bobbing her head from side to side every so often. "I spent the night with Auntie Viv, and usually she comes to get me after breakfast is ready, but she didn't, so I watched cartoons for a long time, but then I got hungry, and I know my mom doesn't like it when I eat sweets in the morning, but like I said, I was hungry, so I got some cookies, and—"
"Annika," Timothy interrupted her when there was no indication that her story was coming to an end any time soon. "I get it."
"So… did my mom send you to get me?" Annika asked.
Timothy opened his mouth, but he didn't know what to say. *Should I tell her that her mom, her aunt, and her uncle are dead?* He looked into her inquiring, brown eyes, so alive and happy and unburdened. He couldn't do it.
"Yep," Timothy said, the word coming out too high-pitched.
Frank threw him a questioning look and mouthed, "What the hell?"
Yeah, I'm not going to take judgment from a thug who almost killed me.
"Great!" Annika put her hands behind her back and swayed so that her nightgown swished. "So… what are we doing now?"
"Well, you're going to get dressed, uh… and you're going to pack up your suitcase, and then… we're going to go." Timothy smiled.
Annika shrugged. "Okay," she said, and then she skipped down the hall.
"Hey, Southie," Frank said, whispering in a harsh tone, "I ain't no expert, but the kid's gonna figure out you's lyin' to her, and she's gonna figure it out pretty quick once we step outside and she sees that dead guy across the street."
Timothy climbed to his feet and looked at the box of Band-Aids. He squeezed his eyes shut. "I know," he said.
"Here," Frank held out his hand and gestured for Timothy to give him the box. He took it and dug out an extra-large Band-Aid. He peeled the packaging off and stepped up to Timothy. "I got ya good," he said as he batted away Timothy's hand and pressed the Band-Aid over the cut. "But it'll be fine. Not nearly as bad as my arm," he said.
"Thanks?" Timothy blinked several times, not sure what to make of Frank bandaging the wound on his neck.
Frank worked his jaw back and forth as he stepped away. "I don't like whatcha did," Frank said. "But… I guess I can see how I mighta forced ya into it." He scuffed his shoe against the floor like a kid being forced to apologize.
"Okay…" Timothy stared at Frank.
"I just get so mad when people think I'm stupid," Frank said, finally. "I know I ain't the sharpest crayon in the box, but I got street smarts. And I'm a good person." He gestured toward the hallway, his expression making it clear that he believed his refusal to kill someone in front of a child was proof of his good nature.
"Yeah, I mean, I think we can all agree that not killing me was the right thing to do," Timothy said.
Frank pursed his lips. "I'm sorry I got so mad, okay?" He glanced at the couch, then looked back at Timothy. He chuckled. "You're tougher than ya look, Southie. You almost got me with that gun." He shook his head and patted his own chest. "Like a roach, I tell ya. I'm unstoppable."
"Are you going to let me get my gun?" Timothy asked.
"Are you kiddin' me?" Frank said, laughing and shaking his head. "Nah." He walked around the couch, bent down and picked up the gun from where it had come to a stop at the foot of the coffee table. "I'll take this as a gift, a gift from one friend to another as an apology, from you to me, Southie, for tryin' to trick me into gettin' nabbed by the cops." He shrugged as he checked that the safety was on before putting it away at the small of his back.
"You threw away my taser," Timothy said. "How am I supposed to get Annika back to my car safely? You saw the guys with guns. It's dangerous out there."
Frank nodded. "All right, all right. You convinced me. As your friend, I'll come with you to your car, and then you can take me to my uncle's place. If I'd known you had a gun and thought about the possibility of you havin' a car, well, I guess we wouldn't have come out here and rescued the girl. So, you're welcome," he said, nodding once in a generous manner. "Besides, I'm not sure I wanna stay in a place like this." He shuddered. "Probably haunted already."
"Where does your uncle live?" Timothy asked tentatively.
"Out near Worcester. He's got some stables out there, and from the way things are goin' down here in the city, I think some country air would do me some good." Frank breathed deeply as if he were already there. "It's a little outta your way back to Wellesley, but you don't mind, right, *friend*?" He narrowed his eyes just slightly, quirking one eyebrow as if daring Timothy to object.
"I guess we're going back to the car together, then," Timothy said. Not that I have much of a choice, not while Frank has my gun. But… at least once we're rid of him, I can get Annika to safety back in Wellesley.
"So… whatcha gonna tell the girl?" Frank asked. "Ya better get your story straight."
"I like stories!" Annika's lighthearted voice interrupted them as she bounced into the room, a pink backpack strapped to her back.
"Well, Timmy over there's got a real good one," Frank said, flashing a toothy grin.
Annika spun around to face him, and Timothy had to work to keep his expression neutral. He struggled over what to say.
"Um, well… you see, things aren't going so well outside," Timothy said.
"Yeah," Annika said, her smile fading. "I heard some people earlier, and they sounded like they didn't feel too good. And there was shouting, and some sirens…"
"Well," Timothy said, "your mom wants you to come with me, and we're going to get to safety in Wellesley with *my* mom. I really think you're going to like her."

"Is Heather there?" Annika asked.

Timothy nodded. "She sure is."

"Is my mom there?"

"I… don't know," he lied. "Maybe."

"What about Auntie Viv and Uncle John?"

Timothy swallowed a lump in his throat. "I don't think they'll be there."

"Okay," she said, shrugging, just accepting whatever he said. She was so trusting, and Timothy hated that he was going to be part of destroying that part of her.

"There are some… scary things outside," Timothy said carefully. "You're going to see some people… sleeping in weird positions. And… um, you might see some people who are hurt or some people who are angry."

Annika frowned and stuck out her lower lip, swishing back and forth like she did before.

"I'm going to need you to do exactly what I say, okay?" Timothy said. "And we will want to be quiet. If we see anyone, we might hide in the bushes or behind a fence or something, but I'm going to keep you safe."

"You ready to go?" Frank asked as he opened the front door.

He wasn't ready. He wasn't ready to expose Annika to the horrors across Mattapan, wasn't ready to risk his life again or go anywhere with Frank, despite the man's friendly, crooked grin. But he held out his hand, and Annika took it. He stepped out into the hot, summer sun with the five-year-old girl at his side. He couldn't stop looking at her as they walked down the front steps, couldn't stop wondering how much longer he could protect her from the truth, couldn't stop wondering if he actually *was* protecting her at all. Maybe he was just protecting himself. Somehow her ignorance, her trusting nature, her childish view of the world made him feel hopeful.

"Who are they?" Annika asked after they cleared the last concrete step. "Are they the angry guys you were talking about?"

Timothy jerked his head up, gasping with surprise as he swung Annika up into his arms. Two men with guns leaned against the chain-link fence.

"Thought that was you turnin' down this street, Frank," one of them said, flicking a cigarette to the sidewalk as he straightened up. "You owe me big, and I want to be paid in information." He raised an eyebrow at Timothy and Annika. "And who do we have here?" he asked, his voice sickeningly sweet.

His companion smiled and brandished his gun. "Looks like leverage."

Chapter 16

Alexander Roman

"Oliver!" A jolt of panic shot through Alex's veins at the sight of his son following Minnie into the fray. He jumped out of the truck, not bothering to close the door behind him, and rushed after Oliver.

Ahead, a portion of the crowd scattered as the police officer made his arrest. Townsfolk ran every which way with yellow bags of goods swinging from their arms. Half of those that stayed watched the argument between the policeman and the brothers unfold, several of them offering their own opinions on the matter. The other half still bickered, shoving their way out of the store, trying to buy the last of the toilet paper off those who'd been lucky enough to grab a package.

Alex caught up to Oliver, panting and grimacing, his body aching and bursts of pain radiating from his ribs. He grabbed his son's shoulder and turned him around, securing one hand on each of Oliver's arms.

"You can't go off like that," Alex shouted.

Oliver's wide, teary eyes made Alex rethink his panicked tone. He pulled his son into a hug, but they were close enough now that neither one of them could ignore the scene unfolding just a few feet away in front of the dollar store. Someone in a yellow apron shoved two people out of the store, closed the glass door, and locked it, turning the open sign around so that it read "closed" instead.

Minnie stood near Samson, and though he was growling pointedly at the guy shouting at the officer, she didn't take hold of his collar. Instead, she stood with her arms crossed, lips pursed as she glared at the man Samson clearly didn't like.

"How come you ain't arrestin' Jane, Willard?" The man shouted at the police officer who had just finished cuffing the man who'd tried to hit him. "She done run off with my brother's property, and you're arrestin' James instead?"

"Put a cork in it, Jerry." Willard jerked James backward toward his police car. Samson stood solidly between the policeman and the cuffed man's brother, barking fiercely. Jerry didn't so much as take a step toward Willard while the dog barred his teeth.

"You stole that toilet paper from Jane, you ass!" A woman with curlers in her hair, her makeup thick and bright, shouted from the sidelines.

"*You* put a cork in it, Ruth!" James shouted as he was tugged toward the police car in cuffs. "She ain't never liked me," he said to the policeman. "You can't trust a word she says."

"Just let him go, Willard!" Jerry said with an eye still on Samson.

"Your brother took a swing at an officer," Willard said. "That ain't no joke. I can't let him off for that one."

"Aw, come on," James said as Willard opened the door, put a hand on the top of his head, and guided him into the back seat. "I was mid swing before I even realized it was you. I was just caught up, is all."

"A few hours in a cell will do you some good," Willard said, wrinkling his nose as he unlocked the cuffs. "Seems to me like you've been drinkin' already today. Good gravy, James, it's not even lunch time." He closed the door on a groaning James and turned back toward the brother. "You better walk to the police station if you've been drinkin', too, Jerry." He put his hands on his hips and pointed to the bystanders. "All y'all better get home. Hunker down and stop causing trouble. You should be ashamed of yourselves!"

The woman in curlers stuck out a pouting lip, and the others had the decency to blush or avert their eyes. The crowd dissipated slowly. Alex raised an eyebrow as two teens passed him and Oliver, one of them mumbling, "That's the most interesting thing that's happened in Red Bud all summer."

Hopefully, nothing more exciting than that is headed your way, Alex thought.

"And Minnie," Willard said, "you can call Samson off."

"Come, Samson." Minnie uncrossed her arms and patted her thigh. Samson perked his ears, relaxed, and trotted over to her. She shrugged at the police officer as Jerry stomped away. "He jumped out of the truck of his own accord, Willard. He likes you."

"He likes dog biscuits." Willard shook his head but smiled and pulled out a bone-shaped cookie from his shirt pocket. Samson wagged his tail and barked excitedly as the policeman walked over and let him snatch the treat. "You're a good boy, Samson." The police officer scratched the dog's ears.

"Hey, while I've got ya here, my friend has some questions. We were headin' to the station, but maybe you know what he's after," Minnie said, nodding at Alex.

Alex stepped forward and held out a hand, which Willard took and shook heartily. "Officer, I don't want to bother you if you need to get that man to the station."

Willard waved his hand in the air. "Nah, he's fine. It's nice and cool in the car. My guess is that he'll pass out here in a minute and snore all the way to the station. My back seat's got a nice indentation of his butt, so he's probably right comfortable."

Alex had never spent much time in a town as small as Red Bud. Things obviously worked differently than they did in Atlanta. *Maybe that means they're not as tight lipped when it comes to information.*

Oliver left Alex's side to wrap his arms around Samson's neck after the dog wolfed down the last of the biscuit. Samson nuzzled Oliver's belly before licking his face. Alex smiled, but the smile didn't last long. The officer was waiting, and he needed to ask some questions. But he didn't want to do it in front of his son.

He turned to Minnie. "Could you take Oliver back to the truck, Minnie?"

"Sure thing," Minnie said. "Let's wait for your daddy in the truck, Oliver. I might need your help gettin' this big ole mutt in the back seat." She smiled warmly as she patted Samson's side, but Oliver looked up at Alex questioningly.

"I'll be where you can see me," Alex said, "but I've got some grown-up stuff to talk to the officer about. If you can be a good helper and get Samson in the truck, maybe we can pick up some ice-cream for later."

"Darn tootin'!" Minnie said, causing Oliver to chuckle. "We've got the best ice cream parlor in the whole state on the square downtown."

Oliver nodded hesitantly. He went with Minnie, but he looked over his shoulder every few steps as they made their way back to the truck. Samson walked beside him, nudging Oliver's hand and drawing his attention a little more fully each time. Alex had never loved a dog so much; the worry and fear in Oliver's eyes abated when Samson was by his side.

"So, what can I do for you, sir?" Willard said.

Alex swallowed hard as he turned to the police officer, trying to find the right words. "Well… my wife, um…" He frowned, his tongue growing thick, the words he needed to say feeling so wrong. "We were at the World's Fair, and…" He trailed off as his chest tightened. He hadn't had to tell Minnie; she'd understood. He hadn't had to say the words out loud yet.

"You need to file a missing person's report?" the police officer asked.

"No. She's not missing. She's… she didn't make it, and we had to leave her, to get out…" Tears rimmed Alex's eyes, and heat rushed into his cheeks. He glanced at the truck, at Oliver, and fought to keep his composure.

Take care of Oliver. That means I can't break down again.

Willard's features softened, and he shook his head. "I'm sorry for your loss, sir. You need to claim the body, that's what you're after?"

Alex nodded. "Do you know anything about how I can go about that?"

"I know it might be a while," Willard said gently. "They'll comb the area, looking for survivors and gathering the dead, but son, it'll be more difficult with the sickness. My guy Terrance led a few volunteers up there, and he said this morning that the process hasn't even started. It's complicated because they can't just send people in. Terrance and the rest aren't even sure they'll be allowed to help. Not to mention the whole city's in chaos. Word is that a lot of sick people poured into St. Louis, causing car accidents and panic when they died."

"So, you can't help me?" Alex asked, his heart sinking.

Willard put a hand on Alex's shoulder. "I didn't say that, son." He pulled out a pad of paper and unclipped a pen. "What was your wife's name?"

"Naomi," Alex said. "Naomi Roman." Saying her name out loud almost physically hurt.

"And, I know this is difficult, son, but can I ask my people to be on the lookout for any defining marks? What did she look like?" His pen hovered above the paper, but his eyes were kind as he waited.

Alex sucked in a shaky breath as he pulled up her image in his mind. He'd been trying so hard not to think about her, about how perfect she was. "She's got black hair, long, but it was braided last night."

He paused. It didn't seem right that it had been less than a full twenty-four hours since his wife's death. Part of him couldn't process that she was gone at all, but the other part felt as if he'd been without her for much longer.

Alex continued, working to speak clearly. He gripped the hem of his shirt, balling the fabric into his hands to keep them from trembling as he described her. "She had hazel brown eyes with a little green in them. She wore a golden cross every day, small with a diamond in the center. She's got a strawberry-shaped birthmark just above her ankle." He wiped away a few tears he couldn't keep at bay. "And, um, she should have my business card in her pocket. She might even have her credit cards on her, now that I think about it." He smiled at her memory. "She never could seem to keep her cards in her wallet."

"I'm the same way, son," Willard said softly.

"She always forgot to empty her pockets. Credit cards, pens, candies. She was worse than Oliver. And half her clothes couldn't go in the dryer. Doing her laundry was a nightmare." He half laughed, half cried out and then ran his hands over his face. He shook his head and took a steadying breath. "Sorry," he said.

"Not a problem, son. No need to apologize. She sounds like a lovely woman," Willard said as he clipped the pen back in place, folded the pad's cover closed, and put it away. "Will you be in town a few days? I can call around, talk to my people that went on up to help, see what I can find out."

"Thank you, officer," Alex said. "I think we'll be staying at Minnie's for now, but I'll let you know if that changes."

"That's good, that's good," Willard said, nodding. "She'll take care of you both. And it'll be good for her, too. She hasn't known what to do with herself since Lauren up and left." He gave Alex's back a good pat. "I'll let you know as soon as I hear anything at all."

"Thank you." Alex sighed as the officer turned back toward his car.

He was about to return to the truck when a country twang rang out from Willard's phone, and the officer pulled it out. "Hello, Terrance? How's it goin' up there? Still a mess?"

Alex paused at the name. The same Terrance he said was part of the volunteer team?

"What?" Willard said, straightening his shoulders, eyes going wide. "But you said they didn't even let y'all inside the fairgrounds." His free hand went to his forehead. "How am I gonna tell Barbie? And Nickie… damn it! They've got kids!" He paused, listening.

Alex took a step forward, frowning as he listened, as the rock in his stomach grew heavier.

"Well, get out of there, Terrance. Come on home." Willard frowned as the man on the other side of the line said something. "What do you mean they won't let you go?" He looked up at the sky. "That ain't right. Let me see what I can do from here. Okay, you take care, and keep away from anyone that doesn't look healthy, got it?" He hung up the phone and hung his head, hands on his hips, unmoving for a moment.

"Officer?" Alex asked. "Was that… was that the man you told me about? The one who went up to the World's Fair with a team of volunteers?"

Willard looked up, a mixture of pain and anger and confusion in his eyes that Alex recognized all too well. "Yeah," he said. "And two of ours caught that sickness we've been seein' on the TV. They're dead." He breathed out in frustration. "Damn it, they're dead!"

Alex froze. His heartbeat thudded in his chest as the seconds ticked by slowly, as if time itself had slowed. A tremor of fear rippled through his body, leaving behind a numb, tingling sensation in his limbs. His knees buckled, and he barely managed to keep his balance. The pieces of the puzzle were coming together, and the full picture was beginning to look more terrifying than he ever could have imagined.

They caught the sickness. They weren't at the fairgrounds last night… that means we've got a worst-case scenario. Alex couldn't deny it, couldn't hold on to the hope that this would be over soon. It's a fast-acting agent, it's deadly, and it's contagious.

Chapter 17

Timothy Peters

Timothy held Annika protectively, turning his body so that while he could still see the thugs, he could also shield the girl if they started shooting. Annika had quickly understood that they were in some kind of danger, and she buried her head in Timothy's shoulder, clinging tightly to him. Frank casually meandered in front of them, putting himself between Timothy and the two men with guns.

"Leverage?" Frank laughed. "Since when does Frank Russo care about anybody but Frank Russo? I broke into that house, tryin' to find somethin' to eat after you lot chased me all over town." He held out his hands, palms upward, shrugging. "You can shoot 'em right this second, and I wouldn't bat an eye."

Timothy glared at the back of Frank's head, but then the man turned to look over his shoulder and winked before spitting at Timothy's feet, making a show of it. Timothy thought he understood, so he played along.

"We don't know this man," Timothy said, his eyes darting from one gun to the next. His own gun was concealed under Frank's shirt. "Please," he added, "just let us go."

The man who'd first spoken worked his jaw back and forth, tapping his gun against his thigh as he seemed to consider his next steps. The other man hung back, deferring, seeming to wait for the first to make a decision.

"Well, Frank," the lead thug said, "we got rid of the Irish, for now, anyway, but we only got so much time before the National Guard shows up, and we've got to lay low again. Ace has plans for CON, and he needs his debts collected. The boss gets what the boss wants. So, I'm gonna bet on the rumors that you've got some weird code of ethics about kids, a code ConMen don't abide by." He waved his second-in-command forward. "Mike, you keep our new friends company, and if Frank steps out of line, you've got yourself one adorable punching bag."

Timothy's eyes widened in horror as Annika whimpered in his arms. "She's only five years old, you sick freak!" he shouted.

Mike pushed past Frank and put his gun to Timothy's head. "Can't we just kill this guy now, Andy? We don't need him."

"That'd be a mistake," Frank said. "The kid's rich." He sighed. "All right, ya got me. I was makin' nice with this wuss 'cause it's easier to hold a hostage for ransom when they think you's on their side. I know you want information, Andy, and I can get that for ya, no problem, but Frank Russo pays his debts in style."

Andy waved Mike off, and Timothy let out the breath he'd been holding in as the thug lowered his gun. Mike's shoulders sagged, apparently disappointed. Timothy looked at Frank, frowning.

How does he come up with this stuff?

"If he's so rich, what's he doing in Mattapan, Frank?" Andy asked.

"Getting' the kid," Frank said as if it were obvious. "You know how it is. Moneybags meets maid, maid gets preggo, and moneybags has a new, shiny apple of his eye. Shit hits the fan, everybody's dyin', maid keels over, moneybags saves the day, satisfies his hero complex and all that. The guy spilled the whole story to me, thinkin' we was gettin' to be friends."

Andy shook his head, grinning. "Frank, you always surprise me."

"Don't listen, Annika," Timothy whispered into her ear. "He's just telling stories." Annika didn't say anything as she squeezed her eyes shut and burrowed her head deeper into Timothy's shoulder.

"You can't trust *him*." Mike scowled.

"Hey," Frank said, "I'm not holdin' back. I swear on my mother's grave." He put a hand in the air, his expression solemn. "Your wish is my command," he said. "Information and cash. It's what we all want, right? And I'm offerin' it to ya on a silver platter."

"You've got my attention," Andy said. "Go on."

"We split the ransom money, fifty-fifty. That, plus the information, and we're square," Frank said. "More than square. In fact, you'd owe *me* a favor."

Timothy's mouth dropped open. Is he playing them or me? Or both?

Andy licked his lips. "How much you think you're gonna get out of him?"

"Well," Frank said, chuckling, "that's the good part. Between him and the kid, I figure it's an easy two, maybe three mill."

"Seventy-five," Andy pointed to himself and then back at Frank, "twenty-five." He raised his eyebrows. "*That* and the information, and we're square. No favors owed."

"What about me?" Mike said, his cheeks flushing red. "And Ace? You really think he's gonna let you make a deal like that without talkin' to him first?"

Without so much as blinking, Andy shot Mike in the chest. The thug didn't even have time to protest. Timothy flinched and ducked to the ground, crouching around Annika's small frame. Mike held his hand to the wound near his heart where blood soaked through his t-shirt, and he fell to his knees, eyes wide in surprise. Andy shot him again, and Mike fell on his face, unmoving.

"What Ace don't know can't hurt him," Andy said, shrugging. "I heard you pulled off a ransom, a pretty big one, back in the day, Frank. If you're doin' it again, I want in. Seventy-five, twenty-five."

Timothy cursed as Annika cried and trembled, as he tried to keep her from seeing the ever-widening pool of blood seeping from Mike's body. *He's playing* me, *damn it.*

"C'mon, Andy," Frank said. "How you figure that's a fair deal?"

"I lost two good grunts today," Andy said, shrugging and nodding toward Mike's body on the ground. "And I killed off those Irish chasin' you. And it'll take some work keepin' this all under wraps so that Ace doesn't find out. He'll kill us both and take one hundred percent if he catches wind of what we're doin'."

Frank clucked his tongue. "You're a businessman at heart, Andy. Gotta love that 'bout you. All right, all right, you got a deal." He shook his head. "Gotta say, you've got some balls. I wouldn't cross my uncle, no way, no how. He'll be gettin' his cut of my cut, I'll tell ya that right now."

"Yeah, well, Ace ain't no capo," Andy said.

"True," Frank said, smiling broadly.

The second Andy relaxed was the second he died. Frank pulled the gun from the back of his jeans so fast, Timothy didn't even notice he'd done it until the loud *crack* rattled Timothy's bones. The thug fell back against the chain-link fence and slumped to the ground. Frank walked over to Andy and wrenched the gun from the thug's grasp.

"I'll take that." He did the same thing with Mike. "And I'll take that, too, thank ya very much." He strutted over to where Timothy still shielded Annika and took a bow, stretching his hands out to either side, each one gripping a gun.

Timothy just stared at Frank for a minute, trying to figure out what had just happened. Then, something Andy had said about Frank's uncle clicked. He scowled. "You're part of the *mob*?"

"Yeah, I mean, sorta," Frank said, straightening up. He checked the safeties on the handguns and then nodded at Timothy's foot. "I'm gonna need that ankle holster."

"How are you *sort of* in the mob, Frank?" Timothy asked.

Frank raised his eyebrows and looked pointedly at his ankle, so he complied and held it out. Frank put one foot forward.

"Really?" Timothy said, staring flatly up at him.

"Yeah, really. My hands are full, nitwit." As Timothy sighed and strapped the holster under Frank's khakis just above the ankle, Frank continued. "Anyone who's related to a capo or a boss is sorta in the mob. I got a fifth cousin three times removed, and he's been workin' for my uncle since he was twelve." He put one of the guns in the holster, left Timothy's behind his back, and stuck the last one by his hip. "This day is turnin' out a lot better than I thought it would," he said.

Annika had been mostly quiet in her terrified crying, but when Timothy had moved away from her to strap on the holster, her cries had gotten louder. After a long, high-pitched wail, she shouted, "I want my mom!"

"Geez, kid," Frank said as he put a finger in his ear.

Timothy stood and picked Annika up. "Hey, you've got to calm down, okay? We don't want more bad men to hear and be able to find us."

That just made Annika wail even louder.

"Amateur." Frank scoffed at Timothy as he reached in his back pocket. "Hey, sweetheart," he said. "How 'bout a cherry flavored sucker?"

She sniffled and eyed the candy, quieting down. Annika reached out and took it, unwrapping it and sticking it in her mouth. She lay her head against Timothy's shoulder, the hard candy clicking against her teeth.

"Where did you get that?" Timothy asked.

"Ah, I keep a few in my back pocket," Frank said. "Got low blood sugar. You ready to go? Andy's got other guys combin' the streets. We'd better get outta here. Those shots were like a neon sign flashin' our whereabouts to everyone in a half mile radius."

"Then, let's go," Timothy said.

"Where ya parked?" Frank asked.

"I'm at a church just a few blocks from where we met," Timothy said.

"Yeah, I know the place." Frank nodded. "Let's go a different way, down some side streets, avoid the main roads, know what I mean?"

Timothy agreed, and he followed Frank through Mattapan. Annika fell asleep after about twenty minutes of walking. He'd encouraged her to keep her eyes closed as they went, and it had had the desired effect. There was so much death and destruction everywhere. Timothy had never been more eager to get back to Wellesley.

It was four o'clock by the time Timothy and Frank made it to the church lot. After he'd put a drowsy Annika in the back and buckled her up, he slid into the driver's seat. Frank had wasted no time getting into the passenger seat, gun in hand, and he was already making himself comfortable by the time Timothy's seat belt clicked into place and he started the car.

"You know how to get to Worcester?" Frank asked.

"Yes," Timothy said as he maneuvered the vehicle out of the little memorial alcove. "But the way out of Boston isn't going to be pretty, and it's going to take forever."

"That's all right," Frank said as he tapped the GPS screen. "I'd love to get to know more 'bout ya, Southie. You seem like an interestin' fella."

Timothy pulled out of the lot and began weaving through the maze of vehicles and debris. He didn't see any moving vehicles at first. At some point since Timothy had arrived, people had begun using all lanes to get out of the city, and while there were some pileups and accidents on what was supposed to be the incoming lane, Timothy always managed to find a way through, thanks in part to holes in the wreckage where a larger vehicle had apparently rammed aside smaller cars blocking the way.

They drove for hours, creeping forward most of the time, though the main highway still had stretches of cleared space. Frank asked all sorts of questions, and Timothy answered as succinctly as he could. If he tried to evade a question, the man got irritated and tried to dig further. For a short period of time, Annika was awake, and Frank talked to her. That made Timothy squirm, though he said nothing harmful. It was a blessing when Annika fell back asleep. Timothy savored the stretches of time when Frank was quiet, staring out the window at the rising smoke and never-ending devastation.

Finally, they turned down a long driveway in the countryside. Ahead, a picturesque ranch and stable sat against a clear blue sky. Frank started digging in the glove compartment, interrupting the relief at almost being rid of him.

"I don't have any more weapons," Timothy said.

"Not what I'm lookin' for." Frank pulled out a pen and a receipt. He squinted at the GPS screen and began jotting down information.

Ice ran through Timothy's veins as he realized what Frank was doing. "Why are you writing down my parents' address?" he asked. The GPS screen showed the most recent places visited, and one of them was labeled "mom's house." Timothy had been too focused on navigating the roads to pay attention to what Frank had been doing.

He finished writing down the address, folded up the paper, and put it in his pocket. "Let's recap the day, shall we, Southie? I *don't* kill ya, though you come into town with a taser and insert yourself right into my life uninvited. Then, I *don't* kill ya when I find out you tried to get me busted. And then, I actually save your Southie, rich kid ass when Andy and Mike come along. And *then*, I decide to pass up a good ransom." He held up his hands. "Now, I know I don't do those anymore, but still... I coulda done it, and I didn't."

That's not exactly how I remember it, Timothy thought, but he kept that to himself. Instead, he said, "Thank you, Frank. We couldn't have made it without you." He tried to sound sincere.

"That's exactly my point," Frank said. "I knew you'd get it."

"Get what?" Timothy asked.

"Well, remember when I said I always pay my debts?" Frank asked.

"Sure," Timothy said, the word scratching against his throat.

"Well, I do. And I got lots o' debts, Southie." He smiled. "But, you see, I also always *collect* my debts. And that's why I needed to know where your ma's at, and your daddy in South Boston, and I even got a few other places from that handy list right there, just in case."

"Because you plan to collect a debt," Timothy said, his body turning numb.

"That's right," Frank said. He looked in the back seat where Annika slept. "I'll find ya when I need ya, but... if I were you, I might find a more suitable place for the kid. I like you a lot, Southie, but chances are, my uncle's guys are gonna come with me, and ya know, I can't exactly stop 'em from doin' whatever they want. If I were you, I might also make sure I was in Wellesley. You wouldn't wanna make the guys angry, makin' them track ya down."

Frank put his hand on the door.

"How long?" Timothy asked. "How long before I can expect you in Wellesley?"

"I'll give ya a couple days," Frank said, nodding at the back seat. "For her."

Chapter 18

Zara Williams

Zara had never been so sure she was going to die. What Mr. Peters had said about the illness, about government contingency plans, about… everything — he was right. His words played on repeat in her head as the police officer held her fast, one hand gripping her shoulder, the other holding a vice grip just above her elbow.

They'll want to control the information… if the authorities come, there will be no getting out. Zara's chest tightened as panic pinched her rapidly beating heart. He was right… they didn't hesitate.

Three of the people in the back of the black truck moaned and rocked, their hands pressed tightly against their eyes or ears or temples. One of them had blood seeping through the fabric of their surgical mask in messy blots around the outline of their lips. The other half of the passengers watched dully, eyes glazed over. A woman lifted her hand toward Zara, but it dropped back to the seat as she blinked far too slowly, a single tear escaping the corner of one eye. The three who were in pain were on their way to a gruesome death, and if the others hadn't been sick when they'd been put in the truck… well, their fates were likely sealed.

This is it. I'm going to die. Zara squeezed her eyes shut, every muscle tensing as the needle prick signaled her demise.

But the second it punctured her arm, the nurse with the needle grunted and cried out in pain, and the officer dropped Zara's arm. She was pushed to the ground as a form barreled into the police officer, knocking him to the ground. His head hit the concrete hard, dazing him. The nurse cowered out of the way, blood streaming out of her nose. Zara trembled, her hands flat on the hot asphalt. She sat up as a drop of blood trickled down her arm from the tiny puncture. The faint blue of a forming bruise was already visible where the officer had gripped her, adding a new mark among her older scrapes and bruises.

She stared at the syringe that had been knocked free, now only half a foot away near the curb. For a moment, she was seven years old again, curled up beneath a shiny metal table on wheels, wires and IV tubing extending from her body, connecting her to machines. The asphalt turned to white tile, and a breeze brought with it a subtle smell of disinfectant. She'd been so afraid, so tired. She'd just wanted to get away, but when she tried to run, she'd knocked over equipment and medical supplies. Vision blurred with tears, her eyes had focused on a syringe on the floor as her mother's voice calmed her cries.

Hey, Zee-zee, it's okay. You're not alone. You're never alone.

The white tile vanished, and Zara tore her eyes from the syringe. The police officer who had opened the door to the truck lunged at Mr. Peters, grabbed his sullied, button-down dress shirt and threw him against the back of the military-style truck. The back doors were still flung open, and Mr. Peters leaned back into the truck for just a moment, his eyes going wide as one of the drugged captives squinted at him. He pushed back against the officer, but the officer was bigger than he was.

"Run, Zara! Take care of Elizabeth!" Mr. Peters said through gritted teeth as he strained to stay as far away from those inside the truck as possible.

Her mind slurred as she processed his words. She looked behind her, frowning at the crowd. Lizzy was nowhere to be seen. The lines toward the doors had deformed and bulged toward the fight.

"Go!" Mr. Peters roared, and Zara's eyes snapped back to him.

She'd been trying so hard to get away from him, but now…

I can't leave him to die.

And he would. They would find out where he'd been, and it would be him inside that black truck instead of her. Zara's mind cleared as her eyes fell back on the syringe. A chill crept over her as she reached for it and wrapped her hand around the small, hard plastic cylinder. She had only one idea, and it went against every instinct.

The officer who'd fallen dazed to the ground stirred, and his movement spurred Zara into action. She scurried forward on her knees, raised the syringe, and injected the needle into the other officer's thigh, plunging the drugs into the man's body. He instantly let go of Mr. Peters, stumbled backwards, and tripped over Zara. He fell to the ground, landing on his rear end and slamming the back of his head on the front bumper of the vehicle behind them. He grasped feebly for Zara.

"What the…" His speech was slow as he frowned and smacked his lips. "You little—"

Zara watched, part of her horrified, as the officer's words were cut off by a loss of consciousness. He fell over onto his side, and blood began to pool under his head.

"No, no, no," Zara lurched forward to help the man.

"No time," Mr. Peters, voice gruff, grabbed Zara by the arm, yanked her to standing, and dragged her into the crowd. She tried to keep her eyes on the officer, relieved to see the nurse come to his aid. But he wasn't moving, and the nurse looked worried. Zara's attention was torn away from the man she'd injured when Mr. Peters pulled his gun and fired into the air.

Zara screamed and flinched away from him, but he didn't let her go. The crowd oscillated in a frenzy around them as shouting filled the air. Cries of pain and terror mixed with crazed jeers and taunts as some fled, trampling over each other, and others rushed the airport doors. Bodies slammed into them from every side, but Mr. Peters held firm, like a bulldozer plowing forward, carving a path for them. His limp only served to make him look more determined.

The authorities clustered together, pulling rioters off one another. Medical personnel huddled together or shrank against the glass windows, shielding their heads with their arms. Meanwhile, the crowd had swallowed Zara and Mr. Peters whole, and if it wasn't for him, Zara would have been swept away. She pushed forward, no longer fighting his direction. When they finally broke through the thickest portion of the crowd, Mr. Peters loosened his grip. Zara took back her wrist, rubbing the reddened skin where his hand had been. She gasped for a full breath and wiped tears from her eyes.

"We've got to keep moving," Mr. Peters said. He put a hand on her back and almost gently pushed her forward. His lips were pale, and a thin sheen of sweat covered his brow.

"I think I really hurt that officer," Zara said.

"He was going to kill you." Mr. Peters didn't seem to give her concerns a second thought.

He was just doing his job. Zara thought of her own father, out in the streets of Boston. Is he being forced to put people in trucks? But then she remembered the officer's face as he'd held her arm. He wasn't being forced. But still, did he think he was sending me to my death? The fact that the nurse was there to help didn't do much to assuage her guilt.

"Don't overthink it, Zara," Mr. Peters said. "You did what you had to do." He grimaced for a split second before regaining complete composure, though his limp was impossible to ignore.

"Are you okay?" Zara asked.

"I will be." He didn't stop. "Elizabeth should be around the corner, if she was smart enough to listen to me this time." His tone was biting.

Zara frowned. He tended to insult her on a regular basis, but he was usually more reserved when it came to Lizzy. "Why did you come back for me?" she asked, still panting as they turned the corner of the huge building.

"Elizabeth told me what happened." Mr. Peters said it like his words should explain his actions, but they only confused Zara more. They kept walking until they reached the back of the terminal where a small passenger jet was docked. The tarmac was still and quiet. Zara followed Mr. Peters, mulling over his words. *What did Liz say to him?* She frowned. *Does she even know what really happened? What I was trying to do?*

When they rounded the back of the plane, Lizzy was just ahead, leaning against the hood of a black BMW, arms crossed, face downcast. She looked up, a look of relief washing over her as she stood up straighter at the sight of them. "Dad! Zee!" She sprinted forward, closing the distance between them. She threw her arms around Zara. "I'm so glad you're okay. When that man grabbed you… I just, I didn't know what to do."

"If Zara hadn't been there, if she hadn't left that note—" Mr. Peters's voice broke, his tone a mixture of both pain and anger.

"What?" Zara asked, dumbfounded.

"I told Dad what happened, Zee," Lizzy said, her smile fading. She blushed as she looked at her dad. "He knows it was my idea. I know you cover for me all the time, but right now, you don't have to. I'm owning up to my mistake."

Zara's mouth dropped open, and she quickly snapped it shut, looking from Lizzy to Mr. Peters and back again. "But the note…" she said, trailing off.

"Yes," Mr. Peters said, crossing his arms and looking down his nose at Lizzy. "Tell me, Elizabeth, what possessed you to crumple it up and throw it away?"

Lizzy swallowed audibly, and the fact that she didn't make eye contact with her father wasn't lost on Zara. "I wanted to prove I could get supplies without your help, Dad. You're always treating me like a little kid, and this whole time, I've just felt so useless. It was Zara who got me to the stage, Zara who got you out of the scaffolding, Zara who drove us here… I wanted to *do* something on my own. Zara insisted on leaving the note for you after she couldn't talk me out of going, but I just… I wanted you to be proud, Daddy." She looked up at her father with big, doe-eyes and a perfectly subtle pouty lip.

Wow. She's good at this. Zara tried hard to keep her expression neutral, to keep the shock out of her eyes, to keep her mouth from gaping. Mr. Peters sighed and rubbed his hands over his face. He put his hands on his hips and looked up at the sky, shaking his head and biting his lip. When he looked back at his daughter, his anger had relented. "I *am* proud of you, Elizabeth," he said softly. "But if you pull anything like that ever again… damn it, Bethie, you could have been killed." His eyes glistened as he pulled Lizzy into a hug and held her to his chest.

"You haven't called me Bethie since I was, like, five," Lizzy said, her own eyes brimming with tears, though Zara couldn't tell if they were genuine.

"Well, it's been about that long since you've called me Daddy," Mr. Peters said. He sniffed, pulled away from his daughter, and put his hands on Lizzy's shoulders. "Promise me you'll be smarter."

"I promise." Lizzy nodded.

He looked at Zara. "And next time my daughter has any crazy ideas, you can't go along with it, got it?"

Zara nodded, her lips sealed in a tight line.

"But," Mr. Peters said, "thank you for trying to look out for her. You should have woken me, but… at least you left the note."

Zara swallowed a lump in her throat, thinking about how she'd drugged an officer to free Mr. Peters. "Is that why you came back for me? Because I… was looking out for Liz?"

"Look, Zara. I know I'm an ass sometimes, but I don't want you dead, okay?" He offered her a small smile, the first he'd *ever* offered. "If something happened to me, I'm going to need you to take care of my daughter." He looked at Lizzy. "No offense, Elizabeth, but you wouldn't make it out here on your own."

Lizzy shrugged. "Yeah, I guess I can't argue with that."

Zara bit the inside of her cheek. Well, now I have some sort of value to Mr. Peters, which is good because it looks like I'm stuck with him until Boston.

She nodded toward the car. "So, where'd you get that?" she asked.

Mr. Peters shuddered. "When I found your note, I had to resort to taking the keys from… one of the lounge guests. I wore a double layer of latex gloves from the First Aid kit and used one of the lounge's golf clubs from the little putting green in the corner of the lounge to hook the key ring that was halfway out of one man's pocket. I doused it in sanitizer and got here as quickly as I could."

"My dad's a genius, Zee." Lizzy stood on tiptoes and kissed his cheek. "And when he's *not* an ass, he's a pretty decent hero."

"Well, you remember that sentiment the rest of this trip," Mr. Peters said, chuckling and putting one arm around his daughter. He pulled the keys out of his pocket. "I think I can handle driving with my left foot," he said. "You girls get in the back. We'll take this service road to the back of the property. There's got to be a way out back there."

Zara didn't know what to do with a Mr. Peters who didn't completely despise her, but she also couldn't forget the man who had murdered two people and degraded her for questioning him on multiple occasions. As he walked toward the car, Lizzy hooked her arm in Zara's and pulled her forward.

"Well, your plan worked," she said. "Sort of."

"What?" Zara asked. "My plan completely fell apart."

"Well, I saved it." Lizzy smiled.

"Oh… yeah," Zara said, "I guess he doesn't hate me anymore. For now."

"Exactly." Lizzy patted Zara's arm as they approached the back door to the BMW. "I'd say he's pretty invested, now."

"Because he thinks all this was your idea, and I was the one who left the note," Zara whispered, her cheeks burning. "He doesn't know it was my idea or that I threw the note away."

Lizzy frowned. "Why did you do that, anyway?"

Zara cleared her throat, her mouth suddenly going dry. "I just… like you said, I wanted to do it on my own. Prove myself."

Lizzy rolled her eyes. "You're not alone, Zee. You're not a team of one. You've got to stop acting like it."

Her words echoed Zara's mother's words from all those years ago, but they didn't hold the same comforting effect. Their so-called team was built on lies and the ability of a murderer to keep his humanity front and center. And Zara was trapped. Even if Mr. Peters had turned a favorable eye on her now, she had no doubt that newfound friendliness hung by a thread.

Do I even want to be on his good side? Assaulting a police officer is the only thing I've ever done that he's approved of. She closed her eyes as the BMW skirted the circumference of the quiet airfield. I'm not sure I wouldn't rather be alone…

Chapter 19

Alexander Roman

Alex stared at the blood smeared across Minnie's name on the side of her food truck. A long, thick streak ended in a handprint just above the last *i*. More blood was splattered like paint on the hubcaps and bumpers, and the undercarriage and grill would have made Alex's breakfast come up if the smell hadn't done that already. The stench had begun to seep out past the barn; it was a mixture of something like rotting meat and garbage that had been left in the hot sun all day, but worse. Someone's black, thick hair had gotten tangled in the grill, and pieces of scalp hung limply from the matted tresses. Minnie swore whoever it had belonged to was dead before she came along, and she said the same thing of the bloody, congealed bits and pieces stuck underneath the truck.

She saved our lives… the least I can do is wash her truck. One hand holding his t-shirt to his nose, Alex squeezed the hose nozzle and water spurted toward the handprint, pummeling the metal and rinsing the blood away. Minnie had provided a long mop and a bucket of soap, but part of Alex wondered if that would be enough for the rest. Still, he worked until the summer sun was straight overhead. He worked, without Oliver for the first time since the incident, and considered his options.

What the officer had said about his volunteers catching the sickness and dying had haunted Alex for a full day. He had called his boss, Dr. Jonah Newton, as soon as he'd gotten back to Minnie's, as soon as Oliver had been preoccupied. The last thing Alex needed was for Oliver to retreat further into his shell, and overhearing what Alex needed to talk to Jonah about was a heavy burden for anyone, much less a ten-year-old boy.

"It's spreading," Alex had said to his boss. "This thing is just getting off the ground. It's not close to being over."

Jonah had been quiet for a full minute, only the sound of his breathing evidence he was still on the line. "We've got a few disease detectives reporting similar findings," he said. "We need you on the job, Alex."

I can't go back on the job. Not right now, Alex thought as he used the mop to clean the truck's grill, actively avoiding looking directly at what he was doing. How can I leave Naomi here? How can I move on with the task of claiming her, of burying her, hanging over my head? And what about Oliver? He needs me right now.

But then another thought nagged at him. What kind of world will Oliver have if this thing isn't stopped?

Naomi's voice answered in his head. What kind of world will Oliver have if he loses us both?

Alex wanted to scream. He threw down the mop and kicked the soap-covered truck. "I didn't ask for this!" He looked up at the sky and shouted, angry. "Why is this happening?"

"No one asked for this, darlin'." Minnie's southern drawl came from behind.

Alex spun to find her with a glass in hand, leaning against the wall of the barn. "How long have you been standing there?" he asked.

"Long enough," she said. "Now, you want some sweet tea or not?"

Alex sighed and picked up the mop, walking over and accepting the glass. "Thanks. I haven't had sweet tea in forever. I usually have it unsweetened."

Minnie scoffed. "You Yankees and your aversion to good food and drink." She shook her head. "Unsweetened tea." She clucked her tongue. "Not in my house."

Alex chuckled and sipped his cold, deliciously sweet drink. "Where's Oliver?" he asked.

"Watchin' some classics and munchin' on popcorn," Minnie said. "Have you made any progress?" she asked.

Alex looked back at the food truck and frowned. "Well, I mean, it seems obviously a lot cleaner to me. Am I missing something?"

"I'm not talkin' about the truck," Minnie said, raising her eyebrows. "I'm talkin' about decidin' what you're gonna do."

"Well," Alex said, "my boss wants me back in Atlanta, and with things going the way they are, it might be safer there, but…" He looked down into his glass, swirling the tea in circles.

"But it don't seem right?" Minnie asked.

Alex nodded and shrugged. "No matter what I do, I'm going to need a vehicle. We can't rely on your generosity forever."

"I don't know 'bout that," Minnie said. "But I do need to tell ya somethin'." She took a deep breath. "I think I'm gonna need to go on down to Nashville, to where Lauren is. I'm afraid if I don't go now, I won't see her again. It seems this plague or whatever it is ain't goin' nowhere. Or rather, it seems like it's goin' *everywhere*."

"Yeah, I think you're right," Alex said. "I understand the need to get to your daughter."

"I won't be kickin' ya out," Minnie said. "In fact, you can stay here, if you want. Use my trusty ol' Ford."

Alex stood up straighter. "Minnie, you don't have to—"

"Now, you listen here," Minnie said. "I'm gonna pack up. I'm takin' Samson with me, out on the road. I'm leavin' tomorrow. If you change your mind, you can come with me to Nashville. It's on the way to Atlanta, and you can get your car rental there. If you need to stay, I've got a spare key. I only ask you look out for the place."

"Why are you doing all of this?" Alex asked. "Why would you trust me to stay here while you're gone?"

Minnie patted Alex on the shoulder. "I've got a gut feelin' like we met for a reason. I done prayed on it, and I just can't leave you and that angel to fend for yourselves, not if I can help it. And besides, Samson is a great judge of character, and he's taken a liking to you both."

"Minnie, I can't take advantage o—"

She held up a finger. "In case you were wonderin', I just sounded *exactly* like my momma."

Alex smiled. "Well, then, I guess I have no choice." He reached out and grabbed her hand, giving it a light squeeze. "Yes, ma'am, and thank you."

Minnie took Alex's empty glass, a big smile on her face. "Well, now that you're practiced in respectin' your elders, I've got another favor to ask before I go."

"Anything," Alex said.

"I need you to take me to get Harvey," she said. "It's a two-person job, and I'd just as soon not bother Willard what with all the hullabaloo in town."

"How big is this dog?" Alex asked.

Minnie laughed. "Oh, Harvey ain't no dog." She winked. "You just drive me, and I'll show you Harvey in all his glory."

"You've got it," Alex said.

Alex and Minnie went back inside and got Oliver ready to go. They'd found some lavender at a naturalist shop near the ice-cream parlor on the square the day before, and Oliver insisted they all moisturize their hands, put on lip balm, and spritz each other with lavender. Part of Alex resisted the thought of making Naomi's signature scent so prevalent, but something about the routine she and Oliver had so loved comforted Alex, made it seem like she was still with them in some way.

They drove into town as they had before, with Samson and Oliver in the backseat. But when they pulled into the Red Bud Veterinarian lot, Minnie had Alex go around to the back of the Victorian-style home. The paved lot turned to gravel in front of a mechanic's shop that sat on a hill behind the house.

"This here is Nolan's shop," Minnie said. "He used to be a mechanic in the army way back when. And that—" She pointed to the house behind them. "—is Madeline's. She's the town's best veterinarian in my opinion." Samson barked, and Minnie laughed. "Okay, in Samson's opinion, too."

"And Harvey?" Alex asked, confused.

"Come on, and I'll show ya." Minnie, bursting with pride, got out of the truck, and Alex, Oliver, and Samson followed her to the side of the shop where a squat, boxy RV was parked. It looked to have once been a top-of-the-line vehicle, now worn but still sturdy. Silver lettering stood out against a black background, reading *The Aurora Roamer* across the part of the RV that extended above the cab.

"Harvey is a camper?" Alex asked.

Minnie tsked. "This here is not your typical camper," she said. "This is an off-road beauty." She ran her hand along the hood of the four-door cab. "He's a little old and ornery, but one day, he'll take me all over these here United States. For now, though, he's gonna take me to Lauren." She smiled. "Lauren's the one that named our first recreational vehicle when she was little. Thought I was saying Harvey instead of calling him an RV, and well… it stuck. This here is technically Harvey the Second."

Oliver grinned and walked up beside Minnie, running his hand along the cab just as she had. Alex smiled and walked its length, noticing a battery charging port next to the gas tank and solar panels on the top. Harvey had been ahead of his time; Alex didn't remember hybrid battery-diesel RVs coming into popularity until five years prior, and Harvey's battery ports looked to be at least ten years old. They didn't make them quite like that anymore.

Oliver tapped the door to the living quarters, and Minnie unlocked it, letting him look around inside with Samson on his heels. She turned to face Alex, leaning back on the outside of the RV and breathing in deeply.

"I know the world's fallin' apart, but I really am lookin' forward to seein' my baby," Minnie said.

"I'm sure Lauren will be glad to see you both," Alex said, nodding at the RV.

Minnie's smile faded. "Actually, she'll be madder than a wet hen. We… haven't talked in a while."

"Do you mind if I ask what happened between you two?" Alex asked, standing beside Minnie and leaning against the vehicle.

"It's a long story," Minnie said. "The long short of it is that I got too big for my britches. I thought I knew best, and Lauren didn't agree." She smiled sadly. "I gotta find her and make it right while I still got a shot at it."

"Well, I guess we better get you on the road, then," Alex said.

"I just gotta settle up with Nolan for fixin' Harvey." She wiped away every trace of sadness and beamed at Alex. "Why don't you take a look inside, and I'll go find Nolan. He should be inside his office, but the lights are all out." She pursed her lips and squinted at the house. "Maybe he's takin' a break with Madeline."

Alex looked at the house. The lights were out there, too. "Are you sure they're open?" he asked.

Minnie nodded. "Should be. It ain't a bank holiday, is it?"

"No," Alex said.

"Well, like I said, maybe he's takin' a break. I reckon they just got the curtains open for some natural light." She walked down the small, gravel hill toward the house. The back door had a little sign hanging from it that indicated they were open. Minnie tried the door, and it opened. "Be right back," she shouted, waving for Alex to go take a look inside the RV.

He turned around, but only got two steps before he heard a scream coming from the house. Oliver stuck his head out of the RV's window, eyes wide, fingers gripping the window frame. Samson barked and scratched at the inside of the door to the RV.

"Stay here, Oliver," Alex shouted. "Don't let Samson out, okay? Keep him safe, bud."

Oliver shrank back into the RV, but as another distressed shout rang from inside the house, Alex didn't have time to do anything but repeat his instructions over his shoulder as he ran toward the house. He flung the door open to a small foyer, the walls covered with pictures of pets and smiling faces. Minnie sat on the floor, turned away from the next room, her hand covering her face. She was trembling.

"Minnie! What happened?" Alex knelt beside her, but she just shook her head and pointed behind her.

Alex looked up into the waiting room beyond. A woman lay across a row of chairs, limp and unmoving. Alex stood and took a step into the room, dread a palpable thing pressing in all around him. He couldn't quite see her face until he took one more step.

"No," he breathed out the word, the blood in his veins turning to ice.

"That's Madeline," Minnie's shaky voice came from behind him, but he didn't turn to look.

He could only stare at the dried rivers of blood forming thick lines from her nostrils and her ears, her blood-soaked blouse, the welt on her arm with fingernail scratches marking the swollen skin, and her eyes… one was missing completely and one bulged like those at the World's Fair. A squawk and the flapping of wings startled Alex as a green parrot flew past his head and landed on Madeline's shoulder. The parrot dropped something from its beak, and it landed on the ground with a wet *splat*. Madeline's other eye looked up at him from the floor. The parrot squawked again, spreading its wings out protectively and hissing at Alex.

He backed away, swallowing bile, but tripped over something big, stumbling and catching himself on a small table. A metal bowl of dog treats clattered as it hit the floor. He'd realized the moment he tripped that the thing on the floor was a body. Alex had assumed when he regained his balance, he would see Nolan, the mechanic, but instead, Willard lay on the ground, dog biscuits peeking out of the top of his pocket. Alex blinked rapidly and turned away only to see a trail of blood leading to the bottom half of another corpse sticking out from behind the counter.

"We have to get out of here," Alex said, an urgency clawing up his throat. He rushed forward toward Minnie and hooked his arms under hers, hauling her to her feet.

"We can't leave them here," Minnie said. "These are my people, Alex. They're *my* people."

He gently pushed her toward the door. "We have to get out. Right now."

"No!" she cried. "What if someone's alive in there?" She tried to push past him.

Alex blocked her path. "Remember what Willard said? This is contagious. I don't know if you can catch it from the dead or if the host has to be living to spread it, but we can't take the chance. We have to get out of here. Think about Lauren."

Minnie shook her head, but she let herself be guided back outside. "It's here," she said. "How did it get here?"

"I don't know," Alex said, "but this is spreading a lot faster than I anticipated." He kept walking toward the RV, encouraging Minnie to keep walking. As soon as he got to the RV, he opened it and stuck his head inside. Samson and Oliver were curled up together on the small sofa. "You okay, bud?"

Oliver nodded, but he looked pale.

"Everything's going to be okay. Minnie is fine. You and Samson are fine. I'm fine." Alex met Oliver's eyes, speaking with as much reassurance as he could muster. "I'm going to talk to Minnie for just one minute, and then we're leaving, okay?" Alex had to be content with another silent nod. He turned back to Minnie. "I think I'm going to take you up on that offer." He took a deep breath. *I'm sorry Naomi.* "It looks like we're all going to Nashville."

Chapter 20

Zara Williams

The countryside might have been comforting if not for the plume of smoke billowing from a crashed plane in the middle of a scorched field. To the north, cornstalks swayed and danced in the summer heat as the sun began to dip below the horizon. Old, two-story country homes with white siding and wrap-around porches dotted the land between crops. There hadn't been a crashed car or dead body on the backwater road for a full thirty minutes. It had started to seem normal, almost.

But then that black plume loomed in the distance, and the closer they got, the more attention Zara paid to it. She'd hoped it was a burn pile when they'd been far enough away. Even a house fire would have been better, more ordinary. The shape of a broken airplane wing emerged through the swirling smoke, and a jolt of despair shot through Zara, adding to the weight of the rock in her stomach. The road ahead was blocked with emergency vehicles as local responders put out the last of the fire, so Mr. Peters turned down another road to avoid the area.

"That looks like a big plane," Lizzy said as she looked out the back window of the car.

"It's definitely a passenger plane," Mr. Peters said. "The wing's too big to be from a crop duster or even a private jet."

"Where's it from?" Zara asked.

"Probably where we just came from," Lizzy said. "I mean, where else?"

"It's not from St. Louis." Zara shook her head. "There were no planes coming in or going out since early this morning. I mean, it could have been more than twelve hours since the last plane left St. Louis."

"And this is too close," Mr. Peters said. He met her eyes in the rearview mirror with an approving look Zara wasn't sure she wanted from him. "It would take thirty minutes for a plane to travel this far, maybe less."

She shook off the uncomfortable feeling and nodded. They were three hours outside of St. Louis, three hours from the chaos and destruction. They'd taken country roads that wound through the state at forty-five miles per hour, slowing as they meandered through smaller towns.

"No, this plane came from another airport, probably a hot spot. Maybe San Francisco." Mr. Peters shook his head. "Unless it's spread to other airports already…"

"It could just be a regular crash, couldn't it?" Lizzy asked. "Like, those happen, don't they?"

Mr. Peters pursed his lips. "There's no sense in holding on to false hope, Elizabeth." Somehow, his sharper tone made the situation familiar, which was almost reassuring.

He just doesn't see me as a threat anymore. Zara chewed on her lip. That's good, isn't it? I mean, we'll get farther if we work together, and then when we get to Boston, I can still turn him in. I can still do the right thing. Her cheeks flushed. And I can turn myself in, too. She could still feel the syringe in her hand, see the blood pooling under the officer's head. I should have found another way.

Zara prayed for the hundredth time that the man she'd drugged and left bleeding from a head wound would be okay. No matter what he'd done, Zara was *not* like Mr. Peters. She didn't hurt people.

As the sun disappeared and the moon took its place, silence fell upon the group for nearly an hour. Eventually, Lizzy began to snore softly, but Zara continued to stare out the window, contemplating how much had changed over the last twenty-four hours. It was hard to comprehend and even harder to accept.

Outlines of distant tree lines separating fields and the occasional porch light twinkling in the dark gave way to streetlamps and sidewalks and businesses as they entered the suburbs of Indianapolis while avoiding the main highways. Mr. Peters veered toward heavier traffic, though, as they got closer to the city.

"Are you getting on the highway?" Zara asked.

Mr. Peters shook his head and pointed to a bright red, orange, and white Pilot Travel Center sign reaching toward the sky. It would be clearly visible from the highway. "We need to stop for the night."

"You don't think we can check into a motel or something?" Zara asked. "I mean, sleeping in the limo was bad enough but—" She scooted forward a few inches, noting how easy it was for her knees to touch the back of the seat in front of her. "It's cramped in here."

"No." Mr. Peters said, not offering more of an explanation.

Zara swallowed any objections. Just… lay low until we get to Boston.

Mr. Peters pulled into the lot and parked at the back, near the side of the station used by semis. "Let's get some sleep," Mr. Peters said. He shut off the engine. "We're running low on gas. It should cool down enough overnight to be bearable in here. I'll turn on the car and blast the AC periodically. In the morning, we'll fill up, grab something hot to eat, and maybe by the end of tomorrow, we'll be back in Boston." He tipped his seat back a tad, crossed his arms, and leaned his head on the headrest.

Zara closed her eyes and tried to sleep, drifting in and out until the sun rose. Still dreary, she barely registered the shouting until Mr. Peters jerked awake and cursed. Zara blinked away the exhaustion and rubbed her eyes clear of morning eye gunk. It had been two hours since Mr. Peters had blasted the air conditioning to keep the inside of the car cool overnight.

"What is it?" she asked, her tongue working against a parched mouth.

"They're fighting over gasoline," Mr. Peters said. "That's not good. It means people around here are starting to panic."

Two men were in a fist fight near the gas pumps. A truck with a tiny utility trailer full of red gas containers blocked two pumps, and a woman hurriedly continued filling the containers while keeping her eyes on the fight.

A cold numbness spread from Zara's bones into her veins. "Does that mean… is that sickness here, too?"

"It could be." Mr. Peters started the BMW, which woke up Lizzy, and he drove to the opposite end of the rows of gas pumps, car sputtering a few times as it ran on fumes.

"What's going on?" Lizzy asked.

"Go inside, use the bathroom, and grab supplies," Mr. Peters said. "Go quickly. We need food, water, bug repellent, maybe a few lighters… camping gear, if they have any, just in case."

"Camping gear?" Lizzy looked like she'd just swallowed something sour.

"Just in case," Mr. Peters repeated, and then under his breath, "This is spreading too fast."

Zara raised an eyebrow. "What did you say?"

"Nothing." He looked over his shoulder after he put the BMW in park. "Buy anything that looks like it could be useful. And don't linger outside," he added firmly. "Or get too close to anyone else. And if you see someone sick, come back immediately."

Zara looked at Lizzy and met her questioning gaze with one of her own. Lizzy shrugged and opened the car door. Zara followed suit. A police cruiser pulled up and parked, causing Zara to freeze in place until he got out and turned all his attention on the fight happening several yards away.

"Come on, Zee." Lizzy nodded toward the sliding doors.

"Sorry." Zara shook her head.

As they walked into the convenience store part of the station, a woman with a newly purchased gasoline can in hand frowned at them and gave them a wide berth.

Lizzy laughed and playfully punched Zara's arm. "You're scaring away the locals, Zee."

Zara scoffed. "It's not just me, princess."

Lizzy's laughter cut short, and she wrinkled her nose as she looked down at herself. "Ugh. You're right." She grabbed a handheld basket near the door and headed straight for the racks of t-shirts and jeans.

"We're supposed to be getting essentials," Zara said as she grabbed her own basket.

"And I *am*," Lizzy said. "It is *essential* that we get out of these clothes." She pulled a t-shirt from the rack that read: Real Men Smell Like Diesel. "What about this one for Dad?"

Zara couldn't help but chuckle. "What about this one? 'It's not Dad Bod—'"

"'—It's a Father Figure?'" Lizzy finished reading the t-shirt and burst into laughter. She grabbed it from Zara and stuck in her basket. "We're getting it, no contest."

"Okay, fine. You get us some clothes and then grab some food, and I'll get some other supplies," Zara said. She pointed at Lizzy. "I'm trusting you with my t-shirt, Liz. In fact, you can get me whatever you get yourself." She raised her eyebrows and turned on her heels.

"You're no fun!" Lizzy said as she turned to the rack of women's t-shirts.

With every minute, Zara noticed more and more people coming into the store, heading straight for the things she needed. She hurried, picking up several items they'd left at their hotel in St. Louis: deodorant, hairbrushes, toothbrushes and toothpaste, and other travel-sized toiletries. She turned down the aisle for electronics to find a short, curly-haired woman putting the last three phone chargers into her basket.

Zara's shoulders sagged. "Hey, um, ma'am? Can I just have one of those? All our phones are dead and—"

"Back off," the woman said, her eyes going wide as she shuffled away, eyeing Zara from head to toe. "No way I'm giving up anything to some homeless b—"

"Hey!" Zara cut her off. "Who the hell do you think you are? I'm not homeless, and next to you, I'm an angel, sweetheart." She put one hand on her hip.

The woman gasped, her frown deepening as she scurried away, all three chargers still in her basket. Zara rolled her eyes and looked at the empty rack where the chargers were supposed to be. The only ones left wouldn't charge any of their phones.

"The camping gear…" Zara said out loud, chewing her bottom lip as a thought occurred to her. She walked as fast she could to a small section meant for campers and clapped her hands at the sight of the solar-powered cell phone chargers. They took forever to charge a phone, but they would work. She grabbed three and then added bug repellant, ponchos, a few lighters, some batteries, two flashlights, and a set of metal sporks. She slung three small, flat backpacks under her arm, nearly cleaning out the section, glad she wasn't paying. Soon, her basket was full. She found Lizzy in the canned food aisle, dumping cans of over-priced ravioli into her basket. She had three t-shirts and three jeans slung around her neck like scarves. When she saw Zara, she set the basket down and grinned, pulling free one of the t-shirts. She held it up.

"I got a pink one with black lettering for me, and a black one with pink lettering for you," she said.

"Sassy but classy?" Zara sighed. "Really?"

Lizzy huffed and strung the shirts back over her shoulders. "Um, those were the best ones," she said defensively. "Would you rather have the ones that say, 'Home is Where the Pants Aren't?'"

Zara wrinkled her nose. "I actually kind of liked that one."

"Oh my gosh, Zee. No." Lizzy gave her a flat stare. "Just, no. Just because the world's going insane doesn't mean we have to, too." She picked her basket back up and looked back at the canned goods.

Zara grabbed some tuna and canned vegetables. "We need something with nutrition," she said as she put them in Lizzy's basket.

"Ravioli has meat *and* tomatoes," Lizzy said, frowning at the mixed vegetables.

"We probably won't even need these, not for long. Your dad just wants to be prepared for worst case scenarios, like the car breaks down on the side of the road or something. We'll be back in Boston tonight." Zara smiled at Lizzy, trying to reassure her.

Mr. Peters appeared at the end of the aisle, approaching them with a nod of approval. "Good job, girls."

"You don't look so great, Mr. Peters. You feeling okay?" Zara asked.

He nodded but undid the top button of his shirt. "I think I just need to splash some water on my face and change my clothes. Let's buy these and change in the bathrooms."

The cashier could barely tear her eyes from the television screen to check them out, clearly annoyed at the amount of things they were purchasing. Though, as Zara looked around the store, she expected they were one of the first of many people stocking up.

"Look, Dad," Lizzy said, pointing at the television as Mr. Peters got out his credit card and swiped it at the machine. "A whole plane full of sick people landed in Indianapolis."

"Not just sick," the cashier said, leaning forward, whispering. "Some of them were already dead when they landed this morning. They shut down and quarantined the whole airport."

"When did this happen?" Mr. Peters asked.

"Plane came in early, maybe five or six this morning," the cashier said. "It came from Denver."

Mr. Peters took half a step backward. "Denver? Are you sure?"

She nodded. "Yep. Some of the passengers were from Los Angeles, switched planes in Denver."

Mr. Peters swallowed audibly, the blood draining from his face. His forehead glistened with sweat, and it soaked through his soiled dress shirt at the small of his back and under his arms. "We need to get home," he said, his voice hoarse. He limped out to the car, threw everything in the trunk but the clothes, and turned to face Lizzy and Zara. "I want to get out on the road in under ten minutes. Can you do that?" He sounded urgent enough that both girls just nodded.

Zara took her jeans and t-shirt, ripped off the tags, and went back inside with Lizzy. It felt good to wash her face, and she did her best with the rest of her body using paper towels, careful not to disturb the newly formed scabs all over her left side. She threw her old clothes away, though Lizzy kept hers, wading them up and sticking them in the plastic bag her new clothes had been in.

"Well, at least we look… better?" Lizzy said, frowning at the mirror.

Zara tried to ignore the barrage of scabbed cuts and green and blue bruises. She was still a mess, but she wasn't as dirty, and that was something. "I'm taking a real shower as soon as we get home," Zara said.

"Me too," Lizzy said. "Speaking of, we should get back before Dad flips. He's, like, on the edge. I've never seen him like this."

"He's better today than he was yesterday… or, you know, the night before." Zara shuddered.

"Do you have to bring that up?" Lizzy asked, anger in her voice. "I mean, come on, Zee. I don't need to be reminded of… of *that*."

Zara wanted to shout at Lizzy, to tell her that she would have to think about it eventually, but she didn't. We don't have time for that. And she's made it clear that she's not going to do anything that would go against her father, so… just go with the flow, Zara.

"Sorry," she said, straining to hold back the things she really wanted to say.

Lizzy exhaled with frustration and stomped out of the restroom without saying another word. Zara followed into the hallway that connected to the bathrooms. Mr. Peters was coming out of the men's room at the same time, but he was leaning on the wall, sweating even more than he had been before.

"Something… is wrong," Mr. Peters said, his speech slurred. Half of his mouth didn't move when he spoke. He fumbled to get something out of his pocket, his keys falling to the floor. That's when Zara noticed his entire right side was drooping.

"Dad?" Lizzy's frightened voice mixed with a sense of urgency. She pulled out her phone, but then screamed in frustration at the black screen. She turned to Zara. "Go get someone to call 911!"

Mr. Peters slid against the wall to the floor. "No," he said slowly. "Can't… stay…" He gasped for breath, a look of confusion and fear emanating from his eyes. He reached for the keys, but they were too far for him to grasp. "Get back to the car…"

"Zee!" Lizzy yelled, her voice breaking as tears rimmed her eyes. She dropped to her knees beside her father, letting her phone clatter to the tile floor.

"I've got it," Zara said, heart racing as she fled down the hallway. "I need to borrow someone's phone!" She shouted. "Someone call an ambulance!"

"Dad!" Lizzy shouted again, the word coming out as a sob.

Zara looked over her shoulder and froze. Mr. Peters slumped, his eyes closing, his body going completely slack as he stopped gasping for breath and the rise and fall of his chest ceased.

Chapter 21

Timothy Peters

Timothy flipped on the lights to the storage room in the bunker and headed straight for the back row, for the stash of weapons he'd thought overkill just the day before. Suddenly, he was insanely grateful that his father hadn't left out guns in his obsessive preparations. Timothy had been itching to take inventory and start making plans to defend their home against Frank since he'd pulled the car into the garage late the night before. But Annika had clung to him, and he couldn't quite bring himself to leave her or to take a weapons inventory with a five-year-old on his hip.

He had insisted that he and Annika stay upstairs while the rest of the family slept in the bunker. He couldn't be sure that they hadn't brought back whatever sickness destroyed Boston, but between his father and the news reports, it seemed whatever it was killed quickly, within four or five hours. And it obviously spread easily. So, he slept on the couch while Annika slept on the love seat knowing that if they made it to morning, they were probably in the clear.

In the morning, Heather had cautiously come upstairs, pure relief on her face when she'd found Timothy and Annika alive, though Timothy was more exhausted than he'd ever been in his life. The morning had been spent trying to make Annika forget the horrors she'd experienced. If it hadn't been for Frank Russo, Timothy would have been able to shield her from all of it. But the little girl had seen two thugs get shot, and even though Timothy hadn't told her about her family, even though he'd gotten her to sleep on his shoulder most of the way through Boston, the things she *did* see were enough to disturb her.

Thank goodness for George. Timothy smiled at the thought of his little brother.

George befriending and playing with Annika was the only reason Timothy was able to get away and come back to the bunker to prepare for what was to come.

A couple of days, and he's coming here with henchmen to back him up. Timothy ran his fingers through his hair. All to collect a debt. What does that mean, Frank?

"Are you ready to tell me what happened yesterday?" Heather's voice, though gentle, startled Timothy.

"I didn't hear you come in," he said.

Heather came up to him and put her arms around him, kissing his cheek and hugging him close. "You've been walking around like you've seen a ghost, and you only brought back Annika. You were so insistent last night that we stay away… I've been waiting all day to get you alone so we could talk." She leaned away, concern etched into her features. "Please tell me there's some other explanation for Annika being here while the rest of the Williams family are not."

Timothy took a deep breath. "No," he said. "Her mom and Zara's parents… they were in the backyard, dead."

Heather closed her eyes, her bottom lip quivering. "That poor baby," she said. "And Zara… how are we going to tell her?"

"I'm not sure, but… that's not the worst of it," Timothy said.

Heather opened her eyes, tears rolling down her cheeks. "What could be worse than that?"

"I met a man named Frank Russo." Timothy told his wife all about the destruction in Boston, how he'd met Frank, and how Frank had bullied his way to the Williams' house. "I would be dead if it weren't for Annika," Timothy said after describing the fight he'd had with the sort-of-mobster. "And then, the guys who'd been looking for him showed up. He ended up shooting them right in front of Annika, and I thought maybe it would be okay in the end. But…" Heat flooded Timothy's cheeks as both anger and embarrassment warred for the spotlight as he recalled his mistake. "He wrote down a bunch of addresses off the car's GPS, and right before he got out of the car, he told me he'd be coming to collect a debt with some of his uncle's men. Frank made it sound like he thought I owed him our supplies. He even recommended children find another place to be because his uncle's men weren't as nice as he is." Timothy scoffed. "That man was unhinged. I can't *believe* I let him in the car."

Heather rubbed her hands up and down his arms. "Babe, he had three guns, and you had a five-year-old and no way to defend yourself. What else could you have done?"

"I don't know," Timothy sighed. "I could have done *something*. I should have killed Frank. I should have gone for the ankle holster sooner, killed him before I even got to the Williams' house."

"Tim, I love you," Heather said. "You're not a murderer, okay? It wouldn't have been that easy to kill him, even if you'd had a real chance at it. You're a good man. You tried to do the right thing."

"I tried to do the *safe* thing." Timothy corrected her. "And now, I *am* going to do the right thing. I'm going to protect my family." He nodded toward the small arsenal.

"What about the police?" Heather asked. "Surely we can get some protection if you report this."

"Heather, I know things look normal right now here in Wellesley, or at least, here in this community, but I'm telling you whatever happened in Boston is going to happen here, and there wasn't an officer in sight, at least not one living. We're too close to escape it."

Heather shifted her weight and chewed on her bottom lip. "They'll get it under control, though, won't they?"

Timothy shook his head. "I don't know. I don't even know if there's a 'they' anymore. Boston is practically in ruins. It took less than two days for that to happen. I think long before anyone gets anything under control, it's going to hit Wellesley."

"Should we just evacuate?" Heather asked.

"My dad said to stay put, and he's got all these supplies for us…" Timothy took a deep breath, considering the option to flee. "With reports coming out of several major cities now, I don't know that anywhere is going to be safe."

"Okay, so we stay, but what are we going to do?" Heather asked.

"I'm debating the options, but we have to protect this bunker. If the world gets as crazy as I think it's going to get, we're going to need this stuff." Timothy glanced around at the room full of weapons, food, first aid supplies, and more.

"Timothy, Frank doesn't know about all of this." Heather gestured to the supplies. "The bunker is made to keep people safe for a long time. We can just hunker down here until they've come and gone. Let them raid the house, think they got everything important."

Timothy shook his head. "I don't know. Frank sounded like he wanted to see me, like he wanted something more from *me* personally to finish collecting the debt. I have no doubt that he's going to take whatever supplies he finds, but he said if I wasn't here, he and those men would come and find me." He shrugged. "If they search the house, they'll see the bunker door. They'll suspect I'm hiding there. It's a steel door in the basement. People don't install those at random."

Heather shuddered. "What could he want from you?"

"I don't know." Timothy leaned his forehead on Heather's, taking comfort in her arms still wrapped around his waist. "I've been trying to figure it out, but all I can think of is that maybe he's planning on cleaning out our bank accounts. Maybe he wants our passwords and whatnot."

"You think it's about money?" Heather asked.

"Yes. He did say he owes people money. Unless he just wants to finish the job and kill me," Timothy said, the blood draining from his face. He pulled away from Heather and sat down on the stool against the wall. "I mean, I guess that could be it. He didn't want to kill me in front of Annika, so he wants me to find somewhere safe for her, and then he wants to kill me."

"Why would a man like that care if a kid sees someone die?" Heather asked.

Timothy shrugged. "He was a strange man, Heather. It was like, one minute, I actually *liked* him. He had a sense of humor. He showed real concern for vulnerable people. And then, it was like a switch was flipped. He just became this monster… but no matter how he acted toward me, I really believe he would never hurt Annika or George."

"But the men he's bringing with him…" Heather looked back at the guns. "We can have your mom and the kids lock themselves up here. If you think the police won't be around to help, you and I are going to have to ward off whoever comes."

Timothy's eyes widened. "What? No way am I putting you in danger. You are going to lock yourself in here with my mom and the kids, and you're going to—"

Heather narrowed her eyes. "Are you telling me what to do right now?"

"Yes?" Timothy winced.

She crossed her arms. "Since when do we work like that, Timothy?"

Timothy sighed. "Since never. I should have asked. This is a conversation we need to have, though. Heather, I couldn't live with myself if something happened to you because of something I did."

"If something happened to me, it would be because of my own darn decisions, thank you very much," Heather said. But then she softened her tone. "Tim, you do realize I couldn't live with *myself* if I cowered in a bunker while the love of my life faced off against actual freaking mobsters?" She reached out and took his hand. "Besides," she said, her expression somber, "you know I'm more likely to die if I have to be locked in a bunker with your mother."

Timothy laughed and shook his head. "I love you," he said.

Heather smiled and nodded toward the guns. "So, are we going to make a plan or what?"

"Yes." Timothy stood beside his wife and put an arm around her. "Yes, we are."

He let his eyes roam across all the weaponry and gear his father had collected and stored in the back of the storage area. There were guns and knives in the gun safe, but there were also cans of mace, flashbangs, and little cameras that matched the security cameras by the front doors, the back doors, and the bunker door. A fourth, wide-angled camera was situated in the corner of the open concept living room. The safe house was connected to all four, giving anyone in the bunker an advantage.

"These cameras are perfect. Mom will be able to see and confirm with her own eyes that it's safe to come out." His eyes landed on a row of walkie talkies on the top shelf beside the gun safe. "These should come in handy," he said, pointing.

"Why do you think he has so many?" Heather asked. "I mean, the whole family is only six people and there are a lot more units up there than that."

"Backups, maybe?" Timothy asked. He frowned, and then an idea hit him. "Or maybe he's got back up, as in other people willing to help us in a situation like this."

"As in, we might not have to do this by ourselves?" Heather asked. "Wouldn't anyone he'd made a deal with already be here?"

"I bet Mom would know," Timothy said. "Let's go ask her. We'll need her to open the safe, anyway." He gestured to the fingerprint pad on the door handle.

Heather led the way out of the bunker, into the basement, and up the stairs. She approached the dining table where Dana, George, and Annika were playing Monopoly. "Hey, Dana, Timothy has some questions for you. Do you think I could take your spot for a minute?"

Dana smiled. "Of course," she said, and then she winked at George. "This is your shot to beat me, Georgie."

Heather pinched her lips together and took a deep breath as Dana got up and joined Timothy. He patted her on the shoulder and kissed the top of her head as she sat down.

"Thanks, babe," he said. Then, he pulled his mother over to the couches where they were out of earshot, assuming they talked quietly.

"Mom, I need to know if Dad invited anyone to come here and help defend the property in the case of a crisis like this. There are a ton of walkie talkies downstairs."

"No," Dana said, shaking her head. "There's no one that I know of."

Timothy's shoulders sagged.

"Why do you think we would need other people to help *defend* the property?" Dana asked. "That seems a little extreme."

Timothy gave his mother an abbreviated version of what he'd told Heather, and then added, "So, I'm going to need you to protect the kids in the bunker. Heather and I will take care of this."

Dana's expression was grim. "I can do that," she said, "but I think I can help you prepare, too."

"We'll need all the help we can get." Timothy shook his head. "I really thought maybe there was a neighbor or something Dad had brought in, maybe someone with another bunker nearby."

"I think if there was, I would know about it," Dana said. "Your father has always kept me informed when it comes to his plans for our safety. However," she added, her eyes lighting up, "we do have neighbors that could be of use. The HOA president was talking about putting together a neighborhood watch. If there are dangerous people coming to our area, I bet we could get some of them to keep an eye out and let us know if they see anything suspicious."

"That's not a bad idea," Timothy said. "Do you know who we could ask?"

Dana smiled. "I think I do. Candice Liddle and Rhonda York." She held up a finger. "Give me a minute. I'll go get the Merlot for Candice and the Bordeaux for Rhonda."

"What?" Timothy asked.

"Trust me, Timmy," Dana said, patting his cheek. "A nice bottle of wine makes a favor go down smoother."

He sighed. "Okay, fine. If that's what you think will get the job done. I'll take them over—"

"Oh, no, no, no." Dana shook her head. "I know these women. If I don't go, it won't happen."

Timothy shrugged and got out of the way as his mother bustled past the kitchen and into their pantry where they had an entire wall dedicated to wine and whiskey. She emerged with two bottles sleeved in black and silver gift bags. He'd noticed the drawer of the bags before, but he'd never really understood why the drawer was kept stocked.

Dana charged toward the front door. "Come on, Timmy. We need to be back before your father's time limits." She'd been vehement about everyone being inside by seven o'clock and had given Timothy an ear full when he'd come in late the night before.

Timothy followed his mother outside, the afternoon sun bright and hot. His parents' house sat a fourth of a mile from the road on a large lot of land on a quiet street that ended in a cul-de-sac. The grass was usually well-manicured, but it had started to grow a bit wild. They walked along the long drive and a mile down the road to the Liddle's Tudor-style house.

"Candice is the President of the HOA this year," Dana said. "She and Rhonda have been trying to find a reason to use their bird watching binoculars for something other than policing neighbors for property violations. They both view the HOA as their little kingdom. They take it all *very* seriously." She rolled her eyes. "I'm shocked no one has come knocking about our grass. It's a full half inch over the guidelines."

Timothy couldn't help the sour look on his face. "I do *not* miss living here," he said. "Isn't Candice…" He paused, trying to think of a nice way to put it. She was Harry Liddle's fifth wife, if he was counting right. "… new?"

"Yes," Dana said, "but your father thinks this one will stick. Harry is quite taken with her."

"I'm sure." Timothy refrained from commenting further.

"She's not too bad," Dana said. "I think there's more to her than meets the eye."

"If you say so," Timothy said as they approached the house, "In any case, when we knock, just keep your distance, okay? Just in case."

His mother pursed her lips, but she didn't argue. She raised her hand, knocked, and stepped back to stand next to Timothy. Candice Liddle opened the door in a Gucci denim dress, hair in long, blonde braids, the rim of a wide-brimmed, floppy hat bouncing gently with her movements. Her leather sandals had cords that crisscrossed up to her knees.

"Oh, did we catch you on your way out?" Timothy asked.

Dana discreetly elbowed him in the side as Candice tilted her head and narrowed her eyes.

"No," Candice said, "Why would you say that?" Her voice was sweet and her smile wide, but there was an edge to her words.

"Timmy just isn't used to seeing a young woman who is always so put together," Dana said, laughing and waving off Timothy's comment. "My daughter-in-law is a peach, really, but she goes for the natural look."

"Ah," Candice smiled and nodded as if Dana's explanation cleared up everything.

Timothy frowned. "Um, Heather is pretty awesome just the way she is, Mom."

Dana laughed again. "Young love, am I right, Candice?"

Candice practically giggled. "Don't I know it. Harry says the same thing about me. Perfect just the way I am." She flashed a very white, shiny smile. "What can I do for you, Dana? Having trouble with your lawn care? I can certainly give you a recommendation. Our guys didn't miss a beat, even with all of this mess the media just keeps blowing out of proportion. My Harry says the footage on the TV isn't even of Boston or the real World's Fair. He says it's from a movie. CGI." She shook her head. "What is the world coming to?"

Timothy's mouth dropped open. He'd questioned some of the reports himself before seeing Boston with his own eyes. It had been an effort to cling to the hope that no disease could spread as quickly and destructively as it appeared this one did. He'd told himself that perhaps the media were focusing on a few really bad situations to make it seem like the world was on fire. But CGI? Fake footage?

Dana's smile faltered. "Oh," she said, looking at Timothy before clearing her throat. "Um, Candice, sweetheart, I'm sorry to say it, but Walter was in St. Louis. He says it's all true. You and Harry should be careful."

Candice quirked an eyebrow. "It can't be as bad as all that," she said.

"I get that the news can make things seem worse than they are, but I was in Boston yesterday," Timothy said. "It's bad. Like, Boston has been destroyed and a lot of people are dead. If anything, the media was underreporting the destruction."

"Hmm." Somehow Candice still looked skeptical. "Well, I'll have to ask Harry all about it when he gets home. He went into the city this morning to check on the office. He was all worried about hoodlums taking advantage of the panic brought on by the media."

"Speaking of hoodlums," Dana said, "my Timothy has it on good authority that they've set their sights on our little community. He… overheard some plans to invade our homes while he was discreetly moving about the city yesterday."

Timothy tried not to look surprised at how easily his mother created the lie.

Candice gasped, her hand flying to her mouth. "Are you sure?"

"I am," Dana said, proffering the gift bag. "Here," she said. "I've brought you a nice Merlot." Candice took it, peering inside as Dana continued. "I was thinking perhaps it's time to get that neighborhood watch started up. We thought we might donate some walkie talkies."

Candice looked from the bag up to Dana and crossed her arms. "Oh, really?" she asked. "What is this about, Dana?"

Timothy frowned and looked between the two women. "It's about the fact that some really bad men might be coming here, taking advantage of the fact that law enforcement has their hands full, and we'd like to ensure the safety of the community," he said.

"I pushed for the neighborhood watch at the last meeting," Candice said, "but *you* said there were other things more important on the agenda, like that eyesore on the Reed's property."

"It's a therapy playhouse," Dana said, "for their autistic daughter. It's very modern."

"It wasn't approved," Candice said, handing the gift bag back. "We already voted on this, Dana. Don't think you can come here, create a problem and offer a solution, playing to the fact that I wanted a neighborhood watch." Candice turned up her nose. "This HOA president can't be bought." She raised both eyebrows and slammed the front door.

Timothy sighed. "Mom, we n—"

She held up a finger to her lips and shook her head once, firmly, before speaking loudly at the door. "I wasn't finished, Candice, dear. I'll give you the neighborhood watch *and* the restriction on brightly painted doors."

Candice opened the door and put her hands on her hips. "I want that statue of the Smith's dead dog gone, too."

"Sweetheart, I think that's something we can all agree on." Dana held the bag out again, and Candice took it.

"Rhonda will need some convincing," Candice said. "For it to be official, that is. I need all three of us on board so that no one will object."

"I've got it taken care of," Dana said, patting the other bag. "But if I donate the walkie talkies, I want to be the first person notified if you hear of any trouble. Deal?"

"Deal," Candice said, shutting the door less dramatically, this time with a smile.

As they walked away, Timothy looked back at the huge house. "Mom, what just happened?"

"I just got you your neighborhood watch," Dana said. "And I got the Reeds their therapy playhouse." She sighed. "Although, I'm not sure that will matter as much if you really think Wellesley is going the way of Boston."

"If people are still going into the city, I can't imagine that it won't," Timothy said. "Even if people stay put, the way dad talked… it just seems inevitable."

"Well," Dana said, shrugging, "With Candice and Rhonda and their little gossiping network, no one is going to come in or out of this place without their knowledge, and now, there's a good chance we'll know Frank is coming before he ends up on our doorstep."

That'll buy us what… an extra ten minutes at most? At least that should give Mom and the kids enough time to get to safety. He rubbed the back of his neck, a sinking feeling in his gut. Even with the guns, the security cameras, and the warning… will it be enough to scare them off?

Frustration and fear coursed through Timothy's body as bleak scenarios of the future ran through his mind. Even if they survived Frank, the sickness was coming for them, and there was no way to prepare, no ten-minute warning, no weapon to scare it off.

We need a miracle, Timothy thought, because that's the only way any of us are going to make it out of this mess alive.

Chapter 22

Zara Williams

Zara sprinted back to Mr. Peters, sliding the last foot on her knees, ignoring the protests of her aching body. She tilted his head back and lifted his chin, leaning down to see if she could feel his breath on her cheek. The air was stagnant. Zara looked for the rise and fall of his chest, but it, too, was still. *He's not breathing! What's next… what's next?* She tried to remember the order of instructions from her training for her lifeguard summer job two years prior. Her memory clicked, and she grimaced briefly before administering two rescue breaths, trying not to gag in the process. She'd never actually done that part on a human being. Then, she interlocked her fingers, leaned over him, and began thirty compressions, pumping against his heart as hard as she could. Lizzy screamed again for help, and a man in a ballcap stuck his head out of the end of the hall under a sign that read: Trucker Lounge.

The moment he saw what was happening, he pulled out his phone. "I gotcha, girls!" he said as he came down the hall. "I'm calling 911."

A few customers had now gathered at the end of the hall, back toward the convenience store. They watched with wide eyes and whispers as Zara continued CPR, counting to keep the rhythm steady. Time blurred, and all Zara knew was how her fingers grew slick with sweat, the slight give of flesh and the resistance of bone, the straining of her cheeks as she blew into Mr. Peters's mouth, and the sound of Lizzy's cries.

Zara focused on Mr. Peters's face as her arms grew tired. His eyes were closed, but his skin sagged beneath his right eye and at the right corner of his lip. It wasn't terribly noticeable, just enough to make his features look off.

He looks more peaceful than that woman he killed at the fair… and Mr. Ludlow. Zara breathed in through her nose, out through her mouth. The groove in the hard tile dug at her knees, but she couldn't reposition herself without losing her rhythm. *Doesn't he deserve to die?* The thought shocked her, and she paused for only a moment before returning to CPR with renewed vigor. *No. I can't think like that. That's not who I am.*

The sounds all around her became a hum, nothing but background noise as she entered a sort of trance borne from repetition and exhaustion. When a hand gripped her shoulder, it startled Zara.

"You can stop, now, hon. We've got it." A woman in a blue EMT uniform gently moved Zara away from Mr. Peters as her partner took over, prepping Lizzy's father for the defibrillator.

Zara scooted against the wall, her arms trembling. Lizzy crawled over to her, tears streaming down her face. She grabbed Zara's hand and sat next to her, keeping her eyes on her father.

"Clear!" the paramedic shouted.

Mr. Peters's chest arched upward as the defibrillator shocked him. The paramedic repeated the shock, and a look of relief came over his face. "All right, we've got a steady heartbeat. Let's get him to the hospital."

Zara closed her eyes and leaned her head back, breathing a sigh of relief. The paramedics worked, but Zara barely paid attention, her mind numbed. She opened her eyes when Lizzy moved beside her to get to her feet. Mr. Peters was on a stretcher, hooked up to an IV. He was mumbling something about having to get back to Boston.

"My name is Sue," the woman paramedic said. "We're going to take good care of your…" She trailed off, a questioning look in her eyes as she glanced from Zara to Lizzy.

"My dad," Lizzy said. "I'm Lizzy, and this is my friend, Zara." She gestured to where Zara looked up at them on the floor.

Sue held up Mr. Peters's wallet. "Can you confirm for me the name of this man?"

"Walter Timothy Peters," Lizzy said. "His birthday is December 12th."

The paramedic glanced at the license inside the wallet and nodded. "Okay, well, your dad is in rough shape, but I think Zara here gave him his best shot." She looked down at Zara. "You okay, hon?"

Zara nodded. "Just… that was intense."

"I'm sure it was," Sue said. "We've got to get going. You girls have a way to get to the hospital?"

Zara turned to look at the keys Mr. Peters had dropped before he'd collapsed. She grabbed them and stood up. "Yeah," she said. "We can follow you."

Lizzy stepped up to her father. "Hey, Dad. We'll be right behind you, okay?"

Mr. Peters rolled his head from side to side. "Got to get back to Boston," he said. "Bethie, we can't stay. It's all wrong."

"I know, Dad." A few more tears rolled down Lizzy's cheeks. "But it's going to be okay." She squeezed his hand.

He grasped Lizzy's hand tightly and tried to lift his head. "How did it get out?" he asked, anger in his voice. "Did you let it out?"

Lizzy pulled her hand away, rubbing her wrist. "Dad, I don't know what you're talking about."

"He's just a little out of it, hon," Sue said. "C'mon, Chad. Let's get this guy to the hospital." They began to wheel Mr. Peters down the hallway. "We're taking him to St. Vincent's," she said. "You know where that is?"

"No," Zara said. "We aren't from here."

"Well, it's a newer hospital, real nice," Sue said. "Just a couple miles north. You got GPS?"

"The car does," Lizzy said.

They entered the convenience store area of the truck stop, and Zara paused. It was twice as full as it was before, and there was a line at the register. People's arms and baskets were full, and many of them seemed agitated.

"You're lucky you're in the outer suburbs instead of in the city proper," Sue said as her partner cleared the way at the front of the stretcher. "The hospitals there are slammed. That sickness got a lot of people at the airport."

"Are there any sick people here?" Zara asked.

Sue laughed and waved her comment off. "Nah. We're an hour from all of that. The metro area is going to be fine."

Like it was in St. Louis? She didn't mention how the metro area was burning and littered with the dead as they escaped the area, though. She didn't want the paramedic to know where they'd come from.

"The news always makes things out to be worse than they really are," Sue said. "You just worry about Mr. Peters, here. That's enough for anybody to carry."

Zara exchanged a knowing look with Lizzy. What they'd seen on the news hadn't exaggerated anything. In fact, the sickness seemed to be spreading fast. As the paramedics loaded Mr. Peters into the ambulance, Zara got into the driver's seat of the BMW as Lizzy stayed by her dad's side as long as possible. Once the back doors of the ambulance shut, Lizzy joined Zara in the car.

"Okay, let's go to the hospital," she said as she buckled up and the ambulance pulled out, lights on and sirens blaring.

"Are you sure?" Zara asked, heat flooding her cheeks as she forced out the words. "I know you want to follow your dad, but… the hospital will take care of him, and he said we should get out of here, that it wasn't safe."

Lizzy crossed her arms. "I thought we were past this, Zee. Are you seriously suggesting we leave my dad after he almost just *died*? Would you leave your dad?"

Zara swallowed hard. "No," she said. "You're right. I just… an hour isn't very far. And I think… I think your dad would want you to be safe." It was the truth, but Zara was using that truth in a way that made her stomach twist in knots.

Lizzy's expression softened just a bit. "I know," she said. "But I won't leave him."

Zara nodded and started the car, punching in St. Vincent's hospital in the GPS. It was a short drive that didn't require the main highways. They turned down a road that led through a residential area to find several driveways full of vehicles in various stages of being packed full.

"They can feel it," Zara said quietly. "Things are going to get worse here."

Lizzy sank into her seat but didn't say anything. She looked smaller, somehow, as she stared out the window. Zara made a few more turns before pulling into the hospital grounds. The building did look new, styled with balconies and black, iron railings on the second and third floors. Three tiny plazas with benches and trees were spaced out along the front of the building. A main entrance was to the far right, and a red Emergency Department sign pointed them around to the side of the building.

They rounded the hospital. A parking garage stood across from a small ED parking lot, a 24-hour blue and white sign attached to the garage above the entrance. A tow truck was moving the last of a few vehicles inside the lot, and some men were setting up white tents in the cleared area.

"What are they doing?" Lizzy asked.

"Maybe setting up a field hospital? You know, like they did in Boston outside the hospitals when that new strain of the flu went through a few years back." It was only a guess, but Zara would bet they were getting ready for a wave of the sickness they'd seen on the news.

"But it's just precautionary, right?" Lizzy asked.

"I think so," Zara said, "but I also think they're going to need it."

Lizzy pointed to another lot, the one the tow truck was pulling cars into. "Do you want to park there?"

"No," Zara said. "We should probably park in the garage. We might be here a while. Plus, it looks more secure than the lot."

Lizzy pulled out her wallet and handed Zara a credit card as they pulled up to a barrier arm. Zara rolled down her window, slid the credit card into the machine, and the arm lifted.

"You think someone would try to steal our stuff at a hospital?" Lizzy asked.

Zara found a spot on the third floor of the garage. "Not usually, if the doors are locked, but… I don't know what's going to happen or how long we'll be here. If things get rough like they did in St. Louis, I think we'd better not make *our* stuff low hanging fruit."

"My dad would probably say the same thing," Lizzy said.

Zara didn't let Lizzy know how that comment stung. *I'm nothing like him.*

She grabbed the solar-powered chargers out of the trunk along with some snacks and water bottles before they left the parking garage for the ED entrance. As they approached, five men and women in scrubs rolled metal carts full of supplies through the automatic doors, passing them in something of a hurry. They were heading toward the white tents.

That seems like more than just a precaution. Zara hugged her middle.

They walked into a hospital bustling with staff. A table was being set up at the entrance, and a large man in scrubs and a surgical mask stepped up to them, holding up a hand.

"Whoa, there, girls," he said. "We just got word. No one comes in without a questionnaire and a temperature check." His name tag read, "Brian."

"We're just looking for my dad," Lizzy said. "An ambulance brought him in. I think he had a stroke and a heart attack."

Brian nodded. "Still gotta ask the questions and take your temperatures."

The other nurses behind him finished setting up the table, and one of them handed him a tablet and a touch-free temperature gun. Zara and Lizzy let him scan their foreheads.

"Temps are normal," he said. "Okay, any headaches, pressure behind the eyes, bleeding from the gums, nose, eyes, or ears?"

"No," Zara and Lizzy answered simultaneously.

Brian tapped the tablet a few times and pointed down the hallway behind him. "Go that way," he said. "There's a service desk, and the ladies there will be able to help you know where to go."

"Thanks," Zara said.

The girls did as they were told, and they were hurriedly directed to a second floor waiting room. The atmosphere in the waiting room was less chaotic. A woman sat by herself in one corner, reading a magazine and tapping feet on the floor in an impatient rhythm. On the other side of the room, a small group sat together playing cards around a coffee table. Two smaller children colored at a nearby table. One wall was covered in floor-to-ceiling windows, casting plenty of light into the space. They could see the white tents on the lawn.

A nurse sat at a small station in a third corner next to a coffee machine. Zara and Lizzy approached her, and she looked up from her computer screen.

"Can I help you?" she asked.

"My dad, Walter Peters, was brought in by ambulance. The desk downstairs said he was taken into surgery, but I don't know anything. We just got here. Can you get us any other information?" Lizzy asked, she looked at the woman's name tag. "We'd really appreciate it, Peggy."

Peggy smiled. "Let me see if I can get a doctor," she said. "Why don't you two have a seat?"

"Thanks," Lizzy said, turning despondently toward the center of the room.

"Let's sit by the windows so we can charge our phones," Zara said.

Lizzy nodded. "I need to tell Mom what's happened."

Zara folded open the solar charger's little golden panels and set it up facing the window. "You want to charge your phone first?" she asked.

Lizzy patted her pocket, and her face went pale. "Oh no." She groaned. "I must have left it at the gas station."

Zara sighed and pulled out her own phone. "That's okay," she said. "I can drive back and get it later. Right now, though, let's charge my phone. We can call your mom. You can talk to her, and I can ask Timothy if he was able to check on my parents."

"But, Zee," Lizzy said, "I was hoping that video I downloaded would give us some clues about Jordan."

"You can log on to the forum from my phone and redownload it after we talk to your mom, okay?" Zara said. "And, like I said, we can always go back to the station and grab your phone. I bet that cashier has it behind the counter already."

Lizzy nodded and sat down as Zara plugged her phone in. "How long will it take to charge?"

"I think we're going to need to give it a few hours," Zara said. "The instructions said a full charge would take twenty hours, so…" She shrugged and sat down, slipped off her shoes, and then lay across the chairs. "I didn't sleep well last night," she said. "Might as well get some sleep while we wait. It feels good to lay with my legs stretched out."

"You go ahead," Lizzy said. "I'm going to wait for the doctor."

Zara nodded, her eyelids heavy. "You sure?" she mumbled, already feeling the tug of unconsciousness. "I can try to wait up with you."

"No, it's okay." Lizzy scratched Zara's head gently, which only made her sleepier. "You go ahead and…"

Lizzy's voice faded as Zara fell into dreams of home. She laughed and painted Annika's nails while her mom and Auntie Rachel sipped red wine on the couch. The smell of her father's cooking wafted in from the kitchen, and soon he was bringing homemade jalapeno poppers, popcorn, and mini quiches for the ladies of the house to enjoy.

"Zara, baby," her mother said, "wake up."

Zara frowned. "What?" she asked, looking up at her mother and aunt. "I *am* awake."

Annika giggled. "You're silly. None of us are awake."

A cold chill swept through the room. When Zara looked back at her parents and her aunt, all the color had drained from the room, leaving everything in black and white. Their mouths were open in silent screams, eyes beginning to bulge, hands pressed against their temples.

Zara jumped to her feet and screamed. "No!"

Her mother's face glitched back into a smile. "Wake up, baby," she said sweetly as Auntie Rachel's skin began to melt. Her father's eye popped out of its socket as he stood over the couch, mouth open, holding a big bowl of popcorn.

"Wake up!" Lizzy's voice tore away the sickening images, and Zara startled awake to a sterile hospital waiting room.

She nearly fell out of the chairs she'd laid across as Lizzy shook her shoulder. "What happened?" Zara asked, sitting up, her eyes darting around the room. The others who'd been waiting were still there, and they were all staring at her.

"You were shouting in your sleep," Lizzy said.

"Oh… sorry," she said loudly enough for everyone to hear. "It's been a rough day." She smiled sheepishly as the woman by herself pursed her lips, quirked an eyebrow, and went back to reading her magazine.

"Don't worry about it," a woman from the group said, offering a smile. She stood up and brought a tin of cookies, pushing it out for them to each take one. "Here. These were made fresh this morning," she said. "Chocolate chip. A classic."

Lizzy grabbed two and handed one to Zara. "Thanks," she said.

The woman smiled again and went back to join her family. Zara took the cookie and nibbled on it. It was delicious — crispy on the outside, chewy on the inside, and chock full of chocolate. She leaned back against the chair, trying to get the images of her family out of her mind. She scooted over to the table and tapped her phone. It was at fifteen percent.

"Hey, I think we can make a call," Zara said.

Lizzy took a deep breath. "I don't know what I'm going to say to my mom."

"Did the doctor come while I was asleep?"

Lizzy nodded. "Yeah. He said my dad had a stroke, and then a heart attack." Her eyes glistened. "He said you saved his life."

Zara flushed. She knew it probably came off as her just being humble, but all she could think about was how she'd almost stopped to let him die. "So, he's going to be okay?"

"They said he's not out of the woods, but he has a good chance." Lizzy's sad smile was small and pitiful.

"I think that's all you need to tell your mom," Zara said. "We can update her again when he's awake and can talk to her himself. Which," she added, "I'm sure will be very soon."

Lizzy nodded and reached for the phone. She dialed and held the phone up to her ear. "Hello? Hey mom… um, something happened. Dad's in the hospital…"

Zara munched on her cookie, trying to be patient as Lizzy explained the situation to Mrs. Peters. The images from her nightmare had shaken her, and all she wanted was to hear that her family was okay. When Lizzy handed her the phone, she took it eagerly.

"Mrs. Peters?" she asked.

"No, it's Timothy." His voice sounded apprehensive.

"Oh. Hey, Timothy. Were you able to check in on my parents?" Zara scooted to the edge of her seat.

"Um, yeah." Timothy paused.

"And?" Zara asked.

"I don't know how to say this," he said. "Zara… they… they caught the sickness somehow. It's all over Mattapan. I… I don't know how, and I'm so sorry."

Flashes of cold and heat flooded her body at the same time, and she began to shiver. "But… they're okay?"

"No." Timothy's voice broke. "I'm so sorry."

Zara's vision blurred with tears and a sob bubbled up from the deepest parts of her. "That can't be right," she said loudly. "You have to go back. They… they have to be okay."

"Zara, your Aunt Rachel was with them, and she… she also didn't make it." Though Timothy's voice was gentle, every word was like a violent punch to Zara's gut. "But we found Annika," his voice sounded more hopeful. "She was alive and—"

The phone line went completely silent.

"And what?" Zara asked, tears streaming down her face. No answer came. "And what, Timothy?" she shouted. She pulled the phone away, wiping away her tears to see that the call had dropped. She tried to dial again, but there was no service.

"Zee?" Lizzy came up behind her and put a hand on Zara's back. "What's wrong?"

"This phone is what's wrong!" A guttural scream ripped from her throat as an uncontrollable rage built inside her body. She threw the phone, and it crashed against the wall, falling to the ground, screen cracked.

"Miss!" Peggy, the nurse from the corner station, stood up and came around the corner. "You need to calm d—"

Zara screamed again as images of her mother and father and aunt flashed in her mind's eye. "It's all wrong," she shouted, falling to her knees, rocking as she held her stomach. The room spun. Her body felt like it was imploding. Her head pounded, her heart raced, and every molecule was teeming with a pain unlike anything she'd ever experienced.

Lizzy knelt in front of her. "Zee, tell me what my brother told you."

"They're all dead," Zara said.

Her words stopped Peggy in her tracks, and her angry expression melted into one of understanding. The woman with the magazine closed it and looked up, brow creased, hand covering her mouth. Zara heard a few gasps come from the family behind her.

Lizzy blinked back her own tears. "Who? Your parents?"

Zara tried to answer, but the words suddenly felt too cumbersome, shaped all wrong to make it past her lips. They lodged in her throat, and she coughed, choking on them.

Lizzy wrapped her arms around Zara. "I'm sorry, Zee." She cried quietly, her tears joining Zara's while still giving her the space to grieve.

Zara couldn't breathe. She couldn't think. All she could feel was pain. The nurse brought her a cup of water and some tissues, staying close to keep an eye on her, and Zara sat in the middle of the waiting room floor, rocking and crying and trying to catch her breath. She vaguely registered the family in the corner, holding hands and praying for her. The thought crossed her mind that her Auntie would have liked that.

Finally, she couldn't cry any longer. She looked up at Lizzy. "Auntie Rachel was with them," she said. "She's gone, too," she whispered.

Lizzy sucked in a breath. "And Annika?" she asked tentatively.

That name was like a tiny spark of hope. "She's alive, he said," Zara sat up and blew her nose. "But then the phone's signal dropped." She looked around. "I'm sorry," she said to the entire room. "I just… does anyone have a phone that works? I just want to know if my cousin is okay."

Each person in the room pulled out their phones, but one by one, they confirmed it. No one had a signal. The nurse checked the landline, but there was no luck there, either.

"I'm sorry," Peggy said. "I'm not sure what's going on." Almost as if on cue, with her last word, the lights in the hospital went out for a just a moment, and then half of them blinked back on.

"What was that?" Lizzy asked.

"I think the power went out and the generators kicked on," Peggy said. "The waiting rooms and hallways only get half power in emergencies."

"There isn't a storm," the woman in the corner said, standing up and looking out the window.

A man in a suit and tie burst into the room, his eyes landing on the nurse. "Peggy, everyone needs to stay put, except to use the bathroom, okay?" He looked around, eyes wide with panic. "For your own safety, please stay in this room."

"Mr. Richards?" Peggy said. "What's going on?"

"There was an incident at the powerplant. Someone there brought this new sickness in to work. We don't know where he got it from yet, but the hospitals in Indy are full. We've got three cases coming here to the triage tent." He nodded toward the window.

Zara struggled to her feet. "Only three?" she asked. "There were more, weren't there? But they're dead?" she asked.

He frowned at her. "How did you know?"

"Gut feeling," she said.

"Yes, well… three are coming here. That's all I can tell you right now." He backed out of the room. "Your loved ones are getting the proper care. The generators are working. We just need everyone to stay put." He left, nodding to the nurse.

The woman in the corner pulled a small, handheld radio out of her purse and began to search the channels. She was met with static over and over again.

"I'm not sure that's a good idea," Peggy said. "I don't think we should—"

"Thirteen dead," a man's voice reverberated throughout the waiting room. "The powerplant is now cordoned off as thirteen body bags leave the scene. Three are being taken to St. Vincent's, and the other thirty employees are being kept at the plant in quarantine, though I have confirmed some of them are ill."

Zara stumbled over to the chairs and lay back down, her back to the other occupants in the room. She ignored the alarmed voices arguing over whether they should stay put. Instead, she began to count the dots in the pattern on the back of the chair.

One, two, three…

"Zee," Lizzy sat next to Zara's head. "What are we going to do?"

Eight, nine, ten…

"Zee?"

Thirteen, fourteen, fifteen…

Lizzy leaned back in her chair, and Zara heard her best friend break down and cry. And Zara would have cried, too, if her burning eyes had any tears left. But they didn't. She had no words. She had no thoughts. Her body had no strength left. She counted away her emotions, and Zara let herself fade into the numbers.

Chapter 23

Alexander Roman

It was dead quiet. Alex sat across from Minnie at her kitchen table, waiting. She hadn't said a word since coming back from Red Bud, her in her RV and Alex following behind in her truck. Oliver had gone straight to the bedroom, crawling under the covers, and Alex had followed him, rubbing his back until he fell asleep. It was only the afternoon, but the emotional burdens of tragedy were like a drug. Alex felt the pull of it; part of him wanted to join his son, to let sleep keep reality at bay for just a little while. Instead, he'd come to check on Minnie and found her sitting at the table, staring blankly ahead, silent, tears rolling down her cheeks. Samson lay at her feet, occasionally raising his head to look at her.

"Minnie…" Alex began, though he wasn't sure how to say what needed to be said, not without sounding harsh. *We need to get as far away from here as we can, and we can't go back to check on your friends.*

Minnie blinked and frowned, turning her head to the kitchen cabinets. She abruptly stood, opened the one above the sink, and grabbed a bottle of bourbon. Two glasses clinked as she pinched them together with her fingers and set them on the table along with the alcohol. She poured a finger in each, plopped one down in front of Alex and threw back the second, swallowing it in one go. Alex followed suit, letting the amber liquid slide warm and prickly down his throat.

"I 'spose we should hightail it outta here," Minnie said, remaining on her feet. "Help me pack up Harvey?"

"That's it?" Alex asked. "You're okay with just picking up and leaving?" It had only been a matter of hours since he'd been set on staying for his dead wife; he'd expected Minnie to want to go back for her people, some of whom may still be alive.

"If it means getting to Lauren before this plague gets her," Minnie said, "then, yes."

Alex nodded. "Okay, good. We need to bring food and water," he said. "Besides a few changes of clothing and my go-bag, pretty much everything else should stay behind. We don't have the time or capacity for extras."

"You're not talkin' about Samson as an extra, now, are ya?" Minnie asked, one eyebrow quirked.

Alex looked down at the dog and couldn't help but smile. "He's anything but. Oliver would never forgive me if we left him behind."

Minnie reached down and scratched Samson behind the ears. "That boy's got sense." She stood straighter. "I've got a good emergency stash of canned goods and about a dozen jugs of water in the barn," Minnie said. "There should be room for all of it in Harvey's storage areas."

Alex stood and put a hand on Minnie's shoulder. "I don't know how I'm ever going to repay you. You've saved our lives."

Minnie looked up at him. "Is the CDC… Atlanta… do you think it'll be safe there?"

"Yes," Alex said. "The CDC has protocols, equipment, doctors, researchers, and even security. Oliver and I will be okay once we're there. I think they'll let me keep him there, at the facility, if things go haywire in the city."

"Do you think they'll let you bring along two more?" Minnie asked.

"I don't know about the dog," Alex said, "but if you can help with Oliver, I think I can make a good case for why you should be able to stay, too. They're going to need me, and I won't be able to work if I don't know that my son is safe."

"I was talkin' about Lauren. Me and Lauren… and Samson, too," Minnie said, eyes pleading.

"I will do everything in my power to make sure you and your family are safe," Alex said. "I swear."

Minnie breathed out in relief, the air whooshing out of her, the creases on her forehead smoothing as a bit of the stress melted from her features. "Thank you," she said. Then, she dried her cheeks with a napkin on the table, rolled her shoulders, and looked Alex in the eye. "Let's get on it," she said. "Nashville is what… five hours from here?"

Alex shook his head. "I have the feeling we should stick to back roads. That's going to add time to the trip."

Minnie nodded. "Then we best get goin'."

Within the hour, Alex and Minnie had finished packing the RV with the essentials, and he was softly sitting on the edge of the bed to wake Oliver. His son held Naomi's macrame purse to his chest as he slept, his features relaxed, his mouth twitching up into a smile every so often. Alex reached out and let his hand rest on Oliver's chest, falling and rising gently with every precious breath. If losing Naomi had almost killed him, he wondered what losing Oliver would do to him.

I'm not going to find out. I'm going to keep him safe. It was a promise to himself, to Naomi, and to Oliver, and behind his declaration was a desperate prayer—unspoken words that were somehow more powerful because he *felt* them instead of said them. If there was a God out there listening, Alex petitioned Him with every ounce of his soul. He *needed* Oliver to live, and that would take a whole slew of miracles.

Oliver stirred, his eyes popping open and his arms stretching above his head. For a moment, there was that light in his eyes that had been there all the time before his mother had died. It was quickly erased as he sat up and looked around the room, replaced by a sad smile as Samson hopped up onto the bed.

"We're leaving," Alex said. He held up a reassuring hand when tears sprung into Oliver's eyes, and his son wrapped his arms around Samson's neck. "Minnie and Samson are going to help us get home, bud. They're coming with us."

Oliver relaxed a little and nodded. He pushed away the comforter and got out of bed, looking at Alex expectantly, the purse in hand as if waiting to follow.

Alex's forehead creased and his eyebrows drew together as he looked at his son. "What do you think about all this, bud? I'd really love to hear what's going on inside your head."

His son averted his eyes and shrugged, his cheeks turning red. He stepped forward and wrapped his arms around Alex's waist, hugging him tightly, squeezing his eyes shut.

Alex sighed and patted Oliver's back. "It's okay," he said. Then he gently pulled away and knelt before Oliver, looking his son in the eye. "I'm here when you're ready, okay?"

Oliver nodded, and Alex took his hand, leading him outside to the RV and letting him buckle up in the backseat of the cab with Samson, who took up a good chunk of the space, the dog's head resting in Oliver's lap. The cab was similar to that of an oversized truck. Behind Oliver, between the top of the seat and the ceiling, a sliding window gave emergency access to the living quarters which contained a kitchenette, a couch, a small table, storage space, a tiny bathroom and shower, and a bed which was positioned over the cab, extending over both the back and front seats. Once they picked up Lauren, it would be crowded but not unbearable, at least not for a short-lived trip.

Minnie came up beside Alex and pointed to a lip in the plastic backing of the driver's seat, a smile on her face. "That there slides down, and there's a screen built in. It hasn't been used in a while, but I think there's still a thing or two on it, mostly music." Her smile faded. "Lauren sure does love country music," she said. "Listened to it nonstop."

"Not a fan?" Alex asked as he slid down the plastic to reveal the small, rectangular screen.

"Nah, I'm a big fan." She smiled. "What's not to like about trucks and love and enjoyin' the simple things?" She shook her head. "Just brought up a few bad memories is all." She hopped into the front seat, sticking the key in the ignition. The vehicle roared to life and then quieted down, becoming a steady rumble in the background. "See if it turns on," Minnie said over her shoulder.

Alex pushed the power button, and the black screen turned blue, then a list appeared of items stored on the device, including the movie and album covers. "Music and a few Disney cartoons." Alex raised his eyebrows and looked at Oliver. "These are old, but they're good. Trust me."

Oliver wrinkled his nose, looking skeptical.

"Look, kid. Snow White, here, she's got superpowers. Animals and dwarves alike hang on her every word. And Mulan? I mean, come on. Just look at that war paint." He tapped the movie poster on the screen. "And there's a talking dragon," he added.

Oliver pursed his lips but then nodded, like he wasn't sure, but he'd give it a try. Alex hooked up the old headphones via an adapter already fixed into the port and gave them to Oliver, turning the movie on. He kissed the top of his son's head, closed the door, and rounded the vehicle.

"Are we good to go?" Alex asked as he slid into the passenger seat, placing his CDC go-bag on the floor at his feet. The padding of the seat was worn down, and Alex shifted his weight to find the most comfortable position before buckling up.

"Harvey's got enough juice to get us to Nashville, no problem," Minnie said. "The solar panels will keep the electricity in the back goin' but they only go so far in terms of stretchin' the fuel. We'll need to gas up before we leave the city."

Alex's stomach dropped. "What are we going to do if there isn't fuel available? I mean, I'm hoping everything is okay in Nashville, but..."

Minnie shrugged. "I reckon we'll have to cross that bridge when we get there."

As Minnie pulled out of the driveway and turned south, the realities of their trip weighed heavy on Alex's mind. He looked back at Oliver, who was rapt, eyes wide and a toothy grin on his face. Samson nuzzled his stomach, and he absently scratched at the dog's ears.

"We'll need to listen to the radio," Alex said quietly to Minnie, "to see if we can figure out what we're driving into, but first, I'm going to call my boss." He dug out his cell phone but frowned. "No service."

"I didn't have service last I checked, either," Minnie said. "I wanted to try to call Lauren, to tell her we were comin' but I couldn't."

Alex dug out his CDC satellite phone from the go-bag. "Well, I guess it's time to switch phones. This should work," he said.

"Can I try Lauren?" Minnie asked. "I tried her before my phone's signal petered out, but she didn't answer."

Alex nodded. "I'm not supposed to let anyone else use it, but I'm guessing this counts as emergency circumstances. I can dial while you drive. What's the number?" Alex punched it in as Minnie recalled it, and then they waited for Lauren to pick up on the other end. There was no answer. "Maybe cell phone service is down there, too."

"You think Nashville's been hit?" Minnie asked, her voice trembling a little.

"I don't know," Alex said. "My boss might." He dialed Dr. Jonah Newton and waited, relieved when he heard a click.

"Alex, is that you?" Jonah's voice was urgent and questioning, which was odd considering Alex's name should be attached to the number he was calling from.

"Yes," Alex said. "Of course it's me. Who else would it be?"

Jonah breathed a sigh of relief. "Well, Laura and Ned had strangers call in their final notes. Some kind of dying wish."

"Do you mean they're both..." He trailed off, looking back at Oliver who was still watching the screen.

"Dead." Jonah's voice was exhausted and cracked. "They're not the only ones. Alex, I think you're the only disease detective we have who was at a ground zero and is still alive."

"What?" The air turned suddenly thick, and Alex's chest constricted. "Who else?"

There was a pause. "Charles and Gerald," Jonah's shaky breath was loud in Alex's ear. "And Ann and Pedro. We sent three teams of two to St. Louis, Boston, and San Francisco. They were to work with our local offices and the local authorities, but... things didn't go well for any of them."

The landscape they drove past seemed to swirl as Alex tried to process the news. Lightheaded, he cleared his throat and reached for a water bottle in his cup holder he'd yet to open. He struggled with the cap, dropping it and splashing water on his shirt.

"Alex?" Minnie glanced at him, keeping an eye on the country road ahead. "You okay?" She began to slow down.

At the same time, Jonah spoke. "I know it's a lot to process," he said. "Do you need a minute?"

Alex nodded at Minnie, gesturing for her to keep driving, and spoke to Jonah. "No, I need answers." Alex's mouth was dry like he'd been chewing cotton. He took a drink, but it didn't seem to help.

"I can tell you what we know," Jonah said. "Does this mean you're coming in?"

"Yes," Alex said. "But I'm going to need to keep my son safe and with me."
"We can accommodate whatever you need, Alex. We've got a few options essential personnel are considering right now for our own immediate families. The labs, the research... we can't leave it, and it doesn't look like there's a safe place to send our loved ones. Atlanta has seen its first case, so... we're thinking we've got about twenty-four hours before the city is in chaos."
"I need to bring two women with me as well," Alex said. "They'll help take care of Oliver. One of them saved my life."
Jonah sighed. "We've restricted our facilities to essential personnel and security and *immediate* family members. We can't let everyone bring in their friends and extended family."
"Please, Jonah. This woman saved my life. Just her and her daughter... and their dog," he added quickly. "I need someone to help me with Oliver."
"A dog? You can't be serious." Jonah's stilted words were followed by a heavier sigh. "Alex, I can probably get an exception for one woman to help you with Oliver. That's it."
"Can the other woman and the dog stay in an RV parked outside?" Alex asked.
"Maybe." Jonah didn't sound happy. "Look, we can figure out the logistics when you get here. Right now, we need to figure out what you know."
"Not much," Alex said. "Not yet, anyway. I've seen the symptoms. It looks like one hundred percent mortality, or pretty close to it. I haven't been able to study it which might be why I'm still alive. I don't have the proper gear to protect me." An image of the woman popped into his head. "I did take note of a particular woman. She died, but her symptoms seemed less pronounced than that of who I assumed was her daughter. They were still deadly, but not quite as extreme. That might indicate the disease is less severe in some which could give us more time to treat the disease between the onset and death. It could even be survivable without medication for a lucky few, though I have no proof of that."
"There's been some speculation that once we understand what's happening," Jonah said, "we'll be able to treat it. I hope that's the case. I'll bring your notes to the team."
"What else do you know?" Alex asked.
"We know the disease kills within three to seven hours, though that window could be less. We haven't figured out the vector. Ann believed it to be an airborne pathogen. We believe Gerald's notes indicated that several bodies he found had one, singular welt that was different from the other welts, one that looked like a bug bite. But we got that information second hand from a stranger reading Gerald's notes, not from the man himself." Jonah took a deep breath. "All the initial infections happened at outdoor events. There's a consensus that the vector is something naturally or artificially occurring in the environment. Perhaps an insect or spore or indetectable gas."
"I would agree," Alex said.
"There's one more thing," Jonah said. "Most infections, especially early on, originated at night and outdoors, which seems to track with the idea of a mosquito vector. That would make the hours of nineteen hundred hours to maybe eight or ten hundred hours the highest risk."
Alex raised his eyebrows. "A mosquito vector? Mosquitos don't carry contagious diseases. And it's spreading too fast to be spread by any insect alone. The disease itself must be contagious."
"We're definitely thinking outside the box," Jonah said. "Whatever this is doesn't follow the rules we're used to. We're working on getting a blood sample analyzed, but anyone who's been able to collect a sample has died before getting the chance to study it."
Alex rubbed a hand over his face. "If we can't study it without catching it..."
"...we'll never find a treatment." Jonah finished his sentence.
"Okay," Alex said. "Well, we're going to have to figure this out together. I hope to be in Atlanta soon, hopefully before the day is out tomorrow. But we're not taking any main highways if we don't have to, so the travel will be slow. We've got to stop in Nashville to find my friend's daughter, the second woman I was telling you about. Do you know anything about Nashville?"
"I haven't heard anything about Nashville since we got a report that a few cases had hit their airport the night of the incident at the World's Fair. There have been so many reports, Alex." Jonah's weary voice somehow sounded even more exhausted. "It's hard to keep track of everywhere this thing is popping up, especially since we lost cell service across most of the country. I'm honestly not sure how long we'll have satellite phones, either. They rely on ground relay stations. The power has already gone out in several regions. The entire eastern seaboard has no power. Relay stations are supposed to have backup generators, but if the technicians get sick or don't come in to work..."
"So this might be the last time I talk to you until I see you," Alex said.
"Alex, this might be the last time you talk to me at all." Jonah sighed. "I know that sounds grim, but—"
Alex cut him off, shaking his head. "Hey, let's just plan on seeing each other soon, okay? Don't talk like that. We're both going to make it out of this."
"You're right," Jonah said after a pause. "You be careful out there."
"Will do." Alex hung up the phone and leaned back against the headrest.
"That sounded rough," Minnie said. "What'd he say about Nashville?"
"It's there, but they don't know how widespread." Alex closed his eyes. "It might be bad, Minnie."
She nodded. "You understand I gotta try to find my girl?"
"You helped me save my son. I'm not going to begrudge you the chance to save your daughter," Alex said.
The countryside rolled past, and Alex meant to close his eyes for only a minute. But they were safe, and exhaustion tugged him into dreams of before he'd lost Naomi. Before his son had been so traumatized, he'd lost the ability to speak. Before the death and destruction on a scale Alex could never have imagined. He dreamed of family and home, his wife's smile and his son's voice. The dream was cut short by the nightmare of reality. He woke to Minnie shaking him. Night had fallen, and they were no longer moving. Moonlight shone off the metallic sheen of vehicles smashed and piled up and abandoned. The glimmering pathway of wreckage led to an angry red blossom that spanned the distant horizon, a halo of fire brightening the dark. Ahead, Nashville burned.

Chapter 24

Zara Williams

Zara traced the white cracks, rough beneath her fingertip, along the surface of the cool, dark screen. The phone was dead. The casing had cracked when she'd thrown it against the wall, shattering the screen. But that didn't matter. Cell service was down. Even if she hadn't destroyed her phone, Zara wouldn't be able to call Timothy back to ask for more information about Annika.

Please… let her be okay. Zara prayed, her heart longing to be there for the little girl she'd grown to love over the past several years. *And Jordan, too. Please. Please, let them be okay.*

Timothy had said Annika was alive, but was she injured? Sick? And he had used the past tense. He'd found Annika, and she *was* alive. *He sounded like maybe he was telling me something good, like she was still alive, like she was going to be fine.* But Zara wasn't sure she could trust her memory. She'd been reeling from the news of her parents' deaths, of her auntie's death. *Was I just holding onto hope? Making up the positive in his voice when he said her name?*

And she still had no idea what had happened to her brother. They'd never gotten to watch the video Lizzy had downloaded onto her phone, but it had sounded like a big deal on the forum. Something happened to Jordan, or he did something big, something his fellow Green Earth Futurists had wanted to leak to the press. Zara glanced at the solar charger. *If the video is on the phone, we could still access it, even without cell service or WiFi. We'd just have to charge it.*

"Ms. Peters?" Peggy, the nurse, walked over and sat next to Lizzy and Zara. "Your father is waking, and the doctors have said you can come see him."

Lizzy breathed out a sigh of relief and then her eyes darted to Zara apologetically. "Zee, I—"

"You can be happy that your dad isn't dead, Liz." Zara's words came out with a bitter edge, something she hadn't meant to do. She put her broken phone on the seat next to her. "I'm sorry," she said in a sincere tone. "I meant what I said."

Lizzy nodded. "It's okay," she said. "You want to come with me?"

Zara shook her head. That was the *last* thing she wanted to do. "Actually… I think I'm going to go back to the gas station and get your phone."

"What?" Lizzy asked, looking out the window onto the lawn of the hospital.

Cars were being towed to make room for more tents. A handful of hospital staff walked around in white compression suits, surgical masks, glasses, and face shields. Hours had passed since the three men had been brought to the hospital from the powerplant. All three lay in body bags on a patch of grass across the road on a black tarp. The six paramedics who had treated them and brought them in had sat off to the side for quite some time, one by one developing symptoms and being brought inside the tent. When the screaming started, it didn't last long. Zara suspected doctors were sedating patients, but once a patient entered the tent, there was no way for her to know what happened to them—until they were rolled out of the tent in a body bag. One paramedic was left, impatiently tapping his foot on the ground, several yards from the tent. He kept putting his fingers to his neck as if checking his pulse.

"Zee, I don't know if that's a good idea," Lizzy said.

Peggy's face had turned ashen the second Zara had voiced her plan. "You really shouldn't leave, Ms. Williams. I… I didn't want to scare anyone, but…" She stood up, retrieved her radio from her nurse's station, and turned it on, flipping through the static. "I was asked not to play this in here because it caused panic last time, so I took it into the bathroom for a few minutes about an hour ago." She kept flipping, passing on the channel she'd stopped at before, the one with a radio personality relaying news about the local situation. She stopped on a station that was in the middle of broadcasting a long beeping sound. The family, who had continued their card games half-heartedly, and the woman, who had been staring at the same magazine page for hours, eyes vacant, turned their attention to Peggy and the radio.

An artificial voice, cold and robotic, picked up after the beep. "This is a warning from the Center for Disease Control and the United States Government. A nationwide curfew is in place from nineteen hundred hours to ten hundred hours. This is for your own safety. Maintain social distance. Do not leave your homes. Do not panic. This station will broadcast more information when it is available. This is a warning from the Center for Disease Control and the United States Government." A long beep ensued once more, and Peggy turned off the radio.

"I'll be back by seven," Zara said. "It's only what?" She looked at the clock on the wall. "It's noon. Plenty of time to drive there and back. It'll take me an hour at most."

Lizzy's brow creased as she watched another body bag roll out of the tent on a stretcher. "What about this disease?"

"It's contained, right?" She looked at Peggy. "The three guys from the plant and the paramedics that were in direct contact with them got sick, but this area hasn't been hit?"

"Well, yes, but that could change at any time," Peggy said. She lowered her voice, her eyes darting to the woman staring at her magazine page and over to the family before settling back on Zara. "As people flee Indy proper, there's a good chance they'll spread this disease. If things are getting worse there… there's no telling how long we've got before we're in real trouble." She shook her head. "I've got to go."

"What? We're trying to convince her to stay here, and you're saying you've got to go?" Lizzy asked.

"You have to stay because of your father." Peggy stood up, not bothering to keep her voice low anymore. Her breathing became quicker, shallower. "I… I should have left hours ago. I've got to get my son and my parents, and I've got to get out of here." She rushed over to the nurse's station.

The woman looked up from her magazine, the vacant expression she'd held for a long time melting into confusion. She shut the magazine and stood up. "You're right." She looked at the door leading to the patient rooms. "I'm leaving, too."

"Don't you have a brother here?" The woman who'd given them cookies stood up, too. "We can't leave our family members here, alone." She looked at the nurse. "And you… the hospital needs you right now. How can you just go?"

Peggy slung her purse over her shoulder, took off her lanyard which held a set of keys, and quickly walked toward the door. "The hospital doesn't need me more than my son needs me. The doctors will stay." She kept her eyes focused on the door, not looking at anyone.

"And I don't even like my brother," the woman with the magazine said. "He's always been a jerk." She followed Peggy out of the room, the door closing behind them.

"Bertie," a man stood up next to the woman, who stared at the door, fists clenched at her side. "Maybe we should—"

"I am *not* leaving Judy here by herself," Bertie said. "I can't believe you would even suggest that, Lionel."

"What about the grandkids?" he asked, nodding to where the two smaller children huddled next to each other, watching with wide eyes.

Bertie's shoulders sagged. "Judy is our *daughter*."

"She'd want them to be safe." Lionel put a hand on Bertie's shoulder.

"You take them," she said. "Get them out of here. Maybe to the cabin up north. I'll follow with Judith as soon as we can." The family had hugged and said their goodbyes, half-heartedly offering positive well wishes.

In less than five minutes, only Zara, Lizzy, and Bertie remained in the waiting room. Hope dwindled even further in the silence that followed as they each stood still as statues, eyes fixed on the door.

Finally, Lizzy broke the trance, throwing her hands in the air. "Great, Zee. Nice. Now who is going to update us on my dad? I don't know what room he's in! How am I supposed to find him?" she asked.

"Are you blaming Peggy's leaving on me?" Zara took a step away from her. "Your phone has the only clue about Jordan on it. I need to see it, Liz."

Bertie took a deep breath. "I'm going to go sit with my daughter. I don't think anyone will stop me. If you come with me, hon, I'll help you find your dad."

"That's really nice," Zara said. "Thanks."

"But what if you don't come back?" Lizzy asked, eyes rimming with tears.

"That's why I need to go right now, before crap hits the fan," Zara said. She went over to the nurse's station where Peggy had set her keys. She unlocked the cabinets lining the wall, rifling through. "I'll bring these gloves and a mask," she said as she set the supplies on the counter. "I'll stay away from people. I'll get the phone and be back before you know it."

Lizzy shook her head. "Zee—"

"That video has something important on it about Jordan," Zara said. "I need to see it. I need to do something besides think about my dead parents, about my cousin who may or may not be okay."

"Fine." Lizzy relented. "But… hurry, okay?"

"I promise. The gas station is like five minutes away. What could go wrong, really? I'll be there and back in a half hour." Zara gave Lizzy a hug and then turned to Bertie. "And thank you for your help," she said.

Bertie offered a small smile. "If we lose our kindness in times like this, we lose everything. I'm just holding onto something good."

"Well, I think that's pretty amazing," Zara said as she walked back over to Lizzy.

"Me too." Lizzy nudged Zara gently. "Go on and get the phone," she said.

Zara nodded, slipped on the gloves and mask, and left the waiting room, some of the numbness of grief thawing as finding the phone gave her a purpose. If Jordan was still alive, the video might give her an idea of where to find him. She skipped the elevators and headed for the stairs, taking them two at a time. She avoided the exit she'd come in earlier as it led straight to the tents outside and followed the signs for another exit. Once outside, she walked to the road that skirted the hospital's parking lots, backtracking toward the right parking garage.

The garage was only half as full as it had been that morning. She found the car and hopped in, frowning as the GPS pulled up a map but had no signal. She could see the city, but it couldn't find the gas station or create a route.

"Well," she said to herself. "The station isn't far. I'll just have to find it on my own." She shrugged and pulled out of the garage, trying to remember the roads she had taken to get to the hospital.

What had taken her a little more than five minutes stretched into ten and then fifteen as Zara navigated the busy roads. Everyone seemed to be fighting to get to the highways, vehicles packed full to the brim. A few homes and businesses sported newly boarded windows and doors.

As she passed one small strip mall that included a grocery store, fighting broke out in the lot. She inched forward in a stream of bumper-to-bumper vehicles. Her palms sweaty, she kept one eye on the road ahead and one eye on the growing crowd of angry people. A car backed out of a parking spot at a snail's pace, honking as they tried to part the mob. But the people turned on the car and began smashing the windows. The car accelerated backwards, knocking several people to the ground and running straight over someone, before crashing into the parked cars behind them. The mob pulled the driver out of the window. Zara looked away as the driver was thrown to the ground and the throng surrounded him.

When she finally reached the gas station, she had to park the car at the edge of the lot because it was full of gridlocked vehicles. The windows were broken out of most of them, and the windows and glass doors of the station itself hadn't fared better. A truck had driven into the side of the building, the back half sticking out onto the sidewalk. Zara turned off the car and got out, staring at the mess before her. Behind, horns blared, and people shouted out their car windows.

Zara turned in a circle, taking it all in. She'd slowly integrated into the chaos, focusing on finding her way to the gas station. She hadn't stopped to really think about what she was getting herself into. Her hands began to tremble, the keys clinking as they hung on her thumb by a keyring.

How am I going to get back? She couldn't imagine trying to cross traffic. Maybe I can merge and then go around the block to turn around…

Down the street, a man, woman, and child with backpacks strapped on went from vehicle to vehicle, the man knocking on windows, begging for a ride. The woman followed, her steps reluctant as she kept hold of her daughter's hand. There were others on foot. A young man jogged past Zara, jaw set, eyes intensely focused ahead. He didn't so much as look at her. A homeless person on the other side of the street clung to a grocery cart that looked to contain everything they owned.

Zara faced the station and stuck her keys in her pocket. She had to get that phone and get back to the hospital. Glass crunched under her feet as she squeezed between vehicles, finding a way through the maze to the front of the gas station. There was no one inside that she could see. Empty, overturned shelves, broken glass, and trash covered the floor. She stepped through the frame of the sliding glass door that had had its glass shattered.

Her heart thudded in her chest at the sight of someone's legs protruding from the tangle of shelving. "Hey!" she shouted, rushing forward. "Are you okay? Hello?" She gripped a shelf and heaved, pushing it out of the way so that she could see the person on the ground. He was dead, eyes open, a puddle of congealing blood creating a halo around his head.

Zara gasped and stumbled backward, tripping and falling to the ground. "What is wrong with people?" she shouted, images from the grocery parking lot surfacing. She thought of what Bertie had said and shook her head, wiping away tears. Apparently, those willing to hold on to the good were fewer and farther between than Zara could have ever imagined.

"They're just trying to survive." A man's voice sounded from behind Zara.

Startled, she yelped and scrambled back to her feet, hand to chest. She almost tripped again, but maintained her footing. "Who are you?" she asked.

The man was short, his glasses black-rimmed and thick. He pushed them up his nose and stepped forward, reaching into the side pocket of his backpack, bringing out a large pocketknife. He opened it and took a step forward. "All I want," he said, "is your keys."

"My keys?" Zara sidestepped along the fallen shelves, trying not to trip again. "Wait, you're the guy with the family on the street." She pointed at him, frowning. "You're seriously going to rob me? What about your kid? You really want her to see you hurt someone?"

He wiped beading sweat off his forehead with the back of his hand. "I won't hurt you," he said, voice quivering, "if you just hand over your keys. And besides, my wife and daughter are outside. I told them to stay put when I saw you come in here after getting out of your car."

"That's my only way out of here," she said, holding out her hands. "Please, don't do this. It isn't right."

"Do you think I want to do this?" he shouted.

"No," Zara said. "Of course not. And you don't have to."

"No one out there was going to help us. No one *for hours* has agreed to help us. My daughter is eight. They don't care." He shook his head. "This is the only way for me to get them to safety."

"Okay," Zara said. "Look, maybe I can drive you somewhere—"

"No! I'm done trying to be nice," he shouted. "Just give me your keys!"

He lurched forward, and Zara narrowly dodged his clumsy swing with the knife. She turned to run, hopping over a fallen clothing rack only to land on a loose shirt, sliding and flailing before crashing to the hard tile. The man was quickly upon her, clawing at her pockets. Zara pushed at him, screaming for him to get off, and his blade sliced at her arm. The skin tugged as the steel cut through skin like butter, and then a piercing pain shot through her forearm in waves. Blood spurted from the wound, splattering the man's shirt. Zara screamed again and held her arm to her chest, recoiling from the man. The second she pulled back, he brought the butt of the knife down on her head. It cracked against her skull, forcing her head to bounce hard off the floor.

"I'm sorry," he said as her body went limp and her vision blurred. He pulled the keys from her pocket. "I'm not a bad person," he said, voice cracking. "I'm so sorry."

The last thing Zara saw before the world blurred into darkness was him running back outside, her keys in his hands.

Chapter 25

Alexander Roman

Columns of black smoke marred the Nashville skyline. Alex stood next to Minnie in the late morning sun at the edge of a city park, arms crossed. The destruction across the river rose above the smaller buildings of East Nashville. Daylight had revealed that the tops of several skyscrapers had been shorn off, and about four of them in a cluster were in various stages of collapse. It looked as if a plane had crashed through them, setting them ablaze. A heavy summer rain in the night had squelched the fires to smoldering.

Alex and Minnie had backtracked the night before, searching for any way into the heart of the city. The Cumberland River cut through Nashville, making their inroads to Lauren's apartment few and far between. They'd ended up in East Nashville, having found no passable way to a bridge while driving the RV. Alex had gotten Minnie to agree to stop and rest so that they could walk into the city the next day. They'd parked off-road in a small park in a cluster of trees, and then he had explored the immediate area, stopping at a thoroughly plundered and abandoned convenience store. Maps had been about the only thing left, though they'd been rifled through and the rack was nearly empty. He'd brought the map and a few pre-packaged brownies that had escaped the apparent mob back to the RV. The area was cleared of all but the scattered dead, but the damage all around them spoke of large numbers of panicked people.

"Are you sure that bridge will lead to your daughter's apartment?" Alex asked, holding up the map.

"I remember it," Minnie said, pointing to the John Seigenthaler Pedestrian Bridge on the map. "It's a straight shot to Lauren's apartment building. She brought me to the bridge when I visited because it's her favorite spot in the whole city. It was maybe a mile from where she lived, so she liked to walk there most days."

"Okay, so… the pedestrian bridge looks to be about two miles south, so we should only be a few miles from Lauren. But from what we saw last night, I don't think we'll be able to take the RV." Alex chewed on his lower lip. It was a long way on foot with a child in tow. They hadn't seen a living soul yet, but it was unlikely it would remain that way. Desperate people weren't always in their right minds. *If we're careful and quiet maybe we'll avoid attention.*

"I can go alone," Minnie said. "I know we don't have a clue about what we're gonna come up against, and I wouldn't blame y'all for wantin' to hang back."

"I'm not sure we're safer here," Alex said. "And besides, we've got to stick together. You could have left me at the World's Fair on my own, and you didn't. I won't let you go in there by yourself."

"I'd have Samson," Minnie said.

"I doubt I could get Oliver to let Samson *or* you out of his sight right now." Alex looked over his shoulder to see Oliver staring at them through the windshield as he leaned over the front seat. It was odd how Minnie and Samson—strangers just a few days ago—felt like family. "In fact," Alex said, a little surprised at how much he meant it, "I'm not sure *I* would be comfortable letting you out of my sight. It just doesn't feel right sending you in there alone."

She offered him a smile. "I appreciate that," she said. Then, she looked over her shoulder at the RV with a contemplative look. "You reckon we should take some supplies? Water, food, maybe the first-aid kit?"

Alex nodded. "That's a good idea. Even if we plan on getting in and out of the city quickly, if we can't find Lauren right away, we might have to find shelter for the night. I want to make sure we're inside by seven, just to be on the safe side."

"This 'cause of what your boss said?" Minnie asked.

"Yes," Alex said, "All we have are theories at this point, but we have to consider even those that are less plausible. This disease isn't behaving normally, and it's unlike anything I've ever heard of." He looked at Minnie. "Is it okay with you if I start setting some more stringent rules for how we as a group handle things? I know setting a curfew is presumptuous, but—"

"Hey," Minnie said, holding up a hand. "You're the expert, not me. Now, if y'all need some advice on makin' proper biscuits, I'll be takin' charge. But I have no idea how to protect against this plague. It's sprouted from the fingertips of the devil himself, and I reckon folks like you will be the key to squashin' it. I'll do the prayin' and you do the sciencin' and we might just make it out of this thing."

Alex put a hand on Minnie's shoulder. "Sounds good to me," he said. "Now, if you don't mind getting a few supplies together, I'll talk to Oliver, and then we can be on our way."

Alex looked back and waved at Oliver to come outside. His son hopped out, Samson following, and shut the door behind him. Minnie went back to the RV, disappearing inside. Alex pulled out one of the brownies and sat in the grass, patting the ground beside him. There was a slightly foul odor in the warm air underneath the scents of oak trees and irises, but when Oliver was near, the smell of lavender overpowered the smell of distant decay; he had sprayed his body from head to toe with the stuff and coated Naomi's purse with spritzes of oil.

"We're going to go farther into the city on foot," Alex said, unwrapping the brownie and handing it to his son. Oliver broke it in half and offered him a piece. "Thanks, bud." He took it, rustled his son's hair, and looked back toward the heart of Nashville. "I'm going to need you to stick close, do what I tell you, and stay away from other people, okay?" Oliver nodded and nibbled on his brownie. "It might be scary," Alex continued, "but the world is going to be scary right now, and I don't think I can hide that from you. I wish I could, but I can't. You've already seen and experienced more than any ten-year-old kid should. I'm sorry for that."

Oliver nudged him with his elbow, and Alex glanced at his son, grateful for the offered smile. Oliver popped a bite of brownie in his mouth and stood up, holding out a hand. Alex took it and chuckled as his son grunted in an effort to help him off the ground.

"Y'all ready?" Minnie asked. She had a backpack on, and she handed Alex a second one. Oliver patted the macrame purse at his hip and nodded. Minnie hooked a leash to Samson's collar. "He won't run off, but I don't want 'im sniffin' at dead bodies." She patted the dog's head. "Me and Samson are set."

"Let's go, then." Alex took Oliver's hand and led the way.

Alex stuck to side streets as they navigated toward the pedestrian bridge. They passed buildings with broken windows at the street level and countless abandoned vehicles. He avoided the bodies strewn across the streets and sidewalks. They became part of the landscape, the areas without the dead out of place. A few of the bodies stuck out, having been carefully placed. One woman, two bullet holes in her chest, her shirt covered with blood, lay neatly with a flower on her stomach. Someone had tied a cloth around the eyes of a man with a welt on his neck, presumably to hide bulging eyes. He saw more than one small bundle, wrapped or covered with care in sheets or articles of clothing, each one with a teddy bear or a toy. Alex averted his eyes from bodies like these, a stab of guilt piercing his heart with each one. He'd left Naomi's body wherever it had fallen, discarded and lost in the wreckage of the World's Fair.

Pushing down his grief, Alex shifted to a more clinical way of thinking. Not everyone had been killed by the disease. In fact, at least one out of every four had been killed by some other means, as far as he could tell. The onset of the symptoms drove people to panic, and in their panic, people died. He noted what he could about the characteristics of those who'd clearly died from the pathogen. Not all of them had a readily visible welt. The welts he *could* see were not always in the same spot. Hemorrhaging seemed to be the most dangerous symptom. That much blood loss that quickly would kill anyone. But for all his study of disease, he couldn't figure this one out.

When we come back to the RV with Lauren, maybe I should walk around and make notes about those who died of the illness. It still made his blood run cold to consider the fact that so many of his colleagues had lost their lives in the pursuit of knowledge about this new pathogen. He didn't want to risk getting too close, especially with Oliver in tow, but the more he knew, the better he'd be able to help once they got to Atlanta.

They passed two bridges and walked under a highway that would have led to a third, but Minnie wasn't sure she could remember the way to Lauren's building if they crossed via an avenue besides the pedestrian bridge, so they kept going. Alex led them past the Nissan Stadium to a walkway that ran alongside the Cumberland River where the pedestrian bridge came into view. The water sparkled in the noonday sun, the river meandering lazily. It was quiet enough that the sounds of lapping water and birds chirping could be heard. The scene might have been peaceful if it were not for the dozen bodies bobbing in the river, the smell of death on the breeze, and the smoke billowing in the distance. A slow melody, picked on a guitar and sung with a sorrowful voice, carried on the wind as they approached.

"Someone is on the bridge, alive," Alex said when they got closer and he could tell where the music was coming from. He brought Minnie, Oliver, and Samson to the bridge's outside wall — an iron lattice fence set into concrete. His stomach churned as the stench of a city filled with the dead somehow got even worse. "Stay here. I'm going to make sure it's safe."

Minnie nodded and sat on a patch of grass, leaning against a short, concrete pillar. She was breathing heavily, and she pinched her nose. "It smells bad enough to gag a maggot," she said. "I don't know how much longer I can stand it." Oliver nodded and copied her, pinching his nose.

"It does seem to be getting worse," he said, "but I expect we'll get used to it the longer we're here." The mournful song continued, drawing Alex's attention. "I'll be right back," he said.

He rounded the wall and approached the entry to the bridge, freezing at the sight laid out before him. The bridge was so littered with the dead that it would be impossible to avoid stepping over them. A solitary, petite figure with a guitar stood at the center near the railing, playing the guitar, singing softly. He was completely exposed to the stranger, but she didn't seem interested in him or dangerous in any sense of the word. He quietly picked his way over the bodies, coming to a stop a few yards away.

The woman sang, drawing out the words to the song in a hauntingly sad, beautiful voice. Her back was to him, her clothes tattered, long brown hair twisting and playing in the wind. There was a cut on the right side of her forehead, crusted over with dried blood. Tears rolled down her cheeks. She didn't seem to register that Alex was even there, but he couldn't bring himself to interrupt her. The lyrics echoed his own grief, and he found himself crying along with her as she sang:

"The shadow of myself
Holds the remnants of you
But this shadow keeps fading
No matter what I do"

She played the last note and was still for a moment before she took off the guitar, carefully leaned it against the ironwork, and stepped up to the railing, taking hold of it with a white-knuckled grip. She looked up at the support beam beside her and reached for it, grabbing hold and lifting one leg to the top of the rail.

Her intentions hit Alex like a punch to the gut. His heartbeat quickened and fear sent a jolt through his body. "Wait!" he shouted, lurching forward, stumbling over a body.

The woman sucked in a breath and spun to face him, eyes wide. She hurriedly wiped her tears away with her hands. "Who are you?" she asked, backing away.

Alex held up his hands, palms outward, trying to show he wasn't a threat. "I… I'm Alex. I heard you singing, and I came to make sure it was safe." He looked back the way he had come. "I have my son with me, and a friend. I… that song. I've never heard it before. It was… I lost my wife a few days ago, and it was… well, it meant something to me."

Her cheeks went red and she looked at the railing she'd been climbing over just a moment before. "It wasn't what it looked like," she said.

Alex followed her gaze, swallowed hard, and looked back at her. "Sure," he said. "I get it. I just… maybe I can help you get home?"

She blinked at him. "Home?" She looked past him to the destruction all around. "This is my home," she said, her voice getting louder. "My fiancé is my home. My friends are my home." She was shouting now. "They're gone! Verity, Lilly, Jared, Missy..." She backed against the railing and sank to the ground, a corpse only a yard away. "And Aaron, the man I loved," she said softly. "Everyone and everything… just gone."

Alex came to sit next to her. "I lost my wife, but we were traveling when it happened. At the World's Fair, actually. Neither one of us had any family, but we did have Oliver."

"Your son?" she asked.

"Yeah," Alex said. A few moments of silence passed. Alex didn't know what to say, but he couldn't leave her alone, not after what he'd seen her almost do. After a while, he looked at her. "That song, where is it from?"

"I wrote it after Aaron died this morning." She shook her head. "He wasn't sick, you know. He got hit by a car when all hell broke loose. I thought… I thought I could save him. I should have been able to save him."

"I keep telling myself the same thing about my wife." Alex sighed. "But it isn't true for me, and it's not true for you."

"You don't know anything about me." She stood up. "I better get back to my apartment." She looked at the railing again. Her jaw tightened, and she turned her back. "There are people there who need me."

Alex got to his feet. "Hey, um… we're here to find someone. Do you think maybe you could help us?"

Her head drooped, and she put her hands on her hips. "We're already stretched thin with our supplies," she said.

"I don't need your supplies. We brought our own," Alex said. "I'm just concerned that me, my son, and my friend will find ourselves without shelter as we search the area."

She faced him again, dropping her arms, seeming to study him from head to toe. Finally, she sighed. "Fine, but you can't stay long, okay? A few days at most."

Alex nodded. "Great," he said. "That would be perfect. I mean, we might find her and be gone today, but it would be nice to have a solid backup plan."

"Where are your people?" She narrowed her eyes, peering down the bridge.

"They're just at the end of the bridge. I'll go get them." He crossed the bridge, stepping over bodies all along the way, checking over his shoulder to make sure the woman stayed away from the railing.

The woman grabbed her guitar, slung it over her shoulder, and followed him slowly, keeping her distance.

He reached the part of the fence where Minnie and Oliver were and leaned over the railing. "Hey," he said. "You okay?"

Minnie and Oliver looked up at him. "We're fine and dandy," she said.

"I think I found someone who can help us," he said, and then more quietly, "and I think maybe she needs to be around people who… aren't dead."

"Ah. I see. Well," Minnie said, hauling herself to her feet with a groan. "We can't keep every stray we come across. There's just no room in the RV, and—"

Samson started barking excitedly at the fence, jumping up and down. Minnie stopped short, her gaze fixed on something. Alex followed her line of sight to where the woman leaned over the fence, frowning at the dog.

"Samson?" the woman said. She looked up, her mouth dropping at the sight of Minnie.

Alex furrowed his brow, looking from the stranger to Minnie, who stared slack-jawed back at the stranger. The woman straightened and turned a glare on Alex.

"Who do you think you are?" she asked. "What kind of trick is this?"

"Trick?" But then Alex understood. *Minnie's daughter loves this bridge.* "I'm guessing you're Lauren?" He recalled the pictures hanging in Minnie's halls. This woman was older and her style had matured, but it was the same person.

"As if you didn't know," Lauren said, sneering.

"Baby girl," Minnie said. "We came to get you. If you'd just give me a minute—"

"You've had *years*," Lauren spat. "I'm not going with you anywhere." She turned on her heel and stalked away, angrily stepping over bodies, fists at her sides.

Alex looked back at Minnie. "This isn't going to be easy."

Minnie shook her head. "Nope, don't look like it will be."

"And you're staying until she goes?"

"Yep."

Alex closed his eyes and took a deep breath as his only way out of Nashville walked away.

Chapter 26

Timothy Peters

Wood splintered as Timothy slammed an axe into the back porch swing. He hit again and again, pouring all his anger and frustration into the motion. Once the swing was nothing more than scraps and long slats of wood, he set to driving long nails through the center of each length. Sweat trickled down his face and soaked through his tank. The sun beat down on his skin, and he breathed in and out, the warm air thick with humidity.

"Here's some water, Timmy," Dana said as she approached him from the house where all the doors and windows were flung open. She handed him a bottle of water.

"Thanks," he said. "How is everything else going?"

"Heather is almost done putting security film on the windows," Dana said. "I've been helping her while the kiddos play board games in the safe room where it's still nice and cool." She patted her forehead with a cloth and shook her head. "I don't know how much more of this heat I can take."

"You should go down with the kids," Timothy said as he took a swig of water. The bunker was hooked up to a generator powered by solar panels on the roof and still had cool air, but the power had gone down that morning all across the community. Cell service was still down, too.

"No, I'm still helping Heather with all your little booby-traps. That security film your father bought is just ghastly. I see why the HOA didn't let us put it up before. It's *tinted*." Dana sighed. "Do you really think all this is necessary?"

"I think it's better to be overprepared than to find ourselves with guns to our heads," Timothy said. "And the tint will go in our favor if someone is attacking from the outside." He'd been excited to find the film, meant as a home security measure to strengthen glass windows, in his father's stash.

"Candice is going to throw a fit," Dana said.

"Candice can shove it," Timothy said.

Dana pressed her lips together disapprovingly but didn't chide him. "What are we doing with those?" she asked, nodding at the strips of wood with nails protruding.

"We're going to put them nails up in the rock beds under all the windows," Timothy said. "What about the muriatic acid?" he asked.

"It's in the pool house," she said, nodding to the little building behind the pool in the backyard. "But are you sure about that one? It's so dangerous. We always leave it up to our guy to clean the pool tiles with it because that one time I tried, I burned myself."

"That's the point," Timothy said. "I'll handle it. I just needed you to tell me where it is. I'm going to put a bucket of it above the front door. If they bust through it, they'll get a nasty surprise."

"I hate that we have to stoop so low," Dana said. "It's barbaric."

Timothy sighed. "Mom—"

"Yes, I know," she said. "Fight fire with fire. You're just like your father."

Timothy blanched. "Don't ever say that," he said, his tone harsher than he intended.

She shrugged and put her hands up, palms outward. "Well, you did take to all his preparations like a fish to water. You do what needs to be done. You get your hands dirty." She looked pointedly at his hands. "Perhaps more literally than your father, but still."

"Mom," Timothy said, "when Dad gets his hands dirty, he does it to protect himself. I'm trying to protect my family."

Dana scoffed. "Is that what you think?"

"I don't want to argue with you," Timothy said, grabbing one of the slats. "I've got work to do. If you want to help, we need to set up some defense stations on the second floor. If you could bring what we have in the gun safe upstairs, that would be great. Then, I'm going to need you to stay with the kids and keep them safe." He walked past his mother, heading for the rock beds under the windows.

"Tim!" Heather rushed outside, holding up her walkie talkie, and Timothy stopped in his tracks, just a few paces from Dana.

"What is it? Does Mr. Finley see something suspicious?" Timothy put a hand to his head. "We're not ready! If Frank is coming now—"

"No," Heather said, "but this barbeque business needs to be shut down."

"What?" Timothy asked.

A crackle was followed by a female voice over the speaker as if on cue. "I've got six filet mignons," she said.

Someone else answered. "We've got twelve brats."

Timothy threw the slat back in the pile and grabbed the walkie talkie. It was set to channel three. "The neighborhood watch is supposed to be on channel one, isn't it?"

Heather nodded. "I accidentally changed the channel when I sat on it, and then I heard this nonsense. They're using the walkie talkies to plan a party or something."

"They can't do that!" Timothy said. "How do they all have walkie talkies, anyway?" He turned it to the channel reserved for the neighborhood watch. "Candice? Hello?"

"Roger, this is Gucci," Candice's voice chirped. "Over."

Heather rolled her eyes. "Is she serious?"

"You have no idea," Dana mumbled.

"Candice—"

"Use my code name," Candice said. "I'm on duty for the neighborhood watch."

"Okay, Gucci," Timothy sighed. "I thought we were just giving walkie talkies to those on the neighborhood watch." There was a long pause with no response.
"Are you done?" she asked. "You're supposed to say, 'over.'"
"Over." Timothy said through gritted teeth.
"Roger that. We got so much interest after cell phones stopped getting a signal. I mean, they're awesome. I was able to fill the watch schedule at the front and back gates in no time in exchange for a walkie talkie. Did you hear about the party? Over."
"Yes, and it's not happening. It can't. Haven't you heard that warning from the CDC over the radio?" Timothy asked. After Candice cleared her voice, he begrudgingly added, "Over."
"Roger. We decided that since everyone has all this meat thawing out and going to waste, a barbeque would be perfect. And besides, no one here is sick. Duh. Over."
Timothy raised his eyebrows. "Candice, that's ridiculous. And stupid. We have criminals coming to our community. There's some kind of disease destroying the nation, and we have no idea how it spreads. Maybe there are asymptomatic carriers. Did you think of that?"
"I'm *not* stupid," Candice said, losing her walkie talkie etiquette. "We could use a morale boost around here, okay? My husband is still not back from the city, and there are others missing. The power is out. It's way too hot. The police weren't answering our calls before the phones went down, and now they're totally MIA. I mean, *that's* ridiculous. Someone went into Wellesley and had to turn right around because of some riot. We've already got a letter to the mayor in the works, and we're all going to sign it at the party. Our community is safe, but we're all bummed. A little steak and wine isn't going to hurt anyone."
"That sounds about right," Dana said, shaking her head.
"Is someone going to be watching the gate during this party?" Timothy asked.
"Of course," Candice said. "I put myself on the schedule for half of it, and Rhonda's husband is going to come to the security booth at the front for a shift so I can go to the party. He doesn't drink, so he never stays long at parties anyway. Although, it would be nice if the *actual* security guards showed up to do their jobs."
Timothy rubbed his hand over his face and groaned. "We don't even know if they're alive, Candice."
"Well, if they are, they are going to lose their jobs," Candice said. "We need dependable security, especially during times like these. I mean, the situation we find ourselves in now, with these criminals threatening to break in, is proof enough of that. Important people live here. We should have some priority."
Heather's mouth dropped open, and she crossed her arms. "This lady is a piece of work."
"I know," Timothy said, "but we need her cooperation." He pressed the button on the walkie talkie to speak. "I really think this party is a bad idea. It's a huge risk, but I appreciate you making sure the gate is manned."
"Then don't come," Candice said. "And you're welcome. These thugs are a bigger threat than this disease, anyway. I mean, before you know it, the government will get it under control, and the power will come back on, and things will be back to normal."
Timothy sighed. There was no use arguing with her. "I hope so," he said. "I've got a lot to do, Candice. I'll talk to you later." He handed the walkie talkie back to Heather as Candice's voice quipped almost cheerfully, "Over and out."
"What are we going to do?" Dana asked. "If this sickness does come here, from what you saw in Boston, from what your father said… everyone I know is going to die if they don't protect themselves."
He handed the walkie talkie back to his wife. "We can't worry about them," he said. "They're so disconnected from reality that reality is going to have to smack them in the face before they accept it."
Heather shrugged. "We tried warning them, Dana."
"These are good people," Dana said. "My neighbors have their faults, but most of them are decent."
"We're not arguing their morality," Timothy said. "But we can't waste energy trying to make them listen, not when we are still setting up our own defenses."
"We'll get them on board eventually," Heather said. "Let's do one thing at a time."
Dana folded her arms and frowned, but she nodded. "All right," she said. "I know you're right." She glanced at Timothy. "You can say what you want, son, but your father would have told me the same thing you just did. I know he would have. I almost heard his voice in your words." She patted Timothy on the arm. "I'm going to go gather those weapons and check on the kids."
Timothy stared at his mother's retreating back, her words rolling through his mind on repeat. "I'm not like my father," Timothy whispered.
"Of course you're not," Heather said. "You're not *exactly* like him, anyway."
"What's that supposed to mean?" Timothy took a step back from his wife.
She closed the distance between them, her tone gentle. "Tim, you're what your father could have been, and he's what you could become. I've heard Dana talk about Walter. He's not always a monster. He's got good in him. He just chooses the bad. That's the difference between the two of you. I have faith that you will always choose what's right in the end." She kissed his cheek. "It's right to protect your family, but I know once the stress of this Frank thing is past us, you won't give up on the people in this community just because they've got their heads in the sand."
Timothy's eyes settled on his wife's face, on those eyes that looked at him with expectation. "Maybe the difference between my father and me is that I have you," he said.
The truth of that statement sunk in, and part of him was overwhelmed with gratefulness for a life partner that helped him choose the right path. But part of him was terrified because he was suddenly positive that without her, he would have followed the path of his father.
Heather smiled. "Well," she said, patting his chest playfully. "You know what they say. Behind every great man—"
"Well, I don't know how great I am," Timothy said, "but I won't argue that you're the best."
"Tim, do you trust me?" she asked, wrapping her arms around his neck, meeting his eyes with her own. "I'm being serious. Do you trust me?"

He nodded. "Of course."

"Then trust me when I say that *I know* you're a good man." She kissed him again and pulled away. "Now, I finished up with the windows. All the glass on the first floor has been reinforced. It won't stop a bullet, but it will make it harder to just break the glass and crawl through a window or the back door. Let's get started on placing these," she said picking up a slat. "We're going to give this Frank Russo hell when he comes knocking."

Timothy grabbed a nail-laden length of wood and followed his wife, pushing thoughts about himself and his father into a very familiar and well-used box in his mind. He focused on the task at hand. No matter how many traps they set or how prepared they were, he couldn't get the sinking feeling out of his gut. All he could do was work and wait and hope. But there were a thousand ways a confrontation with Frank and a crew of mobsters could go badly. A thousand ways everything he loved could be ripped from him. In the end, reassurances rang hollow.

Chapter 27

Alexander Roman

Alex couldn't protect Oliver from everything, but he could protect him from stumbling through a sea of corpses. He breathed a little easier when they were on the other side of the bridge where the bodies weren't as concentrated. Alex had carried his son, letting him bury his head in the crook of Alex's neck, much like when they had climbed down the Wind Breaker's frame. Minnie followed behind, making sure Samson didn't stop to mess with any of the bodies. He followed Lauren as quickly as he could, but she was moving fast, even with a guitar hanging on her back.

"Hey, bud, we're past the worst of it, okay? I'm going to put you down, and you can walk with Minnie for a minute." He set Oliver down, but his son threw his arms around his waist.

"Lauren!" Minnie shouted. "Baby girl, wait!" She stopped beside Oliver, bending over to rest her hands on her knees as she tried to catch her breath. "I'm losin' her, Alex!"

"Oliver, I'll be right back. I promise. I just need to help Minnie get her daughter." Alex knelt in front of his son and cupped his face in his hands. "It's going to be okay. I just don't want to lose Lauren."

Oliver glanced up at Minnie who was crying as she leaned low. He stepped over to Minnie, nodded at Alex, and cupped Minnie's face in his hands, wiping away her tears with his thumbs. She straightened and pulled Oliver into a tight hug.

"If you've got mine, I'll go get yours," Alex said.

Minnie patted Oliver's back. "Thank you," she said to Alex.

Alex bolted down the street after Lauren. "Hey!" he shouted as he caught up to her. "Stop!" He slowed as he passed her and got in front of her, blocking her way. "Please, Lauren. Just talk to me."

"Why? I don't know you." Lauren tried to get past him, but Alex blocked her way.

"I'm a friend of your mother's," Alex said.

"I don't know her, either!" She gripped the strap of her guitar where it crossed her heart.

Frustration built in Alex's chest, and as she raised her voice, he started to raise his. "What are you talking about? She's got pictures of you all over her house, and she talks about you all the time. She came here to help you, and you won't even talk to her?"

"Ha! Of course," Lauren said. "She's been trying to save me my whole life. Well, I've got news for her. I've never needed saving."

"It sure looked like you needed something back there," Alex said, his anger at her stubbornness and hostility toward Minnie making his tongue loose.

She blinked and then averted her eyes. "I told you that wasn't what it looked like."

"Then what was it?" Alex asked. "You felt alone, right? You felt like you'd lost everything. Well, you haven't. You have your mother. Do you really think this Aaron guy would want you to—" A sharp crack split the air as stinging pain blossomed against Alex's cheek.

Lauren's finger jabbed at his chest the second she'd finished slapping him. "Don't you *ever* talk about Aaron."

Alex rubbed his cheek and glanced behind Lauren, sighing with relief at the fact that Oliver wasn't looking. He held up his hands and backed away, trying to even out his breathing. "I'm sorry, Lauren. You're right, okay. I wouldn't want anyone telling me what my wife would have wanted, assuming I wouldn't know. I was upset, and I said the wrong thing."

She crossed her arms and chewed on the corner of her lower lip as she examined him. "Really," she said. "Who are you?"

"I'm Alexander Roman. I work for the CDC, and Minnie saved my life and the life of my son. I'm bringing her with me to Atlanta where I hope it's safe, and she wanted to come get you. I agreed." He spoke softly, reining in his frustrations. "I owe her a lot."

Lauren let her hands fall to her sides. She quirked an eyebrow. "I guess that sounds like a story worth hearing," she said. "But… I just can't talk to her right now, okay? You guys can come back to my place. I'll find you somewhere to sleep tonight, and I'll hear you out in the morning. But I'll hear *you* out. I need some time before I talk to my mother."

Alex nodded. "If that's what you can give, that's what I'll take. I'll talk to Minnie about it, tell her to lay off until you're ready."

Lauren pursed her lips. "She won't listen."

"Maybe she will." Alex shrugged. "She's got her hands full helping me with Oliver."

"If you say so." Lauren turned around, looking in Minnie's direction.

Samson was pulling at his leash, dancing from foot to foot, nose pointed their way. Minnie and Oliver quietly leaned against a brick wall, both of them looking at the ground. Minnie's lips were moving, her expressions animated, and Oliver laughed.

"Go tell her now," Lauren said. "I'll wait here. She needs to understand I need some space before I can talk to her."

"Okay, but you're going to talk to her eventually, right?" Alex asked. "Surely whatever happened between the two of you can't be so bad that it can't be fixed. I mean, the world is falling apart, Lauren. We've got to cling to the people we've got left."

Lauren bit her lip harder and shook her head. "The end of the world doesn't erase the past." She quickly wiped away a tear from the corner of her eye. "But… maybe it can turn the page to a new chapter. Maybe."

Alex smiled. "That's better than nothing. I'll wave you over once I've talked to her." When Lauren assented, he jogged over to Minnie.

"Is she coming with us?" Minnie asked.

"Not yet." Alex comforted Minnie with a hand on her shoulder when her face fell. "But she's going to let us come with her to her apartment. She says she will find a spot for us to sleep tonight, and we can talk tomorrow."

A smile broke out on Minnie's face. "So she's comin' with us tomorrow?"

Alex shrugged. "I don't know yet. I mean, I hope we can convince her. I can't imagine that she'd want to stay here." The broken buildings, the dead bodies baking in the sun, the streets trashed with piled-up and burnt-out vehicles, the stench—it would be insane for anyone to choose Nashville over the CDC facility.

Minnie set her eyes on Lauren. "Let me just go talk to her, and—"

"No," Alex said. "There's a condition. She wants you to keep your distance until she's ready."

"What?" Minnie's smile faded.

"You need to leave her alone for now, okay? It's the only chance we've got to convince her to come with us."

"But—"

"She told me you wouldn't respect her wishes." Alex raised his eyebrows. "Are you going to prove her right? Or are you going to do things differently?"

"Differently?" Minnie flushed and she looked down at the ground. "What did she say?"

"Nothing much," Alex said. "But from what I can gather, you made some mistakes. If you're going to fix this, it needs to be on her terms."

"You're right." Minnie nodded, swallowing hard, eyes glistening. "I'll keep to myself until my baby is ready to talk."

"Good." Alex offered her a reassuring smile. "The first step is getting Lauren to come with us. That's got to be our priority."

Minnie took a deep breath and agreed. Satisfied that she would hold to her word, Alex waved Lauren over. The young woman tentatively approached, arms crossed. She stood for a moment, just looking at Minnie, eyes narrowed as if she expected her mother to break the deal immediately. Minnie stayed silent, though Samson barked and wagged his tail.

Lauren broke her glare and stepped closer, allowing Samson to jump up and place his paws on her shoulders. He licked her face, and she laughed. "Hey, boy! How's it goin'? You miss me?" She scratched vigorously at the back of his ears before pushing him off and patting his side. "I missed you, too." She stood up and looked at Oliver, who was giving her a toothy grin as Samson continued to wag his tail and playfully bump Lauren's legs with his nose. "You must be Alex's son. It's nice to meet you." She held out a hand and Oliver shook it. "I'm Lauren. What's your name?"

Oliver pulled back his hand and scooted behind Alex.

"He's, um… a little shy right now," Alex said.

"Oh, that's all right," Lauren said, her eyes landing on Minnie who clasped her hands hopefully at her chest. But Lauren didn't acknowledge her mother; she just turned around and waved for them to follow. "My building is this way," she said. "It's about a thirty-minute walk."

Alex followed, taking in the city in various stages of disrepair. "I've never been in downtown Nashville," he said. "I've just driven around the city to get to other places. I wish I could see it like it's supposed to be."

"Well," Lauren said in a sing-song tourist guide voice, "here on the left you've got your Country Music Hall of Fame. Down the road, you've got your Bridgestone Arena, home of the Nashville Predators. We've got an Art Museum further down the road, and normally I'd give you recommendations on the best places to get a bite to eat, but unfortunately all these buildings—" She spread out her arms turning around and walking backwards, her pasted on smile falling flat. "—are full of dead people." She turned back around, letting her hands fall and slap her thighs.

Alex sighed as Oliver turned widened eyes on the nearest building. "They're not *full* of dead people, bud. She's exaggerating."

Lauren stopped and looked up at the sky, hands on her hips. Then she hung her head and turned to face them. "I'm sorry, kid," she said. "Your dad is right. I'm not used to being around little people. I shouldn't have said that." She offered him a small smile. "I'm just tired and the world's a little shi—" She snapped her mouth shut and winced. "I mean, the world's a sad place right now."

Oliver regarded her silently, and she just let out a long, slow breath, turned around and kept walking. Alex followed, Oliver at his side, Minnie barely keeping pace a few steps behind. Samson trotted at the end of his leash, taking turns sniffing at Lauren and Oliver. The silence of the city was eerie. Every once in a while, a shout or distant gun shot rang out, echoing off the buildings. Alex flinched at the first few, but Lauren didn't even blink. So, he kept walking, though he kept his eyes open.

The city felt abandoned, but there were little signs of life here and there. An open window with white smoke and the smell of spicy meat cooking. Wet laundry hanging to dry on a balcony. The strumming of a distant guitar. There were still people in Nashville waiting. Alex wasn't sure what they were waiting for. Perhaps they hoped for rescue or wanted someone to come and tell them what to do. Or maybe they were just frightened at the thought of leaving.

"So, what happened here? How long has it been this way?" Alex asked. He hadn't heard the specifics of Nashville's plight on the radio or the news. Jonah hadn't known much past the fact that they'd had a case at the airport.

"Well, from what we can tell, it started with a group of students who came back from the World's Fair on an airplane. It was a nonstop flight, about an hour, and they didn't know they'd caught whatever this sickness is when they landed. It spread out from the airport real quick, and then that happened." She pointed to the rising smoke in the distance. "A plane crashed through those buildings and completely decimated the area. Tonight will be the fourth night since it began. We had some National Guard around for about a day. They set up at the Nissan Stadium football arena that first night in town, and then… well, a bunch of 'em died. Maybe a couple hundred moved over to the Fairgrounds Expo Center, indoors, and I honestly haven't seen much of them since. Yesterday was bad. Everyone who was left here scrambled for supplies, and a lot of them fled the city. That's when Aaron…" She trailed off and slowed her steps, her voice wavering. "He got hurt. And he died from his injuries."

Minnie let out a small gasp, her features twisting into sympathy. She reached out a hand toward Lauren's back, but Alex gave her a firm shake of his head and came up beside Lauren, gently placing his hand on her back instead.

"I'm really sorry for your loss," he said. He looked over his shoulder at Minnie who mouthed her thanks silently.

"It doesn't matter," Lauren said, shrugging him off. "We're here."

She pointed at a building with a modern facade, all rectangles and glass, white panels and wooden slats. It was tall, twenty stories at least. A coffee shop was integrated into the front of it, protruding from the face of the building. Two stories of clear glass panels rose above the shop, exercise equipment visible along the windows. The gym extended past the shop, a white rectangular support anchoring it to the sidewalk and creating a veranda underneath. Lauren led them through the veranda to a set of glass doors next to the coffee shop, which contained five dead bodies slumped over tables.

Two men with guns waited at the lobby desk. The lobby itself was clear of bodies, though long smears of dried blood on the floor indicated it hadn't always been.

"Hey, doc." One of the men raised a hand at Lauren.

"Hey, Garret." Lauren stuck her hands in her jean pockets.

"Found some drifters?" Garret asked.

The second man frowned. "We don't got room for more, doc. You know that."

"Yeah," Lauren said. "But these aren't drifters, Paul. This is my mom and her friend, Alex. And this is Samson." Lauren smiled when Samson gave a short, low bark at the sound of his name.

Paul shook his head. "Still don't got room or food or water to share. You were the one that told us not to pick up strangers so our rations would last."

Garret elbowed Paul. "C'mon, man. She also let the Links' bring in their grandma, and she let *you* bring your sister. She gave us all a shot at shelterin' family. Least we can do is let her momma stay here."

"Oh, she's not staying," Lauren said, shaking her head. "She just wanted to check on me. She'll be leavin' soon. Probably tomorrow."

Minnie opened her mouth, but Alex put a hand on her back, and she closed it.

"See? Ain't nothin' to worry about," Garret said.

"Oh, all right." Paul nodded toward the stairwell at the back of the lobby. "Go on, then. I was just tryin' to follow the rules."

"I appreciate that Paul," Lauren said, smiling at him.

She headed toward the stairwell, opening the door to a wave of hot air. "It's really hot in here," she said. "My apartment is on the fifteenth floor, but we moved everyone left down to the first few floors because of the heat. It's bearable if you keep the windows open, but we close them at night to keep the bugs out."

"That's good," Alex said. "The CDC is recommending everyone stay indoors from seven at night to eight in the morning at the earliest. Each ground zero happened outside at night, and there's a theory that ongoing infections are happening at a higher rate overnight."

Lauren nodded. "I put those puzzle pieces together pretty quick," she said. "I use the excuse of keeping the bugs out for the purpose of keeping our food safe. And there are a lot more flies in the city right now than usual, which with all the dead bodies, can spread other kinds of infections. I mean, it might be contributing to the spread of this one."

"Smart," Alex said, impressed. "Is that why they called you 'doc' down there? Or, are you an actual doctor?"

Minnie paused behind Alex, and Lauren stopped as well, looking over her shoulder at her mother.

Alex shifted his gaze between the two women. "What is it?" he asked.

Minnie cleared her throat and refused to look Alex in the eye.

"It's nothing," Lauren said. "I just… I've told them not to call me that. I'm *not* a doctor." She turned and kept walking up the stairs.

Alex followed, Oliver's hand in his. Lauren exited the stairwell on the second floor. The first several doors on either side of the hall were wide open and a breeze from open windows cooled the floor a few degrees. It was still hot. Sweat beaded on Alex's forehead, and Oliver's hairline was damp. Minnie's face was beet red, sweat rolling down the sides of her face. Lauren's face and neck glistened, but she didn't seem terribly bothered by it.

Each open door they passed led into living areas with bandaged people laying on couches. One room had nothing in it but two dining tables pushed together. Alex paused at that door. A woman cleaned the tables, scrubbing them, white suds tinged red creating a film on the wood. The wooden floor was stained with huge splotches of blood, though it looked like it had already been scrubbed. A small pile of towels, every one of them reddened, was against the wall.

"What happened?" Alex asked.

Lauren had stopped, too, and stood just behind Alex. "That's where Aaron died," she said.

He turned to look at her. "I really am sorry."

"Oh, baby girl," Minnie said. She took a step toward Lauren but stopped, her outstretched hand hanging in the air a moment before she pulled it back. "Sorry," she said. "I just… I'm your momma, Lauren. I made mistakes, but—"

"Stop," Lauren said, firmly and loudly. "I don't need your excuses."

A few people came out into the halls at the sound of her aggressive tone, each one with some minor injury. To their right, a man with a bandage wrapped around his head was watching more intently than the others.

"No, that's not what I meant, baby girl." Minnie held out her hands, pleading. "I'm so sorry for everything."

Lauren turned to Alex. "Look," she said, rubbing her hands over her face and then threading her fingers through her hair, "I don't know if this is going to work. I'm going to find you guys a room, but tomorrow you can go on to the CDC, okay?"

"The CDC?" The man with the bandage around his head stepped forward. "What are you talkin' about, Lauren?"

"It's nothing, Quinten. Just go back and lie down. You need to rest." Lauren barely looked at him.

"Hold on, doc—" Quinten stepped closer.

"Would you *all* stop calling me that?" Lauren shouted. "I'm not a doctor!" She rounded on Minnie. "Are you happy, Mom? You want to talk now?"

Oliver backed away from her, his back to the wall. His lower lip quivered.

Alex held out a hand. "Hey, Lauren. I don't know why that makes you so angry, but you're scaring my son."

Minnie set her jaw. "Don't you throw a hissy fit, young lady. I told ya. I made mistakes," she said. It seemed Lauren's shouting had stirred up some of Minnie's stubbornness. "And I did. I shoulda supported this musician thing no matter how dumb it was. Maybe then you wouldna rebelled and dropped out of your residency."

"Great!" Lauren said, still angry. "Now everyone knows my business."

"I wanna know what you meant by him being CDC!" Quinten said.

"Are they workin' on a vaccine?" A woman on the other side of them asked.

"Do you think they'll have a cure soon?" Asked another.

"Did they send him here?" Someone shouted from one of the rooms.

"Where's the cure? I know they've got somethin'!" Quinten yelled over the rest.

Alex tried to keep track of who was asking what, but soon several people were crowding the hall. Each one seemed to have some sort of minor injury, their faces bruised or bandaged, several of them limping. They began shouting their questions over one another.

"Hey!" Alex roared, and they all quieted. "I don't have a lot of answers. I wasn't sent here, okay? The CDC is working to gather information, and they are working on finding a cure. But that's all the information I have. Please, back up." He held out his hands and gestured for them all to clear a space.

The hall began to clear, but as it did, Minnie gasped, and Samson growled. Alex froze, his heart thumping, pounding in his ears, knees suddenly weak. His stomach lurched, and the whole world shrank to one focal point.

Quinten, eyes wild, held a knife to Oliver's throat. "You got connections," he said, his voice a mixture of desperation, fear, and anger. "I want a cure or a safe place to go, or you ain't seein' this kid again." He wrapped an arm around Oliver's waist and hauled him, whimpering, down the hall, disappearing into a room and slamming the door behind him.

Chapter 28

Zara Williams

Thick, suffocating heat enveloped Zara, making her stomach churn as her eyes fluttered open. One hand lay flat against tile, cool to the touch by comparison. She rolled her head to the side, and the room spun, all blurred images she couldn't quite make out. Her whole body throbbed, her blood pulsating in her veins, muscles twitching with every beat of her heart. She lifted her arm and searing pain shot through it, the intensity of her pulse doubling as if her insides were trying to beat their way out through the skin.

She groaned and blinked slowly, willing the room to stabilize. When she swallowed, she tasted copper, and her tongue brushed up against a gash in her cheek where she must have bitten it. Sweat stung the back of her head, and her fingertips brushed a gash beneath matted hair.

What happened? Zara focused on a shiny metal pole, following the line of it to the top of a clothing rack where t-shirts lay in piles, still on the hangers, loosely connected to the broken and twisted metal frame. A ray of sunshine fell upon the words "I'm with Stupid" in bright red under an arrow of the same color. *Gas station t-shirts.*

Memories flooded over her of scrambling to escape a man in thick-rimmed black glasses. The shiny metal pole of the rack echoed the glint of steel when he'd brandished his knife, and Zara sucked in a sharp breath. Tears stung her eyes as she patted her pockets, moving only her uninjured arm. Her keys were gone. He had taken them.

"No, no, no," Zara repeated as she forced herself to sit up. The motion rocked her, and she heaved to the side, throwing up the contents of her stomach. She scooted away from the mess, using a t-shirt to wipe her mouth. "The car," she said as she got to her knees, the world still swaying. "All our supplies."

Tears rolled down her cheeks as she struggled to her feet. Her equilibrium wasn't quite right, and she almost fell sideways, catching herself on a counter next to a stagnant slushy machine. Her mouth was so dry. She grabbed a plastic cup and shoved it under the machine, pulling the dispenser and letting melted blue liquid, cold but no longer icy, fill up the cup. She drank the too-sweet drink greedily, set the cup on the counter, and then stumbled forward. Her hand grabbed the door frame and she yelped, pulling back immediately. Blood welled from a cut on her palm. She stared at the growing bubble until it popped into a slow-moving line, running along the creases in her hand, dripping to the ground at her feet. The pain was simply an addition to all the other pinpoints of agony from head to toe.

Zara stepped more carefully through the door and squinted across the parking lot to where she'd left the car. She had expected it to be gone, but a sob burst from her at the sight of the empty space. She looked up at the sky.

"How long before dark?" She spoke out loud, though she was alone. In fact, there was no one in sight. The cars on the street, different ones from when she'd entered the station, where empty. The city was quieter, save a shout echoing in the distance, a *pop pop* echoing from the opposite direction. "How long have I been here?" She had no idea. It had to have been hours.

She shuddered, feeling exposed. She hadn't seen that man come after her, hadn't considered him a threat until it was too late. A jolt of fear rushed through her. What if someone was watching her, waiting to hurt her again? She wouldn't be able to put up much of a fight. Zara clumsily darted back into the station.

The place was a mess. She held a hand to her throbbing head as she navigated fallen shelves and racks, trash and broken glass. She spotted a small pocket-sized flashlight poking out from under an empty bag of chips. Zara picked it up and switched it on, grateful for the beam of light as she went further into the station where the daylight couldn't reach. Her palm still bled and stung, so she held the light with her fingers, careful not to grip it too tightly. The last place she'd seen Lizzy's phone was in the hallway next to the bathrooms, but when the hall came into view, it was blocked by the front end of a truck. She vaguely remembered seeing the tail end sticking out of the side of the building. Zara screamed in frustration and kicked at the tire.

"It's got to be here," she mumbled to herself, standing on tiptoes and shining the light over the truck. She searched the ground for the phone, but she couldn't see directly on the other side of the vehicle. Zara pulled the flashlight back, the beam of light sweeping the inside of the truck.

The front seat was occupied by a dead man, head leaning on the blood-spattered window, eyes bulging, face and neck swollen. Lines of blood traced paths from his eyes, his mouth, and his ears. Zara jumped back, hand to mouth, beam of light still focused on the man. She hobbled backwards a few steps before turning to flee the horrid sight. When she dashed into the main room of the station, she had an undeniable urge to hide.

Thieves and murderers walked the streets. The sickness was here. If the people didn't kill her, surely the sickness would. She'd never in her life felt so weak and vulnerable. Vision blurring from tears, a sob escaping her lips, Zara rushed to the front counter and sheltered in the corner, pulling her knees to her chest, holding her arm gingerly. In her panic, she'd tightened her grip on the flashlight, pressing the hard plastic into the cut on her palm, causing the wound to bleed more fervently. Zara peeled the flashlight from her palm and set it on the ground. Her hands trembled when she held them out. The piercing pain in her arm had turned numb as long as she limited movement and was careful not to bump into anything.

"What am I going to do?" she whispered. Once the tears started, they were impossible to stop. Zara sealed her lips, breathing through her nose, her body convulsing with the effort to keep quiet. The last thing she needed was to draw attention to herself.

Get it together, Williams. She squeezed her eyes shut and focused on getting her breathing under control. Tears still ran down her cheeks, but she was able to subdue her sobs. Her body light and her head heavy, she stood, the contrast making her dizzy again. She leaned with her elbows on the counter, and then she saw it — Lizzy's phone was tucked in a corner by an outlet. It was plugged in, sitting on a notepad. Zara reached for it and pressed a side button, laughing with joy as the screen came to life, a picture of her and Lizzy appearing as the lock screen. The time read four o'clock. The notepad the phone had been sitting on read: Belongs to Girl/Dad Taken to Hospital. Zara touched the letters. "Thank you," she whispered, overwhelmed with gratefulness for whichever employee had taken the time to set aside the phone and charge it.

She carefully put the phone in her pocket. Once Lizzy unlocked it, Zara would finally be able to see what had happened to her brother. Or she'd at least get some clues. Even if the video itself didn't have specific information about Jordan, she could see who he was with in the moments before all hell broke loose at the World's Fair. It was the only lead she had on what could be the only family she had left.

She pulled back from the counter, grimacing at the blood smear she left behind. A pair of scissors in a cup caught her attention, and she grabbed hold of them. She made quick work of cutting up a few t-shirts for bandages and wrapped her arm, palm, and head the best she could. She spotted a rainbow purse with a cartoon character she didn't recognize, meant for a little girl, and she picked it up, slinging it over her head and stuffing the scissors inside. The cross strap was too short, and it sat awkwardly a few inches below her armpit. Still, she was less likely to lose it than if she let it hang loose.

Zara chewed on her lower lip as she turned toward the broken glass doors. *I have three hours to make it what… five miles?*

Normally, she could run five miles in under an hour. But she was exhausted, injured, bruised, and nauseous. Three hours would have to be enough. The hospital was the safest place she knew of, certainly safer than the gas station, and that's where Lizzy and Mr. Peters were. So, Zara ventured back outside, willing her heart to stop beating so quickly as she stepped into open air. Still cautious, Zara ran as quickly as she could into the maze of cars, ducking so that she would be less visible from a distance.

Using the vehicles for shields and cover, she stayed on the streets and avoided exposure in open areas. In the few hours since she'd driven through, the suburb had changed. She'd seen the beginnings of anarchy, but now it was in full swing.

Zara covered her face with her t-shirt as she passed a strip mall on fire. Fire blazed out the windows, black smoke billowing into the air. Half a dozen men whooped and hollered in the lot, drinking bottles of alcohol. She ducked low and walked quickly, praying they wouldn't see her with every step.

"Hey!" one of them shouted. "Pretty momma! Come hang out with us." He drew out his vowels in a drunken stupor.

Zara's stomach lurched, and she sprinted away. Low, hearty laughter followed her, and she didn't look back. She just kept running, bouncing lightly off vehicles as she used them to steady herself. Once she was sure they hadn't come after her, she slowed and leaned against a car to catch her breath. A cold sweat broke out across her forehead, and the blood drained from her face, leaving her lips numbed. She heaved blue liquid this time, her arms shaking and her legs threatening to give out.

But she had to go on. For what seemed like forever, her whole life consisted of putting one foot in front of the other. She finally reached the residential area that bordered the hospital grounds, and by that time, she could no longer feel any pain. A steady buzz of pins and needles replaced all feeling. Waves of chill rolled up and down her body as she walked the outer hospital road that lead to the parking garage.

She vaguely registered movement ahead of her as someone crossed the lawn, ignoring a long row of body bags, and heading straight for the tents. It was a man. He strode into one of the tents and then cursed loudly as he exited and entered a second.

"Where is everyone?" he shouted. "I need a doctor! My brother is sick!"

Zara came closer, approaching the tents as he was leaving them for the front door. She poked her head around the canvas, frowning. Two guards with guns stood in between two sets of sliding glass doors.

"Let me inside!" the newcomer banged on the glass, but the guard shook his head. "I need help," the man tried again.

The guards looked at each other. One of them turned back to the man, shouting through the door, "Leave now, and you won't get hurt."

"This is a hospital," the man said, throwing up his arms. "Are you serious?"

The guard who hadn't spoken walked over to one wall and nodded at the guard remaining in the middle. That guard raised his gun and planted his feet. The glass doors slid open.

"No one gets in." The guard shouted. "We will shoot you, sir."

His partner moved away from the wall, pulling his own gun. The newcomer balled his fists at his sides, took two steps forward, and then shots rang out. He stopped and dropped to the sidewalk, blood seeping out from under his body.

The guard who hadn't shot his weapon lowered his and stood up straighter. "This isn't right, Mitch."

Mitch holstered his own gun. "It's survival, Brandt. I know you're young, but these guns are a life saver right now. We're lucky I had 'em."

"We're security guards," Brandt said, staring at the dead body. "Not police. We're not supposed to be killing people."

"Well, people's eyes aren't supposed to pop out of their heads, neither." Mitch stood over the body, hands on his hips as he looked down. "We oughtta move him so he doesn't start to stink."

Zara ducked into the tent and sat on the ground, unable to do more than stay still as the sounds of shuffling and grunting and footsteps commenced outside. She waited, and once they subsided, she peeked outside again. Mitch and Brandt were back inside the sliding doors, waiting. Mitch looked a little too comfortable for someone who'd just shot a man. Zara returned to her seat in the grass.

Thinking was like wading through mud. *I can't go in that way. How do I get inside?* She stared blankly ahead at the white canvas across from her. She had nothing. The sun was low in the sky, and she needed to get inside if she was going to heed the CDC warnings. Head bobbing with exhaustion, she was drawn to the parking garage across the road.

Zara struggled to her knees, and then she hauled herself to her feet. There was a completely enclosed stairwell inside the garage. It would be hot, but it would be safe. She stumbled ahead, looking over her shoulder to keep the tents blocking the line of sight from the garage to the glass doors. Her feet dragged against the concrete as she entered the parking garage. Her head was swimming, and her body craved rest as she threw open the door to the stairwell. It shut behind her, and she breathed in a long, slow breath of hot, stale air. Finally, having reached a modicum of safety, Zara leaned against the wall and slid to the ground. Her limbs trembled with exhaustion as she lowered her body to rest on the concrete. It was dirty and unyielding, but she could be still, she could close her eyes, she could—
A shuffle sounded from beneath the stairs, and a figure clothed in shadow emerged.

Chapter 29

Timothy Peters

Time was running out. Frank had given Timothy two days. If the sort-of-mobster kept to his word, he'd try to collect the perceived debt by the end of the day, which was coming quickly to a close. The outside perimeter of the house was as secure as Timothy knew to make it. The windows were covered in security film that would make it harder for someone to break through them. The tint provided extra concealment of their movements beyond the stylish wooden-slat blinds. A bed of nails waited amongst the bed of rocks, hidden by bushes.

Inside, a bucket of chemical tile cleaner sat on top of an adjustable ladder, flush with the top of the door. Timothy had attached a wire to the top of the bucket and run it to the corner of the door frame. Testing it with water, he'd pushed open the door forcefully, pleased to see that when the door slammed into the ladder, the wire pulled the bucket to splash the contents on the entrance. The chemical would do a lot more damage than a bucket of water. Granted, it would only work if the door was pushed hard enough to rock the ladder, but Timothy expected if the criminals were coming in, they'd be doing it by force.

Timothy was finishing off his last trap at the back door when the walkie talkie came to life. He checked the one at his hip, but it was the one on the dining table that had chirped. That one was so that he could keep apprised of the party situation. He had a bad feeling about it, but he and Heather had agreed that there was nothing they could do.

"Hey," Candice's voice came over the speaker, "Rhonda, you there? Where is Bill?"

"Candy!" Bill's slurred voice made Timothy roll his eyes. A shushing sound from Rhonda ensued, but there was no answer to Candice's question.

"Rhonda, seriously. I want to come to the party. I still have to go home and get dressed. I'm wearing camo."

Timothy chuckled.

"What's so funny?" Heather asked as she came down the stairs.

"Candice is being stiffed at the guard post," Timothy said as he squeezed super glue onto the hardwood floor on one end of the sliding doors at the back of the house. "She wants to go to the party, but apparently camo is a neighborhood watch outfit only." He pressed a flashbang into the glue to secure it to the floor.

He'd dissembled another flashbang according to his mother's instructions and secured a wire to its pin mechanism. The opposite end of the wire was tied securely to a nail he'd driven into the hardwood. If he got his measurements right, he would simply need to replace the pin in the live flashbang with the pin attached to the wire. Anyone coming through the back door would hopefully unwittingly pull the wire with a step inside and set it off. It wouldn't seriously injure anyone, but it would certainly surprise them and disorient them long enough for Timothy to put a bullet in their chest.

The walkie talkie on Timothy's hip crackled. "This is Gucci, over."

Timothy sighed and held the device up to his mouth. "Gucci, just stay at your post. This is more important than a party."

"I know that," Candice said defensively. "I mean… Roger, but I'm calling because two black vans are coming up the road."

Timothy's heart stopped. Heather froze, wide-eyed.

"Are they passing?" Timothy asked.

"No… what am I supposed to do? They're pulling up!" Candice's voice was panicked.

"Keep the walkie talkie on so I can hear," Timothy said. "They won't be able to get inside the gate unless you open it, okay? If it's them, you can run back to your house. Just leave the gate closed."

"They're using the intercom," Candice said.

Timothy's skin crawled at the familiar voice that followed.

"Hey, honey, you're lookin' nice today." Frank Russo was at the gate.

"Candice, that's him!" Timothy said into the speaker.

"Oh," Candice said as if she were waving off the compliment with false modesty, "well, thank you. How sweet."

"Candice?" Timothy asked again.

"If she's pressing the button so you can hear, she wouldn't be able to receive you," Heather said. "Are you sure that's Frank?"

"Yes," Timothy said, "I'm sure."

"I bet your smokin' hot," Frank said in a friendly voice.

"Well, that's a little inappropriate," Candice said, "but yes, I believe my husband would agree with that."

Frank chuckled. "I like you, sweetheart. But I was talkin' literally. Like, with the heat and all."

"Oh. Of course." Candice cleared her throat. "What can I do for you?"

"I'm here to fix the power," Frank said. "Gotta get all your fancy houses back on the grid."

"Really?" Candice said too enthusiastically. "That's *wonderful*. We're having a party right now, all outside, because our meat is thawing. Can you believe that?"

"A cryin' shame," Frank said. "Well, have no fear, sweetheart. We're gonna check in on *every* home and make sure everythin' is up and runnin' before we leave."

"Let me buzz you in," Candice said.

Timothy shouted, "No!" But Candice still couldn't hear him.

"This is Gucci," Candice said quickly. "I'm sure you heard all that. I'm going to go to the party and send someone back in my place, okay? Everyone will want to know the power's coming back on."

"What? Candice, those are the guys I was telling about. Can you hear me? Hello?" Timothy sat up straight, body tense as he waited for an answer. None came. "She switched off her walkie talkie," he said incredulously. "She didn't want to hear my objections, so she just turned it off!" He threw the walkie talkie and it skidded across the floor.

Heather was pale. "Once she let them in, there was nothing she could do for us anyway," she said.

"She could warn people," Timothy said. He glanced at the walkie talkie on the table. "We'll have to warn them. Go ahead while I finish setting this up." He turned back to his project, carefully switching out the pins.

"Hello?" Heather said over the walkie talkie.

"This is Rhonda speaking." Rhonda giggled. "I mean… this is Cosmopolitan… no! Man-hat-tan." She burst into laughter. "None of those are good code names, Bill."

"Rhonda, everyone needs to protect themselves," Heather said. "Those guys we told you about are here, and we think they might try looting other homes besides ours."

"Loot, boot, scoot, root…" Rhonda sounded as if she were rolling on the floor in glee.

"She's really drunk," Heather said.

"Forget it," Timothy said, "Just… make sure my mom and the kids stay in the bunker no matter what, okay?"

Heather nodded and relayed the message to Dana.

"Be careful," Dana said. "I'll keep the kids safe."

Heather clipped the walkie talkie to her belt and threw Timothy the one he'd flung across the floor. "Channel 5? No one should be on that one."

Timothy nodded and set the walkie talkie. He stood up and followed Heather up the stairs, going straight for his parents' room. Heather went to the opposite side of the hallway, to the guest room. Both had windows facing the front of the house. He'd made sure Heather had a handgun she was comfortable shooting and plenty of ammo. He had chosen an AR-15 and had a few magazines loaded and ready to go. Timothy cracked open the window and gritted his teeth at the sound of loud music coming from a few streets over.

"Hey, babe," Heather shouted from across the hallway, "it sounds like we're all ready to party."

Timothy rolled his eyes but smiled. "You good over there?" he asked.

"As good as I can be," she said. "Love you, Tim."

"Love you, too," he said as he grabbed a magazine, inserted it, and gave it a good whack.

Timothy pulled the charging handle to chamber a round as the black vans pulled into the u-shaped driveway and parked in front of the house. The drive was several yards from the front porch with a brick walkway connecting them and flowers in the rock bed leading up to the house. Frank Russo stepped out of the first van, tapped on the window of the second, and said something Timothy couldn't hear. The second van drove around Frank's and continued on down the driveway.

Frank turned to face the house and looked up at the windows. "We don't need them, Southie," he said. "They's got other houses to visit. It's awful nice o' your neighbors to go off and have a party like that, leavin' their belongins' up for grabs. No resistance. In and out." He shrugged. "Easy. I say, let's you and me make this easy, too, Southie."

"What do you want, Frank?" Timothy shouted as he strung his earplugs around his neck and hooked them on his ears to prepare to shoot.

"I figure a life's worth somethin' is all," Frank said. "Two lives, actually. Ya owe me everythin' ya got. And with things the way they are, I'm gonna need it right now, Southie."

"Sorry, Frank. I'm not ready to part with anything just yet. Get out of here before you get yourself killed." Timothy plugged his ears, set his sights, and fired a warning shot.

Frank scuttled away from where the bullet grazed the concrete. Four men hopped out of the back as they drew their guns and the driver stepped out of the front and leveled his weapon at the window.

"Shouldna done that, Southie," Frank said. He turned and walked behind the van, joining the driver behind the engine. He raised his gun and fired a shot that shattered a pane above Timothy's head.

Heather started shooting, and one of the thugs turned his gun her way, eyes wide as if he didn't expect another shooter. Timothy took aim and fired, landing a shot square in the man's chest. He stumbled backwards, hit the van, and slumped to the ground.

"We gotta get in there!" Frank shouted.

Shots rang out from half the men as Frank brought up the rear of a charge on the house itself. Mr. Peters had spared no expense in the security of his front door, and the man who threw his shoulder into it bounced right off.

"The windows!" Frank shouted.

A man picked up a large paving stone lining the walkway and threw it into the window. It cracked, but it didn't shatter. He picked up another and made to smash it into the window closer up, treading into the bushes. He screamed in pain and howled, "My foot!" He hopped away and fell on his rear end, a length of board attached to his foot, the tips of two long nails sticking up through his tennis shoe.

"What the—" Frank scowled up at Timothy. He pointed to two thugs. "Round back you two, and you and me," he said to the driver, "we're gonna break down this door!"

Timothy pulled back from the window and met Heather in the hall. "You ready for this?" he asked. She nodded, face solemn as she put her own earplugs in place.

They reached the bottom of the stairs and Timothy led Heather into the kitchen area. They both crouched below the island, Heather at the center, Timothy at the edge so he could turn and shoot at the door. A thud sounded at the front door, and then again and again until the frame broke and the door swung open. The door slammed into the ladder, and the bucket of muriatic acid dumped onto the driver who charged in first. He threw his hands to his eyes and screamed, pressing his hands against his face and slipping, crashing to the ground.

Frank raised his gun, treading more carefully on the hardwood, but as the two broke into the back, they triggered the trip wire and the flash bang exploded. Frank and the two remaining thugs reared back and covered their ears. Shots fired behind him, but Timothy focused on Frank. He shot, hitting him in the shoulder, and Frank dropped his gun. The mobster fled back out the front door. Timothy turned his gun on the back door to find one man dead and another limping away, fleeing with blood seeping down his thigh. The driver crawled out of the front door, screaming for help. The second van pulled up, and Timothy hurried to the front door, carefully avoiding the puddle of acid.

A man rolled down the window. "You idiot! I thought you had this handled!"

"I'm sorry, Big Blue," Frank said. "I didn't know."

"Get in the van," Big Blue said.

Timothy peeked around the door frame, cocking an eyebrow. *It can't be that easy.*

"But, with all of us, we can take 'em." Frank said, holding his shoulder. Blood seeped into his shirt, the stain widening with every second.

"I don't think so, Frankie," Big Blue said. "I got plenty o' supplies from the nearby houses. We got to get you and our guys to the doc. The Boss would kill me if I came back with his dead nephew. We can come back later."

Sulking as the driver, the guy who'd had his foot run through, and the man who'd been shot in the leg climbed in the back, Frank turned around and shouted, "Hear that, Southie? We're comin' back! And soon. Don't get too comfy in there. We know your tricks. I'll get what I'm owed and burn the rest with you inside!" He piled into the back and the mobsters drove off, tires squealing. They left the other black van behind.

"We did it!" Timothy shouted, pumping a fist in the air. He looked back toward the kitchen, expecting to see Heather there. But she was nowhere in sight. "Heather?" Timothy jogged to the kitchen to face his worst nightmare.

Heather lay on the floor behind the island, blood pooling beneath her, a bullet wound in her side.

Chapter 30

Alexander Roman

Alex stared into the single, dancing flame of the only candle in the hall. He leaned forward, chin resting on folded hands. The heat in the hallway was stifling. The windows had all been shut, and with no electricity, the inside of the apartment building was several degrees hotter than the summer night. Sweat created a thick film over Alex's whole body.

Across the hall, orange light glowed from under the door of the only room Alex cared about in the whole building. It had been hours since Quinten had pulled Oliver inside. Alex had barged in at first, intent on getting Oliver back, but that blade against his son's neck had stopped him in his tracks. Quinten wasn't backing down. He was holding Oliver hostage until he had proof that Alex could get him medicine Alex didn't have.

Minnie had come to sit with him some time ago. She'd brought him something to eat, Samson by her side. The dog had stared at the door with about as much intensity as Alex himself.

"It's hotter than blue blazes," Minnie had said as she lowered herself to the ground. She'd handed him the candle and a matchbox. "It'll be dark soon," she said. "Thought you might want some light."

"Thanks." Alex slumped against the wall.

People had walked between rooms and up and down the hall, but everyone else had been giving him space. A few had thrown him sympathetic glances, but no one seemed to know how to help. Minnie had sat in silence for a long time, somehow knowing that Alex didn't have the capacity for anything else. Alex had gotten lost in that candlelight as night enveloped him, as the doors in the halls closed and people stopped coming out to watch him with pity in their eyes.

"We'll get him back," Minnie said, though why she chose that moment to switch from silent support he couldn't tell.

He wasn't sure he wanted to talk at first, but tears sprung to Alex's eyes, and his inner turmoil just poured out of him. "No matter how hard I try, the people I love most die. And not just in normal ways, Minnie. My wife died a terrible death." He closed his eyes, voice cracking. "My sister died a terrible death, too. I couldn't save either one. They died because I was too weak."

"Now, that doesn't sound right to me," Minnie said. "You're not a weak man, Alex."

He scoffed and wiped away his tears. "I didn't even try with my sister," he said. "I hid under the bed until a firefighter came to get me, cowering while Mary burned alive in the next room. When my wife was dangling in front of me, I tried to save her, I tried to be brave for her, but… I couldn't save her, either. And now, my son…" He buried his face in his hands.

"How old were you when Mary died?" Minnie asked gently.

Alex pushed his palms up to his forehead and let his head rest against them. "About Oliver's age, I guess."

"Do you blame Oliver for not helping to save his mother?"

Alex snapped his head to look at Minnie. "Of course not," he said vehemently.

"Then how can you blame yourself for Mary?" Minnie placed a hand on Alex's arm.

Alex frowned. He'd regretted hiding under that bed every day for twenty years. He'd gone over the situation in his head, imagining what he could have done differently, what he *should have* done differently. *Just like I'm doing with Naomi…*

"Alex, sometimes folks like me shy away from guilt like it's a snake in the grass. I shoulda faced my snake, taken responsibility, and then killed the thing and left it behind in the mud a long time ago. And I'm workin' on that," Minnie said. "But others, like you, take in the snake like it's a pet and nurture it. What you need to do is release that guilt back into the wild. Maybe someone else needs to face it. Maybe no one does. But either way, that venom doesn't belong to you."

Something tight in his chest unfurled a little, but he didn't know what to say. He returned to the silence, drawing his knees to his chest and staring at the candle flame again, waiting as close to his son as he could get without making the madman lose his mind completely. He'd sat in silence until Minnie had patted his arm and stood.

"You chew on that," Minnie said after a few minutes. "I'm gonna take Samson and get him settled. I'm not sure he'd make things better if that man actually opened the door. Maybe Lauren can come back and try again. She's good with people, and she's had a lot of practice with difficult ones." She retreated with Samson in tow.

Not long after, Lauren opened a door down the hall and approached with three bottled waters in hand. She handed one to Alex. "I'm going to see if I can get Quinten to let me in," she whispered. "He's got to be thirsty, and I know your kid is probably thirsty, too. I'm hoping he's calmed down a little."

Alex stood up. "I need my son back," he said.

"I know. Just let me do the talking," Lauren said. "I've known Quinten for six months. He's just panicking. I've never seen him like this."

"He was your neighbor?" Alex asked.

"Yeah. He always had a joke of the day, every morning." She smiled sadly. "I don't know what he's thinking. He's never been quite normal, but this…"

"What does that mean? Did you know he was crazy?" Alex hissed.

Lauren frowned. "He's a bit of a conspiracy nut, but—"

"So, you knew he was dangerous, and you led us right to him?" Alex balled his hands into fists.

"Whoa," Lauren said, holding up her hands, still gripping a water bottle in each. "Back up, cowboy. I've never seen him hurt a fly, okay?"

"That kid is everything to me," Alex said.

"I don't think Quinten will hurt him." Lauren let her hands fall, the water swishing in the bottles at the movement. "Maybe I can talk some sense into him. We need to keep him calm, though. Agitating him isn't going to do anyone any good."

"Fine," Alex breathed out, long and slow. "But I'm right behind you. I need to see my son."

Lauren nodded. "Okay, here we go," she said as she stepped up to the door and knocked. "Quinten? It's me, Lauren."

There was shuffling on the other side. "Does that guy have anything for me? Has he contacted his people?"

Alex closed his eyes and bit his lip. He wanted to scream at Quinten and tell him, again, that his so-called people had nothing to offer. Not yet, anyway. But that route hadn't worked before, and he had no reason to think it would work again.

"No, Quinten," Lauren said. "But I brought you and the kid some water."

"You're trying to trick me!" Quinten said.

"I swear I'm not," Lauren said. "I'd like to give you some water and just check on the kid."

"No." Quinten sounded like a child. Alex half expected to hear him stomp his foot.

"I've contacted my people," Alex said over Lauren's shoulder. She looked back at him, eyebrow quirked. He shrugged and continued with the lie. "But there's no way I'm going to let them bring you anything if I don't know my son is safe."

The sound of metal sliding on metal as a bolt was undone made Alex's whole body tense. The door flew open, and Quinten stood there, his form shadowy and backlit by dozens of candles burning all over the apartment. The sudden light was too much for Alex, and he had to blink several times for his vision to adjust.

Quinten held the knife, making sure Alex could see it while he stepped aside so that Oliver was visible. The candlelight illuminated Oliver asleep on the couch; Alex narrowed his eyes, looking for any sign of injury. But his son's chest rose and fell in a rhythm, and he seemed okay.

"There." Quinten pointed at Alex with the tip of the blade. "You see? He's fine."

"Why don't you let the kid go?" Lauren asked. "Here, take some water. You can come with me, tell me a few of your famous jokes—"

"What good are jokes?" Quinten said. "We're all gonna die!" He pointed his knife at Alex. "They're in on it! *They* have the cure, I know it. This is how they do it. I bet they're sitting in fancy high rises, laughing as the dregs of the earth drop like flies."

A low, angry growl escaped Alex's lips. "Do you hear yourself? Who the heck are *they*? If I'm part of *them*, why am I here?"

"You're a cog in the machine, man." Quinten's eyes went wide, and he backed away, his hands trembling. "Maybe you really don't have what I need."

"That's what I've been trying to tell you," Alex said.

"Then it's useless," Quinten kept backing up until he hit a small kitchen table between the living area and the kitchen. The table was covered in candles of all shapes and sizes. When Quinten bumped into it, one of them fell onto the floor and the rug caught fire, the flames small at first. Quinten put the knife to his own throat. "I can't do this anymore."

"Whoa, Quinten, buddy," Lauren said. "I get it, okay? I was where you are just this morning after Aaron died." Her eyes flickered to Alex, but she kept talking to Quinten. "I was wrong. This isn't the way. We've all got people left."

Alex watched the flames get higher, his eyes darting between them and the couch on the other side of the apartment. Oliver sat up and rubbed his eyes. He frowned at the growing fire and then gasped and scooted farther into the corner of the couch.

Quinten began to cry, his chin quivered, the blade drawing blood at his neck. "You don't understand. No one understands."

"Quinten, give me the knife," Lauren held out her hand. "You're my friend, and I don't want to see you get hurt."

She stepped forward, slowly at first, but when Quinten started sobbing, he let his hand drop a little. His eyes were squeezed shut as tears rolled down his cheeks. Lauren bolted forward and grabbed his wrist. Alex rushed to help her, taking hold of Quinten's forearm from the other side. The knife clattered to the floor.

"Let me go!" He wrenched himself free and fell backward into the table, knocking it over. Dozens of candles were flung to the floor, flames catching everywhere. Quinten scrambled away from them and bolted out the door.

Alex was halfway across the room, passing rising flames, before he realized Oliver wasn't on the couch. "Oliver! Where are you?" He spun, wildly looking for his son.

"There!" Lauren shouted, pointing down a short hallway. "Under the bed!"

"Go! Get everyone out!" Alex shouted. "I'll get my son."

Lauren only hesitated a moment before rushing out into the hall, sounding the alarm up and down the halls. Alex, heart pounding, rushed toward the room. He fell to his knees and looked over his shoulder. Flames were steadily advancing, finding fuel after fuel, consuming and growing. He placed his hands flat on the laminate and lowered himself so that he could see Oliver cowering under the bed.

But then Alex couldn't move. Smooth, cool flooring underneath, hot air pressing in on all sides, a white lace bed skirt, the sound of glass exploding, the cracking and popping of fire… Alex no longer saw his son. He was looking at *himself.* He trembled as high-pitched screams of terror pierced the air, but it was so much worse when they stopped. His sister was dead.

"Mary…" Alex couldn't breathe. The stench of burning plastic permeated everything. He gasped for air. *This can't be real. It can't be real.* He squeezed his eyes shut, but there he saw his wife, battered and broken, launching herself off the metal frame to her death. "Naomi!" Take care of Ollie.

"What if I can't?" He whispered, tears flowing freely. He was broken. He'd always been broken. Every minute he'd held it together, he'd been pretending. It was all his fault. Mary, Naomi, Oliver… It was all his fault.

Two small, warm hands cupped Alex's cheeks. "Dad?" It was Oliver's voice, raw but sweet, the most wonderful sound Alex had ever heard.

Alex opened his eyes. The world spun back to Nashville, to the apartment building, to his son. A voice inside repeated, *It's all my fault,* but those words seemed so weak as he looked into the eyes of his son.

No. That venom wasn't his. But the love he had for his son? That belonged. That was real. That was his.

Alex slowed his breathing and blinked away the nightmare. "You ready to get out of here?" he asked.

Oliver nodded and army crawled out from under the bed. Alex got to his feet and held out his hand. Oliver took it, but the fire was already eating the hall, black smoke billowing into the bedroom, rolling across the ceiling. Alex slammed the door shut. There was no way they were getting out that way, but closing the door slowed the smoke.

"We're only a couple floors up," he said rushing to the window. He unlocked it and yanked it upward, sticking his head outside to see just how far the drop would be. They were on the second floor, and it was at least a twenty-foot drop.

"Alex!" Minnie shouted from a little way down the street. She gestured to the crowd around her, those who had been sheltering inside the apartment building. Minnie and Lauren led the charge as several able-bodied men and women rushed to where Alex was hanging halfway out the window.

"I've got Oliver!" Alex shouted. "But the hallway is engulfed. We can't get out that way."

Lauren held up a hand. "Hold on!" She said something to the crowd, and five of them scurried around the corner. They were pushing a large dumpster, and they positioned it under the window.

A tall man climbed on top, and then Lauren scrambled up with him, proceeding to crawl onto his shoulders. With the height of the dumpster, Lauren's outstretched arms were only a couple feet from the window.

"You're a genius," Alex said, turning to Oliver. "C'mon, bud. We're going to get you out of here."

"What about you?" Oliver asked, coughing and looking at the smoke building up on the ceiling.

"I'll be right behind you." Alex put both hands on Oliver's shoulders. "We're going to get out of this."

Oliver nodded, and Alex carefully helped him through the window. He lowered his son down so that Lauren could wrap her arms around his legs. She lowered him to the top of the dumpster, and then she got off the man's shoulders to help Oliver to the ground. Alex scrambled over the side as the fire invaded the room. He held onto the windowsill, body flush against the glassy surface of the building, said a prayer, and let go.

Chapter 31

Timothy Peters

Timothy paced behind the couch where Heather was stretched out. She was awake, drowsy and pale but alive. The bullet had torn through the outer abdominal wall below her ribs. Skin had been shorn from muscle as a hole had been punched between them. There was an exit wound, and he knew that was good, but he didn't know *how* good. It didn't seem like her internal organs had been damaged, but he wasn't a doctor. And what about infection? And blood loss? The wound still seeped.

Dana hovered over Heather. She had helped Timothy clean the wound with hydrogen peroxide, pack it with gauze, press a towel around the wound, and secure the bandaging with duct tape wrapped all the way around Heather's torso. Her hands had been steady when Timothy's had trembled.

I'll always owe her for that. Timothy paused and studied his mother as she put a third blanket on Heather, tucking it around her like she'd done for him as a child at bedtime.

"Your couch," Heather said, her voice raw. "I'm getting blood all over it."

"Oh, shush," Dana said. "We can buy a new couch." She stood up straighter and arched an eyebrow, eyes sweeping the room. "We're going to need to redecorate anyway."

Heather chuckled but then cried out in pain. "Don't make me laugh," she said.

"I was being perfectly serious," Dana said, though she offered a small smile.

Timothy leaned over the couch and kissed Heather's forehead. He straightened and reached out a hand toward his mother. She took it and squeezed. "I don't know what I would have done without you," he said.

"Despite what you both think," Dana said, "I do love you like a daughter, Heather."

Heather frowned. "Dana, I—"

"No, it's okay," Dana said. "I'm not always easy, and I know that. But, maybe after all this, you two might consider rejoining the family. Fully, I mean. Walter loves you both, too, in his own way."

Heather somehow got even paler as she looked at Timothy.

He sighed. "I don't know," he said. "Maybe I can try again, if Dad can try again."

Dana's eyes glistened as she folded her arms. "Then, maybe something good can come of this mess. If your father makes it home, that is."

"He's a stubborn man," Timothy said. "You know he's always got to have the last word. No way he's going out before you do."

"I suppose you're right about that," Dana said. She let her hands fall to her sides and glanced at the sliding doors hanging off their rails and the front door torn off its hinges. "It's getting late."

"We need to get downstairs," Timothy said. Sunlight was rapidly dissipating. "We don't want whatever it is out there making people sick to add to our problems. The bunker should be secure, and we have more medical supplies down there than we do up here."

"Moving her right now isn't the best idea," Dana said, "but I think you're right. Do you think you can walk?" She asked Heather.

"Not on my own," Heather admitted.

"I've got her," Timothy said, rounding the couch and gathering her in his arms. She was slight compared to him.

She bit her lip as he moved her, squeezing her eyes shut, sucking in a breath and holding it in. "This isn't going to be fun," she said. "Just get me downstairs."

"Dana?" A female voice rang from the doorway, and Candice walked inside, a canister of pepper spray held out in front of her. She wore her hair in a side braid, and she was dressed in a fashionable sundress. She'd apparently gone home and changed into party attire. "I swear I know how to use this thing!" She shouted.

"Candice?" Timothy asked. "What are you doing here?"

She lowered the canister. "Oh. My. Lanta. What am *I* doing here? What is that *dead body* doing in your driveway? I thought Dana was in real trouble."

"So… you came inside to save me with pepper spray?" Dana asked.

"Well, at first I saw the tints on your windows, and I was like, 'Um, no. We voted on this.' But then I saw the broken glass and the open door and the dead body…" She shrugged. "So, yes. But," she raised one finger and pursed her lips, "I also take a kickboxing class," she said.

"That's actually quite sweet of you," Dana said. "And brave."

Candice beamed and flipped her braid over her shoulder. "I *am* the HOA president. I was just doing my du—" Her words cut off as her eyes went wide as saucers. Candice's mouth dropped open and she pointed at Heather's wound. "She's bleeding! Like, a *lot*."

"Thanks for pointing it out," Heather said. "I hadn't noticed."

Dana pursed her lips. "What Heather means to say is that we appreciate your concern. We're taking care of it. She was shot."

Candice placed her hand flat against her stomach. "What happened?" she asked.

"Those guys you let into the community happened," Timothy said, fresh anger boiling at the memory. "You practically invited those criminals to our doorstep."

"That can't be right," Candice said. "Those men were here to fix the power outage."

"Then why is one of them lying dead outside? Why did one of them shoot my wife? You didn't find it odd that their van is abandoned in my mother's driveway?" Timothy raised his voice, and Candice moved her hand from her stomach to her chest.

"Well. It's not my fault." She drew her bright red lips into a thin line. "They tricked me."

Timothy opened his mouth to refute that, but Heather gently patted his chest. "We need to get downstairs."

"She needs to get to the hospital." Candice put her hands on her hips.

"I can't imagine the hospitals are safe right now," Dana said. "I can't imagine they're safe anywhere." She said the last part softly.

"Well, Doctor Patel is at the party," Candice said. "We could at least bring him here to take a look."

"You would do that for us?" Timothy asked, a flicker of hope coming to life inside his chest.

"Of course," Candice said. "I'll go get him."

"When you come back, just come on in and come downstairs. You and Dr. Patel are welcome to stay in the safe room with us tonight," Dana said, "if you want."

"I can't believe that's the rumor about you that turned out to be true," Candice said, sounding almost disappointed. She seemed to realize she'd spoken it out loud and her cheeks flushed red. "I'll go get Dr. Patel." She turned and walked stiffly away.

When she was gone, Timothy continued toward the stairs, letting Dana open the door for him. He carefully took the steps one at a time, trying very hard not to knock Heather against the wall. It would have been dark down there with no power to the house, but the bunker had a floodlight on the outside door that came to life at the movement and lit up the basement. Dana opened the door that led down another flight of stairs. At the bottom landing, she let him into the bunker itself, and Timothy carefully lay Heather on the bed that was still pulled out from the couch.

"Is she okay?" George asked, peeking out from one of the bedrooms. He held the door slightly ajar.

"She'll be okay, Georgie," Dana said. "If you could keep Annika occupied, that would help a lot, though."

"She's already asleep," George said.

Dana walked over to the door. "I think it's time for you to go to bed, too," she said as she pushed open the door. "I'll tuck you in."

"Moooom," George said, shoulders sagging. "I'm not a baby. I want to know what's going on."

"Okay," Dana said. "I'll tell you about it in the morning, when we've all gotten some rest."

George huffed but stepped back into the room. Dana followed and shut the door behind her.

"I think I need some sleep, too," Heather said groggily.

"Okay, babe. I'll be right here for you, okay? Get some rest. The doctor should be here soon." He sat next to her and stroked her hair until she fell asleep, which didn't take long.

Timothy lay his head back, his body sinking into the mattress. It was thin, but he was tired enough that he didn't care. The lights in the bunker were soft, the quiet welcome. He must have drifted off because the next thing he knew, his mother was shaking him awake.

He sat upright, blinking and rubbing his eyes. "What is it?" he asked.

"Heather doesn't look right." Dana rushed over to the kitchenette and ran a rag under water, dashing back to the bed and patting Heather's forehead. "She's shaking like a leaf."

"How long have I been asleep?" Timothy asked.

"Just a couple hours." Dana said. "It's too early for an infection, I think. She's just lost a lot of blood."

Heather moaned. Her expression was twisted with pain, and her breathing was rapid, her face paler than before. "It's too cold," she whispered, teeth chattering.

"What do we do?" Timothy asked. "Where is Candice with Dr. Patel?"

Dana shook her head. "I'm not sure."

"What kind of pain medication do you have down here?" Timothy hopped up from the bed and took a few steps toward the storage room.

"We've only got over-the-counter stuff," Dana said.

Timothy turned to face her. "How is that possible? Dad planned for everything."

"Buying a large stash of prescription medications isn't exactly legal," Dana said as she pulled the blankets up around Heather's shivering chin.

"Blankets," he said. "We do have those." He turned around again and retrieved several. He covered his wife with a few more layers. "I don't know what else to do," he said, voice cracking.

"I have a few Percocets left over in the medicine cabinet in the master bath," Dana said. "Maybe one of those would help?"

"We've got to do something," Timothy said.

A dull thudding on the thick door of the bunker made him snap his head up to look at the intercom system, complete with a little screen, by the door. A floodlight connected to the bunker's power illuminated the basement. Candice leaned her head against the door, knocking, her hair disheveled and hanging so as to conceal her face completely. Dana walked over and was about to pull the lever that unlocked the first door.

"Wait," Timothy said as he approached the intercom screen. "Dr. Patel isn't with her."

"That doesn't mean we just leave her out there," Dana said. "I told her she could stay here."

"No, there's something wrong." Timothy squinted at the black-and-white image. "I think she's sick." Candice slumped forward and scratched vigorously at her neck beneath her hair. Timothy pressed the intercom button. "Candice? Can you hear me?"

She reared her head back, her head bobbing until her eyes settled on the intercom. She stumbled sideways and pressed the button. Her face and neck were swollen and misshapen, a lump visible on her neck as her hair fell back.

"I need help," she said, words slurring. She coughed and dark liquid bubbled out of her mouth and ran down her chin, black against her white skin on the screen. The lack of color made it look like a scene from an old horror movie.

"Candice, did you find Dr. Patel?" Timothy asked. "Maybe he can help you."

Candice shook her head. "Went to party," she said, the words sounding thick. "They… were… dying. Everyone. Dying." She placed her flat palms against the side of her head. "It hurts," she said, her eyes leaking black as she squeezed them shut. "Tried to help… but… I don't know what happened. Woke up. Came here." She opened her eyes, but they were too wide, beginning to pop.

"I can't let you in," Timothy said.

"Timothy!" Dana said. "She's dying. We can't just leave her."

"We have to, Mom." Timothy placed his hands on his mother's shoulders, looking her in the eye, making sure she saw both his firmness and his regret. "We let the sickness in here, and we could get it. George. Annika. We have to protect them."

Dana swallowed and looked back at the screen. She sucked in a shaky breath, nodded, and then turned her back and hung her head.

Timothy turned back to the intercom. "Candice, I need you to move away from the door."

"Please," Candice said, "help."

"Step away from the door." Timothy hated himself for how cold he sounded. He didn't like Candice, but he wouldn't wish that kind of death on anyone.

"Move aside," Dana said as she stepped up to the intercom. She pressed the button. "Candice, my babies are in here," she said. "Please, you are very contagious, and if you die right outside the door, we won't be able to risk leaving for a long time. But Heather isn't doing well, and I don't know if we can stay here. Help me protect my babies."

Candice wiped blood from her chin with the back of her hand. Black lines streaked through the whites of her eyes as they began to bulge. "I… had a baby… once."

Black lines of blood ran down her neck from her ears and streaked down her cheeks from her eyes. It coated her chin and chest. She backed away, dropping her finger from the button, cutting off sound from the basement. Her mouth opened in a scream Timothy couldn't hear. She stumbled into the farthest corner, sinking to the ground, her tiny form on the black-and-white screen convulsing.

Dana began to cry, covering her mouth with her hand, and Timothy pulled his mother into an embrace. They both watched until Candice stopped moving long enough for the floodlight to blink off, plunging the basement into darkness.

Chapter 32

Zara Williams

Zara's eyes fluttered open. Hard concrete had been her bed, but her head rested upon something soft. Sunlight filtered in through the stairwell's one opaque white wall opposite where Zara had slept. Her back was to a concrete wall, and the shadows underneath the stairwell were directly in front of her. A lump moved in the dark. Zara tensed, the air squeezing out of her lungs as she pressed against the concrete.

A grandmotherly voice broke through her panic. "You awake, dear?"

The lump unfolded, and a lantern switched on to reveal a woman with dark grey hair, wrinkles aplenty, and a crooked nose. She had kind blue eyes, though, and while her smile was missing a few teeth, it was genuine. She sat upon a sleeping bag with a few blankets piled up near one end, and butted up against the wall was a small cart on wheels, full to the brim with bulging black trash bags. A ragged old backpack was on the floor next to her.

Zara's racing heart slowed, and she allowed herself to take a breath. She sat up, groaning with the effort. Her head pounded, and her mouth was so dry. She picked up the blanket that had been rolled up and stuck under her head. She squashed her immediate assumption that she was in danger simply for being in the presence of a stranger. *If this woman wanted to hurt me, she could have. There have to be good people left.*

"I guess this is yours?" she asked.

"It is," the woman said cheerfully. "You looked like you could use it."

"Thank you." Zara's voice was scratchy, and she put a hand to her throat, frowning. The movement sparked a stab of pain through her arm and she held it out, grimacing. The t-shirt scraps she'd tied around her wounds were gone, removed when the woman had applied antibiotic cream the night before. She barely remembered that. The cut on her arm was newly scabbed over, but the skin around it was swollen.

"It's rough out there, is it?" the woman asked.

"What?" Zara's mind was still a little fuzzy.

"You were too dazed last night to tell me much, but I assume someone did that to you." She didn't point to her arm, instead opting for a gesture that seemed to encompass Zara's whole body.

"Yeah," Zara said, remembering the man with the black-rimmed glasses. "Someone stole my car. I remember walking through the city… someone was shot outside the hospital…" She squeezed her eyes shut, trying to piece together what she'd seen and done in her exhaustion the night before. "You helped me."

"It was nothing," the woman said. "Just gave you some pain killers and a blanket. Anyone could have done that."

"From what I've seen, I don't think just anyone *would* have done that." Zara leaned her head back against the wall and winced as the wound on the back of her head touched. "I'm a mess," she said.

"I'd say let's get you to the hospital, but…" The woman shrugged. "They're not taking new patients right now. Whoever you saw get shot, it wasn't the first. Old Mitch has lost his mind." Her eyes went wide, she made an "o" with her mouth, and she twirled her finger by her temple. "He's always been a little off his rocker."

"My friends are inside." Zara's stomach sank. "I don't know what I'm going to do." Her hand rested on the bulge in her pocket where Lizzy's phone was securely tucked away. She needed Lizzy to unlock it so she could find out more about Jordan.

"Well, I don't have much, but you can stay with me if you need to." She began digging in her backpack. "Name's Nina," she said as she pulled out a bottle of water. She shifted onto her knees, crawled forward, and held out the bottle.

"Oh no," Zara said, though she couldn't help but stare at the water. "You should keep it. Things are getting bad out there. You shouldn't be giving away supplies."

"It's all right," Nina said, shoving the bottle toward her.

"Maybe just a sip, then." Zara took it and opened the cap, not caring that it wasn't sealed. She took a swig and swallowed. The water was a bit musty, but it staved off her thirst. She handed it back. "I need to figure out how to get into the hospital."

"They've locked and sealed tight all the doors but the main entrance," Nina said. "They even closed the warming and cooling center in the back."

"The what?" Zara asked.

"They got a room in the back for people like me. Keeps us cool in the summer, warm in the winter. And it keeps us out of their Emergency Department waiting rooms," Nina said. "But it's closed now, and there's no way inside except through Old Mitch and that new kid, Brandt."

Zara frowned. "You know the security guards by name?"

"I'm a people person," Nina said.

Using the wall as support, Zara struggled to her feet. "Thanks for the info," she said as she headed for the steps.

"You going somewhere?" Nina got to her feet and shuffled out from beneath the stairwell.

"I'm going to get to my friends," Zara said. "I don't know how, but… I've got to find a way. I should be able to see the hospital better from the top of the garage. I'm hoping I can make a plan from there."

She hobbled up the stairs, focusing on the ascent. Her body was sore from head to toe, and a grimace accompanied every movement. Her right arm throbbed, and sharp pangs coursed through her left hand. Instead of gripping the railing, she leaned against it with her left elbow and side, doing her best to haul herself up one step at a time. She took a break at the first landing, leaning against the wall. *There's no way I'm going to make it up to the top.* She narrowed her eyes at the next flight of stairs. The door at the next landing would take her to the second floor of the garage. *That will have to be high enough.* Footsteps drew Zara's attention to the flight of stairs she'd just come up.

Nina got to the landing and held out an arm. "Come on," she said.

"It's okay," Zara said, "I can do this by myself. You've already helped me a lot. Really, you should be trying to get out of here, like out of the city. Go into the country. Stay away from people."

"Ha! Into the country?" Nina pursed her lips. "Country folk don't want a homeless lady sleepin' in their barn. I'm almost invisible in the city. I can go where I want, and no one bothers me unless I bother them. But I'm bored, and you need help." She held out her hand again and raised her eyebrows.

Zara looked at the stairs again and then back at Nina. "Okay," she said. "Thanks."

Nina wrapped an arm around Zara and helped her up the stairs. The older woman was surprisingly steady. Zara pushed open the door and exited the stairwell. Directly in front of her, a bloodied face with bulging eyes stared at her behind the window of a vehicle that had come to a crooked stop near the stairwell. She gasped and jumped backward, pressing against the door. More bodies lay strewn on the ground and over the hoods of vehicles.

"Oh, it's been like that since yesterday," Nina said. "It's like that on the first floor. Didn't you see when you came in?"

Zara shook her head and swallowed hard. "I was kind of out of it."

"Yeah, it all got kinda crazy when folks found out about the pop-up clinic. Sick people practically swarmed the place. That's when they locked down the hospital." Nina shook her head. "It all went downhill from there."

"But the hospital… the people inside are okay?" Zara asked.

Nina shrugged. "Don't know," she said. "I'm guessing so. Otherwise, who are they guarding?"

Zara turned from the grotesque sight and walked up to the chest-high concrete wall that lined the perimeter of the garage. She ducked, peeking out over the wall at the sight of the security guards at the door. Zara gestured for Nina to get down, too, but she just shook her head and said, "They know I'm here."

"Okay, just, don't look suspicious," Zara said as she turned her attention back to the hospital. She scanned the building, taking note of the balconies on the second floor.

"If the doorways are blocked," Zara mumbled to herself, "maybe I could get inside by way of a balcony? But… how?"

"Can you climb a tree?" Nina asked.

"Normally, yes," Zara said. "Right now… I'm not sure. I could try."

"Well, that tree right there is the closest one to a balcony," Nina said, pointing.

Zara squinted at the tree in question. It was tall enough, but she wasn't sure the branches could hold her weight. "The trunk looks thick, but the branches?" Zara bit her lip, studying it. She could possibly climb up the center of the tree where the trunk and branches were thickest, but by the time the branches reached the railing of the balcony, they were little more than sticks. She could try to jump mid-branch, perhaps, but there was another problem. "It's so close to the entrance. The security guards will see me."

"All you need is a distraction," Nina said, grinning. "And, like I said, I'm bored."

"Why are you helping me?" Zara asked.

"Because you seem like you need it, dear." Nina tilted her head. "Isn't that reason enough?"

"I guess it should be…" Zara backed away from the wall, limping, and stood straighter as she approached the stairwell again. "Do you think you can do this, though? I don't want you to get hurt. That Mitch guy seemed a little trigger happy, if I remember last night right."

Nina chuckled. "Old Mitch wouldn't hurt me, even if he is crazy. We go way back."

Zara opened the door with the tips of her fingers, careful not to grab hold of the handle with her injured hand. "What if I can't climb the tree? My arm, my hand… I'm weak and exhausted. I could barely climb these stairs."

"You could wait with me a few days." Nina offered her hand again.

"No." Zara's hand went to the phone in her pocket. "I need to get inside today. I'm going to have to suck it up and push through the pain." She moved forward and descended the stairs on her own, without Nina's help. It wasn't much, but it made her feel stronger.

Nina went out first, not bothering to keep the tents between herself and the entrance. "Hey, Mitch!" She waved cheerfully.

"Now, Nina," Mitch's voice carried as Zara kept low and ran toward the cover of the tents, quietly coming up beside them and peeking around. The older security guard and his protégé had opened the doors. The man had one hand on his gun but held out his other hand in front of him. "Stay right there," he said. "Don't come closer."

"I'm not sick. I wanted to see if you fine gentlemen wouldn't mind sparing me a few granola bars from the kitchen, maybe a few water bottles?" Nina came at them from an angle so that as Mitch and Brandt came out of the doors, their backs were to the tree that potentially gave access to the balcony.

"I don't think so, Nina." Mitch shook his head, hand still on his gun.

"Mitch, maybe we should let Nina inside," Brandt said. "I mean, it's not like she's a stranger. Everyone around here knows her."

"We only got so much food," Mitch said. "You wanna leave so she can come inside? Split your rations with her? This mess could last weeks!"

"But it's Nina!" Brandt said.

Zara scurried toward the tree as the two men debated. She slipped around it and hid behind the trunk which was just a bit wider than she was. She pressed against the bark, hands on the rough wood, sweat dripping from her brow. No one yelled after her, so she looked around the tree to check on Nina.

The woman tapped her foot, arms crossed, as if she were feeling impatient. She made an arching gesture with one hand, and then pointed to the doors. Mitch unholstered his gun but just held it at his side. He shook his head firmly.

I've got to get up there so Nina can leave.

Zara jumped up and grabbed hold of the lowest branch. Her eyes watered as the bark bit into her palm, reopening that wound. Hanging tightly to the tree branch, she walked up the trunk and swung up onto the branch, straddling it. She sat back against the trunk, legs dangling, and breathed in through her nose, out through her mouth. The quick movements had made her queasy.

Keep going. Get up. Push through it. I'm a survivor, right?

She reached for another branch and pulled herself up into a crouch. She couldn't stand upright. The branches were too close for that, so she crawled upward, leaves rustling with her progress. The sun shone through the leaves to throw patterns of dappled light on her skin and clothes. Life buzzed around her. Two squirrels bounded away, rushing down the trunk at the sight of her. A bluebird cocked its head from a high branch, flitting away when she got too close. Ants marched in lines up and down the tree as if she weren't there, tickling her skin as they crawled across her hand. She shook them off and kept climbing. When the black railing came into view, she almost shouted for joy. The top rail was about five feet from the trunk of the tree. The spindly tips of branches brushed against it but didn't provide much cover. Once she jumped, she'd be exposed and need to haul herself over the railing as quickly as possible. Her eyes roamed from the railing to the ground, and her stomach lurched from the thought of falling.

Mitch's voice rose. "I'm losing patience, Nina!"

That spurred Zara onward. The last thing she wanted was for Nina to get hurt. Even if the woman thought Mitch was her friend, Zara didn't like his tone as he yelled at her. She inched out onto the branch, heartbeat wild in her chest, hands trembling. She tested her weight on the branch, holding out her hands on either side for balance. A gap in the leaves opened up as she neared the railing, and Zara glanced toward Nina and the security guards. She almost lost her balance as she saw Mitch with his gun now pointed at Nina.

I've got to hurry so she can leave. Zara took a deep breath and jumped, arms outstretched. Branches scratched at her cheeks and her arms and tugged at her clothes. When her fingers curled around the rail, she gripped it tightly, gritting her teeth as stinging pain zipped up her arm and her hand started to throb. She scrambled for footing, her foot slipping.

She frantically looked over her shoulder as she kicked at the wall, her shoes scraping against it too loudly. Nina took a step forward in the same moment Zara found a foothold and launched herself over the railing. She hit brick and bit her tongue hard enough to draw blood as she struggled to keep a shout of pain inside. But then a gunshot *cracked* and echoed off the walls of the hospital, and Zara scrambled on hands and knees to the railing. She clawed her way to standing and craned her neck to see. Nina was crumpled on the ground.

Brandt was on his knees beside her, hands on his head. "This isn't what I signed up for, damn it!" he shouted.

"No," Zara whispered. A scream tore at her throat, burst within her chest, but she couldn't let it out. She backed away until she hit a smooth white wall. Her fingernails dug into her skin, and the pain felt right. It felt *necessary*. Her whole body shook with the tension from the scream she kept captive until she slammed her fist behind her into the wall. The tiniest bit of tension oozed out of her, and she turned to face the wall. Zara held up her trembling fist. A drop of blood seeped from her palm. It wasn't enough. Zara stopped thinking. Her knuckles cracked as they hit the wall, and then she hit it again, and again, and again. Each time she pulled her hand away, she left behind a spot of blood. Each shot of pain connected to a source of internal agony.

Mom. Dad. Auntie. Dead.

Jordan. Missing.

Nina. Dead.

Her hands grew numb, but she kept punching.

I'm stuck with Mr. Peters.

The world is ending.

Blood ran down the wall, stark red against the white.

"Zee?" A horrified voice sounded from behind Zara.

She spun, seething, angry tears rolling down her face. Lizzy stood there, her hands covering her mouth, her too-wide eyes staring at her, no—staring *past* her to the blood on the wall. Zara fell to her knees.

"We're all going to die," she whispered, looking up at Lizzy.

"You can't think that way." Lizzy knelt in front of Zara.

"You should leave me behind," Zara said.

"What?" Lizzy's mouth pinched as she narrowed her eyes.

"I'm no good," Zara said. "My parents are dead, and all I ever did for them was drain them of every cent to their name. I—"

"Like, when you had cancer?" Lizzy asked incredulously. "Are you serious? Your parents loved you. They—"

"I wanted to let your dad die," Zara cut her off. "When I was doing CPR, I thought about letting him die."

"Stop it, Zee." Anger laced each word.

"I left my brother, alone, because I was scared." She pulled the phone out of her pocket and stared at it. "I let this nice old homeless lady help me, and now she's dead because of it. She's lying just out there, right now." Zara looked up. "I should stay behind and die. I'm not a good person, Liz."

"I said, stop it!" Liz smacked Zara's face, just hard enough to sting. "You stop talking about my best friend like that."

Zara put a hand to her cheek, frowning at Lizzy. "Didn't you hear anything I just said?"

"I heard a bunch of bull." Lizzy jabbed her finger into Zara's chest. "Your parents loved you. They wanted to keep you alive. I guarantee you they didn't care about the money. And last time I checked, you saved my dad's life. Now, about this homeless woman, I don't know what happened, but I don't see a gun in your hand. Did you pull the trigger?"

"Liz, it's my fau—"

"Did. You. Pull. The. Trigger?" Lizzy raised her eyebrows as if daring Zara to stray from answering.

"Well, no, but—"

"Then, I'm sure that woman made her own choices for her own reasons." She took the phone out of Zara's hand. "And as for Jordan? We're going to charge this thing and figure out where he is." She stood up. "Stop blaming yourself for everything. You're not a burden, Zee. You're my best friend."

Zara struggled to her feet, suddenly even more drained than she'd been last night. She couldn't stay standing, so she stumbled to a bench against the wall and sat down. She offered Lizzy a small smile, though her heart was still aching. "You know that's some Captain-America-level speech giving right there? I didn't know you had it in you."

"You know I have no idea what that means." Lizzy sat next to her. "But I do know I've never seen you go all Hulk like that." Zara quirked an eyebrow and Lizzy shrugged. "I do pay attention to your ramblings about old-school stuff sometimes."

"Well, I'm sorry." Zara held up her hands. They were still a little numb, though the sting was starting to set in. The knuckles were swollen and bleeding. "I guess I sort of freaked out."

"Don't do it again, okay?" Lizzy said. "Promise me."

"I promise." Zara wasn't sure if she could keep that promise. She hadn't known she was even capable of such rage. It had come upon her so suddenly.

"Good." Lizzy held up the phone. "Let's charge this thing."

"It's already charged." Zara leaned over and pushed the button on the side. The screen glowed with their picture. "Someone at the gas station plugged it in."

"Then let's take a look." Lizzy unlocked the phone and tapped on the screen a few times. "Okay. It's in my files." She tapped one more time and then held the phone sideways. The video took up the entire screen. She pressed play.

Zara and Lizzy gasped at the same time. The first frame was of Mr. Peters.

Chapter 33

Timothy Peters

Timothy dabbed Heather's forehead as her teeth chattered. Her skin was cold and clammy, and her breathing was too rapid. For the first half of the night, she'd been either unconscious or awake but nonsensical. Timothy's only hope that she would recover from the shock of blood loss was the fact she'd had a few lucid moments in the past few hours. Her trembling was slightly more manageable. Sleep had claimed her, but it was anything but peaceful. Heather grimaced and arched her back, her arms popping out of the blankets. She blinked a few times, groaning, and Timothy gently tucked her arms back under the covers.

"It's all right." Timothy's hushed voice seemed to soothe her as her pained expression softened a little.

The door to the first, tiny bedroom opened, and Dana quietly walked out. His mother sat at Heather's bedside. "How is she, Timmy?"

"She's... better than she was before." Timothy's shoulders sagged. "I feel so helpless."

"And how about you?" Dana asked. "Are you okay?"

Timothy's chest tightened. "I'm perfectly fine." He ground his teeth. "I mean, besides the fact that my stupidity is what did this to Heather."

"Sweetie, this is that Frank Russo's fault, not yours." Dana reached out and patted Timothy's arm. "If it weren't for you, he and those goons could have killed us all or thrown us out of our own home in the middle of the sickness that killed everyone else."

"If it weren't for me, Frank wouldn't have known where we live." Timothy rubbed his hands over his face a few times to keep the exhaustion at bay. He'd forfeited sleep in order to keep an eye on Heather. "I'm an idiot, Mom. I should have made her stay downstairs with you and the kids."

Dana raised an eyebrow. "No one *makes* Heather do anything."

"I know," Timothy said darkly. "I should have tried harder. She can be so stubborn."

"I didn't say her tendencies were a bad thing, Timmy," Dana said. "I've always respected the way you work with her, defend her, even against me sometimes. She made the decision, and you didn't fight her on it not because you're an idiot but because you love her." She shifted and averted her eyes. "Your father doesn't always understand that, and... I think it hurts us both. Trust me. Letting her make her own decision was the right thing to do."

"Yeah," Heather croaked. Her eyes—sunken in dark circles—fluttered open. "What she said." She smiled weakly. "Don't you make me repeat it, Timothy." She sucked in sharply, her expression contorting in pain. "That Tylenol isn't doing much," she said. "I'm going to need something stronger if we're going to move."

"Move?" Timothy shook his head. "We can't. You can't."

"We have to," Heather said.

"She's right." Dana hugged her middle. "Those men will be back, and we don't know when. If they burn the house, like Frank said he would, we'd be in trouble. The structure could collapse in on the basement, making it impossible for us to get out. And if the house burns, the solar panels will be destroyed. Without those, this bunker won't be able to keep us safe."

Timothy wracked his brain for a way to prevent that from happening, but they'd used all his best ideas for the first attack. "What are we going to do?"

"Your father had a backup shelter," Dana said, "but he hadn't planned on using it so soon after a disaster occurred."

"Another bunker? More supplies?" Timothy perked up a little.

Dana shook her head. "I don't know if there's a whole bunker, or if it's just a secondary place to hunker down. I'm not even sure if he finished with the preparations. He only started putting together a second contingency plan recently."

"Well, what *do* you know, then?" Timothy asked.

"Your father would want us to go to New Horizons Lab." Dana breathed in deeply.

"In the city?" Timothy shook his head. "That's insane. We can't go there."

"It's the only place we can go," Dana said. "Frank wouldn't know where to find us there, and that's the only other place I know of that's sure to have at least some supplies. I'm not sure what supplies or how much. I just know that Walter told me to go there if the bunker was ever compromised."

"There has to be another option," Timothy said.

"Tim," Heather said, "we can't be here when they come back."

He closed his eyes. "We're between a rock and a hard place, aren't we?" He pressed his lips together and stood up. "We've got to figure out how to move Heather without causing her too much pain or re-opening the wound."

"We can make a stretcher of sorts. The twin trundle mattress in the second bedroom is pretty thin," Dana said. "We could break apart the metal frame of the bunk bed for the poles. Duct tape the mattress to the poles?"

Timothy nodded. "That could work. Why don't you and George get started on that while I go up and find that Percocet you said you had in your bathroom?"

"I also might have some left over anti-biotics," Dana said. "We might need to find more later, but I think giving her what we have would be a good idea. What do you think, Heather?"

Heather managed a small nod. "Sounds good to me," she said.

Timothy glanced at the dark screen of the intercom. "I'd better take something to cover Candice with," he said. "George knows her. It might be... traumatizing for him to see her like that."

"Good thinking." Dana rushed into the storage room and came back out with a small, folded tarp. "Use this."

Timothy left the bunker for the basement, taking the stairs between slowly. When he got to the top, he took a deep breath, steeling himself for the color version of a dead Candice. The bolts slid open with ease, and he cracked the door open. The movement brought the floodlight to life, illuminating the open space beyond. He paused for a moment, listening for movement or voices, just in case Frank and his men were already there.

The thought of the mobsters made Timothy's skin crawl. Sweat beaded on his forehead as he stepped into the warm basement and very carefully closed the door behind him. Still listening, he focused on the staircase and soundlessly crossed the basement, setting the tarp down and tiptoeing up the stairs. Candice could wait. He wanted to make sure the coast was clear before he did anything else.

The rest of the house was in utter disarray. Everything was broken. Blood spattered the floor, soaked the couch, and smeared the walls. The floor by the front door was discolored from the chemical spill. A bird was perched on the cracked television, and it cocked its head as he rounded the corner into the kitchen area. He stared for a moment at the pool of congealed blood where he'd found Heather after she'd first been shot.

A vision of seeking Frank out, of choking the life out of him with his bare hands, materialized in Timothy's mind. "Frank's going to pay for this," he whispered, seething.

The vocalization of pure loathing in his voice made him take half a step back. Never in his life had he put so much hatred into someone's name, not even when he was at his angriest with his father. He balled his hands into fists. He wasn't going to take it back. He didn't have the time or the resources to hunt down the man, but Timothy would kill him without hesitation if they crossed paths again. He'd wished over the past couple of days that he had the guts to pull the trigger when he'd first met Frank. Part of him was frightened that he no longer had any question about his ability to do so, but another part accepted it, welcomed it even.

Timothy tore his gaze from the spot where Heather had fallen and focused on the task at hand. It wasn't hard to find the Percocet and Amoxil in the upstairs master bath. The Percocet was almost full, and the Amoxil had six pills left. He looked through the rest of the pill bottles, finding another half bottle of Keflex antibiotics in the back. For once, he was grateful for his father's tendency to never finish a prescription.

He stuck the bottles in his pocket and headed back downstairs and then into the basement, his stomach churning as the light switched on. He picked up the tarp and unfolded it, walking slowly to stand over Candice. She was covered in blood, and bruises peeked out from under the hem of her skirt and her neckline. The welt was visible on her neck, scratched open, still glistening.

"I guess I should say something," Timothy started, looking up at the ceiling, trying to remember the woman who had willingly backed away from the door, the woman who had gone to find a doctor for his wife, instead of the woman who had practically welcomed Frank and his men into the community. "Um… thank you for trying, and uh… if we ever see your husband, we'll be sure to let him know that you died heroically."

Timothy looked back at her to place the tarp, but he paused and frowned. Her eyes were closed, and while her eyelids were swollen and bruised, her eyes weren't popping out of her head. Her lips parted, and her chest moved just slightly. Timothy jumped back, dropping the tarp with a yelp. His heart thundered in his ears, and the blood drained from his face as Candice opened her eyes to slits.

She smacked her lips, dried blood cracking and flaking on her lips and chin. She raised her eyebrows as if she were trying to open her eyes wider, but they were too swollen to allow it. "Is this… Heaven?" she asked, frowning. She blinked and groaned. "No… this must be Hell."

"C-Candice?" Timothy stammered.

Her chin fell to her chest, and one hand weakly flopped against the skirt of her blood-stained dress. Her lip quivered, and she let out a whining, high-pitched cry. "This… this…" She sniffed between words. "This… is… *Armani.*" She let herself slump all the way to the floor and put her arm over her eyes.

Timothy barely registered her words. "You're not dead."

"Why… does everything… huuurrrt?" She sobbed.

His mouth dropped open, and his brain had trouble registering what was happening. No one survived the sickness. Did they? Out of all the radio broadcasts he'd heard, out of all he'd seen, Candice was the only person he knew of to live through it.

"What does this mean?" he whispered. He backed away and sat on the steps, staring at the woman crying on the floor. He ran his fingers through his hair and let out a shaky breath.

Their shelter was no longer safe. The mob was after him. His wife was possibly dying. His only hope of keeping his family safe was to get them to the lab, going back into the chaos that was Boston. And Candice, of all people, had become possibly the most important person on the planet. The world had gone completely mad.

Chapter 34

Zara Williams

A heaviness settled over Zara as the video came to an end for a third time. A lump had formed in her throat from the first few seconds of the first time she'd watched it, and she couldn't get rid of it. Grief lodged itself in her esophagus and refused to budge.

The video had started with an angry picture of Mr. Peters. It had zoomed out, and Zara's heart had skipped a beat at the sight of her brother, Jordan. As the camera continued to zoom out, a row of ten white cubes accompanied by ten individuals in Green Earth Futurist t-shirts could be seen behind him.

"Today," Jordan said, his eyes bloodshot, "the Green Earth Futurists are going to change the world. Over the past few decades, every part of the planet has seen mosquito borne diseases run rampant. Finally, when the problem hit the United States, our country took notice. My own aunt lost a child due to the Zika virus. It's affected everyone I know. The mosquito population has begun killing human beings at a rate of one and a half million per year, and our government placed the responsibility of discovering a way to curb those deaths upon one Mr. Walter Peters, the CEO and owner of Vanguard." Jordan cleared his throat. "Through genome editing at New Horizons Lab, Mr. Peters succeeded in creating a mosquito that could effectively wipe out all mosquitos." Jordan scowled, sweat beading on his forehead. He swayed a little as he spoke as if he weren't feeling well. "But he kept the new breed to himself, even going so far as to incinerate batches of larvae. And why would he do this? Because he cared more about making money than stopping the disease. Vanguard's plan was to hold on to batches of these world-changing mosquitos and release them only upon an exorbitant payment to the cities and countries around the world that could afford it."

The camera cut away to a dark room, and a man Zara didn't recognize spoke. He sat behind a white, plastic table, and a GEF symbol was painted on the wall behind him. "This video was recorded the day the sickness broke out. Note that the team at the World's Fair, led by Jordan Williams, a brave martyr for the cause, had technical difficulties during the actual release of the mosquitos. They opted to shoot a new video in the same area, staging a release for the promotional material hours after the actual release occurred."

"Wait, did he call Jordan a martyr?" Zara had said, snatching the phone and rewinding it to listen to the stranger again. "Does that mean… is he dead?" Zara's eyes were bone dry; she couldn't cry anymore. But the news sucked the life out of her. She had needed a minute before she could continue watching the video.

It picked back up, the video cutting to a close-up of Jordan once more. "With help from those closest to Mr. Peters, the Green Earth Futurists did something about it." He squeezed his eyes shut for a moment. "We stole thousands of…" He coughed into his elbow, shook his head, and looked back at the camera. "… thousands of larvae before they could be destroyed, and…" He coughed again. "Hey, guys?" He backed away from the camera and turned around. "I've got a killer headache, and this cough is rough."

As he stumbled back toward the cubes, the others became visible. Two or three of them were rubbing their temples. One was attempting to stop a nosebleed. All of them, including Jordan, were scratching at growing welts on their legs, arms, or necks.

Jordan put a hand to his side and slowly pulled up his shirt. A purplish red bruise had begun to form there. "What the…" He coughed, this time spewing blood. Jordan fell to the ground and pressed his palms against his eyes.

Zara gasped at the video and looked away. "I can't watch this," she said.

"I'll skip ahead," Lizzy said, voice shaking. "There. It's back to the guy in the basement."

"What… what happened… did you see?" Zara turned to Lizzy.

"Jordan… I don't think he made it." Lizzy spoke gently. "I was fast forwarding it, but I think most of the GEF activists died, too. A few ran off, probably into the World's Fair where they spread the sickness."

Zara swallowed hard, and it hit her like a punch to the gut. Part of her had expected Jordan to be dead; she just hadn't wanted to admit it. She shook her head. "This doesn't make sense. He said the mosquitos were supposed to eliminate the mosquito population, not spread a disease."

Lizzy, face pale, shook her head. "I don't know, Zee. Maybe this guy will explain it." She played the video.

"We at GEF spent *months* organizing this release worldwide. We did everything in our power to save the world only to discover that Mr. Peters and Vanguard were not sending their proprietary world-saving mosquitos to be incinerated," the stranger said. "Instead, they were covering up their real purpose. Biological warfare using mosquitos as a vector. And almost every one of our brave team members who risked their freedoms to spread hope to the world, ended up dying because of Vanguard's secrets. We only have proof of one team's deaths because of a technical mistake. But now, no one can deny what's happened."

Lizzy shoved the phone away from her onto the bench as if it were on fire. She stood up and backed away. "My dad is a monster." Lizzy's cheeks burned red. "Like, he's a super villain from one of your movies. All he needs are tentacles and sharper teeth."

"He knew what this was from the start," Zara said. "I… I *knew* it, and I just… let him shut me down. I let him walk all over me and make me feel like an idiot."

"How could he lie like that?" Lizzy put a hand to her forehead. "Maybe… maybe he has an explanation. Maybe they're wrong about him."

"Lizzy, what about what he said at the gas station when he was totally out of it?" Zara stood up. "He asked how *it* got out. And he's kept us indoors when he knew mosquitos would be active." She shook her head. "He knew, Liz."

Lizzy's forehead creased. "No, he kept us safe, Zee. He suspected but… he was confused by this. I know he was."

"He wasn't confused, Liz. He was scared." Zara scoffed. "He had us leave the fair quickly because he didn't want to be questioned by authorities."

"No," Liz shook her head. "There has to be an explanation. You've seen how quickly this thing spreads. He got us out of there because he was trying to keep us safe."

"Fine." Zara jutted out her chin toward the doors leading back inside. "Let's go ask him ourselves."

"He… he's still sick." Lizzy backed away from the door. "We shouldn't… we can't. *I* can't."

"Then I will. I won't let him get away with this any longer." Zara turned on her heel and marched into the hospital, down the hall, and into the empty waiting room. The pain of her injuries was dampened by pure anger. She burst through the door in the back that led into the area reserved for patients' hospital rooms. "Mr. Peters!" she shouted. "Where are you?"

Bertie stuck her head out in the hall. "Zara?" She hurried down the hall. "You're okay!" She paused and looked her up and down. "Well, you're *here* at least. We should get a nurse to take a look at you. There's still a few around."

"No, thank you," Zara said firmly. "I need to see Mr. Peters."

"Where is Lizzy?" Bertie frowned.

The door from the waiting room opened. "I'm here," Lizzy said. She didn't look directly at Zara, instead nodding reluctantly down the hall. "He's this way."

"Are you girls okay?" Bertie asked.

"Not even a little. Thank you for your concern, but right now, all we need is to speak to Mr. Peters." Zara raised her eyebrows at Lizzy. "Are you going to show me where he is?"

Lizzy closed her eyes, her bottom lip trembling. "Follow me," she said quietly.

Zara's shoes slapped the vinyl flooring. "He has to give us answers, Liz. I know you love him. I know he's your dad. But this is too big to let go."

"I know," Lizzy whispered as she stopped outside a room. She looked at Zara. "You need to be calm, though, okay? Let me wake him. Let me talk. I… I don't want him to have another stroke or heart attack."

Zara stiffened. "We can't just—"

"Like you said, he's my dad. Not yours. Let me do this."

Zara sighed and relented. "Okay," she said. "If you confront him, I'll hang back."

"Thank you." Lizzy pushed open the door.

Zara followed her into the room to find Mr. Peters lying in a hospital bed, his upper body slightly elevated. He was asleep. Cords connected him to machines, and he was hooked up to meds via IVs. His breathing wasn't easy, though it wasn't exactly labored. Zara had never seen him look so fragile. It gave her a moment's pause before she remembered the contents of the video. She hardened herself toward him. He didn't deserve sympathy from her.

"Dad?" Lizzy came up beside Mr. Peters and took his hand.

Zara wanted to shake him awake. She wanted to slap him awake. Anger roiled inside at the sight of him. A part of her protested. *This isn't right. This isn't who I am.* But the rage blocked that little voice out.

Mr. Peters stirred and opened his eyes. "Hello, Bethie," he said, his voice a raw, scratchy whisper. He slowly turned his head to Zara. "Zara," he said, frowning. "What happened to you?"

"As if you care," Zara said.

"What?" He blinked several times, his frown deepening as he pressed a button to further elevate his upper body. "Of course I care," he said. "You saved my life. That's what the nurses said." His eyes were misting. "Thank you. I… I underestimated you."

"Damn right you did," Zara snapped.

"Zee, c'mon," Lizzy pled. "Please, let me do this."

"I'm trying to make things right," Mr. Peters said. "I'm sorry for how I treated you, Zara." He looked to his daughter. "What do you want her to let you do? What's going on?"

Lizzy pulled out the phone and handed it to him. "I downloaded this before we lost satellite signals. We need an explanation."

Mr. Peters took the phone. "What is this?" he asked.

Zara narrowed her eyes. "This is the end of your charade, Mr. Peters."

His face somehow got paler as his lips pressed into a thin line. He played the video. At first, he furrowed his brow in confusion. Then, he shook his head, putting his hand to his forehead and cursing under his breath. He had the nerve to look at Zara with pity when Jordan's death was confirmed. And when it was over, he lowered the phone to the bed slowly. He leaned his head back and breathed out slowly as if he'd been holding it in.

"At least now I know how this happened." He sounded relieved.

"So, you didn't know?" Lizzy straightened up, her eyes brightening for a moment.

He met her eyes for a moment and opened his mouth, but then he shut it again and averted his eyes. "I didn't know how it got out, but… what they said about Vanguard, that's all true," he said. "It's not the whole truth, but it's the start."

"We should leave you here to rot." Zara spat.

"Zee, I asked you to let me do this," Lizzy said.

"I know, Liz, but… I just, I can't. Look at me. I'm exhausted. I've seen more death over the past five days than anyone should see in a lifetime. And I'm on my last leg. I hurt *everywhere* and not just on the outside, in *here*." She pounded her chest. "I've lost everything because of him."

"You're right," Mr. Peters said. "Elizabeth told me about your family. But she also told me that your cousin is alive."

"As far as I know," Zara said. "But that's just it—I don't know, not for sure."

"If she's alive, though, she needs you," Mr. Peters said. "And I can get you home. Regardless of what I've done, you need me."

Zara scoffed. "We don't need you. I can get us home."

Mr. Peters's eyes hardened. "Are you threatening to take my daughter from me?"

"She can't threaten that, Dad," Lizzy said. "But I can. And yeah, I'm having a hard time imaging spending any more time with you right now."

"Can you get to my labs?" Mr. Peters asked, his voice becoming cold. "Do either one of you know how to find scientists who can help undo this? How about supplies along the way? What are you going to do when you run across the kind of people that did that to you, Zara?" He narrowed his eyes at her.

"I... He caught me off guard." Zara tried to speak confidently, but that was only half true. If she had known the man in the black-rimmed glasses was coming, what would she have done? She could have run, maybe, but she'd still have lost all their supplies.

"What if you come across people who want to lock you up again?" Mr. Peters asked. "Have you forgotten that I saved you? Both of you?" He looked at Lizzy. "I've kept both of you alive. You both owe me. And besides—" He sneered "—I didn't unleash this on the world. I tried to destroy it as soon as I realized what it was. Your delinquent brother and those idiot activists, they're the ones to blame. They were the ones that let this out. It's not my fault they were too stupid to know what they were stealing."

"Dad, I can't believe you just said that," Lizzy backed away from him.

"You girls can hate me all you want," Mr. Peters said. "But, Elizabeth, you are *my* daughter. You are going to stay with me. I am one of the only people in the world who can help stop this from killing everyone." He breathed out through his nose, rolled his shoulders, and met Zara's eyes with a steely gaze. "You need me. The whole world needs me."

Zara's insides squirmed. No matter how much she wanted to deny it, Mr. Peters was right. But he was missing one important detail. She stepped forward, banishing her discomfort at being so close to him. She came closer and snatched the phone from him. He grasped for it, but she was too quick. She backed away, out of his reach.

"Here's the thing, Mr. Peters. You're lying in a hospital bed. We know your deepest darkest secrets. I just saw a security guard put a bullet through a perfectly wonderful woman. What do you think he'd do if we told him what we know? If we showed him this video?" Zara raised her eyebrows.

"You wouldn't," Mr. Peters said between gritted teeth.

Zara ignored the shocked expression on her best friend's face as Lizzy looked at her. "Oh, I would. Because while you might be able to fix this mess you've created, you're also a liar. And a good one. I can't trust you when you say you know what to do. I can't trust that you're the *only* person that can fix this."

Mr. Peters's mouth flopped open and closed like a fish.

"So, we're going to reach an agreement." Zara slid the phone in her pocket. "You're going to help us get home, and you're going to do it without being an ass. Preferably, you're going to do it quietly. And when we get to Boston, you're going to fix this because it's the right thing. And then, you're going to go away. Far enough away that I don't ever have to see your face again. Otherwise, everyone is going to know that you were behind this. Got it?"

Mr. Peters worked his jaw back and forth. He reluctantly gave her a curt nod as he averted his eyes. That was enough for Zara.

"Let's go, Liz." Zara didn't take her eyes off Mr. Peters as his daughter did as she asked. She left him there, alone, and led Lizzy back to the waiting room.

"I asked you to let me handle my dad." Lizzy shook her head and plopped into the corner chairs of the room.

"Liz—"

She raised a hand. "I'm not a pawn, Zara. You... you treated me just like my dad treats me. No, it was worse because it came from you." She lay down and turned her back on Zara.

Zara sat in the row of chairs opposite her best friend. "I didn't mean it that way, Liz."

Lizzy didn't respond. Zara turned her back, too, and lay down, frowning. She'd taken the power from Mr. Peters. She'd said what she needed to say. But she didn't feel better. Instead, her options were cut off from her, and the few things she had left—her friendship with Lizzy, her cousin, *herself*—they were slipping through her fingers.

There was only one way forward. Zara had to enter the belly of the beast with the devil by her side.

Chapter 35

Alexander Roman

Alex pulled Naomi's leather journal out of his bag. He'd stashed it there back at the hotel and then had barely given it another thought, but after all they'd been through, he finally knew what to do with it. He opened it and brushed his fingertips over the pages, smiling at the sight of Naomi's handwriting. The pages were full of her thoughts, her notes on natural remedies, and her hopes for the future. Before, he'd barely been able to look at the cover of the journal, much less read the words inside. The journal was a representation of her, a part of her. And that was just what he needed. He found the perfect page and gently tore it free of the journal itself, lovingly placing the book back in his bag before folding the paper and sticking it in his pocket.

He stepped outside of Minnie's RV to a bright summer afternoon to find Lauren and Minnie chatting beneath the branches of a tree. They looked happy together, despite everything that had happened.

Alex, Oliver, Minnie, Lauren, and all those who'd been living in her building had taken shelter the night before in an abandoned building across the street. Alex had stood by Lauren, watching her home burn to the ground. That morning, Minnie had finally gotten to talk to Lauren. Both had asked Alex to stand in as a buffer, just in case, but it turned out that they didn't need him. He stood aside and listened.

"I'll go without ya, if ya want," Minnie had said. "I just… I want ya to know that I'm sorry. And that I'm so very proud to be your momma. You don't need me, Lauren. It's always been me that's needed you. I shouldna put my hang ups on your shoulders. I wish you'd come with me now, not 'cause I wanna control you, but 'cause I think Alex can get ya somewhere safe. Or… if not, if we die, we'd die havin' spent our last days together." Minnie had smiled sadly. "But Baby Girl, I know you'll make the best decision for you, and that's all that matters."

Before Minnie could walk away, Lauren had thrown her arms around her mother's neck and hugged her tight. "Thank you, Momma." She'd pulled back and agreed to walk with them to the park where they'd stashed the RV.

Alex kept his hands in his pockets, the smooth texture of the paper a comfort to him. He laughed as Samson rolled over next to Oliver on the grass, wagging his tail as Oliver vigorously scratched his belly. It was a moment of peace. It was time to remember his wife, to grieve her, and to give her the only burial he could.

"Oliver?" He called out to his son.

Oliver came running, Samson on his heels. The sight of Oliver *not* glued to someone's side, his eyes bright, a smile on his face… it was the best thing Alex had seen in a while.

"Yeah, Dad?" Oliver's voice didn't squeak or break. He sounded more like himself every minute.

But he still needs healing. He's not quite there yet. "I wanted to show you something." Alex brought out the piece of paper. "This is from your mother's journal." He hoped his plans would take his son another step down the road to recovery. How long the road stretched was a different story. *At least I can help him move forward.*

Oliver clutched the macrame purse slung across his chest and stared at the piece of paper. "What does it say?"

"Well, I'm going to get to that." He gestured toward a flower bed where purple irises were in bloom. He got to his knees. "Will you help me carefully dig this up? We've got to be gentle about it."

Oliver nodded, and they both set to work, digging their hands into the rich soil and working the plant free. Alex set it gently aside. He drew in a shaky breath and took the paper in his hands, unfolding it.

"This journal entry is about you," Alex said, and he began to read. "Oliver is getting to be such a gentleman. I hope he grows to be like his dad: gentle in all the right ways, strong when it counts." He swallowed hard. "There is no prouder mom in the whole wide world than me. I hope he knows that. I hope he knows how much I love him." Alex folded the piece of paper and looked at his son. "The journal has a lot of entries, some really similar to this one, and I think you should have it. It's a piece of her she's left behind." He looked back at the hole they'd made.

"You want to bury it here," Oliver said. He looked sadly at the note.

Alex nodded. "Yeah, bud. I want to bury it, and I want to talk about her, and I want to remember her always."

"I can't…" Oliver sniffed and wiped away a tear with the back of his hand. "I can't believe she's gone."

"She's still in here," Alex said, laying his hand across Oliver's heart. "And in here." He put his hand over his own.

Oliver reached for the note. "Can I do it?" he asked.

Alex handed over the paper. "Of course."

Oliver laid it in the hole and covered it with a handful of dirt. "She was the best mom," he said.

"The very best," Alex whispered.

Oliver broke down and sobbed then, and so did Alex, but it wasn't like the tears they'd cried before. These felt different. They felt like the beginning of a road to healing. They held each other for a long time before replanting the iris. Oliver asked for some time alone and went to sit by himself under a tree. He didn't shoo Samson away when the dog came to lay his head in his lap, though, and Alex once again was grateful for the lovable beast.

"You okay?" Minnie asked as Alex stepped inside the RV. She and Lauren had retreated inside to give him and Oliver some privacy.

"I'm okay," he said.

"I think I'm coming with you, after all," Lauren said, "if that's still okay with you?"

Alex smiled. "Yeah, that's all right with me."

Minnie slapped the side of the RV. "Old Harvey is gonna get us where we need to go," she said. "And he's gonna get us there together, as a family."

"As a family," Alex said. "I like the sound of that."

A ringing sound came from Alex's go-bag stashed in a compartment over the bed, and all three of them looked toward the sound with wide eyes.

"What is that?" Lauren asked.

"It's my sat-phone," Alex said, rushing over to the compartment and ripping it open. He dug in his go-bag for the phone and pulled it out. "Jonah?"

"Alex? You're still alive." He sounded surprised.

"Barely," Alex said, "but yes. I'm alive. Oliver's alive. And we're coming to Atlanta."

"I tried calling," Jonah said. "You didn't answer."

"The last twenty-four hours has been crazy. I had to stash my stuff somewhere safe," Alex said. "What's going on?"

Jonah coughed violently, and he groaned. "The CDC… it's been compromised."

"What?" Alex leaned against the elevated bed and slid down to sit on a rung of the small ladder that led up to it. "Jonah… are you sick?"

"I don't think I'm going to make it." A high-pitched whine came through the line, and it took Alex a minute to realize it was Jonah wheezing. "I'm dying," Jonah said.

"No." Alex swallowed hard and shook his head. "Jonah—"

"I have… information. Before I can't talk… you need to listen." A cough and a gurgle interrupted him. "If you make it here, I've left a van full of supplies for you in our facilities, but then, you've got to keep searching for a cure. And we know what's causing it, or… we know how it's being transmitted. Or… we know *a* way it *can be* transmitted. It *is* mosquitos, Alex. We don't know if they are the original cause, but we know they can carry it. And we know it's contagious." Another violent coughing fit was followed by a clattering noise as if the phone had been dropped.

"Jonah?" Alex shouted. "That doesn't make sense. Jonah, are you there?" He raked his fingers through his hair. He blinked rapidly, picturing a page in Naomi's journal, remembering something she'd said once. He put the phone on speaker, slapped it on the table, and grabbed the journal out of his other bag, flipping through it.

"What is going on?" Lauren asked.

"It's bad," Alex said. "My boss at the CDC… he's got the sickness. Atlanta isn't safe." He found the page he wanted and sucked in a breath as he read a list of oils and their uses. "Lavender repels mosquitos." He looked up. "So does heavy smoke. The World's Fair, by the time we were on the ground, there was so much smoke. And then the fire yesterday… combined with the lavender we've been practically dousing ourselves in." He shook his head. "It wouldn't be a complete repellent on its own. We're going to need something heavier. We're just lucky."

"Hon, what in the world are you talkin' about?" Minnie frowned with concern.

Alex put the journal down and placed his hands flat on the table, looking down at the phone. "Jonah, are you there?" He closed his eyes. "Please, pick up. I need more."

Friction and shuffling were followed by rough breathing. "NSA… covering it up… whistleblower."

"A whistleblower came to the CDC?" Lauren asked.

Silence followed. "What did he say?" Alex said. "Jonah, don't give up. You've got to fight. What did the whistleblower say?"

"W-Walter Peters," Jonah said, a tremor in his voice. He gurgled, and his next words sounded like he squeezed them out with the last of his energy. "New Horizons. Boston."

The line went dead.

Author's Note

I have a t-shirt that reads: I am too emotionally attached to fictional characters. It's written in scrawling script, dramatic gold against a dark blue background. I think it was made for readers (and I *am* an avid reader), but it felt like such the perfect statement for me as I wrote this book. When I write, these characters come alive. The more I explore their stories, the brighter they shine in my own mind, the more they become almost like friends (or adversaries!).

Mr. Peters gets under my skin like no other. He needs a serious chill pill. Yes, he's trying to save his daughter and himself (and even Zara, I guess), but geez. He's harsh. Timothy and Heather are #relationshipgoals. They love each other, support each other, and fight for each other. Zara makes me root for her, makes me think of the women and girls in my life who never see that they actually *are* good enough. Alex and Oliver tug on my heart strings. And Minnie… well, I just love her. She makes me laugh. She's a straightshooter, a Southern Bell without all the frills but with *all* the sass.

I have *loved* telling their story, and I can't wait to share the whole thing with the world. But, it wasn't always easy. Writing this book and starting this series was a leap of faith. This was my first venture into Post-Apocalyptic Fiction. This was the first time I'd worked with a publisher and the first time I'd attempted such a rigorous writing schedule. I'm so grateful to say that leap has paid off.

As I continue the series, as I plot and weave story threads and decide where to tie them up, I'm finding a serious love for this genre. I love writing about the best of humanity struggling to shine in the worst of situations. I love exploring the strength of relationships, both the familial sort and the newly forged. Survival, good vs. evil, man vs. nature, man vs. self – that's the good stuff, the stuff that connects to the heart. I've always enjoyed consuming Post-Apocalyptic fiction, but now I love creating it.

If you've made it this far, dear reader, thank you, and I hope you enjoyed every minute of it. Your support means the world to me.

B.K. Boes

Ruination

No Tomorrow Book 2

Chapter 1

Alexander Roman

Alexander Roman stood at the edge of a mass grave in the middle of a dead silent Atlanta. Ten days earlier, he would have been standing at the edge of a high school football field. The air would have been saturated with voices and honking and the everyday cacophony of doors slamming, engines roaring, and tires screeching. Ten mounds, each about seven feet wide, ran the length of the field, and the only sound was Alex's breathing. Two-by-four lengths of wood were planted upright at intervals, crude lettering inscribed from top to bottom. Doublegate Drive. Live Oak Lane. Fairway Circle NE. Names of nearby residential streets.

This was the third makeshift graveyard he'd seen from the road. The other two had been in parks, and he hadn't known what they were from a distance. When he saw the wooden posts and dirt mounds on this field, though, he'd asked Minnie to stop so he could investigate.

The scuffle of shoes on the synthetic rubber track that circled the field made Alex look over his shoulder. Lauren approached. "You okay?" she asked, slowing as her eyes flitted from Alex to the field. "What… what *is* this?"

"A mass grave, organized by street," Alex said. "Someone has been gathering the dead and burying them."

"Military?" Lauren walked up to a post and brushed the letters with her fingers. "This is an organized effort. Can you think of anyone else with the manpower to do something like this?"

Alex shook his head. "No, but we haven't seen a military presence yet."

"Yet being the key word." Lauren dropped her hand to her side and turned to face him. Her long brown hair sat on top of her head in a lazy bun, and it bobbed with her every movement. Dark circles had long since formed under her bloodshot eyes; Alex had woken to her stifled crying every night since leaving Nashville. She'd lost her fiancé just before Alex had found her. The way she carried her burden of grief made him wonder if he'd still be crying in the dark over Naomi's death if it weren't for his son, Oliver.

"You make it sound like it would be a bad thing to run across the military," Alex said. "If they're still here, maybe they can help us."

Lauren snorted. "Yeah, sure. Like the military helped in Nashville? It's every man for himself right now."

"Didn't a bunch of soldiers die? I mean, maybe they pulled back to regroup." Alex crossed his arms. "Besides, whoever dug these graves and marked them put a lot of effort into it. That's a good sign. It means someone cares."

Lauren walked slowly from row to row. "So many people… just gone." She spoke softly as if speaking to herself.

The death count isn't over, not by a long shot. Alex averted his eyes, shifting his weight. He'd had a few days to think about the mosquitos being vectors for disease and about the initial spread of human-to-human contact; if his suspicions were confirmed, a second wave of disaster was going to roll across the world. The first wave was mostly due to the spread of people, the second would be due to the spread of the insects themselves. *Maybe I'm wrong… Please, let me be wrong.*

He offered something positive instead of his misgivings. "Maybe whoever buried these people are trying to put the city back together. Could be civilians. Military. Religious organizations. They could be allies."

Lauren sighed. "No matter who organized this or what their intentions, we should watch our backs." She turned from the mass grave and walked back toward the RV, saying as she passed, "This isn't the same Atlanta you left behind. You need to remember that."

Alex jogged up next to her. "Of course I know that. But I also know whoever has survived should work together. It's the only way forward."

She narrowed her eyes skeptically, stopped, and put her hands on her hips. "Look, organized effort like this means there's some kind of piece-meal governance in place. Could be military, like you're hoping, but it could also be gangs. Their intentions could have been pure, just burying the dead because it's the right thing. Or they could be clearing the way for looting."

"Then why mark the graves?" Alex glanced back at the wooden posts. "They could have just thrown all the dead into one big grave and been done."

"The point is that we don't know. Whoever's in charge, though, they're not going to be following the rules of the old world. That means they're unpredictable," Lauren said.

Alex pressed his lips together and walked with Lauren back to the RV parked on the road. If there was one thing he'd learned about Lauren, it was that she loved playing devil's advocate, and she always assumed the worst was just around the corner. She was the polar opposite of her mother, Minnie Stevens, who had rescued Alex and Oliver at the 2035 World's Fair ten days prior.

Samson, Minnie's ruddy-brown hound and Oliver's new best friend, stuck his head out of the back window of the four-door cab attached to the off-road capable RV lovingly nicknamed Harvey. Lauren rounded the vehicle and slid in next to Oliver in the back seat. Alex scratched Samson behind the ears and hopped into the passenger seat next to Minnie.

"So, what are they?" Minnie asked as she eased the RV back onto the road.

"Minnie said they were a giant's potato garden!" Oliver said, leaning forward. "And I said giants aren't real, and *she* said she bet me a dollar that they *were* real and that a giant potato garden proves it! So, is it a potato garden, Dad?"

Alex savored the sound of Oliver's voice. For five days, he hadn't been sure he'd ever hear his son speak again. "Well," Alex said, "I'd have to say a giant potato garden is a viable option." He looked over his shoulder and grinned.

Oliver narrowed his eyes. "Then, we should go back and dig around for a huge potato. I'm not giving anyone a dollar until I see proof."

Alex had to keep a fake smile pasted in place of his previously genuine one. His stomach lurched at the image of Oliver digging up bodies. "All right, bud. You called my bluff. Minnie owes you a dollar."

Oliver pumped his fist in the air and settled back into his seat with a smile as Minnie picked four quarters out of a tray built into the dashboard. As she handed them back, she looked questioningly at Alex, and he gave her a shake of his head to discourage the line of questioning. She nodded and turned back to the road. He'd have to fill her in later.

Oliver has been exposed to enough. He'll be exposed to so much more… I have to protect him from whatever horrors I can.

"Are we going home, Dad?" Oliver asked. "I want to check on my friends."

Alex closed his eyes and leaned back against the headrest, trying to think of a response. We're not going home. Not now, maybe never. And most of your friends are probably dead or far from here, trying not to die.

"No, bud," he said instead. "I'm not sure home is safe right now."

"Are they all dead, too?" Oliver asked.

Alex turned around and held out his hand, and his son took it. "I don't know," he said honestly. "But they might be." He winced as the words left his mouth.

Oliver's face fell, and he chewed on his lower lip. Samson whined and nudged Oliver's cheek with his nose, and Lauren stared out of the window blankly as if she hadn't heard a word. Minnie guided the RV, but her attention was clearly divided between the road, Oliver, and Alex as she took turns glancing at each.

"I guess if things are never going back to normal," Oliver said, putting an arm around Samson's neck, "it's a good thing we're all together. We're the lucky ones."

Lauren shrank a little more in her seat and wiped away a tear. Sniffing and hugging herself tighter, she put her feet up on the seat and rested her head on her knees, concealing her face from view as she continued facing the window.

"I think we're lucky because the people we loved who are no longer here are watching out for us," Alex said.

"Like Mom?" Oliver asked, perking up a bit.

"Yeah, like Mom."

Lauren let her feet fall back to the floorboards, and she smiled sadly at Alex. She nudged Oliver with her elbow. "From what I've heard of your mom, between her and Aaron looking out for us, we're going to be just fine."

Minnie slowed to a stop as she turned a corner onto the road that led to the CDC. "Uh-oh… that looks like a big to-do we don't wanna mess with."

Lauren frowned at the two military Humvees blocking the intersection ahead. "There's our military. They're obviously protecting the CDC, but… I thought your boss said the sickness wiped out the CDC? And they're kind of far from the actual facility, aren't they?"

Alex pointed east. "There's a hospital that way. They might be securing an entire zone. As for what Jonah said… I mean, he was dying, and he said the CDC had been 'compromised' which I took to mean by the sickness. He left us a van full of supplies *at* the facility, so… there's no way he wouldn't have mentioned a military presence."

"A man smack dab in the middle of dyin' might not be in his right mind." Minnie put her hand on the gear shifter. "We goin' forward or we goin' back?"

"I don't think we're going to have much of a choice," Lauren said.

"What do you m—" Alex swung his head to look at Lauren, who was shying away from the window, and cut off as he saw what she was staring at.

A soldier approached from the tree line on the side of the road, weapon drawn. More men, some of them in black suits, melted out of the foliage. Samson growled, and Alex slowly put his hands up. The soldier closest to Minnie motioned for her to roll down her window.

She stuck out her chin and pressed the button with a grumble and reddened cheeks. "Pointin' weapons at a child," she mumbled as the window inched down.

"What's your business here?" the soldier barked.

Minnie's mouth dropped as if she were utterly offended. She had the look of Southern fire, and Alex leaned forward before she could say anything brash to the man with the gun.

"Sir," Alex said, "I'm a scientist with the Division of High-Consequence Pathogens." He swallowed hard at the blank look on the soldier's face. "We're disease detectives…" He waited a moment, hoping he might recognize the more common term. "My boss was Dr. Jonah Newton. He told me to come here—"

The soldier held one palm up and lowered his gun, stepping back and unclipping a radio from his belt as another soldier took his place. Alex cleared his throat. He couldn't hear what was being said.

"Dad, what's going on?" Oliver leaned forward.

"No one move!" The soldier at the open window shouted.

"Oliver, stay very still," Alex said, his heartbeat picking up.

"He's just a boy, and you're scaring him. What kinda man are you?" Minnie asked in a scathing, motherly tone that made a few soldiers blush. Unfortunately, the soldier closest to her just hardened his expression and set his jaw.

"It's okay, Minnie. We need to stay calm," Alex said softly.

The first soldier stepped back up. "Everyone out," he said. "Slowly, hands visible at all times." Samson growled again, and the soldier added, "Leash that dog and keep him under control, or we *will* put him down."

Oliver gasped and put his arms around Samson's neck. "You can't do that!"

Alex handed the leash to Lauren who hooked it to Samson's collar. "Bud," he said, "you've got to let Lauren handle Samson right now, okay?"

Oliver nodded and let Lauren pull Samson over to her.

"I said everyone out!" the soldier repeated.

The second Alex opened the door, it was flung open and he was grabbed by the arm. "Hold on," he shouted. "Just let me help my son." His eyes widened as another soldier roughly grabbed Oliver. "Hey! Be careful with him!"

The soldier pulled Alex toward the military vehicles. "You're coming with us," he said.

Alex frowned as he stumbled forward. Minnie and Lauren backed away from the RV at gun point, Lauren keeping Samson on a short leash. The soldier who had taken Oliver shoved him at Minnie, who put her arms protectively around the boy.

"Didn't your momma teach you any decency?" She wagged her finger at the soldiers though she kept backing up as they forced her back. "I bet she'd tan your hide right here and now if she saw what you're doin'. All y'all are makin' your mommas ashamed."

"What are you doing?" Alex demanded as the soldier's hand dug into his upper arm, dragging him away from the people he loved. "Why aren't you bringing my family?"

"They're not coming." A flash of a grimace was quickly replaced by lips drawn taut. Behind, them, the RV began to roll forward, driven by a stranger.

They're confiscating the RV… all our supplies? Our shelter?

Alex yanked on his arm, but the soldier's grip held. His heart raced furiously, and a wave of nausea hit as the blood drained from his face. Without the RV, his people would be in serious danger come nightfall. "You can't do this. I need to stay with my son!" Alex shouted, locking his knees so that his feet skidded on the road. Another soldier stepped up and grabbed his other arm, helping to move him forward. "Stop!" Alex struggled to get loose. "You can't leave them out here with no shelter. You can't do this!"

They were almost to the Humvees. Alex threw all his weight to one side, and the two men stumbled just slightly. They were too strong for him to fight against. They shoved him forward, and his body slammed against the side of the vehicle as his captors jerked his hands behind his back, zip-tying them securely. The RV passed by them, and a line of soldiers walked backward, guns trained on his family.

As he was being shoved into the backseat of the Humvee, he heard Oliver calling for him. He craned his neck, catching sight of Oliver as Minnie pulled him back. "Find shelter!" he shouted.

"I will!" Minnie yelled. "Promise!"

"I love you, Oliver!" He was pushed into the vehicle, and the door slammed shut.

Alex couldn't catch his breath as the Humvee roared to life, jostling him as it did a three-point turn and headed toward the CDC facility. He pressed his face against the window, trying to catch a glimpse of his son one more time, but it was no use. His chest heaved as he gasped for air, and his head swam. It had finally happened; he'd lost everything.

Chapter 2

Zara Williams

Zara Williams squared off with Mitch at the door to the outside, her blood boiling. Every time she looked at the man, she saw Nina – the homeless woman who had helped her – lying dead at his feet. The trigger-happy security guard would be banished from the hospital if it were up to her, but it wasn't; nothing was ever up to her. Control of her life had gone out the window ten days prior. Brandt, the younger of the two security guards, and Mitch, the older, had barricaded all other entrances and taken shifts guarding the front door to the hospital. Zara hadn't decided if Brandt had a conscience or if he just had no guts, but he had let her go outside to place mosquito traps the day before. All she'd had to do was bat her eyelashes and give him a smile, a move she'd picked up from Lizzy. But Mitch was sticking to his guns, thankfully only in a metaphorical matter. His gun, the one he'd used to murder multiple people trying to make it to safety, had run out of bullets days ago.

"Let me outside." Zara met Mitch's glare with one of her own. She may have been half a foot shorter, but she had twice as much spirit. Mr. Peters wanted a look at the mosquitos to see if he could recognize any of the hallmarks Vanguard had included in their weaponized species. Apparently, he had no idea which mosquitos had been released; there had been several experiments of various degrees of deadly and disastrous.

"I can't do that." Mitch put a hand on his baton, the only weapon he was actually supposed to be carrying.

Lizzy stood a few feet behind, silent. There had been a time when she would have quipped alongside Zara, making light of the situation or tag teaming with a good-cop-bad-cop routine. Zara missed the way their friendship used to be, before the end of the world had created a chasm between them that seemed impassible.

It's not her fault that her father had a part in all of this. She didn't know… she couldn't have known. Zara pushed away a nagging feeling that Lizzy wasn't telling her everything. Before they'd been thrown into survival mode following the World's Fair, Zara had been surprised to learn Lizzy had gotten close to her brother, Jordan, and the Green Earth Futurists. *Did she get involved with them because she knew her father was up to something?* That question plagued Zara. If Lizzy had suspected something nefarious but kept it to herself, if Lizzy could have helped prevent the death of Zara's family… No. Zara reined in that line of thinking. She couldn't handle that on top of everything else. Lizzy wasn't telling her something, but that something didn't have to be about the apocalypse. *Please let it be about something else.*

She redoubled her efforts against Mitch. "Brandt let me outside yesterday, and it worked out just fine." Zara sidestepped, but Mitch darted into her path again.

"He shouldn't have done that. We agreed. No one in. No one out." Mitch pulled the baton free of its holster on his belt. His security guard uniform was wrinkled but clean – another reason to despise him.

"We also agreed that no one would use unnecessary water." Zara jabbed her finger into his rounded belly. "You don't stink as usual, Mitch. Why is that? How often are you washing that uniform while the rest of us wait our turns?"

Mitch raised the baton. "You little brat!" He swung.

If I'm going down, so are you. Zara leaned in and slammed her knee into Mitch where it could really do some damage. He wheezed, and only then did she notice he no longer held the baton. Brandt stood next to them both, the baton in his hands and his wide eyes trained on Zara.

"I can't believe you just did that." Brandt stood motionless as Mitch stumbled to a chair. Brandt didn't bother to help his former boss.

"What?" Zara crossed her arms. "He was coming at me, so I did what I had to do."

"I didn't mean he didn't deserve it, it's just…" Brandt's face burned bright red. "You're half his size, and…"

"And what?" Zara narrowed her eyes and stepped toward him.

"And you're a nice person, I think?" Brandt backed up, shoulders hunched, baton hanging loosely from his hand.

Great… he's afraid of me. Zara rolled her shoulders and created some distance, trying to loosen up her body and tone down her anger. Brandt hadn't done anything to deserve her ire, but that churning, adrenaline-inducing anger in her gut only seemed to be growing, and controlling it wasn't easy. Still, the anger was better than grief.

Lizzy stared at the ground and mumbled, "If you knew her better, you wouldn't be surprised. She can be brutal."

Ever since Zara had confronted Mr. Peters, Lizzy had been cold shouldered. Sure, she threatened to expose what Mr. Peters had done, that his company – Vanguard – had a hand in the current state of the world, and yes, exposing him would put a target on his back. Maybe Lizzy's back, too. But it had been the only way to claw back some modicum of control over the situation. After losing her parents, her brother, and her aunt to Vanguard's experimental disease-carrying mosquitos, Zara had the right to push back on Mr. Peters's narcissistic dictatorship over her life. He deserved it, and more. If she thought she could survive on her own, if Lizzy would have left her father behind, Zara would be long gone from the hospital just north of Indianapolis. But, neither of those things were true, and both of them grated on Zara every minute of every day.

"I'm only brutal when I'm forced to be." The rising tide of fury pulsing through her veins only raged more intensely. "Besides, you don't have any right to judge me after what your dad did." Lizzy stepped backward as if Zara had shoved her, and Zara immediately regretted her words. She wanted to mend things with Lizzy, not make them worse. *I do want to mend things... right?*

"That's not fair." Lizzy's eyes glistened, and she pushed past Zara. "Let's get these stupid traps and go back to sitting in separate corners, okay?"

Brandt frowned. "What did Mr. Peters do?"

"Nothing. Just, forget I said that, okay?" Zara waited for Brandt to shrug his agreement before following her best friend to the lot just outside the front door. "Liz, wait." She reached out and grabbed Liz's shoulder. "I'm sorry. I didn't mean that. I—"

"You did mean it, though." Lizzy whirled around, tears falling freely down her cheeks. "I hate what he did, but... Zee, he's my dad. I can't help it. I still love him. Part of me wants him to burn in hell, but a bigger part wants to find a way to forgive him. He didn't do it on his own, you know. He never meant for them to be released."

"Are you blaming my brother?" Zara scoffed. Jordan and the organization he'd been obsessed with — the Green Earth Futurists — had released the weaponized mosquitos thinking they were releasing a species that would eradicate disease-carrying mosquitos. Many of them, including Zara's brother, had paid for their mistake with their lives.

Lizzy shook her head. "No, but there are dozens of other people farther up the food chain than my dad is. The government wanted his company to develop this as a weapon." She spread out her arms, gesturing at the world around them — a destroyed city, black plumes of smoke in the distance, a mound of dirt covering a pile of bodies on the edge of hospital property. "This was never supposed to happen. It wouldn't have happened, if the GEF hadn't stolen the experiment in the first place."

"Just because *other* people share in the blame doesn't mean that your dad is free from it," Zara said.

"No, but it does mean he's not solely responsible, and that means something. It has to." Lizzy wiped away her tears with the back of her hand.

Zara wanted to scream. Instead, she turned stiffly toward the bushes lining the parking garage on the other side of the lot where they'd put the mosquito traps. Lizzy followed as Zara strode across the asphalt in the hot summer sun. "I understand if you need to forgive him," Zara said, "but don't ask me to do it, too. And don't ask me to give him a break or be nice to him or try to understand things from his perspective."

"Then don't ask me to hate him," Lizzy said, "and don't hate me because I don't hate him."

Zara stopped in front of a bush and searched for their mosquito trap. "Fine. I guess that's all we can do for each other right now." She glanced at her friend out of the corner of her eye. "Do we have a deal?"

Lizzy reached into the bush and pulled out the camouflaged trap, a green 2-liter bottle, the top fourth cut off, flipped, and inverted into the bottle. A concoction of brown sugar, dry yeast, and water — salvaged from the hospital kitchen — sloshed in the bottom. Several dead mosquitos floated in the mix. "I hate this." She gestured, pointing back and forth between them. "Don't you hate this? We need each other right now, and you're pushing me away."

Zara found the other trap two bushes down and pulled it out. "You know what I need? My parents. My aunt. My brother."

Lizzy's hands trembled as she held her 2-liter trap. "I can't change what happened," she said. "What do you want me to do?"

"I don't know." Zara wiped sweat from her brow and trudged back toward the hospital. "You know what?" She stopped and turned on Lizzy. "I do know. I want you to stop defending him. I want you to tell me you'd leave him behind if we could make it out there on our own."

Lizzy's eyes grew wide. "But we wouldn't surv—"

"I know!" Zara shouted, cutting her off. "I want you to say that if it were possible, you'd leave him behind. I want to know that my best friend would choose me over the man who killed my family."

"Zee, I..." Lizzy hugged the plastic bottle and curled in on herself. "I can't," she whispered. She looked up, teary eyed and voice desperate. "I despise what he's done, but you have to see this isn't all his fault. He's no saint, but he is my dad. And he's done everything he can to keep us safe. Maybe his methods haven't always been great, but he's trying to fix this."

"There is no fixing this." Zara let the words hang between them.

After a few seconds of silence, Lizzy swallowed hard. "Do you mean the end of the world or our friendship?"

"I don't know," Zara said. "Maybe both." There was no stirring of sympathy as Lizzy unraveled and broke into tears. There was only that deep-seated anger, iced over by numbness when she needed control. Before she'd lost everything, she would have been frightened of this version of herself. A tiny part of that old self broke through her icy walls. *This isn't me. This isn't who I want to be.*

"You don't mean that," Lizzy said through her tears.

"I don't want to mean it. Maybe... maybe I just need more time." Zara's attempt at civility was frigid; even she could sense it. But exhaustion was setting in, and she couldn't give any more. Her body was still recovering from the injuries she'd sustained in the first five days after the World's Fair, but it was more than that. Her *soul* was tired. She pushed herself to move, passing Lizzy without so much as a glance. "Let's get back to the hospital."

"Just do it yourself." Lizzy let out a sob, put the trap on the ground, and ran back inside. Zara couldn't blame her. She picked up the trap and followed suit, walking into the hospital with a mosquito trap in both arms.

"What was that all about?" Brandt asked as she passed him. He'd apparently taken up guard duty. Mitch was nowhere to be seen. "Lizzy looked really upset. And what are those?" He pointed at the 2-liters. "Bug traps?"

"Mind your own business, Brandt." Zara snapped at him. She'd agreed not to tell anyone of the mosquitos for the time being. Everyone was staying indoors when the mosquitos were supposed to be active due to the CDC warning that had gone out over the radio. As long as they did that, they would be safe. Zara hated keeping secrets for Mr. Peters almost as much as she hated the man himself.

She navigated the first floor toward the cafeteria where she'd last seen Mr. Peters. The remaining fifteen people in the hospital had agreed to stick mostly to the cafeteria, the gift shop, and the Emergency Department where they each had claimed a room for themselves. Shutting down the rest of the hospital saved energy. No one knew how long the generator would last, but they had all agreed they wanted to keep it going for as long as possible. Zara slipped into the vending machine room that led into the cafeteria and peeked into the room beyond. She didn't want to draw attention or get sucked into a conversation.

Bertie — a woman Zara had first met in the waiting room — sat at a table with her daughter, Judith, and an older woman named Lorrie who was recovering from pneumonia. Dr. Sarah Donald and Dr. Jerry Young sat across the room at a table by themselves, sipping coffees. They were the only two doctors who had stayed when things got bad. They had fought along with two nurses, Brian and Sunny, to keep critical patients alive. Mr. Richards, the only remaining hospital administrator, had done his best to help. Judith and Lorrie had survived while three others had died. At another table, a man named Amos opened a water bottle for his daughter, Sophie, who had her arm in a temporary cast. Mr. Richards and the two nurses weren't in the cafeteria. Zara assumed they were walking the halls for exercise or relaxing in their rooms.

Mr. Peters wasn't there, so she backed out quietly and headed for the Emergency Department, the soft sloshing of the mixture matching the rhythm of her step. When she got to his door, she paused, tension building in her muscles and a knot forming in her stomach. Her palms began to sweat, and a chill rushed down her spine. Nausea swept over her, and she swallowed bile. She couldn't so much as look at Mr. Peters without wanting to throw up. She hated how he made her feel, how she felt his eyes on her as if he were evaluating her for weaknesses.

I can do this. I can face him. He's just a man. Zara took a deep breath, steeled herself, and opened the door. Mr. Peters sat on his elevated hospital bed, eyes closed, head resting on a pillow. He was no longer hooked up to machines, but he still looked weakened to her. That was good. Lizzy sat by his side, looking miserable with reddened eyes, slumped shoulders, and pale cheeks.

Zara set the 2-liters on the small counter next to the sink and nudged Mr. Peters's foot. "Wake up."

Mr. Peters snorted awake. The dark circles under his eyes were more evident when he tilted his head up. He blinked, looking around the room, his gaze landing on the mosquito traps. "Are there any mosquitos in there?"

She ground her teeth. He had to have seen how upset his daughter was, and he ignored her. *He doesn't deserve her loyalty.* She wanted to spit in his face.

"I caught a few. You want to get up off your lazy butt and take a look, *Walter*?" She used his first name, suspecting it would annoy him.

He narrowed his eyes and swung his legs over the side of the bed, standing up and stalking over to the traps. "Let's stick to Mr. Peters," he said as he opened one of two cabinets and brought out a silver tray with medical instruments on top.

"I think Walter will do just fine, thanks." Zara raised her eyebrows. A flash of satisfaction, the only positive emotion she'd felt in days, encouraged her onward. "If you're looking for respect, you should find someone who cares."

Mr. Peters removed the inverted top of the trap and set it aside, peering down into the mixture. He picked up a shiny pair of tweezers and picked out the bugs, one by one. "You remind me of myself when I was young, Zara." He looked at her and smiled. "I'm glad to see you've not lost your fight."

"I'm nothing like you," Zara said, seething. When he smiled wider, when a look of satisfaction came over *his* face, she dug her fingernails into her palms until they pierced her skin. *He's trying to make me lose it.* "That won't work," she said through gritted teeth, although it absolutely was working.

He bent over the specimens, squinting at them. "Sounds like something I would say."

"Stop it, Dad," Lizzy spoke up from her chair, but she didn't move. "Please? Just leave her alone."

Her palms stung and warm blood welled under her fingers as her fists began to shake. *Don't let him win. Hold it in.*

Mr. Peters moved on to the next trap, removing the lid and picking out the mosquitos. "I'm not doing anything. She should be honored to be compared to me. I'm a successful, wealthy —" He paused, holding up a particular mosquito. "No." He whispered the word vehemently as if he were trying to change reality with one word.

Zara loosened her fists, ignoring the stinging of her palms and the drops of blood seeping down her fingertips. "What is it?"

He set the specimen down and backed away from the counter, shaking his head and running his fingers through his hair.

"Dad?" Lizzy stood up. "Are you okay?"

He looked at them both with wild eyes. "I need to find a microscope right now. If I'm right…" Mr. Peters sucked in a breath and reached out for the bed, plopping down hard on its edge. "This can't be happening."

Zara's legs wouldn't move; she'd rarely seen Mr. Peters like this, and it was never a good sign. "How can things get any worse?"

Mr. Peters met her eyes. "Pray you don't have to find out."

Chapter 3

Timothy Peters

"I thought she was getting better." Timothy Peters dabbed a damp rag on his wife's forehead. Heather was sweating profusely, a rash covered her body, and she wore a perpetual grimace. She was floating in and out of lucidity; in her lucid moments, she spoke of pain in her muscles, joints, and head. He'd tried to make the stiff, green couch in the clinic lobby more comfortable with pillows from an exam room, but it didn't seem to help much. The windows were cracked just enough to let fresh air into the sunlit room, but it was stiflingly hot. He didn't dare fling the windows wide open for fear of drawing attention to the clinic.

After Candice had survived the mysterious illness that was killing everyone, she'd suggested they hide out in the Walden Plastic Surgery Clinic in Wellesley. Without enough gasoline to make it to New Horizons Lab where his mother wanted them to go, and with the threat of Frank returning to the gated community, Timothy had agreed to take temporary shelter where there was bound to be some medical supplies and maybe even pain killers.

He had packed up his mother's Dodge Charger and Candice's sparkly, purple Cadillac Escalade with as many supplies from the bunker as he could fit and driven his family, Candice, and Annika to safety. From the outside, the clinic looked more like an office building than a medical facility, and it hadn't been looted or broken into, unlike many of the other businesses in town. Candice said the façade had something to do with privacy for patients; the clinic was a word-of-mouth, high-end clientele business. Or at least, it used to be. It had turned out to be a decent hiding place for the end of the world. They'd found a suture kit, pain meds, and antibiotics and patched Heather up as best they could.

Apparently, our best wasn't good enough. Timothy checked under the gauze taped to Heather's side to find the bullet wound oozing. His chest tightened. *This is all my fault. I brought Frank into our lives.*

Timothy's mother, Dana, sat next to him and put a hand on his shoulder. "I don't know, Timmy. I thought she was getting better, too."

The clicking of heels on tile made Timothy turn toward the hallway. Candice strode into the room in a bright yellow, strapless dress matched by the same color shoes. She'd insisted they bring two of her very large suitcases in exchange for using her Escalade. "The children are eating lunch." She clapped her hands together. "Peanut butter crackers and beef jerky sticks. I would have had a mutiny on my hands, but I added some gummy worms from the vending machine, and I think that did the trick." She stopped at the foot of the couch and put her hands on her hips.

"Did you eat?" Timothy asked, raising his eyebrows at her.

For days after that night she'd almost died, she hadn't eaten a bite. With some prodding, she'd started nibbling on food again. It was hard to tell how ill she was still feeling just by looking at her; she insisted on covering her bruised eyes, the scratches on her neck, and the stretch marks sustained by rapid swelling with layers of makeup. Her long, blonde hair was greasy but brushed and braided, and she'd started dressing in her usual designer clothes and shoes again. Still, there were things she couldn't hide. Her skin sagged a little under her still-bloodshot eyes, which now bulged slightly too far out of their sockets like she was constantly surprised. A scab on the side of her neck couldn't be covered, and she still had splotches of bruising dotting her arms and legs.

"I ate a protein bar, if you must know." Candice stuck her nose up. "I'm not a child. You don't have to check on me."

Timothy sighed. "I was just trying to be nice, Gucci. It's not like you've got a great track record when it comes to discernment." He invoked her choice of a walkie talkie code name, not bothering to hide his sarcastic tone. The woman had practically welcomed Frank and his goons into the gated community just so she could go to a party that never should have happened in the first place; she was easily duped and incredibly disconnected from the hardships of the world. *Annika is more of an adult than she is.* Candice shoved her fists down at her sides — much like a child about to throw a tantrum — and opened her mouth.

Dana cut her off before she could respond. "How did you get anything out of the vending machine? I've been eyeing that candy for days."

Candice pursed her lips and held out her hands to show them her nails. "I broke the last of my nails breaking it open with a chair."

"That's… impressive," Dana said.

Candice raised an eyebrow. "I do what needs to be done. How do you think I got to be HOA president?"

"Through a rigged vote?" Timothy asked dryly.

"Ha. Ha. Very funny." Candice huffed and looked down, frowning deeply at Heather. After a few moments of silence, she walked around to the other side of the couch and touched Heather's forehead with the back of her hand. "She's on fire. She looks awful."

"We know," Dana said.

"We have no idea why the antibiotics aren't working." Timothy rubbed his hand over his face.

"Well, if you ask me," Candice said, "it looks like she's had an allergic reaction to the antibiotics. I had a friend once that looked just like that after taking cefazolin. She got a little infection after fixing up the ladies. The doctor gave her an antihistamine, but I don't remember what kind."

"We had some of those in the bunker." Timothy leapt up and rushed to the plastic bins of supplies he'd brought with him. "I can't remember if I grabbed them. I was so focused on getting us out of there… I know I shoved like a whole shelf of pill bottles into one of these bins."

"There were two shelves of meds," Dana said, helping him sift through the bins. "Hopefully you packed the shelf with the antihistamines."

"Here's the bin!" Timothy ripped off the lid and picked up a pill bottle. "Ibuprofen." He picked up one after another, sorting them on the floor into types. "Acetaminophen. Naproxen. They're all pain relievers and fever reducers."

"I think there were some bottles of Benadryl in with the cough syrups, and there was another spot for creams: antibiotic, burn cream, stuff like that." Dana kept looking through the bins. "Did you pack any of that?"

"I should have taken more time." Timothy groaned and looked back at his wife. "Maybe there are some left in the grocery down the street?"

Dana put the bottles back into the bin, keeping them sorted and neatly packed in rows. "Maybe it would be safer to just go back to the house and see if there's anything left there, if Frank hasn't already ransacked it." She put the lid back on the bin and clicked it closed. "I don't like the idea of stopping in town, not with the gunfire we heard yesterday. My Charger is quiet. I think you can sneak through town without drawing much attention if you stick to side roads."

"My Escalade isn't that loud. It's a hybrid, and it has a lot more room." Candice dug out a key fob from a hidden pocket in the folds of her skirts. "You can use it, and you can also check to make sure Harry hasn't come home. He must be just as worried about me as I am about him." Candice's chin quivered. "My poor Hair-Bear."

Timothy exchanged a knowing look with his mother. There was no way Harry Liddle was still alive. He'd gone into Boston to check on his business, and he'd been missing for nearly two weeks. But Candice spun out at even the implication he might be dead, so Timothy just nodded and smiled. "Um, sure. I can check on your place, see if Harry is around. But your sparkly purple Escalade isn't exactly inconspicuous."

Candice dangled the keys in front of Timothy. "You'll need the room if the bunker still has all your stuff in it. Plus, if Harry is there, he'll want to come back with you."

Timothy sighed and took the keys. "Fine. I guess you're right. Maybe if Frank looted the house, he didn't find the bunker. Or maybe he couldn't get into the bunker. I'll need to bring back as much as I can find." Timothy rubbed his hands over his face, remembering Frank's threats. "Unless he burned down the house…"

"Even if he did," Dana said, "the bunker should still be intact. The first door at the basement level should have protected the stairwell and the second door that leads into the bunker. It only locks from the inside for safety, so it's likely Frank and his guys found the bunker, though it's unlikely they were able to get in. Even without the solar power on the roof in the case of a fire, the keypad should still open the bunker door, though. The bunker wouldn't be ventilated, cooled, or livable, but it should still be there."

The pattering of little feet interrupted their conversation. Annika ran into the lobby with a magazine flopping from her hand. She came to an abrupt stop upon seeing Heather and then spun to address Timothy. "She promised we could read Vogue, but she looks sleepy." Annika held the magazine to her chest and swished back and forth. "We were gonna learn about Fall trends."

"Sweetheart, I don't think Heather is up for reading today," Timothy knelt in front of her. "I'm sorry."

"Well… I know how to read," Annika said, lifting her chin. "I can read to her instead. My mom reads to me when I'm sick." She pointed at Candice. "Candy can help."

Timothy looked over his shoulder. "Candy?"

She smoothed the front of her dress. "My closest friends call me that." She walked forward and held out a hand which Annika took. "Of course I would love to help. Who better to guide young minds when it comes to fashion?"

"Is fruit a Fall trend?" Annika asked. "If it is, can I dress like a banana, too?" Timothy chuckled, his mother snorted, and Candice stiffened and cleared her throat. "What?" Annika looked between the three of them, her eyebrows knit together in confusion.

"It's nothing," Candice said with a smile. "It's just that you, my dear, are more of a blueberry. Dark, rich blues would make you shine even brighter."

"Oh, I like blueberries." Annika tugged on Candice's hand, and they walked together to sit next to Heather.

"I wish Annika didn't have to experience all of this," Timothy said softly to his mother. "She should be reading kids books, going to the park… she should be with her mom." He sighed. "It's not right."

"I feel the same about Georgie, though it scares me to death to think things might get worse for him. If your father doesn't make it…" Dana cut off, licking her lips and averting her eyes. "They're both having their childhoods stolen from them." She paused for a moment before continuing. "You and Heather have taken a liking to Annika, haven't you?"

"I feel responsible for her," Timothy said. "I found her, all alone. She's been a bright spot in all this darkness even though she's lost so much. I just want to protect her from any more pain."

"Well, I'm glad she's here with us," Dana said. "Are you heading out to the house, then?"

Timothy nodded. "I'd better get going. I want to be back before seven."

"Here." Dana grabbed a can of mosquito spray from a bin on top of the stack. "Use this, just to be safe."

Timothy took the metal cylinder, cool to the touch. "You really think Candice is right about the mosquitos?" He glanced at Candice. She'd insisted that the scab on her neck, at first a large welt, was caused by a mosquito bite and that its swelling had been the onset of her symptoms. She'd also said the barbeque wherein nearly all of the Peters's neighbors had perished had been swarmed with weirdly aggressive mosquitos.

"I mean, mosquitos carry illness, right? Maybe whatever this is can be spread that way." Dana tapped the can. "Just use it. It won't hurt you, and it will make your mother feel better."

Timothy patted the gun holstered at his hip; he'd kept it handy every second of every day since driving Frank and his men away from the Peters's home. "This right here makes *me* feel better, but I'll take the spray, too."

He kissed his mother on the forehead, took the mosquito spray and Candice's car keys, and headed for the attached parking garage at the back of the building. When they'd first made it to the clinic, they had siphoned off full tanks of gas from the other cars in the garage, and Timothy had collected more gasoline from cars on the street in the days since. He was doing everything he could to set up his family for survival. He didn't want to fail them again; he couldn't. The plan was to pay New Horizons Lab a visit to see if his mother was right about his father leaving backup supplies at the lab, but first, Timothy wanted Heather to recover. Even then, he wasn't sure about permanently moving deeper into the heart of Boston. Last time he'd visited the city proper, he'd met Frank and almost gotten himself killed more than once.

A few of the cars in the garage still had dead bodies inside, and Timothy gagged as he caught sight of one on the way to the Escalade. Eyes hanging from their sockets, body bloated, flesh rotting, clothes coated in dry, crusty blood, they barely resembled a human being. There was a sickeningly sweet and sour stench lingering in the air, waxing and waning with the breeze in the hot summer air. He pushed past his nausea and hopped into the Escalade. The gated community was on the outskirts of Wellesley, and it didn't take long to get there.

Ash, blackened timber, and a shadow of what used to be were all that was left of his childhood home. Parts of the house had collapsed in on itself. Even parts of the basement were visible. Through the debris, he could make out the entrance to the stairwell leading down into the bunker. The fire had clearly been set days ago; there was no smoldering or smoke. He turned his back on the house, trying to process the fact that it was gone, and something caught his eye.

On the other side of the u-shaped drive, a plastic baggie flapped in the breeze. It had a piece of folded paper inside. In five quick strides, he had the baggie in hand, having ripped it free of the nail. He fumbled with the paper, sticking the baggie in his cargo pocket. *Southie, we'd be square if you hadn't shot me and killed my guys. But you did. And like I said, I'm like a cockroach. You ain't getting rid of me until I collect your debt. I'll find you.*

"Damn it, Frank!" He crumpled the paper and threw it into the wind, roaring into the quiet afternoon. He grimaced at the way his voice echoed, hoping Frank didn't still have his goons keeping watch.

The mobster had attacked his family, shot his wife, and forced him and his family to flee for fear of his return. Timothy wished every day he'd killed Frank when he'd first met him. *At least we brought supplies with us, but… I need those antihistamines.*

"What am I going to do?" He groaned and turned to survey the pile of rubble. He could break into another house and search for the drugs, but there were other things in the bunker he wanted to collect. More food, water, and other supplies.

He walked the perimeter of the wreckage and stopped at the side of the house to look down into the basement where the outer wall was completely gone. The concrete walls of the basement itself stood firm, though it was now filled with burnt timber, metal beams, and scraps of barely identifiable items: a picture frame, mangled box springs, a melted and cracked flat screen television. Parts of the basement ceiling had completely caved in while the frame of the first floor hung precariously over the basement elsewhere. He focused on the entrance to the stairwell leading one level lower where the bunker waited. If he could lower a ladder into the pit, he could make out a pathway to that door and get inside. It wouldn't be easy, but he could salvage what was left of their supplies, including the variety of antihistamines, one of which was bound to help Heather if she was having an allergic reaction to the antibiotics.

He jogged across the street, peeked into the garage, and found what he was looking for. A rock through the window did the trick, and soon he was lowering a shiny silver ladder into the remains of the burned down house. He ducked under beams and shimmied past debris to make it to the stairwell. Sunlight barely reached the bottom of the stairs, but what it revealed made his stomach drop.

"No… how?" Timothy backed up, his eyes wide, his mouth hanging open. "How did you get inside, you bastard?" The door to the bunker was wide open. His mouth ran dry, and his whole body tensed. Rage swelled inside his chest, and his heartbeat thrummed in his ears. He'd won the battle when he'd driven Frank and his men off the Peters' property, but Frank was winning the war. The mobster was relentless, insane, and cruel; Timothy hadn't known he could hate another man so much. He balled his hands into fists, his body trembling with the effort of keeping his anger inside. He couldn't do it. Timothy shouted and swung his fist into a nearby beam.

The beam budged, and the remains of the ceiling overhead groaned and shuddered. Ash floated downward, and Timothy didn't dare to even breathe. His heart stopped. A crack and whine split the air as the structure collapsed completely. Timothy jumped for the protection of the stairwell but couldn't gain his footing. He tumbled head over heels down the concrete steps. The rock-hard edges of the steps bit into his side, his back, his head. He landed at the bottom in a heap, and the last stream of sunlight was cut off by the falling debris, trapping him underground in utter darkness with no escape.

Chapter 4

Alexander Roman

"Let me out!" Alex banged his fist against the solid gray door until his hand hurt. "I want to talk to someone in charge!"

He repeated his demands, shouting at the top of his lungs, peering out of the small ten-inch-square window. The glass was so thick, the hall outside was warped when looking through, and while he hadn't had any luck breaking it, he could occasionally see a young woman in camouflage army fatigues guarding his door.

The room was barely large enough to contain a twin-sized bed with sheets and one pillow, a nightstand, and a thin, three-drawer dresser. A bathroom was attached, also small and cramped, but equipped with a shower. There was nothing else in the room. No lamps, no television, no magazines or books, no clock, not even posters on the wall. Before they'd thrown him into the room, he'd seen an identifying plaque on the wall beside the door which read: Medical Observation Room 3. He'd never been to this floor, sticking mostly to the laboratories and his office.

Alex roared at the lack of response, opting to kick at the door to give his hand a break. Pain exploded in his ankle as his foot twisted upon impact, and he yelped in pain, backing off to hop on one foot, eyes watering. The soldier outside peeked through the window, frowning.

"Oh, that's got your attention, huh?" Alex yelled. "You don't want me hurting myself? Is that it?"

He paused as it dawned on him. They wanted to use his skills. That's why they took him and not Oliver, Minnie, and Lauren. He grinned and launched himself at the door, cracking his head on the window. The soldier flinched and gaped. He did it again, screaming against the pain.

"I'll keep going unless you get someone in charge!" The next crack of his forehead against the thick glass broke the skin. Blood seeped down his face, and though he stumbled forward, he smashed his head into the window again. Blood smeared the glass and dripped down the door.

The soldier burst into action, scrambling to unlock the door. "Stop doing that!" she shrieked. "Are you crazy?" She shouted down the hall. "Get the doc! And… get General Hunt down here, too."

She opened the door, and Alex lurched into the hall, dizzy and vision blurred. The soldier threw her shoulder into his chest, and he hit the wall and slumped to the ground. The hallway emptied as a man in a black suit rushed around a corner and disappeared.

"Don't do anything else stupid," she said, rolling her shoulder and wincing.

"I'll do whatever I have to in order to talk to someone in charge." Alex spoke slowly and deliberately.

"Okay, well, you won." She crouched in front of him. "I've sent for my superior. Now, will you please go back to your room?"

"I want to see my son." Alex squeezed his eyes shut and wiped blood from his face with the back of his hand.

"I can't help you with that, but I can help you to that bed. It's not going to do you any good sitting here in the hall."

"You can't lock me up in the hall."

She chuckled. "Look, sir, the only way in and out of this section of the building is locked, so actually, yeah… we can."

Alex groaned. "I'm not going back in there."

She stood up with a heavy sigh. "General Hunt is going to be livid," she said under her breath.

"Who's Hunt?" Alex asked.

"He's the highest-ranking army officer here," she said. "I was guarding you under his direct orders."

Alex's head throbbed, and his ankle was no better. Blood stung his eyes, and he spit as it seeped into his mouth. The coppery taste made him grimace. "You have no right to keep me against my will."

The hall spun every time he moved his head. Maybe giving himself a concussion wasn't the best of his ideas, but at least it had gotten someone to talk to him.

A man burst into the hall with a green satchel in hand. "What happened here, Corporal Conner?" he barked. "Who did this?"

Corporal Conner nodded at Alex. "He did, doc," she said. "He wants to speak to someone, and he's been shouting about it off and on for hours. I guess he figured out how to get us to respond."

"Well, let's get him to the bed, at least," the doctor said. He hooked one arm under Alex's left armpit and the woman followed suit with his right arm; Alex was too disoriented to resist. Once they'd deposited him on the bed and he flopped onto his back, the doctor motioned toward the bathroom. "Grab a hand towel. I need it damp. Let's get this cleaned up so I can take a look at the wound."

Alex blinked away the brain fog and willed everything to stop spinning. "I have the right to know what's going on, and I want my people safe. I'm not doing anything for anybody until I know they're safe."

"What's he talking about?" The doctor took the towel from Conner when she came back.

"I wasn't told the whole story," Conner said, "but I think he showed up at the perimeter with a kid and a couple of women."

"No wonder he's upset." The doctor used the hand towel to wipe away the blood. "All right, sir, let's get you cleaned up."

Alex swatted the doctor's hand away. "Not until I get answers."

The doctor sighed. "Don't be stubborn, sir."

"I still have rights," Alex seethed.

"That's not how the world works right now, Mr. Roman." A man in a camo uniform with a vertical, three-star general's patch in the center of his chest walked into the room with a man in a black suit on his heels. This man was taller and broader than the one Alex had seen running off to obey the corporal's order.

"How do you know my name?" Alex asked.
The man in the suit scowled. "You're not the one asking the questions."
The general held up a hand. "Back down, Mr. Price."
Mr. Price took a wide stance and flipped back his jacket so that his gun was visible. "I don't work for you, General Hunt," he said. "I work for Mr. Lawson."
So… not everyone is on the same page. Alex observed the two alpha males as the doctor finished with the towel and dug some alcohol wipes out of his bag. Alex couldn't quite tell who the man in the suit was supposed to be, but the two men were rivals, that much was clear in how they glared at each other.
General Hunt adopted his own intimidating stance. He didn't have to show off a weapon to effectively stare down the man in the suit. "Mr. Lawson agreed that you and your men would cooperate with the army. A house divided cannot stand, Mr. Price, and right now, you're in my house. Are you with me or against me?"
Mr. Price closed his suit jacket and buttoned it. "Fine." He took a step back. "But there are just as many of us as there are of you. Who this house belongs to is still up in the air. I don't want a war in the middle of the damn apocalypse, but things need doing, and if you can't get them done, I will."
"If you two are done, I'd like an answer to my question." Alex winced as the alcohol pad stung his wound. His head still pounded, but the room was stable even when he turned his head. "How do you know my name?"
"ID in your wallet. We found it in the RV," General Hunt said. "Now, Mr. Roman, I don't want to hear about any more incidents like this one. You're going to report to the lab as soon as possible and get to work. We need answers about this disease, and you're going to do your job and help us get them."
"Did you kill Dr. Jonah Newton?" Alex asked. He'd thought for sure his boss had died of the sickness, but…
"I don't know who that is," General Hunt said. "When we got here, everyone was dead. They're long buried, son."
"I talked to him five days ago, and he was here. He left a van full of supplies for me so that I could continue figuring out what the heck is happening." Alex let the doctor put a large bandage over his wound, and then he sat up to look at the general.
"We got here three days ago, cleared the dead, and secured the area." General Hunt crossed his arms. "We've got these CDC facilities, several Emory University buildings, and the EU Hospital under our direct protection as of this afternoon. The plan is to hold the area and to consolidate and protect those who can get the good ole U.S. of A. up and running again, and that includes you. We've got a few scientists already working on this, and you're going to join them."
"I have other plans." Alex wasn't about to give the general every bit of information he had, not unless he could come to a place of trust with the man. He frowned. "Why are you here instead of D.C.?"
"D.C. is gone," the general said. "Next in line for the presidency was here. So here we came."
"I'm sorry, what? D.C. is gone?" Alex blinked, sure he hadn't heard right. "Next in line? The president is dead? The Vice President was in Georgia?"
"No. President Coleman was the Secretary of Agriculture. He was visiting family." General Hunt cleared his throat and shifted his weight, looking unsure for the first time since he stepped into the room.
"Are you… are you the highest-ranking general here… or anywhere?" A weight formed in the pit of his stomach. "How much of the government is left?" He narrowed his eyes at the man in the suit. "And who is this Mr. Lawson?"
"That's not your concern," Mr. Price said.
"The point is, son," the general said, "your country needs you."
"Well, I need to know my son and my friends are safe," Alex said. "Your people left them without any shelter. You took our RV and threatened our lives. If they don't find proper shelter, they could die tonight."
"And do you know why that is?" General Hunt asked. "The city is practically empty. Everyone's already dead. There's no one left to spread this thing, and yet…"
"People are still getting sick." Alex bit the inside of his cheek.
If the local mosquito population picked it up and are already spreading it… this is bad. This is really bad. It has to be passed down through the reproductive cycle. Otherwise, with no infected people to feed on, they wouldn't be such a threat. Unless they're picking it up from animals? His head swam with the possibilities. So many dead. So many more deaths to come.
"I'm assuming you've been following previously set CDC guidelines, the ones playing out over the radio for the last week?" Alex asked.
"Absolutely." General Hunt said. "To a T."
"Good." Alex worked his jaw back and forth, considering his options.
He needed to find Walter Peters. His boss had been sure Peters held the key to how to fight the sickness, and if the teams at the CDC couldn't solve the puzzle without the missing pieces Mr. Peters had, Alex was positive whoever had been brought in from the east coast wouldn't be able to figure it out, either.
And how do I know anything I've been told is even true? These guys look military, but… what if this is some kind of coup? I don't know them. I've never heard of Coleman. And why would they be working with some kind of what… private security? Militia? Alex glanced at Mr. Price. He definitely didn't trust that guy. There was too much at stake and not enough information. Information is power. I can't give that to these men until I'm sure I can trust them.
But first thing was first. "I've got information you're going to need," Alex said. "But as long as my people are in danger, my lips are sealed."
The general clasped his hands behind his back. "All civilians we find are boarded at Emory University after a twenty-four quarantine in the hospital. Your people were not left to die, Mr. Roman. They're safe."
"What about the dog?" Alex asked.
The general frowned. "Pets are not our priority right now, Mr. Roman."
"Did you kill him?" Alex held his breath, remembering the threats when they'd first encountered the men with guns.

"I don't know what happened to the damn dog," General Hunt said, tone gruff.

Corporal Conner spoke up. "He's been sitting outside the hospital, sir, staying in the line of sight of the door his people entered through. At least, that's what I heard."

"I want to see them," Alex said. "The dog included. If you want anything out of me, my people come here, with me, and we are *all* treated with more respect than this."

Alex balled his hands into fists to keep them from shaking as both the general and Mr. Price threw glares his way. But he stood his ground. He didn't back down. If these people already had Oliver, Minnie, and Lauren, he had to find a way to get them all together. Only if he knew exactly where they all were could he orchestrate an escape. And with the way things weren't adding up, Alex wasn't about to stay under the thumb of these men any longer than he had to.

"Corporal Conner," the general said, "you will guard the civilian from inside this room from now on. Doctor Miller, administer something to make our guest more comfortable." He turned on his heel without so much as a word about Alex's demands.

"What?" Alex barely had time to register what had been said before the doctor pulled a syringe from his bag, uncapped the long needle, and plunged it into his arm.

Chapter 5

Minnie Stevens

"You lyin' snake in the grass! Tell me where Lauren and Oliver are, right now, little missy." Minnie pulled against the restraints on her wrists.

She was in a hospital room that had been converted with clear plastic to hold two square quarantine bubbles — hers and that of an older gentleman. There was a makeshift hall on the other side of the plastic rooms that ran from the door to the wall. She'd been fine and dandy with the arrangement until they'd refused to tell her where her daughter and Oliver had been taken. They'd lured her to the bubble with slick lies about an exam to check her health. Well, no doctor had come, and the exam turned into the start of a twenty-four-hour quarantine. When Minnie had attempted to leave, they'd restrained her.

Those yellow-bellied tricksters. She used her best if-looks-could-kill stare down. *Ain't nobody keepin' my kin from me.* And that meant both Lauren, her daughter, and Oliver. That boy had grown on her something fierce. As for Alex, well, he'd been taken into the CDC by the military when they'd been carted off to the hospital by those suspicious men in suits. She'd find Alex, too, eventually.

"I'm not lying. I really don't know where they are." The woman — Cheryl, if she hadn't lied about her name, too — held out a glass of water in her blue-gloved hands. "Now, you want this or not?"

Her body was covered head to toe with PPE; the only part of her visible was her eyes, cold blue. But that was all Minnie needed. From the time she was a tiny tike, she could tell if someone was lying just by getting a good look at their eyes, the windows to their soul. And Cheryl's windows were dirty.

Minnie saw red. "You were there when we came in. I'd know your high-pitched, whiny voice anywhere."

"Beg your pardon?" Cheryl narrowed her eyes and thumped the glass on the side table, sloshing water over the lip. "Well, then, you can figure out how to feed and water yourself, thank you very much. I shouldn't even be here. I'm an engineer, for goodness sake." She turned on her heel and stomped out of the room, fists at her side.

"You coulda been nicer." The gentleman, her roommate by force, smiled at her from his side of the plastic wall. A handsome fellow with warm brown skin and kind eyes, he sat on his hospital bed all calm and serene, which meant he couldn't be normal. Who could be in their right mind in such a situation?

"I don't recall askin' you." Minnie repositioned herself the best she could with her wrists restrained as they were. The fact the bed was elevated to a sitting position was a small mercy. At least she could see who she was talking to.

"I don't recall needing to be asked to speak." He chuckled and sat back, propping his legs up on the bed. "They're just makin' sure we don't have that sickness that's killed everyone. And they're all volunteerin'. Just seems to me, you coulda been nicer."

Minnie huffed. Perfect strangers didn't get to tell her what to do. Not anymore. She'd been her own boss for thirty years, and no apocalypse was going to change that. "I'll be nicer when they tell me where my family is."

"You still got family?" He cocked his head at her. "Ain't that nice. I been here longer than you. My time's almost up, in fact. Had time to talk to people, and that lady you just terrorized? Well, she lost her parents. And her best friend. Cheryl ain't so bad if you're not bitin' her head off."

Heat rose to Minnie's cheeks, and she lost a bit of the fire in her belly. "Well... I didn't know that." She heaved a sigh. "I 'spose I'll be apologizin' next time I see her. But she *was* there when we first came in, and she *does* know where Oliver is."

"That may be." He folded his hands in his lap. "While we're waitin' for your chance to apologize, how about we get to know each other? Name's Elijah Dixon."

She pursed her lips. "My friends call me Minnie, but I ain't sure about you yet. No charmin' southern accent is gonna pull the wool over my eyes."

"Charmin'... well, doggone." He laughed again. "I ain't been called charmin' since '27."

"Did your charm get any more answers about what's goin' on here?" she asked, hoping he couldn't see her blush.

"Quarantine. Separated by age," Elijah said. "This is the section for old fogies."

"I ain't old, and I certainly ain't no fogie." Minnie blew a stray, gray curl from her face. "I got plenty of life still left to live."

"I'm sure you do." Elijah continued, "There's a section for kids, and one for young adults, if I understand it right. And everyone will be reunited after a stay of twenty-four hours. Everyone with someone, that is. I got nobody, so..." He trailed off.

"You lose family since the start of this whole thing?" Minnie asked.

"Nah." Elijah shook his head. "I lost my people a long time ago. I guess... I did lose my cat, Puff. But, she's not dead, I don't think. Just... lost."

A pang shot through Minnie at the thought of Samson. "That's nothin' to sneeze at. My dog, Samson... I don't know where he is right now, and I hate that as much as anything."

Talking with Elijah did something to calm Minnie's nerves. She still had the urge to charge down the halls looking for Lauren and Oliver, but Elijah had a soothing way about him. He distracted her, and seeing as how there was nothing she could do about her predicament, she let him do it. An hour passed before the door opened again.

A man in a full-body paper suit, complete with a hood, a mask, and blue gloves strode inside, eyes on a clipboard. He looked up, glancing between the two of them before he settled on Elijah. "Mr. Dixon?"

"That'd be me." Elijah smiled.

"Good afternoon. My name is Dr. Smith." He unzipped the doorway to Elijah's bubble. "You've been here for twenty-four hours. Congratulations. Your quarantine period is over."

"Well, I'd be lyin' if I said I wasn't happy about that." Elijah hopped off his bed. "So, what's that mean, doc? Where do I go next?"

Dr. Smith unclipped a purple wrist band that had been attached to the board. "I see on your chart you've got Type 2 diabetes?"

"I do." Elijah nodded. "I've managed it pretty good, though, doc. Lost the weight, ate real healthy."

"That's wonderful, Mr. Dixon, but access to the right meds and the right foods might be a little harder than it was before. We want to make sure the most vulnerable get some extra attention. If you could put on this purple wristband, it will tell the security guys where you should go." He held it out, and Elijah took it.

"Security guys? You mean those men in suits?" Minnie frowned. She still hadn't figured out who they were. Not military, that was for sure. The two groups didn't seem to like each other very much. "Where will they take him? I think I've gotten used to him. Might wanna check up on him once I'm outta here."

"I'd like that, Minnie." Elijah said as he peeled off the sticker part of the wristband and secured the bracelet around his wrist. "I bet they'll be takin' me somewhere real nice. Ain't that right, doc?"

Dr. Smith shifted from one foot to the other and cleared his throat. "Um, yeah, I'm sure you'll be very comfortable. Do you have any family that need to be notified you'll be lodging at a separate facility?"

"No, sir," Elijah said. "It's just me."

Minnie cocked her head. "Don't you *know* this other facility is comfortable?" The doctor gave her a questioning look. "You said you were sure, but you didn't sound like you knew."

"Well, we've been given instructions. Those still at risk for some health issue or another need to be grouped together so we can better care for them, but I'm not on that medical team. I haven't seen those accommodations. I'm living here in the hospital. I can't leave the building." Dr. Smith sounded bitter as he gestured for Elijah to come out of his bubble.

Can't leave? Minnie frowned. He almost implied he was being kept at the hospital against his will. "And what about me? Where will I be taken?" Minnie asked.

"Most patients are given green wristbands post-quarantine and are sent to the dorm rooms at Emory University, about a mile and half down the road." The doctor took a step toward the door, tapping his finger on the clipboard he held at his side. "Now, I really must—"

"Hold on a sec, doc." Minnie didn't like that some tough-guy Suits were going to take Elijah Heaven knows where. Her gut told her something wasn't right. "That's not too far from the hospital for him to come back and get treatment if need be. It ain't like diabetes is contagious. Why would Elijah need to be separated from everyone else?"

"There's nothin' wrong with a little extra attention." Elijah waved off her concerns.

"Yes, exactly." The doctor perked up a little at Elijah's explanation.

Why's he itchin' to end this conversation? Minnie pasted on a fake smile and nodded graciously. "I 'spose so," she said. "Hey, doc, before you go… you mind undoin' these here cuffs? I'm thirsty as a dog in the desert."

"We restrain people for a reason," Dr. Smith said. "I really shouldn't—"

"Oh, it's all right, I think, doc," Elijah said. "She was worked up before, but she's been good as a church mouse for a long time now. You can't leave her with no water, no food, and no company."

Dr. Smith sighed, but he walked over and unzipped Minnie's bubble. "Promise you'll stay put?"

Minnie crossed her toes under the blanket. "Swear it on my mama's grave." *Sorry mama.*

The restraints were off her wrists a minute later. "Is there anything else?" he said with an exasperated tone as he stepped outside her quarantine space and zipped the plastic back up.

"That'll do it," Minnie said.

"Good. Now, Mr. Dixon, if you could just—"

"I'd like to say my goodbyes," Minnie said, "if you don't mind." She raised her eyebrows and glanced pointedly at the door.

"Fine." Dr. Smith practically ran out the door, giving Elijah instructions on his way out. "Just go down the hall, and a security guy will take you where you need to go."

"Yes, sir. Thank you." Mr. Dixon nodded, grasping his hands meekly until the doctor was out of the room. Then, he turned to Minnie with his hands on his hips. "What in tarnation was that about, woman?"

"We gotta get outta here, Elijah." Minnie pointed to his wristband. "I got a bad feelin' about this. Nobody in the place is givin' straight answers. Those Suits… there was somethin' wrong about them. And it just don't make sense to be separatin' people like that. Monitorin' folks with health problems don't mean isolation."

"Whoa, now," Elijah held his hands up, palms out. "I ain't about to stir up trouble. I'm not fond of the Suits neither, but I'm also not fond of gettin' shot. And who knows? Maybe I'll get a nice room all to myself."

"This ain't a vacation, Elijah." Minnie stepped up to the zipper.

"Now, you stop that." Elijah shook his head and backed away. "I ain't goin' nowhere they don't tell me to go. The city out there is a nightmare. I'll take my chances with the Suits. I'm sorry, but I'm not breakin' the rules. You gotta stay in quarantine."

Minnie grasped the zipper and pulled it an inch. "What I gotta do is find my people. If you wanna be herded off, I guess I can't stop ya."

"I'll shout." Elijah put his hand on the door. "They'll come and restrain you again."

"You wouldn't." Minnie drew back her hand like the zipper was on fire, staring wide-eyed at Elijah.

"Ma'am, I would, too. I'm tellin' ya it's better in here than it is out there. I ain't doin' nothin' to compromise my place here." He raised his eyebrows in a challenge. "I suggest you don't, neither."

"Don't you 'ma'am' me, mister!" Minnie huffed. She hated being called that, as if she were ninety-nine and dying tomorrow. Still, she backed off the plastic wall and plopped back down on the bed, crossing her arms. "I'll stay put until you're gone, then, at least."

Elijah nodded. "Good. It's for your own safety. Everybody's just doin' their best around here. Now, I don't count none of that against ya, and I hope you don't count nothin' against me either. I'd love to see you again, Miss Minnie." He flashed her a handsome grin.

She blushed again. *Dagnabbit!* She pursed her lips. "I wouldn't mind it," she said, her heart fluttering. It had been a while since she'd had butterflies, but she liked the man, even if he was a fool. *Maybe I'll try again to get him to come with me when we break loose from this place.*

Elijah left with a chuckle and a shake of his head. She sat back with a huff and stared at the door through the plastic, counting to three hundred mississippis to give him about five minutes to get clear before she caused a ruckus. Then she cracked her knuckles, took a swig of water, unzipped her bubble, stomped over to the door, and flung it open. Five minutes of chewing nails, and she was ready to spit barbed wire.

Chapter 6

Alexander Roman

Alex was halfway through counting the forty-two ceiling tiles for the hundredth time when General Hunt charged into the room. Corporal Conner, who had been sitting silently by the small dresser keeping watch, leapt to her feet and saluted. Alex sat upright on the bed, expecting the general to have some answers for him. He had demanded to see his people if they wanted him to get to work in the labs; the way they'd knocked him out and then kept him under closer guard hadn't changed his mind. His skill set was the only bargaining chip he had.

"At ease, corporal." General Hunt didn't acknowledge Alex. "The asset is to be escorted to the Blue Room immediately. Let's pack him up and roll him out." The corporal pulled a zip tie out of her pocket and stepped toward the bed.

"Whoa, now." Alex held up his hands. "No need for that. I won't try to run. You've got my son and my friends. I'm not going anywhere."

Conner glanced at the general, who gave her a curt nod. "Bring up the rear, corporal. Make sure he stays in line." He finally regarded Alex. "Cause any more trouble, and things'll get a lot worse for you, son. Peacetime is over. We ain't got time for that crap."

"Yes, sir." Alex stood up, swallowing a groan. His head swam for a moment with the sudden movement, but he found his bearings with a steadying hand on the side of the bed.

Corporal Conner reached out, but the general stopped her. "He can reap what he's sown." He frowned at Alex. "I can't stand drama queens, son. Get it together."

"Lead the way, sir." Alex stood tall and then concentrated on walking in a straight line behind the general as the corporal kept his pace steady from behind. Any time he slowed, she prodded him forward with a hand on his back. He had a few wobbly steps, but he wasn't terribly disoriented; the walls and floor only spun when he moved his head too quickly. A mild throbbing at the site of the wound on his forehead didn't help, either, but he had gotten their attention. That was all that mattered to him.

The general used a keycard to open the door to the stairwell, and Alex tackled the stairs with the help of the railing. Their footsteps echoed up and down the shaft as they climbed four flights, and they emerged into a hallway empty save two men in black suits and another two in military fatigues. General Hunt stopped a few yards from a set of double doors Alex had been through before.

"Stay here." General Hunt marched up to the double doors and went inside.

"Is that where the President is?" Alex asked.

"It is." Corporal Conner settled into a wide stance with her hands clasped behind her back.

"Why aren't they using one of the big fancy offices on the top floor?" Alex asked.

"Too many windows. Not enough security." She shifted her eyes between the double doors, the men in suits, and Alex, though she barely moved a muscle.

"What's with them — the guys in suits, I mean?" Alex whispered. "Who are they?"

"Lawson's guys. Private security." Corporal Conner whispered back.

"That's all you're giving me?" Alex stepped a little closer. "C'mon. I have important information, but I need to know who to trust. You seem like a regular, run-of-the-mill patriot."

She quirked an eyebrow at him. "Thanks?"

"I mean that as a good thing." Alex licked his lips and tried again. "Most of these guys rub me the wrong way, but I've seen humane reactions from you. You seem like a good person, and right now, that means more to me than you could know. Who is Lawson?" He shifted to try to keep her looking at him as she turned her head. "We're on the same team. I just want to give the information I have to the right people. I want to help fix this."

Conner pressed her lips together and crossed her arms. She looked him straight in the eyes for a few long seconds before sighing and dropping her arms. "Lawson's a tech mogul, President Coleman's father-in-law. It's who he was visiting when all hell broke loose. By the time our platoon got here, Coleman already trusted them, wanted them to come along." She said that last part with a soured expression. She looked like she wanted to spit.

"You don't like them. Or worse… you don't trust them." Alex frowned. "Is this Coleman guy any good? I mean, he was the Secretary of Agriculture. He didn't sign up for this. He wasn't even voted into office."

"Doesn't matter what I think," Conner said.

"It matters to me." Alex pressed her. He was about to go into a room where his lack of knowledge could put him at a severe disadvantage.

"I think he's a good guy trusting the wrong people." She averted her eyes, looking at the ground. "Maybe he's over his head. I don't know," she said softly. Then her cheeks flushed red, and she snapped her head up to stare down Alex. "Don't tell anyone I said that, got it?"

"Got it." Alex backed up and sealed his lips.

The double doors opened again, and General Hunt poked his head into the hallway. "Come on in, Drama Queen."

Alex grimaced and glanced at Conner. "He's not going to keep calling me that, is he?"

She cracked a smile. "He does love nicknames."

"Great." Alex sighed and walked past the guards into the conference room. General Hunt took up a position nearby but out of the way.

The huge conference table, big enough to seat eighteen people, had been removed. Alex had only attended a few meetings in the space since he'd started at the CDC, and he'd never realized just how large the room was. The absence of the wooden table and the removal of several abstract art pieces made the thin blue carpet and gray blue walls more prominent. A large desk was centered at the back of the room, and a lanky man, perhaps in his forties, with big round glasses sat behind it. An American flag hung from a pole near the wall on the right. To the left, a second man in a black, pinstriped suit loomed over the room as if he were a permanent fixture. This second man commanded attention. His head was shaved clean, and he had piercing blue eyes with small, dignified crow's feet and a thick, graying beard. He scowled at Alex.

"Alexander Roman?" The man behind the desk stood and rounded the desk, holding out a hand. "Michael Coleman... or, President Michael Coleman?"

Alex raised his eyebrows. "Is that a question?"

Coleman chuckled. "Well, yes, I think it is. At least, for now."

The other man was at Coleman's side in a few long strides. "As far as everyone here is concerned, you are the president, Michael." He spoke forcefully, and the wiry man flinched at his harsh tone.

"This is my advisor and father-in-law, Charles Lawson," Coleman said.

"Thank you for seeing me," Alex said.

Charles's upper lip curled. "You didn't give us much of a choice."

"Yes," Coleman said, nodding as he returned to his chair behind the desk. "I was a little shocked to discover someone with your skillset was making demands at a time like this."

Lawson took up residence right behind him, his hands gripping the back of Coleman's chair. "You haven't made a great first impression, Mr. Roman. The United States needs heroes right now, not opportunists."

Who is in charge here? Alex wasn't sure which man to look at as he replied; he defaulted to the one holding the title of president, but he was tempted more than once to defer to Lawson.

"I'm not an opportunist," Alex said. "I'm a father. We came here seeking supplies my boss left for me in a van. He said the CDC had been compromised, and I'm pretty sure I heard him die over the sat phone. My son and my friends were apprehended when we approached, and we were separated. I was imprisoned—"

"—quarantined, actually," Lawson interrupted. "Not imprisoned."

Coleman cleared his throat and said more timidly, "Your family would have been quarantined as well, at the hospital. You were quarantined here because of who you are. The twenty-four-hour quarantine is due to the full work up and assessing the medical needs of every survivor we find. From what we can tell, this new sickness manifests in four hours or less. That's what my people are telling me, anyway, and so we figured it would be better to get you to work as soon as possible. Your four hours were almost up when you started banging your head on the door."

"I can tell you right now that the four hours is an average, not a definitive number, and that you should probably quarantine newcomers for longer than that." Alex sat back and folded his arms across his chest. Both Coleman and Lawson shrank back from him. "I'm not sick," he added. "I am positive I'm clean unless I've been infected since I've been here by one of you, in which case, we're all probably dead anyway."

Lawson rolled his shoulders and set his jaw, but the president's face was pale as he tapped his fingers nervously on the desk. "We need to know what you know," Coleman said.

"You go first." Alex leaned forward, trying to match Lawson's intensity. "I don't know you. I don't know if what you're telling me is true. General Hunt said something about D.C. being gone. That doesn't make any sense. I don't know if the guys out there are real military, and I definitely don't know if I can trust those security meatheads."

The muscles in Lawson's face constricted and a vein popped out of his forehead. "You little—"

"Hold on, now, Charles," Coleman said, and Alex was a little surprised when the bigger man shut his mouth. "He's asking the right questions." Coleman took off his glasses and rubbed his hand over his face as he sagged back in his chair. "A lot has happened over the last two weeks. I was here, in Atlanta, visiting Charles with my wife and our kids. Those security meatheads protected us, and they did their jobs well. When General Hunt showed up..." Coleman trailed off, breathing in shakily. "I could barely believe what he had to say." He waved General Hunt over to the desk. "He was there. I think he should be the one to fill you in."

The general stepped up to the side of the desk, planted his feet, and looked straight forward. "The sickness hit D.C. two days after it hit Boston." General Hunt spoke in a clear, no-nonsense manner, his tone even and calm. "It's spreading up and down the northeast coast quick. Heavily populated area, lots of traveling and commuting, and there were quick, short flights available to and from all the major cities. The former president boarded Air Force One and was pronounced dead when the aircraft went down after communication was lost. It is speculated that the sickness was on board. The Vice President was killed the following day in a traffic accident. The Speaker of the House, president pro tempore of the Senate, and the Secretary of the Treasury were confirmed dead on the fourth day, all succumbing to the sickness." He hesitated before he continued, the only sign of emotion evident during his recounting. "And then the Secretary of Defense suffered a heart attack after losing four of his five children. The Attorney General was not eligible for the line of the presidency due to the fact he is not a natural-born citizen. Three teams were sent out to track down the three people next in line: The Secretary of the Interior, the Secretary of Agriculture, and the Secretary of Commerce."

"Wait," Alex held up a hand. "So, there was another guy in line before you?" He directed his question at Coleman.

"Which is why I said my presidency is still in question." Coleman nodded at the general. "Thank you, General." Hunt stepped back and fell silent again.

"But the only way to function is to behave as if your presidency is certain," Lawson said.

"Yes, we've all agreed," Coleman sat back in his chair and looked at Alex. "So, that's where we are, Mr. Roman. General Hunt wants to take me to Cheyenne Mountain where the other teams are supposed to meet up and hunker down. I can't leave yet, not until we have answers. The line of the presidency wasn't the only thing decimated. The House, the Senate… they're in shambles. If the government is truly going to rebuild itself, we have to beat this sickness."

"Okay," Alex said, "I'm in. But only if my demands are met. I can't work if I don't know my family is safe. I want them here, in the facility with me. And the dog, too. He's important to my son."

Coleman quirked an eyebrow. "I've given you a lot, Mr. Roman. Give me something that tells me I can trust *you*, and we have a deal."

Alex leaned forward. "My boss, Jonah Newton, and a few other brave souls at the CDC were working on our problem before it killed them. Jonah told me over the sat phone that they'd found a second vector for the sickness. Mosquitos can carry and spread this illness. We need to update the CDC warning that's going out on radio frequencies to include this information."

Coleman nodded. "We will pass that information to our scientists and see if they can corroborate. In the meantime, we have located and are prepared to reunite you with your son, Ms. Lauren Stevens, and… your dog… but we have an issue with the other woman you arrived with."

Alex's heart stopped. "Minnie? Is she okay?"

"Well, we don't know. The military and the security team aren't always on the same page, and the security team is the dominant force at the hospital. We know where she was before there was an… incident… where she broke quarantine. The fact is, Mr. Roman, Minnie Stevens's whereabouts are unknown."

Chapter 7

Zara Williams

Six instruments of destruction were lined up on a tray inches from Zara's hands. Several of the mosquitos caught and killed in her traps were thrown out for their normalcy, but these were different. Larger, with white strips on their legs and an orange diamond on their backs, these little devils were spreading the disease. DV-10... that's what Mr. Peters had called it. He'd said Vanguard had created mosquitos with markers that would allow them to tell which version of virus they carried.

"The combination of this specific genetically modified mosquito and this particular strain of our proprietary virus was too virulent even for the most aggressive of our backers in the government." Mr. Peters studied one of the specimens under the microscope.

"So, what does that mean?" Lizzy hugged her middle as she sat in a chair in the corner. Her voice was small, her eyes reddened, and her posture shrunken.

A pinprick of guilt stabbed at Zara, but she ignored it like she tried to ignore her best friend's hollow, sad eyes. *She's falling apart because I'm making her choose.* Zara closed her eyes and images surfaced of Mr. Peters killing innocent people in cold blood – first a woman at the fair and then his own pilot. She hadn't known it at the time, but he sentenced them to die with his cursed virus and then finished them off early with his own hands. Zara set her jaw, opened her eyes, and focused on the killer insects in front of her. *No... Liz is falling apart because she refuses to make the right choice.*

"The virus is obviously terrible," Zara said, "but you're saying these mosquitos you engineered are also terrible in and of themselves? So, this is going to get worse as the mosquitos multiply? Is that it?"

"Well *I* merely approved the work." Mr. Peters continued to pace. "Someone else—"

"Someone else would have done it if you hadn't?" Zara finished his familiar refrain. "Cut the bull, Walter. What about these mosquitos is so terrible?"

Mr. Peters rounded on her, eyes wide with fury, but something stopped him as he loomed over Zara, his hands balled into fists as he stared her down. Zara didn't flinch, not outwardly at least. She refused to cower in front of him; she'd done enough of that already. The second Mr. Peters smelled weakness, he'd pounce on her and drag her back under his thumb.

"Dad... Zee... please don't..." Lizzy didn't get up, and her plea was laced with exhaustion.

He took a step back, but his features remained taut. "This species breeds faster, spreads farther, and is more aggressive than even the worst nature developed on her own."

"So you decided to make mosquitos from hell." Zara proceeded with a mocking, slow clap. "Congratulations, Walter. Good job. Mission accomplished. I'm sure we could find a gold star somewhere around here if we really put some effort into it."

"Will you stop it?" Mr. Peters shouted. "It wasn't *me*."

"Right. It was a group effort." Zara rolled her eyes. "Which you orchestrated, approved, and facilitated."

Mr. Peters threw up his hands and plopped into a chair next to Lizzy. He buried his head in his hands and just sat there, unmoving, for several minutes. "What's done is done," he said finally. "I can't undo the past, but I'm trying to fix it." He leaned back, and Zara was taken aback by the moisture in his eyes. "Every experiment had a counterproject, a failsafe. There are mosquitos that can eradicate this species. The eggs are frozen at Horizons Lab. There are two other locations housing the failsafe, but the one in Boston is the only one I know how to get to without a plane."

Lizzy sat up straighter. "So, there really is a way to fix this?"

He nodded. "There is, if we can get to Boston and I can dust off some of my lab skills. My hope is that some of the others who have worked on this project have survived and have already begun to implement the counterproject. If they recognized DV-10 and identified the mosquitos, maybe the process has already started."

"If and maybe... that's not good enough," Zara said. "We have to survive long enough to make sure this thing is stopped." She narrowed her eyes at Mr. Peters. "*You* have to survive long enough." Her skin crawled. She *hated* how important Walter Peters was to saving the world he'd had a hand in destroying.

"How long do we have?" Lizzy asked.

Zara snapped her eyes to look at Lizzy. "Until what?"

"Until these mosquitos spread everywhere." Lizzy rested her chin on her knees and looked at her father.

"I don't know exactly." Mr. Peters stood and placed his hands on the silver counter, each hand on either side of the tray holding the mosquitos. "We never planned to release them like this. They were to be weaponized for targeted attacks, viruses that targeted specific DNA sequences particular to a person or maybe a family line. DV-10 was experimental, unfinished, too general. And these..." He rocked back and then slammed his hands on the table, causing the tray to rattle. Then he swept the tray off the table, his hands trembling. "Those mosquitos and this virus are the worst possible combination, of all the experiments, of all the possibilities, they just *had* to steal *this* batch." Lizzy burst into tears and ran from the room, and Mr. Peters watched her go with a look of surprise. "Elizabeth!" He called after her but didn't move to follow. He returned to the chair and sank into it. "How much does she hate me?"

Zara frowned at the door as it clicked shut. "She doesn't." *That's part of the problem.*

"What?" Mr. Peters asked. "How could she not?"

"Beats me." Zara shrugged and changed the topic; she did *not* want to talk about Lizzy with him. "What are we going to do now that you know which mosquitos are out there and exactly what they're spreading? We're going to tell our people, right?"

"The people in this hospital are not *our* people, so no, absolutely not." Mr. Peters shook his head vehemently. "They're safe for now, anyway."

"They deserve to know. *Everyone* deserves to know. We can't hold on to this information." Zara crossed her arms. "I won't do it."

"Telling them will only induce panic." Mr. Peters leaned forward, and the corner of his mouth twitched upward so slightly someone not used to the way he enjoyed passive aggressive behavior might not have noticed. "And you promised my daughter you wouldn't expose me."

Zara narrowed her eyes. *Trying to manipulate me, again, are you?* She let her arms fall back to her sides and loosened her shoulders. She met Mr. Peters's gaze. "Look, I'll give you some time, but either you figure out a way to tell people what they should be afraid of, or I will. And if I do it, I'll include *you* on that list."

She walked out, trying to keep her cool, escaping before Mr. Peters could figure out a way to bait her like he did in his room hours earlier. He sat back and watched her leave, and out the corner of her eye she thought she saw something like pride reflected in his eyes. That made her sick to her stomach. His accusations repeated in her mind. *You remind me of myself when I was young, Zara,* he had said. She'd insisted she was nothing like him. *But I could be.* That thought stopped her in her tracks at the end of the hall, at the bottom of the stairwell. It made her weak in the knees, made her heartbeat throb in her ears. She was changing, evolving into a person she didn't recognize. Her chest tightened, and the air was too thick, too hot. She bolted up the stairs, the throbbing in her head reverberating throughout her body. She burst through the door to the main level where they'd kept the temperature control on. It wasn't cool exactly, but it was more bearable. She put her hands on her knees and just breathed, forcing her mind to quiet.

A stifled sob followed by a series of hiccups interrupted Zara's attempt to gather herself together. She frowned as she straightened and looked up and down the empty hall. She walked slowly in the direction of the sound and stopped outside a small chapel with a dove on the door. She gently pushed the door open and peeked inside. Benches sat on either side of an aisle, and at the front, there was a long, tiered table full of little candles, all long since burned out.

"I'm so sorry," Lizzy's voice came from the front of the chapel, though Zara couldn't see her. "I didn't know. This is all my fault."

Zara stepped into the room and let the door close behind her. "What are you talking about?"

Lizzy bolted upright from where she'd been laying on the bench at the front. "What are you doing here?"

"I heard you crying." Zara walked to the front so she could sit on the bench across the aisle from Lizzy. "What did you mean when you said this is all your fault?"

"I… I've wanted to tell you… I mean, I…" Lizzy's face paled as she stumbled over her words.

"Just spit it out, Liz." Zara gripped the seat of the bench, waiting. *What have you been hiding from me?*

Shouting erupted outside the chapel as footsteps pounded the hallway floor. "Everyone come quick! To the front lobby!" The door burst open, and Brian's broad-shouldered frame took up the entirety of the doorway. "Let's go, ladies!"

"How did you know we were in here?" Zara asked.

The male nurse waved for them to hurry. "Someone is always in the chapel," he said. "I was just trying to find everyone. Where's your dad?"

"I'm right here." Mr. Peters came up behind Brian and slapped his back. "What's going on?"

Brian stepped backward, nearly bouncing on the balls of his feet. "The CDC warning has changed. Dr. Young said everyone should gather in the front lobby ASAP."

"What's changed?" Zara stood and joined Brian and Mr. Peters in the hall. Walter looked almost as pale as Lizzy when she asked the question.

"I'm not sure," Brian said. "I didn't get the chance to hear it before Doc Young sent me to find everyone. He wanted us to meet in the lobby so that whoever's guarding the door can still participate in whatever decisions we make."

Mr. Peters swallowed hard, and his hands trembled just a little before he flexed his fingers. "We'll be right behind you, Brian. Go ahead."

"Yeah, I still need to find Sunny. See you there." Brian went in search of his fellow nurse.

"Do you think they know what really happened?" Lizzy asked as she stepped into the hallway with Mr. Peters and Zara.

"The CDC is part of the government, right?" Zara asked. "And the government commissioned the project, so I'd say it's possible."

"Yes," Mr. Peters said, "but this project was Top Secret and highly compartmentalized. I doubt the people at the CDC know the whole story."

"I guess we're about to find out." Zara led the way down the hall and took a right into the lobby.

Dr. Young paced the width of the lobby by the entrance where Brandt still stood, half turned as he divided his attention between watching the outside and the people in the room. Dr. Donald held a small radio in her hands as she leaned against a wall. Everyone else in the room occupied the chairs lining either side. Zara took a seat next to Amos and his daughter, Sophie, which put plenty of distance between her and Mitch who glared at her from across the room. Mr. Peters took a seat at the back of the room, and Lizzy chose a chair next to her father. Brian and Sunny were the last to join them, and soon all fifteen survivors were accounted for.

"Everyone is here." Dr. Donald stepped up to her colleague, Dr. Young, and handed him the radio. "Do you want to do the honors?"

He took the radio. "We thought, when we heard the updated message, that we should all talk about it, about what to do next." He switched on the radio, and the same artificial, robotic voice came on the radio.

"… Do not panic. This station will broadcast more information when it is available." The end of the message, which Zara had heard dozens of times, culminated in a pause before it picked back up again. "This is a warning from the Center for Disease Control and the United States Government. A nationwide curfew is in place from eighteen hundred hours to ten hundred hours. The disease has been confirmed to be contagious. It can be spread through human-to-human contact and has been confirmed to be carried by mosquitos. Maintain social distance. If you go outside, take precautions against insect bites. Do not leave your homes. Do not panic. This station—"

Dr. Young switched off the radio. "So, the curfew has been expanded an hour, and we now know more about how this thing spreads. The hospital only has enough diesel to run the generator another few days. Once we run out, it's going to be hot in here, and if we can't open the windows for fear of mosquitos, it's going to be unbearable."

"Wait a minute. Mosquitos?" Mitch grunted as he got to his feet. He stomped across the room and jabbed a finger at Zara. "Those traps you set with the 2-liters… those were for catching bugs. Were you catching mosquitos? What do you know?"

All eyes turned on Zara, but she just quirked an eyebrow. "You should be asking those questions of Mr. Peters. He's the one who asked me to catch them. He knows *all about* mosquitos, don't you, Walter?"

"Walter Peters…" Dr. Donald mumbled something to herself and then her eyes went wide. "Are you the Walter Peters of Vanguard? I've been following that project with malaria mosquitos for two years."

A look of recognition crossed Dr. Young's face. "You're right, Sarah. He was speaking at the World's Fair. The whole medical community has been excited about that project. Didn't you three say you were at the World's Fair?"

"That can't be a coincidence." Mitch seemed to forget about Zara as he turned his attention on Mr. Peters.

Lizzy brought her knees to her chest and froze like a stone statue, unmoving, eyes wide and terrified. Zara just sat back and lightly folded her arms. *Let's see how you wiggle your way out of this one, Mr. Peters.*

"All right, everybody," Mr. Peters stood straight and held out his hands disarmingly. "You caught me. I am *that* Walter Peters, and yes, my company was developing mosquitos that could destroy entire species of disease carrying mosquitos. And yes, I was at one of the three ground zeroes in the United States."

"That's awfully suspicious." Mitch pointed at Mr. Peters. "Something isn't right!"

"Is that why the girls have been so upset with you?" Bertie asked, scooting farther back into her chair and putting an arm protectively around her daughter. "The things I've heard Zara say in passing, they didn't make much sense before, but… Walter, did you have something to do with this?"

The way each person around the room tensed and looked at Mr. Peters was satisfying. He was finally going to be seen for the monster he was, and Zara wouldn't have to break her promise to Lizzy for it to happen.

"Suspicious? Did *I* have something to do with the disease?" Mr. Peters chuckled like the notion was amusingly insane, and Zara's stomach dropped as several individuals visibly relaxed. "I would call who I am and what I've been through a stroke of luck, not for me, of course, but for the world. I would have never chosen to put my daughter in harm's way, but being at the World's Fair, seeing how it all started… well, I have been studying how diseases spread through mosquitos for years. I don't know if that's how this disease started – my money is on terrorism," Mitch, Lorrie, and Amos all nodded at that, "but over the past weeks, I've come to suspect mosquitos as a way this disease could spread." He walked the length of the lobby with slow, deliberate steps, meeting the eyes of every person as he went. "With the limited lab equipment here and my background, I asked the girls to help me gather some samples, and the CDC message confirms my theory that one of the reasons cases seem to soar overnight and in the first hours of the day is that the disease is spreading through the mosquito population. I believe the onset of symptoms comes very quickly, within a matter of hours. The pieces all fit."

"Wow," Brandt said. "That makes a lot of sense."

Zara sat up straighter, her mouth dropping in shock. *They're eating this up!*

"You're trying to see if you can use your genetically engineered mosquitos to slow the spread of this new disease." Dr. Donald put her hands on her hips and smiled.

"Better." Mr. Peters grinned. "If I can get back to my lab in Boston, I think I can do more than slow the spread. Vanguard has developed vaccines, medications… humanity isn't done yet, not if I have anything to say about it."

Sweat rolled down Zara's back and her palms became clammy as the people in the room actually cheered and clapped for him. *This can't be happening.*

Men gathered around Mr. Peters to shake his hand and clap him on the back. Zara couldn't handle it; her skin crawled, her stomach churned, and she swallowed bile. Mr. Peters was the last person who deserved to be treated like a hero. The video of her brother dying, where the Green Earth Futurists revealed the truth, was still on the phone Zara had hidden in the cafeteria. She skirted the crowd and headed straight for the hall that led to the cafeteria, her blood pulsing in her veins, her sole focus on revealing the truth.

I can't let him win. She marched past the vending machines and headed straight for the soda fountain. She had slipped the phone into a plastic baggie and taped it to the inside of one of the syrup boxes in the cabinet underneath the machine. Her knees hit the floor, and she flung open the cabinet, reaching inside the far-left syrup box to retrieve the phone. She froze, her heart lodging in her throat. It wasn't there. Her only leverage over Mr. Peters was gone.

Chapter 8

Heather Peters

Heather took her first satisfying breath in *days,* and then she did it again and again, letting the air fill her lungs. Never had something so simple felt so extraordinary. Unfortunately, breathing was the only thing she could do without compounding her exhaustion. Just raising her head off her pillow an inch felt like an Olympic sport. Heavy limbs weighed down her bloated body while sharp pangs shot up and down her side any time she moved.

She squinted at the unfamiliar ceiling and then turned her head to take in a lobby she only faintly recognized. The room was dimly lit as sunlight filtered through shades pulled over a wall of windows. She frowned at the ugly green cushions of the sofa that served as her bed. The wooly fabric was textured and warm beneath her fingertips. There was a pillow underneath her head, but no blankets, which was understandable considering how ridiculously hot it was. A rhythmic clicking echoed off the walls, and Heather strained to angle her head so she could see where a hallway opened into the lobby.

Candice Liddle paraded into the room in a lightweight, pink, sleeveless jumpsuit and gasped when her eyes fell on Heather. "You're awake!" She scuttled over to the couch and perched on the edge of a coffee table, reaching out to feel Heather's forehead with the back of her hand. "I *knew* I was right!"

Heather shied away, her frown deepening. *What is Candice doing here and where is here, exactly?* Flashes of memory surfaced, of seeing Candice's face when she was sick, but at the time, she'd thought she'd been dreaming. The last clear memory she had was of being carried to the bunker in the Peters' house after being shot.

"How long…" Heather started to speak, her voice croaking, her throat raw. She had to stop just to swallow.

"You've been iffy going on six days. I'll get you some water." Candice bounced to her feet and headed for a stack of plastic bins, grabbing a water bottle out of one and returning.

"I dreamed you… died." Heather's recent memories were blurred together with nightmares. She didn't remember how they got to wherever they were or why Candice came with them.

"Oh, I did die," Candice said. "I'm pretty sure, anyway." She twisted off the cap and held the bottle out. "I think I'm going to write a book about it. Or, like, hire someone to write it for me, you know, once everything gets back to normal."

Heather tried to sit up — her mouth was so dry, and the water looked so good — but she was too weak. Her head fell back to the pillow as she tried to process what Candice had said. "What are you talking about?"

Candice knelt on the floor beside her and put a hand under Heather's sweaty neck, lifting her and bringing the water bottle to her lips. "I caught whatever is killing everyone. I think I might have died in your mother-in-law's basement for a minute. I remember the pain kind of floating away as I started to float away, and there was some kind of rainbow light all around me, but then I don't remember anything until I woke up to your husband gawking at me."

As Candice talked, Heather sipped at the marvelous water; warm though it was, it satiated her thirst. She let Candice go on about her so-called encounter with the sickness; the woman had a flair for the dramatic. No one survived. But Heather didn't have the energy to tackle delusions. "Where is Timothy?" she asked. It struck her as odd that her husband hadn't been the one to find her waking.

"He went back to the house to find supplies yesterday, particularly antihistamines for you, but he hasn't come back. Thankfully, Dana and I found what we needed after some sleuthing in the garage… not enough though, I don't think. You might need more antibiotics, but the only ones we have are ones you're apparently allergic to." Candice gently lay Heather's head back on the pillow, set the bottle on the table, and stood. "Dana will want to know you're awake. I'll be right back." She disappeared into the hall again, that bounce in her step annoying. No one had the right to be so cheerful when it was so hot and when everything in the world was just plain wrong.

Heather squeezed her eyes shut. *Wait… he went yesterday?* Her heart lodged in her throat. There were a thousand ways a man on his own could run into trouble as the world fell apart. Not to mention that the one thing she did remember clearly was Frank threatening to come back to the house, which had to have been the reason they'd left the bunker. Several pairs of footsteps padded back down the hall, along with Candice's clicking heels.

Annika was the first to burst out of the hall, a huge smile on her face. "You're okay, you're okay, you're okay!" She hopped in place at the foot of the sofa, but then she paused to really look at Heather. Her nose wrinkled. "*Are* you okay?"

Heather chuckled. "I will be," she said. "I'm feeling a lot better."

George came next, slowing to a casual walk and sticking his hands in his pockets when he saw her. "Hey, sleepyhead," he said. "Don't worry, I've got Monopoly primed for a rematch as soon as you're ready to get creamed."

"Don't be so sure, hotshot. My boot will kick your hat's butt any day of the week." Heather's scratchy, tired tone dampened the playfulness she intended, but George grinned at her anyway.

Dana and Candice came in right behind George. "We were eating breakfast and listening to the CDC update again," Dana said. "I'm so sorry you woke up alone. We didn't want to disturb you, so we've been eating in a staff lounge down the hall."

"What update?" Heather asked. It seemed all she had were questions, and it was getting old fast. She hated feeling helpless *and* out of the loop.

"It looks like they've confirmed mosquitos have something to do with the outbreak," Dana said.

"Which we already knew," Candice said, "because *I* told you when I got sick it all started with the swelling of that mosquito bite, not to mention the swarm of the little devils at the barbeque."

"Wait... Candice really did catch it? And survived?" Heather raised her eyebrows, incredulous. She looked closer at the woman. *Her eyes do look a little weird. And she's wearing more makeup than usual...*

"It's like you people don't hear anything I say." Candice put one hand on her hip. "I was right about the mosquitos. I was right about the allergic reaction. And I'm right about who should go find Timothy."

Dana glared at Candice. "Kids, why don't you go finish that puzzle?"

George's mouth fell open. "But mom, I want to st—"

"Now, George." Dana gave him one of her mom-stare-downs. He huffed and mumbled under his breath, but he took Annika out of the room. Then Dana looked at Heather sympathetically. "Timmy has been out there for too long. I want to go find him, but Candice thinks she should go."

"I'm immune to whatever is killing people. You aren't. It's not rocket science, Dana." Candice pursed her lips.

"I'm his *mother.*" Dana reached behind her and pulled out a gun. "You won't even carry. How are you supposed to protect yourself from everything else? The sickness isn't the only thing out there that can kill you."

"I know how to use that. Harry took me shooting all the time." Candice stuck out her chin. "I just don't see why I would need to carry a gun while you're carrying one. I mean, can you even imagine a holster with this jumper? Where would I put it?" She put flat hands against her hips where the fabric was smooth, no pockets, waistband, or belt in sight.

"Yeah, I think Dana should go," Heather said. She didn't understand Candice at all, but she didn't think the princess could handle it if things got too rough.

Candice *actually* stomped her foot. "You two are being unreasonable. What happens if I die?" She looked between them both and rolled her eyes at their nonresponse. "Exactly. And what happens if Dana dies?"

Heather couldn't help but see her point. "Dana, you know Walter's contingencies. You've got George, and if something happens to me and Timothy, you're the best person to take care of Annika, too. Candice wouldn't be able to hack it with two kids out there. No offense, Candice."

"None taken." Candice held up her hands, palms out. "I love the little monsters, but at this point, I'm more of a cool aunt than a mother figure. And I know nothing about raising kids. Or surviving the apocalypse."

Dana sighed, her shoulders slumping. "Fine." She pulled out her car keys. "Take the Charger, go back to the house, see if you can find him. Don't stop for anyone, don't take any detours. Got it?"

"Cross my heart," Candice made an x over her heart with a finger and then swung it to point at Dana's gun. "Now, you wanna get me one of those bad boys from wherever you're hiding them while I go change into something more G.I. Jane?"

Dana sighed. "Okay, fine." she said. "What are you used to shooting?"

Candice held out her hands several inches apart. "A gun about this big. Harry said it was a good option for my petite hands and that it didn't have too much kick."

Dana winced. "Are you *sure* you know what you're doing with a gun?"

"I know how to shoot it, I swear. And I'm good at it, too. I just don't know all the technical mumbo-jumbo," Candice said.

"Give her some mace and a taser," Heather said. The taser hadn't done much good for Timothy when it came down to it, but according to him, he'd been pinned down and held at gunpoint before he knew what was happening. "The gun can be a backup, or she can give it to Timothy when she finds him."

Dana didn't seem happy about it, but she led Candice out of the lobby, leaving Heather alone again on the sofa. The minimal effort of the interaction had left Heather drowsy. She closed her eyes for only a second, settling back into the cushions. A thin film of sweat covered her body, and she longed for a nice, long, cool bath. A memory surfaced of floating in a lazy river at a theme park when she was a child, and she smiled at the thought of cool water cradling her, moving her gently along a winding path. She let go of her questions, of all the blanks that needed to be filled, of her aches and pains, and just focused on that peaceful moment when she had been oblivious to all the terrible things life would bring her way.

A loud *bang* startled her, and her eyes snapped open. The light in the room had changed, the shadows in different spots. *How long was I asleep this time?* Heather frowned as she rolled her head to look at the hallway. She was still so tired, so weak. "Dana?" She croaked out her mother-in-law's name and eyed the water bottle on the coffee table. She smacked her lips together and reached for the water bottle, her fingers clumsily knocking it over to roll onto the floor with a crackling of plastic and a thud. Heather groaned.

The sound of a door creaking and slamming against a wall was followed by Dana rushing into the room, pulling a stumbling, wide-eyed Annika behind her by the hand, with George beside her; he clutched a folded white sheet to his chest. She dropped Annika's hand, whispered something to George, grabbed the sheet, and hurried to Heather's side.

Heather tried to sit up. "Dana, what's wr—"

Dana unfolded the sheet and lay it over her. "No time," Dana whispered as she kept looking over her shoulder. She was pale, but there was determination in her eyes. "When I saw them circling, I hid our bins of supplies just in case we had to flee, but then they broke in... I have to get the kids out. Play dead, Heather. Put this over your head. I'll come back, I swear. I'm so sorry, and I love you."

"What?" Heather blinked rapidly. A deep voice, too close for comfort, mumbled something Heather couldn't quite make out. "Is it Frank?" Heather asked.

At the sound of the voice, Dana had returned to the children. Annika's lower lip was puckering, and Dana shushed her, taking a moment to look back at Heather. "I don't know who they are," she said as she swung Annika onto her hip and stepped toward the exit. "But if they think you're dead, maybe they'll leave you alone."

"We can't leave her." George stepped toward Heather.

"No, George. Go!" Heather spoke as forcefully as she could manage. "Get out of here!"

George shook his head, tears streaming down his cheeks. Dana grabbed hold of his arm and tugged. His face contorted as he squeezed his eyes shut, balling his fists at his side, and followed his mother out of the lobby. Heather pulled the sheet over her head; pain shot up her side at the motion, stealing her breath and making her eyes water. She wiped away the moisture and then attempted to lay still, taking a few even breaths and willing her trembling body to relax. Heavy footfalls thudded against the tile floor, but whoever had invaded their space didn't seem to be in a rush. Doors opened, objects clattered, and two voices continued to get closer.

"I'm telling you, I saw a kid through that window before the blinds were pulled. Ace said if I find a couple kids, I can trade 'em in for my cousins at The Farm. I gotta get 'em out of there, Digger." As he spoke, his voice got closer.

"Why, man? They're bein' fed, right?" Digger said. "Ain't that better than what we had comin' up?"

"Nah, man. We had family, you know? I can't leave 'em there."

"Awww, how sweet," Digger said in a mocking voice. "Icepick's got a heart." He switched from a sickly-sweet tone to one that was more disgusted. "I thought you were supposed to have a heart of ice or something, man."

"You're an idiot. I got that name 'cause I like to finish people off with an icepick. You seen me do it, Digger." Heather's heartbeat quickened at the sight of a dark form through the sheet as the speaker stepped into the room.

"That sharp metal stick thing?" Digger came closer to Heather. "Hey, man, what is *that*?"

"Looks like a dead body." Icepick dropped a duffel he was carrying and passed Digger.

Heather closed her eyes and tried to be limp and still as the man reached for the sheet. As his fingertips brushed against the sheet at her forehead, a deafening clatter rang through the building. Heather's heart stopped as Icepick straightened.

"I told you, man. There's people in here. Leave the duffel, man. We'll come back for all this loot." He sprinted toward the sound, and Digger ran after him.

"Stop!" Heather pulled the blanket off her head, hoping she could buy Dana a few more moments, but the two men either didn't hear her or ignored her altogether. "No… stop!" She pushed herself onto her elbows and sucked in a breath at the pain. When she swung her feet over the side of the couch, they fell like dead weights, and by the time she managed to sit up, sweat was pouring down her face. Her side flared with searing pain that churned her stomach and made her dizzy.

A gunshot made Heather's heart skip a beat. One of the men shouted in pain, but then more shots reverberated throughout the building. Heather hauled herself to her feet, her legs wobbly as Jell-O, and promptly crumpled back on the couch.

"Come on, Heather. Get it together." She chastised herself as she stood up more carefully. Even if she couldn't stop the men, she would at the very least distract them. She made it four steps from the couch before toppling to the ground. She cursed as she held the wound at her side, her vision blurring as wave after wave of agony coursed through her. Warm, wet blood soaked through the bandages, through her shirt, coating her hand.

Annika's scream as another gunshot permeated the air yanked Heather past her pain and grounded her to the moment. She dragged herself toward the hall.

"Mom!" George's frightened shout gave Heather the strength to keep moving. "Mom! Get up!" His words mingled with a sob, and Annika kept screaming.

"Dana!" Heather meant to shout, but she could only wheeze as she finally pulled herself to the hallway entry.

The hall ended at a T several yards down. The connecting hall itself was dark, but the perpendicular hallway at the other end was illuminated by sunlight. George stumbled into Heather's view, his hands zip-tied behind his back, his nose bloodied. A man stepped up behind him, grabbing his upper arm and forcing him forward.

"Hey, Icepick, shut that girl up." The man who had to be Digger pushed George forward.

"Let him go!" Heather's shout was weak and pitiful. She dragged herself another foot down the darkened hallway.

Digger squinted at the hall and smirked. "Hey, there's another one." He raised his gun.

"No, don't!" George slammed his shoulder against Digger as the shot went off, and Heather curled in on herself at the thunderous sound. No bullet hit, but when she looked back up, Digger had shoved George into the wall and raised his gun again.

"Let it go, man." Icepick stepped into view, Annika's wriggling body under his massive arm. He held her tight as if she were a squirming pup as she whimpered and pushed at him in vain. "Don't waste the bullet."

"You gonna finish her off?" Digger asked.

"Nah." Icepick held up a bloody metal pick with a wooden handle. "I had my fun. I'm in a hurry, man. And that lady ain't gonna make it." He pointed with the icepick down the hall at Heather.

Heather snarled. "What did you do?"

Icepick just laughed, stuck the pick into a slim pocket on his shorts, and patted Digger on the shoulder. "Let's go, man. We'll load up those bins, these kids… Ace is gonna be stoked."

Digger grabbed George by the back of his neck, and the two men walked away with the children in tow. Annika cried out for Heather, reaching for her as Icepick carried her out of Heather's line of sight.

"Stop!" Heather army crawled another yard, leaving a trail of blood on the floor behind her. "Please! Bring them back." She didn't stop until she reached the other hall, but they were gone by the time she got there, though she had no idea what she would have done if she'd been able to catch up to them.

Heather rolled onto her back, her chest heaving, vision blurred from tears, burning fire radiating from her wound to every inch of her body. She rolled her head to the side; Dana lay on the ground near a toppled, three-tiered metal cart. Blood blossomed from several small holes in her abdomen, and a larger gunshot wound gaped in her chest. Above, a sprinkler jutted out of the ceiling, and a bright red lighter lay on the tile floor. Heather groaned. Sprinkler systems didn't require electricity to work.

She tried to activate it, but she couldn't reach it, and the cart tipped. She was trying to help me. A cry bubbled up, and Heather let it out unrestricted as she pushed herself to crawl to her mother-in-law, stopping at the edge of a pool of blood.

"Why didn't you just leave?" Heather sobbed as Dana's vacant eyes stared back at her. Thick blood seeped from Heather's side, trickling to the floor. She was too exhausted to move another inch. Dana's blood found the grooves between tiles and created little red rivers reaching for Heather. Her eyes drooped, and her body, heavy and immovable, was increasingly distant. A weightless, painless state of mind enveloped her, tempted her to let go, to give in, and her ability to fight faded with every passing second.

Chapter 9

Timothy Peters

Timothy held tight to the only source of light he'd salvaged from the ransacked bunker — a small flashlight he'd kept in the drawer of the side table by the pull-out couch where he and Heather had shared a bed.

He'd spent the first hours trapped underground trying to get out. The entrance was blocked by blackened timber and metal beams, all tangled around a burned-up, misshapen refrigerator which had fallen from the floor above. Every attempt to make a hole only made things worse, though he had managed to create small gaps where pinpricks of light shone through the darkness. That was how he knew when night was falling. He'd shut the door at the bottom of the concrete staircase and hunkered down in the pitch black, stifling bunker to try and get some sleep.

When morning had come, Timothy had opted to search the bunker with the flashlight instead of tackling the way out. He'd found a few items under the bottom shelves in the storage room: a bottle of water, a box of granola bars, and a roll of 130-pound IGFA-class fishing line. He shook his head at the line; his father loved to deep sea fish, but it seemed such a frivolous item to stock up on. Frank and his goonies hadn't thought so, however, as they'd stolen the rest of the line and everything else, including all their meds. He put the items with him near the door and waited. When he was certain it was safe, he had opened the door and sat in the doorframe, listening and letting the vestiges of sunlight poking through the wreckage give him some hope.

They'll come for me. I've been gone too long, and they know that. The stale air was too thick, and the faint scent of smoke lingered. *How long before I run out of air?* He reached out to let a sunbeam play on the back of his hand. He had no idea if the tiny holes leading to open air were enough to keep him alive.

A jolt of adrenaline pumped into Timothy's veins as the mess of beams, timber, and debris shifted. He hopped to his feet and grabbed the door, ready to slam it shut if the wreckage fell further into the stairwell. His hand was on the door, and the door halfway shut when a beam of sunlight widened and a high-pitched voice yelped. Timothy paused and frowned in confusion at the familiar sound.

"Candice?" He yelled. "Is that you?"

"Timothy?" Candice's face popped into view beyond the new hole. "Timothy! You're alive! When I saw the ladder, I thought maybe you'd come down here." She clapped her hands and then yelped again, frowning and sucking on a finger. "I got a splinter," she said. "Good thing I already chipped all my nails." Her nose wrinkled. "This pile is not going to be easy to move."

"Where is Mom?" Timothy asked, straining his neck, hoping to see his mother. "And why didn't you stay behind to take care of Heather?"

"It's just me. We decided that since I'm immune and Dana is the best person to care for Heather and the kids, it made the most sense for me to come." Candice disappeared from his view, and she grunted, a series of thumps and clacks echoing outside as if she were throwing bits of debris to the side. "I'm going to remove the little pieces first. There's nothing left from the ground floor to fall on top of the pile, so I think we just need to be worried about it falling farther down into the stairwell."

"Just be careful," Timothy said. "We need to get back as soon as possible."

"Oh, well, we've got a little time, I think." The sounds of debris moving continued as Candice talked. "Dana found some antihistamines in the glove compartment of an empty car in the garage. It's not enough, and we still need to find antibiotics that Heather isn't allergic to, but she seemed a little better when I left."

"I still want to hurry," Timothy said. He was confident that his mother could keep Heather comfortable, but he had a bad feeling he couldn't explain. He'd thought she was getting better a few days ago before she'd taken a bad turn, and he couldn't get the worry out of his system. He needed to see she was okay for himself.

"It's cute that you're all worried about your wife, but I need to take my time, or this thing will cave in while I'm trying to dig you out." Candice's head reappeared beyond the hole, and she raised her eyebrows at him. "Capiche?"

"Yeah," Timothy sighed. "I guess you're right. I've already moved all the smaller pieces on this end. Every time I moved one of the bigger pieces even a hair, the whole thing shuddered. I just didn't want to risk it. Are you sure you know what you're doing? How are you going to move the heavier pieces?"

"I've been playing Jigsaw Jam for, like, a whole year," Candice said. "I'm like Jigsaw Jam royalty. I'm really good at it. I've got this."

Timothy rubbed his hands over his face. Jigsaw Jam was an annoying jigsaw puzzle game for phones that had taken the world by storm. It had the worst sound effects.

"Ding-a-ling-bum!" Candice sang the jingle for winning a round of Jigsaw Jam as she cleared the debris.

"Great." Timothy sighed and backed up, ready to close the door if an avalanche ensued. But, piece by piece, larger holes appeared. None were big enough for Timothy to crawl through yet, but it was a good start.

"Okay… I've cleared all the smaller stuff." Candice poked her head through a larger hole that was cut in half by a metal beam. "I think if I can move this big baby—" She patted the beam. "—we can get you out."

"That thing has to weigh at least fifty or sixty pounds," Timothy said.

"I have to lift it straight out, too," Candice said. "I don't think I can push it to the side without causing debris to collapse again."

"Wait a minute!" Timothy spun around and picked up the fishing line. "This might work. It's one-hundred-and-thirty-pound fishing line, over eight hundred yards of it. If you used a few points of pressure—top, middle, and bottom of the beam—you could run three lines to a trailer hitch and pull the beam out."

"Neither of our vehicles has a hitch," Candice said, tapping her chin. "I think the neighbors across the street had a truck, though. I could go see if it's still there." She disappeared, shouting as she left, "I'll be back!"

Timothy paced in a tight circle on the bottom landing, eyeing the holes Candice had made. She was right, that one with the metal beam splitting it in two was their best bet. It was just above the refrigerator, which was wedged on its back between the walls. He could climb on top of it and squeeze through, as long as the fridge didn't budge.

He breathed a sigh of relief when Candice popped back into view. "I've got the truck!" she said. "You want to toss me the line?"

Timothy did so, and then waited impatiently as Candice chatted as she worked. "I grabbed a pair of shears from their garage. It seems overkill for these little lines, but the only other thing I've got is a pair of nail clippers in my glove compartment, and that won't cut it."

"No, that's good. This kind of line is pretty strong and hard to cut if you don't have the right tools." Timothy pushed away memories of deep-sea fishing with his father. He had enough to worry about without adding to it whether his father was alive. The last he'd heard, Walter Peters had been admitted to a hospital. That had been right before cell service had gone down for good. His mom, Heather, the kids, Lizzy, and Zara… he made room to worry about them because they deserved it.

Before long, the metal beam started slowly lifting as Candice inched forward in the truck. The lines stretched twelve yards over the wreckage of the basement to ground level. Timothy could see the lines if he craned his neck. He bounced on the balls of his feet in anticipation. *Come on… come on… keep going.*

When the beam was nearly perpendicular to the ground, the top line snapped at the knot Candice had tied, and it teetered sideways, coming too close to the wreckage. If it barreled into the two-by-fours and beams sticking out of the doorway to the stairwell, the rest of the debris could slide further into the hole and trap Timothy for longer, maybe forever.

"I am *not* staying down here." Timothy scrambled up the refrigerator, grateful it was wedged between the walls, and headed for the hole. Dust drifted on the air as the beam teetered and touched a two by four that was sticking out of the ball of debris blocking the stairwell. The middle line snapped as Timothy was nearly out, and the beam fell onto the wreckage with a crash, dislodging several pieces of debris. The refrigerator slipped and began to slide. Timothy jumped, launching off the appliance and through the hole as splintered and charred wood, broken kitchen tile, long nails, and metal cascaded into the stairwell. He skidded on the concrete floor of the basement. Shaking, he got to his feet and patted his body, looking for injuries. He whooped and pumped his fist in the air when he found none. "I can't believe that worked!"

"Are you okay?" Candice rushed from the truck to the top of the ladder, her shoulders relaxing at the sight of him.

Timothy picked his way to the ladder by climbing over the fallen beam. "I'm fine! Now we just have to find some meds, and we're good to go."

He ascended the ladder, and he and Candice split up, each one exploring the homes in the gated community, looking for antibiotics, antihistamines, and any other drugs they could use in the future. Timothy was shocked at how much he found, but when Candice met him back at the vehicles, she just shrugged at the four grocery sacks full of random medicines they had gathered.

"This community popped pills like candy. I'm surprised we didn't find more." Candice sifted through her bag. "I found some left over antibiotics in cabinets, but I actually thought this might work." She brought out a box with a dog on it. "It's amoxicillin, but for dogs. I also found like twelve of these." She held up a bottle labeled Moxifish. "It's also amoxicillin."

"You want to give my wife antibiotics for a fish?" Timothy quirked an eyebrow.

Candice shrugged. "My momma used fish antibiotics before I married Harry and I could pay for her to have good insurance. It works. It's the same stuff they give people." She stuck it back in the bag.

"I guess it'll work if we have to use it," Timothy said as he stuck the bags in the car. "I'll take mom's car. You take your own."

They exchanged keys and got on the road, driving as quickly as they could while remaining safe. Timothy knew something was wrong the second they pulled into the garage. The glass door that led inside was shattered. Not bothering to pull into a space, he stopped the car and jumped out.

Candice did the same. Her face was pale, and she held out a gun. "Here. Dana gave this to me before I left. I've got a taser and some mace. I can watch your back."

Timothy nodded and put a finger to his lips. Candice nodded like she understood, and he moved forward with his gun at the ready. The halls were dark where no outside windows provided daylight. His heartbeat thudded inside his chest, pulsated in his ears. Every corner he turned where he found nothing produced both relief and a building dread. Candice followed him with the taser in one hand, but she was too jumpy. He kept one eye on her, afraid she might accidentally deploy the taser on him.

When he turned another corner and Candice cried out, he spun around to shush her only for a startled cry to escape his own lips. His mother and his wife lay in a puddle of congealing blood that spread beyond them both in all directions. It was so much blood. His stomach curdled, and he dropped to his knees, his hands trembling. He couldn't breathe. His chest constricted, his throat closed up, and a chill swept over him.

Candice slowly tore her gaze from the bodies to look at Timothy. "I… I'll check to see…" She swallowed audibly and didn't finish her sentence. Instead, she walked to the edge of the pool of blood.

To Timothy, every step she took seemed to take a thousand years. His vision blurred. He couldn't see the rise and fall of their chests, and his mother… her eyes were wide open, blank and lifeless. The hairs on his arms and the back of his neck stood on end and goosebumps rose up and down his body. *This had to be Frank. How did he find us?*

Candice stepped into the blood, her designer shoes making a wet, squishing sound. She squatted beside Heather and reached out a hand to rest against Heather's back. And then Candice pulled back her hand with a gasp and stood up. "She's alive!"

It took a moment for those words to sink in, but once they did, Timothy was at his wife's side in the blink of an eye. Her blood soaked into his pants as he turned her over. "Her wound broke open. We need our supplies! Go grab them."

Candice sprinted away, leaving bloody footprints behind her, and Timothy ripped off his shirt, pulled up Heather's, and pressed the cloth against the front end of the bullet wound. She'd managed to rip it open, but the patching at the exit wound seemed to still be intact.

Candice came back, shaking her hands, her face screwed up in a frantic panic. "The supplies aren't in the lobby," she said.

Timothy lifted his shirt. The wound had opened, but it didn't seem to be bleeding much anymore. "I think… I think most of this blood is my mom's," he said, bile rising in his throat. He pushed it down and leaned over Heather's face, patting the cheek that wasn't coated in blood. "Heather? Hon, wake up."

Her eyes fluttered open. "Timothy?" she asked, and then her expression twisted, and her bottom lip quivered. She turned to look at Dana. "It's real," she said, voice cracking. "I thought it was a nightmare. Dana!" She reached out, and her fingertips brushed his mother's cheek. "Dana, I'm sorry." She curled into Timothy's chest, but then seemed to notice that half of her body was covered in blood. She shrieked and clawed at the blood, scooting away from him and the crimson puddle. "Get it off," she shouted, crying hysterically as she tore off her bloodied shirt.

"Heather," Timothy approached her with hands held up, speaking gently. "It's going to be okay. We just need to grab the kids and get out of here before someone comes back. Where are George and Annika hiding?"

The question made Heather burst into another round of sobbing. She forced the words out between labored breaths. "Those men… took… them."

Timothy's mouth ran dry, and a new seed of fear blossomed in his chest. "Which men? Frank and his guys?"

Heather shook her head, body heaving as she tried to calm her cries. "He wasn't here," she said. "There were two men. Icepick and Digger. I… I don't know, Tim. They mentioned a guy named Ace and a place called The Farm where he's keeping kids. They… they murdered Dana."

His mother's name sent a sharp pain through his chest, but he closed his eyes, swallowed a lump of grief, and focused on that name. He couldn't focus on the fact his mother was dead *and* get Heather to safety, so he pushed down rising emotions. *Ace…* Timothy frowned at the familiar name, and then he remembered the thugs outside of the Williams' house, the ones who had been after Frank. *They said Ace has plans for CON…*

"I think Ace is the leader of CON," Timothy said. "I ran into some of his guys in Mattapan when I found Annika."

"The gang? Why would gang members kidnap a couple of kids?" Candice asked.

"This Farm… one of them said his cousins were there, that it wasn't a good place to be." Heather leaned her head back against the wall. "Maybe they're using child labor?"

Timothy crawled over to Heather and sat beside her. "What are we going to do?"

"We have to go get them," Candice said, crossing her arms. "We *have to*. Right?"

"Of course, but… how?" Timothy asked. "We don't know where this Farm is. We don't know anything about them except that ConMen hate Frank."

"You know where Frank's place is out in the country," Heather said. "We could give them that location in exchange for the kids."

Timothy shook his head. "Those guys don't have a code, not like Frank, even if his is twisted. They'll just get the information, kill us, and keep the kids."

"We can't just sit here." Candice wiped tears from her cheeks, her makeup smearing to reveal blue vein lines on her cheek that hadn't been there before she'd caught the illness.

An idea came to Timothy, but it was crazy. He squeezed his eyes shut, searching for another solution, but none came. The seed of fear grew roots that invaded his bones and seeped into his blood. He could only see one way forward, and even as he said the words, he could barely believe them. "There's only one person I know who might help us. Only person who might care about Annika, maybe even George. One person who has the resources to find them and fight back. He might kill us, but I don't know what else to do." He looked from Candice's confused expression to Heather, who shook her head, a knowing look on her face. "We have to go to Frank."

Chapter 10

Minnie Stevens

Minnie had stormed the hospital like a bat out of hell, but some lily-livered charlatan had drugged her before she could find her kin. A day had passed since she'd woken up in this new plexiglass prison. They hadn't restrained her, but there was no need. The door was locked from the outside.

The isolation room was only big enough for a cot and a little standing room to one side. There was no bathroom; they'd forced her to use a bedpan. And she'd had no one to speak to since she woke up inside; the nurses gave her food and took her bedpan through a slot in wall. It was downright undignified.

The curtains lining the entire perimeter of the room gave her privacy, but there was nothing she could do with it. She'd tried unscrewing parts of the cot with her fingernails, but it was no use. They'd left her nothing to work with and nothing to do except think, and that was no good. After worrying herself half to death over Lauren, Alex, Oliver, and Samson, she'd moved on to considering her regrets. She wasn't one to feel sorry for herself, but thinking of lost years with her daughter had her moping in no time.

After years of estrangement, she'd finally gotten over her pride and started to patch things up with Lauren only to have her daughter taken from her a few days later. Their falling out had been all her fault; she'd thought being hard-headed about Lauren's education was the right thing to do. Minnie had scraped by and pinched pennies and worked her butt off to send her daughter to a good university, and after that, she'd been so proud when Lauren had passed her MCATs and started medical school. Her daughter was going to be somebody who didn't have to live paycheck to paycheck. It felt like Minnie's life meant something more knowing she'd raised a doctor. When Lauren gave up all that work, moved to Nashville, and announced she was looking to start a music career… well, Minnie about died of shock.

Foolishness. Minnie picked at the fuzz on her blanket, once more feeling the weight of when she'd first realized her mistake. Lauren didn't need her momma's discipline, not at twenty-two years old. She needed me to love her, to try to understand her. She flicked a little gray fuzz off the bed and rolled onto her back. If I'd gone to her sooner, we wouldn't be in this mess. My pride ruined everything. It took the end of the world landing on the doorstep of her food truck to get her to push past that pride. Still, if it hadn't been for Alex and Oliver, she might not have survived long enough to see Lauren again. She would have died back in her hometown along with all her friends. *I've got to find them. I can't lose my family. Not again.*

The door to her pod was unlocked and the curtain pulled back. Dr. Smith walked in with his clipboard, a Suit by his side. "Ms. Stevens, your quarantine is over, and it's time for you to be relocated." He held up a purple wristband. "It looks like you'll be joining your friend, Mr. Dixon."

"I'm strong as an ox." Minnie sat up, got out of bed, and backed up. "You said only people who need extra attention get the purple bracelets."

"You, Ms. Stevens, are obviously dealing with PTSD which has resulted in some dangerous aggression." He frowned and touched his forehead where a flaming red scratch ran parallel to his hairline. He'd been in the hall when she'd broken out of her original quarantine bubble to find her people.

"I'm sorry 'bout that, doc," she said, gesturing to her own face to mirror where the scratch was on his, "but you were between me and findin' my daughter and my friend." Minnie crossed her arms. "You can go get me one of those green bracelets. What you call aggression, I call spirited, and I can tell ya now, that ain't out of the ordinary for me."

"Hmmm." Dr. Smith pursed his lips and wrote something on the paper on his clipboard. "Very well. I think perhaps a more thorough psych exam is in order. I'll still need you to put on the purple bracelet."

"I'm not crazy," Minnie said. "I'm just madder than a mule chewin' bees. Y'all have no right to do any of this. I want to see Lauren Stevens and Oliver Roman right now."

"Put on the bracelet and follow Mr. York, or we'll have to drug you again." He held out the bracelet, and the Suit — Mr. York, apparently — looked like he was ready to tackle her right then and there.

Minnie narrowed her eyes. They had her cornered. There was only one thing to do until she found out what she needed to know. "Fine, I'll go peaceably." She took the bracelet and affixed it to her wrist. "I 'spose it'll be nice to see my good friend, Mr. Dixon."

Dr. Smith visibly relaxed, but the Suit only watched her closer. The way he looked at her, it was like he *wanted* her to give him a reason to put her down. There was something wrong about the Suits, every last one of them. Minnie was going to find out what. She added that to her to-do list, underneath finding Lauren, Oliver, Alex, and Samson.

As she walked the halls, she peered into every room she passed, but she had no luck finding her people. Mr. York led her to a portion of the hospital devoid of military presence. She frowned at that. Up to that point, she'd seen a mingling of the two forces, but only Suits guarded the new halls. He stopped at a pair of double doors and gestured for her to enter. The Suits guarding the doors glanced at her briefly. Once she stepped inside, the door was closed behind her, and the lock clicked into place.

What is this place? Minnie stood frozen at the front of the room, taking in the scene before her. Beds with flimsy dividers between them lined the walls, and in the center of the large room stood half a dozen circular tables. People of all ages — including five children, two of them completely bald — were scattered throughout. The tables were full of people snacking or playing board games. A few sat silently on their cots. Others congregated as they stood. Still more talked over their dividers. Minnie scanned the room and found Mr. Dixon sitting on a cot with a chess board between him and a teenage boy.

Her feet unfroze, and she marched across the room, whispering harshly when she was close enough that he would be able to hear her. "Elijah Dixon, I told you this place wasn't right."

He looked up at her, his eyes wide, and then he smiled. "Well, I'll be. Minnie, what are you doin' here?" His smooth tone and handsome grin, that spark in his eyes that said he really was happy to see her — well, it made her blush.

"There ain't no time for flirtin', Mr. Dixon." Minnie pressed her hands against her hot cheeks for only a second before clicking her tongue and nodding sharply at the center of the room. "You can't tell me this looks right to you. Only sick people are supposed to be here." She pointed at the young man playing chess with Elijah. "He ain't sick. Look at 'im."

"I've got Type 1 Diabetes," he said. "And my name is Rodney."

Minnie worked her jaw back and forth. "Well, fine, but *I'm* not sick, and they put me here. I can't be the only one."

Elijah furrowed his brow in concern. "Well, did they do any tests? Minnie, what if you've got somethin', and they just haven't updated you yet?"

"Oh, stop that." Minnie's temper was mounting. It was painfully obvious that things weren't right. "I've been carted down here against my will after bein' kept in a box and made to tinkle in a pan. I don't need no patronizin' from you or anybody else. I am *just fine*. If this was a place for the sick, I wouldn't be here."

"There *is* some weird stuff happening," Rodney said, keeping his voice low. "I mean, people leave, and they don't come back, but it's not like they left because they were healed."

Elijah rubbed the back of his neck. "How do you know, son? They could have gotten better."

"Shawn had terminal cancer." Rodney gave Elijah a flat stare. "And they didn't once resume his cancer treatments while he was here." He looked across the room at one of the bald children, a girl of about nine or ten. "There's a few cancer patients here that aren't getting any treatment. And what's with those kids being kept here, anyway? Like… did all their family die?"

"It's possible," Elijah said.

"No, I think the kid's onto somethin'." Minnie leaned closer to them both. "I could maybe understand isolatin' contagious people. Or makin' sure people that need a little extra help came into the hospital for checkups or somethin', but this?" She looked around the room. "This ain't right."

"I didn't take you for a conspiracy nut, Minnie." Elijah pointed to the chess board and nodded for Rodney to take his turn. "The nurse said this is just a temporary arrangement."

"Temporary my butt," Minnie muttered. "We all gotta get outta here." She chewed her bottom lip, trying to remember the twists and turns she took to get to this room. It had to have been a cafeteria at some point; it was so large. How many exits? Were the double doors the only one?

"Ms. Stevens?" A woman's voice startled Minnie from behind.

She spun around to find a petite nurse in blue scrubs with that customer-service-smile she'd pasted on her own face too many times.

"Yes?" Minnie asked.

"My name is Tilly, and I'm one of the nurses on the floor today. I have here that you need to see Dr. Terrance." She smiled sweetly, as if Minnie couldn't see that disingenuous glint in her eyes.

"You mean the psychiatrist?" Minnie matched the woman's sweet tone. She'd thought at first that she'd only see their doctor if they could drag her in kicking and screaming. She didn't trust whatever was happening. However, a new course of action came to mind, one where she could gather information.

"Yes, ma'am," Tilly said, her voice cheery. But Minnie saw that flash of guilt in those brown peepers; the nurse, whoever she was, wasn't being straight with her. "Would you like to get settled at your station before joining the doctor in the other room?" Tilly gestured across the room to an empty cot.

Minnie pursed her lips. "How long has this Dr. Terrance been with y'all?"

Tilly hesitated, her smile faltering when Minnie changed the subject. "Oh, he's new," the nurse said, "but he's really done wonders considering the situation. He takes care of the mental health of the people in this room, and he attends the staff. I've seen him myself, Ms. Stevens. He's a wonderful man."

"He's new, you say?" Minnie asked. "So he wasn't with the hospital when the sickness broke out?"

"Oh no. He came here with the security team." The nurse's smile faltered for just a moment. "Well, I mean, he arrived at the same time." *Not supposed to tell me that, huh? I've got you, you little minx.* Minnie smiled at her and then looked over her shoulder, giving Elijah an I-told-you-so glare before turning a smile back to the nurse. "I'll go see him right now, thank you very much." She held out a hand. "Lead the way." *Maybe this so-called doctor will know what's goin' on here.*

The nurse led Minnie to a single door at the side of the room that led into a very small waiting room lined with chairs, but Minnie didn't bother sitting down. She headed straight into the room beyond, slapping open the door with not a hint of decorum, despite Tilly's protests.

"Lawson wants two delivered to the lab—" A man in a lab coat with a name tag that read Dr. Terrance cut off his conversation with a Suit when Minnie entered. He spoke with an accent Minnie couldn't quite place… French, maybe. "Excuse me, ma'am, but—"

"Ms. Stevens to you," Minnie said as she waltzed over to his desk, scowling briefly at the Suit. "Your people wanted me to see you, and I ain't got a lot of patience, so here I am." She plopped down in a chair, set her jaw, and stared daggers at him. "They say I got a problem with aggression."

"I'm so sorry, doctor," Tilly said from the doorway. "She wouldn't listen, and—"

Dr. Terrance raised a hand. "It's all right, Tilly. Just go back to your duties."

The Suit the doctor was talking to when Minnie had walked in cleared his throat. "You want me to stay? Make sure things go smoothly? This one made some trouble yesterday."

"I think we'll be just fine here," Dr. Terrance said. He smiled at Minnie.

She feigned a sympathetic look. "Well, bless your heart, doctor." He relaxed his shoulders, the Southern insult flying right over his head, just like she intended.

He dismissed the Suit and picked up a pad of paper and a pen. "Now, Ms. Stevens, let's talk about you. I'm sure you've had a terrible couple of weeks, just like the rest of us. This is a safe space where we can talk about your feelings. I understand you're angry and don't like how you've been treated in quarantine?"

"I'm not sure who *would* be happy with your so-called quarantine." She tapped her fingers on the arms of the chair. "No one will answer any of my questions."

"Let's see if we can remedy that." Dr. Terrance kept that smile on his face and scribbled something on his paper.

"Well, I have a lot of questions that're ailin' me, doc." Minnie hardened her voice and leaned forward. "Like who the heck is Lawson and why am I bein' imprisoned? Where is my daughter? And Oliver Roman? His father, Alex Roman?" She stood up and put her hands flat on his desk, leaning in so he could see the full ire in her eyes. "And what in blue blazes have you done with my dog?"

He leaned back in his chair, his eyes wide. "Ms. Stevens, if you could just sit down—"

Minnie pointed her finger in his face. "If you don't answer my questions, you buzzard, you maggot—"

"Ms. Stevens!" He shrank back in his chair and pounded a service bell, the sharp *ting-ting-ting* cutting off when she swiped her hand across the desk and flung it to the floor.

"If you don't tell me where my people are, I suggest you give your heart to the Lord right now, before I—"

The door opened behind her, and the Suit stalked over and wrapped his arms around her, pinning her arms to her sides. "Where you want her, doc?" he said.

"Let me go!" Minnie squirmed, but she couldn't get his muscled arms to budge an inch.

Dr. Terrance smoothed his white coat. "Take her to the labs," he said. "She's new. No one will miss her. And take that kid, Rodney, too. We don't have an infinite supply of insulin. I'd rather use him now than have the rest watch him get sick." He smiled again at Minnie, and this time she saw genuine *glee* in his eyes. It sent a shiver down her spine. "We've got plans for you, Ms. Stevens. You see, even troublemakers have the chance to redeem themselves these days. You're going to help us save the world." His bottom lip puckered just slightly, and he spoke in a mockingly regretful tone. "Too bad you won't be around to see it."

Chapter 11

Alexander Roman

Alex didn't have much practice in creating awkward tension, but he sure was trying. President Coleman had invited him to lunch in the room across from his makeshift Oval Office, but Alex wasn't game for making friends quite yet. He still hadn't seen any of his people, and he wasn't going to let a nice lunch change his mind.

"We found your dog," Coleman said as he bit a dainty piece of fish off his fork. "We put him in quarantine inside the hospital, just in case. He was sitting outside the hospital, just like Corporal Conner said. A Rhodesian Ridgeback, right? Responds to the name Samson?"

"He's not my dog. He's Minnie's." Alex didn't touch his silverware or look at the food, which was getting cold on his plate.

Coleman cleared his throat and took a sip of water. "Right. Um... but you said your son was attached to the dog, right? I'm sure Oliver will be happy to see him once the dog is cleared. We haven't concluded if animals can spread the disease or not, so we figured the best route would be to isolate Samson. But, I made sure to throw him a bone, literally." He grinned and laughed at his own joke.

Alex didn't crack a smile. "Oliver is also pretty attached to Minnie."

The president's grin faded. "I'm taking her unknown whereabouts very seriously, Mr. Roman. We will find her."

"Haven't Lauren and Oliver been in quarantine long enough?" Alex asked. "When do I get to see them?"

A knock at the door was followed by Corporal Conner sticking her head inside. "Mr. President, your other guests have arrived."

Coleman smiled. "Ah, excellent timing." He waved for Conner to let the guests inside. "Mr. Roman, I believe this will answer your question."

As the door swung open, Alex's heart leapt at the sight of his son. "Oliver!" He laughed and stood up so quickly he knocked his chair over. He rushed around the table, reaching for his son and smiling at Lauren, who hesitated in the doorway.

"Dad!" Oliver ran to him, colliding with his middle, nearly toppling him.

"I'm sorry, bud. If I could have stopped them from separating us—" He cut off, squeezing his son close, choking up at the reminder of being dragged away.

"I know, Dad. Me too," Oliver said.

Lauren stepped inside the room, her body stiff as she shuffled over to Alex, scooting up against the wall, eyeing Coleman suspiciously. "You okay, Alex?" she asked.

"Yeah," he said. "You?"

Her hair was a mess, dark circles ringed her eyes, and she was pale, but she nodded. "Yeah, but I'll be a lot better when I know what's going on here." She frowned, eyes darting around the room. "Hey, where's my mom?"

Alex shook his head, still holding his son close. "I don't know. I wouldn't cooperate with them until they reunited all of us—" He turned toward Coleman. "—and I still won't."

"Ms. Stevens, can I call you Lauren?" Coleman scooted his chair back calmly and stood.

"No." Lauren said bluntly. "Who are you?"

"I'm President Coleman." He took a few steps and righted Alex's chair.

"Like President of the Chess Club, or...?" Lauren took a step in the opposite direction with every step Coleman made toward her.

"As in President of the United States." Coleman stopped walking. "You don't have anything to be afraid of. I have very few scientists at my disposal. All I want is for your friend here to work with my people to put a stop to the disease that's ravaging our nation and the world. I brought you and Oliver here as an act of good faith. We're even quarantining the dog, and we'll bring him here, safe and sound, as soon as we can."

"Is he serious?" Lauren looked at Alex.

At the same time, Oliver stepped back and said, "Samson is okay, Dad, right?"

Alex addressed Lauren first. "I'll explain later, but yes. He's serious." He looked down at his son. "And as far as I know, Samson is fine."

"But my mom?" Lauren hugged her middle. "Where is she?"

Coleman spoke up, and whether or not he was genuinely sincere, he did a good job portraying himself that way. "We're doing everything we can to find her. She's been... misplaced, but I'm confident she'll be back with you soon. And I'm so sorry for the way our system is set up right now. It's not perfect, and I know that. I'm working with my advisors to lessen the severity of the quarantine experience while maintaining top level security. Unfortunately, we haven't had much time to—"

Lauren stepped *toward* Coleman, her face twisted in anger. "Wait... how do you misplace an entire person?"

This time, Coleman took a step back. "Ms. Stevens, I assure you—"

"Stop it with the political, smooth-talking bull," Lauren shouted. "Be straight with me. I want to know where my mother is."

Corporal Conner and General Hunt burst into the room at the sound of Lauren's raised voice, but Coleman held up a hand to stop them from going for Lauren. "That's enough," he said. "No need to do anything brash. Ms. Stevens has the right to be angry. I would be furious if my child or my wife were missing."

Alex and Lauren exchanged a glance as Alex put himself between his people and the military. "Are you going to do anything about it, or you just going to continue with empty apologies?" he asked.

Coleman gestured to the table. "Why don't I call for a couple more plates, and we can discuss it. I'm open to suggestions about how we can do better." He smiled at Oliver. "I can get you something a little more to your liking. How about a nice cheeseburger and fries?"

Oliver, bouncing with excitement, licked his lips and looked up at Alex. "Can I, Dad?"

"Yeah, bud. Of course." Alex ruffled Oliver's hair, but as he pulled out a chair for his son to sit in, he let his expression go flat as he looked at the president. A nice conversation and some food wasn't going to deter him from the situation with Minnie. He sat next to Oliver, and Lauren sat down next to him as Coleman called for Conner.

"Bring us a cheeseburger and fries for Oliver, please, and another plate of tilapia and asparagus for Ms. Stevens." He settled back in his chair.

"Yeah, I'll take a cheeseburger, too, if you don't mind." Lauren wrinkled her nose at the fish.

Coleman nodded, and Conner left to do his bidding, though Alex did catch a disgruntled look on her face as she turned back toward the door. *Doesn't like being an errand girl. Willing to tell the truth. If I keep her close, she could be an ally.*

"So," Coleman said as he cut his asparagus, "tell me, Ms. Stevens, what can we do better?"

"Ha!" Lauren scoffed. "Pretty much everything."

"This is an open discussion. Please, go on." He stuck a bite in his mouth and chewed slowly, his eyebrows raised in anticipation.

Lauren narrowed her eyes as she sat back in her chair, arms crossed, but when Coleman just waited, she sat up a little bit and gave Alex a questioning look. He shrugged, unsure if she wanted his approval, his opinion, or what. She took that as a sign to launch into all her grievances, which Coleman listened to without interruption as the rest of the food arrived. Lauren continued even as she ate her food, talking with her cheeks stuffed.

Alex observed. He looked for hints of emotion from Coleman, trying to discern if he was sincere or not. His body language seemed engaged with the conversation, and he nodded and made agreeable noises at all the right moments. Corporal Conner had said he was a good guy who might be over his head, and maybe that was true. But he did have something of the slick politician in him; he'd deescalated the situation and got Lauren talking. Alex was no politician, but even he understood that simply *pretending* to listen intently to someone was enough to earn a little trust. When Lauren had said her piece and lunch was over, Coleman walked with them into the hallway.

"I've arranged for you all to have your own set of rooms in a different wing," Coleman said. "I think you'll find them more comfortable. There's a gym and public showers on the same floor. Unfortunately, only the isolation rooms have private bathrooms, but I assumed you'd prefer this to the doors that lock from the outside."

"You assumed correctly," Alex said, a little surprised. "Thank you." He was just starting to feel a little relief when the president kept talking.

"I would like a word, Alex." He put a hand on Alex's back and guided him a few feet down the hallway. "I've shown, I think, that I can be trusted. I put out that updated CDC warning like you asked. I've brought you your son and Lauren, just like you asked. I've even taken steps to reunite your people with the dog. I need something from you, now, Alex."

Alex stopped, refusing to let the gentle pressure on his back influence his movement anymore. "I said what I said. I'm not touching the research until Minnie is found."

"I understand," Coleman said, "but I'd like you to at least go and meet the people you'll be working with. Start building a rapport. Listen to what they've discovered so far. Just start percolating that information. I'm not asking you to be hands on until your friend is safe and sound. I've taken several steps toward you, though, and now I need you to take one, little step toward me."

Alex ground his teeth. The president was being so darn reasonable that Alex was having a hard time coming up with any objections. He sighed and nodded. "Fine. I'll introduce myself. I'll see the lab they're working in. I'll hear what they've got so far. I guess it's only fair."

Coleman slapped Alex on the back. "Good man," he said. "I'm glad we could see eye to eye on this." He rolled his shoulders and buttoned his suit jacket. "General Hunt," he called for the general to join them. Charles Lawson, who had been speaking with a couple of Suits down the hall, came as well, though he wasn't asked. As usual, the president didn't seem to mind Lawson's presence or the way he loomed over him. "Ms. Stevens and the boy should be escorted to their newly prepared rooms near the gym," Coleman said. "Anything they need that we can provide, do it."

"And Mr. Roman will be joining Turner and Ward in the labs." Lawson addressed Coleman like he was giving orders.

Alex blanched. So it was Lawson who really wanted me to meet the scientists.

"Right now?" Alex asked. "I didn't mean I would go *now*. I haven't spent two seconds with my son alone. I haven't seen the new rooms or made sure my son is settled."

Lawson scowled. "It is of the utmost importance—"

Coleman raised a hand, and for a split second, Alex detected annoyance in his expression. "Of course. In an hour, then?" His tone was on the edge of impatience.

Lawson's face grew bright red, and his lips drew into a tight line. He scowled at Alex. "An hour is *another* very generous concession, Michael."

"I don't care if you're his father-in-law, Lawson," Hunt growled. "He's Mr. President to you when we're operating in official capacities."

Coleman pinched the bridge of his nose as his two top advisors glared at each other. "Mr. Roman, please tell me an hour will suffice."

Alex didn't like it, but he nodded. "Fine. An hour is better than nothing."

Part of the second floor had been converted to living quarters. Former offices were cleared of desks, bookshelves, and office chairs, and they were filled with bedroom furniture. Two mismatched twin beds sat in the corners of a room given to Alex and Oliver. The beds, the side tables, the blankets and pillows—everything seemed to be from a different place. Lauren was given a similar room, one she was to share with Minnie once she was found.

"Hey, Dad, look at the games!" Oliver pointed to his side table where a stack of dice and board games sat.

"Why don't you pick out something for us to play this evening?" he said. "I'm going to check on Lauren." He left Oliver to sift through the games, stepping a few feet down the hall to Lauren's open door. He leaned on the doorframe and smiled as she looked up at him. She sat on her bed, spreading her hand over the colorful, patchwork quilt. "This stuff… I think it came from people's houses." She shuddered. "Whoever owned this a few weeks ago is probably dead."

"Or they fled the city and left the blanket." Alex walked in and sat on the bed opposite hers. She was right, though; the things in these rooms were a mishmash of tastes, quality, and colors. They had to have come from homes in the immediate vicinity.

"I can't stay here," Lauren said, tears welling up in her eyes. "It feels like a prison. I need to find my mom and get us out. I understand if you want to stay but—"

"I don't." Alex cut in. "Things aren't right here. I want to find out what they know, and then I want to get to Boston and find Walter Peters."

"Have you made sense of what your boss said yet?" Lauren asked.

Alex shook his head. Jonah had used his last breaths to give him pieces of a puzzle, but there weren't enough pieces to paint a full picture. He'd said the NSA had been covering up something and that a whistleblower had said something about Walter Peters and the New Horizons Labs in Boston. Hearing the name put to the lab had jogged Alex's memory eventually. Vanguard's New Horizons Labs was one of the most innovative private facilities in the country. Alex had read papers written by their scientists, and seeing as how malaria was a huge focus of the CDC, he and his colleagues had been excited about their most recent endeavors.

"I know a little about Mr. Peters and his company," Alex said. "I've read some of the research published by his scientists concerning the theories of eradicating mosquito populations. In the past, the community has been concerned about using technology to cause an extinction event; it's never been done. That slippery ethical slope may start with mosquitos, but… the research and practices perfected in that pursuit could be used for more nefarious purposes. However, Walter Peters's people made some good arguments, and their recent work to begin getting rid of disease-carrying mosquitos has been lauded as possibly one of the greatest scientific contributions to humanitarian efforts in recent history."

"I think I followed most of that," Lauren said with a half-smile.

"Maybe Walter Peters knows his research can be used to curb the spread of this disease," Alex said.

"Or he had something to do with it in the first place," Lauren said.

Alex quirked an eyebrow. "You mean the disease could have started with mosquitos and spread to humans? Don't you think it's more likely it developed in the human population and then began spreading via mosquitos after?"

"I don't know. I'm not a scientist." Lauren kicked off her shoes and lay back in the bed. "Either way, it sounds like this Peters guy needs to be found, if he's still alive. Are you going to tell your new buddy, the President of the United States?" She said the title with air quotes.

"No, not yet. I don't know if I can trust him." Alex stood up, crossed the room, and sat at Lauren's feet. "I have the feeling we're going to need to escape," he said, keeping his voice low. "I'm going to need you to keep Oliver close. Keep an eye on the people. Listen if they start talking. We need to know who we can trust and who we might be able to pull to our side if things go wrong."

Lauren nodded, her expression solemn, and Alex left her to join his son. The rest of the hour flew by, and soon Corporal Conner was knocking. Alex reluctantly left his son with Lauren and followed Conner through the building to a door guarded by two men in suits. Once their identities were confirmed, one of the security guards punched in a code on the keypad next to the door; there was a rubber shield around it so that Alex couldn't see the numbers.

"I'm guessing the code I know to get inside wouldn't work anymore?" Alex asked.

"Price had them changed," Conner said as the door beeped, and she pulled it open. "He's pretty protective of the codes. They change every day. Only his guys have access."

Alex frowned. "The military can't get inside without Price's permission?"

Conner shrugged. "We've got most of the perimeter, civilian security at the dorms, and we share in guarding the President, the hospital, and this building. We're stretched thin. Hunt doesn't like it, but he doesn't have the manpower to argue. Plus, the scientists work for Price. He found them."

That didn't sit well with Alex. He didn't know whether to trust the general or Coleman, but he definitely didn't trust Charles Lawson. That man was power hungry and aggressive, a type A alpha male used to being in control. And Chandler Price, who seemed cut from the same cloth, worked for Lawson.

Alex paused at the sight of Price standing in front of a laboratory door down the hall. "What is he doing here?"

"I told you," Conner said, "they kind of run this part of the show. Hunt wanted me here, and Lawson wanted Price."

"So, the military does want some sort of say in what happens back here?" Alex asked.

"I'm not at liberty to discuss this further," Conner said. She paused and put a hand on Alex's arm. "Look, things around here aren't as stable as they look. Two independent forces are trying to work together. Both of them are used to getting their way all the time. Don't rock the boat, Roman. We've just got to keep it steady until a cure is found, and then we can all go home heroes."

"Sure, whatever you say," Alex said softly. Corporal Conner looked younger in that moment than he'd originally thought, and a wave of pity softened him toward her. Youthful optimism, the idea that normality would return, that they'd be praised as heroes… he didn't want to take that away from her. He suspected the rug would be pulled out from under her feet eventually, but he'd let someone else do it. "I hope it works out like that, too," he said.

Price approached. "Mr. Roman, let's go," he said. "Our scientists are waiting for you. They've got some sort of presentation planned. Your addition to the team is—"

A scream — half cry of terror, half cry of pain — echoed down the hall. Alex jumped at the sound. Corporal Conner's eyes widened, and her body tensed, but Price didn't seem fazed.

"Someone is in trouble," Alex took a step down the hall.

"Oh, no, no, Mr. Roman. Everything is fine." Price gestured toward the laboratory door he'd been standing in front of earlier. "We should go ahead inside. It's a sound proofed lab, so we shouldn't be bothered."

Another scream was cut off abruptly. "No, it sounds like someone is hurt." Alex took a few more steps, but Price grabbed his arm.

"There are infected people that way," he said. "They're being kept in complete isolation, but when they open the trap doors to give them water or they use the intercom to ask them questions, sometimes they're in a lot of pain."

"How is that possible? If you're bringing in infected people, how is the disease not spreading? It's extremely contagious." Alex frowned at the other end of the hall. The screaming had stopped.

"We have a separate entrance for the infected, and there are these plastic bubbles around gurneys. I'm sure Turner and Ward can explain the system they've come up with better than I can," Price said, walking over to the door and pressing in a code. "That whole area is restricted. You can't go back there. I'm sure our people can answer all your questions, though, if you'll come with me."

Alex turned his back on the direction the screaming had come from, ready to confront these scientists and find out what the heck was going on, when another shout, this one angry, stopped him in his tracks. He knew that voice. It had a southern twang, one he'd grown to love. Alex set his jaw and bolted for the restricted zone, straight for the sound of Minnie.

Chapter 12

Zara Williams

Zara gripped the knife's hilt and glared at Walter Peters. He orchestrated the movement of half a dozen people under the hot midday sun, and they did his bidding with stupid smiles on their faces. They were fools. He'd pulled the wool over their eyes, and Zara couldn't do anything about it.

How did he find the phone? The question popped into her mind every time she laid eyes on him. *And why hasn't he lorded it over me yet?* Instead, he was dragging it out, making her squirm. Not admitting that he had it could make her sweat, putting her in limbo, making her question everyone. But she wasn't going to let him have that; she was positive he was the one who found it. No one else would have a reason to keep the discovery a secret. The phone couldn't call anyone, and most of the others had their own useless phones. She ground her teeth and swore under her breath. He wasn't going to get away with what he'd done. *I'll get it back. Wait and see, Walter.*

"Zee, um… we should probably get to it." Lizzy hefted one of the garden hoses they'd brought with them. She let it drop to the ground and began to unroll it. "How long should the pieces be?"

Zara tore her gaze from Mr. Peters and bent over the hose. "We'll need two sections to siphon the diesel," she said. "I'll take care of this part. Why don't you grab a few of those gas cans Brandt and Mitch found at those hardware stores?"

Lizzy headed to a long line of five-gallon gas cans, and Zara watched as she greeted everyone she passed as though they were on some team building trip at camp. They'd decided their next move as a group, and they were all working to make it happen. With the hospital generator running out and with a limited amount of diesel in the vicinity, they had two options. The first was to siphon diesel and keep trying to make the hospital work. But that wasn't a long-term plan. They were on the outskirts of a major city. Most of them agreed the countryside would be safer, and Amos — the father who had been stuck at the hospital with his little girl after she broke her arm — promised they could find a safe haven near a place called Pleasant Home, Ohio. He swore his parents were part of a prepper community that would welcome them all if they would agree to carry their weight.

Zara couldn't stand how they treated Mr. Peters like a savior. Everyone agreed *because* it was on the way to Boston, *because* it would help Mr. Peters save the day. They had plans to get their new hero a better vehicle, to stock them up on food and supplies, and to kiss his butt before sending him off on his blessed mission to save the world. It irked her that Mr. Peters could smooth talk his way out of taking responsibility for what he'd done, even if it *did* mean the three of them were getting exactly what they needed: a way to get to Boston.

If it hadn't been for him, my family would still be alive. And he's not even sorry. She sliced at the hose, gritting her teeth so hard her jaw hurt. I just hope he doesn't find a way to screw them over before we part ways.

Mitch had suggested they take a bus from a school bus yard nearby, and so half their number had braved the outside in the hottest part of the day when there were no mosquitos out, trekking half a mile to where they were now. Twenty bright yellow school busses were at their disposal. They only needed one. Amos had said the prepper community would want contributions, so they had to take out the back seats of the bus and load it up with whatever supplies they could pack from the hospital. Zara was the only one who knew how to siphon diesel from the other busses, and so she had been assigned that task. Lizzy had volunteered to help her, even though they still weren't on the best of terms.

The drive home was over fourteen hours from Indianapolis, and the drive to Pleasant Home only got them four hours closer. But Mr. Peters was all on board with Amos's plan; they thought it was because he wanted to see them to safety. Zara understood it was because he wanted to get rid of them as quickly as possible. Maybe he was waiting until it was just the three of them so he could force Zara to watch him destroy the only piece of evidence she had that he was the bad guy.

I have to get it back. It's what Dad would have done. Zara sawed at the rubber, cutting through. Her father had been a proud member of the Boston Police Department, a man who loved justice. He was dead because of Mr. Peters, just like her mother, her brother, and her aunt. *It isn't right that they're dead and he's alive.*

Lizzy shuffled over with her arms wrapped precariously around three cans and let them drop to the ground with hollow thuds. She grabbed one of the red, five-gallon gas containers and set it on the ground next to Zara. She frowned at the hose. "I thought we only needed two pieces?"

Zara stopped cutting. Distracted by her thoughts, she had cut the hose into seven lengths. "Well, if any of the others get tired of being ordered around by your dad, they can come help us."

"They're getting the bus we've chosen cleaned up and ready to be stocked." Lizzy picked up two pieces of hose. "It's not like they're fanning him with palm leaves or something."

"Right. They're just jumping at his every word. None of them even notice that he's not actually doing anything. He's pointing and shouting and puffing up his chest trying to look important while they do all the work." Zara grabbed two different pieces of hose. A hand towel she'd brought from the kitchen at the hospital hung from her front pocket. She plucked it out and stalked over to one of the busses.

"Zee, he's getting us home. Can't you give him a little credit?" Lizzy asked as she followed with the gas container. "He might not like to get his hands dirty, but if it weren't for him, we'd probably be stuck in some containment center near St. Louis. At this rate, we'll be home in a few days, tops."

Zara scoffed. "I can't believe you're defending him. Again." She jerked the gas hatch open and twisted off the cap, tossing it to the ground. Then she fed one end of the longer piece of hose into the bus's tank before sticking the opposite end into the gas container.

"I just want a little peace." Lizzy leaned against the bus and hugged herself tight. "I can't stand this constant tension. I'll be the first to admit that my dad is a jerk sometimes, and he's aggressive and arrogant and he can be really mean. But in his own way, he loves me, and he's my dad. Plus, he's our ticket home, and he knows how to stop the end of the world. So, he's not all bad, Zee."

"Yeah right. You know he took the phone?" Zara twisted the towel into a little rope and wrapped it around the shorter piece of hose, sticking the hose into the hole and stuffing the towel all around it to keep any air from getting in or out. "It's the one thing we had to keep him in line. He hates me, Liz. Now that I've shown him I'm not going to let him walk all over me anymore, he'll get rid of me first chance he gets." *It's not like I have family that'll come looking for me.* Her cheeks burned hot at the bitter thought and she bit the inside of her cheek, willing away the sudden urge to cry, which was something she had to do more and more.

Lizzy sighed. "You don't have to worry about that." She bumped the back of her head gently on the bus a few times, and then pushed off it. "I don't want to argue with you. I'm going to go help the others. If you want my help and you want to talk about something other than my dad, let me know."

Anger flared inside Zara's chest, but she sealed her lips and turned her head away from Lizzy. She couldn't spend her time on small talk when there were so many huge problems looming over her. The fact that Lizzy thought things could go back to how they were — chatting about boys and gossip and making fun of each other for their quirks — made Zara furious. *She can be that way because as far as she knows, her family is still alive. I've lost everything, and she gets to go back to her giant house and her money and her family.*

Zara put her mouth on the hose and blew hard a few times until she could hear a trickle of gas going into the container. While she waited for the container to fill, she stewed, and by the time she'd filled all three containers, she was miserable and doused in frustration. She lugged the containers to the bus where Mitch, Brandt, Amos, Brian, Sunny, and Mr. Richards were working on the back seats of the bus, breaking them down and using tools from the hardware store to unbolt and remove them.

"Hey, Zara," Brandt said as he hopped off the back of the bus. "You need some help with the gas cans?" He craned his neck. "Where's Lizzy?"

"She was supposed to be helping you guys," Zara said, grabbing two more containers.

"She came by, but there wasn't a lot she could do to help." Brandt frowned as he continued to look around. His eyes went wide in recognition. "Ah, there she is. But… why is she just sitting there?"

Zara followed his line of sight to where Lizzy sat on the ground, leaning against a bus's tire, knees to chest. Lizzy had always needed someone to tell her everything was going to be okay, even when the worst thing in her life was something trivial, like the time she wore the same dress as another girl to a school dance. Zara had never cared about that stuff, but she'd always been able to empathize, to make Lizzy smile and forget her troubles.

That's what our friendship is, isn't it? Lizzy needs comfort, so I give it to her. She needs a laugh, so I tell a joke. She needs someone to listen, and I'm all ears. Zara's stomach churned. Memories of Lizzy telling off Tosha Fisher for stuffing Zara's locker with plastic WalMart sacks surfaced, and a small smile came at how Lizzy had proceeded to wear only clothes from that store for a month. She'd somehow made fifteen-dollar sweaters cool in a prep academy full of rich kids. Zara's smile faded. She did that because it was fun for her and because she hates Tosha. I've just been too stupid to see it.

She turned back to Brandt. "She's not feeling great. I'd leave her alone. If you want, you can help me carry some empty containers to a fresh bus."

Brandt helped her for a while, and by the time she'd filled all twenty containers, it was time to drive the bus back to the hospital with Mitch at the wheel. It was only a ten-minute drive, but it felt agonizingly slow. Everyone on the bus grated on her nerves; even if they didn't know it, they were constantly praising the man who murdered her family. As the bus made its way, occasionally nudging smaller vehicles to the side, the air grew thicker and hotter. They cracked the windows, but the summer air didn't provide much relief. Zara was sick to her stomach. She was tired of the lies, of trying to make Lizzy see reason, of bearing Mr. Peters's presence.

When they pulled into the parking lot, Bertie, Judith, and the two doctors had boxes of supplies stacked near the entrance to the hospital. The four were gathered around the supplies, seeming to organize them into type. The bus wouldn't fit under the concrete awning, so Mitch stopped a short distance from the awning where he wouldn't have to back up to get out. The second they parked, Zara bolted for the bus door.

Mitch had barely reached out to touch the lever to open the door, so Zara grabbed it and opened it for him. "Hey!" he shouted as she jumped to the ground. "I'm getting tired of your attitude!"

Mitch kept shouting at her, but she ignored him and headed for the hospital door.

"Zara, sweetie, what's wrong?" Bertie stepped away from the supplies upon her approach, a look of concern on her face.

"I just need a minute." Zara said as she passed her.

"Hold on, now, Zara." Mr. Peters's voice rang out behind her, deep and authoritative, scolding in tone. "We all need to help get these supplies on the bus."

Zara whipped around, her face growing hot. She spoke through bared teeth. "Don't you tell me what I can and can't do, Walter. Don't forget that I know who you are."

He smiled. "You're being a little dramatic, don't you think? I just think everyone ought to pitch in as we prepare to head East."

"And what exactly have you done?" Zara balled her hands into fists. Her voice got louder with every word, and they echoed under the concrete awning. "You've not lifted a finger. None of this was even your idea. Amos came up with going to Pleasant Home. Mitch came up with buses." She scoffed. "Come on, Walter. Even *Mitch* has done more than you."

"Dear me." Bertie placed a gentle hand on Zara's back. "Honey, Mr. Peters has a lot on his plate. He's planning something much bigger than just getting us all to Pleasant Home."

Zara shrugged off Bertie's hand and stepped away from her. "You don't get it. He's a murderer, not a hero." At Lizzy's gasp, Zara realized she'd let it slip; she'd finally said what she'd wanted to say. Despite the hurt in Lizzy's eyes, she wasn't sorry.

"You're becoming hysterical," Dr. Young said, walking up to her with a no touch thermometer and pointing it at her to get her temperature. She groaned as he shook his head at the normal number.

"I'm not sick!" she shouted, kicking at a rock. It soared toward the window next to the sliding glass doors. A satisfying *crack* was followed by a webbing of fractures on the glass. "I'm just done. I'm done pretending everything is fine. I'm done with *him*." She pointed at Mr. Peters.

Brandt wrung his hands, looking at her like she'd gone crazy. "Zara, Mr. Peters wouldn't hurt anybody."

Zara started laughing, and she started to sound hysterical even to herself. But what Brandt said, what they *all* thought about Mr. Peters—that was the real insanity. She laughed so hard, tears came to her eyes. She took a deep breath, trying to calm herself. "I've seen him kill two people," she said. "No," she corrected, "I'm sorry. In less than two weeks, technically, I've seen him kill thousands. *Millions*. The whole damn world."

Mr. Peters's expression darkened. "Zara is obviously very distraught." He pasted on a look of concern that Zara could see straight through. "She did see me kill two people who were approaching us, both of which were infected. I'm not proud of it, but I had to do it to protect my daughter." He put a hand on Lizzy's shoulder, and she let him use her to gain empathy.

"Tell them the truth!" Zara spotted a larger, landscaping rock nearby. Furious, she retrieved it and held it over her head. She didn't intend to throw it at him, not really. But she *needed* him to stop the lies.

"Put that down, Zara." Walter's voice was full of unnatural gentleness.

The raging tension Zara held within threatened to break her. "No, I won't," she shouted at him.

"I'm sure what he did was a very hard decision for him," Bertie said. "Maybe you should put that down, sweetheart."

"We've all done things we're not proud of," Mitch grunted.

He was doing it again. Wriggling out of being seen for who he truly was. Zara couldn't take it anymore. She hurled the rock at the window, and the fissures widened to the entire width of the vertical piece of glass. When Walter flinched, she thought maybe he'd cave, but his shock disappeared too quickly.

He shook his head at her with pity. "Perhaps you need to go and rest for a little while, Zara."

Why can't they see how fake he is? She screamed and rushed toward Mr. Peters, whose eyes went wide. "Where is the phone, Walter?" she shouted, hands outstretched as she rushed toward him. She was going to rip his clothes apart. It had to be on his person, close to him so that she couldn't find it by searching through his stuff.

Lizzy stepped between her and her father. "Zee, stop!"

Zara shoved Lizzy, and she stumbled out of her way. Zara took two more steps toward Mr. Peters before the crash stopped her in her tracks. Her heart stopped and shame banished her frenzied anger. She must have shoved Lizzy harder than she'd intended. The already damaged floor-to-ceiling window next to the sliding doors was shattered, and Lizzy lay on the inside, her face bloody, her body unmoving.

Zara gasped. *What did I do?* She sank to her knees beside her best friend, trembling. *This isn't me. What is wrong with me?*

Chapter 13

Alexander Roman

Alex barreled down the hall, following the sound of Minnie's curses. The footsteps of two others pounded the floor behind him: Chandler Price and Corporal Jenny Conner. He turned a corner to find a man in a suit, standing with hands folded in front of him, blocking his way. Beyond that bulky, muscled frame, two men dragged Minnie kicking and shouting into a hallway junction and then disappeared down the adjoining hall.

"Sorry, sir, this is a restricted area." The man held up his hand.

He didn't bother with a reply. Instead, he put his head down and charged. The guard sidestepped and hit Alex on the back, causing him to trip and roll. But instead of staying on the floor, he used the momentum of the roll to get back to his feet and kept running.

"Hey! You don't want to go back there!" The man shouted.

Alex looked over his shoulder as he approached the junction. The guard bounced on his feet nervously, but when Price and Conner blew past him, he rolled his shoulders and followed at Price's command. That made three people trained to fight on his tail and two ahead with Minnie. He had no idea what he would do when it was all five of them against just him and a sixty-something year old woman, but he had to stop them from sticking Minnie in a contaminated area. There was no way she was sick; the men handling her wore no protective gear.

Her voice echoed down the hall. "I oughtta tan your hides, the both of you! All y'all are a bunch of turds stinkin' up God's green earth!"

Alex slid into another junction, whipping his head down one way and then the other. The two men had stopped at the end of the hall. They each had an arm hooked under one of Minnie's armpits, saddled with her full weight as she went completely limp, though her southern insults just kept on coming. One of them was keying in a code on a pad. As the door clicked open, Alex burst down the hall.

"Minnie!" Alex's heartbeat kept time with his rapid footfalls, and a cold sweat broke out all over his body. He'd only been through the door they'd opened a few times; beyond it was a hall that connected four Biosafety Level 4 labs. Those were meant to be used in the study of the worst pathogens in the world. "Don't let them take you in there!"

Minnie craned her neck to try to see behind her, finding her feet again. "Alex?" She squinted at him over her shoulder as he sprinted toward her.

"What the—" the taller of the two guards, the one holding the door open, dropped Minnie's arm and pushed it wide. "Get in," he said. The other started to push Minnie into the doorway, but she barred her teeth and sunk them into his shoulder. He shouted and pushed her off, backing up and hurriedly checking the spot under his shirt. "She bit me!"

Minnie fell to the floor as Alex caught up to her. The guard at the door stepped forward to try to grab her, and Alex leapt over Minnie and landed a punch to his gut. He doubled over, and Alex slammed his knee into the man's face. Blood spurted from his nose, but he slammed his body into Alex anyway. Alex stumbled back and tripped over Minnie who was still on the floor. The man who'd been bitten descended on him, straddling him and pulling back a fist, ready to pummel it into Alex's face.

"Garcia, stop!" Price shouted as he approached with Conner close behind. "Don't hurt him!"

Garcia frowned in confusion, but he obeyed the command, giving Alex a shove before letting the collar of his shirt go and standing up. "What's going on, sir?"

Price slowed down and hurriedly helped Alex up. "I'd like to ask you the same question, Garcia." He looked at the other man. "Hall, how about you? Do you have anything to say for yourself?"

Hall stammered, pinching his nose and looking up at the ceiling. "We... uh... we were escorting this woman to Lab Fourteen as instructed, sir."

"Escorting?" Alex said as he helped Conner get Minnie to her feet. "You were dragging her. She's not sick or you two would be covered in protection gear and she would be on one of those gurneys with the plastic bubble surrounding it. Right, Price?" He raised his eyebrows at Price, using the information he'd given just minutes earlier.

Conner backed him up, placing herself in front of Minnie, who was brushing herself off and straightening her clothes in an angry, trembling frenzy. "He's right," Conner said. "Why were these men bringing a completely healthy citizen to the restricted zone?"

"This is a huge, terrible mistake." Price held out his hands, laughing nervously. "In the hour since you've been with your family, Mr. Roman, Minnie was found, and I asked to have her relocated to the main building. I mentioned we would be in Lab Four, *not* Fourteen, and the orders must have gotten mixed up. I didn't mean for her to be brought to the labs at all; I just wanted to inform her where you were, Mr. Roman."

Garcia frowned in confusion, but Hall spoke up. "Sir, we've brought combative patients to this area before." He pointed to the door they'd unlocked. "Two murderers are locked up back there right now. We just thought... you know, with her history and disposition... I mean, she *did* bite Garcia."

"Those are Biosafety Level 4 labs, Price. Why would you be keeping prisoners in laboratories meant to contain dangerous pathogens?" Alex kept his guard up. Garcia had wiped away the confusion on his face, but not before Alex had noted it. They weren't telling him the truth.

"Look, Alex, that Biosafety mumbo-jumbo might mean something to you, but all I saw when we found those labs was a set of cells with multiple fail safes to keep murderers locked up." Price shrugged and held out a hand. "I can show you, if you want."

Something Jonah had mentioned over a month prior popped into Alex's head. "The endemic of mammarenaviruses in South America," he said absently. Everyone looked at him like he was speaking a foreign language. "A team had gotten approval to begin vaccine testing for an often-fatal virus being spread by mice in Venezuela, Argentina, and Bolivia. They were outfitting a level 4 lab for a series of monkey trials."

Conner looked disgusted. "They still do animal testing?"

Alex nodded. "In certain circumstances, yes. Monkey trials give us data that's essential for the safety of human trials. That's what the cells were for. Probably a little cramped for a person, but actually quite roomy for a monkey. They do try to keep them comfortable, and the 'cells' are temperature controlled so they can keep them nice and warm."

Price breathed out a sigh of relief and brought out a handkerchief from his suit pocket, using it to dab the sweat off his brow. "Now that we've gotten that all straightened out—"

"Straightened out? Are you kiddin' me?" Minnie squeezed between Alex and Conner and jabbed a finger into Price's chest. "I don't believe you for one second! The way I've been treated is downright horrendous!"

She was right. Even if there was truth to what Price said, it wasn't adding up. Minnie was a spit fire, but she was no murderer, and the men in suits were, from what Alex could tell, a tight operation. For them to make a mistake like that was so unlikely.

"Of course, Ms. Stevens. What you endured was never our intention. Garcia and Hall will be duly reprimanded," Price said.

"Wait, where are you keeping the infected, if you're not keeping them in there? And now that I think about it, the infected should die in quarantine. If any are living long enough to be brought to this restricted zone, that's significant data." Alex was suddenly very aware of the vents in the hall. Biosafety Level 4 labs had separate ventilation systems, which was why he'd assumed the ill were inside. "If they *aren't* in BSF 4 labs, I'm not sure we're safe."

"Isn't there another set of these labs further down?" Price asked. "Turner and Ward chose where we'd confine them."

Alex nodded. "There is one more block of them. The last door on the left, at the end of this hall?"

"Yes." Price refolded his handkerchief to find a dry spot and dabbed his forehead again. It wasn't warm, but he was sweating bullets. "That's the one. Really, Mr. Roman, any more questions should be directed at Ward and Turner. I'm not a scientist." Price gestured down the hall. "Please, Ms. Stevens, let us take you to your room where you can be with your daughter."

Minnie's eyes went wide. "Lauren? She's here?"

"She's with Oliver." Alex put a hand on Minnie's shoulder and smiled. "They're both fine. Safe. And we've got a set of rooms where we can be close to each other."

Price took a few steps down the hall, encouraging the rest to follow. "Yes, so, let's get Ms. Stevens where she belongs, and Mr. Roman, you can begin your meeting with—"

"Hold on. I agreed to do that meeting before all of this happened. I think I'd like to see Minnie safely back to the rooms." Alex gently prodded Minnie forward with a hand on her back. "I'll meet with your scientists tomorrow. This whole thing has been enough excitement for one day."

Price stammered. "But, Mr. Roman—"

Alex held up a hand. "When I said I would meet with your scientists tomorrow, I meant I would start my work with them tomorrow. First thing in the morning." He held up a hand. "Scout's honor. Minnie has been found. I'll keep my word. I just want to be there for our complete reunification and spend the rest of the day recovering from the last two weeks. This is the first safe environment we've been in since this whole thing started." He smiled, trying to sound convincing. Grateful, even. In truth, the place set him on edge, and he didn't believe everything Price was telling him, either.

"Oh, well..." Price grinned. "I'm sure Mr. Lawson will be pleased to hear that. I'll escort you back to the rooms."

Conner narrowed her eyes. "President Coleman will also be pleased," she said.

"Yes, of course. President Coleman." Price cleared his throat and led them a little way down the hall before turning to address Garcia and Hall, who had stood by mostly silent. "And before I forget, you two are on gravedigging duty for a week." Hall moaned softly, and Garcia's mouth dropped open like he wanted to protest. "It's either that, or you two are out. You can hand over your firearms and have fun with the civilians."

"We'll do our jobs, sir," Hall said.

"Excellent." Price turned on his heel and led Alex, Minnie, and Conner to outside the laboratory wing, to the door with the daily code change. "You've got this, Corporal Conner?" he asked.

"I sure do," she said. "Good luck with your men, Price. I'm sure General Hunt could give you some advice about keeping them in line if you have any more trouble." Her half smile dripped with sarcasm.

"I'll let you know if I need brainless rule followers," he said. "Lawson knows what he's doing. He only picks men with great potential to be on his team."

"Sure," Conner said. "Whatever you say."

Price scowled, turned his back, and marched back to the door, waiting impatiently for the guard to reenter the code for the day. Conner led Alex and Minnie away, back through the halls of the CDC. Minnie kept an eye on the corporal's back as she walked beside Alex.

"It's all right," Alex whispered. "I think Conner is okay."

"Maybe," Minnie said. "But that Price guy? He's full of crap." She kept fiddling with a purple medical bracelet on her wrist, similar to the kind given when someone was admitted to a hospital.

"I agree." Alex slowed his gait so that the gap between them and Conner got a little wider. "Something isn't right."

Conner opened the door to a stairwell and propped the door open so they could enter ahead of her. As they passed, she was oddly silent. Her brow was furrowed, and her contemplative frown suggested she was distracted by deep thought. She quickened her step to pass them and once again led from the front, exiting on the correct floor and leading them to their rooms. Lauren and Oliver were playing Yahtzee on the floor; a doorstop kept the door wide open.

"Thank you," Alex said. "I guess I'll see you in the morning."

Conner blinked and looked at him with wide eyes. "In the morning?"

"Yes?" Alex asked. "You'll escort me to the labs in the morning, right? So I can begin my work?"

"Right." She shifted her weight and bit her lower lip, her frown deepening. She didn't walk away, instead standing awkwardly in place, gripping her right arm with her left hand, knuckles turning white.

Alex and Minnie exchanged a look. Conner wants to say something, but she's holding back. Does she know what really happened back there?

Lauren looked up from the game of Yahtzee. "Mom?"

Minnie sucked in a sharp breath and tears sprang to her eyes. She held out her arms and embraced Lauren as her daughter hopped off the floor and rushed to her. "Lauren, I'm so glad you're okay."

"Minnie!" Oliver laughed and threw his hands up in the air.

Lauren held onto Minnie for several minutes, and Alex smiled as he leaned against the doorframe. When they'd first found Lauren, he assumed Minnie had expected their reunion to be more like this one. They'd not resolved all their differences, if their little tiffs along the way to Atlanta were any indication, but it seemed they were making progress. Oliver hurled himself at them both, wrapping his smaller arms as far as he could around the two ladies' waists. He was still laughing, and that laugh was contagious. Lauren and Minnie pulled away from each other slightly to make room for Oliver, and Alex couldn't help but chuckle as the three giggled together. Lauren looked up, grinning from ear to ear, holding out a hand to Alex, but then she looked past him, her smile immediately fading.

"What is she still doing here?" Lauren asked.

Alex looked over his shoulder to find Conner still there. She jumped a little when she looked at them to find them all staring at her. Then she licked her lips, pushed past Alex into the room, and sat on the bed. "We need to talk. You're right," she said. "Something is wrong. Whatever happened down there… I can spot a liar. I've got a good radar for that sort of thing. Price was lying through his teeth. And so were Garcia and Hall."

"Oliver, why don't you—"

"Yeah, yeah." Oliver sighed. "I'll go into Lauren's room." Shoulders sagging, he left the room.

Alex rustled his hair on the way out and thanked him. His son was getting older, growing up too fast, faster than he should have to. He was no longer completely a child, and while that pained Alex, it was also a good thing. The things they had to face needed maturity to get through. *But for now, he can still be a kid sometimes. One day he'll stay, and the rest of his childhood will be gone.*

"Can we trust this gal?" Minnie asked when Alex shut the door.

"I think so." Alex sat on the bed opposite Conner. Minnie sat on his left, Lauren on his right. "We can trust her enough to listen to what she has to say."

Conner leaned forward, resting her elbows on her knees. "Hunt is a good man," she said. "He brought us here to find the president, take him to Cheyenne Mountain, and piece the country back together. I get why the mission is stalled, but it feels so permanent. And Lawson." She leaned back, shook her head, and whistled. "He's a big part of influencing the president to stay and figure out a cure. But we don't have the right people for that. Lawson is counting his lucky stars that you came along, Roman. He's the one that wanted any CDC personnel that showed up at the gate to be brought into the main building immediately. The other scientists are his, but I don't know their credentials. I've heard Hunt complain about how all Lawson cares about is that his company is going to rake in the money once a cure is found, *if* it's found."

"If there are any people left to pay," Lauren said.

"Except with all the people dead, the pond Lawson is swimming in got a lot smaller," Conner said. "And with his son-in-law possibly being the new president during wartime? Lawson's got the ear of the government, whatever is left of it. I don't trust him, and I don't think Hunt does either."

"Wait, did she say the president?" Minnie asked.

Alex and Lauren filled Minnie in with what they knew, and then Alex turned back to Conner. "I'm going to be honest. We have a lead on a real cure, but I don't trust anyone here to give that information up. Do you think Coleman and Hunt can be trusted?"

"Hunt, definitely. Coleman, yes *if* Lawson is out of the picture," Conner said, nodding her head once and firmly. "But we need to bring them evidence Lawson can't be trusted, and if we do that, we have to be prepared."

Alex frowned. "Prepared for what?"

Conner looked him in the eye. "The military and the private security team would come down on different sides of this thing. I'm not one hundred percent sure about Coleman, but if we bring evidence to Hunt that Lawson and his guys are up to no good, which I think is a real possibility, we need to be prepared for war."

Chapter 14

Zara Williams

Zara was a pariah. She stood on the outskirts of the group not because she wanted to but because every attempt to move closer earned her glares of disdain. Instead of exposing Mr. Peters, she'd made herself look crazy, and she'd hurt Lizzy in the process. Dr. Sarah Donald had rushed to Lizzy's aid after Zara had pushed her into the window. After she'd cleaned the cuts on Lizzy's face, hands, and arms, the doctor had found a suturing kit in the supplies they'd put outside to be loaded into the bus.

Dr. Donald worked on a gash above Lizzy's eyebrow. "How's that numbing cream?" she asked. "Is it working okay?" She slid a curved needle through Lizzy's skin, the thread pulling the skin together as she tightened it.

"I barely feel a thing," Lizzy said with a small smile. She glanced at Zara. "I'm okay. Really."

Zara blushed with shame. Lizzy wasn't even mad at her. She had every right to be, but more than once she'd looked at Zara as if worried about her wellbeing. And on the other side of completely losing it, Zara wouldn't be able to blame her or anyone for being angry with her. On top of physically trying to attack their hero, the shattered window provided an open invitation if mosquitos wanted to venture inside to find a snack. They'd planned to stay one more night in the hospital, but it was too risky. They'd moved their timetable up and planned to leave before curfew. That meant they would have to stay in the hot, cramped bus overnight.

"Thank you so much, doctor," Mr. Peters said as he knelt beside Lizzy, picking pieces of glass out of her hair, acting the attentive father.

"It's my job," Dr. Donald said. "I wish I didn't have to do it, but..." Her smile faded as she looked at Zara. "...at least it wasn't worse."

Zara shrank back and averted her eyes. Mr. Peters had finally won. He had the evidence on the phone, and he had the complete trust of the people around him. Zara had simultaneously discredited herself and created sympathy for him. Even Bertie, who had always been kind, refused to look at her.

Zara stepped up to the pile of supplies and picked up a box. She put her head down and carried it toward the bus, ignoring the way Sunny gave her a wide berth on her way from the bus to pick up another box. Brandt awkwardly speed walked with two boxes in hand in order to pass her. She perked up a bit; if anyone would forgive her, it would be him.

"Hey, Brandt?" Zara tried. "I know I was—"

He started whistling and picked up his pace. Zara sighed and slowed down so she wouldn't arrive at the back of the bus at the same time as anyone else. *I'm never going to live this down.*

Sophie, Amos's little girl, hopped happily off the bus and skipped over to her while holding her arm, which was still in a temporary cast, close to her chest. The little girl had been napping inside the hospital when Zara had lost it, so she hadn't seen what had happened. She jumped and landed with two feet right in front of Zara. "Everyone says you're crazy," she said.

Zara paused and looked over the box to look down at her. "I'm just... having a bad day," she said.

Sophie nodded slowly, expression strangely contemplative for a six-year-old. "Yeah. Well, my dad told me to give people second chances." She shrugged and held out a hand for Zara to shake. "Friends?"

Zara smiled and put down the box, reaching out to give Sophie's hand a good shake. "Friends," she said.

"Sophie!" Amos's alarmed voice came from behind, and he swooped in to pick up his daughter. He frowned at Zara. "I think we've got the loading under control Zara," he said. "You might consider lying down for a bit."

Zara's cheeks burned with embarrassment at how protective he was over his daughter. She would never hurt a kid. *But he doesn't know that. He just knows I freaked out and Lizzy paid the consequences.* She stammered a response. "I... I just wanted to help."

"I think you've done enough." Amos set Sophie down behind him. "Go on back to the bus, Sophie. Why don't you pick out our seat?" She ran along, and then he turned and picked up the box Zara had been carrying. "Really," he said. "You should take a longer break. You're not the only one who needs some time."

Zara swallowed hard. "Okay... I guess I could take a walk."

"Good idea." He turned his back on her and carried the box to the bus.

Zara chewed on her lower lip as she watched him hand the box up to Mitch who stood in the back of the bus. Sunny, Brian, and Amos exchanged a few words, laughing together. She looked the other way, toward the hospital, where Lizzy sat patiently as Dr. Donald wrapped her hand in gauze. Mr. Peters talked seriously with Bertie and Judith. The others were inside looking for more supplies they could bring.

Zara was the only one alone. She had a couple hours before curfew, before they would need to seal themselves up in the bus and get on their way to Pleasant Home, Ohio. She did not want to spend them under the scrutiny of people who thought she was either a troublemaker or an insane person. *I guess I brought this on myself. I shouldn't have tried to go up against Walter Peters. He's always gotten his way.* At one time, she'd thought it was solely because he was rich, but now she understood. Mr. Peters was willing to get what he wanted through any means necessary. He could charm anyone just as easily as he could destroy them. He was a master manipulator and a skilled liar.

She walked away from the hospital to the outer road on hospital grounds, cutting across the lot so she could avoid the parking garage and the body bags next to it. The stench alone was enough to keep her away, but she also didn't need any more sad memories. She would never forgive Mitch for killing Nina. She would never fully forgive herself for getting the kindly old woman involved.

I've made so many terrible decisions. Saving Mr. Peters from the fallen scaffolding had been the beginning of a string of mistakes. I couldn't have left him there, though. Maybe the problem is that there haven't been any right choices to make.

She stepped onto the black asphalt road. It glittered in the sun, heat waves rising above it further down. A squirrel bounded across and skittered up a tree. In the distance, the city was quiet. Cars were parked along the road, almost like stalled traffic. It was almost normal. Except the strange cloud of birds in the air. Hundreds of birds flocked together, moving in waves across the sky, low to the ground. But there was something wrong with them. The black cloud was too black, too thick, too… busy.

Zara stopped and looked up at the cloud as it got closer, frowning at it. The birds closer to the ground had broken formation and seemed disoriented. One of them dropped from the sky, and then another and another crashed to the ground. The cloud hovered closer still, the birds frantically chirping as the cloud undulated, as more of their number crashed to the earth.

One of the birds fell to the ground close enough for Zara to see it, but she couldn't actually *see* the bird. Its head stuck out of a ball of dozens of mosquitos draining its body dry as it twitched; the mosquitos bore orange diamonds on their backs. The bright color stuck out to Zara like a blaring horn, and she scrambled backwards, startled. She looked back at the cloud in horror. The flock of birds was being *attacked.*

Zara spun, her feet slipping. She caught herself on her hands and stumbled forward into a panicked run. Her heart slammed against her chest. If they didn't all get on the bus quickly, they were all dead. She waved her arms as she approached and shouted.

"Hey! Get on the bus!" Zara's feet pounded the pavement. The impact of each step reverberated throughout her body. She repeated her warning.

Some of them stopped what they were doing and looked at her, but none of them moved. Walter Peters jogged out to meet her, blocking her path. "Don't do anything stupid, Williams," he said. "I think we've already established that no matter what you throw at me, I come out on top. Whatever drama this is—"

"They're here, you jackass." Zara panted. "The mosquitos with the orange diamonds on their backs. They're attacking a flock of birds. Never seen anything like it. They're headed this way."

Mr. Peters's face paled. "That's not funny. It's too early."

"I know. But I saw them, Walter. I swear." Zara looked over her shoulder and pointed at the distant cloud of birds. "See how dark it is? If you look closer, you'll see birds dropping."

Mr. Peters squinted, and then his eyes widened, and he cursed. "Let's go." He ran back to the group with Zara. "Get in the bus! The mosquitos with the disease are coming this way. On the bus! Now!"

"We haven't loaded everything yet!" Mitch said.

"I don't care. Leave everything and get on the bus. We've got to shut all the windows and doors." Mr. Peters grabbed Lizzy's hand and yanked her to her feet. "I'm serious. We go right now."

Mitch didn't argue anymore. He just darted for safety. Amos followed suit, picking Sophie up and running for the bus. The others were more hesitant.

"It's too early," Brian said. "They shouldn't be out right now."

"I know. That's the problem." Mr. Peters said sharply. "Now get to the bus."

"I think we should listen," Sunny said, giving her colleague a tug before she got to her feet and started jogging after Mitch, Amos, and Sophie.

"Lorrie is inside. She wanted to get a nap in a bed before getting on the bus. I'll go get her." Brian darted inside the hospital.

"No!" Mr. Peters shouted. Then he grunted in frustration.

Dr. Donald's hand flew to her mouth. "Jerry and Mr. Richards. They're inside, too."

"We don't have time," Mr. Peters said.

A high-pitched, agonized cacophony of chirping and a steady *buzz* murmured in the background, and Zara looked back at the cloud.

"Walter! We have to go."

Mr. Peters picked up Lizzy, who had started to limp toward the bus, and threw her over his shoulder and broke into a run. "Do not go back inside!" he shouted over his shoulder. Dr. Donald followed him.

"I have to get our things! My phone, it has all my pictures." Bertie disappeared inside the hospital.

"Mom!" Judith started to run after her mother, but Zara grabbed hold of her arm.

"Judith, no!" Zara pulled her toward the bus.

Judith shoved Zara off, knocking her to the ground. "I won't leave her! I'll get her inside a room and shut the door tight."

Zara shook her head, choking on her own tears. She scrambled to her feet and darted to the bus. A series of thuds, the flapping of wings, the buzzing of insects — the sounds began to roar as she ran. Dread and pure terror cleared away all other emotion. Ahead, the people inside the bus were shutting the windows. Lizzy, hand flat against the window, sobbed Zara's name. And Mr. Peters held the door open, elbowing Mitch to keep the man from closing it.

"Zee!" Lizzy's sobbing shriek fueled Zara's footsteps.

"We still have time for her. She'll make it!" Mr. Peters screamed. He held out a hand. "Zara, RUN!"

Zara pushed her body to its limits. Every muscle strained. Every step felt like it could be the one to send her tumbling head over heels. She was mere feet from the safety of the bus. Human screams erupted behind her, and Zara made the mistake of looking over her shoulder. Brian swatted away an angry cloud of black, his arms swinging wildly as he howled in terror. Zara's knee gave out on her next step, and she tumbled to the ground, the bus just out of reach.

Chapter 15

Alexander Roman

Alexander prayed he'd made the right decision in trusting Corporal Jenny Conner. If he was wrong about her, the new family he'd cobbled together would soon be blown to bits. She'd come to their rooms early, delivering a breakfast of plain oatmeal for them and a cold Pop Tart for Oliver, who was still asleep. Conner was to escort Alex after breakfast back to the labs where he was to finally meet Lawson's scientists.

"Are we clear on the plan?" He scooped the last bit of his bland oatmeal into his mouth, forcing himself to swallow, chugging a bottle of water to get the thick gruel all the way down.

"Don't worry," Minnie said, winking. "I can pick a lock right quick. Samson'll make good cover." She grinned. "I'll be happier than a frog on a log when I see that big oaf again." Samson was to be reunited with her that day; she'd worked in a way to mention her anticipation of getting him back three times already that morning.

"You remember where I said I keep the voice recorder?" Alex asked.

"Sure do. Middle drawer. I'll have to pick that lock, too." Minnie waved the task off like it was nothing. "Piece o' cake."

Alex hoped it was actually going to be as easy as Minnie thought it would be; no one else knew how to pick locks. His voice recorder was locked away in a drawer in his locked office on the second floor of the CDC building, far away from anywhere any of them had a reason to be. If Minnie was caught, she'd planned to claim she'd gotten lost walking Samson through the halls.

Conner drummed her fingers nervously on her thighs. "And Alex, you'll use the recorder to get the evidence we need to prove Lawson is up to no good?"

Alex nodded. "I just need to make sure they trust me enough to share everything with me. After yesterday, my guess is that they'll give me minimal information to start. I broke the rules when I broke into the restricted zone, so they know I'm not great at following orders."

"Innuendo and suggestions won't be enough," Conner said. "Lawson is the president's father-in-law. We need iron-clad proof of whatever is going on. If we can get that to Hunt, he can convince President Coleman to ditch Lawson, wrap things up here, and head on to Cheyenne Mountain."

"What if Lawson or his guys want you to do something wrong?" Lauren asked.

"I… I don't know," Alex admitted. "I'll have to play it by ear. I'm hoping it won't come to that, or, if it does, it will be a gradual increase in the severity of their demands as they test the waters with me."

Lauren ran her fingers through her hair, her lips drawn taut. She sat back and sat cross-legged on her chair. "I'm still not convinced that Coleman will do the right thing. He has a legit attachment to Lawson."

"We have a responsibility to try," Minnie said. "The room with all those sick people, the purple bracelets, the restricted zone… I got a feelin' about it. I told y'all what that doc said about no one missin' me if I was gone. That man I told you about, Elijah Dixon… he believed them when they said it was all temporary, that they were keepin' the ill together for the convenience of treatment. But I think they're gonna let 'em all die of their diseases, takin' them away one by one. I bet they're lettin' people die alone and out of the way so as to not cause panic, and maybe they're throwin' troublemakers in the mix so they don't have to deal with lockin' them up long term."

"It makes sense," Alex said. "Limited resources mean they can't take care of everyone. If they want to maintain the illusion to the citizens at the dorms that everything is fine, that they've got everything under control, they wouldn't want cancer and diabetes patients dying in the open, exposing their lack of resources."

"All of this is just a bunch of gut feelings based on a mistrust of Lawson, Price, and their guys until we get the proof." Conner stood.

"Dang Suits." Minnie scowled. "They won't get away with whatever they're up to."

"Suits… that's a good name for them. I think Hunt would like that." Conner nodded toward the door. "Let's go expose these Suits, then, Drama Queen."

Alex rolled his eyes as Lauren chuckled. "You've got Oliver today," he said to her. "Just keep him away from trouble. If something goes wrong, take him to the rendezvous point we discussed."

Lauren grabbed a deck of cards. "Don't worry. I've got this. Hopefully, today will be all about Gin Rummy, but if things go bad, I'll get Oliver to safety."

"Thank you," he said to Minnie and Lauren. "If I had to do this all on my own…" He choked up thinking about it.

Minnie stepped forward and wrapped him in a tight hug, squeezing long and hard, and then stepping back. "I feel the same way," she said.

Lauren put a hand on his shoulder. "Me too."

Conner cleared her throat. "I hate to interrupt this love fest, but…"

"Right." Alex followed her out of the room and down the hall.

"So… you guys didn't know each other before this?" Conner asked, quirking an eyebrow at him as she opened the stairwell door.

"No, we didn't, but they've been a godsend." Alex's hand slid along the cool metal railing as they took the stairs. "My wife, Naomi…" His breath caught at her name. "…she would have loved Minnie and Lauren. Sometimes I think maybe she sent them to me because she knew I would need them. I met Minnie just hours after Naomi died. She… really helped me keep it together."

"I guess tough times make for fast friends," Conner said as she reached the landing and opened another door.

"Tough times make for new family," Alex said. "I know it's crazy, but… I feel like I've known Minnie forever, even though I've only known her a couple of weeks. She's like the grandmother my son never had but always deserved. And Lauren, well, Minnie's family feels like my family."

"I get it. I feel that way about Hunt and my platoon." Conner led the way through the maze of hallways to the outer door of the laboratories. "Most of us don't have anyone left out there, or at least, we don't *know* if we do."

"And you?" Alex asked, pausing in the hall.

Conner stopped walking, too. "My family lives in Denver. I thought when I signed up to go to Cheyenne Mountain that I might have the chance to check on them. It's not far from the city. They were still alive when the phones went dead, but…" She trailed off and then gave her whole body a little shake before straightening her shoulders, lifting her chin, and continuing on her way.

Alex kept pace with her. "No use in fretting over what you don't know, right?" he said.

"Right." She gave him a half smile as they approached the outer door to the laboratories. More quietly, she said, "Go get 'em, Queen." Then she addressed the two Suits at the door. "I'm here to escort Mr. Roman to Laboratory Four."

"We got orders to only let him in," one of the Suits said. "I'm supposed to escort him to the lab."

"I'm sorry, what?" Conner put one hand on her hip. "Who gave that order? Hunt wants me on his tail, and I intend to stay there, Zimmerman."

"Lawson doesn't think you can handle it after what happened yesterday, Conner." Zimmerman took a step forward, narrowing his eyes and setting his jaw.

Conner stepped up to him, seeming unfazed as she stared up at him with intensity. "That's *Corporal* Conner to you, Zimmerman."

"You're not getting past us," the other Suit rolled his shoulders. "Don't make a scene."

"We'll see what President Coleman has to say about this." Conner stepped back. "Alex, you want to go in or wait until I'm cleared to enter?"

"He doesn't have a choice," Zimmerman said, eyes wide. "We have orders to escort him—"

Conner put a hand on her gun. "He's in my care until I release him into yours," she said. "If he doesn't want to go—"

"I'll go with them, Corporal," Alex said, holding out a hand between the two. "I'll be fine. I really need to get started on my research."

Conner frowned at him, but he took a step toward the door, and Zimmerman turned his back with a smug grin, ready to escort Alex. He looked over his shoulder and mouthed the words, "Go to Hunt," with an urgent expression, hoping to communicate that he did want her to find a way back into the laboratory area. But this was the perfect opportunity to begin earning the trust of the Suits and their scientists. Siding with them, putting the work first… he hoped it distanced himself from Conner enough to dispel any assumptions that he was cozy with the military just because he had a constant military escort.

A flash of understanding in Conner's eyes was quickly covered over by a look of disdain. "Don't get too comfortable without me, Mr. Roman."

"Wouldn't dream of it," Alex said with obvious sarcasm. He pointed his finger over his shoulder at the retreating corporal. "Is it just me, or is she uptight?"

Zimmerman laughed and patted him on the back while the other man punched in the code to the door. "No, man. It's not just you. All of them are like that. Wouldn't know how to have fun if they were dropped into the middle of a carnival."

Alex shuddered. "Well, I can't blame them there. The World's Fair was a sort of carnival, wasn't it? I can tell you from first-hand experience: that was *not* fun."

Zimmerman gestured for him to go through the door. "You were there? At the World's Fair?"

"Unfortunately, yes." He looked Zimmerman right in the eyes. "That's why I'm willing to do whatever it takes to fight this thing." He decided to let the Suit interpret that however he wanted.

"Then you're in the right place," Zimmerman said, nodding at him with respect. He stopped in front of Laboratory Four.

Alex took a deep breath and pushed open the door. This wasn't a high containment lab, so he wasn't sure what he would find. They wouldn't be testing the pathogen, if they even had any samples of it, not in this lab, not if they had any idea at all what they were doing. What he did find caused him to freeze halfway inside. The steel-clad room was plastered with papers. At the center, two people sitting side by side huddled over manilla envelopes. When Alex entered, they looked up with expressions of surprise. The woman, who was too young to be far out of her graduate studies, immediately began gathering the notes all over the table. Her blonde hair was pulled back in a tight braid that ended at the nape of her neck. Her partner was short and stout, his messy hair curling in wisps of black and gray all about his head. At her shuffling, he stood and put his back to the table, drifting in front of the papers as if to hide them.

The man cleared his throat. "You must be Alexander Roman. I'm Blake Turner, and this is Joanna Ward."

Joanna stuffed the papers back into the envelope. "I'm sure you're used to being the hot shot disease detective, and I'm sure you're not crazy about us taking over your home base, but we never asked you to come here. I don't need some know-it-all taking credit for all my work."

Alex raised his eyebrows at the immediate hostility. "You might not have asked me, but the president and Lawson certainly did. If you don't think I'm needed—"

Blake glared at Joanna before smiling at Alex. "Oh, no, no. Please don't mind her. It's been a stressful couple of weeks. We're all just tired."

She hurriedly stuffed the envelope into a cabinet and used a key on her bracelet to lock it. "I meant what I said." She returned to her associate's side and crossed her arms, brow furrowed deeply. "This wasn't part of the arrangement."

"What arrangement?" Alex asked as he scanned the room, frowning at the papers stuck to the walls like wallpaper.

"You know," Blake said. "The arrangement with Lawson. The whole reason we're risking exposure and cooping ourselves up in this building and consenting to horrendous—"

"Hours," Joanna finished the sentence and elbowed Blake while Alex was pretending to look at the walls. If he wasn't watching them out of the corner of his eye, he would have missed it.

I'll have to dig into this arrangement with Lawson. And whatever else they're trying to hide. He walked the room, squinting at the series of crème and white papers. He read through a crème-colored one. Yersinia Pestis... pCD1, Type III Secretion System... this paper has all the properties of the Black Plague. He lightly touched the white paper beside it for the same bacterium. It contained known treatments, both modern and historical.

"I see you found the CDC's paper records in the archives. You've been trying to narrow down the options because you don't have access to the databases." Alex kept walking the perimeter of the room, noting the information on each paper. "That's clever. With Tier 1 Networks and satellite relay stations down, it could be a while before we can rely on conveniences like the Internet."

"It's been a lot of work," Blake said. "Once we got a sample, we were able to narrow it down to an arboviral disease, but before that we were considering bacteria and parasites." He pointed to the other side of the room. "Over there is where we've been pinning our most recent suspects. All of those can use mosquitos as a vector."

Alex paused as one statement sunk in. "How did you get a live sample?"

Joanna stepped forward and answered as Blake opened his mouth. "From the hospital. Someone showed symptoms while in quarantine, and they got us a blood sample before they died."

Alex tensed. "You haven't been researching the pathogen here, in this lab, right?"

"Of course not." Joanna sneered. "We've been using the appropriate precautions in a Biosafety Level 4 laboratory."

"Okay. Good." Alex walked over to the papers outlining the most likely culprits. "Let's go over to the BSL-4 lab so I can get a good look at this thing."

"We actually thought you'd like to see an experiment we've started." Joanna smiled, but there was a challenge in her tone and expression.

Here comes the first test. Alex opened the door. "Lead the way," he said.

Joanna walked with confidence in her step, and Alex had to walk quickly to keep up with her pace. Blake was huffing and puffing by the time they reached the restricted zone. They passed the first BSL-4 block and headed straight to the end of the hall for the second. Two Suits guarded the entry, and they punched in a code to let them all pass through. On the other side of the door, there was a short hallway with four steel doors. Joanna led them into the first door on the left. That room held several full-bodied, air-supplied, positive pressure suits along with neatly folded cotton jumpsuits akin to long underwear. They all changed into the jumpsuits and lab suits before entering the lab itself. Entering the lab was the easy part; if anything unexpected happened, if Alex wanted to get out of there quickly, leaving would prove more difficult. Exiting a BSL-4 lab required going through three rooms for three different tasks: a chemical shower, removing the suit, and a personal shower. Anything less, and Alex would risk contracting the disease and then spreading it, especially if they'd been growing cultures of it in the lab for research purposes.

The lab contained one eight-by-four-foot glove box; the Class III Biosafety Cabinet was completely enclosed with its own rubber gloves reaching into the cabinet and ducts and pipes reaching to the ceiling from the center to connect the cabinet to the air purifying system. There was another glove box about half the length, the two of them centered in the room. Class II Biosafety Cabinets lined one wall; these were like desks with shields, and their ventilation systems sucked air up into the system to be cleaned. Steel cabinets and refrigeration units lined another wall, and at one end, near the refrigerators, there was an electron microscope. On the other end, a computer sat on a small desk. A door led into a much smaller room where there would be large, climate-controlled cells. Alex had seen similar cells in other labs filled with everything from plants to insects to apes.

Joanna walked over to the smaller glove box and looked inside. "This specimen was fortified with antiviral medication before we infected it with the disease. We wanted to see if it would hinder the virus in any way, make it survivable."

Alex peered inside. A two-foot tall chimpanzee huddled in the center, rocking and chattering. It placed one hand on the top of its head and closed its amber-colored eyes. Alex jerked his head up and took a step back. "He's not sedated." He tried to keep his tone even, but his voice cracked.

When monkey trials were performed, at least at the CDC, they were done after computer simulations, after rodent trials, and when the scientists believed the test subjects would survive. And they always sedated them if there was any chance of pain or discomfort. He looked back at the chimp, and his stomach twisted. He'd worked with chimps before; they were amazing, intelligent creatures. *This isn't right.*

"We don't have time for all the protocols, and we aren't anesthesiologists," Joanna said. "We need to observe this virus in action, up close. We need to test medicines and potential cures."

"It's not ideal," Blake said, "but it's better than using human specimens. We're just lucky that we have a few chimps to work with. They would have died of starvation if we hadn't come along, anyway, right?"

Alex backed away from the glove box. "Of course, but—"

"I told you he wouldn't be able to handle our work," Joanna said.

Alex swallowed his objections. What will you do if they ask you to do something wrong? Lauren's question repeated in his mind, and he felt the blood drain from his face. I have to observe. I have to gain their trust. If this is the test... what are they hiding?

"He already looks like he's experiencing some pain," Alex said. "I'm assuming if you're forgoing sedation, you're also forgoing pain medication?"

"You are correct." Joanna smiled down into the box. "We will gain the most information by observing the full effects of the virus in the presence of the antivirals. We already know and have documented what happens after infection without any preventative measures; this is our first attempt to lessen the potency of the virus. The hope is that we will find less internal degradation and bleeding upon the autopsy of this specimen than we found with the prior."

"If you're expecting him to die, why not start with mice?" Alex asked.

"We only had a limited supply of testing specimens," Blake said. "We *did* start with mice, but by the time we got here, many of those were already dead. And we're not positive the specimen will die; we hope it lives through the infection."

They're going to autopsy him either way. Alex nodded. "I see. That makes sense, I suppose."

Joanna looked up, the only smile Alex had seen her wear fading. "We have some time yet before the virus reaches its peak, which means we have a little time to take a look at a live culture of the virus." She left the box and retrieved an agar plate from the refrigerator. She placed the round disc under the electron microscope. "Go ahead, Mr. Roman. Give this virus a close-up and see if you can tell us something we don't know."

Grateful for the distraction, Alex did as he was asked. He frowned at the live virus and double checked the settings on the electron microscope. "These virions are huge, twice the size of any other virus I've ever studied. Have you sequenced the viral genome yet?" he asked.

Joanna raised an eyebrow. "We have, but we found nothing of consequence."

"I'd like to see it." Alex said.

Blake and Joanna exchanged a look. Joanna shrugged, and then Blake started typing away on the computer. He pulled up the genome and then joined Joanna back at the glove box so that Alex could sit and study the screen. There was something wrong with it, something odd. No connection to the database meant it couldn't compare it to known viruses, but Alex had the feeling it wouldn't have come up with any matches anyway. The software could label the family of virus based on its genome without a connection, and that field read: unidentified. Someone unfamiliar with the software would probably take that to be equivalent to the blank spaces on the report.

A new family of viruses… that's not good. How is that even possible? Alex's eyes widened, and his heart stopped as he held his breath. The protein patterns weren't homogenous. This genome isn't natural… it's been manipulated.

"This virus has been *engineered*," he whispered to himself.

"What was that?" Joanna said from across the room near the glove box.

He spun in his chair. "What?"

"Didn't you say something?" Blake asked.

"Oh… um, yeah." Alex cleared his throat. *Information is my only advantage. Whatever their backgrounds, they don't know enough to see the footprints of CRISPR.* "You're both right. The sequence is odd, but I can't put my finger on why without the database."

Joanna let out a short *pfft* and shook her head. "We told you there was nothing to see. Your type always assumes that everyone else in tangential fields are *sooo* beneath you."

A sharp shriek, muffled by the box, drew Alex's attention. Both Joanna and Blake stepped up to the glove box, staring down into it. Alex hurried to join them on the other side of the box. *I have to observe, make notes. Something. I have to show them I can handle this, otherwise I'll never find out what they're really doing here.* He braced himself and looked down at the chimpanzee.

The poor animal lay on its back, limbs too swollen to sit up any longer. Its amber eyes bulged, and its back arched as it screamed and flung its arms side to side, hitting the sides of the box. Alex bit the inside of his cheek as blood trickled from the chimp's ears, eyes, and nose. He glanced away from the expression of pain, and he was transfixed by the way Joanna and Blake observed the experiment. They didn't even seem to notice he wasn't watching. Joanna's lips were turned up at the corners as if she were holding back a full-blown smile; the excitement in her eyes made Alex's skin crawl. Blake, at least, seemed more interested in taking notes, his brow furrowed in concentration. Alex forced himself to look back at the chimp, trying to find some significant difference in its reaction compared to the people he'd seen with the virus. Red foam formed at its mouth, and one of its eyes broke free of the socket. The chimp twitched, its arms falling with a *thump*. Relief washed over Alex at the creature's death, and then guilt followed. *I'm sorry, little fella. I wish I could have done something…*

The urge to vomit made Alex gag, but he kept his lurching stomach under control. He swallowed hard and forced himself to speak. "No projectile vomiting. Did your last specimen experience that, or do you think the antiviral medicines made a difference?"

Blake grinned. "Good catch, man, but the chimps don't seem to have exactly the same symptoms. Swelling, but no rashes. Internal bleeding and expulsion, but no projectile vomiting so far."

"So, as far as we know, the meds did nothing." Joanna's crazed expression had returned to normal, and she simply shrugged. "I guess we'll see upon autopsy. We've got a long afternoon ahead. Are you two ready to begin?"

"Let's get on it." Blake marched to a cabinet and pulled out a tray with dozens of plastic-wrapped tools on top. He put the tray inside the autoclave to the glove box as Joanna stuck her hands into the gloves.

Alex nodded his agreement, afraid if he spoke, his voice would quiver. Hours later, after they'd shaved the chimp down to observe the skin, cut the animal open to find bruised organs, collapsed lungs, and broken blood vessels, and then proceeded to spend twice as much time cleaning up the mess and disintegrating the body in chemicals, Alex was exhausted, both physically and emotionally. He had to pretend none of it bothered him when inside, he was still writhing, still wondering what they could be doing that was so bad that their test of his limits consisted of such inhumane practices.

Sagging with the weight of the day, Alex was ready to leave. Joanna went first, stepping into the chemical shower room first. Alex was left with Blake Turner, who seemed to be the lesser of two evils. He, at least, didn't seem to enjoy torturing creatures. He seemed all about the science.

"So, I think I like you, Mr. Roman," Blake said.

"I think you're the only one." Alex glanced at the door, looking forward to his turn.

"I agree." Blake stepped in front of Alex. "But we can't wait for Joanna to come around. She's hardheaded, and she's wrapped up in her own future prospects."

Alex suppressed his confusion, keeping his face neutral. No one had any future prospects anymore. *Unless this arrangement they've made with Lawson comes with personal benefits.*

"Right," Alex said, going with his hunch. "Lawson sure does talk a good game."

Blake raised his eyebrows. "So you *do* have an arrangement with him." He pursed his lips. "Better keep that to yourself. Joanna won't like adding another claim to the profits once we do find the cure."

"And you?" Alex asked. "You don't mind?"

He waved off the question. "Are you kidding? Lawson's going to have plenty of power and money to share if he can use the cure for a bartering chip. Everyone's going to want it."

"Right," Alex said again, trying to process the information, wishing he had his voice recorder already. "I agree. So, what are we going to do about Joanna?"

"We're going to make her come around by bringing you fully into the club." Blake slapped Alex's back. "We don't have time for these games she's playing. I have a good sense about these things, and I trust you. The sooner we can get this figured out, the sooner we can find answers. And everyone can't be dead by the time we get them, or else what's the point, am I right?" He laughed, and Alex forced a laugh of his own. "Meet me at the entrance to the labs tonight around eight. Once you've seen the whole operation, Joanna won't have any other choice but to get on with our work."

"Tonight at eight," Alex said. "I'll be there."

Chapter 16

Zara Williams

For at least the second time, Zara was alive because the man she hated most in the world decided to save her. Though the swarm of deadly mosquitos had been too quickly approaching, when she'd fallen, Mr. Peters had come after her, threatening he'd break open the glass on the bus and kill them all if Mitch tried to close the door on him. He'd yanked her up and practically threw her onto the bus before slamming the door shut and ordering Mitch to drive as Brian had run toward them, screaming for them to help him.

Zara would never forget the young security guard, flailing as tiny black killers swarmed every inch of exposed skin. He'd wipe them away to reveal rapidly growing welts, and every time he opened his mouth to shout, he would end up spitting them out, choking on them as they swarmed for access to his blood. Brian had been kind, even if, in the beginning, he'd been complicit in some of Mitch's more heinous deeds.

Isn't that how it always goes? The real monsters always live. She glared at the front of the bus where Mr. Peters led a discussion about their next move. They'd driven back to the bus yard and shut off the bus overnight, hoping to conserve diesel and avoid drawing attention to themselves. Amos, Dr. Sarah Donald, Mitch, and Sunny took turns weighing in. None of them asked for Zara or Lizzy's opinion; they expected the teens to occupy Sophie while the adults made decisions. Lizzy didn't seem to mind sitting in the back of the six remaining rows, playing hand clapping games with a child, but Zara kept her eyes and ears focused on the discussion happening at the front of the bus.

"We should go back for the rest of the supplies," Mitch said.

"We have enough already loaded. We shouldn't go anywhere near that place. The mosquitos inside the building might still be active." Mr. Peters adopted a tone like a loving father explaining something unfortunate.

Sunny looked up at him with trusting eyes as she twisted the corner of her pink scrubs top. "If Walter says we should go on to Pleasant Home, Ohio, that's my vote."

"The more we bring, the more the prepper group is going to feel obligated to let us stay long term," Amos said.

"Sure, but Amos, they're going to take you and Sophie, regardless. Your parents are part of their group, and that makes you their people." Mr. Peters placed a flat hand on his chest. "I'm going on to Boston, and so are Zara and Elizabeth. That leaves Sarah, Sunny, and Mitch. Sarah and Sunny have medical training. They've got a lot of value your prepper group could use, right?"

"That's true," Amos said hesitantly, glancing only a moment at Mitch, who didn't seem to catch that his uselessness meant he'd be the only one they'd need to convince the preppers to take in.

Zara stood up. "What about Judith and Bertie?" All eyes turned to her, and Mr. Peters scowled. "Judith said she would hole up inside the hospital with her mother. There's a chance they could both be fine. If we go back to get the supplies, we could also check to see if they made it."

"Do you think anyone else could have survived, too?" Sunny asked, sounding hopeful. "I mean, Brian looked pretty bad, but... it's not impossible, right?"

A vein in Mr. Peter's forehead popped as he breathed slowly out through his nose. "I'm sorry, Sunny, but Brian is dead. No one survives this sickness once they're infected."

Zara narrowed her eyes. "And how would you know that, Walter?" Everyone turned to look at Mr. Peters and Zara threw him a smile. His study of mosquitos wouldn't explain his knowledge of the survival rate of this particular sickness.

"Has anyone ever seen a survivor?" Mr. Peters asked.

"It's only been two weeks," Zara said.

Dr. Donald nodded thoughtfully. "Yes, the morbidity rate is certainly high, but there's a good chance it's not one hundred percent. At least, we can hope."

"We did leave behind half our people," Amos said. "Even if Brian didn't make it, Bertie and Judith would have been careful. We don't know if Brian reached Lorrie or if she's still safe. And Dr. Young and Mr. Richards... they could have heard the commotion and hunkered down, too. If they survived, we'd be condemning them by leaving them."

"I'm with Walter." Mitch ran his hands along the wheel. He'd barely left the driver's seat since the night before. "We need to get out of here. See if Pleasant Home is any better. Those bugs... they weren't natural."

Mr. Peters patted Mitch's shoulder. "Mitch is right. Now, I'm not an expert on this particular mosquito, as Zara pointed out—" Zara dug her fingernails into her palms to keep from commenting "—but my research on mosquitos leads me to believe that these are, indeed, a new breed. They seem to be rapidly spreading, reproducing, and evolving, which could account for their aggressive feeding behavior. In my professional opinion, going back is too risky."

Zara remained calm in her tone and body language. Another outburst would only put everyone on Mr. Peters's side. "Well, in my opinion *as a human being*, we should at least go back and look. It's only a few miles away, and we are protected inside the bus. Worst case scenario, we decide not to get out and we drive away knowing we at least tried."

"I'm with Zara on this," Dr. Donald said. Amos nodded, but Sunny kept looking between Zara and Mr. Peters.

"How about if we vote?" Amos asked.

"Fine, but let's keep the decision making to the people who have graduated from high school." Mr. Peters raised his hand. "All those for going straight to Pleasant Home?" Mitch raised his hand, and Sunny's hand twitched upward before she shook her head, yanked her hand back, and sat on it. Mr. Peters sighed. "All those for driving by the hospital?" he asked. Dr. Donald and Amos raised their hands while Sunny continued to sit on hers. "Sunny, you have to weigh in."

"I think you're brilliant, Walter, but... I guess... I've worked with Brian for two years." She winced and raised her hand. "I just couldn't live with myself if we didn't at least drive by."

"Fine." Mr. Peters sat stiffly in the front seat. "Let's get it over with."

Mitch groaned, but he complied. Zara plopped into her seat with a smile on her face. It was nice to win a battle every once in a while, even if Mr. Peters was winning the war. Sophie went back to sit with her father, and as everyone settled for the short drive to the hospital, Lizzy sat with arms crossed, despondently looking out the window.

"We're doing the right thing," Zara said. "I'm glad there are people on this bus that have some humanity left."

Lizzy frowned at her. "And what was it when my dad saved your life, *again*?"

"I don't know." Zara snapped. "He must have had a reason, and I'd bet it had nothing to do with the fact it was the right thing to do." She turned away from Lizzy, angry that she'd brought that up. It was driving her nuts that she owed Mr. Peters. *That's probably the whole point. He wants me to be in his debt.*

The bus rumbled to life, and Zara sat half-turned away from Lizzy until they pulled into the hospital. She stood up as they approached, her body swaying as the bus came to a stop. She craned her neck to see out the windows as everyone else was doing the same thing. The boxes of supplies still sat just outside the doors. Brian's body lay face up a few yards from the awning.

"I don't see anyone else," Dr. Donald said. "Maybe they're all still inside?"

"We can't go in there," Mr. Peters said. "The generator should be out of diesel by now, so it's going to be dark inside. There could be infected people, or even lingering mosquitos. They were out too early last night. We don't know what time is safe. The last thing we need is one of us getting infected."

"Well, the swarm is gone, at least." Amos said. "If we park closer to the awning, on the other side away from Brian's body, maybe we can grab the rest of the supplies."

"And we can honk the horn to signal to anyone inside that we're out here. If they're still alive, we can save them." Sunny put a hand on the window, and through her reflection in the glass, Zara spotted a tear sliding down her cheek. "I can't believe Brian is dead. I guess it didn't seem real until now." Zara came up behind Sunny and put a hand on her back. It seemed the whole bus took a moment of silence, and then the moment was gone and everyone started shuffling away from the windows.

"Okay, so we need to all agree." Dr. Donald moved into the aisle toward the front of the bus. "No one goes inside. Let's grab the rest of the supplies, and then we'll honk the horn and wait to see if anyone comes out."

"Sounds good to me." Zara said, ignoring the way Mr. Peters looked at her, like no one cared what she thought. Like she was a child. She scoffed. Sunny was only four years older than her. That wasn't such a big difference.

Zara followed the short line off the bus, stepping into the sunlight. The open air induced a tingling sensation throughout her body, like something or someone was watching, waiting to pounce. A shriveled dead bird lay a few feet from her, and she stared at its pathetic form, images of the black swarm forming in her mind. She took a step back and pressed against the bus. It was only then that she noticed none of the others had moved far from the bus, either.

We have to do this. Zara swallowed her dread and stepped toward the awning. She couldn't force herself to go quickly, and she had to clench her hands into fists to keep them from shaking. The outermost box was a kind of trophy when she reached down and picked it up. It was full of bottled water, and the sunlight shone through each one, dancing off the plastic and creating patterns against the cardboard. She turned around, box in hand, and walked more confidently back toward the others. Her action spurred them to movement, and soon they were all loading boxes. In no more than twenty minutes, Zara was hefting the last one.

That was when she allowed herself to look at the hospital doors. She stood still, the building before her having been her refuge and her prison for seven days. Those were some of the longest days of her life. The first five days after the World's Fair almost blurred together. They were frantic, emotion-filled, terrible days. But the seven days spent inside the hospital were nightmarish in a different way. She'd had time to think, time to fester, her anger and grief boiling in the cracks, widening them and breaking her.

Beyond the glass sliding doors, beyond the broken window beside them, daylight cast shapes into the darkness. Elongated, slanted rectangles of light reached for the chairs lining the walls of the lobby. Inches from the grasp of day, the darkness writhed, and a figure stood from one of the chairs. The only way out was through the broken window. The form limped forward, bloodied sneakers, once white, scuffing the carpet at the edge of one rectangle of light.

"Judith?" Zara smiled, recognizing those cropped jeans, but as Judith came closer, the light revealing more of her body, Zara began to tremble.

Blood caked Judith's clothes, running in wet, glistening streams from her ears, eyes, nose, and mouth. Her eyes bulged. She held one hand against her temple. The other she used to steady herself as she grabbed the edge of the window which was lined with jagged glass. She stepped through, into the full daylight, just six feet from where Zara stood. When she pulled her hand away from the window, fresh blood dripped from her palm.

"Help... me..." Judith gurgled blood, her swollen eyelids twitching as if she were trying to blink.

Zara backed away. "Judith... stop. You're infected. You can't—"

"Zara?" A voice from inside the hospital made Zara jump. It was Bertie. She came through the window. She wasn't as bad off as Judith, but she was sweating profusely, her expression was pinched in pain, and a welt was growing on her arm. "We were safe, but... when we woke up, there were mosquitos in the room. I don't know how they got in." She coughed, and when she pulled her hand away, blood coated her teeth. "But we're not dead, not like everyone else. We just need help."

Zara's vision blurred with tears. She shook her head, hugging the box to her stomach. "No, Bertie. There's nothing anyone can do."

Judith collapsed and her swollen body seized. Bertie fell to her knees beside her daughter as blood began seeping from her own ears.

"Help us," Bertie said. "You have to do something!"

Mr. Peters's voice sounded from behind her. "Zara, get away from them!"

She closed her eyes, tears streaming down her face, but she backed away. Bertie struggled to her feet and lurched forward, reaching out for her. Panic shot through her, electrifying her and urging her to flee. Zara dropped the box and ran to the bus where Mr. Peters ushered her on and closed the doors. Amos, Dr. Donald, Sunny, and Lizzy stared out the window at Bertie, who continued to advance, slowly but persistently. Her pleas for help cut like a knife, and Zara looked away, her cheeks burning with guilt that she couldn't do anything.

"Don't go anywhere yet, Mitch." Mr. Peters strode the length of the bus to the back and began digging through the boxes.

"Walter, I don't think we have anything that can help," Dr. Donald said. Mr. Peters pulled a rifle out of a long box, and the doctor's face went white.

"Actually, we do have something." Mr. Peters took out a box of shells and began loading the rifle.

"No!" Zara shouted. "You can't!"

"It needs to be done." Mr. Peters finished loading the ammunition and pushed the bolt forward, then downward, snapping it into place.

"Where did you get that?" Amos asked. He gently put a hand on Sophie's head and kept her from looking out the window toward Bertie or back at Mr. Peters.

"Mitch and I found more than gas cans when we went out to gather supplies from the store. We needed these hunting rifles for barter and for protection." Mr. Peters walked to the back row of the remaining seats and slid the window down.

Zara rushed to Mr. Peters and pummeled his back with her fists. "You don't have to kill her, you cold-hearted son of a—"

He grabbed her by the nape of the neck, thrust her toward the window, and slammed the rifle butt against her shoulder. "Take it, then!" he shouted. "You're right, I'm always the one who has to do the hard thing. You get to sit back and judge me while I keep us safe, you little brat." He shouted again, squeezing the back of her neck. "Take the gun, Zara."

She raised trembling hands to take the rifle. The muzzle rested on the open window frame, aimed in Bertie's direction. She'd held a rifle dozens of times before on hunting trips with her dad, but the weapon felt foreign in her hands. She'd been taught to *never* point a gun at a person. *Maybe I can empty the gun's ammunition? Scare Bertie off?* She put her finger next to the trigger, but she couldn't bring herself to touch it. Zara had the urge to get away. Every muscle in her body was tense, and her mind raced with possible ways she could get out of the situation.

Dr. Donald's voice broke through Zara's trepidation. "Walter, I don't think—"

"Not now, Sarah," he snapped. "I'm trying to teach her a lesson she's refused to learn." Mr. Peters shook Zara hard when she squirmed. It was a tight fit, the bus seats on either side of her, Mr. Peters directly behind her. She couldn't move. Bertie was out there, crying for help, and with Mr. Peters's hand on her neck, Zara was forced to look at her down the barrel of a rifle. Her heartbeat throbbed in her ears, a cold sweat raised goosebumps up and down her body, and her stomach flipped. Mr. Peters's hot breath sent a shudder down her spine as he spoke in her ear. "I'm tired of you assuming I don't feel anything, Zara. You think I *wanted* to kill Bart? I've known him for years; he drove for my father before me. I've met his children. But I did the right thing by killing him, and I'm not going to lose one second of sleep over it. I won't let people like you judge me for making the right call for me and mine." He snarled, his anger so palpable, Zara could feel it in the air. The hairs on her arms stood on end.

"Come on, Walter." Amos's voice cracked, but he didn't move to help. "Let's just leave."

"What do you think happens when we leave?" Mr. Peters roared, the pressure of his body against her back lessening slightly. "Bertie is going to die a slow and painful death, just like her daughter did. She's barely started, but soon her insides are going to be coming out of every hole in her body, and she's going to be screaming in pain. And if that takes a couple more hours, if she goes to find help in her delirious state, what if she runs across someone healthy who's stupid enough to help? They die, too. So shut your mouths, and let me do what needs to be done."

Every word he spoke was like a punch to the gut. Zara's mind cleared. *He's right.* She settled the rifle in a more comfortable position and aimed. Her hand shook, though, and she couldn't do it.

"Fine, but you don't have to make a kid shoot her," Amos said.

"She was never going to do it," Mr. Peters said. "But she needs to understand. I do these things because I'm stronger than she'll ever be, not because I'm evil incarnate." He kept ranting, moving away just enough to give her room.

I'm not as weak as he thinks I am. Zara steadied her hands, took a deep breath, and let it out slowly.

Mr. Peters continued. "If it wasn't for me—"

Zara fired. She'd always been an excellent shot. Bertie was knocked backward, blood blooming from her chest as she fell to the ground, dead. Zara screamed, pain exploding inside her own chest as she dealt the killing shot. Her throat raw, she steadied herself with one hand on the back of a bus seat, allowing her entire body to feel the agony radiating from her heart. It was only right that she experienced every ounce of it. Then, she brought the gun inside, set it on the seat, and pushed the window back into place. It took effort to regulate her breathing, to hear anything outside of the drumming of her heart. When she turned, everyone, including Mr. Peters was staring at her with wide eyes, some of them mouths open.

Tears streamed down her face as she faced Mr. Peters. "There. It's done." Her voice quaked. "Let's get one thing straight, Walter. I don't need you anymore. You got that? There is a lot that would have happened differently if it wasn't for you, and personally, I think the world would be a better place if Bertie were still here and you were gone." She pushed past him, but then stopped, jabbing a finger at him. "And you know the difference between you and me, Walter? The difference is that I *hate* what just happened. The difference is that I'll think about it every day for the rest of my life. Killing Bart was an inconvenience for you. An unpleasant experience. This will haunt me, and I knew it would, and I did it anyway. *That* is what strength looks like, you bastard."

She plopped into the back seat and scooted up to the window, drawing her knees to her chest and burying her face from view. No one said anything as Mitch started up the bus and everyone took their seats. Zara didn't look up to see their reactions to what had happened. She didn't care anymore. Mr. Peters was right. They weren't her people. She no longer had people. Maybe it was better that way.

Chapter 17

Timothy Peters

The Escalade stuttered and spat, finally dying and rolling to a stop on the country road. Timothy hit the steering wheel with both hands. They were out of gas, but they still had three miles to go – if Timothy's memory was accurate concerning the way to the mobster house where he'd dropped off Frank a week prior. Heather lay in the back seat, softly snoring, and Candice sat next to him in the passenger seat. His mother's absence was like a blaring horn as Candice picked at her nails. *Mom would have already given me three suggestions. How am I going to get the kids back without her?* He squeezed his eyes shut. The only two expeditions he'd made on his own had ended in disaster.

"What are we going to do?" Timothy scanned the horizon. "I don't think Heather can walk the rest of the way, and it's going to get too hot inside the car."

Candice let her hands fall back in her lap. "There was a farmhouse not far from the road a little way back. I can take Heather there, and you can go on to Frank's."

"No, I'll go with you. I'm not sending you two into a strange house without backup." He hopped out of the car and opened the back door, rustling Heather gently to try to wake her.

"What about my suitcases?" Candice asked. Her suitcases and the weapons Dana had hidden in the ceiling was all that was left of their supplies, and Timothy didn't exactly count Candice's shoes, clothes, makeup, and hair products as supplies.

"We're going to have to leave them." Timothy tapped Heather's cheek with his fingers. "Wake up, hon. We need to get out of here."

"I'm *not* leaving my suitcases." Candice gawked at him.

"Well, I'm not hauling them anywhere. I've got the duffel with the guns, ammo, and meds. Those are way more important than your designer clothes." Timothy smiled at his wife as her eyes fluttered open. "Hey, babe. We ran out of gas. I'm going to take you and Candice to a house just off the road, and then I'm going on to Frank's by myself, okay?"

Heather nodded and sat up. Her eyes were red and puffy from crying too much, and she winced at the movement, putting a hand to her side. "I wish I could go with you," she said, closing her eyes. Fresh tears sprang and streamed down her cheeks. "I'm sorry, Tim."

He held her for a minute, as he'd done a dozen times over the last day. "It's not your fault. My mom and the kids… it's my fault for leaving you alone." She didn't contradict him, which he took as a sign that maybe she was accepting that she couldn't have done more to save Dana, Annika, or George.

Candice popped out of the passenger seat, her scrunchy-tied ponytail bobbing, and slid her fancy sunglasses up on top of her head. She stomped to the back, opened the trunk, and took out her suitcases. "You can carry the duffel on your back and help Heather yourself. I'll get the suitcases. I have snacks and drinks from the vending machine those thugs left behind."

Timothy groaned. "Candice, those suitcases are bigger than you are."

"They are not," Candice said stubbornly, setting the duffel on the road next to the suitcases. She closed the trunk and popped the handles up on each suitcase, rolling one in front of her and the other behind.

At least she's wearing sneakers. He rolled his eyes, not willing to waste any more time arguing. He helped Heather out of the car. They closed and locked the doors, but Timothy hated leaving the vehicle on the side of the road. He slung the duffel over his head and carried it crossbody; it was so heavy it almost made him lose his balance. But he put his arm around his wife and trudged forward toward the house they'd seen about half a mile back.

Candice's suitcases rolled in an unwieldy way as she herded them down the road. Timothy passed her easily and didn't wait for her. If he had to, he would come back for her. Thankfully, somehow, she was able to corral her suitcases all the way to the little farmhouse on the patched and bumpy asphalt. Cracked concrete led up to the house, but as Timothy rounded some foliage to step onto the driveway, he saw shadows in the windows. He gasped and backed up, pulling Heather and himself out of sight.

"Who was that?" Heather asked.

"I don't know." Timothy readjusted the weight of the duffel and looked for a place to hide Heather. Bushes lined the road, and between them and a tree in the yard, there was a shallow gravel ditch that ran under the driveway. It was bone dry because of the summer heat, perfect for a temporary hide out. He helped Heather down and set the duffel bag down. The tree's roots reached down into the ditch, creating little ridges in the rocks to sit on. "If you stay sitting, no one should be able to spot you." He popped back up to the road to get Candice.

"What are you doing?" Candice grunted as she awkwardly kicked the suitcase in front of her to free it of a little pothole and simultaneously yanked on the other one behind her.

Timothy shushed her. "There are people inside." He pointed into the ditch. "Take your stupid suitcases over there and stay out of sight."

"You want me to bring these down there? I'll never get them out!" Candice sighed in frustration when Timothy narrowed his eyes and his mouth pinched. "Fine." She hauled the suitcases into the ditch.

Timothy unzipped the duffel and rifled through weapons and pill bottles to find a handgun. It was stored in a holster he could clip to his pants. "I'm going to check it out. Maybe it's just regular people, and we've caught a break."

"Yes, because we're so good at finding regular people." Candice huffed, crossed her arms, and sat back on a root. "Even if they *are* normal, no one is going to share their supplies with strangers."

Heather reached out and put a hand on Timothy's cheek. "Just be careful, okay?"

He kissed her forehead and dropped the keys to the Escalade in her lap. "Promise. Now you two stay here. If I run into trouble, though, don't wait too long to head back to the car for shelter." He glared at Candice. "If you have to make a dash for safety, leave the suitcases."

She put up her hands in a sign of surrender. "If it's between life and death, I'll leave them."

She's important, maybe the only person who has survived this sickness… and she did come to dig me out of the bunker. Timothy sighed as the woman frowned at the dirt smeared on her two-thousand-dollar jeans. Candice is either going to save us all or kill us all.

He crawled out of the ditch and rounded the house, using the trees as cover wherever he could, and came up beside a window. He peeked inside to find a living room with two men lounging on a couch. One was tall and lean, his knees at an upward angle as he sat eating peaches out of a can. The other one had some muscle, though not so much that Timothy found him intimidating. He slurped a large, plastic jar of applesauce. Timothy could barely make out the muffled words as they chatted about their lack of food variety.

A walkie talkie came to life on the coffee table, and Timothy frowned at it. *Is that one of ours?* It looked exactly the same as the ones they'd left behind. They had brought a few with them to the clinic, but those had been in the bins stolen by Digger and Icepick. The rest had been left at the bunker; Timothy had planned to come back to get them. He still had no idea how Frank got into the bunker to steal what they'd left behind.

"Hey, String Bean!" A voice squawked over the little speaker. "Pick up. You hear me?"

The tall man picked up the walkie talkie. "I'm here. Just havin' some lunch. Whatcha want?"

"That sparkly purple car you said drove past half an hour ago—it never came by."

"Me and Reggie ain't seen it come back this way," String Bean said. "We got Pugsie watchin' the road from the upstairs window."

"That's a problem," the voice said. "No connectin' roads between here and there. They didn't just disappear. They either got stuck, or somebody is tryin' to sneak up on us. You know how The Boys in Blue be. Can't leave us alone, even now."

Reggie chuckled. "Them cops ain't got nothin' better to do. Never did, never will. Just playin' games. Who cares who gots the goods in times like these?"

"Yeah," String Bean said, letting the walkie-talkie rest on his lap while he shoved a peach in his mouth. He spoke as he chewed. "Frankie's been real good to people. Sharin' what we've got. Dishin' it out pretty fair, I'd say. Why they's got to butt in?"

Frankie… our Frank? I thought he wasn't far up in the mobster food chain. Timothy concentrated, trying to get every word. And if the police are still operating in some capacity… maybe I can find them, ask them to help?

"They's got to butt in," Reggie said, "because they ain't got nowhere else to do it now the ConMen have Boston." He shook his head. "Real shame, too, that. We's gots rights to the city. Those thugs ain't got no code."

The ConMen have Boston… Timothy's brief hope that the police could help him get the kids back faded. If the ConMen took the kids and the Farm was in Boston, the police wouldn't have any better chance at getting them back than Frank. And Timothy had no idea where the police force was located, anyway.

"String Bean, did you hear me?" The voice on the walkie-talkie chimed in with a frustrated tone. "I said we got a problem."

"Whatcha want us to do?" String Bean put down his can of peaches as he responded.

"Get off your lazy asses and find the damn car." The voice shouted, and both men jumped out of their chairs.

As soon as they find the vehicle empty, they're going to be on high alert. If they put out a search party, we're done. We'll be shot before we even get the chance to ask for help. Timothy ducked back under the window. He ran his hand over his face, his mind running a mile a minute through his options. He landed on something that resembled a plan, though he didn't know if it would work. He couldn't kill any more of Frank's guys, not if he wanted to convince Frank to help.

Timothy hurried back to the ditch, holding his finger to his lips as he slid down. Huddling with Candice and Heather, he whispered, telling them what he'd heard and what he planned to do. "If you stay hunkered down here, I can barter and make sure you'll be safe before coming back to get you."

"Are you sure they won't find us?" Heather asked.

"They'll be going to the Escalade first, and my guess is that they'll fan out from there. That should give me enough time to steal a walkie-talkie and get ahold of Frank, maybe even enough time to come to a deal with him, before they think to look closer to this house." Timothy looked at Candice. "I don't like how late it's getting. We've got an hour tops before we need to get out of here and head back the way we came on foot to try to find shelter. If I'm not back by then, you've got to get Heather out of here. Leave *everything* else behind, except for maybe a couple of firearms and some ammo. Got it?"

"I've got it," Candice said, whispering in a serious tone. "We can always come back for my bags later. They're waterproof, so we should be good."

Timothy rolled his eyes. "Sure, Candice. Just get Heather out. One hour, okay?"

"I said I've got it." Candice sat back, indicating that part of the conversation was over.

Heather stayed close, leaning her head against Timothy's. "Just be careful, Tim. I don't think I can do this without you."

Timothy met her eyes and cupped her face in his hands. "We're going to make it. We're going to find the kids, and we're going to get to that lab, and we're going to ride this thing out together."

"I love you, Timothy Peters, and I know you can do this." Heather kissed him. For a moment, there was just the two of them, and she covered over the gouges in his heart with a balm. He let himself feel whole, feel something other than brokenness in that moment.

Timothy broke the kiss reluctantly, but for the first time that day, he genuinely felt like he could pull his plans off. "I love you, too, babe." He smiled at her and wiped away a few stray tears on her cheeks with his thumbs.

As soon as he heard the rumble of a truck across the driveway, Timothy climbed out of the ditch and headed back for the house, staying low and trying to keep to the shadows of the trees. He kept his eyes on the upper windows this time, noting where the lookout was stationed, looking down at the road. He reached the side of the house, confident he hadn't been seen, and crept to the back where he entered the house through an unlocked back door.

He breathed a sigh of relief when he saw a walkie-talkie on the kitchen counter. He grabbed it and slipped back outside, sitting against the house. He switched it on and held it up. His mouth suddenly felt dry, and his palms began to sweat. The thought of talking to Frank again made his hair stand on end. He swallowed hard and pressed the button to talk.

"Hello?" His voice cracked. He rolled his shoulders, cleared his throat, and tried again. "Hello? This is Timothy Peters. I need to talk to Frank Russo." No reply. He double checked that the walkie-talkie was on. *They would have it set to the right channel, right?* He tried a third time. "This is Timothy. Peters. Is Frank Russo there?"

A few more seconds passed, and just as Timothy was about to try again, the speaker crackled to life. "Southie? You's got a lot o' balls. Where's my guys? You already owe me. Don't think I won't pop one in your skull just 'cause I like ya."

"Your men are fine. They don't even know I'm here." A flood of relief and dread washed over him, and Timothy shifted uncomfortably as the two emotions warred within him. "And I'd say after you burned down my parents' house and took everything we had, we're even."

"Nah, Southie. That was payment for getting you free of the ConMen back in Mattapan. You still owe me for tryin' to stop me from collectin' my debt. You shot me and did a number on my crew."

Timothy closed his eyes and kept his tone even. "Well, I've paid you back for that already. You just don't know it."

"How's that?"

"We had some trouble with the ConMen. They kidnapped Annika and my brother, George. They're just kids, Frank. I could have gone to them and offered up your location in exchange for the kids, but instead, I came to you for help. I know they want your head, Frank. I also know they control the city, and that they would jump at the chance to grab everything you've got. I could have given up your location, and instead of me coming to you for help, you would have ConMen on your doorstep. I guarantee they wouldn't have asked nicely to come inside. But me? I'm just here to ask for help because I know how you feel about men who hurt kids." Timothy's hands were so sweaty, the walkie-talkie slid from his hand when he lifted the pressure on the button. He fumbled to catch it, waiting for a reply.

"Who are you?" A man shouted from the right corner of the house. "You a cop? Where's the rest?"

Timothy looked up to find Pugsie, the lookout, pointing a gun right at him. He raised one hand. "This is just a walkie-talkie," he said. "My gun is holstered at my hip. I'm not here to hurt anyone."

A second voice came from the other side of the house. "What're ya here for, then?" String Bean asked, weapon raised.

Timothy looked down at the walkie-talkie, praying that Frank's voice would come through, that he would accept Timothy's plea for help. *Who am I kidding? I'm such an idiot.* He glanced at the back door. *If I can make a dash for the door, maybe I can run through to the front and escape.*

He gathered up his courage to move, but then the third man, Reggie, came through the back door, gun in hand. Three guns pointed at Timothy's head, and there was no way out.

Chapter 18

Minnie Stevens

It had been decades since Minnie had had so much fun sneaking around, but this time, it was for a good reason and her Pop wouldn't be waiting at home with a switch. Samson sat dutifully behind her on the stairwell landing, keeping still and quiet. Having him back made her family whole again, and her anxieties had lessened significantly since he'd been returned. He nudged her leg with his nose, and she put a finger to her lips, then made a gun shape with her hand and whispered, "Pew, pew." Samson took a few purposefully awkward steps and lay on his side, closing his eyes to play dead. That would keep him quiet for a few minutes at least.

Minnie cracked open the stairwell door and peeked into the hall. She could see Alex's office, the number 202 taunting her. A military man marched down the hall, slow and steady, and Minnie shut the door and started the stopwatch she'd found in the gym lockers. Then, she waited with her ear pressed to the door. Samson lifted his head to peek at her, but she pointed her finger at him again, and he promptly lay back down. There'd been a time after she'd fallen out with Lauren that teaching Samson dog tricks became something of an obsession. She'd never imagined she'd actually have to use the training for something so important.

Several minutes passed before she heard the sound of footsteps. She cracked the door open and saw the same soldier as before. She'd timed the man once before, and both times had been within seconds of each other. *Takes him about six minutes to make his rounds. I've got to get that door open in five or less. I bet I can do it in two.*

She waited a few seconds and then patted her leg. Samson jumped up, and she slipped him a potato chip. She'd thought at first her plan might go awry because she didn't have dog treats, but apparently Samson was a big fan of chips, which was a good thing because that's all she could manage to get. The door opened without a sound; the hall was clear. Minnie slipped out, tugging Samson's leash and rushing to the door. She pulled out Lauren's bobby pins. She'd flattened one, and she'd picked off the rubber nub of the other and sharpened the point. She inserted the flattened one into the bottom of the keyhole and used the sharper bobby pin to find the locking mechanism. A satisfying *click* followed, and she had to bite her lip to keep from whooping out loud.

Momma's still got it. She opened the door and brought Samson inside Alex's office, closing the door behind her as softly as she could. She slipped Samson another potato chip, and he munched happily on it, his tail wagging lazily.

Alex's office was simple and small. A desk stood opposite a line of three floor-to-ceiling bookshelves. There were no windows, and the paintings on the wall seemed like something someone might find in a doctor's office waiting room. Minnie scooted around the desk and picked the lock on the long drawer at the center. Another *click*, and she was in. The drawer slid open, and she grabbed the small, handheld voice recorder.

"Let's see if there's anything else in here Alex might need," she said softly to Samson. He barked a reply, and she winced, making him play dead again as she looked through the remaining drawers. She grabbed a small pack of batteries and a sharp letter opener in a leather pouch, sticking both in her cargo pockets. She looked up, ready to leave, when she spotted a small family portrait on the bookshelves. She walked over and took a gander at the woman Alex had told her so much about: Naomi. She was a fine young woman with long, black hair falling around her shoulders in styled waves. The Roman family looked happy, Oliver between them, a green park and sunshine behind. Alex looked a bit younger, and his eyes didn't hold the same weight Minnie was so used to seeing there. He looked content. Free.

"Nice to meet ya, Naomi," she whispered as she picked up the portrait. "Your boy is right delightful, which I'm sure you knew already, but… lands sake, I sure am grateful to have met him and Alex." Tears sprang, and she imagined her boys like they looked in the picture: happy and whole with Naomi alive and well. "They miss you somethin' awful, but they'll be okay. I'm lookin' out for 'em, but I'd appreciate any help ya can throw my way." She pressed the picture to her chest, took a deep breath, and dried her eyes.

After sticking the portrait under one arm, she checked the time. *Should be safe.* The door opened without so much as a squeak, and she carefully closed it, stepping lightly and praying Samson stayed quiet. But then she turned around, tickled she'd pulled off her mission without a hitch, and ran smack dab into a tall, distinguished gentleman in a uniform. Minnie yelped, her hand flying to her chest.

"Good gracious, General Hunt! You spooked my ghost right out of my skin."

The general frowned and stepped back to give her an inch. "What were you doing in there?" He eyed Samson as he sniffed the general's hand. The man was stiff as a board.

Minnie also threw Samson a little glare. *Way to warn me someone was comin', you stinker.* She pulled out the portrait from under her arm, a white lie springing to her lips. "My friend, Alex, well, he's been tore up about losin' his wife, and he mentioned he'd love this here picture but it was locked away, so since I can pick a lock, I thought to myself, 'Minnie, put that to good use,' and I did." She smiled at the picture, hoping her nerves weren't showing. "I reckon he'll be over the moon to have this back."

General Hunt grunted. "I appreciate the sentiment, ma'am—"

Minnie held up a finger. That wasn't a term she wanted handsome men using in reference to her. He couldn't be more than a few years her senior. No, that wouldn't do. "You can call me Minnie."

His frown deepened. "Ma'am, I—"

She narrowed her eyes and said with more force, "Minnie."

For a military man in charge, he wasn't too hard to fluster. He shifted his weight, his frown deepening. "Minnie, I understand why—"

Got to get him off that right quick or I'm in trouble. Minnie used her sweetest, most innocent voice and threw in a touch of friendly scolding. "A gentleman would introduce himself proper after startin' to use a lady's first name." She pursed her lips and batted her eyelashes a few times.

"But, I..." He squirmed just a little, and she could see him softening up like butter. "You already know my name," he said.
"I know what your subordinates call you," Minnie said. "I ain't in the military, and I ain't your subordinate. I'm just a lady, walkin' her dog, doin' a friend a favor. And you're just a man goin' about his business. Now, are you gonna introduce yourself proper, or what?"
His mouth opened and closed like a fish out of water. Finally, he said, "It's Alan, but no one calls me that here."
"Well, now, won't it be nice to have a friend, Alan?" Minnie smiled, turning up her southern charm. "Are you gonna offer me an arm and take me back to my rooms like a gentleman?"
He blinked a few times but stuck out his arm. "I... um, I guess I could take a few minutes to take you back to your room."
She handed the picture to him, and he took it without question. Her arm hooked in his, she followed his lead toward the stairwell, holding Samson's leash with her other hand. "Samson's a good judge of character," she said, "and he seems to like you. You a dog person, Alan?"
He cleared his throat. "I had a dog when I was a boy," he said. He stepped away from her and opened the stairwell door, gesturing for her to go first.
"Why, thank you," Minnie said. She stepped through and held out her arm for him to take, and they strolled down the steps. "And you haven't had one since? A dog, I mean."
"No," he said. "I never married, and military life isn't conducive to owning a pet otherwise."
Minnie widened her eyes. "Mylanta! Such a catch and never married?"
The faintest blush colored his cheeks. "I'm not very good at relationships."
"Oh, fiddlesticks." Minnie waved away his comment. "It just takes a little work, and I can tell you're no stranger to that." She squeezed his arm, and his blush deepened.
He opened the door for her again when they reached the right landing, and walked her down the hall to her room, his pace picking up. Minnie had to practically jog, but she didn't complain. The faster she got rid of him, the better. He was a nice enough man, it seemed, but she had a whole host of secrets swept under her rug. The last thing she needed was for him to go snooping.
When they reached their destination, he dropped his arm, a relieved expression coming across his face. Minnie let Samson go into the room where he jumped up on the bed and curled up next to Lauren, who looked up from her book and frowned at Minnie. She turned back to face the general.

"Can I do anything else for you?" He subtly tapped the photo frame against his leg as he held it by his side.
"You can give me that picture," Minnie said sweetly.
"Oh, right." He nearly shoved it into her hands. "If that's all—"
"Actually, Alan," Minnie said as she took the picture from the general's hand, "now that we're friends, I would like to ask you a favor."
"Oh?" He swallowed audibly, his Adam's apple bobbing.
"I shared a room in quarantine with a man by the name of Elijah Dixon. I'd dearly love to visit with him, to check on his health. Would you mind poppin' over to the hospital to ask after his wellbeing and let me know how I can set up a visit?" She patted his arm, not waiting for his answer, and stepped inside her room. "Thank you kindly, Alan," she said before closing the door on a man who looked as lost as last year's Easter egg. She held her breath until she heard his footsteps retreat down the hall, and then she let it out slowly.
Lauren quirked an eyebrow at her. "Mom, what just happened?"
"I put the cart before the horse, and then my wheel 'bout got stuck, that's what happened." Minnie breathed out slowly and then tapped her temple. "Good thing I'm quick."
"Did you get the voice recorder?" Lauren asked.
Minnie pulled it out of her pocket. "Sure did. Now, where's Oliver?"
"He's napping in his room." Lauren let Samson put his head on her lap, and she scratched between his ears.
Minnie plopped down on her bed and put the picture and the letter opener on the side table. "He's got the right idea. I think I'll rest my eyes, if that's all right with you."
She lay back and got comfortable, drifting off before she could count six sheep. When she woke, the room was empty, but she heard mumbles through the wall. She stretched her arms as she got out of bed, noting the picture was gone, and joined the others in Alex and Oliver's room. Lauren and Samson were there, and the photo was beside Oliver's bedside where he sat cross-legged playing solitaire with a deck of cards like Minnie taught him the day before. Corporal Jenny Conner was there, too, standing and chatting with Alex and Lauren in a tight circle.
"Afternoon everybody," Minnie said as she closed the door behind her. The three widened their circle to make room for her, but they each had grim looks on their faces. "What's got your goose? Did your meetin' with those scientists fall flat?"
Alex shook his head. "No, actually, it went well, all things considered. I'm meeting with one of them tonight. You did good work with the voice recorder. I'm confident I'll be able to get some proof that Lawson and his guys are trouble."
Minnie patted Alex's arm. "Well, that's great! Y'all don't know how to celebrate good news. Turn those frowns upside down. Everything's comin' together."
The three of them gave each other that look again, like somebody died and they didn't know how to tell her. Her stomach sank, and her smile faded.
"Well, spit it out," she said. "What's wrong?"
"General Hunt had me go to the hospital to check on your friend," Conner said.
"That was fast," Minnie said, her chest tightening a little. "Is he okay? Did somethin' happen?"
"You're sure his name was Elijah Dixon, Mom?" Lauren asked, forehead creased. "It was a really stressful day. Maybe you didn't get the name right?"
"No, I'm positive. Elijah Dixon. I'd bet my bottom dollar on it." Minnie braced herself for the worst. "If y'all don't come out with it, I'm gonna pitch a fit." Nothing she could have done would have prepared her for what came next.

"Minnie," Alex said, "the hospital doesn't have any record of an Elijah Dixon. According to them, he doesn't exist. He was never there."

Chapter 19

Zara Williams

The excruciating pain shooting up Zara's leg gave her something to focus on; it felt right somehow, fitting together nicely with the tightness in her chest and the rocks in her stomach. She'd murdered Bertie. The reasons were good; it had made sense. No one blamed her. Dr. Donald, Sunny, Amos, and Lizzy had each made a point to sit next to her and insist she'd done nothing wrong. That didn't matter. It had been justified. Reasoned out. It was objectively the responsible thing to do. And yet, it had still been so very wrong.

For four hours, she had hugged her knees to her chest and looked out the window, unmoving and stiff, every muscle tense. Her feet tingled with a lack of blood flow, a cramp raged angrily through her calf muscle, and her shoulders and arms ached from the effort of keeping her body scrunched in on itself for so long. The hot, humid air dampened each breath. Even with her tight, black curls pulled into a puff on top of her head, her face and neck were sweltering. She'd pulled her t-shirt hem into a knot at her side, and the small gap at the small of her back between the hem of her shirt and the waistline of her jeggings kept sticking to the faux leather of the bus seat.

The landscape rolled by, and the greenery of the countryside blurred together until houses began to dot the roadside. A small road sign jutted out of the grass between the asphalt and a corn field, reading: Pleasant Home. That was it. No population number, no welcome message. Just a brief notification that, for the blink of an eye on that two-lane road, she was *somewhere.*

Amos directed Mitch to a road with no center line. The bus took up almost the entire road by itself, but for all Zara could see, it wasn't a one-way street. It extended into what Amos called "the boonies" which was nothing but fields, fences, and a house every so often.

Lizzy slid into the seat next to Zara. She'd stayed away for most of the trip, choosing to sit with Sunny. Zara had let their conversations drift past her melancholy state a few times. They talked of nothing important, but Lizzy needed that when she was upset, when she was scared. She needed meaningless chatter and laughter. Lizzy knew how to give up control, roll with the punches, and just let things happen. Zara used to like that about her until she started doing it with the death of Zara's parents, aunt, and brother. Until she used that particular quirk to ignore the fact that her father was responsible for the apocalypse.

"Looks like we're almost there." Lizzy held two bottles of water, one of which she kept for herself, the other of which she proffered to Zara. "How're you feeling?"

Zara unfurled her body, letting her feet plunk to the floorboards. Fingers stiff, she took the water bottle. "I'm tired," she said as she unscrewed the top and took a drink, and she meant it in every way possible – physically, emotionally, and mentally. The sunlight played with the water, casting shapes on the back of the seat in front of her. Just like it had on the cardboard of the box before Judith came out of the hospital. Before Zara shot Bertie in the chest. Zara cleared her throat, capped the bottle, and put it beside her, pushing the memory out of her mind.

"Are you going to stay mad at me forever?" Lizzy slumped in her seat. She'd been doing a lot of that lately, especially around Zara.

"You never care what people think of you, Liz," Zara said.

"They aren't *you*, Zee." Liz wiped the sweat off her forehead with the back of her hand.

"I know you're keeping something from me." Zara noted how Liz shifted uncomfortably. "Do you know where the phone is? Where he's keeping it?"

Lizzy bit her lower lip. "I—"

The bus screeched to a halt. "Amos, you know these wackos?" Mitch shouted from the driver's seat, and Amos came to stand next to him, facing the windshield.

"Well, it's hard to tell with those outfits." Amos put his hands on his hips.

Lizzy popped up with everyone else to look out the window, but Zara kept her eyes on Lizzy for a few moments. *She was going to tell me. She* wants *to tell me.* Zara glanced at the water bottle, conflict pulling her apart. Lizzy wasn't giving up on her or their friendship, and if Zara was being truthful with herself, she didn't want her to. They'd been best friends too long, been through too much to throw away the sisterhood they shared. But the secrets, the love Lizzy still had for her father, and the pure hatred Zara harbored for Walter Peters… it was eating her up inside.

Zara sighed and used the back of the seat in front of her to pull herself up. Her body protested, pins and needles shooting through her feet as blood flow returned in full force, muscles twitching as she tried to loosen them up. Ahead on the road, two men with assault rifles blocked their way. Each wore wide sun hats with mesh nets connecting to what looked like white beekeeping suits.

One of them walked over to the bus's door and tapped the glass with the muzzle of his rifle. "State your business, but don't step out," he shouted.

Mr. Peters stood next to Amos. "Do you recognize him?"

"I think… Hosea, is that you?" Amos opened the door. "We're clean, if that's what you're worried about."

The man in the beekeeper suit whistled as he walked up the steps into the bus. "Well, I'll be darned. Amos Redding! I can't believe my eyes." He held out an arm and the two men hugged, though it looked awkward with Hosea's suit and the rifle in hand. Hosea pulled back. "That can't be little Sophie?"

Sophie shrank into her seat and whimpered. Amos rushed to her side. "It's okay, sweetie," he said. "This is a friend." He scooped up his daughter and turned back to Hosea. "I'm guessing by that get-up you're wearing that you've heard about the mosquitos."

Zara leaned forward, trying to see the newcomer beyond the mesh. Something white caught her attention out of the corner of her eye, and she noted the other man in a beekeeper suit as he slowly circled the bus. He was staring up at them through the windows. *Trying to see if he can spot any signs of sickness. He's a little more cautious than Hosea.* Zara didn't hide the fact that she saw him staring at her. She stared right back and pursed her lips. She couldn't see beyond that mesh very well; it was all shadows. That unnerved her.

"We've heard some tales from travelers," Hosea said. "Swarms of the little buggers that'll suck you dry or make you sick. Either way, they kill you dead. We've seen the sick at our gates; the swarms we've yet to encounter." He patted his hat. "But we're prepared for them. The same night this all started, Thomas rallied everybody together and by morning, we'd all gathered at the compound and started shoring up defenses, pooling resources, that sort of thing. Thankfully, one of our members had killer bugs on his apocalypse bingo and had stockpiled all kinds of mesh." Hosea laughed. "We all thought he was nuts!"

Mr. Peters frowned. "This Thomas… he's your leader?"

Hosea pointed with his thumb at Mr. Peters. "Who's this guy?"

"I'm Walter Peters," he responded, though Hosea hadn't addressed him. He put on what Zara considered his business persona: no-nonsense posture, hard jawline, slightly narrowed eyes, not a smile in sight. "We're here to make a trade."

Hosea snorted. "Amos, where'd you find this lout?" He made stiff movements with one arm and spoke with a robot voice. "Beep-boop-beep. We're here to make a trade." He belly-laughed and slapped Mr. Peters on the arm. Mr. Peters stiffened and that vein popped again.

Zara quirked an eyebrow. *This is who they sent to guard the road?* His companion rounded the entire bus, seeming to stop and take a good look at them all through the windows. Then, he positioned himself so that Hosea could see him and gave him a thumbs up. Zara crossed her arms, impressed as Hosea slung the rifle over his shoulder. *He was distracting us, keeping his rifle at the ready, until the other guy gave the all clear.*

Amos chuckled nervously. "He's, um… kind of an important man, Hosea."

"Sure," Hosea said. "He's real fancy." He looked to the back of the bus. "You've got good sense, Amos, bringing supplies. Thomas will want to talk, but first we've got to get everyone inside the compound."

"Just like that?" Mr. Peters asked, sounding suspicious.

"Amos is our boy, Walter," Hosea said. "He knows the rules, and he'd never put us at risk. Isn't that right?"

"That's right." Amos put up two fingers. "Scout's honor."

"All right, then," Hosea said. "Thomas would kill me where I stand if I let his son stay out here longer than I had to." He put out an open hand, waving it over the occupants of the bus. "Now, I can't promise you can *all* stay; our community is a family, and we don't let just anybody in. But since you're with Amos, I'm pretty sure Thomas'll give you temporary shelter." He stepped down off the bus. "We'll let you pass and radio in to let Thomas know you're coming."

Lizzy looked over her shoulder at Zara and mouthed the words, "His son?"

That one had surprised Zara, too. "I know," she whispered.

"Thanks, Hosea." Amos moved Sophie to his other hip. She seemed more curious now that Hosea put some distance between them as she craned her neck to look at the men in the beekeeper suits.

Mr. Peters shut the doors to the bus and then raised his eyebrows at Amos. "The man in charge is your father? Did I hear that right?"

Amos blushed and nodded. "Well, yes. Sort of. Everyone treats him like he's in charge, even though it's not an official title or anything. It's always been that way."

"Sound familiar?" Zara whispered to Lizzy. She chuckled, and Zara smiled for half a second before remembering the two were at odds. Her smile faded, and so did Lizzy's. But that second had been nice, an echo of what used to be. Her words from before echoed in her own mind. *I'm so tired.*

"And you can get me a meeting with him?" Mr. Peters ran his fingers through his sweaty hair and then dried his hand on his shirt. "We need to get to Boston."

"My father will talk to you," Amos said, "don't worry about that. But, it'll be tomorrow at the earliest before you get back on the road, so let's just get to the compound, get a bite to eat, and get some rest."

Zara slid back into her seat. Lizzy stepped toward the seat Sunny was sitting in, but Zara cleared her throat. An urge to *not* be alone as they entered somewhere new and unfamiliar washed over her. "It's only a few more minutes," she said. "You want to sit here?" She patted the seat next to her.

Lizzy beamed. "Yeah," she said. "That would be nice." She sat down as the bus budged forward and picked up a little speed, Amos directing Mitch as they went.

Trees on the side of the road gave way to a clearing, and farther back from the road, a wall of shipping containers with barbed wire running along the top dominated the open space. A steel-barred security gate stood at the center of the wall. As they approached, two men pulled open the gate, and the bus crept inside the compound. Zara gaped at the containers, which were stacked four high and two deep, creating a secure square of protection for multiple buildings. Each log cabin was complete with a rooftop full of solar panels and shiny steel mesh covering the windows. In the distance, the ground was tilled, sprouting green plants along the back of the compound.

Mitch stopped the bus near the center of the compound where a line of people waited – three men and two women, each one in long sleeves with thick gloves and knee-high galoshes. They each had on sun hats with mesh coming down to tuck into the collars of their shirts, and their frumpy clothing spoke of layers. *They have to be dying in this heat!* Zara looked at her own bare arms, though, and a tinge of insecurity flared up. *At least they have some protection.*

One of them broke the line and approached. Mitch opened the doors. "Everyone off the bus," the man said. He backed off and crossed his arms.

Mr. Peters was the first to get off, followed by Amos and Sophie. Zara wasn't in a hurry. She let the others go first, being the last to step onto the gravel. Mr. Peters was already in an argument with Thomas, the man who'd approached.

"My situation is urgent, Thomas," Mr. Peters said. "If you'd just take a minute to listen, you'd understand why."

"I don't care," Thomas said. "You and your group need to quarantine in that building over night until we're sure you're all as healthy as you claim to be." He pointed to a cabin devoid of any personal touches. Several of the others had painted shutters or plants on the other side of the mesh, different colored doors, and plaques with last names carved into them above those. Thomas didn't flinch under Mr. Peters's insistence. "If my son and granddaughter can follow the rules, so can you."

"We don't have time for that." Mr. Peters shook his head. "We need to leave for Boston first thing tomorrow, as soon as its safe. We're going to need a vehicle—"

Thomas burst into laughter. "There's no way we're giving you one of our vehicles. We don't have enough of them, and we certainly don't have enough gasoline. You're stuck here, friend."

Of course we are. This was going too smoothly. Zara didn't want to hear any more. She trudged toward the building at which Thomas had pointed. Exhaustion hung off her limbs like weights, but at least it dampened the raging emotional currents she'd been fighting. Or perhaps she'd stopped fighting just long enough for the currents to drag her under into the darkness of grief. Before she could decide which it was, before she even reached the door to their quarantine cabin, an alarm, like a blaring horn, sounded throughout the camp. In a matter of seconds, three dozen people poured out of the buildings, each in a layered outfit with gloves, galoshes, and mesh, each with a firearm.

Zara spun around, trying to get someone's attention. The people on the bus were still gathered with Thomas several yards away, and she couldn't hear what was being said to them as the compound leader gestured firmly toward the quarantine cabin. "What's happening?" she shouted to a woman jogging toward the gates.

The woman's reply made Zara's hair stand on end. "We're being attacked," she said. "Get to the quarantine cabin and stay put." She didn't stay long enough to make sure Zara followed her orders.

Mitch bustled by, his arms flailing as he dashed for the cabin. Several black spots appeared over the top of the barbed wire, and Zara squinted at them. *What the heck are those?* She frowned at one of them, focusing on it as it got closer. Lizzy barreled into Zara's side, sending her crashing to the ground, breaking her trance.

Zara pushed Lizzy off and sat up. "What the h—" She cut off as a short, thick crossbow bolt *thunked* into the ground where she'd been standing. Her mouth dropped open, and she yelped as several more *thunks* sounded across the yard. One of them struck Mitch right through the eye, and his head snapped back, his feet flying out from under him as his back slammed into the ground. The bolt stuck out of his head like a flag claiming ground. Zara looked up into the sky as the preppers reached the top of the wall and started shooting. It was too late; another volley of crossbow bolts descended upon them.

Chapter 20

Timothy Peters

Timothy's pulse throbbed in his temples as sweat trickled down the side of his face. He held his breath, expecting a gunshot to go off at any second and a bullet to rip through his body. *I should have gotten Heather out of here first. I should have found a safe place for her somewhere else before coming to find Frank. I should have –*

"Yeah, all right, Southie." Frank's voice crackled over the walkie-talkie in Timothy's hand. "You got my attention."

Timothy sucked in a breath, relieved to hear a reply. The three men pointing their guns at him exchanged glances and lowered their weapons, though none of them put their guns away. "Can I answer him?" Timothy asked.

Reggie grunted. "Go on, then. But don't try nothin' funny. You run, we shoot."

"Got it. No running." Timothy slowly lowered the walkie-talkie to his mouth. "Hey Frank," he said. "Your guys found me, all three of them. Mind telling them to stand down?"

Frank cursed. "String Bean, you idiot! All three of you's on this kid when you know we got bigger fish?"

String Bean's cheeks burned red as he fumbled for his walkie-talkie. "Uh… sorry, Frankie. We didn't know. Thought maybe he was a cop."

"Well, he's not." Frank shouted. "Get Pugsie to bring him to me, and you and Reggie get back on the watch."

The tall, lanky mobster nodded frantically as if Frank could see him. "Yeah, boss. Will do. Sorry, boss." He holstered his gun and nodded at Timothy. "You heard Frankie, Pugs. He wants to talk to this guy."

Pugsie came up to Timothy and removed his handgun from the holster. Then, he poked Timothy's back with the muzzle of his gun. "Let's go, then," he said.

"Where to?" Timothy asked. "You got a car, or…?"

"We're cuttin' across the field." Pugsie pointed to a path carved out of the cornfield that reminded Timothy of an entrance to a corn maze, except it extended straight through.

Timothy walked toward the path, and the other two mobsters returned to their posts inside the house. They walked in silence for several minutes, the yellowed and broken stalks of corn crunching beneath their feet. An earthy scent with a touch of sweetness not quite like honey wafted from the cornfield around him. It was a sharp contrast to the wave of body odor coming from Pugsie every time the breeze picked up.

Timothy decided to keep quiet about Heather and Candice until he knew what Frank wanted to do with him. Time wasn't on their side, but there was still a couple of hours left before he had to worry about their safety. *They should be able to get to the Escalade and hunker down for the night if need be. Surely Frank's guys will stay inside once it gets too close to sundown. Even if they already found it, they couldn't have moved it without the keys or gas in the tank, right?* He chewed on his lower lip. If they'd found the vehicle and broken the windows to get a better look inside, that would render it useless as a temporary shelter. Or if they had excess gasoline and could bypass the Escalade's safeties against hotwiring, they could move the vehicle.

"What's Frank want with you, anyhow?" Pugsie asked, annoyance clear in his tone. "It woulda been easier to just kill you dead and be done with it. I got better things to do with my time than be some babysitter."

"I'm sure you're a man of many talents." Timothy kept walking, trying to speed up the pace without alarming Pugsie. He needed to get this over with. He had to convince Frank to help and then convince him to take in Heather and Candice.

"Yeah," Pugsie said, "I *am*, actually. I gots loads of talents."

"A sharp eye, obviously." Timothy swallowed his nerves, trying to get on the mobster's good side. "Otherwise, they wouldn't have asked you to keep watch on the road." He looked over his shoulder at the man.

Pugsie grinned. "Exactly. I'm a good shot. Stealthy as a cat. And I can knit."

Timothy frowned. "Knot? You can make knots?"

"Nah. I knit. Which is kinda like makin' knots, I guess. But fancier. And what's everybody gonna do when winter comes 'round, huh? We're gonna need hats and scarves and blankets and crap, right? Well, I'm gonna be the go-to guy." He made the sign of the cross and touched a pendant hanging on a chain. "Granny did me right. None of the other guys can knit."

"I sure can't." Timothy craned his neck as the end of the pathway came into view. He saw the sliver of a house through the field. "Is that where we're going?"

Pugsie, still grinning, let his gun down to his side as he nodded. "Yep, that's it." He sniffed and looked sideways at Timothy. "You never answered my question. What's the boss want with you?"

"It's more like I want something from him." The path through the corn field ended. Ahead, a sprawling ranch-style house accompanied a large stable, and beyond that, a pasture with a white fence surrounding green grass, butting up against a pond, made for a picture-perfect landscape. Timothy's heartbeat quickened with every step toward the house.

"I guess that don't surprise me," Pugsie said. "The boss has a soft spot. As long as you're square with 'im, he's fair. Whewee, though… if you ain't square, if you ain't fallin' in line, I wouldn't want no part of that."

"I know what you mean." Timothy walked up the steps and through the front door. Men three times Pugsie's size stood by the entry, hands clasped before them, still as statues except for their eyes. Their eyes followed Timothy, their intense glares almost palpable, burning into his skin.

To the right, a set of glass paneled double doors led into a large office. Bookshelves lined the back wall, and bay windows gave the space plenty of natural light. Frank sat behind the largest desk Timothy had ever seen, his feet propped up on it as he leaned back in an oversized office chair. Frank's short, stocky stature made the desk look even larger. He was tracing the long, thin scar on his left cheek with one finger when Timothy walked in. Seeing him there — clean, in control, put together — was so much worse than seeing him on the streets where he was dirty and desperate. Timothy wasn't sure if his hands were trembling because of the shock of fear rolling over him or because of the boiling rage in his stomach.

He'd blamed himself for what had happened to Heather and his mother. If he hadn't met Frank, if he had killed Frank in Mattapan, if he'd just let Frank take everything instead of fighting back, if he'd never left the clinic to gather more supplies… but clarity came over Timothy as he took in the mobster. It all came back to Frank and Frank's choices. The rage won out over the fear.

Keep it together. I still need Frank's help. Timothy cleared his throat, and Frank seemed to notice him for the first time.

He stood up and clapped his hands together once, a look of pure delight on his face. Frank's bark of laughter made Timothy tense up.

"Southie, my man!"

Timothy nodded once. "Frank. I see you've moved up in the world." He tried not to sound as angry as he felt, but his tone wasn't warm or even kind. It was the best he could do. "I thought this was your uncle's place."

"It was." Frank knocked on the desk's top. "But so many people bit the dust, ya know? My uncle, his sons…" Frank shrugged. "Not all of 'em from this virus or whatever it is, but dead is dead. Turned out I was next in line after that dust settled. I had to bust a few heads to prove myself, but I was pretty riled up after you messed up my crew. That pent up frustration did me some good when I came back. And collectin' that debt—" He whistled, his eyes going wide as he leaned back a little. "Well, those supplies didn't hurt my cause, neither."

"Glad we could help." Timothy balled his hands into fists at his sides and concentrated on keeping calm. "So, we're even?"

Frank scrunched up his nose. "Eh, I don't know, Southie. I gotta say, what you said over the walkie… it piqued my interest. I 'preciate you comin' here instead of to CON." He put a hand to his chest. "I really do, but… I just don't know if that's enough. You killed off some valuable assets."

"You almost killed my wife," Timothy said, "while you were invading my mother's home. And because we had to flee to a place that wasn't secure, my mother is now dead and the kids have been kidnapped."

Frank shrugged. "Fair point. But if that makes us even, are you sayin' you wanna go back into my debt? Southie, you ain't got nothin' left."

"No," Timothy said. "I came to you because I thought maybe you'd help me for the sake of the kids of Boston, for the sake of any kids you might know. CON is stealing children, probably for manual labor, maybe for worse. You told me you had a code. That's what I'm appealing to. If you help me, it'll be because we want the same thing, not because you're doing me a favor."

Frank worked his jaw back and forth as he seemed to study Timothy. "I'm not sayin' no, and I'll tell ya why." He crossed his arms and sat on the edge of his desk. "CON ain't got any kids I'm responsible for. That girl from Mattapan was a sweetheart, but she ain't mine to protect. I wouldn't hurt her, wouldn't hurt any kid, and you know that better than anyone, but I also don't take responsibility when I ain't got nothin' to do with the situation." He held up a hand. "However, CON's got Boston, and I don't like it. That city has had a Russo in play for generations. I don't know I can stand by and let Boston go to hell. On the other hand, though, ConMen outnumber us two to one, at least. You're givin' me somethin' to think on, Southie."

"So, you're going to help?" Timothy asked, frowning. He wasn't sure where Frank was going with his line of reasoning.

"I'm gonna think about it." Frank pushed off the desk. "Meanwhile, I's got a real problem with The Boys. Cops have been pushed outta Boston, too, and they's chompin' at the bit to get my supplies. Nevermind I've been dolin' them out fairly to the people that depend on me. Nah, they wanna be the ones in control, even if they don't have the right."

"So… what does that mean for me?" A spike of adrenaline put Timothy on high alert. Those men at the door were huge. There would be no way for him to resist them.

Frank held out his hand. "This is a big house, Southie. You'll be joinin' me until I figure out what to do with ya."

"My wife and a woman named Candice… I need to make sure they have shelter, too." Timothy was careful to leave out their whereabouts until he got a straight answer from Frank about what joining him would mean.

"Fine. You's can all share a room. No skin off my back. They in that Escalade?" Frank asked.

"No, but—"

Pugsie rushed into the room, his voice high-pitched. "Boss, they've been spotted. Didn't even bother with unmarked vehicles. The ol' black and whites are surroundin' the lookout house."

Frank let out a string of curses. "We gotta get out there in force. Put 'em down for good. This is Russo country. We got the big guns ready to go?"

Big guns? Heather and Candice are still in that ditch. "Frank, a fire fight with the police isn't going to do anyone any good. This is a new world. There's got to be some way to negotiate."

"Ha! Southie, you're a hoot." A dark look crossed his face. "This ain't gonna be no fire fight. The whole place, the yard, the property line… it's rigged to blow. We set a trap, left some bread crumbs to that farmhouse."

The blood drained from Timothy's face, and his stomach flipped. If what Frank said was true, Heather and Candice would be casualties of his war with the Boston Police Department. "Frank, my wife is in the ditch near the road, hiding. Please, you *can't.*"

Frank cursed again. "Southie, I gotta do it. This is my chance to get rid of them."

Another crazy idea popped into Timothy's head. It was a long shot, but it would kill two birds with one stone. "What if I convince the cops to work with you to take out CON?"

Frank gaped. "What? Did you knock your head, Southie? That's nuts."

"You said CON outnumbers you. The police are targeting you instead of them for the same reason, I bet." Timothy licked his lips, hoping the pieces falling together in his head were making sense to Frank. "If you were to team up with the Boston PD, you'd have a real chance at getting Boston back *and* saving the kids. And then you and the cops can work together to rebuild."

Frank pursed his lips. "Or we can duke it out. Let the best man win, once and for all. Loser leaves Boston for good."

"Sure." Timothy just wanted to keep Frank from blowing up his wife along with the police. "Whatever you want."

"Only problem is they'd never go for it." Frank shook his head. "Nah… I gotta stick to my plan, Southie. I might not get another chance."

"Give me an hour," Timothy blurted. "Please? One hour to convince the police to call a truce with the Russo family until Boston is rid of CON. If I can't do it, you can blow the place with me in it, and then you don't have to worry about me ever again. It's a win-win for you."

Frank took a deep breath, his eyes narrowed at Timothy, his lips in a tight line. He quirked an eyebrow. "All right, Southie. You've got one hour."

Chapter 21

Heather Peters

Heather was snatched from the edge of sleep by the whir of tires on the road. The discomfort of the makeshift bed of roots and gravel she'd been leaning against in the ditch had only been made tolerable by her exhaustion. Her body was unevenly sore as she shifted and focused on the sound. When the cars turned into the driveway, she bolted upright, wincing at the shooting pain in her side. The handgun she'd chosen sat next to her in the gravel between roots. She took hold of the grip, taking comfort from the weight of the weapon, and craned her neck as she perched on a slightly higher root, counting the cars.

"Are those police cars?" Candice stood up straight, not bothering to crouch or keep her voice down. Thankfully, the bushes shielded them from full view as long as no one came around to the side of the tree farthest from the driveway.

Heather grimaced as she reached out and tugged on Candice's shirt. "Get down," she whispered. "What's the matter with you? We're supposed to be hiding." Four cars had rolled past, but she hadn't been able to see how full they each were. The unknown numbers and friendliness of the occupants turned her stomach to rocks.

"We're not hiding from the cops." Candice batted away Heather's hand. "Maybe they can help us."

"Just because they have cop cars doesn't mean they're police." Heather's side protested with a dull, aching throb for every second she sat up. "Will you please get down?" Her tone was intentionally sharp. *George has more sense than this woman.*

The thought of George hit Heather square in the chest and tears sprang to her eyes again as they led to thoughts of Annika and then Dana. It was like someone had used a sledgehammer on her heart three times over; she had to fight to stay in the moment. She was getting better at sweeping the grief under a very heavy rug soaked in the determination to get the kids back. That mission kept her going.

Heather blinked away the moisture and refocused. "I'm serious, Candice. Get d—"

Car doors slammed shut and a deep voice shouted, "This is the police! Surrender yourselves, and no one will get hurt."

A gunshot exploded into the afternoon in reply, and then a bombardment followed. A *thwack* sounded above Heather's head, and she ducked as splinters from the tree flew. Candice yelped and ducked.

"The suitcases!" Heather lowered herself to the gravel bottom of the ditch. "Get behind them." She was not going to get shot again.

Candice propped up the two suitcases and helped Heather hunker down behind one of them before taking shelter behind the other. "Weatherproof suitcases are tough, right?" She flinched at every gunshot.

Not bulletproof tough. "We're not a target," Heather said instead. She curled her body in on itself, trying to keep every inch of her behind the suitcase even as she reassured Candice. "And we're below ground level. It would take a ricochet to hit us. But if Timothy is up there…" Her heartbeat picked up. She cursed her wounds. There was no way she could climb out of the ditch on her own, let alone charge four cars full of cops to try to save her husband.

"I'm sure he's fine." Candice put her hands over her ears and squeezed her eyes shut until the last gunshot echoed into open air. She opened one eye. "Hey, I think it's stopped."

Heather held her breath, waiting with gun in hand, praying Timothy wasn't dead. Voices murmured in the near distance, but she couldn't hear what they were saying. Car doors opened and closed. The muscles at her side seized with her efforts of keeping her body small, and she had to bite her lip to keep from shouting in pain.

A small *snap* sounded above, and Heather hesitantly peeked around the suitcase. A German Shepherd stood at the edge of the ditch. It barked and danced on its two front feet. She jumped at the sound and pulled back behind the suitcase.

A deep-set woman's voice made Heather's pulse race. "Good boy, Moose. Who's down there?" the stranger shouted. "Hey, boys! There's somebody in the ditch."

Candice put her hands up over the suitcase she was hiding behind. "I don't have any weapons," she said. "I'm going to stand up."

Heather shook her head. "Candice, don't!"

The insufferable woman ignored Heather and crept out from behind the suitcase, slowly standing. Heather readied herself to open fire if need be. She glanced at the pipe that ran under the driveway. They'd hidden the duffel of weapons and medicine inside the shadows there, but she wasn't sure if she could get to it in time if she ran out of ammunition. *How many people are up there? How many with guns?*

"Hands where I can see them!" The woman at the top of the ditch shouted.

Candice wiggled her fingers; her hands were still held above her shoulders. She raised her eyebrows and there was too much sass in her tone. "My hands are right here. I'd appreciate it if you wouldn't point that thing at me. I'm a taxpaying citizen. Technically, you work for me, ma'am."

Heather sighed. *Not now, Candice. Your tax money is going to get us shot.* Heather peeked out from behind her suitcase and looked up to find the stranger, a woman in uniform, frowning down at them. She looked to be in her forties, petite frame, short brown hair tucked behind her ears. Her uniform had seen better days. Her short-sleeved, patch decorated, navy top was unbuttoned, a plain white tank visible underneath. The hem of her shirt had burn marks on one side, and there was a poorly sewn-up rip in the knee of her navy pants. The German Shepherd looked up at her as if waiting for her instructions.

"Of course," Candice said, "I have the utmost respect for you. My husband and I attended the Boys in Blue Gala, actually, and—"

The policewoman scoffed. "Lady, I couldn't care less right now. I need to know what you're doing in that ditch. You with the men in the house?" She shifted her gaze to look right at Heather. "And don't think I don't see you."

Heather leaned her head against the suitcase and sighed. Surrender was the only route that might end in survival. And they did *seem* like actual police. "She doesn't have a weapon, but I do," she said, speaking loud enough for the policewoman to hear. "I'm going to release the magazine and throw it aside on the rocks in plain view." She removed the magazine and tossed that far out of her reach. Then she took the body of the gun, stuck her arm out from behind the suitcase, and put it down. "I'm going to stand up, too, but I'm injured, so I'm going to need my friend's help."

"Just move slowly," the policewoman said.

A second voice joined her at the top of the ditch as Candice helped Heather to her feet. "Whatcha find, Abrams? A couple o' stragglers?" An older man came into view.

"Not sure yet," Abrams said, keeping her gun trained on them. "One of them had a gun, though." She nodded toward the disassembled weapon.

Heather leaned on Candice, eyeing the newcomer. He was older than Abrams, hair gone completely gray. His uniform was buttoned up, but it, too, had poorly mended rips and burn marks. At the mention of the gun, his lips drew taut. "Cover me while I retrieve it," he said.

"You got it, O'Donnell." Abrams turned her full attention back on Heather and Candice. "You didn't answer my question," she said as O'Donnell climbed down into the ditch. "Who are you?"

"Just two friends trying to get somewhere safe." Heather answered before Candice could. There was no way she was telling them her husband was trying to reach Frank Russo. If Timothy had been taken to Frank at the ranch, he'd be safe for the time being. If he'd been shot, if he was dead already, mixed in with the mobsters — *Oh, dear God, if you're listening, please don't let him be dead* — she and Candice would have a better chance of survival if the police didn't think them connected to what they considered the bad guys. "That Escalade up the road is ours. We ran out of gas, but then we saw men with guns that didn't look too friendly, so we hid here. We were trying to figure out how to get to safety when you showed up."

O'Donnell grunted as he skidded down the side of the ditch. "We're obviously police. Why not come out and reveal yourselves?" He picked up the body of the gun and then headed for the magazine.

Please don't see the duffel in the pipe. Heather intentionally kept her eyes forward so she wouldn't glance at the hiding spot. "It's hard to know who to trust," she said. "Not everyone is who they seem to be at first."

"Ain't that the truth," Abrams said from above. Her shoulders loosened a bit and her expression softened, though she still held the gun pointed at them. When she relaxed, Moose seemed to relax, too. The dog sat on his haunches.

O'Donnell still had a wary look in his eyes. "What's in the suitcases?"

"Just clothes and shoes, mostly." Candice smiled innocently, her hands still raised.

"And what happened to you?" He narrowed his eyes at Heather.

She looked down at her side. The wound had bled through the bandage, and a spot of blood had seeped through her shirt. "I was shot by some of those thugs that have taken over Boston. It's one of the reasons we're trying to get out."

O'Donnell pursed his lips, staring at her for a long moment, and then sighed and nodded. "CON," he spat. "Waste of space, garbage human beings." He glanced up at the policewoman. "Abrams, what d'ya think?"

She lowered her gun, and Moose let his tongue hang out of his mouth, panting in the heat. "It's hard to say with any certainty, but I don't get mob vibes from them, if you know what I mean. We can't leave them in the ditch. I say we put them in a room in the house and escort them to safety once we're done with the Russos."

"Agreed." O'Donnell shook his head at Candice and Heather. "You ladies landed in a bad spot. It might get ugly 'round here real soon. Whatever we tell you to do, you do it. Got it?"

"Got it." Heather and Candice said at the same time.

O'Donnell helped Heather climb out of the ditch, and with a batting of Candice's eyes, he even hauled her suitcases out, though he made Candice handle them from there. He led the way to the farmhouse with Abrams and Moose bringing up the rear. A dozen men and women in uniform dotted the property or could be seen through the windows of the house. Some had already gotten to work patching a few bullet holes in the house with duct tape. They worked with a solemn perseverance. There was no chatter or banter between them. Though none of them wore untarnished uniforms, the clothes all looked clean, and an attempt had been made to mend them.

Heather limped along, the adrenaline from the initial encounter with the police wearing off until she spotted two bodies laid out on the grass beside an empty flowerbed in front of the house. Her heartrate spiked, and the blood drained from her face. She bit the inside of her cheek and made fists with her clammy hands as they neared the bodies. *Not Timothy. Please, not Timothy, too.* The prayer played in her mind over and over again, intensifying with every step. She nearly collapsed in relief when they got close enough for her to see her husband was not among the dead.

"A'ight, ladies," O'Donnell said as he took the steps up the front porch. He opened the door and gestured for them to enter. "Let's get you two settled inside and see if our EMT can do somethin' about your injury."

"You have an EMT?" Heather put her hand to her side, an unexpected hope lifting the tiniest bit of weight off her shoulders.

"I'll take them to Ellis." Abrams squeezed past them on the steps and headed into the house, gesturing for them to follow. Moose trotted inside and sniffed at the floorboards, his nose leading him further into the house.

Candice deflated, looking between her suitcases and the steps. O'Donnell sighed. "I'll get your stuff inside. Just go on and let Ellis take a look at you both." Candice grinned and lightly bounced up the steps, strolling inside behind Abrams.

Heather started forward, but then stopped beside O'Donnell. "Thank you," she said. "We really appreciate your help."

He cleared his throat, voice gruff. "Part o' the job," he said, and then he offered a half smile. "Besides, it's nice to do a little servin' as well as protectin' every once in a while. These last two weeks have been nothin' but one endless fight."

"I hear you," Heather said, returning the smile and leaving him to tackle Candice's suitcases. The front door opened up into a living room, and to the right, a doorway led into a dining room. Abrams and Candice sat at the table with a young woman. "This must be Ellis?" Heather asked.

The EMT, also in a tattered uniform, stood up. "I am," she said, frowning. "Why don't you have a seat." Heather did so, the hardwood chair surprisingly comfortable after sitting on roots and gravel. "Abrams says you've got a gunshot wound?"

Heather nodded and lifted her shirt. "It went all the way through. We found Cefazolin at first, and I was taking that, but I had a reaction to it, so now I'm taking Amoxil and acetaminophen."

Ellis peeled back the bandage and winced. "Ouch. Yeah, we'll need to suture the entrance and exit wound. You're lucky this wasn't worse. It looks like you've done a pretty good job keeping it clean, at least." She got some supplies out of her bag and ripped open a small white packet to pull out a wipe. Ellis cleaned around the wound, and then got out some cream. "I'm going to use this numbing cream. We'll let it sit for about fifteen minutes, and then I'll stitch you up, okay?"

Heather breathed out slowly. "You have no idea how relieved I am. It keeps ripping open. I haven't been able to sit still long enough for it to heal."

"While we're waiting," Candice said, looking from Abrams to Ellis, "you mind telling us what's going on here? Why are you all out here, and who were those dead guys out front?"

"It's a long story," Abrams said, "and we can't really trust you yet. What I can say is that supplies need to be in the hands of those who will distribute them fairly and not in exchange for loyalty to a criminal organization."

"Makes sense," Heather said. "So… I guess if we can't talk about that, what about we talk about something normal? Like… how long have you been an EMT?"

"About a year," Ellis said. "I loved it… until my partner's eyes popped out of his skull and he died right in front of me."

"I'm sorry for your loss." Heather licked her lips and shifted her weight on the chair. "Maybe we should talk about something else." She looked at Abrams. "What were you doing three weeks ago?"

Abrams clasped her hands on the table in front of her and looked down at them. "My niece's thirteenth birthday party. Lissa… pretty sure she's dead now."

"Oh. I'm sorry for your loss, too." Heather chewed on her lower lip. "I guess there's no normal left."

"What do you mean, that you're 'pretty sure' your niece is dead?" Candice asked.

Abrams shrugged. "My sister and her family were alive a week ago, but last I went to check on them, all I found was their bodies. Swollen, eyes popping, you know…" She closed her eyes and swallowed hard, a sour look on her face. "Anyway, Lissa wasn't there. I looked all over, but… she's got to be dead. I left a note at my sister's place telling her to come to the station, and I kept checking the house, but Lissa never turned up."

"I guess we've all lost a lot," Heather said. Everyone around the table nodded in agreement, and Heather felt a sort of bond with these strangers — good people trying to get by, doing their best in the worst of circumstances.

Ellis stitched up Heather's wound, and the conversation turned to all the things they missed. Ice cream, sunsets, cold drinks… Heather found she even missed sitting in traffic, the worst thing about her day being that she would be late. "I even miss *work*," she said, chuckling. She'd never realized before how *good* the everyday, mundane things of life really were.

"Someone is coming!" A policeman from the other room shouted, and the whole house came alive with movement. Moose barked again from somewhere in the house and then bolted through the doorway to the dining room to where Abrams sat.

Abrams patted Moose's head and got up, addressing Heather and Candice. "Stay here. Could be trouble." She left with Moose on her heels.

Heather stood up, anyway, and entered the living room. "We want to know what's going on, too."

"I'm good." Candice stayed seated, and Heather ignored her, charging toward the windows where she could see police gathering outside.

"It's safer here, and you're not in great shape. Come back to the table." Ellis followed Heather, trying to get her to obey, but Abrams was long gone, and the EMT didn't have a gun.

"I just want to look." Heather insisted, making it to the window before Ellis could block her way. Heather froze and her breath caught in her chest. Timothy stood with hands on his head, two dozen men and women aiming their guns right at him.

Chapter 22

Timothy Peters

Timothy's interlocked fingers pressed against the back of his head as men and women in beat-up police uniforms surrounded him, guns trained on his chest. The walkie talkie clipped to his pocket — and super-glued to his cargo pants — felt a thousand times heavier than its actual weight. Frank had secured it there in hands free communication mode so that he could listen in on everything Timothy said. The deal Timothy had made with Frank to try to convince the police to work with the mob included the caveat that the explosive devices on the farmhouse property be kept a secret. He had to get a verbal confirmation with the Boston PD within the next hour that they would consider working with Frank to oust CON from the city. If he failed, Frank would detonate the explosives which were set up to be triggered by a specific radio frequency.

"I'm unarmed!" Timothy shouted. "I'm here as a liaison between you and Frank Russo."

A few of the cops shared looks of bemusement. "And what does Danny Russo have to say about that?" one of the men asked.

Timothy tried to keep his voice even, though a shudder ran up and down his spine as he worked to keep his body from trembling. "Frank is in charge now," he said.

The man squinted at Timothy, his tone laced with disbelief. "Wait, are you talking about Frankie — that wanna-be-mobster nephew? Short, stocky, a scar on his cheek? He's just a lackey, and not even a good one."

Timothy prayed Frank wouldn't take the man's comment as an insult and blow them all to smithereens right then and there. "Most of the Russos are dead," he said. "Frank took over the family business. He's... become more efficient at his job over the past couple of weeks."

"That's hard to believe, but... let's say it's true. Who does that make you?" he asked.

"My name is Timothy Peters. I'm..." He hesitated. *Who am I to these people?* "I'm no one. Just a guy trying to survive. I'm not with the mob, but I did come to seek Frank's help. My thirteen-year-old brother and another kid, a five-year-old girl, have been taken by CON. Frank was the only person I knew who might be able to help."

Murmurs among the police circled Timothy. He picked out snippets among the frenzied whispers of "I knew it was them" and "maybe that's where Lissa is." That was good. If they'd heard of what was happening or knew of children who'd been taken to The Farm, they would be more likely to help.

"You came to the Russos for help, but you're not one of their guys?" A gruff woman's voice broke through the rumble of exclamations. "How do we know anything you say is the truth?"

"If you all could just lower your weapons, we could go inside, and I could explain everything. No one has to get hurt here today. There doesn't have to be a war between the Boston PD and the Russo family. Frank has sent me with an offer." A lump formed in Timothy's throat when none of the officers moved a muscle. "I'll consent to being handcuffed if that makes you feel better. I'm not armed. I just want to talk."

The original speaker put down his gun and stepped forward. A woman called after him. "O'Donnell, are you sure about this?"

He shrugged. "If the Russos don't want bloodshed, maybe that means they're willin' to capitulate. We've lost enough already, don't you think?"

"Let's have Moose check him first," the woman said. The man nodded, and she patted her leg. A German Shepherd dutifully came forward. "Get to work, Moose." The dog approached and sniffed at Timothy, circling him a couple of times before returning to the woman. "He's clean," she said.

Timothy held his breath, hoping no one mentioned that Moose was a dog. *Is he trained in detecting guns... gunpowder? Would he also be able to detect bombs?* His spirits lifted at that, though if Frank made the connection through what he could hear over the walkie talkie, he might blow the place to be on the safe side.

"I'll watch him, Abrams. Don't worry." O'Donnell approached Timothy cautiously, his eyes studying him from head to toe, probably looking for the bulge of a knife.

Abrams kept her weapon up. "Timothy, if you so much as poke O'Donnell with a pinky finger, you're going down. Got it?"

Timothy nodded. "I understand." He put his hands behind his back and allowed the man who seemed to be in charge to handcuff him. The cool metal bit into the skin at his wrists, and he stumbled when O'Donnell shoved him forward. But he wasn't dead, and that counted for something.

"Get to walking," O'Donnell said. "We'll hear you out inside." The rest of the men and women parted, some looking at Timothy with curiosity and some with suspicion.

He made his way around to the front of the house, glancing at the ditch. Two sets of little wheel tracks marked the earth from the ditch to the concrete driveway, dirt skid marks continuing the trail halfway to the front steps. *Candice's suitcases.* Panic seized him, his body tensing. *They came up out of the ditch.* O'Donnell shoved him again, and he turned his attention back to the house, bounding up the steps, eager to see if Heather was inside.

"What did you do with the people who were here?" he asked, rocking just slightly on the balls of his feet as he impatiently waited for O'Donnell to pull open the door.

"They're dead." O'Donnell didn't offer any further explanation.

Timothy breathed out a shaky breath, and he was about to ask to see the bodies when the door opened, and Heather came into view, alive and well. She took a step toward him, and she opened her mouth, but Timothy cut her off before she could speak. "Who are they?" he asked. Heather and Candice both frowned, but Timothy pressed his lips together in a tight line and gave them the very slightest shake of his head.

"None of your business," O'Donnell said. "You two go back to the dining room with Ellis." He gestured for the women to leave. Heather didn't move. Timothy tried to give her another subtle look, but he wasn't sure it was getting through. If the police decided he was a bad guy, it would be safer for Heather and Candice to have no connection with him.

Candice's frown deepened. "But—"

"He's right, ladies," Timothy said, sarcasm intentionally lacing his words. "I'm the big bad wolf in sheep's clothing." He looked at O'Donnell. "Can we get on with this?"

Heather blinked, her brow creasing, and he could see the wheels turning in her head. She nibbled on her lower lip for half a second before tugging on Candice's arm. "Let's go in the other room," she said. Candice didn't seem happy about it, but she let Heather lead her away.

"Have a seat." O'Donnell patted the back of a chair kitty-corner to the couch. Timothy sat, and O'Donnell uncuffed him as soon as the room was lined with cops. A few of their number stayed outside, visible through the windows as they kept watch. "You'd be an idiot to try anything in here," he said. "You know that, right?"

Timothy glanced at the dusty side table, hoping to find paper or a pen. "I'm here as a liaison." There was nothing but an empty candy dish which also boasted a thick layer of dust. "I don't want to hurt anyone, and I certainly don't want to get hurt. I just want to get those kids back."

O'Donnell crossed his muscular arms. "You say that, but if my brother gets kidnapped, the first thing I do isn't gonna be going to the Russos."

Timothy met the policeman's eyes and shrank back a little from the intense glare. The others surrounding him matched his hostile posture and glower. Their burned, patched, and ripped uniforms only served to make their presence more intimidating. And the way that dog watched him didn't help, either.

"I didn't know where to find the police or even if there were police left," Timothy said. "Frank forced me at gunpoint to bring him to his uncle's ranch about a week ago, but he also saved me and the little girl from CON before that. He was the only person I knew who might have the resources to help me." The dusty surface caught his eye again. He needed to communicate with them without Frank hearing it over the walkie talkie.

"If that's true, you've got guts, kid." O'Donnell said. "But you're also an idiot."

Timothy twisted his hip forward so the walkie talkie was in plain view. "Not really," he said. "Frank is reasonable." He lightly touched the walkie talkie and then pointed at it. "He's actually a good listener." Then he put one finger to his lips in a hushing motion before reaching over to the side table and writing the word "paper" and a question mark in the dust.

O'Donnell frowned and stepped forward, reading Timothy's message. He quirked an eyebrow and waved Abrams over to the table, shushing her in the process. "Fine," he said out loud. "Whatever your reasons for goin' to Frank, what made him send you here?" Abrams nodded and left the room.

A tiny bit of tension leaked out of Timothy's body. He was making progress. "I convinced him that the Russos and the Boston PD could work together to take Boston back from the ConMen."

As a few chuckles broke out around the room, Abrams came back with sticky notes and a pen. She quietly handed them to Timothy, and he mouthed a thanks.

"That's a good one, kid." O'Donnell squinted at Timothy as he wrote on the first sticky note: *Frank is listening.* O'Donnell nodded. "Go on," he said. "You've got to have some reason you think your half-cocked plans will work."

"I do." Timothy wrote: *Do NOT react.* Then he handed over the sticky note and gestured for him to pass it around the room. As O'Donnell passed the sticky note to Abrams, who then took it around the room for everyone to see, Timothy continued. "You and the Russos have lost too many to go up against CON individually, but together, you're more evenly matched against the gang, right?"

O'Donnell tilted his head to one side and worked his jaw back and forth. "Yeah, maybe. But once CON is gone, what does Frank think will happen? We're not going to help him take over Boston for the mob."

"That's where the compromise comes in." Timothy bounced his knee up and down as the last of the onlookers read the sticky note. "You'd have a hard time denying that between the Russos and CON, the ConMen are the greater of two evils, wouldn't you agree?"

"I don't really think like that." O'Donnell raised his eyebrows and nodded at the pad of notes.

Timothy wrote: *Multiple bombs, house and perimeter.* "Maybe you should," Timothy said as he handed it over and wrote on the next note: *Agree to stay alive.* He handed that one over as well. O'Donnell took both notes, his eyes widening. "Frank thinks of you that way, you know," Timothy said. "The lesser of two evils. He believes he's the best person to distribute the goods." He wrote as he spoke: *Buy us time.* "CON is using children for labor and who knows what else. When I encountered them, they suggested using a child as a punching bag. If you work with the Russos, Frank agrees it would be a temporary truce. He said afterward, the two of you could duke it out and let the best organization win Boston for good. But the first step is getting rid of CON."

O'Donnell cleared his throat as he stared at the sticky notes stuck to his fingers. "And if we agree to the concept, what do we do next?" He walked around the perimeter of the room and showed the notes to the men and women gathered around.

Timothy wiped the sweat off his brow with the back of his hand and wrote another note. "It's getting late. It won't be safe much longer outside. Frank will give you the night to come up with terms, and he'll take the night to do the same. Tomorrow, Frank would invite a representative back to the ranch with me, and we can discuss what it looks like to take out CON and get back those kids together." The note read: *Can you find and disarm?* He handed it over, nodding at Moose, and held his breath.

O'Donnell waved Abrams over and showed her the note. She narrowed her eyes at Timothy, then whispered something in O'Donnell's ear. He pulled away and gestured for the rest of the officers to join him in the corner of the room. "Give me and my people just a moment, will you? We need to discuss it."

Timothy slumped into the chair. "Sure, but Frank is waiting for an answer. He needs to know right now if you're interested. Just… don't take too long."

The woman grabbed the pen and sticky notes from Timothy and joined O'Donnell and the others as they huddled at one side of the room, whispering. The German Shepherd sniffed at the floorboards around the coffee table, and then sat with his nose pointed at the floor. Timothy frowned at the dog, but then a blur of movement outside the window caught Timothy's attention. A deer bounded through the front yard, weaving around three of the police cars. It was going fast, like it was running from something, and it didn't quite clear the fourth car, bumping into it and then skittering away. The police officer standing at the entrance to the driveway spun around at the sound and then leaned forward to watch the deer flee. Timothy sat up straighter when another deer darted by the house, just a few feet away from the window. Birds lifted from the trees, and the officer looked upward. Moose left the spot by the coffee table to whine at the window.

"We're willin' to talk to Frank. We'll get to making a list of non-negotiables for the meeting tomorrow." O'Donnell pulled away from the group and handed Timothy a sticky note. It read in small letters: *No dice. We're out of here before the bugs come out.* The others started gathering their things. "How do we notify him that we're in?" He handed Timothy another note: *We need time to get off the property. Can NOT take you.*

Timothy stood up, raking his fingers through his hair. *They're leaving?* "You, um… just have to talk to him. I've got this walkie talkie." He tried to keep the panic from his voice. *If they go, and Frank finds out I let them, I'm dead.*

"Great," O'Donnell said. "Give me a few more minutes to gather my thoughts."

Heather's voice came from behind. "Hey, Abrams? Is anyone going to tell me what's going on?"

The woman who'd seemed like O'Donnell's second-in-command took Heather aside into the dining room, shushing her, too. *At least they'll take Heather with them, right?*

But then Abrams stomped out of the room, red in the face. She glared at Timothy, her hands balled into fists. Heather followed, biting her lower lip, and Candice filled the doorway, her hands on her hips, looking annoyed. Abrams whispered in O'Donnell's ear, and he whipped his head to look at Timothy. Heather's eyes flitted between Timothy and Abrams. She sheepishly walked over to Timothy and picked up the sticky notes and pen, writing: *I couldn't leave you.*

He could have screamed. His chest ached as his heart pounded against his rib cage. He shook his head frantically, grabbing the notepad and ripping off Heather's note. He wrote: *Please, Frank will kill us.* By the time he looked up, all the police were already stepping onto the porch and into the yard, heading for their vehicles, except for Abrams who was struggling to get Moose to leave. He jogged to catch up with O'Donnell and shoved the note in his face. O'Donnell batted Timothy's hand away.

Another deer stumbled out of the cornfield and dropped to its knees. Timothy had never heard the normally quiet creatures make a sound, but as it tried to get back on all fours and then fell completely on its side, the deer bleated loudly as if it were in pain. Everyone stopped in their tracks. Timothy's skin crawled as a high-pitched buzzing reached a crescendo. The deer seized, its body shaking.

One of the officers closest to it yelled, "Its eyes! Its eyes are bulging!"

"Get everyone inside!" O'Donnell screamed.

"That's impossible." Shock washed over him as he stared at the deer. "We've still got a few hours. It should be safe."

The walkie talkie at his hip crackled with Frank's voice. "Southie, what's happenin'?"

A black swarm bled through the shadows in the cornfield and into the yard, part of the swarm engulfing the deer. The black coat of undulating mosquitos with specks of bright orange transformed the deer into an alien creature. Timothy took a step backward, the pounding of his pulse thrashing through his body from head to toe. Ice settled in his bones as the black, porous wall of insects advanced. The whole was like a single beast crawling forward, persistent, cornering its prey.

A human scream shattered Timothy's stupor. It was the officer who had been out by the road. He darted inside the house, past Abrams who was staring dumbfounded out the window as Moose tugged on her pant leg with his teeth.

Timothy shouted as he bolted into the dining room. "Heather! Candice! Take cover!"

"Southie!" Frank's voice erupted over the speaker. "Tell me what's goin' on."

"The mosquitos are here," Timothy said. "Right now. Thousands of them."

Frank cursed. "Keep the walkie talkie on ya, Southie. The second I can't reach you, I blow the place. Pugs, get everyone in—" Frank's voice cut off. He would be able to hear Timothy, but Timothy would only be able to hear Frank if the mobster wanted him to.

He guided Heather and Candice toward the hall beyond the dining room. "The bathroom!" he shouted. "Get in the bathroom." He looked over his shoulder to see O'Donnell still ushering people back inside the house. If he didn't cut them off soon, he'd be risking everyone. Timothy wasn't going to wait to find out if O'Donnell did what was necessary.

Once Timothy, Heather, and Candice were in the bathroom, he shut the door, locked it, and stuffed towels from the towel rack under the little crack in the door. Heather sat on the toilet lid, and Candice perched on the lip of the tub. Timothy put his back to the door. Screams of terror pierced the air, and a guttural bellow rang out as someone opened fire.

Chapter 23

Alexander Roman

Alex reached for the stairwell door, his hand curling around the cool metal handlebar. He stopped. Alone on the landing, his shallow, uneven breathing was the only sound. Pulling the door open and meeting with Blake Turner was the next step in his plan to discover and then expose Lawson. The Suits, Minnie's experience at the hospital, the unethical behavior of the scientists, the possibility of people disappearing, and the way Lawson's greed and thirst for power radiated off him painted a picture Alex didn't like. He couldn't trust a government influenced by Lawson and his minions.

If everything went well, the fledgling government would be cleared of corruption. Alex could go on to Boston, find answers, and hand them over to a trustworthy infrastructure. Maybe he could be part of not only eradicating the virus but of rebuilding a country, a home, for Oliver to grow up in. If things didn't go well, Alex would be stuck under Lawson's thumb, or worse. Lawson could hold his people, his son, over his head as leverage. He didn't want to be part of some scheme to use a vaccine as a power play, but if it was between that and protecting Oliver, Minnie, and Lauren… he could see himself compromising for their sakes. He'd hate himself, but he'd do it.

He opened the door and turned toward the labs. The thin, stiff letter opener bumped against his hip. Conner had lent him her mending kit so he could sew the sheath for the opener on the inside of his boxers. He wasn't sure if he'd need it, but it would work as a weapon in a pinch and was a lot easier to hide than a gun, even if he'd been able to get hold of one. Turner didn't seem like the kind of guy Alex needed to fear, but he didn't want to get caught in a fight with the Suits with no way to defend himself.

The voice recorder was in his pocket. Before he turned the corner, he brought it out and started recording. He didn't know what was in store for him or even how much Turner knew about the big picture, but he at least hoped to get some more information on whatever deal Lawson had made with the scientists.

Turner was waiting for him outside the entrance to the labs. "You ready for this, man?"

"Ready as I'll ever be." Alex offered a smile he hoped looked more excited than nervous. The door to the labs was guarded, even at night, but the Suits let them inside without question. "That was easy," Alex said. "I expected some pushback. I don't think I'm supposed to be here."

Turner chuckled. "Oh, don't worry about that. I didn't tell Joanna what we were doing, but we have permission to be here."

"We going to Lab Four or the restricted zone?" Alex asked.

Turner stopped at Lab Three. "Neither." He opened the door.

Alex stepped inside and froze. Lawson and Price stood in the corner of a mostly empty room. They'd been talking in low whispers, but at his entrance, they'd both stopped and turned their eyes on him. Lawson looked down on him in every way. His broad, towering frame was even more intimidating in the smaller room, and his deep, intense scowl made Alex feel like he was in a room with a bull about to charge. Price, on the other hand, had a neutral expression. Not indifferent, just… unreadable. Cabinets and countertops lined the walls, but everything else had been taken out, leaving room for a medical exam chair.

"Sorry, man," Turner said, halfway in and halfway out of the room, his hand on the door. "I wasn't going to go over Lawson's head. When you said you'd made a deal with him already, I went to him to ask if we could bypass Joanna's approval." He winced. "You shouldn't have lied about that, man." He backed out and closed the door.

The air turned thick, oppressive as the room seemed to shrink. A heavy numbness took root in his chest and began to spread. The exam chair left him nauseous. It didn't belong there any more than he did. He stepped backward, goosebumps rising all over his body.

"We can do this the easy way," Price said, pulling a bundle of zip ties out of his pocket, "or this can be an unpleasant experience." His slight smile made Alex's stomach flip. "For you, that is. Go ahead and take a seat." When Alex glanced at the door, Price continued, "My men are guarding this door already, so don't even think about it."

"I've done what you asked," Alex said, his throat dry, his words cracking. His mind raced. *How much do they know about our plans? Did Conner betray us?* "What is this about?"

"You're playing both sides." Lawson's voice rumbled through Alex like thunder. "Trying to see how much you can get. That's not your place."

Alex stammered. "W-what? I don't know what you're talking about."

"Please," Price said. "We know what you're doing here. Sit. Down."

Alex's feet had become weights, and his body resisted every step toward the chair. He perched on the edge of it, every muscle tense, ready to jump up if Price came at him with those zip ties. "I'm not sure what you think you know, but—"

Lawson sneered. "Don't try to pull the wool over my eyes. You're clearly trying to get in on the action, see how much Turner was getting out of this so you could milk it for all it's worth." He shook his head. "And all that family man, good guy crap with Coleman. Buddying up to Hunt's favorite. You want to make sure you have friends everywhere so that when push comes to shove, you've got somewhere to land. But I'm telling you right now, Roman, *I* was the only friend you needed. Now, I don't know if I can trust you. I would have offered you a deal once Joanna judged you trustworthy. You could have been brought into the fold in due time."

They think I'm like them, trying to play the game. Alex swallowed hard. That was better than Lawson figuring out he'd already chosen a side, and it wasn't his. *I have to get them to trust me.* "And can't that still happen?" Alex asked.

Lawson narrowed his eyes. "That's for you to decide," he said. "I can't keep two-faced players on my team."

Alex raised his hands, palms out. "I was scouting the field, that's all. One thing you got wrong about me is that I wasn't pretending to be a family man. I only did what any father with leverage would do. I've got knowledge and skills you need, and I needed to know who had the real power to protect me and mine."

Price shrugged. "It doesn't seem like you've contributed much," he said. "Joanna's report stated you were observant and capable, but that you added nothing new."

"I kept some information to myself until I could decide how to use it," Alex said. "Like the fact that this virus is clearly engineered."

Price cocked his head. "What do you mean by that?"

"It didn't come about naturally," Alex said. "It's got CRISPR written all over the genome." Price and Lawson only frowned. "The virus is manmade."

Price's eyes widened. "Are you sure?"

At the same time, Lawson said, "Ward and Turner haven't said anything about that."

"I'm positive," Alex said. "And they didn't notice it because epidemiology and disease ecology are clearly not their expertise. I'm sure they're doing the best they can, but they're working off limited knowledge. They need me. Turner saw it. Joanna is just stubborn and greedy."

"Ward assures me they will have answers within a few months," Lawson said, shaking his head. "She knows not to lie to me."

"If we had unlimited power, resources, and test subjects, I could maybe believe her," Alex said. "But we don't have any of that. We can't run this place on a generator forever, our resources are finite, and there can't be more than a few chimps left. Every test needs to count. Ward and Turner are wasting their resources hoping to get lucky. I can help them use a more targeted approach that will get results faster."

"Are you willing to commit to whatever it takes? Are you willing to swear loyalty to me?" Lawson asked.

Alex said a prayer that the recorder was still running properly. "I guess that brings us back to what I get out of it. Anyone can see that you're at odds with the military. And the president is trying to hold a balance between your two forces. What happens if Coleman shuts you down and decides to go on to Cheyenne Mountain?"

"Coleman is a puppet," Lawson said, spitting his name. "He's always been soft. This is my operation, top to bottom. He's no president." He scoffed. "There's no longer anything to be president *of*. This is a new world, Roman, and when the dust settles, I'm going to be king."

Alex blinked. *Wow… that's worse than I thought it would be.* "So, you're going to stick it out here even if Coleman wants everyone to leave?"

"If Coleman tries to shut us down," Price said, "we'll cut him off at the knees. We're evenly matched with Hunt and what's left of the military as far as manpower goes, but we've got advantages they don't know about thanks to having control over the labs."

"You can't mean you'd infect them?" Alex asked, unable to keep the horror from his face. "That would be a disaster. This virus spreads fast. There would be no way to protect your own people."

"Calm down," Price said, rolling his eyes. "We're not stupid. These labs provided Turner and Ward with plenty of other options."

Alex's stomach turned. "The CDC has a stash of chemical warfare agents, but we don't keep delivery systems lying around. Those are for study only. Trying to release them would still give you the same problem: your men would suffer, too."

"We share responsibility with the military for guarding our food stores," Lawson said.

"You plan to use biotoxins and blood agents." Alex tried to stay calm. The CDC kept samples of all sorts of dangerous substances found in nature. There wouldn't be enough of one thing to harm the entire military force, but they could put a little cyanide in Conner's oatmeal and a little Ricin in Hunt's and the end result would be the same.

"Eventually, yes. They'll have to die or join us," Lawson said. "I'd like to keep them around as long as possible, though. They are helpful in my efforts to stabilize Atlanta. After all, what's a king without a kingdom? This country will be split up and given to whoever's willing to step up and take it. I'll have a vaccine or a cure or a treatment — whatever works to keep the people in line — and that will draw survivors here, to Atlanta. Whoever stays loyal to me will have important places in our new society, and they'll have first access to medical care."

"So, what do you want, Mr. Roman?" Price asked. "Lawson can make it happen. Ward wanted accolades and free reign to experiment without rules holding her back. Turner asked for riches. Take time to think about it, if you want."

Alex nodded, pressed his tongue to the roof of his mouth, and focused on maintaining some measure of composure. His first impression was that Lawson was insane, but even Hunt admitted that Washington D.C. was dead. The government was gone, and Hunt was trying to pick up the broken pieces to put something similar back together again. *What's more likely? That, with so many dead and a government collapsed, we'll be able to cobble together an effective democracy, or that people like Lawson will lay claim to cities or regions all across the world? And if he's the only one in the country with a vaccine, he'll have the power to do it.*

Alex had so many questions, but one resounded in his mind. He forced himself to look Lawson in the eye. The man disgusted Alex, and looking at him made Alex want to vomit. Still, he had to know. "Why are you telling me all of this if you don't trust me?" His heartbeat quickened at Lawson's response.

"Because, Mr. Roman, you now have two choices. You'll be considering these options here, overnight, and in the morning you'll choose. You can swear loyalty to me and prove yourself through one more test, go on to help discover a treatment for this virus, and then live out your days in comfort, enjoying whatever reward we agree upon. Or, you can refuse and you and your family will unfortunately become infected and die when you successfully escape into the night, too selfish to stay and serve your country." Lawson straightened the collar of his suit and calmly walked toward the door, Price on his heels.

"Why not just let me make a decision now?" Alex couldn't bring himself to look at Lawson again. He wasn't sure he could hide the fear or the rage stirring inside him.

"I want you to stew on the fact that there is no third option," Mr. Lawson said. "If you agree, Coleman has approved my request to free up the military. They will no longer be tasked with your care. Every waking moment, you and your family will be under my… let's call it, *protection.*"

Lawson and Price left, and Alex breathed out, long and slow, wringing out his hands and then running his fingers through his hair. He stood up and dug the voice recorder out of his pocket. It was still recording. He stopped the recording, holding onto it like a lifeline. He paced the room, running through scenarios. The recording wouldn't do any good if he wasn't able to play it for Coleman or Hunt. It wouldn't do any good if he took it to his grave, either. He stopped pacing, the truth sinking into the pit of his stomach, dragging him down to the floor. He leaned back against the cabinets, a shudder running up his spine, his hands clammy as he clasped them together. The only way he could see forward was to keep up the ruse with Lawson. Playing pretend was quickly becoming his reality, and there was nothing he could do about it.

Chapter 24

Timothy Peters

There were people still alive on the other side of the bathroom door. Timothy pressed his ear against the wood, careful not to disturb Heather who was leaning against him. He sat closest to the door, the soles of his shoes flush against the cabinets of the vanity. Heather sat next to him, napping, and Candice next to her had fallen asleep with her cheek on the rim of the bathtub. The small window above the bathtub let in what was left of the daylight, though it would soon be dark, both outside and inside. There had been no voices for hours — just shuffling, the clicking of Moose's nails on the floor, and the occasional snore — not since a shouting match had erupted shortly after the gunshots ended. He'd gathered that O'Donnell had been forced to shoot some of his own men to keep them from getting inside after being attacked by the mosquitos.

"I had to do it!" he'd shouted. "They would have infected all of us!" The anguish in those words had quieted everyone else. "Now… I suggest we all stay away from each other." O'Donnell had continued, "Spread out. If we survive the next four or five hours, we can talk about what to do next."

They'd left Timothy, Heather, and Candice in the bathroom. O'Donnell had even commended them for separating themselves so quickly. Frank had checked in once or twice, just to make sure Timothy knew he was still listening. It was fortunate that Timothy had been holding the sticky notes and the pen when the farmhouse yard had been overrun with mosquitos. He'd brought Heather and Candice up to speed through writing notes, and those notes were now arranged in order on the bathroom mirror above the sink. If any of the police outside survived, he could direct them to the notes. Maybe then they would understand.

Frank could blow the house and the yard, which would probably damage their vehicles, at any time. Timothy counted them all lucky that it hadn't happened already. It was possible he was simply dealing with the aftermath of the mosquitos and hadn't gotten around to obliterating them yet.

What have I gotten myself into? He sighed and pulled his head away from the door. If we stay and the cops go without attacking Frank's supplies, he'll know I warned them off. We're dead. The cops won't take us with them. There's nowhere for us to go. Timothy was startled by a knock on the door, and Heather stirred beside him, blinking and wrinkling her nose as she woke up. Candice snorted and sat up straight with a sharp intake of breath, eyes wide as she looked around the bathroom. Something like recognition flashed across her face, and she slumped, cursing under her breath.

"It's been five hours," O'Donnell's voice came through, exhausted. "We're gatherin' together to… discuss Frank's offer. We'd like your input, if you don't mind joining us. We could do it through the door, but communication might not be optimal."

Meaning we can't write notes. "What do you think, babe?" Timothy asked Heather. "I won't open the door unless you and Candice agree."

"I'm good." Candice yawned and stretched. "I mean, I am im—"

Timothy sat up straight and held out a hand, motioning for Candice to stop. Frank did *not* need to know about Candice's immunity. And, frankly, neither did the police. He didn't trust them yet, even if they seemed better than Frank.

"—imaginative." Heather saved the day, cutting Candice off in the middle of the word. She raised her eyebrows and pointed at the walkie talkie on Timothy's hip.

"Right." Candice blanched and hugged herself around the middle. "Imaginative. I think out of the three of us, I have the best ideas. Obviously. The police could use my input."

Relieved, Timothy leaned back against the wall and slowly breathed out. He squeezed his wife's hand and mouthed the words: *Good catch.* And then out loud, he asked, "And you?"

"I don't want to cozy up to any of them, yet but I think it's probably safe. Maybe we can just maintain a reasonable distance?" Heather stood up and pointed to the mirror and the notes stuck there, nodding at the door. The notes were the only thing he had left to convince O'Donnell and his men to work with Frank. They explained that Timothy really did think the police and the mob working together could be the only way to oust CON from the city. They also explained that Timothy planned to do everything he could to gather information on Frank and his operation that might help the police secure the area once their first task was completed.

"All right, then, O'Donnell. We're opening the door." He pulled himself to his feet. "We'd prefer to keep a little space between us and your men, though. Do you think you can manage that?"

"Won't get any arguments from us," O'Donnell said.

When Timothy opened the door, the officer was several steps down the hall, waiting. Heather and Candice walked out after Timothy.

"Hey, O'Donnell," Timothy said, "I think you've got something on your face. You might want to check it out in the mirror."

"Are you crazy?" O'Donnell scoffed. "None of us are lookin' pretty these days."

"No, you might want to take a look at that," Heather said pointing over her shoulder with her thumb. "You've got a nasty bump."

"I don't see it." Candice squinted at the officer, and Timothy nudged her. *The notes,* he mouthed. Her eyes widened. "Oh, yeah… there it is. Looks infected."

O'Donnell rolled his eyes and stomped into the bathroom, coming up short at the notes stuck on the mirror. He cleared his throat. "Yeah, thanks," he said as he leaned over the sink to get a closer look at the notes. "I guess it's worse than I thought."

"We'll leave you to it," Timothy said, hoping the officer would take the time to read through everything he'd written.

The living room and dining room were full of deflated, solemn officers. Abrams sat cross-legged on the couch with Moose sitting at her feet. Timothy was drawn to the window. He looked outside, twilight painting the sky orange near the horizon, the stars beginning to shine through overhead where orange bled to black. The swarm had mostly moved on from what he could see, though a single mosquito with an orange diamond buzzed just outside the window. They weren't gone, just… less concentrated. The yard was littered with corpses: three officers, the deer, a rabbit, and at least a dozen birds.

"Has anyone seen a swarm like that before?" Timothy turned around to face those in the room.

A few continued to stare at nothing, barely moving a muscle. A few others shook their heads. "I've seen those mosquitos in the city at night, outside the windows of the precinct. I figured those were the ones causing trouble since I've lived here twenty years and never seen a mosquito with that orange marking. But, I've never seen a swarm attack like that." She turned a shade paler, put her feet on the floor, and scooted to the edge of the couch. Abrams scratched Moose behind the ears. "Whatever happened today… I don't get it. The time was wrong. And the numbers. There were *so* many."

Timothy frowned at Moose, who only briefly acknowledged Abrams with a look before turning back to the position he'd been in before, nose pointed down at the floor beside the coffee table. The dog let out a short whine but stayed put. *He was sitting there, exactly there, hours ago, nose pointed to the same spot.*

"Anybody got any food?" Candice asked. "I'm starving."

"We've got limited supplies in the kitchen," the EMT, who Heather had told him was named Ellis, spoke up from the dining room and appeared in the doorway. "I think it might be a good idea for everyone to eat."

"Maybe we three can distribute some dinner." Heather pointed between herself, Candice, and Ellis. "That is, if you think you can forgive us for not telling you we were with Timothy right away."

Abrams scoffed, and a few other officers followed suit, but Ellis only smiled. "These are uncertain times. I get it," she said. "In any case, we're stuck together tonight. Might as well get along." She said the last loudly and in a chastising tone, hands on hips as she swept her eyes across the room.

The three left for the kitchen, Candice and Heather keeping a bit of distance from Ellis as they walked. At the same time, O'Donnell came out of the hallway to the bathroom and sat next to Abrams, speaking softly to her. She scowled at them before stalking to the bathroom, first tapping on another officer's shoulder and gesturing for him to follow her. Timothy frowned again at Moose. He had followed on Abrams's heels earlier in the day, but when she left the room, the dog sat still, shifting his weight and whining, but keeping his nose pointed down.

O'Donnell wrote something on the sticky note pad he'd brought with him from the bathroom, ripped off the top page, and stuck it to Timothy's chest. "You got any suggestions for our terms with Frank?" he asked.

"If you've got ideas for taking out CON, or ways in which you refuse to operate, I'd include those," Timothy said as he plucked the sticky note from his chest and read: *Your plan is the best we got. As long as the others agree, we're in.* Timothy quirked an eyebrow. Just hours ago, they were ready to abandon the area, and they still could if they fled as soon as it was safe outside. He held out his hand for the notes, and O'Donnell handed them over, along with the pen.

"Well, there's not much we wouldn't do these days," O'Donnell said, "but we do wanna minimize casualties, especially innocents. This is a war zone, and I get that, but we need veto power on operations."

Timothy handed him a note that read: *What changed?* "If you ask for veto power, Frank will want the same."

"I'd expect nothin' less. Do you expect any problems with that?" O'Donnell took the same note and wrote below Timothy's handwriting in small letters: *More info. Time to think. Bugs can't be dealt with until CON and mob are out. Your plan is the quickest way.*

Timothy nodded at the note, a weight lifting off his chest. Having a group of men and women he sort of trusted on his side made the coming task less daunting. And it made getting George and Annika back more likely—if Frank didn't change his mind.

"If you and Frank both have the power to say no, you might not like what Frank does with that," Timothy said. "It forces you both to compromise. To get him to agree to an attack plan, you might have to concede to something on the edge of ethical. He won't do anything to hurt the kids at The Farm, I don't think, but he's not going to care about your people. If there are innocent adults at The Farm, I'm not sure he'll care about them, either."

Abrams strode into the room with a little less hostility in her step than when she'd left. "Seems about right for a man like Frank Russo." She stopped and furrowed her brow at Moose. Then, her eyes lit up and she scooted the coffee table back and pulled up the rug underneath. Moose backed up and wagged his tail as Abrams pushed down on one side of a loose floorboard and the other side lifted easily. She removed the length of wood and gasped, her hand flying to her mouth.

Timothy stepped back from the white, plastic brick with a walkie talkie secured to its side. Three entwined wires led to a blue blasting cap. Dusty, washed-out sunbeams, the leftovers of the day, cast the room in an eerie light and caught on the forms of people to throw shadows around and into the hole on the floor. But the device itself seemed to sit atop the shadows. The white of the plastic reflected what little light there was, creating dull imitations of the window's square corner. For a moment, the bomb was the only thing in the room; its presence was so potent, Timothy broke into a sweat, heart pounding, fists clenched, expecting it to fulfill its purpose and obliterate him.

The room had stilled, people turned to statues. Abrams raised a hand in the air and then pointed toward the hall. Timothy got the simple message: she wanted them out. Careful footsteps padded the floor as the room cleared of everyone except Timothy, Abrams, and O'Donnell.

"How about you and me go into the kitchen and grab us a bite to eat?" O'Donnell placed a hand on Timothy's arm.

He jumped at the touch but gathered his wits. Frank was still listening, or he could be. The mobster hadn't checked in for a while, which meant he could have assigned someone else to listen to the channel. Timothy tried to swallow, his mouth and throat like sandpaper.

"Yeah," he said, voice croaking. "I'm starving." He could have kicked himself; his tone hadn't been even or calm.

He let O'Donnell lead him into the kitchen at the back of the house where everyone was huddled. It was farthest from the living room without going outside, and that wasn't an option. Wide eyes and pale faces crowded the ever-darkening room. Soon, the sunlight would be completely gone, and they'd be plunged into complete darkness. Timothy took up a position next to Heather and put his arm around her shoulder. O'Donnell found space right next to him. Any hope of keeping distance from the officers was shattered, and on the fringes of his mind, Timothy spoke a quick prayer that everyone in the room was healthy.

Every second of waiting for Abrams to appear at the other end of the hall was like an eternity. Heather threaded her fingers through his, and Timothy held on tight. *Have we survived all of this just to die now?* He pushed that thought away and focused on survival as if hoping hard enough would result in a good outcome. *Abrams looked like she knew what she was doing. She'll disarm this thing. We'll be okay.* He squeezed Heather's hand. *We have to be okay. We still have to rescue George and Annika.*

The moment Abrams appeared, Timothy's heart leapt. When she smiled and gave the thumbs up, he had to bite his lip to keep from shouting for joy. Quiet exclamations and congratulations worked their way from the gathered people to Abrams, and everyone had a turn scratching behind Moose's ears. But then Abrams took a deep breath and held up a sticky note to be passed around. It read: *We need to search the whole house. Even one more of those bombs could destroy the entire structure.* Then she handed one to Timothy which instructed him and his walkie talkie with an open channel to hide away in a bedroom upstairs after she and Moose checked it.

For Frank's sake, Timothy said, "I'm ready for bed. I'm going to take one of the upstairs twin beds, if that's okay with everyone?"

"Fine by us," O'Donnell said. "We've got a big day tomorrow. I suspect we'll all be asleep shortly."

As Timothy settled into a stranger's bed, sequestered from everyone so they could quietly search the house and disarm any additional bombs, he checked in one last time with Frank. "I'm alone," he said into the empty room. "Are you there, Frank?"

A minute passed before the speaker crackled. "What is it Southie? My man here says you's goin' to bed, that it's been pretty boring over there. Which is good, I'd say. Too much excitement and you'd be in trouble."

Timothy's shoulders relaxed a little. *He hasn't heard anything suspicious, then.* "Just checking in before I go to sleep. Everything okay there?"

"Yeah," Frank said. "I owe ya one for warnin' me about the mosquitos comin' out early. Only lost one guy. How many did the Boys lose?"

"Three." Timothy's stomach churned. "They're ready for negotiations. We're on the right track."

"So far," Frank said. "But don't get your hopes up too much. We'll see how it goes in the mornin'. If negotiations don't work, the only cop that'll survive is whoever you bring with you to the ranch. I'll let ya bring your ladies, I guess, since you tried so hard."

"Thanks, Frank." Timothy said, trying to sound grateful. He hadn't expected Frank to offer him, his wife, and Candice protection. *If the negotiations go wrong, and Frank tries to blow the farmhouse but it doesn't work, he'll know I warned them.* He rubbed his hands over his face. Every so-called right call he made seemed to result in possible destruction. *The only way we make it out alive, the only way we get George and Annika back, is for this to work between the Boston PD and Frank.*

"No problem, Southie. Nightie-night." Frank's sing-song response made Timothy's stomach curdle.

"Good night, Frank." He rolled onto his side to look out the window. O'Donnell's last words to him couldn't have been further from the truth. No one was going to sleep that night.

Chapter 25

Heather Peters

For the second time, Heather huddled in a far corner of a stranger's house waiting to find out if she'd die. The moon hid behind clouds so that the windows yielded no relief from the absolute dark of night. Labored panting, steady wheezing, and quick, shallow gasps – the sounds of people breathing filled the space around her. Her own chest rose and fell with a shudder, the tremor of her chin creating an unsteady oscillation of air past her lips. She was shoulder-to-shoulder with her fellow huddlers. Candice's warm, sweaty skin pressed against her left arm while the back of O'Donnell's uniform, damp and scratchy, brushed against her other. Musk and salt and something sickly sweet created a pungent aroma; she could taste the scent as it settled in her nostrils and on her tongue.

There was no one there to hold her hand. She interlocked her fingers, sticky and too hot, pressing her palms together as she held her hands to her chest like she used to do as a child in Sunday school – except her prayers were desperate pleas instead of platitudes. She wasn't safe. Death loomed outside in the form of nature gone wrong; inside, death hung over her head in the form of humanity's more familiar evils.

Her body complained of the tension held in every muscle. Head throbbing, exhaustion held at bay by adrenaline, her healing bullet wound on fire, Heather stood vigil. She fixed her eyes on the hallway to the kitchen where a soft, white glow emitted from the flashlights the officers had set up all around Abrams and the site of the bomb. The glow shifted, and Heather sucked in a breath. She nearly cried when Moose trotted into the light and Abrams followed with a flashlight.

"It's done." Abrams pulled a kitchen timer out of her pocket and set it on the coffee table. "Moose has searched the house. All the explosives we can get to are neutralized." The policewoman's expression remained solemn as she perched on the edge of the couch and let Moose lay his head in her lap. She stood the flashlight on its end so that the white beam of light hit the ceiling and dimly illuminated the room.

"What's wrong?" Heather asked. None of the other officers looked happy or even relieved. Candice scooted closer to Heather, shrinking against her. "Are we missing something? Shouldn't we be celebrating?"

O'Donnell's footfalls thudded against the floorboards as he joined Abrams on the couch and put a hand on her back. "You wanna go outside and disengage the bombs at the perimeter." He wasn't asking; he was interpreting.

The other officers slowly dispersed from the corner to fill the room, many of them sliding against the wall to sit on the floor. Their postures and expressions spoke of defeat.

Heather frowned. "We can do that in the morning, right?"

"We can wait for a few hours," Abrams said. "I *need* a few hours. I've got to sleep, or I could make a mistake that costs us big time. But we don't know how many bombs are out there. We don't know where the bombs are located. It could take hours to find and neutralize them all, and we won't have hours by the time it's actually safe." A tear glistened as it slid down Abrams's cheek; she leaned over Moose and hugged him to her chest. Her words were slightly muffled with her face buried in the dog's fur, but Heather could make out her words. "I'm sorry, buddy. We have to do it."

Candice shook her head and folded her arms against her stomach. "What's the worst that can happen if we don't check for bombs outside?"

"It could mean all our lives." O'Donnell looked away from Abrams. "It's my fault we fell for this. Frank set us up. I thought that interrogation yielded the results we wanted, but all it did was lead us right into a trap."

"But Frank won't definitely blow up the property, right?" Heather asked, voice cracking as Abrams hugged Moose tighter. "The two in the house we've taken care of, so… why not take our chances that he'll just blow the yard?"

Abrams pulled away from Moose. "He wants *one* of us to accompany Timothy to the ranch tomorrow. If he doesn't like what he hears, he'll get rid of everyone here. I have no doubt he'll have people watching the farmhouse during the safe hours of the day. He'll blow the place if anyone tries to leave. He'll do the same if his people report a lady searching the property with a dog. Timothy's intervention bought us one chance to get out of this: for the deal to work."

"We're on borrowed time." O'Donnell stood up and walked to the window, others making way for him in an almost reverent way. "Frank wanted to kill us the moment we took over this house. He'll be lookin' for reasons this deal won't work. And if he detonates the bombs in the yard, he could damage our vehicles." He swore. "Frank probably set a bomb under that little bridge over the ditch. We'll be stuck here."

Somber understanding settled over Heather. "And whoever lives will be hunted down by Frank's guys. So, clearing the property of explosives is the only way to ensure an escape if one is needed."

"I'll do it, Abrams." O'Donnell turned abruptly from the window and set his jaw.

Abrams stood and shook her head. "C'mon, sir. You know that's not going to happen. Besides the fact you're our leader, I'm Moose's handler. I've been trained more extensively in disarming bombs. There's no question who should be the one to go out there. It's me, hands down."

"This is my fault. It should be my responsibility to fix it." O'Donnell took half a step forward. The dim light cast shadows over his face, but his eyes were alight with determination as they glistened with the slightest evidence of despair.

"It's not your fault, O'Donnell." Abrams turned in a circle, continuing with an address to the rest of the officers. "We all agreed to this raid, didn't we?" A chorus of yes-ma'ams answered. "We voted on it because O'Donnell is the kind of leader to take the opinions of the men and women he's responsible for under advisement. And that's the kind of leader we want, isn't it?" A stronger agreement rang out from the officers. "So, let's give this one a vote. I'm telling you all right now that I volunteer to go out there. I'm the best person for the job. You *need* O'Donnell. All those in favor of letting me do my job, raise your hands." She picked up the flashlight and shone it around the room where every officer had his hand raised, each one looking upon Abrams with clear respect and awe. Abrams turned the flashlight on O'Donnell; trails of tears made clean paths down his smudged cheeks. "All I ask," Abrams said, "is that if you go to this Farm, that you look for my niece, Lissa, and you take good care of her if she's alive."

O'Donnell's answer was gruff but filled with conviction. "I swear to you, Abrams. If Lissa is alive, I'll find her, and I'll protect her."

Abrams let her hand holding the flashlight fall to her side. "Then it's settled. I'm going to lay down, get some rest, and make my peace. I'm going to do it alone, in one of the upstairs bedrooms." She picked up the kitchen timer and put it in her pocket. "I'll set this kitchen timer for three hours. I need to start my search outside in no more than four hours so I can finish before there's too much daylight." She stepped toward the hall and Moose followed. She stopped at the doorway. "Me and Moose are gonna share that jar of peanut butter in the kitchen cabinet. Anybody got a problem with that?"

"It's all yours," O'Donnell said, and then Abrams left the room with Moose on her heels. The officer turned to Heather. "Abrams was right. Your husband gave us our first shot at getting out of this alive. I was wrong to try to leave you three here. If you wanna come with us, you are welcome."

"Thank you," Heather said. "We just want to get the kids back. If that means going with you, we'll do it. If that means staying with Frank, we'll do that, too." She offered a small smile. "For what it's worth, I hope it means sticking with the Boston PD."

"Our forces are too small to oust CON, but..." He glanced at the hallway where Abrams had gone. "A promise is a promise. No matter what, I'm goin' after Lissa, and the first place I'll check is this Farm. It'll be a long shot, but I'll do what I can to help you get your people back." O'Donnell addressed everyone in the room. "A'ight, squad, I want you to get some rest. Tomorrow will be here in a few hours, and the rest of the day is going to be long." He sighed as he lowered himself to the floor and lay on his back right where he was, leaving the couch and chair for others.

Candice crawled into a chair and curled up into a ball, resting her head on the arm. "You going to update Timothy?" she asked as she yawned.

Heather nodded. "Yeah. He'll want to know what's happened. I doubt he's gotten any sleep."

"I don't know if any of us will really get any sleep," Candice said. "I'm exhausted, but... sleep seems so far away."

"It won't happen if you keep blabbin'," O'Donnell said from the floor.

"Sorry," Heather whispered. She walked past Candice and put a hand on her arm, whispering, "Just try to rest. If I'm not down here when Abrams comes, go upstairs, and get me, okay?"

Candice agreed, and Heather trudged into the dark hallway and up the stairs as officers retrieving their flashlights from the kitchen clicked them off and found places on the floor all around the house to rest. She had to creep along the second story hall, running her hand along the wall until she found the last door on the right. She lightly knocked, and when she opened the door, a bright light shone in her face. She groaned and put up her arm to cover her eyes.

"Oh, sorry." Timothy redirected the flashlight. He grabbed the sticky notes, which they were running low on, and wrote: *What's going on?*

She sat on the bed next to him, taking the pen and notepad. We found the bombs in the house. Abrams is going to have to go out with Moose in about four hours to disarm the bombs in the yard. She then explained on a new note how O'Donnell, Abrams, and the other officers had come to that decision and why.

Timothy bit his lip and ran his fingers through his hair. She could see the tension in the way he held his body. If he could have screamed, she suspected he would have. Heather pulled back the covers and slid underneath, gesturing for Timothy to come to her. He couldn't hold her, not with her side the way it was, but they could hold hands. They could be close to one another. Having him there was a balm to her soul, one she desperately needed to keep going.

Heather drifted in and out of sleep over the next few hours, never fully sinking into complete rest. The creak of a door down the hall, the click of Moose's nails on the hallway floor, and the passage of white light under the bedroom door told her it was time to get up. Timothy got up with her, showing her a note: *I have an idea. I'm coming downstairs with you, but I need you to warn everyone to keep quiet about Frank.*

Heather nodded and wrote: *Give me a few minutes.*

She navigated her way downstairs to find Abrams in the middle of the kitchen, surrounded by her companions. Candice stood with Ellis on the outskirts of the circle. "Timothy wants to come downstairs. He says he has an idea," Heather said. "No one talk about Moose or the bombs, okay? Actually, Frank probably expects us to be sleeping, so try not to talk at all."

Everyone nodded, and a few minutes later Timothy came downstairs with his flashlight in hand. He went straight for Candice's suitcases which were in the corner of the dining room. Heather followed behind, and the rest followed behind her, crowding the dining room as Timothy unzipped the luggage. Several officers clicked on their flashlights and set them up on the table to give the room plenty of light.

Candice's mouth fell open, and she put her hands on her hips, eyes wide as she watched Timothy rifle through her things. He pulled out her sunhat, which he had to reshape, and a sheer, flowing, white top. Candice gasped when he knotted the long sleeves. He then stuck the sunhat inside the shirt, the top of the hat poking out through the head hole. Timothy slipped it on his head and tucked the hem of the shirt inside the collar of his t-shirt.

Heather smiled. *You clever, wonderful man.* She looked around the room and the others were smiling, too. Timothy looked ridiculous, with the arms of the shirt hanging down like ears, but it looked like it would protect Abrams's head and neck.

Timothy took off the makeshift mosquito net and put it on the table, bringing out the notepad. Heather stood next to him, reading over his shoulder. *Layers. Maybe gloves from the coat closet?*

The farmhouse came alive with the search for things to protect Abrams, and by the time they were done, Abrams looked like some make-believe creature with the layers of bulky clothes and two sets of gloves and the sunhat-sheer-top contraption. She made the rounds, hugging and whispering her goodbyes. Then she took up the little tool kit of pliers and wire cutters she'd had in the utility belt of her uniform, put the flashlight between her teeth, and faced the door. Her pocket bulged with the stainless steel one-cup measuring scoop they'd found in the kitchen to help her dig for the explosives, and a bag was slung over one shoulder with the bricks of C-4 she planned to throw into the cornfield. She and Moose slipped quickly outside while everyone else shone flashlights all around the door to look for any bugs that might try to slip inside.

Heather put an arm around Timothy's waist as the officers gathered at the windows. He'd given them hope, and she loved him that much more for that. He smiled, the first smile she'd seen on his face in a long time. It was too dark outside to see more than Abram's shadowed figure and the beam of her flashlight, which revealed ominous black specks hovering in the air wherever it shone.

After a while, Timothy left so that everyone could speak out loud without the possibility of Frank hearing every word they said. Heather hated that he had to go, but a swell of pride in all he'd done in the last twenty-four hours made her smile. Candice returned to her chair, and Heather sat on the couch next to Ellis. Several officers, including O'Donnell, stayed at the windows, but others settled back on the floor. Soft snores picked up as a few men and women fell asleep. Her own eyes drooped. There was nothing to be done except wait as Abrams and Moose searched for the bombs, dug them up, and then disarmed them.

"Maybe everything will be okay," Ellis said.

"Yeah, maybe." Heather leaned back and sank into the couch.

She was jerked awake by a string of curses from O'Donnell's mouth. Heather bolted upright. "What's wrong?" Sunshine filled the room, and from the view out the windows to her right, there was no swarm to be seen. "What time is it?" She whipped her head around to look at the clock on the wall. *9:22… we made it! But… why is everyone upset?*

Ellis was standing, her hand to her mouth, and Candice was wiping away tears. Officers lined the windows facing the front yard, O'Donnell at the center. His hands were clenched into fists at his side, and he was shaking.

"What happened?" Heather stood up and craned her neck, trying to see between those at the windows. Ellis only turned her back, buried her head in her hands, and wept. Candice didn't answer either, instead devolving into more intense tears.

Footsteps pounded the stairs and Timothy rushed into the room with a sticky note in his hand. "Hey, everyone," he said, his tone urgent. He slowed, his look of panic mixing with one of confusion. He handed Heather the note. It read: *Drone coming in from over the cornfield.*

Oh no. Heather sprinted to O'Donnell and squeezed her arm between him and another officer, putting the sticky note practically in his face. He backed up, cheeks wet with tears, scowling at her until he read the note.

He hung his head. "Then the jig is up."

"No," Heather whispered. She pointed out the window. "We just need to—" She cut off as she looked out the window where Abrams stood facing the house, just a couple yards from the windows. Heather's eyes went directly to the thing most normal about Abrams's appearance: her hands. She'd taken off her gloves. Her fingers were swollen and red. Moose paced behind her, his whine audible even from inside the house.

"No." Heather's voice shook. "Why did she do that?"

O'Donnell stepped back to the window with Heather, the other officers making room. He put his hand flat on the glass as if reaching for his friend. "She couldn't use her tools properly with the gloves on."

"I'm sorry," Abrams shouted, her voice muffled through the glass. The policewoman's trembling, bloated hand reached for the sheer top and the sunhat, pulling them off and letting them drop to the ground. Tears of blood ran rivers from her bulging eyes to her chin. She coughed, blood spurting from her mouth.

"No!" O'Donnell shouted. "Don't say that. You're a hero. You hear me? A damn hero." His voice cracked and he leaned his forehead against the glass.

Suppressed sobs rose from all over the room as Abrams fell to her knees. "Make it out," Abrams said, words garbled. "Survive. All… of… you." Her face contorted a little more with every word until she finally brought her hands to her temples and screamed between gritted, bloody teeth.

Then a voice broke through, pulling Heather's attention from Abrams. "Touching," Frank said. "I see you's been workin' all night, diggin' up my hard work and ruinin' all my plans."

Heather's head spun. Frank's drone was watching them. He knew what they'd done. She stumbled to her husband and held onto his arm.

"I wonder," Frank said, sounding amused, "if you found every last one. That attic ain't easy to get to. I guess we're gonna find out."

"No," Timothy said. "Frank, please. Let's just talk about th—"

A deafening explosion burst from above, the ceiling buckled, and then beams cracked and split. Timothy threw Heather to the ground and covered her with his body. She screamed, though she could no longer hear anything. It was as if someone had jabbed sharp pencils in her ears. Debris fell all around them, smoke filled the air, and then the ground rumbled as a second explosion rocked the farmhouse from somewhere outside. Timothy's body went limp, pinning Heather to the ground.

Chapter 26

Minnie Stevens

Minnie pressed her tongue against her clenched teeth and narrowed her eyes at the Suit with the gall to stand in her way. Alex had never returned, and she'd planned to get Lauren and Oliver to a more secure location when Corporal Jenny Conner arrived with their breakfast. Instead, the Suits had shown up, and now Minnie needed, more than ever, to get the two to safety. If Alex had disappeared like Elijah, Minnie had to do whatever she could to protect his son. "My daughter is takin' that boy to get some exercise, and you're gonna let her — *if* you know what's good for ya."

"Ma'am, you, your daughter, and the boy need to stay in your rooms." He gestured to the other Suit at the opposite end of their block of the hall. "We have our orders to keep you confined to this area. You can walk this section of the hall if you need some exercise."

She scoffed. "Son, you'd better go lookin' for your missin' paddle cause your brain ain't makin' it upstream with just one."

He frowned. "What does that mean?"

Minnie huffed. "This hallway ain't enough room for a boy to run. That gym is sittin' useless. Let him and my daughter go. What harm is it gonna do?" She didn't mention that she knew for a fact that the women's locker room had a separate exit from the gym. With any luck, the egghead standing in front of her wouldn't realize she was trying to find an opportunity to leave him in the dust. The men's locker room bordered an outer wall, so as long as Munez didn't have some weird habits, she hoped that layout detail had escaped his attention.

"Ma'am—"

"Stop callin' me that." Minnie crossed her arms, but then her heart leapt at the sight of Conner turning the corner of the next hallway intersection, stomping her way toward them. She grinned. "I expect my good friend Alan Hunt has sent someone to straighten out this tangle you've created."

His frown deepened. "Your good friend?" He sounded too skeptical for her liking.

"That's right." Minnie crossed her arms and quirked an eyebrow, daring him with her stare down to question her integrity again.

Conner started shouting like she was a drill sergeant while she was still several feet away. "Back up, Munez! These people are under the protection of the military."

The Suit turned halfway to look at her. "I don't think so, Conner. We have orders directly from—"

"*My* orders come directly from President Coleman. He trumps Price every day of the week." Conner stopped inches from Munez, standing toe-to-toe, looking up at the Suit with a fire that made Minnie smile. The corporal whipped a paper out of her pocket and shoved it under Munez's nose. "Signed orders for you and your buddy to clear the area."

Breathing too heavily through his nose as he pinched his mouth into a tight line, Munez snatched the paper and unfolded it. "We were told not to leave them alone under any circumstances."

"Am I invisible, Munez?" Conner put her hands on her hips. "You're not leaving them alone. You're leaving them with me. These people are important to Mr. Roman, who is one of the most essential assets we have in this building. The president takes his preferences seriously, and right now, that means I chaperone them. *Not* you."

The other suit jogged up to them. "Maybe we should go check with Price. He told us to stand guard, but he also said to avoid trouble."

Munez sighed and handed his companion the paper. "How about you go talk to Price, and I'll stay here." He held up a hand as Conner opened her mouth. "You can stay, too, okay? If he comes back with confirmation, I'm out of your hair."

"Fine." Conner glared at the other Suit and barked, "Get on it, slow poke!"

He jumped a little before hurrying away down the hall. Munez took up his previous position and nodded toward where the other Suit had been standing earlier. "Why don't you go over there while we wait?"

"If I heard right, our very important guests wanted to visit the gym for a little exercise." Maintaining eye contact with Munez, Conner nodded toward their rooms. "Why don't you go get Lauren and Oliver. We're going on a little field trip."

"What?" Munez said. "We have orders to keep them here."

Conner dismissed his objection. "I have orders to make them comfortable."

"I'll get Lauren and Oliver," Minnie said, grinning at Conner and then throwing one last scowl at Munez. She pushed open the door where the two were playing cards. At the sight of her, Lauren started packing the cards back in their box. Samson stretched and yawned.

Minnie walked to the bed with as much normalcy as she could muster and spoke softly. "It's time to go," she said. "You two need to get to the safe spot Alex told us about. Not sure how it's gonna happen yet, but Conner will help us."

"Any word on Alex?" Lauren asked, brow creased.

Minnie shook her head. "Not yet, but I haven't had much chance to talk to Conner." She put a gentle hand on Oliver's head. "We might not be coming back here, so grab what you need."

"What if Dad can't find us? We have to stay here." Oliver shrank back from her, scooting farther onto the bed.

"Your dad told me where to go if you needed to be taken somewhere safer," Minnie said. "He knows exactly where we're goin'. In fact, he might go there first lookin' for us when the time comes."

Oliver chewed on his lower lip and seemed to consider it before finally nodding. "Okay," he said. "We better go wherever Dad told us to go."

"That's right," Minnie said, smiling, though her heart broke for the boy. *What if Alex isn't coming back? Will it break the boy completely?* He'd spent most of the first week she'd known him completely silent after the death of his mother. If he lost his father, too, Minnie was afraid Oliver wouldn't come back from that.

"You think we'll have to escape into the city?" Lauren whispered as Oliver hopped off the bed, grabbed his mother's macrame purse, and slid the picture and frame inside.

"Depends on what happened to Alex," Minnie leaned closer and whispered very softly. "I don't like that he didn't come back last night. When we get to the gym, you've got to get Oliver out through the ladies' locker room exit. I'll stay and help Conner distract the Suit."

"Does she know what we're planning?" Lauren asked.

"She'll catch on. She knows about the rendezvous point, and Alex trusts her. We'll have to trust her, too, and hope she goes along with it." Minnie rubbed the back of her neck and took a deep breath. The longer she didn't know what had happened to Alex the previous night, the more nervous she became. But his absense also stirred up a determination to follow the plan.

Oliver returned to Lauren's side and took the little deck of playing cards. He plopped it in the purse before slinging it over his shoulder. "I'm ready," he said, patting the bag at his hip.

Minnie ruffled his hair. "You sure are." She grinned and held out her hand. "Will you escort me, good sir?"

Oliver giggled and hooked his arm in hers. Minnie whistled for Samson, and the dog wagged his tail as he followed the three of them into the hall where Conner and Munez were still debating. Minnie just turned the opposite way, putting her finger to her lips, signaling Oliver to be quiet as they walked away.

"Hey!" Munez shouted. "We haven't decided we're going yet."

"What are you going to do about it?" Conner asked. "Are you going to take me down and then tackle a grandma to keep them from stretching their legs?"

Munez heaved a frustrated sigh. "You're impossible. Just… take the lead to the gym, and I'll come up behind to make sure they don't slip their detail."

Conner offered him the first smile Minnie had seen on her face since she'd arrived. "That's the first reasonable thing you've said, Munez." She backed away from him until she was in front of them all, waiting to turn her back.

"The dog can stay," Munez said.

"What do you have against dogs?" Minnie asked. "Samson needs exercise, too." She grinned when he rolled his eyes but didn't object further.

"Hey, Conner, the least you can do is call this in," Munez said from the back. "I'd do it, but you know, there's that whole thing where Hunt commandeered the walkie talkie supply for the military."

Conner sneered at him over her shoulder. "We've got the perimeter, Munez. We're more spread out. And, in case you forgot, *we* brought the walkie talkies here in the first place."

"Are you going to call it in or what?" Munez nearly spat the words.

Conner unclipped her walkie talkie and put it up to her mouth. "Breaker 1-9. This is Corporal Conner."

General Hunt's voice answered. "10-4. Go ahead."

"I'm taking the Brady Bunch to the gym, sir. I've got Munez following behind."

"Roger that."

"The Brady Bunch?" Minnie asked. "Is that your code name for us now?"

Conner stopped at the door to the gym and held it open for them. "For your group as a whole, yes. The general loves his nicknames, and you all *are* a wholesome, blended family. He wants us using the codes on the walkie talkies for the president, the doctors, your group… no one is listening, but old habits die hard."

"Ain't that the truth." Minnie ushered Oliver into the gym in front of her. "All right, now, Oliver. You and Lauren get changed in the locker room." She clarified, speaking to Conner, but making sure Munez could hear. "The general was nice enough to provide us with shorts and t-shirts. We've been keepin' them in the locker rooms." She rolled her shoulder. "Too bad I'm a little bent out of shape. I think I'll just relax in the café corner." She pointed to a little nook with vending machines and a coffee station, all of which had been long emptied. There were a few tables and sets of chairs. Minnie headed that way while Lauren guided Oliver toward the women's locker room. Oliver patted his leg for Samson to come with them, and the dog followed, glancing at Minnie only briefly, seeming to ensure she had no objections.

"Wait a minute." Munez held out a hand and took a few long strides toward Lauren and Oliver. "Why are you taking the boy in there? Shouldn't he be going to the men's room?"

Lauren paused, her mouth opening and closing, her eyes too wide. *She looks guilty as sin.* Minnie pursed her lips. *I suppose she's never been good at keepin' secrets.*

Conner stepped up and put a hand on Munez's chest. "Lay off, Munez. No one else is in there. It doesn't matter which room he uses."

Munez still looked skeptical. He was eyeing Lauren. Bless her heart, the fact that she was hiding something was written all over her face. "Conner, what if she tries to get out through the vents or something? Go in with her."

Well, I guess he doesn't know about the separate exit. Minnie gave Conner a smile. "That's fine with us," she said.

"And what about the dog? No need for him in the locker room," Munez said.

"Actually, he's been somethin' of a therapy dog for Oliver," Minnie chimed in. "He calms the boy. Oliver has been through a lot."

Munez sighed. "Fine. Just… hurry up in there, Conner." He nodded at Minnie. "I'll keep an eye on her."

Conner scoffed. "I'm more concerned that she keep an eye on *you*. Minnie, you'll be all right out here with this guy?"

"Of course," Minnie said. *Just go… we're bringin' too much attention to the locker rooms as it is.* "I'll watch him like a hawk." She took a seat at one of the tables. "Come on, now, Munez," she said. "Take a load off for a few minutes."

Munez walked over but stood with a wide stance, facing the locker rooms on the other side of the gym, locking his hands behind his back. "I'm good where I am."

"Suit yourself," Minnie said. "I was just tryin' to be friendly."
Munez didn't look at her. "Sure you are."
"No need for a smart mouth, young man." Minnie settled in the chair, studying him. He was latino, thickly built, not too tall but not exactly short.
"Ma'am," Munez said, taking his eyes off the lockers to look at her, "you haven't said a friendly word to me since I got to your door this morning. I'm just doing my job." He returned his gaze to the other side of the gym.
Minnie watched him for a few more minutes. He'd been as stubborn as a mule all day, but he *had* tried to be polite. "I s'pose I get a little high and mighty sometimes," she said. It was as close as she was going to get to an apology.
He looked at her sideways. "I had orders," he said. "I work security. I don't always know *why* my orders are what they are, but I do know it's my job to keep people safe."
Minnie raised an eyebrow at that. *Safe, huh? Either he's lyin' or he's in the dark.* She chewed on the inside of her cheek, thinking. If he *was* in the dark, she wanted to know; if the Suits weren't all bad, maybe they could bring some of them to their side if things went all cattywampus. *There's only one way to find out. Listen to his side of things.*
"Tell me," Minnie said, leaning back in the chair, "I've heard about this dustup between your people and the military from Conner, but I'd like to know what you think of it. Why're you two always fixin' to mix?"
"They think they're better than us," he said without hesitation. "A lot of us are ex-military. We were burned by that experience and decided to use our skills elsewhere. They don't like that the President wants us here, that this is our home turf, and that they need us."
Minnie nodded slowly. "I see. And what do you think you're doin' here?"
"What do you mean?" Munez asked. "We're stabilizing Atlanta for the survivors. That's pretty obvious."
"You done any rotations at the hospital?" Minnie asked.
"No. Price only has senior members of the team stationed there." He shook his head. "You ask weird questions."
"You're not the first person to accuse me of that." Minnie pressed her lips together, the possibility of there being good men mixed in with the Suits reorienting her view of their plan.
"It's been too long," Munez said. "I'm going to check on them."
"You can't go in there!" Minnie stood up so fast she knocked her chair over. She swallowed hard at her overreaction. "It's a ladies' locker room," she said more calmly. "It wouldn't be decent."
Munez cocked his head, looking at the overturned chair. "Something is going on." He unlocked his hands from behind his back and strode toward the locker room.
Minnie followed on his heels, her heart lodging in her throat. He paused at the door, hesitating with one hand on the doorhandle. He cracked it open. "I'm coming inside," he said. "Is anybody indecent?"
There was no answer. Minnie's mouth fell open, surprised he'd taken the time to ask. "Look, Munez, I'm sure—"
"I'm coming in," Munez repeated before pushing the door open with force and marching into the locker room with one hand on his gun holster.
Minnie yelped as the door slammed against the wall. She rushed in, hands held out. "Now, let's not be hasty," she said, her voice trembling. She couldn't take her eyes off his gun and how he looked so prepared to pull it out.
"Where the heck are they?" Munez rounded on Minnie, yelling.
She looked around, part of her anxiety easing at the sight of the empty room. That relief only lasted a second as she stopped scanning the room and came face to face with Munez. He stood over her, muscles tense, and a scowl on his face.
A dull pounding came from somewhere off to the side, around a partition wall. "Maybe they're over there?" Minnie pointed.
He stalked over, and Minnie followed. Conner was pounding on the thick glass of a sauna door, the handle having been tied and secured with resistance bands to a hand rail on the wall next to it. Her forehead rested on the glass, and she was looking down as if she hadn't heard them.
"Conner!" Munez leapt forward, pulling a pocket knife out and sawing through the bands. They snapped, and he pulled the door open.
Conner stumbled out, sweating up a storm, leaning on the wall and taking deep breaths. "Lauren used the dog to threaten me, get me into the sauna. They turned it on to a barely tolerable level after securing the door. I think they were trying to buy time once you came in."
"Well, that doesn't sound like Lauren at all." Minnie crossed her arms. *What is she up to?*
"Why didn't you pull your gun?" Munez asked.
Conner pointed to a bench along the wall. Minnie hadn't seen the gun there when they'd turned the corner around the partition wall. It lay next to Conner's walkie talkie. "They disarmed me," Conner said. "And the dog was *not* friendly."
"Well, now, *that* doesn't sound like Samson," Minnie said, and then she added, shrugging, "unless you provoked him, that is."
Munez let out grunt of frustration. "Where did they go?"
"There's a side exit I didn't know about. Goes out into the hall," Conner said. "You can still catch them if you run."
"What?" Minnie stood with her arms spread wide. "I don't think so. You're going to have to get through me, Munez."
"I knew you were in on something suspicious," Munez said, turning on Minnie, shouting. "Do you know how much trouble we'll be in?"
"Calm down," Conner said, "they're still in the building. They have to be. They're not going to leave Minnie and Alex."
Minnie sucked in a breath. She's going to tell him about the rendezvous point! "You little—"
Conner interrupted her. "Go, Munez! I can't. I need a second to recover, and somebody's got to watch her." She pointed at Minnie.
Munez balled his hands into fists. "I don't want to draw my gun on you, ma'am, or push you aside, or do anything to hurt you. But you need to move. Now."

Minnie licked her lips, glancing at Conner, who gave her a wink and mouthed the words, "Let him go." She reluctantly moved aside and Munez bolted for the center of the room, whipping around until he found the second exit, and then running for it. Minnie put her hands on her hips. "What in tarnation?"

"We can't let the Suits think I'm in on this. It will escalate things between them and the military." Conner straightened up and popped her back, grimacing. "All of this was Lauren's plan. Well, most of it. I put my gun and the walkie talkie on the bench to explain why I didn't use either one. The downside is, you're probably in some trouble. But, Lauren, Oliver, and Samson had plenty of time to get out of the area."

"I guess I was fixin' to be in trouble anyway," Minnie said. "Thanks for helpin' them get out. You had even me goin' there for a minute. I thought maybe you'd been spinnin' tales all this time."

"If I convinced you, then hopefully I definitely pulled one over on Munez." Conner, still breathing a little heavy, walked over to her gun and walkie talkie. She holstered her gun, smiling and shaking her head. "As if I'd let someone take my gun."

Munez burst back into the locker room by way of the gym entrance. "That door doesn't have a way to open it from the hall," he said, running his fingers through his hair. "I can't believe this." He jabbed a finger at Minnie. "You kept me talking to distract me, let the time go by. You *knew* they were going to escape. Why? Where did they go?"

"I'm not at liberty to say." Minnie stuck out her chin and pursed her lips, realizing she had some leverage. "To *you* that is. I would like to speak to Alan Hunt."

Chapter 27

Zara Williams

Zara touched the numbered strips of paper affixed to the cork board in the prepper community's town hall. Eight lines of a choppy poem kept her mesmerized; each one had been written on three separate crossbow bolts for the preppers to find. It had been a puzzle, one the community had put together overnight while Zara had been quarantined with the rest of the survivors from the hospital. They'd forced Zara and her companions into the cabin and locked them out of the way, promising to bury Mitch.

It had only been a few hours since they'd let them all out, but Mr. Peters had gotten his audience with Thomas Redding despite the aftermath of the attack from the day before. He'd barely waited until after they'd all gathered around the mound that was Mitch's grave before securing the meeting.

The funeral had been awkward. Zara's first impression of Mitch had been when he'd murdered Nina, and he'd not improved much upon his character since. But he'd contributed to their group, nonetheless, and everyone had tried to say something kind, even Zara. His unexpected death had served to remind her how quickly she could lose someone. *I have to figure out how to mend fences with Lizzy, how to let go of our disagreements.*

She turned her attention back to the strips of paper. Walter was going on half an hour arguing for a vehicle to take them to Boston, but the cork board had drawn her and pushed away everything else. Zara had overheard conversations about the poem in the mess hall, but seeing it had made it more real. It wasn't elegant, but it was frightening. It read:

Mother Earth judges.
Only we know who is
Worth her mercy.
Join us to see
Who will perish
And who will relish
Life after the end.
All else are condemned.

Lizzy came up beside Zara and gently bumped against her. "This is crazy," she said, nodding to the poem. "What do you think it means?"

Zara shrugged. "Somebody phoned it in when they learned about poetry in high school?"

Lizzy chuckled. "It's not great. Is 'judges' supposed to rhyme with 'who is'?"

"The 'all else' is especially dramatic," Zara said. "And the whole 'Mother Earth' thing? Do you think they're hippies?"

"Aren't hippies, like, all peace and love and stuff?" Lizzy wrinkled her nose.

"It's a cult." Thomas's voice cut into their banter as he broke away from his conversation with Mr. Peters. "And they are to be taken seriously, well written poetry or not." He turned back to Walter. "For the last time, we don't have the gasoline to spare. We don't have a vehicle to spare even if we had the gas. You're going to have to find another way."

"And what exactly do you suggest?" Mr. Peters raised his voice and gestured wildly. "We should click our heels and wish for home? We need your help. That bus doesn't have enough gas to make it to Boston, and even if it did, I'd be shocked if it made it there in one piece. I am trying to stop this sickness from getting worse. I am maybe the only person *in the world* who can do it."

Thomas scoffed. "You're awfully full of yourself. There's no way your company is the only one working on these genetically modified mosquitos. And if it was, there's no way you're the only person who understands it. There's probably somebody working on it right now. Our first priority is keeping the sick out and surviving inside our compound."

"You're only saying that because you don't understand what's coming," Mr. Peters sounded like an enraged animal, his voice a near growl. "Those walls won't keep the mosquitos out when they get this far. You've been spared because you're so far from an epicenter, and you've barely seen the worst of this sickness because you're so far from a major city. All you've seen is the straggling survivors. But let me tell you, *most* of the world is dead. And if I don't get to Boston, that number is only going to get worse."

"If he told Thomas the truth," Zara whispered, "he'd see why your dad is the best person to fix this mess."

"I know." Lizzy chewed on her lower lip, keeping her eyes on her father. Her cheeks turned red.

"We can force him to tell them, Liz." Zara stood in front of her friend and pled with her softly so that the others in the room wouldn't be able to hear. "If you know where he's keeping the phone, tell me now. I'm afraid he's turned it on to let the battery run out."

Lizzy shook her head and turned away, her eyes misting. "Can't you let it go?" Her shoulders dropped. "I'm going to get some air." She left Zara standing there, once again choosing her father's reputation over the right thing. Zara wanted to scream. *It's like she's actively pushing me away. How can I mend our friendship when she won't see reason?* She scowled at Mr. Peters. *We do have to get to Boston.*

Zara strode across the room with intentional steps, eyes fixed on Thomas. He stood at one side of the table, arms crossed, expression hard, and Mr. Peters stood at the other end of that table, hands pressed on the surface, leaning over as he continued his aggressive verbal assault.

"You're nothing but a backwoods control freak," Mr. Peters said between gritted teeth.

"And you're nothing but a city-slicker who thinks the world revolves around him." Thomas wasn't backing down. "I've known people like you my whole life. You think money is everything. Well, guess what? I've got just as much money as you do. I spent it building this compound to keep my friends and family safe, and you spent yours on what — fine wine, a second home in the mountains, a few hookers when your wife wasn't looking? Your kind make me sick." Thomas spat in Mr. Peters's face. "You've got no power here."

Walter wiped the spit off his cheek with the collar of his shirt. "You uncivilized—"

Zara slammed into the empty table and shoved it, overturning it to create a clatter that had both men staring at her in seconds. "Enough! You're both acting like spoiled brats."

"Excuse me," Thomas said. "I will not have a child talk to me that way."

"I'm not a child, Mr. Redding. Maybe a few weeks ago, you could have said it and gotten away with it, even though I'd already survived leukemia and worked harder to get into a good school than most adults work a single day in their lives." Zara shook her head, speaking with more conviction than she'd realized she even had. "But now? You don't get to call me a child. Not after I survived the World's Fair. Not after I lost my entire family except *maybe* my cousin. I've been beaten and robbed in a gas station, witnessed the death of so many people I've lost count, and yesterday, I shot a woman in the chest, a woman I cared about, in order to save other people I'll probably never meet. I'm almost eighteen; I'm not ten. Got it?"

Thomas raised his hands in surrender. "Got it." His tone actually contained some modicum of respect, which almost threw Zara off completely.

It apparently did the same to Mr. Peters. "That's it?" He gaped. "You're just going to let her talk to us that way? If anyone is a spoiled brat, it's her, let me tell you—"

"I don't want to hear another word you have to say." Thomas cut him off and gestured for Zara to continue. "Her on the other hand, well… she interests me."

Zara blinked a few times, her momentum stolen by sheer shock. "Right," she said, clearing her throat. "Like I was saying, you two aren't getting anywhere with this whole macho man bullcrap." She looked at Mr. Peters. "He isn't going to give us a new vehicle, but he seems willing to let us use the bus, right?" She looked to Thomas who nodded. "Great. So then, the problem is the gasoline. Since Thomas knows the area, and he's obviously done a lot of thinking in terms of preparing for the world to end, maybe instead of insulting him, we should ask him if he has any ideas."

Thomas crossed his arms and smiled at Zara. "I like you," he said before turning a frown on Mr. Peters. "Now that someone is speaking to me like I'm a human being, I think I might have something. There's an ad of sorts going out over CB radio. A man is ferrying people over the mountains and back via a small passenger plane in Clearfield, Pennsylvania. He only goes to small airstrips where he knows he can refuel, and people have to barter for a flight. One tank of gas in that bus should get you to Clearfield, but it's a long shot. He might be dead. He might be stuck somewhere. The message is on repeat, and we first stumbled over it a week ago. He won't answer any transmissions."

"That sounds like a whole lot of *nothing*," Mr. Peters said with a look of disgust.

"It's not nothing, Walter," Zara said. "We'd need to figure out the gas and something to barter. If we get there, and the guy is still operating, we get closer to home. Maybe he'll go to Boston itself. If we get there and he's not operating, we search for more gasoline for the bus, siphon it off, and get home that way."

"That's preposterous when we could load up a couple of the gasoline tanks we brought here and make it home that way," Mr. Peters crossed his arms.

"You're not taking that gasoline. It's part of the deal with the rest of your party; it's their way into this community." Thomas shook his head. "I'll let you take one tank full. The rest stays here to run the generators and provide power for the extra people who will be staying on the compound."

"I guess we have a plan, then," Zara said. "Can we stay here until we figure out the gas and the bartering chips? Where do you suggest we search?" When Thomas didn't look at her, his eyes steady on Mr. Peters, his eyes growing darker with every second, Zara added, "This isn't just about him. It's about me, it's about my cousin who *is* a child and needs me. It's about his daughter, who is actually a nice person. And he's not wrong about his labs. His company could be the one to fix this."

Thomas worked his jaw back and forth, staring intently at Mr. Peters. When he pulled his gaze away, it seemed to take some effort. He sighed when his eyes landed on Zara. "We've used the two vehicles we do have to gather supplies from abandoned towns within a sixty-mile radius. That includes Akron and Cleveland. If you want to claim a seat on a scavenging team, I can allow you to keep a small portion of each bounty in exchange for your work. Except gasoline. I'm afraid I can't part with more than one tank, no matter how much we bring back. It's too valuable to our people."

"Great." Zara nodded. "Thank you." She winced at the overturned table. "Sorry about that," she said. "I might have gotten carried away."

Thomas smiled. "Perhaps." He put a hand on her shoulder. "You're sure you don't want to stick around here?"

"If it wasn't for my cousin, I'd be tempted," Zara said. "You have no idea what it's like to travel with this guy."

"Funny." Mr. Peters crossed his arms, his clouded expression growing darker.

Thomas quirked an eyebrow. "I don't think she was joking." He nodded toward the door. "Now, I've got bigger fish to fry." He looked at the cork board. "This cult is causing us real issues. Your friend was the first person they've killed, but their messages have gotten increasingly dark."

"They're using bows and arrows," Mr. Peters scoffed. "You have guns. How hard can it be?"

"Just because they've been using bows and arrows doesn't mean that's all they have." Thomas shook his head, never taking his eyes off the board. "In fact, we're pretty sure they have some weapons that could do serious damage. They've been in the area for a long time. They call themselves Heirs of the Mother, but they started as part of the Green Earth Futurists. They only came out as the Heirs of the Mother after everything collapsed."

Zara blanched. "The GEF? They were just a crazy group of college students." Her brother's face surfaced in her mind, and her stomach churned. She hadn't expected to hear the name of the group he'd gotten so wrapped up in, the group he'd died for, the group that ignorantly released the mosquitos.

"That was a huge segment of them," Thomas said, "but they've been around for decades. They had whole communes dedicated to living off the grid and decreasing carbon footprints and whatnot. Several of them came to prepper meetings in the area to learn how to live without modern technology so they could be more green or whatever." He rubbed the back of his neck. "The first message they sent to us was all about how they knew the Mother's secrets. They think she manipulated humanity to bring about the end. Actually, their first message said something cryptic about tiny, black angels of death." He sighed. "I actually had one guy go off and join them after the CDC's message was updated to include the bit about mosquitos. He thought the Heirs of the Mother predicted it."

Zara's stomach lurched. They saw the message on the GEF forum. How much do they know?

Mr. Peters took half a step back, almost like someone had shoved him. "These Heirs of the Mother… what do you think their endgame is here?"

A chill went up Zara's spine. She'd always assumed that the Green Earth Futurists' motives had been pure even if the outcome had been disastrous. But that was before she knew a segment of them were crazy cultists.

"They've always believed humanity was a burden, that nature would figure out a way to oust us eventually. Now, though, I think they want to be part of it." Thomas took slow steps toward the board until he was standing in front of it, looking up at it like Zara had been several minutes before. "I think they want to get rid of anyone who doesn't want to join them, and I think they view us a threat to recruitment. We're competition." He shook his head. "We're not really… I mean, we won't accept just anyone, and we have limited space here in the compound. But if I'm right, that's how they see it. I have to figure out how to prevent something worse from happening." He took a deep breath and let it out slowly. "I don't know what to do with them, but I'm going to have to figure it out soon."

They want to be part of it… Zara swallowed bile. *Did they know what they were doing by releasing those mosquitos? Did Jordan know?* She remembered his face on the video before he died, as he died. He'd been terrified and shocked. There was no way he knew, but… he wasn't the only one involved.

Mr. Peters had gone pale, and the anger had completely drained away. "While we're here, maybe we can help you with them."

"Well, you certainly changed your tune." Thomas cocked his head at Mr. Peters. "I thought you wanted to get out of here as soon as possible."

Mr. Peters put a hand on Zara's shoulder and squeezed it too tightly. "Sometimes this young woman surprises me." He held out a hand, and Thomas took it. "I apologize for earlier. I… have had a very rough couple of weeks. When I didn't get what I was looking for from you, I viewed it as you putting my daughter in danger, and that wasn't fair."

His calm, cool, and collected side is back. Zara rolled her shoulder, loosening where he'd gripped her. At least with Thomas.

Thomas nodded. "I guess I can understand that, as long as you don't cause any more trouble."

"I think you and I are on the same page, now," Mr. Peters said. "If you'll excuse me, I think she and I need to have a talk about our new plans."

Zara's whole body was numb as she left the building, and Mr. Peters led the way through the compound toward their temporary shelter, a shed-like building with enough room for a triple bunk. Her eyes on his back, Zara only had one thought: *What if I was wrong? What if Walter Peters isn't the only one to blame?*

Chapter 28

Minnie Stevens

Minnie may have started the fire, but it was Corporal Jenny Conner who was feeling the heat. Conner stood at attention as Alan Hunt loomed over her; the only sign of her distress was a bead of sweat rolling down the side of her face. It pained Minnie to see the corporal take the verbal lashing on the chin. Munez, on the other hand, didn't seem to mind half as much. He remained with Minnie in the corner of the room, nodding in agreement with Hunt every few words.

Hunt was inches from Conner, and his face had turned a bright shade of red. "You're telling me that after you insisted it was imperative for our people to have watch over the Brady Bunch, after I called in a favor with the president, you proceeded to *lose* them?" His voice filled the room to bursting. "Why would they escape their detail? Now, I have to consider them a security threat. What do you have to say for yourself, Corporal?"

"I apologize, Sir," Conner said, never slouching or looking away from her superior. "However, I would say that a little boy and a halfway trained doctor turned musician are barely cause for concern. There's nowhere for them to go, anyway. My guess is that they're on the premises and will come out of the woodwork once they no longer feel threatened."

"Threatened? They've got protection, food, entertainment. They've been living in what amounts to a damn hotel room in times like these." Hunt scoffed and turned his attention on Minnie. "Ms. Stevens—"

Minnie held up a finger, using her sweet voice. "Oh, no, hon. It's Minnie, remember? I swear we've been over this before."

Hunt went from having his knickers in a knot to having bees in his britches. He spoke with a measured tone and clipped words, and his cheeks were only half a shade paler than the fires of hell itself. "Where did your people go and what are their intentions?"

Minnie gulped. *I guess I'm all out of Southern charm.* "Their intentions are to stay safe," she said, all pretense gone. She glanced at Munez. "I'd feel more comfortable speaking with you if *he* weren't here."

Munez did a double take. "I'm not going anywhere," he said. "I was told to keep watch on Mr. Roman's people, and until I hear differently from the man I work for, I intend to follow orders."

Hunt threw Munez a stern look. "Son, there's one way in and one way out of this office, but there's about a hundred ways I could kick you out of it. I admire your steadfastness to what you perceive to be your duty, despite the fact you've seen written orders from President Coleman to the contrary. However, this is my office, and you *will* step outside."

Munez, his eyes a tad too wide, cleared his throat and grimaced. "Yeah, I… I can wait outside. But I'm not leaving her in your care completely until I can confirm that the orders I saw were legitimate."

"I'm going to pretend you didn't just imply I'm a liar," Hunt growled.

A barely audible sound like a balloon being deflated came from Munez's parted lips as he took a step back. "I'll be out in the hall." He scrambled with as much dignity as Minnie imagined a man could muster under the circumstances, and he was out the door in a matter of seconds.

"Now, Ms. Stevens. You have the floor. This better be worth my time." He crossed his arms and perched on the edge of his desk.

Minnie licked her lips, hoping she was doing the right thing. "Conner, I think it's time we brought the general in on our suspicions."

The corporal's eyes grew wide, and she started shaking her head frantically, but Minnie continued. "I know you wanted to wait until we had solid evidence, but… Alex didn't come back last night, and if they've disappeared him, we're not gettin' squat."

Hunt raised an eyebrow at Conner, his thin-lipped glower apparently more intimidating that his previous berating as the corporal shrank back. "My patience is growing thin," he said.

"I can explain," Conner said, "I… just need you to hear us out without drawing any conclusions until we're done. Lawson's people are up to something."

"Hold your horses, now." Minnie held up a hand for Conner to stop. "Before we get into all of that, I think we oughtta start with askin' Alan here the same questions that got us goin' in the first place. It'll help him see where we're comin' from." Minnie took a deep breath. "My suspicions first sprouted legs at the hospital durin' my quarantine where I met Elijah Dixon."

Hunt shook his head. "I thought we already established that there is no Elijah Dixon."

"No, there most certainly was." Minnie raised her eyebrows. "I spent hours with the man, and I talked to him over a period of two days. He was real, and no, I didn't get his name wrong."

"Is that all that has you people spooked? One man's disappearance that could be explained by a missing record or a misheard name?" Hunt didn't look impressed.

"That's just the start of it. Have you been to the place they put people with purple bracelets?" Minnie asked. "How much time have you spent in that hospital?"

He shifted his weight. "We don't have much of a presence at the hospital. Lawson and Price gave us most of the perimeter in exchange for their presence at the quarantine center."

It had irked her that the military had ignored the treatment of all those deemed too ill to join the others at the dorms, but if the operations there were nefarious, Minnie supposed it made sense. "I'd bet my last nickel it was their idea to split it up that way, wasn't it?"

"I had no problem with their request." Hunt moved his hands to his sides where he could grip the edge of the desk. "I *wanted* control of the perimeter."

Conner spoke up, a deep frown forming on her face. "They knew you would," she said. "And it gave them the perfect opportunity to get rid of anybody that would make our fragile control look weak."

Hunt's brow creased. "What are you talking about?"

"Minnie said there was a room at the hospital where citizens with purple bracelets were being squared away, many of them left untreated," Conner said. "We think perhaps Lawson didn't want people getting worried as cancer patients, diabetics, and others with historically fatal illnesses died off in the dorms. We think they threw troublemakers in with the ill for a similar reason: to keep the dorms quiet and lulled into a sense of security."

"That doesn't make sense." Hunt pushed off the desk to stand up. "We have joint teams bringing in whatever we can find from the other medical centers in the city. I know for a fact we have diabetes medications. We might not be able to provide most cancer treatments, but who wouldn't understand that? Not to mention the fact that we have a brig over on the campus, one that's been used for disorderly dorm residents."

"Maybe they're up to worse than we thought," Conner said, "worse than abandoning people to the city to cover up a lack of resources."

Hunt shook his head. "This is all pure conjecture."

"And what about when the head shrink in that room had me hauled off?" Minnie shuddered at the memory. "He said to take me to the labs. Now, Alex said he coulda been talkin' about the area, the cells *in the midst of* the laboratories. But, I never bought that. The way that man looked at me… he also said no one would miss me and that they had plans for me, that I wouldn't be around to see it." She put a hand to her chest. "Everyone can think I exaggerated that, that I misheard Elijah Dixon's name, that the things I heard and saw don't make much sense — but I'm startin' to think maybe they don't make sense because no decent person would imagine what they're really up to."

"Which is what?" Hunt asked. "What do you think they're doing?"

"I don't know," Minnie said reluctantly. "But I think it has somethin' to do with their work to find a treatment or a cure."

"Alex said the scientists have some sort of deal with Lawson," Conner said. "He brought a voice recorder from his office to a meeting with Blake Turner last night, but he never came back."

Hunt narrowed his eyes at Minnie at the mention of the voice recorder. "You were grabbing the recorder when I caught you in the halls."

Minnie blushed. "I was," she admitted. "But that's beside the point. Alex went to get evidence, he disappeared, and then this mornin' Lawson and Price tried to take watch over us. That doesn't sound the least bit suspicious to you?"

"Unfortunately, it does sound suspicious. Not damning, but definitely worth looking into further." Hunt sighed and rubbed his temples.

"First thing's first," Minnie said. "We need to find Alex. If he's got that evidence, and they found out, he could be in danger. He could have everything we need to prove that Lawson and Price are up to no good."

"And if we find Mr. Roman and he has no evidence," Hunt said, "will you and your people put your rogue investigations to rest and let me handle it?"

"If Alex is safe and he's found nothin' to back up our worries, then yes, I s'pose we'd have no choice. But—" Minnie stuck out her chin and squared her shoulders. "—I won't be tellin' no one where Lauren, Oliver, and Samson went until I know it's safe."

Hunt worked his jaw back and forth, but he finally nodded. "All right, Ms. Stevens. But, we can't go find Mr. Roman just yet. We need to brief the president."

Conner took half a step toward the general, her expression alarmed. "Sir, what about Lawson? He's almost always with President Coleman. If he's there—"

Hunt held up a hand. "Lawson and Price are overseeing some sort of breakthrough in the labs today. They informed us this morning neither one of them would be available unless there was an emergency, which now that I think of it, their last-minute absence coupled with Alex's disappearance adds to the suspicious nature of their activities."

Minnie's heart skipped a beat. "Do you think Alex is in danger?"

"I don't think so. Alex is a valuable asset. But…" He trailed off, shaking his head. "I can't guarantee anything while he's in Price's custody."

"Well, I'm tired of bumpin' my gums while my friend could be in trouble, so let's get the president on board and get on with it." Minnie marched to the door and swung it open. Munez stood outside, ear turned to the door. He stumbled back when she opened the door, a look of shock on his face. "Land's sake!" Minnie crossed her arms. "What are we gonna do with him?" She shuffled out of the way as Hunt growled and stalked forward.

Munez raised his hands. "Take me with you!" he said.

Hunt paused, eyes narrowed. "What was that, son?"

"If you think Lawson is doing something wrong, I want to know about it." Munez spoke earnestly, hands still up in surrender. "I'm serious. When I was in the military, I was sent places to do things I didn't believe in. I chose Price's security company because I thought I would be protecting people, straight and simple, no politics. Just keep some guy and his family from getting shot or kidnapped or whatever."

Hunt still didn't look pleased, but his posture relaxed just a bit. "If you make one wrong move, I'll knock you out and lock you up. Got it?"

Munez nodded. "Got it."

"Conner, keep an eye on that one," Hunt pointed at Munez, and then proceeded across the hall and down a couple doors to the president's makeshift oval office. He put a hand on the door, but paused, looking sideways at Munez. "Son, maybe some other time you and me can have a sit down over your time in the military, if you mean what you said. There's pride to be found in your service."

Minnie gave Munez a motherly pat on the back as he stared at the general with surprise. "I've been thinkin' since our chat in the gym that maybe you're not a low-life snake in the grass. I hope I'm right."

She followed Hunt to find the president making notes on a map of the city pinned to the wall. He turned at their entrance and smiled at Hunt's introduction of her. That smile faded as Minnie launched into her tale, and all she could do was hope that the one man who could stop her in her tracks with a word would instead help her get Alex back.

Chapter 29

Zara Williams

Zara wrenched her arm from Mr. Peters's grip. "I'm not going anywhere with you right now." She took a step in the opposite direction from their small cabin. She couldn't handle being cooped up in that small room with Walter, not when they'd both learned the Green Earth Futurists included crazies who were trying to *participate* in the end of the world.

"Oh yes, you are." Mr. Peters tried to grab hold of her again. "You need to explain a few things."

That was exactly what Zara was afraid of; he thought she knew something. *He probably thinks Jordan and his friends did this on purpose.* His hand gripped her upper arm too tight.

Zara shouted as loud as she could. "Let go of me, Walter!" She pulled against him, but he dragged her a few steps toward the cabin. She struggled to get free, digging her heels into the dirt only to be yanked forward.

He was winning the fight until a young man stalked out of a nearby dwelling with a gun. "Hey!" he shouted. "She doesn't want to go with you."

"Stay out of this." Mr. Peters stopped dragging Zara toward their cabin to tell him off. "It's none of your business."

"I'm making it my business." He aimed his weapon. "We don't tolerate abuse of any kind here."

"How old are you, *boy*?" Mr. Peters scoffed. "You shouldn't play with your daddy's guns. That's not a toy, and this isn't abuse. I'm responsible for this girl, and she has some explaining to do."

"I'm nineteen, asshole." He switched off the safety. "And my *dad* taught me to shoot. I'm not half bad. Also, that so-called girl isn't a toddler, and from what I understand, she isn't even your daughter. Let her go."

Zara swallowed hard, her heartbeat racing in her chest. Mr. Peters had never hurt her, not really. He'd saved her life too many times for her liking. But he was angry. And he thought she was keeping important information from him. He'd killed people, and if it weren't for Lizzy, Zara was sure he'd have killed her or left her for dead a long time ago. She did *not* want to be alone with him.

The sound of a door slamming made Zara look toward their cabin. Lizzy was running toward them, her eyebrows knit together, jaw set, eyes focused on her father. Zara expected her to plead with the stranger to put the gun down, but instead she went straight for Zara's captive arm, trying to free her.

"Let her go, Dad!" Lizzy shouted.

"Elizabeth, stop making a scene and go back to our cabin." Mr. Peters frowned at his daughter. He spoke with his usual fatherly restraint — condescending but gentle, at least compared to his usual tone.

"No." Lizzy punched her father in the arm. It didn't do much besides make his frown deepen. "You're being a bully. Just let her go." Lizzy kicked Mr. Peters's knee.

He yelped and dropped Zara's arm. "What the—"

Zara stepped back, holding her arm where his grip had been, mouth agape at the scene before her. Mr. Peters hopped back on one foot, favoring his left knee, and the young man with the gun re-holstered it at his hip. Lizzy kicked her father's other knee, and he held out his hands, though he didn't grab Lizzy like he had Zara.

"What is wrong with you?" He shouted.

"What is wrong with *me*?" Lizzy kicked again, but he dodged. "What is wrong with *you*? You can't treat my best friend that way." Her voice quavered. "Just leave us alone!" She started crying, but it wasn't timid or reserved. She wasn't curled up in a corner. She was raging. She screamed and charged her father, but Zara lurched forward and grabbed Lizzy around the waist, picking her up off the ground as she kicked toward Mr. Peters. Walter flinched, the anger in his expression completely melted away.

"Liz, stop. It's okay." Zara stumbled backward and had to set Lizzy back on the ground. She put her arms around her friend, clasping her hands at Lizzy's collarbone. "Look at him, okay? He's done."

Mr. Peters stared at Lizzy, his shoulders slumped, his mouth parted as if he wanted to say something but couldn't. The dark circles under his eyes were more prominent due to the paleness of his cheeks. He reached out a hand, slowly, toward his daughter. "Elizabeth, I—"

Lizzy screamed and doubled over, breaking Zara's hold. Mr. Peters pulled back, sucking in a sharp breath as Lizzy shouted, "Don't! Just… go!"

He pressed his lips together and his eyes darted to the young man and then to an older woman who'd come out behind him. Zara followed Mr. Peters's gaze as he looked beyond her. She turned to find several residents had come out of their homes, many of them with weapons. They were watching with grim expressions. Walter Peters turned and left them in the middle of the compound yard, disappearing without another word into the little cabin.

"Are you okay?" Zara asked, positioning herself in front of Lizzy.

"I should have stood up for you a long time ago." Lizzy wiped her tears away. "I'm sorry."

A spark of warmth in Zara's chest brought tears to her eyes. "I shouldn't have wanted you to hate him. He *is* your dad. He wouldn't have left just now if he didn't love you."

"I know." Lizzy wrapped Zara in a hug. "But that just means I have the ability to do something about the way he acts. I didn't get that until now."

Zara squeezed Lizzy tight and smiled. It felt good to have her best friend back. She pulled away, wiping away her own tears, and addressed the young man who had first come to her rescue. "Hey, thanks," she said. "You didn't have to step in like that."

He shrugged as his mother patted his back with a knowing smile. "Kyle wouldn't be Kyle if he hadn't tried to help. I raise my boys right." She kissed her son's cheek and went back inside.

Kyle blushed and scratched his head. "Well, I have a supply run to get to, so… I guess I'll see you two later?"

Zara grinned. "Actually, Thomas said we need to start going on supply runs to earn our keep and earn a little extra to take with us when we leave. Do you think you'll have room for two more?"

"Uh… yeah, I guess so, if Thomas said so. We're not going far, just out to West Salem. It's only five minutes. Really small. Completely abandoned. We've still got the dollar store to clear out." He started walking toward the back wall of the compound, and Zara and Lizzy followed. "It was just going to be me and Carol today, but you two won't take up much room."

"Carol?" Lizzy asked.

"Yeah. She's our… inventor? I don't know. She has all sorts of crazy ideas." He gestured toward the wall of shipping containers. "That was her idea. It gives us *tons* of storage and great protection. She came up with the wall a few years ago." They walked in silence for a few minutes until they got to the wall. A door had been inserted into it, and Kyle paused outside. "Give me a minute. I'm going to fill Carol in. She's not a huge fan of newbies."

Zara and Lizzy exchanged a look. "Are you sure it's okay that we come?"

Kyle nodded. "Yeah, just… let me butter her up first." He stepped inside the shipping container and closed the door behind him.

Zara nudged Lizzy with her elbow. "He's cute, right?"

Lizzy put her nose in the air. "I'm more mature than that now."

"Oh, really?" Zara laughed. "I find that hard to believe."

"You're right," Lizzy scrunched up her nose, and then they both laughed.

"I missed this," Zara said, catching her breath.

"Me too." Lizzy bumped Zara with her hip, but then she frowned. "What was that with my dad, anyway? I can't believe he grabbed you like that." She lifted Zara's short sleeve. "He didn't really hurt you, did he?"

"Oh, right. You left before Thomas told us about the Heirs of the Mother being part of the Green Earth Futurists." Zara nodded when Lizzy's mouth fell open. "I know. It's nuts." She told Lizzy everything she remembered about what Thomas had revealed.

"Is he sure?" Lizzy started to breathe a little heavier. "I mean, I was part of the GEF for a little while. I never met anyone who was part of a cult."

"Yeah, well, I think your dad thinks Jordan knew what they were doing." Zara whispered, keeping her voice low. "And I think he assumes I knew, too, because Jordan was my brother. And these Heirs did know about the mosquitos before the CDC announced them, so they must have still been a part of the GEF. They must have seen that post on the forum."

"That's ridiculous!" Lizzy licked her lips, still breathing too fast, too hard. She held out a hand and steadied herself against the side of the shipping container. "Jordan would never… *I* would never… the GEF members I knew were all good people."

Zara felt a weight lifted. She had been sure her brother couldn't have been part of anything truly nefarious, but hearing Lizzy say it was soothing to her soul. Lizzy dry heaved, holding her hand to her stomach.

"You okay?" Zara came up behind Lizzy and gathered her hair while Lizzy heaved again, this time losing part of her breakfast. "What's wrong? Are you sick?" She looked around, searching for any signs of mosquitos.

"No… I just…" She didn't look at Zara as she wiped her mouth with the back of her hand. "It's just a lot to take in. I mean, what if… what if *someone* did know what they were doing? Not Jordan or his friends, but… like, their superiors or something?"

Zara rubbed Lizzy's back in circles. "Hey, so what? I mean, we can't change it now, right? It just means people suck. We've known that a long time. Your dad, the GEF, these Heirs of the Mother… maybe they all hold some responsibility." She shrugged. "Maybe even I hold some responsibility. Jordan and I weren't close, and I think that was my fault. I always took up so much attention, with the cancer and then prep school. Mom and Dad always compared us, like I was some kind of superhuman and he was just a troublemaker. If he didn't want to get away from home so badly, maybe he'd still be alive."

"Don't say that, Zee." Lizzy took Zara's hand. "Jordan wanted to go to that school. He wanted to be part of the GEF. That didn't have anything to do with you. And he loved you."

Zara nodded and smiled a little. "I know." She patted Lizzy's back. "You sure you're okay?"

Lizzy nodded. "Yeah." She cleared her throat and her eyes flicked away from Zara. She had that look again, like she was hiding something.

Stop it. You're being stupid. Zara shook it off. Even if she is hiding something, I have to trust her. She wouldn't hide anything that would hurt me. She let go of the assumption that Lizzy knew where the cell phone was. It seemed suddenly ludicrous that Zara had blamed Lizzy at all for her father's actions. I'll get the phone back from Mr. Peters. Ugh… I've been a terrible friend.

She was about to apologize when Kyle came back outside. "Okay, you two ready?" He looked at Lizzy. "You don't look so great."

Lizzy gave him a weak smile. "I was just more upset by that fight with my dad than I thought."

Kyle nodded slowly. "I guess most people would feel that way. I can't imagine if my dad acted like that."

"I should be used to it by now." Lizzy played it off with a laugh, but Kyle only looked at her with pity. Her laughter trailed off awkwardly.

"Okay, then." Zara pulled Lizzy behind her and they entered the shipping container. "Are we here to get supplies, or…"

The two shipping containers that made up with width of the wall had been combined and turned into a sort of garage. Doors led into the containers on either side, and a thin staircase led upward to the second ring. They had been fused together and renovated on the inside to include concrete flooring. Two mid-sized cars were parked facing away from them, and the outside wall of the compound had been converted to include garage doors. Nice though it was, it was stifling hot inside.

"We're not taking these." He led them to the end of the container and opened a door into another, adjoining garage-like room. This one had five four-wheelers with open trailers attached. "Since we're not going far, we're taking these. We can each have one."

"It's the only reason I'm not mad you're coming." A woman with long, braided blonde hair, graying at the temples, shut the door to a cabinet and threw a set of bungee cords in the back of each trailer. "Four people means twice as much space to bring back supplies."

"You must be Carol." Zara held out a hand as Carol approached.

She used one finger to push her huge, round glasses up the bridge of her nose. She did *not* take Zara's hand. "We have to get on the road." Her voice was even and flat. She pointed to the wall where a half dozen homemade beekeeping-like suits hung on the walls. A motorcycle helmet accompanied each one. "We wear those at all times, just in case. If the mosquitos hit while we're out, we need to be prepared."

Lizzy swallowed hard. "I thought this area hadn't seen the mosquitos yet."

"Not yet," Kyle interjected in a friendlier tone. "But better safe than sorry, right, Carol?"

Carol frowned. "Yes, of course." Then she stiffly walked over to the suits and brought down a motorcycle helmet. She pulled thick fabric out of the hollow of the helmet. It was enough to drape over the wearer's shoulders. "This goes under the suit. Have you ever driven a four-wheeler before?"

"Yes," Zara said, and the same time, Lizzy said, "Nope."

"Do you mind sharing?" Kyle asked. "That would be safer. We don't have time to teach you."

"Four is better than two." Carol shook her head. "You promised a one-hundred percent increase, Kyle."

"Carol, a fifty percent increase is still pretty great," Kyle said. "Plus, Thomas is on board."

Carol cocked her head like she was thinking about it, and then nodded. "Fine. Fifty percent is better than zero." Then she shouted, "Mandy!"

A girl about Zara and Lizzy's age scurried into the room, smiling. "Hey, strangers!"

"Hello," Zara replied, returning the girl's smile.

"Mandy." Carol continued to speak in a monotone voice. "We're leaving."

"Right." Mandy pulled out a set of keys from her pocket. "I'll get the padlocks."

"Padlocks?" Zara asked.

"The garage doors are padlocked to the floor so no one can get in from the outside. Ever." Mandy flashed a sweet smile at Kyle; he blushed back at her but smiled sheepishly.

"How do we get back inside?" Zara looked between Mandy and Kyle. *Well, I guess he's taken.*

Mandy turned toward the garage doors as she sorted through a key ring. "We do a knock with a certain rhythm on the garage door. I'll be back here in four hours, and I'll stay until you return, waiting."

"We only knock if it's all clear." Carol grabbed a suit and stepped into it, keeping her clothes on. "If the crazies follow us, we lead them away."

"Has that ever happened?" Lizzy asked.

"No," Kyle said, waving his hand reassuringly.

"There's a first time for everything," Carol said as she put her arms into the suit. "You three better get suited up. There are gloves in the pockets. Two sets. Medical gloves and then leather gloves on top."

"It gets uncomfortably hot," Kyle said. "You sure you guys want to come?"

"We have to start sometime, and I definitely don't want to stay here all day," Zara said.

Lizzy agreed, and before long, they were all suited up, helmets on. After Carol stuck a few more things in her trailer, including some tarps and a crowbar, it was time to go. Mandy opened the garage door, and they exited the shipping container wall one at a time, trailers rumbling over the grass behind. Zara wished she could feel the wind on her face; instead, she was trapped inside layers of clothes, gloves, and a helmet. Lizzy pressing against her back made it even more uncomfortable and way too hot. She steered the four-wheeler, following Kyle who followed Carol. Zara's teeth chattered as they rolled over uneven ground, and she was grateful when Carol led them onto the road. It was flatter, at least, though the gravel road threw up a lot of dust.

Guards in suits with mesh hanging from their hats greeted them at the end of the road, parting and waving them through. Kyle had been right when he'd said West Salem wasn't far. In fact, once they got on a country road labelled 301 in Pleasant Home, it was a straight shot north to the tiny town. They passed by a subdivision and a trailer park before entering a small business district a few blocks in radius. Zara pulled into the lot of the Dollar General store behind Carol and Kyle, parked, and patted Lizzy's hands which remained clasped tight around her middle.

"You can let go now," Zara said.

"Are you sure?" Lizzy didn't budge.

"We're not moving anymore." Zara twisted to try to look at her friend, but Lizzy was holding her too tight.

"Are you sure?" Lizzy repeated.

Zara laughed and pried Lizzy's fingers apart. "Yes, I'm sure. We were going under the speed limit. Only like forty miles an hour."

"Yeah, but we were *outside* in the open air going forty miles an hour." Lizzy leaned back and patted down her body.

"You would *not* like riding on a motorcycle." Zara chuckled and climbed off the four-wheeler.

Lizzy followed suit, wobbling a little when her feet hit the ground. "I don't plan on trying it any time soon."

Carol approached them and lifted her face shield. "No time to waste. Load up food first. Not the stuff in the refrigerated section. That's already gone bad."

Zara lifted her shield, too. "It's okay to take this off?"

"You can lift the shield. That's easy to snap down if you need to. Don't take the helmet off, just in case." Carol turned on her heel, picked up the crowbar from her trailer, and marched to the door, smashing the glass.

Zara breathed in deeply and stretched her back by twisting right and then left, looking over her shoulder. There were a few businesses across the street, one of them a pawn shop. She smiled and tugged on Lizzy's arm and pointed to the shop. "I bet we could find some things worth trading in there."

Lizzy wrinkled her nose at the rundown pawn shop. Its sign looked like it had started falling off the building a long time ago. "In there? Are you sure?"

"Have you ever been in a pawn shop?" Zara walked toward the shop. "They're full of random stuff, a lot of it useful."

"I guess it wouldn't hurt." Lizzy followed, picking up a brick when they got closer and handing it to Zara. "You'll need to break the window."

Zara took the brick and threw it through the glass door, shattering it. She found another brick and smashed the remaining shards out of the frame before stepping inside, shoes crunching the glass. "Jackpot," Zara said, grinning ear to ear. Rifles, guns, and knives took up an entire wall of the shop.

"Hey," Kyle's voice sounded from behind them, "what are you guys doing?" He stopped and gaped at the discovery. "Whoa. I guess we should have looked in here. I'll help you load these up. Thomas is going to be super excited."

"What about the jewelry?" Lizzy had gravitated toward a glass case full of rings, necklaces, and earrings.

"I don't know if we need to bother with it," Kyle said.

"We can take the wedding rings at least," Zara said. "People will still want to get married. It could be a great bartering chip with that guy who flies the plane."

Kyle shrugged. "A small bag of rings or whatever won't take up much space. Might as well."

"I'll leave my dad's information at the register." Lizzy hopped over the counter and ripped off paper from the old receipt roll on the cash register. She found a pen and started writing.

"No one is ever going to come back here for this stuff." Kyle shook his head. "That's a waste of time."

Zara shrugged. "Maybe not. If it makes her feel better, I think it's nice."

"Are you going to leave your dad's information at every place you go?" Kyle laughed. "That's nuts. This stuff doesn't belong to anyone anymore."

Lizzy frowned and stopped writing. "He's right." She put down the pen. "The world is never going back to normal."

Zara chewed on her lower lip. "Maybe the world won't," she said, walking over to the jewelry case and smashing the brick through it. "But we will." She pulled out one ring with a blue sapphire setting in the shape of a butterfly and another with a ruby and onyx setting in the shape of a ladybug. She held out the butterfly. "Lizzy Peters, will you officially be my very best friend for life… again?"

Lizzy laughed and took the ring. She glanced over her shoulder at Kyle, wrinkled her nose, and quickly ripped off the gloves on one hand. "Ah-ha!" she said when it fit on her thumb. "It fits. I would love to swear to always be your BFF, Zara Williams."

Zara couldn't help but laugh as Lizzy motioned for her to take her glove off as well. "Fine," she said under breath. "Just for a second."

Lizzy took the butterfly ring from Zara and tried it on all of Zara's fingers until it slid perfectly onto her pinky finger. "You, Zara Williams, are the cheesiest girl I know, and I wouldn't have it any other way. Best friends for life?"

Zara gave her a thumb's up. "You got it, dude!"

"Is that from that old sitcom from like a million years ago?" Kyle asked, looking at the two girls like they'd gone nuts. "What was it… Full House?"

Lizzy laughed. "I have no idea."

"Hey!" Kyle frowned and sighed. "C'mon guys. Put your gloves back on."

Lizzy was already doing so, slipping both pairs over her ringed finger. "Calm down," she said. "We're not stupid."

Zara followed suit, the ring under the gloves signaling a fresh start. For the first time since the day of the World's Fair, Zara felt light. Lizzy started singing some modern pop song Zara only knew the chorus to, and so she belted out a few lines every time they came around, dancing as she filled a sack with gold and silver. She tried not to think about how she hoped the jewelry would pay for passage to Boston. As they loaded the trailers first with items from the pawn shop and then with canned goods from the dollar store, Zara pushed away everything that had happened in the last two weeks. She'd almost forgotten what it was like to have fun. She even got Kyle to join in, twirling her and Lizzy in the aisles.

Reality settled back in soon enough. Once they were loaded up, Zara got back onto the four-wheeler. Lizzy climbed on behind her, and they started back toward the compound where Walter Peters waited for Zara. She wouldn't be able to escape once curfew fell, but the idea of a confrontation with Mr. Peters didn't sound so bad anymore. She had her best friend back by her side. They'd figure out whatever life threw at them together.

Chapter 30

Alexander Roman

There is no third option. Lawson had left Alex with those words, and after an entire night of racking his brain, Alex had come to the horrible conclusion that if he couldn't get evidence to the president and to Hunt, Lawson was right. *Actually, even if I do get the recording to them, if Lawson and Price's men have as much power as they think they do, delivering the evidence just might be my death sentence – and Hunt's and Coleman's.*

The safest, sanest course of action was to do as Lawson wanted. Except, there was one massive problem. Alex didn't think he really could create a vaccine or treatment, not before the generators failed or the sickness found a way in, and certainly not ethically with the way Ward and Turner operated. If he played along with Lawson's plan, there was a good chance he'd simply be buying time. And if, by some miracle, a vaccine, treatment, or cure *was* discovered quickly enough, he'd be part of creating a new dictatorship.

If only I could get to Boston and talk to Walter Peters, or even just someone at New Horizons, we could stop the spread of the disease through the mosquito population. He'd had all night, alone, to think about it. His best guess was that the world was suffering from a terrorist attack gone very, very wrong. The mosquito population's ability to carry and spread the virus must have made for the perfect storm. The virus was released worldwide in key locations, and then the mosquitos picked it up and made it worse, intensifying the virus's spread wherever human carriers went. Surely that was an unintended consequence… The work Vanguard was doing with their subsidiary laboratory to eradicate disease carrying mosquitos could be the key to significantly slowing the virus. It has to be. That has to be why Jonah wanted me to go to Boston.

The fact that Dr. Jonah Newton and his team of top-notch scientists not only failed to create a vaccine before the disease killed them but that Newton had used his last breath to tell Alex to find Walter Peters had to be taken into account. Alex respected Jonah's wisdom, knowledge, and abilities more than any other person he'd ever met. *Jonah knew the answers wouldn't be found fast enough here.* Questions niggled at the back of Alex's mind that he couldn't answer; as they festered, they left him with a gut feeling that Jonah knew more than he'd had time to say. *Why did he believe Walter Peters was the answer? What did that whistleblower say, exactly?*

Something Lauren had said days prior popped into his head. *Or Walter Peters had something to do with it in the first place.* He'd dismissed her comment, chalking it up to her consistent role of devil's advocate. Lauren tended to be pessimistic, and he hadn't wanted to consider that New Horizons – a laboratory lauded as one of the best humanitarian companies in the country – would have something to do with releasing such a monstrosity of a virus. He shook his head. *No… even if they had developed the virus, why release it in the States? They all live and work here. That doesn't make sense.* He tucked Lauren's comment away once again. All throughout his training, he'd always been told when hoofbeats approached, it was unwise to look for zebras when the likely culprit was a run-of-the-mill horse. It was best to attack the problem from the simplest and most plausible angle first.

Alex sighed from his spot on the floor and tapped the back of his head on the empty cabinets. The medical exam chair had sat empty all night; there was no way he was going to be found sleeping in that thing. If they were going to zip-tie him to it, they were going to have to fight him first. He had no idea what their plans for him entailed. Lawson had mentioned one more test, but he'd left out any details.

The sound of a metal lock sliding out of place made Alex scramble to his feet. He winced with the movement; his shoulder and back were full of kinks due to his time sleeping on the unforgiving, rock-hard flooring. He touched his outer thigh where the letter opener was sewn to the inside of his boxers. Its weight provided some comfort. The entire room had been emptied of anything that could have been used as a weapon – he hadn't even been able to find a pencil. The handle of the five-inch letter opener reached almost to the top of his waistband. It wasn't a perfect weapon, but it would do in a pinch. Hopefully.

Joanna Ward stepped into the room and let the door shut behind her. "Hello, Mr. Roman." Her voice was cold, her expression steely. "I hear you've been keeping secrets."

"About the obvious CRISPR red flags?" Alex stared at the door, expecting more people to come through it, but it didn't budge. "I would have told you eventually," he said.

"You just needed to find the best way to make me look the fool first?" Her words dripped with venom as her lips curled into a near snarl. "Well, congratulations. Despite everything I've done for Mr. Lawson, all the progress I've made, he now questions my abilities because some know-it-all caught an inconsequential detail I missed."

"I wouldn't call it inconsequential," Alex said. "At the very least, it's a demonstration of why you need me. I'm trained for this."

Joanna narrowed her eyes. "So am I. My career might have taken a turn into the mundane, but I know what I'm doing. You might help us find out the *what* when it comes to this virus, but I'm going to find out the *how* when it comes to the cure. Everyone is going to know my name by the end of this, and you're just going to be a footnote in history."

Alex shrugged. "Hey, I'm not here to rain on your parade. All I want is to keep my family safe and to build a better future for my son."

"And secure a place in Lawson's new world," Joanna said.

"Sure. I'd rather be chilling in a penthouse than dead on the streets. You've got me." Alex crossed his arms and tried to give off a vibe of indifference as Joanna walked around the exam chair, her shoes clicking on the floor. "What do you want, anyway?" he asked. "I thought Lawson said I had some sort of test to complete. Are you part of that?"

She laughed, the sound sending a shiver down Alex's spine. "No," she said. "I asked to be the one to come and fetch you. Lawson, Price, and Turner are waiting for us."

"Okay… then why aren't we leaving?" Alex asked.

She made her way around the chair and perched on the edge of the seat. Then she slid into it, crossed her legs, and tapped her fingers on the arms of the chair. "I needed you to understand something before we moved forward. This is *my* project. I am the visionary here. If you threaten my place again, I'll find a way to hurt you. And considering that you came with three lovely attachments, I don't think I'll have to look very far to find your vulnerabilities."

Alex clenched his hands into fists at her threat, every muscle in his body tensing. He had to keep his cool, make her think he was on her side; it wasn't easy. He bit the inside of his cheek to stop his immediate counterthreat, breathing in and out through his nose slowly, calmly. "Okay, Joanna. I get it. Like I said, I'm just here to keep my family safe. Whatever you want me to do, I'll do it." *I have to get out of here. I can't live like this, someone always threatening to harm Oliver or Minnie or Lauren.*

Once he passed the test Lawson had set up for him, he had to get the recording to Hunt. People like Lawson, Price, and Ward couldn't be allowed to take over. If they somehow figured out a treatment, they would bleed the population dry in exchange for their lives. And if they never did figure it out, they would practically enslave any living soul who might — like they were doing to him. Either way, humanity lost.

Joanna smiled. "If we understand each other, I think we can move on." She stood up and opened the door, gesturing for him to go first. "We're going to the BSL-4 labs. I believe you know where they are."

Alex stepped out into the hall in between two Suits. He caught a glimpse of the door out, and then forced his feet to walk away from it. Trying to escape wouldn't work, not with so many guards stationed throughout the area. And if he tried now, any chance he had of maintaining his cover of compliance with Ward — and therefore Lawson — would be gone. Every step away from that outer door was like swimming deeper into the dark depths of the ocean while the last bit of oxygen left his lungs. He pushed forward anyway.

Get it over with. When I'm outside their territory, I can flee. I can find Hunt or Conner. I can get my family out of here somehow. For now, do what they want.

Ward took the lead, and Alex followed her to a block of BSL-4 labs he hadn't been inside since his arrival. They were the same ones the Suits had been taking Minnie to when he'd stopped them a couple days back. He frowned as he stepped past the block entrance and into the single hall that led to four laboratories.

"I thought these were being used to imprison criminals. What are we doing here?" he asked.

Joanna gave him a tight-lipped smile and opened one of the steel doors. "You're about to find out," she said in a sickly-sweet voice. "Lawson, Price, and Turner are already inside."

He followed her inside. "I guess it's time to suit up?"

She gestured toward the full-bodied, air-supplied, positive-pressure suits. "Take your pick."

Alex grabbed a folded cotton jumpsuit and an air-supplied, positive-pressure suit. He began to change into the jumpsuit, his stomach churning as he folded his pants and made sure the shape of the slim voice recorder didn't show through the fabric. His letter opener would be hidden underneath underwear, a jumpsuit, and an airtight protective suit. It had provided him with some measure of comfort up to that point, but as he changed, its weight against his thigh mocked him.

In a BSL-4 lab, he would be trapped with four morally bankrupt souls who would expect him to comply. Would they force him to infect a chimp? It made sense for them to keep the remaining specimens in one of these labs. Joanna could have noticed how uncomfortable their experiments had made him in the first place. Or they could force him to personally put biotoxins in food meant for his family if he chose not to comply. They could have concocted all sorts of loyalty tests that would make Alex sweat. As he went through the motions of preparing to enter the lab, his heartbeat steadily picked up pace. His suit filled with air and puffed out a bit from his body, the speakers crackling to life as he switched them on at an outward switch on the neck of the suit. He prepared himself; whatever they wanted him to do, for the sake of his life and the lives of his family, he *had* to do it.

When he entered the lab, Lawson stood next to the larger eight-by-four glove box, leaning against it, his own suit puffed out around him. He held a clipboard in one hand, and he was flipping through the pages. Price stood next to him, his normal stance — hands clasped at the front — almost comical in the positive pressure suit.

Turner was preparing a tray next to the glove box, arranging tools in order of size. He smiled at Alex through his helmet's clear face shield. "Hey, man. Sorry about before. You know how it is. Gotta do whatcha gotta do. We cool?"

Alex held back the biting remarks on his tongue and instead pasted on his own smile. "We're cool, Blake. I get it."

"Awesome." Turner continued arranging the tools.

Alex breathed deeply as he walked over to the glove box, peering down inside, expecting to see a chimp. It was empty. Relief flooded over him for only a moment. *What am I doing here, then?*

Joanna entered in her own suit, securing the door behind her. That door had no handle on the laboratory side, and it blended in with the wall when it closed. The room seemed to shrink, the walls closing in. Alex focused on breathing normally. His insides twisted and writhed, adrenaline pumping through his veins, overloading his system, making his stomach flip-flop.

Lawson finished with the clipboard and let the hand holding it drop to the side. He held out his other hand toward the climate-controlled cells attached to the lab. "Please, after you, Mr. Roman."

Price opened the door to the cells, and Alex walked toward the doorway. His heart pounded. Something wasn't right. Would they stick him in a cell? His feet were heavy as lead and getting heavier with every step. Ward, Lawson, and Turner were right behind him. They could block him in, and he'd be stuck. To his family, he'd just be gone.

No, they still need me. They have my family to hold over my head. That's where their threats lie. That thought made him pause. His family had already been threatened multiple times. Lawson could have taken any one of them and put them in these cells. His heart thrashed against his ribcage, but his feet lightened. He closed the gap to the doorway quickly, rushing to see what was waiting beyond it.

His first reaction was utter relief. Oliver, Minnie, and Lauren were not there. His next reaction was pure horror because there *was* a person trapped in a center cell, enclosed by clear walls that offered no dignity. It was an older man, and he lay on a bench at the back of the cell. He sat up when Alex entered, and their eyes met.

No. Alex couldn't breathe. He couldn't swallow. He drifted toward the door to the cell, eyes locked with the prisoner's sad gaze.

"You were right," Joanna said, her voice too distant in Alex's ears for how close she was. "We have run out of chimps. We're going to get closer to a cure faster using human specimens. Sacrifice a few to save the many."

"We play hard ball here," Lawson said, handing him the clipboard. "This is his chart. Look it over. We need to take everything we know about him into consideration before we begin."

"Has he already been infected?" Alex asked. The man's wrinkled face contorted, and a tear slid down one cheek at Alex's words.

"Nah, poor guy," Turner said. "You've got this one start to finish."

The clipboard could have been a thousand pounds with how he struggled to hold it up. Alex stared at it, blinking, trying to get the words to come into focus. *My family... if I don't... how can I?*

"Is there a problem, Mr. Roman?" Lawson asked. "Are you unable to do what needs to be done? This is about saving the human race. Losing one old man who wouldn't even be alive today without modern medicine is worth it." Lawson tapped on the glass, a look of pride on his face. "And he'll have a legacy. His name will go down in history books as a volunteer that helped save the world. I'll make a memorial or something."

Alex's mouth felt like he'd stuffed it with cotton. The first line on the medical chart had come into focus, and he hadn't been able to move past it. The man in the cell, the man Lawson wanted Alex to infect with the virus — his name was Elijah Dixon.

Chapter 31

Timothy Peters

Timothy came to, ears still ringing, gasping for breath before he even opened his eyes. Sooty air clogged his throat, and he coughed violently, spitting out the acrid taste of ash. He blinked away grime, eyes stinging. His vision cleared as someone shoved him.

"Tim!" Heather was halfway pinned underneath him. As she spoke, her voice slowly overpowered the ringing. "Get up. Are you awake? Tim?" She shoved him again.

He grunted and pressed his hands against the floor to push himself off her. He heaved himself to a sitting position, his chest tight, his head spinning. "I think I'm okay," he said, his own voice sounding muffled in his ears. He patted his body, glad to find it in one piece. He was also glad to find the walkie talkie Frank had used to eavesdrop broken open, only the back half of it still attached to his cargo pants. The sticky note pad and pen was still in his pocket. *Guess I won't be needing those anymore.* He turned his attention to his wife. "How about you? Are you hurt?"

"I'm fine." Heather sat up, favoring her injured side, and scooted closer to him, touching his chin and gently moving his head to the side. "The back of your head was hit." She scooted some more and leaned forward, pulling back with a gasp. "Your back is torn up and burnt. Can't you feel that?"

He frowned; his body was numb, his head light. "I don't think so. How bad is it?"

She grimaced. "Don't worry about it right now." She got to her feet. "Can you get up?"

He blinked rapidly and shielded his eyes from the sunlight. He was sitting on the floor of the living room in the farmhouse, but there was no ceiling. Some walls remained standing; others had been blown outward or had chunks missing. A beam was angled over them, lodged in the splintered floor. *It must have shielded us from the debris.*

"Tim?" Heather held out her hand.

He took it and struggled to his feet, using her hand and the beam to gain his feet. A blown-out window created a framework for viewing the front yard. The four police cars remained untouched; they'd been far enough from the blasts to escape damage. Closer to the house, O'Donnell, uniform even more tattered than before, limped into view and draped his singed police uniform button-down shirt over Abram's body. Abram's dog, Moose, whined at her side, but he didn't seem ill. *That's odd. The deer, the birds… they were affected.*

The wall to Timothy's right was gone, opening up to a view of a crater at the edge of the cornfield. Everyone had been in the living room, most of them crowded near the windows when Frank had detonated the bomb in the attic. It hadn't been enough to bring the house down, at least not yet. What was left of it could collapse at any moment. Officers tended to each other, many of them out on the lawn already, a few searching the rubble at the back of the living room.

"Where's Candice?" As if on cue, a frustrated grunt followed by a squeak came from behind them. He turned to find Candice falling backward as she dislodged a suitcase. Timothy rolled his eyes, but he couldn't help a relieved smile. "We should get out of the house before the rest of it falls in on itself," he said. "Candice, let's go."

She sniffed as she got to her feet and lugged the suitcase toward the front door which hung on its hinges. Candice held her head high though her clothes were covered in dirt and soot, her hair was singed, and blood soaked through her expensive jeans from a wound on her knee. Her forehead boasted a goose egg, and small cuts littered her body. "I've already decided to let the other one go," she said, a pained look on her face as she nodded toward her suitcase. "I couldn't find it."

Heather shook her head as Candice made her way outside, and then she and Timothy hobbled toward the right-hand side where the debris created less of an obstacle course to the yard. "I think most of us made it," she said as they hopped off the floor of the house into the grass.

"I found her!" One of the officers searching the debris in the house shouted. He frantically threw aside chunks of plaster and wood.

Timothy held out a hand and stopped a woman officer jogging past him. "Who are we missing? Who's still in there?"

Her face was grim. "Ellis," she said. "I think he's found Ellis."

"Oh no." Heather bit her lower lip and craned her neck to see back inside the house.

Timothy watched with his wife by his side as four officers in singed and bloodied clothes, their bodies bruised and covered in lacerations, pulled Ellis out of the rubble and carried her to the grass. He gasped when the officers stepped away, huddled together, and held each other. Ellis stared back at him, her eyes lifeless.

"She was good to us," Heather said.

Timothy's heart broke for the officers gathering around the second of their own lost in one morning. "There are enough people dying in the world without us killing each other." A surge of anger tempered by sadness flowed through him. *Why can't people stop taking from each other?*

Candice limped up beside them, her chin quivering. "What are we going to do now?"

"We're gonna kill Frank Russo." O'Donnell's gritty, angry voice carried across the yard, causing everyone to turn and look in his direction.

Timothy was about to object when the squeal of tires on the road interrupted him. He craned his neck to see Frank and a dozen men get out of several vehicles. They all had guns in their hands. And none of them had just been knocked out and banged up by a bomb. Even so, O'Donnell balled his fists and squared his shoulders like he was preparing for a fight.

"No, no, no…" Timothy softly repeated as he limped forward. O'Donnell stepped toward Frank and his men, and Timothy shouted. "Stop!"

O'Donnell growled. "He killed Abrams and Ellis. He's gotta pay."

"If we don't deescalate this, Frank will be responsible for killing *all* of your officers," Timothy said. O'Donnell was larger than he was and had escaped injury. The rage in his eyes would have had Timothy clamping his mouth shut a few weeks ago. But he was positive attacking Frank would get them all killed. "Take a second and *look* at your people."

He drew in a sharp breath and unfurled his hands as he scanned the yard, but then the resolve in his eyes seemed to redouble. "Frank isn't just going to leave. We have to—"

"—survive." Timothy cut O'Donnell off, surprising even himself with his stern, quick response. The other officers were gathering around O'Donnell, drawing their guns, eyes flitting from O'Donnell to Frank's men. When Timothy spoke, they all seemed to gravitate toward him. "Abrams's last request was that we get out of here. Ellis was a healer. She would have wanted the same. If we engage Frank, we die."

O'Donnell's expression remained hardened until Heather spoke. "I seem to remember you swore to Abrams that you would look for Lissa at The Farm. Are you going to break that promise?"

His face fell, and O'Donnell glanced at Abrams's body. "What do you suggest, Peters?"

"Let me talk to Frank." Timothy took a deep breath. "I think I know what to say."

"I'm coming with you," O'Donnell said.

"Fine, but… just let me do the talking. Frank has this thing about owing debts or being square. He'll… appreciate an argument centered around that." Timothy's skin crawled as he limped forward. He hated the familiarity of Frank's face, the way he smiled as Timothy came closer. The mobster had tried to kill Timothy over and over, and yet… the man didn't seem to harbor any hatred toward Timothy. Frank seemed to *like* Timothy, and somehow that made interactions with him so much worse. *What kind of person is so ready to murder people they actually like?*

"Southie!" Frank said, holding out his hands like he was ready for a hug as Timothy walked across the little bridge over the ditch. "You're alive. You know, you and me got that in common. A couple o' roaches. Ain't nobody gettin' rid of us that easy."

"Can't argue with you there," Timothy said. "I'm hoping we can both live a little longer."

Frank shrugged. "I don't know 'bout that, Southie." He smirked at O'Donnell. "Shoulda known you cops weren't good for it when it came to your word."

"We were gonna negotiate," O'Donnell said. "That part wasn't a lie. We just didn't want bein' blown up to be hangin' over our heads."

Frank laughed. "Yeah, okay. I get it." He pointed at Timothy. "It's his fault, really, then, ain't it? If he hadn't told you, you wouldna dug up my explosives. We woulda had a nice talk, and then we'd be sailin' to Boston ready to get rid of CON." He held up his hand, palm out and fingers spread wide, sweeping it in front of him with a mocking expression. "The Russos and the Boys, skippin', holdin' hands. Besties for life. Can't you see it?"

"Yeah, right. Until you didn't like what they had to say." Timothy crossed his arms. "We both know you were looking forward to pressing that detonator."

"You know me too well." Frank grinned and dropped his hand, showing all his teeth. "In any case, I'd like to get on with my day, so I think we're just gonna kill all of yous and break for lunch." He raised his gun, and O'Donnell had his own weapon trained on the mobster in seconds. The mobsters and cops each followed suit.

"Wait," Timothy said, holding out his hands and stepping between O'Donnell and Frank. He looked at Frank. "The way I see it, you and me are even. You and the cops are even. Call it a truce. Let us go free those kids from CON. The cops won't come for your supplies ever again."

Frank narrowed his eyes and worked his jaw back and forth. "How d'ya figure we're all even?"

"We were even when I came over here with the walkie talkie, right?" Timothy said.

"Yeah, sure," Frank said, "but then you betrayed me."

"And then you bombed me." Timothy raised his eyebrows, daring Frank to argue with that.

"I guess you got a point." Frank nodded at O'Donnell. "And them? They came here to steal my stuff. They been givin' me problems for days." He smirked. "Years, really, even when things were normal. I ain't lived a day in my life where the cops and the Russos were on good terms."

"Well, first, they didn't steal your stuff," Timothy said. "And even if they *were* going to, again… you tried to blow them up."

"They killed two o' my guys. What 'bout that?" Frank pursed his lips.

"You killed two of theirs." Timothy licked his lips. "And you injured every single one of them."

"Huh." Frank pushed out his cheek with his tongue and narrowed his eyes at Timothy. He dropped his gun back to his side, though his men kept theirs aimed. After several very long seconds, Frank shrugged. "Yeah, okay." He eyed O'Donnell. "On the count o' three, everybody put their guns down. Deal?"

O'Donnell nodded and motioned for his officers to put their guns down. "Deal."

Frank counted to three, and everyone very slowly lowered their weapons. Then Frank pointed at O'Donnell. "You get outta my territory. Don't come back."

"We won't," O'Donnell said.

Before Frank got back in his car, he pointed down the road. "We'll pull back toward the ranch, but we'll be watchin' to make sure you leave. My guys'll follow you to the highway." He didn't wait for a reply before ducking into the back seat of a black car with tinted windows.

Frank's men did as he said they would, and within minutes, Timothy stood with O'Donnell on the little bridge as they retreated up the road.

"That's not the last time Frank Russo will bring us trouble, is it?" O'Donnell said.

"I'd be shocked if it was." Timothy winced as he limped back toward the vehicles. His back was starting to sting, the skin tight, a sharp tingling sensation spreading over his shoulder blades.

O'Donnell slowly walked to one of the vehicles and opened the driver's door. "Let's load up," he said. "Leave the dead. We can't risk bringin' Abrams's body, and Ellis… we don't have time to bury her."

"What about Moose?" one of the officers asked.

O'Donnell looked at the dog who was still sitting by Abrams's side. "I doubt we'd get him to leave her, and even if we could, we don't know if he's infectious."

Heather bit her lower lip and said softly to Timothy, "That poor dog. He saved us, too, and we're just leaving him? It's not right."

Timothy squeezed his wife's hand. "O'Donnell is right. And Moose will be okay." He kissed Heather's forehead.

After Candice somehow convinced one of the officers to stick her suitcase in one of the trunks, Timothy and Heather joined her in the back of O'Donnell's car. Timothy had to lean forward to keep his back from bumping the seat as they drove off, but despite the pain, he was flooded with relief. It didn't happen the way he'd thought it would, but he was leaving with help. He could only pray the small force of police officers would be enough to get George and Annika back.

Chapter 32

Alexander Roman

Time had slowed. Alex's heartbeat thudded in his ears, the sound muffling everything else. He took hold of the sharp pencil lodged in the clip of the board he held before him, pretending to use it to guide his reading. Another beat of his heart thrashed against his chest and pounded in his head. Alex glanced up from the medical chart. Elijah Dixon. Minnie's friend. By all accounts, a kind and optimistic man, lonely without his cat. A normal, innocent man. A survivor. Alex's temples pulsed. The old man had barely made a sound or moved a muscle since slowly sitting up to keep his eyes on Alex and the others. His tears weren't accompanied by pleas for mercy or trembling, only by a sorrowful gaze.

"Your first step is to administer the sedative." Joanna stepped against the wall so that Blake could hold out a syringe toward Alex. "Price will help you hold him down, if need be."

Price cracked his knuckles. "He doesn't look like he'll cause too much trouble."

Alex's tongue was stuck to the roof of his mouth. He cleared his throat and looked at the syringe in Turner's open palm. He stepped up to it and reached out with a barely steady hand to grasp the sedative. The hall in front of the row of four cells was crowded, and even though the positive-pressure suit provided him with a clear, three-hundred-and-sixty-degree face shield and plenty of oxygen, a claustrophobic anxiety settled over him and his head was too light, his body too heavy. Turner offered him an encouraging smile that only served to make Alex's stomach churn. His fingers closed around the syringe.

Price pressed a button on the outside of the cell and the door slid open. "If he tries anything, I'll hold him down." Then he looked to Elijah. "Let's make this easy, shall we?"

"Yeah, man," Turner said, "don't make it worse, okay? Just go with it. It'll be over soon."

Joanna pinched her lips together but didn't speak, and Lawson stepped back against the wall, his body settling as he watched Alex with something of an eager anticipation. Alex took the clipboard with Elijah's medical chart, the pencil, and the syringe into the cell, stepping past Price and putting everyone but Elijah behind him. The old man looked up at him, unmoving, eyes misty.

This isn't right. I'll never be able to look Oliver in the eyes again. "Mr. Dixon," Alex said, "I'd like to do a quick examination before we get started."

"That's not necessary," Joanna said. "We have all the information on his medical chart."

"If I'm going to do this," Alex hissed over his shoulder, "let me do it my way."

"Let him work, Ms. Ward," Lawson said.

Alex held the syringe in two fingers as he grasped the clipboard with the same hand. He came closer to Elijah. "I swear I'll make this easy for you," he said. "As quick and as painless as possible." *Four of them, one of me. They'll kill my family… infect them or torture them. I have to do this, don't I?* He reached out with his free hand. "I'm just going to check your lymph nodes." His gloved fingers pressed against Elijah's neck, warmth seeping through the vinyl gloves. Alex's own heartbeat raced at the feeling of Elijah's pulse.

"Please," Elijah whispered, finally speaking. "I don't want to die."

Alex pulled back his hand. The churning in his stomach had spread; his whole body writhed inside. *I can't. I won't.* He breathed out slowly, his only course of action becoming clear to him. *I'm probably going to die, but at least I'll take a few of these bastards with me. And if I'm dead, my family have no value as leverage. Maybe they'll just move Oliver, Minnie, and Lauren to the dorms and forget about them.*

He pulled out the pencil and wrote: *Run. Get as far as you can. Minnie says hi.* "Mr. Dixon, there are no allergies checked off on this list," Alex said. "Just to be sure, can you double check it for me? I wouldn't want your experience to be any more painful than it already has to be."

"This is ridiculous." Joanna's clipped words interrupted Alex.

"Do you want our results to be skewed because of an unforeseen complication?" Alex asked. "Or are you just so reckless you don't even care?"

"Joanna," Lawson said, "I told you to let him work."

Alex showed Elijah the chart and tapped the pencil next to his note. "You have no other allergies, correct?"

Elijah frowned and wiped away moisture from his eyes with trembling hands. His frown deepened as he leaned slightly forward toward the chart. "I… yes, that's right."

"I know this is difficult," Alex said, pulling the clipboard back, "but I need you to comply. Are you ready?" Price is the biggest physical threat. And then there's the problem of getting trapped inside this cell if anyone closes the door. His very bones thrummed with apprehension and a prickling sensation circulated throughout his body. Minnie… take care of Oliver for me.

"I'm ready," Elijah said.

Alex nodded, gripping the clipboard in one hand and taking the still-capped syringe in his other. He took a deep breath, and then as quickly as his suit would allow, he whipped around and flung the clipboard through the open cell door right at Ward's head. It wouldn't hurt her, but it did do as he hoped it would. She yelped and dodged out of the way, a look of surprise on her face. In the same movement, he leapt forward and slammed into Price's middle, pushing him into the hall and ramming him against the wall. They slid to the floor, grappling. Price's fists pounded Alex's back as Alex clung to his midsection. As Price tried to get Alex off of him, Alex grasped at the snaps on the side of Price's positive-pressure suit that hid the zipper just beneath the underarm.

"Turner!" Ward screamed. "Get more sedative."

One snap came undone. As they struggled, Price's elbow jabbed into Alex's shoulder blade, the impact pushing Alex into the wall. His head bounced off the wall, and he winced at the smarting pain. He managed to rip another snap apart before Price threw Alex to the floor. On his way down, he almost hit Elijah's legs as the old man tried to shimmy toward the doorway into the laboratory area.

"Do something," Lawson growled, and Joanna sidestepped Alex as Price straddled him. She grabbed a fistful of Elijah's clothing, and the two began to struggle.

"Turner!" Joanna screeched. "What the hell are you doing?"

"I'm going as fast as I can! I dropped the key," Turner shouted back.

Price's hands went for Alex's neck, but the positive-pressure suit and the air pumped into it created too much of a bubble for Price to clamp down and cut off Alex's air supply. Whatever training Price had, he wasn't adapting to the puffy suits very well. He bore down, teeth clenched, brow creased in concentration. A surge of hope emboldened Alex at Price's inability to reach his neck through the suit, and he snatched the zipper, jerking it down. A steady stream of air rushed out of the hole, but Price didn't seem to notice. Alex used his thumb to dislodge the cap on the syringe. He plunged the needle into the hole in the suit and pushed past the resistance of the cotton jumpsuit underneath. Price's eyes widened as he flinched away from Alex's hand, and at that moment, Alex plunged the sedative into his body.

"What did you do?" Price screamed as he scrambled away, getting to his feet and backing away, trying to see the hole under his armpit. He stepped into the open cell, frantically clawing at the side of his suit.

Chest heaving and heart pounding, Alex got to his feet, his eyes on the button that closed the door. He leapt for it, his palm slamming against it to close the door on Price. He glanced at Elijah who somehow managed to shove Joanna in the farthest of the four cells and close it tight. She was on the ground inside the cell, holding her ankle. Just as Alex opened his mouth to ask if Elijah was okay, Lawson grabbed a fist full of his suit and yanked him backwards. Then Lawson tried to open the door to Price's cell, and Alex threw all his weight into the older man, knocking Lawson against the wall.

Lawson growled and slammed Alex face-first into the closed door of the cell so that his face stuck to his shield. As Alex batted at his face, Lawson said, "You ungrateful idiot. You could have had whatever you wanted. You could have—"

A blur in Alex's periphery was accompanied by Lawson's howl of pain. Lawson let go and stepped away, his hand searching his own back. Elijah was there, grimacing, and when Lawson turned in a circle as he swatted at his back, Alex raised his eyebrows at a scalpel pinning his suit to his back, the air puffed out around the metallic tool. Not wasting another second, Alex pushed Lawson into the third empty cell and closed the door.

"Where did you get that?" Alex asked, breathing heavily.

"It was on a tray outside the door." Elijah shrugged.

"Turner!" Ward yelled from her cell, drawing his name out in a tone that was half plea, half spite.

"I got it," Turner entered the hall, holding up the syringe over his head like it was a prize. He looked wide-eyed at his three companions in cells and then turned his attention on Alex and Elijah. He gulped and lowered his hand. His eyes flicked to the nearest cell where Joanna sat.

"Don't do it, Turner," Alex said. "None of this is right, and you know it."

"Sorry, man." Turner flung himself toward the button to open the cell door, but Alex barreled into him and knocked him into the lab, falling on his back, Alex on top of him. The syringe skidded across the laboratory floor as Alex and Turner fought.

"Get the syringe!" Alex yelled. He could hear Elijah shuffling past, and he got to work on Turner's snaps and zipper. He pinned the weaker man down on his stomach. Alex laid on top of Turner's back as the suit deflated once the zipper was undone, and then he grasped Turner's hands and stopped him from flailing.

"What do I do?" Elijah asked, voice trembling.

"Inject him where I unzipped his suit," Alex instructed. "Don't move, Turner, or I'll have to knock you out."

"Okay, okay. Don't hurt me, man. I was just trying to help people." Turner whimpered.

"You weren't tryin' to help me." Elijah scoffed and then plunged the sedative into Turner's body.

Alex stayed put a few minutes until Turner was out cold, and then he dragged the scientist into the last cell and closed the door. "I can't believe that worked." Price and Turner were splayed on the floor, unconscious. Lawson was taking his punctured and deflated suit off in quick, angry motions, the bloodied scalpel lying at his feet, and Ward sat against the wall of her cell, her suit still on, wincing in pain and prodding at her ankle. Ward and Lawson had some choice words for him, so he gestured for Elijah to go back into the laboratory where they could close the door to the little hall. Alex noticed one last capped syringe Turner must have dropped. He picked it up and rubbed the back of his neck, a wave of dread washing away the moment of relief. *One dose of sedative and a letter opener against how many security guards in the halls?*

"We're home free!" Elijah clapped his hands together.

"Not quite." Alex walked toward the exit. "We still have to get out of this lab, get passed the guard at the entrance to this lab block, make it out of the restricted zone which is also heavily guarded, and then make it out into the main building where we need to find someone we can trust." His stomach sank. "It'll take a half an hour just to get out of this lab. We have to go through the chemical shower, undress completely, take personal showers, and then get dressed again in new clothes." He looked at Elijah. "You'll have to wear Lawson's clothes. They'll be a little too big, but I think they'll fit well enough."

"How are we going to get past all those guards you were talkin' about?" Elijah asked.

Alex closed the remaining gap to the door, threw the lock, and opened it. "I have no idea."

Chapter 33

Minnie Stevens

It turned out this new president wasn't as lily-livered as Minnie thought he'd be. Once she'd finished her story, he'd launched into a series of questions aimed at all four of them: Minnie, Hunt, Conner, and even Munez. His questions to Minnie had centered around Elijah Dixon and her experience at the hospital. He'd been sorting through and clarifying the information for at least half an hour. Minnie tapped her fingertips against her thigh. *The good Lord rewards those who wait. Be patient.*

"This room in the hospital was guarded only by Charles's security personnel?" President Coleman stood up from his chair.

"Yes," Minnie said, the tempo of her tapping picking up. "But from what Munez here said earlier, I don't think they're all in on that part."

"That's right, sir," Munez said. "Only senior members of the security team guard that room. It's the same with the restricted zone in the laboratories. It made sense to me at the time. Senior members have more experience, and obviously the restricted zone is important. We were told that wing of the hospital was also of utmost importance, but what goes on there is on a need-to-know basis."

"Need-to-know?" Coleman shook his head. "A room full of sick people?" He paced the length of his desk. "That doesn't make a whole lot of sense." He paused and pointed at Hunt. "Lawson had Price negotiate for sole protection over those two areas?"

"We've got better communications and vehicle support, so I believed it would be better for my people to guard the perimeter where the men have to be spread out," Hunt crossed his arms.

"Lawson done pulled the wool past y'all's eyes right down to your knees, tied a knot, and then sent you to skippin'." Minnie tapped her foot to the same rhythm as the drumming of her fingers. "And now he's got Alex who knows where doin' who knows what."

"We don't know how bad this is yet," General Hunt said.

Minnie leveled a glare at him. "Alan, you've got more than a lick of good sense. Don't patronize me. People don't go through this much trouble to steal a cookie out of the jar. Lawson's out for the whole kit and caboodle."

"I agree," President Coleman said. "He's definitely up to something. I have a bad feeling about it, too." The president paced for a few, long minutes in silence, stopping to stare at the ground every few seconds.

Minnie could barely stand still. *We've done enough talkin'.* "Beg your pardon, Mr. President," she said, "but we've done enough talkin'. It's time to *do* somethin'."

President Coleman stopped pacing and faced them, and Minnie spotted courage and determination in his eyes. It made her wonder if the president was about to stand up to his father-in-law for the very first time.

"With the disappearance of Mr. Roman coinciding with his attempt to gather potentially incriminating evidence against my father-in-law, and with the strange and sudden absence of Lawson and Price this morning, and with their hasty actions in regards to keeping Mr. Roman's family under lock and key, and the suspicious disappearance of this Elijah Dixon, I believe it is imperative we find Alexander Roman and ensure no harm has come to him. I have been... concerned about my father-in-law for quite some time. He's the kind of man who would do anything to get what he wants, and he's never met a roadblock he couldn't flatten with money, influence, threats, or a combination of those three. My wife can't be in the same room with him for more than ten minutes anymore."

"So he ain't even a wolf in sheep's clothing." Minnie frowned. "He's a wolf, plain and simple. Why'd you keep a man like that around? Family or not, Mr. President, it don't seem right."

"Ever heard of keeping your friends close and your enemies closer?" Coleman asked. "Whatever he's up to, he would have done it under my nose or outside my purview all together. Plus, we really did need his security force." He looked to Munez. "I'm under no illusions about Charles's influence over you and your companions. I'm frankly shocked that you are here to begin with."

"Mr. President, a quarter of us have only been with Lawson for six months, me included. Another quarter have been with him only a year. Price's company was on the upswing, adding new teams and growing in number. I've got friends — no, brothers — among those men, but there's always been this divide between the new and the old guard." Munez pressed his lips together and shook his head. "Many of us are patriots, sir. Good men trying to make a living with the skills we've been given. But the ones that have been with Price the longest... they seem to be the ones who *enjoy* it when things go south, Price included. It's like taking out a threat makes them come alive so much so that they are always looking for one." He averted his eyes. "They look out for us, though, and I guess... it was easier to ignore the things about them that made me uncomfortable."

"We've all been there," General Hunt said, "but not all of us find the strength to do something about it."

"You could accuse me of the same," Coleman said. "I've put up with my father-in-law for twenty years with barely an off-hand comment every so often to make myself feel better."

"I appreciate that, sirs." Munez lifted his head and set his jaw. "I've always wanted to protect and serve. If I can help do that, I'm all in."

"Well, if Price is the kind of man who enjoys hurting people, it's no wonder he and Lawson get on so well. The pair of them have the potential to cause trouble." Coleman stood up straighter and set his jaw. "General Hunt, you have your orders. I want Alexander Roman found. I want Charles Lawson and Chandler Price brought to me. They have some explaining to do."

"There's no way the old guard is going to let you arrest Price," Munez said. "If he decided to resist, there would be a fight on your hands."

"Then it looks like you'll need to gather your men for a show of force," Coleman said. "But if at all possible, make it *show*, General Hunt. I don't want bloodshed."

"If there's a possibility of a fight, we need to get you and your family to your personal quarters where you can lock yourselves up and avoid the action," Hunt said.

Coleman started gathering papers and notebooks and stuffing them into a briefcase. "Ever since we survived the first days after the sickness hit Atlanta, my wife has barely left the room and won't let our children out of her sight. I can't say I blame her." He closed the case and clasped it shut. Then, he opened one of his desk drawers and pulled out a holster with a gun. He secured it to his belt. "Hunt, leave the two men you've got guarding my personal quarters with me and my family. The rest of the military force is at your disposal."

Minnie clapped her hands once. "Great. Let's get this show on the road."

"Hold on." General Hunt held up a hand. "Minnie, you can't come with us. If there's an altercation—"

"You just try to stop me, Alan Hunt. I triple dog dare you." She narrowed her eyes at him. "You just ask Munez here how useful I can be when dealin' with a Suit."

Munez shrugged. "She is good at distracting people."

"And she's got a lot of good ideas," Conner added.

Hunt sighed. "You'll stay back and out of the way?"

"Scout's honor." Minnie held up three fingers in a Girl Scout's salute. "Now, let's stop wastin' time. Y'all are like a herd of turtles."

Coleman smiled. "You heard the lady, gentleman."

It wasn't twenty minutes later that the president was secure with his family, and Hunt was calling for reinforcements on the walkie talkies. "10-17. I repeat, 10-17." Hunt spoke as he walked.

"What does that mean?" Minnie whispered to Conner.

"It means he's got something urgent," Conner replied before hurrying ahead and opening the door to the staircase.

Hunt didn't miss a stride as he led them all down a flight of stairs. "All available, 10-22, location 3."

"He wants all available soldiers to report in person to the main lobby," Conner said, still translating, keeping a slower pace with Minnie.

"That's what I'm talkin' about." Minnie waved for Conner to go ahead as Hunt and Munez had gained speed. "Go, Jenny. I'll be fine. I'll catch up."

The corporal jogged to catch up with the men. Minnie clung to the railing and flew down the steps as fast as she could without tumbling head over heels. The other three were soon out of sight and the sound of a door opening and closing resounded up and down the stairwell. Her knees ached, but she kept pushing, sweat beading on her forehead, a prayer on her lips with every step.

More doors opened and closed and the patter of shoes filled the stairwell as half a dozen men and women in fatigues carefully bypassed Minnie on the stairs, one or two pausing to ask if she needed help. She waved them off just like she waved off Conner. *I may be gettin' old, but I've still got enough fight in me to make it down a flight of stairs on my own.*

She made it to the main floor landing and opened the door, yelping as a young man jogged right past the doorway. She avoided colliding with anyone, and by the time she got to the lobby, Hunt was already giving directions for them to head to the laboratories.

Minnie only had a few minutes to catch her breath as she leaned against a wall. She was sweaty, her heartbeat was wildly pounding inside her chest, and she was exhausted, but Minnie smiled at the hope swelling inside her chest.

As the group made their way to the labs, Minnie followed behind. *We're comin' for you, Alex. Hang in there.*

Chapter 34

Alexander Roman

"Don't come out until I come to get you." Alex put a hand on Elijah's shoulder. "They might recognize you, and I'm not sure that would work in our favor." The two men were separated from the guards in the main hall outside the block of BSL-4 labs by one thick, steel door. Alex had retrieved his pants, relieved to find the voice recorder untouched in his right-hand pocket, and he had access to the sharp letter opener without the positive-pressure suit to hinder him. In his left pocket, Alex had stuck the last prepared sedative from the lab.

"Good luck, son." Elijah tugged on the slightly-too-large sleeves of Lawson's blazer jacket. "Thank you for what you've done for me. No matter what happens, you're a good man, Alex."

"Let's hope that's enough." Armed with the sedative and his letter opener, Alexander pulled open the door into the main hall outside the block of BSL-4 labs. His hair was still wet from the showers, and his cool scalp contrasted sharply with his burning hot ears. A shiver ran down his spine as he stepped between the two Suits standing watch — Garcia and Hall, if Alex remembered their names correctly. They had been the men who had dragged Minnie to these very labs. Alex's stomach flipped. He hadn't had time to think about it, but the puzzle pieces slid into place as he took in those faces once more. *They were going to do to Minnie what they were going to do to Elijah.* A flash of shame fell over him as Elijah's last words to him resounded in his mind. Even if it had only been for a moment, Alex had considered sedating Elijah and going through with what Lawson had wanted him to do. *I'll have to save the soul searching for later…* He clung to the fact that he had ended up doing the right thing, cleared his head, and focused on the task at hand.

Bruises where Alex had slammed his knee into Hall's face two days prior peeked out from underneath a bandage over the bridge of Hall's nose. He scowled upon seeing Alex, and then his eyes squinted and watered as he gingerly touched his wound. His voice had turned nasally since the last time they'd spoken. "Where's everybody else?" he asked.

"I thought you two were on grave digging duty," Alex said, his hand grasping the syringe in his pocket.

"Starts tomorrow," Garcia snapped. "Hall asked you a question."

Alex had tried to remain calm as he put a little bit of distance between himself and the guards. Out of arm's length, he turned and bolted down the hallway, sprinting as fast as he could toward the next intersection. He had only one plan, and it depended on *not* running into any more guards before he implemented it. Garcia yelled after him, but Alex kept running, his feet pounding, every slap of his foot against the floor sending a jolt up his body. He skidded around the next corner and slid to a stop, doubling back a few steps and pressing his back against wall.

Alex pulled out the syringe and fumbled with the cap, popping it off just as Garcia rounded the corner and passed him. Alex lunged at the guard, sinking the needle into his neck and plunging the sedative into his body. He yanked out the needle and threw the syringe far from him as he turned on his heel and ran back toward Hall. Behind him, he heard a groan and a thud. He glanced over his shoulder to see Garcia following him in a zigzag pattern, bumping into the wall on occasion.

Looking back was a mistake; Alex ran right into Hall's rock-solid arm, and his feet flew out from under him. He landed hard on his back, his head bouncing off the floor. Alex groaned as his vision blurred. Hall landed a kick to Alex's side, and Alex curled in on himself, coughing as the wind was knocked out of him.

"Garcia!" Hall's foot struck Alex's back. "What did you do to him, Roman?"

Alex fumbled for the letter opener; the handle was just beneath his waistline, but with every kick, he found it harder to concentrate. Garcia fell to his knees not far from Alex and then face planted on the ground.

Hall's boot battered Alex with every word. "What. Did. You. Do. To. Him?"

"It's just a sedative," Alex said, the world spinning as he finally grasped the handle of the letter opener and yanked it out of the sheath that had been sewn to the inside of his boxers. He couldn't concentrate well enough to aim, so he swung the sharp point as hard as he could in Hall's direction. The metal tool sunk into flesh and then hit what Alex could only guess was a femur. He tore it out and Hall screamed. Alex rolled onto his stomach and army crawled less than a foot before Hall grabbed a fistful of Alex's hair.

"You're dead," Hall hissed. The guard forced Alex up to his knees. Alex clumsily swung the letter opener again, but Hall slapped it from his hand and pulled out his gun. "I don't care if they want you alive. I'll just tell them I had no choice."

Light and dark bled together, shapes moved down the hall, and the floor, walls, and ceiling swayed. Maybe if he kills me, Elijah will be able to use it as a distraction to flee. Maybe they'll leave Oliver alone. Maybe it won't be for nothing. Alex's whole body ached and throbbed. He'd used the last of his strength to stab Hall. He readied himself to die, smiling at the thought of holding Naomi in his arms once again.

A familiar voice broke through the haze, pulling Alex back from the brink of letting go. "You let go of him right this second, or I'll boil your hide and then feed it to ya one bite at a time!"

"Minnie?" Alex squinted and blinked, trying to clear his vision. Hall let go of his hair, and Alex slumped to the ground, barely supporting himself with his arms as he tried to figure out what was happening. As his vision cleared, Alex frowned. About a dozen people in fatigues stood behind Minnie, Hunt, and Conner… and was that a *Suit* standing next to Conner? *I must have hit my head harder than I thought.*

"Munez? What are you doing?" Hall asked.

"I'm trying to do the right thing, Hall." Munez nodded toward General Hunt.

"Are you crazy?" Hall limped forward two steps before Hunt drew his weapon and pointed it at him, stopping him in tracks. Hall put his hands in the air. "Look, Mr. Roman attacked me and Garcia." He pointed to Garcia who lay unconscious against the hallway wall. "He went into the labs with Price, Lawson, and the other two scientists, and he came out alone. I was just doing my job."

"Well, I'm here now, on orders from the President," General Hunt said. "I'm to retrieve Roman and take Lawson into custody."

Several Suits appeared in the intersection behind the military personnel, and one of them spoke. "You outnumbered us at the door, Hunt, but now we're evenly matched, and I've got more coming." Alex's heart skipped a beat as he saw through the crowded hallway the ten or so Suits pull their weapons. The military did the same, and Conner pushed Minnie to the center.

"This is pointless." General Hunt shouted, his voice reverberating up and down the hall. "Lawson and Price are under suspicion of treason. Like it or not, we're taking him in, wherever he is. And we're taking Mr. Roman with us, too."

Hall pulled his weapon and pointed it at Alex's head. "Didn't you hear my friend? More of us are on their way. We can stay in a holding pattern until they get here, but eventually, there will be enough of us to haul your butts out of here."

Alex licked his lips and dug in his pocket for the voice recorder. At least one Suit had changed sides which meant maybe more of them would do so if they knew the truth. Whatever miracles Minnie had worked to get Hunt and his people to the restricted zone in full force couldn't go to waste. He lifted the voice recorder above his head in the dead silence as all the men and women with guns glowered at each other, none of them really paying attention to him. He pressed the play button, and it began where he'd paused it the night before, right before the incriminating evidence.

His own voice filled the silence. "Anyone can see that you're at odds with the military. And the president is trying to hold a balance between your two forces. What happens if Coleman shuts you down and decides to go on to Cheyenne Mountain?"

Every eye turned to Alex, and he turned up the volume as loud as it would go.

Lawson's next words were accompanied by several gasps. "Coleman is a puppet. He's always been soft. This is my operation, top to bottom. He's no president. There's no longer anything to be president *of*. This is a new world, Roman, and when the dust settles, I'm going to be king."

By the time the recording ended, several of the Suits had lowered their guns. Alex's head had cleared, though he still felt light-headed and nauseous. Hall had lowered his gun when he noticed some of his fellows on the other side of the hall doing the same, but when Alex struggled to his feet, Hall raised it again.

"Don't move." Hall's voice trembled. "This doesn't change anything. Not for me. Those of us who were the most important already knew most of that."

"Oh?" Munez said. "And what about the rest of us?" More of the Suits lowered their weapons.

"If Lawson thinks of the President of the United States as a puppet, what do you all think that makes you?" Alex shouted loud enough that everyone could hear him, and he took one more step toward Hunt. Minnie peeked at him through the crowd, brow knitted with worry.

"Shut up," Hall yelled. "And I said don't move!"

Alex stayed still, but he didn't stay quiet. "They were willing to do human experiments," he said. "They were going to infect actual human beings with this virus, as many people as it would take, in order to somehow try to find a treatment. But even after that, they were going to use it to control people. And don't for a second think they wouldn't use the disease to threaten people, either. They already have. They threatened to kill my child, my ten-year-old son. Lawson is only interested in making himself a kingdom to rule over. You heard it in his own words." All the suits who had lowered their weapons holstered them and moved to join Hunt's group.

"It looks like we outnumber *you* now," Hunt said.

Munez stepped toward Hall, but he spoke loud enough for everyone to hear. "Most of the others coming to back you up are newer to Price's team. They weren't in on this like you were, Hall. Do you really think they're going to side with you?"

"Traitor!" Hall spit at Munez and then turned his gun on him. A single gun shot rang out, and Alex flinched, ducking against the wall. He turned to see Hunt with his weapon drawn and Hall on the ground, bleeding. Hunt now had twenty men and women backing him. The remaining four on the other side of them raised their hands in surrender, each one placing their weapons on the floor.

Hunt turned to Alex. "Where is Lawson, Mr. Roman?"

"He's locked in a cell in one of the BSL-4 laboratories beyond that door." Alex used the wall to get to his feet, and he stumbled to the steel barrier, reaching for the handle. "Price, Turner, and Ward are all in cells, too. Price and Turner are out cold from a sedative shot, just like Garcia over there, though they might be awake by now, I'm not sure."

"You detained four people by yourself?" Hunt sounded shocked.

Alex opened the door. "No, not by myself."

Elijah stood in the hallway, hands up, eyes wide, but when he saw Alex, he grinned. "You did it?" It was clearly a question.

"Yes," Alex said, waving the older man into the hallway. He stepped back and nodded at Elijah as he came into view of Hunt, Minnie, Conner, and the rest. "I couldn't have done it without his help."

"Elijah?" Minnie pushed through and held out her arms, closing the gap between them and throwing her arms around Elijah's neck. "You're alive!"

"Barely," Elijah chuckled.

"Now, didn't I tell you this place was trouble?" Minnie pulled back and put her hands on her hips.

Elijah quirked an eyebrow. "Didn't I tell *you* it would all work out fine in the end?"

"You're insufferable," Minnie said, blushing.

Alex couldn't help but smile, but then General Hunt grunted and stalked forward. "Enough of that. There'll be time for a reunion later. We've got work to do." He started barking orders, taking names of Suits who'd joined them, and having those who hadn't cuffed.

Is he… jealous? Alex shook his head. Minnie really was something else. "Are Oliver and Lauren okay?" he asked.

"Right as rain, I suspect," Minnie said. "I got them to safety before Conner and I got to Hunt."

"How did you manage all of this?" he asked her.

"Well," Minnie said, smiling wide, "It wasn't easy, mind you, but Southern gals know how to get things done."
Alex laughed and drew her into a hug. "I can't wait to hear all about it."

Chapter 35

Zara Williams

Zara munched on a granola bar as she stared up at the ceiling from the top bunk. "He'll be back any minute," she said with her mouth half full. She rotated the ladybug ring on her pointer finger with her thumb. It calmed her, helped her remember that she wasn't alone anymore.

Lizzy's voice came from below. "You think it'll be bad?"

"I don't know." Zara shifted to her stomach and hung her head over the side of the bed to look at Lizzy. "That note he left didn't leave much for us to go on." When Zara and Lizzy had gotten back from their trip into town, they'd had very little time before curfew. She'd walked into their cabin expected Mr. Peters to be there, waiting to interrogate her about Jordan and the Green Earth Futurists. Instead, she'd found a note: *I'm staying the night with Amos's family. Don't wait up.*

Lizzy took a bite of her own granola bar. "Maybe he was invited to work out the details of our arrangement with Thomas."

"Yeah, or maybe he decided to tell Thomas all about my brother's connection to the GEF." Zara groaned and pushed herself back onto the mattress. "It *is* weird… that the Heirs of the Mother knew about the mosquitos before anyone else. And their connection to GEF… I mean, it makes sense. What if the Heirs were part of it? What if they planned all of this, and then my brother and his friends were duped into being part of it?"

"They could have just had access to the video, Zee." Lizzy stood up and peeked over the side of Zara's mattress. "Even if it's worst-case scenario, it wouldn't make it Jordan's fault any more than it's mine."

Zara frowned. "What did you have to do with it?"

Lizzy's cheeks turned red, and she averted her eyes, her voice becoming small. "I have something to tell you, Zee."

What has she been hiding? Zara reached out for Lizzy's fingers gripping the edge of the mattress. *Is it about the phone? Does she know where it is?* "It's okay," Zara said. "You can tell me."

The door opened, and Mr. Peters stepped inside the cabin. "I trust you girls had a good night?" His voice was steely, his expression hardened.

"We had a good run into town," Zara said. "I think we've got a good start on gathering items to barter for a plane ride."

"Zara had us go into a pawn shop, Dad. It was great. Loaded with guns and jewelry." Lizzy smiled, though her light tone was badly forced.

"I heard. I spent the night talking over the specifics of our stay here. Percentages of our commission. What kind of work we're expected to do in exchange for housing and food." His slow, measured footsteps thudded on the wooden planks as he walked closer to them. His eyes were set on Zara. She swung her legs over the side of the bunk and hopped down to the ground, resisting the urge to squirm. Mr. Peters continued, "We also talked about these Heirs of the Mother. I talked to Thomas about who they were before the mosquitos were released. About their connection to the Green Earth Futurists. Seems they're not just a local group. The GEF started out as a more palatable figurehead organization and grew like wildfire across college campuses. Thomas had some very interesting conversations with one of them about a year ago; they started coming to prepper meetings, and he got the feeling they were planning something big." He glared at Zara. "I wonder what that could have been. Thomas seems to think they were just going to blow up some government building. What do you think, Zara?"

Lizzy stepped in front of Mr. Peters, cutting off his eye contact with Zara. "Dad, we need to move on from this. Does how all of this happened actually matter anymore? Zara is getting over the fact that your company created this virus and these mosquitos in the first place. If she can move on—"

"Hold on, Liz. I never said that." Zara stepped up to stand beside her. "Just because I'm letting go of your need to justify his actions doesn't mean I'm letting him off the hook."

Mr. Peters's face contorted in anger. "I was doing the job my country asked me to do. It wasn't my idea. And I used it as an opportunity to do good. I was going to wipe out malaria all over the world. Zika Virus, Dengue, Yellow Fever — gone because of me."

"Yeah, well, instead the human race is almost gone because of you." Zara clapped her hands in mock praise. "Good job, Walter."

"I want to know what you and your brother had to do with this." He jabbed a finger into Zara's shoulder, pushing her back a step. "I had the experiments under control. How did they get in? Did you let them into my house, Zara? I had a book in my safe with passcodes. Did you find your way in? Copy the pages and hand them over to your brother?"

"No," Zara said. "It's not my fault you messed up your security."

"How did you do it?" Mr. Peters screamed, spit flying from his mouth. "The Heirs *knew* what had happened before the CDC announced it. They *wanted* it to happen. It's no coincidence that one of their members is connected to me. Is that why you became Lizzy's best friend? To get to me? How long has this been going on?"

"You're going crazy, Walter. Jordan wasn't part of the Heirs of the Mother." Zara's fingernails dug into her palms.

"The GEF and the Heirs are the same thing," Mr. Peters roared, and both Zara and Lizzy flinched back from him.

But Zara quickly got over her instinct to shy away. She gritted her teeth and stood toe-to-toe with Walter Peters. She'd had enough of his accusations. "I don't know *anything* about the Green Earth Futurists, and Jordan didn't know anything about these Heirs of the Mother. You *have* the video, Walter. Why don't you watch it again and tell me my brother knew what was coming? He was clearly shocked when he got sick."

Walter opened his mouth to respond, his face red and that vein popping on his forehead. But then he stopped, his eyes searching hers as if she were playing a trick on him. "You... *don't* have the phone?"

"Of course not." Zara crossed her arms, her resolve faltering. "You took it back at the hospital."

"I didn't, actually." Walter laughed, but his laughter frightened Zara more than his anger. He cut off abruptly, a smile still on his face. "All your leverage is gone." His lips tightened into a thin line, his eyes narrowed at her, and he lurched forward. His hands closed around Zara's neck as he pushed her back against the wall. "Tell me what you know."

Anger fled in the presence of fear as Mr. Peters pinned her in place. "I swear I don't know anything," Zara said, her voice hoarse.

"Dad!" Lizzy pummeled her father's arm. "Stop it! It wasn't Zara."

"She's been lying to you, Elizabeth. Using you." Mr. Peters was seething. "She wormed her way into our lives for these sick bastards. Vanguard has been a target of the GEF for years. I always suspected it was her that leaked those pictures of me for their flyers. They knew too much about me, about Vanguard and New Horizons. She gave them the missing pieces to the puzzle they wanted to build."

"That's not true!" It was getting harder for Zara to speak. Mr. Peters wasn't cutting off her airway yet, only holding her firmly in place, but the longer he held her there, the tighter his grip became.

"You're a liar." Mr. Peters yanked Zara forward an inch or two and then slammed her head against the wall.

He's going to kill me. Zara pulled at Mr. Peters's hands and tried to kick at him, but he was too close to give her foot any momentum. "Let me go." She rasped the words, her vision blurring.

"It was me!" Lizzy yelled.

Zara scratched at Walter's arms as the back of her head throbbed. "Get help," Zara said, ignoring Lizzy's attempts to distract her father.

"Elizabeth, don't you dare. Can't you see what she's done?" Mr. Peters's hot, sweaty hands squeezed tighter around Zara's neck.

Lizzy pounded her fists against her father's arms and back. "I said, it was me! I gave Jordan your passcodes. Let her go."

"Don't be ridiculous." Mr. Peters's grip loosened enough for Zara to gasp for air, and he looked at his daughter with wide eyes.

"We were together," Lizzy said. "I joined the GEF more than a year ago because it was important to him. They *did* recruit me because of you, but I wanted to impress Jordan. I thought — Jordan thought — releasing the mosquitos would get rid of diseases all across the world. Your company was going to charge a crazy amount of money, and poorer countries wouldn't be able to afford it. I thought I was doing the right thing."

Mr. Peters dropped his hands from Zara's throat and stepped back, shaking his head at his daughter. Zara slumped to the floor, touching her neck, tears streaming down her face. She looked up at Lizzy. "What are you talking about?" Zara asked, not wanting to believe the implications of what Lizzy had confessed.

Lizzy licked her lips, her eyes flitting between Zara and her father. "Neither one of you would have approved of me and Jordan, so we kept it between us. It was mostly just for fun, not anything serious yet. I... thought maybe it *could* be serious, one day."

"It was *you*?" Mr. Peters stepped back again. "You gave them pictures of me for their flyers? You fed them information about my company? About our lives? And that book in my safe... the passcodes to get into the building, to log into my computer at work, the encryption keys for my files... that was you?"

"I copied the pages a little bit at a time and gave them to Jordan over a period of several months," Lizzy said. "Daddy, I'm sorry."

Mr. Peters held up his hand. "No. You betrayed me. Don't ever call me that again. You can stay here, the both of you. I don't want anything to do with either of you."

"You don't mean that." Lizzy's voice broke.

"Don't I?" Mr. Peters swallowed hard, set his jaw, and turned his back toward the door.

"I defended you," Lizzy said. "You made mistakes, too, Dad. I even took the phone, to keep you safe. I'm sorry for what I did, but you can't just leave me here."

Mr. Peters paused with his hand on the door, but then he shook his head. "You're dead to me, Elizabeth." He walked out, slamming the door behind him.

Zara blinked, her brain replaying the things Lizzy had said, over and over, trying to make sense of it. "You took the phone?" she whispered.

Lizzy sunk onto the bed, hugging herself tight. "Yes. I just... if I hadn't given Jordan copies of that book, none of this would have happened."

"If they wanted the information, Liz, they would have found it another way." A numbness sprouted in Zara's chest. "I could have forgiven you for that. But the lies?"

"I didn't know how to tell you about the phone. I knew you'd be mad." Lizzy got to her knees in front of Zara and took her hands. "Please, I was wrong. I made a lot of bad choices, but you're my best friend. I need you to try to understand."

Zara jerked her hand away from Lizzy's. "You dated my brother behind my back, Liz. You knew about his juvie record, and you *helped* him commit a crime. I'm sorry, but you had nothing to worry about. Your father wouldn't have pressed charges against you, but he would have *buried* Jordan if he'd gotten caught."

Lizzy scooted closer to Zara, her eyes pleading. "I... I didn't think about it that way."

"You didn't *think*, Lizzy." Zara struggled to her feet, using the wall for support. "You lied to me. Jordan, the phone, your involvement with the GEF and what they did..." Zara shivered as the numbness reached her bones, chilling her from the inside out. Lizzy had sworn she wouldn't date Jordan without Zara's blessing. She'd *never* talked about the GEF or about *how* involved she'd gotten; Zara had just assumed she'd gone to the meetings to impress Jordan, just like she joined clubs at school to get some guy's attention just to drop the club when she lost interest in the guy. Best friends were supposed to tell each other everything.

"I didn't *lie* about most of that. I just... didn't tell you." Lizzy got to her feet. "Please, Zee. I was afraid to tell you. I was afraid to tell anyone. It's been killing me ever since we watched that video, and I realized what part I'd played."

"I can't believe I thought you were my friend." Zara took off the ladybug ring and shoved it at Lizzy who fumbled to keep it from dropping on the floor.

"I *am* your friend." Lizzy sobbed and reached for Zara.

Before she could even think it through, Zara slapped Lizzy across the face. "No, you're not." The certainty with which she said the words sent a jolt through her body. She didn't mean them, even after what Lizzy had done, but the urge to get away banished every other feeling. Zara sprinted to the door and flung it open.

Mandy, the girl who had been assisting Carol in the garages, was on the other side, her fist raised as if about to knock. "Oh, hey," she said, holding up a small bag. "I'm just runnin' errands for Thomas. I got your loot." She smiled wide, but then wrinkled her brow. "Hey… are you okay?"

Zara hurriedly dried her eyes with the back of her hand and took the bag from Mandy, opening the drawstring to look inside. A handful of wedding rings clinked together inside. She stuffed the bag into her back pocket. *I'm going to need these if I'm going to barter my way onto that plane.*

Mandy peeked into the room beyond Zara where Lizzy cried. "Is she okay?"

"No. I've got to go." Zara sidestepped Mandy who entered the cabin. She heard the stranger coo comforting words before she got out of earshot. Part of her was relieved at Mandy's appearance. She couldn't deal with feeling sorry for Lizzy.

Zara had only one thing on her mind: distance. She couldn't stay anywhere near Lizzy or Mr. Peters one second longer. *I'm so stupid. Even when I didn't like the way she was acting, I trusted her.* She headed toward the garages. *I have to get out of here. Maybe I can go on another supply run.*

She flung open the door, looking around for Carol. "Hello?" She walked from container to container. "Carol?" There was no answer. *If I can't trust Lizzy, who can I trust?* She wiped away more tears and pressed her hands to her throbbing temples. She'd always considered herself a good judge of character. Not anymore. *I have no one but me.* She leaned against the wall, and an image of her cousin, Annika, formed in her mind's eye. *No, that's not entirely true. I still have her, but… she was so far away.* "That whole family is messed up," Zara whispered. "I can't leave her with them."

Zara grabbed one of the beekeeper-like protective suits off the wall along with one of the sunhat-mesh combinations. Leaving temporarily wasn't enough. Her skin crawled with the idea of staying at the compound, of being forced to travel with Mr. Peters and Lizzy all the way to Boston. *They won't let me go on my own. They only have the bus we brought to spare.* She pulled the suit over her clothes, a decision made. She secured the mesh, tucking it into the suit.

A little board with hooks was attached to the wall beside a few lockers. Zara grabbed the keys to the padlocks on the garage doors. She also grabbed a key to one of the four wheelers, but she put them back almost immediately. If she took only a suit, and she went on foot, she'd have protection. *Maybe they won't come after me for just a suit.* She could find a vehicle eventually, or maybe a bike. Farmhouses dotted the countryside; she could find shelter every few miles if she needed it.

She had to go through a few of the padlock keys to find the right one, but eventually she managed to find the right key. The padlock clicked open. Zara worked quickly, her heartbeat racing, adrenaline racing through her body. She had to get out before someone came back to the garages. There was no time to think, no time to backpedal or question herself.

Zara left the padlock keys on the workbench against the back wall of the garage, along with a note: *I'm sorry I left. I only took one suit. The garage door is unlocked.*

She lifted the garage door manually, and then closed it from the other side, pushing down as hard as she could to make sure it *looked* closed from the outside. And then, before she could change her mind, Zara turned away from the compound and ran for the cover of the nearby trees.

Chapter 36

Alexander Roman

Alex leaned forward in the improvised oval office having just finished laying everything he knew out on the table for President Coleman. After a long night's sleep, he'd labored over the meeting, over if he could trust Coleman and Hunt. Minnie and Lauren had agreed in the end that trusting Coleman was the only way forward. He'd shown himself to have integrity when it came down to the wire, and they needed his help if they wanted to leave Atlanta with the supplies they came there for in the first place.

General Hunt stood to the president's righthand side, frowning as Alex wrapped up the last of his revelations about Walter Peters and New Horizons Labs in Boston. The president himself rested his elbows on the arms of his chair, his hands folded in his lap, his expression neutral. He'd asked a few questions along the way, but he'd mostly just listened.

Alex continued, hoping he'd made the right decision in trusting these people. "I believe Jonah and the team who died here would have instructed me to continue their work if they thought they could find the answers fast enough. Instead, Dr. Newton used his last words to tell me to go to Boston and find Walter Peters. My suspicion is that New Horizons Lab's developing technology in the field of mosquito population control has something to do with it."

"You believe eliminating the mosquito as a vector for the virus is essential to stopping its spread?" President Coleman frowned. "What about person-to-person spread?"

"We can take measures to stop further person-to-person spread after we make it safe to go outside again in the mornings and evenings," Alex said. "We can't even begin to stabilize and rebuild under these conditions."

The president nodded. "Yes, I think you're right. We can take what we've learned here, and all that you've told us, to Cheyenne Mountain where what's left of our best and brightest are gathering."

General Hunt stirred from his statuesque stance. "You're ready to move on, Mr. President?"

"Thought I'd never leave?" Coleman chuckled. "I wasn't sure either, but… I think it's time."

"I'm glad to hear that, Mr. President," General Hunt said.

Coleman hung his head for a moment before looking back up at the general. "We need to know if I really am the next in line, if I'm *actually* the president. I have temporary authority until that's confirmed. And this information Mr. Roman has revealed needs to be shared."

"Can you put it out on the radio waves along with the CDC warning?" Alex asked.

The president shook his head. "I'm afraid sharing it with everyone with access to a radio would be a bad idea."

General Hunt grunted and gave a curt nod. "I concur. We don't know who is out there listening, if there are more Charles Lawsons. Nut jobs and narcissists tend to survive catastrophes. Besides that, it could cause panic or a rush for Boston that would result in complications you don't need, Mr. Roman."

Alex sighed. "People hear an answer might be in Boston, and they flock there whether their presence is helpful or not."

"Not to mention that people have the tendency to do stupid things when they're angry and afraid," General Hunt said.

"Yes," President Coleman said, "the *right* people need to know. And those people are at Cheyenne Mountain. We've got to tell them the old-fashioned way: in person."

"There's one more thing," Alex said, "You can't leave this place completely unprotected before destroying the dangerous samples stored here. Most of them wouldn't survive for long once the generators shut off, but you can't take the risk of someone getting to those samples first."

"We've had a crew carefully incinerating samples since last night," President Coleman said. "After hearing the potential plans my father-in-law had for them, I didn't like the idea of their availability."

Alex raised an eyebrow, impressed at the forethought. "Good. And what are you going to do with Lawson, Price, Ward, and Turner?"

The president sighed and rubbed the back of his neck. "I don't know. Our justice system is a little… scarce these days." He looked to General Hunt. "Do you have any recommendations?"

"I believe you would be justified in sentencing them to treason and executing them, sir," General Hunt said. "This could be considered war time, and they are traitors to our country."

President Coleman winced. "I can't do that, General. Besides the fact I don't know my official status yet, Lawson is my father-in-law. Ward and Turner might still be useful, though whatever uses they may have, they'd have to be utilized under strict supervision."

"And Price?" Alex asked. "What are you going to do with him and those of his men involved in their plans? There were at least half a dozen highly trained and skilled men still loyal to him when it was all said and done."

"Is there any way to take them all with us, bound and guarded?" President Coleman asked.

"Traveling with ten prisoners isn't going to be easy, sir," General Hunt said, "but if you insist, we can make it work. We'd need to issue a shoot-to-kill order upon any escape attempts, considering their crimes and potential threat to the security of the nation and its people. I would suggest leaving Price's men, the ones who came over to our side, here in Atlanta with what supplies we can spare. It wouldn't be wise to put them in a position wherein they'd have to watch their former friends dragged across the country in cuffs. You could offer them pardons for their unknowing participation in treason in exchange for their commitment to serving the community we've gathered in the dorms and at the hospital."

President Coleman nodded. "I like that idea. I could create an executive order declaring a new position for Munez here in Atlanta. Maybe a City Executor? I think we can trust Munez to keep things stable around here until a new, proper government can be set up."

"I agree, sir. At least, I don't see many alternatives," General Hunt said. "Once we arrive at Cheyenne Mountain and establish who is in authority, we can either take next steps there or hand the prisoners over to whoever is in charge."

"It sounds like we have a plan, then, gentlemen." President Coleman stood up, pushing his chair back and holding out a hand toward Alex, which he took. "You've done a great service to your country, Mr. Roman. I'm not sure how we'll ever repay you."

"Thank you, sir," Alex said, feeling light for the first time since they arrived at the CDC. "All I need is to get on the road with the RV that we came here in, plus the van of supplies Jonah left for me. I know this is quick, but I'd like to leave today."

"General Hunt, can you arrange for that to happen ASAP?" President Coleman asked, and General Hunt responded with a grunt and nod. "Mr. Roman, once you have answers, please know that you will always have an ear to listen at Cheyenne Mountain. My guess is that we're going to be headquartered there for quite some time."

"I might need your help one day," Alex said. "In fact, I'd be surprised if I didn't. The task ahead feels… daunting. But, knowing I can come to you makes it a little less so."

Minutes later, he breathed a sigh of relief as he left Coleman and Hunt. The meeting couldn't have gone better. *It's about time something went right.* He actually smiled on his way to his room where Oliver, Minnie, Lauren, and Samson were waiting. Hope coupled with optimism filled him to the brim; it was such a foreign feeling after the events of the past two weeks, but he welcomed it gladly.

When he turned the last corner into their hallway, he slowed as he approached Minnie and Elijah. "Good morning, you two," he said.

Elijah took a deep breath and tore his eyes away from Minnie. "Mornin', Alex. I was just comin' to say goodbye. Minnie said you'd be leavin'."

Alex nodded. "Today, hopefully."

"Can't lie," he said. "I was hopin' Minnie might stay a while longer."

Minnie took Elijah's hand. "That'd be nice, Elijah, but I've got to go with my people." She kissed his cheek, they embraced briefly, and then Alex came to stand next to her as they watched Elijah walk away and disappear around the corner.

"You could stay, you know." Alex grinned at her. "Or you could go with General Hunt. I think both of them might be sweet on you."

Minnie pshawed. "Neither one of 'em could handle me."

Alex shrugged. "Maybe, but I wasn't kidding about staying here. It's probably safer to hunker down in one spot, get into a routine, and build something of a life. There will be trained men looking out for the community, and they've already got systems in place for gathering supplies." A sudden heaviness fell on Alex, and he glanced at the closed door that led into the makeshift bedroom where Oliver was. "Do you…" He trailed off, swallowing a lump in his throat. "Do you think it would be safer for Oliver… to stay here, with you?" His stomach turned to rock. He hated the idea of being separated from his son.

"Alex, the worst decision I ever made was pushin' Lauren away. I thought I was doin' what was best for her, forcin' her to choose the safest career path," Minnie said. "The situation is different, but I'd say Oliver is better off with you than he would be here. We don't know the future. This could become a place of hope for survivors, or it could all fall apart because the wrong people bite the dust." She shook her head. "And besides that, I'm not plannin' on leavin' you to your own devices. In case you didn't notice, I saved your butt."

Alex chuckled. "That you did." His smile wavered. "You and Lauren and Oliver and Samson… you have options that don't include traipsing up the east coast to one of the three ground zeroes. Things are bound to be worse there than they are here."

"Maybe. Or maybe it'll get worse here in the coming days. Like I said, we don't know." She quirked an eyebrow at him. "Unless you've got a crystal ball you've been hidin' from me?"

"I kind of wish I did," Alex said. "I don't know if accepting your coming with me is the right choice or if I'm just being selfish."

"Hogwash," Minnie pursed her lips. "We're in this together, Alexander Roman. I don't want to hear another word about it. Got it?"

Alex nodded, and she swiped her hands together as if washing them of the conversation. "Okay, then. When are we gettin' on the road? It's not like we got a bunch of stuff to pack."

"Hunt is having the vehicles pulled around. It should be safe out by now," Alex said. "When they're ready, he's sending Conner up to get us. It shouldn't be long." He opened the door into the room where Lauren and Oliver sat cross-legged on the bed, a pile of cards between them. They were laughing and flipping cards quickly into the pile.

Oliver slapped a card and yelled, "Slap Jack!" Samson barked and wagged his tail furiously. Both Oliver and Lauren turned to look at Alex.

We came all this way back home and now we have to leave. Alex folded his arms, trying to think of the best way to tell Oliver. "Hey, bud. We need to talk."

Oliver began gathering the cards and putting them back in their box. "Are we getting out of here?"

"That's what I wanted to talk about." Alex sat on the bed after Lauren stood to make room for him. "We're not just leaving this building. We're leaving Atlanta."

Oliver stuffed the deck of cards into his mother's purse and slung the bag over his shoulder. "Okay," he said, grabbing the photo he'd put back on the side table. "Can we bring this?"

Alex took the picture. "Yeah, but… are you going to be okay? I mean, I know you were looking forward to coming home to Atlanta."

Oliver shrugged. "I just want us to all be together."

Alex drew his son into his arms and hugged him tight. "Me, too, bud."

A knock on the door signaled Conner's arrival. "I have some things that belong to you." She handed back Minnie's keys and the three wallets that had been confiscated upon their arrival before leading the way to the lobby and out into the warm summer day. Minnie's sturdy, off-road RV, lovingly nicknamed "Harvey," was hooked up to a trailer almost as long as the RV itself.

The hood was up, and Hunt peeked out from behind it. He slammed it shut. "Oil's been changed. Tires have been checked. Gas is full to the brim, and there is more in the trailer."

Conner patted the side of the trailer. "We transferred everything from the van into this trailer. There's plenty of nonperishable foods, water, and a lot of equipment." She held up a finger. "Oh, and…" She hurried to the back door of the four-door cab and opened it. "…this was in the front seat of the van." She handed Alex a thin briefcase.

"What is it?" Alex asked.

"I'm not sure, but a piece of paper was sitting on top of it with your name on it." She fished a folded paper out of her pocket and showed it to Alex; his name was written on it with the flourishes of Dr. Jonah Newton's handwriting.

"Come on, Samson!" Oliver bolted to the cab, and Samson bounded behind him. The two jumped into the back seat. "Are you guys coming?"

"I guess I'm driving," Minnie said.

"Ms. Stevens?" General Hunt stepped up to Minnie and tugged once on his collar. "If we ever have the pleasure of meeting again, I think... well, I..." He swallowed hard. "Things aren't right for it now, maybe not ever, but..." He trailed off, his cheeks red.

"Maybe you'd like to try some of that hard work that goes into relationships?" Minnie asked.

"Yes." General Hunt's shoulders relaxed, and he sounded relieved that Minnie had found the words for him.

"I wouldn't mind a nice stroll and some proper sweet tea," Minnie said.

The general grinned, and Alex quirked an eyebrow. "I don't think I've ever seen that man smile," he whispered to Lauren.

Lauren smiled and shook her head. "He has no idea what he's getting himself into."

"Nope." Alex patted Lauren on the back and took a few steps toward the RV, the briefcase in one hand.

"I call shotgun." Lauren sped past him, throwing him a smirk.

Alex groaned and climbed into the back of the cab next to Samson who managed to lick his face before he even got his seatbelt on. He couldn't help but laugh, even if there was dog slobber in his ear. They were all together again, and they were back on the road. Though he wouldn't have chosen the way it happened, Alex had not only helped stabilize what was left of the government, he had also managed to inform them and garner their support.

As they pulled out of the CDC complex, Alex scratched Samson behind the ears. "You've got to be some kind of good luck charm," he said.

Minnie navigated the cleared streets through Atlanta, following signs the military had placed along a route out of the city. "We don't need good luck charms as long as we have each other." She smiled through the rearview mirror, and Alex caught her throwing a wink at Oliver. "Although, Samson's always been kinda special, now that I think on it."

Samson curled into a ball between Alex and Oliver, his head resting on Oliver's lap. His rear end pushed Alex's legs to make room, and his foot bumped the briefcase he'd put on the floorboards. He'd nearly forgotten about it in the pure relief and excitement of moving on from the ordeal at the CDC. He retrieved the case and opened it, frowning at the single manilla folder inside. A dry scraping of skin on paper sounded as Alex flipped the folder open.

"Who's that, Dad?" Oliver asked as he craned his neck to look at the picture attached to the top page.

"That is Walter Peters," Alex said, his frown deepening, his heartrate picking up speed. The pages were redacted, black lines taking up most of the page, but that picture was labelled with red pen. And in the same chicken-scratch handwriting were four words — underlined in the margins — that wiped away every ounce of Alex's foolish optimism: *Peters can't be trusted.*

Chapter 37

Zara Williams

Zara had only been walking for an hour when a distant explosion rumbled through the air. She spun around, frowning at the black plume of smoke rising from the direction of the compound. "What in the world?" Zara chewed her lower lip. "Nope. Not my problem. It's probably some sort of weapon's test. No big deal."

Another explosion sounded and a second plume of smoke rose next to the first. The threats made by the Heirs of the Mother surfaced, and Zara's heart skipped a beat. *What if Lizzy is hurt?* Zara bit her cheek at the thought. "Why should I care?"

She turned her back, but she couldn't take another step. Zara groaned. No matter how angry she was at Lizzy, she *did* care. Then a thought rammed into her chest like a wrecking ball. She'd left the garage door unlocked. She'd had to in order to get out in secret with the stolen suit, and she did close it behind her, but…

What if the Heirs had someone watching? They were planning to attack. What if I gave them the perfect opportunity? Zara had been so wrapped up in getting out, that possibility hadn't occurred to her. As she'd walked, the panic had eased off, though her resolve to get home by herself had remained. The possibility of Lizzy and the people at the compound being in danger changed everything. Zara switched directions and headed back toward the compound, which was about three miles away. A third explosion went off, and she broke into a jog.

"What did I do? What did I do?" Zara's legs were moving too slowly. Sweat trickled down her face as she navigated the uneven ground of a soybean field. When she'd suited up, it had seemed like a good idea. She hadn't wanted to get caught out in the open without protection once the mosquitos came out, even though the area hadn't seen the swarms yet. She had planned to walk as far as she could for as long as she could. But as she made her way back to the compound, she wished she could take it off. The summer heat was overwhelming as she tried to run, and the suit and hat became even more stifling the more she picked up speed.

Zara alternated between running, jogging, and walking, a stitch growing in her side as she approached the final leg, a wooded area on the outside of the compound. Through the trees, columns of black smoke twirled, reaching for the sky. When she finally broke through the tree line, she gasped. Her fear was confirmed: the garage door she'd left unlocked was wide open, and the space that had been filled with four wheelers was empty. A body lay in the center of the concrete floor, but she didn't see anyone else.

She hurried to the garage, keeping her ears open. It was too quiet. When she reached the open door, she slowed and entered cautiously, scanning the room for danger. But it was just her and the body on the floor. Zara walked up to it, a lump forming in her throat as she recognized Carol. The woman's glassy eyes stared lifelessly, her arms and legs splayed in odd angles. Blood pooled around her body, and a bullet wound in her stomach left her shirt covered in red.

Zara walked around Carol's body as the sunlight coming in through the open garage door shone on silver. The keys she'd used to unlock the padlock still acted as a paper weight for the note she'd left. *No one saw it.* She reached out and tugged on the paper, letting the keys clink back to the table. Her hand trembled as she stared at her own handwriting. *This is my fault.*

She crumpled up the paper and let it fall back to the counter. *What would they do to me if they found out?* Panic seized her, and she quickly peeled off the suit and hung it back in its place on the wall. She grabbed the balled up paper and shoved it in her pocket, shame bringing tears to her eyes as she faced the door into the compound itself. She took a step toward it, as ready as she'd ever be to face whatever was on the other side, when it opened and a figure stepped through.

Zara yelped and grabbed a screwdriver on the countertop, holding it out in front of her. She couldn't seem to catch her breath. The air, too thick, pressed in on her, holding her in place. All she saw at first was the barrel of a gun pointed at her, but then it was lowered, and she was able to focus on Kyle's face. She dropped the tool and leaned on the counter, her chest heaving as she tried to regulate her breathing.

"You're alive," Kyle said, coming up beside her and placing a hand on her back. "What are you doing in here?"

Sweat stung her eyes and salted her lips. She had a hard time forming any other thoughts except, *What did I do?* "I… um… I was hiding." She lied, appalled at the words that came out of her mouth. *Is this how Lizzy felt when she lied to me?* It was a terrible feeling.

"Might have saved your life." Kyle closed the garage door and put the padlock back in place. "Mandy must have forgotten to lock this one after our last run. She's either gone or dead, now, though. I guess that's punishment enough for her."

"Gone or dead?" Zara blinked away tears. "Have you seen Lizzy? Or Mr. Peters?" *If he dies, does the solution to all of this die with him?*

"Mr. Peters is alive. I saw him, but… I haven't seen Lizzy. She might not be here." Kyle came up to her and put an arm around her. "Come on. Let's get you some water. You look terrible."

"What do you mean Lizzy might not be here?" Zara let him guide her out of the shipping container, but she stopped a few steps in. Several of the cabins were nothing but blackened timber. A few members of the community were still putting out some of the fires. The bigger buildings — the mess hall, the food storage, and the town hall — were all smoldering and blown to bits.

"It's likely the Heirs took some of us with them. We don't know why. It was so chaotic, no one really saw exactly what happened, but there aren't enough dead bodies to make up for the missing people." His voice cracked and his eyes misted. "Ten dead. Three missing. I guess we could still find their bodies in the rubble, but… someone did see at least one person with a bag over their head, their hands tied, being led away when the Heirs fled."

Zara shook her head in disbelief. None of it seemed real. "I can't believe this is happening." She hugged her middle, trying to hold onto something, to ground herself.

"They waited for the patrol at the top of the wall to pass by, and then they basically just threw the door open and waltzed right in. They caught us completely off guard. Blew our buildings, shot up our people, set a few cabins on fire, and then they were gone. It happened so fast. I didn't even register what had happened until it was over." Kyle guided her further into the compound, passing huddled groups, crying and holding onto each other, many of them holding children tight.

"That's our cabin." Zara pointed at a blackened, half-standing cabin. Mr. Peters stood outside of it with his hands on his head, just staring at it. He swung around, and upon seeing Zara, he rushed to her.

"Zara, you're alive," he said, his sooty cheeks marked with the path of tears from his eyes to his chin. "Where's Elizabeth?"

Zara shook her head. "I don't know." Dread swelled in her chest as she looked back at the cabin. "I… left her. I was angry."

Mr. Peters turned back to the cabin. "The bodies… I can't tell if any of them are her. There weren't any in the cabin, not that we could find."

"Where…" Zara swallowed bile. "Where are the bodies?"

"They're this way," Kyle said solemnly. He led her around the town hall to a row of corpses, several of them burned to a crisp. The air smelled of charcoal and burnt meat with a sulfur undertone that reminded Zara of when she'd burnt her hair with a flat iron. She fell to her knees and heaved, losing her breakfast.

"What is it?" Mr. Peters asked, pleading. "Do you recognize Elizabeth? Is she one of them? Why can't I recognize my own daughter? What have I done?"

His cries echoed Zara's own thoughts. She held out her hand and let Kyle pull her to her feet. "I… don't know. I think… that one is her same size." She pointed at the last body at the end. One burdensome step after another, and she was soon standing beside the body. The flesh was blackened, with patches of angry red. There was no hair, no identifiable features. The clothes had been burned away. "Where was this one found?"

"I'm not sure," Kyle said. "I think these burned ones were in the bombed-out buildings."

"Well, what would she have been doing in one of those?" Zara asked. "I mean, right, Mr. Peters? Maybe she was taken."

"Yes, yes." Mr. Peters nodded. "Taken. We… we have to get her back. Thomas… where is Thomas?" He swung his body around, yelling for the leader of the prepper community.

But then something glittered in the clenched fist of the burnt hand. Zara took half a step back. *No…* She knelt, looking more closely. *No, no, no.*

"What is it?" Kyle asked, kneeling beside her.

"There's something in that hand. I… I need to know what it is." Zara sat on the grass, trying not to breathe through her nose, her eyes fixed on that glitter.

Kyle nodded and pried the fingers open. The palm was blistered, but not completely blackened, and the two rings that fell from the hand were bloodied but recognizable. A butterfly and a ladybug.

"These rings are from the pawn shop…" Kyle picked them up and held them reverently in his hand. "I think… I think she'd want you to have them."

He held them out to her, and she took them, holding them close to her heart. Zara drew her knees to her chest, tears streaming down her face. "The last thing I said to her was that we weren't friends. I knew it was a lie when I said it, but I didn't take it back."

"I'm sure she knew," Kyle said. "She was holding onto these rings when she died. She hadn't given up."

Mr. Peters stopped yelling for Thomas. "What are you two talking about?"

Kyle turned and approached Mr. Peters with a gentle posture. "Zara found the friendship rings she gave to Lizzy in that hand. So, I'm sorry Mr. Peters. I'm really sorry. I think it's safe to say that this is Lizzy."

Mr. Peters half-heartedly pushed Kyle aside. "You're telling me that is my little girl?" he asked. "Zara, are you sure?"

Zara couldn't figure out how to form any more words. She nodded, though, and that sent Mr. Peters to his knees. He crawled in front of Zara to Lizzy's head, gingerly touching the corpse. His body visibly trembled. "I didn't mean it, Bethie. I didn't mean it." He lay down in the grass, rocking, repeating the same words over and over and over again.

And Zara wept. She wept for Lizzy, for her parents, for Jordan, for her aunt. She wept for the world. She wept until Kyle had to drag her into the safety of a small structure that hadn't burned to the ground while two others had to do the same for Mr. Peters.

But when she woke, something was different inside her. A resolve had taken the place of her guilt. Unlike when she'd discovered the deaths of her family members, Lizzy's death was like the last nail in the coffin of who Zara used to be. She sat up on her pallet on the floor, made up by Kyle's mother as a makeshift bed, knowing exactly what she needed to do.

"Zara, you're awake." Kyle was at her side with a pitying smile and a glass of water before she even got the blankets off. "How do you feel?"

Mr. Peters sat in a chair in the corner of the living area, rocking back and forth, as he'd done all night. He mumbled Lizzy's name and apologies in a cycle, sometimes stopping to say, "It doesn't make sense. I did everything right. I had the power. Me. I earned it. It doesn't make sense, Bethie. I'm sorry. I didn't mean what I said." And then he'd continue, never stopping. He seemed… broken, never raising his voice, always mumbling the words, eyes searching empty air.

Zara took the water and drained the glass in one drink. She handed the empty cup back to Kyle. "I feel like I've got a job to do." She forced herself to look at Mr. Peters. "Lizzy was a lot of things, but she never gave up." She took a deep breath. "I won't let the deaths of the people I loved be for nothing." *And there's only one way I know to find redemption.* "I have to get that man to Boston."

Chapter 38

Lizzy Peters

Three words had saved Lizzy's life. They'd come to her in a panic as a man had loomed over her with a gun. Kneeling on the ground outside her cabin, she'd screamed the greeting the Green Earth Futurists had always started their online meetings with. "Restore the Mother!" She'd sounded ridiculous, even to herself, but her instincts had been right. Mostly.

"Who are you?" the man had said.

She'd peeked from behind her upheld arms, trying to think of how best to answer, when a second bomb destroyed the town hall. She'd thrown herself to the ground and covered her head. The next thing she knew, the world went dark as someone wrenched her arms behind her back and put a cloth bag over her head.

She didn't know how much time had passed, only that she was in a moving vehicle with a flat, hard surface. From the roominess of the space and metallic *thrum* when she kicked the side, she assumed she was in the bed of a truck. There was no wind, though, which meant it was enclosed. That was good, considering the dangers of being exposed to open air in the evenings.

Lizzy rolled onto her side, trying to stabilize her body while her hands were tied behind her back. It wasn't easy. She slid when the truck slowed or sped up, and she could feel every bump in the road. Her head bounced, sometimes hitting the floor hard.

She wasn't holding out hope that anyone would come to rescue her. After what she'd done, she couldn't blame them. Her father would go on to Boston and save the world. He'd probably become famous. Her mother and Timothy would miss her, surely, but they'd get over that once her father told them what she'd done. And Zara would find her cousin, probably striking out on her own. Lizzy couldn't imagine Zee traveling with her father any longer.

I hope Zee gets those rings. That had been Lizzy's last act of friendship. Zara could use them to barter on her way home, if she chose to go it alone like Lizzy suspected she would. Zara would have never accepted them from Lizzy, so she'd given them to Mandy to pass along as a neutral party.

The truck rolled to a stop, and Lizzy tensed as doors slammed shut and footsteps sounded outside. The scraping of hard plastic and a burst of fresh air from above made her scrunch into a smaller ball. The truck bed bounced up and down as someone climbed in, and then someone was cutting the zip tie around her wrists and pulling the hood off her head.

A woman with bright blue eyes, wizened crow's feet, and a kind smile sat on her knees before Lizzy. They were in a large concrete room, the daylight being shut out by two massive doors closing. The woman's next words sent a shudder down Lizzy's spine despite the warm, inviting tone. She smiled, leaned in, and whispered, "Welcome home."

Attrition

No Tomorrow Book 3

Chapter 1

Timothy Peters

Stinging pain clawed at Timothy's back with every bump of O'Donnell's police car as they drove away from the farmhouse to police headquarters in Boston. Timothy was covered in soot, the taste of ash still thick in his mouth. His body ached, and his back was stiff, the skin taut and tender. As the adrenaline and shock wore off, the pain steadily increased. Debris that had flown at him when Frank's hidden explosive was detonated had tattered the back of his shirt, and flame had burned the skin in patches.

"Are you sure you're okay?" Heather asked from beside him. She sat in the middle of the backseat, Timothy on one side, Candice on the other.

"I don't think the burns are too bad," Timothy said, downplaying the pain a little. "I was really lucky." That part was true. Frank had tried and failed to kill him three times, he'd survived being trapped in the bunker, and he'd not gotten sick. Yet.

"We were all lucky," Heather said.

"It wasn't luck," O'Donnell said as he followed the other three police cars in front of him. "It was Abrams." His voice was gruff but laced with emotion at the mention of his fellow officer. If it hadn't been for Abrams and her dog, Moose, searching the farmhouse and property and then disarming several explosives, Frank Russo would have obliterated every single one of them. Instead, they'd only lost Ellis, their EMT. Of course, Abrams had died from exposure to the sickness, and they'd lost her, too.

Timothy nodded along with Heather and Candice. "Abrams was a hero," he said. "I'm sorry for your loss."

O'Donnell grunted, and his reflection in the rearview mirror revealed his motion of scratching his cheek was more of a cover for wiping away a stray tear. "We've all lost lately," he said.

Timothy swallowed a lump forming in his throat as an image surfaced in his mind; he'd found his mother dead in a pool of her own blood, shot and stabbed by the members of CON who had kidnapped the kids. George and Annika's faces coalesced in his mind's eye, too. *No, they're not lost yet. We're going to find them and get them back.* He didn't want to think about Lizzy and his father, either. He had no idea if they were still alive. Even if they were, he had doubts he'd ever see them again. The world had gone crazy. Getting across Boston without resources was hard enough, never mind trying to cross half the country. *One thing at a time. I can't do anything about Lizzy and Dad. George and Annika, though… they're within reach.*

He shoved down hopelessness and grief; he couldn't afford debilitating emotions. He still had people who needed him. And he still had to do something about Candice. He had no idea why she'd survived the sickness. He'd kept that a secret and convinced Candice to do the same, at least until they found someone who could do something about it. He didn't particularly like Candice, but he also didn't wish her ill. He didn't want her to become a lab rat or be forced to put herself in danger; he could see someone like Frank using her when he couldn't use his other men for fear of them dying. Like her or not, he felt some responsibility for her. She'd proven herself to be helpful… or at least, she'd proven she *could* be helpful when she wanted to be.

Timothy winced as O'Donnell wove around vehicles, hitting a pothole in the process and causing his back to bounce against the seat. Parts of Boston's streets had been cleared, cars and trucks and buses shoved to the sides of the road to create a straight way through, but there were still plenty of places where one had to get creative to move forward. He sucked in a sharp breath and tried to offer Heather a small smile as she threw a look of concern his way. "I'm okay," he said.

"You saved me from the brunt of that blast." Heather leaned over and kissed his cheek. "Thank you."

"I'd do it again in a heartbeat." He returned her affection, kissing her forehead.

Candice sniffed, her eyes tearing up. "You two make me miss my Hare-Bear. Do you think he's out there, somewhere?" She looked longingly out the window. "Maybe he found a way to the yacht in the harbor. It's practically a floating house. He'd be able to survive for a while there."

Heather took Candice's hand in her own. "I'm sure he's out there missing you, too."

The women shared a smile. *I guess Candice is growing on Heather.* Timothy didn't contradict his wife, but he couldn't bring himself to give the woman false hope, either. Harry Liddle was an older man, twice Candice's age. He'd gone into the city to check on his business when all hell broke loose, and he hadn't been heard from since, not even before cell service was lost. He'd had plenty of time to return to Wellesley before Timothy had been forced to flee with his family, Annika, and Candice.

The northern end of Roxbury rolled by, the buildings and sidewalks of Columbus Avenue abandoned of all life. The dead sat stiffly in vehicles, lay in awkward angles on the ground, and rested in the nooks and crannies of the city's porticos, balconies, and verandas. As the procession of police cars slowly made its way past the community college, faces appeared in one of the windows. Timothy put a hand on the glass of the police car window, leaning forward, trying to count how many people were inside. Five men and women watched, and one of the women pressed her hand against the glass, too. Their eyes met for a split second, and a sense of solidarity blossomed in Timothy's chest. He could see it in them, just like he was sure they could see it in him: they were survivors, but not the proud, triumphant kind. They were lost and frightened and torn apart and pretending not to be.

Timothy looked away from the college campus once those faces were out of sight, searching for other signs of life. On the other side of the road, corpses scattered the ground among the skeletons of blackened trees in Southwest Corridor Park. He avoided looking into the parked vehicles, having learned earlier on in their venture that the roads had become a graveyard, the vehicles their crypts.

A bright flash of red stood stark against the gloom in the scorched branches, and Timothy frowned, stooping to look out Candice's window. A very large, bright red parrot stretched its wings and flapped them a few times before taking flight. He twisted to look out the back window but lost sight of the bird. *Someone's pet must have gotten loose.*

"We're almost to headquarters," O'Donnell said, his voice pulling Timothy's attention away from the exotic bird. "We left behind some of our guys to hold the building and continue reaching out over our radios. It's been a week since we left, though. When we set out, we were going station to station, but… one thing led to another. We helped a few groups of citizens out of trouble and heard of the Russos and CON eatin' up resources, hoarding them. I knew where the Russos were. Only problem was the Russos got wind of us coming. They got eyes and ears in Boston even now."

"I wish that surprised me," Timothy said, "but Frank is a relentless son of a—"

O'Donnell slammed on the brakes as the brake lights of the car ahead turned bright red. He came within an inch of rear-ending his fellow policemen. Those in the other vehicles started getting out of their cars. "Hold on a sec." O'Donnell put the vehicle in park and stepped out.

Candice craned her neck around the driver's seat headrest. "Police Headquarters is right there. Do you think there's a problem?"

"Stay here." Timothy grabbed the doorhandle.

"What are you doing?" Heather asked. "O'Donnell said to stay put."

"No, he asked us to hold on a second, and I did." He opened the door. "I'll be right back. Whatever is going on involves us, and we have the right to know about it."

The summer sun beat down on him and reflected off the white patches on the police vehicles. He raised an arm as he stepped forward to block the glare, but then he paused as he approached the front of the procession. A concrete barricade blocked the road and extended into the parking lot to their left. It seemed to wrap around the back of the massive building. Three officers in heavy gear — helmets, face shields, bullet proof vests — pointed assault rifles at O'Donnell and his men, who had their hands raised.

O'Donnell's voice was like that of a father giving advice to his son. "Let's be reasonable," he said. "We're brothers, not enemies. My name is Captain Pat O'Donnell. Homebase is the Thirteenth, but we gathered here at headquarters pretty quick after the crap hit the fan. Figured with so many dead, it'd be best if we all regrouped."

One of the officers in gear shook his head. "Had some posers four days ago that approached the barricade, all dressed in uniform. They infiltrated us too easily, killed a couple guys, stole supplies and weapons. I don't know you. Got to wait for confirmation."

"I understand that, son," O'Donnell said. "Maybe we oughtta put the guns away, though?"

"Come on, Burke." The only woman among the three in gear lowered her weapon and nodded at the police cars. "Those other guys didn't have shops. Duncan said he's been waiting for an O'Donnell to come back."

"I have to be sure, Murphy," Burke said, keeping his gun trained on O'Donnell. "I need Duncan to come down and confirm. They can wait a few minutes for him to get here."

"Andy Duncan is an excellent lieutenant and an even better man," O'Donnell said. "We can wait." He addressed his own men. "Let's keep our cool." He held out a calming, open hand to one officer in particular whose fingers rested on the hilt of his firearm. "Webb, no need for that." The officer dropped his hand but kept his eyes on Burke.

The third officer on the other side of the barricade lowered his weapon. "C'mon, Burke," he said. "The man knew Duncan's first name. He's legit."

Burke hesitantly lowered his weapon. "We're still waiting on confirmation before we let any of them through."

Timothy took a cue from O'Donnell and stayed perfectly still. Burke may not have his weapon pointed at any of them anymore, but he still looked ready to use it.

Within five minutes, a man jogged out from the building, slowing to a stop with a grin on his face. "Captain, sir." He hopped the barrier and met O'Donnell with a handshake. He then turned to the rest, slapping Webb on the shoulder, then moving on to hug, shake hands, and pat the backs of the rest. All three in gear, including Burke, finally relaxed as they witnessed the reunion. "You guys have no idea how good it is to see you. Did you get the supplies?" He looked around them to peer inside the cars. "Where's Abrams? I'd figure she'd be the first out here to tell me I was wrong about you leaving."

O'Donnell cleared his throat. "Abrams didn't make it," he said. "We lost Ellis, too."

Duncan's smile faded and he took half a step back. "Sir… I…" He shook his head. "I know how close you and Abrams were. And Ellis… she was a good one. Damn it. We need good people like them right now."

"I know," O'Donnell said. "You were right, Andy. We never shoulda left."

Duncan looked up at the captain, eyes wide. "No, sir, I didn't mean… I would never…" He swallowed hard. "This isn't your fault, sir."

O'Donnell pressed his lips together and looked down at his feet for a moment before sighing and nodding toward the three who had greeted them. "I see our communications are working as intended. Why don't you introduce me to these fine officers?"

Duncan stood up straight, nodding. "Yes, sir." He pointed to the man who'd held his weapon aimed the longest. "This is Eric Burke." He pointed to the other man and the woman. "Scott Torres and Vicky Murphy. They were all on the beat in Chelsea. Showed up the day after you left."

"How are things across the river?" O'Donnell asked.

Murphy rolled her shoulders and shook her head. "Just as bad, sir, but I think things are just as bad everywhere."

"And how many have we added to our numbers, Duncan?" O'Donnell asked.

Duncan set his feet a shoulders' width apart and gave a short report. "About a dozen from all over Boston, and a few as far as Cambridge to the north, one from Milton to the south. That makes twenty-seven, besides whoever you brought back with you. Not a ton, sir, but better than when you left."

O'Donnell nodded. "What d'ya think about lettin' us through the barricade?" He raised his eyebrows, and the three in gear hurried to move a section of the barrier. "We'll talk more inside. We've got a lot of work to do, Duncan. We can't just stay here, holed up at headquarters."

"What's that supposed to mean?" Duncan frowned.

"It means we took an oath to uphold the law and protect the people," O'Donnell said, "and I know exactly how we're gonna do it. I've got a story to tell, Duncan. I just don't wanna do it out here." He patted Duncan on the shoulder, and then he turned around. "Let's go," he shouted as he walked toward the end of the procession.

His officers jumped to return to their vehicles. When O'Donnell spotted Timothy outside, his expression soured. "I told you to wait in the car," he said.

Timothy walked with him to the last police car. "I appreciate your help," Timothy said, "but I'm not one of your men. I don't have to follow your orders, and I want to stay in the loop."

O'Donnell stopped and faced Timothy. "We worked together back at the farmhouse," he said, "but that—" he pointed at the police headquarters "—is *my* house and those are *my* people. If you want our help, I have to know that I can trust you to follow *my* orders. I'm going to rescue Lissa if she's out there, if she's at this Farm with your brother and that little girl. But if you want to tag along, if you want to be part of my team, you gotta do what you're told. Got it?"

"Yeah, I understand," Timothy said. He needed their help if he wanted to find George and Annika. *I guess this is another hierarchy… but it's better than Frank's.* He shuddered at the thought of the Russos and what it would have been like to be subject to Frank's whims until the kids were safe and sound. But this hadn't been what he'd had in mind either. He'd pictured partnering with O'Donnell and going after CON as a team. His stomach sank as he crawled into the back seat with Heather and Candice.

It didn't matter what he did. Timothy was always under someone else's control. His actions were always dictated by a man more powerful, more knowledgeable, more capable. Every time he took his life by the horns and tried to ride it out, it threw him to the ground and stomped all over him. Shucking the family business had left him in a dead-end job. Finding Annika had brought Frank into his life. Fending off Frank had almost gotten Heather killed. Leaving for supplies had gotten his mother killed. And he'd barely made it out alive after trying to get the Russos to work with the Boston Police Department.

"What's wrong?" Heather asked as Timothy closed the car door, and O'Donnell started up the engine.

"Nothing." Timothy smiled, unwilling to lay more burdens at his wife's feet. But the truth was that his luck had carried him through the last week. *Despite* his mistakes, he was still alive. *Despite* him, the people he loved were still alive. The truth was that luck wouldn't last forever.

Chapter 2

Alexander Roman

Peters can't be trusted. Dr. Jonah Newton's warning scrawled in red ink nagged at Alex as he navigated the smaller roads of North Carolina's countryside. The beloved voices of Oliver, Minnie, and Lauren bounced around the cab of the RV Minnie had lovingly nicknamed Harvey, but Alex couldn't concentrate on what they were saying. That ominous message took center stage while other worries played second fiddle.

They'd left the CDC in Atlanta the day before, driving five hours before pulling off the road, hiding Harvey in an empty barn, and hunkering down in the RV's living space. The four-door cab, the compact but well-arranged living space, and the vehicle's off-road capabilities made it perfect for traveling cross country. However, they were also hauling an enclosed trailer with extra gasoline canisters and supplies from the CDC. It was a gold mine on wheels, which meant it was a perfect target for the desperate or the downright unsavory. The RV wasn't easy to maneuver, and it wasn't winning any races any time soon. That stirred in Alex a sense of vulnerability. He had chosen country roads and avoided cities, even if it added length to their journey. But he couldn't let go of the feeling that he had to be on high alert at all times. Those concerns, layered over his worry about their destination, made for poor sleep and a wandering mind as all the what-ifs circulated in his head, his thoughts always coming back to that note and Jonah's last words on the sat phone.

Jonah used his final breath to tell me to go to New Horizons in Boston and find Walter Peters. He glanced at the glovebox where he'd stuck the file folder with the photo, the redacted report, and a map of Boston with New Horizon's location pinpointed on it. They'd found that in the supplies Jonah had left for them at the CDC. *The file must have been given to Jonah by the government whistleblower. But then why send me to someone he knew wasn't trustworthy?*

The only explanation was that Walter Peters and his company could help, but Alex would need to keep an eye on him. *Maybe Peters is like Lawson. Maybe he's just out for power.* He'd experienced it more than once in his lifetime: the humanitarian work at big companies like Vanguard were often sparked by the more common man. If Walter Peters had only taken credit for publicity's sake, or if his humanitarian work was just a means to an end for his public-facing persona, the real Walter Peters could very well be like the man who'd attempted to carve out his own little seat of power in Atlanta.

"What do you think, Dad?" Oliver asked, his voice breaking through Alex's thoughts from the backseat of the cab.

He raised his eyebrows and looked over his shoulder. "About what?"

"Daaaaad." Oliver drew out the word and ended with a frustrated huff. "Aren't you listening?"

Alex looked at Minnie in the passenger seat beside him, raising his eyebrows and throwing her a smile. "A little help, please?"

Minnie chuckled. "We were all playin' a game called 'Would You Rather.'"

"Ah!" Alex said with as much enthusiasm as he could muster. He couldn't stop worrying, but he could protect his son from the same spiraling thoughts. "One of my favorites. What was the question?"

Oliver perked up, scratching Samson's ears. The dog sat between Oliver and Lauren, his head on Oliver's lap as usual. "Would you rather be able to talk to all animals, *or* be able to speak all foreign languages?"

Alex smirked. "I would rather be able to speak all foreign languages—" He held up a finger. "—*because* research shows that animals communicate with each other. What is language if it's not communication? So, being able to speak *all* foreign languages would mean I would also be able to talk to animals." Samson barked, and Alex shrugged. "See? Samson knows what I'm talking about."

"Showoff," Lauren muttered from the back seat with a smile. She quirked an eyebrow, giving him a pointed look in the rearview mirror.

"Yeah, Dad." Oliver laughed. "That's cheating. It's supposed to be one *or* the other. Not both."

"I can't help it if I'm brilliant." Alex flourished his hand in an exaggerated motion. "This brain is no joke."

Oliver laughed again. "You *are* a showoff."

"I love you like a son, Alex," Minnie said, patting his shoulder with a grin, "but stick your nose up any higher, and we'll be able to see just how big that brain of yours is just by lookin'."

Alex grinned. "Only if you could see past all the boogers."

Oliver devolved into a fit of giggles, and Lauren rolled her eyes. Minnie just shook her head and said something about how he'd never pass for a Southern gentleman. Alex pulled himself fully into the present; it felt so *normal* and so *good* to laugh and joke around with his son. A part of him ached that his wife, Naomi, wasn't there with them, but another part believed in some ways she actually was. He felt her presence in his son's laughter, in the lightness of his heart as he joked with good friends. *You would have loved Minnie and Lauren, my love.* The worry cleared to the edges of his mind as he made room for the people he still had left.

A sign of three white boards announced their arrival in a town called Stem. Though Alex didn't spot a population number, the sign boasted six insignias, almost like achievement patches on a boy scout's vest announcing his accomplishments. They were apparently very proud of their two churches and their 4-H club, those being the largest insignias of the six. Alex had diverted their path from cities, but this little town didn't seem to pose a threat, even if there were survivors there. *Maybe we'll run into someone friendly.*

His spirits were high as a few houses appeared, set back on large lots. The road forked, and he chose the path straight ahead as he continued to play silly road trip games with his son. The road sidled up to a railroad track, the sun shining down on the countryside. He could almost imagine that the world wasn't in chaos out there, with the birds flitting from tree to tree and the fields sprouting green shoots. But another quarter of a mile, and a loud pop sounded. They bounced, with a loud *thud* coming from one tire, and the vehicle wobbled.

"Harvey's gone and popped a tire," Minnie said as Alex came to a stop. "No bother, though. We got a spare."

"Well, I'm having too good of a time to let this get me down. I'm sure we all need a bathroom break anyway, and there are plenty of trees around. Plus, Samson could use a little stretch." Alex smiled over his shoulder at Oliver. "Keep the dog on the leash, though, bud. We don't want to waste time chasing him down if he gets too spirited."

"He'd never do that." Oliver pursed his lips. "Samson is the best dog that ever lived."

"That he is," Minnie said. "But even the best dogs get too excited sometimes."

"I'll keep him on the leash." Oliver sighed and hooked the leash onto Samson's collar before he opened his door. "Sorry, boy. You can't run free today." Samson hopped to the pavement and tugged Oliver down the road a little way, sniffing everything, tail wagging furiously.

"I'll change the tire. You two keep an eye out for anything suspicious." Alex got out of the car along with Minnie and Lauren. He headed to the back of the RV where the spare tire was kept.

Lauren shuffled along the road behind the RV toward a line of trees. "I've got to pee," she said. "I'll be right back."

Alex slid the tire rack out from under the RV and retrieved the spare and set it beside the RV. He frowned at the flat tire. "We must have hit a nail or something." He scratched his cheek and crossed his arms, stepping back from the RV. "Hey, Minnie? I just realized I don't know what I'm doing. This has to be more complicated than changing the tire on a little car, right?"

Minnie stuck her head around the front of the vehicle and gave him a flat stare. "Same idea, but it is a little different," she said. "You need me to do it?"

"How about when Lauren's done relieving herself, she can keep an eye on Oliver, and then you can teach me how it's done. That way I can do it myself if it ever happens again." Alex joined her, smiling at Oliver as he let Samson tug him in zigzags.

"That's what I like about you," Minnie said. "Not too proud. Some men could be as lost as the Easter egg nobody finds for years, but they wouldn't admit it if the Easter Bunny himself slapped him with a basket."

Alex laughed. "Minnie, has anyone ever told you you're an absolute gem?"

She pasted on a haughty look. "I do believe they have." Her haughtiness gave way to a playful smile. "Now, where is that daughter of mine?"

Lauren's voice answered as if on cue. "Hey, Alex? You should come look at this."

Alex furrowed his brow as he rounded the vehicle. Lauren was several feet from the back of the added trailer, standing in the middle of the road. As he passed the end of the trailer, he noticed the back tire on it had blown as well. *That's odd. Two tires?*

"Hey," he said, "you ever have two tires blow at the same time?"

"I think I know what happened." Lauren pointed at the pavement.

Alex's heartbeat picked up as he got closer and bent down to investigate. He hadn't seen these on the road when he was driving. He'd been too distracted, enjoying life a little too much. The metal was almost the same color as the grey road. It looked like someone had taken a very small hollow pipe, cut it up, and bent the pieces at ninety-degree angles, welding them together in pairs. The tips of the pipes had been cut, sawed to sharp points.

"Tire spikes," Alex whispered, his mouth running dry. He bolted to standing. "We have to get out of here."

Lauren looked at him with widened eyes. "What? Where would we go? We can't drive Harvey, not with two flat tires."

Alex spun around. "Come on. Go and grab Oliver and Samson and lock yourselves in the back. Get low and stay away from the windows." He yelled for his son as he sprinted toward where Minnie watched him from the front end of the vehicle. "Oliver, get into the RV!"

Oliver paused from where he was several yards away, and Samson barked. "What did you say, Dad?"

"What is it, Alex?" Minnie asked.

Beads of sweat rolled down Alex's neck, and his heartbeat pounded inside his chest. "Get over here, now, Oliver!" He took Minnie by the elbow as Lauren rushed past him toward Oliver and Samson.

"I'll get them to safety," she said. "Get the tires changed."

"Hurry, Minnie." Alex spoke hushed, frantic words. "The tires weren't an accident. I think we've fallen into some sort of trap. There were tire spikes on the road back there."

Minnie's face went pale. "We'd better hurry, then. There's a compartment there on the side with what we need. We've got to block the tires and jack up both sides. We've got the spare from the trailer and the one from the RV. They ain't gonna take us anywhere fast, but at least we'd be movin'."

Lauren pulled Oliver and Samson behind her, her eyes on the door into the back of the RV. Samson trotted along, seeming without a care in the world until his ears twitched and his nose snapped to one of the houses sitting back on a lot. The dog growled. Alex followed Samson's pointed gaze, his blood running cold.

"Dad, who are they?" Oliver's voice quivered.

Six men in bright orange jumpsuits walked toward them in a line. They didn't seem in a hurry. Two of them had handguns. The rest held weapons of different sorts: two crowbars, a baseball bat complete with nails jutting outward, and a long-handled axe.

Alex set his jaw. "There's no time to change tires."

"What are we gonna do?" Minnie asked. "Those jumpsuits… are those prisoners?"

"We run," Alex said. "They won't chase us down if they get what they want."

"We can't replace those CDC supplies, Alex." Lauren's voice was low and trembling.

"We also can't replace our lives, and those men don't look friendly." Alex looked at his son. "Let's cross the tracks. I think the town is that way. We might find shelter and a vehicle."

Oliver patted his mother's purse which always hung at his hip and nodded once. Alex confirmed with a glance that both Minnie and Lauren were with him. The men were still walking at an unhurried pace.

"Let's get out of here." Alex waved for Minnie to go, and she started at a jog. Oliver followed close behind. Lauren tugged on Samson's collar hard to get him to stop growling and move. Alex followed last, looking one last time over his shoulder at the approaching men. They were all focused on the trailer. Not one of them paid any attention to their fleeing victims. Alex bolted around the front of the RV and almost ran straight into Lauren's back. Minnie and Oliver had frozen, too. Alex's temporary relief that the men hadn't been focused on them was banished as a flood of adrenaline filled his veins. Four more men were approaching from across the tracks.

"This way, then." Alex took a step north, but he only had to look to see that fleeing that way wasn't a choice, either. Three men walked toward them from that direction. His stomach knotted as he positioned himself in front of Minnie, Lauren, and Oliver. They backed up against the RV, and Samson came up beside Alex, tugging at his leash, growling. "They're not in a hurry," Alex said, "because they've got us boxed in."

Chapter 3

Lizzy Peters

Whispers mocked Lizzy from within. *I'm a liar, a monster. Just like my dad. I deserve to be trapped here.* She sat on a hard metal bench in an underground concrete room, her elbows resting on a cold metal table. A small bowl of oats proffered curling steam and the scent of cinnamon. Lizzy kept her head down. There was no way out of what she'd gotten herself into.

Strangers in plain brown clothing chattered amongst themselves, throwing suspicious glances at her. Their whispers scorned her, too. Lizzy caught words like *unworthy, fraud,* and *outsider.* They gave her table a wide berth.

Lizzy's position among the Heirs of the Mother was unclear. She'd been welcomed the night before into a windowless, grey world of the very people who'd almost killed her. The very people who *had* killed others at the compound. She had no idea if Zara or her father were still alive.

I should have kept my mouth shut. But when the intruders had come after her, she'd shouted the mantra she'd heard over and over again in meetings with the Green Earth Futurists. *Restore the Mother.* Lizzy scooped up a spoonful of thick oatmeal and let it plop back into the bowl. *I'm such an idiot.*

She'd recently discovered that the GEF was a front to make the Heirs of the Mother more palatable. And she'd fallen for it all to impress a boy she never should have been involved with in the first place: Jordan Williams, Zara's older brother. Since learning about GEF's origins, Lizzy had no doubt that the information she'd supplied them, the information that allowed them into Vanguard's records, into her father's safe at home, had been used to bring about the end of the world.

Her father had been a shrewd businessman, fulfilling a contract with the government. Jordan had been gullible and idealistic, just like most of the GEF. But Lizzy had just been stupid and thoughtless. *I should have let them kill me at the compound. I can't escape this place. I can't become part of it, either. And if I did escape, where would I go? My father and Zara hate me. Mom and Tim and George… once they find out, they'll hate me, too. I betrayed them all.*

Hot tears burned her eyes, and she quickly wiped them away. Lizzy pushed the bowl away and stood up, immediately reminded that she wasn't completely alone when the man who'd escorted her to the cafeteria stepped forward. He'd introduced himself as Orion, but Lizzy wasn't convinced that was his real name. Every name she'd heard in the lair of the Heirs was connected to nature in some way: the name of a star, a flower, a bird, a tree. It was just too weird to be a coincidence. She suspected most of them gave themselves new names when joining the Heirs. Or they were born into it, and their parents really were so far gone that even the names of their children were dictated by the Heirs.

"If you're finished," Orion said, "the Mother wants to see you."

Lizzy had to stop herself from scrunching up her nose in confusion. *They call the earth Mother, right?* "Oh," she said. "Yeah, I um… I can do that. Do we need to go outside? Like… give a message to the Mother through the tree spirits or something?" She swallowed hard. *That went too far. Who does that?*

Orion smiled. "No, although some of us do enjoy that type of meditation on Wednesdays at noon."

Oh. My. Goodness. "At noon… right. Yeah, that'll work for me. My schedule is totally clear." Lizzy returned his smile.

He laughed and *booped* her nose like she was five years old. "I love a sense of humor," he said. "But we shouldn't keep the Mother waiting."

Lizzy's smile faltered. "Yeah, sure. Lead the way." She followed behind him, suddenly hyperaware of her heartbeat as the room quieted. Everyone in the commissary froze, and all eyes turned on her as she left the room for an empty concrete hallway.

Her mind raced as fast as her increasing pulse, and she wiped her sweating palms on the brown trousers she'd been given the night before. *It's fine. I mean… they're insane, and this guy is probably leading me to some weird ritual where my heart's cut out – like in that ancient, stupid Indiana Jones movie Zara made me watch last summer.* She took a deep, shaky breath. She was alone. Her dad and Zara weren't there to save her or tell her what to do. So, she did what she always did. She followed. Orion brought her to a door at the end of a hallway, and then he stood off to the side.

"You want me to go in there?" Lizzy pointed to the plain steel door set into the concrete.

"Knock, and she will allow you in when she's ready." Orion clasped his hands in front of him.

Lizzy hesitantly walked up to the door and raised her fist. She knocked, glancing at Orion out of the corner of her eye as she did. The sound echoed down the hall. Lizzy waited, but there was no reply, so she raised her hand again.

"No," Orion said, a note of scolding in his tone. "She knows you are here. She'll come when she's ready."

"Right." Lizzy cleared her throat and took a step back. "Sorry." She folded her arms and waited. *What kind of game is this?* The minutes ticked by with no answer. *Am I supposed to just stand here forever?* She was about to ask Orion if he was *sure* whoever was inside the room heard her when the door opened. Lizzy jumped, the movement startling her, and stepped backward.

A woman in a nude-colored, floor-length, wrap dress opened the door. Her long black hair was fashioned into a single, thick braid which fell over her shoulder. She wore no makeup or adornments, but she boasted a natural, subtle beauty.

"Orion, you may enter with her. I may need your help." She didn't look at the man, instead keeping her eyes on Lizzy, though she didn't speak to her. She only retreated into the room, leaving the door open.

Lizzy forced her feet to move forward. The room beyond was bathed in a warm light, and though it was set up like a cozy office, with a sitting area opposite the desk and bookshelves lining the back wall, Lizzy's skin crawled. She waited for the next odd thing to happen. She didn't have to wait long.

A hiss startled Lizzy, and she jumped away from the door, her hand flying to her chest at the sight of a very large snake staring straight at her. It only helped a little that the thing was behind glass. Half of the entire wall next to the door was a window into a large terrarium for the creature. Lizzy bumped into the back of a sofa and nearly toppled over it.

"Please, have a seat." The woman's voice drew Lizzy's eyes away from the snake. She had taken a seat in a wing-backed chair and was looking at her expectantly.

Lizzy's hands were trembling, so she balled them into fists and tucked them under her thighs as she sat on the small couch. "So, you're… the Mother?"

"My name is Autumn Griffin," the woman said. "I am the Mother of the Heirs, just like my birth mother was before me."

Great. Generational crazy, then. "Okay," Lizzy tried not to shrink back from her.

"The mantra you spoke, the one that alerted my people to your knowledge of our ways, what does it mean to you?" Autumn asked.

"It means that… I want the earth to be healthy?" Lizzy didn't mean for it to come out as a question, but it did.

Autumn smiled. "It means that Mother Earth deserves to be restored to a time before humanity ravaged her."

"Yeah," Lizzy said, "that's what I meant. But, um… you said it better."

"You pretend to be an Heir." Autumn leaned back in her chair, her tone more curious than angry. "It was very clever, and I'm glad you did it. I believe the Mother has brought you to me, Elizabeth Peters."

Lizzy's heart stopped. She'd never told them her name. Her mouth opened, but no words came out. *What do I do? How does she know me?*

"You were an important part of the Cleansing, Elizabeth," Autumn said. "Did you think I wouldn't know your face? You, dear girl, were our Plan A."

Lizzy felt the blood drain from her face, and her head swam. "I… I didn't know what you would use that information to do. I didn't know my father's company had created something so dangerous."

Autumn smiled brightly. "So you know, then? You know what you did?"

"I know I betrayed my father." Lizzy felt cold. She wanted to huddle in the corner of the couch, bury her head in the cushions.

Autumn offered a sympathetic look. "You betrayed a bad man, Elizabeth. To us, you're a hero. We could have been forced to wait too long. We could have been pushed to more extreme measures. You aided the Mother in Cleansing herself of the wickedness of humanity." She scooted to the edge of her chair and reached out a hand to rest on Lizzy's knee. "And now you're here, and you can make sure nothing gets in the way of the completion of the Cleansing."

Lizzy shook her head and batted away Autumn's hand. "You're insane!" In her periphery, Orion frowned and stepped toward her, but Autumn stopped him with a look.

"Your father is one of the few people in the world with ready knowledge about how to curb the Cleansing." Autumn set a steely gaze on Lizzy, her previously friendly smile gone. "It's a miracle that you ended up here, Elizabeth. It's a miracle from the Mother, and she's begging you to help her. Where is he?"

Lizzy's eyes had gone so wide they stung. Her mouth was like sandpaper, and the air seemed to be doubling in thickness with every quick breath. "He's dead," she said, hoping Autumn would believe the lie. "He died at the World's Fair."

Autumn's smile returned, but there was something menacing about the way her eyes narrowed just slightly. "If you know what we used the information to do, you know because he told you. And he wouldn't have done that before the World's Fair."

Lizzy searched for an answer, and one came tumbling out of her mouth. "I read the same files I gave you access to. I knew what I was doing when I betrayed him. That's how I know that the sickness was created by New Horizons Lab as part of a government commission. My father is dead."

"So, you knew what we were doing, and you said nothing?" Autumn's expression didn't change, and neither did her voice. Her words were accusatory, but her tone was even, like she was chatting on the porch with a friend.

If they think I'm one of them, they won't hurt me. The lie formed in her mind quickly. She tried to remember the name of the most radical member of the GEF, someone who might have been an Heir.

"Yes. I knew." Lizzy swallowed her doubts that this line of reasoning would work and went all in. "I'm not here because of some miracle. I wanted to find you. Poison Ivy… I don't know her real name, but… she told me about the Heirs. I was looking for you. I'd heard your people were raiding the area."

Autumn narrowed her eyes and sat back again in her chair, proceeding to simply stare at Lizzy for what seemed like an eternity. Lizzy stared back for a time, but eventually, her nerves got the better of her and she turned away, clasping her hands in her lap and twisting at her fingers.

Finally, Autumn stood. "I don't believe you, but I suppose a test of your devotion to our cause would settle the matter."

Lizzy nodded. "Sure," she said. "What do you want me to do?"

"Follow me." Autumn exited the room from the same door Lizzy came in through and opened a door in the hallway to the right. Lizzy followed behind, Orion on her heels, into the room on the other side of the glass terrarium. The room was smaller, the snake a prominent feature. And in the center of the room, a man was gagged and tied to a chair. Lizzy gasped at the sight of him and backed up, only to have Orion block her from leaving.

"I know it's not original," Autumn said as she walked along the glass, her finger gliding across the surface of the terrarium, "but this beautiful creature is Venom. He's an Australian Inland Taipan. Not easy to acquire, but I've found we make a good team." Her finger lifted from the glass and she turned, placing her finger on a small table by the wall. She picked up a syringe. "Venom provides me with a natural way to rid the world of bad people. It's a sort of poetic justice; they destroy nature, and she destroys them. Just like the mosquitos." She ungagged the man, who coughed and spit, cursing with dry, rasping words. "This man, and two more who have been found guilty and are being held here now, sat on the board of directors for an oil company that has had its fair share of oil spills. Millions of innocent animals slain because people like this man couldn't bother to put the safety of the Mother before their own greed." Autumn uncapped the syringe. "Elizabeth, upon your word, justice will be served. Tell me, should he die for his crimes?"

The man leaned his head away and wriggled against his ties. His attempts were all in vain. "I'm sorry. Please, I just… I need to get out of here. I need to check on my kids." Tears rolled down his cheeks. "Please, please, let me go."

Autumn smiled at Lizzy and raised the syringe in the air. "Elizabeth? I await your word."

Lizzy's breaths came in short bursts, and her vision blurred with tears. "No," she said, "the… the Cleansing is done, isn't it? I mean… so many have died."

Autumn's smile turned sad. "I can't say I'm surprised at your response. But a problem remains; not *enough* of the *right* people are dead." She looked back at the man and without ceremony plunged the venom into his arm.

Lizzy sucked in a breath. There was no hiding the way she trembled. Orion wouldn't let her back out of the room, so she pressed against the wall.

"If you'd been converted to our way of thinking, you wouldn't have hesitated to give the word for this monster to meet his end. You'd understand that we're not trying to destroy humanity. We're trying to save its soul, and then we'll rebuild our species into a more peaceful society." Autumn shook her head and replaced the syringe on the tray. "Tell me the truth, now, Elizabeth. You've never been one of us, have you?"

Lizzy shook her head as she sank to the ground and hugged her knees to her chest. "I want to go home," she said. "Please? Just let me go." Her voice broke as she echoed the dying man's words.

Autumn gently brushed the man's hair out of his eyes as his body began to jerk in sharp motions. "Elizabeth, you call me insane. You lie to my face. You try to twist the message of the Heirs as you sit in the comfort of *my* home." She turned away from the convulsing man. "But, no matter." She walked over to Lizzy and knelt in front of her, wiping away her tears with the back of her hand. "You'll come around, Elizabeth. Eventually."

Chapter 4

Zara Williams

Zara watched the evidence burn. The crumpled paper twisted in the flames, unfurling enough for her to make out her own handwriting just before the fire consumed it, turning it to ash. The day before, she'd left it on the counter in the garage, weighed down by a padlock key, thinking it would be discovered shortly after she'd fled the compound in a stolen protective suit. Instead, it seemed the Heirs of the Mother had seen Zara leave alone and infiltrated the compound through the unlocked garage door. Everyone thought Carol, the woman who cared for the equipment in the garages, was responsible. Twelve people had died, including Lizzy Peters, Zara's best friend, and Sunny, the nurse they'd brought with them from the hospital. From that group, only Zara, Mr. Peters, Dr. Sarah Donald, Amos, and his daughter, Sophie, were still alive.

The butterfly and ladybug rings Zara and Lizzy had exchanged at the rekindling of their friendship just a couple days prior hung on a chain around Zara's neck, the weight of them pressing against Zara's heart. As the last of the note burned away, Zara clutched the rings in her hand, letting the gemstones dig into her palm. She focused on an ember floating up into the late morning sky and breathed in deeply of the warm summer air.

"Hey, Zara." Kyle sat next to her on the little stone bench surrounding the fire pit which had been started that morning to burn trash from the wreckage all around them. "You okay?"

Zara tucked the rings under her shirt. "Considering what happened yesterday? Yes. Although I can't say the same for Walter."

Kyle reached for a stick and poked at the fire. "He's still in a trance, still whispering her name."

Zara furrowed her brow. "When I found out my parents and my aunt were dead, I was like that… totally broken. I could barely function. And then I found out my brother was dead, too, and I just got so angry. But now… my best friend is dead. I told her we weren't friends anymore." Zara shook her head, her shoulders slumping. "She'd just confessed to lying to me about some pretty major stuff, and I was so mad at her."

"You have to believe she knew you didn't mean it." Kyle put the stick down and put a hand gently on her back. "You guys were like sisters. Sisters fight. You can't let this destroy you."

"That's just it." Zara looked right at Kyle. She'd cried the night before when she'd first found out about Lizzy's death, but there had been no tears since. "I *should be* devastated, but… after grieving my family, after spending so much time so angry… I'm just done. This is the world now. If I break every time something bad happens, I won't live to see it get any better. I won't get home to my cousin, who may be the last family I have left. I'm sad about Lizzy, and I'll never forgive myself for my last words to her, but I'm *not* devastated." She took a deep breath. "I don't know how to feel about that."

"It sounds to me like you've just had a lot of practice grieving," Kyle said.

"Yeah." Zara stood up. "I guess I have. I think I'm going to find Walter, see if I can do anything to help him. We need to get out of here, back to Boston."

"You could stay." Kyle stood up, too, and he took half a step toward her. "We could use you here."

A stab of guilt ran through Zara, and she was almost grateful for it. *Maybe I'm still normal. Still human.* She offered a small smile. "Like I said, I have to get back to my cousin. And Mr. Peters has two sons and a wife back home." *And he's still got to fix this mess.*

Kyle shifted his weight and ran his fingers through his hair. "Maybe you could come back, you know… with your cousin?"

Zara held out her hand, and he took it. She gave it a light squeeze. "Maybe," she said. *But probably not.* She couldn't live in the compound knowing what she'd done, and they wouldn't let her if they ever found out. *More secrets. I guess we all keep them.* "But right now, I need to find Walter. Do you know where he is?"

Kyle squeezed her hand back, returned her smile, and let her go. "He's where you left him, probably." Kyle stepped back and gestured toward the wall of shipping containers — four high, two deep — with barbed wire at the top.

The barrier that surrounded the compound had seemed so impenetrable the first time Zara had seen it. The hollows of the wall had been acting as garages and storage, but they served a third function after the Heirs had attacked: living spaces. Not all of them were suitable for living inside, and none of them were fancy, but they would do the job until the members of the community could rebuild their cabins and other buildings. It had been a relief to Zara to learn that Thomas, the man who ran the place, kept duplicate stores of supplies in those walls. Her actions hadn't left them completely defenseless as well as down a dozen members.

Zara made her way to the wall, passing working members of the community. Half of them were finishing digging graves, and the other half worked to clear debris, including Amos. Dr. Sarah Donald was tending to injuries in a tent Thomas had set up for her. She was frowning at someone's ankle, poking and prodding. The flaps were open, and as Zara passed by, she caught the doctor's eye and they waved at each other. In the distance, Sophie played tag with a few other kids her age.

The children playing were the only part of the scene that resembled normalcy. Everyone else looked exhausted, even though they'd been forced to shelter inside and rest all night. It would take them twice as long to get the area cleared and rebuilt with only part of the day deemed safe for outside activity. Zara wasn't sure the compound would be back to its former glory even if that hadn't been the case. Everything would have to be built by hand and from scratch.

She paused at the sight of the bus on the other side of the compound, beyond where the children played. *Their vehicles were stolen. What if they won't let us take the bus now that they need it?* Zara's stomach sank at the thought, but she kept moving. That was a problem for later. *Right now, I need to deal with Walter. Before I can get him home, I need to get him out of bed. I owe Lizzy that much.*

The entrance to the garage was the only way into the livable areas of the wall. Zara slowed as she passed a dark stain in the center of the concrete. That was where Carol had died. *She doesn't deserve to be blamed.* But telling Thomas and the rest of the community that it was all Zara's fault wouldn't do anything but get her and Walter kicked out; if Walter Peters died because they couldn't reach shelter, or because they ran into someone who was infected, the whole world would pay the price.

She put her head down and headed for the thin staircase that led to the second level of shipping containers. They hadn't bothered to convert the second level into one large room like they had for the garages below. Instead, these containers were separate rooms, connected by doorways. Supplies had been stuffed into other spaces, and the room the staircase led to was filled with bedrolls. Walter was the only person still there. He'd set up his bedroll in the far corner, and his back was to Zara as she approached. He was shriveled. Defeated. Unimposing. He was nothing like the Walter Peters Zara knew.

"Hey, W—" Zara cut herself off. She'd started calling him by his first name because she'd known how much it angered him. It didn't seem right as he grieved his daughter. She cleared her throat. "Mr. Peters?" There was no answer. Zara sat on her own bedroll which was next to his. "I know you're hurting, but... we need to talk."

He shuffled and then rolled onto his back, letting his head loll to the side to look at her. "You don't have to pretend to be nice to me, now, Zara."

"I'm not pretending." Zara looked into his eyes, tried to break through their glossy stare. "We both know you have to get to Boston. And soon."

Walter's eyes ticked upward, and his mouth parted slightly as he stared at the ceiling at one of the battery-powered lanterns hung in intervals. Each one had a cord hanging down from it with an on and off switch attached. He seemed to be concentrated on the light.

"My daughter burned to death after I told her I didn't want anything to do with her."

"I know." Zara swallowed the lump forming in her throat. "I said things I regret, too."

"I'm... not a good person." He frowned. "I thought I was. I thought I was just doing what had to be done. But I'm just like *him*."

"Just like who?" Zara leaned over and put the back of her hand against Walter's forehead, checking to make sure he wasn't feverish. His skin was clammy and sweaty, but he didn't seem any warmer than she was. The renovated portion of the wall was fitted with a cooling system run by the generator. Thomas had ordered it be run in bursts to conserve energy, but it wasn't terribly hot inside.

"My father." Walter looked back at Zara, his tone flat and distant. "I inherited his demons, but I tried so hard to kill them. And they were gone for so long. I loved my wife and my kids. I never touched them, never hurt them. I was *there* for them. But the demons were just waiting to come out." His eyes filled with tears that spilled over and ran down his temples, dripping to the pillow. "You were right about me, mostly. Except for the part about not caring, of moving on and never looking back. I see their faces in my dreams. Even the woman at the fair, the one I didn't know."

His words pierced Zara. Twenty-four hours ago, she would have relished his admission that he was a monster, but as she listened, she remembered how he'd saved her and Lizzy several times over the last weeks. Her own demons showed their faces in her mind's eye. She'd stewed in anger and bitterness, shot a woman she cared for in the chest, lambasted her best friend, and then caused the deaths of a dozen people with her recklessness. "Mr. Peters," Zara said, "we all have demons. Whatever your father did was his problem. You're no saint, but... maybe you're not as bad as I thought you were."

"You don't understand," Walter said, propping himself up on one elbow and reaching for Zara with his other hand. He gripped her ankle, looking up at her as though pleading. "I'm *worse*. The things I've done since the World's Fair, those things are the real me, Zara. Playing a husband and father, pretending at being a philanthropist... *that* was the lie." His features twisted in agony. "I want to die, Zara. I deserve it. You can do it. I know you want to."

"What? No!" Zara tried to pull her ankle away, but he held on tighter. She slapped at his hand, tears springing to her eyes as she remembered momentarily considering backing off of CPR when he'd had a stroke. "Let me go, Walter!"

Zara pried his fingers off her ankle and scooted back from him. Walter's expression faded to something neutral again, and he slunk back to the ground, lying once more on his back. She scrambled to her feet and took a few steps back, running her fingers through her hair. His haunted voice still rang in her head.

"Mr. Peters..." Zara tried again, her voice trembling. "You have to make it to Boston, and you have to fix what's happening in the world. You said you had a way to fix it. That wasn't a lie, was it?"

He squeezed his eyes shut. "If I go back, I'll have to tell Dana that I lost her, that I got her killed."

"No, you won't." Zara took a deep breath. "It wasn't your fault."

"The mosquitos, DV-10... I'm responsible for that." Walter sounded exhausted. "I couldn't find a way to bring her home safely. It *is* my fault. Control slipped through my fingers, little by little until it cascaded through, and I lost her."

"You lost control the second someone else decided to steal what you created." Zara cautiously sat back on the bedroll. "The lies, the cover up, the anger, and the secrets... you were trying to control the situation, but they only made things worse. You weren't the only one doing that. Lizzy did it. I did it." She bit the inside of her cheek as she thought of the note. "Dang it, I'm doing it now." She looked straight at Walter. "I unlocked the garage door. I left, and when I heard the explosions, I ran back as fast as I could, but... if it wasn't for me, the Heirs wouldn't have had a way inside."

Walter frowned at her. "You were trying to get back to Boston by yourself?"

"Yes," Zara said. "I abandoned Lizzy, and I lied when I got back." She stood up again. "I have to tell Thomas. I can't live like this anymore. There's a line between telling a lie and *being* a liar, between doing a bad thing and *being* a bad person. If I don't want to cross it, I have to take responsibility."

"No," Walter said, struggling to a sitting position. "I let the demons out, and I drove you to it. I drove Lizzy to lie and hide and carry burdens on her own. If I had been the kind of father she could talk to, if I had been a good man..." He let out a long breath. "No, you can't put yourself in danger. I can't let you. I owe Elizabeth that much."

Zara smiled sadly at how closely his words resembled her own thoughts when she'd come to help him. "Then come with me, Mr. Peters. Thomas and the people here are good people. Come with me, and we can both tell the truth." She stepped toward him and held out her hand. "Thomas is going to kick us out, or worse. We're going to have to scramble for shelter and supplies, and it's going to be hell. But… we'll be free."

He looked down for a moment, his lips pressed tightly together, a contemplative look on his face. "Maybe," he said, "it's time for me to try something different." He looked up and took her hand, letting her help him to his feet.

Chapter 5

George Peters

George finally understood why his mother never let him stay when the action started. When she tried to shield him from the news; when she sent him to the other room under the guise of watching Annika; when she made him babysit while they all prepped the house for invasion; when she forced him to stay in the bunker when Timothy and Heather fought off Frank and his crew… his mother had known that George wasn't grown up like he'd wanted to be. He would have messed things up, just like he had in the clinic. He'd told his mother he could help, and for once she'd let him. When George had crawled on top of the rolling medical cart to set off the sprinklers with a lighter, he had tried to be quiet. Instead, he'd knocked the tray over, alerted Digger and Icepick, and gotten his mother killed. He could still see her sputtering for breath every time he closed his eyes. He had no idea if Heather was dead, too.

His cheeks turned hot, shame bubbling up inside of him at the thought of explaining to his family what had happened. *They're all going to hate me.* At the same time, his chest hurt every time he thought of his mother. He missed her so much; that word people used sometimes — heartache — he understood that for the first time, too. It was like someone was slamming a sledgehammer into his chest over and over, waiting until the pain had faded a little before taking another swing.

He pressed his hands flat on the metal floor of the U-Haul he'd been shoved into a few hours before and took a deep breath. The air was hot and stale, and breathing deeply only made his hands and legs more jittery. He wanted to bang on the doors, to get out and run. There were too many kids crammed into the space. It was too dark, the only light coming from a large flashlight hung from the ceiling. It rocked back and forth with the movement of the vehicle.

After Digger and Icepick had taken him and Annika, the thugs had left the two of them tied up in a room while they ran "errands." Eventually, they'd brought George and Annika to an abandoned grocery store. There, other men stuck them in a back room with a dozen other kids. George and Annika had been loaded up into the U-Haul along with the rest; he hadn't lost her, and that was the only thing saving him from a complete meltdown. It was another reason he couldn't run. *I'd probably die if I escaped on my own, but trying to drag Annika with me? I'd get us both killed.*

And there was no way he could let that happen. The little girl had become part of the Peters family over the past weeks. He'd known her in passing ever since she'd been adopted by Zara's aunt, but she felt like a little sister to him after all they'd been through. And she needed family, even if she didn't fully understand that hers was gone forever.

"George?" Annika cuddled up to him. "I'm thirsty." She swayed and bumped him as the truck jostled them.

"Here, take the last of my water." He handed her the water bottle he'd been given as they'd been shoved into the back of the truck. It had one drink left. He'd been saving it, but Annika needed it more than he did. Besides, she was the only person in the world who didn't think of him as useless.

"Are we almost there?" Annika asked after draining the water.

"I don't know," George said.

"Where are we going?"

George sighed. "I don't know."

"Are we going to that Farm place those men talked about?"

"Maybe." George rubbed his hands over his face, trying to clean off some of the grime.

Annika was quiet for only a moment before launching into another question. "What is The Farm?"

"Annika," George said, trying to keep the frustration out of his voice, "I don't know *anything* right now."

"Okay," Annika said, drawing her knees to her chest and resting her chin on top of one. She looked at him from the corner of her eye, opened her mouth, and then shut it again.

"What is it?" George could tell she wanted to say something else.

Annika wrinkled her nose. "I'm hungry."

They'd all been given one granola bar early that morning, but that was it. "I don't have anything to give you." George didn't like how the older kids were scowling at Annika, so he added in a whisper, "I think we should try to be quiet."

Annika nodded, and rested her head on George's shoulder. When the truck slowed to a stop and the engine stopped rumbling, she sat up straighter, and so did George. A wave of uneasiness fell over the truck as kids started shuffling and whispering, many of them scooting toward the back of the truck. George grabbed Annika's arm and tugged her away from the door.

"Aren't we getting out?" Annika asked.

"I don't know," George said, his heartbeat picking up. What are they going to do with us? Will they separate us?

"I don't want to be scrunched." Annika resisted being pulled toward the other kids.

George wrapped his arms around her waist and did his best to pick her up. "Just do what I say, Annika."

"I don't want to!" Annika kicked in the air as George lifted her. "I want to get out!"

"Stop it!" George grunted as Annika struggled. "I don't know what they want," he said. "I'm trying to protect you. I don't want them to hurt us."

Annika wrenched away from him, but she stood still, tears rolling down her cheeks. Then she lurched forward and wrapped her arms around his waist, letting him walk her to the back of the truck without another word. George didn't know what to think about that. Sometimes he didn't understand her.

He put a protective hand on Annika's shoulder, warm bodies crowding him. One of the kids started crying, and one of the older kids shouted for them to shut up. Metal scraped against metal, and the door slid upward. It caught the cord the flashlight hung from, the light wobbling like crazy as the door took all the slack of the cord, pushing the flashlight until it was pulled taught and pointing to the back wall. Daylight flooded inside the space, and George momentarily shielded his eyes.

Annika clung tighter to him, and a few of the girls yelped at the sight of two men. One of the men pulled a built-in ramp out of the U-Haul and set it into place, taking up position at the bottom while the other man stalked up into the truck. Yelps turned to terrified screams. A few of the kids started sobbing. Even the bigger kids George's age huddled away from the man. George hugged Annika tighter and pressed his back into the person behind him, shuffling his feet to keep from being pushed forward.

The man came about a foot into the U-Haul and then stopped, crossing his arms and narrowing his eyes. "Bunch o' sniveling crybabies we got here, Big Mack," he said over his shoulder.

George's muscles went rigid as the sounds of heavy breathing and whimpering took the place of the screams. He could feel Annika's heart pounding through her back as he pressed his hand against her. His own pulse raced, ticking in a too-fast rhythm; his heart lodged in his throat.

"Even sorrier than the last batch." Big Mack scowled at them from the ground. "But we got uses for every bag o' bones."

"That we do." The man's features were all sharp angles, covered with a layer of fat freckles, sitting beneath a shock of bleach-blond hair. He was thin but toned, and despite how short he was, his ice-blue eyes made for an intimidating stare down. "I want all you kids off this truck. If I have to make you move, you won't like it, so I suggest you get on it right now."

"Hey, Ruger!" Big Mack's voice boomed into the truck. "If this batch needs incentive, I can get creative." He grinned. "Maybe the last one out is left in the coop overnight?"

"Ah, the coop," Ruger said fondly. He smiled at them. "You see, kids, the coop is what it sounds like. A nice, big chicken coop with nice, big holes in the wire. Plenty of room for those mosquitos to mosey on through, take a bite, leave you with eyes buggin' out of your head."

Annika hugged George tighter, and his shirt grew snug as she balled the material in her hands. He glanced at the other kids, and suddenly he was glad he was at the front of the group. *Would they really do that? Leave a kid out to die?* Icepick and Digger came to mind, and he suddenly had no doubts. These adults weren't like the ones he was used to. If they had boundaries or lines they wouldn't cross, he hadn't seen them yet.

George bent his head down to whisper in Annika's ear. "Be ready to run." She shook her head, burying her face into his torso. She was so stiff.

Ruger chuckled. "Nah," he said. "I wouldn't do that to ya on your first day. We can save that one for later. I like to keep it in my back pocket. How about instead, the last person on the truck doesn't eat?" He looked back at Big Mack, who shrugged.

"That'll do, I guess," he said.

Ruger joined Big Mack at the bottom of the ramp, his footsteps clanging against the metal surface. The two men stood off to each side of the ramp, facing the kids. "Okay, kids," Ruger said. "Let's have a little race. Last kid inside the truck misses their next three meals."

George's stomach growled. He'd not had anything but a granola bar in the last twenty-four hours. Other kids' hands pressed against their stomachs, and soft groans of trepidation rose amongst them.

George rubbed Annika's arms to try to loosen them up. She was holding on too tight. "Come on," he whispered anxiously. "You have to let go of me so we can run."

"I want you lined up against that wall when you come out," Ruger said, pointing to a bright red building with white-framed windows. "Don't try to run past that. There's nowhere to go, and if you try to escape, we really will need the coop tonight. Got it?" He waited as George and a few others nodded. "Ready, set… go!" Ruger clapped his hands on the last word.

There was a moment of hesitation before the huddled mass of kids unfurled and broke apart in a panic. The kid behind George shoved him hard, and George tried to run forward, but he tripped over Annika who was still stiff as a board. George was shoved again, and he and Annika fell to the ground. He flung out his hands, catching himself and managing to not crush her beneath him.

"George!" Annika curled up and put her hands over her head as another kid tried to leap over him, feet slamming into George's side instead, sending them both sprawling. George landed on his side beside Annika, but he quickly scrambled to his feet, throwing his shoulder into another boy who tried to barrel over him.

"Come on, Annika!" George grabbed the back of her shirt, ignoring her sobs, and yanked her to her feet.

She spun around, her eyes wide and teary. Her lip puckered and trembled, and she was still frozen stiff. He bent down and grabbed her around the legs, throwing her over his shoulder, and rushed toward the ramp. Most of the kids were out already. George glanced back. There was one more kid still huddled in the corner. *We can make it!* He was *so* hungry, and he couldn't let Annika go another day without food.

It took a moment, a few more steps toward the ramp, for his brain to process the image of the last kid, a little boy around Annika's age, crouched in that corner. *Was he bleeding?* George slowed his steps and came to a stop at the edge of the truck's back end.

Big Mack frowned at him, and Ruger quirked an eyebrow. "You coming, kid?" Ruger asked. "I ain't got all day."

George looked back at the little boy. There was a gash on his forehead. He squatted with his arms wrapped around his knees, and he was rocking back and forth. He looked terrified. George let out a long sigh. He set Annika down, her feet on the ramp, his still on the truck.

"Stay here," George said. "I'll be right back. I'm going to get the other kid, okay?"

He jogged to the back of the truck. It had been less than a minute since Ruger had forced them to all enter a free-for-all. It hadn't taken long for them to turn on each other. George wasn't going to be that kind of person. He knelt in front of him.

"I'm George," he said. "What's your name?"

"J-J-James." The boy stopped rocking.

"C'mon, James." George held out his arms. "Let's go." He picked up the boy — he was actually lighter than Annika — and carried him to the ramp, setting him down. The second the boy's feet hit the ground, he turned around and bolted for the wall. Annika looked up at him and smiled, and George smiled back. He looked up at Ruger. "There," he said, holding out his arms. "I'm the last person on this truck."

"Well, that spoils the fun." Big Mack scoffed and walked away toward the line of kids.

Ruger seemed to study George before responding. "Who is this girl to you? Your sister? Cousin?"

"A friend," George said. "Like a sister," he added. Annika held out her hand, and George took it, joining her on the ramp.

"One day, that kind o' moxie might get you somewhere," Ruger said, "but today, you've got to learn that you're not in control." He wasn't smiling anymore, and his tone was serious. "For the next twenty-four hours," Ruger said, "you *and* your friend go without."

"What?" George's mouth dropped. "You can't do that!"

"I can." Ruger nodded toward the wall. "Join the others, the both of you."

George bit his tongue, but he was raging inside. He'd failed Annika, but it wasn't for lack of trying. *Is that how it'll always be? Trying and failing to make myself useful?* He pressed his lips together and walked down the ramp, still holding Annika's hand. But when he passed by, Ruger stopped him with a firm hand on his shoulder.

George couldn't quite place the look on Ruger's face, something similar to when a parent tries to teach a child, but… different. Like when adults were explaining something to another adult. His words sent a shudder down George's spine, not just because they were frightening but because he *understood* the lesson.

"Don't try to bend the rules, kid," Ruger said. "Today, it makes you hungry. Tomorrow, it might make you dead."

Chapter 6

Alexander Roman

Alex didn't like the odds — thirteen men, thirteen *convicts*, against three adults, a child, and a dog. He'd learned he could fend for himself when push came to shove *if* the people he loved weren't being immediately threatened. He'd also nearly committed murder and found out the lines he *was* willing to cross to protect his family were a lot farther than he'd previously assumed.

He held up his hands, standing between Minnie, Lauren, and Oliver and the men in orange jumpsuits. "We don't want trouble," he said. "Just let us go. We need to get moving if we're going to find proper shelter."

One of the convicts eyed Lauren and brandished a handgun. "You can take the kid and the old lady," he said, "but leave *her* behind, and you've got a deal." A few of the other men looked past Alex; they were practically salivating. Samson growled, barring his teeth.

"You yellow-bellied snakes!" Minnie stomped up to stand beside Alex. "You ain't touchin' my daughter. No way, no how."

"Yeah, that's not going to happen," Alex said. "She comes with us."

A man with glasses held together by tape stepped out of line; he was the only one who didn't seem ready to pounce on Lauren. "We're here to get supplies." His shoulder twitched upward just a tick, and he blinked rapidly for a moment. "We need food. Water. Medicine."

"Shut up, Ben." The first man to speak seethed. "We got other needs in mind." A chorus of agreement circulated amongst the convicts. The speaker focused back on Alex. "Look," he said. "You three can save yourselves. No one here *wants* to kill a kid. We'll do it, but we'd rather not. We won't go looking for you. But if you stay, we'll get what we want anyway, and you'll all be dead." He raised his weapon. "Your choice."

Alex's stomach sank. He looked over his shoulder at Lauren, but she was staring at Oliver, her lips pressed into a thin line. That wasn't fear on her face; it was determination. She looked up, a fierce glint in her eyes.

"Get Oliver and my mom to safety." Lauren held up a hand when Minnie opened her mouth. "I can't let you all die."

"Dad?" Oliver looked up at him with wide eyes. "We can't leave her."

Alex looked into the eyes of his son. The last thing he wanted was for Oliver to lose another person he loved. And then there was Minnie. Alex wouldn't be able to make her leave Lauren, and they'd lose her, too. *No one can make that woman do anything.* Alex felt time slow as he looked back at Lauren.

"You saved me once," Lauren said, voice cracking. "Let me save you and Oliver now."

"You're not talkin' straight," Minnie said. "You—"

The loud rumble of multiple engines ripped through the air. Every single convict startled, most of them whipping their heads around, wide eyes searching in all directions.

"It's *them*," one of them shouted. "They found us!"

Ben balled his fists together in front of him and knocked his knuckles in an anxious gesture. His face contorted. "I told you," he said. "I told you they'd come for a big group. I told you we should stay underground. I told you, I told you, I told you."

"Shut up, Ben!" The man who'd been leading them yelled. The convicts were now focused on the north end of the road as two motorcycles rounded the bend.

"Don't talk to me now," Ben said to no one in particular. "Not now. Not now."

The motorcycles kept coming in staggered pairs. "We can take 'em," the leader said. "Hold your ground."

Alex didn't care who the motorcycle gang was or why the convicts seemed so afraid. An overwhelming sense of relief fell over him, but then adrenaline kicked in. The convicts were temporarily distracted, but that wouldn't last forever. He grabbed Oliver. "C'mon!" He shouted. "Let's get out of here!"

He urged Oliver to run in front of him. "Go, buddy! Don't stop!" They ran back the way they'd come. "Watch out for the spikes," Alex yelled as he narrowly missed one. He glanced back to make sure Lauren and Minnie were following. Minnie was huffing and puffing, but they were both—

A piercing pain shot up through Alex's foot. He shouted as he tumbled forward, hitting the pavement hard. He caught himself on his forearms, skidding a few inches. Eyes watering, he held in a scream by biting his lip, though he couldn't stop an agonized groan. The taste of copper flooded his mouth as he drew blood.

Oliver slowed down and half turned toward him. "Dad!"

"Don't stop!" Alex shouted. "I'm fine! Keep running, Oliver!"

Lauren and Minnie caught up to him, and Minnie kept on toward Oliver with Samson by her side. "I got 'im, Alex!"

Lauren stopped, looking back nervously as the convicts stood together to face off against the motorcycle gang. "Things are going to get ugly," she said.

Alex grimaced as he sat up and took a look at his foot. A crude tire spike protruded from the sole of his shoe. He sucked in a breath. "Damn it," he breathed. "I'm such an idiot."

"We can debate that later," Lauren said. She knelt beside him. "I'm going to take it out, but it's going to hurt. A lot. You'll have to fight through the pain to run, but it's our only choice."

A gunshot shook the air and the sound vibrated through Alex's chest as shouting and more gunshots broke out on the other side of the RV. A man in orange fled for the field, but he was quickly tackled by a man wearing a leather vest over a white t-shirt and jeans. The biker threw two punches to the face with fingerless leather gloves, and the convict went limp.

Lauren yanked the spike out of Alex's foot. He sucked in a sharp breath, and a wave of nausea swept over him. The world spun as he held his breath, trying not to scream in pain so as to avoid drawing too much attention.

"Don't pass out on me," Lauren said, flinching and ducking her head as more gunshots rang from the near distance. She threw the spike aside, stood up, and held out a hand. "Get it together, Alex. We've got to go."

Alex nodded, newly formed beads of sweat dripping down his face as he took her hand and let her help him to his feet. He leaned on her, putting all his energy into moving forward. Ahead, Minnie, Oliver, and Samson turned off the road into a gravel driveway, hustling toward a house.

As Alex and Lauren reached the same driveway, Alex's head began to clear. The pain was still intense but so was the adrenaline. He found a way to walk on his heel that minimized the pain of the puncture to the front of his foot. Blood seeped into his shoe and a wet, sucking noise sounded with every step. The warm, thick substance made his heel slip and slide inside his shoe so that he could never quite land in the same way twice. But he managed to keep going, to make walking bearable.

Minnie ushered Oliver into the house, handing him the leash so that Samson could follow him, and then she held open the front door, waving for them to hurry. "That's it," Minnie said. "Keep a'comin'."

"Just a few more steps," Lauren said as she helped him limp through the front door.

"Is there a basement?" Alex asked, panting. "We need somewhere to hide." He moved away from Lauren, using the walls to help him balance. He pulled back the curtain just enough to peek outside. "We're not far from the fight."

"I'll check!" Oliver dropped Samson's leash and disappeared down the hall. Samson came to sit by Alex, sniffing at his foot, whining a little and nudging Alex's leg gently with his nose. The clicks of doorhandles and the whine of hinges signaled Oliver's search had begun in earnest.

Minnie leaned over and rested her hands on her knees, breathing hard. "If you'd told me a few weeks ago that we'd be runnin' into some stranger's house uninvited, tryin' to escape a bunch of criminals as a bunch of bikers went hog wild on their butts, I'd have said you were crazier than a soup sandwich."

"What do you think happened out there?" Lauren asked, leaning against the front door. "I mean… whoever those bikers were, they saved me from… from…" She swallowed hard. "They were going to…" Her cheeks blushed and her eyes glistened with tears. "I can't even say it."

Minnie was wrapping Lauren in a hug in a second flat. "You don't have to, sweet pea. It didn't happen."

Lauren hugged her mother, her head resting in the crook of Minnie's neck. "Momma… if it was between me and all three of you, though—"

"Shush, now," Minnie said. "We weren't going to let that happen."

Once again, however, Alex had been close to compromising in ways he never would have even considered himself capable of a few weeks before. When he was safe and untested, before the world made a turn for the worse, it was easy for him to conjure up perfect responses to theoretical dangerous situations. He'd hear stories on the news about people being attacked or about people surviving natural disasters, and he'd judge the reactions as brave or stupid, courageous or cowardly. But when facing those same situations, he was finding out quickly that the line between those things was a lot thinner than he'd once imagined, and it wasn't always so black and white in the moment. Despite Minnie's assurances, when those bikers had shown up, Alex had been debating what to do. He hadn't *wanted* to leave her there with those convicts, but…

Thank goodness I didn't have to make a decision. He nodded at Lauren, meeting her eyes with his own and offering a small and somber smile. Her solemn nod back at him as her chin rested on Minnie's shoulder communicated that she knew what he was saying. *Thank you for being willing to sacrifice yourself for us.*

Alex checked outside again, hoping no one would notice the curtain if he was careful. In the near distance, a man in orange ran at full speed past the house on the road, a look of terror on his face as a biker drove past him and wacked him on the back with a crowbar, the same one that had been used to threaten Alex and his family.

"Whoever those bikers are," Alex said, "they're a gift from Heaven."

"We don't know anything about the bikers. Don't assume they're friendly." Lauren pulled away from her mother. "They could have been just as bad. We may have stumbled into a turf war."

"You don't have to worry about that," Alex said. "The people I trust these days are right here."

"Well, whatever they're fightin' over, we just need to steer clear of it, and we'll be fine," Minnie said. "Right?"

"I hope so," Alex said.

Samson huffed and pointed his nose down the hall where Oliver had gone, and then his ears perked up and he took a few steps before barking again. Alex frowned at the dog and looked down the hall.

"Oliver?" Alex no longer heard evidence of his son searching for a door to a basement. He limped away from the window, avoiding the blood smeared on the floor in the rough shape of his shoeprint. "Bud, did you find anything?"

When no answer came, Minnie stood up straighter. They all three exchanged a frightened glance. *Something isn't right.*

Alex bolted down the hall. "Oliver! Where are you?"

He came up short as he ran into the kitchen at the back of the house. A man in an orange jumpsuit had Oliver, one arm around his neck. But he wasn't paying attention to Alex. He was staring at the other side of the kitchen where a back door led out into the yard. Standing in the doorway was a hulking biker with a scowl on his face. The three men were locked in a triangle.

"Let the kid go," the biker growled. He pointed a finger at Alex. "That your dad, boy?"

"Yeah," Oliver squeaked out.

"Whatever is going on between you two," Alex said, "leave us out of it. Just let my son go."

"Can't do that," the convict said. "He's my ticket out."

"Not true," the biker said. "I ain't lettin' you go. You hurt the kid, I'll kill you with my bare hands. Let him go, give yourself up peacefully, and I'll take you back to the lineup without harming a hair on your head."

The convict sneered. "Not a ch—"

Samson zoomed into the room, nearly knocking Alex over. The convict yelped and threw up his other hand, backing into a corner of cabinets as Samson's teeth snapped at him. He let go of Oliver and tried to climb up onto the counter.

Alex grabbed Oliver and pulled him back into the hall where Minnie and Lauren waited. "Go! Lock yourselves in a bedroom. I'll get Samson." He turned back to the kitchen as Minnie and Lauren whisked Oliver away.

The convict was standing on the counter, backed against the wall, stooping over because he was too tall to fit. The biker crossed his arms and chuckled, seeming to enjoy the show.

"Samson," Alex said, patting his thigh. "Come here, boy." Samson gave one last growl and snap of the teeth as if to warn the convict from trying to hurt his people again. Then he licked his snout and trotted back to Alex. "Good boy," Alex said as he scratched Samson's ears.

The convict was still on the counter. "I wasn't really going to hurt the kid," he said.

"Yeah, sure." The biker was still chuckling. "You got about half of what you deserved. Now, get down off the counter. You're coming with me." He pulled zip ties out of his pocket. The convict warily got off the counter, shuffling quickly over to the biker when Samson looked at him and snarled just a little.

As he put the zip ties on the convict, the biker nodded at Alex. "Name's Ned. I'm guessin' you were these scumbags' target?"

Alex nodded, though didn't feel like being friendly with the biker just yet. "I'd say that's accurate," he said.

"We've been trackin' these convicts for about a week." Ned pulled the ties tight and patted the convict on the back hard enough to make him stumble forward a step. "They escaped the prison two weeks ago. Not all of 'em are much of a danger, but there were about a hundred in the supermax building."

"We had to escape!" the convict said. "The prison guards gave up and left us there to die."

"That don't mean you gotta team up and start terrorizing survivors," Ned said. "Now shut it until the lineup. You caused me enough of a headache already." He looked at Alex. "I know you don't know me from Adam, but I suggest you and your family come with me. We can help you."

"And who are you, exactly?" Alex asked.

The biker grinned. "We're just a bunch of guys who love ridin' hogs and hate seein' good people get hurt. We call ourselves Zion's Angels."

Chapter 7

Timothy Peters

Timothy paced the room that had been delegated for him, Heather, and Candice. Chairs had been stacked and tables folded, and everything had been moved to the walls so that three cots could be centered in the space. O'Donnell had insisted they stay at police headquarters, squashing opposition. It seemed many of the police officers wanted the building to remain a center for lawmen and women only, a base of operations for the professionals. The compromise had been that the three were cordoned into a small section of the building previously dedicated as a break room for members of other emergency services to use when at the station. They had no access to police records, weapons, or resources, not that Timothy cared. The police had even positioned a guard to sit in the hall connecting the room to the rest of the station.

"It feels like we're being kept prisoner." Timothy paused his pacing to look into the hall where the guard chowed down on a granola bar.

"They don't know us," Heather said. "It makes sense from their perspective. We need to trust that O'Donnell is talking to them about going after the kids."

"They can't stop me from coming." Timothy crossed his arms, wincing a bit at the tug of skin on his back. Another EMT had treated him with prescription strength burn cream and pain killers. It still stung, but it was manageable.

"No one said they would try." Heather stood up from her cot and put a hand gently on his chest. "Timothy, just sit down, okay? Have some water. Eat a granola bar. You need to rest if you're going to be able to go after the kids."

"I can't rest *until* those kids are back with us." Timothy was still focused on the guard outside. He was itching to march into the hall and demand O'Donnell come and tell him what the heck was going on.

Heather's calm and gentle voice should have been soothing, but it only aggravated him. "Timothy—"

A surge of anger bubbled up inside him. He shrugged off Heather's hand. "I can't believe you aren't more eager to get them back." He knew it was the wrong thing to say the second he said it, the second his wife's chin trembled, and she backed away, becoming smaller.

"Hey! You're being a butthead." Candice frowned at him. "She wants those kids back just as much as you do. *I* want them back, too. We're all worried about them. We all want to go shouting at the top of our lungs, searching the city. But that would be stupid."

Timothy blushed at Candice's reprimand because he knew she was right. He was taking out his frustrations on the one person who he could always count on. He sighed and pulled Heather closer, kissing her forehead. "I'm sorry," he said. "I shouldn't have said that. I didn't mean it."

Heather relaxed into him. "I know you didn't," she said. "We're all on edge."

"Not you," Timothy said. "You're perfect. I don't know how I would have gotten through any of this without you."

Heather kissed him softly. "I'd hug you tight, but I don't want to hurt your back." She offered a small smile. "Don't worry, Tim. We'll get George and Annika back." Her smile faded, and she looked away from him. "We have to get them back. For us. For them. For Dana."

A pang went through him at the mention of his mother, but he also recognized that look in Heather: guilt. And that hurt him, too. He tilted her chin up and met her eyes, repeating what he'd already said dozens of times. He'd say it a hundred more, if he needed to. "What happened to my mom wasn't your fault."

Tears sprung into Heather's eyes. She nodded and buried her head into his chest, but he wasn't sure she really believed it. He rested his chin on Heather's head, stroking her hair. Candice was looking at them, her own eyes glistening. Timothy's eyes blurred; he held his emotions at bay, but it required a constant building to brick them out. Sooner or later, the dam would break. He just couldn't let it happen. Not yet.

A knock at the door barely gave them time to gather themselves before O'Donnell barged in. He stopped short, his mouth snapping shut as he took in the scene. "I… uh… didn't mean to interrupt anything, but we're gettin' ready to discuss what to do with CON. I had to fight to get you in the room, Timothy. We need to go. Now."

Heather stood by Timothy's side, lifting her chin. "Candice and I need to know what's going on, too," she said. "We are part of this team."

"I agree." Timothy crossed his arms. "They're coming. And going after CON was our plan to begin with, not yours. There shouldn't be any fight over our inclusion. If there's any hint that we're going to be kept from full participation, we'll go get George and Annika ourselves and let you guys do what you can about CON on your own."

O'Donnell sighed. "It doesn't work like that," he said.

"Like what?" Candice stood up and came to stand beside Heather. "You have no right to keep us prisoner."

"No," O'Donnell said, "I meant, I can't speak for everyone. We've got dozens of precincts represented here, many o' them from surrounding jurisdictions. We're poolin' resources, and there's a lot o' good that comes from that. But we're also experiencin' some… difficulty in chain of command. No one is high rankin' enough to just call the shots. I don't know how many o' them will even join my men in going after CON. They won't stop us, not after our promise to Abrams, but we might be on our own."

"Let's be clear," Timothy said. "We are working with you, not *under* you. We call our own shots. And if you and your guys are all that come with us, we'll make it work. We made a good team back at the farmhouse. We'll make a great team here in the city."

O'Donnell grunted. "Damn it. I hated your guts when we first met, but I'm startin' to like you, son." He sighed. "A'right. Fine. All three of you with me."

Timothy exchanged a look of solidarity with Heather and Candice. They'd stood together and gotten what they wanted. Candice was right. We all want this. We all have to go after it together, and I've got to have their backs. I know they have mine.

O'Donnell led them down the halls of the large building. All the doors were open to almost every room, and natural light spilled into the space from the abundance of windows. They were all on the first floor due to the heat. It was bearable, but only just. When they walked into a conference room with skinny tables and chairs facing a podium at the front, they were each handed a water bottle. Timothy followed O'Donnell to the front of the room and sat down with Heather and Candice in the second row.

Chatter increased upon their arrival. The section of seating O'Donnell had led them to was filled with members of the 13th Precinct. Timothy still didn't know all their names, but he recognized Karl Webb, Lucy Freeman, and Arnold Penn from the farmhouse. He also recognized Lieutenant Andy Duncan from the day before. He was the man O'Donnell had left in charge when he'd left with a team to investigate the Russos and try to confiscate their stolen supplies. In the back righthand corner, Timothy spotted the police officers who had been in full gear at the barrier: Eric Burke, Vicky Murphy, and Scott Torres. Burke still looked on edge. He fidgeted with his fingers, eyes darting back and forth across the room as if waiting for an enemy to pop up out of nowhere. Murphy put her hand on his back and whispered something to him, and Burke leaned back, relaxing only a fraction.

Burke wasn't the only officer who looked like they'd been through hell. Every single one of them had tattered uniforms, some worse than others. Most of them had visible cuts and bruises, and if Timothy had to bet, he'd say the rest had injuries covered over by their clothing. But it wasn't just appearances that spoke to the state of the officers in the room. Some had haunted eyes and pale cheeks, and they stared ahead, barely acknowledging their fellows. Others rocked just slightly or displayed some other tick, such as tapping the table with their fingers or pulling at their hair. Still others were like Burke: stiff and alert, searching, eyes wide as if expecting something terrible to happen at any minute.

But they were all there. They were all in uniform. They were all at least trying to keep their oaths to protect the city. They don't have to be here. Who's making them? Who would judge them for going to look for their families or just abandoning their posts all together? It's been weeks since everything collapsed, and none of it is getting better any time soon.

"A'right ladies and gentlemen," O'Donnell said as he took the spot behind the podium. Another man with captain's stars on his shoulder joined O'Donnell. "In case any of you don't know me yet, I'm Captain Pat O'Donnell of the Thirteenth."

"And I'm Captain Hal Winters from the 14th in Brighton," the other captain said. "We're here to talk about CON and to update Captain O'Donnell and his crew concerning what we know so far, since they were out on a supply run that was, unfortunately, unsuccessful." Winters emphasized the last part of his sentence, and Timothy got the distinct impression the captain wasn't thrilled with having competition for rank.

Captain O'Donnell set his jaw, his lips forming a thin line. "Though our mission was unsuccessful, we *did* discover that some of Boston's children are being kept and used for labor… or worse. And at least one of those children may be Sergeant Abrams's niece. There could be more children we know and love under CON's thumb." He cocked his head, sparing a glance at Winters before addressing the room again. "Are there any other officers who are missing children?"

Two officers raised their hands; one of them was Vicky Murphy. O'Donnell pointed to the first. "What's your name?"

"Officer Paul Landry, sir," the young man said.

"And who are you missing?" O'Donnell asked.

"My sister, sir. Wren. She's seventeen. She went to check on her boyfriend, and I never saw her again. Mom is dead; Dad won't leave the house in case Wren comes back. I should have gone with her." Paul choked up, his hand shaking before he balled it into a fist to steady it. "I don't know if she's been taken by CONmen."

"But you believe it to be a possibility?" O'Donnell's expression was one of empathy though he stood above and over the room. He was broad shouldered and imposing most of the time, but as he spoke to his fellow officers about their loss, he transformed into someone more fatherly.

"I do, sir," Paul said firmly.

"And you, Murphy?" O'Donnell asked. "Who are you missing?"

"We haven't been able to find my son's body," Murphy said, expression pinched as if she were trying to hold herself together. Timothy knew that expression too well. "He's six, and he was with the babysitter. If you're going after CON, I want in."

"Me, too." Paul looked over his shoulder and nodded at Vicky, who returned the gesture.

The two spoke with conviction, and the murmurs started up again. Timothy picked up bits and pieces of a dozen conversations over the pros and cons before Captain Winters's high-pitched whistle drew them all back to attention.

"That's enough," Winters shouted. "Now, here's the truth: we don't know if those kids are actually with CON or if they just haven't been found. Anyone who chooses to go with O'Donnell's precinct needs to be aware of what they're getting themselves into. Murphy. Landry. I understand your grief, but we need every officer we can get right now, and going after these kids could be a suicide mission. Even if we all go, we don't know if we're outmatched. We don't know where Ace is situated. And for all you who don't know, Ace has been running CON since its inception. He's rammed his gang up through the ranks in Boston, and he didn't hesitate one second to use this disaster to solidify his hold on the city. He's got Boston by the neck. She doesn't belong to us anymore, and I have to question whether rescuing kids is going to be the thing that gets her back." He pounded a fist on the podium. "We need to wage a guerilla war on CON and get our city back under our control before we do anything else."

Timothy's heart sank at the outburst of support among the officers. *O'Donnell was right. The police are fractured.* Despite the fact that Timothy would go after George and Annika regardless of numbers, the more officers that went with them, the better chance they had.

Officer Landry stood up so fast he knocked his chair over backward. "How do you know getting those kids back won't cripple CON? We don't know what they're being used for."

An officer Timothy didn't recognize stood up on the opposite side of the room. "Yeah, Landry, but — and I mean no offense — how likely is that? First, we gotta kill as many of those bastards as we can. And *then* we can go in and rescue those kids when their forces are weakened."

Murphy stood up. "That could take weeks," she said. "Months even. My son could be dead by then."

An older officer scoffed, not bothering to get up out of his seat. "We can't make these decisions based on an emotional woman."

Burke shot up out of his chair. "Murphy is top notch, you old coot. She's right. What happens when they decide to use children as bait and shields? I saw it overseas, man. Bad guys go there eventually when the heat's turned on too high."

"That's crazy," another officer shouted. "You want us to risk our lives based on *what ifs*? We're not overseas. We're in Boston, for goodness sakes."

"No," Torres shouted. "We want you to risk your life based on your *oaths*."

The room exploded, though most of the officers seemed to be on the opposing end of the argument. Those who wanted to go after the kids first were definitely the minority.

Heather put a hand on Timothy's arm. "This is going to come to blows." She nodded to where Burke was nose to nose with the older officer who'd accused Murphy of being too emotional.

"Can we do anything?" Candice pressed against the wall, looking wide-eyed all around. "We won't be able to get out of here without a few knocks if this gets ugly."

Timothy glanced at the door at the back of the room. Candice was right, and while Timothy was on the mend, he wasn't quite ready for a fist fight with a trained officer. Not to mention the majority of men and women in the room were armed. Timothy turned to O'Donnell, who was in a shouting match with Winters.

"I need to get their attention," Timothy said. "I just… I don't know how." He stood up on the chair and shouted, but no one spared him a glance. He tried again and waved his hands. "Hey! Everyone! Hello?"

A shrill scream pierced the noise. Timothy nearly fell off his chair as he hurried to cover his ears. Candice stood a foot away, fists straight down at her sides, her eyes shut tight, a blood curdling shriek coming out of her wide-open mouth. Every single person in the room covered their ears and stopped arguing to glare at Candice. Her scream tapered off, and she took a deep breath.

"Well. I haven't done that since I had to stop a brawl at a party my senior year of high school." She flashed a toothy grin. "Now, if you are all done acting like teenagers, my friend here has something to say."

Timothy blinked a few times, still unsure what the heck had just happened. Everyone now glared at *him*. "Right," he said. "Uh… thank you, Candice." He tried to find his bearings. "Look," he said, "the world as we knew it is gone. We can't bring it back, but we can try to maintain what's left of humanity. And we can try to save the future. That starts with our children. No children, no future. Period. From what I understand, gangs like CON have always exploited young people. They bring them in, they make them feel like the gang is part of their identity. Those kids might be dead in a few months, or they might be brainwashed into turning against us. We wait, and we could be shooting kids in the street to keep them from shooting us. Kids we love. Kids we could have saved. We wage an all-out war, CON won't be the ones killing those kids. It will be *you*. Do you really want that?"

All eyes were still on Timothy as he stepped off the chair. It was quiet for several minutes before Winters stepped back up to the podium.

"I say we give O'Donnell and whoever wants to go with him a week to free those kids. One week, and then we start dismantling CON whenever and however we can." He looked to O'Donnell. "CON has been charging local survivor groups for protection basically from CON itself. They hit every group on the regular. We know where they'll be tomorrow. Don't know what time, just that they'll be there. It's a lead on finding CON's base of operations. What d'ya say, O'Donnell?"

O'Donnell furrowed his brow and then stepped forward, meeting first the eyes of his squad, who nodded their agreement, and then to Timothy, who nodded his. O'Donnell got a signal from Murphy, Burke, and Torres and a nod from Landry, as well. Then he held out a hand to Winters. "It looks like we have a plan," he said.

Winters shook it. "God help you, Captain," he said. "You're going to need it."

Chapter 8

Zara Williams

"So, it wasn't Carol's fault," Zara said. "It was mine. I practically threw the door open for the Heirs of the Mother and welcomed them in. I didn't mean to, but… I guess that doesn't matter now."
Thomas sat slack jawed, his eyes darting between Zara and Mr. Peters. He sat behind a table he was using as a desk in a cabin he'd converted into a temporary town hall. He'd listened to them in silence as they recounted everything from Vanguard's involvement in the outbreak to their speculation that the Heirs may have used the Green Earth Futurists to carry out their plans to Zara's mistake in leaving the garage door unlocked in her angry frenzy to flee the Peters family. Once Zara had started unloading the story, the words wouldn't stop. And Mr. Peters backed up what she said and took responsibility for what he'd done. Thomas now knew everything that had happened to her since the World's Fair.
"So…" Thomas said after a long pause. His features were tight, and his body was tense. The tone of his voice was barely restrained, as if he were on the edge of shouting. He pointed at Mr. Peters. "You destroyed the world" — his finger swung to Zara — "and you destroyed my community."
"She didn't destroy anything," Mr. Peters said. "She was acting under extreme duress, and she made a mistake. If you want to blame someone for those who died, blame the Heirs of the Mother."
"And," Zara said, "it was probably the Heirs who stole Vanguard's research. It would explain a lot. You should also keep in mind that the research was something the government wanted done, and it would have happened whether or not Mr. Peters's company had taken the job. So, I guess… it's not really his fault, either. Not completely."
"No." Mr. Peters leaned forward, making a slicing motion with his hand. "My company created this disease and developed the new species of mosquito. I approved every step. I convinced myself that because it was a commission from the government and because another company would do it if I didn't, that I was doing the right thing. I was wrong."
"Why didn't you tell me this sooner?" Anger flared in Thomas's eyes. "I would have sent you on your way days ago."
Mr. Peters shifted his weight, his jaw working back and forth. "I told you we needed to get to Boston. I told you my company had resources to get rid of the mosquitos."
Walter is losing patience. Zara cleared her throat. "We weren't completely honest, but we were doing what we thought we had to do at the time. And we told you why we needed to get back to Boston, even if it was a simplified version."
"Oh really?" Thomas was shouting now. He put his hands flat on the desk and stood up. "I had no idea that this mosquito was engineered to be deadly. I was never told you knew *exactly* what this disease was. Nobody ever mentioned that you had no doubt you could fix this *because you freaking created it.* I thought you were just an optimistic rich guy trying to throw money at a problem!"
Mr. Peters stood up abruptly. His hands clenched at his sides, and he was visibly trembling with anger. "We're telling you now," he said.
He's holding back, but he's not very good at it. Zara stood up more timidly. "Thomas, we know this is a lot of information to process. We decided to tell you everything because we thought we could trust you and because we need your help. We need that bus to get to Clearfield. We need supplies to barter for a plane ride across the mountains."
"Zara is right," Mr. Peters said, voice still on edge. A little louder, and he would have been shouting. "We can't afford to get stalled over and over again on our way. Travelling by foot is out of the question, and even if we could get there in the bus, we seem to attract trouble. We need to get to Boston quickly, without any more detours."
"Oh, okay." Thomas threw up his hands. "So not only have you brought a plague upon the entire earth and gotten my people killed through your recklessness, you also want to rob us of our only remaining vehicle? You realize that the Heirs took our vehicles?"
"Yes," Zara said, "but for the good of literally everyone, we need the bus and the supplies. We might need to barter the actual bus to get the plane ride."
"So I have no choice but to let you take it." Thomas rubbed his hands over his face. "Just… get out."
Mr. Peters started to speak again, this time with a more controlled tone. "Thomas—"
"I said get out!" Thomas yelled and pointed at the door to the cabin. "Go somewhere else. I need to think."
Mr. Peters held up his hands and took a step back. "Let's go, Zara," he said.
Zara followed him outside, her heart pounding. "He's really angry."
"Of course he is," Mr. Peters put hands on his hips and looked up at the sky. "I almost lost it on him. I don't think I'll ever get used to this."
Zara cocked her head. "People hating you?"
"No," Mr. Peters said, "telling the truth and then not arguing about why I was right."
"So… being humble?"
"Yes." Mr. Peters started walking toward one of the debris piles. "If I go back to that bedroll, I might spiral again. I need to do something worthwhile. I'm going to help."
"Really?" Zara quirked an eyebrow. "Manual labor, huh? Maybe you really have changed."
He eyed her. "I can't tell if your sarcasm is in good humor or if you are just making fun of me."
"Good humor," Zara said. "This time, anyway."

Zara pitched in alongside Mr. Peters, helping to clear the burned-out husk of one of the cabins. They worked alongside community members for an hour until Kyle showed up, going from person to person, pointing to the garages. He came up to Zara and Mr. Peters with a solemn look on his face.

"Thomas is calling a meeting in the garages," Kyle said. "He says you need to prepare yourselves to give the same story you told him to all of us."

A chill went down Zara's spine, and her stomach lurched. She glanced at Mr. Peters who looked three shades paler than she'd ever seen him. She'd been prepared for Thomas to reveal everything they'd told him, for the compound community to hate her, but she hadn't been prepared to tell them what she'd done herself. Bearing one person's shock, anger, and judgment was nothing compared to shouldering the same from dozens all at once.

"What is it?" Kyle asked. "What did you tell Thomas?"

"Go on, kid." Mr. Peters dusted his hands off on his pants. "You'll find out soon enough. We'll be right behind you." When Kyle retreated to the garages in the wall, Mr. Peters faced Zara. "This is going to be tough. Are you up for it?"

"Not really, but… if it's what we need to do, I'll do it." Zara hugged her middle and faced the garages, willing herself to take a step forward.

"Thomas is right," Mr. Peters said. "They've given us shelter, the Heirs breached their wall because of us, and they're about to lose some important supplies. They deserve to know why. And they deserve to hear about it from us." He walked purposefully toward the wall. "Come on, Zara. We've got a story to tell."

Zara caught up to him. "Lizzy would be proud of you," she said.

"Too little, too late." Mr. Peters said gruffly.

"Not for George," Zara said. "Even Tim still needs a father."

"I'm not a better man, yet, Zara." Mr. Peters reached the door first and opened it, gesturing for her to go through. "I'm just trying to be."

"One step at a time," Zara said as she stepped over the threshold into a room full of people, all staring at her and Mr. Peters. *Here goes nothing…*

But this time, telling the story was so much harder. When she'd been talking to Thomas alone with Mr. Peters, she'd been talking quickly, letting the words pour out of her. It had almost been cathartic. She knew Thomas would be angry, but she'd been holding the truth in for so long, it felt *good* to get it out.

Though it was a shortened and more concise telling, Zara had to pull every word from her mouth as if she were pulling her own teeth out by the roots. She focused on the people she knew: Kyle, Amos, and Dr. Donald. Their expressions went from confused to shocked to angry and then hurt. She could see it on Kyle's face: how could she let him blame Carol for her mistake? And the question burning in Amos's and the doctor's eyes: how could you lie to us for so long? When she uncovered her own lies, their expressions had revealed that the deception was perhaps the biggest betrayal, worse than making a mistake.

Tears rolled down Zara's cheeks, and she wiped them away. Her cheeks were hot and her throat raw. "I'm sorry," she said. "I'm really sorry." Her chest felt like it was caving in from the pressure of the anger-infused air.

"As am I," Mr. Peters said, contrite but far less emotional. He had maintained a businesslike tone throughout, as if he were reporting to a board an unfortunate slip up that he would turn around next quarter.

Thomas, who had been standing to the side, faced them. He no longer seemed angry, but he did seem exhausted. "I have another question," he said. "Can you stop the spread of this DV-10 if you can get to Boston?"

Mr. Peters nodded. "We have the countermeasure mosquitos that can wipe out the new species over a few generations of breeding in the wild. And we have the research for DV-10. You have to understand, it was never meant to be released. It would never have been approved. It was scrapped. We had no idea the research had been stolen. It was copied, and the actual mosquito species… to get samples of those, the culprit had to have someone actually in my labs." His eyes got wider, and he paused for a brief second.

Zara's expression mimicked his. The Heirs had someone on his staff? A shock of numbness rolled over her. They had to have been planning for this for years. And they had to have known exactly what would happen.

"Sorry," Mr. Peters said, clearing his throat. "I… I only just realized that this conspiracy must have been brewing under my nose for years." He gave his head a little shake. "Anyway, we have enough information, I believe, to synthesize a cure or a treatment. If I can't do it, I'll find someone who can."

Zara felt so small in that moment. *I have no redeeming skill, only my mistakes. What value do I have?* She looked down at her feet. She wanted to run up the stairs to her bedroll and throw the thin blanket over her head.

Thomas addressed his community, turning to them. "I was furious when they first told me how they'd lied. How Zara had provided the Heirs easy access to our compound." He took a deep breath. "But I had some time to think. The Heirs of the Mother are the real enemy here. Walter's story begins with greed and Zara's culminates in a reckless moment that cost this community dearly. But in their story, I see two people who have lost, who have fought tooth and nail to get back to their families, and who have come forward to tell us the truth." Thomas pointed back at them. "They could have stolen that bus full of supplies. We are too weak to really stop them. Instead, they came forward. Zara confessed to clear Carol's name." He turned to Zara and Mr. Peters. "It might take a while before I forget, and I may never like either of you very much, but… I can forgive you for what you've done. I've always believed — I've always told my children — that who we were yesterday isn't who we have to be today if we are striving to be something better tomorrow." He took a deep breath. "So, I forgive you. And I want to help you get to Boston, so as long as my people can see it the same way I do, you can take the bus and the supplies you need to barter for a plane ride across the mountains."

Sophie wriggled out of Amos's arms and pushed her way through the crowd, bursting forward to wrap her arms around Zara's leg. "I forgive you, too, Zara."

Zara rested her hand on the little girl's head, her vision blurring with tears. "Thank you, Sophie," she whispered.

"I'm with Sophie," Amos said with a small smile.

"Me too," Dr. Donald said.

"I forgive you, too." Kyle didn't smile, but he offered a small nod of acknowledgement.

As murmurs of forgiveness spread and some came forward to shake hands or offer a hug, some shouted their dissent and marched out the back door. The anger and hatred on their faces she could understand; she couldn't wrap her head around the kindness being shown her. Mr. Peters seemed to be having a hard time with it, too. He awkwardly accepted their forgiveness, brow furrowed as he stuttered his thanks. It was as if he had forgotten to how to shake, fumbling to grab outstretched hands.

Little by little, the crowd cleared, going back to their work. Thomas was the only one left. He breathed out slowly, his whole body deflating. He put a hand on Zara's shoulder. "You did good, kid." He looked her in the eye. "I meant what I said. Don't let one mistake define you, even a mistake as bad as this one was. You're a hell of a negotiator. One of the most intelligent, sharp young ladies I've ever met." He pointed at Mr. Peters. "You might think he got you this far, but from what I heard, you had a lot to do with it."

Tears still rolling down Zara's cheeks, she nodded. "Thank you," she croaked.

"Thank you, Thomas," Mr. Peters said sincerely.

Thomas crossed his arms. "You can thank me by getting rid of those mosquitos and finding a cure for DV-10."

"I swear, I won't stop until it's done." Mr. Peters paused and then cleared his throat. "The only other thing I ask of you is to allow me and my family to come back some day to visit Lizzy's grave, maybe have her moved back to Boston."

Thomas nodded. "I can allow that," he said. "Now, we need to teach you to drive a bus, and then we need to get you loaded up and out of here. It's about time you two made it to Boston."

Chapter 9

Alexander Roman

Alex, Minnie, and Lauren had agreed to go back to the RV with Ned and the captured convict. When they arrived, Ned made the convict stand in a line where another biker slipped on some reading glasses and walked the line of zip-tied captives, writing down names in a little notebook. Two delivery vans Alex hadn't seen before had parked behind the motorcycles.

Ned came back to examine the RV's tires alongside Alex who had started setting up the jacks with Minnie's instructions. "You got family you're tryin' to get to?" He took a silver Zippo lighter out of his pocket, flipping the lid open and closed to produce a rhythmic clicking.

Alex set the second jack in place; the other was ready to go on the other side of the RV, and he'd already unhooked the trailer. They needed to jack up both sides of the RV to keep the large vehicle from tipping as they put the spare tire in place. "We're trying to find someone." Alex left it at that.

Telling anyone too much of their mission could turn out badly. Back at the CDC, Alex had discovered that there were people out there willing to exploit others and cross a lot of lines in order to find a cure; those kinds of people were after the power it would lend them. But even if Zion's Angels were good people, President Coleman and General Hunt had warned that survivors swarming Boston and clamoring for answers might not help in the process of finding a cure, either.

Ned shrugged, his Zippo still clicking away. "It's smart not to trust everyone you meet. I get it. I won't press further, then." He slipped the lighter back in his pocket, kicked the flat tire on the RV, and then pointed at the flat on the trailer. "This old bucket of bolts needs fixing up. I see you got one spare. Do you have another for the trailer?"

Alex looked between the two tires. "We only have the one. But the spare wouldn't get us far even if we left the trailer. We need proper tires for both. I was going to put on the spare, hunt for the tires, and then come back for the trailer."

Ned eyed the trailer with a frown. "You're travellin' with too much. In times like these, you don't need as much as you think you might. This trailer is weighin' you down, makin' you a target."

"Is that why you're itchin' to help?" Minnie narrowed her eyes and put her hands on her hips. "You wanna see inside that trailer? See if it's good for stealin'?"

"What? No." Ned took a step back from the RV and trailer, his hands held up, palms out. "I'm offering friendly advice. For your own good, leave the trailer and go find your friend."

"Look," Alex said, "that trailer isn't filled with photo albums. I get what you're saying, but those supplies are things we *need*."

"It's our business," Minnie said. "Stop pokin' your nose in it. For all we know, you're tryin' to part us with our things so you can use our stuff to barter."

"We're not like that," Ned said earnestly. "I swear to you, we aren't. Even before this mess, the Zion's Angels Hog Club just wanted to help people. We were all given the chance to turn our lives around in our youth, and with God's help, we did. We volunteered as a group with underprivileged and at-risk kids. We were on disaster relief teams. Whatever we could do to pay God's love forward, we did it." He offered a smile. "Never been a better time for a little love than right now, don't you think?"

Minnie seemed to be searching Ned's face for some sign that he wasn't who he said he was. Then, she dropped her arms. "Well, all right. I'll give you the benefit of the doubt. For now." She looked at Alex. "He's got sincere eyes, Alex."

Oliver wrinkled his nose and cocked his head. "Why are you in a club all about pigs?"

Ned barked a laugh. "No, kid. We're all part of the Harley Owners Group. H. O. G." When Oliver gave him a blank expression, he grinned and nodded toward their rides. "The motorcycles, kid."

"Oh... that's cool." Oliver's eyes brightened. "Hey, Dad? Can I ride one?"

"No." Some things were still simple. Alex ruffled Oliver's hair as his son frowned and crossed his arms. He turned to Ned. "Thank you for what you've done for us. I don't mean to be rude, but there's only so much time in a day. We really need to get this tire changed. Lauren, can you—" He sighed as Ned jogged around to the other side to help. "Ned, we can—"

"Just let me help you, man," Ned shouted from the other side of the RV.

Alex glanced at Lauren and Minnie, who both shrugged. "I like him," Minnie said.

"It can't hurt to let him help us a little," Lauren said. "I mean, there's enough of these Zion's Angels to just take our stuff if that's what they wanted. If they're serious about helping, I'd say... why not let them?"

"One of you keep an eye on whatever is going on with the line up, then. We need to know if they're up to something." Alex met Oliver's eyes and nodded toward the long strip of grass on the side of the road. "Oliver, why don't you play with Samson? Stay close to the road, but get some energy out, okay?"

"I'll keep an eye on Oliver," Lauren said.

"And I'll play the nosy old woman," Minnie said, "even though I'm *not* an *old* woman." She walked in the direction of the line up with her hands clasped behind her back as if she were out just to stretch her legs.

Alex and Ned worked together to change the tire and get the RV ready to go. Ned didn't ask any more questions about the trailer or try to convince him to leave it. He seemed to understand that Alex didn't feel like sharing any more information because he did most of the talking, mostly about how he missed his barber shop in Raleigh.

"Bein' a barber is like bein' a bartender, except without the drinkin'," Ned said. "My regulars would come in and get things off their chest, and I would get to do what I could to help them. It was a good, simple life." They finished putting the spare on, and Ned brushed off his hands on his jeans. "Anyway, we should have what you need in town to get back on the road."

"You're set up in Stem?" Alex asked.

"This tiny town?" Ned shook his head. "Nah. We're in Butner, southeast of here. Not too far. It's still on the small side, but it'll have what you need. If it don't, Durham isn't far."

"You two done?" Lauren asked, jogging up to the RV. "Oliver says he's ready for lunch."

Seconds after Lauren returned, Minnie did, too. She nodded toward the biker with the glasses and a notebook. "What's your friend up to?" she asked Ned.

Alex resisted the urge to slap his forehead. What happened to the covert Minnie who got my voice recorder out of my office?

Alex took a closer look at the lineup. Five other burly bikers, imposing with stern expressions, stood guard over their captives. But the man taking notes had a professional air in his walk and stance. If it weren't for the leather vest and skull tattoo — and the orange jumpsuits and zipties of the convicts — the biker would have looked like upper management checking in with employees.

"That's Wyatt," Ned said. "We found paper records of the convicts and wrote down their names and what they done to get locked up. He's got a list. When we track down groups like this, we round them up and see who we got."

"What do you do with them?" Alex asked.

"That's a big part of the problem," Ned said. "Some of us are takin' shifts at the supermax. All the fancy stuff don't work, but the cells still lock. So, the most dangerous of the convicts can go back where they belong."

"And the others?" Minnie asked.

"Well, not all of them are dangerous, and there's only so many of us. Some in lower security areas got locked away for non-violent crimes. The new prison complex down near Raleigh was more like an experiment. The state's been switching up how they do things with the prison system ever since I can remember," Ned said. "The new supermax was separate from the medium security, and that was separate from the minimum. But it was all in the same general area. They did it to rotate employees. You see, they'd get burnt out real quick on the supermax. They were trying to go for less turnover."

"You sound like you know a lot about it," Lauren said.

"My brother was a security guard," Ned said. "Found his body inside the supermax, head caved in."

"Sorry to hear that," Minnie said.

Ned nodded. "Thank you, Ma'am."

"Call me Minnie." She patted his forearm. "This is Alex, Lauren, and Oliver." She placed a hand on Samson's head. "And this one is Samson."

Alex held back a grimace. He'd tried to protect their information, but Minnie had given away their names without a second thought. *I'll have to talk to her about that later.*

"Mighty fine dog you have there." Ned held out a hand and Samson sniffed it, his tail wagging.

Lauren cleared her throat. "So… what do you do with the ones that weren't put away for violent crimes?"

"We give 'em a chance to work with us back in town. We've got a small community of survivors. If they went away for money launderin' or drug possession, for example, we put 'em to use. First offense will get them sent to Raleigh. There's a sort of government still standing, and they're takin' the manageable convicts for labor. They're also givin' us a few supplies to keep us going so they don't have to track down the escapees." Ned scowled at the lineup. "It's like the Wild West in the countryside except our bandits wear orange jumpsuits. We've even got our own infamous criminal in the making: Jesse King. He messed with my brother a few times in the supermax. He's the one that killed my brother."

"How do you know?" Alex squinted at the convicts, starting with the man who'd threatened Oliver and stopping at the other end of the line on the man who'd tried to get the others to take the stuff and let Alex and his family go.

"The tip of my brother's pinky finger was sawed off." Ned's face grew a shade paler. "I hope that part happened after he was already dead." He shuddered. "Jesse King is a serial killer. He always chopped off the last bit of the pinky finger and kept it. My brother told me about him, but he was arrested over thirty years ago. We don't know what he looks like, just his name."

"How do you know he's not dead?" Alex asked.

"Found a body a couple days back with no pinky fingertip," Ned said. "It has to be him."

"Well, that's *not* going to help me sleep tonight," Lauren said, visibly shuddering as she held her pinky finger.

"Maybe we should go with Ned here." Minnie put both hands on Oliver's shoulders. "We can put the spare on old Harvey and then go lookin' for a permanent one tomorrow first thing."

"Yeah," Lauren said, "it might be better to be in a larger group until we're ready to keep going. Strength in numbers and all that."

Alex was outnumbered. "I hate to leave the trailer," he said.

"Is there a place we can sleep, Ned?" Lauren asked. "If so, maybe we can pack some of the stuff in the trailer into the RV."

"There sure is," Ned said. "We've got about two dozen survivors in the elementary school gym. We set up shop there."

"Ned… can we have a moment?" Alex asked.

"Sure," Ned said. "I'm going to help load up these men into the vans. One goes back to Butner with us, and the other heads out to Raleigh."

Once Ned was gone, Alex crossed his arms. "I can't believe after all we've been through that you two are so willing to trust a stranger."

Minnie pursed her lips. "I'm an excellent judge of character."

Lauren shrugged. "I don't *trust* them, Alex, but we need them. It seems they know where to get the tires we need. They've got a place for us to sleep so we can pack away our supplies into the RV and leave the trailer mostly empty."

"I don't want them asking too many questions about the supplies in the trailer," Alex said. "If we go, we pack the stuff after they've left and meet them at the school."

"Agreed." Lauren nodded once. "We should keep watch, too. One of us stays awake at all times, and we huddle together in the gym. We're not there to make friends. We're there to make it through the night."

"Okay," Alex said. "If Ned agrees, we're good to go. If he tries to insist on unloading the trailer after I make it clear we don't want help, we insist he leave with the rest of his friends and instead of going to Butner, we load up what we can into the RV and suffer being cramped inside the cab until we can find a new one."

With a plan in place, Alex jogged over to where Ned was helping zip-tied convicts up into the back of a delivery van. None of them seemed happy. Only one of the convicts had their zip ties cut, and he was standing next to the other van. The freed man was the same one who had tried to get the others to back off.

"Hey, Alex, did you decide what you wanna do?" Ned was taking the elbow of a convict, helping him stay balanced on a step ladder up into the back of the van. Another biker on the other side of the ladder did the same. "In case it helps, these guys are bein' taken to Raleigh." He nodded to the lone freed man. "Only that one is comin' with us to Butner. His name's Ben Polk, and he was a banker. Embezzled a bunch of money. No money to speak of where we're goin'. Besides, he says he only had a few months left of his sentence."

"Makes sense, actually," Alex said. "He tried to help us... or at least, he didn't want to hurt us."

"Good. I think that one's got a shot at bein' a good man," Ned said. "That is, if he survives all this end-of-the-world crap. So... you guys coming with us?"

"Yes and no. If you can give me directions to the elementary school, we'll load up what we need from the trailer *on our own*" — he emphasized those three words — "and we'll follow."

"Sure thing," Ned said without hesitation. "I'd offer to help you load up, but as your friend said earlier, whatever's in there ain't my business." He helped the last of the zip-tied men up into the van and took the step ladder as the other biker closed the doors on the convicts. Ned pointed up the road. "It looks like you need to go back the way you came a few miles. You'll turn left onto Central Avenue which will take you into town. Then you'll turn left again on East D Street. Your last left will be on South Eighteenth. It leads straight to the school." Ned slapped Alex on the back. "Got it?"

"Yeah," Alex said. "It sounds pretty straightforward."

Within five minutes, the bikers were rumbling away on their bikes, followed by the van, and Alex, Minnie, Lauren, and even Oliver were helping move things from the trailer to the living space of the RV. The gas cans fit into the luggage compartments on the outside of the vehicle, and they loaded food, water, and several duffle bags and storage bins full of specialized equipment from the CDC.

"I can't believe we're being forced to take another detour," Alex said as they got into the cab. "It feels like we'll never get to Boston."

"Well, at least this time, the detour is more straightforward," Lauren said. "I mean, we're just getting a couple new tires, right? What could go wrong?"

Alex pulled the RV around and started down the road toward Butner. "I don't know," he said, "but I hope we never find out."

Chapter 10

George Peters

George had never been so hungry. He'd already been starving when Ruger had punished both him and Annika for his stupid heroics. His stomach complained loudly throughout the night, refusing to let him rest. Annika had cried herself to sleep, not for the first time since they'd been kidnapped. She'd scooted her sleeping bag right up to George's. James — the little boy he'd saved from being the last kid on the truck — had set up on the other side of Annika.

The night before, Big Mack and Ruger had ordered all the kids into a large room attached to a kitchen. George hadn't had much time outside to examine the area, but when they'd been ushered into the space, he'd remembered attending a birthday party at the event center after it had been newly renovated a few years before. The CONmen had taken them to Franklin Farm at the Franklin Park Zoo, which made Icepick and Digger's reference to "The Farm" make a lot more sense.

The darkness of night gave way to dawn as George listened to the breathing and soft snores of the other children. He hadn't crawled into the sleeping bag; it had been far too hot. But he was grateful for the soft barrier between him and the floor. His stomach growled again, the pit of his stomach twisting, begging to be fed.

At least I know where I am… for all the good that does. George had never really paid attention when being driven there, or anywhere really. He'd never had to know how to get around Boston; he'd never been in the city alone.

Annika rolled over and snuggled closer. James had sneaked half of a bologna sandwich to them the night before, though George had given all of it to Annika. The boy had pulled it out of his pocket, flattened and warm, as a thank you gesture, and he'd stayed nearby ever since.

Whatever CON was going to do with them, it was better than being stuck with Icepick and Digger. It seemed once his punishment was over, George would receive actual food instead of a cheap granola bar or candy at random. Big Mack and Ruger had provided the kids with the sleeping bags, and Ruger had told them they'd have three square meals a day in payment for their work. Then, the kids had been left alone, locked inside with nothing to do and nowhere to go. Ruger and Big Mack had come back with one more truck load of kids before the day had been out, calling them the "last batch." One of them had also had their dinner withheld. The two CONmen had retreated to the upper level of the event center when the clock on the wall had reached seven. The doors were locked, but George doubted anyone would have risked going outside after that.

As daylight slowly brightened the room, other kids began to stir. Some sat up, but most of them lay there in silence. George remained one of the latter. He didn't move for fear of waking Annika next to him. His own eyes burned with lack of sleep. *I just have to make it to dinner. I'll get some food, and then I'll be able to sleep. I hope.*

It wasn't long before footsteps pounded the stairs behind a door, and Ruger burst into the room. "Up, up, up!" Ruger shouted, clapping his hands three times. George sat up with the rest of the kids, gently waking Annika, as well. "It's time for breakfast. Losers from yesterday's races, you're last in line." He put his hands on his hips and narrowed his eyes as he scanned the room. Then he pointed at George. "Our resident hero and his little friend, however, are sitting this one out. As you watch them drool over your food, remember: don't try to find loopholes or be clever. Do what you're told. That's your only job. Do that, and we'll take care of you."

George's cheeks burned hot. Several kids looked sidelong at him. A few of them sniggered. Annika let out a small whimper beside him. Her lip quivered. "It's okay," George whispered. "It's going to be okay."

Annika nodded, but then she buried her head in her hands and sniffled, anyway. George couldn't blame her. He was barely keeping it together, and he was more than twice her age. Ruger unlocked the door to the kitchen, and in a few moments, a metal door slid upward to open a serving window. He could only sit and watch as kids went through a line to grab prepackaged gas station pastries.

James came back and pinched off pieces of his honey cake and slipped them to Annika, glancing at Ruger before handing them over every time. Annika tried to give George a piece, but he declined. She needed it more than he did. More footsteps down the stairs signaled Big Mack's arrival, and he burst into the room rubbing his eyes like he'd just woken. He hopped up on the counter next to where Ruger slid pastries across to kids in line, and the two CONmen chatted quietly.

Ruger waited five minutes after the last kid had taken their breakfast before coming to stand at the front of the room. "Okay, crybabies. It's time to sort you into groups. We got jobs that need filling. But first, you need to understand CON and what your life is now." He clasped his hands behind his back and slowly paced back and forth, keeping his eyes on them, while Big Mack leaned against the wall. "First thing you've got to know is that Ace is the boss. What he says, goes. You'll know him by the Ace card he always sticks in the ribbon of his bowler hat." He gestured vaguely to his own head. "It's like an old-timey hat. Point is, Ace calls the shots."

Big Mack lazily pushed off the wall. "And Ace wants things done. We got a new world, a new Boston. Things are different than they were before. We need people to wash the clothes, scavenge for food, clean the water, things ain't nobody had to worry about before. That's where you kids come in."

Ruger held up a finger. "But don't think you're not gettin' something out of this. You're joinin' a family where everybody pulls their own weight. It might not seem like that at first, but you'll get to appreciate it. You got protection in CON. You got food and water. You'll get some down time, days off. Friends, even." He put an arm around Big Mack's neck. "We all gotta pull together in times like these, you know?" He let go of Big Mack and clapped his hands. "So, today you find out your place in our new world. I'm gonna come around and tap you on the head. You get tapped, you come up to the front." Ruger started walking around the room, tapping the youngest among them.

George grabbed hold of Annika's hand. *He's going to separate us.* Ruger got closer, tapping huddled children and directing them to the front of the room. Annika scooted closer. Ruger tapped James on the head and then reached for Annika. She squealed and ducked, wrapping her arms around George's middle. He hugged her tight, leaning over her head as if covering her head would stop Ruger from selecting her.

Ruger squatted in front of them, looking George in the eye. "Kid, don't be a hero. You gotta learn to pick your battles. She won't be harmed. I swear. You'll still get to see her. CON is a family. You're both in the family, now."

"I *have* a family," George said, "and it's not CON."

"It will be," Ruger said. "Tell your friend here to get up in line. If she don't, there are worse places for her, places I can't guarantee she'll be safe."

George's heart jumped into his throat. *What does he mean by that?* Whatever he meant, Ruger's expression was so sincere, it was disturbing. The man wasn't threatening George or Annika. He was giving out the facts, plain and simple.

George nodded. "Give me a second," he said.

Ruger nodded and stood up. "You got until I'm done choosin' out her group." If George wasn't mistaken, the CONman walked a little slower as he went on to tap the next child.

"Annika," George said, unsticking her from him, "listen to me. I think it's safer for you to go with that group of kids at the front. I swear I will come find you if they don't bring us back here together tonight, okay? They're going to have you washing clothes or dishes or something."

Annika pouted. "I don't wanna go."

"You *have* to," he said. "We have to do what they say. For now, anyway. If we don't, we could end up hurt."

"Like your mom?" Annika asked, her eyes wide.

George swallowed hard, the image of his mother gasping for breath surfacing for only a second before he pushed it away. Even that second was nearly too much. It stole his breath away, made his heartbeat pound in his ears.

"Okay, George." Annika stood up. "I'll go."

"Thank you," George said.

She joined seven other children around her age. By the time Ruger was finished choosing Annika's group, there were eleven children around five or six years old standing at the front of the room.

"This is our odd jobs crew," Ruger said, smiling down at the children. "Today, Ace wants every hole in the sidewalks and grass that could hold standing water to be filled with sand. Mosquitos breed in standing water, so eventually, we need this entire zoo to be free from it. You'll work on that during the hours it's safe to be outside. Tomorrow, you'll work on hand washing and hanging laundry. Every day, you'll have something different, and the work will rotate." He opened the door and a woman in her twenties came inside, all braids and tattoos, a midriff t-shirt under overalls.

"All right, little CON ladies and gents," she said, "we're about to put in a hard day's work. Me and my ladies outside are gonna make sure you're taken care of today. Don't try to run, do as you're told, and everything will be just fine." She held out a hand to the closest child, who looked up into her smiling face and hesitantly took her hand. Annika glanced at George as she was led outside, but she looked more curious than frightened, which made George feel a little better.

Once the kids were out of the room, Big Mack rubbed his hands together and licked his lips. "Now it's time to pick our newest Butterflies for the Tropical Forest."

Ruger's expression went flat, he pressed his lips together, and he stepped back against the wall as Big Mack walked around tapping the oldest girls in the room on the head. The smile he gave the girls made George's stomach sick. The girls lined up at the front of the room just like the smaller children had. The four of them held hands, huddling shoulder to shoulder.

"Not a bad batch," Big Mack said, elbowing Ruger playfully. He walked up to the girls and caressed one on the cheek. "Pretty, pretty butterflies."

"Hold up," Ruger said, stepping forward. He had not offered Big Mack so much as a smile. "Any of you girls know how to shoot a gun?" One of the girls shyly raised her hand. "What's your name?"

"Lissa." She spoke loudly and the sound of her own voice seemed to startle her.

"How good are you, Lissa?" he asked.

"I… went hunting with my dad?" Lissa said it as a question. "I… um… I went to the range a lot with my aunt, too."

"You ever gotten a kill while out hunting?" Ruger asked.

"Best was a five-point buck," she said, her posture straightening a little. "And we like squirrel for jerky."

"What're you used to shooting?"

She lifted her chin. "A 243 Winchester for deer and a Browning 22 for the squirrel. My aunt bought me a Glock 43 for the range."

Ruger nodded. "That's my girl." He smiled at Big Mack. "That one stays." He looked at the other girls. "You three have any special skills we need to know about? Anything at all?"

The three glanced at each other. One of them raised her hand. "I can sew," she said. "Like, real clothes. I couldn't afford to stay on trend, so… I learned to make things. Pants, skirts, shirts, hats… pretty much whatever."

"Sounds useful to me," Ruger said. "Sit back down." The girl sat back on the floor, hugging her middle.

Ruger raised his eyebrows at the other girls, but they only looked at him with wide, frightened eyes. Neither of them spoke up.

"Fine," Big Mack scowled before turning a greasy smile on the remaining two. "Now, let's get you girls settled in the Tropical Forest."

"Wait up," Ruger pointed to the girls. "Ages?"

"Oh, come on, Ruger." Big Mack's shoulders slumped.

"Ace said no one under fifteen joins the Butterflies." Ruger crossed his arms.

"No one ever asks." Big Mack grumbled.

Ruger approached the girls. "Ages. How old are you?" One was sixteen, the other thirteen. Ruger guided the thirteen-year-old away and sat her down next to Lissa and the girl who could sew. He didn't look at Big Mack or the only girl left when he spoke. "Go on," he said. "Take her where she needs to go."

George frowned at the way Ruger's features pinched, the way it seemed he held his breath until Big Mack pulled the girl outside. George wasn't a little kid. From the way Big Mack had leered at the girls, he'd figured out pretty quickly what a Butterfly did for CON. He was disgusted, but he wasn't surprised. His school had focused an entire week on raising awareness for human trafficking. What he didn't expect was Ruger's reaction to it.

Ruger has a conscience. He's got a code, maybe, like Frank? Codes can be used. George tucked that nugget in the back of his mind. Weeks ago, when his big brother had come back from Mattapan with Annika, George had eavesdropped through the vents in the bedroom next to the supply room in the bunker. Most of what they said was mumbles, but he'd caught enough to know that if it weren't for Frank's code about kids, Tim would be dead.

"Who here besides Lissa can shoot a gun?" Ruger asked.

George raised his hand. He'd never gone hunting with his dad, but both his parents had taken him to the gun range on multiple occasions. He'd joined the skeet shooting club at school, too, and he was a pretty good shot. He glanced around, counting four other hands, all boys.

"Good," Ruger said. "I'll be keeping an eye on you six." He pointed at George. "Especially you, Hero. Today everyone in this room will be scavenging. The six who can shoot will need to earn trust through hard work and a good attitude. Once I know you're ready to graduate from the scavenging team, you'll start training with the CON Guard. Now, all of you — up! up! up!" He shouted, clapping his hands. "On your feet! We're going into the city to find supplies."

George stood quickly and he filed outside with the other kids. A dozen guards waited outside, each one with a rifle or handgun. There were men who looked to be as old as George's dad and a girl who looked to be Lizzy's age, maybe a little younger. All of them wore tank tops with a CON tattoo on one arm.

Ruger separated the kids into groups, assigning guards to each one. "Hero, you're with me," he said, pulling George into his group. "You, too, Lissa." He pointed at the girl who could sew. "You… what's your name?"

"Charity," she said.

"You're with me, too." Ruger also chose the thirteen-year-old girl who he'd saved from becoming a Butterfly. She said her name was Poppy. The CONman finished up his group of scavengers with a boy named Clyde who was a little older than George. One of the younger guards joined Ruger. As the other guards in teams of two chose their scavengers, Ruger crossed his arms and addressed George and the others he'd chosen. "I expect you five to obey, and I expect you to live. In case you haven't noticed, Boston ain't what she used to be. Today is about finding supplies to help us *all* live a little longer. You each have a part to play. You got it?"

George nodded, and a flare of excitement got his blood pumping. The stakes were real. He was going out into the city to do something important. *For CON. I'm being used by CON.* That thought dampened his mood, made his cheeks burn with embarrassment. *How could I be excited about working for the bad guys?*

But then another thought fanned the flare of excitement into a flame of something else, something darker. *If I do things right, Ruger will make me part of the guard.* A plan formed, one he was sure his father would have come up with if he'd been in George's position. *I'll learn what I can about surviving in the city. I'll become part of the guard. Then, I'll get a gun. With a gun, I can escape with Annika. I can survive and protect us both.*

George fell in line behind Ruger and marched into Boston. He wasn't a kid anymore. He was a Peters, and Peters men always did what had to be done.

Chapter 11

Lizzy Peters

The darkness was complete. Pervasive. All encompassing. It seemed like it might be eternal, too. Lizzy had no idea how long she'd been sitting in the pitch black with a cold, metal water bottle in one hand and a bedpan an arm's length away; she wrinkled her nose as she caught a whiff of the waste inside it. The wall was to her back, the hard concrete floor underneath. Their solidness grounded her, reminded her that there was more to the world than the darkness.

Shortly after Autumn had killed a man in front of her, she'd given Lizzy some warm tea. Lizzy had refused to drink it until Orion had stepped forward under Autumn's orders to force it down her throat. She'd downed the small cup of tea to avoid being manhandled. The next thing she knew, she woke up in the dark with the water bottle clipped to her belt and the bedpan next to her feet, both of which she had to identify by touch alone.

No one responded when she called out. She'd cowered for the first hours of her confinement, waiting for Autumn to come back and kill her. But then some of the shock wore off, and it was clear that death wasn't coming. At least not yet. They wanted something from her. They wanted to know where her father was, what his plans were, how to stop him from stopping the end of the world. That's when she'd tried to find a way out.

Lizzy had never realized just how disorienting darkness could be. She'd stumbled forward with her arms outstretched, sliding her feet forward a few inches at a time until she'd found the wall. It was smooth and hard and cold, like the rest of the room. She searched, finding first the seams of the door, then the hinges, and finally the doorknob. It wouldn't budge no matter how she pushed or pulled, and the handle would not turn, locked from the other side.

Screaming for help and pleading for someone to turn the lights on only made her throat raw. She gave up, eventually, taking up residence against the opposite wall with her only two resources: the water and the bedpan. Once she'd grown quiet, it seemed right; the silence *belonged* in that room. Even the whisper of her feet brushing the floor was out of place. Lizzy was deep within the belly of the void where time was no longer certain, and life was reduced to remembering to breathe.

Until the lights turned on. Brilliant white banished the dark, searing Lizzy's eyes. She gasped and threw up her arms to block the invasion, curling away from the harsh onslaught. Her stinging eyes watered as she dared to open them, blinking rapidly and squinting as her eyes adjusted. Metal sliding against metal as the door was unlocked and the click of the door opening sent Lizzy's heart to pounding.

A woman with raven-dark hair in a braid stepped over the threshold, standing aside with hands folded in front of her, holding a knapsack. At first, Lizzy thought it was Autumn, but as her face came into focus, Lizzy realized it was a different woman, younger and a bit shorter. The canvas knapsack was embroidered with flowers, and she wore plain, taupe slacks under a tunic of the same color. Lizzy was drawn to the brightly colored thread of the flowers on her knapsack. Greens and pinks and oranges, beautifully done and so colorful amidst the grays and browns of everything else. Never had something so simple captivated her so thoroughly.

The woman focused warm blue eyes on Lizzy, her smile full and welcoming. "Hello, Elizabeth," she said.

Lizzy cleared her throat, but she didn't speak. She was distracted by another figure who entered the room with a plastic tote in his hands. This one she definitely recognized: Orion. She shrank back against the wall. "Leave me alone," she croaked. But then she immediately regretted saying it. Her stomach lurched at the idea of being plunged back into the void.

"No one is going to hurt you, Elizabeth," the woman said, still smiling. "You're a special young lady, treasured by the Mother."

Lizzy frowned, unsure of how to respond to the woman's words. *Are they all as crazy as Autumn?*

Orion stalked over to where Lizzy still sat scrunched up next to the far wall. She flinched away from him as he set the tote down and opened it, but he only pulled out a new bedpan and water bottle. He also pulled out a lid, snapped it onto the used bedpan, and stuck it in the tote along with the old water bottle. He left the room, and three more men entered. One carried a folding table, the other two highbacked, cushioned chairs. They set them up and left.

"My name is Azalea." The woman sat down at the table and placed the knapsack on top. "My mother sent me. I believe you met her yesterday." She gestured to the other chair. "Please, come and sit."

"What do you want?" Lizzy asked.

"To talk." Azalea's smile never faltered. "Mother sent me because she cares. She would have sent someone else if you weren't so important."

"Why didn't she come herself?" Lizzy slowly stood, keeping her back to the wall, her eyes on the door. *If it opens again, could I escape this room?*

"Mother is a very busy woman," Azalea said. "That she talked to you in person at all is a great honor."

Lizzy's legs felt like Jell-O. Her feet tingled, and her body trembled as her legs supported her own weight. *How long was I sitting here?* "Is she your actual mother? Or are you calling her that because you're nuts?"

Azalea frowned. "The title of Mother of the Heirs has been passed from woman to woman in my family. We aren't crazy, Elizabeth. We're dedicated to preserving the Earth. The Mother guides each generation, nurtures us all. One day, that will be my privilege."

"So, she's your actual mother?" Lizzy gave her a flat stare. *Do these people ever just answer a question?*

"She gave birth to me," Azalea said, "if that's what you're asking."

Lizzy stayed where she was, her eyes fixed on the knapsack. "Is there food in there?" she asked, stomach growling.

"Oh, no. You're fasting, silly." Azalea playfully rolled her eyes and dismissed Lizzy's question with a nonchalant wave of her hand. She then pulled out a wooden box, unfolding it to reveal a checkerboard. "I thought we might play a game. It's hard to sit in here, doing nothing for so long. I thought a little company would help you understand that we're not your enemy." She reached back inside to pull out a black bag and a red one, placing the red bag closest to the chair opposite her. She dumped black checker pieces from the bag she kept onto the table.

"You people murdered my friends at the compound and then murdered another man right in front of me and then locked me in this room for who knows how long… you've pretty much ticked all the right boxes for an enemy." Lizzy stepped forward, putting her hands on the back of the chair.

"You've been in here for about twenty-eight hours," Azalea said. "Barely more than a day." She finished placing her pieces. "I see you're no longer lying to us about your feelings. That's progress, Elizabeth. I'm so proud of you." She gestured again to the chair. "Please. Sit down."

She wants to talk? Fine. Lizzy sat down, her body sinking into the cushions. She despised how comfortable it was. "You people are evil, and I'm never going to give you what you want."

Azalea clucked her tongue and frowned momentarily. "Elizabeth, those are some outlandish accusations. Evil? Really?" She reached over and dumped the contents of the red bag onto the table, placing Lizzy's pieces on the board. "You're one of us. If we're evil, you're evil, too. And that's just not the case."

"I'm not one of you." Lizzy crossed her arms.

"Did you not provide key information that enabled the Cleansing? When the time came, did you not know exactly what to say to catch our attention?" Azalea quirked an eyebrow. "Do you believe yourself to be a bad person?"

"Yes." The word was instinctual, visceral. Heat crept up Lizzy's neck, and tears stung her eyes. *I guess I really am done lying.* "I'm a liar. I was being selfish when I gave you that information."

"How does your father feel about that?" Azalea asked.

"He hates me, and so does Zara." Lizzy spit out the words before she could consider them. She sat up straighter as Azalea raised her eyebrows. "He hated me, I meant. He *hated* me. He's dead."

"Hmmm." Azalea moved a checker piece, but she didn't comment on Lizzy's mistake.

Lizzy moved her own piece just to keep from talking. *I'm such an idiot.*

"You're not hated here." Azalea moved another piece, right where Lizzy could take it.

"I deserve to be hated." Lizzy jumped Azalea's black checker and put it to the side.

Azalea's expression turned sympathetic. "No, Elizabeth. You don't. Deep down, you know what you did was right. You knew what you were doing."

"No," Lizzy said, "I knew nothing of your plans. I was lying when I said I did."

"No, part of you knew." Azalea spoke matter-of-factly. "And that part brought you to us. You're an Heir at heart, and soon, you'll be an Heir in mind and body, too." Azalea offered a small smile. "You're a hero here, Elizabeth. That's what will define you. Your actions were essential to start the Cleansing."

There was no use in arguing, so Lizzy just continued to play the game with Azalea, gathering her pieces easily. Once the game was over, and Lizzy had won, she sat back, allowing herself to look Azalea in the eye. "What are you going to do with me?"

Azalea plucked pieces off the table and put them back in their bags. "We believe in you," she said. "When you believe, too, we'll take the next steps. But it won't be easy. I think you're resisting who you are because the real evil — the old world, your father, your misguided friends — they've misled you. But you were brave. You found the truth, but the truth is so different that it feels like a lie. We'll remedy that." She folded up the board and stuck everything back in her knapsack.

The men came back into the room and advanced on Lizzy. She yelped and tried to stand, but two of them were holding her down before she could get on her feet. Orion zip-tied her wrists and ankles to the chair, wrapping a rope around her chest and tying it tight behind the chair. Lizzy yelled for them to stop, but none of them reacted. Their eyes were devoid of empathy; none of them even looked at her.

"Let me go!" Lizzy squirmed, but she was securely tied down.

When the men moved away, Azalea was standing in front of her. "You're not the only Heir who ever needed a little help to find themselves, Elizabeth." Orion came back once more, wheeling a cart with a television into the room. "Once you understand us, once you understand the *good* you've done, you'll be thanking me. I promise."

Orion placed a set of over-the-ear headphones on Lizzy's head, and then Azalea stepped out of the way of the television. "What are you doing?" Lizzy shouted, eyes wide, adrenaline shooting through her veins. Images began to flash on the screen. Falling trees and scattering animals. Sea turtles with pinched middles, deformed from being caught in plastic rings. Penguins covered in oil, lying dead. Images not unlike ones she'd seen in school. Just when Lizzy was about to scoff, a piercing, angry scream burst through the headphones. She wanted to rip them off, but she couldn't. The images got more gruesome, and she detected real *pain* in the screaming. A field of dead goats, guts bursting in the hot sun. Child-sized corpses littering cracked and dry ground. And the screaming wouldn't stop.

Chapter 12

Alexander Roman

Alex leaned back against the side of the school building, watching Oliver play tag with other kids his age. Samson barked and ran in circles around the children. It was the most fun he'd seen his son have since before the Ferris Wheel incident at the World's Fair.

Zion's Angels had gathered a small, safe haven at the school, protected by burly men in leather, most of them boasting multiple tattoos. The bikers could hold their own, as Alex had witnessed when they'd rescued him and his family from the convicts, but he got the distinct impression they'd rather be sharing a beer with a friend or rolling down a country road on their Harleys.

The door to the school banged open, and Ned strolled outside. He seemed to spot Alex as he raised his eyebrows and waved, striding in his direction. Three or four kids ran by, and Ned put his hands in the air and roared, taking several huge steps toward the children in exaggerated motions. They giggled and squealed, scattering as Ned caught one of the little boys, swung him up high in the air as he burst into laughter, and then set him back down. The biker's wide grin got even wider. The children scampered away, returning to their game of tag with renewed vigor.

Ned approached Alex with a bounce in his step. He pulled his Zippo lighter out, rolling it in his hand a few times, snapping the lid open and closed in a rhythmic clicking. "You ready to head on out and find a tire for your rig?"

"I was ready yesterday." Alex pushed off the wall. "How far is Durham?" They'd checked the closest tire shop the previous afternoon and only found a replacement for the trailer. The RV needed off-road capable, specialized tires. It had irked Alex that they'd had to stay the night, but there was nothing to be done about it.

"Durham proper is twenty or thirty minutes, but I'm hopin' we find what you need at a shop along the way." Ned put away the Zippo, stuffing his hands in his pockets, and looked up at the sky. "We got plenty of time before we got to hole up again. You grabbed some breakfast already?"

"We did," Alex said. Minnie and Lauren were inside, sipping their increasingly rare cups of coffee. The Zion's Angels had made a large pot of it over a campfire the second it was safe to go outside, and the ladies had treated their cups of joe like liquid gold. Alex had left them to enjoy their drinks and let Oliver run around outside. "Minnie and I are both coming. Is it okay if Lauren, Oliver, and Samson stay here?"

"All right by me," Ned said. "The new guy, Ben Polk… he's coming, too. It's my turn to keep an eye on him."

Alex frowned. "He seems… off. I'd prefer he not come."

The convict — an embezzler, according to Wyatt's records — was in his mid-forties. Calm and calculated most of the time, he had episodes where he would twitch and scratch at his arms. Other times he would murmur as if talking to someone who wasn't there. The strange behavior was subtle enough that one had to be actively watching the man to catch it.

Ned shrugged. "He's a little quirky, but beggars can't be choosers. If we can trust him, we can use him. I'll keep an eye on him. Don't you worry about that. And maybe he just needs a little time out of the slammer. Prison isn't exactly the best place to develop normal social skills."

Alex sighed, but he didn't argue. *This isn't my operation. Let it go. Move on. Get out of here.* He called to Oliver who ran over to him with a big smile on his face.

"Yeah, dad?" Oliver bounced on the balls of his feet, clearly ready to return to playing with the other kids.

It seemed almost normal. Alex hated to inject real life into his son's break from reality, but he had no choice. "Oliver, I'm going to leave with Minnie to find a tire so we can get out of here, okay?"

"Can't we stay here for a while?" Oliver asked. "I really like it here." He looked around Alex and grinned at the biker. "Hey, Ned!"

"What's up, little man?" Ned gave him half of a salute.

"I'm sorry, bud, but we really have to get to Boston." Alex gently put a hand on Oliver's chin and turned his son's head so that he could look into his eyes. "I need you to listen. Lauren will come out here to watch you. If she tells you to come inside, you drop whatever you're doing and go inside."

"Dad, none of the other kids have adults hovering over them." Oliver crossed his arms, his smile disappearing as he huffed.

Oliver's attitude took Alex by surprise. It had been weeks since his son had done anything but obey and obey quickly. *He's getting used to all this.* Alex couldn't tell if that was good or bad.

"Oliver, this place might seem safe, but nowhere is completely safe right now. We need to move on to Boston. For now, Lauren will be keeping watch while I'm gone, and you *will* listen to whatever she says. Either that, or you can go inside right now and stay there." Alex pressed his lips together and raised his eyebrows. "What will it be?"

"This place isn't so bad," Oliver said. "It's better than St. Louis or Nashville or Atlanta! Mom would have let us stay here!"

The assumption about what Naomi would have done hit Alex hard. He rubbed the back of his neck. "Oliver…" He sighed. *How do I make him understand?*

Ned stepped forward and knelt in front of Oliver, his hulking figure somehow displaying gentleness. He looked up at Alex. "You mind if I butt in?" Alex shrugged and nodded, and Ned continued. "Oliver, I gather you lost your mom to all this mess?"

Oliver nodded and swallowed audibly, his eyes brimming with tears. "A few weeks ago," he said.

"Well, those kids know how you feel. Most of them don't have parents left to hover over them and worry about their safety."

Oliver looked back at the other kids, pulling up the collar of his shirt and drying his eyes. "They don't?" His frown turned contemplative.

"All but two of 'em," Ned said. He pointed down the side of the building to where a woman sat on a bench, partially hidden from their view by a tree. "Kiki's mom watches her from over there, and Pete's dad, well… I don't think he's *ever* done much in the way of watchin' over the boy. Even so, us Zion's Angels, we keep our eyes on 'em through the windows." Ned stood up. "This place is as safe as we can make it, but that's not sayin' much these days. We're all sittin' on pins and needles, sleeping with one eye open. Your dad knows what's best for you, kid, and I bet he knows what your mother would want, too."

Oliver looked up at Alex. "I guess Mom would have wanted us to do the right thing, to keep going." He sighed. "I just miss the way things used to be."

Alex drew his son into a hug. "I know this is hard. I just need you to keep listening so that we can all stay safe, okay?"

Oliver nodded. "Okay, Dad. Do you want me to go inside?"

"No. It's okay to play for a while longer," Alex said. *This might be your last chance for a while.* Oliver ran back to join the others, hesitant at first, looking over his shoulder at Alex every few seconds. The other kids soon seemed to take his worries off his mind, however, and Oliver chased after another kid, hand outstretched to tag him, laughing as he barely missed touching him.

"He's a good kid," Ned said. "This is hard on everyone. How the kids are getting' by when us adults are barely makin' it, I'll never know."

"And I don't think it's even close to being over," Alex said. "Sometimes I wonder, if we live through this, how long will it take for him to recover? For us *all* to recover? Or is this just the new normal?"

"Only God knows," Ned said, pulling out his Zippo again, clicking it open and shut. "But it seems like the damage is here to stay. I don't know how the world recovers from this. From what we saw on the news before everything went dark, the sickness was showin' up worldwide. Ain't no U.N. or foreign powers coming to help us out if things are as bad everywhere as they are here." Ned snapped the lid on the lighter shut one more time. "All I know is, we can't let people like Jesse King be the last ones standin'." He scowled when he said the name of the serial killer who he suspected of murdering his brother.

"Amen to that." Alex gave Ned a friendly pat on the shoulder. "Let's go get that tire."

When Alex and Ned walked back into the building, Alex found Minnie tipping back her mug to drain the last of her coffee. She set the cup down as he approached and smacked her lips. "I woke up this mornin' movin' slower than molasses in January." She stood up, put her hands on her back, and stretched. "I miss having a good, hot cup every morning with homemade biscuits and bacon."

"Mmmm. Bacon." Lauren looked into her empty cup and sighed. "I'm really starting to miss regular breakfasts."

The new normal. Alex smiled, remembering the last so-called regular breakfast he'd had with Naomi and Oliver the morning they'd left for St. Louis. It was nothing special. Scrambled eggs. Coffee for him, tea for Naomi. Toast with strawberry jam. *It was simple. Mundane.* An ache settled in his chest. He could almost see their kitchen table bathed in natural light from the bay window, hear the laughter as he'd wiped off a glob of jam from Oliver's nose. *I wish I'd savored it.* Instead, he'd pushed to get out the door in an effort to make it to the airport early.

"I guess our coffee break is over." Lauren stood up beside Minnie, pulling Alex into the present. "I'll go out and watch Oliver. You two get that tire so we can get back on the road."

"Right." Alex took a deep breath, clearing his mind of the past. There was no use dwelling on what had been; it would only paralyze him. Already the ache had grown to a dull throbbing, his stomach turning to rocks. *I can grieve the past when the future is secure.* "Ned, go get Ben, and we'll meet you out front."

Ned gave another lazy, half salute and turned toward the kitchen, whistling. Alex and Minnie walked Lauren outside and then rounded the building to the front where three white delivery vans were parked. Ned and Ben were leaning against one, talking. Or rather, Ned was talking. Ben was zipping and unzipping a light jacket.

"I'm tellin' you," Ned said, "you're gonna be sweatin' bullets in that thing."

Ben zipped it up to his neck and then dropped his hands. "I like the jacket," he said. "I'm keeping it. Are we leaving or not?"

Alex and Minnie frowned at each other as Ned shook his head and double clicked a key fob. The van unlocked, and the biker sighed one last time at Ben before opening the back. "You two mind riding in the back? These vans are all we got besides a few school buses and the bikes. It's not ideal but…" He grimaced at Ben who was whispering something Alex couldn't quite make out. "… I think it's best that one ride up front with me."

Alex looked inside the back of the van. There were no windows except a grate at the center behind and between the driver and passenger seat up front. Two benches ran along the sides, but it was empty otherwise. He and Minnie exchanged cautionary looks. Minnie crossed her arms and raised her eyebrows at Ned. "That grate's about as useful as an ash tray on a motorcycle."

"Yeah, that's not going to work for us," Alex said. "I can't see where you're taking us from back here."

Ned chuckled and shook his head. "Then you and Minnie sit in the front. Me and Ben will ride in the back. Would that work for you?" Ned tossed the key fob at Alex.

Alex barely caught the fob; he hadn't expected Ned to hand them over. "Are you sure?"

"Yeah, man." Ned motioned for Ben to get inside. "You don't trust people. I get it."

"And you trust me?" Alex asked.

"No," Ned said. "I trust the Big Man upstairs." He pointed to the sky. Then he shrugged. "Plus, you left your kid here. I doubt you're going to try to steal my van and leave him behind."

Alex nodded. "Okay, then. You good with this, Minnie?"

"Right as rain," Minnie said as she headed toward the passenger side door.

Ben stuck his head inside the back of the van and shook his head. "I don't like it," he said. "It's too… white. It's too white, like solitary." He knocked on the wall of the space inside, his lips moving as if he were talking to himself. Then he nodded and said abruptly, "Yeah, okay." He climbed inside the van and sat down on the bench.

"You were in solitary? For what?" Ned asked.
"Got in a fight," Ben said. "The other guy started it."
"If you say so." Ned looked up at the sky, shook his head, and climbed up after Ben.
Alex pressed his lips together, pushing aside the shudder that went up his spine at Ben's strange behavior. There was no way Alex would want to be alone with that man, even if it was only partially alone. But Ned had already insisted Ben come with them, and Alex had no doubts the big biker could handle the wiry convict.
He shrugged off the uneasy feeling and hopped in the driver's seat. "I'm just driving southwest?" he asked through the grate.
"Yep." Ned said as Alex turned on the vehicle. "South on 85. Stop wherever you want, if you think you'll find what you need there. We got a full tank, but keep an eye on it."
Alex pulled out of the parking lot of the elementary school and headed toward the highway. He wove through the vehicles, most of them empty. However, the first glimpse of a rotting corpse with its eyes bugging out of its head sent his stomach to lurching and encouraged him to keep his eyes on the road.
"I'm guessing this area was hit by the sickness coming in at the airports, like Atlanta was?" Alex asked.
Ned's voice came from the back through the grate. "Yep. Private plane landed from Washington DC, a senator and his staff. Raleigh didn't know what hit 'em until it was too late. Spread like wildfire. But to be honest, we'd still have a lot of our loved ones with us if it weren't for the panic. Lots of looting and violence."
"I imagine it was the same most places," Minnie said, looking out the window at the abandoned businesses with windows shattered and doors hanging on their hinges. "Not even a month has gone by and look where we are. This country is unrecognizable."
"At least we haven't seen any of those swarms yet," Ned said. "I suppose they're coming, eventually, but… man, I wish they wouldn't."
"Swarms?" Alex frowned. "What are you talking about?"
"You haven't heard?" Ned asked. "Swarms of very aggressive mosquitos. People comin' from up near Boston told us they started showin' up a week or two ago. If they swarm you, you're good as dead unless you're covered head to toe. One guy described it as a pack of mosquitos, a deadly black cloud with a mind of its own."
"That's not normal activity for mosquitos, not here." Alex frowned. He'd discovered during his stay at the CDC that the disease was manmade, but this was the first time he'd considered a new possibility. If true, it increased the sinister nature of what was happening. "I mean, occasionally, swarms of mosquitos have been known to occur after hurricanes here in the States, and there are even reports of hundreds of livestock deaths as a result of anemia after being swarmed, but… roaming swarms that seem to *hunt*? And no underlying cause for the increase in numbers? It just doesn't make sense."
For an engineered disease to be released at the same time a natural emergence of a new species of mosquito takes place… that's too coincidental. His thoughts turned to Walter Peters, to his company's research concerning mosquitos and how to eradicate them.
His thoughts were interrupted as Minnie pointed at the side of the road where a large billboard proclaimed a discount on RV supplies.
"I reckon we can find what we need there," she said.
"All right," Alex said, squinting at the sign. "Randy's RV Repair, here we come." He pulled off the highway via the exit and backtracked half a mile to get to the store. He and Minnie got out and reached the back as Ned was hopping to the ground. A small square building was separated from a larger garage by a narrow alleyway. There wasn't much else in the area.
Minnie pointed toward the glass window of the store front where stacks of tires created a nice display. "There!" she said. "One of those would do nicely."
"Hold on a minute," Ned said. "This isn't too far from the prison." He reached into his leather vest and brought out a handgun. "I'll check to see if it's safe. Look in a few windows, scan the area… you three wait here." He walked toward the alleyway with his gun pointed down and away from the path of his feet.
"I've been here before," Ben said. "With the others from the prison. Right after we broke out."
"Anything we should know about?" Alex asked.
"That's not a very specific question." Ben peeked around the back of the truck.
"What do you mean by that? Are your friends set up inside?" Alex raised his voice, his heartbeat picking up. *Is Ned walking into an ambush?*
"All my friends are right here." Ben waved vaguely in Minnie and Alex's direction. "The other guys from the prison weren't my friends."
"That wasn't an answer." Alex jogged forward a few steps but skidded to a stop at the sound of Ned's cry echoing down the alley.

Chapter 13

Zara Williams

Zara stretched out her legs on the faux leather bench seat of the old school bus. The windows revealed the Pennsylvania countryside through a veil of dust and grime as the bus rattled its way toward Clearfield. Pleasant Home, Ohio, and the compound lay more than three hours in the rearview along with Lizzy's grave.

It had been quiet from the time she and Mr. Peters set foot on the bus, but it wasn't the tense, unbearable quiet she'd endured in his presence before. Zara didn't know if it would last, but Mr. Peters seemed to have buried the man she'd grown to hate when he buried his daughter. He'd been broken, and he wasn't trying to glue the pieces of himself back together like they'd been before. They had that in common. He wasn't the only one changed by the events of the past weeks.

She wasn't the Zara trying to prove herself to the world anymore, the young woman busting her butt to get scholarships so she could one day justify all the pain and financial trouble her family had gone through to see her survive childhood cancer.

She wasn't the frightened Zara surviving the beginning of the end of the world as she knew it, either, allowing a bully to stir up insecurities and dictate her every move.

But she also wasn't the Zara consumed by a mission to see Mr. Peters pay for the deaths of her family, blinded by hatred and anger and grief. That Zara had been on the cusp of becoming like the man she despised. Zara didn't have the energy to be that person anymore. The burdens of anger and hatred had fallen from her shoulders when Mr. Peters had owned up to his part, when he'd stopped resisting responsibility. If justice knocked on his door, she believed he would accept it. She wasn't sure she could ever *like* Walter Peters, but she could work with him to get home.

Zara didn't know who she was becoming, what version of herself would develop from the wreckage of the past weeks. But there was hope in the unknown, in the possibilities. Somehow knowing the kind of person she *could* be but didn't *want* to be made her embrace the pieces of her that were strongest.

There was only one thing still nagging at her: guilt. Thomas and several members of his community had openly forgiven her. "But how do I forgive myself?" she said.

"What was that?" Mr. Peters asked from the driver's seat.

Zara blushed. She hadn't meant to speak loud enough for him to hear. "I don't understand how they could have forgiven us. I'm glad they did, but… how did they do it? And how…" She trailed off, about to ask him what she'd asked herself moments before. It was harder to say, though, and she clamped her mouth shut.

"How do you forgive yourself?" Mr. Peters asked.

"Yeah." Zara pulled her knees to her chest.

"If you figure that one out, let me know," he said. "I could use the advice. In the meantime, I think we're finally here." He pointed ahead.

Zara sat up straighter and peered through the windshield. Ahead, a sign welcomed them to Clearfield, population 5,873. Under that, a hand-painted sign on a slab of plywood read: Flight Auction at Courthouse. "That's what we're looking for," she said. More hand-painted signs led them to follow the highway across a river, turning immediately right after the bridge onto North 2nd Street.

Mr. Peters slowed the bus, frowning at the barricades blocking the road ahead. Beyond them, pedestrians roamed downtown. "I guess everyone left has consolidated here," he said. "The rest of the town up to this point seemed deserted."

Just before the barricades, there was a parking lot next to a large old stone building reminiscent of a church. "Maybe we can pull in there?" Zara pointed to the lot.

Mr. Peters shook his head. "There are too many RVs, trucks, and SUVs crammed into that lot. Most of them are hemmed in on all sides." He pulled over to the side of the road. "This will be fine for now."

"Okay," Zara said, crossing her arms. "Next steps? We need to gather information at the courthouse about the flight auction."

Mr. Peters frowned at the street beyond the barricades. "We can't leave the bus unattended. Even with the bike locks for the doors, it wouldn't take much to bust a window and get away with some valuables." He stood up and scooted around Zara, heading to the back of the bus.

Zara followed him past the six rows left in the bus; the back half was empty save three crates, four small gas canisters, and two large hiker backpacks, each one with a sleeping bag roll attached. He'd designated the latter for the things they wouldn't trade. "So one of us stays here to guard the supplies, and the other one goes into town to gather information on the auction."

Mr. Peters grabbed one of the backpacks and unzipped one of several pockets to pull out a holstered handgun. He held it out for Zara. "We'll both need to carry while we're here. Actually, it might be a good idea for us to carry from now on."

The weight of the gun in her hand made her stomach lurch, but she took it anyway. She swallowed hard, for a moment unable to look away from the weapon. Shooting handguns at the range had been a favorite pastime of hers, something she could do with her father, just the two of them. She was a good shot, too. But the last time she'd held a gun — a rifle — she'd shot a woman she cared about. Bertie had been sick with DV-10, not thinking clearly, trying to get herself and her daughter on the bus. If Zara hadn't pulled the trigger, Mr. Peters would have; she did it in the heat of the moment, with Mr. Peters breathing down her neck, yelling in her ear about how she couldn't handle doing what needed to be done.

"Zara?" Mr. Peters sounded hesitant. "Did you hear anything I just said?"

Zara shook her head. "Sorry. I got distracted." She wrapped the band of the holster around her waist and secured it at her hip. She didn't want to talk to Mr. Peters about Bertie and how she wished he wouldn't have put her in that position in the first place.

"If you're not in the right frame of mind to carry a gun—"

"I'm fine." Zara set her jaw and met his eyes with her own, a familiar tension flaring within her.

Mr. Peters put up his hands in surrender. "Okay. If you say so. Just be careful." He grabbed the other backpack and retrieved his own gun, securing it around his waist. "I'm going to go into town—"

"I think I should go." Zara interrupted him. "I'm more approachable."

Mr. Peters sighed. "You're also more vulnerable."

"Let's say a bunch of guys come around this bus and see we've got crates in the back and there's only one person — skinny, little ol' me — between them and our only bartering chips. I'm vulnerable everywhere, Walter." She grimaced; she hadn't meant to fall into old habits. "Sorry," she said. "Mr. Peters."

"You're right," he said. "We should go into town together."

Zara's body relaxed a little, the tension dissipating. "None of those RVs or other vehicles had broken windows." She offered a small smile. "Worst case scenario, we've got each other's backs, but we lose everything we brought with us."

"That's old hat," Mr. Peters said, smiling back. His expression turned more serious. "But… I think you hit on what I was thinking. We can recover from loss of stuff. If one of us dies…" His voice caught, but he continued with a soft rasp of emotion. "…we can't fix that."

"Then we're agreed," Zara said gently. "We go together, everywhere, until we get home."

Zara helped Mr. Peters stash their backpacks under the front bench seats, away from the crates. Then she twisted the bike lock through the handles of the skinny doors at the front of the bus while Mr. Peters grabbed a few small items from the crates they could use to barter with for information, if it came to that. They hopped out of the back, and Mr. Peters locked the padlock Thomas had installed on the outside.

Zara stayed alert as they walked past the barricades. It wasn't crowded, per se, but it was the most people she'd seen gathered in one place in weeks. Mismatched old brick buildings gave the street plenty of character. Lines hung between windows in the alleyways boasted drying laundry. A few people on horseback trotted across the intersection ahead. They walked by a bar, the door open, the bar full of patrons. One man slid a package of cough drops across the bar and received a fresh glass of honey-colored liquor. Mr. Peters stopped at the window which was plastered in posters and papers.

Zara came up beside him and read over the postings. "Guns for hire. Safety in numbers. Don't go into the mountains alone. Are they trying to scare people into hiring them?"

A man who'd just stumbled out of the bar slammed his hand against the window, startling Zara and making her jump back. "It's th' truth," the man said, words slurred. "S'not safe." He pushed off the walls, hands swinging to grasp hold of Zara's arm.

"Don't touch me!" Zara swatted away the drunk man.

But she didn't have to fend him off. Mr. Peters stepped between them and took hold of the man's wrist, towering over him. "You've had too much to drink," he said.

The man cowered and whimpered. "I was warnin' her," he said. "S'not safe."

"He's right." A man with a gun holstered under each arm leaned nonchalantly in the doorway. He unsnapped one of the holsters, clearly ready to pull his weapon. "That sorry heap is Fred. He's from Scranton, further into the mountains. Arrived in Clearfield barefoot, in nothing but his underwear, about four days ago, covered in blood. Said it belonged to his wife."

Mr. Peters let Fred go, and the man scampered away, still whimpering. "What else did he say?"

"Nothing new." The man let his hand drop, leaving his gun holstered. "The mountain roads are hard to get through on foot. Steep roads. Bandits can sneak up on smaller groups pretty easy. All they got to do is block the road and pounce. On the other side, those mosquitos have been reported at all hours. Clearfield is the last safe spot on the way East. At least for now."

"And who are you?" Mr. Peters crossed his arms.

"You can call me Nolan." He reached over to the window and tapped one of the signs that advertised guns for hire. "That's me and my boys."

"You've gotten people to the other side safely?" Zara stepped forward.

"We started out on the other side and got a caravan through to Clearfield safely," Nolan said, "but we've not gone back. Not yet. Not a lot of people going toward the worst of it. And everyone who is wants to win that ridiculous auction."

Zara raised her eyebrows and exchanged a look with Mr. Peters. "What do you know about that?"

"You too, huh?" Nolan shook his head. "The kid who flies the plane holds an auction every week. Mondays, Wednesdays, and Fridays he flies East on a little private plane. Auction is on Sunday. Three winners get a one-way trip. He's got a nice little operation going, at least until he runs out of fuel at that little airport outside of town."

"What day is it?" Zara asked, frowning. It had been a while since the date had actually mattered.

"It's Wednesday," Nolan said. "You've got four days."

"That's not soon enough," Mr. Peters said. "Where can we find the pilot?"

"He's flying across the mountains right about now. He's got another winner booked for Friday, too. The soonest you're getting out of here by flight is going to be Monday." He got a hungry look in his eyes as he leaned forward a little. "What did you bring to barter? Maybe my boys and me can help you out?"

"Thanks, but we'll talk to the pilot first," Mr. Peters said. "If he's coming back tomorrow, we might convince him to take us sooner."

"Not going to happen," Nolan said, his expression turning a shade darker. "Your best bet is to go with me and my guys."

"I'm not fond of repeating myself," Mr. Peters said. "We'll consider your offer *after* we talk to the pilot."

Nolan sniffed and folded his arms. "Fine. We're at the firehouse on Van Valzah, just a few blocks from the courthouse. This place is full of people waiting for a ride on his plane. Dozens enter his auction; three come away happy. Meanwhile, my crew is ready and willing with Humvees and weapons."

"We'll find you if we need you." Mr. Peters put a hand on Zara's back and guided her away from Nolan, back toward the bus.

"Why not take Nolan up on his offer?" Zara asked when they were out of earshot.

"I don't trust him," Mr. Peters said. "In business, you learn to read people, and that guy is underhanded. I can smell it on him like I could smell the whiskey on Fred."

"Four days *is* too long, though. And it might be longer. What if we don't get a spot this week through the auction? We can't stay here indefinitely, defending our supplies, hoping we get a ride before they're stolen or the pilot runs out of gas." Zara wanted to scream. *Will we ever get home? Why can't anything ever just work out?*

Mr. Peters opened his mouth as if he were about to respond, but then his eyes widened and he shouted, "Hey! Stop!" He broke into a sprint toward the bus. Zara's stomach dropped. Strangers were trying to get inside; one of them held a bat, ready to swing at the glass. And Mr. Peters was charging them, one man against four.

Chapter 14

Alexander Roman

Alex threw Minnie the keys. "Get in the car and get ready to run, with or without us." He pointed at Ben. "You – get back in the van if you don't want to be left here."
Minnie rushed to the driver's side as Ben mumbled to himself, zipping and unzipping his jacket. He didn't seem interested in getting back in the van. But Alex couldn't worry about the convict, not when Ned could be in trouble. Minnie was safe inside the van with a means to escape; that's all that mattered to him.

He darted toward the alleyway, his mind racing. If Ned was in real trouble, there wasn't much he could do about it. But the biker had saved his life and the lives of his family. He had to try to help. Slowing before he reached the corner of the building, Alex crept the last few feet before peeking around to the back. Ned stood with his hands on his knees, his head bowed low, breathing hard, but Alex couldn't spot any immediate threat. There was a back door with a sign above it that read 'repair waiting room', but it was closed. And there was an odd stench in the air.
"Ned?" Alex whispered loudly. "What happened?" He slowly came out into the open, scanning the area for any movement.
Ned straightened up and ran his fingers through his hair. "There's a bunch of dead guys in the waiting room," he said.
Alex furrowed his brow. "The sickness?"
Ned shook his head. "No… they… they…" And then Ned heaved and fell to his knees, losing the contents of his stomach to the pavement.
Alex frowned and rushed to the door, throwing it open. He had to see for himself. If it was the sickness, and it had somehow gotten more gruesome… he gagged at the sickening odor of the dead. The little waiting room held four corpses in prison jumpsuits, but none of them had welts or bulging eyes. Instead, they had gaping wounds, their insides spilling onto the floor. Blood spattered *everything*. Trails of dark crimson led down the hall as if the bodies were dragged from other parts of the store. Beams of sunlight filtered in through a high window, shining off the silver butt of an axe head still buried in one of the corpse's skulls, the handle at a forty-five-degree angle to the body.
A shock wave that left him numb radiated through Alex's body, and he froze with one foot inside the room, his hand holding the door open. He'd stopped breathing in that moment, and when he did suck in a shaking breath, the stench knocked him back from the massacre, his shoe noisily unsticking from the partially-dried blood on the floor. The door swung closed, and Alex turned away, hand to mouth as he willed his stomach to calm.
Ned had mostly recovered, though he still looked too pale and a sheen of sweat shone on his forehead. "Did you see it? The tip of the pinky finger on the closest man… it was sawed off." Ned's voice shook. "This was the work of Jesse King."
"I wasn't looking at their hands." Alex leaned against the wall of the building, fighting to maintain composure. The wave of numbness gave way to his quickening pulse; the tips of his fingers tingled as his hands trembled.
"King has to be stopped." Ned's eyes were glued to the door, horror painted in his expression as if he could still see beyond it. "No one deserves to die like that."
A shot of pure terror seized Alex's thrashing heart, squeezing it so hard, he thought it might burst. "Ben said he was here with other convicts, and I left him back there with Minnie." That fear was like a jolt of electricity, springing him toward the alley. He ran back in the direction he'd come.
"Alex!" Ned's footsteps scratched the pavement behind him as the biker ran to keep up. "It was King, not Ben!"
Alex burst into the parking lot. Minnie sat in the driver's seat, engine rumbling and both hands on the wheel, staring at the alleyway. She sat up straighter when Alex got nearer, as if she were waiting for him to give her a signal to tell her what to do. Ben sat next to her in the passenger seat. He didn't belong there. He was supposed to be in the back, away from Minnie. All Alex could think about was how Ben had avoided answering his question about his time at the shop with the other convicts.
"Hey!" Alex yelled. "You get out of there! Get away from her!" He ran up to the passenger side door and yanked it open. Then he reached up and grabbed hold of Ben's jacket, forcing him out of the van. "Did you know what we would find? Did you have something to do with it?" Ben grinned, and Alex could have sworn a flash of pleasure shone in his eyes. Alex growled and threw Ben to the ground, straddling him. "What happened in there?" Ben's grin had only widened, which lit a fire in Alex's stomach. He drew back his fist, ready to punch the smile right off Ben's face.
"Whoa, Alex!" Ned wrapped his arms around Alex's middle and lifted him off Ben. "Come on, now. He wasn't doing anythin' wrong. We don't know anythin' yet."
"Alexander Roman! What in Sam Hill are you doin'?" Minnie had come around the front of the van to scold him.
Ben scrambled to his feet, his grin gone. He pointed at Alex. "He attacked me! You saw it. You *both* saw it!"
Ned set Alex down on his feet and put himself between Alex and Ben. "Alex is bent out of shape, Ben. We just saw four men, dead. Murdered, actually."
"You said you were here before," Alex shouted. "Four men don't axe themselves to death. What do you know?"
Ben scratched the back of his left hand with his right and shook his head. "I don't want to be here. I'm going back inside the van."
Ned held out his hands. "Ben, hey… just hold on a minute. I know Jesse King was here. Do you know where the man is?"

Ben grimaced. "What do you want with Jesse King?"
"I want to bring him back to prison," Ned said, "where he belongs. He killed my brother. And he's killed a lot of other people, too."
"Your brother was an inmate?" Ben asked, touching his ear to his shoulder, still scratching at the back of his hand.
"No, he was a security guard," Ned said.
Ben stopped scratching the back of his hand and shook his head, mumbling something indecipherable. "I liked the security guards."
Alex wanted to scream at Ben, that sickly amused grin pasted itself into Alex's mind, but no one else had seen it. So, he kept his tone under control as he listened to his instincts. "Ned, he knows something."
"Land's sake, Alex." Minnie put a gentle hand on Alex's forearm. "Calm down."
"You didn't see what happened back there," Alex said. "Minnie, those men were *butchered*." Alex pointed at Ben. "And he was here."
"He didn't say he was here when *that* happened." Ned pointed back at the building. "If he had been, King would have slaughtered him with the rest."
Ben cleared his throat. "I know where Jesse King wants to go," he said.
That got everyone's attention. Ned snapped his head to look at Ben. "Where?"
"He's going to Brooklyn," Ben said. "To find his sister."
"And how do you know that?" Alex crossed his arms.
"Jesse King told me so." Ben stood up a little straighter, rolling his shoulders as if to work out the kinks that had made him screw them up so tightly.
Ned nodded. "I guess I'm goin' north, then. King can't be allowed to keep killin' people, and that's exactly what will happen if we leave him out here. We need to find him, and then we put him back where he belongs. In prison, where he can't hurt anyone else." Ned chewed on his lower lip for a moment. "I can't ask the guys to abandon the mission here, though. I'll have to go on my own. Wyatt'll want to come. And Asher, maybe. We'll need a way to get there besides the bikes. They're no good for long distances anymore. Too exposed to the elements."
Alex's jaw dropped. "You're ready to go off to New York City on *his* word?" He nodded at Ben who acted affronted at Alex's suggestion he wasn't trustworthy.
Ned pointed north. "If he's here, Zion's Angels will keep lookin' for him. They'll find him. But if he goes north, he'll continue to wreak havoc on what remains of humanity. I have a fire in my belly, Alex, and it won't be quenched until Jesse King is back behind bars or dead."
Alex shook his head, but he kept his mouth shut. It's not our business. We just need to get back on the road. We have to find Peters and figure out how to stop this disease and these mosquitos.
Then Minnie piped up. "Once we get the tire fixed," she said, "you can come with us. We can drop you off near the city. It'll be a tight fit, but it's only an eight-hour drive. There ain't seatbelts in the back, but there's room."
Alex ran his hands over his face. New York City was on the way to Boston, but he had planned to give The Big Apple a wide berth. "Minnie, I don't want to get close to the city. Even the suburbs will be dangerous. And it's way more than eight hours when you stay off the main highways, which will be more dangerous and more congested the closer we get to any city."
"Harvey is *my* RV," Minnie said, raising her eyebrows and putting her hands on her hips. "And besides, we owe Ned."
Ned looked at Alex with pleading in his eyes. "It would be nice to travel in a bigger group. Might be safer for the both of us, actually. You don't have to go too near the city. You can drop us off at the edges of the suburbs. Ain't no country to speak of there, no way to get caught without shelter. We'll be fine."
Alex sighed, but Minnie was right. Ned wasn't asking for much in exchange for all his help, and if they didn't have to drive into the city itself… "Okay," he said, looking at Minnie. "You're right. Ned and his friends are welcome to travel with us any time."
"We might not even have the need to go all the way to the city," Ned said. "We found a body fresher than these just three days ago. It was less mutilated, but it was Jesse King's work. That means he was still in the area three days ago."
"He likes it here," Ben said. "He likes the people in North Carolina."
Alex joined Ned and Minnie in staring at the man. Ben shifted his weight from foot to foot, scratching at his hand again.
"Jesse King doesn't like people; he likes choppin' 'em up," Ned said.
"That's just what he told me." Ben shrugged.
"Apparently this serial killer is a real chatter box," Alex said, his words intentionally dripping with sarcasm.
Ben nodded, dead serious. "Oh yes. He can be very social. Charming even. I bet those guys in there didn't even see him coming. They all loved him."
"Okay, that's good to know, I guess," Ned said. "Anyway, if he's traveling on foot, he'll have a head start, but we'll catch up to him. If he likes people, he'll want to stop where they're gathered. I know of a few survivor camps along the way. The man is on a killin' spree. I doubt he'll be able to go long without killin' again. We might even find him before we reach the city. We might just stop him from committing his next murder."
Ben nodded, scuttling up to Ned's side. "I want to come with you, Ned."
"Absolutely not," Alex said.
"Do *you* know what Jesse King looks like?" Ben asked. "Because I do."
"He's got a point," Ned said. "We don't know what he looks like. He's got to be fifteen or twenty years older than the only photograph I've ever seen of him. And that was on the news so long ago, I don't know I could recognize him even if he looked the same."
"Plus, you're my new friends." Ben grinned again, and Alex shuddered. There was a sinister undertone to his smile, but it seemed only Alex noticed it.
"I suppose there would be room for four in the back of the RV," Minnie said, sounding more skeptical than she had when offering to bring only the bikers.
"We'll be out of your hair as soon as the big city is within our reach," Ned said. "Or as soon as we get wind of King elsewhere."

Alex pointed at Ned and then at Ben. "You keep him away from my family. I don't want him so much as looking at Oliver."
"Understood," Ned said.
"Let's get this tire, then." Alex looked back at the storefront window where the tire they needed was stacked in a display just beyond the glass. They'd found what they needed, but they'd also been saddled with three bikers and a convict. *One step forward, two steps back. The new normal.*

Chapter 15

Timothy Peters

Timothy prepared himself to cross the maze set before him. He'd followed O'Donnell and the small team of police officers, starting behind police headquarters, skirting the edges of the northern tip of Southwest Corridor Park, and coming to the threshold of a wide-open space where there was no cover from buildings and any cover from foliage had been eliminated due to a fire long put out. Ahead of him, the remnants of the chaos looked more like a war zone than like the city Timothy loved. Small, decorative trees had been burned leaving only blackened branches. An entanglement of vehicles, many of them burned out, many more with corpses still inside, acted as a barrier to their destination. Corpses in various stages of decay lay on the ground or across the hoods of cars, and the stench was overwhelming in the hot summer sun, every breeze carrying with it something like rotten eggs and garlic wrapped in moldy, musty cloth.

"We'll want to stay low." O'Donnell pointed to a nearby body that was clearly fresh, a middle-aged man with three bullet holes in his chest. "CON would take us out in a second if they saw us."

Murphy, the female officer from Chelsea who was looking for her son, pulled out her binoculars. She'd insisted on coming, and her buddies, Burke and Torres, weren't going to be left behind. It seemed those three were inseparable. Besides the officers from Chelsea, O'Donnell had brought two of his own from the 13th: Karl Webb and Lucy Freeman. Timothy had convinced Candice and Heather to stay at headquarters and find out whatever they could about the plans to take out CON if O'Donnell's mission to save the kids failed. They would need to know what to expect if the police went to war with CON.

"CONmen aren't the only ones we need to look out for." Murphy scanned the area with the binoculars. "We've seen normal everyday people do crazy stuff to get a leg up in this mess."

Torres was standing backwards, his eye on where they'd come from. "We've got guns and bullet proof vests. That makes us targets just as much as it makes us capable of defending ourselves."

Burke clenched his fists at his sides, standing back-to-back with Torres. "Anybody could be a perp."

"We've been living this, too," Freeman said. "You're not the only ones." She narrowed her eyes at the Chelsea officers.

"And Captain O'Donnell knows what he's doing," Webb added.

"Hold on, now," O'Donnell said. "We're all the same team. We need to remember that."

Timothy pressed his lips together. He'd never been on a team so divided. If either Murphy or O'Donnell found the kids they were looking for in the midst of a survivor group like the one they were on their way to visit, what little support Timothy had garnered would vanish. *We're the only ones who know for certain our loved ones are with CON.* Timothy squirmed at the thought, not because he was afraid he'd lose support but because the possibility made him hope those children were either captured or so lost they'd not be found any time soon.

"We've got more than a mile to go before we reach the library." O'Donnell pointed at a gap in the vehicles that revealed a curb. "The sidewalks aren't clear, but they're better than the center of the wreckage. When we get to Dartmouth Street, we'll need to turn left, so let's stay left all the way down Route 28 so we have to cross less of this mess."

Timothy fell in line, in the center, as he'd agreed when they'd first set out. O'Donnell led, the officers of the 13th behind him, and the officers from Chelsea brought up the rear. Timothy ducked low as he followed so that his head was always below the tops of the vehicles. It took them an hour to traverse the streets of Boston the rest of the way to Central Library where survivors had formed a community.

When they reached the intersection just before the library, O'Donnell stopped and veered into a hotel's portico, trying the door and finding it unlocked. He swung it open and stepped inside, all seven of them cramming into the bit of sunlight making it past the awning and into the lobby.

"The library is just ahead," Burke said. "Why are we stopping?"

"Because they're expecting CONmen to show up today." O'Donnell crossed his arms. "I don't want to walk into a shootout with the gang just yet. Our uniforms, the vests, even our department-issued guns give us away."

"So, what do you want to do, sir?" Freeman dabbed the sweat from her brow with her wrinkled, tattered sleeve.

"I'll go." Timothy pulled at the Velcro of his vest. "I'll go in, no vest, no gun. I'll play a survivor on the street who heard about their community if I see CONmen there. If it's clear, I'll come back and get you."

Murphy shook her head and pulled out a long, thin whistle from her pocket. "We used these to communicate a bit on the way from Chelsea to headquarters. If the coast is clear, use three short bursts to let us know, and we'll come to you. If it's not, don't use the whistle, and we'll know to stay back. If you get into trouble, though – something you don't think you can get out of on your own – blow on the whistle long and hard."

"Got it." Timothy wriggled out of the heavy vest.

"We should spread out and cover the exits," Burke said. "That way if CON is already inside, we can follow them when they leave, try to find their base of operations."

"I like it, Burke." O'Donnell nodded firmly and then placed a hand on Timothy's shoulder. "Are you ready for this? Don't try to follow them yourself, okay? If they're in there, you keep your head down and leave the rest to us."

"I can do this." Timothy handed over his vest and gun. "You're sure I can trust the survivors in there?"

"No," O'Donnell said, "I'm not. I wouldn't trust anyone farther than you can throw 'em."

"Works for me." Jitters worked their way from Timothy's chest into his hands as he walked back outside and faced the library across the street. He jammed his hand into his pocket to feel for the whistle. He had very limited means of communication with the only people he trusted within a mile, but it was something, and the feel of the cool metal cylinder lent him a bit of comfort.

Timothy stepped forward as the others fanned out into the street. O'Donnell crouched beside the large wheel of a truck where he had a clear line of sight to the front entrance. Timothy kept going, scanning the area but staying visible, back straight. *If anyone is watching, maybe they'll notice the idiot taking no precautions instead of the others.*

He was gaining confidence, his steps surer when a high-pitched bleating startled him. He nearly jumped out of his skin as the bleating turned to a rumbling bellow that echoed around Copley Square. "What the—" His eyes grew wide as in the near distance three giant, shaggy creatures with two humps on their backs clopped their way across the intersection on the other side of the library. "Are those *camels*?" He was so shocked, he spoke out loud to no one in particular. He looked around out of instinct, but only caught O'Donnell peeking around the truck, waving him to go on.

"Okay," he said softly to himself. "Camels in the middle of Boston. No big deal." He shook off his shock and focused back on the library.

Six stone steps led up to the ornate main entrance: three doors with arched glass windows set into the granite face of the building. American flags hung above his head, flapping in the breeze. Timothy tried the first door, but it was locked. The double doors at the center opened up, though, and he walked into the pink marble entry complete with a statue in a little alcove and three pairs of bronze doors Timothy was familiar with from previous trips to the building. Oil lanterns made a pathway into the lobby, dimly illuminating the doors with a flickering light. They were open inward, making the gorgeous, sculpted depictions of women in flowing robes easy to pass by, but Timothy had always loved the doors, and as he passed through the center, his eye was drawn to the woman etched into the metal to his righthand side, elegantly representing the concept of Wisdom.

I could use some more of that these days. He sighed, a moment of sadness falling over him at the memories of field trips to the library as a child and the tours he'd enjoyed as an adult exploring the beautiful architecture. It seemed frivolous in the chaos of the times that he'd ever had the pleasure of finding a peaceful reading nook inside the building being used as a shelter for survivors. *Even good memories are colored dark.*

"Joining your buddies?" A woman stepped out from behind a column in the lobby and into the light of the lanterns, her tone decidedly *not* friendly. She had a baseball bat, but it rested on her shoulder. She didn't seem like she was about to attack him, despite her icy glare.

"My… *friends*?" Timothy frowned, and then his eyebrows shot upward. "They're here already?" The words were out of his mouth before he realized how decidedly unwise they were.

"You're not a CONman?" the woman asked, narrowing her eyes.

"Uh… what?" Timothy said awkwardly.

Her brows knitted together. "What?" She shook her head. "Who are you?"

He cleared his throat. "I… um…" He grasped for the story he was supposed to tell. "I'm just a guy," he said. "A survivor and… um… I heard about you guys, thought I could maybe join."

"Heard about us from who?" She let the baseball bat fall from her shoulder, catching it with her other hand and holding it parallel to the floor.

"Other… people?" Timothy wanted to slap himself. *I really am an idiot.*

"I don't know if you're with CON, and you're messing with me, or if you're just some lucky bastard who's managed to stay alive." She bounced the tip of the bat up and down in her hand and took a menacing step toward him. "Here's the thing. I don't have time for games, and we can't take on any more survivors. It's hard enough on us as it is, with CON collecting a tax every week on what we scavenge." She nodded toward the door. "So, no matter who you are, how about you turn right around and leave us be?"

I have to at least find out where the CONmen are. Find out how many of them there are.

"Okay," Timothy whispered and stepped closer, trying to keep his voice as low as possible. "I'm not *with* CON, but I'm looking for them. They have my brother and a little girl I care about."

The woman sighed, her posture softening a little. "That's a fool's errand."

Timothy was about to continue his arguing when footsteps echoed down the grand staircase into the lobby. He looked up to find a group of four men, each with backpacks on, coming down the stairs, coming in and out of pools of light from the lanterns placed every third step. The man who reached the lobby first had a CON tattoo wrapped around the front of his neck. He nodded at Timothy but spoke to the woman.

"Hey, Linda. Who's that?" He walked over to the woman, his gun lazily tucked into the side of his jeans.

Linda let the bat fall to her side. She started to scoot away from the CONman, but he put an arm around her waist and pulled her to his side. She didn't fight it, but she didn't look happy about it, either.

"He's just a guy," she said, smiling at Timothy. "A survivor who thought he could take up space here."

The other CONmen walked by, headed toward the door. "Hey, come on, man," one of them said. "We all love to have a little fun, but we need to get going. We've been here too long. Still got another stop before we're done."

"Oh sure." The thug let go of Linda and followed his fellows with sagging shoulders. "When you wanna poke holes in somebody with an icepick, it's all 'we got time,' but when anybody else wants to take it slow, suddenly we're crunched for time."

Timothy stumbled back half a step, his body turning cold. *Icepick?* The image of his mother's body drenched in her own blood, small holes dotting her abdomen where the monster who'd killed her had stabbed her. As the men left the building, Timothy snapped out of his stupor in a rage. He turned on Linda, no longer caring if she attacked him.

"That guy… that was Icepick? You know him?" Timothy asked, his voice raised.

Linda furrowed her brow. "Yeah, that's him. A real scumbag. Why?"

"Because," Timothy said, turning back toward the door, "I'm going to kill him." His heartrate skyrocketed like water coming to a boil, anger overflowing the walls he'd built to keep his grief in check.

"Whoa, stranger," Linda trotted up beside him, her eyes wide. "You want to think about this? You can't attack them. There's four of them. One of you."

Timothy stepped forward with purpose. "I don't care." Just as he put his hand flat on the door to push it open, one of the CONmen outside shouted and pointed to the right where O'Donnell had been hiding. Then all four of them pulled their guns. Timothy flinched as the first shot rang out.

Chapter 16

Lizzy Peters

They wouldn't let her shut her eyes. The agonized screaming penetrated her mind, echoed there, and came out of her own mouth in a whimpering cry. Despite the cool temperature of the room, sweat rolled down her face, her neck, her back. Horrible images played on repeat, and when she squeezed her eyes shut against them, Orion held her eyelids open. There was no escape. Her heartbeat pounded against her rib cage, her wrists and ankles were cut and bleeding from her constant attempts to free them from the zip-ties. She couldn't think beyond the screaming.

"Make it stop," she cried for the hundredth time. The words scraped the lining of her throat, the pain the best indication she was speaking. The noise from the headphones drowned out even her own voice.

Every muscle in her body was taut with tension, and it had been that way for what seemed like hours. Sprinkled into the images of oil-slicked animals and human corpses and dry, cracked earth were photos of men in suits. She didn't recognize two of them, but one of them was the man Autumn had killed. The fourth was her own father. She could hear his voice in her head, beneath the screaming, every time his face appeared on the screen.

You betrayed me. I don't want anything to do with you, Elizabeth. You're dead to me. His voice was always followed by Zara's. I can't believe I thought you were my friend. You're not.

At first, she flinched at the memory of their words, she pled for them to forgive her. But hours passed, and eventually, the sight of her father and the accompanying voices enraged her. "I can't change it!" She spat. "Neither of you are perfect!" She shouted at them, cursing them.

And then the screaming stopped. The television screen went black. Heartbeat pounding in her ears, blood pumping furiously, lungs gasping for air, stinging pain shooting from her wrists and ankles, Lizzy whipped her head wildly to try to see behind her. *What are they going to do to me now?* Orion reached for her head, and she snapped at him with her teeth. He wagged a finger at her and plucked the earphones off.

Quiet rushed over Lizzy, though the screaming was still lodged inside her brain, just like the images. There was a surety inside her that both could reassert themselves at any moment. She didn't need the television or the headphones anymore. They were forever carved into her mind.

Azalea walked into the room with a brass bowl and knelt in front of her. "Elizabeth, you look terrible." She lifted a cool rag and dabbed at Lizzy's forehead. "You poor, poor girl. Let me help you."

"You did this to me!" Speaking and being able to hear herself felt like a trick. She still couldn't quite catch her breath, and she jerked her head backwards, eyes wide, waiting for the headphones to be put back.

"No, sweet Elizabeth. Our Elizabeth. You've done this to yourself. I don't want this for you. I respect you. I'm your friend." Her voice was soothing and gentle. She looked so sincere. The cool rag felt so good as it wiped away the grime of sweat and tears. "Don't you want some water to drink?"

Lizzy nodded. "Yes, please," she said, desperate. *Pathetic. I'm so pathetic.* She didn't care. "Please?"

"Of course." Azalea lifted the metal water bottle to Lizzy's lips and tilted it so that the water dribbled into her parched mouth.

Lizzy drank greedily, savoring every drop. Azalea smoothed away the strands of hair stuck to her forehead, smiling. When she was finished, Lizzy smiled back at her. "Thank you."

Azalea kissed the top of her head, and then she knelt beside her hands, frowning at the zip ties. "You've hurt yourself, my friend." Concern etched her features. "I'm going to cut these loose and apply a salve to make the wounds hurt less and heal faster. I can trust you, can't I, Elizabeth?"

Lizzy's mind was muddied. Thinking was like swimming against the current. Every ounce of her begged for rest. "I just want to lay down and sleep," she said.

"I want that for you, too," Azalea said. "Orion? Please, get the salve and bring in a cot. Grab a fresh set of clothing while you're at it. These are soiled."

Lizzy blushed. "I'm sorry. I didn't realize—"

"Hush. It's okay," Azalea said. "I understand. You've been through a lot."

Azalea cut Lizzy's ties loose. She glanced at the door, but she was *so* tired. And she had no idea how to get out of the underground compound. Orion rolled the cot into the room with a fresh change of clothes, salve, and bandages on top. Lizzy let Azalea help her clean up, apply the salve and bandage her wrists and ankles. Lizzy could barely lift her arms, and her body trembled with pure exhaustion when she stood up. She *needed* Azalea's help, and the young woman was so gentle, so kind.

She doesn't seem so bad. Lizzy frowned at the thought. No… she left me here with Orion. She knew I was being tortured. Just because I need her right now doesn't mean she's my friend.

Azalea helped Lizzy to the cot and let her lay down. Lizzy's eyes drooped as her head hit the pillow. "I'm so tired," she said.

"I know." Azalea stroked Lizzy's hair. "You can sleep soon, daughter of the Mother. You belong here. We want you to be happy."

Lizzy nodded and closed her eyes, but Azalea gently patted her cheek. "I need to sleep," she said. "Please let me sleep."

"I will," Azalea cooed. "Just tell me what we need to know," she said softly. "Tell me about your father. Tell me what he has planned. Was he with you when we found you?"

Lizzy was barely able to form complete thoughts. "No," she said. "He's dead. He died at the World's Fair."
"Tell me everything you know about your father's work." Azalea's thumb worked circles at Lizzy's temple, relieving some of the tension.
"I don't know anything," Lizzy said, her eyelids heavy.
"What about the men we have in holding?" Azalea asked. "The men who served on the board of the oil company. What do you think about them?"
A hint of agonized screaming surfaced in the back of Lizzy's mind, and her eyes popped open. "They're bad men," she said, frowning. *They are, aren't they?*
"Good. Yes, they are bad men." Azalea moved on to Lizzy's other temple. "And your father? Is he a bad man?"
Lizzy wanted to say that he was, but she hesitated, her frown deepening. "He… he's dead."
"Is he a bad man?" Azalea asked.
"He's… my father. Please, I just want to go to sleep." Lizzy met Azalea's eyes with her own. "Please?"
"Almost time," Azalea said. "Tell me, if I gave you the chance to rid Mother Earth of bad men, would you do it?"
Lizzy's heart started beating faster. "No," she said. "That's not my place."
Azalea pulled back her hand. "It seems you still need time, Elizabeth." Her voice wasn't as soft, and Lizzy blinked rapidly to clear her mind and focus. The young woman was frowning down at her. "Don't worry. I understand. I'm not angry."
She leaned over Lizzy and pulled a strap over Lizzy's chest, and before Lizzy could process what was happening, Azalea had secured the strap and was moving on to another. Lizzy was barely able to voice her objection. She was starving, she was weak, and she was exhausted. Orion came back with a little speaker and a small round table. He set it up at the head of her cot.
"Thank you for all your help, Orion," Azalea said as she pushed the play button on the portable Bluetooth speaker. Lizzy recoiled at the action, expecting the screams to return, but all that came out was the sound of a babbling creek. "Get some rest, Elizabeth."
As Azalea left the room, the sounds of nature were accompanied by Autumn's voice. "You belong with the Heirs, Elizabeth," the Mother of the Heirs said, her voice calm and soft, inviting Lizzy to rest. "You are special to us. No one will ever take care of you like the Heirs of the Mother. The Earth needs you, Elizabeth. The world needs to be cleansed of all those who would harm her."
Lizzy fell asleep to the sound of Autumn's voice, surrounded by the beautiful songs of nature, of birds and creeks and rustling leaves; it rid her mind of the remnants of screaming. Part of her whispered that something wasn't right, but exhaustion won, and Lizzy welcomed the Mother's comfort.

Chapter 17

Timothy Peters

Timothy moved behind the stone between doors, watching CONmen shoot toward O'Donnell through the window. His jaw clenched, the rage still twisting him in knots. Icepick and Digger, the men who'd killed his mother, the men who'd kidnapped George and Annika, were mere yards from him.

"Get back," Linda hissed from beyond the etched bronze doors, peeking around to wave him over. "You're going to get shot."

"As soon as those CONmen move, I'm going out," he said. "And then I'm going to chase them down."

"You're crazy," Linda said. "You're going to get yourself killed!"

The CONmen were shooting and moving away from O'Donnell's position, almost out of sight. The shooting stopped as they ducked behind a row of cars and disappeared around the corner. Timothy ignored Linda's warnings and burst out of the library, rushing to the right, where O'Donnell had been.

Timothy didn't have time to feel relieved when O'Donnell stood up from behind the truck, unharmed. "Give me my vest and my gun!" Timothy shouted.

O'Donnell frowned but reached down to the ground, picked up Timothy's things, and handed them over. "Son, they're long gone. No need to be afraid. I don't think they're coming back."

Timothy strapped the vest on and holstered the gun at his side where the vest was designed to keep it. "I'm not afraid. I'm going after them."

"Oh, no you're not," O'Donnell said. "They don't know about Webb and Murphy who are hiding out right where they're running. Our guys will follow. Don't worry. We won't lose them."

Timothy was seething. "The men who murdered my mother and kidnapped the kids are in that group. I *have* to follow them. I—"

"Tim, stop. You're not thinkin' straight." O'Donnell put a hand on Timothy's shoulder. "You can't go after them."

"We can follow them, you and me." Timothy licked his lips, his heart still bursting inside his chest, pumping adrenaline through his veins so that he nearly exploded with the need to act.

O'Donnell frowned. "Tim, I—"

Gunfire broke out in the distance. Timothy whirled around, but he couldn't see where it was coming from. "They saw our guys hiding or following." He turned back to O'Donnell. "We can at least follow at a distance. Come on, O'Donnell. What if Webb or Murphy are hit?"

O'Donnell looked down at his feet as if he were studying the pavement, his expression full of conflict. Then he looked up. "A'right," he said. "Let's go."

Timothy broke into a run toward the opposite corner of the huge, block-long library. O'Donnell's footsteps pounded the decorative sidewalk beside him, but Timothy kept his eyes on his destination. He pulled up short at the corner, chest heaving, the healing burns on his back stinging despite the ointment applied that morning. Still, he was full to the brim with energy, his rage fueled by his mother's blood. He'd pushed aside the anger, managed to keep it locked away, but seeing those men had broken the dam.

O'Donnell risked a glance around the corner. "I can see the CONmen," he said as more gunshots rang out. "Follow closely." Crouching, he ran to the cover of the wreckage on the street.

There weren't as many vehicles on this one-way avenue. Timothy pointed to what was left of a bus stop. The frame of it was still there, the glass mostly broken out, but there was a solid advertisement panel that would provide some cover. O'Donnell nodded, and the two men rushed to the vertical sign. Neither the CONmen or the officers seemed to notice their advancement as Timothy and the captain darted from the sign to crouch behind a city bus that had tipped and lay on its side, blocking the street. Timothy and O'Donnell leaned against the top of the bus.

"The line of fire is on the other side of this bus," O'Donnell said. He crept along the bus toward the church on one side of the street, and Timothy followed as another round of gunfire filled the air with blood-curdling explosions.

"Webb? Webb! Talk to me!" Murphy's voice rang out as the gunfire ceased.

Timothy looked over O'Donnell's shoulder, craning to see beyond the bus. He spotted the top of Murphy's ponytail for half a second as she moved behind a two-foot stone wall, shouting for Webb to respond.

"Not another man," O'Donnell said between clenched teeth. He moved forward, stepping in front of the windshield of the overturned bus. His eyes were on the wall where Murphy and Webb were trapped.

"Not so hot, now, are ya?" A voice from the other side of the street made Timothy's blood boil. "There's four of us, babe. Two of you." He laughed. "Well, maybe only one." His voice sounded like it was getting closer.

Murphy shouted a curse at him, but she didn't show herself. O'Donnell set his jaw and met Timothy's eyes. "You got my back?" he asked in a whisper. Timothy nodded and unholstered his gun. The thug's shoes scraped the pavement close by, his pace slow but steady as he headed toward Murphy's position.

O'Donnell shouted. "Let's make this a little more fair, shall we?" He strode out from behind the bus, his gun drawn, and Timothy stepped into the open behind him ready to shoot just in time to see the captain blow a hole through the thug's head at nearly point-blank range. Blood and brain matter erupted from the man's head, and he dropped, leaving a pink mist hanging in the air.

On the other side, the thugs had come out from the hole they'd used as cover: the entrance to the underground Copley rail station. All three of them flinched, shock evident in their expressions, as Timothy and O'Donnell opened fire. Murphy joined them, and they managed to kill one more thug. The other two practically threw themselves down the stairs that descended underground. Timothy advanced beside the officers to the threshold, all three with guns trained on the shadows.

When they got to the top of the stairs, part of a sentence echoed up at them. "... out of here, Icepick... not worth it!" Evidence of a flashlight's beam danced in the darkness below for a second before the sound of rapid footsteps hitting concrete indicated the thugs were fleeing through the underground system.

"Look!" Timothy pointed to drops of blood leading down the stairs. Neither of the dead men were the ones he was after. "One of them is hit. They're leaving a trail. We've got to go after them."

"We've got to get Webb back to headquarters," Murphy said, shaking her head. "He's injured. I think he'll live, but... we've got to figure out a way to get him back. Maybe the survivors in the library will help us?" She kicked the backpack still stuck on the man fallen by the entrance. "They'll be happy to have half the supplies back, at least."

O'Donnell turned his back on the entrance to the station. "Worth a shot." He and Murphy jogged toward the low wall, leaving Timothy by the stairs.

"No!" Timothy shouted. He caught up with O'Donnell, ripping free the flashlight strapped to his vest before the captain could object. "I'm going after them."

"Tim, don't!" O'Donnell yelled at him as he darted after the thugs, but Timothy didn't listen.

Neither officer followed him, and Timothy was fine with that. He understood. They had a friend to save. But he wasn't about to let his mother's murderer get away *and* lose out on their original plan to follow CONmen to find out where they were holing up.

The blood trail led down the tracks toward the Hynes Convention Center. The track itself was nearly flush with the platform, so the trail was easy to follow. When he saw their light ahead, he turned off his flashlight, gripping it tightly in one hand as he stumbled after them. He didn't want them to see him coming. They weren't going fast, their shadows in the ball of light indicating one was leaning on the other. Their mumbled voices and noisy footsteps reverberated off the walls of the tunnel. Timothy stepped as lightly as he could, carefully trying not to trip as he walked several yards behind.

He raised his weapon, his first instinct to take them by surprise, shoot them both from the shadows before they had time to react. He'd made the mistake of not pulling a weapon on Frank when they'd first met; he didn't want to make the same mistake again. But a quiet, sensible voice inside his head reminded him of George and Annika. *I'll follow them to wherever CON is hiding, and then I'll kill them.*

The next station was perhaps a half mile from Copley Square. When Digger and Icepick reached the next platform, Timothy crept forward slower as they stepped off the tracks and onto the platform, taking their light with them. He listened as he reached the tunnel's end.

One of them cursed. "Idiot! Don't touch the arm! I swear, Digger, use your head."

"I'm just tryin' to help you up the stairs."

That must be Digger.

"I'll use the railing."

And Icepick. He walked forward, a hand on the wall, until the wall gave way to nothing. He searched the dark, but he couldn't see their light. Their voices were getting farther away. He hadn't used the trains often, perhaps only a handful of times in his life. He tried to remember what the station looked like. He put his hand over the end of the flashlight and turned it on, the light shining through his hand, emitting a faint glow. There were stairs around the corner, leading up to Boylston Street according to the sign. He clicked off the light again and traversed the stairs in the dark, following distant voices.

"Hey, man, this exit is never open," Digger said. "Only used it that one time I tried dating that runner and the place was packed for Marathon Monday."

"Ha!" Icepick barked a laugh. "That was somethin'. I still can't believe she gave you the time of day. It's no problem, though. We'll just bust the windows."

"With what?" Digger asked.

A gunshot rang out, and Timothy ducked. He was halfway up the stairs where the remnants of natural light could be seen above. Glass breaking was followed by a few loud *thumps*, and then the daylight got brighter.

"See? What did I tell ya?" Icepick said, the sound of the door slamming following his gloating.

Timothy continued all the way up the stairs, through the small lobby and to the doors, carefully staying in the shadows. By the time he got to the doors, Icepick and Digger were at the end of the brick sidewalk that led to a set of stairs that Timothy assumed led to Boylston Street. When they exited onto the street, he quietly followed. Above, through a gate that lined the street, Timothy spotted the two thugs. His heartbeat skyrocketed. If he could see them, they could certainly see him. It would just take a look over their shoulder, down at the path leading from the station.

An old brick archway in the wall beside the stairs to the street provided a spot for him to hide. He slipped to the other side of the wall, watching until they were far enough down the road. He stepped out behind the wall and ran up the steps, ducking behind cars the second he was on Boylston Street.

He followed, ducking and weaving, trying to ignore and avoid the dead, turning left on Fenway, skirting the Back Bay Fens. He caught up to them, close enough to hear their conversation again just after he passed the Museum of Fine Arts. Timothy was running out of steam. His back stung, his muscles ached, and he was thirsty. When Icepick stopped to lean against the hood of a car ahead, Timothy didn't mind the respite. He sat against a tire of a truck and dug out a few over the counter pain killers from a small pocket in his vest. He'd hoped he wouldn't need them, but if he couldn't fix his exhaustion, he could do something about the pain.

"Help me out, man." Icepick's voice drew Timothy's attention. He carefully peeked to see the thug taking off his shirt and handing it to Digger. Icepick's face was pale, and his arm was bloody. "I need you to rip this into strips. Wrap the wound. We can fix it up better when we get back."

"You gonna make it all the way back?" Digger did as requested, creating strips of dingy cloth, once white, and helping his friend tie the strips around the wound.

Timothy perked up. *Back where?* He licked his lips, and his heart lodged in his throat. If they revealed the information he wanted to know, he could kill them and be done with it. The police headquarters weren't far. He'd make it back before curfew.

"It's just a few miles," Icepick said. "I mean, as long as we don't run into The Boys again."

"Or Stripes." Digger shuddered. "It's not fair. Ace should let us put the thing down."

Icepick shrugged. "Everybody's got a weak spot. Ace loves animals, you know?"

"Loving 'em is one thing," Digger said, "but lettin' 'em loose where we might run into them?"

Icepick sighed. "At least he kept the lions."

Digger laughed. "Yeah. It's like those gladiator stories up in the zoo these days. Maybe one day they'll make a movie out of it."

"Stop actin' like you're educated," Icepick scoffed. "What do you know about the Colosseum?"

Digger looked affronted. "Lots, actually."

Timothy frowned. *He kept the lions? Let the other animals loose? The parrot... the camels...* His eyes widened. *Franklin Park Zoo?* His jaw dropped as he put the pieces together. *CON has the kids at Franklin Farm!* Or at least, that would make the most sense. They'd called the place they were taking the children The Farm. He grinned. *Now those bastards can die.*

But then a sound he hoped he'd never hear again sounded in the distance — a consistent, high-pitched buzzing. Birds he hadn't noticed before took to the air as far as the eye could see. A buzzard that must have been feasting on a corpse a few yards away, previously hidden by vehicles, squawked and flapped his wings, frightening Timothy and making him bump his head on the car he leaned against.

"What was that?" Icepick's voice sounded from behind, but Timothy barely noticed. And the thugs didn't seem to dwell on it very long, either.

"Icepick... we gotta run!" Digger shouted.

Timothy shot up to standing, no longer caring if anyone saw him. A black swarm was rolling over the top of the rubble, coming straight for him.

Chapter 18

George Peters

George's plan to earn the trust of the CONmen so that they'd give him a weapon lent him some energy, but he wasn't sure that was enough. His stomach growled and ached; he eyed Ruger's backpack ahead. They'd all been given water bottles out of that bag, and George had seen food, too. His own backpack was still empty, though they'd trekked several miles north through the streets of Boston. *Maybe by lunch time, he'll let me eat.*

It was hard to focus on anything besides his hunger and the act of putting one foot in front of the other. He'd never been so weak and tired in all his life. There were moments he questioned the reality of his situation. The scene around him was more like that of a video game than Boston: the streets cluttered with cars, some crumpled and piled up, others just abandoned; a block of blackened rubble where several homes had burned to the ground; dead bodies mingling with debris like Waldo in one of his pictures — all George had to do was look hard enough at any point in their trek to find one.

Ruger led the group along streets where each building had been marked with an X, either green, yellow, or red. The yellow ones seemed to be occupied: smoke snaking from a chimney, clothes drying on the porch railing, the lonely sound of a violin, muffled as it breached the walls. In a few of these yellow-marked homes, George spotted gaunt faces peeking out from behind curtains.

George wasn't sure exactly where he was. The area was residential, with most of the structures being houses. But he'd only rarely ventured beyond the city's main attractions. His home, his school… they'd been separate from the bustle of the big city. He'd been assigned a project once where he'd had to create a map of Boston's major neighborhoods, but he didn't remember much of it. That life was so distant. *Grades, girls, sports… why can I remember what Jenna Yardis likes for lunch, but I can't remember the stupid map?*

George glanced back just briefly. He wanted to keep both of his captors on his radar. Cash — the younger CONman who'd joined Ruger at the zoo — brought up the rear. He kept to himself and barely said a word, but George felt the man's eyes on his back as they walked. Both CONmen carried handguns and rifles slung over their shoulders. Neither could be trusted, despite Ruger's occasional display of decency.

George trudged forward in the middle of the group. Ahead of him, Lissa and Charity carried backpacks like his while behind, Poppy and Clyde pulled suitcases. The whirr and clicks of the wheels mixed with the scuff of shoes on pavement. An occasional bird sang, too, but it was mostly quiet. Until Clyde decided to run.

A loud *clack* sounded, and George looked over his shoulder to find Clyde's suitcase on the ground, the older boy bolting, weaving through the cars on the street, heading for a gap between houses. The four kids huddled closer; the others seemed to be watching Clyde. George kept his eyes on the CONmen. Neither panicked. Neither seemed angry. Cash sighed and readied his rifle, glancing at Ruger, who nodded. Then a gunshot rang out, two of the girls screamed, and Clyde dropped. George took half a step back, staring at the empty air where Clyde had been. A dull roar filled his ears, the sounds of Poppy and Charity crying muffled in the background. Lissa didn't make a sound, but her features twisted in anger.

They didn't try to stop him. They just killed him. He swallowed hard, though that didn't clear the lump in his throat. When we escape, we'll have to be smart about it.

"Go check," Ruger said, and Cash let his rifle hang once more on his back before pulling his handgun and stalking toward where Clyde had fallen. Ruger turned to George and the others, his lips drawn to a thin line, his eyes intense. "Don't make us do that to you," Ruger said. "Run, and you're dead. Simple as that."

"Nobody made you kill Clyde." Lissa's voice shook with rage.

Ruger sighed and pinched the bridge of his nose. Then, he closed the distance between himself and Lissa, bending over to meet her eyes. He was only inches from her, but she didn't back down, though her hand trembled at her side. George tensed, his first instinct to defend Lissa. He held back, though. *It's me and Annika. If I get killed, nobody's left to make sure she's safe.*

"We have rules." Ruger's no-nonsense tone, firm with an edge of something like fatherly concern, sent a shiver down George's spine. "Rules keep us all alive. You're *lucky* to have been brought into CON. We're survivors. Always have been. You're being given the chance to live, to be looked after, to become part of something bigger than you. But you're also needed. Ace can't do what needs to be done without grunts, supplies, and soldiers." He pointed back to Clyde. "That ungrateful idiot killed himself. If I let him get away, I'd be telling all of you it's okay to run off. And Clyde would have died out there on his own, anyway, just like you would if you tried to run." He jabbed her shoulder with his finger, but then he backed off. Lissa trembled but held her head high. "You can handle Clyde's load, Lissa. Maybe carrying twice as much will help you see how selfish it was for that kid to run."

Lissa stomped over to the suitcase, grabbed the handle from the ground, and glared at Ruger. "I'll do what you want," she said. "But you *didn't* have to kill Clyde."

A half smile turned up the corner of Ruger's lips. "Maybe when you're leading a team, you'll understand, Firecracker."

Lissa's eyes narrowed, but she didn't say anything else. Cash returned to the group, exchanged a look with Ruger, and they continued another half mile until they reached a house not marked. George craned his neck to look down the street. None of the houses from that point on were marked.

"First provisions we find can be lunch. Lissa and George come with me," Ruger said. "Poppy and Charity, go with Cash." The two girls squirmed, throwing wide-eyed glances at the CONman. "Keep in mind, Cash, these girls aren't Butterflies. Got it?"

"Got it, boss." Cash nodded toward the first house. "Come on girls. Let's learn the rules of entering an unmarked house."

Ruger waved for Lissa and George to follow him. "We got three types of marks. Red means it's been checked and it's no good. Dead bodies inside, too many to clear safely, or the windows are broken, so it's not safe from the elements. Green is good to go, but it's been picked over. So, those make good shelter should the need arise. Yellow means survivors are livin' there. There ain't a ton of those. Most survivors are gathered in groups in bigger buildings, but there are some that refuse to leave their homes. Ace leaves them be. Some of 'em are family members of CONmen. Others are informants. A few are disabled. If they got a yellow mark, though, they've got protection." He pointed to the white house ahead, a porch above the balcony. "We go house to house until our bags are full, then we head back."

"Aren't these houses locked?" Lissa asked.

Ruger pulled out a black zipper pouch. "Good question. Yeah, they're locked. We don't break the windows. We pick locks. A broken window leaves one less safe place at night."

Lissa crossed her arms. "You got bump keys in there or actual picks?"

Ruger raised his eyebrows. "You know how to use either one, Firecracker?"

"Yeah, I do. My aunt says to be prepared for anything. She bought me a kit when I was little, and it was all over from there."

"Your aunt sounds like a badass," Ruger said, handing over the black pouch. "Show me what you got."

Lissa took the pouch, leaving the suitcase upright beside her. "She's a cop." She unzipped the pouch and chose her tools.

George frowned. "She's a cop, but she bought you a lock picking kit? Isn't that... weird? Like, aren't those for criminals?"

Lissa started working on the lock. "Knowing how to pick a lock properly can save property damage if you lock yourself out or you got to get into someone's house for a legit reason. Like, one time, I had to pick my grandma's lock to get inside when she didn't answer her door. She'd fallen and broken her hip."

"I'd keep the part about her being a cop to yourself," Ruger said. "Ace don't like The Boys, and it'll call your loyalties into question."

The lock clicked and the door opened. "Loyalty out of fear isn't real loyalty," Lissa said. "It's just fear."

"I'd keep that to yourself, too." Ruger put his hand on the door and pushed it all the way open. "I can't keep you from the Butterfly House if you make too much trouble."

Lissa frowned and her cheeks burned red. "Fine. I get it."

I don't. Why does he care? George followed Ruger inside as the man cautiously drew his handgun.

"I don't smell anything especially pungent," Ruger said. "That's a good sign. Floor is dusty, no sign of footprints other than ours." He called out. "If anybody is here, we won't hurt you if you show yourself." There was no answer.

"Is that true?" George asked, his stomach growling. Following the conversation almost took too much effort. He was losing the ability to filter himself.

"That I wouldn't hurt someone?" Ruger asked. "Yeah, I mean, we got a society to rebuild. Everybody can be part of the new Boston if they follow the rules. Everybody can play a part."

Lissa scoffed but didn't say anything, and Ruger seemed to ignore it. "We need to check every room," Ruger said. "Search the house. Pick up anything useful. Start upstairs and work our way to the kitchen."

He led them through the first house, picking up the scraps that were left. Whoever had lived there hadn't left much of use behind besides some canned goods and a few items in the medicine cabinet. They put the canned goods out on the table: three cans of mixed fruit, half gone peanut butter, and five cans of vegetables.

"Pick a can," Ruger said. "Both of you. It's been about twenty-four hours, Hero. Let's eat, and then we'll get on to the next house."

George grabbed the can closest to him and ripped off the top, guzzling the slightly sweet water and then dumping the canned corn into his mouth. He filled his cheeks, chewing with his eyes closed, swallowing with satisfaction. He opened his eyes to find Ruger shaking his head as he popped off the top to a can of fruit and Lissa frowning at him as she held a can of peas in her hand.

"I'm really hungry," he said before tipping more corn into his mouth.

After they'd finished their food, they packed the rest away in Lissa's suitcase, which held cans of spray paint in the outer pockets, and in George's backpack. They moved on, house after house, the afternoon slipping away. Only two houses were marked red: one had five dead bodies gathered in the living room and the other had several broken windows. The others they marked green.

When their bags were almost full after finding a score of alcohol which Ruger carefully wrapped in bath towels and packed away, he cracked his knuckles and patted both George and Lissa on the back. "Last house of the day. I think we're done."

Just then, a scream echoed from across the street. Ruger's handgun was at the ready within seconds as he motioned for George and Lissa to follow. George's backpack was heavy; it was a struggle to even jog across the street. Ruger took the steps to the front door two at a time, and Lissa followed. George was last, but before he took the first step up to the door, another scream made him pause.

"It's comin' from outside!" He shouted. "Around the back. It sounds like Charity." He dodged to the side as Lissa set her jaw and bounded down the steps, slipping between the houses, mumbling darkly about Cash.

"If he's hurt her..."

George didn't hear the rest. Ruger nearly knocked him over in his pursuit of her, but he maintained his feet and then followed, huffing as he hoisted his heavy backpack and tried to run.

"Hey! Firecracker! Let me go first," Ruger shouted, but Lissa was already bursting into the backyard.

George tried to prepare himself as he stepped into the open for something grotesque or crass, but there was no way he could have expected what greeted him. He came to an abrupt stop beside Lissa and Ruger. To the side of the yard, Charity and Poppy stood behind Cash who had his gun pointed at... a snarling *tiger*?

"Don't shoot it!" Ruger yelled.

"Are you crazy?" Cash shouted back, not taking his eyes off the huge feline. "It's lookin' at me like I'm a steak dinner."

"Ace wants it free. He gave us orders not to shoot any of the animals he let out." Ruger picked up a decorative brick lining the flower garden behind the house and threw it at the tiger. It hit the beast's rump, which made the thing scramble and back up, teeth barred. Cash closed the shed door, then, and the tiger focused completely on Ruger, George, and Lissa.

"What do we do?" George blinked, his body frozen as the tiger took a step toward them.

"Don't run." Ruger had his handgun pointed at the thing. "If we run, it will chase us, and one of us won't make it. If I shoot at the ground—"

"You could just make it angry," Lissa hissed.

But then the tiger changed posture. It straightened from its prowling advancement, ears twitching. It gave Ruger one last snarl before bounding away. George ran his fingers through his hair and then leaned against the back of the house.

"It's fine, Cash!" Ruger shouted. "Stripes is gone."

Cash opened the door gingerly and looked around before throwing the door open all the way. "That stupid tiger is going to eat somebody. He's probably already eaten somebody. It's ridiculous that we can't just shoot the thing. What the h—"

Ruger held up a hand, cutting off Cash in the middle of a rant George hadn't known the quiet man was capable of. "Why *didn't* he attack?"

"He was scared off," Lissa said, "but not by us." Her sweaty, red cheeks turned a shade paler.

George pushed off the wall. "Do you guys hear that? What is that?"

A buzzing drifted over the air, high-pitched. Lissa, Cash, and Ruger all had the same look of terror. But George had never heard anything like that, and both Charity and Poppy looked as confused as he felt.

"That's a swarm," Lissa said, her voice cracking.

"Ruger…" Cash swallowed hard, his Adam's apple bobbing as his eyes grew wide.

Acid burned George's throat as his food threatened to come back up. "A swarm?" he asked. "Like… the mosquitos?" He'd heard a few of the kids telling stories at The Farm, but… *That can't be real, right?* But the way the CONmen and Lissa were looking at each other, George wasn't so sure.

Ruger put his hand on Lissa's back and pushed her back toward the street. He reached out and tugged on George's shirt. "Hurry! Go back down the street. We've got to find a house with a green mark." He gave George a shove that sent him stumbling. "Run, you idiot! Run!"

Chapter 19

Timothy Peters

Timothy ran. Digger and Icepick turned left at the corner ahead; their backs had already been turned, their feet pounding the pavement when he'd stood up, revealing himself the last thing on his mind. If they'd noticed him, they hadn't paid him any attention. The swarm advanced like a monster, tendrils made up of hundreds of mosquitos reaching, searching for blood. He followed Fenway, turning right instead of left. He didn't want to get caught between two monsters.

The buzzing filled his ears, reverberated throughout his body, became the only sound he was capable of hearing. He was already so exhausted, but he pushed his body harder. His feet came down hard on the pavement, heavy like weights. Sweat stung his eyes, blurred his vision; it seeped into his burns and cuts, plastered his clothing to his body, and coated his skin so that even the slightest breeze sent a shiver down his spine. One step after another, weaving around vehicles, watching the ground ahead, jumping over debris and the occasional body, Timothy finally slammed into the door of a building that didn't have broken windows immediately noticeable. He yanked on the doorknob, but it wouldn't budge. He looked back.

The swarm was too close. It bulged toward him. Panic fueled him further, and he burst into a sprint down the sidewalk of Fenway until he came to an ornate stone entrance beneath a portico. It's wooden double doors with glass panels were blessedly intact. He stumbled up the steps. *Please, let this one open. Let this one open.* He grasped the handle, his slick hand nearly slipping, and yanked on the door. It gave way, and he threw himself inside, shutting the door tightly behind him. He threw the locks, imagining the thugs trying to barge into his sanctuary.

His heartbeat thrashed in his ears, his blood pulsating through his body as if it might violently burst from his veins. His lungs burned as he desperately tried to satisfy them, the hot, thick air falling short amidst his shallow, quick breaths. Timothy leaned against the wall and focused on slowing his breathing. *Don't pass out. Calm down. You're safe.*

Timothy pushed off the wall, squinting at the white lettering facing the street on the glass of the door, having to read it backwards. "Simmons Main College Building." He wiped the sweat off his brow, but it was no less hot inside. Sweat dripped from his fingertips as his hand fell back to his side. Outside, specks of black with spots of orange invaded the air. A soft *thud* sounded as a mosquito slammed into the glass. Timothy stepped back as another followed, and then another.

What if they can get in through the cracks in the door? He licked his lips, tasting the salt, as he turned around in the small entryway. A white rack stood full of pamphlets, so he grabbed fistfuls and started wedging them around the door. There were no cracks large enough for him to notice sunlight creeping in, but the action of stuffing the pamphlets under the doors made him feel a fraction of safety.

Once pamphlets jutted from all around the doorframe, he turned around to see exactly where he'd landed. He stood inside a small, enclosed, square entryway, blocked in by another set of doors, glass framed in white, and two arched windows on either side, both looking into sitting areas belonging to the larger lobby. Sunlight only reached so far through the windows. But the warm rays, dust dancing in their light, touched disaster.

His stomach dropped as his eyes adjusted to the bigger room outside of the entryway. A numbness swept over him, a dull roar filling his ears. Bodies of the young, once bright-eyed college students ready to explore independence, carpeted the floor, occupying every chair. They were rotting, eyes bulging or hanging from their skulls, skin sloughing off the bones. But the goosebumps covering him head to toe and the ice running through his veins were due to the *way* their bodies sat, the way they lay on the floor. These people hadn't died in panic, crawling over each other to escape or running away. Timothy fell to his knees, tears joining his sweat.

A row of five lay just outside the glass doors, the soles of their shoes nearly flush with the glass. In between each body, clasped hands rested as if they had decided to die just like this, together, holding hands. Other corpses snuggled and still others lay with folded hands tucked under their cheeks. One sat in a bright green chair, head bowed with one eye hanging from the optic nerve, a small silver cross dangling from their bony fingers, sparkling in the light. The grotesque scene mingled with evidence of humanity, of love and faith. It spoke to what had been lost.

Timothy groaned as tears ran down his cheeks and the image of his mother's dead body surfaced yet again. He lowered himself onto his side; his aches and pains were magnified by his stillness and coalesced with his inner turmoil; the intensity peaked and then ebbed, leaving in its wake pure exhaustion, weight, and numbness.

Every blink of the eye brought with it a shifting in the daylight, and time passed as he drifted in and out of consciousness. Night came and went, as did the soft *thud* of mosquitos against glass and the distant buzzing of passing swarms. One last blink brought him into the next day. Still, he lay unmoving. Lifting a limb, sitting up… these were things he *used* to do.

I could choose to be done, choose to die in this graveyard. There was a split second when he believed that would be better.

That split second jump-started his heart. Images of Heather overlaid images of his mother. *She still needs me.* He put one hand flat on the cool tile floor. *George and Annika still need me.* Timothy pushed hard, lifting the weight of his body to sit up. His eyes flitted from one corpse to the next, stopping on the sparkling silver cross. *It's not time to give up. Not yet.*

"They had no choice." He took in bulging eyes, popped welts, and bloody shirts. "I'm *not* sick. And I'm not done." Timothy crawled to his feet, dug out a few more pain killers from his vest pocket, and swallowed them in one dry, uncomfortable gulp. "I have to go to the zoo, confirm my suspicions."

There was nothing he could do on his own. He wouldn't be getting George and Annika back that day, but he could bring solid information back to police headquarters.

He stepped closer to one of the windows into the lobby and searched the walls, squinting until he found what he was looking for: a clock. The second hand still ticked away as if nothing had changed. It was past ten in the morning. Timothy took a deep breath, took one more moment of silence in the midst of the dead, and then left the crypt for the daylight.

He set his jaw and started walking south, keeping to the sides of the streets where there was ample opportunity to duck into an alleyway or a building. And he kept his senses on high alert. Every sound earned a second of pause. The hours of safety he'd been relying on didn't seem so reliable anymore. Other people, CONmen or otherwise, could get in his way or complicate his mission. And if Ace had taken over the zoo and let wild animals into the city, he apparently needed to keep an eye out for fangs and claws.

He kept his pace slow and manageable, even as the pain killers kicked in. His stomach growled as he passed some townhomes, and he cautiously explored the homes for a safe place to find something to eat. He didn't make it past the first door due to the stench that bespoke corpses, but the second home seemed empty, at least downstairs. He purposefully didn't look at the portraits on the walls and he avoided the toys scattered on the floor. Fruit rotted in a ceramic bowl on the counter, bread molded on a cutting board, and a gallon of milk sat out next to a box of cereal.

"Maybe they made it out. Left in a hurry." It was eerie, walking into the middle of a set scene, a lovely morning in a cozy home coated in dust and rot.

He opened a few cabinets before finding a can of peaches with a tab opener on the top. He grabbed a few granola bars, too, and stuffed them in his pocket before getting back out on the road. The juice in the peaches helped quench his thirst, and he downed them all within just a few minutes. He held onto the can until he reached a trash receptacle, and then he couldn't help but chuckle as he noted the millions of pieces of debris and trash scattered all around him.

"Hey! What's that?" A voice rang out, and Timothy ducked low, afraid someone had heard his laughter.

He hunkered down behind the cars, peeking between gaps to try to spot who the voice might have belonged to. A rickety squeal of wheels sounded not too far away, but they were still out of his line of sight.

"Those are giraffes, dumbass." Another voice joined the first.

Timothy blinked and frowned, instinctually looking up and peering around the vehicles. Sure enough, three giraffes were feeding on trees in the near distance. *How did I miss that?* His mouth dropped open at the sight of safari animals in the middle of a destroyed Boston. Regardless, the voices weren't discussing him, and that was really all that mattered. He turned his attention back to them, searching to see who had been speaking. They sounded very young.

The front of a grocery cart emerged through the gaps in the vehicles on the other side of the road, followed by a boy of about twelve and another boy that seemed slightly older. Neither were George, but if they knew something… Timothy nearly revealed himself to ask some questions when a third figure, much taller, came into view. He had full sleeves of tattoos on both arms, a CON tattoo standing out to Timothy like a flashing warning sign.

"Keep moving." He grunted. "Getting caught out on supply runs happens, but when it does, we got to get back ASAP. Got it? You two got other chores to take care of. Ace runs a tight ship."

"Aw, c'mon. I'm sooooo tired." The younger boy slumped as he pushed his cart.

"You got sleep last night," the CONman said. "Don't make me stick you in the coop."

"He's not complaining." The older teen, who was pushing his own cart, moved ahead of the younger, and tried to push his own load while pulling the other. "Right, Jay?"

"Right," Jay said, pushing harder. They were moving out of sight. "I'm not. I swear. I'm sorry."

The CONman laughed, but it had a mocking edge. The voices fell silent after that laugh dissipated, and Timothy took his opportunity to follow them. He wasn't disappointed. They led him the rest of the way to the zoo entrance. Timothy stayed out of sight, choosing to hide behind a convenience store as the CONman led the two kids into the park surrounding the zoo. He didn't dare cross the street and follow them further. The area was too open, and he spotted at least two men with guns stationed along the road at the edges of the park. *I should gather more information, figure out what kind of security they've got.* He made his way down Seaver Street behind the buildings, counting the men with guns as he crept between buildings to peer across the street every chance he got. He took the long way around whenever he hit parking lots or open spaces, always staying in the shadows. When he reached the Blue Hill Avenue and Franklin Park Street intersection, he stopped, having counted seven men standing guard. Going any closer to the main entrance would be too risky; there wasn't enough cover in the park surrounding the zoo.

He was just about to begin his trek back to the intersection when another group of children pushing carts and hauling backpacks, accompanied by two CONmen, caught his attention further south. Timothy's breath caught as they came closer, as the gait of one of the boys drew him in. The closer the group got, the surer Timothy was. Guarded by thugs with assault weapons, surrounded by other vulnerable children, unreachable though only yards away, George turned the corner toward the zoo.

Chapter 20

George Peters

George couldn't get the image of the swarm out of his head as he followed Ruger back into the zoo the following morning. He'd watched it roam the street through the window of a stranger's bedroom and seep into the open window of a yellow-marked house across the way. Blood-curdling screams had followed, and George had thought surely whoever had been inside was dead. But an hour after the swarm had moved on, in the waning daylight, a middle-aged man had stumbled out onto the porch, crumpling to his knees as he vomited blood down the steps. His hands had slipped in the crimson liquid, and he'd fallen, stretched out across his steps, face down. The man had crawled to the sidewalk and then rolled over onto his back, screaming and holding his hands to his eyes. He'd screamed for a long time, his voice going hoarse before it died in the midst of bloody gurgling. The man had arched his back, clawing at the sidewalk, blood spurting and bubbling from his lips, eyes bulging, before finally going limp. And George had watched every second; he hadn't been able to tear his eyes away, even long after the man was dead.

Sleep had been tumultuous, nightmarish images of the dying man melding with the memory of his mother, of his father, of Timothy and Heather, of Annika, even of himself. When he woke, he woke to exhaustion. Lissa, who'd slept on a trundle next to him, didn't look much better. Charity had crawled into bed with her at some point, the company perhaps setting her at ease. Poppy was curled up on an extra-large bean bag chair, eyes wide open. George wasn't sure she'd slept at all.

When Ruger and Cash had fed them, and it seemed safe enough outside, they went as a group to recover the suitcases. Lissa and Poppy had left them behind when it came time to run. Neither CONman seemed to blame them. They trekked back to the zoo at a quick pace, Ruger and Cash both walking with guns in hand, keeping an eye out for Stripes.

George breathed a sigh of relief when they walked under the cast iron gates of the Franklin Park Zoo and headed for The Farm. *Never thought I'd be happy to be back here.* The desire to check in on Annika gave him a burst of energy, but before they reached The Farm, Ruger pulled him and Lissa aside as Cash led Poppy and Charity ahead.

"You two are comin' with me." He turned his back as if expecting them to follow without asking questions.

George exchanged a look with Lissa.

She shrugged. "Worse places to be." She followed.

"I want to see Annika," George said, not moving. "I need to make sure she's all right."

Ruger stopped, put his hands on his hips, back still turned, and looked up at the sky as he took a deep breath. Then he turned around. "Look, Hero, they don't work the little kids as hard. She's fine. She'll see you later today. Chances are, she's already being put to work." He raised his eyebrows. "You can be stubborn about this, earn another day of no food for both you and your little friend, or you can just come with me."

George balled his fists at his sides. He had to clamp his mouth shut to keep from talking back, but he managed. Without saying a word, he nodded his assent.

"Good. I don't want to keep the others waiting." Ruger led the way through the zoo to the back entrance typically referred to as the Giraffe Entrance, just because it was near the exhibit that used to hold the creatures.

"Can you at least tell me where we are going?" George asked.

Lissa slowed as they approached the huge white-domed structure known as the Tropical Forest. "Isn't that where you send the Butterflies?" she asked.

Ruger waved a hand toward the structure which was heavily guarded. "Yeah, but don't worry about it, Firecracker. We ain't goin' in there."

"That's where Ace is?" George eyed the men with guns outside the entrance. He recognized Big Mack, but he didn't see Digger or Icepick.

"The Boss set up shop there, yeah." Ruger kept walking. "But we're goin' to the abandoned bear enclosures for some target practice. We're gonna see what you can do."

George's heartbeat picked up pace as he passed through the exit. *They're going to give me a weapon.* A cold sweat broke out on the back of his neck, and his stomach lurched. Being handed a gun was essential to his plans to escape. *But could I actually use it against Ruger?* Digger and Icepick, the thought of them enraged him, but the other men — as much as he disliked them — he couldn't drum up the same level of hatred.

Two pillars on either side of him held up sculptures of people in clothing that reminded him of Greek statues. The one on the left depicted four people, the most prominent being a man with an axe in the crook of his arm and the other a woman holding a vase propped on her thigh. They both seemed to be staring at George, judging him, shaking their heads at his foolish plans. "He's no more than a little boy," he imagined her saying. To the right, a boy held out his hands and turned his face away to look at a woman behind him as if he were disgusted at George's weakness.

Stop it. They're just sculptures. If he remembered right from his field trips, they had originally been at a post office or something. They had nothing to do with him, with his situation. He chuckled at himself, looking up one last time at the stone woman, but shuddered at how she looked down on him and hurried after Lissa and Ruger.

Just keep it together, and maybe you'll actually do something right for a change. George chewed on his lower lip as they walked beneath the tree branches on Playstead Road. When they got to the stadium, they turned right down a smaller paved pathway, and then left once more to where the Old Bear Dens were situated. Once, he'd seen a homemade apocalyptic short film that used the abandoned enclosures as its set; it had been produced by one of Timothy's college friends as part of a filmography project. *And here we are, during the actual end of the world…*

His mother had forbidden George from venturing into the woods to find the place last time they'd visited the zoo. She'd heard the secluded spot was a favorite of addicts. She'd been furious to learn that Timothy had gone with his friend to help film, even though it had been during the day. George missed her so much, he even missed her chastisements, the way her brow would furrow, and she would whisper-yell while they were out in public, ready with a quick smile and a high-pitched but polite, "Good afternoon," for passersby.

The abandoned enclosures spoke of a once-grand display. Rusted out gates, parts of them missing, high stone walls, old and dry pools filled with foliage, a beautifully carved depiction of two bears standing on hind legs, between them the date: 1912 — the bones were just enough to form a framework for the imagination to go wild.

But Ruger didn't lead them into any of the enclosures, instead walking around them into the wooded area where several balloons filled with something that made them sag hung from trees. Below, pumpkins were placed on stools. Two other CONmen were there, none of whom George recognized, along with the four other kids who had raised their hands the previous morning to indicate that they could shoot a gun. The other CONmen seemed to be waiting on Ruger to start the show; they all deferred to him immediately, nodding with respect and letting him take the lead upon his arrival.

Ruger instructed the six kids to line up, and George did as he was told, standing at the end of the line next to Lissa. Ruger then retrieved a handgun from one of the other CONmen. "We've got one compact gun here for you all to share. One at a time, you can come up, show us what you can do." He patted his still holstered gun. "Now, in case any of ya get any bad ideas, me and my friends here each have our own weapons, and we will be ready to put you down if you point the weapon anywhere but straight ahead at those targets." He pointed at the balloons and pumpkins. "The balloons are filled with sand, and we've set up a sort of pulley system to make them swing on their ropes. I wanna see if you can hit a still target, but later on, I'll test your skill with a moving one." He walked over to an empty stool and laid the compact handgun down, pressing on it with one finger. "There's no optic on this one, and we've got a nine-round mag loaded. Safety is on. Any questions?"

George glanced down the row of kids. They seemed older than him. He was the shortest, the scrawniest. But he was a good shot, and he *needed* to earn Ruger's trust. The sooner he could do that, the sooner he could get on guard duty, and the sooner he could get himself and Annika out of there. He raised his hand.

Ruger narrowed his eyes. "What is it, Hero?"

"Can I go first?" George asked.

"All right," Ruger said, waving George forward. He patted George on the back when he came near and smiled down at him. "I like the initiative. Give it all you got." George reached for the gun, but Ruger grabbed his wrist before he could grasp the grip. "You understand, if you try to use this against us, you're dead."

"I'm not stupid." George took the gun in hand. "You mind giving me a little bit of space?"

Ruger chuckled and stepped back. "Have at it, Hero. You got three shots to hit something."

George raised the gun, using the sight to take aim. His immediate instinct was to go for one of the larger pumpkins that sat closer to him, but he had something to prove. Some of the only real quality time he'd ever had with both parents present was at the range. He breathed in through his nose and out through his mouth, repeating to himself the things his dad taught him. *Keep your finger off the trigger until you're ready to shoot. Breathe. Right foot back. Bend the knees just slightly. Be ready for the recoil.* He set a bright red balloon in his sights and fired.

The deafening *bang* rang through the air, startling George. He was used to wearing earmuffs to dampen the sound. It took him a second to realize he'd missed. He swallowed hard and lowered the gun a few inches, staring at the red balloon which was still fully intact. His mouth ran dry. *What if I mess this up, too? What if I fail?*

"Hey, Hero," Ruger said quietly enough that the others wouldn't be able to hear. "You've got this."

George snapped his eyes toward Ruger, who gave him an encouraging smile. He blinked several times, not sure what to do with that. He didn't want to feel *encouraged* by a criminal who'd starved him and a six-year-old girl for twenty-four hours. But Ruger's expression was genuine. Ruger shifted his weight, bringing his thumb and his forefinger to his chin, watching intently as if he really wanted George to succeed. George had seen the same stance, the same intense but eager look from his father on the shooting range.

He nodded once and refocused on the red balloon. He took another steady breath, took aim, and pulled the trigger. Sand exploded from the red balloon. "Yes!" George shouted, more out of relief and instinct than anything else. It felt good to hit the mark, to celebrate something, even if it was a small victory. He put the safety back on and put the gun back on the stool, smiling as he turned to Ruger who had his hand up, and not even thinking, George followed through on a high-five with the CONman.

"That's it, Hero! Good job. You can keep training." Ruger was smiling wide, his blue eyes which had seemed so ice-cold before sparkling with approval.

George's smile faded, and his cheeks burned. The moment of connection with the man made him sick to his stomach. He pressed his lips together and looked away when Ruger gave him a friendly pat on the shoulder.

Then a voice that George recognized shouted from behind the line of kids. "I ain't never thought *that* kid would make the guard."

Icepick. George's embarrassment was replaced instantly with rage as he spun to see a stocky, bald man with thinning eyebrows elbow his way through the line of kids, though he could have easily walked around them. Icepick chuckled as the kids stumbled out of his way.

George took two steps back as Icepick came forward. The stool with the gun on it was between him and Ruger. *I could shoot Icepick before anyone could shoot me.* His fingers twitched toward the gun, but he held himself back. *That would leave Annika alone.* But he had to fight it the closer Icepick came.

"Icepick, what the hell are you doin' here?" Ruger's lips drew a thin line, his smile gone, and he crossed his arms.

He eyed Lissa and licked his lips. "Big Mack sent me. Said if the girl doesn't pass, she'll need an escort to the Butterfly House."

Despite Lissa's tough demeaner, she shrank back a little bit. "I guess you wasted your time, then," she said, her chin raised but her voice just shaky enough to cause Icepick to grin.

The gun on the stool called to George. *He deserves to die. He killed my mother. The way he's looking at Lissa…* The other CONmen were watching the altercation between Icepick and Ruger with anticipation, half of them smiling along with Icepick, the other half frowning with Ruger. *They're distracted.* The only thing keeping him from grabbing the gun and putting a hole or two in Icepick's torso was Annika.

Ruger scowled and within a few strides stood between Lissa and Icepick, standing toe-to-toe with his fellow CONman. "Kid's right. Waste of time. If she fails, which she won't, *I* will escort her where she needs to go."

Icepick raised an eyebrow. "Nah, brother. This is Big Mack's domain, handed to him by Ace. I'll be taking her." He craned his neck to look at Lissa again and winked. "I had a rough night. Could use some stress relief. And looks like she could use some breaking in."

Lissa's mouth dropped, and she backed up further. That was it. The rage tearing through George reached its peak. As he reached for the gun on the stool, Ruger frowned at him, and Icepick started to turn. But then Ruger did something that stopped George from grabbing hold of the gun. He threw a punch, hitting Icepick square in the jaw. The stockier man was caught off guard and hit the dirt.

The shock of what Ruger had done, the silence that followed, the way the other CONmen tensed and began to turn on each other as if ready to break into two camps — those for Ruger and those for Icepick — rattled George out of his rage, and he tucked his hand behind his back. Ruger stood over Icepick, who was apparently just as shocked as George.

"The girl is mine," Ruger said between clenched teeth. "She's part of my crew, and she's gonna ace this test. I've seen her out in the city. She was ready to face down a damn tiger while Cash was shaking in his boots. We need her in the guard."

Icepick put up his hands. "Fine," he said, smiling as his lip welled with blood. "I'll let you have her, then. But if she fails, you'll have to take the Butterfly assignment up with Ace. His orders, not mine."

"You let me handle that," Ruger said, "and get the hell off my range."

Icepick chuckled as he stood up, shaking his head. And then he threw his own punch, right to Ruger's jaw.

Ruger stumbled back, but he didn't fall. He worked his jaw back and forth, wincing. "We good, now?"

Icepick shrugged. "Yeah, man. We're good." And then he left, his footfalls heavy through the wooded area.

George's feet felt planted in the soil as he watched Icepick leave. I did the right thing, not shooting him. I can do that later, when Annika is safe.

Ruger rubbed the back of his neck. "Lissa, you can go last." He put a hand on her shoulder, stopping her when she passed. "You can do this, okay? Just get Icepick out of your head. If you can shoot like you can sass, you've got nothing to worry about."

She nodded, though she looked just as confused as George had felt when Ruger had given him encouragement. "Yeah," she said. "Um, thank you."

"Sure thing." Ruger turned back to George. "You, come with me." He pointed at Caleb, the boy at the other end of the line. "You, take your turn." He nodded at the other CONmen who had seemed to relax when Icepick retreated. "You've got this one, boys. I'll be right back."

George stepped tentatively toward Ruger until the CONman grabbed the back of his neck and forced him to walk faster, leading him into one of the bear cages out of sight of everyone else. "What are you doing?" George's voice shook. *He saw me reach for the gun. Is he going to kill me himself?*

Ruger threw him to the ground, and George caught himself on his hands, sharp rocks digging into his palms. His eyes watered as he sat up and turned to face the CONman.

"I guarantee you that didn't hurt half as bad as what I took for you on the chin," Ruger said, his voice a deep growl as he jutted a finger toward his already bruising jaw. "What the hell was that, Hero? Reaching for that gun would have gotten you shot."

George set his jaw and narrowed his eyes. "Icepick doesn't deserve to live. I could have done one good thing before I died."

"You would have left your friend to rot just so you could, what? Defend the honor of your crush?" Ruger threw his hands up in the air. "You stupid, idiotic, lovesick—"

"What?" George's face scrunched in confusion. *He thinks I have a crush on Lissa?* "No, he doesn't deserve to die because of that — well, maybe he does — but that's not why I hate him."

Ruger stopped ranting and looked down at George. "Then… what is it? Why would you do something so stupid?"

"Icepick killed my mom." George looked down at his hands, the welling blood nothing compared to the rivers Icepick drew from his mother's body. "He stabbed her to death. Like, over and over." Tears blurred his vision. "He and Digger were the ones who took us from our family."

Ruger let out a heavy sigh that puffed out his cheeks, and he squatted in front of George, letting his hands dangle from his knees. "Icepick is a bastard. I'll give you that. He *enjoys* killing. He killed her in front of you?"

George scoffed. "Yeah, like you ordered Cash to kill Clyde."

Ruger shook his head. "Don't pretend that's the same. Clyde was shot once, and he was dead. His suffering was minimal, and it was necessary. And no one enjoyed it." He ran his fingers over his short, white-blonde hair.

George hated that he agreed, but in the end, he wished his mother had simply been shot. What Icepick had done to her had been horrifying and drawn out and so, so bloody. "Fine. It's a little different."

"It's a lot different, and one day, you're going to understand that." Ruger stood up. "Clyde was brought into the fold, and his decision to run was a betrayal of every CONman, including you."

George shook his head but didn't respond. Arguing wouldn't change Ruger's mind, and George couldn't change that Clyde was dead.
"Look, Hero," Ruger said, "One day, you'll get a chance to get your revenge, okay? But you gotta be smart about it."
George's eyes snapped to Ruger's. "What? Are you… saying I *should* kill him?"
Ruger shrugged. "Yeah, I guess I am. He's a psycho. But, you gotta wait, be patient. Earn your right to be here. Show you've got value. One day, in a year or somethin', you'll get a chance. Just… make it look like an accident, you know?"
"I… can't believe you just said that, but… thanks?" George blinked a few times, unsure of what to do with the fact that he'd just gotten Ruger's blessing to murder his fellow CONman.
"Look, we need good soldiers. Ace needs good soldiers. Before all this, Icepick was an enforcer Ace used to scare the crap out of people. He'd send him with strict instructions, keep a leash on the destruction. But… things are different now. Nobody's gonna see your mom on the news. If Icepick is left unchecked, he's just gonna bring havoc to Ace's new Boston." Ruger reached out and took hold of George's forearm, helping him to his feet. "Just don't get caught, Hero. Okay? Keep your head down. Don't bring attention to yourself. And… make sure you're ready when you take the plunge. Killin' ain't as easy as it looks." Ruger shrugged. "Or maybe it shouldn't be."
"Yeah," George said, emotions warring inside. "Okay. I'll be careful."
He patted George on the back and began leading him out of the ruins. "You're going to make a great CONman, kid. I can see it."
No adult had ever treated George like he was capable, like he was useful. George fought against it, but he could feel something of a bond growing between him and Ruger. *What if my family are all dead? What if CONmen are the future of Boston, like they say? What if I can save Annika by being one of them?* George swallowed hard. Maybe things weren't as black and white as he thought they were.

Chapter 21

Zara Williams

Fending off the four men who had gone after their supplies had been the first of many problems in the short time Zara and Mr. Peters had been in Clearfield, Pennsylvania. They'd scattered quickly enough when they'd noticed that they were faced with *two* gun-wielding opponents against their baseball bats and tire irons, but Mr. Peters hadn't trusted that they wouldn't be back. It had taken them the rest of the afternoon to find a safer place to park their bus, eventually pulling behind an empty farm supply store.

That morning, they'd driven to the airfield and waited. The pilot was supposed to return, at least in time for him to take his Friday winner back across the mountains. So far, Zara and Mr. Peters had done very little but wait in silence. They sat in different rows, on different sides of the bus, each with legs outstretched on a bus seat, leaning back against the window. Zara played with the rings she wore on a chain, a butterfly and a ladybug, as her thoughts swirled around her head.

Time to think wasn't exactly what Zara needed. Or maybe she did, but it was definitely not what she *wanted.* She still couldn't quite wrap her head around all the changes that had happened over the past few days. And when she had long enough to think about it, everything since the World's Fair seemed an insane nightmare.

I need to do *something.* She tucked the rings under her shirt, sat up, and rifled through her backpack, counting out supplies: six water bottles, a box of protein bars, beef jerky, dried fruit, baby wipes and other toiletries, a flashlight, a sheathed knife, spare socks, a small first aid kit, a box of matches, and duct tape.

"This isn't going to last long," she said, taking into account the food and water. "Especially the water. I mean, two days at most in this heat."

Mr. Peters stayed seated, leaning his head back against the window. "That was the deal. Besides what we brought for barter, Thomas allowed only a few days' provisions."

"What happens if we don't get a flight for weeks?" Zara smoothed stray curls away from her face, wishing she could take a shower. She retrieved a baby wipe instead, cleaning off her face and the back of her neck. "We could scavenge some more, maybe, but with the number of people we saw downtown and the size of the town to begin with, Clearfield has to be mostly picked over by now."

Mr. Peters looked toward the back of the bus. "Let's hope there's still something to be had out there. I'd hate to dig into our bartering supplies to trade for food and water in town."

Zara pressed her lips together and repacked her backpack, sliding it under her seat. She hugged her middle, bringing her feet back up to rest on the seat, tucking her knees under her chin. Mr. Peters didn't say anything else, which wasn't unexpected. He wasn't the type to give out false hope, even if he was trying to be nicer.

"We can't do anything about the pilot," Mr. Peters said after a stretch of silence. "But I did bring a deck of cards. We can at least stop wallowing."

"Who says I'm wallowing?" Zara was *definitely* wallowing, but she'd hoped it wasn't so apparent.

Mr. Peters pursed his lips and narrowed his eyes at her, but then he relaxed. "Well, *I* am, at least. Do you want to play?"

Zara sat up, letting her feet plop to the floor. "Yeah, why not?" *Anything is better than just sitting here.*

"Lizzy loved poker. What about you?" Mr. Peters asked.

Zara quirked an eyebrow. "She liked *poker*? I've never seen her play."

"Well, I guess it was mostly a family thing. Or… a me and her thing." His shoulders sagged. "Actually, it's been… I don't know… a couple of years since we've played together. I guess we won't ever get to do that again." His face fell, and he breathed in deeply. "You know, I've lost people, but this… this is different."

"I know how you feel." Zara didn't mean to sound bitter, but she could hear it in her voice. *I've lost everyone who matters to me except my cousin, and she might be dead, too.*

"Zara…" Mr. Peters wiped the sweat off his own face with his sleeve. His brow furrowed as he looked down, eyes searching. Just when he seemed to have found what he wanted to say, a *bang* sounded in the distance, followed by a rushing, dull roar.

Zara sat up straighter, peering out the window as a plane approached the one and only landing strip of the small airfield. "He's here!" She stood up and pointed outside.

Mr. Peters twisted to look outside. "I guess the biggest negotiation of my life is about to go down." He stood up and tugged on his short-sleeved, plain blue t-shirt, smoothing it before running his fingers through his hair. He cracked his knuckles and rolled his shoulders, then faced Zara with a set jaw and determination in his eyes. "How do I look?"

Zara took in the dark circles under his eyes, his reddened cheeks, the sheen of sweat and dark spots under his armpits, and his wrinkled attire. A ripe odor emanated from him, but Zara wasn't so sure she was any better. She smiled anyway. "You look great," she said.

He reached under his seat and grabbed his gun holster, securing the band around his waist in plain sight. "Can't be too careful. You got yours?"

Zara retrieved her own. "You sure these are necessary?"

He nodded once, firmly. "Yes," he said, and then he headed toward the front door of the bus. "Let's go, then. We can do this."

"We as in… we? Or we as in… you?" Zara jumped down onto the tarmac.

"Zara, you did a great job with Thomas at the compound. You could make a hell of a politician or CEO one day." He looked down the runway where the plane touched down.

Zara smirked. "As if there will be companies to run and elections taking place."

Mr. Peters threw her a flat stare. "What do you think Thomas was? The downtown area here, with their trade and barter? The pilot's whole flight auction? There will *always* be someone buying, someone selling. And there will *always* be positions of power and leadership."

"You have a point," Zara said, but she still wasn't sure exactly how involved he wanted her to be in the upcoming negotiations. She did *not* want to stir the pot with him. He was about to go into Mr. Peters Executive Mode, and she wasn't sure how much of his old self was tied to that persona. She'd seen it with adults all the time. Even her dad had been different in subtle ways when wearing his police uniform: more reserved, alert, tense. But for Mr. Peters, the man in the suit, the man in power… he'd been a shark and a bully.

Just play it close to the vest. Maybe don't say much at all. I mean, he's got more experience. If he stays levelheaded, he's our best shot at moving forward. But there was one more thing she had to ask before the plane came to a stop.

"We're sticking to the truth, right?" Zara asked. "We're not covering anything up?"

Mr. Peters cleared his throat, hesitating. But then he nodded. "Yeah, the truth. One hundred percent." He let a few moments go by as the plane rolled their direction and came a stop, the propellers slowing. "But," he said over the noise, "let's be smart about it. Maybe just let me decide how much we tell him. The whole truth might scare him off."

Zara's eyes widened, and she opened her mouth to speak, but before she could object, Mr. Peters was raising his hand and jogging toward the small plane. She rubbed the back of her neck, her chest feeling suddenly tight. She swallowed hard as she followed, catching up with Mr. Peters as he approached the pilot.

The pilot was young, early to mid-twenties, muscled though shorter than Zara and thinner. His eyes were nearly as dark as his black hair, which was somehow styled despite the whole end-of-the-world thing. His clothes were high-end casual, touches of leather nodding to recent trends. He plucked aviator sunglasses from his shirt pocket and put them on, his step full of swagger in his designer sneakers. And then he pulled out a gun from behind him without breaking stride and pointed it straight at them before coming to a stop. He held it in a side grip, which made Zara quirk an eyebrow. *Somebody thinks they're hot stuff.*

"There will be no negotiations," the pilot said. "Answer is no, I do not do extra runs. I don't care if you're trying to reach your sick mother who's babysitting your son *and* your diabetic dog. Whatever. The auction rules apply to everybody." Then he lifted his sunglasses with his free hand and smiled at Zara. "Hey, babe. What's up?"

Zara narrowed her eyes. "My name's Zara, actually."

"Kai. Kai Lee." His smile widened.

"Well, *Kai*, what's up is that you look ridiculous." Zara crossed her arms. "You're not in a movie, man. Shooting a gun like that makes your aim stupidly unpredictable."

His smile faded and he looked at the gun, frowning. "Really?" he asked, his voice a little too high pitched.

"Yeah, really." Zara rolled her eyes.

He cleared his throat, his deeper tone returning. "Whatever, babe." The pilot stuck the gun back out, his stance awkward. He gripped it vertically this time. "I'm close enough that I can put a hole in your old man easy."

Zara was about to correct the assumption that Mr. Peters was her father when Mr. Peters looked at her and shook his head subtly, whispering, "Stick to what's important." He turned back to the pilot. "My name is Walter Peters. We've brought a bus and supplies for barter."

"Great." The pilot sniffed. "Enter the auction. If you beat out the rest, I'll take you next week."

"We need to get to Boston faster than that," Mr. Peters said. "I have the ability to stop this sickness from spreading, but my labs are in Boston."

"That's a new one." The pilot waved his hand toward the bus. "Look, just enter the auction, dude. Like I said, no negotiations."

"He's not lying," Zara said. "His company created the disease. It's called DV-10, and it spread at first through genetically modified mosquitos, then person-to-person." She continued even though Mr. Peters shot her a wide-eyed stare and mouthed for her to stop. "He's trying to get back to Boston where—"

Kai threw his head back and broke out into a fit of hearty laughter. He took off his sunglasses and slipped them into his pocket, wiping his watering eyes with the back of his hand. "Aw, man, that's a good one. Girl, I'm not the one pretending to be in a movie. That sounds straight up ripped from some sci-fi Hollywood flick."

Mr. Peters's mouth was drawn in a thin line. He was glaring at her now, but when he turned back to Kai, his expression changed to a more charming smile. "While it does sound outlandish," he said, his voice strained. "It is true."

"Sure." Kai shook his head, his smile fading again. "Look, you either get in the bus and get out of here, or I kill you now."

Zara pressed her lips together and breathed out through her nose. Frustration built tension throughout her body as she glowered at the arrogant young man. "You do realize that we both have guns."

"Zara," Mr. Peters said her name sharply and held out a hand, motioning for her to stop. "Kai," he turned back to the pilot. "Let's just talk about this. Maybe we can bring out a nice bottle of whiskey—"

Kai pointed the gun at the ground and fired a shot, making both Mr. Peters and Zara jump backwards. A spark flew, and it ricocheted, grazing Zara's leg. She screamed, more out of rage and shock than actual pain. It *did* hurt. A lot. But she'd endured worse, and it had only nicked her.

The pilot cursed and held up his hands. "Oh, crap. I didn't mean to hit her."

"You idiot!" Zara shouted. "You don't know how to use that thing." She hopped on one foot, her eyes watering. "You could have killed me!" She bit the inside of her cheek and stuck her leg out to examine the wound. Her skin had split, a shallow groove extending across her outer left calf. Blood trickled down her leg.

Mr. Peters had pulled his own weapon immediately after Kai had fired and was now properly aiming at Kai who still had his hands up. "You reckless little sh—"

"I'm sorry!" The pilot cut Mr. Peters off, his eyes wide. "Look, you kill me, you've got no one to fly the plane. But I can't just take you, okay? I've got a client booked for tomorrow. I've got a system. If I break the rules, I can't come back here. It would be chaos. People would be constantly coming to the airfield, threatening me. I can't negotiate. All I can do is tell you to enter the auction on Sunday." He nodded toward the bus and continued talking, the words pouring out of his mouth in a panicked flood of information. "The bus is a nice touch. I can use that to trade. High value categories are weapons, vehicles, alcohol, medicine, and clean water. Most people that enter the auctions have vehicles, so that won't put you over the top. You bring the goods, I'll schedule you for Monday's flight at the auction." He was breathing fast by the time he was done, all signs of his previous arrogance replaced with fear.

Mr. Peters worked his jaw back and forth before abruptly lowering his gun. "Fine. You've got a deal. I'm going to help her back to our bus and tend to her wound. Are we good?"

Kai nodded. "Yeah, man. We're good." He winced at Zara. "Sorry, babe. I—"

Zara lurched toward him, seething and limping. "If you call me *babe* one more time—"

Mr. Peters stepped easily between her and Kai. He looked at the pilot. "Her name is Zara. Show some respect, *dude*."

Kai gulped. "Yeah, right. Zara." He reached into his jacket pocket, and Mr. Peters lurched toward him. But he only pulled out a package of Twizzlers. "Hey, dude. It's just a peace offering." He held it out slowly to Zara. "What do you say, babe — uh, I mean… Zara. Truce?"

"You think candy is going to make up for shooting me?" Zara narrowed her eyes.

"I mean, maybe. Like, it barely touched you, right?" Kai's face pinched. "I think saying I *shot* you is a little extreme. It was more of a scratching, really."

Zara put one hand on her hip. "You want to say you scratched me with a *bullet*?"

The pilot grinned. "Yeah. So… Twizzlers?"

Mr. Peters raised his eyebrows at Zara. "He's an idiot. Back to the bus. Let's go."

Zara limped toward Kai and snatched the Twizzlers. She clenched her jaw, glaring at Kai one last time before turning back to Mr. Peters who let her lean on him to make it back to the bus. She winced with every step. The outrage seeped from her and the stinging, burning pain took its place by the time she'd climbed back onto the bus and taken a seat. Her calf, her sock, and her shoe were bloodied as she hoisted her leg up to rest on the seat. She leaned over and stuffed the candy in her backpack, ignoring Mr. Peters's eyes as they followed the package.

"What? I love Twizzlers." Zara huffed and crossed her arms.

Mr. Peters dug out the First Aid kit. "You're lucky you weren't more seriously injured. What were you thinking, antagonizing him like that?" He covered the wound with gauze. "Hold this."

She scoffed. "He was a total nitwit." But she pressed the gauze to the wound to staunch the bleeding, grunting at the pain of putting pressure on it.

"Yes, Zara, he was. That doesn't excuse *you*." Mr. Peters retrieved a packet of baby wipes and then removed her shoe and sock.

Zara reached out and grabbed the baby wipe with her free hand. "I can clean my leg, okay?"

She wiped away the blood, snagging a few more wipes before she was done. She did allow Mr. Peters to bandage it, changing out the gauze for a fresh pad and wrapping medical tape around her calf to keep it in place. The wound was only a few inches in length, perhaps an inch in width; she'd never had an injury so small hurt so badly.

"Now do you see what I mean about telling people the whole truth up front?" Mr. Peters asked. "It sounds crazy unless you establish some facts first. Like who I am, exactly, and what I know."

Zara chewed on her lip. "I thought…" I thought you were trying to hide the truth to protect yourself again. I thought you wanted to lie. I thought you were—

"You thought I was turning into the old Walter Peters?" He nodded as if he understood. "I should have given my reply to your question more attention." He sighed. "This is my fault."

Zara swallowed a lump in throat as her words and actions in the conversation suddenly seemed so foolish. "Well, I did sort of poke the bear. I shouldn't have been so aggressive. I should have taken the fact that he had a gun more seriously."

Mr. Peters didn't contradict her or try to smooth over her mistake. He just moved on. "We'll do better next time. We just need to figure out how to get all those high-end items. We've got the vehicle and a crate of whiskey. Thomas let us take only enough gasoline to get us here."

"And we can't give up our guns," Zara said. "We might need them on the other side of the mountains."

Mr. Peters nodded in agreement. "We're short on water, too. We need what we have."

"And we don't have enough medical supplies to part with those, either." Zara looked back to the crates. "We've got jewelry, a few good hunting knives, fishing supplies, the whiskey, lye soap… what else?" She scrunched her nose as she tried to remember what else Thomas had parted with.

"Candles, seeds, and batteries." Mr. Peters sighed. "All good stuff, but if we can trade some of it for the stuff Kai really wants, it sounds like we're a shoe in."

"If he was telling us the truth." Zara's stomach sank. They had no way of knowing for sure. "What will we do if we trade for the right stuff or scavenge to find it, and then Kai doesn't agree to take us? We *have* to get through those mountains."

Mr. Peters rubbed his hands over his face and took a deep breath. "I guess we've got three days to figure it out."

Chapter 22

Lizzy Peters

The hollow pit that was Lizzy's stomach growled and twisted her gut as she blinked away sleep. The sounds of the Mother of the Heir's voice alongside gentle sounds of nature still played at her bedside. It was dark, pitch black as it had been before, but she was strapped to a cot instead of left to cower in the corner. And the soft sounds of the recording were so much better than either the complete silence or the agonized screaming.

Lizzy tried to shift her weight. She didn't know how long she'd been lying on her back in the same position, but her hips and shoulders and neck were sore. It wasn't possible to change positions no matter how hard she tried. Five straps held her securely in place; her forehead, chest, waist, thighs, and calves were restrained.

Her wrists and ankles still stung, a reminder of being zip-tied to a chair, forced to watch those terrible images on repeat while her ears were bombarded with those awful, never-ending screams. She'd been left alone with Autumn's voice ever since.

At least I'm not exhausted anymore. She was parched and starving, though. *Maybe when Azalea comes back, she'll give me another drink.* She chewed on her lower lip, wishing the young woman would appear. Azalea had never laid a harmful hand on her. She'd only comforted Lizzy and asked questions. *She's a lot better than Orion. Definitely better than Autumn.* A twinge of guilt at that last thought confused Lizzy as Autumn's kind words played over the speaker.

"You are wanted here, Elizabeth," Autumn said. "You belong with us."

Lizzy's cheeks burned as the image of her father, the business headshot used in the video she'd been forced to watch, surfaced in her mind. His voice echoed in her ears. "I never wanted you or your weakness, Elizabeth."

Tears blurred her vision. *He never said that… did he?* He'd said she'd betrayed him. *And I did. I gave Jordan the passcodes from the book in his safe.* He'd said he didn't want anything more to do with her. *And I deserved that.* And she could hear him in her head, voice dripping with vitriol, saying she'd never been wanted, saying she was weak, but she couldn't picture him saying the words, not like she could with the rest. When she remembered what had happened in that cabin with Zara and her father in the moment of her confession, she could see the hurt and betrayal in his eyes. But she was remembering other things he'd said, too, and all she saw when she tried to picture those memories was that business headshot.

Before she could consider the disparity further, the door opened and the room was flooded with light. She grunted and shut her eyes against the sudden change, and it took several minutes before she could blink away the spots in her vision. By then, the recording of Autumn's voice had been turned off.

Orion came up beside her, undoing the straps. The sight of him made Lizzy suck in a sharp breath. She balled the sheets in tight fists as she started trembling. He smiled down at her. "Be good, Elizabeth, and everything will be just fine."

Lizzy nodded frantically. "O-Okay," she said, hating the way her voice shook. "I'll be good. J-Just don't make me listen to the screaming again."

"Oh, I hated that one, too," Orion said, still smiling, shaking his head like he was fondly recalling some silly childhood game. "In the end, though, everything we do here helps us come closer to the Mother." He paused as he was halfway through unbuckling the strap at her waist, his smile disappearing. "You would like to be closer to Mother Earth, wouldn't you?"

Lizzy's dry mouth felt like cotton balls had been stuffed inside. "Yes," she croaked. "Of course." *That was the right answer, wasn't it?* Her muscles tensed head to toe until Orion's smile returned and he finished removing the strap, moving on to the one at her thighs.

"We do that by obeying Mother Autumn." He sighed happily. "She is so in tune with the Mother. She's the embodiment of the Mother. No one else has her passion for justice."

Lizzy sat up as the strap at her thighs was removed, licking her lips as Orion moved on to the last strap. She rubbed the back of her neck and stretched her arms in different directions. It felt so good to be able to move.

The clatter of wheels entered the room through the open door, and Lizzy frowned at the large basin being brought inside the gray concrete room. "What's that?"

The basin was oval-shaped, gray and metallic, like a tub on wheels, with latches circling the rim. There was a mesh-like line about two inches thick three-quarters of the way up the side; it circled the basin, which was perhaps four feet high, three feet wide, and six feet long.

She searched the hands of the men who'd come inside, looking for a set of headphones. There were none. The men who'd brought it in left again, returning shortly, each one holding an oval-shaped lid. The top half of the latches were welded to it.

"W-What is that for?" Her heartbeat quickened. Her stomach twisted, the hunger suddenly staved off in the midst of trepidation as two men approached her. She hopped off the cot, planning to fight them off, but her body betrayed her and she crumpled to the ground instead.

"You need to understand," Orion said. "Some people learn through gathering information, but that didn't work for you. So, we're taking a more hands-on approach."

Lizzy scooted away from the men. "Don't touch me!" She crawled a few feet before one of them hooked their arms under her armpits and lifted her. The other man grabbed hold of her feet, her feeble kicking only a minor inconvenience. "Stop!" She yelled, but the word came out more like a rasping squeak. Lizzy arched her back, twisted, pulled and pushed, but nothing she did even made them pause.

They lowered her into the basin, and she managed to wriggle free of the man who held her upper body before he meant to let her go, but all that did was cause her head to hit the side of the basin. The lid slid over the top before she could regroup. It was dark except for what light the mesh line three-quarters of the way to the top let in. There was one larger hole on the other side of the basin, set within the mesh.

Lizzy hit the inside of the lid with the palms of her hands. "Let me out! I want to talk to Azalea!" The hard surface of the basin was unforgiving as she shifted, kicking and hitting every side. She peered through the mesh, but the two-inch view through a metallic crisscross pattern didn't reveal much. "Azalea? Are you here?"

Outside the basin, a black box was set within an inch of her metallic prison. A piercing scream emanated from the box, the speaker, and bounced off the inside of the basin, reverberating throughout Lizzy's body. She jerked away from the familiar, terrifying sound only to find another speaker had been set up on the opposite side of the basin.

"No, please!" Lizzy cried out and covered her ears, barely able to muffle the screams amplified by the basin all around her.

And then something thick and wet touched her foot. Lizzy screamed and yanked her foot away. Her chest heaved as she squinted at the place where the larger hole in the mesh used to be. A tube jutted into the basin there, pouring a black, thick liquid into the tub. A sickly-sweet scent reminiscent of gasoline filled Lizzy's nostrils. The waxy oil kept coming, filling the bottom of the tub, seeping through her linen pants.

"Stop!" Lizzy screamed, her voice cracking. Tears rolled down her cheeks as she pressed her palms against her ears and pled for mercy. She grimaced and bore the deafening screams as she pounded her fists on the sides of the basin, but she could only handle the sounds for so long before she had to cover her ears again.

As the oil level rose, she repositioned herself on her knees, her head touching the lid. It sloshed up to her waist and kept coming until the oil almost immersed her. They stopped pumping the stuff into the basin when it reached the mesh. She sobbed, her head tilted back, her chin held up away from the surface of the oil, her hands covering her ears.

Images of birds covered in black oil, of animals eviscerated by manmade machines, of human corpses littering the ground because of project oversights, of cracked and parched lands accompanied by bony children with cracked, parched lips, of *those men* sitting all the while in their pristine suits, smiling and lining their pockets while Mother Earth screamed — those images barraged her.

"I don't want to die. I don't want to die." She whispered it over and over and over again, until she was screaming it. Her voice joined the voices of agony echoing inside the basin. She squeezed her eyes shut, so exhausted, her body so weak. She tried to lean against the side of the basin, but she slipped, yelping as her head was swallowed by the oil.

The screaming stopped as her whole body submerged. She held her breath. If she was going to die, she would do it there, suspended in the thick liquid. It enveloped her, warmed her, kept the screaming out.

But then hands were gripping her arms, her legs, pulling on her everywhere, lifting her out of the oil and into the light. Her body hit the mattress of the cot before she could even register that she was free. A towel quickly dried her face, rubbing away the oil, though it dripped from her body everywhere else. Lizzy filled her lungs with air and opened her eyes to find Azalea, brow furrowed, hurriedly grabbing more towels, wiping away the oil.

"There, there," Azalea said, and Lizzy realized she was still crying and trembling. "It wasn't real crude oil. You'd be dead if it were. Just regular canola, colored and thickened a bit. A few spritzes of gasoline through the mesh to give you the full experience."

Lizzy smiled up at Azalea, overwhelmed with joy at seeing her face. Azalea never harmed her. Azalea always brought comfort. It was when she left Lizzy alone that things went wrong. "Thank you for getting me out of there," she said.

Azalea offered a small smile. "Do you see how evil those men are? Can you imagine the real stuff? Fumes making you dizzy, slowly killing you, and real crude oil burns after a while."

"That's terrible." Lizzy's eyes drooped. "I need water."

"Of course, sweet Elizabeth." Azalea helped her sit up. "We've got water and hot tea and a nice, soapy bath waiting for you right down the hall. Doesn't that sound nice."

Lizzy nodded eagerly. "Yes, yes, please. I'm so thirsty."

Orion rolled a wheelchair up to the cot, and Azalea helped her into it. Then she pushed her out of the gray, concrete room into a gray, concrete hall. She was still coated with oil, her hair slicked back, her clothes plastered to her body. Her face maintained a thin layer of the stuff, her eyelids heavy, her lips waxy, her ears still a little bit muffled.

A man opened a door for Azalea a few doors down, and Lizzy was rolled into a gray, concrete bathroom with a drain in the middle of the floor. There was a shower head in one corner, and a large claw-foot bathtub in another. Next to the tub was a bamboo table with water and a cup of tea.

"Why don't you clean up in here, and I'll wait outside, okay? I suggest the shower first, and then maybe a nice soak with the bubble bath." Azalea smiled at Lizzy. "Then us girls can have a nice talk."

"Okay," Lizzy said, relief relaxing her at the thought of being left alone in the bathroom.

Once Azalea was gone, Lizzy rushed to the water, guzzling it quickly, wishing there was more once she'd drained the bottle. She moved on to the tea, chamomile with a bit of milk. It soothed her raw throat. She undressed and showered, washing and rinsing her hair three times before the oil was mostly gone. It was an effort to remain on her feet, and a few times, she had to lean against the wall, but in the middle of the fog of hunger and exhaustion, all she could feel was gratitude for the hot water and the soap.

Eventually, she filled the bathtub, including a healthy dose of the bubble bath provided. It smelled of lavender and when she stepped into the warm water and sank into the foamy bubbles, she couldn't help but laugh. She leaned her head back and closed her eyes.

A knock on the door startled Lizzy awake. She whipped her head back and forth, her body tensing immediately. The bubbles were now no more than a thin film over the water, and the water itself was lukewarm. *How long have I been in here?*

Azalea opened the door and peeked inside. "Elizabeth? Are you ready? I've brought you a towel and new clothes, and your room is set up for your return."

Lizzy licked her lips and nodded. "Okay," she said. "I guess... just set them down on the table there, and I'll get dressed."

Azalea did so, and Lizzy reluctantly got out of the bath, dried herself, and pulled on another set of linen pants and a tunic. She was still tired, but she could stand without her legs shaking, and she could think. "It's going to be okay," she whispered to herself. "If Azalea is there, they won't hurt me."

She paused. *Azalea is one of them…* But she couldn't drum up hatred for her. She was actually eager to talk with her, eager to see if Azalea had brought her food. *If anyone in this place is going to bring me food, it'll be her.* That thought made Lizzy rush to open the door. It had been days since she'd eaten.

Azalea waited there, smiling sweetly and gesturing back toward the gray, concrete room. "I'm so glad you're feeling better."

Lizzy kept tabs on the others, the men ahead and behind. They parted to either side of the door when they reached the right one. Azalea waltzed right in without breaking stride, but Lizzy paused at the threshold, cautiously peering inside to find the basin gone, the room clean, and a new cot situated at one end with fresh blankets and pillows. There was no food anywhere in sight.

"Azalea, please… I don't want to be in here." Tears sprung to her eyes again. "I'm so hungry. I… I just want to have something to eat. I swear, I won't cause trouble if you just let me out. Give me a room. I'll work for food. I'll do whatever you want?"

Orion nudged her hard from behind, and she stumbled inside, her heart lodging in her throat at the sound of the door slamming behind her.

Azalea sat on her cot, scooting up to the wall and leaning against it. She patted the sheets next to her. "Come, Lizzy. We can talk about food in a minute."

Lizzy chewed on her lower lip, tears spilling onto her cheeks. "Why are you letting them do this to me?"

"Do what?" Azalea spread out her arms. "Look, Elizabeth. You're clean, you've been given a place to rest. All despite your hurtful rebellion against us. Why are *you* doing this to *yourself*? We want to give you a nicer bed, a nicer room. Do you know how Orion cries at night, worried for you? We all want you to see that you belong here, that when you helped us with the Cleansing, you were fulfilling your destiny. What happened to you today was a pale imitation of what has been happening to Mother Earth for *hundreds of years*."

Lizzy stared at her, wide-eyed. She didn't know what to say. She didn't want to risk Azalea leaving, because if she left, they could come back. If she left, all chances of getting her hands on something to eat would vanish. So, Lizzy walked across the cold, gray concrete floor and sat on the cot beside Azalea.

Azalea took Lizzy's hand in her own. "You are special, Elizabeth. Please, you can stop all of this. Just tell me about your father's work."

Lizzy squeezed her eyes shut. Her father's voice came alive in her head. *Worthless. Weak. I want nothing to do with you.*

"He's dead," Lizzy whispered, though it lacked conviction. Emotions warred inside her. He was her father, and she was his Bethie. She remembered crawling into his lap and feeling like it was the safest place in all the world. But she also remembered how he could kill without hesitation, how he pressured Zara into shooting Bertie, how he would snarl and spit and say the meanest things.

"What about the other men?" Azalea asked. "The two men I told you we have waiting for justice to be served? Do they deserve to die like the man my mother poisoned?"

Yes. They're bad men. Lizzy pressed her lips together. *No, that's not right, is it?* She didn't say anything.

"If you were given the means to carry out justice, if we put that needle in your hands, would you do it?" Azalea asked.

Lizzy opened her eyes and stared at Azalea. "You wouldn't ask me to do that, would you?"

Azalea sighed. "One more question," she said. "Is your father going to Boston? Is there something there that can curb the progress we've made, slow or stop the Cleansing?"

The countermeasure mosquitos. My father can create a vaccine. "I don't know. My father is dead." Lizzy nearly choked on the words, unsure why they felt wrong.

Azalea scooted off the cot, leaned in and kissed Lizzy's forehead. "No restraints tonight, I think. You're closer, Elizabeth. But not there yet." She turned her back and took a step toward the door.

"Wait!" Lizzy sat up straighter. "Please, I just need something to eat. Anything."

Azalea paused and looked back at Lizzy. "Fasting strengthens the soul. It gives us the strength to do the right thing. Our bodies, our greed for satisfaction, it leads us to make selfish, wrong decisions. You need more time, Elizabeth." She walked over to the side table and pressed play, Autumn's voice filling the air.

"You are loved here, Elizabeth. Mother Earth needs you to do the right thing." Autumn spoke slowly and yet there was so much passion in her words. Her voice was calm yet full of purpose. "Listen to the sounds of nature. Let it soak into your mind and heart and body." The sound of rushing wind followed, and despite how hungry she was, it calmed Lizzy's nerves.

Azalea left, but no one else came in. It was time for rest. There was no use fighting it. Lizzy laid down and let her head rest on the pillow. Affirmations and soft words and gentle sounds flooded her mind. It was a nice change of pace.

"You belong here," Autumn's voice said. "All you have to do is accept us, accept yourself."

And as Lizzy drifted off to sleep, she smiled.

Chapter 23

Timothy Peters

"You can't still be angry with me." Timothy looked from Heather to Candice and then back to his wife. "I found George. I'm sure Annika is there, too." The three of them were once again cooped up in the little break room with their cots back at police headquarters. He stood before the two women who sat cross-legged on the cots, facing him, a wall of disapproval.

"But you don't *know*." Candice crossed her arms. "You should have stayed until you caught sight of her."

Heather narrowed her eyes at Timothy. "No, you should have never run after those men in the first place. I can't believe you risked your life like that."

Timothy sighed and rubbed his hands over his face. Heather had sobbed at the sight of him when he'd shown up the day before. She'd thought him dead. But once she'd hugged him and kissed him and poked and prodded and reapplied salve to his back, she'd slapped him across the face for leaving her to think he was dead for an entire day. And she'd been angry ever since.

Candice had understood why he'd followed Icepick and Digger. She hadn't blamed him for getting caught overnight at the college or for checking his suspicions at the zoo. She was angry with him for not staying *longer*.

And O'Donnell wasn't happy with him either. He'd disobeyed orders, not followed his lead. It didn't matter to the captain that Timothy was *not* an officer. That seemed to make his decisions worse. He sighed. *Basically, everyone is mad at me. Great.*

"I did what I thought was right." Timothy sat next to Heather. "I can't lose my brother. And he and Annika are only there because of me." He met her eyes with his own, willing her to understand that he had no choice.

Heather's eyes softened. She took his hand in hers. "They're there because of Frank and because of those two CONmen."

A knock on the door was followed by O'Donnell's gruff voice. "We need to talk."

Timothy squeezed Heather's hand, hopped off the cot, and opened the door to find O'Donnell brooding in the hall, his frown deeper than usual. "Hey," Tim said, shoving his hands in his pockets. "Is it time for another strategy meeting?"

"That's done." O'Donnell shook his head once.

Timothy's eyes widened and his jaw dropped. He looked over his shoulder at Heather and Candice who both stood and approached the door. Timothy looked back at the captain, stepping into the hallway as Candice and Heather took up the space in the doorway. "I thought we agreed that me, Heather, and Candice would be included in those."

"I thought you had a good head on your shoulders." O'Donnell narrowed his eyes. "Until you ran into Copley Station alone, like a mad man, and left me and Murphy to get Webb to safety on our own."

Timothy grimaced. He hadn't thought of Karl Webb, the officer who'd gotten shot. "How is he?"

O'Donnell grunted. "Don't know, exactly. There was a trauma nurse holed up in the library, and she said it wasn't a good idea to carry him back here. She dug out the bullet, stitched him up, gave him a bed, but I don't know much else yet."

"I'm sorry," Timothy said. "I am. But I *did* find the information we were looking for."

"You found The Farm, where they're keepin' the kids," O'Donnell said. "We don't know for sure that's where the CONmen are *all* gathered. We don't know that's where Ace set up his base. But we're going to find out. Today. It's reconnaissance *only*. No engagement."

"Great," Timothy said. "I'll be ready to go in five minutes."

O'Donnell set his jaw. "I do not need your reckless behavior on this mission. We had that meeting without you to *discuss you* and what to do with you. There are quite a few who want to lock you down, put you on a tight leash. They think you should let us handle the bad guys."

Candice snorted. "Like last time? If it weren't for Tim, you wouldn't even know where to go today."

"Tim has a good eye. He's smart, and he gets things done. We agreed to work with you, but we don't answer to you." Heather crossed her arms. "He's going with you."

Timothy raised his eyebrows at the two women who had been berating him moments before. *I guess when push comes to shove, we've got each other's backs no matter what.*

He looked back to O'Donnell. "George is my brother, and Annika… well, she's become part of the family, too. I *am* sorry that Webb got hurt and that you had to leave him at the library. But I'm not sorry I chased those men. I need to get those kids back." Conviction swelled up inside Timothy, stirring up his passion for keeping those he loved safe.

"Will you let me finish?" O'Donnell gave Timothy a flat stare, and when he nodded, the captain continued. "Though quite a few are upset by your brashness, you've also earned some respect. You've got heart, and you followed through, and you had the smarts to at least come back here and get help instead of rushin' in at the first sight of your brother. That tells me you're a little rogue, but you're not stupid." He held up one finger. "But I meant what I said. Recklessness can get you or somebody else killed. You got it?"

"I'll do my best," Timothy said, very intentionally *not* making any promises.

"Fine." O'Donnell looked as if he barely stopped an eye roll. "Vest. Gun. Ammo. Five minutes. South barricade on Tremont." He abruptly turned and marched back down the hall.

Timothy breathed out long and slow. "Thank you," he said to Heather and Candice, "for speaking up and having my back."

The same intense stare Heather had used on O'Donnell was turned on Timothy, though her eyes glistened just a little. "You listen to me, Timothy Peters. Captain O'Donnell knows what he's talking about. You heard him. Don't be reckless. And *don't* leave me to think you're dead for any length of time." She blinked and a tear rolled down her cheek.

"Heather, I'll come back to you, okay?" Timothy wrapped her in a hug. "I'll be careful." He pulled away from her and dried her tears with his thumbs as he cupped her face in his hands. "We're going to get through this. We're going to get the kids back, and then we're going to ride this out with whatever supplies my dad left for us at New Horizons. And we'll do it together."

Heather nodded, leaning her cheek into his hand. "Together. Always." She lifted up on tiptoes to kiss his cheek and then hugged him one more time before stepping back. "Candice and I will continue to take the temperature of the cops here. I haven't gotten much out of them, but they seem to be awfully chatty with Candice."

"It's a gift." Candice flashed a smile, her makeup covering over nearly all the signs that she'd had the sickness. Her eyes still bulged just slightly, but if one hadn't known her before, it might have seemed simply a unique feature. Always dressed well, always put together. That was Candice Little.

"They're itching to do something about CON," Heather said. "And there's rumors the Russos are extending their influence in the northwest corners of the city."

"They're not happy about either," Candice said. "Once this week is done, it's going to be all out war here. Three more police officers from down south arrived yesterday. The more their numbers grow, the more confident they're getting."

Timothy's stomach dropped. "This city will be torn apart if CON, the Russos, and the police go head-to-head. We can't let those kids be caught in the middle of it. Not just George and Annika… all of them."

Candice gathered Timothy's bulletproof vest, which was already equipped, the gun holstered and the pockets filled with survival items. She handed it over. "Find my little blueberry," she said. "I miss her."

"I miss her, too." Timothy smiled at the memory of Annika assuming Candice was dressing to imitate fruit. Candice, who'd been a banana in her bright yellow dress, had settled on blue as the little girl's most flattering color. Annika had brought a lot of sunshine to otherwise gloomy days. And so did George, always so willing to help, ready with a joke to lighten the mood, board game master and practical joker extraordinaire. They reminded Timothy of what he was surviving for — the future of humanity. *We need them just as much as they need us.*

Timothy strapped on his vest, wincing a little as he tightened it against his back. He found O'Donnell exactly where he said he'd be, along with Lucy Freeman from the 13th, Paul Landry, and the crew from Chelsea — Murphy, Burke, and Torres. As Timothy approached, he sensed tension between the officers as they exchanged glances.

"Watch your backs," Burke said. "He won't do it for you."

"Come off it, Burke." Landry, the officer whose sister was missing, scoffed. "It's not like he left Webb alone."

"You weren't there," Burke snapped.

"I was," Murphy stepped forward, holding out a hand toward Timothy. "You took fire, and you gave fire. And you found The Farm. That's all I care about. I just want to get my son back."

Timothy took her hand and shook it. "That means a lot to me." He nodded at Burke. "I know I might not have handled the situation perfectly the other day, but I did my best. I did leave the team, but I didn't run from danger. I ran toward it. I might be brash, but I'm not a coward."

Torres patted Burke on the back. "Give him a shot," he said. "He's not trained like us. He's a civilian."

Burke pursed his lips, glancing at Murphy who gave him a subtle nod. He didn't apologize or take back his statement, but he didn't say anything negative, either. *I guess I'll take what I can get.*

O'Donnell dropped a backpack at Timothy's feet. "You carry the food and water. We'll keep watch for trouble. Stay centered with the group, just like we talked about last time. You think you can handle that?"

Timothy nodded. "Yes, sir, I do." He slung the bag on his back, and he followed O'Donnell, Freeman, and Landry, the three Chelsea officers taking up the rear. He trudged ahead over the next couple of hours, quiet and observant, following O'Donnell's lead.

He was getting used to the way Boston had been trashed and burned and looted. Spray painted yellow, green, and red marks marred most of the buildings the closer they got to the zoo. Trash and debris were scattered everywhere.

What he wasn't used to yet were the wild animals. A bright yellow parrot perched in a tree. Monkeys playing on a porch swing, pushing each other off to get a turn, climbing the ironwork railing when they got tired of swinging. Six goats hopping the tops of parked cars. Timothy smiled at the little creatures bounding from vehicle to vehicle as if they had somewhere important to be.

"Hey, what's with those?" Murphy's voice from behind Timothy caused everyone to stop.

"Whatcha talkin' about?" O'Donnell asked frowning in the direction she was pointing.

Timothy didn't see it at first, but then the light caught on clear plastic nailed to a tree. "It's a… plastic baggie."

"That's the fifth one I've seen," Murphy said.

A note in a bag, nailed to a tree. It struck a chord with Timothy, but he couldn't place the familiarity.

Burke stepped toward the tree. "There's a paper inside."

"We should leave it be," O'Donnell said. "These X's on the houses, those are marked by CON, and the baggies could be, too. If we disturb them, we'll give ourselves away."

I've seen this before. Outside the house in Wellesley.

"No, CON didn't do that." Timothy passed Burke and approached the tree. "This is Frank." He yanked the baggie off the nail. "You counted five of these, Murphy?" The others crowded closer to Timothy.

"Yeah," Murphy said. "All on this street."

Timothy reached inside the baggie and pulled out the note. "Frank is sending a message, but he didn't know how to contact us directly." He stared at the folded piece of paper, part of him wanting to wad it up and throw it away, the other part curious.

"I thought we were done with that maniac," O'Donnell said. "At least for a little while. We don't have time for his games."

"He's like a cockroach," Timothy said, repeating Frank's own description of himself. "Hard to kill, keeps coming back."
"Who's Frank?" Torres asked.
"The newest head of the Russo family." Freeman shuddered. "He's nuts. Nearly blew the Thirteenth to bits."
"The Russos, as in the mob?" Landry's widened eyes settled on the note. "How do you know that's from him?"
"He left a note for me exactly this way once, after he burned my parent's house to the ground. The last note I got from him in a bag nailed to a tree was a threat." Timothy rubbed the back of his neck, his heartbeat picking up as he held the note.
"Well… open it." O'Donnell motioned for Timothy to hurry.
Timothy took a deep breath and unfolded the paper. He frowned. "It's not in English."
O'Donnell snatched it from him. "What the heck is this? He turned it around for the others to see. Does anyone know what this means?"
"It's Italian," Landry said. "I recognize that word. *Tredicesimo.* Thirteenth." He shrugged. "Uh… I'm not sure about the rest. Maybe… 'see you' or 'meet you.'"
O'Donnell cursed. "The Thirteenth is my precinct. That has to be what he means. What does he want?"
"Uh… there's more to it, but I honestly don't know much Italian," Landry said. "I had an app on my phone that was teaching me, but I hadn't put much time into it. I was planning a vacation."
"What if he wants in?" Timothy looked up at O'Donnell.
"Like he wants to work together?" O'Donnell scoffed. "After Abrams and Ellis? No."
"Shouldn't we see what he has to offer?" Timothy held up his hands, palms outward, trying to be as noncombative as possible. "I mean, they had weapons. Drones. They could help."
"Are you crazy?" Freeman put her hands on her hips. "Have you forgotten the last time we tried to even have a conversation with them? They're criminals."

"I'm not saying we trust them," Timothy said. "I'm saying we use them. Or at least find out what they're doing at the Thirteenth."
O'Donnell spit and cursed again. He shook his head, hands on his hips. Finally, he grunted and looked up. "Fine. Timothy, Freeman, we've got experience with the Russos. We can head over to Jamaica Plains, check out the precinct. See if there's anything to this note."
"We can continue with reconnaissance," Murphy said. "See what we can see. We can meet you back at headquarters."
"I don't like it," O'Donnell said, "but we've got to make sure the Russos aren't up to something. The last thing we need is for Frank to surprise us the day we attack CON."
Timothy put his hand on the hilt of his gun, the presence of it and the vest comforting. "This roach is a slimeball," he said. "If he's playing with us, if he gives us any reason at all, I'm going to kill him."
O'Donnell patted Timothy on the shoulder. "You and me, both, kid." He shook his head. "You and me, both."

Chapter 24

Zara Williams

Zara and Mr. Peters walked into the courthouse expecting it to be full of people looking to sign up for the flight auction. Instead, they were met with a graying, wrinkled woman behind a counter, her hair pinned up in a bun, her thick glasses sitting on the edge of her nose. No one else was there.

"Can I help you?" She was barely tall enough to see over the high counter as she approached from the other side, but she bobbed upward, apparently using a step stool Zara couldn't see. Her desk nameplate read: Rita Dimmesdale.

"We're here to put our names in for the flight auction," Zara said, frowning at the empty room.

"Oh, yes. Of course." Rita hopped down the step stool and ducked below the counter. "Where did I put that clipboard… ah! Yes. Here it is." She stepped back up and slid the clipboard across. "Put your name and the number of people in your party. Mr. Lee only accepts parties of five or less, unless children are involved, in which case he may be able to take on six."

Zara frowned at the paper as Mr. Peters took the clipboard. "There are only six other parties on this list."

"Is this everyone who is trying to get a flight east?" Mr. Peters asked.

Rita chuckled. "Oh yes," she said. "No one wants to go *east*. Well… almost no one. But those who do really only have a few choices. The flight auction is supposed to be the safest." She smiled.

Mr. Peters scribbled down their names. "How do we enter the items we have to trade?"

"Oh, you do that Sunday." Rita pursed her lips and scooted her glasses up her nose. She held up a finger, stepped down, rifled through something, and reappeared once more with a slip of paper. "Here you go, dear." She slid it across the counter. "Instructions are at the top. He'll need to know *what* you've got and *how much* you've got, all in U.S. measurements, please."

Zara quirked an eyebrow as Mr. Peters shifted into a more relaxed posture and leaned an elbow on the counter. She held back an eye roll as his voice dripped with charm.

"How lucky Mr. Lee is to have such a competent manager," Mr. Peters said. "If I was still in business, he'd be in trouble. I'd offer you a job on the spot." He flashed her a grin.

"Oh, stop." Rita blushed and smiled. "I'm just a clerk. Been here serving this community for thirty years. I'm no manager."

"Are you kidding?" Mr. Peters leaned back as if surprised. "You're obviously a seasoned pro."

Wow. She's drinking this in. Zara watched the woman as she blushed again.

"No, I promise," Rita said. "Just a clerk. But, this side business of Mr. Lee's *has* been fun. I never thought little Kai Lee would make much of himself. A little disaster has a way of booting you out of your living room. He's become quite the entrepreneur without those virtual reality games to scramble his brains. And he's been taking care of me and my family, just for helping him organize these auctions." She leaned over, whispering. "Don't tell, but his mother was a good friend. I might have done it for free if he hadn't offered to be so generous!"

"So, you're a gem *and* you're savvy. Well, don't sell yourself short. I'm sure you're worth every penny," Mr. Peters said. He changed subjects just slightly as the woman beamed over his compliments. Zara couldn't help but be impressed as he continued. "Since you seem like the kind of woman who knows what's happening around town—" The woman batted away his compliments with a smile as her blush deepened. "—I'm wondering if you might be able to point us in the direction of the best spot to trade goods." Mr. Peters finished by leaning forward and offering her a wink.

"Oh, well." Rita put her hand to her chest and then leaned forward, too. "Don't tell, but… the downtown area is full of trade, of course, but the fairgrounds are the best spot. Downtown is where the locals trade with outsiders. The fairgrounds are where locals trade with locals. Just don't tell anyone I sent you. They won't turn you away if you've got goods and just *happen* to stumble upon it. Just cross the river at Nichols Street, follow that road west a bit until you get to Park Street. That'll take you straight to it. It's only about a twenty-minute walk from here, a few minutes' drive."

Mr. Peters graciously excused himself and Zara, and they walked out of the courthouse knowing exactly where they needed to go. The wind had picked up, whistling through the alleyways.

"That was impressive." Zara crossed the street with Mr. Peters, both of them keeping a good distance from strangers. Families and couples clustered on the streets, keeping the same precautions. The downtown area was bustling, compared to everywhere else Zara had been since the World's Fair, but that wasn't saying much. At any one time, Zara could only count about a dozen people in her purview, the wind tugging at their hair and clothes.

"That was nothing." Mr. Peters hopped up on the sidewalk and turned in the direction they'd left the bus.

"I didn't know you could be so diplomatic." Zara babied her wounded leg. The stinging pain reminded her a little of a badly skinned knee, but it was manageable.

"Before I was the boss, that was my whole life." Mr. Peters frowned. "I just got used to being the one with the information, the one with the power." He turned a corner and slipped between houses.

"So, which is the real Mr. Peters? The charmer or the boss?" Zara asked it like she was joking around, but there was too much truth in the implications. It was a loaded question, and she realized that when Mr. Peters stopped to look her in the eye.

"Neither," he said. "The charmer is a manipulator. The boss is a no-nonsense hard-ass who doesn't care who he hurts to get things done. I don't want to be either of those men."

"Then… who do you want to be?" Zara asked hesitantly.

"I want to be the man Dana thinks I am." His faint smile was tinged with sadness. "No, I guess I want to be the man Dana thinks I *can* be. She's never been fooled; she just… did her best to bring out the best in me."

Zara just smiled. Dana had always been kind to her. She'd always wondered how a woman like that fell for a man like Mr. Peters. But lately, sometimes — just sometimes — he reminded Zara of her own father. *Dad would have known how to sweet talk that clerk, too.* A pang of grief pierced her for a second, but she carefully tucked the pain away. The anguish over losing loved ones no longer consumed her, but it didn't feel right to ignore it, either. She'd settled on packaging it up to unwrap later.

Mr. Peters's eyes glistened, but he sucked in a long breath, rolled his shoulders, and kept moving. "There was never any pulling the wool over her eyes, but she loves me anyway." The sadness in his expression deepened. "I've been going over how to tell her about Lizzy. How to tell Timothy and George. I don't know how I'm going to do it."

"I'll tell them the truth. It was my fault," Zara said. "She'd be alive if I hadn't let those crazies into the compound."

They reached the bus, which was hidden behind a home with thick trees lining the property, and Mr. Peters unlocked the back door.

"You don't know that. They were planning to attack the compound, and we would have been there when they did. They had explosives, Zara. They may have been a small offshoot of a larger beast, but they had the means and the will to take out Thomas's people and steal their supplies."

"Yeah, maybe." *I just wish I hadn't made it easier for them.* She tucked those feelings away, too. Grief and regret were powerful, and she'd already let them control her once. *I'm going to have to pull the string and unbox them eventually. Maybe one day I'll be able to do it without breaking.*

Zara climbed inside and took her seat, and Mr. Peters started up the bus and followed the clerk's directions. Within five minutes, they were parked on the edge of a field that had been equipped with a paved road around its circumference, a stage and bleachers, some tennis courts, and a little inroad down the center with a line of trucks backed up to it on either side.

Mr. Peters stopped at the entrance to the inroad. He set his jaw, leaning on the wheel to look out the window at the people milling between stations of goods. "We're after weapons and meds, water if we can find it. Gasoline, maybe, but we can always venture out and siphon that from abandoned vehicles."

"Gasoline cans, then?" Zara asked. "We can't siphon it if we can't store it."

"Good thinking." Mr. Peters switched gears and drove to the end of the line, parking the bus to join the rest. "Let's open up for business. You want to go down the line and tell them what we have and what we need? I can open up the back, see if anyone comes to us for a trade. We should be able to see each other if you stay on the road."

"Works for me." Zara walked to the back of the bus, opened the door, and hopped to the ground, gathering her hair into a ponytail to prevent the wind from tossing it in her face. A dozen shoppers explored the offerings of twice as many stations in the little marketplace.

Mr. Peters hopped to the ground as four of the nearest Clearfield citizens, one of whom had been manning the nearest station, approached.

A man in jeans and a plaid button-up shirt crossed his arms and scowled at them. "You two aren't from here, are you?"

Zara cleared her throat. "Um… no, but we do have things to trade."

A woman pressed her lips together. "This is meant to be a local market."

"We're sorry to impose," Mr. Peters said. "We won't spread word if that's what you're worried about. We stumbled across this place and thought we might be able to trade."

The locals exchanged glances, a few of them shrugging and returning to their trucks. The man crossed his arms. "You swear not to lead a bunch of outsiders here, and we'll let you stay."

Mr. Peters held up three fingers. "Scout's honor."

"We're all armed," the man said, not bothering with a smile. "Don't try anything stupid. We don't know you. Get what you came for and leave."

"You got it," Zara said. "We appreciate the opportunity."

He returned to the nearest station just as a little girl bounced up to him with a bag of candies. The same frown fell on the girl, and she stuck out her lower lip. "Lola Jane," he said. "I told you to trade Mrs. Hallifax our soap for her acetaminophen."

"Did you hear that?" Zara whispered, elbowing Mr. Peters. "Mrs. Hallifax has meds."

"I *did,* Dad." Lola tugged on her hair as the wind played with it, too.

"Then where did you get that candy?" He looked up and down the line. An older woman waved and smiled, popping a little hard candy into her mouth.

"Mrs. Hallifax wanted me to weed her garden. You said nobody gets nothing for free anymore, so I neg-nego-shee-aid-ed for candy." Lola hugged the bag and returned her father's frown with a formidable one of her own.

Her father's lips worked into a small, proud smile before he sighed and ruffled her hair. "Well, all right, then. But one candy per day, max. And brush your teeth after. There's no dentist anymore."

Lola beamed as she skipped to a stool and sat down with her bag of candy. The second her father looked away, she popped one into her mouth and grinned.

"I guess Mrs. Hallifax is your first stop," Mr. Peters said with a chuckle. "And if you have to negotiate with Lola, keep your wits about you."

Zara cracked her knuckles. "I've got this." She headed straight for Mrs. Hallifax, her eyes widening as she approached the woman's stand.

Two young men with rifles stood on either side of the truck, each of them stepping forward at the sight of Zara. Mrs. Hallifax, a woman in her fifties or sixties, light blonde hair in a single braid over one shoulder, wore a jean dress with bright sunflowers embroidered along the collar and hem. She sat by a chalkboard which had a list of medications in two columns and a decorative border of cartoonish pills wearing smiling faces. Mrs. Hallifax was cross-stitching, periodically reaching for a small, round candy from a little bowl beside her on a small table.

Zara kept an eye on the two young men. They looked a lot alike. *Brothers, maybe?* One of them scowled at her and the other one smiled.

"Good afternoon," Mrs. Hallifax said, not bothering to look up from her cross-stitch.

"Good afternoon," Zara repeated, trying to sound friendly but professional. The list of medications was long and included a few antibiotics, oxycodone, and diazepam. "I'm here to trade—"

"Looking to get on a plane?" Mrs. Hallifax said, still calm, still busy with her craft.

Zara cleared her throat. "Um… yes, but—"

"There's a reason I'm not downtown where all you leachers are gathered."

Zara swallowed hard. "I… I'm just trying to get home.

Mrs. Hallifax looked up at her. "These drugs are for locals."

The young man who had smiled at Zara stepped up. "Come on, Mom. We can help her out, right? Just a little?" His eyes turned dreamy. "I mean, what about those stories you told us? Always help a stranger." He looked right at her. "Might be an angel in disguise."

Wow. How original. Zara managed to smile back at him as she bit back her reply.

"Good gracious, Lawrence." Mrs. Hallifax backhanded his arm. "I didn't raise you to bat your eyes like that at some stranger."

"Come on, Mom. It's bad karma to turn her away. What if I was stuck somewhere, trying to get home?" Lawrence turned puppy dog eyes on his mother.

Mrs. Hallifax sighed. "Fine." She pointed to the chalkboard. "No asthma or diabetes medications. Those we need. I'll trade limited amounts of some of the rest, but I won't let you clean me out of anything. That's only *if* you have something I want."

"Sounds good to me," Zara said. She started with some of the lesser items. "We've got jewelry and lots of seeds for planting a garden. Cucumbers, peppers, tomatoes, green beans, lettuce…"

Mrs. Hallifax quirked an eyebrow. "I'll take whatever seeds you have. I don't need jewelry. What else you got?"

Zara bit the inside of her cheek. *I can't give up too much. We still need other supplies.* "Are you sure? What about wedding bands and engagement rings?" She indicated what Zara assumed were both the woman's sons. "Surely these two will need something like that eventually. We've got some really nice ones."

Mrs. Hallifax narrowed her eyes. "All right. I suppose there's no harm in dreaming."

"Yep," Lawrence said. "No harm in that."

"She's leaving, dimwit," the other man said.

"Shut up, Jerry." Lawrence snapped.

"Anything else?" Mrs. Hallifax asked with a sigh. "These meds are valuable. What you've offered so far is only minimally so."

"Fishing supplies," Zara said. "Nets, poles, line, bait and tackle."

Mrs. Hallifax nodded. "All right. Bring the fishing supplies, the jewelry, and the seeds. We can come to an agreement once I see how much you've got." She waved at Jerry. "Lend her the wagon."

Zara accepted the wagon with thanks and headed back to the bus, but as she did, her eyes were drawn to a new structure opposite where they'd parked, a tent with a sign out front that read: Clearfield Watch.

"What's that?" she asked as she approached Mr. Peters.

"I don't know, but… I heard a few words of chatter as they were setting up that tent." He nodded toward Lola's father, who still eyed them with suspicion. "I asked our friendly neighbor, but all I got out of him was that the Clearfield Watch was a local law keeping group."

Zara shrugged. "Well, I've got a drug deal to make." She paused. "Wow. Never thought I'd hear myself say those words."

Mr. Peters shook his head and laughed, but then his expression changed as his eyes focused on something behind Zara. "What is he doing here?"

Zara turned to see the man from the bar, Nolan, walking toward the tent. He walked with purpose, three men following close behind. One of the men behind him was struggling to keep straight several full sized, floppy poster boards as the wind tugged at them. A gust tore one loose, and it tumbled toward Zara. Without thinking, she rushed forward and grabbed hold of it, only intending to help the man recover it. It flapped as Zara picked it up, and she frowned at the sketch. Her eyes were drawn to a paragraph over the side.

But before she could decipher the words, the poster was snatched from her, and Nolan was rolling it up. "Thanks, but I've got it," he said.

"No problem." Zara smiled wide, though her stomach was twisting in knots. As Nolan walked back toward the tent, Zara returned to Mr. Peters.

"What's wrong?" Mr. Peters straightened up and stared daggers across the road at Nolan's back. "What did he say to you?"

"Nothing, really." Zara's chest tightened. "But… that poster… I think there was a sketch of the airfield on it." She felt the blood drain from her face. "I think they're up to something, and I think it has to do with our ride home."

Chapter 25

Timothy Peters

Timothy hid with Captain O'Donnell and Officer Lucy Freeman behind a pile-up in the center of an intersection. He'd found his own inconspicuous position to examine the target building. A tattered flag hung over a Boston Police sign with the words: Jamaica Plain Neighborhood Station. It wasn't anything like the huge, modern headquarters, all steel and reflective glass. Over the doorway of the small station, blue lettering labelled it District E-13. All the shades were drawn on the windows of the brick building. But it was what he could see through the glass front doors that told Timothy they were in the right place. A man sat behind the glass, a gun at his hip, knitting needles in hand and a half-finished blanket on his lap.
"Pugsie." Timothy shook his head as he recognized the lackey guarding the door.
"Is that guy knitting?" Freeman squinted at the entrance to the building.
"Yeah. He wants to start a legit business." Timothy shrugged. "Guess it's never too late to follow your dreams."
O'Donnell grunted. "Smart man. Winter isn't going to be fun without the power."
"At least the mosquitos will be hibernating or whatever." Freeman shuddered, and then she looked between Timothy and O'Donnell with wide eyes. "Right? I mean… these mosquitos will go away when winter hits?"
Timothy shrugged. "I hope so, but… they are different from any species of mosquito I've ever seen. I'm not going to get my hopes up."
"Well, let's take this whole end-of-the-world thing one step at a time, shall we?" O'Donnell straightened up. "They'll be expecting us. We should show ourselves."
"Are you sure, sir?" Freeman shifted uncomfortably. "This could be a trap. Lure us here. Shoot us before we get to the door."
Timothy shook his head. "I don't think so. We're even."
"You really think that matters to a guy like Frank?" Freeman asked.
"I'm not saying we trust him, but Frank put those notes out for a reason. He wants to talk." Timothy straightened up next to O'Donnell. "I'm betting he wants to talk to me."
"Lead the way, then, Peters." O'Donnell held out a hand toward the station. "We've got your back."
Timothy pulled on the straps of his bulletproof vest and patted his gun. "Okay. Let's go." He stepped into the open and cautiously approached the front door of the station with Freeman and O'Donnell on his heels.
As they approached, Pugsie put his knitting needles and his project into a wicker basket on the floor. The lackey opened the door for them. "'Bout time you got here. Frank's been sayin' it was only a matter o' time before you showed your ugly mug." Pugsie slapped Timothy's arm like they were old pals.
"Hey, Pugsie." Timothy kept one hand on the hilt of his gun. "Do you know what he wants?"
A loud bout of laughter echoed down the hall. "Ho! Is that who I think it is?" Frank turned a corner surrounded by a wall of guards. "Southie! Captain!" He stopped a few feet from them and winked at Freeman. "Good afternoon, doll. Name's Frank Russo. I don't believe we've met."
Freeman spit. "We've met. I was at the farmhouse. You killed my friends."
"Oh, don't be sour, baby." Frank flashed a toothy grin. "It's a new day."
Timothy's stomach churned; the anger radiating from Freeman and O'Donnell was nearly palpable. "They're still grieving, Frank. Let's not make light of their loss."
Frank sniffed. "Yeah, okay. Whatever. I invited you to work with me because I thought that was all water under the bridge, ya know? Got to thinkin' about that little girl, about the kids my people are missin', and I thought, 'Frankie, maybe Southie was onto somethin' after all.' Was I wrong?" He narrowed his eyes and pulled his gun from his holster. All six men surrounding him followed his lead, and suddenly Timothy was staring down the barrels of multiple guns. Frank yelled louder. "Well, Southie? What's it gonna be?"
Timothy had been too shocked at Frank's sudden shift to pull his own weapon, but both O'Donnell and Freeman had their weapons trained on the two men in front of Frank. Timothy put his hands up and looked back at his companions. "How about everyone just calms down? This is about the kids." He looked back at Frank. "Right, Frank? You're the kind of man who protects children. We're the same in that regard. All of us."
Frank sniffed and worked his jaw back and forth. "You really know how to get me worked up.
Why ya gotta do me like that?" He lowered his weapon.
"I'm sorry." Timothy raised his eyebrows. "Can you order your guys to lower their weapons, too?"
Frank lifted his chin stubbornly. "You first."
"Guys?" Timothy met O'Donnell's eyes and then Freeman's. "Let's try this again." Both police officers lowered their guns but neither holstered them. Frank gave the order, and his men did the same, all but one tucking their guns away. Timothy wiped sweaty palms on the front of his shirt and offered an unsteady smile at Frank. "Why don't you and two of your guys come outside with us? Three of us, three of you. Nice and even. Then, we can talk about why you put up those notes for me to find."
"There ain't nothin' to talk about. I got a proposition. You take it or you leave it." Frank snapped his fingers and a man behind him handed him a large shoe box. "In case you missed it, Ace set up at the zoo. I got what The Boys like to call a CI up in CON's ranks, so I got the goods when it comes to information. You ready to soak up my genius, Southie?"
"Sure." Timothy waved his hand for Frank to continue.

"And *you*, Captain?" Frank rocked from heel to toe and back again, looking expectantly at O'Donnell.

Frank's tone was far too cheerful, his wide grin sending goosebumps up and down Timothy's arms. At any second, the mobster could change moods. *How could I forget how this feels? Waiting for him to explode or do something completely nuts?*

The burly captain crossed his arms and set his jaw. Frank narrowed his eyes. There was a moment of tension. Timothy lightly elbowed O'Donnell and threw him what he hoped was a subtle glare. *C'mon. Just go with it.*

The captain sighed. "Fine. Go on, Einstein. We're listening."

"Good." Frank patted the shoulder of one of the men in front of him and then stepped through the wall of guards to stand in the front, the box still in hand. "This station is right around the corner from the zoo, within spittin' distance, if you will. I decided it makes a perfect base of operations, so—"

"This station belongs to me," O'Donnell cut in, his tone harsh. "This is *my* house." Frank's men pulled their guns again at the captain's outburst.

"Well, that's debatable." Frank chuckled. "Seems like you abandoned it. Went on to a new house." His smile faded into a hard line. "Either way, it's mine now, until I choose to leave it."

"Let's hear him out, O'Donnell." Timothy said softly. "We can fight over property later."

O'Donnell ground his teeth. "Fine," he said again, pushing the word out with what seemed like great effort.

Frank cracked his neck, continuing with less enthusiasm. "We set up here. I take the lead. You're my backup, not the other way around. Your guys get the kids out. We do the dirty work of wiping CON off the face of the planet. My guys are goin' straight for the Tropical Forest Pavilion."

"And after?" O'Donnell asked. "What happens after that?"

"Any kids that belong to us are returned to us," Frank said. He handed the box to Timothy. "We sent in a drone, got some pics. You'll see nine kids' school photos in there; we confirmed at least four of 'em are at The Farm. There are more pics you can bring back to your people. Maybe you'll spot the kids you're lookin' for, too."

"Keep going," O'Donnell said. "What happens once CON is taken care of?"

Frank shrugged. "We give it a three-day truce. Then, we duke it out over the city. Best man wins." He winked. "It'll be me."

Freeman shook her head. "There's no way we're going to get enough cops willing to follow a Russo's lead."

"She's right." O'Donnell nodded toward the officer.

Frank scoffed. "Well, I ain't followin' *your* lead."

Timothy cleared his throat. "How about the police stick to their chain of command, and you stick to yours? The BPD gets the kids to safety. Frank, you and your men go for Ace, like you wanted. Everyone can meet up here, at this station. The Tropical Forest Pavilion and The Farm are on separate sides of the zoo. You both attack on the same day, same time, working parallel. Neither gets in the other's way. The kids that don't belong anywhere get taken to refuge communities. Truce lasts from now until three days after the attack."

Frank shrugged. "I can live with that."

"I think I can convince my people to agree," O'Donnell said.

"And where does that leave you, Southie?" Frank asked.

"My family only cares about getting our kids back. We want no part in your war." Timothy held up his hands, palms outward.

"You wanna be Switzerland, is that it?" Frank asked.

"I guess that's accurate," Timothy said. "I'm betting most of the survivors in this city won't want anything to do with this. Most of us probably just want to continue surviving."

"Well, ain't that precious?" Frank pointed at Timothy. "Look here, Southie. One o' these days, you're gonna realize everybody's got to pick a side. Just make sure you bet on the right horse." He stared flatly at O'Donnell. "Now, I'm sure you cops gotta vote on this or something stupid like that." He shooed them with a wave of his hands. "Go do what you gotta do. I want a firm answer by tomorrow at noon. I'll send a guy to you since you came to me this time. And then we gotta come up with a plan of attack, one where we can both do our thing without gettin' in each other's way."

O'Donnell led the way outside, marching quickly with fists at his sides. A vein popped out on his forehead, and every step was rigid. "Who does he think he is? The lunatic!"

Timothy struggled to keep up with the captain with the large shoe box in both hands. He jogged awkwardly. The lid wasn't taped down, and he had to keep his thumbs on top to stop it from flying off. "O'Donnell?" He followed through the debris in the streets. *Why is he going so fast?* He looked down at the box. *I have to see if Annika is in any of these photos.* "Hey, can we stop for a minute?"

But there was no evidence that Timothy's pleas were even registering with the captain. He stormed on, back toward headquarters. "One of these days I'm going to kill him with my bare hands. I'm going to wring his neck." He continued muttering and fuming, walking way too quickly for Timothy's liking.

With every step forward, Timothy's body complained a little more. "Hey, O'Donnell? Can we slow down?" He was tired, and he was certain he couldn't keep up the same pace all the way to headquarters, especially with the box in both hands. When he tripped and stumbled forward, barely keeping the box from spilling all over the road, Timothy shouted. "Captain! I'm trying to talk to you!"

The bigger man turned on Timothy and roared. "What is it, Peters?"

Freeman stood by, her expression clearly indicating she wasn't about to get involved. Timothy stared at the captain, his mouth hanging open. "I… I just wanted to slow down." He lifted the box a few inches. "This thing is a little awkward. And we have time. We don't have to rush. And… we got what we wanted, right? Maybe we should take a second to calm down."

"*Calm down*?" O'Donnell spat. "I'm about to make a case that we work with the Russo family, a crime syndicate I've been working *against* my whole career." His voice kept getting louder with every word. "And once we're done ousting their competition, they're coming after me and mine. I don't even know if Abram's niece is at The Farm! She could be dead. Everyone is dying, Peters. Don't tell me to calm the hell down!"

"We can look through the pictures in this box," Timothy said. "We can find the girl you're looking for. We—"

"Stop it with this *we* business." O'Donnell poked Timothy hard in the shoulder with his finger. "That crazy bastard was right about one thing. The war that's coming once this truce ends… that's not going to be the kind of fight where you can just bow out. I'm not going to let the Russos have Boston. If you're not for that, Peters, you're against the BPD. And that's not a place you're going to want to be."

Timothy's throat closed up as his heart pounded in his ears. He could only stare back at the captain, unable to say anything. When O'Donnell let out a frustrated sigh and turned back toward headquarters, continuing his march, Timothy's feet stayed glued to the pavement. He tipped the box so that the lid was pressed against his chest, the papers inside shifting and the cardboard bowing as he hugged the box tight.

The city was already broken. It was haunted, saturated with loss, filled with corpses. Debris littered the streets. Wild animals roamed the concrete jungle, and black clouds of death waited to emerge from the shadows. *This morning I would have said things couldn't get much worse.* Timothy sucked in a sharp breath as images of a true war zone flitted through his mind. *I would have been so, so wrong.*

Chapter 26

Zara Williams

While Zara and Mr. Peters continued to trade goods, more locals showed up to gather in the tent across the road. The deal with Mrs. Hallifax got them a variety of drugs, both over-the-counter and prescriptions. They made another trade with a man further down the line, batteries for ammunition, and a third trade of candles and matches for water jugs and gas containers, though it was made crystal clear that siphoning gas or gathering water from inside Clearfield city limits might get the two of them shot.

"I guess that's a wrap," Zara said as she slid a crate of ammunition next to the rechargeable batteries they'd kept. She was inside the bus, stacking their supplies neatly, as Mr. Peters loaded what they'd traded for through the open back door.

"Everyone here is packing up their stuff." Mr. Peters lifted a large, empty water jug and slid it through the door. He set it next to nine more jugs. "I'm glad we got here when we did. We might not have had time to get what we needed otherwise."

"Yeah..." Zara chewed on her lower lip as she watched a line of men and women headed for the tent which was still standing and filling with people. "I'm worried about what they're doing."

Mr. Peters glanced over his shoulder. "Me too..." He turned his back to Zara. "Maybe I'll just go and check it out, see if I can overhear anything."

Zara walked to the end of the bus. "I don't think that's a good idea. It seems like strictly a locals thing."

"Nolan isn't local." Mr. Peters crossed his arms.

Their neighbor, Lola's father, was passing by on his way to the tent and apparently overheard. He paused, put his hands on his hips and hung his head, and then approached Mr. Peters. "Nolan was invited. You weren't. Don't go near that tent. Not everyone around here is as friendly as I am."

Zara raised her eyebrows. The man had done nothing but throw disgruntled glances at them since they'd arrived. Lola skipped up to her father and hugged his middle, smiling up at him. He placed a loving hand on her head.

"Lola, go sit in the truck, windows up, until I get back from the meeting, okay?" The man urged her toward the truck, though his little girl gave him a convincing chin tremble.

"I want to stay with you, Dad." Lola blinked her glistening, sad eyes.

"Lola, hon... this is for adults, okay? You can eat half that pot pie we got from Mr. Phelps."

"And... more candy?" Lola stuck out her lower lip.

Man... she's adorable and she knows it. Zara crossed her arms and leaned against the doorframe of the back door of the bus.

"All right. Just one more." Her father kissed her forehead. "I won't be long, okay?"

"I'll be all alone." She batted her eyelashes, a single tear escaping one eye. "I wouldn't be alone if you'd let me keep that kitten."

Her father sighed and pinched his nose. "Fine. If you go and stay in the truck and show me you can be responsible, I'll let you keep the kitten."

Lola squealed and grinned. "You're the best dad in the whole world!" She stood on tiptoes and reached up. Her father bent lower, and she wrapped her arms around his neck and kissed his cheek. "Thanks, Dad!" She turned skipped back to the truck, not a tear in sight.

Her father's smile faded as he looked back at Zara and Mr. Peters. "You gotta pick your battles," he said. He pointed over his shoulder at the tent. "And this isn't one you're going to want to fight. Just get in your bus and leave."

Mr. Peters put his hands up in surrender. "Okay. You've got it. I'm going to finish loading up what we traded for, and then we're out."

The man nodded. "Good." He turned on his heel and headed straight for the tent.

Mr. Peters smirked. "That little girl has him wrapped around her little finger. Reminds me of Bethie at that age."

Zara smiled at the thought of a little Lizzy giving Walter Peters a run for his money. And then she sat up poker-straight. "I have an idea."

"What?" Mr. Peters put another jug on the bus, and Zara slid it into an empty spot along the wall of the bus.

"We need to know what's going on in that tent, right? I mean, they could be trying to take over Kai's business. Or run him out of town. Or they could know something about Kai that we don't. We could use that information, right?" Zara knelt so that she was eye-level with Mr. Peters.

"Depends on what it is, but yes. We could use it to barter for an early ride out of town if it's good enough." Mr. Peters shook his head. "But there is no way we can get in there without being noticed and possibly shot. They don't want us there."

"*We* can't, but *Lola* definitely could. Even if her dad caught her, I mean, you saw... she'd be able to get out of it. No harm, no foul." Zara turned around and headed toward her backpack.

"Okay, but how are you going to get her to do it?" Mr. Peters finished loading up the last water jug and climbed up into the bus.

"She'll take a bribe, if it's good enough." Zara pursed her lips as she surveyed what they had left to trade. "We've got jewelry." And then she clapped her hands together once. "Ah! I know." She rushed to her backpack and pulled out the package of Twizzlers Kai had given her, holding them up like a prize. "Lola will love these."

Mr. Peters shrugged. "I guess it's worth a shot, but... we can't just stick around, waiting for her to sneak over there and come back with a report. They'll notice."

"Pretend like there's something wrong with the bus." Zara nodded toward the engine.

"I guess I could stall for a little while that way." Mr. Peters pressed his lips together and walked the length of the bus to peer out the window toward the truck Lola currently occupied. "She could also say no and then tell her dad we tried to bribe her."

"Maybe. But… if we get a bad response, we can just lay low until the auction." Zara shrugged.

Mr. Peters nodded. "All right. I think it's a good idea. Better take both the jewelry and the Twizzlers. Just in case she doesn't like one or the other."

"Who doesn't like Twizzlers?" Zara scoffed, and then her eyes widened at Mr. Peters's look of disgust. "You don't?" He shrugged, and Zara shook her head in mock disbelief. "Just when I was starting to like you."

"They're not even real licorice," Mr. Peters said.

"I'm going to pretend we never had this conversation." Zara smiled at him in good humor, and then she grabbed the jewelry and the candy. "I'll be back." She exited the bus via the front door and walked around the engine so as to not draw too much attention from those in the tent.

She stopped at the edge of the front of the bus, peeking around it to take a good look at the tent across the road. The chatter was hushed but increasing, and she saw several people looking over their shoulders at their bus, though she was pretty sure she was mostly hidden from their view. About three yards away, Lola sat in the front seat of her father's pickup truck. The little girl was singing into a flashlight, her eyes squeezed shut as she belted out a note.

"Okay," Zara whispered to herself. "If I can just make it to the other side of her truck without being spotted, I'll be golden. Slip into the back seat, do a little negotiating, get the info."

She glanced at the tent again, waiting until all heads turned toward the front as Nolan whistled to get their attention. Zara darted across the empty space, heart pounding as she ducked behind the front of the truck. As she'd predicted, the other side of the truck had no line of sight to the tent. With the bribe tucked under her arm, she rose to see through the window. Lola was staring right at her, eyes wide. Zara held up the Twizzlers, and the little girl licked her lips.

"I'm going to open the back door." Zara kept her voice low but exaggerated the way she mouthed the words to make it easier for Lola to understand her through the window.

"What?" Lola yelled. "I can't hear you!"

Zara flinched and held a finger up to her lips, shushing the little girl. She quietly opened the back door of the truck and slipped inside, keeping her head low. "Hey, Lola," Zara whispered.

"Why are you whispering?" Lola turned around in her seat to sit on her knees.

"Uh… I guess I don't have to." Zara cleared her throat. "I was wondering if you might be able to help me out."

"For the Twizzlers?" Lola asked.

"Yes. I need to know what's going on inside that tent." Zara held up the bag. "You can have the entire bag of Twizzlers if you go over there and then report to me and my friend in the bus what they say."

"My dad told me to stay here." Lola eyed the small bag of jewelry. "What's in there?"

"Some very nice jewelry. I might be able to throw in a pretty ring or a set of earrings." Zara opened the bag, digging through it to find a sapphire ring. She pulled it out.

"That's pretty." Lola reached out for it, but Zara held it back.

"You have to do the work first," Zara said.

Lola scrunched her nose. "I don't know… this is risky business. My dad could ground me for life. I mean, you're a stranger. As in, *stranger danger*."

Zara grimaced. "Yeah, totally. I get it. It's important for kids to stay safe, and most strangers are definitely to be avoided." She held up her hands, one of them holding the bag of jewelry, the other the Twizzlers, as she shrugged. "You're right. I'll just take this stuff back to my bus."

Lola stuck out her hand, palm outward. "Wait!"

Zara shook her head and reached for the door handle. "Oh, no. You had some very good points."

"No, I didn't!" Lola leaned between the two front seats. "Please? I can do it!"

"You can?" Zara paused with her hand on the doorhandle. Part of her felt a little guilty for tricking Lola into cooperating, but she'd done worse. A lot worse. And they really needed to know what was happening in that tent.

"Yes. But I want the *whole* bag of Twizzlers. And I want to pick out my own jewelry." She crossed her arms.

"Well… I guess if you swear to me you'll be safe around the bad kind of strangers, which is pretty much everyone else, besides me and my friend and anyone your dad says you can trust." Zara settled back into the seat. "Like, if a stranger asked you to go somewhere with them without your dad's knowledge, that would be bad. We just want to do business with you. It's different. You see?"

Lola nodded. "So… you just want to know what they're saying?"

"That's right. And then you can choose your own ring, and you can have the whole bag of Twizzlers." Zara opened the bag and held a red rope out for her. "In fact, you can have one right now."

Lola snatched it and bit into the candy. "Yum." She smiled. "How long should I stay?"

"We just want to know what Nolan has to say about the airfield and about Kai Lee." Zara pointed to the bus. "I'll stay here unless I see your dad coming, and then I'll have to leave. If that happens, I'll leave the Twizzlers for you anyway, for your efforts."

Lola nodded. "Got it." She hopped out of the truck, slamming the door behind her.

Zara winced at the sound, but when she peeked through the back window of the truck, she didn't see anyone looking their way. Lola sneaked into the tent successfully right before two men started untying the flaps on either side of the opening. They closed it, each one scowling at the bus. *Let's just hope they don't see Lola.*

Zara glanced back at the bus. Mr. Peters was already outside, fiddling with the hood. It swung upward, the hinges at the front of the hood instead of the back, and Mr. Peters retrieved a collapsible step stool. He proceeded to pretend to examine the engine.

Only another ten minutes passed before there was a disturbance at the tent. Lola reappeared with her father holding her upper arm, a deep frown on his face. Lola's expression was one of stubbornness as her father let her go and pointed toward the truck.

Great. There's no way she heard enough to know what's going on. Zara stayed low, watching the scene in the truck's passenger side mirror. Lola crossed her arms and stomped away, and her father reentered the tent with a very similar but more reserved march. Lola stopped, glanced over her shoulder at the closed tent, and then turned back toward the truck with a smile. She skipped the rest of the way, hopping into the truck with gusto.

"All right," Zara said. "A deal's a deal." She passed the Twizzlers up. "It's okay. You tried."

"I *crushed* it." Lola pulled a folded piece of paper out of her pocket and held it out with a proud grin, her chest puffed out and her shoulders straight. "This is the paper Nolan passed around."

Zara handed over the Twizzlers, exchanging them for the paper. "Okay, well… at least it's something."

"Is it enough for some jewelry?" Lola asked.

"Let's see." Zara unfolded the paper and began to read, and then her mouth fell open. She handed the bag over to Lola. "Pick whatever you want." Lola grabbed the bag with a squeal, and Zara sank back into the seat. The paper was a voting ballot, outlining Nolan's propositions.

"I'll take this one. And this one. And this one." Lola plucked rings out of the bag and slid them on her fingers.

Zara's hand trembled, and her heart beat furiously inside her chest. "Lola, I need to go." She held out her hand.

"One more." Lola pulled an emerald ring out and then handed the bag back. "You said I could have whatever I wanted." She held up her hands and wiggled her fingers. Each one had a ring on it, most of them too big for her.

"Um… that's not what I meant, but sure. I have to go. Just tell your dad we gave them to you after we couldn't trade them." Zara took the rest of the jewelry and opened the door as Lola did a double fist pump. She didn't have time to argue any further.

As Zara rounded the truck and approached Mr. Peters, he closed the hood of the bus and stepped down from the stool. "Well, that took less time than I thought. Did she get anything at all?"

Zara forced the words out past a lump in her throat. "The townspeople don't want strangers here at all. They're afraid of the virus." She pushed the paper at Mr. Peters. "This is a copy of a contract. Nolan's changed his business model."

Mr. Peters frowned as he read over the contract. "He's going to set up a perimeter around the city to keep out unapproved visitors. They'll pay him, provide for him and his men, and in exchange they act as a sort of security." He looked up at Zara. "So what?"

Zara stepped forward and turned over the paper. "Look at their plan for ensuring Kai doesn't continue bringing people to Clearfield."

Mr. Peters took a half a step back. "They can't do that."

"It's already signed by the mayor and the police chief." Zara indicated the bottom signatures. "They're going to leave us without a safe way across the mountains. They're going to murder Kai Lee."

Chapter 27

Timothy Peters

Timothy stared at a picture of George aiming a gun. The picture was from far away, but he could tell it was his brother from the shirt he had on; Timothy had seen him in that same shirt when he'd spotted him entering the zoo days before. Five kids stood in a line behind him, and O'Donnell had thought one of them could be Abram's niece, Melissa. That definitely helped their cause.

I'm coming for you, George. Just… hang in there. Timothy's vision blurred, and he quickly wiped away the tears and gathered himself together, praying his little brother wasn't forced to do anything he couldn't recover from.

Candice had found a closer picture of Annika. She was shoveling dirt into an empty fountain along with several other little boys and girls. Murphy had pinned her hopes on the picture of the back of a boy in the distance of one photo. Landry hadn't been able to find any pictures that resembled his sister, Wren, but he was holding out hope.

Frank's box of pictures had not only provided hope that loved ones lived. They also provided data about CON, about how they'd set up at the zoo. Several of the more well-known gang members, including Ace himself, were identified. That took care of the BPD's skepticism about the zoo being the best place to concentrate their efforts.

The official meeting to discuss the mission to coordinate with the Russos wasn't for another hour, but Timothy had already heard bickering over it all morning. Not everyone was on board with Frank's proposal, nobody liked it, and alternative plans of action were being thrown around left and right. Timothy wasn't even sure where O'Donnell stood anymore, not exactly. He'd made a promise to Abrams, and he *was* going to try to get Melissa out of there. If he focused on just Melissa, O'Donnell could probably snatch her from CON's grip with the help of the 13th. Getting more than one kid, especially going after all of them, would be a lot harder. Where O'Donnell stood on the matter drastically affected the goal of the mission. However, his disposition toward Timothy, Heather, and Candice had changed.

He's definitely not crazy about me right now. Timothy had stuck to his guns in regards to the fact he wasn't interested in fighting a war; he just wanted his brother and Annika back. *After that, the BPD and Frank can fight over Boston all they want.* Of course, he hoped O'Donnell pounded Frank into oblivion, but Timothy had his own people to worry about. *I can't lose anyone else.*

But that hadn't sat well with the captain, or any of the officers, really. Timothy was willing to live with that if it didn't cloud their judgment concerning how important it was to rescue those kids. He didn't want to make enemies. Once the war started, he hoped he and his people could fade into the background where no one would notice. *Lay low. Survive. It'll work. It has to.*

"Hey, Tim, you got a second?" O'Donnell's voice interrupted Timothy's thoughts. His shoes clopped against the hallway floor as he approached.

Timothy pushed off the wall he'd been leaning on just outside their breakroom-turned-bedroom and tucked the photo into his pocket.

"Is the meeting starting early?" Timothy glanced at the clock on the wall.

"No." O'Donnell planted his feet at shoulder's-width and looked at Timothy like he was prepared for a fight. "We want you guys to take a walk."

"What?" Timothy frowned. "You want us to go outside?"

"Go hunt for supplies. We're low on these things." He plucked a paper from his shirt pocket and handed it to Timothy. "See what you can find."

"But the meeting—"

"You need to skip this one." O'Donnell didn't leave room for negotiations. "The department needs to discuss this on our own. Worst case scenario, it'll be the Thirteenth, Landry, the Chelsea cops, and you three."

Timothy sighed in relief. So, O'Donnell hasn't changed his mind on that front.

The captain continued, "Best case, the whole department goes in on it. But Frank's guy will show up in a couple of hours, and the decision about the BPD's involvement is ours to make. Not yours. We can't trust you to stay out of it if you're in the building, and we need supplies. Two birds. One stone."

Timothy pinched the bridge of his nose. His shoulders sagged. He looked down at the list. *We're not going to be here, with the BPD, at this time next week if all goes well. We'll need our own supplies again.* And then his spirits lifted as an idea entered his mind. *Maybe this is a good thing. We need to scout out New Horizons. See if it's good to go for shelter or if we need to find someplace else. Take an inventory of what Dad left behind.*

Timothy shrugged and looked up at O'Donnell with more confidence. "Fine," he said. "I guess it's a good idea for us to take a turn scavenging, anyway."

"Now, Tim, I don't want to h—wait… what?" O'Donnell furrowed his brow. "No more arguments?"

"Nope." Timothy stood up. "I'll grab the ladies, and we'll get out of your hair."

"Well, good." O'Donnell gave Timothy a rigid nod. "Try to be back before curfew. But if you get stuck out there, get to shelter and come back in the morning. Don't be stupid."

Timothy forced a smile. "I'll do my best."

O'Donnell turned around, but then stopped. "You're a good man," he said. "I hope you make the right choice when it comes time to fight."

"Thank you, O'Donnell," Timothy said. And I hope when I make the choice to protect my family, you'll accept it.

Once the captain had left, Timothy returned to the room where Heather and Candice were and explained the conversation he'd had with O'Donnell, including his thoughts about going to New Horizons Lab to ensure it was a safe place to hide.

"I can't believe they're kicking us out." Candice huffed and blew her hair out of her eyes.

"They're not kicking us out for long." Heather shrugged. "We're coming back."

"Well, what if we want to listen in on their meeting?"

"We don't have a choice." Timothy strapped on his bullet proof vest and gestured for the ladies to do the same. "They want to make the decision as a unit, and we're not part of that. I think it's good that they're seeing us as separate."

"Well, it's ridiculous that they even have to debate it." Candice followed suit, though she made a face at the vest before layering it over her wrinkled, stained, designer t-shirt. "This is a no-brainer. I can't believe a bunch of cops have to discuss whether it's a good idea to rescue dozens of kids from the likes of CON."

"It's not that simple." Timothy handed the ladies their empty backpacks. "I believe Frank will honor the truce, but I understand why O'Donnell and the rest have their doubts. There are all sorts of worst-case scenarios being thrown around that make staying out of it seem the wisest choice." He secured his gun. He was the only one of their party to have one; ammo was low, and the BPD hadn't spared more than one firearm for the trio.

"Half of them are just mad that they'd be doing the rescuing instead of the shooting, and the other half are cowards." Candice threw up her hands in frustration before throwing a few necessities into her backpack and slipping it on. "What's worse than children being abused and turned into CONmen?"

Heather tightened the straps of her vest and backpack. "Well, it might be worse if we showed up and Frank double crossed us. The kids would still be in the same spot, and we'd be dead."

Timothy shook his head. "I know that's a theory some of the cops have come up with, but Frank isn't going to make the same deal with CON that he did with us. The only way Boston is freed from CON is if we combine forces to match theirs. The Russos would lose against CON on their own. He has a chance of taking down the BPD, though. It makes more sense for him take his chances with us after CON is gone."

Heather raised her eyebrows. "It would also be pretty terrible if we helped get rid of CON and then Frank turned on us immediately. That truce is going to be important recovery time to get the kids settled and prepare for what's coming next."

"Frank needs the same prep time," Timothy said. "And I think that's one of the reasons he suggested we get the kids. I mean, we'll have some of their kids, too. The truce works for both sides. They're trusting us to save their family members." He pointed with his thumb over his shoulder toward the door. "Speaking of preparing for what's to come, I think we better get moving."

They kept mostly quiet as they made their way outside and began their trek to the west. Timothy led, about eighty percent sure he was going in the right direction. The building was near Newton, a suburb of Boston, in the neighborhood of Brighton. He estimated it would take them a little more than an hour, at least, to find the labs if he knew exactly where to go. The problem was he only knew *mostly* where to go. He could see the building in his mind's eye: utilitarian and gray, barely any windows, tucked behind a medical diagnostics complex also owned by Vanguard. Timothy fell into a rhythm, step by step advancing toward the goal, keeping his eyes open for complications, keeping his ears on high alert to avoid trouble.

Candice groaned after three quarters of an hour had passed. "What's the name of the place we're going again?"

"New Horizons Lab," Timothy said.

"Right." Candice took small, quick steps to keep up with them. "How much do you think your dad left for us there? Dana didn't seem to know much about it."

"I know just as much as you do." Timothy noticed a rotting arm hanging out of a car window ahead, so he diverted to the other side of the road. "He wasn't finished making it a backup location, so I'm not expecting much. I'm just hoping the building will make a decent shelter to ride out this upcoming war between the mob and the police. We need to get George and Annika and then hide. We can't tell anyone where we're going, okay?" He looked directly at Candice.

"Hey, I'm great at keeping secrets." Candice put one hand on her hip.

Heather looped her arm in Candice's and pulled her forward. "Don't pick on Candice. There's enough division going on right now. We should be focusing on the tasks at hand. Once we scope out New Horizons, we'll need to gather supplies. I'd like to get back today and find out what happened at that meeting."

Timothy kept walking and scanning the area ahead. "Me too. We're almost there, I think." He pointed to an intersection ahead. "I'm pretty sure that's the right street." He paused in the center of the intersection and looked down the road on either side, spotting a familiar building. "Let's go left." They walked a few more blocks before Timothy spotted a grouping of buildings with the logo of Vanguard Diagnostics on their signage. "There! New Horizons is right through this lot!" He beamed with the accomplishment of finding the place and turned, expecting Heather and Candice to be just as excited. Instead, they were staring open-mouthed at something down the road.

"What are you guys looking—" Timothy's question died on his lips. A dozen zebras were stampeding between vehicles, headed straight for them at full speed. And then a *tiger* leapt onto the top of a car several yards behind the last zebra, sprinting after its prey. Candice gasped and bolted for the diagnostics complex, shrieking at the sight. Her movement barely registered as Timothy's whole body had been turned to stone. His brain misfired at the terrible, majestic predator bounding after its exotic prey in the midst of smashed and abandoned cars and black pavement, accompanied by a backdrop of brick and glass.

"Tim…" Heather put a hand on Timothy's arm. "I think we should run."

Timothy blinked, willing his body to move past the shock, and his body went from zero to one hundred in mere seconds as adrenaline flooded his veins. "Get to the lab!" He put a hand on Heather's back and nudged her to movement. They sprinted after Candice, who seemed to be going in the right direction. Still, Timothy shouted so she could hear. "New Horizons is on the other side of these buildings, across the lot!"

Timothy reached the drive that connected the street to the parking lot behind the diagnostics buildings as the pounding of hooves combined with the thumping of zebras sideswiping vehicles. Ahead, Candice reached the entrance to New Horizons and turned around to lean on the building.

As they entered the parking lot, Timothy slowed to a jog beside Heather. "I can't believe that just happened."

"I know." Heather came to a stop and put her hands on her knees. "My heart is pounding." She took a few deep breaths and then stood up. "Boston isn't what she used to be, huh?" She started laughing, and Timothy couldn't help but join her.

Until Candice shrieked again, screaming, "Behind you!" She waved her arms frantically.

Timothy frowned and looked back at the drive. There, the tiger prowled forward, freezing in a crouch when Timothy turned toward it. "Heather… run."

"If we run, it will catch one of us." Heather shook her head. "Aren't we supposed to like, try to seem scarier than it is?"

Timothy pulled out his gun. "I'll stay to keep its attention. I'll shoot it if it comes too close."

"Tim—"

"Go," Timothy said.

Heather retreated, and Timothy slowly walked backwards, his gun drawn, aimed at the tiger. He didn't want to waste his bullets, so he waited, hoping the creature would turn tail and go back to his zebra hunt. *I guess we looked like easier prey.*

"The door's locked!" Candice's voice echoed against the buildings.

Timothy tensed. He'd imagined there would be a keypad, but he'd hoped the locking system would have been disabled when the power went out. *What would my dad's code be?* "Try some dates," he yelled. "Birthdays, Mom and Dad's anniversary…"

Timothy was alone in the middle of the lot, slowly making his way toward the building. The tiger skulked forward, its eyes fixed on him. His heart slammed against his ribcage repeatedly as he stepped backward. Fear churned his stomach even as awe kept him enraptured. Huge paws soundlessly carried the tiger, all muscle and power. The creature broke into a run, teeth barred.

"No!" Timothy shouted as a visceral reaction caused him to step back faster. He tripped and fell as he pulled the trigger, landing hard on the asphalt. The loud bang of the shot rang in his ears and reverberated off the buildings. Timothy's head bounced off the ground and the gun skidded several feet from his hand. The tiger slid to a stop and crouched, but just for a second.

"Tim!" Heather screamed from somewhere behind him, and a slam as if the door had been swung open against the building sounded. He scrambled for the gun as the tiger sprinted forward. His head swam as his knees scraped against the asphalt. *I'm going to die.* The gun was almost in reach, but so, too, was the tiger. And then an explosion louder than a gunshot was followed by a whistle, and Timothy curled in on himself as bright red sparks shot in a line above him. The tips of shoes touched his back, and two legs pressing against him. The whistle continued, and five more explosions too close for comfort rattled his bones. His brain registered what he was hearing as he protected his head from the flying sparks, but he could barely believe it. *Where did Heather find fireworks?*

Finally, the fireworks ran their course. He peeked from between his arms. There was no tiger in sight. He relaxed and rolled onto his back. "Heather, you beautiful—" His mouth dropped.

Standing above him was a scruffy man in a white lab coat, boxers, and an undershirt. He was holding the capsule of a large roman candle, and he smiled a toothy grin down at Timothy. "I've always wanted to do that," he said. "I mean, *something* like that." He snorted. "Who could have guessed the opportunity to frighten a tiger with fireworks would ever present itself here in Boston, eh? I mean the stats on that have to be pretty staggering. One in a billion." He held out his free hand in an offer to help Timothy up. "Name's Theodore Finch."

Timothy grabbed the man's hand. "Uh… thank you. My name is—"

"Timothy Peters." Theodore's smile widened. "I know who you are."

Chapter 28

Alexander Roman

Though he'd made sure to give Washington D.C. and Baltimore a wide berth, Alex passed more pockets of survivors and more travelers than he had since leaving St. Louis weeks prior. As he passed the third small group trekking the smaller country roads bordering Maryland and southern Pennsylvania, Alex kept his foot on the gas, not bothering to give their waving so much as a glance.

"Dad? Why aren't we stopping to help people?" Oliver's voice piped up from the backseat.

Alex turned the rearview mirror so he could see his son, who was craning his neck to watch the travelers get further and further away. Samson pressed his nose against the window as he stepped over Oliver's lap, obscuring Oliver from view. His son wrapped an arm around the dog's neck and coaxed him to lay down, scratching his belly as Samson complied.

"We don't know them, Oliver." Alex shifted his eyes between the road and the mirror, trying to gauge what his son was thinking, how he was handling the situation. Minnie sat in the passenger seat next to him, and she threw him a sympathetic look.

Oliver cocked his head to the side, pursing his lips thoughtfully. "That never stopped you and Mom before." In the rearview, Alex could see Oliver's hand go to the purse his mother had made. He never let that bag out of his sight.

Lauren, who sat beside Samson and Oliver in the back seat of the cab, patted Oliver's knee. "Things are different now, kid."

"Why?" Oliver asked. "I mean, if there are more people in trouble, shouldn't there be more people trying to help?"

Alex's heart ached. He'd taught Oliver to always be kind, to have empathy for those in need. How can I explain this to him? All he sees is us hoarding supplies and running from anyone who looks like they need help.

"Well, sure, bud," Alex said. "In a perfect world, where we could trust people, that's exactly how it should be. But… we're not in a perfect world. I wish we were. I wish we had unlimited resources and that I wouldn't be risking our lives by stopping for every person who waved for us to help them. But the fact is, even good people do bad things when they're scared and desperate."

"But we're good people, and we're not doing bad things." Oliver shrugged. "Wouldn't we want help if we didn't have Harvey?" He patted the seat of the RV as he used the vehicle's nickname. "I mean, the bikers helped us, right?"

Alex nodded slowly. "Well, yes, they did." He hesitated, not wanting his son to lose faith in people all together. *It was more like they were hunting the people attacking us, but yes, they did help us.*

"And we're helping them, too." Lauren stuck a thumb over her shoulder, pointing toward the attached RV. Ned, Wyatt, Asher, and Ben were crammed back there, separated from the cab. "We're going out of our way to help them get where they need to go."

Minnie twisted in her seat to look back at Oliver. "You ever heard the saying, 'The squeaky wheel gets the grease?'"

Oliver shook his head. "No."

"Well," Minnie said, "it means some problems need fixin' faster than others. Used to be that everybody had a squeaky wheel once in a while, and other people could step in and let them borrow some grease. But nowadays, everybody's got a dozen squeaky wheels and there's a grease shortage. You get what I'm tryin' to say?"

Oliver wrinkled his nose. "Not really."

Alex sighed. "Bud, Minnie is saying that we only have so much we can give, and right now, most of what we have has to go to our own survival. One day, things will be better, but until then, we have to protect ourselves. That doesn't mean we never help. It just means we have to be more careful about who and when we help."

"I guess that makes sense." Oliver's face fell and his shoulders sagged.

"Hey, bud?" Alex met his son's eyes in the mirror. "You think I'm a good person, right? You trust me?"

Oliver nodded.

"Okay. Then, how about this. I promise you that we will help the people we can, when it's safe and when it won't take away from what we need to survive. But you have to trust me to know when that is." Alex smiled as Oliver perked up a little bit.

"Okay, Dad." Oliver returned the smile and turned his attention to Lauren. "Hey, you want to play 'I spy?'"

"Sure, kid." Lauren rustled Oliver's hair, and the two started playing in the back seat.

Alex turned his attention back to the road, talking to Minnie quietly. "That road sign back there said we're about thirty minutes outside of Lancaster. I've been there before. I'm pretty sure that means we're a little more than an hour outside of Philadelphia."

"So, how far from New York City?" Minnie asked. "Three… four hours?"

"Something like that." Alex chewed on his lower lip. "I think we need to find a safe spot to pull over, restock on water, food, and gas, if we can. I'd like to keep what we have as reserves. We're out of what Zion's Angels sent with us."

It had taken them a day to repair their vehicle, retrieve their trailer, and prepare to leave the school where Zion's Angels had set up, and they'd already travelled a full day since. Every time Alex had started to see too many people, he'd gone further into the countryside in the hopes of getting as close to New York City as possible without running into any more trouble. The night before had been hard. Alex, Minnie, Lauren, Oliver, and Samson had stayed in the cab, turning the vehicle on for air conditioning when it got unbearably hot. The three bikers and the convict had slept in the living quarters. Ned had suggested switching spots for the night, but Alex wasn't letting Ben anywhere near the driver's seat. No one had slept well, and they'd all started the day hot, sticky, and sore.

"I think we should also find shelter for the night. Maybe a convenience store," Alex said. "We could use a map."

"It'll be hard to find somethin' that hasn't been picked clean." Minnie shook her head. "I guess we can try, though."

"Just keep your eyes open for a good spot," Alex said. "We'll have to fill up the gas tank and stretch our legs soon."

Alex turned off the little highway onto a country road, going east and then north again in an attempt to get away from foot traffic. When he'd not seen a soul for another hour and there were more fields and trees than houses, Alex relaxed and looked for a place to stop. The next city limits sign they came upon looked promising.

"Bernville, population seven hundred and two," Alex drummed his fingers on the steering wheel. "If she's got a gas station and we don't see anyone, I think we've found our spot."

A few minutes later, they were parked in the lot of a small gas station attached to a mechanic's garage. Alex jumped out, and Ned stepped down from the entrance to the RV shortly after. He absent-mindedly clicked his Zippo open and shut as he surveyed the area, and then he slipped it back in his pocket before addressing Alex.

"Too many windows broken to make a shelter." Ned squinted at the gas station convenience store and garage.

"There's not much in Bernville. Maybe one of the houses will do?" Alex turned in a circle, noticing a nice brick home across the street. He turned back toward the station. "We should check this place out. See if we can find anything left, especially a map or vehicle repair tools in the garage."

"I agree. Let me and Asher go on in and make sure the place is clear." Ned pulled a handgun from the holster on his belt. "You might wanna keep the vehicle runnin' in case we need to make a run for it."

Alex nodded. "Sounds good to me." He did as Ned asked, but it didn't take the bikers long to come back and report that the station and garage were empty. They all stepped outside, each one stretching their arms. Even Samson yawned and stretched all four legs.

The inside of the small gas station was a mess. Shelves were tipped, trash littered the floor, and the refrigerated drink section had been ransacked, the glass doors shattered. But few people owned maps anymore; gas stations and rest stops were the only places Alex had seen one in years. If it hadn't been for that, he wouldn't have suggested looking inside the ransacked store. He headed for a magazine rack that lay on its side, its contents heaped on the floor.

"What are we looking for?" Oliver asked.

Alex squatted so as to not touch the floor; there was too much glass to kneel. But as he sifted through the pile, he spotted what he needed. He leaned over and plucked a map from the mess. "One of these." He handed it to Oliver. "Have you ever even looked at a paper map?"

Oliver frowned as he flopped it open, trying to figure out how to unfold it. "I mean… I've seen maps on posters. Does that count?" He held it up in front of him as he folded out another portion and wrinkled his nose. "There are a lot of lines. How do we know where we are?"

Alex stepped over and folded the map back into a rectangle. "I'll show you later. Right now, let's get what we can out of this place."

His shoes crunched glass along with everyone else's as they searched for supplies that might have been left behind. Everyone except Ben. The convict just stood in the corner, whispering to himself, periodically continuing to scratch his arms raw. Alex kept Oliver close and kept one eye on Ben while they searched.

"I think we've got everything left here." Alex held up the map. "At least we found one of these. Navigating the countryside hasn't been easy."

"I got three bottles of water." Minnie hugged the bottles to her chest.

Lauren stood up from behind a mess of broken shelving. "And I found a beef jerky stick, a bottle of soda, and a few bags of chips."

Asher was in the garage, but Wyatt and Ned had discovered a can of ravioli and a few chocolate bars.

"Not much here." Wyatt dusted off his hands and straightened his leather vest before scooting his glasses up his nose. He pulled a little notebook and a pen out of an inside pocket of his vest. "Do you have inventory, Mr. Roman? We can make a list of the items we need to find to replenish your supplies." His tattoos and leather somehow didn't clash with his accountant-like vibe.

"We'll take what we can find." Alex had an inventory, but he didn't want to show it to men he barely knew. Their reasons for getting to Boston were on a need-to-know basis, and the equipment in the trailer would bring questions he didn't want to answer. Word that a cure could be around the bend in Boston would only cause a gold rush Alex wasn't sure they could handle. Too many complications were never a good thing, and people always came with complications. Once the cure or a vaccine was found, he'd be the first one to scream it from the rooftops, but until then, he needed to avoid adding problems to his already full plate.

Wyatt nodded thoughtfully. "All right, then. I assume we've stopped early so we can do a little scavenging?"

Alex nodded. "I figured some rest and the chance to resupply would help us get where we're going. The closer we get to the coast, the closer we come to more densely populated areas. Scavenging only gets riskier from here. And we're getting closer to where the sickness first emerged on the east coast. We're going to run into more of it. Notice how everyone we come across is going either south or west? We have to be careful."

"Agreed." Wyatt started scratching his pen on the paper. "Water and shelf-stable foods should be at the top of the list. If you don't mind, we'd like to take a little of those things for ourselves if we can find enough."

"You help us find supplies, we'll split 'em, fair and square," Minnie said.

Asher came in from the entrance to the large garage space. "There are a lot of tools and things left here that I think would come in handy should we break down. I'm going to pick out some essentials." He held up a coiled tube and a hand pump. "I found one of these, too. It's a siphon kit. Should work on the actual pumps out front."

"That's a good find," Wyatt said. "I can siphon as much gasoline as we can fit into the empty gas containers. Maybe we can find a few more containers lying around, too."

"Sounds perfect," Alex said. "Lauren, do you want to go house to house with me to the north? Ned, do you want to take Ben and see what you can find in the homes and businesses to the south?"

"Sure thing," Ned said. "Let's go, Ben. We've got plenty of time."

Minnie put her hands on her hips. "Well, this ain't a place to lay your head. I'm not one to twiddle my thumbs, neither. I'll follow Alex and Lauren, see if we can find an empty house to hole up in overnight. Me and Oliver can spruce up some sleepin' arrangements."

"Looks like we've got a plan." Ned clapped his hands and grinned. "We make a good team. Let's get 'er done."

They split off from there, each one to their assigned tasks, the scavenging teams grabbing backpacks from the RV. Alex led the way to a house across the street that seemed intact from their angle. A walk around revealed no broken windows, and no corpses could be spotted from peeking through the glass. But the doors were locked.

"Let's see if we can get inside without breaking anything. Maybe there's a spare key somewhere?" Alex felt around the top of the doorframe.

Minnie and Lauren felt around in the potted plants, Samson sniffing at the parched bushes and flowers and wagging his tail like they were playing a game, but it was Oliver who tipped over a ceramic frog and found the key. "Dad! Look!" He held out the key proudly.

"Good job, bud." Alex took the key, unlocked the door, and cracked it open, waiting for the telltale stench of dead bodies. The air was stale but otherwise fine, so he stepped inside. "Let me make sure it's all clear."

Just inside, on a long, thin wooden table, a lonely note read:

June Bug,

We waited as long as we could. We had to get your brothers out. Go to Aunt Sue's. See you soon.

Love, Mom and Dad.

A thin layer of dust covered the paper, as it did every surface. The house was otherwise clean, though. Dishes put away, beds made. Whoever had left hadn't left in a hurry. *I'd have waited as long as I could, too, if I'd been waiting for Oliver.*

Alex returned to the front door. "It's all clear. No one's been here in a while."

Minnie took Oliver's hand, and Oliver tugged on Samson's leash. "We'll get set up in here, gather anything that was left behind. You two go on."

Oliver patted his mother's purse; the thing was always slung across his shoulder. "If you find any more chapstick, I'm almost out."

"I'll keep an eye out, but we need to stick to unopened packages only, okay, bud?"

"I know, Dad." Oliver rolled his eyes like Alex had said the most obvious thing in the world.

There goes that preteen spirit. Alex sighed as Oliver plopped down on the couch and groaned a complaint about the heat.

Alex and Lauren headed north. The homes in the little town were mostly spread out on larger lots. There was no sign of life. Death was another matter. Simply cracking open the door to a house with corpses inside was enough to make Alex nearly sick to his stomach. They stayed away from those, moving on quickly.

"This one is good, I think." Alex stepped inside yet another home, Lauren following close behind. It was an open concept floor, the kitchen to the right, the living room area to the left, stairs in the back left corner. Clothes were strewn across the furniture. The fridge door was left half open. The counters were a mess. It was a sharp contrast to the well-kept house they'd first entered. "These people left in a panic," he said as he scanned the counter for anything worth keeping.

Lauren rifled through a cabinet. "Yeah, I hope Mom is finding better supplies than we are. Most of these houses are a mess." She plucked a bag of rice from the back of the cabinet and stuffed it in her bag.

"She's quite capable," Alex said. "If there's something to be found, she'll find it."

"Yeah... I guess she is." Lauren shrugged and stood on tiptoes to move a box of cereal.

"I'm glad you two made up, that you decided to come with us," Alex said.

"Well, she apologized, and it *is* the end of the world." Lauren found a can of okra, making a disgusted face at it before dropping it in her bag.

"I never really got the details on that," Alex said, and then he blushed. *Idiot. You don't know her well enough to be asking.* He tried to back pedal. "I mean, you don't have to tell me. It's not my business. Minnie is just so awesome, and you're awesome, too, and I just thought it was so odd that you were so mad at her, and..." He was talking faster and faster until Lauren stopped what she was doing to throw a flat stare at him. "Sorry," he said. "Never mind."

Lauren shook her head and moved on to the next cabinet. "It's fine. I guess you're like family now. It'll eventually come out, and it's not a secret." She turned around and leaned against the counter. "Mom always told me from the time I was little that I could be anything, a doctor, a lawyer, the freaking President of the United States." She crossed her arms and frowned.

"That doesn't sound so bad," Alex said.

"Well, I wanted to follow my passion for music, and when she said I could do anything, what she meant was I could do anything as long as it was sure to make good money. She had it hard most of her life, and she didn't want that for me." Lauren shook her head. "We fought about it all the time. I ended up studying medicine because it was what she wanted, but I dropped out during my residency. I didn't want to be a slave to my career. I didn't love it. I could barely tolerate it. I should have never studied medicine in the first place. I lied to myself for a long time because I knew Mom would never accept what I wanted. Residency shook me to the core, though. I realized just how much I wanted to be a musician, an artist, and not a doctor."

"So... what happened when you told her?" Alex leaned forward.

"She cut me off completely. I guess she thought it would make me go back to the residency. She thought I was ruining my life." Lauren's eyes glistened. "Music made me happy. And then I met my fiancé, and I was even happier. Eventually, she tried to come back into my life, but at that point, I was so angry with her for cutting me off in the first place that I never let her back in."

"Wow. That's nuts." Alex rubbed the back of his neck. "I'm sorry that happened."

"Me too." Lauren turned back to the cabinets. "Maybe keep that between us, though. One day, I think we'll have to dredge it back up and maybe deal with some of the details, but for now... things are good. I don't want to mess that up."

"Of course. I won't say a word." Alex went back to the island, dumping a small pack of batteries from a drawer into his bag. Then, a flyer on the countertop caught his attention. A glass was tipped over on top of it, and it was smeared and crinkled as if water had pooled on it and then dried. He frowned and moved the glass, carefully unsticking it from the countertop. "Lauren..." He looked at her, a spark of hope flaring up inside. "We've got a change of plan."

Chapter 29

Timothy Peters

Timothy had never seen so many fireworks in one place. The lobby of New Horizons was full of crates marked with black lettering indicating they were dangerous. "Where did you get all of these?"

"I found the big ones in a city warehouse. I'm pretty sure they were for the Fourth of July show," Theodore said as he pulled on some jeans. "The smaller ones I bought in New Hampshire months ago. I was pretty excited about that roman candle. It was the biggest I thought I could get away with, living out in the country."

"Because they're illegal?" Candice quirked an eyebrow. "You were going to have an illegal fireworks show?"

"I mean, could you really call it a show?" Theodore shrugged. "It was just going to be for a few neighborhood kids. Roman candles, sparklers, poppers, snakes, smoke bombs... nothing crazy."

"Well, I guess we should be grateful you had a rebellious streak." Heather patted the top of a large wooden crate. "You wouldn't have been able to use one of these to scare off that tiger. You would have just blown us all to bits."

Theodore chuckled. "Well, I do have a degree in molecular biology. I'm not stupid."

"What were you going to do with them, then?" Candice frowned at the crates.

"I don't know." Theodore straightened his lab coat. "But, I wasn't going to leave them in a hot warehouse to explode and proceed to burn down Boston. I thought maybe if good news came over the radio, I could put on a show for survivors."

"Wait..." Timothy straightened up. "I just realized this building is cool."

"You're right," Heather said. "How are you keeping the power on? I didn't hear a generator outside."

"Oh, this building is self-sustaining, to a point." Theodore pointed upward. "Solar panels on the rooftop, top of the line, really efficient. They give me enough juice to use a few lights every once in a while, keep the building's temperature bearable, and keep the security system intact. That's how I was able to see you in trouble outside. I saw it on the cameras."

"How long have you been here?" Timothy ran his fingers through his hair. Theodore's presence was a lot to process. He apparently worked at New Horizons and knew Timothy's father, recognizing Timothy from some company picnic two years prior.

"I came here with my stuff pretty much as soon as possible. I mean, I had to. You know..." He paused and looked sideways at Heather and Candice before looking back at Timothy and speaking more quietly. "... because of the government project."

"What?" Timothy had no idea what he was talking about.

Theodore grimaced. "Oh, well... if you don't know, I really don't think I can tell you."

Candice rolled her eyes. "As far as we know, the government is pretty much gone. It's at best taking a sabbatical," she said. "It's not like they'd care."

"Oh, they would." Theodore held up his hands and shook his head. "I'm not touching that subject unless I am a thousand percent sure the government is gone. I'm just here to do my work and figure out how to stop what's spreading."

"Stop... wait, what?" Heather stood up straighter.

Timothy's heartbeat skipped in his chest. "Did you just say you might be able to stop what's spreading?"

"Maybe." Theodore shrugged. "I don't know yet. Where is Mr. Peters? I could use his expertise."

"You think *my father* could help you stop this?" Timothy shook his head. "My father is a corporate suit."

"No, your dad built this company with his own two hands. He actually participated in Project—" Theodore cut off, chuckled, and then wagged his finger. "Almost got me. I really can't talk about this anymore. Where is he?"

"I don't know." Timothy's mind was reeling. "He was in St. Louis with my sister and her friend when everything first happened. Last we heard, he'd gotten as far as Indianapolis, but he'd had a heart attack. For all we know, he's dead."

The words came tumbling out of his mouth like he was talking about the weather. He'd gotten so used to pushing thoughts of his father out of his mind before the world was ending that after the devastation, that habit was already in place. They hadn't spoken in years until the phone call weeks prior in which his father had told him and the family to lay low and stay inside; his father had known about the curfew before the radio announcement. He'd chalked it up to having government contacts, and Timothy hadn't thought of it since. And Timothy had chosen to tell himself that his father was alive because if he was, Lizzy was alive, too. He was a lot of things, but Walter Peters would never let something happen to his only daughter, his Bethie.

His own admission that his father might be dead rang in his ears. *Am I giving up on them?*

"Well, for all our sakes, let's hope he's not dead." Theodore crossed his arms. "If you don't know about the project, then what are you doing here?"

Timothy let out a long, slow breath as the image of his mother lying dead on the floor, soaked in blood filled his memory. He closed his eyes. "My mom..." He choked on the words. It was so much harder to talk about his mother's death. It was a surety; there was no hope in it, and thinking of it plagued him with horrific images.

Heather stepped forward. "Dana told us that Walter had started putting together a backup shelter here for his family. We don't know how much of the supplies are left. We wouldn't blame you for using them up, but—"

"Whoa, whoa, whoa." Theodore held up his hands. "I haven't used up anything." He nodded toward the hallway. "But I think I know where those supplies might be." He started walking, obviously expecting them to follow.

Timothy squeezed Heather's hand, and they followed after Candice who hadn't hesitated to follow Theodore. They climbed the stairs to the third floor. Most of the lights were turned off, Timothy assumed to save power, but there were a few nightlights to guide them in the otherwise dark halls and stairwell. On the third floor, Theodore led them to a corner office.

"This is your dad's office. He was here maybe a day or two per week, except recently when New Horizons' focuses began to bring in new potential for Vanguard. He started coming in more regularly." Theodore approached the wall of bookcases behind the desk. "I combed this place looking for supplies, and I found something odd behind the books."

"You were looking for supplies behind books?" Candice gave Theodore's back a flat stare and then raised her eyebrows at Timothy and Heather, mouthing the words, "Do you believe him?"

Heather shrugged, and Timothy rolled his eyes. *What, now she's Nancy Drew?*

Theodore didn't miss a beat as he removed a stack of books and turned around to set them on the table. "These are survival books." He held up the top book titled, *Off the Grid.*

"I guess books *can* be great supplies." Timothy spoke to Theodore but threw a glance at Candice.

Theodore set the book back on the desk and then turned back to the empty spot on the shelf. "When I pulled them off, I noticed a crease in the wood where there shouldn't be." He stepped back to reveal a little panel swung outward to reveal a keypad. "I don't know what, but there is definitely something hidden away behind this bookcase. Until you said something, I assumed it was like a safe for cash or documents, but maybe it's something more."

A rush of excitement made Timothy break into a smile. "That looks like the keypad in the basement!"

Theodore frowned and pointed at the ground. "I don't think there's a basement here."

"No," Timothy said. "My parents had a bunker, and the entrance was in the basement." He stepped around the desk and began to press the buttons. "Let's try the same code from the bunker."

A click and the soft grinding of metal sounded when Timothy entered the last number. The bookcase moved just slightly, and with a light tug on the right side, it swung open like a door. Behind it, there was a concrete stairway leading downward. Small, recessed lights in the ceiling lit up near the top of the stairs.

"Tim," Heather said, "did we just find a second bunker?"

"I shouldn't be surprised," Candice said, her tone breathy. "But I didn't expect that."

"Your dad is my hero." Theodore stepped over the threshold and descended, the lights coming to life as he passed. He stopped a few steps down and looked back at them. "Are we going to check out the Batcave or what?"

Timothy nodded and took the first step. *This could be exactly what we need to stay under the radar during the war between the BPD and the Russos.* Four sets of footsteps slapped against the concrete of dozens of steps, descending into what was surely a basement. Timothy's heart raced as they neared the bottom. *We can build on whatever my dad started, add to the supplies. We can—*

He stepped into the light of a very large, very empty concrete room.

Theodore's shoulders sagged. "Bummer."

Heather turned around in a circle, scanning the entire area. "There's nothing here."

Candice pointed. "What about those knobs?" She hurried over to the wall and slid back a metal panel.

Timothy followed after her, hoping for something useful. "It's a security feed." A series of screens were embedded behind the panel.

"Same feed as the one upstairs," Theodore said from over their shoulder.

"Dana thought there would be more than this." Heather hugged herself.

Timothy walked back into the center of the room. He'd not expected much, but it looked like all his father had had time to do was create the foundation for a second bunker.

"I mean, it's probably safe, though, right?" Candice asked. "That's better than nothing."

"There's hardly anyone left in the whole world," Theodore said. "What are we going to need a safe room for?"

"War," Timothy said. "We're going to need it because by this time next week, Boston is going to be a war zone."

"And there *are* still people out there," Heather said. "Without a societal structure, there's enough people to pose a threat."

"Well, you guys are the first people I've seen in weeks," Theodore said. "I mean, I haven't really been anywhere, but still… the radio has been silent, and I've been glued to those security cameras."

"That's a good thing," Timothy said, "it means this area is probably farther away from any of the survivor camps. Less people means we'll be safer."

"Tim," Candice said, "we don't have weapons or food or water here… at least not enough for six people."

"Six people?" Theodore took a step back. "What I gathered was for *me*. And also, there are only three of you. With me, that makes four."

Heather waved off Theodore's comments. "We'll be coming back here with two kids."

"And this is my father's building," Timothy said. "Which means it's mine now. You can stay, but we're sharing supplies."

"What?" Theodore shook his head. "No way. I've been living here on my own for weeks."

"We'll help find food," Heather said. "And weapons and water. Once things get nasty, you'll not want to be on your own, anyway."

"You leave here, and I lock the doors." Theodore crossed his arms. "I won't let you back in."

"You can't do that!" Timothy stepped up to Theodore, toe-to-toe.

Though Timothy wasn't usually an intimidating guy, Theodore was smaller and even more wiry. Still, the man puffed out his chest. "Can't I? I saved your life from that tiger, and this is the thanks I get?"

Heather stepped up and put a gentle hand on Timothy's arm. "Babe, let's settle this cordially, okay?" She looked at Theodore. "Look, we can work together. It'll be better that way. And what if Walter Peters does show up? You really want him to find out that you turned away his son and his daughter-in-law?"

Theodore wavered for a moment, but then he set his jaw. "There are other buildings right across the lot."

"They aren't equipped with solar panels and a safe room." Timothy tensed further and balled his hands into fists.

"I need to be able to concentrate on my work," Theodore said. "You can't just barge in here and—"

"I had the sickness." Candice shouted. "I had it, and I recovered."

Timothy swung around to look at Candice, his eyes wide. They had agreed, for Candice's safety, not to bring that up.

Heather shook her head. "Candice, don't—"

"That's impossible." Theodore stepped away from Timothy and toward Candice.

Candice stuck out her chin stubbornly. "It happened. My skin used to be taught and smooth like a baby's bottom. My eyelids are all droopy now." She moved her braid so that it no longer covered her neck and began to rub furiously at the spot where the welt had been when she'd first been infected. "The skin is still flaky and healing where that welt was. See?"

"Is she telling the truth?" Theodore didn't take his eyes off of Candice. "If so, she could be very helpful in my work."

Timothy met Heather's eyes with his own. He didn't know what to do, and he certainly didn't like the way Theodore was looking at Candice, like she was some perfectly cooked steak served up for dinner. *I can't believe I'm feeling protective of Candice.* He cleared his throat and moved to step in front of her. "She's not a guinea pig."

Theodore sucked in a breath. "So it's true." He rubbed his hand over his face. "Okay," he said. "I won't fight you. You can stay here, and we can work together, no problem, if you agree to let me test her."

Candice scoffed and slapped Timothy's arm, motioning for him to get out of her way. She stomped up to Theodore and poked a finger in his face. "If you ever try to make a deal about me and my body without my consent, I'll wring your neck. Capisce?"

Theodore nodded furiously, excitement shining in his eyes as he did a poor job of hiding his smile. "Yeah, okay. Fine. Whatever you want. If you agree to testing."

"If you think you can find a cure or a vaccine to this thing by poking and prodding me, and you hand over the codes to the building, and you promise to play nice with my friends, I'm in." Candice crossed her arms.

"I think I love you." Theodore made to throw his arms around Candice, but she batted him away.

"I don't think so," she said. "No touching unless I approve first."

"You got it." Theodore clapped his hands together. "Should we get started?"

"What?" Candice's mouth dropped open.

"We're not staying," Heather said. "We're coming back after we get the kids we told you about. It's going to be a few days."

"She shouldn't be going anywhere." Theodore shook his head. "She's too important. If she dies, the answers die with her."

"I'm quite attached to one of the kids," Candice said. "My little blueberry is in danger right now, and I'm not going to let anyone stop me from being part of her rescue." She stomped passed him and started up the stairs.

Theodore's mouth opened and closed, and he began to object. "But—"

Heather narrowed her eyes at him. "She's survived this long. We won't let anything happen to her." She followed Candice up the stairs.

Timothy made to go upstairs, too, but Theodore stopped him with a hand on his arm. "Surely you see how ludicrous that is? DV-10 has become far more than anyone could have expected. It wasn't meant—"

"Wasn't meant?" Timothy did a double take. "What are you talking about? DV-10? You've got a name for it?"

"Uh… yes… I had to name it something." Theodore stammered over his words and stepped back, rolling his shoulders like he was trying to relax. It wasn't working. His forehead was furrowed, his movements stiff.

"Did you *expect* this disease? Did you know it was coming?" Timothy's eyes widened, and it clicked. "Did my father know?"

"Well… I mean… I can't really talk about this." He scurried by Timothy, headed for the stairs.

Something visceral came over Timothy, and he snatched the back of Theodore's lab coat, flinging him backward so that he fell on the ground. Timothy stalked forward. "Answer my questions. Right. Now." He stood over Theodore, leaned over, grabbed him by the scruff of his shirt and roughly pulled his face closer.

"I can't—"

"You can be afraid of a government who probably doesn't know you're still alive and may not be in existence at all, or you can be afraid of me." He slammed Theodore back to the ground, straddled him, and drew back a fist.

"We knew it existed, but we thought it was secure." Theodore threw up his arms to cover his face.

"How did you know?" Timothy growled.

"It was created here, okay? We created it." Theodore's voice had turned to a high-pitched whine. "I'm sorry. It wasn't supposed to get out. That strain… it was supposed to have been destroyed."

Timothy shoved Theodore away, stood, and backed away. His lungs were on fire as he tried to catch his breath, and his limbs tingled, on the verge of going numb. "Vanguard created this sickness?" Timothy backed away. "My father…" He couldn't complete the thought. "Why?"

"It was a government contract." Theodore sat up, gingerly touching his chest and neck. "But Vanguard didn't release it. And what's out there now is worse than DV-10 should be. The way it spreads… I think it has something to do with the mosquitos evolving outside the lab. Or whoever released it, maybe they altered the mosquitos or DV-10 or both."

Timothy's heartbeat thrashed in his ears. His chest was getting tighter by the second as he tried to process what was being said. His hands trembled, and heat crept up his neck onto his cheeks. Shame seeped into his bones, and his stomach lurched.

"Babe?" Heather's voice sounded from behind.

Timothy turned to see Heather stooping below the ceiling on the staircase. "Everything okay?"

The urge to hide the ugliness of what he'd learned took over, and Timothy forced a smile. "Yeah. Everything's fine. We'll be right up." He swallowed bile. *We don't lie to each other.* But he couldn't tell her. It was for her own good. *Knowing won't do any good. He's probably dead, anyway. Nothing we do can change what's been done.*

Heather frowned, but she nodded and went back up the stairs. He waited until her footsteps receded, and then he turned on Theodore, who had gotten to his feet and was brushing himself off. The man flinched and backed up, hands raised in surrender, as Timothy advanced.

"This stays between us." Panic coursed through Timothy's body, but he channeled it into something like a growl. *If people found out, my family would be ostracized. I can't let that happen.* "If you ever tell another soul, I'll kill you." As the words left his mouth, Timothy believed them; he'd meant them as an empty threat, but a part of himself that he'd buried back in college was rearing its ugly head. It had always been there, the potential to be like his father, but he'd tried so hard to never let that side of him out.

Your father would have told me the same thing… I heard his voice in your words. His mother's words from weeks prior, when they'd been preparing the house against Frank's inevitable attack, resurfaced. He'd sworn he was nothing like his father, and yet even Heather had said she'd seen Walter in him. *You're what your father could have been, and he's what you could become.*

"I swear," Theodore said, his voice quivering, "I won't say anything. I shouldn't have said anything to you in the first place. If the wrong people come knocking, it's best they don't know I revealed the project, anyway."

Timothy nodded once and stepped aside, nodding toward the stairs. Theodore sprinted toward them, and Timothy watched him go. When he was out of sight, his breathing turned shaky. He wanted to scream, but he held it in. He'd lied to Heather. He was going to lie to her again.

It's for the best. To protect everyone involved. He wiped the sweat off his forehead. Besides, I have more immediate concerns.

He had a place to retreat, to flee the coming conflict. All he had to do was rescue George and Annika and get them all back to New Horizons. He could make sure that his family survived. Timothy pushed out everything else — his grief, his shame, his fear — and put everything he had into the next step, and then the next, until all that remained was pure determination.

Chapter 30

Alexander Roman

"You sure about this?" Ned's features pinched as he read the flyer. "Flemington, New Jersey?"
Alex pointed at the paper. "A *National Guard Armory* in Flemington. It says right here, 'Need help? We're trained for this!'"
Ned frowned as he read. "Shelter, provisions packages, medical attention, a hub of information. Rescue missions into NYC and surrounding area." He sighed and folded the flyer, handing it back to Alex. "I'm not sure about this."
"It's only a little more than an hour away," Alex said. "We can drive up there and drop you off close enough to walk to the armory. You boys can join a rescue mission into NYC for safe passage. Or maybe they've heard something about a maniac serial killer. Either way, they're better equipped to help you from here than we are."
Wyatt craned his neck to see the paper. "There are no dates on here. How probable is it that this armory is still operational? Things change quickly these days."
Asher scratched his head. "Why drop us off? Don't you guys need to restock, too?"
Minnie snorted. "This ain't our first rodeo. We ain't goin' near a place like that with our trailer and the RV." She looked down at Samson, who lay at her feet. "Isn't that right, boy?" He stood on all fours and looked up at her, wagging his tail.
Alex threw Minnie a subtle glare. *I'm trying to get them to go. Dropping them at this armory will save us at least a day!* He didn't want to get any closer to New York City than he had to, either.
He turned his attention back to the bikers. "You four have nothing to lose," Alex said. "The problem we had in the past was showing up with a bunch of valuables. You should be perfectly safe. And we don't need to restock if it's just the four of us again." Samson barked, and Alex shrugged. "Fine. The five of us." He scratched the dog's ears.
Lauren crossed her arms. "Mom is right. I mean, how can you even consider going near a military base? The last time we encountered a *hub* like that, we almost lost everything, including our lives."
"A National Guard Armory isn't a base. It's completely different," Alex said. "We'll drop them off far enough from the armory that they won't even know we were there."
"What if there are bad guys there?" Oliver looked with concern at the burly bikers. "We can't leave them there if we don't know it's safe."
Ned reached out and put a hand on Oliver's head. "Don't worry, little man. We can take care of ourselves."
"I gotta disagree. Little man makes a good point." Asher shook his head. "If it's not legit, and you guys leave us there, we'd be stranded. We were thinking you were going to drop us a lot closer to the city. Not smack dab in the middle, but the outskirts at least."
"We can hide out at a distance from the armory, then," Alex said. "One of you come back to the RV in the morning once it's safe. We'll wait for you to confirm everything is fine before leaving the area."
Ned looked like he was about to agree when Ben let out a whine. "Nope, nope, nope. They could lie to us," Ben said. "They could leave us. I'm not going."
"He's right, too." Asher shrugged at Alex. "Sorry, man, but I don't know you."
"I think we can trust him," Ned said. "He trusted us, didn't he?"
Wyatt shook his head. "I'm with Asher."
"Okay. I get it," Alex said. "How about I go with you? Minnie, Lauren, Oliver, and the dog can stay in the RV somewhere safe and a good distance from the armory. We can drive there now, find a hiding spot. I'll go with you to the armory, make sure it's all good to go, and I'll return. If we leave now, we should have plenty of time. It's what… one o'clock? We get there at two-thirty. That gives us four or five hours to confirm the armory is safe and to get me back to the RV."
Ned scrunched his shoulders and raised his eyebrows at his friends. "C'mon, guys. He's really tryin' here."
Wyatt pushed his glasses up his nose. "Those arrangements are satisfactory."
Asher made a fist and pointed at Wyatt with his thumb. "What he said."
Ben was off in his own little world again. He'd stepped several steps back, and he was shaking his head in quick, small motions, but he wasn't even looking at them. He was looking at nothing and mumbling at no one.
"You still haven't convinced *us*," Lauren said.
Alex pressed his lips together and glanced at the bikers. To convince Lauren and Minnie, he'd need to address their concerns as related to their previous experience in Atlanta. He wasn't sure they could do that without revealing too much about who they were and what they were doing. The last thing he wanted was to dredge up questions.
Maybe I can trust the bikers. His eyes landed on Ben who was chewing on his nails, mumbling incoherently, eyes darting over to nothing every few minutes. That dark grin no one else had seen after they'd found those butchered men surfaced in Alex's memory. He shuddered. *Yeah… I'm not telling him anything.*
Alex held up a finger. "Hold on a sec, Ned. We've got some personal business to discuss." He took Oliver by the hand, gestured for Minnie and Lauren to follow him, and crossed the lot. Once situated out of easy earshot, he kept his voice low just in case. "Guys, if we go in as nobody, if we have nothing, there's no danger. Most people in Atlanta were just sent to the dorms where they were provided for."
Minnie put one hand on her hip. "Except for the lab rats, you mean?"

"They don't have labs like that at the National Guard. They train for disaster relief and have drill weekends. It's very likely that this flyer is accurately depicting the situation. National Guard members live and work in their communities. It makes sense that survivors would rally there and offer search and rescue." Alex put a hand on Minnie's shoulder. "This is what we need, a place to drop off our guests where they'll have provisions and maybe even get a little help in their search. And then we can go on our way, having paid them back for their kindness."

Oliver looked up at Alex. "So… this is what's best for Ned?"

Alex nodded. "Sure, bud. It's best for everyone."

Lauren glanced at Oliver and then back at Alex. "What if something… you know… *happens* to you? We shouldn't separate."

Her attempt at talking over Oliver's head didn't work. He moved closer to Alex, looking up at him with big eyes. "I don't want to separate from you, either."

Alex knelt beside his son and looked him in the eyes. "It's safer for you if you stay hidden. I'll be fine. I'll get in and come out. If the flyer is telling the truth, I'll even come back with some supplies. I'll only be gone for a few hours."

"And if you're gone longer?" Minnie asked.

Alex sighed and stood up, rubbing the back of his neck. "I should make it back before curfew, but if I'm not back in three days max, leave the area." Oliver gasped and hugged Alex's waist tight. He patted his son's back. "But that's *not* going to happen."

Lauren shook her head. "You're too important, Alex. This entire road trip is to get *you* to Boston. If the bikers need assurance we won't leave them stranded in a bad situation, I should be the one to go, not you."

"No." Alex cut the air with his hand. "I'm not sending a woman alone into an unknown situation, no matter how safe it seems, with three bikers and a convict who might be nuts."

Lauren narrowed her eyes, crossed her arms, and met his eyes with her own. "I'm not sending a single father and the man who could possibly *save the damn world* alone into that same situation." She raised her eyebrows, her lips forming a thin, determined line.

"As I live and breathe," Minnie said, "I've never seen two people more stubborn. The both of you go, and I'll stay hidden in the RV with Oliver."

"Fine." Lauren held out her hand for Alex to shake. "I'm good with that."

Alex sighed and shook her hand. "You Stevens women are impossible to argue with, especially when you're on the same page."

"Thank you," the two ladies said in unison.

Alex shook his head, but he couldn't help but smile. He'd come to care about both of them, and even if they'd ganged up on him, Alex wouldn't change who they were for anything. He had never felt alone in helping his son deal with the grief of losing his mother, and he would never be able to repay Minnie and Lauren for that.

They hadn't unpacked much, so it only took them a few minutes to load up the meager supplies they'd found and get back on the road, headed to Flemington. A little more than an hour later, they were driving through farmland, searching for a spot to hide the RV. There were hand-painted signs along the main roads directing people toward the armory. Alex veered off onto the smallest country roads going in slightly the wrong direction to avoid running into travelers. Withering, yellowed fields that had gone thirsty for too long stretched out on either side. About fifteen minutes into the middle of nowhere, Lauren spoke up.

"Hey! What about that?" Lauren tapped the window from the backseat.

Alex stopped the vehicle and glanced at a burned-out husk of a brick house surrounded by a small outcropping of trees and overgrown foliage, at least a half mile off the road. The driveway was overgrown with weeds, and vines snaked up the house, bright green against black. "That looks like it's been abandoned for a lot longer than a matter of weeks. I didn't even see it before you pointed it out."

"Exactly." Lauren beamed. "It's perfect. It kind of blends in, right?"

"It looks haunted," Oliver said.

Minnie chuckled. "I suppose it does. I'd bet my bottom dollar no one would think to look there for supplies."

"Let's go check it out." Alex pulled down the drive, the vehicle and trailer bumping mercilessly on the unkempt gravel road riddled with potholes. He inched along slowly to avoid damage.

"Pull around back," Minnie said. "Let's see if there's any way to hide this hulk of metal."

Alex drove around and found the back of the brick house completely missing. The front and sides still stood, though the walls were blackened and crumbled. But the inside of the house was gone, the debris cleared away and nature allowed to take its course. All that remained was a concrete slab with weeds growing through the cracks. It looked as if someone had begun the demolition after a house fire years ago but never finished it. Trees and bushes and vines made a perfect veil drawn across the front and sides of the house. More trees lined the yard, separating the little plot of land from the corn fields.

"If we park back here, no one will be able to see," Lauren said.

Alex pulled into the middle of the house and parked. "I guess we'd better get walking. We're about five miles from the armory."

He hopped out of the cab and stretched, squinting at the bright summer sunshine. The bikers and the convict stepped out of the RV, each one with the loaded backpacks they'd brought. Ned approached Minnie as Alex was nearby giving Oliver a hug goodbye. He held out a handgun, grip first.

"What in Sam Hill?" Minnie put her hands on her hips.

Ned blushed. "If you're stayin' with the kid, I think you should have it. Just in case. Wyatt and Asher both have one. We'll be fine."

"I can't take your gun," Minnie said. "What if you get separated from the others in the big city?"

Alex gave Oliver one last squeeze and approached. He held out his hand, and Ned handed the gun to him. "Thank you, Ned." He gave it to Minnie, and she reluctantly accepted it. "We could use a gun down the road, Minnie. And I'd feel better knowing you've got some way to defend yourself should someone discover this place."

"Oh, all right." Minnie's eyes glistened as she looked up at the big biker. "You've got gumption, Ned. And integrity. It was a blessin' to know you."

Ned's blush deepened. He cleared his throat and slipped his Zippo lighter out of his vest, clicking it open and closed, like he just couldn't accept a compliment like that without hiding behind something to do. "Well, thank you, but I'm just doin' what I think the good Lord would want."

"I know," Minnie reached up and patted his upper arm. "You keep at it," she said. "The world needs good people right now."

Oliver walked up to the biker. "I'll miss you, Ned." He threw his arms around Ned's waist, and the biker's eyes glistened.

"You're a good kid, Oliver." He knelt in front of him and handed him the Zippo. "Hey, why don't you hold onto this for me? Being able to start a fire can be the difference between life and death sometimes, kid. I've got another one at home, but... I think I'd like you to have this one to remember me by."

Oliver's eyes brightened. He looked back at Alex. "Dad? Can I?"

Alex nodded. "Go ahead. But don't try to use it yet. Maybe Minnie can teach you how while we're gone."

"Promise." Oliver put the Zippo in his mother's purse at his hip.

"All right, now stop dawdlin'. You should be gettin' on the road." Minnie shooed Ned and Alex. "You're burnin' daylight, now, go on!"

Lauren stepped out of the RV with her own backpack, tightening the straps as she went. She gave Minnie and Oliver hugs goodbye, and Alex joined her as she followed the bikers and Ben back toward the road. They all walked quickly, sometimes jogging to cut down on travel time.

The road was lined with trees most of the time, and wherever there was evidence of society, there was also evidence of destruction. Homes that sat just yards off the road were burnt or broken into or marked with a red circle with a line through the center. A few of the homes had mounds of dirt in the center of their lawns, wooden crosses at their heads, some labelled with names, others left without.

Eventually they came to a crossroads. Homes and restaurants were clustered there, about a dozen that Alex could see from the center of the intersection. A few of the buildings were little more than burnt rubble, and several more had been looted. But there was a larger building — plain off-white stucco with black awnings — left unscathed. Painted on the side of the building between two windows were the words:

If you hear a hum,
it's time to run!
No need to fear.
Hide in here.

Ned stopped and looked back at Alex. "Remember them swarms I was tellin' you about? That's what they're talking about."

Alex frowned and studied those words as Ned and the rest studied the map against the instructions on the flyer. It's so prevalent here that they have temporary shelters set up. If it gets this bad everywhere... how will any of us survive?

It was clear in the lab in Atlanta that the disease itself had been altered using CRISPR, and the more he thought about it, the more he was leaning toward the possibility that the mosquitos themselves were *also* modified. Their quick breeding, overt aggression, the distance they seemed to roam, and the new behavior of swarming to attack *could* have been a natural evolution, but that was much less likely than human intervention.

He had told Lauren and Minnie about the marks of CRISPR on the disease's genome, but he'd not brought his newer suspicions to light yet. *I can't spread misinformation. I need more proof. I need to study the mosquitos themselves.* It was his suspicion at first that his former boss, Dr. Jonah Newton, sent Alex to Mr. Peters because of Vanguard's work and extensive studies on mosquito species. But after the warning that Peters wasn't to be trusted... *Peters could have had something to do with this. The whistleblower was from the government. What if Vanguard was the company commissioned to carry out the research? Their humanitarian projects would be the perfect cover for a secret bioweapon project like this.*

He shuddered and breathed out the words: "I still can't believe it."

Lauren walked up beside him. "Believe what?"

"That we did this to ourselves." He shook his head. "Human beings orchestrated this."

"Does that really surprise you?" Lauren scoffed. "I'm shocked we didn't kill ourselves off sooner."

Alex couldn't argue with that. "Which way are we going?"

Lauren shrugged. "Ned's lost, and we all miss GPS."

The door to the stucco building swung open, the screech of hinges making Alex jump. The two bikers with guns pulled them and aimed. Ned roughly put the map away and took several steps toward Alex and Lauren while keeping his eye on the door, a protective aura to his advancement. Alex held up his hand against the bright sunlight to find a man in camo fatigues with his hands up.

"I'm just coming out to give you directions," the man said. "I'm with the National Guard. You looking for the armory?"

Ned nodded at his companions, and they holstered their weapons. "Sorry about that," he said to the soldier. "We found a flyer. We *are* lookin' for the armory. We were hopin' to participate in some of the search and rescue missions into New York City."

The man did not put his hands down but rather maintained a calm, open posture. "You've got people in the city?"

"Something like that," Ned said. "We're lookin' for someone."

"Well, I'm telling you right now, they'll let you take the guns with you into the city, but they'll make you check them in at the door. You won't be allowed to carry inside the facility. If you're okay with that," the man slowly pointed south, "go down to the next intersection and then turn left. You're about a mile from the armory."

"Thank you, sir," Ned said. "And thank you for serving."

The man lowered his hands and nodded in acknowledgement. "Be safe out there. I haven't heard about any swarm sightings over comms, so you should be good to go."

Ned led the way as they followed the soldier's instructions, and Alex picked up his pace in unison with the bikers. They turned where instructed and soon found two armored vehicles blocking the road. A man and a woman, both in uniform, exited one of the vehicles.

"I was starting to think we'd not have anyone come today." The man smiled at them but held out his hand. "My name is Vince, and this is Amy. We're happy to meet you, but if you could stop right there, we'd appreciate it."

Alex stopped at the rear of their group and observed. Ned was leading this expedition, and Alex wasn't going to butt in unless he had to.

"We're all healthy," Ned said.

"We hope so." Amy sounded sincere. "We're still going to need you to quarantine for four hours. There's a house across from the armory that makes for a good quarantine spot. It's been kept up and stocked with food and water, so you should be good for the night. Unfortunately, you'll need to stay there longer since curfew is just in a couple hours."

"There's some card games and board games under the coffee table," Vince said. "If you want, you're free to follow us. If you know of another shelter you can reach or you'd rather pass on through, we'd be happy to escort you across the premises to our southern perimeter. If you stay with us, any weapons on your person need to be removed now and checked in. You will get them back any time you exit the premises."

"We're hopin' to join you on a search and rescue mission into the city," Ned said. "We're lookin' for a serial killer by the name of Jesse King. We'd like to bring him back to the prison he escaped from."

The two soldiers raised their eyebrows and looked at each other. "That's a new one," Amy said. "You law enforcement?"

"Just some guys tryin' to do the right thing," Ned said. "King came from our neck of the woods in North Carolina. He killed my brother, and when I heard he was coming to New York City, I had to come after him."

"If he's in our neck of the woods now," Vince said, "then we're glad to have you. We'd be happy to assist you in any way we can."

"Yeah, the last thing we need around here is a serial killer." Amy visibly shuddered. "But for now, how about getting that quarantine over with?"

"We'll be ready for that in just a moment." Ned whispered something to Asher and Wyatt. The two bikers nodded, and the three of them looked back at Alex and Lauren. "These people seem top notch. We feel comfortable with you two goin' on back."

Alex nodded. "Well, I'm glad we got to know each other, Ned. Asher, Wyatt, you, too." He eyed Ben, who had kept quiet and made the trek in a trance, whispering to himself as he kept up with Ned. Alex swallowed his discomfort with the convict one last time, glad he'd never have to see the man's face again.

Lauren smiled. "We wish you all the best of luck."

Alex waved to the soldiers. "We'll be headed back, actually," he said. "We just wanted to see our friends to safety. We've got other plans."

"Are you sure?" Vince asked. "You don't need anything? Would you like a supply pack, at least? We can give you each a small bag of canned goods, two water bottles, a pack of Band-Aids, and a tube of anti-bacterial cream. It's not much, I know, but we're trying to assist everyone as much as we can."

"Yeah," Alex said. "That would be great if you've got it."

Amy jogged to the back of the vehicle. Asher and Wyatt handed over their weapons, and they started to follow Vince between the vehicles and on to quarantine. Amy came back, two plastic sacks in either hand. Alex met her halfway, and as she handed him the sacks, the walkie talkie at her hip crackled to life.

A voice filled the air, speaking between gasps of breath as if the person were running and hyperventilating at the same time. "Swarm spotted. Half a klick west. Headed our way."

Alex stared at the device, his blood running cold. It seemed for that moment they were all frozen in time. And then, Amy broke into a whirlwind of action. She turned on her heel and sprinted back to the vehicle, shouting over her shoulder. "Go with your friends! We've got six minutes, tops!"

"Let's go, let's go, let's go!" Vince shouted as he, too, broke into a run. Ned, Asher, Wyatt, and Ben followed.

Alex cursed as his heart lodged in his throat, and he dashed after the bikers, Lauren at his side.

Chapter 31

Lizzy Peters

Time felt different in the grey, concrete room with nothing but a cot, a bedpan, and a side table with a speaker that would play Mother Autumn's soothing voice. Lizzy drifted in and out of sleep, every movement taking more effort than the last. Her hunger was just a dull ache, which was better than the sharp gnawing pain of the first several days, but she was so tired. She'd had nothing to eat since being brought to her concrete jail. She'd been given water and tea in intervals, but not enough to stave off dizziness, exhaustion, a dry mouth, and cracking lips.

She'd thought perhaps they would leave her alone after they'd allowed her to bathe, but twice since, she'd been strapped to a chair and subjected to terrible images, headphones clamped over her ears to deliver the screaming of a dying Mother Earth, flashes of men in suits mingling with the destruction.

Sleep was full of nightmares, and she couldn't avoid it, no matter how hard she tried. The men from the video were always in her dreams, her father among them. They tortured her and laughed at her weaknesses. Zara was there, too, in the worst nightmares. She would stand by and watch, expression flat, looking right through her, not even flinching at her pain. And so, Lizzy struggled to avoid sleep, staring blankly at the wall, her back to the door, inevitably failing only to jerk awake to the nightmare of her prison.

The sound of metal sliding against metal, a click, and a soft whine of hinges announced someone entering the room. Lizzy tensed but didn't look to see who it was, muscles freezing from head to toe. She sucked in a deep breath, balled her hands into fists, and curled her body in on itself. Lizzy waited, heart thumping, her pulse taking over her body, immersing her in evidence that she was still alive, reminding her that she was fragile. All thought and emotion melted into the *thrum* for several wonderful, empty moments.

And then a scratchy, black sack was pulled over her head at the same moment that many sets of hands grabbed hold of her. She let them take her without so much as a word of protest. Her throat was too dry for speaking, anyway. They set her upright, and her legs wobbled when she tried to put her weight on them. The hands didn't let go, lending her support.

At least they're helping me. Lizzy followed the guidance of those hands. They weren't rough once it was clear she would comply. *Be good, and it will be fine. Azalea will come, eventually.*

Twists and turns led to an incline, and then a staircase. Another door opened, and something Lizzy wasn't sure she'd ever experience again washed over her: fresh air, a breeze, gentle sunlight on her exposed skin. She gasped and then laughed at the pleasure of the summer air filling her senses. There was a garden nearby, livestock, too. Earthy, sweet scents of nature filled her with joy.

They walked over flat, hard ground until another set of steps greeted her. These, she guessed, were wooden as they bowed beneath her weight. She licked her lips, anticipating the moment they would remove the sack from her head. Little dots of sunlight penetrated the cloth, teasing her with the promise of daylight.

Tight restraints tied her to a pole of some sort. She could feel it through the back of her shirt, the texture uneven and roughly cylindrical. It pressed against her back as the ropes secured her, but they'd tied her down before. That wouldn't be the worst of whatever waited for her, but for some reason, she could only revel in the experience of being outside again. There was no fear of what they would do to her. Azalea will come. A calmness she didn't understand filled her up. Even Orion… would he really let something bad happen to me?

Mother Autumn's voice recited the same message in her mind that she'd heard countless times. *You are wanted here, Elizabeth. You belong with us. The Heirs of the Mother love you.*

The cloth bag came off, and Lizzy smiled wide at the blue sky, at the beautiful clouds floating by. It was so quiet, except for the chirping of birds and the rustle of leaves. "It's so wonderful out here," Lizzy whispered.

Orion stepped in front of her, his brow slightly furrowed. "Mother Earth is healing."

"That's good." Lizzy really meant it.

His eyes dropped to a gas mask in his hands. Azalea had said that Orion cried at night, worried for her. *He's never yelled at me, not like my dad. He's always soft spoken. And he does look sad.*

Lizzy wanted to reach out to him, but she was bound too tightly. Instead, she offered him a smile. "What's wrong?"

He took a deep breath. "This one is going to be hard."

Lizzy frowned and looked down, noticing the logs leaning against the platform all around her. "Is this what I think it is? Like… a pyre to burn people alive?" She looked up and looked around. "Where is Azalea?"

"She's not coming." A tear slipped down Orion's cheek, and then he was pressing the gas mask to Lizzy's face, reaching to secure it.

"What?" Lizzy's voice was muffled. "Orion… what are you doing?" Panic reared its head, all sense of calm evaporating.

"What has to be done." The straps yanked strands of her hair as Orion put the mask on her.

"Does Azalea know what you're doing?" Lizzy's voice squeaked. She tugged in vain at the ropes, but only for a few seconds. She was too weak to keep trying. "What about the Mother?"

Orion didn't say anything as he fitted headphones over her ears and retreated back down the steps. She twisted her head, looking for Azalea. Or Autumn. Her gut told her they would never let her die.

Lizzy blinked away tears. It's a test. It's just a test.

Men in taupe, linen clothing gathered in front of the pyre with torches, and Orion lit each one. The men walked slowly to take up positions all around the structure. And then they set fire to it. The sounds of nature were joined by the crackling of wood. A barrage of voices screaming burst from the headphones and filled Lizzy's mind. Images washed over her, images of burning forests, of blackened corpses, and of burned flesh, pink and raw and peeling. Four faces, smiling and smooth shaven and well dressed, joined those images.

"I hate them!" she screamed. "I'm nothing like them!"

The flames licked the platform, rising higher, bringing with them a dry, intense heat. But she could breathe. *The mask… they wouldn't give me a mask if they were going to kill me, would they?*

"Azalea?" Lizzy hoped her muffled voice carried beyond the flames. They were getting too close. "I know you won't let me die. I know this is a test. Mother Earth has been burned, and you want me to experience the fear of fire."

Yes, that's it. That's the test. Lizzy swallowed a lump in her throat. "I understand! You've never failed me, Azalea. Please… Orion? I'm sorry. I'm so, so sorry."

Sweat rolled down her body, and embers burned into her clothes, seeping into her skin, pinpricks of white-hot pain. "Restore the Mother!" She screamed at the top of her lungs, repeating the mantra over and over, letting the words tear at her throat. They were important words. They needed to be heard. They'd saved her before, shown the Heirs that she was worth saving. They'd do it again, she was sure of it.

A white cloud enveloped the pyre as a loud *whoosh* overtook the sound of crackling fire. When the cloud cleared, the same men who had been holding the torches held fire extinguishers, and the pyre was covered in white foam. The men parted, and Azalea stepped through, coming to the edge of the pyre, pride in her eyes.

Orion brought a ladder to where the steps had been and laid it down so that he could use it as a sort of bridge onto the platform. He removed the mask from Lizzy's face with tears in his eyes. "I hold no grudge," he said. "You are one of us."

Lizzy's body trembled as Orion undid the ties. Without the ropes to hold her up, Lizzy collapsed to her knees. Her vision blurred with tears. Orion had to scoop her up in his arms and hand her to another man at the edge of the platform, and that man put her in a wheelchair.

Azalea knelt in front of her. "You're so tired, Elizabeth." She gently brushed away sweaty strands of hair from Lizzy's forehead. "Let's get you cleaned up, okay?" She stood and walked behind the chair to begin rolling Lizzy across the concrete, back toward a steel door set in the side of a hill.

"What about the bag over my head?" Lizzy looked over her shoulder at Azalea.

"I don't think that's necessary anymore." Azalea smiled down at her. "Do you?"

"No." Lizzy relaxed into the chair. "Do I get another bath?"

"You've earned one," Azalea said. "And I think we can move you to a more comfortable room."

"Really?" Lizzy smiled, her heart skipping.

"Yes," Azalea said. "You'll be moving in with me, where you'll be safe and comfortable."

"Thank you." Lizzy's voice caught on the words, gratitude filling her up to bursting. Tears of relief ran unchecked down her cheeks. "I knew you would come for me."

"I will always come for you, Elizabeth." The sincerity in her voice comforted Lizzy. "You are a daughter of the Heirs. My sister, so to speak. Sisters don't abandon each other." She wound Lizzy down a ramp and through the halls.

"I had a friend once who I thought was like a sister to me." Lizzy twisted her fingers together, the memory of Zara knotting her stomach. "I made a mistake, and… she didn't want me around anymore."

Azalea stopped in front of the same bathroom Lizzy had used before. "That doesn't sound like a very good friend." She circled the wheelchair and knelt once again, cupping Lizzy's cheek in her hand. "How many mistakes have you made since coming here? You've lied. You've hurt us with your accusations and assumptions. You've tried to undermine everything we believe in by keeping important information to yourself." Her voice was gentle and knowing, never condescending. Concern and hurt saturated her words. "You've been selfish, Elizabeth, even though we've invited you in. All you had to do was be honest with us."

Lizzy frowned. *Why do I always make the wrong decisions?* "I'm sorry," she said. "I thought… I thought I was doing the right thing."

"But was it?" Azalea asked.

"No." Lizzy shook her head.

"And did I leave you, even after all of that?"

Lizzy smiled. "No."

"Exactly." Azalea stood up and kissed Lizzy's forehead before wheeling her into the bathroom. "Now, do you think you'll be okay on your own in here? Can you stand?"

Lizzy stood, though her balance was a little shaky. "I think I'll be okay."

"Good." Azalea stepped toward the door. "I'll be right outside if you need me."

Lizzy nodded her thanks. Once again, fresh clothes, hot tea, and cool water were waiting for her. A warm bubble bath had already been drawn. She undressed and slipped in, the warm water relaxing her muscles. She sipped the tea, which rested on a bamboo bath tray, but she didn't stay in the bath as long this time.

She was too eager to see her new room. Surely, there will be food now, and plenty of water. And no more screaming.

Exhausted but clean and hydrated, Lizzy dressed in her linen clothing and opened the door to find Azalea sitting with hands folded in a chair by the door.

"That was quick." Azalea stood upon seeing her.

"I didn't want to keep you waiting, and… I'm really tired."

"Of course." Azalea looped her arm in Lizzy's and led her down a series of hallways, *away* from that terrible, barren concrete room she'd been held in before. Every step in the opposite direction was a reassurance that she was doing the right thing.

Azalea's bedroom was simple but comfortable, and Lizzy had a real bed with a fluffy pillow and a wonderfully soft comforter. "What about something to eat?" Lizzy sat on the bed, gingerly touching the clean, fresh linens.

"That will come," Azalea said, "but your fasting period isn't over. Not quite yet."

Panic rose as immediate tears burned Lizzy's eyes. "But… I thought… isn't it over? The testing?"

Azalea sat beside her. "You trust me, don't you?"

Lizzy swallowed a lump in her throat. "Yes."

"You must wait." Azalea took Lizzy's hand in hers.

"But—"

Azalea snatched her hand away. "You are ready to move on, aren't you? I thought you were, but if you can't—"

"I'm sorry." Lizzy grabbed for Azalea's hand, desperate. "I swear, I'm ready."

Azalea smiled and squeezed her hand. "Good. You see, tomorrow, our doctor will be tending to you. You'll get all the ice chips your heart desires. And some mineral tablets to help with the muscle cramping and to prepare you for the feast."

"The feast?" Lizzy perked up at that.

"Oh, yes. Once you've finished your last test, there will be a great feast in your honor." Azalea patted Lizzy's knee.

"One more test?" Lizzy asked, her nerves getting the best of her.

"Oh, this one will be easy, I think." Azalea waved it off. "Don't worry about it. You focus on being strong and start thinking about anything and everything you need to tell us."

"Okay." Lizzy chewed on the inside of her cheek, hoping Azalea couldn't see how nervous the idea made her. Azalea was her guardian angel, her true friend. And yet, Lizzy's heart still snagged on the thought of giving up her father, on putting him or Zara in harm's way.

She snuggled down into the bed, and Azalea turned off the lights. The darkness caused Lizzy's heartrate to skyrocket, though. She squeezed her eyes shut. *It's not the same. Azalea is here. Everything is fine.*

And then there was a click, and a recording began to play. Rustling leaves, soft wind, birds chirping. Lizzy could almost feel the sun on her face. Mother Autumn's voice, gentle and soothing, calmed her heartbeat. "You belong," she said. "You're home."

Lizzy rolled over, and her body relaxed into the mattress. Her eyelids fluttered as she listened, and peaceful sleep wasn't far behind.

Chapter 32

Alexander Roman

Alex bolted in through the front door of the little white house across from the National Guard Armory, and he slammed the door shut behind him, throwing the bolt and securing the chain lock. A layer of sweat covered every inch of his body as he stumbled on shaky legs toward the back of the house. The threat of the swarm and the rush of adrenaline left him trembling, but safety was not sure, yet.

"Look for any other entrances and lock them tight. We don't know who else is out there, who might try to seek shelter here." Alex reached the back door and locked it, too, comforted by Asher's "yes, sir" and the sound of his footsteps toward the entrance from the garage.

Lauren leaned against the counter, breathing deeply to steady herself. "Mom and Oliver…" She pressed her lips together, her face falling a shade paler.

"Minnie is smart," Alex said. "Even if they left the RV to stretch their legs, they wouldn't go beyond that little yard. They know to stay hidden, and the swarm is coming from the opposite direction. They might not even see it."

Lauren nodded in silence, but the color didn't return to her cheeks. Alex wasn't so sure he looked any better. His heartbeat slowed only a fraction, his body only beginning to relax, when he detected the distant, high-pitched hum.

He straightened up. "Do you hear that?"

"Yeah," Lauren whispered. Eyes focused on the direction from which the sound originated, she walked back to the front of the house. Alex followed. Asher and Ned stood in front of the couch, staring across the room at the bay window. Wyatt was a few steps in front of them, short enough to not block their view. Ben was pressed against the front door, standing on tiptoe to look out of the square window there, his fingertips under his chin, drumming the pane lightly as he whispered.

Lauren knelt in front of the bay window, resting her arms on the bench, her chin on her interlaced fingers. Alex sat on his knees beside her, hands resting on his thighs. The view of the road was obscured by a great weeping willow, its long, elegant branches brushing the ground. Small animals flocked to it: squirrels, racoons, cottontails, and small rodents, all disappearing under its dome.

The sound was getting louder by the second, filling him with dread. It seeped into his brain like an anesthetic, slowly numbing his body. Ben's whispers, the unsteady breathing of his companions, and his own thumping heartbeat created a terrifying song that crescendoed as the hum of thousands of mosquitos drowned them out.

The willow tree trembled. Birds scattered, and an erratic, living cloud of blackness seeped through the green. Panicked animalistic shrieks pierced the steady hum. Squirrels scrambled from the curtain of leaves only to be overwhelmed with a black blanket, and when the dark lifted, all that remained was a welt-covered corpse, small and shriveled.

In his line of work, as a disease detective, his colleagues had gone to problem areas in Texas and Louisiana to deal with swarms of mosquitos after hurricanes, to consult on the resulting anemic cases of livestock and ensure the human population protected themselves. Those species didn't tend to carry disease, but they were a problem, nonetheless. Video documentation of these events showed loosely gathered swarms, busily flying in all directions, mindlessly seeking blood.

This swarm was different. As tentacles of tightly knit blackness with specks of bright orange reached for these small creatures trying to escape, Alex couldn't help but see a monster. The swarm overcame the tree in mere moments, the illusion of their oneness broken upon the window as they covered it, causing the rest of the occupants in the room to gasp and step back.

Alex looked closer. They were larger than the average mosquito with an orange diamond on their backs, only visible when one flew away. Their legs and underbellies bore white stripes, like the tiger mosquito, which was a very aggressive species that was not nocturnal. *But the size, the orange coloring… these aren't tiger mosquitos.* "I've never seen anything quite like this."

Wyatt cleared his throat. "You act as if you know a lot about these things. You some kind of insect fanatic?"

"No," Alex said, "a disease detective. I—" He paused and closed his eyes. *And I have a big mouth.* He'd tried so hard not to invite questions about who he was or where he was going. *Well, that cat's out of the bag.* "Mosquitos have long been the deadliest animal on the planet. More than a million people every year die from mosquito-borne illnesses."

Ben rocked back from the window in the door and scratched at his arm. "Breaking records. Breaking all the records. They've killed *way* more than a million this year. Maybe someone should tell them they've met their quota."

Wyatt laughed out loud. Asher groaned, and Ned grimaced. Lauren shook her head, and Alex just stared at the convict. Ben laughed nervously along with Wyatt as if he didn't understand what was so funny.

"This kid," Wyatt said, "he's got a dark sense of humor."

Ned cleared his throat. "So, you're a disease detective? Does that mean you know what's goin' on? Have you ever heard of this sickness?"

Alex shook his head. "No, unfortunately, I have no idea what this disease is or how to fight it. I just know it's new and unusual." *And manmade.*

Wyatt cocked his head to one side and narrowed his eyes. "What—"

"I'm exhausted," Lauren said. "I think we better get to bed. I mean, tomorrow, we all go our separate ways. We've got long journeys ahead of us."

"Separate ways?" Ben's eyes went wide. "We should stay together. We're all friends."

"Ben… the deal was that Alex and Lauren would go back to the RV." Ned rubbed his hand over his face. "Now, I need a bed, preferably in a room with curtains." He shuddered at the bay window where the mosquitos were thinning, the swarm moving in a different direction now that they'd gorged themselves on the available blood.

Wyatt and Asher nodded in agreement, and the three of them headed toward the staircase at the center of the home. Ned put a hand on Ben's shoulder as if to lead him upstairs, but the convict crossed his arms and backed away.

"We're friends," Ben repeated. "We should stay together."

"No," Ned said slowly. "They're goin' back. And you do understand that when this is all over, you'll not be taggin' along everywhere we go?" Ben shook his head, red creeping up his neck, but Ned just gave him a gentle push upstairs. "Let's talk about this later, okay?"

Ben stomped up the stairs with the bikers, and Alex and Lauren followed the group upstairs. There were four bedrooms, each one with a bunkbed. Ben and Asher took one, the convict still fidgety and upset. Wyatt and Ned took another. Alex was about to follow Lauren into the third bedroom when she turned in the doorway and pointed across the hall.

"But… I think we should stay together," Alex said. "We're not sleeping in the same bed. What's the difference between bunkbeds and the cab or the RV?"

"Uh, it's not just the two of us?" Lauren closed the door halfway. "Besides, this is my one shot at having a room all to myself for who knows how long."

Alex sighed. "Okay, well if you need anything—"

Lauren rolled her eyes. "I know where you are."

She shut the door, and the telltale click of a lock provided Alex with some assurance she'd be safe. He didn't expect any of the bikers to do anything untoward, but it was better safe than sorry. And also, there was still Ben, and although no one else seemed leery of him, Alex had that devilish grin of his stuck in his memory forever. He turned toward his room, stopping to listen to the muffled arguments of the convict in the bedroom adjacent to his. It seemed Asher was doing his best to remain calm, simply repeating that they needed sleep and could talk about it later.

I'll be glad to leave this mess behind. His own room was small. He locked the door and stripped to underwear, glad that Lauren had insisted on separate rooms. It had been forever since he'd been comfortable while asleep. He slipped under the fresh blankets and relaxed into the clean sheets and pillow, breathing in the scent of laundry soap. It contrasted sharply with his own body odor. He hadn't noticed how bad it was. The fact that they all stank was a little comforting. He pulled the scented sheet up around his nose and smiled. Sleep came easier than it had in a long while. They were secure; the National Guard was just across the street and the house had been cleared by them. Not everything had gone to plan. Alex would have preferred to be back at the RV already. But he figured he'd still saved them some time. When it was safe, he and Lauren would split, and they wouldn't have to worry about getting Ned and his guys closer to the city. They could finally reach Boston.

Alex woke to bright sunlight streaming through the window. A little battery-operated clock at his bedside read 9:30, but he didn't jump right out of bed. He had time to breathe, time to think. He'd dreamed of his wife, Naomi, the night before. Not of her death, but of her life. It was refreshing. Normal, even. They'd sat over a cup of coffee and talked through a boring schedule, one that weeks ago he would have considered a chore. He'd do anything to get that back; the mundane routine of partnering with Naomi to raise their son had been such a gift.

I wish I could tell her that. I miss her so much. Alex let tears slide down his cheeks for a few minutes before wiping his eyes dry and rolling out of bed. His feet hit the cool hardwood floor. A few minutes to let his own grief express itself did him some good, and he pulled on his clothes with a sad smile. He left off his socks and shoes for the time being, reveling in the idea of washing them in bottled water from the kitchen. *Maybe I'll bring up a couple bottles and wash the rest of me, too.*

He opened the door to find Lauren's wide open across the hall. He peeked inside. She wasn't there. *Probably grabbing breakfast.*

Wyatt and Ned's door was open, too, though Ben and Asher's door was still closed. A line of something thick and wet glistened as it slowly rolled out from under the door. Alex frowned and stood over it. *Is that… blood?* His head snapped up at the door, his heartbeat suddenly wild within his chest.

"Asher?" He turned the doorknob and pushed. It was locked. More blood seeped from under the door, tickling his toes and making the floor slippery. "Asher!" He threw all of his weight against the door several times until the frame cracked. "Asher, can you hear me? Ben? Are you in there?" Alex pushed hard one more time. Wood splintered, and he stumbled inside as the door ripped free of the frame. He skated into the room on blood, barely keeping his balance.

Ben was nowhere in sight. Asher was crumpled on the floor, eyes wide and unblinking, his throat cut open, his body covered in slashes and blood pooled beneath him, seeping toward the door due to the slightest slant of the floor. But that wasn't what made Alex freeze in horror. Asher's arm was stretched out onto the floor, his hand opened, palm upward. One of his fingertips had been sawn clean off.

Chapter 33

George Peters

George grabbed two granola bars and two apples from the counter. Lissa behind him did the same, and the two navigated the rows of sleeping bags to the far corner of the room where Annika and James waited. Ever since George had taken James's place on the truck that first day at The Farm, saving him from punishment, the little boy had stuck close by. Lissa had taken to James once she'd discovered his mother was a cop just like her aunt.

George didn't mind the two. He even liked them. But he hated the growing feeling of obligation. As he sat next to Annika and handed her breakfast, he avoided eye contact with James and Lissa. Two days ago, his plan had been to escape the zoo with Annika. Then, he started to wonder if his best option was to join the CONmen and take advantage of Ruger's protection. He hated that, too, the way he *didn't* hate Ruger.

The man had protected several girls from the Butterfly House. He'd protected George, kept him from getting himself killed in a vain attempt to shoot Icepick. And then he'd given him advice on *how* to get revenge the smart way. The last two days of training under Ruger had been good days. George had been treated more like a young man and less like a little kid. Ruger believed in him, believed he could help make something good out of the new Boston.

But at the same time, George wanted the *old* Boston back. He didn't want to go out in the name of Ace, threatening people with a gun to their face if they didn't do what they were told. He didn't want to be part of an organization that even *had* a Butterfly House. Ruger had promised George could train Annika so that she would never have to be taken there, but that would mean training her to hurt people. He didn't want that, either.

Why does this have to be so confusing. There are no good choices. George munched on his apple, wishing he could see a sure way out. Tim and Heather and Candice are still out there. They'll be looking for us… won't they? It had been almost two weeks since he'd last seen them. Are they even still alive?

"Got a lot on your mind?" Lissa tapped George's knee. "You've been chewing that same bit of apple for like three minutes."

George swallowed. "Just thinking about the day ahead." He hadn't been, of course, but once he came up with the excuse, anticipation made his heart skip a beat. Ace himself was supposed to come and assess the guards in training. Ruger said it was just a check-in, but he'd seemed agitated the day before, and George had the feeling Ace's visit was more than that.

Lissa leaned in and whispered. "Annika said you have a plan to get out of here. Is that true?"

George did a double-take and then glared at the little girl, Ace momentarily forgotten. "I told you not to talk about that."

Annika shrugged. "We need help, and I like her."

He rubbed his hand over his face and groaned. "Swear you won't tell anyone else," he said. "It's really important."

"He's right," Lissa said. "We should keep this between us four."

"What about everyone else?" James's small voice was sad as he surveyed the rest of the room.

"Maybe we can come back for them." Lissa squeezed James's arm. "We can find my aunt. The Thirteenth isn't far from here. I think we could make it and ask for help."

"My mom would help, too," James said. "But I don't know where she is."

George frowned at Lissa. "Don't make promises we can't keep." Every bite George took tasted a little blander. He put the apple down, half eaten. "Every adult we've ever known might be dead."

Annika brought her knees to her chest, but it was James who sniffled as his eyes welled with tears. "My mom isn't dead," he said defiantly, wiping his nose with his sleeve. "She's looking for me."

George sighed. "Sorry, James. I… I'm just tired."

"But you'll be okay today?" Lissa asked. "I mean, we've got that assessment. Whatever that means."

"Yeah, I'll be fine." George picked up the apple and finished it, though he'd lost his appetite. He didn't want to get hungry or feel weak later on. Ace was like a king amongst CONmen. If he decided he didn't like George or thought George too weak, he could shoot him on the spot and no one would blink an eye. *Well, maybe Ruger would blink, but I doubt even he would do anything to stop it.* Of course, the more likely scenario was that George would just ruin his chances of being in the guard, which would make escaping a thousand times more unlikely. *No pressure.*

The rattle of the lock on the kitchen door being undone from the other side was followed by Ruger swinging the door open and striding inside, stretching and grabbing himself a granola bar. He had a small stack of paper tucked under one arm. The room went quiet at his presence, most of the children shrinking into themselves. "Guard trainees!" Ruger's voice called out as he whipped out the papers, held them up, and slapped them on the counter that separated the main room from the kitchen. "I got an agenda for you to prepare for your assessment right here. Other groups will be getting their own assessments later on. In about an hour, we'll be headin' out, and I want you all prepared. Come up and grab your sheet." He patted the papers, leaned against the counter, and ripped open the granola bar package, eating a third of it in one bite.

George hopped up from his sleeping bag, and Lissa followed suit. They joined the other four trainees in line. George grabbed the last two sheets, handing one to Lissa. They were normal copy paper covered in Ruger's chicken-scratch handwriting.

"Hey, Firecracker." Ruger nodded toward Lissa, his expression serious. "You got something to prove today. Keep your head on straight. Got it?"

Lissa frowned. "Don't we *all* have something to prove?"

Ruger shrugged. "Yeah, but... I'm gonna need you to put in a little extra. Show Ace what's what. Think you can do that?"

"Um, sure." Lissa pressed her lips together, her face turning pale.

George made to follow her as she turned her back, but Ruger put a hand on his shoulder. "I got a word for you, too, Hero. Don't do anything stupid. No matter what happens, keep your cool." George nodded, and Ruger lifted his hand, relaxing back against the counter and shoving another third of the granola bar into his mouth.

George caught up to Lissa and kept his voice low. "What was that about?"

Lissa put one hand to her stomach. She looked like she was going to be sick. "What did he say to you?"

"Something about keeping my cool today, no matter what." George frowned and looked back over his shoulder at Ruger who was stuffing the last bit of the granola bar into his mouth.

"I'm the only one he told to put in extra effort." Lissa reached her sleeping bag and sank down onto it. "George, there's only one difference between me and the rest of the trainees."

George sat beside her. "Well, yeah. You're a girl, but..." He trailed off, Lissa's pale face and frightened eyes spurring him to come to a conclusion about what she was thinking. *The Butterfly House.* "Ruger already stopped them from taking you twice. He won't let them."

"He won't let *Ace*? Are you kidding me? No one stops him from doing anything." Lissa's harsh whisper turned some nearby heads, and a little warmth came back into her cheeks.

George swallowed hard and looked at the paper Ruger had handed out. "Well... he gave us this to help us prepare. He said you could prove you belong, right?"

"It's just what we've been doing the last two days." Lissa squinted at Ruger's handwriting. "Run a quick mile. Shooting range while we're still catching our breath. And then Ace is going to ask us each a question."

There were a lot of notes under the last activity. George read them out loud. "He'll come up with a scenario for each of you, ask you what you would do, and your answer will help him determine if you're on the right track. Remember, CON are your people, and the buck stops with Ace. The New Boston will be all about working together to survive and rebuild. Too many cooks in the kitchen ruin the stew. Ace's vision for the future is the only one that matters. Blah, blah, blah. And then he's got a list of questions Ace has asked before."

George shrugged. "So, we tell him what he wants to hear. That's nothing new."

"He's going to judge me more harshly," Lissa said. "Otherwise, Ruger wouldn't have said anything. You saw the way Icepick looked at me the other day." She shuddered. "What if Ace is more like that guy than he is like Ruger?"

George chewed on the inside of his cheek for a minute, not knowing what to say. She's not wrong. These guys aren't the good guys. And if Ruger told me to keep my cool, at least part of him suspects Ace is going to do or say something that I won't like. He rested his elbow on his knee, and his head on his raised fist. But he gave us this paper for a reason, too.

He looked up at Lissa. "Let's go over answers to these questions," he said. "I mean, it couldn't hurt, right? I'll ask, you answer. We can try to come up with the best answers together."

Lissa took a deep, shaky breath. "Okay, yeah. I mean, that's better than doing nothing." She took his hand and squeezed. "Thanks, George."

Heat crept up his own neck. It wasn't embarrassment, exactly. *What is wrong with me?* His stomach flipped, and his brain stopped working properly for a second. He shook it off, literally; he pulled back and shook out his arms. At Lissa's confused frown, his cheeks turned hot, too. *Okay... now I'm embarrassed.* His mother had told him one day he'd get the "warm fuzzies." He'd thought she was nuts. *Is this what she meant?*

"George?" Lissa wrinkled her nose. "What... I mean... you're being weird."

Annika and James giggled at him from the far side of their sleeping bags.

"Yeah." There was no point in denying it. "Sorry. I... um..." He got to his feet and started shaking out his whole body. "This is how you get the blood flowing to your brain. I do it before tests. Gets the nerves out." He took a few deep breaths and sat back down. The movement *had* actually helped him refocus. "Okay, let's do this."

He sat down again, and for the next hour, he and Lissa studied the questions Ruger had provided as samples. Lissa straightened up over time, answering with more confidence toward the end. They brainstormed what Ace would want to hear based on things Ruger had said, their own experiences with CONmen, and not a little bit of speculation based on what they'd seen in movies and television. It wasn't a fool-proof method, but when it was time to get up and follow Ruger to the old, abandoned bear enclosures, they did so with steady steps and heads held high.

They passed the rusted gates of the once great cages for the shooting range of sand-filled balloons and fresh gourds. Ruger's helpers — long standing members of CON — were waiting, as usual. But this time, they stood on either side of a high-backed, red armchair where a man reclined with an air of authority that included an unsettling intensity. Ace wore a bowler hat with an Ace of Spades playing card sticking out from behind the thick ribbon. Behind him, a white Ferrari, clean and shiny, reflected the swaying leaves of the trees overhead.

George and Lissa lined up where they always did along with the four others they'd been training with — Caleb, Gavin, Omar, and Albert. They faced the range out of habit, their backs to Ace.

"All business? I came here to see you." An unfamiliar voice spoke from behind George with slow, deliberate pronunciation. "Turn around and face me."

George did as he was told, turning with the others, keeping his head down, trying not to stare. He didn't want to draw attention to himself. But out of the corner of his eye, he spotted two men he hadn't expected to be there: Big Mack and Icepick. George's stomach twisted into knots. He couldn't help but throw a glance at Lissa beside him. She was breathing hard. *She must have seen them, too.*

Big Mack handled the Butterfly House, and as far as George could tell, Icepick had joined Big Mack's lackeys shortly after George and Annika had been brought to The Farm. The hierarchy within CON was still fuzzy to George, but he had nailed down the basics. Ace was at the top. Men like Ruger and Big Mack were middle management, in charge of certain functions of Ace's empire. The majority of CONmen were lowly, their duties meted out by whoever had claimed them as part of their team.

How is Lissa supposed to do well when they're here, staring at her? His blood boiled. It's not fair… they're sabotaging her!

Ace abruptly stood, and the men closest to him flinched. He seemed to like that, the corners of his mouth turning up in a subtle expression of satisfaction. Ace walked right up to Lissa, and George's heart leapt into his throat. The man was broad-shouldered and tall, his buzz cut making his thick eyebrows more prominent. He studied Lissa, his dark eyes never leaving hers. She didn't look away, though. Silence stretched on, and George had to force himself not to squirm. There was no indication Ace was paying him any mind, but the intensity with which he stared her down and her audacity to meet him toe-to-toe charged the air with a dreadful anticipation. The sound of shoes scuffling on the gravel as the other trainees shifted their weight interrupted the quiet. Ace stepped back, his eyes still on Lissa. "Ruger, I've got things to do. New plan." He held up a finger. "Big Mack, let's have it."

"This oughtta be fun." Big Mack smirked and nodded at Icepick who brought a small duffel bag to Ace.

Ruger, his eyes wide, stepped forward, too, though he wasn't asked to do so. "Ace, they've only been training a few days. We talked about this."

Ace grinned and shrugged. "Your thing was boring."

"Ace—" One glance from his boss stopped Ruger cold. He cleared his throat and looked away.

"Good. Now," Ace nodded toward the bag. "I brought some toys. Knives. Some big. Some small. All of them sharp."

George had the urge to step away; he ground his feet into the gravel instead. The guards were watching. Running would only get him shot. Whatever was about to happen, there was no getting out of it.

Chapter 34

Zara Williams

Zara hated waiting. She'd never been good at it, and the end of the world hadn't changed that one iota. "He's *got* to be here soon." She groaned and let her head hit the back of the bus seat repeatedly.

"The auction is today." Mr. Peters shifted in the seat across the aisle. "He'll be here."

Zara dug the ballot Lola had stolen for them out of her pocket, studying it for the hundredth time. "Surely not *everyone* wants to kill him. He's one of them, isn't he? They've known him his whole life."

"Fear and anger make people do crazy things." Mr. Peters looked sideways at her. "I think the last few weeks have proven that a thousand times over."

Zara pulled her knees to her chest and hugged her legs. She rested her chin on her knee and looked sideways at Mr. Peters. She held out the paper. "Sure, but this? It's nuts!"

Mr. Peters shrugged. "The clerk at the courthouse said Kai was a troublemaker before all of this. And it's not like he's changed much since." He waved toward the bandage wrapping Zara's calf. "I mean, he shot you."

Zara quirked an eyebrow. "I wasn't debating whether or not he's a blockhead. He's definitely a world-class idiot. But I wouldn't want him dead." She sighed and put the paper down on the seat next to her. She'd read it a hundred times already. It was a ballot with the title: Clearfield Watch, Nolan Security Meeting #3. Below the title, a short paragraph explained that ballots would be counted and then burned. There was also a summary of the minutes from the last two meetings.

From what Zara and Mr. Peters could tell, at the first meeting, they had concluded that outsiders were the biggest threat to their survival and that Kai Lee was making it worse.

The second meeting had discussed Kai's refusal to stop, and Nolan had been invited. Three people had presented options for dealing with Kai, and Nolan had presented his plan for securing Clearfield from outsiders, laying down what his men expected in exchange for their safety.

The third meeting had been a final vote on not *if* they should kill Kai but *how* and *when*. There were two possibilities. Mr. Phelps put forth they do it at the airfield in secret. Nolan put forth they do it at the auction, publicly, to take swift and precise control of the town.

Zara shook her head. "I just don't get how they could be so calloused. Clearfield has been fine, and Kai might be a terrible person, but he's helping people."

Mr. Peters leaned over and grabbed the paper from the seat beside her and looked over it again. "I don't know… I get where they're coming from. It looks like they tried to reason with Kai first."

Zara reimagined her encounter with Kai. "He's not exactly the reasonable type, is he?"

"No, he's not. If he hadn't accidentally shot you, we wouldn't have gotten any helpful information out of him at all." Mr. Peters tapped the paper with his finger. "And all the attention he brings *is* attracting outsiders. These people have already lost a lot. If I were them, if it were between the life of one troublemaker and the security of my hometown and everyone else in it, I don't know… maybe I'd vote to kill him off, too. If we didn't need his help, I'd leave Kai to his fate and find us another way safely over those mountains."

"Why not just kick him out?" Zara asked.

Mr. Peters shrugged. "My guess is that they're convinced he'll keep using the airfield. It's outside of Clearfield proper, in the countryside. For him, this airport is a small, safe, known entity. Kai could have realized the risks of moving his operation and made it clear he wouldn't be kicked to the curb without a fight. Plus, if he's dead, they can raid his supplies."

Zara winced. "I hate to think that's a motivator for them, but honestly… people are messed up."

The whine of an airplane engine cut off Mr. Peters's nod of agreement, and they both jumped up and scrambled outside. Zara held up her arm to block out the sun, relief flooding over her at the sight of Kai's plane landing.

"How do we approach him without spooking him?" Zara asked.

"We let him come to us." Mr. Peters backed up and leaned against the bus. They'd parked it to block the only road onto the little airstrip. He patted his gun and nodded at hers. "Be prepared to use these. If he pulls his weapon, I might just kill him myself, save the people of Clearfield the trouble."

"Let's not get trigger happy," Zara said. "If we don't convince him to flee and take us with him, getting to Boston is going to be a lot harder."

"Not impossible."

"But harder." Zara narrowed her eyes at Mr. Peters, who shrugged and relaxed his shoulders. She sat on the bottom step of the entrance to the bus, and they waited.

A few minutes after the engines died down, the door between the wing and the cockpit swung open and the stairs were let down. A man stepped out and reached back toward the plane to help a woman come down the stairs as she clutched a toddler on her hip. The child's face was buried in the woman's messy, thick braid, his arms wrapped tightly around her neck. Behind her, an older couple followed, and the younger man helped them in much the same way. They were dirty, their clothes tattered and faces smudged, and they all sagged with exhaustion. But when all five of them were on the ground, they gathered in a group hug and a mixture of sniffles and laughter carried over the tarmac.

Zara couldn't help but smile and imagine wrapping Annika in a big hug, though her smile faded almost as quickly as it had appeared. She could see in her mind's eye the perfect picture: her entire family — Mom, Dad, Jordan, Auntie, and Annika — laughing and hugging and *together.* But she would never have that again.

"Too bad that won't last long," Mr. Peters said.

"What do you mean?" Zara glanced at Mr. Peters, and she saw the same longing she felt reflected in his eyes. *At least he's still got most of his family… I hope.*

"Their relief. Their happiness." Mr. Peters blinked rapidly and drew in a deep breath as he turned away, deftly wiping away moisture from his eyes.

"They'll get it back," Zara said, "after we get you back to Boston so you can fix this." She set her jaw and forced herself to look at what she was fighting for. *I still have Annika. And there are still plenty of people out there — families like that one — who need this to end.*

Kai Lee appeared in the doorway of the plane. He glared at Zara and Mr. Peters as he descended the little staircase. He stomped toward them, his fists thrust down at his sides. His leather jacket and perfect hair did little to assuage the childish anger rolling off him in waves.

Zara grimaced. "I can't believe we have to depend on *that* to get us to Boston. Look at him. He's like a toddler."

Mr. Peters grunted and pushed off the bus, standing tall, his feet planted a shoulder-width apart. "Let's just save his life and get this over with."

Kai approached with a fury, waving his hands in dramatic gestures as he spoke. "Look, dude, I won't be bullied." He stopped a couple yards from the bus. "You people think you can threaten me, bribe me, pester me to death — well, it won't work. The auction is today. Like, a couple of hours. I already told you, if you bring the goods, I'll put you on the schedule." He barely stopped his rant for a breath. "What happened? Couldn't find the right stuff? Well, I don't care. Boo-hoo. Better luck next time."

"Are you done?" Zara crossed her arms and raised her eyebrows.

"Yeah, I'm done. Now, get out of here and stop blocking the road." Kai turned on his heel and started to walk away.

Mr. Peters took a step forward. "The Clearfield Watch is going to kill you."

Kai paused mid-step and turned around, his eyes narrowed at Mr. Peters. "What did you say?"

"I said, the Clearfield Watch is going to kill you."

Kai scoffed. "You really think I'm going to fall for that?"

"It's true," Zara said. "There was a meeting. They're going to either kill you here, at the airport, or today at the auction. Since they aren't waiting for you here, I'm guessing they're planning on doing it at the auction."

"Nolan got involved," Mr. Peters continued. "Clearfield doesn't want outsiders coming in anymore. They want to lock the town down, and apparently, you wouldn't listen when they asked you to stop using the airstrip."

Kai folded his arms across his chest and shook his head. "You two are unbelievable. I grew up here. Clearfield loves me." He paused, looking up at the sky for a moment before shrugging. "Well, it's more like they love to hate me. And to be fair, I haven't always been the ambitious, responsible type. But they would never kill me off."

Zara pulled out the ballot and held it out. "Then what's this?"

Kai frowned and stepped forward, yanking the paper out of her hand. He held it up, and his eyes shifted back and forth as he read. He crumpled up the paper, shoved it into his jacket pocket, and smiled at them, though his confidence was clearly waning. "What else you got, babe?"

Zara pinched her lips together, her blood boiling. "My name is Zara."

Mr. Peters held out a hand, indicating that Zara should calm down. "What do you mean? That clearly says they're planning to kill you."

"So what? You hooked up a laptop and a printer to a power source, got a little creative, and printed your best attempt at tricking me into taking you early. There are a few places in town with generators." Kai's smile returned. "Might have worked if I hadn't known these people my whole life. But, dude, even if most of them don't like *me*, they all legit loved my mom. They would never hurt me."

"They're not who you think they are," Zara said. "We're telling you the truth. They're scared, and you didn't listen when they told you to stop."

Mr. Peters took a step forward, his business, no-nonsense posture relaxing into an empathetic one. "Kai, under normal circumstances, I'm sure you're right. But these are not normal circumstances. My guess is that they'll have Nolan do it, and they'll be ashamed of it for the rest of their lives. But they'll also justify it. Please. Don't go to the auction."

"Whatever, dude." Kai shook his head. "You know what? *You* don't bother coming to the auction. Find another way over the mountains. I'm not taking you. I don't care what you've got to barter." He unholstered his gun and backed up, facing them. "Now, I've got a family that paid me to get them safely into town. I'm going to do that, and then I'm going to that auction. I've got a business to run."

"Kai—" Zara cut off and put her hands in the air when the pilot aimed directly at her. She stepped back. "Fine. We'll lay off."

He lowered the gun but kept it at his side as he approached the family and ushered them into the hangar.

"That didn't go well." Mr. Peters rubbed the back of his neck. "That kid is going to get himself killed."

A Jeep pulled out of the hangar, loaded up with the family, Kai in the driver's seat. He drove straight for them, and then went off road around the bus to continue on his way, shouting as he passed, "You better be gone by the time I get back!"

"What are we going to do?" Zara followed Mr. Peters around the bus, and they stood side by side, watching the Jeep drive off into the distance. "You don't know how to fly a plane, do you?"

"I had a pilot, remember?"

"Yeah, I remember." Zara grimaced at the memory of Mr. Peters bashing the pilot's head in with a car door after he'd shown up infected with DV-10. She understood now that he'd been forced to kill the man or risk his own daughter's infection.

"Why would I know how to fly a plane?"

Zara shrugged. "I don't know. Rich guy stuff. You hired people to do things you could do for yourself all the time."

"Point taken." Mr. Peters sighed. "You ready to go save that idiot's life?"
Zara gave Mr. Peters a half smile. "You got a plan?"
"A plan to somehow get Kai away from a mob of people who want him dead and then whisk him back here where he can fly us across the mountains?" Mr. Peters shrugged. "I've got a plan. Sort of."

Chapter 35

Alexander Roman

Alex burst into action, the bottom of his feet coated in rapidly drying blood, sticking to the wood floors as he ran back to Lauren's room to make sure he hadn't missed anything. He threw back the comforter on the bed and did a quick turnaround, scanning every corner. The room was empty. Seconds later, he was bounding down the stairs, panic flooding his veins.

"Lauren?" Alex shouted.

"Kitchen!" Lauren's reply was followed by a scream.

Alex reached the bottom of the stairs, his feet snagging on living room carpet as the blood congealed like glue. He searched frantically for something — anything — he could use as a weapon. Sweat rolled down his face, stinging his eyes, tasting of salt. His vision blurred as his heartrate skyrocketed. It had been mere moments since discovering Asher's body, but a moment too long, and he'd have to tell Minnie her daughter had died on his watch.

"Alex!" Lauren shrieked.

He had no choice. He bolted empty-handed through the living room and into the kitchen, tripping over something, skidding across the floor, and slamming into the cabinets on the other side of the room. Alex scrambled to his feet. He'd stumbled over Wyatt's body. The biker had a long slash across his abdomen. The slightest rise and fall of his chest indicated he wasn't quite dead. Ned stood in the corner of the kitchen with hands outstretched, legs slightly bent, his body a shield for Lauren who was backed up against the wall. Ned had a deep cut in his forearm, and it dripped blood on the floor. Ben stood in the middle of the room, a meat cleaver in one hand, blood saturating his clothes. None of it looked to be his own.

No, not Ben. Alex snarled. "Jesse King." Ned blinked at Alex, and then turned wide eyes on the convict. Alex pulled himself up to standing, wincing at a pain in his back as he leaned against the counter. The horrific scene was reflected in the glass of the coffee pot just inches from his face. The smell of fresh, hot coffee blended with the mineral scent of blood and the stench of sweat and body odor.

"It can't be," Ned whispered.

"Really?" Lauren said from behind Ned. "Because it seems pretty possible to me."

Alex turned around, still leaning against the counter. "Asher's dead. The tip of his finger was cut off." He pointed at Jesse. "I knew there was something wrong with him."

Jesse shook his head. "No, no, no. There's nothing wrong with me." He waved the meat cleaver in the air.

"You've killed people!" Lauren's high-pitched voice seemed to agitate Jesse further. Her words tumbled out of her mouth. "You lied about who you were, and you killed Asher. And maybe Wyatt. And you're trying to kill us!"

Jesse ran his fingers through his hair. "No, no, no. I'm keeping us together." He twitched and whispered in a harsh tone to no one in particular. "I didn't mean to draw it out," he spat. "I usually wait for the perfect moment. I make sure to have the perfect tools. I'm sorry. I'm sorry!"

"Who… who are you talkin' to?" Ned asked.

"Your brother. And Ben. He was another inmate. Very nice to me. When I heard you were looking for me, he said I could use his name." Jesse tapped his temple. "They're all with me forever. And that's where you belong, Ned. You're my friend. We're supposed to stay together."

"All the people…" Ned swallowed audibly. "… the people you killed are in your head?"

"None of you understand! I have to *make* you understand!" With a crazed shout, he raised the cleaver and lurched toward Ned, swinging with a two-handed grip.

Lauren scrambled from behind Ned, and the big biker squatted low at the last second, grabbing Jesse around his middle and attempting to tackle him. Jesse followed through on his swing, lodging the blade in Ned's back. Though the biker screamed and dropped, scrambling away with the cleaver still lodged between his shoulder blades, he managed to fling Jesse backward.

Alex saw his chance. He grabbed hold of the coffee pot and slung scalding liquid into Jesse's face. Swirls of steam danced off his skin as the convict screamed in pain, and Alex reared back and swung again, this time smashing the coffee pot against Jesse's face. His screams cut short as he passed out. Alex dropped the pot and straddled Ben, patting him down for any other weapons. Steam still rolled off the convict's face, and his skin was red hot, blisters already forming. Blood trickled from a gash on his head where the broken glass of the pot had gouged him.

"I don't think he's got anything else on him," Alex shouted. "Lauren? Are you okay?"

He looked over his shoulder to find Lauren kneeling beside Ned, who was face down on the floor, the meat cleaver sticking out of his back. Tears streamed down her face as she gingerly touched the biker.

"Lauren." Alex spoke calmly, though his insides were raging with the urge to help Ned and Wyatt. "We can check them both in a minute. I need your help. I need you to find rope or zip-ties or… anything I can use to tie this lunatic up."

Lauren pulled back her trembling hand and nodded, rising on shaky feet and leaving the room without a word. Alex heard her rifle through drawers in the next room, and then the next. "I can't find anything!" She shouted. And then, "Wait! I think I have something."

After a series of grunts, Lauren came into view, pushing a large trunk. She got to the doorway, climbed over the trunk, and dragged Wyatt out of the way, apologizing repeatedly as she placed him next to Ned. She hopped back over the trunk and pushed it into the kitchen from the other side.

"It's got a lock, and look!" Lauren positioned the trunk so that it faced Alex. "It's got a key in it." She unlocked the trunk and opened the lid. "It's heavy… do you think he'll be able to breathe in here?"

"I guess we'll find out." Alex held Jesse down at the shoulders as he straddled his stomach. "We can look for a better solution after we lock him up and take care of Ned and Wyatt. Besides, the National Guard should be by to check on us soon."

Lauren nodded. "Okay. Let me get all these blankets out." She piled quilts and crocheted blankets on the floor.

Alex glanced back at the bikers. Ned groaned and his fingers twitched. "Ned! Can you hear me?"

Jesse King sucked in an agonized breath. His swollen, red eyelids opened to a slit, and he moaned. Alex pushed down harder as the convict woke, trying to ensure he stayed put, but the man's steadily growing panic peaked as he thrashed and dislodged Alex's grip. Jesse's arms and legs swept the floor as he squirmed. Broken glass from the pot clinked across the kitchen tiles.

"Get off!" Jesse's swollen lips garbled the words.

The convict grabbed a shard of glass, and Alex wasn't fast enough. A sharp pain sprouted from where Jesse stabbed Alex's upper arm. Jesse pushed Alex to the side, threw himself on top of Alex, grabbed another shard, and raised it for a second strike.

"Alex!" Lauren screamed as she dove for the convict, barreling into him and knocking him sideways off Alex. Lauren rolled across the tile, bumping into Wyatt's body.

In a rage, Jesse stumbled forward, the shard of sharp glass now aimed at Lauren. Alex scrambled to his feet, and fighting through the pain in his back and his arm, wrapped his arms around Jesse, stumbled backward toward the empty chest, and threw the man toward it. He sank into it, his knees hooked on the edge so that his legs hung out, but his body wedged inside. The convict struggled to get out, but before he could make much progress, Alex landed a punch to the side of his inflamed face. He went limp for a second time.

Alex lifted Jesse's legs, repositioning the man so he could stuff him into the trunk. He shut the lid and sat on top. He turned the key, locking it in place and then slid onto the floor, breathing heavily. Lauren crawled over to him and plopped down next to him, leaning her head on his shoulder.

"You okay?"

Alex winced at the glass sticking out of his bicep, at the blood trickling down his arm. "Yeah," he said. "I think I'll be okay."

He struggled to his feet and was about to check on Ned and Wyatt when the front door opened. There was a straight line of sight through the living room from the front door to the door that led into the kitchen. Amy and Vince, the National Guard soldiers from the day before, strode in and pulled their weapons at the sight before them. They quickly marched into the kitchen, their eyes flitting over the chest, the pile of blankets, the mess of broken glass and blood, and Wyatt and Ned laying on the floor.

"What the—?" Vince pointed his gun at Alex. "You okay, ma'am?"

"Are you talking to me?" Lauren frowned up at him.

"Yes, ma'am." Vince nodded at Alex. "Did he hurt you, too? Where are the others."

"I didn't hurt anybody," Alex said. "I mean, except for the guy in the trunk."

"Say that again, sir?" Amy turned wide eyes on the trunk. "There's a man in the trunk?"

Lauren nodded. "Ben… or Jesse King, I guess. He's the one that tried to kill us."

"That serial killer you were looking for?" Vince lowered his gun. "He found you… here?"

"Isn't Ben the name of one of your guys?" Amy asked.

"Best I can tell," Alex said, "Jesse King assumed the name of a man he killed. It sounded to me like he, I don't know… hallucinates his victims."

Lauren nodded. "Before you got here, he was trying to explain it. Like… we would be happy to be murdered with a meat cleaver if we only understood we would be with him for forever." She shuddered. She nodded toward Ned and Wyatt. "They need help. Please, we need to help them."

Amy called for paramedics and back up on her walkie talkie and then knelt beside the two men, both of whom were still breathing but were out cold. "We'll make sure they get medical attention, but we're going to need the two of you to come with us and answer some questions."

"And you're going to have to do it slowly," Vince said. "Where's the sixth guy that came with you?"

Alex's stomach twisted. "Asher. He's dead. He was rooming with Ben… I mean, Jesse." He let out a long, shaky breath. "I can't believe we didn't see it. Ben sent us to New York City. He admitted to being there at that tire shop. The way he was always whispering to no one. That *smile*."

"I don't know what you're talking about." Vince nodded toward the living room. "But you're going to have a seat and start from the beginning."

As more of the National Guard arrived — soldiers to remove Jesse King from the trunk in cuffs and paramedics to tend to everyone's wounds — Alex and Lauren told Vince and Amy everything they knew. By the time they were done, Ned was awake enough to confirm that Ben was Jesse King and that Jesse had been the aggressor.

"We're going to take them over to the armory," the paramedic said as Ned and Wyatt were ferried out of the house on stretchers. "We've got a doc that should be able to help." She looked at Alex's arm. "I think we can probably handle that, but you need to come with us. Let us stitch you up in the infirmary."

An hour later, Alex's arm was stitched up, and he'd been given meds to ease the pain in his back, which the paramedic suspected to be a pulled muscle. "We were lucky," Alex said as he sat down next to Lauren in the infirmary waiting room. "Again."

"Or we were unlucky and we're just really good at getting out of pickles." Lauren shrugged. "What are we going to do? We can't leave Ned and Wyatt like this."

"No," Alex sighed, "I don't think we can."

Lauren quirked an eyebrow. "I thought you'd argue with me."

"Well, I made a promise." Alex leaned back in the chair. "I told Oliver that if it was safe, if it wouldn't take away from our ability to survive, I would always help people in need. Ned and Wyatt are our friends, and they're hurt. We can at least wait a few more hours, make sure they're okay. Minnie will wait three days from when we left."

"What about saving time?" Lauren asked. "You had a plan, and it included getting back to the RV as soon as possible."

"You know what Minnie told me the last time I mentioned my plans to her?" Alex looked sideways at Lauren.

"What?"

Alex smiled and leaned back in the chair, imitating Minnie's southern drawl. "The best-laid plans happen only if the creek don't rise, and it *always* rises. But we've got the best crew and a sturdy boat. The only plan worth its salt these days is to keep on paddling."

Chapter 36

George Peters

George's blood ran cold despite the heat. The glimmer of stainless steel demanded all his attention as the duffel bag of knives was overturned in a pile. Puffs of white rose from the dusty gravel, dimming the reflection of sunlight on dozens of sharp edges. A hollow roar, like white noise, filled his ears as his heart froze in his chest.

Ace's voice broke through that noise, and George tore his gaze from the weapons to look at the CONman king. His lips were moving, words forming. George concentrated on the information, doing his best to process through molasses-slow comprehension.

"It'd be best if nobody died," Ace said, "you know, with so many people dead already. We're kind of changing things up around here. Life is more precious than it used to be. But, hey," — he held up his hands — "things happen. No judgment." He paced for a few moments, hands clasped behind his back, lips pursed as if considering his next words. "I wanna see passion. I wanna see the fight to survive. Bullets ain't gonna last forever. Ruger's already told me you can all shoot. That's good. But what happens when it's man to man, when you're out there, forming a new Boston out of blood and sweat and pure grit?"

Ruger pinched his lips together, his blue eyes turning icy, his muscles tensing all over. He stepped forward but then set his jaw and clasped his hands behind his back. George had never seen such fury behind anyone's eyes, nor such restraint.

Ace glanced at Ruger and smiled. "Now, I *did* say it'd be best if nobody died." He turned back to the six kids. "Everyone chooses their weapons. I'll pair you up. The first to draw blood wins and gets to go on to the shooting range to show me what you've got after you've been under a little pressure. It means nothing to me if you can meet your mark on a full belly after a full night of sleep. Now, the three of you who lose the duels have another chance at drawing first blood in a fight, all three of you in the ring, so to speak. Again, the winner goes on to shoot, and then we're back to a one-on-one knife fight. Last one to get cut gets a new test. If he, or *she*, fails, there will be consequences. At the very end, I'll have a question for each of you." Ace clapped his hands together and raised his eyebrows at Big Mack. "Now, doesn't that sound like fun?"

"You bet, Ace." Big Mack grinned. "I even brought popcorn."

"What do you think, Ruger?" Ace turned to face the closest thing George and the other kids had to an ally.

"It's definitely *you*, Ace." Ruger's forced smile was stiff, his body still tense as his tone betrayed his anger.

"You see?" Ace sauntered over to Ruger and put a hand on his shoulder. "This is why I love you, man. I know you think I'm being reckless. But you get it. Loyalty above all else." He patted Ruger's arm. "Good man. And don't you worry. Your little proteges will be all yours again in an hour." He turned a sinister grin on the kids. "Maybe less."

He's crazy. George glanced at the other kids. Caleb and Omar didn't bat an eye, but Lissa, Gavin, and Albert were all shifting nervously. *What are we going to do? We can't hurt each other.*

"Alright," Ace said. "Pick out your weapons. No fighting until I pair you up and give you the go ahead."

Caleb and Omar stepped up with confidence, each one kneeling beside the duffel bag and surveying their options. George approached the pile of knives more cautiously. He stood at the edge of the pile, Lissa standing by his side. Gavin and Albert approached the weapons as if they were a pile of live snakes.

"We should choose small ones," George said softly as he knelt beside Caleb. The others knelt or leaned in to listen. George moved aside a larger knife to pick up a pocketknife, the blade only a couple inches in length. "The shorter, the better. It won't make wounds too long or too deep."

Omar scoffed. "Won't that just make Ace angry? He said he wanted to be entertained."

"George is right," Lissa said. "The point is to draw first blood, not to kill each other. I propose some ground rules. No stabbing, for instance."

"Who made you the boss?" Caleb picked up a five-inch blade with a leather hilt, some kind of hunting knife if George had to guess. "You want to make it easier so you can win. How do we know you two love birds won't trick us into grabbing baby knives and then you switch yours out for big ones?"

George shook his head. "Maybe this is a test of loyalty to each other. Did anyone consider that? What good is an army if they don't trust each other?"

Caleb took a deep breath and put down the longer blade. "I guess you got a point. We shouldn't be making enemies of each other." He picked up a smaller blade. "And maybe it's a trick, like you said… like reverse psychology or whatever. See who's a team player and who's not."

"I'm going last." Omar stood up and crossed his arms. "No way I'm getting tricked. If any of you pick a longer knife, I'd be screwed."

"I'm good with this one." Caleb stepped back into line with the pocketknife he'd chosen.

George dug through and found his own pocketknife as did Lissa, Gavin, and Albert. *This is good. Maybe it's a test of loyalty, maybe not. But they need to see that we won't turn on each other regardless.* He felt proud of his fellows as the five of them lined up. Ace pursed his lips and nodded at them as if he understood what they were doing. He looked mildly impressed. *This was the right move.* George breathed a little easier for about two seconds.

Then it was Omar's turn. He grinned and chose one of the longer hunting knives. "Suckers," he said as he passed the others to take his place at the end of the line.

"Traitor." Lissa hissed at him.

George could only scowl at Omar. He didn't know what Ace had wanted of them, and neither did Omar. But choosing the same sized weapons would have started them all out on the same playing field, making it harder for Ace to single them out and decide one of them was unworthy.

Ace clapped his hands slowly as he walked the line. "Very interesting choices. It looks like five of you are all about teamwork. One of you has a little more… ambition, shall we say?" He chuckled. "I love a good twist. Let's see what happens." He surveyed each of them, narrowing his eyes as if studying them intently. And then he assigned pairs, pointing at them and directing them to face each other.

George held his breath. Gavin and Albert were the first pair. George's skin crawled. He didn't want to be placed with Omar, but he didn't want anyone else to get stuck with him, either. Air wheezed out of his lungs as Lissa and Caleb were paired, leaving him with Omar. *At least Lissa will probably survive. As long as I make sure Omar is taken out of the fight by winning this duel. He's the most dangerous of us. He's only out for himself.* He was simultaneously relieved and terrified.

It's okay. I can do this. His shoes crunched gravel underfoot as he faced Omar. His mouth went dry as he compared his pocketknife to his opponent's hunting knife. All he had to do was get Omar to draw first blood without killing him. And put on a little bit of a show. CONmen didn't react well to straight-up heroics. *Go on the defense. Don't make it too obvious I'm letting him win. If they don't catch on, and if I don't die, Annika won't be starved again for my actions.*

Omar was about six feet from George. He was older, bigger, and stronger. Whereas the other kids, besides Caleb, looked unsure in their stances, their grips either too tight or too loose, Omar looked perfectly comfortable with his weapon. The textured metal handle of George's knife dug into his sweaty palm. He was afraid to loosen his grip too much for fear of it slipping.

Ace returned to his red armchair, the white Ferrari still shimmering behind it as sunlight danced between leaves and bounced off its surface. His bowler hat was his crown and his Ace of Spades card his signet ring. It was an odd set up — luxury and gravel, red velvet and baggy jeans.

"Your referees will settle any disputes on who draws first blood," Ace said as one CONman joined each of the three pairs. "Once blood is drawn, the fight is over. Have fun, kids."

George's throat was tight. He licked his lips and turned from looking at Ace to face Omar, hoping to plea one more time for him to show some restraint. He didn't have time. Omar rushed forward, knife held over one shoulder as if he were planning on skewering George right through the heart. George spun away with a yelp as Omar plunged the weapon downward.

"What are you doing?" George yelled. He glanced at the other pairs, all of which had paused at Omar's sudden lurch forward. They stared at the bigger boy as he stumbled past where George had been, regained his footing, and faced George again.

"You can't just dodge me," Omar said as he repositioned his grip. "Fight back, Hero."

A few yards away, Albert stared open-mouthed at Omar and his knife clattered to the rocks. Gavin, holding his knife gingerly, stepped forward and nicked Albert's arm.

"Ouch!" Albert jumped back, his hand flying to the cut.

Gavin looked apologetic as he threw his knife to the ground and wiped his hands on his pants. The referee rolled his eyes and nodded at the firing range. Gavin gulped, blushing toward his opponent, and then trotted off to the range.

George hardened his resolve. *I can't let Omar face Albert. He'll kill Albert for sure.* He glared at the boy across from him. "Just because I'm quicker on my feet doesn't mean I'm not ready for a fight. Don't blame me because you missed."

Omar lunged forward with a grunt, his face contorted in anger. George bounced away again, this time lightly pushing Omar as the bigger boy passed. Gunshots in the near distance made George flinch. He rolled his shoulders, focusing on Omar.

"All brawn and no brains?" George bent his knees slightly, getting ready to move quickly again as Omar regained his footing. He took a moment to check on Lissa, his stomach dropping as Caleb caught her wrist as she thrust her knife at his arm.

"You're always pretending you're better," Omar growled, "but you're not. You're going to do the same messed-up stuff all of us are going to have to do to survive."

George was trying to keep one eye on Lissa as she struggled against Caleb's hold. She swung her fist at Caleb's face, but he blocked that with his other hand, the one that held the knife, and slid his knife downward, cutting Lissa's forearm. A short but intense scream left her lips as Caleb backed off, leaving her to hold her bleeding arm to her chest.

"I'm not trying to act better than you, Omar." George's heart was pounding in his ears. He couldn't focus fully on his opponent. Blood soaked Lissa's shirt and dripped on the gravel. The wound looked more serious than George thought such a small knife could inflict. Caleb's mouth gaped as the referee told him to go to the shooting range. He reluctantly left Lissa as Albert knelt beside her. George looked back at Omar. *This needs to end.* "I just *am* better than you are."

Omar scowled and rushed toward George, swiping his blade back and forth as George jumped back again and again. George fell backward onto the gravel, his elbows and forearms skidding across the rock as he tried to keep his head from smacking the ground. Omar raised the knife and plunged it downward as if trying to pin George to the ground. George rolled out of the way, and Omar's knife lodged itself into the dirt beneath the gravel. He scrambled to his feet, his eyes watering at the pain up and down his forearms. His skin was shredded, bits of gravel sticking in the tiny wounds, gouges running down the back of each arm, blood running in rivulets to his fingertips.

George held up his arms and looked at the referee. "Looks like he drew first blood."

"That doesn't count," Omar yelled as he yanked his knife from the ground.

"First blood is first blood," Ruger shouted.

The referee looked to Ace who shrugged an agreement. "All right, kid," the referee said to Omar, "go on to the shooting range."

Omar threw his knife to the ground and shoved George to the side as he passed. "Coward." He spat and stomped away to follow Caleb and Gavin. A second round of shooting had already begun. *Caleb is almost done with this test. Maybe he'll talk some sense into Omar.*

George took a deep breath and jogged over to Lissa. She'd used her knife to cut her t-shirt and then ripped the bottom half of it off. "Let me help." George reached out and took the makeshift bandage and wrapped it around her arm. The cut was still bleeding, and Lissa's face had lost a lot of its color.

"I don't want to do this." Albert's high-pitched, nervous whisper drew George's attention.

"Just nick me like Gavin nicked you," George said. "Once they give the go ahead, I won't stop you, okay? I trust you."

"Really?" Albert squeaked.

"Yeah," George said. "Just be careful."

"Thanks, George." Albert's tremble faded.

"I won't let you do that," Lissa said. She held her good hand to her stomach and heaved as if she were going to be sick. Sweat beaded her forehead and her whole body shook, but she recomposed herself. "I have something to prove, remember? I need to win this fair and square. Don't dodge me like you did Omar."

"We'll make a show of it," George whispered.

"You're not fooling anybody," Lissa hissed. "I have to fight through this, George. Do. Not. Go easy on me."

"But—"

"Enough chatting," Ace shouted. "Time for the last bout."

"I mean it, George," Lissa said as she backed away and picked up her fallen knife.

"Let's go," the referee said, backing up.

George's eyes were still on Lissa. She nodded at Gavin, and the younger boy stepped forward and quickly scratched George with his little knife. George flinched and drew in a sharp breath.

"Sorry," Gavin said as he threw away the little knife and held up his hands in surrender.

"It's okay. Good luck at the shooting range." George looked back at Lissa as Gavin scampered away. The kid wasn't a bad shot, as long as his nerves didn't get the better of him. The referee rolled his eyes at Gavin's back, but didn't say anything, much to George's relief. He had enough to worry about at the moment.

Lissa stood before him, blood soaking her shirt, dripping off her elbow, determination in her eyes though she had lost all color in her cheeks. It was time for them to do the unthinkable. It was time for them to fight.

Chapter 37

Zara Williams

"We were hoping to find you here," Mr. Peters said as he walked into the courthouse clerk's office.
Zara followed, glancing nervously down the empty halls before closing the door behind her. It turned out the plan depended on the good will of a little old woman, the only person they knew for sure wouldn't want Kai dead. The pilot wasn't there yet, or at least, his Jeep was nowhere near the courthouse. He'd taken his passengers into town to get them settled, and Zara and Mr. Peters had beaten him to the courthouse despite taking time to quickly stash their necessities in the plane's cargo hold in case of a quick getaway. But Kai could arrive at the courthouse any moment, and when Kai did get there, Zara expected things to get ugly.
"Well, hello, there Mr. Peters." Rita used her stepstool on the other side of the counter so she was tall enough to lean her elbows on the surface. "The auction is down the hall, up one floor, turn left, and there's a nice big courtroom dead center of the building. That's where Mr. Lee likes to hold the auctions." She furrowed her brow, pushed her glasses up her nose, and glanced at the clock on the wall. "Usually, there's more people here by now. So far, it's just been the new guys… Nolan and his crew. The locals come for the party. Mr. Lee compensates them to bring homemade baked goods, and he's always got plenty of drink to go around. Fancy stuff… wines, ale—"
"Rita," Mr. Peters stepped up to the counter and slapped the ballot down. "We're here to get Kai out of here before he's murdered."
Rita squeaked as her hand flew to her mouth, her widened eyes magnified behind thick glasses. "What?"
Zara scooted the paper across the chest-high counter. "I'm sure they've kept you out of it since you'd never agree. It's the Clearfield Watch. They've gotten out of control."
"We found this at the fairgrounds," Mr. Peters said. "They were having a meeting there, and it looked suspicious. I won't pretend our motives are completely selfless; we need Kai. So, we came to you. We have to find him before they do."
"Nolan, specifically," Zara said. "If he's already here, we need to catch Kai before he goes to that auction."
Rita's trembling hand picked up the paper, and she proceeded to gasp repeatedly, each one sharper and louder than the last. When she lowered the paper, the good-natured woman they knew was gone, replaced with a Rita Dimmesdale that made even Mr. Peters take a step back. Her glare was reminiscent of, and yet a thousand times more intimidating than, Zara's mother's glare, the one that kicked in when she was about to defend one of her children. Rita reached under her desk and pulled out a rifle that was almost as tall as she was high. She rested it on her shoulders, her features pinched and her face growing red.
Zara and Mr. Peters each took a giant step backward. Zara's mouth dropped open at the transformation. Rita was apparently a woman one should *never* cross. At first, Zara assumed the townspeople would have left her out to spare her. *Maybe it's the other way around. They're protecting themselves.*
"They've crossed a line," Rita said, her normally cheery voice now hardened. "That Clearfield Watch has been trying to run this town since before the illness. That they'd even think of harming a hair on that boy's head — I won't stand for it."
Mr. Peters picked his jaw up off the floor and blinked several times before he could get the words out. "Um, okay… I guess we're a team of three."
"Kai stops by here to get the list of participants every auction before he heads upstairs," Rita said. "They'll know that."
Mr. Peters nodded. "We're going to pull our weapons, too, okay?" He slowly placed a hand on his gun, telegraphing his intentions.
Rita frowned. "You're a sweetheart, Mr. Peters, but don't go asking permission in times like these."
Zara shrugged and pulled her gun. "Rita, I must say I like this side of you."
"Thank you, dear," Rita said.
At that moment, the door opened, and all three of them took aim at the door. Kai yelped and held up his hands, eyes wide. He looked from Mr. Peters and Zara to Rita, his frown deepening. "What in the—"
Rita lowered her gun. "Son, you've really gotten yourself into a pickle, haven't you?"
Kai turned on Mr. Peters and Zara as they lowered their guns. "Are you here to threaten *Rita*? I can't believe—"
"No, we're here to save your ungrateful butt," Zara said.
"Not that again." Kai groaned. "Mrs. Dimmesdale, they're nuts. That paper is fabricated nonsense. You don't have to worry."
Rita pursed her lips and marched down the step stool, the tip of her hair and her rifle visible as she rounded the counter and came through a swinging door. She softened her features just a little as she spoke. "Kai, I believe them. People have been avoiding me. I've noticed, but I just thought they were mad at you for not listening to them when they asked you to stop with the auctions. But I've been watching that security feed you set up under the desk. The only people who have come through the front doors are Nolan and his crew."
"You have a security feed?" Mr. Peters asked. "That's great. We can find them. They're probably waiting for him with guns ready."
Kai shook his head. "We keep the use of power light here. The security feed is just a baby monitor I set up so that Mrs. Dimmesdale could always see who comes inside." He shook his head. "I just… I don't believe it. I'm part of Clearfield. I'm bringing in good business." He looked at Rita. "Remember when I went looking for Clearfield residents who got stuck? I'm *saving* people. For the first time in my life, I'm doing something meaningful." He set his jaw. "I'm going to go talk to them." With determined step, Kai strode back into the hall.
"Wait!" Mr. Peters lurched forward, as did Zara and Rita. They all three followed Kai, pouring into the hall at the same time that Nolan and three of his men burst into the hall through a door opposite the clerk's office.

Kai was standing still as a statue, hands up. "I want to speak to the Clearfield Watch," he said.
It was a standoff. Nolan and his three men, all with guns, facing down Zara, Mr. Peters, and Rita. Kai was armed, but he hadn't pulled his gun.
Zara's heartbeat skyrocketed as she scooted forward and tugged on Kai's shirt. "Get behind us, idiot!"
"We're here for Mr. Lee." Nolan had his gun trained on Kai. "The rest of you should go, now, before you get hurt."
"Didn't anyone hear what I said?" Kai let his hands drop, his voice rising. "I want to speak to the Clearfield Watch. They wanted to scare me into compliance. Fine. I'll talk through a compromise."
"Too late for that," Nolan said.
Zara tugged harder on the back of Kai's shirt. "Kai… get behind us. Right. Now."
But Kai didn't move. Mr. Peters walked sideways, his gun pointed at Nolan, moved in front of Kai, and backed up. Zara grabbed Kai's arm, and together, she and Mr. Peters forced him to move back.
"They're not going to shoot me," Kai said. "They're just trying to scare me."
"Wake up, hon," Rita said. "If they wanted to do that, they'd be here to negotiate."
"The old lady is right," Nolan said. "Your time is up, kid. This is my town, now."
Zara, Mr. Peters, and Rita formed a half circle around Kai, moving as one, circling in the hall to get their backs to the front door. Nolan and his men moved with them in the double-wide hall.
"Don't come a step closer," Mr. Peters said, "or we'll open fire."
"Well, then, we'd all be in trouble," Nolan said. "I didn't come here to get rid of you, and my guess is the Clearfield Watch wouldn't be too happy with me if I shot Rita. Unlike Kai, here, people like her, even if some of 'em are a little afraid of her." He smiled at the old woman, who just scowled in return. "You almost saved his life without even knowin' it. But I'll kill every last one of you if I have to."
Kai mumbled something from behind them, and then spoke louder. "You're lying!" he shouted, his voice cracking. He pulled his gun and tried to step forward, though Mr. Peters held out an arm and blocked him from stepping through their line of defense. "Clearfield is my home."
"Keep back," Mr. Peters said. "If they shoot you, this is over. Stay behind me."
"Kai," Rita's voice was firm but empathetic, "you need to accept what's happening, or we're not going to make it out of this."
Zara kept her gun aimed at one of Nolan's lackeys, who in turn had his gun trained on her. "A shootout right here, right now is only going to get all of us killed or severely injured."
"We're not letting you go with him," Nolan said. "Not now. Not ever. That little punk has gotten in my way for the last time. He's half my age and not half as smart. He can pilot a plane. So what? He's a pompous, entitled nobody."
Kai scoffed. "Sounds like somebody's jealous. I'm a Clearfield gem. This town should be thanking me."
Zara rolled her eyes. "Really, man? Not the time."
Nolan growled. "I'm going to enjoy putting a bullet in your brain."
Zara stayed in step with Mr. Peters and Rita, the three of them continuing to make progress pushing Kai toward the old, wooden door with decorative glass panels. There was a portico outside, and a few stone steps. Then, they'd just need to make it to Kai's Jeep, wherever that was. Their bus would be too slow to outrun whatever Nolan would be driving.
"Go," Rita said. "It's time for the three of you to make a run for it."
"I don't think so," Nolan said.
Zara sucked in a breath as the man she was facing off against put his finger on the trigger. She pulled hers first, the explosion echoing off the hallway walls and ceiling. Gunshots erupted all at the same time, the stench of gunpowder filling the air. The noise itself knocked Zara back a few paces, vibrating her bones, leaving her ears ringing. It was over in seconds. Nolan and his three men were dead. And Rita lay on the floor, a bullet wound below her left collarbone.
"Mrs. Dimmesdale!" Kai knelt beside her, brushing back her hair. "I'm going to go get help. Hang in there."
"No…" Rita wheezed. "You have to run. Get out of Clearfield."
Mr. Peters put a hand on Kai's shoulder. "We'll tell someone on the street to come and help her. She'll be okay."
Zara's vision blurred with tears. She barely knew the clerk, but she didn't like the idea of leaving her behind, either. "Nolan's dead. He can't hurt Kai anymore."
"They'll still come…" Rita winced, holding her breath and tensing for a moment. "They'll still come for you."
"I'm getting help, and I'm not leaving until we know you're okay." Kai stood up. "I'm going to go get Dr. Cundiff or Mrs. Hallifax. She's a nurse, right? One of them will be able to help." He turned and ran for the door before anyone could stop him.
"Zara, go. Stop him. Or help him." Mr. Peters took off his button-down shirt, leaving himself in a yellowed undershirt, and pressed the fabric to the wound. "Whichever is quickest. We can't let him go on his own. Too many people want him dead."
"I'm on it." Zara sprinted after Kai, busting through the door only to skid to a stop, narrowly avoiding a collision with the pilot.
"You were right," Kai said, his voice small.
Zara stepped out from behind Kai, frowning, to discover the Clearfield Watch surrounding the entrance to the courthouse, every single one of them armed.

Chapter 38

George Peters

Lissa held her injured arm to her chest, the blood already soaking through the cloth wrapped around it. Her pleas for George to make the fight real still rang in his ears. If he didn't do as she asked, she could be seen as too weak for the guard. And that meant she'd be sent to the Butterfly House.

"You know I'm right." Lissa said.

"Yeah," George said, his heart dropping at the look in her eyes. *She can't go to the Butterfly House.* "Okay," he said. "Are you ready?"

Lissa pointed her knife at George. "I'm not a clumsy oaf like Omar," she said. "I can do this."

"I know you can." George took a deep breath and made himself charge Lissa.

She stepped into his charge and her head collided with his nose. The bone cracked with a sickening *crunch.* The taste of blood in the back of his throat made him gag and spit as his vision swam and sharp pain shot up through his skull. His knife slipped from his hand as he stumbled. Her knee rammed into his side, and George didn't have to pretend to fall to the ground. He groaned and rolled onto his back, holding his arms over his face. His head was exploding with blinding pain, and blood dripped from his chin, but he could still hear Lissa.

"If his skinned-up arms counted, that does, too."

A slow clap once again resounded, and George heard Ace's voice, though he couldn't yet focus enough to *see* anything. "Well, *that* was a surprise," he said, his voice getting closer. "Go on to the range, girl. I'm still watching."

George sat up and squinted at Lissa as she dropped her knife. "I figured a broken nose wouldn't run the risk of this." She nodded to her arm, held gingerly to her chest. Her eyes watered, and she was way too pale. Blood still dripped from her elbow, slow but steady. "Good luck, George." She turned her back and walked with an unsteady gait toward the range. She'd sounded exhausted.

But she's safe. He blinked rapidly and pulled the hem of his shirt up to his nose to try to stop the bleeding. He could already feel it beginning to swell. Ace looked down at him, shaking his head and clicking his tongue.

Ruger jogged over to stand next to Ace. "Ace, this one is a good one, I swear. He'll pass whatever test you put him to."

Ace smiled. "He reminds me of you, Ruger. Loyal to a fault." He looked down on George. "When we were kids, you were like him, protecting me when no one else would."

"He *is* like me," Ruger said. "And I think he'll be good for CON. He just didn't grow up on the streets like us. He needs some more experience, that's all."

Ace nodded. "All right," he said. "Let's see what he's got. Go get that first kid, the one that went nuts."

"Omar?" Ruger frowned.

"Yeah, that's the one." When Ruger hesitated, Ace raised his eyebrows. "Go get him, Ruger." As the CONman obeyed, Ace turned back to George. "You did good today, kid. I liked your gumption. You're last because you chose to be last. I need people who understand what it means to sacrifice for the greater good. You can see how Boston needs leadership, can't you? You can see how she needs me?"

George wanted to throw up on Ace's shoes, but instead he nodded, his voice nasally as he tried to speak despite his broken nose. "Yes," he said, remembering the answer to that question he and Lissa had practiced. "The city is falling apart. CON can build it back better."

"Good." Ace smiled and clasped his hands behind his back, straightening as Ruger brought Omar back. Lissa, Albert, Gavin, and Caleb followed, lining up at Ruger's request to watch whatever Ace had in store.

George struggled to his feet and managed to stay there despite the urge to hurl and curl up in a ball on the ground. His head pounded, his face was numb in some places and pulsing with pain in others, the coppery taste of his own blood made his stomach revolt, and his arms stung where they'd been shredded by gravel.

"Omar did well on the shooting range," Ruger said. "He hit every target."

"Yeah," Ace said, "he was probably feeling pretty good about himself."

Omar looked smugly at George. "If he hadn't cheated, I would have shown you what I can do."

Ace raised his eyebrows. "Oh, really? You would've what? Stabbed him in the gut?"

Ruger cleared his throat and gave his head a subtle shake, but Omar didn't seem to notice. The boy raised his chin. "Yeah, I would've gutted him."

Ace chuckled and nudged George with his elbow. "I did say no judgment, didn't I?"

Nose throbbing, George could only stand by and pinch his nose. Where is he taking this? Is he going to give Omar another shot at me?

"Here's the thing, though," Ace said. "What happened to the girl, it could have killed her if the cut had been lower, around her wrist. *That* was an accident. Our boy… what's his name?"

"The boy who fought against Lissa first was Caleb." Ruger held up a hand. "But we don't know that Omar meant to—"

"Don't try to defend a turncoat." Ace's tone lost its levity.

Omar blinked, his glare at George disappearing as his eyes widened in shock. "A w-what?" he stammered.

"A turncoat." Ace clasped his hands in front of him. "Your fellow CONmen came up with a plan, one that would mean most of you lived, if not all. Even the pansies participated. But you decided to go rogue. To play to power instead of loyalty." He reached behind his back and pulled out a gun. "That was the wrong move, my friend. I don't need more of *me* in CON, men grasping for my seat, trying to show off all the time. I need more of him." He nodded at Ruger. "Even more Big Macks and Icepicks. They play the game as a team. They don't turn on each other, even when they want to rip each other's throats out. They're brothers."

"But… but George is soft! He's not loyal to *you*." Omar beat his chest with his fist. "I can be loyal. I can be a CONman."

Ace held out the gun toward George. "Is that true, George? Are you soft, or can I count on you to play on my team?"

Whispers and gasps from the four kids lined up a few yards off to the side drew George's attention. Lissa stared at him wide-eyed, still pale, a look of concern on her face. Albert and Gavin looked at each other with uncertainty, and Caleb's lips formed a thin line as he hung his head and averted his eyes.

George took half a step back, away from the gun. "What are you asking me to do?"

"You can't be serious." Omar's panicked, high-pitched voice raised goosebumps on George's arms.

"You took it too far, kid," Ace said. "And you're right." He nodded at George. "I need to see he can do this." He grinned at Omar. "Thanks for your service." He pushed the gun at George.

"Take it, George," Ruger said, resignation in his voice. Omar whimpered and moved away from Ruger only for Ruger to grab his arm and pull him back into place.

"No." George pressed his palms against his thighs. "I'm not going to shoot him. He's not a threat to me now."

Ace shrugged. And then he shot Omar point-blank in the head. The movement was so quick, George barely had time to take a breath before he saw what Ace was doing. George shouted and held out a hand, but it was over in a flash. Omar was crumpled on the ground with a gaping wound in his head. No longer able to hold the contents of his stomach, George turned to the side and heaved.

Ace sniffed, holstered his gun, and patted George on the shoulder. "We'll work on it, kid." He pointed at Ruger. "He needs to be able to kill when I ask him to. I meant what I said, about seeing the potential, but the things I do here today, I do for you. I'm counting on you to make it worth it."

Ruger nodded. "I'll get him ready. I swear."

"If you don't, I'll have to find another place for him," Ace said. "We'll always need grunts."

"And what about Lissa?" Ruger asked.

George, body trembling from shock and exhaustion, snapped his head to look at Lissa. She gulped and took a few steps forward, nervously shifting her weight back and forth.

"The girl can stay in the guard," Ace said. "You were right about her, too."

Ruger let out a sigh of relief. "Thank y—"

"But she's gotta do her part to rebuild New Boston, too." Ace interrupted Ruger and waved his hand behind him. Big Mack stepped forward, a sinister grin spreading on his face as his eyes locked on Lissa. "I'll make her one of mine. She can live in comfort, share a room with Jade and Rachel, and still train for the Guard." He winked at her, and Lissa's chin quivered. "We gotta think long term. There's only one way CON survives. One way Boston survives. Repopulation."

George listened in horror. He limped over to Lissa, who was trembling as she held her arm. He stopped in front of her, and their eyes met.

"I tried so hard," she whispered, her eyes glistening, tears rolling down her cheeks.

"I know. This isn't your fault." George set his jaw and turned around, trying to think of something — anything — that might change Ace's mind.

"Don't do this, Ace." Ruger clenched his teeth. "Lissa belongs here, with the Guard."

"I agree. Mostly." Ace raised his eyebrows. "But if you think this will cause problems between us, I'll just let Big Mack have her for the Butterfly House. Out of sight, out of mind. I'd never let a girl come between us, Ruger."

Ruger closed his eyes, his whole body tensing once more. "No," he said, his shoulders sagging. "It won't be a problem."

"Good." Ace waved a hand, and two men walked past a sulking Big Mack and Icepick, heading straight for the line of kids.

George shook his head. "No," he said, standing in front of Lissa. "You can't do this."

Caleb, expression solemn, took a step back and away. He looked down at his feet and stood still as a statue. Albert took one step toward George as if to stand with him, but Gavin pulled back on him and shook his head. They both threw sympathetic glances at George and Lissa but joined Caleb.

George balled his hands into fists, still unsteady but willing to fight. "I'll distract them," he whispered over his shoulder. "Run, Lissa."

She shook her head. "What can you do? We have no power here. If I run, I die. If I make a fuss, I'll be sent to the Butterfly House." She stepped around George. "This is the best it gets for me."

"I'll get you out," George whispered. "I promise I'll try."

Lissa offered him a half smile. "I know you will." Then she held her head up high, strands of hair plastered to her forehead, face drained of color, her arm held close, and as the two men approached, she spoke as if she had some kind of authority. "I'll go where you lead me," she said loudly. "I won't resist."

Ace smiled broadly, and George's stomach turned. "All right," Ace said, holding up a hand to cause the two men to pause. "Our chariot awaits, then." He bowed and waved his hand toward the Ferrari. "You will need to be cuffed and I think I'll take you home in the trunk so as to not dirty the seats. Also, I just don't trust you, yet. But don't worry, it'll be for five minutes tops. We'll head straight home."

Lissa didn't struggle as one of the men cuffed her hands behind her back. George didn't know what to do. *This can't be happening.* He breathed in deeply, but it didn't help. The air was too thin. His lungs burned. There had to be something he could do. He stepped forward, his head still pounding, finding it hard to think through his next steps. *I can't let them take her.*

Ruger stepped in front of him and put both hands on George's shoulders. He leaned in and spoke quietly in George's ear. "What did I say about doing something stupid. Let me handle this." He pulled back and turned to Ace. "Do me a favor?"

"I've already done you a few today," Ace said.
"One more?"
Ace ran his tongue over his top teeth and then pursed his lips. "You can ask," he said.
"Give her a few days with Jade and Rachel to calm her nerves. Let her eat a few nice meals, enjoy the benefits of being one of yours. Just a few days for the ladies to help her understand that this is a good thing."
Ace shrugged. "Sure," he said. "I'll give her three days." He slunk off to his fancy white car as his men popped the trunk. Lissa climbed into it of her own accord, and soon gravel crunched under the wheels as the luxury car spun out of sight.
"I hate this place." George was dazed, but anger was starting to peek through his shock.
"Yeah." Ruger still stood beside him, still sagged more than usual.
George scowled. "I hate *you*."
Ruger sighed and nodded slowly. "Yeah. Me, too, kid. Me, too."

Chapter 39

Zara Williams

Zara stepped in front of Kai, slowly, hands raised, palms out. She was still ramped up from the shootout in the hall and the urgency to get Rita medical attention, and it took effort to move calmly into the line of fire. But they wanted Kai dead, not her. It was the only thing she could think to do to keep those with guns from taking aim and firing. The young pilot had lost his cocky flair. He stood silent and still before the mob, his expression slack as his eyes seemed to search faces that were surely familiar to him.

He wouldn't even see it coming. He's in shock or something. Zara didn't have time to feel sorry for him. She and Mr. Peters had tried to warn him he was in danger. *At least he finally believes us.*

Once she was positioned in front of him, she whispered over her shoulder. "Is there another way out of the courthouse?" As far as she knew, only one entrance had been left unlocked, and they'd just come through it. Kai didn't answer. Out of the corner of her eye, she thought she saw his eyes glistening. "Hey, *dude.* Snap out of it. I know this isn't fun, and I know it hurts, but we've got to survive right now."

"Where's Nolan?" A man stepped forward, one Zara recognized from a trading booth with freshly made pot pies. Mr. Phelps, if she remembered correctly. He had a tire iron in hand.

Zara narrowed her eyes at him. "Well, he's dead, but he shot Rita Dimmesdale, so I'm pretty sure he deserved it." She couldn't help but spit the words. *The nerve of these people. Asking after the man they sent to murder Kai.*

Mrs. Hallifax, the woman who'd sold Zara meds, shoved her double-barrel shotgun into Lawrence's hands — her more friendly offspring — and rushed forward. "Oh, Rita! Oh, no, no, no." Her face was contorted with worry, her voice a high-pitched whine. As she hustled past Zara and Kai, Zara heard her mumble under her breath. "What have we done?" Her other son, Jerry, only scowled at Zara as he'd done at the market. He had a baseball bat resting on one shoulder, and he looked like he wanted to use it.

The rest of the armed Clearfield Watch broke into harsh whispers, shuffling as they argued amongst each other. Zara strained to pick out what they were saying, but it was hard to distinguish their voices.

"We've come this far…"

"Rita didn't deserve…"

"… this was all a terrible idea…"

"If we don't stop Kai now…"

Their voices got louder and louder, and they became less and less focused on Zara and Kai. She looked back at the pilot again. "Kai, are you with me? We need to figure out what to do."

"I thought…" Kai trailed off, his eyes haunted. "They were supposed to be my family. I've known them my whole life…" He sucked in a breath, and his lips formed a solid line. Kai turned back toward the courthouse. "I'm going to see how Mrs. Hallifax is doing with Rita."

"What? You can't leave me out here!" Zara wanted to scream at him as he stuck his hands in his pockets, ignoring her, and entered the building. She turned back to the divided mob. If she went inside, her people wouldn't know if the Clearfield Watch decided to charge in. If she stayed, she could give them all a few seconds to hide should she see any signs of their advancement.

Maybe I can calm them down, or… make a case for letting Kai go. She grimaced. If I can find anything positive to say about that idiot. He loves Rita, at least. That's something.

"Hey, where'd Kai go?" A voice broke through the chaos. It was Jerry, Mrs. Hallifax's son. More people echoed him, and they all seemed to remember their common goal, turning their shouts on Zara.

Mouth dry, sweat dripping down her face, heart thrashing, Zara took a deep breath. "If you'd all just quiet down—"

"He's going to get us all killed!"

Zara didn't see where that comment came from, but she shook her head. "No! He's not. He'll come with us, and he'll never come back."

Jerry pointed his bat at her. "You can't promise that," he shouted.

Lawrence, cheeks bright red, elbowed his brother. "Stop it, Jerry! Let her speak."

"He's going to bring in the illness one of these days," Mr. Phelps said. "That kid has always been trouble."

Zara wiped the sweat off her forehead with the back of her hand. "This disease can be carried by both people *and* mosquitos. You won't be able to keep it out—"

Jerry levelled his bat in his hands and took a step forward. "No reason to invite it in!"

"It's a reason to cherish the people we have left!" Zara shouted.

"No one wants you here," Jerry seethed.

"Shut it, Jerry." Lawrence nodded at Zara. "She's got a point. Haven't enough people been killed?"

"Yes." A mournful voice rang out from behind Zara as the door behind her swung open. "We've lost enough," Mrs. Hallifax said. "Rita is dead."

Zara's heart sank. Her throat tightened, and her vision blurred. "Oh no," she whispered as Mr. Peters led Kai outside, a hand on his back. The door closed behind them. "Kai… I'm sorry."

Tears ran freely down the pilot's cheeks, but he was once again silent. He glared at the mob, balling his hands into fists at his sides. Zara may not have liked Kai, but she knew what it felt like to lose people.

She put a hand on his shoulder. "It's going to be okay. We're going to get you out of this, and her death won't be in vain. She loved you, Kai." He didn't respond or take his eyes off the crowd, but his hands started to tremble. Zara cupped her hands over his fist. She didn't know what else to do.

Mrs. Hallifax spared her a glance that was, for once, kind, and then she turned back to the crowd. "It's our fault," she yelled. "We did this. We should go," she said. "My boys and I won't be part of this."

"Sorry, Mom." Jerry stood up straighter. "You don't speak for me. I'm going to make sure our family survives, and that means Kai's got to go."

"Didn't you hear her?" Lawrence asked. "Mrs. Dimmesdale is dead because *we* sent Nolan after Kai."

Mr. Phelps shook his head. "She's dead because the newcomers interfered! Because Kai brings trouble on himself. It's not our fault."

"What about Nolan and his friends?" Another man shouted. "He's been here longer than the newcomer. We've had drinks with him. He helped us till a garden!"

A woman added her voice to the dissent. "Yeah, if those newcomers had left things alone, Kai would be the only one dead. One dead is better than four!"

"We should get rid of all of them!" Jerry shouted.

Mrs. Hallifax gasped. "Jerry! You take that back."

"Go home, Mom." Jerry hefted his bat. "Let's go, people. Let's get this over with." He took two steps forward before his brother, Lawrence, slammed the butt of the shotgun into Jerry's back.

All hell broke loose. The mob turned on each other, throwing punches and tackling those of opposing viewpoints. Mrs. Hallifax took half a step back, eyes wide. She turned around and leaned one hand on the brick wall of the courthouse, hanging her head and closing her eyes. "You three should go, now, while they're distracted," she said, her voice small. "It might be your only chance."

Zara exchanged a look with Mr. Peters, and he nodded.

"Kai, we need to get out of here. They're talking about killing all three of us, now. Are you ready?" Mr. Peters asked.

Kai tore his glare from the mob and stepped to his right, shaking off Mr. Peters and Zara. "My Jeep is this way." He didn't say anything else, but his movements were stiff.

Zara knew that look, that posture. He was angry like she'd been angry. It was already eating him up from the inside out. *No matter what he's done, he didn't deserve this.*

Mr. Peters put a light hand on Zara's back indicating that she should go first. She did, jogging to keep up with Kai as Mr. Peters brought up the rear. They skirted the edge of the mob, and Zara had to jump back as a man was thrown into the bushes. The man doing the throwing was on their side and waved at them to go.

Zara and Mr. Peters darted past, and as they caught up to Kai, a voice carried over the noise behind them. "They're trying to give us the slip!" And another voice, "Stop 'em!"

Kai turned into an alleyway a few paces ahead. Zara skidded around the corner, looking back to see the mob too close for comfort. Kai jumped in the driver's seat, and Zara got in behind him. Mr. Peters took the passenger seat.

"Hurry, Kai!" Zara twisted in her seat and watched as the mob oozed into the alley.

"I'm trying!" Kai shouted as the vehicle came to life with a whirr.

Jerry fought to the front of the fight, his mother's shotgun in hand, and took aim. Lawrence was charging him, hands outstretched, but he was several paces from being able to stop him.

"Get down!" Zara pressed her body to the seat as Kai stepped on the gas. A loud *bang* echoed through the air, but the Jeep was still moving, and the shot had somehow missed. Zara peeked over the seat as the vehicle left the alley on the other side. Lawrence had made it. He straddled Jerry, the two brothers in a wrestling match, as the shotgun lay on the ground.

"That was close." Mr. Peters turned to look at Zara. "You okay?"

Zara sat up and took a deep breath and nodded. Kai sped through the streets, taking sharp turns onto roads already cleared for traffic. They passed smaller roads where abandoned cars, wrecks, and fallen trees had been left alone.

"You sure you know how to get to the airfield without running into any roadblocks?" Mr. Peters asked.

"Yeah," Kai said. "I helped clear these roads." Then, he muttered, "Ungrateful bastards." He took another sharp turn, making his way along a zigzagged northeast route.

In the middle of his turn, Zara caught a flash of white out of the corner of her eye. A large white truck whipped around a corner and sped after them. "Someone is chasing us," she said, the urgency in her tone filling her to the brim with panic. A man leaned out of the bed of the truck, a familiar shotgun pointed their direction. "Jerry is with them. He's going to shoot!" Zara ducked again, and right as the shot exploded, Kai made another turn and she slid off the seat and onto the floorboard.

"We're on the road that leads to the airfield, now," Kai said. "There's no more turning, just a straight shot. You two better return fire, or we're in trouble." He pushed a button above him, and the soft top of the Jeep rolled back.

"Great." Zara pried herself from the tight space and climbed back onto the seat.

Mr. Peters unholstered his gun. "I'm going to use the ammo I do have pretty quickly. How far are we from the airfield?"

"About five minutes, but I've got some weapons in the back that should give them a run for their money," Kai said. "We need to stop them in their tracks, not just slow them down. I'm going to need a few minutes to get in the air once we get there."

Boom. Another shot rattled Zara to the bone, but it missed like the first one.

"Ha!" Kai snorted. "Jerry couldn't hit the broad side of barn."

"I'm not complaining," Zara said as she leaned over the back seat, her eyes widening at the three rifles, an ammo can, and a green metal box with the words *Cartridges for Weapons* stamped on top. It all looked military grade. She frowned and opened it. "Are those *grenades*?"

Kai laughed. "Yeah. One of those should do the trick. You know how to work one?"

"I mean, not besides what I've seen in movies and television." Zara closed the lid. "I'm not touching those."

Kai scoffed. "You just have to make sure you've got a clean pathway to throw the thing, keep pressure on that lever, pull the pin, and chuck it. Even if you don't hit the truck, you might scare them off."

Behind them, the white truck swerved as the man in the passenger seat climbed out to sit on his open windowsill, taking aim at them with a handgun.

"We've got a second shooter!" Zara shouted.

Mr. Peters, already turned around in his seat on his knees, popped up through the open roof, one hand slapping the outside of the Jeep and holding on to keep him steady as he fired his handgun. "Get down, Zara!"

The back window shattered as Zara ducked. The exchange of gunfire continued, the *pop, pop, pop*, freezing her in place. She waited to feel a round tear through her. But then the shooting stopped.

"One down," Mr. Peters shouted. "Zara, get me one of those grenades. Carefully. Kai is right. We need to get rid of them before we get to the airfield."

Zara trembled as she unfurled herself, forcing her stiff body to obey against its will. Her chest tight, her throat closing in, her ears ringing, she leaned over the back seat. Behind them, the man who'd been shooting the handgun from the passenger side window hung out of the truck, unmoving. The truck kept swerving as the driver shouted, looking over his shoulder as Jerry leaned in the back window and shouted back. He slowed only for a second when his lifeless buddy flopped out of the window, hitting the pavement hard. The truck bounced as the back wheel ran over the man's chest. If the bullet hadn't killed him, the truck certainly had. Still, they kept coming, once again lurching to a higher speed.

"Zara! I'm out of bullets." Mr. Peters shouted. "I need a grenade. Right. Now."

Zara tore her gaze from their pursuers and opened the box, swallowing bile as she reached for one of the round, black grenades. She picked it up like she would an egg, with a firm but gentle grip. Her heartbeat throbbed in her chest and thrashed in her ears, drowning out the ringing. She held her breath until she was able to deposit the grenade in Mr. Peter's outstretched hand, and then she let out a woosh of air and pulled back her hand, trembling.

Mr. Peters popped back up through the sunroof, pulled the pin, and threw the grenade. It bounced once on the pavement and hurtled toward the truck, which swerved. For a moment, Zara thought the grenade must have been a dud, that the truck would pass by without getting hit. But then a sound like a lightening strike tore through the air, and the back, right end of the truck lifted, twisting the vehicle as it flipped onto its top, throwing Jerry through the air and into the ditch.

Zara's mouth hung open as they sped away, the white cloud and wreckage growing smaller. *This is the world now. Killing to survive.* She turned around in her seat and hugged her stomach.

Kai turned into the airfield's drive and parked in front of the hangar. "You two get your stuff, and I'll grab my go-bags."

"We already put two backpacks and some of what we traded for in your cargo hold," Mr. Peters said. "You left it unlocked."

"Pretty confident we were going to make it back here, huh?" Kai hopped out of the Jeep.

Mr. Peters did the same, and then opened the back door for Zara. "We like to plan for the worst, hope for the best."

Zara slid out of the back seat, numb and exhausted. "To be clear, we somehow manage to always land just on this side of not getting ourselves killed."

"Well, thanks." Kai opened the trunk, slung the rifles crossbody, picked up the ammo can with one hand and grabbed the handle of the metal box with the other. "I would have been dead by now if it hadn't been for you two."

"We need to get out of here. Where are your go-bags?" Mr. Peters asked. "We can grab them for you."

Kai put down the ammo can, shut the trunk, and dug keys out of his pocket. "Over there, in that cabinet." He threw them to Mr. Peters, who wasted no time, going straight for Kai's supplies. Kai jogged with his weaponry to the plane to stow his supplies.

Zara followed behind him, waiting for him to hand her a bag, filing away the images of Rita dying on the floor and of the three men who were either dead or severely injured to her collection of violent memories.

"Hey, you okay?" Mr. Peters handed her a duffel bag after taking one himself.

"I don't know," Zara said. "I guess before all of this, I thought people were… better. It sounds stupid now."

"No, it's not stupid." Mr. Peters put a hand on her shoulder.

"I just want this to be done. I want to be home."

"You know that Boston is probably just as screwed up, don't you?" Mr. Peters spoke the words gently, but he voiced something Zara hadn't wanted to think about.

It hit her hard. "Boston isn't the end of this, is it? It's just the next death trap."

"Probably." Mr. Peters offered a small smile. "It might not be the end of this nightmare, Zara, but I'm hoping it's the beginning of the end."

"No time to chat," Kai said as he jogged up to them, grabbing a third duffel out of the cabinet. "Let's get out of here before more Clearfield thugs show up."

Minutes later, the cargo hold was full, and Zara was boarding the plane with Mr. Peters. Kai bounded up the steps and secured the door as Zara chose a seat, relaxing into the soft, plush leather.

Kai stopped in the doorway between the passenger seating and the cockpit, and he winked at Zara, some of his characteristic flair returning. "You and me are gonna be friends, babe. I can feel it."

Before she could say anything else, he ducked into the cockpit. Zara narrowed her eyes and crossed her arms. They'd just saved his life, and she already wanted to kill him.

Chapter 40

Timothy Peters

Eleven days. It had been eleven days since Timothy had said goodbye to his brother, George, and left to find supplies in the original bunker at his parent's house in Wellesley. Eleven days since he'd suffered Annika's countless, wonderful curiosities. Since he'd hugged his mother, taken the life in her eyes for granted.

Every day made it a little harder to hold on to hope. Small victories were always followed by epic failures. *That changes today.* Timothy set his jaw and adjusted his bulletproof vest, checking his gun and extra ammo were secure.

Candice and Heather were on either side of him, all three of them outfitted with gear. Ahead and behind, O'Donnell's recruits crowded the lobby of police headquarters. At noon, they would attack through the southeast entrance closest to the The Farm. Frank and his men would attack through the northwest entrance closest to the Tropical Forest Pavilion. Working together but independently, they were going to squash CON and save the children.

When Timothy had returned with Candice and Heather the day before, O'Donnell had convinced three quarters of the police force to help save the kids from The Farm and from CON. That victory should have uplifted Timothy. It should have given him hope. But it was dampened by what he'd learned, by the lies that now existed between him and his wife.

His father had betrayed them all. Walter Peters hadn't known about the safer hours of the day because some government higher-up had clued him in. He'd known because he'd been part of creating the disease. DV-10. The Peters' legacy. It made Timothy sick to his stomach.

"Tim?" Heather nudged him gently with her elbow. "It's going to be okay. We're going to get the kids back."

Timothy offered a weak smile. *If only that was all that I was worried about.* "I know," he said instead.

Candice took a deep breath, her banana-yellow silk blouse peaking from beneath her vest. A matching, shiny hair tie secured her braid. She had a second silky scrunchy — blue as a blueberry — around her wrist. She'd brought it for Annika. "They'll be okay, won't they?" Candice asked.

"Yes," Timothy said with more confidence than he felt. He lowered his voice. "And once we get George and Annika, we need to head to New Horizons. We need to get out of the middle of things as quickly as possible, slip away where we won't be found or expected to choose sides. You two are clear on the plan?"

Heather licked her lips and leaned in, speaking quietly. "And you're sure that's the right move?"

Candice leaned in, too, her eyebrows arched. "Of course it is. Those kids need some peace and quiet."

"They won't get much peace and quiet if the war over Boston reaches New Horizons," Heather said.

Timothy rubbed a hand over his face. "We talked about this, Heather. We've done enough fighting over the past weeks."

Heather pressed her lips together, her knitted brows betraying her doubts. "I know you, Tim. You're not being truthful with me. If you want to keep fighting—"

"What?" Timothy shook his head. He swallowed hard. He should've known he wouldn't be able to hide something from her without her sensing something was wrong. *Maybe it's better she think I want to go on fighting the Russos than she know this whole mess is my family's fault.*

"Light the torches!" O'Donnell shouted. "It's time to move out!"

He avoided answering by shuffling forward with the rest. As dozens of them filed outside, police on the edges of their group lit mosquito repellant bamboo torches. Since the safe hours were no longer guaranteed to keep them from swarms, O'Donnell had procured a large stash of the torches, hoping the citronella oil would encourage mosquitos to snack elsewhere. In addition, designated DEET sprayers began coating the crowd in more deterrent the second they were outside.

Timothy coughed, his eyes watering as a mist of chemicals engulfed him. "If that doesn't do it, we're in trouble."

"I can taste it." Candice gagged and waved her hands in front of her face as the woman with the DEET can liberally doused her. "Surely that's enough. Save some for everyone else."

"Thank you," Heather said as the woman left them for the row of police in front of them. "We need to stockpile that stuff, too," she said when they once again were able to walk at a near distance to the others. "It's a good idea. We shouldn't be going anywhere these days without chemical deterrents."

"One thing at a time," Timothy said.

But she was right. One impossible task followed another. Rescue the children, and then start from scratch. No supplies. Limited weapons. With a war raging outside. He pushed the future away.

One thing at a time. He repeated to himself as he marched west, toward George and Annika.

Chapter 41

George Peters

George ground his teeth, looking over his shoulder in the direction of the Tropical Forest Pavilion. If Ace held true to his word, Lissa would be there, unharmed for a little while longer. He was running out of time to do something about her predicament, but he had no idea how to help.

Ruger walked beside him around the perimeter roads of the zoo. Ace's stupid tiger had been spotted, and it was the job of the CON guard to ensure the animal was frightened back into the city. The last thing George needed was for Annika to be in danger of being eaten by the creature, so he'd gone willingly, despite the urge to rebel after what had happened to Lissa.

Caleb, Albert, and Gavin walked ahead in a line, all eyes on the streets, looking outward into the city. More guards were stationed at the entrances, but the tiger was more likely to jump a fence by way of a tree if it wanted inside, and so that's where the guard patrolled for the time being.

"I know you're mad at me, kid." Ruger didn't look at George. His eyes continued to search the wreckage and debris. "I did the best I could. Ace was doin' me a favor, putting Lissa in with his ladies instead of in with the Butterfly House girls. She won't like it, but… it's better. Trust me."

"Oh sure." George spat. "Is that what you're going to tell me when the same thing happens to Annika down the road? You told me she'd be safe, but that's not true. You can't protect any of us. Not really."

Ruger's cheeks burned red. He pressed his lips together and walked on in silence. A twinge of guilt pierced George, but he promptly batted it away. What he said wasn't entirely fair. Ruger *had* tried to protect them. But it was also true. The CONman had failed. His heart wasn't as black as Ace's or Icepick's, but it was still stained.

Gunfire erupted somewhere beyond their field of vision, and George froze, as did the others. "Did someone find the tiger?"

"Maybe." Ruger frowned. And then an explosion of gunfire rang through the air. The other three boys moved closer. "Something is wrong," Ruger said. "That sounds like back-and-forth fire. And it sounded like it was coming from the Northwest entrance."

George's heart leapt. The entrance in question was near the Tropical Forest Pavilion, not far from their position on Seaver Street. *Is someone rescuing us?* And then an explosion vibrated the ground beneath his feet. "Wait… the crew that Annika is on… where were they today?"

"All right, boys," Ruger shouted, ignoring George's question, waving at them to leave the street and head into the trees. A walkway led from Seaver Street to Pierpont Road where the entrance nearest to the Tropical Forest Pavilion stood. "Let's check this out. Use the trees for cover as we approach the parking lot. Follow me." Ruger stepped lightly and quickly, darting into the trees.

George followed, Caleb, Albert, and Gavin close behind. They flitted from tree to tree, following Ruger's lead until they approached the parking lot. Ruger had them stop and gather, as they witnessed the shootout happening several yards away. White vans provided some cover for a group of men with guns. CONmen returned fire from behind the giant, thick concrete pillars that held up the enormous statues on either side of the entrance. One of the pillars had a bite taken out of it, George assumed from the larger explosion he'd felt from Seaver Street. He squinted at the attackers, kneeling beside Ruger. And then he saw a familiar face.

"That's Frank Russo," George said, fear and anger flushing through his veins all at once.

Ruger did a double take. "Frank Russo? How do you know anything about Frank Russo?"

"My family's had trouble with him." George's stomach sank. "He knows Annika. He wouldn't hurt her, but he'd take her. He'd use her as a pawn against my brother."

"Annika is nowhere near here," Ruger said. "She's with the laundering team at The Farm. Keep your head on straight. Right now, if we're under attack, we need to help defend Ace's position. We can't be worried about anything else. You understand?"

George shook his head. "Every CONman is going to be thinking the same thing. Please, I have to get to Annika. Make sure she's safe. She's my responsibility."

"Your responsibility is to CON. Lissa is in the Tropical Forest Pavilion," Ruger said. "You care about her, too, right?"

"Everyone is protecting that building." George narrowed his eyes. "When we get inside the zoo, I'm going straight for The Farm."

"You'll do what I say." Ruger raised his voice, his tone harsh. "Whoever is supervising those kids will get them inside and make sure they're safe. You're coming with me, kid. No more arguments. If we stop Russo in his tracks here, he'll never even get close to her."

"Fine," George said through gritted teeth.

Return fire from the CONmen ceased. Ruger cursed as Frank Russo's men charged into the zoo, Frank strutting forward at the back, surrounded by big burly lackeys. Albert whimpered as he crouched behind George and Ruger. Gavin tried to comfort him, but Caleb stood on the other side of Ruger, clearly waiting for instructions. Ruger glanced at the cowering boy, cursing again.

"Albert, Gavin," Ruger said, "you stay here and keep an eye on the entrance. If another wave of men come to attack, blow your whistles to warn us. Think you can do that?"

Gavin fumbled to take out his whistle, nodding furiously, something of relief in his expression. "Y-yes, sir. We can do that."

Ruger shook his head but turned his attention to George and Caleb. "You two, follow me. You should be able to pick out CON from the Russos pretty easily. You see khakis, shoot to kill. They aim at us, we pull the trigger first. Got it?"

George nodded along with Caleb, but his mind was still on Annika. *What is Frank Russo doing here? Would it be better or worse for him to win this fight?* George had no idea. All he knew was that whatever happened — whether CON or the Russos ruled — he had to stay with Annika and make sure that she was safe.

Ruger led the way into the zoo, stepping over slow-moving rivers of blood and chunks of concrete. George was oddly unafraid. His heartbeat thundered inside his chest, but it wasn't from fear. Adrenaline pumped through his veins and kept him steady, kept him moving. A thrill enveloped him, and he raised his gun when Ruger did.

But then shooting erupted in the distance, from the other side of the zoo. George froze. "Annika," he whispered, taking steps forward when Ruger started to veer off to the left, toward the Tropical Forest Pavilion. The mountainous building, which once held a variety of tropical animals, was close.

"Hey, Hero," Ruger whispered harshly. "What did I say? Stay on me. Don't even think about it."

"You heard that," George said, shaking his head, jutting a finger in the direction of The Farm. "The Russos are attacking at the other entrance, too. What if they don't know there are kids? They could spray the area with gunfire. We have to go. *I* have to go." He backed up toward a smaller pathway that arced away from the Tropical Forest Pavilion and bypassed the mobsters.

"Don't." Ruger aimed at George.

"Are you going to shoot me?" George kept walking backward, hedging his bets that Ruger had some good in him. "Because I'm not trying to rebel against CON right now. I'm just trying to protect our people. Annika is part of CON, too, isn't she? Isn't that what you've been telling us?"

Ruger pressed his lips together, shifting his eyes between George and the path that led ahead to the Tropical Forest Pavilion. "Damn it, kid. There's rules. Why can't you get that?"

"You lost my trust," George said. "This is your chance to get it back. You say you hate it when one of us is put in danger. Prove it. Let me go and help CON protect those kids."

Ruger breathed out through his nose, a heavy and frustrated breath. "Fine." He lowered his gun. "Caleb, go with him." He pointed at George. "Don't get a big head about this. And remember that I mean what I say. I really am trying to do my best by you."

George nodded once. "Thanks, Ruger."

"If you try anything stupid, if you try to run…" Ruger hardened his voice. "You'll be hunted down. You understand?"

George nodded again. "I understand."

Ruger sighed and took off toward the Tropical Forest Pavilion, leaving Caleb to jog over to George. "I can't decide if you're an idiot, if you're just lucky, or if you're a genius," Caleb said.

George took off at a run, and Caleb kept pace without a moment's hesitation. "I'm probably just an idiot," George said.

Caleb snorted. "Yeah, maybe. Let's go get your friend, Hero."

They sprinted the length of the zoo until they got to an old restaurant CON was using to house food and other supplies. Outside, metal basins with soapy water dotted the grass, linens and clothes strewn about as if everyone there had left in a hurry.

"They must have taken them back to the barn," George said, referring to the meeting space the children had been using as their shelter. They ran the rest of the way, reaching the front door of the barn as the shooting nearby died down. George burst through the door to find one of the women who supervised the smaller children, Shannon, aiming right at him. A dozen kids were curled up behind her on the floor, most of them hiding in sleeping bags.

"Geez, George," Shannon said, jerking her gun upward. "I almost shot you."

"Where are the others?" Caleb asked as he closed the door behind him.

"I'm the only one that stayed. Everyone else had to go help. But now that you two are here, I've gotta go where the action is. You two can take care of a bunch of kids, right?" Shannon didn't really give them the chance to respond. Her words came quickly as she approached the door and opened it. "Stay here with the kids." And then she was gone.

"George!" Annika popped up from beneath a sleeping bag and held out her hands to him, her eyes watering and chin quivering. The little boy, James, peeked out from his own sleeping bag nearby, though many of the kids stayed curled up with their blankets over their heads.

"Annika, are you okay?" George knelt beside her.

A string of words poured out of Annika's mouth as she looked up at him. "People are fighting, and Shannon said we're in danger, and James scraped his knee when we were running, and it was really scary, and my sleeping bag is too hot!"

George hugged her tight. "It's going to be okay. We're going to make sure you're safe."

"How?" Caleb asked. "What if those mobsters come in here guns blazing?"

A few whimpers rose from around the room. George dried Annika's tears with his thumbs and tried to put on a brave face for her and the other kids. He stood up and threw a glare at Caleb.

"What?" Caleb shrugged.

"Let's be a little more discreet about the worst-case scenarios, okay?" George turned in a circle, trying to decide what to do, searching for anything that might help them keep the kids safer. "Maybe we should have them all go into the kitchen area."

Caleb nodded. "Yeah… that might be better. Maybe they can shield themselves with pots and pans and stuff."

"Okay, kids," George said, clapping his hands together to get them to look at him. "Come on. Get your sleeping bags. You're going to go sit in the kitchen."

Caleb jiggled the door into the adjoining room. "It's locked." He jumped up on the counter between the rooms and slid into the kitchen that way. He held out his hands. "Hand me the kids. I'll get them situated."

One by one, George helped the kids hop up onto the counter and slide across into the kitchen. Caleb grabbed pots and pans and cookie sheets, instructing the kids to cover their heads with them if they heard anybody else enter the room. Then, he joined George in the larger room, and the two crouched below the front windows of the building beside the door.

"Do you think we'll have to deal with the intruders?" Caleb asked, his gun at the ready. "Maybe they'll look through the windows, see the room is empty, and keep going."

"I don't know what's going to happen." George peeked over the windowsill, spotting someone in head-to-toe black gear in the distance. He ducked back out of sight and switched off the safety on his handgun. "But if they come knocking, we'll be ready."

Chapter 42

Timothy and George Peters

Timothy stepped over a dead CONman and then reached back to help Heather and then Candice. A crooked line of dead bodies blocked the entrance to the zoo. It wasn't pretty, but it was less death than he'd anticipated. Gunfire and the occasional explosion had drawn a good portion of the CON guard to the opposite end of the zoo before the Boston Police had approached the southeastern gate. Once the opposition was dead, police in gear moved deftly over the grounds toward The Farm.

"They're going to scare the kids." Candice cleared the dead bodies as if she were daintily stepping over something uncouth on a nice night out. She wrung her hands, which she'd found time to manicure over the past few days.

Timothy scanned the area as they jogged after the BPD toward Franklin Farm, which was just to the left of the entrance. A series of buildings made to look like barns, and a couple actual barns, made up the children's area of the zoo. He walked quickly, one hand on Heather's back, his eyes and ears open. If gunfire broke out again, he wanted to be able to shield her and get her to safety. But, so far, the only movement in the area was that of the police officers.

O'Donnell called several of his lead men and women to him. After a few seconds, they dispersed, and O'Donnell waved Timothy over. "The grounds here at The Farm are clear. We're going to start clearing the buildings. You and yours come with me and mine."

Timothy nodded, and soon he, Heather, and Candice were following O'Donnell, Freeman, and Landry to the Meeting Barn, a place normally used for things like birthday parties for kids. The cops from Chelsea – Burke, Murphy, and Torres – passed them on the way to the petting zoo barn. It was quiet save for the shuffling of feet and the distant gunfire. Timothy hoped it stayed that way.

O'Donnell approached the white double doors, peeking through the glass panels for a second time before he tugged on the doorhandle. "It's locked." Using the butt of his gun, he broke a glass panel and then reached in to open the door.

Timothy stood back with Heather and Candice, keeping an eye on the larger windows off to the left. The second the doors opened, two figures popped up in the shadows beyond the glass, both of them raising weapons. "O'Donnell!" Timothy shouted. "Watch out!"

O'Donnell, Freeman, and Landry raised their weapons, crouching and aiming. "Police! Drop your weapons!"

"They're just kids, Chief!" Freeman shouted.

"How do we know you're police?" One of the figures shouted, gun still raised.

Timothy frowned. That voice was familiar. He squinted at the shadowed figures through the windows.

The same voice spoke a second time. "I saw Frank Russo. I know he's here. You can't have the kids."

O'Donnell growled. "Lower your weapon, kid, or I will shoot."

Heather put a hand on Timothy's shoulder. Her furrowed brow warped into an expression of recognition, and she voiced the thought just as Timothy put a name to the voice. "Tim," she breathed in a panicked tone, "that's George!"

A rush of adrenaline as his heart leapt into his throat propelled Timothy forward, hand outstretched. "O'Donnell, don't shoot! That's my brother!"

***

"Tim?" George blinked at the sound of his brother's voice, barely able to believe what he was hearing.

"You know these guys?" Caleb's gun dipped lower as he shifted uneasily on his feet.

And then Timothy burst into the room, putting himself between George and the men who'd been aiming at him. "Lower your weapons!" Timothy shouted. "Didn't you hear me? That's my brother." He glanced over his shoulder. "George, put your gun down. Your friend, too."

George lowered his gun, switching the safety back on. He nodded at Caleb to do the same. "It's okay," he said. "We can trust him."

Caleb breathed out shakily and holstered his gun. "So… you guys really are the police?"

"Yeah, kid." O'Donnell lowered his weapon. "How did you two get guns?"

"We're being trained for the CON guard," George said. "I've been earning their trust. I figured getting a gun would be my best shot at getting me and Annika out of here."

Timothy's mouth gaped a little. "Wow, George. That's a really brave thought." He stepped forward and wrapped him in a hug. "I'm proud of you, buddy."

A mixed flood of emotions made George hesitate. He was shocked and happy to see his brother alive, but… it had been almost two weeks since someone had talked to him like he was a little kid. He couldn't go back to waiting on the sidelines for someone to believe he was ready for the action. Heather and Candice popped into the room, and Heather joined in the hug.

Candice looked around the room, seeming dismayed at the empty sleeping bags. "Where's Annika?"

He pulled away. "The kids are in the kitchen," he said.

"Blueberry?" Candice shouted, bounding toward the counter that separated the kitchen from the larger room.

Annika's small voice squeaked a reply. "Banana?" Her eyes peeked over the counter, and upon seeing Candice, Annika squealed and jumped up and down. The other kids curiously peeked over the countertop, too, though most of them were more wary than excited.

Candice went straight for the door, which Annika ran to unlock from the other side. In seconds, the little girl was wrapped in a hug of her own. George felt a piece of himself melt in relief. He was no longer solely responsible for Annika. She was safe.

The other kids slowly filtered out into the room. The cops who'd first come in called to more police, and soon a woman flew into the room, eyes wildly searching. "James?" she called, and the little boy George had saved from punishment that first day at the zoo ran to her.

It's over. George breathed out slowly, but then he remembered Lissa and the mobsters.

"Wait…" George frowned at Timothy. "I *did* see Frank over at the other side of the zoo. Is he working with you?"

"Sort of, bud." Timothy patted George's shoulder. "Don't worry about it. You're safe now."

Anger at being dismissed rushed over George. "Tim, what's going on over there? There are other kids, older kids in the Tropical Forest Pavilion. My friend, Lissa—"

"Lissa Abrams?" The leader of the police, O'Donnell stepped toward George. "Lissa is over there?"

"You know her?" George looked around for an older woman who might share some of Lissa's features. "That's right. She said her aunt is a cop. Is she here?"

"No," O'Donnell said. "She's… dead. But I promised to find Lissa. I've got to get to her. Where is she?"

"I don't know for sure," George said. "Ace made her one of his… ladies. That's what he calls them." George's cheeks burned red. "It just happened yesterday. I don't think she's been forced into anything yet."

O'Donnell's features pinched and his hands balled into fists. "If that sick bastard touched her, I'm going to skin him alive." He began barking orders. "Landry, if the older kids are over there, maybe you'll find your sister, Wren. Come with me. Murphy, Burke, Torres, you stay here…" He continued rattling off names, and within moments he'd separated the police into those who would take the smaller children out of the area and those who would forge on to rescue the older children.

When O'Donnell and his team began their march toward the Tropical Forest Pavilion, George made to go after them. Timothy put a hand on his shoulder. "What do you think you're doing?" he asked. "We need to get all of you kids out of here."

George shook off Timothy's hand, ignoring Heather's raised eyebrows. "You have no idea what I've been through the last two weeks." He backed away and pointed northwest. "My friends are over there. And so are my enemies. The man who killed mom. Ace. I'm not leaving this fight until it's over."

Timothy's mouth dropped open a second time. "George, you listen here—"

"No, *you* listen." George shook his head. "I'm going. You can come with me if you want to help me. But I'm going." There was no time to argue, no time to explain further. He turned his back and jogged after O'Donnell and the Boston police.

He hadn't gotten very far when Timothy jogged up beside him. "Heather says I shouldn't try to stop you." He didn't sound like he believed that was the best route to take.

"Are you going to listen?" George kept pace with the police in front of him as they got closer and closer to the sounds of fighting.

"Have you ever tried arguing with Heather?" Timothy offered a small smile as he glanced sideways at George. "Plus, you're too heavy for me to throw over my shoulder."

George snorted and smiled, grateful to have his big brother by his side, a little shocked that Timothy wasn't doing more to stop him. His smile faded, however, as they approached the northwest side of the zoo, now turned war zone.

* * *

"George, get down!" Timothy grabbed his little brother by the arm, forced his head down, and covered him with his own body as bullets pinged off the colorful metal surrounding them. He'd followed O'Donnell and his team into a butterfly-themed pergola just before a battle between mobsters and CONmen came to a head at the end of the decorative zoo structure.

"We don't have time for this." George grunted and jerked free. "We have to go around." He sprinted back the way they had come, barely flinching as a bullet sparked off a metal butterfly affixed to the fence.

"No, wait!" Timothy sprinted after his brother, glancing over his shoulder to find O'Donnell, Freeman, Landry, and two other officers he didn't know running toward the minimal shelter of playground equipment on the other side of the pergola. There, some of Frank's men were exchanging gunfire with CONmen sheltering behind trees across the road to the north. A few of the CONmen had apparently spotted O'Donnell and his men and turned some fire on the pergola. It seemed O'Donnell was siding with the mobsters, upholding their temporary alliance. Timothy spared a hopeful prayer that Frank's men were just as much sticklers for agreements as Frank was. Ideally, the two forces wouldn't have crossed paths during their attempt to defeat CON.

Ahead, George veered into a viewing alcove once reserved for the giraffes. He hopped the log fence and began climbing the short, chain link fence on the other side. Timothy skidded into the wooden barrier and reached out to grab at his brother's shirt, to keep him from launching himself into the enclosure. On the other side, a steep and rocky ditch bit into the ground.

"George, stop! Just wait a minute." Timothy's fingers brushed the fabric of George's shirt, but he didn't manage to grab hold.

"We have to get to Lissa and get her out of there." George jumped, falling out of sight.

Timothy's heart burst with fright. He hopped the wooden fence and leaned over the metal one, relief flooding him as he saw George begin to scramble up the rocky embankment. "We can get to your friend with the police as backup," Timothy said. "Please, come back. We'll wait for the shooting to die down, and then follow O'Donnell to the Tropical Forest Pavilion."

"The main pathways are going to be full of fights like that one." George struggled up the incline, rocks dislodging beneath his feet with every step. "We can cut through the enclosures, get to the Tropical Forest without resistance, grab Lissa, and then get out of there."

"It won't be that easy." Timothy groaned as he realized his brother was not returning. He looked down into the ditch. "If I twist my ankle or something…" He carefully straddled the metal fence and lowered his body until he was hanging, his feet still too far from the ground. "Here goes nothing." He let go, hit the ground, and fell backwards onto the rocks.

"You okay?" George asked.

Muttering a curse under his breath, Timothy got to his feet. His tail end had not appreciated the rough landing, and his hands were a little scraped up, but he was otherwise fine. "I'd be better if we weren't doing something crazy." He climbed the rocky ditch, still unsure how he ended up there. "George, I'm an adult. You're twelve—"

"Thirteen," George said. "I turned thirteen, actually. While I was with Icepick and Digger, right after… after Icepick killed mom."

Timothy joined George on the grass at the top of the ditch. "I guess you're right. Thirteen." Timothy put his hand on George's shoulder. "You know that wasn't your fault? What happened to mom, I mean. It was mine. I never should have left—"

George shook his head. "No. It wasn't my fault. It wasn't yours either. It was Icepick's. And if I see him while we're looking for Lissa, I'm going to kill him."

Timothy blinked, his mouth running dry. "George, no. You're still a kid."

"What — you're going to do it, then?" George scoffed and walked away, heading in the direction of the Tropical Forest Pavilion. The white dome of it could be seen through the trees on the other side of the enclosure.

"I don't know." Timothy jogged after George. "If he was an immediate threat, yes. I'd be lying if I said the idea of hunting him down wasn't appealing, but—"

"But I'm too young?" George spun on Timothy. "I've been keeping myself and Annika alive for almost two weeks. I'm not going to let you keep me from doing what I know is right anymore."

Timothy balked. "When have I ever—"

"When Frank attacked us at the house, I could have helped. I'm a good shot, Tim, and you knew that." George jabbed his finger into Timothy's shoulder. "Maybe if you'd had an extra gun on your side, Heather wouldn't have gotten shot. And I should have been carrying when Icepick and Digger came for us. Instead, our weapons were stashed away, and we had no time to get to them."

"We were trying to protect you." Timothy ran his fingers through his hair. The sound of the gunfight still raged too close for comfort. "We can hash this out later, okay? I… I can see why you're angry with me. I just don't know what to do about it. Now that both mom and dad are gone, I *have* to protect you."

George shook his head. "No, that's where you're wrong. You're not my parent. You're my brother. And I'm not the same kid I was before. I can make my own choices." He turned his back and sprinted across the grassy field.

Timothy's heart cracked. George was right. He was *not* the same, and there was nothing Timothy could do to erase the terrible things that had forced him to grow up so fast in such a short amount of time. But no matter how brave or passionate his little brother became, he would always be his little brother. Timothy forged ahead, determined to keep George safe, whether he wanted him to or not.

Chapter 43

Heather Peters

It wasn't over, not by a long shot. The kids were lined up, policemen and women surrounding them, ready to take them to safety. Timothy had run after George, leaving Heather, Candice, and Annika to meet them at a nearby church where they would be able to continue on together to New Horizons. There, they would all be safe from the coming war over Boston. He'd been reluctant to leave, but Heather knew her husband wouldn't be able to live with himself if he'd let George go on his own. And besides, she and Candice made a good team. Heather had no doubt they could get Annika to the lab, as long as they could escape the zoo unscathed.

"Where's Mary?" Annika craned her neck to look down the line of children from her perch on Candice's hip. "I don't see her."

Ahead, Torres shouted, "Everyone ready?"

"Wait a minute!" Candice shouted, patting Annika on the back, reassuring her. "We think there might be a kid missing."

"We need to go." Burke turned his head to look in the direction of nearby gunfire.

Murphy, who now held her son, James, in her arms, put one hand on Burke's arm. "Give it a minute."

Burke drew his lips into a thin line, met Murphy's eyes, and then looked to Torres, who nodded. The three Chelsea cops were as tight knit as ever. Heather doubted anyone but Murphy or Torres would have been able to change Burke's mind.

"Who are we looking for?" Burke barked at Candice.

"What does Mary look like, Annika?" Candice asked.

"She's my size. Blonde hair. Lots of freckles." Annika wiggled free of Candice's grip and stood on her own two feet, walking down the line of kids. Most of them looked exhausted. Some whispered among themselves as Annika asked after Mary. When she got to the end of the line, Annika put her hands on her hips. "Nope. Not here."

"When did you last see her?" Heather asked.

Annika wrinkled her nose as if she were trying hard to think. Then she shrugged. "In the kitchen?" She didn't sound too confident.

Heather sighed. "Okay, I'll go check." She glanced at Burke. "Wait just a minute, okay? I'm going to see if the little girl is hiding somewhere. Maybe she got frightened."

"Just hurry. You've got one minute." Burke shifted his weight, his features pinching as a shout rose from somewhere nearby. He turned to give orders to the other cops. "Be ready to engage as we retreat. Murphy will lead the kids, and the rest of us will create a wall of protection ahead and behind. We're heading to the pre-disclosed safe house two blocks east. No rest until we get there. Eyes open. Stay alert."

Heather bolted back into the building in which they'd found the kids, rushing to the kitchen. It was empty. "Mary?" She called out and listened. A soft whimper sounded from a cabinet under the sink. Heather knelt and opened the door to find a little girl curled up inside, her cheeks stained with tears. "Hey, sweetheart. I've come to get you. It's going to be okay." Heather held out her arms. "Come on, honey. We need to get out of here."

Mary shook her head furiously.

"You know Annika, right?"

The little girl nodded.

"I'm Heather. I'm Annika's friend." Heather gestured for the girl to come out. "Please? We have to go before the bad men come back."

Mary hesitantly slid out of the cabinet, and Heather scooped her up. She locked her arms around Heather's neck, her legs around Heather's middle, and Heather ran back outside. "I've got her!" she shouted, taking up position once again beside Candice and Annika.

"Let's move out!" Burke shouted.

Mary wouldn't let go, so Heather carried her forward. Annika walked beside Candice. Behind them, a row of cops kept an eye on their backs. Ahead, nine kids shuffled forward, the cops blocking them in on the sides herding them in the right direction. Murphy held her son at the front of the group of kids, and another line of police protected them from the front.

The exit wasn't far, and they were soon there, coaxing children to step around the dead CONmen they'd left on the ground upon entry. Heather's heart lightened at the sight of the street ahead. They were leaving the fighting behind. *Just a couple blocks to –*

A gunshot rung out, not from behind, but from ahead. Heather flinched and covered Mary's head, as Candice crouched with Annika. At the front of the group a man in gear cried out as his leg gave way.

"Take cover!" Burke shouted.

The concrete walls of the entrance were just behind them. "Go back!" Heather prodded Candice. She tugged on a few of the children nearby. "Hide behind the wall. Hurry!"

Most of the cops hurried to the front to shield them while Burke and Torres rallied with Murphy to help get the dozen children safely behind the wall. Heather pressed her back against the concrete, her heart racing. The way the path curved didn't allow for her to see past a building and trees, but the sounds of the fight coming closer were getting louder by the second.

"Who is shooting at us?" Candice checked Annika from head to toe repeatedly.

"CON might have had a few men in the city," Murphy said. "Unless it's the Russos going back on their deal."

Heather shook her head. "Their kids are here, too. They wouldn't do that."

"I hope not." Murphy moved to the edge of the wall and peeked out. "The shooters look to be in CONman streetwear. Our guys are pinned down. We can't go back into the zoo." She stepped back and put her hands on her head, squeezing her eyes shut. Then her eyes popped open. "We're going to have to risk exiting there." She pointed north. The entrance was essentially a pair of concrete arches, connected by several yards of fence.

"That's too close to the fire," Heather said. "Whoever is shooting will see."

"Not if we're quiet and quick. They are too focused on our guys returning fire. We can stay close to the fence, move between it and the trees until we're far enough from gunfire that we don't have to worry. We'll double back through the streets in a wide arc to make it to the safehouse." She wiped the sweat off her brow and glanced down at her son, James. "If we stay here, CONmen will surround us, and then it will be too late. The window for escape is narrowing."

"It's risky," Torres said.

Burke glanced back at the inside of the zoo. "So is staying here."

"I think we should go," Heather stepped up to the Chelsea cops.

Candice joined her. "Me too." When Burke and Torres quirked their eyebrows, Candice scoffed and gestured to herself and Heather. "We get a say, whether you like it or not."

Torres put his hands up in surrender. "Okay, fine. If all four of you think it's worth the risk… let's do it."

Heather grabbed Mary and took responsibility for a few other kids as the other adults did the same. Encouraging the kids to play quiet as a mouse, they hurried along the chain link fence to the other concrete structure of doorways. All the while, the shootout continued too close for comfort. These arches weren't in the direct line of fire, but as they reached them, a stray bullet hit a tree just on the other side of the fence, sending chips of wood flying as a sharp *thud* encouraged Heather to run the last few steps, practically dragging the two children she had by the hand, and pressing against the concrete wall.

"Are you sure about this?" Torres asked as they all took shelter. "Once we leave the protection of these concrete walls, any one of us could be hit by a stray bullet or a ricochet."

Murphy held her son tighter and glanced over the other kids. "Maybe we should—"

A distant shout drew Heather's attention. Back in the zoo, a group of four CONmen were jogging down the pathway, and one of them was pointing directly at them. Heather's heart leapt into her throat. "We don't have a choice," she said, pointing out the approaching threat.

"Take the kids." Burke hardened his voice and set his jaw. "I'll hold them off as long as I can."

"Burke, no—" Murphy's voice caught, her eyes glistening.

"Go!" Burke shouted.

Torres teared up, too, but he grabbed two of the smaller kids, one on each hip. "You bigger kids are going to have to run. You can do this."

Heather grabbed Mary who was still frozen with fright. The girl buried her head in the crook of Heather's neck, her stiff arms locking. She tried to loosen Mary's grip just a little so she could breathe. Candice wrapped Annika in her arms, and Murphy kept her son in hers. With Torres carrying two, that left seven of the bigger kids, each somewhere around ten to twelve years of age.

Panic clawed at Heather's chest as the second shootout between Burke and the approaching CONmen began. She, Candice, Murphy, and Torres urged the kids through the exit, most likely leaving Burke to die. Heather's feet fell heavy on the ground. Mary's whimpers added to the frantic beat of her heart. She couldn't breathe as she tried to run and, at the same time, keep track of Candice, Annika, and the children running on their own. It was chaos.

As they approached the four-lane avenue chock full of abandoned vehicles, Heather's eyes were on the other side. If they could slip through the maze of wreckage and disappear into the city beyond, they'd escape immediate danger, have the chance to recoup. Heather and Candice could take Annika and make a run for the safety of New Horizons while Murphy and Torres could lead the other children to the safehouse in relative peace.

Heather kept as low as she could, ducking behind vehicle after vehicle. Down the road, Heather spotted a few CONmen behind trees, facing the zoo, exchanging fire with the Boston police. None of the CONmen so much as glanced their way as they guided the children across the road. *We're doing it! We're escaping!*

Candice and Annika ducked behind a vehicle a few feet away. Candice pointed to her ear and scrunched up her face, mouthing, "Do you hear that?"

Heather frowned. The popping of gunfire persisted, but that didn't seem to be what Candice was talking about. An animalistic bawling had joined the cacophony. It seemed to be coming from the direction they were heading. They were sneaking through an intersection, heading for a road that was perpendicular to the one that outlined the zoo's perimeter. Just past the intersection, a creature raised its head, wicked horns pointing at the sky. Several beasts were munching on a long strip of grass and bushes planted in the median.

"Are those… wildebeests?" Heather counted at least a dozen.

Murphy, who was closer to the other side of the intersection, popped up to look, groaning as she sank back to the pavement. She turned to face Heather. "Wildebeests are aggressive. We'd better go that way one block instead. It'll make our loop larger, but I don't think we have a choice."

"Everyone get down!" Torres, who was bringing up the back, shouted.

Heather whipped around as Torres fired a shot, just in time to see a CONman take a bullet to the chest, knocked on his back before he was able to take aim himself.

"They must have gotten past Burke!" Murphy yelled. "Everyone move!"

Murphy chopped the air with her hand repeatedly toward the only remaining safe direction. To their left and behind, CONmen were a threat. To their right, the wildebeests were an unknown, possibly dangerous.

There was no way to move deftly, to stay low as Heather traversed the debris. She ran into obstacle after obstacle, needing to lift kids over crunched car bumpers and slide across car hoods to move forward. The CONmen who'd gotten past Burke were on their tails, bullets sparking off car hoods and shattering windows, releasing the stench of weeks-old corpses. Heather gagged as she scrambled forward, her eyes watering.

Farther back along the road, where the rest of the BPD were still fighting the first group of CONmen they'd encountered, an explosion sounded and the ground beneath Heather's feet shook with the blast. She stumbled and fell against a vehicle, her hand falling through the broken window, sharp glass cutting her hand as she gripped the sill to stop Mary's body from slamming into the car. An overwhelming, rancid odor of decay washed over her as she came face-to-face with a grey-green corpse in a women's business suit, the mouth hanging loosely, maggots infesting every orifice, eyes missing completely.

Heather screamed and reared backward, falling to the ground while trying to keep Mary from getting hurt. The little girl cried out as Heather pushed her to the side and wretched, her whole body shaking as she tried to steady herself on hands and knees. Her ears were ringing, her head swimming from nausea, when Torres's arms wrapped around her middle and lifted her, forcing her to her feet.

Heather's eyes widened as she saw above the tops of the cars. The few CONmen that had made it past Burke and come after them were screaming and running toward them, the herd of wildebeests right behind. One was head-butted by one of the creatures, a horn spearing him as the beast tossed him aside to be trampled. Another tripped and his screams rang out as the wild animals overran him. The wildebeests had been frightened by the explosion, and were stampeding straight for them, leaping over the lower parts of the debris, somehow always finding a way to keep speeding along.

"Don't just stand there! Run!" Torres shouted. "Get to the side, to those buildings!" He picked up Mary and pointed to where Murphy stood in a cluster with a bunch of the kids under the portico of an apartment building.

Instinctively, Heather ran after Torres, fear muddying her thoughts as the herd of wildebeests neared, as the stench overwhelmed her, and as the image of the decaying corpse had completely unnerved her. But when she reached the sidewalk, finally clear of the wreckage, she realized her oversight.

"Where is Candice?" She was breathing too fast, too heavy. She was so dizzy, but she spun around and tried to focus her vision.

"Candice? Annika?" She shouted and scanned the four-lane avenue, spotting them farther north in the median. A CONman was struggling with Candice to take Annika from her. "No! Hold on. I'm coming!" Heather lurched toward them, but Torres grabbed her around the waist again and flung her backward.

The lead wildebeest bounded past her, barely missing her. The CONman shouted in surprise at the oncoming stampede, apparently having been too focused on retrieving one of CON's slaves. He dropped Annika's legs and bolted. Candice hugged Annika to her and sprinted for safety. Even from a distance, Heather could see the terror on her face.

Heather screamed in agony as a wildebeest leapt over the hood of a car right for Candice and Annika. A blur of powerful muscle and bleating beasts followed. In seconds, the herd had fled the area, having trampled the spot Candice and Annika had been standing.

Chapter 44

Timothy and George Peters

Timothy crouched beside George at the edge of a tree line, staring aghast at the Tropical Forest Pavilion. They had ventured across the giraffe enclosure, across an access road, and around a fenced-in garden only to hide in the foliage, blocked again by fighting. Though the entrance was mere yards away, the concrete plaza was fraught with hand-to-hand skirmishes. Dead bodies, a mixture of CONmen and mobsters, littered the ground. A blood-spattered sign riddled with bullet holes announced a reopening after renovations. The building itself had been damaged, and it didn't look any safer indoors. Bats flitted around a gaping hole in the side of the dome, and pops of gunfire were accompanied by screams and shouts from within.

"Where is your friend?" Timothy asked, keeping his voice low. He didn't see a way through to the twisted, mangled doors without attracting too much attention.

"I don't know. I've never been inside." George's tone indicated he didn't think that was a problem.

Timothy grabbed George by the shoulder. "What do you mean? I thought you said you knew what you were doing."

"I said I knew what I needed to do, and I'm doing it." George shrugged off Timothy's hand. "I'm going in there, I'm going to find Lissa, and I'm going to get her out."

Sweat soaked Timothy's shirt, beaded on his forehead, and dripped off his chin in the summer heat. His heart beat furiously, and a rock formed in his stomach as a smaller explosion sounded from somewhere inside the building. Someone began screaming in pain.

"This is crazy," Timothy said. "We should wait for O'Donnell. We've each got one handgun. That's it. It isn't enough." *And you're just a kid.* He kept that last thought to himself. Their conversation earlier had been repeating in his head. *Arguing about how he's not an adult yet will just drive him further into danger, and he won't let me go with him.*

"And what if Lissa is killed while we're out here waiting for your friends to get here?" George didn't bother to keep his voice down.

Timothy hushed him, glancing nervously at the men fighting nearby. The last thing they needed was for someone to start shooting into the trees or come after them. *Would they even be able to tell which side we were on?* He was wearing police gear, but George was dressed in street clothes similar to those worn by CONmen.

"This is reckless," Timothy said. "You're not thinking about all the angles." He gestured toward the plaza beyond the trees. "We can't possibly fight our way through that mess." The tangle of rivals – punching, choking, tackling – would be impossible to navigate without injury. Timothy shook his head. "And once we're inside… George, we're going to get ourselves killed."

"Then stay here." George stood straight and took one step onto the concrete.

Timothy threw his arms around George's waist and pulled him back down, frantically checking to see if anyone had spotted his brother. "Will you just listen to me? I didn't come all this way to rescue you just to lose you now."

George pushed Timothy away. "Let me go!"

"We should be smart about this. I have an idea of how to get inside." Timothy let go. "I'm telling you, George: this is a bad idea. But if I can't stop you, I'm going to help you."

"Fine. What's your idea?" George tugged his shirt down, clearly irritated that Timothy had forcibly stopped him.

Timothy pointed to the entrance. "The doors lead into a tunnel that goes underground and into the Pavilion. There's a grassy patch above the tunnel, see?" He pointed to shrubbery growing above the entrance. "We can make our way up there, and drop in front of the doors, bypassing all this fighting."

George agreed, and they carefully and quietly climbed the hill that led up to the space above the tunnel, and then they lay on their stomachs, crawling to the edge to look down upon the entrance below. The concrete structure upholding the tunnel was blackened, and the front doors lay twisted and mangled on the ground.

"I'll drop first," Timothy said.

George pulled his weapon, his attention turning to the riot below. "If anyone comes at you, I'll take care of it."

Timothy blinked at his little brother, his mouth slightly agape. George really had changed in the weeks since he'd been taken. He didn't know how to feel about that, except that it pained him. No matter how much George wanted to grow up, no matter how much George *needed* to grow up, a sense of his brother's loss of childhood weighed heavy on Timothy.

This isn't what Mom wanted for him. The thought coalesced as a tight ball of tension in Timothy's chest. But it wasn't the time, and so he buried the regret and sadness beneath the mountain of their current goal: rescuing Lissa.

"They're too busy fighting each other," Timothy said. "Just… be careful. If we can avoid drawing attention to ourselves, that would be great."

George rolled his eyes. "I'm not a trigger-happy idiot."

Timothy sighed and pinched the bridge of his nose, but he didn't say anything. Instead, he carefully lowered himself over the edge, hanging just a moment in front of the final "T" in the "Tropical Forest" lettering affixed above the entrance before dropping onto shattered glass, the pebbles crunching under his feet. He stepped over twisted metal, unholstered his gun, faced the battle, and waited for George to follow.

Within seconds, his brother had dropped beside him, and his gun was once again at the ready. "I'll watch for people coming from inside," George said, pointing the weapon down the dark tunnel. "You make sure no one comes at us from behind."

Timothy nodded and put his back to George's. They slowly walked into the dark. If there had been power to the building before the attack, that power was now gone. Timothy carefully stepped backward, and George inched forward. The tunnel wasn't terribly long, and the natural light filtering in from the destroyed front doors was enough that George was able to see corpses or debris and warn Timothy to step over them.

They reached the double doors leading into the rest of the building just as the door burst open. Timothy spun around, putting one arm instinctively across George's chest, pushing him back. He also got out of the way as a CONman ran screaming into the tunnel, the door closing behind them. The man didn't bother with Timothy or George at all. His footsteps pounded down the tunnel toward the daylight, and he shouted, "The tiger's got in! It's out for blood!"

Timothy's mouth ran dry. "What...? The tiger is *here*?"

"You know it?" George asked.

"Yeah. It tried to eat me." Timothy shuddered as the memory brought up images of being stuck in the college foyer, only glass to separate him from the dead.

"It was spotted this morning." George reached for the door handle. "There has to be something wrong with it, right? If it's coming after people in the middle of all this chaos? I thought wild animals were spooked by that sort of thing."

"That's a good point." Timothy's stomach soured further, and he put his own hand on the door to keep it closed. "It may be diseased, or... maybe infected with DV-10."

"DV what?" George asked.

Right. No one knows it's got a name. That it was... created. Timothy swallowed bile. "The sickness," he said. "I heard someone on the radio call it DV-10." He hoped George couldn't see the slight grimace he made as he eked out the lie. "I've seen it kill animals, but... it might not affect every species the same. Come to think of it, I've not seen one dead cat."

"Huh..." George shrugged. "Okay." He tugged on the door. "Are we going in or what?"

Another scream erupted from somewhere beyond the door. "There's an actual tiger, possibly diseased, running around and attacking people, CONmen and mobsters fighting for their lives, and you *still* think it's a good idea to not wait for backup?"

George's only answer was to heave a sigh and grab the other door handle, twisting it and throwing open the door before Timothy could stop him.

* * *

Timothy was starting to really get on George's nerves. If it was Annika or Heather or even Candice stuck inside the Tropical Forest Pavilion, Timothy wouldn't have hesitated. *Or is that why it took him so long to find me? He's too afraid, or he overthinks everything, or...whatever it is, I'm not going to let Lissa die here because I didn't help.*

George's pulse quickened at the thought of Lissa in mortal danger. She was the first friend he'd had since the world fell apart; his friends from before were most likely dead or gone. He'd already sat idle while Ace forced her into this position in the first place.

"... you *still* think it's a good idea to not wait for backup?" Timothy was never going to stop lecturing.

George opened the door and stepped into the space beyond, ignoring Timothy's frustrated sigh. Above, the gaping hole in the Teflon-coated cloth dome let in strong rays of sunlight. The bats dipped in and out, chirping as if furious they'd been disturbed. Whatever explosion had ripped a hole in the dome had reduced the walls to rubble. Bodies — a few fresh, a few charred — were scattered in with the debris.

But even with the destruction, George could see why Ace had chosen that building. The specially made dome let in natural light but protected from the elements. It made for less power usage. Ahead, beyond the rubble, another world waited, a jungle in the midst of Boston. Arching tree trunks with vines hanging loosely, exotic plants, slabs of stone, and rich, natural colors made the place come to life, even in its ruin.

George crept through the rubble and reached that intact jungle, pausing to listen. A door labelled "maintenance" was to the left while an open pathway led deeper into the pavilion, toward all the noise. "I guess we're going that way."

"I guess so." Timothy raised his weapon and stepped quickly to get a few feet ahead of George.

George hung back and let his brother have his illusion of protection. The gun felt too heavy in his hands, and his body was pulsing with nervous energy. But he focused on remaining steady, on keeping his fear to himself. If Timothy knew how his stomach flipped and how his chest tightened, he would try harder to stop George.

They turned a corner and came to a large exhibit that was curtained from the inside. Muffled shouts seemed to be coming from the other side, and several bullets had pierced the curtains to make webs in the thick glass. George walked up to one of the holes and tried to peer through, but could only discern blurred movement. "I bet that's where Ace set up," George said. "He's obsessed with the zoo. And he's really weird. I bet he's playing out some kind of king of the jungle fantasy."

"Look." Timothy pointed to a door meant to blend in with the wall. It was flung wide open. "That might lead to an access point for that exhibit."

George sprinted to the open doorway but slid to a stop at the threshold. A dead man lay halfway propped against the wall just inside the hall. George swallowed hard, refusing to wretch. "He was *not* killed by a bullet." The body was mauled but not eaten, freshly exposed muscle and entrails bulging and hanging from flesh torn apart.

Timothy turned his face to the side, the color drained from his cheeks and lips. "The tiger?"

"I'd say that's a good guess." George grimaced, but then movement caught his eye at the other end of the hall. It was Icepick, running past a hallway intersection toward the exhibit George and Timothy were meaning to investigate. With a guttural growl, George stepped into the hall, over the dead body, and followed the man who'd murdered his mother.

"What are you doing?" Timothy whispered.

"That was him. Icepick." The sounds of fighting echoed from the direction Icepick had gone, and George ran after him. He burst into a large exhibit, Timothy right behind him. A discarded gun slid a few inches as George accidentally kicked it, spinning the weapon and revealing it held no magazine. It wasn't the only discarded weapon.

At first, George scanned the chaotic battleground for Icepick. He found him not far off, near the back wall of the exhibit where the faux mountain included a few small caves. The mobster Icepick was fighting came at him with a knife, but Icepick moved to the side, his sharp metal stick in hand, and in three sharp stabs, blood was spurting from the mobster's neck in three different spots. The injured man fell to the ground, the knife skidding toward one of the caves. He held his throat, eyes wide with terror as he rolled onto his back. Icepick finished him off the same way he'd finished off George's mother.

George growled. He wouldn't be able to get a clean shot from where he was. He couldn't jeopardize the truce between the BPD and the Russos. There were too many people in between. *But I* am *going to kill him.*

Icepick wiped the fresh blood from his weapon and charged another mobster who had a CONman in a headlock. George gripped his gun, ready to find the shot, when bound hands reached from the shadows of the cave to grasp hold of the fallen mobster's knife. Lissa emerged from the shadows and began cutting the ropes that tied her down. He shifted his focus and headed straight for her, the first hurdle a mobster who'd turned a sleezy grin at George.

***

The manmade habitat was a battleground, and at the highest point, on an elaborate treehouse, Frank Russo and a man with an ace card stuck in the ribbon of his hat were at each other's throats. *Frank's found his prey.* That's what Timothy was focused on when George sprinted into the fray.

"George!" Timothy's breath caught in his throat as George charged a mobster with a bit of a belly, but his little brother ducked and twirled, completely avoiding the meaty fist.

The mobster grunted, but when George kept running, he shouted, "Coward!" and then turned his eyes on Timothy. "Hey, you're one o' them cops, ain't ya?" He pointed at Timothy. "Three days, and you're mine." He grinned broadly and then went after another CONman.

Timothy only had a second to sigh in relief before someone threw their weight on him from behind and locked their arm around his neck in a vice-grip. He dropped his gun, the clatter of metal on rock signaling the loss of his only advantage.

***

"Lissa!" George holstered his gun, stepped over a corpse, and dropped to his knees beside her. "Are you okay?"

She startled at his voice, glancing up with wide eyes. She held the knife awkwardly as her hands were bound. "George? What are you doing? They'll kill you if anyone sees you helping me. Go. Fight." She cut the final strand of a rope that had connected a thick, leather anklet to a post screwed into the rock. "I'll be fine. I'm getting out of here. I understand if you can't, you know, because of Annika—"

"No, Lissa. You don't understand. The Boston Police Department is working with the mobsters to take out CON." He held out his hand. "Let me help you with the ones around your wrists."

Lissa didn't argue as he took the knife from her, instead craning her neck and searching the chaos. "I knew my aunt would find me. I *knew* it. Did you see her?"

George shook his head. "I don't think so. The man looking for you was named O'Donnell."

"Pat?" Lissa furrowed her brow. "If my aunt's not here, she must be hurt. She must have sent him." A sudden gasp escaped her lips as she sat straighter and shouted, "George! Behind you!"

George reacted out of instinct. Knife in hand, he slashed as he rolled to face whoever was coming at him. Digger had been reaching for him, most likely to pull him away from Lissa and into the fight. He let out a shocked cry as George's knife came at him, pulling his outstretched hand back. George's blade still met its mark. He felt the slightest tug of resistance as he sliced through Digger's skin from elbow to wrist. It wasn't a deep cut, but he yelped in pain and stumbled backward.

"You little sh—"

George didn't let him finish. He barreled into Digger, launching himself with every ounce of strength he had. He was able to knock the CONman flat on his back.

"What side are you on?" Digger raged. "Ace is gonna kill you."

"I'm on *my* side." George held the knife to his throat before he could move another inch, and the CONman froze, disbelief playing out on his face as George leaned closer. George was lighter and physically weaker, but he'd taken Digger by surprise and one slip of his wrist could end the man. "You were there when Icepick killed my mom." A burst of pure fury coursed through his veins. His body trembled, intoxicated by it. "You could have stopped him."

"I'm sorry, man." Digger held his hands up, his fingers shaking. "Look, you ever tried to stop Icepick when he gets that way? Truth is, I didn't do nothin' to your ma. Maybe I coulda been nicer to you and the girl after, but that ain't the same as killin' your ma."

The surety he had in that moment of fury was dampened by doubts. I was there when Ruger killed Clyde. Does that mean I'm responsible?

Digger's hands wrapped around George's wrists, and he threw George off like he was a ragdoll, using both his arms and his knees to launch him into the air. The knife fell to the ground, and George's back slammed against a small rock, knocking the wind out of him. His lungs refused to draw in breath, and George clutched his chest as he lay on his side.

Digger picked up the knife. "I'm gonna save Ace the trouble and kill you myself."

"Stop!" Lissa shouted. "George, get away!" She tugged on the rope that was attached to her other ankle.

George's lungs burned as he started to breathe again, but he was lightheaded. He scrambled backward, his motions sluggish, as Digger raised the knife over him.

"Icepick's been tellin' me I just need to test out his methods. Stabbing people to death, I mean. Let's see what all the fuss is about." He plunged the knife downward. Only then did George think of his gun.

But then Ruger was there, having slid on his knees to catch Digger's arm before the knife rammed into George's body. He wretched the knife free, kicked the inside of Digger's knee, and plunged the knife into Digger's chest as the man fell forward. Ruger pushed the man to the side as he gurgled blood, twitching for a few moments before falling still.

George stared at Digger, the knife protruding from his chest. "Ruger… you… you killed him."

Ruger grabbed George by the scruff of his neck and forced him to standing. "What the hell, kid? How many times do I have to tell you not to do stupid stuff?"

"What?" George blinked a few times, still unsure what had just happened and why.

"I saw you go at Digger. He wasn't about to kill you, idiot. He was trying to get you focused on the fight." Ruger ran his fingers through his bleach-blond hair and cursed, glancing around at the ongoing fight. "I don't think anybody was payin' attention. Don't talk about this, okay, kid? It was a mobster who done Digger in. Got it?"

Something behind Ruger caught George's attention. Frank had wrapped a length of free-hanging climbing rope around Ace's neck.

"Uh, Ruger…" George pointed as Frank kicked Ace off the treehouse platform.

The CONman leader fell only a short distance before swinging. Ace was alive but struggling against the rope around his neck. He was grasping for it, trying to lift himself up on the rope to stop it from choking him. Ruger cursed again and left George, sprinting toward the treehouse as Frank slapped his hands together as if dusting off his hands after a hard day's work.

George stumbled over to Digger's corpse. He had to put one foot on his chest for leverage just to yank the buried knife out of the man's flesh. He wiped the blood off on Digger's shirt before bringing it back to Lissa.

"Do you think Ruger can save him?" Lissa asked.

"Who, Ace?" George glanced back to see Ruger scrambling up the ladder, Ace still sputtering and grasping. "Maybe. We'll be gone soon, so I guess it doesn't matter." He turned back and sawed through the rope that bound Lissa's hands.

"Where are the rest of the BPD?" Lissa asked.

"We left them behind." The rope snapped one strand at a time. "They were fighting their way here, but my brother and I were able to sneak around the fighting to get here quicker."

"Your brother is a cop?" Lissa frowned. "You didn't tell me that."

"No," George said as he cut the final strand. He sat back as Lissa rubbed at her wrists. "He's not. He's just a regular guy. I don't really know how he got mixed up with the police."

"He doesn't sound like a regular guy," Lissa said. "It sounds like he did a lot to get to you."

A twinge of guilt pricked George's heart. "Where is he, anyway?" George had assumed his brother would follow him, but he hadn't slowed down to figure out why he might not have. "Oh no…" George dropped the knife and stood up. A CONman had Timothy around the neck, and his brother managed to kick hard off the ground, sending them both reeling backward through the open door, into the hallway and out of sight. Nearby, Icepick finished off another victim. Blood spattered his face, his chest, his arms. A wicked grin formed as he stalked toward the door, his ice pick at the ready. Timothy's gun was left behind on the ground, useless.

Chapter 45

Ruger

Ruger flew up the ladder. He would not let Ace die that way, strangled, hanging above his men, beaten by a fat mobster in khakis. The Russos were nothing more than unsanctioned politicians and sleazeball businessmen. Sure, they had plenty of access to hitmen and cleaners. They were old money, old ideas. But they hadn't gotten their hands dirty, not *really* dirty, in a long time. CON was fresh, a different kind of family. They did what had to be done, not just for themselves, but for their neighborhoods. Ace had gotten a little off track since the world collapsed, but his vision of a New Boston — that was the old Ace. The Ace that wanted power for the man born and raised in the projects. Nobody was really themselves these days.

Ruger was case in point. He'd just offed Digger to save a recruit. *Put that in a box for later. Right now, I've got bigger problems.*

He reached the platform, rushed the edge, and leapt, grasping hold of the thick branch to which the rope strangling Ace was affixed. He heaved and climbed on top of it, hugging the top of the branch. *Those pull ups are finally paying off…*

"Hold on, Ace, I'm coming," Ruger shouted as he shimmied toward the top of the rope. Ace was moving less, and he was no longer fighting to grab hold of the rope. "Ace, don't you die on me!"

Ruger reached the rope, his heart racing. They were higher up than he'd originally thought. If I cut the rope, will he survive the fall? It's what… two stories? What if he breaks his legs? Can someone die from that without a hospital?

Questions assaulted him, but Ace was dying. "I'm sorry if this is the wrong decision," Ruger said as he pulled out a pocketknife, leaned over the branch, and began cutting the top of the rope. "If you can hear me, don't lock your legs. Ace?" He desperately searched for signs that his oldest friend was still alive. "Ace, come on, brother."

Brother. Before CON, there had been Ruger and Ace. Ruger's own mother had died when he was born, and his father had been a useless drunk who only lifted a finger when he felt the need to beat Ruger half to death.

But Ace's mother… she'd been a life saver. A single mother, working two jobs, sometimes three, she let Ruger stay over whenever he liked. And she always had food in the fridge. She'd asked after Ruger's grades and talked him through his first breakup. If she'd lived, Ruger and Ace would have had very different lives. It was her death that birthed CON, a new gang of young men who were sick of their mothers and sisters being shot in the streets with bags full of groceries and babes in arm. CON had grown and wiped out those who'd claimed their streets only to ruin them.

Ruger and Ace had had their disagreements over the years, perhaps more in the last one, certainly too many in the last weeks, but they were still brothers. Even if Ace had instituted policies that more and more resembled those of the gang that had killed his own mother. Even if his vision for CON had strayed. Even if Ruger was constantly running interference, trying to keep some of what they had built together alive. Even if Ace had been cutting him out, little by little.

He severed the rope, and Ace fell, his body dropping, a dead weight thudding to the ground, unmoving. Ace's eyes stared lifeless up at Ruger. Mere seconds of an intense desire to see those eyes blink ended with a sense of relief that caught Ruger off guard. He turned his head, ashamed.

"Hey, you." Frank Russo leaned against a post in the center of the platform, arms crossed, a stupid grin on his face. "You wanna come 'ere, let me do you in, too?"

Ruger straddled the branch and looked out over the fight below. The mobsters were winning. The police force was on the way. Ace was dead. CON wouldn't survive.

"What happens when all the CONmen are gone?" Ruger asked.

Frank raised his eyebrows. "Good question. We's got a truce. Three days. And then the Russos are gonna do the same to the BPD that we've done to you. We're gonna rule Boston, and we're gonna make her shine again."

"A New Boston." Ruger repeated the mantra Ace had been using for years. It had become more tangible since the sickness started, since Boston fell into chaos, but that had always been the dream.

"Yeah," Frank said, narrowing his eyes. "You could say that."

"If the police win that fight, even if we're able to get rid of this sickness, get rid of the swarms… Boston will never be free from their self-righteous bull." Ruger met Frank's gaze. "With what's left of CON working under you, in exchange for Roxbury and Mattapan, you could win."

"Eh, I don't need ya." Frank shrugged. "Besides, I like Roxbury and Mattapan."

"We'll give you ten percent of whatever wealth we create," Ruger said. "Food, clothing, weapons, whatever… you're the king of Boston. I'm the Lord of Roxbury and Mattapan."

Frank barked a laugh. "You's a smart one, ain't ya? Gettin' all medieval on me." He cocked his head and gave Ruger half a grin. "Twenty percent."

"I can work with that." Ruger nodded.

Frank's grin broke into a smile. "Then I'd say, it's a deal."

Chapter 46

Timothy and George Peters

As they fell to the ground in the hall outside the exhibit, Timothy was able to break apart from his attacker. He rolled away and gained his footing, using the wall as support. His vision had gone a little blurry as the CONman had tried to crush his throat. The CONman, however, didn't seem to need time to recover.

But then a man covered in blood walked into the hall. "I've got this one, Lenny."

"Yeah, sure, Icepick. Whatever you want." Lenny, though he was larger and had more muscle than the newcomer, nervously scrambled away. He disappeared back into the exhibit where the fighting continued.

"You're the man who killed my mother." Timothy lifted his head, determined to look the murderer in the eye.

"I've killed a lot o' people." Icepick said, the whites of his eyes standing in stark contrast to the blood spattered on his skin. "You'll have to be more specific."

"Stop!" George slid into the hall, a gun in hand and another in its holster, and then sidestepped warily once Icepick's eyes were on him. The three of them stood in a triangle, a length of hallway to each man's back, the doorway back into the exhibit between George and Timothy. "If you touch my brother," George said, "I'll—"

Icepick laughed, the sound echoing down the halls. "Your *brother*? Man, I should have just killed you and that girl when I had the chance, taken the loot and counted my lucky stars. Your family is too much trouble."

George aimed. "You're right. You should have."

Timothy held up his hands, his stomach lurching at the idea of his little brother crossing that line. "George, no!"

Icepick took the moment of distraction to turn tail and bolt down the hall. George fired, but he missed. Sharp pain pulsed through Timothy's chest with each heartbeat as inner conflict threatened to tear him apart. He wanted Icepick dead; he just didn't want George to be the one to do it.

"Why would you do that?" George shouted. "I had him! I was going to end this!"

"No, you were going to do something that you could never come back from." Timothy held out his hand. "Give me my gun. I'll go after him. I'll kill him."

George growled and stepped into the center of the hallway. Icepick was nearing the opposite end. He raised his weapon, let out a guttural scream, and fired several shots, all of them missing as his body trembled. Timothy covered his ears as the shots reverberated off the walls. Icepick turned a corner, unscathed, and George ended his round of shots as the gun clicked, the magazine empty. George tossed the empty gun to the ground and pulled the second.

"Would you listen to me?" Timothy shouted, his frustration with George more potent than ever. "You're not thinking clearly. Give me the gun." He forcefully held out his hand.

George gave him one look, his lips in a tight line, his eyes glistening. Timothy thought he might give the gun over, but then his brother shook his head and pursued their mother's killer. Timothy had no choice but to follow.

* * *

This was what George had wanted, what he had promised himself he would do. But even as he squeezed the trigger, vision blurred through traitorous tears, he had mixed feelings when Icepick escaped around the corner. Doubts muddied his mind as he exchanged the spent gun for the new one, and Timothy's words tapped into his desire to run away. George almost gave Timothy the gun.

But then an image surfaced: his mother's body twitching, her hands vainly pushing at Icepick — his face, his arm, his chest — as she tried to escape his onslaught. Her blood draining, spurting from each new puncture as he ripped his wretched tool from her flesh. The way she stopped fighting as the life left her eyes. The way Icepick looked so *satisfied*.

That man deserved a worse death than what George could deliver with a gunshot, but he could give him at least that much. So, he gripped the gun firmly and dashed after the murderer. His shoes pounded the floor, and Timothy's slapped the tile behind him, offbeat. The corner was just a few more paces. He had to get there, get to Icepick before Timothy could stop him. He had to—

George turned the corner and slammed into Icepick's back. Timothy, who followed close, grabbed hold of George's shirt, their momentum sending them both careening into the wall. His shoulder collided with the hard surface. He cried out as the gun slipped from his hand and went skidding across the floor. Icepick stumbled forward onto his hands and knees, the gun within his reach. But that was not the worst part.

A rich, deep, undulating growl chilled the air. Icepick was on all fours, face to face with a snarling tiger. The creature's mouth foamed pink. Its fur was matted with blood, but there was no sign of injury. Its yellowed fangs barred, its muscles tensed in a prowling crouch, the tiger gnashed its teeth as another slow rumble emanated from its throat.

"H-help m-me." Icepick stammered.

George pushed off the wall an inch, slowly, to regain his composure. "Timothy? What do we do?"

Icepick scooted back a few inches, still on hands and knees, and the tiger roared. The CONman yelped, shaking visibly. And then he seemed to notice the gun for the first time. The second his hand reached for it, the powerful beast lunged, its huge paws wrapping around Icepick's shoulders, its teeth sinking into his neck and shoulder.

Timothy tugged on George's arm, and he snapped out of his shock. He had the urge to run, but his brother backed away slowly. The tiger no longer faced them, and so the two brothers turned the corner as quietly as they could. Once around the corner, George didn't have to be told to run for it, the dead, mauled corpse coming to mind. The creature wasn't killing to feast. They both bolted for the exhibit where the fighting was taking place. Three-fourths of the way down the hall, George's stomach curdled at another roar. He glanced back to see the tiger bounding after them.

"It's coming!" George screamed.

Though they'd had a head start, the creature was fast. It was gaining on them.

"I'll get the door," Timothy yelled.

George couldn't help a long, drawn-out scream as he finished the last yards of the hall and threw himself through the doorway. He rolled on the stone, coming to a stop facing the doorway. Timothy turned to grab the door handle as the tiger leapt, soaring through the air. But Timothy slammed the door shut, and a *thud* signaled the tiger making impact. It roared again, but they were safe. From the tiger, at least.

Wait… why is it so quiet in here? George swallowed hard as Timothy turned to face the room with a look of utter confusion on his face. George turned and gaped. O'Donnell and his small team of four other officers in full gear had finally arrived, and they were facing off against their enemy, the CONmen. Lissa was with the BPD, free from her chains. George would have been relieved. Except the mobsters were standing with the CONmen, and Ruger and Frank Russo stood at their head, unified.

* * *

"Frank, what is going on?" Timothy's heart was still racing from escaping the tiger. He'd expected to slam the door shut and turn into another fight, but instead, he'd found the room quiet. And it looked like the fears over Frank's trustworthiness were being confirmed.

"Hey, Southie." Frank winked at Timothy. "Good o' you to join the party." He gave half a wave to George as he stood up and moved cautiously back beside Timothy. "And lookit here. The littlest Peters. I don't know as we've formally met."

"You burned my house down." George's tone was matter-of-fact, almost monotone.

"That I did." Frank chuckled. "Good times. Simple times. It seems things are about to get a little more complicated, though."

"Wait a minute, kid." Ruger narrowed his eyes. "Are you workin' for the other side?"

If Timothy wasn't mistaken, a look of shame crossed George's face. "I'm with the actual good guys, Ruger — my family and the police. And Frank was my enemy before I even knew you. I can't work with him."

"Ouch." Frank placed a hand on his chest. "You've hurt my feelings."

"Hold on," Timothy stepped in front of George, hoping his little brother would take the hint and keep quiet. "George isn't with the BPD. I'm not either. Me and George, Heather, Candice, and Annika… we're all retreating and staying out of this." He gestured between Frank and the BPD.

"Yeah, yeah." Frank waved him off. "Switzerland. Southie can't handle the heat. I still say you'll have to pick sides, but that's a conversation for another time." He smiled at O'Donnell.

O'Donnell scowled back. "We had a deal, Frank. We work together to take out CON. We held up our end. The kids are safe. And now, what? You're gonna turn on us at the last minute?"

"I told them Frank Russo kept his word," Timothy shouted. "I thought you and me were even."

"Ah, but I *do* keep my word." Frank tutted. "And we're not even. I think I might owe ya one, Southie." He turned to O'Donnell. "CON, as it was, no longer exists. I'm gonna send my guys to collect our kids, and our kids only. Then, you and yours can get outta here, go back to your headquarters. You can pretend like you can win the city, or you can pack up and skedaddle. Whatever. You've got three days, just like I promised."

"Except instead of splitting CON's resources," O'Donnell said, "you're keeping them and the manpower for yourself."

"Now, now." Frank held up his hands as if defending himself. "Resources weren't never mentioned in our deal. We're absorbin' CON, so naturally, what's theirs is ours. I suggest you don't violate our truce by tryin' to steal from us."

O'Donnell balled his hands into fists. Through gritted teeth, he gave orders to his small team. "We've done what we came to do," he said, placing a hand on Lissa's shoulder. "The kids are safe. Move out, back to the rendezvous point. We'll make sure the Russos are reunited with their own, and then we're out." He glared again at Frank. "We've got a city to save, and we've got three days to make sure we know *exactly* how to clean out the sludge."

Ruger stepped forward, striking an intimidating pose despite his shorter stature. His ice-blue eyes were cold. "George and Lissa are CONmen. They belong with me."

Timothy's heart leapt into his throat. He looked back at George, whose eyes had gone wide at Ruger's suggestion that he was one of them. "Don't worry," Timothy said. "They're not going anywhere with you."

O'Donnell growled. "I'll kill you before I let you take her again, you dirty little—"

Frank gave Ruger a hard pat on the back. "My new friend here don't understand how all this works yet. You'll have to forgive 'im." Frank narrowed his eyes at Ruger, and their eyes met for a moment before Ruger stepped back, seeming to submit. "You can keep your kids, just as we agreed."

"I think it only fair that those who trained under me decide for themselves where they want to go," Ruger said. "At least let them choose. Many of them don't have families left. CON was the start of something real to them." He alternated his gaze between Lissa and George.

"Yeah, a'right." Frank shrugged. "Ruger, you go on with Pugsie and Joe to get our kids." He raised his eyebrows at O'Donnell. "I'd say, if the kids don't belong one way or the other, it makes sense to let 'em decide."

O'Donnell worked his jaw back and forth for a few seconds before finally answering. "Fine. Teens only. If a teen decides to come back with CON, we wouldn't want them fighting for us, anyway. But *no one* will be forced into anything they don't want to do."

"Let's start with you two," Ruger said. He looked to Lissa. "I'm sorry I let Ace take you. You know that's not what I wanted. You've got potential. You can be yourself with me, with CON. I promise you, you won't regret staying."

"I won't deny that you did what you could to protect me and the other girls," Lissa said. "And I'm actually grateful for that. But I never intended to stay." Her face fell for just a moment before pointing at Frank. "I found out that my aunt died because of him. I'm staying with Captain O'Donnell, and I'm going to fight for the city my aunt loved."

"And George?" Ruger turned, and though Timothy tried to stay in between the CONman and his brother, George stepped forward, resisting Timothy's urges to stay back. Ruger continued. "You're the kind of young man I want CON to be built upon. You're brash, but you've got guts. I can make something out of you, Hero."

Timothy's blood boiled at the audacity. "How dare you even speak to my brother. George will *not*—"

"I can speak for myself." George walked slowly toward the gap between the two groups. "Ruger, I *do* think you've got good in you. And I believe if I were to join you, you would treat me like a brother." He stopped in the center of the gap, facing Ruger.

Timothy frowned, his stomach dropping. *No... what is he saying?*

"The problem is," George continued, "I already have a brother."

Timothy breathed out in relief.

"And I don't need another man thinking he knows what I need." George backed up, taking up a position beside Lissa.

Timothy went cold. He can't be serious. Can he?

"I'm joining Lissa and the BPD." George clasped his hands behind his back and lifted his chin. "I don't want to fight you, Ruger. If CON should be joining anyone, they should be joining the police. I'm guessing you've negotiated something with Frank. I'm sure O'Donnell would be able to meet the offer, maybe make one better."

Timothy's jaw dropped. O'Donnell blinked and took half a step sideways, eyeing George. A murmur broke out among the men and women on both sides.

O'Donnell cleared his throat, recovering from some kid making an offer on his behalf a lot quicker than Timothy anticipated. "I'm open to discussion," he said, his tone stiff as he faced the CONman.

Ruger laughed. "Open to discussion? Right." He shook his head. "George, these Boys in Blue... they're not who you think they are. With me, you get what you see. No secrets. No pretend. If you stay with *them,* do yourself a favor and grow a pair o' eyes in the back of your head. You're gonna need 'em. And don't think for a minute that their uniforms make them somehow better, more moral. Wait and see, Hero. And then come crawling back to someone you can trust." He pounded his chest with his fist.

"You don't know what you're talking about." Lissa shouted, stepping forward only to have O'Donnell stop her with a hand on her shoulder. "My aunt was a good person. She protected people. And these were her friends."

George took Lissa's hand, and the girl seemed to calm down just a little. "No one is perfect," George said, "but I'm going to take my chances with the people who *didn't* sanction my kidnapping."

Timothy had had enough. "George, you are *not* fighting in this war over Boston. You're coming with me. End of story."

"I'm sorry," George said, his voice firm. "The captain said no one would be forced into anything they didn't want. I don't want to go with you and hide. I want to fight."

"O'Donnell—" Timothy started.

"The kid's right." O'Donnell crossed his arms. "We're gonna need every able-bodied man we can get."

"He's a kid! Barely thirteen!" Timothy threw up his hands. "This is insane!"

"If he's good enough that CON wants him, he's good enough to stay with the BPD. We need him," O'Donnell said. "We need you, too, but you're not willing to do the right thing."

"The right thing is to protect my family," Timothy shouted.

"Well, it looks like we're done here." Frank shrugged, ignoring Timothy's outburst. "We sent out enough men that the rest of our numbers should know what's goin' on by now. I gotta get all these newbies acclimated." He ordered Pugsie, Ruger, and Joe to go with O'Donnell and meet back at the Jamaica Plains station, which made O'Donnell's face go a shade redder. Still, the captain didn't do anything more as Frank retreated, leaving the three behind. He had his men open the door, guns ready, but the tiger was already gone, nowhere to be seen.

"Let's finish this," O'Donnell said once Frank had left, exhaustion and frustration lacing his words. He addressed Ruger, Pugsie, and Joe. "You three go first. We're meetin' up at the Roxbury YMCA. You can take your kids from there."

The three reached the doorway, and Timothy stepped between them and O'Donnell, holding out his hands. "You can't do this," he said. "You can't let George do this."

"How about you try talking to me?" George said, his tone hardened. "I'm making this decision, not him."

"The kid's right." O'Donnell shrugged. "I'd be proud of him, if I were you. He's making the right call."

Timothy shook his head. O'Donnell would never understand. He had conflict in his blood. He'd been a soldier and then a policeman. It was all he knew. "George, what about Annika? Heather? Don't you care about any of us?"

"Of course I do." George put a hand on Timothy's arm. "I failed mom. I wasn't even able to kill the man who murdered her. This is how I'm going to make up for it. When I'm with you, you hold me back. You make me weak, Timothy. I can't stay with you."

Those words hit Timothy square in the gut, mostly because he wasn't sure if he believed them to be false. He couldn't speak, couldn't come up with a reply or an argument to make George stay. And so, George moved on without him. Fifteen minutes later, Timothy left the zoo for the church where Heather, Candice, and Annika would be. *If anyone failed today,* he thought as he made his way through the streets alone, *it was me.*

Chapter 47

Heather Peters

"What do you mean, you can't do anything?" Heather wanted to scream, wanted to shake Murphy until she changed her answers. They stood in the main aisle of a sanctuary, and her voice resounded off stained-glass windows and wooden beams. The children they'd saved were sitting, some sleeping, on the platform between the pulpit and a baptismal. A large cross hung over the room, affixed to the wall above. Afternoon daylight shot colorful beams through the stained glass.

"If Ellis was still alive, maybe… but even then…" Murphy's solemn expression held no hope as she looked upon Annika's battered form. Candice lay in the next pew, one row up, softly sobbing. She was bruised, a head wound bleeding, at least a few ribs broken. She'd apparently passed out as she'd tried to shield Annika when a wildebeest hoof made contact with the back of her head. After that, they could only guess that Annika had tried to protect *her*, as they'd found the little girl curled around Candice's head.

Heather, Torres, and Murphy had worked together to get them to the church, Murphy and Heather carefully carrying Annika and Torres helping Candice. The original plan had been for Murphy and Torres to take the rest of the children along to the YMCA down the street where they would hand over the Russo children.

"You have medicine. The salve you've been giving to Timothy… I've seen stitches and pain meds." Heather was grasping, and she knew it.

"We all have some basic training," Torres said. "But she's got to have internal bleeding. You need an actual doctor."

"You need a surgeon." Murphy added. "There might be one alive among the survivors, but we don't have time to find them and bring them to you."

A squeal of hinges made the two cops react, and both of them had their weapons drawn and facing the entrance to the sanctuary. It was Timothy. Heather let out a half laugh, half sob, relieved and thrilled and joyous to see her husband alive and intact. She ran to him, down the aisle, and threw her arms around his neck. He barely hugged her back.

She pulled away, frowning, searching behind him. "Tim… where's George?" Tears stung her eyes. *He's dead, too.*

"He stayed with O'Donnell." Timothy's eyes pinched as if he didn't understand the words that were coming out of his own mouth. "He… he wants to fight, and… I couldn't make him come with me." He blinked a few times at Heather, seemingly in shock.

"But he's alive?" Heather pushed, her voice trembling.

Timothy nodded, and then his frown deepened. "Who's crying? Is that Candice?" He straightened, some life coming back into his eyes. "And why would you bring Murphy and Torres here? And where is Annika?"

Candice's cry became louder at the sound of Annika's name echoing off the high ceilings. Heather took Timothy's hands in her own. "Tim, there was a stampede. Wildebeests. Candice and Annika were caught in it, and…"

Timothy pushed past her, stalking down the aisle until he got to the pew where they'd laid Annika. Heather followed, tears falling again for the little girl. She rested on plush red cushions. One knee was swollen, every inch of skin scraped and bruised. Murphy and Torres explained what they'd already said to Heather. They spoke in soft, empathetic tones, but Timothy answered harshly.

"Leave," he said. "Go and prepare for your war."

"Tim… maybe we should go back with them," Heather said. "I mean, they might not be able to help Annika, but they have pain meds. They could—"

"I'm not going to let her die!" Timothy turned on Heather, and she backed up, her mouth gaping at the way he shouted at her. "They already said they can't help her. They're not doctors. They don't know what's going on. We can get Annika to safety, and Candice, too. And then, I'll go out and find a doctor. There's got to be one somewhere."

"Tim…" Heather trailed off, unsure of what else to say.

He softened his voice and closed his eyes. "Heather, if we stay with the Boston Police, we're all dead. CON has joined Frank."

Both Murphy and Torres shouted, "What?!"

Heather gasped and stepped back to plunk into a pew. CON and the mob had joined forces against the BPD.

"We have to get back," Torres ran his fingers through his hair. "Are they attacking now?"

Timothy shook his head. "Frank is keeping his word. There's still the three-day truce."

"Keeping his word?" Murphy scoffed. "He was supposed to get rid of CON!"

"He did, according to him. They're no longer the same CON. He hung their leader and chose a new one from among their ranks. They worked out some kind of deal." Timothy walked to the front of the church, approaching two flagpoles, one that held the American flag and the other that held the Christian flag. "We can make a stretcher out of these. We need to get moving, Heather. If we hurry, we can get Candice and Annika to safety. I can run to the library, see if there's a doctor among those survivors."

Heather looked up. "Tim, I don't know if Candice can make it without help."

Candice sat up, swaying a little too much. "I can do it," she said, though her weak words didn't sound very convincing.

"Wait a minute," Torres said. "You can't just drop a bomb on us like that and leave. What else do you know?"

"Nothing much," Timothy said. "You should go to the YMCA with the kids. The Russos will be wanting their own."

Murphy's little boy, James, got up from his spot and came to his mother, tugging on her arm. "Mom, I don't want to leave Annika. She's my friend."

"I know, sweetheart," Murphy said. "But… we have to go. Annika is with her family. They'll help her the best they can. Help me get the other kids ready, okay?" Little James reluctantly went with her as she started rousing the sleeping children.

"You should come with us." Torres crossed his arms. "You won't make it long out there on your own."

"Timothy," Heather said, "maybe—"

"We'll make it longer out there on our own than we will in the center of the attacks. And wherever the BPD is *will* be the center." Timothy cut her off, and Heather clamped her mouth shut. "You can't help us, not any more than giving her meds to make her comfortable."

Heather was still trying to process what was happening. *Maybe Timothy is right.*

"Well, if you change your mind…" Torres shrugged.

"Heather, come on. I need material to tie to these poles to make a stretcher." Timothy finished taking off the flags and laid them on the pulpit. "We have to hurry."

"The nursery," Heather said, popping up to her feet. "I bet we can find some blankets there."

Timothy put the two poles in the center aisle and went over to Candice, putting the back of his hand to her forehead and checking her over. Torres and Murphy began herding the children back out through the entrance.

"Hey," Timothy said before they could leave. "Look out for my brother, George, will you?"

"Sure thing," Murphy said. "If he's joined with us, we'd keep an eye on him with or without your prompting."

Timothy gave them a quick nod and a thanks as Heather stood up. *Get it together. Blankets. We need to move.*

It didn't take her long to find the nursery, and just as she expected, there were fresh blankets waiting in a cupboard. She threw aside the stretchy, crocheted variety. And she couldn't stomach the blankets themed after the zoo or the safari. "Sheep and rainbows it is," she said to herself as she gathered several sturdier blankets. They weren't very big, but neither was Annika. "They'll have to work."

When she came back into the sanctuary, it was just her, Candice, Timothy, and Annika. She felt the absence of George acutely, but there was nothing to be done about it yet. She could go and find him before the war started, convince him to come back with her. For now, they only had one idea to keep Annika alive: get her to safety and bring a doctor to her. It was a long shot, but it was all they had.

Chapter 48

Lizzy Peters

"That's for *me*?" Lizzy touched the colorful, soft dress. It was a deep red with orange and yellow flowers embroidering the hem. "I thought we only wore stuff like this." She tugged at her taupe tunic.

Azalea laughed. "We do, most of the time. But sometimes, for special occasions, we wear something more festive. This is a handspun silk dress. Very expensive in the old world. Rare, because people stopped learning to use what Mother Earth gave us, turning instead to manufacturing." Her smile faded. "It's sad, really."

"Yes," Lizzy nodded, curbing her enthusiasm. "Very sad."

Azalea patted the dress fondly. "Anyway, today, you are to be celebrated. The doctor has given you the all-clear for the big feast."

"But I still have to pass one final test?" Lizzy asked.

"Of course." Azalea put an arm around Lizzy. "But, I have no doubt that you'll be just fine, Elizabeth. I really think you've come a long way. The Mother is so proud."

Lizzy beamed. The last two days, since she'd finally understood, since she'd stopped being so stubborn, had been peaceful. Comfortable. While she'd not been given any food, she *had* been given plenty of water and tea, even a little bit of goat's milk. The doctor had given her some vitamins, too. She was hungry; there was no denying that. But the dull ache became bearable after she'd been provided enough nutrients and water to keep her muscles from constantly cramping, and she'd regained some of her strength.

"Help me put it on?" Lizzy asked. She stood, her legs shakier than she would have liked. All the testing they'd put her through had contributed to her exhaustion. But she could stand on her own now, and there was something… spiritual about it. Never had she been so grateful to be using her own two feet.

Azalea helped Lizzy pull her tunic up over her head. "What is this expression?" she asked. "Smiling and thoughtful. What are you thinking?"

Lizzy blushed as the cool underground air washed over her bare skin. She reached for the dress. "Nothing… it's silly."

Azalea's lips pinched. "When I ask you a question, Elizabeth, you should answer." Her tone only had the slightest bit of chastisement in it.

I suppose I deserve that. "Sorry." Lizzy blushed deeper, hugging the silk to her chest. "I was just thinking that I used to take so much for granted. Being strong enough to get dressed on my own, for instance. Or having a full belly. I never thought about what I was taking when I fueled my body, you know? I just took whatever was in reach, whatever felt good."

Azalea nodded slowly. "And now?"

"Now, I'm more grateful, I guess."

Azalea took the dress from Lizzy and began unbuttoning the back. "You've really absorbed what we've been trying to teach you, haven't you?"

Lizzy nodded. "I have."

"And you understand that for humanity to be pure, to be free, Mother Earth must be cleansed?"

Again, Lizzy affirmed Azalea's statement fervently. Her new friend — no, her new sister — bent low, opening the dress wide so that Lizzy could step into it. She used Azalea's shoulders for balance as she did so, and Azalea pulled the dress up. Lizzy slipped her arms into the three-quarter sleeves and pulled the modest V neckline up around her shoulders.

Azalea motioned for Lizzy to turn around so she could button the back. "Today, you will prove your statements, not just with words, but with your deeds. And tomorrow, you will begin the process of telling us everything we need to know."

Lizzy chewed on her lower lip as Azalea moved her braid over her shoulder to continue buttoning the dress. "Why haven't I been required to tell you everything already? I mean… isn't that what you've wanted me to do the whole time?"

"Yes. But we want you of sound mind and spirit, devoted and truly part of us before we sift through your memories for every last bit of relevant information." Azalea patted her back. "All done," she said, stepping around to face Lizzy.

"What would have happened if things hadn't clicked?" Lizzy asked, frowning. "If I had never come to understand, I mean."

Azalea took her hands gently. "Elizabeth, you have a good heart. Those with good hearts always come to understand."

"But… if I hadn't?" Lizzy asked.

"We believe everyone, even a person with evil in their heart, understands the truth in their death, in their last conscious moments, when their body releases itself to become nourishment for Mother Earth. She is merciful upon them, allowing their deaths to have meaning even if their lives were spent in destruction."

"You would have let me die?" Lizzy asked.

Azalea cupped Lizzy's cheeks in her hand and smiled. "Death seeds life, as Mother Earth intended. With the nourishment of sacrifice, she will reclaim the ground humanity defiled, and one day, she will bless us, her children, to live once more on the surface, in harmony with her instead of in rebellion against her. It is better that those who intend to harm her die in service to the greater good. You and I, we are Heirs of the Mother. Our fate is service in life *and* in death."

Lizzy listened in awe. Tears burned her eyes. "You worked so hard to give me life. All those things the Mother let Orion and the others do to me… it was to open my eyes, to bring me into a family."

Azalea caressed Lizzy's tears away with her thumbs. "Restore the Mother, Elizabeth. And in so doing, restore ourselves."

Lizzy pulled Azalea into a hug, hearing Mother Autumn's voice in her mind, as loud and clear as it was in the night. *You belong here. You are one of us. You are valued. You are loved.*

Azalea pulled away. "Are you ready for your final test?"

"I've never been more ready for anything." Lizzy's body thrummed with anticipation. She would endure one more test, and then she would feast with her family.

Azalea led the way, out of their shared bedroom, and down the hall, twisting and turning through the underground, concrete complex. Tantalizing scents of freshly baked bread and savory spices pulled Lizzy like a hook through her nose; she had to work hard not to sprint past Azalea. Her stomach growled, and she licked her lips, almost tasting soft, fluffy rolls and butter.

The entire community waited for Lizzy in a large, open space. When she walked through the doorway, they were on their feet, clapping for her. To the right, three tables strung together boasted so many dishes that it overwhelmed her. Lizzy laughed, her hands clasped together at her chest, her eyes misting with tears again.

Azalea led her past tables of smiling faces to an opening in the tables that surrounded an open center. It was then that Lizzy's smile faltered. She froze in place, her clasped hands transforming to claws at her throat, fingernails digging into her skin.

At the center of the room, a man was tied to a chair, and Mother Autumn stood to the side, a metal tray in her hands. At the sight of the man, terrible images flitted through Lizzy's mind; he had scorched the earth. His hands had blood on them. He had relaxed into his bed made of money as Mother Earth suffered.

The room fell deathly quiet. Azalea gently guided Lizzy to stand before Mother Autumn, before the man who brought screaming to Lizzy's ears. Even without the headphones, the screaming of victims — man and animal, earth and sky, Mother Earth herself — enveloped Lizzy, sunk into her bones, and curdled her stomach. Her fingernails scratched their way to her ears. She tried to cover the noise, to stop the pain-filled screeches, but though she squeezed her head between her hands until she thought she might burst, they did not stop.

The man was saying something, shaking his head furiously. Sweat rolled down his face, past his guilty eyes, sorry only because he'd been caught. Lizzy wanted to scream, too. She wanted to join her voice with that of the dead, so loud in her mind. But Mother Autumn stepped in front of the man, and she reached out, her cool touch soothing Lizzy's burning skin.

"Elizabeth, remove your hands from your ears." Somehow, her voice broke through the screaming. "I know how to make it stop."

Something about her voice dampened the screaming. Mother Autumn's very presence had the power to push back the horrible images. Elizabeth swallowed, her throat burning as if it might close up and refuse to allow air into her lungs. It took great effort to pry her hands from her ears, but she did it, for the Mother.

"Good, Elizabeth." Mother Autumn held out the tray. "Will you deliver justice for Mother Earth?"

Lizzy trembled, the syringe on the tray becoming her focus. "That's… venom?" she asked, thinking back to when the Mother had cleansed a man from the earth when she'd first arrived. *I refused to give her the word, refused to deliver justice. Why did I do that?* Lizzy grasped at that memory, a sense of *wrongness* creeping in at the edges of her heart.

"It is." Mother Autumn smiled reassuringly. "This is your final test."

Her voice was so soothing, so welcoming. *One more test, and I can eat. One more test, and I prove that I belong.* Lizzy reached out and her hand closed around the syringe. The screaming voices receded a little more.

Mother Autumn moved aside so that the man was in full view once again. "This man is guilty of conspiring to murder Mother Earth through neglect, through outright destruction, and through complicity. We demand justice. Tell me, Elizabeth, should he die for his crimes?"

Lizzy held up the syringe. Such a small tool for such a lofty task. The man was begging, but his words sounded like drivel to her. Nonsense. A tiny part of her old self emerged as she took a step toward the man, as she closed her hand around the syringe.

"Please," the man said, that one word breaking through his panicked babbling.

Don't! This is wrong. It's wrong! Lizzy frowned and stopped.

"Restore the Mother!" Azalea shouted from behind her, and then the room swelled with the mantra, every voice lending to its power. When something is dirty, it needs to be cleansed. Lizzy felt the voices of her brothers and sisters bolster her. You're not weak, anymore. You can do what needs to be done.

Lizzy bent close to the man and looked him in the eye. "It's better this way," she said, thinking back to what Azalea had told her about death. "You'll see. Your death will do the world more good than your life ever did."

She plunged the syringe into his neck, delivering the venom, delivering justice. Whatever was left of her old self died. She pulled out the syringe and stepped back, watching as the man began to choke, his lips and tongue swelling. Soon, he would no longer be able to feel pain or inflict it on others.

The screaming was gone. Elizabeth closed her eyes and let the mantra fill her up. "Restore the Mother!" She joined her voice to those around her, and her doubts and questions melted away.

Mother Autumn, her beautiful smile shining down on her, took the syringe and handed it and the tray to Orion. She led Elizabeth to the table and let her fill a plate with a variety of delicious foods, everything from warm bread and seasoned chicken to pie and cookies.

A fiddle began an upbeat tune, full of life and laughter. Elizabeth sank her teeth into a buttered roll, and then she savored the juices of her chicken drum, and then she licked her lips of Mother Earth's sweet, sugary gifts. It was euphoric, every bite bursting with intense pleasure. Rich wines were offered, and she drank freely. A communal cup was passed from person to person, and Azalea explained that it would enhance her connection to the Heirs, to the earth herself. No gift of Mother Earth was denied her, not among her brothers and sisters.

And then Elizabeth danced, her spirit light, her feet flying. She was free from guilt. Free to be herself. No shame. Acceptance on all sides. She floated on air, never having experienced such pure joy and beauty. She spread her arms wide and absorbed the colors, the music, the melodic mantra; it was wonderful.

Tears streamed down her cheeks. Why, oh why did I ever resist this? This is what home is supposed to feel like. I belong. I am loved. I am free. And there was nothing she wouldn't do to keep it that way.

Chapter 49

Alexander Roman

They were two days later than Alex would have liked, but they were finally in Boston. It was good to know that Ned and Wyatt would be okay and that the National Guard would help the bikers find their way back home. Despite his original misgivings, Alex had grown to like them, and if it hadn't been for Ned, he would have been forced to return to Minnie without her daughter. That would have crushed Alex after all Minnie had done for his own son.

Put people before the mission. Alex glanced over his shoulder at Oliver, who was pressing his forehead against the window, watching the broken city pass by slowly. *Maybe if I'd been more interested in helping Ned to begin with, I would have dug into my intuition about Ben – er, Jesse.* He shifted in the passenger seat, rubbing his hand over his face. *I was so wrapped up in* not *getting involved that I let a serial killer travel with us.*

He vowed to do better, to show his son that one could have a heart and be a good person, even when the world was falling apart. It seemed the disaster that unfolded worldwide had pushed people to be either the best or the worst versions of themselves. The people surrounding him — Oliver, Minnie, Lauren, and even Samson — had kept him from losing himself in his fight for survival. But, he'd had some close calls.

If I were on my own, would I have participated in the shady experiments at the CDC? Would I have tried to help Ned at all? When I woke to all that blood, would I have fled the house instead of trying to save whoever was left? The uncomfortable truth was that he didn't know. All the more reason for me to choose to be better, from here on out.

"Whatever's happening south of here has finally died down," Lauren said from the back seat. "I was worried we'd have to get close to it, but I haven't heard any explosions for at least an hour."

"Someone must have been fighting over supplies," Alex said. "Military maybe. We just need to steer clear of trouble."

"I'm gonna have to reroute again." Minnie slowed the RV, pointing ahead to where a semi lay blocking the road completely.

Alex got out the map that had been in the file folder in the briefcase Jonah Newton had left behind. It was a rudimentary, hand drawn map of a part of Boston, and the Vanguard complex where New Horizons Laboratory was located had been circled. The problem was that the map only included main roads, and they'd not been able to stick to those.

"It's getting late," Lauren said. "Do you think we'll make it in time? Maybe we should just find a spot to park and wait until morning."

"I don't know." Alex turned the map and then squinted at a road sign up ahead. "I think we're close."

"Hey, look!" Oliver pointed past Lauren out her window, and Samson perked up beside him as if trying to see what Oliver was talking about. "There's people!"

Minnie frowned. "They look like they've been galloped too hard and put away wet."

"They don't look like they've got the sickness," Alex said.

"They're coming from the direction of the conflict." Lauren leaned forward and tapped her mother's shoulder. "We should go on. There are plenty of buildings here for shelter. They'll be fine."

"No!" Oliver's face pinched with worry. "They need help, and maybe they'll know exactly where New Horizons is."

Alex sighed. *Wasn't I just telling myself to put people before the mission?* He looked closer at the group weaving their way through a street their RV would never be able to navigate for the abandoned vehicles. There was a man in tactical gear. *A policeman, maybe?* Except both women with him were wearing similar gear, and one of them had a bright yellow, shiny blouse under her bulletproof vest. That one was limping along, a look of pure agony on her face. The other two appeared to be carrying a makeshift stretcher. They had to lift it up over head as they squeezed through a tight spot. *The lump in those blankets is so small, and… the stretcher must be light.*

"Oh, good Lord!" Minnie gasped. "I think there's a child in that stretcher!"

"That's exactly what I was thinking." Alex looked back at his son, and Oliver's round, pleading eyes won. "Okay. Let's at least offer help. Lauren?" He turned around and looked at her. "Come with me. You've got medical training. You can assess the injuries better than I can."

"I… but…" Lauren trailed off when Oliver turned the same expression on her. "Fine. But we should bring weapons. Just in case. And approach cautiously. They might be weirdos, even if they *are* hurt."

Oliver sat back, satisfied, as Alex got his gun out of the glovebox and hopped out of the cab of the RV. When he closed the door, the group noticed them, pausing. They looked terrified, so he kept his gun holstered and raised his hands as he approached.

"Hey, friend," Alex said as they got within a couple yards. "We're just here to offer some help. My name is Alex, and this is Lauren. She's got some medical training."

"Yeah," Lauren said, clearing her throat. "I've been through medical school and some residency. It looks like you guys could use some medical attention."

The woman with the bright yellow blouse cried out. "Yes," she said. "Please."

Lauren took that as permission to come closer, and she did so, coming right up to the stretcher. Alex came closer, too, making sure to always be in arms-reach of Lauren. He caught the man eyeing his gun, and he put a hand on the hilt, ensuring the stranger couldn't rip it from its holster.

"Can you set her down?" Lauren asked, the pole under her armpits, her hands reaching down toward the girl. "Gently. I want to take a better look. It's hard to do with her hanging like this."

The two did as they were asked. The woman who'd been trailing them leaned against a car, moaning from pain. The man stepped around the stretcher and came closer to Alex.
"We appreciate the help," the man said. "But it looks like you're coming into Boston with that RV and trailer. You must have really done some zig-zagging to find a path this far into the city."
"Yeah," Alex said. "We were in St. Louis when the sickness hit, and then we went down to Atlanta, and now we're here. It's been a long, long journey. We weren't going to let a few parked cars stop us from getting where we need to go."
"That's a strange way to get to Boston from St. Louis." The man narrowed his eyes.
"Long story." Alex shifted uncomfortably. "We're actually looking for a specific place. It's important. It's called New Horizons—"
The woman gasped from her spot on the ground, looking at him, and at the same time, the man rushed Alex and pushed him against a truck's hood. Lauren popped up, pulled her gun and had it at the man's temple before he could make a grab for Alex's gun.
"Back off," Lauren said, her tone hardened.
The man worked his jaw back and forth, his lips taut, his eyes searching Alex's — for what, exactly, Alex couldn't say. He let go and stepped back. "Why are you looking for New Horizons?"
The woman stood up. "You came from St. Louis? Did Walter send you?"
"Walter Peters?" Alex asked, rubbing his chest.
The man and the woman looked at each other. "Do you know my dad?" The man eyed Alex suspiciously. "Did you work with him?"
"No... wait, you're his son?" Alex motioned for Lauren to put away her weapon.
"Yes," the man said. "My name is Timothy, and this is my wife, Heather." He pointed to the injured woman and child. "That's Candice and Annika. If my father sent you, does that mean he's still alive? What about my sister?" He whipped his head around to the RV. "Are they with you?"
"I'm sorry, but no," Alex said. "Your father didn't send me. I was sent to look for your father. I'm one of the only scientists left from the CDC. I believe your father and New Horizons are the keys to ending this nightmare."
Timothy hung his head for a moment before looking Alex directly in the eye. "I'm not sure there will *ever* be an end to this," he said, "but I hope you're here to prove me wrong."

Calamity

No Tomorrow Book 4

Chapter 1

Zara Williams

"I can't believe you two talked me into this," Kai said.
Zara quirked an eyebrow at him from the seat behind the pilot's chair. She'd joined him in the cockpit to try to get some rest apart from Mr. Peters's incessant snoring. "I can't believe you're still complaining about it. We saved your life."
"That was ages ago, babe."
"It was yesterday, you idiot." Zara smacked Kai on the back of the head. "And stop calling me that."
Kai rubbed his head. "That hurt."
"Good. Now shut it so I can get some sleep." Zara crossed her arms and leaned into the back corner of the cockpit. The five-point seatbelt gave her some support, and she'd brought a pillow to stuff under her head. It was still hard to get comfortable.
Kai had originally flown them to a small, single airstrip on the eastern side of the mountain range and planned to leave them to go it on their own from there. It had taken half a day of pestering to get him to agree to take them closer to Boston. His business was gone until he could pinpoint a new route and set up in a new town on the western side of the mountains, one preferably without a town nearby. It wasn't like he had anything better to do. And Zara and Mr. Peters *had* saved his life.
Zara only had a few minutes of silence before Kai spoke again. "We're not far, you know," he said. "You'll get half an hour, at most."
She groaned in frustration. "Just be quiet! I want a nap, not a full REM cycle."
Kai looked over his shoulder. "Are you one of those STEM girls? All smart *and* sexy?"
Zara grimaced. "Is that supposed to be a compliment?"
Kai shrugged. "Yeah."
"You're a terrible person." She unbuckled her seatbelt. "I think I prefer the rumbling of Mr. Peters's nostrils to your…" She paused to gesture vaguely at him. "… everything."
"Whatever, babe." Kai sniffed and looked away. "The ladies love them some Kai Lee."
"I'm sure." Zara scoffed. "Everybody loves people who talk about themselves in the third person."
Kai looked over his shoulder again. "Hey, you know what your problem is?"
"What?" Zara put her hands on her hips. "Enlighten me. Clearly you know more about me than I do."
Kai pointed at her and opened his mouth, but before he could say anything, a strong gust of wind caused the plane to rock. He grabbed hold of the controls as Zara stumbled. "Sorry about that," he said as he cleared his throat. "Looks like we might have a storm brewing."
Zara kept one hand on the back of the empty co-pilot's seat to keep herself steady. The sky was noticeably darker than the last time she'd paid attention to it. The clouds seemed to be growing blacker by the second. "Is it safe to fly through that?" she asked.
"I don't know," Kai said. "It's whipping up pretty fast." Another gust of wind hit, and then a sudden downpour of pelting rain ensued. "We should land, maybe. What do you think?"
"Why are you asking *me*?" Zara frowned.
"I've never flown through a storm like this." Kai's tone was laced with panic, which didn't inspire much confidence.
"Didn't you learn about this in pilot school or something?"
"Pilot school?" Kai scoffed. "It's flight training."
Was that an attempt to change the subject?
"Kai," Zara asked, her heart rate picking up speed, "how long have you been flying?"
"Three months."
Zara had no idea if that was just sort of bad or really bad. "But you went to flight training, or whatever?"
"Ehhh," Kai wrinkled his nose and made a so-so motion with his hand. "Basically."
"Kai!" Zara's heart thumped harder. "What does that even mean?"
"I had some lessons. A lot of good lessons. I worked on the planes first. I was an assistant to the mechanic. I know planes, okay?" He leaned over the cockpit display, seeming to study the different indicators, controls, and screens. "Maybe I can go above the storm."
A bright flash of light hit the nose just outside the cockpit windshield, and a sound like an amplified shotgun blast rattled Zara's bones. She screamed as the plane shook and her knees buckled. She lost her balance as the engine died. Her hands and knees hit the floor hard, and her forehead barely missed slamming into the seat of the chair she'd been sitting in moments earlier. She didn't see what Kai did to get the engine going again as she turned to sit on the floor and gather her wits.
"You okay?" Kai shouted over the sudden and increasing roar of wind and rain.
"What happened?" Mr. Peters burst into the cockpit, barely keeping upright as the plane was jostled by the storm. "Zara, are you hurt?"
"This storm came out of nowhere," Kai said.
"I'm okay," Zara said, though her body trembled. She assessed herself, but the only thing off was a smarting pain in her wrist. "I might have sprained my wrist, but… it's nothing serious."
"Did we lose the engine for a minute?" Mr. Peters reached out a hand toward Zara. "I thought… it sounded different." He pulled her to standing.
"Yeah, but I know what I'm doing. It's fine." He laughed nervously. "I mean, half the controls aren't working at the moment, but other than that…"

"What?" Zara screeched. She sat again to keep from falling as the wind pushed and pulled at the aircraft.

Mr. Peters steadied himself with one hand on the ceiling and one hand on the wall. "It doesn't seem fine, Kai."

"It's no biggie. We just have to, you know, make an emergency landing." He kept messing with the cockpit display. "You should get buckled in, Walter."

"No biggie? Are you serious?" Zara could have strangled him.

"Landing gear isn't working," Kai said. "And visibility is shot. It's going to be a bumpy landing."

Walter's face went a shade paler. "Again, doesn't sound fine."

"Have you ever landed without landing gear?" Zara couldn't tear her eyes away from the increasingly violent storm outside. The plane continued to jerk unpredictably.

"Nope." Sweat beaded on the back of Kai's neck. "I've never been caught in a freak storm, never been hit by lightning. Looks like today is a day of firsts. You two should buckle up."

Zara's stomach somersaulted. "We're going to die."

With that, hail began to assault the plane. It's chaotic hammering added to the overwhelming cacophony of the storm. Zara grabbed hold of the five-point harness, slipping her arms through the loops. Mr. Peters sat across from her, doing the same.

"Damn it!" Kai shouted. "How am I supposed to find a safe strip?"

"Again," Zara said shrilly, "*why* are you asking *us*? You're the pilot!" Her hands were shaking. She couldn't get the harness buckled.

"Zara, look at me." Mr. Peters's voice was firm and calm. He left his seat to kneel in front of her.

Swallowing bile, she focused on Mr. Peters's face. His expression had hardened. Once, she would have seen the set of his jaw and the slight narrowing of his eyes, she would have heard that no-nonsense tone, and she would have labelled it a symptom of his ice-cold heart. But she understood him better than that after all they'd been through.

"We survived ground zero at the World's Fair," he said as he took over the harness, buckling her in. "A stroke and heart attack. Being beaten down over and over again. Crazed mobs. Disease left and right. A freaking barrage of arrows. The loss of someone we both dearly loved." His steely gaze somehow transferred a little bit of collectedness into Zara. "We can survive this, too. But we need to help Kai stay calm and do his job."

She nodded. "Yeah, you're right." She took a deep breath, ignoring the way fear shivered up her spine. "You can do this Kai."

"I'm not so sure," Kai said. His hands shook as they flew over the controls. "I'm trying to get some of this working again, but even if I do, if we land in the wrong spot… it could tear the plane apart."

Mr. Peters tightened the straps on Zara's shoulders. "Do your best, Kai." He stood up and began stumbling back to his seat.

"Hold on!" Kai shouted as the tops of trees came into view. He pulled back, and the plane leveled out, flying low, the stray tip of a tree slapping the underside. "If we can just find a field—"

"Kai, watch out!" The ground took a sharp upturn, the rising wall of forest becoming visible through the torrential downpour only as they came upon it.

Kai yanked back on the throttle and the plane tipped. Mr. Peters, still on his way to his own seat, was thrown through the open door into the back of the plane.

"Walter!" Zara screamed.

"We're too close!" Kai said through gritted teeth.

She tore her gaze from the door to the windshield, horror coursing through her. The plane's increasing altitude was outmatched by the crest of a mountain before them. Metal crunched and tree trunks battered the plane, cracking the windshield. All the while, the wind and rain and hail were relentless in their attack. The bottom of the plane hit the raised ground and bounced off rock. Kai's head slammed forward on the wheel, and then he went limp. Ahead, a ridge formed out of the swirling rain. The plane hit the top of the mountain, and then the plane rent in two, the screeching of metal unbearable.

The darkness of the storm, the howling wind, whipped through the door where Zara had last seen Mr. Peters. "No!" Her voice was stolen by the gale. Not even she heard her cry.

For a moment, the windshield revealed swirling, black clouds through a sheet of rain. And then the cockpit was spinning — she was spinning — and everything was a blur.

Glass sprayed her as the top of a pine broke through the cracked windshield, missing Kai but flinging splinters everywhere. Zara screamed, her throat raw, and tried to cover her face with her arms. Slivers of wood pierced her skin. The tree bent forward and snapped, the top of it still jutting through the windshield. Again, the cockpit was tumbling down a decline and Zara couldn't tell which way was up.

And then the ruined ball of metal slammed into something, but whatever it was gave way. Disoriented, Zara willed her head to stop spinning.

"Kai," Zara croaked. She flopped her hand over the seat to touch the pilot's shoulder, wincing as she agitated the jagged splinters protruding from her arm. "Are you alive?" *Please be alive.*

She concentrated as she reached for his neck, as she sought a pulse. His skin was cold. It was so dark, and Zara still couldn't think straight. A steady, concentrated stream of water hit her hand as she searched for signs of life. Frigid water pooled around her ankles, too. Zara frowned in confusion. Her ears were still ringing, her stomach still sick. She blinked to clear her vision.

Yes, that *was* water at her feet. Water sprayed through the cracks on the windshield and around the protruding treetop, too. Rain and hail came through the door, perpendicular to the front of the plane. The door was pointed toward the sky, the windshield toward…

Zara snapped her attention back to the front of the plane. "Water…" She mumbled. "We landed in water."

Kai groaned, and the sound yanked Zara out of her shock.

"Kai, wake up!" Zara pulled on her harness, fumbling with the buckle. Water was coming in through the cracks at the front, but the door was still exposed to open air. "We have to get out of here." Her buckle clicked and slid apart, and she frantically freed herself from the shoulder straps, screaming in pain as she again bothered one of the larger slivers of wood protruding from her arm. She yanked three splinters from her arm, each one as long as her finger. Her eyes watered, and she bit her lip so hard, she tasted copper.

Rain from above and squirting water from the windshield below soaked her. The blood welling from minor wounds all over her body bubbled up only to be washed away, running in pink streams down her arms and legs.

Freedom from the harness produced a problem she hadn't considered. What had been her left-hand side had shifted to *downward*. She no longer leaned against the back of Kai's seat; gravity pushed her against it.

"Kai…" Zara whimpered his name, desperate to hear a response. "Please, I need you to wake up."

I won't be able to haul him up and out of the door, not in this condition. Zara looked up, shielding herself as a large hailstone flew toward her. It hit her back as she curled away from it.

The water was coming in slowly through the windshield. They would sink, eventually, but if she waited much longer, Kai would be under water. Or the glass would break, and the water would gush in too quickly.

Zara didn't know much about the buoyancy of planes, but she had to do something. Maybe if I put my weight near the door, the cockpit will level for a moment. Maybe it'll act like a boat long enough for me to get Kai out.

She carefully got to her knees, using the walls and ceiling of the cockpit to steady herself. The back of Kai's seat served as a platform as she struggled to her feet. Kai groaned again as her movements jostled the pilot's chair, but she kept going. Once standing, she took a deep breath, bent her knees, and jumped for the doorway above her head. It was close enough that she was able to hook her armpits over the edge.

But the cockpit didn't level. Zara's heart lodged in her throat. Once outside, she could see how far the cockpit had already submerged. It was barely afloat, most of it underwater, and her plan backfired. Her weight caused the bottom edge of the doorway to dip below the surface, and then water gushed into the open space.

Zara yelped as it pushed her back into the cockpit. She hit the back of Kai's chair, tumbled over it, and slammed into the windshield. Cold, relentless water overwhelmed her.

Chapter 2

Walter Peters

Walter stirred at the creaking of metal. Eyes peeling open to darkness, he sucked in a breath, confused as panic set in. His whole body ached, and a sharper pain emanated from his knee and his shoulder. The back of his head throbbed.

And he was soaked. A gray and gloomy daylight revealed an onslaught of hailstones and sheets of rain beyond a crudely circular opening. As the ringing in his ears abated, the cacophony of wind, rain, and hail took over.

Where the hell am I? "Bethie?" he shouted, and then a pang shot through his chest, compounding his physical pain. *Elizabeth is dead. Get it together, Peters.* Another wave of panic rolled over him as a different face flashed before his eyes. "Zara?" he shouted as loudly as he could, the effort straining his lungs. "Zara, can you hear me?"

A flood of memory overwhelmed Walter. He was in a plane. The back half. Zara had been strapped in behind Kai in the cockpit when the plane had torn apart. He'd been thrown into the back just before a horrendous crunch of metal, just before the sky appeared where the cockpit should have been. That was the last thing he remembered, being tossed like a rag doll, body slamming into chairs, rolling head over heels, fingers slipping on wet leather upholstery.

More than ever, he wished he could get back that moment after waking, that split second when Elizabeth was alive, when he was still in Wellesley, when all he had to do was roll over to find Dana beside him.

Wishing for the impossible isn't going to help. He pushed away the bubbling emotion; he needed to be strong, to find Zara and Kai, to get them all to safety. *Just take the next step, Walter.* He focused on breathing steadily. *What's the next step?*

He used his good arm to push himself to a sitting position. A searing hot surge of agony burst through his left side and radiated throughout his body. Bile stung the back of his throat as his head spun. He arced his body in an awkward position, desperate to relieve the pain. It ebbed enough for him to catch his breath when he laid back down, but his left side was still on fire, still pulsing.

Breathing heavy, Walter gingerly reached with trembling fingers to search for the source of his pain. The wetness of his shirt was thick and warm all along his left side. It was a sharp contrast to the frigid dampness that caused him to shiver where he lay. As he carefully prodded, he felt along the outline of a jagged piece of metal, roughly triangular. A sharp edge pricked his finger, and he pulled back, gasping.

I must have been hit by debris. He tried to incline his head to get a view of his injury, but it was too dark in the shadowy recesses of the mutilated plane. Using his one good leg and his one good arm, he scooted himself toward the middle of the plane, out from behind the deeper shadows of the passenger's seat to his right. He leaned against the bathroom door. Everything still spun just slightly, and he tried to ignore the rocking sensation as he refocused his eyes.

Damn vertigo. He swallowed hard and held his forehead in his hand. *I can't think like this.*

Rivulets of water ran down the aisle from where the cockpit had been shorn off the rest of the plane. What little daylight fighting through the storm made for poor illumination as Walter moved himself into its path, but it was something. He could make out the placement of the debris and its size, or what he could see of it. It seemed a corner of the triangular fragment had embedded itself somewhere above his kidney.

"Do I pull it out?" he mumbled to himself. It didn't go all the way through to his back. In fact, from what he could tell, it didn't seem that deep at all. "It's a lot of blood, but… it could seem like more, mixed with all this water."

He chewed on his lip as he studied the incline in front of him. If he was going to find Zara, he would need to get out of there. The tilt of the plane would make it difficult, but not impossible, to army crawl his way up. He couldn't do that with the debris implanted in his side.

"Would too much movement push it deeper?" Talking out loud filled the air with something other than the pounding of hail and the pinging of rain on the plane's hull.

The same creaking that woke him sounded again, and the plane groaned. The rocking sensation returned. *That's* not *vertigo. It never was.* He'd disturbed the balance of the plane.

And then the plane *moved.* Walter pressed against the bathroom door, a scream lodged in his throat, every muscle tensing. What he imagined to be trees slapped the side of the plane, and the sound of limbs snapping and foliage splintering joined the discord of the storm.

A jolt ran through Walter as the back of the plane made impact and the sky became visible above. He put his good arm out, bracing for the structure to flip, but instead it slammed back to the ground, the incline slightly sharper than it had been before.

Walter leaned his head back against the bathroom door and let out a slow, shaky breath. "I have to get out of here." Hailstones fell through the opening, most of them missing him, hitting seats or the walls on either side of him, but a few struck him, adding a frigid sting to his pains.

He tested the stability of the plane with a slight shift of his weight. Nothing. *Okay, that's good.* Walter scooted up the aisle, his knee protesting as he tried to use both feet to steady himself. He was able to haul his body in front of the seat and then pull himself into it, but it took every ounce of strength, and though he avoided putting his full weight on his left side where the injuries — shoulder, side, and knee — were concentrated, it was still excruciating. He bit his lip hard enough to taste blood, his heartbeat thrashing in his ears at the effort.

The plane groaned again, and this time, instead of sliding backward, it began to tip onto its side, the side Walter had occupied. The structure quivered, and Walter gripped the armchairs as it crashed to the ground. Gravity pulled him out of his seat, and he curled his knees and good arm hitting the wall-now-floor, trying to protect his side. He hit harder than he'd anticipated, his knee screaming in pain upon impact and giving out. At the same time, his hand slipped on the wet, smooth surface. The triangular debris pierced his side further, clawing its way deeper.

He rolled to his right, blinding pain causing him to bite his tongue hard enough to sheer a layer of it clean off. He screamed, blood running down his throat, coppery and hot. It was too much; blackness crept into the edges of his vision.

And then his eyes popped open as he drew in a deep breath, gasping for air, choking and spitting blood. He'd lost consciousness, but he didn't know if it had been minutes or hours. The storm still raged. *Minutes, then. Hopefully.*

The pathway to the outside was no longer on an incline. "I can do this." Concentrating on keeping all his weight on his right side, Walter used his good arm to pull himself toward the opening. That cursed metallic creaking seeped into Walter's bones again as he pulled himself along the windows under the overhead compartments.

"No!" He pulled harder, faster. I have to get out! I have to find Zara!

He was nearly there. He could make out bushes and tree trunks through the gloom. He reached, hooked his elbow on the next window, and pulled, dragging his body behind him, using his uninjured leg to wriggle forward. The pattern continued as the structure shuddered: reach, hook, pull; reach, hook, pull. He was mere inches from making it outside when the plane rocked.

Ignoring the protests of his body, the way his nerves fired in agony, the sharp jabs of pain threatening to overwhelm him, Walter launched himself out of the opening, aiming to land on his right side, careening into a mess of thorns and foliage as trees snapped and the plane rolled down the mountain, the sounds of crunching metal resounding through the air.

Tiny spikes etched trails of blood on his face, his arms, his legs. Walter wrenched himself free of the shrub, slipping and falling on his back in the mud. The rain and hailstones continued to assault him, but he lay there, motionless besides the rise and fall of his chest.

Breathing: that was all he could manage as the adrenaline seeped from him. The blackness edged back into the corners of his vision, his head lolling to the side, blood drooling from his lips. He surrendered to the ebb and flow of consciousness; the longer he did so, the more deadened he became to the pain.

A high-pitched whine sounded at his feet, but Walter didn't have the strength to lift his head. Something licked his hand, the tongue rough and small. And then a sharp yip suggested a dog had found him, somehow, in the midst of the storm. The yipping continued, and Walter tried to blink away the exhaustion.

If there's a dog, maybe… maybe there's a person. He tried to form words, to yell for help, but the sounds were garbled as they passed his swelling tongue.

"Nugget?" A woman's voice broke through the noise.

Walter's second attempt to speak was no better than his first, but he was making sounds. He'd never thought much of praying, but he did so then, as he felt the life draining from him so close to being rescued.

"Nugget!" The woman's voice was both relived and chastising. "You silly dog. Going *toward* a noise like th—" She gasped. "Saul." She said the name as if there was no question, and then Walter was looking at a face behind a plastic mesh. The woman knelt over him.

"Saul, it's me. It's Carol. I knew I'd find you out here. I *knew* it."

Walter couldn't frown, couldn't contradict her. *Am I that banged up? That unrecognizable?*

"It's okay, hon." Carol gently stroked his hair away from his face. Her touch stung as she agitated cuts and bruises Walter had barely been aware of before. She shouted over the din. "I'm going to get you to safety. I just… I need help. I'm going to be back, I promise. I'm going to grab LeeAnn and Heath. We have time before the swarm comes out. They don't fly in the rain, not this kind of rain, anyway."

Walter heard the dog yip again as the woman picked him up. She reassured him she'd be back once more before retreating, and though Walter tried to fight the constant tug on his mind to let go and rest, he couldn't. He surrendered while the storm still raged.

Chapter 3

Zara Williams

Zara fought against the gushing water with everything she had, fumbling with Kai's buckled harness. The water consumed the empty space, hungry to force every bit of air out of its domain. Kai's chin was barely above water.

Finally, the straps loosened as the buckle snapped apart. She tugged Kai upward, relieved that his legs didn't catch, that he floated. The water, pouring in through the doorway, pushed his body against her, the current strong.

"Wake up!" Zara slapped at Kai's cheeks.

And then the windshield broke, tearing away from the cockpit, sucking Zara out with it. She instinctively sucked in breath, but it wasn't enough. The back of her head slammed against the inside of the cockpit before she was sent into the expanse of water beyond. It hurt, but she barely had time to consider it as Kai's body hit her hard and rolled over her. She tumbled, weightless and terrified. She desperately sought to reorient herself, her eyes stinging as she opened them to peer through the murky water.

Kai! She searched frantically and spotted a figure below her. Zara used her arms and legs to push herself through the cold depths toward him, and by the time she reached him, her lungs were burning. He'd hit a sandy bottom, arms floating above his head, bubbles escaping his lips.

Zara hooked her arms under Kai's armpits and pushed off the ground to give them some momentum toward the surface. She kicked wildly as she hoisted him upward, but as she was about to break the surface, Kai twitched. Still making progress toward the surface, she glanced down to see Kai, wide-eyed with fear, cheeks puffed out, look up at her. His mouth opened in a silent scream, and he began to thrash.

No! You idiot! You're losing all your air! Zara shook her head vehemently and grasped at his shirt, trying to keep hold of him as he twisted away from her.

He flailed, suspended for a moment. Zara tried to grab him — his hand, his arm, his shirt, even his hair — to yank him to the surface. His hand slapped her cheek, and then he tried to throw his arms around her neck, tried to push himself upward. He only succeeded in pushing her down.

Zara had no choice. She wrestled herself free of him, pushing and kicking until he no longer held her down. Zara raced upward, her head pounding, her lungs begging for oxygen. When she broke the raging surface, she gasped, feeling as though someone had hit her chest with a sledgehammer, but she was able to breathe.

Waves tossed her back and forth. Rain and hail hit the frothing surface all around her. Wind buffeted her face and made it harder to suck in air. Still, she twisted and turned, watching the water, hoping to catch sight of Kai breaking the surface. *C'mon, Kai. Fight to the surface.*

Salty tears joined the rain streaking down her cheeks. She was so tired. Her arms and legs ached. She had sustained lacerations from the splinters and glass. The pain in her wrist, intensified as what had started out as a sprain or a fracture had become something more, was almost welcomed. It kept her aware, let her feel something in the cold water.

As she searched, she made out trees. They didn't seem too far. Guilt racked her as she decided whether to swim for the shore, to save herself, or to dive again and look for Kai. *I only have the strength to do one.* Sobbing, she made for the shore.

She'd managed only a few strokes when something bobbed up with a great splash several yards from her. "Kai!" Her voice barely carried in the terrible noise of the storm. She swam in his direction, careful not to get too close lest he, in a panic, push her under the surface again. "Kai!" She screamed his name as she got closer.

He whipped his head to look at her, a wild look in his eye. "Zara!" He coughed and struggled as the waves moved him back and forth.

"The shore!" Zara screamed, exaggeratedly pointing in the direction she'd seen trees. "Swim for the shore!"

He nodded and turned in the right direction. Zara didn't check on him again as she fought against the mini waves toward the tree line. Every stroke of her arms drained a little more energy. Every kick simultaneously brought her closer to life and closer to death; the difference between the two was one mistake, one cramp, one pause that lasted too long.

When she reached a low, concrete sidewalk that bordered the lake, she laughed out of sheer relief. A black fence with two metal rungs between each post provided perfect handholds for her to haul herself out of the water. She crawled onto the sidewalk, hysterically happy to be on solid ground.

"Hey!" Kai grasped a rung, but his hand slipped. "A little help?"

Zara quickly closed the distance and helped Kai get onto the sidewalk. He rolled onto his back, and she lay beside him. She didn't even care that the rain hadn't let up, that smaller bits of hail still pelted her, stinging with every hit.

"We're alive!" Zara laughed again. It bubbled out of her. She couldn't believe they'd both survived. She slapped Kai's arm. "You almost killed me, you idiot. Like three times in the last hour."

Kai coughed and spit water. He didn't look in the mood for laughter. "I'm sorry," he said. "I… I'm really sorry." He sat up. "We've gotta find shelter."

"I don't want to move." Zara shook her head. Her body felt light, and when she tried to sit up, the world swayed, and her stomach flipped. "I don't think I should be going anywhere."

Kai got to his feet, a gust pushing him to stumble back a few steps. "We have to. Once this storm clears, the mosquitos are going to be out in force. It's only the winds keeping them from swarming right now." He held out his hand. "Come on, Zara. I mean it."

Zara let him help her to her feet, but it wasn't pleasant. She hurled, but only water and bile came up. She wiped her mouth with her arm. "I just want to lay back down."

"Zara, you're delirious." Kai pulled her along the concrete path. "We have to—"

"Find shelter. I know. I think I hit my head, down in the cockpit. I feel… funny." Zara laughed again and stopped walking. "I don't think walking is a good idea." She bent her knees toward the ground, but Kai stopped her, grabbing both shoulders, and forcing her to stand.

"This isn't good," Kai said. "Stop trying to sit. You don't know what you're doing. Just do what I say, okay? Keep walking." He reached out for her.

Zara batted at his hand weakly. "You're starting to sound like…" She stopped and jerked her arm from Kai's grip. "No… Mr. Peters." A sudden shot of adrenaline made her heart feel as though it might burst from her chest. "Walter!" She turned back toward the lake and pointed at the dark shape of the mountain on the other side of the lake. "He's that way. We… we have to find him. We have to—"

"No." Kai took Zara's cheeks between his hands and forced her to look at him. "He wouldn't want that. We have to get to safety. Tomorrow, we can try to find some protective gear, and we can go into the forest looking for him. Right now, it's too dangerous. We've got miles to search."

Zara blinked, her exhaustion making it harder to process his words. "No," she said, her body sagging into Kai. "No, we can't leave him. He has to save the world."

"What?" Kai shook his head and pulled her once more down the sidewalk. "Come on, Zara. I didn't fall for that before, and I'm not going to fall for it now. You can't just make crap up when you want me to do something."

"It wasn't a joke. Or a lie." Zara put one foot in front of the other. Part of her knew Kai was right, that they had to find shelter. She didn't have the strength to resist him, not for long, and not effectively. She'd have to follow the path around the lake to get to the mountain, anyway. "He knows how to stop them," she said. "He made them."

"Made who?" Kai kept tugging her through the rain, the wind pushing at their backs.

"The mosquitos. In his lab. I mean, his scientists probably did it… but he took the job." She shook her head, and the motion made her dizzy. Never in her life had she wanted so badly to just lay down and sleep.

"You're crazy." Kai hooked his arm around her back and under her armpit, halfway holding her up, though he seemed to struggle to keep her walking. He was shivering and limping and there was a gash in his forehead, fresh blood continuously washed away by the rain.

They came to an intersection, and a sign pointed the way to the parking lot. Kai turned right, away from the mountain. Zara shook her head in protest, but that was all she could do. If they found shelter, she could sleep. She could lay her head down and rest. The part of her that wanted to go right that minute into the unknown forest to search for Mr. Peters wasn't strong enough to do anything more than lament her compliance.

Though it had been several minutes of putting one foot in front of the other — who knew such a simple task could take so much effort? — Zara returned to their previous conversation. "I'm not, you know."

"Not what?" Kai sighed.

"Crazy. Or lying." She had to make sure he understood. They couldn't leave Mr. Peters to die.

"Okay, fine," Kai said. "What job, then? What are you talking about?"

"Mr. Peters owns a lab. The government hired him to create a weapon. And it got out. Probably because a bunch of crazies in an environmentalist group stole them." Zara started to cry, hot tears stinging her tired eyes. "I hate them. Those bastards. Stupid GEF or Heirs of the Mother or whatever."

"Heirs?" Kai chuckled. "Now you really sound like you're crazy."

"I'm not!" Angry, Zara pushed at Kai unsuccessfully. "The Heirs of the Mother killed my best friend!"

Kai frowned. "Geez. I'm sorry, okay? I… I just… this whole thing is just nuts."

"Yeah, it is," Zara said sharply. She gestured to the empty air all around her. "The world is crazy now. It's all going to sh—" She gagged as a sudden wave of nausea washed over her, and she hurled; this time more than just water came up.

Kai rubbed her back as she heaved. "Okay, you're right," he said. "Everything's crazy. I can't argue with that."

Zara gasped for fresh air, her mouth burning from her stomach acid. She again began to sink to her knees, and Kai stopped her. "I don't care if I die. If Mr. Peters is dead, we're all dead, anyway. Just leave me alone." She wasn't sure she believed that, but she was *so* tired. And her head was swimming. And her body ached.

"Don't you give up on me," Kai said. "Not after you saved me down there." He hauled her up again.

She cracked a half smile. "You owe me *again*." She poked his chest.

"Yeah, babe—I mean, Zara." Kai held up one hand in defense of her glare. "I do owe you, okay? That's why you've got to keep going."

"Fine," Zara said as she allowed him to continue guiding her. The wind was lessening as they turned another corner. She knew that wasn't good, but she couldn't remember why. *Isn't that nice? Not having to fight against the wind?*

"Go faster," Kai said, panic lacing his words. "The wind keeps the mosquitos at bay, remember?"

"Oh, yeah." Zara nodded. "Right. Well… good thing there's the parking lot." She pointed up ahead, her arm drooping almost as soon as she raised it.

They hobbled another several yards to a parking lot full of cars, trucks, and a few campers. Kai led them to a small, silver airstream hooked up to a truck and tested the door. It opened.

"Let me check to make sure there aren't any bodies." He leaned Zara against the camper. "Don't fall asleep. Don't sit down."

Zara nodded, though she thought his ask was going a little too far. She felt so strange, almost like she was watching herself from somewhere else. Her body was abuzz with pins and needles. She eyed the step that led into the camper and licked her lips. She took a step forward, planning to sit down, but Kai popped his head back out.

"All clear," he said, holding out a hand. "Come on up."

He helped her up the steps into the tiny compartment and closed and locked the door behind her. It was hot and humid inside, but it was safe and dry. There was a small bed to the right, and Zara stepped toward it.

"Wait." Kai pushed past her to some drawers under the bed, pulling them out. He rummaged through them and pulled out a large shirt and some boxers. "Change into these in the bathroom real quick. You're going to get sick if you stay in those clothes."

Zara wrinkled her nose. "These aren't my clothes."

Kai rolled his eyes. "I know," he said, impatiently. "Just do it. Please?"

"Fine." She dragged her feet across the floor, removing her shirt on the way to the little door that led into the cramped bathroom. She dropped the torn, bloodied, wet thing on the ground.

"Wait until you're *in* the bathroom, dork." Kai's voice followed her into the tiny room. "Geez. You must have hit your head hard. Walter is going to kill me if you die. You hear that?" Then in a quieter voice that Zara barely overheard. "If he's alive to do it, that is."

"He's alive!" She shouted as she tried her best to undress and don the oversized t-shirt and boxers without falling over. The fact the room was small made it easier for her to lean on surfaces to maintain her balance. Once dressed, she threw open the door, stumbling into a kitchenette countertop. "He has to be alive! I told you, he has to save *everyone*!"

Kai frowned at her, deeper this time. He helped her to the bed, and she let him, though she kept repeating her words. He *had* to understand. They couldn't give up on Mr. Peters. Not now, not ever. She plopped into the bed, wincing as she lay her head on the pillow. Zara turned so she lay on her side instead, her eyes drooping before she even registered Kai kneeling beside the edge of the mattress.

"We're going to talk about this more after you're… normal again," he said, pulling a blanket up around her. "If you're telling the truth now, you're going to have a lot of explaining to do then."

Zara nodded, her body becoming heavier by the second. The last thing she heard before drifting off was Kai's whisper. "Please, God. Please… let her live."

Chapter 4

Lauren Stevens

Lauren Stevens leaned over the little body of her first trauma patient in years, checking her vital signs. Annika's injuries were worrisome; without the proper equipment, she'd only been able to make likely diagnoses: a concussion, blunt kidney trauma, a knee fracture, and multiple lacerations and contusions.

"How is she?" A weak, hoarse voice came from Lauren's second patient, Candice. She was far better off than the little girl with a milder concussion, a few bad lacerations, and a few broken ribs. Lauren had assumed her to be the mother at first, but she'd learned that wasn't the case.

Lauren walked over to Candice's cot. They were set up in a research and development laboratory of some kind, the walls lined with stainless steel cabinets, the room sterile and cold. In the absence of a hospital, it was a good option for patient care. Lauren had arranged for the two cots to be moved, and she'd organized what little supplies she had over the past twenty-four hours to the best of her ability.

"She's… not great," Lauren said truthfully. Bedside manner hadn't been her strong suit during her residency. "I'm doing what I can. I'm most concerned about internal bleeding, her kidney, specifically."

Candice looked up at Lauren with concern etched into her features. "But that woman, Minnie… she's donating blood."

Lauren hugged her middle. She hated giving bad news. When she'd quit her residency to pursue her passions of music in Nashville, she'd thought she'd left behind the weight of trauma care forever. *I was never cut out for this.*

"My mom was able to donate once because she's a universal donor but donating again too soon would make *her* sick. Not to mention we only had one field blood transfusion kit." As she spoke, the door opened, and Timothy entered. Lauren hadn't pegged him yet; he had a constant suspicious glint in his eye, and his expressed gratitude for her treatment of his friends had been stiff.

He came to stand by Annika's bed, gently squeezing her hand. His sharp, hardened tone contrasted strangely with his soft touch. "Where did you get that anyway? The transfusion kit?"

Lauren shrugged. "From the CDC facility."

Alex had opted to tell Timothy more than he'd told Ned and the bikers, seeing as how Timothy was the son of the man they were looking to find. Before the bikers, they'd been reticent to give out information to the people occupying the CDC. It was nice to not be keeping secrets, for once.

"Right." Timothy nodded, his jaw set. "The same guys that basically kept you prisoner gave you all these supplies and then just let you go."

"Yep." Lauren put her hands on her hips. "I assume you're here to get the list of things I need to save the lives of your friends. You want that, or do you wanna play twenty questions?"

Candice chuckled and winced in pain, holding her breath and then letting it out slowly. "That hurt," she croaked, eyes squeezed shut.

"You okay?" Lauren grimaced, imagining the pain of fractured ribs with only over-the-counter pain medications to dull the agony.

Candice nodded and then looked at Timothy. "I like her," she said softly.

Timothy, who had stepped forward in concern, relaxed at her words, shaking his head. "You would," he said.

"Stop being an ass," Candice said.

Timothy pressed his lips into a thin line, quirked an eyebrow, and held out a hand. "The list?" he asked.

"It's okay," Lauren said, passing him and patting him on the shoulder. "I know some people just can't help themselves." She grabbed the list off the countertop and handed it over. "I've listed these in order of importance."

"An ultrasound machine? Another doctor or surgeon?" Timothy gawked. "IV Fluids, rapid blood type testing kits, O negative blood… where are we supposed to find this stuff?"

"The items at the top are all long shots," Lauren said.

Timothy frowned. "But you said you put them in order of importance."

Lauren raised her eyebrows. "So you *were* listening." She sighed. "Look, maybe you can find an ultrasound machine at an OB/GYN clinic. The IV Fluids are salt water and should be stored in a dry place; they don't have to be refrigerated. The O negative blood… maybe you could find those at a hospital with a generator still kicking, but I'm not sure that one's realistic. If you could find some rapid blood type testing kits in a hospital lab or maybe an air ambulance, I could test Annika's blood type and see if maybe we have more donors in our group that would match her. You're looking for something called an EldonCard Kit. My mom can't give any more blood for a while. I mean… the sutures, transfusion kits… a lot on that list can be found in hospitals."

"I'm afraid they'll be picked over," Timothy said. "But we can check, and we can take this list to Police Headquarters. They might be able to spare some of their supplies."

"And you can try to get George to come back." Candice pursed her lips. It wasn't a question.

"George… that's your little brother?" Lauren asked.

"Yeah." Timothy folded the paper and stuffed it into his pocket. "We might be away until tomorrow." He glanced at Annika. "Will she make it until then?"

Lauren wiped away all hints of sarcasm. "I'll do whatever I can to keep her alive. The transfusion put some color back into her cheeks, but I can't do anything about continued internal bleeding or brain swelling or… any number of things. Not without those supplies, and even then, I might not be able to do much. We might need to look for a surgeon."

Timothy blanched. "How long does she have, worst case scenario?"

"I can't answer that," she said. "I can say if the trauma isn't too bad, the kidney will heal on its own within a few weeks, as long as we keep her blood pressure up. If it's worse, I'm hoping she doesn't go into kidney failure. Once I see signs of that, it could be as little as a few days before she's gone. We'd definitely need a surgeon at that point." Lauren shook her head. "That's not the only concern, though. She's woken up a few times, which is a good sign, but she's not out of the woods as far as the brain injury is concerned, either."

He nodded solemnly, absorbing the information and taking it in stride. "We'll be back tomorrow, as early as we can, with as many of these supplies as possible." Timothy kissed Annika's forehead. "We'll go back out every day if we have to." His voice caught. "I can't lose anyone else."

Lauren swallowed a lump in her throat as hot tears sprung to her own eyes. Those words hit too close to home. She held the emotions at bay as she thought of her fiancé. He'd perished in Nashville weeks ago, before her mother and Alex had found her. So many friends were just gone. She walked over to Timothy, still leaning with head bowed over Annika, and put a hand on his arm.

"I swear to you, I will do everything I can for her." She offered as much confidence and hope in her tone and expression as she could muster.

He stood up straighter. "Thank you." He looked around her to Candice. "Take care of her, too. She's grown on me."

Lauren stepped back a little as the two friends exchanged a look; it was clear that they'd been through a lot together. She smiled at him, and he returned the sentiment. They didn't say anything, but it didn't seem like that was necessary. Lauren had been too busy working to stabilize Annika to share in storytelling, but the group they'd joined seemed as close to each other as she and her mom had become to Alex and Oliver.

The door opened again, and Heather stuck her head inside. Her eyes landed on Annika, a pained expression crossing her features, before she spoke to her husband. "Tim, you ready to go?" She gave Lauren a small wave. Heather had slept on the floor on a pile of blankets, much like Lauren had, and she'd offered an extra hand throughout the night. "How are you doing?" she asked.

"I could use something to eat," Lauren said. "A few miracles would be nice, too. Other than that, I think I'm golden."

"I'm hungry, too," Candice said.

Lauren smiled. "Good. You've not had anything to eat since before the accident."

"The stampede, you mean?" Candice quirked an eyebrow. "It was no accident. I'm pretty sure those wildebeests meant every kick."

"We'll make sure something is brought in for you both before we head out," Timothy said as he joined his wife at the door.

"I think we've got protein powder we can mix into some oatmeal," Lauren said. "That would be ideal, I think. Carbs, protein, vitamins."

"Yum," Candice said.

"Listen to the doctor," Timothy said, pointing at her and using a chastising voice.

Lauren didn't bother to correct him; she'd already tried a dozen times. She sighed as the two left, leaving her once again alone with her patients. With no monitors, no alert system, she couldn't take her eyes off the little girl for long, and she hadn't stepped outside the makeshift clinic except to use the bathroom.

It wasn't long before her mom bustled in with a tray holding two steaming bowls of protein-infused oatmeal. "Peaches and cream," Minnie said. "A little bit of vanilla protein powder, too." A bulging cloth sack hung from one arm, and she lifted her elbow just a smidge. "I brought some of that fancy electrolyte water we found, too."

"Thanks, Mom. Just set it down on the counter." Lauren helped Candice sit up to minimize the pain of moving with fractured ribs. She retrieved a bowl and held it out. "See if you can manage to hold the bowl. I know it sounds weird, but you might be too weak."

Candice scoffed and reached for the bowl. "I can feed myself, thank y— oh." She grimaced as she tried to hold the bowl but had to rest it on her lap. A trembling hand grasped the spoon and the oatmeal plopped back into the bowl as she tried unsuccessfully to transfer a bite into her mouth.

"I'll help you for a few days," Lauren said.

"Now, don't be silly. You're doin' enough." Minnie stepped forward and swatted Lauren's hand away from the bowl on Candice's lap. "I'll help her eat. I can do that much."

"Mom—"

"Hush. Go get your oatmeal." Minnie brought a bite to Candice's lips.

"Well, I guess I won't fight you on it." Lauren kissed her mother's cheek. "Thanks."

She took her bowl and settled on a pillow, leaning against the cabinets to eat. The oatmeal was mushy and slightly too sweet, but it soothed her hunger pangs. "How are Alex and Oliver?" she asked.

"Oliver is right as rain," Minnie said. "Him and Samson have made themselves at home."

"Samson's your dog, right?" Candice asked between bites.

Minnie nodded. "Yep. A Rhodesian Ridgeback. Loyal and sweet as can be, except when his people are threatened."

"And Alex?" Lauren asked after swallowing another lump of oatmeal.

"He's been holed up in a lab with… what's his name?" Minnie raised an eyebrow at Candice, withholding the next bite as she waited for an answer. "The other scientist?"

"Oh, Theodore?" Candice asked.

Minnie nodded. "That's the one. Him and Timothy, though Timothy seems to come and go."

"We don't know Theodore well," Candice said. "We only met him a few days ago. But I'll be spending a lot more time with him once I'm able. He wants to study me." She shuddered. "What's Tim doing in the lab, though? He doesn't know anything about diseases."

"Well, I don't know. If he just met him, maybe he don't trust him." Minnie frowned. "Why does he wanna study you?"

"I got the disease that's killed everyone," Candice said. "But… I didn't die."

Lauren blinked at that, dropping her spoon back into her bowl. "Say what now?"

"Lands sake!" Minnie's mouth dropped open, and she took a step back. "When?"

"It's been weeks," Candice said. "I swear I'm not contagious."

Minnie took a tentative step closer. "I 'spose they wouldn't be crazy enough to keep company with someone whose gonna get them sick." She glanced at Lauren questioningly.

Lauren nodded. "I think it's okay," she said, getting to her feet. "But… that's good, right? Does that mean you can help them find a cure?"

"Or a vaccine, apparently," Candice said. "I mean, my blood can. Maybe." She shrugged.

Lauren smiled. "That's the best news I've heard in quite a while."

"Well, I'll be darned." Minnie excitedly scooped another spoonful of oatmeal. "We gotta take care of you, little miss." She shoved the bite forward. "Open up. And I'm gonna get you some of that fancy water, too."

Candice ate the oatmeal – not that she had a choice in the matter now that Minnie was whole heartedly involved. "If you want me to be okay," she said once the oatmeal was gone, "take care of her." She nodded toward Annika. "She's important to me." Candice's shoulders drooped; she looked and sounded exhausted.

"She's in good hands," Minnie said.

Lauren sighed, the pressure of saving the girl growing by the second. "I'm doing everything I can." She stood up again as Minnie gathered the bowls and unloaded the water bottles onto the countertop. Lauren focused on Candice. "For now, let's get you some hydration, and then I think it's time for you to rest some more, okay?"

Candice didn't argue. She drank her fill, and gratefully accepted Lauren's help in lowering her back down to the mattress. It was only moments after her head hit the pillow that she fell asleep.

"I'm proud of you, hon," Minnie said, wrapping her arms around Lauren.

Those words stung; she knew her mother hadn't meant them to hurt, but they hadn't spoken for years after Lauren had dropped out of her residency. Minnie had insisted since then that she was proud of Lauren outside of her pursuits of a medical degree, too. Her mother had said pushing Lauren away had been her biggest regret in life. And she *had* come to Nashville to find her when the world fell apart. They'd come so far in mending their relationship over the past few weeks.

But practicing medicine, having her mother there to express pride over it… old feelings stirred. "I know I'm needed in this way," Lauren said softly, "but you know I'm not a doctor, Mom, right? You know that's not who I want to be. I mean, we should be going out and looking for surgeons or trauma physicians, if there are any left nearby." She lowered her voice even more, glancing at the sleeping Candice. "I'm not qualified for this."

"Hon, right now, you're the closest thing we've got." Minnie cupped Lauren's cheeks in her hands. "I know you're not a doctor. I know you wish this hadn't happened, that you didn't have this on your shoulders. Truth be told, I wish you didn't have to carry it, either. If we can find someone to take that burden, I'll gladly help you hand it over. In fact, I'll go out into the city and help find whoever it is you need." She held Lauren's gaze. "But that still don't stop me from being proud of my baby girl. I've been bursting with pride ever since Nashville."

"You'd do that? You'd go out and try to find a surgeon or a trauma physician?" Lauren's heart leapt at the thought of not having to handle the pressure alone. She'd give anything to hand the medical decisions over to someone with experience and more training.

"If that's what you want." Minnie nodded firmly.

Lauren threw her arms around her mother's neck and squeezed. "Thank you, Mom."

Minnie hugged her back, and when she pulled away, she offered a confident smile. She retrieved the tray with the dishes stacked in the center. "I'll talk to the others and come up with a plan. Now, you get some rest while these two are asleep."

Lauren nodded and walked her mom to the door. And then she settled once again on the pillows and blankets on the floor. She didn't sleep, though. She couldn't. Sooner or later, something would go wrong. She could only hope that when it did, she wouldn't be expected to save Annika alone.

Chapter 5

Timothy Peters

Sweat beaded on the back of Timothy's neck as he listened to two strangers trying to figure out how to save the world. One of them, Alexander Roman, had travelled from St. Louis to Atlanta and then back north to Boston, hoping to find Timothy's father, Walter. The other, Theodore Finch, had been at New Horizons, his father's company, for weeks trying to figure out how to undo the atrocities ravaging humanity.

Theodore also held secrets Timothy could never let anyone else discover. Vanguard had created the sickness, DV-10, and the mosquitos meant to be the original delivery system. His father had known about it, approved it, even helped to envision it.

Despite what was happening with Annika, Theodore and Alex had started talking shop almost immediately. Timothy had been forced to intercede, to pull Theodore aside.

"You can't let my family be connected to the creation of this disease," Timothy had said.

Theodore had snorted. "I would never. I'm not stupid. It's as much a government secret as it is a company one."

Timothy quirked an eyebrow. "You weren't supposed to tell *me*, but you did."

Theodore looked affronted, his mouth flopping open and closed as he stammered, "Well, y-yes, but you… you *threatened* me. I had to tell you."

Timothy ground his teeth together, doing his best to keep his voice down. "You let details slip before that. You have to do better this time."

"What do you want me to say, then?" Theodore asked. "I *do* have to tell Alex as much as possible. He can help us. And I'm not good at elaborate lies."

Timothy took half a step closer, crossed his arms, and tried to imitate Captain O'Donnell's best glare. The Boston Police captain was bigger, stronger, and more intimidating than Timothy would ever be, but the posturing seemed to be working as Theodore shrank back. "It doesn't have to be elaborate. It only matters that we cover up the origin of DV-10." Timothy narrowed his eyes. "Be creative."

Theodore groaned and rubbed his temples for a moment before his eyes lit up. "Maybe we could say Vanguard was commissioned to counter a foreign threat. The government gave us information, and we started working on counter measures. That would explain a lot of our current resources without revealing the truth."

Timothy nodded slowly. "It sounds plausible to me."

"Fine. That's the way I'll spin it, then." Theodore breathed out, some of the tension in his shoulders dissipating. "I don't want to be connected to the creation of this thing any more than you do."

"Good," Timothy had said. "If we play our cards right, we can all come out of this unscathed."

And then Theodore had continued to lay information at Alex's feet. Timothy watched the newcomer carefully, searching for signs of suspicion. He picked up on hints here and there that the disease detective knew something wasn't quite right. But so far, Theodore had fielded questions well, directing Alex away from the knowledge that Walter Peters and Vanguard — and scientists like Theodore — had created the nightmare they were all living.

But he couldn't monitor them forever. Half of what they said went right over his head, anyway. When the two scientists had taken a break, Timothy had gone to check on Candice and Annika and talk to Lauren about what she needed to do her job.

An hour later, he walked the ruined streets of Boston, Heather by his side and an impossible wish list in his pocket. He tried to let go of the anxiety twisting his stomach into knots. *I have to trust Theodore. All he has to do is keep one detail from slipping. The rest he can share freely. As long as Alex doesn't dig too deeply…*

"Tim, are you okay?" Heather paused a few steps ahead of him, letting him catch up to her.

"Yeah… it's just… Annika. I'm worried about her." The half-truth left a bitter taste in his mouth. He'd never lied to his wife; it was a pact between them. *Maybe I should tell her. But… then she'd have to keep the secret, too. The fewer people who know about this, the better.*

Images of angry mobs hunting his family down haunted him. It wouldn't matter that only Walter had anything to do with the scandal. DV-10 had destroyed the world. There would be justice-seekers holding to the eye-for-an-eye mantra. Timothy, Heather, George, and Lizzy, if she was still alive, would all suffer simply because they were connected to Walter.

Before he'd had a falling out with his father, on Timothy's wedding day, Walter Peters had given Timothy a piece of advice.

"Sometimes, omitting a truth that would only cause stress or pain is the most loving thing a person can do for their spouse," he'd said as he'd straightened Timothy's tie. "There are plenty of burdens the two of you will share together. Every once in a while, you'll need to shoulder one all by yourself."

At the time, Timothy had been disgusted with the idea of destroying the transparency he enjoyed with Heather. He was *still* disgusted by it, but he'd done it, anyway. He was becoming his father; part of him recoiled at that, but another part was dumfounded by the sudden understanding of the man he'd sworn off years ago.

"Timothy?" Heather waved a hand in front of his face.

"Sorry." Timothy focused on his wife, forcefully pushing away thoughts of the past. "What were you saying?"

Heather's concerned expression wasn't lost on him. "I was saying we are all worried about Annika, but I need you to stay with me, Tim. We've got to work together, to keep hoping things will be okay. If we operate in the space of the worst-case scenario, it'll turn into a self-fulfilling prophecy."

Timothy sidestepped, making his way through the mess of vehicles. "Annika is hurt. George is going to get himself killed. Mom is gone. Dad and Lizzy might be gone, too. What's left of the world is falling apart. This feels pretty worst-case scenario to me."

Heather stopped and sat on the hood of a car, hanging her head. "Tim, this is the first time in weeks I've had hope. George might not be with us, but he's safe. O'Donnell will look out for him. And yes, Annika is bad, but we've got someone with medical training caring for her. Not to mention the fact that a guy from the CDC showed up to help Theodore with this vaccine. We've got a safe place to lay low, and we've got a solid plan. I *need* to believe things are looking up."

He heard the desperation in her voice, and his heart softened. "I can try harder to focus on the silver lining. Things could be worse. I can see that. And I can see where we've been lucky. I just… I miss my mom. I miss my sister. I even miss my dad, and I'm afraid for George. I'm afraid for all of us, all the time."

"I know. I'm afraid, too." Heather stood and came to him, wrapping her arms around his neck, pulling him close. "Just… have a little faith with me, okay?"

He welcomed her embrace, sank into that feeling of home. It was easier to find hope there, in her presence, with her love so palpable. Timothy pulled back just enough to give her a kiss. "You, Mrs. Peters, are my favorite person."

She smiled up at him. "Likewise, Mr. Peters."

He stepped away and held out his arm. "How about you and I check some of these things off our list?"

Heather slipped her hand into the crook of his arm. "Don't mind if I do."

They walked together through the city, testaments of destruction wrought weeks ago present at every turn. But the scene was growing familiar; it was sliding on a scale from surreal to normal more quickly than he would have thought possible. The wild animals, though… they still inspired awe. Timothy couldn't help but stop and stare as they came upon a small herd of giraffes amongst a cluster of trees nestled against a stone bridge. The overgrown grassy area led into Olmstead Park where the giraffes would have space to roam and access to fresh water.

"I don't think I'll ever get used to that," Heather whispered.

Timothy frowned as he noted fast-growing vines snaking their way up the stone bridge on either side. Tufts of green grew out of cracks in the sidewalk and road. He spotted moss forming on the bumper of a nearby car. "How long do you think it'll take for nature to take over?" he asked.

"What?" Heather furrowed her brow.

"The police and the mob are fighting over a city that nature is already starting to consume. We'll be able to keep pockets of it maintained, but the rest? There are so few people, so few resources." He shook his head. "They both want an empire, but whoever wins is going to end up with nothing more than a village."

"No, whoever wins will end up with a string of villages, and they'll claim power over each one," Heather said. "It matters who wins, Tim. O'Donnell and the BPD are going to treat survivors better than Frank Russo. They're not perfect, but they're better. That matters."

"But does George have to be part of it?" Timothy started walking again; there was so little time. He could have watched the giraffes for hours. Part of him longed for a break, and maybe if George was safe, if Annika hadn't been hurt, if war wasn't about to erupt across the city, if…

Staying positive was going to be hard. He glanced at his wife, whose forehead crinkled in growing anxiety, the corners of her mouth pinched. "I'm sorry," he said. "There I go again."

"You need to talk about this before we get to headquarters and see George, don't you?" Heather walked beside him, looking sideways at him.

"I guess I do," Timothy said. "I can't help but think that if I could just say the right thing, George would see sense and come back with us. We need him."

Heather sighed. "I love you, Tim, but you have to accept that you and George are on different paths right now."

"You're siding with him?" Timothy blinked. He'd expected comfort. Maybe a little brainstorming. "He's a kid, Heather."

"I know George is young. I know you want him safe." Heather shook her head. "What he went through, being captured and trained by CON… it made him grow up fast. I don't like it, but he's a teenager. We can't drag him home kicking and screaming. And O'Donnell won't put him directly in harm's way, not any more than he'd be if he were with us, anyway." Heather gave him a pointed look. "Don't pretend he would be completely safe with us."

Timothy worked his jaw back and forth, annoyed. "He'd be safer. And we'd be together."

"You can't control what he does," Heather said. "All you can do is choose to be proud of him or choose to push him away."

They walked a little longer in silence as Timothy digested Heather's words. The world had changed too fast, and it was demanding he change with it. The social constructs modern technology had afforded them were crumbling. He'd been fighting toward restoring life as he once knew it, or at least, fighting toward something similar.

"It's never going to be the same, is it?" he asked.

"There are freaking giraffes in the middle of Boston," Heather said with a wry smile, and then more softly, her smile fading, "No. It's not."

***

"I'm sorry," O'Donnell said in his Bostonian accent, voice deep and authoritative, his posture stiff as he glanced over the list Timothy had given him. "We can't spare anything. We need what we have for the upcomin' conflict. I can barely spare the time for this conversation, let alone weapons or gear."

Timothy bit his tongue, trying to keep his cool. The captain had been cold toward him ever since it had become clear he wasn't joining the fight. It didn't help that Timothy's plan to get rid of CON by using Frank Russo had resulted in Frank making a deal with Ruger, who was the gang's newest leader.

Heather's hand slipped onto his knee under the table, and she gave him a look that said he should remain calm. "Please," she said. "Our family is just trying to survive."

O'Donnell worked his jaw back and forth, his eyes softening slightly. He cleared his throat. "Is that little girl still alive?"

No thanks to you. Timothy opened his mouth to voice his thoughts, bitter though they were, but Heather spoke first.

"She is. We actually had the fortune of running into someone with medical training, a woman who'd gone through school and a bit of residency," Heather said. "She's watching after Annika, keeping her alive. We're trying to bring back supplies that will help."

O'Donnell took another look at the list, seeming to read it more carefully than he had the first time. He looked back up at them. "You two think you can speak on behalf of this woman?"

Timothy and Heather exchanged a look, and then Timothy took a gamble. "Maybe. I guess it depends on what you want."

O'Donnell grunted. "We're down medical personnel, and we're gonna need 'em. If she can be on standby for an emergency, we can let go of one Glock, some ammo, a couple bulletproof vests, and some walkie talkies, provided you keep one of 'em tuned to our frequency so we can communicate."

"One gun?" Timothy scoffed. "What about the medical supplies? Food and water?"

"You gotta scavenge for your own food and water. And we don't have enough medical supplies to give you a bandaid, kid. Don't push it. This is a good deal."

Heather folded her hands on the table and leaned forward. "Our medical emergencies supersede yours. If we need her, she stays with us. If we can spare her, we'll escort her here and back."

"And no calling her into or through active war zones," Timothy added. "We all have to keep her safe."

O'Donnell quirked an eyebrow. "Fair enough. But if it becomes a pattern, if she can't *ever* come when we call, the deal's off and you bring back what we gave you."

Timothy nodded. "Deal."

"Now, you two gotta go. Take your stuff from the breakroom you were stayin' in last week. I'll have someone meet you at the door with the supplies." O'Donnell stood, his chair screeching across the floor.

"I want to talk to my brother before I go," Timothy said.

"To try to take him with you?" O'Donnell shook his head. "I don't think so. He's made his decision. I'll take care of him, Peters. I won't put a teenager on the front lines."

"I want to see him so I can tell him I love him, O'Donnell." Timothy stood and met the other man's eyes with his own. "Please."

The police captain gave him a curt nod. "I'll have him bring you the supplies at the door, then."

Timothy and Heather nodded their agreement and left for the breakroom that had been their temporary home while staying with the BPD. Lucy Freeman, one of the cops who'd been at the Russo farmhouse when they'd first come across the police, escorted them. She had always been friendly, for the most part, but she barely said a word as she led them to the door and stood watch in the hall. Timothy caught a few scowls out of the corner of his eye as they walked by other officers. It seemed O'Donnell wasn't the only one at the BPD who thought Timothy's decision to bow out of the fight was the wrong one.

Timothy walked into the little room, glancing at the cots still set up and sat on the edge of what had been Candice's bed. He kicked at the suitcase at his feet, open and brimming with designer clothes, feminine products, and makeup. "It figures this is all we have left. Maybe we can convince Candice to unpack these, and we can use the cases to haul supplies." He leaned over and zipped the open suitcase. "When this all started, we had food, weapons, walkie talkies, medicine… even after Frank burned down the house and raided the bunker, we still had *some* supplies. We've lost everything."

Heather sat down next to him and lowered her voice. "What about the duffel bag, Tim? Do you think we could go back and get it?"

Timothy frowned. "What are you talking about?"

"The duffel of guns and ammo. There were some meds in there, too. Antibiotics. Pain killers." Heather glanced at the door, her voice no more than a whisper.

His frown deepened. "Didn't O'Donnell take it when he found you?"

Heather shook her head. "We hid it in the drainage pipe that ran under the little bridge over the ditch. When we saw the cop cars coming to the farmhouse, Candice and I didn't know if we could trust them. Then, there was all the crazy afterwards. The swarm. The bombs. I was dazed, and there was no opportunity to get the duffel back. We sort of trusted O'Donnell at that point, but Frank and his guys were there, watching us as we left."

Timothy's eyes widened. He'd assumed O'Donnell had absorbed their weapons into the BPD's stockpile. "So… those weapons might still be there?"

Heather nodded. "Yes, but… they're close to the Russo estate."

"Sure, but Frank and his guys are here in the city. I mean, he's got a stockpile out there. There's got to be guards surrounding the estate, but the farmhouse was a mile down the road. He'd have no reason to watch it after it was destroyed." Timothy stood, smiling. "Finally," he said. "Some good news."

Heather grabbed the handle of one suitcase. "We have to find the other things on our list, though," she said. "Weapons are important, but… we need food, water, and medical supplies first."

"Maybe we can split up. If I can get Alex to come with me, and maybe Minnie can go with you—"

"No," Heather said. "We can't take Alex away from the work he's doing. And we can't risk him. He's working on the only long-term solution we've got. And you can't go by yourself."

Timothy grabbed the handle of the other suitcase. "Let's get out of here, talk to the others, and then see where we are, okay?"

"Okay, but you heard me, right?" Heather raised her eyebrows. "You are *not* going by yourself. I think we've learned by now none of us should be doing anything alone."

Timothy swallowed hard, embarrassment making his cheeks burn hot. His trip alone into Mattapan to check on Zara's family, his mission to recover what was left of the bunker after they'd fled his childhood home, and his chase after CONmen through the city — none of them had gone as planned.

He rubbed the back of his neck. "Yeah, I heard you. Every time I go to do something on my own, I screw it up."

Heather closed her eyes briefly as she breathed in and out through her nose. "That's not what I meant. The point is that what happened to you happened not because it was *you* but because you were alone."

Timothy nodded, but the weight of inadequacy still clung to him with the sharp claws of shame. He let that feeling linger. *I have to do better, make smarter calls, be quicker on my feet.*

Freeman crossed her arms as they reemerged from the breakroom with Candice's suitcases in tow. She led them down the hall toward the lobby. "You sure you don't want to join your brother?"

Timothy sighed. "We're sure."

The policewoman pursed her lips and looked at him sideways as they walked, and then she shrugged. "Well… I saw you in action, Peters. I've been thinking, and I can't come to terms with the idea that you're a coward, not after you ran after those CONmen outside the library. I might disagree, and you might be brash, but I'm calling a truce between us." She opened a door that led into the lobby and waved them through.

Timothy glanced at the entrance to the building, mixed feelings running through him at the sight of his little brother. "Thanks, Freeman. I really appreciate that."

Freeman held out her hand. "You still got friends here." She offered a small smile. "All of you do."

Timothy returned the smile. "Be safe out there."

"Will do." Freeman shook Heather's hand, too. "The captain will come around. Give him more time. He knows not every survivor is up for what we do. I mean, we've had years of training on the job. We might hold a special place in our hearts for people like your brother who want to help, but that doesn't mean we don't understand your position. I mean, even some of us are bailing, and for good reason. Those cops from Chelsea decided to hightail it out of Boston after Murphy got her son back."

"All three of them?" The seed of an idea began to sprout in Timothy's mind. "Do you know where they are? Have they already left?"

"They left about an hour ago, I think." Freeman shrugged. "If I had a kid, I'd get out of here, too."

Timothy's shoulders sagged. He'd hoped they would still be in the area. "Thanks, Freeman. We'll see you around."

Freeman left after farewells, and Timothy turned toward the exit, toward George. *I guess it's time to let my little brother go.*

Heather took his hand, squeezing it gently. It was time to say goodbye.

Chapter 6

Theodore Finch

Theodore Finch was going to make something of himself. He'd been top of his class, breezing through his Masters in Genetics. Getting a job at Vanguard had been a dream come true, at first. Walter Peters was on the edge of advancing research, always pushing the envelope. Theodore had followed Walter's rise in the field of research long before he'd been hired. Afterward, Vanguard and New Horizons had become his entire life.

And then he'd spent a decade being passed over, keeping his head down, doing the work, and never being recognized for his talent. Heat still flushed his cheeks at the memory of the Senior Scientist chastising him months ago.

"You're going to have to realize that here, you're a little fish in a big pond." She'd talked down to him, her tone slick with unwanted pity. "I get it. You've worked hard, but you have to have more ambition. Get your Ph.D. and move up the ladder wherever they're hiring."

He'd blanched. "I'm working on getting accepted into a program, but I want to work here."

"We're an elite team, Theodore," she'd responded. "Our senior staff are the best of the best. You're not there. But that doesn't mean you can't have a promising career at another research facility. Maybe somewhere where the stress isn't so… intense."

Those words haunted Theodore right up until the day everyone had died. Then, he'd been the only one on staff left, which by default made *him* the senior scientist. The arrival of a CDC disease detective hadn't changed that. In fact, Theodore viewed it as an opportunity to solidify his position. If and when Walter Peters returned, he would have so much to offer that Mr. Peters wouldn't be able to deny him his due. He wouldn't be a footnote in history; everyone was going to know the name of Theodore Finch. He just had to play his cards right.

Theodore gingerly sat in the office he'd claimed as his own, right beside Walter's larger corner office. He'd taken Jim Brown's name placard off the wall outside the door, leaving it blank. The plush office chair beckoned him to make himself comfortable, so he slid back and let himself relax. He swished his legs back and forth and then gave himself a quick twirl, chuckling as he tucked his feet under and let the chair spin.

He caught his breath as it slowed to a stop. "I've always wanted to do that," he said quietly to himself. There was no one to tell him he didn't deserve the office with the nice chair and oak desk, that he was too socially awkward or didn't know when to stop talking.

"I wonder how much time I have before Alex gets back." He chewed on the inside of his cheek, making some approximate calculations. Alexander Roman had wanted to get a firsthand account of Candice Liddle's story, of how she contracted and survived DV-10. And he'd needed to check on his son, his friends, and even that little girl he'd only just met. Theodore glanced at the photo of Dr. Brown and his wife, smiling wider than he'd ever smiled at work. "Alex is a bit of a bleeding heart, as you'd say, isn't he?"

That would work in Theodore's favor. The last thing he needed was another man willing to take a confrontation to blows, like that Timothy Peters. Of course, Tim had seemed nice enough at first, too. Once he'd figured out Theodore knew more about the sickness than what was normal, he'd gone crazy, going so far as to threaten Theodore's life.

"Best to keep my guard up." Theodore sighed and tipped the photograph facedown.

He stood up and sauntered over to the liquor table. Dr. Brown had loved his bourbon. He'd been in charge when Walter Peters had been off site, which was most of the time.

"I guess it's my bourbon now." Theodore threw back the bourbon as he imagined Dr. Brown would have done. It *burned.* And it got up his nose. And that was like fire filling his nasal passages. Eyes watering, hacking and coughing, Theodore put the glass down and squeezed his eyes shut. He pinched the bridge of his nose, willing the pain to subside.

He stumbled to a package of water bottles he'd left beside the desk and ripped one free. He took a long drink and then plopped back into the office chair. A few more moments passed before his eyes stopped watering. "Guess I should get back to work," he mumbled.

He pulled out the bottom drawer to his left where he'd kept his notes, sifting through them to categorize information into the kind he could share, the kind he should modify to fit the new narrative, and the kind to leave out: like the fact they had two cryopreservation labs, one to store the eggs of countermeasure mosquitos and the other to store the eggs of mosquito vectors of DV-10. Theodore couldn't access either one, which would reveal that he wasn't as high up the food chain as he'd allowed the others to believe. And the existence of hundreds of modified eggs wouldn't look great, either.

Theodore shuddered to think what would happen to him if the information got out to the wrong people. The government would kill me if they found out I was alive, that I knew what they'd done. And everyone else would kill me if they found out I'd had a hand in the creation of DV-10. His hands shook as he separated the notes into three piles. The truth was, Timothy hadn't needed to threaten Theodore at all.

"Me and my big mouth." Theodore's stomach churned. Pressure brought out the worst in him; it always had. It was one of the reasons his superiors had thought he wouldn't make it at New Horizons, or any subsidiary of Vanguard, for that matter.

The papers in front of him slowly but surely fell into the appropriate categories. He took two of the stacks and shoved them back in the drawer where he intended them to never see the light of day. The rest he could share.

It wasn't really lying. He was omitting some truths, but it was all for the greater good. "A few white lies, and we'll have a vaccine in no time. Maybe even some treatment options." In the end, Theodore was certain the truth would only distract Alex and hamper their work.

He lifted the photograph and imagined Dr. Brown would finally be proud of him for "growing a pair." It had been his favorite piece of advice.

A knock on the door caused Theodore to jump up, and the frame clattered back to the desk. He glanced down at the drawer to make sure it was closed, straightened up the approved stack, and cleared his throat. "Come in." He spoke too loudly, and when Alex poked his head inside, Theodore's voice cracked as it went too high. "How is everyone?"

"They're all as good as can be expected," Alex said.

Theodore gestured to the liquor cart. "Care for a drink?"

"No thanks," Alex said. "I'm ready to get back to work."

"Right." Theodore said. "Absolutely." He held up the stack of papers. "I've got more information for you. I dug these notes out, and I've been sorting them…" He blanched. He hadn't intended to say that part. "… um, sorting them into what's relevant," he said quickly, trying to cover his misstep.

Alex stepped forward, let the door close behind him, and crossed his arms. "Theodore, we need to talk."

Theodore instinctively looked down at the drawer again, and then he winced. *I shouldn't have looked.* He swallowed a lump in his throat and pasted on a smile. "We certainly do. We have a lot to talk about. A lot of work to do." He took a step away from the chair, but Alex held up a hand and he froze.

"No," Alex said. "We need to talk about keeping secrets. I knew more about New Horizons and Walter Peters than I've told you."

Sweat formed on the back of Theodore's neck, sending a cold shiver down his spine. He held his breath.

"As a federal agency, the CDC became privy to—"

"I knew this would happen!" Theodore's heartrate skyrocketed. All pretense of keeping secrets, of being bolder and having more ambition, vanished, immediately replaced with panic. He stepped backward. "Please. I know it seems like the best thing to do is to just clean up the mess. Get rid of anyone who knows. But I swear I won't tell." He shook his head and stammered as he corrected himself. "I-I mean, I told Timothy, but his father is the head of the project. And he hasn't told anyone." The words tumbled out of his mouth, barely giving him space to breathe.

Alex blinked slowly, and Theodore recognized his confusion too late. His expression turned dark. "I was going to tell you about a whistleblower who warned us not to trust Walter Peters. I thought you should know in case he came back. Since I thought you were just boots on the ground, just a man trying to do his job." Alex narrowed his eyes. "Are you telling me that New Horizons created this 'mess'?"

"Oh." Theodore deflated, at first relieved, until… "You didn't know." Fear bloomed, this time faster and farther. "He's going to kill me. He said he would." He wrung his hands. "This isn't good. It isn't good."

"Who are you talking about?" Alex asked more gently than Theodore anticipated. "Who threatened you? Was it Walter Peters?"

"I don't even know if he's alive." Theodore's legs trembled, and he was afraid his knees would buckle at any moment. He inched back to the chair and sat. "I'm such an idiot."

"Look, I won't let anyone hurt you," Alex said. "I can tell you want to fix this, and we are going to need you. Tell me who threatened you, Theodore."

He looked up at Alex, his eyes widening. "Really? You'd protect me?" Whatever he'd expected, it hadn't been kindness. And Alex had said he was needed. After only a little more than a day, one of the most important scientists left alive in the world had recognized Theodore's worth. Tears sprang to his eyes. "It was Timothy Peters. He threatened me. He said the whole world would hate him and his family just for being connected to Walter. I can't say he's wrong."

Alex let out a long, slow breath, his cheeks puffing out as he took a seat on the other side of the desk. "Why can't things ever just go well?" He rubbed his temples. "Do you think Timothy can be reasoned with? I get that he's afraid. I get that he wants to keep this a secret. But withholding information wasn't smart, not when it came to me."

Theodore reached for a tissue and blew his nose. "I agree," he said. "I don't know if you'll be able to reason with Timothy or not. He threatened my life when I revealed his father had spearheaded Project Pinpoint. I really didn't get any farther than that when he lost it. I don't even think I mentioned the name of the operation."

"Project Pinpoint?" Alex asked, leaning forward. "What was the point of all of this? Why did the government commission such a dangerous project?"

Theodore snorted, realized his reaction was inappropriate, and swallowed hard, wiping any amusement from his face. "Well… the government has pretty much always commissioned dangerous projects. Project Pinpoint was a Top-Secret initiative from the Department of Defense, meant to explore the possibility of bioweapons and covert delivery systems. Eventually, we were to attempt to create a disease that would target a specific individual's DNA variants, but we were starting off with an experimental ethnic bioweapon derived from Dengue. It was never supposed to get out; it wasn't targeted enough yet. Obviously. It's been killing everyone. We're dealing with DV-10 or perhaps an evolved form of it that's worse."

Alex rubbed at his temples. "This is insane. Covert delivery systems? You created this species of mosquito, too. I had my suspicions. There's no way any species we've known of could have evolved to be this… aggressive. And the swarming? The distance they can travel? None of it is normal."

"I wasn't on that team," Theodore said, "but… yes. Both the disease and the vector came out of this lab. Though how it was distributed in a coordinated attack all over the world, I have no idea."

Alex sat upright. "Wait, does that mean you have countermeasures here? Surely you wouldn't have created something like this without having contingencies."

Theodore winced. "We have a starting point for a cure for DV-10, but we hadn't come up with anything substantial, which is why we originally sent the samples for that iteration to the incinerator."

"Okay…" Alex seemed lost in thought for a minute before he continued. "And what about the mosquitos?"

Theodore shrank into his chair, his mind racing. *I can't let him know that I wasn't even close to being in charge.* "Well, like I said, I wasn't on that team. But… we do have countermeasure mosquitos that if hatched, brought to adulthood, and released, would eventually breed with the vectors for DV-10 and render them unable to reproduce. They'd eventually die out. We kept the mosquitos the same once we perfected them; the disease was another matter. We could never get it quite right."

"Excellent!" Alex said, and then he frowned. "Why haven't we already released these countermeasure mosquitos?"

"Because I don't have access to the cryopreservation lab where they're kept." He cleared his throat, reiterating his previous excuse. "I wasn't on that team. From what I understand, the lab itself and each cryopreservation pod is secured with codes only a few people knew, one of them being Walter Peters, the others being dead. If we mess with them and a failsafe kicks in, if the cryopreservation pod is damaged…"

"We lose the countermeasure altogether." Alex slumped. "Okay. Then… I guess we work on the vaccine."

Theodore breathed out in relief. "Good. And what about Timothy? Are you going to tell him you know everything?"

"I've worked with people willing to resort to violence, willing to cover up anything to save their own skin. I won't do that again." Alex's lips formed a firm line.

"What are you going to do?" Theodore asked.

"I don't know yet," Alex said, "but whatever it is, I guarantee you Timothy isn't going to like it."

Chapter 7

Timothy Peters

Timothy hooked his arm around George's neck and pulled him in for a hearty hug. "Take care of yourself," he said, "and we're not far. Don't forget that."

George returned the hug. He'd been reluctant when Timothy and Heather had first approached, but once it was clear Timothy wasn't going to try talking him out of staying, they'd eased into a less awkward conversation.

Timothy and Heather had brought George up to speed on Annika and Candice as well as on the newcomers. Timothy decided to also bring George in on the basics of what Alex and Theodore were working on, making sure he understood the time wasn't right to make it widely known they were working on a vaccine. They needed to work in peace until they made some progress.

By the end of the conversation, Timothy had been forced to come to terms with the fact that George really had grown up while being held captive by CON, that perhaps he'd already started that process a long time ago. Timothy had just been too wrapped up in himself and his own problems to see it.

Heather took her turn saying final goodbyes, wrapping her nephew in a gentler embrace. "Listen to O'Donnell. Remember that fighting isn't the only thing they're going to need. If they have you scavenging or running supplies or whatever, that's just as important. Somebody has to do it."

"Yeah, I know." George pulled back and offered them a smile. "I might stop by and check on Annika. You'll send word if anything changes with her, right?"

"Absolutely." Timothy clapped George on the back.

George patted the handle of the dolly he'd used to haul their supplies to the door. A small backpack sat atop two bullet proof vests laying flat. He grabbed the top handle of the backpack and moved it aside. "You've got your ammo and walkie talkies in here. I put some water and food inside. It's not a lot." He nodded to the bullet proof vests. "You two might as well wear those now. Couldn't do any harm, and it's the easiest way to transport them." He patted the Glock holstered at his side and nodded to Timothy. "And I can hand over this baby once your vest is on. You can secure it in the built-in holster."

Timothy picked up the top vest and handed it to Heather before putting on the second. "I can't believe you got O'Donnell to throw in a little food and water. He was being a bit of a hard ass earlier."

George shrugged. "He wasn't thrilled, but he allowed it. I don't know him as well as you do, but I think he doesn't understand why you won't join the fight." He quirked an eyebrow and lowered his voice. "Maybe he would, though, if you explained more about what you're doing at the lab."

Timothy shook his head. "That's one thing Alex explained that I think I agree with one hundred percent. If too many people know about it, the lab will be flooded with survivors trying to get first in line."

George shrugged. "Okay, if you say so. I won't say anything."

Timothy secured the last strap of his vest and held out a hand for the gun. "It's important you stay quiet about it," he said. "I mean it."

George rolled his eyes as he handed over the Glock, the look a shadow of his old, childlike self. "I get it. Geez. I can keep a secret."

"We know," Heather said with a small smile as Timothy holstered the gun. "Thank you for coming to say goodbye. We love you, George." She hugged him one last time, the bulky vest getting in the way.

"I love you guys, too," George said, stepping back and opening the door for them. "Be safe."

Timothy took a deep breath, reminding himself again that he'd decided to let George stay without any further protests. It was hard to walk away. It went against every instinct. But he did it, hauling one of Candice's suitcases behind him, keeping his eyes on the road ahead.

Heather pointed down Tremont Street. "I think we should stop by the Brigham. The hospital complex might have some of what we're looking for."

"Good idea." Timothy followed her around the corner.

The jingle of a bell stopped him in his tracks. He reached out and took hold of his wife's upper arm, stopping her and putting one finger to his lips. Up ahead, the door of a shop was wide open. He signaled for her to duck, and they both crouched behind a nearby car. Timothy peeked over the top of the hood to inspect who they might be up against, his hand resting on the gun holstered at his side.

Three adults — one woman, two men — and a child exited a thrift shop. The woman, her back to Timothy and Heather, smoothed the child's hair from his forehead and removed a tag from the back of his shirt. She straightened and proceeded to pull her hair back into a ponytail, fitting a ballcap over her head and pulling her hair through the hole at the back. The men also wore ballcaps, pulled down over their eyes. Each adult sported a handgun holstered at their hip.

"Isn't that Murphy?" Heather whispered.

Timothy did a double take. He'd never seen the three Chelsea cops out of their worn-out uniforms. But the kid, James, was clearly recognizable once Heather had made the connection. "Yeah," he said, his earlier ideas concerning the three cops coming to mind. "This is perfect."

Heather frowned. "What do you mean?"

"I mean, I think I can convince them to help us get our weapons back." He grinned and made to stand up, but Heather put her hand on his shoulder and stopped him.

"What makes you think they'll help us? They could just take the guns and ammo for themselves." Heather shook her head. "Torres and Murphy seem trustworthy enough, but Burke? That guy is only interested in protecting himself and his friends."

"The three of them are close." Timothy took Heather by the shoulders and met her eyes with his own. "Murphy and Torres keep Burke in line. If they agree, he'll agree."

Heather cast a worried glance in the direction of the three cops, but she sighed and nodded. "Okay. If you say so."

"This is going to work." Timothy smiled and stood up, holding his hands in the air. "Hey!" He shouted.

Burke and Torres had their weapons trained on Timothy in the blink of an eye. Murphy was a second behind them, having first stepped in front of her son.

Timothy sucked in a breath. "Whoa!" he said. "It's just me. It's Timothy Peters."

Murphy and Torres lowered their weapons, but Burke didn't budge. "Come on, Eric," Murphy said. "It's fine. It's just Peters."

The coldness in Burke's expression didn't change as he lowered his weapon. "What do you want?" he asked sharply.

Heather peeked up over the car. "We were on the way to the hospital to look for supplies."

"We saw you," Timothy said, "and I wanted to talk with you."

"Well, come on." Murphy waved them over. "I'd rather us not shout. The less attention we draw, the better."

Timothy exchanged a look with Heather, and they both came out from behind the car to weave through the mess of vehicles over to the sidewalk in front of the thrift shop. "I've never seen you three in street clothes."

"We're done with being cops," Burke said. "We're going to look out for each other, and that's it."

Murphy pursed her lips and glanced disapprovingly at Burke as she rested a hand on her son's head. "We've decided to protect our little family," she said. "Like you are. I can't risk James's life by playing O'Donnell's game. Boston is just a place. We can find a new home. I can't replace my son."

"We wish the Boston Police Department the best of luck," Torres added, "but if O'Donnell sent you to talk us into staying—"

"Oh, no. Not at all." Timothy shook his head. "We're in the same boat as you. We aren't about to go to war. It's all we can do to survive without fighting the Russos and what's left of CON."

"So, what?" Burke glared at him. "You just wanted to pop in and say hello?"

Timothy laughed, but it had a nervous edge to it. "No. We… uh…" He swallowed hard, suddenly nervous.

"We have a problem," Heather said, "and we think maybe we can work together for the benefit of both our groups."

"We're not interested." Burke half turned his back but paused as Murphy spoke up.

"We can hear you out," Murphy said. Both men groaned, but she raised her eyebrows at them. "If it weren't for Timothy, I wouldn't have James back. It was him, Heather, and Candice that convinced the BPD to go after those kids."

"They did it for their own, not for us," Burke said.

"Doesn't matter." Murphy set her jaw and crossed her arms. "I want to hear him out."

"Fine." Torres gestured for Timothy to continue as Burke sagged in resignation.

Timothy's heart leapt; he couldn't have asked for a better solution. All he had to do was present his plan in the best possible light. "We know where a stash of weapons and ammo are hidden, out in the countryside. O'Donnell only spared us one gun, and I'm not comfortable with that, not with the war over the city about to start. I don't want to go it alone, but we don't have enough people for some of us to search the city for supplies while others go out and retrieve our weapons." Timothy nodded toward their guns. "You three surely could use backup weapons and ammunition. If even just one of you could come with me, we can split the weapons. There's a duffle bag full of them. Handguns, rifles. There's some meds in there. We could maybe part with a bottle of antibiotics."

"If it was going to be an easy job, you wouldn't need us," Torres said. "What's the catch?"

Timothy tried not wince as he told them the rest. "It's close to the Russos, what's left of them out in the country, that is. Remember the farmhouse O'Donnell told you about? The one where we ran into his squad?"

The three of them nodded. "We remember. It was quite the story," Murphy said.

Heather shifted beside Timothy. "Candice and I hid the duffel bag before O'Donnell and Abrams found us. We didn't know they could be trusted, and by the time we did, Frank was there, watching. We had to leave it behind."

"I can't take my son anywhere near the Russos," Murphy said.

"You and James can stay in our safehouse," Timothy said.

"Why share half?" Burke narrowed his eyes.

"It's simple," Timothy said. "We have three guns and very little ammo right now. Half of that duffle bag is better than nothing."

Burke, Murphy, and Torres exchanged looks, and then Torres nodded sharply to their right. "Give us a minute," he said.

Timothy nodded, and the three Chelsea cops huddled a few yards away, whispering amongst themselves. It didn't seem like much of an argument. Burke kept shaking his head, and his frown only deepened as Murphy cut the air with sharp hand gestures. When they came back, Murphy held out a hand.

"We'll do it," she said.

Timothy took her hand and shook it, grinning. "Thank you."

"You helped get me my son back," Murphy said. "I don't think the BPD would have done what they did if you guys hadn't pushed them. And James told me your brother, George, protected him while he was at The Farm. I'm indebted to you and your family, Peters."

"And if she's indebted," Torres said, "so are we."

Burke grunted but nodded his agreement. "We owe you." He held up his index finger. "To a point."

"Do you guys mind helping us search the hospital for a few things on our list before we head back to the safehouse?" Heather asked. "It's just right down the road. We can split some of that, too, although we really need to keep things like blood transfusion kits."

"Sure." Murphy shrugged. "We don't know how to use something like that, anyway."

* * *

The smell of death still lingered everywhere, but Timothy had been steeped in it for so long he barely noticed anymore. When he pried open an automatic sliding door leading into the hospital's emergency department, however, he gagged and stepped back; the dead inside had been rotting for weeks, the stench compounding without any ventilation. A wave of hot air whooshed over him, carrying notes of something like spoiled milk and hot, rancid garbage and long-forgotten, slimy, raw chicken.

Behind him, a collective sound of disgust rose from his companions. Torres stumbled to some bushes and lost his breakfast. Burke's face paled, and his cheeks puffed as his lips pinched.

"It's so bad my eyes are watering." Heather groaned as she wiped moisture from her eyes. "It can't be safe to go in there. Don't diseases fester in situations like this?"

"And in a hospital where there would have been plenty of people already sick..." Murphy shook her head as her son buried his head into her shirt, covering his nose. "We're not going in there."

"Maybe," Timothy gagged again as he opened his mouth to speak; he *tasted* the stench. He pushed the door closed again, backed away, and headed toward the street. The others followed. Once he could open his mouth without his stomach lurching, he tried again. "Maybe there's another way in."

Torres, his face still drained of normal color, shook his head. "Not without protective gear. Heather is right. That place is a cesspool of disease." He glanced at Murphy and Burke. "You two thinking what I'm thinking?"

Burke nodded once. "If the BPD hasn't picked them clean."

Murphy shook her head. "I didn't see any biohazard supplies at headquarters. I think they've been too busy to think about it. The supplies would be good to have, anyway."

"What are you talking about?" Timothy asked.

"Aftermath services," Torres said. "They clean up crime scenes and whatnot for the police."

Burke grunted. "Biohazard suits and respirator masks *would* be nice."

Murphy nodded toward the hospital. "But none of us should step foot inside that place, or any place like it, without some protection. Layers would be helpful tools against the swarms, too."

"Alex brought some PPE with him, he said, but there wouldn't be enough for all of us." Heather frowned and folded her arms against her stomach. She scanned the faces of Torres, Burke, and Murphy. "You three know how to get to one of these facilities?"

They nodded in response, and Murphy pointed eastward. "It's downtown. We know the place."

"Another thing to add to our list." Timothy sighed heavily. He chewed the inside of his cheek as he glanced at the sky and tried to gauge the position of the sun. "We don't have much time left to gather supplies. I'd hate to come back with so little."

"What about the ambulances?" Heather pointed to several of the emergency transports in the emergency department bay and then gestured toward some more mixed in with the mess of vehicles on the street.

"It's worth a shot," Timothy said.

"We'll check that one." Torres pointed at the street. "You two try the closer one over there."

Timothy and Heather agreed, and a few minutes later, Timothy was opening up the back of the nearest ambulance, relieved to find it empty of corpses. He stepped up into the vehicle as Heather investigated the compartments that opened on the outside.

"I think we could pile some things onto this rolling cot and get some supplies to New Horizons that way," Timothy said as he started investigating.

"There's all kinds of things out here!" Heather's voice was accompanied by the sound of her rifling through the compartments. "Tim! There's a whole cooler of bottled water."

Timothy scooted around the cot, sliding open cabinet doors and opening cabinets. Two bags, one a smaller black backpack and the other an oversized blue one, rested on a built-in bench on the other side of the cot. He reached over and pulled the bags onto the cot, sat down, and unzipped them. "This is a gold mine. Splints, gauze, bandages..." He opened another compartment. "I don't know what all of this is, but it looks important." His heart skipped a beat at the sight of a clear compartment with medication. "I found meds!" The excitement picked up as he moved on to the bigger bag.

Heather's voice came from outside. "I've got an axe and a pick. Those could be useful. And bolt cutters!"

Timothy sifted through clear packages full of tubes and equipment he couldn't identify. "I hope some of this will help Lauren." He opened the largest compartment to find more equipment separated into kits. One of them was labelled. "Hey, I think this is an IV kit! That was on the list."

"I wish the streets were clearer," Heather said. "We could roll a few of these ambulances to the lab." She came around back, stopping to peer inside.

"We'll just have to take what will fit on these cots." Timothy tidied up the contents of each bag, zipping them back up. "There's a defibrillator there," he said, pointing to one stored behind clear plexiglass cabinet doors. He opened another cabinet and peered inside a container. "And these look like suture kits."

"Let's get this cot out and start loading it up," Heather leaned into the back of the vehicle, tugging on the cot. "There has to be a release somewhere. Ah! There it is." The cot rolled forward. "There's a touchpad here," she said as she struggled to keep the cot up. She breathed a sigh of relief as the legs of the cot lowered. "It's still working."

Timothy began handing items to Heather, and she stacked them on the cot. "I'm going to secure this stuff," he said once they were finished loading everything, including the axe and pickaxe and the cooler of bottled water. "Why don't you check on the others?"

Heather returned a few minutes later. "They had the same idea," she said. "They're loading up another cot as we speak."

"The lab is only a couple of miles from here," Timothy said. "We can load up a cot for each of us. It wouldn't be terrible to have the cots themselves, too, for sleeping on."

Over the next hour, their group worked in teams to scavenge from four ambulances. It was mostly basic supplies. Even the medications were things like aspirin, EpiPens, and Diazepam. But they did find vials of morphine and lidocaine, along with syringes, and a ton of equipment that Timothy hoped would be helpful but couldn't identify.

They rolled the supplies through the streets of Boston, taking it slow so as to not draw too much attention. By the time they arrived in the parking lot of New Horizons, Timothy was exhausted and ready to plan the next steps, both for retrieving their weapons and for searching the city for needed supplies.

"Stay here for a few minutes," Timothy said as they rolled to a stop. "I need to explain to everyone else what's going on, that you guys are staying temporarily, and only to help us."

"Why are you staying in a laboratory?" Burke's signature frown was on full display.

Timothy paused and exchanged a look with Heather. Alex and Theodore had made it clear they shouldn't bring anyone else into their business of finding a vaccine. They wouldn't appreciate him bringing Burke, Torres, Murphy, and James to their front door. They'd be downright angry if they learned he'd let them in on their secret. And Timothy agreed; the last thing they needed was a crowd of survivors clamoring to be the first recipients of a vaccine, especially since they had nothing to give yet. *And I've got my own secrets to keep…*

The door opened, and Alex stepped outside. He didn't look happy to see them, but his appearance gave Timothy the opportunity to dodge Burke's question. "Hey, Alex." He gestured to the newcomers. "I can explain. They're here to help. I trust th—"

"One thing at a time," Alex said, crossing his arms. "First, we need to talk about you."

Timothy blanched. The way Alex was looking at him… *What did Theodore do?*

"What are you talking about?" Heather asked.

Alex's demeanor hardened further. "Your husband is a liar, and neither of you are getting back into that building until we've had a little chat."

Chapter 8

Walter Peters

Walter's eyes cracked open. His body was stiff. Areas of throbbing agony competed with sharper jabs of pain all over his body. Dull, rhythmic pulsing emanated from his knee, his shoulder, and his head. The pain in his left side reminded him of the embedded metal debris. Gingerly, he lifted his hand and probed the spot, his breath catching at the pain of movement. There were bandages where the wound had been, and for the first time since waking, he realized he was shirtless. Walter focused on steady breathing as he returned his hand to his side.

Where am I? He tried to take in his surroundings. A thick comforter lay beneath him, and he curled his fingers against its warmth. A mattress cradled his broken form. He imagined it would be comfortable if it weren't for his injuries. Above him hung the still blades of a ceiling fan. The room was dimly lit, sunlight pouring in from the windows. The storm had let up, and he could no longer hear the sounds of rain or hail or thunder.

The storm. His heart skipped a beat. *Zara and Kai.*

The events of the plane crash rushed back to him, and he remembered the beginnings of shock on Zara's face as he was thrown into the back of the aircraft. He could almost hear the terrible sounds of rending metal, of the storm thrashing against his almost-tomb. He groaned, the urge to find Zara stronger than his pain for a split second. He raised his head, the room spun, and his stomach lurched. He barely had the energy to lift his head off the pillow.

"You okay, mister?" A small voice sounded from the floor, and then a little girl popped up, her curly blonde hair bouncing as she jumped three times to close the distance to the bed. Her jumping brought yipping from the corner of the room.

And then he remembered the dog who'd found him and the woman who'd called him Saul. Walter cleared his throat and carefully turned to look at the little girl. Perhaps seven or eight, she was covered in freckles, and her brown eyes shone with curiosity.

"Quiet, Chicken!" she said over her shoulder.

Walter smiled. "I thought…" His voice was raspy, barely audible. His tongue was a bit swollen, too, as he'd bitten off a sliver. He cleared his throat and tried again, his words only a little garbled. "I thought his name was Nugget."

The little girl laughed. "No, silly. Nugget is his brother. They don't even look alike."

"Your dogs are named Chicken and Nugget?" If he hadn't been so exhausted, he might have chuckled at that.

"I named them myself." She puffed out her chest and grinned.

"And you are?" Walter asked.

"LeeAnn." She looked over her shoulder as if looking for someone. She turned back to him and lowered her voice. "What's your name?"

"Walter," he said.

"Mom thinks you're my dad," she said, still quiet. "You look like him about as much as Nugget looks like Chicken."

Walter slowly moved to touch his face. He felt a few scratches, but he couldn't imagine it was bad enough that he could be mistaken for someone else, not someone the woman knew so well, anyway. "How long has it been since you've seen your dad?" he asked.

The girl shrugged. "A long time. Before all the bad stuff happened."

"I'm sorry." He paused for a few moments before he asked his next question. "Did your mom bring back anyone else?"

LeeAnn shook her head. "Just you."

"LeeAnn!" A hiss from the door startled Walter. It was a tall, wiry teenage boy. "What are you doing?" He stalked forward and pulled the girl back.

"I'm just talking to him, Heath! Stop being a bully." She stuck out her tongue at him.

"I'm not!" He kept tugging her back, looking suspiciously at Walter. "We don't know him. And… mom doesn't want us bothering him." That last part was said with some measure of discomfort.

"Heath, was it? You're her brother?" Walter interjected, trying to sound as nonthreatening as possible.

"None of your business," Heath snapped.

"Yes, he's my big, dumb brother," LeeAnn said, crossing her arms and scowling up at him. "He's no fun anymore."

"LeeAnn, the world has literally ended!" Heath raised his voice. "It's time for you to grow up."

"I'm eight!"

"Hey," Walter said, trying to redirect the conversation. "I just want to know what's going on. LeeAnn seemed to think your mom is confused about who I am." He winced as he tried to sit up again. It wasn't any better the second time, and he quickly lowered his head.

"Yeah." Heath's cheeks burned red, and he threw a glare at his sister. "She's… not okay. My dad is…" His expression changed, a mix of concern and empathy in his eyes as he looked at LeeAnn. "He's missing. He worked on the radio satellites at the top of the mountain, and that's where he was when… when…" Heath sighed and rubbed the back of his neck, going silent.

"And your mom has been looking for him?" Walter asked, the situation becoming clearer. *Her grief must be breaking her.* He understood that. And then a little bit of hope flared in his chest. "So… are we still near where she found me? Is that why we're here?"

Heath nodded. "Sort of. This is the Log Cabin. It's a fancy restaurant and a venue for things like weddings. My parents got married here. We're still on the mountain, just not at the peak."

Maybe Heath can go out and look for Zara. Walter opened his mouth to try to convince the young man, but the woman who'd found him entered the room before he could get the chance. *Carol, wasn't it?*

"What are you two doing in here? Get out right this minute!" She shrieked, pointing back to the hall. A little dog at her feet pranced into the room, its nails clicking on the hardwood. The two dogs, Chicken and Nugget, greeted each other with short, high-pitched yips and wagging tails.

"Mom, it's nothing." Heath stood between himself and LeeAnn, almost protectively. "We were just about to let him rest."

"It's my fault," Walter said, hoping to get on Heath's good side. "I was making a fuss."

Heath glanced at Walter before tugging his sister toward the door. "I'm going to take LeeAnn downstairs and play cards or something."

"Good." Carol put her hands on her hips. "Go on. Let your father rest."

The two kids exchanged a look, and Heath pressed his lips together, shaking his head just slightly at his little sister. From his vantage, Walter thought he saw a warning in his eyes. They hurried out, Heath calling the two dogs to follow. Carol stayed, shutting the door and leaning her head against it, sagging.

"I'm sorry, Saul," she said. "They just missed you. I know you need your rest." She pushed off the door and sighed. Then, she turned around. "Do you need anything?"

"I need you to find the others who were in the plane," he said gently but firmly.

She shook her head. "I don't know what you're talking about, Saul."

"Your name is Carol, right?" Walter asked.

She put a hand over her heart. "Are you trying to hurt me? Why would you ask that?"

"I'm not trying to hurt you." Walter shifted so he could better look at her, grimacing as he did. She held out her hands, gasping at his pain, but he tried to reassure her with a smile. "Carol, my name is Walter Peters. I was flying to Boston with two young people, a young woman named Zara and a young man named Kai. I need to find them."

His heart ached at the thought of Zara, the only piece of his daughter he had left. He'd not been a good father. He'd practically abandoned Bethie in her last hours. He'd thought the least he could do was get her best friend back to Boston. Taking care of Zara had felt almost like taking care of Elizabeth the way he'd always wanted to.

And now I've lost her, too. The pain of that possibility was worse than his physical pain. Beyond his prayerful promises to his dead daughter, Zara had become something more to him. He'd seen her strength, admired her tenacity. Bethie's death had unlocked a part of him he'd put away a long time ago. Every waking moment since she'd been killed, he'd wished he'd been able to show her the love she deserved when she was still alive, but he couldn't. And so he'd channeled his fatherly affections toward Zara, and in turn, he'd found some healing in their relationship. After all, Zara had lost her father. Neither could replace what the other had lost, but they'd found they could seal up some of the cracks if they worked together.

Carol shook her head. "You're just tired, Saul. You're talking nonsense."

"No, Carol. My name is Walter. Walter Peters."

Carol wouldn't look directly at him. "Stop it!" She shook her head, stepping backward. "I don't know why you're doing this to me. I spent weeks looking for you. Nugget sniffed you out. He led me to you." She crossed her arms and raked her fingernails along them, from elbow to wrist, over and over again. "I knew you couldn't be dead." Her eyes darted up to him only briefly. "I know what I said the last time we saw each other wasn't fair. I'm sorry, Saul. I… I was upset. I wouldn't leave you, not really."

Walter's impatience was growing despite his empathy for the woman. *Zara might not have much time, if she's still out there. She needs shelter. She has to be hurt.* He wracked his brain, pushing through the throbbing pain, to come up with an angle that would snap Carol out of it. *I have to make her see her husband is probably dead. Or somewhere else.*

He used his negotiating voice, calm and neutral, not unkind but not weak. "Carol, what made you think to look on the mountain?"

"That's the last place you went." Carol lifted one shoulder, touching her ear, her hands trembling slightly. "There are buildings for shelter. I figured if you'd broken your leg or something, you wouldn't be able to get to me, to the kids. We waited at home that first week, but… things were getting bad in town." She smiled, her eyes glistening. "I brought the kids here, left a note at home. This place was always special to us."

It didn't seem the right time to correct her, to assert again that he was not her husband. He didn't want to affirm it, either, so Walter chose his next words carefully. "Don't you think it would be almost impossible for a man injured so badly that he couldn't make his way off the mountain to survive?"

"Well, no. You're alive." She chewed on her lower lip and repeated herself, her voice almost a whisper. "You're alive. I found you."

Walter sighed, the pounding of his headache too much. "Carol, please. I was in a plane crash," he said. "If you were nearby, surely you heard or saw something? You had to have seen the wreckage."

"I don't want to talk about this anymore." She hurried over to a vanity against the wall, her back to Walter. She rifled through the contents of a drawer.

His bubble of forced calm burst, made more fragile by his pain. "I am not your husband," he said. "There are people out there who need help. You have to go look for them. They need your help."

"You're sick, Saul. All that time spent in the woods. You've caught something." She turned around, a syringe in hand. "I brought these with me from the clinic. Once I saw what was happening, that all the nurses were dying, all the patients — *everyone* — I packed a bag and got out. This should help you rest." She walked forward with a determined, quick step.

"No!" Walter's throat was raw as he tried to shout. "My name is Walter, Carol." He couldn't move. He tried a third time, but the pain was too great. "You have to stop!"

She plunged the needle into his upper arm. "This will make you feel better, Saul. You'll come back to me. I know it."

A flood of tingling relief washed over his body. The pain was still there, beneath the surface, but his eyelids drooped, and the medicine worked. Without the aching misery, his exhaustion was brought to the forefront. "You have to find her. You have to find Zara." He managed these last words as numbness spread over him. He couldn't help but embrace it.

She gently kissed his forehead. "I'll take good care of you, Saul. Don't worry. I'll never let you out of my sight again."

Chapter 9

Timothy Peters

Timothy clenched his fists on his lap, his nails digging into the palms of his hands. Alex, Theodore, Lauren, and Minnie had refused to let Heather and Timothy back into the building. Candice was nowhere to be seen, but he doubted anyone had asked her opinion.

Or they told her, and she despises me because of my dad, just like I knew people would. He bit the inside of his cheek, muscles tightening with every word as Alex laid bare all of Timothy's secrets.

He and Heather sat with Alex in a first-floor conference room of one of the Vanguard buildings across the lot from New Horizons. It was a small mercy that Alex had asked the former cops from Chelsea to wait in the lobby.

Apparently, Alex and Theodore had had quite the chat while Timothy had been gone. They'd opened up the building and moved supplies enough for two into the space. And Theodore had changed the security codes to get into New Horizons. He and Heather were locked out. It was his family's building, and these newcomers had taken it from him within mere days of their arrival.

"From the look on your face, Heather," Alex said, "it seems you didn't know about this."

"Is it true?" Heather asked, her words laced with hurt. "Did you know that New Horizons created the disease? The mosquitos? Did you threaten Theodore's life? Keep vital information from the only people we know of who could possibly create a cure or a vaccine?"

Timothy's mouth ran dry. He dared to look at Heather, to meet her eyes with his own. She was crying, tears sliding down her cheeks, eyes brimming. There was hurt and anger in her expression, but there was also the thing he'd most feared: disgust.

Heather clenched her jaw and said through gritted truth. "Answer. Me. Did you lie to me?"

He closed his eyes and hung his head. "Yes," he whispered.

Heather gasped for breath, suddenly seeming unable to breathe. She stood up so fast her chair toppled over behind her. He stood up, too, reaching out for her, but she batted him away, putting both hands on top of her head and retreating from him.

"This was what I was afraid of," Timothy said, pleading. "What my father has done, it's the most terrible thing I've ever heard of anyone doing. The whole world is going to hate me if they find out. They're going to hate *you* because you're connected to me, to my father. George, Lizzy, Candice, Annika – anyone who associates with the Peters family will be fair game. I mean, look! You're even disgusted by what my father's done, Heather."

"Of course I am," she said, her anger flushing her cheeks. She raised her voice. "But I didn't *have* to be disgusted with *you*. You made that happen all on your own!"

"Heather, I was trying to protect you and me and all of us. Please–"

She stepped forward and punched him in the arm. It didn't hurt, not really, but the action stung. "You idiot! I'm your wife. We're supposed to be in this together. We could have talked about this. Maybe – *maybe* – we would have decided to keep parts of that a secret from the world, but you decided to keep it a secret from *me*. I can't believe you. And threatening a man's life?" She shook her head. "Who *are* you?"

Timothy's own eyes burned as his vision blurred with tears. "I'm sorry," he said, his voice breaking. "I was afraid." He sat back in his chair and put his head in his hands. "I've made so many bad calls. I've lost so much. I'm so tired of losing. I'm so tired of being afraid. I'm just *so* tired."

Several silent minutes passed. Timothy fought to control his emotions, fought against the tears. With everything out in the open, with the way his wife had looked at him, with the admission of his mistakes and his fears – his defenses against the state of the world, against his grief and pain, had crumbled. He was weak and helpless, and there was no way to deny it any longer. There were no excuses left.

"What does this mean?" Heather's voice broke the silence. She wasn't talking to him. When he looked up at her, she was staring at Alex. "What my husband has done hasn't changed our situation, not really. We have things that need to be done. People that need us to work together. And the lab belongs to the Peters family. We have an obligation to be involved, to right the wrongs done by members of our family. We let you into our space. You can't just boot us out."

Timothy looked between Alex and Heather. Neither of them seemed to care what he thought, so he didn't say anything. He didn't have the right.

Alex shook his head. "I've worked with people I don't trust, and I'm not doing that again. At least not without some boundaries. But I admit we're in a tough spot. Lauren won't leave her patients. Minnie is watching over Oliver and taking care of a lot of the basics for everyone – delivering food and water, acting as a pair of helping hands for Lauren, laundry, babysitting… And she's not going out there on her own to scavenge, even if we didn't need her here." He shifted in his seat, clearly not happy with his next words. "The truth is, we need you if Theodore and I are going to have time to do our work. We need supplies, especially considering what you've told us about the upcoming conflict."

"Okay, so let's talk boundaries," Heather said. "But we have some conditions."

Timothy's jaw dropped just a little. Heather had always been strong and no-nonsense. But with the police and with Alex, she'd shown herself to be a talented negotiator. Of course, he'd known she often got her way with him, but he was beginning to think she'd missed her calling as a lawyer.

Alex snorted. "You don't have a leg to stand on when it comes to making demands."

Heather leaned forward. "Except you're right. You do need us. There isn't enough food and water, weapons and ammo, or medical supplies to last long. We were starting from scratch, so even if you did plan on stealing what we've already gathered, it wouldn't set us back very far. And in case you didn't notice, we came here with three tough-as-nails ex-cops. They're on our side, and I don't think you want things to get nasty." She quirked an eyebrow and waited.

Alex narrowed his eyes. "I'm listening, but you're on something if you think I'm going to let you and your buddies inside the lab. I don't trust you as far as I can throw you."

Heather nodded, throwing a glare at Timothy. "I understand. We can stay here, in this building."

Alex crossed his arms. "Go on."

"You can't stop us from seeing Annika and Candice."

"I'm not letting him inside." He pointed at Timothy but spoke about him as if he weren't there. And then they started talking fast, going back and forth, setting terms.

"Fine. Let me in twice a day, if I'm around. I need to be able to check on them."

"Okay. I can do that."

"Any supplies we gather stay here in this building with us. If you want us gathering supplies, we need to know we'll have access to them. We'll let you take what you need day by day."

Alex frowned. "Except for medical supplies or supplies we need for our research. And water. We split the water, fifty-fifty."

"Agreed. You have no access to any weapons we gather, unless we say so. If you want your own weapons, you'll have to figure that out yourself," Heather said firmly. "No negotiating on that one."

"What if someone attacks the lab?"

Heather shrugged. "We'll defend you. But I don't think that's going to happen. You'll stay locked up in there, doing your work, right? If anyone is going to get attacked, it'll be us. There will be far more opportunities for someone to see us coming and going with supplies."

"Then how are you going to keep our supplies safe?" Alex asked. "You'll not be here a good portion of the time, if you're out on missions to gather what we need. What's to stop someone from breaking in and taking whatever they want?"

"This building has the same security as New Horizons," Heather said. "And the solar power has clearly kept the locks working. I didn't see any broken windows."

"Fair enough." Alex conceded the point.

"We also need to bring you in on a few things from our trip today," Heather said, her expression growing grim. "I'm not sure you're going to like some of it."

She proceeded to tell Alex about their deal with O'Donnell to escort Lauren to help should they need medical attention. She was quick to add in their stipulations that she not be put in danger, and that their own medical emergencies would come first. "We got high-quality, long-distance walkie talkies, bullet proof vests, a gun, and some ammo out of the deal," she said. "We're going to need that stuff, at least until we get our own weapons and ammo, which we need to talk about next."

"You've been making deals all over the place. I can't speak for Lauren, but I don't think she'll object, not with the conditions you put on the deal." Alex shook his head. "Do you know where we can find weapons?"

"We do." She glanced at Timothy for the first time since they'd started negotiating. "Tim, Burke, and Torres are going to retrieve them. To that point, we don't need our friends knowing all about my husband's indiscretion."

"More secrets?" Alex asked.

"From outsiders? Absolutely." She worked her jaw back and forth. "That wasn't the problem. I'm sure there's plenty of stuff you've not told us. Things you've done or plan to do or things from your past you don't feel like sharing. The problem was that my husband lied to me and resorted to threats to keep those lies. The fact he lied to you was only a problem in my book because of the work you're doing. It was selfish and wrong. And it won't happen again." The last part she said sharply with a quick glare at Timothy.

Timothy's cheeks burned hot. "I swear, Heather, I—"

She held up a hand to cut him off. "Our friends are kept in the dark. It's the only way we can know they won't turn on Timothy and take the weapons for themselves. Got it?"

She's really angry. Timothy's heart skipped a beat. Is she going to be able to forgive me?

Alex nodded. "Fine."

"And one more thing," Heather said.

Alex smirked. "Well, I wouldn't want you to hold anything back."

"I need Murphy to come with me to gather supplies in the city. We also need to check out the hubs of survivors, know where our human resources are — doctors, surgeons... it would help to have a list of everyone and their skills, even gardeners and grandmas who still can their own food." Heather took a breath. "But that means we'll need to leave her son, James. Obviously, he can't stay here. He'll need to stay with your son and with Minnie. He's a good kid. No threat at all."

Alex nodded. "That's not a problem. Got anything else?"

Heather shook her head. "I think that covers it."

Alex stood up and extended his hand to Heather. "Then you've got a deal."

She got to her feet and shook his hand. "For what it's worth, I'm sorry."

Alex licked his lips and studied her for a minute. "I believe you." He gestured toward the door. "We should get your friends set up, get all those supplies put away."

"Grab one of the walkie talkies," Heather said. "And then you can go back to the lab. We've got it from here. I'll come and check on Candice and Annika in a bit. I expect you to update us over the walkie talkies should anything change with them at any minute."

"I can do that." Alex started toward the door and stopped. He turned around and faced Timothy. "For what it's worth, while I don't trust you right now, your ability to admit you were wrong goes a long way. I've met power hungry monsters without a decent bone in their body, and they justified their positions until the very end. It's a good first step that you were able to shut up and let Heather take the reins. It's the only reason I agreed so easily."

Timothy nodded once. "I'm… sorry," he said. "I really am."

Alex left, and Heather deflated, sitting across from Timothy, leaning back into her chair with a heavy sigh. She looked more tired than angry, but the anger was still there. Timothy waited. She had the right to speak on her own terms.

"How am I supposed to trust you?" Heather said at last. "What did you do, Tim? What did you do to us? I need you, and… now I'm alone."

"I made a mistake." Timothy's heart broke at the hurt in his wife's eyes. "I made a few mistakes. I see that now."

He reached out again, but Heather abruptly stood and backed away. "I need time, Tim. I know you were scared, but you were wrong in what you did. And I know you know that, but… I just…" She shook her head. "I need time. And space."

Timothy wet his dry lips, desperate. "Heather, either one of us could die out there tomorrow. Please. I love you so much. I'm so sorry."

"I love you, too," Heather said, her voice softer. "And if something happens, I do want you to know that. I'm not saying I can't forgive you, but I need time." She walked out of the room without another word, leaving Timothy more broken than he'd ever thought possible.

Chapter 10

Kai Lee

Kai groaned and stretched as sunlight found a crack in the blinds and pierced the darkness inside the camper. A sharp pain shot down the back of his neck. He'd left the bed to Zara, choosing to curl up on the poorly cushioned bench behind a small table.

His neck wasn't the only body part protesting the arrival of morning. His entire body was stiff and sore, and his head pounded harder by the second as he forced himself to sit up.

"Zara?" he asked, his throat raw, his voice barely audible.

She didn't respond. Kai winced as he stood and limped over to the bed. Zara was sprawled across the mattress, tangled in the blanket, an ugly bruise on her cheek. He sat on the edge of the bed, careful not to disturb her, comforted by the clear rise and fall of her chest. He vaguely remembered waking underwater, flailing desperately, his hand hitting her hard. A lump formed in his throat. He had done that. He'd hit Zara as she'd tried to save him, after he'd crashed the plane in the first place.

Kai hung his head, looking away from her. His father's last words to him rang in his ears. He'd come to the trailer park to give Kai's mother a taste of what he'd do if she took him to court over raising child-support payments. Kai had only been fifteen at the time, but when his father had backhanded his mother, he'd stepped in and pushed the bigger man with everything he had. It hadn't been enough. Before he knew it, Kai had been shoved to the floor, and his father was standing over him with a look of disgust on his face. You're nothing, he'd said. And you'll always be nothing. Remember that, boy. You're no hero.

It hadn't been the first time his father had said something like that, and it hadn't been the last. And it seemed no matter how his mother tried to weed those words from his mind over the years, they always found a way to take root and grow again. Normally, Kai worked hard to at least look like he was worth his weight, but another screw up was always just around the corner to remind him that maybe his father had been right after all.

He buried his head in his hands. Things had been going so well. He'd built something that made him important, something that helped other people. Flying people over the mountains had given him purpose. When his hometown turned on him, it had crushed him, but at least someone had still needed him.

And then I failed Zara and Walter, too. A wave of nausea washed over him at the thought of Mr. Peters. He was likely dead. Kai glanced at Zara. *How am I going to convince her to move on?*

Part of him suspected he'd have to show her Walter's dead body before she agreed to leave the area. She'd been so insistent the day before, going so far as to make up stories about mad scientists and secret government conspiracies. In his exhaustion, he'd almost believed her.

He sighed and looked around the camper. "I'm starving," he mumbled, reminded of all the food they'd lost when the plane went down. The hold had been stocked with supplies, both his and those of his passengers.

Kai stood again and hobbled to the tiny kitchen. There were some dried and canned goods in one of the overhead cabinets; the other was filled with plasticware and minimal cookware. He grabbed a box of cookies and popped one in his mouth. One taste made him realize how hungry he actually was, and he grabbed a handful of the sweet treats and shoved them in his mouth. They were chewy and chocolatey and delicious. A soft groan interrupted Kai's breakfast. He lowered the box to see Zara squinting at him.

"Hey, babe," Kai said, his mouth half full. "You're awake!" He swallowed hard at her scowl. It was hard for him to remember how pretentious she was. "Right. Not babe. Zara. Sorry."

She grunted as she tried to sit up, her hand flying to her head as she immediately laid back down. "Look, Cookie Monster, the least you can do is use my name. I saved your life."

Kai set the box of cookies down and wiped his mouth with his arm, suddenly very thirsty. He grabbed a can of mixed fruit, popped the top, and sipped the juice. "You're right," he said. "I said I was sorry, okay?" He took another drink and then held it out for her. "You want some?"

Zara blanched and shook her head. "I can't even think about eating. I feel terrible."

"At least drink some of the juice," he said. "You need some hydration."

"Fine," she said. "Is there another can, though? I don't want to drink your slobber."

He gave her a flat look but grabbed another can and brought it over to her, sitting at the foot of the bed as she slowly sat up and leaned against the windows at the head. He tipped the can back, slurping up a slice of canned peach. It was surprisingly refreshing. "We need more supplies," he said. "There's not enough here to get us past a couple of days."

Zara popped the top of her can and gingerly sipped. "We need to find Mr. Peters." She closed her eyes and leaned her head back. Even her lips had grown pale. She groaned.

"We need supplies first, food and water." Kai plucked a cherry out of his can with two fingers and dropped it in his mouth, savoring it. "And we need protection before we go searching the forest. I told you, the mosquitos here are worse than on the other side of the mountains." He reached up and patted the silver interior above his head. "This baby is hooked up to a truck. We might be able to take it into town, find something that works."

Zara sat limply, not having brought the can to her lips after her first sip. "He might be hurt." She swallowed audibly. "He's out there without protection, and he can't die."

"Yeah, yeah. He's got to save the world." Kai rolled his eyes. "You're really sticking with that, aren't ya?"

"It's true, Kai." Her voice was barely above a whisper, but the way she looked at him when she said it made a shudder go up his spine.

"What's true exactly?" Kai asked. "You weren't making much sense last night, and you're not giving me much to go on. You want me to risk my life to go save some old man who's probably already dead—" He winced at the abrupt words, but they were true. He kept going. "I'm sorry, but it's a miracle we survived. He was on his own. And he spent the night in the forest. Once the rain and hail and wind died down, those mosquitos were probably out in force."

"I know," Zara said softly. "But I have to try to find him. With or without you." She lowered herself to the mattress, lying on her side, tears sliding down her cheeks as she held the open can of mixed fruit which remained mostly untouched. Her eyelids drooped. "We have to… to find…"

Kai pressed his lips together as she drifted off again. He leaned closer, alarmed at her loss of consciousness, but she *was* breathing. "We have to find help. That's what we have to do."

He took the can from her and slid off the bed, placing the two cans on the counter. This time, he searched in earnest, pushing past his aching body. He found a first-aid kit, pain reliever, and discovered — much to his chagrin — that the small table lowered to latch into the seat of the bench and create a second, small bed once a couple small cushions were placed correctly. But he couldn't find what he was searching for: a set of keys to the truck. His best friend had always kept spare keys hidden in his camper, and the way he talked, the practice was commonplace. By the time he'd searched every inch of the inside of the camper, he deemed it was late enough in the morning to risk venturing outside.

"There's got to be a spare somewhere. A magnetic box, maybe." He shook out his nerves as he glanced back at Zara. She was still pale. Still breathing. But he didn't know how long that would last. "We can't stay here." Kai grasped the handle. "I'll be quick about it."

He burst outside, slamming the door shut behind him, dropping to the ground to look up under the camper. A whimper escaped him as he forced himself to hop back up; his body was not ready to move like that. He leaned against the camper's exterior as he made his way quickly around to the other side, preparing to drop again and search the undercarriage.

Below the truck's passenger-side door lay a human skeleton picked clean besides fragments of bloodied clothing and the hair still clinging to the top of the skull. Several of the bones were missing, but the rib cage was still intact, though it was spread too wide. Hot, stinging bile rose at the back of Kai's throat. He'd seen corpses plenty of times over the last few weeks, but he'd not run into a skeleton as of yet. Scavengers had to have come along and had their fill. Something about a person being consumed like that made Kai sick. He stumbled a few feet and lost what little he'd eaten.

When he gathered himself, he turned back toward the truck. He'd intended to avoid looking at the skeleton, but a glimmer caught his eye. He groaned as he tentatively stepped closer. A set of keys wedged near the spine had caught the light of the sun, and there was a fob that very well could belong to the truck.

"Really?" Kai ran his fingers through his hair and wet his dry lips, an anxious energy causing jittery movements. He sighed heavily, Zara's face, drained of all energy, flashing in his mind's eye.

Disturbing the dead had not been on his to-do list that morning, but he reached out with his foot and nudged the skeleton's rib cage aside, stepping on the set of keys and scratching them across the gravel toward him in one swift motion. He reached down, flicked away one of the shiny keys, and pressed a start button on the fob he suspected belonged to the truck. It stuttered to life.

"Finally. Something goes right." Using two fingers, he plucked the keys from the ground and hurried around the camper, popping inside for a moment. Zara was still out cold. There was a small dry erase board by the door. Kai grabbed the attached marker and wrote a note in case Zara woke while they were still traveling: *Don't worry. We'll go back. Getting help/supplies.*

A few minutes later, Kai was rumbling down the road, crossing a small bridge over a major highway, searching for signs of a nearby town. The country road lined with trees ended in a T with a small highway. There were no signs to indicate what lay to the north or south, but left with only two options, he turned right and continued southbound. The road was mostly clear with the exception of a few pileups and abandoned vehicles. He circumvented most of them easily, though there was one stretch where dozens of vehicles had crashed into each other. A thin pathway had been cleared through the mess, but Kai was only barely able to fit the truck and camper through it.

He was soon passing picturesque homes sitting farther off the road, and then the residential area became a bit denser until he passed a small decorative sign which read: Holyoke. Smaller letters underneath read: Birthplace of Volleyball.

"Huh. Learn something new every day, I guess."

After that, Kai passed several ransacked businesses; there wasn't a soul in sight. Holyoke seemed to be a mid-sized town, too small to be called a proper city, too big to be a small town. Still, there was enough there to give Kai hope of finding what he needed: food, water, and protection from the elements. His heart leapt when he caught sight of a hospital sign.

"If there's a place people haven't ransacked, maybe that's it," he said aloud to himself.

From what he'd heard over the weeks from the passengers he ferried over the mountains, hospitals were either places people feared to go or they'd turned into strongholds for survivors. It all depended on what went down when the crap hit the fan. Some communities had rallied around the medical supplies and kept the virus out of the hospitals while others had allowed those resources to perish along with everyone scrambling to save the dying.

He turned next to a sign pointing the way toward the emergency department. The road was completely clear of vehicles until he got to a line of them positioned horizontally in order to block entry into the medical complex. Ahead, two individuals decked out in head-to-toe beekeeper suits stalked outside of the emergency department doors, rifles in hand.

"I guess we know what decision old Holyoke made." Kai sighed. It wasn't bad; the fact they'd gathered at the hospital meant any supplies within were safe to retrieve. He wouldn't have to worry about sifting through a cesspool of disease and rotting corpses to get to them. He turned off the engine and opened the truck door, preparing his usual charm. Just because it hadn't worked on Walter and Zara didn't mean he hadn't seen positive results from most people. Kai plastered on his best disarming smile as he exited the vehicle. He had one foot on the ground when the first shot was fired.

Chapter 11

George Peters

George sat at the back of the briefing room next to Lissa. Of the six chosen to train under Ruger, they were the only two who'd decided to join the Boston Police Department after the battle at the zoo. Gavin and Albert had opted to join one of the survivor camps, and much to George's shock, Caleb had opted to stay with Ruger. George suspected that if Ace had still been alive, if Ruger hadn't been the one to take over CON, Caleb would be sitting with them in police headquarters. Ruger inspired a sort of loyalty, despite the fact he was on the wrong side of the fight. Omar, their sixth member, had been shot by Ace for being a 'turncoat' after the six had been forced to fight one another in one of Ace's twisted tests.

The room was brimming with police officers. George had never felt more out of place. Even in CON, he'd had a small group of people who were like him. But it was different at headquarters. Even Lissa, who'd grown up around police due to her aunt being one of them, fit in. She'd grown up around some of the officers who'd served with her aunt. She understood the way they talked, the way they thought. George was an outsider, welcomed but not yet proven.

And though he had a lot to prove, it only made him want to fight harder. At least at the BPD he was treated like an asset, like an adult. He had the option of joining the fight. He'd earned at least that much.

The door at the back of the room swung open, and Captain O'Donnell strode through, a dark look on his face. His lieutenant, Andy Duncan, trailed after him, as did Officers Lucy Freeman and Arnold Penn. They were O'Donnell's most trusted officers, his inner circle, officers from the thirteenth precinct. A hush fell over the room as the four entered, and the pressure of anticipation filling the room pressed against George's chest.

O'Donnell stood front and center as the other three took seats in the front row. A huge map of Boston pinned to the wall behind him served as a backdrop. "I'm gonna get straight to the point," the captain said. "Lieutenant Duncan has returned from his most recent mission with both good and bad news." He took a deep breath. "The bad news is pretty bad. Karl Webb is dead."

A few gasps went up around the room. George had only heard of Webb, never having met the man himself. He'd been injured in a shootout between CON and the police outside the library. Timothy had been there, and George had heard two completely different tales about the incident. His brother had either been an idiot who'd gotten Webb shot and then abandoned the team, or Timothy was a brazen daredevil who flirted with danger and got exactly what he'd wanted: the location of CON's base of operations. George assumed both stories had some truth to them.

Lissa's hand had gone to her mouth at the announcement, and she'd closed her eyes. "Not another one," she whispered.

"I'm so sorry," George said softly. "Did you know him?"

Lissa nodded. "A little." She smiled sadly. "He participated in the Guns and Hoses hockey annual charity event every year. My aunt loved it. She would always bring snacks for the guys on the team. Got the whole family tickets. She said Webb was going to get us the win this year." Her smile faded. "He seemed like a really nice guy."

"Webb was a dedicated police officer, just like so many we've lost, but he died protectin' Boston from the scum who want to take what's left o' her and destroy this city for their own gain." O'Donnell's gaze swept the room. "Which brings me to why we're here. What's left of Boston is her people, and we've got to get them out of harm's way before Frank Russo makes his move. We got a day and a half, people. That's not a lot of time."

O'Donnell stepped aside and indicated the map on the wall, pulling a marker out of his pocket and drawing a line from a point on the Charles River, through the city, ending at Carson Beach. "These four miles are our front line. We're workin' on buildin' a force of both police and civilians willing to fight, and we've got several checkpoints to secure." He circled the places on the map as he named them. "Fenway, the Museum of Fine Arts, Headquarters, District B-2 Police Department, Southbay, and the state police in South Boston."

O'Donnell faced them again. "Obviously, this building is already secured. We've already got a small force in Roxbury at B-2 as well, run by Captain Hal Winters." He laid his hand flat over the area of Boston behind the line, hemmed in by water on all sides. "We're callin' this the green zone. I don't want to lose one inch of this ground."

The room erupted in protests and counterprotests. George sat back, many of his thoughts being vocalized all around him. He couldn't even pinpoint who was saying what.

"We don't have enough men to cover four miles!"

"He said we've got civilian support."

"Enough to defend *four* miles?"

"What about the Russos? Where is their front line?"

"Every civilian who's old enough to fire a weapon should be fighting with us. We're putting our lives on the line. Why shouldn't they?"

"What's the point of protecting them if we get them all killed? They aren't trained! Why are we even including civilians at all?"

Lissa crossed her arms and scowled. "I can't believe these guys. O'Donnell's not even done, and they're already tearing apart his plans."

George frowned. "They've got a point, Lissa."

She turned her scowl on him. "We don't know that yet. He hasn't finished."

He gulped and shrank a little under her intense scrutiny. "Yeah, I guess you're right." He wasn't about to argue with her after that withering glare.

"Enough!" Captain O'Donnell roared, and the room fell silent again.

Lissa sat back with a satisfied nod of her head. George, on the other hand, stuffed his heart back down into place after it had jumped into his throat.

"The enemy is, by all accounts, still centered in and around the zoo two miles west of here, but they're spreading north and south. We're callin' their territory the red zone for now." O'Donnell slammed his hand onto the map. "It seems they're settin' up their front line, and we've got to do the same or else risk them encircling us and coming at as from all sides. But securing our own front line leaves a whole swathe of Boston between us and them. We're callin' this the white-hot zone. That's where this war will be fought and won, and that means we need to get as many survivors out of that area as possible. Now, Lieutenant Duncan has a few things to add at this point, so shut up and listen up." He nodded to Duncan in the front row.

The lieutenant joined O'Donnell at the front of the room. "Yesterday, I went on a mission to find survivor groups already in our green zone that could possibly absorb refugees." He pointed at the map behind the line O'Donnell had drawn for their own forces. "I started at the library, since we knew about them already, and information I gathered there led me to a community downtown at Boston City Hall and another one at the convention center in Seaport. At each of the major survivor camps, I was able to recruit civilians who will be meeting us at one of the checkpoints the captain just mentioned, and I confirmed with their leaders that they are willing to take on more survivors in exchange for our protection and, when the Russos and what's left of CON is gone for good, provisions."

O'Donnell stepped forward again as Duncan took his seat. "While the cease-fire is still active, I am sending a few of you into the white-hot zone to clear it of civilians. You'll be provided protective gear and weapons, but these are only for self-defense. We don't need this war to start early." He nodded a second time to the front row, and Freeman stood up, clearing her throat as she turned to face them.

"We are working on some solutions to our problems as far as mobility is concerned," Freeman said. "We believe there is only one or two swarms of the deadly mosquitos roaming the city, but there is no way to confirm that. We've only cleared one pathway through the city over the last few weeks, and that's not going to be enough. A full-sized vehicle isn't going to get us where we need to go. Motorcycles are better, but they leave us exposed to the elements." She took a deep breath. "That leaves us with the beans."

A groan went up all around the room, and George frowned, leaning over to whisper to Lissa. "Did I hear her right? What are the beans?"

Lissa chuckled softly. "They're tiny solar-powered cars, only big enough for one person. Parking enforcement officers use them and so do officers patrolling the parks."

Freeman held up her hands. "I know, I know. They're not the most reliable if it's not sunny outside, especially without the ability to plug them in to a charging port, but we're in the middle of summer here, and they should be fine for our purposes. They're enclosed, they're small enough to drive on sidewalks, and they might be slow, but they're faster than walking." She grimaced. "We've also rigged up some full body suits for those walking through the city. There are only so many beans available. But please take advantage of what we've got, people. We need every last one of you, and a swarm is no joke. We need plans that go beyond running and hiding, hoping you pick a safe building." She nodded back to O'Donnell.

"I've got a few last notes before we dismiss." The captain took a deep breath. "As Duncan has already said, we've got recruits planning to man our other checkpoints. Some are veterans and National Guard members who are more equipped for what's coming, but many of them are just brave Americans protecting their city and the people they love. By all estimations, with these recruits, we're about evenly matched with the enemy."

Murmurs with more of a positive note filled the room, and George exhaled in relief. When CON and the mob had decided to work together instead of wiping each other out, the BPD had found themselves outnumbered.

O'Donnell continued. "Individual assignments are coming your way. Team leaders already have their orders and the names of those who will join them. Be safe out there." He took a step to the side, and the room stirred, but then he held up a hand. "One more thing," he said. The captain quieted for a moment as if contemplating his next words. Then, he let his gaze settle on his officers, and yet somehow, it seemed he was speaking directly to George. "Stay strong. Believe not only that we're on the side of liberty but also that good can and will triumph. If you give in to fear, to doubt and self-preservation and cowardice, the Russos win before they've even fired a shot. Let's show those bastards that they're messin' with the wrong city."

A slow, steady clap began and then the room burst into applause as O'Donnell walked down the aisle and left the room. George joined in, but he wasn't quite as enthusiastic as Lissa. She was beaming, adding her whistle into the cacophony of support for the captain's last words. The noise died down, and she threw George an excited smile as team leaders began calling out names.

"You ready for this?" she asked. "We're going to take Frank Russo down, what's left of CON, too."

"Well, not by ourselves, but..." George looked around as small teams began to filter out of the room together. The room was thinning fast, and his heart began to sink. "I haven't heard our names yet. What if we aren't assigned a team?"

"Why wouldn't they put us on a team?" Lissa asked.

"I don't know." George shifted his weight from one foot to the other, avoiding eye contact. "What if they just put us on scavenger duty or something?" *That's what my brother would do, what he probably asked O'Donnell to do.* He didn't mention his thoughts out loud, though. He wasn't about to admit that his own brother could have relegated them both to menial tasks.

Lissa frowned. "I'm talking to Freeman." She stepped out of their aisle and shimmied her way toward the front of the room where Freeman still spoke with Duncan and Penn in hushed tones, their expressions serious.

George made to follow, whispering sharply, "I don't think that's a good idea. We should wait for her to finish whatever she's doing." But Lissa only stopped when she was close enough to Freeman that she could have patted her on the back. George stopped short, paling a little as Lissa's mere presence clearly interrupted the conversation.

"I didn't survive CON and choose to be here so I could scavenge," Lissa said. "I want an assignment."

Duncan crossed his arms and exchanged a look with Freeman. "Scavenging *is* an assignment, Lissa. And it's an important one."

Freeman quirked an eyebrow. "I scavenged two days ago with a team. Are you saying helping to provide food and water for your fellows is beneath you?"

Lissa stuttered and took half a step back. "N-no. I mean, I'll do my scavenging rotations just like everyone else, but—"

George cringed as Lissa's shoulders slumped. He stepped up beside her. "We just want to make sure our names are on more than one rotation list."

Penn shook his head, a smirk on his face. "Rookies." He nodded to Freeman and Duncan. "Good luck with that."

"Oh, they're not my problem," Duncan said, grinning at Freeman. He nudged her with his elbow. "I can't believe you volunteered."

Both Duncan and Penn left, and Freeman's expression darkened as she narrowed her eyes at George and Lissa.

"Volunteered for what?" Lissa asked, tone more tentative this time.

"To take you two with me on my team." Freeman pursed her lips and examined them both. "Be ready in ten. Meet me at weapons checkout." She pointed at them. "And don't make me regret this."

Chapter 12

Heather Peters

Heather stepped out from behind a truck with her hands raised as she approached the library, Murphy following her lead. She walked slowly toward the front doors, set within the granite building beneath arched windows, and just as she expected, someone stepped out.
"Stop right there," the man said, drawing a handgun but leaving it pointed toward the ground.
"We're here to talk." Heather was still a few yards off, so she raised her voice, hoping her words were clear enough. "We'd rather do it inside, where it's safe."
"Who are you with — the Russos or the police?" He seemed to ignore her request entirely.
"Neither." Murphy replied. "But Captain O'Donnell is a good friend."
"What do you want? We told the police we'd take some of their refugees, but we didn't expect anyone for another day at least." He narrowed his eyes. "I don't see any supplies with you. We were promised any refugees would each come with supplies."
Heather shook her head. "We're not here to stay, just to talk. We know a trauma nurse is taking care of Karl Webb. We wanted to talk to her, specifically."
"Webb is dead," the man said abruptly. "Valerie isn't here. She was the nurse taking care of him."
Murphy cursed, and Heather glanced at her to see the lines at the corners of her mouth and eyes tighten. "He was a good one," she said so that only Heather could hear. "This is exactly why we can't stay here any longer than we have to. James needs me."
"We'll head on to the cleaners' soon enough," Heather said, just as quietly. "I just don't want to miss the opportunity to gather information."
"Speak up, ladies!" The man's hand twitched at his side as if he were considering raising his gun. There was panic in his voice.
"Sorry," Heather shouted. "We have an injured little girl back at our own camp. We wanted to speak with Valerie. Where is she?"
He rolled his shoulders, scanning the distance behind them. His nervous energy was contagious, and Heather resisted the urge to obsess about their surroundings. There was no hum in the air, no reason to be jittery. Not at the moment, anyway.
"Valerie is at City Hall," he said. "Webb's death hit her hard. We heard there's a surgeon downtown, and she wanted to go over Webb's case with him, figure out if she did anything wrong."
Heather's heart leapt. "There's a surgeon alive, in Boston?"
He scowled at her. "Isn't that what I just said? You want anything else, or are you going to continue wasting my time?"
Murphy took half a step forward. "You're being a real d—"
Heather put a hand on Murphy's shoulder to stop her. "We need to keep relations amiable," she whispered.
"What was that, lady?" The man's frown deepened. "What did you call me?"
Murphy flashed a smile at him. "Thanks for you help," she said. "You've been a darling."
He quirked an eyebrow, but her words seemed to throw him off. "You two better get on, now. There's nothing here for you."
"Just one more thing," Heather said. "We were hoping, for when things are settled around here again, to make a list of skills people have. Maybe we can start to rebuild the city if all the survivors work together."
He scoffed. "I tell you what, sweetheart. If things ever *settle*, you come back, and we'll get right on that."
Heather narrowed her eyes, the urge to finish Murphy's original insult strong. Instead, she controlled her impulse. "All right, then. We'll see you around."
The man retreated back into the building. Murphy backed up, still facing the library, refusing to turn her back on strangers until they were farther away. Heather did the same for Murphy's sake, though she doubted the man would try to harm them.
"To City Hall, then," Heather said when they finally turned around and began their journey in earnest.
"You think they'll be any friendlier?" Murphy's tone suggested she doubted it. "We should just get the protective suits and head back to Vanguard. I don't want to be out here. It's dangerous."
"If there's a surgeon at City Hall, I need to investigate that," Heather said. "Lauren has mentioned several times that she's not qualified to care for Annika if things get worse than they already are. She specifically mentioned that Annika might need surgery. And if it were James, I would make sure you had access to whomever could help."
Murphy clenched her jaw but nodded, conceding the point. "Fine." She didn't seem to want to talk after that, and so they walked in silence.
Which was not good for Heather. Every second not occupied by doing something gave her another second to fume against Timothy. The way he lied to her. The way he threatened Theodore like an insane person. The way he'd kept vital information secret. She would have expected that sort of behavior from Walter, but Timothy?
I've seen more of his father come out in him over the past weeks than I ever thought possible. Heather remembered Dana's words, how she'd said Timothy was more like Walter than he would have liked to admit. And she had seen it, too, but she'd hoped it was only the good parts he was emulating. She let out a frustrated growl and kicked at a rock, sending it bouncing across the pavement in front of them. *I didn't marry a younger version of Walter. I fell in love with Timothy because he bucked against what he knew was wrong. How could he do this to us?*
"Need to get something off your chest?" Murphy asked.

"Sorry," Heather said, heat rushing to her cheeks. She couldn't tell Murphy everything. Tim had been right that it was expedient to keep some of the information within their inner circle. And she barely knew the woman, but... she *did* need someone to talk to. "Tim and I are having some... difficulties."

Murphy laughed, and Heather glowered at her. Murphy held up her hands in mock surrender. "Hey, I'm just glad to see the dream couple are human after all. You two have weathered some pretty crazy stuff. You've been so lovey-dovey, I was starting to believe you two were robots or something. So, what he'd do?" Her smile faded. "He didn't cheat, did he?"

"What? No!" Heather recoiled. "Of course not."

"Well, it can't be that bad, then," Murphy said, shrugging.

"He lied to me. About something important." Heather looked straight ahead and crossed arms. "We swore we'd never lie to each other."

"Ah. So, he broke your trust in a different way. Well, do you still love him?"

"Yes," Heather said without having to think about it.

"Does he still love you?"

"Yes."

Murphy furrowed her brow. "Did he apologize?"

Heather didn't keep the annoyance from her answer. "Yes." This was a mistake. How could she possibly understand without the full context?

"Well, then... I guess, be mad if you've got a right to be," Murphy said, "but don't hold out too long. I mean, for all you know, he's dead already."

Heather blanched and rounded on Murphy. "How could you say that? How could you put that thought in my head? What if I said that about James?"

Pain flashed behind Murphy's eyes. "Then, you'd be right." Her voice cracked a little. "For all I know, James *could* be dead. Every minute we survive is a miracle these days. So many things could go wrong..." She trailed off, swallowing hard and averting her eyes.

"Well, they're both alive," Heather said. "We can't live our lives always assuming our loved ones could be dead or dying. There's no sense in that."

"I agree," Murphy said. "But it does put things in perspective. The last thing I said to James was that I loved him. I hugged him until he squirmed out of my arms, and then I tickled him and bottled up his smile and his laughter and tucked it away for the journey." Murphy gave Heather a sympathetic look. "I'm just saying, no matter how mad you are at Timothy, if you two are still in love, if you know you're going to forgive him eventually, anyway, you might as well get it over with. You don't have time to brood about it."

"What if I can't forgive him?" Heather asked, voicing the concern out loud for the first time.

Murphy raised her eyebrows. "That must have been one hell of a lie."

"It was."

"I don't know, then," Murphy said. "I just know that after all you've been through, if it were me, I'd fight real hard to figure it out."

Heather thought about the conversation as they walked briskly through the city toward the downtown area. She wasn't about to throw away her marriage over one mistake, but it *was* a big mistake, to her, anyway. And she'd seen it in Tim's eyes when he'd confessed: he had *known* it was wrong, and he'd done it anyway. It terrified her to think Timothy could end up as brutal and cruel as his father and grandfather had been before him, that those traits were just waiting to be unlocked beneath a kind and gentle surface.

At their pace, it only took them about twenty minutes to reach City Hall from the library. Heather prepared for much the same welcome as they'd received before, and she and Murphy both ensured their hands were raised as they crossed Congress Street and approached the first-floor entrance.

Two men strode out of the building. One was short but stocky and well-built. The other was tall with a beer gut, head shaved clean, sporting a very long beard.

"Stop," Beard said, holding out one hand, drawing his gun with the other.

Heather sighed. *Déjà vu.*

This time, Murphy took the lead. "We're friends of the Boston Police. Not here to stay. Just to talk."

Short and Stocky frowned. "Who are you here to talk to?"

"The surgeon. And we're looking for Valerie, too. Is she still here?" Heather asked.

"Yeah, there's a surgeon. His name's Dr. Linden." Beard lowered his hand. "You know Val?"

"Not quite," Heather said. "We know of her. We'd also be interested in speaking to whoever is organizing your operation. Is there a council of some sort? Or is one guy calling the shots?"

"We got a bunch of accountants running the show," Short and Stocky said. "I guess they'd be some sort of council."

Beard assessed them both, looking them up and down. "We've got a few tents set up in the plaza," he said. "That's where newcomers stay until we're sure they're not sick and until we know we can trust them. We've been setting up a few dozen to prepare for the refugees that might be on their way over the next few days." He looked at his companion. "Zane, why don't you show these ladies to one of them, and I'll go see if anyone wants to talk to them."

"Sure thing, Matt." Zane nodded for Heather and Murphy to follow behind. "Keep a bit of distance, if you don't mind," he said. "Can't be too cautious these days."

Heather nodded. "No problem," she said as she followed him around the side of the massive concrete building.

Matt paused at the door as they passed by on the sidewalk toward the plaza. "I can't guarantee anyone will come out and talk to you," he said.

"We appreciate you trying," Heather said, giving him a grateful nod as he entered the building.

They entered the large plaza, which previously had been used for large events and a regular farmer's market, to find several small tents underneath large offset patio umbrellas with thick, sturdy mesh walls hanging from the edges. The mesh looked added on, and the bottom of the screens were weighted with sandbags.

"Wow," Murphy said, taking in one of the structures. "This is impressive. Why not just set up a bunch of tents by themselves? You must have raided every home improvement store in the city to find the materials to make these."

"Barry — that's one of those accountants we were telling you about — well, he thought it would be better to have two layers of protection. Said last time he went camping, mosquitos got inside the tent. They're sneaky, he said." Zane was almost cheerful as he led them to one of the structures. "Anyway, you should be safe in here, even if the swarm comes by. There's repellent spray inside each tent. You can spray that through the mesh if you need to, but I'd suggest getting in the tent."

"How long are we going to be waiting?" Murphy asked.

Zane shrugged. "I don't know. I guess it depends on what everyone's doing right now." He unzipped the outer net on the first empty structure and let them inside, zipping it up again after them.

"Well, if someone doesn't come soon, we'll have to check back another time," Heather said. "We want to coordinate human resources, know who has what skill so that down the line, we can work together to rebuild."

"Sounds like a good plan," Zane said. "I'll mention it when I go back inside." He left them there and re-entered the building without so much as a glance back.

Heather retrieved the spray, but neither of them opted to stay inside the tent, instead standing behind the mesh barrier to watch for someone to come meet them. To Heather's relief, it wasn't long before a woman exited the building and came toward their structure. She stopped on the outside of it, keeping her distance, clearly more comfortable with them while they were behind the mesh.

"I'm Val," she said. "You wanted to talk to me?"

"And the surgeon," Heather said.

"Well, I'm what you've got. Dr. Linden is busy." She crossed her arms, looking nervously to her left and to her right. "I don't like being out here longer than I have to. Say whatever it is you came here to say."

Heather frowned. "Are you the only one coming out here to talk to us?"

"I'm not good enough?" Val shrugged. "Fine. Go back to wherever you came from." She started to leave but paused when both Murphy and Heather called for her to wait.

"We have a little girl who got caught in a wildebeest stampede," Heather said. She blinked and shook her head. "That does *not* get less weird the more I say it."

"Okay," Val said. "So, she's injured? How badly?"

"We have someone with a little medical training. She dropped out of her residency, so she doesn't have any surgical experience, but she thinks Annika has blunt kidney damage," Heather said. "She says that there's a chance Annika might need surgery to remove the kidney, but—"

"Whoa," Val held up both hands, palms outward, her eyes wide. "That's major surgery. You'd need Doctor Linden for that, not me."

"Do you think he'd help us?" Heather asked.

"If you were able to get her here, maybe," Val said. "I don't think he'd turn you down, but he's made it pretty clear to everyone: he's not going anywhere. He set up a surgery in City Hall, and the guys have helped him get fully stocked. There's a generator and solar keeping the lights on in this place. I think there's only a handful of buildings in the whole city that have that, and to my knowledge, they're all occupied. Or full of corpses, like the hospitals. That's why Linden set up at City Hall."

Heather's shoulders sagged. "I guess if it was an emergency, we could try to get her here, but… it's like ten miles, and there's definitely not a clear pathway to travel by car."

"Is there anything else I can do for you?" Val asked.

"Just… when you get back to the library, and when you're here, can you talk to people about working together? Really thinking through their skills and coming up with ways they could support a whole community?" Heather hoped Val could see the value in her proposition. "Long term, Boston will need everyone working together. We can't live in pure survival mode forever. We've got to start figuring out how to be self-sustaining. Things aren't going back to how they were before. We need gardeners, tailors, cobblers, bakers, herbalists… any skill could be useful."

"I think people need to think one step ahead at a time right now," Val said. "It's going to be a while before they can envision any sort of routine. We need to deal with this whole green zone, white-hot zone thing, the whole war between the police and the mob, before we get caught up in moving past survival."

Heather frowned. "I know about the conflict, but… what zones? I haven't heard of that yet."

"The Boston Police are moving everyone from the designated war zone behind their front lines," Val said. "They've drawn a line from Fenway, through Roxbury, all the way to Carson Beach. I guess the other side has drawn a similar line a few miles west, with the zoo at the center. That strip in the middle is going to be the war zone. They're calling it white-hot and the mob's territory red."

Heather groaned, her stomach dropping. "We're in the war zone, then."

Murphy had gone pale. "Well, I mean, you guys can move, right? You can set up on this side of the line."

"Maybe," Heather lied. Her heartbeat quickened, and her knees trembled. She sat on the ground, despite her attempts to keep her cool. She couldn't reveal why that was a lie, why they *had* to stay at Vanguard, at New Horizons Laboratory. But they had no other choice. The lab they needed for everyone to survive was smack dab in the middle of the war zone, and there was nothing they could do about it.

Chapter 13

Walter Peters

Keeping track of time was nearly impossible when Carol kept dosing him. But Walter was pretty sure at least one night had come and gone since being brought to The Log Cabin. He stirred, this time making sure not to make a fuss. He didn't want Carol to give him any more of whatever it was she was using to drug him.

"You sleep a lot." LeeAnn was in his room. Again.

"You talk a lot," Walter said, unable to keep a slight smile from his lips. "You aren't supposed to be in here."

LeeAnn's bottom lip stuck out just a bit. "You don't like me?"

Walter blinked at her big, round eyes and protruding lip. Even he couldn't disappoint that face. "Of course I like you," he said, his voice still grating.

His entire body was still sore, and the wound in his side was still very tender. Carol changed the bandage three times a day and ensured it stayed clean. She tended to him well, despite her mental breakdown. If it was up to her, at least he would live long enough to make an escape.

He couldn't say the same for Zara. Carol had mentioned the mountain had many buildings, and he could only hope Zara and Kai had taken shelter in one.

"I like you, too," LeeAnn said, popping up from where she'd sat playing Pick-Up-Sticks. "Heath is just boring now, and Mom is…" The light in her eyes flickered. "… different. You're interesting."

"I'm just new," Walter said. "I'm probably more boring than Heath."

"That's impossible," LeeAnn said, cutting the air with her hand. "Heath is the ultimate booger. He's a sticky blob on the couch. Barely moves." She said every word with emphasis.

The door opened and the sulky teenager slunk inside the room. "You in here, LeeAnn?" He scowled when he spotted his sister.

"He's moving now," Walter pointed out. "He doesn't seem so bad." He winked at the girl.

"Stop talking to her," Heath said. "LeeAnn, get out of here. We're about to leave, and Mom is going to get mad if she knows you were in here again. She can't keep an eye on you constantly. Everything we do now takes a hundred times longer. Laundry, dishes, cooking… and we've got all kinds of new things we've got to do. You could help with some of it, you know, instead of playing games."

LeeAnn rolled her head in an exaggerated fashion to look at Walter as if to say: *told you so!* Then she crossed her arms, stuck out her tongue, and started toward the door. Heath turned around, too, but something he'd said registered with Walter.

"Wait! You said you guys are about to leave. Where are you going?" Walter asked.

"We're going into town," Heath said. "There are some people left at the hospital. Mom wouldn't join up with them at first because she wanted to look for Dad. Now, she's saying the less exposure to other people, the better." His perpetual frown deepened. "I don't think we're ever getting out of here."

Hope blossomed in Walter's chest. "Heath, I understand why you can't go looking for Zara and Kai, but you can tell someone else about them, see if they can go search for them."

Heath shook his head. "My mom never takes her eyes off me. I think she's afraid I'm going to run away again."

"Again?" Walter asked, unable to stop himself from asking, though that line of questioning had nothing to do with what he needed.

The boy looked ashamed. "I ran away a few times before all of this." He gestured vaguely around him. "I was being stupid. I thought my parents had too many rules. I mean, I didn't *run away* run away, but I would hide out at friends' houses sometimes. I wouldn't do that now, though. Not with Dad gone, and Mom… the way she is. I wouldn't leave LeeAnn alone, no matter how annoying she is."

Behind him, LeeAnn's head poked around the corner of the doorway. Walter spotted her smile, but he didn't draw attention to her. She'd chosen to eavesdrop, but he *wasn't* her father. They met eyes for a moment, and the little girl froze as if waiting for him to tattle on her. Instead, he only let his gaze linger for a moment before turning back to Heath.

"You're a good brother," Walter said. "And a good son."

"You don't know anything." Heath shook his head, a look of disgust on his face.

"I know you love your family just as much as I love mine. And Zara is like a daughter to me." Walter tried again. "If she's hurt—"

"Kids?" Carol's voice resonated throughout the hall, and Walter heard her mounting frustration before he saw it on her face. "How many times do I have to tell you to leave your father alone?" Carol appeared in the doorway, hands on hips. "Heath, really. What are you doing?"

"We're just talking, Mom," Heath said.

"Go get in the car," Carol said. "I thought about letting you two stay here, but I can see I can't trust you to let your father rest."

"We won't bother him," Heath said, pleading in his voice. "I don't want to go into town, Mom."

"Don't argue." Carol's tone brooked no argument. "Get. In. The. Car."

Heath sighed, and his whole body sagged as he walked, as if he were literally dragging himself out of the room. Carol took a few steps inside as her son passed, and then she turned to survey Walter. Behind her, Heath grabbed LeeAnn by the hand and tugged her away. The little girl waved at him before she was pulled out of his line of sight.

"Saul, you really shouldn't encourage them to stay in here. You need rest." Carol came closer, carefully sitting on the edge of the bed next to him.

Her nearness made him uncomfortable, but Walter swallowed the feeling and resisted the urge to scoot away. She wasn't a bad person. He could tell that from their interactions. But she was definitely broken. And she wasn't his wife. The familiarity she showed toward him was a pale imitation of what he shared with Dana.

"Sorry," he said, not contradicting her this time. All he wanted was for her to go away without drugging him. "I'll rest. I promise."

"Good." Carol leaned over and kissed his forehead. "We'll be back in a couple of hours. I'm going to restock on well water from the Fischer's farm and then I'm going into town to grab some essentials. I want to make sure you've got the right medications."

"Okay." Walter chose his next words carefully, glancing at the wheelchair in the corner. Carol had used it to help him to the adjoining bathroom; so far, those short trips were the only opportunity he'd had to get out of bed. "What if I have to go to the bathroom?"

Carol looked thoughtful. "I hadn't thought of that." She pursed her lips. "I suppose it wouldn't hurt to let you use the wheelchair. We're on the second floor. It's not like you can use it to roll away." She spoke as if talking to herself and then chuckled absentmindedly. She retrieved the wheelchair and positioned it by the bed. "You've got water," she said, nodding to the glass on his bedside table. "You need anything else? Pain meds?"

Desperate to distract Carol from injecting him with anything else, he shook his head. "No," he said too quickly. At the slight narrowing of her eyes, he widened his smile. "A book maybe? A magazine? I'd like to do something besides lie in bed and sleep."

Carol pursed her lips. "I've got just the thing." She left the room for a few minutes and came back with a large, thin book. It was a coffee table tome for amateur Massachusetts historians. "How about this."

"Perfect." Walter forced a smile as he took the book. "I'll see you when you get back."

Carol returned the smile, hers more genuine. She patted him on the arm and left the room again, this time shutting the door behind her.

Walter breathed out, relieved. She hadn't drugged him. He lay there patiently until he heard another door open and shut, until he heard the rumble of an engine. He stayed still for a while after silence returned, listening for any signs that he was not alone.

When he was satisfied that Carol and her children were gone, he steeled himself and slowly sat up, scooting himself gingerly back to lean against the headboard. Pain shot up his side, but he couldn't stop there. Grimacing, he moved one leg and then the other over the side of the bed. His legs trembled with the effort. He eyed the wheelchair, questioning whether he could successfully transfer himself from the bed.

Dozens of images of where Zara *could* be ran through his mind. Lying broken and bleeding on the forest floor, waiting for death. Huddled in some dirty, dark corner of an abandoned park bathroom. Dead inside the ruins of the cockpit. Dead, eyes bulging, body covered in blood. Dead, body shredded by some wild animal. Dead, fallen in a twisted heap off a cliff while looking for him. Dead. Dead. Dead.

Walter squeezed his eyes shut. There were so many ways she could have died already. Because he'd been stuck here. Because he'd not been strapped in, with her when the plane went down.

And then he saw Lizzy's eyes as he'd last seen them. Sad and hurt and pleading for him to love her no matter what. And he did, but… he hadn't shown her that. He'd abandoned her, and she'd died.

He couldn't do the same to Zara.

"She's alive," he said aloud, willing it to be true despite the chances that it wasn't.

And if she was alive, he knew she wouldn't be idle. Zara wouldn't leave the area until she'd searched for him. There would be no body in the wreckage, and so she'd keep looking. Until she *did* wind up dead.

Walter reached for the handles on the wheelchair and swung his body awkwardly into it, using what little strength he had to get situated properly. By the time he was sitting normally in the chair, he was sweating and shaking, but he unlocked the wheels and slowly pushed himself to the door.

He reached out and wrapped his hand around the cool-to-the-touch, vintage glass doorknob. "Please be unlocked," he whispered as he twisted. It gave way, and Walter pulled, relief flooding him as the door clicked open.

By the time he rolled into the hall, he was even more exhausted, sweaty, and sore. He wheeled himself toward the staircase but stopped at an alcove with a display memorializing an old version of The Log Cabin that had burned to the ground. A poster explained how it had been rebuilt, but that wasn't what Walter was staring at. An open-faced 3-D model of the building was encased in glass.

The wedding party suites, where Walter had been put, was on the *third* floor. Eyes widening, a vague memory of lying on a stretcher, of Heath arguing with his mother as he helped her haul Walter up the stairs, surfaced.

His stomach sank. He'd planned to sit on the floor and scoot down the stairs one at a time, but that had been when he thought he was only one flight up. It had seemed foolhardy in his current state but not impossible. Once downstairs, he'd hoped he'd be able to walk around using the walls for support. There was nothing wrong with his legs, besides the bruising and a few pulled muscles and his overall weakness. Maybe he could find a set of keys to a car or even a golf cart. As long as he didn't break open the wound at his side and vertigo didn't hit from his concussion, he'd be golden. Sort of. But adding another flight of stairs felt like adding a mountain. Especially after everything seemed to take him ten times the amount of effort and time.

A lump formed in his throat. *I can't give up. I have to get out of here.* He was slow, and he wasn't sure how long he'd been at his attempt to escape. But he knew Carol wouldn't be gone more than a couple hours, tops.

Walter rolled to the stairs and carefully — painfully — managed to lower himself to the floor. Breathing hard, he scooted to the edge of the first step and sat there for a moment, gathering his wits. His heartbeat pounded within his chest. Every muscle screamed at him, begging him to stop. Sweat created a sheen across his bare chest and arms and made the sweatpants Carol had dressed him in cling to his legs.

Before moving farther, he checked the bandage at his side. It held, and the outside of the bandage was still white and crisp. Carol had changed it that morning and checked the sutures. It was still early, but it was healing nicely, she'd said. But the wound *hurt* more than it had since waking. He'd half expected to see blood seeping through.

The meds she's been giving me must have been dulling the pain. Moving around like this… it's going to hurt. I just have to accept it and keep going.

Walter grimaced, holding his stiff and swollen knee out straight as he lowered himself one step. He focused on breathing and moved down one more. Halfway down the first flight, he had to stop as his body was shaking so violently that his teeth chattered. Nausea washed over him as he leaned his head against the wall. The room spun, and it wouldn't stop. The edges of his vision clouded.

Fear clawed at the inside of his chest as perched on the step, the room spinning, his stomach lurching, sweat drenching him head to toe. If he could just make it to the landing, he could rest and then try for the second flight. Walter grasped at the railing above his head, trying to use it to keep himself steady, but the edges of his vision clouded.

His limbs were cold, and his face flushed hot. He lowered himself another step and then he tipped too far to one side. He grasped feebly for a handhold but found none. And then he was falling, body slamming against the edges of several steps before he came to a stop on the wide landing, his back careening into the wall, one hand stretched out above him, dangling over the first step of the next flight.

Walter gasped for breath as agony washed over him. He sought out his wound, trembling fingers coming away sticky and warm and wet. All plans to escape fled his mind, and plans to stay awake, to keep breathing took their place.

Chapter 14

Timothy Peters

Timothy sat behind the wheel of a Vanguard company car, navigating through the city via the only route that led out of Boston. It had been cleared weeks ago by the BPD when they'd driven out of the city to strike at the Russos and take back what they'd viewed as goods stolen from the city. The mile between New Horizons and the path had not been cleared, however, and Timothy, Burke, and Torres had spent most of the morning changing that.

He'd welcomed the work, though it had been nerve wracking as they'd kept their eyes and ears open, ready to take shelter in the car should a swarm of mosquitos or a wild animal approach. Heather hadn't spoken to him that morning, and he hadn't pushed. She was right; he was wrong. All there was to do was to wait for her to forgive him. And to not do anything stupid in the meantime.

The silence in the car afforded him too much time to think, to wonder if he'd effectively destroyed his marriage, which was the only good thing he had left. Torres and Burke weren't exactly the company he would have chosen to keep him occupied, but Timothy had little choice in the matter.

"So…" Timothy said, shifting uncomfortably as Burke glared at him from the back seat. He glanced at Torres, who wore a more neutral expression. "Where are you guys headed after this?"

"North." Burke grunted the word, his upper lip curling.

"Right…" Timothy swallowed hard, the silence that followed awkward.

"North*west*." Torres offered Timothy a smile. "We don't want to end up in a big survivor camp, but we figure a smaller one would welcome our skills and provide a safe spot for us. We've got some ideas about where to go. We're going to look for a place with friends or family, but we don't know who's left alive. I mean, everyone we know can't be dead." Burke grunted again, and Torres amended his statement. "Probably."

"That's all you need to know," Burke said. "We're making a clean break from Boston."

Timothy nodded. "I get it."

"I was thinking," Torres said, "do you think we could take this car?"

Timothy's guard went up. "That's not a good idea. We might need it."

"You've got that off road capable RV," Burke growled. "Don't be greedy."

"That doesn't belong to us. It belongs to Alex, Minnie, and Lauren. And I don't know that we're going to be sticking with them long term." Timothy licked his lips. He did *not* want the conversation to take a turn into an argument, but he also couldn't promise valuable resources. Then he had an idea. "Hey, I know a place that has a ton of great options for you to choose from as far as vehicles go. My parents' neighborhood in Wellesley. Most residents died pretty early on, and there's dozens of vehicles for the taking."

"A camper of our own would be great," Torres said. "You don't mind heading out there after we retrieve the duffel bag?"

Timothy shook his head, relieved at the positive note in Torres's voice. "Not at all. I'd be happy to take you out there."

"Let's focus on getting in and out of Russo territory first," Burke said. "And keep the chatting to a minimum. We're not friends, Peters."

"Life of the party, back there, isn't he?" Timothy rolled his shoulders. Burke's attitude wasn't helping his tension.

"He's really just shy," Torres said, throwing a wink to the back seat. "He loves people."

"Fine," Burke said, his glare focused on the rearview mirror where Timothy could see it. "You wanna chat? Wanna be friends? What are you really doing at Vanguard?"

"What?" Timothy cleared his throat, racking his brain for a quick response. "My father owned that block and all the buildings on it. We thought he might have left supplies there."

"That explains why you went there in the first place," Burke said, "but not why you're staying. You've got just as much reason to leave as we do."

"It's a self-sustaining building." Timothy tried to keep the nervousness from his voice. "We're not going to find that out in the countryside. And we're not country folk. We love Boston."

"Which is why you lived in Wellesley?" Burke narrowed his eyes.

"Heather and I lived in South Boston. My *parents* lived in Wellesley." Timothy gave Torres a pleading look, hoping the kinder man would show him a little mercy.

"All right, Burke," Torres said with a sigh. "You win. We'll all sit in silence and brood. But don't think you can get away with this when we're traveling with James. That kid will call your bluff and play twenty questions, no problem."

"That won't be an issue," Burke said, "because I *like* James."

Timothy didn't prod for any further conversation. He drove in silence, growing more wary and watchful the closer they got to the farmhouse.

"What do you think is the best approach," he asked, finally breaking the silence. "Should we walk in? Move more quietly?"

"No." Burke shook his head. "A quick grab and dash would be better."

"I agree," Torres said. "I'll hop out, retrieve the duffel from the drainage pipe, and then we need to hightail it out of there."

"What if we run into Russo's men before we get the bag?" Timothy asked, turning onto the country road that would lead to their destination.

"You drive," Burke said. "We'll shoot."

Timothy groaned. "Your Plan B is a high-speed chase?"
Burke scoffed. "Got a better idea?"
Timothy worked his jaw back and forth, trying to come up with something. "No, I guess I don't."
"You're the one who invited us out here," Torres said. "If you want to go back—"
"No," Timothy said. "You're right, Burke."
An intimidating suspicious glare from the back seat was all the reply Timothy got. He kept driving, eventually perking up at the sight of a few familiar landmarks.
"We're almost there," he said as the ditch on the right-hand side of the road started to run deeper. And then he saw it. The farmhouse, blown to bits. It looked like a monster had taken a bite out of one side. And there was a small graveyard where the front lawn used to be. "This is it," he said quietly, remembering those who had died there, especially Abrams, who had sacrificed herself to disarm Frank's bombs planted around the outside of the house.
"Be right back." Torres jumped out of the car and quickly descended into the ditch.
Timothy stared at the crosses marking the graves, a few of them painted blue. He wasn't all that surprised that Frank had ordered the bodies respectfully buried and marked. The mobster had a weird code of ethics for a criminal. He refused to harm children, for one. He kept his word, and he was always concerned about debts, both what he was owed and what he owed to others. And, apparently, he honored the dead.
"Incoming," Burke said, his tone urgent. He pointed ahead, and Timothy's blood ran cold at the sight of a truck coming their way.
Burke slid to the passenger side of the car and opened the door. "C'mon, Torres! We've got company."
As if on cue, Torres's head popped up, and he climbed out of the ditch, the duffel bag strapped crossbody. He threw it into the front seat next to Timothy as the truck came to a stop not far down the road. A man hopped down from the bed, a rifle in hand, dressed in khaki slacks and a button down, which was almost a uniform for Frank's men.
"What did you take from the ditch?" he shouted, leveling the weapon at them. "Whatever it is belongs to the Russos!"
Torres slid into the back seat with Burke. "Go, Tim," he said. "Turn around and *go*." He rolled down his window and pulled his own gun.
Timothy was already moving seconds before Torres managed to close the door behind him. He whipped the car around, tires squealing. As the car turned, Torres fired, hitting the man just as he fired his own shot. The mobster reeled back, the rifle shot blasting high. He toppled over and lay motionless on the ground.
Shouting erupted from the other men in the truck, but Timothy only glimpsed them as he finished his turn and sped off in the other direction. They left their man in the road and followed after him, gaining speed quickly. The next shot didn't miss. The bullet tore through the back window, leaving a hole, the glass spiderwebbing from it. Timothy cried out and swerved as the bullet thudded into the passenger seat headrest.
"Torres!" Burke shouted.
Timothy, eyes wide, caught Torres grimace in pain through the rearview mirror.
"It just grazed me," he said. "I'm okay."
"Bastards." Burke growled, leaned out his window, and fired several shots at the truck.
Torres barely lost any time as he, too, returned fire. Timothy didn't know whether to swerve to avoid getting hit or to stay straight so that Burke and Torres could aim better. His heartbeat pounded in his ears, and he flinched as another bullet completely shattered the back window. Torres and Burke began firing through it instead of out the side windows.
"Hold steady, Tim!" Torres shouted.
Relieved to have some instruction, Timothy sped down the bumpy country road in a straight line, though the potholes didn't make for a smooth ride. Heart racing, he could feel his pulse in the palms of his hands as he gripped the steering wheel tight enough for his knuckles to turn white.
All he could think about was leaving Heather, the last thing he ever did to her a betrayal. *Please, that can't be the end of us. She deserves better.*
The gas pedal was flush with the floor. The car couldn't go any faster. Cornfields blurred by on the sides of the road. They were fast approaching the end, where he'd need to turn. Slowing could mean their death as the truck would surely catch up to them, maybe run them off the road if they didn't manage to kill them with bullets first.
And then Torres let out a whoop, and Timothy glanced in the rearview just in time to see the truck behind them swerve and launch into a cornfield, hitting nose down, the back of the truck flipping upward, the truck landing upside down before skidding to a stop.
"Yes!" Timothy pounded the steering wheel, elated for only a moment before remembering he was about to run out of road. "Hold on!" he shouted, slamming on the brakes.
The car wasn't slowing fast enough. He had no choice but to turn sharply, and the back of the car drifted. They rotated once, twice, three times before coming to a halt. Timothy just sat there, eyes wide, sweaty hands frozen on the wheel, breathing heavily.
Torres had slammed into Burke during the rough turn, and the two had to untangle themselves from each other. Burke reached up and slapped Timothy's arm, jolting him out of his shock.
"Good driving, Peters," he said. "Maybe you're not so bad, after all." He punched Torres in his good shoulder. "You okay?"
Torres nodded. "It stings, and it's going to hurt for a while." He took off his t-shirt and a white undershirt, put the t-shirt back on, and ripped the undershirt into strips.
Burke immediately started helping without being asked, wrapping his friend's arm where the bullet had grazed him. "Peters, we should keep going."
"Yeah," Torres said. "I don't like driving around in this thing. We'll need to pick up more than one vehicle in Wellesley."
Timothy heard them, but the pounding of his heart was thrumming in his ears, competing for his attention. He worked on steadying his breath.

"Hey, Peters. Snap out of it." Burke hit the back of Timothy's seat, jostling him a little.

"Sorry." Timothy shook his head and loosened his grip on the steering wheel.

Wind whistled through the car as they made their way to his parents' old neighborhood in Wellesley. As he passed through the gates of the community, he prepared himself to see his childhood home again. Frank had burned it to the ground and stolen everything his father had left for his family in the basement bunker.

The house — and the streets surrounding it — had plenty of good memories, despite the bad ones that mostly involved Timothy's dealings with his father. The neighborhood reminded him of better times. Times when his only real worries had been akin to a test grade or navigating his father's aggressive expectations. He'd walked those streets with Heather. Played horseshoes with Lizzy in the backyard. Gone house to house trick-or-treating. Mowed neighbors' lawns for summer cash. It had been home for so much of his life that it was hard to come back there and be reminded of the death and destruction.

He frowned as he turned onto his parents' street and slowed. "Um… guys?"

"What's wrong?" Burke asked.

Timothy pointed to a van parked right out in front of the Peters' burnt and collapsed house. "I don't recognize that vehicle. Someone is here."

"You said the mob knows about this neighborhood?" Burke asked.

Timothy nodded. "They've attacked and scavenged the area before."

"Park on the side of the road here," Torres instructed. "Get one of the guns from the duffel. We don't know who we're up against."

He did as he was told, letting the two ex-cops take the lead as they approached the van. Torres and Burke approached the driver's side while Timothy came up on the passenger side. They all three opened the doors of the van to find it empty. He swept his gaze across his parents' property, not seeing anything of note.

Timothy looked back to talk to Burke, who was framed through the center doors of the van, both sides slid open. Torres rummaged through the front seats. Timothy was about to ask what they should do next when a figure emerged from the house opposite.

"Behind you!" Timothy yelled just as the figure — a young woman — raised her arm in the air and fired a shot. Another figure followed her outside as she started yelling.

"That's our van," she said. "Our supplies. Step back!"

Timothy ran around the van to join Torres and Burke, both of whom had their weapons trained on the two young women. But then Timothy froze. He couldn't believe his eyes.

"If you don't lower your weapon," Burke said, "we will shoot you both. We don't have time for games. And we don't know who you are."

"No!" Timothy turned on the safety of his gun and set it down. He held out his hands and carefully walked in front of Burke, standing between him and someone he thought he'd never see again.

The young woman recognized him, her eyes going wide. "Tim?" she whispered, as if she didn't believe it either.

"You know this guy?" the stranger spoke, hesitating and lowering her gun just slightly.

Timothy smiled, tears brimming his eyes, his words catching on pure, joyous emotion. "Hello, Lizzy."

Chapter 15

Zara Williams

Zara fumed. She still felt like she'd been run over by a truck — and then beaten with a bat — but Kai had added imprisonment to her troubles, and she wasn't happy about it. It was a clean prison, a hospital room, actually, but it was a prison, nonetheless.

"You can't stay mad forever," Kai said, leaning back in a gray recliner. The material was synthetic, something easily wiped clean, pulled taut over the minimal stiff cushions, and it made noises with his every movement.

"Can't I?" Zara asked sharply. The headache that had been nonstop since the crash had eased somewhat, but there was still pressure at her temples, a slight pulsing. They'd given her pain medication and something for nausea, and the rest had done her good. But she wasn't about to admit that to Kai.

Kai sat up abruptly at her reply. "You were sick. We had no supplies."

"We left Walter out there, Kai." Zara crossed her arms.

"Yeah, yeah." Kai waved her off. "He's important. Blah, blah, blah. You were about to explain why we should risk our lives to find a man who's probably already dead when you passed out." He pointed back at himself. "I had to decide whether to listen to the ravings of a concussed crazy woman or go into town and try to gather supplies so we can *both* live."

Zara pinched her lips together, angry that he had a point. She hadn't been able to explain to him her reasoning. And she *had* passed out. And they didn't have protection from the elements or food and water. And under normal circumstances, even she had to admit that searching for a man who fell from a plane into plague-infested wilderness wasn't the wisest of choices.

But these were not normal circumstances. She eyed Kai. How do I explain to him what's going on? Where do I start?

"I guess I could start from the beginning," she said.

"What?" Kai asked.

Zara snapped. "Do you want to hear what's really going on or not?"

"Fine. Weave your tale, princess." He scoffed. "You act like you and Walter are part of some grand scheme to fix everything. Well, news flash, babe. There's no fixing this." He waved his arms around randomly.

"Maybe not," Zara said, hoping he could see how serious she was. "But unless we find Mr. Peters and get him to Boston, we might never get to a place where we can start over. That's the closest we're ever going to get to 'fixing this'."

He still looked at her like she was crazy, but she explained anyway. She gave him a basic run down of everything she knew. There was no point in keeping any of it secret. She needed him to understand how important it was to find Walter. Kai listened, nonchalantly at first. But he steadily became more serious, and by the end of her recap, he was staring at her with his mouth slightly ajar, all signs of sarcasm vanished.

"You're serious?" he asked. "Like… really, really serious? Because none of that was funny."

"I'm telling you the truth," she said. "Everything I know. We can't tell anyone else, though, okay?" She leaned forward, emphasizing every word. "If we can get Walter back to Boston, he needs to work without interference. Mobs of desperate people seeking a cure wouldn't exactly make his work easier."

Kai sat back again, not saying anything for several minutes. Then he swallowed audibly, his brow furrowed. "What if Walter is actually dead? I mean… that's the most likely scenario, right?"

"I don't know," Zara said. "If that's the case, I'll probably go on to Boston alone. I mean, my cousin is still alive. Or at least, she was the last I heard. And maybe we can find people who can help? Maybe there are other scientists out there who would know what to do with the information and resources at New Horizons Laboratory." She shuddered at the possibility she'd have to figure out what to do without Mr. Peters. "But I don't want to leave here until I have proof that he's dead. Because he's our best shot. Everything else will just be grasping at straws."

"Whoa." Kai shook his head. "That's… insane." He raised his hands. "I mean, I believe you. I don't think *you're* insane. Just the situation. It's nuts."

"You understand why we can't tell everyone?" Zara asked.

Kai nodded, much to her relief. "Yeah. I get it. I won't say anything." He made the motion of zipping his lips and throwing away the key. "And you won't be alone, you know. I'm going with you to Boston."

Zara didn't know why — Kai was brash and cocky and annoying — but his offer made her feel better. "You're not going to figure out a new business? You seemed to really like ferrying people back and forth. And it was good work, Kai. Even if your hometown didn't see that. You were helping people."

Kai shrugged. "My plane is trashed. I could find another one. Might go ahead and do that one day. But this is bigger." He grinned. "Plus, I've always wanted to save the world. Like, years down the road, they'll be making movies about me. Maybe I'll even get a historic nickname." He spread out his hand in front of him as if seeing the name in lights, whispering dramatically. "The Eagle of the Apocalypse. Sky Captain Kai. The Dashing Aviator."

Zara broke into a fit of laughter, and she couldn't stop, Kai's mockingly offended expression making her laugh even harder. He eventually joined her, both of them wiping tears from their eyes as they tried to catch their breath. Zara's sides hurt and her head pounded from the mirth, but she didn't regret it.

A knock on the door brought her back to reality, though, and she straightened, ready to rush whoever it was so they could escape. They'd stuck her and Kai inside, posting a guard at the door while they "decided what to do with them." She didn't have time to wait for them to deliberate. But Kai seemed to know what she was thinking.

"I've got this," he said as he stood and readied himself. "If they want to keep us here, I'll tackle, you run."

"How about we work together?" Zara asked. "I'm not helpless. You and me can tackle together, run together, watch each other's backs."

Kai grinned at her. "You're kinda hot when you say stuff like that."

Zara rolled her eyes as she came to stand next to him. "Shut up, you idiot."

The door opened, and a young woman entered. She was tall and thin, not lanky exactly, more… wispy. Her blonde hair was poker straight, somehow well-kept and shiny despite the trying times. She held up her hands, clearly trying to look nonthreatening at the sight of Kai and Zara poised and tense. "You two can come out now," she said. "The mayor wants to speak with you."

Kai smoothed his shirt and sauntered forward. "Well, that was easy." He nodded to the woman. "Hey, babe. I'm Kai."

She flushed red and batted her eyes. "Willow," she said, holding out her hand.

Kai took it and *kissed* it. "Nice to meet you."

Zara wrinkled her nose and smacked him on the back of his head. "You just can't help yourself, can you?"

"Ouch!" He rubbed at the spot, but quickly recovered his smile for Willow. "She's a little cranky. You know, with the concussion and everything."

Willow smiled back, and Zara crossed her arms. A feeling of immense dislike for the woman washed over her, and then Zara recognized the reaction for what it was. *Oh. My. Goodness. I'm jealous? Over that moron?* She almost smacked herself. *The world really is ending.*

She shook off the feeling, burying it as a momentary lack in judgement, and stuck out her hand, too. "Zara."

Willow smiled sweetly. "I'm sorry we had to put you in here. We're a little cautious these days. Early on, we tried to help whoever came across our doorstep, but that didn't work out so well for us."

"Look, babe," Kai said, his disarming smile on full display. "If anyone understands that, it's me. You try to help people, you know? Do the right thing. And they just turn on you like a pack of rabid wolves."

"Yes," Willow said as if he had read her mind. "Exactly."

"Well, we're not like that," Zara said quickly. "We aren't going to take up much of your time, either. We just need—"

Willow held up a hand. "Oh, I'm not the one you need to talk to about that. The mayor is waiting to speak to you, though."

Zara sighed and gestured for Willow to lead the way. "After you."

Willow led them to the lobby where a woman in a pant suit waited, a box at her feet. The woman did not offer her hand.

"The mayor, I presume?" Kai said, bowing with a flourish of his hand.

"Um, yes," the mayor said, frowning at Kai. She seemed taken aback and annoyed as she continued, barely missing a beat. "I've put together a little care package that should get you to the next town," she said in a no-nonsense manner. "You can keep the truck and camper you took from the park. The family that owned it is dead. But we don't want to see you here again. Deal?"

At that moment, a woman and two kids, one a teenager, the other much younger, entered the lobby. The little girl skipped to the corner where a miniature set of a table and chairs was set up, seeming to know the place well.

The woman nodded at the mayor tersely. "Helen."

The mayor nodded back. "Carol. I hope things are going well for you up at The Log Cabin?"

"We're just here to get a few things," Carol said, her tone holding no love for Helen. She looked into the corner. "LeeAnn, stay there, okay? We'll be right back."

"Okay, Mom," the little girl said as she plucked a blank piece of paper from a pile and began coloring with the assortment of crayons.

As soon as Carol had moved on, her teenage son sparing them one curious glance before following after her, Helen looked back at Zara. "Do we have a deal? I don't want to see you milling around Holyoke."

"Actually, we can't go. Not yet." Zara rushed to explain before Helen could add words to the flash of anger behind her eyes. "We actually survived a plane crash, at the top of the mountain, and we're missing someone."

The little girl in the corner gasped and looked up, wide-eyed. Zara frowned but continued. She might have gasped, too, if someone had told it to her when she was that age. She ignored the way the girl watched her with rapt attention, focusing instead on the mayor.

"We have to look for him, and once we find him — dead or alive — we'll leave," Zara said. "We came into town for food and water, but also hoping to find something to protect us as we search the forest where we crashed."

The mayor pinched the bridge of her nose. "He's probably dead. You know that, right?"

"We survived," Zara said. "Who's to say he didn't, too?"

"We don't have any gear we can spare," Helen said. "We found a few beekeeper suits we've been using when we absolutely need them, but we've mostly been keeping close enough to shelter that we don't have to worry about it."

A bit of hope flared, and Zara spoke too eagerly. "If we could just borrow one of the suits—"

"I said we can't spare what we've got." The mayor gestured again to the box. "We can't spare any more food and water than this, either, so I suggest you not stay in town long."

"We *have* to look for him." Zara was practically begging, but she didn't care. She had nothing to bargain with except human compassion.

"Do you know where we could get beekeeper suits?" Kai asked.

Helen worked her jaw back and forth as if thinking about it. "I know of an apiary north of here. The people who owned it were in town for a demonstration; they died, the suits in their car. There should be half a dozen more suits at their place. They offered beekeeping classes and had this whole thing about harvesting your own honey. You basically paid them extra to do it yourself."

Kai scoffed. "What a rip off."

Zara frowned, more concerned about something else. "Why haven't you already retrieved those suits?"

"We tried a week ago, but our people never came back." She licked her lips and surveyed them for a minute. "If I tell you where they are, you have to bring them back here after you're done with them."

Kai nodded, clearly about to agree.

Zara cut him off. "You think there's something dangerous out there, or you'd have already sent someone else. If we risk our lives to get those suits, we're keeping at least three of them." She shrugged. "Two, if Walter didn't make it." She swallowed the immediate swell of emotion at saying those words out loud.

"Fine," Helen said. "But you'll bring the other suits back?"

"For another box of food and water? Yes." Zara held out her hand. "*Now* do we have a deal?"

"I guess we do," Helen said. "Just follow 91 North a few miles. You'll see billboards for the apiary. It's not too far."

Kai bowed again and picked up the box. "Thank you, Your Majesty, Mayor Helen, Ma'am."

Helen grimaced. "Don't ever call me that again."

Zara shook her head at Kai. Before she turned to leave, she couldn't help but notice the little girl was still watching her with wide eyes. She offered a little wave, but LeeAnn yelped and ran out of the room. Zara shrugged. Stranger danger was probably a good motto to live by these days.

Chapter 16

Theodore Finch

Theodore was certain he'd done the right thing. Secrets had never really been his forte. Timothy could be angry all he wanted, but Alex wouldn't let anything bad happen to Theodore. His new friend valued him, worked with him, asked him for opinions. It was *wonderful*. For the first time, Theodore was necessary.

He carried the caddy full of vials of Candice's blood with the utmost respect and care. In his hands, he held clues that would help Alex create a vaccine or a treatment, perhaps a cure. Candice's antibodies combined with the knowledge already contained about DV-10 in New Horizons' files would surely be enough.

When he entered the lab, Alex was hunched over one of the files Theodore had brought him earlier. "How is Candice?" he murmured without taking his eyes off the file.

"Oh, the blood draw went fine." Theodore set the vials down on the counter. "I'll stick these in the centrifuge," he said.

Alex glanced at Theodore. "I'm glad the draw went well, but I asked after Candice, not the work."

"Right." Theodore smiled and shook his head. He forgot how sentimental Alex could be. "She seems about the same. Worried for the girl, mostly. Her own injuries seem to be mending, though."

Alex nodded. "I think we should all be worried about Annika."

Theodore began sliding the sample tubes into the centrifuge. He didn't want the girl to die. He liked children. They were honest and good. But he couldn't drum up the same amount of concern for her as everyone else. He didn't know her. Her death would not affect their work. In fact, with one less mouth to feed, and one less child who needs so much attention, objectively they'd be better off. He'd never admit that out loud. No one would. But it was true.

"I'm sure Lauren will take good care of her," Theodore said, trying to say something socially acceptable.

"She's not equipped to handle anything more serious," Alex said. He shook his head. "I wish I could go out and look for a surgeon or qualified doctor myself."

Theodore snapped his eyes to Alex, holding his breath. *That would jeopardize our progress!*

"If this work wasn't so important, I would do it right now." Alex ran his fingers through his hair and sighed deeply.

Theodore just breathed out. *At least his priorities are straight.* He set the centrifuge to spin.

"Theodore, can you do me a favor?" Alex asked.

Theodore brightened. "Anything."

"I'd really like to figure out how to get into the cryopreservation pods." Alex stood and stretched. "You know more about this building than anyone. There's got to be information written down somewhere, in someone's office. I just keep thinking about it, and even if we are able to produce a vaccine, it's unlikely it will be one hundred percent effective for a person's lifetime. In fact, its effectiveness could run out in a year, maybe less. It's an excellent line of defense, but DV-10 will continue to wreak havoc until the mosquitos created to spread it are eliminated. Instead, these mosquitos are multiplying. We also don't know how many *other* species of mosquito can spread this disease, so I think it's time to take the leap."

Theodore frowned. "I'm not sure I know what you're talking about."

"New Horizons has the countermeasure mosquitos, and those should be our first priority in terms of release, but they've also developed modified mosquitos meant to eradicate other species, correct?"

"Yes, that was the cover for our research." Theodore nodded. "So… you want to get rid of *all* mosquitos?"

Alex nodded. "I've thought that route would be the best route since I first heard of the possibility many years ago."

"And what about the argument that it would upset the ecosystem?" Theodore asked.

Alex laughed, though there wasn't much amusement in the sound. "The ecosystem is already screwed. Plus, I've always been of the opinion that other insects would fill in the gaps without spreading so much disease."

Theodore licked his lips. He'd already searched Mr. Peters's office and Dr. Brown's, but he didn't want to disappoint Alex. "I'll comb over this building, top to bottom," he said. "Maybe I've missed something."

"Good man," Alex said. "I really appreciate it."

The praise did not fall on deaf ears. Theodore soaked it up. It was about time someone appreciated him.

"I'll go start looking now," he said, smiling wide. He left the lab and headed upstairs. He'd start in Dr. Brown's office first.

As he walked, he considered what it would take to release the countermeasure mosquitos. There were plenty of obstacles, but it was a good route. A necessary one, if they wanted to create an environment where humanity could rebuild again.

They'd need to find the codes to open the cryopreservation lab. Then, they'd need to find codes for each pod. And that was just the easy part. It would take two weeks to bring the eggs to adulthood. They couldn't release them just anywhere, either. They'd need to make sure they were released close to where a swarm frequented so they could infiltrate and begin to breed. Then, they'd have to wait. Genetic malformations would work their way through the population, and eventually, the mosquitos would die out.

It was a major undertaking, and it would have to be done all over the world. But the prospect filled Theodore with pride. He imagined centuries from the disaster, his name being in history books as part of the team that saved the world.

If only my colleagues could see me now. He scoffed at the memory of what the Senior Scientist on Project Pinpoint had said to him. *Who's the small fish in the big pond, now?* No one would ever know *her* name.

He whistled as he worked, searching every drawer, opening every journal to search every page. He hadn't thought to close the door.
"What're you doing?"
A child's innocent, curious voice made Theodore jump as he was checking under the desk for any hidden compartments. He hit his head on the desk, hard, and grunted, squeezing his eyes shut and trying very hard not to yell. There was a boy in the doorway, the only notable thing about him some sort of macrame purse he carried. There was a dog just about as big as him sniffing the floor at his feet. It was Alex's son, and the last thing Theodore wanted was to ruin things with his new friend.
"You're not supposed to be in here," he said between clenched teeth.
"My name is Oliver," the child said as his eyes roamed over Dr. Brown's hunting photos and memorabilia. "And this is Samson." He gestured lazily to the dog.
"Yes, I know," Theodore said. "Where is your... nanny?" He wasn't sure that was the right word, but he couldn't remember the woman's name.
Oliver wrinkled his nose. "I don't have a nanny. Minnie is my..." He paused and tapped his chin. "... my adopted grandma." The dog barked as if in agreement.
"You're adopted?" Theodore asked.
The child laughed. "No," he said. "I adopted *her*. To be my grandma. Weren't you listening?"
"Apparently not." Theodore sighed. "I'm trying to find something, so—"
"What's your name?" Oliver asked. "I told you mine. It's only fair."
"It's Theodore. Now—"
"That's a cool name. I like it." Oliver grinned. "It's classic. Like Theodore Roosevelt."
Theodore blinked. "Well, thank you."
"What are you looking for? I can help." Oliver puffed out his chest a little. "I'm a pretty good finder."
"I'm looking for a set of very important numbers. The man who used to have this office wrote down *everything*. He didn't have a good memory. But I can't find the journal or paper or... whatever he wrote these codes on." Theodore shook his head. "I doubt you'd be able to—"
"What about that?" Oliver pointed to one of the photographs, getting up close to the wall. He couldn't reach the one he was indicating.
"The picture of the dead ducks?" Theodore asked.
"No, the frame. If you look from my angle, it's fatter than the others, and there's a keyhole. Maybe it's a secret box." Oliver smiled and clapped his hands together.
"What?" Theodore hurried over to the wall and removed the photo frame, turning it over to find a locked compartment on the back, large enough to fit a thin journal. His eyebrows shot up and he laughed. "I can't believe you found this!" He practically skipped to the long, thin drawer at the center of the desk and opened it, retrieving a little key he had been curious about for weeks. He almost clapped himself when the lock clicked and the compartment opened to reveal a notebook. It was exactly what he'd been looking for. "The old man knew he wasn't supposed to be writing down important codes, but he did it anyway. Bless him."
He hugged the notebook to his chest, and then he looked down at Oliver. His smile faded. *If I'd had more time, I would've found it. Now I have to share the credit with a child?*
"Say, Oliver? What do you say we keep this between us? I... I really wanted to find the journal on my own, and you sort of stole the wind out of my sails, if you know what I mean."
Oliver thought about it for a moment. "So... you want everyone to think you found it?"
Theodore grimaced. It sounded petty, but he was just being honest. "Yes."
"Is that a real duck call on that shelf?" Oliver pointed over his shoulder.
Theodore frowned. "I think so."
The boy walked over, plucked it up, and blew in it, hard. An annoying sound came from the instrument, like a duck's quack but long and drawn out. Samson barked again, and Oliver laughed as he pulled it away from his mouth. "If I can keep this, I won't tell anyone I found that for you."
Theodore shrugged. "Sure," he said.
Oliver slipped the duck call into the purse at his side, waved goodbye, and left, the dog trotting along at his side.
"Well, that was easy." Theodore opened the notebook again and searched for the right codes. He found them, and his entire body filled with excitement. He rushed to give Alex the good news. While he was making the vaccine, Theodore would be carefully cultivating the mosquitos. The two of them made the *best* team.

Chapter 17

Walter Peters

Walter woke to an ear-piercing shriek. He blinked his eyes open as the pounding of feet on stairs was accompanied by a string of incomprehensible words. The floor was hard, every point of contact with his body a source of shooting pain. It took a few seconds for him to put together where he was – the landing between flights of stairs.

"Saul?" Carol dropped to her knees beside him. "What are you doing here? What happened?"

"Is he okay?" Heath asked, his voice unsteady.

Walter groaned as he turned his head to see Heath standing a few steps down, his brow furrowed. At the bottom of the stairs, little LeeAnn clutched her hands beneath her chin, bottom lip trembling, tears streaming down her cheeks.

"I don't know." Carol was panicking, her hands shaking as she cupped his cheeks in her hands and had him look back at her. "Saul, say something. Are you okay?"

"I am *not* Saul." Walter's frustration warred with his pain. He wanted to shout, but the words came out weakly.

Carol slapped him across the face, but it didn't seem like something she'd planned to do. It was more like she was trying to bat away his words. She immediately started sobbing. "I'm sorry, Saul," she said. "I'm so sorry." She kept repeating herself, crying hysterically, smoothing back his hair and begging him to forgive her.

It was LeeAnn's crying and Heath's helpless stare that made Walter give in. He had to make Carol stop, for their sake. He reached with limp hands to grasp Carol's, and she reverted to a whimper once he was holding them. "Carol, it's okay," he said. "I forgive you. I'm sorry about this. I thought I was getting better. I wanted to surprise you, but I got dizzy and fell. This is my fault."

Carol shook her head. "No, no, Saul. Oh, you poor thing." She smiled. "You've always been so ambitious." She looked up at Heath who was staring at them both with something like horror written in his features. "Heath, go get the stretcher. You need to help me get your father back to his bed."

Heath didn't move. "Mom," he said, swallowing audibly, his eyes glistening, but he didn't say anything else to her. He looked at Walter. "I'm sorry," he said.

Carol frowned and repeated her earlier command. "Heath, go get some towels and damp rags. This blood isn't going to clean itself. And my suture kit. Some antiseptic, too, and then I'll need your help getting him back upstairs. Just put on some cartoons for LeeAnn."

Heath hesitated, but then he retreated down the steps. At the bottom, he picked up LeeAnn and carried her away.

"Blood?" The word registered and Walter craned his neck to see a small pool of congealing, dark red on the floor at his side, and when he moved, the floor beneath him was a bit sticky.

"You reopened the wound," Carol said, examining him. "But don't worry. I'll clean you up and patch you up. Can you sit?"

Walter let her help him, and he leaned against the wall. The oversized landing was wide enough that he could remove himself from the drying blood. When Heath returned, Carol started cleaning his wound, and Heath began cleaning the mess Walter had created.

"Now that we've got the mess cleaned up, I'm going to need you to lie down," Carol said.

Walter complied, slowly lowering himself to lay flat on his back, his knees in the air, his toes to the wall. Carol held a towel to his wound as he moved. Her touch added nausea to his pain, and he had to deliberately keep from swatting her away. Whether he liked it or not, he needed her help.

"This is going to hurt," she said.

Carol opened her kit, and Walter closed his eyes, turning his head away from her and from what she was about to do. His wound was already a source of agony, but as the needle pierced skin and tugged torn flesh back together, Walter sucked in a breath and couldn't help but flinch.

"Hold still," Carol snapped. "This is your fault. This is better than the alternative. And remember, the kids will hear if you make too much noise."

Walter clenched his teeth as the next stitch set his skin ablaze, but he didn't let himself make a sound. Carol was right, and he couldn't get Heath and LeeAnn's reactions to finding him like that out of his mind. While the kids were his best bet at getting out of the situation, he didn't like frightening them.

"Where's the bandages?" Carol asked after restitching his side, searching the wicker basket Heath had used to bring up supplies.

"I don't know," Heath said. "I couldn't find them."

Carol closed her eyes, pinching the bridge of her nose. "I'll get them myself," she said, her tone more exhausted than harsh.

The second she was turning the corner at the bottom of the stairs, Heath came close to Walter, whispering. "I'm sorry," he said. "But… you have to stay in the bedroom until you're better, okay? My mom and LeeAnn can't handle finding you dead."

Walter met the teenage boy's eyes and tried to get his point across. "I *have* to go looking for Zara and Kai. If you don't want me doing it, maybe you should because—"

"They're alive," Heath said. "They were at the hospital when we stopped by to get supplies."

"Do not lie to me," Walter growled.

The small pitter-patter of footsteps made Walter go stiff until he saw it was just LeeAnn hurrying up the steps.

"Go back downstairs." Heath waved her off.

LeeAnn stuck out her tongue at her brother and turned to Walter. "It's true. Heath isn't lying."
Walter sat up straighter out of excitement, but then winced at the pain of doing so. He eased back against the wall. "How do you know it was them? Did you tell them I was here?"
Heath averted his eyes. "No," he said. "I was with my mom the whole time. I only realized who they were after I heard the mayor talking about them surviving a plane crash. They were gone by the time we were leaving."
LeeAnn lowered her voice and tip-toed nearer. "I drew a picture," she said, whispering. "It was of you in bed, and I put your name on it."
Heath's eyes widened. "Did you give it to anyone?"
LeeAnn shook her head. "No… I promised Mom I wouldn't say anything about you." Her cheeks flushed and chewed on her lower lip. "Drawing isn't *saying* anything, right?"
Heath sighed, but Walter smiled and reached out to pat LeeAnn on the back. "No, LeeAnn. That was exactly the right thing to do. Thank you," he said. "That was very clever."
She looked up at him, brightening. "Really?"
Walter nodded reassuringly and then turned back to Heath. "Were Zara and Kai okay?"
"They seemed fine to me," Heath said. "Bumps and bruises. I think Zara was worse off. She looked paler. Willow said she had a concussion."
"Where are they staying?" Walter nodded. "I need to get word to them."
"I don't know much, just that they're going to go out to the honey farm to get some beekeeper suits so they can search for you." Heath was about to say something else when Carol appeared at the bottom of the steps.
"LeeAnn, please, honey. Go watch your cartoons." Carol shooed the little girl off, and immediately started bandaging the newly restitched wound.
Walter longed to ask Heath more questions as the boy and his mother helped him up the stairs and put him back in bed. He lay down, defeated and grateful for the mattress at the same time. He tried desperately to think of an excuse to keep Heath in the room, but Carol was too quick, too insistent on his rest.
"You've got to be in more pain after that fall," she said, her back to him as she began preparing a syringe with the medicine she'd drugged him with a few times already.
"I really don't need that." Walter shook his head. "Carol, I don't want it."
"You're not making the best decisions, Saul." Carol turned, the syringe ready in one hand, a sad smile on her lips. "Were you really trying to surprise me?" she asked.
Walter cleared his throat. "Of course." A nervous energy built in his chest with her every step as she neared.
"Maybe," she conceded. "But part of me is worried you were trying to abandon us. Maybe to get back at me for threatening to leave you."
"What? I would never do that." Walter tried to remain calm.
"I think," Carol said thoughtfully as she stopped just beside the bed, "we're going to need to rebuild trust. I've done so much to prove my loyalty to you, to prove how much I love you, to apologize for what I said before the sickness hit."
She jabbed the needle into his arm too quickly for him to do much about it besides flinch. He wasn't about to hurt her, and he was in too much pain; his reflexes were slow. Walter's heartbeat, pounding wildly, picked up pace.
Carol continued. "It's time for you to do your part, Saul. When I said I was leaving, I told you why. I needed more from you. I needed you to care about me as much as you care about the kids. I needed attention and honesty." She kissed his forehead as the drug began taking effect, his heartbeat slowing and his body feeling light. "Until I'm convinced you can do that, I'm going to have to keep a much, *much* closer eye on you."
Walter's eyes drooped. He didn't fall asleep right away, rather he succumbed to the out-of-body feeling. The pain relief was wonderful. And as Carol settled into a chair against the wall, opening a book, making herself comfortable, Walter had an inkling that her presence was bad, that he should be coming up with a plan, but then as exhaustion began to win out, her form morphed as his vision blurred, and suddenly, it was Dana watching over him instead. He smiled as he fell asleep, comforted.

Chapter 18

Zara Williams

Zara sat up front with Kai this time as they traveled north on the major highway. It was between small towns, and the stretch was mostly clear. Her head still swam if she turned it too quickly, and she had zero appetite despite not eating for almost two days. She did sip on a bottle of water, though she had to do it slowly or else risk nausea.

Kai turned off at the exit for the apiary; the mayor had been right. There were billboards and signs everywhere pointing to the place.

"Are you nervous?" he asked.

Zara looked sideways at Kai. "You mean because those people didn't come back?" She shook her head. "No. I bet they just decided to go do their own thing. Helen didn't seem the kind of woman to bend. I don't know if I'd want to stay at that hospital, just waiting for supplies to run out, depending on someone else to decide my fate."

"Yeah, or they ran into bad people. Or a swarm. And they're dead." Kai turned again, following a big, yellow arrow with the words "Honey Farm" on it.

"I guess I wouldn't be surprised," Zara said. "Let's just get these suits and get out of here as quickly as we can. I want to search for Walter before the end of the day. If we've got the suits—"

"Wait," Kai said. "You want to… what? Spend the night out there?"

Zara nodded. "Why not?"

"There's more than just the swarms we have to worry about," he said. "That mountain is bound to have big cats and bears and coyotes and—"

"I get it." Zara cut him off, crossing her arms. "People go camping all the time where there are wild animals. I mean, come on. It can't be that bad."

"I've heard stories that say otherwise," Kai said. "Some animals die from the swarms, from the sickness. Some of them go crazy. I guess not all animals go one way or the other, but this sickness seems to play Russian roulette with animals. It just doesn't affect them the same way as it does humans."

"Fine. So a crazy bear doesn't sound like my idea of a nice camping trip. Still, we have a camper. We have the suits. We can at least drive the camper deeper into the forest and search from there, and with the suits, we don't have to worry as much about the hours we're out, right?"

Kai shifted, clearly uncomfortable. "Sure. I guess."

"Good." Zara nodded, satisfied. Kai was a lot easier to get along with when he just did what she wanted.

It wasn't long before Kai was pulling the truck and camper beneath an ironwork archway and into the Honey Farm. It was a rustic and charming place. A large, old home with a wraparound porch stood on a hill in the near distance, and a shop made to look like a barn sat closer to where visitors entered. A paved pathway curved away from a gravel parking lot in front of the barn and led into a lush flower garden.

There was one car in the lot, parked directly in front of the shop. Kai pulled around in the truck, pointing it toward the exit instead of parking. "I'd rather not have to back up with the camper attached if we have to leave in a rush," he said.

"Fine with me." Zara opened the door, ears perked as she listened for any unusual noises. The gravel crunched under her feet as she surveyed the area. "You think that car belonged to whoever the mayor sent out here?"

"Maybe." Kai walked over to the car, peering inside. He pulled away and shrugged. "It's empty."

Zara pointed to a sign in the window that read: Beekeeper Classes, Saturdays at 2:00. "I bet the suits are in there somewhere."

"I have a bad feeling, Zara. Let's get this over with." Kai walked over to the glass door and tested it; the door opened easily, but he immediately reared backward. "It really smells in there."

Zara approached the door and wrinkled her nose. The air was hot and rancid. "That's disgusting." She pulled her shirt over her nose. "But we need those suits. Just… try not to breathe." She walked into the space beyond. It was dimly lit by the sunlight streaming in through the windows. All sorts of beeswax and honey products were neatly displayed on shelves throughout the store. A slight breeze stirred the putrid air, and Zara, eyes watering, looked up. "Look." She pointed to several broken windows. Some merely had holes as if someone had thrown rocks at them; others had entire panes missing. "This isn't a safe space." A tingle up her spine made her shudder.

Kai stopped short under an open doorway. He backed away, face pale. "I found the people who came here from town, I think."

Zara hurried over and peered inside. Two men were lying at odd angles on the floor, each one halfway dressed in a beekeeper suit. Glassy eyes bulged from their skulls, and their skin looked ready to pop from a build up of fluid. They were covered in ugly welts. Swallowing bile, Zara stepped into the room. "It looks like they were attacked here."

"Like they were trying to suit up to escape." Kai glanced up toward the broken window. "We need to get out of here."

Zara stepped gingerly around the corpses, hugging the wall to avoid them the best she could. She had her eye on a set of lockers at the other end, two of which hung open, empty. "I bet the suits are in those."

Kai stood still in the doorway, frozen, still looking up toward the broken window in the shop. "Zara…"

She was right. Six lockers held one suit each, including thick workers gloves and bulbous, structured hoods complete with hat-like inserts and mesh veils. She glanced back at Kai. "We need a trash bag or something to put these in."

It seemed to take Kai a moment to register her statement, but when he did, he nodded and tore his gaze from the shop's broken window. "I'll see what I can find."

Zara took suit after suit and folded them up on a nearby bench, stacking the gloves on top and then creating a new pile for the hoods. Kai returned with black trash bags tucked under his arm, face paling as he stepped around the bodies and handed one to Zara. She stuffed the suits into two of them and handed one to Kai.

"Let's get out of here," she said.

Kai didn't have to be told twice. They exited the changing room, but when they entered the shop, Kai stopped. Zara ran into him.

"What the—"

"Quiet." Kai whispered. "Do you hear that?"

Zara frowned. It took her a second, but then a sound that curdled her stomach rose from somewhere outside. It was the lethal hum of a swarm.

"Run!" Zara gave Kai a push, and he stumbled forward, recovering and looking nervously at the door. "What are you doing? Go!"

"What if they're out front?" he asked.

As if answering his question, the buzzing sound got louder behind them. Zara looked over her shoulder. Black, writhing clouds seeped through the holes in the windows, and as if reaching with tentacles outstretched, the swarm oozed toward them.

"Kai, go!" She didn't have to urge him.

He sprinted toward the glass doors, his gait uneven as he fished through his pocket with one hand and held on to the trash bag with his other. Zara looked over her shoulder, adrenaline flooding her system at the sight of the swarm. She was gripping her own trash bag so tightly that her nails bit into the cheap plastic. The weight of the suits stretched the bag too low. Frantic and not wanting to slow, she tried to gather the ripping bag. Instead, she tripped over it, still running full speed, and collided with Kai, sending them both crashing through the glass door.

She skidded across concrete, tangling with Kai, pebbles of glass embedding into her skin. Kai gained his feet faster than she did, and he yanked her up, pressing the keys into her palm.

"I'll get the bags." He slung one over his shoulder and wrapped his other arm around the broken bag. "You get the car door."

Zara nodded, whipping around to face the truck, unlocking it using the key fob. The world spun. Her stomach lurched. *Not now.* Zara groaned as it seemed the ground itself tilted. She stumbled forward even as Kai passed her. The keys slipped from her hand, clinking against gravel. The pounding in her head that never really went away reasserted itself, a dominant beat as the buzz of the swarm competed for her attention.

Her knees buckled, and the sky rotated. She toppled and rolled to a stop facing the shop. In the midst of her vertigo, she could make out the monster creeping closer, the swarm of death opening its maw, hungry for a taste of *her*.

And then two arms scooped her up, and her head lolled against Kai's chest. He grunted as he took her the last few steps to the open truck door, and he tossed her inside the back seat. Kai scrambled in after her, slamming the door shut behind him.

Breathing heavily, Kai maneuvered in the space between the front and back seat so that he was leaning over her. "Did they get you?" He frantically lifted her arms, checked the back of her neck, examined the exposed skin on her legs.

Zara closed her eyes against the swirling world, against the thrashing inside her skull and the feeling that her throbbing veins were attempting to break past her skin. The sound of rain hitting the window made her frown. She opened her eyes; the window was dark and writhing.

"They're trying to get in," Kai said. "Where are the keys?" He grasped at one of her hands and then the other.

Her wits were slowly returning, but as they did, her nausea increased tenfold. "Kai… I dropped them."

He groaned and sat on the console between the two front seats. "Then we're stuck here until they either go away or find a way inside."

* * *

When the buzzing sound of the swarm distanced itself, Zara noticed not because she'd been watching the window but because their hum had so ingrained itself into her head. She sat up, the world only rocking a smidge.

"Kai." She leaned forward. "They're gone."

He was already sitting poker straight, one hand on the door handle. "I know. I'm waiting until they're further away. The bags are just outside the truck. The keys are a few more steps away. I'm going to go fast, okay? The second I open this door, I need you to open yours and grab the bags. Think you can do that?"

Zara scooted over to the window and looked down. One of them was close enough she could probably grab it just by leaning out of the truck. The other was beside it, a few inches away. "Yes. I can do it."

"You sure? I don't want you to collapse again."

Zara took a moment to gauge herself. "Yeah. I think… I think the fall through the glass messed me up. Scrambled my brains a little more than they already were."

Kai looked back at her, a slight smile working its way through his obvious exhaustion. "Is that your official diagnosis, Dr. Williams?"

She returned the smile, though she didn't have the energy to laugh. "I'm ready when you are," she said instead, putting her hand on the door.

Kai nodded and then he was darting outside. Zara opened the door, stepped down as quickly as she could, and threw the two bags into the back seat. She climbed in after them, her stomach flip-flopping and bile rising in her throat. It was only a moment later when Kai jumped back into the car, visibly relaxing for the first time since they'd gotten trapped. He started the car and hit the gas, clearly as eager as she was to get out of there. By the time they drove back to the empty lot at the edge of the park where they'd first found the truck and camper, it was getting late.

Kai hopped out and opened Zara's door. "Let's get in the camper," he said.

"Okay." Zara slid weakly out of the cab of the truck. "I'll change into a suit and then—"

"Are you kidding me?" Kai shouted.

Zara's eyes went wide. "Kai, we have to—"
"I will go looking for him tomorrow, Zara. Get in the camper. Lay down. Rest." He took her by the arm and led her toward the camper's door.
"You're not my boss." Zara yanked her arm away, the sudden motion forcing her to lean against the side of the camper for support.
Kai looked at her incredulously. "You can't even walk straight." His voice was still a few octaves too high for her liking. "I almost died out there. You almost died. Again. We almost died *again*. Doesn't that mean anything to you? You have a concussion. It's not a bump on the head, Zara. If you don't rest, it will get worse. But noooooo," he drew out the word, his expression crazed. He threw up his arms and paced in front of her. "Zara, Queen of Stubbornville, doesn't want to rest." He laughed. "Oh, no. That would be practical. That would take time. That wouldn't put her life at risk, and hey—" He flashed her a grin and swung his arm in front of him with his thumb up "—it's not a good day unless she almost dies a hundred times."
Anger boiled inside and spilled over. "You have no right to talk to me like that. You're the one that crashed the plane. We're here because of you."
"You and Walter basically commandeered my plane!" Kai shouted.
"We saved your life!" Zara wobbled a little as she stood straighter.
"Well, I guess we're even because I saved your life after the lake *and* out at that farm." Kai stuck out his chin. "And the plane crash wasn't my fault. The plane broke."
"Because you didn't know what you were doing." She seethed. "And you don't know what you're doing now."
"Maybe not," he said, "but neither do you."
Zara pressed her lips together and stepped toward the door to the camper. "I'm putting on a suit and I'm going to look for Walter." She grasped the handle and pulled open the door.
"No, you're not." Kai put a hand on the door and slammed it shut, leaning against it.
She pulled weakly on it, but it was of no use. He was too strong. "Let me in!"
He jutted a finger in her face. "You're going to go back to sleep. And you're going to rest tomorrow." He pointed back at himself. "I'll go out and look for him. This isn't up for debate."
"I don't need you," Zara spat. "If I want to go out tomorrow, I will. What's it to you, Kai? Why do you even care?"
His entire face turned red. "Because I care about you, Zara!" he shouted. "I *like* you. A lot. And yes, you're strong and independent and wonderful, but you're not invincible. I think we learned that today at the farm, don't you?"
A retort rose to Zara's lips faster than she could process what he was saying, but then she shut her mouth, her anger replaced with shock.
"If you'll let me, I will go out and look for Mr. Peters. If he survived last night, he's likely to survive tonight. Or maybe he's somewhere else. Or maybe he's gone. Whatever the case, I will go out there and search every inch of the plane crash for you if you will just listen to me and rest."
Zara blinked. Did he say he cares about me? That I'm... wonderful?
She spoke more softly. "Kai—"
"No!" He was still riled up, still ranting. "Let me finish. Do you really want to survive everything you've gone through just to die because you wouldn't take a few days off? I swear to you, I will find him. I just can't..." He trailed off, his eyes glistening as his voice caught. "I can't..." He stopped again and let out a frustrated sigh.
"Lose anyone else?" Zara asked gently.
"Yeah." Kai nodded. He worked his jaw back and forth, letting the silence linger. "I'm sorry I yelled."
Zara let out a long breath. "I'm sorry, too. You're... right." She nearly choked on that last word. "I'm in no shape to go out searching. At least not tomorrow. Probably." He raised an eyebrow, and she clarified. "I was being stubborn, but I *do* know my own body. I was going to push, just like I pushed all day today, but that did almost get us both killed. I won't do it again. I promise."
"Yeah, okay." Kai nodded. "You're right, too. I don't have the right to force you to do anything."
Zara smiled just a little. "You'd go out and search for me?"
Kai shrugged. "I need the exercise."
"And I'm... what was it that you said? Wonderful?" Her smile widened.
He smiled back a little sheepishly. "Slip of the tongue."
"Right." Zara stepped up into the camper. "Well, just in case you meant it, you're not so bad yourself." She paused and then feigned a moment of consideration before adding, "Sometimes."

Chapter 19

Timothy Peters

Timothy was horrified. Lizzy had said only a few words since uttering his name when they'd first met, but Azalea had filled him in on everything she knew. The two of them had been captured separately but sold to the same human traffickers, amateurs taking advantage of the situation, by the sounds of it. Azalea claimed to have broken them both out before they could be sold off to the highest bidder.
The three of them sat around the dining room table of the house across the street from what was left of the Peters home. Burke and Torres had gone to search out two vehicles in the wealthy Wellesley neighborhood, targeting the homes with campers.
After the initial shock of seeing Lizzy, Timothy had tried to wrap her in a hug, but she'd shied away from him, apologizing while she cowered. It had broken his heart. It seemed after losing their father and Zara, after being captured, she'd broken. Only Azalea seemed to be able to calm her nerves.
"So then, once you were safe, Lizzy told you how to get here?" Timothy asked. He glanced at his sister. She sat very close to Azalea, a shadow of the girl he knew.
"Sort of," Azalea said. "She wrote it down. Like I said, she doesn't talk much. She's spoken more today with you than she has since we first met."
Timothy nodded and gently addressed Lizzy. "But Dad and Zara were alive the last time you saw them?"
Lizzy flinched but nodded. She pulled out a paper and wrote something down, passing it to Azalea. She read it out loud. "Lizzy says she doesn't know if they are dead or alive. She thought they might be here."
Timothy sighed and shook his head. "No sign of them here or in the city at the Vanguard buildings. I think when Dad finds his way back, he'll check the house and then those properties."
Again, Lizzy wrote a message. This one seemed to be a few lines long, but when Azalea read it off, her question was short. "How is everyone?" Azalea closed the notebook and handed it to Lizzy, her action seeming to suggest Lizzy put the pad of paper and pen away.
Timothy frowned initially, not liking how deferential Lizzy was being, but then the question hit home. His stomach curdled. *Lizzy doesn't know about Mom.*
He took a deep breath. "Well… Heather and George are okay. Annika is injured, but we're trying to take care of her." He hesitated. From the way Lizzy was behaving, he wasn't sure she could handle the news about their mother.
"Mom?" Lizzy's voice was barely above a whisper. Her eyes flitted to Azalea momentarily, and the young woman reached out and put a hand on her shoulder.
He couldn't avoid it now. "Mom… she…" Timothy steadied himself. It still hurt to say it. "She's gone, Lizzy. I'm so sorry."
Lizzy's eye twitched and her hands made tight fists on the table. And then she gave the table one, hard pounding with both as she barred her teeth. It startled Timothy, but what she said next startled him even more. "It's *his* fault."
"Look," Timothy said, "I blame myself, too. I should have taken better care of her, but—"
"No," Lizzy seethed. "Not you." Her eyes flashed with a murderous anger that made Timothy shudder.
Azalea wrapped an arm around Lizzy and made her sit back in her chair. She leaned over and whispered in Lizzy's ear. Again, Timothy frowned. He'd expected tears or denial or questions, not an outburst of anger.
"Then, who are you talking about?" Timothy asked gently.
Lizzy calmed at Azalea's whispers, but she didn't answer. Azalea shushed her, brushing stray hair from Lizzy's face. The stranger's motherly disposition toward Lizzy was odd, but if it hadn't been for her, Timothy wasn't sure Lizzy would have survived. So, he tucked away an uneasy gut feeling.
I've been jaded by these last weeks, he thought. They've just been through a lot together. Lizzy's broken. She needed someone to act as the glue. She'll get back to herself eventually, now that she's home.
"I think she means your father," Azalea said. "She wrote out some wild story of him being responsible for what's happened. The disease, the mosquitos. All of it. I think it's pretty clear she's had a mental break."
Timothy blinked. "You know?" he asked, leaning toward Lizzy. "Dad told you?"
Lizzy stared at him wide-eyed for a moment, but her shocked expression morphed into something more like snarl. "How long have you known?"
Timothy swallowed hard. He'd never seen Lizzy so… crazed. "I only found out a few days ago. I learned it from the one remaining scientist at New Horizons Laboratory in the city."
Azalea raised her eyebrows. "So, it's true, then?" she asked.
"Yes," Timothy said. "I can explain it more later." It did seem Azalea would be staying with them long term. And they owed her for bringing Lizzy back to them. "But we're not shouting it from the rooftops," he said, looking over his shoulder at the front door to the house. "The two people with me don't know, and I need to keep it that way."
Azalea nodded, but Timothy only barely registered it. He couldn't take his eyes off his sister. Lizzy was trembling. She ripped out her notebook and began to scribble furiously. Her jaw was clenched, her knuckles white as they gripped the pen. Horror washed over Timothy at the sight of his sister like that. She was unhinged.
"Azalea," he said slowly, "what is she writing?"

Azalea was leaning over Lizzy's shoulder, reading as Lizzy's pen flew over the pages. Finally, Azalea reached out and put a hand on Lizzy's, making her stop the frenzied writing. "That's enough," Azalea said calmly. She took the notebook and, one by one, tore out the pages and stuck them in her own pocket, speaking to Timothy as she did. "Lizzy needs rest. I think it would be best to get her to this lab where you're staying."

"What did she write?" Timothy repeated.

Azalea smiled sadly and shook her head. "It's all gibberish. Don't worry about it."

That didn't sit right with Timothy. "She's *my* sister," he said. "I want to see the notes." He held out his hand.

"She's practically an adult," Azalea said, "and she deserves some privacy. These ravings don't make sense. It's mostly illegible. And it wasn't written to you."

Timothy blinked. *Well, isn't she brazen?* "Look, Azalea, I'm grateful to you for taking care of her, but she's my responsibility now. You need to understand that if you're coming with us. We can just as easily leave you h—"

"No!" Lizzy shouted. "I stay with her."

Timothy stared at her for a moment. "Lizzy, she's not your family."

"Yes. She. Is." Lizzy's glare challenged Timothy to say otherwise.

But it wasn't the time. Lizzy had attached to Azalea, and it seemed clear: pushing away Azalea would be pushing away his sister. He held up his hands in surrender. *My first priority has to be getting Lizzy back to the lab, getting her to safety.*

"Fine. I'm sorry. We won't leave you here," he said. "I shouldn't have said that. I just… I don't know you. And Lizzy clearly needs help."

"I agree," Azalea said. "We both want what's best for her. I care about her a lot, Timothy."

"Okay, then I guess we have the same goals." He stood up. "A good night's rest in a safe space will do you both wonders. Just remember to keep quiet around Torres and Burke. They're going to be leaving town for good in the next day or two, so you shouldn't have to worry about it for long."

"I can do that," Azalea said.

It wasn't long before Burke and Torres returned. They rolled up with an SUV and a camper, and Burke handed the SUV over to Timothy.

"We loaded the vehicles with some supplies we found in a few houses on the edges of the neighborhood, ones that weren't as picked over," Burke said. "The duffel is in the back of the SUV. We can split the weapons and meds when we get back to the city." He eyed Azalea who sat beside Lizzy on the front steps of the house. "You think we can trust that one?"

"I don't know," Timothy said honestly. "But I can't imagine she'd cause too much trouble."

Burke grunted. "It's not my business, but I don't like her. Your sister is too dependent on her, and she's eating it up. Isn't normal."

Timothy shook his head. "You're right. It's not your business. Azalea and Lizzy have been through a lot together. Until today, Lizzy thought she may have lost everyone she's ever known. I think she just needs some time in an environment where she can rely on more than just one person."

"That explains your sister," Burke said, raising an eyebrow.

"I barely know Azalea," Timothy said. "But I'm capable of keeping my eye on her. Don't worry about it, Burke." He offered a smile. "It's nice to know you care, though."

Burke scoffed before heading toward the camper. "We'll lead the way," he said over his shoulder.

"Fine with me," Timothy called back.

He hurried back inside, thinking of his father and Zara. They'd been alive the last time Lizzy had seen them. It was possible they were still on their way. Just in case, he took a page out of Frank's book, grabbing paper and a baggie from the neighbor's house, along with a nail he ripped out of the wall and a hammer from the garage. He scribbled a note, stuck it in the bag, and nailed it to the tree in the front yard.

By the time he climbed into the SUV, Lizzy and Azalea were already in the back seat. When Timothy glanced at them through the rearview mirror, Burke's misgivings about the girls repeated in his head. They put words to some of what he had been feeling, confirmed that something wasn't quite right. There was hardly anything he could do about it, though. He couldn't even put his finger on exactly *why* Azalea made him wary, besides a few actions that could easily be put down to not trusting a complete stranger. He sighed, stepping on the gas to follow Burke and Torres back to the city, hoping time would prove him wrong.

Chapter 20

Heather Peters

Heather was exhausted as she and Murphy trekked the last leg of their journey. She'd not been able to get the knowledge of New Horizons Laboratory's precarious location out of her mind since she'd learned of it. Their mission had gone to plan. They had one of Candice's suitcases full of hazmat suits and knew where a doctor was located should Annika need one. But still, it felt like she was returning with bad news.

When the fighting starts the day after tomorrow, we're going to be in the crosshairs. They had one more day to gather as many supplies as they could before stepping outside would draw unwanted attention to what they were doing there, not to mention the added danger.

All of that fled her mind when she and Murphy delivered the suits to the Vanguard building across the lot from the lab. She stopped short, the suitcase she'd been rolling behind her falling flat. Beyond the glass of the conference room sat a ghost.

"Hey!" Murphy lost her balance as she avoided colliding with Heather, stumbling a few steps before righting herself. "What's the matter with you!"

Her shout caused the figure in the conference room to turn her head, and Heather gasped. She wasn't hallucinating. Timothy appeared around a corner, water bottles and bags of chips in hand. She met his eyes.

"Tim, I'm seeing this right?" she asked, her breathing quickening.

"It's her," Timothy said with a small smile. "She was at the house in Wellesley."

Heather looked back, and Lizzy had moved to the doorway. She took a few quick steps forward, laughing. "Lizzy! I'm so happy to—" She stumbled to a stop as she noted Lizzy's sudden stiffening. Lizzy shrank back and another young woman Heather noticed for the first time came up behind her. Heather threw Timothy a confused look.

"She's been through a lot," Timothy said. "Go slow. She's not big on physical contact right now. I got one hug, but… that was it."

Heather nodded, a lump forming in her throat. *Poor thing.* She glanced at Lizzy and lowered her voice. "And your dad? Zara?"

Timothy's smile faded and he shook his head. "They were separated. Just… don't ask her too many questions. It's hard for her to talk about it. I'll fill you in after I get her settled."

Heather nodded and reached for the water bottles. "Let me help." Their dispute would have to wait. Making Lizzy comfortable was all that mattered at the moment. Her eyes widened at a sudden thought. "What about George? Someone should tell him."

Timothy shrugged. "I delivered a message to O'Donnell via the walkie talkie he gave us, but George wasn't there. He'd gone out with a team to help clear what the captain called 'the red-hot zone.'" He sighed. "That's an entirely different conversation."

A bit of relief washed over Heather. She didn't have to be the bearer of bad news; they already knew. "I actually heard from someone at City Hall."

Behind her, Murphy cleared her throat. Heather turned, her cheeks reddening as she realized she'd completely forgotten about Murphy. The ex-cop had the suitcase in hand.

"I'll put these in storage," she said. "We can go out and scour the hospital tomorrow before things get hairy here."

"Yeah, thanks," Heather said. "Are you sure you guys want to stay that long?"

Murphy furrowed her brow, her body tensing. "I don't know that we have a choice. We don't have a vehicle."

"We actually brought back a camper for your crew to take," Timothy said. "You can load up and get out of here before the fighting starts."

Tension left Murphy's body, her muscles visibly relaxing. "That's a relief. Thank you."

Timothy shook his head. "If we hadn't gone out to find the camper, I wouldn't have found Lizzy and Azalea."

Heather took note of the name. If Timothy brought her back with Lizzy, he probably planned for her to stay a while. "I'll see you in a bit," Heather said.

Murphy nodded and took the suitcase, leaving Heather and Timothy to turn back to Lizzy who still watched them from the doorway. Her friend, Azalea, was watching, too; Heather thought she saw a flash of overt interest in the stranger's expression when she turned to look her way, but it quickly vanished. If she'd been eavesdropping, though, Heather couldn't blame her. She'd do the same if she'd been dropped into the middle of a large group of strangers.

Heather followed Timothy over to the conference room, handing the bottle of water to Lizzy, her eyes welling with tears. "I'm so glad you're here," she said.

Azalea put a hand on Lizzy's back, and the two met eyes for a moment. Lizzy turned and offered a small smile, stepping forward and wrapping her arms around Heather's middle. "Me too," she said softly.

Heather was more than happy to accept the embrace, hugging Lizzy close but loosely enough that her sister-in-law could easily pull back when she was ready. She had to force herself to keep her hands to herself, not brushing away the hair from Lizzy's forehead or reaching for her hand; if Lizzy was traumatized, if touch was hard for her, Heather wanted to ensure she let Lizzy set all the boundaries. But it was hard; the brief hug had been confirmation that what she was seeing was real, that someone she loved and thought lost was back.

"Timothy's going to fill me in later," Heather said. "You can tell me whatever you want, but it's okay if you don't want to explain what you've been through again."

Lizzy chewed on her lower lip, averting her eyes. It was Azalea who answered, though. "That's thoughtful," she said. "Thanks. I think we're just going to eat and then get some rest."

Heather nodded, but a thought occurred to her. "Have you seen Lauren? She's got some medical training. It might be a good idea to have her look you both over."

"That won't be necessary," Azalea said, her tone sweet but firm, as if she had the authority to speak for both of them.

Heather frowned. "Well, if *you* don't want to take advantage of our resources, Azalea, that's fine, but I think Lizzy—"

Lizzy shook her head and stepped closer to Azalea. "I need rest," she said.

Heather blinked but didn't say anything more. "Okay," she said, nodding. "If that's what you want. But if you change your mind, just let me know."

"She won't," Azalea said, hooking Lizzy's arm with her own and leading them to the table. They both sat and opened their water bottles and chips.

Heather threw a concerned look at Timothy, who only shrugged and sat at the table. Heather followed suit. "We'll be out most of the day tomorrow," Heather said. "We have to make sure we have plenty of supplies. The day after, there's going to be a conflict in the city, and we won't want to go outside these buildings if we don't have to."

Azalea swallowed a bite and then cocked her head. "Why *are* you separated into different buildings?"

Timothy glanced at Heather before leaning forward. "It's a long story. There's a... conflict... between me and Alexander Roman. He's working on something important in the lab, and we decided it was better for me to remain here where we're keeping a stash of supplies."

Close enough to the truth, I suppose. Heather pursed her lips. She wasn't sure about revealing everything with Azalea present, either.

"So, the lab isn't in this building?" Azalea asked, her voice nonchalant.

"No." Heather's frown deepened. It was an odd question. "Why do you ask?"

"No reason," Azalea said. "I'm just trying to get the layout of the place. I like to know where I am and who I'm with." She pinched another chip between two fingers and popped it into her mouth, seeming to be in thought as she chewed. "So, you two, and those three cops are hanging out here, in this big building, guarding the weapons and supplies, while some other people are working on the cure or the vaccine or whatever in the lab?" As Heather raised her eyebrows, a little surprised that Azalea already knew so much, the young girl nodded at Lizzy. "She told me on the way here what her dad wanted to do once they got back to Boston."

"Oh," Heather said, "well, then, yes. That about sums it up."

"Tim here already told us to keep our lips sealed around Burke and Torres," Azalea said. "I'm assuming we need to add the woman who came in with you to that list?"

"Yes," Heather said, her cheeks warming. It didn't feel quite right keeping the truth from the Chelsea cops, but in the end, she understood and agreed with the reasons they'd decided to do it.

Azalea nodded. She glanced at Lizzy, frowning. "You know, Lizzy is looking paler than I thought. Maybe we should spend some time over at the lab, let this Lauren look us over."

"You don't have to go, too," Timothy said. "You can stay here. I don't think it will take long."

"Lizzy wants me to go with her," Azalea said.

Heather looked at Lizzy, trying and failing to make direct eye contact. "Is that true?" Lizzy nodded but didn't say anything else. An unease settled in the pit of Heather's stomach at the exchange, but she couldn't put her finger on what exactly bothered her so much. Azalea seemed to be in tune with what Lizzy wanted, and Lizzy didn't seem to *want* to speak for herself, but... it was so unlike Lizzy.

"If that would make you more comfortable," Heather said, somewhat reluctantly, "I'm sure we can arrange it."

Lizzy murmured a thanks, and when the two girls had finished eating, Heather and Timothy led them to an office that had been cleared and furnished with two cots, blankets, and pillows. They left the two young women to rest, and Heather walked beside Timothy as they retreated down the hall. She took his hand in hers.

He quirked an eyebrow at her, glancing down at their intertwined fingers. "I'm not complaining," he said. "But... does that mean...?"

"That I've forgiven you?" Heather asked. He nodded, and she sighed. "I'm... close. I'm still mad at you, but..." She stopped and turned to face him, placing her hands on his cheeks. "You promise not to *ever* keep things from me?"

"I swear," he said, his eyes pleading with her to believe him.

"And you swear not to threaten the lives of the people we're working with?" Heather asked.

"Yes." His voice was firm and certain.

"I can forgive you, Tim," she said, hearing the hurt in her own voice, "but I need you to understand it might be a while before I can trust you."

"I understand. I deserve that." Timothy swallowed audibly, a tear escaping one eye. "I'd really like to hug you now."

Heather wrapped her arms around his neck and stood on tiptoes, breathing out long and slow as her husband wrapped his arms around her. She'd missed that more than she'd admitted to herself. He felt like home. Even if she was angry at him, she needed him. In truth, that fact was *why* she'd been so angry.

When they pulled apart, she took his hand again, and they continued down the hall, back toward the conference room. Timothy filled her in on everything he'd learned about where Lizzy had been and what had happened to her.

"But most of this information came through Azalea?" Heather asked, the feeling something was off returning.

"Yeah," Timothy said. He hesitated. "Call me crazy, but... I don't think I like the way Lizzy does whatever Azalea says."

Heather nodded. "I don't think you're crazy. I'm a little worried about it, actually."

"Do you think we should try to separate them?" Timothy asked.

"I don't know. I don't think so. It might make Lizzy pull away from us even more. She seems so... dependent on Azalea. Maybe it's just a trauma response," Heather said.

"I had that thought, too," Timothy said. "She's been through so much with Azalea. We just have to give her time to reacclimate to us, her family. Eventually, though, I think we'll need to get her alone to really talk to her. Right now, it might just frighten her."

"We've got too much to deal with to figure it out right now," Heather said. "But when we're safe, when we've got our supplies and there's a lull, we need to come back to the conversation, figure out what to do to help her recover."

Timothy nodded. "I agree. That'll take some real thought and careful action. It might take weeks or months… maybe years for her to get back to her old self."

Heather shrugged. "I can't say it will be different for any of us, really. We're just lucky we've been together this whole time. We keep each other grounded. The most important thing is that Lizzy is safe, that we've got her back."

Timothy put his arm around her shoulders, and she leaned into him. She tried to put her worries for Lizzy on the back burner; there was nothing she could do about it for the time being, and there were plenty of more immediate problems to take front and center. But the sense that something with Lizzy wasn't right lingered for the rest of the day.

Chapter 21

George Peters

George secured another duffel bag onto the back of a donkey and patted the animal on the neck. "I bet he's from the petting zoo at Franklin Park." He looked over the animal to where Lissa was hooking a bag to the other side. "This group is lucky to have found him."

"As long as he gets their stuff to the green zone," Lissa said, eyeing the beast warily. "I know donkeys are built for this kind of thing, but I remember this guy from when I visited the zoo with my cousin. He was stubborn. The zookeeper was trying to move him inside, and he was not having it."

"Yeah, but Blaze here *loves* me." Hadley, a member of the survivor group Freeman's team had spent the night with, cooed as he rubbed the donkey between the eyes. "Don't you, boy? Yes, you do."

"You named him Blaze?" George eyed the animal skeptically.

"Name your truth," Hadley said. "I want him to be fast." He shrugged.

"Suuure." Lissa drew out the word and seemed to be holding back an eye roll.

"Don't listen to her, buddy." Hadley continued to pet the donkey for a few more moments before taking the reins and clicking with his tongue. Blaze moved forward, hooves clopping on the road, not a bit of hesitation in his step. Hadley looked back at them. "See?"

Lissa laughed. "Alright," she said. "You got me."

Hadley led the donkey laden with his group's supplies to the dozen people waiting a few yards off, and soon George was waving as the third survivor group they'd talked to in the white-hot zone the day before headed east toward City Hall.

Freeman came up beside George. "You two ready? We've got one more day to clear the area. This group pointed us toward a smaller one about half a mile south, in Roxbury."

George frowned. "That's a little close to the zoo, isn't it?" Reports of the Russos and CON spreading hadn't been encouraging. They were definitely creating their own front line, just like O'Donnell had said.

"Yes," Freeman said, "but as long as we don't cross into Dorchester or Jamaica Plain, I think we'll be safe."

A high-pitched, nonthreatening honk sounded from behind them, and George turned to see Paul Landry pull up in one of the tiny solar powered vehicles known as beans. "Time to load up," he said. "I hate wasting daylight."

"He's got a point." Freeman sighed and headed toward the three little vehicles parked a few yards away in front of the community center where they'd found Hadley's group. "You two follow close, okay?" She paused to point at George. "But not too close. I don't want a repeat of yesterday."

George's cheeks warmed, and he rubbed the back of his neck. "I think I have the hang of it now," he said apologetically. Only ten minutes into driving one of the beans, he'd tapped Freeman's vehicle in a one-mile-per-hour fender bender. It hadn't hurt anyone, but it had startled her and made her wary of him driving.

"I hope so," she said. "Now let's get out of here."

George approached his own vehicle. It was a one-seater, and it *did* sort of resemble an upright bean. It could only go a maximum speed of thirty miles-per-hour, and it wasn't comfortable. But it was safe. And if he left the air-conditioning on low, he got a slight reprieve from the summer heat without depleting the battery too quickly. Apparently on cloudier days, they'd have to forego the cooler air, even if it was hot, but for the moment, the sun was out, and the sky was clear; he gladly took advantage of that.

He slid into the seat, and pushed the ignition button, chuckling at the way the smart car puttered to life. *Lizzy would think this thing is adorable.* He smiled at that thought. The evening before, O'Donnell had sent a communication through their radios: Timothy had found Lizzy. George didn't know much else, just that she was alive and safe. That was enough for him. He wanted desperately to see her. Part of him had wanted to ask for permission to hop in a bean that morning and go to Vanguard, but the mission was too important. Besides that, he was sure Timothy was taking good care of her.

George followed, last in line as the tiny cars moseyed through Boston, zigzagging through the streets, fitting between narrow spaces, and taking advantage of the sidewalks. The next group of survivors they'd targeted was supposed to be holed up in an elementary school near Horatio Harris Park. They drove through a well-maintained neighborhood of old homes, but when they got closer, Landry stopped a block away, bringing their procession to a halt.

He got out, looking back with a frown on his face, a worried expression taking shape. Freeman exited her vehicle, as did Lissa, so George got out, too, walking up to where Landry and the others were gathered.

"There are men with guns up there," Landry said. "The last group didn't say anything about guns."

George squinted ahead, his heart sinking. "I recognize them. They're CON."

Lissa nodded. "I recognize them, too." She pointed, visibly shuddering. "That one's called Big Mack. He's a piece of work."

"Great," Freeman said, shaking her head. "If they're forcing people to join them, we can't have that. We have to do something."

"What about the cease-fire?" Landry asked.

"We have to at least try to help," Freeman said, nodding as half a dozen people appeared on the sidewalk, including a small child. "It's people like that we're fighting for. We won't open fire. Pull your weapon, let them know we're armed, but don't engage unless they shoot first." She looked back at George and Lissa. "You two stay here. If there's shooting, stay put."

Lissa gaped. "We can help," she said. "There are three of them and four of us. Numbers matter."

George crossed his arms and stood his ground, too. "We brought guns," he said. "We know how to shoot them. CON would have used us in a situation like this, and you shouldn't hesitate."

Freeman worked her jaw back and forth, seemingly in thought. "Fine, but let us do the talking, okay? And stay behind us. And don't point your weapons at anyone. You two remember the SUL position I showed you?"

George nodded, as did Lissa. He unholstered his gun carefully, keeping the safety on, and pulling the gun close to his torso but pointing it down and slightly outward. He ensured his index finger was *not* on the trigger, rather pointed along the outside of the gun. His free hand rested overtop. Lissa did the same, both of them demonstrating that they'd listened when Freeman had shown them the fixed position the day before. She'd said it was a nonthreatening position that communicated the *ability* to engage with force without the *intent*.

"Good," Freeman said, her expression serious, her tone no-nonsense. She held her gun differently, arms extended at chest level, gun pointed a little more straightforward. "This is a low ready position. I might teach it to you eventually, but for now, stick with the SUL. Do not try to imitate us. I know you think you know what you're doing, and you might be able to shoot and hit a target, but these are people. It's different. Just trust me."

Landry examined their grips and nodded. "If anyone is going to shoot first, it will be one of us." He pointed between him and Freeman. "Be ready to shelter behind a vehicle if that happens, and then shoot back to defend yourselves. Hopefully, it won't come to that."

George nodded again, not daring to argue. His heartbeat picked up as Freeman and Landry took the lead. Approaching people with a gun drawn *did* feel different from target practice — more... immediate; something bad could happen any moment, and if it did, it was life or death.

Big Mack, thickly built, average in height, stood to the side of a stone staircase that led to the sidewalk from the school's front door. He perched on a short, cobblestone retaining wall. On the other side, George recognized Cash. He was a quiet man, followed orders without question. George's first encounter with Cash had been when he'd shot a kid for trying to escape on a food run; Ruger had only had to give the order. Cash hadn't hesitated. Following behind the half dozen civilians was a woman, Shannon. She'd helped with the smaller children when they'd all been kept captive at the zoo.

"What do we have here?" Big Mack pushed off the wall and sauntered toward them, the first to notice their approach. He craned his neck to raise his eyebrows at Lissa. "Hey, sweetheart, you change your mind? Want to come back? I sure could use my own butterfly these days." He winked at her. "I know you miss me."

George's stomach curdled, and rage pulsed through his body. Ace, the previous leader of CON, had cultivated what he called the Butterfly House, where young women were exploited and forced to do unspeakable things. He ground his teeth together at the memory of seeing Lissa tied up, emerging from the shadows of a habitat cave at the zoo in her attempt to free herself. He glanced at his friend. She was stiff, her eyes glistening, clearly holding back tears behind her fury.

Lissa glowered, her voice guttural as she spoke. "I'm no butterfly, Big Mack. You come near me again, and I'll show you my teeth."

George frowned. *Again?* His heart dropped.

"That's not going to happen," Freeman said, her tone dark, "because to get to you, he'd have to come through me."

Big Mack raised his hands in mock surrender. "Fine, fine. Since you ain't here for fun, what *are* you doin' here?"

"We're here to talk to them." Landry nodded to the civilians behind Big Mack, all of whom were looking at them.

A few of the men and women scowled at Landry and Freeman. The others seemed curious or amused. George frowned at that. *They're not scared. And they don't look relieved to see us.*

"You're wasting your time." A man in sweats and a t-shirt walked up to stand beside Big Mack. He focused on Landry and Freeman. "We don't need you to save us. Never have. Never will."

Freeman sighed and relaxed her muscles. "So you're not being coerced? You know who these people are?"

"Why?" The man stuck out his chin, anger flashing across his features. "Because we're not capable of understanding our own situation?"

"No," Freeman shook her head. "These are CONmen, and they're working with the mob to take over Boston. It's a complicated situation. There are safe communities downtown, one of them at City Hall."

Shannon laughed. "Safe? You mean locked down, old world communities. The Russos are giving CON Roxbury and Mattapan once we beat your asses. We're gonna live how we want, with our own rules. Ruger's got our backs." She spit on the ground, turning a glare at George and Lissa. "At least, for those of us who ain't traitors."

George shook his head, scoffing. "Traitors? You kidnapped us. We weren't *ever* CONmen."

"Your friend, Caleb, disagreed," Big Mack said. "But then again, he's got guts."

George masked the hurt at hearing Caleb's name. He'd liked Caleb. If he was being truthful, George liked Ruger, too. But leaving CON and joining the BPD was so clearly the right thing to do. He couldn't imagine what Caleb was thinking, siding with the bad guys.

Freeman and Landry glanced at each other, and then Freeman looked back at the other civilians. "All I need is a visual confirmation that you're all going with these idiots of your own volition. If not, you can come with us."

"Who says you're in charge in here, doll?" Big Mack asked.

"Her name is Officer Freeman," Landry said. "And there might be a cease-fire, but don't tempt us."

The man who'd joined Big Mack laughed. "You have some balls. Look, we're all going exactly where we want to go. You four can get out of here with your savior bull crap."

"Again, I just need visual confirmation." She waited, eyes on the other five civilians. One by one, they each nodded, except for the child, who simply clung to his mother. "Fine," Freeman said. "We'll leave."

"What?" Lissa stepped forward as Freeman and Landry backed up. "What about that kid?" She looked at the mother, pleading. "CON is no place for kids. We've seen them use kids for slave labor, and worse. Do you want your son trained to kill other human beings? Do you want him to treat women like nothing more than baby machines to rebuild the population?" She pointed at Big Mack. "Do you want your son to turn out like that bastard?"

The woman narrowed her eyes. "I know what's best for my son," she said. "And siding with the losers in a fight ain't it."
"Lissa," Freeman put a hand on Lissa's shoulder. "We should go."
Lissa set her jaw and looked back at the kid. "But—"
"We're leaving." Freeman was firm in tone and expression. "Now."
"Lissa, we can't force them," George said softly.
Lissa's gaze drifted to Big Mack, and her expression soured. She turned stiffly, and Freeman addressed the civilians. "One last chance. I wouldn't bet on Frank Russo and Ruger winning this fight. We love this city, and we only want the best for her people. We've got resources, too. We've got just as many fighters. Better weapons and—"
Big Mack scoffed. "Ha! You don't know what's comin' at all, do ya? I almost feel bad for you." His greasy smile turned George's stomach. "Almost."
"What's that supposed to mean?" Landry asked.
Big Mack grinned. "Grenades. A couple missile launchers. Frank got hold of some military grade sh—"
"Shut your big mouth," Cash stepped in, growling. "Ruger'll kill you himself if he finds out you told them anything about what we've got."
Big Mack paled. Then, he turned on Freeman and raised his weapon. "Then, we'll just shoot them. They can't go back and blab if they're dead."
George reacted, aiming at Big Mack's head. But in that same moment, everyone with a gun had chosen a target. The civilians had retreated, and the man who'd stepped up before was ushering the others away and around the corner. George shifted, not knowing where to look. Shannon's gun was trained on him. Cash was alternating his aim between Landry and Lissa.
Adrenaline flooded his system, and the back of his neck flashed cold as a shiver ran down his spine. Beads of sweat formed on his forehead, rolled down his face, stung his eyes. He blinked it away and licked his lips, tasting salt. Heart pounding in his ears, he focused, his senses heightened. The smell of death lingered in the air, more pronounced than it had been seconds prior. The brush of his finger against the safety on his gun, the subtle click that followed: the sounds echoed in the moment of silence.
"Stand down," Landry shouted.
Shannon spoke, a warning in her tone. "Big Mack, the cease-fire—"
"We can't let 'em go back," Big Mack said. "You heard Cash."
Cash licked his lips. "How about we all just keep our mouths shut? Then we can all leave today, live to fight tomorrow."
"Don't be a moron," Shannon whispered sharply, her gun still pointed at George. "There are four of them. We're outnumbered."
"She's right," Freeman said. "This wouldn't be a win for you, but we'd also probably lose someone. So, how about we all just back up? You three follow those civilians, and we'll let you go."
"Deal," Cash said. He raised his hands, pointing his gun upward. Shannon followed suit, and the two backed away.
"Let's go, Big Mack," Shannon said. "For real. We're not backin' you up on this one. It's not time."
"Yeah, we'll get 'em tomorrow," Cash said as he approached the corner, Shannon right behind him, both of them backing up slowly.
Big Mack ground his teeth. He was sweating profusely, dark circles forming under his armpits, sweat dripping from his chin. He let out a long, slow breath and took a step back. "All right," he said, finally lowering his weapon. "Fine." He grinned again as he stepped backward, and then he looked straight at Lissa and grinned. "See you soon, sweetheart."
Lissa roared and the explosion of one, two, three gunshots accompanied her scream as she stepped forward with every shot. George flinched at first, then could only stare open-mouthed at Lissa as she stood over Big Mack who'd been knocked off his feet onto his back. Blood bloomed across his chest as he sputtered, eyes blinking rapidly. Lissa lowered her gun and stared down at him. No one moved. Until everyone did. The next seconds were a blur.
"Get down!" Freeman shouted, rushing forward, grabbing Lissa by the shoulder and shooting at Cash and Shannon as they, too, opened fire.
Lissa stumbled backward, and George leapt for her, grasping her by the wrist and pulling her behind a nearby vehicle, forcing her to the ground. She sat there, eyes vacant, breathing rapidly, tears falling freely. He didn't have time to address whatever had just happened. Gunshots filled the air, and he crawled around her, peering around the hood of the car. Shannon went down, body twirling and hitting the sidewalk hard. Cash's arm extended around the corner of the retaining wall, firing off shots in the general direction of Freeman and Landry. The second he dared to look, Landry landed a bullet between his eyes.
George breathed out in short-lived relief. Freeman and Landry checked pulses and retrieved the CONmen's guns. George sat beside Lissa, not knowing what to say. She didn't offer up any explanation, either. It seemed all she could do was silently cry. Her whole body trembled, but other than that, she didn't move.
"What the hell was that?" Landry stalked around the car to face them. "Are you kidding me, Lissa? You just ended the cease-fire early. And right after we found out that we are *not* prepared to handle what the Russos are about to throw our way." He shouted louder with every word. "Those civilians saw us gun down those CONmen. They're going to report back, and then it's over. We're in deep sh—"
"Landry, enough!" Freeman cut him off as she approached. "Look at her. Think about what she said. You know that look just as well as I do."
Landry blinked at Lissa, and his eyes went wide in recognition. He shook his head and looked away from her, nodding. "It was still the wrong move," he said.
"Yeah," Freeman said. "It was." But then she knelt in front of Lissa and met her eyes. "But sometimes what we have to do and what we should do don't line up."
"He wasn't supposed to touch me," Lissa said, "but… he did. And he would've done it again. I know he would have."
George swallowed bile. "Then he deserved what he got."
"Nobody's going to argue that," Landry said, rubbing the back of his neck. "But, we've got to get back to headquarters. Things are going to get ugly sooner than we thought. We have to warn everyone."

Freeman held out her hand. "C'mon, Lissa. We've got you, okay? It's done. It's over."
Lissa nodded and took Freeman's hand, letting herself be hauled up to standing. George stood, too, following at a close distance. He glanced one more time behind him at the bloody scene before climbing into the tiny smart car, and it hit him: he'd just witnessed the first shots in the war over Boston, and what was promised to come next would be a thousand times worse than any of them had anticipated.

Chapter 22

Lauren Stevens

Lauren held her breath as she tilted Theodore's blood testing card back and forth. She'd discovered Annika's blood type to be A positive, which had given her hope at first; it was a very common blood type. But so far, she was the only match besides her mother, who was a universal donor.

Theodore stood by, still rambling. He hadn't stopped since coming in to get his blood tested. "And that's how I found the hidden codes," he continued. "Hours of searching. And now, we can get into that lab and..."

Lauren sighed and let the card fall to the table. "You're not a match," she said. "You can go."

He looked disappointed, but Lauren was almost positive it was because he couldn't tell her, *again*, how he'd saved the day by finding the codes behind the picture frame. "That's too bad," he said. "Well, I should get back to my work," he said.

Lauren offered a smile. "It sounds like you and Alex are our best bet," she said. "Good luck today."

"That we are. We'll have the world back up and running in no time." He smiled back and patted on her shoulder awkwardly. "Don't worry. You're... um... doing good work, too." He waved his hand over the makeshift clinic. "I'm sure it will be remembered in the history books. Might even get a few sentences out of it."

Lauren did a double take. *That's what he's concerned about right now?* Plastering on a smile, she put a hand on his back and guided him to the door. "Well, wouldn't that be nice," she said, giving him a nice pat as she opened the door wide. "You go land those extra paragraphs in your lab."

Theodore chuckled. "Pages, I think you mean." He shook his head as he left, still chuckling.

When she let the door swing shut behind him, she turned and sighed. "Did you hear that?"

Candice rolled her eyes from where she sat on her cot, answering with a raspy voice. "Every word. I think I might have a few choice sentences to contribute to his section in the history books, if anyone wants to ask."

Lauren gave her a wry smile. Candice was getting stronger every day, but she had a ways to go before Lauren would be comfortable with her leaving care. Not to mention, she'd grown to enjoy Candice's company. But the situation quickly made Lauren's smile fade. She walked over to Annika and gently took her wrist to take her pulse.

"At least he's helping," Lauren said, shoulders sagging. Annika's pulse was there, but it wasn't strong. "If she needs surgery, we're going to need at least one more donor if we're going to do it safely. Surgery can require up to four units."

"What about me?" Candice asked. "You haven't tested me."

Lauren chewed on her lower lip, trying to figure out the best way to explain. "The truth is, Candice... we don't know enough about DV-10. You recovered, and it's clear you're not spreading it through air-borne transmission. But we do know that patients with Dengue, which is the disease used to create DV-10, have to wait six months to donate blood. Alex informed me of it the second he found out we were testing blood donors. That was his area of expertise at the CDC."

Candice's face fell, and she closed her eyes. "So, even if I was a match..."

"Your blood may make Annika sicker," Lauren said. "It could kill her."

"We need to find more donors," Candice said, opening her eyes and staring at Annika.

"These tests don't take long," Lauren said, nodding at the stack of EldonCard Kits on the counter. "Maybe, if we have to take her to City Hall to this surgeon, people there will be willing to get tested."

"You could teach me how to do the test," Candice said, perking up a bit. "I mean, if we do need to rush her there, chances are the doctor will need you. I could help if I knew how to test people."

Lauren nodded. "Not a bad idea. We can—"

The door opened again, and Lauren turned as Heather poked her head inside. "You have a minute?" Heather asked.

"Yeah," Lauren said. "You coming to check in on Annika?"

"Not exactly." Heather held open the door, and two young women entered, putting a hand on the shoulder of the taller redhead. "This is Lizzy, my sister-in-law." She pointed to the shorter of the two, a woman with black hair and pale skin. "And this is Azalea. They've been through a lot, and we wanted to make sure they were okay. I thought maybe you could look them over?"

"Um, sure. Why don't you two sit down." Lauren gestured to two rolling office chairs that had been brought in for visitors. Azalea moved first, and Lizzy followed. When they sat, Lizzy moved her chair closer to her friend. "Who wants to go first?" Lauren asked.

Azalea cleared her throat. "I will," she said as she slid off her shoe. "We did a lot of walking."

When she took off her sock, Lauren grimaced at a wound on the back of her heel. It seemed to be infected. "That doesn't look good at all." She walked over to her stash of supplies from the ambulances and grabbed some antiseptic, a scalpel, antibiotic ointment, and a bandage. She returned to get a better look. "I'll need to drain it, clean it, and wrap it, okay?"

Azalea nodded. "Thank you," she said. "I appreciate it."

"I'm kind of surprised you weren't limping. This has to hurt," Lauren said.

"I've experienced much worse." Azalea waved off Lauren's concern.

Lauren raised her eyebrows, impressed at the pain tolerance. "Still," she said, "we need to make sure you've got proper shoes and socks. That's likely what caused this wound. Especially in times like this, we need to take care of our feet." Lauren worked to drain the pus as she talked.

Beside Azalea, Lizzy brought out a plastic bag of berries and popped a few in her mouth. She was so quiet, and she pulled in on herself every time Lauren glanced at her.

"Where did you get blueberries?" Lauren asked, trying to lighten the atmosphere.

Lizzy didn't answer, her mouth full.

Azalea shrugged. "We found them," she said. "I haven't eaten any. We were saving them, but Lizzy was too hungry. Couldn't wait for lunch."

Lauren snapped her head to look at the berries frowning, her days as a teen camp counselor coming back to her. "You found them? Where?" She dropped her supplies and snatched the bag away, peering inside. She picked up one, and her stomach dropped as she bit her fingernail into the fruit to examine the seed.

"What is it?" Heather asked. "What's wrong?"

Lizzy's face contorted, and she hugged her middle. "I don't feel well."

A memory clicked and Lauren flew into action, her chest tight with panic, adrenaline shooting through her veins. "It's moonseed. Poisonous. Sometimes fatal. How much has she eaten?" She rushed to her stash, grabbing activated charcoal suspension.

"I don't know." Azalea's voice shook. "Maybe a few handfuls?"

Heather flattened one hand against her stomach, the other against Lizzy's back as the girl bent over and groaned in pain. "Lizzy?" She looked up, eyes wide. "What do we do?"

Lauren spun around and sprinted back to Lizzy as the girl's hand went to her chest and she gasped. "Help me get her to the floor, on her side, not her back!" Heather and Azalea did as they were asked. "Moonseed is supposed to taste terrible. I don't know how she could have gotten through more than one or two bites." Lauren tried to breathe steadily as she broke the seal on the activated charcoal. Lizzy was in a ball on the floor, every muscle tense, the veins in her forehead popping from strain. "Lizzy, you need to drink this charcoal. It will absorb the poison."

Heather helped steady Lizzy's head as Lauren administered the black liquid. "Swallow it, Lizzy. You have to swallow it." It dribbled out of her mouth. "I'm grabbing another bottle. She didn't get enough."

"Here!" Candice shoved another small bottle of the substance at Lauren, wincing with the effort it had taken her to walk across the room. "I saw her spitting it out. Figured you might need it."

"Lizzy," Azalea said, her voice resiliently calm. "You need to take the medicine Lauren is giving you." Lizzy nodded, the words registering, and her eyes seemed to refocus on Lauren.

"Okay, hon. You need to swallow all of it." Lauren successfully administered the activated charcoal. "Let's try to sit up. Heather, maybe she can lean against you."

Heather nodded as she sat behind Lizzy, and the three of them helped Lizzy sit up and lean back. Azalea positioned herself close enough to take one of Lizzy's hands. For half an hour, Lizzy alternated between strained stillness, when every muscle seemed to seize as she grimaced in pain, and restless rocking, when she would hold herself tight, eyes closed, skin sweaty and pale. Finally, she came to an exhausted rest.

"Okay," Lauren said, breathing out slowly. "We need to bring in another cot. I want her to stay here, with me, for a little bit. I don't know how long. I would just feel more comfortable monitoring her. The activated charcoal should have done its job, but I don't know how much of the poison was absorbed before we administered the medicine. She's likely to feel unwell for a while."

"Thank you," Heather said. Lizzy still leaned against her. "I want to stay, but… we are all going out to scavenge at the hospital." She glanced at Annika's still form. "We have so much we hope to find. We need everyone we can get."

Lauren nodded. "It's okay. She'll be fine here."

"I'll stay with her, of course," Azalea said.

Lauren shook her head. "There's already too many people in this room."

Lizzy shook her head and reached for Azalea. "Please," she whispered, grasping her friend's hand. "I want her here."

Lauren sighed. "I guess… we can set you up in a nearby room? You can check on her regularly, but I really need this room to be for patients only."

Azalea nodded. "That should work."

"Lizzy?" Heather asked, throwing a slight frown at Azalea. "What do you think?"

Lizzy nodded. "I'll be sleeping anyway, probably."

Three patients. It hit Lauren hard, all that she was responsible for. I'm not cut out for this. I'm not a doctor. I never wanted this kind of responsibility.

All the focus she'd had during the emergency, every ounce of calm she'd managed to maintain, melted away and her hands began to tremble, just as they had after every trauma she treated early in her residency. She'd felt the same rush of illness after she'd stabilized Annika, but experiencing it twice in such a short amount of time did something to her. Her chest heavy, her head pounding, a flight response kicked in.

"I'll go grab a cot," Lauren said. "I'll be back in a few minutes."

Lauren walked across the room, the urge to be anywhere else fueling every step. The second she was out in the hall, her walk turned into a sprint as she put distance between herself and a room full of patients relying on her to make them better.

She turned and was met with a dead end. Lauren sucked in air, her lungs burning; she couldn't get a satisfying breath, no matter how deeply she breathed. Lauren stumbled to the wall and leaned against it, old fears and insecurities surfacing, along with memories of her last day of residency.

A bloodied form, small and mangled. When Lauren had first gotten to the boy, he'd been breathing. He'd been alive. But no matter what she did to try to undo the damage done by falling three stories with nothing but concrete as a landing pad, the boy had steadily slipped away. She'd failed him. And she'd had to tell his parents. It was the worst day of her life. She'd never felt more helpless, and she'd never managed to step into a hospital as a doctor again.

Lauren leaned her head against the wall behind her. Years of therapy had helped her realize that while it was true medicine wasn't right for her, what had happened wasn't her fault. But being back in the position of caring for patients ripped open all the wounds she'd thought healed. The difference was that she didn't have the option of walking away, no matter how desperately she wanted to.

Chapter 23

Timothy Peters

Metal screeched as Timothy yanked two grocery carts apart and rolled one to Heather. "These should do it. If we each push a cart, we'll gather a nice stockpile from the hospital." He rolled two more carts to Burke, Torres, and Murphy.

Burke, expression flat, except for his usual slight frown, lifted one of Candice's suitcases into his cart. It contained the protective gear they needed for their scavenging trip. "These hazmat suits better work," he mumbled.

Timothy blanched. "Is there a chance they won't? I mean… they were your idea."

Murphy elbowed Burke in the arm. "He's just grumpy. Of course these will work. The masks and suits are made for this sort of thing."

Torres quirked an eyebrow. "Not *exactly* this sort of thing. There are hundreds of rotting bodies in that hospital."

"Fine." Murphy shrugged. "But they were made to protect people from the dangers of cleaning up after corpses. We aren't even going to be touching them, hopefully. Right?"

"Right." Heather nodded once, but her tone lacked confidence.

Burke grunted again, but Murphy only turned her cart around to face the hospital down the street. "If we're going to do this," Murphy said, "let's get it done. We could use a few medical supplies, boys. And whatever our fair share is that we can't use, we can trade down the line. I want to get James out of here before things get ugly, and I want to do it knowing we can take care of him."

Mention of Murphy's son seemed to be all Burke and Torres needed to move forward without any further comment. The three former Chelsea cops took the lead, pushing their carts toward Brigham and Women's Hospital. Heather and Timothy exchanged a glance.

"You don't have to come," Timothy said for the hundredth time. "Going into that hospital isn't completely risk free. If we both die…"

"George and Lizzy would be alone," Heather said, nodding and pushing her cart ahead. "I know. But we don't want to make this trip more than once if we don't have to. We need to grab everything inside that hospital that could help Lauren, or even that surgeon down at City Hall, save Annika. Even with the five of us going in, we're going to have to pick and choose what we bring back. And George clearly can handle himself these days. He'll be okay no matter what."

"That's all true." Timothy followed, his stomach twisting in knots as they wove between vehicles. "But what about Lizzy?"

"If Lizzy needs anyone," Heather said over her shoulder, "it's you, not me. You're her brother. She was happy to see you. I can barely get her to talk to me. I was so useless when she got sick from those berries or wild grapes or whatever they were."

"Heather, there was nothing you could have done. We're just lucky Lizzy agreed to see Lauren in the first place." Timothy came to a stop as the three ahead did so as well. To their left, the red and white emergency department sign hung in the shadows of a concrete overhang.

"Time to suit up," Burke called, voice gruff as he unzipped the suitcase and yanked two suits out of it. He threw one to Heather who threw it back to Timothy, and then Burke gave Heather her own. They each had a gun and ankle holster, and they each took them off and rested them on the handles of their carts while they dressed.

Timothy slipped one foot into the suit and then the other, leaning on the cart when he needed a little balance. "You all know our top priorities?"

Murphy pulled up her suit and stuck her arms into the sleeves. "An ultrasound machine, portable. More transfusion kits. Any and all meds we find outside of a refrigerated system. Suture materials. And saline."

"We're focusing on the meds." Burke zipped his suit up to the neck. "That's what we can take with us. That's what we're looking for."

Murphy gave Timothy an apologetic smile. "Burke's right. But if we see any of that other stuff, we will bring it to you."

"Or just tell you where to find it," Burke said.

Murphy looked over her shoulder. "Or *bring it to them*, Burke. C'mon. The sooner we all get out of there, the better, right?" Torres nodded at Burke, and the man just grunted in reluctant agreement.

Heather caught yellow booties as Burke tossed a couple pairs their way. She handed one pair to Timothy. "Burke must be fun at parties," she said under her breath.

Timothy chuckled as he slipped the booties over his shoes and up around the pant legs of the suit. He grabbed his ankle holster and secured it over the boot. Next came two layers of latex gloves, and then each of them put on a full-face respirator mask with a circular filter attached to one side. Timothy pulled the hood of the suit up and pulled the strings tight so that it overlapped the shield by a few centimeters, leaving no gap. The last piece of equipment was a headlamp secured just above the mask with an adjustable strap. As he followed the others to the sliding door, his nose wrinkled at the memory of the stench from the last time he'd cracked it open.

Burke and Torres worked to pry open the doors again, and when they managed to roughly force the doors open, Timothy was relieved at how little of the stench permeated the respirator mask. He switched on his headlamp, his beam of light joining four others as the five of them pushed their carts into the lobby of the hospital.

"I say we start in the ED," Murphy said. "We might find most of what we need in there."

Timothy agreed and followed, bracing himself to find something similar to what he'd seen when trapped in the foyer of the college several days prior. There, it had been clear: those who'd died had chosen to do so together. They had held hands as they'd died. The ability for humanity to come together even in their last moments had been hauntingly, tragically, terribly beautiful.

The hospital was nothing like that. There were a few scattered bodies in the lobby and sitting area, but when they followed the signs to the emergency department, Timothy stopped short. Heather gasped beside him, and Murphy turned her head. Burke and Torres were as frozen as the rest of them.

Corpses were piled against the double doors as if they'd died trying to get inside. At first, the decomposing bodies were like a grotesque tumor growing out of the ground, discolored flesh and stained clothing and oozing fluids melding together under the buzzing, crawling cover of hundreds of flies.

But then details distinguished themselves from the gore. A corpse on the bottom of the pile, hands like claws trying to dig his way out from under the mob. Another, knees resting on someone's back, reaching over the others toward one of the two glass windows; the flesh had fallen away at their fingertips, tapered bone resting against the glass. A woman, Timothy assumed by the purse still hanging on her shoulder, supported in her outstretched palms a smaller corpse as she leaned on the outside of the pile.

"She wanted whoever was on the other side to see her child," he whispered, vision blurring with tears.

"I think..." Torres said. "...maybe we should find a different way."

Timothy was the last to turn. Heather walked past him and rested a hand on his shoulder. He blinked away tears, tearing his eyes from the evidence of bygone chaos, to look into the eyes of his wife. She offered him strength, offered him comfort in her solidarity. Despite what he'd done, despite the lost trust between them, Heather was there for him. Always.

She's stronger than I am. He hung his head. *She would have handled the truth better than me.* In that moment, he couldn't pretend anymore. He couldn't justify his lie. *I didn't do it for her.* And it was clear to him: he'd known that from the first moment he'd decided to cover up the truth about his father and about the disease.

"I'm sorry," Timothy said softly. He looked back at Heather. "For everything." He'd said it before, but he could say it a thousand times and find a new depth of meaning to the words.

"I know." The sadness in those words betrayed her meaning. It didn't change what had happened, no matter how much they both wanted it to. "Come on, Tim. We need to find our way into that emergency department."

Timothy nodded, useless words that would only sound hollow on his lips catching in his throat. He and Heather joined the others back to the lobby. He cleared his throat. "There should be a back entrance to the emergency department," he said. "At least one, maybe more."

"Should be this way," Burke started toward the hallway that would border the emergency department.

Their lights uncovered new horrors with every step. Decaying bodies sprawled out or huddled, flies and maggots eating away at them, crawling through blackened lips, holes in cheeks, or exploring empty eye sockets. Weeks gone, these bodies were well on their way to becoming skeletons, white bone visible where skin and muscle had fallen off. The corpses secreted brown fluids, and Timothy gagged and swallowed bile when the carpet *squished* underfoot.

But then his light swept over a body down an adjoining hall. "That one is... new."

"What?" Heather, who was ahead of him, turned to look at him.

Timothy pointed. "That body," he said. "It's fresh. And... it was infected." Though swollen, with eyes bulging and blood streaking from every orifice, the fresh corpse wasn't even discolored yet, and with no welts visible, it seemed he'd caught it from a person rather than the swarm. Somehow, that was more terrifying than the hundreds of weeks-old, rotting bodies.

"Hey, guys," Heather said, voice trembling. "I think we might have a problem."

Burke stopped at the front of the line. "What are you two doing?"

"Tim found a fresh body," Heather said, raising her voice so that they could all hear her. "People are coming in here, unprotected."

Murphy left her cart to examine the new corpse. She stood over it, sweeping her light over it, head to toe and back again. She pointed at the feet. "There's a syringe still sticking out between his toes. He's a junkie."

Torres crouched beside the body and pointed to a small glass vial. "Fentanyl." He pulled his gun as he stood back up.

"He's already dead," Timothy said, frowning at the way all three former police officers tensed. "He's not going to attack us."

"If word got out that there's Fentanyl in this hospital, junkies will flock here," Burke said. "Those who are still alive, that is."

Heather gaped. "But it's clearly not safe."

"Doesn't matter," Murphy said. "Addiction like that hinders a person's ability to think clearly. They'll do anything for a fix. They're surprisingly resilient, too," she said looking down at the corpse, "until they're dead, at least."

"We need to fill these baskets and get out of here," Burke said as he stalked back to his cart with long, determined strides.

Timothy followed the line around the next corner. The back entrance to the emergency department was open, the door bent and broken, crowbars and sledgehammers scattered on the ground. Beyond, the ground was littered with supplies. A few carts with drawers all pulled out were tipped over or left in the center of the aisle.

"If they were looking for drugs," Heather said, "maybe they didn't take much else." She bent over and picked up a handful of packaged gauze. "We will need to sanitize the outside packages of everything we find here, but we probably would have needed to do that anyway." She tossed the gauze into her cart.

"They probably wouldn't take a portable ultrasound machine," Timothy said. "At least there's that."

"Let's fan out," Murphy said. "Search every room."

"I'll take that back corner." Timothy headed that way, stopping at a door labeled for hospital supplies. It was cracked open. He pushed it open fully, finding a mess of overturned metal shelves. "Bingo," he said as he spotted a few yellow totes full of saline IV bags. He put them in his cart, as well as suture kits, transfusion kits, and IV start kits.

"I found an ultrasound machine!" Heather shouted, both relief and excitement in her voice.

Timothy turned to find Heather rolling out a stand. "Will you need to roll that whole thing back to Vanguard?"

She frowned. "Well, we'd need to detach everything, including the screen." She examined all around it, and then nodded. "I just need a multi tool." She eyed the nurses' station at the center of the department and hurried over, rummaging through.

"I'm going to go on to the next room." Timothy rolled past the station toward an admittance room. He glanced to his right, stomach churning at the sight of the doors they'd first approached. On the other side of the glass windows were bony hands and the faces of corpses. He looked away only to be met with four white-coated corpses sitting against the half wall of the nurses' station, staring straight ahead at the doors. And then he spotted, in the pocket of one of the doctors, a silver clip. "Heather, I think that's a pocketknife. It might be a multi tool."

He approached, hesitating a moment before reaching for the dead man's pocket. He plucked the tool free, relieved to see it was a Swiss Army Knife. He walked it over to his wife and handed it to her, and she proceeded to go about dismantling the ultrasound station and putting the equipment in her cart.

It took them another fifteen minutes to clear the emergency department of the remaining supplies, but there had been very little in the way of medications left in the emergency department. They agreed on exploring further until the carts were full. In the space of another two hours of grueling work, traversing corpse-infested halls and rooms, they had no more room in their carts and made their way back to the building entrance.

Timothy pushed his cart outside behind the other four. He was about to take off his mask when a figure appeared from the shadows. Another rose from behind a vehicle. A third and fourth man came out of hiding. In seconds, they were surrounded by eight men, the hospital at their backs with nowhere to run.

"Told ya they'd come out," one of the men said, his hands visibly shaking, eyes wide and bloodshot as he stepped into the light. He had a crowbar in hand.

Burke, Torres, and Murphy already had their guns unholstered and at the ready. "Don't come any closer," Murphy said. "We don't want to shoot you, but we will."

"You ain't the only one with a gun." A man on the left raised a sawed-off shotgun. Two more revealed their own firearms, a handgun and a rifle. "Just give us what you got, if you don't want trouble."

Of the eight, at least half of them were shaking. All of them looked crazed and desperate enough to be dangerous.

"Three guns," Murphy said, barely loud enough for Timothy to hear. "Two crowbars. Two hammers and a spiked baseball bat."

"Go for the guns?" Torres asked under his breathe.

"I've got left." Burke growled.

One of the strangers shouted. "What're you saying? Don't mess with us!"

"Middle." Murphy switched off the safety of her gun.

Torres nodded. "Now!"

Timothy lunged for Heather, covering her with his body as gunfire filled the air.

Chapter 24

Kai Lee and Zara Williams

Kai batted away a branch as he made his way through Mount Tom State Reservation. The trail he'd chosen was a bit overgrown, but it was the beekeeper suit that made the trek hard. He'd gone out first thing that morning. The back end of the plane had left a trail of flattened brush and small, broken trees down the backside of the mountain. Once he'd found the first sign of the crash, it hadn't been difficult to track.

"There you are," Kai breathed out in relief as he spotted the wreckage through the mesh of his helmet.

The wings had been shorn off, and the body of the back end of the plane was battered. Kai looked up the mountain at the trail the hunk of metal had left as it had slid to its final resting place in a ditch. He closed his eyes and took a deep breath, preparing himself to find Walter Peters's dead body.

"Okay," he said. "I can do this. If I don't find him — and really confirm it's him — Zara will insist on coming out here herself." He opened his eyes and turned with determination toward the plane.

He had to take big, awkward steps through the brush, focusing on maintaining balance, as he approached the edge of the narrow ditch. Kai leaned over, assessing the slope, and his foot slipped. He shouted as his backside hit dirt, and he tumbled over brush, bouncing and then hitting the bottom of the ditch hard. Groaning, he rolled over and looked up at the tall, skinny trees ending in poofs of broad leaves; his feet pointed toward the wreckage. He sat up to face the shadows of the inside of the broken plane, its twisted metal frame bent in on the cusp like a monster's wide-open maw completed by jagged, uneven teeth.

Daylight pierced the darkness in some places, finding its way through small punctures in the sides, providing some light. It had landed so that the seats were upright. Kai swallowed hard as he got to his feet and took a hesitant step forward. He walked the center aisle slowly, gathering fresh courage with every step.

Smeared blood ran across the ceiling above the overhead compartments, and more blood had soaked into the floor at the back of the plane near the bathroom. But there was no body. Kai's hand shook as he reached for the handle to the bathroom door, and his heart pounded as he flung it open. But still, Walter was nowhere to be found. He wasn't in the plane, and Kai hadn't found his body in the woods as he'd tracked the wreckage.

Kai looked back at the smeared blood, frowning. "What happened to Mr. Peters?" he mumbled. He examined the blood more carefully, finding drops on the seats below and lines of dark red running down the compartment doors.

"If that's his blood," he said, "if the plane had been turned almost upside down… maybe he crawled out." Kai raised his eyebrows at the possibility. It would mean Mr. Peters was alive when he left the plane. "At least the compartment doors are still closed." He sighed as he opened each one, pulling out a messenger bag that contained ammo and a small gun safe with a biometric lock, keypad, and a keyhole. He'd lost the key ages ago, and he'd set the code when he was half drunk, without writing it down. Only he would be able to open it using his thumbprint, though he wouldn't be able to do so with gloves on, and there was no way he was taking off any of his protection until he was safely indoors, especially for the particular gun inside the safe: an old .44 magnum American Derringer.

It had been one of Kai's first trades, only a few days after disaster struck his hometown, and it had been the worst trade he'd made so far. He'd given up good food and bottled water for the weapon only to find out it was practically useless — for him, anyway. The first and last time he'd fired it, the kickback had been so violent, he'd sprained his wrist and the weapon nearly recoiled right into his skull. Of course, if he absolutely had to shoot it again, he'd brace himself a little better, but it wasn't something he wanted to experience again.

"Still… better than nothing, I guess." Kai sighed and slung the bag over his shoulder before going back outside.

He examined the plane. The sides of the ditch hugged it like a hotdog in a bun. The doors to the cargo hold were completely covered by dirt. If they'd stayed shut during the crash, Kai would be able to recover three military-grade rifles, ammunition, food, water, and first aid supplies, plus whatever Walter and Zara had stashed there before they'd come to save him from the crazies of Clearfield. But that was only *if* he could dig around the side of the hold enough to gain access.

"I'll need a shovel for that," he said. "And more time than we've got." It made him sick to his stomach, all those supplies buried just out of reach, but he decided to leave them for the time being.

Unable to find any more clues as to Walter's whereabouts, Kai left the ruins of his broken plane to climb back up the side of the ditch and make his way through the forest the way he'd come. He kept his eyes open for signs of a body. Zara would want more than speculation if he was going to convince her to stay put and get better.

* * *

Sitting still was going to kill Zara long before her concussion. It was hot inside the airstream, even with the windows open, the screens shut tight to keep out the bugs and more importantly, mosquitos. Of course, if she heard the sound of one of the swarms again, she'd be closing and locking the windows regardless of screens. She'd already practiced doing it quickly and then locking herself in the tiny bathroom. After half a dozen drills, though, her headache had become too much, and vertigo had set in.

Her cheeks still flushed hot from embarrassment when she recalled collapsing at the apiary. The more she thought of it, the more she had to accept that Kai was right to ask her to stay put. *I don't know which annoys me more: the rest or Kai being right.* She sighed and readjusted her pillow.

The sound of a motor in the distance startled Zara. She sat up too quickly, the room spinning slightly before settling back into place. She steadied herself with one hand on the ceiling, the other on the wall, as she blinked away the dizziness so she could listen. Carefully scooting toward the window, Zara watched the road that led away from the lot. It wasn't long before a little white car appeared.

Panic tightened Zara's chest. If the newcomer wasn't friendly, she wouldn't be able to defend herself, not very well, anyway. She couldn't wait to find out one way or the other. She stood up, straightening little by little, praying slow movements would be enough to keep the world from tilting. Stepping lightly so as to not rock the camper, Zara made her way to the kitchen drawer to pull out a long, sharp knife. She settled on the floor underneath the little table, knife at the ready.

Maybe they won't bother me at all. She held the knife tightly, pointing it outward, fighting down nausea. Just keep it together. They could be looking for something in particular. Or maybe they want easy loot. The door is locked. She winced as that thought led her to realize the windows were still open. She had no idea if that would be enough to signal that someone was inside.

The rumble of the engine died, and a car door slammed. The crunch of gravel neared, and then a knock on the door made Zara jump.

"Hello? Zara? Kai? It's Willow."

Zara frowned. "What are you doing here?" she asked, loud enough for the woman to hear. "I thought the mayor didn't want you guys leaving the hospital."

"She doesn't," Willow said. "But I found something I thought you should see. And I told her I'd bring back the suits, if you two were still alive. Is… is Kai here? Or is it just you?"

"Just me." Hiding the truth wouldn't do any good. The camper was too small to really hide the fact that she was alone.

"Is he okay?"

Zara pursed her lips, remembering how the two had flirted. "He's fine," she said. "He's looking for our friend. He'll be back soon."

"I don't really want to stay out here." Willow's words were laced with nervous energy. "Can I come inside?"

The young woman had seemed nice enough back at the hospital, but Zara had doubts about welcoming her with open arms. She made her way to the door, leaning against it. "How do I know I can trust you? You could take everything we've got, including the suits we were promised."

"I told you, I didn't come out here for that. The suits were just an excuse." Willow was silent for a few moments before she continued. "I think I might know where your friend is. Open the door, let me in, and I'll show you. We have enough at the hospital. The little bit you took didn't make a dent in our supplies, okay? I just want to help."

Zara bit her lower lip as she reached for the door handle. The prospect of information leading to Walter was too much to ignore. She gripped the knife with one hand and unlocked the door with the other. She backed up a few steps. "Okay, you can come inside."

Willow opened the door, hesitating at the sight of the knife in Zara's hand. She still stepped inside, though, closing the door behind her. The woman's shoulders relaxed a bit, apparently more comfortable with Zara's knife than being exposed outside. She dug a paper out of her pocket and unfolded it. "Little LeeAnn drew this." She held out the paper. "I thought it strange. Her father has been missing, and at first glance, I thought maybe she was pretending he was in a hospital, but… then I noticed that." She pointed to misshapen letters written in crayon. They were somehow smooshed together and stretched at the same time.

Zara squinted at the handwriting, and then her eyes widened. "Walter," she whispered. The name was misspelled — W-A-L-L-R — but it was close. Zara snatched the paper and held it closer, examining it.

"Maybe," Willow said hesitantly. "Carol was acting even stranger than usual when they came by, and she seemed irritated when I was recounting the tale you and Kai had spun about a plane crash. She couldn't get out of there fast enough once I started talking, and her son, Heath… he had this look, like he wanted to say something but couldn't. I didn't think much of it until I saw this. Those poor kids have been locked up with their crazy mother for weeks."

"Where?" Zara looked up, hope blossoming. Her body itched to move, to go and find out if Walter was alive.

"Out at The Log Cabin," Willow said. "I can draw a map for you. It's not far. It might be nothing, though. I mean, it's just a picture, and those letters are hard to decipher."

"Can I keep this?" Zara asked, holding up the paper. Willow nodded, and Zara folded it up and stuffed it in her pocket. She pointed to a small dry erase board on the wall by the door. "Will that do for a map?"

Willow followed her gaze, turning to look at the board. "Yeah," she said. "I think so." She grabbed the marker attached to the side and began to draw. "I think if you're driving this big old rig, you'll want to go through town. Get to Northampton Street — that's the road you drove in on before, I think — but you've got to turn way before you get to the hospital. Take Bernis Road all the way over to 141 — that's Easthampton Road — and go right until you get to The Log Cabin. It'll be on the left." She capped the marker, put it back in its place, and turned around. "Now… the suits?"

"Oh, right." Zara rotated in the small space and opened the closet doors to get the backpacks full of beekeeper gear. "We found the guys you sent out there, by the way." She handed the backpacks over, grimacing. "They're dead."

Willow's face paled, but she nodded. "We figured so. The swarm?"

Zara nodded. "It almost got us, too. We were lucky."

Willow slung one of the backpacks over her shoulders and picked up the second. "Thanks for letting me know. I hope you find your friend." She half turned back toward the door but paused and looked back at Zara. "When I said Carol is crazy, I meant it," she said. "She's… unhinged. She can be violent. I think she's had some sort of mental breakdown. But… before all of this, she was a good person. And those kids haven't done anything wrong, okay? Don't hurt them."

"We wouldn't hurt kids," Zara said, shocked that Willow would suggest she might.

"Just be careful. For your sake, and for theirs."

"Sure," Zara said. "We will."

Willow nodded before scurrying to her car, throwing the bags inside, and then leaving just as abruptly as she'd arrived. Zara returned to the bed, resting as she'd promised Kai before he'd left. She watched the door, waiting for him to return. The second he did, she wanted to be ready to go investigate The Log Cabin.

Chapter 25

Theodore Finch

Theodore set the environmental control cabinets to the right sequence of gradually increasing temperature. He'd carefully removed the countermeasure mosquito eggs from cryopreservation and submerged them in trays of water. Dr. Brown's notes suggested ideal conditions for hatching the eggs could be reached by sprinkling one crushed fish food tablet and a tiny bit of active yeast in each tray. He'd followed the notes carefully, satisfied that the eggs would soon hatch, and he could move on to rearing larvae in a few days at most.

In the meantime, his partner, Alex, would be synthesizing possible vaccines and testing potential treatments. It was good to be on a team again, this time with someone who valued his work. Of course, he knew all too well what would happen if he failed, if he messed up one too many times.

Theodore ignored the tension in the pit of his stomach, the shudder that ran up his spine. "That won't happen," he said, promising himself. He wouldn't take the opportunity to reinvent his career lightly. Alex didn't know of his mistakes, his missteps, his character flaws. Theodore could be anyone he wanted to be; everyone who knew otherwise was dead.

Of course, old habits had surfaced with Timothy. But his survival instinct was the least of his flaws. If the only bad thing anyone remembered about him was that he did whatever was needed to stay alive in order to save the world, well… that was okay by him.

His work well on its way, Theodore shrugged off his lab coat and slipped off two layers of nitrile gloves. It was time for a well-deserved break. A snack. Maybe some whiskey. And a nap. He left the lab, ensuring the door was closed and locked behind him. The lab Alex worked from was on the way; he popped in to ask if he wanted to join in.

"Thanks," Alex said, "but I'm good. I've still got a lot to do today. Maybe I'll take you up on that whiskey once I've made significant progress."

"Well, I understand," Theodore said, offering a sympathetic smile. "I've been so efficient with my tasks, I suppose I'd assumed you'd be further along."

The corners of Alex's mouth twitched, but then he smiled. "Thank you for your work, Theodore. I've really got to get back to this."

Poor man. Jealous of my progress. Can't stand it, probably. We've all been there. Theodore patted the man on the back. "That's the spirit. Keep at it."

He left Alex to toil away. He would have offered to help, but that kind of work wasn't his specialty. Of course, neither was the work he'd already accomplished, but no one needed to know that. Dr. Brown's notes were impeccable. By the time he was done studying them, Theodore would be the expert, perhaps one of only a very few still left alive on the planet. He grinned at that as he pushed open the door to his office. But his smile didn't last long.

"What are you doing in here?" Theodore frowned at the young woman sitting in *his* office chair with her feet propped up on *his* desk. She didn't seem bothered in the least by his question or his presence. That didn't surprise him much. She was gorgeous, after all, and pretty people didn't play by the same rules as people like Theodore. Women like her were used to deferential treatment.

Well, this is a new world, and I don't plan on deferring to anyone unless I want to. Theodore's frown deepened. "Go back downstairs," he said hotly. "I don't appreciate you barging into my office and—"

The woman — he couldn't remember her name — puckered her lip. "Theodore," she said, taking her feet off his desk and sitting up straighter, "don't be like that. I wasn't *barging*. I was *waiting*."

"Waiting for what?" Theodore crossed his arms.

"For you," she said, moving to perch on the edge of his desk and gesturing to the office chair. "I wanted to talk to the man who was going to save us all."

Theodore's mouth dropped open momentarily before he snapped it shut. He stared at her, trying to decipher if she was making fun of him or not. He'd never had a woman pay any attention to him, but then again, he'd never been a hero, either. And now he was. Of course he was. It dawned on him slowly. Women paid attention to power and fame, and he would be famous. If she was smart, why *wouldn't* she find him worthy of her attentions?

"Well, then," Theodore said, cautiously optimistic as he strode across the room to sit in his chair. He looked up at her, drinking in her raven locks, inviting blue eyes, perfectly smooth skin, and her many other… delightful attributes. "Remind me again of your name?"

"Azalea," she said, clearly disappointed he hadn't known it already.

Theodore smiled. He knew just the thing to drive her mad. He *did* remember Timothy's sister's name. She'd been important, someone of note. Women hated to be looked over in favor of another. "And how is Lizzy?" he asked. "I heard she had a little hiccup." He feigned genuine interest and searched Azalea's features for any hint of jealousy. And he found it: the slight pinch of her lips, the twitch of her left eye, the way she cleared her throat.

"She's fine," Azalea said, her answer short. "I wouldn't have left her alone if she were in any real danger."

"What a good friend you must be." Theodore rested his elbows on the arms of his chair and folded his hands. "So, Azalea, what can I do for you?"

She smiled, and she somehow became even more gorgeous. She leaned closer. "Oh, I was hoping I could learn more about what I've gotten myself into around here."

"I see," Theodore said, smiling at her obvious train of thought, "and you thought because I'm one of only two men here working on the cure for what ails the world, that I could protect you."

She opened her mouth in surprise, blinking a few times. "Y-yes," she said, her smile widening. She'd clearly not realized how perceptive he could be. "Precisely."

"Well, you've made a good choice, but I must ask, why not go to Mr. Roman?" He was almost ready to give her what she wanted, but he had to make sure she wasn't toying with him. Alex was more traditionally handsome, and if there was any competition, it would be him.

"The other scientist?" Azalea frowned.

"Yes," Theodore said, waving for her to continue, to answer his question. If she was seeking protection from a powerful man, Alex had to be in the running. He needed to know if she'd gone to him first, if she planned to play them both. It wouldn't be a deal breaker – he was a man with needs, after all – but it would change how he interacted with her and how hard he made things on her.

Azalea laughed, her tone airy and light. "Why would I go to him? He's got a son. And he doesn't know how to have any fun, not like you. He's so boring."

Theodore chuckled. "That is true," he said. "I was just thinking so on my way up. The man can't even stop for a nice glass of whiskey."

Her eyes widened. "That sounds delightful." She looked over at the liquor table. "I can pour us both a finger or two."

Her wicked smile won him over. "Oh, why not?"

Azalea popped up from her perch with youthful energy. His eyes lingered as she poured their drinks; she didn't rush, and he didn't mind. She returned to sit closer to him, handing him his drink. "So," she said, "can I ask you anything I want?"

He sipped his drink and nodded. "Curiosity is the sign of real intelligence," he said. "Go on. Anything."

"At the entrance, there were all these crates and boxes. Were those what I think they were?"

Her playful smile glossed over her woefully stupid question. He decided to ignore any signs of idiocy. From the looks of things, her assets lay elsewhere, and that was just fine. He had enough brains for the both of them. And besides, he deserved to have some fun.

"The fireworks?" he asked. "Oh, yes. Loads of them. I brought them here from a city warehouse. If I'd left them where they were, in the middle of summer, with so many hooligans running around and the heat, they would have combusted or been set afire weeks ago."

Her eyes widened. "So, you basically saved the city from burning to the ground."

He shrugged and sipped at his whiskey. "Basically," he said.

"Is saving the world becoming your hobby, Mr. Finch?" Azalea leaned even closer and traced his jawline with her fingertip.

"I suppose it is." He chuckled, finishing off his drink and letting her take the glass to refill it. When she brought it back, he took another sip. "You'd not believe the work I'm doing. I'm not even sure you'd understand it. But it is fascinating. And I'm good at it. And when I'm done, the world will remember my name."

"I had a feeling about you," she said, moving from the desk to his lap. He didn't stop her. It was actually quite pleasing. "Tell me everything, Theodore. Even if it goes over my head, I just love to hear you talk."

A warmth settled in the pit of his stomach as he downed the last of his second glass of whiskey, and his head and limbs buzzed with the beginnings of numb relaxation. He grinned and slid his hand along the small of her back. "I don't mind if I do."

Theodore started talking, more generally at first, but eventually getting into the specifics of his work. Every time he thought she would surely be getting bored of his rambling, she asked him another question. It was so nice, being heard and recognized. Even as the whiskey did its work and his tongue became loose and his words slurred, Azalea seemed captivated. And so Theodore kept going, every gasp of awe and playful touch and praising word making him crave more.

By the time his eyelids were drooping and his head swimming from the effects of the liquor, he had told her everything. Part of him recoiled at that. No one besides him and Alex was supposed to see the codes to the building and to the cryopreservation pods. He wasn't supposed to share the location of the empty bunker below New Horizons. But it was all going in one ear and out the other with a woman like Azalea. He was just impressing her, showing off a little. Every man deserved to do that once in a while, deserved to have a pretty woman hang on his every word. And he was finally getting the chance. Finally, Theodore Finch was getting exactly what he deserved.

Chapter 26

Timothy Peters

Within seconds, the three addicts with guns had been taken out by the trained ex-cops from Chelsea. But it only took that long for the other five to get close enough to do some damage. A man with dark circles under his eyes and several missing teeth charged Timothy and Heather with a spiked baseball bat. Timothy pushed his wife behind him as he stooped to retrieve the gun in the holster around his ankle.

His gloved fingers clumsily grasped at the snap. He looked up; the man was too close, and he couldn't get a grip on—

Heather stepped out from behind him, weapon raised, and fired. The man jerked backward as the bullet grazed his shoulder, but then he let out a blood-curdling scream as his eyes went wide and he gnashed his teeth. He showed no signs of slowing. Finally, Timothy pulled his own gun. Heather dodged a swing of the nail-ridden bat, and Timothy fired, landing a hit square in the man's abdomen. The assailant dropped to his knees, the bat clattering to the concrete as his arms went limp. Trembling, he stared at the gushing wound in his stomach as if confused, and when he looked up, blood seeping from his lips, there was a clarity in his eyes that hadn't been there before. He blinked and toppled over, rolling onto his back, gurgling something unintelligible. Tears streamed from his eyes, and then his body went still as his bloody mouth gaped open and shut.

Heart racing, pulse reverberating in his ears, pumping adrenaline through his body, Timothy turned his gun on another man with a crowbar. He stood over Torres, who looked to be unconscious, lying on his back. Timothy was about to shoot, but Murphy aimed and fired before he had the chance. The bullet hit above the man's right eye, and his head snapped back, his body a dead weight as he dropped to the ground. Torres was out of the fight, but his chest still rose and fell; he was still alive.

"My gun's jammed!" Burke's shout drew Timothy's attention.

Another crowbar-wielding man swung for Burke, and the weapon caught on the ex-cop's suit and ripped a long hole through it. A second attacker came at Burke with a hammer, lodging the claw into Burke's back. He roared and swung, punching the hammer wielder squarely in the face, sending him reeling to the ground. As the first man jumped on Burke's back and held him in a choke hold, Timothy raised his firearm, intending to shoot.

"No!" Murphy shouted, sprinting toward her friend. "You'll shoot Burke!"

She took hold of the thug on Burke's back and flung him off, though not before he was able to tear off Burke's full-face respirator mask. The man slammed into the hospital wall and fell with a stomach-churning, wet crunch upon an oozing corpse. The addict screamed as he rolled away covered in blackish brown gunk. He raked his fingers across his face, smearing the tar-like secretions, trying to wipe them away. As he made to regain his feet, snarling back at Burke and Murphy, Timothy took aim and fired, the bullet tearing through his thigh. He dropped back to the ground and held his wound, howling in pain and fury.

The last attacker relentlessly held to Burke whose face was now completely exposed. Though he was smaller and weaker, the man had a vice grip on Burke's suit. Murphy had her arms around the addict's waist, pulling him as he held on, as he bared his teeth at Burke. There was no reasoning, no humanity in his red-rimmed eyes, only a wild, animalistic fervor. Burke, hands still gloved, clawed at the man, but the attacker managed to sink his teeth into Burke's palm, creating a third point of contact. No matter what Burke did, the man would not let go of his suit or his hand.

"We have to do something!" Heather shouted.

Timothy spun around, grabbed the spiked bat, and lunged at the tangle of friend and foe. He swung, landing the spikes into the addict's upper left arm. The man screamed, his teeth releasing Burke's hand, and his left hand losing its grip. As Murphy threw the attacker away from them, Burke stumbled back and tripped over the still-howling, gunk-covered man on the ground behind him, twisting to catch himself, face slamming into the same crushed sack of bones and rotting flesh near the hospital wall.

Two shots signaled the crazed addict's death as Murphy stopped him from coming at them a second time, but Timothy barely registered that. Heather stepped toward Burke to help him, but Timothy stopped his wife, dread a thousand-pound weight on his chest as Burke scrambled to his feet, frantically cleaning off his face with his sleeve. Timothy couldn't look away from the last of their attackers, the man he'd shot in the thigh, the man who was covered in the same human fluids as Burke.

"What are you doing?" Heather asked, frowning at Timothy as he held her back with his arm.

Timothy's voice caught in his throat; words eluded him as horror ran ice-cold down his spine. He nodded at the man who'd stopped screaming, stopped holding his bleeding leg. Fresh, bright red blood leaked from his eyes, his ears, his nose; it ran over the darker secretions creating a forking pattern on his cheeks. He gasped for breath as his eyes went too wide, as they bulged. Already, signs of swelling were evident in his limbs. Chest heaving, body convulsing, he gurgled blood.

Murphy closed the gap between herself and the dying addict and put a bullet between his eyes. Timothy jumped at the sound, the boom of gunfire somehow echoing more harshly off the concrete all around them than the gunshots before it. Lips pressed together in a firm line, she looked up at her friend, her hardened gaze softening.

Burke's usual stoicism was replaced by pure terror as he stared at the man at his feet. He backed away, tearing off his tattered suit, using every bit of clean fabric on the inside to scrub the muck off his face. Timothy and Heather took a giant step backward, but Murphy shuffled a few steps forward, her hand outstretched.

"Burke," she said, her voice cracking.

"No!" Burke roared. His breathing was panicked, quick and heavy. "Stay back. Don't come near me. Think about James."

Murphy pulled back her hand, but she didn't retreat. "Maybe you're okay," she said. "Maybe—"

"You know that's probably not true," Burke said. "Give me space, Murphy. I mean it." Though he trembled, he managed to make his voice firm.

Murphy did as he asked, but neither of them broke eye contact. Timothy watched, his heart racing. He looked at his wife, at the woman whom he loved with all his heart. *It could have been her.* He reached out, and she took his hand. He breathed through the respirator, more grateful for it than he'd ever been. And then they all stood still in the midst of the dead, Burke at a safe distance, until Torres groaned from where he lay a few yards away.

"I guess we won?" Torres sat up slowly. "That was a doozy. At least we got the sup—" He cut off as he looked their way, frowning at them. "What's going on?" He got to his feet and blinked several times, holding the side of his head with one hand. He reached to pull of his respirator.

"Don't!" Timothy shouted, holding out his hand.

"Whoa, Torres, slow down. Peters is right." Murphy approached him. "Keep your respirator on."

He let go of the edge of his respirator, and Murphy helped him to the hood of a car where he sat, confusion written in his features.

"What does Burke have all over his face? And why doesn't he have his gear on?"

"Those bastards ripped his gear off," Murphy said. "And..." She swallowed hard and looked over her shoulder at Burke. She couldn't seem to finish.

"We think he fell into an infected body," Timothy said. "Same as him." Timothy pointed to the addict who'd shown signs of DV-10 before Murphy had shot him.

Torres snorted, shaking his head. "That guy clearly died from a gunshot to the head. And the thigh. I mean... c'mon, guys. This isn't funny."

"It's not a joke," Murphy said.

"Burke?" Torres stood straight again, his voice desperate, his stance unstable. He reached out, and Murphy let him lean on her shoulder.

Burke nodded once. "It's likely. I don't feel sick, yet, but..." He breathed in deeply. "You four take these carts back to Vanguard."

Murphy shook her head. "We're not leaving you here."

Timothy tensed. "We have to get these supplies back," he whispered to Heather.

She gave him a look, one that he'd seen many times before. "Just wait," she said softly.

"I'm not going to risk your lives," Burke said, frustration creeping into his voice. "Go now, before more trouble comes our way."

Timothy felt some tension melt away. He hated it, but Burke was right. They had to go. They had to leave him.

"No." Murphy crossed her arms.

"Murphy's right," Torres said. "We stick together. We don't even know for sure that you're infected."

"C'mon, Torres. It's just a matter of time," Burke waved toward the corpses.

Murphy raised her chin. "With all we've been through, you really expect us to just walk away?"

"For James? Yes." Burke's voice went hard. "We all love that kid, but you're his mom, Murphy. You're responsible for keeping him safe."

"We're a team," Murphy said, a sob escaping her after she'd spoken.

Torres turned away from them both, leaning on the car, hanging his head.

"He can follow at a distance," Heather said. All eyes turned on her. "If he's sick, we'll know soon. If not, he'll be nearby when it comes time for everyone to get to safety inside. And it's possible that he's fine. That man was probably infected hours ago, right? That's how it usually happens. Maybe it wasn't that corpse that infected him."

Timothy's stomach churned. "Not always," he said. "Think back to the farmhouse. That cop out on the driveway that got left behind. That deer. They died within minutes. Abrams had longer, but... not by much."

"They were attacked by a swarm," Heather said. "It's different. It's hundreds of bites within a few seconds."

Murphy nodded. "Heather's right." She looked at Burke, pleading in her words. "Follow us, Burke. We'll keep our distance. You won't endanger us."

"Fine," Burke said, "but I'm not going anywhere near anyone for at least a day. We'll need to wait to leave until tomorrow." He nodded toward the carts. "Now let's get out of here. I won't touch anything, just in case." Burke started walking away, skirting their group and leaving the carts where they could all grab one.

Torres grabbed both his and Burke's. "I see how it is," he said, offering a small smile. "You just didn't want to do the work of hauling these back."

Burke snorted and shook his head. "That would be more your speed, Torres."

"Ain't that the truth." Murphy joined in, and soon the three were bantering as usual, though Timothy didn't miss the undertones of heartbreak and fear. Burke's life hung in the balance, and only time would tell which way the scales would tip.

Chapter 27

Zara Williams and Walter Peters

Zara woke with a start as the door to the camper slammed shut. Kai entered, his beekeeper suit smudged with dirt from head to toe. A bag was slung over his shoulder, but other than that, he'd not brought back any of their supplies. He slid off the wide-brimmed hat and mesh net that covered his face; skin glistening with sweat, cheeks bright red, he looked at Zara with an expression she couldn't read. She sat up, placing her feet on the floor, squeezing the edge of the thin mattress in an attempt to prepare for whatever he was about to say.

"I didn't find anything," Kai said at last. "I mean, I found the plane, what was left of it, anyway." He hefted the bag. "And I found this old gun, barely worth having. But I didn't find Walter's body."

Tension whooshed out of Zara, her arms going slack at her sides. "That's good," she said softly. "That means there's still hope."

Kai raised one hand. "Hold up," he said. "It's a big forest. We don't know anything yet. I don't want you to get your hopes up. And I don't want you even thinking about going out there tomorrow. I'll go looking again, but you still need to rest."

Zara shook her head. "No. We have another lead. If you couldn't find him out there, I think I know where he might be, and I think he's alive." She dug LeeAnn's drawing out of her pocket, unfolded it, and handed it over to Kai.

After setting the bag on the floor and his gloves on the narrow counterspace of the kitchenette, Kai took the paper, frowning at it as he turned it right side up. "What is this?"

"Willow stopped by," Zara said. "A little girl left that at the hospital. Willow thought that drawing might be Walter. The mother – I think her name is Carol – she's lost it, and it's possible that she wouldn't have told others about finding Walter. She's paranoid, doesn't trust people. Anyway, the family is staying at some venue called The Log Cabin." Zara nodded toward the dry erase board where Willow had drawn a map. "Willow left directions. I think we should check it out."

Kai sighed and let the drawing flutter down to rest on the counter on top of his gloves. "Zara, it's been a long day. I don't think it's a good idea. Can't we go tomorrow?"

"What if he's there?" Zara tried to keep the sharpness from her tone, but her words came out clipped.

"Then he's safe for another night," Kai said. "I'm tired, Zara."

Frustration ignited inside Zara, her chest tightening, angry heat creeping up her neck. "Because you've been doing everything *I* wanted to do. If you'd have let me go out there, maybe you wouldn't be so tired. I thought about unhooking this trailer and driving out there myself. But I knew you'd hate that. I promised to rest, and I kept my word. But you're back, I've rested, and if you don't take the wheel, Kai, I'll do it myself." She crossed her arms, her breath more labored after her speech than she liked.

Kai plopped down on the bench seating of the little eating area. He stared at her for an uncomfortably long moment, so long that she cleared her throat and readjusted herself, her mood softening at the way he seemed to be searching her for answers to unspoken questions.

Finally, he stood and took the beekeeper suit off, folding it up and sticking it in the closet with the other two they'd kept. Zara was quiet. He wasn't objecting further, and she wasn't going to argue anymore until he gave her a reason. Kai walked over to the dry erase board and took it off the wall, studying it silently. Then he turned to face her.

"You want to ride in the truck or back here?" he asked. "I don't want to leave the trailer unattended. It's finders-keepers these days."

Zara smiled, relieved. "Really? You're not going to push back anymore?"

"It's not like you've given me much of a choice," Kai said, but then he shrugged. "Then again, I didn't give you much choice when it came to staying here today, so… I guess this makes us even. Besides, it'll take us maybe an hour at most to drive there, check, and then come back here or find another spot to park this rig. If he's there, we can stop worrying about him, and you can chill out. If not, nothing changes."

"Thank you, Kai." Zara carefully stood, grateful that the world didn't spin. "I'll sit in the truck with you."

Within a few minutes, they were buckled up, Kai in the driver's seat, Zara beside him. Zara held the dry erase board at the edges so as to not smear Willow's directions as Kai pulled the truck and camper out of the lot. He drove a little faster when they reached town, cutting across the northwestern corner of Holyoke as quickly as possible. The mayor hadn't seemed keen on the idea of them sticking around.

Not far out of town, Zara sat up, pointing as they rounded a slight bend in the road. "There! I think that's it."

Kai turned into the lot of the building, more a log mansion than a cabin. It was a charming, three-story venue with a restaurant on the first floor. A large wooden sign designated it the place they were looking for: The Log Cabin.

"It's getting late," Kai said as he parked out front. "Let's hurry this up."

Zara nodded, hopped out of the truck, and followed Kai up to the front door. But before they could get there, a woman – the same one who'd come to the hospital as they'd been speaking to the mayor – burst outside with a rifle in hand. Kai stepped slightly in front of Zara, stopping her in her tracks.

"Who are you?" Carol pointed the rifle at them, her tone harsh.

"Carol, right?" Zara said, standing on tiptoes to look around Kai's shoulder. She put a hand on his arm and gently pushed him aside. He didn't resist, but his muscles tensed as if he wanted to.

"How do you know my name?" Carol didn't lower her weapon.

"We're friends of Willow's." Zara offered a small smile.
"I don't have supplies to spare," Carol said. "Get back in your truck and go back to wherever you came from."
"We don't want your supplies," Kai said. "We're looking for someone."
That seemed to upset Carol more than the possibility of them asking for supplies. "I said," she shouted, "get back in your truck."
"Mom?" A teenage boy stuck his head outside, his brow furrowed.
"Go back inside, Heath." Carol's finger lowered toward the trigger, and she repeated her demands to Kai and Zara, raising her voice, shouting at them to leave.
Heath came to his mother's side, gently putting his hand on her arm to coax her into pointing the rifle at the ground. "C'mon, Mom. They're not causing trouble. Let me talk to them, okay?"
"Don't go anywhere near them," Carol snapped, keeping her eyes on them.
"Ma'am," Zara said, "we are just looking for our friend, Walter. Please, we—"
"It's just me and my kids here." The barrel of the rifle flew upward again.
Heath's face paled at Zara's words, though. He looked at them, stepping back out of his mother's periphery. She was so focused on them that she didn't seem to notice her son's actions. Heath shook his head, his eyes flitting between them and the gun. He looked terrified, his hands visibly shaking as he waved for them to leave behind his mother's back.
Zara frowned and exchanged a look with Kai who seemed as confused as she felt. But there was something about Heath's actions and expression combined with Carol's wide, desperate eyes and harsh tone that turned Zara's stomach. The air was thick with tension, and the longer they stood there, the more certain Zara became that Carol would actually shoot them if they didn't leave.
And then Carol pointed the rifle slightly upward and fired. Zara flinched and ducked, and Kai lunged for her in the same instant, hunching over her. He pushed her backward toward the truck. Zara didn't resist. She shouted in alarm as Carol aimed her gun back at them.
"We're leaving," she shouted. "We're going, okay? Don't shoot!"
"You've got five seconds before you're dead," Carol shouted.
Zara scrambled for the safety of the truck.

***

The sound of gunfire was like someone had gut punched Walter out of his half-asleep state. He'd been drifting in and out of consciousness since he'd fallen down the stairs and been returned to his comfortable prison. Carol had faithfully kept him mostly pain free with injections of whatever drug she'd been using, and Walter hadn't had the capacity to fight her over it. The idea that he could escape when he was better was poor consolation, but it was all he had.
Carol wasn't in the chair by the wall. She wasn't anywhere to be seen, which was a welcome break from his new normal. Walter frowned at the sound of shouting. *That* was *a gunshot, wasn't it?* He sat up straighter, trying to see as much as he could from the bed, but from his angle, all he could see was the road. He couldn't even see the parking lot.
"We're going, okay? Don't shoot!"
The voice was shrill and desperate, frightened maybe. And it was familiar. Walter worked through the brain fog the drugs had induced, working to embrace the feeling that he should know that voice.
"You've got five seconds before you're dead!"
That was Carol.
"Chill, lady! We said we're outta here."
"Kai, unlock the doors!"
A shock of understanding, like a shock of electricity, shot through Walter's body. "Zara!" he shouted, flinging his legs over the side of the bed as the sound of vehicle doors slamming made a knot grow in his stomach. "I'm up here!"
His body did *not* want to cooperate. The window was only ten steps from the side of the bed, but it felt like a mile. The wheelchair was removed from his reach. He used the side table as a crutch and then moved to leaning on the wall. Every step was a victory, but he was so slow.
The sound of an engine and the squeal of tires propelled him the last few steps. He slammed against the window, hands flat against the smooth, glass surface. There they were: Kai and Zara in the front seats of a truck as it sped away, hauling a silver airstream camper behind it. He barely caught a glimpse of them. "Zara, wait!" he shouted, his voice cracking, eyes blurring with desperate tears. His fingers fumbled with the window, trying to unlock it, but it was no use. The truck and camper pulled out of view. He sank to his knees, resting his arms on the windowsill of the tall glass pane, the moment of hope lost.

***

"She's nuts!" Kai shouted as they pulled out of the lot.
Zara was still trembling. "Willow was right," she said. "Carol *is* unhinged." She hugged herself tightly and leaned against the door, but then she realized they were going the wrong way. "Wait, where are you going?"
"I don't know," Kai said. "Away from the crazy lady with the rifle?"
"Do you know how to loop around, get back to where we came from?" Zara asked. "We need to go back. We know where the wreckage is from the lot."
Kai smacked the wheel with one hand, shouting with frustration. "I'll have to double back," he said. "I was so focused on getting out of the line of fire…" He pulled over, turning in his seat to look back. "I don't think she's following."
Zara breathed out a long, shaky breath. "What was that about, anyway. Did you see her son? The way he looked at us?"
Kai nodded. "Yeah. I think…" He chewed on his lower lip for a minute, clearly hesitant to finish his sentence. "I think she's got Walter."
Zara raised her eyebrows. "Why wouldn't she be happy for us to take a sick man off her hands? You heard her. She said she doesn't have enough supplies to go around."

"Yeah, but I just… I have this feeling. Her son knew who we were. And before we mentioned Walter, she wasn't violent. The kid got real nervous when we talked about Walter, like he expected that to set his mother off."

"Okay, then… we have to go back." Zara shook her head. "We get that gun you brought back from the plane, and we use it."

Kai shook his head. "We can't," he said. "It's not a good gun. It's got a kick like a horse, and it's unwieldy. I brought it back for emergencies. Like, the absolute last option. Neither one of us is experienced enough to use it."

"You don't know that about me," Zara said, crossing her arms. "I know what I'm doing when it comes to firearms."

"I know you do, but Zara… I'm telling you, you could hurt yourself more."

"I want to go back." Even she could pick up on the childish lilt of her words, the stubbornness in her tone, but she didn't care.

"Zara—"

"Go back, Kai. If Walter is there, I want to know." Zara doubled down. "We could be minutes away from knowing if he's alive. Just drive closer. We can get out, creep closer, try to sneak inside."

Kai ground his teeth as he lowered his forehead to rest on the wheel. He groaned. "You're impossible."

"I know," Zara said. "I'll walk from here, if I have to."

"How about this: we drive by, slowly if that woman isn't outside, faster if she is. We park the truck on the other side of the place, farther down the road, maybe hidden somewhere, so that we don't have to worry about doubling back if we sneak up to the building and make her angry again. I don't want things to go south and our only option is to bypass The Log Cabin all together. We don't know the area; it could take forever to find our way back to the lot."

"Okay, deal." Zara nodded. "Let's do it."

Zara steeled herself as Kai pulled the truck around and drove back the way they'd come. If Carol was still outside, she prepared herself to duck, braced herself for gunfire. But when the building came into view, no one was outside. She breathed a sigh of relief, and she pressed her hands against the glass, studying the building.

Kai drove slowly, as he said he would if it was safe. "See anything?" he asked.

Zara scanned every window, pressing her lips together as she squinted whenever she caught sight of a shape. And then she stopped at a window on the third story. There was someone there, leaning his head against the window. "Stop!" Zara shouted. "Stop the truck."

Kai put on the brakes. "What is it?"

Zara pressed her hand against the window, willing the man to look up. He startled, sitting up straighter and swinging his head to look behind. He moved away from the window in a hurry. In the second that she could see his face, even from a distance, she recognized him.

They had found Walter.

Chapter 28

Timothy Peters

"It's been two hours." Murphy stood just inside the door to the camper they'd brought back from Wellesley. "How long are we going to make him stay out there?" She grabbed a bag from Timothy and turned to stash it inside.

Timothy had volunteered to help her load their share of the supplies after everything had been sanitized. Torres was resting where Lauren could keep an eye on him after his concussion, and Burke was self-quarantining. The gruff ex-cop had decided to camp out on the edge of the lot, far from any of them.

"He said a day, and I'm not planning to argue with him." Timothy handed her the last duffle bag. "It's smart for him to stay away from everyone. Even if he didn't catch *the* disease, it doesn't mean he couldn't have caught *a* disease. I mean, he fell into the juices of a rotting corpse. That can't be good."

Murphy gave him a flat stare as she took the bag. "Thanks for the optimism, Peters. I should come to you about my problems more often."

Timothy winced. "Sorry."

"It's fine." She sighed and ran her hands over her face, patting her cheeks a few times. "I'm exhausted. It's about time for us to hole up for the night. I think we're going to do it here, in the camper. James needs to get used to it." She nodded to the walkie talkie clipped to Timothy's pocket. "Do you think we could have that for the night? I'd like to be able to communicate with everyone while we're out here."

"Sure," Timothy said, handing it over, and she clipped to it her belt. "We've got one in each building and a third tuned in to the police department. This one is for stuff like this. I'll get you two an extra meal for the night, too, and for the morning, on us. Hey, James, how do you feel about Pop Tarts?" He frowned as he looked to the side where Murphy's son had been moments before. The boy had insisted on helping, and his mother had allowed it, considering he'd been stuck inside for days and the camper provided quick shelter. James had been drawing with chalk on the asphalt for half an hour, but the chalk was scattered and the boy vanished. He took a step back, turning in a circle. "Where *is* that kid?"

"What?" Murphy hopped out of the camper, her eyebrows knit together as she whipped her head back and forth. "James! Come out. We are not playing right now, bud."

Movement caught Timothy's eye, and he looked up to the top of the camper. "Um, Murphy?" He pointed at the little face peeking over the side.

Murphy's shoulders sagged, and she pinched the bridge of her nose. "This kid is going to give me a heart attack," she mumbled under her breath. She looked up and put her hands on her hips. "James, we see you."

"Aw, nuts!" James popped up on his hands and knees. "This is a good hiding spot, isn't it, Mom?"

Murphy crossed her arms. "How did you even get up there?"

"There's a ladder. Duh." James crawled across the back of the camper.

Timothy followed Murphy around. She squeaked as James shimmied backward off the top where the ladder was and rushed forward, holding up her hands, fingers reaching impatiently. As soon as James's waist was in her reach, she snatched him from the ladder and set him firmly on the ground.

"The world is dangerous enough without you doing stuff like that, James," Murphy said. "I didn't let you come out here so you could fall and break an arm."

James scrunched up his face, clearly displeased. "You used to let me climb trees all the time!"

"Does that look like a tree to you?" Murphy pointed at the camper.

"No." James stomped one foot. "It looks *shorter*. And so it's safer. I climbed one as big as that building at Grandma's!" He pointed to the Vanguard building across from New Horizons Laboratory. It was twelve stories.

"Oh, for goodness sake," Murphy said. "You did not, James."

Timothy chuckled softly, and both James and Murphy gave him death stares. Their expressions looked so much alike, he had to choke down another laugh. He cleared his throat and held up his hands. "I'll fill the tank so you're all ready to go tomorrow."

Mother and son continued to argue as Timothy grabbed the gas can Alex had agreed to give away and worked to fill the truck's tank. Gasoline was valuable, but more valuable was getting Murphy, Torres, and Burke, if he survived, out of Boston. The last thing Timothy needed — and Alex agreed for his own reasons — was for anyone else to find out what they were doing there and the story behind it.

"I told James to pick up the chalk and get in the camper," Murphy said as she came up behind Timothy. The sounds of huffing and puffing could be clearly heard on the other side of the camper. "I've seen some of his old self come out the last few days, like he was before… all of this." She sighed and smiled tiredly. "It's been good. I missed him, even the tantrums."

Timothy set down the gas can and closed the fuel door on the truck. "He's a good kid," he said. "And the tantrums, they're normal for a kid his age."

Murphy nodded and looked out over the lot, toward the edge where Burke sat on the hood of a parked car, back to them. His plan was to sleep in the back seat. They hadn't checked on him since they'd arrived at Vanguard a couple of hours prior. Burke had seemed like he wanted to be alone, and it wasn't like anyone could get close enough to him to really keep him company.

"James wanted to go hug Burke before we settled down in the camper," Murphy said. "I had to tell him no, of course."

"Maybe Burke will be okay," Timothy said.

"Maybe." Murphy shook her head and patted Timothy on the shoulder. "Thanks for your help," she said. "I think it's time to call it a day."

She and Timothy walked together to the end of the camper. She turned to go around to the other side, and Timothy crossed toward Vanguard's main building. Behind him, the door to the camper clicked open and shut. He was several yards from the camper when, out of the corner of his eye, he noticed Burke moving. Timothy glanced toward the distant man as he pushed off the hood of the car. Even from afar, he looked worn out, his feet scraping the ground as he walked out into the street. His gait was unusual for him, his shoulders too hunched, his arms hanging too loosely. He turned to face east and then stilled.

Timothy frowned. "What is he doing?"

The slam of the camper door startled Timothy, and he spun to see Murphy storm out of the camper. "James!" she shouted. "I swear, if you don't get your butt in this camper…" She bent low, looking under the rig.

Timothy cast his gaze around the lot, looking for signs of the boy. There were a few vehicles parked here and there, abandoned weeks ago. A small form darted from behind one and started running — toward Burke.

"Hey!" Timothy shouted. "He's going for Burke!"

Murphy spun around, gasping. "No! James, stop!" She broke into a run.

Timothy was right behind her when he realized James was only speeding up. Ahead, Burke seemed oblivious to what was happening. He still faced east, the shouting behind him apparently not registering. James was getting too close to Burke; Timothy wasn't going to catch up to him. And the closer he got, the more he was sure: there was something wrong with Burke. But then Murphy burst forward with more speed than Timothy thought she was capable.

James held out his arms toward Burke's back as he closed the distance between them. He was only yards away from wrapping his arms around him. "Burke! I want to stay with you!" His voice was small but stubborn.

Murphy reached him, going so fast, she had to grab hold of him and stumble to a stop, falling to the ground with her son in her arms, positioning herself so she fell on her side, so that James didn't hit the ground at all. He struggled against her, but she had him firmly around the waist.

"Stop it, James." Murphy sounded more desperate than she did angry. She glanced at Burke's back as Timothy approached, coming to a stop. She and James were one point in a triangle between them, Burke, and Timothy. "Burke? Please… tell James he can't stay with you." She pled with her friend as she maintained her hold on her son.

And then Timothy caught sight of Burke's hand; it was trembling, swollen at his side. "Burke… are you… are you okay?" He was already three or four yards from the man, but he took a few steps back anyway.

James cried out. "Let me go, Mom! I want to stay with Burke!"

Burke twitched. The back of his neck was blotchy, the skin stretched too taught. "Quiet," he said, his voice raspy and wet. He coughed harshly, and then Burke turned around.

James stopped fighting his mother and shrank into her. Murphy cried out, and Timothy sucked in a sharp breath. Thick blood made rivers down his face. His eyes had begun to bulge; he could still blink, but there was little life left in his gaze. At this point, most people Timothy had seen suffering from DV-10 were screaming in pain. Not Burke. Every inch of him was trembling with effort. His body twitched, and when he spoke, he was clearly focusing on every word, pushing past the agony.

Bloody spittle sprayed the air with every word. "Do—you—hear—it?" There was an urgency in the words.

The blood drained from Timothy's face, and a chill swept over him. The sound he had learned to fear the most was a steady undertone to the near quiet of the empty city. It was growing louder, that dizzying hum. Down the street, the black swarm seeped around a corner. Timothy's heart leapt into his throat.

Burke, his back to the swarm, spoke again. "They slow when they feed," he said, and his body shook more violently with every syllable. He turned, his movements stiff as if his legs weighed a hundred pounds each. After a wheezing breath inward, Burke seemed to focus all of his pain, all of his determination, every ounce of his being into one, drawn-out scream which resulted in one word: "Run!"

"We love you," Murphy said as she scrambled to her feet, tears streaming down her cheeks. "We love you, Burke." Sobbing, James clinging to her, she sprinted back toward the camper.

Timothy's lungs burned as he ran. He took one last look over his shoulder as they crossed the lot. Burke ran into the black undulating cloud, his scream a battle cry. And he was right. The swarm *did* slow. It engulfed him, fed off of him.

Timothy tripped and rolled, quickly regaining his feet and continuing his mad dash toward safety. Burke's last moments gave them the precious seconds they needed to reach the camper. Murphy flung open the door, and Timothy climbed up after her.

"Seal the windows!" she shouted as she tossed James to the bed.

Timothy worked with her, ensuring they were safe. "The walkie talkie!" he said, holding out his hand. "We have to warn the others to stay inside."

Murphy nodded, unclipped the device, and slapped it into his hands. She rushed to her son, sitting on the edge of the bed, and holding him, rocking back and forth, fresh tears falling.

"A swarm is here," Timothy shouted into the walkie talkie. "Stay inside. Do you copy?"

A few agonizing seconds passed. "Are you safe?" Heather's voice came in over the speaker.

"Yes. Me, Murphy, and James are in the camper. Burke…" He paused, swallowing as the sound of Burke's name brought a sob from Murphy. "Burke's dead. He… he saved our lives." He closed his eyes. "Alex? Lauren? Are you hearing this?"

A crackle sounded, and then: "We hear you," Lauren said. "I'll make sure everyone in the lab knows."

The swarm reached the camper, flowing around it, thousands of mosquitos buzzing and clinking against the windows, like black rain with a mind of its own.

* * *

Murphy, Torres, and James didn't wait to leave; once the swarm had passed, though it was nearing evening, they had made the decision. They were already packed, and there was nothing keeping them there anymore.

"I have to get my son out of this city," Murphy said. "There's only death here." She choked on those last words, having to pause, eyes glistening as she seemed to swallow grief. "You shouldn't stay either."

Timothy and Heather stood just outside the door to the Vanguard building where Murphy had pulled up the truck and camper. James sat inside the cab, in the back seat. Torres sat next to him; whether his pale complexion was from his concussion or the pain of losing his friend, Timothy wasn't sure.

"If you find a place that's much different," Timothy said with a sad smile, "send us a postcard. Maybe we'll follow you there."

"You got it." Murphy offered a half smile in return. "But seriously, I hope we cross paths again."

Timothy looked away, heat creeping up his neck. "If it weren't for us, Burke would still be alive." He looked back up at her. "I'm sorry we asked you to help us."

Murphy shook her head. "No. Don't do that. We made our choices. We needed supplies. We needed weapons. Burke's time had come, and whether we were here or elsewhere, there's no guarantee he would still be alive. Not in the world we live in today."

Timothy couldn't help but glance in the direction where Burke's corpse still lay. His body would stay there until they could wrap it in a tarp and bury it in the nearby city park. Alexander Roman had laid down some specific rules for handling Burke's body, and they simply didn't have the time to carry the process out that day.

The CDC disease detective had also seemed quite concerned about the possibilities for *how* Burke got sick with DV-10 in the first place. Alex had come to the larger Vanguard building to receive a debriefing after he'd heard about Burke's death. He'd been quiet, mostly, asking questions, prompting for more details occasionally, but listening with a sharp ear, writing down everything Timothy, Heather, and Murphy remembered from the time Burke had his respirator taken off to the moment of his death.

"I already knew from studying the virus that dead bodies would be a problem," Alex had said. "It's a capsid virus, after all, but I was hoping it wouldn't be able to survive in a corpse for longer than seven days. With the way you describe the condition of the corpse, it had to be older than that. Maybe three weeks or more, though in this heat… perhaps less."

"So… how long can DV-10 last after someone infected has died?" Timothy had asked.

"I don't know," Alex said. "This virus is more adaptable than any I've ever seen. It's evolving, and I'm afraid it's only getting more resilient." He sighed. "That means we won't be able to use those hazmat suits for longer than I had anticipated, not until we find enough cleaner in which to soak them. We have to kill any virions left on the surface of the fabric."

It hadn't taken long after that for Murphy to decide she, Torres, and James were leaving sooner rather than later.

Timothy turned his attention from Burke's corpse and the darker thoughts that accompanied it back to Murphy, who had come in for a hug with Heather. When she pulled away, she reached out a hand, and Timothy grasped it.

"Thank you for being so kind," he said. "And we wish you the best of luck."

"Same to you," Murphy said before climbing back into the truck and pulling away.

"I'm exhausted." Timothy rubbed his hands over his face. "It's time to call it a day." He turned toward the door, entered the code to get inside, and swung open the door.

"Agreed." Heather walked in ahead of him, but she didn't walk in the direction Timothy assumed she would. She started toward the room *he* was sleeping in. They hadn't shared a bed overnight since he'd ruined everything by lying to her.

"Are you…?" Timothy hesitated. "Are we…?"

"Going to sleep together?" Heather asked.

Timothy nodded.

"Are you complaining?" she asked.

He raised his eyebrows. "Not in a million years."

"Good. I think… after Burke… I just want to move forward." She hooked her arm with his.

That night, Timothy held his wife close. The warmth of her, her very presence, was comforting and wonderful and exactly what he needed. And yet, even she couldn't smooth the knots in Timothy's stomach completely. He sought sleep in those early hours of the night, but the memory of Burke's death wouldn't leave him.

He was wide awake when the walkie talkie that was kept open to the Boston Police Department crackled to life. "Timothy, are you there?" It was George's voice.

Timothy slid his arm out from under Heather's sleeping form very carefully so as to not wake her. He hurried to the walkie talkie, grabbed it, and quietly left the room. "George? Everything okay?" he asked.

"No," George said, the pause afterward unbearably long. "We made a mistake," he said. "We broke the peace between us and the Russos."

A lump hardened in Timothy's stomach as he anticipated George's next words. The time for war was near, but they were supposed to have half a day left, maybe more, depending on when Frank started counting. They needed that half a day.

"They have military grade weapons," George said. "O'Donnell is afraid we're going to be outgunned. The Russos and what's left of CON are about to hit hard and fast, so you guys need to hunker down, consider moving into the green zone."

Timothy listened and tried to process what his brother had said. "We can't do that, George."

There was another long pause. "Yeah," George said, "I know."

Timothy didn't know what to say. All he could think about was his little brother running headlong into danger, of that danger coming to their doorstep. Again. *It never ends,* he thought.

"Hey, Tim?" George's voice was laced with emotion. "I love you. I… I just wanted to say that. Can you tell Heather and Annika? And Lizzy…" He made a frustrated noise. "I wish I could have seen her."

Tears sprung and spilled over. "You *will*," he said. "You'll see her. And dad, too, once he makes it back." Timothy closed his eyes. "I love you, too, George. We all love you." His voice cracked as his words echoed those of Murphy as she'd said her final, rushed goodbyes to Burke.

One by one, good people were being picked off, by nature and by man. All he could hope for was that for once, history wouldn't repeat itself, but all he could think about was how likely it was that it would.

Chapter 29

Lauren Stevens

Lauren was relieved to have one less patient in her makeshift clinic. Torres hadn't taken up much of her attention, but his mere presence had added pressure she'd barely been able to handle. She leaned against the counter, sipping on a water bottle and munching on crackers, trying to keep up the illusion that she was just fine while her insides continued to writhe with the anxiety of responsibilities she'd sworn off long ago.

Annika had been awake less often the last twelve hours than Lauren would have preferred. The girl's progress seemed stagnated. Lauren had been ecstatic to receive an ultrasound machine, and she'd searched for any complications immediately. There were a few concerning signs but nothing requiring immediate attention, though Lauren had found a stronger antibiotic for Annika at the sight of a slightly swollen right kidney.

Candice was getting better by the day; all she needed was rest. Lauren had been pleased with her progress. Candice could walk on her own, though she was clearly still sore. The woman wouldn't leave Annika, though, and Lauren hadn't suggested it. It was good to have another set of eyes on the girl so that Lauren could eat, sleep, and use the restroom.

She had suggested, however, that Lizzy go back with her brother. The toxic fruit she'd eaten was almost certainly out of her system, but Lizzy hadn't agreed, insisting she was still feeling off. Azalea had been overly protective of Lizzy, pushing to keep her there. Lauren couldn't exactly blame either one of them. They'd been through a lot together, and Lauren wasn't going to fight them.

Lauren offered Azalea a small smile from across the room as the young woman sat idly by Lizzy's side; they were both on the ground. Lizzy was wrapped up in a sleeping bag, napping. Azalea didn't return the smile, instead folding her arms and shifting her gaze back to Lizzy.

Perhaps they feel comforted by being near medical help, Lauren thought as she shook off the urge to ask them to leave again. *They'll go eventually.* The thought also crossed her mind that Lizzy might not be ready to be around her brother. After being trafficked, escaping, and travelling under dangerous conditions, it wouldn't be surprising if the girl just needed some space to mentally heal.

It was getting late. Day and night were almost irrelevant, or it seemed that way while Lauren was stuck mostly in the same room, sleeping in short intervals, always on guard. She finished her crackers and stepped over to Candice, placing a gentle hand on her shoulder as the woman slept.

"Hey," Lauren said. "Candice?"

Candice woke with a start, sucking in a deep breath. "Annika? Everything okay?"

"Yeah," Lauren said quickly. "Everything is fine. I was just hoping you could keep an eye on things so I could rest."

Candice rubbed her eyes. "Right. Of course, yes. How long have I been asleep?"

"About four hours," Lauren said.

"How long do you need?" Candice sat up slowly, her movements stiff. "When should I wake you?"

"Give me as long as you can," Lauren said, "unless something changes with Annika. Then, wake me immediately."

Candice nodded. "Sure thing." She glanced at Annika. "How is she? What should I be looking for?"

"Any change, really." Lauren turned toward her own pallet of blankets on the floor. "Swelling in her legs or feet, labored breathing, any signs she's in pain… don't wake her, but if she does wake while I'm sleeping, ask her how she feels."

"I can do that." Candice slid off her cot and shuffled over to Annika. "Hey, Blueberry," she whispered, softly placing her hand over Annika's. "I'm going to be keeping an eye on you, okay?"

Lauren smiled at the sweet gesture and settled onto her blankets, pulling out a set of earplugs from her pocket. She turned toward the cabinets and tried to find some semblance of comfort. Squishing the earplugs into place, Lauren closed her eyes, pushing aside every feeling except for exhaustion.

It seemed only seconds before she was being shaken awake. A muffled voice filtered through the earplugs, and Lauren blinked away sleep. She rolled over, brow furrowed, to find Candice on her knees, leaning over her. Lauren plucked the earplugs out as Candice's teary eyes registered.

"What is it?" Lauren sat up, eyes darting to Annika.

"There's something wrong." Candice's voice trembled. "She woke up, and she was okay. She wanted to sit up for the first time since the accident, so I helped her, and… and..." A sob shook Candice and she covered her mouth. "…something's wrong," she repeated.

Lauren pulled herself to standing and rushed to Annika, her hands flying over the girl as she tried to diagnose what was wrong. Annika was pale, and her hands and feet were ice-cold. Her abdomen was distended. She'd broken out in a sweat from head to toe, and she whimpered, her eyelids drooping, her groaning constant.

"My stethoscope," Lauren muttered, heart pounding as she swung toward the counter, frantically snatching the medical tool and returning.

Annika's heart was racing, and the sound of it made Lauren's heartbeat speed up to match. Her lungs burned as she held her breath. When she pulled back Annika's shirt, a long dark bruise spread across her left side, just under the ribs.

Lauren's hands shook, and she placed them flat on the cot, willing her body to steady. Throat closing, chest tight, she focused on one point, on a speck of dust on Annika's sheet. Everything else blurred, and her body was too light. A cold sweat sent a shiver down her spine. A whooshing sound filled her ears, and her stomach roiled within her.

It was happening again. She was going to lose her patient. There was nothing she could do.
"What is it?" Candice asked.
Azalea and Lizzy were standing in the distance, watching with horrified expressions, when Lauren looked back up. She refocused, breathing in and out intentionally, evenly. Candice deserved an answer, so Lauren forced the words out, letting them sour her mouth.
"Internal bleeding. I think... I think it's a delayed splenic rupture. She might have burst her spleen when she tried sitting up and moving around."
"What does that mean?" Candice stepped forward, smoothing back Annika's hair as the girl moaned louder. "It's okay, sweetheart. Hang in there." She looked back at Lauren, her desperate voice firmer, harsher. "What—does—that—mean?"
"It means..." Lauren swallowed bile. "I can't help her."
Candice deflated as if Lauren had punched her in the gut, folding in on herself, air rushing out of her as she breathed a cry of agony.
"No, no, no, no..." She whispered, shaking her head. "What about Dr. Linden at City Hall?"

Lauren bit her lower lip. "If we can get her there in time, maybe..."
"Then let's go." Candice marched over to the counter and snatched the walkie talkie. "Heather! Heather, are you there?" She'd stifled her cries, and while her voice wasn't completely stable, her words were understandable.
"Candice?" It was Timothy. He sounded wide awake despite the early morning hour. "Heather is asleep. What is it?"
"We have to get Annika to City Hall. Now. She needs the surgeon."
Lauren backed away from the cot until her back hit the wall, and then she sank to the ground. *I can't do this. Not again.*
"Are you sure?" Timothy asked.
"Yes." Candice started stuffing water and granola bars in a backpack.
"Okay," Timothy said. "I'll wake Heather. We'll be over in a—"
A distant *boom* was accompanied by the ground shuddering beneath them. Lauren gasped and scrambled up, leaping to steady Annika's cot as Candice did the same. The other woman put a protective arm over the girl, leaning over her. Azalea and Lizzy both shrieked and ducked, covering their heads with their hands.
"What the hell was that?" Lauren asked, shaken out of her stupor.
"It sounded like an explosion," Candice said.
"You guys all right?" Timothy's voice shouted urgently over the walkie talkie.
Candice rushed to the device she'd dropped in the heat of the moment. "Yeah," she said. "We're fine."
"We were going to tell you this morning, but we got word last night that things were going to heat up sooner than expected. I just thought..." Timothy paused. "Hold on," he said. "We're getting something over the BPD walkie talkie."
The door slammed open, and Minnie barged inside, followed closely by Alex and Oliver. They were wide-eyed, having clearly just woken. Samson followed them into the room, pacing and whimpering near the boy, stopping every few seconds to perk up his ears and listen.
"Land's sake!" Minnie wrapped Lauren in a hug. "You okay, baby girl?"
"I'm fine, Mom," Lauren said. "But Annika isn't. We have to get her to the surgeon at City Hall."
"You're not going anywhere," Alex said. "That sounded like a bomb or something. Isn't that war over the city supposed to start soon?"
"We were supposed to have more time." Candice held the walkie talkie with a vice grip, staring at it as if willing more information to come through.
"Right before you got here, Timothy said something about the conflict starting early." Lauren pressed her lips together, shifting her weight back and forth anxiously. They all turned their eyes to Candice and the walkie talkie.
"We've got news. We're coming over." Timothy's voice sounded grim.
Candice set the walkie talkie on the counter. "No matter what is happening out there," she said. "I'm getting Annika to City Hall. They're in the green zone. It will be safer there, anyway."
Lauren nodded. "Okay, okay." She was reeling with thoughts on how to safely transport the girl. "The roads aren't clear between here and City Hall. The swarms are going to be more active at this time of day. We're going to need to be careful when transferring her or else risk her bleeding out more quickly..." She let out a frustrated breath. "What are we going to do?"
"We're going to come up with a plan," Alex said.
Candice shook her head. "We can't sit around and *talk* about this. We have to *go*."
"Hold on, hon," Minnie said in a motherly tone, "the last thing we need is to poke a hornet's nest with a short stick while we're tryin' to get this baby to where she needs to go."
"You don't even know her!" Candice raised her voice. "If she was *your* daughter, we'd already be gone."
Samson positioned himself between Candice and Minnie, curling his lip at Candice's shouting. Oliver patted his thighs, shushing the dog and beckoning him over. Samson obeyed reluctantly after Minnie reinforced Oliver's command with a shooing gesture and a simple, "Hush now."
"Calm down." Alex's firm words did not go over well with Candice.
The conversation devolved into Candice, Minnie, and Alex all speaking at once. No amount of Oliver's efforts seemed to be able to stop Samson from adding to the noise as he barked and whined. Anxiety continued to build up inside Lauren's chest until her heart threatened to burst. When Timothy and Heather barged in, they stopped short, eyes wide at the shouting match. Then, they added their voices to the mix, their pleas for peace only making things worse. In the far corner, Lizzy cowered with her hands over her ears, and Azalea stood next to her, whispering into her ear, perhaps trying to calm her.

Lauren couldn't take it anymore.."Stop!" she screamed. "Everyone shut up!" She pressed one fist against her chest and steadied herself with one hand on the wall. "Annika will die if we don't do something." They all fell silent, including Samson, and turned to look at her. Panic welled as she dug her fingernails into her sweaty palms. She looked at Timothy. "We need more information. Did you get anything from the BPD?"

Timothy nodded, clearing his throat before hesitantly speaking. "Um, yeah. It's not good. Headquarters has been hit with some kind of missile. After suspicions were raised about that kind of fire power in Frank's hands, O'Donnell had already evacuated to a nearby building, but... they lost a lot of supplies. They're preparing a counterattack right now. It's not safe out there."

"I don't care," Candice said. "I'm getting Annika to that surgeon."

Heather nodded, her eyes going hard with determination. "Me too."

"I'm with you," Timothy added. He looked to Alex. "We could use more protection on the way, at least until we get into the green zone."

"I can't leave the lab," Alex said. "And I won't leave Minnie and Oliver." His son wrapped his arms around Alex's waist and hugged him tightly. "But we can put our heads together, figure out how to get you all there quickly and safely."

Timothy nodded. He looked over his shoulder at his sister, who was clearly still unstable, and turned back with a pained expression. "I agree that someone should stay here," he said. "Lizzy and Azalea aren't in any position to keep themselves safe should the lab come under any sort of attack."

"Dad?" Oliver turned frightened eyes up at his father. "Are they going to bomb us?"

Alex shook his head. "No," he said. "That wouldn't make any sense for them. They're fighting the Boston Police Department, miles from here. They probably won't even come that close to us. Not tonight, anyway."

"Let's just go," Candice said. "We can strap her to the cot, roll her across the city. Tim, you can scout out ahead, find suitable hiding places, and Heather, you can come up behind. Me and Lauren can push this thing. If a swarm comes, we hurry to hide until they pass and then continue on our way."

"That's too dangerous," Alex said. "Are you guys sure one of the vehicles can't get through?"

Heather shook her head. "Not until you get to Interstate 90. We'd have to clear a pathway ourselves for at least a mile."

"Maybe," Timothy said, "but we'd have the shelter of the car close by."

"That would take too long," Candice said. "What if we get stuck? What if we have to double back too many times?"

"No plan is going to be perfect," Timothy said.

The back and forth started up again. Lauren's head spun. The tightness in her chest was only getting worse. There were too many people in the room, too many voices, too many opinions. And all the while Annika was dying. The fact that she wasn't dead yet was a sign that the bleed was slow, but she had several hours at most before she absolutely *needed* surgery. And even then, Lauren and Minnie were the only blood donors. If Minnie was staying, Lauren would need to find three or four donors at City Hall.

"It's too much," she whispered, vision blurring with tears. She turned and fled the room, fled the arguments and the desperation and her dying patient. She turned down one hall after another until she met a dark dead end and curled up on the cool, smooth floor, letting every pent-up fear and emotion pour out of her through her tears.

She only lay there a few minutes before she heard Alex's voice. "Lauren?" He sounded worried. His footsteps pounded the tiled halls, as his voice came closer. "Lauren? Where are you?" His form took shape at the end of the hall, a beam of light shooting out from a small flashlight as he ran up to her, coming to his knees beside her. "Hey, are you hurt? What's going on?" He placed the flashlight on the floor, standing it up so that it illuminated them in a soft glow, and coaxed her to sitting as she continued to sob.

"I... I..." Lauren pounded her chest and squeezed her eyes shut. "I think it's a panic attack."

"What do I do?" Alex asked.

She couldn't answer. There was nothing much he *could* do. After a few seconds of her cries, he shimmied up to her and pulled her to his chest, letting her lean on him.

"It's okay," he said. "We're going to be okay." He smoothed away her hair from her face and just let her cry, repeating over and over again the same reassurances.

After a few long minutes, through the tears and in the quiet of the dark hall, the weight began to lift, and Lauren's breathing came more steadily. She pulled away, wiping her eyes and nose with the hem of her shirt. "I'm sorry," she said. "I haven't had a panic attack like that since..." She fell silent, a pang shooting through her at the memory of the boy who'd died years ago, the boy she was supposed to save.

"Since when?" Alex asked. "You're one of the strongest people I know, Lauren."

She shook her head, a small laugh escaping her at the absurdity of that. "Alex, I've been here. My last patient was a boy Annika's age. He died because I made a mistake, and history is repeating itself. I missed the injury to her spleen. I was so focused on her concussion, on her kidneys, on everything else, that I missed it."

"It sounds like you had your hands full," Alex said.

"That's not the point." She pulled her knees to her chest and rested her forehead on them.

"I think it is." Alex sighed. "Lauren, you kept that girl alive. She would have died days ago if it weren't for you. And you told them that they needed to find a surgeon, that you had your limits. If it weren't for you, we'd have no options right now. We wouldn't know where to take her."

Lauren looked up at him. "I don't know if any of that will matter. What if she dies?"

"Then she dies." Alex said the words heavily. "Just like Naomi died. Just like your fiancé. Just like billions have died in this new, miserable world. But I know you, Lauren. You're not a quitter. You fight for the people you care about, and you're going to fight for her, too. If she dies, it won't be because you didn't do everything in your power to save her."

His words hit home, peeling back some of her doubt, but her confidence still waned. "You're right, I guess," she said simply, quietly.

"Damn right, I'm right," Alex said. "You're the girl who took care of your entire apartment building when crap hit the fan."

She shrugged. Anybody would do that, if they could. We worked together, she thought.

"You survived Nashville. Survived losing the love of your life," Alex said.

Lauren nodded slowly. *So did you, Alex,* she thought. But, then again, Alex was the bravest man she'd ever met. Comparing herself to him stirred up courage.

"You helped save everyone, including the *President of the United States*, in Atlanta," Alex said. "And then, you helped save my son from a bunch of escaped convicts, and you helped take out an actual serial killer. You're a badass, Lauren Stevens. No one and nothing can take that away from you."

"You're right," she said with more conviction, a flicker of belief in those words fanning the embers of determination to flame. "I didn't know who I was when I lost that boy all those years ago. I didn't really know who I was when you and I met, but… you're right. I know who I am now." She got to her feet. "I'm a survivor and a fighter."

Alex stood up next to her. "There's the woman I know and love."

Lauren quirked an eyebrow at him and cocked half a smile.

Alex cleared his throat. "Uh… the woman *we all* know and love."

Her heart warmed; the two of them were both too close to having lost the people they'd loved for years for anything truly romantic to develop between them — not anytime soon, anyway. But there was affection between them, a deep friendship forged through the hottest of fires.

Lauren punched Alex's arm. "We all love you, too, big guy."

He laughed softly and shook his head. "Now, are you going to save this little girl, or what?"

Lauren took a deep breath. "I'm sure as hell gonna try."

Chapter 30

George Peters

The sun was still low, still leaking deep purples and pinks into the sky. Black, billowing smoke marred nature's artwork as the Boston Police Headquarters burned. There had been few options for shelter nearby when George and his team had returned with news that they'd killed CONmen, that the war was coming early, and that Frank Russo had gained access to military-grade weapons.

The gaping hole which showcased the fire licking the walls inside headquarters was final confirmation: the BPD was outgunned. Or at least, they would be until Frank ran out of things like actual missiles.

George leaned his forehead against the glass window of a building so new, it hadn't had the chance to be filled with corpses. Deflated balloons littered the foyer. Streamers still hung from every doorway. The furniture was all new, in pristine condition despite the thin layer of dust coating everything. From the banners hung across several doorways, it was clear the building was a new extension of a high school right next to it. Though separated by some distance, a parking lot, and large highway, there was a clear line of sight to the burning building.

"Maybe it wasn't such a bad thing, what happened yesterday." Lissa announced her presence by plopping her duffel bag on the ground next to George, leaning her back against the window, and nudging George with her elbow.

"How's that?" George didn't look away from the burning building.

"If we hadn't, a few hours from now, that—" She pointed dramatically at headquarters. "—would still have happened, except we would have been inside." She lightly kicked her duffle bag. "Instead, we all got out, and we got to save some essentials."

O'Donnell had ordered everyone to pack up a duffel, dress in full gear, and add a rifle slung over their shoulder in addition to the Glock at their hip. Their duffel bags were stocked with food and water, ammo — both for their handguns and for their XM-15 rifles, a change of clothes, a pepper ball launcher, pepper balls, and several cans of DEET. They'd each carried a ballistic shield on their short trek to the building across the way as well.

"Yeah, maybe you're right," George said, tearing his eyes from the smoke to look at Lissa. He offered a small smile. He wasn't sure he agreed, but she didn't need his objections to her interpretation of events. She'd been through enough without blaming herself for losing the majority of their supplies.

In truth, the actions of George, Lissa, Freeman, and Landry may have spurred Frank to his reckless attack in the early morning when the swarms were known to be more active. George imagined O'Donnell and everyone at headquarters would have been better prepared to defend the line had things gone as planned.

"Do you think O'Donnell and the rest will be back soon?" Lissa asked.

As if in answer, a line of black-clad policemen trudged into view across the lot. "Looks like it," George said, counting the number of men returning. "O'Donnell took five with him, right?"

Lissa nodded. "Yeah," she said, tense for a moment as her finger poked the window in a line as she quickly whispered her own count. "They didn't lose anyone."

The two of them weren't the only ones to flock to the foyer. Calls echoed down the halls as men and women who'd stayed to guard their only remaining supplies spread the word that their friends were returning. The next ten minutes only filled the air with tension as George waited silently with Lissa and a room full of anxious cops.

The silence remained as O'Donnell pushed open the door and five more followed inside after him. They closed the door to the outside, locking it so that it sealed them safely inside. The five stayed by the doors, and O'Donnell walked into the center of the foyer as a circle formed at the edges of the room.

"It was one man," O'Donnell said. "Frank sent one man on a suicide mission to take us out. We caught up to him, shot him, and got a few pieces of information out of the man before he took his last breath." The captain turned in a circle, slowly, taking his time as if recognizing every person in the room as he spoke. "They had two missiles. Two launchers. And they used 'em both. It seems their second attack, which according to their own man was a strike against our southernmost post at the state police station, was more successful. If the man was tellin' the truth, we've lost two dozen at that post." He let the round of gasps settle before he continued. "I'd hoped to steal one of their two-way radios to continue gatherin' intelligence incognito, but the man warned them and then shot clean through his radio before we could get to him. He seemed rather proud about that, before he bled out."

Murmurs circled the room until one voice spoke up louder than the rest. It was Landry. He stepped forward, his voice pained. "What else do they have? Who was their supplier?" he asked. "Who gave that monster weapons like that? Once we put the Russos to bed, we're gonna need to go after the supplier, too. Or else they're just going to resupply the next mobster or thug."

Sounds of agreement followed, and for a moment, O'Donnell seemed to lose the room as opinions were thrown around in quick succession. Everyone seemed to know the best way forward, how to best put Frank Russo in his place. Voices became higher pitched, louder. A few disagreements broke out into arguments.

George shook his head and glanced at Lissa. "We're never going to win if we can't keep it together."

Lissa nodded at O'Donnell. "Just wait. He's just letting them get it out of their system."

He looked back at the captain, observing him more closely. He stood with hands on hips, foot tapping the floor impatiently, jaw set in a hard line. O'Donnell was waiting like a parent would wait for a toddler's tantrum to run its course.

"If he doesn't say something soon, these people are going to lose it," George whispered.

"He knows what he's doing." The confidence in Lissa's voice wavered as someone on the other side of the room pushed another man, sending him crashing to the ground.

But then Freemen stepped between the two, holding a hand out toward the aggressor. "Really, Jenkins? You're going to play Nate like that? Your brother, one of the only men left on God's green earth that you can trust?"

Freeman raised her eyebrows, stood firm, and stared Jenkins down. Though she was shorter and smaller than the man, he stepped back and raked a hand over his face, regret clear in his expression. The whole room had stilled, though a few nearby the almost-fight helped Nate to his feet.

"Sorry, Freeman," he said.

"C'mon, Jenkins. You know who to apologize to." Freeman stepped to the side.

Jenkins hung his head. "Nate, man… I'm sorry."

Nate stepped forward and held out a hand. Jenkins took it and the two men pulled each other into a hug that was more like a chest bump with a nice back pounding. Handshakes around the room ensued as others who'd been arguing moments before settled their differences.

Freeman patted Jenkins and Nate each on the shoulder and gave them each a smirk. "Now," she said, "let's leave the plans up to someone who knows what they're doing." She nodded at O'Donnell who acknowledged her with a grateful nod of his own.

"We need to get on the walkie talkies, send out a message to our people. We need scouts fanning out into the city, and we need to know where Frank and his men are," O'Donnell said. "They might be thinking to break through our front line and surround us on all sides. Frank and his cronies aren't gettin' away with this, d'ya hear me?"

"Yes, sir!" The sentiment repeated around the room, out of sync, some answers more enthusiastic than others. George mumbled his reply at the tail end, still not sure how they were going to fight against Frank. Their enemy had called himself a cockroach in the past, and George couldn't agree more. It seemed he just couldn't be killed.

O'Donnell's expression hardened, and he raised his voice. "We've got this. We're men and women of the BPD. We've survived hell to get here, and we can survive Frank Russo. Do—you—hear—me?"

George listened, something about the way O'Donnell exuded confidence and surety absorbing into him. He joined his voice to a more unified, "Yes, sir!"

"Boston is on the line, ladies and gentlemen!" O'Donnell shouted. "I'm ready to kick some ass. Are you?"

This time George roared his answer with the rest: "Yes, sir!"

"Okay, then. Let's get some scouts on the move, get some chatter on those lines." The captain clapped his hands several times in quick succession. "Let's move, move, move!"

The room burst into motion, and soon men and women were streaming out of the foyer, heading toward the rooms in which they'd stashed their own supplies. George and Lissa returned to the window, kneeling in front of their duffel bags and pulling out their walkie talkies. But a shadow loomed over them before George could attempt to send a message. He glanced up to see O'Donnell standing with arms crossed, looking down at them.

"Sir?" George asked.

"You two are stayin' with me. Wherever I go, you go. Got it?" O'Donnell narrowed his eyes at them both. "I don't want no heroics, either. You do exactly what I say, when I say it."

George only nodded, but Lissa let out a squeaky, "Got it."

"You want us to try reaching the other teams?" George asked, holding up his walkie talkie.

"That'd be fine," O'Donnell said. "But don't you go out with the scout teams, understand?"

George nodded, as did Lissa, and then the captain turned and walked away, heading for a room at the end of the hall. Through the open doorway, George spotted several of them putting on their gear.

"That means he's not leaving us here," Lissa said, grinning at George. "He said we stay with him."

"What if he stays behind?" George asked. "He could get updates through the walkie talkies, give out orders from here."

Lissa shook her head. "He could've done that with the team who tracked down the man who blew up headquarters. He didn't stay behind at the zoo, either. Or before that, when he and the thirteenth planned to raid Frank's supplies out in the country."

George's eyes widened. "I guess you're right." He couldn't smile about it. He wasn't happy to be going out into a war zone. But he was relieved he wouldn't be forced out of it, either. The obligation and desire to defend Boston, to defend the people he loved the most, was a strong feeling unlike anything he'd ever experienced. He couldn't imagine sitting out, not after all he'd been through.

Lissa held up her own radio. "Let's raise some voices on these things," she said.

George turned the dial on his own walkie talkie, checking the channels he knew were designated for different checkpoints along their front lines. Each line was already full. He stopped at the channel meant for the group stationed at the state police building, sad at the thought of so many of their men and women dead on the other end.

"What if not everyone is dead?" George asked.

Lissa shook her head. "I heard Freeman in the hustle after O'Donnell's speech. They tried to raise them several times already. It's pretty certain no one's left."

George frowned at the walkie talkie in his hands. He sighed and held it up to his mouth, pressing the PTT button. "Your deaths won't be in vain," he said. "We're going to beat the Russos and what's left of CON. Rest in peace." He released the button and set the walkie talkie down. Lissa quirked an eyebrow at him, but he only shrugged. "They deserved someone to say something. We can't exactly have a funeral right now, so…" He trailed off, hoping no one would be speaking final words over his dead body any time soon.

"Hello?" A voice came in over the walkie talkie, followed by a hacking cough. "Is anyone there?"

George's eyes went wide. He stared at the device for a moment, mouth agape.

"Please… I know… I know I heard something." Whoever was on the other line — a man, if George was hearing correctly — sounded weak and desperate.

"Pick it up!" Lissa shouted, crawling the few feet between herself and George.

He snapped out of his shock and raised the walkie talkie again. "Um, yes, there's someone here. Who is this?"

Lissa waved her hands at him. "What are you doing?" she hissed. "We have to—"

"What if it's one of Frank's guys?" George asked. "Just… go get O'Donnell. He needs to hear this."

Lissa popped up from sitting and ran down the hall, nearly tripping as she did.

"My name is Detective Jack Carr, badge number one-six-zero."

That sounds pretty official. George licked his lips and looked up as O'Donnell strode out of the room down the hall and made long, quick strides his way. Lissa was behind him, and so were several other officers.

George stood and walked to meet O'Donnell. "Can you repeat that, detective?"

The voice on the other end did as he was asked, and O'Donnell was there to listen. He held out his hand, motioning for George to hand over the walkie talkie.

"Detective Carr, this is Captain O'Donnell. It's good to hear your voice."

"Likewise, captain." Another harsh cough followed. His next words had more of a wheezing quality. "I think… I think I'm the only one left. I heard—" He coughed again, the fit lasting longer. "—I heard them talking. I jumped from the building, landed in rubble, broke my leg… they didn't see me. From what they said, I thought they'd hit more checkpoints."

"They tried," O'Donnell said. "And they took out our building, but… we cleared out before they got us. I thought for sure they'd put all their focus here." The captain's voice broke, and a shadow of deep regret fell across his features. "I thought they'd retaliate at headquarters. I didn't think they even knew about your checkpoint, Carr."

"We didn't either, sir," Carr said, words coming out slowly in between wheezes and coughs. "When we got the warning… last night… that there would be trouble… we didn't expect it… so soon, not here… I guess we were all wrong, huh?"

George felt the blood drain from his face at the way Carr's voice was fading in volume. "We've got to send someone to get him," he said. Behind O'Donnell, saddened faces of several officers averted their eyes, and more of them shuffled uncomfortably.

"Hang in there," O'Donnell said. "We'll come for you when we can. We just…" He closed his eyes and seemed to force out the words. "We've got to find out what's going on out there, detective. For the sake of everyone, we need to know what Frank Russo is doing."

"Don't," Carr said. "Not gonna… make it… But I… I heard their plans. The smaller forces… the ones that took out checkpoints… they're returning to the zoo. That's… where… Russo is… waiting." A wetter, choking sound followed, and then a groan of pain.

George's heart leapt and lodged in his throat as he waited for more, but the silent seconds dragged on. He didn't move, didn't breathe, praying that Detective Carr's voice would come through one more time.

"Detective," O'Donnell said, "are you still with me?"

"Russo… going to…" Carr was weakly gasping for breath, and his words were only barely recognizable. "…City Hall."

O'Donnell frowned. "City Hall? Are you sure? Why would Frank go there?"

"Hos-hostages."

George let out the breath he'd been holding in and stumbled back half a step. He'd gotten word not long ago that his family were on their way to City Hall, to a surgeon for Annika. *No, no, no.* He shook his head and reached for the wall to steady himself. Lissa was at his side in a second, a hand on his shoulder. He'd told her about Annika, and now it seemed she sensed the fear coursing through him.

The captain's eyes had gone wide at Carr's revelation, and every officer in the hall had gasped. Whispers filled the air until O'Donnell held up a hand to silence them. "Carr… you still with me?"

There was nothing. The captain tried again. Still, only silence was returned. He walked stoically to George and pressed the walkie talkie into his chest. George took it, the pressure pulling him out of his racing thoughts about his family.

"What are we going to do?" George asked.

O'Donnell stepped past George and turned to face them all. "Do we have confirmation that the other checkpoints are solid? I don't want to base all our plans on one dying thug's word, especially after Detective Carr mentioned hearing something about more checkpoints being hit."

Freeman stepped forward. "We heard back from Fenway and the Museum teams. They had to fight off smaller teams of CONmen, it looks like. But they succeeded in driving them away. We haven't heard from B-2 or Southbay. They're not picking up, which I don't like, sir."

O'Donnell cursed, his hands balled into fists. "It sounds to me like Frank sent out small teams with weapons to strike first at each checkpoint. The bastard we caught lied when he said he was the only one. He must have just fallen behind the others. He said he'd ditched the launcher, but now…" He cursed again. "We can't be sure they've only got two missiles. We can't be sure of anything that man said."

Landry stepped up beside Freeman. "If the Russos and CON are gathering at the zoo, they're either headed this way, straight through to City Hall, or they're about to be."

O'Donnell grunted. "Send word. I want everyone that's left at the other checkpoints to head toward the zoo immediately. We're gonna cut those bastards off so they don't get anywhere near the civilians in the green zone."

"I can go ahead, sir," Freeman said. "I run the Boston Marathon every April, train for it the rest of the year. Give me a walkie talkie, and I'll sprint my way toward the zoo. I'll find out if they've left, and if they have, where they've gone. I know the city, sir, where they'd go to get to City Hall from Franklin Park. I'll report back, and you can make plans from there."

"You think you can get there quick enough with all your gear? With protection?" O'Donnell asked.

Freeman lifted her chin, her voice steady. "No, sir. I'd have to go without all of that. Just me and a walkie talkie."

"I can't ask you to do that," O'Donnell said. "We can send a scout in a bean, if there are any left undamaged."

"They were too close to the building when it blew, sir. Some were in the attached garage. They're gone, sir." Freeman began to strip off her gear. "Sending a runner is the only way."

Landry put a hand on her arm. "Freeman, you don't have to do this."

"Yeah, Landry," Freeman said, "I do."

O'Donnell nodded. "She's right," he said. "It's our best bet at getting information quickly." He took a deep breath. "If we fail—"

"We won't fail, sir," Freeman said.

George straightened, some of his strength returning. The best chance his family had was for O'Donnell's plan to work, for them to stop Frank and Ruger and the rest before they even reached the green zone.

"Freeman's right," Landry said. "We're with you."

A chorus of agreement rose from the rest, and George added his voice to the mix. He'd stayed with the Boston Police Department for precisely the task ahead. It was time for Frank Russo to be taken down. Even cockroaches could be killed if the grinding boot was determined enough.

Chapter 31

Zara Williams

Zara slammed her shovel into the root, once, twice, three times. Finally, the stubborn thing cut through. She leaned against the side of the airplane, sweating obscenely beneath her beekeeper suit, attempting to help Kai dig a hole in the ditch with the shovels they'd taken from the local hardware store. Their weapons were mere feet from them, but with the way the airplane was wedged between two walls of dirt, rock, and roots, they were unreachable without a lot of hard work.

"You okay?" Kai asked for the thousandth time. He paused his digging; his expression was shadowed by the dim light beneath the canopy and the mesh hanging from his hat, but Zara could imagine the way his brows knitted together just slightly when he was worried.

"I'm fine," she said, "and if you ask me that one more time, I'm going to take this shovel to your head instead of these roots."

He held up his hands. "I'm just watching out for myself," he said. "I don't want to have to carry you out of here if you pass out."

Zara smirked. "Are you calling me fat?"

He walked right into that one, she thought.

He dropped his hands and straightened up. "What? No. I… I wasn't… I mean—" He swallowed audibly. "I was calling myself a wimp."

Zara chuckled. "Oh, really?" She leaned her whole body into the handle of the shovel and scooped up a big pile of dirt.

"Yep." Kai went back to digging, working quicker than he had before. "I'm no bodybuilder, Zara. I'm a businessman. Never set foot in a gym my whole life."

"Nice save," Zara said. She threw dirt to the side, as far from the cargo hold as she could.

A few minutes passed as she and Kai worked in silence, digging relentlessly. She had been feeling better that morning. She hadn't experienced dizziness in hours and her headache was a dull thrum instead of a persistent thumping. Her thoughts were clearer, her body stronger. And her hopes were high. Walter was alive, and they knew where he was. That alone had lifted her out of the worst of the muck she'd been wading through the last few days.

The only problem, she thought, is that he's under the roof of a crazy lady. With two innocent kids. And she's probably just going through a mental break. And she has a gun. She sighed to herself as she remembered Willow's plea for her and Kai to keep Carol and her kids safe. So… more than one problem.

"Hey," Zara stopped digging and looked up at Kai. "Maybe we can just use that gun you found, the Derringer? I know it's got a hell of a kick, but we won't have to fire it."

Kai shook his head, the mesh swishing around his face and neck. "They've got guns that work," he said. "Guns that are accurate. That .44 magnum is more likely to give *me* a concussion than it is to hit the mark."

"I told you what Willow said, Kai. We can't hurt them. Walter looked okay from what I saw of him, for the condition he must be in. He's hurt. They're taking care of him. I know Carol threatened us, but maybe if we try again—"

"We are trying again," Kai said. "This time, we're going to try with a couple of M27s."

"We can't hurt them," Zara repeated, letting the shovel drop and crossing her arms.

Kai groaned. "Zara, come on. Do you want to get Mr. Peters out of there, or not? She very clearly was willing to shoot us both. And from the way her son, Heath, acted, she's hiding the fact that they have Walter. I don't know why, but maybe it's because she found out who he is or that he knows how to fix this whole end-of-the-world thing."

Zara blanched. "Walter wouldn't tell her that, not without knowing he could trust her. We've been careful with that information."

Kai scoffed. "Well, you told me."

"Because we had to trust you," Zara said. "We needed you to know why it was so important for us to get to Boston. But it's not like we announced it to everyone we met." She shook her head. "No. Carol *is* hiding Walter, from us and from the people in town who know her. I don't know why, but that much is clear. And it has to be something else, something to do with her mental break. Walter knows how to keep a secret. Trust me."

"When he's in his right mind, maybe," Kai said, "but we don't know what kind of injuries he has. They could be a lot worse than what we got. The fact that he hasn't gotten out of there to come find you tells me that they have to be pretty bad."

That bubble of dread, that she'd lost Walter Peters, returned. *What if he* is *hurt? What if he's dying?*

"What does she want with him?" Zara whispered, racking her brain for an answer. It just didn't make sense.

"What was that?" Kai grunted as he lifted another shovel full of dirt and tossed it to the side.

"I'm just tired," Zara said.

"Me too, but we need to go into this prepared, and—"

"No," Zara said. "I'm tired of this." She waved her arms around. "I'm tired of the whole collapse of civilization, the end to all normalcy. I'm tired of crazy people and fending off bad guys and losing people." Her voice caught in her throat, and she paused, trying to gather her thoughts. "Kai," she said after a few silent moments, "I don't want to become the bad guys in the story those kids tell years from now."

Kai buried the tip of the shovel into the dirt and left the handle sticking upright as he walked over to her and leaned against the side of the plane. Even through her suit, the weight of him lightly pressing up against her brought a comfort to Zara she didn't quite understand. She could better see his face through the mesh as he was closer. He looked at her, eyes searching as if he could find the answers to his questions by studying her face long enough.

Finally, he looked away and cleared his throat, breaking the moment. "We could leave Walter there," he said. "For a few days, a few weeks… however long it took for us to convince the locals to intervene on our behalf."

Zara shook her head. "Walter doesn't think we have that kind of time, not if we're going to stop the rest of the world from dying."

"We could go in without weapons," Kai said. "If we sneak in, maybe we can get him out without them noticing."

"From the third floor?" A sinking feeling at the obvious lack of choices mixed with a warmth at how Kai was trying, how he'd listened to her and stepped outside of the box instead of barreling ahead with what he thought was best. Zara leaned against Kai, hooking her arm with his. It felt like a natural thing to do, and he didn't object or pull away. "If we go in without weapons, we risk all three of us getting killed."

"I'm all ears," Kai said. "We need the food and water stashed in the cargo hold, and we'll need the weapons later, so… maybe we can just keep digging? See if we come up with anything else?"

Zara offered him a sad smile. "I don't think there's going to be an easy solution."

"Never is," he said, smiling back at her. He let go of her hand and wrapped his arm around her shoulders. "But you're not a quitter," he said. "And you're not a wimp, not like me. You're smart. You'll think of something." He squeezed her shoulder and then stood up, leaning over to pick up her shovel. He picked it up and handed it to her.

Zara took it, her smile remaining. She watched Kai's back as he walked to his own shovel. No matter how he got on her nerves, he always managed to make her like him.

"What?" Kai said, catching her staring at him. She blushed, but then he patted down his suit, and said mockingly, "Does this suit make me look fat?"

Zara laughed out loud and shook her head. "Nah. I think it showcases your physique perfectly."

He flexed, striking a pose, and she laughed harder. "Okay, muscleman, stop showing off. Let's get back to work."

It took them another thirty minutes to move enough dirt to get into the cargo hold. In that time, Zara thought through every scenario she could dream up, imagined whole conversations with Carol in which she tried to make the woman see reason. There were too many instances in which things didn't end up well for Zara, Kai, and Walter.

They loaded up wheelbarrows they'd gotten from the same hardware store as they'd gotten the shovels. By the time they were done with that, both of them were breathing heavily, and Zara felt like her lungs might burst from the effort of digging and then pulling the supplies up and out of the ditch. She grabbed a water bottle from their freshly recovered stash, sat next to a tree, leaned back, and pulled the mesh away from her face.

"Here's to the hope that we don't get hit with a swarm in the five minutes we need to rehydrate," Zara said, holding out her water bottle to Kai, who'd followed her lead and sat beside her. They knocked the bottoms of their bottles together, and they both guzzled the contents. The warm, clean water slid down Zara's throat, quenching her thirst. It was gone in mere seconds. She leaned her head back and let the light breeze caress her face for a moment before pulling the mesh back down and securing it.

"So," Kai said, "any thoughts about what you want to do?"

Zara nodded. "I think we should load these supplies into the camper. Park it somewhere near The Log Cabin but out of sight. We need to stake out the place. See if there's any way we *can* sneak in. I mean, they left Walter there when they went to the hospital, right? Maybe they'll leave him again."

Kai nodded. "And what about the guns?"

"We only use them if we absolutely have to," Zara said, "and then, we try not to kill anyone. We've got to get Walter out of there, and we've got to get him to Boston. But we've also got to sleep at night."

"All right, then," Kai took a deep breath and stood up, holding out a hand to help Zara to her feet. "I'm with you all the way, babe." He blanched. "Uh, sorry. Old habits."

Zara smirked. "Just don't do it again." She elbowed him lightly as she passed by toward her wheelbarrow. The truth was, his slip up didn't bother her quite as much as it used to.

***

Dressed once more in the beekeeper suits, Zara huddled with Kai in the cluster of trees beside The Log Cabin. They'd parked in a small commuter's lot less than a quarter of a mile down the road. Zara was just starting to get antsy when the door to The Log Cabin opened and Heath — who had to be just a few years younger than Zara at the most — came outside hauling a large bucket.

"What's he doing?" Kai asked.

Zara shrugged. "I don't know." Then her eyes widened. She smacked Kai's arm.

"Ouch!" He frowned at her, holding his arm.

"Look! He's coming this way." Zara pushed Kai, urging him to step deeper into the woods. "We don't want him to see us."

"Okay, okay." Kai moved back with her, and then they both turned to watch as Heath stepped into the trees.

Heath came a few steps into the wooded area and then dumped the contents of the bucket, grimacing as he did so. "Gross," he grumbled, gagging as what appeared to be human waste sloshed out of the bucket and into the brush.

Zara swallowed hard. "This is it," she whispered.

Kai shook his head, but she was already standing up, hands raised high, moving slowly. She didn't want to startle Heath, but he jumped and dropped the bucket, nonetheless.

"It's okay," she said. "I just want to talk."

Kai stood up next to her. "We don't want to hurt you," he said.

"Who are you?" Heath whipped out a pocketknife and held it out, hands trembling.

Zara stepped closer. "We came by yesterday," she said. "These are beekeeper suits. We're just trying to protect ourselves." She did her best to sound friendly. "You shouldn't be out here without some kind of protection."

Heath glanced between them, lowering his knife but keeping it in hand. "I'm only out here for a minute when I dump our toilets. You can hear a swarm coming. I'm close enough to run inside." He raked his fingers through his hair. "What are you doing here? If my mom sees you, she'll kill you. She wasn't kidding."

"We can't leave town without our friend," Zara said.

Heath sighed. "She won't give him to you," he said.

"Why?" Kai asked.

"She thinks…" Heath hesitated, and his cheeks turned red. "She thinks he's my dad, Saul."

"Okay," Kai said, "didn't expect that one."

Heath grimaced. "I know it sounds crazy, but… she's not hurting him. I mean, she's drugging him to keep him from trying to run, but it's for his own good. He almost killed himself falling down the stairs when we left him here the other day. But don't worry. My mom was a nurse. She knows what she's doing. He's fine. I swear. Just… just go, okay?"

"Heath… Walter is *not* fine. And he needs to get to Boston. He has family there," Zara said. "His actual wife is there. He's got kids." Zara took a deep breath, thoughts of Lizzy bringing tears to her eyes. "I have to get him home."

"Maybe you could talk to her, Heath," Kai said. "Maybe you can convince her to hand Walter over to us. All you'd have to do is talk to him to know that we're telling the truth. He belongs with us."

Heath shook his head. "It's not happening. My mom just isn't in the right frame of mind to even talk about this. If you try to take him… I don't know what she'd do." He took a step backward, waving them off. "You need to leave."

Zara's heart jumped into her throat. Her chest tightened. She could feel him closing them off, see the panic in his eyes. She didn't want to storm the place with guns, didn't want to endanger Heath or his little sister. She was about to plead with the boy one more time when Kai stalked forward.

"Hey, what are you doing?" Heath held up an arm to cover his face as if afraid Kai might punch him, but Kai only grabbed his wrist, spun him around, and put him in an arm lock. "Mom!" Heath shouted. "Mom, help!"

The wiry kid struggled, but Kai was stronger than he was. "Stuff your glove in his mouth," Kai said. "Quick!"

Zara stared open-mouthed for only a second before Heath started shouting again. Out of instinct, she rushed forward and did as Kai said. "What the hell, Kai? What are we doing right now?"

Kai clamped a hand over Heath's mouth, securing the glove. Heath still struggled, but he couldn't make much noise. Kai pulled him further into the trees, back toward their camper. "Help me," he said. "We're going to pull this off without shedding one drop of blood."

Zara followed, glancing nervously back toward The Log Cabin, looking for any signs that Carol had heard, that she was following.

"What are you talking about?" Zara hissed. "Now *you've* gone crazy!"

"No," Kai said. "I'm solving the problem. She's going to want her kid back, Zara. And we're going to give him back, completely unscathed, as long as she gives us Walter."

Chapter 32

George Peters and Frank Russo

A cloud of bug repellent surrounded George as he trekked through the city with O'Donnell and his team. They'd all drenched themselves in the stuff after dressing in full gear. Still, those ahead and behind checked for access to buildings in case they needed a quick escape from the open air. They'd heard from Freeman ten minutes prior, and she'd left twenty minutes before that.

"They're still at the zoo," she'd said. "I don't know what's holding them up, but they seem to be waiting for something. We've got a good chance of cutting them off."

All of them had been ready and waiting, and all O'Donnell had to do was lead the way. He had George and Lissa follow at the center of their group, protected by a ring of three dozen police officers. More were on the way, coordinating movements by way of walkie talkies.

As George walked, he kept his eyes and ears open. He watched the sky, specifically. It seemed animals always knew when a swarm was coming, that they started to flee before people could even hear the buzz of danger coming their way. Adrenaline flooded his body, made his heartbeat quicken. Just ahead or just behind, something life-threatening could be waiting.

"Remember when we could, you know… go on walks and stuff without being afraid?" Lissa asked. "I miss that."

"Me, too." George took a break from vigilance, for only a moment, so he could offer Lissa a smile. "It's crazy. All these weapons, and we're still not safe."

O'Donnell paused a few yards ahead, and so did the rest of them.

Freeman's voice came over the speaker. "Found out what they were waiting on. One of the men with a missile launcher returned, and they started kicking it into gear. He must have gotten held up after leaving Detective Carr's location."

"Probably a swarm," Lissa whispered.

George frowned. "Should we be worried?"

"We should always be worried," she said, "but he was coming from near Carson Beach. If he thought it safe to come to the zoo, my guess is that the swarm he ran into isn't coming this way."

Freeman continued her report after a few more seconds of silence. "They've pulled up a garbage truck. I think they're going to use it to plow through the wreckage. Lots of vehicles rolling up behind it. They're starting to load up."

"Report if you see any intel on weapons," O'Donnell replied.

"Besides the missile launcher… lots of automatic rifles. A couple of large crates with red lettering… could be grenades. About forty men and women cramming into seven vehicles behind the garbage truck. I think Frank and Ruger are in a truck at the back of the procession."

George swallowed hard. If they were waiting on the missile launcher, that means they must have more missiles.

A few moments of silence were followed by another voice on the speaker. "This is Lieutenant Lowell from the Fenway team. We've just picked up the team from the museum, and we're headed your way."

Okay, that's something, George thought. At least we won't be outnumbered, even if they do have missiles and grenades.

"That's good news, lieutenant. Between all of us, Frank's asking for trouble," O'Donnell said.

"Yes, sir," Lowell said, tone enthusiastic. "Just let us know where you want us."

"Stand by," O'Donnell said. "Freeman? What's happening?"

"I'm waiting to see… they're pulling out… okay, I think they're going to stick to the widest roads instead of the most direct route. They're heading northwest on Seaver."

"Got it," O'Donnell said. "Hold on. I think I've got an idea." He held out a hand to his right, and Landry, who'd walked next to him the whole time, pulled out a map from his back pocket and handed it over. O'Donnell unfolded it and held it up, seeming to examine it.

"They're going slow, sir," Freeman said. "There's a lot of vehicles to move. I'm going to try keeping up with them."

O'Donnell grunted and folded the map back up. "Keep me in the loop, Freeman. You know where the Fort Hill Tower is?"

"Sure do, sir," Freeman said.

"You listenin' in, Lowell?"

George exchanged a look with Lissa. "Sounds like he's got a plan."

"He always does." Lissa grinned.

"I am, sir," Lowell said. "I know where Fort Hill is, too."

George moved closer to O'Donnell as the captain turned around and invited them all in. Anticipation made him bounce slightly on the balls of his feet.

"Good." O'Donnell's expression hardened. "This is what we're gonna do. Seaver turns into Columbus, right? Well, on Columbus, before it runs up next to Fort Hill, we need to stop them in their tracks. Lowell, you and your team corral them into Highland Park, and we'll set up in the surrounding homes, waiting. We'll use the park as a killing ground. But we've got to get them off track by just a block, make them leave their vehicles."

"We've got this," Lowell said. "If we take out whoever's driving the garbage truck, they won't be able to push through the wreckage, and if we open fire from the west, we can drive them east, into Highland Park."

"Exactly," O'Donnell said. "And Freeman? You've got to be our eyes out there. Let us know if they stray."

"You got it, sir," Freeman said.

O'Donnell hooked the walkie talkie back onto his utility belt. The captain's determined, confident demeanor seemed to emanate from him and soak into George's skin. He stood a little taller, ready for the fight to come.

* * *

Frank reclined his seat and put his feet on the dash, enjoying the cool air coming through the air conditioner. It would be a while before they got where they were going, and that was just fine with him. He wasn't in a hurry. There was no way the cops could win, not with his rock-solid plan in place. He had the manpower. He had the weapons. They had the same old, tired defenses.

Been one step ahead all my life, Frank thought. That ain't gonna change now.

He glanced at Ruger who drove their car. Over the last few days, it had occurred to Frank that it might be harder than he originally anticipated to stamp out the idea of CON, to make Ruger and his people think of themselves as belonging to the Russos. He was a man of his word — he'd give Ruger Roxbury and Mattapan once this was all done — but he had them agree to pay their dues of twenty percent for a reason. The whole of Boston was going to belong to him, and then he'd get her straightened out. Boston needed a strong hand to pull her out of the mess she was in, and Frank had some ideas.

First thing's first. I gotta get rid o' those swarms. And then we gotta seal off the area. Make some trade routes to other surviving communities. Get some prep in for the winter before it's too late. He listed off ideas in his head for how he could make all of that happen. He wasn't just a pretty face. Frank Russo was about to show the world that he knew how to make things happen, too.

The procession was slow as the garbage truck up front worked to push vehicles out of the way. As Ruger put on the brakes, and their car came to a halt, the lowlife dared to turn his ice-blue gaze onto Frank. He could always tell when the man was looking; it never failed to send a shiver down his spine.

"Keep your eyes on the road," Frank snapped, flicking his hand toward the windshield. "We gotta keep watch."

"They don't know we're coming," Ruger said, voice even and calm. There was no respect there, no fear.

Still don't know his place. Frank put his feet on the ground and snapped his seat up to sitting. "You think they don't know? Ha! Them cops know by now. And they know we got missiles." He shook his head. "We took out two o' their checkpoints, includin' their most important one. Hopefully that O'Donnell character is returned to dust by now, but they still had plenty o' other cops elsewhere." He jutted his finger at Ruger, the fact that he didn't flinch slightly infuriating. "What they *don't* know is where we're goin'. They're gonna think we took out that station by Carson Beach so we could flank 'em. That we took out O'Donnell's because it was the strongest checkpoint. We gotta get through their line and then make a straight shot for City Hall before they realize what's up."

"Yeah," Ruger said flatly. "Thanks for the recap."

"You're awful cocky," Frank said, scowling, "and I don't like it. You want this deal to work out, you gotta start showin' me my due respect. Got it?"

Ruger pressed his lips together, and Frank didn't miss the way his knuckles turned white on the steering wheel. His muscles flexed, and his right eye twitched.

"You wanna say somethin'?" Frank shouted. "Or you wanna stick to our deal?"

"I'm a man of my word, *boss*," Ruger said between clenched teeth. He added that last bit begrudgingly, but it was a start.

"Good." Frank nodded. "Me, too. Don't you worry, Pretty Boy." He added a little sarcastic flair to his new nickname for the man. He wasn't sure it would stick, but for now the name took Ruger down a notch. *Maybe when he's a little more seasoned, I'll give him an upgrade.* "I'll take care o' you and yours if you just do what you're told."

Ruger grunted and turned back to the road. They only moved a few feet before they had to stop again, and just when Frank was about to go nuts, the *pop, pop, pop* of gunfire interrupted the monotony. He straightened up, craning his neck.

"Where's that comin' from?" he asked, keeping his voice even despite the uptick of his heartbeat. He put a hand on the handle to the car door.

"Let me check, boss," Ruger said, holding out a hand. "Stay put. Get down. I'll come back and give you an update."

There didn't *seem* to be any spite in those words. The thug even managed to look sincere. *He was Ace's second-in-command. Maybe it's his instincts kickin' in.* But there were other options, too, like a double cross. Ruger's loyalty was unproven.

"I'll do what I think best." Frank shoved Ruger's hand away. "You go first, I'll come behind." If Ruger wanted to protect him, Frank wouldn't argue with that, but he would rather it be as a shield. If he let Ruger go out there all heroic-like while he cowered in the car, it would only bolster the man's hardened image. *Nah, I gotta let 'em all see: Frank Russo is just as badass as some street thug.*

Ruger reached into the back seat and pulled up the bulletproof vests they'd brought with them. "Put this on, at least. Let's grab rifles from the trunk, too."

Frank scoffed. "I give the orders, Pretty Boy."

The gunfire picked up ahead, but neither of them could see. Ruger was clearly losing patience. Frustration laced his next words. "Then what the hell are your orders?"

Frank grinned. "I'm gonna put this vest on, and then we're gonna grab a couple rifles from the back." He opened the car door, sliding out of the car, staying low, chuckling at Ruger's incredulous expression. *Just because I'm a badass doesn't mean I can't have a sense of humor.*

It only took them a minute to don the vests and grab their rifles. Frank slung his over his shoulder, opting to take out his handgun instead. Ruger raised his rifle like he was a soldier, leading the way, acting as a shield while Frank followed.

Along the procession of a dozen cars, Frank's men emerged from their vehicles, following his example, heading toward the sounds of gunfire. Men from the front, closer to the garbage truck, met them halfway.

"What're you idiots doin'?" Frank shouted. "What's happenin' with the garbage truck? Why ain't they pushing through so we can get outta here?"

Pugsie wrung his hands, flinching at the continuing sound of gunfire. "The road's blocked by a semi-truck, lots of cars behind it. I don't think the garbage truck can get through so easy. And besides, they shot Gill through the windshield."

Frank growled. Gill had been driving the garbage truck.

A young man — Caleb, one of Ruger's guys — spoke up. "They're high up. Snipers." He was clearly addressing Ruger. "Shooting long range. No one came close for hand-to-hand engagement." He threw a look at Frank, as if it were a last-minute thought.

"It's an ambush, damn it!" Frank said. "How'd they find us?"

"Doesn't matter, boss," Ruger said under his breath. "We need to get out of here. Anyone near that garbage truck is going to get a bullet in their head." He turned to look at Caleb. "That's why you all retreated back here, right?"

Caleb nodded, and murmurs of agreement rose from the others who'd retreated to the back half of the procession.

"Gill ain't the only one they got," Pugsie added. "But they ain't shootin' back here. Maybe they can't see as good from wherever they are?"

Frank growled and slammed a fist against the hood of a car nearby. He looked up, taking a deep breath. *A little setback, is all. I can't let it get to me.* He rolled his shoulders, calming himself and working through his options. A new plan to get to City Hall fell into place.

"Okay, okay. They're comin' at us from the northwest. We gotta move east, and then start back up toward City Hall. And we'll have to move fast. Grab the big guns, gentlemen. Let's go!"

Ruger nodded, his expression approving, and Frank noticed a marked difference in those who'd come with Ruger from CON. They trusted him more than they trusted Frank. They needed Ruger's approval to follow orders, and that wouldn't do. Frank was going to have to do something about that.

* * *

George kept his eyes to the west from his spot atop the Fort Hill Tower. Highland Park was little more than a fan-shaped patch of grass and walkways. The old water tower was a historical landmark in the corner, seventy feet high and made to look more like a medieval turret than anything. It had spiral stairs curving around the old, disused tank at the center and windows dotting the height of it.

"I can't believe they stuck us up here," Lissa said, pacing behind him as the sounds of nearby gunfire continued.

"It was smart," George said, "even if it means we can't be directly in the action. O'Donnell just wants us to be safe. At least he gave us something to do." He tapped the window. "Look, Lissa."

She came over to the window. "It's working," she said.

George held up his walkie talkie. "They're on the way," he whispered.

Below, O'Donnell, Freeman, Landry, and several other officers had their backs to the trees. They faced the tower. The highway was beyond the park, a couple rows of triple-deckers and a smaller road between them. Closer gunfire broke out as snipers stationed just to the north and south funneled Frank's men directly east toward the park.

"Get out of full view," O'Donnell hissed over the walkie talkie.

George and Lissa simultaneously stepped to the side, each of them only barely peeking. More officers waited in the surrounding homes, ready to charge the park on all sides once Frank and his men were at the center.

"Wait… what is he doing?" Lissa asked.

"I don't know." George frowned as Ruger rushed to the front of the oncoming enemy and held out his hands. Then, George's stomach knotted. "Ruger knows something is wrong. He's smart, Lissa."

The color drained from her face. "Do we warn O'Donnell?"

"We have to wait," George said. "If we do it too soon, we'll give away their location." He cursed, wishing he could do something besides just watch.

* * *

"What the hell, Pretty Boy?" Frank growled. "They're gunnin' for us. We got to go!"

"Gunfire drove us east," Ruger said. "Then more snipers were waiting for us, keeping us corralled right toward this park. It's wide open, Frank."

Frank swallowed hard. *Damn it. He's right.* He loosened his shoulders, forcing a laugh. He'd cultivated a certain… crazed persona… that would allow him to cover over his mistakes with eccentricity. Of course, sometimes he enjoyed that a little too much. Sometimes the crazier he acted the more he felt like himself. But he had no time to contemplate that. He had to recover.

He exaggerated his laughter. "Good," he said. "Good. Pretty Boy's got a brain." He cut off his laughter. "He stopped us too soon, though." He looked around at the surrounding triple-deckers. "See those houses? You think there's not men up there now? We're gonna get shot standin' here in the street." He pointed ahead, to the trees. "We gotta take cover under the trees, regroup where they can't target us, observe and find out where the snipers are. Then we raid 'em, one by one. Take 'em out."

"We need to charge to the north," Ruger said, shaking his head. "They *wanted* us to go east."

"Ha! Hear that, fellas? He wants us to run *toward* their snipers." Frank narrowed his eyes. "We take cover under the trees. Like I said. We go north, and we're dead. We don't know how many snipers they got. I ain't about to risk that." A fresh sweat broke out over Frank's entire body. He wasn't entirely sure he was making the right call for his men, but it certainly was the only way to maintain his authority. He was already working up how to spin it if things went south.

Ruger set his jaw and stepped aside, frustration clear in his expression despite his compliance. Frank said a silent thanks to Ace. Whatever he'd done to break Ruger had worked. The man's obedience had won out so far over and against his defiance. Still, Frank didn't like the way the man glared as he followed orders or the way those from CON, like Caleb, looked to Ruger instead of to him. That kind of loyalty might have been enough for a thug like Ace, but for a refined boss like Frank? No. His blood had a history of authority. He was born to lead, and he'd finally been given the opportunity. Nobody — not some wanna-be hero cop or some overly zealous thug from the streets — was going to take that from him.

Frank stepped forward, leading the way toward the cluster of trees that lined the park's edge. He raised his handgun, approaching slowly. And then he spotted it: the sun caught metal, maybe the clip of a pocketknife. It was a twinkle, only a second, and then there was the slightest movement and it was gone, but it told Frank what he needed to know.

"Spread the word," he whispered. "They're on the other side of the trees." Instead of coming in fast, Frank led his men with caution. Half of them went left, the other half followed him to the right. He made sure Pugsie was with him; he had their missile and launcher. His men all had their guns on the trees. Frank watched carefully, ready to shoot at the first sign of the Boys in Blue.

* * *

On edge, not knowing what to do, George was close to full blown panic. "O'Donnell is expecting them to pass by unaware," George said. "The snipers around the park aren't going to shoot until they've got clean shots at the center of the clearing." He balled his sweaty hands into fists. "They're sneaking up on our guys!"

"Forget this," Lissa said. "We have to do something, and a message over the walkie talkie will only tell Frank's guys exactly where to shoot." She jumped in front of the window and started wildly waving her arms. "O'Donnell is watching. Get his attention! He'll know something is up."

George stood behind Lissa, jumping and waving, hoping it was enough.

* * *

O'Donnell's voice rang out into the silence as Frank and his men approached the trees the cops hid behind. "Do it now!" the captain shouted, and then men and women were whipping their guns around tree trunks and shooting at them.

Frank took cover between two trees, pulling Pugsie and the artillery he carried into safety with him. His men returned fire, but the police picked up ballistic shields and started moving back into the clearing. Behind them, a sniper began shooting *into* the trees. Frank cursed as a bullet took one of his guys in the face just a few feet off, blood spurting everywhere, his body hitting the ground like a hunk of lead.

But Frank saw where that shot came from. He peeked out from behind his shelter and spotted a fallen cop, laying on his shield. Frank took a deep breath and lunged forward, sliding to the ground, pushing the body off the shield, and picking it up to cover himself. Ruger ground to a halt beside him, firing a shot behind Frank and coming back-to-back with him.

"I know where one of the snipers is," Frank said. "I'm gonna take this shield, and I'm gonna take a few guys, and we're gonna go get 'im."

"Someone is up in the tower," Ruger said, firing off a few more shots. "They've got a central, bird's eye view. I'm going after them. I'll shoot out a window, too. It's a perfect spot to take out the other snipers. It's thirty feet higher than the surrounding rooftops."

"You do that," Frank said. "See ya on the other side."

"You got it, boss."

The force of Ruger's back against his lifted, and two more men took his place: Gino and Savi. He pulled Caleb to his side, too, so as to separate the kid from Ruger. He needed to see a real man in action to understand who exactly he should be following. Frank charged forward, signaling for Pugsie to come with him, making his a force of five. That missile launcher was about to come in handy.

* * *

"Ruger's coming for the tower!" Lissa's voice was high-pitched, grating with nerves. "He must have seen us, too."

George's stomach sank as he dug out his earplugs from a small pocket in his bulletproof vest. "We can't let him up here. It's too good of a vantage point." He stepped away from the window. "Put in your earplugs."

As soon as they both had some ear protection, George raised the rifle and fired. The bullet pierced the glass, leaving a fist-sized hole, the glass splintering outward from there. George used the butt of his rifle to knock out the rest, and then he brought his rifle up. He aimed, but Ruger was so close. George leaned out of the window. Images flashed in his mind's eye of Ruger, proud of him, encouraging him, teaching him. George pushed past his emotions; he had to protect his people. Ruger was on the wrong side. He put his finger on the trigger, positioning himself, aiming the barrel of his rifle downward at Ruger, but his shot missed, and the man slipped inside, unharmed.

George stepped back. "He's on his way up! I missed."

Lissa took aim at the top of the stairs. "Get ready," she shouted. "We've got to get him on the way up."

George shook it off, trying not to let the failure get to him. But then, out of the corner of his eye, he saw another man running toward the tower. He almost took aim and fired, but then he realized it wasn't the enemy. "O'Donnell is coming after Ruger."

The captain sprinted away from the skirmish toward the tower faster than George had ever seen him run. He was leaving the fight, turning his back on the enemy, exposing himself to a well-placed shot because George had been distracted by his complicated feelings toward Ruger. George narrowed his eyes and raised his weapon toward the stairs, along with Lissa, determined to do whatever needed to be done.

* * *

Frank stood over the dead body of the sniper and gave him one last kick. "A'ight," he said stepping to the window. "Now it's time for some fun." He looked out over the battlefield and then held up a rifle, looking through the magnifier. He found another sniper across the way, focused on taking out his guys. Frank fired, and the man spun out of sight, dropping his rifle out of the window.

Caleb opened another window, aiming toward the clearing. "I'm gonna take out some of those bastards," he said.

Frank grinned. "Have fun, Sharpshooter."

The kid flashed a smile before taking aim and meeting his first mark, taking out one of the policemen below. Frank came up to him and patted him on the back.

"Looks like Sharpshooter it is," he said. "How d'ya like that, kid?"

"Not bad," Caleb said, standing a little straighter, his smile widening.

That was exactly what his nicknames were for, to make men feel what *Frank* wanted them to feel. He gave the kid another pat on the back. "Let me see another one."

Caleb turned toward the park and raised his rifle, but then he frowned. "Didn't Ruger run into that tower a minute ago?"

"Yeah," Frank said. "Why?" He looked out over the battle and looked through his magnifier again as none other than Captain O'Donnell entered the tower. "That woulda been a good shot, Sharpshooter. Next time, take it."

Caleb blushed. "Sorry."

"Not a problem." Frank held out his hand. "Pugsie, load up the launcher. We've got a police captain to take out."

"But Ruger's in there!" Caleb said. "You can't— "

"Excuse me?" Frank turned a hardened look on the boy. "O'Donnell's a freakin' thorn in my side. He shoulda been dead already. I thought he was. There's only room for one cockroach in this town, one man with nine lives, and that's me." The fact that Ruger would be taken out played into his decision, of course. He'd keep his word. Ruger's people would still get their swathe of Boston, still have the illusion of autonomy. But they'd be Frank's people, sure as the morning comes.

* * *

"I'm unarmed," Ruger's voice came before the sight of his open hands at the top of the stairs. "I set down my weapons at the bottom of the stairs."

George hesitated, glancing at Lissa. She, too, shifted uncomfortably. Ruger continued up the stairs, hands held high. There was no sign of any weapon on his person as he emerged into the small, circular room.

"Why?" George asked.

"We should just shoot him," Lissa said.

"You won't do that," Ruger said. "I disarmed myself because I don't want to hurt either one of you. I saw it was you up here, and I came to talk."

"You're not going to talk us into coming back with you or switching sides," George snapped. "We made our choice."

"Yes, you did." Ruger's words were laced with distaste. "It was the wrong one, but I'm not here about that, either. You two need to get out of here. The cops won't take care of you. This might seem like a safe position, but I saw you. I'm in your corner, and one day, you're gonna see that. You're gonna come back to CON where you can have real power, real respect."

"Respect?" Lissa's voice trembled. "I didn't feel respected when Big Mack assaulted me."

Ruger frowned and then his eyes widened in understanding. He cursed. "You shot him?" he asked.

Lissa raised her chin. "I'd do it again."

"Good." Ruger spat on the floor. "Good riddance. I'm not about that kind of treatment of our people. Things'll be different with me at the forefront of CON. I swear. And I want people like you in our community. We have to rebuild, and we have to do it different. I think you two can help me do that."

"I've got somethin' to say about that, you bastard." Captain O'Donnell's voice preceded his weapon as he cautiously traversed the steps upward, pointing his handgun at Ruger.

"He's unarmed," George said. Neither he nor Lissa had lowered their weapons, but he didn't plan to shoot a defenseless man.

"I'm not so sure that matters to a man like that, kid," Ruger said, nodding at O'Donnell.

The captain scowled. "If it didn't, you'd be dead already."

"Maybe you and me should have a little old-fashioned brawl, old man." Ruger's lopsided smile was full of confidence.

George shook his head as Lissa objected. "No," she said. "He's twenty years older than you are."

O'Donnell lowered his weapon. "I'm not worried about it," he said. "I win, you leave these kids alone for good. Understand?"

Ruger lowered his hands, his smile turning into a full grin. "Understood."

* * *

"See?" Frank growled, watching through the broken window of the tower as Ruger surrendered to the enemy without a fight. "He's betrayed us." He nodded at Caleb to take a look himself.

"No," Caleb said, shaking his head after taking a look, "you don't understand. That's George and Lissa. My bet is that Ruger is trying to turn them. He cares about them."

"Ha!" Frank barked a laugh. "He's got you fooled. Pugsie, hand it over." He motioned and Pugsie did as he was told, laying the heavy missile launcher into Frank's hands.

"No!" Caleb stepped forward.

"Hold him!" Frank shouted, and within seconds, Gino had his hands on Caleb's shoulders, holding him in place.

Frank held up the missile launcher and pointed it toward the tower. He wasn't about to let anyone else have this victory. No, it would be him, Frank Russo, who took out Captain O'Donnell *and* Ruger, the last true leader of CON.

But just before he fired, there was a grunt from Gino and Caleb careened into him, knocking the missile off course.

Gino held his head back as his nose spurted blood. "He head-butted me, the little bastard!"

Frank cursed, but then the missile struck the base of the tower, and it tipped backward, toward the houses on the far side of the park. It toppled into a triple-decker, and Frank laughed. The tide was turning. The Boys were fleeing, and his guys were cheering on the grass. Frank had been tested and found worthy.

"It's done," he said, elated. Still laughing, he turned toward Caleb, who stared dumbfounded at the wreckage of the tower where his beloved leader had suffered his inevitable fate. Frank pulled out his handgun and shot Caleb through the temple before the kid even knew what was happening. His laughter cut off at the sound of the shot. "Sorry, Sharpshooter, but the last thing I need is another Ruger."

Chapter 33

Zara Williams

"Wait!" Zara held out a hand, her stomach lurching.
Kai slammed on the brakes. "What is it?" Kai asked, hand already going from steering wheel to the back seat where the rifles were.
"I just… are you sure about this?" Zara pulled on her seatbelt, which had locked in place at Kai's sudden stop. It wouldn't budge, and the air felt too thin, too hard to breathe. They were only a few yards from pulling out behind the tree line and coming into sight of The Log Cabin, so she unbuckled and let the seatbelt snap back, the metal part clinking against the door as it did so. She took a few shaky breaths, trying to calm herself.
"We already talked about this." Kai sighed and brought his hand back to the wheel.
Heat rose to Zara's cheeks, nerves distracted by a burst of frustration. "Yeah, *after* you kidnapped Heath."
Zara was still having trouble grappling with the fact that she'd helped tie another human being to a table leg after gagging him and forcing him into their camper.
"Do you want to just let him go?" Kai answered her, matching her tone. "I mean, I guess we could do that. Sure. Just untie him, let him go back to Mommy, and then we can be like, 'Hey, crazy lady, I know you want to kill us, but maybe you could do as we ask, instead? Pretty please with a cherry on top?" His words were laced with sarcasm, but there was also something desperate there, too.
Zara pinched the bridge of her nose. *He's just as lost as I am. At least he's* got *a plan that might actually work.* She took a deep breath and looked Kai in the eye.
"Swear we won't actually hurt him," she said.
"Of course we won't," Kai said. "We're just getting Walter back. That's it."
"What if she won't trade?" Zara asked. "Heath said his mom thinks Walter is her husband. And she's not exactly thinking clearly. We have no idea what she's going to do."
Kai let his forehead hit the steering wheel, and he groaned. "Zara, if that happens, we'll drive away, and then we really will let Heath go. Simple as that. We'll find another way." He turned his head, eyes pleading with her. "But this is the best plan we've got right now. And I think it will work. And if it does work, no one will get hurt, and we'll get Walter back."
Zara squeezed her eyes shut, grimacing as she nodded. "Yeah, okay. You're right. Do it." He'd only barely stepped on the gas when she shouted again, "Wait!"
"*What?*" Kai shouted back.
"Are you sure he's tied up well enough?" Zara glanced over her shoulder, biting her lower lip. "I mean, if we're doing this, we can't have him busting out of the camper, coming at us from behind while we're trying to negotiate."
Kai smirked. "Come on, Zara. I know how to tie a knot."
"Okay, okay." Zara gestured at the road. "Go on, then."
"You sure this time?" Kai asked.
"Yes," Zara snapped. It was a lie. She wasn't ready. She didn't want to do what they had to do. So many things could go wrong. But Kai was right. Carol had left them little choice.
Kai pulled the truck and silver airstream into the lot of The Log Cabin and parked parallel to the front door. He reached for a rifle, handed it to Zara, and retrieved one for himself. "They're just for show, unless she fires first," he said.
"I don't feel good about this," Zara said.
"Me either." Kai reached for her hand and squeezed it lightly. "Let's get Walter back, okay?"
Zara nodded. "Okay." She stepped out of the truck on wobbly legs, and by the time she'd come around the truck to face the front door of The Log Cabin, Carol was already bursting through the door, her own rifle at hand.
"I told you two—" Carol began, but then she cut off at the sight of their weapons. She smiled wryly and shook her head, lowering her weapon. "So you've come for my supplies, after all. Well, I don't have time for this. Go on and take them. My son has lost his mind, went for a walk or something, and I—"
"We didn't come for your supplies," Kai said, raising his weapon. "We have Heath."
Carol frowned and took half a step back. "You… you what?"
Zara cleared her throat, following Kai's example, raising her rifle. "We have your son," she said. "And we will give him back in exchange for Walter Peters."
Carol shifted her weight, the color draining from her face. "I told you, there's no one here by that name."
"We saw him, Carol. In the third story window." Zara took a step toward her. "We don't want to hurt anyone. We just want our friend back."
Carol shook her head, whispering to herself, eyes glazing over with madness. The door opened, and it was only then that Zara realized it had been cracked since Carol came outside.
The little girl — LeeAnn — ran forward, a foot or two past her mother, tears in her eyes. "Please don't hurt my brother," she said.
Her little voice, those big, innocent eyes… they pierced Zara through the heart. Hot tears sprung to her eyes. "No, honey," she said. "We're not going to hurt him."
"Not if we get our friend back," Kai said harshly, giving Zara a wide-eyed look that said, *What are you doing?*

"You can't have Saul," Carol said. "I just got him back."
"Mommy? It's not Daddy." The little girl came to Carol and tugged on her mother's arm even as the woman raised her weapon again. "Please… it's not Daddy. He wants to go with them. He told me they're his friends."
Carol pushed her daughter away, her eyes still crazed. Spittle came out of her mouth, her words clipped. "Stop it, LeeAnn. Stop it. Go inside." She didn't seem to notice that she'd pushed her daughter to the ground.
LeeAnn scooted a few inches away from her mother, drew her knees to her chest, hugged them tight, and hid her face, her hair falling down over her eyes. Her sobs shook her whole body. Zara couldn't handle it. She let her gun down.
"What the hell, Zara?" Kai shifted his weight nervously.
"There's a little girl crying on the ground, Kai." Zara pointed, exasperated and sick to her stomach.
And then the door to the airstream burst open. Zara whirled around, and instinct had her raising her weapon in that direction. It was Heath, and he had Kai's old .44 magnum American Derringer pointed right at them.
It was Zara's turn. She glanced at Kai incredulously. "What the hell, Kai?"
"Get away from my mom!" Heath shouted.
Kai blanched, looking over his shoulder, keeping his rifle aimed at Carol. He shuffled sideways, putting his back to Zara's. "So… it seems I overestimated my knot tying abilities." He cleared his throat. "But I have no idea how he got that gun out of the safe. The only way I have to open it is by thumbprint."
"How did you get the gun?" Zara asked.
Heath scoffed. "It was inside a messenger bag, and there was a key in a small zipper pocket. You don't have to be Sherlock to figure that one out."
"Really, Kai?" Zara gritted her teeth.
"I thought I lost that key ages ago!" Kai groaned.
"Just get in your truck and go!" Heath shouted.
"No. I can't do that." Zara bit her lower lip hard, but she did the only thing she could think to do. She lowered her weapon and put it on the ground in front of her.
"Zara, pick up your rifle." Kai turned to the side, head whipping back and forth between Carol and Heath.
"We don't want anyone to get hurt!" Zara balled her hands into fists, anger making her chest go tight. "Why can't you just give us Walter and let us go on our way?"
Carol grimaced. "I said, there's no one by that name here. Son," she shouted, "we have to take care of these two, or they'll never leave us alone."
Zara shook her head at Heath. "Don't listen to her," she said. "You know she's not right in the head. She needs help."
"I'll take the boy," Carol said. "You take the girl. Don't let her innocent act fool you, Heath. She's going to come back, kill me in my sleep, and take your father. She's probably that whore he was sleeping with, come back to finish the job and tear our family apart."
"What?" Zara almost laughed at the absurdity. "Heath, come on. Your mom has lost it."
"I know," Heath said, raising the gun, pointing at her with trembling hands. "But she's my mom. And if you take that man, I think she's going to lose it for good. She's been more like herself these last few days than she has been in weeks. I think…" Heath licked his lips and lowered his voice, glancing toward his mother. "I think she'll kill herself if you take him."
Zara's heart sank. "Heath… you can't let her keep doing this."
"I'm going to take her out," Kai said over his shoulder.
"What did he say?" Heath shouted, pointing his gun more ferociously. "I heard you," he said. "Don't you dare hurt my mother!" His entire face screwed up with tension, sweat rolling down the sides of his face. He bit his lip, and the look in his eyes turned harder.
"Kai, get down!" Zara dropped to the ground as Heath bared his teeth and a loud *boom* shook the very air.
But the Derringer was too much for Heath. As soon as the gun went off, it reared backward and slammed into Heath's forehead. He went down, knocked backward by the force, the gun skidding across the lot as he fell and lost his grip on it. Zara dropped to the ground, picked up her rifle in one hand, and scrambled on her knees for the Derringer. She reached it without trouble, noting the way Heath's thumb jutted at a weird angle as he groaned in pain and slowly moved his head back and forth.
Adrenaline like electricity pulsing through her veins, the handgun beside her, she spun around to sitting and raised her rifle toward Carol. Everyone on the parking lot was on the ground. Kai was sitting much like she was, wildly switching aim between Carol and Heath. But he seemed to realize just as quickly that the two were no longer a danger.
"Are you okay?" Zara asked breathlessly.
Kai nodded. "You?"
"I'm fine." She frowned at Carol, who hadn't moved from where she lay on the ground. "Oh no…" A growing dread filled Zara up, choking her, preventing her from saying anything further. LeeAnn crawled over to her mother and poked her in the shoulder. The woman still didn't move.
Heath slowly sat up. He turned to the side and wretched, groaning again and holding his head. "What… happened?" he asked, clearly confused. And then his eyes widened as he looked across the lot as his mother. "Mom?" he shouted, ignoring both Zara and Kai as he stood on unsteady legs and haphazardly made it to where Carol lay, a growing red stain on the front of her shirt becoming more prominent by the second.
Kai scooted away when Heath passed, but he lowered his weapon, too. Zara got to her feet and came to stand by Kai, who stayed sitting, shoulders slumped.
"It's all my fault," Kai whispered. "I'm sorry, Zara."
Zara let her rifle hang at her side as Heath and LeeAnn sobbed over their mother. She wilted, her vision blurring with tears.
Heath let out a haggard sob. "I shot my own mother." He knelt beside Carol and reached tentatively for her. And then he snapped his hand back, looking around at them with wide eyes. "She's still alive!"

Zara sucked in a breath and walked forward, her strides long. There was still a chance she could keep from becoming the bad guy. Even if it was slim, she was going to take it. "We can get her to the hospital," she said as she approached. "We can—"

The sound of her own name, shrilly, desperately repeated over and over again made Zara snap her head up. It was Walter. *Didn't Heath say he almost killed himself trying to get down those stairs by himself?*

"I'll help you get her inside the camper." Kai stepped forward. "Zara, go get Mr. Peters."

"Don't touch her!" Heath put a protective hand over his mother. He was still crying, and his assertive command was followed by an unsure frown as he studied the two of them.

Zara tore her gaze from the front door, choosing to ignore Walter for just a second longer. She crouched so she could look at Heath right in the eye. "We *never* wanted to hurt anyone," she said. "And if you'll notice, we never fired a shot." She held out a hand and rested it gently on Heath's shoulder as he sucked in a breath at those words. "I'm sorry we took you and tied you up. We were desperate, and we needed to get our friend back. My guess is you would have done the same for someone you loved." He averted his eyes, and she continued. "I do *not* want your mother to die. I wouldn't be able to live with myself if we didn't try to save her. So, you can remain suspicious of us, or you can let us take your family to the hospital in town where they might be able to keep her alive."

Heath glanced at his little sister before looking back at Zara. "Okay," he said. "Let's go. We have a stretcher inside. I think it would help move her."

As Zara rushed inside and followed the sound of Walter's voice, Kai went with Heath to get the stretcher. She found the stairs and took them two at a time. On her way up, she heard a *thump* and the shouting stopped. An urgent, jittery sensation shot through her, and Zara sped up, nearly tripping over her feet.

"Mr. Peters? I'm coming!" When she rounded the top of the stairs, she didn't have to guess which of the bedrooms he was in because he was laying in the doorway of one of them, breathing heavily. Zara's heart leapt into her throat, and she rushed to him. "Walter!"

He looked at her, a slow, exhausted smile spreading. "Zara?" He frowned. "Did I die? Are you dead?"

"I'm fine," Zara said. "You could have just watched through the—" She glanced into the dark room to find the windows blocked out by what appeared to be paint. "Oh..."

"She saw me at the window... said I was trying to plot my escape again."

Zara nodded and looked back at him. He was pale, bruised and broken, barely able to speak a sentence without breaking for more air. "You look terrible."

He laughed and then winced. "I think that's mostly the drugs. I have the feeling I might be able to at least walk if it weren't for that."

"She's been drugging you?" A flash of anger lit a fire in Zara's belly, and she shook her head. "Maybe she deserves what she got."

Mr. Peters frowned. "What happened?"

"We kidnapped Heath. Tried to exchange him for you. They both went crazy. We weren't going to hurt them, but... Heath ended up shooting his mother. We're going to get her to the hospital as soon as we get you downstairs and into the truck." She reached for him. "Come on. Let's see if we can get you to your feet."

Mr. Peters shook his head. "Help me to the bed, but then you go. You can come back for me. Don't let Carol die. She's all those kids have left, and... she's broken. It doesn't mean she can't be fixed."

"I can't leave you here," Zara said, fresh anger at how Walter had been treated surfacing. "She doesn't deserve the help we *are* giving her."

Mr. Peters reached up, put his hand against Zara's cheek, and spoke gently. "Neither one of us deserved forgiveness after Lizzy's death. After the destruction of that compound. But we got it. We got second chances, Zara."

Zara swallowed hard and closed her eyes, sighing, the sting of that truth causing hot tears to spring up. She wiped them quickly away, nodding her agreement. "Okay," she said. "You're right. To the bed, then, and we'll come back for you as soon as we've taken care of Carol."

It was hard to leave him there after all she'd been through to find him, but he was safe. He was alive. Her family was okay, but another family needed her help. As she rushed down the stairs, Heath's desperate eyes and LeeAnn's terrified expression spurred her on. If Carol died after Heath had shot her, no matter how accidental it was... and for LeeAnn to lose her mother... well, Zara understood both kinds of pain, and she wouldn't wish either of them on anyone. She burst out of the front door of The Log Cabin as Kai was shutting the door to the airstream.

"Where's Walter?" he asked. "We're ready to go."

She reached the truck, shaking her head. "He's staying. Too injured to come quickly, and he wants us to save Carol. We can come back for him."

Kai licked his lips and glanced at the building. "You sure?"

"Yes," she said.

"Okay," he said. "Let's go save the life of the woman who just tried to kill us."

Chapter 34

George Peters

The sounds of fighting had died down a while ago. George leaned back against rubble in the preserved pocket of space wherein he found himself trapped with Lissa, O'Donnell, and Ruger. He wasn't sure how long they'd been there; it could have been hours, for all he knew. Lissa sat beside him, more bruised and battered than George, but alive, nonetheless. It was dark, besides O'Donnell's flashlight. He'd ordered George and Lissa to save the batteries on their own small flashlights, and he had immediately started examining the debris, looking for a way out. Meanwhile, he and Ruger wouldn't stop arguing.

"That's not the way out. Stop digging near the tank," Ruger said. He stomped over to O'Donnell and knocked on the top of the old water tower tank which had made up the core of the tower.

One thing they'd agreed upon was that when the base of the tower had been hit, the tank and cast-iron spiral stairs around it had kept the structure from buckling downward. It had remained a foundation for the room at the top as the tower tipped, and halfway down, the power lines had caught them, slowing their decent. They'd all sustained minor injuries, and they were stuck inside a cavern made of debris, but they were alive. For the time being.

"It's more stable over here," O'Donnell said, grunting as he removed a chunk of debris. "This tank ain't gonna collapse." He put his hands on his knees, coughing hard.

George shook his head. "Captain, maybe you should take a break. Are you sure you're okay?"

"Yeah, old man. Have a seat. Let people like me do the real work, like you always have." Ruger smirked.

"Shut up, Ruger," Lissa snapped.

"Look, Firecracker," Ruger said, "you don't have to like me, but you do have to respect me."

O'Donnell barked a laugh as he stood up straighter. "That's rich, comin' from you."

"Oh? And you think you're worthy of respect? I've seen guys get a beat down for jaywalking from Boys like you. Families forcibly evicted by your brothers 'cause some slumlord has the so-called right to do it." Ruger crossed his arms. "Nah, you don't get to judge me."

"I'm sure you've seen some bad apples, Ruger," O'Donnell said, rolling his right shoulder and rubbing his upper arm, "but don't think for one second that when the law is used by evil men to do unkind things, those who have to enforce it are excited about that."

Ruger sneered. "Tell that to the kids spending holidays in shelters. And I've seen more than *some* bad apples in your lot."

O'Donnell turned to face Ruger, towering over the CONman. "Now who's got room to talk? CONmen are lowlifes. They don't care about nobody outside their little group. They steal and murder and rape—"

"I ain't never raped nobody!" Ruger got closer, looking up at O'Donnell as if he weren't an entire foot shorter.

George tensed. "If things get ugly," he whispered to Lissa, "stay out of the way."

"I see how you left out the murderin' bit," O'Donnell shouted.

Lissa leaned closer. "Where do we go? There's no room."

Ruger's voice filled the small space. "And why do you think we gotta steal and kill? It's survival out there on these streets. Always has been, long before everybody died off." Ruger jutted his finger in O'Donnell's face. "You and yours failed me and mine generations ago, and that left us no choice but to fend for ourselves."

O'Donnell growled, but he did nothing more than stare at Ruger for several more minutes, still standing over him, jaw clenched. "Bah!" He stepped back and let out a long, frustrated breath.

George relaxed just a little at the captain's actions. It seemed he was trying to deescalate the argument.

Ruger's cocky smile held a note of disgust. "See? You can't even deny it."

"Maybe law enforcement failed parts of the city," O'Donnell said. "But we ain't the only ones that failed. We can't be held responsible for the bad decisions of every man and woman who decides to skirt the law or ignore it completely."

"But you can be held responsible for yourselves, for your own so-called bad apples," Ruger said.

O'Donnell sighed. "We're not gonna agree on who's more to blame for the darker aspects of this city," he said. "But I tell ya what, I can say this: we *did* have bad apples. Hell, we had entirely rotten trees. But those weren't the cops who stayed. The fact is, here and now, the men and women in uniform who survived *and stayed* are good ones, every last one of 'em. They're out there riskin' their lives to save Boston from the likes of Frank Russo. And don't you dare try to tell me that between me and him, you really think he's the better of us."

George nodded at that. He couldn't imagine a city run by Frank. The mobster was too unstable, too self-serving. It would be a dictatorship of the worst kind.

"That doesn't matter," Ruger said, a little more calmly. "We're going to be free and clear once this mess is over. CON and anyone who wants to join up, we can live in peace." He pointed back at himself. "And when I'm in charge, things are gonna be done right."

"Is that what Frank promised you?" George asked from his dark corner. He couldn't keep the sarcasm from his voice.

"Now's not the time, Hero," Ruger said. "But yeah, that's what he promised. We pay him twenty percent of our resources; he leaves us alone. And if there's anything good about Frank Russo it's that he sticks to his word."

George laughed, thinking about his brother's dealings with the mobster. "Oh sure. Except he gets to define what his words *really* meant after the fact. Your interpretation doesn't matter. And if you go back on what *he* thinks is your deal?" He whistled and shook his head. "Be ready. He'll come after you, and to get even, he'll take everything you've got. I can almost guarantee it. The first time you can't get him twenty percent, he'll count your deal done, and your freedom will be gone—" He snapped his fingers. "—like that."

"You act like you know him," Ruger said, narrowing his eyes at George. "You said something that made me think that back at the zoo, too."

"It's his brother," O'Donnell said nodding at George. "Tim got into trouble with Frank, and... I've never seen anyone understand Frank like he does. Timothy Peters can actually negotiate with him, anticipate what he's going to do. From what I've heard, George has hit the mark. You can't trust Russo."

George stood up. "Did he know you were coming into this tower?" he asked. Ruger didn't answer, but the look in his eyes said enough. George shook his head. "Frank wouldn't let a finite resource like a *missile* be used up without his direct consent. You know I'm right."

Ruger cursed, stringing together obscenities into colorful nicknames for the mobster. He paced the small space, running his hands over his head. "He tried to kill me." He looked up and around at the dimly lit cavern. "Maybe he already has."

"Maybe not," George said, "if you two can actually work together."

The two men scoffed at the same time, as if the notion was insane. But George had been able to see it from the time he'd trained under Ruger when Ace had been in charge of CON. With Ruger and O'Donnell working together, Boston could actually see some peace.

Ruger shook his head and backed away. "You don't know what you're talkin' about, Hero. You're young and idealistic and sometimes that means you're stupid, too. People like him and people like me don't do anything *together*."

O'Donnell pursed his lips, staring at Ruger's back as the man started moving the rubble again. George turned to Lissa, about to suggest they help O'Donnell near the tank, when her eyes went wide. At the same moment, out of the periphery of his vision, George spotted a blur of movement as O'Donnell leapt forward. A rumbling of rock accompanied the captain's shout. George barely had time to process what had happened as O'Donnell slammed into Ruger, knocking him out of the way as a piece of rubble above his head dislodged. The slab fell on top of O'Donnell, pinning his legs to the ground.

"No!" Lissa lurched forward, the first to have her hands on the heavy debris. "Help me!"

George was right behind her. O'Donnell groaned. Smaller bricks had come down with the larger slab, and there were gouges in the captain's arms, neck, and face. George began clearing the smaller bricks.

"We won't be able to move him if these are still piled on top," he said, flinging the bricks aside.

Lissa nodded, tears welling and spilling onto her cheeks as she followed suit. "We're going to get you out of there," she said.

"Ruger!" George looked up. "We're going to need your help to get the slab off his legs."

The CONman was staring wide-eyed at the captain, confusion written in his expression. He opened his mouth but shut it again, looking up at the gaping hole in the debris — full daylight visible — and then back down at the captain as if he couldn't believe what he was seeing.

"Why did he do that?" Ruger asked.

O'Donnell groaned louder and coughed. "Get it off me," he moaned. "I can still feel my legs. That's a good sign, but it hurts like hell!"

"Ruger!" George shouted again. For a moment, he thought Ruger was staring at the hole, contemplating whether he should escape right then and there.

"Hey!" Lissa's shrill voice drew Ruger's gaze. "Are you going to help or what?"

Ruger blinked, and then he was moving, taking up position beside Lissa. "On the count of three, we all lift," he said.

George set one foot on either side of O'Donnell's chest. Lissa stood by his side, and Ruger stood opposite George, feet positioned on either side of the captain's legs.

"One. Two. Three." Ruger finished his count, and they all heaved at the same time, managing to move the slab aside.

O'Donnell scooted out from between George's legs, huffing as he positioned himself against the more stable rubble, holding his thigh.

Ruger stepped up to him. "Why did you do that?" His tone was harsh, hostile, even.

"You're welcome." O'Donnell scowled, his teeth gritted in pain.

"Step off, Ruger." Lissa came to O'Donnell's side. "He could have just saved your life."

"I know," Ruger said. "And I want to know why. What does he want?"

O'Donnell laughed. "I didn't save your life to get somethin', ya idiot."

George stepped between Ruger and O'Donnell. "He's a good apple, Ruger. And now you've seen it with your own eyes."

Ruger shook his head. "Nah, I don't believe it for one second." He shoved George to one side and knelt in front of O'Donnell. "What do you want, old man?"

"Peace!" O'Donnell shouted, the effort bringing on another coughing fit. "I want the people of Boston who survive to live in peace."

"Under your rules," Ruger said.

"There's a council forming at City Hall," O'Donnell said. "I don't wanna be in charge of the whole damn city. I wanna help support the right people so *they* can do it."

"A council, huh?" Ruger laughed. "Yeah, right. Representatives who come from the same stock as you, probably."

"You do realize," O'Donnell said, "that with the number of people left alive, coupled with the supporters you've got, that *you* could get a seat on the council? This isn't the old government. It's new and untested, and it'll look completely different from anything we've had before. You could work *with* the rest of the survivors in town to make this place better instead of supporting a crazy man just so you can grab a corner of Boston he won't let you keep anyway."

"What?" Ruger sat down hard, staring at O'Donnell like he'd grown another head. "You can't be serious."

"He is," Lissa snapped. "You've got people who will follow you. People who would want you on that council to represent *their* interests. You just wouldn't have complete control over everything. You'd have to be on a team, and you'd have to care about what other people need, too."

"They're both right," George said. "And even if you don't want to join up with City Hall, there's nothing stopping you and CON from setting up your own survivor's camp in Mattapan or Roxbury or wherever, just like the one at the library."

"Nobody's stopping any of the survivor camps from self-governance," O'Donnell said. "But we can't let one group enslave another or destroy what little chance of peace we've got as they try to set up a dictatorship."

George looked Ruger straight in the eye. "You were so used to enabling Ace's power-hungry, selfish ways, that when Frank Russo came around, you switched masters instead of becoming your own."

"That's not true," Ruger whispered, though he hung his head, and there was no conviction in his voice.

"It doesn't have to be," George said.

Ruger worked his jaw back and forth in silence, and then he shook his head, cheeks and neck red — with anger or embarrassment, George couldn't tell — and he climbed out of the hole, disappearing into the daylight.

"I guess it's up to you two to help me outta here, then," O'Donnell said through gritted teeth. "Pretty sure I've at least fractured somethin' in my pelvis, though… not sure I can walk." He shook his head. "Maybe it's best if you get outta here. Go to wherever your brother is hiding, George. Timothy will take care of you both."

"No," Lissa said. "We're not leaving you here to die."

George pushed away the disappointment building at Ruger's actions and shook his head. "I agree. We can't do that." He sighed and looked around the cavernous space. "But we can't lift him out of here without some help. Everyone probably thinks we're dead. The battle has moved closer to City Hall by now, but… we can go there, get someone — anyone — and bring them back here to help us."

"I'll climb out, get a few supplies, and I'll come right back," Lissa said to O'Donnell. She glanced at George. "Somebody needs to stay with him."

George nodded. "Let's go. We need to get him out of here as soon as possible."

Lissa gave him a leg up, and George climbed outside, turning around and leaning back into the rubble to pull her out. They scooted carefully down the remaining few feet of brick and rock. And then Ruger came running around a corner, an orange stretcher under one arm.

"He didn't run," George said.

"I remembered a firetruck down the street, when we were approaching the park," Ruger said, hefting the stretcher as he approached. "It won't be easy, but I think between the three of us, we'll be able to get him out of there."

Lissa smiled. "Well… I guess I'm still capable of being surprised."

George stretched out a hand toward Ruger. "Give me a corner of that thing," he said, "and let's get O'Donnell out of there."

Chapter 35

Timothy Peters and Lauren Stevens

Timothy slammed his hand on the steering wheel and growled. "This *cannot* be happening!"
Ahead, smoke rose high in the air, and the sounds of gunfire signaled the battle over Boston had reached far into the green zone. It had taken them forever to push their way through the danger zone, entering what was supposed to be a safe area around Fenway. They'd taken the path of least resistance, Timothy driving a truck out front, using it as a battering ram to clear a path when there was none. Heather drove the minivan behind them, taken from a car lot not far from the lab. Candice and Lauren were with her, monitoring Annika and keeping her as steady as possible. It had required them to go so slow, but Timothy had gained hope with every yard. The sight of smoke had dashed that to pieces.
He roughly grabbed the doorhandle and flung it open, stalking back to where Heather was already rolling down her window. "You hear that?" He pointed, frustration and fear and anger swirling inside, coming out of his mouth in the form of a bitter tone. "You *see* that? The battle is all the way up to the Boston Common, for crying out loud."
Heather blanched. "Do you think… does that mean it's not going well? I mean… what about George?"
The thought heaped anxiety into the mix. "I don't know," he said. "I can't imagine O'Donnell would allow the fighting to get so far if things were going well." He paced, raking his fingernails across the back of his neck. *I have to get Annika to City Hall, but… if George is so close, fighting a losing battle, can I leave him?*
Timothy turned and slammed both fists onto the top of a nearby car. He hung his head between his arms, letting the sting of the impact radiate up and down his arms. Behind him, the minivan door clicked open and closed. The weight of Heather's hand rested lightly on his back.
"Get us to City Hall, Timothy," Heather said. "Go around the fighting, and then we can handle Annika. You've got to go help George."
Her words confirmed what was in his heart to do. Timothy pushed off the car, turned, and wrapped his wife in a hug. "How did you know what I needed to hear?" he asked.
"We both love George," she said, squeezing him right back. "If I could go with you, I would. But if the fighting is this close to City Hall, I want to be there in case it reaches us while Annika is in surgery."
Timothy's chest tightened; there was no winning. Everyone he loved was in danger, and he could only be in one place at a time. He rested his head on Heather's as he let out a long breath. "Can any part of this scenario *not* be terrible?"
Heather pulled away slightly and held his face between her hands, looking up at him. "I love you, Timothy Peters. And that's about as *not terrible* as it gets right now."
Her words brought a small smile to his lips. "I love you, too."
The minivan's side door slid open. "I heard everything," Candice said, nodding to Heather's window, which was still rolled down. "And I get it, I do. But we need to get Annika to Dr. Linden right now, okay? You two can get all kissy on us later, after we've all survived this."
"Right," Timothy said, letting Heather step back and return to the driver's seat of the minivan. "We're almost there, but we'll have to take another detour to avoid the Common. Just follow me."
He hopped back in the truck and pushed forward.

* * *

Lauren checked Annika's vitals for the hundredth time that hour. The little girl was hanging in there, but every second was precious. With every minute, the chances of her ultimate survival decreased. Lauren could only hope that it wasn't as bad as she feared, that the surgeon would know exactly what to do.
Annika rested, stretched out on the backseat of the minivan. Lauren and Candice had folded down the middle bucket seats and used them to sit facing the girl. Candice did as instructed, constantly keeping Annika's bottom half as still as possible. While going slowly was agonizing and time was working against them, Lauren wouldn't have wanted them to go too quickly even if the pathway had been completely clear. Annika needed stability.
A low rumble filled the air, mixing with the sounds of warfare in the distance. Lauren snapped her head around to look out the window. She still couldn't see anything beyond the row of buildings to their right, besides the growing plume of black smoke a few blocks away. "That didn't sound good," she said. "Are all the big bombs Frank's?"
"Unfortunately, we think so," Heather said.
"I can't believe the fighting has reached the Common." Candice didn't take her eyes off Annika, ensuring with steady hands that the girl wasn't jostled too hard as the vehicle moved.
"And how far is the Common from City Hall?" Lauren asked. She was the only one of them not from Boston; she'd never even *been* to Boston before.
"Like a ten-minute walk," Candice said.
Lauren's stomach lurched, and her heartbeat picked up. "That's… too close."
"Yeah, we're going to have to skirt the park to get to City Hall. We will get close, but if we keep a couple of blocks between us and them, hopefully we'll get there safely," Heather said. "If I know O'Donnell, he'll be doing everything he can to keep those bastards from getting to civilians."

Lauren nodded. There was little to do besides wait for them to arrive. The tension in the air was palpable as they came closer to the fighting, as they drove mere blocks from where men and women were killing and being killed. Brick buildings gave way to more modern high rises, the occasional symbols of history in the form of historical buildings sitting stubbornly untouched in the midst of the twenty-first century. All the while, the sounds of gunfire and explosions reverberated down every street.

A growing knot in her stomach kept Lauren stiff and on guard. Her heartbeat pulsed, hard and fast, loud in her ears; she could feel the rhythm from her fingertips to her toes as if her body was a clock, counting down the seconds until she ran out of luck. She made sure her breathing was steady, though she couldn't do much about the beads of sweat rolling down her face, or about the cold shot of fear racing through her veins.

I said I could do this, she reminded herself, and I can. I have to. But another voice surfaced. It was easier to believe in myself before knowing I'd be facing a war zone on top of losing another patient.

"Lauren?" Candice's voice broke through Lauren's thoughts.

She blinked, realizing the van had stopped moving. "Are we there?" She looked around, heat rising to her cheeks as she saw Heather at the open side door. "Sorry," she said, the need for action enough to distract from her nerves, at least temporarily.

"Are you okay?" Heather asked as Timothy came up beside her.

"Yeah, I'm fine." Lauren scooped her arms under Annika. "Let's get her inside." Annika was light in her arms. She passed the girl to Candice, who pivoted on the top of the folded-up bucket seat and held her out to Timothy. Candice was still too weak from her own injuries to carry the girl herself, or else Lauren suspected Candice wouldn't have let Annika be carried by anyone else.

"No," Heather said, reaching out for Annika. "We've got it from here," she said. "Remember?"

Timothy glanced uncertainly at his wife, and then his gaze shifted to Candice and finally to Lauren. "Are you all *sure*?"

Lauren nodded. "My guess is they need all the help they can get. And if the fighting reaches City Hall in the middle of surgery…" She trailed off, averting her eyes. She really didn't want to think about that; surgery without a modern and fully equipped operating room was challenge enough.

"Okay, then I'm out of here." He kissed his wife, lingering for only a few seconds, and then he was gone.

Heather held out her arms, and Candice transferred Annika safely into her arms. The girl was in and out of consciousness, pale and sickly. Her small groan of pain both terrified Lauren and made her move faster. She scrambled out of the van behind Candice but then took the lead.

"You said they made you wait last time, didn't you?" Lauren asked Heather as the three women hurried forward together.

"Yes," Heather said, holding the little girl close. "They had these tents and nets set up in the plaza."

Ahead, a small group of people exited a side door entrance, each one loaded down with backpacks, sleeping bags, and a variety of smaller bags.

"Hey!" Candice shouted. "Wait!" She sprinted ahead, holding up her hands. "Where are you going?"

Lauren followed, leaving Heather to carry the child at her own pace. Only a short and stocky man paused to address them, frowning at first. The others hurried away.

"We can't take on anyone right now," he said, but then as Heather neared, his eyes widened in recognition. "Heather, right?"

"Zane?" Heather stopped beside Lauren. "What is going on?"

He took one look at Annika and shook his head. "If you're here for the surgeon, Dr. Linden is packing up. We all are. We've stockpiled working vehicles in the garage across from the plaza. The fighting is getting too close. We're out of here."

"What?" Lauren didn't mean to shout, but her objection was loud enough to make the man jump.

"Don't blame me," he said.

Lauren pointed back toward the sounds of fighting. "More than just Annika might need medical care," she said. "What about the nurse… Val, wasn't it?" She glanced at Heather for confirmation, and the woman nodded. "Where is she?"

"Helping the doc pack the most important stuff," Zane said. He shook his head. "I'm sorry." Then he turned around and continued on his way.

Lauren's legs turned to Jell-O, and she held out a hand, steadying herself on the side of the building. A cold sweat broke out all over. She couldn't bring herself to look at anyone, so she squeezed her eyes shut. *Will they expect* me *to try and save her on my own now?* The thought made her nauseous.

But when Candice spoke, the way her voice held no fear made Lauren open her eyes. "This isn't over," Candice said, fire in her eyes. "I'm going to find that surgeon, and he *is* going to help us." She turned on her heel, flung open the door, and barged into City Hall, everything from her stride to her expression daring anyone to try and stop her.

* * *

Timothy ran hard — rifle at his back, gun holstered at his hip — until he reached the corner of Tremont and Park Street. Breathing hard, he edged around the curved corner of the building, trying to get an idea of what he was facing. The east end of the park was clear, the smoke billowing at the other end, toward the public gardens. He took off toward the fighting, running through the center of the park, ignoring the pathways, until he reached Charles Street, which cut between the Common and the Public Gardens.

He pulled his rifle around into a ready position and bolted across the street, adrenaline running high as he crouched low and sheltered with his back against a stone pillar next to an open iron gate. Timothy raised his rifle, peering through the scope, searching the grounds. Still, he could see no one.

So, O'Donnell hasn't let them get too far into the park. They're holding their ground. Timothy moved onto the pathway, keeping low as he moved quickly. His hope was rekindled. He hadn't heard a larger blast in some time. *Maybe the worst of it is over. If Frank used all his big guns already, maybe we can still win this.*

As he approached the garden's lake, just before the bridge, he spotted a group of men and women to his right in a small grass clearing. He slowed and frowned. They weren't moving. He sucked in a sharp breath as he realized they were dead.

"Hey! Get away from there!"

The shout from behind startled Timothy, and he swung around, rifle raised, coming face to face with…

"Freeman?" Timothy lowered his weapon as Officer Lucy Freeman did the same. She was covered in grime and blood, her hair matted, her uniform even more tattered than it had been previously.

"Timothy, what are you doing here?" Freeman waved for him to get off the path. "It's not safe here." She nodded at the small suspension bridge that continued the walking path. "Over the bridge is where we're holding the line."

"I know it's not safe," Timothy said. "We needed to get Annika to City Hall. There's a surgeon there. We heard the fighting close by, and… I needed to come and see if I could help my brother."

Freeman pressed her lips together for a moment, just staring at him, and then said, "Follow me, Peters." She led him past a giant, sprawling tree, its thick branches arching over the pathway, to a clearing beyond a decorative fountain. Half a dozen men and women were sitting or lying on the grass, though these were all clearly alive. "This is where we're dragging our wounded, for now," she said. "That clearing you came to first… obviously that's for the dead."

Timothy stepped forward, his heart lodging in his throat. "Is George…?"

"He's not here," Freeman said, but something about the way she said it wasn't comforting.

"Where is he?" Timothy asked.

"I'm sorry," Freeman said. "We think… George is dead, Tim."

Timothy staggered backward half a step. "No," he said. "He can't be. O'Donnell said—"

"O'Donnell died trying to keep his promise." Freeman reached out and put a hand on Timothy's shoulder. "I've got to get back to the battle. We're keeping the enemy from crossing Arlington, but we need all hands on deck." She patted his shoulder and dropped her hand. "Stay and fight or go back to City Hall and get your people as far away from here as possible. I don't know how long we're going to hold."

As Timothy processed the news, his fear and anxiety melted away. Frank Russo and CON had taken everything from him. His mother. His childhood home, supplies and security… they almost took Heather. Annika might be dying because of them.

And now they've taken George, those bastards. Timothy ground his teeth, a low growl coming from the pit of his stomach as an animalistic rage reminiscent of when he'd threatened Theodore surfaced. But that anger was more alive, more virulent than it had ever been. Part of him, a small part, screamed at him to stop, to think. But grief and rage were more powerful a combination. He made himself a promise: *They will not take anything else from me.*

"I'm coming with you," he said, "and this time, I'm going to kill Frank Russo, even if I have to choke the life out of him with my bare hands."

Chapter 36

Candice Liddle and Lauren Stevens

Candice was used to getting what she wanted. She'd wanted to marry Harry Liddle since she first laid eyes on him, and she did. She'd wanted to be HOA president, despite being young and new to the neighborhood, and she'd made it happen. Getting Harry to agree to a two-month European tour for her fifth wedding anniversary? Piece of cake. Finding a way to get her name on the client list of top designers on the East Coast? A little harder, but she'd done it.

And those were things she'd only cared about a little. Annika was different. Annika was her little blueberry, the little girl who'd captured her heart more completely than any man ever had. There was a time Candice had anticipated being a mother; a miscarriage had dashed that dream, until those same motherly instincts had been brought to the surface once again by a motherless little girl whose smile made Candice's world sing.

Dr. Linden didn't stand a chance.

Candice barged into City Hall, Heather and Lauren right behind her. She gritted her teeth against the sharp pain emanating from her fractured ribs at the action. "Stay by the door," Candice said. "If I don't find them first, don't let that nurse, Val, or the surgeon leave."

Heather settled Annika on a nearby lobby couch. "What do you want us to do? Tackle them?"

Candice set her jaw and made sure to make eye contact with both women before she said firmly, "If that's what it takes." She was in pain. She was exhausted. She was scared. Threats were not beyond her at the moment.

Lauren cleared her throat; her face was pale, but the woman nodded, almost too eagerly. "We can't let them leave," she agreed. "We need them. I am *not* a surgeon, and that's what Annika needs."

"Hopefully I can find them before they even finish packing," Candice said. She glanced at Annika, her determination solidifying further.

And then she turned and strode through the halls with her head held high. She did her best to ignore her aches and pains, to walk with purpose, like she owned the place. She was good at that, even when she didn't belong. She'd been doing it her whole life. Eventually, most people conceded to the loudest, the boldest, the richest. Candice was convinced that was because no one *actually* knew what they were doing; following someone who at least looked like they knew something gave people peace of mind.

After blocking the way of a few men on their way out, insisting they give her directions before letting them move on, she opened a door into a large conference room which had been converted to a medical area. Cots not unlike the ones their own group had found were arranged in groups of three on each side of the entrance. On the far end of the room, shower curtains and what appeared to be a custom wooden frame created a room within the room. Low voices, the clinking of metal, and the sound of a zipper indicated the people she was looking for were beyond the curtains.

Candice took a deep breath, rolling her shoulders and picking at her Santorelli top to make the folds lay right. *Never hurts to look your best when you're trying to change minds,* she thought as she shook out her hair, grimacing at the greasy feel of it, but reminding herself that no one was getting regular showers these days.

Marching forward, she reinforced her confidence with every step. Candice threw back the curtain and assessed her targets. The woman was mid-thirties, the man perhaps in his mid-sixties. They were both stuffing backpacks full of food and water. The medical supplies hadn't been touched yet, it seemed.

"Kelly, I—" The nurse spun around, jumped at the sight of Candice, and let out a small squeak. "Who are you?"

"Dr. Linden, I presume?" Candice arched an eyebrow and stared directly at the man.

That got the surgeon's attention. He looked up from his own backpack and frowned. "Yes," he said, voice monotone, "that's a good question. We don't have time for distractions, girl."

Candice's cheeks burned red with anger. "That's *Mrs.* Liddle, thank you very much," she said, her words clipped. "And this isn't a distraction. It's an emergency."

"Of course it is." Dr. Linden sighed. "What? Let me guess: you want to make sure you've got birth control pills before the clinic is packed up?"

Candice narrowed her eyes. She wasn't going to let some old codger talk to her like that. "I'm here because a little girl needs surgery, and you're the only one who can do it. Her name is Annika."

The doctor pursed his lips. "No, no," he said. "We're all leaving. I—"

"I wasn't asking," Candice said.

The doctor bristled, but Val licked her lips and looked at her colleague. "Maybe we could just have a look?"

"That battle is nearly at our doorstep!" He shook his head vehemently. "I will not—"

"They're not going to kill a doctor," Candice said. "They would need you just as much as anybody else."

"Will you stop interrupting me?" Dr. Linden shouted.

"No." Candice didn't leave any room for him to continue. "But I'll tell you what I will do." She strode forward and stood toe to toe with the man. He was about her height, but he cowered lower when she approached. She knew his type. They weren't used to people daring to stand up to them; doing so threw them off. Candice glowered. "If you don't help, and Annika dies, I will hunt you down and kill you myself. And nothing will stop me, not even that disease." She smiled, intentionally putting a little crazy in her eyes. "It's already tried to kill me, Dr. Linden, and I'm too stubborn. I will find you, and I will end you."

Dr. Linden gulped, shrinking further. "I-I could m-maybe take a look," he said.

"I'm sorry, wait," Val said, holding up a hand, "did you say you caught the disease and *survived*?"

"We can talk about that later," Candice said, keeping her eyes focused on the doctor. "I'm going to go get my friends and Annika, and you two are going to be *right here* when I get back. Got it?" She quirked an eyebrow at the doctor, waiting for him to nod before turning on her heel, back toward the door. "I suggest you two start preparing for a surgery," she said over her shoulder as she left them there, all her projected confidence not enough to still the swirl of nerves inside. Once the door had shut behind her, she broke into a run.

* * *

Lauren paced the hall, trying to remember who she was and of what she was capable. Alex's encouragements from earlier had given her the strength to get Annika to City Hall safely, even in the midst of skirting a war zone, but the prospect of going through all of that just to find out the surgeon was gone or leaving had nearly crushed her. She *couldn't* perform the surgery on her own, even if she wanted to. She was too inexperienced.

Not to mention the fact there's no anesthesiologist. That thought alone made Lauren shudder, nevermind all the other complications. She wasn't even sure a surgeon with decades of experience could save Annika at this point.

"Hey, Lauren?" Heather stood up from sitting on the arm of the couch and walked over to her. "You know this isn't all on you, right? No one is going to expect you to do this surgery, no matter what happens with the surgeon."

She paused her pacing and blinked at Heather. "I just… I guess I assumed…" She trailed off for a moment, a weight lifting off her shoulders. "Really?"

Heather offered a small smile. "Yes, really. You've done your job. We're grateful. Annika wouldn't have made it this long without you." She cast a sad look at the girl, who lay almost motionless, her only movements a tensing of her muscles every few moments as she grimaced and whimpered. All color had drained from her face, and she trembled slightly as if freezing cold.

Lauren let out a shaky breath. "That's good because I'm at my limits. I've done the best with the limited training I've had, but—"

Candice rounded the corner, nearly sliding into the wall as she did. "Come with me! The surgeon is preparing now." She knelt beside Annika and squeezed the girl's hand. "Heather, can you carry her? I'm still not up to it." She kissed Annika on the forehead and moved aside.

Lauren almost insisted Candice wait there, that she sit still while they got Annika where she needed to go, but then Lauren thought better of it. There was no way Candice was leaving Annika's side, not unless she absolutely had to. Instead, Lauren let Candice lead the way.

As they navigated the halls, Lauren kept an observant eye on their surroundings. There were still dozens of people packing their things, but some of them didn't look like they planned to go anywhere. From the looks of things, offices had become homes, and not everyone was willing to leave *another* one so quickly.

That's good, Lauren thought. We might need a few people for blood donations.

Within minutes, they were entering the makeshift clinic with a DIY operating room at the back. It wasn't perfect, but it was something. A woman was setting up the surgical tray while an older man leaned against a counter, muttering to himself. Lauren nodded to the nurse, Val, with respect and then approached the doctor.

"Dr. Linden, my name is Lauren Stevens." She waved over to where Heather was placing Annika on one of the cots nearest to the operating room. "I've been caring for Annika the best I can, but I believe she's had a delayed rupture of her spleen. If I'm right, it's been several hours since the rupture, so we don't have much time."

Dr. Linden pursed his lips. "I'll do the diagnostics, Ms. Stevens." He stalked over to Annika. "What happened, exactly?"

Candice immediately launched into the story of how Annika had been trampled by wildebeests as Dr. Linden examined the girl from head to toe. "We need imaging," he said, shaking his head.

"I brought a portable ultrasound," Lauren said, "just in case, but… I thought you'd already have something."

"Well, we don't," Dr. Linden said flatly.

Lauren frowned. "You've been doing surgeries here, haven't you? How could you not have imaging?"

"I've been stitching people up," he said, "but nothing quite as involved as repairing or removing a spleen. This place isn't really set up for that sort of thing. I've been acting more as a primary care doctor than anything. I haven't done a proper surgery since before all of this happened." He gestured vaguely all around him.

"But you *will* do the surgery." Candice didn't sound like she was asking a question, and it was clear that the doctor didn't mistake it for one.

He pinched the bridge of his nose. "Surgery might not be the best idea. We can't put her under during the procedure," Dr. Linden said. "She will be in extreme pain, even with painkillers."

"She'll die if you don't do this." Lauren didn't keep the pleading from her voice. "Please, Dr. Linden. We don't have any other options."

Dr. Linden looked back at Annika, the first hint of compassion touching his expression since Lauren had first walked in. "Yes," he said. "I'm afraid she will die."

"That's not an option," Candice said. "Heather can go get the ultrasound machine, right?" At Heather's nod, Candice continued. "If there's any chance you can save her, you have to try."

"I'll go get the ultrasound," Heather said. "It'll only take a minute. We parked right outside."

"And she might need blood transfusions, as well," Lauren said. "I can gather volunteers to stay and donate while you get started." She took one step toward the door, a sliver of hope that her efforts had not been in vain prompting her to action.

"Hold on." Dr. Linden held up both hands, speaking sharply. "You all need to understand what we are about to do. This surgery has a good chance of killing her. There's no guarantee that she will make it. And on top of that, if she dies, her last moments will be filled with agony unlike anything any of us could imagine. I'll need a person at her head and a person at her feet, holding her down. It won't be pretty, and this won't be for the faint of heart."

Candice set her jaw and narrowed her eyes at the surgeon. "But there's a chance you can save her?"

Dr. Linden sighed. "We can make her comfortable before Val and I leave the area for safety."
Lauren's heart sank. Is he saying that because he wants to get out of here or because he believes that's the best option?
Candice stood up, the cold stare down she gave the surgeon making even Lauren shift uncomfortably. "Are you or are you not a man who is good at his job?"
"What?" Dr. Linden looked affronted and irritated at the same time. "Of course I'm good at my job."
"Then answer my damn question," Candice said. "Is there a chance you can save her?"
Dr. Linden spluttered. "Well, I never—"
"Answer—the—question." Candice spoke through clenched teeth.
Lauren held her breath as she waited for the surgeon to reply.
"Yes." Dr. Linden worked his jaw back and forth, reluctantly finishing with, "There is a chance."
Candice nodded. "Good," she said. "Then we're going to take it."

* * *

Candice brushed away hair from Annika's forehead; her fingers trembled, and she had to lay both hands flat on the operating table on either side of the girl's head. She focused on Annika's face, purposely avoiding a glance at her strapped-down body. Heather stood at her feet, ready to help hold her still, just as Candice stood at her head. Lauren had gone to check the blood types of those who had stayed and to start gathering donations.
Dr. Linden and Val finished scrubbing their hands over a bowl of water. They slipped on blue surgical gloves and took their places: the surgeon at Annika's side, Val at the surgical tray.
"The lorazepam and the morphine should stave off some of the pain, and we've applied local anesthetic, but she's still going to feel this. With the dosage of lorazepam we gave her, hopefully, she won't remember it." Dr. Linden held out a hand toward Val without looking at her. "Scalpel."
The nurse handed him the scalpel, and Candice leaned forward on Annika's shoulders. "It's going to be okay," she said softly as Heather pushed down on Annika's feet.
Annika groaned and twisted slightly, her eyes still closed, a tiny frown forming in her sleep at the resistance of the bands tying her down. She'd been too sickly to stay awake or speak over the last day. As the surgeon's scalpel touched Annika's skin, Candice prayed, desperation and fear clawing at her insides at the first line of blood. She clenched her jaw as the surgery began, redoubling her efforts at remaining calm, closing her eyes as they welled with tears, because at that moment, Annika's first screams filled the air.

Chapter 37

Timothy Peters

Timothy embraced rage-filled anticipation as the cowards fighting for Frank Russo fired their weapons from behind trees in the Commonwealth Avenue Mall. He stood his ground, the iconic George Washington statue several yards behind, rifle at his back, handgun drawn, ballistics shield in arm, officers and civilians to either side of him. Freeman had given him the full gear of a fallen cop, and then she'd left him at the front lines to continue dragging wounded back to the clearing.

"The launcher!" Landry shouted from beside Timothy. "Everyone, focus fire on the launcher!"

Timothy whipped his head back to the enemy to see a man rushing to the middle front, the missile launcher in hand. "Why haven't they used it before now?" Timothy shouted over the sounds of gunfire.

"Might be their last one!" Landry shouted back as he dropped his ballistics shield and swung his rifle around, taking aim and firing. The man with the launcher went down. "They're trying to wear us down, make us run out of ammo before they cross."

"Will that work?" Timothy asked, flinching as a bullet made impact with his shield. It sent harsh vibrations through his arm.

"It's not a bad plan," Landry said. "Another one's going for the launcher." He raised his weapon to shoot, but then cursed. "I'm out."

The second man had reached the launcher and was setting it up, one knee on the ground, the launcher propped on his shoulder. Landry wasn't the only one who was out of rifle ammunition. Timothy dropped everything else to raise his own. It was the best way to take out a specific man from so many yards away. He got the man in his sights and fired. But at the same moment his target buckled in on himself from Timothy's shot, an explosion from the launcher left a puff of smoke.

"Get down!" Timothy shouted, turning to Landry just in time to see the missile hit squarely in his chest, making him fly backward. It was as if a jet engine passed mere feet away, and Timothy had to drop everything to cover his ears. He watched in horror as Landry hit the base of the George Washington statue and the missile detonated, a ball of fire and smoke obliterating the officer, cracking the statue's base. "Landry!" He stumbled forward a few steps, his brain taking a few moments to catch up to what he'd seen: the officer was dead. "No!" He screamed, his mind going straight to George, who Freeman said had died in a missile blast as well. He whipped around in a rage, running forward, twisting the rifle to his back, and reached for his shield.

A roar went up all around him as Frank Russo's men broke the line and charged the gardens. Men and women on both sides met in a clash of battle cries and gunfire. But Landry had been right. From the amount of hand-to-hand combat and discarded weapons, many of them on both sides were out of ammunition.

One thought dominated Timothy's mind: I'm going to find Frank Russo, and I'm going to kill him.

Adrenaline pumped rage and grief through his veins, a crazed energy unlike anything he'd ever experienced saturating his body down to the bones, oozing from his pores, gushing through his mouth in the form of an inhuman howl. He *could not* let Russo and his men reach City Hall. He *would not* allow anyone else to be taken from him.

Timothy rushed the nearest mobster who'd raised his gun at someone else, slamming into him with his shield. They both crashed to the ground, but Timothy recovered faster, picking up his shield and smashing it into the man's face until he passed out, features bloodied beyond recognition. Timothy wrenched the mobster's gun free of his grasp and fired it at another man who was rushing his position. Timothy's aim was true, and the second mobster fell with a growing blood stain at his chest.

And then he spotted him: Frank Russo, bringing up the rear, surrounded by men. He was still in the middle of Arlington Street, and it seemed those huddled around him were definitely *not* out of ammunition.

He can't get away with it. Not again. Timothy ground his teeth together. *My only shot is to get him to fight me one-on-one.* Knowing Frank's ego, the way he relished personal grudges, Timothy had a shot at egging him into a battle he could win.

"Frank Russo!" Timothy shouted as loudly as he could, trying to get Frank's attention.

Only a few strides forward had him face-to-face with a CONman. Timothy didn't hesitate, dodging the thrust of the gangster's knife. Timothy shoved his shield forward hard enough to knock his opponent off his feet, and without pausing for more than a second, he brought the edge of the shield down on the man's wrist. Bones crunched and the man dropped his knife, roaring in pain, curling forward toward the injury. Timothy smashed his boot into the gangster's face, and his head snapped backward, blood spurting from his nose.

The next man in his way scurried away before Timothy reached him. "Frank Russo!" Timothy shouted again.

This time, Frank frowned in his direction. "Southie? Is that you?"

"You killed my brother!" Timothy raised his shield and braced against the bullet of one of Frank's guards.

Frank stepped forward and put a hand on his man's shoulder. "Don't shoot," he said. "Not yet." Then to Timothy, "Stop there, Southie. I got five guys ready to blow your brains out. You ain't gonna win nothin' here. Why don't ya go back to your hidey-hole where you belong?"

"What about George?" Timothy scowled. "I heard what happened. He was in that tower you took out. He was a lookout, Frank. He wasn't even in the fight."

Frank shrugged. "I wasn't exactly aimin' for him. O'Donnell was in there. He was… an unfortunate casualty."

"You still killed him," Timothy said, and then he went forward with his plan, hoping it would work. "That means, you owe me."

Frank chuckled. "Does it now? All's fair in love and war, or somethin' like that, right?"

"Oh?" Timothy shouted. "And what about your code? George was still a kid, Frank. He was only thirteen!"

Frank's smile dissipated, and he seemed to study Timothy a second before continuing. "I am sorry about that," Frank said. "Let's say I see your point, you and me having a history and all. What do ya want, Southie?"

"You and me, no guns," Timothy said, dropping his shield and laying his handgun on the ground. "Let's finish the fight we started the day we first met."

Timothy was trembling with pure energy borne of hatred and anger. His breathing came hard, his lungs burning. Every heartbeat reverberated throughout his body. The memory of that day chafed him; he had missed so many opportunities to end Frank. He had fallen for the mobster's code, even liked him a little bit after he'd refused to kill Timothy in front of Annika, after he'd turned on those CONmen and got Timothy and Annika safely to his car. But the humanity he'd thought Frank had displayed was a lie, a manipulation to get to Timothy's supplies. Not killing Frank that day had resulted in Heather being shot, in losing most of the supplies in his parents' bunker, losing the bunker itself, having to move to the place where his mother was brutally murdered and George was kidnapped… letting Frank go again was not an option. He was a disease, and Timothy was ready to eradicate him for good.

Frank frowned. "You mean that fight where I about slit your throat? You wanna continue *that* fight?"

"That's the one," Timothy said as he removed his rifle, laying it beside his handgun.

The mobster chuckled and rolled his shoulders. "A'ight, Southie. This might be the last request you ever make o' me. That okay with you?"

"I plan on it being the last request you ever grant to anyone," Timothy said, "so, yeah. That's okay with me."

Frank's chuckle turned into a fit of laughter so robust that tears welled at the corners of his eyes. He finally took a breath and nodded. "You got it, Southie. I'm growin' tired of this thing between you and me, anyway. I like you, I really do, but you're a thorn in my side, kid."

"Then you agree?" Timothy asked. "No guns?" He glanced over his shoulder at the battle raging behind them. It was only Frank's guys surrounding him now. They had pushed the officers back several yards. "And if I win, you need to order your men right now to let me go after you're dead."

"You've grown some balls, I see," Frank said, raising his eyebrows. "Okay, okay." He raised his hands and spoke loudly. "If Southie here manages to kill me dead, you all gotta let him go, *but* you gotta let him go away from the fight. Not toward City Hall. I don't want him joinin' the fight again."

Timothy paused, trying not to show any signs of worry. If he was forced to go *away* from City Hall, he'd have to make a wide loop to avoid Frank's men to get to his wife and friends. They might even chase him to ensure his complicity, and they would definitely be on the lookout for him. He might not get to Heather in time to help her.

But that was a risk from the moment he left City Hall to join the fight. She knew that, and she was armed. His wife, Lauren, and Candice… those three were smart. They would know what to do should the fighting reach their doorstep. And Timothy *would* come to their aid. He'd just have to be smarter about how he got there. And everyone would be safer with Frank dead, even if the battle continued.

"You got a deal," Timothy said.

"Give us some room, boys," Frank said, handing over his guns to some of his lackeys. "Don't interfere. Let us men have it out." His guard created a line between Frank and the fight that was progressing through the public gardens.

Timothy took one more look behind him. Officers were holding the bridge over the shallow lake, and more were stationed along the edge of it, shooting at those mobsters and CONmen trying to cross the water which was only a few feet deep. Some of them were using the swan boats as cover as they pushed forward to the other side, but bullets pierced the swan boats easily, and it looked as if the BPD could hold their position for a while yet.

He turned his back on the fight and stepped past the line of mobsters to face Frank Russo for the last time. And then Frank pulled out a large pocketknife. Timothy faltered to a stop, and he couldn't keep the surprise from his expression.

"You said no guns." The mobster grinned.

"You know what I meant," Timothy growled.

"I know what you *said*." Frank shrugged. "We can call it off, Southie, if you want."

"Not a chance." Timothy balled his hands into fists.

"Have it your way." Frank's posture went from indifferent to dangerous in the blink of an eye as he lunged, the blade of his knife snapping outward, glinting as it caught the light of the sun.

The mobster slashed once, twice, three times, each one barely missing Timothy's flesh as he jumped backward and to the side. The knife caught on his shirt twice, leaving long, thin holes in its wake. On his next lunge forward, the mobster gritted his teeth, clearly irritated at having missed his mark. Timothy dodged, but instead of moving away, he leaned to the side, grabbed hold of Frank's wrist with one hand, and then slammed his elbow into Frank's nose with his other arm, drawing blood following the crunch of breaking bone.

But then Frank's fist connected with Timothy's ribs, over and over until he lost his grip on Frank's wrist. As the mobster moved back, his blade sliced across Timothy's forearm and left a shallow mark in his bullet proof vest. Warm blood welled at the gash and dripped down Timothy's arm as the stinging pain of the wound settled in.

Frank jumped from foot to foot like a boxer, seemingly energized after the exchange. He cracked his neck, smiling as blood made rivers down his chin. He lunged again, but feinted and went low, plunging his knife into Timothy's thigh. He wrenched it out again, and Timothy howled in pain, falling to his knees as his pantleg became heavy with blood.

At Frank's next strike, Timothy pushed aside the pain, letting his anger fuel him. He knocked Frank's arm aside and pushed his entire body into Frank's legs, flipping the man over his back. Timothy continued his momentum, rolling away from the mobster, his thigh burning hot as sharp stabs of agony traveled up and down his leg with every movement. Frank landed awkwardly, shielding his head and flipping onto his back, hitting the ground with a thud and a grunt.

Timothy tried to get up, but his leg prevented him from moving quickly. Frank turned and charged, knocking Timothy back to the ground before he was able to gain his feet. Timothy threw up his hands and stopped Frank from putting the blade to Timothy's throat. The struggle seemed to last for hours as he pushed against Frank's force, blood dripping from the mobster's chin onto Timothy's face. The blade was coming too close, and Frank wasn't letting up. He bared his teeth, pushing downward, knife parallel to Timothy's throat.

"C'mon, Southie," he grunted. "Give it up, and maybe I'll let your little wifey live when I find her. Heather, wasn't it?"

Timothy scowled. "Keep—her—name—" He allowed Frank's hand to come a little closer, hoping the mobster would think it was him weakening. "—out—of—your—mouth—" He stopped pushing only upward and moved Frank's hand closer to his face. "—you—bastard." Timothy clamped his teeth into Frank's hand, biting down as hard as he could.

Frank screamed, his eyes going wide. As Timothy tasted blood, the mobster dropped the knife, and then Timothy shoved him aside, spitting and reaching for the knife. As Frank made to jump back on top of him, his hand closed around the metal hilt and he twisted, the knife sinking into Frank's stomach. Timothy kept pushing until his hand was flush with Frank's body.

"Even cockroaches have to die, eventually, Frank." He yanked out the knife and plunged it in a second time.

Thick, warm liquid soaked into Timothy's clothing before he was able to push the mobster away. Frank spluttered, shock written all over his features. He rolled to the side and coughed, blood dribbling from his mouth. Timothy crawled away, unable to put any weight on the leg Frank had stabbed earlier. He collapsed onto his side, drenched in a mixture of his blood and Frank's. He focused on breathing as adrenaline waned and left him weaker than he'd ever felt in his entire life. Heartbeat thrashing wildly inside his chest, head pounding, body protesting every movement for the pain, Timothy watched the life drain from a man he should have killed a long time ago.

Frank Russo was finally dead.

Chapter 38

George Peters

George and Lissa carried O'Donnell's stretcher near the feet while Ruger carried from the head. They tried not to jostle the man too much. George winced every time the captain grunted in pain, but there wasn't much they could do about that. The man couldn't walk, but they had to get him and Ruger both to the fight. It was their only chance of turning the tide, of getting the CONmen to switch sides. The long greenway of Commonwealth Avenue Mall was a mile and a half, a straight shot to the battle. Stepping foot onto the pathway going down the center bolstered George; it was the last stretch of their journey, the only way forward. George concentrated as they passed statue after statue, men of war cast in stone, each one seeming to truly understand the determination that drove George to keep going. He blinked away the stinging sweat from his eyes as he pushed forward. His arms ached, and his whole existence became putting one foot in front of the other. But there was no stopping. As long as he didn't entertain the idea of rest, he could keep pushing himself beyond what he thought his body capable. The best chance to end the war over Boston was literally in his hands; that was all that mattered to him. It was how he was going to save the people he loved.

He and the others hadn't spoken since first starting the trek toward the Common, but George felt like a cog in a well-oiled machine. They were in sync, each person seeming wholly focused on the mission. But as they neared the end of the mall, passing the last statue before reaching Arlington Street, George noticed a small group hanging back from the main fight. It seemed two people were battling each other, alone behind a line of men, completely separated from everyone else. And as the battle came to an end, both men lying on the ground, one of them surely dead, George recognized the one still living.

His mechanical movements forward faltered. "Timothy?" he whispered, his chest heaving, his lungs starving for air, body begging for rest.

"Is that your brother?" Lissa asked almost at the same time.

They slowed to a stop. "What is it?" Ruger asked.

"Set the captain down," George said, nodding ahead to the open iron gates leading onto Arlington Street.

The three of them lowered the stretcher, and O'Donnell frowned at George, craning his neck toward the battle. "Did you say Timothy is up there?"

George nodded. "He's hurt," he said, glancing over his shoulder. The men who were in a line were now surrounding Timothy and the other man. One of them kicked Timothy in the back, and that's when George realized they were not on his brother's side. "Hey!" George broke into a run, ignoring his aching muscles. "Stop!" He drew his handgun. It was the only weapon he had left. His rifle had been lost in the fall of the tower.

Two sets of footsteps were soon behind him, and Ruger grabbed George's shoulder, pulling him to a stop. "Get down, Hero," he whispered harshly, shoving George behind the stone pillar next the gate. "Don't draw attention. Just wait a minute."

George shook off Ruger's hand. "My brother is in trouble," he hissed.

"Ruger's right. Something's off." Lissa peered around the pillar. "I don't think they've noticed us. The mobsters are all fighting, except for those two."

Ruger took a look. "One of them is Jovie. He's my guy. The other is Pugsie… he's not a fighter at heart. Probably born into all this." Ruger shrugged. "Makes a mean knitted cap, though."

George pressed his lips together, pushing down the urge to barge forward and get his brother out of what was clearly a dangerous situation. But as he scanned the scene again from his spot behind the gate, he realized that while one of the mobsters *had* kicked Timothy, the four of them were mostly focused on each other. And they were arguing loudly enough for them to hear as the sounds of the battle in the public gardens became less and less filled with gunfire.

"I say we finish off Peters and then these three. Be done with it. Join the fight," one of them said.

"We can't do that." Pugsie shook his head, glancing furtively at the dead body. "Frank said to let him go."

"Frank's dead." The first mobster sneered. "I'm next in line. I'm the oldest cousin. You's should be listenin' to me now."

George sucked in a breath as he connected the dots. The dead man was Frank, and from a distance, before he'd realized who the two were, George had witnessed his brother putting an end to the man who'd wrought so much pain in their family.

"Nah," another man shouted. "Frank promised *me* the seat when he was done with it, Lyle. You're dumb as rocks. Nobody's gonna follow you."

Pugsie took a step back, fidgeting with his hands. Jovie crossed his arms and watched the four argue, breaking into a grin as they began to skirmish, shouting loudly about who deserved to lead in Frank's place. And then one of them turned his gun on the rest.

He turned his weapon on Jovie and Pugsie. "I'm takin' Frank's place. You two got anything to say about it?"

Jovie scowled but shrugged. "I've got no horse in that race, man. Do what you want."

Pugsie shook his head vehemently. "You know me," he said. "I'm not a leader."

The victor scoffed as he put his weapon back in its holster, and the second he did, Ruger stood up, stalked forward, and landed three bullets in his back. At first, Jovie was on his toes, drawing his weapon, but he soon dropped his arm, eyes wide. George cautiously stood and approached, Lissa following, as Jovie held out a hand toward Ruger, a smile slowly spreading.

"Ruger?" Jovie laughed. "Frank said you were dead."

"Good to see you, too, Jovie," Ruger said. "Frank lied."

George reached Timothy, keeping Jovie and Pugsie in his line of sight as he knelt over his brother. "Tim?" he whispered, glancing down, his stomach lurching at the amount of blood covering him.

"George?" Timothy blinked slowly at him, seeming confused. "I thought you were dead." He reached up to touch George's face, flinching when his fingertips met flesh. "You're alive!"

"Yeah," George said, offering a small smile. "I'm okay."

Lissa came to her knees beside Timothy, examining him from head to toe. "I don't see any serious injuries, besides the stab wound at his thigh."

"Most of this blood isn't mine. I'll be fine." Timothy pulled George closer, and despite his crimson-soaked clothes, George allowed his brother to hug him tight.

Jovie and Ruger embraced mere feet from them, and Jovie looked hopeful for a moment as the two continued their own conversation. "What about Caleb? Is he alive, too? Frank said he died with you."

"He's not with me," Ruger said, cursing. He pointed at Pugsie. "He wasn't in that tower. Is Caleb dead? You're always with Frank, Pugsie. I know you know."

Pugsie gulped. "Frank's been bananas for weeks. He shot Caleb point-blank. I was there, and I was shocked. Not like the old Frank at all. I don't think he woulda done that before, not to some kid who'd come under him like that."

Lissa cursed under her breath, hanging her head, and George felt a pang of regret for the loss of life as he pulled away from Timothy's hug. He hadn't agreed with Caleb's decision to stay with Ruger, but he'd always hoped Caleb would join the good guys one day.

Timothy grimaced as he struggled to a sitting position. "I don't think I can walk," Timothy said, his top half wobbling. "And I'm dizzy." He let out a long breath and slowly laid back on the asphalt.

"Ruger," George said, interrupting the two older men, "we need to do something about Tim. He's hurt."

"We helpin' the enemy now?" Jovie narrowed his eyes. "What's goin' on, Ruger? I thought those two kids abandoned CON."

"It's complicated, but I think Pugsie can speak into this, too," Ruger said, turning to the mobster. "Frank knew I was in that tower, didn't he?"

Pugsie nodded fervently, not hesitating for a second. "He did." He made the sign of the cross and looked up toward the sky. "I'm spillin' all your secrets. Sorry, Frank."

Ruger turned to Jovie. "I should've known it would happen, but the Russos turned on us. I don't think they ever planned to do what they promised, not really."

Jovie ran his fingers through his hair. "Then what are we doin'?"

"We're gonna stop this war," Ruger said. "I've got a plan to give CONmen a future, Jovie. You've got to trust me, though."

Jovie sniffed and licked his lips, looking down at the ground for a second. "You know I trust you," he said. "You always looked out for me, better than Ace ever did." He nodded. "I'll do whatever you say, Ruger."

"George," Timothy whispered, "we can't trust them."

"It's okay, Tim," George said. "Ruger helped me bring O'Donnell to safety. I'm going to need you to trust me, not him, okay?" He held his breath.

It had always been a question in his mind, whether or not his brother really trusted him. It seemed Tim had *allowed* George to stay with the BPD because he couldn't force him to return to New Horizons Laboratory. But Timothy had never acknowledged the things George had gone through to make that decision, not really. He'd never understood what he'd learned and what it took to get that knowledge.

"Okay," Timothy said, a touch of reluctance in his tone. "I'll trust you. We just… we have to stop that battle from getting to City Hall."

George exhaled some tension; he was willing to take whatever he could get. "We will," he said, looking up at Ruger again. "What are we going to do?"

"Jovie, you wanna take a look at that leg?" Ruger asked. He looked at George. "My man here has been our resident nurse for the last two years. He knows what he's doing. He's tended to plenty of wounds of all types."

"Yeah, alright," Jovie said, sighing, clearly not understanding why he was suddenly helping the man he would've killed a few minutes prior. He knelt beside Timothy, his attention going to Timothy's thigh. "This is where he was stabbed. I don't think Frank got him good anywhere else." He ripped the hole in Timothy's pantleg wider to reveal the gash in his thigh. "It's still bleeding, but there's no gushing. That means it didn't hit the artery."

Timothy groaned in pain as Jovie's motions jostled his leg. "That's good, right?"

"Yeah, that means you'll be fine. Probably." Jovie took off his t-shirt, leaving only a tank underneath. "Try to stop the bleeding. This needs to be stitched for sure, and we don't got nothin' to do that with here." He handed the shirt to George. "Put pressure on the wound. It'll hurt."

George nodded. He pressed down on the wound, grimacing as Timothy shouted in pain. "Sorry," he said.

"It's got to be done," Timothy said between clenched teeth.

Ruger turned toward the battle in the near distance. "We need to get our guys to turn on the mobsters," Ruger said. "It sounds like everyone is out of ammo. I haven't heard a shot in at least five minutes. That should help."

Jovie came to stand next to him. "We can do it, together," he said.

George looked up at them both. "Someone needs to tell the BPD what's going on," he said. "The fallen officers might have walkie talkies still on them. If I can get to one of them, I can try to raise Freeman or Landry. They'll listen to me, and everyone else will listen to them. They need to know that O'Donnell is alive, and that CON is turning on the Russos."

"Landry's dead," Timothy said. "He was hit with one of those missiles."

George blanched, and out of the corner of his eye, he noticed Lissa take a slow and shaky breath at the news. "Freeman, then," he said, "if she's still alive."

"What should I do?" Pugsie asked.

Lissa stood up and looked at Ruger. "Can I trust him?"

Ruger looked at Jovie, who shrugged. "I ain't never seen him do anything but follow orders."
Timothy spoke through gritted teeth. "I'd say that's accurate."
Pugsie smiled and stood a little taller. "I'm a good grunt. Frank used to say that all the time."
Lissa quirked an eyebrow at Pugsie. "Okay, then… maybe you and me can chat about your aspirations while you help me with O'Donnell. If we get one of those walkie talkies, we won't need to raise anyone specific to get the rest to listen. They'll all listen to the captain."
"You're right," George said, feeling the idiot for not thinking of that himself. "I'll find one and bring it back here. You fill in O'Donnell, but… maybe bring Timothy back there instead of bringing the captain up here. There's more protection behind those trees."
"So," Ruger said, "George, you and O'Donnell get that message out to the Boys. Me and Jovie will get to our guys one by one."
George started to stand, but Timothy grabbed hold of his wrist. "Be careful out there, George," he said. "I love you."
"I love you, too," George said, squeezing Timothy's hand before letting it go. "Don't worry, okay? I'll be fine."
Ruger walked over and slapped George on the back. "This kid's resilient," he said. "You ain't got nothin' to worry about." He grinned at George. "C'mon, Hero. Why don't you put some credentials behind that nickname?"
George nodded and faced the public gardens. "Let's go."

Chapter 39

Lauren Stevens

Lauren worked in the silence, both grateful and terrified of the lack of Annika's screams echoing down the corridors of City Hall. She hoped that Annika had passed out, but that wasn't the only explanation possible.

"We're all done," she said as she pulled the needle out of the volunteer's arm, a woman by the name of Regina. Lauren had gathered enough blood from donors; she needed to get what she had gathered to the operating room. Annika would need it, if she was still alive.

"You think that kid is going to be okay?" Regina asked.

Lauren nodded, though there was no surety in her voice. "I hope so."

"Are *we* going to be okay?" Regina looked nervously toward the direction of the Common. The sound of battle had also gone quiet.

"I… I think so," Lauren said, praying that if the lack of gunfire meant someone had won, it had been the good guys. "I guess we'll find out soon." She stood up. "Thank you for your donation," she said. "I've got to get this to Annika."

Regina nodded, looking pale. "I was tired of running," she said. "If someone comes to kill us, I think… maybe I'll just let them."

Lauren placed a hand on Regina's shoulder. "We're all tired," she said, "but you're a good person. Don't give up, okay? And besides, I don't think anyone wants to kill the people left here, even the Russos. What good is having control over a city if there are no people left?"

Regina acknowledged Lauren's words with a small smile. "Good luck, with the girl I mean."

Lauren hurried to the clinic, holding two precious units of blood. When she got there, and she quietly pulled back the curtain, she paused, taken aback by the gory scene. The surgeon worked over a long incision in Annika's side; if Lauren had to guess, he'd needed to use older methods in order to work under the conditions granted to him, mainly the lower visibility and the lack of equipment for a laparoendoscopic procedure.

With no suction, there was blood *everywhere.* Candice stood at the head of the operating table, a haunted look in her eyes, eyes puffy and red, tear tracks down her cheeks. Heather only appeared marginally better at the foot of the bed. Even Dr. Linden and Val were pale.

"I was able to do a partial splenectomy." Dr. Linden took a moment to glance at Lauren as she came near. "She lost a lot of blood. She's going to need that."

"He's just got to sew her up, now," Val said. "That incision will take a while to close."

"Will she be okay?" Lauren asked.

"If we pump her full of antibiotics and give her some blood to help with what she's lost, I think so," Dr. Linden said. "Physically, at least, she'll recover." He started to remove the retractor. "But mentally… I just hope she doesn't remember today." His expression was grim. "I'd like to forget the experience, too, actually. Having a patient semi-awake… the screams…" His voice caught and he swallowed hard.

"I'm sorry," Candice whispered. "I didn't know it would be like that."

Dr. Linden sighed as he removed blood-soaked rags from around the area, balling them up and throwing them in a pile on the ground. "You would have forced me to do it either way," he said, and when Candice's mouth dropped open to say something else, he continued, "but I don't blame you. I would have done the same if it were my child, truth be told. You stood by her side through it. Not everyone would have the strength to do that, even for their own blood. You're a good mother."

Candice blinked, seeming still in shock. "I… I'm not her mother."

"Oh? And who is, then?" Dr. Linden asked.

"She's gone," Candice said. "Died from the disease."

Dr. Linden asked Val to hand him the suturing supplies. He pinched together one end of the wound and began to stitch it closed. "Well, you could have fooled me. As far as I'm concerned, you're her mother, Mrs. Liddle."

"He's right," Lauren said.

Heather added a smile and a nod. "You've cared for her just as well as any mother would."

Candice looked down at Annika, her fingers trembling as she cupped the girls head gently in her hands. She kissed Annika's forehead and didn't offer any further rebuttal.

"Let's get the transfusion started," Dr. Linden said as he continued to stitch the wound. "Grab a towel over there to help make a place for firm footing."

Lauren looked down, understanding immediately what the surgeon meant. She grabbed a towel and dropped it on the floor, using her foot to sop up blood and wipe an area mostly clean so she could stand near Annika. She rolled the IV pole a little closer and hung the blood next to the saline, preparing for the transfusion.

Soon, fresh blood was being administered, and Lauren could step back. She was about to ask if there was anything else she could do when there was a knock at the door to the clinic. Lauren's eyes went wide. "I better get that," she said. "A lot of people can't handle seeing this kind of thing. The last thing we need is someone fainting." She closed the curtains behind her before approaching the door. Her shoes left bloody prints on the floor, but there was nothing she could do about that. She opened it to find Regina outside.

"There are some men here," Regina said. "They're hurt. I think they need help."

Lauren swallowed hard. *Who's side are they on?* But that didn't matter, not if they were there seeking medical attention. She nodded.

"The clinic is…" She glanced over her shoulder at the bloody prints, at the closed curtain. "… occupied. But I can see them in those tents outside in the plaza."

"Okay," Regina said. "I'll tell them to wait out there."

Lauren closed the door and returned to the others, frowning at herself. *Did I just offer to treat* more *patients?* She found that, for once, her skin didn't crawl at the thought. Heather's reassurances, Alex's words, they reassured her, bolstered her. She could do what she could do, and that was enough. Neither she — nor anybody else — could expect her to do anything more. But suddenly she found that she didn't want to do anything *less*, either.

"There are some men outside, injured. I'm going to go out there and see to them," Lauren said. "Where do you store your PPE?"

"There's a set of plastic drawers just outside the curtains, to your right. Take what you need," he said as he concentrated on closing the wound.

Lauren grabbed two layers of everything except the goggles: gown, gloves, mask, and hair and shoe covers. She marched down the halls with a backpack full of supplies, bracing herself to do whatever needed to be done, regardless of who was asking. Showing herself as a value to the winner of the war would not only protect her, but everyone she cared about, too.

Her heartbeat quickened as she stepped outside and turned toward the tents with their umbrella and mesh second layers. She rounded the first tent, holding her breath as she peered past the mesh to the man sitting in the unzipped entrance. She exhaled at the sight of a tattered police uniform. The man had a bloodied arm where it seemed a bullet had grazed him, and his shoe was off, a very swollen ankle bulging beneath a sock. The arm that hadn't been grazed was hanging at a funny angle. He was rocking back and forth ever so slightly, grimacing and concentrating on getting through the pain.

Lauren unzipped the mesh and stepped through, zipping it behind her. "My name is Lauren," she said. "I'm going to help you." She knelt beside his limp arm first, examining it.

"I'm Officer Numan," he said between gritted teeth.

"You got a first name?" Lauren asked.

"Keith."

"Okay, Keith, your shoulder is dislocated. We're going to need to pop it back into place. I'm going to need you to lay down and relax the best you can." She readjusted herself as Keith did as she asked, prompting him again to relax his muscles before she continued, relaying her actions to the officer as she worked. "This is going to hurt, but once it's done, you'll feel better. I'm going to need you to work with me. I need your elbow at about ninety degrees." She took hold of his wrist and helped him move his arm. "That's it. I'm going to pull outward, rotating your shoulder, and I'm just going to give it a little push and—" She placed her hand in position and pushed, a soft *thud* sounding as Keith cried out and the shoulder popped back into place. "—there it is."

Keith moved his arm, relief in his expression. "Thanks, doc."

"I'm not a doctor," Lauren said, "but I do know enough to help every once in a while." She smiled at him. "I'm going to take a look at that ankle now." She moved to his foot as he sat back up. "So, you're with O'Donnell, right? What's going on down there? I haven't heard gunfire for a while."

"Everyone ran out of ammo," he said. "Those of us who were too injured to do much were ordered to flee back to City Hall, get some treatment if there was anyone here to do it. Send someone back to the battlefield, if possible."

"So the fighting is still going?" Lauren deflated.

"Yeah… it's bad. We're holding, but I don't know for how long." Keith rotated his arm again. "You think you can patch up my ankle so I can put weight on it? I need to get back there."

Lauren shook her head. "You won't be able to put weight on this for a while. It's definitely broken. You'll need to stay here, elevate it. I'll go inside and see if I can find some pillows or something, once I check out the others." She moved up to the bullet wound, taking a look, making sure it was just a graze. "Okay, I think you're good for now." She took out some pain medication from her backpack and handed over a hefty dose of acetaminophen. "Take this. It will help."

She moved on. There were four other men and two women who had made it to the plaza from the Common. She gathered as much information as she could, but the only thing she could really confirm was that the battle was too close to call, and that if it were to swing one way, those injured who'd fled upon Freeman's orders were under the impression it would swing in favor of the enemy. They needed a miracle to turn the tide.

Chapter 40

George Peters

George spotted the black ballistics shield across the field of the dead. He ran for it, a mixture of conflicting feelings warring inside. It seemed the BPD had systematically pulled their dead behind their front lines whenever possible, and he'd yet to find a body with a walkie talkie. And so he prayed the shield would be accompanied by the officer who'd fallen alongside it. But it felt wrong, to hope for that, and so when he approached and finally found what he was looking for, he couldn't feel anything but regret as he unclipped the officer's walkie talkie. Whoever it was hadn't been stationed at headquarters; George didn't recognize him. He deserved reverence, but George didn't have the time to give it. He simply whispered a thanks before turning his back on the corpse.

He started back toward Arlington Street. The sound of footsteps pounding the sidewalk made him tense, and he looked behind him to see a member of CON coming in his direction. It was Virginia, one of the women who'd been in charge of keeping the younger kids busy with odd jobs at the zoo. At first, George hesitated. She'd worked alongside Shannon, who'd died in the shootout after Lissa had opened fire to kill Big Mack. But she didn't look angry when she approached; in fact, she offered George a grin.

"I hear we're on the same side again," she said as she jogged up next to him.

George kept pace with her, the walkie talkie in hand. "How many have Ruger and Jovie gotten to?" he asked.

"I was the first," she said. "I was about to go back in, charge the bridge. A rifle makes a pretty good bludgeon, if it needs to be one."

"What did Ruger say to get you to retreat?"

"He didn't have to say much. Told me Frank turned on us. The fact he's alive backed it up. Plus, he's always been a favorite in CON. Ace and him were tight. It was always Ruger you went to if you wanted something you knew Ace would just say no to," Virginia said.

George nodded. He'd gotten that impression. Ruger had done plenty of things George hated, but he'd also been protective once he considered someone part of CON. He always did what he thought needed to be done for the good of the group. He wasn't always right, but even George had found himself liking the man by the time he was rescued.

"What did Ruger say you were to do, once you got to Arlington Street?" George asked.

"He said to form up, protect O'Donnell, wait for him to give further instructions," she said. "You know more?"

George held up the walkie talkie. "I'm getting this to the captain, and he's going to instruct his men to let CONmen retreat, pass a message to the ones still engaged in the fighting that Ruger is alive and to look for him in the fight."

They reached Arlington Street. Virginia slowed. "I'm going to wait here," she said. "You go on, Hero."

But George hadn't waited for her permission to keep going. He was already nearing the other side of the street, running through the gate onto the Commonwealth Avenue Mall. O'Donnell had moved from the stretcher to lie on the grass. Timothy was nearby, sitting propped against a tree. Lissa knelt beside the captain, and Pugsie sat next to Tim, helping to keep pressure on his wound.

"I've got it!" George held up the walkie talkie as he dropped to his knees on the other side of O'Donnell. "You ready, sir?"

O'Donnell's gruff determination came through in his tone. He was clearly in pain, but he didn't let that stop him. "Give me that thing." He grabbed it and spoke into it. "BPD, this is Captain O'Donnell speaking. Does anyone copy? Freeman, are you there?"

"Why aren't they answering?" Lissa asked.

"They don't know for sure it's me," O'Donnell said. "I gotta give 'em somethin' to confirm it." He thought for a moment before speaking again. "O'Donnell, badge number two-two-one." Still nothing.

"Someone could have gotten that off your body," he said.

O'Donnell grunted, glancing at Lissa. "Abrams, badge number one-eight-one."

George pumped his fist as the crackle over the speaker was followed by a familiar voice. "Sir, this is Freeman. It's good to hear your voice."

"Likewise," O'Donnell said. "Now, everyone listen up. Ruger helped get me out of that collapsed tower. We've had a chat, and it turns out he could see straight through Frank Russo just like the rest of us. He just had to look a little longer. And, by the way, Frank Russo is dead, and good riddance. We gotta let CONmen retreat. Focus on the mobsters. That should leave you in the majority, and then I'm ordering you to kick ass and finish this. Do you copy?"

"Copy that," Freeman said. Her acknowledgement was followed by at least a dozen more. Every reiteration made George's smile a little wider. He stood straighter and took a look out onto Arlington. More CONmen had joined Virginia. Their plan was working.

Within another half an hour, Ruger and Jovie were returning with the last of CON. George ran out to meet them.

"It's done, Hero," Ruger said. "All our guys are out. There's about three dozen cops left against half as many mobsters. We took care of a few on our way out."

It didn't take long for what remained of the BPD to follow, six mobster prisoners being pushed along with them. They were a ragged group, uniforms stained with blood and mud, faces bruised, and more than a few of them walking with a limp. Freeman led them, slowing at the edge of the public gardens.

George approached, the BPD in front of him, CON to his back. "O'Donnell is injured, but he's safe and alive," he said.

Freeman's entire body sagged, though she made an attempt to straighten her shoulders. "How do we know we can trust them?" She nodded to Ruger and his men.

"They've cooperated so far," George said. "And I think Ruger is going to try to take them legit."

Freeman scoffed, and a low rumble of voices traveled through the group of officers and civilians who'd fought against the Russos and CON that day. "What does that mean?" Freeman asked.

George looked at her seriously. "It means we have a chance to move forward, but we've got to put the past behind us."

When Freeman's eyes flitted to George's left, he turned to see Ruger approaching. He stopped beside George. "CON calls it truce," he said. "We're done acting like lapdogs. My people are setting up in Roxbury and Dorchester. Anybody who wants to join CON's camp is welcome, and we won't infringe on anyone else."

Freeman quirked an eyebrow. "No more safety taxes on civilians?"

Ruger shook his head. "Not unless they choose to live within our borders, and then it's just contributions for the good of the whole. We won't be forcing anybody to stay, but there are plenty of civilians who will be happier with us than they would be with you."

George exchanged a look with Freeman, thoughts of those they had met who'd chosen CON over the BPD's protection in the green zone confirming Ruger's assertion.

Freeman didn't argue. "Then Boston belongs to all of us?" she asked.

Ruger nodded. "Boston belongs to all of us."

He held out a hand toward Freeman, who looked at it for a moment, contemplating before grasping it in her own and shaking. To George's left and right, handshakes closed the gap between the two groups. For the time being, it seemed, the city was at peace.

"We've already sent some of our wounded, the ones who could get there on their own, to City Hall to be looked after. We hear there's some medical personnel there," Freeman said to Ruger. "But we've got plenty of wounded that were unable to make the trek. What about you?"

"I don't know," Ruger said. "I just got here, really. I was late to the fight." He looked to Jovie, who nodded.

"We need to comb the battlefield, look for survivors," Jovie said. "We weren't as organized as you were," he admitted to Freeman. "We didn't have orders to pull back the wounded."

"Frank didn't care about the wounded." Ruger sniffed and nodded at the mobsters. "What are we gonna do with them?"

"They surrendered, so… I guess we'll stick them somewhere until we can figure it out," Freeman said, scratching her head. "There's not enough of them to cause trouble."

"They got families out in the country," Ruger said. "More men, too. Not a lot, but… give it some time, and you might have another war on your hands, once they figure out who's next in line to take Frank's place. We should get rid of them, and then go find whoever's left of the Russos and get rid of them, too."

"No," George said firmly. "You have to do things differently, Ruger. Remember?"

Freeman pursed her lips. "I get your reasoning, Ruger," she said, "but the kid's right. They get a trial, eventually. And their families? The women and children… we gotta give them amnesty."

Ruger raised his hands and then slapped them together as if dusting them off. "It's your problem, then," he said. "We're out."

"What about running for council?" George asked.

Ruger shrugged. "The whole world is the wild west, now, Hero. I don't know that there's gonna *be* a council like O'Donnell's hoping for. What I do know is that CON is going to set up, build something that can last, and we won't bother nobody if they don't bother us. When it comes to somethin' mutually beneficial, we'll help for the good of the city. That's about as 'legit' as I get, kid."

Freeman nodded. "If that's what you want, we won't stop you. We just want a safe Boston. Don't mess with that, and you won't see our faces ever again."

"Sounds good," Jovie said, smirking.

"Yes, it does," Freeman agreed. "Now, let's get the wounded to City Hall."

***

George let Timothy lean on him, anticipation building as they neared City Hall. Ahead, two officers and Lissa carried O'Donnell on a stretcher. "You think Annika is okay?" George asked.

"I hope so," Timothy said as he hobbled forward. "She was in bad shape, though."

"So… you took out Frank." George looked at his brother sideways.

"Yeah. I did."

"I saw the last bit of the fight," George said. "From a distance, but… it was pretty badass."

Timothy offered a small smile. "Not as badass as what you accomplished today. I'm proud of you, George."

Those words produced a warmth in George's chest, and until Timothy had said them, he hadn't realized how much he'd wanted to hear them. "Thanks," he said.

"Mom and Dad would be proud, too." Timothy looked ahead, his tone sad.

"You think Dad's dead, too, don't you?" George asked.

"I think… it's been a long time since we last heard from him." Timothy squeezed George's shoulder. "But Lizzy made it. Who knows? Maybe Dad is on his way."

"I miss him," George said.

"Yeah," Timothy said. "Me too. And I don't even like him." They walked a few more feet in silence before his brother spoke again. "I don't think I can really put into words how glad I am that you're alive. You know that, right? You know how much I love you?"

George nodded. "Yeah," he said. "I know."

"I need you to promise me something." Timothy stopped hobbling forward, forcing George to do the same. He motioned for George to look at him. "I know you've found a purpose in working with O'Donnell, but if something ever happens to me, I need you to step up and protect the family. That includes Candice and Annika, now, too, but especially Heather."

George blinked, the weight of the request settling in. "Yeah, Tim," he said. "Of course." He smiled and gently punched his brother's shoulder. "But you're not going anywhere, okay? You have to stick around for at least another few decades."

Timothy chuckled. "I plan on it," he said as he turned back toward City Hall and allowed George to help him move forward again.

It was another ten minutes before they reached City Hall. Those carrying O'Donnell had gotten far ahead of them, arriving a few minutes earlier so that when George and Timothy staggered into the plaza, Lauren — who was dressed head to toe in PPE — was already taking a look at the captain. Lissa stood nearby, hugging her middle, watching Lauren poke and prod.

"How is he?" George asked.

Lauren looked up. "I think he'll be okay," she said. "It's a pelvic fracture. Nothing we can do really, besides pain killers and anti-inflammatory meds." She eyed O'Donnell. "And lots of bed rest. Like eight weeks, at a minimum."

O'Donnell cursed. "Now *that* will kill me."

Freeman chuckled. "Don't worry, sir. Your voice carries. You can still give orders from bed."

O'Donnell scowled, cursing under his breath, grumbling.

"And Annika?" Timothy asked.

"The last I checked, she was doing just fine," Lauren said, her gaze drifting to the building looming over the plaza. "It was a hard surgery, though. Bloody. And painful." She sucked in a shaky breath and shook her head before her eyes seemed to catch on Timothy's leg. "What happened there?"

"Stab wound," Timothy said. "Needs stitches. And probably antibiotics."

Lauren nodded reaching out to take Timothy's weight from George. "I'll help you to one of these tents and get you taken care of," she said. "We'll all need to stay overnight here, at City Hall. I think we can move people inside, as long as they've had no exposure to a swarm or to any of the dead who've died from DV-10."

"I can go around, ask some questions, start getting people moved," George said.

"That would be great," Lauren said as she helped Timothy to one of the last remaining empty tents. "The plaza can remain our triage center for now. So far, I haven't seen anyone with suspicious symptoms. If I do, I'll let you know, and those will stay out here."

"I'm guessing we won't be able to return to the lab today," Timothy said.

"No," Lauren agreed. "You might need to stay here a while. I'd suspect Annika would need to stay for a few days, minimum."

"Which means Candice and Heather will be staying," Timothy said. "I guess we should make ourselves comfortable." He shook his head. "Someone is going to have to go back to the lab and tell our people there what's happened."

"I'll do it tomorrow," George said.

He looked out across the plaza as more of the wounded arrived. The day's work wasn't over, and though he was exhausted, he was also relieved. A lot of people had died that day, but it was finally over. The people of Boston were safe, at least from each other.

Chapter 41

Zara Williams

Zara watched Walter from the bench seat of the little dining area of the airstream camper as it bumped along the road back toward town. He rested on the bed, grimacing every time they hit a pothole.

Once Zara and Kai had gotten Carol and her kids to the hospital, they had gotten Willow to come back to the Log Cabin with them. Walter had insisted they write down a list of the meds Carol had used on him. They were all stored in an unlocked drawer. And then Zara, Kai, and Willow helped get Walter down the stairs and into the camper. Zara had opted to stay with Walter on the drive back into town. She hadn't wanted to leave Walter's side.

"Do you need anything?" Zara asked. "Food or water?"

He shook his head. "Not now," he said. "I'm okay. Carol… well, she wouldn't have let me go without."

"I'm still trying to wrap my head around what happened," Zara said.

"Me too." Walter winced as the airstream was jostled by another bump in the road. "I know it sounds crazy, but I do hope that Carol is okay."

Zara cocked her head at Walter. "You know, Mr. Peters, you've changed a lot over the past couple of weeks."

"I've *let go* of a lot the past couple of weeks," Walter said. "After Bethie…" He closed his eyes, his voice catching on his nickname for his daughter. "I don't know who I was trying to be before, but who I am now, that person maybe she would be proud of."

"I think you're right," Zara said, tears welling at the memory of her best friend.

"And… I think you can just call me Walter from now on. Mr. Peters is starting to sound weird." He offered her a smile.

"It's not too… informal or disrespectful or something?" Zara quirked an eyebrow.

"I'm not trying to impress anybody anymore," he said.

Zara smiled. "Walter it is, then," she said.

The camper came to a stop, and Kai was soon opening the door. "You two ready to get this guy inside and patched up?"

"I'm telling you," Walter said, "the worst thing Carol did was give me too many meds to keep me compliant. She was a nurse, and she knew what she was doing."

Kai stepped up into the camper. "Still won't hurt to have a doc take a look, right Zara?"

"Exactly," Zara said, standing up. "C'mon, let's get you to an actual hospital bed."

"Willow is grabbing a wheelchair, old man." Kai backed up to the bed and squatted low. "Get on," he said.

Walter frowned. "He's not serious."

Zara cracked a smile. "I think he is."

"I don't know if I like this whole thing between you two, like you're becoming friends or something," Walter said, pointing between the two of them, a half-smile forming. "What happened this week?"

Zara glanced at Kai, heat flooding her cheeks, though she didn't know exactly why. The truth was she didn't really know what had happened between them. "I think we've just grown to trust each other," she said.

"And maybe become friends," Kai said, shrugging, and then with a joking smile, "Jury's still out on that one."

Zara shook her head, turning her expression serious. "Are you going to make him squat like that all day?"

"He can't carry me," Walter said. "He's a twig!"

"Am not!" Kai readjusted his stance a little wider. "I could carry you for miles."

Walter shook his head but managed to slowly sit up, grimacing and sucking in a breath every few seconds. He reached with trembling arms to wrap them around Kai's neck. "This is humiliating." He hoisted himself onto Kai's back.

Kai grunted, his voice strained as he took a step forward. "Yeah, this is fine." A vein popped in his forehead. "Totally fine."

Zara stepped aside until he'd passed, and then she made a face as she supported Walter from behind, having to lift him from his butt cheeks.

Walter groaned. "Okay, *now* this is humiliating."

"I don't think anyone's going to argue with that," Zara said as she helped Kai get Walter down the few steps onto the ground.

Willow was already waiting, and she and Zara helped ease Walter into the wheelchair. All of them seemed to breathe a collective sigh of relief. Kai straightened and cracked his back, making a few jokes about Walter's weight as Willow rolled him inside. Zara followed, feeling lighter than she had in a long time. It seemed they were finally going home. All she wanted was to find her cousin, Annika, and hold her close, to be in a safe place where she could stay and recover from the past month.

As they passed by a waiting room, Zara caught sight of Heath. She paused. "Hey, I'll be along in a minute, okay?"

Walter's eyes flitted from her to Heath. "He needs a friend," he said.

"I know," Zara said.

"Take all the time you need." Walter smiled at her.

"You want me to stay?" Kai tensed a little at the sight of Heath, but Zara shook her head.

"I don't think he's a danger. He was scared. He made a mistake. And we *did* kidnap him." She waved him off after handing him the list of meds. "Go with Walter. I'd feel better about it if you did. And make sure the doctors see that list. It could be important during treatment."

"Okay," Kai said, his posture still indicating he wasn't completely happy with her decision.

But he let her do what she knew was best. He left with Walter, and she watched him go for a minute, trying to decipher the feelings swirling inside about him. *He trusts me. And that means something.* Zara chewed on her lower lip, and then smiled as Kai turned and gave her a salute before turning the corner. The expression on his face made her chuckle.

She took a deep breath and turned toward the waiting room, switching her thoughts from Kai to Heath. He was only a few years her junior, maybe fifteen… but those years made a big difference. Heath fidgeted with his fingers, tears falling as he sat silently. She would have placed a bet, with the expression on his face, that he was blaming himself for what happened.

"Hey, Heath?" Zara walked into the room and sat across from him.

He snapped his head up and wiped away his tears with quick, harsh motions. "What are you doing here?"

Okay, maybe he's blaming us, too. Zara cleared her throat. "We didn't want anyone to get hurt," she said. "I… I hope you know that. And we're sorry if we didn't handle things right. We needed to get our friend out of there. We need to get him home to his family." *And to his lab where he can maybe save the world.*

Heath shifted and crossed his arms. "I don't want to talk to you."

A pang went through Zara's chest at the clear hurt and fear in his eyes. "Well, that's fine," she said. "I understand. But I also wanted to make sure you knew that this wasn't your fault."

"So, what?" Heath shouted. "It's not your fault. It's not my fault. Whose fault is it? Hers? She wouldn't listen! My dad wasn't even a good guy. He cheated on her. He never came to any of my games. He got drunk at LeeAnn's last birthday party." He jutted a finger at no one in particular. "But when he died, *she* went crazy. We needed her, and she might as well have left us, too."

Zara listened, her heart breaking, waiting for him to finish. "I'm sorry, Heath. It sounds like you've been through a lot."

"Whatever." Heath sat back and crossed his arms again.

"I can leave, if you want," Zara said. "But, I can also stay and just sit here. You don't have to be alone. Or I can go find LeeAnn and help her."

"She's with friends," Heath said. "She probably doesn't want to talk to you either." And then under his breath, "She sure as hell doesn't want to talk to me."

"I'm sure that's not true," Zara said.

"You don't know her," Heath snapped. "And you don't know me."

"Maybe not. But I do know you love your sister. And I know you love your mother. You probably even love your dad, despite his faults." Zara leaned forward, speaking gently but firmly. "And I also know that what happened to your mom wasn't really anyone's fault. It was a bad situation that got worse. It was an accident, Heath."

He swallowed hard, his Adam's apple bobbing. Fresh tears glistened and rolled down his cheeks, and he promptly wiped them away.

"I was trying to kill you," he said. "Why are you being nice to me?"

"You were trying to save your mom," Zara said. "In this case, I think maybe that's different. I think maybe you were scared, no thanks to us." What Heath had said before he pulled the trigger echoed in her mind. "Remember what you said to me? That you were afraid of what your mother would do to herself if we took Walter?" She tried to make her voice as gentle as possible. "My parents are both dead, Heath. I think there was a time when I would have done *anything* to save them."

"I'm sorry about your parents," he whispered.

"I'm sorry about yours," Zara said. "But you know what? Carol is still alive, and there's a chance she'll make it."

Heath nodded, but he seemed to shrink at her words. "I am so angry at her," he said, his voice small. "But I'm also so scared *for* her. I don't want her to die."

"I know." Zara moved to sit next to Heath as he broke down completely. He leaned on her shoulder, and she let him sob without interruption, rubbing his back, remembering what it had felt like when she'd found out her parents had died. She settled in, deciding then that she wouldn't leave Heath's side until news came about his mother.

Eventually, he sheepishly pulled away from her, the anger gone from his eyes. An hour later, Kai came to check on her, and he ended up staying. The three of them found a deck of cards in the nurse's station, and they played for an hour more.

When the mayor, Helen, came to the doorway and cleared her throat, all three of them stood up. Zara held her breath as Heath stepped forward.

"Do you have news about my mom?" he asked.

Helen nodded, a tired smile on her face. "She's going to live," she said. "Thankfully, we haven't had many traumas, our generator stayed strong, and our people are good at what they do. She was lucky."

Zara exhaled as Heath threw his arms around Helen's neck and hugged her tight. The woman didn't seem to know what to do with that, holding her arms awkwardly for a few seconds before deciding to return the embrace.

"I guess not every story has a bad ending these days," Kai said.

She nudged his side with her elbow. "Oh, I don't know. I'd like to think we'll survive this mess. Maybe even find happiness again."

"Yeah, maybe." Kai put his arm around her shoulders and gave her a light squeeze. "You think we should go check on Walter?"

Zara nodded. "Yeah," she said. "He's probably wondering what happened to us."

They said their goodbyes to Heath, who was about to find LeeAnn and tell her the news anyway, and they navigated the halls to Walter's room. When they entered, he was snoring, tucked into the sheets, seeming relaxed.

"I think this couch folds down into a bed," Zara whispered.

"I can stay in here with him, if you want to take one of the more comfortable hospital beds in another room," Kai said.

"No, I want to stay with him." Zara found the lever and converted the couch. "I think I'm ready for bed."

Kai opened a cabinet and brought her fresh sheets and a tiny pillow. "All right," he said. "Sleep tight, babe." He winked at her, and she hit him with the pillow.

He feigned injury to his arm. "Careful, Zara. I'm fragile," he whispered.

"Go." Zara stifled her laughter as she pointed toward the door.

But before he could leave, a young woman entered, pausing at the sight of them. "You two are with him, I guess?" she asked. "I'm a nurse. Name's Amy. Trying to keep track of the few patients we have right now by myself, so I might not be able to come by as often as I'd like. Any questions?" She moved as she talked, checking Walter's vitals without waking him.

"How's he doing?" Zara asked.

"Well, I'd imagine he'll be doing a lot better after the drugs Carol was using on him are out of his system. I mean, he still needs a lot of rest and antibiotics and painkillers, but a good portion of the weakness was fatigue from the cocktail she was giving him."

"We really need to get out of here," Zara said. "First thing tomorrow, if possible."

"I wouldn't recommend it," Amy said, "but his wounds have been tended for what, three days now?" She shrugged. "We can give you some antibiotics, show you how to change the bandage, give you instructions for care. Honestly, we don't have the staff to do much but check in on him and hope for the best, anyway."

"Then, I say," Walter opened his eyes, his voice hoarse, "we get on the road to Boston tomorrow. We're not far, and I need to be home."

"Whatever you say, boss," Kai said, nodding.

Zara came up to Walter and took his hand in hers. "Walter," she said, "We're so close. We are *finally* going home."

Chapter 42

Theodore Finch

It was early morning, but Theodore didn't care. He woke with a smile. Things had never been better for him, and they could only look up as long as he kept himself safe. His mosquito eggs were hatched just the night before. Well, not all of them. Half of them. Maybe a little less than half. But he'd smudged the numbers a little so that no one would ever find out the real percentage. It wouldn't be fair otherwise; he was using Dr. Brown's notes, after all. It wasn't *his* fault if the stuffy old man had made a few mistakes in his calculations. Everyone would still be asleep, and he deserved an extra hour or two with all the work he'd put in, but Theodore was too energized to stay in bed. He rolled out of his cot, whistling a tune, hoping that Azalea would be up and about.

He'd run into her early in the morning when he'd gone for a pee the day before. She'd said she was an early riser, and he counted that in her favor. He still flushed over the night they'd spent together, though he didn't remember much of it. She'd been enthralled by him, though, of that much he was sure. And ever since, she'd been embarrassed by her hussy-like behavior, avoiding him, making him play cat and mouse with her.

Well… he didn't mind that too much.

He looked for her in the break room they'd designated their cafeteria. Not finding her there, he opted for a granola bar, stashing an extra one in his pocket. The rules about only taking one were ridiculous. He was saving the world, and that made him hungry. No one would hold an extra granola bar against him once he successfully released those mosquitos into the wild, flying to join the swarm only to sabotage the modified species with defects that would eventually make them go extinct.

Picking up his whistling again as he walked the halls toward the cryopreservation pods, Theodore enjoyed the quiet. The entire building only had a handful of people in it besides himself. Azalea and Lizzy were still there, moved into a room of their own while the other building was empty. They'd not wanted to be alone, they'd said, but Theodore knew Azalea had wanted to be nearer to him. And then there was Alex, Minnie, that dog, and Oliver, the annoying little boy who had turned out to have his uses.

I would have found that journal eventually, Theodore reassured himself.

The others had been gone for a little more than a full day, trying to save that little girl who was probably dead already. People always wasted resources when they got their emotions involved, but Theodore stayed out of it. He hadn't liked them being in the lab, anyway. What use do they have? Maybe that Lauren would be good to have around, but the others? Me and Alex, Lauren if you don't mind a nervous nurse, and Azalea for her… entertainment qualities… that's all we need here. He pursed his lips, his frustration weighing him down, stopping his whistling tune.

He ruminated on how best to bring up his suggestion of moving everyone *except* those who were useful over to the other building. He was in the middle of a very convincing speech in his head when he turned a corner and stopped short. The door to the cryopreservation lab was open. When he came nearer, his heart nearly stopped. He gasped and rushed into the room, mouth agape at the atrocities before him.

"Who did this?" he screeched.

Before him, every tray he had filled with larvae had been taken from their drawer, sat on the floor, and bleach — *bleach!* — bottles were strewn on the ground. Horrified, he hurried to each one, finding his larvae dead.

He shook his head, backing away slowly. It was his worst nightmare come true. Someone had broken into the lab and sabotaged his work. Dashed his newly revived career to bits! Ruined his life forever!

"No, no, no… who? *Who?*" Theodore growled, kicking at one of the trays and sending water solution and dead larvae spilling across the floor.

And then a memory of that night with Azalea came rushing back, something he'd forgotten until that very moment. He reached out, stumbling until he found stability leaning against the wall. He had told her about the cryopreservation pods, about the process of hatching the larvae and transferring them to water trays where they could grow into pupa. But, to her own admission, his work had gone over her head.

Was she pretending? The thought made Theodore gasp for breath. "She wouldn't have…"

But he didn't know her, not really. And she was the *only* person who could have done it. Alex was too altruistic to ruin Theodore's work out of jealously, though the possibility did occur to Theodore. He dismissed it quickly. It didn't make any sense. No, it *had* to be Azalea. She was the only person to have seen the codes.

"Well, *I'm* not taking the blame for this." Theodore was seething.

He stomped out of the lab, intent on finding the woman. Her room wasn't far, just across the building. Theodore was going to find her and make her confess. And then he was going to bring her to Alex and make her confess to him, too.

"That witch! That temptress!" Theodore cursed her with every step. But then a strange smell hit him on the way. He stopped, his eyes widening. "Is that… gasoline?"

He followed the stench, putting aside his mission for the moment. The closer he came to the lobby, the stronger the smell became. And then he heard voices. Two of them. Both women. One of them was definitely Azalea. His anger resurfaced, and he nearly charged into the lobby, but what she was actually saying caught him, making him slow and then stop altogether to listen.

"It's the right thing to do," Azalea said, her voice coaxing, smooth and alluring.

"But what about the boy?" That was Lizzy. "He didn't do anything to deserve this."

"His father has brought this upon himself," Azalea said, "working against the Cleansing, working *for* the likes of your father."

Theodore peeked around the corner in time to see Lizzy's expression darken at the mention of her father. *What are they talking about?* He frowned. None of it made any sense.

Azalea held out a box of matches. "Strike the match, Elizabeth. I've laid the groundwork. It's time for you to do your part. Restore the Mother."

"Restore the Mother," Lizzy repeated, taking the box in her hands, looking at it as if it were a puzzle box.

"Set fire to this place." Azalea's gorgeous smile sent a shiver down Theodore's spine. "We'll flee through the front door to the other building, watch it burn from there. If the Mother wants the boy to live, he'll live. If not, he'll return to the earth. Dust to dust. Just like the rest of us."

Lizzy looked up from the box, looking into Azalea's eyes. "The Cleanse must continue."

"That's right, Elizabeth." Azalea reached out and tucked Lizzy's hair behind her ears. "And you're going to help, aren't you?"

"I'm going to help," Lizzy repeated again, almost as if in some sort of trance.

"You're both crazy!" Theodore said, speaking out loud before he thought better of it. But once he'd drawn attention to himself, he figured he might as well stop the insanity. He strode forward and held out his hand. "Give me those matches. Gasoline. Fireworks. This place will go up like a bonfire." He *tsked,* fully expected Azalea to cower at his presence.

But instead… she *laughed* at him. "Oh, Theodore," she said, tossing her black locks over her shoulder. And then she pulled a knife from her pocket, and with one quick thrust, buried the blade into Theodore's throat.

He stared at her, shocked. He couldn't speak. She viciously yanked the blade out, and he fell to his knees, desperately trying to stop the bleeding.

"Do it, Elizabeth," Azalea leaned over and wiped her blade on the shoulder of Theodore's shirt, the one not covered in his blood.

He collapsed onto his side, dizzy, gasping for air as his mouth filled with thick, coppery liquid. He couldn't wrap his mind around what was happening. Rolling onto his back into a puddle of gasoline, he panicked, gargling, thrashing, trying to scream and failing even at that.

Lizzy struck the match. "Azalea told me how you touched her," she said. "You're just like *them.*" And she dropped the match next to him, backing away quickly. As they fled out the front door, fire leapt up to lick at Theodore's skin. But he didn't have long to endure the excruciating pain. His last coherent thought was of deep regret; no one would ever know his name.

Chapter 43

Alexander Roman

At first, Alex thought the smell of smoke was left over from his nightmares. He'd often dreamt of the night he'd nearly lost Oliver in a fire in Nashville. It had been one of the worst days of his life and one of the best. It was that day that Oliver had begun speaking again after the death of his mother.

But as he came fully awake, he coughed, the very real smell of smoke leaving a nasty taste in his mouth. And Samson was at the door, whining. Alex bolted upright. "Minnie!" he shouted, springing up and shaking the woman awake.

"Jiminy Christmas, Alex, what is it?" Minnie smacked at him, but then she opened her eyes and sat up. "Who's been grillin' plastic?" She coughed and waved her hand in front of her face.

"I think the building is on fire," Alex said, raising his voice over Samson as the dog started to bark. He threw back the covers on Oliver's bed and scooped up his son.

"Dad? What's going on?" Oliver asked sleepily.

"Minnie, there's a fire exit at the end of the hall. It has no way in from the outside, so it's been left unblocked. Take Oliver. I'm going to get the others." He passed Oliver to her.

"Mom's purse!" Oliver reached back toward the bed.

Alex spun, snatched the macrame purse and handed it to his son. Oliver hadn't been without it since the World's Fair. He slid the strap over his head and wrapped his arms around Minnie's neck.

"Alex," Minnie said. "You gotta come with us."

"There are other people still here. I've also got to grab my research," Alex said firmly as he hooked Samson's leash onto his collar and slid the handle over Minnie's wrist. "I didn't come all this way to lose the answers we've found. Go on. Right now."

He opened the door to what they'd claimed as their bedroom, an office on the first floor, near the lab he was using to work on the vaccine. Minnie stepped through, holding Oliver close, Samson by her side. She hurried toward the emergency exit as Alex stepped out into the smokey hall, rushing after her. He opened Theodore's door, finding it empty.

"He's not here," he shouted back at Minnie.

"Prob'ly made it out, Alex!" she shouted.

"I'll be right behind you after I get the girls," he shouted. "Go!"

Minnie did as she was told, hustling outside with Oliver and Samson. Oliver had his head buried in her shoulder, but Alex still caught his muffled voice, crying for him to come, too. But if there were people still inside and if he could save the research...

He ran down the hallway that connected to where the two young women were staying, but he only made it a few yards when an explosion rocked the building, followed by a loud whistling almost like... a series of pops made Alex curse. "The fireworks in the lobby," he growled as a green glow illuminated the hall.

More explosions followed, the smoke thickened, and one thing became very clear: he couldn't make it to the other side. *There's an exit there, too,* he reassured himself. *Azalea and Lizzy will get to it. Or maybe I can wrench open the door from the outside with a tool from the other building.*

He said a silent prayer for them as he turned and ran back toward the lab, throwing the door open. There were papers strewn everywhere, left in the same cluttered mess he'd convinced himself he'd organize later. He grabbed a plastic bin full of clean towels and dumped them out before rushing to the cork board on the wall and removing the papers he'd pinned up first. And then he started grabbing handfuls of paper and stuffing them in the bin before securing the lid back in place. It was only a few minutes worth of work, but when he opened the door again, the smoke was much thicker.

Alex got to his hands and knees, keeping his head below the billowing smoke, pushing the bin toward the exit. His eyes watered, his throat burned, and his heartbeat thrashed in his chest, pulse pounding against his temples. Every foot of ground was a victory. Finally, he reached the emergency exit. Hand searching above his head, he found the bar to open the door and pushed. It opened and smoke poured outside. Alex scooted out with the bin, coughing and squeezing his eyes shut against the increased onslaught of heat and smoke.

Hands hooked under his armpits, dragging him; Alex didn't let go of the bin's handle, helping the person dragging him by pushing himself with his feet. He opened his eyes again after he'd been deposited farther from the building. He lay back on the parking lot, looking up at Minnie as Oliver jumped on top of him, hugging him tight. Samson came up to him, too, nudging him with his nose and planting a few slobbery dog kisses on his cheek.

"Couldn't get to the girls?" Minnie shouted over the volatile sound of too many fireworks going off at once.

Alex shook his head grimly and sat up, prompting Oliver to stand. "Let's get to the other building. The swarm probably won't come near this amount of smoke, but we should get inside to be safe."

He led the way, punching in the code on the key pad. Behind him, the lab burned while colorful bursts brightened the still dark sky. Smoke blended in with the night, concealing the stars. Alex opened the door into the Vanguard high rise. When he did, Azalea and Lizzy were waiting for him.

"You made it out!" Lizzy clasped her hands together below her chin.

"So did you!" Alex laughed. "I tried to get to the other side of the building, but it was blocked by the fire."

"See?" Azalea said to Lizzy, though her expression remained neutral. "I told you. The Mother is gracious."

Lizzy nodded, tears in her eyes as her smile widened. Alex frowned, not understanding Azalea's reference. He exchanged a look with Minnie.

"Kids these days," she mumbled. "Can't understand 'em half the time."

"Hey!" Oliver looked up at her.

Minnie ruffled his hair. "Not you," she said, smiling. "Well, it's a good thing there weren't a lot of people inside the lab tonight." She looked around. "Is Theodore here?"

Azalea shook her head. "No," she said. "We didn't see him come out, either."

"Minnie?" Oliver looked up at her, eyes glistening. He turned his eyes to Alex. "Dad? Should we go back for him?" His lower lip stuck out, trembling.

Alex's heart broke. "No, bud. He... he's gone. If he didn't make it out, we can't go back in there for him. I'm sorry. I did check his room, and he wasn't there. Maybe he made it out." It was doubtful that Theodore would have escaped without coming straight to the other Vanguard building. But the possibility seemed to make Oliver feel better.

"I'm going to get Oliver cleaned up and settled with a bite to eat," Minnie said, taking his hand. "It's a good thing we stored so many of our supplies over here." She glanced at Samson. "I reckon you'll want something to eat and drink, too, won't ya?" The dog barked once, wagging his tail, and Minnie led the way toward their supplies.

"I'll be right behind you," Alex said, and then he turned back to Azalea and Lizzy. "Did you girls see or hear anything?"

"What do you mean?" Azalea asked.

"I mean..." Alex sighed. "It's just odd. Something caught those fireworks on fire, but... I don't know, the way the fire burned, the smell of it... and the sprinkler system didn't turn on."

Azalea shifted. She looked uncomfortable, but only for a split second. "Must have been something wrong with it," she said. "Did you check to make sure it was working before?"

"Well, no..." Alex frowned. "I mean, the water in the building was working, though."

"Those systems have to be maintained, don't they?" Azalea asked.

"Probably." Alex shook his head and bit the inside of his cheek. *She's right,* he thought. *I don't know enough about these things. I'm just tired, maybe. Putting too much thought into this.* He sighed and was about to leave when Azalea stepped nearer to him.

"What's that?" She pointed at the small bin Alex was holding.

He hefted it. "Research," he said. "It's important, related to what we've been working on." He wasn't sure how much the young women had been told or how much they would understand.

Azalea cocked her head, and if Alex wasn't mistaken, there was the barest hint of frustration in her tone. "Did you get everything you needed?"

"No, unfortunately." Alex held the bin a little closer as Azalea eyed it. "We lost too much in that fire. What I salvaged is useless without the tools and materials going up in flame."

The frustration Alex had thought he'd seen was replaced by what seemed to be real sympathy. "That's too bad," she said. "Lauren told me you were close to a solution to what's happened, with the disease and the swarms." She stepped closer, twirling her finger around the ends of her long, black hair. "You must be devastated," she said, reaching out and lightly touching his arm. "I'm sure it would go right over my head, if you were to explain it, but if you ever wanted to talk..."

Is she flirting with me, or am I going crazy? A shudder went up Alex's spine, and he tried to keep his expression neutral. If she *was* flirting, he didn't want to embarrass her. He stepped back and cleared his throat. "Um, I'm good, thanks," he said awkwardly. "You two girls let me know if you need anything."

He glanced at Lizzy as Azalea stepped back, crossing her arms a little too sharply. Lizzy's smile had faded at the first sound of Theodore's name. She had remained silent throughout the rest of the conversation, the corners of her mouth twitching, her eyes narrowed just slightly. And then she'd seemed to smooth out her expression bit by bit until it mirrored Azalea's. It didn't sit right with Alex, the way the two were acting.

They've just been through a traumatic event. And so have I. Now's not the time to be analyzing them. Alex tried to shake the feeling.

"I'll see you two later," he said. "I've got to help Minnie with Oliver." He left the two girls standing there, and he could feel their eyes on his back as he walked away. "Stop it," he mumbled to himself. "Not everything is a conspiracy." He shook his head. *The craziness at the CDC and the way Ben... Jesse King... tricked us... it must be getting to me.*

He found Minnie and Oliver in one of the storage rooms; she was rummaging through boxes of food. "I swear, I'm about to ask the good Lord for a rock and a staff. I'm parched!"

Alex frowned. "What?"

"Oh, nevermind," Minnie waved him off and kept searching.

Oliver stood by a window, staring up at the fireworks. Alex came to stand next to him, placing a hand on his shoulder. "You okay?" he asked. "I know that was scary."

He shrugged. "Not as bad as the Nashville fire. Or the Ferris Wheel. Or the swarms. Or—"

"Yeah, okay, I get it." Alex shook his head. "We've been through a lot, haven't we?"

Oliver nodded. He pointed out at the burning building. "What does that mean, Dad? Didn't we come here for that place?"

"I don't know what it means, yet," Alex said, trying not to sound as worried as he felt.

He stared out the window with his son by his side. The truth was, he was terrified. He'd saved words on paper. Knowledge. But… he hadn't saved enough of it. He'd barely gotten started sorting the information. And without the countermeasure mosquitos, he wasn't sure a vaccine by itself would save humanity. The distribution of a vaccine would present so many complications, even if they were able to produce it without the samples of DV-10 they'd had access to at New Horizons. Everything became a thousand times harder without the lab. Alex's heart sank. He had the feeling he was watching their last real hope go up in flames, and there was nothing he could do about it.

Chapter 44

Zara Williams and George Peters

"Well," Zara said, "this is bad." She stared out the truck window at the Peters' home in Wellesley… or what was left of it.
"Hey!" Kai twisted in his seat at the sound of the airstream door opening. "Zara…"
"I've got it," Zara said, quickly hopping out of the cab and hurrying toward Walter as he stumbled out of the camper.
"We've got to check… to see if they're in there…" Walter leaned against the silver body, tears rolling down his cheeks.
"Me and Kai will check," Zara said gently. "You can't, Walter, okay?"
"I have to—"
"No," Zara said firmly. "What happens if you fall into the wreckage? You can barely walk."
Kai was already out of the truck, coming around to help her. "She's right, man," he said. "We will go look, okay?"
Walter nodded, his entire body trembling, from fear or weakness Zara wasn't sure. She and Kai helped him to the cab where he could watch them search upon his request. He leaned the passenger seat back a bit, a haunted look on his face as he stared out at the ruins of his home.
"Just wait here," Zara said before closing the truck door. "We'll be back."
She took a deep breath and turned her back, facing what could be a graveyard of people she'd known for years. And Annika, her cousin, could have been with them. "If Annika is gone," Zara said, "I… I don't know what I'll do. She was the last family I had left."
Kai, who stood next to her, threaded his fingers through hers, and squeezed her hand. "I'll be here," he said. "And so will Walter. Do you want me to go look on my own?" He looked sideways at her. "I understand if you don't want to risk coming across your cousin."
Zara swallowed hard. "No," she said. "If she's in there, I'll need to bury her, anyway." She took her hand back, grateful for Kai's presence as the two of them walked forward. But then something odd caught her eye. "What's that?" She pointed to the tree in the front yard.
Kai jogged over to it, and she followed more slowly. He ripped a baggie off a nail and held it out to her. "There's a note inside."
She took it and ripped the paper out, her heart leaping with hope as she opened it and read out loud, "We're safe. At New Horizons." She looked up at Kai. "It's signed by Tim!"
She whirled around holding the note up in the air. "They're alive!" she shouted, running back to the truck. She threw open the cab door, stepped up onto the bar, and threw her arms around Walter. She leaned back at his flinch and grunt of pain. "Sorry," she said, too excited to sound actually sorry. She shoved the paper in his face. "Look!"
He took the note and stared at it, a smile spreading as he breathed out a sigh of relief. "Tim," he said, and then he laughed, reaching for Zara again, but winced at the movement. He grasped her arm instead. "They're okay, Zara. They're alive."
"We just have to get to New Horizons, then," Zara said.
Kai got back into the driver's seat, smiling across at her. "Let's go find your family."

* * *

George could see the plume of smoke a mile away, and the closer he got to the Vanguard properties, the more certain he was that it was coming from one of those buildings. He had left City Hall midmorning, cautiously moving through the city as quickly as he could, keeping his eyes and ears open for signs of a swarm.
He'd stopped a few times along the way, investigating potential safe havens. The people at City Hall had been stockpiling green spray paint, marking doors much like CON had when they'd been scavenging the city. George left a green circle on the doors of those places he'd found clear of corpses, using them for a resting spot on his way to New Horizons.
He'd had a bad feeling when he'd first noticed the smoke, but his stomach had knotted and a feeling of dread had settled on him the closer he'd come to it. When he entered the lot, the blackened husk of the lab smoldering before him, he slowed to a complete stop, staring. His only thoughts were of Lizzy. He'd not seen her since she'd arrived. He'd been too wrapped up in what had been happening between the BPD and the Russos. The sound of a door opening behind him drew his attention.
"George?"
He turned to see Lizzy running toward him, and he wiped away the welling tears. "Lizzy!" George sprinted forward, meeting her halfway, throwing his arms around her.
Lizzy laughed and pulled away from him, cupping his cheeks in her hands. "You look taller," she said. "Are you okay?"
George nodded. "Yeah," he said. "I'm fine." He couldn't keep the smile from his face as he drew her into another hug, squeezing tight. "I've never been so happy to see anyone in my whole life."
"I'm happy to see you, too."
"What happened?" George asked.
Lizzy pulled away again, her smile faltering. "What do you mean?"
George frowned, pointing over his shoulder. "Oh, I don't know," he said sarcastically.
Lizzy pursed her lips. "It was a fire," she said, her tone sharp.
"Well… is… is everyone else okay?" George stumbled over his words, his frown deepening. "Why are you being so weird?"

"Everyone is fine." Lizzy's expression cooled, and she nodded toward the Vanguard building she'd just exited. "Except Theodore," she said, the corner of her lips twitching upward, a flash of something like satisfaction crossing her eyes. But it was gone as quickly as it had come. "We think he died in the fire," she said.

"That's... terrible." George took half a step backward. He hadn't seen Lizzy in a long time, but... there was something off about her, something *wrong*. "But Alex, Minnie, and Oliver... they're inside?"

"And Azalea," Lizzy said.

"Oh, right. Your friend, right?" George offered a small smile, despite his twisting gut. She nodded curtly, becoming colder toward him by the second. "I'm... I'm so happy you all made it out. It's too bad about Theodore. I didn't really know him."

There was awkward silence. George waited for Lizzy to ask about Tim, Heather, and Annika, but she just stared at him as if she were studying him, trying to decide something. He was about to offer up the news about what had happened anyway when a man came out of the Vanguard building and sprinted up to them.

"Alex, right?" George asked, sticking his hand out to shake the man's hand. "I'm George. Lizzy filled me in on what happened, the fire and Theodore. I'm sorry."

Alex nodded in acknowledgement. "Yeah, it was quite the morning." He glanced at Lizzy, but his gaze didn't linger. "I guess you've got news?" he asked George. "Is Lauren okay?"

George nodded. "Yes, she's fine. Tim, Heather, and Candice are all okay. Annika is recovering from surgery. There's more, but... we better get inside."

Lizzy was already turning toward the building, and George and Alex walked behind her. "Is your sister always like that?" Alex whispered.

"No," George said. "I mean, she's been through a lot, but... she's definitely different."

"I'm sure she just needs time," Alex said.

George nodded, hoping he was right.

***

Zara had held on to hope and excitement even after they'd spotted the smoke. That slowly dissipated the closer they came. A pathway was clear to the Vanguard properties, which would have been a good sign. But it quickly became clear that the smoke was coming from the place they were going.

"No," Walter's voice cracked. "No. No. No." He repeated the word as they pulled into the parking lot.

"Walter... this is recent," Zara said. "Like, really recent. Maybe they made it out. Maybe they're in the area."

Kai looked grimly back at her after putting the truck in park. "Just like back at the house?"

Zara nodded. "Stay here, Walter."

"We should grab the rifles," Kai said. "This is the city. We have no idea how that happened, and there's bound to be survivors here. Someone could have burned the building on purpose."

Zara hated to admit it, but Kai was right. She helped him retrieve their rifles, handing one to Walter to protect himself should someone come up on the truck while they were investigating the area. She stood in front of the smoking building.

"What kind of trouble did they get into?" Zara frowned. "I mean, the house burned down... now the lab? These were both targeted, right? I mean... it's too coincidental for them to both have burned down like that. The Peters aren't idiots. They wouldn't have let their shelters burn by accident."

Kai shrugged. "I don't know. What I do know is that we can't go inside that building. It's not safe."

Zara groaned and turned, shielding her eyes from the sun as she looked across the lot. It was then that two men emerged from the Vanguard building across the parking lot. "Kai!" She raised her rifle.

Kai reacted just as quickly. They both moved forward, positioning themselves in front of the truck and camper. Zara wasn't about to lose *another* set of supplies. The truck door opened behind them.

"We've got this, Walter," Zara shouted as the two approached.

"No," he said from behind them. "That's George!"

"What?" Zara squinted. The shorter man wasn't a man at all. He was a teenaged boy. The hair was too long, and his expression was too hard, but then she saw it. "George?" she shouted. "Is that you?"

Behind her Walter groaned in pain, and Zara turned to see him trying to get out of the truck on his own. She let her rifle fall, putting the safety back on and slinging it across her back so she could help Walter to the ground.

"Dad? Zara?" George's voice rang out across the lot. "It's okay, Alex. They're with us!"

Zara held out a hand as George rushed forward. "Woah, there," she said. "He's hurt pretty badly. Be gentle."

Walter reached out anyway, though, and took George's hug gladly. "It's okay," he said. "My son," he said. "You're alive." Tears streamed down his face, and he kissed the top of George's head.

"And this guy?" Kai asked, pointing at the older man Zara didn't recognize.

George pulled back, smiling ear to ear. "That's Alex," he said. "He's from the CDC."

Walter's smile faltered, and Zara's did too, probably for the same reason. Alex had lowered his weapon, but he didn't look friendly.

"Walter Peters," Alex said, "I've been looking for you."

"You know," Walter said.

"I do." Alex licked his lips. "I don't think he does—" He pointed at George. "—but Tim and Heather know, too."

Zara looked between them. She knew this would be an awkward conversation, but she couldn't imagine a worse start to it. George pulled back from his father, frowning.

"I promise, I will tell you everything, George," Walter said, "but I only want to do it once. I need everyone, your mom and Tim and Heather, all together. I've got a lot to tell you including..." His voice faltered. "...about Lizzy."

George's face had gone white. "Mom didn't make it," he said.

A pang shot through Zara's chest. "Walter," she said, "I'm so sorry."

Walter staggered backward. "Dana…" he whispered, clutching his chest and sitting hard on the step bar of the truck. "Dana," he said again, closing his eyes, his face contorting in grief.

But then George said something that Zara couldn't quite comprehend at first.

"But Dad," George said, "Lizzy… she's alive. She's *here*."

Zara stared at him, shaking her head. "No, she died at the compound." She dug out the two rings she'd worn on a chain ever since, one a butterfly, the other a ladybug. She held out the butterfly as if it were hard and fast proof. "We saw her body. She was holding this, and I gave her this ring."

George shook his head. "I don't know anything about the ring," he said. "But I do know that Lizzy is inside that building right now."

Walter had stopped crying, and he stared up at George with the same incredulous look Zara imagined she wore on her own face. "Are you sure?" he asked. He stood up, wobbling on his weak legs. "Bethie!" he shouted.

"Hold on, Walter," Kai said, coming up beside him to try and provide some support, and George followed suit, coming to his father's other side.

Zara turned toward the building and sprinted for it, her heart beating wildly. "Liz!" she shouted, not quite believing George, but unable to ignore his claims.

And then there she was, stepping outside into the sun. Zara laughed and sped up. "Lizzy, I thought you were gone." Tears blurred her vision, and when she was only a few feet away, she realized that Lizzy hadn't moved since spotting her. "Lizzy," Zara said, remembering the last words she'd spoken to her best friend. "I'm so sorry," she said. "I was being an idiot. I swear, I didn't mean any of those things. And your dad, he didn't either." She desperately held out the two rings. "Look! I kept them. And I wore them every day."

"I'm glad you're alive," Lizzy said, little emotion in her words as another young woman Zara didn't know stepped out of the building, placing an arm around Lizzy's shoulders.

"Hi," Zara said, thrown off by the woman. "I… uh… me and Liz were talking," she said. "I don't mean to be rude, but—"

"My name is Azalea, and I know all about you, Zara," the woman said. "And all about him," she nodded, indicating Walter, who was limping forward with Kai and George on either side. Alex followed close behind.

"Who are you?" Zara asked sharply as she faced her again, anger flaring at the interruption, at the way the woman looked at her.

"I'm Elizabeth's best friend," Azalea said, "and I would *never* abandon her."

The words struck Zara in the chest like a hammer, knocking her back half a step. She swallowed a lump in her throat and turned her eyes back to Lizzy. If she could only talk to her… "Lizzy," she started.

"No," Lizzy said. "I *am* glad you made it, Zara, but I need some time before I can talk to you." She scowled at her father, who was still several yards away. "And I *refuse* to talk to *him*. Tell him that for me, Zee. I don't want him anywhere near me." Her voice caught on the words, but the emotion was very clearly one of anger, hatred even.

Azalea guided Lizzy back inside. "If you want your friend back, Zee—" She spat Zara's nickname like it was a curse. "—you'll do as she asks."

And then they were gone. Zara sucked in a breath, her chest tight, and then a sob escaped her lips, and she was crying. She turned her back, holding out a hand to stop Walter. "You can't," she said, trying to gather herself together, to speak clearly despite the fact that she couldn't stop herself from weeping. "She doesn't want to see either of us right now."

Walter shook his head. "No," he said. "She… she's my daughter, Zara. She *has* to talk to me." He got a determined look in his eye.

But Zara could feel it. They couldn't push her, not yet. "No," she said firmly. "Walter, you have to trust me. She's glad that we're alive, but… she thinks we abandoned her. She doesn't know how you've changed, how I've changed. Think about the last words we said to her. We can't force this, Walter. We can't."

Fresh tears fell down Walter's cheeks, but he nodded. "Okay," he said hoarsely, his face falling.

George was very obviously confused. "Whatever is going on here, we need to talk about later," he said.

"I agree." Alex stepped forward, addressing Walter. "But I have to ask you one thing before we do anything else, Walter." He pointed toward the building. "I was able to save some of the research, but the countermeasure mosquitos are gone. The samples of DV-10 are gone. And I wasn't even able to save all of the research."

Walter swallowed audibly, looking over his shoulder at the lab. "You want to know if that means there's no hope left."

"Yes," Alex said. "I want to know if the solution to the end of the world burned down with that building."

Walter turned to look Alex in the eyes. Zara waited for him to answer, her palms going sweaty, time seeming to slow as her heart pounded in her chest. From the way everyone else had their eyes on him, she wasn't the only one waiting in rapt anticipation for his reply.

"There's one last option," Walter said, his tone far from reassuring. "Another lab, but…" His body sagged between George and Kai. "It's a long shot," he said. "And none of us are going to like it."

Fortitude

No Tomorrow Book 5

Chapter 1

Alexander Roman

Alex took hold of his rifle, the cool metal hard in his hand. The comfort it brought him struck him as odd, but only for a moment. That was the way the world worked these days. He scowled as he called out, grabbing a second rifle and a handgun. "George! We've got company!"

He marched through the first level of the Vanguard high-rise. As he entered the conference-room-turned-dining-hall, George had already abandoned his breakfast and pulled on his shoes. Lizzy and Azalea sat back in their chairs, exchanging a glance that was more curious than nervous. Alex tried to ignore their indifference and the way neither offered to help. Minnie had Oliver by the hand, waiting for his instruction.

Alex handed Minnie the handgun. "Take Oliver to an inner room, away from the windows." He nodded at the two young women. "You two can go with her, if you want."

Azalea quirked an eyebrow. "We're fine right here," she said. "We haven't finished our breakfast."

Lizzy had sat up at Alex's suggestion, as if she were ready to follow Minnie, but at Azalea's words, she relaxed again and bit off part of her granola bar. His skin crawled at the strange reaction, but he shrugged it off. It wasn't the time or place. And their odd behavior wasn't exactly his business, until it affected his family, of course. Then, he'd *make* it his business. But for the time being, he buried the feeling that something was off with the two young women.

Alex held out a rifle toward George. "You ready?"

George took it and nodded. "How many?"

"I'm not sure." Tension tightened Alex's muscles. "Hopefully, we can just scare them off."

Alex led the way outside, slipping out and ensuring the door closed behind them. It locked automatically, the only way back in through a code on a keypad. They'd lost a lot, but everyone and everything that was important to Alex was inside that building. He meant to keep it safe.

The summer breeze brought with it the stench of a rotting Boston, something Alex had started to get used to. But a particularly foul stench was added to the mix. A plume of smoke still rose from New Horizons Laboratory, and the smell of burnt plastic and chemicals emanated from it. There was the undertone of burnt flesh, too, something Alex wasn't sure if he was actually still detecting or if it was a phantom smell brought on by the knowledge that Theodore Finch had likely been burned alive. Whatever the case, he pushed past the nausea and made his expression and his stride as intimidating as possible.

And then something unexpected happened. One of the newcomers called out George's name.

"Dad? Zara?" George dropped the muzzle of his rifle. "It's okay, Alex. They're with us!"

Before Alex could object, George was sprinting forward. And then Alex processed exactly what George had said. *His dad? Walter Peters?*

Alex stopped a few feet short of the newcomers, examining them. There was a young woman, Zara presumably, and a young man. The older man, the one George had thrown his arms around, was clearly weak. *Must have been injured recently,* Alex thought.

The three exchanged quick greetings, and then the young man, a snarky-looking guy in a worn-out leather jacket, had the nerve to look at Alex suspiciously. "And this guy?" he asked.

"That's Alex," George said. "He's from the CDC."

Alex did not miss the look of shock that crossed Walter's face. If he wasn't mistaken, there was a bit of fear in his eyes as well. After all he'd discovered about the man, Alex kept his guard up. Mr. Peters had been key in producing the genetically modified mosquitos and the disease they carried – DV-10. The mosquitos had evolved into nightmarish pack-like swarms, devouring humans and animals alike. The disease and the subsequent panic had wiped out most of the population. From what Alex knew of humanity, he expected Walter to either seek a way to gain power through the tragedy or seek to rectify mistakes he decided to own. That seemed to be the way it worked; people were either at their best or at their worst when crap hit the fan, and there was no way to tell which way they'd go until they took a step.

"Walter Peters," Alex said, keeping his voice even. "I've been looking for you."

Understanding fell across Walter's face. "You know."

Alex kept his initial reaction to himself. What you've done? Who you really are? Yeah, you greedy bastard.

Alex narrowed his eyes. "I do." Alex licked his lips. "I don't think he does, but"—he pointed at George—"Tim and Heather know, too."

George pulled back from his father and looked at Alex questioningly. A stab of regret made Alex wish he'd been more tactful. George was a good kid. He didn't deserve to have a bomb like that dropped on him. Timothy should have been the one to reveal that Walter was behind the disaster that had ended the world as they once knew it.

Walter chimed in, his voice pleading. "I promise I will tell you everything, George," Walter said, "but I only want to do it once. I need everyone, your mom and Tim and Heather, all together. I've got a lot to tell you, including…" He choked on the next words. "…about Lizzy."

George's eyes went wide as his face went white, and he met his father's gaze. "Mom didn't make it."

The news of his wife superseded the lies Walter Peters had to confess, and Alex understood. The already weakened man crumpled at the news. The instant grief there as he moaned and called for Dana brought tears to Alex's eyes. He knew that pain. His own wife, Naomi, had been taken from him not that long ago. Alex swallowed hard and turned his back on them, taking a few steps back toward the Vanguard building to allow them some space. It felt like a distinctly personal moment he had no right to take part in. Not to mention the fact that his own emotions demanded he take a minute to gather himself. Wrapped up in thoughts of Naomi, Alex only barely registered talk of Lizzy being alive.

Soon, Walter and Zara were rushing past Alex toward the Vanguard high-rise. Alex frowned when Lizzy stepped outside, and Azalea behind her. *So, they weren't so uninterested. They had to be watching this whole time.*

George and the other man, Kai, if Alex had caught his name correctly, passed Alex, too. He closed the distance more slowly, watching as Lizzy coldly turned away from Zara and her father while Azalea stood at her back. When the two young women went back inside, Azalea whispering into Lizzy's ear as she punched in the key code, Zara and Walter were left in their pain.

"Whatever is going on here," George said, obviously still confused, "we need to talk about it later."

"I agree." Alex stepped forward, addressing Walter. He had some sympathy for the man, despite what he'd done, but there were larger matters which needed to be addressed. "But I have to ask you one thing before we do anything else, Walter." He pointed back at the burnt-out lab. "I was able to save some of the research, but the countermeasure mosquitos are gone. The samples of DV-10 are gone. And I wasn't even able to save all the research."

Walter followed Alex's gesture to stare at the lab. "You want to know if that means there's no hope left."

"Yes," Alex said. "I want to know if the solution to the end of the world burned down with that building."

Walter met Alex's eyes with his own, his tone laced with pain and grief and uncertainty. "There's one last option. Another lab, but…" He sagged against George and Kai, who were offering his broken body support. "It's a long shot," he said. "And none of us are going to like it."

Alex braced himself. "Go on," he said. "There's very little I've had to do lately that I've actually *liked*."

"The government had us send backups of everything, even the countermeasure mosquitos, to a top-secret lab. You know the global seed bank?" Walter asked.

Alex nodded, but he explained further at the blank looks of George, Zara, and Kai. "Yeah. It's in Norway, a place where frozen seeds are stored from all over the planet. It was meant to ensure the survival of a wide range of crops should there be a worldwide crisis." He pursed his lips. "It might come in handy once we get all of this mess sorted out."

"Exactly," Walter said. "Well, there's something like it, but it's for cures to diseases. We hadn't found the cure yet, but they'd wanted to store all the information we did have in case…" He gestured vaguely around him. "… something like this happened."

Alex shook his head, bile rising, burning his throat. He had to take a minute to dampen the burst of anger and disgust. "You're saying the government knew that this was a possibility so much so that they stored information about it in this… cure bank, or whatever it is?"

Walter's cheeks flushed, having the decency to at least appear ashamed. "Yes."

Alex balled his hands into fists. "They thought the risk was worth the power they'd gain. Is that it?"

"Yes." Again, Walter gave a simple answer, and it earned him a modicum of respect. Alex despised those who tried to sugar coat evils or make excuses for them.

"And you and your company just… went along with it. The dollar signs outweighed the potential for catastrophe? Or rather, the dollar signs outweighed the potential for *you* to experience something tragic." Alex couldn't help the rising volume of his voice. "I've looked at the research. I know DV-10 wasn't the final version, wasn't supposed to get out, but entire people groups could have been targeted with this research. You just knew it wouldn't be *your* people, so you didn't care."

Walter hung his head. "Yes. I wish that I could say otherwise, but behind all the excuses, all the statistics that said something like this was less than one percent likely… the answer to your questions is, 'yes.'"

"Am I the last to know?" George asked, his brow knit in anger, his tone sharp.

"George, I—" Walter started, but didn't get far.

George wasn't talking to him. He was talking to Alex. "Answer me," he said.

"I think so," Alex said. "But, to be fair, you weren't really here. You were with the police department, fighting your own war. Your brother didn't want to bring you in on something you could do nothing about, something that would weigh you down."

The teen turned to his father. "Like you said earlier, when Timothy and Heather get back, you've got some explaining to do." Walter opened his mouth, but George held up a hand. "I can't right now. I love you, Dad, and I'm glad you're alive, but… I need a minute."

George turned abruptly and disappeared inside the Vanguard building without another word. No one tried to stop him.

Walter sank to his knees, hunched over, hugging his middle. Kai crouched beside him, one hand on his shoulder. Zara knelt.

"You're not that person anymore," Zara said. "They'll see that eventually."

"We should get you back to the camper," Kai said. "I don't know that we're safe inside."

"No one will harm you," Alex said. "No one will harm *any* of you. Walter is too important, despite what he's done."

"Then we should get him to a place where he can rest," Zara said. "We're all exhausted, and he needs to heal."

"One more question," Alex said.

Zara was about to object when Walter shook his head at her before looking up at Alex. Tears ran down his cheeks. He looked defeated, beaten down. "I'll answer."

"You said none of us are going to like it," Alex said. "Why? Where is this place?"

"I have a name. Barlow Scientific Research Bank." He shook his head. "I don't know where it is. Just that it exists. We're going to have to find whoever is left of the government, somehow, find someone who was part of DARPA. The headquarters were in Arlington. If—"

Alex shook his head. "No, no one important is left on the east coast. We took the long way here, through Atlanta, to try to get answers at the CDC. Part of the government, the new president... or *possibly* the new president, Coleman... he told us, before he took a small army west, that there was nothing left of the government in D.C. or anywhere nearby. Everyone left in every branch, in every agency, was to meet at Cheyenne Mountain in Colorado."

"Then that's where we need to go," Walter said. "If we have any chance of saving humanity, we have to find out where that research bank is located."

Alex reached out a hand to help Walter up. "We're going to need to send for Timothy and Heather, and we're going to need to figure out how we're going to make it all the way to Colorado. We're running out of time, and the scariest part is I don't know how much we have left."

* * *

It was decided. Alex was silent; the last hour had been full of noise. He needed a minute to sit with the knowledge of what they had to do next, and he wasn't the only one. Timothy and Heather held hands at the opposite end of the conference room table. Beside Timothy, his father leaned back, dark circles under his eyes, breathing too heavily for the little exertion the conversation had required. Zara and Kai glanced at Walter in unison, both of them with concerned etched into their features. Candice sat next to Heather, anxiety coming off her in waves, a continuation of the already expressed worry the woman had for the little girl, Annika. Lauren sat between Candice and Alex, silently tapping her fingers as if counting. Alex expected she was considering the medical supplies they would need for the upcoming journey. George frowned into his lap, working his jaw back and forth.

Minnie reached out and patted Alex's hand from her seat beside him. "We've got a plan," she said. "All we can do is take the next step. As long as we're together—"

"I'm not going," George said, looking up to meet the shocked gazes of his family members.

"Like hell you're not," Walter said, his voice too weak to sound intimidating.

"You can't stop me." George looked at Timothy, pleading in his eyes. "I'm not the same kid you left behind."

Timothy sighed and rubbed his forehead. "He's right, Dad. George can make his own decisions."

Walter sat up and set a fist down on the table in a lackluster manner. "I'm not leaving my teenage son in Boston while we travel halfway across the country during the end of the world."

"I've been on my own before," George said. "And this won't even be that. I'll have Captain O'Donnell and the BPD. I'm part of them, now. I fought to keep Boston from falling into the hands of the mob. I believe in rebuilding this city."

"No," Walter said.

"If you try to force me," George said, "I'll get away, and I'll come back to Boston."

Walter opened his mouth again, but Timothy held up a hand. "Dad, you haven't been here. I have. I'm telling you something I had to learn the hard way: you can't make George do anything. The world is different now. Being a teenager is *different* now. It has to come with more responsibility. And like George said, he won't be alone."

Heather spoke up, keeping her tone gentle. "Walter, Boston is probably safer than most places right now. There's been a solidifying of power, and it's gone into the right hands. Who knows what we're going to face out there? George should stay."

Alex listened, finding it hard to disagree. Months ago, he would have balked at the idea, just like Walter. But he'd heard what George had been through, what that kid had done. He was tough, and O'Donnell wouldn't let anything happen to him. He stayed out of it, though. It wasn't his fight.

Walter sat back, shaking his head. "How can I leave you?" he asked. "After you've just found out what I've done, after fighting so hard to get back to you..."

George licked his lips. "What you did can't be changed," he said. "I'm not sure how I feel about it, how I can forgive you, but... I still love you, Dad. I just... I can't go."

That seemed to be settled, but it brought up another issue. "And what about the rest of us?" Alex asked. "Walter and I have to go. Minnie, Lauren, Oliver, and I... well, we've made a pact. We don't split up."

Minnie nodded firmly, as did Lauren.

"But the rest of you," Alex said, "it's up to you. You can stay here. This building is pretty secure. Boston is safe, for now. Or as safe as any place can be. I wouldn't blame any of you for sitting tight."

"I've come this far," Zara said. "I'm not giving up now." She smiled at Lauren. "And if Lauren is going, Annika would be best served by staying with someone who knows how to treat her."

"Agreed," Candice said, her back stiffening. "We had to force that doctor to do Annika's surgery. Now that she's on the mend, we need to keep her with someone who cares about her recovery."

"I don't think the surgeon is coming back to Boston," Lauren said. "Before we left City Hall, I heard a rumor that he was leaving, didn't appreciate being forced into treating someone. Annika should be fine if we take the right supplies and I keep an eye on her."

"Well," Kai said, throwing a grin Zara's way, "I go where she goes."

"Azalea? Lizzy?" Alex asked. "You two don't have to come. I think it might even be better if you stayed with G—"

"No," Azalea said, a little too quickly. She looked at Lizzy, giving her a nudge with her elbow.

"If most of my family are going," Lizzy said, "I'm going, too." She leaned forward to look at George. "But I will miss you."

George nodded, returning the sentiment. "You'll come back," he said, clearly making it a point to look at her, his father, his brother, and his sister-in-law. "You'll all come back. And when you do, Boston will be even safer. Once you figure out how to stop this disease, these mosquito swarms... you do your part, and I'll do mine. One day, we'll have our home back."

Alex couldn't help a sad smile. *Home... I guess I don't really have one of those anymore.* He glanced at Minnie and Lauren, then thought of Oliver who was doing a puzzle in another room. *No... I do have a home. It's just not a place.*

"So, we leave within the next day or two," Walter said.

Everyone nodded in agreement. They would make their way to Cheyenne Mountain, to the place the government was supposed to be set up, and then they would search for answers as to where the Barlow Scientific Research Bank was located. And then they'd hit the road again. But between Boston and Colorado, between Colorado and wherever else they needed to go, there would be more hardships, more danger. Added to that was the fact that there were no guarantees. They could find Cheyenne Mountain empty. There could be no trail to the research bank.

But we have to try, no matter the risk, no matter the outcome. Alex sighed again and leaned back in his chair. "You were right, Walter," he said. "This is one hell of a long shot. But if there's a chance, there's no other group in the world I would want to bet on to get it done."

Chapter 2

Lizzy Peters

3 Weeks Later

Lizzy let the sway of the old camper and the feel of Azalea by her side distract her from the misery of being stuck inside a small space with her father. The only thing saving her sanity at the moment was that he was asleep.

She would have preferred to be in the airstream with Candice, Lauren, and Annika; instead, she and Azalea had been stuck in what Minnie lovingly called "Harvey the RV" with Walter and Alex's kid, Oliver. Meanwhile, Harvey's cab was full, with Alex at the wheel and Heather, Timothy, and Minnie as passengers. Kai and Zara drove the smaller truck hauling the airstream. Neither cab would have been less awkward. The only person in Lizzy's family she felt comfortable around was George, and he was back in Boston.

The dining table in the RV had been lowered and snapped into the bench seats to create a flat surface. A few extra pillows created a second, very small bed space. Lizzy and Azalea took up two-thirds of it, and Oliver sat on the side closest to the primary bed, which extended over the top of the four-door cab. Walter hadn't seemed to mind the space, which barely had enough height for him to sit up. The entire camper was a tight fit.

Azalea and Oliver had been drawing pictures for an hour, using clipboards and paper and colored pencils they'd grabbed from a craft store in Missouri. She was up to something with the way she'd been catering to the boy, but Lizzy hadn't gotten enough time alone with her to really understand. She'd opted out of the drawing, blaming car sickness. The truth was, she didn't *want* connections with people she'd never see again, people likely to end up dead as collateral damage. Of course, not everyone was like Oliver; not everyone was innocent.

An absent-minded movement of her hand to her pocket brought Lizzy's fingertips to the smooth cardboard of a matchbook. She'd kept it with her the last two weeks to remind her of what she was capable. A thrill unlike anything she'd ever experienced had shot through her veins when she'd dropped a match on Theodore Finch, a sorry excuse for a human being. As the flames had consumed both man and building, the screams of Mother Earth had quieted into contentment, the roaring crackle of fire a soothing replacement.

The sounds of agony had returned, though, upon her father's arrival in Boston. No one else could hear it except for Azalea. No one else had been given the gift of the Mother's voice. But Lizzy's eyes had been opened to the evils her father and those like him had wrought. The only chance earth had left — the only chance humanity had left — was to return evil men to dust and start over. It may have taken extreme measures for The Heirs of the Mother to make her understand, but what blind man wasn't willing to go through a little pain in order to see?

And so, over the past three weeks, Lizzy had waited, biding her time as their little caravan travelled the lands of a decaying nation. Azalea would know the right time to act, like she always did. And once they'd ensured Walter and Alex could not continue their plan to prematurely end The Cleanse, they would return to the underground compound and wait for Mother Earth to welcome the Heirs back to her surface.

It was hard, in the meantime, being surrounded by people she once trusted. Zara's presence was particularly unnerving, sometimes confusing. There were times her former best friend reminded Lizzy of happier times, but always there was a stab of pain following closely after. Zara had abandoned Lizzy, refusing to have compassion for her as she'd dealt with her father's sins. Zara had been the first to throw away their friendship.

It had been a cruel irony to discover that Zara had been right about Lizzy's father all along. They never should have helped him. It was almost laughable how the roles had reversed. Zara was quick to defend Lizzy's father, and Lizzy wanted nothing more than to be rid of him.

Azalea shifted beside Lizzy as she raised the clipboard on her lap to show to Oliver. "What do you think?" she asked.

Oliver laughed. "What is it?"

Lizzy frowned at the paper on the clipboard, leaning into Azalea to get a better look. "It looks like a… bear, maybe?"

"It's my dog, from when I was a kid. Dusky the husky." Azalea turned the clipboard a quarter to one side and then the other.

"Was he really fat?" Oliver asked. "And what about his tail?"

Azalea puckered her lower lip and plopped the clipboard onto her lap. "I forgot that part."

Lizzy chuckled. "You forgot his tail? How do you forget to put a tail on a husky?"

"Okay, okay," Azalea said, her tone light and good-humored. "So, I was never going to be an artist." She nudged Oliver with her elbow. "What did you draw?"

Oliver held up his clipboard. He'd drawn purple irises in a flower bed. "Do you like it?"

"Oh, yes," Azalea said. "They're so pretty. Are they your favorite type of flower?"

Oliver shrugged. "I guess. Me and Dad buried a note my mom had written next to flowers like this. We couldn't bury *her* because…" He trailed off, hanging his head.

Lizzy allowed herself to feel the sympathy clawing at her insides. "My mom died, too," she said. "I don't really have anything of hers to bury, but if I did, I think I'd like that."

Oliver offered a small smile and wiped away moisture from his eyes. "We could make a list," he said. "A list of things you loved about her. We could bury that."

The thoughtfulness of his idea struck Lizzy hard. She stared at him a moment, wishing she could snatch him up and take him to the Heirs of the Mother where he could grow up safe, where he could one day be part of the new world.
"That's a good idea," Azalea said, placing her hand over Lizzy's, giving it a soft squeeze. "But Lizzy might not be ready for that."
"My dad helped me a lot." Oliver glanced at Walter, who hadn't budged in hours. "Maybe he can help you?"
Lizzy tried to keep the vitriol from her voice, but she wasn't sure she succeeded. "My dad isn't that kind of dad," she said.
Oliver opened his mouth to say something else, but the RV slowed, grabbing his attention. Together, they watched as it turned off the highway and stopped. Lizzy was grateful for the distraction. She wasn't as disciplined as Azalea.
Azalea twisted around and looked out the window. "Looks like a church."
"We should be close to Colorado Springs," Lizzy said. "Why would we stop now?"
"Let's find out." Azalea scooted forward off the bed.
A final, loud snore and a sharp intake of breath signaled Walter's wakening. "How long have I been out?" He yawned and stretched, swinging his legs over the side of his bed.
"A *really* long time," Oliver said.
Walter climbed down and raked his hands over his face. "After the past month, I guess this old body is just worn out. My injuries are so much better, but… I still feel like I've been hit by a truck."
"Everyone has been through a lot, Walter," Lizzy said. "And you're not *that* old."
He sighed. "Lizzy, when are you going to start calling me dad again?"
"Not any time soon. And I'd rather go by Elizabeth, now, thank you." Lizzy turned her back on him and strode the few feet between her and the door. She was about to reach for the door handle when it opened, Alex on the other side.
"Whoa," he said. "I thought we had a procedure in place. Don't open this door until I give the all clear. You have no idea why we've stopped."
"Sorry," Lizzy said. "I… I wasn't thinking."
"My son is in there," Alex said, and not kindly. "Don't let it happen again. This time, we've just chosen a spot for the night. We thought it best not to go too far into the city just yet. But next time? Who knows? People are crazy these days. Trust me. I know."
Azalea came up behind Lizzy. "She said she was sorry." She gestured toward Walter. "It can get a little emotional in here. Maybe if we could switch with one of the other—"
"We talked about this," Alex said. "Annika still needs her space. She can't share a bed until she's healed up a little more. Lauren has medical training. Candice is like a mother to Annika. You could sit in the truck with Zara and Kai, but that's not suitable for you, either, is it?"
Lizzy's cheeks burned hot. *Who does he think he is?*
"C'mon, Alex," Walter said. "She's a teenager. Back off a little. She's going through a lot."
Rage at her father's audacity to insert his opinion — to downplay her emotions because she's just a *teenager* — made Lizzy ball her hands into fists at her sides. It was only Azalea's touch on her back that kept her from expressing that anger through choice words.
Alex eyed her, but when she didn't say anything, he glanced at Walter and sighed. "Sorry," he said. "I get a little protective when Oliver is involved."
"I get it," Walter said. "It's fine."
Oliver squeezed past Lizzy and Azalea and hopped down the steps. "Lizzy's nice," he said. "But she doesn't like her dad. If I didn't like you, it would be hard, I think." He made one last jump, landing on the asphalt outside. "But don't worry. You're the best."
Alex smiled at his son and ruffled his hair. "Why don't you go help Minnie take Samson for a walk? After that, we're going to settle here, in this church for the night." When Oliver had bounded away, he turned back to them. "Sorry. Again. Oliver didn't mean anything by that." He rubbed the back of his neck. "Kids, you know… they speak their minds."
"It's fine." Lizzy stepped down and into the lot, Azalea close behind. "He's not wrong. About my dad, that is." She kept walking, not bothering to give Alex any more of her time.
Azalea was by her side in seconds flat. "Elizabeth," she said, keeping her voice low. "Alex is the last person we want to antagonize right now. We don't want him suspicious of us. He's smart, and he's also the man most important to their mission, besides your father. We need him to trust us."
"He's already suspicious," Lizzy said. "The way he talks to me… I hate it."
Azalea put out a hand and gently brought Lizzy to a stop, standing in front of her, meeting her eye to eye. "Please tell me I wasn't wrong about you."
Lizzy's heart nearly stopped. She shook her head, swallowing a lump in her throat. "No," she said. "You weren't wrong. I can do this."
"This isn't just about you, Lizzy. We worked so hard to show you what you could be. We worked so hard to give you the chance to do some good for the Mother." Azalea squeezed Lizzy's arms tighter and leaned even closer. "Do you hear the screams?"
At those words, flashes of photographs and videos — horrendous accounts of a dying world — cycled through Lizzy's mind's eye. She squeezed her eyes shut, adrenaline flooding her system. She could feel the straps holding her down, remember the pitch black of a lonely concrete prison. The sun's warmth was reminiscent of dancing flames licking at her feet. The kiss of a slight breeze on her skin turned to oil sloshing into a small basin in which she'd been trapped. And the screaming permeated all of it.
"I hear them." Lizzy's voice cracked. She wanted to shy away, but how could one run from the earth itself?
"Don't you want the pain to stop?" Azalea's voice broke through the chaos in her mind.
Lizzy nodded, her chin trembling. All she wanted was for the pain to stop. A sob escaped her, and then another. Hot tears stung her eyes.

"Look at me, Elizabeth." Azalea's tone was forceful. It was a command, not a request, and Lizzy obeyed. "As long as you're with me, as long as you're on the right path, the screams can be quieted." She lightened her grip and pulled Lizzy into a hug, allowing her to cry into her shoulder. Azalea stroked Lizzy's hair, speaking softly, her words dampening the awful screaming as she mimicked the soothing message of her own mother, leader of the Heirs. "You are loved, Elizabeth. You belong to the Heirs. You belong to Mother Earth, and she needs you. You've heard her screams, now listen to her comfort. Hear her gentle breeze, the sound of birds nearby. Listen and soak in the possibility of what will be after The Cleanse: an earth free of humanity's afflictions."

The Mother's voice quieted, and Lizzy rested in Azalea's embrace. "Thank you," Lizzy said, pulling away after several long minutes. "I'm sorry. I'll do better." She flushed in embarrassment; she was so weak. "Sometimes I think you'd be better off if you left me, just like everyone else."

"You're forgiven," Azalea said. "And I would never abandon you. I'm the only one who can help you, Elizabeth. And the Mother chose you. She brought you to us."

Lizzy wiped away her tears. "So, we need to get Alex to trust us? Is that why you've been doing so much with Oliver?"

Azalea nodded. "His son is a gateway to that trust." She looked back at the two vehicles where the others were congregating outside, talking amongst themselves. "But he isn't the only one we need, Elizabeth. We need all of them to trust us. The future is undecided. Any one of them could be the key to unraveling their plans." She looked back at Lizzy, sympathy in her eyes. "Even your father."

Lizzy's stomach turned. "I can't pretend to like him," she said.

"You don't have to." Azalea wrapped an arm around Lizzy's shoulders. "He's trying to prove himself to everyone," she said, "and he's going to try to use you to do it. He needs them to believe he's a good person. You see that, don't you? How he's pulled the wool over their eyes? He doesn't love you, not really. He loves himself, and he can't stand for his own daughter to hate him. What does that say about him?"

"That he's a bad man," Lizzy said.

"Exactly." Azalea smiled. "All you have to do is make him think there's a *chance* you'll forgive him one day. That's enough to satisfy his need for a cleaner image, at least for now. You'll see. He won't do the hard work that a father who loved his daughter would. As soon as he can say he's respecting your boundaries, that you're coming around, he will."

"He's always been more hands-off," Lizzy said. "That sounds like him. Taking the easy route with his family. Saving all of his effort for work."

"But you don't need him," Azalea said.

"No, I don't." Lizzy straightened her shoulders, feeling more confident.

"So, you'll stick to the plan? You and me, we gain the trust of every one of them, and then when the opportunity presents itself, we throw a kink into their plans. Whatever it takes, we stop them. We save the earth from ultimate destruction at the hands of the greedy."

Lizzy took a deep breath. She wasn't as strong as Azalea, but she could do this with Azalea by her side. "Whatever it takes," she repeated. "Restore the Mother."

Azalea rewarded her with a proud smile. "That's right, Elizabeth. Restore the Mother, indeed."

Chapter 3

Minnie Stevens

Catching rain in a sieve was easier than confessing sins in the apocalypse; there were too many rain drops, and a new downpour was bound to happen before the day was done. Minnie tried, of course. Her only hope was if the good Lord accepted the divulgence of categories, but he never seemed the type to nitpick a repentant heart, so she gave it a go. She was in a church, after all, and everyone else was asleep.

"For lyin'… especially to Oliver about the state of things," she said quietly, looking up at the cross and the stained glass, both illuminated by moonlight filtering through floor-to-ceiling windows. The place was untouched. Not a corpse in sight. There had even been canned food in the kitchen and bottled water. "For stealin'… I done stole a whole host of things, but I'm pretty sure most of the original owners are dead. So, maybe that don't count. I've had some nasty thoughts, too, I'm sorry to say. Hateful ones. I sure ain't been lovin' my enemies. Some of these people who made it this far, I'd like to strangle myself." She grimaced. "You're gonna have to keep workin' on me with that one."

The sound of the door opening gave Minnie pause. She turned in the pew to see a figure enter, but, due to the dim light, she couldn't quite tell who it was until he spoke.

"Oh, sorry," Walter said. "I couldn't sleep."

"Lookin' for a place to pray?" Minnie waved him over. "Don't be shy. There's room for both of us."

Walter walked forward, still limping slightly. "No… I, um… wasn't looking to pray." He glanced at the cross. "I don't know what I believe about all of that. I mean, I used to believe there wasn't a god. And then, everyone died, and I've had mixed feelings about it. I've prayed, maybe out of desperation. I don't know if we've just been lucky or… if it's something more. But…" He leaned against the end of the pew Minnie occupied. "Anyway, I was just looking for a quiet place to think."

"Well, this'll do it." Minnie gestured vaguely around at the sanctuary.

Walter smiled, but there wasn't any heart behind it. "Thanks, but I don't want to disturb you," he said.

"Nonsense." Minnie patted the bench next to her. "You go on and sit."

Walter obliged, settling into the pew at the very end. Minnie smiled and closed her eyes. She'd yapped her gums long enough, anyway. It was time she had a good listen and sorted out her thoughts. But before long, Walter was fidgeting, and when she cracked an eye, she caught him looking at her like he wanted to say something.

"Sometimes," she said, "we think we want to be alone with our thoughts but what we really want is to talk to somebody about them."

Walter shook his head, his smile a little more genuine. "You're very kind, Minnie. And observant."

"And smart, and creative, and—" She flushed and held up a hand toward the heavens. "—boastful. Sorry 'bout that." That got a chuckle out of the man, and Minnie scooted closer, nudging his arm. "Spill it. I got ears. Might even have some advice."

"There's a lot on my mind," Walter said. "I don't really know where to start."

"Are you worried this hairbrained plan ain't gonna work?" Minnie asked.

There was no point beating around the bush on that one. The plan they'd come up with back in Boston after the lab had burned to the ground was crazy.

Walter plastered on a look of mock shock. "What?" He waved his hand and pshawed. "Finding out where the government kept their top-secret laboratory will be a piece of cake."

"At least you know the name of the place, right?" Minnie asked. "Better than nothin', at least."

Walter sighed. "Barlow Scientific Research Bank." He shook his head. "It could be anywhere."

"It could be at Cheyenne Mountain," Minnie said. "Ain't no use frettin' over matters until you got all the facts."

"I can see why Alex likes you so much," Walter said. "But I'm afraid planning for the worst is in my nature. If it's as you say, if the government really has set up at the Cheyenne Mountain Complex, there's a chance we can find someone who knows where the laboratory is or at least knows how to find it, but…" He licked his lips and looked down as he slowly wrung his hands.

"It's our last shot," Minnie said. "Yeah, I know." That feeling she hated, the one that made her stomach knot and raised goosepimples on her arms and sent a cold streak down her spine, tried to take hold of her. She squeezed her eyes shut and gave her head one good shake. "Nope," she said. "We can't go there. Givin' up before we got all the information wouldn't be losin' hope; that'd be givin' it away."

Walter looked at her as he flattened his palms on his thighs, his trembling hands stabilizing as he rubbed them against his jeans. "We're lucky to have you," he said. "Maybe I did need to talk." He leaned back in the pew and let out a long, slow breath. "Maybe you can chat with Lizzy sometime. I think she needs to talk, too, but… not to me. If my wife were here…" His nerves seemed to be dissipating, replaced with melancholy at the mention of his wife and daughter. When he next spoke, his voice was small. "I haven't been a good father," he said. "But you? You seem to know what you're doing."

Minnie scoffed at that. "That's 'cause you just met me. I ain't sayin' I was always a crap parent, but let me tell you, I made my share of mistakes. Big ones, actually. It took the end of the world for me to finally make 'em right. I hadn't seen my girl in years when I first met Alex. I was bein' bullheaded. Thought I knew best. Thought Lauren should do what I wanted as if I was entitled to see her life go a certain way just 'cause I raised her." Her heart ached at the thought of the time she'd missed, the hurt she'd caused.

"I never would have guessed," Walter said. "You two seem so close."

"We've been closer," Minnie said, thinking back to when Lauren was a preteen, back before Minnie had tightened her grip on her daughter's future. "We love each other, that's for sure, but the baggage ain't gone. We've just agreed to unpack it a little bit at a time, together." She shifted in the pew, laying a gentle hand on Walter's shoulder. "When it comes to your daughter, just keep bein' there for her, keep showin' up. One day, she'll notice you never stopped tryin'."

Walter nodded, the moonlight streaming in through the windows catching on his glistening eyes. She sat with him for a moment longer, until he seemed like he'd be okay on his own, and then she let him be, walking the hall back to the Sunday school classroom she, Alex, Lauren, and Oliver had claimed.

On the way, she passed by the office Azalea and Lizzy had chosen as their temporary sleeping quarters. A short, frightened scream erupted from behind the door, and Minnie's heart leapt within her. She hurried to the door and reached for the doorhandle only to pause at the sound of Azalea's voice inside. Minnie couldn't make out the words, but the tone was sharp. She glanced up and down the hall, confirming she was alone before stepping closer and holding her breath as she listened.

It hadn't been the time or the place to mention to Walter her concerns about his daughter, but she *did* have concerns. That Azalea character set off her bullcrap alarm more often than not; she was the kind of gal who used her smile as a weapon and kind words as a tool. Lizzy, on the other hand, well… Minnie couldn't put her finger on what was wrong with her, but there was *definitely* something off surrounding the way she and Azalea interacted.

Minnie could only make a word or two of their whispers. Something about nightmares and mothers and being patient. She shrugged and backed away, shaking her head at herself. *What did you expect?* She looked up at the ceiling and pursed her lips. *Guess I better add eavesdroppin' to my list, if you're up there listenin'.*

With a sigh, she made her way down the hall to her room. The end of the world was making her paranoid. She chuckled at herself. *Might as well change my name to Nancy Drew.*

* * *

Minnie pinched the bridge of her nose. There were too many cooks in the kitchen, and that was always a recipe for disaster. Alex and Walter had called a meeting first thing after breakfast, and that was the last thing they'd agreed upon. Lauren, Timothy, and Heather all had their own ideas about next steps, too. Minnie was just relieved Candice had opted to stay with Annika and Oliver in another room, and that the girls, Azalea and Lizzy, had so far kept to themselves, watching from the sidelines. She'd not given too much input herself, mostly because getting a word in would require more energy than she currently wished to part with.

"We need you to stay safe. Both of you." Heather gestured between Alex and Walter.

"She's right," Timothy said. "Without you two, this plan to stop DV-10 is futile. No one else can do what you two can do."

"Not to mention," Lauren added, raising her eyebrows at Walter, "that *you* still need your rest."

Walter crossed his arms. "We need to scout the area before we make our next move. Whoever goes should be the person most qualified. No matter who we find at that facility, I'll be able to talk to them. I've made deals and negotiated all my adult life."

Alex shook his head. "We won't need negotiations. General Hunt knows us. That's why one of my people should go. I'm the best person for that job. The general and several of the soldiers would recognize me."

"They'd recognize me, too," Lauren said. "And mom."

"Whoa, now," Minnie said, holding up her hands. "You need someone quick on their feet. I'm good with the kids. I ain't about to go runnin' up and down no mountain. Not today. Not if I don't have to."

"Finally," Heather said, "someone with some sense. We need to play to our strengths."

"We also need to prepare," Timothy said. "What if we get up there and the people you thought were going to be there aren't? You have no idea if this supposed president and his people even made it to Cheyenne Mountain. They all could have died on the way. Or gotten there to find the government had relocated again."

Minnie held up a hand and interjected as soon as she saw that stubborn look cross Alex's face. "C'mon, now," she said. "The man's got a point. You'll all be as old as me and I'll be buried out back before we finish this argument unless y'all start listenin' to each other."

"Fine." Alex sighed but nodded. "You're right, Tim. We don't know, but if President Coleman, General Hunt, Corporal Conner, or any of the others *did* make it, which I believe to be likely, we'll have a better chance at them taking us seriously should I come along. They know who I am. They know I worked for the CDC. And frankly, even if they didn't make it, my job title still gives me more sway than anyone else here."

"That's fair," Walter said. "If we're all honest, I don't think we can argue with that. Alex should go."

Everyone nodded, Heather reluctantly. "Fine, but if he's going, that's two reasons Walter should stay: he's the other person who knows the most about how to stop DV-10 *and* he's still recovering from his injury."

Walter pursed his lips but after a few seconds sighed and shrugged. "Okay," he said. "Point taken. I'll stay."

"And I'll go in his place," Timothy said. His wife closed her eyes for a moment, her entire body sagging, but she didn't object.

"Y'all done fightin' like cats in an alley, as if riskin' life and limb was the last bit o' tuna in the dumpster?" Minnie raised her brows and put her hands on her hips. "I swear, if it makes you lot stayin' back feel any better, maybe some crazies will attack the church while Timothy and Alex are out havin' all the fun."

Walter smirked and shook his head. "She's right," he said. "There's plenty for all of us to do. I guess I've been so used to diving headlong into danger that *not* doing so doesn't seem right anymore."

"I'm sure that hits home for all of us," Minnie said. "Now we've got our next steps, I say let's get it over with." She looked between Alex and Timothy. "What do you two need in order to go scout out the military facility up the mountain?"

"We'll need to detach the truck from the airstream camper and use it to get closer," Timothy said. "I don't want to stop in town, at all. We should try to avoid any settlements, get there without notice, if at all possible."

Alex nodded. "We can take a few days' worth of supplies and two of our hazmat suits, just in case. Some binoculars from the CDC stash in the trailer behind Minnie's RV. And we'll take a couple of radios. The terrain might make the signal spotty, but if we can update you, we will."

"Well, nothin' ever gets done by just sittin' and talkin'," Minnie said, shooing them all into action. As the rest headed out the door, she grabbed Alex by the arm, speaking in a low voice. "You be careful, now, Alex," she said. "The world might need you, but so does Oliver. So do me and Lauren. You got it?"

Alex offered a small smile. "I got it," he said.

She hung back, watching him follow the others outside where they could unhook the airstream and bring supplies inside. The church would act as a temporary base of operations until they found out whether General Hunt and President Coleman had actually made it to Cheyenne Mountain. Despite her outward confidence, Minnie had to calm her twisting stomach at the thought of all that could go wrong.

Two things'll happen in the next couple of days, she thought. *We'll be ridin' high, our plans goin' off without a hitch, or we'll be lost.* She forced herself away from considering the possibility that they'd travelled all that way for nothing. Because if they had, if there was no one at Cheyenne Mountain who could help them, the countdown to the real end for them all would begin.

Chapter 4

Alexander Roman

The closer Alex drove to the city, the more tense his body became. His grip on the steering wheel tightened, and with every glimpse of civilization, he swept his eyes across the landscape to either side of the road, keeping an eye out for trouble. Buildings and trees made his chest tighten; it wasn't so long ago that a group of escaped prisoners had set upon him and his family on a road not terribly unlike the current one.

"It's changed everything, hasn't it?" Timothy spoke for the first time since they'd left the rest of their group behind at the church. "We can't even drive through open countryside without anticipating some sort of disaster."

Alex glanced at him. Timothy looked as tense as Alex felt. "It won't be this way forever."

"I don't know," Timothy said. "For us, maybe it will."

"Maybe." Alex conceded the point. After spending a few weeks cooped up in a cab with Timothy and his wife, he'd learned the man wasn't the kind to forego practicality for wishful thinking. His wife, Heather, balanced him out, adding hope to whatever reality Timothy observed.

Alex had mostly gotten over the bad first impressions Timothy had made weeks ago at New Horizons in Boston, but there were definitely still things about the man which irked him. *Two peas in a pod… isn't that what Minnie would say? That I don't like him because he's too much like me?* He sighed. *Well, we can't both expect the worst. That's asking for things to go wrong.*

"Even if we never get over what we've been through," Alex said, trying his hardest to find the silver lining, "at least our grandkids will grow up better, right?"

"What about Oliver and Annika?" Timothy asked.

"Well… I'm pretty sure they're past the point of no return. They've seen too much." Alex's throat tightened. "And I guess if we don't get this right, our grandkids will be screwed, too."

Timothy swallowed audibly. "Heather would say something about how we don't know the future and how we should hope for the best."

Alex nodded. "Yep. And Minnie would give me some Southern mom advice that I don't quite understand but makes me feel better, anyway." He chuckled, trying to lighten the mood. "Women, am I right? Always proving how much we need them…" A pang shot through him at the thought of his wife, Naomi, but he kept that to himself; Timothy didn't know much about her, just that she'd been lost.

"Ain't that the truth?" Timothy cleared his throat, and Alex thought for sure he caught the man drying his eyes quickly with the collar of his shirt.

"So," Alex said, rolling his shoulders as he purposefully loosened his grip on the steering wheel, "how are we going to find this place?"

"We probably start there." Timothy pointed in the distance to the mountain looming on the left.

"That's a big mountain," Alex said. "The only thing I know about the facility is what I learned on *Stargate SG-1*, and I doubt that's going to be accurate." He caught a questioning look from Timothy out of the corner of his eye. "It's an old television series. My dad was a big fan. I love some of those old sci-fi shows."

"Right. Well," Timothy said, "I say we skirt town as best we can, stay away from anywhere that might still be more populated. Head toward the mountain range, see if we can find anything."

Alex nodded. "Sounds like a plan," he said, "but man, do I miss GPS."

"Well, we made it across half the country with old school maps," Timothy said. "The ones we have are too zoomed out, not specific enough for finding something in a city, but maybe we can find a map of Colorado Springs somewhere, like a library, or something."

"That's not a bad idea," Alex said, "but then we'd have to find a library. Our best bet for *that* would probably be downtown."

"Maybe for the largest one," Timothy said, "but this city is big enough to have a few. Let's keep our eyes peeled. If we have to go downtown, we will, but at that point, we're going to probably run into survivors."

"A last resort, then," Alex said. "I don't want to mess with locals until I have a better idea of what's going on around here."

"Agreed."

Alex followed their plan, taking roads that kept to the outskirts of Colorado Springs while still heading toward Cheyenne Mountain. It took an hour of driving around abandoned residential streets, the eeriness of them making the drive more somber by the minute, before they came across a small concrete library, square and unremarkable, with shriveled flower beds out front.

"It looks abandoned," Alex said as he parked the truck and searched for evidence of people. "Still, I think we should use caution." He patted the gun and holster on his hip. "You ready?"

Timothy nodded, pulling his own gun free as he opened the passenger-side door. Alex grabbed his flashlight from the side pocket of his backpack. The two of them approached the building cautiously, but the doors were unlocked and the inside seemed as abandoned as the streets surrounding the library.

Alex ran a finger along a librarian's desk, leaving a trail in the dust. "Let's take a look around, see what we can find." He looked up, scanning the walls. When he saw nothing immediately helpful, he clicked on his flashlight and explored anyway.

It wasn't long before they found exactly what they were looking for. On a wall in a dark and dusty computer lab was a large, framed, color map of the city. "It's old, but look—" Timothy pointed at the edge of the map. "—I bet this is it."

Alex focused the light just to the side of where Timothy was pointing. Where the city map stopped, there was a dark green area going up into the mountains, labelled as Cheyenne Mountain State Park, but just on the edge, wedged in the mountains, there was an area shaded yellow.

"It's not labeled," Alex said, "but I think you're right. It's clearly something, and it's on the edge of Fort Carson. It makes sense that it would be connected to a military base."

"It's our only lead." Timothy gave Alex a pat on the shoulder. "Let's give it a try."

* * *

When they approached Fort Carson, Alex had halfway expected to run into a military force. Instead, he was met with the same ghost town feel as the rest of southern Colorado Springs. They drove through checkpoints unhindered, coming out on the other side of the base to find Norad Road, which wound up the side of the mountain. But when they reached another security checkpoint closer to Cheyenne Mountain, Alex groaned.

Skeletons that looked picked clean by scavengers dotted the area, the concrete beneath them stained brown with old blood. Tatters of clothing still clung to them in bits and pieces, but most of it was gone, and what was left was unrecognizable. It was the first sign of conflict they'd come across since arriving in Colorado Springs. He'd hoped the city had escaped the most violent impulses of desperate survivors. It was, after all, a city saturated with military men and women and their families.

"That's not a good sign," Alex said.

"We don't know what it means." Timothy leaned forward in his seat, squinting. "It doesn't look recent."

"So whatever the fight was about, it's been won," Alex said.

"They could have died from DV-10," Timothy said. "It might not have been a fight at all."

"I guess we're going to have to find out." Alex rubbed his hands over his face, weighing their options. He glanced at the parking lot to his left. It was full, with only a few spaces empty. "We should park, take our backpacks, and go in on foot. The truck will blend in with the other vehicles in the lot. It'll still be there when we return, but driving ahead will only draw attention to ourselves if anyone is out there."

"Okay, but I don't think we should take the main road." Timothy glanced at the tree cover to the right.

Alex nodded. "And we'll need to suit up, just in case." He nodded to the back seat where they each had a hazmat suit. "I don't want to run into a swarm out here unprepared."

The truck slid into a parking space at the back of the lot overlooking a vista that Alex would have found awe-inspiring under different circumstances. Cheyenne Mountain State Park extended as far as he could see. There was no time to enjoy it, though, and he was soon stuffing himself into a hazmat suit beside Timothy. Once they were both suited up, they took turns spraying each other down with mosquito repellent. They strapped belts around their waists, complete with holsters and guns.

Alex situated his backpack full of supplies. His peripheral vision was hindered by the full-face respirator mask, and he had to turn his shoulders to talk to Timothy. "You mind if I lead the way?"

Timothy gestured for him to go first. "By all means," he said. "I'll keep an eye on our backs."

Alex crossed the lot, and then the road, avoiding the dead. He stepped into the trees, going only a few steps before realizing there was a chain-link fence and a house on the other side. "I say we follow Norad Road," he said, turning toward the mountain and pointing ahead. "Use the trees for cover."

Timothy nodded, and Alex led the way. The road took on a U-shape, and Alex chose to cut across a grassy, rocky area dotted with pines, taking a shortcut and meeting up with the road again on the other side. They kept walking in silence following Norad Road until Alex spotted another, larger parking lot. He cut across rocky land again, Timothy on his heels, both of them keeping low.

As they crossed the lot, Alex noted a few corpses in vehicles, but there was no sign of the living. It was quiet, the only sound the whistling of wind.

"Is that a sub shop?" Timothy asked from behind him.

Alex shushed him and whispered, "Is that really relevant?"

Timothy shrugged. "Just… whenever I think about a top-secret facility built into a mountain, I don't think about finding a sub shop right outside it. I mean, I guess everybody's got to eat."

Alex pursed his lips. "Well, this *is* it," he said, turning back and pointing between two buildings. "You can see the entrance to the north tunnel right there."

"No one is here," Timothy said.

"Maybe…" Alex stood up straighter. "Maybe they're all inside."

"Do we just… go into the tunnel?" Timothy furrowed his brow, his tone skeptical.

Alex shrugged. "I've never gone up to knock on someone's nuclear blast door," he said. "I don't know how this works."

"Let's get closer," Timothy said. "Worst-case scenario, someone pops out and tells us to go away, right?"

"No. Worst-case scenario is someone shoots us dead before asking any questions. The world is crazy right now, and if the only government we have left is in there, the people guarding them might be a little trigger happy," Alex said.

"Use your title," Timothy said. "You said they'd recognize your name, right? And if they didn't, if the people you're looking for aren't here, your job would give you an in."

"It's likely." Alex took a deep breath. "Okay, I'll go, but you stay here. If there's trouble, run. Get away from here, okay? I can take care of myself."

Timothy nodded and ducked low. "If you say so. Just be careful. I don't want to go back and tell your son that you got shot."

"I don't want that either." Alex rolled his shoulders, gathering up a little courage.

He left his backpack behind and jogged from the edge of the lot to the space between the two buildings and pressed up against the wall, trying to make himself look small despite his hazmat suit. There was a wide-open space, no cover, from there to the tunnel entrance, and the tunnel itself was dark.

A scuff sounded, startling him, but when he looked back at the lot, he saw no one, not even Timothy. Heart racing, palms sweating, he took a risk as he stepped past the building and toward the tunnel.

Alex slipped his respirator mask upward to sit on the top of his head. He needed his voice to be clear and to go far. "My name is Alexander Roman," he said, his voice echoing off the mountain rising sharply above the tunnel entrance.

White lettering etched in the rust-red metal archway stuck into the side of the mountain read 'Cheyenne Mountain Complex.' Chain-linked fences with barbed wire spirals on top lined the road leading up to the tunnel. He imagined how intimidating it would have been with armed guards everywhere.

"I worked for the CDC," he shouted. "I'm here to help. Is anyone here?" He walked forward slowly, his nitrile-gloved hands raised high, trying his best not to look like a threat.

And then a figure bled out of the darkness of the tunnel, stepping out into the daylight. At first, Alex was relieved, but then his chest tightened as he took in the man's appearance. He wore plaid and jeans and cowboy boots, and he carried a hunting rifle. He did have a military-grade weapon slung on his back, its muzzle sticking up over one shoulder, but his beer gut and lazy stride didn't speak of someone trained in the military. A woman and three other men followed the first out of the tunnel and into the light.

Alex swallowed hard, keeping his hands up, though they trembled slightly. He was completely exposed. *What was I thinking? Who are these people?*

"You're not from around here, are you?" the woman said, brandishing her handgun.

"No," Alex said. There was no point in lying about that. "I'm not."

"What are you doing up here, then?" The man in plaid narrowed his eyes at Alex.

A layer of sweat broke out across Alex's forehead, and his stomach lurched. His instincts told him to bend the truth. "I… well, I thought maybe the military could help me, and when I didn't find anyone in Fort Carson, I thought maybe someone would be here. Like I said, I'm from the CDC. I'm trying to help stop this disease that's killing everyone."

The woman worked her jaw back and forth and leaned closer to the man who'd come out first. "Might be useful, Mark."

"I don't think so, Carrie," Mark said. He snapped his head back to Alex. "No one gets in just by walking up and making claims about who they are. You won't find a soldier in sight. Not anymore. The disease took most of them out, and we had bigger numbers."

Alex swallowed hard, his mind racing. He needed more information, but he didn't want to push. Mark didn't seem in the mood for a nice conversation. But, he had to try to get more out of him, and then he and Timothy needed to get the hell out of there.

"And who are you, exactly?" Alex asked, keeping his tone curious and light. "I mean, you wouldn't happen to need someone like me, would you? I'm sure it's safe in there."

"You're not listening," Mark said.

And then another woman ran out of the tunnel, waving a walkie-talkie in the air. "We found another one in the lot!" she shouted. "He's not alone! He's not alone!"

And just like that, Alex had five guns aimed at his chest.

Chapter 5

Alexander Roman

"Don't shoot!" Alex couldn't keep the pleading from his voice and hoped it didn't come across as weakness.

He held his gloved hands higher, spread out his fingers, and pushed down the rising panic working to get the best of him. His gun rested uselessly in its holster at his hip. He'd not pulled it, thinking doing so might have gotten him killed before he could make introductions. But he was questioning that line of reasoning with five guns aimed directly at him. His feet itched to run, and adrenaline in the face of having no defense made every molecule of his body writhe with the urge to flee. His mind fought against the natural flight response, recognizing it for what it was. He wasn't a runner, and besides that, running would just get him and Timothy killed. The fact that they had found Timothy meant there could be even more strangers with guns waiting to pounce.

"We don't want trouble," he said, his hazmat suit rustling in a slight breeze.

Behind him, Timothy shouted. "Let me go! We didn't do anything wrong."

Alex carefully, slowly backed up a few steps and turned so he could see Mark, Carrie, and the unnamed four people accompanying them on his left; to his right, a sixth stranger approached with Timothy roughly in hand. The newcomer had zip-tied Timothy's hands and removed his respirator mask. He threw the younger man to the ground. Timothy hit hard, grunted, and rolled, wincing as he got to his knees. The concrete had skinned his cheekbone. He didn't have his backpack, and neither did his captor.

Maybe that means he hid our supplies before they found him, Alex thought.

"If you aren't looking for trouble," Mark said snidely, "then what exactly are you looking for?"

"Look," Alex said, "we wanted to come someplace where we could be of use. That's all. We thought we'd find the government here. It *is* a government facility. Who else is going to be working on a way to fix all of this?"

Mark scoffed. "Well, that was your first mistake. This place doesn't belong to *them* anymore."

"Them, who?" Timothy struggled to his feet.

"Elitists." Carrie spat on the ground, and the rest of her people nodded in agreement.

"Those greedy bastards," Mark said. "They thought they were so smart, thought they could get away with saving themselves and letting the everyday man rot. Well, this disease didn't play favorites."

He grinned and cocked his head to one side as his fellows encouraged him on with affirmations. Alex exchanged a look with Timothy, and he felt his insides curdle at the thought of his friends who'd been headed to Cheyenne Mountain weeks prior.

"Their mistake was adding onto the complex," Mark continued. "They made an underground paradise for the rich — the politicians, the doctors, the lazy 'investors and entrepreneurs' who just inherited their wealth." He scowled at having to name that last group, throwing up air quotes to reinforce exactly what he thought of those kinds of investors and entrepreneurs. "But they used regular Joes, just like me to build it." He laughed. "As if some NDA piece of paper was going to stop us from spreading the word about a safe place when crap hit the fan."

"So…" Alex swallowed hard and tried to sound impressed. "… you guys managed to overcome a military presence? That must have been some fight."

Carrie shrugged. "We had a few things going for us, mainly the fact that this place wasn't fully manned when things went south, and the disease got in before we did."

A man who'd remained silent up to that point, a man who was clearly in tip-top shape, spoke up. "And not every soldier was happy to hear our orders were to protect the politicians and let women and children die on our doorstep. They made something of a hotel in that mountain — a swimming area, restaurants, apartments with screens in the windows to display whatever scenery you'd want — and the only criteria for getting a spot was money." He nearly growled, and his eyes darkened. "The second they ordered me to turn away my sister and her kids, I was done. I didn't sign up to betray my family. I signed up to protect them."

Mark nodded. "We got in with suits like what you're wearing now. Cleared it out, sanitized it. The new living quarters were still mostly untouched. And we did it fast, before that new guy claiming to be the president came to town." A collective chuckle rose all around. "What a joke. As if we're just going to roll over and give up our newfound freedom just because some Washington nobody thinks he has a right to rule."

Alex's heart leapt with hope but immediately lodged in his throat. His gut told him to hide the fact that he knew President Coleman. He forced a bit of nervous laughter. "A new president, huh? Did he give you any trouble?" Silently, Alex prayed the question was enough to learn if his friends had been killed in a conflict.

"Nah," Mark said. "We already held the mountain, and if they'd wanted to take it from us, they'd be turning the whole town against them just for trying."

Timothy cleared his throat. "So you've got the support of Colorado Springs, even though they don't get to come inside? Seems lucky."

Mark shrugged. "Not really. There's a system in place. A raffle. But the people that get inside, they're not going to be of the same breed as those we took this place from. We don't want politicians or smooth-talking executives. The rest of the world can worry about preserving that lot. We want to make sure the culture of the blue-collar worker, the soldier who's in it for the people and not the power, the little guy running a mom-and-pop business, the nurses who're used to the grind — we want those kinds of people. And it seems so does what's left of Colorado Springs."

"Well," Alex said, "I can assure you, I'm just a regular guy. So is Timothy."

"It's admirable," Timothy added, "what you're doing here. Without the people who know how to work hard and long, without the people who understand sacrifice, we might as well kiss the world as we knew it goodbye, forever."

Mark worked his jaw back and forth. "Yeah, well, that was your second mistake. The world as we knew it is already long gone. You said you want to be of use, that you want to find a way to fix this." He shook his head. "There's no fixing it. There's only accepting it and trying to find a way to live with a new normal. And here, that means building a safe community inside Cheyenne Mountain."

"And how are you doing that?" Timothy asked. "You can't cut yourself off from everyone. Eventually, you'll run out of supplies."

"We're building a second community in Colorado Springs, one that'll work to supply this one. One where the new American dream is to get inside this mountain, and to do it, you've just got to work hard and contribute." Mark smirked. "It's more American than these good United States have been for a long time. The process starts at The Broadmoor World Arena."

"Okay," Alex said. "Then we'll go there. How about that?"

Mark pursed his lips. "How do I know you are who you say you are?" he asked. "How do I know there aren't dozens of people waiting to try and infiltrate this place?"

"All I've got is my word," Alex said. "It's just me and him. We didn't bring anyone else."

"We should take their weapons," Carrie said. "Always need more of them."

"Agreed," the soldier said, and the rest voiced their support.

Timothy's expression screwed up in defiance and outrage, but Alex shook his head once and firmly. "That's fine," Alex said, hoping that Timothy followed his lead. It would make the trek back to the church riskier, but they had more weapons there. It was a small price to pay if it meant getting off that mountain alive.

Timothy let out a slow breath. "Fine," he said. "But then you'll let us go?"

Mark nodded. "I think that's a fair deal. Spread the word if you come across anyone else new to town. We don't want visitors."

"Fair enough." Alex nodded at his weapon. "You want to take this off me, or should I hand it to you?"

"Chad," Mark said to the man who'd found Timothy in the lot, "relieve them of their weapons, please and thank you."

Chad did as he was asked. Alex's belt lightened significantly as his gun was removed, and a fresh desire to get back to the truck and to the safety of the church outside of town settled heavy in its place.

"I'd like my respirator mask back, though," Timothy said, nodding at his which was hanging from Chad's arm. "I don't think that's too much to ask."

"You can have it back," Mark said, nodding at Chad who then handed the respirator to Timothy. "The swarms… they're getting bigger. We wouldn't wish a death like that on anyone."

Timothy slipped his full-face respirator mask back on. "You mind telling us where this arena is? It's not like we can Google it."

Mark smirked. "Sure thing," he said. "It's northeast of here. Go out past Fort Carson, go north on 115, and then hang a right on Cheyenne Meadows. You'll run right into it, and you'll know it when you see it. These days, it's hard to miss."

"We should be going, then." Alex lowered his hands, re-situated his own mask, and backed up, Timothy following suit. Neither of them turned their backs until they were clear of the group by several yards. "The supplies?" Alex whispered once out of earshot.

"Under a black Subaru," Timothy said. "Follow me. We'll grab them and then pick up the pace back to the truck."

After retrieving their supplies, Alex led with a faster pace than when they'd approached. Just because they hadn't seen people watching when they'd first pulled up didn't mean no one had been there. By the time he reached the truck, he was damp with sweat beneath his suit. He wanted to rip off his gear, but the first thing he did was check that the doors were still locked. Timothy, however, was almost out of his suit by the time Alex had begun taking his off.

"So, your friends," Timothy said, "it sounds like they're still alive."

Alex nodded. "Alive, maybe. But this is not the situation I was hoping for. Even finding a government we didn't know and couldn't trust would have been better than this."

"Maybe they just had to relocate," Timothy said. "Maybe we can still find the information we need."

"If they're still in town," Alex said. "Mark seemed to indicate those left in town weren't fans of the so-called elitist government."

"You think they ran your friends out of town?" Timothy asked.

"I have no idea." Alex finished stripping off his gear and threw everything into the back seat of the small cab. He slid into the driver's seat as Timothy slid into the passenger seat next to him. "I don't think we'll find them at that arena, though."

"Maybe not," Timothy said, "but if there are people there, maybe someone there knows where to find your friends."

Alex's stomach felt full of rocks. "We'll have to tread lightly. From the sound of things, we don't want to openly support President Coleman."

"Should we go there now?" Timothy asked.

Alex turned the key, the engine roaring to life. He backed out of his space. "My first thought is to go back to the church, update everyone, and then come up with a plan."

Timothy shook his head. "We're coming back with nothing except bad news. We should at least stop by the arena, see what's going on there. Our people know we're likely to be gone for a couple of days. They won't worry, and they should be safe." He looked over his shoulder out the back window. "Plus, if they have someone following us or if they have someone at the arena reporting back to them, it won't look good if we don't show up."

"I hadn't thought of that," Alex said. "You make a valid point."

"Well, I learned a few things back in Boston. Things like crazy people like to have complete control over what they've claimed as their territory. I wouldn't put it past those guys at the complex to try and keep tabs on us. I don't want to lead them back to the church, to our families." Timothy's tone was grim, full of regret. "I've done that before," he said. "I've led the wrong people straight to the people I love. It's a mistake I'll never make again."

Alex felt the weight of his warning. "So, when we do go back, we need to make sure we're not followed." He shook his head. "I wouldn't have thought of that, either."

"Well, from the sounds of it, you were constantly on the road or trying to be," Timothy said. "That's different from choosing to hunker down in one spot, to trying to make a place more permanent. I guess you and I just learned a few different tricks."

"Let's hope so," Alex said. "Maybe if we put our heads together, we can actually do this thing."

"I hope so," Timothy said. "For our families."

"For our families," Alex agreed. "So, next stop: Broadmoor World Arena. Let's hope we find some answers there."

Chapter 6

Zara Williams

Zara sat cross-legged on the floor of the church's lobby, a rifle at her knees and a book in hand, a view of the parking lot stretching beyond the tall, narrow window just in front of her. There was one entrance to the lot, and it was Zara's turn to keep an eye on it. She had the blinds pulled down to provide cover but the slits open just slightly. There was little chance anyone from the road would notice her behind the blinds. The church sat too far off the road, and their vehicles were parked behind the building. It was a good place to lay low, but if someone *did* turn into their lot, she'd see them and sound the alarm.

She looked up from her book when the shuffle of shoes on carpet sounded down the hall. "Hey, Minnie," she said.

"Afternoon," Minnie said, her southern drawl making Zara smile. "I reckon it's about my time to keep watch."

"Really?" Zara got to her feet, realizing how stiff she'd gotten from sitting in one spot for too long. "I guess this book made the time pass." She bent down and picked up the rifle.

Minnie grabbed a nearby lobby chair and scooted it close to the window. "I can't be sittin' on the floor like that. My old bones would throw a fit." The older woman positioned the chair where Zara had been sitting. "Whatcha readin'?"

"I found it in that corner library." She nodded down the hall. "It was weird, finding it there. I mean, I'd heard of C. S. Lewis, but I'd never heard of this book. Most of the books in the library here are theology and philosophy books." She wrinkled her nose.

"Philosophers, bless their hearts. I do think I prefer my cookbooks." Minnie nodded at the book in Zara's hands. "But that looks a bit more lively."

Zara showed her the cover. "Well, it was nice, doing something normal. I haven't sat down to read a book in forever." She glanced at the rifle; it and the tension in her shoulders made her amend her statement. "I mean, it was *almost* normal."

Minnie frowned, squinting at the book and reading the title. "*Out of the Silent Planet.* Space Trilogy? Huh." She sat in the chair, settling back into it as if trying to find the most comfortable position. "That's the gentleman that wrote Chronicles of Narnia, right?"

Zara nodded. "Yeah, but this one isn't for kids." She shrugged. "It's a good read."

"I ain't one for sittin' and readin'," Minnie said. "I used to like to bake in my free time. Travel in my RV. Tend to Samson. Watch old television shows."

Zara lit up. "I love old TV. Everything from Happy Days to Star Trek to those old, cheesy superhero shows."

"A kid your age?" Minnie raised her eyebrows in surprise. "Well, dy-no-mite! We might have more in common than I thought."

Zara laughed. "J.J. from Good Times," she said, nodding. "Aired in the 70s. That's a *really* old one."

"You know your stuff," Minnie said. "I'm impressed."

"It was a hobby, sort of," Zara said, her grin fading into a sad smile. "You know, before all of this. I guess… I wonder if those old sitcoms are just… lost."

"Now don't let happy memories become dark clouds, not when they're tryin' so hard to stay fluffy," Minnie said.

Zara shrugged and held out the rifle for Minnie, who took it, checked the safety, and rested it across the arms of her chair, muzzle facing away from Zara, at the wall. "Things just won't stop changing. The second I think I have things figured out, it turns out I don't."

Minnie sighed and made a motion with her hand, encouraging Zara to go on. "Alright, little lady. Lay it out for me. Get your thoughts out in the air where you can take a good look, see which ones are for keepin' and which ones need rearranged and organized."

"I don't want to bother you," Zara said hesitantly, though something about the woman made Zara feel safe, like there was a grandmotherly circle of protection around Minnie's person in which anyone could divulge their secrets and their thoughts without judgment or backlash.

"Well, it's no bother." Minnie looked at her expectantly.

"It's just…" Zara bit her lower lip. Reading had allowed her mind to rest, but the second she'd put the book down, all the what-ifs and the need to figure out solutions to her problems had resurfaced. A myriad of emotions had plagued her day in and day out, but everyone already had so much to deal with that she'd kept it all buried.

"I promise I don't bite," Minnie said, prodding her gently.

Zara took a deep breath, and then it all came pouring out. "Well, there's my cousin, Annika," she said. "She's my only remaining family, and I expected her to need me, you know? I fought so hard to get back to her, but when I got here, it was like… well, maybe she forgot about me. I mean, I'm glad she's bonding with people, that she's got people to look out for her, but…" Zara paused, wincing. "It's just selfish, I guess. I thought she needed me, but maybe I needed her, and now we're together, but not really, and I'm sad, but I don't know why because she's happy, and shouldn't that be enough?" Running out of breath, Zara paused to catch it.

"That's a lot to—" Minnie started, but Zara's mind was moving too fast, and the woman *had* told her to lay it *all* out.

"That's not it," she said. "Lizzy won't speak to me. She was my best friend. I thought she was dead. I thought the last thing I'd ever said to her, that last terrible thing when I threw away our friendship, would be the end of it forever. And now that I have the chance to make it right, I can't. I don't blame her, either. But I miss her."

This time Minnie quirked an eyebrow. "Anything else?"

"Walter's got his family back," Zara said, leaning against the wall next to the window, her shoulders sagging. "Kai likes me, but he doesn't need me. And I guess that's it. That's what's bothering me." Her voice trembled, and she fought back tears. "No one needs me. Not anymore. Not really."

"Well, that's a load of crap," Minnie said.

Zara frowned and snapped her head up to look at the woman. "What?"

"You heard me," she said, her voice firm but not unkind. "We all need each other these days. It's true even for your friend, Lizzy. It's especially true for that little girl, Annika. But guess what, sweetheart? The person who needs you most, the person who can't survive without your love and attention? That person is *you*."

Zara blinked. "Me? I can't be my own friend."

"And why not?" Minnie asked. "What do we do for our friends? We love 'em. We take care of 'em. We accept 'em despite their flaws and encourage 'em to be better. Human beings are so good at bein' their own worst enemy. Well, I say it's about time we start bein' our own best friends."

"Okay, I get what you're saying," Zara said, "but that doesn't fix my problems."

"Be kind to yourself," Minnie said gently, "and maybe you'll find enough energy to work through all that. Fightin' yourself, tearin' yourself down… that's hard work. It's exhausting. You'll be surprised at what you can do, what you can *see* about life, about others, when you invest in a little self-worth."

"So, like… that whole 'it starts with me' mantra," Zara said, shaking her head. "Fake it 'till you make it? All that sort of cheesy, self-help stuff?"

"Look," Minnie said, "I can tell you all day long that your cousin loves you to the moon, that she talks about you when you're not around, that I heard her tell Candice the three of you girls should have a sleepover. I could tell you how I've noticed that boy Kai always askin' your opinion because he values it. I could talk about how Walter thinks of you like a second daughter, how it's clear to everyone that you've got our backs. I could remind you that you pull your weight around here, and we all know it." She shook her head. "I could talk forever, but until you start talkin' to yourself, not one word will stick. Might as well hold yourself together with wax. The minute it starts to get hot, you'll just melt."

Zara mulled over Minnie's words. "I've just made so many mistakes," she whispered.

"So you're not perfect. That doesn't define you." Minnie leaned forward and squeezed her arm softly. "Thank the good Lord none of us are defined by our mistakes."

"You're really good at this," Zara said. "You're like a real-life Yoda. Except Southern."

"And better lookin'," Minnie added.

Zara chuckled, her sadness fading a bit. "Definitely."

"You go on, now," Minnie said. "Go grab yourself somethin' to eat."

"Thanks, Minnie." Zara stepped forward and leaned over, giving the woman a light hug. "I mean it. Thank you."

Minnie beamed up at her as she pulled away. "Well, I'll be! Aren't you a sweetheart. Anytime, Zara. Anytime at all."

She left Minnie to watch the lot, heading through the sanctuary which was a shortcut to the other side of the building where the kitchen was. Sunlight poured through the stained-glass windows, casting bright colors over the room, the spectrum of the rainbow displayed in patches and patterns, touching her as she walked, warming her skin, lifting her spirits. Her focus shifted from what was happening *to her* to what she could do about it.

Zara paused and stood for a moment in the wide-open space. It was quiet there, serene. She glanced at the door but didn't move toward it. She'd allowed herself to read, but only when she was on guard duty, as if dedicating time to herself and her desires was a waste of time. *Maybe it's okay to take a minute to myself, to relax, just this once.*

Zara settled into a pew, cracked open her book, and let herself be at peace.

* * *

Waking refreshed from a nap was just as much a novelty as reading a book had been. Zara slowly blinked her eyes open, rubbing her bleary eyes. The book was wedged between her hip and the pew. She lay still, planning to allow her brain get back to work at its own leisure.

And then Lizzy's face peeked over the back of the pew, looking down at her. "Are you finally awake?"

Zara gasped and nearly fell to the ground. "Geez, Liz! You about gave me a heart attack." She sat up, looking around. "Where's Azalea?"

"Around," Lizzy said. "Not here."

Zara quirked an eyebrow. Lizzy hadn't been more than a few inches from Azalea since she'd returned. It was like the two of them were joined at the hip.

"I know you don't like her," Lizzy said.

"What? No, I just…" Zara avoided eye contact. Lizzy could always tell when she was lying, keeping things from her. Denying the truth had driven a wedge between them in the past, made Lizzy start keeping things from her.

Lizzy pursed her lips. "You don't have to like her, Zee."

Zara startled at the use of her old nickname. It was the first time she'd heard it in weeks, and Lizzy had only used it once, when they'd first met again back in Boston. The sound of it made tears spring to her eyes. She smiled. "If you like her, maybe I'll learn to like her."

"Maybe." Lizzy sat back, her body language cold and subdued. But she was talking to Zara, and that was progress.

Don't push it, Zara thought. Be cool.

She wanted so desperately for Lizzy to forgive her, but Minnie had been right. Zara couldn't control anything but her own actions, her own thoughts. She focused on that.

"So, how's it going?" Zara asked.

Lizzy shrugged. "Fine."

Zara frowned. *If she doesn't want to be here, then what is she doing?* She waited a few more moments and then noticed Lizzy's eyes flick to the front right corner of the sanctuary. Zara followed her gaze to find the door barely cracked, a sliver of Azalea's face visible. The young woman's eyes widened, and the door shut.

"You're here because she asked you to be." Zara stood up and backed away from Lizzy, trying to keep her tone calm. "What does she want?"

Lizzy narrowed her eyes. "What do *you* think she wants?"

"What kind of answer is that?" Zara crossed her arms. "Look, I don't know what you've been through. I'd like to know. I'd like to be there for you. But one thing I do know is that I've never seen you follow someone around like a puppy dog, begging for approval. There's something about her, Liz, something that makes me worried for you."

"You don't know anything about her." Lizzy's voice was ice. "And you're right. You don't know what I've been through or how Azalea has helped me." She stood up. "You know what she wanted? For me to talk to you, to mend our friendship. She's listening through the door because she's a better friend than you ever were. She makes me feel safe, Zara, because I know she'll forgive me if I need her to, unlike you. I made one mistake. I hid that cell phone because I was trying to protect my father, and you threw away *years* of friendship over it."

Zara's anger and frustration with Azalea was squashed at those words, replaced by a pang of regret. "I know," she said, "but I didn't mean it."

"Didn't you?" Lizzy asked. "Where did you go after that argument?"

Heat flooded Zara's cheeks. She looked down at her feet and closed her eyes. "I… left the compound. I thought I could make it back to Boston on my own."

"That's how they got in." Lizzy wasn't asking a question.

"How did you know?" Zara swallowed hard.

"That's what you're worried about?" Lizzy's voice raised an octave. "I would have never been taken if it weren't for you."

"Liz, I'm sorry," Zara said, stepping forward, her body crumpling in on itself as tears sprung to her eyes. "I'm so, so sorry."

Lizzy held up a hand, signaling for Zara to stay back. "No. You know what? I can't do this." She stepped out into the aisle and headed for the door, pausing and looking back at Zara. "You know what's funny? I don't regret it. What happened, it opened my eyes. It made me stronger. It gave me a new family, one that will never turn their backs on me. They—"

"Elizabeth." The door in the corner of the sanctuary opened, and Azalea stepped through, Lizzy's name spoken like a command. "That's enough."

Lizzy turned to Azalea, and without a word, hurried to her side. She whispered something, her body language, the movement of her lips indicating an apology. And then she rushed out of the sanctuary leaving Azalea still standing there.

Zara frowned, her shame interrupted by confusion, both at what Lizzy had said and Azalea's reaction to it. "Who do you think you are, ordering her around like that? And who is *they*?"

Azalea smiled at her. "Lizzy and I formed a bond with some of the other women who'd been trafficked. They do feel like family."

"I… guess that makes sense." Zara hugged her middle. "That doesn't answer my first question."

"Lizzy can get out of control sometimes," Azalea said. "She gets angry, and I seem to be the only person who can stop her from taking things too far."

Zara shook her head. "That doesn't sound like Liz."

"Maybe she's not the same person you once knew," Azalea said. "Maybe she needs friends who will accept where she is right now."

Everything Azalea said was logical; it was put together, wrapped up with a bow, able to explain away the feelings that something wasn't right. But those feelings wouldn't go away. They only intensified.

"Liz is like a sister to me," Zara said. "Of course I accept her, but… even if a person changes, they don't lose *every* part of themselves. The Liz I love, the core of who she's always been, is still in there."

"Maybe," Azalea said, stepping forward, her tone even and calm. "But you can either help or hinder her healing. Who she is on the other side of that is up to her, isn't it?"

"Yes," Zara said. "Up to *her*, not you."

Azalea chuckled condescendingly, as if Zara were a child who'd said something ridiculous. "Of course. But she trusts me. She loves me. We share a very strong bond. I'm the only one capable of truly being there for her, and if you loved her as much as you say you do, you'd support me as I do my best to enable her healing."

"You're not the only one capable of that," Zara said. "Her father and I—"

"Betrayed her," Azalea said harshly. "Moved on without her. And before that, you played tug of war with her emotions, tried to make her choose sides. You both lied to her, devalued her opinions, and took advantage of her kindness."

Zara shook her head and swiped away the tears rolling down her cheeks. But she didn't say anything. How could she? Azalea wasn't wrong.

"You're jealous. That's why you don't like me," Azalea said softly, stepping even closer.

Am I? Zara looked up at Azalea, but she still couldn't bring herself to say anything.

"I tried today to initiate a healing between you and Elizabeth, and you screwed that up," Azalea said. "But if you trust me—" She stepped close enough to put her hand on Zara's arm. "—maybe I can help you rectify that."

Her touch sent a shudder down Zara's spine. What is wrong with me? She's trying to help… isn't she?

"How?" Zara asked, her voice catching.

"I'll keep talking to Elizabeth," Azalea said, "but I'm going to need you to let go of her completely. If she wants to come back, to be your friend, she will when she's ready. Trust me, Zara. Live your life. Work on yourself. Leave Elizabeth to me. I promise, I won't let her throw away important relationships."

Part of Zara rejected that idea. How could she give up on Lizzy? Not to mention, she wasn't sure she could believe a word that came out of Azalea's mouth. But another part kept hearing the truth in Azalea's words, how she'd hurt her best friend so badly. And she *was* trying to focus on herself, on her own perspectives. Wasn't that how she would become a better person? A better friend?

She nodded, unable to voice an agreement as she fought against the guilt and pain of all her regrets. She combated the negative self-talk the best she could, as Minnie had suggested. *I'm not that angry person anymore, that person who said those things to Lizzy, but she needs time to see that.*

"Good." Azalea patted her arm, turned, and followed after Lizzy.

Zara plopped back down on the pew, reassuring herself everything would be fine, that in time, she'd get her friend back. She sat there for a while, thinking over the two very different conversations she'd had that day, before the doors behind her opened, and she turned to see Walter coming down the center aisle of the sanctuary.

"Hey," he said. "What are you doing in here?"

"Recovering from a conversation with Azalea," Zara said.

He joined her, sliding into her pew. "I had a conversation with Lizzy this morning that left me feeling sort of the same way," he said.

Zara quirked an eyebrow and tilted her head at him. "That's how it started," she said. "I woke up from a nap, and Lizzy was here. I just happened to spot Azalea halfway through our conversation. She came out, Lizzy left, and she told me to trust her with Lizzy, as if she was Lizzy's keeper."

"Do you think Azalea was eavesdropping when Lizzy talked to me this morning?" Walter asked.

Zara shrugged. "I wouldn't be surprised."

"Does she… make you uncomfortable?" Walter winced as he said it.

Zara nodded. "Yeah, and I have no idea why exactly. She told me maybe I was jealous, and honestly, maybe I am. But, if it's not just me…" She took a deep breath. "Maybe she *is* throwing shady vibes."

"Or maybe we *are* jealous." Walter sat back in his seat. "I mean, she was there for Lizzy after we… after we…" He didn't seem able to continue.

"I know," Zara said. "I'm having a hard time trusting myself right now, too. I've been feeling a little lost after the lab burned down, you know?"

Walter nodded. "Like after all of that stuff we survived, our bad luck just followed us home?"

"And it'll follow us out here, too?" Zara asked.

"Yeah."

Zara and Walter fell silent for a long while, just sitting in the sanctuary as the light through the stained-glass windows shifted slowly.

Zara finally broke the silence. "That's silly. We're not cursed, Walter. It's the end of the world as we knew it. No one is having *good* luck, right?"

Walter nodded. "In fact, you could say our survival *is* good luck."

"Exactly." Zara nudged him a little with her elbow. "It's going to be fine," she said. "Lizzy will be fine. Years from now, this will all be stories around a campfire."

"We'll all be together again in Boston," Walter said.

"And there'll be no more swarms, no more DV-10," Zara leaned back and tried to imagine it, tried to tell herself the nightmare would one day end; the problem was, all the positive words, the hopeful thinking — they were as hollow as the sound of Azalea's promises. She didn't really believe a word of either.

Chapter 7

Alexander Roman

"I think we found it." Alex stopped weaving through the debris where the evidence of chaos gave way abruptly to cleared pavement just a few yards ahead. The road behind was littered with abandoned vehicles left at odd angles. "If we go any further, we'll be sitting ducks. It's wide-open space." Alex couldn't help but notice a dozen hiding places; there was plenty of cover surrounding the wide swath of empty pavement between them and a fortification which lay on the other side of the highway. "I was hoping we could sneak up, take a look, but…"

"It doesn't seem like they want anyone to get too close without being noticed," Timothy said. "Maybe we should sit tight and see if anyone comes or goes."

Alex put the truck in park and leaned back, threading his fingers through his hair and resting his hands on his head, trying to think through their next move. Just past the intersection, a wall made of crushed cars rose to the same height as the streetlights. To the far right, a crane sat still in the distance, near the place the wall curved away from the road. A break in the wall was centered with the intersection, and metal barricades blocked an entrance. Beyond that, a large, high-end, hexagonal deer stand had been erected as a guard tower of sorts. Alex's suspicions were confirmed when he noted movement behind one of the rectangular, horizontal windows which was one of a string that seemed to circle the structure. The words "For the People" were spray painted on the wall to the left of the entrance, and to the right, the message read, "Workers and Families Welcome."

"Do you think they've seen us?" Alex asked, pointing at the structure beyond the scrap-metal wall.

As if in answer to his question, the door to the deer stand opened, and a man rushed down the steps.

"It looks like we've been spotted," Timothy said, leaning forward, frowning. "What is he doing?"

The man hurriedly opened a gate in the barricade, and his gaze fell in their direction. At first, Alex had hoped he was welcoming them in, but his expression definitely didn't exude friendliness. The man looked over his shoulder, back into the parking lot beyond the wall and jumped back a few paces. Alex's stomach dropped as four figures on dirt bikes zoomed past the guard before he closed the gates again. They sped straight for Alex and Timothy.

"Crap!" A shot of adrenaline launched Alex's heart into his throat.

"Back up!" Timothy shouted.

"I'm trying," Alex shouted back as he put the truck in reverse.

But it was impossible to quickly escape while driving backward through the maze of vehicles. The dirt bikes overtook him easily. The second he spotted one of them stop and pull an assault rifle off his back, Alex slammed on the brakes.

"What are you doing?" Timothy twisted in his seat, panic written on his face as his eyes flitted from one rider to the next.

"We can't outrun them, not like this. There's no space to turn around." Blood pulsed through Alex's ears, making it harder to think.

Timothy balked. "So, we're not even going to try?"

Alex shook his head. "No, this is the best way. They look like shoot first kind of people," he said. "Put your hands in plain view. Let's give them a reason to ask us a question." Alex rolled down his windows and slowly stuck his empty hands outside. Then, he shouted as loudly as possible. "We're not here to cause trouble!"

One of the riders took off his helmet and tucked it under one arm. By that time, he was the only one of his group who'd not aimed a weapon their way. "You with the military?"

"No," Alex said. "We're just travelers looking for somewhere safe. We went up the mountain first. Mark told us where to find you." He hoped the name drop would gain him a modicum of trust, but the stranger's expression didn't soften.

"If Mark sent you, why didn't you approach the wall? You got something to hide?"

Alex shook his head. "Of course not."

"Then why'd you try to run?"

Alex snorted. "A bunch of guys on dirt bikes with rifles were coming after us."

"Didn't you see the sign?" He pointed over his shoulder to the welcome message. "You stopped and sat here, like you were spying, for ten minutes straight. If Mark told you who we were, what was the problem?"

Alex exchanged a look with Timothy and then shouted out the window. "We've run into people who say one thing and mean the other," he said. "Can a man not get ten minutes to think anymore?"

The man pursed his lips and then worked his jaw back and forth. "You got any weapons?"

"We don't," Alex said, his hands spread wide outside his window.

"All right," the stranger said. "Go on and get out of the truck. Put your hands up, flat on the vehicle. We'll pat you down. If you're good to go, then we can talk."

"You sure about this?" Timothy whispered. "What about the truck? We need it."

"We don't have a choice," Alex said just as softly. "There are four of them, all armed. Hopefully, they won't steal our stuff."

"I don't feel great about this," Timothy grumbled.

"Just do as they say for now. We'll figure it out as we go." Alex slowly opened his door from the outside and stepped onto the pavement. He left the door open, turned toward the truck, and grasped the edge of the truck bed, waiting. On the other side of the truck, Timothy did the same. Alex kept an eye on what was going on behind Timothy, the same way he hoped Timothy was watching his back.

It didn't take long for two of the strangers to pat both Alex and Timothy down, finding nothing. They turned off the truck, pocketed the keys, and searched the vehicle but didn't take any of their supplies. Then, the four of them converged at some distance from Alex and Timothy to speak in hushed tones.

"What are we going to do?" Timothy asked from the other side of the truck. Neither of them had taken their hands off the edge of the truck bed, and they still faced each other.

Alex shook his head. "I don't know, but I'm not sure we should go inside." He nodded just slightly at the gate and wall so as to not draw attention.

"Well, I'm positive about that," Timothy said, whispering. "We still need to find your contacts. This is a big city, and we know they're not here."

"Agreed." Alex spoke out loud as he worked through the possibilities. "I suspect, with the way we were greeted, the people inside aren't free to come and go as they please. If they've got an us-versus-them mentality with the military, and they're concerned about spies, my guess is they're also concerned about a takeover. If they're smart, that means limited freedoms, especially for guests. We go in there, we're not coming out any time soon."

Timothy leaned over the edge of the truck bed, his tone urgent. "Then let's run," he said, nodding to the truck doors, which were still wide open. "We don't have the keys, but we can grab our bags and get lost in that neighborhood behind you, circle the city, find our way back to the church."

Alex shook his head. "Even if we could get away without being shot, these people are connected to the ones at the mountain," he said. "If we can find out more about what happened at the Cheyenne complex, we might get a few clues as to where to look for Coleman, Hunt, and the rest."

The group of strangers finally broke apart, and all four approached. The same man who'd spoken first spoke again. "You can move freely," he said.

Alex moved at a snail's pace, keeping his hands where they could be seen. He didn't want to spook anyone. They all still had weapons; the fact they weren't aimed his way *at that moment* wasn't of much comfort.

We have to play this smart, he thought. Get out of here before they make us go beyond their wall and get some information, if at all possible.

Alex cleared his throat and forced a smile. "So, introductions?" He held out a hand toward the man who'd done the speaking. "I'm Alex, and this is Timothy."

"Jarod," he said, grasping Alex's hand briefly. The other three had their helmets under their arms just like Jarod by that point. Jarod was the oldest of them by far, the bit of gray at his temples and wrinkles at his eyes setting him in his forties. He pointed to the others, naming them quickly. "This is Milo, Perry, and Sam."

"So..." Timothy looked at Alex and then back at Jarod. "Can we get our keys back?"

"Aren't you coming inside?" Jarod asked. "Why would you need your keys? This community is safe. That's what you were looking for, right?"

Alex and Timothy exchanged a look, and Alex frowned at Jarod. "We wanted to check it out," Alex said, "but we by no means have decided to stay."

Jarod crossed his arms. "We get newcomers more often than you'd think, Alex. Stragglers who tried to stick it out on their own in the city for too long. Travelers who're coming in from all over the great state of Colorado, just trying to survive. But they're all desperate, and unless they're passing through, trying to get to someone who's probably dead anyway, they're clamoring to get into the arena." He narrowed his eyes. "There's something off about you two."

Alex tried not to squirm, but the way Jarod stared him down made it hard. "We just want some more information," he said.

"We still don't understand exactly what happened here," Timothy said. "Mark made it sound like Colorado Springs had something of a rebellion against the local government. I mean, we're new to the area, so maybe we don't understand, but... why go against the military? Aren't they here to protect us?"

Milo, a ginger headed man, tall and thin, his jaw a hard line, his eyes a cold blue, scoffed at Timothy. "The soldiers who were loyal to the people have joined our cause," he said. "We even got a few officers on our side. The rest... they weren't protecting us. They had orders to protect politicians and socialites. It was all about money, who had it, who didn't. They expected us to feel lucky if we were chosen to do their grunt work up in that mountain, even if it meant leaving our friends and family to die out here."

"That's terrible," Alex said, considering how to show empathy for their situation, how to frame his words so that they trusted him a little more. "Aren't you afraid they'll try to take the mountain back? I mean, are their forces *that* depleted?"

"They took a hard hit," Jarod said. "They got some reinforcements when Coleman came to town, though. From what we've heard, they picked up soldiers and added to their numbers as they travelled up from Atlanta, thinking they'd be greeted with some kind of parade." Jarod scowled. "They weren't happy to find Cheyenne Mountain under our control. Set up at the Air Force Military Academy, took over the whole northern corner of the city."

"So, they've left you alone?" Timothy asked. "They haven't tried anything, then? Maybe they won't. I mean, maybe they're not so bad."

Alex winced at the way all four of the men threw disgusted looks at Timothy. "What he means is," Alex said, "you guys seem to be in control. It doesn't seem like you have much to worry about."

Milo spat on the ground. "Tell that to the four teenage boys we sent out hunting. Those monsters took them out just for trying to get some fresh meat. Shot them in cold blood. Laid their bodies in the intersection on the pavement in the middle of the night as a warning." He shook his head. "Nah, they're coming for us eventually. They're biding their time. And we've seen their spies scoping out the mountain, scoping out this place." He pointed over his shoulder. "They want their mountain complex back, and if we get too comfortable, they'll kill off anyone who dares to stand up to them, just like they murdered those boys."

Alex listened in confused horror. "Are you sure?" he asked. He thought back to Atlanta, to what he knew of Coleman and Hunt. They were good men, men who helped Alex shut down a maniac, men who wanted to protect people, not hurt them.

"Sure about what?" Jarod asked.

"Coleman and Hunt would *never*..." Alex sucked in a breath, realizing what he'd said too late.

"We didn't mention General Hunt's name," Milo said.

Timothy cleared his throat. "Mark mentioned him," he said quickly.

"Nah, I don't think so." Jarod's frown deepened and the other three men had their hands back on their rifles. "You talk like you know the man. He would never *what*, Alex? Murder innocent teenage boys? How would you know that?"

The heat of the day was suddenly scorching as sweat formed on Alex's forehead. He took half a step back, looking from Jarod to Milo to Sam and Perry. His mouth opened and closed, but it was as if he'd never spoken English a day in his life. He couldn't quite form a coherent thought, much less speak one.

"I think we better go inside," Jarod said. "Have a longer talk." He paused to look Alex up and down. "Or we can just shoot you now and be done with it."

Alex tensed, every muscle in his body frozen as he kept his eyes on the raised rifles. The four men stood nearly shoulder to shoulder, a wall of deadly suspicion. His mind raced for an explanation, but he could find none. His mouth ran dry as the only option became clear: they'd have to risk going with these strangers, behind their wall.

"Okay," he said, his voice croaking. "We'll go with—"

Out of nowhere, Timothy lunged forward, ripped the rifle out of Sam's unsuspecting hands, and threw his entire body into the man, which in turn created a domino effect, all five of them stumbling to the ground. Alex, just as shocked as anybody, shouted in alarm and ducked as one of the rifles went off. Perry's rifle skidded to just within an inch of Alex's foot. He reached out for it, snatching it as Perry's fingers grazed the stock. Alex righted himself, taking quick and haphazard steps backward, still working out of instinct rather than thought.

Beside him, Timothy recovered his feet quickly, reorienting the rifle to aim at the four strangers. His eyes were wild as he panted, chest heaving. "Not again," he said. "Never again."

The four men had piled on top of one another and were quickly untangling. Weapon in hand, Alex aimed at the strangers while throwing his own scowl at Timothy.

"What the hell, Tim. You could have gotten us both killed," he growled.

"I played it safe with Frank Russo," Timothy said, that crazed look still in his eyes. "That got my mother killed, got my wife shot, ruined everything. We lost *everything*. I'm not letting these macho assholes think they can walk all over me."

Flustered confusion gave way to an angry growl as Jarod pushed Perry off of him and got to his feet, raising his rifle. Milo still had his weapon, too, and while Jarod was enraged, he seemed to have some control over himself. Milo, on the other hand, let out a long string of curses and threats, feet moving constantly, finger tapping the trigger guard impatiently.

"We can take them," Milo said. "There's four of us, two of them, even if they have our weapons!"

Jarod gritted his teeth, the malice in his eyes suggesting he might authorize the reckless move. But then, a crackling radio and a voice interrupted the showdown.

"Jarod! Come in!" The voice sounded urgent. "Jarod!"

"Get my radio, Sam," Jarod ordered gruffly, not taking his eyes or his aim off of Alex and Timothy.

Alex followed suit, the standoff intense as he and Tim took slow steps backward, weapons raised, and Jarod and Milo stood their ground. Sam grabbed a handheld radio from the back of Jarod's belt and spoke into it.

"It's Sam. We're a bit... busy."

"Tell Jarod to stop messing around out there," the voice said. "We've got bigger problems. You know that King Soopers we've been fixing up with solar so we can use the freezers? The military has found it. We've gotta send everybody we can spare or else we're gonna lose our assets there."

"Damn it." Jarod spat. "Sam, tell them we're on our way."

Sam did as he was told, but Milo shook his head. "What about them?"

"Don't have time to work this out," Jarod said, clear disgust in his expression. "We've got to do everything we can to get those freezers up and running so we can stockpile for the winter."

"He's right," Perry said. "Those bastards will take all our hard work if we don't show them we're willing to defend what's ours."

Alex frowned at the exchange. They really *were* afraid that Coleman would authorize stealing from them. They really believed Coleman and Hunt were the bad guys, and if what they said was true...

Are we backing the wrong guys? Alex's stomach churned.

"All right," Jarod said, clearly talking to Alex and Timothy as he took out their truck keys and threw them on the ground. "Let's make a deal. You take your truck and get out of here. I don't ever want to see your face again. We'll take your weapons. Set them down, nice and slow. Do as I ask, and I'll call it all even, forget my plans for interrogation. Deal?"

"Deal," Alex said without hesitation. "You'll never see us again." He and Timothy laid their guns on the pavement and backed away. None of the four strangers seemed happy about it, but they grabbed the weapons and left Alex and Timothy where they'd found them. The second they got back on their bikes and rocketed away, turning north and out of sight, Alex breathed out slowly, hands trembling as he picked up the keys.

Timothy turned to face him. And without really thinking about it, Alex threw a punch, landing his fist across Timothy's jaw. It wasn't his intention to really hurt the man, but he'd gambled with Alex's life.

"Don't you *ever* do anything like that again," Alex said. "I have a *son* who needs me. You might be willing to throw everything away, to leave your wife, to let Candice and Annika and Lizzy and all those that need *you* down, but I'm not."

Timothy straightened and, before Alex knew what was happening, threw a punch of his own. Alex's head snapped to the right and the force of the impact left his jaw throbbing. He worked his jaw back and forth as he righted himself.

"You're not in charge, Alex," Timothy spoke firmly, his voice raised. "I've played that game before, where you do everything you can to stay alive, where that priority outstrips everything else. And guess what? I stayed alive, sure, but the bad guys, they found a way to my family. I'm never going to let that happen again."

Alex rubbed his jaw, just as Timothy did. They stared at each other for a few seconds before Alex dropped his hand and rolled his shoulders. "You and me, we can talk about your reckless behavior another time. Right now, we've got to get out of here." He didn't wait for a reply, rounding the truck and hopping into the driver's seat.

Timothy slid into the seat next to him, clearly still fuming. It took some maneuvering, but Alex got them out of there, weaving backward through the mess of vehicles. Timothy was silent as Alex took a long, indirect route through the city, going south.

"I don't think anyone is following us," Alex said eventually. "I think it's safe to go back to the church."

"Are you asking my opinion or informing me?" Timothy asked coldly.

"Asking," Alex said, not bothering to keep the frustration from his tone. "C'mon, man. What you did back there was reckless by anybody's standards."

"The world isn't what it used to be," Timothy said. "Sometimes being reckless is the only way we're going to survive. You heard Jarod. He had plans to interrogate us. What does that even mean, Alex? Do you really think they would have let us go?"

"I… don't know, if I'm being honest." The admission was harder to say than Alex could have anticipated.

"Look," Timothy said. "You're used to calling the shots. I get it. But you're not running the show, Alex. You don't get to decide how we handle everything. And in situations like that, when we have no time to prepare or come to a consensus, you're going to have to deal with the fact that we won't do exactly as you want. Just because you lead, doesn't mean we'll follow."

Alex pressed his lips together, purposefully keeping his mouth shut. He wanted to argue, to insist that Timothy was wrong, that they should follow his lead. But part of him realized Timothy had a point. He'd not considered these new dynamics, except to get mildly frustrated with the drawn-out negotiations wherein the entire group had a say.

"We're never going to get anywhere like this," Alex said. "There's a chain of command literally everywhere for a reason: the military all the way down to a mom-and-pop store on the corner. When no one is in charge, you're inviting chaos. You're inviting failure, Timothy."

"And who's to say that person in charge should be you?" Timothy asked. "Going inside, in my opinion, was a larger risk than doing what had to be done to get out of there immediately."

"I don't know the answer," Alex said after a long pause. "There are a lot of things I guess I need time to think about right now."

"No kidding," Timothy said. "Like if your buddies in the military are actually killing teens in cold blood? Like if they're stealing resources and kicking average people to the curb? I'm not sure I want to fight for that."

"Yeah," Alex said. "Stuff like that."

"You do realize that's not solely your decision, either?" Timothy asked.

Alex glanced at Timothy as he pulled the truck onto a country road that would lead them to the church. "Whether or not I want to work with Coleman and Hunt?"

"No," Timothy said, "whether or not you'll get *our* support."

Alex turned his eyes back to the road, but he didn't answer. Timothy's words lingered in the air and repeated over and over in his mind. Up to that point, he'd taken for granted how easily he and Lauren and Minnie had worked together. The roads and towns they'd travelled through on the way to Colorado had been mostly empty, and they'd done a good job of avoiding trouble.

Walter was essential in moving forward, in finding the lab and working with Alex to make right all that Walter and Vanguard had done wrong. Alex just didn't believe he could do it on his own, not after spending time in both Atlanta and in Boston working through the problems on his own and failing.

There's no way Walter will leave behind family, Alex thought. But what if… what if our downfall doesn't come from the outside? What if we can't work together? He gripped the steering wheel tighter as new fears rose up and secured a choke hold on his fledgling hope. He'd been so busy worrying about the threats coming from the outside, he hadn't stopped to consider one simple reality: they didn't need an outside threat to destroy them. If they couldn't find a way to work together, they'd do that all on their own. And they'd take the world's last hope of survival down with them.

Chapter 8

Heather Peters

The second she was given a moment's peace, Heather's body rebelled against her. The most exciting thing that had happened over the last couple of weeks had been her relationship with Timothy returning to something like it looked like before.

And that *was* exciting. Timothy had started down a darker path in Boston, and it had scared the crap out of Heather. She'd been worried that even if they both survived the swarms and DV-10 that their marriage wouldn't. Timothy was her person, her best friend, and trusting him was a cornerstone of her stability when everything else was crumbling. To see her trust in her husband begin to erode was akin to knocking out the last pillar holding up her sanity. It had been a balm of reassurance when the cracks between them received some tender-loving care, when they'd started to knit together again.

But if it wasn't one thing, it was another, and Heather had been experiencing the most intense bout of exhaustion she'd ever had, not including after she'd been shot. She groaned as she shifted on her pile of blankets and pillows. Her nap had been interrupted by an unpleasant bout of heartburn.

"Great," she said, rubbing her chest as she sat up and leaned against the wall. "I'm getting old."

"What was that?" Lauren walked through the door, a guitar in hand, and frowned at Heather. "You don't look so great."

"I know," Heather said. "I said I'm getting old." She patted her chest. "Heartburn."

"Ah," Lauren nodded. "Probably those greasy potato chips we had for lunch." She shrugged. "I had a little heartburn, too. I mean, it was worth it, but our bodies haven't been eating a lot of grease lately."

"My heart doesn't burn at all," Annika looked up from the child-sized table where she and Oliver were working on a puzzle of Noah's ark they'd found, Samson lazing under the table at their feet. The girl was getting stronger every day. She still slept a lot, had a noticeable limp, and took daily pain meds, but she was healing nicely. It was a miracle she'd lived through so much.

Oliver pursed his lips. "Mine either, but she did say it happens to old people, and we're kids."

"Oh, right," Annika said, throwing a concerned look at Candice. "Does your heart burn?"

Candice sat next to Annika on one of the miniature chairs, scrunched knees to chest but still managing to look put together, the signs of the times subtle: the way her skin sagged beneath her eyes just slightly, an effect of surviving DV-10; the few scars and scabs marking her previously flawless skin; the little holes in her designer blouse and the faded blood stain at the ankle of her skinny jeans. Compared to Heather, Candice could have been a model out of a magazine.

Candice quirked an eyebrow at Annika. "I'm not *old*, Annika."

"You're not?" Annika looked genuinely surprised, and Heather couldn't help but chuckle.

Candice huffed a little. "No, I'm not."

Samson raised his head to look at her, a small whine almost making it seem he was voicing skepticism at her claims. Heather's chuckle turned into a full-blown laugh as Candice scowled at the dog, stood, and cleared her throat.

"This puzzle is almost done," Candice said. "I think I'll go find another." She only took a few steps before Annika had jumped up and hobbled quickly to her side.

Annika grabbed Candice's hand and looked up at her, eyes big as she leaned against her. "Can I come?"

Candice's expression softened. She smiled and nodded toward the door. "Of course you can, Blueberry."

A warmth came over Heather at the exchange, and she shook her head as the two left. "That girl has Candice wrapped around her little finger."

"Done!" Oliver grinned as he stuck the last puzzle piece into place.

"Good job, bud," Lauren said as she sat next to Heather, leaning against the wall and propping the guitar across her crisscrossed legs. "You might want to go with the ladies to pick out the next puzzle. I saw a lot of rainbows and princesses out there."

Oliver made a face. "Why would anyone want to do a puzzle with princesses?" He didn't wait for an answer, popping up from the little table and rushing out the door. Samson grunted and followed on the boy's heels.

Lauren laughed as Oliver and the dog scurried out, and then she gave Heather a sideways glance. "Really, though… you look like you're dealing with more than just heartburn."

"I've been really tired," Heather admitted. "I think the past months have been so hectic that my body just hasn't been allowed to rest. First, there was the outbreak and our family being away when it happened. The stress of that was just the beginning, you know? Frank Russo, CON… even dealing with the Boston Police had its stresses. Not to mention George and Annika's kidnapping, my mother-in-law's death, the war in Boston when I thought I might lose everyone I had left…" Heather leaned her head back against the wall and breathed out slowly, terrifying memories bombarding her. "Now that no one's chasing me, now that I know where my loved ones are, now that they're relatively safe… I guess my body is just grinding to a halt."

"Could be," Lauren said. "It takes time to recover from that much stress. We're all dealing with that." She picked at the guitar, leaning one ear closer as she played a few chords and adjusted the tuning pegs. "You need something to destress, something besides napping."

"Is that why you've got that guitar?" Heather asked.

"Yep. Found it in the sanctuary, up on stage. It's just what I needed to destress. Everyone needs something right now. It's why I encouraged Candice and the kids to work on those puzzles, why I was glad Zara found something in the library." Lauren strummed the guitar, winced, and shook her head. "Not quite," she said, her expression turning to one of concentration as she returned to adjusting the guitar.

"Any bright ideas for me?" Heather asked.

Lauren shrugged halfheartedly as she turned the pegs again. "What did you like to do before?"

"I don't know," Heather said. "Cook, when Dana wasn't anywhere nearby."

Lauren quirked an eyebrow. "Your mother-in-law?"

"Yeah," Heather said, smiling sadly. "She babied her kids, always wanted Timothy to have the best, and when it came to food, *her* way was always the best way." Her mother-in-law's criticisms had been too much sometimes, but she'd give anything to have Dana back. The two of them had grown closer in the short time between the start of trouble and Dana's death. "I guess, truthfully," Heather said, "her deserts blew mine out of the water nine times out of ten."

"Well, we don't have a ton of options when it comes to cooking, but… maybe you could get creative with what we do have." Lauren strummed the guitar, the sound harmonious and lovely, and she grinned. "That'll do it. Perfect." She began to play a soft, light melody that reminded Heather of a bright, carefree day in the sunshine.

"Maybe I'll have a look," Heather said, the music making her instantly more relaxed. "But first, I think I'd like to hear you play a little while. I miss music."

Lauren seemed more than happy to oblige, and Heather let the music distract her from her exhaustion. But it wasn't long before the pounding of feet in the hall interrupted Heather's brief reprieve.

Oliver burst into the room, holding the door open. "My dad and Timothy are back!" Samson barked excitedly in the hall behind him.

Energy flooded into Heather, and she was on her feet in seconds. "Are they both okay?"

Oliver nodded. "Yeah, I think so."

Lauren laid the guitar on the ground and stood, too. "Are they alone?"

Oliver nodded again and waved for them to follow. "C'mon. Dad told me to get everyone into the sanctuary." He bounded away with the dog, calling Minnie's name down the hall.

Heather and Lauren exchanged a look. "Sounds like they've got news," Heather said.

Lauren shook her hands out and rolled her shoulders. "No matter what it is, we'll be okay." She spoke so softly Heather was sure she was talking more to herself than to anyone else.

Heather grasped Lauren's hand. "Even if it's bad news, I think we've proven we can get through just about anything. Alex and Timothy are here. They're safe. Whatever else is happening, you're right. We'll be fine."

Lauren nodded. "Right. Let's go." She pulled Heather out into the hall, still holding her hand.

Heather's stomach fluttered when she and Lauren entered the sanctuary to find Timothy and Alex near the front. She broke free of Lauren's grasp and jogged down the aisle toward her husband, relieved to see him in the same shape as when he'd left. Timothy turned from Alex, his serious expression breaking into a smile. She threw her arms around his neck and hugged him tightly for a moment before letting him pull away just enough to kiss her.

"Gross!" Oliver's voice echoed behind her, and she and Timothy grinned at each other.

Heather turned around in time to see Minnie bop Oliver on the head lightly as they entered the sanctuary with Samson. "Ain't nothin' gross about love," she said. "We need more of it, if you ask me."

Annika limped into the sanctuary beside Candice as Minnie held the door open. Heather glanced at the front pew where Lizzie and Azalea already sat. Behind them a few rows, Zara, Walter, and Kai were side-by-side.

"Well," Alex said, "we're all here." He held out an arm as Oliver came to lean against him.

Candice held up a puzzle box. "Oliver, Annika, do you two want to work on this new puzzle you picked out?"

"That would be really helpful, bud," Alex said, rustling his son's hair. "Why don't you take Samson, too?"

Oliver shrugged reluctantly. "I guess…" He sighed and, with slumped shoulders, walked over to Candice and took the box. "C'mon, Annika. Let's go back to the room with the little table."

Minnie held up a hand. "Hold up, now," she said, pulling a brightly colored package out of her pocket. "Not without these." She held out a single package of candy.

"Whoa!" Oliver brightened immediately. "Thanks!" He tugged on Samson's collar. "Let's go, boy!"

"You share, now, ya hear?" Minnie shouted after the kids as they hurried away with the dog in tow, puzzle box and candy in hand.

Heather shook her head. "Where *did* you find a package of Skittles?"

"And more importantly," Lauren said, "are there more?"

Minnie chuckled. "Let's just say the church secretary seems to have had a sweet tooth." Her expression turned, though, as she looked past Heather and Lauren. "Speakin' of candy, Alex, you look like someone licked the color off a jaw breaker and then made you chew it. What's wrong?"

Heather frowned, following Minnie's gaze and noticing Alex's face becoming paler by the second. She turned to her husband. "Tim? You didn't find them, did you?" It was more a statement than a question.

Timothy shook his head. "No, but… we did find someone, and it wasn't pretty."

"I think we should all have a seat," Alex said, gesturing to the pews as he sat on the steps leading up to the stage. He nodded at Timothy, who joined Alex after leading Heather to sit on the front row a few feet down from Lizzy and Azalea.

Heather settled in, listening intently as Timothy and Alex launched into a summary of what they'd discovered. The tension in the room built, and more than once, Heather's mouth dropped and she had to glance at the others to get confirmation that what she was hearing was as crazy as it sounded. By the end of their account, Heather was sitting poker-straight, her muscles tense as she tried to process it all. The news about the Cheyenne Mountain Complex being occupied by a hostile civilian force was bad enough, but the rumors about Coleman and Hunt authorizing the deaths of innocents was somehow worse. When Alex and Timothy finished, the sanctuary fell silent for several minutes.

"I'm having a hard time *not* sympathizing with these civilians," Heather said. "Would we have done any different? The government tried to lock them out of the only safe place, and then more people in power show up, people they don't know, and murder a bunch of teens after being denied what they wanted." She shook her head, her mouth running dry. She met Timothy's gaze and saw her own feelings reflected in his eyes. "How can we work with people like that? We fought hard to be the good guys in Boston. We can't sacrifice our integrity."

"I don't believe one word of those rumors," Minnie said, slapping the back of the pew in front of her. "This Mark sounds like a snake, and the people at the arena weren't exactly angels. We *know* Coleman and Hunt. I don't know these other fellas from Adam's house cat."

Heather frowned at Minnie's sure tone, at the red creeping into her cheeks. It was as if the woman was offended by even the idea that Coleman and Hunt were bad faith actors. "Minnie, you barely know these people," she said, "and most of us here have never met them."

"Minnie's right," Alex said. "I don't know if I can believe Coleman or Hunt would work against the people. They helped right some pretty big wrongs once they figured out they were being led astray."

Timothy quirked an eyebrow. "So, they have a history of getting into bed with the wrong kind of people?"

Heather nodded along with her husband's words, and she was glad to see Walter, Zara, and Kai had similar expressions of skepticism.

"We have to go into this with our eyes open," Walter said. "We can't trust *anybody* outside of this group, not completely. We might need Coleman and Hunt to get our information, but there's also the chance that we could get the information without them, if it's locked away somewhere inside the mountain complex."

Lauren shook her head. "No. The fact is, we know Coleman and Hunt, even if we choose to be cautious around them. We know much less about these strangers."

"Except," Alex added, "that Timothy and I definitely burned our bridges with them."

Timothy nodded and shrugged. "That *is* true. They won't be giving us information any time soon."

"But you didn't tell them about us?" Azalea asked, speaking for the first time.

Timothy shook his head. "No."

Alex grimaced. "Well… that's not exactly true. Timothy hinted that he had a family to protect."

"But they still don't know our faces or anything about us?" Azalea calmly crossed her legs, her tone nonchalant.

How can she be so indifferent to all of this? Heather blinked at Azalea's cool tones, at the slight upturn at the corner of her mouth. It wasn't the first time the young woman had acted that way in an otherwise tense moment. *It's almost like she enjoys conflict.*

"I guess not," Alex said.

"Then maybe we have two routes to explore," Azalea said.

Walter stood and exited his pew, coming to the front where he could face them all. "What matters right now is finding out where Barlow Scientific Research Bank is located without giving anyone the chance to disrupt our plans. The fact is, we don't know who we need, and I repeat: we can't trust *anybody*. This is too important to leave in the hands of power-hungry men."

"You would know," Lizzy muttered loud enough for everyone to hear.

Walter took half a step back as if he'd been punched in the gut, and the room went silent. A lump formed in Heather's throat as her father-in-law stared at his daughter, his expression sickly.

"Elizabeth," Azalea said, her light tone somehow carrying a stern reprimand, "we talked about this—"

"No, it's okay," Walter said, holding up a hand, his voice cracking with emotion. "She's right. I *was* a power hungry, greedy man who stopped at nothing to build his own little empire. I sacrificed everything that was good in my life, including my own conscience, to do it. And that's why I know, without a shadow of a doubt, that men like the man I *used* to be can't be trusted. Even if their goals align with ours, even if those goals are *good*, there's a certain kind of person who can sully that journey in their desperate need to come out on top."

"And you're not that kind of person anymore?" Alex asked.

Walter turned to look at Alex, his eyes glistening. "I hope not," he said.

Zara stood, and Kai with her as if in support. "I *know* he's not," she said.

Heather met her husband's eyes. He sat still, neither defending his father nor attacking him. *It's okay to be on the fence,* she thought, willing Timothy to feel her support. He relaxed a little as he looked at her, and she offered a small smile. Walter had spent years pushing Timothy away, and Timothy had spent years gladly stepping back. It was only recently, during the past few weeks, that the two men had started talking again.

"Okay," Alex said, "let's say I believe you, Walter. What do you suggest?"

Walter swallowed audibly, giving his head a little shake, clearly gathering himself. "Ideally, we all stay together, and whether we can trust Coleman and company or not, they are most likely to have the information we need or to know where to find it. We get that information, and then we decide on our next move. We stay flexible. We keep our trust and our loyalty limited to those in this room right now. Once we have the next piece of the puzzle, we decide together what our next steps will be."

"So," Heather said, "we're approaching Coleman. But how? If it's true that they're shooting people on sight, we should send a familiar face."

"It should be me," Alex said.

"One of us should go," Walter said. "You guys might not spot red flags. You want to believe these are good people."

Heather had only a moment to be relieved that her husband would be staying behind when Timothy volunteered himself… again.

"I'll go, then," Timothy said. "That way, if we run across the same people, we won't burn anybody else. We need some of us to be able to get into that arena without suspicion, if it comes down to that."

It was almost comical. Heather had imagined things going differently in Colorado. They'd had their fill of war and loss in Boston, and after weeks of traveling with little gone wrong, she'd thought perhaps the end to the nightmare was fast approaching. She almost laughed at that notion as she leaned against the hard pew, a growing sense of dread building in her chest.

Heather closed her eyes, the heartburn from earlier returning with a bout of nausea. The relative peace of the last couple of weeks was over before she'd had the chance to enjoy it. Once again, she and those she loved were being thrown into the fray, and she could feel it in her gut: it was only the beginning. The cycle of danger and risk taking, of clinging to hope and surviving by the skin of their teeth had begun again, and there was nothing she could do to stop it.

Chapter 9

Alexander Roman

A night in the relative safety of the church had done little more than provide Alex with enough time to second guess himself. He believed that the people he'd worked with in Atlanta – specifically Coleman, Hunt, and Conner – were trustworthy. But they weren't the only players. And they *had* chosen poor allies in the past. As they ventured nearer to the city, Alex said very little. He only drove about fifteen miles before he turned off the two-lane highway into a shopping center parking lot on the outskirts of Colorado Springs.

"We're nowhere near where we need to be," Timothy said. "We're only halfway to where we need to go."

"I know." Alex parked the truck in the lot between two cars. A skeleton still holding on to bits of flesh stared back at him from a vehicle facing his. Alex averted his eyes, purposefully *not* focusing on the insides of the surrounding cars. It had become almost habit, the way he glossed over the dead, the way he actively ignored them. But it was the only way he'd found to avoid becoming paralyzed by the mere number of corpses left rotting everywhere.

"Then what are we doing?" Timothy frowned.

"Yesterday, we didn't know where we were going. We needed mobility and speed. Today, we have more information, and we won't have to traipse all over the city looking for Coleman and his people." Alex used a firm voice, Timothy's dissent from the day before still fresh in his mind. He didn't want to argue about what needed to be done. "So, we need to walk in this time."

Timothy's pronounced blink was followed by a moment of silence. "We still don't know much about this place." He ran his fingers through his hair, sighing heavily. "Lay it out, Alex. What are your reasons for dragging this out and putting the two of us in more danger?"

Alex shook his head. "We won't be in more danger. There are hostiles in the city. Going in quietly will draw less attention."

"And the swarms?" Timothy asked. "We've got protective gear, sure, but… I don't really want to test it over fifteen miles. At the mountain, we knew the round trip from our truck to the complex would be a couple hours at most. I don't want to get caught by a swarm even in the gear. I mean, what if the little devils find a way in?"

"I agree," Alex said, "and if there's a swarm, Plan A is always to run and take shelter. Plan B is to hope the gear protects us from them *as* we seek shelter. The less time we're exposed to the swarm, the less likely it is we'll get bitten. That doesn't change what we need to do."

Timothy let out a frustrated sigh. "Walking another fifteen miles into the city is going to take forever. Not to mention the fact that our gear is going to hinder our movement and slow us down even more."

"Yes, but there's also the issue of gasoline," Alex said. "We need to siphon a fresh supply sometime soon, but for now, we should save what we've got and use it only as necessary."

"Why?" Timothy shook his head. "Can't we keep doing what we've been doing?"

Alex shifted uncomfortably in his seat. They'd been resupplying their gasoline as they drove across country, taking what was left in the vehicles abandoned or occupied by the dead. And there were a *lot* of opportunities to do so. It had worked so far, but it wouldn't work forever. The only vehicle they had with solar power was Minnie's RV, and while it stretched their fuel, the solar was mostly for the use of the stove, bathroom, and air conditioning. And there was the simple fact that not all of them could even fit inside the thing.

"No," Alex said, "I don't think we should rely on our current methods. Survivors are hoarding, gathering gasoline locally, stockpiling it, and adding fuel stabilizer. It works for them, and it'll keep them in business for a couple of years, but even that won't last forever."

"We've got fuel stabilizer, too," Timothy said.

Alex sighed in frustration. Timothy was referring to a few bottles they'd been lucky enough to trade for along the way. "Not enough of it," Alex said, "and I don't know we'll be able to find any more. You saw it just as I did these past weeks: cities and towns are nearly finished consolidating their resources. Stores of all types are picked clean, and survivor communities are stingy with their goods. The fact is, we've got a limited supply of gasoline with no guarantees of finding more. The gas sitting in vehicles, left untreated, will start to go bad very soon."

Timothy rubbed his hands over his face and let out a frustrated grunt. "It's not going to be easy, getting back to Boston, is it?"

Alex shook his head. "No, it's not. Honestly, wherever we end up after this, wherever this research bank is, we might be there for a long while. And when it comes to spreading a vaccine, to releasing the countermeasure mosquitos…" Alex paused. Admitting the complications out loud for the first time made his stomach twist into knots. "The simple logistics of transporting them are going to be a huge hurdle. We're looking at possibly years of work just to stabilize the globe. And then who knows how long to build society back up. We might not see that in our lifetimes."

Timothy had gone pale, his lips pressed in a thin line. He looked at Alex, and his eyes seemed to be searching for something, perhaps a sign that Alex was exaggerating. Finally, the other man closed his eyes, shoulders sagging, and nodded reluctantly.

"Then we do what we must to survive," he said. "I guess that's nothing new."

"We do it for kids like my son," Alex said, "like Annika. We do it for their kids, for the next generation."

"Yeah, of course." Timothy rolled his shoulders back and reached for the door handle. "We've got a long walk ahead of us," he said. "Let's gear up." His tone lacked passion and conviction, but he was moving.

Alex nodded, grateful he didn't have to do any more to convince Timothy. He wasn't sure he could blame the man for his pessimism. Neither of them would likely live to see the world restored to what it once had been. Alex got so much motivation from the thought of Oliver living on to have his own children in a peaceful world, from Alex's grandchildren living in a society rebuilt. Without that, he was certain his own ambitions would fall short of his current, fiery conviction to fight to fix the world; it would be so much easier to join a survivor community and enjoy what time he had left with his son. And if his wife, Naomi, were still alive...

I wouldn't blame Timothy if he and Heather bowed out of this fight, Alex thought. Not that he would voice that opinion any time soon. He needed all the help he could get.

Alex got out of the truck and retrieved his gear from the back seat: suit, gloves, respirator, backpack. He and Timothy both had fresh handguns at their hips once their gear was on, and Alex had suggested they keep unloaded backups and ammunition in their backpacks.

"All set?" Alex asked, his voice filtered through his mask.

Timothy gave him a thumbs up, and the two of them started walking northwest. They stuck to residential areas whenever possible. The houses and trees provided plenty of potential places to hide or take shelter. They took a ten-minute break every hour, on the hour, but Alex was quick to urge them onward.

They knew very little about where they were going, except for the general direction. The longer they walked, the more anxiety took hold of Alex's body. It wasn't just the physical exertion that was draining him, either; it was the burden of setting his senses to high alert, his heartbeat racing at every sound, his ears waiting in anticipation, his body ready to bolt at any moment.

Colorado Springs seemed abandoned wherever they went, but Alex caught movement out of the corner of his eye constantly. Sometimes it was a bird or a cat. Other times, he could have sworn he saw someone draw back a curtain only to disappear when he looked their way.

And Timothy walked on, mostly quiet. The way any attempts to strike up conversation fell immediately flat and the way the other man tensed at every sound, Alex assumed he was on edge, too.

I wish Minnie were here, Alex thought. She'd know how to dissipate some of this tension. For the first time in hours, he smiled. Or Lauren... she'd be strolling down these streets like she was a tourist or something. He sighed. When he was apart from his newfound family, it became painstakingly clear that they were largely responsible for the way he'd been holding himself together.

That moment of levity brought to him by thoughts of loved ones ended when he heard a scream. Alex stopped so suddenly, he nearly tripped over his own feet. "Where did that come from?"

Timothy turned with quick, jerky motions, first east, then west. "That way," he said, pointing west as another cry split the air.

Alex took one step in that direction before Timothy stopped him with a hand on his chest. "What are you doing?" Alex asked.

"Are you sure you want to go *toward* the trouble?" Timothy asked. "We don't have time."

"I promised my son that I would always do whatever I could to help people in need," Alex said. "We have to at least check it out."

"What if it's the crazies from the arena?" Timothy stepped in front of him. "It's a bad idea."

Alex pushed him aside, careful to only use the force necessary to move the man out of his way. "What if it's the people we're looking for? Or someone who would help us?" He strode forward with determined steps.

Timothy followed. "If it looks hairy, we need to agree before moving in. Got it?"

"I might not be 'in charge' of you or anybody else, but I make my own decisions," Alex said. "And if it's the right thing to do, I'm going in."

"Well, I don't want to die because you have some savior complex," Timothy said harshly.

Alex paused. "Excuse me?" He jabbed a finger into Timothy's shoulder. "Just because you're a coward—"

"Hold on, now, cowboy," Timothy said. "I'm out here. I'm doing the thing we need to do. I've fought hard to survive this long, and I've fought hard to protect the people I love. I just don't want to throw all that away for a stranger!"

A third scream made Alex bite his tongue, turn his back on Timothy, and pick up the pace. He reached the end of a residential street and stepped onto the grass of what looked to be the backend of a school grounds. A football field stretched left to right in front of them. On the righthand side, four people in army fatigues ran around the corner of a school and entered the field at a dead run.

"They're military!" Alex looked back at Timothy.

"Yeah, okay, but they're running from someone. Just hold on a minute." Timothy craned his neck. "I don't see whoever is chasing them yet."

Alex took a step out onto the field, squinting at the four soldiers. And then his heart leapt. "Conner?" He took another step forward. "I know her!" He waved his arms. "Jenny! Corporal Jenny Conner!"

Timothy came up beside him. "Alex, wait... do you h—"

"We can trust her," Alex said. "I know it. We have to help. We don't have time to play around. The people we've been looking for just fell into our laps." He sprinted toward them, waving his hands and calling for Conner.

Timothy yelled from behind him. "What the—Alex! Stop!"

Ahead, the two soldiers who noticed him, including Jenny, stumbled to a stop. The two in the lead kept running.

Alex slipped off his respirator so that she could see his face better. "Conner, it's me! It's Alexander Roman."

Conner waved off her companion. "Go, Warren! Run!" The man didn't need to be asked twice. He dashed after the others, who were entering one of those classroom trailers on the other side of the field. "Alex," Conner was breathing heavily, her eyes wide. "We have to run. Right now."

Alex pointed back at Timothy who was still at the edge of the grounds. "Whoever is chasing you, we can help." It was then that a low hum chilled Alex to the bone. His throat constricted as Conner confirmed his fears.

"We just lost a soldier to a swarm. It's coming this way." Conner stepped forward and grabbed Alex by the forearm. "Let's go!"

"I'm right behind you," he said. "I just have to get my friend."

"There's no time!" Conner bit her lower lip, her eyes glistening. "Damn it, Alex. I have to go." She turned and ran.

A black cloud came around the school building, undulating with life and promising death, moving twice as fast as the last swarm Alex had escaped. He stumbled backward a few steps, shocked by the mere size of the swarm. The center was thick and black and teeming, perhaps twenty feet in height, a halo of more loosely packed mosquitos surrounding it. Specks of bright orange from the diamonds on their backs added dimension and living patterns.

The memory of studying the creatures behind the safety of a window flashed in his mind's eye. He had the same, horrified thought as he'd had then: *That is* not *natural.* The dense swarm, the movements that mimicked purpose, the rate at which they must be reproducing... none of it was normal.

Buzzing filled the air, and the screaming he'd heard earlier echoed in his mind. The monstrosity prowled forward as if hungry, masses of mosquitos unfurling from the center, reaching like appendages.

It had been mere seconds since he'd spoken to Conner, since the swarm had become visible. Alex's heartbeat was like a series of punches to his chest, and his entire body throbbed as pounding filled his ears.

"Alex! Move!" Timothy's frantic shout pulled Alex out of his stupor.

He willed his legs to move, and he cried out as he started to run back toward Timothy. "Go!" Alex screamed. "Find shelter!"

Timothy took one step back but then rocked forward again, shaking his head. "Run faster! I can't leave you."

Alex put everything he had into pumping his legs faster, but the ground was uneven and his suit and backpack were cumbersome. He gathered a breath, too winded and panicked to shout anything profound. "I said, go!"

Then his foot caught on the uneven, grassy field as he ran. Alex soared through the air and hit the ground rolling, his full-face respirator flying. He came to a stop, but he couldn't catch a breath. The wind had been knocked out of him when he'd hit the ground. The swarm was coming. His respirator, the thing that would cover his face and protect him was out of his reach.

And then Timothy was there, snatching up the respirator and falling to his knees beside Alex. He slapped the respirator onto Alex's face and tightened the straps before pulling up Alex's hood and cinching the drawstring so that the suit overlapped with the full-face mask.

"Time for Plan B," Timothy said.

Alex struggled to his feet as Timothy helped him, and then they both broke into a run toward the residential area, the swarm on their heels. The hum was loud and angry, all-encompassing. Tendrils of the monster wrapped around Alex's chest, the black line breaking as he ran through it, mosquitos clinging to his suit. He swatted at them with panicked movements, revulsion making his stomach turn. All he could do was pray the gear was enough as the black cloud overtook him.

Chapter 10

Alexander Roman

Alex slammed into the front door of the first house on the street, turning the handle as the swarm surrounded him and Timothy. He stumbled into a foyer, the black cloud pouring into the room, angrily filling the air with a mind-numbing buzz. His mask was covered with mosquitos crawling and searching for blood. He had to wave them off rather than swatting them; he'd learned quickly that doing so would only leave guts smeared across his only window to the world.

"Sprint down the hall, as fast as you can," Alex shouted. "Get to the door at the end."

Timothy did as he was told, and Alex followed, breaking through the densest part of the swarm. He gained a few seconds on the army of insects. Heart racing, sweat stinging his eyes, Alex ran. Timothy was through the door first, holding it open. Alex raced inside a bedroom, turning to see Timothy close the door just before the bulk of the swarm was able to get inside. Still, there was a crack under the door. A steady stream filtered into the room.

Alex spun around, pausing only momentarily at the sight of a corpse in the bed, laying on top of the comforter. The withered, dried, gray skin clung tightly in spots, white bone showing through in others. Mold grew on what was left of a feminine nightgown and spread out from the body.

He grabbed a blanket folded on an ottoman at the end of the bed and rushed to the door, stuffing the fabric into the crack. But plenty had already made it inside.

"What are we going to do?" Alex shouted, standing up, swatting at the air, searching for anything in the room that might help them.

Timothy hurried to a dusty side table by the bed, tearing the drawer out so quickly, it ripped free of the table all together. The contents went flying. "There!" Timothy pointed as a candle lighter hit the ground and skidded under a dresser.

"They hate smoke," Alex said, understanding. "It'll kill them if they get caught in it too long."

"And we've got respirators. We can leave through there," Timothy said, pointing to a quaint six-paned window. "What's left of the swarm inside will die. The rest will get far away from all the smoke."

Alex stepped toward the dresser but hesitated. "A fire could spread, and there'd be no one to put it out."

Timothy was at the dresser in two, long strides, pushing it aside. "We have people who need us," he said. "The city is mostly abandoned."

It was hard to think in the midst of what amounted to hundreds of mosquitos still surrounding them, but one word made him nod and step forward to help: *Oliver.*

Once the dresser was out of the way, Timothy picked up the lighter. "We need something flammable."

Alex spun toward a vanity in the opposite corner of the room. The surface of the vanity was covered with perfumes, hair products, and makeup. "Most of this stuff is highly flammable," he said. And then he barked a laugh and held up a dusty cannister. "Aerosol hairspray!"

Timothy grabbed the perfumes, glass clinking. "We can soak the bed with these."

"We make this place ready to burn, fry these suckers, and then get out through the window," Alex said. "Our respirators will mitigate the smoke."

The longer they exposed themselves to the swarm, the more likely they'd get bitten or the mosquitos would find a way through their gear. Alex didn't want to think about the possibility that it had already happened and they were just unaware.

We'll find out soon enough, either way, he thought. But in the meantime, this is our best bet.

"Help me with these," Timothy said as he emptied a bundle of perfumes onto the ottoman. He unscrewed the first one and poured it out on the bed.

Alex did the same, grim as he poured perfume over the corpse. His rubber gloves made his fingers clumsy, but he and Timothy managed to empty all six of the bottles while the swarm inside the room darted rapidly every which way. Then, Alex picked up the hairspray and lighter once more.

"Over there, next to that window," Alex said. When Timothy was safely up against the wall beside the window, Alex put his finger on the candle lighter's trigger and prayed there was some juice left. He clicked, and the flame dancing on the end of the long black tube made him shout with joyful relief. He held up the cannister and sprayed, pointing away from him and toward the bed.

The flame caught and exploded outward. The bed was immediately blazing. Alex lifted the improvised torch and swept the room with it, singeing mosquitos as he backed up next to Timothy. Smoke quickly filled the room. After a minute, Timothy opened the window, and the two of them fell over themselves to get outside, smoke billowing out of the window behind them. Timothy started to get up, to run, but Alex reached out and stopped him, grasping his ankle.

"Wait," he said. "We don't know where the majority of the swarm went after we shut that door. If they got out, they'll flee the smoke. We don't want to tempt them again. We need to stay near the fire for now."

Alex rolled onto his back in the grass, breathing heavily, drenched in sweat inside the suit. Timothy collapsed onto the ground next to him. They lay there, yards away from the house they'd set on fire, as smoke made the air hazy and blacked out the sky directly above. Pure exhaustion settled in as adrenaline faded. Alex had walked for hours with Timothy before the swarm had shown up, and he was certain he'd gained a few bruises when he'd taken that tumble on the football field. His body was sore and depleted.

"I think there's enough space," Timothy said after a long while.

Alex let his head loll to the side so he could look at him. "What?"

"Between the houses," he said. "I don't think the fire is going to spread. There's no wind."

Alex nodded. "That's good," he said, and after a few more minutes, "hey… thanks."

"For what?" Timothy asked.

"For being a cowboy," Alex said.

Timothy laughed. "Yeah… I guess I need to work on that savior complex."

"Well," Alex said, keeping his tone flat. "Nobody's perfect."

Timothy laughed harder, and it seemed contagious. Alex started laughing, and he just couldn't stop. The two of them lay sprawled on the ground, a house on fire, smoke everywhere, in their hazmat suits laughing like maniacs. Alex could only stop after his vision had long been blurred by tears and his sides hurt.

"Alex!" A female voice interrupted them, shouting over the roar of the fire.

Alex sat up and turned, finding Conner and her three companions looking between them and the house on fire several yards away. The flames raged, and black smoke billowed into the sky. Conner and the other soldiers were farther from the house than Alex and Timothy, and it didn't look like they wanted to get any closer.

"Conner," Alex stood, his exhausted legs trembling a little as he put weight on them. He helped Timothy to his feet, and the two of them approached.

"Whoa, stop right there." One of the soldiers held up a hand, and the two other strangers put hands to weapons. "That swarm was all over you."

Alex looked straight at Jenny Conner. "Conner, maybe tell your guys to back off."

"That's *Sergeant* Conner," the man said.

Alex quirked and eyebrow. *So she's been promoted?*

For a minute, he wasn't sure if Conner would help them or not. She stared at him with pursed lips for too long before she finally relaxed and held out an open-palmed hand toward her companions.

"Alex is a friend, okay? And they've got protective gear," she said. "High quality hazmat suits. I don't see an inch of exposed skin, do you, Warren?" She looked at the other two, looking first at a taller, lanky man and then at a short, stocky one. "Yeomen? Potts?"

"Doesn't matter," Yeomen said. "We can't get too close until they've gone 24 hours."

Alex held up his hands as Conner crossed her arms, seeming ready to dissent. "No, it's okay. We can still talk, right? As long as we stay a good ten feet apart and we keep our gear on, it would be nearly impossible for us to spread DV-10 if we *did* catch it. Which I don't believe is the case."

"He's a CDC guy," Conner said. "If he's here, it's for something important." She looked at him, quirking an eyebrow. "Right?"

"Yes." Alex nodded reassuringly. "I swear, President Coleman is going to want to know what's happening."

"Let's move a little farther from the smoke," Conner said.

"Not too far," Alex said. "The smoke is what's deterring the swarm from returning."

"Clever." Conner nodded, looking up at the smoke with interest.

"Dangerous," Warren said. "Reckless, even. I doubt they examined their surroundings to determine if starting a house fire was the smartest solution."

"Considering this is the last house on the row," Timothy said, "and the fact that we were trapped by a swarm, we didn't have much choice."

Warren's features hardened. "And if the fire spreads? If the wind picks up? We don't have the capability to stop a city-wide fire."

"It's contained for now," Conner said. "Potts, why don't you radio this in. We'll need someone to watch the fire, at least. Give a warning should it start to spread."

Potts nodded and did so. Then, the group moved into the cul-de-sac at the end of the street, the air hazy but seemingly bearable for the soldiers who didn't have the luxury of respirators.

"You feeling okay?" Alex asked in a low voice.

"So far," Timothy said. "You?"

"I'm tired, but… I don't think I'm experiencing any symptoms." Alex took a deep breath and rolled his shoulders. "Let me do the talking," he said.

"We've both got things to say," Timothy said. He stepped just slightly ahead of Alex, stopping and projecting his voice through the mask. "What were you four doing here?" he asked. "Scavenging, or…?"

Alex sighed as all four soldiers smirked. "Tim—"

"Alex trusts you, Conner," Timothy said. "But before he starts talking and lays everything out on the table, I need to trust you, too."

"And who are you, exactly?" Conner asked.

"He's a friend," Alex said. "He's just—"

"I'm the son of Walter Peters," Timothy said. "And I'm here on his behalf."

Conner raised her eyebrows and the three others whispered amongst themselves. "The Walter Peters you were looking for, Alex?"

"Yes," Alex said.

"Where is he?" Warren asked.

Potts interjected next. "Did he have any answers?"

And then Yeomen: "Do you have a vaccine? A cure?"

Alex shook his head. "I see you've been spreading the word about what we've been up to in Boston," he said. "I thought we asked for discretion." His nerves were suddenly on edge.

"It got out among the soldiers," Conner said. "But they've all sworn not to say anything to civilians. And news that there's hope has boosted morale, Alex. You have no idea how hard it's been. We have so little in the way of answers."

"I'm pretty sure I have a good idea how hard things are right now," Alex said, not bothering to temper the irritation in his tone.

"Can we get back on track here?" Timothy snapped at Alex. "I need to know we can trust them." He turned to the soldiers. "What were you doing out here?"

"Patrolling," Conner said. "We try to keep the hostiles a good distance from our home base."

"And you do that by what? Shooting them on sight?"

"What? No, of course not." Conner's affronted expression was exactly what Alex wanted to see. "We only shoot in self-defense."

"We were told you murdered some teens who ventured into the forest north of the city to hunt." Timothy wasn't letting up. He sounded like an interrogator. "We were also told that you laid their bodies out on the street as a message to civilians at the arena."

"Is that what they're saying?" Conner's face had gone a shade paler at Timothy's words.

Potts spat on the ground. "Those lying sons of—"

"Why have you been talking to *them*?" Warren interjected.

"We came across them first," Alex said quickly, not wanting Conner to get the wrong idea. "We went to the Cheyenne Mountain complex. Met Mark, lost a set of weapons, and were directed to the arena. We'd only planned to scout out the arena, but some guy named Jarod led a posse out to surround us. If it hadn't been for some conflict they had to address, my guess is we'd be locked up somewhere inside their new compound."

Conner narrowed her eyes. "And that's whose word you're taking?"

"I know you just as well as I know them," Timothy said.

Conner shook her head and put her hands on her hips, looking at the ground for a moment before responding. "Okay, fine. Fair enough. There were five of us. We were patrolling, as I said. The swarm came up on us. We ran to the nearest pre-determined safe spot: that trailer on the other side of the field. The school is full of bodies. It isn't safe. A lot of these houses have corpses, too. We've got a few places we know are clear, and that's where we go when we need safety. On the way, we lost Redding. She was a good soldier and a good friend."

"We're sorry for your loss." Alex put a hand on Timothy's arm, squeezing through the hazmat suit. "Is that enough for you?" he asked.

Timothy shook his head. "I also need to know about those kids that were gunned down. It didn't seem like Jarod was lying about that, even if he did seem like a macho jerk."

"Those kids weren't out hunting for food," Potts said. "They were hunting *us*."

Conner nodded. "Maybe they'd been sent out to hunt deer or something, but that's not what they were doing. They killed one of ours, but then our guys took them out. It wasn't until after the shoot out that we realized they were so young."

"Not that their age would have changed much," Yeomen said. "They made it a survivor's game. Them or us."

"It's all that nonsense that's being spewed at the arena, at the complex," Conner said. "Some soldiers even fell for it. They're making a whole lot of good people out to be the enemy just because of their jobs before Day Zero."

"When we realized those kids were just teenagers," Warren said, "we returned their bodies to the arena. We didn't do it to send a message. We did it so their families could have closure, if they had any family left."

"How about now?" Alex asked. "Are you satisfied?"

Timothy crossed his arms. "And what about the stories of civilians being left to die while the only safe place was left to the elites?"

Conner snorted. "You mean the Cheyenne Mountain Complex? The place Mark and his guys had to clean out after everyone inside *died*? That safe place?"

Alex blinked. He hadn't considered that. "So… it's not safe?"

"Under proper protocols, sure," Conner said. "But all that happened before we even got here. I don't know what went wrong. The rumor is that someone sick and important came in before they started showing symptoms and the disease spread that way. If they were high enough in the chain-of-command, they might have been let inside even if they'd had symptoms. In the first days of this thing, no one really knew what was going on. We're really cautious now, but then?" She shook her head. "That's how a lot of people died: getting too close to people they knew."

"You've asked enough questions," Warren said. "It's time we asked some of our own. What were *you* doing out here?"

"Looking for you," Alex said.

"What happened in Boston?" Conner asked.

"We made some progress, but…" He winced, knowing the coming news wouldn't go over well. "The lab with all the research… it burned down. Most of our progress was lost, except for the notes I was able to save."

Conner gasped at the mention of the lab burning down, and the soldiers took a collective step back as if the words had slammed into them like a tidal wave. "Is the research you saved…" Conner gulped, as if she were afraid to finish her sentence. Still, she squeaked out the rest. "… is it enough?"

"No." Alex answered honestly. They didn't have time to beat around the bush. "That's why we're here. Walter Peters knows duplicates of the research, and more of what we call the countermeasure mosquitos, were stored elsewhere, at a place called Barlow Scientific Research Bank. But we have no idea where it is."

"And you knew government agents who survived would come here," Conner said.

"Exactly." Alex nodded eagerly. "And if anyone knows where the research bank is, we suspect they'd be here."

"I don't know for sure," Conner said, "but… I think you did the right thing. It's classified information, but again, those rumors are hard to keep quiet. We need to bring you back to the academy and arrange for you to meet with President Coleman."

Alex's heart skipped a beat at the sliver of hope Conner had dangled in front of him. "Okay, let's do it," he said, and then he looked at Timothy who had thrown him a glare. "I mean, I think we should go. What about you?"

Timothy sighed. "Yeah," he said. "We should go."

"We've got to get moving, then," Conner said. "It's a long walk. My guess is that we'll need to deposit you at a quarantine trailer on the edge of academy grounds. I'll brief the president, and I suspect he'll want to talk to you first thing in the morning."

Relief washed over Alex, mixed with a growing sense of anticipation. "We'll be ready for him."

Chapter 11

Alexander Roman

Alex undressed outside a small quarantine trailer and left his clothes, hazmat suit, and backpack on the ground, as instructed. A large, burly man in uniform watched from several yards off, scrutinizing him, making sure he followed directions. Perhaps fifty yards down the small dirt road, Alex could make out Timothy getting the same treatment.

He couldn't blame the military for their precautions. His hazmat suit and face shield had smeared mosquito guts all over them. Alex eagerly reached for the bucket of water and soap and scrubbed his skin vigorously, looking for any signs of welts beginning to form. He couldn't see his back, of course, but he stretched himself to be able to cover every inch in soap. It took a while to wash his body clean, and by the end of it, he was shivering despite the comfortably warm summer sun and his skin was red from the coarse sponge.

"What now?" he asked, teeth chattering.

The soldier guarding him grunted and pointed at the trailer. "Quarantine," he said. "Twenty-four hours."

Alex grimaced. "So, we'll be here all night and a good chunk of tomorrow?"

The man shrugged. "If you're not dead."

Alex glanced at his gear and clothing, his stomach lurching. *If I've caught DV-10... no, no use in thinking that way.* He took a calming breath as he rubbed his arms for warmth.

"What are you going to do with our supplies?" he asked.

"What can be saved will be sanitized and returned to you... if you're not dead."

"Yeah, you don't have to add that little caveat to every answer," Alex said. "I get it."

"Get inside the trailer," the soldier said. "I'll lock the door from the outside. There's a fresh change of clothes, a mattress, bedding, food, water, and two business buckets, labelled one and two. I think you get the idea." He quirked an eyebrow.

Alex grimaced. "Yeah, I got it."

"If you're not dead—" He ignored Alex's sigh. "—in the morning, we will collect the fertilizer. Got it?"

"Anything else?" Alex asked.

"Your briefing with the president will be tomorrow evening, but we've supplied a pad of paper and a few pens. Write down anything you think we ought to know. You can present your notes yourself, if—"

"If I'm not dead," Alex said, frustration lacing his tone. "And if I *am*, someone will deliver my notes to President Coleman."

"Exactly," the soldier grinned. "You're catching on." He nodded at the trailer. "Good luck," he said. "I hear you might be someone important."

"Yeah," Alex said. "Thanks. I guess."

He turned and entered the trailer, closing the door behind him. The sound of metal sliding against metal and a padlock clicking into place told him he was stuck inside until someone let him out. There was no window, though a battery-operated lantern sat on the floor next to the mattress, its bright white glow touching every corner of the space. Two MREs and two stainless steel water bottles sat next to the lantern on the floor, and there were, indeed, two buckets on the floor opposite the mattress, each one labelled and equipped with what appeared to be pool noodles on the rim for comfort and large, plastic drum covers fitted over top. Alex guessed the covers were to keep the smell contained should he need to use the improvised bathroom.

"Better than nothing," he said as he reached for a folded set of nurse's scrubs on the bed.

He dressed and then sat, pulling a blanket around him and setting the pillow between his back and the wall. His next step was to write down relevant information, but as he picked up the legal pad and a pen from beside the lantern, he wasn't sure where to start.

"I bet Timothy isn't writing anything at all." Alex tapped the pen against the paper as he thought out loud. "Maybe I should just write a letter to Coleman. Be honest. Lay everything on the table." He grimaced. "Except Timothy probably won't want me to mention the location of our families. But... how can I not? If we die, Walter will need access to the military's resources."

It took a good five minutes of debate with himself before Alex decided his only choice was to trust the people they came to Colorado to find. "Besides, he said, General Hunt was sweet on Minnie. He'd take care of her and Lauren and Oliver, and Minnie wouldn't let anything bad happen to the rest."

Satisfied with his reasoning, Alex started his letter, detailing what they'd found in Boston, the fact that the lab had burned along with the research, and what he knew about the research bank. Alex ended the letter with directions to the church and instructions to send Conner if General Hunt couldn't go himself. He trusted Conner, and she'd helped them before. There was no reason to believe she wouldn't again. Plus, Minnie and Lauren already had a good working relationship with her.

Once he'd finished writing, Alex stood up and searched his body for welts one more time before laying down and turning off the lantern. The trailer went dark. It was so quiet. And it was safe. Though the mattress wasn't of the highest quality, he could have been sleeping on clouds for the way his exhausted body welcomed its comfort.

But sleep had become the ultimate commodity. Alex drifted off to sleep only in short bursts, waking suddenly with an anxiety that clenched at his heart and made him sick to his stomach. Every chill down his spine or tickle in his throat brought on panic that had him switching on the light and searching his body once again. And his mind refused to let go of all the nerve-wracking unknowns, all the things that could go wrong while he waited for his quarantine to be up. Timothy could have succumbed to DV-10 already, or hostiles could have come upon the church and attacked in search of supplies.

Alex didn't know how long he lay there in a never-ending cycle of what-ifs that had him drifting into nightmares and waking to frantic thoughts, but eventually, he couldn't take it anymore. He sat up, grabbed the pen and paper, and flipped to a clean sheet to write more letters.

His first was to Oliver, and it was full of hopes and dreams, warnings and advice, and all sorts of stories of family history. The more he wrote, the more he realized how much he'd never told his son, how much Oliver might want to know one day, and how much information could die with Alex. It was long, and some of it was a rambling mess, but it gave him some comfort to think Oliver would have it should he die, that day or any day in the future.

Don't forget me, Oliver, he wrote. Don't forget your mom or the stories I've written for you. But also, let it all go. Don't cling to the past. Step forward into the future, your future, with boldness and kindness and bravery and love.

As Alex finished that first letter, tears sprung, warm and bittersweet. Warring emotions swirled inside: joy at the thought of his son and grief at the thought of never seeing him again, hope for his future and dread for what the world would throw at him. He signed the letter, his heart aching, and then he sat back and just breathed.

But something about the experience of writing to someone he loved had been therapeutic and life-giving. For the time it took to pen the letter, he'd not obsessed over his health, over every feeling in his body that could be a sign of something bad settling in. He picked up the paper and pen again.

His next letter was to Minnie. She was the glue that had held him together. Without her, he'd never have survived so long. From that first moment when she'd decided to let him and his son into her food truck, Minnie had been a constant rock. It took an enormous burden off him, to realize as he wrote the letter how he knew without a shadow of a doubt that Minnie would look after Oliver if he were gone.

Stay you, Minnie, he wrote. Teach Oliver to be a good person. Use that Southern charm — or should I call it Southern spice? — to continue making his world a better place.

When he'd finished that one, he moved on to write to Lauren. She would be there for Oliver, too. He imagined whether he lived or died, both Lauren and Minnie would be in his son's life forever. A smile formed as he wrote asking Lauren to teach Oliver everything she knew: everything from music to critical thinking to medical knowledge.

You're so smart, Lauren. Smarter than you give yourself credit for. Don't let anyone tell you otherwise. You're wonderful, just as you are, he wrote.

His pen hovered above the page as he reread the last few lines. Sitting there in the white, unnatural light of the lantern, leaving all that he had on a page, his heart had taken over, and a stream of his true thoughts and emotions had spilled out of him in the form of ink and letters and tear drops.

He knew what it was to lose someone he loved; he still ached for Naomi on a daily basis, still reached for her in his sleep, still thought to tell her first when anything happened, good or bad. But this was the first time since the nightmare started that he'd stopped to consider what he'd gained: a bond with two women, a love for them forged through fire — literally. And he'd never been closer to his son. When weighing all the love he held against all the grief, it became clear to him that love tipped the scale just enough to make life bearable. Part of him had died with his wife, but Oliver and Minnie and Lauren had breathed life back into him.

Once those three letters were finished, Alex was spent. His mind emptied, his emotions dealt with, he was able to lie down and finally sleep.

***

When Alex next woke, he grasped consciousness as if being handed a gift from God himself. He had his aches and pains, but there was nothing out of the ordinary. There was no way to tell how long he'd been quarantined, but he was starting to accept the likelihood that he was not sick.

Alex held onto that possibility with cautious optimism as he opened an MRE labelled "Vegetable Crumbles with Pasta in Taco Style Sauce." Several individual packets were inside the larger one, and he tried to hold skepticism at bay as he read more labels, which included: crackers, chunky peanut butter, raspberry applesauce, vegetarian taco pasta, jalapeño cashews, and a chocolate-flavored "nutritious energy bar." There were condiments, salt, utensils, and even some toilet paper. He set that aside for use later, frowning at the buckets across the room. He also set aside the packet labelled "flameless ration heater." The FRH would need water to heat the food, and he wasn't prepared to part with any of that quite yet.

Alex picked through the options and decided to eat the taco pasta followed by the applesauce. It wasn't bad, even at room temperature, and before he knew it, he was opening the rest of the food. He'd been a *lot* hungrier than he'd thought, and it wasn't long before he'd devoured every bit of the MRE. He chugged half of a water bottle, too.

After he'd eaten, he paced the trailer, and when he no longer wanted to do that, he relaxed again on the bed. His time in quarantine, sequestered in the quiet, went on. He ended up getting more sleep than he thought possible in the new world of endless fighting and danger.

When the door finally rattled with the accompanied sound of the padlock being unlocked, Alex was ready. His body was refreshed and renewed, but his anxious mind wanted to see Timothy and get the ball rolling with the president.

There was a knock on the door. "You dead?" the voice of the soldier from the day before boomed on the other side.

"Nope," Alex shouted back. "I'm still kicking."

"Stay back," the voice said before the door swung open.

Daylight filtered into the trailer, and Alex squinted at the fuller color of the outside. The white light of the trailer's lantern had left everything looking a bit washed out. He stood back until the soldier waved him forward, and as he stepped out, he was given a thorough once over. While the soldier examined him from a safe distance, Alex looked down the road toward the other trailer. Another man was approaching.

"I'm fine," Alex said. "Not even a sniffle."

"Yeah, all right," the soldier said, nodding. "Well, nice to meet you, Mr. Roman. Name's Kenny. Most people around here call me Major Willis, but Kenny's just fine, seeing as how you're a civilian."

"I get a name now?" Alex nodded in appreciation as he kept Timothy's trailer in his periphery. The other soldier was knocking.

"Well," Kenny shrugged. "You're not dead. Didn't make sense to go through introductions yesterday. No use coming to like a person hours before they're gone. I've had enough of that."

Alex cleared his throat. "I guess… that's one way to look at it." He shielded his eyes from the sun, tension building inside, tightening his chest as he watched what was happening down the road. He held his breath. *Come on, Tim. Come out.*

The door to the other trailer opened, and Timothy stepped outside. Alex put one hand on his chest and leaned over, his other hand on his knee. He straightened up and ran his fingers through his hair, laughing with relief.

"He's okay," Alex said out loud.

"Looks like it," Kenny said. "Why don't you go inside, grab your notes. We've got to get you two to your briefing."

Alex couldn't keep a grin off his face as he hopped back inside and picked up the legal pad. He held it close as he stepped back onto the dirt road.

"I… um… might have written a whole lot more than just notes to the president," he said. "I about used all the paper left on the pad. Most of it is for my son." He ripped out the first few pages and handed them over. "These are for the briefing."

"Nah, you can keep those for now," Kenny said. "They might want them after the briefing, but I'm sure you can keep the rest of the paper. Let's get going, then. We don't want to keep the president waiting." He started walking.

Alex followed, matching the soldier's quick pace down the dirt road. Timothy jogged to meet him halfway, seeming just as relieved to see Alex as Alex felt about seeing Timothy.

"The gear worked," Timothy said, grinning.

"We were lucky." Alex gave Timothy a hearty pat on the back. "I don't know that the swarm would have let up without the smoke."

"All that matters is that we're alive." Timothy returned the pat with a punch to the arm. "We make a good team, when we're not arguing."

Alex laughed, and shook his head, and the two of them followed the soldiers to where a four-seater golf cart with solar panels on the roof waited for them. It was enclosed in plastic that zipped up where doors might be. Alex got into the backseat with Timothy and the two soldiers took their seats in the front. As the cart ambled forward on the dirt road, Alex looked down at the legal pad where his letter to President Coleman started. His notes sobered him a bit, and his smile slowly faded. He had a lot to tell and a lot to ask. The briefing ahead was perhaps the most important meeting of his life. In a few hours, he would know if there was help to be found in Colorado Springs, and if there wasn't, he'd have to face a future devoid of all hope.

Chapter 12

Alexander Roman

The Michael Coleman of Colorado Springs was not the same guy Alex had left in Atlanta. Back then, the man had been finding his place. He'd been somewhat insulated inside the CDC as his father-in-law had sought to wield the power of his office. Coleman had been unsure of his position, not knowing if he truly was next in line for the presidency. But the man who sat at the head of the conference table listening as Alex recounted the relevant details of what had happened since they'd last seen each other… well, *that* Michael Coleman had clearly learned to fill the shoes of his predecessors. He was confident, used to giving orders without checking with a shadow looming over his shoulder, used to being accorded respect. While kindness still shone through in his greeting, President Coleman had become a leader.

General Alan Hunt was there, too, on the president's right-hand side. Two others, a man and woman, were also in the room. They'd been introduced as Dr. Chase Pullman and Colonel Lola Holland. They sat on the president's left, while an additional armed guard stood silently by the door. Alex and Timothy sat on the opposite end of the long conference table. A skylight lit the interior room with a soft daylight glow that seemed counter to the tension building as Alex's story unfolded.

When he had no more to say, Alex sat back in the office chair. "So, can you help us?"

Coleman sat still, his fingers laced on the table before him. "I think that's a long and complicated answer," he said.

Alex exchanged a look with Timothy. "I'm sorry, sir, but… we came all this way," Alex said. "We can handle long and complicated."

"I'm sure you can." Coleman gestured to the two strangers at the table. "I invited Dr. Pullman and Colonel Holland to this meeting because they were part of the office at the Department of Defense that dealt with the commissioning of Project Pinpoint."

Alex straightened. He'd first heard the name of the project in Boston, but the last time he'd been around Coleman, Alex had been the one with more information. *How much does he know?* He was about to ask, hopeful that he was about to get some answers.

But Timothy spoke first. "So you were the ones who hired my father's company to create this disease and the mosquitos in the first place?" His tone was harsh.

"Well," Colonel Holland said, "we didn't come up with the idea on our own, and we certainly didn't allow a failed, deadly experiment to leak into the world."

Dr. Pullman was less haughty as he spoke. "I was on the Chemical and Biological Defense medical team, but I wasn't involved in Project Pinpoint directly." He scooted his chair a few centimeters from the colonel.

Alex put a hand up as Timothy took a breath as if about to respond. "How long have you been in Colorado," Alex asked, "and why didn't you come to Boston? Surely you knew that was where the research was."

"I did," Holland said. "I also had a family to get to safety and a promised spot inside that mountain complex."

A sudden burst of anger shot through Alex's body, and his cheeks flushed with heat. "I have a family, too," he said. "So does Walter Peters. We both risked our lives and the lives of our children to get to New Horizons Laboratory in order to work on a solution to DV-10 and these damn swarms."

The colonel quirked an eyebrow at him. "Congratulations," she said. "I see that worked out wonderfully. How long were you there, exactly, before you let the lab burn down?"

Timothy stood up so fast his office chair on wheels slammed into the wall behind them. The guard by the door stepped forward, raising his weapon. Alex was on his feet in the blink of an eye, one hand on Timothy's chest the other held out toward the guard.

General Hunt grunted. "Sit your ass down, son." Even in the dim light, Alex could make out the muscles in his neck and arms tightening.

"He's right, Tim," Alex said through gritted teeth, not thrilled with letting the colonel get away with her jab.

President Coleman waved off the guard. "That's not necessary," he said. "They're unarmed."

"She has no idea what we've been through," Timothy said under his breath. "We've sacrificed everything and—"

"I know," Alex said, keeping his voice low. "But we need them."

"They haven't given us anything of value." Timothy scowled, but he retrieved his chair and sat down, hard. "And they've just admitted to being cowards."

"Now," President Coleman said, "you've had your say, Mr. Peters. That really *is* enough from you. I can have you removed, if you'd like. I allowed your presence due to your father's importance, but you don't have to be here."

"He should be here," Alex said. "It's important that Walter trust the information we bring back to him, and he trusts his son. Walter barely knows me."

"I won't tolerate outbursts," President Coleman said, and then he looked at the colonel, "or backbiting."

Holland's cheeks reddened and her lips pinched before she let out a begrudging, "Yes, Mr. President."

President Coleman turned his eyes on Alex and Timothy and raised his eyebrows. "Well?"

"Yes, sir," Alex said as calmly as he could as Timothy muttered the same. Alex added for good measure, "Mr. President."

"Now, listen up," General Hunt said gruffly. "We're on your side, damn it."

Timothy was calmer, but his voice still held an edge. "We'll see," he said.

"The fact is," the president said, ignoring Timothy's comment, "we were hoping to tackle this problem from two fronts. I'd counted it a blessing that Colonel Holland made it to Colorado Springs once I found out what she knew." He paused, seeming to calculate before he spoke. "The fact is, the colonel informed me of the project and of Barlow Scientific Research Bank shortly after I arrived." He looked at Timothy. "I don't know what Mr. Roman has told you, but when he left Atlanta, we didn't know much more than rumors and speculations." He sighed. "My first thought after learning all about Project Pinpoint was to send a team of skilled individuals to Boston to help you, but Colonel Holland convinced me that working on two fronts to solve the problem would be wiser."

Alex nodded slowly. "So, you've sent a team to the research bank already?"

"No," President Coleman said, looking at the colonel. "We have a problem. Several, actually. The first is that the research bank is in Antarctica."

"Excuse me?" Alex blurted at the same time that Timothy cursed.

Alex stared at the president, and then looked at the others in the room, hoping for some sign that Coleman was trying to be funny.

"He's serious," General Hunt, his no-nonsense expression serious as ever, said flatly.

"That's *so far away*," Alex said. He breathed out, deflated and daunted by the idea of even attempting to cross the Southern Hemisphere.

Timothy's tension seemed to melt in the face of shock. His shoulders slumped. "How are we supposed to get there?"

"Actually," Holland said, "we have a theory of how we might be able to get *to* Antarctica. That's actually not as hard as you might think, not right now, anyway, when the fuel for our planes is still viable."

General Hunt scoffed. "You mean if we can find *two* pilots who can fly the only aircraft in Colorado Springs that can make a nonstop flight to Christchurch?"

Colonel Holland sighed. "Yes, sir," she said. "That's what I mean."

"As in New Zealand?" Timothy asked. "Why would we need to go to Christchurch?"

"Christchurch is a gateway to Antarctica," Colonel Holland said. "If we land there, we can possibly pick up a plane that's more suited to landing on ice in McMurdo. And there might be personnel still alive there or supplies that could help us survive our mission."

"You said we have several problems," Alex said, his stomach sinking.

Colonel Holland nodded. "Even if we can get on the continent, we wouldn't know where to go once we arrived. And seeing how the continent isn't known for its forgiving nature, that's a much larger problem. We've not been able to contact any of our stations. Long-distance communications around the world are gone."

"We have no idea of the condition of those who live on the continent," President Coleman said. "If a supply plane landed with DV-10 on board, they could all be dead."

"Excuse me, Mr. President," Colonel Holland said, "but even if most of Antarctica is compromised, I believe the crew at the research bank have a better chance of still being alive. Their location is Top-Secret, and they only take in supplies once a year. Before communications were cut off, messages were sent to all of our Top-Secret facilities warning them to stay put and stay safe, that there was a worldwide plague, and that they should hunker down. Barlow was told specifically that the research they protected could be vital to a treatment or vaccine."

"So," Timothy said, "what happens if those people *do* die? Or abandon the research bank?"

Colonel Holland nodded as if the question was anticipated. "Facilities like this one are created with the worst-case scenario in mind. Barlow was created with the capability to go into a sort of sleep-mode. Its backup power is always kept at full strength, and with no human intervention and using very limited energy, the facility can maintain cryopreservation pods for eight months. The most important databases will remain functional for a year."

"But it all comes back to one thing," General Hunt said. "We have assets, albeit nearly unreachable assets, but Antarctica is a big place, and Colonel Holland does not have the coordinates needed in order to find them."

"How do you know *about* the research bank without knowing its location?" Alex asked.

"My duties as the Deputy Assistant Secretary of the DASD did not include memorizing coordinates of every facility we have around the world." She shuddered. "Washington was... chaotic. It fell hard and fast. Fires took out a lot of infrastructure. Panic made everyone crazy. The chain-of-command was lost as everyone just... died. I uploaded as many files as I could to a thumb drive, and I got out of there with my family."

"And with me," Dr. Pullman said. "I was alone at the facility, and the colonel allowed me to come with her."

"He and I were possibly the only ones on staff still alive," Colonel Holland said. "It didn't make sense to leave him behind."

"The coordinates are on the thumb drive, then?" Timothy asked. "That's great, right?"

Colonel Holland looked down, for the first time losing her confident assertiveness. "It was lost on the way here," she said. "I kept it on me at all times. I was vigilant, but... there was an altercation on a bridge. My daughter fell into the river below, and I went after her without a second thought. I was able to pull her to shore, but when I did, the thumb drive was gone."

Alex didn't much like the colonel, but a part of him softened toward her. "Any parent would have done the same," he said firmly.

"I agree," President Coleman said.

General Hunt grunted his approval, and Dr. Pullman reached out a tentative hand and gave the colonel a very awkward pat on her shoulder. He pulled back like he'd touched fire when she gave him a sideways glance.

"If there's one thing I understand," Timothy said, "it's fighting for family, Colonel."

She swallowed audibly and lifted her chin. "I appreciate the sentiment," she said, looking at each of them. "I truly do. But the important thing now is that we need those coordinates."

"Where are they?" Alex asked. "I'm assuming with the way you're talking that there is a way to get them."

President Coleman nodded. "There is. The Cheyenne Mountain Complex has an internal offline database where important information is stored. The computers that run it can't even access the internet. We believe that the coordinates to Barlow Scientific Research Bank can be found in that database."

Alex sat back and tried to process the overwhelming odds against them. "So… we have to find a way inside the complex, log into the database to find the coordinates, figure out how to get to Antarctica, travel to the research bank, finish the research, and then somehow administer the treatment and release countermeasure mosquitos worldwide." He let out a long, slow breath. "Is there *any* good news?"

"Oh, yes," Dr. Pullman said, grinning. "Swarms shouldn't be able to thrive in Antarctica due to the temperatures." His grin faded. "However, neither would we without the modern equipment that makes life on Antarctica tenable, especially this time of year. There's no daylight, extremely low temperatures, hostile weather, and no natural food sources."

"So, then," Timothy said, "when we do get there, instead of the swarm trying to kill us, we'll be fighting against nature itself to survive?"

"Yes." Dr. Pullman nodded matter-of-factly. "Now, things are a little more friendly come late October and through February, but we certainly can't wait another three months just to get *started* on finishing the research. Every month means a smaller worldwide population, more time for the swarms to multiply, and less probability of success when it comes time to rebuild."

"Great." Alex rubbed his hands over his face.

"But," Colonel Holland said, "while it will be dangerous, the supplies and people we could gain in Christchurch would make it possible."

"We need to take things one step at a time," President Coleman said. "The first thing we need to do is get those coordinates. The second is finding a couple of pilots."

"I do have an update on the latter," General Hunt said. "After interviewing the surviving local airmen, I discovered there's a retired pilot who was something of a doomsday prepper. Went off the grid ten years ago. We're still looking for a second pilot, though."

"I wish we could find more than just two," President Coleman said. "It's such a specific skill set, one that we may need." He shook his head. "But we have to do what we have to do."

"Actually," Tim said, glancing at Alex with a furrowed brow. "Isn't Kai a pilot?"

Alex nodded slowly. "He's flown small aircraft, from what I understand."

General Hunt leaned forward. "Perhaps he knows enough already to be of some use."

"We'd have to wait on the opinion of the expert," President Coleman said. "Have we sent anyone to retrieve this pilot?"

"Conner's team is recovering from their loss," General Hunt said, "but they're the best we've got for the job. The sergeant has requested to lead the team that retrieves the rest of Alex's people, though, and I'm keen to let her do it first. It should be a quick, easy job, and her team needs a boost in morale."

"Good." The president nodded. "That's all we can do about that for the time being. Now, about getting into the complex to retrieve those coordinates…"

Alex rolled his shoulders and settled into his chair. We've only gotten everyone caught up and on the same page, he thought. This meeting is just getting started. Now begins the real work.

Chapter 13

Minnie Stevens

Minnie never understood how anyone in their right mind could use the word 'dog' slanderously. In her mind, dogs had a lot going for them. They were loyal, kind unless taught differently, empathetic, protective of those they loved… the list went on. Of course, there was a bad apple every now and then, but for the most part, dogs were good people. *Actual* people, though… well, they were a different story. Nine times out of ten, one could count on a dog being friendly. Nine times out of ten, one could count on a person hiding away something ugly. Nasty dogs bared their teeth in warning; they didn't hide their nastiness. Nasty people tended to smile and pat you on the back two seconds before sticking a knife in it.

"When this is all over, Samson," Minnie said, "let's me and you take a vacation." She reached down and scratched her dog between the ears.

He looked up at her with a whine and big, puppy dog eyes.

"Fine," Minnie said, "Oliver can come, too."

Samson barked twice and nudged Minnie's leg with his head before turning and tugging on his leash to keep walking. Minnie sighed but smiled as she let Samson keep going in the lot behind the church. He loved his daily walks, and he seemed quite satisfied to sniff at the decorative trees and mulch, mark his territory, and mosey on to next concrete planter.

Minnie was satisfied, too. The sun was shining, and she could see far in every direction, besides just behind her where the church blocked her view. If a swarm were to come that way, she'd be able to spot it in plenty of time to get back to safety. Zara watched the front, knew that Minnie was out walking the dog, and would warn her if there was trouble coming that way.

And it was quiet. Not the tense kind of quiet that made Minnie's stomach churn and her mouth run wild, like the silence between those girls – Lizzy and Azalea – and Walter and Zara. Still, that was better than the snooty noises Candice made every morning while digging through her ridiculous suitcase, complaining about the state of her clothes and makeup.

"For goodness' sake," Minnie had said just that morning, after many mornings of keeping her annoyance to herself. "Nobody cares, Candice. We all got holes in our clothes. And you're the only one still paintin' her face." It became clear real quick that she'd made a mistake. Not because she'd been wrong, either, but because Candice was too hoity-toity for down-to-earth advice.

Candice had proceeded to huff and puff for a good spell about "standards" and how there was nothing wrong with "self-care even at the end the world." In the end, Minnie decided the woman was probably just holding on to something to make her feel normal.

"All right, then," she'd said. "Bless your heart, don't have a cow. I'll not say nothin' about it ever again."

Minnie wrinkled her nose as she thought about the conversation. "I guess it ain't my place to judge," she muttered, glancing up to the sky. "So help me, it ain't my place. Everybody's got a vice. I guess bein' a bit of a priss ain't no worse than me actin' the judge."

That had always been her weakness, judging people. Thinking she knew best. It about ruined her relationship with her daughter forever. And she *was* better than she used to be. She'd grown a lot in past years, but sometimes that old habit reared its ugly head. *Other* people weren't the only ones hiding their ugly.

Minnie took a deep breath of coveted fresh air. The outdoors was a different kind of sanctuary, one that allowed for self-reflection in wide-open space, where she could acknowledge the bad, dig it out, and let it float away on the wind.

Samson's ears perked up, and he took a few steps back toward the church building before freezing in place, every muscle tense. A low growl emanated from his throat, and Minnie's heartbeat picked up.

"What is it?" She asked.

The back door to the church opened. "Mom!" Lauren shouted. "Get inside! A vehicle is pulling in. It looks like the truck Alex and Tim were driving, but it parked on the edge of the property. Hasn't come any closer, and it's making me suspicious."

Minnie jumped into action, pulling Samson's leash to get him to go inside instead of rushing around the building where he clearly wanted to go. When she reached the door and slipped into the church, she pulled out a key in her pocket and locked the door from the inside. She'd found a master key in the office where she'd found the candy.

"They wouldn't lead anyone hostile this way," Minnie said.

"Probably not." Lauren picked up a rifle she'd left leaning against the wall. "But better safe than sorry. And I said the truck *looks* like ours. If Alex and Tim step out and they don't look like they're under any duress, we're all good to go. But with that story of Tim leading that mobster back to their bunker… I'm just not willing to take any risks."

Minnie nodded, aware of the handgun on her own hip. She never went outside without it. The swarms would give her warning. Bad guys might not. "You need me with the kids?"

Lauren shook her head. "Candice has them. If it's people from Atlanta, we'll need friendly faces."

Minnie's heart skipped a beat as she thought about General Hunt. Alan had been a little sweet on her, and she'd not minded one bit. The gentle giant gave her butterflies like she was a teenager with a crush. Heat flushed to her cheeks, and she looked down at herself, suddenly wishing she'd asked Candice for some help instead of getting annoyed with her.

Lauren smiled. "Mom, if he's here, he's not going to care that you're a little scuffed up. Do you think he'll be any different? There's not a lot of opportunity these days for pressing clothes or curling hair. Honestly, it's just impressive that we've all had sponge baths this week and our clothes are sort of clean."

Minnie nodded. "I guess no one smells that bad if *everyone* stinks to high heaven."

"That's the spirit," Lauren said. "Now, let's go."

Minnie, with Samson by her side, followed her daughter through the halls of the church to the front doors where Zara, Kai, Walter, Azalea, Lizzy, and Heather waited. Zara, Walter, and Heather were all armed. Outside, Minnie watched the truck. It was impossible to know exactly *who* was inside from that distance, but she could make out three individuals. They were talking animatedly, using a lot of hand gestures.

Finally, though, the person in the back stepped outside. They were in full gear, including fatigues, bulletproof vest, and a helmet. They held their rifle at the ready and moved forward in quick, measured steps. The other two stepped out, too, each of them with their own vest, and followed behind the soldier. It wasn't long before Minnie could confirm the two who'd been in the front of the truck were Alex and Tim.

"Everyone who's armed, come with me," Lauren said. "We're going to meet them in the lot."

Minnie handed Samson's leash to Walter and followed Lauren's lead again, as did the other three who were armed. When they stepped outside, the soldier stopped for a moment and then lowered their weapon and took off their helmet.

The woman yelled out two names: "Lauren? Minnie?"

"Land's sake! Jenny Conner, is that you?" Minnie shouted.

"It's okay," Lauren said, gesturing for them all to put away their weapons as she flipped on the safety on her rifle.

"She wouldn't let us just come up," Timothy said once the gap between them was closed.

"I followed precautions," Conner said, giving him the side eye. "Just like they did."

"Fair point," Alex said.

Timothy shrugged and put his arm around his wife's shoulders. Minnie stayed quiet as Lauren and Conner made small talk on the way to the church building. She was trying to figure out some way to bring up the general in conversation.

He's a busy man, Minnie thought. Of course he couldn't come here himself. A sick feeling washed over her. Unless something happened to him.

But then Lauren, bless her soul, brought it up for her. "So, how are the people from Atlanta?" she asked. "Hunt and Coleman? Are they okay, too?"

Conner nodded as they slowed and Walter came out to hold open the door. "Yeah," she said. "They're great, all things considered. President Coleman and his family made it safe and sound, and General Hunt helped him set up and take command of what was left of the military here." She held up a finger, her eyes widening. "Oh! I almost forgot." She started digging in her pockets until she pulled out a folded envelope. She handed it to Minnie with a wink. "This is for you," she said.

Minnie blushed and cleared her throat, snatching the note and putting it in her pocket. Lauren waggled her eyebrows at her. Minnie scowled and lifted her chin, marching inside.

"I think you just left my mom without any words," Lauren said as she followed. "Impressive."

Conner chuckled. "Well, General Hunt is almost downright *talkative* when it comes to her. I don't think I knew what it meant when books talked about someone's eyes twinkling until seeing him when Miss Minnie Stevens is brought up."

"Oh, enough of that," Minnie said as the entire group gathered in the church's lobby, though she couldn't help but grin as she nudged Lauren's arm. She took Samson's leash from Walter.

"She's right," Conner said. "It's time to move beyond pleasantries."

"We should gather in the sanctuary where we can all sit," Alex said.

Minnie tucked away her excitement about the letter. The expression on Alex's face gave her a bad feeling that whatever they wanted to talk about wasn't going to be pleasant. The group moved into the sanctuary, and the three new arrivals stood before them. Minnie settled with Samson at her feet as Alex and Timothy gave a detailed account of their last couple of days. When they got to explaining their situation and all the roadblocks in their way, the very air around them seemed to get heavier and thicker with every word. By the time they were finished, Minnie's mouth had dropped open and Samson, seeming to sense her tension, had sat up and rested his head in her lap.

"Does anyone have any questions so far?" Alex asked.

"Sure," Minnie blurted, "like how're we supposed to make fried chicken when we've only got the feathers?"

Conner wrinkled her brow. "I'm sorry… what?"

Minnie sighed in frustration. "I thought when you left we'd be a step or two away from the end of all this, but now… good grief! We've just been warming up. We've still got a whole race in front of us."

Lauren cut in. "I think what my mom is trying to say is that we have a list of things that need to be done and no way to actually do them. You say we need to get into Cheyenne Mountain to get these coordinates, but you don't say how that's even possible. You talk about getting to freaking Antarctica by way of *New Zealand* like it's an option, but… again… how?"

"We do have some answers," Alex said. "But we wanted to get out the basic plan before going into the how because… well, we don't think you're going to be thrilled about the options."

"I've come with Alex and Tim for more than just protection," Conner said. "I'm not going back to base, and I hope I'm not going alone." She looked right at Lauren, and Minnie shook her head before the woman even said a word. "Lauren, I want you to come with me to the arena. We're both young and of child-bearing age. You can go in as a nurse. I'll use my background growing up on a farm. I can make preserves, can vegetables, garden, sew, and I know a bit about breeding and keeping chickens… my family kept alive a lot of old school skills."

"What does being of childbearing age have to do with it?" Lauren asked, her face going pale.

The blood drained from Minnie's face. "Yeah, what *does* that have to do with it?"

"The people who hold the mountain are looking for working-class people, and they're looking to protect the ability of the population to regrow," Conner said. "The women who are accepted have to agree to attempt pregnancy either via the natural way or the redneck way."

"Like a turkey baster?" Minnie shouted. "Hell no! My daughter ain't steppin' foot in that backwards, hillbilly, no-good den of snakes!" She scooted closer to Lauren and put an arm around her daughter's shoulders, and Samson added a few good barks for emphasis.

"Every woman has a timetable of six months," Conner said, putting her hands up as if to calm her. "They say everyone gets the chance to acclimate and decide if they want to commit before becoming a permanent part of the community. The six months is a probationary period for everyone, both men and women. We'll be out of there long before anyone would expect us to do anything we don't want to do."

Lauren swallowed audibly and squeaked out, "It's okay, Mom. I'm okay with that."

"What?" Minnie narrowed her eyes at Conner. "Who's 'they' and how do you know 'they' won't force somethin' on my baby girl?"

"We have sources inside," Conner said. "They're reliable. I swear. I wouldn't go in there myself if I didn't believe that."

"I'll do it," Lauren said. "But... why a nurse and not a doctor? I have knowledge beyond a nursing degree. I could pass as a family doctor."

"A nurse will have a little more freedom," Conner said. "They want working-class people, and they view doctors as highbrow, even the ones who probably weren't. The doctors are watched closely, and they have a high workload. There's only two of them for the entire complex. They might *want* a third, but you'd have no time to do the work we actually need to do."

"We can go, too," Azalea said. "Lizzy and me. We're of childbearing age."

Minnie turned with the rest of those present to stare at Azalea, who sat with Lizzy behind them all. The girls didn't often speak, but Minnie hadn't taken them for fools. Lizzy had a moment of shock flash across her features, but it was gone almost as quickly as it had appeared. Goosebumps ran up and down Minnie's arms. It wasn't the first time Azalea had spoken on behalf of Lizzie like that.

Minnie looked back at Conner, expecting the woman to immediately decline. *Those girls have no business going undercover.*

Instead, Conner frowned and asked, "Do you have any other skills?"

"We're alive," Azalea said. "We survived. And we're young. And we're healthy. We can volunteer for cleaning duties. No one wants to do that, but maids are invisible. It would be perfect for someone trying to gather information."

Minnie shook her head. "Are we so desperate that we're willing to send in a couple of girls?"

"We're both legally adults," Azalea said. "And even if we don't get into the complex via this lottery, we can help gather information at the arena."

Walter shook his head. "That's a bad idea."

Conner grimaced. "I'm sorry, but... the more the merrier."

"Lizzy is still dealing with a lot of trauma," Walter said. "She should—"

"I'll make my own decisions," Lizzy said.

There was a few minutes of awkward silence before someone else spoke up.

"And where do the rest of us go?" Heather asked.

"That leads us to the problem with the pilots," Conner said. She looked straight at Kai. "I hear you know how to fly."

Kai shook his head vehemently. "Look, babe, I'm not getting into a plane any time soon."

Conner quirked an eyebrow. "You can call me 'sergeant.'"

Zara elbowed him hard, and the young man winced. "Sorry. But still, I can't fly."

"You can't or you won't?" Conner asked. "You would only be assisting if we can get the retired pilot to come back in for one last mission. And he'd train you to fly the plane that would take you to New Zealand."

"I won't," Kai said, leaning back and putting an arm lazily over the back of the pew. He didn't elaborate.

Conner crossed her arms. "We need you," she said.

"Kai... maybe you should think about it," Zara said softly.

Kai looked at her for a moment before letting his arm drop back beside him and slumping forward. "Fine," he said. "I'll think about it."

"My team is going without me to find this guy," Conner said. "I was hoping you'd go with them. He's more likely to come back with them, to agree to our plan, if there's proof we have a second pilot."

"I'll go with you," Zara said with a small smile.

Kai glanced at her and then back down at his lap. "Yeah, all right," he said.

Minnie's heart was breaking. All these young'uns with the weight of the world on their shoulders. They deserve to have the chance to heal. Instead, we're pushin' them into the fire after pullin' them outta of the frying pan.

"So," Alex said, "Conner, Lauren, Azalea, and Lizzy will go to the arena, enter the lottery, and get into the complex to steal those coordinates. Kai and Zara will go with Conner's team to find and convince this retired pilot to come back with them and fly us to New Zealand. The rest of us go back to the military academy where we'll be safe, where me and Walter can continue to study the research I saved and speak with Colonel Holland about what we plan to do once we get to Antarctica. Is everyone okay with that?"

Heather stood up. "No," she said. "I think... I think I want to go with the women heading to the complex."

"What?" Timothy shook his head. "Why would you want to do that?"

"She said the more the merrier," Heather said.

Timothy glared at Conner. "Tell her this is insane."

Conner held up her hands. "I'm not about to tell a grown woman what she can't do, not when she's right. The more people we have inside coordinating with each other to find what we need, the quicker we can get those coordinates and get out of there."

Timothy crossed his arms. "I can't go with you. We said we would stay together."

Minnie frowned as Heather's eyes glistened. *There's more going on here,* she thought.

"Conner, do they have a functioning medical facility?" Heather asked.

Timothy scoffed. "What does that m—"

"They're looking for women who can have babies. Does that mean they have a gynecologist?" Heather asked.

Conner's frown deepened. "Yeah, they do."

Minnie's mouth dropped open. *Oh. My. Good. Gravy.* A revelation hit her before it was confirmed.
Timothy set his jaw. "Heather, I won't let you—"
"I think I'm pregnant," Heather shouted.
Minnie closed her mouth and squirmed in her seat. Everyone fell completely silent as Timothy took a few steps backward, almost as if someone had punched him in the gut.
Heather blushed but continued. "I'm *really* late, and I've had a lot of symptoms. It hit me this morning. I didn't think it was possible, but… if it is, I need to make sure it's not ectopic, like the last one."
"Pregnant women don't need to enter the lottery," Conner said softly. "They'll make you take a test at the arena, and if you *are* pregnant, they'll take you in, no more questions asked. But… it might be hard for you to get out."
"You have a history of ectopic pregnancy?" Lauren asked.
"Just one," Heather said. "And two other miscarriages."
"She needs to go," Lauren said. "If they have a gynecologist, she needs to be seen."
Timothy ran a trembling hand through his hair. "Yeah," he said. "Okay."
Heather got up and came to him, wrapping her arms around his neck. "I'll be fine," she said.
Not one bit of their new plan sat right with Minnie, but she couldn't see a way around any of it. "All right, now," she said. "We've all got our marching orders." Empathy washed over her as Heather turned and leaned into her husband's side. "But it's too late to pack up and get on the road today. I think we all need a little time to process this mess, anyway."
"Minnie is right," Alex said. "We'll head out in the morning, after everyone's gotten some rest. In the meantime, we should grab something to eat. We brought some MREs from the academy, one for each of us."
The group began to disperse, but Minnie stayed put as the sanctuary emptied. "I'll be along in a minute," she said, scratching Samson's head. When the room was cleared, she breathed out long and slow. "I'm gettin' too old for this, Samson."
She reached into her pocket and pulled out Alan Hunt's note. She opened it, unfolded the paper, and smiled at the short message: *When the time's right, I'm here, Minnie Stevens. Yours Affectionately, Alan.*
Minnie held the note to her chest. It wasn't much, but from a man like General Hunt, it was everything. It wasn't so much that she loved the man that made her smile. It was more that she thought she *might* if she were given the opportunity. She tucked the letter away again, smiling at the hope it represented. And then she stood and stepped into the aisle. She had one night left with her daughter before they'd be separated again. She wasn't about to spend it moping in a corner.

Chapter 14

Heather Peters and Zara Williams

The unfamiliar highway in Colorado Springs was quiet. Heather waded through air thick with tension. There was the ever-present fear of the swarms, of course, but another familiar terror plagued her, one she'd first encountered a decade prior, one she'd thought she'd never have to deal with again.

Three times she'd been pregnant, and yet she'd never held a child of her own in her arms. She didn't know if this time would be just as dangerous as the last, which had been an ectopic pregnancy, or if she'd lose the child in a month or two. But she didn't dare consider any other option; to hope would only lead to a heartache she wasn't sure she could survive again.

But if she could get to a functioning medical facility inside Cheyenne Mountain, she could at least get answers.

"You okay?" Jenny asked, looking over her shoulder. The soldier was in plain clothes, dirtied and torn to appear worn over time and travel. She led the way, Heather behind her, Lauren a few paces behind Heather, and Azalea and Lizzy taking up the rear.

Heather took a few quick strides to catch up to Jenny. "This is just a longer walk than I thought it would be," she said.

Jenny glanced at her sideways. "We couldn't let the boys take us any closer. We can't risk being seen with them. Our story has to stand. We're just a bunch of women, banded together for safety, trying to find our way to a new home."

"I know," Heather said. "I'm not complaining."

"Well, I *am*," Lauren said as she matched their pace. "My feet are killing me."

Jenny quirked an eyebrow at Lauren. "That's because you've been spoiled, riding in your mom's RV all the time."

"Hey," Lauren said, "Harvey is like a member of the family."

Jenny smirked. "I can't believe you named your RV."

"Well, I did it when I was a little kid," Lauren said. "I thought my mom was saying 'Harvey' every time she said 'RV,' and the name just stuck."

Heather's first thought was, *Kids are adorable.* And her second thought was to bury the first. The last thing she wanted to do was talk about kids.

She looked out into the distance, adjusting the weight of her backpack, focusing instead on scanning the area ahead. They needed to keep an eye out for swarms.

"Hey!" Heather pointed at a green road sign ahead. "It says, 'World Arena, Broadmoor, Next Right.'"

Jenny nodded. "Yep. Looks like we're almost there."

Heather couldn't see anything beyond the trees lining the highway on the left, and the right was nothing but farmland. It took a few more minutes for the tree line to fall away for buildings to take their place. Before long, they spotted a wall of crushed cars with no gate in sight. A silvery white, circular building peeked over the top of the wall.

"If it weren't for that," Jenny said, pointing at the crushed cars, "we could just cut across the highway, cut through that little wire fence, and be where we need to go. But from what our inside source tells us, armed guards keep watch all along the perimeter, especially here where the highway leaves them vulnerable."

"So we take the long way around," Heather said. "At least we're close."

They walked a little further, taking Exit 138 off the highway and into the city. Colorado Springs was large, but it was so spread out that it didn't have the same crowded feel as Boston. The streets were often wide, lawns were plentiful, and the sky was wide open. There was just so much *space*.

When they made their final turn, they did so onto a road that had been cleared of debris and abandoned vehicles. The wall of crushed cars came into view again, this time from the other side of the building.

Jenny paused and turned, holding up a hand to indicate Heather and Lauren should stop.

"Tim said not to hesitate, to go right up to the gate," Heather said.

"We need to wait on them," Jenny nodded toward Azalea and Lizzy. "We need to approach all together."

When they'd caught up, Azalea hooked her arm with Lizzy's. "What are we waiting for?" she asked.

"You," Jenny said. "Is everyone on the same page? Everyone remember their story?" She paused and looked from woman to woman. "Real quick, let's repeat them. Remember, the best lie is one that has some truth to it, okay?" She cleared her throat. "I'm a born-and-raised farm girl with Little House on the Prairie skills."

Heather nodded. "I'm a widow, likely pregnant, travelling with my sister-in-law and her best friend." She smiled at Lizzy.

Lizzy raised her hand. "Said sister-in-law, fresh out of high school, just trying to survive."

"And I'm Elizabeth's best friend from school," Azalea said. "My whole family's dead, and Heather was kind enough to bring me along."

Heather couldn't help but wince at that. It seemed so odd, like Azalea was stealing Zara's story. But Lizzy didn't even bat an eye. That was even more unsettling. Heather knew a lot had happened between Lizzy and Zara, but their friendship had been so strong before. It broke her heart that they were no longer friends.

"And I'm a nurse," Lauren said. "Met up with you guys a couple weeks back. I have no one left, either."

Jenny nodded. "Good," she said. "Okay, let's go, all together. Remember, we've been traveling together for weeks. Act like it." She gave Azalea and Lizzy a look. "Don't trail behind. Pretend we've all bonded, okay?"

Azalea flashed her a smile. "We've got it," she said. "Now we should keep moving before they get suspicious."

"She's right," Heather said. "We don't want them reacting to us like they reacted to Tim and Alex."

They turned as a group and approached the entrance, the junkyard wall rising on either side, metal barricades closing the gap, the message "Workers and Families Welcome" spray painted to their right, "For the People" spray painted to their left. There was a hexagonal deer stand, just as Tim had described. But there was also a bus parked off to the other side, and when they approached, men with guns stepped off the bus one at a time and lined up. They didn't approach, but they also didn't look too friendly. Dirt bikes were lined up beside the bus.

To their left, another man, this one unarmed, stepped out of the elevated deer stand and made his way to the ground. He wore a paper protective suit, gloves, a paper mask, and eye goggles. He had something small and white in his hand. "You ladies alone?" he asked while maintaining a safe distance.

"We are," Jenny said. "We need help. Shelter. We've been travelling for weeks."

Heather swallowed hard. Jenny didn't sound desperate enough. *Didn't Tim say they expected desperation?*

"Please," she said, letting her voice crack. "We heard this is a safe place for women, a place someone who's pregnant can get medical care. We ran across a man who'd been here but was denied entry to the mountain. He told us he didn't get lucky with some sort of raffle, but that we might."

The man raised his eyebrows. "Is one of you pregnant?"

Heather nodded. "I think so. I haven't been able to find a test."

The man held up a forehead thermometer. "Don't move," he said. He scanned each of them in turn, reaching with a fully outstretched arm. "No fevers," he murmured, looking them each up and down as if examining them.

"We have skills," Lauren said, voice laced with panic. "I'm a nurse." She put her hand on Jenny's shoulder. "Our friend can do all sorts of old timey things. Like canning and raising chickens and stuff. She won't shut up about growing up on a farm."

"Forget about skills," Lizzy said, stepping up, almost sounding like her old self. "Didn't you hear my sister-in-law might be pregnant? She's had bad experiences before. We heard you might be able to help, but if not, we need to find someone who can."

Good, Heather thought. We need to layer it on.

"No, no," the man waved his hands out in front of him. "We can help. There *is* a raffle, but if you're pregnant, at least you won't have to mess with that." He pointed back behind the deer stand. "All five of you are gonna have to quarantine for twenty-four hours in the back of one of those semi-trucks. There's a jug of water, some buckets for your business, a battery-operated lantern, and a box of protein bars in each. We can't spare more than that. All five of you to one," he repeated firmly. "I'll follow behind and lock you in. We'll open the door tomorrow."

Heather sighed, but she followed the man's directions, just like the others. She and the others climbed into the back of the semi-truck, the empty container barren but clean. Jenny turned the lantern on, and Vincent shut them inside, the metal doors clanging shut with a finality that made Heather's insides squirm.

"Well, this will be fun," Jenny said, tone laced with sarcasm.

"I think that went well," Lauren said, "didn't it?"

"As well as can be expected," Heather said.

"Agreed." Jenny glanced at Azalea and Lizzy. "Good job back there, Lizzy."

"Yeah," Heather said. "You were convincing."

Lizzy shrugged, her expression indifferent. "I just told the truth." She threw down her backpack and sat with a huff. "I don't like being cooped up like this." She glanced at the lantern, which threw a white light on everything. "We can keep that on, right? I won't be able to sleep if it's off."

"Of course we can," Heather said. She was about to step forward and sit next to Lizzy, her heart breaking at her nervous posture.

But then Lizzy flinched at her movement and Azalea took up residence at her side. "I'll be right here," Azalea said.

Lizzy nodded and leaned her head on Azalea's shoulder. She didn't look at Heather after that, and as the rest of the women settled, too, Heather found a spot on the plywood floor, using her lumpy backpack as a pillow. It was going to be a long twenty-four hours.

* * *

Zara could feel Kai's fear as if it were seeping out of his pores and saturating the surrounding air. It had been like that since the day before, when he'd agreed to "think about" assisting in the flight to New Zealand.

There really wasn't a choice; Zara knew that, and she believed Kai did, too. They *had* to convince the veteran pilot to take on the mission, and they *needed* Kai to help fly the plane. But the illusion of choice was important, and so she didn't push the matter further. Not yet anyway.

She was scared, too. The thought of getting back into a plane, of flying again… it made her heart pound loudly in her ears, made her blood run cold and her hair stand on end. The sounds of metal creaking and breaking, the tumultuous head-spinning tumble down a mountainside, the crash into a watery tomb, all while a storm raged, pelting them with freezing rain and hail—Zara would never rid herself of those memories.

She shuddered and took a breath. Just don't think about it, she told herself. That's not going to happen again, and if Kai is going to do this, he's going to need someone to be strong with him.

It was odd, the two of them having time alone. Walter had opted to sit with Timothy in the front of the truck that pulled the airstream. He'd wanted to talk to his son, apparently, and test his ability to ride sitting up. He'd been feeling better the last couple of days, the lingering fatigue seeming to ebb with a couple days of rest in one spot at the church. In the larger, four-door cab of Minnie's RV, Alex had driven, and Minnie had shared the cab. Candice had stayed in the back camper with Oliver and Annika.

Kai sat opposite her on the bed in the back of the airstream, his legs stretched out, inches from her own. His head rested on a pillow he'd stuck behind his neck, and he wore his aviator sunglasses. But he wasn't asleep; Kai wasn't a snorer, exactly. He was more of a… snorter. But he'd been quiet since they'd left the church and started toward the city, toward the Air Force Academy grounds where he and Zara would meet up with a team to go find and bring back the pilot. No, Kai was hiding behind those glasses, and Zara decided to let him.

If he doesn't step out of this state on his own, she thought, *I'll give him a nudge.* But she hoped he'd do it on his own. There was a time when she would've shoved him forward, bombarded him with the facts of what they had to do, of his responsibilities, of what was *right.* That approach was what had ruined her friendship with Lizzy. She knew that now, after having lost her best friend, first physically and then figuratively. She'd pushed and prodded and forced her opinions, all of which were driven by her anger and hatred and grief, onto Lizzy until her friend had shut down, until she'd started keeping things from her. And then Zara had fled, her escape allowing an enemy in, her selfishness and anger resulting in death and loss. Lizzy had been taken, scarred, and hurt. From start to finish, it had been Zara's fault.

As her mind turned to her regrets surrounding Lizzy, as they followed a roundabout route north and then west, an abandoned and broken cityscape passing by the airstream's windows, Zara was brought to thoughts of Azalea.

Despite having been in the same caravan as the woman, Zara barely knew her. Part of her was glad that Lizzy had someone, and sometimes it did seem like Azalea was trying to help Lizzy mend fences. But Zara couldn't bring herself to trust the stranger. And she hated how Azalea controlled Lizzy's actions. Zara had never seen Lizzy Peters—confident, bold, flirtatious, bully-taming Lizzy Peters—apologize so often and for so little. It was unnerving, but it was also no longer Zara's business. Lizzy had made that very clear.

"Are we going for a world record?" Kai spoke without moving a muscle.

"What?"

"You've sighed like fifty times in the last ten minutes." Kai tilted his head downward and looked out over the top of his aviator sunglasses.

"Oh." Zara pulled her knees up to her chest and shrugged before wrapping her arms around her legs. "I was just thinking of Lizzy. Of how she won't even ride in the same vehicle as me anymore. Of how I've lost the right to raise my concerns."

"About Azalea?" Kai asked.

Zara bit her bottom lip and winced. "I'm trying not to be judgmental."

"Yeah, all right," Kai said, pulling off his glasses. "I'll do it for you."

Zara chuckled. "What? Kai, c'mon."

"She's creepy as hell," Kai said. "And she acts more like a parent than a friend when she's around Lizzy. And if you want to talk judgmental, I'm pretty sure her neck has permanent damage from how often she turns up her nose."

"You're not helping," Zara said as she threw a pillow at him.

He batted it away and grinned. "I don't know, you haven't sighed once since I started talking. All I'm seeing is a big fat grin."

Zara purposefully turned down the corners of her lips, but it was impossible to keep them that way. It was good to see him interacting, and it *was* a little cathartic to hear her own thoughts about Azalea echoed in someone else's words.

"Still," she said, "I'm trying to be open-minded. It seems like Azalea has been there for Lizzy, like Lizzy needs her right now. Even if she is creepy."

Kai pointed at her. "You admit it! I knew I wasn't the only one who saw it."

"Stop!" Zara laughed and lightly kicked Kai's leg.

He put up his hands in surrender. "Fine," he said, and then his tone evened out into something more serious. "But, seriously, Zara? You may have lost the right to be close to Lizzy, but if you think Azalea crosses the line sometimes, you haven't lost your right to speak your mind, especially if it's done out of concern for your friend. I mean, make sure it's necessary, you know? Like, if you're just jealous or if you think Lizzy really is benefitting from having Azalea around, then keep it to yourself. But if it *is* necessary, letting Lizzy lose herself to some high-strung know-it-all with control issues is its own kind of betrayal."

Zara frowned and pressed her lips together, giving Kai a small nod of agreement. "Yeah, I guess you're right. I honestly don't know, though, if I'm right about Azalea or if my instincts are totally off. Because I *am* jealous. I miss my best friend."

"Well, I'm here for you, babe," Kai said.

It used to drive her nuts when he called her that, but he didn't do it anymore unless he was trying to lighten the mood. Now, it almost bothered her more when he called *other* women "babe." She grinned, having decided that his use of the term was more playful than disrespectful these days.

She winked at him. "Back at you, stud muffin."

It was Kai's turn to laugh. He put a hand to his chest. "I feel like you and me have reached a new level of our friendship."

"Yeah, well… don't go crazy, okay? I still prefer my name." She sat back and let Kai lead the conversation into small talk, grateful for the distraction. She needed it, and it seemed he did, too. He wasn't anything like Lizzy, and their newer friendship wasn't the same, but she felt like she could be herself around him, like he had her back.

The spread-out city buildings gave way to a mostly flat landscape as the road they were on crossed over a major highway. A solar farm appeared to the far right, and the mountains dominated the distance on the far left. They passed a short, concrete wall with overgrown hedges growing behind it and lettering on its front which read "U.S. Air Force, United States Air Force Academy."

"Looks like we're here," Zara said, though when she looked out the window, she could see nothing but yellowed grass, short trees, blue sky, and mountains. The vehicle slowed briefly, and then pulled through a checkpoint, armed men in uniform waving them through as another soldier in a solar-powered golf cart pulled out in front of the caravan. It seemed from the quick passage they had been expecting the little caravan of RVs and were leading them somewhere. Alex had described his own quarantine experience in a little trailer farther out, but Conner had told them General Hunt had arranged for their quarantine to be a little more comfortable.

It was another minute or two before office buildings and parking lots started appearing on the left-hand side of the road. The base was its own small town, butted up against the mountains on the edge of Colorado Springs, complete with schools, office buildings, and amenities. The only thing missing was people. It wasn't until they reached the northern corner of the grounds that Zara started seeing evidence that the base was occupied by more than just the soldiers who'd been guarding the entrance.

When they finally came to a permanent stop, Zara scooted off the bed first, stepping toward the door but waiting in the narrow walkway next to the tiny kitchen. Alex had made it clear: neither of them were to go outside until he'd given them the all clear and opened the door himself. It was the rule for both Minnie's RV and the airstream. She was able to see a bit through the windows and determined they'd pulled up to a duplex.

A loud exchange between Alex and the soldier who'd led them there ended with the soldier driving away. A minute later, the door to the airstream opened.

Alex stuck his head inside. "Looks like Conner was right. We get VIP treatment this time. Let's get inside, get settled, get some rest. Tomorrow is going to be a long day for everyone."

Zara took a step toward the door but glanced back when she heard the sound of Kai plopping down onto the bench of the tiny kitchen table. He looked up at her, that fear emanating from him again, face pale, brow knit.

"It's going to be okay," Zara said softly.

Kai swallowed hard and nodded, but he didn't get up.

Zara held out her hand. "C'mon," she said. "I bet they've got new foods in that duplex."

His smile wasn't convincing, but it was there. He stood up. "You always know what to say to make me feel better." He took her hand, and Zara squeezed it once before letting go.

Stepping onto the solid ground of the military base dissipated the levity Zara and Kai were able to find inside the airstream. As she took in the sight of their group, those missing from it were all too noticeable.

The following day, it would be her and Kai leaving. She'd have to enter unknown lands with three strangers and a half-baked plan. And their mission wasn't the only essential one. There were too many moving parts, too many potential points of failure.

Just don't think about it, she told herself for the second time that day.

But the words came with a knot in her stomach. The mantra repeated in her head too often, ringing hollowly, carrying with them an underlying note of unease. She wouldn't be able to ignore it forever. The end was coming, and it was fast approaching. The question was whether it would be the end of disaster or the end of everything and everyone Zara loved.

"Hey," Kai said, nudging her lightly, "it's going to be okay."

She smiled at her own words returned to her. They were either true or a comforting lie, and Zara had no idea in which category they belonged.

Chapter 15

Heather Peters and Jenny Conner

Heather listened to the sounds of the other women breathing. It was hard to tell exactly how long they'd been inside the shipping container, but the end of their quarantine *had* to be reaching an end soon. They'd tried to keep sane by doing things, instead of just sleeping. Jenny had even led them in a yoga routine at one point to "keep them calm and levelheaded." But the others had also done a lot of sleeping.

Except Heather couldn't sleep. She wanted answers, wanted to stop the scenarios of what could be from spinning through her head, one right after another.

A clang of metal made her sit up straight, and when the container door swung open to let in sunlight, she threw up her arm to shield her eyes. It was so much brighter than the dim lantern light.

Lauren groaned. "You could have warned us," she said. She was sitting upright, too.

Jenny was already on her feet near the door, her backpack on the floor nearby. Azalea blinked and yawned before turning to wake Lizzy. The man who'd come down from the deer stand the day before squinted through goggles into the container. He wore the same protective gear as the day before.

"Everyone all right?" he asked.

Heather nodded. "We're all fine," she said as she got to her feet.

"You can come out, now," he said. "But I'll need to check your temperature again. Hop out, line up." He wiggled the thermometer in the air. "It'll only take a second."

Heather grabbed her backpack and followed Jenny and Lauren outside. Azalea and Lizzy were the last to leave the container. The men with guns were watching them from outside the bus again. As their temperatures were taken, Heather kept an eye on them, remembering that they'd been told those with symptoms could be shot on the spot.

But after he'd checked the last woman, the man with the thermometer turned and shouted over his shoulder. "They're all good, Jarod. Let's get them to the arena."

The oldest man nodded and gestured to a young redheaded man, tall and thin. The second man walked toward them while the rest filed back on the bus.

"I'm Vincent," the gatekeeper said, and then he pointed to the man approaching. "And this is Milo. He's going to take you ladies to the arena doors and hand you off to our welcome team." Vincent moved a metal barrier. "Let's go, now. We don't want to tempt the swarm."

Heather shuffled past the barrier with the others. "Thank you," she said, to both Vincent and Milo.

"Just doing my job," Vincent said, smiling. "Good luck, ma'am. If you've got a bun in the oven, this is the place to be."

"Follow me," Milo said, flexing a little as he gestured. He seemed to only be talking to Azalea and Lizzy as he walked backward. "Sorry about the guns, ladies." He had a rifle slung across his back, the strap across his chest. He tugged the strap with one thumb. "They're just a precaution. We want to make sure whoever comes inside is safe. And with me around, you have nothing to worry about." He winked past Heather, Lauren, and Jenny, clearly aiming his charm at the younger women.

Heather glanced back at Lizzy. Her sister-in-law used to be boy crazy, used to lap up attention, especially from tough, macho guys like Milo. And while Azalea winked back, Lizzy only blushed and looked away. That was good, in a way. Heather didn't want Lizzy flirting with a guy like Milo. But it was just another reminder of how much she'd changed.

Milo turned around and led them to a wall of glass doors and windows beneath lettering that read, "Gate B." He waved, and the door on the far right was opened. Another armed man opened the door and held it open until they were all through, Milo included. Daylight filtered in through the glass doors, and the concourse, which curved away from them, was lined with people, all of whom seemed busy with one chore or another: mending clothes, peeling and chopping potatoes, sorting through boxes. Farther down where the wall of glass ended, the crowd thinned significantly. Eyes flickered in their direction, but most of them returned immediately to their task.

Milo turned around again and spread out his arms like he was showing off his own apartment. "Pretty sweet, isn't it? I'll show you aroun—"

"Milo!" A woman, round in face and body, with a long, black braid and a cheery smile, bustled through the crowd. "You stop flirting with these girls. Go on and do your job. Let me do mine."

Milo sighed. "C'mon, Gran. Can't I get this one?"

"No." The woman reached up and tugged hard on Milo's earlobe. "Go on. I mean it."

Milo rubbed his ear and scowled, but he still muttered, "Yes, ma'am," as he scurried back outside.

"Now," the woman put one hand on her hip. "You ladies can call me Gran, just like Milo, just like everyone else. I take care of people around here. Now, do you all got names, or should I make some up?"

Heather couldn't help but smile. "I'm Heather," she said, and then she pointed to each of her companions in turn. "This is Lauren, Jenny, Azalea, and Lizzy."

Lauren stepped forward and put a gentle hand on Heather's back. "Heather believes she might be pregnant. It's one of the reasons we decided to come here."

Gran's eyes widened. "Is that so?"

Heather nodded. "I haven't been tested, but… I think so."
"Okay, then," Gran said. "Let's get you all checked in and then get Miss Heather to our clinic."
Heather and the rest followed Gran to the first concessions built into the concourse. Instead of burgers and fries, canned foods were stacked behind the counter. A line of a dozen people waited for service as a man with a clipboard ran a pen down the side of the top page. He was young, perhaps late twenties, fit and lean. His movements and attitude were stiff and no-nonsense, and he was almost studious in his examination of the list.
"Helen…" he said to the woman at the front of the line, "Ah, there you are." He flicked his wrist as if making a checkmark on the paper, turned around, and grabbed a small can of Vienna sausages and a can of corn. "See you tomorrow. Next!"
The woman, Helen, made a face as she picked up the Vienna sausages, but she took both cans. "Thanks, Andy." She skulked off, and the next person stepped up.
"You lot wait here," Gran said, patting the countertop on the far right where there was no line. She hurried over to a door in the concourse wall, and she soon entered the other side of the concessions shop with a clipboard in hand much like Andy's. She slid a short stack of papers across the counter along with four pens. "Andy, when they're done filling these out, I'll need you to add their names to the list and get them an allotment of food. I've got to take that one to the clinic." She beamed as she pointed at Heather.
Heather's cheeks warmed as Andy looked up from his clipboard and raised his eyebrows at her, smiling. A few in line to get food did the same, watching her with expressions of excitement and even awe.
I guess they know what it means when a woman is sent straight to the clinic after arrival, she thought as she tried to swallow her discomfort.
"Good luck," a middle-aged woman said softly from her place in line, offering an encouraging smile and nod.
But it didn't *feel* encouraging. The reaction left Heather with a dry mouth and a knot in her stomach. Part of her understood before she'd come that part of the mission of those who'd taken over the complex and the arena was to rebuild the population, but she hadn't expected what appeared to be reverence for her situation. It would have made her a bit uncomfortable, to have eyes on her, to have people she didn't know invested in her health and the health of her baby, even if she wasn't expecting something to be wrong with the pregnancy.
"Are you creeped out?" Lauren whispered. "I can insist on coming with you."
Heather cleared her throat as the heat in her cheeks intensified.
Andy jumped a little and concern washed over his features. "Let me get you a water bottle." He hurried through the door at the back of the concessions where Gran had entered. The door swung both ways, and he was in and out of the back room quickly. He handed her a plastic water bottle with the Broadmoor World Arena logo on the side. "You can get it filled at the clinic," he said. "They run the water supply."
"Um… thanks," Heather said, her voice more of a croak.
"Seriously," Lauren said, "do you want me to come?"
"Oh, no," Gran said from across the counter. "You've got to stay and fill out paperwork. I'll help Heather fill hers out at the clinic, but you've got to stay here. When it's time for you four to get your allotment of water, you can come on over and check on her."
"It'll be fine," Heather said. "I'm just going to pee on a stick." She smiled, trying to reassure her friend.
"Okay," Lauren said skeptically. She lowered her voice as she pulled Heather into a hug. "But if anything is off, you scream, and we'll come running."
"I will," Heather whispered back.
Only a few minutes later, Heather was following Gran, leaving behind the only people in that place she truly trusted.

* * *

As Heather followed Gran down the concourse, Jenny started filling out paperwork while trying not to pay too much attention to the military's inside source: Andy Munez. He'd been an enemy once, a man on Chandler Price's team back in Atlanta. But when he'd found out that Price and Price's boss, Charles Lawson, planned to use the disease to control the population and that they were sanctioning human experimentation, Munez had switched sides and ultimately helped take Price and Lawson down when he convinced several of his fellow guns-for-hire to join General Hunt. Since then, he'd integrated well into the military, proving his integrity and loyalty on numerous occasions.
Lauren stepped closer to Jenny with her own paper and pen, leaning over her paperwork as she whispered at Jenny. "*Munez* is your inside source?"
Jenny startled a little at that. "Hush!" she whispered harshly, glancing around them, relieved to see no one paying them any mind. Azalea and Lizzy were huddled together, filling out their paperwork halfway between them and the line. The counter was long enough to afford some privacy.
"Sorry," Lauren said, wincing. "I just… are you sure we can trust him?"
Truth be told, Jenny had forgotten that Lauren knew Munez. He'd guarded Lauren, Minnie, and Oliver on Price's behalf, and Lauren hadn't been privy to all the good things Munez had done, both in Atlanta and in the interim. "Yes, we can," Jenny said. "Trust me if you can't trust him."
"Okay," Lauren said. "I do. Trust you, I mean."
Jenny swallowed an uprising of guilt and nodded. "Good. Let's get this paperwork done so we can check on Heather."
But her words stayed with Jenny: *I do. Trust you, I mean.*
And Lauren could trust her about Munez, but there were things Jenny had to keep to herself, things she wasn't sure Lauren would understand. Her mission was complex and top-secret. She was the only one on the team of volunteers who understood the full scope of why they were infiltrating Cheyenne Mountain.
I'm doing my job, and the mission is what's best for everyone. Jenny obliterated any doubt she had with the fact that she trusted General Hunt and President Coleman. They would never do anything that wasn't in the best interest of the people.

She leaned closer to Lauren. "We don't know him," she said. "Got it?"

Lauren nodded. "Got it."

Jenny returned to filling out the information they were asking her for: name, place of birth, last place of permanent residence, and medical history, including a box to check if a female was open to bearing children for the sake of the community. She fudged the truth, counting her last place of permanent residence as her parent's farm and outright lied about her willingness to get pregnant. The last section included listing any and all useful skills.

By the time all four of them had finished, Munez had finished with his list. "I've got to check on a few things in inventory before taking you ladies over to the clinic to gather your friend," he said. "After we get her, I'll assign you a spot in the concourse to settle down. We should have enough sleeping bags for you." He was nothing if not thorough. That part of his persona wasn't made up.

"What about the lottery?" Jenny asked. "What do we have to do to enter?"

Munez didn't even look at her as he gathered their papers. "You'll be entered based on your skill sets and willingness to contribute to the community," he said.

"You mean our willingness to pop out babies?" Lizzy asked, crossing her arms.

Jenny froze. Andy was on their side, but neither of the girls knew that.

Andy blinked, his mouth dropping open slightly. "Well… that *is* one way to contribute, but—"

"We're okay with that," Azalea said. "We both are. Right?" She looked at Lizzy, a hardness behind her eyes that made Jenny frown.

Lizzy smiled. "Yeah," she said sweetly. "I was just messing with you."

Andy cleared his throat and stammered. "Um, okay. Well…" He clipped their papers to the board in his hands. "I'm going to come around into the concourse and get you settled." He disappeared into the back room.

Jenny breathed out. Andy was doing an excellent job maintaining his cover. That was the only reassuring thing about the exchange.

"What the hell was that?" Lauren asked.

"She's just nervous," Azalea said.

Jenny took a step toward Lizzy. "Are we on the same page here, or not? Our goal is to get into that mountain complex, not hand out sass to the people running this place," she said quietly, keeping details to a minimum should anyone hear.

"I'm sorry," Lizzy said, looking only at Azalea.

"If you're not sure it will help," Azalea said, "then just keep it to yourself, okay?"

Lizzy nodded, and Jenny sighed. She backed off and held out a hand as Lauren opened her mouth as if to speak again. "Everyone slips up sometimes," she said. "Let it go." It occurred to her that perhaps Lizzy's father had been right, that the young woman wasn't ready for their mission. *I can't do anything about it now,* she thought.

Andy stepped through the doorway into the concourse. He barely gave them a gesture to indicate they should follow and began to walk in the same direction Gran had taken Heather half an hour before. Jenny let Lauren, Azalea, and Lizzy go ahead of her, and she took up the rear. People had taken up little squares of floor space in the wide, curving hall. About half of them had very small tents set up, and the other half had rigged blanket tents around chairs and boxes and other found items.

The clinic was set up next to the last window in the wall of glass that looked out onto the parking lot, the junkyard wall rising in the near distance, blocking out the city beyond. Rolling curtain stands created two blocked off rooms, and Heather was seated outside one of them. A man with a stethoscope around his neck was frowning down at her, asking if she was okay, and then his eyes flicked upward, stopping on them as they approached.

"Andy," the man said. "I assume you're here for Heather?"

Andy nodded. "What's the news, Matt?"

Heather barely moved. She seemed frozen in her chair, except for the fact her hands trembled. Lauren knelt beside her, speaking softly, and after a moment, Heather looked up at her, seeming to come out of some sort of daze.

"Is she okay?" Jenny asked.

"I think she's in a bit of shock," Matt said. "I was excited to give her the news, but she's seemed… a bit off since she heard the test was positive."

"Are you even a doctor?" Lauren stood up and crossed her arms. "What's her blood pressure? Heart rate? Do you have any idea how far along she might be? Did you even get her medical history?"

"I'm a surgeon, actually," Matt said. "The people around here don't use honorifics. They like to keep things down-to-earth, but I *am* a doctor. And I've got her history. Gran helped her fill it out."

"Did you read it?" Lauren asked.

"It was just a pregnancy test," Matt said. "I know what I'm doing. I was an attending at St. Francis. And you? I'm guessing you're a nurse, right? Is that why you think you can talk to me like that?"

"Yeah," Lauren said. "I am, and I've been taking care of Heather for a while. If you had read her history, you would have seen what she's been through, and maybe you would have been less *excited* and a little more sensitive."

Matt blinked and then a look of understanding came over his face. "Miscarriages?"

Lauren nodded. "One ectopic, two that just didn't make it."

"Most women who are pregnant are just excited to be able to get into the mountain…" Matt sighed. "I'm sorry. You're right. I should have read her history."

"So then," Andy interrupted, "my guess is that we need to get Miss Heather up to the mountain to receive further medical evaluation as soon as possible?"

Matt nodded. "That's procedure, yes." He threw a sympathetic look at Heather as she rose to her feet to stand beside Lauren. She was still very pale. "Depending on the viability of your pregnancy, you may not be able to stay in the complex. If something is wrong, you'll receive proper care, and then you'll be returned here to be entered into the lottery just like everyone else."

"That seems harsh," Jenny said, genuinely surprised. "You'd send her back while she's so emotionally vulnerable?"

"Again," Matt said, "that's the procedure. I don't make the rules."
"We make very few exceptions when it comes to who gets into the mountain, who gets living quarters," Andy said. "We have to. It's the only way this works. Pregnancy is one of those exceptions. Highly skilled people we need are another." He looked at Lauren. "If you're a nurse, we need you up at the mountain."
"I could use her here," Matt said.
"I was told the next two nurses to come through get an immediate pass," Andy said.
Matt threw up his hands. "I don't get you people. I'm one of your best assets, and you keep me here, in this arena, running check-ups and pregnancy tests. It's ridiculous!"
"We already have two surgeons up at the complex," Andy said. "We also have a family doctor. You're not needed. And, frankly, the fact that you still think so highly of yourself and think you deserve special treatment is one of the reasons you're stuck here."
"Sure," Matt said, "but smartass nurses are in high demand."
"Smartass nurses are the backbone of hospitals," Lauren said. "Good doctors and *surgeons* know that."
"Fine. Take these two up to the mountain and leave me here to wipe noses and hand out aspirins." Matt shook his head.
"That's the plan," Andy said as he flashed the doctor a smile. "Now, let's move on, ladies," he said. "We've got places to be."
Jenny took up residence at Heather's left-hand side as Lauren stayed at her right. "We're with you, Heather," she said. "It's going to be fine."
Heather glanced at Lauren. "At least I'm not going there alone," she said, "but what about the rest of you?"
"Don't worry about it," Jenny said. "I'll figure it out."
Andy stopped at the first empty space along the concourse wall. The daylight barely reached so far, and the darkness of the concourse beyond where the light reached began only a few yards down. "Jenny, Azalea, and Lizzy will be assigned this spot," he said. "We'll get you a lantern and a few basic supplies."
"Tents?" Jenny asked.
Andy shook his head. "Those with tents brought them in, I'm afraid, but we do have blankets, and you're free to take a lantern and explore to try to find materials with which to raise a tent. There's scaffolding making up the stage on the floor of the arena, but there aren't windows in there. It's pretty dark, so just be careful."
"So… you don't have access to a generator, then?" Jenny asked.
"Nope," Andy said.
"But the mountain does?" Lizzy asked.
"Yes." Andy nodded. "It's got generators and an entire *lake* of diesel fuel to run them, plus they installed a solar farm on the other side of the mountain dedicated to providing power to the complex. They'll be fine for a long time up there." He shrugged. "And we will be, too, but we'll have to do it without modern amenities."
"How long before our friends will join us at the complex?" Lauren asked.
"I don't know," Andy said. "Maybe never. We have a system, and it prioritizes the needs of the mountain community. It's a special place, one we want to protect."
"Wait," Lizzy said, "do *you* live there?"
"Yes," Andy said. "I stay overnight here sometimes, but I have a small apartment at Cheyenne. I help run this place along with Gran, though she opted not to accept an invitation to live in the mountain. My job is to be a liaison and to ensure that the *right* people are accepted into our community."
Azalea smiled at him. "I can see why they'd choose you," she said. "You're so… reassuring. And obviously a good judge of character. The way you put that doctor in his place, well…" She gently touched his arm. "I'm confident you'll make wise decisions where we're concerned."
"Maybe we can talk more about that later," Andy said, the corners of lips turning upward slightly. "Right now, I've got a job to do."
That smile and tone of voice annoyed Jenny — flirting with young women wasn't part of his mission — but she supposed he might be staying in character.
Or all of this might be getting to his head. That thought made her stomach sink.
He'd been feeding them information intermittently on a secure channel via an encrypted radio, but he'd been inside, playing his role, for weeks. He'd gotten into the arena and proved himself quickly through providing information on an untouched store of goods. The military had secretly stocked a backroom in a warehouse before sending him inside, and Andy had leveraged the information perfectly.
He turned to Lauren and Heather. "You two ladies can come with me. We are going to get you up to that mountain ASAP. The medical staff will want to see you right away, Miss Heather."
Heather nodded. "Can we just have a few minutes with our friends to say goodbye?"
"Sure," Andy said. "I'll meet you back by the door to the outside."
He left then, briefly throwing a look at Jenny, a slight nod that was barely detectable. It was the first time he'd acknowledged her, there in the gray and murky light of the far side of the concourse. She met his eyes, relief flooding her. That look reminded her of the Andy she knew. But she didn't return the nod. She didn't want to raise questions with the other women or give away who her inside source was just yet. Lauren knowing was enough for the time being. Jenny wouldn't have even told *her*, despite trusting her, if she'd not met Andy back in Atlanta.
When he'd gone, Jenny huddled with the others. "Heather, Lauren, you've got this. Try to find out where the offline database is. I know that's going to be hard without raising suspicion, but do your best. Play yourselves off as fascinated with the complex. Ask a lot of questions. That's the best way to find a natural segue into asking about the database."
"What do we do if we get that information?" Lauren asked.
"Sit tight." Jenny spoke firmly even as she kept her voice in a whisper. "I have a high clearance log in. When I get there, I'll handle it."
"Why not give us the log in?" Lauren asked. "That way if you don't get inside, one of us can get the information."

"I know that seems like an option to you," Jenny said, "but it's not. I'm under strict orders not to give that information away. I have to be the one to get into the database." There was a good possibility they'd only have one shot at the database, and Jenny needed information Lauren didn't know about yet. Again, Jenny's chest constricted just a little at the half truths she spun, but she wasn't about to blow her mission just because she was squeamish.

"What if I'm sent back?" Heather said. In the dim light, Jenny barely caught sight of a tear rolling down Heather's cheek.

Jenny reached out and took Heather's hand; the woman wasn't talking about the mission. "They have a good medical team there," she said. "You're going to be okay."

The others, even Azalea and Lizzy, offered support and words of encouragement. As they said their goodbyes and Lauren and Heather walked back toward the door to the parking lot, Jenny breathed deeply, maintaining the calm confidence she'd worked hard to build before coming to the arena. She had a lot of work to do, and she was glad that Heather and Lauren were a part of it. They were good women, trustworthy and reliable. Part of her wanted to tell them everything before they left so that they knew exactly what they were doing, but she couldn't. She wouldn't betray the trust of her leaders. And besides, they would find out eventually, when it was said and done and behind them. Jenny could only hope that it all went down as planned, that she'd be able to look back on her decisions with pride, and that when her friends found out, they would forgive her for dragging them into a full-scale invasion and takeover of Cheyenne Mountain.

Chapter 16

Zara Williams

Zara narrowed her eyes at Kai and threw him a ruthless smile. She leaned forward and put one hand flat on the table between them. "Go. Fish."
"Aw, man!" Kai reached for the center pile, but his hand froze, hovering as a voice sounded outside.
"Quarantine is up!"
Zara stood from the kitchen table and hurried to the window at the front of the duplex. Walter joined her, discarding a book on the coffee table in front of the couch and pressing his hands on the window. Three solar-powered golf carts had pulled up. One soldier stood on the driveway with a bullhorn.
"Everyone outside for a quick briefing," the soldier said into the contraption, his voice booming.
Zara turned to look at Kai. He'd not joined her at the window, opting instead to hang back. "We better get out there," she said.
He nodded, expression resigned.
Walter walked over to him and put a hand on his shoulder. "You're going to be great, Kai," he said. "This pilot is going to handle the heavy lifting. And he's going to train you. It's going to work out."
"I haven't said I would fly again," Kai said.
"Yeah... I know." Walter patted him on the shoulder and then walked out the front door.
"C'mon," Zara said. "Let's see what the next step is, okay?"
"One step at a time." Kai took a deep breath and ran his fingers through his hair. "Let's go." He motioned for Zara to go first.
All ten of those who'd taken up residence in the duplex were soon on the lawn. Alex immediately recognized the man with the bullhorn. Zara folded her arms and listened, wondering if any of the soldiers present were part of the team she and Kai would be joining.
"Kenny!" Alex spread out his arms in greeting. "You're not dead!"
Kenny grinned. "Not yet," he said. "Glad to see you're still kicking." He addressed the rest of them. "You lot can call me Kenny, just like Alex, here." He pointed to the other two soldiers who were unzipping the protective plastic around the carts they'd driven. "That there is Cadet Hogan Sumner and the other one is Cadet Shelly Lindt."
Zara relaxed a little. None of the names were familiar. "It looks like we won't be leaving base just yet," she said quietly to Kai. "What were the names Conner gave us? Yeomen, Warren, and..." She frowned.
"Potts," Kai said.
"Major Willis?" The woman—Cadet Lindt—pointed at the back of her golf cart. "Should we unload?"
"Yep." Kenny gestured toward the boxes as Lindt and Sumner unloaded them. "These are supplies. The general wants you lot well taken care of while you're with us."
Walter stepped forward. "Is that all you've come to do? Give us supplies?"
Kenny clasped his hands behind his back. His friendly demeanor with Alex shifted. He loomed over Walter. "You must be the famous Walter Peters," he said.
Walter faltered. "Um... yes, I am."
Zara winced at the way Kenny narrowed his eyes. Timothy and Alex had both been there to debrief the president, and Kai was clearly too young to be Mr. Peters. The rest of them were women. It wasn't surprising that Kenny had picked Walter out, but it was unnerving the way the major stared him down.
"Not a big fan," Kenny said.
"Oh." Walter swallowed so hard Zara could hear it from where she stood. He practically *gulped*. He laughed nervously. "Well, me either, actually."
"Should we be worried about Walter?" Kai whispered.
Zara bit her lower lip, body tense as Kenny stood rock solid and unmoving until Walter's laugh petered out. But then Kenny barked a laugh that made her heart jump into her throat.
"I'm just messing with you." Kenny slapped Walter's arm so hard, the man stumbled. "Mostly, anyway. I mean, everyone knows you screwed us all over, but it's not like you did it alone."
"Uh..." Walter was pale as he seemed to grasp for what to say next. "Thanks?"
"No problem." Kenny let his eyes sweep over the group. "Most of you are staying here, but we're going to need Walter, Alex, Kai, and Zara to hop in a golf cart and come with us. We've got some research up and running that Dr. Pulman wants to show off, and you two—" He pointed at Zara and Kai. "—need to meet up with your team. Everything you *need* will be provided, but if you want to take anything else with you, now's the time to grab it. You won't be coming back here."
Zara's hand went to the two rings hanging around her neck: the ladybug and the butterfly. They had once been a symbol of her friendship with Lizzy. It was the only sentimental thing she had. "I think I'm good." She glanced at Kai. "You need anything?"
"What about weapons?" Kai asked.
Kenny nodded as if he appreciated the question. "If you've got them, bring them."

"I'll go grab our holsters and handguns," Kai said. He disappeared inside the house for a few minutes and reappeared with two holstered weapons. He handed one to Zara.

She took it and wrapped it around her waist, the weight of it on her hip familiar.

"I'm also looking for Minnie Stevens," Kenny said.

"That'd be me," Minnie said.

"Oh, no," Kenny said, "you're much too young." He winked at her, strode forward, and stuck out his elbow. "General Hunt asked me to escort you, as well. I believe the good man has had stars in his eyes all morning."

Minnie blushed. "Well, goodness gracious." She glanced at Candice and Timothy. "You two don't need me, do you?"

"We've got the kids, Minnie," Candice said.

"Okay, then…" Minnie took Kenny's arm and let him escort her to one of the golf carts.

He turned around and said over his shoulder, "The rest of you pile in."

Zara and Kai got into the back seat of the golf cart that had just been emptied of supplies while Alex and Walter got into the second cart. Timothy started taking the supplies into the duplex as the soldiers zipped up the plastic doors of the back seats.

Cadet Lindt took up the driver's seat. "This'll take a bit," she said. "These things are slow, but the solar power saves gasoline." She turned around, and the cart lurched forward.

It was quiet as the little convoy rumbled through the Air Force Academy grounds. Zara peered through the plastic, taking note of the layout of the base. The mountains stood tall to the west, reaching toward fluffy white clouds set against a bright blue sky. Like Colorado Springs, the base was spacious and spread out, patches of grass and trees plentiful. They soon left the residential area behind and entered the northernmost section which was apparently where the actual academy was built. They passed by a long, thin building called Harmon Hall and pulled into a courtyard.

Cadet Lindt drove right up to a building with a tall, backward-leaning triangle of shining steel and glass atop a concrete base that was flush with the ground. Black fencing sectioned off what appeared to be a sunken outdoor area on three sides of the structure, and a row of men and women waited where a set of concrete steps receded behind them.

Kai sat next to her, silently rubbing his right thumb into his left palm, the only outward sign of the nerves she knew he was doing his best to overcome. He hadn't said a word since leaving the duplex.

Cadet Lindt unzipped her plastic door. "Welcome to Polaris Hall," she said as she stepped outside and reached for the zipper of Zara's door.

"We'll be there in just a second," Zara said, holding out her hand and giving the cadet a pleading look.

The woman looked past Zara to Kai and then back again. "A second," she said, offering a small smile.

"Thanks." Zara scooted a little closer to Kai, who hadn't yet looked up from his hands. "Hey, I know—"

"No, you don't," Kai snapped, looking up sharply. "I almost killed us on the way to Boston. I mean, Walter still has a limp! And we were lucky. Now you people want me to fly again, and all I can think about is that storm and landing in that lake and thinking I'd killed Walter even after you and I survived the crash. And back then, I didn't even really know who I almost killed! The people going to New Zealand, they're going to be the world's most important people, and if we crash in the damn *ocean*, there won't be any coming back from that."

Zara tried to keep her voice calm. "I was there, too, Kai. *I'm scared, too.*"

"But, what?" Kai's breaths came more quickly. "We don't have a choice? Because we do. We can refuse to go."

"We do that," Zara said, "and everything—everyone—we love will die without hope."

Kai squeezed his eyes shut and quickly wiped away the moisture there. His hands balled into fists on his thighs. "I can't do this," he said.

Zara laid her hand over his fist. "You can," she said. "We can do it together."

Kai took a few more moments to unfurl his fist, to relax his body. He took a great shuddering breath and looked at Zara. "When we met, I was pretending. I was stupid, and I thought if I acted brave, I would become brave. But it never happened. I don't want to do this, Zara. Every part of me wants to run."

"When I first met you," Zara said, "you would have never admitted that to me. You're braver than you've ever been. Doing the right thing despite fear, *that's* brave. And you're not alone, anymore, either. You've got me."

Kai swallowed hard. "The next step?"

Zara nodded. "Together."

She turned and unzipped the plastic, stepping out and moving aside for Kai to follow. He slid out slowly and slipped on his aviator sunglasses. When he rolled his shoulders back, she smiled. His cool-kid persona was a shield, but underneath, she could see a young man becoming more than any hotshot wanna-be could ever dream of becoming.

One day, you'll see that, she thought.

Alex, Walter, and Minnie were already standing near the soldiers lined up at the entrance to Polaris Hall. As Zara and Kai approached, another man, tall and broad shouldered with hardened features, walked up the steps set into the ground behind the line to join them. The soldiers gave him deference, and Minnie blushed furiously.

"That must be General Hunt," Zara whispered as she and Kai came to a stop beside Walter.

"It is," Walter said, glancing their way. "You two okay?"

"Right as rain," Kai said.

He didn't look convinced. Zara shrugged, and Walter let it drop. Alex stepped forward and held out a hand, which the general took. After a hearty handshake, and another one with Walter, the general cleared his throat and sidestepped to stand in front of Minnie.

"I was hoping," the general said, "that we could talk after a few things get settled. I've set up one of the meeting rooms. I thought perhaps we could have lunch."

"I'd like that very much," Minnie said.

The general nodded to Cadet Sumner who then escorted Minnie down the steps. Then, the general turned to look at Zara and Kai. "You two will be going with one of our best teams, sans Conner, of course." He gestured to the end of the line, and three men stepped forward. "They—"

"Hold on a minute." Alex was looking to the far left, toward Harmon Hall where four men with shackled feet shuffled forward, old reel mowers in hand. An armed soldier led them and another brought up the rear. "Is that Lawson?" He shifted, squinting. "And Price? What the hell are they doing out here?"

One of the men grinned as they came closer and raised his tool as if toasting with a glass. "Mr. Roman!" He lowered the mower. "It's been a while. Care for a rematch?"

The soldier at the front turned and rammed the butt of his gun into the man's stomach, and while it made him double over, he managed to maintain a smile.

"You're done, Price," Alex shouted back. "How do you enjoy being Lawson's pet, now?"

The man behind Price scowled and spat toward them, though he was too far for the spittle to reach. "You're a fool, Mr. Roman."

"That's enough!" General Hunt shouted. "Get them out of here."

Zara frowned and exchanged a look with Kai. "Aren't those the guys they took out in Boston?" she asked in a whisper.

Kai nodded. "I think so."

Over the weeks travelling from Boston to Colorado Springs, they'd all heard summaries of what they'd each endured since Day Zero. If Zara remembered correctly, Lawson was the president's father-in-law and also the man who'd orchestrated a plot to use DV-10 to control Atlanta and gain power. Price had been his muscle as the owner of a guns-for-hire operation.

Alex turned back to General Hunt. "Well they seem fat and happy." He didn't sound pleased.

Hunt narrowed his eyes. "We've got them and the two surviving mercenaries loyal to them using old grass cutters to keep our area looking sharp. We had to give them something to do, let them get some sunlight. And yes, we feed them. I'm pretty sure we're the good guys, Alex."

Alex's scornful laugh made the general stiffen further. "They should be locked away," Alex said. "They're dynamic and intelligent, General Hunt. They know how to talk their way into what they want. And they're all highly trained in combat. You've got *two* men on them? Really?"

"If you're suggesting we'd allow them to escape, I'd have to take issue with that." The general stood a little taller, as if he wasn't already towering over Alex. He spoke sharply, his tone that of a man who was challenged often.

Alex shook his head. "They tried to kill me. They threatened my son. They used the deaths of millions as an opportunity to gain power amongst the survivors. I thought when you took them prisoner, they wouldn't see freedom ever again, and yet here they are, strutting around like they own the place."

A new voice entered the conversation as another man in a similar uniform to General Hunt walked up the steps. "Now, I think *I* take issue with that," the man said.

Hunt's jaw tightened and his eye twitched. "General Boreland, we agreed you weren't needed today."

"Oh?" the man asked. "Is that the way we do introductions now?" He cast a charming smile, looking at each of them in turn, starting with Alex and ending with Kai. "Since I was so thoughtfully left unbothered the last time Mr. Roman was here, I thought it time we met."

Alex's angered demeanor had dissolved in favor of something more cautious as Boreland reached out a hand. He took it but glanced questioningly at General Hunt instead of saying anything to the newcomer.

"This is General Boreland," Hunt said. "He was here, running things, before the president arrived. He and I share the same rank."

"Don't be modest, Alan." Boreland's tone had a note of bitterness to it, if Zara wasn't mistaken. His smile widened as he patted the general on the arm. "This man here is the right arm of the United States government." Before Hunt could respond, Boreland continued. "Now, about your comment concerning our prisoners… as the person who's been so graciously handed the task of overseeing their stay, let me assure you, they aren't going anywhere."

"Speaking of your duties," General Hunt said, "I believe the perimeter inspection was to begin shortly, was it not?"

"Oh yes," Boreland nodded. "The perimeter inspection. That, my friend, was exactly what I was about to do. I just wanted to make sure our guests knew they could come to me should they need anything at all."

"Thank you," Alex said, though the way he shifted indicated he was as uncomfortable as Zara.

"Not at all." Boreland's smile lacked warmth as he said his goodbyes. "Can't keep our border patrol waiting much longer." As he walked off, Zara stared after him, frowning as he pulled a flask out of his pocket and drank deeply of the contents.

"Um, General Hunt, sir?" One of the three men Zara and Kai were to team up with stepped out of line.

"Yes, Potts?" The general grunted.

"Permission to get these two integrated and prepped, sir? We need to get out of here ASAP."

"Permission granted." Hunt nodded. "Return quickly, and return with that pilot in tow. Understood?"

The three of them answered in unison, "Yes, sir!" And then Potts gestured for Zara and Kai to follow. "We've got a lot to do and a long way to go."

Kai stepped closer to Zara, and she put a gentle hand on his back. "We're ready," she said. "Lead the way."

But as they left Alex and Walter with Hunt, she looked back, unnerved by the interactions between Alex and Hunt and then between the general and Boreland. The knot forming in her stomach was heavy; hints of instability made her nervous.

Situations and relationships, allyships and enemies — everything was prone to quick and volatile change when the end of the world was fast approaching. They were already in a fragile state. It wouldn't take much to throw everything into chaos. Zara picked up the pace. The sooner they were off to New Zealand, the better.

Chapter 17

Minnie Stevens

Beautiful, steaming, aromatic, *hot* coffee. Eggs and flatbread. Mixed fruit, drained and displayed in nice little dishes. Minnie had slaved over breakfast that morning. It was the first hot breakfast any of them had had in ages, and all Alex could talk about was his meeting from the day before, which they'd all heard about already.

"The entire time Dr. Pullman was showing me their setup, all I could think about was what Price said." Alex cut through his eggs again and again. He'd not eaten one bite, but he'd managed to make an unholy mess on his plate. "Did I tell you what he said? He said, 'Care for a rematch?' Ha! What does that even mean?"

Minnie opened her mouth. "Well—"

"What *does* that mean?" Alex repeated. "You think they're planning something?"

Minnie sighed. "Will you let me get a word in, or have you figured out how to make a conversation work with only one person talking?"

Alex frowned, and Oliver chuckled. The boy had finished his breakfast several minutes ago, when it was still hot, but he'd stuck around like they were sitting on the story rug and Alex was the teacher. Timothy was there, too, listening intently, working his jaw back and forth. Minnie could almost see his wheels turning, mulling over the implications of everything Alex was saying. Candice and Annika, on the other hand, had skedaddled as soon as they'd had their fill. Sounds of dice and laughter could be heard on occasion as the two played a game in the other room.

"This is my one chance to give Annika something *normal*," Candice had said that morning. "We're here, in this house, with food and water and protection, for a short time." And then Alex had come in, ranting and raving like a man obsessed.

"Sorry," Alex said. He grimaced, looking at the empty seats Candice and Annika had left. "I scared them off, didn't I?"

Timothy shook his head. "It's fine," he said. "Candice wants to pretend like everything is fine, and Annika needs the distraction, I think. She's worried about Zara, going out there again on her own."

"That's right," Minnie said. "They're cousins. I forget sometimes."

"Candice has taken her under her wing," Timothy said. "She's like a second mother to that girl. Or an aunt, as she likes to say. At least they're out of bed." He said that last part with a bit of spite.

"Walter has been a little down and out since Lizzy left, hasn't he?" Minnie asked. "I guess I can't blame him. He's left George behind in Boston. Lizzy won't hardly talk to him. Zara and Kai, well they seem important to him, too, and they're away. That's a lot of people to be missin'."

Timothy scoffed. "Sure, except he's got a son right here. But that's the story of my life. That man has never figured out how to be a father to me."

"He cares," Alexander said. "I can tell that much."

There was a stretch of silence as they all paid a bit more attention to their wonderful, hot breakfasts.

After a few minutes, Oliver's shoulders sagged a bit. "I think I'm going to go join in on the game," he said.

Alex reached over and ruffled his son's hair. "Why so disappointed?"

"I don't know. I thought you were going somewhere with your story about Dr. Pullman showing you the lab, about seeing Mr. Lawson and Mr. Price again. I thought, well… I thought there would be some kind of fight." He perked up. "Was there a fight?"

Minnie chuckled as Alex frowned. "No," he said. "There wasn't a fight. Why would you want there to be a fight? Oliver, violence isn't our first go-to, okay?"

"Sure," Oliver said. "That's what good guys are supposed to say."

"No, that's the truth." Alex spoke firmly, clearly not as amused as Minnie was. "Son, if I never had to fight another day in my life, I'd be a happy man."

Oliver grinned. "Just like the heroes in the comic books."

"Oliver—"

Minnie cut Alex off with a gentle hand on his arm. She looked at Oliver. "Why don't you go play, like you said?"

"Okay." Oliver shrugged, slid out of his seat, and hurried into the other room.

She turned her attention to Alex. "Oliver's not turning into a crazed murderer just yet, Alex."

"She's right," Timothy said. "He's just being a boy."

Minnie quirked an eyebrow. "He's bein' a kid," she said. "A kid who looks up to his daddy. You're his hero, and he's seen you fight for what's right over and over again. We've shielded him from some of it, but the kid's got eyes and ears. He knows what's what."

Alex shifted uncomfortably. "I don't like that he's seen so much death and violence. It's not right."

"On that, we can agree," Minnie said. "It's not right. It just *is*. But Oliver will be okay. He's got a good head on his shoulders and good people all around him."

"I know." Alex sat back and looked down at his plate. "My eggs are cold."

"I can heat 'em up," Minnie said. She reached over and grabbed his plate before he could protest. "You can do the cleanin' up part." She winked at him, and he settled back in his chair.

"You got it," he said.

Timothy leaned forward. "About Price and Lawson… I don't like it, either. I also don't like this Boreland character you've spoken about. He sounds like bad news."

Alex sipped his coffee. "I'm more worried about Price and Lawson."

Minnie put some fresh wood chips in the giant cast-iron pot and set the metal grate back over top after re-lighting a fire. The window was open, the bug screen firmly in place, and the smoke was drawn outside. She scraped the eggs back into the pan and set it atop the grate.

"Those two would try to convince you they could win a race with their feet cut off," Minnie said. "Arrogance is in their bones, Alex. I don't know that I'd give them another thought."

"They *are* prisoners," Timothy said. "You said their feet were shackled and they were forced into manual labor."

"It was just the *way* he was taunting me." Alex shook his head. "Maybe you're right, but I'm still going to keep an eye on them."

"We can all do that," Minnie said. "Ears to the ground, eyes on watch, for Lawson and Price, sure, but also for *any* trouble."

"Did you pick up any signals when you were with Hunt?" Alex asked.

"Oh, plenty," Minnie said, grinning. "There were signals flyin' all over the place."

Timothy laughed, but Alex rolled his eyes. "I mean about what's going on around here."

Minnie sighed. Alex could be strung tighter than a banjo sometimes, especially when he thought there might be danger lurking somewhere nearby. The problem was, there *was* danger lurking nearby *all the time*. The man was going to die of an anxiety attack long before the apocalypse did him in.

"No," Minnie said as she dumped the eggs back on his plate. She slid it back onto the table in front of him. "I wasn't there to catch gossip. My net was too busy catchin' butterflies." Her stomach fluttered at the thought of the general. She laid a hand on Alex's back. "You ever think maybe Candice has the right idea?"

"What do you mean?" Alex shoveled a bite of eggs into his mouth.

"She's enjoying time with someone she loves," Minnie spoke gently. "If you want Oliver to think about something other than the fight, if you want to prevent *yourself* from going crazy, maybe spending more time with him while we're safe will do you some good."

Timothy picked up his own plate and Oliver's. "I'll clean up," he said. "Why don't you go join in on the game?"

Alex ate the last of his eggs in two quick bites and sat back. "I guess it couldn't hurt."

Minnie smiled as Alex thanked Timothy for cleaning up and left the room. She handed over the chore gratefully. "I think I might join in, too, if you don't mind, Timothy."

"I don't mind at all," he said.

"You should join when you're done, too."

His face fell. "With Heather gone… I don't know that I feel like playing a game right now."

"She's gonna be okay," Minnie said, offering a bit of comfort.

"Yeah, I hope so," Timothy said. "I've made a lot of mistakes in our marriage, but… she's the best thing that ever happened to me, you know? I don't think I'd want to face this world without her."

"She's in the company of strong women," Minnie said. "My Lauren and that Jenny Conner… well, you couldn't ask for better. They'll look out for them, and for your sister, too."

"Lizzy…" Timothy breathed out slowly and raised his eyebrows. "I don't even know what to think about her. I do worry about her, but she's like a stranger these days."

"She'll come back to herself," Minnie said, "or somethin' close to it. Just give her time."

"People keep saying that." Timothy smiled sadly.

"Because it's true. Time is a healer like no other. It can't close a wound on its own, but it can get pretty darn close."

Timothy frowned. "I thought the saying was, 'Time heals all wounds.'"

"It is." Minnie shrugged. "But I'd say Time needs a little help from Love. Together, they can heal anything. But on their own, well… I'm not so sure."

Timothy seemed to think about that for a minute before responding. "Huh," he said after a few seconds. "I think you're right."

"Honey," Minnie said, "whether I was right wasn't in question."

He chuckled as she winked and left him to the chore. When she entered the living room to find Alex, Oliver, Candice, and Annika gathered around the coffee table playing a game, Samson popped up from the corner of the room and trotted over to her, looking up with his big, brown eyes.

"I guess it's time to go outside?" Minnie asked.

Samson barked and wagged his tail. She grabbed his leash, hooked it onto his collar, and opened the front door to find a wall of a person just standing in the doorway. It was a gut reaction, a reflex. As a wave of shock at the unexpected raced from head to toe, Minnie's fist was flying before she even registered who it was that had decided to spook her. She landed an upward punch to the nose, her being at least a foot shorter than…

"Alan?" Minnie gasped and pulled her hand back to cover her mouth.

The general stumbled back a step, holding his nose. "Good heavens, woman!" he bellowed.

"What are you doin' sneakin' up on me like that?" Minnie winced at her harsh tone. "Did I hurt you?" she asked more timidly.

Samson stepped forward, sniffing at the general with a low whimper as if investigating whether the man was okay. He stood up straighter, blinking rapidly and wriggling his nose.

"That was a good hit," Alan said. "It smarts."

"I'm sorry," Minnie repeated.

"No," Alan waved his hand, dismissing her apology. "No, no. I said it was good, and I mean it. It wasn't enough to break the nose, but definitely enough to stun a man. You might need that one day."

"Well, I didn't do it on purpose," Minnie said.

"That's also good," Alan said, cracking the smallest of smiles.

Minnie blushed. "What *are* you doing here?" She leaned back a little and glanced through the doorway as laughter filtered through the house. "Alex is relaxing for once. I don't wanna interrupt that."

"I'm not here for him," Alan said. "I came to see you."

"Oh… well…" Minnie's cheeks grew hotter, and a proper response escaped her. *I'm like a schoolgirl around this man.* She chided herself. *Get it together!*

"Were you about to take Samson out on a walk?" he asked, looking down at the dog and scratching him behind the ears.

She nodded and swallowed the lump in her throat. "As a matter of fact, I was. Except I was just going to the front yard, not too far from shelter, of course."

"We can walk together," Alan said. "I'll have my driver follow us at a near distance, and we can walk the street. If there's danger, we can hurry to the golf cart."

Minnie smiled. "I like a man with a plan," she said.

He stepped back and made room for her to come outside. She shut the front door behind her, and Samson pulled forward excitedly as she and Alan started walking. The general gave instructions to the soldier who had driven him there, and as they made their way down the street, the little golf cart followed. They made small talk at first, but what Alex had said about finding out more information kept nagging at the back of Minnie's mind.

"I'm pleased to hear you enjoyed those eggs," Alan said. "I'll have to take you down to the chicken coop sometime. It's a sight, seeing all those chickens running about inside. We decided to keep them in the gymnasium."

Minnie nodded. "To keep 'em safe from the swarms?"

Alan nodded. "Precisely. It creates a wretched stench, but we've kept them in the smaller gym to ensure they're not killed off, by a swarm or by another predator. It seems this DV-10 isn't deadly to *all* animals, but it seems to kill off birds quite easily. Dr. Pullman thinks it has more to do with the fact that the swarms consume the birds. Those mosquitos are unnatural, hungry, and aggressive."

"Unnatural… that's an understatement," Minnie said, shuddering. "Walter says they've already become something more than what they were originally designed to be. They didn't expect the swarmin', for instance."

"Yes, I thought that particularly interesting when I read the research," Alan said. "I'm glad Walter and Alex are here, that we've got some sort of plan. Dr. Pullman should be able to take what they've got and run with it, even after they go off to New Zealand. We can work on treatments while they retrieve the countermeasure mosquitos."

Minnie nodded and hesitantly prodded further. "And your team here, they're good? All in sync?" she asked.

Alan stopped walking and glanced down at her. "You're asking if there is dissent in my ranks?"

"Yes, I suppose I am," Minnie said.

"Alex told you about Boreland." Alan wasn't asking.

"He did. Just so you know, he'll probably tell me most of what happens. He's… like a son to me." She cleared her throat. "He also told me about Lawson and Price and those two mercenaries still loyal. I know they're prisoners, but…" She trailed off at the expression on Alan's face. She couldn't tell what it meant. His brow was wrinkled, just slightly, and his lips turned down at the corners. He'd gone tense, but the man was good at keeping his emotions in check. Every sign of what he could be thinking was subtle.

"Boreland is… problematic," Alan said. "He was here, running the show, before we got here. At first, I thought maybe he'd challenge the president, try to keep power, but… he ended up stepping aside after some persuasion. I thought he understood our forces were better melded together."

"Does he still understand that?" Minnie asked.

"He's never fully gotten on board," Alan said. "There are a lot of cadets and soldiers who trust him, men and women loyal to him. His reputation… the things he's done in the past… you can't just oust a man like that."

Minnie thought she understood. "He's a snake in the grass. Is that what you're sayin'. Everyone knows he'll bite if you cross him?"

"No," Alan said. "He's saved a lot of lives in his career. Organized a lot of successful missions. He's got experience in the field, experience behind enemy lines. If it hadn't been for an injury and a failed mission that left him… unwilling to return to his previous duties, he wouldn't be here."

"I see," Minnie said, "so he's actually earned a spot at the table, and he don't like bein' second fiddle."

"Something like that." Alan nodded. "I gave him responsibilities, but he took it as a demotion. He doesn't like that he doesn't have President Coleman's ear."

Minnie nodded. "And Lawson and Price?"

"Honestly, I don't give them much thought anymore," Alan said. "They're under constant guard, and we have new problems. Big problems."

"Fair enough." Minnie mulled over how she might encourage him to think about the two troublemakers more often when a little voice sounded behind them and Samson turned around, barking and trotting the other way.

"Minnie!" Oliver ran up to her. "We finished our game. Hey, Mr. Hunt, General, sir!" The boy grinned up at the general.

Alan cleared his throat. "You can call me Alan."

"Cool!" Oliver's smile widened.

"What are you doin' out here?" Minnie asked, pulling Oliver in for a hug.

"I thought I'd come help walk Samson, and when I came outside, I saw you all the way down here. I thought it might be my only chance to get this far down the street!"

Alan laughed, a sound Minnie didn't get to hear very often. "An adventurous spirit. I love it." He gave the boy a serious look. "I could use a partner this afternoon when I make rounds. If your dad says it's okay, what do you think about stepping into a general's shoes for an hour?"

Oliver bounced on the balls of his feet, his face lighting up. "Really?" He patted his mother's purse, always hanging around his neck, resting against his hip. "I'm ready. I've got a duck call and a lighter and lavender — that helps repel mosquitos — and all kinds of things." He pulled out the Zippo lighter Ned the biker had given him on their way to Boston. "See?" He tried to ignite the lighter, but it clicked repeatedly without producing a flame. He frowned. "What's wrong with it?"

"Might be out of fluid," Alan said.

Oliver groaned and dropped it back in the bag. "Well... I can still help."

"I'm sure you can," Alan said. "I tell you what, I think I might be able to get hold of some refills for that Zippo, too. I'll give them to you as payment for helping me out this afternoon."

Minnie held up a finger. "*If* Alex says it's okay," she said.

"Right," Alan said, nodding firmly. "You better go ask, soldier."

Oliver jumped a couple of times in the same spot. "He'll let me go," he said. "I know it!" He turned and sprinted away.

Minnie winced. "I don't know that he will," she said. "Alex has been worried about the things Oliver is being exposed to lately."

"Let's head back," Alan said. "I can explain it to him. I thought maybe the boy would enjoy giving a few orders to the men, exploring the base a little. All with plenty of safety precautions in place. Perhaps you can come with as Alex is meeting with Dr. Pullman this afternoon."

"That sounds lovely," Minnie said.

The two of them walked back to the duplex, and Oliver was already eagerly making his case. Alan inserted a few of his own thoughts, and surprisingly, Alex agreed.

"I guess if Minnie's there," Alex said. "Just an hour or so, though, and then I want you back here, okay?" He offered Minnie a small smile and then thanked Alan before the general left, promising to return after lunch to escort Alex to their research center and pick up Minnie and Oliver for a little adventure.

"I'm glad you're letting Oliver go," Minnie said as they stood on the stoop, watching Alan's golf cart retreat down the street.

"You were right," Alex said. "Playing with Oliver, seeing him smile, hearing him laugh... it made me realize that Candice has a point. We need to take opportunities to live while we're trying to survive."

"Well," Minnie said, a little reluctantly as she didn't want to spoil the mood, "you were right, too. I was able to ask Alan about your concerns, and I didn't get very far, but Boreland seems like a rabble-rouser."

"I knew it," Alex said. "He tried to downplay it, but I had a feeling. I'm going to talk to Hunt—"

"Now, now," Minnie said. "Let's stick with honey and leave the vinegar at home. Let me talk to Alan first."

Alex pursed his lips and then sighed. "Okay," he said. "I trust you."

Minnie nodded and patted Alex on the back as he re-entered the house. She looked back at the golf cart as it turned a corner far down the street and disappeared. A bad feeling in her gut set her on edge. She shook her head. "Well... at least we had a nice morning," she said. "I guess it's time to buckle down and prepare for another whiplashin' storm."

Chapter 18

Lizzy Peters

Lizzy leaned against the concrete wall in the dim light of their designated spot in the arena concourse. Their little square of space was the last one in a line of survivors. The elderly couple to the left had used what seemed like scaffolding, zip ties, and blankets to create a teepee of sorts. To the right, the concourse continued, empty and increasingly darker along the way.

The air was thick with the scent of body odor. Everyone had been given a packet of baby wipes with which to bathe, but many people were apparently doing their best to make their supply stretch. Lizzy had tried to clean up the night before but morning had brought an oil-smudged feel to her skin and crusty corners to her eyes. There wasn't much ventilation to be had, and the mere presence of so many people cooped up together created uncomfortable humidity.

But that wasn't the only source of discomfort. Lizzy pressed her lips together and maintained a neutral expression as Azalea approached with two plastic cups of mixed fruit. Heather and Lauren had been taken to the mountain the day before. Meanwhile, she and Azalea were stuck in the arena with Jenny Conner, waiting to be chosen in a lottery. Azalea hadn't liked that, and when Azalea wasn't happy, neither was Lizzy.

Only one person could create the calm she needed to feel safe, to keep the screaming in her mind at bay, to stop the nightmares. It was how Lizzy knew Azalea was right. Only someone good and pure could counteract the chaotic agony that Lizzy's mind had become. She was too weak to do it herself, but Azalea… well, she was strong and connected to Mother Earth, selfless in her protection of Lizzy, in her patience even as Lizzy battled confusion.

Except, the longer they were away from the Heir's underground compound, the more often Azalea displayed her frustrations and the less time she had for soothing Lizzy's inner turmoil.

It was Lizzy's fault, really. She let her emotions get in the way too often. Instead of playing her role, she antagonized, first her father and then Andy, the person in the arena who could be key to getting inside the mountain.

I just had to say something snarky about their program for women, Lizzy thought.

Azalea had given her the cold shoulder overnight for her misstep, and her distance had allowed the nightmares in.

But as the other woman sat beside Lizzy and handed her a fruit cup, she smiled. Lizzy's body relaxed a little. Perhaps her punishment was over.

"I'm sorry again about yesterday," Lizzy said as she took the cup.

Azalea reached out and tucked Lizzy's hair behind her ear. "You won't do it again."

"I won't," Lizzy said. "I swear." She craned her neck, looking for Jenny. "Where is Conner?"

"She's with Gran, trying to show off how helpful she can be," Azalea said.

"Should we be doing that, too?" Lizzy asked.

"Maybe." Azalea peeled back the plastic lid and sipped the juice. "I don't think Gran is the way in, though."

"Andy?" Lizzy tasted the syrup of her own fruit cup, savoring the thick, sweet liquid.

"He seemed to be the one who decided Heather and Lauren could go straight to the mountain," Azalea said. "I think he runs the lottery, too, or at least has something to do with it. He came back this morning."

Lizzy chewed on her lower lip as a weight settled on her shoulders. "I'm such an idiot," she whispered.

Azalea picked a bright red cherry out of her cup. She held it out. "You like cherries, right?"

Lizzy nodded and took it. "Thanks," she said.

"I'm here for you, Elizabeth," Azalea said. "I'm here to fix your mistakes. I'm here to make sure you don't make any more big ones. What happened yesterday is an inconvenience. I have some ideas to make it right." She patted Lizzy's knee, and then she plucked a diced pear from her cup and popped it into her mouth.

"What are you going to do?" Lizzy asked.

Azalea swallowed and leaned closer. She always got a glint in her eye when she revealed her plans, like a kid about to dig into a cake. "Just a little old-fashioned sabotage."

Lizzy was grateful for the dim light as she furrowed her brow. She didn't want to keep questioning—she was loyal, after all—but sabotage could mean a thousand different things. It could put them both in danger.

It could put Heather in danger. Lizzy frowned at the thought. There was no denying she still loved her brothers and Heather, even if she despised her father, even if she hated that they were enabling Walter Peters and his inflated ego. But The Cleanse effectively put everyone in danger, even her and Azalea. Lizzy had come to accept that, come to understand the selfless bravery of the Heirs. *We must make sacrifices,* she told herself. *Dust to dust. Restore the Mother.*

"Aren't you going to ask me how?" Azalea leaned back against the wall so that she was shoulder-to-shoulder with Lizzy.

"I trust you," Lizzy said. "Do you want me to do anything?"

Azalea finished off her fruit cup, her mood suddenly lighter. "Follow my lead. Do as I say." She leaned closer. "My plan is two-fold. Andy is a man, and men do all sorts of things for accommodating women. All I have to do is work my charm on him and plant seeds of doubt in his mind about the others."

"That didn't work on Alex," Lizzy said.

Azalea's smile faltered. "I didn't try that hard."

"Right," Lizzy said quickly. "Of course."

"I wrapped Theodore Finch around my little finger," Azalea said as she sat up straighter. "And that's what I'm going to do with Andy."

Lizzy nodded emphatically, her insides curling at Azalea's tone. She'd said the wrong thing again. "I know you can do it," she said. "I'm not doubting you."

Azalea breathed deeply. "Calm down, Elizabeth," she said, leaning back again, shrugging away from Lizzy.

"Sorry." Lizzy's cheeks burned hot. She dug her fingernails into her palms, squeezing her fists tightly, finding an anchor in the pain as her nails pinched skin. Her chest became tight, and the screaming at the back of Lizzy's mind got just a little louder.

Azalea glanced at Lizzy's hands, sighed, and reached out to lay a gentle hand over one of Lizzy's fists. "I forgive you," she said, her voice becoming smoother. "You're so important to me, Elizabeth. I need you to keep your wits about you. Can you do that for me?" Azalea scooted around to face Lizzy. "C'mon, open your hands. Look at me and breathe."

Lizzy did so, allowing Azalea's voice to soothe her. Once she was calm again, Azalea slid back into place beside her, and there was silence for a while. Lizzy closed her eyes and focused on maintaining control. It was half an hour before Azalea spoke again.

"Tell me you can still do this," Azalea said. "I'll give up our best shot at ensuring The Cleanse continues if you can't. We can opt out of the lottery, ask to leave. They won't keep us here. We can go back to the Heirs and admit our failure."

Lizzy's stomach turned. "No, I don't want to do that."

"If the people here see you losing it like that—" She glanced down at Lizzy's hands. "—if you question them too many times, if you question *me* too many times, I'll have no choice. Do you think they want a ball of anxiety in their new utopia? They're looking for strong women who can add to their strengths."

"I won't let my weaknesses derail us," Lizzy said.

Azalea looked at her for what seemed like forever. Finally, she nodded. "I believe you." She took a deep breath. "Now, do you think you can handle hearing the rest of the plan?"

A sudden exhaustion settled over Lizzy's entire body. That was good. When her emotions ran high, sometimes they overwhelmed her until she shut down, until she couldn't feel anything but a tired ache in her bones. Not feeling anything enabled her to follow the plan without question. It was her emotions that usually got her into trouble. It was happening more and more in recent days, that overload followed by periods of blissful apathy. It hurt less, and she'd learned to give in to it, to look forward to it, even.

"I'm listening," Lizzy said. "You said something about planting seeds of doubt?"

"About Lauren and Jenny," Azalea said. "Our story is that we've been traveling together for weeks, right? I'm sure they'd like to know that Lauren had been training to be a doctor but never became one. And we might speculate why that could be, why she would lie about her training. Was she kicked out of her program? Does she even know how to do the things she says she does?"

"And Jenny?" Lizzy asked.

Azalea waved off the question. "She'll be the easiest one to cast in a bad light. She screams military. A story or two about how she's done things only trained soldiers would think to do, and they'll be keeping a closer eye on her."

"What about Heather?" Lizzy no longer felt a pang at her sister-in-law's name on her lips. She embraced the numbness overshadowing guilt and anxiety and fear.

"We can't do anything about her. If we call her into question, we call ourselves into question. They know she's your family." Azalea shrugged. "She wouldn't be able to do much on her own, anyway."

You might be underestimating her, Lizzy thought, but she kept the sentiment to herself. Azalea didn't want to be questioned.

"I'm going to go find Andy," Azalea said, "but while I do, why don't you get some more rest? You look like you could use it."

Lizzy didn't need much convincing. She leaned sideways and lay with her back to the wall. Azalea covered her with a blanket and kissed her forehead.

"This is it. If we succeed here," Azalea said, "they're done, and we can go home."

Home. Lizzy mulled the word over as she watched Azalea retreat down the concourse in search of Andy. *Acceptance. Love. Community.* The Heirs of the Mother were home, more so than any other place, but thoughts of the underground bunker didn't give her peace. She didn't long for it like she used to long for her home in Wellesley. Her numbness only deepened. Lizzy let the feeling saturate her, let it seep into her fingers and toes, let it slow her heartbeat and quiet her mind. It was good, to feel nothing. She closed her eyes and slept, and not one nightmare claimed her.

Chapter 19

Zara Williams

One page of notes. That was all Zara had on Lieutenant Colonel Joel Blythe, the retired pilot they had to convince to join their mission. It wasn't a lot of information. Sixty-eight years of age, Blythe was retired eight years and had isolated himself nearly that long. He'd received an award, the Distinguished Flying Cross, in his younger days in a rescue mission turned sour; Blythe had lost half his crew while successfully evacuating nearly one hundred American citizens from a war zone. He'd been married twenty years, no children. His wife had died of cancer five years before his retirement. That was it: a list of facts that told Zara very little about who Blythe actually was.

Zara tapped her fingers on the legal pad in her lap as the golf cart ambled past striated red-and-cream rocky walls, the insides of mountainous hills which had been cut through for paved roadways long ago. The sharply rising and falling landscape all around them was covered with a blanket of shrubs, and the sky was bright and blue. As long as she didn't pay too much attention to the corpses in half the vehicles they passed or think too long about how a swarm could be lurking beyond the next curve in the road, the beautiful scenery was a silver lining, a comfort, even. It was nice to know she could still find beauty in the world, but it wasn't enough to distract her from the matter at hand.

She held up the legal pad and looked at Kai. "This isn't much to go on."

Kai opened his mouth to respond, but Yeomen spoke up from the driver's seat first.

"It'll have to be enough." Yeomen guided the solar-powered golf cart around a burnt-out husk of a small car, following the cart ahead of them where Warren and Potts led their group of five people and two carts. They traveled down Highway 24, headed northwest further into the mountain.

"Zara's right," Kai said from beside her. "How are we supposed to convince a man to leave the safety of his off-grid cabin to go on some crazy mission to New Zealand and then Antarctica? The only personal details here are that his wife is dead and he has no kids. So... he basically has no one to fight for."

"If you can't convince him," Yeomen said, "we've brought sedatives. He's coming with us one way or the other."

"Wait, what?" Kai straightened, going rigid. "I didn't sign up to kidnap this guy."

"I didn't either," Zara said. "You can't force him to fly the plane. Sedating him and bringing him against his will isn't going to help."

Yeomen shrugged. "We have our orders. He's not crazy about us airmen. If anything, I'd say he'd be on the side of the civilians when it comes to the conflict happening in the city. I wouldn't mention that, by the way. I hear he's traded wild game for meds at Cheyenne. He's clearly biased."

"Why didn't you mention this when we were talking over our mission last night?" Zara asked. "We had plenty of time this morning while we were waiting for these golf carts to charge. I mean, we were holed up in that little house on the edge of the city for like twelve hours."

"We were sleeping most of that time." Yeomen kept his eyes on the road.

"So, what?" Kai asked. "You and your friends decided to keep your full plan under wraps until we were stuck in this golf cart with no way to opt out?"

"Yes." Yeomen's tone didn't contain an ounce of remorse or even embarrassment. "Again, we had our orders."

"Whose orders?" Zara asked. "We'd like to know who it is exactly that we should be wary of trusting."

Yeomen's eyes flicked to the rearview mirror and then back to the road. "I'll keep that information private, then."

"Was it this General Hunt?" Kai was still stiff, and his voice increased in volume.

"Lower your voice." Yeomen's words carried a calm severity, suggesting little choice in the matter. "If you convince Blythe to come with us, our secondary orders will be rendered null and void."

"This is messed up, man. What makes you think he'll even listen to me?" Kai didn't comply with Yeomen's demands that he lower his voice.

"General Hunt thinks you'll remind him of himself when he was young," Yeomen said. "And like I said, he's not going to be happy to see men in uniform. He'll respond better to civilians."

"And why is that?" Zara scoffed. "Have you kidnapped him before?"

"I have no idea why this nut job decided to hate the people who made him or why he became a hermit," Yeomen said, his cool and collected façade cracking. "Again, I'm following orders. At this point, we have about the same amount of information."

"At this point," Kai spat, "I'm about to hightail it out of here."

Yeomen slammed on the brakes and the cart lurched to a stop. He turned around in his seat, and the hard certainty in his eyes made Zara shudder. "You do that, we sedate *you*. Then, instead of trying to reason with Colonel Blythe, we go in with Plan B to start. You seem to be forgetting what is at stake here. The truth is, you and Blythe aren't being asked. You're being told. The entire *world* needs you two to fly that damn plane, and you're going to do it, either of your own accord because it's the right thing to do or because we have to do something to convince you, like lock up your girlfriend here until you return. And that could be a long time for that firecracker to be in cuffs."

Zara had had enough of *that*. She leaned forward and gave Yeomen a quick, sharp slap. "Don't *ever* threaten me again." He grabbed her wrist, but she continued. "You don't know us," she said. "If we have to, we'll save the world another way and leave you and yours on the wrong side of history. We don't need you. You're just the easiest route to our endgame."

And then Kai's handgun was pointed at Yeomen's head. "I'd listen to her if I were you," Kai said coldly. "That firecracker doesn't go out without a fight."

Zara's heart leaped into her throat as she looked at the gun. They'd all brought weapons, but they were a last resort in case they ran into trouble. They weren't supposed to be using them on each other. She maintained her composure, meeting Yeomen's glare with one of her own, but she was faltering. Her words had come out of rage and a little bit of false bravado. She wasn't sure how much of it was true, just that she needed Yeomen to believe every word, especially since Kai had decided to raise his gun.

"You wouldn't dare," Yeomen said, seething as he stared down the barrel of the gun. "You've gotten too big for your britches, boy."

"Yeomen!" Warren's voice came in over the soldier's handheld radio that was tucked in a pocket on his military-issued vest. "What the hell are you doing?"

Zara looked past him to see the other golf cart turning around to come back for them. She tensed. With Kai's handgun pointed at one of their own, she didn't know what would happen. But something hadn't sounded quite right with Yeomen's threats.

I'm not the only one bluffing, she thought.

"Kai, put the gun away." She sneered at Yeomen; her wrist was still in his grip. "If you want to sedate us, go ahead. I'm sure General Hunt would love to know how quickly your mission failed. My guess is that this colonel isn't going to mess around when it comes to his own safety. You can't kill him, but he can kill you." She smiled despite the way he was crushing her wrist. "Have fun with that."

"Yeomen!" Warren shouted through the plastic barrier as Potts stopped their cart nose-to-nose with the one Zara and Kai were in. He unzipped his plastic door and stepped out while drawing his own weapon. "Put your gun down, kid," he said. "And Yeomen, let her go. Right. Now."

Yeomen shoved Zara backward, finally releasing her. She rubbed at her wrist. It was sore, but it didn't appear to be broken or sprained.

"I'm okay," Zara said to Kai. "Put it away."

Kai lowered the weapon but didn't holster it. Warren came around to Yeomen's door, unzipped the plastic, grabbed Yeomen by the collar, and yanked him out. He kept his weapon drawn the entire time.

"Someone explain." Warren's reddened face made the vein popping on his forehead more pronounced.

"Yeomen let us know that you have no problem sedating us if we're not cool with kidnapping some guy we've never met," Zara said. "And he threatened to keep me prisoner in order to force Kai to go forward with your plans. Is that how you all operate? Because Alex was under the impression you were the good guys."

Warren cursed under his breath and threw a dark look at Yeomen. "You're an idiot." He shook his head and addressed Zara and Kai once again. "Look, our secondary orders are to detain Blythe without hurting him if he refuses to come with us. That much is true. But we were never given the green light to do anything to either of you."

"You really think," Yeomen said, "that if those two tried to run off and abandon the mission, that General Hunt wouldn't forgive a little bit of creativity?"

"Shut the hell up," Potts said as he, too, got out of the other cart. "Man, without Conner here to reign you in, you sure go cowboy real quick."

"These two are practically children," Yeomen said, throwing up his hands. "And we're out here seeking the help of a traitor, hoping a couple of civilians can what? Appeal to his morality?" He scoffed. "We're all going to die."

Potts whistled. "Okay, maybe less cowboy and more doomsday." He held out his hands in front of him, palms down. "Look, Blythe isn't a traitor. He's neutral. The guy has been out of the loop and on his own for a long time. He's just out here trying to survive. And c'mon, Yeomen, sending a young pilot and his girl to plead the case… it's the best play we've got. We're not playing to his morality, we're playing to his empathy, not to mention his nostalgia."

"Hunt believes these two are capable based upon Mr. Roman's evaluations," Warren said. "They weren't even supposed to know Plan B, Yeomen. What made you decide to let that cat out of the bag?"

Zara's mouth dropped open, and she exchanged a look with Kai. "Hey," she said. "You know we're standing right here. We should have been told everything from the beginning. This is supposed to be our mission, too. Kai and I should have had a say."

"That's not how the military works," Yeomen said. "We follow orders."

"We aren't in the military," Kai said, "and we're not following anyone's orders. We're here because we believed it was the right thing to do."

"Yeah, and you're making us question that." Zara shook her head and pointed between her and Kai. "We need to take a break and talk about this."

"Well, we're not too far from the area Blythe's settled," Potts said. "His home base is off the beaten path, and we don't know exactly where he is. Once we turn off the highway into the general vicinity, we'll need to search for his cabin. How about you two stay put in the golf carts while we do that. No need for you to go traipsing over possibly dangerous terrain when we don't know exactly where we're going."

Warren nodded. "You two can hash it out then, although things haven't actually changed. This is still the right thing to do, and without you two, it could get ugly. But either way, whether you're in it or not, you have my word neither of you will be sedated or harmed in any way."

"Well, we're not riding the rest of the way with that maniac," Zara said, gesturing to Yeomen.

Yeomen made fists at his sides, but Potts gave him a small shake of his head and stepped forward. "I've got you," he said. "Yeomen can ride with Warren."

It was still tense when Zara and Kai agreed and slid into the back seats once again, but Potts brought with him an entirely different atmosphere. He was lighthearted and chatty, and though he claimed not to have any kids, it seemed he'd spent time developing his dad-joke skills. The small talk was inconsequential for the next hour or so until Potts followed Yeomen and Warren off the highway and onto a smaller, two-lane road.

"So, what are you two young'uns planning on doing once things settle down?" Potts asked.

Zara was still feeling a little tense, but the man was trying hard, and while he'd been part of the lie, he and Warren hadn't threatened them. *It can't hurt to get on their good side,* she thought, *just in case Yeomen does something crazy and we need protecting.*

"Well," Zara said, "college is out of the question, I guess. Boston seemed nice. Maybe I'll go back there."

"I hated college," Potts said, navigating through a very small town with perhaps a dozen abandoned homes. "I wasn't too bad at the sciences, but math? Man, I *lost count* of how many assignments I failed." He chuckled. "Get it? Lost count? Math?"

Zara laughed, more at how amusing Potts found himself than the actual joke. Kai rolled his eyes even as he cracked a smile. The golf cart rumbled along, but it was beginning to slow. The same had happened the day before just as they'd called it quits and set up camp for the night inside an abandoned home. It meant the battery didn't have much left.

"How about you?" Potts asked. "What's in the cards for Kai Lee?"

Kai shrugged. "I wasn't doing much with my life before all of this. I guess I just want to keep helping people. The last couple months… it's the first time in my life I've done anything important."

"If this pilot thing works out," Potts said, "there will be plenty of opportunities for you to do that, you know? Once the government has some more stability, we'll need to assess the state of the country, deliver aid, figure out how to heal our nation… the fastest way to do that will be by air."

"You really think a country the size of the United States is going to be able to recover from this?" Zara asked. "I mean, people are setting up their own local governments now. There are so few survivors."

Potts shrugged. "I don't know what it'll look like." He sighed. "But I sure hope we'll be able to find that American spirit again. Maybe even one more like we see in the history books but without all the bad stuff, you know? Like the prejudice and whatnot. I like to think the United States 2.0 will be up and running again someday, maybe in ten years, maybe in a hundred. Like the Old West, a new frontier of possibilities."

"So, then, you're an optimist," Kai said.

"A dreamer," Potts grinned into the rearview mirror. "We gotta believe in something if we're going to make it, kid, and I want to believe in the future."

The future… Zara thought about that as Potts kept the conversation going with small talk and the occasional pun. The only future she'd allowed herself to think about was the immediate one. Looking out a year or five or ten, she saw nothing. Everything she'd thought she'd become, all of her own dreams, had been ripped away. It had seemed selfish and childish to dream beyond survival, but Potts was right. If they were successful, there would come a time when surviving wasn't the only thing that mattered. *What am I going to do with myself then?*

They drove through a pine forest, the occasional rocky outcropping breaking up the tree line. Their path eventually branched off again onto a downward-sloping dirt road. It wound through the thinning forest leading them farther into the middle of nowhere. Finally, the golf cart came to a stuttering stop. There were no signs of inhabitants anywhere nearby.

"This is as far as she'll take us for now," Potts said. "Good news is I think we're pretty close." He spoke into his radio. "Hey fellas, I ran out of battery."

"We're on our last leg, too," Warren said. "But we're about where we need to be anyway. I think we can go on foot from here."

"Copy that," Potts said. He addressed Zara and Kai as he patted the steering wheel. "These babies use solar power faster than they can gather it. She won't be going anywhere for the next few hours."

"Will it take that long for you to search?" Zara asked.

"I don't know," he said. "Maybe."

"What about Yeomen?" Kai shifted in his seat as he eyed the golf cart ahead of them. "I know you said we're safe, but… the things he said…"

Potts turned around in his seat. "My guess is that Warren has talked Yeomen down by now. I know you don't like Yeomen. He's a hot wire sometimes, I won't deny that. But the man is… complicated. He's scared, and he won't admit it. He wants to barrel through this mess and get things done, and when something is clearly out of his control, he gets uncomfortable. But he's a good soldier. He follows orders, and with Warren as our lead on this mission, you two have nothing to worry about."

"If you say so," Zara said, still not completely convinced as the two other men exited their golf carts.

"I do," Potts said. "Now, I'm trusting you two not to run off while we're searching the area. Remember how I said this was dangerous terrain?"

Zara and Kai nodded in unison.

"Well, I meant it. It's not just about potential swarms, either. You could get lost, get dehydrated, and die from exposure. There are plenty of cliffs, plenty of snakes, and we've heard there are some predators in the area becoming bolder, acting erratically."

Zara couldn't help but look out into the trees. "What kind of predators?"

"Bears. Mountain lions. Also Moose." Potts nodded in affirmation as Zara threw him a questioning look. "You heard me. Moose aren't predators, per se, but they're mean S.O.Bs. They'll stomp a man to death twice over just for the fun of it."

"Okay," Kai said. "So watch out for the wildlife. Good to know."

"That's not all," Potts said. "You can't count out the possibility that Blythe isn't the only hermit out here. Personally, these days I'd rather run into a snake than a stranger." He raised his eyebrows. "So, I'm serious. You two stay put." He pointed to the duffel bag tied down to a rack at the back of the little vehicle. It was outside the plastic barrier, but it wouldn't take long to access and return to safety. "There's food and water in there, if you need it. When we find the cabin, we'll come back for you. Got it?"

"Agreed," Zara said.
"Whatever we decide to do," Kai said, "I suggest you talk to your boy, Yeomen, about respecting it. He might be acting out of fear, but that's not exactly an excuse. And it's definitely not comforting."
"Fair enough," Potts said.
He unzipped the plastic next to the driver's seat, stepped out, and sealed Zara and Kai in again. As the three soldiers walked into the forest, Warren and Potts both maintained serious expressions and firm body language as they spoke to Yeomen. Zara didn't know what they were saying, exactly, but Yeomen was nodding solemnly. They were out of sight within a few minutes.
"How long do you think they'll be?" Kai asked.
"I have no idea," Zara said.
"I don't like them." Kai bounced his knee as he kept his eyes on the point where the three soldiers had disappeared into the trees.
"Warren and Potts aren't that bad," Zara said as she settled back in her seat. "I kind of like Potts."
"Potts would still kidnap this guy," Kai said, "and that can't happen. Guys like General Hunt sometimes think with brute force first and their humanity second. His orders are just going to make things worse."
"What can we do about it?" Zara asked. "I mean, besides trying to get Colonel Blythe to come with us on his own?"
"We can tell him what they've got planned," Kai said. "I need him to trust me. *We* need him to trust me. Yeomen was right about one thing. I don't like it, but I do have to fly again. There isn't another way. But we need Blythe." He smiled at her. "You were right, too, though. We don't need the military. If Blythe is with us, we can get to New Zealand and on to Antarctica."
"I guess I hadn't thought of it that way," Zara said. "But now that you say it... it's more important that we earn Blythe's loyalty than it is we play nice with General Hunt's men."
"So, we approach Blythe with the absolute truth, start to finish," Kai said. "We make it clear that he's with us, not them, if he decides to do this."
"We can figure out access to the plane and fuel, if we have to," Zara said. "But it would be easier if the military were still on our side when we were ready to fly it. And that would make training you easier, too."
Kai chewed on his lower lip for a moment before speaking again. "Okay. Plan A: we tell Blythe everything, convince him to come with us and the military peacefully. We all work together. Plan B: if Blythe can't work with the military after finding out what *their* Plan B was, we convince him to come back peacefully and we separate from the military when we get to the city. Maybe we go back to the church."
"That all assumes we're able to convince him to come at all," Zara said.
"Yeah, it does." Kai grimaced. "I have no idea what to do if he just flat-out says no."
"I guess we'll handle it if it comes up. I mean, if he does say no, those three are going to try to force him. It might mean a serious fight." Zara rubbed at her temples.
"We're a good team," Kai said. "We'll figure it out."
"Okay," Zara said. "I'm not sure I'm one hundred percent confident, but it is what it is." She reached for the zipper on the door handle. "Let's stretch our legs and grab something to eat. I'm starving."
"Hey, one more thing," Kai said.
When she looked back at him, he had a giant grin on his face. She returned a flat stare. "What is it?"
"When they called you 'my girl,' you didn't correct them."
Zara groaned. "Are you serious right now?"
He shrugged, that silly grin still on his face. "Hey, I just want to know if you didn't correct them because you had other things on your mind or if it was because there was nothing to correct."
"I'm not doing this right now," Zara said as heat flooded her cheeks. The truth was, she wasn't sure. But she didn't want to admit that to Kai, not yet, anyway. "Didn't you hear me say I'm starving? If you don't help me find some food, I'll slap you next."
He put his hands up in mock surrender. "Okay, okay," he said. She unzipped her door and had one foot on the ground when Kai added, "But just so I'm clear, that's not a 'no, I'm not your girl,' right?"
"Kai!" Zara turned around and swatted at him, her fingertips barely making contact. She couldn't help but smile as he pretended to be hurt. "Good grief, I—"
Both of their smiles were wiped clean off their faces as a scream cut off their conversation. Zara sucked in a breath, scurried completely back inside the cart, and hurried to zip the plastic closed. She reached for Kai's hand, and he squeezed hers tight as they both watched the tree line for any sign of what that scream had meant. The only answer they received was that whatever was happening was bad. Another voice screamed, followed by gunshots, one right after another. Zara flinched with each burst of sound.
"Kai... they wouldn't shoot at a swarm," Zara whispered.
Potts came tumbling out of the trees, rolling onto the dirt road several yards ahead of the carts. He came to a stop, righted himself and frantically slung his backpack into the dirt beside him. When he pulled a fresh magazine out and slammed it into his handgun, Zara's entire body went rigid.
"Kai... what—"
Potts raised his gun, but before he could fire, a beast of gray and white fur leapt out of the trees and landed on top of him. One gunshot went wide, and the wolf got hold of his wrist. Potts screamed in agony and his gun dropped to ground, throwing up a puff of dust. He struggled, punching and kicking. The wolf let go and turned his teeth onto Potts's neck. Blood spurted from his wrist, and again from his neck, as the wolf let go to maul fresh flesh. It seemed more intent on shredding the man than killing him for food.
Zara screamed. "We have to help him!"
"No!" Kai wrapped his arm around her and pulled her back before she could reach for the zipper. "Zara, look." He pointed to the tree line.

Another snarling wolf prowled forward, its muzzle, jaw, and mane thick with blood. Its eyes bulged, bloodshot but focused on her. Its matted fur was patchy in places, and though it limped from what appeared to be a gunshot wound in its hind leg, the creature did not whimper. It emitted a low, rumbling growl, and then it reared its head back and howled. Within seconds, it was answered with another howl… and then another… and another. Crazed and bloody, the beast stepped closer.

Chapter 20

Jenny Conner

Jenny had rarely been immersed in such complete darkness. She held a tiny flashlight in front of her, shielding the beam so as to make the light a little smaller. It was important that she see what was just ahead of her, but too much light could attract unwanted attention. She followed Andy's directions into the darkest recesses of the arena. She was to meet him in what was once a locker room and claim to be searching for materials with which to build a tent if she ran into anyone on her way.

So far, she hadn't met a soul. She turned into the last hallway, if she'd followed directions properly, only to come face to face with a rat. It squeaked at her, and she squeaked right back, and loudly. Her hand flew to her mouth as her heart jumped into her throat. When the initial shock of seeing the rodent had passed, and the creature had scurried away, she stood frozen for a moment, listening, her mouth clamped shut, praying silently that no one had heard her. It would be disastrous for some other explorer to attempt to come to her aid when she was so close to the meeting spot.

There was no sound besides the scurrying of little claws on the hallway floor. Jenny let out a long slow breath. Adrenaline still had her heart pumping, though, as she walked the last few yards to the doorway for which she was looking. She slipped inside, her body deflating at the relief of having made it.

"Hey, Jen." Andy was very suddenly right by her side, speaking into her ear.

She flailed and yelped much louder than she had squeaked. Andy laughed, and she punched his arm a little harder than she intended.

"Ouch!" He rubbed at the spot.

"You scared me!" Jenny whisper-yelled. "What the hell? What if someone heard?"

"No one comes down this far," Andy said. "You might have run into someone closer to the concourse, but here? Everyone is afraid of finding dead bodies."

Jenny shone her light around the room. "Are there? Dead bodies, I mean?"

"Not in this room," Andy said. "But I wouldn't go opening up doors willy-nilly." He walked over to a bench in front of a row of lockers and straddled it, placing his flashlight so that the beam shone upward, creating a circle of light on the ceiling. He patted the bench. "Ready for a debrief? I've got an interesting story to share."

"It better be good, Munez," Jenny said. "I still have to search for something to bring back for this tent I'm never going to build." She'd come here on his request, after he'd slipped her a note with her fruit cup that morning.

He reached under the bench and pulled out a thick, hefty cloth folded into a bulky square. "It's a panel from a stage curtain," he said. "It should do the trick."

Jenny pursed her lips as she took the bundle and stashed it back under the bench. "Okay, well… thanks." She swung one leg over the wooden plank and sat down across from Andy. She sighed. "Now, what's this about?"

"Your friend, Azalea," Andy said.

"What about her?" Jenny balanced her own flashlight next to Andy's, the cone of light combining with his. It still wasn't a ton of light, but it was enough for her to see his expression, and that alone created the first stirrings of anxiety in the pit of her stomach.

"What do you know about her?" Andy asked.

"Not much," Jenny said. "Lizzy is the daughter of Walter Peters—"

"Wait… *the* Walter Peters?"

Jenny nodded. "Right… you haven't gotten the full update on what's going on back at base." She filled him in on the basics about who was with Alex. The mission to get inside the mountain and reclaim it for the government had been in the works for a while. Andy already knew about that, but the mission to get information on the location of Barlow Scientific Research Bank was new.

Andy whistled long and low before shaking his head. "That's *nuts*! Do you think they'll be able to pull this off?"

"I'm choosing to have a little faith," Jenny said. "Alex is… a determined guy. And these people he's with, they're solid. Most of them anyway." She sighed. "Azalea and Lizzy… I know the least about them."

"Okay, go on." Andy crossed his arms and settled as if listening intently.

"Lizzy was kidnapped by some cult when Walter Peters was trying to get back to his lab in Boston. She and Azalea were taken with the intention of human trafficking, but they escaped. I don't know how, exactly, just that they did. They found their way to Boston together." Jenny bit her lower lip and frowned. "It seems, from what I've gathered via Heather, that Lizzy hasn't been herself since returning. She's super attached to Azalea, and she practically ignores the people she's known forever, even family. I mean, she seems to really hate her dad."

"Understandable," Andy said, shrugging. "Both hating her father and attaching to a girl who shares her trauma."

"Sure," Jenny said. "That's what everyone is telling themselves. And Lizzy *does* act like she's been traumatized, but…" She winced, unsure she wanted to voice her thoughts about Azalea.

"But Azalea doesn't?" Andy asked.

"It feels gross to say that," Jenny said. "I don't want to discredit a victim. No one does. I mean, there are moments when I think she's definitely been through *something*, but there are other moments when it seems she's manipulating the situation."

"Sometimes people who manipulate and grasp for control are acting out of long-term abuse or trauma," Andy said. "It could be that her life wasn't all roses and cupcakes before this disease destroyed the world, you know?"

"It could be," Jenny said.

"But regardless of the reasons behind the way she's acting," Andy said, "I think she might be a danger to our mission. We have to separate ourselves from her backstory and look at what she's bringing to the table right now. And I don't think it's anything good."

Jenny waved off the comment. "I don't think she can do any real damage, even if she's a little off."

"I think she can," Andy said. "That's why I asked you to meet. She approached me, alone, in the inventory room. I don't know how she got back there without being noticed, but she was waiting for me."

Jenny frowned. "And?"

"She came on to me, trying to get her and Lizzy's name bumped up the list in the lottery."

"She doesn't know you're on our side," Jenny said. "She's trying to get us into the mountain. That's what she's supposed to do. I would have never asked her to do it in that way, but I don't see the problem."

"She wasn't trying to get you *all* in, just the two of them," Andy said.

A spike of confusion culminated in indignation. "Are you serious? So she threw herself at you to make a deal, and she left me out of it? She's trying to leave me behind?"

"That's the thing, though. She didn't throw herself at me. The way she did it… it was calculated, like she'd been trained," Andy said. "She was charmingly innocent. She subtly played to my ego. She was smart about it."

Jenny's stomach turned. "She *was* subjected to human trafficking. I don't know how long she was enslaved to the traffickers. It could have been years. Maybe she was forced to do that sort of thing, to get information or something."

Andy nodded. "Maybe, but… it's not just that. She wasn't trying to leave you behind, Jen. She was trying to cast doubt on you and on Lauren."

"I'm sorry, what?" Jenny's mouth hung open for a moment as she thought of the implications. "How?"

"She mentioned that you had a lot of stories from a lot of different places, indicating you'd moved around a lot. She called you stiff and too precise, said you'd tried to convince their group to find the military first, but you were outvoted." He shook his head. "She talked about it like you five were *really* travelling together for the last month, like the story you gave her to feed to us was reality. If I hadn't known it was a cover story, I wouldn't have caught the lie."

"She tried to suggest I'm military," Jenny said softly. "Why would she do that?"

"I don't know, but with Lauren… you should have heard her talk about Lauren." He raised his voice a few octaves and mimicked Azalea. "She said something once about her residency." Andy flipped back imaginary hair. "And I was, like, nurses have residencies? I thought that was for doctors. But don't worry, she didn't lie. She's totally not a doctor. She dropped out or was kicked out… I didn't really get the full story on that one." Andy went back to his normal voice. "Azalea is a pro at information manipulation, Jen. I don't think she's just some average girl from Ohio or wherever she claims to be from."

"Okay…" Jenny breathed in and out, trying to calm herself. A swirl of emotions warred inside her: fury, confusion, fear. "What did you do?"

"I played along," Andy said. "I did my best to keep my cover intact."

"Good." Jenny nodded. "That's good. What about Heather? Did she say anything about Heather?"

Andy shook his head. "No, and I think it's because part of your story includes the fact that Lizzy is her sister-in-law. Calling Heather into question would call Lizzy into question, and that would call Azalea into question. That's a domino effect she was trying to avoid."

"Let me think for a minute." Jenny looked up at the ceiling, focusing on the circles of light cast by the flashlights. She rubbed her thighs until the friction made her hands warm. The movement helped her think. She ran through the scenarios again and again in her head, trying to anticipate the possible outcomes of each route forward. Her body filled to the brim with the tension of not knowing what to do, and so she slid off the bench and paced a small section of the floor.

"Carving a rut in the floor isn't going to help," Andy said. "And you probably shouldn't stay down here too much longer. We don't want Azalea or Lizzy to come looking."

Jenny stopped and faced Andy. "We have to do what she asked. Let her and Lizzy go to the mountain. Put their name at the top of the list."

Andy shook his head. "What? No way! That's insane."

"It's the best way forward," Jenny said. "Those two are either damaged and self-destructive because of their trauma or they're outright trying to sabotage this mission."

"Yeah," Andy said, "which means we need to get them out of here before they blow your cover."

"And what do you think will happen if we try to do that? If we try to kick them out? Or if we try to trap them here in the concourse indefinitely?" Jenny raised her eyebrows.

Andy leaned his head back and sighed, a look of understanding falling across his face. "They could start to suspect *me*, too. They know we have an inside source. They just don't know who it is or whether they're here or at the mountain."

"Not just that," Jenny said. "Azalea could work her magic on someone who would listen. You're not the only guy who comes down here from the mountain right?"

Andy groaned. "The next guy coming down here, he'd definitely trade a few favors for a bump up in the list."

"If *we* send them there, we can assign them their task, right?" Jenny asked, holding her breath. Her plan hinged on Andy's answer.

"I assess skill sets and place people who win the lottery, yes," Andy said.

Jenny clapped her hands once, grinning. "Good. Okay, what's the most isolated job you could possibly give them up at the mountain?"

"Laundry duty." Andy grimaced. "It's grueling, too. Exhausting."

"Perfect!" She always got a rush of excitement when she solved a problem, and fresh energy coursed through her body. "If they're too tired to make trouble, all the better."

"And what about you?" Andy asked.

"We're going to have to leave me here, in the concourse for at least a few more days. Azalea and Lizzy need to think they manipulated you into getting them bumped to the top of the list. When you send me up, I'll tell them all I had to do was flirt with you. Azalea obviously thinks that's all it takes. She just doesn't think I have the skillset to get away with it." Jenny tapped her chin with her forefinger. "Speaking of that, did she offer you anything? It would be... unethical, to say the least, should you accept any of her advances."

Andy made a disgusted face. "I would never. She made suggestions that if, in six months when her trial period was over, I wanted to be her baby daddy, she wouldn't object. I acted like I was interested because I thought that's what she wanted to hear, but I swear, I won't ever touch her. She's too young for me, anyway."

"Good." Jenny nodded. "I hate to say it, but keep acting interested—" She raised a finger. "—to a point."

"I can do that," Andy said. "Do I need to get a message to Heather and Lauren about them? Warn them not to trust them?"

Jenny put her hands on her hips and looked down at her feet, thinking before shaking her head. "No, I don't think so," she said. "I don't know how Heather would react to suspicion being thrown on her sister-in-law."

"You're probably right on that," Andy said. "Besides, I guess putting Azalea and Lizzy on laundry duty will effectively keep them so busy and isolated, they shouldn't be much of a problem. They won't be able to do much in terms of helping us or hindering us."

"What's to stop them from sneaking off in the middle of their duties?" Jenny asked. "I need to know what to watch for."

"During the trial period," Andy said, "it's a one strike and you're out policy. If they want to stick around, they're going to have to complete their assignments."

"I think that should keep both our covers intact for now," Jenny said. "You gave in to her manipulations, and I had to stay back. I won't be considered a threat, and meanwhile, hopefully Lauren and Heather are able to pinpoint the location of the offline database."

"And if they're stuck in laundry," Andy said, "it'll be hard for them to spread stories or gain the ear of anyone with influence."

"Hard but not impossible," Jenny said. "I'll have to re-examine the situation once I'm inside. This is only a temporary patch on a rather large leak. It will become clear pretty quickly whether these two are self-destructive or saboteurs."

"They could get you and Lauren in a lot of trouble," Andy said. "This is risky for all of us. I don't know what they'd do if they found out who we really are, but I wouldn't take execution off the table, Jen. We can call it all off, you know. I could leave with you, and the general could find another way to breach Cheyenne Mountain."

Jenny shook her head. "No. You've worked too hard to just throw away weeks' worth of undercover work. And I'm not sure there *is* another way in. And even if we could find another way in, we couldn't do it soon enough. Alex and his people need the information in that database."

"Okay, so... we take the risk?" Andy asked.

Jenny nodded firmly. "We take the risk."

Chapter 21

Zara Williams

Four diseased, deranged, and deformed beasts surrounded the golf cart, the clear plastic barrier the only thing protecting Zara and Kai. The screams of the rest of their team had ceased. Potts's body lay mangled and bloodied down the road; the beast who'd mauled him to death seemed to have lost interest when the man had died.

At first, the beasts had approached the cart to sniff at the plastic, yellowed teeth dripping red as they snarled at the barrier between them and their prey. Zara was crammed between Kai and the front bench as she sat on his lap to get as far from either side of the cart as possible.

Her body wouldn't stop trembling. "What are they doing?" she whispered.

"I don't know," Kai said. "But they aren't killing for food. That much is clear."

"Potts said some of the predators in the area were acting weird," Zara said, "but he didn't say anything about them being diseased."

"We have to get out of here," Kai said.

Zara jumped as one of the wolves nearer to the cart gnashed its teeth at her and growled. "The cart doesn't have any battery left."

"It might have some. We've been sitting in the sun with the power off for at least half an hour." He patted her, urging her to move. "I'm going to get into the front seat and try to drive us back the way we came."

"Even if we do get this thing started and drive a little way, those are *wolves*. Don't they, like, track prey for miles?" Zara asked.

"We can't just sit here and do nothing," Kai said.

"Maybe one of the others is still alive." Zara glanced at Potts's body and quickly looked away. He was the only one of the three soldiers she'd actually liked.

"I don't think so. They would have come back for us, or at least come back for the safety of the golf cart." Kai patted her again. "Move, Zara. I'm going to try to get us out of here."

She was stiff as she slid to the side, closer to the plastic barrier than she would have preferred. The wolves took notice of their movement, and one of them came close, teeth snapping, sliding against the plastic. The barrier wasn't solid; it pressed toward her as the wolf put weight against it.

"Hurry," Zara said, her survival instincts making her squirm at the close proximity to the beast.

Kai climbed over the front bench seat into the driver's side, and she centered herself again, though the wolf didn't stop biting at the plastic. It's attempts to break the barrier left smears of blood all over it.

"It won't turn on," Kai said, pressing the button over and over again.

Then the wolf snarling at Zara pulled back and turned to look at the tree line. The other three wolves did, too, their ears perked as Warren stumbled out of the tree line, his right arm limp, his jaw broken and hanging oddly beneath a gaping hole in his cheek.

"Warren!" Zara shouted. "He's alive!"

Warren fell to his knees in the dirt, his eyes glazed, his shirt soaked in blood. Sounds came from his mouth, but they were impossible to discern. All four beasts now had their eyes on him.

"We have to help," Kai said. "Stay inside."

"What?" Zara turned from looking at Warren in time to see Kai already slipping through the driver's side door. "No!" She leaned over the front seat, her fingertips brushing his back as she tried to grab him from behind.

He was outside, zipping the door up behind him, gun drawn, before Zara could do anything about it. She gave him a pleading look, afraid to shout again for fear of drawing attention to him. Behind her, a gunshot made her duck and yelp. She turned to see Warren, still on his knees, a gun in his left hand, struggling to raise it again. None of the wolves seemed to have new wounds.

Zara's instinct was to first look for something to hide behind. If Warren was going to shoot in his current state, it wasn't out of the question for a bullet to find its way lodged in *her* skull by accident. But there was nothing to shield her. The cart was perpendicular to Warren, the open sides exposed except for the plastic barrier which would be no help against a bullet.

Warren's trembling arm swung upward as one of the wolves lunged, and he fired in rapid succession. The first bullet hit the cart, ripping through one layer of plastic and *thumping* into the driver's seat where Kai had been. Zara screamed and made herself small on the back bench of the cart, drawing knees to chest and covering her head, peeking out to see Kai striding forward as he opened fire on the nearest wolf. The first shot hit the beast in the leg, and it growled and jumped for Kai. His next bullet penetrated the wolf's skull, and it went limp mid-air, falling to the ground and skidding on the dirt.

When she looked back at Warren, one of the wolves lay dead inches from him. Another beast approached, though, and Warren looked as if the act of raising his arm, of merely staying upright, was one of the hardest things he'd ever had to do. Sweat beaded his forehead, and his expression, even with his broken jaw, reflected pain. An agonized, low cry emanated from him as he focused on the prowling wolf and raised his gun again.

Zara hugged her knees tightly as the soldier pulled the trigger, but then her mouth hung open in horror as nothing happened. Determination in Warren's eyes turned to panic. The gun was either jammed or out of ammunition; Zara couldn't tell from where she was. The deranged animal leapt for Warren.

"No!" Kai shouted as he finished with the third animal in time to also witness the fourth rip into Warren.

Zara's vision blurred with tears, her cheeks hot and wet, her body shaking. Kai emptied his gun into the fourth wolf, and it gave him one last snarl before collapsing on Warren's lower body. Kai dropped his gun and rushed forward, his arms outstretched as if he planned on pushing the animal off of Warren.

"Stop!" Zara shouted between sobs. "Don't touch it!" Her voice shook, and unfurling her stiff body was akin to unfurling thick, metal wires. Her own limbs resisted her movements, but she forced herself to reach for the zipper, her stomach lurching at the smeared blood as she peeled away the plastic door.

Kai had listened to her, pulling back his hands and kneeling by Warren's upper body. "He's gone," Kai said.

Zara stood from the cart for only a second before leaning back against it, avoiding the bloody spots. The four dead creatures—matted and bloody fur, bulging eyes, a crazed quality to them even after death—were something out of nightmares. She'd thought she'd seen the worst the end of the world had to offer, but it seemed the apocalypse wasn't done revealing new and terrorizing realities.

"They didn't whimper," Zara said, the afterthought somehow making it all worse. She glanced again at Potts's body, then at Warren's, then at the mangled wolves' corpses. Her stomach heaved, and she turned aside and wretched into the dirt.

When she had recovered, she glanced back at Kai, gathering herself, planning to go to him, provide some comfort. But most of all, she wanted to get out of there. She pushed away the terrible thought that they had no idea how to get back to the city. *One thing at a time,* she told herself.

Kai still knelt by Warren. He hung his head, just staring. Zara managed to get to her feet, to steady herself. She took a step forward, but then she froze. A fifth beast prowled out of the tree line, eyes on Kai.

Zara's heart lodged in her throat, stifling the warning she so desperately wanted to scream. She fumbled for her own gun, but her hands were still trembling. "Kai!" She managed to cry out his name, and as the wolf pounced, as she finally freed her gun from its holster, a shot rang out.

Kai scrambled away from the wolf, but he had dropped his gun, and Zara hadn't even had the chance to aim her weapon. She stared at the dead creature, as did Kai, and then they looked at each other.

"What…?" Kai's unfinished question was answered by a gruff voice.

"You two don't belong here."

Zara jumped and turned to see a man coming from the direction of Potts's corpse. He was dressed head-to-toe in camo, complete with a camo ball cap and black shoes. An automatic rifle was in his hands, the barrel lowered, but his body language that of a man willing to re-engage at any moment.

Kai scrambled to his feet. "Yeomen! We have to find Yeomen."

"There's a third man that way," the stranger said, pointing into the woods. "Dead. Military, though." He narrowed his eyes at them. "You two are just kids."

"C-Colonel Blythe?" Zara stammered, and then she took half a step back as he raised his rifle. Apparently, she'd said the wrong thing. The man scowled. "Who are you, and how the hell do you know my name?"

Zara raised her hands, and Kai stepped between her and Blythe. "We're not a threat to you," Kai said. "C'mon, man. We just want to get somewhere safe."

"Tell me what you're doing here," Blythe said.

"These golf carts lost battery power," Zara said. "They need to charge, probably for several hours before they're ready to go. Please, if you help us, we can tell you everything we know."

"You'll tell me something right now, or you two are on your own." Blythe didn't lower his weapon, and his expression was hard as stone. He didn't seem to be bluffing.

"We don't know how to get back," Kai said. "Please—"

"I don't care," Blythe shouted. "You've got one minute to tell me why I shouldn't leave you here. Who are these men you came here with? Who are you, and how do you know my name?"

"We were looking for you," Zara said quickly. "We need your help back in the city, but it's a long story with a lot of details. It won't make a lot of sense if we try to summarize it."

Blythe frowned. "Give it a try."

"There are people who can make things right," Kai said. "People who know how to get rid of these swarms. People who are working on a cure or a vaccine for this disease. But the last piece of the puzzle is far away, and we need a pilot."

"The government needs a pilot, you mean?" Blythe scoffed. "They took the most important part of my life from me. I sacrificed having a family. I wasn't even *there* when my wife died. I was thirty minutes late. Flew halfway around the world to miss her last moment by thirty damn minutes. And now what? They want me to risk my life again? How do you even know this 'last piece' is actually the last piece? They have a talent for always having one more thing they have to ask of you, you know."

"It's not the military that's putting this puzzle together," Zara said. "It's a couple of talented scientists and a bunch of nobodies like us who are trying to get the right people to the right place."

"We're using the government," Kai said. "Not the other way around."

Blythe barked a laugh and lowered his gun, shaking his head. "Sure, kid. Sure." He ran his hand over his face and sighed. "So, what? I'm supposed to believe they sent you as my escort?"

"No," Kai said. "I'm a pilot… sort of. But I need training, and I can't fly the plane we need to use by myself. I can assist you, if you agree and come back with us. They sent me with the team, and Zara volunteered to come with me because she knew I needed her support. Flying again sort of scares the crap out of me." He took a deep breath. "We planned to warn you when we found you that the soldiers who came with us were planning to kidnap you if you refused to come, but you don't have to worry about anything like that anymore."

Blythe took a few moments of silence before responding. "Why tell me that now?"

"Because," Kai said, "those orders can be given again to different soldiers. And I need you to trust me. We'll tell you the truth, everything we know, but we need to get to a shelter sooner rather than later."

"Give us the chance to make our case," Zara said. "You could literally help us save the world."

"Don't get your hopes up," Blythe said, sighing. "I'm not going to leave a couple of young idiots on their own out here. C'mon." He waved for them to follow. "It's a bit of a trek through the woods to my cabin. I don't want to get caught by a swarm... or by more diseased animals."

Zara blanched. "There are *more*?"

Blythe shrugged. "Most animals a swarm attacks just die. Sometimes, though, an animal survives. My guess is one of these wolves was swarmed, survived, and brought the disease back to its pack. Maybe the one who survived died a long time ago, and these were the ones who contracted it after the fact." He visibly shuddered. "But what this disease does to those it doesn't kill... I've seen a man go feral, just like these wolves did. It makes them crazy."

"You've seen *people* like that," Zara asked, horrified as she looked at the nearest wolf.

"I had to put a neighbor down a few weeks back, a man with a homestead," Blythe said. "Whole family died, but he survived a swarm. At first, I thought it was a miracle, but... he went nuts after a few days. If I hadn't killed him, he would have killed me." He scowled again. "What makes you think anybody can fix this mess?"

"Not fix it, really," Zara said. "But stop it from getting worse."

"And give it a chance to get better over time," Kai said.

"Sounds like a long shot. I'm not interested," Blythe said. "In the morning, you two can go back to the city. I'll give you directions. In the meantime, you can both keep your mouths shut. I've given enough. Your people can find someone else to help you. I can't be the only guy left in the world who can fly a damn plane." He turned his back, motioning for them to follow.

"We have a miracle," Zara said quickly. "A woman who survived and didn't go crazy. Her name is Candice Liddle. It's not as long of a shot as you think."

Blythe stopped and looked back at her, raising his eyebrows at her. "Are you serious?"

Zara nodded, and he seemed to contemplate that for a moment.

"Maybe I'll give your story a listen," he said. "I've been bored out of my mind for weeks." With that, he turned and started walking.

Kai and Zara exchanged a look. It was a first step, but it was nowhere near success. Still, they weren't out of the game, yet.

She looked once more at the dead. "What about them?" she asked, loud enough for Blythe to hear even as he walked away.

He didn't even look back. "Leave 'em," he said. "We don't have time to bury them. Staying out here with no real shelter within a quarter mile would be a bad move."

"He's right," Kai said. "I don't like it, either, but he's right." He walked over to her and wrapped his arm around her shoulder. "Let's go."

It didn't feel right, but Zara wiped away a few stray tears and let Kai lead her away from the bloodied dirt road littered with the corpses of men and beasts.

Chapter 22

Alexander Roman

Alex sat on the steps of Cadet Chapel. Its structure was just as interesting as Polaris Hall, which was sort of catty-corner to it. Both buildings had a good amount of natural light in their design. As Alex thought about it, he looked out over the other buildings, nodding with approval. There were a lot of glass walls throughout the campus. That was an advantage in a time when electricity was a quickly fading commodity. The chapel itself was like an accordion made out of giant, steel triangles. It was tall and about eight times longer than it was wide.

Walter sat next to him, quiet as he'd been all day. The two of them were waiting on Dr. Pullman to arrive and escort them to the laboratory already set up on the premises. Apparently, he'd put together a team and come up with some exciting developments which Alex and Walter had to "wait and see" so as to avoid "spoiling the surprise." It wasn't a cure, or anything close to it. Alex had gotten that much out of the man, but when showing him around the day before, Pullman hadn't wanted to reveal their big project until his teammates were there to share in the glory.

In the meantime, that meant Alex got to watch Oliver as General Hunt made him his assistant for an hour. Hunt and Minnie stood a few feet beyond the bottom of the staircase with Oliver, and a dozen twenty-somethings in uniform stood at attention in two blocks of six. Minnie squeezed Oliver's shoulders and turned toward Alex and Walter, coming to join them on the steps.

"Alan set up a little fun for Oliver," Minnie said as she sat. "Those are volunteers. Those angels are gonna follow Oliver's orders, sorta like a game of Simon Says."

General Hunt's voice boomed and echoed as he spoke. "All right, ladies and gentlemen! Your drill sergeant today is the great Honorary General Oliver Roman." He looked down at Oliver, and Alex saw him wink.

Oliver straightened up and puffed out his chest. He spoke with overly distinct pronunciation, drawing out his vowels. "Aaah-ten-shun!" he shouted.

"Sir, yes, sir!" The dozen soldiers replied in unison.

Oliver turned around, his mouth open, his eyes wide. "Dad, they're *listening* to *me*," he said.

Alex chuckled. "You'd better give them orders before they get bored."

"Oh, right!" Oliver grinned and hopped around to face the soldiers again. "Time for exercises!" He paused and tapped his cheek with one finger. "Stand on your right leg!"

They all did so, a few of them able to keep a straight face while others showed hints of amusement around their eyes and mouth.

"Um… hop five times!" Oliver shouted in a voice that mimicked the general's.

When they had done as he asked, the soldiers continued standing with their left legs bent. Oliver seemed to be thinking about his next order, taking a few more seconds than the last time. One or two soldiers wobbled. General Hunt leaned over and whispered something.

"Oh, right! You can put your legs down," Oliver said. "Now… let's do twenty push-ups!" He got down to the ground with the soldiers and began to do his own push-ups, counting loudly as he completed each one.

"Mr. Roman? Mr. Peters?" A voice came from the bottom of the staircase to Alex's far right. It was Dr. Pullman. A four-person golf cart waited a few yards off.

"Oh, sorry," Alex said, popping up from the stairs. "I was distracted." He pointed at his son. "Oliver hasn't had this much fun in forever."

Dr. Pullman glanced at Oliver and General Hunt. "Yes… well, that's somewhat unconventional, but… why not?" he said, offering a small smile.

Alex craned his neck, squinting at the cart. "Will Colonel Holland be joining us?"

The doctor shook his head. "No, no," he said. "She's more of a director, less of a hands-on contributor. She works out how to get resources, what to do with our advancements, things like that."

Walter stood. "I guess it's time to see what they've cooked up," he said as he descended the remaining six steps to the ground.

Alex glanced at Minnie. "Get him back to the house when they're done?"

Minnie nodded. "One hour, as promised."

"Thanks," he said. "Oliver deserved some fun. Be sure to thank the general and those soldiers for me, okay?"

"Will do. You go do what you can to bring us closer to the end of this mess," Minnie said.

As Alex walked down the steps, Oliver glanced back at him and waved goodbye enthusiastically, the smile on his face so wide that Alex could see all his teeth. Alex waved back, reluctant to miss out on all that joy. But he had a job to do, so he followed Pullman and Walter to the golf cart and climbed into the back with Walter. Pullman sat in front, along with Cadet Sumner, who was in the driver's seat.

"The lab is set up in what used to be the Air Force Academy Medical Clinic," Pullman said as the cadet pulled the cart around and headed west. "It's a bit out of the way of the other buildings which are currently occupied, and it's got sterile rooms which could be converted into laboratories."

Alex frowned. "That can't be safe," he said. "We need a BSL-3 laboratory at a bare minimum." He shared a concerned look with Walter, who had stopped staring off at nothing as Pullman had described where they were headed.

"Beggars can't be choosers these days," Pullman said. "The nearest BSL-3 lab is over two hours north of here at the state university. I'm told there's one in Cheyenne Mountain, but we don't have access to that, now, do we?"

"We can't work with DV-10 without the proper precautions," Walter said.
Pullman bristled and looked back at them. "I'm not an idiot," he said. "We can work with information and models via interactive computer simulations. It's not ideal, I'll give you that. We're limited to examining methodology and hypothesizing instead of direct analysis, but it's better than nothing. And there are safer organisms we are studying which we believe could be of help going forward in our fight against this disease. Not to mention the fact that should we *need* to work with DV-10, we would follow complete isolation protocols for researchers and move ahead. There are some risks we must take."
Alex shifted uncomfortably. "Are there live samples of DV-10 at the lab now?"
"No," Pullman said briskly. "You would have been warned ahead of time if there were."
"Okay," Walter said, his tone one of a peacemaker. "We understand. We didn't mean to insinuate you didn't know what you are doing. We apologize."
Alex sighed. "Walter is right," he said. "I'm sorry. I'm sure you've heard of my encounter with Lawson's people in Atlanta. They were deceptive bastards, and they weren't in it for the right reasons."
Pullman glanced back at him again, but this time he looked... *nervous*. "I've heard," he said. "I hope that you'll come to understand that I run a tighter and more moral ship than Lawson ever did."
"I believe you," Alex said, though the look on Pullman's face still bothered him.
"But I also need you to understand," Pullman said, "that we have to work with what we have for the time being. Colonel Holland and I assess the risks for everything our research team does, and it's not *all* risk-free. That's just the nature of researching in these harrowing times."
"What could you be doing that's so risky if you're not experimenting with live DV-10?" Alex asked.
"You will see when we arrive," Pullman said. "But keep an open mind, both of you." He turned back around, and as Cadet Sumner navigated the base, it seemed clear Dr. Pullman was done with the discussion for the time being.
Eventually, they pulled up to another building with a glass façade—those seemed to be the preferred aesthetic at the academy—and Pullman unzipped his plastic doorway.
"You two stay here for a moment," he said. "I'm going to prep my team for your arrival. They requested to be... notified. They are a little anxious to see you, Mr. Roman."
Alex frowned. That's odd, he thought. Why would they be anxious to see me? What kind of reputation do I have?
Cadet Sumner turned around once Pullman was out of sight. "Hey," he said. "I need to... uh... relieve myself. I've been carting Pullman around all day, and I haven't gone in seven hours."
"By all means," Alex said.
"Thanks," Sumner said. "I'll be right back." He left Alex and Walter alone, jogging to a decorative tree several yards off.
Alex turned to Walter, speaking quietly. "What do you think they're doing in their DIY lab?"

Walter leaned closer. "I don't know. Perhaps something to do with killing off the mosquitos?"
"Aren't they engineered to withstand the usual pyrethroids?" Alex asked.
Walter nodded. "The cuticle that would normally absorb pyrethroids was engineered with extra protections to prevent the insecticide from penetrating to the nervous system."
"So that the biological weapon released upon an enemy couldn't be wiped out with a simple store-bought spray," Alex said.
"Exactly," Walter said. "But that doesn't mean harsher chemicals wouldn't do it. It's just that those are normally just as harmful to people."
"I have a bad feeling," Alex said. "I just—"
He froze as the doors to the clinic opened and Pullman stepped out with two people trailing behind. One of them was a blonde, her hair in a tight, short braid. She was young, put together, confident. There was defiance in her step and distaste in her eyes as she narrowed them toward Alex and Walter. The other was the opposite of her, an older man, short and stout. His mess of curly hair had gone almost completely gray since Alex had last seen him.
"No." Alex growled, an immediate revulsion upending every ounce of decorum he had left.
"What is it?" Walter asked. "Do you know them?"
He reached for the zipper and yanked at it. "Yeah, I know them."
"Okay..." Walter put a hand on Alex's arm. "Hold on a minute," he said. "Don't do anything rash."
Alex scoffed and shook off Walter's hand. He pushed aside the plastic and stepped outside, striding forward. His entire body was alive with rage, a sort of hot, seething buzz intoxicating him from head to toe.
"I don't think so," he shouted, pointing at the two newcomers.
Dr. Pullman raised his hands, palms outward, in a calming motion. "Now, Mr. Roman, please calm d—"
"No way in hell I'm working with them." Alex stopped inches short of the three. His hands had become fists at his sides, and it was taking every ounce of self-control not to throw a punch.
The woman puckered her lower lip. "Alex, what's the matter?" she asked. "Chimp's got your tongue?"
Flashes of memory fueled his anger: a lab that was more like a prison, an innocent, intelligent animal, living and breathing, subjected to the virus. He'd watched that chimp writhe in pain and then realized later that the same experiments weren't just happening on chimpanzees; they were happening on human beings. Alex roared and reared back his arm, fist at the ready, all thought of propriety fleeing at her nasty reminder of why he hated her so damn much.
But then Walter was at his side, holding him back. "Alex!" he shouted, taking Alex's face between his hands and forcing him to look at him. "What is wrong with you? You're not the type to punch a woman."
Alex pushed Walter away and turned his back to all four of them, trying to catch his breath, trying to calm down. He clenched his fists so hard at his sides that his arms trembled.

"C'mon, Joanna," the man said quietly, "was that necessary?"

"It was just a joke," she said, her tone amused.

Alex turned back around. "*She* isn't a woman," he said between gritted teeth. "She's a monster. And so is he."

Pullman stepped forward. "Mr. Roman, if I may—"

"You may *not*," Alex said. "I want to speak with President Coleman. Right. Now."

Walter's furrowed brow and incredulous expression only intensified. "Alex, who the hell are these people?"

Alex narrowed his eyes at the two scientists he'd hoped to never see again. The two scientists he'd assumed dead or chained. If Lawson had been the head of the operation in Atlanta and Price the heart of it, those two had been the hands. Hands covered in blood. Hands that had tried to dip *his* hands in blood. He could barely get their names out of his mouth without spitting. "That's Joanna Ward and Blake Turner." He threw a glare at Pullman. "And if I don't get a word with the president right now, we're going to have a serious problem."

Chapter 23

Lauren Stevens

Lauren shot to her feet and backed up against the wall as a flurry of white suits and blue gloves appeared on the other side of the windows of their quarantine prison. "Heather!" She poked her companion with her foot, but she didn't take her eyes off the three people staring straight at her through face shields and glass. They gestured to each other, clearly conversing, though she couldn't tell what they were saying.
Heather groaned. "I think I might puke."

"That's the baby talking, right?" Lauren chanced a glance at Heather, who looked white as a sheet.
"Yeah, I think so," she said.
"Well, push it down," Lauren said, grimacing at her own harsh tone. "Stand up and try not to look like… like *that.* I think they're here to make sure we're not sick."
Heather grabbed the bottle of berry-flavored antacid chewable tablets she'd been gifted the night before, shook out one, and popped it into her mouth. "They know I'm pregnant," she said. "Everyone knows pregnant people get nauseous."
Lauren glanced nervously at Heather and then back at the three. *I hope she's right,* she thought. *I don't want to stress her out, but…*
She tried to keep her tone even. "I just don't want to give them a chance to keep us in here any longer," she said, smiling and waving at the strangers who examined them from a safe distance. None of them acknowledged her.
Twenty-four hours prior, they'd been shuffled into what used to be a sandwich shop outside the North Portal entrance to the Cheyenne Mountain Complex. They'd spent the night and a good portion of the day locked away with a few supplies to keep them alive and well, if not comfortable. The lobby had become a sort of observation box; someone had come to check on them every so often, peering inside, confirming they weren't dead, and leaving without much interaction.
It was apparently a last precaution before letting anyone new come inside the complex, even if they'd been cleared at the arena. They were acting out of an abundance of caution, and it was hard to argue. Their people had only had eyes on Lauren and Heather for less than forty-eight hours. If something had been missed down at the arena, if they'd somehow been exposed to the disease on the ride between the arena and the complex, well… Lauren wasn't going to begrudge them a day to ensure their population was kept safe. DV-10 was new and tricky, and besides that, it wasn't the only deadly disease out there.
Lauren reached out a hand toward Heather, keeping one eye on the door where a man in a hazmat suit was sliding a key into the lock. "C'mon," she said. "At least get up off the floor. That sleeping bag isn't comfortable anyway."
Heather accepted her hand, and Lauren helped her to her feet as the woman held the bottle of tablets to her chest like they were a treasure someone might snatch away. Heather chewed and swallowed and held up the bottle, frowning at the tiny words on the back. "It says I can't take more than five in twenty-four hours." Heather closed her eyes and leaned against the wall beside Lauren. "Oh, but that one is helping. I miss stuff like this." She once again hugged the bottle close.
The door opened, and the man, his suit a puff of white around him, entered. Lauren stiffened but didn't say anything as he approached and pulled an infrared thermometer out of a fanny pack. He held it up to Heather's forehead and then Lauren's.
"Excellent," he said. "I do apologize, but I must ask you both to let me do a quick examination, from head to toe." His cheeks reddened behind his plastic face shield. "I need to confirm there are no welts or rashes."
"As in… you want us to *undress*?" Lauren asked.
"Well… yes." He shifted and waved for his companions to come inside. Another man and a woman came near with a sheet and held it up between them to block out the window. "My name is Stellar, by the way," he said, flashing them a nervous smile. "Stellar service makes for stellar smiles." He cleared his throat. "I'm a dentist."
One of his colleagues rolled her eyes as she held the sheet up high. "We're both nurses," she said, nodding to the other man. "It's okay, ladies. We just need to make sure you're good to go, and then we're going to get you inside where you belong."
The examination was fast, as promised, and there was no leering or disrespect on the part of the three strangers. Lauren kept an eye on them all while Heather was looked over, and Heather did the same for her. Stellar didn't touch them, only leaned in occasionally to squint at a spot. It helped Lauren's comfort level that each stranger was in a puffy suit that made their movements cumbersome, but all the same, Lauren was glad when they were done and dressed.
"Okay, then," Stellar said, sighing with relief, "you're cleared."
Two short, high-pitched honks came from outside as the two nurses were folding up the sheet. One of them nodded toward the window. A small, blue electric car had pulled up outside.
"Looks like it's time for you two to go," he said. "Leave everything here. We'll take care of it."
Lauren hooked her arm in Heather's, and they walked outside together, leaving the three strangers as they began spraying down surfaces. "These people are thorough," Lauren whispered. "Lots of redundancies, doing things just in case. It's not good for us."
Heather frowned. "Why not? I mean, at least we know we won't be exposed to anything."

"All of these extra precautions could mean they keep such a close eye on everything and *everyone* that we won't be able to slip away," Lauren said. "That offline database isn't going to be easily accessible."

"Jenny said to keep our ears open and wait for her," Heather said. "That's all we have to do for now, right?"

"It would be nice if we could do more," Lauren said. "Just because we find the database doesn't mean we have to do anything about it, but the quicker Conner can break into it and get that information, the sooner we can leave. Right?"

Heather bit her lower lip and her frown deepened. Lauren's breath caught as she waited for confirmation from her friend only to receive none. Heather broke away from Lauren, still holding the bottle of antacids in one hand as she reached with her other hand for the doorhandle of the little car.

"Heather," Lauren said, coming around her and putting her hand on the door to keep it closed for a second longer. "Right?"

"I don't know," Heather said, yanking the door open and sliding into the car before Lauren could say anything else.

Lauren ducked her head inside, staring at Heather who had slid to the seat behind the driver. *What did she mean by that?* Of course, Lauren couldn't ask her that, not with the driver sitting right there.

"Name's Carrie," the driver said, turning around in her seat and offering a smile. "Why don't you come on in and shut that door." It wasn't a question.

"Sure," she said. "Sorry." Lauren squeezed into the seat beside Heather and shut the door behind her. There wasn't a ton of room, and her knees touched the back of the seat in front of her. She tried to catch Heather's eye, but the other woman was avoiding eye contact. Heather picked at the hem of her shirt, her body tense.

"It's a tight fit," Carrie said, "but this little car is great for getting us where we need to go. Electric, you know. Powered by the mountain's generators."

The car lurched forward, and Lauren ignored the urge to find out exactly what Heather had meant by her previous comment. They turned around and approached a tunnel entrance which read "Cheyenne Mountain Complex" in white lettering on a rust-red arch.

A few yards inside, Carrie slowed to a stop in front of a wall of silver mesh. "Stainless steel insect screens," she said. "We put this up at both the north and south portals," she said. "There are a few of them between here and the complex."

"Has it held up against a swarm yet?" Lauren asked.

"Sure has," Carrie nodded. "And the one time a swarm tried cozying up too close, we blasted fire through the mesh. Killed a good portion of the swarm, and the rest never came back."

Heather cleared her throat and looked up from her lap. "Impressive," she said as a man on the other side of the mesh cranked a contraption that lifted the barrier slowly. "How did you guys know how to do that?"

"Are you kidding?" Carrie grinned at them in the rearview mirror as she moved the car under the mesh and into the dark tunnel beyond. "We've got all kinds of tradesmen. Welders, construction workers, electricians, carpenters—you name it, we've got it."

The car's headlights illuminated a simple two-lane road surrounded by roughly hewn rock. Their pathway curved to the left as they continued driving.

Lauren leaned forward and attempted a curiously impressed tone. "I heard down at the arena that it was a construction crew who took over the mountain from the government. Is that true?"

"Yeah," Carrie said. "But it wasn't just one crew. I was an electrician. Still am, I guess. They had us sign NDAs, paid us a decent wage, and had us build onto what was already here. Apartments, pretty nice, if you ask me. It was a decade-long project. Some of the finishing touches weren't completed, actually, though those things are mostly cosmetic."

"So, you know the place pretty well?" Lauren asked, a little jolt of excitement running through her body.

"You could say that." Carrie shrugged. "It's not like they let us go exploring, though. Even now, we don't use the whole facility."

Lauren did her best not to let her disappointment show.

"It must have been crazy, working on a secret project like that," Heather said.

Carrie nodded. She was driving slowly, perhaps twenty miles per hour. The tunnel stretched out in front of them, dark save for a distant light that grew larger the closer they came. "That building we added," she said, "it was being sold off, apartment by apartment, to people with big money. It was survival insurance, in case something like this happened, I guess. At the time, I thought it was stupid, like I was happy to take the check, but I thought they were throwing away money. Now, I guess I'm glad those greedy bastards had cash to burn."

"Did any of them ever show up?" Heather asked.

"The ones who paid for the apartments?" Carrie asked. "No, not one of 'em. My guess is they're all dead. If one of them did come around, we'd point them to the military and say good riddance. We don't need their kind, solving all their problems with money. What good is that now?"

"So..." Lauren chose her words carefully. "That addition to the complex, that was the catalyst that sparked the conflict between the military and the regular people of Colorado Springs?"

"You could say that," Carrie said, "but honestly, the real problem started when that so-called president came to town. See, people like me teamed up with some disenfranchised soldiers, people who left this place after being told to abandon their own families. We were going to attack a couple weeks after the disease hit Colorado Springs, but there was no need. This plague did the job for us. All that was left was to clean the place out and set up camp. By the time the leftover force up at the academy realized what we'd done, it was too late for them. This place came with plenty of defenses, and we brought plenty of our own."

"And when this new president came," Heather asked, "what did he do?"

"Oh, he asked if we'd leave, all polite-like at first," Carrie said. "They did bring a small army, but we'd held this mountain for weeks by the time they'd arrived. More and more soldiers had joined our ranks. We were set, and we weren't about to just hand over our safety to a bunch of people looking down their noses at us."

"They didn't try to take it by force?" Heather asked.

"We made it clear we would give them a run for their money," Carrie said. "And to be honest, we're in here protecting women and children. Blue-collar workers who deserve to have the upper hand for once. I think they know that."

"That's optimistic." The sarcastic words were out of her mouth before Lauren could stop them. She swallowed hard. "Sorry," she said. "I'm a bit of a cynic."

Carrie laughed. "Yeah, well, I don't blame you. Look, at this point, we actually outnumber them, and we have a more defensible position. They're going to have to stay right where they are. We're a tough bunch. You'll see. We're not going down without a fight."

Lauren could understand that. She even admired it. Well, as long as we can get our information, these people can have this place. At least for now, she thought. What the military does here after we're gone is none of my business. She rolled her shoulders back and breathed out slowly. A little voice in the back of her mind objected. Part of her did care. Part of her wanted these people to have their safe haven. But another part of her understood: this was a government facility with sensitive information stored within. The second the government could, they would take the place back. She had no doubt about that.

She set aside that line of thought and contemplated their conversation. She needed to find a way to segue into learning more about where the database might be, but the more she thought about it, the more she realized the topic was going to be hard to bring up, especially if the current residents weren't using the entire facility.

Carrie continued with small talk about the inner workings of the complex as they slowly drove in fits and starts through the tunnel, encountering two more mesh barriers before Carrie announced they were almost there. Lauren guessed it had only been a mile and a half, maybe two, from the entrance, but the stops in between made it hard for her to tell by time alone.

Ahead, white lights shone from the ceiling, and Carrie turned into a smaller side tunnel underneath them. There, a huge blast door slowly moved as the creaking of metal echoed up and down the tunnel. Once it was open, Carrie guided the car through the doorway and stopped. A second blast door was sealed, blocking their way.

"Two twenty-ton blast doors," Carrie said. "We'll have to wait for them to close the first one before they open the second."

"This place is *solid*," Lauren said. "The mesh barriers add a lot of security, not just from swarms, either."

That made her stomach turn over. What if we need to escape? Or we need to be rescued?

She looked at Heather, wondering if she was thinking along the same lines, but she didn't seem bothered at all. In fact, the more Carrie talked and the further they went into the mountain, the more *at peace* Heather seemed to be. Her shoulders had lost much of their tension, the lines around her mouth and forehead had smoothed, and her fingers had stopped picking at the hem of her shirt.

Carrie nodded. "And you saw the curve in the main tunnel, the one between the north and the south portals?" She looked back at them.

Lauren nodded. "Yeah, I did. I knew there was a blast door in here somewhere, but I guess I thought it was closer to the entrance."

Carrie nodded. "Yeah, me too, before I came here. You see, it's built so that if there's a big blast, only twenty percent of it will hit that first blast door. The rest of that energy will just flow right through the main tunnel and out again on the other side."

"The security is… really nice," Heather said.

"Sure is," Carrie said as the second blast door, thick and full of bolts and wires, slowly opened. "And it'll be the perfect place to raise a kid, away from all the turmoil out there." The car moved forward again, creeping through the second blast door once it was opened.

Lauren pressed her lips together, trying not to furrow her brow. *Is that why she's being weird? Does she… actually want to* stay *here?* But that thought was crazy. She had Timothy and Candice and Annika out there, all people she loved. There was no way these people would let Timothy in, not after what had happened when he'd approached the mountain and then the arena. And they'd kept her safe so far. They could keep her child safe, too.

Carrie parked the car in a tiny lot, and the three of them stepped out. A white building, about two-stories tall, greeted them, four government seals displayed proudly on its face. Lauren followed Carrie to the entrance beneath a blue awning that read: Welcome to Cheyenne Mountain Complex.

Inside shared a lot of the same qualities with other government buildings: a check-in desk behind sliding glass windows, old furnishings, bland walls, a few American flags. There were some outlines on the walls where Lauren assumed photographs had once been, perhaps portraits of high-ranking officials or the former President of the United States.

The check-in process was quick. Their paperwork from the arena was there, and they were asked to check over it for any mistakes. They were also given badges which had white squares taped over printed photos; they were attached to long, yellow lanyards.

"These belonged to staff before they all bit the dust," Carrie said. "They'll let you through the main doors, into the halls and whatnot, but you won't get higher clearance badges until you've been here a while and are sure you want to commit long term." Carrie pulled on her own lanyard, a green one, and used her badge to open the first door.

Lauren slipped her lanyard over her head. She and Heather followed Carrie into a hall. "So," Lauren said, "will we be staying in these apartments you had a hand in building?"

Carrie shook her head. "Those are reserved for permanent residents," she said. "You'll be staying in suites reserved for staff. They're not much, but they have a bathroom with a shower."

Lauren missed a step and stumbled a bit before regaining solid footing. "A shower that *works*?"

Carrie chuckled. "Yep. But you'll have to keep your shower time to a maximum of seven minutes, twice a week and three minutes, twice a week."

Heather looked at Lauren directly for the first time since they'd gotten into the car outside the sandwich shop. "I call first dibs."

"All right," Lauren said, holding up her hands in surrender. "That's fine with me."

They made small talk as they navigated the halls. The white walls and white floors reminded Lauren of a hospital hallway. There were a lack of windows, of course, but everything else about the building was so normal it was easy to forget they were inside a mountain. They passed a cafeteria called the Granite Inn where a hot dinner was served every other night, and Carrie pointed down a hall here and there to fill them in on some of the amenities available to them, which included a convenience store currently used to dole out rations and a workout room.

When they finally reached their destination, Carrie unlocked a heavy, black door and swung it open. "Here you are," she said, handing over the keycard. "Remember, your badge can get you into the halls. You can go down to the shoppette, the Granite Inn, or the gym any time. But right now, I suggest you two get a nice, warm shower. We've got a few sizes of slacks, tees, and underthings in the dresser drawer. I imagine you'll both find a good fit." She put a hand on Heather's arm, offering a smile. "I'll be coming back to get you in a couple of hours. The baby doc wants to see you before the day is out."

Heather's face went a shade paler. "That soon?" she asked.

"Don't be nervous," Lauren said. "It's a good thing."

"Are you okay?" Carrie asked. "I can take you now, if you want."

"No, I'm fine," Heather said quickly. "It's just… I haven't had the best luck with my pregnancies in the past. I'm a little scared of what the doctor will find."

A look of understanding fell across Carrie's face. "I see. Well, don't worry yourself yet. I've been through a few miscarriages. I know it's tempting to let bad thoughts take over. I'll say a little prayer for you and the baby."

"Thanks," Heather said, her smile small and unconvincing.

"Let's get settled," Lauren said, stepping inside the suite and holding the door open for Heather. "Remember, you called dibs on that shower."

"I'll see you two in a bit," Carrie said before saying her goodbyes and leaving them to their business.

Lauren shut the door and leaned against it, taking in the room. It was small with a bunk bed on one side, a single desk under a window, and one dresser for them to share. A picture of wind sweeping across tall grasses hung on the wall where a window might've been. It was a nice touch. It didn't make up for the fact that they were underground, but it was pleasing to look at, nonetheless. There was an open door that led into a hotel-like bathroom.

Taking a deep breath, Lauren pushed off the door and approached Heather, trying to keep her tone gentle. "Hey, before you clean up, I think we should talk about what you said before we got in that car."

"No," Heather said. "Not right now." She walked over to the dresser and started rummaging through the clothes.

"What?" Lauren blinked, a little shocked by Heather's abrupt answer. "Are you serious? I really think we should talk about whatever is going on inside your head. We have a mission, and—"

"I said I didn't want to talk about it right now." Heather picked out a few items and headed for the bathroom.

Lauren stood in her way. "I'm sorry, but there's a good chance I'm risking my life here. I need to know that we're on the same page."

"I can't." Heather shook her head and sidestepped Lauren. "I don't even know what I would say. I need to think, and I need some time."

"Heather—"

"No!" Heather walked into the bathroom and shut the door.

Lauren stared at the door for a few moments, trying to process what Heather had said and the fact that she wouldn't say anything else. Confused and discouraged, she walked over to the bunk bed and sat on the bottom mattress. When she'd agreed back at the church to the mission, she'd thought she'd be going in with a team. As creaking pipes and the sound of spraying water emanated from the bathroom, a chill went down Lauren's spine. She was surrounded by strangers, locked away in a secure facility below ground with no way out, and the one friend she thought she had was possibly flaking out on her. She was alone, and one thought dominated her mind: *This is* not *what I signed up for.*

Chapter 24

Alexander Roman

Alex paced the small conference room, keeping his distance from President Coleman. Rage had boiled over, lost a little steam, and settled into a roiling simmer since he'd first laid eyes on Ward and Turner.

Walter Peters waited for him outside the room. "I trust you on what we should do," Walter had said when they'd arrived at Polaris Hall. "This seems to be between you, those scientists, and the president. I don't know them like you do, but I do know you have a good head on your shoulders. I'll follow your lead."

Alex had been grateful for that. The more time he spent with Walter Peters, the more he liked the man. So, Alex had listened to the president's explanation, and he was turning it over in his mind, trying to come to some sort of understanding.

But no matter how he thought about it, one thought kept surfacing. He stopped pacing and turned to face the president. "That's not good enough," he said. Though he'd tried to keep his voice respectful, it was clear even to him that he'd failed.

President Coleman quirked one eyebrow, and the two soldiers on either side of him shifted forward at Alex's tone. "And what would you have done?" Coleman asked. "We needed them to conduct more research. I couldn't just sit around and hope that you were figuring it out. And clearly, I was right."

Alex bristled. "I have done more to find a treatment or cure for this disease than anyone else out there, even Walter."

"But do you have any answers?" President Coleman asked.

"Do they?" Alex shot the question back at the president as he slammed his palms against the conference table and leaned forward to meet the man's eyes.

"For a cure or a treatment? No." President Coleman shook his head just slightly, keeping his cool. "But they haven't just been focusing on that. Did you even give them the chance to talk?"

"Of course I didn't," Alex said. "They were experimenting on the most vulnerable survivors in Atlanta. The old and frail, the young and weak. Ward and Turner are sludge at the bottom of the barrel." He pushed off the table and ran his fingers through his hair, not believing he even had to remind Coleman of who he'd decided to work with. "They almost got Minnie killed. They threatened my *son*."

"Perhaps we should have warned you ahead of meeting them," President Coleman said. "You can blame me for that. There were a few options of how to proceed, and I thought maybe telling you up front would have prevented you from going at all. I was hoping you'd listen to the work they've been doing and decide to stay."

"Well, you're right about one thing," Alex said. "I would have *never* agreed to meet with them. I'm starting to question whether I should have so much faith in *you* at this point. You're working with criminals. Again. And you don't seem to understand the gravity of the kinds of moral compromises those two could lay at your feet. You're trusting their judgment, and that makes me question yours. You're either stupid, or you've pushed the line of what you're willing to do, how far into the morally deficient territory you're willing to go."

President Coleman's eyes hardened, and he stood slowly, without rush, but with the assuredness that comes with power. "When we first met," he said, "I was frightened. I allowed my father-in-law to guide me, to speak for me. I didn't know who I was." He mimicked Alex's earlier pose, his hands flat on the conference table, leaning forward, except he did it with a measured precision. "I know who I am, now, Mr. Roman. I'm the President of the United States, and I will *not* tolerate your disrespect. Bring to me your dissent, your questions, your ideas, but do *not* dare to disrespect me by attacking my character."

Alex worked his jaw back and forth, eyeing the soldiers on either side of the president. The rest of Polaris Hall was filled to the brim with men loyal to Coleman. He could have Alex and his people locked up at any time, and there would be nothing Alex could do about it.

"Is that a threat?" Alex asked.

"No," President Coleman said, sitting back down, a flash of exhaustion crossing his features. "If you can't be for me, for the United States, I don't have the energy to deal with you. Go back to the duplex, wait for your people to return with the location of the lab in Antarctica, and then leave. You and your people can be confined to living quarters." He folded his hands in front of him. "Or, you can see reason, work with Ward and Turner, and help us move forward while you wait for those coordinates."

The president looked sincere, and Alex relaxed a little. He believed Coleman when he said there was no threat in his words. *Maybe I did cross the line,* Alex thought. But he still didn't know what to do.

"How can I work with them?" Alex pulled out a chair and sat down. "They're *bad people*, Mr. President."

Coleman nodded. "I'm not going to argue with that. What I will say is that they, unlike you, have no actual freedom. Dr. Pullman and Colonel Holland oversee everything they do, and I believe we are in good hands when it comes to them. Ward and Turner aren't allowed to do *anything* without permission. They can't even go to the bathroom without a guard. You might not have noticed because you were so worked up, but they have chains at their ankles, the same as our other prisoners. And at the end of the day, they are stashed away in isolation, behind locked doors. If you work with them, you will have seniority. More than that, you would have *authority.* I would expect you to keep an eye on them, to keep them on the straight and narrow. If they put one toe out of line, by all means, cut the damn thing off."

Alex drummed his fingers on his thigh as he thought through the implications of that. "I do like the sound of keeping those two in my sights," he said. But there was another thing still bothering him. "What happens to them, if this all works out? Do they get immunity from their crimes?"

"We will have trials for all of our prisoners when we have the capacity to do so," Coleman said. "My guess is that won't be any time soon, but I can tell you that the evidence against them is damning and we've made no promises of immunity."

"It makes my skin crawl to even think about being in the same room with them," Alex said, shaking his head.

"I know the feeling." Coleman looked down at his hands. "I don't like it either, Mr. Roman. But the fact is that we don't have a pool of scientists to pick from these days. And we have to use everything and everyone we've got, regardless of how it makes us feel to work with them. Ward and Turner can advance our cause. They can help bring about an end to all of this."

Alex nodded. He couldn't deny that. Turner and Ward had been studying DV-10 in a lab longer than Alex had. Whatever they were, they were also skilled. "Okay," Alex said. "Fine. I can't believe I'm saying this, but... I'll work with them until it's time for me to leave."

"Thank you," President Coleman said. "Now, I believe Dr. Pullman is waiting back at the lab. There are some things he needs to show you, and I think you're going to be impressed. Maybe even excited to have a hand in working on them. We haven't been idle these past weeks, Mr. Roman."

Alex stood, his stomach in knots. *I hope I'm doing the right thing,* he thought. But the truth was, he wasn't sure, and that scared him more than anything.

* * *

"Right this way," Dr. Pullman said as he led Alex and Walter through the halls of the clinic.

"You're sure about this?" Walter asked.

Alex paused. Dr. Pullman came to a stuttering halt and looked back at him, and both men waited for him to reply. "No," Alex said, and before Dr. Pullman could object, he raised a hand, "but I think it's our best option. We can change our mind at any time. If I see too much I don't like, we can back out, go back to the duplex, and let these people ruin themselves by themselves."

"I assure you," Dr. Pullman said, "no one is *ruining* anything."

"I hope you're right," Alex said. He looked at Walter. "Before we go into working with Ward and Turner, I want to make one thing very clear: we can't trust them. Not even a little. Keep your eye on them at all times. Watch your back. Tell me if you see or hear anything that makes you uncomfortable."

Walter nodded once. "I can do that."

"For heaven's sake," Dr. Pullman said in an exasperated tone. "Stop being so dramatic. They are just people. They have shackles about their ankles. They are only given materials I pre-approve. What could they possibly do?"

Alex shook his head. "I don't know," he said. "That's the point. What I *do* know is that there isn't a line they won't cross. Especially Joanna. Blake Turner is greedy. Maybe he'll stay in line as long as he feels it's in his best interests. But Ward? That woman did terrible things, and she *liked* it. She did it because she wanted fame and power and because inflicting pain amused her."

"Oh, come now," Dr. Pullman said. "She's made some bad decisions, but—"

"No." Alex stepped closer to Dr. Pullman. "I saw her eyes gleam in anticipation as she watched a chimpanzee bleed out, screaming in pain. The thought of human experimentation excited her. If it meant she'd be remembered, if it meant she'd have power and glory, she'd cut out your heart with a smile on her face while insisting it was for the greater good. And I mean that literally."

Dr. Pullman swallowed hard, shrinking before him. "You've made your point," he said. "I know that she's a criminal. They both are. I suppose... well, all my time spent with them is about the science. Facts and hypotheses and numbers and observations."

"That's part of the problem," Alex said, glancing at Walter to make sure he was listening. "Bad people don't come out of the gate cackling and rubbing their hands together like some cartoon villain. They think they're justified. They think *they're* the good guys, but they're always partway in the shadows."

"And until something forces them into the light," Walter said, "they seem okay to everyone else. But they know." His voice cracked, and he looked away. "They know who they are." He rolled his shoulders back. "I know how to spot people like that, Alex. I used to *be* like that."

Alex shook his head. "Maybe you were greedy and self-interested, Walter, but when push came to shove, you did the right thing."

Walter shook his head. "It took me believing my daughter had been burned alive to really change. And I have changed, but... I wish it had been sooner. I'll live every day of the rest of my life trying to make up for it."

"See, that, right there," Alex said, pointing at Walter and looking at Dr. Pullman. "Regret. Penance. Have you ever heard either Ward or Turner say anything like that?"

Dr. Pullman shook his head. "Like I said, it's been all about the science. I... haven't really talked to them about anything else."

"Because they care more about the science than anything else, including people," Alex said. "There's no humanity in that."

"All right, all right," Dr. Pullman said. "We'll all three keep a close eye on them."

Alex nodded. Three of us. Two of them. Better odds, he thought.

Still, there was a tightness in his chest as he followed Dr. Pullman and entered a hall of open doors. They stopped outside an exam room that had been stripped of all medical equipment. It reminded him of one of the rooms back in Atlanta. There were papers strung up everywhere. Ward was inside, looking between a notebook in her hands and the papers stuck with magnets to the metal cabinet doors. She sat on a rolling stool, her legs crossed, a manacle on her exposed ankle, a chain linking it to her other foot. There was a soldier in the corner of the room, standing with hands clasped in front of him as he watched Joanna. Dr. Pullman cleared his throat, and Ward looked over at them.

"Is Alex done throwing his tantrum?" she asked.

Alex clenched his jaw, but it was Dr. Pullman who spoke. "Joanna, I'm going to have to ask you to behave. Alex has seniority here. The president has given him the right to boot you back to confinement, and I won't argue with him if he feels it's necessary."

Ward flashed a smile. "I'll be on my best behavior," she said.

"That'll make things a lot less interesting." Blake Turner stepped out of another room down the hall, followed by his own guard. The chain between his ankles rattled as he walked.

"That goes for you, too," Dr. Pullman said.

Turner feigned offense. "I'm always on my best behavior," he said, the corners of his mouth turning up into a grin.
Alex scoffed. "Like when you led me to a night of torture and threats under false pretenses?"
"Oh, that?" Turner waved off Alex's comment with just a momentary glimpse of discomfort. "I was following orders."
"That's all you have to say?" Alex crossed his arms.
"Look, man," Turner said. "You're the one giving the orders, now, right? You and Dr. Pullman, Mr. Peters, here, Colonel Holland and President Coleman… I'm a company man, okay? I do what I'm told. The people doing the telling this time around are people you like."
"I think," Walter said, "we should just get to work. None of this banter is going to get us anywhere but another fight."
"Wise words," Dr. Pullman said, clearing his throat. "Have you two set up the presentation we talked about?"
"I'm always prepared," Joanna said, standing up and joining them in the hall.
"Excellent." Dr. Pullman gestured for Joanna and Blake to go first. "Lead the way to the conference room," he said.
Ward and Turner—and their guards—started down the hall. Alex preferred to have them in his line of sight instead of behind his back.
The small conference room looked to have once been a break room. A table only large enough to seat six was centered there, and a whiteboard on an easel was set up at one end. Ward and Turner took seats on one side of the table, Alex and Walter on the other. Dr. Pullman stood to one side of the board. The guards once again settled into the corners of the room.
"We have been working on something I believe you'll find quite fascinating," Dr. Pullman said. He started writing a list on the board, speaking as he did so. "The normal chemicals used to kill off mosquitos don't work against these swarms," he said. "These are the ones we've tested in the field." He marked them out and turned back to face them.
Walter nodded. "I was explaining that to Alex yesterday. These mosquitos were engineered to be resistant to the absorption of those chemicals. Their nervous system is more protected than nature intended."
"Genius, really," Ward said, leaning forward with that gleam in her eye that made Alex's stomach churn. "I do wish I had been part of this project before it all went to hell." Alex glared at her, and she scowled, sitting back in her chair. "Can't I compliment the man?"
"Considering what the project led to," Walter said, "I'm not so sure anyone could interpret that as a compliment."
"You need to work on your people skills, Joanna," Turner said.
"Anyway," Dr. Pullman said, "we moved on to look at chemicals that might degrade the exoskeleton."
"Which is also engineered to be resistant to such efforts," Walter said.
"Yes," Dr. Pullman said as he wrote another list on the board. "We made progress when we started looking at a piranha solution to see if we could somehow stabilize it enough to use fog as a delivery system." He eyed Walter. "A piranha solution is—"
Walter sighed. "—a powerful mixture of sulfuric acid and hydrogen peroxide capable of decomposing organic matter quickly. I may have been a corporate suit, but I didn't start out that way."
Alex shook his head. "But that's insane. Piranha solutions have to be mixed carefully, used immediately and cautiously, and then neutralized. One misstep, and we'd have an explosion on our hands. Even if we could somehow get it to a swarm safely, whoever was delivering it would be on a suicide mission. That stuff would eat through a hazmat suit."
"Yes," Dr. Pullman said, "but the solution is much safer to handle when it's cold." He turned and wrote a formula on the board. "This formula is a sort of super-cooled piranha-adjacent solution. We believe it would do the trick."
Alex frowned at the formula. "Sure, but that doesn't address delivery, and we'd still have to ensure no one would be hurt in the process of delivery. A hazmat suit wouldn't stand up to that, either."
"Fire extinguishers," Turner said, grinning. "Refillable fire extinguishers. There are fire protection equipment supplier shops in the city. We could find the equipment to refill extinguishers there. We'd have to transfer some things to the shop, set up some basic safety precautions, and hook up a generator, but then we could fill fire extinguishers with that solution. It would stay stable and cool in the pressurized canister, and the moment it hit air, it would turn to a thick fog."
"Precisely," Dr. Pullman said. "And we have skilled workers here in the mountain who believe they could create a timed-release system with those extinguishers, perhaps two or three working together in a contraption."
"People would have to set it up," Turner said, "but the timer would give them time to escape before the fog was released."
Alex exchanged a look with Walter. "Do you think that could work?"
Walter looked back at the board. "We'd have to test it, of course, but… maybe."
"Still, though," Alex said, "I don't get how this could be effective against a swarm. You set up one of these contraptions, and what? Have a person sit by hoping a swarm comes along and stays put long enough to be killed by the fog? The swarm will go after that person. If they flee the area, the swarm will follow."
Dr. Pullman smiled and turned around, erasing the board and writing a new formula on the board. Alex looked at it, but his frown only deepened.
"What is that?" he asked.
Walter sat back in his chair, his eyes wide. "It's an artificial pheromone."
"Now imagine the contraption also has a device that releases that," Ward said. "We attract the swarm, and then we kill it off."
"It could work," Walter said.
"It could go terribly wrong." Alex ran his fingers through his hair as all the scenarios of failure went through his head. "The fog could drift and kill people. These formulas haven't been tested. The chances of an explosion are still fairly high, and not just when the fog is delivered, but in the creation of the solution, in the filling of the extinguishers… pretty much at every step of the process."
"But you can't deny that it could work," Joanna said.
"We realize it needs testing and refinement," Dr. Pullman said. "But we think we could possibly kill off entire swarms this way. It's not a worldwide solution, but it could make safe zones, give us a weapon against them that works until, hopefully, you and your team come back with the countermeasure mosquitos that will wipe them out for good and a treatment or a cure."

Ward shook her head. "Even the countermeasure mosquitos will take time to work through the swarms. That's not an immediate solution. It's a long-term one. We estimate there are two, maybe three swarms in this area. This could effectively make Colorado Springs safe within a few days' time."

"C'mon, man. It's at least worth looking into," Turner said.

"There are so few left in the city," Dr. Pullman said. "And the fear, the knowing that there's nothing anyone can do about these swarms, it's part of why there's this cold war going on between the military and the civilians. We need to show the people that we are on their side."

"I think he's right," Walter said. "Desperate times, and all that."

Alex closed his eyes. He had a bad feeling about it, but part of him saw the possibilities. It was too complicated and dangerous to be a widely used solution to the problem, but if it worked, if they could perfect it, they could buy time for the people in Colorado Springs.

"The experiments happen far away from any population center," Alex said.

"Agreed, of course," Dr. Pullman said.

"Okay," Alex said. "Let's get to work."

Chapter 25

Lauren Stevens

The privacy of a real shower was enough to push Lauren's worries aside, even if only for the moment. The targeted streams of water were like dozens of little fists massaging her back and pounding the tension out of her muscles. Dirt and grime loosened from her scalp to her toes, leaving her clean and refreshed. The steam cleared her sinuses and fogged the room, reminding her of a time when her biggest concern for the day was booking the next gig on some tiny stage in a coffee house in Nashville.

A quick pang of grief over the past wasn't too hard to bury; she was practiced at it, efficient. She shut down thoughts of anything and everything and cleared her mind. She focused instead on the warmth prickling her skin, on the sound of trickling water that tasted of minerals when she licked her lips. For once, she allowed herself to just *be*.

A sharp *ding* filled the air, and after only seven minutes, Lauren forced herself to turn the shower off. She pulled back the curtain and reached for a towel, drying off before stepping out and turning off the alarm. Seven minutes allotted time in the shower wasn't much, but it would be hard to leave behind when it was time for them to skip out on their trial inside Cheyenne Mountain.

Lauren held the little alarm clock in her hand, her gaze shifting from it to the shower and then to the door. *Hard to leave behind…*

On the other side of that door was Heather. They still hadn't spoken about Heather's disconcerting hints that perhaps she wasn't planning to leave the facility at all.

Maybe, Lauren thought, she's just not thinking straight. She's just worried.

She sighed and pulled the towel tighter around her body. The room was still warm, the steam still curling up toward the ceiling. Out there, beyond the door, Heather's cool stare and icy silence waited. She hadn't wanted to talk when she'd been finished with her shower, and Lauren had only made things worse by pushing her. She wasn't sure she could get Heather to say a word. She wasn't sure she should even try.

She said she needed time, so give it to her. Stop being impatient, Lauren chided herself. Wait until after the doctor sees her to figure out how to approach this.

Lauren turned toward the mirror and wiped it clear. "You can do this," she said quietly. "Even without Heather. Conner will be here soon. You're not alone." She squinted at her reflection. "But you *are* a mess. Good gracious. What has the end of the world done to you?"

She touched what seemed to be a permanent new wrinkle between her eyebrows. A long, thin scar graced her chin, and for the life of her, she couldn't remember how she got it. Her face had been scratched up more times than she could count. She was thinner than she'd ever been in her life. Her collar bones jutted out, and an old bruise was fading on her shoulder, large and yellowed. Her skin from head to toe was dry and evidence of her most recent sunburn was visible in peeling patches. She'd glimpsed herself in windows and little visor mirrors over the last weeks, but she'd not really stopped to look.

Turning from the mirror with a bit of a defiant huff, she grabbed her clothes and dressed, avoiding the mirror and reminding herself that even badasses get wrinkles.

Then, she faced the door once again, bouncing on her heels. It was game time. She had to be strong when she rejoined Heather. She had to be cool and collected. Heather needed support, not judgment. She could do that. Heather would come around eventually.

Cold air rushed over her when Lauren opened the door. Heather was lying on the bottom bunk, her legs crossed at the ankles, her hands resting on her belly. The floor was cold and hard. Lauren still had socks in a bunch in one hand, and she crossed the room to sit on the bed at Heather's feet.

"This is nice," Lauren said as she put on her socks. "The room, I mean. The shower is amazing." After a few more minutes of the silent treatment, she grabbed boots from the foot of the bed. "I can't believe they had my size," she said, nudging Heather. "How do yours fit?"

"If I stuff socks in the toes, they're fine," Heather said, still not looking at her.

But an answer was better than nothing. Lauren offered a smile. "Maybe we can get another size."

"Maybe." Heather sat up and slid her legs over the side of the bed, scooting to the edge to sit next to Lauren. Her face fell, and she hugged her middle. "I've just been sitting here, thinking about what's coming, about the ultrasound." Her eyes glistened as she looked back at Lauren.

"It's a lot to deal with," Lauren said. "But it's going to be okay."

"I know we're not really here for *me*, that we're supposed to be on this mission," Heather whispered, "but I can't think of anything else. And I can't stop thinking about what will happen if the pregnancy is fine. How can I go back out there when I know this place is safer? But then… what about Tim? I can't leave him out there, and I don't think they'd let him in here."

Lauren swallowed her immediate answer in favor of a few seconds of thought. *Support. Not judgment.*

"Hey, listen to me." Lauren put an arm around her. "First, we *are* here for you. We're here for two missions, as far as I'm concerned. Let me worry about finding the offline database. You take care of yourself, got it? And second, who knows what these people will allow. Maybe you can blame the arena incident on Alex. He wouldn't mind. He's not sticking around. Anyway, it doesn't matter, not yet. So, stop worrying about all the what-ifs and just take the next step."

Heather chewed on her lower lip and nodded half-heartedly. She opened her mouth as if to say something else, but a knock on the door made them both jump a little. Lauren half stood, bumping her head on the top bunk.

"Ouch!" Lauren grimaced, her eyes watering as she rubbed the top of her head.

"That should be Carrie." Heather stood more gracefully. "You okay?"

"It smarts, but yeah, I'm fine." Lauren blinked away moisture and used the collar of her shirt to dry her eyes. She waved for Heather to go on and open the door.

"Good morning, ladies," Carrie said, holding up two stainless steel tumblers. "Coffee anyone?" She winked at Heather. "I've got decaf for you."

"Um, thanks," Heather said, reaching for the tumbler.

Lauren groaned with longing as she stepped forward and grasped the warm tumbler in her hands. "A shower *and* hot coffee? You're an angel, Carrie."

"I've also got these." Carrie waggled her eyebrows as she pulled a bundle wrapped in cheesecloth out of a messenger bag at her hip. She handed it to Heather and then brought out a second bundle to hand over to Lauren. "Fresh flatbread sandwiches. Scrambled eggs and goat cheese."

"What?" Lauren's mouth dropped open as she untied the bundle carefully to get a look at the sandwich for herself. "Where did you get goat cheese?"

"Goats," Carrie said.

Heather chuckled. "You have goats down here?"

"This place has everything." Carrie gestured around the building. "When they built those apartments, they set up a specially ventilated wing for small livestock and a space for hydroponic gardens. There weren't any animals or plants yet when we arrived, but we've had some experienced homesteaders on the job for weeks. They sourced some goats and chickens — that's all we've got so far of the animals — and some heirloom seeds for the gardens. We don't have much in the way of fresh vegetables yet, but we've got a bit of goat cheese and we've got some eggs."

Lauren took a bite and a shudder of absolute delight ran down her spine. "This is delicious."

"Well, if you can eat and walk, I'd appreciate it," Carrie said. "We've got Heather here last up on the doctor's roster. I don't want to keep her waiting."

"And Lauren can come with, right?" Heather asked. "For emotional support?

"Sure," Carrie said. "I think they'd like to show her around the building, anyway. That's where she'll be assigned."

"When do I start?" Lauren asked before taking a bite.

"In the morning," Carrie said.

Lauren swallowed. "That's fast. I was hoping for more time to get settled."

Carrie shrugged. "You live and eat here, you work."

"Of course. That makes perfect sense." Lauren smiled as she kept any traces of disappointment out of her voice. She'd hoped to explore a little right away, but she could poke and prod in conversations, too. "Lead the way, then."

Lauren and Heather followed Carrie out into the hall, closed and locked their door behind them, and the three women once again navigated the complex until they reached medical services. Stellar was there, with a clipboard, behind a desk. He stood up when they came into an area with a row of cots, curtains tied off on the walls between them.

"Evening, Stellar," Carrie said, nodding to the dentist.

"Ah," he said. "Good to see you both!"

Lauren quirked an eyebrow at the man who'd examined them at the sandwich shop, but Heather was the one who voiced what she was thinking.

"I'm sorry," Heather said. "Are *you* the doctor who will be doing my ultrasound? Didn't you say you were a dentist?"

"Oh, no," Stellar said, laughing so hard he had to wipe a tear from his eye. "No, no. Not me. Teeth are my forte. Simple exams I can do, but delivering a baby? Goodness, no."

"I'll be helping you out today," a voice said from the far side of the room.

Lauren turned to see a woman in a white coat, hair pulled back in a high bun, striding forward with quick, sure steps as she held her own clipboard before her. Two fingers pushed her reading glasses back up her nose. She didn't look up at them as she stopped a few feet away; by the way her eyes shifted back and forth, she was reading. Finally, she looked up from her clipboard, looked between the two, and raised her eyebrows questioningly.

"And which of you is Heather?" she asked, her tone polite but to-the-point.

Heather raised her hand. "That would be me." She gestured to Lauren. "This is my friend, Lauren."

"The new nurse?" the woman asked.

Lauren cleared her throat. "Looks like it."

"This is Ingrid," Carrie said.

"*Doctor* Gregory," she corrected. With a disapproving look from their guide, the doctor coughed, shifted uncomfortably, and smiled at them. "Ingrid is fine."

"That's right," Carrie said, as if she'd corrected a child. "What's good enough for the nurses is good enough for the doctors." She patted Lauren on the back.

"Yes," Dr. Gregory said with a tight smile. "Of course it is."

A stranger poked his head into the room. "Hey, Carrie! I've been looking for you."

"What is it, Hector?" Carrie asked.

His lip curled at the sight of Lauren and Heather.

Carrie sighed. "You're the most paranoid—" She cut herself off, put her hands on her hips, and smiled at them. "Be right back, ladies."

When she'd gone, Lauren jumped on the opportunity to make friends with someone who might have information. "So, Dr. Gregory," she said, "what's with them insisting we call you by your first name?"

"You heard her," the doctor said. "Their whole motto is that no one deserves more respect than anyone else, regardless of career choices or how much money they had in the bank before this absolute disaster." She rubbed the back of her neck.
"I've worked in hospitals," Lauren said. "I get it. Professional distance lets you do your job, right?"
Dr. Gregory pointed at Lauren with enthusiasm. "Exactly! They don't get it. I'm not saying they have to call me 'doctor' anywhere else but here, in the clinic, where I do my work, so I can be in the right headspace."

This might be a way to break down barriers fast, Lauren thought.
"Maybe they just need to see that using your title doesn't change who you are or your disposition toward them," Lauren said.
Carrie returned with a huff, mumbling something about Hector, but her smile resurfaced when she took her place in their circle again.
"Sorry about the interruption," she said. "Any questions so far?"
"Would it be okay," Lauren asked, directing her question at Carrie but keeping an eye on Dr. Gregory, "if when I'm on duty, I refer to her as Dr. Gregory? I actually prefer it."
Dr. Gregory looked at her, eyes a little wide. Her surprised expression morphed into one of appreciation.
Carrie frowned. "I guess so, as long as it's *your* decision, and not forced on you because she thinks she's a big shot."
"For goodness' sake," Dr. Gregory said. "You people—"
"See?" Carrie jutted a finger in the doctor's face. "You don't see yourselves as one of us."
"Because *you* don't see me that way!" She put her hands on her hips. "I'm just trying to do my job. I'm helping people. I've even saved a few lives since I've come on board. You need me, but you hate me. How does that make any sense?"
"You don't see Stellar bragging like that, acting all high and mighty," Carrie said.
Stellar looked up sharply and put his hands in the air. "Oh... I don't think—"
"He's a *dentist*." Dr. Gregory threw up her hands in frustration. "He's important, and I'm glad he's on staff, but can he deliver your babies?"
"Oh, no." Stellar shook his head, going pale.
"We've got ourselves a midwife," Carrie said, sticking out her chin.
"Can the midwife do a c-section?" Dr. Gregory crossed her arms.
"I said we needed you. What more do you want?" Carrie raised her voice.
Lauren raised her hands, one palm facing Carrie, the other facing Dr. Gregory. "Maybe she just wants a friend."
Heather nodded. "Sounds to me like we all just want to belong somewhere."
Dr. Gregory's chin trembled. She looked up at the ceiling, and her eyes glistened. She quickly wiped away a tear. "I've lost everyone, too, you know, Carrie," she said softly, her voice strained.
Carrie worked her jaw back and forth, and then her expression softened a little. "Yeah, well... maybe we just got off on the wrong foot. Me and some of the guys are gonna play cards two nights from now at The Granite Inn. It's a weekly thing. I think I can talk them into giving you a place at the table." She nodded at Heather and Lauren, too. "You all might as well come by, too."
"Really?" Dr. Gregory straightened.
"Yeah," Carrie said.
"We'd love that," Lauren said.
Carrie pointed at the doctor. "But I'm not calling you Dr. Gregory. It's Ingrid all day and all night. That's how I refer to my friends, by their first names, thank you very much."
Dr. Gregory smiled. "I can live with that."
Carrie shifted as if she were uncomfortable. "Are you gonna take Heather back to take a look at her baby, or what?"
"I'd like Lauren to come with me," Heather said.
"Okay, sure." Dr. Gregory dabbed her eyes with the collar of her shirt and smiled at them. "Follow me, please." As she led them down the row of beds to the last one, she glanced at Lauren. "I've been trying to get them to see me as a person for weeks. Thank you."
"Sometimes people just need a new perspective," Lauren said. "I'm glad I could help."
Behind them, Stellar piped up. "I like cards," he said.
"Fine," Carrie said with a sigh. "You can come, too."
Lauren glanced back to see Stellar nearly clap his hands before Carrie gave him a flat stare that made him stop his hands mid-air and pat the front of his shirt instead. She chuckled. "We all have to learn to get along," she said. "There aren't a ton of people left."
"I couldn't agree more," Dr. Gregory said as she stopped and gestured to the bed. "Let's get a look at your baby, Heather. I'm sure you're anxious to see how the little one is faring."
Heather took a deep breath and climbed up on the bed as Dr. Gregory unsnapped the loop around the curtain and pulled it out to create a little room within the room. The doctor proceeded to walk around the bed and prepare the ultrasound machine next to it. Lauren came nearer to Heather and took her hand, squeezing it, hoping her presence offered her friend a bit of comfort.
"I wish my husband were here," Heather said quietly.
"I'm sorry for your loss," Dr. Gregory said as she squeezed a bit of jelly onto the transducer. She sat there for a moment. "Let me know when you're ready."
Though Timothy was alive, Lauren realized in that moment that Heather *had* lost something, even if it wasn't as big as losing him. She'd lost the chance to share the moment with him, whether it ended in joy or in grief. Lauren bent over and wrapped Heather in a hug.
"I'm here," she whispered. "You're not alone." She pulled back, and Heather nodded at the doctor.
"I'm ready," she said.

If there was something wrong, Heather would be given medical care and then sent back to the arena. And then Lauren would be the one alone in a place full of people she was planning to deceive. She'd have to wait until Conner got a spot inside the mountain, and for all she knew, that could take a while. She wasn't sure she could keep up the ruse for that long. Her heartbeat picked up at the thought of having to pretend, having to spend weeks inside the mountain while having no idea if her mother, Alex, and Oliver were still safe or even alive.

She focused on the monitor as the doctor pressed the device to Heather's stomach. So much was riding on one, tiny heartbeat. Lauren held her breath and listened.

Chapter 26

Zara Williams

Zara sank back into the couch as silence fell over the small cabin. She and Kai were finished filling Lieutenant Colonel Joel Blythe in on everything they knew to tell.

"But this Candice Liddle," Blythe said, his elbows resting on his knees as he leaned forward on his own chair across from the couch, "she got sick right away? Back when this was new? Were there even swarms yet?"

"I mean… we weren't with her when it happened," Zara said. "But, yes, this was early… in the first week, I think."

Blythe worked his jaw back and forth a moment before shaking his head. "It makes sense that these mosquitos, that this disease was created. It makes even more sense that the government had a hand in it. It's too quickly evolving. The fact is, if she'd gotten sick today, there's a better chance she'd have died or gone nuts, like my neighbor. Whatever advantage she's given to the efforts of finding a treatment… well, it's probably too late to use it. What if it's not relevant anymore because this disease is changing?" He stood up and rubbed his hands together as if washing his hands clean. "This isn't my fight. It's not yours, either, from the sounds of it."

"Are you serious, dude?" Kai asked, standing to come eye-to-eye with Blythe. "It's *everybody's* fight. And I'm sorry, but there's no way you know more about this disease and what's going to work than the scientists back in the city."

Zara nodded. "Kai is right. Alex and Walter know what they're doing. You have to help us."

"No, I don't." Blythe turned his back and crossed the room to the small kitchen that took up the far side of the cabin. "You're young, and you think the world is yours, that you can do anything. I'm too old for that crap."

Kai looked down at Zara, his expression incredulous. But she shook her head subtly. "We shouldn't push him too hard, not yet," she whispered. "We have all night and the morning to convince him."

"That's not a lot of time," Kai said.

Pots clinked as Blythe reached for one hanging from a rack over the sink. "You two hungry?" His tone and body language sent a clear message: he was done talking about their mission.

"Starving," Zara said, meeting Kai's eyes and nodding toward the small table between the living room area and the kitchen. "Let's just spend a bit of time with him," she said quietly. "Give him the chance to maybe trust us a little."

Kai sighed and held out a hand to help her up off the couch. She took it, and they transferred to the table, which was made of wood but reminded Zara of a card table in size and shape. They sat on wooden chairs that were sturdy and simple, handmade by the looks of them, just like the table, just like the cabin and much of the furniture within.

"How about some mac and cheese with some ground venison?" Blythe asked.

"As in, deer meat?" Kai asked, his expression and tone skeptical.

Blythe looked over his shoulder at him with raised eyebrows. "Shot the buck myself. It was healthy. No need to worry about that." He patted his thin, five-foot fridge. "Been off the grid with a hybrid solar-wind-turbine system for years. The meat's fresh, already cooked, too. All I need to do is stir it into the mac and cheese and heat it up. Shouldn't take long."

"That's… not what I'm worried about," Kai said.

Zara chuckled. "I think he's just never had venison, but it sounds pretty good to me."

"You've had venison?" Kai wrinkled his nose.

"My dad liked to hunt," Zara said. She smiled sadly at the thought of him.

"He's gone, too, I'm guessing?" Blythe asked.

Zara nodded. "My whole family except for my cousin, Annika. They're all gone."

"And you?" Blythe asked, glancing back at Kai as he used a hand pump at the sink to fill the pot with water.

"My family's gone, too," Kai said, "but I only ever had my mom to start, and she died a while ago."

"Before Day Zero?" Blythe asked.

Kai nodded. "Yeah," he said. "And she was a single mom, working a lot. The best mom I could ever ask for, but… I had to take care of myself more often than not."

"Seems we're all out here fending for ourselves," Blythe said, turning back to his pot and setting it on a wood-burning cook stove. There was a small cubby on the bottom filled with split wood. There were also two glass doors, one in the middle where Blythe placed two logs and struck up a fire, and below that, there was a small oven. "That's what the world is now," Blythe continued. "Every man for himself. Not that it was much different before."

"Nah," Kai said, "that's where you're wrong. See, Zara and Walter, they're family now. We look out for each other. Even the rest of the gang—Alex and the rest—we're all in this together."

"Kai's right," Zara said. "We're not alone, and if you join us, if you help, you won't be alone, either."

Blythe stiffened, but his back was turned. Zara couldn't see his face. "Maybe I like being on my own," he said. "No one else to worry about. No one else to lose."

"No one else to love," Zara added softly. "No one else to love *you*."

Blythe turned around. "I had that once, and I ruined it."

"This could be your last chance to have a second chance at family," Kai said. "You really want to pass that up?"

Blythe cleared his throat and turned his back again, opening a cabinet and pulling down two boxes of mac and cheese. "The water needs to come to a boil," he said, his voice gruff. "I'll be back in a few." Without looking at them, he strode past the table and living room area to an open door on the other side of the cabin. He slammed it shut behind him.

"How do you think that went?" Kai asked.

"I was going to give him more time before diving back into why we're really here," she said. "I don't think he's ready to keep talking about it. But the conversation just... went there." She shrugged. "I guess it could have been worse."

"How?"

She winced. "He could have killed us back at the road. Or refused to let us come at all. Or refused to listen once we got here."

"Okay, so he listened, so what?" Kai asked. "He doesn't want to do this."

"Neither do you," Zara said, and then she looked down at the table where she fidgeted with her fingers. "Neither do I, not really. No one wants any of this."

"Then how do we get him to come with us?" Kai folded his arms on the table and let his head drop onto his arms as he groaned.

"You and I are doing this because we have people we care about," Zara said. "That's all it takes. A tiny bit of caring." She looked back at the closed door to what she assumed was Blythe's bedroom. "He didn't yell or get angry, Kai. He got emotional. I think he got uncomfortable because he *does* care, even if just a little. He wants human connection, or at least, he doesn't want all possibility of human connection to be wiped out."

Kai looked up. "He still hates the military."

"This isn't about them," Zara said.

"I don't know if he sees it that way."

Zara sighed. "Maybe that's what we have to change then. Make him see *us* and not *them*."

The two of them waited at the table, the conversation turning to other things, less stressful things. Zara felt the tension in her shoulders and the knot in her stomach ease as Kai got her talking about old movies and television. He made her laugh, distracted her from her exhaustion.

When the water on the stove started to boil, Zara left Blythe to his room. She was no cook, but she could throw together boxed mac and cheese with a little pre-cooked, ground venison in the mix. The savory scent of cheesy noodles and meat filled the cabin, and only then did Blythe reenter the common area.

"I see you're not entirely useless," Blythe said as he crossed the room to the kitchen. "I'll take it from here." He grabbed three out of four bowls from a cabinet, filled them one by one, and plopped them on the table.

"You're welcome," Zara said as she pulled one of the bowls closer.

Blythe handed out spoons, pulled a couple levers on the wood-burning stove, and then sat hard on one of the chairs in front of the last unclaimed bowl. "I heard you two laughing about something while I was in my room," he said. "Haven't heard that sound in a long time. What was so funny?"

"We were talking about old movies and television," Zara said. "I love all of it, from the black-and-white sitcoms to the sci-fi space operas. Kai's never seen half of my favorites. I was trying to explain the difference between Star Trek and Star Wars."

Blythe nodded, shoveling a heaping spoonful of hot noodles into his mouth. He swallowed and gave Zara a hard stare. "Who's your favorite captain? Picard or Kirk?"

Zara raised her eyebrows. "Oh, do we have a fellow Trekkie at the table?" She tapped her chin. "Janeway, actually," she said.

Blythe straightened. "Janeway? Are you kidding? You're going Janeway before all of them? Even Sisko?"

"An unconventional opinion, sure," Zara said. "But Janeway was real. She had to be, disconnected from everyone and everything she'd ever known. Everyone else had to follow the rules. She made up her own. I identify with her now more than ever."

Kai laughed. "Wow. You two are nerds."

Zara and Blythe gave him a similarly scathing scowl. "You're just mad because you're boring," Zara said.

"What she said, kid," Blythe said. "What kind of hobbies did you have, anyway? First-person shooters, I bet. You look like the type."

"Okay, okay," Kai said, raising his hands in mock surrender. "You got me. But what's with these old shows, anyway? What drew you in?"

"There was something charming about media back then," Zara said.

"Agreed," Colonel Blythe said. "These days it's all reality shows."

Zara nodded. "Or the complete opposite. Philosophy wrapped up in drama and bad endings."

"It's not that bad," Kai said. "There are plenty of good action movies."

Zara scoffed and quirked an eyebrow at Blythe while pointing her thumb at Kai. "This guy. Can you believe it?"

Blythe cracked a smile. "I got enough juice to plug in my little T.V. for one episode of *Next Generation*. It's one of the few DVD collections I kept after going off-grid."

"Really?" Zara sat up straighter, smiling so wide her cheeks hurt.

"What's that?" Kai asked.

Zara smiled at him. "Star Trek. Picard. You're going to love it. What do you think?"

"I'm down," Kai said, shrugging.

After dinner was done and cleaned up, Blythe disappeared into his room again and reemerged holding a small television screen and a DVD player. Zara and the colonel debated for at least twenty minutes on which episode they wanted to watch. He popped some stove-top popcorn, and the three of them settled down for forty-five minutes of one of Zara's favorite episodes: "The Inner Light."

Zara leaned into Kai, letting him put an arm around her as the story played out on screen. Blythe munched away on popcorn in his chair, and for that hour, Zara let herself be carried away on the winds of story. When the episode came to a close, she sat up and stretched.

"Yeah, okay," Kai said. "You nerds are right. I enjoyed that."

"You just need to accept the fact," Zara said, elbowing him playfully, "that I'm usually right."
But then her smile faded as she looked over at Blythe. He was staring at them, his eyes misty. When he caught her looking at him, he sucked in a breath and stood up quickly, turning to the kitchen and putting his snack bowl on the table. He sat down on a wooden chair, his back to them.
"What's wrong?" Zara asked. "Blythe, are you okay?"
She looked at Kai, and he shrugged. Zara picked up her snack bowl and Kai's and walked slowly to the kitchen, placing them in the sink. She turned around to face Blythe, who was looking at his feet. He seemed so focused on the floorboards, his eyes searching as if trying to find a pattern in the wood.
I know that look, Zara thought. He's lost in the dark, and he's seen a light, but he doesn't know if he can trust it.
Zara folded her arms and gave him time. It was something she had learned the hard way: people couldn't always be pushed; sometimes the truth of reality had to slowly draw them into acceptance.
Kai stood up and opened his mouth, but Zara held up a hand and shook her head. Instead of speaking, Kai came to sit at the table opposite Blythe. They waited together until the colonel let out a shaky breath and finally looked up from the floorboards.
"For a minute there," he said, "I forgot. It was just so normal. And… I looked at you two, and I thought of my wife, and…" He swallowed hard. "I just don't think I can go back to the military."
A spike of panic gave Zara's stomach a jolt. "You're not going back to the military," she said, keeping her voice even. "You'd be joining our people."
"I'm safe here," he said. "And it's easier to survive when you're on your own, when you don't have to worry about anyone else."
"Is that your only goal?" Kai asked. "To survive? Is that really living?"
"You two are fighting for your futures," Blythe said. "But what am I fighting for? I've had my shot, and I don't deserve another one."
He's talking himself out of it, Zara thought as Blythe's expression smoothed and the emotion started to dissipate in his eyes.
"Tell me about your wife," Zara said. The question tumbled out of her mouth, a gut feeling pushing her in that direction. She couldn't put a finger on exactly what was holding Blythe back, but she knew it had something to do with how he instantly worked to suppress his emotions, either by running from the situation or changing the subject.
Blythe blanched and blinked as if surprised by her request. "What?"
"Your wife," Zara said again, hoping she was on the right track. "What was she like?"
He shook his head. "I can't do this." He stood up and turned as if to flee back to his room, but he froze in place when Kai spoke up.
"My mom worked harder than anyone I've ever known," Kai said. "Even when she was exhausted, though, she made sure to hug me every morning and every night. She'd wake me up at midnight just to hug me, to whisper that she loved me." He breathed in slowly and closed his eyes for a moment. When he opened them, his expression was sad but also a bit wistful. "I miss talking about her."
Zara offered Kai a small smile as she came closer to him and put a hand on his shoulder. "My dad was tough as nails, but he was most at peace when helping other people. And my mom, her laughter could fill a house, and it was contagious. They never let me feel alone." She looked up at Blythe. "Even when I was practically living in the hospital because of my leukemia. They were always there for me."
Blythe turned back around to face them. "You… you had cancer?"
Zara nodded. "Yeah. I used to think it was the scariest thing I'd ever experience." She laughed a little at that. "I blamed myself for so much, for my parents' debt, for the way my brother got into so much trouble. He needed attention, and it was all eaten up by me and my illness."
"That wasn't your fault," Blythe said. "My wife… she used to feel the same way. Guilty for being sick. It wasn't her fault, either."
"I know that now," Zara said.
"She was smart," Blythe said. "Brilliant. This cabin was a design she came up with. She loved creating things that made other people smile. Even in the hospital, as she was dying, she made little crocheted flowers for the nurses, for the other people who were sick."
"She sounds like she was kind," Kai said.
"And beautiful." Blythe closed his eyes. "Even after chemo took all of her hair, she was gorgeous. Her eyes had a sparkle to them until the end." He let out a long breath and opened his eyes, tears sliding down each cheek. He walked over to the couch and sank into it, covering his face with his hands for a few moments, his shoulders shaking. Finally, he leaned back and wiped his face clean. His eyes were red and puffy, but he nodded. "She'd want me to help," he said. "Even if it's a long shot, if there's any chance that this could work, she'd want me to try."
Relief flooded Zara's body, and she felt as though she might collapse as tension bled out from every pore. On shaky legs, she reached one of the chairs at the table and sat down. She was suddenly so exhausted that she could barely speak. She hadn't realized how much fear she'd been holding in until she was able to let it go.
"So, you're coming with us?" Kai asked.
Blythe nodded. "I guess I am, kid. I guess I am."

Chapter 27

Minnie Stevens

Minnie lay awake on one of two beds in a room lit only by moonlight coming in through two six-pane windows. Alex and Oliver slept on the other bed, and Samson had made himself comfortable on hers.

Alex's summary of his day kept repeating in her mind. President Coleman and her very own hunk of a man, Alan Hunt, were letting Ward and Turner waltz around free and clear like they didn't lock Minnie up and try to experiment on her.

Well, they are shackled, she thought. Maybe it's more of a shuffle than a waltz. But still. Those two are pigs.

She shifted and rolled onto her side. Alex had explained what they were working on: a system that would lure a swarm and then kill it off. It was more of a Band-Aid than it was a solution. It wasn't reproducible except through a team of specialists, and it had plenty of risk. But it was something. If it worked, Colorado Springs could be made safe, even if only temporarily.

But Ward and Turner were the last people Minnie would ever trust to do something good. *What are they up to, playing hero?* Something wasn't right about the whole situation, and it made Minnie squirm. *You can put perfume on a pig, but that don't mean you've made a lady out of it*, she thought.

It was possible that they were just doing as they were told in order to enjoy the benefits of a little freedom, but their presence combined with that of Price and Lawson made Minnie want to hightail it out of Colorado Springs as soon as possible. She sighed and closed her eyes, intent on getting a bit of sleep.

Samson shifted, and she opened one eye to peek at him as he whined. The dog lifted his head and looked toward a window. He huffed a bit, letting out a short, low bark. Minnie shushed him and looked over at Alex and Oliver. He hopped onto the floor and trotted over to the window, barking again, this time a little louder.

"Shush. You're going to wake them," she whispered sharply.

Samson looked back at her, whining. Well, that wasn't like him at all.

"What is it?" Minnie pushed off her thin blanket and sat up.

And then a loud *boom* reverberated through the air, and the entire house shook. Minnie instinctively threw herself back on the bed and covered her head, but it was over just as soon as it had begun.

Alex snorted awake, and Minnie caught the outline of him flailing as he sat up, startled. "What the hell?" he shouted. "Minnie, are you okay?"

"I'm fine." She sat up again, shaking a little. "What was that?"

Oliver snatched a flashlight from the side table and turned it on. "Dad? Was that an earthquake?"

"I don't think so, bud," Alex said. His face was illuminated by the flashlight as his son turned it on him. Eyes wide, he sat on his knees on the bed and tried to peer past Minnie out the window.

"It sounded like an explosion." Minnie got up as Samson started barking again. He'd stood on his hind legs, his paws against the window facing the street. Her mouth dropped open when she reached the window and looked in the direction of the academy campus. A bright orange glow lit the sky. "Alex…" she said breathlessly. "Something's hap—"

The glass before her shattered, accompanied by the sound of gunfire. She flinched and stumbled backward, noticing dark figures on the street before she tripped and fell onto her back, her head bouncing off the floor.

Bullets shot through the window and the wall, shattering more glass, pinging off the metal bedframe, thudding into wood and mattresses. The shock of impact with the floor had stunned her, and she threw up her hands, body trembling. She forced herself to unfurl and army crawled a few inches, trying to see in the dark as wood splinters and glass sprinkled her.

It was too dark, and she was too low. The flashlight had been dropped, and it shone uselessly under her bed, pointed at the wall. A heavy thump sounded from the other side of the room.

"Alex?" Minnie shouted. "Oliver?" Her voice cracked. She wasn't far from the flashlight, so she went for it, but as she passed one of the side tables, another bullet whizzed overhead and struck a porcelain lamp. The heaviest part of it rolled off the edge and hit Minnie in the same spot she'd slammed against the floor just moments earlier.

Dazed, she curled into herself. Oliver's cries mixed with another bombardment of gunfire. Shouts from elsewhere in the house reached her through the floorboards. *Protect us*, she prayed. *Protect Oliver.* She repeated the plea over and over again as another explosion sounded in the distance.

And then it was quiet.

Minnie didn't move at first. She couldn't quite believe it was over. Her ears were ringing, and her throat was raw. *Was I screaming?* she thought. She couldn't remember.

Her forearms stung when she finally stirred. When she lightly touched her arms, she found bits of glass embedded into her skin. Some of it flaked off, having barely broken through. She had to pick out a few longer slivers.

The floor was slick and warm. *Blood? It can't all be mine.* She hadn't been hit by a bullet, and while her arms were scraped up badly, none of the glass had gone deep enough to draw that much blood.

She looked up at the beam of light from the flashlight and reached toward it, her fingertips brushing the metallic tube. She inched closer, grimacing as the movement sent little jolts of pain throughout her body. Once the flashlight was in hand, she scooted back from under the bed and sat up.

"Oliver? Alex?" Minnie whispered, her heart beating so hard she thought it might tear through her chest. The next second of silence was an eternity as she held her breath, prayed for a word, a sound, anything.

"Minnie?" Oliver's small voice pulled Minnie further out of her shock.

She got to her feet, her legs wobbly. Her foot slipped, and she turned the flashlight on the floor beneath her. There was so much blood. She limped forward, searching. When she reached the space between the two beds, her light revealed Oliver, still on the floor, and Samson, who was covering part of Oliver with his body.

Oliver had his arms wrapped around Samson's neck, and his face was wet with tears. "He's still breathing," he said, squinting into the light.

A spark of hope kept Minnie from collapsing as she looked at her dog, her most loyal friend. A trail of blood trickled from beneath Samson and Oliver, running under the bed to the place where she had curled up and frozen.

"It… It's going to be okay," Minnie managed to say as she knelt slowly. "Are you okay, Oliver?"

Oliver nodded. "I'm fine," he said, his brow knitted. "We need to do something about Samson." And then his eyes went wide. "And Dad…" he whispered, and then he shouted, "Dad?"

That one word carried with it a terror that seized Minnie by the throat, nearly choking her. She looked up from Samson, who was indeed still breathing, and shone the flashlight under the second bed to where Alex lay. The light hit his face, and he winced, groaning and putting his hand up to cover his eyes. Minnie shifted the light so it wasn't shining directly on him.

"Oliver?" Alex blinked several times. "Are you okay?"

"Are you?" Oliver asked.

"I think so," Alex said. "I got nicked on my upper arm, but… it's nothing. Minnie, what about you?"

"I don't know," she cried as she looked back at Samson. "Scrapes and bruises, I think."

Alex sat up. "What is it, then?"

Minnie stood taller on her knees as Alex got to his feet. "It's Samson. Come help me? He's a big dog."

Alex crawled over the bed and surveyed Oliver and Samson, his entire body deflating at the scene. "Samson… shielded him. He shielded my son."

Oliver nodded. "Yeah," he said. "I just froze in a ball, and Samson, he laid on top of me like this, licking my cheek, until he… until he stopped… and… and…" Oliver hugged the dog tighter.

Samson opened his eyes and whimpered, moving off of Oliver to lay on the floor. Minnie scooted to him, stroking his head. "It's okay," she said. "Let me see…" She shone the light along the dog's body. "That's a good boy," she said, cooing and talking softly as she checked for injuries.

Meanwhile, Alex pulled Oliver off the floor and onto the bed, looking the child over head to toe much like Minnie was doing for her dog. "I don't see anything serious." Alex gathered Oliver into his arms and held him close, let him cry into his shoulder.

"I see one bullet wound," Minnie said. "On his flank. I think… if we can get someone to get it out, clean it up, bandage it… I think he'll be okay." But her stomach was sick at the sluggish way Samson moved. "He's just lost a lot of blood." She pulled a sheet off the bed and pushed on the wound. "We need to stop the bleedin'." Samson squirmed and nipped at her when she put pressure on it, but he was too weak to fight it.

Footsteps pounded the stairs outside, and Minnie tensed, looking up at Alex. "Someone's comin'."

"Oliver, get behind me," Alex said, looking wildly about the room. He grabbed the alarm clock off the side table and reared his arm back.

Timothy burst through the doorway, followed closely by Walter. They both had flashlights which they shone on Alex first. "Whoa," Timothy said, holding out his hand, palm outward. "It's just me."

Alex breathed out and put down the alarm clock. "Candice and Annika?"

"They're fine," Walter said. "We checked on them first. Their bedroom is at the back of the house. Whoever attacked did it from the front. They're gone now."

Timothy took in a sharp breath. "I see lights coming from the street!" He rushed to the window.

Minnie's heart jumped into her throat. "Are they back?"

"I think…" Timothy paused. "It's the golf carts."

"The military's come to check on us," Walter said, the relief in his voice reflecting Minnie's own.

"A little late for that," Timothy said.

"To be fair," Alex said, "it seems they got hit, and it wasn't pretty. I'm surprised they got here as fast as they did, actually."

"We heard the explosions." Walter walked over to the broken windows, peered in the direction from which the golf carts had come, and whistled. "That doesn't look good at all."

Minnie's thoughts went straight to Alan, and she bit her lip as she continued to put pressure on Samson's wound. *Please… let Alan be okay*. Her prayers seemed to do some good before, so she kept at it.

"I think that's General Hunt getting out of the cart," Timothy said. "It's hard to tell in the dark."

But seconds later, Minnie heard the front door slam open, and Alan's gruff voice called out. "Minnie? Where are you? Minnie!"

"We're up here!" Minnie shouted.

Several sets of footsteps thundered up the stairs, but Alan was the first to enter. He had a lantern in hand and held it up, illuminating the entire room for the first time. Debris was scattered everywhere: broken glass, splintered wood, the fluff from the mattresses and pillows. "Minnie, you're okay?" he asked.

She nodded. "I am, but Samson… he's shot." She choked up. "He saved Oliver," she said.

A woman paused in the door with a backpack. "Anyone in here need my assistance, sir?" she asked.

Alan looked back at her. "I've got a top priority patient for you, Sergeant Till," he said, nodding toward where Minnie knelt next to Samson.

The sergeant rushed in but paused, her eyes scanning the people in the room.
Minnie scrambled back a bit as Walter and Timothy came over to push aside the bed, giving them more room.
Sergeant Till looked back at Alan. "The… uh… dog, sir?"
"Damn straight," Alan barked.
She jumped a little and then scuttled forward, kneeling next to Samson. Minnie stood up as Till spread a mat on the floor beside Samson and got to work. She pulled out a needle.
"What's that?" Minnie asked.
"Just a sedative," Till said. "So I can work on removing that bullet."
"Will he be okay?"
Till's lips pressed together as she administered the drug. "I'm not a veterinarian," she said, "but… I think I know enough to help. It doesn't look like the bullet hit any organs. It's lodged in his rear, which is good. It's the blood loss we need to worry about," she said glancing at the bloodied floor. "We'll have to hope I got here in time for that."
Minnie stepped back and sat on the edge of the bed. Alan came to her, sitting gently, barely disturbing the mattress. He put an arm around her, and she leaned into him.
"What happened?" she asked. "Who would shoot up a house that has children in it?"
The rest of the room went absolutely silent besides the medic's movements. It seemed no one breathed as they waited collectively for an answer.
Alan's expression darkened. "It had to be the civilians from the arena."
"What?" Timothy asked. "Why would they do that?"
"Who else would it have been?" Alan's clipped words brooked no argument.
And it was a good point. The civilians in Colorado Springs were mostly consolidated into the group running the arena and the mountain complex. They were certainly the largest, best supplied of the survivor groups, and they *did* have a beef with the military.
"Have they done anything like this before?" Alex asked.
"No," Alan said. "But it could be in retaliation for what they think happened with those idiot teens."
Walter came closer. "How would they have gotten past your surveillance?"
"We've got only human eyes and ears, for the most part," Alan said. "We use a few drones to scout out the city on occasion, but we're down to mostly human patrols to keep an eye on our borders. And at night?" He shook his head. "It's insane that they risked it. The swarms are out in full force."
Minnie glanced back at the broken windows, her anxiety spiking again. "Speaking of," she said, "we need to get out of here, Alan. This place isn't safe anymore."
The general nodded. "Agreed. We're going to move you to Polaris Hall tonight."
"It wasn't hit?" Timothy asked. "We heard the explosions. Saw the fire."
"They hit one of our food stores," Alan said. "And the other explosion was in an empty building. We think maybe they thought we were storing weapons there. Bad intel, maybe?" He shook his head. "I don't know. We lost three men, which hits hard these days. We don't have a lot of men to speak of."
The medic looked over her shoulder, a pained expression smoothing as she spoke to the general. "We'll need to be careful transferring the dog," she said. "I'm going to get a couple guys to help."
"Go ahead, Till," Alan said. "I think other injuries can be tended when we get everyone to safety." He glanced at Alex. "If you agree, that is. I see you were hit."
"I would appreciate something to numb the pain," Alex said. "But otherwise, yes. It can wait half an hour."
Till dug around in her bag and brought out a paste and a pill bottle. "This is topical cream. It will numb the area. And this is a painkiller." She handed them to Alex on her way out. "I'll be right back."
Alan stood. "Let's get all of you to a safer location."
"Give us a few minutes to pack our stuff," Alex said. "We'll be out front in a minute."
"Minnie," Alan said, turning to her. "I—"
Sergeant Till rushed back in. "Sir! There's a fight on the front lawn."
Alan stiffened. "Are the civilians back?"
"No, sir." Till shook her head, grimacing. "It's Cadets Sumner and Hallifax."
Alan cursed and growled before addressing Alex. "A few minutes, then," he said. "I've got some heads to knock, it seems." He stormed out, the medic scurrying after.
"Land's sake," Minnie said, standing and shuffling over to the window. The brawl on the lawn looked serious. "Those two have their stingers out." She frowned down at them, gasping as the two grappling men pushed off each other and one shadowy figure decked the other.
"General Boreland has the right idea!" one of them shouted. "We can't let this slide, Sumner."
"Boreland is a drunk has-been," Sumner roared. "Those are *civilians*, not the enemy, Hallifax."
Hallifax scoffed and threw his hand wide across the distant glow of burning buildings. "Oh really? Because it seems like we're dealing with an enemy right now."
"Hey!" Alan stomped outside, and the two young men faced him, both of them clasping hands in front of them. "Are you two idiots done? Here we are, sitting ducks for the swarms, and you two are duking it out instead of doing your damn jobs."
Sumner shifted his weight from foot to foot and pointed at Hallifax. "Sir, he's talking some nonsense about doing whatever it takes to get the mountain back. Boreland—"
"That's General Boreland to you Cadet!" Alan shouted, getting right up into Sumner's face.
"See?" Hallifax said. "Even General Hunt understand—"

Alan stepped over to loom over Hallifax. "Don't pretend to know my mind, Cadet. I'm disgusted by your behavior, the both of you! Who here decides our next move?" The two of them mumbled something, and Alan looked between them. "I can't hear you, Cadets!" The two answered loudly in unison: "The President of the United States, sir!"

"That's right," Alan stepped back, though Minnie imagined he was no less intimidating to the young pups before him. Every word remained laced with authority. "Whatever options General Boreland and I bring to the table, it's the *president* who will give the final order. And we will obey, won't we?"

"Yes, sir!" they said, again in unison.

Minnie stepped back from the window and looked at Alex, who had come to the window to listen with her. "This ain't good," she said. "I don't know exactly what they're talkin' about, what this Boreland wants them to do, but… it's not good, Alex. I know it."

"You don't think they'll retaliate, do you?" Timothy asked. "Heather, Lauren, and Lizzy are still with the civilians." He added as if it were an afterthought, "Azalea, too."

Alex shook his head. "No," he said. "They have people on the inside, too. They won't do anything to put our people into harm's way, not when they know what's at stake."

"Or at least," Walter said, "they won't do anything crazy until we have the information we need, until our people and theirs are out of there. If the president actually has the power his position is supposed to carry, that is."

"President Coleman does have control over his own forces, right?" Timothy asked.

Alex shifted uncomfortably. "I… don't know," he said. "He seems to. I think so."

The three of them stood there for a long second before they broke apart, none of them adding any more to the conversation. Minnie packed her things, the question Timothy had asked still lingering in her brain. As they all, including Samson, were ferried away from the duplex in the little golf carts, Minnie couldn't help but think through the implications of Alex's answer to that disturbing question. If there's a question of the president's control, she thought, who exactly is his opposition?

Chapter 28

Heather Peters

Heather held the ultrasound picture gingerly, careful not to smudge the image or wrinkle the shiny paper. She'd set a battery-operated lantern in the corner, the white light turned down to a soft glow. Never had a tiny grey blob been so beautiful. And so incredibly frightening. Laying there, warm beneath blankets, she felt the missing presence of her husband more acutely than she could have imagined. All she wanted was to show Timothy that picture, to share with him the sound of their baby's heartbeat, to hear him tell her it was all going to be okay. Lauren had done that last part, but it was clear she wouldn't approve of the thoughts occupying much of Heather's headspace the last couple of days.

And why would she? Heather asked herself. How could she understand? Do I even understand what I want?

She looked up at the bottom of the top bunk, listening to Lauren breathe. It was early, but Heather hadn't been able to sleep any longer. She hadn't wanted to disturb Lauren, though, and since they'd both had showers the day before, neither of them were allowed another quite yet. And so the only thing left for her to do had been to think, and all she *could* think about was the life growing inside her.

This is my last chance, she thought. My last chance to bring a baby to term, to have a child of my own.

It was crazy, of course. She knew that. The world was churning with death and destruction. Any day could be her last, and resources were tight.

Out there. She glanced around at the little suite. *In here, though…*

There was still the fact that Timothy had made himself unwelcome, but the people she'd met so far seemed like good people.

If I can befriend them, make them understand what Tim was doing up here, why we went to the military… we're only after information. And that information will help make their world a safer place. She put a hand on her belly. The people here want to protect mothers and children.

But Lauren was right about one thing: they were there for another reason. After considering it all morning, Heather had come to a decision. She wouldn't jeopardize their mission to get into the offline database. Both her personal agenda and the agenda of the group relied on building friendships within the community, and she saw no reason she couldn't attempt to diverge from that after Lauren, Conner, Lizzy, and Azalea were safely out of the complex.

Or… maybe Lizzy and Azalea would want to stay. Antarctica is no place for two young women, right? That thought encouraged Heather even more. This is the right thing. For me, for Timothy, for the baby. For the girls. I mean, maybe Candice and Annika could stay, too.

The picture of the people she cared about being accepted into the mountain complex, of them all living safely, happily… it made Heather smile.

I'd just have to convince Timothy to stop fighting. She sighed at that, but then smiled again. Or convince him to fight for something else. We helped bring Boston together. Maybe we could do the same for Colorado Springs, bring the civilians and the military to a peaceful resolution.

The truth was that Walter and Alex *needed* to go to Antarctica. Kai, too, since he was helping to fly the plane, but the rest of them had already done so much. What more could they do?

Lauren snorted and mumbled something unintelligible in her sleep. Heather bit her lower lip, took one last look at the sonogram, and carefully slid it back into its envelope. She grabbed the lantern, got up, and crossed the room to store it in the top dresser drawer. When she turned around, she lifted the lantern, let the glow illuminate Lauren's sleeping form.

She'd never stay, even if she could, Heather thought. She'll want to go with Alex.

The two of them—Alex and Lauren—had both lost life partners, Lauren her fiancé and Alex his wife. It was clear to Heather, though, that they'd developed a special sort of bond over their time together. And while it could take months or years for them to move on from what they'd lost and embrace what they had found, Heather believed the two of them belonged together, if they could both survive the trials ahead.

Lauren blinked and groaned. "Heather," she said, "what time is it?"

"Six-thirty-ish," Heather said.

Lauren threw her blanket over her head, her voice muffled. "How long have you been up?"

"A while." Heather turned and set the lantern on the dresser. "Couldn't sleep."

"I think we're supposed to use that lantern for, like, going to the bathroom and stuff," Lauren said.

"I know." Heather shrugged. "I just… I was looking at the sonogram."

Lauren peeked out from the blanket, her hair a mess, and smiled. "That was pretty cool, huh? Hearing the baby's heartbeat?"

Heather laughed. "Yeah, it was pretty cool. Amazing, actually." Her smile faded. "Kind of scary, though, too."

"We're going to figure it out," Lauren said. "I promise, we're going to do whatever it takes to support you, okay?"

Even if that means helping convince these people to let me stay? But she kept that thought to herself. Instead, Heather nodded. "I appreciate that," she said.

"Well, I think at 6:30 we can turn on the lights," Lauren said. "Might as well get ready, go down to The Granite Inn for breakfast."

Heather walked over, flipped the light switch, and then turned off the lantern. To conserve energy, the complex had a lights out policy from 10 p.m. to 6:30 a.m. That was all well and good. Any use of electricity or plumbing was a luxury for which Heather was grateful.

The two of them took another half hour or so to dress and navigate the halls to the little cafeteria. Breakfast was modest: bread, butter, and canned fruit. The woman handing out the food gave Heather a big smile and added a boiled egg to her plate.

"For the baby," she said.

Heather raised her eyebrows. "News travels fast around here," she said.

"It sure does," the woman said, her smile widening. "Pregnant and nursing women get the best care we can afford. Will you be going to the Expecting Mothers Circle?"

"Yeah," Heather said, "that's the plan."

As she and Lauren took a seat, Lauren eyed Heather's egg. "I think you and I are going to have two very different days."

"I have no idea what to expect," Heather said. "Carrie said my job here is to grow a baby, and that expecting mothers are only able to participate in limited work. Nothing physically stressful, I guess."

"Meanwhile," Lauren said, "I've got a ten-hour shift ahead of me at the clinic."

Heather chose her words carefully so as to not sound suspicious to the others eating breakfast nearby. "I think we'll both be in a good position to make new friends," she said.

"Honestly, I'm hoping I'll get word about our old friends while working in the clinic," Lauren said. "I'm... anxious for them to get here."

"Me too," Heather said. "I'm also looking forward to that card game Carrie invited us to. It seems like a good opportunity to get to know people."

Lauren nodded. "Seven o'clock tomorrow. For tonight, though, I think we just lie low."

"Yeah," Heather said. "Sounds like a plan."

When the two of them had eaten breakfast, they parted ways, Lauren to the clinic and Heather to the Expecting Mother's Circle, which was in the newest facility. All the buildings were connected, the hallways making the entire complex seem almost like one big building. But the transition into the newest facility, Building Sixteen, was clear.

White walls turned to a pleasant cream color. The floor became faux wood. Art pieces hung in intervals, and there was a pleasant vanilla scent as she entered a lobby. A woman behind a desk stood at Heather's arrival.

"Heather?" she asked.

"Um, yes," Heather said. "And you are?"

"Jewels," she said. "I'm working hospitality today."

"Nice to meet you," Heather said.

"You're here for the Expecting Mothers Circle?" Jewels asked.

Heather nodded.

"Right this way." Jewels gestured for Heather to follow.

"So..." Heather said. "Hospitality, huh? I guess that's your job down here?"

Jewels smiled at her. "No, actually. I'm an architect. But everyone who becomes a permanent resident has hospitality in their regular work rotation. No one here is above serving the community in humble ways."

"I like that," Heather said.

"Me too." Jewels turned down another hallway. "It's what this place is about. Equal treatment for everybody. Making sure no one gets a big head. Even Mark does hospitality."

"Mark?" Heather asked. "Who is he, again?"

"Kind of like our leader, I guess." Jewels shrugged. "He was a supervisor over the construction of this building, and he was the one who organized everyone in the beginning. If it wasn't for him, we wouldn't be here. A lot of us would probably be dead. He still refers to himself as a supervisor, when he uses titles at all."

"And he does hospitality?" Heather asked, quirking an eyebrow.

Jewels laughed. "Yep. Delivers fresh sheets from the laundry, checks in on residents, guides newcomers like I'm doing now, delivers food to anyone who can't make it to the diner for one reason or another. He even cleans the lobby bathrooms."

"I guess I'm impressed," Heather said. "Leaders don't usually do those types of things."

"That's the point," Jewels said. She stopped in front of a pair of wooden doors. "Here we are!" She smiled and opened the door for Heather. "Have fun."

Heather walked in to find a circle of women sitting on various types of pillows, all of whom were in various stages of pregnancy, she assumed. A few of them had clearly gotten pregnant before Day Zero, but there were some whose flat stomachs put them in the same trimester as Heather. They were conversing amongst themselves, but several of them turned their heads to look at Heather as she approached.

An older woman, perhaps in her sixties, though fit and toned, sat on an exercise ball. She was part of the circle, though clearly not pregnant. "Heather!" The older woman spread her arms in greeting. "Welcome. I'm the midwife. You can call me Vivian." She made a parting motion with her hands. "Make some room, ladies!"

Heather offered a small wave and a smile, her cheeks growing hot at the attention. "Thanks," she said as she sat between two women, one of whom was *very* pregnant.

"I think we're all here," Vivian said, clapping her hands. "Let's do some quick introductions for Heather's sake, then we'll move on to a little light yoga."

Heather paid attention to names as the other seven pregnant women introduced themselves and revealed how far along they were and how long they'd been at Cheyenne Mountain.

"And Heather," Vivian said, "tell us a little about you."

"Well," Heather said, swallowing hard. "I'm new, obviously." She laughed nervously. They were all so… happy, so far removed from the anxious reality of the outside world. They laughed with her, encouraging her to continue. "I'm about five or six weeks along," Heather said. "I'm… really glad to be here. It's a little surreal, though. I've been in pure survival mode for so long. This place is nothing like the mess out there."

Vivian nodded, her expression sympathetic. "It might take a while for you to let go of that feeling of being unsafe all the time," she said. "Stress isn't good for your baby, though, so we're going to do our best to help you relax and feel at home in our community."

"Thank you," Heather said. "I… I don't know what else to say, except that: thank you *so* much."

The women moved on to the yoga, each woman grabbing a mat from the corner of the room. Heather did her best to follow Vivian's movements, and at the end of it, she felt better than she had in months. A short break was called, and Heather filled a stainless-steel water bottle Vivian had gifted her with water from a dispenser.

"Heather?"

A voice spoke up behind her, and she turned around. "Um, Emily, right?" Heather asked.

"That's right," Emily said. "I just wanted to invite you over. My husband and I thought you might enjoy a private lunch tomorrow in our apartment. Mark thinks he can swing a few steaks to welcome you to the complex."

"Mark, as in… the supervisor, Mark?" Heather asked. Her heart leapt. Making friends with the leader of the civilians would go a long way. If anyone knew where the offline database was located, she suspected it would be him. Emily looked at her questioningly, and Heather added quickly, "Jewels mentioned his name on the way here."

She nodded. "Ah, yes. I see. Mark likes to go by just 'Mark' unless he's leading his team, and then he's fine with 'boss.'"

"Noted," Heather said. "So, do you guys invite all the newbies over or just the ones with morning sickness?"

Emily chuckled. "Well, nothing against your friend, Lauren, but since I'm pregnant, too, I sort of asked Mark about you. If you stay, our kids will be friends, and… I just think we should be friends, too."

Heather nodded. "I'm in," she said. "Carrie did invite Lauren and I to a card game tomorrow at The Granite Inn, but that's not until seven at night."

"Aren't you the social butterfly?" Emily tapped Heather's arm playfully.

"Not usually," Heather said. "I'm usually the last one to make friends."

"Well, not here," Emily said. "Every woman in this room wants to get to know you, Heather. You're going to be surrounded by friends, safe and sound with your baby."

Vivian called an end to their break, and Emily looped her arm with Heather's, pulling her back toward the yoga mats. Heather let the woman lead her, hoping what Emily said would stand up to the test if they ever found out what Heather was really there to do.

Heather sat with Emily in a circle of women, each spot complete with a small basket of sewing supplies and pieces of clothing. The midwife explained their next activity would be mending clothes for the children already inside the complex.

Heather made herself comfortable, picking out a pair of small socks. Her baby was healthy. She and Lauren were making connections with the right people, people who could know where the database was, people who could have some influence when it came to letting Timothy inside.

For once, things were going well. Of course, she had to lie to everyone, to Lauren about her intention to stay, and to everyone else about her intention to steal information for the military. And she wasn't very good at telling lies. There was also the fact that if something went wrong with her pregnancy, the thing that set her apart and made her special, the thing that made her worthy of inviting over for lunch, would be gone, and she'd be sent back to the arena. And if they were caught? Heather wasn't sure what the civilians would do.

Stress isn't good for the baby, she thought as she pushed away the negative thoughts threatening to disturb the hope she'd managed to latch onto. Instead, she let that hope take root.

Heather found the little hole in the toe of the tiny sock and got to work, imagining the article of clothing was for her own child. Her resolve doubled as she mended. No matter what it took, Heather was going to find a way to make the civilians see that her family belonged within the safety of that mountain.

Chapter 29

Alexander Roman

Alex leaned against the doorway of the office-turned-animal-hospital, watching Oliver sit next to Samson, reading out loud a copy of *The Call of the Wild* by Jack London. General Hunt had found it in the campus library upon Oliver's request. The main character was a dog, and Oliver had thought Samson would like it. The dog lay on a pallet of blankets, his head on Oliver's lap, licking Oliver's hand every so often.

A gentle pressure on his back alerted Alex to Minnie's presence as she patted his back and looked past him into the room. "Peas in a pod, those two," she said. "Sometimes I wonder if Samson's forgotten whose dog he is." She smiled up at him. "Sometimes I wonder if Samson is even still *my* dog."

Alex chuckled. "I think you'll always have a place in his heart, but c'mon, Minnie." Alex gestured toward his son. "Nobody can compete with Oliver. He's just too cute."

Oliver looked up from his book. "I'm too old to be cute, Dad."

Alex folded his arms. "To me? Never." Before Oliver could protest further, Alex continued. "But I suppose I can try a few different descriptors. What would you like me to talk about when I'm bragging about your attributes?"

"And before you answer," Minnie said, shaking her finger at Oliver, "understand that it's just the natural way of things for a father to brag on his boy. It's gonna happen."

Oliver wrinkled his nose. "Ugh. Fine." He let the book fall to his lap and rested a hand on Samson's head. "Do you have any other options for me to choose from?"

"Besides cute?" Alex asked.

"How about winsome?" Minnie asked. "Downright charming. Maybe throw in a little handsome while you're at it."

Oliver sighed and looked down at Samson. "This is embarrassing."

Samson looked up at him sympathetically.

Alex laughed. "That's just a rite of passage," he said. "Honestly, I'm glad. Maybe that means not *everything* about our life right now is completely abnormal." He shrugged. "Every kid thinks their parents are a little embarrassing at some point."

Oliver pursed his lips. "I didn't say a *little*, Dad."

It was Minnie's turn to laugh as Alex's jaw dropped in mock offense. She patted Alex on the back. "*That's* a rite of passage, too, my friend."

Oliver laughed, too, and when the laughter had died down, he smiled up at them. "I guess winsome is fine," he said. "I don't mind a little bragging. Just... don't overdo it."

"No promises." Alex walked across the room and bent down to kiss the top of Oliver's head. He scratched Samson's ears while he was at it and then knelt to look his son in the eyes. "I'm going to be gone most of the day. You listen to Minnie, okay?"

Oliver nodded. "I will." A little worry crept into his eyes as he looked back at him. "Be careful, Dad."

"That I can promise, bud." Alex leaned in and hugged his son. "I'll see you later." After he pulled away, he pointed at Samson. "And you keep healing up. We need you."

Samson offered a small, gruff bark and wagged his tail just slightly. Alex returned to Minnie, said his goodbyes to her, and met Walter at the entrance to Polaris Hall. They'd all stayed there after their previous accommodations had been destroyed by the shooting. Alex's arm still hurt, but the bullet had only grazed him. The medic had stitched the wound closed and dressed it, applying some numbing cream that worked to lessen the pain quite a bit.

"You ready for this?" Walter said as Alex approached.

"I don't particularly feel like working with Ward and Turner today, if that's what you're asking," Alex said. "I might actually be excited about the potential of this project if it wasn't for them."

"Well, I *am* excited," Walter said. "This lure and toxin system could clear the area of swarms."

"I know." Alex tried to ignore a shudder that went up his spine. "But with Ward and Turner involved, I can't help but think they're going to find a way to ruin it or corrupt it. Their ideas back in Atlanta, their goals to find a vaccine or a cure, weren't the problem. It was their methods, how far they were willing to go to do it."

"They have oversight now," Walter said. "Don't worry about it so much. We're alive. We're doing good work. They'd be doing this with or without us; at least this way, we can keep an eye on them, even if only for a little while. Besides, when our people get back from the mountain, we'll leave all this behind. It won't be our problem anymore."

"Yeah," Alex said, nodding. "You're right."

"You two ready to go?" Cadet Lindt asked as she came up from behind them. "I'm supposed to escort you to the bus."

"Good morning, Cadet Lindt," Walter said.

"You can call me Shelly," she said.

"Well, Shelly—" Walter spread out his arm for her to go first. "—lead the way."

She nodded and stepped between them, opening the doors which led to a concrete stairway. Alex followed, keeping step with Walter, up the staircase and into daylight at ground level. They loaded up into a golf cart, and Shelly drove them through the base to where a bus waited. It seemed Cadet Hogan Sumner had escorted Ward, Turner, and Dr. Pullman. There were three other young men in military uniform, plus the older Major Kenny Willis, who approached them once their carts were parked.

"Mr. Roman!" Kenny said enthusiastically. "You're not dead!"

Alex chuckled. "Not yet. Good to see you're still kicking, too."

Kenny scoffed. "Of course I am." He pointed his thumb back over his shoulder. "But this lot might kill me off today. They're... testy."

"What does that mean?" Walter asked.

"Politics." Kenny shrugged. "I guess it's just human nature to pick sides, but I'd thought we'd banded together a little tighter than this, what with all we've been through. Ever since President Coleman showed up..."

"What?" Alex asked when he didn't finish his sentence.

"Well," Kenny cleared his throat, smiled, and waved off his previous comment. "Nevermind," he said. "The point is, I'm over all this infighting. Everyone's too anxious these days."

Alex looked past the major. There was a subtle tension between the soldiers, the way one of them had joined Lindt and Sumner and the other two had hung back, arms crossed and scowls on their faces. Ward and Turner stood behind the two opposite of the cadets, and Dr. Pullman stood by himself, off to the side, studying a paper map. The doctor seemed oblivious to the division, though Ward's expression was one of pure amusement. Turner looked nervous as he occasionally whispered in Ward's direction.

Does this have to do with that fight on the lawn last night? Alex thought.

"Sumner got into it last night over something to do with the mountain complex and General Boreland," Alex said, "but I don't recognize those two."

"They weren't there," Kenny said.

Walter shifted from foot to foot. "Are you saying this is a widespread disagreement?"

Kenny shrugged. "Like I said, human nature. Everybody's picking sides."

"That can't be good." The tension in Alex's body increased along with the urge to leave the base all together. But they had to stay. Not only were their people in the Cheyenne Mountain Complex, but they needed President Coleman to let them take that plane, if Kai and Zara ever returned that was. His stomach churned as thoughts of the two—and the lack of any updates— only increased his anxiety.

"It is what it is," Kenny said. "But rest assured: soldiers follow orders. As long as that stands, we're gonna be fine."

"It sounds like there's disagreement about who should be giving the orders, though," Walter said. "Boreland or Hunt, right?"

Kenny waved off the concern. "Nah. The president is Commander-in-Chief. What he says goes. Period. That's the way it's always been. And it's not like he's disrespected Boreland, like some people seem to think. They're just squabbling because they need something to squabble about. Times are tough. Tensions are high. They're angry and scared, and they need somewhere to direct their emotions. That's all this is."

Alex nodded and shrugged. "Maybe," he said, though Kenny's explanation didn't make him feel any better.

"Well, let's get on that bus." The major turned and approached the divided soldiers, shouting, "Load up before I get the hankering to see you schmucks do pushups!"

The three soldiers and two cadets scurried onto the bus, followed more slowly by the three scientists. Alex and Walter boarded the bus next, and Kenny came up behind them, taking the driver's seat. The back seats had been removed to make room for supplies, including a generator about the size of an air conditioning unit. If they found the right spot, the work to convert a fire protection supply shop into a lab would begin. The soldiers would stand guard to protect against civilians, and some of them would be required to keep guard through the night. That meant the facility had to be secure and safe from swarms.

"All right, Dr. Pullman," Kenny said. "Where am I going?"

Pullman looked up. "I've marked every fire protection supplier in the city according to the phone book." He shook his head. "Never thought one of those would come in handy again." He turned the map around to show a series of marks. "I say we try the closest one on Briargate Boulevard first, and then go from there. It's likely that my information is outdated as the phone book is old, but I'm hoping one of these has been in business long term. All we need is to find one with the equipment to refill extinguishers, preferably one with a stash of extinguishers, too."

"Sounds like a plan," Kenny said. He turned the ignition, and the bus rumbled to life. "We got limited time, though, doc. I'm supposed to get you back here within five hours. All we're doing today is scouting out a location and setting up a guard to ensure the location stays secure."

Alex sat back as the bus lurched forward and slowly gained speed. The road noise and rattle of the bus droned on in a steady, mind-numbing way that left Alex's eyes drooping. He'd not slept much after being woken by flying bullets the previous night. There were conversations, low and quiet, voices adding to the monotonous euphony, but Alex couldn't make out what they were saying. He leaned his forehead on the window and let his eyelids close, telling himself he would just rest his eyes for a moment.

He was woken by the sudden jolt of something slamming into the back of his seat. He sat up with a sharp intake of breath. The bus had stopped. Out the side window, there was a small building with a sign that indicated they were at their destination. Groggy, Alex blinked a few times, looking to Walter who was on his feet facing the back of the bus. His eyes were wide. Kenny was no longer in the driver's seat; he wasn't even on the bus.

"What happened?" Alex asked as he got to his feet.

Sumner got up from the seat behind him, shuffled into the center aisle, and charged a knot of soldiers halfway down. They were all fighting. Ward and Turner were at the very back of the bus, and Ward was grinning, watching eagerly. Dr. Pullman was scrunched up on the third seat, knees to chest, covering his head with his arms.

"The major suited up and went to check on the building," Walter said. "He's been gone maybe ten minutes. And then this fight broke out."

Lindt ducked under the swinging fist of a man who had to be twice her weight. Alex almost stepped forward, an anger brewing at the sight of a man attempting to strike a woman. And then Lindt threw her open palm upward into her attacker's face, and the man's nose *cracked*, a fountain of blood unleashed. He stumbled backward and held his shirt to his nose, pinching it between two fingers, eyes watering.

"Hey!" Alex shouted. "Get it together! Stop it!" Not one of the soldiers or the cadets acknowledged him. Alex sighed and looked back at Walter. "Do you know what it's about?"

"Boreland. The mountain." Walter shrugged. "I only caught bits and pieces."

The side door to the bus cranked open, and the major stepped up into the bus. He shut the door behind him and took off his hazmat helmet, his face red and twisted in anger. "What the hell is going on here?" he shouted.

The writhing tangle of men and women froze, and then they all pushed each other away and stood apart, each one straightening their uniforms. All of them had physical signs of the fight: an eye starting to darken and swell, a fat lip, a broken and bleeding nose, a scratch across one cheek.

Kenny's heavy, measured footfalls down the aisle and his low, growling voice sent a shudder down even Alex's spine. "Someone better explain before I throw you all out and go back to base to get some *disciplined* soldiers. You lot can fend for yourselves out there if you can't behave. You understand me?"

The soldiers and cadets answered in unison: "Yes, sir!"

His back now to Alex, the veins on his neck popping, his voice still dark and low, Kenny spoke again as if through gritted teeth. "Then one of you better tell me right now what this is about."

"We're sick of people disrespecting General Boreland," one of the soldiers said.

"Is that right, Tawdry?" Kenny asked. "I'm guessing you're talking about Lindt, Sumner, and Ponte?"

"Yes, sir," Tawdry said. He nodded at his companion. "Me and Coors are loyal. Those three are turncoats."

Kenny crossed his arms. "Is that right?"

"Liars!" Lindt pointed at the two who'd been sitting with Ward and Turner when they'd left. "We take orders from the president. They're talking treason, Major Willis."

Coors and Tawdry each took one step toward the other side, but Kenny shouted, "One more step, and you're out on your asses." He sighed. "Lindt, what are you talking about?"

"General Boreland has started saying we should charge the complex, sir," Lindt said. "President Coleman's orders are to stand down, and General Hunt—"

Coors scoffed. "General Hunt knows nothing about our city or the conflict with the civilians. If the president and his entourage had arrived just a few days later, General Boreland would have already taken the complex back."

"Yeah, right," Ponte said. "Maybe if he could walk straight. Too bad he can't go without a drink every two seconds."

"He wasn't like that before they came into our territory and pushed him out!" Tawdry raised his voice.

"No, he wasn't like that before Lawson and Price started getting to him," Ponte responded, his voice going higher. "I care about General Boreland. He was a good man. But those two have gotten in his head!"

"Hold on," Willis shouted. "Boreland *is still* a good man. You all need to cool it, acting like there's some big division up top when the president is working with *both* generals and taking *both* of their opinions into account."

Alex startled at the mention of Lawson and Price, his heartbeat racing. "Wait," he said as he finished processing the implications, his eyes going to Ward and Turner at the back. Turner looked away, but Joanna met his eyes with a haughty gaze. Alex swallowed hard and looked back at the soldiers. "What do you mean, Lawson and Price? They're imprisoned. How are they getting into his head?"

"They're not!" Tawdry said. "It's a stupid rumor."

Sumner shook his head. "No, it's not. I've seen him visit them."

"He's in charge of them, you idiots!" Coors yelled.

"Is he in charge of bringing them extra rations?" Sumner asked. "Since when did supervising prisoners include having lunch with them? He's grasping at power, trying to get dirt on the president through his father-in-law."

"Hold on, now!" Kenny said. "All of you, sit the hell down and take a breath. This is ridiculous. General Hunt and General Boreland are on the same team. And they're both advisors to the president. President Coleman has known General Hunt for longer, that's all, and I'll hear no more accusations thrown around about anyone." When none of them moved, he shouted, "I said, *sit*." They all slid into the bus seats, each one looking a little defeated.

Alex stepped into the aisle. "Kenny, wait. Lawson and Price are dangerous. If there are rumors that General Boreland—"

Kenny rounded on Alex, his expression hardened. "I'm trying to do something here, Mr. Roman. We can't complete this mission if we're all at odds with each other. And rumors are just that: rumors. I won't abide them."

Alex's heart was still beating loudly in his ears, his stomach was churning, and beads of sweat had broken out across his forehead. He lowered his voice to a whisper. "Kenny, if it's true—"

Kenny cut him off. "—you can talk to the powers that be when we get back. I have a job to do, and so do you. Now are we going to do this or not? I can turn this bus back and you can scratch your plans all together."

Dr. Pullman finally unfurled. "No!" he squeaked. "This is *essential*."

Walter stepped forward. "We're good," he said. "You're right. This isn't the place. We'll look into it when we get back."

Alex knew they were right, that talking about it would only stir trouble in a place where nothing helpful could be done, but he hated pushing the topic to the back burner. It made him sick to his stomach, made his hair stand on end. Because sometimes rumors were true.

"Good." Kenny rolled his shoulders back and took a deep breath before letting the air out slowly. "Now, the building is cleared. It seems safe. No cracks or broken windows. No dead bodies."

"Good, good," Dr. Pullman said. "I need to get off this bus. Let's go inspect, shall we?"

Kenny stepped back into the space between two seats and gestured toward the door. "The front door was unlocked when I got here. My guess is that it was abandoned when crap hit the fan and whoever was working here forgot to lock up."

Dr. Pullman stepped into the aisle and started making his way to the bus doors. Alex hung back next to Walter, processing, trying to get his head in the right space to do the work ahead.

"I guess the fun's over," Joanna said as she walked the aisle. She didn't seem the least bit disturbed by what had happened. "Time to get to work."

Turner followed behind her, his shoulders hunched slightly, and he didn't look at Alex as he passed.

Maybe he knows something, Alex thought. If he does, between him and Joanna, he's the one that would crack. If I can get him alone…

Alex followed after Turner, his mind split between the project and finding out more about the conflict between those who trusted Boreland and those who trusted Hunt and Coleman. The rest disembarked, each one staying in line as Kenny had ordered, but the tensions remained. Whatever was going on, Alex didn't like it. If things got bad, there was nowhere to go, not until Lauren, Heather, Lizzy, and Azalea returned from the mountain.

And if the last two months are any indication, Alex thought, it's not if there's trouble, it's when.

Chapter 30

Alexander Roman

They'd gotten lucky. The first supplier they'd scouted had what they needed. They unloaded what they'd brought and started moving things around in the shop, creating space for what would be a little laboratory where they could create the mosquito lure and the toxin. Despite their good fortune, Alex's mood had only darkened. Joanna Ward was glued to Turner's side. She wouldn't let him out of her sight long enough for Alex to attempt to pry more information out of him. He was certain that if he could get Turner alone, he would find some answers as to whether the rumors about Boreland were true.

As they were wrapping up, Alex decided to try one more thing to get the man alone. Eyes set on Turner, he stepped away from the table where he and Walter had just finished arranging the tools they'd use the next day.

"Wait," Walter said, grabbing Alex's upper arm and forcing him to pause. "Do you really think that's a good idea?"

Alex pulled his arm free. "We need answers."

"We can get them back at the academy, like Kenny said." Walter crossed his arms. "This place is a powder keg. It's been ridiculously tense all day, and the major has been working hard to keep everyone civil."

"I'm not going to talk to any of these hothead soldiers," Alex said. "I'm after Turner. He knows something."

"Except those hothead soldiers might just step in if you go after him," Walter said.

Alex looked over at Turner who was examining the equipment they'd be using to refill the extinguishers. The man was low to the ground, tapping and moving tubes, his expression one of concentration. Ward was several feet away, berating Lindt for misplacing something; she had turned her back on her co-conspirator.

"She's distracted," Alex said. "I'm going in." He made a beeline for Turner and squatted beside him. "Hey, Blake. What are you looking at?"

"We need a user manual for this system," he said, standing up and looking around the room. "I think I understand the gist of it, but we need to make sure we do things exactly right. I also want to make sure these tubes will stand up to the toxin."

Alex nodded. "Agreed. We wouldn't want to rupture a pressurized extinguisher."

"Especially with our Piranha Solution 2.0." Turner stood and ran his fingers through his hair. "As for the tubes, we might need to risk it. Replace the tubes if they wear down too quickly. Use extreme caution as we work."

"It will be most dangerous after it's turned to fog, when it's released from the extinguisher," Alex said as he got to his feet. "As long as we use precautions, we should be reasonably safe as we create the system."

"I'd still like to see that manual," Turner said.

"I'll help you look for it," Alex said.

Turner narrowed his eyes at Alex. "Why are you being nice to me?"

"I'm just trying to do the work." Alex nodded across the room at an office. "There's a filing cabinet in there. I bet that's where it is."

"You can't stand the sight of me, and now you want to go on a little egg hunt with me?" Turner shook his head. "What do you want?"

Alex did his best not to scowl. He glanced around and lowered his voice. "I need to know what's going on with Boreland. You've said before that you're just a company man, that you're not a monster. Well, prove it. Tell me what's going on so I can protect my family."

"Look, man," Turner said, also lowering his voice, "all I can say is that Lawson is a smart guy. He knows how to get to people. He knew how to manipulate Coleman back in Atlanta. Hell, he even knew how to manipulate you."

"And he knows how to manipulate Boreland? Is that what you're saying?" Alex asked.

"I don't know." Turner shrugged. "I haven't seen him since we got here."

"Has Joanna?" Alex asked.

Turner swallowed hard and looked away.

Alex's stomach sank as Turner remained silent. "Blake, has she been allowed contact with him?"

"Excuse me, Alex, but I think my colleague and I need to chat." Ward's voice broke into their conversation as she stepped into Alex's periphery. She took Turner by the elbow and tugged him away, but Alex grabbed hold of the man, too.

"We weren't done," Alex said, his voice low, nearly a growl.

"Yeah, you are." Coors came up behind Alex and gave him a push away from Turner and Ward. "They're just doing their jobs."

Tawdry looked up from across the room. "What's going on?" He joined Coors in a few long strides. "Why don't you leave Joanna and Blake alone? Let them do their jobs. Maybe that will leave you with the time to actually do yours, Mr. Roman."

Alex gawked at the two soldiers. "You do realize that these two are *criminals*, right?"

"Innocent until proven guilty," Coors said.

Alex threw up his hands. "We're way past that point, fellas."

Coors crossed his arms. "It seems to me they've been doing everything they can to make this city safe. Isn't it true that they came up with this whole idea in the first place? They were going to get rid of the swarms in Colorado Springs way before you got here."

"We have worked *so* hard," Ward said, her lower lip puckering just slightly. "All I've ever wanted was to put right what's gone horribly wrong."

"She's lying," Alex said. "All she wants is free rein to conduct sick experiments."

"Oh, I think you have me confused with Mr. Peters over there," Joanna said, giving a little wave to Walter who was still where Alex had left him across the room.

Alex looked over his shoulder at Walter, who looked confused at the attention. He waved back, and Alex groaned. "Walter is trying to redeem himself, and you know that."

"So," Tawdry said, "he can have redemption, the guy who rubber stamped DV-10, but she can't?"

"My thoughts exactly," Ward said, placing her hand over her heart.

"You *enjoy* other people's pain, Joanna," Alex said. "I can see right through you."

Turner had gone back to avoiding eye contact while Ward seemed like she couldn't get enough of it. She clearly feigned offense, though the two soldiers didn't seem to recognize the act for what it was.

"Just back off," Tawdry said. "You see a criminal. We see two scientists who we need to be at their best. You're here for a minute, but you'll be gone soon. We need them."

The front door of the shop opened, the bells still tied to it ringing. "The surrounding area seems clear," he said. "No civil—" He stopped and frowned. "What's going on here?"

"Mr. Roman was just about to start minding his own business," Coors said.

"I for one," Ward chimed in, "have been deeply offended by his accusations. I don't think I can work like this, Major Willis."

Kenny's expression darkened. "A word, Alex. Right. Now."

Alex worked his jaw back and forth, but he nodded and followed Kenny back outside and onto the bus. "You can't summon me like a kid to the principal's office, Ken—"

"The hell I can't." Kenny rounded on Alex.

Alex narrowed his eyes, doing his best to keep his tone calm. "Look—"

"No, *you* look." Kenny poked Alex's chest with his finger. "It's my job to make sure this goes off without a hitch, that you all get back safe and sound. I told you, we aren't talking about rumors today. I need peace, and I'm going to get it, either through cooperation or through duct tape. Got it?"

Alex blanched. "You don't understand."

"I do, believe it or not." Kenny raised his eyebrows. "Did you ever think maybe it's *you* who doesn't understand? It's not safe anywhere anymore. We get in a fight, let our guard down, those civilians could come at us. Those soldiers and cadets lost friends in that attack. Emotions are high. That makes us all vulnerable. When we get back, you can take up your grievances and ask your questions with the president. Not with my people. My people need to unite, or division could be the death of us."

He's right. The thought hit him like a punch to the gut. He'd been brash and arrogant. Even if he'd gotten answers out of Turner, he wouldn't have been able to do anything about it until they got back to base. In the meantime, the only thing he managed to accomplish was to force Tawdry and Coors to step in on behalf of the two scientists, further solidifying the alliance between them.

"I… didn't look at it like that." Alex's cheeks burned hot. "I'm sorry. I'll leave your people out of it. But when we get back, I do need to speak to President Coleman."

"That'll be up to him," Kenny said.

Alex nodded. "Fair enough."

"Good." Kenny nodded. "Now, we've unloaded everything we brought. Coors and Sumner are staying behind to stand guard, and Coors is going to get started hooking up the generator. Hopefully, having to work together will be good for those two knuckleheads. The rest of us are going back."

Alex didn't argue. He needed to get back to base and direct his questions and concerns at someone who could do something about them. The two of them went back inside the shop, and Alex helped wrap up their task for the day. The shop was ready for them to come back, set up their lab, and get to work.

The bus ride back was quiet. Tawdry sat with Ward and Turner. Lindt sat closer to Alex and Walter. Dr. Pullman remained on his own, scribbling in his notebook, seemingly unconcerned about the implications of the rumors about Lawson and Price gaining the ear of General Boreland.

"The second this bus stops," Alex said softly as they approached the academy, "we need to find Hunt and get an audience with the president."

"All right," Walter said. "Just don't go demanding things. Be more diplomatic, you know?"

Alex frowned. "What?"

Walter sighed. "You have to know when the situation calls for vinegar and when it calls for honey."

"You sound like Minnie," Alex said. "Look, this isn't a business deal, Walter. This is serious."

"Whatever you say." Walter held his hands up as if in surrender. "Let's just ignore how your whole cowboy thing backfired less than an hour ago."

"Now you sound like Timothy," Alex said.

"If I sound like both Minnie and Tim," Walter said, "doesn't that mean you ought to listen? Both of them are better people than me, and if I'm not mistaken, they've both earned your trust."

"So have you, Walter." Alex leaned his head back and sighed. "I've just got this feeling in the pit of my stomach… whatever's going on, I don't think it's something we should take lightly."

"Then don't," Walter said. "Just be smart about how you approach it. Remember who you are. Remember who you're talking to. Think about their needs. The best thing you can do is to align what you want with what they need. Make it their idea and guide the conversation gently. You don't have the power or the position to bulldoze through this one."

"That sounds easier said than done," Alex said.

Outside, the bus passed the perimeter guard. Small columns of smoke still rose from the two locations the civilians had bombed. Kenny parked on the outskirts of the base where the golf carts from that morning were still waiting for them. They switched modes of transportation, Lindt driving Alex and Walter, Tawdry driving Ward and Turner, and Kenny driving Dr. Pullman. Alex was deep in thought about what Walter had said as they turned onto Chapel Drive.
"Do you hear that?" Lindt asked.
Alex frowned and refocused his attention. "Is that… shouting?" he asked.
Walter nodded. "I think so."
Lindt stiffened. "I'm going to park in front of Harmon Hall. We should proceed with caution, just in case there's been another attack."
Ahead of them, Kenny seemed to have the same idea. The two parked in front of the long building that mostly blocked their view of Polaris Hall, and Tawdry pulled up behind them. There was a throughway under the second floor, right at the center of Harmon Hall, that let them see a crowd in the courtyard beyond. They were clearly agitated. Alex immediately reached for the zipper, his hands shaking as he thought about his son.
Lindt turned in her seat. "Whoa, hold on a second, Mr. Roman. You need to stay behind me and Major Willis."
"My son is in Polaris Hall," Alex said, continuing to open his door.
"I know," Lindt said. "But we don't know what's going on, and we're the ones with the weapons."
Ahead of them, Kenny got out of his cart, leaving Dr. Pullman behind. The doctor didn't seem eager to move, and the major wasn't giving him orders to get out. Instead, Kenny walked quickly back toward their cart. Behind, Tawdry was already out. Alex scowled as Ward sat back in her seat and waved at him, a smile on her face. It seemed the two scientists weren't getting out of their carts, either.
Walter had already unzipped his side and was stepping out when Kenny raised a hand and repeated Lindt's warning. "We're not rushing in there," he said. "Cool your jets." He pointed at Tawdry. "Soldier, we can't leave our charges unattended."
Tawdry nodded and said, "Yes, sir. I'll take Dr. Pullman back to the other cart, escort the scientists back to the clinic where it's for sure safe."
"Good thinking," Kenny said. He looked at Alex and Walter as if contemplating what to do with them.
Outside, Alex planted his feet firmly next to Walter. "I'm not going anywhere," he said.
"Figured as much," Kenny said. "Tawdry, leave Mr. Peters and Mr. Roman here. Take the others." He quirked an eyebrow at Alex. "Don't make me regret this."
Every heartbeat pulsed through Alex's entire body, thrumming in his ears, making the veins in his neck throb. "I'll follow your lead, but if my son is in danger, don't try to stop me from getting to him."
"That goes for me, too," Walter said. "We've both got family in there."
"We'll help you get to your family, if it comes to that," Kenny said. "All I hear right now is something akin to a minor riot. I don't see an enemy, and no one is running. They're congregating. Something has happened, but I don't think your family members are in immediate danger."
Alex exchanged a look with Walter, and they nodded to each other. Alex restrained himself, following Lindt and Major Willis through to the courtyard. Behind, Tawdry drove away with Pullman, Ward, and Turner.
Kenny seemed to be right. There was definitely something wrong, but the only people in sight were soldiers, and no one had any weapons drawn. About twenty soldiers blocked the staircase that descended into Polaris Hall and a group of at least that many were shouting, demanding answers.
"They're separated into two sides," Alex shouted over the din.
"Is this about Boreland and Hunt?" Walter asked.
"Maybe," Lindt said.
Kenny shook his head. "What is going on? You three, stay here." He stalked forward and marched right between the two groups. He *was* intimidating, but not even he could fend off that many people.
"What is he doing?" Alex took a step after him, but Lindt put out a hand, indicating he should stop.
"Let's just follow orders for now," she said.
"What the hell?" Kenny shouted as the soldiers and cadets began to quiet at his presence. "All of you, shut up and get yourselves together."
Those guarding Polaris Hall did as asked, and about half of those on the other side fell back a few steps and quieted.
"The attack was *their* fault!" A young man shouted as he pointed in the direction of Polaris Hall.
"Your fellow soldiers?" Kenny asked, confusion written all over his face. "Son—"
"No, sir!" the man said. "The newcomers. The civilians. They led the enemy right to us."
Alex looked at Walter, his stomach churning. "They're talking about us," he said quietly.
"They were almost killed in that attack!" Kenny shouted. "You're spouting nonsense! The president has vouched for the whole lot of them. They sent their own into that mountain undercover to help us. They're willing to risk their lives to end this nightmare for the rest of us!"
The soldiers behind him mumbled their agreement, but dissent rose from the hostile group.
"I can't make out what they're saying," Alex said as their shouts melded together.
"Something about dead soldiers," Walter said.

Lindt frowned and looked back at them. "They're saying none of you were really hurt in the shootout, that it was all for show." She shifted uncomfortably.
"That's ridiculous," Alex said. "Our dog was almost killed."
"Yeah, but none of you were seriously injured," Lindt said.
Walter's mouth gaped. "You… you don't believe them?"

Lindt's cheeks reddened. "No," she said, "of course not." But her tone said otherwise.

"Quiet!" Kenny yelled. "What the hell brought this about? Why are we suddenly turning on our own?"

A woman from behind him stepped forward. "There was an incident, sir. Of the party that went to bring back the pilot, only the two civilians returned. They're in quarantine, and General Hunt has gone to speak with them through the trailer doors."

Alex took in a sharp breath. "Zara and Kai are back?"

He spoke a little too loudly and someone at the back of the hostile group turned around, recognition blooming in his expression as he met Alex's gaze.

"Hey!" the soldier yelled. "There's one of them! Maybe they can explain how three trained soldiers are dead while two untrained civilians came back alive."

Another of the hostile soldiers turned. "Are your people in the mountain going to betray Conner?"

A barrage of angry questions and accusations were pelted in their direction as the crowd turned toward them.

"Who are you, really?"

"It's your fault our friends are dead!"

"What did they promise you?"

"Admit it! You're working with the arena!"

"Walter Peters is a terrorist!"

"Once a terrorist, always a terrorist!"

A dozen soldiers surged toward them. Lindt took long strides forward, holding up her hands, demanding that they stop. She was easily pushed aside.

Alex took a step back. "No!" he shouted back. "You're wrong. We're on your side!"

"Alex," Walter said, tugging on his arm, "we have to run!"

But it was too late. The mob pressed in, the anger palpable. They were surrounded.

Chapter 31

Minnie Stevens and Alexander Roman

Someone had poked the hornet's nest, and Minnie would be darned if she was going to let Alex bear the brunt of their stinging fury. She'd left Oliver and Samson with Candice and Annika at the first sign of trouble. Timothy had already been there, pacing at the bottom of the concrete staircase at the entrance to Polaris Hall.

"Do you know what's got their panties in a twist?" Minnie had asked as a few soldiers burst out through the doors, ran past her, and joined their fellows at the top of the stairs.

"No," Timothy had said. "I've been listening to their shouting, and all I can say for sure is that some of them are protecting the president—" He'd nodded back inside where President Coleman was calling the shots, safe and secure for the time being. "—and by extension, us. The other half, the mob… they're angry. At Coleman, at *us*, I think."

"Land's sake! What for?" Minnie had put her hands on her hips.

Timothy had shrugged. "I'm trying to listen to find out."

The two of them had crept up the stairs until they could peer over the top step into the courtyard. Slowly, Minnie started to understand: the issues Alan was having with Boreland, the fight on the front lawn after the shootout, the things the mob was shouting.

They'd become suspicious after the house had been destroyed in a fire fight that hadn't killed any of Minnie's people, and then when Zara and Kai had returned sans their soldiers, the mob had formed, their suspicions fanned to flame. And it had some connection to the division amongst the soldiers concerning the two generals, though Minnie wasn't exactly sure why Boreland would target them with his nasty rumors.

Maybe he's just grasping at straws, trying to find some way to regain power? Minnie thought.

And then she spotted Alex and Walter behind the angry crowd. She willed them to leave, but they were noticed, and the mob turned on them.

Timothy straightened from his crouched position once the word "terrorist" was thrown at his father. "I've got to help," he said.

"What're you gonna do?" Minnie asked.

"I have to get my dad and Alex inside Polaris Hall, try to get a few of these soldiers guarding the entrance to help." Timothy started up the stairs. "You should go back inside."

Minnie snorted. "I ain't no damsel, Timothy Peters," she said.

But Timothy was already at the top of the steps, trying to get a few of the soldiers to come with him. Minnie took another look, trying to assess how she might help get Alex and Walter to safety, but part of the mob had already surrounded them. As Timothy, Major Willis, and a few other soldiers left their posts guarding the entrance, fighting their way toward Alex and Walter, Minnie looked back inside as the right thing to do dawned on her.

She turned and threw open the door, marching through Polaris Hall on a mission. Sunlight poured into the center of the building through a pyramid-like ceiling of glass and steel. The president was surrounded by people in uniform. The tension was palpable as Minnie strode right up to them. A young man stepped in front of her.

"Sorry, ma'am," he said. "You can't come any closer."

Minnie narrowed her eyes and looked past the soldier. "President Coleman," she shouted. "I'm fixin' to talk to you!"

Coleman startled at her shout and turned to look at her. Dark circles under bloodshot eyes spoke of a man who hadn't been sleeping well. He sighed and held up a hand to a man who was talking quietly beside him, and then he walked over to Minnie.

"I have a man outside who's communicating with me," Coleman said. "I swear to you, we are going over our options."

"You need to go out there and put these rumors about us to rest," Minnie said.

"I can't do that," Coleman said. "Even if I wanted to, my security team wouldn't let me. I can't put myself in that kind of danger. And that mob out there isn't the only thing I'm dealing with. General Hunt is out at the quarantine trailers, trying to get information about what happened to our soldiers."

"So, that part's true?" Minnie asked. "Zara and Kai are back?"

Coleman nodded. "And the pilot," he said. "Please, Minnie, go get somewhere safe and—"

"Sir, General Hunt says he's got more information." The man who'd been speaking to the president previously held out a handheld radio, and the president took it.

"What have you got for me, Alan?" Coleman asked.

Alan's voice came in over the radio. "It seems our soldiers were attacked by a pack of diseased wolves," he said. "The pilot helped rescue Zara and Kai. They later convinced Blythe to come back here, but it sounds like they had no choice but to leave the bodies in the wilderness. They did, however, bring back their dog tags." There was a pause.

"Have them finish their quarantine periods, then," Coleman said. "We have a situation here, General. A mob of sorts, soldiers misdirecting their grief, blaming Alex and his people, accusing them of working with the civilians at the arena. Find Boreland. He needs to convince them to stand down. They respect him. They'll listen to him."

Alan cursed before accepting the order with a firm, "Yes, sir."

"That'll take too long," Minnie said. "Alex and Walter are in hot water. By the time Alan gets here, they'll be boiled and served up on a platter!"

"I'm doing what I can," he said.
"Sir," Minnie said, "sometimes, you gotta skin your own skunk."
He wrinkled his nose. "I'm sorry… what?"
"These rumors have made a stink, and you've got to kill 'em off before your entire house reeks," Minnie said. He sighed like he was going to object, and so she pointed back toward the exit. "Go out there and *talk* to them."
President Coleman shook his head. "I told you, I can't."
"Oh, fiddlesticks! Don't be a coward." Minnie pointed back toward the entrance. "You want some good ole' American unity? Prove to them that you're worthy to call yourself president. Remind them of who they are—not hoodlums or anarchists. No, sir! Those men and women might be scared out their damned minds, but they're still Americans who chose to serve their country. Give them back their courage."
President Coleman's eyes widened. "What would you have me do?"
Minnie couldn't help the exasperation in her voice or the volume that came with it. "Get your butt out there and make a damn speech!"
Coleman took half a step back. Minnie cleared her throat as she noticed a few mouths agape at the way she'd raised her voice to the president.
She added, "Mr. President. Sir."
The president looked past Minnie, nodded once and firmly, and turned back to his people. "Somebody get me that bullhorn."

* * *

Alex didn't know how many people had hold of him. Hands grasped his arms, his shoulders, pulled at his clothing. People shouted at him, overwhelming him with questions and accusations. He couldn't make out most of the words anymore. All he could really focus on was the noise and the angry faces and the pain. A few of the soldiers who'd been guarding Polaris Hall had entered the fray to attempt to subdue those who'd attacked him and Walter, but the majority of them had stayed back, and he understood: the president was inside. If the crowd turned against him, they had to stop it. That didn't stop Alex from shouting for help. He'd been pushed to the ground and yanked back to his feet more than once, and he'd gotten a few jabs to his ribs and jaw. Adrenaline kept him moving, kept him fighting, but it didn't take long for him to lose track of his allies.
"Walter?" Alex shouted, struggling against the hands that pulled him in all directions. "Kenny? Lindt?"
Fear gripped his insides, turned his mind to mush. It was hard to think straight. The soldiers around him argued amongst themselves even as they attacked him. Fighting back was futile, but he frantically pushed and clawed at the mob, trying to stay alert and on his feet.
"I'm on your side!" Alex shouted. "Stop!"
Finally, someone *else* pushed away one of his attackers. It was Kenny. "You've all lost your damn minds!" he shouted, ramming his elbow into someone's face and then throwing a punch at another man.
Timothy was right behind him, shoving and making room. "Where's my dad?" he shouted.
"I lost him," Alex said.
"There!" Timothy pointed behind him. "They're hurting him!" He ducked as a soldier swung, and Timothy tackled the man, throwing them both to the ground.
Not alone anymore, Alex's mind thawed from the numbness which had claimed it. He was trembling, slowly regaining his composure as the two other men defended him. He looked back at where Timothy had pointed. Walter was on the ground, in the fetal position, and three soldiers were kicking him.
"We have to get to Walter!" Alex shouted.
Timothy regained his feet as three more soldiers joined them, defending them. "Let's move together!" he shouted. "Get to my dad!"
They formed a tight triangle, back-to-back, as they inched toward Walter. No longer facing the right direction, Alex couldn't see what was happening, if Walter was still on the ground or if he'd managed to get away. He concentrated instead on keeping people back and hoping none of them decided to take it to the next level and pull a weapon. So far, they'd kept the fight to fists.
Alex spread out his arms as he stepped backward, keeping up with Timothy and Kenny. Many of the soldiers had turned their focus on each other. As one man approached Alex, another stepped between them, pushing the first man back, saying something about how they'd gone too far. Smaller brawls had broken out, distracting the mob from Alex's group as they made their way to Walter.
"Get off him!" Timothy's voice made Alex turn to see they'd reached Walter. Timothy was already engaging those who'd been kicking him.
Kenny threw aside one of Walter's attackers, the much younger man hitting the concrete and rolling a few feet. Alex rushed forward and tackled the third man, jumping over Walter's curled-up form and slamming into the man's midsection. As they fell, the man took hold of Alex and jammed his knee into Alex's stomach. When they hit, the other man extended his leg and pushed, sending Alex sailing overhead. His breath was stolen from him when his back hit the ground; he gasped but couldn't make his lungs take in air for several terrifying seconds. When he finally caught a breath, he looked up, a bit dizzy, and saw the man he had tackled getting to his feet and drawing his handgun.
Just as he pointed it in Alex's direction, his face red with fury, a loud voice boomed across the courtyard.

* * *

Minnie's heart jumped into her throat and stuck there; someone had a gun pointed at Alex, and he didn't look to be in a position to defend himself.
The president raised the bullhorn to his mouth. "Your president is speaking!" he shouted. "Stand down and stand to attention, soldiers! This is not who you are. This is not who *we* are."
When the soldier with the gun lowered it, Minnie nearly collapsed right then and there out of pure relief. He still looked mad as a bat out of hell, but his weapon was no longer pointed at Alex.
The shouting quieted as the men and women in the crowd, both those who'd come to protest and those who'd come to defend against them, turned toward their president.

I was right, Minnie thought. *They just want some leadership, some answers.* She looked up at President Coleman who stood on a small platform they'd brought from inside, surrounded by his Secret Service agents, the bullhorn raised. *Now all he has to do is give them enough to keep 'em calm.*

"I assure you," President Coleman said, "if Alex Roman or Walter Peters are involved with the arena, I will personally see to it that they are put on trial."

Minnie's mouth dropped. *That is* not *what I meant.*

"But," he said, emphasizing the word, "there is no evidence thus far to suggest they are anything but loyal to the United States of America." A few *boos* echoed back at him. "However," Coleman continued, "far be it from me to disregard your concerns. There will be an investigation conducted, in which both General Boreland and General Hunt will have input."

Okay, Minnie thought. *Well… Alan wouldn't steer us wrong. He's playin' to the crowd, both sides.* She chewed the inside of her cheek as she surveyed the soldiers. They were still listening, and that wasn't something to sniff at.

"I must remind you, though," President Colman said, "of their mission, a mission that I have approved and believe is the only way to rid ourselves of DV-10 and the swarms for good. It is true Joanna Ward and Blake Turner, both of whom have been found guilty of treason, are working out their penance by finding a temporary solution to the swarms. But you must understand: that won't be enough to ensure the survival of the human race. What Alex and Walter are setting out to do, *that* is our only hope of building a future, of rebuilding the United States of America and the world."

The crowd mumbled amongst themselves, the sound of disagreement getting louder with every passing second until another voice boomed throughout the courtyard. Minnie took half a step forward as she recognized it. She wanted to go to him, but hung back, relieved to see him and, at the same time, taken aback by the look on his face.

Alan Hunt looked like he could pickle a cucumber just by staring at it. He marched through the crowd with General Boreland and a few other soldiers coming up behind him. The mob parted, all those within spitting distance of Alan shrinking back, flinching as he passed them by. Minnie had never seen him quite like that.

He stopped in front of the president, his calm voice a stark contradiction to the powerful waves of authority rolling off him. "Mr. President, sir." He nodded respectfully. "If you would allow us, General Boreland and I would like to say something."

President Coleman nodded. He looked relieved, too—and a little intimidated. "I would welcome it, General Hunt." He handed the bullhorn to one of his bodyguards who then handed it to Alan.

Alan handed it to General Boreland, and Minnie caught a flash of something in Boreland's eyes as he took it: anger and fear, maybe a little pride. But when the man spoke, he kept it short and to the point.

"I've spoken to General Hunt," Boreland said, "and he and I are on the same page. Listen to him, cadets and soldiers alike. President Coleman was right when he said this is not who we are. I'm ashamed. Those of you who learned how to be a soldier right here on this campus: I taught you better than this." He handed the bullhorn back to Alan.

"We're all fighting for the same thing," Alan said. "We all want the country we loved, the country we gave up everything to serve, to survive and come back stronger than ever. We can't do that if we can't work together, if when conflict arises, we turn on each other like rabid dogs." He took a breath, let those words sink in, and then turned and handed the bullhorn back to the president.

President Coleman looked out across the courtyard. "There you have it. Your leadership is united, brothers and sisters. If you don't follow suit, you might as well say goodbye forever to our country, to our dreams of rebuilding, and to our future. I implore you to remember who you are, to band together, and to fight against our real enemies: this disease, those damn swarms, and all those who would stand in the way of eradicating them!"

Several loud whoops were accompanied by a round of applause, and then General Hunt and General Boreland turned toward each other and shook hands. Those soldiers who'd been fighting against each other began to do the same, opposite sides agreeing to peace, at least for the time being.

Minnie skirted the crowd until she came to where Alex and Timothy were crouching beside Walter who was sitting up with his head in his hands. Alex stood as she neared, a look of concern on his face.

"Oliver is fine," Minnie said.

He breathed out slowly, walked over to her, and wrapped his arms around her. "What are you doing out here?" Alex asked. "You shouldn't have stepped outside Polaris Hall."

Minnie waved off the comment. "If I hadn't, you'd be sorry," she said. "I may have had a hand in President Coleman deciding to give that speech."

Alex gave her a tired smile and shook his head. "Why am I not surprised?"

"Is Walter going to be okay?" Minnie asked.

"I think so," Alex said. "He's banged up, definitely needs to be checked over by the medic, but he's talking and thinking clearly, says he's okay."

"Are *we* going to be okay?" Minnie looked back at the dissipating crowd.

"That, I don't know," Alex said.

She nodded and stepped closer to Alex. The raging river had receded before it had swallowed them up, but her head was swimming with a thousand ways they could drown in two feet of water.

Alex placed a hand on her back. "We need to get out of here," he said softly. "I've got a bad feeling, Minnie."

The knots in her stomach twisted tighter as she caught sight of Boreland going back inside Polaris Hall with Alan and the president.

"Alex," she said, "if anyone's on the same page, it's you and me."

Chapter 32

Lizzy Peters

Lizzy could sense the anger rolling off Azalea in waves despite her smile as Carrie explained what exactly the two young women would be expected to do while on laundry duty. To conserve energy, they were not to use the washing machines which made for quite a bit of work. Their days would alternate between laundering, making soap, ironing, mending, and delivering clothes.

"It's a hard rotation," Carrie said. "Ten-hour days. We usually don't start newbies out there, but I guess good ole' Andy wanted to give you girls a chance to prove yourselves right off the bat. He must think you're up to it if he assigned you here."

Azalea's tone sent a shudder down Lizzy's spine. "Good old Andy," she said, eyes cold above a plastered smile.

Carrie didn't seem to notice. "So, all that's left for you to do today is visit the laundry and meet some people. We don't put you straight to work the same day you get out of quarantine."

Lizzy nodded and offered a small smile. She and Azalea had been taken to a room that morning and allowed to shower and change into fresh clothes. When Carrie had come knocking, Azalea had been in good spirits, but she'd been under the impression the two of them would be able to roam the complex under the guise of housekeeping services.

The second Carrie had started explaining laundry duty, though, Lizzy had felt the air go thick with Azalea's displeasure. It was strange how she could read the other woman's most subtle movements, anticipate her moods. Her happiness revolved around Azalea's. Her *sanity* revolved around it, too. When Azalea wasn't happy, the screaming voices in the back of Lizzy's head got louder.

"Will we be visiting the laundry now?" Azalea asked, that fake smile still present, her voice still too high-pitched.

Carrie nodded. "Yep." She waved for them to follow. "Let's get this done."

Lizzy stepped into the hall behind Azalea, their door clicking closed. They had each been given a keycard on a lanyard that would get them into their room, the laundry, and a few places meant for the general population to share. The limited access had made Lizzy's stomach churn. Azalea wasn't going to let that stop her from preventing Conner from getting the information about Barlow Scientific Research Bank.

What will she want us to do? Lizzy thought. Her next thought was of her sister-in-law. So far, Azalea hadn't suggested doing anything to put Heather in danger, and Lizzy was glad for that. She still felt a connection to her brothers and by extension, to Heather. They were innocent, even if they would never understand what the Heirs of the Mother were trying to do.

Lizzy walked quietly. She wanted to ask about Heather, but she was afraid it wasn't the right time, that Azalea wouldn't approve. So, she kept her head down and her mouth shut. That was usually the best course of action.

Carrie took them by The Granite Inn, pointing it out. "That's where you'll get your breakfast," she said as she continued on their way. "Pay attention to the route we take. You'll need to remember it for tomorrow morning."

"And what time should we arrive to start our work day?" Azalea asked.

"Be at the laundry by seven," Carrie said. "Bright side is you've got permissions to turn on the lights early. Five in the morning. And you'll be expected at breakfast no later than six-thirty."

Azalea cleared her throat, making a shudder go down Lizzy's spine. "Lovely," she said. "Ten-hour days, so… that means we'll be there until five?"

"Sure does," Carrie said.

"And what are our duties after that?" Azalea asked.

Lizzy looked up and held her breath. She wants to know when we'll be free to interfere with Conner's plans.

"Once you're done at the laundry," Carrie said, "you can do whatever you want, as long as you stay in the areas you've been approved to be in: The Granite Inn, your room, the Shoppette, the library, the gym." She shrugged. "Your keycard will get you into those places. There might be events, too, if you're interested."

"Excellent," Azalea said. "I'm all for a hard day's work, but I honestly was looking forward to building friendships in a safe environment, you know?"

"I do know," Carrie said, smiling and looking over her shoulder at Lizzy. "Hey, Heather and Lauren are going to be playing cards with me and some guys tonight. I don't know that we've got room at the table for more players, but you two feel free to come along, meet some people."

"We'd love to," Azalea said. This time her smile wasn't as forced. Her shoulders had relaxed, and Lizzy could practically see the wheels spinning behind her eyes.

A little of the weight on Lizzy's shoulders lifted. Heather was healthy, and Azalea's mood had shifted for the better. On top of that, Carrie had given her a reason to ask after Heather. "So, Heather is okay?" she asked. "I haven't seen her yet."

Carrie nodded. "She's doing just fine. Baby is good, too, from what I understand." She turned another corner and stopped in front of a door. "Here we are, at the washing room."

She pushed it open to reveal a room with six large, black rubber bins filled with water. Each bin had its own attendant, and each man or woman was busy either stepping in sudsy water, wringing out clothes, or scrubbing stains.

"Hey, Carrie!" A redheaded woman plopped her foot into the water and waved. "Are these the newbies?"

"Hey there, Lyla!" Carrie smiled and waved back. "Sure are. I thought you'd be in here. You wanna come on out and show these ladies around? Tell them where to go in the morning?"

"Sure thing." Lyla lifted a foot, shook it off, and stepped onto a towel on the floor, continuing the process with her other foot afterward. "This here is the wash room," she said. "Stepping on the clothes is our version of agitating the clothes to get them clean." She patted her thighs. "You'll get some shorts like mine to wear for that. We treat stains here, set aside clothes that need mending, and put them on a cart like this one. The water we use also gets put through filtration so we can reuse it." She walked over to a cart full of wet clothes. "Why don't you follow me? I'll show you the rest of our laundering system."

Lyla wheeled the cart across the hall, into another room where lines had been hung in rows. Clothes were pinned up, and a worker retrieved the cart from Lyla and delivered it to a free line to begin hanging them up. There was another room for hanging bedding and towels. A third space was reserved for making soap, and a fourth was for mending, ironing, and folding.

When they had finished their tour, Lyla led them back into the hall. "It makes for a hard day's work," Lyla said, "but it's good work. It keeps everyone clean and comfortable." Then the woman smiled past Lizzy, Azalea, and Carrie to wave, her grin widening.

Lizzy turned around to see a young man coming down the hall, a clipboard in hand and a pencil stuck behind one ear. When their eyes met, he missed a step and stumbled before regaining composure.

"Whoa there, Nick," Carrie said. "You okay?"

The man cleared his throat. He was still looking at Lizzy, and it made her squirm a little. There was nothing disrespectful about that gaze. There was a time when she would've thought it sweet. His following smile was accompanied by a curiosity in his eyes.

"Yeah, I'm fine," he said, cheeks reddening a little as he cleared his throat. "I… um…" He blinked and turned his eyes from Lizzy to Lyla and Carrie, though he did look back at Lizzy a time or two as he spoke to them. "I just came down to inform you we'll be doing some electrical work in this building in a couple of days."

"Again?" Lyla wrinkled her nose. "Didn't you just finish with that a couple weeks ago?"

"That was the inspection," Nick said. "There's not much work to be done, but it'll need to happen at around three in the afternoon. I just need to make sure you and yours clear out so we can turn off the electricity to this building."

Lyla let out a big sigh. "Yeah, okay. In two days, you say?"

Nick nodded. "Yes, ma'am." He looked back at Lizzy. "Now, Carrie, while I'm here, maybe we can do some proper introductions?"

Carrie smirked. "Sure, kid. But I do have other responsibilities. Now that they've gotten a tour, I got to get them back to The Granite Inn for lunch. Unless…" She smiled wider. "You wouldn't happen to want to escort them, Nick, would you?" She winked at him, and the meaning in her expression wasn't subtle.

Lizzy's own cheeks warmed. It seemed she wasn't the only one who'd noticed Nick's attentions directed at her.

"I'd love to," Nick said, holding out his hand to Lizzy. "Nicolas King."

Lizzy's first instinct was to shrink away. She took half a step back, but Azalea's hand on her back stopped her. She froze, looking over at her friend. Azalea put pressure on her back, pushing her back toward Nick.

"Introduce yourself," Azalea said softly.

"I…" Lizzy licked her lips, confused. *Why does Azalea want me to encourage him?* "Okay," she said, taking Nick's hand and letting him shake it. "I'm Elizabeth Peters."

"And I'm Azalea Griffin." Azalea let Nick shake her hand but pulled it away quickly. She wasn't giving off the usual flirtatious vibe she tended to emanate when she thought a man might be useful to her. That confused Lizzy even more.

"Well, I'd be happy to escort you two to The Granite Inn, maybe even get my lunch at the same time, if you don't mind the company," Nick said.

Azalea pressed on Lizzy's back again, but she was so confused. Lizzy looked at Carrie. "Is there a bathroom around here?"

"Sure is," Carrie said. She pointed at the only door in the hall they hadn't entered during their tour of the laundry system.

Lizzy mumbled her thanks and hurried toward it. Behind her, as expected, Azalea dismissed herself and followed. When they entered the bathroom, Lizzy turned to find Azalea's face mere inches from her own.

"Don't waste this opportunity," Azalea hissed in a low voice as she grabbed hold of Lizzy's upper arm. "Nick is obviously into you. We can use that. He's an electrician. That means he's probably got access to *everything*."

Lizzy cowered as Azalea squeezed her arm. "You're the one who knows how to get information out of people," she said.

"He was clearly interested in *you*," Azalea said.

"Why do we need access to more areas?" Lizzy asked. "What if the others find out? They'll want me to use him to get to the database."

"That's fine with me," Azalea said. "We can get to it first and destroy it, or use him to catch Conner in the act of breaking into the database. Get her and Lauren kicked out. They're going to figure out a way to get access. It's far better if we control the means."

Lizzy swallowed hard. "Conner and Lauren… but not Heather, right?"

Azalea narrowed her eyes. Then, she let go of Lizzy's upper arm and took a step back, folding her arms and taking in a deep breath, a look of contemplation on her face as she seemed to study Lizzy for several long, uncomfortable moments.

"Who is your family?" Azalea asked.

"You are," Lizzy said quickly and without hesitation. "You and the Heirs of the Mother."

Azalea nodded. "And who is Heather?"

Lizzy looked away and down at the floor. "You know I care about her," she whispered. "You didn't throw suspicion on her at the arena for me."

"I did that because our story connects us to her in a stronger way than it does to Lauren and Conner." Azalea took a step forward again and reached out, placing a finger on the bottom of Lizzy's chin and applying pressure until she forced Lizzy to look back up at her. "You are weak, Elizabeth, but… I understand. Do as I say, help me gain as much control over this situation as possible, and I'll do my best to keep Heather and her baby safe." She came closer and wrapped Lizzy in a hug, guiding Lizzy's head to her shoulder. "If you care," she said, stroking Lizzy's hair, "then I care."

Lizzy relaxed and squeezed Azalea's middle, relief flooding her. "Thank you," she said.

"Now," Azalea said, "I'm going to need you to gain Nick's trust so we can use him to stop Conner and protect Heather." She pulled away, both hands on Lizzy's shoulders, and looked into Lizzy's eyes. "Do you think you can do that?"

"Yes," Lizzy said. *I think so*, she added in her head.

If it had been a year prior and she'd set her eyes on some young man at school, there would have been no question. She would've had him taking her out on a date by the end of the week. But that was back when she was living in denial about who her father was, who *she* was. Back when she'd foolishly trusted her own judgment. Back when she'd been blind to the evils of humanity all around her. Back when new relationships weren't likely to end with death sooner rather than later.

"The universe is working with us, with the Heirs, to finish the Cleansing, Elizabeth," Azalea said. "I see the hesitation you try to hide from me, the lack of confidence. But those who work toward our goal will survive and live in harmony with the earth instead of in domination over her. What we do here is bigger than us, and it is *right*. Let that alone give you confidence. We will not fail."

"You're right," Lizzy said, nodding, gaining a bit of strength from her words.

"Restore the Mother," Azalea said, her warm blue eyes still locked onto Lizzy's.

"Restore the Mother." The mantra calmed Lizzy and cleared her mind of worry, helped her focus on Azalea's instructions.

"Let's get out there and get to work on Nick, shall we?" Azalea asked. "We need to know just how much access he has without raising any suspicions."

"I think I have an idea," Lizzy said. "Heather is supposed to be in the new building, in some sort of pregnant lady group, right? If I can convince him to take me to her, I can see what kinds of doors his keycard opens. I can ask him questions about the facility in a more natural way."

"If you can be subtle enough… I think that's a great first step," Azalea said. "I don't think he's supposed to take us there. If you can get him to bend the rules a little now, that's a good sign for us later."

Lizzy rolled her shoulders back, smoothed her hair, and straightened her shirt. "I can do this," she said.

"Yes," Azalea said, smiling. "I believe you can."

Chapter 33

Minnie Stevens

It may have been a new day, but yesterday's worries were still fresh in Minnie's mind. Once the mob had settled and dissipated the day before, the fight had picked up again in a conference room inside Polaris Hall. It was a quieter fight, more subtle, like the dead quiet that seeped into one's bones before a tornado ripped through. Despite their show, Alan and General Boreland were at odds, each one vying for different routes forward. President Coleman had listened to each and his nondecision had only left everyone in Polaris Hall with a feeling of unease.

Alan was the more sensible of the two. He wanted to wait for Conner and the rest to come back from the complex before doing anything else. He also didn't blame everyone at the arena for the attack, bringing up the point that if the military was beginning to fracture, the civilians might have fractured completely already.

General Boreland on the other hand was adamant that there was no evidence from their inside sources that the civilians were fighting amongst themselves. Their source also hadn't confirmed civilians had driven the attack, either, but their source hadn't denied it flat out. That seemed to be as good as confirmation for the trigger-happy general. He wanted a counterattack, sooner rather than later.

The only good thing that came out of it all was that the two generals agreed to have an amiable public relationship, to at least pretend to be on the same page. The only reason Minnie knew any of what had happened after they had sequestered behind closed doors was because Alan had briefed Alex with her standing in the room. He trusted her, and he trusted Alex, and she loved him for that.

Still, the knowledge didn't do much for her health. She'd barely slept, and she'd prayed a dozen times already that morning for her daughter and the team at the complex to show up with the information they needed to leave Colorado Springs.

"Minnie, are you listening?" Alex asked.

Minnie looked up at him from where she sat. They'd been given a small table with two chairs to put in their temporary room at Polaris Hall. It was just her and Alex there; the others were in an adjoining room, the one where Samson was still recovering. Oliver was probably reading to the dog, and Candice and Annika were most likely working on a puzzle. Their options for keeping busy were far fewer than when they were stuck in the duplex.

"Sorry, Alex," Minnie said. "I zoned out. You were explainin' what you were goin' to do today, right? Preparing for the big test where you'll see if your swarm trap'll work."

"And then I told you to watch your back," Alex said, "and General Hunt's, too. I know he comes to see you often, and that's great. I mean, if anyone here is going to protect us, it's going to be him. But I'm worried, Minnie. The rumors that Boreland and his lot started, the fact that Boreland has been friendly with Lawson and Price... things around here could get a lot worse." He looked at the door, his features pinched.

"You don't like leavin' us," Minnie said.

"How do you read my mind like that?" Alex asked.

"Alex, sometimes your thoughts are written on your face, easy as readin' a book." Minnie shook her head. "Don't worry. We won't leave Polaris Hall. Alan will look out for us, and I'll keep my ears open so as to look after him. We've been in quite a few pickles over these last months, and I'm sorry, Alex, but you didn't get out of 'em all by yourself."

Alex sighed. "I know that," he said. "I know you're capable. I know you and Candice will do whatever it takes to protect the kids, but... one day, we're going to run out of luck, Minnie."

Minnie scoffed. "Luck? Is that what this has been?" She shook her head. "Maybe, if it was once or twice, but I'm startin' to believe destinies are real, and ours is to see this thing through to the end."

"I can't count on faith," Alex said.

"Fine. I've got enough for the both of us." Minnie reached out and patted Alex's hand. "Now, go on and do what ya gotta do. Make up that contraption. Get ready to kill off a swarm. If you help with that, it'll go a long way around here, make some of Boreland's people maybe realize we're here for the right reasons."

Alex nodded. "All right," he said. "I'll see you tonight. Be careful today."

"Always," Minnie said. She stood up and shooed him toward the door. "Go on," she repeated. "We'll be fine."

She followed him out the door and into the next room where he said his goodbyes to Oliver. When he finally left, it was just Minnie, Candice, Annika, Oliver, and Samson. Walter and Timothy, who were staying together in what amounted to a broom closet, had left their little corner of Polaris Hall already, Walter to prep for his and Alex's trip and Timothy to see if he could help the soldiers with anything. Minnie could see the man writhing in his own skin when he had nothing to do. She suspected too much thinking time led Timothy to worry about Heather to the point of driving him crazy. Thinking about Lauren did that to her, after all. The only reason she was half sane was because Oliver was such good company. He gave Minnie someone to care for. With Candice taking charge over Annika, Timothy didn't really have that.

The other thing keeping Minnie sane was the fact that Alan visited every day. She never knew when he'd come by, but he always did, and he always got them a little bit of sun, even if it was only in the recesses of Polaris Hall's outdoor sunken patios.

She didn't have to wait long. He showed up about eleven in the morning, a paper sack of food in hand.

"Thought I'd deliver lunch myself," he said as he opened the bag and pulled out two colorful, shiny packages. "Look what I've got here." He held them out to Oliver and Annika.

Annika hopped her way over to grab one. "Fruit Roll-ups!" Annika squealed.
Oliver's eyes brightened. "Thanks, General Hunt!"
"I don't suppose you brought one for me?" Candice asked with a half-smile and a tone that suggested she was kidding around.
Alan—the Lord bless him—brought out two more and grinned. "Momma bears need carbs, too," he said.
Candice raised her eyebrows and took the snack. "I think you're one of my favorite people," she said.
Minnie chuckled. "Well, you're definitely one of mine." She took her snack and nodded at the bag. "I'm guessin' this ain't all you brought for lunch, though."
"It isn't," he said. "I've got peanut butter sandwiches and Jell-O cups for everyone. I thought maybe you'd all like to go outside on the patio while we eat. Samson, too."
Samson raised his head and got to his feet, whimpering at the word "outside." Minnie walked over to him and scratched his ears. He'd been able to move around okay, and the wound on his upper flank seemed to be healing properly. He babied it and didn't like for it to be touched. His walk was a little lopsided, and he wouldn't run or jump, but Minnie had high hopes he'd be back to himself sooner rather than later.
Alan led their little group through Polaris Hall with the bag of food in hand. Minnie and the rest followed while chewing on their fruit snacks. Hers was strawberry, and she'd forgotten how sweet food like that could be. She puckered her lips as she chewed, and her mouth watered at the chewy goodness.
Pure sugar and direct sunlight put Minnie in a good mood as they ate their lunches outside at a picnic table. There had been a soldier or two out there when Alan had ushered them in, but they'd left within minutes. Others had come to the doors since and turned back. Thoughts about why that might be dampened Minnie's spirits, but she kept it to herself until Candice and Annika finished their lunches.
"I'm headed inside," Candice said, nodding to Alan. "I appreciate the food and the sun."
"Sure thing," Alan said.
Candice looked over her shoulder to where Oliver and Annika were drawing on the patio's concrete squares with chalk. "You mind if she stays out here with you for a while? I could use some me time."
"That don't bother me one bit," Minnie said. "It'll be good for 'em to stay outdoors for a while longer."
Once Candice had gone, Alan took Minnie's hand and spoke softly. The kids were on the other side of the patio, but Minnie was grateful he was thinking about their little ears. While she couldn't keep the kids from the terrible things going on around them, she would do everything within her power to protect the moments where they were able to just be kids.
"How are you holding up?" he asked.
"About as good as a one-footed bat with missing toes," Minnie said, "but I 'spose that's to be expected."
Alan smiled. "Always honest. I love that about you."
"Well..." Minnie said, "I ain't so sure you're gonna like what I got to say next. It's about Boreland and what's been going on."
"Even if I don't like it," he said, sitting back in his chair and pinching the bridge of his nose, "I better hear it. You won't keep it to yourself, and you're usually right, so..." He dropped his hand and sighed. "Say your piece."
"And that's what I love about you." Minnie's heart warmed. It would be hard to leave Alan when the time came. *Figures I'd only find the perfect man in the apocalypse,* she thought. She nodded toward the doors. "Have you seen people comin' up to the glass, gettin' one look at you, and turnin' tail?"
He looked over his shoulder and shrugged. "I guess so, but subordinates can be insecure around someone of my rank. It's a relationship I'm not sure you understand."
"Well, then," Minnie said, "General Boreland don't understand it neither. I've seen him out here chattin' up a storm with his *subordinates.*"
Alan bristled. "I talk to my men, Minnie."
"But do you get to know them?" Minnie asked. "Do you talk to them outside of givin' orders? Are you friends with any of 'em? You've got loyalty from many of the soldiers here, but is that loyalty out of duty or love?"
"I can't be *friends* with cadets," Alan said. "And I am friends with some of the older soldiers, some of the officers. I think."
"You *think* you're friends?" Minnie didn't hide her skepticism.
Alan ran his hands over his face a few times, groaning, and then rolled his shoulders. He looked at her like she just asked him to eat something sour. "You're saying that Boreland is making friends, and I'm not, and that could go badly for me if Boreland makes a move I don't like."
Minnie smiled and patted his hand. "Exactly."
"I'm not a people person," Alan said.
"Oh, stop it," Minnie said. "You know how to think about other people, put them first. You also know how to *listen*. That's all it takes to be a friend."
"Anything else?" Alan asked.
"Alex wanted me to make sure you knew of the rumors involving Boreland and those low-life prisoners you've been using for lawn care." Minnie gave him a pointed look. "You've shrugged off the danger of their presence before, but I'm hopin' yesterday's display will make you wake up."
"Boreland is in charge of the prisoners," Alan said. "He's a stubborn old coot, and he's a drunk, but he's not treasonous."
"Maybe not on purpose," Minnie said, "but Alex heard the soldiers talk about him and Lawson and Price havin' nice little lunches together, kinda like us out here on this patio. He's not just droppin' off food, Alan. He's stickin' around for long chats."

Alan pressed his lips together and looked up at the sky, seeming to take a minute to think through what Minnie had said. Finally, he nodded and looked back at her. "A soldier told me a few days ago he'd seen Boreland bringing coffee to the prisoners, three cups, that he went into their quarters and stayed a while before leaving. The man who told me hadn't seen it himself. I was hoping it was just that: a rumor. But… if Alex heard something similar, well…" He shook his head. "Lawson is a smooth talker, and Boreland didn't see firsthand what he orchestrated in Atlanta. Maybe I'll have a nice, long talk with the general."

"Maybe," Minnie said, "you should start havin' nice, long talks with your soldiers. Shore up your loyalties. Prepare for the worst."

"I'm not going to dismiss Boreland's integrity just yet, not entirely," Alan said. "He had a good reputation before all of this. I respect him, even if I don't like him."

"Do you think he feels the same way about you?" Minnie asked. "Because I don't. I think he's full of himself and can't see past his own nose."

"I hear you," Alan said. "I do."

"You'll watch out for yourself, then?" Minnie asked. "Don't go lettin' some yellow-bellied snake stab you in the back."

"I don't think you'd let that happen," Alan said with a small smile as he took her hand again. "I'll think about what you said, think about how I can connect better to the men and women under my command. And I'll have a talk with Boreland, too. I won't take those rumors lightly."

"Promise?" Minnie asked.

"I promise." He brought her hand to his lips and kissed it softly.

"Gross!" Oliver said.

Minnie hadn't noticed him coming up to them until his exclamation. "That ain't nothin', Oliver. Trust me. You'll understand in a few years." She shook her head at his scrunched features and twisted mouth as he pretended to gag. "Did Annika go back inside?"

Oliver nodded. "Yeah. Just now. Can I stay outside a little longer, though?"

"A little longer," Alan said, "but when I have to go back to work, so do you. I've got to get your dad's friends out of quarantine today. You've got maybe ten minutes."

"Thanks!" Oliver jumped over to Alan and threw his arms around the general's neck, giving him a quick squeeze.

Alan's eyes went wide, and he looked like he didn't quite know what to do with himself. When Oliver pulled away, he cleared his throat a few times and mumbled, "Uh… that reminds me, kid. I got you something." He reached into the paper bag and pulled out a four-ounce black metal container of lighter fluid. "This is for that Zippo you've got. You have it on you?"

Oliver nodded and reached into the bag he always wore crossbody. He brought out the lighter, and at Alan's request, handed it over. Alan showed Oliver how to refill the lighter and then handed the black container to Minnie.

"Now, I'm going to let Minnie keep the fuel for you, and she can help you refill it when necessary." He pointed at the lighter that Oliver held up before him. "That there should last you a couple weeks, but the fuel does evaporate, so be aware of that. It's an excellent tool, but you've got to be careful with it. Keep it bottom down in your bag when you carry it around, and put it somewhere safe the rest of the time. Don't practice lighting it inside where you could catch something on fire, either."

Oliver nodded. "I won't. And I'll be careful. Can I practice lighting it now?"

Minnie chuckled at his enthusiasm over the simple tool. He'd been wanting to learn how to use it ever since Ned the biker gave it to him. "Okay," she said, "but then I think we'll store it in our room on the table, safe and sound, along with the lighter fluid."

Oliver nodded again, and as Alan taught him how to light the little silver contraption and tips on starting a safe fire should Oliver ever need one, Minnie had mixed feelings. It was her opinion every kid needed to know simple survival techniques, and even though Oliver was young, she counted him responsible enough to handle the lighter with the supervision of the adults in his life. She'd even thought about getting him a pocket knife to go with all the little knickknacks he kept in his mother's old purse. It was also good to see Alan connected with Oliver; it reassured her that the general *could* be likeable to someone besides herself.

But it was bittersweet.

Oliver should be learning this stuff from his own dad, she thought, out on campin' trips and whatnot. Not at an Air Force academy where he's barely sheltered from danger. Not after bein' shot at. Not because he fears for his safety and the safety of the people he loves. But that was the world they lived in, and even if they succeeded in their mission to Barlow Scientific Research Bank, Minnie wasn't sure that would change anytime soon.

Chapter 34

Zara Williams

As the golf cart ambled onto academy grounds, Zara swallowed hard at the damage that had been done since they'd left. Two buildings had been made into rubble, but it was the way people stopped and stared that left Zara with an uneasy stomach.

"Some of these people really think we're the bad guys," Zara whispered as a young man in uniform stopped to spit on the ground as they passed him.

General Hunt had given them a quick summary of the mood on base, but he hadn't gone into much detail, insisting that they would be debriefed shortly while demanding that they hand over their own information immediately. She didn't really understand what was going on beyond the fact that there had been an attack and that some people blamed them for it. She hadn't connected the dots yet as to exactly *why* she and her friends would be blamed, but she suspected the president would do that for her during the debriefing.

Kai squeezed her hand. "Don't worry about it. It can't be that bad, right?"

Zara gave him a flat stare. "Based on how many soldiers are staring us down as we pass, I'm not so sure."

"C'mon," Kai said. "So we have some haters. Who cares, right?"

"Yeah," Zara scoffed, "we're basically rolling like celebrities."

"Exactly. Look at all this security," Kai said, his tone lighthearted. "Just a couple of celebs going to see the President of the United States." Another soldier gave them the finger from a safe distance, and Kai waved. "They're just jealous," he said with a grin.

He wasn't fooling her. She could see the concern in his eyes no matter how he tried to hide it with his cool-guy, thick-skin routine.

He was right about one thing, though. They did have quite the escort. General Hunt had come down to the quarantine trailers himself when they'd been released. He and another soldier were with Blythe in another cart. Major Willis drove Zara and Kai, and he, too, had a soldier by his side for backup. In addition, a third cart with four soldiers brought up the rear. That was eight soldiers to protect three people.

"I still don't understand what's going on," Zara said loudly enough for everyone to hear clearly.

Major Willis glanced back at her over his shoulder. "People are angry," he said. "It'll blow over, but until then, just stick with us, and you'll be fine."

"We shouldn't need protection," Zara said. "We almost got killed bringing Blythe back here so that we can get to where we need to go so that *everyone* can get rid of DV-10 and these swarms. We even brought back both of your stupid carts."

The major nodded, keeping his eyes on the road. "I hear you, kid, but right now, it don't matter what *should* be. It just matters what *is*."

The golf cart pulled to a stop outside Polaris Hall. The soldiers bringing up the rear were out and surrounding them before Zara had the chance to even touch the zipper on her plastic door. She stepped out, and they ushered her forward toward the steps descending from the courtyard into the building. She was shuffling down the stairs with Kai and Blythe within seconds, emerging into Polaris Hall to a sunlit room and a round of applause.

Zara missed a step as the warm welcome startled her. She bumped into the soldier ahead of her. "Sorry," she said, wincing.

Kai leaned over, speaking through a smile as he awkwardly waved. "Are these people trying to give us whiplash? I thought everyone hated us."

"Not everyone blames you," Major Willis said quietly as they started moving again through the building. "To be honest, it would be better if everyone was on the same page, even if it meant everyone wanted to boot you out. But differing opinions formed after the attack, and now half of us are in awe of Alex and his crew while the other half think you're all a bunch of fakers."

Ahead, General Hunt led Zara, Kai, and Blythe into a conference room lit by a large skylight. Major Willis didn't stay, and all but two of the soldiers escorting them left with him. Those two each chose a corner and stood silently.

Zara paused at the sight of President Coleman at the head of the table. She froze, started to bow, but stopped herself. *No, that's not right,* she thought as her cheeks went red. She settled on a half salute, half wave.

"Just stop," Kai whispered, wincing. "You're making it worse."

The president stood upon their entrance and smiled, ignoring Zara's awkward attempts at propriety. "It's good to see you three," he said. "Have a seat. I've asked for some hot tea and fresh cookies. They should be here soon. You deserve it."

"Cookies and tea?" Blythe scowled. "That's where your priorities are right now?"

President Coleman's smile faltered. "Lieutenant Colonel," he said, "I understand—"

Blythe raised his voice as he cut off the president. "You don't know jack sh—"

"Blythe!" General Hunt rounded on him. "This is President Coleman's house. You show him respect. You were taught better than that, soldier."

Blythe didn't back down. "I'm not a soldier. Not anymore."

"Something in you still is," Hunt said. "Who you become after that many years of active duty doesn't leave you just because you retire. I suspect it was that part of you that made you do the honorable thing and come back here to help."

Blythe narrowed his eyes, still mere inches from Hunt. "Who I was died with my wife," he said. "And it was the part of me that loves her still that made me come here."

Hunt looked like he might say something else, but the president spoke first. "Alan, give the man his space. Joel, that's your first name, right? Would you prefer to be called Joel?"

General Hunt backed off.
"Everyone just calls me Blythe."
"Okay. Blythe, please, have a seat." President Coleman gestured to the empty chairs. "Zara, Kai—you, too."
Kai tugged on Zara's hand. She swallowed hard and followed him to the table, looking back at Blythe to give him a pleading glance. He sighed and grabbed the nearest chair, sitting down hard as Zara and Kai took their seats.
"We gave you all the information you needed through the doors of those trailers," Blythe said. "And then we wrote it all down three ways. You got our accounts of what happened. We need to get to work, Mr. President, not sit around wasting time with redundant debriefings."
"I would agree with you," President Coleman said, "but I need to ask you three some questions now that you're all here together. There was a bit of a commotion yesterday. Alex and Walter got caught up in an angry mob due to some rumors—"
Zara sat up straight and put her hands on the table. "Are they okay?" She hadn't meant to interrupt, but she hadn't seen Walter yet.
"Yes," the president said, "they're okay."
She relaxed a bit. "Good," she said.
"How much did you tell them, General?" The president turned his attention to Hunt, who had taken a seat at his right hand.
"Not much," the general said.
"As I requested." A voice boomed into the room from behind them.
Zara jumped in her seat and turned to see General Boreland striding into the room. *What is he doing here?* she thought.
He sat at the president's left-hand side, nodding as he did so. "Mr. President."
"General Boreland," Coleman said, "you're a little early. I was planning to give them a few minutes to get acclimated."
"No disrespect, sir," Boreland said, "but I'm not about to give them more time to think before their interrogation, especially not time together where they can straighten out their stories."
Zara's mouth dropped open, and she looked from Blythe to Kai and then back to the president. "I'm sorry… *what*?"
"What she means," Blythe said, "is what the actual hell is this man talking about? I didn't come here to be interrogated."
Boreland raised a hand. "Now, Lieutenant—"
"Call me Blythe," he growled.
"All right… Blythe. If you did nothing wrong, you have nothing to worry about." He rested his elbows on the table and leaned into the statement, staring at Blythe as if to challenge him.
"This place hasn't changed," Blythe said. "None of it has. It's the end of the world, and we're still dealing with this bull." He pointed at General Boreland. "I *never* liked you, Boris."
Kai looked at Zara and mouthed the words, "*Boris Boreland?*" He chuckled softly.
She elbowed him. "Not now," she mouthed back.
Boreland leaned forward. "The feeling is mutual, Lieutenant Colonel."
"Well, then, maybe I should go home." Blythe stood up, his chair rolling backward so fast it slammed against the wall.
Zara stood up, too, a spike of panic puncturing her stomach. "Blythe, you came here for us, not for them. Please… don't leave. We *do* need you."
"Please, man," Kai said. "This is bigger than some idiot in a uniform."
Boreland moved to speak, but the president held up a hand and shook his head. The man fell silent but the hard set of his jaw, the vein popping in his neck, and the seething look in his eyes spoke volumes.
But Blythe didn't turn toward the door. He pressed his lips together, his eyes on Zara. She met his gaze, her heart beating louder with every passing second. *Please stay,* she thought, willing him to sit back down.
Finally, he nodded once, pulled his chair back up, and sat once more at the table. "Fine. But I don't like it." He crossed his arms. "You hear that, Mr. President? I object to this interrogation."
"Your objection is noted," President Coleman said, "but please understand that I fully expect this to be settled in your favor, and soon." He nodded at Boreland. "You may begin, but keep it civil."
"And remember," General Hunt said, "they're innocent until proven guilty."
Boreland sniffed and turned his attentions back on Zara, Kai, and Blythe. "Your story is that three highly trained soldiers were killed by rabid wolves, and yet you two—" He pointed at Zara and Kai. "—managed to survive that encounter without so much as a scratch?"
"We were in the cart when they first attacked," Zara said.
"You expect us to believe three of our best were taken out by dogs?" Boreland raised an eyebrow.
"They were huge," Kai said. "There were a lot of them, and they didn't seem fazed by pain at all."
"I suspect this pack was let loose from a zoo," Blythe said. "They were too large to be from around here. And they weren't dogs, Boris. They were *wolves*. They were *diseased* wolves. Crazy. Vicious. Out for blood."
"And yet you three survived," Boreland said.
"Barely," Zara said.
"Warren, Yeomen, and Potts took several wolves out," Kai said, "but there were too many of them."
"Those were three of our best," Boreland said. "Maybe if one of them had been taken out, I could believe you, but all three?"
"Come on, Boris," Blythe said, "unless you've added a training exercise to prepare soldiers for coming across a pack of wolves, a pack that works together to take their prey down, this isn't that unbelievable."
"These answers aren't good enough," Boreland said, leaning forward.
"What? Do you think *we* killed them?" Kai said with half a laugh and a lot of sarcasm.
Boreland quirked an eyebrow. "Maybe you wanted to take the credit for bringing back our lieutenant colonel, here. Or maybe Blythe is working with the civilians, too." He narrowed his eyes at Blythe. "You haven't been much of a fan of the military these days. Maybe this entire farfetched plan to go to Antarctica is a ruse."

"That's enough." General Hunt laid his hands flat on the table and stood. "Mr. President, calling into question the mission to Barlow Scientific Research Bank is going too far. We can't spread doubts about that, too. If that mission is sabotaged, it's all over for all of us."

Boreland threw up his hands in an exasperated manner and shouted, "That's what they want you to think!"

President Coleman shook his head. "I agree with Hunt on this one," he said. "Alex would have no reason to lie to us."

"No?" Boreland asked. "Not even if helping take us out would get him and his entire crew a spot at Cheyenne Mountain where they can live in safety? That place and scientists like Joanna Ward and Blake Turner who can clear the air of swarms… that's the only way anyone in Colorado Springs survives long term."

Zara was so taken aback by the outlandish theory that she laughed out loud. "Are you serious? You're saying we came all the way from Boston to take sides in your little fight?"

"It's hardly little," Boreland said. "How many places do you know of like Cheyenne Mountain? Powered by diesel and then solar after that. Electricity. Hot water. Hydroponics. Livestock. Defenses like no other. That place is pure gold. Heaven on earth. Maybe you came here looking for the president, hoping for special treatment, and then when you found out who had the most power in Colorado Springs, you decided to flip."

"That's insane," Zara said. "We would never do that."

"And we're supposed to take your word for it based on what?" Boreland stared her down, the corner of his mouth turning up ever so slightly. He raised his eyebrows as if waiting for an answer, but Zara couldn't give him one.

The fact was, he was right. She had no *proof* that his theory was wrong. All of their actions could be used to support the truth or could be twisted to support the lie.

"You're wrong," Kai said, his voice raw.

Boreland looked like a man who'd just won a game of chess. "Prove it."

"Hunt is right," President Coleman said. "That's enough."

Boreland's smile disappeared. His eyes snapped back to the president. "Sir, I—"

"No, General Boreland." President Coleman cut the air with his hand. "I suspect I know whose been feeding you these wild theories, and I won't stand for it."

"Mr. President, if I may," Boreland said, "Mr. Lawson knows he made mistakes. But he did it for the right reasons. He was trying to make a safe place. He was trying to save—"

"He was trying to save his wealth and power," Hunt said. "That's it. He was orchestrating a system by which human beings were sacrificed to create a treatment that he planned to use as a tool of enslavement. He was trying to be a damn tyrant."

"My father-in-law is not to be trusted. Period." Coleman's tone brooked no argument. "Alex, on the other hand, showed great integrity in Atlanta. I trust him, and I need you, General Boreland, to trust me. If you can't do that, I can't have you on my counsel."

Boreland balled his hands into fists on the table, his voice strained. "Sir, let me interrogate them for real. I'll get them to confess."

Zara's throat tightened, and she took Kai's hand. Goosebumps sprung up on her arms and legs, and she shuddered.

"You mean you want to torture them until they say what you want to hear," General Hunt said.

"Hold on," Blythe said, "I don't think so. These kids are just kids. I mean, technically they're adults, but c'mon, Boris."

"You're blinded," Boreland said to Hunt as he rose to his feet. "Blinded by that southern b—"

Hunt slammed his hands down on the table. He was around the president in a flash and had Boreland by his collar before Zara could even register what he was doing. Hunt spoke through gritted teeth. "I wouldn't finish that sentence," he said.

President Coleman stood and smoothed his button-down dress shirt and tie. "Alan, let him go. That's not how we do things." After a few seconds of no movement, he said again, "Let him go. Now."

Hunt let go with a little push, sending Boreland stumbling backward so that he had to catch his balance with a hand on the wall. Hunt backed up, breathing hard.

"You will not be questioning anyone any further, General Boreland," Coleman said. "Do not spread these unsubstantiated, dangerous lies. I will assign the prisoners to Major Willis from now on. Your duties as far as they are concerned are no more."

"Your offer to have me here in the first place was just for show," Boreland spat. "Mr. Lawson was right about you. You're weak. You were never meant for this role."

The president stared at Boreland, a frown forming and deepening as his eyes went from Boreland to Hunt, and then to Zara and Kai. He took a deep breath and then let it out slowly. "I don't want to do this, General Boreland, but you're too unstable." He looked straight ahead, his voice turning cold. "Alan, please restrain him. I want him secure and under constant watch until we can determine what to do with him. He does not leave Polaris Hall. The people here are loyal, and we don't need word of his confinement spreading. Let's say he's come down with something contagious. No one is allowed to visit."

"You can't do that," Boreland said, his words clipped.

"I can drag you kicking and screaming," Hunt said, "or you can come with me and keep the scrap of dignity you have left."

"You can't keep this a secret," Boreland said. "And we all know Coleman won't kill me. If he was capable, Mr. Lawson and Mr. Price would be gone."

"Are you complaining?" Hunt asked. "Because I might be able to convince him to let me do it myself."

Boreland smirked. "This isn't over."

Hunt grabbed Boreland by his upper arm. "You're right," he said as he pushed Boreland forward, "but it's not going to end well for you." With the help of one of the soldiers in the corner, Hunt led Boreland out.

President Coleman sank down in his chair as soon as the door was shut, the hardness in his eyes replaced with exhaustion. "I had hoped that letting General Boreland be part of this process would give him a voice, make him see that he could be part of this. I hadn't expected… I thought the rumors about him and Lawson had been exaggerated…" He ground his teeth, his expression turning sour. "I've underestimated my father-in-law again."

"I have no idea what's going on," Blythe said, "but someone needs to tell me who Lawson and Price are and why Boris is so wrapped up in what this Lawson guy has to say."

Zara had heard the tale in its entirety once, and she'd heard bits and pieces from Minnie, Oliver, Lauren, and Alex at different times over their long journey from Boston to Colorado Springs. But she still found the president's version of events fascinating as he explained it to Blythe.

"So, Lawson and Price are definitely the bad guys," Blythe said after the president was done. "Got it. But why would Boreland listen to them? I've never liked the guy, but he's not stupid."

"My father-in-law is brilliant," Coleman said. "He can read people as easy as I can read a book. He knows what to say to appeal to them, to make them *want* to believe him. I mean, I believed him for a long time." The president paused and his face fell. "Too long," he said. "If it hadn't been for Alex, I would have never broken away from him, and I would have never found my voice as President of the United States."

"How long can you keep him here without causing another riot?" Zara asked.

Blythe wagged his finger at her. "She raises a good point. Zara and Kai explained the mission to me, but it's my understanding we can't leave until we have the coordinates and until I teach Kai enough to be my co-pilot. He already has some knowledge, but it isn't going to be nearly enough. I'd normally want a co-pilot with years of training." He pointed with his thumb over his shoulder at the door. "It sounds to me like we don't have a lot of time."

"There are plenty of contagious illnesses that last for a week or more," Coleman said, "but you're right. You won't have a lot of time. And my suggestion is that once Conner gets back here with coordinates, you all need to get out of here as soon as possible. When word gets out that I've confined Boreland, well, things are going to get ugly around here."

"Then we need to get to work," Blythe said.

President Coleman leaned forward. "Then tell me what you need to get this operation off the ground and into the air."

Chapter 35

Heather Peters

"You ready for lunch?"

Heather plopped down on her yoga mat. "Give me a sec, Em," she said. "I thought all this walking I've been doing the past weeks had gotten me in shape, but moving *this* way is a whole other ballgame. I'm using muscles I didn't even know I had."

Emily laughed. "Well, you'll be thanking us later. There are no epidurals to be had, save for the emergencies, and yoga is supposed to help with a natural birth… or that's what Vivian says, anyway." She nodded to the midwife who was across the room.

"I hadn't thought about that," Heather said, groaning, "the no epidurals part, I mean." She still had seven or so months before she had to give birth, but it didn't seem like long enough to prepare.

"It'll be fine," Emily said as she rolled up her own mat. "Women have been giving birth since the dawn of time without meds."

And women have been dying, too, Heather thought, though she kept that to herself.

"But there *is* the option for a spinal block if there're complications, right?" Heather asked. "For a c-section, I mean?"

Emily shrugged. "Sure, but that's a last resort. We've got to save what we have for absolute emergencies. Between our midwife and our baby doc, though, I think we've got ourselves a pretty good team. I wouldn't worry."

Heather got to her feet with a sigh. "That's a lot easier said than done." She rolled up her own mat. "But being here…" She straightened up and looked around, a genuine smile spreading. "Being here makes me a lot *less* worried than I was out there."

Emily put a hand on Heather's arm. "Good. Let's keep it that way." She nodded toward the door. "I'll meet you in the hall, and we can go up to my apartment. Mark is making up some steaks in a big cast iron skillet. I just want to ask Vivian a few questions about natural remedies for heartburn first."

Heather put away her mat and made small talk with the other women on the way out the door. They usually all went down to The Granite Inn together for lunch, and as the rest of the ladies did just that, leaving Heather alone in the hall, a face Heather hadn't expected turned a far corner.

"Lizzy?" Heather smiled wide. "You made it!"

A man trailed behind her, looking slightly nervous. Lizzy jogged forward, leaving him behind and approaching Heather.

"Carrie told me you and the baby are okay?" Lizzy asked.

Heather nodded. "Yep. Nothing to worry about. Not yet anyway." She opened her arms, and Lizzy stepped into them. The genuine warmth in Lizzy's eyes was encouraging. It wasn't often that Heather caught glimpses of the old Lizzy. As she squeezed her sister-in-law tight, she noticed Azalea wasn't there, and part of her was relieved. "When did you get here?" Heather asked.

"We got out of quarantine this morning," Lizzy said as she pulled away.

"You, Azalea, and Conner?" Heather asked, perking up a little. She hadn't been sure if the three would arrive all at once or one at a time.

"Just me and Azalea," Lizzy said, her smile fading and that reserved nature resurfacing. "I don't know when Conner will be sent up."

"Oh." Heather frowned. "That's a little odd, isn't it? That you two made it in, but she didn't?"

Lizzy shrugged, and as her expression became more guarded, as the light of happiness bled from her eyes, Heather knew she'd said something wrong.

"I'm sure it will be fine," Heather said. "Conner will make it."

That didn't seem to be the right thing either. Lizzy mumbled her agreement and then folded her arms, her shoulders hunching slightly. Heather tried again, changing the subject.

"And who is this?" Heather asked, smiling at the young man who was still a couple yards away.

"Oh," Lizzy said, smiling before she turned her head to look at him. "That's Nick." Lizzy waved, and Nick crept forward. "He's a little nervous because I don't think I'm technically supposed to be in this building." She slid her arm into the crook of his elbow. "But he knew how much I needed to see you, and he escorted me, anyway."

"Not supposed to be here, indeed." Emily's voice came from behind Heather. "Nick, what do you think you're doing?"

"Emily!" Nick gulped and straightened, stepping away from Lizzy. "I just… she wanted to see her sister-in-law, and I thought… I mean…"

Emily walked up beside Heather, shaking her head. "A pretty girl asks you to jump off a cliff. Would you do it?"

"I told her five minutes," Nick said. "Just to see Heather. Please don't tell Mark."

Emily laughed. "Oh, stop it," she said, waving away Nick's nervous tension. "It's not like you let her into a private apartment." She smiled. "I'm glad you brought her."

"You… are?" Nick asked.

"Sure," Emily said. "Heather needs less stress, and I'm sure that seeing her loved one safe and sound is very helpful."

"It is, actually," Heather said quickly.

"Don't worry about it, Nick," Emily said. "Let's give Heather a minute with Lizzy, and then you can escort her back."

Nick let out a long breath as some of the tension went out of his shoulders. "Yeah," he said. "Sounds good." He touched Lizzy's shoulder and smiled before departing with Emily down the hall a little way.

Lizzy looked after him, smiling until he turned his back. Then, she breathed out and looked back at Heather. "I'm glad he's not in trouble."

Heather smirked. "He's sweet on you, isn't he?"

"Yeah, and…" Lizzy lowered her voice. "… we can use that. He's an electrician. On the way here, I found out that he has access to practically *everywhere.*"

"You mean, you're just using him?" Heather asked.

"I mean, he's a nice guy," Lizzy whispered, "but… you know…" She looked around at the empty hall. "We can't stay."

Heather stepped forward. "Conner can't stay," she said, and a protective instinct urged her to say more. "You and Azalea could, though. Our family could be safe here."

Lizzy's eyes widened. "Are you serious?"

"It's not the craziest idea," Heather said, her hand going to her stomach. The image of her and Timothy and their baby living safely in Cheyenne Mountain flashed before her once again. "Just make sure you don't burn bridges, okay? If we can somehow work out a way to stay *and* to get Conner the information she needs to bring back to Alex and your dad… why not?"

"They'll never let Tim come inside," Lizzy said.

"You don't know that." Heather's clipped tone was snappier than she'd intended. She took a deep breath. "I'm sorry," she said.

"It's okay." Lizzy reached out. "It's not crazy. I just… didn't expect that."

"I know." Heather took Lizzy's hand. "Just keep an open mind, okay?"

"I'll ask Azalea what she thinks," Lizzy said.

"You know you don't need to run your opinions by her, right?" Heather asked.

Lizzy bristled and yanked her hand back. "She's my friend, and she looks out for me."

"Okay." Heather held up her hands and tried to use a calming voice. "I'm sorry. I didn't mean anything against her. I just… I worry about you."

"Well, I'm fine." Lizzy was clearly shutting down again, distancing herself. "Azalea and I were invited to the card game tonight," she said in a calm, monotone voice. "I'll see you there. I better get back." She turned around without so much as a goodbye and started walking away.

Heather shook her head and followed, picking up her pace. "Lizzy, wait," she said as she came around her and blocked her way forward.

"Azalea is waiting for me," Lizzy said, trying to sidestep Heather.

"I'm glad you're here," Heather said, "and I love you." She cupped Lizzy's cheeks in her hands and tried to convey all of her love through that touch, willing her sister-in-law to understand that Azalea wasn't the only person who cared about her. It seemed Lizzy had forgotten that lately.

"I know you do," Lizzy said after a moment. She offered a very small smile. "I love you, too, even if you do get on my nerves."

Heather laughed and pulled Lizzy into a hug. "I'll see you tonight," she said. "Good thinking with Nick, just… be careful. And open yourself up a little. It's okay to make new friends here." She gave Lizzy one last squeeze before letting her go.

"See you tonight." Lizzy ducked around Heather before she could gauge how the younger woman felt about what she'd said.

As Lizzy rejoined Nick and the two retreated, Emily came up to Heather, lightly clapping her hands, her expression excited. "I think there's a little romance brewing," she said in a sing-song voice. "Did you tell her to go for it? Maybe they've got l-o-v-e in their future."

Heather blinked slowly. "Em, they just met. I told her to keep an open mind, but love?"

"Things move fast around here," Emily said. "Even though we're safe, we've all learned not to waste time. And the more couples we have, the faster we'll be able to rebuild the population."

"She's too young to be thinking about babies!" Heather said.

The look on Emily's face made Heather realize her mistake. They'd made it very clear at the arena that if Lizzy and Azalea stayed after the sixth month trial period, they'd be expected to try for a baby.

"Is she? She's legally an adult, right?" Emily asked.

"I mean, yes," Heather said hesitantly. She wasn't very good at hiding her true feelings, but she tried anyway.

"Look, things have changed." Emily looked ahead, a smile on her face. "What we need now is growth in order to secure our future. Lizzy knew that when she put her name on the list to come up here. She knows that one of her greatest assets is the fact that she's of childbearing age." Emily looked sideways at Heather. "You knew that, too."

Heather cleared her throat. "Yeah," she said, putting forth what she suspected Emily wanted to hear. "I guess you're right. I just need to stop thinking about her as the little girl we used to take for ice cream. She's old enough to make her own decisions."

"That's right," Emily said, patting Heather's arm approvingly. "And if she decides to pair up with Nick, I promise you she'll be just fine. He's a good man. Kind and hardworking and even a little empathetic."

"Right…" Heather said, smiling. *So… the basic requirements for being a decent human.* She didn't want to talk about it anymore. The thought that their expectations of Lizzy might keep her from staying made her heart sink and her stomach churn. "Anyway, we should get going. You know, Mark and his steaks. Wouldn't want to keep him waiting."

"Oh!" Emily put a hand to her mouth, her eyes wide as if she'd forgotten about her husband and their lunch. "You're right. We should hurry."

She took Heather by the hand and tugged her down the hall. Heather kept up, all the while thinking about how she could both charm Mark and Emily *and* get information out of them at the same time. For the first time in her life, she wished she was a better liar.

* * *

"What we're doing here," Mark said as he sat down to his plate of steak and potatoes, "will go down in the history books. Preserving the middle class, the blue-collar worker, is of utmost importance. And fostering a safe environment to rebuild the population?" He reached out and laid a hand over his wife's hand. "It's perhaps the most important thing being done right now in the entire world."

"I'm certainly grateful for that," Heather said as she looked down at her plate: a filet mignon with butter and herb fried potatoes. She stuck a potato with her fork and took a bite, the flavors exploding in her mouth. She closed her eyes and savored it. "This is delicious," she said. "I haven't had a meal like this in ages."

"The potatoes we'll have in plenty for as long as we're here," Mark said, cutting a bite of steak and holding it up. "But this…" He ate the piece of juicy meat and smiled. "Mmmm-mmm. This is a dwindling luxury. We've got a freezer full of beef for special occasions, but once it's gone, it'll be goat and whatever we can hunt: venison, most likely."

"Well, thank you for having me," Heather said. "There aren't enough words to describe what it means to me to be welcomed like this."

"Well," Emily said, "this isn't just a welcome."

"That's right," Mark said, "I like to get a little input from the people of Cheyenne Mountain on our path moving forward. I want this place to be *ours*, you know? I want people like you to have a say. That's the whole point of what we're doing, right?"

Heather raised her eyebrows. "Oh? What kind of input are you looking for?"

Emily smiled as she swallowed a bite of her food. "That's up to you," she said. "What are your hopes for this place?"

Heather cut into her steak, using the action of eating to delay her response. When she'd swallowed the bite, she gathered her courage. *This is my shot to steer the conversation…*

"Well," Heather said, "I love your priority of preservation, and your comment on making history made me think about education. This might be one of the few places left in the world where kids are going to school."

"Top priority," Mark said. "Book learning right alongside old school apprenticeships. Even the doc and the nurses are going to need to take on students eventually. Got to keep knowledge alive and well."

Heather nodded earnestly. "Yes, exactly. I want my kid to contribute in a meaningful way. Being safe isn't enough for mental health. We need to learn and grow as human beings."

Mark grinned. "Absolutely. I love to hear a mom talking about raising her kid right."

"Well, concerning that," Heather said, "I was wondering how much of a priority history will be in teaching our kids. The library is so small."

"We haven't gotten all that worked out yet," Mark said, "but we've got ideas and resources we've not tapped."

"Oh?" Heather asked. "Like what?"

"Libraries in town, for one," Mark said.

Heather did her best to keep her disappointment in check. She'd hoped education sources would lead Mark to talk about exploring the offline database. There had to be relevant historical documents there. She tried a different tactic.

"It's too bad that some skills will be lost entirely, though, don't you think?" Heather asked.

Emily frowned. "Like what? We've got everything we need to survive."

"I'm just thinking about the things we've lost," Heather said, "the internet, computer skills, the ability to store vast amounts of information in a small device. I mean, books take up so much space. Imagine the information we could hold if we had working computers again."

Mark nodded thoughtfully. "There are computers here in Cheyenne Mountain, you know. There's even an entire database of information we haven't even tapped. Most of it I think would be useless now. Records of government workings and whatnot."

Bingo, Heather thought, straightening up, not having to feign interest. "That kind of storage space could be useful," she said.

"Maybe," Mark said, "but we've already thought about it, and the experts we have here have all agreed that even with the solar farm on the side of the mountain, powering up computers and electronics too often will drain our power too quickly. Not to mention that the computers here are all very, very old. We only have one guy who knows anything about how to repair them, and according to him, they'll eventually be unusable, probably sooner rather than later, without proper maintenance."

"That's too bad," Heather said. "So, they're basically just taking up space?"

"Yep. Basically," Mark said, "the entire floor where the database is stored is a pile of junk. We haven't had a need for the building yet. It's mostly kept dark, but eventually, we might have to just dump the whole thing."

Heather tried not show too much excitement. She was on the right track, getting good information, but she could ruin it if she caused suspicion. Still, an idea popped into her head, one that could solve their problem. "Do you think," she said slowly, "that maybe the database is part of why the military wants this place? I mean… if it holds government secrets… maybe you could use it to trade with them."

Mark sat back in his chair. "Huh. Maybe so. The information is encrypted, so we don't know what's on it. We don't have anyone with hacker skills. Just a guy who said he could wipe the database clean should we ever want to use the computers for anything. Now I'm glad we didn't do that."

Heather breathed out, a shudder going up her spine at the thought that wiping the database had been an option. "Yeah," she said. "That would have gotten rid of a potentially huge bargaining chip."

"You know," Mark said, "I like you. I'll talk to my guys about your idea. See if we can't use the database somehow in our relations with the military."

If they traded the information, maybe we could get at it without all the sneaking around, Heather thought. Maybe when Conner gets here, I can convince her to get a message to the military. If they're willing to barter… maybe there could be peace after all in Colorado Springs.

Mark seemed to be mulling over her suggestions as Heather was trying to come up with a way to get more information on the exact location of the database. She was about to open her mouth when Emily opened hers.

"On the other hand," Emily said, "who knows what's in that database."

Mark frowned at his wife. "What do you mean, babe?"

"Well, you're always telling me how the military is full of dangerous secrets. If we hand over that database, what if we're handing them a way to get into the mountain that we don't know about? Or the location of some secret stash of weapons?" Emily shrugged. "I know it sounds crazy, like conspiracy theories or whatever, but..."

Mark nodded. "No, you're right," he said. "There's no way we can hand over that information without knowing what we're giving them."

Heather deflated a little.

"If it's encrypted," Emily said, "maybe it's better to wipe the computers after all."

"No," Heather said too quickly.

Both Mark and Emily looked at her with surprise.

She cleared her throat. "I mean, it seems to me that someone should at least *try* to decrypt it. Maybe if we don't have anyone who can do it now, we will find someone to do it in the future. Peace between the mountain and the military could be worth the wait, right? What if wiping the database makes them angry?"

"I don't know how they'd find out," Emily said, shrugging.

"Well," Heather said, dampening her frantic feelings the best she could, "you do allow people to leave here after six months if the place isn't for them, right? I mean, what if someone left and told them?"

"We wouldn't make it common knowledge," Mark said, "but rumors do get around." He sighed. "I'll have to think about it, consult with my people. For now, though, enough about that. I don't like to talk logistics when I'm entertaining guests."

Heather swallowed further objections to the idea that they wipe the database. *I'll only sound desperate... raise suspicions.*

But as they finished their lunch, all Heather could think about was the fact that she'd potentially started a conversation that could result in the permanent loss of the location of Barlow Scientific Research Bank. If that happened, it wasn't just their immediate mission that would be all for nothing. Their hopes of saving the world could be dashed with just a word from the man sitting at the table with her. And Heather would be partially to blame.

Chapter 36

Lauren Stevens and Heather Peters

Lauren's second day of working as a nurse under Dr. Gregory had gone much the same as the first. The complex did have other nurses, but they all had various duties. Two of them—Jessi and Wesley—stuck with Stellar and helped him with his responsibilities. Another nurse, Betsy, was on a house call rotation, mostly checking on reported sicknesses in kids, and another named Lola clocked in for the night shift. Apparently, if a resident was ill, that illness had to be reported and screened by a nurse before they were allowed to seek medical attention. The hard truth of it was that any contagious illnesses, such as the flu, required a person to be quickly taken away and into quarantine topside. Even a runny nose was enough to lock down a family in their rooms until any possible signs of illness were gone. Lauren was grateful she didn't deal with that side of medical care in the complex. Her job was to help Dr. Gregory with noncontagious patients.

And so far, it had gone well. Their last patient of the day was a man who'd sustained a laceration on his forehead from tripping and hitting his head on a metal bar. He was being held for observation, and after a few stitches, was resting comfortably.

"You ready for this card game, Dr. Gregory?" Lauren asked as the two of them waited for Lola who would keep an eye on their patient for the next twelve hours.

"You can call me Ingrid when we're done with work," the doctor said, "and we're basically done." She sighed. "Carrie would rip my head off if you used any honorifics outside of this clinic." Then she offered Lauren a small smile. "And besides that, I think you and I are going to be friends."

"Me, too, Ingrid," Lauren said, smiling.

"As for the card game," Ingrid said, "I'm honestly nervous."

"Not very good at cards?"

"Not very good at people," Ingrid said. "At least, not *these* people."

"I don't know," Lauren said, "it sounded like Carrie was willing to give you a shot. Just loosen up and be real with them."

The door to the clinic opened, and Lola came in, offering a small wave. "Hey, guys. What have we got?"

The doctor gave Lola a few instructions for their patient before the two of them left the clinic and headed toward The Granite Inn together. As they came upon the door, Stellar was approaching from the opposite direction.

He patted his button-up plaid shirt and tugged on his collar. "What do you think?" He asked. "Do I look okay?" He smiled wide and said between his teeth, "Anything in my teeth?"

Lauren leaned back as Stellar leaned in. "Um, no, you're good," she said.

"You look great, Stellar," Ingrid said. "Don't be nervous." She glanced at Lauren and then back at him. "Just be yourself."

Stellar rolled his shoulders. "Be myself," he said. "Yes, yes," he muttered, and then he turned toward the door, walked through, and bellowed, "Hey-oh! Are you ready for a *stellar* game?"

A few awkward laughs came from inside, and Lauren blinked a few times before laughing softly and shaking her head. "You know, I don't even mind his bad jokes. He kinda grows on you, doesn't he?"

Ingrid winced as Stellar continued talking in puns. "I mean, eventually, but... first impressions can be rough."

Lauren gestured for Ingrid to go first through the door. "Well, he did make it a little easier on you," she said. "Make your entrance, stop the madness with a smile and a 'hello.' They'll love you for it."

Ingrid let out a breath, smiled, and stepped through the door. Lauren followed.

"Hello, everyone," Ingrid said, interjecting as Stellar chuckled at his own joke.

"Ingrid!" Carrie said, more enthusiastic than usual. She waved for the doctor to come and sit. "And Lauren! So glad you two could make it."

Most, if not all, of the players were already there, including Heather and...

"Lizzy and Azalea," Lauren said, crossing her arms. "I'd heard from Stellar that you two had gotten out of quarantine. I've been waiting all day to see you!"

"We're not playing," Azalea said sweetly. "We just wanted to get to know some of our new friends." She and Lizzy were sitting close to the round, foldable card table, just behind Heather.

Lauren quirked an eyebrow as a young man sitting next to Heather looked over his shoulder at Lizzy with a smile. "Well, okay, then," Lauren said, cracking her knuckles and sitting on Heather's other side. She looked around the table. "Let's get to playing."

"I've never seen somebody so eager to get smoked," Carrie said to a round of laughter.

"Go easy on the newbies," one the men said. He waved at Lauren from across the table. "First thing's first. Introductions are in order. My name is Van." He pointed at the man sitting next to Heather. "That's Nick and the guy next to him is Otis, both on the maintenance team. You know Ingrid and Stellar and Carrie. Those two hard headed louts are Hector and Ash. They're guards. You might have seen them on your way in by one of those steel mesh barriers."

Lauren nodded. "It's nice to meet you all," she said. "Did Heather do introductions for us already?"

"Carrie took care of that," Heather said.

"There sure are a lot of you," Hector said, chewing gum as he spoke. "Some of the folks down at the arena have been down there for ages. How'd you manage to get up here so quick?"

The table went silent as Hector stared at Lauren and her friends, his eyes narrowed. His fellow guard, Ash, seemed just as skeptical. Nick, the young man who had smiled at Lizzy and seemed to be giving her quite a bit of attention, frowned at Hector. "You know that Lauren is a nurse and Heather was already pregnant when she got to the arena. Most of the people still waiting don't have what it takes to be up here or they're not cleared because they don't have the skill set to be useful."

"Yeah," Otis said, "they're just good stock."

"And those two girls?" Hector asked, pointing at Lizzy and Azalea.

Nick bristled. "They're hard workers. I can tell. Smart, too."

"Andy knows what he's doing, Hector," Carrie said, elbowing him. "Stop being a grump." She crossed her arms. "They just travelled with the right kind of people out there. There's another one of them coming up. She should be in quarantine now. From the sound of it, she's going to be pretty helpful when it comes to caring for our chickens. A farm girl, Andy says."

"Jenny's coming?" Lauren asked, perking up. Her heart leapt. *I won't be alone in this mission.* She immediately looked at Heather, who smiled at the news but didn't seem as excited.

And then she caught movement out of the corner of her eye and looked to see Azalea standing, her expression neutral but her hands in fists at her sides. Azalea's chair had squeaked when she'd stood, and everyone had looked in that direction.

Azalea cleared her throat. "I… um… I'm going to be right back. Bathroom break." She turned and was out of the room before anyone could say anything else.

Lizzy's face was red as she sat on the edge of her seat, looking after Azalea, seeming ready to pop up and follow the other woman if only she were asked. But Azalea didn't so much as look back at Lizzy, and once she was out of the room, Lizzy scooted back in her chair. Lauren tried not to bring any more attention to the pair, though the interaction bothered her.

There is something going on there, she thought for the hundredth time.

"It will be nice to have everyone together again," Heather said, bringing the conversation back into focus. She leaned forward and looked right at Hector. "Carrie is right, by the way. When I found out I was pregnant, I made sure the people travelling with me out there were intelligent and useful and ready to have my back just like I'd have theirs. No offense to the people down at the arena, but most of them were just lucky to have shelter. They were too old or weak or incompetent. They were also mostly loners." She pointed back to Lizzy. "I had my sister-in-law before I found out I was pregnant. I still had people I loved, people to protect. That makes a difference in how you fight and who you choose to be around."

Hector stared back at Heather, and for a moment, Lauren thought things might turn ugly. But instead, his expression changed suddenly from suspicion to pure delight. He howled with laughter and slapped the table. "All righty, then, momma bear! That's what I like to see. A little spunk and a lot of fight." He nodded at Carrie. "Maybe Andy does know what he's doing."

"Enough chit-chat," Otis said, seeming to emulate Hector's mood again as he grinned widely, "let's play."

A few whoops around the table were followed by Carrie acting as dealer. Azalea eventually came back, cool and collected and quiet. Lauren's tension eased the longer they played. She could tell Carrie, Otis, Hector, Ash, Nick, and Van had a bond. The group joked with each other nonstop, poking and prodding at each other in the way only good friends could. It made Lauren feel like she was at a family gathering, just having fun, which made the sudden spike in adrenaline so much worse when Hector brought up the military.

"Can't trust them," Hector said. "They're coming for us eventually. I know it."

"This again?" Carrie waved off Hector's remark, but several of the others didn't seem to think it was something to be taken lightly.

"He's right," Nick said.

"As someone who spent years as a soldier," Ash said, "I second that sentiment."

Okay, Lauren thought, stay cool.

The conversation was either an opportunity or a curse. They could find out information, or they could slip up and reveal that they weren't who they'd claimed to be. Alex and Timothy had done it when they'd first ventured into Colorado Springs. They'd mentioned General Hunt with too much familiarity, or so they'd said.

"Just a matter of time before they try to take the mountain back," Hector said, shaking his head.

Carrie ground her teeth. "Let them try," she said.

"They're not getting through us, though," Ash said.

"That's right," Hector nodded. "We're the ones that made this place what it is."

As the conversation spun into a bashing session complete with talks of military and government conspiracies, Lauren tried to find a way to steer the conversation. She kept coming up blank. She looked over at Heather, expecting to see her just as stiff as Lauren felt. Instead, Heather cleared her throat and leaned in.

* * *

"Okay," Heather said, "but what if they *do* find a way in? Or what if they don't but they do something like cut off incoming supplies gathered at the arena?" She licked her lips. *Here goes nothing,* she thought. "Don't we need a way to barter with them, to make peace?"

"Make peace?" Hector did a double take and stared at Heather. "You really think they're interested in that?" His question was laced with skepticism and disbelief. "Nah. I don't think so."

"Heather's got a point," Azalea said.

Heather looked behind her. Azalea had been quiet since she'd come back from the bathroom. Heather had almost forgotten that she was there. Of course, Nick had been bringing Lizzy into the lighter conversation at every chance earlier in the night, but no one had talked to Azalea and she hadn't inserted herself into the conversation, either.

"Thank you," Heather said.

Azalea stood and walked forward, taking up the space between Heather and Lauren. "I mean, what are we going to do if all those defenses don't work out?"

Heather's mouth dropped. That's not the point I wanted to emphasize!

"What if they, for instance, destroyed the solar panels that are going to keep this place viable long term?" Azalea continued.

"They wouldn't do that," Lauren said quickly. "Then they couldn't take this place for themselves. It would be useless after the diesel runs out."

"True." Azalea shrugged. "But some people are just like that. If they can't have something, no one can."

Heather's mouth ran dry. She wanted to scream at Azalea and ask her what the hell she thought she was doing. Instead, she tried to redirect the conversation again. "My point was that we need to find a way toward peace."

"Maybe we should prepare for both," Carrie said. "Let them decide: war or peace?"

"Or maybe we should take them out first," Otis said.

"That could just provoke them." Nick's eyes were wide, and his words carried a note of alarm.

"Kid's right," Van said. "We have vulnerable people here, including kids. Mark wouldn't risk them just to throw the first punch. If he thought like that, he would've already done it."

"We do have some plans in place if they decide to attack," Ash said. "We'd get the mothers and children out, take them back to the arena if our defenses were breached. That place is more fortified than the military can imagine. The rest of us would be required to take up arms and defend."

"How would you do that? There's only one way in," Heather blurted out, not meaning to egg on the direction of the conversation but suddenly picturing how she could evacuate in the case of the complex becoming an active war zone.

"There's an escape tunnel," Ash said. "It's a bit claustrophobic, only wide enough for one person, and it's a bit of a climb. The hatch on the surface only opens from the inside so that no one can get in that way, and the hatch down here only opens from the outside. No one who tries to come in through the tunnel would actually be able to unless someone inside opened the door."

"It's definitely for emergencies only," Carrie said. "If you go out that way, you better be sure you're ready to get out because you're not coming back."

Heather's head was throbbing. She met Lauren's gaze with her own. *Say something useful!* she thought, though she wasn't doing a good job of that, either. Her plans to control the conversation had backfired again, and anxiety over her future, over her family's future, was becoming so intense, she couldn't think straight.

"Unless the military has someone on the inside," Azalea said. "That could ruin everything."

"Enough!" Heather stood up, knocking her chair over. "Stop it!" she shouted at Azalea. Sweat beaded on her forehead, and every heartbeat brought with it the sensation of her entire body *pulsing*. "Just stop, Azalea! What is wrong with you?"

The young woman's eyes widened, but there was a spark of something like satisfaction in the tilt of her lips. Lauren stood, too, and the people around the table had gone deathly quiet. Suspicion had returned to Hector's eyes, and two of the men whispered something Heather couldn't hear through the *whooshing* in her own ears.

And then Heather's stomach lurched. The room spun. Everything and everyone became blurry, and she was slightly aware of Lauren's voice, giving her instructions she couldn't decipher. She lost her dinner on the card table, and then she stumbled sideways. Someone caught her, but she wasn't sure who. Blurry shapes moved quickly in the odd juxtaposition of light and dark. She'd broken out in a cold sweat all over, her limbs had gone numb, and her heart fluttered. The only thoughts she could manage as her body shut down was a wordless prayer for her baby in the midst of pure terror.

Chapter 37

Lizzy Peters

Lizzy was alone in the dim light of the only private room in the clinic. Heather slept soundly as machines beeped and whirred at her bedside. Lizzy stared at the bright lights, the beacons of a time slipping away, a time The Cleansing had tried to erase completely.

The Cheyenne Mountain Complex was an oddity, the last vestiges of a society hanging on by a thread. Those settlements still surviving on the last of the world's gasoline would soon run out. Perhaps there would still be low-performing electronics for a while yet, what with the widespread use of solar power on RVs and even some homes and other buildings. But even those would fail eventually, and who would replace them? What materials could be used to repair them?

Of course, the complex she found herself in could last for a long time as it was. They had specialists and extra solar panels and innovators. The Heirs of the Mother had a complex that was similar to it. Azalea's mother, Autumn… she talked of a time when they would leave the complex, when Mother Nature would be finished with The Cleansing, when it would be safe to come outside and live and work and rebuild. The Heirs would let the complex go, then, would allow it to fall into disrepair. The clinging to some modern conveniences were essential to their survival for the time being, a necessary evil.

Or so they say, Lizzy thought, wondering for the first time if the Heirs would ever actually give that up. Will it ever be safe to live outside if we stop those who are trying to make it safe?

It wasn't time, they said. Not enough of the wrong kind of people had perished.

Lizzy studied the curve of Heather's chin, the rise and fall of her chest, the flat of her stomach beneath the blankets. Her pregnancy wasn't showing yet, but there was new life there.

Is Heather the wrong kind of people?

No. She didn't believe that. Her father, well… he had brought his fate upon himself. But Heather? She was innocent.

Lots of people who died were innocent…

Lizzy gripped the arm of her chair. Images of oil-slicked waters, of the aftermath of natural disasters, of dead children scattered on the dirt after a genocide in some third world country. The Heirs had shown her the truth: innocent people had always been the victims when it came to the consequences wrought by humanity's greed and destruction.

As the images rolled through her brain, horrific and increasing in gore, just as they had been shown to her over and over and over again, the phantom weight of the headphones the Heirs had made her wear pressed against the sides of Lizzy's skull. The screaming, always present in the back of her mind, quieted only by her faithfulness, by Azalea's soothing voice, got louder and louder and louder. Her heartbeat picked up, and her mouth ran dry. She gripped the chair tighter as the air became too thin. No amount of breathing seemed to satisfy her. Lizzy's lungs burned as the piercing screams rang in her ears and an unbearable weight settled on her chest.

Lizzy closed her eyes and concentrated. Restore the Mother, she thought. Restore the Mother. I will not be part of the problem. Sacrifices must be made. Restore the Mother.

It wasn't working. She needed Azalea's voice. It had been her soothing tones that had comforted her after having the truth drilled into her, after the others had done the hard work of opening her eyes.

She had to get out, get to Azalea. Lizzy stood, dizzy, her vision blurry with tears. It had been foolish to ask Azalea to go the night before. She couldn't remember why she'd been so angry. Azalea had pushed Heather's anxiety to the brink of collapse, but she'd just been doing what was necessary.

Lizzy opened the door and stumbled into the clinic, her breathing too rapid. The room spun. She first laid eyes on Lauren.

"Lizzy?" Lauren was at her side. "What is it?"

"Azalea," Lizzy said, calling out, weakly pushing Lauren away. "Azalea?"

She wasn't able to focus her vision, but a lump on one of the beds stirred. Lizzy fell to her knees. Lauren was still saying something, the panic in her voice coming through while the meaning of her words failed to register.

And then that blessed voice broke through the pounding of her heart, the screaming in her head. "Elizabeth." Azalea was kneeling in front of her, holding her face in her hands. "Look at me."

Lizzy knitted her brow as she blinked away tears. Azalea's face came into focus. She crooned calming words, and the screaming faded.

"I'm sorry," Lizzy said. "Don't be mad at me. I'm sorry." She desperately clawed Azalea closer, grateful that her lifeline didn't pull away, clinging to her. "I shouldn't have been angry," Lizzy whispered. "I shouldn't have—"

"We're not alone," Azalea whispered into her ear. It was a gentle warning. "But you are forgiven. Be calm, now. You see? I didn't leave you."

Not like my father. Not like Zara.

Trembling, Lizzy nodded as she rested her head on Azalea's shoulder. No matter how she messed up, Azalea didn't leave. Lizzy pulled back, her breathing steadier, the screaming quieted, but she didn't let go of Azalea's hand. Not yet.

Lauren was watching them from the edge of a cot, her mouth in a thin line, her face pale. There was a look in her eyes Lizzy couldn't quite decipher. There was confusion there, certainly, but there was also something else… a fearful caution, maybe? That wasn't good.

What did I do? Lizzy thought as her cheeks burned hot.

She swallowed hard, glancing at Azalea and then back at Lauren. "Sorry," she said. "I… had a nightmare."

Azalea reached out and smoothed away stray hairs sticking to Lizzy's forehead before also addressing Lauren. "When we were with those traffickers, we went through a lot together," she said. "Sometimes we need each other to remember our nightmares aren't real."

"Of course," Lauren said, "don't think any more about it. I, um… I can get you some water, Lizzy, and then… maybe it's best you go back to your room." She pushed off the cot and walked into a supply closet off the main room, coming back with a bottle of water.

Lizzy got to her feet, suddenly very tired. "That's a good idea," she said.

Lauren came back and handed her a bottle of water. "I'll come for you if anything happens with Heather."

"Thanks," Lizzy said.

"I've got her from here." Azalea smiled at Lauren, hooked her arm in Lizzy's, and led her out into the hall.

They walked to their room in silence, and Lizzy was okay with that. She needed time to think. Azalea would ask questions once they were alone, once she was sure no one would overhear. Lizzy needed to give the right answers.

Once they were back in the privacy of their little suite, Azalea closed the door and sat with her on the bottom bunk, their handheld lantern set between them. They sat cross-legged, facing each other. An unnatural white light illuminated them both. It made Lizzy cold, made her long for the warmer light of the sun.

Azalea's tone was gentle. "I'm glad you saw reason, Elizabeth. I was worried last night. You were… thinking of betraying me, weren't you?"

Lizzy's eyes went wide, and she sucked in a breath. "What? No! I swear. I would never, I just… I was angry, yes. I thought it was your fault that Heather collapsed. But, I was wrong. I thought about it, and you know what you're doing here. I'm the one who's lost. I need you."

"I know," Azalea said softly, meeting Lizzy's gaze with her own, "and maybe I can believe you, but… I need more. Sometimes I think you weren't ready for this, for what needs to be done. You're so new to the truth. But we needed you to be ready, and so we just hoped that you had what it took. Tell me what I need to hear, Elizabeth. Tell me we didn't make a mistake."

A lump formed in Lizzy's throat. "I *am* ready," she said. "I was thinking about Heather, about her innocence in all this. I was thinking about all the innocents who've died during the cleansing." She looked down at her hands and fidgeted with the hem of her shirt. "I got overwhelmed," she admitted, embarrassed. She looked up at Azalea and tried to put all her conviction into her words, to make Azalea see that she *understood* what was important. "But that's why the Heirs started The Cleansing. This is the last time masses of innocents will die. When The Cleansing is over, when Mother Nature is free of humanity's interference, those who are left will be able to live without the greed and selfishness that leads to suffering. That's why it's worth *our* suffering now. I know that." She looked away again. "It's just hard sometimes."

Azalea reached out and turned Lizzy's chin so that they were looking at each other again. "It gets easier when you keep repeating our purpose to yourself. Keep moving forward. Do whatever it takes."

"Restore the Mother," Lizzy said.

Azalea nodded once, seeming satisfied. "Restore the Mother."

"Now what?" Lizzy asked.

"The seeds of doubt I've planted in the minds of the people here will sprout and bear fruit," Azalea said. "We just have to tend the soil, water them a little, and be ready to harvest when the time comes." She squeezed Lizzy's arm and smiled. "In other words, I have plans, and they start with you and Nick."

* * *

Lizzy peeked into The Granite Inn, scanning those sitting at tables, hoping to see the man for whom she searched. She was renewed thanks to Azalea and rearmed with conviction and purpose. And she was equipped with a plan.

"There you are," she whispered as she spotted him. Lizzy entered the room and sat down across from him. "Hey, Nick," she said.

He looked up from his lentil stew. "Lizzy! What are you doing here? Is Heather okay?"

Lizzy nodded. "Yeah," she said. "It was a drop in blood pressure. Very sudden. Due to stress. I guess all that talk of the military finding their way in got to her. She's banking on this place, on the safety it provides for her baby."

"So the baby is fine, too?" he asked.

"Yes, as far as we can tell." Lizzy allowed her smile to falter. "Of course, it's been hard. I've been worried about both Heather and the baby. I was so grateful when Carrie said I could have a mental health day."

"We take care of each other, here," Nick said. "Are you spending most of the day down in the clinic? Isn't Heather still there?"

Lizzy nodded. "She is, but I spent all night there. Went back to my room for a nap, and I've just gotten up. I'm starving. I was hoping to catch you here, to have lunch."

He pointed at his bowl with his spoon. "I just got started. It's pretty good. I've got about twenty minutes left on my lunch break, if you want to grab a bowl."

"I'd love that." She went to the counter, retrieved a bowl of soup, and returned to sit across from Nick. The soup was warm and earthy. She took a few bites, enjoying the savory goodness of it, thinking about what she needed to do next, how to engage in the right kind of small talk to get what she wanted. "So," she said, "tell me more about what you do around here."

Nick shrugged. "I go around checking on electrical wires, repairing them. Stuff like that."

"How many people are on your team?" she asked.

"There's a few. I do most of the inspections," he said. "We check on all the buildings regularly. You don't want a little problem turning into a big one, you know?"

"That makes sense," Lizzy said.

"You also don't want to waste electricity. We're working on the buildings we don't use yet right now, cutting electrical to certain spots, rerouting it. We want to make sure that when we do need to use those buildings, it's updated to match what we've done in the rest of the place."

"Like only having every other light working in the halls?" Lizzy asked.

"Yeah," Nick said, "like that."

"Do you like your work?" Lizzy asked.

Nick swallowed another bite and shrugged. "Sure," he said. "It's nothing fancy, but it's work, and I like to keep busy."

"What's in those other buildings anyway?" Lizzy asked. "Why haven't we started using them yet?"

"They're full of junk, mostly. Well, it's junk *now*, anyway. The computers are all encrypted, and even if we could get into them, I'm not sure why we'd want to," Nick said. "Although, I guess there's talk of trying to break the encryption on some kind of database. Mark hasn't decided what to do with it, yet. I'm supposed to go by there tonight and boot the database up, make sure the computers are still working."

Lizzy's heart jumped into her throat. She raised her eyebrows, trying to mask her excitement with a look of curiosity. "Could I come with you?" she asked. "I used to hang out with hackers. Even dated one once." She cleared her throat as an unexpected wave of regret washed over her. She was talking about Jordan, Zara's brother. He'd unknowingly helped start The Cleansing and died in the process. Whether she wanted to admit it or not, she still missed him. She cleared her throat. "I picked up a few tricks," she said. "Nothing that could get past military-level encryption, of course, but…" She shrugged. "I do know how to search a place for passwords. You'd be surprised how often people write them down and stick them under a keyboard or just keep them on sticky notes on their monitors."

That wasn't a lie. She'd been the one to find her father's passwords to enable the Heirs to steal information that led to their eventual stealing of DV-10 and a batch of mosquito eggs. She hadn't known what she was doing back then, that she was helping to start The Cleansing. She'd thought she was just helping the Green Earth Futurists with their comparatively tame agenda.

I was always meant to be part of this, Lizzy thought, the notion of destiny comforting her conscience.

Nick chuckled. "I think people down here would have been a little more careful," he said. "But yeah, sure. You can come with me. That area isn't restricted so much as it's just unused. Like I said, it's really just a bunch of junk."

"I would love that. I could really use a distraction from worrying about Heather," Lizzy said.

"It would be my pleasure to distract you anytime," Nick said.

He grinned at her, and Lizzy smiled back, this time genuinely. It had been a while since she'd had the attentions of a guy, but the art of flirtation was starting to come back to her. She'd forgotten how fun it could be. Of course, back then, she'd had Zara around, always reining her in, telling her what to do.

Ironically, she was pretty sure Zara would like Nick quite a bit. He wasn't her usual type. Part of what had attracted her to Jordan had been his rebellious nature, the way he'd fought against big corporations through joining the Green Earth Futurists. He hadn't known just how much of an impact he would make.

No, Nick wasn't like that. He was a rule follower. That much seemed obvious to Lizzy. But he'd set his eyes on her, and he was sweet and kind. It was a shame she'd have to break his heart when she left, but as she smiled back at him, she felt some of her old self emerge, that part of her that liked to have a little fun.

"Well," Lizzy said with a playful smile, "it would be *my* pleasure to let you distract me."

"You know," Nick said, "I hope you don't mind me saying this, but you've got a pretty smile."

"I don't mind," Lizzy said. "Staying here after the sixth month trial period is starting to look better and better, you know," she added, and they both knew what she was talking about. If she stayed, she'd need a partner or a sperm donor, one or the other. She'd be expected to have a baby, contribute to the population. Everyone knew that.

"I hope you do stay," he said with so much earnest honesty it almost made Lizzy feel bad about leading him on.

She reached out and slipped her hand over his hand. "I think we should get to know each other better over these next months, you know? I'm feeling a connection between us. Do you feel that, too?"

He nodded. "Yeah," he said. "I've been waiting… *praying*… for someone like you to come here."

"Maybe God still answers prayers, after all, then," she said.

It really should have been harder. But she could see it in his eyes: she'd caught him, hook, line, and sinker. Azalea's plan was working, and Lizzy was playing her part like a pro.

Chapter 38

Alexander Roman

"I really hope this works," Alex said.

He bent over and squinted through the glass jars at the thick, black substance, something they'd labeled simply, written in all caps on the jar lids: BAIT. They'd dyed it that color to ensure any traces of it could easily be seen and dealt with. No one wanted that stuff exposed anywhere nearby. It was their swarm lure, and if it worked, it would draw a swarm into their trap where they could then release Piranha Solution 2.0, a deadly fog that would hopefully eradicate the mosquitos.

"We could use the win, that's for sure." Walter picked up one of the jars. "If we can give everyone some good news, maybe it will make them stop talking about us like we're the enemy."

"If Ward can bear to share the credit, that is," Alex muttered.

"Now, now," Joanna said as she came up from behind him, "don't be mean. I don't want to see you hanged. Or shot. Or whatever they'd do these days." She brushed his temple with the tip of her fingers. "That mind is too valuable."

Alex stood up and smacked her hand away, repelled by her touch. It made his stomach sick to have her touch him in any way that mimicked the way his wife used to touch him.

Joanna mocked offense, puckering her lips and shaking her hand as if he'd hurt her. "Well, *someone* can't take a compliment."

As often happened when she was around, rage bubbled up in the core of Alex's being. He gritted his teeth and held his tongue. The president and General Hunt had admonished him to cool things between himself and the two wayward scientists. Every time he engaged in a spat with one of them, word got around that *he* was the hostile one, that *he* was being uncooperative. Ward and Turner came out looking like victims of his vindictiveness, and no matter how much he hated them, he couldn't have that.

"I'm sorry I slapped your hand," Alex said, keeping his tone even. "I shouldn't have done that."

Ward smiled at him, reached out, and laid a hand on his arm, letting her touch linger as she spoke. "I forgive you," she said. "We're a team now, after all, aren't we?"

Skin writhing beneath the cold, hard pressure of her hand, he nodded and forced a smile. He didn't pull back, no matter how much he wanted to. Soldiers were watching them as they worked, looking for signs of strife. A few of them had stopped their work just to keep an eye on him after he'd slapped Ward, and as he allowed her to touch him, they slowly returned to their work.

"We'd better get things ready," Walter said as he casually walked around Alex and stood between him and Ward, forcing her to pull her hand away. "We don't have all day."

Alex breathed out, meeting Walter's eye with a grateful and subtle look of gratitude. The other man seemed to understand. He nodded and maintained his position between Alex and Ward, acting as a buffer.

"Blake is supervising the installation of the extinguishers inside the container," Joanna said. "I'd better go help him. You two suit up. I told the soldiers that you volunteered to coat the inside of the container with the bait, you know, to earn you two some brownie points." She grinned as if she expected that to rankle Alex.

"Wouldn't have it any other way," Alex said instead, satisfied as her smile fell and she turned up her nose before trudging up the little hill in the park they'd chosen for their experiment.

"She really is a piece of work," Walter said once she'd gone.

"You have no idea." Alex reached for the protective suit on the bottom shelf of the rolling cart they'd loaded up with jars of bait. They'd each wear a hazmat suit with another plastic layer overtop that had been made just for the experiment at hand.

"Blake doesn't seem so bad, though." Walter grabbed a suit, too.

"He's dangerous, too," Alex said. "Don't let his laid-back personality fool you. He's all about his own survival. He doesn't care who he has to hurt to protect himself."

"Sure," Walter said, "but he doesn't go out of his way to be malicious, not like Joanna."

Alex shrugged. "Doesn't matter. He doesn't play as many games. So what? He'll still stab us in the back if he as half a chance."

"Well, neither of them will be our problem for much longer." Walter put on two layers of blue vinyl gloves. "As soon as our people get back from the mountain, as soon as Kai and Blythe can fly, we're out of here."

"Amen to that." Alex slipped on his suit over his clothes and zipped it up. "I just wish they would hurry. I don't know how much longer I can stand working with Ward and Turner."

"I was thinking more about the fact that half the base thinks we're basically domestic terrorists," Walter said.

"I can't even pretend to understand that." Alex put on booties that fit over his shoes and pulled up to his knees. Then, he grabbed the plastic layer he'd put together himself, made from disposable grocery bags, which would fit over his hazmat suit. It was sort of like a hospital gown he could slip over his arms and tie at the back, except it included fingerless gloves and it draped over his feet. When they were finished coating the floor of the container with the bait, they'd both ditch their outer plastic. They couldn't risk any trace of the bait being on *them* when the swarm showed up. It was important every drop remained inside the box where they planned to trap the mosquitos.

"I don't get it, either," Walter said, "but people who are desperate and angry don't always think straight. Trust me. I've been there. The anger drives you to action. The desperation drives you to *stupid* action."

Alex sighed. "Well, maybe, like you said, success here today will go a long way toward settling things." He nodded at the container at the top of the little hill. "Let's take these jars up there, see how the extinguisher installation is coming along."

Alex and Walter each took two jars, and they walked up the hill. The plywood container was long and wide enough for two men to work side-by-side. The extinguishers were mounted to the walls, their nozzles hung from the ceiling so that they faced the back floor. Wires ran to the opening, and one side of the box was propped up with two wooden stakes so that it looked sort of like an awning. It was a trap door of sorts, attached by hinges at the top, and the wooden stakes were removable.

"Ah, the heroes of the hour," Blake said as they approached. "I believe we're about ready."

"Okay, Turner," Alex said. "Let's go over this one more time."

"Right." Blake nodded. "So, the rest of us will observe from our trailer. We should be safe there. You two will dump the bait in the box, remove your outer plastic, leave it in the container, check each other's suits for any contaminate, and then retreat in your hazmat suits to the bottom of the hill. The lure should be strong enough to keep the swarm's attention away from you, though I suspect being inside the hazmat suit will also dampen your scents."

Alex nodded. "Okay. We go to the bottom of the hill, lay on our stomachs, keep low, and wait, right?"

Blake pointed at Alex enthusiastically. "Exactly. And when the swarm comes and it's mostly in the box, you two come up here, remove the stakes, let the door slam closed, and then latch it closed from the outside."

"When the stakes are removed," Joanna said, stepping up to them and joining the conversation, "their ties to the wires will trigger the extinguishers."

"And we'll have to close the door fast," Walter said. "Piranha Solution 2.0 will eat right through our suits if too much of it gets out."

"Exactly," Blake said. "Let's kill off the swarm, not each other."

Joanna smiled. "At least for today," she said lightly. Turner was the only one who chuckled. She sighed. "You two have no sense of humor."

Yeah... the problem's not us, Alex thought, though, for the sake of peace and appearances, he kept that to himself.

"We latch the door at six points," Alex said, "and that should seal the toxins in."

"Yes," Blake said. "There's a rubber seal here," he said, pointing to a black seal they'd glued to the door, "that matches the seal here." He pointed to another black line on the door frame. "It will seal the swarm in with the toxins."

"And then you two," Joanna said, pointing between them, "retreat to the second trailer. The piranha solution in the fog *will* get out as you do these things, and it *will* get on *you*. There's no stopping that. But the quicker you complete the task, the less of it will contaminate your suits. Still, you'll need to run back to the second trailer, get inside where it's safe, and get the suits off and in the steel barrel we've set up there. It's got water in it to dilute the chemicals."

"Then, it'll be time to see if we've done it or if we've just made a swarm very angry," Blake said.

"Where is Major Willis?" Alex asked as he glanced around the site. He spotted the major as he stepped out of the second trailer, the one Alex and Walter would flee to after trapping the swarm. Alex waved him over. "Any word from the scouts?"

Kenny nodded. "Reports all rolled in five minutes ago. Everyone is positioned. No one has seen a swarm in the vicinity. Two drones are scanning the area. You should have plenty of warning."

"Good," Alex said. "Then we're ready to test this system out."

The major whistled loudly and made a circle in the air with his finger. "Round up!" he shouted. "Back to the trailer!"

The three soldiers double-checking wires followed Major Willis along with Ward and Turner. Alex and Walter were left with four jars of bait. They set to work. The second they opened the first jar, the countdown began.

"We need as large of a surface area as we can get." Alex put the mouth of the jar against the wall. A little goop slid down the wall, but as he moved the jar back and forth, pressing the mouth against the wood, it smoothed the substance. He worked quickly as Walter did the same beside him. Soon the back wall of the container was coated in black. They did the same to the sides of the container and the floor at the back.

"Looks good to me," Walter said as he put his jar down.

Alex nodded and took a step back. "Agreed. Let's—"

"A swarm's comin' your way, gents." Kenny's voice came over the speaker of a radio he'd left behind. Get out of there. You got five minutes, tops."

Alex put his jar down, too, and stepped back from the black substance as he removed his outer plastic layer. He hadn't gotten any of the stuff on him, but he left the layer on the floor as he stepped out onto the grass in his hazmat suit. Walter had moved just as fast, and they gave each other a quick check before rushing to the bottom of the hill where they could lie in wait.

A minute passed before the telltale buzz of the swarm sent a prickling up Alex's spine. "We're safe in our suits," he said, just as much to remind himself as to remind Walter. "Timothy and I were trapped with a swarm inside that house, and our suits kept them out."

Walter looked at him through his visor, which fogged around his mouth as he breathed too hard. "It's a lot harder not to run away than I thought it would be."

"Will you be able to run *toward* them when the time comes?" Alex asked.

"I... I think so." Walter's stammering didn't sound convincing.

"We can do this," Alex said. "We can do it together."

Birds erupted from the tops of the tree line at the other end of the park, squawking and beating their wings, zipping ever upward. The swarm seeped through the foliage. Swirling tentacles broke from the main mass and reached for straggling birds, over taking them, engulfing them, and then retreating as little corpses fell from their grip.

The swarm crept forward, a writhing black mass, condensing and expanding like a caterpillar, parts of it thick and opaque, other parts thinned out to let the daylight through in pinpricks. It arced toward the ground, levelled, and then surged toward the container.

"They shouldn't move like that," Walter whispered, fear tempered with a touch of awe lacing his words. He lay on his stomach, propped up by his arms, watching.

"Maybe one day we'll figure out how they evolved so quickly," Alex said. He couldn't look away from the swarm, either.

The closer the swarm got, the harder Alex's heart beat within his chest. *Please work,* he thought. *Go toward the bait. Go inside the container.* His clothes stuck to his sweaty body beneath the hazmat suit. Sweat beaded on his face, stung his eyes, and salted his lips as he willed the swarm to go after the bait. *They're not intelligent. They're instinctual. If the bait is formulated correctly, they'll be attracted to it first.* His reassurances were overshadowed by the nonsensical feeling that the swarm was more like a roaming predator than anything else.

But the swarm did as they'd predicted. It flowed up the hill, pulsated around the entrance, and then entered.

Alex scrambled to his feet. "Let's go!" he shouted.

Walter was right beside him. When they got to the container, Alex couldn't help but look inside the box. In the shadows, the surfaces which had been covered in bait were squirming with mosquitos. The middle of the container was full of zigzagging, agitated black. Dots of bright orange colored the mass, the markings more noticeable as close as he was.

"Alex, the stakes!" Walter shouted.

Alex shook himself free of the mesmerizing swarm and turned to tackle his stake. The both of them removed the poles holding up the door at the same time, and it fell down, thudding as it made contact with the frame. Alex threw his weight against the door, as did Walter. The whipping of wires and the whooshing of the extinguishers told Alex the mechanisms for releasing Piranha Solution 2.0 had worked.

"There are still a few lagging mosquitos outside," Walter said as he smashed one gloved hand against the wood, leaving behind a smear of bug guts, and reached for a latch with the other.

Alex pressed his lips together and squinted, trying to see how many had been left out of the container. He looked back at where the door met frame. White smoke-like tendrils leaked from it. "Spread the residual fog," Alex said, waving his hand around to disperse the toxic fog.

It took only seconds before the air was clear of the oversized, deadly mosquitos, but in those seconds, Alex could already see the top layer of vinyl gloves starting to melt. He and Walter latched the door closed.

"My gloves!" Walter shook his hands. "The fog is eating through them!"

"Get to the trailer," Alex said, already stepping in that direction. "Hurry! We have to get this gear off, and quickly. As he turned to focus on where he was going, he noted two spots on the outside of his visor where the plastic had become distorted.

How long before it eats through our air filters? Alex picked up the pace. They were out of range of the fog, but the chemicals that had gotten on their suits would keep eating away at them.

"Take off your helmet, first!" Alex shouted as he slammed into the trailer door and then ripped it open.

He and Walter scrambled inside the trailer. Walter closed the door behind them as Alex started ripping off his helmet and suit. Walter did the same. The air smelled like burning plastic. That wasn't good. The fumes alone could kill them.

"Gloves last," Alex said, "so that you don't accidentally touch the piranha solution."

They each had their gear off and thrown into the steel barrel within thirty seconds. It was half full of water, and they had to push their clothes down to cover them. Alex slid on the lid to the barrel and looked over at Walter.

"You okay?" he asked.

Walter was trembling, but he nodded. "I think so. You?"

Alex leaned on the barrel as the adrenaline faded and his legs turned to noodles. He stumbled backward and plopped onto a twin-sized bed. He held up his hands. "I don't see or feel anything that would have me worried."

Walter walked over to the window and looked out. "Do you think it's working?"

Alex glanced at the barrel where their hazmat suits were soaking. The water would dilute the solution enough that it would become a powerful irritant, but not quite as dangerous. But even the barest hint of the solution had begun eating through their suits, through materials made to withstand extreme conditions. "If it's not working," Alex said, "we're in trouble. Because if that solution doesn't destroy their exoskeletons, nothing will."

Chapter 39

Jenny Conner and Lizzy Peters

Jenny was finally inside the complex, and things were *not* ideal. The others had been there too long without her. She had very little information about what had been happening in her absence, and she needed to talk to Heather and Lauren.

I have to let them know what happened with Azalea and Lizzy at the arena, Jenny thought, determined to reveal that the two youngest of their group were at best unstable and at worst saboteurs.

She had been debating it, gone back and forth on her options. There was definitely the possibility that Heather would stick up for Lizzy, and there was very little evidence that Lizzy herself had done anything suspicious. But she followed after Azalea like a puppy, and there was no doubt in Jenny's mind that Azalea was up to something. It had taken her a while to come to that conclusion, but the more she thought about Andy's assessment, the more she'd come to believe that there was more to Azalea than she wanted everyone else to think.

At first, Jenny had thought only to tell Lauren. But no... Lauren and Heather are tight. She'd tell Heather, and then I would look like the one trying to cause trouble.

And so, the plan was to find her people, gather them all together, and confront Azalea—and maybe Lizzy, too—so that Jenny could get the truth out there, whatever that was. Why Azalea would want to keep Jenny back at the arena and hurt their chances of finishing their mission successfully was a mystery. It didn't make a lot of sense. But if Azalea hadn't approached Andy, the military's inside man, what she'd said about Jenny very well could have gotten her thrown out at best, shot and killed at worst.

At the moment, Jenny waited on the edge of a mattress on the bottom bunk in a room she shared with a woman she didn't know. Her roommate would be about her daily duties, and Jenny would have to play the part of hopeful complex resident later. For the time being, she could just be herself, prepare for whatever came next. She'd showered, as would be expected of her, and then perched on the bed, hands resting on her knees, back straight, eyes on the door, mind racing with all the possible outcomes of a confrontation.

When Carrie knocked, Jenny was ready. She opened the door with a smile in place. "I'm so excited to be here," she said. "I can't wait to see my friends, see what they've been doing."

"About that," Carrie said, "I wanted to let you get settled before worrying you too much, but Heather's down at the clinic. She's okay, it seems, but she did have a little... episode last night. Your friends are actually with her now."

Jenny's hand went to her chest. "The baby?" she asked.

"Seems fine," Carrie said.

She blew out a breath of relief. "Can I go see them?"

Carrie nodded. "Sure can," she said. "I'll take you to them. They've all got the day off as they were up all night, waiting to see how things panned out. Lauren went ahead and helped out with the night shift. Lizzy sat by Heather's bedside until real early this morning. Word is she had a panic attack or something, and Azalea took her back to their room for a rest. But I expect they'll all be back at Heather's side today. I'm sure they'd all be glad to see you."

"I don't have to start work until tomorrow, anyway, right?" Jenny asked.

"Well," Carrie said, drawing the word out a little, "not technically. Normally, I'd give you a tour of the agriculture department and let you get to know your fellow workers, but I think we can hold off on introductions until tomorrow."

Jenny thanked her and then followed her to the clinic. As they walked the halls, she thought through her plan again. I don't want to upset Heather, not if she's feeling unwell, but... this is important. We need to decide what to do about Azalea, at least. Maybe I'll hold back my suspicions about Lizzy for the time being, focus on Azalea.

When she walked into the hospital room, Jenny nearly tripped over her own feet. Unlike the last time she'd been in a room with the four ladies, she walked into intimate laughter as if they were all old friends. She walked into a room where she immediately felt like the outsider, despite the way Lauren greeted her.

"Jenny!" Lauren hopped up from a chair on the other side of the hospital bed where Heather was sitting up, a Jell-O cup in one hand a spoon in the other. Lauren wrapped her arms around Jenny's neck and gave her a hug. She pulled away. "Heather's been sharing her Jell-O. We haven't had so much fun in ages."

"Watch," Heather said, grinning as she dipped her spoon in the Jell-O and cut away a small portion. She held the spoon back as Lauren opened her mouth and bent her knees, and then Heather launched the orange blob. Lauren caught it, and all four of the women in the room let out a cheer.

Jenny wasn't feeling so jovial. She smiled, but her heart rate was picking up and her palms were sweating. *If they've bonded further, this thing with Azalea and Lizzy is going to be a harder pill to swallow.*

"You want to try?" Heather asked.

Jenny held up a hand and shook her head. "Um, no thanks," she said. "I'm... um... well, I actually wanted to talk to you, all of you, about something."

"Right to business?" Lauren asked. She sighed. "I guess you're right. It's just been so stressful, and when Heather woke up feeling well, her baby's heartbeat strong... the good news just put us all in a good mood, you know?"

"I get it," Jenny said, "but we do need to talk."

"We *are* glad to see you," Heather said. "We were worried when you didn't come up with Azalea and Lizzy."

"Well, I finally made it," Jenny said, flashing a glance at Azalea to see if the young woman would react. Andy had given off the impression that Jenny wouldn't be coming to the mountain complex if he had anything to do with it. "It was a close call," she said, "but I'm here."

Azalea smiled, as did Lizzy; neither of them seeming surprised or upset.

"We found out you were in quarantine last night," Heather said, "before I made a mess of things."

"I got carried away," Azalea said, waving off Heather's comment. "It was my fault Heather fainted. I got so wrapped up in playing Nancy Drew that I about blew our cover here." Her cheeks turned red. "I'm an idiot. I've apologized a thousand times, but I don't know if I'll ever forgive myself."

Jenny's mouth ran dry. "Oh?" she asked. "What did you say, exactly?"

"That's not important," Heather said. "We need to put last night behind us."

"Do we?" Jenny was trying to keep calm. She couldn't keep her eyes off of Azalea. "Because this isn't the first time our friend here has let something slip that might blow our cover."

The room went quiet, and Heather and Lauren frowned. Lizzy froze, and Azalea smiled.

"I'm not sure what you're talking about," Azalea said sweetly.

"Down at the arena," Jenny said. "I had to wrangle myself out of trouble. I was interviewed a dozen times—interrogated, even—because of something *you* said, Azalea. They kept referencing some conversation you had with Andy, who by the way, was rooting for me to get kicked out altogether. He was also under the impression that Lauren was trouble because *someone* told him that she had been a resident, that she had lied about her history in the medical profession."

Keep it to Azalea, Jenny thought as her gaze drifted to Lizzy. Though the Peters girl averted her eyes and twisted at her fingers, which bespoke guilt, it was pretty clear that Jenny was walking on thin ice with her accusations against Azalea.

Lauren's frown deepened, and she looked from Jenny to Azalea. "Is this true?" she asked. "Did you talk to the people at the arena about me and Jenny?"

Azalea's smile faded, and for the first time since Jenny had known her, the woman looked uncomfortable. She squirmed in her chair as all eyes fell on her. Jenny crossed her arms and waited for her reply. There was no way she could wiggle out of that one.

* * *

Lizzy's blood ran cold. In the midst of Heather's fainting spell, Lizzy's own panic attack, and the initial phases of Azalea's plan for Lizzy to get to the database through Nick, she'd put thoughts of Jenny's return on the back burner. She glanced at Azalea to try to decipher if she'd done the same.

At first, Lizzy thought perhaps Azalea had been caught off guard. She'd certainly been so the night before when mention of Jenny's arrival had kept her quiet most of the night. But when Azalea brought her hand to her mouth and tears started rolling down her cheeks, Lizzy was certain her friend knew exactly what she was doing.

"There has to be an explanation," Heather said sternly, throwing a chastising look at Jenny. "Azalea, just tell us what happened."

"I'm so embarrassed," Azalea said, her voice squeaking. A sob broke loose as she covered her face with her hands.

"This is ridiculous," Jenny said. "You guys can't be taking this act seriously."

Lizzy twisted at her fingers. There was a lump in her throat that seemed to be cutting off her ability to speak. *I should say something, help Azalea, but… what if I make it worse?*

"I… I…" Azalea stammered, the tears flowing freely, and looked up at them, wide eyes flitting from person to person. "I was trying to move things along. I thought flirting with Andy would get us somewhere, but once I got him alone, I just… I just…" She nearly wailed, the sound making Lizzy jump.

"Hush," Jenny said sharply. "You're going to draw attention to us." She went to the door and looked out through the narrow glass pane.

"Take a deep breath," Lauren said, grabbing a tissue and handing it to Azalea.

Azalea nodded and blew her nose. "Sorry," she said more quietly. She dabbed her eyes with the tissue. "I started talking, and I got so nervous when I realized I'd put myself in a room, alone, with a man I didn't really know. The idea was to flirt to gain favor, but I didn't think it through to the end, to what would be expected of me."

Heather sat up straighter. "Did he… do anything to you?"

Azalea shook her head. "He put his hand on my thigh, but then I just started talking and talking and talking. I… I said too much. When I saw talking about you guys made him back off and listen, I couldn't stop myself." She burst into fresh tears. "I was hoping it hadn't had any real effect."

Lizzy watched as Lauren's uncertain expression melted into one of sympathy. *How does she do it?* Lizzy thought. She finally unfroze and reached out a hand to rub Azalea's back.

"Please, Jenny," Lizzy said, "don't be mad. We went through a lot, out there on our own. Azalea has made mistakes, but her heart was in the right place."

"It really was," Azalea said, "I'm not like Lizzy. She's so good at this kind of thing. Just today, she convinced a maintenance guy to give her access to the database."

A shock went through Lizzy's entire body. She tried to control her expression, blinking rapidly and working to keep breathing normally. *What is she doing? I thought we were keeping that a secret.*

She'd assumed Azalea had wanted to destroy the database. That would be harder if they brought Jenny into the picture. But Azalea had always been a step ahead of everyone else, and mentioning it was an excellent distraction from the very accurate accusations being thrown at Azalea, so Lizzy played along.

* * *

Jenny's mouth dropped open. "What are you talking about? You found the database?" Despite the fact that she suspected she was falling prey to the bait of classic misdirection, she couldn't help but bite.

"It's nothing," Lizzy said. "I thought we'd probably see you soon, so I was keeping it to myself until then. Nick is supposed to boot it up tonight, make sure it still works, and he said I could come with. I told him I thought it would be fun to look for a password, even if it was unlikely someone would have written it down, sort of like a treasure hunt. I'm not sure if we can even use it as an opportunity."

"Okay, hold on a minute." Jenny pinched the bridge of her nose, trying to think about what to do. *Tonight? That's a tight timeline.* She shook her head. "I want to talk about that, but we need to work out what really happened with Azalea. One slip-up like that… fine. Okay. But two? What happened last night?"

Heather sighed. "I don't think we should rehash this," she said. "Azalea is clearly distressed. Maybe we just let her sit out, you know? She's not made for all this lying and sneaking around. This amount of stress is clearly giving her enough anxiety that she can't think straight."

Except, according to Andy, she wasn't stressed at all… and Andy would never come on to Azalea like that! She's just going with that story because she doesn't know Andy is our inside guy. Jenny took a deep breath as she debated whether to reveal Andy's position. Would it make a difference? Or would that just endanger him?

Lauren walked over to Jenny and put a hand on her arm. "I think we should talk outside, give Azalea some room."

"Lauren," Jenny said, "I—"

"I mean it," Lauren said, and something in the way Lauren looked at her made Jenny nod and follow her outside. Lauren was the only other person who knew Andy was military. She was the only one who'd been there in Atlanta.

Lauren waved across the room. "Hey, Stellar," she said to the man behind the desk, the man who'd come to examine Jenny after quarantine.

"Oh, hello, hello," he said cheerfully, waving back.

"Where's Dr. Gregory?" Lauren looked around the long room, which was empty.

"She's on a late lunch break," Stellar said. "Can I do anything for you?"

"Oh, no, we're just fine," Lauren said, still smiling. "I'm just going to chat with my friend over here. We're trying not stress out the pregnant lady, you know?"

Stellar nodded gravely. "Oh, I get it. Last night was a scare for all of us."

Lauren pulled Jenny into the far corner of the clinic, pushed her into the corner, and lowered her voice. "Heather's not going to let you attack Azalea," she said.

"I'm trying to get to the bottom of this," Jenny said. "Something's not right with that woman."

"I know," Lauren said.

"I didn't buy that crying act. And Andy would never—" Jenny paused, Lauren's agreement registering for the first time. "Wait, what?"

"I don't trust her, either." Lauren glanced back over her shoulder and shuddered. "For weeks, I've been telling myself that I'm overreacting, but… I can't do that anymore." Lauren ran her fingers through her hair and looked back at Jenny. "But Heather is fragile right now, and she needs everything to be okay. Azalea is tied so closely to Lizzy… I don't know what's going on between them or what Azalea is trying to do, but I want to know. I *need* to know. What was Andy's side of that story?"

Jenny gave Lauren the best rundown she could in a short amount of time. There was no telling when the other doctor might return, when their whispering might encourage eavesdropping, no matter how quiet they tried to be. So, she spoke in rushed whispers.

"Andy said she seemed like she knew exactly what she was doing," Jenny said after summarizing what he'd told her about his interaction with Azalea. "She wasn't giving him that information because she was rambling and scared. She was giving it because she wanted to cast doubt on you and on me."

"She has no idea that Andy is on our side," Lauren said.

"Exactly." Jenny licked her lips and leaned against the wall. "And if he wasn't, if he hadn't told me what happened, I would have believed every word of her story. Whatever is going on, it seems pretty clear to me that Azalea is a good liar and even better at manipulation." She paused as that sank in. She looked at Lauren. "Tell me what happened last night."

"The conversation turned toward the military and what they would do to get the complex back," Lauren said. "Azalea didn't take it there, but once the topic had been brought up, she encouraged it in the wrong direction. Some escape hatch was mentioned, one that can only be opened from the inside, and Azalea mentioned that if the military *did* have someone on the inside… well, the implications were enough to plant seeds of paranoia."

"Damn it," Jenny said. "That hatch is important. If we needed to use it…"

"You knew about the hatch?" Lauren asked. "The military isn't planning on invading that way, are they?"

Jenny shook her head. "It's only big enough for one person at a time to come through. Maybe a small team could come in that way, if Andy could let them inside, but a plan to take back the mountain would have to include a lot of puzzle pieces."

"But they're not planning on doing that, right?" Lauren shifted from foot to foot. "We were told this mission was about information. That's all it is, right? I mean, these people are good people. They're just trying to survive up here."

"Yes," Jenny said. "Of course. We're here for the location of Barlow Scientific Research Bank. That's it."

It was a lie, but Jenny had to tell it. Her stomach fluttered at the deception. *Here I am trying to expose Azalea's lies while I tell a few of my own.* Jenny hated the thought, hated misleading Lauren. But orders were orders.

Lauren's body relaxed, and she leaned against the wall, too. "So, we know Azalea didn't want you or me here, and we know from last night that she wants the people here to be wary of the military."

"But *why*," Jenny asked. "She has to know the mission to the research bank is more important than anything else right now."

Lauren pressed her lips together for a few seconds and looked down at her feet. Finally, she raised her head. "I think I know what's going on."

Jenny quirked an eyebrow. "Please, enlighten me."

"Heather wants to stay here," Lauren said, "and I think Lizzy and Azalea do, too."

Jenny pushed off the wall. "What?" she asked too loudly. She looked back at Stellar who raised his head at the sound of her voice. She smiled at him and waved awkwardly before lowering her voice and turning back to Lauren. "Heather can't stay here. She has to know that. I mean, is she planning on living here without her husband?"

Lauren shrugged. "I think she thinks she can convince them to let Timothy inside." She raised her hands, palms out. "I know it's nuts. It would never work. But she's desperate for a safe place for her baby, and I don't blame her."

"I guess that's another thing we'll have to talk about," Jenny said, shaking her head, "but what does that have to do with Azalea and Lizzy?"

"Heather wants them to stay, too. Or at least, she wants Lizzy to stay. What if they're on the same page as she is? What if they want to stay, but they know you and I wouldn't agree?" Lauren raised her eyebrows. "Don't you think Azalea might be trying to get rid of us so that they can all stay here where they have food and running water and electricity? Hell. They even have yoga and game nights."

Jenny considered Lauren's theory, tapping her fingers against her thigh and chewing on the inside of her cheek as she did so. "Okay," she said, "I could see that. It makes sense. But just because their motivations might be understandable doesn't mean we can let them ruin our mission."

"So, we keep an eye on them," Lauren said. "Heather is older and wiser. She's not going to jeopardize our mission for what she wants, and maybe Azalea and Lizzy don't want to do that either, not really. We just… we need to get this over with. We need to get that information, be done with that part, and then deal with their desire to stay."

Jenny nodded. "One thing at a time," she said. "That's always a good plan." She looked back at the door to the private room where Heather waited with Azalea and Lizzy. "Let's go back in there and see where this Nick guy can take us."

* * *

When Jenny and Lauren returned, Lizzy expected conflict, but she was more disturbed by the lack of it. Jenny had simply asked Lizzy to explain more about Nick and about their planned trip to the offline database that night.

"Okay," Jenny said. "This is it, then. We need to discuss our strategy. We're going to get that information tonight."

"So… you're not mad?" Heather asked. "About Azalea's mistakes?"

"We still need to talk about that, but I think it can wait," Jenny said. "This is more urgent."

So Azalea's act worked, Lizzy thought.

"But," Lauren said, "Jenny and I think Azalea should sit out on this one. Completely. Azalea can go relax in your room while Lizzy makes a way for Jenny to get inside."

Lizzy tensed. *Will Azalea be okay with that?* She glanced at her and frowned. Azalea was smiling, and it seemed genuine.

"That's a good idea," Azalea said. "You two have been so forgiving. Thank you."

What is she up to? Lizzy rolled back her shoulders and tried to match Azalea's relaxed posture. How are we going to destroy the database before Jenny gets to it?

Once the soldier found her way to where she wanted to go, she would be able to get the location of the research bank. She had the encryption key. She was the only one who did. Their only chance of stopping it, that Lizzy could see, was to flat out get rid of the database. Would Azalea want to set fire to it? Blow it up somehow?

"Okay," Jenny said, "then I say we iron out a way for Lizzy to let me inside. I think I'll bring you with me, Lauren, if you'll come. I could use back up, just in case."

Lauren nodded. "Yeah, absolutely."

Jenny nodded. "Good. Nick will have a keycard that can get us in, but we won't want him to realize it's missing. Do you think you can distract him, Lizzy?"

"I think so…" Lizzy said as she looked at Azalea, looking for clues as to what she should be saying, what she should or should not be agreeing to.

But through the whole conversation, as they planned their information heist, Azalea barely contributed. She listened, leaning forward, clearly interested, but she stayed quiet. When their plans had been made, Azalea asked Lizzy if she was hungry, a sign that she wanted to talk.

"Yeah, we could go down to the Shoppette and see how much snack food they're willing to part with," Lizzy said.

It was a good long walk, one that afforded her and Azalea a few minutes of empty hallway.

"What are we going to do?" Lizzy asked, whispering despite there being no one else in sight. "Jenny is going to get to the database before we do."

"Don't worry about it," Azalea said, grabbing Lizzy's hand and squeezing it. Her smile was warm. "Trust me, Elizabeth. By end of day, all our problems will be solved."

Lizzy wanted to ask more questions, but Azalea was in such a good mood. She didn't want to spoil that. Lizzy smiled and absorbed Azalea's happiness. Whatever Azalea had in mind, it would work. It always did.

Chapter 40

Zara Williams

Zara, Kai, and Blythe had set up camp in the same building as the flight simulator. The president had hooked up a generator to the building, and they were to use it only when necessary. Their cots and supplies were in the lobby where they could get by with natural daylight, only needing power when the simulator was up and running.

A rotating guard of soldiers loyal to the president were at the door at all times, day and night. They hadn't met any trouble yet, but General Boreland's detainment was still a secret and they hadn't even been working for twenty-four hours. There was still plenty of time for things to go sour.

Zara didn't have much to do those first hours. Kai was reading and rereading the C-17 Globemaster III flight manual. Blythe wanted him to study the panels, knobs, switches, and buttons before stepping foot inside the simulator. Zara had picked up some textbooks that looked mildly interesting, just to have something to do. She lay on her stomach, a history text open to the middle section on World War II, reading.

"Half of these are comms," Kai said, looking up from the manual.

Blythe was relaxed on his cot. He'd been reading through a manual, too. He didn't look up from his book as Kai groaned about how many items on the dashboard would be useless.

"There's no one out there to hear us," Kai continued. "And navigation? Are we even sure it's going to be accurate?"

Blythe let his manual fall forward, and he sat up. "Damn it," he said. "I don't know."

"Wait," Zara said, "you don't know if the plane's navigation system will work?"

"GPS won't work, not properly, anyway," Kai said. "GPS satellites lose their accuracy if they're not kept on track by stations on the ground. Ferrying people across the mountains through dead air space is one thing. Crossing an ocean without navigation? That's a whole other ball game."

"The plane has an independent navigation system that will help us, but without those satellites sending accurate information…" Blythe rubbed his hand over his face. "We're going to have to use some old school techniques to find our way." He sighed. "There was life before GPS, you know. And there were planes, too. Even transoceanic flights. We just have to return to the basics."

"How are we going to do that?" Zara asked.

"We're going to need a few things," Blythe said, "and I'm going to need you to learn how to help navigate us. I can chart the route before we leave. There might even be some old records, charts, and maps here at the academy that will help. But I'll need to teach you how to check to make sure we're on the right track as we fly."

"Me?" Zara shook her head. "I don't know anything about this stuff."

"You're going to have to learn," Blythe said. "Alex and Walter are busy right now."

"There's Timothy," Zara said in a high-pitched tone. "I'm not a pilot or a navigator or whatever."

"Neither is he, and I trust you. You can do this," Blythe said. He paused. "But you make a good point. Let's get this Timothy guy down here to learn some good old-fashioned navigation. You two can check each other's work while we're up in the air." He hopped off his cot to a folding table that had been set up for them. There were books and papers and pens spread all over it. He picked up a pen and a scrap of paper and scribbled some things on it before handing it to Zara. "Here. You can get that to the president, tell Timothy we need him, and get started learning how to navigate."

Zara took the list, staring at it with an increasing dread as she read it out loud. "Maps, Colorado Springs to New Zealand," she said, "self-contained doppler navigation system, look in the on-site museum?" She looked up at him. "Are you serious?"

"I am," Blythe said.

She looked back at the list. "A compass and… star charts? Where are we going to find those?"

"The library here on academy grounds should have plenty of star charts," Blythe said. "I figure we can use a couple different methods to check our whereabouts." He tapped his cheek, looking past Zara at nothing. "We don't want to find ourselves over nothing but water with no fuel left in our tank," he mumbled.

"I can't be responsible for that!" Zara thrust the list back at Blythe, but he didn't even look at it, much less take it from her.

"Hold on," Kai said. "You *can't* be responsible for navigation, but I can be responsible for helping to pilot the plane?" He raised his eyebrows at her. "I'm sensing a double standard."

"That's different. You already know something about flying," Zara said.

"Yeah, but I'm terrified of getting back into a cockpit, and you know it." Kai turned to his co-pilot. "Blythe, do you know enough to teach Zara or not? She won't have to just figure it out, right?"

Blythe nodded. "I do. Like I said, I'll be able to chart the route. I'll just need Zara and this Timothy fellow to check our position periodically to ensure we're staying on track."

"And we can do that with this stuff?" Zara asked, waving the note around. "This is crazy!"

"It is most definitely crazy," Blythe said. "And I won't be surprised if we all die. But we're all gonna die eventually, anyway, sooner rather than later if this world has anything to say about it."

Zara's hand was still outstretched, note in hand, but when Blythe didn't take it, she let her hand drop. "Fine," she said, shoulders slumping. "I'll get the stuff we need." She sighed, her footsteps heavy as she approached the guards at the door. "Hey, Lindt?"

Cadet Shelley Lindt smiled at her as she approached. "Hey, Zara," she said. "What do you need?"

"A ride," Zara said, holding up the list. "We need a few more items Blythe didn't think to ask the president for earlier. And we need Timothy Peters."

"I can radio the team," Lindt said, holding out her hand. "We can't leave our post, but the president's orders are that you three get whatever you ask for."

Zara shrugged and handed over the list. "Works for me," she said.

Lindt frowned as she read the list over the radio. "You think you can handle that? Over."

"Ten-nine. Say again?"

Lindt repeated the list.

"Message received. Um..." There was a long pause. "We'll... uh... get back to you soon. Over."

"Heard," Lindt said. "In the meantime, it looks like Blythe's team needs one more player. They're requesting Timothy Peters be escorted down. Over."

"Shouldn't be a problem. Over."

"I'll be waiting for an update on those supplies," Lindt said. "Over and out." She shrugged at Zara. "That's all I can do at the moment. When the shift changes, I can check up on these things myself."

"I'd appreciate that," Zara said. "Thanks."

"No problem." Lindt offered a smile. "What you guys are preparing to do... it's nuts, but... it gives me hope that maybe one day things won't be so bad."

"Yeah," Zara said, "me too." She reached out and squeezed Lindt's arm. "What you're doing is pretty brave, too, you know. You're keeping the United States alive."

Lindt locked arms with Zara for a moment before they both let go. Zara returned to Blythe and Kai, giving them the news that the supplies were being searched for and that Timothy would be on his way soon.

"Well, then," Blythe said, "I think it's time to do a couple rounds in the simulator."

Kai's face went pale. "What? I'm not ready for that."

"Of course you are," Blythe said. "It's just a simulator." The man didn't give Kai a chance to object further as he moved off to ask the guard to turn on the generator for the next hour.

"Hey," Zara said as she noticed Kai making fists with his hands and then shaking them out over and over again, "you're going to be great."

"Simulators look like real cockpits," Kai said, keeping his voice low. "I haven't been in a cockpit since... since..."

"I know," Zara said. "I was there, too." The back of her throat tasted of bile as she thought about their crash. During a raging storm, Kai had clipped the top of a small mountain, ripping the plane apart and hurtling them into a lake. They'd barely survived. "But this time, you've got a seasoned pilot teaching you the ropes, flying with you. And besides, we've survived one plane crash. Who's to say we wouldn't survive another?"

Kai gave her a flat look. "Last time we weren't far off the ground. This time we'll be thirty thousand feet up."

Zara swallowed, but her mouth had run dry. Her words scratched at her throat and squeaked as she spoke. "Thirty thousand... yeah, okay... that's pretty high."

"Thanks," Kai said, tone laced with sarcasm. "I don't know why I didn't come to you sooner."

"Okay, okay, give me a second." Zara took a deep breath, banished every thought except the one that Kai needed encouragement, and faced him, putting both hands on his shoulders. "Kai Lee, you are the most arrogantly confident man I've ever met."

Kai blinked. "You need to work on your speeches, babe."

Zara brought a finger to his lips and hushed him. "I'm not done," she said. "Ever since we first met, you and I have run headlong into the craziest situations. You've gone in with your head held high and a smirk on your face, and while it drives me nuts, that attitude also gives me courage. Because you're just as smart as you are confident, Kai. You learn from your mistakes. You grow and tackle the next big thing with everything you've got. And that's what you have to do now. You've cleared a dozen mountains since that one got the best of you, and you'll clear this one, too. I know you can do this. I wouldn't step foot on the plane if I didn't have faith in you, but I do, and I will. And I'll learn this navigation thing so that I can have your back up there." She smiled up at him. "You're not alone, anymore, Kai. We're going to do this together."

His eyes glistened, but he sniffed and shrugged. "Yeah, okay. That was pretty good."

Zara wrapped her arms around Kai's middle and pulled him close, resting her head on his chest, listening to the steady beat of his heart. "I told you I just needed a second." She channeled her best J.J. from the classic series, *Good Times*, in a whispering dramatic shout that required some shoulder movement. "My speeches are dy-no-mite!"

"You're a nerd." Kai chuckled as he held her still.

"I know." Zara squeezed him tight and then let go. She pulled away and smiled at him. "Are you ready to kick this simulator's butt?"

Kai pulled out his aviator's sunglasses from his shirt pocket and slipped them on. "You know it."

"You two are adorable, but adorable ain't gonna mean a damn thing up in the air," Blythe said from behind them.

Zara cleared her throat, her cheeks going red. She and Kai exchanged a glance. She, at least, had almost forgotten Blythe was even there. For a moment, it had just been the two of them. Someone she cared about had needed to hear everything was going to be okay, and Zara had zeroed in on that, blocked everything else out.

"It's a good thing, too," Blythe said, a small smile breaking his serious expression as he pointed back at himself. "Because otherwise, this ugly would get us all killed."

Kai snorted, and Zara covered her mouth as a burst of laughter escaped.

Blythe nodded toward the door that led deeper into the facility. "Now, let's get this thing done," he said. "The three of us, we're going to get the right people to that research bank, and it all starts here and now. We've got a lot of work ahead of us." He pointed at Zara. "You take up one of these manuals," he said. "It wouldn't hurt for you to familiarize yourself with the plane while we're back there practicing on the simulator."

Zara swallowed her objections. She didn't want to learn about the plane or how to navigate. It would mean that her limited knowledge could be called upon one day to do something with it. But her desire to have Kai's back overwhelmed her more selfish instincts. She picked up the manual, her fingers tingling at the feel of the cardboard cover, and smiled, putting on a brave face as Kai left the lobby with Blythe, both of them heading for the simulator. All the reasons she couldn't possibly do the things Blythe asked of her formed a lump that sat at the base of her throat, put weight on her chest, made it harder to breathe.

Someone, she thought, needs to give me a pep talk.

She looked down at the flight manual, groaning to herself as she sat back down on her cot. The truth was, she wasn't sure she could scale the mountain ahead of her, and shoving metaphorical walking sticks at her wasn't going to help.

Chapter 41

Lizzy Peters and Jenny Conner

"Now, this building might not be restricted," Nick said, "but access to the generators most definitely *is*." He flashed a grin at Lizzy as he unlocked a door with his keycard. "This is where we'll be. Take that lantern and have a blast searching for passwords under keyboards. I'll be back shortly, after I turn on the power to this section."

"Don't be too long," Lizzy said, smiling back at him. "What do you think they'll give us if we do find a password? Maybe one of those steaks?"

"You know, I'd take that," Nick said. "A nice dinner with Mark and Emily, steaks and potatoes, and a little notoriety? Count me in."

Lizzy laughed for his benefit. She leaned against the doorframe, holding the door open as she waved him off down the hall. When he'd turned the corner, she looked back over her shoulder the way they'd come and whistled quietly. Jenny and Lauren peeked around the far corner, and the two of them scurried down the hall and to the door. They went in ahead of Lizzy, and Lizzy looked down the hall each way one more time to confirm no one had seen them before she slipped inside and let the door close.

"I can't believe this area isn't restricted," Lauren said.

"The database is useless to everyone in this building except for us," Jenny said. "To them, it's just a bunch of old servers and computers."

Lizzy held up the lantern to reveal part of what looked to be a large room with rows of servers to the left and several desks to the right.

"Here," Lizzy handed the lantern to Jenny. "You two get to work as soon as the lights turn on. It's about a ten-minute walk from here to the generators. I'll buy you some time, pretend I got scared and left the lantern in here on my way out. I'll wait for Nick outside the generators, stall him as long as I can."

Lauren put a hand on Lizzy's shoulder. "Thanks, Lizzy. This is going to get us what we need so we can get out of here."

Jenny nodded, but she didn't say anything. There was still a note of suspicion behind the woman's eyes every time she looked Lizzy's way.

She's got good intuition, Lizzy thought. Just not good enough.

"I'll see you back at the clinic when we're all done here," Lizzy said. "Good luck getting the coordinates."

She left the two women in the section of the complex where the offline database was stored, but she didn't follow after Nick. Instead, she took a deep breath and looked the other way, toward the hall that would lead her to The Granite Inn. It was getting late. Carrie and her friends would be hanging out there, eating dinner and having a good time. That was where Azalea's plan would begin to take root.

* * *

"Lizzy is cooperating," Lauren said. "That's good, right?"

"Yeah," Jenny said, though every fiber in her being told her something was off. She held up the lantern as she walked over to one of the desks. "But if we're right and Azalea and Lizzy and Heather all want to stay here, what are we going to do after we get these coordinates?"

Lauren shrugged and sat in a rolling chair behind the desk. "Maybe we let them."

Jenny shook her head. "We can't do that." She couldn't add what she was thinking, that everything inside the mountain was about to change.

"Why not?" Lauren asked. "Would it be so bad to let Heather and her family try to find some peace here?"

"We can't leave them behind," Jenny said. "For their own safety, we have to convince them to come with us. The second Heather tries to get them to include Timothy, and we both know she will, they're going to connect them to the military. It'll be over for them."

It'll be over for the civilians, period, she thought. All I have to do is get the schematics and the location of that weapons bunker in the side of the mountain, and the military will have the resources and the knowledge to take this mountain back.

Of course, Jenny prayed the civilians would do the right thing. Once their defenses were breached, for the sake of their families, they would have to back down. And it wasn't like President Coleman would kick all of them out. Once the military was in control, the families could come back. She'd seen his plan. The complex could hold a lot of people. There was no reason it couldn't be shared, and it was only right that the President of the United States and his council would take the helm.

Still, there were a lot of stubborn people inside the mountain. Jenny expected there to be pushback, probably even violence.

She would prefer Lauren and Alex and their whole crew be on their way to New Zealand when that fight started. It was clear that Lauren and Heather had grown attached to the civilians, and Jenny couldn't blame them. But the military needed their most important asset back. They needed the protection it afforded, the information it protected, and the resources it provided.

President Coleman had tried diplomacy. He'd tried to be reasonable. Mark and his guys were just too stubborn. It was time to force them off their pedestals and expand the reach of the complex to include everyone left alive in Colorado Springs, not just a select few Mark deemed worthy.

Jenny found a light switch on the wall and turned it on so that when the power to the area was restored, they would know immediately. Then, she opened a panel on each server to inspect it.

"I was told we'd need to flip on the servers one at a time to get it up and running," Jenny said. "I'll need your help to get them all on as quickly as possible. It will take a few minutes for it to boot up. It should only take me another minute or two to find what I need and download it to my drive. And then you and I are going to shut it all off as fast as humanly possible." She shook her head. "We'll risk losing information in the database if we do it that way, if we don't go through proper shutdown procedures, but we'll have what we need, and we can't let Nick know we were here."

Lauren opened a panel on the next server. "It would be suspicious to find everything up and running," she said.

"On the upside," Jenny said, "if he boots up the servers to find error messages all over the place, he might consider it a lost cause and leave the database alone. I get the feeling there's plenty there that they could use against us, plenty that could just make them even more angry at the military."

"I don't want to know," Lauren said. "I just want to get these coordinates and get out of here."

Then the lights came on overhead, sending a jolt of adrenaline through Jenny's body. She threw the first switch. "Hurry! Get them all turned on. We've got work to do."

She sprinted to the next panel and threw another switch as Lauren did the same.

* * *

Lizzy sprinted through the halls toward The Granite Inn, repeating what Azalea had told her to say. She didn't quite understand it, not yet, but she had faith.

"You don't need all the details," Azalea had said not two hours earlier. "Trust me, and you, me, and Heather will be safe. Lauren and Jenny will no longer be a problem. You and I can go home, and Heather can stay here, if she wants."

Lizzy's eyes had brimmed with hot tears of relief. "You figured it out for Heather?" she had asked.

"You're important to me," Azalea had said, "and Heather is important to you. I should have worked that complication into my plans from the beginning."

And so Lizzy did as she was told. She trusted Azalea, and instead of going to stall Nick, she'd started off at a dead run through the halls to The Granite Inn where she was most likely to find Carrie. She burst into the dining area, scanning the tables wildly for her target.

"Lizzy?" Carrie stood, a look of concern on her face. "What is it? What's wrong?"

"You have to help me," Lizzy said. "Jenny and Lauren... I think they're doing something they shouldn't."

"What are you talking about?" Carrie walked toward her, frown deepening, hands held up in a calming fashion.

Lizzy gestured with her hands, infused her voice with panic, just as she'd practiced with Azalea. "I was with Nick in the buildings we don't use, just hanging out, having some fun. I just... I wanted to get to know him." Tears slid down her cheeks as she worked herself up. "He went to the generators to turn on the power. I'm not allowed there, so I stayed behind. Jenny and Lauren showed up..." She shook her head, covered her mouth with her hand, and squeezed her eyes shut.

"Lizzy... you need to finish your story." Carrie's tone was soft but urgent. Several others had stood and gathered around.

"I've never really liked either of them," Lizzy said between great sobs that shook her body. She was really getting into the performance. "Heather's so trusting, but Azalea and me, we've always thought there was something off about them. Now they're going to ruin everything! They're going to get Heather and her baby kicked out!"

Carrie put her hands gently on Lizzy's shoulders. "No one is going to kick Heather out if she had nothing to do with whatever is going on. But Lizzy, you haven't said anything that tells me Jenny and Lauren are up to no good."

"They forced me to let them inside the room with... I think Nick said it was the database?" She sniffed and got out the rest between her bouts of crying. "Jenny said some guys named Coleman and Hunt were going to be happy with them, that they were finally getting the information they needed for the military to take back the complex." It was the perfect thing to say, the thing that played to all their fears. Everybody in the room tensed, and a few gasps and murmurs rose to accompany Lizzy's cries. "Jenny wanted to tie me down, but I just ran... and I came here. I didn't know what else to do. They didn't follow me. I think they're planning on doing something fast and then escaping through that hatch you were talking about during cards."

"Okay," Carrie said, holding up her hands, her tone hard. "It sounds like we've got a couple of military rats playing the long game." She spat on the floor.

Stellar stood up behind the muttering crowd. "Excuse me," he said, "but Lauren? She's a good nurse. I can't believe that—"

"She had me fooled, too, Stellar," Carrie said. "We've got to go, right now, and stop whatever it is they're doing." She raised her voice. "I need four of you to come with me. The armory is on the way. We'll load up, just in case, but we need those ladies alive, you hear? We need to know exactly what they were doing here." She turned back to Lizzy. "You've done the right thing, Lizzy. Now, I don't know the parts we don't use as well. It'll be faster if you take us to them. Think you can do that?"

Lizzy nodded, and within seconds, she was leading Carrie and four men down the hall, thinking of how she was going to convince Heather to go along with the new narrative for her own sake.

* * *

It took longer than Jenny thought it would for the database to boot up. She tapped her fingers impatiently on the desk as Lauren paced in front of the first panel she would turn off the second Jenny signaled that she had the information they needed.

Finally, the application on the computer monitor indicated the database was live, and Jenny started opening folders, searching for the right information.

"Ha!" She pumped her fist. "I think I found something."

She scooted back and took off her shoe, shaking a thumb drive out onto the desk. It had been in the toe of her boot all day, something Andy had managed to smuggle under her mattress before she even set foot in her assigned room.

"Hurry," Lauren said. "I don't know how long Lizzy is going to be able to stall Nick."

"I'm going as fast as I can. Just stay by the panel and prepare to flip the first switch. We'll need to turn off each one, and fast, as soon as I say the word." Jenny stuck the flash drive in place.

"What is that?" Lauren turned and looked at the door. "Is that... is that shouting?"

Jenny snapped her head up as the shouting got louder. "That doesn't sound like Nick." A hollow formed in the pit of her stomach. Something had gone very wrong.

* * *

When Lizzy turned the final corner, she didn't have to act anymore. She frowned and stopped short. In front of the door that led into the room with the database, Nick lay motionless, a pool of blood eating up the white tile all around him.

"Nick!" Lizzy screamed, real tears springing to her eyes. Carrie grabbed her arm and said something about stopping, but Lizzy tore away and ran forward. She stopped at the edge of the blood and then backed up into the wall, shaking her head. "No," she said, "no, no, no."

He stared lifelessly at the ceiling, the flesh at his neck split, the wound gaping open. There was no rise and fall of his chest. Her body shook uncontrollably.

Why? He was so nice to me. He didn't do anything wrong. Azalea… why? She didn't understand. This wasn't the plan. This wasn't… Then, as she stared horrified at Nick's empty eyes, it hit her. She was going to do this the whole time. This was the plan.

As Carrie swiped her keycard, as five citizens of the complex burst into the room beyond the door with weapons drawn, Lizzy's chest tightened until she couldn't breathe. She hadn't wanted Nick to get hurt. She hadn't wanted Lauren and Jenny to get hurt, either, not really. She'd wanted them gone, out of the way.

But not this, she thought as her lungs burned. I didn't want to frame them for murder.

She couldn't seem to take in a breath. The pool of blood kept expanding. It touched the toe of her shoe. She stumbled sideways but tripped on her own feet as a gunshot rang through the halls. Lizzy reached out as she fell, catching herself with her hands, but one of them landed in the blood. She screamed and scrambled away.

She'd killed before, but those men had deserved it. This was different. Nick… Nick was *good.* Lizzy held up her trembling hand, coated in blood. The stain was more than skin deep; it was one she wasn't sure she could ever get out.

Chapter 42

Lizzy Peters and Jenny Conner

For once, Lizzy's anger was louder than the screaming voices in the back of her mind. She walked the hall with fists balled at her sides. She controlled the way she walked, her expression, everything about her outer presentation. No one could know the boiling rage bubbling in the pit of her stomach, no one except for Azalea herself, the person who'd stoked Lizzy to such all-consuming anger.

She managed to open the door to their room with a measure of normality, but when she saw Azalea lounging on the top bunk, a book in hand, relaxing as if the night were any other night, Lizzy lost it. She slammed the door closed, her breath hot, her cheeks burning.

Azalea arched an eyebrow as she looked up from her book. "I assume everything went to plan? Lauren and Jenny are out of our way?"

"You murdered Nick," Lizzy said, a growl behind her words.

Azalea snapped her book shut. "Keep your voice down."

Lizzy's fingernails dug into her palms. "He wasn't an oil baron. He wasn't trying to stop The Cleansing." Her vision blurred with tears that overflowed and scorched her cheeks as they slid down to her chin. "He was nice to me. Nick was just a regular guy."

Azalea slid off the top bunk, turned around, and reached out to wipe away one of Lizzy's tears. "I can see you're upset," she said. "You and I used Nick for a purpose, and that purpose had run its course. He had to go, Elizabeth. I was protecting you."

Before Lizzy fully realized what she was doing, she had slapped Azalea across the cheek. "Do *not* tell me you killed him for me. I didn't want that."

Azalea spun and grabbed the post of the bunk bed for support. She took a moment, staring at the floor, seeming to gather herself before getting to her feet and meeting Lizzy's gaze with her own steely one. "But I did do it for you," she said, "and you know it."

The tone she took flipped a switch somewhere deep inside of Lizzy, made a modicum of doubt appear, made the very air whisper accusations in her ear. The voices in the back of her mind, the ones that tortured her, wouldn't let her forget her purpose… the shock of finding Nick dead and the subsequent anger had made them strangely silent. But that tone from those lips reawakened them.

"You aren't mad at me," Azalea said, those words coating Lizzy's skin and seeping in to douse her fury in confusion. "You're mad at yourself."

"What?" Lizzy swallowed hard, her head beginning to pound as her heartbeat picked up speed.

Azalea cocked her head ever so slightly, narrowed her eyes, pursed her lips. "When we used Theodore back at New Horizons, when we were done, you lit the match that set him on fire, did you not?"

"That was different," Lizzy said. The room seemed to shrink, the whispers became moans, and her anger was replaced with straight up fear.

"It was the same situation, Elizabeth," Azalea said. "I told you Nick was a tool, a means to an end. I used the same language as when I spoke of Theodore. What did you think we would do with him? Let him go and allow him to tell everyone here that he let you inside, that he didn't see anyone following you two? He would have thrown doubt on our story, Elizabeth. When I killed him, when I sent you to get Carrie instead of doing it myself, I saved you from having to kill Nick. I knew you were too weak to do it, so I took care of it for you, to protect you and to protect Heather."

Lizzy shook her head and stepped back, her legs wobbling. "I didn't know you were going to kill him," she said.

"Didn't you?" Azalea asked.

The voices in Lizzy's head, the voices of dying people, of a dying earth echoed her: *Didn't you?*

"Or," Azalea continued, "did you just not think about it? Perhaps you avoided accepting the only possible outcome of what you were doing? What else could have given the people here absolute reason to believe us, absolute hatred for Lauren and Jenny? What else could have immediately given your story credit? What other end would have made you the one who tried to save the complex? I assume when you returned to find Nick dead on the floor, you were able to give them a nice show of mourning him, did you not?"

"It wasn't a show," Lizzy said as the room spun. She sank to her knees. They were screaming now, drowning out her own thoughts, overwriting them, only allowing Azalea's voice to break through.

"You have a soft heart," Azalea said. "I can't blame you for that. But think about it, Elizabeth. They saw you truly distraught by Nick's death. They would never believe you had anything to do with it."

"I didn't," she whispered as Azalea knelt in front of her. "I didn't know…"

"Tell me the truth, Elizabeth," Azalea said gently. "You knew. I saved you from having to do it yourself."

Nothing made sense. Lizzy shook her head, but she could no longer voice her denial.

Azalea's hands cupped Lizzy's cheeks, her touch soothing the bite of sharp screams. "Ensuring The Cleansing runs its course is hard, isn't it, Elizabeth?"

"Yes," Lizzy whispered, leaning into that touch that soothed the voices.

"I have always steered you in the right direction, haven't I?"

Lizzy nodded. "Yes." The admission quieted the screaming further.

"You want to be worthy, don't you? To be strong?" Azalea asked.

"I do," Lizzy said.

"And I lend you that strength, don't I? Am I not the one who quiets the agonizing screams?" Azalea's voice became cold. "Should I let the voices have their way with your mind?"

"No," Lizzy grabbed hold of Azalea's hands as they lifted from her cheeks. "Don't leave me alone. I… I can't quiet the voices on my own."

"Because you need me," Azalea said. It wasn't a question.

"I need you," Lizzy said, nodding.

Azalea kept her hands on Lizzy's cheeks, her fingers at Lizzy's temples. The voices were back to whispers. "And you're grateful that I killed Nick, aren't you? So that you didn't have to do it."

The words sank in as she could finally hear her own thoughts, and she imagined what it would have been like to have killed Nick with her own two hands. *It would have been unbearable*, she thought. "You did it for me," she said.

"Yes, I did it for you." Azalea drew Lizzy closer so that her head rested on Azalea's chest. She stroked Lizzy's hair as she cried, the anger at Azalea redirected to where it belonged. "Next time," Azalea said softly, empathetically, "when we let a man near, a man we plan to use and discard, let's make sure he deserves judgment."

Lizzy sobbed harder. It's my fault, she thought. I got Nick involved.

"It's okay," Azalea said, hushing her like a mother hushes a child in pain. "I'm here. You can always come to me, Elizabeth. You belong with me. I will love you no matter how many times you make mistakes."

"I'm sorry," Lizzy managed between the heaving of her chest, between the sobs that shook her whole body.

"I know," Azalea said, still stroking her hair. "Now, we need to talk about what to tell Heather so that she doesn't suffer the same fate as Nick. She needs to believe that Jenny killed Nick, that you and I are innocent in all of it. She'll believe you, Elizabeth, and because of that, she will be saved. If she falls in line, the people here at the complex will feel sorry for her. They'll embrace her further, and then she won't be a threat to The Cleansing. We can let her go, leave her to be happy here."

Still crying, fear pulsing through her, Lizzy pulled away and looked up at Azalea. "You have to help me save her," Lizzy said. "Please, you have to help me."

"I will," Azalea said. "Heather is going to be okay as long as you do what I say."

Lizzy threw her arms around Azalea's neck. "Thank you," she said. "Thank you, thank you, thank you."

As Azalea hugged her tight, Lizzy calmed. Shame over how she'd brought Nick and Heather into the mess of preserving The Cleansing culminated in a deep gratefulness that Azalea was there to do the right thing. Azalea would lead them to victory in their mission. Azalea would work out how to keep Heather safe from the fate of all those who would interfere with The Cleansing.

All Lizzy had to do was follow and obey, if only she could stop shaking.

***

Jenny still wasn't sure exactly what had happened. She sat dazed in a room devoid of all furniture. Lauren sat beside her. They both leaned against the wall, their hands zip-tied and resting in their laps. There was a battery-operated lantern in the middle of the room and two water bottles but nothing else. It had been at least fifteen minutes since the two of them had been shoved inside.

"It just doesn't make sense," Lauren said, her voice filling the empty room. "Nick… he's…" She trailed off.

"Dead," Jenny finished for her. "Lizzy didn't seem to have done it. Either that, or she's a hell of an actress."

"But you think Lizzy had something to do with Carrie finding us there," Lauren said.

"Don't you?" Jenny asked. "She was supposed to be with Nick. When those guys dragged us out, accusing us of killing him, she was looking at his body like she'd just discovered it, not like she was there when it happened."

"I just… I can't believe she'd set us up," Lauren said. "And you're right. There's no way Lizzy killed Nick."

"Who did?" Jenny looked over at Lauren. "We're in real trouble here, and we need to decide what we're going to tell them when they come to question us."

Lauren leaned her head back against the wall. "It looks like we killed him to get into that room."

"I know." Jenny breathed out, long and slow. "Maybe we stick with the truth. We don't know who killed him."

"And the reason we were in that room?" Lauren asked.

"Again, the truth. We were sent here to get coordinates of a research bank that may hold the cure to the disease." Jenny pulled her knees up and rested her bound wrists on them. "It's the only thing that makes sense, and it's true, so… maybe we can get them to believe us."

"Okay," Lauren said. "But I think we should leave Heather out of it."

"We can't leave Heather out of it without leaving Lizzy out of it, too," Jenny said, shaking her head. "If we leave Lizzy out of it, we can't tell the whole truth, and the whole truth is the only thing that will make sense right now. We were here for information. Lizzy got us into that room. We don't know what happened after that."

Lauren sat silent for a minute. "I am going to have to deny Heather had anything to do with this, and if that means protecting Lizzy, too, that's fine with me. You agreed that she couldn't have killed Nick. Whatever happened, even if Lizzy had some fault in it, I can't let Heather and her baby take the fall."

"And how do you know," Jenny asked, "that Heather *wasn't* involved? Do you really trust her that much?" Frustration was settling in, and it was hard for Jenny to keep her tone calm.

Lauren nodded without hesitation. "She's fought just as hard to find a cure as I have. I won't say anything to endanger her. She's my friend."

"If you don't tell the truth, and I do, that will just make us look more suspicious." Jenny tried not to raise her voice, but it didn't work. "They might kill us, Lauren. We need to be on the same page."

Lauren looked at her and emphasized every word. "I. Won't. Implicate. Heather."

Jenny gritted her teeth to keep from shouting. Tension built inside of her; she felt like a balloon ready to pop. She closed her eyes and started counting to herself, an old childhood exercise that allowed her to deflate her rising anxiety.

Finally, she looked at Lauren again. "Fine. Let's just see what they think happened. Let me do the talking. I won't bring Heather into it, okay?"

Lauren didn't have the time to agree or offer any further dissent. The door opened, and Carrie entered with Mark on her heels. He crossed his arms and looked down at them, a disgusted look on his face.

"Do either of you have anything to say?" he asked.

"I'll tell you everything," Jenny said, "but first, I want to know what *you* think happened tonight."

Mark scoffed at her. "You're in no position to be making demands."

"That's the only request I'll make," Jenny said. "I swear it."

Mark shook his head at them and jutted his finger at Jenny. "You followed Lizzy and Nick, and when Nick went to the generators, you forced Lizzy to let you in that room. She escaped. That was the first thing that went wrong with your plan. The second thing that went wrong was that Nick returned sooner than you expected. And so you killed him."

"We did not kill Nick," Jenny said.

"We didn't even know he was dead until we were dragged out into the hall," Lauren said.

"You think we believe that?" Carrie stepped forward and spat at their feet. "Nick was a good one. He had a bright future here, and he was my friend. You're going to pay for this." She lashed out, kicking Lauren's shin.

Lauren cried out, and Mark put a hand on Carrie's arm. "The time will come," he said. "Right now, we need information."

Carrie turned and pounded the wall with her fist, leaving behind a dent.

"I swear to you," Jenny said. "We did not kill him."

Mark put his hands on his hips and looked up at the ceiling, shaking his head as if she were a kid claiming to have not stolen a cookie while her shirt was covered in crumbs. He looked back down at her. "What were you doing in that room?"

"We were sent here by the President of the United States to find the coordinates of a research bank which we believe holds the key to getting rid of DV-10 and the swarms," Jenny said evenly, doing her best to infuse her statement with all the sincerity she could muster.

Mark raised his eyebrows. "DV-10? Is that what they're calling it?"

"It is." Jenny nodded once. "Mark, my mission was to get in, get the information, and get out. That's it."

"And what about her?" Mark nodded at Lauren. His expression was grim. "Heather? Lizzy and Azalea?"

"Mark," Carrie said, "Lizzy was shocked by Nick's death. She was the one who warned us. She—"

"I know what we think happened," Mark said. "But their original story was that they'd been travelling together for weeks. That doesn't mesh with the idea that Jenny and Lauren were working alone."

Jenny swallowed and looked at Lauren. Her temple throbbed as the pressure inside the room built. She'd wanted to stick with the truth, but that wasn't working. She looked down at her hands, zip-tied, the lines at her wrists digging into her skin. Racing thoughts made her heartbeat quicken, and there was a whooshing sound in her ears.

Think of something, Jenny. This is it. Be smart.

There wasn't enough time to come up with a full-fledged, convincing lie. But if she could work in enough truth, the lie would be easier to remember. An idea came to her, started working itself into something tangible. She looked back up at Mark.

"I was a soldier before all of this. I really am from Ohio, and I really did live on a farm growing up." Jenny took a deep breath. The next part was where the lie came in. She had to make it convincing. "When everyone started dying, I left my unit and went home, to my family. They were all dead. Before I'd left, though, we'd gotten the call to Colorado. After finding my family dead, I wandered for a bit, not sure if I wanted to try to find my unit again. Everything seemed so… hopeless."

"Let me guess," Mark said. "That's when you met Lauren, Heather, Lizzy, and Azalea."

"Yes," Jenny said.

"Okay, fine." Mark crossed his arms and looked at Lauren. "Why don't you let her tell a little bit of this story, then?"

Jenny looked at Lauren and nodded. "Go ahead," she said. "Tell them how I kept the truth to myself."

She caught Mark narrow his eyes in her periphery, but she didn't care. She had no choice but to drop the hint, hope Lauren kept them on the right track.

"Jenny was helpful. She knew how to do a lot of things we didn't," Lauren said. "She didn't tell us a lot about her past, and we didn't ask. That subject can be painful for a lot of people these days."

Good, Jenny thought.

"And how did you find yourself here in Colorado Springs?" Mark asked.

"I brought them here," Jenny said quickly. "Like I said, I knew my unit had been headed here before I left them. Lauren and the rest didn't have any real direction, and so I took the lead."

Mark sighed. "Okay, go on."

Jenny licked her lips and coughed. She reached for the water bottle to give her time to think through what she had to say next. She had to meld the lie they'd told together with the new lie she was creating in that moment. Jenny quickly thought it through to make sure it lined up right, and then she continued.

"I liked them, and I thought we would all be safe here," Jenny said. "When we first got to the city, though, I slipped away and approached the military. I wanted to know if my new friends would be welcome there. Instead, I found out all about the mountain complex. They convinced me to go back to Lauren, Heather, Lizzy, and Azalea, pretend to be a civilian, infiltrate the complex."

"And you just trusted them?" Mark asked.

"I'm a soldier. I was given orders." Jenny shrugged. "They got me updates and information through a dead drop in the city, and then I found further instructions in my supplies at the arena."

"I knew it," Mark said. "We've got a mole there." He looked at Carrie. "We'll have to investigate that further."

Sorry, Andy… Jenny thought. Indicating her orders were given anonymously was the best she could do to protect him.

"That doesn't explain Lauren," Mark said, turning to her. "Why were you in that room?"

"I found out she was trying to get information on a cure," Lauren said, "and I volunteered to help. I found a coded message, figured out she was keeping a secret. But we didn't tell Heather. She's my friend, and she's pregnant. We couldn't put her in danger."

Jenny nodded, relieved that Lauren had said something smart. "That's pretty much it," she said. And now maybe I can keep the rest of it a secret, she thought. No one, not Mark and not Lauren, has to find out about my secondary mission.

"We only wanted to help the government get rid of the virus," Lauren said.

"We didn't know you," Jenny added. "But once we got here, we ended up liking you quite a bit. We were going to get the information and then just leave you alone."

"We would have never hurt anyone," Lauren said.

"Except you threatened to detain Lizzy," Carrie said. "You were going to tie her down."

Jenny cursed to herself. *Is that what she told them?* She pushed aside her rising desire to retaliate and throw doubt on Lizzy. *Lauren won't go for it. It wouldn't work.*

"But we weren't going to hurt her," Jenny said instead. "I swear to you we were never going to hurt anyone. And we didn't kill Nick."

Mark crossed his arms and looked down at the floor. For the next few minutes, he shifted his weight back and forth, sometimes looking up at them, sometimes at the ceiling. He didn't speak, and the silence was driving Jenny insane.

"I don't know what parts of your story I believe," Mark finally said. "I need some time to think. Carrie, let's go. I want the door locked and an armed guard outside."

"Can do," Carrie said.

Without another word, the two left, closing the door behind them.

"How do you think that went?" Lauren asked.

"As well as could be expected."

"Lizzy didn't even try to protect us," Lauren said.

"Yep." Jenny closed her eyes and took a deep, calming breath. "There's no doubt about it now: she betrayed us."

"What are we going to do?"

Jenny scooted over and stretched out, letting go of her anger for the time being by focusing on the practical. "I'm going to get some sleep. You should, too, if you can. There's no telling when we'll get another chance."

It was hard to sleep. Jenny drifted in and out, and she suspected Lauren did the same. But the short bouts of rest she did get were invaluable. When a knock sounded at the door, it woke her from the middle of a hazy dream she couldn't quite remember. Jenny sat up and rubbed her eyes as a shadow of a man filled the doorway.

"You two are lucky Mark isn't going to let you starve."

Jenny recognized that voice. Her heart leapt. "Hello, Andy," she said.

Beyond the door, a guard looked into the room.

"Hello to you, too," Andy said, dropping the tray of food so that the sandwiches fell apart, the pudding splattered, and the spoons skidded onto the floor.

Nice touch, Jenny thought.

"Oops," Andy said. He looked over his shoulder, exchanged a grin with the guard, and then the guard turned back around. Andy crouched and shoved the tray closer to them, his expression serious. "Hang tight," he mouthed.

Jenny offered him a small smile, and so did Lauren. But he didn't return it.

"Charge at me," he whispered, barely loud enough for her to decipher.

As he got to his feet, Jenny got to hers. "We're starving, you bastard," she shouted. "We didn't do anything wrong." She ran at him, slamming her shoulder into his chest.

He stumbled a few steps backward as the guard looked back and took a step in. "I've got this, Marv," Andy said. He pushed Jenny to the wall, hard.

Lauren squeaked in what sounded like genuine alarm. "Stop! You're going to hurt her!"

Andy came up behind Jenny and put his elbow at her neck, mashing the side of her face into the wall. "Maybe she deserves it," he said, and then he leaned in and whispered in Jenny's ear something that made her blood run cold, made her breath catch. "Execution is on the table, Jen. Be ready. If I can get you out, I will."

He let her go with another shove, and on his way out, he stepped on one of the sandwiches that had already come halfway apart. Jenny pressed her back against the wall, feeling the blood drain from her face as the guard smirked and closed the door, leaving them once again in the insufficient light of the small lantern, alone and awaiting their judgment.

Chapter 43

Heather Peters and Lizzy Peters

The morning found Heather comfortable beneath her blankets in the quiet of the clinic's private hospital room. She blinked slowly, not wanting to give up her dreams yet. She'd been in a reality where she and Timothy and their baby were welcomed into the complex. Mark and Emily had been there, welcoming them with the keys to their very own apartment. But that wasn't reality, not yet, and so Heather stretched and allowed the dream to fade away completely.

We'll get there, she thought as a smile spread on her face.

She pressed her call button, expecting Lauren to respond.

Dr. Gregory opened the door instead. She flipped on the lights. "You're awake," she said. "Good, good." She busied herself with looking over the monitors, but she seemed... distracted? She didn't look at Heather or ask her the usual questions.

"Good morning, Ingrid," Heather said. "Is everything okay?"

Ingrid pushed a few buttons. "The baby looks healthy," she said. "You probably need to use the bathroom, right? I can get your breakfast, too."

"Where's Lauren?" Heather asked as she swung her legs over the side of the hospital bed.

Ingrid helped her take off the leads from the fetal monitor to the machine. "She won't be here today," the doctor said. Her voice cracked, and she frowned as if it were painful to say.

"Is she okay?" Heather frowned.

"She's physically just fine."

"You're worrying me, Ingrid." A spike of concern pierced through Heather's chest. *Something's wrong,* she thought.

"Carrie wanted me to tell her when you were awake," Ingrid said. "Go about your business, and then I want you back in bed."

Heather reached out and grabbed Ingrid's arm, stopping her as the doctor turned to leave. "Tell me what's going on."

"I can't," Ingrid said. "I have orders."

"Orders?" Heather shook her head. "That doesn't make sense." An anxious burst of energy made her shake out her hands. "What about Lizzy and Azalea? Where are they?"

"Lizzy will be by to see you later today, I'm sure," Ingrid said. "I'm sorry. I can't tell you any more."

"But they're all alive?" Heather asked.

"Yes," Ingrid said.

"Okay." Heather let the doctor go. "I guess... I guess I'll wait for Carrie, then."

Ingrid nodded once and left. Confused, clinging to the knowledge that her sister-in-law and her friends were alive, Heather moved through the first twenty minutes of her day in something of a haze. Every moment boiled down to the simple action of *not* thinking about all the things that could be wrong.

Her heart jumped into her throat when a quick knock was followed by Carrie sticking her head into the room. "Are you... feeling up to visitors?" Carrie asked.

"Please, come in," Heather said, sitting up, smoothing the blankets draped over her legs.

She expected Lizzy or Lauren to be behind Carrie, but instead, it was Mark. Heather frowned as the two of them offered her a greeting and a few niceties.

"I know something is wrong," she said, her words firm and pleading at the same time. "Please, just tell me what it is."

Carrie and Mark exchanged a glance. Carrie arched an eyebrow at Mark, and his lips drew a tight line. She crossed her arms, her expression seeming to say she wasn't backing down on something while Mark took a deep breath, nodded, and looked back at Heather.

"There's been an incident," Mark said. "Lauren and Jenny are in detainment."

Cold dread settled in the pit of Heather's stomach and spread out from there, numbing her as she tried to process what Mark had said. A thousand questions flitted through her brain, but she chose the one that was safest for her. "What... what happened?"

She listened in silence as Mark told her what had transpired the night before, and the numbness only became fuller, more... all-encompassing. He told her that either Jenny or Lauren, or perhaps both of them, were responsible for Nick's death, that they'd threatened Lizzy and gained access to a room with the database Mark had told her about when she'd eaten with him and Emily. Lizzy had escaped, warned Carrie, and a group of them had gone to confront the two women only to find Nick with his throat slit.

That doesn't make sense, she thought, trying to parse the lie from what she knew to be true.

"We got a partial confession from Lauren and Jenny," Mark said. "It seems Jenny was the brains behind the operation, working for the military on her own at first. Lauren was dragged into it under some pretense of trying to find coordinates to some research facility where the military thinks they can find a cure for the illness." He leaned back in his chair. "It's my belief that Jenny was the one who killed Nick, but that Lauren was an accomplice, whether she had a direct hand in his death or not."

Heather shook her head. Her voice was barely above a whisper, but she couldn't seem to speak any louder. "I've known Lauren much longer," she said. "I *know* she would never hurt anyone."

"But Jenny?" Mark asked.

"I thought I knew her, but..." She really looked at Mark for the first time since he'd started talking. "I need to talk to Lizzy."

Carrie shifted in her chair. "I went by there this morning," she said. "I thought you'd want to see her. I'm gonna have to take Ingrid down with me when we're done here, though. Lizzy was… she wasn't all there. Azalea said she didn't sleep, and she was… clearly disturbed by what she'd witnessed. Poor girl."

"Okay, then… I need to go to her," Heather said.

"Before any of that," Mark said, "I need you to tell me now. What do you know about Jenny's involvement with the military?"

"Nothing," Heather said, the lie coming to her lips instantly. "I'm still trying to wrap my head around it. But right now, I'm more worried about my sister-in-law. Finding Nick like that… she was sweet on him, you know? I need to see her."

And I need to get to the truth, she thought.

"We're going to have to talk about this again," Mark said, "but… Carrie and Ingrid have convinced me that we need to take it slow, for the sake of your health and the health of your baby." He stood. "If you get permission from Ingrid for an outing, I have no problem with your going to see Lizzy. My only warning is this: your association with Jenny and Lauren has you on thin ice here. If it weren't for Lizzy's quick thinking in warning Carrie, you would have been under heavy suspicion, along with Lizzy and Azalea. As it is, you three will be watched, but…" He glanced again at Carrie. "A lot of people down here see Lizzy as a hero, and I'm leaning in that direction, as well. If you do see her, thank her for her quick thinking. It might have saved you."

Heather nodded. "I… I will," she said. "Thank you for coming to tell me yourself."

"I'll send Ingrid back to evaluate you and give you the all clear to speak to Lizzy," Mark said.

"She's, um… not very responsive, from what I could tell," Carrie said. "She might not be ready to talk, but I'm sure your being there would bring her some comfort."

Mark and Carrie left Heather, then, and after a few seconds had passed, she threw off her blankets and started getting dressed. With or without the doctor's permission, she needed to talk to Lizzy and Azalea.

* * *

Not thirty minutes after Mark and Carrie's visit, Heather was knocking at Lizzy's door. She didn't let up, her knuckles wrapping on wood until Azalea opened the door.

"Heather," Azalea said. "Aren't you supposed to be resting?"

"Mark and Carrie came to see me this morning." Heather pushed her way inside, not waiting for Azalea to move or invite her in. "What the hell is actually going on?"

"I wasn't there," Azalea said, gesturing to the bunk bed. "You're going to have to ask Elizabeth."

Lizzy sat knees to chest in the shadowed corner of the bottom bunk, blankets pulled up all around her. She was still, and she stared straight ahead. There was no movement to recognize Heather's arrival, not even a glance her way.

"Lizzy?" Heather approached and sat on the edge of the mattress, her heart breaking. "Have you slept?"

"Not that I can tell," Azalea said. "I drifted here and there, but I tried to stay awake for her. I never saw her actually fall asleep."

"I was talking to Lizzy," Heather snapped. Azalea's presence grated on her, though she couldn't put a finger on why that was.

Azalea put her hands up, palms out. "Sorry," she said, "but she'll barely talk to me. I don't think you're going to get much out of her."

"I'm sorry," Heather said softly. "I shouldn't have snapped at you. I'm a little on edge. Thank you for being with her through the night."

"Of course," Azalea said. "I'd do anything for Elizabeth."

Heather turned back to her sister-in-law and reached out to put a hand on Lizzy's arm. "Hon, please… talk to me. What happened?" She waited for a minute, but Lizzy didn't acknowledge her. "You let Lauren and Jenny into the room, like you were supposed to. But something went wrong after that. Please, tell me."

Lizzy sat there, still as a statue. And then she whispered, "Jenny killed Nick."

Heather blinked and her breath caught. Hearing it from Mark was one thing. She hadn't counted anything he'd said as absolute truth. There was too much he didn't know. His story didn't make sense with what Heather knew to be true. But when Lizzy said it, when she confirmed that Jenny had killed Nick…

Heather swallowed hard. "Did you see her do it?"

Lizzy finally looked at her. She nodded slowly, and tears brimmed her eyes and spilled over onto her cheeks. "Yes," she whispered. And then she broke down and sobbed, her cries raw. "Don't make me talk about it."

"Okay," Heather said, hushing her as she hurried to her and wrapped her arms around her. "It's okay. You don't have to say anything else right now. It's okay."

Heather couldn't push Lizzy, not when she was so fragile. But something had happened after Lizzy let Jenny and Lauren inside the room with the database, as they had planned all together, something that Lizzy hadn't told anyone, something that would have made her go to Carrie and endanger their mission.

The truth was, it wasn't okay. Not even a little. Everything was falling apart.

* * *

Lizzy leaned against Heather and cried. The tears were real. She cried for Nick. She cried for her mistakes. She even cried a little for Jenny and Lauren, for having to sacrifice them to save Heather, to save herself and Azalea.

As Heather whispered comforting words, her chin resting on the top of Lizzy's head, Lizzy caught Azalea's eye. There was affirmation there. She was doing a good job. They hadn't quite figured out how to explain what happened to Heather, the only person besides Lauren and Jenny who knew Lizzy had let the two women inside that room on purpose.

They'd wasted too much time talking about what to do when Lauren and Jenny disputed their story. Lizzy had been shocked to find out that they hadn't. They'd denied killing Nick, but they hadn't denied Lizzy's lies about how they got into that room. Azalea guessed they were trying to protect Heather because if Lizzy's lies were uncovered, Heather would be next in Mark's crosshairs. It didn't take a genius to figure that out.

Lizzy didn't mind playing the traumatized, distraught, barely able to speak victim. She didn't *want* to speak. She didn't *want* to tell any more lies. And her heart really was breaking. Maybe she would stay in that role until it was time for her and Azalea to leave, to go back to the Heirs of the Mother, to live out the rest of their days in peace.

Ensuring The Cleansing runs its course is hard, isn't it, Elizabeth? Azalea had asked.

And it was true. The sacrifices they had to make were meant for the strong of mind and body and spirit. It may have felt like moving forward after making such sacrifices would be impossible, but Lizzy was confident in Azalea's promises.

The truth was, it would be okay. She just had to hang on a little while longer. Everything was falling into place.

Chapter 44

Alexander Roman

Alex thought there was absolutely nothing that could destroy the excitement of their successful experiment from the day before. They'd killed off a swarm. The bait had worked, and so had the toxic fog, though it had been dangerous for him and Walter. Their suits had been ruined by the stuff, and longer exposure could have been very bad for them. But as long as they moved quickly and could sacrifice a few hazmat suits in the process, Alex was fairly certain they could manage to wipe out the remaining swarms in the city.

But Alex had been wrong. Every ounce of his happiness was stolen from him as he sat in a room full of his friends, listening to General Hunt recount the latest news from Cheyenne Mountain.

Lauren had been caught breaking into the database with Jenny, and somehow, they'd been accused of murder.

"My Lauren didn't do that," Minnie said, interrupting not for the first time. "It had to be that Jenny character. Y'all have to tell those civilians that. Or let me do it. I'll go right down there myself and—"

"You will not," General Hunt said.

"Alan—"

"Minnie, let me finish my report." It was the softest Alex had ever heard the general's voice. "I promise you: we're not going to let them rot. And Sergeant Conner is one of mine, remember? I don't think either of them actually killed anyone. Our source says they deny it, and I believe them."

The general went on to explain that it seemed Lizzy had betrayed them. She'd told the civilians Jenny and Lauren were in the room.

"It's possible that Lizzy killed this man herself," General Hunt said.

"No." Walter slammed his hand on the table and stood. "My daughter didn't kill anyone."

"He's right," Zara said. "She's been weird lately, but she wouldn't hurt anyone. I don't think she'd even kill someone in self-defense. What about Azalea? Where was she?"

Walter wagged a finger at Zara. "Good question." He looked at the general expectantly.

"As far as we know," Hunt had said, "Azalea was not involved, and neither was Heather. Neither of them were anywhere near the scene of the crime."

Timothy visibly relaxed, but then he tensed as Hunt continued.

"Heather was at the clinic. She... apparently had a fainting spell." He held up his hand as Timothy stood, too. "She and the baby seem to be fine." He looked around the room, the muscles at his neck bulging. "Can I please finish telling you all what I know, in its entirety, before I have any more interruptions?"

Alex put a hand on Minnie's arm. "It's okay," he said. "Let the man finish." He looked around the room. "I know we're all worried about our people, but I'm sure President Coleman and General Hunt would never let anything happen to them." He looked at Hunt as he said the last part, his voice firm.

"Thank you, Alex." General Hunt took a deep breath. "Heather, Azalea, and Lizzy all seem to be fine where they are. The civilians are sympathetic to them. As I said, Heather was in the clinic, under medical watch. Azalea was in her room. Lizzy was the one who alerted the civilians. It's only Sergeant Conner and Lauren who are in any danger."

"Danger?" Minnie asked. "You said they were detained, but... in danger? What do you think they're gonna do to my baby girl, Alan?"

"It doesn't look good..." General Hunt paused, looking at Minnie, clearing his throat, and then looking down at the table. "...they're talking execution."

Minnie gasped, and Alex's heart leapt into his throat. He immediately reached out to put an arm around Minnie, his focus on her as her eyes welled with tears. But his own vision blurred, too. The thought of losing Lauren... it made him sick. It made him want to charge into that complex and get her out of there, no matter what it took.

General Hunt moved from the head of the table the moment Minnie started to cry. "We're going to get them out." He knelt beside Minnie. "I won't let them kill your daughter, Minnie. I'm going to get her back for you."

"How?" Alex asked. "You got her into this mess. How are you going to get her out?"

"There's an escape hatch," Hunt said. "We're sending a small team down through it. Our inside guy... he's been there too long. We can't leave it up to him, not entirely. He's going to let the team inside the complex through the escape hatch, and then it will be up to them to get the sergeant and Lauren out. It's risky, but... it's the only way."

"What about my daughter?" Walter asked.

Timothy nodded and leaned forward. "And my wife?"

"I'm afraid we're going to have to leave the other three there," Hunt said. "They do not seem to be in any immediate danger."

Walter, Timothy, and Zara all started talking at once, putting forth objections, their voices increasing in volume with every syllable.

But why? Alex thought. They should be calling it quits, figuring out another way to get the coordinates. And then it hit him.

"You want them to try again," Alex said, almost to himself.

"Wait, what did you say?" Walter cut the air with his hand and Zara and Timothy quieted. "Alex, *what did you say*?"

"I said—" Alex looked at Hunt. "—they're going to ask an at risk pregnant woman and two young women barely old enough to be called adults to try again for those coordinates."

Minnie pulled back from General Hunt. "Alan?"

The general sighed and stood. He looked exhausted just then as he closed his eyes and nodded. "Alex is right."
"There has to be another way," Walter said. "They went in there as support, as distractions."
"You need to try bartering again," Zara said. "Talk to the civilians."
Timothy nodded. "Give them something—whatever they want! You have to get our people out of there."
"We're not leaving without them," Alex said. "We won't leave them behind. And we don't have months, General Hunt. They're right. We need to consider alternate means of getting those coordinates."
"I wish there was another way," General Hunt said, "but there isn't. The civilians won't listen to us, and they are more suspicious of us than ever. We *have* to get my sergeant and Minnie's daughter out of there, ASAP. After that, we need to lie low."
"Didn't you hear me?" Alex asked. "We don't have time to 'lie low.'"
"We'll have to make time." General Hunt returned to the head of the table. His movement seemed to signal that he was getting back to business. "Heather, Lauren, and Lizzy have months left before they would have to solidify their citizenship within the civilian community. As of now, they are safe there. If we give them some more time to integrate and earn trust, eventually, they will be able to get back into that room and get the coordinates for us."
"This is insane," Walter said.
"We need to be on our way sooner than that," Alex said. "The longer we allow these swarms to reproduce and grow worldwide, the harder it is going to be for us to eradicate them."
"I can't change what's happened," General Hunt said. "We have our orders. We have our plans. This is not a brainstorming session, Mr. Roman. It's a debriefing, to let you know what's going on. And it's a courtesy. Don't make me regret it."
"Alan!" Minnie stood. "Only a fool wouldn't listen to Alex right now."
General Hunt didn't look at her. "I'm following orders," he said.
"I never took you for a coward, Alan," Minnie said, her voice breaking. "I hope I'm not wrong about you." She slid her chair back. "I've heard enough. I need to check on my dog." Tears sliding down her cheeks, she marched to the door and left.
"She's right, General Hunt," Alex said.
"I'm going to get Conner and Lauren out of there," General Hunt said. "That's priority number one. The rest..." He sighed and shook his head. "Whatever we do, it's going to take time. You need to figure out what that means and how to make that work." He pointed between Alex and Walter. "That's your job, not mine."
Walter rubbed his temple. "General H—"
"This meeting is adjourned," Hunt said. "I have work to do." He turned stiffly toward the door and walked out without another word.
"I need to check on Minnie," Alex said.
"Alex," Walter said, "this isn't okay."
"Not okay?" Timothy threw up his hands. "My *wife* is in there. His *daughter*."
"And Azalea," Zara spat. "She has to be the one who killed that man." She wiped away tears from an angry face.
Kai took Zara's hand, the motion seeming to calm her. He hadn't said anything, and he stayed quiet.
"We don't have proof of that," Alex said. "We don't know a lot. Let's just... hold off on making judgments until Jenny and Lauren are back."
"That's not good enough," Walter said. "I've left my daughter in danger before. I won't do it again. I won't!"
He shouted those last words and slammed his hand so hard on the table it made even Alex jump a little. Walter's hand shook from the impact. Tears slid down his cheeks, dropped from his chin. He let out a frustrated, angry sound and then stormed off, slamming a couple of rolling chairs against the wall as he left. Zara and Kai followed after him, calling his name.
Timothy shook his head. "Someone has to tell Candice," he said. "Maybe Minnie can keep an eye on the kids while I fill her in. There's nothing to be done right now. I don't want the kids to overhear and worry." He didn't wait for Alex to respond before he, too, left.
And then it was just Alex in the little conference room, alone and powerless. He needed to check on Minnie and Oliver. He needed to talk to Walter, to make sure the man would be able to continue their work. They couldn't abandon it, no matter how emotional they were. Doing so could put them in danger. The soldiers and cadets needed to see Alex and Walter as men working for their good.
But he couldn't leave the room, not yet, not when his mind was spinning and his heart was racing and his hope was nowhere to be found.
He wasn't sure how long he'd been sitting there when the door slammed open and General Hunt stormed back in with a string of muttered curses coming from his lips. He paced for a few moments before seeming to notice Alex was even in the room.
"You're still in here?" He huffed and pointed toward the door. "You need to go talk to Minnie."
Alex scoffed and shook his head. "Even if I wanted to, I wouldn't be able to convince her you're doing all the right things."
"Not for that, you idiot," the general said. "To make sure she's okay. She's a jewel, a diamond that shines for everyone else all the time. She's always comforting everyone else, and now that her daughter is in trouble, she needs somebody else to do the comforting." He cursed again. "I can't do it because she won't let me, but she'll let you, so get on it, young man!"
"You're right," Alex said as his words rung true. He stood. "But before I go, be honest with me. What's the likelihood we're going to be able to get Lauren out of there?"
General Hunt shifted his weight from one foot to the other and worked his jaw back and forth before meeting Alex's eyes with his own. "It's not looking as good as I'd like it to," he said. "We've lost a lot of our most experienced soldiers in a very short time span. A lot of those who are left are still green. Some of them should still be in the academy or in training. Not one of them has ever crossed into enemy territory like this."
"But you have," Alex said.
"I can't go," Hunt said, his face falling. "The president needs me here. He... didn't approve my request, and I understand why, even if I don't like it."
Alex nodded. So, he already tried to go in there himself. He really does love Minnie, doesn't he?

"And there's no one left? What about Major Willis?"

General Hunt shook his head. "He's got a good head on his shoulders, but no… he doesn't have experience in rescue missions behind enemy lines. To be honest, I don't have a lot of it, either." He rubbed his hand over his face. "General Boreland, though…"

"We can't send him in there," Alex said.

"He has experience organizing these types of missions," Hunt said. "Before he came to this academy, he earned a lot of respect, rescued more than a few airmen stuck behind enemy lines. It's why there's so many people who can't see past his current… lack of good judgment."

"We couldn't trust him," Alex said.

"Maybe if we offered him something, we could," Hunt said.

"If he's listening to Lawson and Price, we shouldn't be giving him anything." Alex wasn't backing down on that one. He stood tall, infusing his voice with conviction. "We can't use Boreland."

"Even if it's our best shot at getting Lauren and Sergeant Conner out alive?" Hunt asked. "Boreland may not respect President Coleman, but he is a patriot, and I think I have an idea."

Alex cut the air with his hand. "I can't think of anything—"

"An election," Hunt said.

"What?" Alex had to keep his jaw from hitting the floor.

"President Coleman wants one anyway, but we can use it to convince Boreland to do the right thing. We'll tell him the truth, that once Colorado Springs is safe again, once there's peace between the civilians and the military, we'll have an election for the offices of President and Vice President, and we can promise him Secretary of Defense. It's one of the ways the president is considering bringing the civilians and the military together, to make a cabinet where differing viewpoints can all have a voice."

Alex frowned. "What if Boreland runs for office?"

"Then he runs." Hunt shrugged. "But I think he'll want Secretary of Defense. It will give him the power he wants, the position and respect. He wants to be heard. And I also believe he'll respect a vote. Right now, he doesn't accept President Coleman, but if he's elected fair and square, he'll have no choice."

"So, he does this mission for us," Alex said, "and he gets what he ultimately wants."

Hunt raised his eyebrows. "I think it's our best bet."

"Okay," Alex said, barely believing the words he was saying, "I guess… if you're sure… we can support you in that."

"I'll bring it to the president," Hunt said. "Now, you go. Be there for Minnie. She needs someone right now."

Alex nodded and took a few steps toward the door. Then he stopped, one last question popping up. "What happens if the rescue doesn't go well? Or if the civilians get angry about it after the fact?"

The general's expression turned grim. "Alex, there's a hundred ways this could end in war. Every step we take could be the wrong one. Let us worry about that. What I need you to focus on is getting ready to get out of here."

A sour taste formed in the back of Alex's mouth. Unease made him take half a step back as his body went tense at the general's tone.

"Because if there *is* a war," Hunt said, "you don't want to be caught up in it."

Chapter 45

Heather Peters and Jenny Conner

Heather remained in the private hospital room. Her own room was being searched due to it also having been Lauren's room, and the room Lizzy and Azalea were staying in was fully occupied. Not to mention the fact that the doctor was more than okay with monitoring Heather for a while longer. If the private room were needed, other accommodations would be made, but for the time being, it was the best place for Heather to be.

She hadn't heard any more about Jenny and Lauren. No one seemed willing to talk to her about it, either because they didn't want to add stress to a pregnant woman who had collapsed just two days prior or because they didn't quite trust her. And she could tell which was which, too. There was a world of difference between a look of compassion and a look of suspicion, even a subtle one.

An hour after Heather woke that morning, Azalea brought Lizzy to see her. She guided Lizzy inside and brought her to a chair at Heather's bedside. Heather's heart ached at the sight of her sister-in-law. She looked better than she had the day before, but she still had a dazed look about her, as if she were sleepwalking with her eyes wide open. Her eyes were bloodshot, and she seemed smaller with the way she constantly folded in on herself.

"Hey, Lizzy," Heather said softly, offering a smile. "I'm glad you came to visit."

Lizzy looked up at her with a wisp of a smile, the ghostly imitation of one. "How are you feeling?"

"I'm doing great," Heather said, and physically, that was true. Emotionally, she was a wreck, but Lizzy needed to worry about herself. "What are your plans today?" She looked at Azalea when Lizzy did the same.

"Lizzy is pretty tired," Azalea said. "I think she'll stay in our room most of the day, but I'm trying to get her out at least around meal times."

"That's a good plan," Heather said. "Thank you, Azalea, and if you need help, I'm here."

Azalea looked around the hospital room and quirked an eyebrow. "I think you need the rest just as much as she does. This whole situation can't be easy on you. I barely know Jenny or Lauren."

Heather bit back the tears that threatened to undo the calm persona she'd put on for Lizzy's sake. "It is hard," she said. "I don't think this is the best time to talk about that, though." She smiled again at Lizzy.

"Of course," Azalea said.

"Focusing on Lizzy might actually help us both," Heather said. "If there's anything I can do—" A knock on the door startled her. She cleared her throat. "Yes?" she asked loudly enough for whoever was on the other side of the door to hear.

Emily poked her head inside. "Hello? Can I come in?" she asked, her smile a sympathetic, sad one.

"Um, yeah." Heather nodded to Lizzy and Azalea as Emily stepped inside. "You've met my sister-in-law, Lizzy. This is her friend, Azalea."

Emily offered a small wave. "Hello, ladies. I'm actually really glad you're here. I was going to have Heather pass the invitation along, but I'm happy to speak to you in person."

"Oh?" Heather sat up a little straighter and exchanged a glance with Azalea and Lizzy. "What invitation?"

"Mark would like you three to come to dinner," she said. "As a thank you to Lizzy for being so quick on her feet, for warning everyone before those… those…" She shook her head, her face screwing up into a look of disgust. "… those *traitors* killed anyone else."

Lizzy brought her knees to her chest and hugged her legs tight. Heather scooted to the edge of the bed and reached out, her hand resting on Lizzy's shoulder.

"Lizzy still isn't really able to talk about that," Heather said. "I'm not sure it's a good idea—"

"Oh, I'm so sorry," Emily said. "You poor thing. I won't say anything else about it, and we won't talk about it tonight, I swear." She made a zipping motion across her lips.

"I don't know…" Heather trailed off and looked at Azalea. She'd never liked the dynamics between Azalea and Lizzy, but Azalea seemed to have her finger on the pulse of what Lizzy really needed. Heather, on the other hand, felt completely lost when she tried to help her sister-in-law.

"Maybe it would be okay," Azalea said, "if she gets enough rest today."

"Wonderful," Emily said. "You three have been through so much. Mark and I just want to assure you that this can still be your home." She walked over to Heather and lowered her voice, though Heather wasn't sure why. Lizzy could certainly still hear. "He might want to have a bit of a private chat with you, Heather, just to see if you can give us even a little information that will help us decide what to do with those criminals."

"Sure," Heather said, just wanting Emily to go so she could make sure Lizzy was really okay with a social activity so soon. "As long as Lizzy is left out of it."

"I'll make sure Mark knows." Emily winked and patted Heather's arm. "I've got to get going, but I'll see you around 1800 hours?"

Heather nodded. "Sounds good." But the second Emily had gone, she turned to Lizzy. "You do *not* have to go to this."

"I… I don't know," Lizzy said. "Can I think about it?"

"Yes," Heather said. "Absolutely. Just meet me here at 1730 if you want to go."

"I'm going to get Lizzy some breakfast, and then we're going to head back to our room. She barely slept last night. I think I'm going to ask the doc if she has anything that could help with sleep." Azalea stood and stretched. "We could both use it."

The two left, and Heather was glad to be alone. She, too, was exhausted. She was about to drift off to sleep when a knock was immediately followed by the opening of her door. A man walked in with a tray of food.
"Oh, I already ate breakfast," Heather said.
He set the tray down. "Do you remember me from the arena?"
Heather frowned. "Um, yes, now that you mention it. Andy, right?"
He nodded. "I'm the inside man," he said.
Heather's eyes widened. "Oh." She didn't know what else to say.
"I can't tell you much," he said. "All I can is this: you three will have to sit tight for a while. And you need to have witnesses tonight, to give you an alibi."
"You're getting them out?" Heather whispered.
"Have an alibi." He looked over his shoulder. "And do not tell the others who I am, for everyone's safety. Got it?"
Heather nodded. "Yes," she said. "And believe it or not, Mark and Emily invited us to dinner tonight, so... who better to corroborate an alibi, right?"
"That's perfect," Andy said. "Make sure you're all three there."
"Okay. I will. I'll figure out how to ensure Lizzy and Azalea come with me."
"You have to do it without telling them about me."
"Can I tell them *someone* met with me?"
He shook his head. "No."
Heather frowned. "That doesn't—"
"I mean it," Andy said. "You have to trust me."
Heather sighed. "Fine. I won't tell them anything about you or this meeting."
He nodded, seeming satisfied.
"Can you... can you tell Lauren to tell Timothy that I'm okay here? That they're treating me well? And... tell her to tell Timothy that I heard the baby's heartbeat." Heather bit her lower lip and waited for a reply, hoping he would agree, even though she knew it was a frivolous request.
He looked at her a moment and then gave her a quick, small nod. "I can do that," he said.
"Thank you."
"Stay safe." He left just as quickly as he had come.
Heather leaned back and breathed out long and slow, relief flooding her body. "Good luck," she whispered into the empty room. "Take care of Timothy and Candice and Annika..." It was half prayer to God, half admission to herself. A tear slid down her cheek as her hand rested on her belly.
The thing that had kept her awake most of the night resurfaced. The conflict between the civilians and the military wasn't working in her favor. There was a very real chance she'd never be able to convince the civilians to bring Timothy inside. If that were the case, if it were between the safety of her baby and seeing her husband again, Heather would stay, no matter how painful it would be.

* * *

"Save your friend, Ms. Conner," Mark said, "if that's even your real name. If it was you who killed Nick, then maybe you both don't have to die."
Jenny closed her eyes. She was so very tired. They'd come for her in the middle of the night and taken turns questioning her, making sure she had no opportunity for a moment of sleep. It was Mark and Carrie before her at the moment, but others had come, some of whom she'd seen around the complex but could not name.
"I didn't kill Nick," Jenny said for the hundredth time. "Lauren didn't kill him, either. I don't know who did it."
"You're lying," Carrie said.
"I'm not." Jenny leaned forward to lay her forehead on the table. Her head was pounding and her eyes burned. But Mark leaned forward and pushed her head back up before it touched the hard surface.
"I don't think so," he said. "You rest when you tell us the truth. Let's say you didn't kill him. It had to be someone. Who are you working with? Is there a murderer walking free in my complex?"
"I don't know," Jenny said. Her eyelids drooped, and Carrie kicked her chair. Jenny groaned.
"Was it Lizzy, then?" Mark asked.
Carrie frowned and pressed her lips together disapprovingly, but she didn't say anything.
Jenny decided to try something different. She smiled at him, or attempted to. She couldn't tell if she was pulling off the vibe she needed to present. "You know what? Yes. It was Lizzy. She killed Nick and set us up. She's a murderer. Better watch your back, too. She's probably out there sticking strangers with butter knives right now."
Mark rolled his eyes. "I'm getting sick of this."
"Me too," Jenny said. "Let's call it a day."
"She'll confess," Carrie said, narrowing her eyes. "We just have to keep her awake long enough to destroy her ability to think straight."
Mark nodded and clasped his hands behind his back. "We have volunteers ready to keep you awake as long as it's needed," he said. "Carrie and I have duties to which we need to attend. If I leave here, I won't be able to monitor whoever comes in here next. I've given them some basic rules. I wouldn't want to debase ourselves, but... I've only restricted the worst of human tendencies. I will not punish them if I come back to find a few bruises on that pretty face of yours."
"Does that go both ways?" Jenny asked. "What will you do if my keepers come away with a few bruises? A broken nose, maybe? A few bite marks?"
Mark scoffed. "No one is going to untie you from that chair, Ms. Conner."
Jenny shrugged. "I like a challenge."

Mark's hands balled into fists, but he didn't strike her. "I'll be back for another round of questions in a few hours."

He and Carrie left Jenny alone in the room, but she expected someone else to come in any moment. She closed her eyes and put her head on the table. Whoever came in next would no doubt force her to sit up, but even if it was just a few seconds, she needed to close her eyes. Her breathing deepened, and her entire body drooped.

And then she woke to a gentle, repeated slapping of her cheek.

"Jen, wake up."

She lifted her head under the guidance of a hand, and despite herself, she whimpered. "Please," she whispered, her voice hoarse. "I need to sleep."

"I'm sorry, but I can't let you sleep any more."

She opened her eyes, and they burned. Her entire body ached worse than before she'd fallen asleep. She smacked her lips as her blurry vision refocused. "Andy…" she said with a sigh.

"Jen, I need you to listen." He brought a water bottle to her lips. "I volunteered for an hour. We have maybe twenty minutes left."

Jenny drank deeply, hungrily. The water only served to highlight how dry her mouth and throat had gotten. She held the last of the water in her mouth, savoring its cool and quenching nature.

"Are you listening?"

Jenny nodded, her cheeks full of water.

"You're getting out tonight, if everything goes as planned," Andy said.

She swallowed reluctantly. "And the others?"

"Lauren goes with you. The other three have to stay."

"I don't know if we can trust them," Jenny said. "Lizzy and Azalea, obviously, but I have some doubts about Heather, too. She's blinded by her desire to protect her baby."

"We don't have much of a choice," Andy said. "We need those coordinates."

"And the schematics," Jenny said.

"That's on hold for now," Andy said. "Unless you think Heather would help us with that?"

Jenny shook her head. "No, I don't think she would."

"That's what we thought."

"So, tonight… I can hold out until then."

"I know you can." He looked down at his hands, let a moment of silence pass. "Heather wants you to tell her husband that she's okay, that the baby is healthy, and that she heard its heartbeat. It… didn't sound like she wanted him to come after her any time soon."

Jenny nodded slowly. "That tracks. She… wants to stay, I think."

"I guess she has no choice, now," Andy said.

"Look out for her?" Jenny asked.

"Yeah, sure. I'll… do my best." Andy looked at the door. "We have ten minutes." He looked back at her and his lips became a thin line, his eyes full of regret as he grimaced. "You know what I have to do?"

"To maintain your cover? Yes." Jenny nodded. "Don't have too much fun."

He looked away from her. "If anything, I'm going to have to hold back my breakfast from making a reappearance."

"Hey," Jenny said. "It's okay. Just don't break anything."

Andy closed his eyes. "I'm sorry."

"I know." She braced herself as Andy backhanded her across the cheek.

Chapter 46

Alexander Roman

Permission had been granted and negotiations had concluded. Alex wasn't sure how he felt about it, but General Boreland had been let out of detainment.

"It ain't right," Minnie said, dropping her sandwich on the plate before her. "I can't eat."

"Me either." Candice stared down at her plate.

It was the first time in days that all the adults had taken a minute to speak without the kids present. Oliver played with Annika in the next room, though Alex suspected he wasn't happy about being left out. It was just… Oliver loved Lauren, and Alex didn't want the boy to worry over something none of them could do anything about. Part of Alex wished *he* didn't know, that he could just welcome Lauren back when she arrived without the gnawing worry over her current predicament.

"Minnie, maybe it's not as wrong as it feels," Alex said, grasping for some hope. "I mean, I can understand why they did it. Hunt and Coleman were right. Their offer was received well. Boreland agreed."

"Well, Lauren'll pitch a fit when she learns they used her as a reason to give that man power," Minnie said. "After she learns what Boreland said, what he did, stirrin' up trouble, lettin' Lawson and Price have their two cents." She clucked her tongue and shook her head. "It's bad news, Alex. I can feel it in my bones."

Timothy slid his plate away from him. "At least they're going in for Lauren," he said as Candice put a hand on his back.

"I can't believe they're just leaving Heather in there," Candice said.

"And Lizzy," Walter said. "I should have never let her go."

"You didn't have a choice," Zara said. "No one was going to stop her from doing what she wanted to do."

"Yeah, man," Kai added. "Don't be so hard on yourself."

"Not an option," Walter said, "not when your daughter's life is on the line."

Alex didn't mention Azalea, and he noticed no one else did, either. There was something about her that he'd never liked. And between all those who'd gone to the complex, he knew her the least, trusted her the least. He didn't know why she *would* kill a man, but he had to admit he wouldn't put it past her. She was cold and calculating and… he had no concrete evidence to think anything negative about her.

And neither does anyone else, he thought. Except for Zara, no one has even mentioned the possibility that she was the murderer.

The whole thing reminded him of Theodore, about how the man had disappeared. He was either dead and burned alive in that lab fire, or he'd run away for some reason. The way Lizzy and Azalea had been waiting for him after he'd escaped the fire still weighed on him. That look Azalea had given him, like she was *angry* he'd gotten out… it made him shudder. He had no proof, just a gut feeling.

"Well, we won't be around when Boreland gets that power," Alex said. "At least we won't have to deal with the fallout of this deal they've made."

Minnie shook her head. "Thank the good Lord for small mercies."

"You think he's left already?" Walter asked.

Alex looked at the clock on the wall. "Boreland and his team should be leaving about now." He poked his sandwich and shook his head. "I can't sit around and do nothing," he said. "Walter, do you want to go to the lab? We could double check our plans and our supplies."

Walter shrugged. "Might as well. I gave those soldiers instructions on how to store the piranha solution and the bait, and Pullman should have been there to guide them, but I always like to check things myself."

"I thought all that stuff was being made down at the facility in the city," Minnie said.

"It is," Alex said. "But we're storing it up here where we have access to consistent and proper temperature control."

"Well, while you all are out there," Candice said, "me and my little blueberry are going to work on making an inventory of everything we plan to take with us."

"Are you sure you're the best person to do that?" Timothy asked.

Candace bristled. "What's that supposed to mean?"

"Candice, you've hauled two suitcases of designer clothes and makeup across the country in the middle of an apocalypse," Timothy said. "Paring down to the essentials isn't exactly your forte."

"Now, hush," Minnie said. "Oliver and I are gonna help out, and I've come to think Candice knows a thing or two about how to keep our sanity in all this. Some sense of normalcy and pamperin' can go a long way when you ain't got runnin' water."

Candice put her hand over her heart. "Minnie," she said. "Thank you. That's the sweetest thing you've ever said to me."

Minnie stood and nodded toward the door. "Let's get on it," she said. "I'm gonna wriggle out of my own skin if I don't do somethin'." She and Candice left together, heading to the next room to get the kids.

"Everyone else good?" Walter asked. "I think it's best for everyone to keep busy, keep working toward our goals."

"Me and Zara and Timothy will be with Blythe, training," Kai said.

"How's that going?" Walter asked.

"Great." Zara gave them all a flat look.

"That… doesn't sound optimistic." Alex didn't bring up the possibility that they would need to flee the city sooner rather than later, but he was thinking it. *No need to make anyone panic any more than they already are,* he thought.

"Considering Blythe is the only one who actually knows what he's doing…" Kai shrugged. "It's going pretty well, I'd say."

Zara rolled her eyes. "We're becoming real Christopher Columbuses over here. Star charts and everything."

"Columbus didn't use radar," Kai said.

She smacked his shoulder. "I know that."

"And Tim?" Walter asked. "You're doing okay down there with Blythe?"

"It's better than sitting around," Timothy said. "It keeps my mind off of Heather and the baby, but Zara is right. We're over our heads."

"Hey, guys," Kai said, "c'mon. We'll get the hang of it."

Zara mumbled an unconvincing agreement, and Timothy shrugged.

"Well, good luck today," Alex said. "Just... do your best. There's a lot riding on what you're doing."

The three of them sighed at the same time but nodded as they picked up their sandwiches to go, saying that Blythe was waiting on them. That left just Alex and Walter.

"Who should we get to take us?" Alex asked.

Walter shrugged. "I guess we'll find out once we make a request to General Hunt."

Alex nodded but didn't say anything. The general had known the morally gray side of what he'd suggested with Boreland, and he might have even been right about it, but Alex was still uncomfortable, still unsure if he could keep the distaste about the subject from his expression. It made him reluctant to approach General Hunt at all.

But in the end, Walter was right. Their request would have to be brought before the general in order to get an unplanned escort, and an escort was the only way he and Walter were getting to the lab on base. They weren't allowed to go anywhere without one.

They found the general on the recessed patio, just outside the glass doors, alone. He sat still as a statue, looking up into the afternoon sky. "We won't have word until Boreland gets back," he said. "No long-range communications."

"We know," Alex said. "We were hoping we could go to our lab to keep busy while we wait for him to return with Jenny and Lauren."

"We need an escort," Walter said.

General Hunt nodded. "I'll do it," he said. "It's only a few minutes away, and it'll be hours before Boreland and his team return. I can't concentrate on anything else, anyway."

"Doesn't the president want you here?" Alex asked.

"When Boreland returns, our perimeter guard will radio us, and we'll all have to come back immediately," Hunt said. "But... it feels like the whole world is standing still until that happens, and Minnie still isn't talking to me." He stood and straightened his uniform. "I'll have Lindt come with us. She's a good one, that cadet. Eager, ready to serve."

It only took a few moments for the four of them to load up in a golf cart and be on their way and another five minutes to find themselves outside the Air Force Academy Medical Clinic where their lab was set up.

"Looks like Pullman is here," Walter said as Cadet Lindt parked next to another golf cart.

"He basically just lives here," Cadet Lindt said.

General Hunt grunted with some disapproval. "Ward and Turner should be here. Dr. Pullman requested them today."

Alex pursed his lips but kept back his complaints, which wouldn't do any good. He wasn't really in the mood to deal with Ward and Turner, but if he stayed out of their way, they generally stayed out of his. And they *had* cooperated, actually helping with the experiments quite a bit. He couldn't deny their contributions, even if he did count them both as bottom-of-the-barrel scum.

As they walked through the front doors, Alex frowned, and he wasn't the only one. All four of them stopped. "Where are the guards?" Alex asked.

There were always guards stationed at the door, but there were also supposed to be extras in the halls when Ward and Turner were present.

General Hunt pulled his weapon. "It's too quiet," he said. "I don't hear anyone."

Cadet Lindt followed suit, though she looked a little like a deer caught in the headlights. She kept looking between her gun and the general, readjusting her stance as her eyes became wide as saucers.

Alex was acutely aware of his lack of a weapon. He exchanged a look with Walter as the two of them positioned themselves squarely behind the two holding guns.

"Stay here," General Hunt said. "Better yet, get down and behind those chairs. Make yourselves small and be quiet."

He and the cadet started slowly moving forward. Alex followed Walter into a corner, both of them crouching in a space between commercial couches with blue plastic upholstery.

"Do you see anything we could use as a weapon?" Alex asked, glancing around the room the best he could from his mostly concealed spot.

"We could break off the legs of that wooden side table." Walter nodded toward the square piece of furniture. "But I don't think that would do us a ton of good in a gun fight."

"I should have brought my gun," Alex said, "even if we were asked not to carry."

Walter shook his head. "Seeing us with weapons could have triggered a fight with Boreland's supporters."

A loud curse from General Hunt echoed down the halls, and then there were footsteps pounding the linoleum floor. Cadet Lindt appeared around the corner.

"There's no one here except Dr. Pullman," she said, "and he's down. I've got to go get a medic." She rushed outside.

Alex stood and Walter was right behind him as he jogged through the halls to where General Hunt was kneeling over Pullman. The man was waking, wincing as he touched a knot on his forehead.

"What..." Pullman tried to sit up, but then he swayed and the general guided him back to the floor.

"Stay still," Hunt said.

"What happened?" Walter asked.

But Alex's eyes were on the far side of the room where the refrigerator had been left ajar. He sucked in a breath as he quickly moved forward, skirting the general and Pullman, diving for the refrigerator with his heart lodged in his throat. He threw open the door.

"No," he whispered.
"What's wrong?" Walter asked. "Is it ruined?"
Alex stepped aside to let Walter see. "Half of it is gone." His stomach twisted into knots. The missing guards, the absence of Ward and Turner, the way Pullman had been knocked out on the floor, and the fact that Boreland had just been let out to lead a small contingent of soldiers: it was all adding up to something he didn't want to think about.
"Why would it be gone?" Walter stared at the half-empty shelves, his face going pale.
"They took Joanna and Blake with them." Pullman's voice was weak as he lay stretched upon the floor, one hand at his head, the other on his stomach. He sounded as if he were holding back waves of nausea as he spoke.
"Someone kidnapped Ward and Turner?" General Hunt asked.
"No." Pullman moaned. "Ward and Turner knew they were coming and... and..." He turned to the side and retched. He spit when he was done, and between panting breaths, continued. "Joanna left a letter for Alex," he said. "She left it on the counter."
Alex caught sight of the white envelope, marched over to it, and ripped it open. He read it out loud: "Alex, you had such great potential. If only you had backed the right man from the very beginning. On the bright side, I've decided you deserve at least a footnote in the history books." There was a lipstick stain in the shape of a kiss, and she'd signed her name below it. "Joanna." He crumpled the paper in his hands.
"What does that mean?" Walter asked.
Alex looked at General Hunt who seemed to understand just as well as he did. At the same time, he and the general voiced their suspicion with equal amounts of disgust. "Lawson."
"Again," Walter said, an edge to his tone, "what the hell does that mean?"
"It means we need to go to the detainment center," General Hunt said.
"What are they up to?" Alex asked. "Do you think they're even going to the complex?"
General Hunt licked his lips. "I don't know," he said. "He must have soldiers with him that are loyal to him, but I can't imagine they'd be enough of a force to raid the mountain."
"The arena, maybe?" Alex asked. "Force a war with the civilians?"
"Could be," General Hunt said, "but we have no idea what he's really up to, and the only clue we have is that Lawson probably put a bug in his ear, laid out a plan that would ultimately end in Lawson being freed."
Walter looked between them. "What if he *is* going to the complex? My daughter is in there!"
"We can't go up there with a force," General Hunt said. "For all we know, we'd be playing into Boreland's hand. He could be trying to get *us* to start the war. Can you imagine what the civilians would think if soldiers just showed up on their doorstep claiming they *might* be in danger?"
"We need to make Lawson tell us what's going on, and fast," Alex said. "If we know what Boreland is up to, we can make an informed decision on next steps."
General Hunt nodded once and firmly. "I'll radio the president on the way, update him and get approval for a full interrogation." He looked down at Pullman. "Doctor, you're going to need to stay here. Lindt will be back with a medic."
"Go," Pullman said, the word more of a moan than anything else.
"We should have Timothy meet us," Walter said. "His wife is in that complex, too. My son has just as much of a right to know what's going on as I do."
"Can do," General Hunt said, already on his way out the door. "Let's move."

Chapter 47

Alexander Roman

It had been months since Alex had seen that look in Lawson's eyes, as if he were king of the world. It was that look that telegraphed Alex and Hunt had been right: Lawson had given Boreland a plan, and the misguided general was carrying it out like a puppet on a string.

But they had no idea what that plan entailed, and until they did, there was very little they could do to stop it. It was getting late in the day, and every second seemed like a step toward disaster.

Lawson had been brought in handcuffs and ankle shackles to Polaris Hall. Major Willis stood at one side and Ponte, the soldier who'd stood with Lindt and Sumner when the fight had broken out over Hunt and Boreland on the bus, was on the other side. They didn't let Lawson sit, pushing him forward when he tried to lean against the wall behind him.

Alex, Timothy, and Walter stood to one side of the room, and Coleman sat at a desk with Hunt standing behind him to the right. The small room in Polaris Hall had a skylight that allowed for the center of it to be well lit while the corners remained in shadow.

Alex was glad the president hadn't afforded Lawson the privilege of meeting in a conference room as if it were a meeting between equals. Hunt had advised the president remain in Polaris Hall due to the unknown nature of Boreland's orders to those loyal to him on the base. The glassy fortress was safe; at least, they believed it to be so. He was also glad the president allowed the three of them to be there. He suspected Hunt had something to do with that.

"I don't know what you're talking about," Lawson said, much too smugly.

President Coleman raised the note left by Ward. "Joanna left us a little clue that says maybe you do."

"And what do you think, son?" Lawson asked.

"I'm not your son." President Coleman kept his voice cool and matter-of-fact.

"Come now," Lawson said. "You may be weak and incompetent and shortsighted, but you're family."

"That's the only reason you're not dead," Coleman said.

Lawson grinned. "And one day perhaps I'll be able to return the favor."

Goosebumps ran up Alex's arms. *He thinks that day is coming soon,* he thought.

General Hunt scowled. "Sir, I think we should move on to the methods we discussed earlier."

President Coleman's expression was grim, but he nodded. "He isn't giving us a choice. Do it."

Lawson laughed as Hunt drew his handgun and walked across the room toward him. Alex blinked at the weapon and looked back at Coleman. The way Hunt stalked toward Lawson spoke of a man ready to fire, but Alex had never seen Coleman approve such methods. *Desperate times call for desperate measures,* Alex thought. Months ago, he would have been shocked at the thought of threatening someone with a gun. He would have insisted such a tactic was barbaric and unnecessary in all situations. But he found himself almost comforted by the determined look on Coleman's face and the general's threatening stride.

The general stopped in front of the man and screwed on a silencer. "This'll still be loud," Hunt said, "but it shouldn't cause anyone damage to their ears." He looked over his shoulder at Alex, Walter, and Timothy. "You might want to cover your ears anyway."

Alex raised his eyebrows and exchanged a look with the other two men. They all three covered their ears. The conversation became slightly muffled, but it was still understandable.

"You'd never," Lawson said, still chuckling. "You don't have it in you." He looked past the general as if he didn't see Hunt at all. Instead, he focused on Coleman. "You might put me in chains and make me participate in labor that's beneath me, but that's as far as you'll ever go, and I know it—"

A gunshot reverberated around the room. General Hunt stood a few feet from Lawson, the gun pointed downward. Blood spurted from Lawson's foot upon the bullet's impact. The older man looked down at his foot in shock, his body absolutely still, his eyes wide, his jaw dropped. As blood started seeping from beneath his foot, the man sucked in a breath and then screamed, his entire body so tense it trembled. And then he was nearly hyperventilating. The soldiers behind him didn't stop him from leaning back on the wall as he backed into it.

"You shot me!" Lawson shouted and cursed between breaths.

"You still have one good foot," Coleman said. "And I'll get you medical attention immediately if you tell me what's going on."

"It's too late to stop it," Lawson seethed. He sank to the floor and struggled to yank off his shoe with the way his hands and ankles were bound.

"Your knee comes next," Hunt said. "That one you might not recover from."

Lawson looked up at him as he tried to put pressure on the top of his foot. "You wouldn't." He didn't sound as confident that time. For the first time, Alex recognized pure fear in Lawson's eyes.

"You're endangering the people of the United States of America," Coleman said. "The soldiers under my command are divided. Boreland is misguided. And civilians who, whether they like it or not, are my responsibility could be in grave danger. I will risk your life for theirs ten times out of ten."

Lawson swallowed so hard that Alex could hear it from yards away. He looked up at General Hunt. "This would have worked a lot better if you'd chosen the right side," he said.

"I did," Hunt said, "and I think things will work out just fine as soon as you tell us what Boreland is doing."

"Like I said, it's too late for you to stop it." Lawson managed a grin though he was sweating profusely and still breathing too hard.

Hunt raised the gun again. "You have until the count of five. One."

"You can't do this," Lawson shouted.

"Two."

"Michael." He looked past the general again, his hands still holding his foot, blood still dripping from it. "My daughter will never forgive you for this."

"She knows," Coleman said.

"Three."

Lawson shook his head. "Stop it! Don't you know who I am?"

Alex scoffed at that. *Does* he *know who he is?*

"Four."

Lawson screamed, and as the sound of his frustration dissipated, he said through gritted teeth, "Fine. I'll tell you what you want to know."

General Hunt lowered his gun. "I won't count next time," he said. "I'll just blow your kneecap to oblivion."

"Michael, please, get this man away from me, and I'll tell you. I'll tell you everything." Desperation had crept into Lawson's voice.

"General, give him a bit of space." Coleman folded his hands on his desk.

"I didn't want this division." Lawson licked his lips. His face went a shade paler with each passing minute. "Boreland was behind the attack on base. The main target was *you* and *yours*." He glared at Alex.

Alex frowned, his heart skipping a beat. "What are you talking about?" he asked.

General Hunt blinked a few times and then his face slowly became twisted in anger. "You had Boreland blow up those buildings? Had him shoot out the house?"

"He made a terrible mess of it, didn't he?" Lawson grimaced. "He was supposed to make *sure* no soldiers were killed. Framing Ms. Minnie Steven's death on the civilians was the perfect plan. It would have united you all against them, and it would have given Boreland a chance to shine. He knows that complex, knows this city."

"And his success would be yours," Coleman said, nodding slowly.

Alex's fingernails bit into his palms. "You bastard," he said.

General Hunt raised the gun again, his face red with rage. "I should put a bullet between your eyes."

"General Hunt." President Coleman stood and spoke an authority that echoed through the room. "Stand down. Right. Now. I don't want him dead, not if we can help it."

The general moved the gun to the side and fired. Alex flinched, as did Walter and Timothy beside him. Lawson screamed and curled away from the shot, which had gone into the floor a few inches from him. Hunt roared and crouched to become eye level with Lawson. "I serve at the pleasure of the President of the United States of America," he said. "And you're damned lucky that I do."

Lawson somehow managed to whimper and cower while throwing a hate-filled glare back at the general.

"General Hunt," Coleman said, "I understand your rage, but he won't talk if he thinks we'll kill him afterward. I'm giving him my word that if he cooperates, if he tells us everything he knows, that he will live, so far as it be on me."

Hunt stood, spat on Lawson, and took several steps backward. "Yes, sir. I apologize, sir."

"So," Coleman said, "I suspect you blew the food stores to make the men desperate. That much worked out the way you'd planned. But the botched assassination required that you spread the lie that Alex and his crew were working with the civilians. If you couldn't unite us for the cause which you deemed the best course of action, you wanted to divide us with a line you could draw."

Lawson nodded weakly, not taking his eyes off of the general. "Yes," he said, the word cracking as it passed his lips. "One way or the other, I needed Boreland to go after the complex, win it back for the military. Once he'd done that, he agreed to reveal my strategic help and to back me as president. I was to make him my VP."

Walter took a step away from the wall. "Does that mean Boreland is going after the complex now?"

"Yes," Lawson said.

"How?" General Hunt's voice made Lawson curl in on himself, flinching way from it as if the man could fling bullets with his words.

"He took one tactical vehicle, a handful of operatives, and a couple of scientists with their bait and toxins. But that place is fortified. Locked down and protected even from swarms."

"You already gave us a way in," Lawson said. "Like I said, it's too late to stop it. And when Boreland gets that mountain, he *will* gain power."

Alex frowned. "I don't understand." He looked between the general and the president, who were looking at each other, some understanding seeming to pass between them.

"The escape hatch." President Coleman's voice was barely above a whisper. "Munez is going to open it from the inside to let our rescue team in."

General Hunt looked back at Lawson. "You would devise the deaths of all those people?"

At first, his question didn't make sense, but then, Alex's breath caught as Hunt's assumption registered. "The bait… you're going to lure a swarm down the escape hatch?"

"My daughter," Walter said, reaching a hand to Alex's shoulder, sagging as it seemed his knees weakened.

"They're going to wipe out everyone inside," Alex said, "and then clean it up with the toxin."

"It only seems fitting," Lawson said. "Isn't that how the civilians took the complex in the first place?"

"They didn't let the swarm in!" Alex shouted.

"That's not how the history books will read," Lawson said.

"When?" General Hunt growled.

"Whenever you scheduled your inside man to open that door." Lawson smiled. "Like I said, it's too late."

"No," Coleman said. "It's not."

Lawson frowned. "It's been at least an hour since Boreland left, and he's got signal blockers with him. You won't be able to communicate with your inside man."

"But our man doesn't open that hatch for another forty-five minutes." The president swelled to his full height and set his jaw. "We can still stop this. We have to approach the complex with a force, but we have to do it in a way that doesn't scare them into attacking."

"White flags, hands raised," General Hunt said.

"We need to bring every last bit of the toxin and bait," Alex said. "We might need it to lure the swarm somewhere we can destroy it."

"Agreed," President Coleman said.

"And I'm coming with you," Alex added.

"As am I." Walter crossed his arms.

"Me too," Timothy said without hesitation.

General Hunt nodded. "I think we could use you three on the approach. The civilians don't like soldiers."

"Go," the president said. "Go now. We don't have a second to lose."

Chapter 48

Alexander Roman, Heather Peters, and Andy Munez

In a procession of one Humvee and a military truck, each with white sheets on poles affixed to their backs, Alex fidgeted in the back seat of the Humvee, unable to do anything but wait as they travelled up the only access road to the complex. They were going as quickly as the curving pavement and wide vehicles would allow, but it wasn't fast enough. If Boreland stayed on track, they would be approaching the complex within a hair's breadth of the time Andy was supposed to be opening the hatch to let the rescue team inside. Walter sat to Alex's left-hand side, and Timothy took up the passenger seat in the front. Walter was still and unmoving, except for his lips. Eyes closed, he moved his lips constantly as if in prayer. Alex had said a few prayers himself in the tense quiet of the drive up. Timothy, on the other hand, made all kinds of small noises as he tapped his fingers and bounced his feet on the floorboards. He seemed unable to do anything but fidget.

General Hunt drove with a determined intensity. Despite being the president's righthand man, he'd insisted he couldn't let the job fall to anyone else. He'd agreed to trust Boreland, blamed himself for that, and made it clear he couldn't put their futures into another's hands a second time. The president hadn't argued.

The sun was on the way down, the time of day getting dangerously close to the swarms' most active. And with the abundance of animals and trees and moisture in the forests at the foot of the mountain near the complex, the possibility of an unknown quantity of nearby swarms was not far from Alex's mind.

It can't end like this, Lauren, he thought.

The past months had been intense, and the bonds formed even more so. The thought of losing Lauren caused an ache in Alex's body he couldn't quite explain. He would have to bring Minnie the news, tell the woman who had been a rock, a salve, and a hero to him and to Oliver that he hadn't been able to save her daughter. It was only because of Minnie that Alex and Oliver were even alive. To fail her in that way would be... unbearable.

And then there was his son.

Oliver can't lose another person he loves. Alex closed his eyes and his stomach twisted at the image of trying to comfort his son if Lauren were to perish.

But the way her death would affect Minnie and Oliver wasn't the worst of it. Her death would affect *him*, and somehow, he couldn't bring himself to picture surviving with his new found family without Lauren there. She would leave a hole in their hearts, a hole in *his* heart, right alongside the larger one his wife had left months ago.

It was confusing, holding onto the deep and abiding love he held for his wife even after she'd been gone for months and then recognizing a budding love for a woman he'd just met but knew so well. Lauren was not his wife, could never hold that same place in his heart, but there was an undeniable connection made more apparent by the prospect of losing her.

As they came upon the parking lot wherein Timothy and Alex had parked and continued on foot the first time Alex had come up that mountain, Alex sat up straighter and pointed between the two front seats.

"There!" he shouted. "It's one of our vehicles."

"I see Boreland. He's talking to another soldier," Timothy said.

"That's Tawdry," Walter said, craning to look over the general's shoulder.

There were six soldiers congregated around green metal containers. They were arming themselves with bullet proof vests and weapons. General Hunt turned off into the lot with a growl. "They've not gone up yet," he said. "We made it in time."

But as the general rushed the military truck Boreland had taken and screeched to a stop so that Boreland and Tawdry had to dive out of the way, Alex's heart sank. "Where are Ward and Turner?" He desperately looked around the lot.

"They have to be here somewhere." General Hunt pushed the door open. "Boreland!" he shouted. "I trusted you, you traitor!"

Alex was out into the open just as quickly. *Where are Ward and Turner? Where is the bait?* His heart rate increased with every second he didn't find what he was looking for.

Soldiers moved to block Hunt's way as Boreland and Tawdry recovered from diving to the ground to avoid being rammed by the Humvee. At the same time, Hunt's force of a dozen men and women disembarked the military truck and came up behind them, weapons trained on the soldiers protecting Boreland.

Boreland looked incredulously at Hunt. "I'm the traitor? You've let a bunch of plumbers and electricians steal and keep our only remaining secure location! If this government is going to survive, it's going to be inside that mountain. It's us or them, and I'm choosing us, damn it!"

"Where are our chemicals?" Alex asked. "Where are Ward and Turner?"

Boreland's triumphant sneer solidified Alex's terror.

* * *

It had taken some work, but Heather had convinced Lizzy to come to dinner with her at Emily and Mark's that night. Azalea had backed Heather's insistence that they attend, which had made it easier to leave the meeting with Andy and the fact that they needed an alibi out of the conversation.

They approached the hospitality desk at the newest building in the complex, and a woman Heather vaguely knew by the name of Megan gave them a pass to go up to Emily and Mark's apartment. It was odd, entering the building but *not* going to the Expecting Mother's Circle.

As they approached the door, Heather stopped and turned to face Azalea and Lizzy. Her sister-in-law had barely said two words that day. Grief still had her stuck in shock and disbelief, it seemed.

"Remember, Emily promised you wouldn't be dragged into any questioning tonight, okay?" Heather said as she gently took Lizzy by the shoulders. "Try to relax, enjoy the food. You don't have to say anything. They know you're still..." She searched for the right words. "... really sad."

"We won't let them push you," Azalea said.

Heather nodded her agreement.

Lizzy nodded. "Okay," she said. "Thanks." She offered a small smile.

"Great. Okay." Heather turned back toward the door, walked up to it, and knocked. "Here we go."

Emily opened the door with a full grin and some pretty convincing suburban housewife vibes. "Heather!" She leaned in for a light hug and then gestured for them to enter. "Azalea, Lizzy, I'm so glad you came." Her hand went to her belly. "I hope you don't mind lasagna," she said. "My pregnancy cravings are out of control these days." She laughed lightly.

The kitchen was just past the entry hall, and Heather walked in to find Mark pulling something out of the oven. "Vegetable lasagna with goat cheese," he said. "No meat, this time, I'm afraid, but I'll be damned if it isn't delicious."

"It smells great," Heather said.

"Well," he said, "we also have a very small, but very delicious cake for dessert. We wanted to thank Ms. Peters appropriately." He put on a sincere look. "We will all miss Nick, of course, but who knows what could have happened if you hadn't rushed to The Granite Inn like you did."

Lizzy shifted uncomfortably, and Emily came up behind her and put an arm around her shoulders. "Oh, you poor thing. Mark, be a little sensitive, hon. Let's not talk about that."

"Right, of course," Mark said. "We'll keep the conversation light. Around the dinner table, at least." His smile seemed a bit stale, as if he'd brought that particular one out of his inventory a few too many times. "You and me can have a little chat later, right, Heather? Maybe after dessert. I've got a small but private office here."

"Of course," Heather said. "I'd be happy to help in any way, though I'm not sure I could tell you anything you don't already know."

"We'll see about that." Mark clapped his hands together and took the dish to the table. "Come, sit. Let's eat." He took the seat at the head of the table as Emily served the food.

Heather glanced at the clock as she picked up her fork, trying to behave naturally. Any moment, there could be alarms blaring, signaling the escape of prisoners. She took a bite, smiled nicely, and waited.

* * *

Andy left the collection of buildings for the rocky cave wall where the escape hatch was placed. His first few footsteps echoed there, where the rocky ceiling above returned every sound. It was like an alarm, telling anyone listening that he was on his way. He pulled up short and took a deep breath. In that quiet, in that moment, he could feel his heartbeat pumping blood through his body, could feel the throb of his knuckles where he'd busted them. His feet rooted to the spot, he held up his hand opening and closing it.

An image of Jenny's bruised cheek surfaced. He shook his head and wiped sweat from his brow. Knocking her around had been one of the hardest things he'd had to do in a while. The damage to his own knuckles hadn't come from that. Andy had slammed his fist against the table until he'd left a mark on himself after he'd made sure Jenny had some marks herself. It had done the trick. No one had suspected he'd spent most of his time with Jenny letting her sleep. Still, he'd hated what he had to do.

He slipped off his shoes and moved forward more quietly. The hatch wasn't guarded; it was checked on patrols. Although it was an alternate entrance, it wasn't viewed as such and for good reason.

Andy would have to open the first hatch, which only opened from inside the cave, and then he'd have to leave that hatch open while he climbed to the surface to open the second hatch which could only be opened from inside the tunnel. The risk of the open hatch down below being closed by a patrol was real and ever present in the back of Andy's mind. Should that happen, not only would the rescue mission fail but his cover would be blown. He wouldn't be able to return, and they'd have no one left inside to help their cause.

But it was the only way to get Jenny and Lauren out, so he'd agreed. If the worst happened and he was found out, at least he would be back with the military and suspicion would be more permanently removed from Heather, Lizzy, and Azalea. They'd assume he'd killed Nick, and the military would still have the opportunity to get a message to Heather. He wasn't sure how, but there was always a way. Another plant, maybe? Andy shook his head. They'll be more suspicious after this. He chewed on the inside of his cheek.

Their best bet was for him to complete his part of the mission. As he neared the hatch, a flashlight swung on the other side of the cavern and footsteps pierced the air. The cave was dimly lit by battery operated lanterns every several yards, but the patrol still used flashlights. They were to sweep the shadows as they went.

Andy moved deeper into the shadows, ducking into a shallow hollow where the rock curved just slightly. He put his back against the rough, unworked surface of the cavern wall and stilled himself. As long as the patrol didn't look backward and shine the flashlight behind them as they passed, the cavern rock should hide him.

As expected, the guard lazily swung the flashlight back and forth, sighing as he passed Andy's hiding spot, not bothering to look back. From his bulky shape, Andy was pretty sure it was Ronald, an older member of the complex whose skills amounted to being related to a set of brothers who'd worked for Mark before Day Zero.

Once Ronald was out of sight—he'd continue along the outside of the building and then retrace his steps a dozen times that night—Andy left the shadowy recess and hurried toward the metal staircase that led to a metal platform where the hatch was set into the rock. He opened it as quietly as he could, wincing at the squeal of hinges but hearing no evidence of Ronald rushing back to investigate. He slipped inside the tunnel and covered the locking mechanism with a sock so that it wouldn't click closed.

Hatch barely open, hopefully unnoticeably so, Andy pinched a small flashlight between his teeth, grabbed a rung, and began the climb.

* * *

"Stand down," Hunt shouted. "That's an order. We don't want to hurt any of you. That's not what we came here to do. Don't force your brothers and sisters to fire."

Alex backed up with Timothy and Walter, watching as the two forces faced off against one another. Hunt stood at the front of his dozen men while Boreland hid behind his seven. Boreland's people hesitated but kept their guns trained on Hunt's soldiers.

A few of Hunt's men plead with the opposite side.

"Stand down, Ivan," said one.

"Come on, brother. You're on the wrong side," said another.

"I don't know what you've been told," Hunt said, addressing Boreland's people. "But I'm hoping it was a lie. I'm hoping you didn't come here knowing you would be sentencing the people in that mountain to die."

Boreland scoffed. "They know what they're here for. They're here to save their country, and sometimes, that means eliminating our enemies."

"Those people aren't our enemies," Hunt shouted. "They are citizens of the United States of America, people we all swore to protect. There are children in there!"

One of Boreland's soldiers, a woman Alex didn't recognize, holstered her weapon and held up her hands. She stepped forward slowly, and when Hunt nodded his consent, she turned and joined his men.

"Sorry, General Boreland," she said. "I wanted to back you. I respect you, but… this isn't right."

Two more of Boreland's men followed her to Hunt's side. That left four against Hunt's fifteen.

"You have one more chance," Hunt said to those four. "Do what's right." When they stood their ground, defiance written on their faces, Hunt ground his teeth together. "If you want it on record that you stuck with Boreland, that's fine. Surrender your weapons, lie on the ground with your hands behind your head, and be prepared to be detained. Or else, you will be shot."

The four did as they were told, and Hunt's soldiers quickly moved forward to zip-tie their hands behind their backs, haul them to their feet, and hold them firmly in place.

"You're too late," Boreland said, his chin too high for Alex's liking. He'd not surrendered any weapons, and he still stood tall. "Everything is already in motion."

Two soldiers approached Boreland, disarming him and cuffing him, but Boreland didn't seem fazed.

General Hunt grunted. "What are you talking about Boreland? It's over. We got here before you made your move."

"Except you didn't," Boreland said. "Ward and Turner are already at the hatch, along with my eighth man."

"We have to warn the civilians," Alex said, looking up at the mountain.

General Hunt towered over Boreland and spoke through gritted teeth. "Where's the signal blocker?"

Boreland licked his lips. "I won't tell you, Alan. This is the only way."

"Innocent people are in there!" Walter shouted.

"I'm doing what's necessary." Boreland sneered. "I'm doing what none of you have the stomach to do. Billions of innocent people are dead. A few more won't make much difference, not if we get control of that mountain back. We can rebuild from there."

"We don't have time to get to the hatch." Alex grabbed a fistful of his own hair, cycling through their options. "It's got to be a twenty-minute hike, minimum."

"Sir, I know where the jammer is. I'll disable it." The woman who'd first stepped out of Boreland's line to join Hunt jogged to the military vehicle and disappeared behind it.

Tawdry, one of the four soldiers who'd stood with Boreland, narrowed his eyes. "Coors is up there, and he won't let you stop him. We're going to be heroes."

Alex shook his head. "By killing civilians in their own homes?"

"That mountain isn't supposed to be theirs in the first place," Tawdry said.

"He's right," Boreland said. "Coors is going to lure that swarm in. It doesn't matter who does the clean up afterward. We've already won."

"So, what?" Alex asked. "You're sacrificing Coors?" He looked at Tawdry. "You're okay with that?"

Tawdry sneered. "He'll be slathered in that repellent. The swarm won't touch him."

Alex frowned. "Repellent? There's bait and there's toxin. That's it. We never made a repellent."

Tawdry shook his head and looked up at the mountain, a fearful expression taking over his defiant one. "No, that can't be true. There was a jar labelled repellent and another one labelled as the bait. Coors is going down that hatch, but he'll be safe. He'll be covered in repellent."

The back of Alex's throat burned with bile as he looked at Boreland. "You're sick," Alex said. "That man is going to die with the rest of them."

"No," Boreland said. "Ward and Turner assured me—"

"Ward and Turner," Alex said, "are criminals who experimented and killed human beings for research back in Atlanta."

"Lawson said they only experimented on animals," Boreland said. "He swore that Coleman had lied to make him and his people look more sinister than they are."

"He doesn't know," General Hunt said. "This poor fool has been deceived."

"Coleman was telling the truth," Alex said. "I was there."

Boreland swallowed. "I don't believe you."

"Alex," Walter said. "We have to warn them, right now."

"Someone get me a radio," Hunt said. "As soon as she disables the—"

"General! Look!" Timothy shouted and pointed.

Alex turned to follow Timothy's finger. There, far away but still distinct, a swarm snaked its way over the treetops and toward the mountain.

***

Andy was sweating profusely by the time he reached the top of the tunnel and the second escape hatch, but he'd done it. He'd heard no echoing of the first hatch being shut, no shout to indicate someone had found the hatch below open.

The mission to get the rescue team inside was almost halfway over. He and the team would have the climb down with which to contend, and then he'd have to leave them to their mission, hoping it went well. And if it did, his cover would be intact. He could go on, helping Heather obtain the necessary information.

He reached for the latch and opened the second hatch. "Hello?" he whispered as he stuck his head outside. The sun was low on the horizon, and there were two people in hazmat suits waiting with a man slathered in some sort of black substance.

"Andy Munez?" the woman in one of the hazmat suits asked.

"Yeah," he said, frowning. "Are you… the rescue team?"

"I'm Coors," one of the soldiers said.

"You're it?" Andy asked, still three-fourths of the way inside the tunnel.

"He's good at his job," the woman said. "We will be waiting up here for him and the two women we're rescuing. We'll make sure they get back safely."

"What's that stuff he's covered in?" Andy asked.

"Repellent," she said. "We only have enough suits for us. He has another jar with him. It will ensure the swarms don't bother us on our way down the mountain."

"Since when do we have effective repellent?"

The woman sounded impatient as she answered. "Since now."

"Okay…" Andy had a lot more questions, but he didn't have the time. "I guess… let's get going."

"We'll leave the hatch open," the woman said, "unless we see a swarm, in which case, we'll close it and take cover."

"Right…" Something didn't seem right, but he couldn't say why. "Follow me," he said. "Be careful. You didn't put that stuff on your hands, right?"

Coors held up his hands. "Nope."

"We don't have much time. Let's go." Andy started the climb back down the tunnel.

Coors followed after. The descent was easier, took less time. When Andy reached the bottom landing, he was grateful to see the slit of dim light outlining the hatch. He opened it and peered into the cavern.

"I think we're clear," he said.

Coors hopped off the rungs. "Let's go, then."

"That stuff reeks," Andy said. "Someone is going to smell you. Maybe you should wait here, and I should get Jenny and Lauren."

"I've got my orders," Coors said, "and I'm not defenseless." He patted his holster. "Don't worry about it."

Andy shook his head. "I don't know, man. Something is off."

Coors pulled his weapon and pointed it at Andy. "Move," he said. "Show me the way inside the complex."

"Whoa!" Andy put his hands up. "C'mon. That's not necessary."

"I've got a job to do, and you're standing in my way." Coors nodded toward the hatch. "Go. Make sure it's clear."

"Damn it," Andy said. "I'm just trying to help."

"I don't want to have to say it again," Coors said. "Move."

"Fine." Andy opened the hatch. When Coors followed him out, he frowned as the man opened the hatch wide. "Ronald isn't the sharpest crayon in the box, but even he is going to notice that. We should close it."

"No." Coors gestured toward the small metal staircase which led to the cavern floor. "We leave it open. Orders from up top."

"That doesn't make sense," Andy said.

"I'm authorized to use force," Coors said, "and that includes you, if you don't cooperate. We're running out of time. Just move."

Andy shook his head and breathed out in frustration. "Fine."

He led Coors down the stair and started toward the complex. This isn't how I pictured this going, he thought. This isn't right. Why is he acting like this?

"Will you please put that away?" Andy asked. "You need my keycard to get inside, and I'm starting to regret letting you in here."

"Is that a threat?" Coors nudged Andy's back with the weapon's muzzle.

Andy turned around. The door to get inside the buildings was just ahead, but he had a bad feeling. "What's going on?" he asked. "This doesn't feel right."

And then Coors shot him. At first, Andy didn't register what had happened. The pain wasn't immediate. Instead, it was as if a force punched him so hard it knocked him off his feet. Vibrations rippled through the muscles in his chest. He landed on his back, staring up into the dark. The air became too thin, or… was it that his lungs couldn't suck it in? He gasped for breath as Coors reached down and unclipped his keycard from his pocket.

Coors didn't say anything as he marched toward the door, swiped Andy's keycard and opened it. The sound of footsteps broke through Andy's numbness, which seemed to affect everything: his hearing, his lips, his limbs. It was all he could do to simply get enough air to stay aware.

"Hey!"

Ronald? Andy wheezed. He wanted to warn the man, but nothing happened. He couldn't make the words come out.

Coors fired two shots, and Andy heard the sound of a body hitting concrete, a thud and it was over.

Stop, Andy thought. He wanted to scream, wanted to ask what Coors was doing.

All he could do was watch as his periphery became pitch black. He focused on the light of the open doorway, on the hallway beyond, on the blurring form of Coors. He took out the jar they'd said was repellent, unscrewed the lid, and poured it out in a long line down the hall.

And then there was a sound behind him that made Andy go through the effort of turning his head and body so that he could look into the dim light, into the shadows that led back to the hatch. He'd heard that sound before. It was amplified by the echoing nature of the cavern. A buzzing that was unmistakable.

A lantern cast a circle of light several yards away. The darkness beyond it got *darker,* like a curtain had been pulled to block out the lantern light further down. And then the circle of white was swallowed by a writhing black monster.

Andy sucked in to scream, but the air caught and then blood bubbled up into his throat, and all he could do was gurgle and cough.

With every last bit of strength, he turned back toward the door and reached for it, willing it to close. He slid in his own blood, one inch and then two, but it wasn't enough.

Coors rushed out of the hall and stepped aside as the first black tendrils reached over Andy and toward the door. He just stood there, though. The man didn't run. He didn't even scream, not until the first tendril of the swarm engulfed him.

Why didn't he run? Andy asked himself as he felt the brush of dozens of mosquitos on his skin, as his vision was clouded with the little black and orange devils, as his ears filled with their constant hum.

The swarm oozed into the complex as pressure built up behind Andy's eyes, as hot blood blocked his airway, as he lost control of his body, as his muscles began to jerk and tremble and heave.

He couldn't breathe. He couldn't move. He couldn't stop it.

It was over.

The swarm would devour them all.

Chapter 49

Alexander Roman and Heather Peters

General Hunt thrust the radio into Alex's hands. "They won't believe it if I tell them."
The signal jammer had been disabled and the detainees loaded into the back of the military truck Boreland had used. Everyone left was looking at Alex: fifteen soldiers, two friends on the brink of panic, and one very stern general.
"Will they even hear us?" Alex asked.
"The radios they have are military," General Hunt said. "They use code, just like we do, to communicate, but we *have* been listening in, and we do have access to their frequencies. The only problem is we can only get through to those at the gate and the arena. The radio signal won't reach to the complex itself."
Alex looked down at the radio and nodded. He looked back at Hunt. "While I'm talking, we have to load up the toxin Boreland took along with the hazmat suits, and we have to get up to that mountain."
"You heard the man!" General Hunt shouted.
Everyone started moving, and Alex raised the radio as he headed back to the Humvee. "Cheyenne Mountain Complex, come in. This is an emergency. Is anyone there?"
A voice crackled over the speaker. "Who the hell is this?"
"My name is Alexander Roman. I'm a scientist. I don't have time to explain this, but a swarm may already be inside your facilities, and if it's not, it will be soon."
The response was accompanied by laughter. "What? Are you crazy? Nice try. Let me guess, you've come all the way here to save us? Or are you just hoping we'll all run outside into your loving arms so you can protect us?"
"I'm being serious. This isn't a joke. The lives of everyone down below are in danger." Alex got into the passenger seat as Timothy and Walter loaded up in the back and the general took the driver's seat again. "Please, you have to check with whoever watches the escape hatch. If they're still alive, maybe it's not too late. You can close the hatch."
The laughter died down. "The escape hatch can't be opened from the outside."
Alex took a deep breath. There was no use in sugar coating it or playing games. "The military has an inside man, Andy Munez, and he thinks he's letting a rescue team in for their operative, Jenny Conner, and her aid, Lauren Stevens. A rogue faction has found a way to lure a swarm down the hatch, and the president has ordered us to stop them."
"Andy ain't no turncoat."
"He's been working for the military since he first came to you, before that even," Alex said. "Wherever he's supposed to be, you won't find him there. Please, before it's too late, send someone to that hatch."
"All right, all right. No harm in checking, I guess." The voice did not sound urgent enough. There was a brief pause.
"I'm on my way with a toxin that will kill the swarm," Alex said as the Humvee swung back onto the road and began the climb at full speed. "Everyone needs to take shelter. I'm talking to the guards at the gate, right? You need to be prepared to let me in without any resistance."
"Can you believe this guy?" another voice added his two cents. "They're either running out of ideas to get inside, or they're just plain messing with our heads."
"Just send someone to go and look!" Alex shouted.
"I did. It'll take a minute," said the original speaker, amusement still lacing his tone. "We got a phone hooked up that connects to the complex. Radios work up here. Radios work down there. They don't work in between. I made a call. Now I'm waiting for an answer."
Alex sighed and shook his head as the radio fell silent.
General Hunt slammed his hand against the steering wheel and cursed under his breath. "It's too late," he said. "I can feel it."
"We have other problems," Walter said. "It's not just about getting inside."
"Go on," the general said. "Any problems that can be worked out now should be."
"After we get inside, how are we going to deploy the toxin?" Walter asked.
"What do you mean?" Timothy sounded on the verge of breaking down. "We just blast the swarm with the stuff!"
"The swarm has to be contained," Alex said. He looked over his shoulder. "The toxin, too. It can kill people just as easily as the swarm. We can't let it into the air filtration systems."
"They're supposed to have a biosafety lab, right?" Walter asked.
"Yes. It would have separate air filtration," Alex said, nodding. "That would be perfect."
"We'll need their help," Timothy said. "We don't know where anything is."
"I doubt we'll get much push back if they find themselves trapped in there with a swarm." Alex looked back at the radio and sighed in frustration as he shook the device. "What are they doing?" He willed someone to speak, to tell him what was happening inside the complex. But all he could do was wait as the Humvee sped ever upward along the curving road.
And then the radio came to life. "We've just lost Otis. He was sent to check," said the voice. "He used his last breath to let us know the swarm is already inside. I've got Carrie on the phone. I'll put it on speaker."
"We need to evacuate," came Carrie's voice. "Get everyone out."

"No!" Alex shouted. "No, they could swarm you in the halls. Have everyone secure themselves in a room where they can stuff blankets or something in any doorway cracks. Hunker down, and let us inside, and we'll take care of it."

"I have to talk to Mark," Carrie said. "Don't you say another word to that man until I give you the word, Hector."

"Yes, ma'am." The original voice, Hector, Alex assumed, said nothing more after that.

"What?" Alex wiped the sweat from his brow. "You have to do what I say! Is everyone taking shelter?"

There was no reply.

"Hello?" Alex asked, desperate for an answer. "Hello? You have to listen to me!"

He was met with only silence.

* * *

Heather slowly ate her piece of chocolate cake. It was delicious, but every bite swallowed meant she was one step closer to having to go talk with Mark in his office.

She looked at the clock again. Shouldn't they be escaping by now? Maybe their absence just hasn't been noticed yet…

Heather reached for her water, and an urgent knock on the door almost made her spill it.

"Mark!" It was Carrie's voice. "Mark! Open up!"

Mark was already halfway to the door. He swung it open. "I told you to only interrupt me in case of an emergency."

Carrie barged in, and Heather craned her neck to see down the short entry hallway. The woman was coated in sweat, and her eyes were wide with terror. She spoke so quickly, Heather had to strain to catch all of it. "We've got a swarm in the complex, come through the escape hatch, and some guy named Alex telling us to hunker down and not evacuate, and it got Otis, Mark. It got Otis, and Ronald, too, we think. He was guarding the hatch."

Heather stood up. "A swarm, in the building?" she asked. *That doesn't make sense. How did a swarm get inside?*

"Do we evacuate or do as this guy says and hunker down?" Carrie asked.

Mark looked back at his wife. "Evacuate," he said.

"No!" Heather shook her head and came around the table. "Those swarms will come for congregated people, and if everyone heads for the gates, they will be swarmed."

Mark swallowed hard. "Do you have this Alex guy on the phone?" he asked.

"Yeah," Carrie said. "Turn on your radio. Stay here, where it's safe. I'll go down to communications and put him on speaker. You can talk from the safety of your home."

"No," Mark said, "I'll come with you."

"Mark!" Emily shrieked. Tears ran down her cheeks in rivers. "Please, don't!"

"You can give the order from here, Mark," Carrie said, raising her eyebrows.

Mark nodded. "Okay. Go. I need to talk to Alex." As soon as Carrie left, Mark started issuing orders. "Seal the crack under the door with towels or blankets or something."

Emily was sobbing, backed up against the wall.

"I'll do it," Heather said, rushing for the bathroom. She pulled out a few towels and ran back to the front door, stuffing them under the crack.

"You have to let us in."

Heather froze on her hands and knees in front of the door. That was Alex's voice. She finished sealing them in and slowly sat up, listening.

"How do I know I can trust you?" Mark asked.

"You don't," Alex said. "But I can promise if you don't let us in, you'll die in there. We have a toxin that will kill the swarm. All we need is access to the biosafety lab."

"That building isn't even hooked up to electricity," Mark said.

"Okay," Alex said. "I can work with that. The important thing is that the toxin is released in a place that isn't connected to the complex's main air filtration systems. We're pulling up now. You have to order them to raise the mesh barriers."

"Who is 'we'?" Mark asked.

There was a moment of hesitation. "I'm with General Hunt and a small force who came here to stop the rogue faction that lured the swarm into your complex to begin with."

"I'm not letting the military inside," Mark said. "They'll just use this as an opportunity to take this place. Not to mention the fact that there's no way I can verify your story or confirm that you and General Hunt weren't the ones who let the swarm inside."

"That's not what happened," Alex said, "but let's say it was. Would you have a choice?"

"I won't let an army into my complex," Mark said.

"Will you let a few nonmilitary men inside?" Alex asked. "I have two friends with me, a fellow scientist and his son. They both have experience fighting off these swarms, and I trust them. Believe it or not, Mark, I'm not and never was with the military. They're just the ones who gave me refuge."

Heather's stomach twisted, and she covered her mouth as a gasp escaped her lips. *No… Tim, stay away! Don't do it!* She got to her feet and reentered the open dining and living room area, every step like lifting cinder blocks with her ankles.

"Fine." Mark leaned against the wall, shoulders sagging. "Just the three of you. Carrie, you still there?"

"Sure am," Carrie said.

"I'm issuing a Code Black. Everyone needs to hunker down, except for you, if you're willing. Someone needs to guide Alex to the lab, someone with high enough clearance that their keycard can get them into any room. Get to our hazmat suits first and protect yourself before meeting them at the gate."

"I've got this." Carrie sounded ten times less frenzied than she had when she'd been at Mark's door. "I know this place like the back of my hand."

And then an alarm sounded over the speakers in the hallways. In between its wailing, a male voice said: "Code Black. Code Black. There is a swarm in the complex. Take shelter. Do not try to escape. Block the cracks under the doors. Report any sightings of the swarm to Carrie's frequency. Code Black. Code Black."

Mark pushed off the wall and crossed the room to where Emily still cried and trembled on the other side of the dining room table. She rested her hand on her belly and leaned into her husband.

"It's going to be okay," Mark said. "I won't let anything happen to you or the baby." He held her, and the sight was bittersweet. There was nothing he could do to back up that promise, and yet Heather wished Tim were there to comfort her with the same words.

Then she remembered she had two people in her care, two younger women who would need her. *Azalea and Lizzy…* she thought as she stepped forward, a sudden guilt at having forgotten them registering with a sharp stab in her gut. But then her step faltered, and she came to a stop.

Azalea was whispering something in Lizzy's ear as one hand, knuckles white, squeezed Lizzy's forearm. As the sirens continued their screams out in the halls of the complex, Heather's heartbeat quickened. Her own internal alarm bells rung as the wrong emotion flashed across Azalea's face. Her glimpse of it was brief, but it was there.

Confusion wrapped Heather up, made her freeze on the spot. *That's not fear,* she thought. *That's rage.*

Chapter 50

Lizzy Peters and Heather Peters

A swarm... the Mother's judgment has come. Lizzy hugged herself tight.

The Heirs of the Mother had given the earth the means by which to cleanse herself, and it seemed there was no place she couldn't reach with the instruments they had given her. Like a sculptor carving away excess clay and making fine lines, the Mother used the swarms and the disease as chisels and detail tools. The Heirs had begun The Cleansing; the earth herself would finish it.

The question of who it was that would perish, who it was that would face judgment, surfaced and sent Lizzy's stomach to churning. It was the good, the pure at heart, who would go on to rebuild a society that could live in harmony with the Mother as her children instead of as her enemies.

The voices rattling in the back of Lizzy's head, screaming for justice to be done, accused her as often as they accused others. It was Azalea's devotion, her goodness, that quieted them, that assured them Lizzy was on the right path and could be left alone.

But it was hard to follow the right path. The things that used to be good were no longer so, and actions she'd once thought unthinkably evil had turned out to be necessary. There was no trusting herself. Her eyes had been opened to the truth, but it was so tempting to squeeze them shut again, to take the easier route, to allow her old self a little room to unfurl in the deepest parts of her heart where she'd been packed away.

There were moments when she questioned. Too many moments.

And every time she questioned, the voices screeched at her, reminded her of bloodied ground, of desolate landscapes, of the death and destruction wrought by man, of the inevitable doomed future the human race had been hurtling toward.

With the screams, her skin crawled with the memory of oil up to her neck. Her body remembered the heat of flames licking at her legs, of smoke rising and blocking out the sun, filling her lungs. The shadows stretched for her, threatening to swallow her in darkness for days on end.

It was better not to question.

And yet...

Lizzy lifted her gaze to where Heather cast a sympathetic look at Emily, who sobbed in a corner while her husband comforted her. There was fear in Heather's eyes, too, and her hand lifted to her own stomach. There was new life there, untouched by humanity's influence. She had to be terrified, and yet she had the room to care about others.

Heather should live, Lizzy thought, and the voices didn't protest.

Azalea's hand drew Lizzy's eyes away from her sister-in-law and to Azalea's ever-tightening fingers gripping her forearm. Emily still sobbed, and Mark talked over her, offering useless words which only served as a distraction from reality. Heather was still focused on them.

"This has to end," Azalea whispered sharply. There was no sympathy in her eyes. There was only the familiar fury that inspired the voices in the back of Lizzy's mind to stir.

Lizzy didn't move, didn't speak. She caught Heather moving in the periphery of her vision. She'd stepped toward them but hesitated.

"If Alex and Walter get inside this complex," Azalea said as she leaned close, her words hot on Lizzy's ear, "they won't leave without the coordinates to that research bank. And I *will not* go halfway around the world to make sure they don't succeed in ending The Cleansing. This. Ends. Tonight."

Her first instinct was to ask how, but there was only one way the two of them could do anything about their problem. "You want us to go out there," Lizzy said.

"It's the only way."

Azalea's fingers pressed into Lizzy's muscles, squeezed her bones, sent a numb tingle down her arm. It would leave a bruise, but Lizzy was sure not to pull away. She'd experienced much worse.

"Their luck has run out." The venom in Azalea's voice sent a shudder up Lizzy's spine. When she was like that, intensely determined and wholly enraged, every fiber of Lizzy's being was prompted to obey lest Azalea turn on her and stoke the agonizing screams to their full power.

But despite the way her insides clawed at her, begged her not to, Lizzy put forward one request. "Protect her," Lizzy whispered. "Please. I need Heather to survive."

Azalea's features pinched in disgust or disappointment, perhaps both. "Again and again, you put that woman above what must be done."

"Not above," Lizzy said, "but just below."

Azalea narrowed her eyes and let go of Lizzy's arm. "The Mother will protect her should she be deemed worthy. I cannot worry about her *and* you *and* our true purpose."

"But you will not harm her directly?" Lizzy denied the urge to hold the spot where Azalea's hand had left behind an aching throb.

"No," Azalea said, "nor will I knowingly put her in harm's way. For you, Elizabeth."

Lizzy nodded, understanding it was the best Azalea could promise. She couldn't argue further. If all Lizzy had done meant anything at all, The Cleansing could not be disrupted. She'd become a liar and a murderer, and she would sacrifice her own life should the time come for it. The cause was just as much hers as it was Azalea's. It had to be. She wasn't a monster. She was a protector.

Finally, Emily's sobs subdued, and the room fell quiet enough that their whispers would surely be noticed. Lizzy sat back and waited for Azalea to make a move.

* * *

Why aren't they afraid? Heather asked herself as the two young women ceased their whispering as Emily quieted. She didn't know the answer to her question, and that made the question feel urgent.

Emily had sunk to the floor when she'd broken down, and as she gathered her wits, Mark helped her to her feet. "I'm sorry," Emily said, still trembling, hiccupping as she dried her eyes with the collar of her shirt.

"It's okay," Heather mumbled, almost out of habit, as her worries threatened to overwhelm her. Tim was going after the swarm, there was something wrong with Azalea and Lizzy, and she kept hearing Ingrid telling her that anxiety wasn't good for the baby.

It was too cold, and yet Heather's face and neck were coated in a thin layer of sweat. She wrung her hands together, twisting at her fingers, trying to overcome her thoughts with physical discomfort. Time felt both too slow and too fast, and she couldn't quite catch her breath. But the last time she'd been stressed to the max, she'd collapsed into a worthless heap. She couldn't do that, not again.

Heather focused on her breathing and walked back to the table, sitting down with her hands flat on the cool wooden surface. She closed her eyes, willing her heartbeat to slow.

"You okay?" Lizzy asked, her voice too calm.

"Heather?" That was Emily's voice.

Heather opened her eyes and reached with a trembling hand to take a sip of her water from dinner. That cold, purified liquid was soothing.

"I'm fine," Heather said, offering a smile she knew wasn't convincing but was the best she could do.

Emily turned to her husband. "Mark, what are we going to do?"

"We're going to take it one step at a time," Mark said. "We're going to get through this." He guided his wife to the table and then returned to the radio Carrie had left behind. He raised it and spoke. "Carrie, where is the swarm now?"

"I got a report not a minute ago that it was spotted in building three," Carrie said.

"And our guests?"

"They're on their way through the access tunnels. Should be almost to the blast doors."

"Keep me updated, Carrie, and stay safe." Mark looked up at Emily. "We have time."

"What are you talking about?" Emily asked.

Mark marched to a cabinet on the other side of the living room area. After punching a few buttons, the cabinet clicked open, and Mark pulled out a handgun. He grabbed a magazine from a top shelf, closed the door, and turned around.

Emily sniffled. "Mark, what good is a gun against a swarm?"

The sight of him with the weapon wasn't helping Heather as she fought against a rising anxiety that could cripple her. "I have to agree," Heather said, "I think I'd feel more comfortable if—"

"It's not for the swarm," Mark said. "Emily, you and I need to go. The swarm isn't here, yet. If we hurry, if we go through building seven to eleven and back down to building one, we can reach the blast doors and get out that way. I can run things from outside, where you'll be safe."

Heather's stomach lurched. She shook her head. "Mark, no. We need to stay put."

"If everyone tried to get out, I'm sure that would lure the swarm," Mark said. "But two people?" He shook his head. "We can make it if we run. The swarms are slow and—"

Heather stood. "They've gotten faster, Mark. It's not a good idea."

"I don't know about this, hon," Emily said. "What about everyone else? We can't leave them."

"Yes, we can," Mark said. "You three stay here. I don't want you following and adding to our scent."

"I don't think that's how it works," Heather said.

"You know, I'm glad you showed your true colors, Mark."

Azalea's voice drew Heather's attention. She looked over her shoulder, frowning as Azalea picked up her fork and scraped the remaining icing off the cake in front of her. She stood, and Lizzy stood next to her.

"Sit down." Mark growled, and Heather's heart lodged in her throat at the sight of his gun pointed at Lizzy. She placed herself between Mark and the table, specifically between the gun and Lizzy.

* * *

The protective stand Heather took made Lizzy double her resolve. She couldn't watch Heather die. There was an untainted and undeniable love between them, a family bond. Unlike Lizzy's father, Heather had never done anything to harm that bond. In fact, she'd only ever nurtured it. Even before Day Zero, Heather and Tim had been a refuge for her and for her brother, George.

"I won't hurt you if you don't give me a reason to," Mark said. "All three of you, sit down. You can stay here, in our apartment. I suggest you go back into the master bath, stuff towels under the bedroom door and the bathroom door, take some food and water with you. That's three barriers between you and the swarm should it get this far."

"Then why don't you take Emily back there?" Heather asked. "We'll stay out here, if you want."

Mark's eyes flicked upward. He looked at his wife. "Just trust me, Emily. We have to go."

Lizzy frowned and searched the area in which she'd seen Mark briefly glance. "The vents…" she said. "You're afraid the swarm will come through the vents."

"It's possible," he said. "What's to stop them? And even if they don't come through the vents, I don't trust the military. By their own admission, it's their fault the swarm is even down here."

Lizzy's stomach fluttered. *If we get rid of Alex and Walter, then we can kill off this one swarm, can't we?* She glanced at Azalea's back. The swarms were multiplying faster than the Heirs could have dreamed possible. One less wouldn't do anything to hinder The Cleansing. *I can convince her,* Lizzy thought. *Azalea will help me save Heather. I know she will. And then we can go home.*

"They aren't part of the military," Heather said. "You heard Alex say that just as I did."

"And you believe that?" Mark shook his head. "I can't *not* let him in if it means the people down here might be saved. But I also don't want to risk my life and the lives of my wife and child should they be lying."

Azalea came around the table, licking the icing off her fork. "Men like you always run when things get hard," she said. "I knew you weren't as pure as you pretended to be. Abandoning your community to save yourself…" She *tsked*. "What ever happened to the notion that a captain goes down with his ship?"

Heather held up a hand, gesturing for her to stay back. "Azalea, stop. You're not helping."

"I never pretended to be pure or whatever," Mark said. "I'm just trying to protect my family." He pointed his weapon at Azalea as she inched forward. "Stay back. Don't take another step."

"Okay, that's enough," Heather said. "Just put the gun down. We won't stop you."

Mark shook his head. "I'll put it down when you three sit, and if I see you in the halls following us, I'll kill you."

Lizzy scowled. "You're just like him," she said, remembering how her father had killed, not even sparing their family pilot who Lizzy had known since she was small. "Hiding behind protecting your family, all the while grasping for power. You want to get out of here for you most of all. Your love for them is a lie."

"You don't know him!" Emily said. "He's a good man. Mark, if you want to go, then let's just go."

"Lizzy, who are you…" Heather paused as a confused frown turned into an expression of understanding. "Your father loves you, Lizzy. That wasn't a lie."

A twisting in her stomach at those words brought moisture to Lizzy's eyes. Part of her wanted that to be true, and another part recoiled at the thought that it might be. If someone like *that* loved her, what did that say about *her*?

"Mark, let's just go." Emily took a step toward the door.

"Not until they sit the hell down," Mark shouted, jutting the gun in their direction.

Heather raised her hands. "Okay," she said, backing up and sitting again. She looked at Lizzy. "Please, Lizzy. Just sit down. Azalea? Just do what he says."

But Azalea didn't listen, and neither did Lizzy.

* * *

Heather repeated herself, the alarm in her voice not lost on her. "Do what he says. Sit down."

But Lizzy and Azalea positioned themselves so that they made a triangle with Mark. Emily watched from near the entry hall with a confused look that Heather imagined mirrored her own. Heather was about to get up and physically move Lizzy back to a seat at the table when Lizzy started talking.

"There's blood on your hands," Lizzy said. She was no longer the girl who could barely speak due to grief. She was a young woman staring down a man with a gun, an almost crazed look in her eyes. "You're just like him, like *them*."

That was the second time Lizzy had said that. She and Walter had a falling out, and for good reason, from what Heather understood, but she'd not seen such hatred from Lizzy before. And she had to be talking about Walter.

Except, she thought, who else is she talking about?

"What are you talking about?" Mark couldn't point the gun at both of them; they were too far apart.

"You didn't hesitate to threaten us," Lizzy said, "and you meant it. You've killed before."

"Most have, these days," Mark said. "Those of us who are left have had to do what was necessary."

"Heather, what is going on? What are they doing?" Emily's voice was high pitched and nervous.

"I don't know," Heather said honestly, looking from Lizzy to Azalea and back again.

"We're doing what is necessary." Lizzy took a step toward Mark.

He pointed the gun at Lizzy, and Heather stood. "No!" she shouted.

* * *

Lizzy flinched, but Azalea smiled. Heather's movement was one more distraction for Mark. He didn't seem to notice Azalea.

While his gun was trained on Lizzy and Heather, Azalea moved fast, plunging the fork into Mark's thigh. As he screamed and bent forward, she turned into him, spinning low, slamming her elbow into his groin, and then punching up, landing a blow to the bottom of his chin. She ducked under the hand holding the gun as he swept it toward his chest, perhaps to trap her against him. But she was like water slipping through the cracks as she flowed away from him and then back again, sinking her teeth into the man's wrist. He screamed again, dropped the gun, and Azalea dove for it. She aimed it at him once she had it, his blood at the corner of her mouth, as Mark sat hard on the ground, a half moon, bleeding wound on his wrist and a fork sticking out of his thigh. His hands trembled around the utensil's handle.

"What the hell?" He looked up, his eyes wide with shock.

Emily had screamed and was hyperventilating again, backed against a wall, seeming to struggle between a desire to move forward and help her husband and the need to stay as far from Azalea as possible.

Azalea cocked her head, glanced at the gun, and flipped the safety off. "I guess we're lucky you weren't planning on actually using this thing." She backed up next to Lizzy, the gun raised.

"Who are you?" Mark asked.

"I'd like to know the same thing." Heather looked between Azalea and Lizzy.

"I think," Azalea said, gun in hand, "it's time for you to find out."

* * *

"Just give me the gun." Heather held out her hand. She tried to keep it steady but failed miserably.

"Why would I do that?" Azalea's eyes lit up with amusement.

"Because whatever is going on, this is not the way we do things," Heather said. "We should let Mark and Emily go, if that's what they want."

"What is this?" Mark was sweating, his voice strained. "What kind of games are you three playing?"

"I'm not playing any games," Heather said, keeping her eyes on Azalea. "I don't know what she's doing, but all I want right now is for her to stop." She took a step forward, keeping her hand out. "Please, Azalea, just give me the gun."

Azalea pointed the gun at Mark. "If you take one more step without me giving you permission, I'll shoot him."

"Please," Emily said between shuddering breaths, "don't hurt him."

"She wouldn't do that," Heather said, glancing at Emily. "She's bluffing."

"She's not," Lizzy said.

"I slit Nick's throat," Azalea said, "and I actually liked him. Shooting Mark would be a walk in the park."

"What?" Heather's mouth ran dry. "That's not true." But the words were hollow. She looked at her sister-in-law but she saw no surprise, no denial. "Lizzy? You… you knew?"

"It had to be done," Azalea said, "just like Theodore."

Heather snapped her eyes back to Azalea, her vision blurring. "You killed Theodore, too?"

"Not me specifically," Azalea said.

"He deserved it, Heather," Lizzy said. "He was a pig. He was more than happy to share all kinds of information while he put his dirty paws all over Azalea."

"Information?" Heather's knees were weak. She reached behind her to feel for the chair and slid into it, her head reeling. "*You* killed Theodore?"

"He was the second man Elizabeth brought to justice, and he won't be the last," Azalea said.

"No… this doesn't… it doesn't make sense." Heather's temples throbbed. She put an elbow on the back of the chair and propped up her head with her hand as tears burned her eyes. "You… you burned down the lab, too, didn't you?"

"She's smarter than she looks," Azalea said.

Lizzy came to her, knelt in front of her, looked up into her eyes. "You don't understand, but you will. One day, you will, after The Cleansing is done, when you and Tim and the baby are living in a world with a fresh start."

Heather tried to process what Lizzy was saying, but it didn't make sense. "You mean, after we get rid of DV-10 and the swarms?"

"No," Lizzy said, "after the swarms and the disease have done their jobs, after they've cleansed the earth of people like my father."

Emily starting sobbing again.

Mark looked horrified and confused. "What is she talking about? Someone tell me what's going on."

Azalea jutted the gun in his direction. "I wouldn't say anything else, if I were you."

He flinched and cowered, curling over his thigh, careful not to touch the fork.

Heather couldn't find the right words. She shook her head at Lizzy. "You don't know what you're saying. We're trying to *stop* the swarms. Everyone is trying to stop them."

Lizzy pressed her lips together. "Only those who don't understand."

The sincerity in her voice, in her eyes… that was almost as bad as the revelations being dropped on Heather one right after another.

"I wasn't trafficked, Heather," Lizzy said, "I was rescued. Rescued from my father, from blindness. I was given a purpose by the Heirs of the Mother."

Heather was still trying to piece together the puzzle, but with her head swimming and her heart pounding, it was difficult. "You mean the people Walter thought killed you in the first place? What purpose?"

"The Cleansing," Lizzy said, smiling.

Bile rose to the back of Heather's throat. "What did they do to you?"

"We helped her see that the world needs to start over," Azalea said, "and it starts with making sure Walter Peters fails in his attempts to right his wrongs."

Lizzy's smile faded, and she blinked a few times. "My father could never wipe away those stains. They were set far before Day Zero."

"What are you going to do?" Heather asked. "Why are you telling me this now?" She looked at Azalea. "What is the point of this?"

"We're going to stop Alex and Walter," Azalea said.

"Timothy is with them." Heather barely managed the words. "Are you… are you going to hurt him?"

Lizzy shook her head. "I don't want to," she said.

"That's not an answer." Heather's chest ached. She reached out and cupped Lizzy's cheek with her palm. "You don't have to do this."

"It's time for us to go," Azalea said, and her harsh tone seemed to snap Lizzy to attention.

Lizzy pulled away, stood, and returned to Azalea's side.

"Mark, where is the lab here in the complex?" Azalea asked.

Mark cursed. "I'm not telling you that."

"If I have to shoot your wife," Azalea said, "I will."

Mark paled and looked at Emily who was a trembling mess against the wall, sitting knees to chest, still crying. At Azalea's words, Emily shook her head and hugged her middle.

"I'm not a patient person." Azalea swung the weapon toward Emily.

Heather sucked in a breath and scooted to the edge of her seat as Mark shouted his objection.

"No!" he said. "No, please don't. I… I have a map. It's in the desk drawer of my office." He reached his right hand, bloodied from the seeping wound where Azalea had bitten him, into his pocket and pulled out a small key on a keyring. "Here." He held it out.

"Elizabeth." Azalea spoke her name as an order that Heather's sister-in-law clearly understood.

Lizzy took the keys and hurried across the room to disappear inside Mark's office. It didn't take her long to come back with a map. She unfolded it as she walked to the dining table. After pushing back dishes, she laid it out and studied it.

"There." Lizzy poked the map with one finger. "I can get us there." She put both hands flat on the table, looking at Azalea with a triumphant expression.

"Please," Heather said, leaning forward across the table, reaching out to cover Lizzy's hand with her own. "You could die out there. This isn't who you are, Lizzy. You don't really want your father and Alex gone."

Lizzy yanked her hand away, folded up the map, and stuck it into her pocket. She didn't respond to Heather, instead addressing Azalea. "Let's go."

"One last thing," Azalea said, "so that we aren't followed."

Heather threw her hands over her ears as the gunshot filled the room with a deafening *bang* and blood blossomed from Mark's chest.

Chapter 51

Alexander Roman and Heather Peters

Alex, Walter, and Timothy had left General Hunt and his soldiers to storm the escape hatch and close it lest a second swarm descend upon them. According to Mark's demands, not one soldier was let past the gate. The mesh barriers had been opened for Alex all the way down the tunnel, but as they passed through, the barriers were lowered behind them again, a many-layered cage sealing them underground.

They reached the blast doors where three guards paced, where one man stood by a landline telephone tapping his finger impatiently on the receiver. A fifth guard worked at a circular metal plate bolted into the wall next to the outer blast door.

A bright white bulb created a cone of light that cast shadows across faces etched with worry. Everyone paused to look at them as Alex parked the vehicle, frozen as if in a photograph documenting some fateful day in history.

Alex's hands still gripped the wheel. There was still space between preparation and action, time wherein potential for success or failure loomed large in their rivalry. "You guys ready for this?" he asked.

"This is crazy," Timothy said.

"It's the only way we're going to save them," Walter said. "It has to work."

Alex turned in his seat to look at the men who'd journeyed with him halfway across the continent, who'd fought for so long to not only survive but protect. "We can do this."

Walter nodded. "I'm ready."

"Me too." Timothy took hold of his door handle and pulled so that his door clicked open.

Alex pushed aside his doubts. There was no room for them. What had to be done needed confidence. Second guesses could mean their deaths. He stepped out of the vehicle and into the tunnel. That transition seemed to breathe life back into the scene before them, and people started moving again.

Unsure of who to address, who was in charge among that particular group of civilians, he made his voice loud enough for all to hear. "We're going to dress in our hazmat suits and get ready to infiltrate. We'll need to open the doors."

The man working at the flat metal plate looked over his shoulder briefly. "We're not doing that," he said. "You three are going to have to go single-file through here. It's meant for emergencies, and I'd say this qualifies. I'm almost finished opening it."

"We haven't been able to reach Mark," the man at the phone added, "but Carrie should be on the other side of this hatch in one of our suits. She'll help guide you to the place you need to go."

"Do you know what's going on in there?" Alex asked.

"It's been ten minutes since we've heard from Carrie," he said. "More than that since we've heard from Mark."

Alex nodded and rounded the vehicle to the trunk. He, Timothy, and Walter layered their suits over their clothes as they spoke.

"A lot can happen in ten minutes." Timothy shook his head as he pulled his suit on.

Walter had already stepped into his. He slipped his arms into the sleeves and shrugged his suit onto his shoulders. "I'm hoping the bait kept the swarm nearby for a while, but they would have moved on by now, I would think. They'll be looking for blood."

"What if the swarm splits up, branches out?" Timothy pulled his zipper up to his neck.

"These swarms have displayed a tendency to behave as a unit." Alex pulled on a second layer of gloves and secured them over the suit's wrist cuffs.

"I still don't understand their evolution," Walter said. "It's maddening."

Alex pulled on his helmet, choosing to keep his thoughts to himself. There was a reason the government commissioned secret experiments involving biological weapons. No matter how much human beings liked to think they understood biology, there was still too much they didn't know. Messing with the makeup of nature, playing God like that… there was always a risk they'd take it too far. But Walter knew that. And he'd paid dearly. Bringing it up wouldn't have helped.

Alex secured his helmet and put one hand on Walter's shoulder and another on Timothy's. "Let's kill off this swarm and get our ladies out of there."

He turned back to the vehicle and pulled out a box containing three fire extinguishers and all the materials they'd need in order to set up a trap for the swarm inside the lab. Then, he followed Timothy and Walter over to where one of them was removing a circular plate. He leaned into the little tunnel.

"Carrie? You there?"

"Yeah. Ross? That you?"

"Sure is."

"You got those scientists ready to go?"

Ross looked back at them. "Yep. Hey, we haven't heard from Mark in a hot minute. Can't raise him on the phone."

"I don't like that at all," Carrie said.

"You seen the swarm yet?"

"No," Carrie said, "but I've heard screams and had a few reports on the swarm's movements. I don't think it's in building three anymore. Pretty sure it's in building four."

"What does that mean?" Timothy asked.

Ross stood back and gestured for Alex to go through. "Carrie will explain as you go. Just listen to her, and maybe you'll make it out alive. I'm gonna seal this back up once you're through, so… good luck in there."

Alex walked up to the hole in the wall, swallowed a lump in his throat, and set the box inside. He pushed it into the dark as he crawled forward toward the light on the other end. Scuffling sounded behind him as the discordant rhythms of the three of them moving inside the small concrete tube created an angry whisper.

Carrie took the box when it reached the end of the tunnel, placed it on the floor, and stepped back to leave Alex room to crawl out into the open. Once Walter and Timothy were standing outside the tunnel, she closed the circular door and bolted it shut.

"Follow me," Carrie said as she turned and started across the paved concrete, following the road leading out from the blast doors.

"Give us a basic layout," Alex said. "Where are the labs compared to where the swarm is?"

"The main entrance is near the center of Building One," Carrie said. "Buildings One and Four create a backwards L-shape, with Four being the bottom line." She held up her right forefinger and thumb, pointing to her thumb as she talked of Building Four. "If the swarm is there, we should have a clear path to Building Eleven which extends from the top of Building One." Carrie tapped the tip of her forefinger before dropping her hand. "But the grid is interconnected, and it's easy to go from one building to the next. The swarm could come at us unexpectedly from a different direction. I'm relying on limited reports from people hunkered down and frightened out of their minds."

They approached a white building, rising between cavern walls. Carrie led them up a small set of stairs and, using a keycard, opened the door. She held it open for them. Alex walked in first and waited in the small lobby for the other three to come inside.

"You said earlier you've heard screaming," Walter said as he passed her. "Is the swarm infiltrating rooms where people have blocked off access to the best of their ability?"

"Nah." Carrie's voice was strained, her expression behind the clear shield of her helmet pained. "I think people are panicking and trying to run. I don't know how many we've lost."

"Let's focus on how many we can save," Alex said.

"I really hope that's what you actually came to do." Carrie set her lips in a straight line and marched past, leading the way once more, turning right when they had navigated through what seemed to be an office for personnel check-ins.

"What's that supposed to mean?" Timothy asked.

"It means we're all a little short on trust these days."

Carrie didn't offer anything else, but Alex had a good idea of who she was talking about: Jenny and Lauren. And he'd revealed that Andy had been military, too. He'd managed to keep Heather, Lizzy, and Azalea out of it so far, but that, too, would have to be revealed. There'd been a time when he'd hoped he'd leave Colorado Springs like they'd left Boston, but as he hurried down the hall of the complex, his only remaining hope was that he, his family, and his friends simply made it out of Colorado Springs, period.

At the end of the hall, after they'd traversed what Alex assumed to be the space between buildings where the floor turned to grates and the walls to metal foil for a mere yard or two, they came to a steel door. Carrie swiped her keycard and held it open.

"Here we are," she said. "The wing reserved for you science-y types. It's one of the smallest buildings, but it's a dead end, closed off. Even if you got the swarm past this secure door and closed it tight, we could at least get people out."

A scream echoed in the distance, and all four of them turned their heads back the way they'd come. Alex stared for a solid five seconds, not daring to breathe, praying he wouldn't see a swarm coming their way. When the scream died and the eerie stillness returned to the hall, Alex let out a shaky breath.

"That sounded closer than I'd like," Walter said.

"I don't think we have much time." Alex marched through the open doorway with the box in his arms. "Let's get the tox fog ready to do its job."

* * *

Lizzy and Azalea were gone, and Heather was left with a dying man and the shell of his wife. Emily had shut down after crawling across the floor to her husband's side. She hummed a sad song that Heather thought may have been some sort of lullaby as she stroked Mark's hair away from his face with the light touch of trembling fingers.

Heather straddled Mark with a towel she'd grabbed from the bathroom closet pressed against his wound. The bullet had gone straight through the right side of his chest, leaving a hole in the couch several paces behind him. Towels lay beneath him, too, soaking up blood. Mark was in shock, staring up at his wife, breathing labored.

"Emily, I need you to snap out of it!" Heather said. She looked over her shoulder. At least Lizzy had closed the door, keeping towels still stuffed into the crack; they didn't have to worry about a swarm coming into the apartment while she struggled to keep Mark alive.

Emily didn't answer. She just kept singing. Mark blinked slowly at Heather, lifted his hand, grunted with the effort and lay it on top of Heather's.

"Why… help?" Mark asked.

Heather looked from Mark to Emily and back again, her eyes blurring once more with tears. She squeezed her eyes shut, banishing the moisture, gaining control. She met Mark's eyes with her own. "From the second I came here," she said, "I wanted to be part of this place, for my baby, for me. What you did, building this community, making them safe… I admire that."

Mark frowned. "You're… part of it, of *them*," he said, wheezing.

Heather shook her head. "I swear to you, I had no idea what was really going on with Lizzy and Azalea. And as for the rest…" She licked her lips, tasting the salt of sweat. "Mark, I can't explain it all right now. I need to get you to someone who can help."

Mark breathed out and closed his eyes. It seemed he didn't have the strength to say anything else.

"Emily," Heather said sternly, "do you want your husband to live? Because I can't do this by myself."

Emily looked up at her, and there was a flicker of life in them, of the Emily Heather had come to know. She nodded.

"Good," Heather said. "I need fresh towels, duct tape, and some sheets."

Emily bent down and kissed Mark's forehead. He hadn't opened his eyes since closing them a minute earlier. She got up and Heather heard the soft padding of her footsteps as she moved around the apartment.

"Wake up, Mark." Heather patted the man's cheek.

He groaned.

She slapped his cheek a little harder. "Come on. Don't die on me."

Emily came back, holding the materials to her chest as she sank back to her knees. "What now?"

"We replace the towels with fresh ones," Heather said, "duct tape them in place to staunch the bleeding. Then, we need to roll Mark onto one of these sheets and get him to Ingrid."

"In the clinic?" Emily hugged her bundle tighter. "What about the swarm?"

"It's either that, or he dies," Heather said.

"You… you'd risk your life for him?"

Heather looked down at Mark, at a man who probably hated her. At a man who'd turned her husband away, who would deny her a home should he survive. At a man who loved a good and kind woman. At a man who was about to be a father. At a man who was dying because Heather hadn't seen through Azalea, hadn't seen what was wrong with Lizzy.

She nodded. "Yes," she said, and she held out her hand for a fresh towel.

* * *

Alex set up the last of the extinguishers carefully, setting the wires and triggers as the soldiers had done just days ago in the park. The lab was a sea of stainless steel and reinforced windows leading into another lab just beside it. There was a door that connected the two, perfect for what they needed.

The hall past the steel door that led into that wing of the complex had dead-ended at a T. On the right and the left were entrances to decontamination rooms, both of which led to the connected biosafety labs.

The set of doors leading into the decontamination room and then into the left-hand lab would be left open, and the bait would be generously poured out on a steel table at the center of the room. They would wait in the adjoining lab, watching through glass, until the swarm entered, and then Alex would come around in his suit, grab hold of the trigger wires leading into the decontamination room, pull them taut to set off the toxic fog, and then shut the outer door as quickly as possible.

"Okay, I'm done," Alex said, backing up and letting Walter double check his handy work.

"I think we're good," Walter said.

"Time for the bait?" Timothy stood over the steel table in the center of the room, two glass jars filled with the black substance in hand.

"What if this doesn't work?" Carrie asked from where she stood in the open decontamination room.

"Let's think happy thoughts," Alex said.

"In other words, we'd be screwed?" Carrie crossed her arms.

"Basically," Walter said.

"Here we go." Timothy opened the jars as Alex and Walter stepped back. He carefully poured the black goo out, letting it spread across the large table. He set the jars down and stepped around the table to approach them. He lifted his arms and turned in a circle. "Am I clear?"

"I think so," Alex said, squinting at the man's suit, searching for any black spots.

"You're clear, son," Walter said, gesturing for him to join them in the decontamination room. "Now all we have to do is wait for the swarm to fly into our trap."

"I'm going to wait outside the steel door that leads into this wing," Carrie said. "Once the swarm enters, I'm shutting you all inside. I'll let you out *if* the swarm is killed off and *after* you've spent twenty-four hours quarantining."

"Great," Alex said, sighing. "I guess that's fair."

He didn't like it, but he understood it.

"And the second that door is closed, my first priority will be evacuation," Carrie added. She held up her handheld radio. "I've had a lot of bad news coming over this channel today. I'm looking forward to giving out something good."

The four of them exited the first decontamination room, and Carrie headed down the center hall toward the steel door. Alex, Walter, and Timothy headed toward the second decontamination room on the other end of the short hall at the top of the T-shaped corridor. But as they started to enter what would be their safe room, Carrie's shout was followed by a sharp *crack* that reverberated through Alex's chest. He covered his ears and ducked low out of instinct.

"Carrie?" Alex shouted as he gathered his wits, turned, and ran for the hall. He slid to a stop at the scene before him. "What the—"

Azalea and Lizzy stood over Carrie's still and lifeless form. The gun was in Azalea's hand, and she was smiling. Lizzy was just behind her and to the right, staring at Carrie, her expression blank. Behind them, the straight shot through the complex had turned black with a writhing swarm in the distance.

Chapter 52

Walter Peters and Alexander Roman

Walter threw his arm around Timothy's shoulders and pushed him down at the sound of the first gunshot. It was an instinctual movement, one that happened as his heart leapt into his throat and he sucked in a sharp breath. That moment, where he guarded his son's body with his own, where he was hyperaware of Timothy's body heat, of the movement of breathing Walter could feel through his hand on his son's back, lasted only seconds.

He guided Timothy to the wall for protection even as Alex called out Carrie's name and sprinted the few steps to the center of the shorter corridor to look down the longer hall that stretched toward Building One.

Walter inched to the corner as Alex's eyes grew wider.

"What the—" Alex cut himself off, just staring.

Alex's expression made Walter want to see. He peeked around the corner.

"Bethie?"

Relief washed over him. Lizzy had been on his mind since entering the complex. In truth, she'd been on his mind almost constantly since she'd volunteered to go with Jenny Conner. It had been so hard to resist the urge to keep her with him, to never let her out of his general vicinity ever again. But he'd given her what she asked for, what he thought she needed. Space. From him.

Walter stepped out into the hall, his relief turning sour. Lizzy was a wisp of herself, a ghostly representation of the teenager he'd come home to back in Boston. There were dark circles under her eyes, and the light in them was gone. Before she'd left with Jenny, there'd at least been the fire of hatred.

She looks... empty, Walter thought as his heart broke for his daughter.

He had to go to her, to wrap her up in his arms, lead her to safety. "It's not safe out here," he said.

Azalea shifted her weight beside his daughter, and Walter looked at her, blinking as the full scene before him finally registered. She had a gun. Carrie's body was on the floor. In the distance, a swarm was swirling down the hall toward them.

"Lizzy," Walter said, his tone urgent as he stepped forward, "get away from—"

Alex shoved Walter just as Azalea raised her weapon and fired a second time. His hands met the hard tile with a stinging slap, and the impact on his knees sent sharp pains shooting through them. Both Alex and Timothy hooked an arm under Walter's armpits and dragged him back to the safety of the corner, behind the wall.

"No," Walter shouted, shaking them off and getting back to his feet. The sharp pains in his knees turned to dull and persistent ache. "Lizzy, run!" He scrambled back toward the open hall, but unwelcome hands held him back. "Stop it! My daughter—"

"—is with Azalea," Alex said, grunting behind Walter, his arms around Walter's waist, "and Azalea just killed Carrie."

"I know!" Confusion clouded Walter's ability to think as he realized Timothy was tugging back on his upper arm. "Your sister is out there! What are you doing?"

"Mr. Peters," Azalea's voice sang out the words as the buzzing of the swarm came ever closer. "We've got a proposition for you."

"Let Lizzy go!" Walter shouted. He swatted at his son and at Alex. "Let *me* go!"

Timothy stepped in front of him so that he could see the pain in his son's eyes as he said, "Dad! You can't. She's got a gun."

He couldn't figure out why everyone kept stating the obvious but kept missing the most important part. "Lizzy is with that lunatic!" Walter clawed at Alex's interlocked fingers at his waist.

"Dad," Timothy said, his voice cracking, "Lizzy is *with* her."

The emphasis on *with* made Walter freeze, made his blood run cold as Timothy's meaning pierced him. He shook his head, but he couldn't voice his dissent. The past weeks, the way Lizzy had clung to Azalea's side, their strange behavior... he'd known something was off for a long time.

When he hadn't struggled for a few more moments, Alex let go. "The swarm is coming. We have to—"

"Daddy?"

His little girl's voice, her calling out to him, erased everything else. Walter set his jaw and pushed Timothy aside, stumbling out into the open hall. He was ready to charge forward, to rescue Lizzy from Azalea no matter what it took. He would get Lizzy to that safe room, even if it cost him his life.

But it wasn't Azalea holding the gun any longer. It was his daughter. His baby girl. And she was pointing it straight at him.

* * *

"Walter!" Alex lunged forward and, for a second time, grabbed hold of Walter and pulled him out of the way of gunfire. The bullet barely missed Walter, but as Alex slammed the man against the wall, he could see that Walter finally understood what was happening. Behind the shield of his suit, Walter's eyes were glassy. "My daughter just tried to shoot me," he whispered. "She had the gun, and she took the shot."

"I'm sorry," Alex said. "Just... don't move."

He put his back to the wall next to Walter. Timothy was on the other side, speaking softly to his father in a reassuring tone.

"What is going on?" Alex shouted. "Why did you shoot Carrie?"

"She would have been an obstacle," Azalea said.
"Lizzy?" Timothy shouted. "Why are you doing this?"
"You know who our father is, what he's done," Lizzy said. "The better question is, why haven't you done it already?"
"Our proposition," Azalea said, "is this, Mr. Peters: let us have you and Alexander Roman, and I'll leave your son alone. He can kill the swarm that's coming, and you will be survived by all of your children."
"Who are you, Azalea?" Alex shouted. "Who are you really?"
"We are Heirs," Lizzy said, "and we're cleansing the world."
"No," Walter whispered.
Alex frowned at Walter. "Do you know what the hell she's talking about?"
"It's a cult," Walter said. "The one that I thought had killed Lizzy in the first place. The one that supposedly sold Lizzy after kidnapping her from the compound. They didn't *sell* her. They *brainwashed* her."
"They opened my eyes," Lizzy said, her voice just around the corner.
The gun appeared first, and Alex only had a split second. He grabbed hold of it and yanked so hard it flew out of his hands and skidded on the floor. He pulled Lizzy forward, too. She was thin and light. It didn't take much effort to grab her and throw her back toward Timothy and Walter. But then Azalea's elbow collided with his ribs, knocking the air out of him.
"Get her inside," Alex wheezed.
Timothy and Walter grabbed hold of Lizzy's arms and dragged her kicking and screaming toward the second decontamination room.
"Azalea!" Lizzy screamed. "Help me!"
But Azalea was going for the gun. Alex leapt forward and caught her legs as they both hit the ground. Her hands were mere inches from the gun, but Alex reached up, grabbed a fistful of hair between his gloved fingers, and yanked her head back. She yelped and her outstretched hand came back to scratch at him as he slid her body back away from the gun.
"Barricade the door!" Alex shouted. "I'll take care of the swarm."
"Elizabeth, don't fail me!" Azalea screeched. "Do something!"
Lizzy struggled harder, but Alex was relieved to see there was little she could do against two full-grown men. Timothy and Walter pulled her into the room and shut the door.
"You have to die!" Azalea twisted and slammed her fist into his face shield.
Alex grabbed hold of her wrists and pushed her back. He brought his knee up between them and kicked her as hard as he could. For a moment, he was free of her, and he crawled toward the gun. His gloved hand wrapped around it, and he rolled several times, away from Azalea who coughed as she got to her feet, looking at him as if he were her prey.
He got to his feet, too slowly in that suit, breathing heavily. "Just stop," he said as he glanced down the hall. The front of the swarm was almost to the steel door. "You can still make it to one of these side rooms. Save yourself."
"The Mother will save me," Azalea said between gritted teeth. "She will reward me when I get rid of you for good."
She charged Alex, a crazed scream bellowing from her as she ran forward. He didn't want to shoot her. She was so young, and if Lizzy had been brainwashed, she could have been, too.
Alex turned and threw the gun as hard as he could. It soared through the two open doorways of the decontamination room and clattered to the ground beyond the steel table.
He made to punch Azalea across the face, hoping to stun her, knock her out. It wasn't ideal, but at least then he might have time to drag her to safety before deploying the toxins. But Azalea ducked under his swing and barreled into him, knocking him off balance.
He stumbled backward into the decontamination room. He hit the wall, and immediately Azalea was on him like a cat, clawing at his suit. The sound of a zipper made Alex's heart skip a beat. He threw her off of him and re-zipped the front of his suit, frantically checking to make sure it was secure.
And then she was on him again, this time slinking around to his back. Before he knew what was happening, her legs were wrapped around his middle, and she was yanking off his helmet, throwing it to the ground.
"Get off!" Alex bent forward, grabbing hold of her hair again, and pulled as hard as he could. She screamed as her hair gave way and Alex pulled his hand away with a fistful of black, a bit of scalp still hanging from the ends. Revolted, he threw it from him. "Stop!" he shouted. "Just get off of me!"
The buzzing was outside the door. He was running out of time. Alex threw himself to the floor, landing on his back, on Azalea, and she went slack beneath him. He rolled off and reached for his helmet, putting it back on as he got to his feet.
When he turned around, she was standing again, that look in her eye, as if getting to him was the only thing that mattered. She rushed him, and this time, Alex had had enough. Adrenaline flooded his veins and with one last heave, he grabbed hold of the woman and launched her away from him. He hadn't been thinking about where he was throwing her, and he took half a step forward, his mouth dropping open as she landed on the table, slid across the goop, and hit the floor on the other side.
He took two steps forward, intending to do something, to figure out a way to save her from a death no one deserved.
But then tendrils of black shot forward, coming from behind him. The hum of the of the swarm was hungry and furious as it surrounded Alex, unable to penetrate his suit. He threw up his hands, startled by the onslaught, though in the back of his mind, he'd known it would hit at any moment.
Azalea slowly stood beyond the table, facing him, coated in the black goop. "You *have to* die!" She screeched the words as the swarm engulfed her.
Alex hit the ground as the last gunshot went off, as Azalea's screams for his death elongated into agonized screams of terror. Alex crawled through the black swarm as it flowed over him, around him, exploring his frame only to move on when it couldn't penetrate his suit.
And then the air around him was clear.

He stood and turned around and took a step back at the thing of nightmares in the room beyond. Azalea screamed in pain, but she didn't struggle against the swarm. She held up her arms, every inch of her skin covered in black and bits of orange, writhing and pulsing and alive with death. The shape of her melded with the monster, the parts of the swarm around her like an extension of her. And then she opened her eyes, the whites of them stark against the frenzied black and white teeth shone in the shape of a smile.

Fear shocked Alex into action. He triggered the trip wires, and a hissing sound built over the noise of the swarm as toxic fog shot into the room all around Azalea. Alex lunged forward and threw the door shut as puffs of white snaked into the decontamination room. He backed away, slamming the second door shut, too.

It was over.

Adrenaline left him, and he sank to his knees.

Chapter 53

Heather Peters

The evacuation was complete.
Their fate remained uncertain.
Heather sat in the darker recesses of the tunnel, in a stretch of road between mesh barriers reserved for the enemies the civilians didn't know what to do with yet. She stretched her back and leaned against the wall, trying not to think about how she'd been categorized as the enemy.
Thinking, that's the real enemy. Heather pictured a void in her mind and willed it into being, welcoming the numbness that exhaustion offered. It was the first moment of peace she'd had all night, the first moment she'd not feared for her immediate safety.
When Timothy sat next to her, she just leaned her head on his shoulder. They stayed there like that for a while, and she pretended in those moments that everything was okay.
"Dad finally fell asleep," Timothy said.
Heather sighed and sat up. It was time to talk, time to stop pretending. When she'd first seen him that night, when he'd found her in the clinic after she'd helped Ingrid save Mark's life, she'd been a mess of emotions, clinging to him, exhausted, relieved. They hadn't spoken much since, in the hurried movements of evacuation, in the aftermath when the civilians had decided who would be allowed to go where.
"Are you okay?" Heather asked.
"No."
Timothy looked at her, but she couldn't make out much of his expression. The overhead light in their section of the tunnel didn't reach far, and while they weren't in complete darkness, her surroundings were reduced mostly to shapes and interpreting them relied upon her imagination. She could hear the ache in his voice, though, and so she sought out his hand with her own. When she found it, she slipped her fingers between his and squeezed.
"Someone should be with her," Timothy said. "She's sick. She's terrified. She won't stop mumbling and rocking and crying."
"I know." Heather glanced at the far mesh barrier, the one that separated them from the enemies the civilians *had* known what to do with: Ward, Turner, Jenny, Lauren, and Lizzy. They were guarded by men with guns. "Lauren is there, at least."
She knew they weren't the right words as soon as they left her mouth, but there wasn't anything she could say to make it better. At first, Lizzy had been hysterical, screeching for Azalea, begging for the screaming to stop, even though she was the only one doing it. The sound of her agony had echoed through the tunnel, slowly falling off in volume until it was a whimper, and then dissipating completely. She was put away from them, behind a wall of guards, bound and possibly gagged. Heather hadn't known which was worse: hearing her and knowing that she was at least alive or the quiet that made the urge to check on her unbearable.
Not knowing how to comfort her husband, Heather cuddled up to him.
"Lizzy tried to shoot Dad." The words were small and distant, as if Timothy had removed himself from them even as he said them. That was something new, something horrible. She'd thought all the terrible things had been revealed already. The possibility—no, the likelihood—that there were little details left unsaid that would add darker shades to the story of what had happened that night sent a wave of nausea over Heather.
She closed her eyes and breathed out slowly, shaking her head. "I think... I think she asked Azalea not to hurt me." She offered it as a sign of hope, that perhaps Lizzy wasn't totally lost. It was something new that was good, something to bring balance.
"I hope that's true." Timothy shuddered beside her. "Dad said the Heirs of the Mother are some kind of cult. I just... I can't help but wonder what they did to her to make her like this. And why—" He cut off and covered his mouth, falling silent.
"Why we didn't see the full damage that had been done sooner?" Heather asked.
"Yeah." Timothy squeezed her hand and then pulled away, covering his face with both hands and rubbing up and down before sighing in frustration.
"Azalea. That's why." A burning heat flared in the pit of Heather's stomach as she said the woman's name. "She had Lizzy on a tight leash. I can see it now. I thought—we all thought—she was helping, but she was controlling Lizzy instead." It seemed so obvious after the fact. "You can't blame yourself." Even as she said those words to Timothy, she thought again, *I should have seen it.*
"This whole thing is a mess," Timothy said. "We don't have the coordinates. We can't leave here without Lizzy and Lauren, anyway. There could be a war on the horizon. I can't handle another war. Is that all that's left?"
Maybe, Heather thought, but she stopped herself from saying the wrong thing *before* it came out that time.
The scuffing of shoes on pavement made Heather look up. Alex approached. "Mind if I sit?" he asked. "Hunt and his soldiers are a little too somber for my tastes."
"We're not much better," Timothy said.
"Yeah, but I like you guys a lot more," Alex said, an attempt at levity in his voice.
"Might as well sit," Heather said. "How are Hunt and his men?"
"Besides being zip-tied and forced to sit in the dark in their tighty-whiteys?" Alex asked. "They're fine, I guess."

Heather looked past Alex as he moved to sit. On the other side of the tunnel, the general and six of his men congregated, their hands zip-tied. When they'd returned from closing the outside escape hatch with Ward and Turner in tow, they'd been given safe quarter for the night only after being stripped of everything but their boxers and t-shirts and agreeing to being cuffed.

"You're sure the rest of Hunt's men took Boreland safely back to the academy?" Heather asked.

Alex shrugged. "Those were their orders. They seemed a lot less resistant after they'd learned Ward and Turner had lied to them about there being a repellent, and when we left them, they had already been bound hand and foot. My guess is that Boreland and those who stuck with him are back at the academy and locked away."

"But we don't know what happened when they got there," Timothy said.

"I really don't want to think about all the what-ifs," Alex said.

Heather shook her head. "Neither do I."

"Things aren't all bad," Alex said. "Heather saved Mark's life. We risked our lives to kill that swarm. That has to count for something."

"Maybe it will be enough to get those coordinates and let us leave with our people," Timothy said.

Those words hit Heather like so many blows with a sledgehammer. Her dream of staying behind, of her child growing up in safety… they were dead. Part of her had known it the second Azalea shot Mark in the chest. But she'd held that knowledge at the edges of her mind, banishing the thought every time it resurfaced.

There was no denying it as Timothy gave it voice.

Heather pulled away from Timothy. "I'm going to try to get some sleep," she said, grateful for the shadows as tears slid down her cheeks. She curled up on the rough, chill pavement, one hand over her belly, and silently cried herself to sleep.

* * *

The sound of metal grating and clinking woke Heather the next morning. Emily waited on the other side of the rising barrier with her hands on her hips and a host of armed men and women behind her.

"Your president has come to get you," she said.

A dozen flashlights shone into the darker spots where the tunnel's overhead light didn't reach. The flashlights cast a wavering, dull yellow light about the place.

Heather sat up as General Hunt struggled to his feet, his hands still bound. "You're letting us go?" he asked.

"He's come with who we understand to be the primary guilty parties, some guy named Lawson and another named Boreland and a handful of soldiers. He's agreed to let us have them, and those two scientists you brought back, too." As Emily spoke, the armed men and women filled the space, surrounding them all, prodding them to get up. "You can take Lauren and Jenny, as well."

"What about Lizzy? I'm not leaving without my daughter," Walter said as he was pulled to his feet.

"She's an accomplice to Mark's attempted murder and to Carrie's actual murder," Emily said, crossing her arms. "She's to receive the same punishment as the others, whatever that will be. I've got my money on a firing squad."

Heather stepped forward. "Emily, please—"

Two men stepped in front of her—Hector and Ash, two men she'd played cards with days earlier—and scowled.

"It's okay," Emily said. "Let her through."

They moved aside reluctantly, and Heather walked between them, shrinking beneath their glares. She reached Emily, reached out, thought better of it, and clasped her hands at her chest. "Please, Emily. Lizzy didn't know what she was doing. She's sick. That woman, Azalea, she poisoned Lizzy's mind somehow. I don't understand it, but I know that the person you saw last night wasn't my sister-in-law."

Emily's expression softened. "Did you ever consider that the person you once knew is no longer who she is? That maybe the girl we saw last night *is* the real Lizzy?"

Heather shook her head. "If you'd just look at her, Emily… she's pathetic. Shut down completely. She needs help, not punishment. And besides, she wasn't the one who hurt people. Azalea killed Nick and Carrie. Azalea shot Mark."

Emily licked her lips and took a deep breath. "You saved Mark's life. You helped me when I was frozen with fear, afraid I'd lose my husband, afraid I'd die right then and there. I owe you." She nodded to the surrounding men. "Let them have Lizzy."

The next mesh barrier was raised, and several civilian guards entered that section, presumably to retrieve Lauren, Jenny, and Lizzy.

"Thank you," Heather said. "Thank you, Emily. You have no idea—"

Emily held up a hand. "We're not friends. Just take your people and go."

General Hunt frowned. "A simple exchange of prisoners? That's it?"

"Your president also brought a bus load of supplies we desperately need now that our home has been rendered unlivable," Emily said. She worked her jaw back and forth as she glanced down the tunnel in the direction of the blast doors which were perhaps a tenth of a mile from where she stood. "Mark has agreed to a sit down when Ingrid has gotten him back on his feet. That's when our next steps will be determined."

"You mean that's when we make peace or go to war," General Hunt said.

"That's right," Emily said, "and we're all pretty angry right now, so I'd enjoy your little interlude of peace."

Heather exchanged a look with Timothy. They couldn't stay for another war in another city. They had to get those coordinates and get out of Colorado Springs.

"Hey!" Walter's shout drew Heather's attention. He stalked toward two men who were dragging a limp Lizzy, bound hand and foot. "Be careful with her!"

The two of them smirked at each other, stopped walking, and let go of Lizzy, dusting their hands off and stepping back. Lizzy dropped to the ground, not bothering to catch herself. Her head hit concrete and bounced.

Heather gasped and rushed forward with Timothy. Her father-in-law scooped down to pick her up, but his touch seemed to trigger something in her. She came to life, screaming, "Don't touch me!" Her nose was bleeding from where she'd hit the concrete. Timothy knelt beside her, and she scrambled into his arms.

"Bethie…" Walter whispered the name, his eyes welling with tears.

"Walter," Heather said, "it's okay. Let Tim take her."

She put an arm around Walter, and as Timothy lifted Lizzy, Walter turned into Heather and buried his head in her shoulder. He broke down, not for the first time in the last twelve hours.

Jenny and Lauren were brought out, too. Alex rushed to Lauren's side, throwing his arms around her and holding her tight. That lasted only a moment. The two of them separated and averted their eyes, both of them suddenly very awkward. Jenny joined Hunt and the rest, looking exhausted as she cracked a half-hearted joke about her fellow soldiers in their underwear.

The protests of Ward and Turner followed them all as they began the trek up to the surface where Emily had said the president and his people were waiting. The desperate pleas of the scientists eventually faded, and all that was left was the shuffling of feet.

When they reached the surface, President Coleman was indeed waiting, and he wasn't alone. It seemed he had brought almost everyone he had, and they were all armed to the teeth. Several military vehicles lined the access road to the complex.

So, Heather thought, he brought gifts and threats.

All that mattered to her was that it had worked. He'd gotten them out.

Heather stepped up into the bus Coleman had brought, and Walter was settled next to her, leaning against the window. Timothy slid Lizzy into a seat and sat next to her while she still clung to him like a small child clings to a parent when they're frightened. When they were all safe, Heather thought the weight that had settled upon her on the climb up through the tunnel would dissipate.

But it didn't. It only got heavier.

Chapter 54

Minnie Stevens, Walter Peters, Heather Peters, and Alexander Roman

Minnie rolled over on her cot, blinking away bad dreams she couldn't quite remember. They *were* nightmares, though. The sweat on her brow, the knot in her chest, the way the darkness of the room closed in on her, the way she felt as though she'd barely slept: all signs of the devil's touch on her dreams.

She had the urge to check on Lauren. Minnie retrieved the flashlight set on the table between the head of her cot and the head of Lauren's. When she clicked it on, she made sure her hand covered the light so as to not disturb her daughter's sleep. Sitting up, she held out the dimmed light, and some of her nerves calmed.

Lauren snorted in her sleep, and Minnie smiled. Her muscles relaxed, and she clicked the flashlight off again. No light came in under the crack in the door. It was still night. She made herself comfortable again, but sleep was elusive.

The past weeks had been rough. They'd taken a toll on her, on everyone, really.

The first week after Lauren had returned from the mountain, the entire base had been a tangle of angry cats. There'd been so many arguments, Minnie and Alex had prepared to just leave the city. If Coleman's people couldn't get it together, if they were going to fight amongst themselves, there was no way the base would be safe if the civilians declared war.

But as more information became widely known, as Alex and Heather and Jenny had told their stories, things had settled. The second week had been one of strategies. A committee consisting of the president and all those involved came together to create a document detailing everything they knew about the events that had transpired. President Coleman had sent that with a second installment of gifts to the civilians. He'd also requested a meeting for negotiations.

The third week had been one of preparation. Those who'd delivered the gifts had returned with a message: Mark accepted the president's invitation, but it would have to be on neutral ground. He'd requested that Heather be present, which had come as something of a shock to her, it seemed. A spot for a meeting was chosen, and the work had begun. From what Minnie understood, the president had some lofty ambitions for those negotiations.

At the first sign of sunlight creeping under the door, Minnie tip-toed to the door and slipped outside. There weren't many people up and about yet, but as she'd grown accustomed to expect, Alan's figure stood facing the glass windows looking out onto one of the recessed patios. Minnie padded barefoot across Polaris Hall and came up beside him. He put his arm around her, and they stood there together, as they'd done nearly every morning since he'd brought Lauren home to her. There was at least one thing, it turned out, she would miss when they left Colorado Springs behind.

* * *

Walter waited impatiently as morning ticked by. He had a lot to do. An escort would take him to the lab to work with Alex on the project set before them by the president. His presence would be required that afternoon at the negotiations between the military and the civilians. There was so much riding on that meeting.

But he didn't care about any of that. Before going to the lab, he was allowed to stop by to visit his daughter. That was what mattered most. The day before, she had let him inside her room. She had allowed him to sit at her bedside. She had *looked* at him. He'd wept with relief the whole way to the lab afterward.

"Hey." Zara came up to him and handed him a steaming mug of tea. She had been working all morning with Blythe and Kai. Timothy would come with Walter's escort and work with them for the rest of the day.

Walter had taken up residence there after only a few days of being back. He hadn't been able to stand being around people who wanted Lizzy imprisoned forever, locked up like a criminal. They said it was for her own safety and the safety of others, that they didn't know what to do with her, otherwise, that letting her roam freely after what she'd done wasn't an option. Even Timothy and Heather had agreed to her confinement. She was comfortable enough, fed and clothed. She'd even been given books and crayons and paper, though it didn't seem she'd touched any of that.

"I'm hoping she'll let me inside again today," Walter said.

"Walter, what if they agree to give us the coordinates today?" Zara asked. "There's talk of leaving soon."

"You mean, what are we going to do about Lizzy?" Walter looked at her, and she nodded.

"They want to leave her here," Zara said. "We can't do that. Not again."

"I won't," Walter said, "but... I can't ask you to—"

"Walter, don't shut me out of this." Zara lowered her voice, though Blythe and Kai were yards away, talking over a map. She grasped a chain around her neck and pulled it outside her shirt, cradling the two rings in her hand, a ladybug and a butterfly. "I abandoned her once, too. What happened to her..." She swallowed hard and worked her jaw back and forth, her eyes glistening. But then her expression hardened. "I won't leave her, either."

Walter nodded and put an arm around Zara. He loved that girl, the girl he'd once despised, like she was his own daughter. "Where there's a will," he said, "there's a way. And there are no two people left on this world that are as stubborn as we are."

* * *

Heather rubbed her sweaty palms on her pants as she bounced her knees up and down. She didn't belong there, with the military, with Alex and Walter and Timothy, as they waited inside an ornate church building for Mark and his people to show up.

Why do they want me here? The question rolled around in Heather's mind on repeat.

The church they'd agreed upon was different from the one they'd hidden out in when they'd first approached Colorado Springs. It had tall ceilings and fancy, padded chairs and a stage that looked well suited for concerts. It also had lots of natural light and big rooms and a dozen exits. The first church had been cozy and lived in; the second was almost imposing, which, she supposed, fit the mood of the meeting to come.

For the time being, she waited in the sanctuary with the rest of the people from the base who'd come there. General Hunt and President Coleman paced in front of the stage, talking in hushed tones. Two soldiers stood at attention nearby. There were other soldiers stationed in the buildings nearby, but they'd agreed to only two for the negotiations. Alex leaned against the open doorway in the back of the sanctuary, staring at the entrance, waiting. Walter lay flat on a row of chairs midway up the sanctuary. He'd kept to himself that day, and Heather could practically see the wheels in his head turning.

Probably thinking through all the possibilities for this meeting, Heather thought, though when asked for input, the man had precious little advice to give.

Timothy sat next to her. He put a hand on her knee, and she stopped bouncing it. "It's going to be fine," he said.

"Emily made it clear," Heather said. "We're not friends. She and Mark probably hate me. I just... I don't understand what they want with me. What if they want me to face some sort of punishment?"

"That's not going to happen," Timothy said sternly.

"They've read our accounts," Heather said. "I sent a letter with mine, addressed to Emily, apologizing, but... I lied to them. I helped Azalea get inside. I worked with Andy, who, even if he didn't mean it, let that swarm inside the complex."

"That wasn't your fault." Timothy's expression darkened. "That was Lawson and Boreland. Ward and Turner. Not you."

"I know, but—"

"If they read the reports," Timothy said, "they know why you were there in the first place."

Heather pressed her lips together and sat back, breathing in deeply through her nose. She wasn't quite convinced.

"Look." Timothy softened his voice. "Hopefully, they came here with the bigger picture in mind. Their only shot at long term survival is for our mission to succeed."

"We should have just told them from the start," Heather said.

"Alex tried, remember?" Timothy shook his head. "They didn't believe us when we approached them the first time."

"What if they don't believe us now?" Heather asked.

But before Timothy could answer, Alex's voice interrupted them. "They're here."

Heather stood and turned, rigid from head to toe, holding her breath. Hector and Ash came through the doors first, followed by Mark and Emily, followed by three more men. Mark's arm was tied to his body, and Emily held the thick binder that President Coleman had sent to them, the one with pages and pages of reports and accounts.

They stopped halfway down the aisle as President Coleman, General Hunt, and their two soldiers approached. Emily glanced at Heather, but Heather couldn't tell what her expression meant. She didn't look angry or disgusted, but the look was too brief to analyze much further.

"Mark," President Coleman said, "it's good to see you're recovering."

"We need to speak to Heather Peters," Mark said. "Alone."

Heather's heart stopped. She staggered sideways, reaching for the back of the next row of chairs to stay steady.

Timothy cut the air with his hand. "No way," he said. "She's not going with you anywhere."

"It's okay," Heather said, putting a gentle hand on Timothy's arm. "I'll talk with them."

"One of you can speak to her in the lobby," President Coleman said, "but the rest of you stay here. If anything happens to her, we'll see it as an act of war."

Mark nodded and looked at his wife. Emily turned without a word, and it was obvious to Heather that she was meant to follow. She scooted out of the row, whispering to Timothy that she'd be fine. Within seconds, she was closing the doors to the sanctuary, turning to find Emily plopping the binder down on a thin entryway table. She pulled out a single paper from the front pocket and turned around, holding it up.

"Is this true?" Emily asked.

Heather frowned and stepped forward, squinting at the paper. It was her apology letter. "Yes," she said. "Every word."

Emily nodded and held the letter between her hands, seeming to read over a few lines before turning and placing it back in the binder.

"I've been thinking about that day," she said as she turned back to face Heather. "About what you said to Mark when he was bleeding on the floor of our apartment."

Heather thought back. "You mean when I said all I wanted was to stay there, to raise my family there?"

Emily nodded. "We have a favor to ask of you, Heather."

Heather shifted her weight and swallowed hard. "I'm listening."

* * *

Alex placed the last chair and sat across from one of the civilians. They'd decided to stay in the sanctuary, to create an oval of sorts in the wide aisle down the middle where they could all face each other. Mark was positioned at one tip of the oval, the president at the other.

He still didn't know what had gone on with Heather and Emily behind closed doors. When they'd come back, Heather had called Timothy into the lobby, and when they'd returned, Timothy's face had gone pale. The color was returning to his cheeks as they sat down, but Alex hadn't liked the whole secret exchange.

"We have a lot to discuss," President Coleman said. "Did you read everything we sent over?"

"Every word," Mark said. "In fact, I read it out loud to the entire community." He looked at Alex and Walter. "It's quite the story."

"It's all true," Alex said.

"Maybe." Mark lifted his chin and narrowed his eyes at the president. "You left something out, though, didn't you?"

"I... don't know what you mean," President Coleman said.

"I'm going to give you one shot to tell me the truth." Mark leaned forward. "Your operatives weren't just there to get those coordinates, were they?"

Alex tensed and looked at the president. Coleman's expression was unreadable, but the general's had darkened considerably.

"Sir," General Hunt said, "I—"

President Coleman cut him off with a raised hand. "No," he said. "We were looking for a way inside, a way to take the complex back."

Alex's mouth dropped open. He looked to Mark to see what the man would do, but he merely leaned back and nodded.

"Good," he said. "That's a good start. If you'd lied to me, we would have left."

"How did you know?" President Coleman asked.

"There were file folders of documents pulled up on the computer when we caught Jenny and Lauren," Mark said. "The contents were encrypted, but the file names gave some of them away as schematics. I put two and two together."

"Can I ask you a question and receive an honest answer?" President Coleman asked. When Mark nodded, he continued. "What did you do with the prisoners we handed off to you?"

"They're dead," Mark said. "Capital punishment. Is that a problem?"

Coleman shook his head once. "No," he said. "Although they could have been useful one day."

"Isn't that what led to their betrayal in the first place?" Mark asked.

"That's fair," Coleman said.

"We assume Lauren and Jenny are free." Mark quirked an eyebrow. "What about Lizzy?"

Alex put a hand on Walter's shoulder as he shifted forward, opening his mouth. At his touch, Walter clamped his mouth shut.

"She's confined," President Coleman said.

"We want her to stay that way," Mark said. "Indefinitely. She's dangerous, even if it's not her fault."

Walter shrugged off Alex's hand and ground his teeth, but he didn't speak, much to Alex's relief.

"So, then," President Coleman said, "can we trust each other?"

Mark glanced at Heather, and she nodded. Then he looked back to the president. "The proposal you sent with the accounts was intriguing," he said. "Will your people back it?"

"They will," President Coleman said. "I put the proposal to a good old fashioned vote before sending it over."

"So, I become your Vice President," Mark said, "and you create a cabinet that includes your people and mine. And you'll actually give us the power that those positions afford?"

"Absolutely," President Coleman said. "We clean up the complex, move in, run it the way it should have always been run: together."

"We had rotations," Mark said. "People cycled through hospitality, guard duty, laundry, all of it, even me. It worked. It created a sense of community. I want that system to continue."

President Coleman frowned. "I don't think you and I will have the time to—"

"It continues," Mark said. "People in leadership don't go through the whole rotation, but I don't care how busy you are, you can find some time every once in a while to serve the people with your hands."

The president sighed. "All right," he said. "Agreed."

"We have one more request," Mark said.

"Go on." President Coleman waved for Mark to continue.

"We want Heather Peters to be a liaison between us," Mark said. "She and her husband stay behind when the rest of them fly off in that plane. We believe that Heather understands us, and if they stay, we feel there is a greater likelihood that Walter Peters will make sure any treatments or countermeasures he finds will be brought to Colorado Springs quickly."

"Timothy," Walter said, "Heather... is this something you want?"

"Yes," Heather said quickly. "We've agreed to it."

Timothy looked down at his hands. "I'm not giving up the fight, Dad," he said. "I'm just going to do it from here, where my wife and child will be safe."

"What about the work you've been doing with Blythe?" Alex asked. "Don't they need you?"

"I was a backup," Timothy said. "You don't need me. I think it was just something to distract me from what was going on with Heather."

"He's got other skills that he can utilize here," Heather said. "He's an out-of-the-box thinker. We can do a lot of good if we stay."

"Okay," Walter said.

"Then we agree to that as well," President Coleman said. "I think we have a few more kinks to work out, but... what do you say, Mark? Do we have peace in Colorado Springs?"

Mark stood and walked halfway across the oval, extending his hand. "I believe we do, Mr. President."

Chapter 55

Zara Williams

"I'll come back for you," Zara said as she knelt in front of her cousin, Annika. "Just like I did before."

Annika nodded and hugged Zara around the neck. The little girl looked up at Candice, who stood beside Zara, tears streaming down her face. "What about you, Banana?"

Candice smiled and lifted Annika in her arms. "You know I will, Blueberry. You go to school and get even smarter, okay? By the time I get back, I bet you'll be running this place."

She put her down, and Annika wiped away Candice's tears with her little hands. "I'll teach them all about seasonal colors, and I'll make sure no one ever wears socks with sandals."

Zara chuckled and shook her head as Candice drew her in for another hug. "That's my girl," Candice said.

The two of them had decided leaving Annika behind was the best thing for her. Where they were going was dangerous, and Annika had already been through so much. With Heather and Timothy staying, she had people to stay with, too. If Candice hadn't been a survivor of DV-10, if Walter and Alex hadn't thought they might need her blood down the line, Zara was sure the woman would have stayed behind with Annika.

They weren't the only ones saying their goodbyes.

At a respectable distance, the soldiers who'd brought them to the tarmac along with all their supplies, waited patiently, but General Hunt wasn't with them. He was speaking with Minnie in the near distance, and he looked a mess. They both did.

But if Zara had learned one thing about Alex, Lauren, Minnie, and Oliver, it was that they stuck together, no matter what. They wouldn't even leave their dog behind. She admired that. She wasn't sure she agreed with bringing a kid with them, but it wasn't her decision.

Closer to her, Timothy pulled away from Walter. "We'll take care of Lizzy," he said. "I'm sorry she couldn't be here to see you off."

Zara tensed. The subject of Lizzy as they were about to leave made her sick to her stomach. Walter nodded, but he didn't say anything.

"That's okay," Zara said. "I saw her earlier, said my goodbyes."

"You've been busy today," Heather said, "especially going back and forth between the plane and the academy."

"Not really," Zara said, frowning. "Most of the packing was done yesterday."

"Oh." Heather looked confused. "I saw you from a distance back at the academy this morning, in a golf cart with Kai and some bags, leaving, I assumed for the plane. But then I talked to you like an hour later in Polaris Hall."

Zara realized what Heather must be talking about and laughed it off. "Right," she said. "Yeah, I forgot. I brought a few last-minute bags to the plane earlier this morning. I *have* been busy. So busy the whole day just kind of blends together."

Heather shrugged. "I can't blame you for that. My brain has been rebelling against any and all proper function lately." Her hand went to her stomach. "Mom brain already, I guess."

Zara leaned in and hugged Heather. "Take care of yourself and that baby," she said.

Goodbyes were over; it was time to board the plane. Blythe and Kai were already in the cockpit, had already brought the plane to life. Neither of them had any goodbyes to make. Timothy, Heather, Annika, and General Hunt retreated back to the line of military vehicles as Zara, Walter, Candice with her suitcases, and Alex and his friends walked up the huge aft ramp and into a fully stocked cargo hold. They had everything they needed and more for the journey ahead: food, weapons, and equipment. Zara grabbed hold of a remote on a long coil that was affixed to the wall, pressed a big red button, and the ramp lifted to a close.

Before it cut off their view completely, Zara saw a distant vehicle speeding toward the tarmac. She stepped back as the ramp shut. Whatever happened next down there was behind her. She said a prayer for those they'd left behind, that they'd all still be alive when they next set foot in Colorado Springs.

The plane started to move, and Zara strapped herself in with the rest of them. It was a smooth takeoff. Alex whooped and clapped, and Zara grinned, joining in the celebration. They had finally left Colorado Springs. They had mapped their route and gotten coordinates to Barlow Scientific Research Bank.

"Next stop," Alex said as he unbuckled his harness, "New Zealand!"

Zara gave him a hearty whistle as she unbuckled her own harness and stood to stretch. "I better go see if there's anything I can do to help," she said, but she didn't really need the excuse. No one was paying much attention to her except for Walter. She caught his eye, nodded, and proceeded toward the cockpit.

She quickly slipped inside once she reached the door and closed it behind her. "Everything okay up here?" she asked.

"As well as can be expected," Blythe said.

Kai turned to look at her. "Did they suspect anything?"

Zara shook her head. "I think someone from the academy was coming with the news right before we took off, but… there's nothing we can do about it now."

She knelt before the seat behind Kai and smiled—despite the completely blank expression returned to her—at the figure dressed in an outfit very similar to her own. "It's going to be okay, Lizzy. I've got you. Now and forever."

Remnants

Chapter 1

Zara Williams

eye, putting every ounce of fire she could muster into her glare. "Don't touch her, Alex, or I swear—"
"You'll what?" Alex looked past Zara and jutted his finger past her. "She should be in Colorado Springs."
Zara narrowed her eyes. "They were going to keep her locked up forever."
"I couldn't leave her again, Alex." Walter put a hand on Zara's shoulder and gently tugged her away from Alex. He nodded back at Lizzy. "Be with her," he said softly. "Let me handle this part."
Zara nodded. The look in Walter's eyes was enough to break through the stubbornness that otherwise could have kept her blocking Alex all day. She understood that look. She'd seen it many times, and it broke her heart.
He *couldn't* be with Lizzy. She still recoiled at his touch.
"Hey, Liz," Zara said as she turned her back on Alex and sat next to Lizzy, putting an arm around her. She'd pulled her knees to her chest when the yelling had started, burying her face in her crossed arms, whispering something unintelligible. When Zara touched her, her entire body went rigid until she peeked above her arm to see it was Zara. She went back to her mumbling.
It hadn't been hard to hide the slight-of-frame, quiet wisp of a girl that Lizzy had become. The huge C-17 Globemaster had a crew compartment just behind the cockpit, and no one had disturbed Zara, Kai, and Blythe during the flight. Zara had given them updates but had insisted they leave the compartment alone, since they'd not known when they were in the middle of calculations.
When Lizzy had come out into the cargo area after landing, those who hadn't known hadn't been happy.
"Walter," Alex said, "we can't take her with us to Antarctica. I mean, look at her."
The cargo hold of the plane was split. Blythe and Kai stood behind Walter, beside Lizzy and Zara. Lauren and Candice stared wide-eyed, their gazes alternating between Alex and Walter and Lizzy. Minnie had pulled Oliver to the other side of the long cargo hold, though that couldn't have done much to keep the kid away from the argument. Shouted words pinged off the insides of the plane as if they were determined to find every ear. Samson occasionally added his bark to the conversation, though Minnie hushed him every time.
"You know what happened to her last time I left her behind," Walter said. "I wasn't going to do that to her again. What if it had been Oliver?"
"We know very little about what happened," Alex said, "except that some cult made her crazy. And I *am* thinking about Oliver. That girl nearly got me killed."
"That was Azalea," Lizzy said.
Alex raised his eyebrows. "The way I remember it, Lizzy took a shot at Walter's head. She's dangerous."
Lauren cleared her throat and stepped up beside Alex. "We can't change it now," she said. "I say we come up with some rules. We can confine her somehow—"
"No." Walter sliced the air with his hand.
"Weren't you listening?" Zara asked. "That's the whole reason we didn't leave her in Colorado Springs!"
"Oh, no!" Candice gasped. "Wasn't that part of the deal? What if taking her sparked some sort of fight? The civilians wanted her locked up! I left my Blueberry back there! Annika was supposed to be safer, not thrown into another war."
Walter held up his hands as the thought spread like wildfire and the others started naming all those they'd left behind. "My son and daughter-in-law, along with my grandchild, are back there, too. We left a fake note from Lizzy saying she had to escape and go out into the mountains where she could meet the fate she deserved."
"It was just to keep you safe," Zara whispered, in case Lizzy was listening. She couldn't tell if the argument was registering or if it was just the noise that had made Lizzy curl up and hide her face.
"Even if they suspect we took her," Walter said, "they'll have something to fall back on. Timothy and Heather didn't know. Both sides wanted peace by the time we left. It'll work."
Candice threw her hands in the air and turned around. "I just can't right now. I'm going to see if Minnie has any words of Southern wisdom to calm me down because right now, I could kill you myself." She marched down the length of the cargo hold.
"It was selfish," Alex said. "You shouldn't have done it."
"I'll agree to disagree," Walter said.
Lauren touched his arm, and Alex met her eyes. "We need to talk about what to do now, Alex, not what should have been done."
He sighed and looked back at Walter. "Fine," he said.
Blythe cleared his throat. "The first thing we need to do actually has nothing to do with all this." He waved his hands in their general direction. "We need to confirm that we've landed in the right spot."
"I thought you said you were sure this time?" Alex pinched the bridge of his nose.
They'd first landed in Brisbane, Australia and had to recalculate their route to Christchurch. Overshooting the islands from the United States had been a possibility. Blythe, Kai, and Zara had done their best to navigate them across the ocean, but they'd had to use antiquated techniques. Finding themselves in Brisbane had been somewhat of a relief. They could have ended up in India or worse if their calculations had been farther off. It would have only taken a few small mistakes.
"I said I was *pretty* sure," Blythe said. "I mean, I'm sure we're in New Zealand this time, at least."

"Okay," Alex said, "I guess… let's check it out. We'll need to find the United States Antarctic Program, see if we can find anything to update us on the state of McMurdo Station."

"We have the coordinates of Barlow Scientific Research Bank," Zara said. "Why do we need to know anything about McMurdo?"

"Because it's possible," Alex said, "that there's still a functioning population there. It's winter there. From what I understand, it's been dark for months, and there were no scheduled supply drops during that time, which means DV-10 might not have found its way down there. We need to know what—or *who*—we're up against."

Walter nodded. "You're thinking of trying to find records of communication with the base."

"Or records of rescue missions," Alex said.

"I'd also like to look for their protocols on landing," Blythe said. "If no one is there to clear a runway, it might be rough. And we might have to dig the plane out of the snow and create our own runway after we get there."

Zara's shoulders sagged. "Well, that sounds like fun," she said flatly.

"We'll do whatever we have to do," Alex said. "For now, let's gather information and plan the next leg of our journey."

Zara stood and tapped Lizzy's arm. "C'mon, Liz. Let's get some fresh air, stretch your legs."

"You should stay here with her," Alex said. "I don't think—"

Zara narrowed her eyes at him. "She needs fresh air and a little bit of sun. I'll watch her, okay? Me and Walter will take full responsibility for her. She's a stick, Alex. She can barely walk, much less attack anybody. If I have to, I'll sit on her to keep her from hurting you, okay?"

Alex worked his jaw back and forth and let out a frustrated sigh, but he didn't object again. He simply joined Blythe at the front side door as they worked to open it. Knocking metal and a *pop* of air signaled the opening of the door. A set of stairs unfolded into the bright sunlight.

Blythe and Alex walked out cautiously, and Zara stayed quiet as she approached the door with Lizzy in tow. They were all listening for the buzz of a swarm. Alex ventured farther onto the tarmac and turned all around. He jogged out of sight and then came back.

"Looks clear," Alex said. "I don't see signs of anything living."

Zara coaxed Lizzy down the steps, and her friend lifted an arm against the sun, squinting and moving slowly. "There we go," Zara said. There were other planes on the tarmac, some pulled up to the building, some left out, either abandoned or full of the dead. Zara tried not to think too much about how many corpses were likely in a one-mile radius of her current location. Airports had been such a central part of how DV-10 had spread that most of them were likely permanent burial grounds.

She led Lizzy away from the others, letting her lead the way, until she just stopped and plopped down on the tarmac. She lay on her back and stretched her arms and legs out.

Zara chuckled. "What are you doing?" she asked.

Lizzy looked at her and smiled. She tapped the ground, and Zara sat beside her. The ground was warm and comfortable, and there was a freshness in the air that Zara hadn't expected. It was perhaps seventy degrees, and the blue sky above was dotted with clouds. As she looked up at them, Lizzy's hand touched hers and she linked her pinky with Zara's.

She's coming back, Zara thought, smiling at her best friend.

"It's not bad out here," Zara said, turning her head to look at Lizzy.

Lizzy shrugged and looked back at the sky. "The voices are quiet."

Zara's smile faded as the spell of normalcy disintegrated. She didn't know what to say to that. Lizzy hardly ever said anything, but when she did, it was often about "the voices." From what Zara and Walter could gather, she heard screaming in her mind. It seemed worse when Walter touched her. It was only recently that Lizzy could even look at her father without problems.

The jingle of Samson's collar was a welcome interruption. The reddish-brown ninety-pound dog bounded toward them, pulling Minnie behind him on his leash. Oliver followed behind her, laughing at the way Samson jumped and wagged his tail, pointing his nose at Zara and Lizzy. The dog looked ecstatic to be off the plane.

Zara sat up and reached out for Samson as he came up to her, catching his head in her hands and rubbing his ears vigorously. He licked her face, barked, and then made like he was going to investigate Lizzy.

"Whoa, now," Zara said, "I'm not sure she's up for that." She laughed as she blocked his way and gave him a few more ear scratches.

"He can sense she needs some love," Minnie said. "That's my guess, anyway." She made his leash shorter, though, and tugged hard. "Come on back here," she said.

"I don't mind."

Zara whipped her head around to look at Lizzy. She was still laying on the ground, but her thin arm was reaching out for the dog, and she was smiling.

Minnie gave Samson's leash some slack, and he approached Lizzy by crouching low and scooting up to her, his butt high in the air, his tail continuing to wag. He sniffed at her head, and then gave her cheek one big, wet kiss.

Lizzy *laughed.* It was musical. It was perfect. Zara laughed, too. *I knew it was right to bring her,* she thought.

"I missed that sound," Zara said, scratching Samson's rump in appreciation.

"Samson's a people person," Oliver said, piping up from a safe distance. "He knows the good ones from the bad ones."

Zara raised her eyebrows at the boy. Sometimes she forgot that he wasn't exactly a little kid anymore. He was an observant ten-year-old at the beginning of his tween years, and he'd been forced to grow up a lot in the last few months.

"That's kind of you to say," Zara said. "Thanks, Oliver."

Minnie lowered her voice. "Alex just don't like surprises is all. He'll think about it for a while and come to terms with it. Just give him time."

Zara nodded. "Probably didn't help that I got so angry."

"Maybe not," Minnie said, "but he was no angel. I love him like he was my son, but if there's one thing he should be able to understand, it's a father's need to keep his child close."

"Thanks," Zara said.

Several yards behind her, Alex waved his hands and shouted, "We're here!" He jogged up to them. "We're in Christchurch. We found a sign on the building."

"Well, now what?" Minnie asked.

"We find the United States Antarctic Program," Alex said. "It's supposed to be somewhere at the airport."

Samson's ears perked up, and he backed away from Lizzy, pointing his nose toward the buildings. At first, Zara thought he was looking at Oliver, who had gotten out the little duck call he'd gotten in Boston. The boy started blowing in it as his dad and Minnie talked. He laughed at the quacking noises, opening and closing his hand around the device to change the pitch.

But Samson walked a few paces past Oliver, his nose still pointed, ears at attention. He seemed to ignore the obnoxious sounds coming from the duck call. Zara followed the dog's gaze as Minnie and Alex discussed how they'd go about finding the right place.

Kai and Blythe burst around the corner of a building, running toward them, waving their hands.

Zara frowned. "What the—"

Samson barked, and Alex and Minnie turned.

"Hush, Oliver," Minnie said, reaching out and patting Oliver's hands so that he would stop twisting the duck call.

Zara stood. "What is Kai yelling about?"

"Minnie, get Oliver back to the plane," Alex said.

Closer to the plane, Walter and Candice stood at attention. Walter raised his hand to shield his eyes as he looked in Kai and Blythe's direction.

"Let's go!" Alex shouted. "Back to the plane! Zara, get Lizzy, and get back. We need to arm ourselves."

A heavy thump in Zara's chest was followed by another, harsher beat. Her heart felt ten times heavier as, beyond Kai and Blythe, a horde of people emerged, running just as hard after them. Zara took half a step back, a cold shock hitting her like a wave.

"Liz…" Zara swallowed hard and willed her body to move. She unglued her feet from the tarmac. Every forced movement was like oil to her joints, and within seconds, she was pulling at Lizzy's arm, tugging hard. "Get up!" she shouted.

But Lizzy wasn't cooperating. She laughed as if they were playing a game. Alex, Minnie, Oliver, and Samson were already halfway back to the plane. Walter was running toward them, shouting for them to move. But Lizzy just laughed harder.

"Get up," Zara said, "or Walter is going to have to throw you over his shoulder."

Lizzy stopped laughing and looked up at her as if she'd threatened to put snakes in her bed. She got to her feet, her expression dark as Walter approached.

"Let's go," he shouted. He reached for his daughter, and she practically snarled. "Fine, I won't touch you, but you have to *run*, Elizabeth. You have to *run*."

Zara stepped behind Lizzy and gave her a little push. "I'll be behind you," she said. "Go, go, go!"

As Lizzy's walk turned to a jog which turned to a proper run, Blythe and Kai reached the plane and rushed inside. Seconds later, they emerged with Alex, Lauren, and Candice, all of them armed.

Less than an hour in New Zealand, and already the threat of death was upon them.

Chapter 2

Stella Sharpe

Day Zero, About 3 Months Ago

Stella Sharpe pulled on her outer layers, stuffed her hair under a beanie, and braced herself as she opened the door. The cold didn't shock her like it used to, but it did take her breath away for half a second. She followed the familiar path between buildings, her boots crunching snow underfoot as the wind pelted her with tiny flecks of ice.

It was dark. It was *always* dark.

When Stella had first come to McMurdo Station, she hadn't planned to winter there, in the months of perpetual night and below-freezing temperatures. But it hadn't taken much for her new best friend, Tabitha, to convince her to stay when the opportunity presented itself. In the summer months, the station was well-populated with at least eight hundred people. There were researchers and scientists, of course, but there were carpenters and electricians and service staff and cooks. It was a small town with all the needs of one. Regular people with regular jobs just living life. The winter was the same, except there were only one hundred and fifty of them, and some of the amenities—like the hair salon—were closed.

It was odd for a country girl from the Midwest to associate June with winter. As she pushed her way through the frigid climate toward the large blue building which housed McMurdo's cafeteria, she thought back to the humid heat of the Junes back home. She honestly didn't know which was worse, but at least at McMurdo Station, there were people who cared about her. She hadn't had that for a long time, not since her last living relative, her aunt, had died a terrible death following a blood infection.

That was what made her stay: the people. And not just Tabitha.

When the warmth of Building 155—nicknamed Big Blue by residents—washed over her, Stella stomped her feet and shook out the cold. She continued down the main hall to the galley. Big Blue was at the center of life at McMurdo Station. It was home to the cafeteria, the weight room, the recreation board, and the general store.

The cafeteria was buzzing. It was a little after noon, and most of them congregated there midday for some good food and better company.

The smell of burgers, fries, fresh bread, and savory soup set her mouth to watering as she immersed herself in a room full of chatter, clinking silverware, and laughter. She unzipped her coat and slid the beanie off her head. The room was kept cool enough for everyone to be comfortable in winter clothes, but it was too warm for outer gear.

"Stella!" Tabitha called out to her from a circular table near the television hung on the wall.

As Stella wove her way through the cafeteria, she said her hellos and returned some jokes and pretended not to notice when Adam Parker winked at her after looking her up and down. Out of one hundred and fifty people, he was the only one she didn't like. The others kept him in line. Everyone had to work well together in a place like that. If Adam were to make too many people too uncomfortable, he'd not be invited back to the station and his remaining time would be unpleasant to say the least. Still, Stella wouldn't want to be alone with him.

She approached the table, having only smiles for her best friend. Abby was there, too, with Charlie on her arm, leaning close to her, making her giggle with whispers in her ear. Romances at the station were usually a whirlwind of drama that Stella had no interest in wasting time on, but Abby and Charlie were different. They'd been together for years, even when they had to work far apart. The two of them were adventurers and McMurdo was simply one they'd been lucky enough to go on together.

"I'm so hungry," Stella said as she slid her coat over the back of her chair. "Are those tater tots?"

Tabitha popped one in her mouth. "Yep. They're salty and delicious."

Abby tapped a chicken breast red with spice. "These are a little dry."

"Good to know," Stella said. "I'll be back." She eagerly found herself a plate and loaded it up with spaghetti and meatballs, bread, and a pile of tater tots. There was always a lot to choose from, but Stella gravitated toward certain dishes. She liked consistency.

"Tots with spaghetti?" Lincoln, one of the serving staff, plopped a tray of vegetables into place as Stella passed. He raised an eyebrow at her.

"Hey, don't knock it," Stella said. "These are two of my favorite things. It's not my fault that the world hasn't figured out that spaghetti's perfect pairing is from the breakfast section."

He chuckled and shook his head. "You do you," he said.

"Right back at you."

Stella returned to the table in high spirits. As she shoveled a huge twirl of spaghetti into her mouth, she noticed Abby's soft laughter die with a small push at Charlie's arm.

"Hush," she said. "Look." She pointed at the television where their only American news station was playing.

Tabitha frowned, got up, and snatched the remote off the Velcro strip on the wall. "Hey, quiet!" she shouted.

Stella read the ticker as Tabitha turned the volume up: *Possible terrorist attack in motion: Boston, St. Louis, San Francisco.* The news anchor, an older man in a white shirt and blue tie, placed his hands flat on the desk before him and looked away from the camera.

"We're getting news," he said, "of similar attacks in Toronto, London, Paris…" He kept going, listing city after city.

"What kind of attack?" Stella asked.

The immediate area had quieted at Tabitha's request and were glued to the screen, but the rest of the cafeteria didn't seem to notice. Stella stood up and banged on the table. "Hey!" she shouted. "Guys! Something is wrong."

The room quieted as Tabitha turned the volume up even higher. Stella sat back down and turned her gaze back to the screen.

Lincoln walked into the seating area, confusion all over his face. "What's going on?"

He looked at the screen for not more than a few seconds before rushing back to the kitchens and returning with the cook staff.

It was a biological attack, they assumed, but no one was taking credit. Whoever had done it had been coordinated. Stella's food went cold as she watched video clips from the World's Fair in St. Louis.

It was a shaky video taken by a teenager, it seemed. The girl screamed as her friend stumbled backward, dropped to the ground, and covered her eyes, screaming in pain. There were visible welts growing larger on her neck and arms. The broadcast switched to a steadier camera which seemed to have been taking footage of the fair from a drone. Stella gasped, along with nearly everyone in the room, when a plane which had been part of a fireworks show, sparks shooting from its wings, plowed into a huge Ferris wheel.

Shock numbed Stella's body more effectively than the cold outside ever could. She hadn't known until then that she could be so numb and feel so much agony and horror at the same time. Her stomach twisted as the report went on, but she couldn't look away.

Every once in a while, someone who didn't know what was going on would meander into the tension, call out some joke. It only took them a few seconds to fall silent. Before long, the entire room was packed.

No one moved. Everyone watched.

The mounting horror was contagious. A few started sobbing. Cell phones were limited at the station. At the best of times, a phone call might not get through. Still, several tried, cursing at their phones as they were denied access to family and friends.

Tabitha switched news stations a couple of times. There weren't many television stations available, and they were mostly news and sports. But every channel had opted to cover the worldwide catastrophe.

An hour went by like that, in a tense, hushed, terrible bubble that felt more like a nightmare than reality.

And then the screen went a fuzzy gray. Despite the terrors displayed there, a visceral reaction at having more information cut off from her made Stella stir and snap at Tabitha. "Did you turn it off?" she asked.

Tabitha shook her head, her cheeks wet with tears, her nose red. "No," she said.

More grumbles rose from across the room until everyone was calling out suggestions for fixing the television.

A familiar whistle cut through the air, and Stella turned to see the Winter Operations Manager, James Linden, taking his fingers out of his mouth. "I had our communications team cut access," he shouted.

Stella crossed her arms and mumbled a curse. Others weren't as reserved. A few outright booed.

But James didn't seem fazed. "I need to talk," he said, "and nobody is going to hear me if you're all trying to get the news back on."

"Then talk!" Adam said, his over-the-top indignation matching the time he was angry the kitchen was serving French Fries a few days prior.

"Sit down," James said, his tone stern, "and quiet down, and I'll give everyone the information I have."

Stella licked her lips and sat as she exchanged a look with Tabitha. *Does he know more than what the news is telling us?*

"As you all know," James said, "something terrible is happening out there. No one knows what it is, not yet. And please, understand that the news is going to sensationalize everything to get more views." He took a deep breath. "We are sitting on an ice shelf, people. It's dark. The weather's bad. We don't have access to evacuation protocols, not for another few months when the temperature goes up with the sun. That means we need to remain calm, we need to do our duties as always, and we need to be patient. I will allow access to the news for two hours over lunchtime every day. I suspect, in a few days, we'll start to see reports rolling in about how this tragedy is being contained. Until then, we have to work together, support each other, and do our best not to freak out. We need to survive, okay? And we can only do that as a team. Got it?"

Mumbled agreement rose in patches across the room. Stella nodded, the speech only going so far to calm her nerves.

"Now," James said, "I'm going to need all of you to get back to work."

Groans accompanied the sliding of chairs and the clink of silverware as people all across the cafeteria started cleaning up after themselves.

Stella looked down at her plate of cold food. She couldn't waste it, but she wasn't hungry. "I think I'm going to box this up and take it back to my room. Heat it up later." She glanced at Tabitha. "You want to stay over tonight?" she asked. "I don't think I want to be alone."

Tabitha nodded. "Yeah…" She drifted off, drying her eyes with a napkin. "I just… I don't know how I'm going to work today knowing Cal is out there."

Stella closed her eyes, berating herself for not thinking of it sooner. "Oh, Tab, I'm sorry." She opened her eyes and reached out to take Tabitha's hand. "I'm sure Cal is fine."

Calvin Mensa, Tabitha's fiancé, was a pilot. He flew supplies to stations all over Antarctica. His involvement had been part of what had attracted Tabitha to McMurdo in the first place. Tabitha gave Stella a small smile and mumbled a polite thanks, but Stella could tell her attempts at making her feel better hadn't exactly worked.

"Hey," Stella said, "meet me back at my dorm room at the end of the day, okay? We're going to be fine. We'll watch a DVD on my laptop. Distract each other. Chocolate and wine. Straight up comedy, no romance." She waggled her eyebrows, trying to put away the fear writhing in her chest in favor of following James's advice.

"Okay," Tabitha said, her smile a little more genuine.

Abby clung to Charlie's arm. "I'll come over to your place," she said.

He nodded, his brow furrowed. "Wouldn't have it any other way."

"You think it's really going to be okay, like James said?" Abby asked.

"Of course." Charlie kissed her forehead.

Stella didn't contradict him. Around the room, similar conversations were happening, but there was an undertone of tension and uncertainty in every expression, in everyone's tone. She got up from her table, going through the motions as if it were a normal day, every movement hollow.

* * *

For the fifth night in a row, Stella waited for Tabitha after the day's duties were done. But that day was different. That day, they hadn't been able to connect to any news station. The internet was down for good, it seemed. Satellite communications were gone. They could still communicate by HF radio with the nearest stations due to the radio towers between them, but the stations farther from them had gone dark.

McMurdo had always been isolated, but it had never *felt* that way as much as it did that day. Stella was stuck at the edge of the world while everywhere else fell apart.

There had been no good news since that first day. No indication things were getting better or ever would. News anchors had increasingly seemed strung out, panicked, and on the verge of losing it. The killer disease had spread all over the globe, much of it done the first twenty-four hours as people carried it by plane to their homes.

No one knew exactly how it spread. Some people dropped dead within an hour of their first symptom. Some people progressively got worse over many hours. No one knew how long the disease incubated. No one knew of a treatment. No one knew *anything*.

There was a slight knock before Tabitha entered. Her eyes were red and puffy. Dark circles under her eyes accompanied exhausted frown lines and a pale complexion. She closed the door behind her, walked over to where Stella sat cross-legged on her bed, and plopped down beside her.

"What if this is it?" Tabitha asked. "We can't make it here if we don't get resupplied. And if no one comes to get us…"

A spike of fear prompted Stella to shake her head in frantic denial. "Don't say that. We just have to make it to sunup, a little past that. Then, someone will come for us. Cal will come. He won't let us die down here."

"What if Cal is dead?"

"He's not."

"What if he is?"

Stella swallowed a lump in her throat as she shook her head. She couldn't say it again, couldn't keep voicing opposition when she wasn't sure she was right.

Tabitha cried softly, and she buried her head in her hands. "If Cal is gone… if the whole world is gone… I can't go on, Stella. I can't do that."

"What is that supposed to mean?" Stella scooted back on the bed and turned to face her friend. "Tab, you can't say stuff like that. I need you, okay?"

She wouldn't look at Stella. "People are talking about it," she said. "It would be better to die on our own terms than to starve to death in the cold."

"No," Stella leaned forward and took Tabitha by the shoulders. "No," she said more firmly. "I'm serious, Tabitha. It's been less than a week. Sure, it looks bleak, but we don't know what's going on out there. I know that this blasted darkness makes it hard to hold on to hope in the good times. I know depression can creep in more easily here than maybe anywhere, but Tab, you can't give up on me. Okay? Promise you won't do anything stupid."

Tabitha pressed her lips together, tears still rolling down her cheeks, and looked away.

Stella raised her voice, panic coursing through her veins. "Please," she said. "Hold on. For me. We're going to be okay. We have to keep it together until the outside world comes to get us. And someone will. I'll bet you a year's salary that it'll be Cal. Two years, Tab. I swear it."

Tabitha rolled her eyes and let out a long breath. "You don't have that much money." She smiled a little, and it gave Stella some hope.

"I'll sell my boat," Stella said. "When we get back to the States, before you marry that goofball, I'll sell the boat my aunt left me, and I'll take you on the best bachelorette getaway in history. Paris. Shopping. Lots of baguettes."

Tabitha laughed. "You swear on your ex's dog's life?"

Stella gasped in mock offense. "Fluff is *my* dog."

"He lives with Jarod."

"Only because I allow it." Stella raised her right hand. "I swear on Fluff's life that I will take you to Paris." She reached out and squeezed Tabitha's hand. "But you have to get through this with me first, okay?"

Tabitha nodded. "Okay." She flopped onto her side. "I'm tired," she said. "I think I just want to sleep tonight."

"Sounds good to me." Stella laid down, too, her head on the opposite side of the twin-sized bed. "Just don't stick your feet in my face this time."

"I'm not responsible for what I do when I'm asleep." Tabitha raised her head and stuck out her tongue. "Besides, your feet are way worse."

Stella grabbed one of her pillows and threw it at Tabitha. She caught it, laughing, and stuffed it under her head. After reaching for the lamp on her side table and turning it off, Stella made herself as comfortable as she could. It was good—no *essential*—for Stella's sanity to be with someone, to not be alone. But even so, she stared into the dark for a long time before she fell asleep, thinking about what Tabitha had said. She couldn't shake the feeling in her gut that all her visions of a normal future were nothing but smoke and mirrors.

Chapter 3

Alexander Roman

The horde of perhaps twenty shouted as if they were running into battle. The sun hit the heads of axes, and several of them carried wooden spears. A few had bows and quivers strapped to their backs.

Walter and Zara rushed Lizzy back to the plane. Oliver was inside, safe for the moment, and Alex had a small army at his back. But as their attackers came nearer, as they shook their weapons and howled, the first thing that threw Alex off was the fact that he didn't spot even one firearm among them.

The second thing that made him lower his weapon was the fact that they looked to be all *children*.

"Alex?" Lauren said nervously beside him. "Are those kids?"

"I think so," he said.

"What in the Sam Hill?" Minnie stepped back.

"Axes and spears can kill just as easily as guns," Kai said. "What do we do?"

The group of warrior-like children, ranging it seemed from Oliver's age all the way up to perhaps sixteen, slid to a stop, whooping and hollering until the tallest of them stepped forward, raised a bow with an arrow knocked, and drew it.

"Surrender your supplies," he shouted, his New Zealand accent thick.

Alex swallowed hard. Kai was right. It didn't matter if they were kids; their weapons could still kill every last one of them. The boys could be grandstanding, but could he risk his life and the life of his son to find out? On the other hand, could he bring himself to shoot a child? Some of them seemed no older than Oliver.

"Where are your parents?" Alex asked.

"Americans, eh?" the boy said, not lowering his weapon. "Goodonya for makin' it this far. Reckon you'd find a safe paradise among the Kiwis, did ya?"

"Uh…" Alex tried to process the foreign nature of the familiar words. "We're not here to stay, if that's what you mean." He put a hand to his chest. "I'm Alex, a scientist. I used to work for the CDC, and—"

"Not interested," the boy said. "You gonna give us whatcha got? Or are we gonna have to take it?"

Several of the boys, even the youngest ones, bared their teeth. The smallest of them stood on tiptoes and spread out their arms wide as they growled.

Minnie tsked. "You must think the sun comes up just to hear you crow. Just go back from wherever you came from."

"None of us want to hurt you," Lauren said, "but we will. Just go, now, and we'll forget all about it, okay? We have guns. You have sticks. Think about it."

"Yeah, nah, mate. We gotta live," the boy said. "I got mouths to feed, and I bet there's heaps of food in that there aeroplane. And if you were gonna shoot us, you'da done it already."

Alex glanced to his right and to his left at his people, each one clearly hesitant, and then he looked at the boys, each one clearly eager. Some of them looked as if they *wanted* a fight.

"Back up," Alex said. "The rest of you get back on the plane. I'll be the last in. We'll just wait them out."

"Don't think so, mate." The leader of the group loosed his arrow, and it zipped across the gap between them, hitting Minnie in the thigh.

She grunted and stumbled back, eyes wide as she looked down at her leg where the shaft of the boy's arrow protruded. "Son of a biscuit! He shot me with a stick!"

"Mom!" Lauren lowered her gun and reached out to steady Minnie. Walter rushed to her side, too, providing support so that she didn't fall to the ground.

Alex's senses heightened, and he trained his gun on the boy who'd shot Minnie. He was so *young*. Alex hadn't really expected the boys to be any real danger. The reality that they were was sinking in through Minnie's agonized, sharp breathing.

"Don't make another move," Alex said. "I *will* shoot."

"I'm going to kill 'em!" Kai raised his gun, but Zara put a hand on his arm.

"We can't kill a bunch of kids," Minnie said between gritted teeth. "Alex, I swear, don't put that kinda blood on my hands."

Walter nodded. "We'll figure out our supplies later."

Alex held up one hand, his heart beating wildly. "Okay," he said. "Let my son come out of the airplane, and then you can go in, get whatever you want."

The leader sniffed. "That's more like it," he said. "Sorry about the old lady." He shrugged. "Just had to show ya I meant business."

"Ihaka!" one of the smaller boys shouted and pointed. "They're here."

The leader—Ihaka, apparently—stepped back. He cursed, throwing some insult at the group that Alex couldn't quite decipher. Then he smiled at Alex. "Today's your lucky day," he said. "Ya see, *those* blokes will sink one right between my eyes if they get half a chance." He grinned. "Good luck." He turned and started shouting, "Back to the motorway! Retreat!"

Alex blinked, not sure if their leaving was good or bad. Across the tarmac, another group, this one of adults, was coming their way. Half of them split off to follow the boys, and the other half continued toward the plane.

"Minnie, can you walk?" Alex asked. "We need to get inside the plane, barricade ourselves inside."

"Wait," Walter said, "they're raising a white flag."

Alex looked back at the group. One of them had unfurled a white sheet and had lifted it over their head, waving it in the breeze as it fluttered behind them.

"I still think we should get everyone inside." Alex waved for them to hurry.

"We have medicine and a doctor," came a loud voice over a bullhorn. "We come peacefully. Please! Wait!"

"That's an American accent," Lauren said. "Maybe we can trust them."

"I'm getting Lizzy to safety," Zara said as she led her friend up the steps and into the plane.

Kai and Blythe followed. "We'll get the engine running," Blythe said, "just in case."

"I'll stay and talk to them," Lauren said.

"No, I won't let you face strangers alone." Alex shook his head.

Sweating and grimacing, Minnie growled at her daughter. "Inside. Right now."

Lauren pursed her lips. "I'm an adult, Mom, and it makes sense. You don't *need* me. I'll face them, ask them what they want, feel it out. They're American. They're offering help. We shouldn't throw that chance away, especially with those miniature Mad Maxes running around."

Alex ran his hand through his hair and looked back. They didn't have much time. "We'll all get in, retract the steps, leave the door open. I'll—"

"And I," Lauren said, "will negotiate. I'll keep my weapon ready. You can stand right next to me, out of the way."

"Lauren—"

"The plane can take off if something goes wrong," Lauren said. "If you want me anywhere near safety, just agree so we can get on with this."

"You're so stubborn some—"

"Thanks." Lauren raised her eyebrows at him. "Now, help me get my mom into the plane."

Acceptance settled in Alex's stomach, and he switched gears, moving fast, as did everyone else. Just as the newcomers reached the plane, Lauren finished retracting the steps. She stood, tall and proud, her gun lowered just slightly but ready to fire. As Alex stood just to the side, behind the protection of the fuselage, he was caught by the beauty in the way she stared down the oncoming strangers. She was strong and brave, and he was hit by an overwhelming sense of trust in her abilities.

He shook his head, heat flooding his cheeks. His next thought went to his wife, but... he only saw her smile, heard her tell him she wanted him to be happy. *I'm not ready for that,* he thought as he looked back at Lauren. *And neither is she.*

"Don't come any closer!" Lauren shouted.

Alex peeked around the doorframe. The group kept at a reasonable distance, and they did not raise their weapons. Instead, they raised empty hands, all but the woman with the bullhorn who stood out front. A man behind her draped the white sheet over his shoulders before showing his hands to be free of any weapons.

"My name's Captain Winona Whitlock of the USS Bancroft," the woman said. "That's a mighty nice C-17 you've got there. Looks like a United States aircraft."

Lauren looked down at Alex. "What do I say?"

Alex shrugged. "I wouldn't lie. That's not gotten us anywhere good in the past."

She raised her voice, shouting, "We're here on the orders of the President of the United States," she shouted.

Captain Whitlock squinted up at them. "You wouldn't be here to rescue us by chance?"

"Not exactly," Lauren shouted. "Not yet."

"Look," the captain said, "I swear to you, we will not hurt you. We just want to talk to you, help you if we can. My crew was out to sea when crap hit the fan. We mostly survived, and we've teamed up with some survivors here on the South Island. We've got a camp, food, medical attention... let's get you safe before those boys come back."

"What do you think, Alex?" Lauren asked. "I really want to get that arrow out of my mom's leg. I don't think it hit the artery—it's pretty close to the outer layer of skin—but she's going to need a safe spot to recover. We're going to have to worry about infection after we get that thing out."

He stood up straighter and addressed them all. "They know the area and they're willing to help. I think we should make an alliance. Agreed?"

"Seems like our best shot," Zara said.

"Let's do it," Walter said. "Maybe they know where the USAP is."

Candice shrugged. "I'm just along for the ride."

Minnie groaned. "For Pete's sake! Just get this over with!"

Oliver sat next to her, arms wrapped around Samson's neck as the dog whined at Minnie's injury. Alex wanted to go to him, wanted to take him away from the worry and from Minnie's pain, but there wasn't time.

Lauren turned back to the door. "Okay. We're willing to trust you. We've got one injury," she shouted.

Captain Whitlock nodded and waved a man forward. "Lower the stairs," she said. "I'm sending our medic up, but it would be mighty nice if you could give the rest of us shelter, too. I'm assuming you've run into the black clouds?"

"We call them swarms," Lauren shouted.

"Well, you never know when they'll pop up," the captain said.

"We need to protect our vulnerable if we let them on board," Walter said.

"Zara," Alex said, "will you take Lizzy and Oliver into the crew compartment? Lock the door."

"I can do that." She nodded and got to convincing Oliver to leave Minnie's side. For once, Samson didn't go with Oliver. He sat right next to Minnie.

Alex stuck his head outside. "Come on up," he shouted. "All of you."

"Yes, sir," the captain said. She unclipped a walkie-talkie, said something, and then smiled up at them. She was the last of her people to board the plane, and Alex closed the door after her. As her medic got to work, Lauren by his side, both of them working to help Minnie, Whitlock looked sideways at Alex. "I bet you've got some tale to tell. Why exactly are you here in New Zealand?"

Minnie bit down on something from the medic's saddlebag. The medic broke off the tip of the arrow on the other side of her leg and pulled the shaft free. She screamed and passed out.

Alex grimaced, his stomach turning at his friend's pain. He took a deep breath. "It's a long story," he said, "but I think I could use a distraction."

* * *

"So, the President of the United States is some guy named Michael Coleman?" Whitlock quirked an eyebrow.

Alex nodded. "Yep."

"And you're on a mission to Antarctica so that you can find some backup fix that's stored in a secret government lab because—and correct me if I'm wrong—*our government* is responsible for the creation of these black clouds and the disease?" She whistled when Alex nodded again. "That's a tough pill to swallow."

"I know," Alex said. "But it's true."

He'd told the captain the highlights of their story, everything that would help her focus on the task at hand. There were a lot of specifics he left out, things that would've taken a lot longer to explain.

It would take days, maybe weeks, to lay out everything that's happened over the past few months, he thought. He could barely believe all the twists and turns, and he had lived through them.

Captain Whitlock and her people had settled down inside the huge cargo hold of the C-17 alongside Alex's people. With Whitlock's promise that they would return the favor, Alex and Walter had agreed to allowing them all to refill their water bottles and canteens. Those in Whitlock's group who'd gone after the boys at first had returned and were laughing and chatting with everyone else. They'd apparently chased the kids far from the airport.

"I'd like to know a little more about you," Alex said. "You said something about being out to sea?"

She nodded. "A research vessel, the U.S.S. Bancroft. Brand-spankin' new. She's a beauty. I've been working with the United States Antarctic Program. Had a few oceanographers doing their thing when the news started rolling in. We came closer to the island, but the city was burning and the few reports we received said it wasn't safe to come in. We were equipped with supplies for another month, so we just stayed on board."

"What about your families?" Alex asked.

Whitlock's face fell. "I let those who needed to go return by boat, told them if they left, I wouldn't be able to let them back on board, for the safety of the rest of the crew. One of them came back, anyway… they came back with their wife and kids in a dinghy they stole." She swallowed audibly and shook her head, her eyes glistening. "Hardest thing I ever had to do was tell them I couldn't let them on board. They begged me, and so I said if they weren't sick in a few days' time, if they stayed on that dinghy next to the ship, that I'd let them on then, but…" She trailed off and let out a shaky breath.

"They didn't make it," Alex said. It wasn't a question. He could see it in her eyes.

"Don't think any of them that left for their families made it," Whitlock said. "The rest of us either didn't have anyone or didn't have anyone in New Zealand." She gave him a sad smile. "I had a daughter back in the States. Before you got here, I had the luxury of pretending she made it to some pocket of safety, that maybe the U.S. had gotten ahead of it somehow, that we'd be rescued."

"You never know," Alex said. "She might still be out there."

"Maybe."

And then the entire plane shuddered and rumbled. Alex stood up. Adrenaline flooded his system. Vibrations filtered through the floor and into his body. "What is that?"

His people had similar reactions, each one looking wildly about as Whitlock's people chuckled. It ended, and Alex waited, knees bent, arms out, confused as to why the others hadn't been more concerned.

"It's just a little bitty earthquake," Whitlock said. "Didn't last more than twenty seconds. You can sit down. It's fine."

"Are they common here?" Alex asked.

"They don't call this place the Shaky Isles for nothing," Whitlock said. "I heard a local once say that the land has waves just like the sea."

"Do we have to worry about that?" Alex dried his sweaty palms on his thighs as he sat back down.

Whitlock shrugged. "We don't feel the majority of the earthquakes, from what I understand. A lot of them are small, like that one, just enough to be felt. If a big one comes, just find cover if you're inside. If you're outside, get away from the buildings."

"Good to know," Alex said. He leaned back and smiled at the captain. "Well, I appreciate your help. If you want to give us directions to a few places where we can look for information regarding McMurdo Station, you can go. We can handle the rest from here."

Whitlock shook her head. "I'm afraid that's not going to work for us."

Alex frowned. "What's that supposed to mean?"

"The way I see it, the safest way south is by ship, and my research vessel is capable of breaking through the ice to get you there. You're lucky, too. It's just barely the time of year where the station is sort of accessible."

"We don't have that kind of time," Alex said.

"Maybe not," Whitlock said, "but there won't be a runway for you to land on if you go by plane. It'll be covered in snow. We've lost communications with McMurdo. There's no way to ask them to clear the way for you."

"So, we'll land in the snow and dig our own runway to leave, if necessary."

"Too dangerous. You could land in the wrong spot, get stuck. Or worse, get *sunk*."

Alex sighed. "I guess you'd know," he said.

"Whoever is essential can go down on my ship," Whitlock said. "The rest of you can stay here."

Alex glanced at Oliver and Lauren who were playing cards beside a sleeping Minnie with Samson by her side. "We've got a thing about staying together."

"Look," Whitlock said, "you have no idea what's waiting for you down there. Antarctica isn't *meant* for us. Your son could die simply from being outside too long without the right gear. There aren't natural resources. We have no idea if the stations are even functioning, if the disease found its way down there somehow… I won't take a child down there, and you shouldn't argue. Besides, your friend, Minnie, needs to stay behind."

Alex looked away from his son, his heart breaking as he realized the captain was right.

She continued. "When you've got what you need, you can reunite and get New Zealand squared away."

"We've got people back in the States," Alex said. "You do, too. We can't stay here long enough to implement the countermeasure or create enough meds to cover the remaining population."

"That makes no sense." Whitlock shook her head. "We'll get to the States, but we should start curing the world on the way."

Alex quirked an eyebrow. "We?" he asked.

She shrugged. "I didn't survive this nonsense for nothing. That research vessel can safely take your vaccine and these countermeasure mosquitos all over the world." She patted him on the back. "Think about it. It's the best way."

Alex sat back as Whitlock stood and made the rounds with her people, checking in with them. A lot of what she'd said made sense. He wasn't sure about all of it. He'd promised Oliver that he'd never separate them again. And the plan had always been to make the States their first priority. But could they really ignore the survivors on that side of the world while they were so close?

Hard decisions lay just ahead. He could only hope he had the wisdom to make the right ones.

Chapter 4

Stella Sharpe

About 2 Months Ago

Twenty days of total isolation had done a number on Stella and the rest of McMurdo's population. A team from another station had radioed them on Day Seven, telling them that despite the weather and despite the danger, they were going to the radio tower to attempt to boost the signal, to try to get into contact with ships or nearby islands. On Day Ten, McMurdo lost radio signals with other stations. Their best guess was that something had happened to the tower that the team had been unable to fix.

Slowly but surely, Stella became one of one hundred and fifty who were falling apart even as they all worked to keep the station running. She lived two weeks of her life in a haze, going through the motions, her mind numb. It was better not to think, not to allow questions. The days blurred together. No one spoke of anything except the same small talk that avoided every possible mention of the world outside.

Even nights with Tabitha had gone silent. They no longer watched movies or played cards or tried to pass the time through distractions. She came, and they slept, and that was it. Stella didn't want to be alone, and she wasn't; she didn't have the capacity to hope for anything better.

But then a switch had flipped.

The cafeteria was as quiet as usual. James tried the television, as he did every day at noon, to no avail. Stella watched him approach the television, her breath caught in her throat, every muscle tense, willing that satellite signal to be there again with everything she had. When there was nothing but fuzzy gray on every channel, she breathed again, held back the tears, and stuffed a biscuit in her mouth. It tasted like ashes. Everything tasted like ashes these days.

Tabitha slipped into the chair next to her, and she was *whistling*, a soft and happy tune. "Hey," she said, and she sounded like she had before the world had abandoned them while it fought for its life.

Stella frowned. "Hey." She didn't have the strength to sound enthusiastic.

"You better eat up," Tabitha said. "I've been talking to the others, and we're going to put on the Midwinter Mile Race. You need your strength."

Stella groaned. "What? Tab, no. No one is up for that."

Tabitha picked up a cookie and took a bite. "I need this, Stella. One last hurrah, you know?"

"One last…" Stella's frown deepened as she noticed Tabitha had only gotten desserts. "What are you talking about? And you're going to make yourself sick. What is with you, Tab?"

"What's with me," Tabitha said, "is that I can't live like this anymore."

Stella was tired of that conversation. "Tab—"

"And so, if we're going to live, we should *live*. The Midwinter Mile Race is a tradition. We were going to do it before and so we're going to do it now." Tabitha took another bite. "This cookie is delicious." She picked up another of the same kind on her plate and held it out. "Want one?"

"Tab, who is going to run a race *now*? Who is going to organize it?" Stella pushed the cookie away.

"I am, and so are Abby and Charlie and a few others."

Tabitha smiled. Stella had almost forgotten what it looked like to see someone smile. She sat back and looked out across the cafeteria. Others were in markedly better moods as well.

"What the hell is going on?" Stella looked down at her food. "Did someone drug my tater tots?"

Tabitha laughed. "No," she said. "Some of us have just decided to make the best of what time we have left."

Stella blinked slowly. "You keep saying stuff like that. What does that mean?"

"It means, life is fragile. We can learn at least that much from what's happened, right?" Tabitha turned very serious and touched Stella's arm. There was pleading in her eyes, in her voice. "Stella, do this with me. For me. We're sad all the time. We need something fun, something good." She held out the cookie again.

Stella hesitantly took the treat. "I guess so," she said, and she nibbled the cookie. For the first time in a while, food tasted like it used to. She tried one of her tots. "Okay," she said as she squirted ketchup on her plate. "I'll do the race."

Her spirits were lifted as others, like Tabitha, started chatting and joking around. The cafeteria slowly filled with a lighter spirit that Stella didn't understand but didn't want to question.

Over the next several days, McMurdo Station was abuzz with people preparing for the race. The kitchen always put together a special dinner for the occasion, something they planned well before the time came. The lamb chops and lobster would have been ordered months ago and delivered on the last plane before the dark winter season.

And it was good to have a goal. Stella found herself racing between buildings when she had to go out in the cold. For the first time in weeks, she and Tabitha went back to the gym. Abby was leading her rumba classes again, and the room was fuller than it had ever been. Stella left classes sore all over, not just from the dancing but from the laughter.

What had happened, the last reports they'd gotten, it all seemed so far away. Stella clung to that feeling. She pushed away her distress every time it threatened to tear down her newfound joy of living in the moment with her best friend. The upswing in mood was contagious. Ping pong battles resumed. Beer and popcorn and community movies returned. As long as she actively ignored everything outside of McMurdo Station, life was good again.

On the day of the race, Stella and two dozen others stepped to the start of the race around the station. They were bundled from head to toe in multiple layers. It was fifteen degrees below freezing, and they had to run in their awkward gear as fast as they could, ending at the cafeteria where they would celebrate Midwinter Day with good food, karaoke, and an open bar.

Of course, Midwinter Day was long past. No one mentioned that, though Stella had to put it out of her mind a few times. Midwinter Day had come and gone in the middle of that haze, after news from the outside world had been lost.

Today isn't about that, Stella thought as she took off in the snow, laughing as she trudged forward, as Adam Parker, who had sworn he'd win, lumbered as she ran past him.

Small crowds awaited them at intervals, cheering loudly, their voices carried on the cold, biting wind. By the time Stella reached Big Blue, building 155, she was freer than she'd been in ages. She threw up her arms and whooped, high-fiving Charlie, who'd come in first.

Tabitha waited at the finish line, jumping up and down every time someone crossed, clapping her gloved hands together in a motion that made no sound beneath the increasing howl of the wind.

Stella laughed and ran to her, helping her welcome runners past the finish line and into Big Blue where the fun of the day would continue.

"Saving the best for last," Adam Parker said as he crossed the finish line.

Stella shrugged. "Yeah, why not," she said. "Congrats, Adam."

His face was covered to keep him warm, but his eyes smiled. "Thanks, Stella," he said. "You know, if you ever want a night cap—"

Stella held up a hand. "Adam, don't push it."

"Yeah. Yeah, I felt it was too much as I said it," he said.

She laughed and shook her head. "I can't stand you."

"But you still love me." Adam pointed at her with two thick, gloved fingers. "Eh? Eh?"

"We still love you," Tabitha said. "Now, let's go eat."

The food was the best Stella had ever had at the station. Lincoln served alongside his fellow kitchen staff, his chest puffed with pride, and a big smile on his face. It had been weeks since mealtimes had been like they used to be: full of conversation and compliments to the chefs.

Once the food was consumed and the tables cleared to make space for a dance floor, karaoke started and the bar opened. Stella danced and drank and forgot, and it was wonderful.

Until the celebration wound down, until James took the microphone.

"He looks serious," Stella said, chuckling as she elbowed Tabitha.

Tabitha held up a pink-colored shot and threw it back. "Just listen," she said, wobbling a bit.

Stella held her friend steady. "Whoa, how much did you drink."

"Enough." Tabitha smiled, but it didn't reach her eyes. "I'm sorry, Stella."

Stella frowned as James started talking. "What for?"

She nodded toward the front. "Listen."

"—but it's time," James said, "to come clean."

The laughter around her had died down, but Stella had missed James's opening sentence. Her mind was fuzzy from the alcohol, but she zeroed in on what he was saying, concentrating.

"We know what happened to the team that went to boost the radio station," James said. "I didn't want to scare everyone, didn't know how to say it, but… they were able to contact a ship, a cargo ship."

Voices erupted, and Stella turned wide-eyed to Tabitha only to see that she wasn't surprised. "You knew?" she asked.

Tabitha nodded. "We had to keep people who'd try to stop us out of it, Stella."

"Out of what?" Stella's blood ran cold, and her heartbeat quickened.

"They were dying," James said. "They'd stopped to look for survivors and caught the sickness we saw on the news. One man left breathing at the wheel. He said the whole world is a ghost town, everywhere they went, every radio communication they managed to secure confirmed it." James let out a shaky breath. "After communicating the truth to the stations around Antarctica, as far as we understand it, the team let themselves freeze to death. No one is coming."

"We don't know that," Stella said, and others shouted it, too, but James just shook his head.

He raised a shot glass with pink liquid inside and threw it back. "Our doctor, who has volunteered to stay with those who choose to live, put together these shots. She's back at the bar, and she'll mix one up for you, if you so choose. Those of us who knew already what we wanted, we've already taken the medicine. We're going to drift off to sleep after one last good night."

Stella sucked in sharply and looked at Tabitha, shaking her head, eyes going to that empty shot glass. "One last hurrah," she whispered. "No… no, no, no…" Hot tears burned pathways down her cheeks.

James continued. "Those who want to hold on to false hope, we'll leave you with our portions of supplies." He nodded and lifted the empty glass. "To the rest, maybe we'll see you on the other side."

Shouts of horror rippled throughout the room as friends realized who had taken a shot of the deadly pink mixture. More frantic, high-pitched shrieking filled the room as people tried to convince others not to go to the bar. Still others, after a moment of silence, walked right up to the doctor and held out their hands, throwing back the concoction quickly.

Stella could only stare at Tabitha. She couldn't process it, couldn't understand. "What have you done?" she asked, her voice breaking. "What about Cal?"

"Cal is dead," Tabitha said. "I know it. He's one of a few pilots who could fly in at this time of year. He'd risk his life to get to me. I know he would. If he were still alive."

"You don't know that," Stella shouted.

Tabitha's eyelids drooped, and she stumbled sideways. Stella stepped forward and caught her before she fell, easing her to the floor. As she sobbed, Tabitha smiled up at her.

"Try to understand," Tabitha said. "This place isn't meant for living. And if you're right, which I know you're not, I will have given you extra time. You can have all the tater tots I would've eaten."

"No!" Stella held tightly to her best friend. "How could you leave me like this? Tab, what have you done?"

She rocked back and forth as Tabitha's breathing became shallower. All around her, the nightmare was mirrored. Wailing and sorrow filled the room where music and laughter had been just moments ago. And as Tabitha slipped away, Stella's keening joined the mournful choir.

Chapter 5

Minnie Stevens

"What in the ever-loving tarnation is *that*?" Minnie recoiled even as Alex and Walter held her up, causing them to tighten their grip on her.
"That's transportation," Whitlock said.
Zara snorted. "I think I love it."
"Oh, hush," Minnie said. "How am I supposed to ride that thing?"
She looked the contraption up and down. It was one of those touristy things, a pedal pub, she thought they were called. But they'd covered it in a clear, heavy plastic shield that hung from the roof and cinched around rainboots that seemed to be glued to the pedals. There was a bench at the back and long benches on either side. A total of twelve sets of boots and pedals surrounded the floorboard. At the front, there was a steering wheel set high behind a seat front and center.
"This isn't our first time transporting someone with an injury," Whitlock said as she unzipped one corner, pulled back the plastic, and pointed to the floorboard where part of a stretcher, minus the legs and wheels, had been crammed into the contraption while in an upright position.
"You want me to crawl in there?" Minnie asked. "I couldn't do that if I hadn't been shot through with a stick!"
Alex shrugged. "Why don't you try it?" he asked. "It doesn't look too uncomfortable, once you get yourself in."
"All you have to do is sit in the driver's seat, rotate, and then ease down onto the stretcher," Whitlock said. "It doesn't work for every injury, but we've had people with leg injuries worse than yours do it."
Minnie huffed. "I guess there ain't no two ways about it."
Minnie's leg hadn't stopped throbbing since she'd woken from having the arrow pulled out. Putting pressure on it produced a white-hot fire like the devil's own breath, so she reluctantly followed Whitlock's directions with Alex and Walter helping her along the way. She strapped herself in to keep herself stable.
As she made herself comfortable, Whitlock gave everyone else instructions. They were to climb in, crawl to the last available spot, slip off their shoes, and stick their feet in the rainboots. Whitlock got into the driver's seat once everyone was settled.
The contraption started moving through the streets of Christchurch. Minnie gritted her teeth when they hit an occasional bump in the road. She tried to stay as still as possible. Lucky for her, there were antibiotics and painkillers in the supplies they'd brought from the States. It would have been nice for the painkillers to do more than take the edge off, but she'd said more than once that beggars can't be choosers, and Minnie wasn't one to preach a thing but expect a special dispensation when it came to herself.
No, she'd tough it out, and she'd do it with dignity.
Everyone started pumping their legs all around Minnie, and the movement created a rhythmic sound that helped her relax as they travelled the foreign streets. When they arrived at a small indoor shopping center, Minnie found out the hard way that getting out of the contraption was harder than getting in. Alex and Walter had to lean over the tabletops above her head and pull her up so she could use the wooden slats on either side as crutches to aid her in hopping back to the driver's seat.
By the time she'd gotten out, Whitlock had already gone inside and returned with a wheelchair, which she offered for Minnie's use as long as she needed it.
The first order of business was getting settled. For the last couple days, most of their supplies had been relocated from the plane. Alex had marked clearly what could be shared with the locals in exchange for temporary shelter and what they'd need to take with them down to Antarctica.
The news that half of their group would be staying behind had been a hard pill to swallow, but Minnie had had little choice in the matter. She was dead weight with her injury. Zara had put up a bit of a fight, but it was nothing to what Minnie expected out of Oliver. The boy still didn't know. Alex had requested time to figure out how to tell him.
Alex wheeled Minnie down a vast hall with skylights running down the center. People milled about or sat outside of shops-turned-homes, mending or weaving or peeling potatoes. Small children ran up and down the hall, laughing as they played tag. A mother called out for them to be careful as they skirted an older man who was carving something with meticulous care. A young woman sat at his feet, reading a book.
"Well, this is right nice," Minnie said softly.
"It's home," Whitlock said. "I'll be sad to leave it. We've become attached to each other around here." She pointed at the center of the hall, beneath the largest skylight, a dome that let in all the natural light they could possibly want. "That's the communal kitchen," she said. "We get our grub three times a day there from our food team. They cook up whatever we manage to grow, hunt, or scavenge."
Oliver turned around in a slow circle as he walked with the rest of them. "Where are we staying?" he asked.
Whitlock stopped in front of a door with no windows, not like the majority of shops with glass fronts and curtains. "This will have to do for four of you for tonight," she said. "There's another one for the rest of you down the hall, a little bigger." She made a motion and one of her people led Walter, Zara, Kai, Blythe, and Lizzy down the hall. Whitlock opened the door with an apologetic look. "I know it's not much. It was an office. But it's what we have for temporary guests. Those of you who are staying can work out one of the empty shops to your liking over the next week or so."
Oliver frowned, and Minnie grimaced as the boy looked up at his father. "Who's staying?" he asked.

Whitlock's eyes went wide. She cleared her throat. "Well, uh… I'll be around if you need me. Sounds like you've got some talking to do."

"Thanks," Alex said. There was an edge of annoyance to his tone.

"Dad?" Oliver's frown deepened.

"Let's get settled," Lauren said, gently guiding Oliver into the room, "and then we can talk about it."

The room was equipped with four bedrolls lining either side. A six-by-four-foot aisle made just enough room for them to breathe and do little else. Minnie had to leave the wheel chair in the hall just outside. Alex helped her hop to a bedroll and make herself as comfortable as possible before lighting the lantern on the floor at the center of the room and closing the door for privacy.

Minnie lay flat, relief flooding her body at the thought of no more movement for a while, and Lauren took up the other bedroll on her side of the room. Samson lay right next to Minnie so that she could rest her arm on his back. The poor dog hadn't left her side since he'd seen her injured, which was a change of pace. He'd been glued to Oliver for months. She supposed he was just going where he was needed most.

Alex leaned against the wall with Oliver snuggled up to his side. "I have something to tell you," he said. "And I know you're not going to like it, but I need you to listen until I'm done…"

Minnie's heart hurt for the boy as the situation was explained to him in full. The confusion and pain in his expression was hard to bear. When his father had finished, he jerked away.

"Dad, you promised we'd stay together," Oliver said.

"Come now, Oliver," Minnie said. "Your father just explained that the captain can't take us all. He wouldn't leave you if he had any other choice."

"And besides," Lauren said, "I'm going with him. I'll keep an eye on him, and you can keep an eye on my mom."

Alex looked up at Lauren. "Whoa," he said. "Walter and I have to go. Candice, too. We might need her blood if we reach that research bank. But you don't have to come, Lauren."

Minnie twisted her head, doing her best not to move her leg as she tried to get her daughter in her sights. "Didn't you hear him say how dangerous this is gonna be?"

"I did." Lauren crossed her arms. "I'm going. One more person isn't going to hurt anybody. You need more people on this trip that you know you can trust."

Oliver stood in a hurry, his face scrunched in anger. "If she can decide to go, so can I!"

"Captain Whitlock won't take you," Alex said. "You're just a child."

"I'm not!" Oliver's chin quavered, and he hastily brushed away a tear. "You can't leave me here!"

"Oliver," Alex said, "I wouldn't if I had a choice. But you'll be safe here. And Minnie can't go. She's injured. Do you want to leave Minnie and Samson behind?"

Oliver turned, flung open the door, and ran into the main hall without another word. Samson whined and lifted his head. Minnie hushed him and told him to stay put.

When Alex made to get up, Minnie held up a hand. "Alex, why don't you let Lauren follow him. Give him some time to process, and then she'll bring him back when he's ready to talk."

Lauren was out the door, closing it softly behind her, before Minnie was even done speaking. Alex rubbed his face and groaned.

"That didn't go well," he said.

Minnie chuckled. "Well, I don't know what you expected, but I think that was about as good as it was gonna get."

He gave her a flat look. "It's not funny."

"I know, I know," Minnie said. "It's just… it is what it is. This is a mud pie, and no matter how long you bake it in the oven, it ain't gonna come out like fresh fruit."

"What if he's right? What if I'm making a mistake?" Alex asked.

"You listened to people who know the area better than you do," Minnie said. "You're leaving your son in a safe place with people who will look out for him. You know I will, but if Zara, Kai, and Blythe are staying, too, they'll watch our backs."

Alex scoffed. "I have the feeling Zara and Kai are going to be preoccupied with Lizzy, and we barely know Blythe."

"They'll still be here," Minnie said, "and Zara and Kai are good ones. Blythe, too, I think. He's a little rough around the edges, but…" She trailed off. She was going to say, "but so is Alan, and he's one of the best there is." Somehow, though, she couldn't quite manage to mention his name out loud, not yet. She missed him something fierce.

"But what?" Alex asked.

"Nothin'," Minnie said, managing a smile. "Give Oliver a minute. He'll come around. Go and do what you have to do, and when you get back, we'll be here. I won't let nothin' bad happen to Oliver."

"I know you won't," Alex said.

"Now, when do you have to go?"

"Tomorrow." Alex rolled his shoulders and glanced at the doorway, that look telling her he was still contemplating going after his son. "It's about an hour and half by bicycle to someplace called Lyttelton Port. That's where the U.S.S. Bancroft is docked."

Though she was getting more exhausted by the second—losing a lot of blood did that to a person, even a couple days later—she was determined to keep Alex busy until Lauren brought Oliver back. "Well, then, tell me everything you know about your upcomin' trip."

Alex took a deep breath. "I don't know much. It's going to be about ten days at sea, I think."

"Then tell me again what you're lookin' for at the research bank, what you hope to find," Minnie said.

"More information on a cure," Alex said, "or a vaccine. I have notes on what I've learned about it, but I'm hoping they got farther than I did with more brain power and less stress. And cryopreservation pods like at New Horizons Laboratory. We need those countermeasure mosquitos. If we can breed them and release them…"

Alex went on, and Minnie listened. He went through different scenarios of how the world might be rid of the disease and the swarms. She'd heard it before, but Alex always got excited when he got into the specifics of how it all would work. As she'd anticipated, it kept him occupied until the door clicked back open.

Oliver slipped inside, and Alex stopped talking. "Sorry I left," the boy said.

"That's okay." Alex patted the bedroll next to him.

Oliver sat and looked up at Alex. "You promise you'll come back?"

"I promise," he said. "Do you promise to be here when I do come back?"

"Yeah." Oliver leaned his head against Alex's shoulder.

Minnie smiled, but there was a sadness inside. She was happy to see father and son spending their last hours together as was proper, but no one could make those kinds of promises and be sure to keep them. She reached her hand over her head as Lauren sat back down. Lauren took her hand and squeezed it. "You okay, mom?"

"I will be," she said, and it didn't matter that she knew the words would be meaningless; she asked for them anyway. "Promise you'll come back to me?"

Lauren kissed Minnie's forehead gently. "I promise."

Chapter 6

Stella Sharpe

About 1 Month Ago

Blood welled as Stella yanked a thick splinter from the palm of her hand. The red bubble grew, burst, and then trickled down her wrist, making a tiny river down her arm.

When sixty of their number had chosen death a month prior, there had been no blood, and death had been clean until a week after that when the doctor had taken her own concoction, the last of it. Death since then had been red.

Stella honed in on the warmth of the new blood, the heat around the site of the wound. It turned cold as it travelled down her arm, tickling her skin like it had come out to play.

"Your arm!" Abby squeaked and then she was there with a towel, holding her wrist, wiping up the red, staining the white cloth. "Stella?" She waved her hand in front of Stella's face.

Stella blinked and tore her gaze from the dirtied rag. "Sorry," she said as she pulled back from Abby and took the care of her wound into her own hands. "It was a nasty splinter. I guess… I guess I got distracted."

Abby sighed and sat. "You should be more careful."

Stella looked down at the cross she'd been sanding down. It was made from wood she'd cut herself at the carpentry shop. "This makes eighty," she said.

"I know." Abby picked up the sandpaper. "Maybe I should finish this one. You look like you could use some sleep."

"Yeah…" Stella nodded, but she didn't move. She *did* need to sleep, but every time she tried, she devolved into a mess of tears. When she did manage to slip into the realm of nightmares, she never woke rested.

"Maybe ask Lincoln for some of that tea he was talking about the other day," Abby said. "Charlie tried it last night, and it worked wonders."

Stella stood, the movement making her head spin. She wobbled and reached for the table to keep from toppling.

"When was the last time you ate?" Abby asked.

"I don't know," Stella said.

"Go talk to Lincoln. Get some food. Get some tea. Get some sleep." Abby raised her eyebrows. "I'm serious."

Stella nodded and forced her legs to carry her around the cafeteria table and past the rows of empty buffet-style serving stations to the kitchen.

An off-tune whistle of some country song greeted her before she caught sight of Lincoln. He was no longer just a server. Half the kitchen staff were gone by their own choosing. He sprinkled salt and some green herbs on a tray full of French fries, his body half turned away from her, his ears covered by headphones. He swayed to music Stella couldn't hear, and then he picked up a wooden spoon and belted out a long note, throwing back his head and spreading out his other arm.

Stella yelped at the sudden sound, her hand going to her chest as her heart leapt. Lincoln startled and dropped the spoon before tearing off his headphones, his cheeks going red.

"I didn't know anyone was coming back here," he said.

"No, it's fine." Stella laughed. "You just scared me."

He wiggled his hips. "Didn't know you were coming for a show?" he asked.

She laughed harder. The movement of her shoulders, the contraction of her stomach, the sound coming from her own mouth, the effort it all took: it broke the haze that she'd been living in since the last death by suicide three days prior. Laughter was like hot water washing over an icy shell that had kept her stiff and unable to feel.

But then she could *feel*.

Her hands trembled as sorrow thawed and injected itself once again into her veins, carrying its heavy load through to the tips of her fingers. The warmth of laughter turned too hot, burned her eyes, her cheeks, as tears spilled from her dry, bloodshot eyes. Her shoulders shook with the effort of sobbing, and her knees buckled.

Lincoln was at her side, wrapping her up in an all-encompassing embrace, providing support with a frame twice the size of hers. It was a good ten minutes, perhaps more, before she was able to catch her breath. She gently pushed away and leaned against the stainless-steel countertop, her exhaustion ten times worse while she somehow felt a little better.

"I'm sorry," she said, her throat raw. "I totally lost it on you." She smiled up at him. "Thanks for… you know… being here, I guess." She winced as she reached for a paper towel to clean off her face.

Lincoln leaned against the countertop next to her and shrugged. "I can handle it," he said. "You okay?"

"No."

"Me either." Lincoln bumped her with his elbow. "You want some fries with that breakdown?"

"Absolutely." She blew her nose and took a deep breath as Lincoln pulled up two stools in front of the tray of fries.

He gestured toward the empty stool. "I added some of my own seasoning. Salt, pepper, and basil."

"They smell good," she said as she sat and picked one of the floppier ones to pop in her mouth. Her stomach growled. "I haven't eaten in like two days," she said.

"I've got some protein if—"

Stella held up a hand, palm facing him. "Protein later. These are delicious."

He shrugged. "Whatever floats your boat."

She stuffed more fries in her mouth, the savory goodness reminding her just how hungry she really was. "This," she said, pointing down at the tray, her mouth half full, "this floats my boat."

Lincoln chuckled. "Noted. I'll make sure to keep the fries coming, then, for as long as we have them." His smile faded as Stella stopped mid chew and looked down at the tray. "Sorry," he said, "I didn't mean—"

"No, it's fine," Stella said. "We're just like four or five days from first sunlight. In a few weeks, it'll be warmer. The station will be accessible." She nodded, more to herself than to him. "Yeah," she said, "I'd put money on us being here for maybe another couple months at most."

"Stella..." Lincoln's voice cracked. He looked away from her, but then he nodded. "A couple months... yeah, okay. What are you going to do when we're rescued?"

Take Tab to Paris, she thought. But it didn't take more than a second for her to remember that Tabitha was gone.

"Go find my dog," she said instead. "Fluff. He's been with my ex too long. It's my turn to take him."

"I'm going to get a job closer to my mom and sisters," Lincoln said. "I'm going to take my nieces to ice cream every week."

"I'm going to climb a mountain," Stella said. "Always wanted to do that."

"See Las Vegas." Lincoln grinned. "Never been."

"Oh, you'll love it," she said. "I loved the magic shows."

"I was thinking show girls." He waggled his eyebrows.

She snorted. "Yeah, okay, heartbreaker. Gonna whisk someone of her feet?"

"Maybe someone'll whisk me off mine," he said.

The door to the kitchens burst open and Abby slid to a stop. "There's a plane! It's circling."

A spike of adrenaline shot through Stella's body. "We've got to get a runway cleared."

"We're already on it," Abby said. "Charlie went with some of the others. They're going to clear the runway enough for the plane to land and then bring whoever is on board back here."

"What kind of plane is it?" Lincoln asked.

"Small. A twin otter, but what else can land safely this time of year?" Abby clapped her hands, her eyes swelling with tears. "We're saved!"

"Have we checked the radio signals?" Stella asked. "We should be able to talk to whoever is flying."

"Adam went to the air traffic control tower," Abby said. "He's communicating with the pilot now, telling him to land in Williams Field."

"Should we go to the field?" Stella stood, and Lincoln made for his outer gear which hung on hooks on the wall.

Abby shook her head. "No, they said to wait here. Everyone that doesn't know how to work the airfield is to meet here to welcome the newcomers and hear whatever news they bring." She held up a handheld radio. "They're going to update us periodically."

"Everybody is going to want some snacks," Lincoln said, springing into motion.

"More of those fries?" Stella asked.

"You bet." Lincoln winked at her.

Stella laughed, and it was light and filled with a hope she wasn't sure she'd ever feel again.

"We need to find everyone," Abby said, "let everyone know."

"I'll come with you," Stella said. "For once, we can spread some good news."

Once their outer gear was pulled on over their clothes, Stella and Abby hustled, shouting with joy in the streets despite the frigid cold and dark sky that had dampened Stella's spirits as of late. Each new person they found joined in their mission to spread the word.

When Stella and Abby returned to Big Blue and entered the cafeteria, it was buzzing with an energy that hadn't been there in a long time.

The smell of fries and mozzarella sticks mixed with the crunch of chips and popcorn. Excited chatter about going home filled the air until Adam Parker appeared, a bottle of whiskey in hand.

"What's goin' on?" he asked, his speech slurred as he shouted above the noise.

The room quieted as all eyes turned on him.

"Not even you can ruin this," Stella said. "A twin otter is landing at Williams Field as we speak."

"So what?" Adam took a long swig.

"So," Abby said, "we're getting out of here."

"On a twin otter?" Adam scoffed and hiccupped at the same time. "Those seat like twenty people." He swept a lazy arm over the cafeteria. "They'd bring a bigger plane if they wanted to rescue us."

"A bigger plane wouldn't be able to land," Lincoln said.

"You're all hatching your eggs before you count," Adam said.

Several booed him, but Stella stood and pointed back toward the door. "You're drunk, like you have been for weeks. Just get out of here, Adam."

"It's not good," he said, pulling out a chair and sitting instead. He leaned toward Becky Steiner who pulled back and waved her hand in front of her nose as he talked. "You'll see. Nothin' but bad news."

Anger stirred in the pit of Stella's stomach as others shouted at Adam to shut his mouth. She marched over to him and grabbed his arm, yanking it hard. "Let's go. You're going to bed. You can be on the last plane out of here, for all I care."

"Leave me alone!" Adam shrugged her off.

He was like a cancer, killing off the hope in the room. The chatter turned worried, and Stella's fury flared brighter. She *needed* that hope, everything in her clawing to keep it close. She snatched the whiskey bottle from Adam, and that got him out of his seat. But when she wouldn't give it back, he shoved her backward.

It was just then that everyone went quiet. Stella flailed as she tried to keep her balance, and the smell of whiskey burned her nostrils as she dropped the bottle, shattering the glass and spattering the floor with liquor. She slammed into something hard but moveable, spun, and caught herself with her hands and knees on the floor.

"Stella?"

That was a new voice. *No,* she thought. *A voice I used to know.* She froze as tears sprung to her eyes. She curled her fingers into fists on the floor. The pure rage she'd had for Adam turned upon this newcomer.

Stiffly, she got to her feet and looked into his face, confirming her suspicions. "Why didn't you come sooner?" she growled.

Calvin Mensa, Tabitha's fiancé, stared at her, confusion written all over a face worn with exhaustion, bruised and battered from who knew what.

"She thought you were dead." Stella pushed him. "She would have stayed if she knew you were coming! Where were you?" She was shouting now, even as Lincoln came up behind her and gently pulled her back.

"Stella," Lincoln said, "that's not his fault."

Calvin looked between Lincoln and Stella, and his eyes grew wide. "Tabitha?" he asked, his voice hoarse.

Hatred stirred for the man until she saw him break. He sank to his knees, and his tears softened her heart. "I tried," he said. "I'm here, now. I tried." He covered his face with his hands, and she noticed a gash on one of them. Between that and his face… someone had hurt him.

Stella closed her eyes. "I'm sorry, Cal," she said, the softness in her voice prompting Lincoln to let her go. She knelt in front of him. "I don't know what I was thinking."

Cal let his hands slide back to his lap. "What happened?" he asked.

"We've lost about half our number in the last month," Stella said.

Fear flashed across his features. "The disease? It's here?"

She shook her head. "No, not the disease we saw on the television months ago, if that's what you mean."

"If that's what I—" He looked around the room, and Stella followed his gaze. Everyone was looking at him, listening, on the edge of their seats, tense and alert. "What do you all know?"

"We know what was said on the news the first several days," Stella said, "and then a team from another station received a communication from a ship. They said there would be no rescue mission, that everyone was dead."

He nodded, and the fact that he didn't deny her statement sent a cold shudder down her spine. "Cal, they were wrong, right? I mean, you've come here to evacuate us?"

Cal laughed, the sudden sound startling Stella. She jumped back from him, hopping to her feet. He just kept laughing. Adam and the dozen or so men who'd brought Calvin here exchanged nervous glances behind him. Lincoln whispered a curse, and murmurs erupted across the cafeteria.

"Cal…" Stella spoke his name hesitantly. Part of her didn't want him to continue. The other part had to know what was going on.

Finally, Cal stopped laughing. He winced and touched an ear, his fingers coming away with blood.

"Are you okay?" Stella asked. The weather in Antarctica was extremely dry. Bloody noses were commonplace, but she didn't think that could affect someone's ears.

"We were," Cal said, "when we left."

Stella looked up at Adam. "Who is he talking about?"

"Hell if I know," Adam said, taking a step away from Cal. "He was the only one who came out of the plane."

"I'd been trying to convince the team in Punta Arenas to organize a rescue mission for months. We thought we were lucky, thought the tip of South America was a safe haven. Last I'd heard, it hadn't spread beyond Brazil." He shook his head and looked up at her, a creeping red rash spreading up his neck. "We were wrong. As soon as it hit our area, I was able to convince them to flee with me, but in the air… one of them had already been infected. I fought to throw them off mid-flight, and I won."

Stella gasped, and she scrambled away from Cal, as did everyone else. "Why did you come here?"

"I had nowhere else to go," he said. "And I thought," his voice was strained, "I thought if I could just see her one more time…" He pressed his palms against his eyes and groaned. "I think I have a fever," he said. "It's *so* hot."

Stella shook her head, noticing a sheen of sweat on Adam's forehead, the redness of his cheeks she'd originally thought were due to the cold outside. She remembered years ago how crazed her aunt had become after falling seriously ill with a blood infection, how the fever and sickness had taken all sense from her.

He's not thinking clearly, she thought. He can't think clearly.

"We're all dead anyway," Cal said, every word pushed past gritted teeth. "There's no escaping it." He leaned forward. "It hurts!" he shouted. "It's getting worse!"

Stella turned and shouted, "Everyone get away from him!"

But she didn't need to tell anyone. People were already scrambling toward another exit. Calvin started screaming, and he raked his fingers down the side of his face as his eyes bulged.

Lincoln pulled at Stella. "C'mon! We have to get out of here."

She turned with him, and she ran. She followed the crowd through Big Blue, Cal's screams following her, panic urging her onward.

"I left my gear," Stella said as they approached a door to the outside.

Lincoln pulled up short. "Me too," he said, panting.

Some burst into the cold, risking frostbite to get as far away from the disease that had killed the world as possible. Others had brought their gear and hastily layered it over their clothes.

"There's gear in the general store," Lincoln said, looking over his shoulder.

They weren't the only ones who'd forgotten their gear in the cafeteria to realize that, it seemed. Others were headed in that direction already.

"We should hurry," Stella said.

It was a madhouse as two dozen people fought for gear in the general store, but Stella and Lincoln managed to grab coats, hats, gloves, and scarves. Her long underwear and trousers would have to do to protect her legs.

When she finally made it outside Big Blue, she made for her living quarters, allowing Lincoln to trail after her. But she only made it a few yards when screaming erupted in all directions. She stopped, heart thrashing inside her chest, her breath coming in short bursts.

It was hard to see what was going on in the dark, but those screams were ones of pain. "Lincoln…" she said. "Do you think it can spread that fast?" She walked backward, away from the sounds.

"Maybe we shouldn't go to the dorms," he said. "Maybe we should go somewhere no one else will think to go."

She nodded, still moving away from those agonized screams. Her heel hit something on the ground, and she tripped, falling backward. She yelped and landed in the snow, her legs resting over… a dead body.

Stella screamed and kicked and crawled in the snow, frantic to get away from that unmoving mass, that bloodied face. It was Adam. He had been with Cal from the moment he'd stepped foot on Antarctic snow. His mouth was open, frozen blood, bright and already edged with frost, coated his lips and chin. One of his eyes hung from its socket.

"Stella…" Lincoln backed away from her. "I'm sorry," he said, and then he turned and ran away from *her*.

She sat there in the snow for only a moment longer as the cold seeped through the two layers protecting her legs. *Move,* she thought, and the tenth time she repeated the word to herself, her body obeyed.

But as she sought a hiding place, the screams continued. The darkness was more pervasive than it had ever been. And a pressure started to build behind her eyes. It was too late. The thing that killed the world had reached the edges of it.

Chapter 7

Alexander Roman and Stella Sharpe

Alex caught his mug before it slid off the galley table as the U.S.S. Bancroft rocked. Ten days at sea, and he had never appreciated land more thoroughly. He'd been seasick for days, and just when his stomach had started to acclimate, they'd hit rough winds. Oliver was constantly on his mind, as was Minnie.

Walter sat beside him, Candice and Lauren across, and Whitlock stood with arms crossed, as sturdy as ever, despite the way the floor pitched.

"We haven't been able to raise anyone on the closer-range radios," Whitlock said. "That's not a good sign. I was hoping the station would be isolated from the disaster, but…" She shook her head. "At this point, I wouldn't count on it. We could see through our binoculars a field of crosses that wasn't there before. That, to me, is bad news."

"Could they have been evacuated?" Alex asked.

"If so, it happened within days. The area is only just now accessible." Whitlock shrugged. "It's possible, but the crosses make me think that disease somehow found its way here. Maybe someone flew in to attempt a rescue despite the dangers."

"The crosses could be a memorial," Alex said. "Like the ones on the side of the road after a car crash. Maybe they're just remembering their loved ones who've died."

"Would they even know what's happened?" Candice asked.

"Not all of it," Whitlock said. "They would have had access to news in the beginning, just like the rest of us, though. A memorial isn't out of the realm of believability."

"So," Walter said. "We don't know what we're walking into. We could be bringing them the worst news of their life."

"Or," Alex said, "there could be no one there at all."

"Or," Lauren said, "we could be walking into a mass grave."

"Exactly." Whitlock put her hands flat on the table and leaned in as if to emphasize her next words. "You four are going to feel it out, let us know what's going on. You'll have handheld radios that should reach me here on the ship as long as you remain close by. Once you update us, we'll decide if we need to organize an evacuation, allow the crew some land time, or get the hell out of here."

"What's that supposed to mean?" Alex tensed. "We didn't come all this way just to turn around and quit."

"It means," Whitlock said, "that if the disease is here, and you have no help to get where you need to go, you'll have little choice in the matter. You can't wander around Antarctica. You'll die. If you find diseased bodies, you find an empty building, quarantine for a couple days, and then we're out of here."

Walter shook his head, as did Lauren, but Alex raised a hand and neither of them spoke. "Let's just see what we find," he said.

He had no intentions of leaving without what they'd come for, but it seemed Whitlock wasn't in the mood to argue. Plus, it was all speculation until they had more information.

"Let's get you four ready to go," Whitlock said. "We'll be docking soon."

* * *

Stella snuggled deeper under her blankets. Thirst nagged at her, but she didn't reach for the water bottle on the floor just a foot or so from her head.

Maybe today, she thought, I'll have the strength to die.

For days after waking, after she'd lost consciousness in the throes of a disease that she was sure would kill her, she'd fought to recover. Stella had survived on the small food and water stores in the chapel where she'd chosen to hide. It was a small building on the outskirts of McMurdo, near the pier, one of the newer buildings the regulars had campaigned for not five years prior. It had solar panels for the summer months and a generator for the winter months.

When walking for a few minutes no longer felt like it would do her in, she'd ventured back into town, certain she would find others. She'd been wrong.

It took days of searching before she'd admitted it to herself: she was the only one left.

The next day, she'd stripped herself naked and, in the dark of winter, stepped into below freezing temperatures. Death by freezing seemed more appealing to her than jumping from a rooftop. But only a few steps into the snow, and the sky became a shade lighter. The sun didn't quite make an appearance, but it was as if God himself had reached out to her through the daylight, asking her to hold on just a while longer.

It hadn't seemed right to leave her friends lying in the cold, on the floor or in the snow, and so she'd burned every body that was left in the station's incinerator. It was meant to incinerate waste, but it did the job. With every single body, she said a few words. It was the best she could do under the circumstances, even though it felt like precious too little.

It had taken days. Days of burning flesh and ash and tears and nice words that no one but her could hear.

After that, she'd gone back to the chapel and waited, for what, she didn't know. Another sign, perhaps. But after a while of that, she'd had enough.

Stella dreamed of dying, but every day, she gave in to her weaknesses. No matter how hard she tried, she hadn't been able to kill that last spark inside that wanted to live.

It was ridiculous. She was only prolonging her death. And yet…

Stella cursed, threw back the sleeping bag, and grabbed the water bottle. Water slid down her throat, cool and refreshing, and she hated it. Hated herself. She screamed and threw the bottle across the room. She screamed again, let all the breath out of her lungs, screamed until her throat hurt.

Devolving into a mess of tears and wailing, Stella brought her knees up and rested her forehead on them. When she could cry no longer, she slumped back onto her sleeping bag and just breathed, looking up at the slanted ceiling as light poured into the sanctuary through stained-glass windows.

"I have to end this," she whispered. "No one's coming. Everyone is dead."

She thought back to her plan to walk out into the Antarctic wilderness, to just die by exposure. Her body would go completely numb.

"I wouldn't feel it," she said, "not after the cold takes over."

And then a long burst of noise filled the air. It startled her, and she sat up, listening as the horn blast faded.

"What the—"

It sounded again.

Stella climbed out of the sleeping bag and to her feet, wobbling a little on unsteady legs. She held up her arm and shielded her eyes from more direct sunlight as she opened the door to peer outside.

There was a ship in Winter Quarters Bay. She blinked and rubbed her eyes, but when she looked again, it was still there. It wasn't a hallucination.

Stella shut the door and backed away. The last time she'd thought she was being rescued hadn't worked out very well.

"But what do I have to lose?" she asked herself.

She shook her head and started to pace, tapping her fingers on her chin.

"What if I'm still contagious? What if *I* infect *them*?"

It had been weeks since she'd been sick, but she had no idea how it worked.

"I'll tell them to leave," she said. "I'll keep my distance, and I'll make them go."

And then, once they were gone and safe, she would end it, knowing she'd done one last good thing.

* * *

Alex was the first to step foot on the snowy pier. With his many layers, the cold was bearable, though Whitlock has said their thermometer read zero degrees. Apparently, they were lucky it was so high.

The sky was clear, though a bit of wind swept flurries of snow across the landscape. Small mountains, black in contrast with patches of white snow, surrounded the bit of flat area where McMurdo Station was constructed. The ship blocked part of the town from view, but from the pier, he could see drab, rectangular buildings of brown and green, with one pop of brighter blue peeking between. The most interesting building was a white chapel set on the outskirts of town. It didn't look as rundown as many of the other buildings, and its shape alone, with a central tower, made it just as unique as the blue building further along.

"It's a bad sign," Walter said as he walked up beside Alex, "that no one's come to see who we are."

"Let's not jump to conclusions." Candice straightened her coat.

Lauren was the last to join them on the pier. "Do we just stroll into town?"

Alex shrugged and started walking. "I don't see any other options."

Behind them, Whitlock called for the gangway to be lifted. There was only one way forward. He led the way over a bridge barely visible beneath the snow. There had to be a road somewhere, but it wasn't marked or visible.

Another bad sign, Alex thought.

But he kept going.

"Look!" Lauren jogged up beside him, her boots crunching snow, and pointed.

A figure came out of the chapel, waving their hands in the air as they approached. Alex picked up speed.

"The station isn't abandoned!" he shouted, relief flooding his body. He smiled and waved back as he and the other three made their way toward the figure.

But the closer they got, the clearer the figure's voice became. When they were perhaps fifteen feet apart, a woman's voice shouted: "Stop! Don't come closer!"

Alex held out his arms on either side, stopping Lauren and Walter. Candice bumped him from behind.

"We're not infected!" Alex shouted back.

"I might be," the woman said. "It's not safe. Everyone else is dead."

"That doesn't make any sense," Lauren said, keeping her voice low.

Walter and Alex exchanged a look, and Walter mumbled, "Not unless…"

"She's a survivor, like me," Candice said, her voice breathy.

"We could compare your samples," Alex said, "figure out commonalities. I still don't know exactly why you survived, Candice."

Walter cupped his hands around his mouth and shouted. "How long have you been alone?"

"It doesn't matter!" she shouted back. "Go away!"

Alex frowned. "How long?" He emphasized each word.

It took a moment, but she responded, "About four weeks, I think."

"Let me talk to her," Candice said. "Follow, but follow slowly. If she's been alone that long… she's probably pretty spooked."

Alex nodded. If anyone could relate among them, it would be her. He let her take the lead, and he kept half a dozen paces behind.

"What are you doing?" the woman shrieked, taking a few steps back.

"It's okay," Candice shouted. "I had it, too, months ago. I didn't die, just like you. You're the only other person like me that I've met, actually. But it's okay. You're not contagious, not at this point."

The woman shifted her weight from foot to foot. "Are you sure?"

"I was with the CDC," Alex said. "I've been studying this disease since the start."

The stranger lifted her hands to her head and rocked on her heels, shaking her head, mumbling something to herself.
"My name is Candice Liddle. What's yours?"
Alex stopped and let Candice keep moving forward. "Let's not make her nervous," he said softly to Walter and Lauren. "She looks frightened."
"Alone out here for four weeks?" Lauren hugged her middle. "I can't imagine."
"Hon," Candice said, "what's your name?"
"Stella," she said at last. "Stella Sharpe."
Candice was within a few feet of the stranger. "You're gonna be okay," she said.
Stella shook her head. "I'll *never* be okay."
Alex's heart broke at the pain in her words. Candice slowly reached out with her thickly gloved hands, cautiously pulling the other woman into a hug. At first, Stella's hands hung limply at her sides, but after a moment, she hesitantly lifted them to hug Candice back. And then she squeezed tighter, and a sob echoed into the cold Antarctic air.
After a few minutes, Stella pulled away. "Sorry," she said. "I just… I thought warning you away would be the last thing I ever did." She cleared her voice and walked forward, Candice by her side. Dark circles under her eyes and greasy hair beneath her hood echoed the desperation in her voice. "What's going on out there?"
"I'm not going to lie," Alex said, "it's bad. Most people are gone. There are pockets of survivors almost everywhere, though, and we came here because the answers to saving those who are left lie in Antarctica."
"What?" Stella shook her head. "What are you talking about?"
"There's a secret research bank," Walter said. "It holds the countermeasures to the disease, to the swarms."
"What are swarms?" Stella asked.
"Is there somewhere we can go to talk?" Alex asked. "Somewhere warmer? We can fill you in, but it's a lot of information."
"We can go back up to the chapel," she said.
And so, Alex and his friends followed Stella through the snow to the little white chapel. It was cold inside, as if Stella hadn't bothered with warming it up. A strong whiff of body odor came from a very thick orange sleeping bag on the floor.
"I've been saving power," Stella said as she pressed a few buttons on a small panel on the wall. "It'll warm up, but it'll be slow. Sorry."
"It's okay," Alex said. "We'll keep our gear on until it gets bearable."
She nodded and grabbed some folding chairs from where they were stacked against the wall. Once they were situated, Alex gave her a summary of current events. He explained why they were there. She asked expected questions, and he and Walter answered them. It always took people a minute or two to process the fact that the government had commissioned the disease and the swarms. Somewhere in the middle of their story, the room warmed, and they all got more comfortable.
When they were done, Stella told them about her life the last three months, about a mass suicide that took the life of her friend, about a man who'd come to them, delirious, and sick, about the last four weeks, living alone and afraid, angry and longing for death herself.
"That sounds… terrible," Candice said when Stella had finished.
"It was," Stella said.
"I have some medical training," Lauren said. "Do you mind if I look you over?"
"I'm going to radio Whitlock," Alex said after Stella had agreed to Lauren's examination. "She needs to know what's happened here, and we need to come up with a plan. Walter, do you want to come with me?"
"Outside?" Walter asked.
"Yeah," Alex said. "We can give Stella a little privacy for her examination."
He and Walter left the chapel after putting their coats back on, and Alex radioed Whitlock to fill her in on what they'd learned.
"So, the disease found its way here, too," Whitlock said.
Alex held the radio to his mouth. "Yes, but I'm hoping the survivor can help us find what we need."
"We should leave," Whitlock said. "It's not safe."
"We won't go near any of the bodies," Alex said. "This is our only chance to secure the future of humanity. We have to get to Barlow."
There was a long pause. Too long. Alex frowned and looked at Walter.
"They can't seriously be considering going back after all that we've done to get here," Walter said.
"That's what it sounds like," Alex said. He spoke into the radio again. "Whitlock? Are you still there?"
The speaker crackled. "We have enough supplies to stay here forty days."
"Okay," Alex said. "How many of your people can you spare?"
"My people aren't trained for this kind of mission," Whitlock said. "I can't risk their lives, and we need every single one of them if we're going to make it back home."
"We have to find the research bank, conduct experiments, and transport what we need back here," Alex said. "What if we run out of time? I have no idea how long that's going to take."
"It'll have to take forty days or less," Whitlock said.
Alex wanted to throw the radio as frustration made his skin crawl.
Walter put a hand on Alex's arm. "We're going to have to do our best," he said.
"Fine," Alex spat into the radio. "I'll update you when we know more." He roughly put the radio back in his pocket.
"Alex, we don't even know if Stella *can* help us." Walter looked back at the chapel. "She's unstable, and she said she was a general assistant. I don't even know what that means. It sure doesn't sound like someone who knows how to get us to the research bank."
"Well," Alex said, "she's all we've got. We made it to freaking Antarctica, Walter." He turned back toward the chapel, stepping toward it with determination. "I'm not going to let anything stop me now."

Chapter 8

Zara Williams

Zara flung curtains aside, losing her balance as bright red fabric entangled her. Lizzy's cries ate away at her insides. She stumbled into the makeshift room at the back of the shop in which they'd made a temporary home. Her hand stung as she whacked it against the wall, but she kept her head from hitting, too. She regained her feet but immediately fell to her knees beside Lizzy.
"Liz! Stop it!" Zara grabbed hold of Lizzy's wrist as her fingernails scraped long gouges down one arm.
Lizzy's eyes were closed. She was sweating, twisting and turning. "Restore the Mother! Restore the Mother!" She screamed the words over and over.
Zara struggled against Lizzy's surprising strength, attempting to prevent her friend from harming herself. "Lizzy! Wake up!" She slapped Lizzy across the face, harder than she'd intended. Her hands flew to her mouth as Lizzy's eyes popped open.
"Azalea!" Lizzy shouted, breathing hard, looking in all directions. She held up her hands and rubbed at her wrists, whimpering. "It burned," she said in a small voice. "The smoke… the flames."
"Liz," Zara said, "there's no fire. You're safe."
Lizzy touched the wound on her arm and winced. It was bleeding, the skin around the gouges already inflamed, pink and raised and angry. "I'm sorry," she said.
"No, it's okay." Zara crawled over to Lizzy and wrapped her arm around her best friend's shoulders. "It was a nightmare, that's all."
"No, Zee, it was a memory," Lizzy said, "or partly." She closed her eyes.
Zara's stomach pinched. "They burned you," she said, knowing it was a possibility, hoping that the burn marks Lauren had found on Lizzy's legs had been from something else.
"They tied to me to a stake," Lizzy said, "outside. Set fire to a pyre. It was a test," she said, "and I passed. I… I did exactly what they wanted me to do." With a trembling hand, she wiped the sweat off her forehead. "But in the dream, I called out the right words, and Azalea didn't come because she was already dead."
Those sick bastards, Zara thought, but she kept her anger to herself. She'd learned when Lizzy first started opening up that any sign of anger shut her right back down again.
"I'm sorry that happened to you," Zara said instead, trying her best to keep her tone even and empathetic. She couldn't let her fury at *them* leak into her conversations with Lizzy.
"I should get a bandage or something," Lizzy said, holding up her arm. Blood welled up in long lines and then spilled over the edges of swollen skin in thin, delicate lines.
Zara hopped up and grabbed one of the towels they'd been given for bathing. It would have to do. She would bleach it later. "I'll go get some antibiotic ointment," she said as she handed the towel over. "Will you be okay while I go find some."
Lizzy nodded. "Yeah. I'm not going to sleep again any time soon."
Zara slipped outside the curtained area to find Kai pacing not far from it. Blythe was unmoving behind a folding table set up along the wall. It was full of maps and equipment, just like what they'd set up back at the academy in Colorado Springs. The three of them were at it again, mapping possible routes to areas likely to still be populated. They needed something to do, there in a place that was not their home, with people who clearly saw them as guests and guests only. And besides, the routes and calculations could be useful when Alex got back.
Until then, the four of them shared a small shop in the indoor shopping center. They set it up with two smaller curtained rooms in the back corners, one for the ladies and one for the gentlemen.
Zara had been relieved when they'd gotten a space bigger than a closet. New Zealanders, or Kiwis, as they preferred to be called, treated their guests well.
Kai stopped moving and faced her, crossing his arms and mouthing, "What was that?"
"It was just a nightmare," she said, not bothering to keep silent.
Kai gave her a flat look. He took her arm and pulled her out into the hall. Blythe raised his eyebrows and ducked his head as they passed by. "We can hear everything," he whispered. "She's hurting herself now? You can't be the only one taking care of her. Ever since Walter left—"
"It'll be fine." Zara sighed and pinched the bridge of her nose. "I'm sorry I cut you off. Kai, I just want to bandage her up, okay? I'm too tired to have this conversation."
"That's the point I'm trying to make," he said. "You're barely sleeping. You need help."
"She needs me right now," Zara said, raising her voice. There were others in the massive hall, of course, but she didn't care. She didn't have the capacity to use much of a filter.
"You can't keep punishing yourself for what happened at that compound when those lunatics took her," Kai said.
"Why don't you let me worry about me," Zara snapped. She held up a hand. "We'll talk about this later. I'm going to get some bandages for Liz."
"Zara—"
"She's bleeding, Kai. I'm not going to let her get an infection." Zara walked away without another word. Sometimes, it felt like she and Kai were an old married couple, bickering like that, even though she wasn't sure they were a *couple* at all.
More thoughts for another day. She sighed at herself.

Those lining the halls—sitting in lawn chairs, bent over laundry, minding their children—they watched her as she walked with sideways glances as if perhaps if they only stared at her in short intervals, she wouldn't notice. And the way they looked at her…

It occurred to her that it was likely everyone nearby might be able to hear Lizzy's outbursts, too. The walls of the shops were thin. She could hear mumbles through their own walls when someone was talking in the next room.

She bit the inside of her cheek. The last thing they needed was for everyone there to think Lizzy was crazy.

But what can I do about it?

She didn't have an answer. Her shoes slid across the smooth floor, the soft *swish-swish* whispering to all those she passed how exhausted she truly was. Lifting her feet so as to avoid the sound was too much effort.

At the center of the great hall, beneath the domed skylight, she found the person for whom she was looking: Mateo Boone, a local who seemed to command the respect and deference of everyone else in Whitlock's absence. She hadn't been *told* that he was in charge, but he certainly knew how to get things done.

"Hey, Mateo?" Zara approached him.

He was talking to the woman who organized the food team. "How many?" he asked.

"As many as I can get, I'd say," the woman responded.

Zara cleared her throat.

Mateo looked at her and frowned. "Well, don't you look knackered?"

Zara blinked. "Um… thanks?"

The woman laughed. "He means, you look like you've been hit by a bus."

"Oh." Zara shrugged. She couldn't argue with that.

"Watcha need?" Mateo asked.

"My friend, Lizzy… she needs some antibiotic ointment, maybe some gauze to wrap her arm. She scratched herself up pretty good." Zara swallowed and avoided direct eye contact, hoping Mateo wouldn't ask how she was injured.

"You'll want to go ask Nyree about that," Mateo said. "She's in charge of our medicinal stores. Hers is the shop with bright yellow curtains, on the left." He pointed down the hall, opposite of where Zara was living.

"Thanks," Zara said.

He nodded once, picked up a clipboard, and went on his way. He was a busy man, always moving from person to person, with that clipboard in hand.

Zara walked the rest of the way down the hall and stopped in front of the shop Mateo had indicated. The gate was up, which she'd found meant whoever occupied the shop didn't mind visitors, but the curtains were drawn across the opening, so she knocked on the glass.

A few seconds later, a curtain was pulled back and a young woman a few years older than Zara looked her up and down. "Zara, is it?" she asked, her tone curious.

Zara nodded. "And you're Nyree?"

"That's me." Nyree smiled warmly.

"Mateo said you might be able to help me," Zara said. "I need some antibiotic ointment, if you have it, and some gauze or bandages or something to wrap my friend's arm. She has three scratches, maybe three or four inches long each."

"Ah, yes. Your friend is having a lot of trouble, I hear." Nyree tied back the curtain and motioned to a wooden stool whose gnarled legs and varying shades spoke of a handmade piece. The sunlight from the hall made the yellow curtains glow, and there were candles placed about the room for more light. "You can have a sit while I see what I've got."

Zara entered the space, freezing for a second at the sight of an older man behind a wooden table. He looked up at her and smiled a halfway-toothless grin. Every square inch of his face was wrinkled, but there was a life in his eyes that sparkled. Stacks of wood piled high behind him, and a small, circular piece of wood was at his fingertips.

"Hello." Zara offered a small wave.

"Kia ora," he said.

"That's a Maori greeting," Nyree said without looking back at her.

"Oh," Zara cleared her throat and tried to repeat the words. "Kia ora." She slid onto the stool. "You're a woodworker?" she asked.

"A master carver," the man said. "My name is Mahaka. Nyree is my granddaughter." He tapped a jade necklace hanging from his neck. "I used to work more in pounamu, but my stone carving equipment requires electricity." He smiled down at the wooden piece—a fish hook, it seemed. "But wood has its own beauty, each piece its own history."

Nyree ran her finger along a row in a shoe organizer and plucked a tube from one of the pockets. "Here we are," she said. "And…" She pulled an off-white roll out of another pocket. "…you can use this like gauze." She retrieved a small jar and handed that and the roll over to Zara. Then, she squeezed some of the ointment into another jar that was even smaller, grabbed a handful of cotton swabs, and handed those over as well. "Use the antibiotic ointment sparingly," she said. "Layer it on first, once a day using the swabs. Keep the wound moist at all times with coconut oil—" She pointed to the small jar filled with a solid white substance. "—which has antimicrobial properties." She indicated the roll of fabric. "That's the best we can do for a wrap. It's repurposed fabric, torn into strips, and bleached. Bring it back every night. I'll clean it, and you can take a fresh roll."

"Wow," Zara said, "thanks. This is perfect."

"Now, what about you?" Nyree asked. "What do you need? A good sleep, I think." She turned back to her shoe organizers and pulled out a small cloth bundle. "Loose leaf tea," she said as she added that to Zara's bundle. "Drink it before bed. It will help."

Zara frowned at it. "Do I plop the whole bundle in?"

Nyree wrinkled her nose. "Don't you have a strainer?"

"A what?"

Mahaka chuckled and shook his head.

"Stop by the kitchens, see if they have a strainer about," Nyree said. "It's a little metal thing with holes in it. You fill it with the tea leaves, and then let it sit in the hot water for a bit until it's done."

"I'm more of a coffee girl," Zara said.

Nyree clucked her tongue as if she were an old woman chastising a child. "Coffee won't help you sleep."

"Okay," Zara said, "I'll try it. Thank you." She slipped off the stool, her hands full, and hesitated. It wasn't that she didn't want to go back. It was only… would she ever be able to rest there? Would Lizzy ever get better?

"Your friend…" Nyree said cautiously. "She has been through something terrible, eh?"

Zara nodded.

"And you… you have, too?"

Zara looked at Nyree and frowned. "Not like her," she said.

Nyree shrugged. "Does one person's pain make another person's pain smaller?"

"Sometimes," Zara said.

"Perspective," Mahaka said from behind her, "does not make pain less. If your pain hurts *you*, it is big enough to care about."

Zara looked back at him, stared at him for a minute. "I don't know how to help Lizzy," she said. "That's part of my pain." She lifted the load in her hands. "Taking care of her helps, besides the fact that I owe it to her."

"Still, healing is needed for you both," Mahaka said.

Nyree put a hand on Zara's shoulder. "When you come back tomorrow to get fresh bandages, make some time to talk to us some more. A master carver does more than make shapes out of stone or wood. What he crafts carries meaning. Maybe we can help."

"I don't know what that means, exactly," Zara said, "but I can use all the help I can get." She smiled. "You two would get along with Minnie."

"Sweet as," Nyree said. Zara must have looked confused because Nyree's smile widened. "I'm agreeing with you," she said. "I've already decided Minnie's to come to dinner soon. I took over her care when the medic left with Whitlock, and I like her a lot." Nyree led Zara back to the hall with a gentle hand on her back. "Let me know if you need anything else."

"I'll see you tomorrow," Zara said, "and thanks again."

She walked the hall slowly, her hands full, and she thought about what Mahaka and Nyree had said about her own pain. Of course, Kai had been trying to say something similar, in his own way.

When she reached their living quarters, she stopped on her way to the partitioned room where Lizzy would be to kiss Kai's cheek.

"What's that for?" he asked. "I thought you were mad at me."

She shrugged. "I had some time to think about it," she said, "and you're not wrong."

"You mean I'm right?" he asked.

"I mean, you're not wrong." She narrowed her eyes at him, a smile tugging one corner of her mouth.

He laughed. "I'll take it," he said.

She let her smile take over, and let Kai kiss the top of her head. Admitting she needed help, that she needed healing, wasn't easy when she'd been downplaying her own hurt for so long, but it was also freeing, to think that she wouldn't always carry the same heavy burdens.

Maybe, she thought, sometime soon, it'll be time for the whole world to heal.

Chapter 9

Stella Sharpe

Stella scoffed. "I think I'd rather not." Every muscle in her body had tensed as Alex had rolled out a map and started asking her questions. When it became clear he thought she was going with them, she had planted her feet firmly and crossed her arms.

"We need you," Alex said. "We don't know anything about the terrain, not to mention the fact that your blood in comparison with Candice's could help me confirm what to bring back. There could be information at Barlow detailing vaccines for dozens of strains of DV-10. I'll need to conduct experiments to know which vaccine will work for the strain that was released."

"I've been here, alone, for weeks. I've seen all my friends die." Stella's cheeks warmed as her stomach turned. "I can't stay here."

Walter, at least, had the decency to *look* apologetic as he spoke. "That ship isn't leaving here for another forty days," he said.

"Better on that ship than out there," Stella waved in the general direction of the map. "Do you have any idea how crazy your plan is? How likely you are to die? All you have is a point on a map, in the middle of nowhere, I might add." Her voice pitched higher with every word. "How do you know this research bank is still functional?"

"It has to be," Alex said.

"It's all we've got left," Walter added.

Lauren and Candice stayed out of it. Stella hadn't been able to figure those two out yet. Neither of them seemed to have much to say. They let Alex and Walter run the show.

That wasn't exactly Stella's style.

"I've never heard of this Barlow Scientific Research Bank," Stella said, shaking her head. "There are very few year-round stations on this continent, especially when you start moving inland."

"But there are stations which are built to be self-sufficient for many months," Alex said.

"Yes," Stella said. "Every permanent station has the capability to be self-sufficient." She straightened. "Oh, no…"

Shame pierced Stella's chest as she looked at the map. She leaned over it, her fingers brushing the paper.

"What is it?" Alex asked.

"There are still people out there," Stella said.

"That's what we've been saying," Walter said. "Barlow is supposed to be manned year-round. It's a secret facility, so it's not surprising you've never—"

"No," Stella said, "I mean, here." She pointed at Admunsen-Scott South Pole Station. "And here." Her finger slid to Concordia. "And here." Again, to Vostok. "There are small crews that winter-over in every year-round station. I've been so wrapped up in McMurdo… it's been so long since we've had contact with others… I don't know why I didn't think about it before." She looked up. "We have to do something. We have to get them out."

"No," Alex said, "we have to get to Barlow."

Stella backed away from the map, her priorities changing as quickly as her mind could process her own thoughts. "Those coordinates are in the Transantarctic Mountains. We would have to cross the Ross Ice Shelf along the South Pole Traverse for three hundred and seventy-five miles, and then veer *off* of the approved, safe route and travel in unknown conditions for two hundred miles. If you want me to help you with that, you're going to have to help me give those people a shot."

"How are we supposed to do that?" Walter asked.

"I don't know," Stella said. "But most places don't expect a resupply for another month or two, and my guess is that they've been rationing. Everyone had access to the news for five days."

"Stella," Alex said, "there's nothing we can d—"

"We can talk to Captain Whitlock," Lauren said, stepping up. "Maybe they can think through a rescue mission."

"Let me talk to this captain," Stella said.

Alex sighed and unclipped his radio from his belt, handing it over. "She's not easily persuaded."

Stella held the radio to her mouth as an idea came to mind. "Captain Whitlock? This is Stella Sharpe speaking."

"Heard," came the reply. "Stand by." And then, a few minutes later, another voice said, "This is the captain."

"There are possibly hundreds of people left alive on this continent," Stella said. "Some of them are hard to reach. We got hit with the disease because someone who was sick brought it here, but we're isolated. The other stations along the coasts could be just fine."

"We're not equipped to rescue the entire continent," Whitlock said.

"I understand that, but Alex needs my help, and in exchange, I need you to help me. Maybe you can explore the coastal stations closer to McMurdo. Maybe you can use that fancy ship of yours to send out a signal, try to reach the South Pole station, tell them to meet you at McMurdo in forty days. Do *something*."

"We did do something," Whitlock said. "We're here, aren't we?"

"That's it?" Stella asked, her mouth dropping open.

Alex shrugged as if say, "I told you so."

Stella narrowed her eyes and pressed the button on the side of the radio. "So, you're telling me that instead of trying to save more lives, you're going to what? Just sit on your asses for forty days? I thought I might be the last person alive on the entire planet. For weeks, I was alone and cut off from everyone and everything. This place was going to be my grave. I had nothing." She paused for a breath, the passion in her chest growing as she willed the captain to really *hear* her. "You have an entire ship. You have forty days. And you're saying that you can't send a few signals? Mosey along the coastline and check out a few stations? Is that the kind of person you are?" She let the button go and waited.

"Not bad," Alex said, nodding.

The speaker crackled to life. "We can send out a signal, but I can't guarantee it'll be heard."

"Better than nothing," Stella said.

"And I can check out these nearby stations," Whitlock said. "I won't expose my crew, though. I can see what I can see from the ports, try to raise survivors on the radio."

"Deal." Stella nodded at Alex. "Thank you, captain."

"Well, no one's ever accused me of sitting on my ass," she said. "Don't want to start disappointing my momma now."

Lauren smirked. "I guess we've found our new speechmaker."

Candice smiled and shook her head, and Stella frowned.

"Alex usually makes the speeches around here," Walter said.

"Okay, okay," Alex said, making a settle-down motion with his hands. "We've all made a speech or two over the last few months."

Stella handed back the radio. "I meant every word of it."

"We always do," Alex said.

Candice took her hand and patted it. "You're going to fit in just fine."

"So," Alex said, tapping the map with two fingers. "Can we get back to this?"

"It's almost six hundred miles," Walter said. "There's no hiking that."

"Not if we want to get back here anytime soon." Lauren stepped up to the table.

"The first explorers did it," Stella said. "They got to the south pole on dog sleds. Of course, a whole lot of them died…"

"Do you know how to stay alive out there?" Candice asked.

Stella nodded. "I know enough. I think. We'll have to use the snowcats," Stella said. "It's the only way I can think of to *maybe* get us there fast enough."

"What are those?" Alex asked.

"They're like tractors. It's usually how they take supplies up to Admunsen-Scott." Stella bit the inside of her cheek as she started to make a list in her head of what they'd need. "Of course, once we get to the mountains here—" She pointed at the map. "—there might not be a path forward for the snowcats."

"Don't tractors take fuel?" Candice asked.

"Yeah," Stella said. "We've got AN8 stored in buried chambers. It freezes at minus seventy degrees Fahrenheit. Those chambers never get below minus fifty-five. Luckily, we should stay in the positive single digits most of the time, no lower than minus ten. It'll be safe to lug around our fuel."

"Sounds straight forward enough," Alex said.

"No," Stella said, "that's just the beginning." She licked her lips. "I barely know what I'm doing out there. You guys have to swear to me that you won't do anything without asking. And do everything I tell you to do."

"Scout's honor." Alex raised two fingers.

"You're the boss when we're on the road," Walter said.

"I need a pen and paper," Stella said. "I've got to start making lists." She walked to the back of the sanctuary, through a door, and into an office. She didn't go in there often. It was mostly books. But she found what she was looking for and came back with a pad of paper and a pen, scribbling items, one after another.

"How long before we'll be ready to leave, do you think?" Alex asked.

"A few days at least," Stella said, her mind spinning with all they had to do. "We'll have to scour the station for the supplies we need."

"Give us lists," Walter said, "and tell us where we can find things, and we'll get it done."

That gave Stella an idea. She looked to the wall where a map of McMurdo was framed. "Get that map," she said. "Lay it out on the table. It's got building numbers on it. I can include numbers next to every item so that you know where to look."

Candice and Lauren were on it before she'd finished her sentences. Stella ripped off the top paper. "This is a list of clothing items every person needs. You have some of it, but you'll need more. If you can replace anything on your body with something wool, do it. We've got the Skua Thrift Shop and the General Store in Big Blue." She pointed to the buildings as Lauren laid the map out over top the continent map. She handed the list to Alex.

"What about bodies?" Alex asked. "It's so cold, the disease might be preserved on the dead."

"I've burned them," Stella said. "They're… gone. I had to bring each one to the incinerator. Figured it would be better than letting their bodies rot inside or stay frozen like statues."

They all stared at her then, and she frowned back as they exchanged glances.

"H-how many?" Lauren asked.

"All of them. All that were left, anyway." Something pricked Stella's heart, something that reminded her how horrible it had been, how horrible the experience must *sound* to someone who hadn't survived by shutting off their emotions. She tried to make it better. "Sixty-nine," she said. "The other eighty were dead and gone before the disease got here. I told you all about what had happened after you told me your story. This isn't news."

"The numbers," Alex said, "those are new to us."

"I'm sorry," Candice said.

And that's when she recognized that look in their eyes: pity. Four people who had seen their share of death and destruction pitied *her*.

"I can't…" Stella swallowed hard. Even the tiniest crack in the walls she'd put up leaked enough pain to make her vision blur with tears. "I can't process all of that… emotionally," she said. "I need to just keep moving, for now, until we get back, until I'm safe, until I have time."

One by one, they nodded. They changed the subject. They started moving, started working. They seemed to understand that pushing her even a little would break her. Physical work, she could handle. Give her hundreds of miles. Give her freezing temperatures and dangerous winds. Give her impossible odds.

She could handle that as long as no one asked her how she was really doing on the inside.

Stella stored that look they'd given her away, chose not to think about it, not to think about anything except her new purpose. It was good to have a purpose again. She wouldn't go out a pathetic mess of greasy hair and tears.

She *was* going to do one last good thing, only it was going to be bigger than warning away a few innocent people. She was going to help save *everyone*.

And then, she would rest alongside her friends, there in a frozen little town on the rim of the world.

Chapter 10

Oliver Roman

If his dad couldn't keep promises, nobody could.
Oliver didn't blame him, not really. When he thought about how he'd been left behind, it sometimes made him angry, but it was easy enough to understand why his dad had done it. Minnie needed someone, after all, and no matter how nice Zara, Kai, and Blythe were, they didn't love Minnie like Oliver and his dad and Lauren did. Plus, those three had Lizzy to take care of, and that was enough for *anybody*.
Still, something had changed inside Oliver over the past couple of weeks. He felt older, but not in a good way.
Why does everything have to be confusing? he thought as he stared up at the ceiling of the little room he and Minnie and Samson shared. The others had gotten one of the empty shops, but Minnie had insisted the room they'd first been put in was good enough for them. And it was plenty of space for two people and a dog, especially when the entire hall outside their room was free to roam. They'd gotten real cots, even if they were low to the ground, and a chair for the corner, and even a game of checkers. Oliver couldn't argue that it was enough space, and yet…
I just want to be alone sometimes, he thought. None of this is fair. I miss my old room. I miss my mom. I miss my friends and my school and my basketball hoop.
But those were childish thoughts, weren't they? His dad was out in Antarctica fighting polar bears or something to save the world, and all he had to do was put up with being bored.
Are there polar bears in Antarctica? he thought. No, that wasn't right. He'd learned that last year in school. Polar Bears were north not south.
He sighed and sat up. His legs itched to move, to do something. He'd been glad when Minnie had gone on a walk with her cane, glad that Samson went with her. Not glad to be rid of them, just glad to have time by himself. He'd had that, and he didn't want it anymore, though.
I'll go find Minnie and Samson. Maybe get a snack. He stood up, and his stomach grumbled at the thought of food.
That was a change he'd been able to easily identify: he was hungry *all* the time. He bent his knees and straightened them again, trying to see if he could tell whether he was growing taller like Minnie had said the other day. Door knobs seemed at about the same height.
I'm always going to be short.
That soured his mood a little. Shoulders slumped, he took a step toward the door right when Minnie opened it, huffing and puffing as stronger light poured into the place.
Oliver jumped back and yelped, and then his cheeks warmed at his reaction, at being startled so easily. He laughed it off. "You scared me," he said.
Minnie hobbled in without closing the door and sat on the chair. "Were you gonna leave without turnin' off the lantern?" She narrowed her eyes at him, and despite the way she couldn't catch her breath, she managed to keep her scolding voice on point. Samson trotted in behind her, wagging his tail and sticking his head under Oliver's hand so that he would scratch it.
"Sorry," Oliver said, shrugging as he gave in to Samson's demands for attention. "Are you okay?"
"Fit as a fiddle," Minnie said.
"You're breathing pretty hard." Oliver frowned at her.
"Child, I'm fine as frog's hair split four ways," she said.
Oliver wrinkled his nose. "That's a weird one."
She leaned back, hung her cane on the chair's back, and breathed out one impossibly long breath. "Woo-hee," she said. "I ain't gotten that winded from takin' a walk in… well, never, I'd say."
"Does your leg still hurt?" Oliver asked.
"A little," she said. "But two weeks have done it some good. It'll be sore for a while, and I ain't gonna run no marathon anytime soon." She barked a laugh. "I 'spose that particular feat wasn't in my future anyhow."
Oliver shook his head. He couldn't help but smile. How does she always do that? Make everything seem okay even when it's not?
"I've got news for ya," she said.
He backed up and sat on his cot, his chest feeling lighter as he let Samson crawl on top of him to lick his arms and tug on the hem of his shirt. He laughed and pushed the dog playfully, rolling off his cot and onto the floor, wrestling with Samson. "What's that?" he asked as he avoided a slobbering tongue to his face.
"They got a school here," Minnie said.
Oliver sat up and made a face like he'd just been forced to eat asparagus. "That's not good news."
"Sure it is." Minnie had that look, like arguing with her wouldn't do much good. "I asked if you could go on and join 'em, and the teacher—Mrs. Zhang—she said she'd love it if you joined. There's not a lot of kids, maybe a dozen."
"No thanks," Oliver said.
"Well, I guess I ain't really askin'," Minnie raised both eyebrows and stared him down.
Oliver groaned. "Minnie, I don't want to."
"You've been sittin' around doin' nothin' for too long," she said. "It ain't good for a boy your age."
"I'm pretty sure most of my life over the past few months hasn't been good for a boy of any age," Oliver said.

"Don't you sass me." Minnie tsked. "I told Mrs. Zhang you'd be there in a bit, and you'll not make me a liar, you hear? I'm worried about ya, boy. You need somethin' to occupy your thoughts, somethin' other than whatever's gotten you so down lately."

Oliver closed his eyes and flopped back on the floor. Minnie was worried. About him.

Take care of Minnie, Oliver thought.

"Okay," he said. "Fine. I'll try it." He opened his eyes and arched his back so he was looking at Minnie upside down. "But if I hate it, do I have to keep going?"

"We ain't gonna be here long," Minnie said, a little more softly, and there really did seem to be concern in her eyes. "This is your shot to be a kid, Oliver. Get out there and be with others your own age. Have some normal interactions while we're somewhere safe."

"When do I have to go?" Oliver asked.

"Soon as you brush your hair and change your shirt." Minnie made a face. "We ain't raisin' no hooligan."

He groaned again as he rolled onto his stomach and reached under his cot for one of his folded shirts. He pulled it out, stood, and stomped over to the corner where they'd put up a divider to dress behind. There was a mirror there, as well, and it served well as a changing room. A little bit of deodorant and few brushes with a comb, and he stepped out to get Minnie's approval.

"Is this good enough?"

Minnie smiled. "Those girls won't know what hit 'em."

"Miiinnniieee. Gross!" Oliver shuddered. Everyone said one day soon he'd start thinking about girls in a different way, but he didn't think so.

Minnie just laughed.

"Where is it?" Oliver asked, sighing, trying to push away the frustration at being laughed at when he didn't think it was very funny. He picked up his bag—the one his mother had made, the one that held all his treasures—and fitted it crossbody so that it rested against his hip.

Minnie stood and slowly moved to her cot, lowering herself with the help of the wall. "Go right when you step out the door, then all the way down the hall. They're the only shop without curtains."

"You need anything before I go?" Oliver asked.

"Nah," Minnie said. "I'm gonna take a nice long nap. Leave the lantern on, though. Otherwise, I can't see worth a hoot if I need to get up."

He did as she asked, and he shut the door behind him as he stepped out into the wide hallway. The natural light gave the impression that when one breathed in, there should be a fresh smell to the air, but instead, he got an odd mixture of body odor and stew from the kitchen area.

Oliver didn't move for a minute. The hallway wasn't crowded, exactly, but there were people, some walking, some hanging out together, some working. They were all strangers. He felt small, even smaller than usual. He lowered his head and turned to his right, forcing his feet to carry him forward.

The further he walked, the more irritated he got. He wasn't a little kid anymore. Wasn't he old enough to make some of his own decisions?

I don't want to do this, he thought. I don't want to. I don't want to. I don't—

"Oliver?"

A voice behind him made him turn quickly, his shoes squeaking on the floor. It was an older woman, small but sturdy, dark eyes curious, smile friendly.

"The class is here," she said, pointing over her shoulder. "Your... grandma?"

Oliver shrugged. "Might as well be," he said.

"Well, she said you'd be coming, so I've been keeping an eye on the hall. I'm Mrs. Zhang." She held out a hand, inviting him inside.

Oliver took a few steps and then stopped at the sight of a dozen pairs of eyes staring right at him through the glass. A lump formed in his throat, and he gripped the long handle of his mother's bag.

"You can do this," his mom's voice echoed in his head. "You can do *anything*."

Oliver nodded once, and strode right through the door, finding a seat at the back on the floor and sitting cross-legged behind everyone else.

Mrs. Zhang continued to the front of the room, and she had everyone introduce themselves, including Oliver. He didn't say much, just what she told him he *had to* say, and he got it over with as quickly as he could. She smiled at him warmly, even though he rushed through her questions, and he decided she wasn't so bad.

The lesson wasn't so bad either. She was reading *The Swiss Family Robinson* out loud, stopping to talk about vocabulary words. After the chapter was done, she used the events to give them all word problems to solve. Oliver was able to solve them in no time at all. It was actually sort of fun.

When she was done, and she dismissed the class, Oliver was in better spirits than he'd anticipated. Though Mrs. Zhang excused herself, she encouraged the kids to stay and chat in the room that was set aside for them. Apparently, students could come there any time just to read or play board games with each other or study.

Maybe Minnie was right, Oliver thought as he stood at the back of the class. The older kids, a group of six, were congregating in the middle as adults came to collect the younger ones.

He cautiously walked up to them and just stood there for a minute, hoping that maybe if he was there long enough, he would *seem* like part of their group and someone would talk to him.

A boy named Will scoffed at something one of the girls had said about liking the book. "It's boring," he said. "I'm keen to pitch it in the rubbish bin if I get half the chance. I've done more interesting things in real life!"

The other kids groaned. "We've heard all your stories, Will," the girl, Ava, said. She looked through the middle of two other kids right at Oliver. "Maybe he's got new ones," she said.

The crowd parted, and Oliver took half a step back, looking from one person to the next. "Me?" he asked.

Will crossed his arms. "He doesn't have anything," he said. "Look at 'im!"

That made Oliver's jaw clench and his hands tighten into fists. "I have lots of stories," Oliver said.

Ava nodded and pointed at him. "See? He's come halfway around the world, Will. What have you done besides fight off the lolly factory boys in a parking lot?"

"Who are they?" Oliver asked.

"Those kids that attacked your plane," Will said. "They live in the lolly factory down the way. Everyone knows that. Are you stupid? He doesn't know anything! And yeah, I did fight 'em off! They were savages!"

"That story gets bigger every time he tells it," another girl said, thought Oliver didn't see which one had said it.

Niko, another boy, chimed in. "First time it was two boys. Last time it was twenty!"

Five of them roared in laughter while Will's face grew five shades redder. "That's not true!" he shouted. Then, he crossed his arms and looked at Oliver. "Fine. Tell a story, little Oli."

Oliver blinked at that name. His mother had called him that, and no one had since. "Don't call me that," he said.

"Why not?" Will's smirk came back. "A wittle baby nickname for a wittle baby boy." He laughed. "Seems right to me."

"I'm not a baby!" Oliver yelled.

"Then, tell a story," Will said, grinning at him like he'd already won.

But Oliver had plenty of stories. He lifted his chin. "A plane crashed right into a Ferris Wheel I was on, and I got out of that." Never mind that he clung to his father the whole way down. "I've been in *two* fires. I have a friend back in the States who's a biker as tough as they come. And I even met a serial killer."

The other kids' eyes went wide, all except for Will's. He puckered his lips and used a voice like he was talking to an infant. "Did you do it all with your wittle bitty purse, baby Oli?"

"I said not to call me that!"

Oliver lunged forward, grabbed Will's shirt, and pulled as hard as he could. The other boy swung around, tripped over his own two feet, and fell to the ground. His back to the other kids, Will's angry expression twisting tighter on his face as he got to his feet with fists at the ready, Oliver froze.

What did I do? Panic welled up inside. He hadn't meant to do that, had he?

"Oliver Roman!" Minnie's stern voice demanded attention. She was in the doorway, staring wide-eyed at him like he'd grown horns and a tail. "Tell me I did not just see you push that boy to the ground." She hobbled in with her cane, her gaze fixed on Oliver.

Will's glare softened to a smile. "Your nanna come to get you, wittle Oli? Just like the littles?"

Minnie's cane whipped out and hit Will's shin hard. She didn't even look at him. He yelped and hopped back, gaping at Minnie. Oliver started to laugh, but the look Minnie gave him told him it would be better for him to keep it in.

"So sorry," she said, still not giving him enough attention to even glance at him. "My cane's a slippery sucker." She narrowed her eyes. "Oliver. We're leaving. Right now."

She stepped to the side, and he quickly walked out into the hall. She followed him, whispering harshly.

"What in Sam Hill are you doin', Oliver? I can't believe—"

"He made fun of my bag," Oliver said, "and he called me a baby, twice."

She licked her lips. "Just because he's a bully don't mean you have to be."

"He wouldn't stop calling me Oli. My mom is the only one who calls me that," Oliver said. He looked down at his feet and corrected himself as his heart grew heavy as a rock. "She's the only one who *called* me that."

"I understand, Oliver," Minnie said, her harsh tone gone, "but you can't go around pushin' pe—"

"You don't understand!" Oliver shouted. He shook his head, turned, and ran. There was nowhere to go, not really, but his feet pounded the smooth, shiny floor, anyway. He would have run for miles if he could have. Instead, he turned into a dark hall no one used, curled up in a corner, and let the tears flow freely where no one could see.

Chapter 11

Alexander Roman

Alex stood before a never-ending white landscape. Despite his three layers, each one Stella-approved, the cold was pervasive. There would be no escaping it out there, where he had to go.

"It's time to go," Stella said as she came up beside him.

"It's going to be a fight," Alex said, "every day out there. A fight against the very land and air." It settled on his chest like a weight: those elements were larger and more powerful than he could ever be.

"We won't be fighting it," Stella said. "We're accepting it, going with the grain and not against it. Out there, you have to work yourself into the fabric of Antarctica to survive."

Alex laughed. "What, as in... become one with the land?"

She didn't find that funny. "Or you can, you know, just die."

He cleared his throat. "Sorry."

"Look," Stella said, "clichés like that come from a grain of truth. If that's too mystical for you, then just do what I say, and maybe we'll all pull through this."

Alex nodded. "Okay," he said. "Acceptance. Going with the grain. Got it."

She looked more annoyed than anything as she turned and he followed. Just behind them, their supplies waited. A large snowcat with wide continuous track wheels stood stark against the snow with its bright red paint. A sled-like contraption was hooked up to the back of it with all their supplies. Walter and Lauren were checking the straps, and Candice was already sitting up in the backseat of the snowcat.

"You sure it's right to travel with the tents like that?" Alex asked.

Secured atop the sled were two tents, already set up, one a little bigger than the other. He and Walter would share one, and the ladies would share the other.

"The weather is going to be unpredictable," Stella said. "If the winds pick up too much, and I think a blizzard might be coming in, we've got to get those tents set up and anchored quickly. Then, we've got to build little walls out of snow blocks, and we might have to do it all in under an hour. We don't have someone to tell us what we're riding into."

"Can't we just stay in the snowcat if the winds pick up?" Alex asked.

"Sure," Stella said, "if we wanted to sit in one spot for twelve hours and use up our fuel to stay warm." She quirked an eyebrow.

"Okay, okay," Alex said, holding up his hands. "I just thought—"

"Look, you can't travel when the winds get up to over a hundred miles per hour. You can't see where you're going and run the risk of falling into a crevice, and there *are* crevices out there, outside the South Pole Traverse. Where we're going, there's no approved track."

Stella walked forward again, heading toward the back of the supplies where a long, weird bag of fuel—that was the only way Alex could describe it—was attached to the sled. "To stay warm without electricity, we'll have to stay wrapped up in those sleeping bags we brought. We'll also need to have a spot to melt snow. It's not too hard to do, even in a windstorm, if all you have to do is reach out your front door and fill a pan."

She rounded the back of their supplies, fuel included, eyeing everything carefully. Alex stayed a step behind.

"And you think it'll take us about four days to reach where we have to go?" he asked.

Stella shrugged as she stopped, reached over the sled, and pulled a strap tighter. "These new snowcats can go eighteen to twenty miles per hour. If we travel eight hours per day, we should eat about a hundred and forty-four miles in that timeframe. If we can do that, we can make it in four days. Then, you'll have to search the area. I have no idea how long it will take for you to actually *find* this research bank."

She stepped up on the foot ladder and grabbed the driver's side door, yanking it open, and shouting over her shoulder, "Everyone load up!"

Alex let Lauren into the middle seat and squeezed into the back left corner. Walter took the front passenger seat, for the time being. They'd decided they'd rotate that position.

"I still don't get why I couldn't wear my own clothes," Candice said. "I mean, under the outer gear. These are so bulky I feel like I can barely move!"

As the snowcat roared to life, Stella shifted it into gear, and it lurched forward. "Jeans are useless out here," she said. "Wool keeps you warm. It keeps you alive."

Candice huffed a little and crossed her arms. Alex still didn't know what to think about her. Sometimes she showed immense courage, and sometimes, she acted more like a teenage girl than a grown woman. Lauren had tried to explain some of it to him, though she didn't seem to *really* understand it either.

"She grew up with nothing," Lauren had said once. "Her stuff is like a security blanket. A way to control her life, even if it's just a little bit."

He tried to have empathy with that and remember all the things he liked about Candice. She had a good heart, and she'd not given him a word of complaint about the fact that he needed her solely to experiment on her. A truly shallow and selfish woman wouldn't have been so easy to work with in those regards. And she'd proven herself willing to sacrifice her life for others in the past months. He could overlook a few oddities for that.

"So," Stella said after they'd started moving, "I'm not going to sit here in silence for eight hours every day. Anybody got any ideas?"

"We could play Hot Seat," Lauren said. "Everyone gets a turn. There are five of us, right? So if it were my turn, the four of you would all ask me a question, and I could only refuse to answer one of them."

Walter winced. "That sounds like it could get… too interesting."

"Never Have I Ever?" Candice asked.

"That one is more fun with alcohol," Stella said.

"Would You Rather is safe," Walter said, smiling, his voice softening. "My family used to play that one." He rolled his shoulders back and gave his head a quick shake. His eyes glistened for just a moment, and then he smiled genuinely. "C'mon. Who has a good one?"

Alex sighed. "Okay, let me think… Would you rather… have a chef or a maid?"

Walter shrugged. "I've had both, but I guess… a chef. No… a maid."

Candice reached forward and tapped Walter's shoulder. "We're samsies," she said.

Alex, Lauren, and Stella groaned together, each of them, even Stella, managing to throw looks at Walter and Candice.

"What?" Walter asked.

"Nevermind," Alex said.

"How about Three Truths and a Lie?" Stella asked.

Alex pinched the bridge of his nose before leaning his head back on the headrest.

"All right," Lauren said. "I went to medical school. I quit my residency to become a singer. And I love hot pretzels."

Alex wrinkled his nose. "Who doesn't like hot pretzels?" He turned around in his seat. "Who *are* you?"

Lauren laughed. "You're not supposed to give it away!"

"Wait," Stella said, "You're a doctor?"

"No," Lauren said. "I never got my license."

Stella shrugged. "Like that means a whole lot now. That's good to know."

"I mean, it *does* mean a whole lot. It means I don't have the experience," Lauren said.

Walter shrugged. "I don't know. You've gained a lot of experience over the last few months."

"Yeah," Candice said, "if it weren't for you, Annika would be dead."

"I didn't perform the surgery that saved her life." Lauren shook her head.

"You kept her alive until we found someone who could." Candice took hold of Lauren's hand and squeezed it.

Alex lightly bumped her with his elbow. "Don't sell yourself short," he said.

"Okay, fine," Lauren said. "Enough about me. You're up next."

The game continued on like that for some time, often diverging into long conversations as they got to know Stella and each other better. Still, the day dragged by too slowly. With every lull in the conversation, with every break, Alex's mind raced.

There was so much to worry about: his son, Minnie, Lizzy and whether she was crazy, their mission, and the list went on.

When he was sufficiently stiff, Stella stopped the snowcat for the last time that day. "We've travelled as long as we're gonna," she said. "The wind is picking up. Nothing too terrible, but we'll want to hunker down for the night. We won't be able to travel again until it settles just a little. Hopefully by morning, we can move on."

All around them, there was nothing but miles and miles of snow, a dazzling white and barren land. Stella had insisted they all bring sunglasses, and she'd been right. Alex looked out over the rim of his glasses and squinted against the brilliant reflection of sun on snow. He slid out of the snowcat, his boots sinking into icy fluff that crunched under his weight. The wind buffeted him, stealing his breath with its chill. Alex secured his wool cowl up and over his nose. They all got to work, compacting snow in a circle several yards from the snowcat, positioning their tents, anchoring them with long spikes, and then further securing them by piling up snow around the edges. Next came the walls of snow bricks, about chest high, set to protect their tents from the wind.

By the time they were done, every inch of Alex ached. Each step, each *movement*, was a struggle against the gale. "Is this what you meant?" Alex shouted. "Is this a windstorm?"

Stella laughed. "No," she said. "This is just Antarctica on an average day out here." She waved for him to come over. "Before we get settled for the night, we need to melt some snow for drinking water, boil it for a bit, too. Go grab the portable stove and the backpack with our food."

Alex nodded and trudged over to their supplies to grab the black box that contained the burner and butane, along with the backpack. Stella let them take their food and ordered them into their tents, insisting she'd bring them water when it was ready.

Inside the tiny tent, he and Walter stripped down to their long underwear and climbed inside thick orange sleeping bags that covered every inch of either man with some room to spare.

"So far, so good," Walter said.

"Except for this wind." Alex shied from the walls of the tent. They whipped in the harsh winds, the sound of beating plastic growing louder by the second. "I know Stella said this is normal, but…"

"It's a lot," Walter said.

Alex nodded. "I hope she knows what she's doing."

"It's hard to trust other people, isn't it?" Walter asked.

"When we know hardly anything about them?" Alex asked. "Yeah, it is."

"She clearly knows more than we do about surviving out here."

A resistance tugged at Alex's chest, a defiance heavy as stones and just as hard. "We still need to keep our guard up."

Walter laughed softly. "That's just like you, Alex."

He bristled. "What's that supposed to mean?"

"I don't know if you've always been like this, but you have control issues," Walter said.

Alex ground his teeth. "I don't think I'll be taking advice about that from you."

"Oh?" Walter laughed again. "Alex, I know what I'm talking about. I was worse than you'll ever be. I can recognize that need to control the situation from a mile away."

"I'm letting Stella do her thing," Alex said. "I'm not impeding her."

"I know," Walter said, "but it's taking every ounce of self-control to do it. Isn't it?"

Alex didn't answer that particular question. "There's nothing wrong with asking questions and making sure you're following the right person."

Walter shifted in his sleeping bag, only his face visible. "All I'm saying is that constantly making life and death decisions is exhausting. It'll drain you dry and leave nothing left of who you want to be. If you have the chance to hand some of that over to someone else, do it. Share the burden. Because the truth is, no matter how much you grasp for control, you'll never actually have it. Control is an illusion. No matter what you do, nature or other people or circumstances can cause all your plans to crumble."

"We've done okay so far," Alex said.

"We've survived by the skin of our teeth and by adaptation," Walter said. "And not all of us have survived."

That much was true. A pang pierced Alex's stomach at the thought of his wife. Walter had lost his wife, too, and they'd lost plenty of friends along the way, seen plenty of death, had plenty of plans fall apart at the last minute.

"Clinging to control only hurts you when it falls apart," Walter said. "You'll be too busy grasping at it as it slips through your fingers to see that you have to adapt instead of fight."

Alex's earlier conversation with Stella, about fighting with the land as opposed to accepting it, echoed in the back of his mind. If Minnie were there, she'd say the similarity wasn't a coincidence, that he should listen or risk her boxing his ears.

After Stella brought them fresh water and night chased the daylight away, Alex lay in the midst of the howling wind and rustling tent. Walter's snoring indicated he'd found a way to sleep through it, but for Alex, the noise outside matched the noise inside his head. There was no rest for him, not even when he dreamed.

Chapter 12

Oliver Roman

Oliver sat on the floor in the empty, dead-end, little hallway where no one would bother him. At least, no one had bothered him over the last four days. Hours spent there with a book and his mother's bag at his side had proved better than his other options. He'd not gone back to that so-called "school." Mrs. Zhang had been nice enough, but the other kids made him seriously doubt Minnie's claim that he needed friends his own age.

He didn't know what to do about Minnie. She kept pushing him to go back, to try again. He loved her, but she was wrong about school. Lately, it seemed all adults wanted to do was tell him what to do when all he wanted was for someone to listen.

"I'm old enough to decide who I want to be friends with," he mumbled to himself.

Besides, there were other ways to learn. Mrs. Zhang had said he could borrow books from the classroom any time, whether he came to school or not, as long as he returned them. He had an old encyclopedia he'd been lugging around for a few days. It was full of information.

"I don't need a teacher or a school or friends."

He picked up the book, stretched out his legs, and flipped it open. The far corner of the dead-end hall was dark, but when he sat closer to the main hall, a solid beam of sunlight from the skylights reached him and illuminated the pages so that he could read.

Maybe education was important, even at the end of the world, like Minnie said, but he could educate himself. All he needed was the right books, and he'd be set. There were no holes in his reasoning. He was sure of it.

"Oliver?"

He sat up straight and looked up from his book to see Ava peeking around the corner. He stared at her, unsure of what to say. "Uh... yeah?"

"Can I come sit with you?" Ava asked.

Oliver's mouth dropped open just a little. "Sure?"

That shouldn't be a question, he thought.

He coughed into his elbow. "I mean... yes, sure."

Ava clasped her hands behind her back until she reached him, and then she sat quickly and sat very close. "I'm sorry about Will," she said.

"I don't care about *Will,*" Oliver said, a bitter taste in the back of his mouth at the mention of him.

"Oh." Ava chewed on her lower lip for a second. "Well... then you should come back."

"I'm not staying in New Zealand long," Oliver said. "When my dad gets back, we're leaving. I think I'd rather be by myself until then."

Her lower lip puckered out a little. "I can go," she said.

Oliver's eyes went wide. "I didn't mean that," he said. "I just don't want to be around some of those other kids, especially Will. He's not nice."

"I know," Ava said, "but I think it would be nice to get to know you better, and everyone else is nice. Even Will isn't so bad after he gets used to you."

Oliver's palms started to sweat. He scratched the back of his neck. "You think the other kids would want me around?" he asked.

She nodded. "Come back with me? Give us Kiwis another shot?"

"Okay," he said, his next thought being: *Wait... what?*

"Great!" Ava hopped to her feet. "We're hanging out right now."

Oliver got to his feet, adjusted his bag, and followed her into the main hall, leaving the encyclopedia behind, but he wasn't sure exactly *why* he was doing it. He liked the way she looked at him, but that was stupid, and he knew it.

I should say I'm sick... just turn off and go back to our room. Or say I forgot that Minnie needed me to do something.

But he didn't do any of that. He followed Ava down the hall and into the classroom. It was the weirdest feeling, seeing all the older kids congregated in the same spot again—déjà vu. His stomach cramped, and his mouth went dry as he approached. He shifted the bag behind him, not because he was ashamed of it, he told himself, but because he didn't want to deal with Will making fun of it.

"Not this bloke again," Will said.

"Be nice," Ava said sharply.

"Yeah," Niko said. "Be nice, Will."

Will's eyes narrowed, but then he shrugged. "I'm just not a big fan of liars."

There it was again: a sudden burst of anger. A bit of fire was added to the twisting in his stomach.

"I'm not a liar," Oliver said.

Will rolled his eyes.

"I'm not!"

"A serial killer? Really? And two fires? I don't see any burns." He crossed his arms and looked at Oliver as if daring him to prove his previous claims.

"My dad got me out. Both times. Doesn't mean I wasn't there." Oliver's hands balled into fists. *I shouldn't have come back,* he thought.

"Well, blow me down," Will said, tone laced with sarcasm. "I knew you were full of codswallop, telling those stories like they were yours. Your dad did those things."

"I did, too," Oliver shouted. "It was me and him, together."
"Will, stop it," Ava said. "Why do you care what he's done? So what if he hasn't done anything scary? You haven't. No one really believes you fought off the lolly factory boys."
For some reason, that hurt. He didn't want Ava defending him because she thought he was making things up, too. "I wasn't lying," Oliver said again, more insistent than ever.
"What do you mean no one believes me?" Will crossed his arms, apparently ignoring Oliver. "I'll go out there, with the black clouds and everything, find me those boys and bring back a whole bag of lollies." He puffed out his chest and started toward the door.
"No, don't," Ava squeaked, her eyes wide. "You'll get yourself killed."
Will turned around. "I faced 'em before. I'll do it again."
"It's dangerous out there," Niko said. "You can't."
"Can too," Will said. "It's just an hour's walk east, an eyesore my dad calls it. Bright colors. Tacky. I'll find it, easy. Those boys chose it because it *looks* grand. But it's not. Just like they're not. I'm not scared of 'em." He turned around and marched into the hall.
Oliver swallowed hard. "He won't really go out there?"
"He's so brave," Ava said in an annoying, breathy voice.
"What?" Oliver nearly shouted at her. "He's being an idiot!"
But Ava didn't seem to hear as she followed him. Most of the others did the same.
Niko sighed. "We better stop Will. That's what he wants."
Oliver frowned. "What do you mean?"
"He wants us to follow him and beg him not to go."
"So, he won't really go, then?" Oliver asked. "Then why chase him at all? He just wants attention."
"Because what if he *does* go out there, just out of pride? Then we'll all feel bad about it." Niko shrugged. "At least, that's why I'm going after him." He gave Oliver a hearty pat on his shoulder that nearly made him lose his balance, and then Niko jogged out into the hall.
Oliver wasn't going to go after them, not if someone paid him a million dollars. *The adults won't let them get anywhere near the doors,* he thought.
But he didn't hear a commotion, didn't hear any mothers or fathers or grandparents chastising. He walked out into the hall, turning right and then left, looking for the others. He saw a flash of blue, the color shirt Niko had been wearing down by the little hall that led to the roof access.
The garden was up there, but kids weren't allowed. Only a few adults ever went up to tend the vegetables.
That's a stupid way to go out, Oliver thought. What if someone is up there? And how would he get to the ground?
But then Niko's words came back to him. Will didn't care that there might be someone up there or that they might get caught in that hall. He didn't really want to leave. He just wanted to be stopped. He wanted to prove that he *would* go without actually having to do it.
Oliver balled his hands into fists. If they're all going to just give him what he wants, I'll make sure he either goes or proves that he would never.
It was hard to walk and not run, but he didn't want to draw attention to himself or to the other kids. The last thing he needed was for everyone else to think he was a snitch.
Half the adults were out in a scavenging party, and the rest were looking after little kids or doing chores. When he passed by the door to the room he shared with Minnie, he held his breath as if Minnie might be able to tell it was him passing by if he breathed too loud. But there wasn't so much as the sound of her stirring beyond that door, or Samson either, for that matter.
When he reached the entrance to the little hall where the other kids were, he slipped inside after glancing around to make sure no one was paying attention. The little hall was just a little wider than the width of Oliver's full reach, fingertip to fingertip should he stretch both arms wide, and there were offices down its length.
The farther he went, the darker it got. He walked around a corner where the narrow hall went behind the shops, and ahead, through a glass window in a door, light shone into the darkness. Hushed voices leaked through the crack under the door.
Oliver narrowed his eyes, marched right to it, and yanked it open. Will, along with Niko and Ava and three other kids, froze at the sound, each one turning at the same time to face the door with startled expressions.
Several of them had small, handheld flashlights they must have been keeping in their pockets. They were in a stairwell with only one flight leading straight to the rooftop.
When it seemed they realized it was only Oliver, and not an adult, most of them relaxed.
"What are you doing here?" Will scowled.
Oliver drew up to his full height. "I came to see you off," he said.
"He's not going anywhere," Ava said.
"I thought he was *so brave,*" Oliver said, immediately regretting it as, even in the dim light, he could see Ava's cheeks turning bright red as she shrank a little.
Will gave her lopsided smile. "Did you say that?" he asked.
"No!" Ava said quickly.
One of the other girls snickered, and Ava elbowed her.
"I wasn't talking about Ava," Oliver said, trying to recover. He hadn't meant to embarrass her. He wasn't even sure why he'd said it like that, why her saying Will was brave bothered him so much. "I was talking about you. You said you weren't scared, and I wanted to see it for myself."
"I was about to go up right when you came in," Will said.
"Then go!" Oliver pointed up the stairwell.
"After you," Will said, gesturing toward the stairs. "Or are you too afraid without your daddy? He's probably going to die out there, you know. That's what my dad says."

"Shut up!" Oliver lunged for Will, grabbing his collar. The other boy was half a foot taller, but Oliver pushed and knocked him off balance.

Will stumbled. "Eh! Get off!" He wrenched himself free, and then reared a fist back over his shoulder.

And then the door at the top of the stairs opened. Will straightened and backed away, and the other kids gasped and stepped back against the wall. Oliver had frozen at the sight of Will's fist about to come straight at his head, and it took him a second to recover. He swallowed hard and quickly wiped away a few stray tears before facing the newcomer.

Light poured down the concrete steps, and a woman with a lantern in one hand and a basket overflowing with greens in the crook of her arm stood at the top. "Will? Is that you?" She closed the door behind her. "What are you doing here?" She didn't sound pleased to see him, though Oliver wasn't sure why she wasn't mentioning the rest of them.

"Sorry, Mom," Will said. "I was just looking for you."

Oliver's mouth dropped open. His mom? He knew she'd be here! So, if we didn't stop him, she would!

"And you brought all of your friends?" She took the steps carefully, glancing down before moving forward with each one. "I told you that you weren't allowed back here, and there's no way you're going to the rooftop."

Will cleared his throat. "Oh, I wasn't—"

"Don't you lie to me," his mother said. "We'll talk about this later." She reached the bottom step. "All of you better move, now, before I decide to tell whoever's responsible for you what you were up to."

Oliver was pushed out into the hall as the five others scrambled to do as they'd been told. Back against the wall, he let the others fly down the dark hall without him, beams from their flashlights dancing wildly in the dark until they turned the corner. Niko dropped his but didn't stop to pick it up. Oliver followed more slowly to avoid catching up with them. He picked up Niko's flashlight and shoved it into his pocket. He'd give it back later, when Niko wasn't around Will.

He returned to his encyclopedia in the dimly lit space where he could be alone only to find that he couldn't stop thinking about what had happened. Once again, the book lay open on his lap, but the words faded and the page blurred. He couldn't focus on it, not with so much frustration swirling around inside.

Maybe they're right, he thought. My dad's brave, but he's just dragged me from place to place, hasn't he? What have I done, really? He still sees me as a baby, won't let me do anything. Minnie won't let me make my own decisions, either.

But Oliver could do all sorts of things, if he was given the chance. And he was just as brave as his dad. He imagined Ava's face if he brought her a bag full of lollipops, and then he imagined Will's. Both images made him grin.

"Will might be afraid," Oliver whispered to himself, "but I'm not."

He pushed the encyclopedia aside and stood. If he wanted to make friends, he had to make it so that Will couldn't make fun of him. What better way to do that than to accomplish the very thing Will had failed to do?

He placed a hand on his bag, his mother's handmade purse, a part of her that was always with him. Inside, trinkets of his past, proof that he had been through plenty of danger already and survived, gave him courage.

It wasn't hard to sneak back to the stairwell. Again, no one noticed him. He was just a kid to everyone, not someone to watch, not someone to ask for help. A helpless kid his dad had left behind.

"I'll be fine," he said as he shone Niko's flashlight up the stairwell at the dull gray door that led outside.

Will had said it was an hour's walk east, that it was an obvious building, bright and unique. If he went quickly, he could cut the time in half. And his dad had taught him how to listen for the swarms, how to find shelter if he heard one coming. He had been through worse than walking through a city. Worst case scenario, he'd have to hide from a swarm.

Still, lifting his foot to take the first step was like lifting a heavy stone. A tingling sensation rolled through his body as he climbed the stairs, as his heartbeat quickened. By the time he reached the top landing, his hands were trembling.

With some difficulty, he dug out the lavender oil he kept in his bag and dabbed some on his neck and arms. That would at least make him a little less appetizing to a swarm. It made him feel better, made him feel like his mother was watching out for him.

He reached out and grasped the metal handle but didn't twist it. *Minnie will be so mad if she finds out,* he thought. "I'll be back before she knows I'm gone," Oliver said, nodding once and then opening the door, stepping out onto the rooftop.

It was quiet. A slight breeze rustled green plants in an assortment of containers. The air was crisp and cool but not chilly, and the sun touched everything with a vibrancy that encouraged colors to pop. He wasn't allowed outside often anymore. He missed it.

The rooftop stretched out before him, the dome not far from the door, skylights like a dotted line running down the center. Oliver avoided those as he scanned the rim of the building for a fire escape. It wasn't hard to find.

He looked up at the sky. It was after midday, so the sun was on its way to setting in the west. That gave him a good idea of which way he had to go if he was looking for a building east of him.

Moving quickly before he could chicken out, Oliver ran to the rusty, old metal handles clinging to the edge of the roof not far from him. He peered over the edge to the ground below, and not seeing anyone nearby, grasped the ladder's handles and descended as quickly as he could.

Speed was the most important part of his plan. He first bolted across the lot, the fear of being caught mixing with a thrill he hadn't expected. Oliver ran through empty streets, leaving traces of fear behind with every yard, gaining the sensation of freedom in its place. He laughed and stretched his arms above his head as he ran faster and faster. No one told him to stop. No one chastised him or tried to hide him away under the claim they were trying to protect him.

When a stitch in his side made him stop, Oliver sprawled out on a sidewalk. His cheeks hurt from grinning so widely, but he didn't care. There was nothing he couldn't do in those abandoned streets: sing, dance, hop, skip… who was going to stop him? Who was going to make fun of him?

He closed his eyes—listening for swarms, of course—and just enjoyed the moment. The sidewalk was rough beneath his palms, warmer than the air around him. A gentle wind brushed his skin, rustled his clothes. He touched his mother's bag at his side.

He imagined he was outside his old house, back in Atlanta, laying on the sidewalk with the sounds of the neighborhood all around him. If it were a Saturday—he didn't know what day it *actually* was, but Saturdays were his favorite—dad would be mowing the back yard, and mom would be at a hair appointment. She'd bring him back a bear claw from the donut shop next to the salon, exchange the treat for a hug when she got back. And he would hug her *so* tight that she would laugh. Dad would grill burgers for dinner and let Oliver flip them when it was time after giving him the same lecture Oliver had heard a hundred times before. It would be normal and boring and wonderful.

A kick to the bottom of Oliver's shoes sent a jolt of panic through his body as he sucked in a breath, opened his eyes, and sat up. Part of him expected to see Minnie standing over him with her cane, threatening to wallop him with it, but instead, it was a face he didn't recognize. A boy maybe six or seven years older than him, which meant he was practically a man.

"What do we have here, boys?" he said, his gaze flicking upward, looking behind Oliver. His half-grin made Oliver shudder.

Oliver scrambled to the side, the boy who'd kicked his foot to one side, and a dozen more boys to the other. "Who are you?"

The group of boys laughed, hooted and hollered like he'd said something hilarious. They were of a wide range of ages, none of them seeming younger that Oliver. The first boy he'd seen was the oldest.

"You can call me Ihaka," the boy said. "We'll have to do proper introductions later."

Oliver shook his head, terror flooding his entire body. He stood on weak legs and hugged his middle to keep his shaking to a minimum.

"I..." Oliver's words were stuck and his mouth was dry. It was like trying to talk through a mouthful of cotton balls. "I have to go." It was all he could manage.

He only made it two steps before Ihaka's hand gripped his shoulder. A panicked whimper escaped his lips as he twisted away, but then two more boys were on either side of him, their hands holding him tight.

"Let me go!" Oliver struggled, but more boys surrounded him. He kicked, but they grabbed his ankles, took hold of his legs, lifted him off the ground. And then, as he screamed for help, there was cloth in his mouth, tied securely around the back of his head.

He'd been free. There had been no one to constrain him. No one to tell him what to do. No one to help him, and no one to save him.

Chapter 13

Stella Sharpe

"This is the end of the line for the snowcat," Stella said as she parked the vehicle. She pointed ahead to where two mountains met, where black rock tapered as if the mountains had interlocked fingers. "Your coordinates are just on the other side of that range."
"We just leave the snowcat here?" Alex asked.
"It's not like anyone's going to steal it," Stella said.
"How many days should we prepare to be out there?" Walter asked.
"I'd say five," Stella said. "If we don't find what we're looking for, we can come back here, get some more supplies, and head back."
"Five days?" Candice's voice sounded weak.
Lauren shrugged. "Maybe we'll find the research bank sooner than that."
"Well, we won't find it until we start looking." Alex opened his door, and the cold sucked the warmth out of the snowcat's cab.
Within half an hour, Stella was leading the way up the foot of the mountain, planning to take a ridge that seemed to cut around it, hedged on one side by a rock wall and on the other by a slope. There was minimal snow accumulation there, on that path, compared to the valley, where snow was blown and caught and possibly quite deep.
And it did seem a path, whether natural or created, she couldn't tell. "Look for signs of human interference," she shouted over her shoulder to the others who followed in her footsteps. "Flags or reflectors, markings of any kind. If we're going in the right direction, we should come across something eventually. The smallest thing could lead us to your research bank."
She trudged on. After days of talking and trying to be social, Stella enjoyed the quiet trek. It was nothing but her and the hard work of taking the next step. The cold was familiar. The daylight made it all bearable. Her body had been stagnant too long. Every muscle yearned for the next movement after spending weeks alone and in a darkness of her own making. She welcomed the rest for her mind, though. The games, the talking, the questions… she had grown weary of that after the first day. It wasn't that she didn't like Alex, Walter, Lauren, and Candice; it was just the opposite, and she couldn't risk coming to care about anyone else.
It wouldn't be completely dark for some time. The days were getting longer. There was only complete darkness for a few hours per night, with an ever-shortening near-dark twilight making travel only unsafe for about eight or nine hours. In just another two weeks, the continent would be completely free of true darkness for the season. Daylight would lengthen, slowly taking over the twilight until it was light outside twenty-four-seven. Eventually, by January, the temperatures would rise to the low to mid-thirties.
Except this year, McMurdo Station will be abandoned in the months when it's the most tenable. Stella pushed those thoughts away. It saddened her to think the station—or really, the entire continent—would possibly never see a human presence again.
The ridge took a sharper curve around the mountain, and Stella stopped as their path narrowed and dead-ended ahead. To her left, nestled between several mountains, was a larger valley of ice and snow. A six-foot drop from the ridge revealed a rocky plateau which was large enough for a camp. A light wind dusted the level rock with snow, but it didn't accumulate, instead drifting down a gentle slope of at least one hundred feet which reached all the way to the valley below.
"Why are we stopping?" Alex asked, his breathing labored.
"This is a good camping spot," Stella said.
"Where do we go from here?" Walter asked.
"I'm not sure." Stella shielded her eyes against the reflection of sun on snow as she scanned the landscape. "We can follow this slope toward the neighboring mountain, but I don't want to go down into the valley itself. There could be lots of pockets in that snow, and if we fall through, we aren't getting out. I want to stay on the rock."
Lauren gestured toward the valley. "What if the research bank is down there?"
"That's all snow and ice," Stella said. "If they built a secret facility, it would be tucked away inside the mountain, not down there, in the ice."
Stella slid her backpack off, sat on the edge of the cliff, turned, and lowered herself to the rock six feet below. "Someone hand me the bags," she said. "Then, help the ladies down first. Walter next. Alex last."
Lauren looked down at her and scoffed. "Candice, Walter, Me, and then Alex," she said. "If you're thinking about sending us down weakest to strongest." She shrugged at Walter. "No offense."
Walter lifted his hands and shrugged. "You're almost half my age. No arguments here."
"None here, either," Candice said. "I need all the help I can get."
"Fine," Stella said. "Let's just get moving, okay?"
The others lowered their backpacks, and then, one by one, Stella helped each person from her place below while Alex helped them from above. Stella had instructed them to bring bivouac bags instead of the tents. They were lighter and easier to carry, perfect for travelling on foot through terrain that wouldn't be amenable to tents that needed to be anchored down. They weren't as comfortable as tents, but they'd do. Complete with a breathable patch over the face and weather-proof material, they slipped over their sleeping bags and kept them both dry and warm.
After a dinner of oatmeal cooked over their single burner along with some dried fruit and nuts, Stella settled for the night. Whistling wind and Walter's snoring made for a restless night. When morning came, she was still exhausted.
"Everything hurts," Candice said, groaning.
Stella's stiff muscles protested as she packed up her things. "My guess is we're all feeling it," she said.

Alex stretched his arms. "Walking it out is our only option."
"I won't be able to keep up yesterday's pace," Walter said.
"Won't have to," Stella said. "Today will be slow and methodical. There's no facility in plain sight, which means they've hidden it somehow. We're going to have to pay attention. Explore."
Candice turned in a slow half circle, squinting into the distance. "Don't you think we'd be able to see flags or reflectors from here? Maybe we're at the wrong spot."
"She's right," Lauren said. "Something like that would stand out here. It's all black and white for as far as I can see."
Stella shook her head. "I was thinking about that last night. If it's a secret facility, maybe they didn't want anything visible by plane or exploratory parties. We need to look for things like… I don't know, maybe camouflaged camera lenses? Honestly, the ridge we came in on could have been manmade. It was a smooth path, even if the incline was rough at spots."
Walter let out a slow breath. "This feels impossible."
"It's not," Alex said sternly.
Stella questioned the conviction in his voice, but she kept that to herself. To her, finding the research bank was looking more and more like a lost cause. She wasn't willing to give up. It would do her no more harm to look for the entire forty days, out there in the wilderness. There was nothing left to lose. But for the others?
We won't be out here long, she thought. *Ten days, max.* If Tabitha had been there, or even Lincoln, she would have placed a bet on it.
A nostalgic smile at the thought of her friends faded with the images of their faces after death: Tabitha's serene, Lincoln's agonized. Bile rose at the back of her throat as she closed her eyes and focused on what she had to do next.
I can't live with these memories, she thought as hot tears came despite her efforts to keep them at bay. A gentle squeeze through her coat made Stella open her eyes.
"Hey," Lauren said, keeping her voice low, "are you okay?" The others were still packing their gear. It didn't seem anyone else had noticed her lapse.
Stella blinked away the tears, drying them quickly with her gloved hands before they could run down her cheeks. "Yeah," she said. "Bad memories." She breathed in cold air. "I haven't teared up in weeks. I don't know what came over me. Sorry."
"Don't apologize," Lauren said. "I think not feeling anything is scarier, you know? That's when…" She swallowed hard and averted her eyes. "That's when we should be worried. When we start to feel again, we start to heal."
"Yeah, well, I'm not there yet, and I'm not sure I want to be," Stella said, her tone sharp. The anger in her own voice shocked even her. She closed her eyes. "Sorry. Just… I don't want to talk about it."
"It's okay," Lauren said. "I've been there."
Stella looked back at Lauren. It was clear the other woman was just trying to help, but that statement did nothing but make her stomach burn and her face flush red. "You don't know me, Lauren, and you don't know where I am or what I'm thinking."
"I know that look in your eyes," Lauren said. "I recognized it the first time I talked to you. It gets better. You just have to hang in there."
Stella stood up, flinching away from her. "You don't know me," she repeated. "And just because I gave you a summary of the last three months doesn't mean you know what happened to me, either. I'm sure you've lost people. I'm sure it hurt. But don't pretend to know what it's like to watch your friends take their own lives. To see every last person you love die a month later. To be left alone—" Her voice broke. "—in the dark. To think you're going to die without ever seeing another human being again. You don't know what *that* is like."
Lauren stood slowly and nodded. "You're right," she said. "That must have been terrible."
But that wasn't any better than when she'd compared their experiences. Stella scoffed, not really understanding her own fury, part of her knowing it wasn't fair to direct it at Lauren. She just couldn't bring herself to say anything else, to do anything else except walk away. It was only then that she realized the others had picked up on the conversation. They quickly looked away as she stalked past them, too.
"Let's go," she said. "We have a long day ahead of us."
She carefully left the level rock for the slowly declining slope, walking parallel to the valley below instead of toward it. Though she didn't look back, the scrape of boots and whispers on the wind told her the others were following. Unable to handle interactions of any kind, Stella just kept moving across the black and white landscape, walking for what seemed like forever, putting one foot in front of the other, going until her thighs begged her to take a break. Still, she pushed harder. The movement numbed her thoughts, numbed her pain, gave her a way to ignore emotions she didn't want to wade through.
"Stop!"
The word echoed all around her, and Stella's foot slipped. She skidded a few feet down the slope before stopping herself. "What the—" She turned her head back to shout at whichever one of the four following her had frightened her like that, but they were all staring up and to the left. Stella followed their gaze to see a man in full gear standing on a ridge about ten feet above.
Alex raised his hands. "We've stopped," he shouted. "Are you with Barlow Scientific Research Bank?"
The man nodded vigorously. "Yes! Good grief. I thought we were going to die up here. Are you here to rescue us?" the man asked, cupping his gloved hands around his mouth as he yelled down to them.
Alex exchanged glances with Walter, and Stella cursed as she scrambled back to her feet. "Yes," she said, and then she made her way to Alex, Walter, Lauren, and Candice, all of whom were looking at her like she'd grown a second head.
"Why would you say that?" Walter asked.
"Because it's true. Mostly." Stella shrugged. "We're not going to leave them here."
"She's not wrong," Candice said.
"But we're not just here to rescue them," Alex said. "It's a lot more complicated than that."
Behind her, the man shouted, "There's a way up over this way."

"We can get into details later," Stella said. "Right now, we need him to show us where this facility is. You don't know what instructions they've been given. If you say anything else, he might disappear."

"I doubt it," Lauren said. "He's obviously desperate to get out of here."

"Which is why," Stella said, "he's going to let a rescue party in."

Walter sighed. "She's right," he said. "It's not a lie. The rescue just isn't immediate."

Alex licked his lips and looked up and past Stella. "Let's go, then. He's going to injure himself if he points any harder."

When Stella turned again, she raised her eyebrows. The man was jumping up and down, throwing his hands toward a spot around a bend in the rock. As the others walked that way, Stella froze as a thought hit her: *We did it. We actually found it. Or… it found us?*

Either way, she hadn't been holding out hope that their mission would be a success. Not a lot in her life had gone well lately. The victory somehow made her earlier actions toward Lauren feel wrong. She caught up to Lauren and touched her elbow. The other woman stopped.

"I'm sorry," Stella said. "And don't tell me not to apologize."

"I wasn't going to," Lauren said.

Stella cleared her throat. "Oh. Well, good. Because I wasn't nice. I don't really… um…" Her next breath was shaky. "I don't really understand myself right now, so I won't ask you to understand me, either. I'm just sorry."

"Forgiven and forgotten." Lauren made to turn, but Stella held out a hand.

"Wait, that's it?"

"Yep." Lauren quirked an eyebrow. "Is that a problem?"

"No." Stella shifted her backpack and tugged on the straps. "I… um… thank you."

Lauren smiled at her, stepped back, hooked her arm with Stella's, and tugged her forward. She didn't say anything, and that was exactly what Stella needed at that moment. For the first time in a long time, hope flared inside, a warm and dangerous flame. Only time would tell if it would thaw her so she could heal or burn her up from the inside out.

Chapter 14

Minnie Stevens

Oliver was gone.

He'd been gone for at least twenty-four hours.

If there was ever a time Minnie needed the good Lord to come through, it was right then and there. She prayed and paced, her cane thumping the floor with every step. Samson sat on his haunches, watching her, his head moving back and forth as she walked. She hadn't left the set of glass doors that opened onto the parking lot all day and neither had her dog. The search party hadn't let them come, and truth be told, they'd been right, though she'd hated to admit it. She was turtle-like and needy, what with her leg and her age seeming to have caught up to her over the past weeks. She'd never felt so *old* and tired.

So, she'd stayed. And paced. And hoped for the boy to come back.

Down the main hall, Minnie spotted Zara coming her way. The girl had enough on her plate, and yet, she'd taken time to check on Minnie every hour. It was a nuisance and a blessing.

"You should sit back down." Zara put her hands on her hips and nodded to a chair they'd made her use off and on that day.

"I don't like bein' told what to do." Still, Minnie hobbled to the chair and sat down hard, putting her cane between her legs and resting her hands and chin on top. She could practically hear her bones sigh in relief. "I'm as useless as those fake pockets hoity-toity companies put in their clothes." Samson laid near and rested his head on one of her feet as if to comfort her.

Zara raised her eyebrows. "Minnie, *no one* is as useless as fake pockets."

She pursed her lips. "I'm bein' serious. Here I am, sittin' while Oliver is out there somewhere, alone. Maybe hurt. Maybe lost. I don't know." She sucked in a breath. "I don't *know,* and it's the worst feelin'."

"You know this isn't your fault," Zara said.

"I do *not* know that." Minnie sat back in the chair, leaning the cane on one leg and crossing her arms. "I weren't lookin' after him like I shoulda been. Maybe he felt lonely. Or maybe he was mad at me for makin' him go to school."

"Minnie, you only made him go once." Zara touched her arm. "We don't know why he left, but we'll find him, okay?"

"What if we don't?" Minnie looked into Zara's eyes. "What if I have to tell Alex that I lost his little boy? What if we never find him?" Her chin quivered. "What if he's d—"

"Don't say that," Zara said, and her tone was firm enough to make Minnie stop.

She hadn't wanted to say it, anyway. Too bad she couldn't keep herself from thinking it.

"Oliver is smart," Zara said. "He's going through a lot. On top of all the coming of age crap that every kid goes through, he's recently lost his mom, the world is on the verge of ending, and his dad left him."

"Alex didn't *leave* him, leave him," Minnie said. "Oliver knows he's coming back."

"Does he?" Zara asked. "And yes, Alex *did* leave him. It doesn't matter that it was for a good reason. I guarantee it still hurts."

Minnie's arms dropped to her sides. Zara was right, and Minnie had *known* it long before she'd said it. But Minnie didn't like to dwell on problems she couldn't fix.

"Did I do it again?" Minnie asked in a soft voice.

"Did you do what?" Zara asked.

"When Lauren was growin' up, I ignored a lot of what she felt. I always knew best, always focused on the answers to our problems that made sense to me. It pushed her away. Took away years of her life she coulda been doin' somethin' she actually loved." Minnie let the tears fall without hindrance. "Did I do that to Oliver? Try to fix his problem my way?"

Zara took Minnie's hand and squeezed it. "Maybe," she said. "I honestly don't know. But either way, him running away like that, it's not your fault. Kids do stupid things at that age."

Minnie blinked away her tears and her eyes drifted back to the doors, to the parking lot beyond. Six figures were approaching. Minnie bolted upright, making Samson skitter back, and got to her feet.

"They're back," she said. "Do you see Oliver?" She squinted, hoping to see a smaller person's legs between that of the adults approaching the building.

But when they entered, most of them avoided looking at her. Amir and Harlow came up to her, holding hands, their eyes sad. The couple had been one of the first to volunteer for the search party.

"I'm sorry," Amir said. "We didn't find him."

"That doesn't mean he's not out there," Harlow said.

"You'll go back out tomorrow?" Minnie asked.

The two exchanged a look, and then Amir's expression turned apologetic. "Every scavenging party will keep an eye out for him," he said. "But Mateo said we can't dedicate any more time or resources to a search."

Minnie scowled. "Where is he?"

"Minnie," Zara said cautiously, "aren't you always saying it's better to catch flies with honey?"

"Well, I'm fresh out," Minnie said. "Where is Mateo?" She turned around and shouted down the long, wide hall. "Mateo! I got a bone to pick with you! Where are ya?"

Heads turned and voices quieted. Minnie shuffled down the hall, Samson's nails clicking behind her. About a fourth of the way down, as she shouted for the man to show himself, Mateo came out from one of the shops-turned-homes with a frown.

"You!" Minnie stopped and pointed at him.

He furrowed his brow and made a calming motion with his hands. "Minnie, what is it?"

"You're gonna keep searchin' for Oliver until he's found. You hear me?" She didn't bother keeping her voice down.

Mateo relaxed his shoulders and gestured to the shop to his left. "Why don't you come in," he said. "We can talk about it in the comfort of my home."

People were gathering, inching closer. "Let 'em stare!" Minnie said. "I don't give two shakes of a rat's tail. I don't got nothin' to talk about. If it was one of your kids, you'd not stop, and you won't stop now."

Mateo squared his shoulders. "Our scavenging parties will continue to keep an eye out, Minnie. There's still a chance we'll find him. But every day we dedicate to finding a child that may not want to be found is a day we're not taking care of everyone else."

"What kind of hogwash is that?" Minnie asked. "Of course he wants to be found. He's out there waitin' to be found."

"You said he took all his bits and bobs with him," Mateo said. "Isn't that right?"

"Bits and bobs?" Minnie narrowed her eyes. "You mean his momma's purse?"

"He doesn't go anywhere without it," Mateo said. "You told me that. And it has everything in it that's important to him."

"What does that have to do with anything?" Minnie asked.

"If he took it, he left on purpose."

Minnie scoffed. "He always has that bag with him," she said. "And even if he did leave on purpose, that don't mean he weren't plannin' to come right back."

"Then why?" Mateo asked. "Why did he go? And if he's not answering our calls, how do you suggest we find him? There's a whole city out there, Minnie. And there are only so many of us."

Samson whined at Minnie's side and licked her hand. She looked down at him, and then she looked over at Zara, who had followed her. And then the floodgates opened, and the sobs came out, and she couldn't stop it. She had no ideas, nothing to say, no way to find Oliver.

Mateo came to her, supported her with strong arms, and led her to a table at the center of the hall, near the kitchen under the dome. "Mind your own," he said to those around them, and the crowd dispersed. When she was seated, he sat next to her. "I'm sorry," he said. "I am. But I swear to you, it wouldn't be different if it were someone else's kid."

Zara put a hand on Minnie's shoulder. "It would be if it was yours," she said.

"Then," Mateo said, his tone sincere, "I'm glad I'm not a father because my orders are the best for everyone." He stood, pulled a clean cloth out of his pocket, and slid it across the table to Minnie. "I've had Harlow start making hankies," he said. "You can have that one."

Minnie took it, but she didn't look at Mateo. The tears were still coming, and she'd never felt more hopeless.

Zara took the seat Mateo left. "Kai and I will go out tomorrow," she said. "Maybe Blythe, too. We'll find him."

Behind her, a boy Minnie recognized from the classroom, the same one she'd seen Oliver fighting with, was staring at her, and there was such a look of pity in his eye. "I'm makin' a scene," Minnie said, sniffling. "I'll get on back to my room."

And she *was* tired. She was exhausted, actually. Zara got her a piece of flatbread and some fresh water, helped her back to her room, and left her alone with Samson. Minnie gave the dog a bit of her water and dished out a cup of dog food they'd brought from their own supplies. All the while, though she got quiet, she kept leaking her grief all over the place. Her eyes stung and her cheeks were chapped by the time she finally lay down and the tears stopped coming.

Sleep was like trying to kill a gnat buzzing around her head. Every time she thought she was close to snatching it, it slipped through her fingers and taunted her for another twenty minutes. The problem was, when her eyes were closed too long, she saw Oliver. And she didn't see him in memories. She saw him as he *could* be: huddled in a dark corner, crying for help, wondering what was taking her so long to find him.

Samson let out a gruff, short bark and startled Minnie awake as she was just on the cusp of sweet unconsciousness.

"Dagnabbit!" Minnie groaned and rolled to her side, slapping the floor beside her low-to-the-ground cot for the lantern. When she found it, she clicked the button, and the electric light came to life. "Samson, if you gotta pee, use the puppy pad for now, okay? I gotta get some sleep."

But the dog was sniffing an unevenly torn piece of paper. He licked it, and it stuck to his nose. Samson shook his head and sneezed, and the paper fell back to the floor.

"What in Sam Hill is that?" Minnie sat up and scooted off the cot, lowering her bottom gently to sit closer to the paper. She picked it up by the corner with two fingers, wrinkling her nose at the slobber. The writing was smudged a bit, and it was messy besides. She could barely make it out. She read it out loud. "Lolly Factory Boys." She dropped her hand and looked at Samson who cocked his head at her. "What is this?"

She struggled to her feet, using the wall and her cane, and when she was finally standing, she went to find Mateo again. "Mateo!" she shouted when she was still yards from him.

The man looked at her with apprehension. "Minnie, I told you—"

She shoved the paper at him. "Who are the Lolly Factory Boys?"

"What?" He took the paper. "Where did you get this?"

"Someone stuck it under my door. Don't know who."

He licked his lips. She could see the wheels turning in his head as his eyes examined the paper again. "It's what some people call that group of boys who attacked you at the plane," he said.

Minnie's eyes went wide. She hadn't thought of it before, but they'd all been so young. "You think they have Oliver?"

"They could," Mateo said, "but if they do, there's no getting him back."

Minnie pshawed. "I'll go get him myself, thank you very much."

"No, you won't." Mateo shook his head. "I don't know what to do with those boys. They'd rather die than be reasonable, and I won't have my people going near them. We've killed one or two, but it was out of necessity, and both people who did it almost went mad from the guilt. It's not easy to kill a kid, Minnie."

"Then we won't," Minnie said. "We'll just go see if they've got Oliver."

"You don't understand," Mateo said. "They're just as likely to kill *us* just because we hesitate when it comes to hurting kids. When we stay away from them, they generally stay away from us. Every skirmish we've had with them has ended badly for both sides. They know we'll fight them if we're forced to, which is great, but none of us want that."

"Let me go by myself, then," Minnie said.

Mateo eyed her cane. "You can't do that."

"I'll get Zara and Kai to come." Minnie lifted her chin.

"What are you going to do if you find him there?" Mateo asked.

"Bring him back."

"How? Are you going to kill a bunch of kids to get to him?"

Minnie sighed in frustration. "No. Course not."

"Then what?" Mateo made a show of waiting for an answer he very well knew she didn't have.

"We'll make a plan," Minnie said. "You ain't got no idea how good we are at that."

"You're not dragging any of my people into it."

"Fine." Minnie waved him off and started toward the shop where she could find Zara. "I don't need any of you, anyhow."

"Minnie," he called after her "this is a bad—"

"I don't care," she hollered, determination making her steps sure. And then, more for herself, she added, "I'm gettin' Oliver back, come hell or high water."

Chapter 15

Alexander Roman

"It's time to talk."
Alex looked up from his coffee. "Robert, wasn't it?" he asked.
It had been an interesting twelve hours or so since Robert had let Alex, Candice, Lauren, Walter, and Stella inside Barlow Scientific Research Bank. They'd found five technicians, trained to keep the facility running, maintain consistency with certain long-term experiments, and do nothing else. Apparently, the scientists didn't winter-over. Alex had, then, found only part of what he'd hoped for at the facility. Having others familiar with DV-10 and the mosquitos would have been ideal.
But when do we ever get the ideal these days, he thought.
Robert leaned against the doorway, arms crossed, eyebrows raised. Tall and broad-shouldered with muscles stretching the fabric of his t-shirt, the man had no problems infusing his words with authority. "The others are waiting in the lounge." It wasn't an invitation. It sounded like an order.
But Alex had been through too much and was too tired to give any feelings of intimidation a chance to settle. "I'd like to finish my breakfast. I didn't get up early to play twenty questions. I got up early because I needed a minute to myself." Alex took a sip, hot liquid soothing his throat, warming his hands through the mug. It had the slight aftertaste of hazelnut.
"You've had a minute," Robert said. "We gave you all night." He glanced around the kitchen. "Where are the others?"
"I gave you the basics last night," Alex said. "I can answer more of your questions, but I also need to get to work." He bit into his granola bar, took his time chewing, and swallowed. "The others are still resting, and I'm not disturbing them. There's no need, except for Walter."
Robert pushed off the doorframe and stood straighter. "We've been up all night, Alex. Not one of us has been able to sleep, and we've all got more questions. You're in our house, now, and we need some answers." A hint of fear and desperation bled through Robert's macho display.
Alex sighed. "I guess I have some questions, too," he said as he finished the last of his coffee. He wasn't going to give in to a bully, but he also wasn't going to hold out on a desperate man for his own comfort. "I'll get Walter, but I'm leaving the others alone. The two of us should be enough."
Robert nodded. "Fine. I'll get a cup of coffee and a quick breakfast for your friend. Meet us in the lounge."
Minutes later, Alex was filling Walter in on his morning conversation with Robert. "They're impatient," Alex said, "and I get the feeling they won't be showing us to what we need until they get what they want."
Walter, already dressed, stepped out into the hall and closed the door behind him. "It's not surprising," he said. "It seemed last night that they knew even less than Stella had when we first met her."
"Are you saying *I'm* the one who's being impatient?" Alex asked.
"I didn't say that." Walter grimaced slightly. "But now that you bring it up…" He started walking down the hall, and Alex kept pace. "They've been holding on to a thin thread of hope. For them, ignorance really was bliss. For the last few months, they've been able to tell themselves it was possible their friends and family were fine. We cut that thread last night. I wouldn't be surprised if some of them are still in denial."
Alex couldn't argue with that, and he prepared himself to respond to the technicians with a little more grace than he had given Robert that morning. They navigated the halls until they got to a lounge, a room whose entrance had a double-wide doorframe without a door. Couches were arranged around a television to the right, and to the left, there was a pool table, a card table, and a few bookshelves stuffed with movies, books, and boardgames.
The technicians were gathered closely. Robert paced behind a loveseat where three women were crammed together, and the last technician, Zac, if Alex recalled correctly, sat cross-legged on the floor, facing the loveseat.
Robert seemed to notice them first. He stopped his pacing. "Coffee and granola bar are on the side table," he said. "You can sit there." He pointed to another loveseat facing the one occupied.
Zac turned around and scooted to the side, remaining on the floor, and the three women whispered amongst themselves as Alex and Walter made their way to the indicated loveseat.
A woman with colorful patterned socks lifted her knees to her chest and hugged her legs. Her voice croaked as if she'd been crying enough to make her throat sore. "How sure are you about everything that you told us last night?" she asked.
Alex sank into the old cushions and took a moment to really look at the people in front of him. She wasn't the only one who looked exhausted and worn. Every one of them, even Robert, showed signs of a difficult night.
"What did you say your name was?" Alex asked gently.
"Cat Daily," she said.
"Nice to meet you, Cat." He gestured toward the men. "Robert, I know. And you're Zac?" The man on the floor nodded. "And you two?" he asked the women. "Farrah and Anise?"
They nodded, but Cat broke in, her tone agitated. "Answer my question."
"I'm sure about all of it," Alex said.
Walter nodded. "We both are. Everything we told you is true."

"You can't know that," Farrah said, brushing dark curls from her face, planting her feet more firmly on the floor, and leaning forward. "You said communications are down everywhere. You haven't been everywhere, right? You can't know that no one has found a way to fix this."
Zac added his voice, uncertain though it was. "You haven't even been west in the United States," he said. "You haven't been to Europe or Asia or Africa or South America or—"
"That's fair," Alex said, cutting him off because he was getting more frantic with every word. "But I saw how things played out in the Midwest. It followed me to the South. And from all accounts, the same thing happened on the east coast. We travelled to Colorado. Same story. New Zealand. Same story. McMurdo Station. Same story."
"The patterns seem clear," Walter said. "Not to mention that when we flew to New Zealand, we checked for signals. Nothing from Hawaii. Nothing from East Asia. Nothing from Australia. There seem to be pockets of survivors everywhere we've gone, but nothing is the same as it used to be. The swarms are everywhere, and we know from the days when the news was still coming in from all over the world that the sickness had reached every continent."
Anise sniffled and pulled out a tissue that seemed already well used. "But you can't *know*," she said weakly. "Everywhere... every*one*?"
"It's a well-educated guess," Walter said, "but unfortunately, it's a good one. I'm sorry. I'm truly sorry."
"The disease was created in the United States. Engineered. So were the mosquitos that have evolved to form these dangerous swarms." Alex looked at Walter. "As far as I know, there is no evidence that any other country had access to the research."
"That's correct," Walter said.
"And you know that," Robert said, glaring as he put both hands on the back of the loveseat and leaned forward, "because it was your company that spearheaded this DV-10."
Walter nodded. "Yes. Vanguard was commissioned by the government—"
"Excuses." Robert pushed off the couch, muscles tight, and he pointed at Walter. "You're responsible."
"I am the only one involved who is left, as far as I know," Walter said. "I am willing to take that responsibility on myself. It's one of the reasons I've tried so hard to get here."
"Whatever happens, even if you're successful," Cat said, "you can't come back from that. There's no redemption."
"I know." Walter looked down at his hands.
"Look," Alex said, "you can't say anything to him that hasn't been said already. He knows. But we need him to help me if we're going to save what's left out there."
None of them seemed to like that. Very few people did, at first. Alex hadn't. For a long time after meeting Walter and finding out what he'd done, he'd sworn justice would be done when it was all over. But his opinions had shifted. He had a new perspective.
"I was furious with him," Alex said. "I hated him at first. But I don't anymore. His penance is in the fact that he lost his wife, that he may never see either of his sons ever again. He's punished himself more than anyone ever could, and he carries all of that pain with him every day. Walter will fight to do the right thing until the second he dies. If I've learned anything about him at all, it's that he's not the same man who accepted that government contract."
"And we're just supposed to take your word for it?" Zac asked.
"For now," Alex said, "yes."
"When are we leaving Barlow?" Anise asked, her voice so soft, Alex nearly missed what she'd said.
"When I have what I need," Alex said. "We've travelled the world to find this place because we hope that the missing pieces to a vaccine are here."
"And," Walter added, "there should be cryopreservation pods somewhere, a lot of them."
"There are two hundred," Robert said. "From what I understand, they hold all manner of specimens. I maintain them."
"Are they still in good working condition? Has this place ever lost power?" Walter asked.
Alex held his breath until all five of them shook their heads. "That's good. That means the eggs should still be viable."
"How is this place run?" Walter asked.
"We have gasoline resupplies," Zac said, "twice a year. Enough to run the place on. And there's a nuclear power supply only to be used if the research bank is abandoned. It can keep this place operational and ready to be reoccupied for about twenty years."
"Twenty years?" Walter's mouth dropped open.
"It's similar to what's used in a nuclear submarine," Zac said. "The only reason subs have to resupply is because of the people on board who need things like food and fresh water. You ever heard of the seed bank up north?"
Alex nodded.
"Same thing," Zac said. "There are other banks, you know, if the rumors are true. You hear stuff when you work in places like this. Technology and information and research, all preserved. Not just by the United States, either."
Alex looked up at the ceiling, processing. That was information he hadn't known he'd needed to hear. "So, then, maybe we can rebuild one day after all. Maybe all the advancements we've made won't be completely lost."
"That's a discussion for another time," Walter said. "First, we need to focus on what we came here to do."
"We're not done," Robert said.
"This is going to take time." Alex stood. "We can talk more, but not right now. Right now, we need to start looking for information related to DV-10."
"He's right," Cat said, looking over her shoulder at Robert. "We can't leave here until they've done the work they came to do. I want to go home, Rob."
"I agree with Cat," Zac said.
The other two girls nodded, and Robert sighed, throwing up his hands in apparent reluctant agreement.
"Robert," Alex said, "I need your help to find which cryopreservation pods hold the mosquito eggs. Meanwhile, maybe one of you can show Walter to your database or a laboratory? He can search for files on DV-10."

"I can do that," Cat said.
"What about the others?" Anise asked. "The women you came here with?"
"Maybe they can answer more of our questions," Farrah said.
"For now, I'd like to just let them be," Alex said. "Stella, especially. She's been through a lot recently."
"But," Walter said, "we are going to be here for at least a couple weeks, I think. I'm sure, eventually, they'd be open to questions."
"We won't push," Farrah said.
"Robert?" Alex gestured toward the doorway. "Lead the way."
The technician grunted with dissatisfaction but stalked toward the hallway anyway. Alex followed as Cat stood and smiled at Walter. He had the feeling his friend was going to have an easier time with his guide.
Robert led Alex to a stairwell, flipped on the lights, and descended several flights before coming to the first door. He opened it, and they entered a smaller room that was cold but bearable. "The pods are kept deep underground," he said, grabbing gear off a hook that reminded Alex of a firefighter's suit. "It's frigid in there." Robert nodded to a glass wall. "You'll need to wear outer gear, just like if you were outside."
Alex approached the window to look out onto a sea of blinking lights. Overhead bulbs came to life, and the pods were revealed. Rows of them stretched across stainless steel floors.
"You'll need to search here," Robert said, tapping a desktop. "Find the numbers assigned to the pods you're looking for, and I'll take you to them."
"I'll need to examine them," Alex said, "grow a few to maturity in a controlled environment. You have labs?"
"The best," Robert said. "This place is designed to work with the deadliest diseases and their cures. But, if DV-10 is spread by mosquitos… is it safe to allow these to mature?"
"These won't carry the pathogen. They're strictly intended to breed with the population and create generations of malformed mosquitos who will eventually render the species completely infertile."
A fresh energy pumped through Alex's veins. He smiled at those pods, at the possibilities. It had only been months. If the mosquitos making up the swarms were still genetically close to the mosquitos in those pods, the countermeasure would work.
What if they're not? Alex pushed the thought away. They have to be, he thought instead. The swarms are only a handful of generations beyond the ones in those pods. And I have so much information already. I've done so much research. We're already so close.
In Atlanta and then in Boston, he had gathered pieces, sliding them into place one at a time. He was so close to seeing the bigger picture, to finding the answers.
He turned and marched to the desk, sitting with anticipation as the computer whirred to life. "Let's finish this puzzle," he said. "Let's get to work."

Chapter 16

Oliver Roman

Escape was not an option. There were too many of them, and he was locked away, and when he was not, he was guarded. No amount of begging or negotiating persuaded Ihaka to let him go, either. Oliver was trapped.

The large dog cage enclosing him provided just enough room for him to sit up, if he didn't mind slouching a bit, if he didn't mind wires pressing into his skull. The contents of his bag bit into his hip, but he didn't dare take it off for fear someone would take it. His legs and back ached. He was only allowed out of the enclosure to go to the bathroom and only on Ihaka's schedule.

I'm so stupid, Oliver thought for the thousandth time. I should have never left.

His plan to prove himself to Will and Ava and Niko and the rest seemed so childish in hindsight. Even Will had been smart enough to know not to go out into the city.

What made me think I could do it? He crossed his arms and squeezed fistfuls of his grimy shirt tight enough to make his hands tremble. Warmth flushed his cheeks as he thought back to that moment of freedom he'd felt, when he'd let his guard down and let his imagination wander. He groaned softly to himself. *So stupid!*

A door opened somewhere he couldn't see, and voices poured into the large factory, hoots and laughter echoing off the walls. Black wires obstructed his view, cut it into squares. There was a narrow field of vision from his cage which was positioned under a set of industrial metal stairs. Large vats were behind him, blocking that way completely. But through the wires and under a set of conveyer belts, he could see the legs of at least a dozen boys.

There must have been a clear space over there, beyond the factory equipment. The boys always settled in the same spot. When they sat, sometimes Oliver could see faces. Sometimes, he was sure some of them looked back. They never responded to him. Ihaka made sure of that.

What they meant to do with him, Oliver still didn't know. Wild theories had raced through his mind at first. Perhaps they were cannibals. Or maybe they had another prisoner somewhere, and they'd make Oliver fight to the death. Those kinds of stories had to come from somewhere. History was full of them… or, at least, Oliver assumed it was. Like the gladiators and the ancient people who sacrificed children and the cannibals he was sure he'd heard about in the deepest parts of some rainforest somewhere. He'd seen it in movies, read about it in books.

Well, whatever they want with me, Oliver said, I won't let them have it.

The sound of footsteps nearing sapped his courage. Oliver twisted, trying to see who was coming, expecting it to be Ihaka. A new boy appeared, though, one he'd seen but never talked to. He plopped down on the concrete floor outside the cage, leaned back on skinny arms, and grinned.

"Kia ora, mate," he said.

Oliver frowned. He remembered someone else saying that at the shopping center. "Hello?" he asked, confused about the friendly tone.

"How's it going?" he asked.

"What?" Oliver blinked a few times. "I'm in a cage."

"Oh, yeah," the boy said. "That's gotta stink."

Oliver shifted the best he could, trying to get a view beyond the newcomer. "Where's Ihaka?"

The boy scoffed. "Aren't you gonna ask my name?" He raised his eyebrows in anticipation.

"Okay… what's your name?" Oliver narrowed his eyes and cocked his head, waiting for the punchline or the trick.

"Etera," he said. "Nobody's got your name yet. What is it?"

"Why do you want to know?" Oliver asked.

"Because. You won't be in that cage much longer. Fact, Ihaka said you're getting out today." Etera leaned forward and started picking at the underside of his nails. "I told him he'd kept you in there too long. I wasn't in there but a few hours."

"You were put in this cage, too?" Oliver asked.

"Oh, yeah." Etera waved the question off like it should have been obvious. "Strength of will test. Good one, too. Usually, we let boys out when they stop crying. You did that yesterday."

"A test?" Oliver's mouth dropped open. "Are there any more tests?"

"Sure," Etera said. "One more big one."

"What is it?" Oliver asked. "And what's it for?"

"It's to see if you're brave enough and tough enough to join the *hapu*," Etera said.

"A hapu?" Oliver wrinkled his nose. "What's that?"

"It's our clan," Etera said. "We never had an American boy before, though. We've been placing bets on if you're going to pass."

"Pass what?" Oliver raised his voice. He was getting frustrated. Etera always said just enough to give Oliver another question.

"Whoa, mate," Etera said. "Don't be so loud."

"I wasn't—I mean, you're not answering my questions," Oliver said.

"Still." Etera shrugged. "I'm not yelling."

"I'm not yelling either!" Oliver said.

"Are too."

"Am not."

"You're raising your voice."
Oliver groaned. "That's not yelling."
"Then what is it?" Etera leaned forward, seeming genuinely interested.
"It's… it's… not yelling." Oliver crossed his arms. "It's a step below yelling."
"Huh." Etera pursed his lips. "Well, the rest of us want to meet you before you go on to the next test. Ihaka said I can let you out if you promise not to try to escape."
Oliver's head started to pound. "What happens if I do?"
"Probably have to kill you."
"Okay. I won't." Oliver crossed his heart. "I swear."
"Goodonya." Etera stood and started fishing in his pockets. "I know I have the key somewhere," he said, screwing his mouth up tight and squinting as if in concentration. "Ah! Here it is." He dramatically yanked out a little key. "Before I do, though, still need your name."
"It's Oliver."
"Oliver. Oli for short?" Etera asked
"No," Oliver said firmly, defiantly. "Don't call me that."
"Yeah, all right," Etera said. "Oliver, then."
"Why didn't you just let me out when you first got here?" Oliver asked, his body aching to stand up.
"Proper introductions, mate," Etera said as he unlocked the cage.
The hinges on the cage's door squeaked as it opened, and Oliver crawled out quickly, hopping up and taking a few steps back from Etera, gripping the bag's strap across his chest. "I'm not going back in."
"I know," Etera said, looking at him like he was crazy. "That test's over. Didn't I say that?"
"No," Oliver said. "I mean… maybe?"
"That's on me." Etera gave Oliver's arm a hard pat that made him lose his balance.
He stopped himself from tipping over with a hand on the side of a conveyer belt. "So… I'm just supposed to go meet everyone? Pretend I wasn't just locked in a cage for days?"
Etera simply nodded once. "Yep. We all had to do it. It's worth it, in the end. We'll show you." He took a slight bow and gestured for Oliver to go ahead of him. "After you," he said.
Oliver cautiously walked forward, and Etera joined him, walking just slightly behind, swinging his arms and walking like he was having one of the best days of his life. It was impossible not to look over his shoulder every few seconds. Oliver's insides were crawling, warning him to be on the lookout for danger, and besides that, the boy's mood seemed so out of place. He couldn't stop glancing.
Oliver stopped on the other side of the conveyer belts and stared at the group of boys lounging on huge pillows and sleeping bags. Sunlight poured in through large windows along the wall. A mound of candies in shiny, multicolored wrappings stood about as tall as Oliver; the foot of the candy mountain was at arm's length for the boys closest to it. One of them leaned back, grabbed a handful and started tossing them to the other boys.
"Oi!" Etera held up an open hand. "I'll take one, Leo."
The boy with the handful tossed one across the room, and Etera caught it. "You want one, Oliver?"
"No…" Oliver's mouth watered despite himself.
Etera had to have spotted the lie. He grinned widely at Leo. "Throw me one for Oliver here." When he had another candy in hand, he grabbed Oliver's wrist and put the colorful wrapper in Oliver's hand. "Take it," he said. "You won't regret it." He popped his own in his mouth and tossed the wrapper away. "Delicious."
Ihaka stepped out of a room to the left, making Oliver's breath catch. "Oliver, is it?" he asked.
Oliver nodded but said nothing. He wanted to run, but Etera's words earlier kept him in place. The sun seemed to catch on the edge of knives and axes and spears amongst the boys to remind Oliver that they could and would hurt him.
"Have a sit, then," Ihaka said, gesturing to the haphazard circle of boys on the floor.
Etera gave Oliver another generous pat on the back and plopped into a bean bag chair. "C'mon," he said, nodding to a round, empty pillow beside him.
All eyes were on him as he sat down, sinking into the pillow. He let his legs stretch out in front of him, unwilling to fold them up after being stuck in the cage. Ihaka sat on the opposite side, never taking his eyes off of Oliver. It made him squirm.
"What do you want?" Oliver asked.
"We just want to get to know ya," Ihaka said, leaning back on one elbow. "You haven't touched your lolly. Not hungry?"
Oliver opened his hand and looked down at the blue wrapper. "The candy?" he asked. "It's not a lollipop."
"A lolly can be all sorts of sweets," Etera said. "Just the Kiwi way of sayin' it."
"Well, if I was hungry," Oliver said, "a candy wouldn't do much, would it?"
Ihaka laughed. "Fair enough," he said. "Hey, Coop!"
The boy to Ihaka's righthand sat up straighter. "Yeah?"
"It's about time we cook tea," Ihaka said. He smiled and leaned forward, bringing his hand to his mouth. "That's the evening meal, for you Americans."
Coop hopped up, rapped two other boys on the head with his knuckles, and all three of them left the circle, heading for an open doorway.
Etera pointed to Oliver's candy. "That there's your appetizer."
"Don't be rude," Ihaka said. "There isn't much to go around these days out there." He shrugged. "In *here,* though… we like to share with our brothers."

Oliver wet his lips and looked down at the candy again. He unwrapped it and slipped the candy in his mouth. It was incredibly sweet, but it only made his stomach growl for real food.

"Tell us about yourself," Ihaka said. "Why would an American come all the way here in a time like this?"

Oliver moved the candy from one side of his mouth to the other; it clacked against his teeth. Everyone was looking at him, so curious, but all he could see was Will's expression of mockery when he'd told him the things he'd done before coming to New Zealand.

He decided to give as little information as possible. "I came here with my dad," Oliver said, "and some friends. They just drag me wherever they go. Except..." He looked down at his hands, the hurt of his father's leaving returning.

"Except what?" Etera asked.

"My dad left me here this time," Oliver said.

"Sounds like he gapped it to me," Ihaka said. "Ain't comin' back."

Oliver tensed. "You don't know anything about him."

"Relax," Etera said, "it's a good thing." The others around the circle nodded. "We only take ones that don't got connections."

"Who says I want to stay here?" Oliver asked.

"Why were you out there by yourself?" Ihaka asked, ignoring Oliver's reply. "Answer me that."

"I was..." Oliver hesitated. He was embarrassed about the truth, but he couldn't come up with a better answer. He deflated a little. "I was trying to find this factory, to take candy back to the other kids. I thought it would help me fit in."

Laughter erupted from every boy except for Ihaka. The older boy stood and made a quieting motion with his hands. The others cut their giggling off immediately. "That's enough," Ihaka said. "He braved the *taniwha* and our *hapu* just to get some lollies for a bunch of randos."

Etera leaned in and whispered, "The *taniwha* is the monster, the black cloud."

Ihaka continued. "That's the kinda boy I want around here. Imagine if we gave him something real important to do! Now imagine he was doin' it for us because he cared about us." Several of the boys' eyes went wide. Ihaka nodded with respect. "Oliver's got guts. I won't have nobody laughing about that."

Oliver nearly choked on his candy. *What is going on?* he thought. He'd expected Ihaka to be like Will, to take every opportunity to make Oliver feel smaller.

A whistle signaled Coop's return. He and the other two boys carried a large bin between them. "Saltines and marmite, cookie times, and burger rings for everyone!" He dumped the contents of the container in the center of the group.

Oliver jumped at the sudden frenzy to grab food. Etera threw a few things at him, and all he could do was block his face and let the packages fall to his lap. He looked down, suspicious of the strange snacks as the other boys settled back down, plastic crinkled, and a comment about how the Cookie Times should be heated inspired several boys to voice their agreement.

Ihaka brought out a marker and wrote on his packages before passing the marker around. "Don't eat too much in one sitting," he said. "We won't give out more rations until tomorrow night. It'll be like that every day. You'll see, if you're still around in a few days."

So, they might let me go? Oliver relaxed a little bit.

He examined the packages. "I've never eaten any of this." He held up the jar of marmite. "How do I eat it?"

"With the saltines," Etera said, "like this." He dipped a finger into his jar and pulled it out to reveal a dark brown substance that looked the consistency of honey. He slathered it on a cracker and popped it in his mouth.

Oliver did the same, but when he popped it in his mouth, he nearly spit it out. "It's salty! It's *really* salty."

Several boys chuckled, and Ihaka had someone throw him a bottle of water. He took a grateful sip and tried the marmite again. He was *very* hungry. It wasn't so bad the second time around, when he wasn't expecting it to be more like jam.

"It's time you told us about yourself," Ihaka said. "It's how we do things here, before you're tested again."

Oliver set aside the marmite and opened the Cookie Time package. "And after I'm tested... I can go?"

"Depends," Ihaka said. "Don't think you'll want to, though. What's waiting back there for you? You said your dad is gone. No mum, right?"

Oliver shook his head. "No, but... I have people who will be worried." He thought of Minnie, guilt making his skin prickle. She was probably out there looking for him.

"Let me guess," Ihaka said, "the same people won't let you be your own man, will they? They're not your parents, but they act like they own you." He shrugged. "Truth is, not even parents own us, do they? These people you think are waiting for you, they don't let you do nothin', do they? I even heard they make those kids go to school. As if books are gonna help us now."

Oliver shifted uncomfortably. Ihaka's words hit close to home. Minnie, and even his dad, treated him like he was a baby. Hearing Ihaka call him a man stirred a desire in Oliver to hear it again. He'd been through so much, survived so much.

I could have gone with Dad, Oliver thought. If he'd given me a chance, I could have helped.

"Where'd your dad go, anyway?" Etera asked.

"It's a long story," Oliver said. "You find out where he went, then you ask why. For that, I'd have to go back to Day Zero."

"Sweet as," Ihaka said. "Go on."

Oliver took a bite of the big, prepackaged cookie. "I don't think you'd believe me."

"We will," Ihaka said.

He sounded like he meant it. He also sounded like he wouldn't stop asking until Oliver gave in.

Might as well get it over with.

Will and the others had assumed he'd been lying about so much; the strangers before him would surely do the same. The only reason Will believed his dad had gone to Antarctica was because the adults all confirmed it.

So, Oliver told his story, from the beginning, the best he could. He used the items in his bag as proof. And something crazy happened. The more he talked, the more awe he saw in the eyes of the boys around him. Ihaka leaned in, and though he didn't seem as enraptured as the others, he looked at Oliver with a growing respect.

Telling the story started to energize Oliver. The boys asked questions. They gasped and oohed and clapped at all the right times. They believed it all, even though some of it wasn't quite true. Oliver had not been with his father when he'd stopped Ward and Turner, the first time or the second, and he'd not been there when his dad had saved Lauren from the serial killer. Half of the story he told were events he'd merely heard about, much of it by eavesdropping when he shouldn't have been.

And it *worked.*

"And that's when I decided Will was a chicken," Oliver said, embellishing a little. "I pushed him aside, and I told him, 'You might not have the guts to go out there, but I do.' And then, I escaped the adults. Not one of them even saw me. I got a little distracted once I was out there, but if you hadn't found me with my guard down, I would have done it. I could have snuck away with a whole bag full of candy."

"Just poor luck, then," Etera said, nodding. "We all got poor luck sometimes."

Ihaka held up a finger. "Or was it his best luck yet?"

The other boys murmured amongst themselves and nodded.

"Without that slip, Oliver wouldn't be here, now, would he?" Ihaka sat back and shook his head. "It's fate, I think. He's meant to be here. If I'm right, he'll pass the test, no problem."

"Are you ready to tell me what the test is?" Oliver asked.

"Depends." Ihaka raised his eyebrows. "What do you think about us?"

"Honestly?" Oliver asked.

"Yeah." Ihaka gestured for Oliver to continue.

"I think the cage was terrible. I don't understand it, and I don't think it's right. But…" He hesitated. He was still soaring from the rush of having so many boys hanging on his every word. "I guess you're all right, besides that. I think we could be friends, as long as you don't put me back in the cage."

"The tests are to see if you're man enough to join the *hapu*," Ihaka said. "They're meant to be hard. They're meant to challenge you. But we didn't starve you, right? Let you out to go to the loo."

"Sure," Oliver said. "But still, that's not how I'd say I usually go about making friends."

Ihaka's voice turned firm and passionate. "We're not trying to make friends," he said. "We're trying to forge brothers. We need strong men for our *hapu* to survive."

Oliver swallowed hard. "And you think… you think *I* could be what you're looking for?"

Ihaka nodded. "I do, mate. If you pass the next test."

"Which is?" Oliver prompted again.

"It's a test of trust," Ihaka said. "When we go out there, we have to know that you have our backs, and you have to know that we have yours."

"So, what?" Oliver said, offering a half grin. "Are we doing one of those trust falls?"

Ihaka shook his head slowly, and the other boys' expressions became grim. "In three days' time, the choice will be yours: face the *taniwha*, the black cloud, and become our brother or fight me to the death in an attempt to leave."

A cold anxiety sprouted in the pit of Oliver's stomach. He met Etera's gaze, looked from boy to boy, hoping for a sign that Ihaka was joking. He was only met with confirmations. No matter what he chose, in three days, Oliver would be forced to come face to face with death.

Chapter 17

Zara Williams

"It was risky," Kai said, "bringing her out here."
"Keep your voice down," Zara whispered sharply.
A few yards away, Lizzy lay in the middle of the road as she'd done on the tarmac back at the airport. As far as Zara could tell, the warmth of the pavement comforted her somehow. She, Kai, and Blythe sat on the curb, eating their lunch after a couple hours of searching for Oliver.
Kai balanced his flatbread on one knee and raised both hands. "Sorry," he said.
Blythe kept his eyes on Lizzy, frowning at her as he chewed his meager lunch. "She doesn't seem to be listening," he said.
"It doesn't matter." Zara kept her voice at a whisper.
It was true, of course. Lizzy hadn't so much as twitched at Kai's comment. Still, Zara didn't want her feeling like a burden. She'd been emotionally manipulated enough by those crazies.
"Kai's right, though," Blythe said, still not lowering his voice.
Zara sighed. "Look, what was I going to do? We had to come out here to look for Oliver. I couldn't leave her with Minnie. She's struggling as it is. And what if Lizzy had one of her nightmares?"
"There are lots of nice people back at the mall." Kai tore off a piece of his bread and popped it into his mouth.
"Like that natural remedies woman and her grandfather," Blythe said. "You said you liked them."
"I do." Zara's stomach rumbled, but when she picked at her own bread, it stuck in her throat and left her mouth dryer than before. She tugged on a curly fly-away brushing her forehead and twirled it around her finger. "They're helping me help Lizzy, but that doesn't mean I want to leave her with them. They're strangers to her."
"And what if a swarm comes?" Blythe asked.
"You had to lead her to safety back at the plane when those boys attacked," Kai said. "There's no guarantee she'd even have the self-preservation to run if a swarm shows up."
"I know," Zara said. "But Blythe, you're a big guy. You can throw her over your shoulder, right?"
Kai scoffed. "What about me?"
Zara reached over and patted his hand. "You're the best, Kai, but…" She shrugged.
Blythe laughed. "I think she's trying to say you don't have the right physique."
"Thanks." Kai gave him a flat stare. "I didn't quite catch that."
Blythe gave him a hearty pat. "Always glad to clear things up." He turned to Zara. "Yeah, if something happens, I've got your friend."
Kai sighed. "I'm underappreciated."
Zara shook her head, smiled at him, and stretched upward to kiss his cheek. "You're not," she said. "I wouldn't like you so much if I didn't know for sure I could depend on you."
He cracked a small smile and waggled his eyebrows. "Tell me more, mi amore."
Blythe rolled his eyes and ate the last of his flatbread. "We better keep moving."
"I'm not done receiving compliments, thank you very much," Kai said.
"Later, okay?" Zara squeezed Kai's hand, and he shrugged at her with a that's-acceptable-I-suppose sort of expression on his face. Zara ate the last bite of her food and hopped to her feet. "I'll get Lizzy."
She closed the distance and looked down at her friend. Lizzy's eyes were closed, but the way she lay with her fingers interlocked over her belly told Zara she was most likely awake. She looked so peaceful. A pang of guilt stabbed at Zara as she squatted and tapped Lizzy's shoulder.
"Hey, we're going to keep going," Zara said. "It's time to get up." She examined the area, not seeing Lizzy's flatbread anywhere. "You ate your lunch, right?"
Lizzy opened her eyes and looked at Zara with confusion at first. But a few seconds later, she blinked rapidly and sat up, the confusion gone. "Did we find him?" she asked.
"Oliver? Not yet." Zara frowned. *Does she not remember?* she thought, but pointing out missteps like that only served to frustrate Lizzy, so she kept the question to herself.
"Okay." Lizzy got to her feet, cupped her hands around her mouth, and yelled, "Oliver!"
Zara stood. "That's it. Just keep close to us."
The four of them picked up the search again until Zara's throat was raw from shouting. Minnie had wanted them to find some candy factory, and they would, if they had to, but Mateo had made it clear that he didn't want them going near it. A few more days of searching the immediate area seemed the best thing to do, anyway. If Oliver had been captured by the rogue boys, he was likely alive and would remain so, according to Mateo. If he was alone, wandering the streets, lost and living off what he could scavenge, however…
Minnie hadn't liked that, but she'd agreed to searching the city in an ever-widening radius from the shopping center. Of course, she hadn't had much choice in the matter. There was no way Minnie could get out there and tackle searching for Oliver herself. Eventually, they would get to the factory, but it would take some time. Zara, Kai, and Blythe could only manage so much, especially with Lizzy.
They made their way back to the shelter after another couple hours and no Oliver.
When the shopping center came into view, Lizzy paused, frowning. "But… we haven't found him, yet," she said.

Zara hooked her arm with Lizzy's and gently prodded her forward as Kai and Blythe continued into the parking lot. "I know. We'll go back out tomorrow."

"Why did he leave?" Lizzy asked.

The question sent a pang through Zara's chest. That was the fifth time she'd asked that question. Zara didn't know what it meant, why Lizzy couldn't remember entire conversations.

"We don't know," Zara said. "Hey, um… how are the voices today?"

"Still quiet," Lizzy said. "They haven't gotten loud in weeks. That's good, right?"

"I think so," Zara said, though she'd feel better if the voices were gone all together. She didn't say that, though. Lizzy did better when they focused on the positive.

Minnie welcomed them with a determined set of her jaw. "You didn't find him because you didn't look in the right spot."

Zara, Kai, and Blythe exchanged glances, and Zara let them take Lizzy on to rest in their shop-turned-home so that Zara could talk to Minnie. It was the same routine every time they came back.

"We've been through this," Zara said. "We don't know Oliver is at this factory, and looking there has to be a last resort. We don't want to cause conflict."

"I should go myself." Minnie huffed and leaned on her cane.

"If he's there, he's safer than he would be if he were wandering lost in the city," Zara said. "What if we sneak up on that factory and get into a fight? What if that makes it so we can't search the city anymore for fear of those boys retaliating? If Oliver isn't there, we've just sabotaged our chances of actually finding him."

"So we sneak up real careful-like," Minnie nodded once and firmly. "Ain't no rocket science. We just gotta be careful."

"Minnie, Mateo is already dubious about letting us go out and continue to look for him at all. He sees it as us refusing to carry our weight around here. If it wasn't for Alex and what he's doing, we might have been kicked out for insisting."

"Who cares? I sure don't." Minnie crossed her arms.

Zara licked her lips and looked up at the skylight, trying to figure out how to say what had to be said. She took a deep breath and met Minnie's eyes with her own. "If they don't come back," Zara said, "this is our home, now. You understand that, right?"

"Don't be ridiculous." Minnie pshawed.

"I'm not. If they don't come back, what other choice will we have except to stay here for whatever time we have left?" Zara softened her voice. "I'm not giving up, Minnie. I'm just trying to take into account all possible outcomes. If they don't come back, we're all dead eventually, but we'll need to make the best of the rest of our lives. I'm not going to spend my last days traipsing across the planet, trying to get home, and neither will the rest of us. We'll have a couple years, if we're lucky, and I'm going to spend them finding as much happiness as I can piece together. That means staying here, with these people."

Minnie stared at her like she'd grown another head. "You're tryin' to make tea without sugar. It ain't right. There's no givin' up, not now, not ever. We can't go around spoutin' nonsense like that! Alex and Lauren *are* comin' back. And when they do, I'm gonna have Oliver back, safe and sound."

"I hope so," Zara said. There was no use in repeating herself or insisting that she wasn't talking about giving up. Minnie wouldn't accept it; she was too stubborn. Zara suspected she'd hold out hope for Alex and her daughter to return until her dying breath, even if that was a year or two away.

But I can't do that, Zara thought.

Minnie threw up a hand. "You ain't listenin'."

Funny, Zara thought, I could say the same about you.

"I am," Zara said, instead. "And we will go back out tomorrow, and we will keep looking. No one is giving up. I promise."

After a frustrated sigh, Minnie clucked her tongue, turned as sharply as she could with her limp and her cane, and mumbled to herself as she hobbled away. Zara watched her go for a minute, part of her glad that the woman still had so much fire left, even if it meant arguments. And even if she didn't agree with Minnie's outlook completely, Zara did need people in her life to remind her to hold on to hope.

Her body was sore, begging her to rest, but Zara stopped at the shop with the yellow curtains anyway. "Nyree?" She knocked on the glass. "Mahaka?"

The old master carver was the one to pull back the curtain, his broad smile crinkling his wrinkles even further so that his delight reached eyes, accentuated by crow's feet that somehow made him seem filled with life rather than tired. Features that on others made them seem old and tired were somehow transformed in Mahaka, as if his age were simply a compounding of his peace and joy.

"Kia ora," he said brightly.

Zara smiled back at him. "Kia ora."

Behind him Nyree waved her inside. "Come," she said. "We have been waiting for you."

"Is it finished?" Zara asked as Mahaka stepped aside to let her in.

He nodded, turned around, picked something up, and faced her again with his hands clasped near his heart. "This *taonga* was carved with a desire for healing and new beginnings." He held out his hands, cupping the wooden pendant on a leather string, offering it to Zara.

She picked up the necklace, its polished surface smooth beneath her fingers. She cradled it much the same way Mahaka had. "And what about the kara.. karakia?" she asked, stumbling over the word.

"Ah, the blessing," Mahaka said. "You remembered."

As Zara had come to get fresh bandages and calming teas for Lizzy the past several nights, Mahaka and Nyree had explained more about what a master carver's work was really about. The tradition of gifting taonga reached back into Māori history, and while they were often created from pounamu, a jade stone native to the island, Mahaka's modern stone-working tools could not be used without water and electricity. The master carver continued his work with woodcarving tools, instead. He believed the sentiments behind the taonga were the most important.

"You may say a *karakia*," Nyree said. "It is a prayer of sorts, an imbuing of intentions. If you follow a faith, you may bless the gift with that in mind."

"What do I say?" Zara asked.

"What does your heart want this gift to represent?" Mahaka asked. "Give it meaning with your own desires."

"Do I have to say it out loud?"

"No," Nyree said with a gentle and encouraging smile. "Bless it however you want."

Zara nodded, closed her eyes, and blessed the pendant to the best of her ability. A peace came over her. "Thank you," she said, holding the taonga to her heart.

Mahaka bowed his head slightly. "May you find what you're looking for."

Nyree held back the curtain as Zara turned to go, both she and her father sending Zara off with encouraging smiles. When she got back to her temporary home, she felt lighter. There were no guarantees that any of them would survive, that they would find Oliver, or that Walter and Alex would come back with the answers they'd sought. There was something freeing in the acceptance of what could be coupled with focus on life in the moment.

She passed Kai and Blythe who were working at the navigation table and headed straight for the partitioned area she and Lizzy shared in the back left corner. Lizzy was laying under a blanket on her floor pallet, hands tucked under her chin, eyes wide open, a blank expression on her face.

"Liz?" Zara sat on the floor in her line of sight. She tucked some of Lizzy's hair behind her ear. "I have something for you."

She held the pendant out, the leather string dangling from her hand. It was in the shape of a *koru*, a spiral Mahaka had said mimicked a furled silver fern frond. Carved along the flat spiral, butterflies and lady bugs played. With Zara's other hand, she brought out the chain on which she kept the rings she and Lizzy had chosen in an abandoned pawn shop months ago, rings that were supposed to symbolize a promise of forever friendship, a promise Zara had broken.

Lizzy propped herself up and took the pendant, staring down at it, saying nothing. A lump formed in Zara's throat, another in her stomach. She'd thought about what to say, how to express herself to Lizzy in a way that made sense, but practiced words were lost to her.

"I…" Zara began but had to clear her throat. She shifted her weight, scooted a bit closer, and started again. "That was made by Mahaka. I told you a little about him. He made me a *taonga*. It's a special custom with the Māori, a gift. That shape symbolizes new beginnings and healing and peace." The weight of the two rings in her hand was heavier than it should have been. "When we chose these rings, I thought I knew what friendship meant. I thought I knew what sisterhood meant. But… I only knew part of it. I made mistakes, and I got wrapped up in grief and anger, and I left you alone." Her vision blurred, and she blinked away tears.

Lizzy reached out and took Zara's free hand. She squeezed it, pulled back, and put the leather string around her head, looking back at the pendant. Lizzy didn't say anything. She had few words most of the time, but her actions gave Zara the courage to finish.

"The lady bugs and butterflies are supposed to represent a new version of what we had before. Like, Zee and Liz 2.0. I… um… blessed it with a prayer. I know that sounds silly, but—"

"It doesn't sound silly," Lizzy said, still examining the pendant.

Zara smiled. "Well, I tried to… I don't know… infuse it with the love I have for you, a sister's love that can't be broken. It can only be made stronger. I learned that through losing you, Liz, and I'll always regret not seeing it before. You and I will always be best friends. It doesn't matter what you do, what you've done, what you're going through—as far as it depends on me, I won't leave you alone ever again."

Lizzy looked up at her. "I love it, Zee."

"You do?"

Lizzy opened her arms and threw them around Zara's neck, hugging her tight. "You know I forgive you, right?"

Zara swallowed hard. The fact was, she *hadn't* known that. "You don't have to," she said, her voice cracking.

Lizzy pulled back and sat on her knees, holding Zara's hands. There was a lucidity about her that Zara only saw on occasion. It happened more and more as time went on, but it was still rare enough that Zara could clearly see the difference between it and her usual detachment. Lizzy's hands trembled a little as she spoke. "If you can love me after what I did—"

"That wasn't your fa—"

"I still *did* terrible things," Lizzy said. "Whether I was… brainwashed or whatever… it doesn't change the fact that with my own hands, I killed people. I tried to kill my dad, Zee. I… I loved Azalea." Her face paled, and a visible shudder ran up and down her body.

"No," Zara said, "you were hurt by Azalea. It was Stockholm Syndrome, or something. I'm not an expert in cults, but you can't blame yourself for those things."

Lizzy shook her head. "I don't blame myself, not really, not anymore. But… I can't separate myself from it, either."

Zara bit her lower lip, unsure of what to say.

Lizzy just smiled, a bit of sadness coloring her expression and a bit of… hope, perhaps? "All I know is, if I'm ever going to heal from what happened, if those voices are ever going to go away, if the nightmares will ever stop, it will be because you didn't give up on me. You and…" She swallowed, the words seeming to come out reluctantly. "…and my dad."

Those last words shocked Zara a little. She hadn't pushed on the issue of Walter. Whatever the Heirs of the Mother had done to Lizzy, it had been centered around fostering a hatred—a *repulsion*—of her father. And Lizzy hadn't gotten to know the new Walter, the Walter who had stripped way his cruelty in exchange for real compassion, who in the wake of believing his daughter dead, had finally found his humanity. Those words were the first time Lizzy had said anything positive about her father since her return.

"Will you tell me a story?" Lizzy asked. "One of those movies you used to love so much? I miss hearing you talk about them."

Taken off guard by the request, Zara wrinkled her brow. "You used to say they were for nerds."

Lizzy shrugged. "I always secretly thought they were cool."

"What?" Zara laughed and playfully swatted Lizzy's hand, pretending to be offended. "You made fun of me all the time!"

Lizzy laughed, and the sound was beautiful. "I know. I'm sorry."

"Okay, okay," Zara said, scooting closer to the wall so she could lean against it. Lizzy did the same and rested her head on Zara's shoulder. "I know a good one. It's got a lot of parts to it, but it's fun. There are superheroes and robots and mythical gods and monsters and the *best* villains..."

The story unfolded as Zara recalled the details, but it wasn't the story itself that filled her up with a hope for the future; it was the feeling of the bond between her and Lizzy reknitting. It was Lizzy's laughter. It was the promise that the story of Zee and Liz wasn't over yet, not by a long shot.

Chapter 18

Oliver Roman

Metal dug into Oliver's wrists as he tugged against handcuffs. The chain wrapped around the leg of a conveyer belt; he was most comfortable hugging the pole so that his arms could rest on his knees, but he had to sit with legs crisscrossed around the metal rod. The boys were mostly out there, roaming the streets of Christchurch, doing what, Oliver couldn't say. Anytime they left the factory, Ihaka cuffed Oliver there, leaving only Etera to guard him. It wasn't as bad as the cage—not nearly as bad—but he was still a prisoner. At least, he would be until he was forced to choose: the swarm or Ihaka's fists. He still wasn't sure which had a higher chance of survival. He might be able to hide from a swarm, but could he beat the older, bigger boy? In a fight to the death, could he *kill* another human being?

No… he thought. *I couldn't.* And he knew it with every ounce of his being, and he wished with all his heart that his dad was there, or Minnie or Lauren, or even Samson. He missed them all, knew that if they were there, they would protect him. *Because I can't protect myself*… He hated that thought, hated the truth behind it.

Etera's steady snoring was interrupted by a drawn-out series of snorts. Oliver froze, wide eyes focused on the boy who slept out of reach on a pile of blankets. He stopped tugging on his chains.

Don't wake up… don't wake up…

Oliver's silent pleas seemed to work. Etera heaved a sleepy sigh, rolled over, and his rhythmic snoring returned. One more time, Oliver examined the floor and the underside of the conveyer belt, looking for something to pick the lock on the handcuffs. No luck. Not that he actually knew how to pick a lock.

I've seen movies, he thought. I just have to find something to stick in that little hole.

If he couldn't face Ihaka or the swarm, his best option was to escape when the majority of the boys were gone. He looked up at the screws holding the leg to the underside of the conveyer belt. Oliver stuck the fingernail of his thumb in the head of the screw and pushed, trying to loosen it. A sharp pain shot down his thumb as his nail split from skin. Oliver jerked back, clenching his jaw against the urge to shout. He breathed out slowly, shakily, and sucked on the broken nail as it started to bleed. The pressure eased the pain, but his thumb throbbed.

The slamming of a door and echoing hoots and hollers made Oliver straighten and fold his thumb into his hand where he could keep pressure on it. Etera jerked awake, sitting up and rubbing his eyes. He blinked rapidly, shook his head, and looked at Oliver.

"Hey, mate," he said. "Let's keep my nap between us, eh? I was right knackered."

"Sure," Oliver said, glancing up at his cuffed hands. "Maybe since they're back, you can let me go?"

"Oh, yeah-nah, mate," Etera said. "I gotta wait for Ihaka to give the say-so."

Oliver sighed and waited. He had full view of the area the boys used the most, with their sleeping bags and blankets and food and belongings spread out in a large circle. There was one for him, too, and he was allowed to use it whenever there were so many of them present that there was no way he could escape. He was allowed to sleep there as long as he agreed to be handcuffed to Etera overnight.

Eventually Ihaka strolled over, clearly not in a hurry. "You keen to join us, Oliver?"

"Well, I don't want to stay chained up like this," Oliver said.

"Go on, Etera." Ihaka said.

"Sweet as." Etera popped up and walked over to Oliver with an upbeat stride. He bent low as Oliver lifted his hands high and unlocked one handcuff and then the other. He took the cuffs and tossed them to Ihaka.

Oliver rubbed his wrists. "Thanks."

Ihaka gestured for Oliver to come near, and he did. The leader of the rogue boys slung an arm around Oliver's shoulders. He started walking slowly toward the pallets on the floor where boys were already lazing about, some of them nibbling on their rations from the day before. "Coming near to the end, mate. Tonight's the night."

Oliver missed a step, but Ihaka squeezed his shoulders tight so that he didn't fall. "Can't I have another day?"

Ihaka reached out, pressed his palm against Oliver's heart, and let his hand rest there for a moment. "You'll make the right decision."

Oliver's heartbeat raced beneath the weight of Ihaka's hand. If the older boy could feel it, he didn't let on, though Oliver couldn't imagine the thumping that pulsed from his chest to his toes would be unnoticeable.

"So…" Oliver swallowed, and the action hurt. Nausea made him sway, and the room suddenly seemed colder. "I can't have more time?"

Ihaka shook his head, and Oliver couldn't tell if the sympathy in his expression was sincere or not. "You've had enough time. More than some others. I was hoping you'd come to me first, tell me you wanted to be one of us." He shrugged. "But she'll be right. You'll see. I have faith in you."

"She…?" Oliver glanced around the room, looking for a girl. It was hard to process Ihaka's words when his pulse thudded in his ears.

Ihaka laughed. "Just an expression. Means it'll all work out."

"When?" Oliver asked. "When do I have to decide?"

"After tea," Ihaka said. "Coop's getting it together now. You got the right to select someone to inherit your possessions, including rations, should you not make it through the night."

After dinner. Oliver took a deep breath. That only gives me an hour, tops.

"Wait, my possessions?" he clung to his mother's bag. "I don't want any of you to have this bag. It was my mother's."

"Fair enough," Ihaka said. "What d'ya want us to do with it? Bury it with you?"

"No!" Oliver shook his head. "I don't want to die. I'm not going to!"

"That's the spirit," Ihaka said. "Have a think on it." He passed him off to Etera.

"Sit down, mate," Etera said. "Eat a little. Gain some strength."

Numb, Oliver settled on his pallet of blankets next to Etera. There was no way out. The time for escape had passed. There were too many of them, not enough time.

"What do I do?" Oliver whispered.

"I ain't supposed to say," Etera whispered back, "but choose the *taniwha.* Choose trust."

The urgent tone Etera used snapped Oliver to attention. He grasped Etera's wrist, still whispering. "What does that mean?"

"Can't say," Etera said. "Rules are rules."

The food came—more crackers to go with his marmite from the day before and prepackaged foods Oliver had never heard of, including something called pineapple lumps which were much chewier than he expected and covered in chocolate. He only ate a few of those, opting for more of the salty cracker and marmite duo. They had to have more nutrients in them than the candies.

As he forced himself to eat, Oliver weighed his options. Ihaka was too strong. Even a pat on the back from him nearly sent Oliver sprawling. And there was something about the option to face the swarm that was more than it seemed. They kept talking about how it was a test of trust. How it would make him one of their brothers.

Does that mean there will be a way to survive? Oliver looked at Etera. He wasn't a bad person. He even seemed nice most of the time. And he'd said to choose the swarm, the *taniwha.*

But if he did die…

I can't let Minnie and the others keep looking for me.

He thought of how terrible it had been not to be able to bury his mother, how burying just that piece of paper that held her words had brought healing to both him and his dad.

"I want Etera to have my rations," Oliver said out loud, and the others quieted and looked at him, including Ihaka.

"Not a bad choice," Ihaka said. "And your… bag?"

"I want you to leave my body and the bag as close to the place my friends are as you can," Oliver said. "They need to know I died, and they need to be able to tell my dad for sure."

"If you choose the *taniwha,*" Ihaka said, "we won't touch your body. It'll have to stay where it is." His eyes flickered to Oliver's bag. "But if you leave it with us, we will leave the bag in plain view with a note."

Oliver nodded. "Okay," he said, and he slipped the bag over his head, setting it beside him.

Ihaka quirked one eyebrow. "Does that mean you've chosen the *taniwha?*"

Oliver nodded once, firmly, despite the way his stomach threatened to empty the contents of his meager meal. "I have."

Ihaka grinned so that even his eyes squinted, and the air filled with wild, oscillating shouts as the boys clapped their hands, threw down their rations, and got to their feet. Some of them even howled. Oliver shrank back, head turning wildly at every new sound like a weather vane in volatile winds.

And then they closed in on Oliver, hands grabbing at his legs, his arms, hooking into his armpits, hauling him up, up, up, and over their heads.

"Put me down!" Oliver's shout was lost in all the noise, but he shouted again anyway. "What are you doing? Where are you taking me?"

He bounced as they carried him out of what had to have been the factory's largest room, the only room he'd ever spent any amount of time in. He yelped as they nearly dropped him a few times on the way up a flight of stairs, and then the bigger three of the boys took him by head, middle, and feet as they entered a much narrower stairwell.

Oliver twisted in their grasp, though his intention was to see better and not to be let loose. If they dropped him, he'd more than likely spill down the steps like a bowling ball, toppling the boys coming behind. With every step, it was becoming a long way down, longer than he was willing to risk. Ihaka led the charge, pumping his fist in the air, practically skipping up the steps. The faces of the boys all around him were exuberant, not malicious, and when Oliver listened through his panic, he heard the occasional boy chanting his name, rooting for him.

The upward sloping ceiling gave way to dirty glass panels. He could see neither the sun nor the moon in the overcast twilight. The boys set him down, and good-natured slaps and punches to his arms and back along with smiles and encouraging words had Oliver frowning as he backed away.

"Are you guys crazy?" Oliver asked, holding out his arms, trying to create as much distance as possible between him and the others. There were outdoor tables and chairs within the glass enclosure. It was large enough to hold them all if half the boys remained standing. The city stretched out on all sides of the rooftop beyond the brown-tinged panels. It would be dark within an hour if Oliver had to guess.

"We're not crazy," Ihaka said, "we're alive. We've all faced the *taniwha* either out there or up here. It is a privilege." He tapped on a door handle in the glass wall, and Oliver noted the hinges running along one side. It would have blended in perfectly with the wall if not for the hinges and handle. Ihaka strode forward, grabbed Oliver by the wrist and pulled him to the door. "It will come," he said. "Face it. Do not turn your back on it. Stand just outside the door, and do not run. Do not try to find a way off the rooftop. Do not sit idle. Be on guard. Listen for the sound of the monster, as will we. And remember, this is about trust and courage."

"That's it?" Oliver shook his head as Ihaka opened the door. "How can I just stand there if a swarm is coming at me?"

"Trust." Ihaka shoved Oliver outside. "No more talking."

Oliver couldn't catch his breath despite the fresh air. He turned around, searching the view of the city for any signs of a swarm. He was sweating despite the cooler weather. Two lumps in the shadowed corner of the rooftop made Oliver gasp and step back as he recognized the shape of arms and legs.

I'm going to die, he thought, and the words repeated in his head, faster and faster, until the words became a feeling, a pressure upon his chest and shoulders, a weight so heavy that he trembled with the effort of holding it.

His back was flush with the glass wall, and he pressed his hands flat against the gritty, dusty surface. The air stilled. Oliver looked over his shoulder to see Ihaka and the other boys standing still, a sea of eyes waiting. Ihaka gave a slight nod back toward the city, and Oliver understood.

Don't turn your back on the taniwha. Oliver ran Ihaka's instructions through his mind over and over again. He checked to make sure he was close to the door, his eyes flickering down and to his left, reassured by the door handle.

The longer he stood there, the clearer his thoughts became. His heartbeat slowed, his chest stopped heaving, and his skin cooled as a breeze brushed his sweaty body. The shuffling of feet or the occasional sound, such as a sneeze or cough, kept the presence of the boys behind the glass in the forefront of his mind.

Oliver eyed the corpses in the corner. The darker it got, the more their outlines blended with the shadows. He imagined his body on the top of the pile, rotting away, an example to the next boy to stand on that rooftop with the factory boys at his back.

But Ihaka had said the test was about trust, that it was a way to become brother to the other boys, to join their *hapu.* It didn't make sense for them to bring him up there just to watch him die. He had to remind himself of that more than once as his legs tired.

And then, after twilight had turned to night, after the moon had shown its face, parting the clouds to shine upon the city, a buzzing rose in the near distance. A large light flickered to life behind the glass, and several beams swept the dark. The boys remained silent within the enclosure. It was just that telltale, high-pitched hum and the sound of Oliver's heart pounding.

Oliver pressed closer to the glass as he searched with the beams of light. The sound of the swarm came nearer and nearer still until a black tendril swam through the yellow light yards out from the edge of the rooftop. Oliver gasped, and his knees buckled. His first instinct was to turn and grasp the door handle, but he didn't do it. That wasn't what Ihaka wanted.

Be brave. Face the taniwha. Oliver, keeping one hand on the glass and carefully remaining mere inches from the edge of the door, lifted a leaden foot and turned to face the swarm as every beam of light coalesced onto the spot where it had first revealed itself.

Writhing blackness crept to the edge of the rooftop. Deeper shadows outside the scope of the light obscured the view of the moonlit city. Slow but sure death spilled onto the rooftop, and Oliver bit the inside of his cheek to keep from screaming. He couldn't keep the tears at bay though, nor could he do anything about the way his body trembled.

Half a step back, but he did not run. A glance at the corpses, but he did not scream. Blurred vision, but he did not shut his eyes. Oliver resisted every urge as his lungs tightened. He gulped for air, but it only filled his lungs with fire. His ears filled with the numbing call of the swarm, the hum that birthed dread and played death's song.

Tendrils reached for him like a claw in the night, but at the very moment Oliver was certain he could no longer face the monster, the door opened and Ihaka's hands yanked him back. Etera closed the door, and the swarm slowly swallowed the glass enclosure.

Oliver's clenched jaw would not unstick. His body would not stop shaking. Blinking away the tears did little good; they were in endless supply.

He was fixated on the black, writhing swarm on the other side of the glass until Ihaka's face filled his view. Numb, realizing for the first time that he was being held up on either side by Coop and Etera, Oliver stared at Ihaka, unable to process the sounds coming out of his mouth. He was smiling a proud smile, and when he held out a hand, the shouts of the boys all around him erupted, overtaking the sound of death. He was lifted again, carried on the shoulders of many boys.

They left the monster behind like it was nothing. By the time Oliver was deposited back on his pallet of blankets, a prickly feeling had returned to his arms and legs. His eyes stung, but the tears came slower. When Ihaka spoke again, Oliver heard him, and he was able to barely process what he said.

"You faced the *taniwha,* and we returned your bravery by risking our lives to open the door. We live together. We perish together." Ihaka raised a fist high, and the other boys followed suit.

No one seemed to notice Oliver's stillness, his inability to move or speak, as every one of them danced and twirled and raised their voices in defiance of the monsters that roamed their city. Time meant nothing. It slipped by and stood still at the same time.

Until Etera squatted in front of him. "Hey, cuz. You did it, bro!" He shouted above the din of celebration.

Oliver frowned at him as Etera snapped his fingers in front of Oliver's eyes. "What did you say?" he asked.

"You're one of us," Etera said again, shoving a glass bottle into his hand. "Have an L&P."

Oliver looked down at it, his frown deepening. "What is it?"

"A fizzy drink." Etera said it like Oliver should know. "Like a cola." He reached out and twisted off the top. "Limited supply. Celebrations only." He winked.

Oliver tipped back the drink and let the mineral-lemon fizz wake him up. "It's been a long time since I've had something like this."

"Don't just sit there, then," Etera said, tugging on his arm.

The feeling of Etera's hand on his skin, the sweet taste in the back of his mouth, they were like anchors that drew him fully back to reality. Oliver got to his feet, and he held out his free hand in front of him.

"I'm alive," Oliver said.

"Just now figurin' that out?" Etera laughed.

Oliver grinned. "I'm alive!" Relief flooded his veins, made him feel light.

Etera howled, and a series of shouts and hoots rose all around them. And then they were shouting Oliver's name again. Oliver turned in a slow circle, taking in for the first time the extent of the joy surrounding him. They were celebrating *him*: his bravery, his victory.

"That's it, mate!" Ihaka shouted. "You're a survivor. You're one of us now." A cheer cut through the last of Oliver's shock, severing it from him and allowing a burst of pride to take its place.

Their movement was contagious now that Oliver was paying attention. How could he not move? How could he not howl into the big empty space? How could he remain silent when he was *alive*?

Every movement Oliver made, every sound, seemed to fuel the boys around him. Laughter bubbled up from deep within, from a place he'd forgotten existed. The boys made their own music with raised voices and danced in styles Oliver had never seen.

The test was over, but Oliver sensed a new beginning. No one before Ihaka, before Etera and Coop and the rest of the boys, would have trusted that he could face a swarm. With the *hapu*, Oliver wasn't a little boy. He wasn't helpless. He was equal. He was free.

Chapter 19

Alexander Roman

Blood filled the vial in Alex's hand. He removed the needle from Stella's arm and set it aside next to three others just like it. "That's it," he said, pressing a bandage into place.

He'd called Candice and Stella to the small clinic near the laboratories, hoping comparing their blood would help him in his endeavors. He'd studied a sample of Candice's blood back in Boston, but she'd been the only known survivor. Alex was sure he was missing something.

Stella put a hand over her inner arm. "I feel like a lab rat," she said.

"You get used to it," Candice said, shrugging.

"Neither of you are lab rats," Alex said as he gathered the vials. "Your contribution is valuable, but you're people first. Always."

Stella didn't look convinced. "It's just… I can't explain it. All of this is surreal. The blood work, being special for not dying… I can't wrap my head around it."

Candice sat beside her on the hospital bed. "Because it doesn't feel like you should be valued for surviving when everyone else died? Because you never thought the most important thing you would ever do would be this?" She shook her head and chuckled sadly. "You can't take pride in it. It's not something you did. It's not even something you wanted."

"Yeah," Stella said, and the two women exchanged a look as Stella took Candice's hand and squeezed it.

"At least we're not alone in it," Candice said. "I feel less like a freak with you around."

Alex slipped the tubes into a carrier one at a time. "I get that me and Walter and Lauren can't fully understand your experiences," he said, "but I hope you understand that we're here for you when you need us."

"I know," Candice said, offering a small smile.

Stella dropped Candice's hand, shifted uncomfortably, and hopped off the bed. "I'll be around if you need me," she said.

"You okay?" Alex asked.

She just shook her head, and he thought he caught a glistening in her eyes before she put her head down, shoved her hands in her pockets, and left the room.

"Was it something I said?" Alex quirked an eyebrow at Candice.

"I don't think so." Candice frowned at the door. "Maybe it has something to do with the people she lost, with having to learn to trust people she barely knows. Plus, the past several days here have made her stir crazy, I think. She doesn't talk much. Keeps to herself. But I see her pacing a lot, and… did you see her fingernails? They're atrocious."

"I don't think now's the time to be criticizing her beauty routine," Alex said.

Candice gave him a flat stare. "That's not what I mean. She's chewed them down to the skin, made them bleed. She's anxious. Bottling up her experiences. If Stella doesn't talk to someone so she can process whatever is going on in her head, she's going to implode."

"Oh." Heat crept up the back of Alex's neck. *Why didn't I notice that?* he thought. And then he asked, "What do we do?"

"I'm going to take care of it," Candice said, determination settling across her face.

"How?"

"First, I'm going to keep those vultures from picking her apart," Candice said.

"You mean the technicians?" Alex asked.

She nodded. "Yeah. I get that they have a lot of questions, but I'm trying to keep them away from Stella. She can't handle it. I don't think she's even processed the whole thing. Before she can help anybody else, she needs time to accept what happened." Candice started toward the door. "Good luck, Alex. The sooner we get out of here, the better."

"Agreed." Alex picked up the tube carrier. "And good luck to you, too, Candice. Stella is lucky to have you."

He turned to the door on the opposite side of the clinic after she'd left. It opened into the hallway where the labs could be accessed. The BS-4 lab waited for him beyond a small locker room and a decontamination room. Alex suited up in a white pressurized biohazard suit and brought the blood samples into the specialized lab. As usual, his eyes first darted to the freezer where samples of DV-10 were kept. The presence of the disease sent a chill up his spine every time he was near.

Alex focused on the task at hand as he slipped the vials into the centrifuge and sent them to spinning. Petri dishes and serums needed to be prepared so that he could look at the blood under the high-powered microscope.

This was different sort of work than what he'd been doing the past five days. It had taken time to find DV-10 in ultra-cold storage, but besides that, he and Walter had gone through all their past research—everything they knew—and come up with plans for experiments. They'd gotten research started on the countermeasure mosquitos, too. The way to making the world right again was anything but simple, but Alex was more confident than he'd ever been that they were headed in the right direction.

The next hours were filled with painstaking work. Every step had to be done right so that samples wouldn't degrade before he got the answers he needed. With every hour came progress, and even the tiniest bit fueled Alex to keep going.

When a hiss sounded, Alex nearly jumped out of his skin. The seal on the door was broken, and another figure in a biohazard suit walked in.

"The pupas are coming along well," Walter said behind the clear plastic covering that enclosed his head. His suit was pressurized, like Alex's, and was puffy with air. "If they keep developing to adulthood, I'd say that's proof enough that the eggs are all viable."

Alex nodded. They'd taken a small sample of eggs from half the pods to test their viability. It was excellent news. "And have you found the instructions for transfer?" he asked.

"It's not going to be easy," Walter said, "but with the help of the technicians, I think we'll be fine. The facility has specialized sleds and the pods can each be fitted with solar panels to keep them at the right temperatures."

"Do we also happen to have another vehicle?" Alex asked.

Walter shook his head. "No, and that's going to be tricky on the way back. But you know how Stella had us travel with the tents already assembled and strapped to that sled? She says we can take turns riding in those."

Alex groaned as he remembered cold nights stuffed in an oversized sleeping bag. They wouldn't get frostbite, but those tents were small. It would be a tight fit between the snowcat and the two small tents.

"What about you?" Walter asked. "Anything to report?"

"Yes, actually." Alex frowned. "What time is it?"

"It's getting late, actually. Everyone else has eaten dinner." Walter walked over to the steel counter and glanced over a series of Alex's notes. "Wait…" He picked up Alex's latest notes and took his time reading them. He looked back at Alex. "Can I take a look?" He pointed at the microscope.

Alex nodded. "Yeah." He gestured to the microscope and the computer next to it. "I've been running simulations on my findings. You can take a look at those, too."

Walter stepped up to the microscope and studied the sample, and then he replayed the simulations Alex had pulled up on the monitor. "Have you tested it on the virus?"

"I was just about to." Alex grinned. "You want to do it with me?"

"Hell yes!" Walter stood and clapped his hands once. "This is promising. If this works…" He trailed off, shaking his head, smile so wide Alex could see all his teeth.

Walter's excitement unleashed Alex's. He'd been so focused that he hadn't stopped to *feel* the implications of what he'd found. "Let's prep the pathogen, then," he said. "I have a small sample that should be ready to stabilize and test."

They worked together to formulate a serum based on the most successful simulation, and then they prepped a sample of DV-10 in a biosafety cabinet where an air vacuum could remove any trace of the virus and run it through the independent air filtration system should it escape during the process.

Walter slid the petri dish with the live virus under the microscope in the cabinet. "You ready?"

Alex nodded, holding his breath as he slipped his gloved hands into the cabinet and, using a dropper, introduced the pathogen to human blood and then immediately administered the serum. He looked over to the monitor where the microscopic view was revealed. His lungs burned as he fixated on the screen. A tingling sensation crept from his core to his limbs, and every muscle went rigid. He let out a shaky breath.

"C'mon, c'mon," he whispered.

And then, it happened. The pathogen slipped away from healthy cells, unable to bind to them, and as antibodies covered the surface of the harmful microorganism, it began to shrivel.

"It worked," Walter said. His jaw dropped, and he stared at the screen.

Alex did much the same as the virus was destroyed, as the healthy cells were allowed to live. And then laughter bubbled up, spilled out, and he threw his hands into the air. Walter faced him and started to laugh, too. They hugged each other the best they could in their puffy suits.

When the elation settled back down to excitement, Alex's first thought had him hurrying to clean up. "I have to tell—" He paused. He was about to say Lauren's name. "—everyone. We have to tell everyone," he said instead.

That wasn't new. As of late, when things went well, Lauren came to mind first. It was the same when he had a bad day or when he needed to talk something out. He still didn't know what to make of his growing affections for the woman, but he no longer outright rejected them, either. It wasn't time for romance, and he was still healing from his wife's death months ago, but…

Maybe the time will come, he thought. Maybe dreaming of a future is more realistic than it has been in a long time. I don't love Lauren, not like that, not yet… but I could, one day.

By the time he and Walter had finished clean-up and decontamination, Alex's cheeks were sore from all the smiling. By the time he and Walter met the rest of the inhabitants of the research bank in the lounge, he was bursting at the seams with the good news.

"This better be good. We were all about to turn in," Robert said as he sat on the loveseat arm next to Anise, Cat, and Farrah. Zac took up residence at their feet, as usual.

Candice and Stella took up the other loveseat, and Lauren stood behind it. Alex looked at her, and she chuckled softly and shook her head at him.

"What's going on, Alex? You look like you just won the lottery," Lauren said. "I don't know if I've ever seen you smile that big."

"I was finally able to identify and replicate the antibodies that enabled Stella and Candice to survive infection," Alex said. Blank expressions were returned to him, so he tried again. "We have a treatment."

Lauren took a step toward him. "Are you sure?"

"Yes," Walter said. "It may not be the entire solution, but it's a start. I wasn't sure we'd ever get this far. It helps us understand next steps, gives us options for fighting DV-10."

Lauren laughed more fully, and suddenly, she was throwing her arms around Alex's neck. He embraced her tightly and lifted her off the ground, spinning her once. She laughed, and his heart fluttered as he set her down and she backed away, still smiling but a bit shy. Her cheeks reddened, and she cleared her throat.

"That's great," she said.

Candice popped up to her feet. "We should celebrate," she said. "It's been too long since we've been able to do that."

"Wait a minute," Robert said, holding out a hand as his friends started to get to their feet. The ladies stopped mid-rise and sat back down.

"It's good news," Anise said.

"Is it?" Robert crossed his arms and narrowed his eyes. "He said it's just a start. Why is that? If it's a treatment, why can't we be done here?"

Alex's smile faded as Walter frowned beside him. "Because," Walter said, "there's no way this treatment will fix what's happened in the world."

"The virus works too quickly," Alex said. "The treatment will work to stop the virus, but it's not a vaccine that will prevent illness. It has to be administered after infection. From the moment the sickness develops, it starts to damage organs. Some people are dead within a matter of hours. Others within a day. And if someone gets caught in a swarm? They're dead within minutes from viral overload."

"Exactly," Walter said. "This treatment will save lives, but only if someone has only momentary exposure to a swarm or they catch the virus from a carrier, either a person or possibly an animal. We still need the countermeasure mosquitos to get rid of the swarms."

"And we need a vaccine," Alex said. "This is a step, and it's an important one, but we still have work to do."

Robert scoffed. "I'm going to bed. I'll celebrate when I'm home." He dropped his arms and stormed out of the lounge.

Cat stood and rolled her neck. "Look, we've got a nice whiskey that's waiting for a good time. When you've figured out these countermeasures and a vaccine, maybe we can pop that cork, but for now, I'm with Robbie." She left the room, too.

Alex deflated. "We've been working on this for a long time," he said. "I wasn't one-hundred-percent confident we'd even get here. This is good news."

Zac shrugged and looked over his shoulder at Anise and Farrah. "We could get the M&Ms."

Farrah and Anise exchanged a look, smiles slowly spreading across their faces.

"Looks like a yes to me," Zac said.

"They've always been pessimists," Anise said.

"No." Farrah used air quotes as she said, "*Realists*."

The three technicians laughed as Zac got to his feet. "Candice is right. We should put on some music, eat some candy, and celebrate."

Stella slowly got up from her seat. "I'm happy for you," she said. "It's great news, but—"

"Oh, no, you don't!" Candice raised her eyebrows. "You're going to stay for at least half an hour."

"I can't," Stella said.

Farrah was already at a cabinet, rummaging through a drawer and pulling out bags of candy. "Sure you can," she said.

Stella stepped toward the door, but Candice grabbed her arm.

"You need to let yourself be happy," Candice said softly.

"The last time I participated in a celebration," Stella said sharply, "half my friends died by suicide."

Alex blinked. He hadn't connected those dots. Everyone had gone quiet at Stella's words, and Candice had let go of her arm.

"Okay," Candice said. "You can go. I'm... I'm sorry."

Stella didn't seem to know what to do with an apology. She strode quickly toward the door, hugging her middle.

Candice took a step forward, but Alex stopped her. "Let me," he said. "You've proved to her that you're here to support her. You've done it all day. All week. She needs to know that you're not the only one."

Farrah came up to him and held out a bag of candy. "Chocolate won't hurt," she said.

"All right." Candice nodded. "Go on." She shooed him toward the door with a wave of her hand.

"Thanks." Alex took the candy and jogged after Stella, having to turn a corner to find her. She was walking fast. "Hey," Alex said. "Wait just a minute."

Stella looked back and groaned, and though she slowed, she didn't stop walking. "I'm not coming back. Can't you leave me alone?"

"Yes," Alex said, "but I'm pretty sure you don't want to miss out on these." Trying to match her pace, he dangled the bag of M&Ms between two fingers.

Stella stopped and pursed her lips before grabbing the bag. "Fine," she said, and then she added, "Thanks."

"No problem." Alex met her eyes with his own. "Stella, I know it seems like things will never be better. But if you just hang on, there *will* come a time when happiness won't feel so foreign."

"It's not foreign," Stella said. "It's repulsive. How can I celebrate *anything*? Everyone I loved is dead."

"I know." Alex took a deep breath. "Your pain is real, and it's hard, and it's terrible. We've survived by holding on to each other, and I'm telling you right now that you are invited into our circle. You can hold on to us."

"So I can lose more people I care about?" Stella asked, shaking her head.

"So that when we all make it through this and the world is put right, you have a home," Alex said. "Because I'm not stopping until that's true. And neither will Walter. And there are so many people out there who will fight alongside us. I've met them. I know them. I believe in them, and I believe in us."

Stella worked her jaw back and forth and nodded ever so slightly. "Okay," she said.

Alex quirked one eyebrow. "Okay?"

"Yeah," Stella said. "I heard you." She offered a very small smile and lifted the candy. "Thanks." And, with less panic in her step, Stella continued on her way.

Alex watched her go down the hall until she stopped at her door and entered her room. "We're going to be okay," he whispered to himself, a promise sent into the universe. "This is a start to a new beginning."

Chapter 20

Oliver Roman

All Oliver had to do was run. It was just him and Etera; the others were out of sight, scavenging other houses. The back door was mere feet from where he stood. He clung to the strap of his mother's bag, felt the weight at his hip. His chance was slowly slipping away. Etera's footsteps had him just above where Oliver stood in the kitchen. The door called to Oliver, and he imagined slipping off his backpack with the meager supplies he'd gathered that day for the *hapu* and finding his way back to Minnie.

Back where he would be treated like a child. Where Will would bully him. Where all he had to look forward to was his father returning. Where the possibility his father might never return was on his mind more often than not.

Or he could stay where he was trusted to do hard things. Where he was accepted by everyone. Where his ideas meant something. Where there was fun and adventure to be had.

Oliver stepped away from the door.

"Hey, cuz, what'd'ya think?" Etera burst into the open concept kitchen and living area from the stairwell near the front door, wearing a large sunhat, about a dozen scarves, and perhaps as many sundresses layered over his clothes. He put his hands on his hips and sashayed as his accent changed and his voice became high-pitched. "I'm here for tea and biscuits. An English lady out for a stroll."

Oliver laughed as Etera started dancing in the ensemble, using moves that had been popular on social media before Day Zero. The more he laughed, the more dramatic Etera's movements, and the more exaggerated he became, the harder Oliver laughed. Etera started flinging the extra garments off as his dancing became wild, and Oliver set his backpack on the kitchen island along with his mother's bag so that he could join him.

Twisting and jumping and diving for the items Etera tossed, Oliver caught scarf after scarf and created streamers of color as he twirled. He picked up the sunhat and jumped up on the couch, bouncing as he threw the hat like a frisbee. By the time Etera had discarded all of the extra clothes, Oliver was out of breath. He collapsed on the couch, and Etera did the same in an overstuffed chair.

"This is the life," Etera said, sighing.

"It's a lot better than sitting in a dark hallway reading encyclopedias," Oliver said.

Etera lifted his head and his features pinched. "What? Why would anyone do that?"

"It was better than going to school with Will," Oliver said.

"That bully?" Etera asked.

"Yeah."

"Bro, I can't believe you ever wanted to go back there."

Oliver shrugged. "I don't anymore," he said, and he felt a pang of guilt. "I just worry about my friend, Minnie. She's like… my grandma, I guess."

"Your gran is still alive?"

"No," Oliver said, "my real grandparents died a long time ago. My dad and I met Minnie on Day Zero, and she helped us. She's been with us ever since. We helped find her daughter, Lauren, and well… we were supposed to all stay together, always." A sour taste in his mouth made Oliver frown. "Until my dad decided to leave me and Minnie here and go off with Lauren."

"Well, is this Minnie safe?" Etera asked.

Oliver nodded.

"Well, then, cuz, stop worryin' about her."

"It's more like I don't want *her* to worry about *me*." Oliver shrugged. "I wish I could get her a note, but if I went back there, she wouldn't let me leave."

"Let's have a think on it," Etera said. "We'll figure it out. You're one of us, now."

The front door opened, and Oliver sat up to see Ihaka enter the house. "You boys r—" He pursed his lips and looked at the mess of clothes. "Etera, you're a bad influence." He grinned. "I like it."

"What's life without a bit of fun?" Etera stood and winked at Oliver.

"We'll get back to gathering supplies," Oliver said.

"Hold on, now," Etera said. "Ihaka, our brother's got a problem."

Ihaka quirked an eyebrow. "What's that?"

Oliver shook his head. "It's nothing."

"Yeah-nah, we can't do that." Ihaka crossed his arms. "If something's bothering you, we'll fix it, if we can. That's what we do for our brothers."

"It's his gran." Etera nodded at Oliver. "She's at the shopping center. He doesn't want her to worry about him."

"I'm afraid," Oliver added, "that she'll come looking for me, and I don't want that either."

Ihaka nodded slowly. "That wouldn't be good for anyone. We don't like strangers around here. We gotta send her a message."

Oliver put out his hands. "Whoa, what does that mean? I don't want to hurt her."

"Hurt her?" Ihaka laughed. "Why would we do that?"

"Well, you said…" Oliver blinked a few times. "What did you mean by sending her a message?"

"The kind you write," Ihaka said.

"Oh." Oliver's cheeks ran hot.

"Look," Ihaka said, "we're orphans, but a few of us got relatives out there. The *hapu* isn't for them, but as long as they leave us be and let us be our own men, she'll be right, I say. But from time to time, they need a little communication to understand they're not changin' who we are. Most of the time, they let it go with a little promise we'll be careful." He grinned. "Might be the only promise most of us ever break."

"Yeah, that would be great," Oliver said. "I just don't want to think about her out there looking for me."

"I got just the thing." Ihaka waved his hand toward the door. "Follow me."

Oliver grabbed his mother's bag and fell in line behind Ihaka and Etera. Just outside the house, in the yard, a wagon full of supplies waited, but Ihaka didn't stop there. He led them past the privacy fence toward the house across the street. A low decorative wall lined the property, and tall bushes and trees acted as a sort of fence to mostly block the house. Oliver had noticed most of the houses were like that: concealed behind bushes, trees, or fences.

They followed a driveway around the back of the house to a single-car detached garage. Ihaka rolled up the door. "Didn't know if we'd have a use for these," he said as he walked in and kicked a cardboard box. "But I'm thinkin' they'll be perfect for what you wanna do."

Etera got to the box first. "Choice!" He bent down and retrieved a tall, thin metal can.

"Spray paint?" Oliver asked.

"It'll do the trick. Paint a message across some cars in the car park." Ihaka picked up the box, and Etera put the can back. "Here, you carry it back to the wagon."

Oliver took the box. "When can we do it?"

"On the way back," Ihaka said. "Still got some work to do out here, but us three can swing by that way while the rest go on home."

That put Oliver in high spirits over the next few hours as he and Etera continued rummaging through abandoned homes. When they were done, their backpacks went on top of other supplies in a shopping cart for Coop to push back to the factory. Oliver, of course, kept his mother's bag slung crossbody. Ihaka, Etera, and Oliver branched off from the others toward the shopping center. Each of them carried a can of spray paint.

"Stay on the footpath," Ihaka said, pointing down at the sidewalk. "Keep your ears open. You hear a *taniwha* or the sound of people, and we hide in one of the buildings. Got it?"

Oliver nodded and crept forward quietly. When they were across the street from the parking lot, Ihaka bent low and hurried to a vehicle, crouching behind it. Oliver and Etera imitated him.

"If you leave a message on the side of a car," Ihaka said, "their scavengers will see it."

Oliver nodded and got out his can of spray paint. "I've got this," he said, staying low to the ground as he ran over to a spot where three cars were lined up. It seemed two of them had been parked nose to nose and a third had backed into one of them, all three crunching together to create one long canvas.

He held up the can, realizing he didn't know what he was doing, and found the instructions. After a quick read, he shook the paint, its rattle making his heartbeat louder—what if someone heard?—and then popped the lid and started painting his message. It was sloppy, but he was certain it was readable.

He stepped back, a weight lifting from his shoulders. Then he looked back to see Etera and Ihaka spray painting cars, too. He'd thought they'd brought the cans as extras, but they both seemed pretty focused on their own messages. Oliver crouched low again and joined Etera, who was closest.

Oliver read Etera's message out loud as the boy finished and stepped back. "Will is a—" He scrunched his nose. "What does that mean?"

"Nothing good," Etera said. "Kiwi name callin' gets real creative." He leaned over and signed his own name.

Oliver shrugged and looked over at what Ihaka had written. It read: Don't give me a reason, Mateo. It was signed with a simple "I."

"What does that mean?" Oliver asked.

"Mateo is my oldest cousin," Ihaka said. "He knows what it means, and that's all that matters."

It didn't seem like something Ihaka wanted to expound upon.

"Ready to get out of here?" Etera asked.

Ihaka nodded, and Oliver did, too. He gave the shopping center one more look before he followed his new friends into the unfamiliar streets of Christchurch. When they'd been jogging for about half an hour, Ihaka finally stopped.

"Should be far enough not to run into anyone we don't want to," Ihaka said. "Still, keep your ears open, mates."

Oliver bent over and put his hands on his knees, trying to catch his breath, and Etera plopped down on the sidewalk. Ihaka put his hands on his head, and took a few deep breaths, but he didn't seem fazed by the trek at all.

And then Ihaka said in an urgent whisper, "Look!"

Oliver followed Ihaka's finger to a playground overgrown with tall grasses, wild flowers, and bushes in need of a trim. A slide stood over the area, its bottom lost in the weeds.

Etera sat up with a groan. "What is it?" he asked.

"A Cap'n Cooker just trotted right into that playground," Ihaka said, clear excitement lacing his words.

Oliver wrinkled his nose. "A what?"

"A wild boar," Etera said loudly; his excitement wasn't as contained. He whooped loud enough to make Oliver jump.

"Quiet down," Ihaka hissed. "If they're movin' into the area, we don't want to spook them."

"Why?" Oliver asked as Etera whispered an apology and pretended to zip his lips.

"Because," Ihaka said, "they're *meat*."

"Real meat?" Oliver's mouth watered. "Boars are pigs, right? Does that mean… *bacon*?"

Ihaka and Etera nodded in unison, their smiles widening by the second.

"My dad taught me how to butcher them," Ihaka said. "He used to take me hunting all the time, but I've never seen one in the city."

"My uncle hunted," Etera said, his voice barely low enough to be called a whisper. "I don't know how to cut one up, but I know how to eat one!"

"We've gotta go back to the factory," Ihaka said. "I bet with all of us and our spears out here, we'll be feasting on boar before we know it."

They tip-toed past the park, and Oliver thought he heard a few grunts coming from the tall grasses. Once they were clear, all three broke into a run again, back to the factory. Ihaka interrupted the rest of the boys in the middle of sorting the food and supplies they'd gathered that day to give them the news.

"Real meat?" Coop's hand went to his stomach, and then he turned toward the stockpile of weapons against the wall. "Let's go get 'im now!"

Five others took steps in the same direction, but Ihaka held up his hands. "We'll go tomorrow," he said. "I'm knackered. Plus, it'll be dark before too long. For tonight, I think everyone can pick one can of whatever you want from the stockpile. Eat up, get some good rest, and tomorrow, we'll go out in full strength to hunt."

Oliver cheered with the rest. He had seen a few cans of something called Wattie's Cheesy Spaghetti, and he was hoping it would be something like the spaghetti he was used to. It would be cold, of course, but it still sounded better than the dozens of cans of beans. He rushed to the stacks of canned goods, looking for yellow and red, grabbed the thing he was looking for and pumped his fist.

"Excited about that, eh?" Ihaka asked from behind him.

Oliver turned and nodded. "Just have to wait in line for the can opener."

"First," Ihaka said, "I want you to come with me."

Oliver frowned and looked down at his can.

Ihaka chuckled. "Don't worry," he said. "It'll only take a sec."

Oliver's shoulders drooped, and his stomach grumbled, but he followed Ihaka, anyway, after asking Etera to keep the can for him.

Oliver perked up when he was led into a small room off the factory's foyer that he'd never been in before. Boys came and went from there on occasion. They always seemed sad or contemplative on their way out.

"I've been meaning to ask what this room is," he said as he stepped over the threshold. Dimming sunlight from the foyer windows reached into the room, but it didn't do much for seeing. The walls and corners were shrouded in shadows.

Ihaka stepped to the middle of the room at the edge of the light's reach. He pulled a matchbook out of his pocket and lifted both arms. The strike of a match revealed an oil lantern hanging on a chain. The wick took the flame, and a flickering orange light illuminated the darkness. Thin tables lined three walls, and there were items strewn across them.

Oliver slowly walked the length of one of them, noting the odd collection. There was a wallet, a family portrait in a frame, a few pieces of jewelry, and more. "What is this place?"

"The Remembrance Room." Ihaka walked over to a replica of the Eiffel Tower that stood only about half a foot tall. "This was my sister's," he said. "She was at uni in Paris. Sent this to me last year. Promised to take me there one day." He picked it up and smiled sadly at it. "She's probably dead. Even if she's not, I won't ever see her again."

"I'm sorry," Oliver said, and his hands gripped the strap of his mother's bag.

"I've noticed you like to keep that close," Ihaka said.

Oliver looked down at the bulk on his hip. "It was my mom's," he said. "And I showed you some of what's in it. Useful stuff."

"Memories," Ihaka said.

"Yeah."

"The past." Ihaka returned the Eiffel Tower to its place. "You're one of us, now, and our *hapu* looks to the future. We can't be stuck in the past."

"There are things in here I could use," Oliver said.

"Have you ever needed them?" Ihaka asked. "Is there anything in there that's useful for survival that can't be replaced?"

Oliver opened his mouth but quickly shut it again. Everything in the bag was either sentimental or replaceable or both. "I've carried it with me for months, ever since… ever since…" He swallowed hard. "… since my mom died."

"Look," Ihaka said, "I'm not saying you have to get rid of it. I'm saying, why not make a memorial out of it? Leave it here, on a table where you can come see it and remember any time you want. But you won't be carrying the past around your neck, and maybe you'll be able to move on from it."

Oliver frowned and clung onto the bag tighter.

"What is it that's stopping you?" Ihaka asked. "Is it your dad? You said he left you, abandoned you."

"He'll come back," Oliver said.

"If he lives." Ihaka leaned against one of the tables. His tone wasn't unkind, just matter-of-fact.

"I want him to live."

"Do you think taking that off will jinx it or something?"

Oliver slowly shook his head. "No," he said, and heat crept up the back of his neck. Maybe part of him *did* believe that.

That's stupid, he thought. Only little kids think like that.

"What happens if your dad comes back?" Ihaka asked. "Will you leave the *hapu*?"

Oliver's first instinct was to answer, "Yes," but he couldn't say it. He let Ihaka's questions roll around in his head for a few more moments.

"Leaving the *hapu* would be a mistake," Ihaka said. "We need to know that we can rely on you, and you need to know you can rely on us. Take me, for example. The *hapu* has made me stronger. I don't cry at night. I'm not scared of the *taniwha*. I can fend for myself. No adult tells me I'm too young or too stupid or too immature. Don't you want that for yourself, mate?"

Oliver nodded, and his grip on the strap loosened.

"So, I ask again," Ihaka said, "when the time comes, are you with us or will you abandon us?"

The *hapu* had shown him he was brave and capable and on his way to becoming a real man. He had experienced the intense thrill of facing a swarm and the overwhelming pride that followed. He had made his own decisions, been trusted to do important tasks. They listened to him when he'd expressed concerns about Minnie.

And none of them had made promises they couldn't keep.

Oliver lifted his chin. "I'm with you," he said.

"That's what I like to hear!" Ihaka stepped forward and gave Oliver a hearty pat on the back. Then, he waved toward the tables. "Pick a spot. Any spot. Make a right nice memorial, and then, leave the past behind."

It was hard at first to lift the bag over his head, to carry it to an empty spot. He didn't take the things out of it. That didn't seem right. The bag and all the contents told a story, his story, and he wanted it to stay that way. He arranged it nicely, though, smoothing out the bumps and making sure the items lay in an orderly fashion within the bag. When Oliver stepped back from it, Ihaka stood next to him and wrapped an arm around his shoulder.

"Ready for that spaghetti?" he asked.

Oliver took a deep breath, and it came out slow and easy. The longer he stayed with the *hapu*, the lighter it seemed his burdens got. He could forget about the pain of loss and focus on the adventures ahead. He turned his back on the past and stepped into his future.

Chapter 21

Minnie Stevens

"No, sir," Minnie said, shaking her head at the spray-painted message. "That ain't gonna work for me." She read it again, hardly believing her eyes. It said: I'm safe. Don't look for me. Love, O. It had to have been written late the day before, after the scavenging parties had come inside.
"At least he's alive," Zara said as Lizzy stood by, quiet as usual, chewing on her lower lip.
"Yeah," Kai added. "Could be worse."
Minnie didn't miss the way Zara elbowed him. She raised her eyebrows at Blythe, daring him to tell her it was all fine and dandy. He held up his hands and took a step back. She nodded, satisfied that at least somebody knew when to hold their tongue.
"How am I supposed to believe that he's safe when they left those, too?" Minnie pointed to the other messages, both more ominous than Oliver's.
Kai walked over to the one about Will, that kid who bullied Oliver. "Well, this one's accurate," he said. "Speaks to their credibility."
"Kai!" Zara wasn't so subtle about her elbow to his ribs. "You're talking about a kid!"
He held his ribs and mumbled an apology. Minnie agreed with Zara in theory, but a part of her sure wanted to blame that kid for Oliver's disappearance. *It wasn't some knuckle-head kid that didn't see Oliver needed more attention.* That thought wasn't new, but it didn't sting any less than the first time it had crossed her mind.
"This is proof he's with those factory boys," Blythe said as he watched Mateo and a few of his friends standing near the last message, one that seemed a warning directed at him.
"What does it mean, anyway?" Zara asked. "Don't give him a reason to do what? And who is 'I?'"
Lizzy cleared her throat and added in a soft, barely audible voice, "Mateo was angry at the message, but he wasn't confused. Not even a little."
"You're right," Zara said, frowning. "That's weird."
"I think," Blythe said, "that it's proof there's more to the story between the people we're staying with and Oliver's new friends. That note seems personal."
Minnie narrowed her eyes. "Darn straight," she said, "and I'm gonna find out *exactly* what's goin' on."
Her leg still gave her a bit of trouble, but she was moving faster by the day. The cane helped keep her steady, but she relied on it less. There was really only pain when her foot landed a certain way. She zeroed in on Mateo, and made a beeline for him.
The man crouched in front of the car with the message written just for him. Amir stood behind him, arms crossed, whispering something to a man named Flynn whose eyes flickered up to her. He stepped forward and tapped Mateo on the shoulder, nodding at her.
Mateo stood and faced her as she came nearer. "Minnie, I know you're going to want to go after Oliver," he said, "but—"
"But nothin'!"
"It must be upsetting to see that I was right about Oliver not wanting to be found, but—"
"You're fishin' in a puddle of mud," Minnie said. "Even if Oliver *did* write that—and I ain't convinced he did—he don't know what's best for him, and it won't stop me from goin' to that factory." She pointed to the message directed at Mateo. "What's that mean?"
He did a doubletake and then glanced at the side of the car with a frown. "I don't think that's something you—"
"If you're about to tell me it ain't my business," Minnie said with a bit of a growl, "I think you best remember my boy is with the person who wrote it."
Mateo closed his eyes for a second and deflated. He looked back up at her. "My cousin, Ihaka, wrote that. He's... a troubled kid. If not for the apocalypse, he would be in a youth detention center right now."
Minnie's heart skipped a beat. "Is that like juvie?"
He shrugged. "I don't know how it stacks up to American systems," he said. "He beat up some kid at school, said he didn't mean to hurt him so badly, but..." Mateo trailed off and averted his eyes.
"But what?" Minnie put some oomph behind her question. He wasn't going to leave her with questions again.
"There was one eye witness, and she insisted Ihaka was out of control," Mateo said. "His dad... he was ten years younger than my dad, but the two of them grew up in the same house. Drug abuse, physical abuse, maybe worse... my own father struggled with anger, but he got help, and he never succumbed to addiction. Ihaka's dad continued the family legacy." Mateo looked back at the message. "Don't give me a reason. That's what my grandpa would say and what Ihaka's dad would say, and it was almost always followed by a beating. I only know about it through what my dad told me."
"Would he hurt Oliver?" Minnie asked.
Mateo shrugged. "I honestly don't know. I've never seen him actually hurt anybody, and he always insisted that the incident started in self-defense." He clasped his hands behind his back and looked down at his feet. "But that message is telling me that it won't take much for him to make my life a living hell."
"Well," Minnie said, "it don't say nothin' about me." She turned back toward Zara, Lizzy, Kai, and Blythe.
"Are you crazy?" Mateo was blocking her path before she'd made it three steps. "You can't."
Minnie leaned on her cane and looked up at the man, meeting his gaze with her own. She didn't say anything, not yet. All she did was stare hard.

He swallowed, the sound audible, and hesitation flashed across his features. "You saw my cousin's message. I can't help you."

"Didn't ask you to," Minnie said.

"If he thinks I sent you—"

"I'll tell him you tried to stop me." Minnie didn't look away, didn't bat an eye. She stood her ground.

Mateo ground his teeth and worked his jaw back and forth. He finally looked away first, and spent a full thirty seconds seeming to search the sky for answers to his problems. When he looked back at her, he looked defeated. "If Alex comes back and finds out I actually did stop you, I run the risk of him skipping New Zealand in his attempt to right the world. If I don't stop you, I run the risk of my cousin starting some kind of guerilla war against us or sabotaging our supplies or…" He sighed. "It doesn't matter. That's a smaller risk than giving your friend a reason to leave us alone to battle the black clouds forever."

Of course, Alex wouldn't do that, no matter what Mateo did. Even if Oliver were to be lost for good, Alex would never leave an entire country to suffer. But Minnie didn't mention that. Mateo was on the verge of letting her go get Oliver. She could tell him when she got back.

"Go," Mateo said, shaking his head. "But if you can get to Oliver without being seen, please, do that."

Minnie nodded. "Can do," she said, and then she gestured toward her friends. "Them three'll wanna come with me. Look after my dog while we're gone?"

"Sure," Mateo said. "If there are any of you lot I don't mind having around, it's Samson."

Minnie patted him on the shoulder. "I'm an acquired taste," she said. "You'll love me eventually."

A reluctant smile pulled at one corner of his mouth, and he shook his head, letting out a long breath as he stepped aside to give in to her demands. She passed him to approach Zara, Lizzy, Kai, and Blythe, all of whom were staring wide-eyed at her.

"You don't lose many arguments, do you?" Blythe asked.

"Never," Minnie said.

Kai frowned. "I mean, when you asked Mateo the first time—"

Minnie narrowed her eyes at him. "That argument ended a minute ago."

"I guess we know where we're going today," Zara said. "Are you sure you're up to coming with?" The young woman eyed Minnie's leg and cane.

Minnie lifted the cane. "This makes a good weapon, I reckon. And you've seen me out and about the last couple days. I'm movin' easier and faster."

"It's a longer walk than a lap through the shopping center," Blythe said.

"You sayin' I don't know what I can do?" Minnie asked.

Blythe raised his hands. "I would never."

"Good." Minnie quirked an eyebrow at Lizzy. "Real question is should Lizzy come along?"

"I've come searching every other day," Lizzy said, edging closer to Zara.

"She'll be fine," Zara said reassuringly.

Kai and Blythe agreed halfheartedly, but it was good enough for Minnie. She didn't have time to argue, and chances were, she'd need them.

Minnie turned east. "Let's get on it, then."

If gumption alone could have determined Minnie's speed, she would have been able to run the whole way there. Unfortunately, Blythe's point proved truer than she would ever admit out loud. Just thirty minutes of walking was like running a marathon, and by the time the factory was in sight, she was huffing and puffing behind the others. She managed to pretend she was taking her time on purpose for a good while, but her white lies caught up with her.

"Are you sure you're okay?" Zara asked.

"I'm just dandy," Minnie said between breaths, all the while thinking: *The only way I'd feel better is if I died right here.*

"We should, um…" Blythe looked at Minnie. "…*all* take a break before getting any closer."

"Let me see if this office building will work," Kai said before jogging over to a one-story building with the windows still intact. He came back out a minute later, waving for them to join him. "It's all good in the waiting room at least," he said. "Pretty dusty, too. I don't think anyone's been in here in a while."

Zara hooked her arm with Minnie's. "Let me help?"

Minnie leaned on her cane for support. Once she'd stopped moving, her body had settled into her exhaustion. The factory was so close, and yet, if she pushed herself, there was no way she'd be able to sneak up on those boys so that she could find Oliver without making a fuss. There was also the fact that if Zara insisted, she was in no condition to resist.

A gnat could bowl me over, she thought.

And so, she let Zara lead her into the office building behind Blythe, and when she found a chair in the waiting room, she couldn't help the sigh of relief that escaped her lips.

"Who wants some water?" Blythe asked. He slipped off his backpack and handed out bottles. "Do we want to talk about a plan?"

Minnie took a long swig of lukewarm water that somehow tasted like heaven. "I don't know how we're gonna sneak into a factory we ain't never even seen up close."

"So, we observe for a bit," Zara said as she sat next to Lizzy on the floor. She nudged Lizzy's water bottle closer to her, as the other young woman hadn't yet touched it. Lizzy took the hint and took a sip.

"Maybe we can go up to a few rooftops surrounding the factory, try to see through the windows?" Kai asked.

"Could work," Blythe said. "We could also—" He cut himself off and cocked his head. "Do you hear something?"

Minnie listened as they all went completely silent. There were voices outside, hoots and hollers. She forced her aching body up and out of the chair. "Maybe some of 'em are outside."

The windows were tall and skinny with blinds that covered them well. They each chose one, except for Lizzy who shared a window with Zara. Minnie's was closest to the door. At first, she didn't see anything. And then a parade of boys with spears and axes and bows and arrows came trotting by like they owned the city.

"Does anyone see Oliver?" Zara whispered.

Minnie scoffed and looked over at Zara. "He wouldn't be with those hoodlums unless they had him on a tight leash!"

"Isn't that him?" Blythe asked.

"What?" Minnie whipped her head back to the window and carefully peeked between the blinds. Sure enough, Oliver was at the back of the group, a big smile on his face, and an actual spear in his hand. "What in the Sam Hill is goin' on?"

"Looks like he's... having fun," Kai said.

"Nonsense!" Minnie snapped. But she watched as Oliver—the boy she loved, the boy she'd promised to protect—shouted with the rest of them and raised his spear. "They've brainwashed him."

"Maybe," Lizzy said, "but it takes a lot of effort to brainwash someone."

"How would you kn—" Minnie stopped herself from finishing the common retort, her cheeks flushing hot. She peeled her eyes away from Oliver and winced at Lizzy. "Sorry."

Zara pursed her lips at Minnie and gave her a flat stare, but Lizzy only shrugged and looked back outside.

"He's stopping," Blythe said with a hint of excitement in his tone.

"Oliver is?" Minnie pulled back the blinds a little too roughly. They crinkled and popped, and she made too large of a hole, but all the boys except for Oliver were past her window. Oliver had stopped to tie his shoe. He knelt with his spear on the ground beside him. "We don't have time!"

She grabbed the door handle before anyone could object, and she cracked it open. "Psst! Oliver!" she whispered.

His head jerked upward and swiveled until his eyes landed on her. For a moment, his mouth dropped, and then he shook his head as his eyes widened. "Stay there," he whispered back, and his tone was harsher than she would have liked. He stood up, looking ahead at the boys who didn't seem to notice he wasn't following, and then he pressed his lips together and turned toward the door. He hurried over, pushed his way inside, and shut the door behind him.

Minnie gathered him in her arms. "Oliver! I knew you—"

"Stop!" He pushed her away, not hard, but enough for her to know that he didn't want to be hugged. "I told you not to come looking!"

"So," Zara said, "you did write that message."

Minnie opened her mouth, but no words came out. It wasn't often that she found herself speechless.

"Who else would have done it?" Oliver threw up his hands.

"You want me to throw him over my shoulder?" Blythe asked.

Oliver gasped and backed away from all of them. "No!" he shouted, and then he lowered his voice. "I'm not going back."

"Oliver..." Minnie shook her head. "I can't believe what I'm hearing."

"Is my dad back?"

"What?" Minnie's whole body was numb. She could barely process what Oliver was saying. She shook her head once his question registered.

"So, he's still gone," Oliver said matter-of-factly. "If he ever comes back, tell him to come see me, but other than that, you all should go back to the shopping center and leave me alone."

"I don't think Minnie is capable of doing that," Kai said.

Oliver looked up at her, and she recognized real *defiance* in his eyes. "If you force me to go back, I'll run away again. I like it with Ihaka and Etera and Coop. I can just be me, and my opinions matter, and they let me do important stuff, and no one breaks their promises."

Minnie's heart broke. "Oliver, we talked about this. Your dad had no choice."

"Maybe," Oliver said, "but that doesn't change the fact that he told me he would never leave me behind, that we would all stay together, always, and then he decided to go off without us."

"Oliver," Minnie tried again, "let's just talk about this."

"I don't have time," Oliver said. "If Ihaka notices I'm gone, he'll come looking, and you all could get hurt." He made fists at his sides, and his voice was angry. "You shouldn't have come, not after I warned you."

"But..." A lump formed in Minnie's throat, and it hurt to swallow. "I love you, Oliver. You should be with people who love you."

Oliver's fists unfurled, and his shoulders lost a bit of their rigidity. He sighed. "I love you, too, Minnie. But I need to stay."

"Have they hurt you?" Lizzy asked. "Did they..." She hugged her middle. "Did they try to make you hurt anyone else?"

Oliver shook his head. "No. I have my own sleeping bag, my own rations, and I can make my own choices."

"What about the spears?" Zara asked.

"We're hunting pigs," Oliver said.

Kai looked impressed until Zara looked at him. His expression quickly returned to disapproval.

"Those boys tried to steal our supplies when we first got here," Minnie said. "How can you say they won't ask you to hurt anyone? They shot me with an arrow!"

"But you're okay," Oliver said. "Ihaka is a good shot. He didn't want to actually kill you."

Minnie blinked a few times. Again, no words seemed sufficient.

"Just because they haven't asked you to do something violent," Zara said, "doesn't mean they won't."

"Ihaka won't make me do anything I don't want to do now that I'm part of the *hapu*," Oliver said.

"The what?" Minnie asked.

"Their tribe." Oliver put his hands on his hips. "I have to go back."

"I can still throw him over my shoulder," Blythe said.

"No," Minnie said. "You heard him. He'd just run off again. And I believe he ain't bluffin' one iota." She hated what she was about to do, but something in her gut told her it was the only way. Oliver was adamant. He was angry about being separated from his father. That she should have seen more clearly before he'd run off in the first place. "Those boys have survived a long time on their own. Oliver ain't safe anywhere, truth be told. No one is. But if he's with people who know how to survive, well… I guess that's the most important thing."

"He's too young to be making these decisions," Blythe said.

"I'm not," Oliver said.

If we hold on tight, he'll slip right through our fingers, Minnie thought. She'd made that mistake with Lauren, and it had resulted in so much rebellion and even more damage to their relationship.

So, her options were to let him go and try again another day or tie him up, gag him, drag him back to the shopping center, and lock him away so he wouldn't run off again. And the second option would only result in the boy finding a way back to the factory. She knew it would. He was too smart. And then, she would *never* get him back.

She walked up to him, cupped his face in her hands, and spoke gently. "Don't let them change your heart, Oliver," she said. "I'm not giving up on you comin' back, but I won't force you, either."

Oliver stepped back hesitantly. "Okay," he said, and he gave her a small smile. "Be safe. I'll see you around." He slipped back outside and closed the door behind him.

Vision blurred from tears, Minnie rushed back to the window to see him pick up his spear and wave to a boy about his age who seemed to have come back to look for him.

"Are you sure that was the right thing to do?" Zara asked.

Minnie let her tears flow freely. "I hope so," she said, and then, in a sincere plea to the heavens, "Dear God, I hope so."

Chapter 22

Oliver Roman

Oliver dragged his feet the closer they got to the park where the wild boar had been spotted. The day had been full of promising adventure, and from the moment he'd woken, Oliver's insides had squirmed with the thrill of the upcoming hunt. He'd never hunted anything before, much less with a spear, but it was a man's task and something he would have never been allowed to do before; that alone was enough to make it worthwhile.

But his spirits had been dampened the second he'd looked up to see Minnie calling his name. A rush of emotions had coursed through him during their talk: frustration and anger at her for coming to look for him; relief to see her up and moving about; worry over his father and a renewed irritation at the fact Oliver had been left behind. Despite that, he had managed to say his piece and keep it together.

Maybe this time, she'll listen, Oliver said, although doubt immediately crept in. His mood soured further. When did they *ever* listen?

"Hey, cuz!" Etera's voice made Oliver look up. "You keep falling behind like that, and you're going to get lost." The boy had left the group ahead and was jogging toward him.

A moment of panic came with the thought, I can't let anyone know Minnie is anywhere near here.

He forced a smile and picked up his pace to meet Etera. "Sorry," he said. "I was so excited about the hunt that I barely slept last night." Oliver jogged past Etera, slapping his arm as he did. "Now who's behind?"

Etera laughed and the two of them raced to catch up. Oliver nearly collided with Coop, and Etera did collide with Oliver, making him yelp.

Ihaka craned his neck as he hushed them from the front of the group. "We're almost there," he whispered harshly. "You'll scare them off."

Several other boys gave Oliver, Etera, and Coop dark looks.

"Not my fault," Coop said, holding up both hands.

Oliver stood straighter and swallowed another laugh. "Sorry," he whispered.

Etera nodded in agreement. "Ol' Oliver gets carried away sometimes, mates. He won't do it again."

Oliver's mouth dropped. "Seriously?"

"Very rarely," Etera said.

"Gather up," Ihaka said, keeping his voice low.

Oliver joined the other boys—they numbered seventeen in all—in a circle around Ihaka. Their leader slowly turned as he spoke, and it seemed to Oliver that he took the time to look at every person.

"There's no guarantee the boar will be in the park," Ihaka said. "But I plan on having a barbe tonight. We'll need to work together. Find any grassy areas nearby and quietly scout them out. Keep in groups of three or four. You don't want to corner one of them pigs on your own, but in a group, with our weapons, we can kill it before it gets the chance to charge. Don't hesitate to strike. You understand?"

Oliver nodded along with the rest as he gripped his spear tighter.

"The Cap'n Cooker might not go down easy," Ihaka continued. "Aim for the heart to kill it quick. Otherwise, you'll make it mad, and it'll run you over. Watch out for the tusks. They'll be the death of you, if you're not careful."

Oliver's mouth ran dry. He hadn't thought about the fact that the boar could hurt *him.* A few of the other boys had hesitant or fearful looks on their faces, too.

"Find a safehouse near where you're scouting before you do anything else. If a *taniwha* comes about," Ihaka said, "run to your shelter." He pointed to a house across the street. "That one is good to go. We've hidden there plenty of times."

A chill travelled up and down Oliver's spine. The swarms tended to be least active at that time of day, but there were never any guarantees. The mission to bring back meat was riskier than Oliver had first anticipated. He'd only been thinking about the adventure, not the danger.

Ihaka knows what he's doing, Oliver thought. *He's led the* hapu *for a long time and kept all these boys alive.* He shut away his fear in the back of his mind and refocused on the task at hand.

"Coop, Etera, and Oliver," Ihaka said, "You come with me to the park." He divided the rest into groups and sent them in different directions. When it was just the four of them, Ihaka set his gaze up the road where they had last seen the boar enter the park. "Follow me."

Oliver mimicked Ihaka's slow, creeping gait along the tall bushes that lined the perimeter of the park until they reached the entrance. The grass was knee-high, and it swayed in a light breeze. Playground equipment dotted a park enclosed by overgrown greenery. There were four entrances, one for each side.

"Me, Etera, and Coop will hide low," Ihaka said. "Oliver, take the top of the slide. It's the highest point. If you see a pig, point to it. We'll be watching, and we'll get to it."

"Sweet as." Etera rubbed his hands together. "I hope we're the ones to catch it."

Coop licked his lips. "I can taste it, mates."

"That's the spirit," Ihaka said. "Oliver, you ready?"

"I am."

"Good." Ihaka nodded, seeming satisfied. "Now, if you see a *taniwha*, shout and run to the safehouse."

Oliver turned toward the slide with determination. He bent low and stepped as softly as he could through the grasses until he reached the ladder. Climbing the rungs felt like climbing the mast of a ship, like he was in some old pirate story where the lookout acted as the eyes of the whole crew.

The breeze tousled his hair. At first, his heartbeat thrashed his chest and thumped in his ears. His palms became slick with sweat, and every one of his senses seemed hyperactive. The flutter of a bird's wing had him turning his head. A strange scent in the air had him narrowing his eyes, searching for the source, hoping it was a boar. He could taste the air, a bit salty perhaps from the sea not far off, and his skin prickled with expectation. His eyes darted from Coop to Ihaka to Etera, each one hiding, quiet and unmoving, their spears poking up out of the grass.

Just as his heartbeat slowed and the lack of action had him tempted to find shapes in the clouds, a series of grunts to the right, near the swings, had Oliver back on edge. In his periphery, Oliver noticed the other boys direct their attention in that direction. But he had the best view.

A boar parted the grasses. It was black and hairy and *huge*. It had to weigh more than Oliver himself. It was larger than Samson. When it lifted its head, shook its snout, and snorted, its curling tusks were on full display.

Oliver pointed enthusiastically, and Ihaka, Coop, and Etera moved in on the boar from different directions. As they neared, Ihaka thrust his spear toward the boar, just below the shoulder, but the thing moved, and Ihaka's weapon lanced the pig's side instead. Coop jumped out in front of it, and the thing hesitated only a moment, long enough for Etera's spear to pierce it from the other side. The boar squealed and charged Coop, who stood frozen.

"Coop!" Oliver shouted. "Move!"

But the boar was already tossing the boy into the air and out of its way. Etera went after Coop, and Ihaka went after the boar. Oliver watched from his perch, realizing that the boar was going to pass the bottom of the slide. Without really thinking about it, Oliver stuck his legs out in front of him, tucked the butt of the spear under one arm, and pushed himself over the edge of the slide.

At the same time, Ihaka let out a loud whistle that echoed throughout the park and beyond. It was a call for the rest of the *hapu* to come back.

Oliver whooshed downward on the slick slide. Halfway to the bottom, he could no longer see the top of the boar's head as it was covered by the tall, yellowed grass. Rustling grasses were his only indication that the pig was still heading his way. He prepared to hop off the slide and—without hesitation, as Ihaka had said—spear the boar and end the hunt.

As he was almost to the bottom of the slide, a piglet ran close enough that it wasn't concealed. Oliver frowned. The little creature was too small to make any noticeable trail through the grass. It squealed, and Oliver realized that some of the sounds he'd heard before hadn't been the big boar at all, but rather a piglet, like that one.

I can't kill a momma boar, Oliver thought. It just didn't seem right.

When he reached the bottom of the slide, he was going so fast that he flew off the edge, his feet hitting hard and bouncing him forward. Spear still pointed outward, he shouted in shock as it embedded itself with force into the side of the larger boar as it ran from Ihaka. The pig didn't stop, though, and as the spear head remained buried in its flesh, the spear handle broke against Oliver's side. He spun and hit the ground with a grunt, his side throbbing. Another piglet ran right into him, and instinctually, Oliver took hold of it as he tried to catch his breath.

Whoops and hollers sounded all around him. Footsteps pounded the ground. The others had come back to the park. Oliver held the piglet tight—why exactly, he wasn't sure. He'd just killed its mother, its protector, and he hated that. As it squirmed in his arms, he sat up, wincing at the pain in his side. It would bruise, he was sure, but he didn't think anything was broken.

He froze when he rose on his knees so that he could see over the tops of the grasses. A circle had formed, boys crowding with their spears, jabbing over and over, though the frightened pain-filled squealing had subsided. Surely the pig was dead, but none of them seemed to notice. Others ran around the park, swinging their axes or poking the ground with spears.

What are they doing? Oliver thought.

"Got one!" A boy a few years older than Oliver named Paul thrust his spear into the air. There was a piglet on the end of it, blood dripping down the shaft.

Oliver gasped, and his stomach turned. Killing a boar for meat was one thing, but slaughtering the piglets was a whole different ball game. He looked down at the little wiggly pig in his arms, and then he made for the tall bushes lining the park's perimeter, crawling through the grass awkwardly as he held the creature to his chest. Knees scratched and sore, he breathed a sigh of relief when he reached the bushes.

"I'm sorry," he whispered as he set the piglet down. It scurried away, through the bushes, and he could only pray that it didn't come back before the *hapu* had gone. He wasn't sure if it would survive on its own, if it could find another momma boar willing to take it in, or if he was saving it just for it to die without its mother. But it was the best he could do.

Oliver stood and faced the ongoing chaos. Etera caught his eye, still in the vicinity where Coop had been thrown.

"Coop!" Oliver shouted. He ran toward Etera. *I can't believe I forgot about Coop!*

"Hey, bro!" Etera's panicked expression softened with relief. "Coop's lights out. I can't get him to wake up."

Oliver dropped to his knees beside Coop and tried to think of what Lauren would do. "Did he hit his head?"

"I reckon," Etera said.

"Okay…" Oliver chewed on his lower lip. "I don't think we're supposed to move him."

"What?" Etera furrowed his brow. "I already did that."

"Oh… well, I don't know. I'm not a doctor." Oliver poked Coop's arm. "Hey, Coop?" He leaned over the boy's face and put a finger under his nose. "He's breathing, at least. That's good, right?"

Coop groaned. "Did I get him?" he asked as he blinked his eyes open.

"Oh yeah," Etera said, nodding as he lied. "You got him good."

"Can you sit up?" Oliver asked.

Coop lifted his head and slowly propped himself up on his elbows. "I'm keen to stand up, but… why's everything spinning?" His speech was a bit slurred.

"I don't think that's good," Oliver said. "Sounds like a concussion for sure."

"Coop, you gotta lean on me and Oliver, okay, mate?" Etera stooped low. "We gotta get you back to the factory."

"Yeah, nah." Coop laid back down. "I think I need a sleep."

Oliver tapped Coop's cheek. "You can't! You don't want us to leave you here."

"The *taniwha* will get you for sure," Etera said. He grabbed hold of Coop's upper arm and pulled. "C'mon. You're coming with us whether you like it or not."

Oliver copied Etera's actions and helped get Coop to a sitting position. "You have to help us get you to your feet," Oliver said, grunting with the effort of pulling the boy up.

Coop groaned again, but with jerky motions, he got to his knees, and then to his feet, all with Oliver and Etera's help. The rest of the boys were lifting a bloody carcass onto the backs of two boys, straddling the beast across their shoulders and using paracord to secure it. Two more stood behind them, holding up the dead animal with their hands. With the four of them carrying the beast, it looked as if they might be able to get the boar back to the factory. Two others had piglets hanging limply from their spearheads. More than half of them were splattered with blood.

Ihaka raised his fist into the air and howled with victory, and everyone else, save Oliver, Etera, and Coop, followed suit.

"We're feasting tonight!" Ihaka shouted. "Back home, boys! We've got a boar to prepare."

It was only as the others were filtering out of the park that Ihaka seemed to notice Oliver and Etera limping forward with Coop hanging between them. He frowned and jogged over.

"Oi, Coop! You okay?" Ihaka asked.

"We think he has a concussion," Oliver said.

Ihaka grimaced and rubbed the back of his neck. "You get first pick of the meat, Coop. How's that?"

Coop grinned, but then his head lolled forward and he heaved, losing the meager contents of his stomach.

"All right, then," Ihaka said, stepping back, his features screwing up into a look of disgust. "Well… let's get him back." He pointed between them. "You two are doing a fine job. I'll send two more to help carry him back. Oliver, you're in charge of getting 'em all home."

"You're the biggest," Oliver said. "Can't you help?"

But Ihaka had already turned his back. He jogged away as if he hadn't heard Oliver's question. Two boys left the main group and came to help, though, and it was a lot easier to carry Coop without his feet dragging and tripping them up.

It was a long trek back to the factory. It took three times as long to get there as the trip to the park had taken, and Oliver's smaller group kept pace with those carrying the boar. Ihaka had scouts branch out from their position with instructions to whistle should a swarm come near. But they were lucky, and they made it to the factory without incident.

Once Coop was settled on his pallet of blankets, Oliver breathed a sigh of relief. The two boys Ihaka had assigned to help them left the second Coop no longer needed carrying, but Oliver and Etera sat beside him.

"We should keep an eye on him, eh?" Etera asked.

Oliver nodded. "Yeah… he's asleep… I don't think there's much we can do about that, but we should make sure he lays on his side. I remember my dad's friend, Lauren, had Annika on her side a lot when she was injured. Said it was so that if she threw up, she wouldn't choke on it."

"That's smart," Etera said. He looked from Coop to Oliver. "Hey… thanks for helping me with Coop. Everyone else was so excited about the boar, they didn't even notice him."

"Yeah…" Oliver glanced across the big factory floor to where Ihaka was giving instructions for butchering the pig and making a roasting pit with the materials they already had. All the boys were gathered around, those who weren't doing something, leaning in to learn. "It was crazy out there. I knew we were going to kill the boar, but… the way they did it…"

"I didn't like it, either," Etera said. "The piglets…" He shuddered and shook his head as if to shake the memories away. "But we got the meat, eh? It's part of surviving now."

"I guess so," Oliver said, shrugging.

Just then, the ground beneath him rumbled and shook. The whole building rattled. Oliver laid his hands flat on the ground on either side of him, about to push himself to his feet, but the shaking stopped. The boys preparing the boar and the fire pit had quieted, too, but when the small quake ended, they just went back to their task.

"Not used to that, are you, cuz?" Etera asked, chuckling.

"Earthquakes?" Oliver asked. "No. I'd never felt one until I got here. They don't seem that bad, though. It just throws me off."

"We haven't had a big one in a long time," Etera said. "In school, before all this happened, I remember there were rumors a big one was supposed to come along anytime."

Oliver shrugged. "They say that about a fault line in the Midwest, too. It's been over a hundred years since the last big one, and it's supposed to be overdue."

"Is that where you lived?" Etera asked.

Oliver shook his head. "I'm from Atlanta. That's in the South, but we only lived there a few years before Day Zero."

Coop coughed and said weakly, "That quake woke me up. Anybody got some water? I'm dying of thirst."

Oliver popped up to his feet. "I'll get some," he said. "You keep an eye on him."

He left Etera and Coop for the water stores in a room adjoining the factory's foyer. They were kept at the front of the room so that no one had to navigate the piles of boxes, bags, and canned goods that made up the rest of their supplies. Water bottle in hand, he paused in the doorway, looking across the foyer to the Remembrance Room. He slowly closed the distance, an urge to see his belongings pulling him there.

It was dark inside. He turned on the lantern and stood over his mother's purse, remembered how she'd crocheted the macrame pattern and sewn the lining herself.

Don't let them change your heart, Oliver, Minnie had said.

Images of Ihaka and the other boys wildly butchering the boar and piglets, reveling in spilled blood, turned his stomach. They'd gone too far, turned the hunt cruel as they'd allowed the animals to suffer, and more than one of them had *liked* the violence. Ihaka certainly had. Oliver didn't know what to think about that. These were his friends. He'd become part of the *hapu*.

"I'm surviving on my own," Oliver whispered to the purse, as if the people he loved could hear. "Mom is gone. Dad left me. So many people are dead. I can't sit around and wait for it to happen to you, too. Ihaka is helping me learn. He lets me *do* things."

Don't let them change your heart. Minnie's voice again, but he could hear the words coming from his dad, from his mom.

Oliver sighed. "I won't," he said. "I promise."

He turned the lantern off and left his memories where they belonged—in the past.

Chapter 23

Alexander Roman

Five days of grueling work, of twelve-hour days, of failure after failure, experiment after experiment, and when the vaccine finally came together, Alex could only stare at the results in utter shock. He blinked, ran the simulation again, and started the process of testing the vaccine with physical samples. Another few hours, and the simulation was proven accurate.

"It works," Alex said aloud to no one. He was alone in the lab. A laugh bubbled up from deep inside, and Alex threw both his hands up as far as the puffy, pressurized suit would allow. "It works!" he shouted.

Or at least, it worked in the lab.

"It needs testing," Alex said. "We have to make sure it's safe."

The vaccine would teach a body to resist DV-10, but without human testing, there was no way to know for sure it wouldn't kill that body in the process. After all, he'd had to use DV-10 in the making of the vaccine. There were no rats to test it on, and they didn't have time for the usual testing protocols. They had to be back to McMurdo Station before their ship was forced to leave them on the frozen continent.

"I have to find Walter." Alex cleaned up the lab, and in an hour, he had decontaminated his suit and stepped into the locker room where he hurried to dress.

I can't tell anyone, not yet, Alex thought as he left the BS-4 lab behind. Except for Walter.

Truth was, if he didn't need Walter to check his work and confirm for him that the vaccine was as far as they could take it in the timeframe they were given, Alex wouldn't be rushing to find him at all. Because what had to happen next…

I can't have any arguments, he thought as he navigated the halls toward the lounge.

It was past dinner, again, and he knew he'd find Walter either there or on his way to stop Alex from "overworking" himself, as Walter liked to call it. And maybe Alex *had* been overworking, but what choice did he have? Walter could check his work, confirm the results. He could understand the numbers and the science. But he wasn't the one who'd personally consulted on and worked in the process of creating vaccines. That was Alex, and it was him alone.

It has to be me, alone, to take the next steps, too. Alex repeated the sentiment with every few steps. It has to be me. It has to be. I can't let anyone else do it.

He turned the last corner into the hall that led to the lounge and ran straight into Walter. He'd been so absorbed in thought, the jolt of their shoulders colliding made him shout. He put a hand to his chest. "Walter! You scared me."

Walter rolled his shoulder. "Geez, Alex. You almost took my arm off."

"Sorry," Alex said. "I just… I need to show you something."

"I was on my way to find you," Walter said. "I know we're on a timetable, but you can't keep going like this. You promised me yesterday that you'd be done by eight." He raised his eyebrows. "Well, it's eight-thirty, and—"

"And—I—have—to—show—you—something." Alex put his hands on Walter's shoulders and lowered his voice. "This could be it, Walter, but I need you to check my work."

Walter blinked, and his mouth opened and closed without any words coming out. Finally, he managed, "You mean, this could be *it,* it?"

Alex nodded while maintaining eye contact. "This time, the work is worthy of an all-nighter, if that's what it takes."

Walter let out a long breath and slowly nodded, "Okay," he said, "but you need to get at least a few hours of sleep, while I catch up, read your notes, study the simulations. You can catch some z's on the locker room bench for all I care. We just need your mind to be fresh. I can tell just by looking at you that you're exhausted."

Alex let out a frustrated sigh and ran his fingers through his hair. "No," he said. "I can't sleep, not while—"

"So, what?" Walter asked. "You're just going to sit there while I read?"

Alex pinched his lips together. He *was* tired. Really tired. And he wouldn't be able to do much until Walter had caught up. "You'll wake me for the live experiments?"

"Of course." Walter's tone suggested a promise.

"Fine." Alex gestured down the hall. "After you, then. I'll sleep in the locker room, like you said."

"I was mostly joking about that," Walter said.

"Well, I'm not." Alex gestured again with more urgency. "I don't want to be far. We'll need to do several tests tonight, and I don't want to waste time."

"Okay," Walter said, "but if I come across anything that suggests we need to rework this significantly before moving on to the next phase, we break for the night and pick it back up together tomorrow."

"Deal," Alex said.

"At least grab a blanket and a pillow from your room on the way," Walter said.

Alex shrugged and agreed. It wouldn't take away from the time, not by more than a minute, and the more he thought about a nap, the more his muscles and bones reminded him just how much he needed one.

The two of them made their way back to the lab after a quick stop at Alex's room. Walter proceeded to suit up, and Alex situated himself on the floor rather than the bench. He wasn't a still sleeper, and he suspected trying to sleep on the skinny bench would land him on the ground anyway.

The floor was hard, but he'd slept on worse. The pillow, at least, gave him some comfort. He closed his eyes and focused on breathing steadily, slowly. It took his heartbeat slowing for him to realize just how fast it had been beating. As the pressure in his temples eased, an ache settled in its place. The urgency of the day had had him going a hundred miles per hour since he'd stepped foot in the lab that morning, and he'd not allowed himself a break. Even while forced to grab a bite to eat or drink, his work had been running nonstop through his brain. The stress had become so normalized that rest felt *wrong*.

Still, the longer he lay there and reached for sleep, the closer it came until he was able to grasp it. Or rather, it was able to grasp him. One second he was focusing on clearing his mind, and the next, he was being gently shaken awake.

"Alex?"

He blinked, eyelids heavy, and cracked open his eyes to see Walter crouching beside him in a deflated hazmat suit, the helmet removed. Alex's tongue was thick in his mouth, and his body was weighted down by resistance to consciousness.

"How long have I been asleep?" he asked, the words slow as mud.

"A few hours," Walter said. "I wanted to be sure before I woke you."

Alex struggled to sit up and then leaned back against lockers, facing Walter. He ran his hands over his face and tried to rub away his exhaustion. "And?" he asked as he leaned his head back.

"And I think you're right."

Walter's response was like a shot of adrenaline to Alex's system. He sat up straighter. "So, then, we get to work?"

"We get to work." Walter stood and held out a hand.

Alex grabbed hold of it, got to his feet, and reached for a suit.

* * *

"It's done," Alex said. "We've brought it as far as we can take it without human trials."

It was six o'clock in the morning. He and Walter had been at it all night, testing and retesting, running simulations, looking for lethal mistakes. They had crafted several doses, but as Alex met Walter's gaze and found his expression as grim as Alex felt, he knew the other man understood what the next step had to be.

"One of us needs to test it," Walter said.

"It has to be me," Alex said.

Walter shook his head. "No. This is something I have to do. Besides the fact that it was my company that developed this disease, my kids are older than Oliver. He still needs you."

"Your kids need you, too, Walter."

"I know."

Alex licked his lips and swallowed hard. He'd been preparing himself for the trial since the previous day. "I can't let you risk your life with an untested vaccine I created."

Walter set a firm stance, drew himself to his full height, and used a tone that made Alex shrink. "I'm not giving you a choice," Walter said.

"Walter—"

"No. This is mine to carry." Walter was like ice: calm and cool but unyielding. "I won't argue about it. I *will* be the one to test that vaccine."

Alex knew that Walter had been the CEO and founder of Vanguard, that the man had been known as a ruthless businessman, but he'd been weak and injured the first time Alex had met him, and even once his strength had been regained, Walter had been a changed man. It had been hard to imagine him as the ambitious cutthroat he'd once been.

Until that moment when Alex caught a glimpse of the man who wouldn't take no for an answer.

"Wow," Alex said, scoffing halfheartedly despite an undeniable feeling of intimidation. "Are you trying to bully me into letting you have your way, Walter?"

"Don't be stubborn," Walter said.

"Me? What about you?" Alex raised his voice. "Just because you think you deserve punishment for what happened doesn't mean you actually deserve it. You know just as well as I do that there were dozens of people at the top, people *over* your head, who made DV-10 happen."

"I stopped trying to shift the blame months ago," Walter said.

"Exactly. Because you're a good man." Alex pointed at him. "You have three children alive and well, and you have a grandchild on the way. Not to mention Zara and Kai."

"What about Oliver? Minnie and Lauren? They love you just as much. My mind is set on this, Alex." Walter sighed and the man Alex was more accustomed to shone through. "This isn't about punishment. It's about redemption. I *need* to do this. For myself as much as anybody else."

The way Walter looked at Alex stirred him, prompted a shift in his thinking. It clicked, and Alex understood, even if just a little. It was still hard to accept. Alex turned away from Walter and walked a few steps, looked straight ahead at nothing while his thoughts were full of everything. When he turned back to face his friend, he nodded slowly.

"Okay," he said.

"Thank you." Walter nodded back and then offered a small smile. "And if I do die, don't worry. You'll get to test the next iteration of the vaccine yourself."

"I have full confidence that you'll take all the glory," Alex said.

"Let's just hope it will be worth it." Walter glanced at the vaccine dosages. "Even if it doesn't kill me, there's no guarantee it would save me if I were exposed to DV-10 in the wild. With the mutations ongoing and—"

"Don't think like that. It's the best we can do," Alex said. "And it's a good starting point for anyone who might take up the work after us, even if we miss the mark, which I don't think we have."

"You're right." Walter breathed out long and slow. "That's a relief, isn't it? That our work so far would outlive us, that we've brought it to a place where another competent scientist in the field could run with it, keep improving it."

Alex raised his eyebrows as his shoulders suddenly felt a bit lighter. "I hadn't thought about that," he said, "but yeah… it does feel good."

"I'd like to write a few letters," Walter said, "say some last words. If I don't make it, you'll give them to Elizabeth and Zara and Kai? You'll find Timothy and George again?"

"I will do everything within my power," Alex said.

Walter nodded. "Good," he said. "We should set me up outside. I can use the gear we brought. It'll be safer out there, just in case our miracle vaccine isn't so miraculous."

"You should stay separated from us for forty-eight hours, just to be safe," Alex said.

"We only have fifteen days left until the ship has to leave the continent," Walter said. "If this doesn't work, you'll have to find out what went wrong and then come up with something better. Not to mention the five or six days it's going to take, minimum, for us to get everyone and everything back to McMurdo. Can we spare two full days?"

Alex moved toward the door. He had supplies to gather, and Walter had letters to write. They had to start the trial as soon as possible.

"We don't have a choice," Alex said. "We have to work quickly and pray what we've done is enough."

Chapter 24

Alexander Roman

Alex stepped out of the protection of Barlow Scientific Research Bank and into the frigid air of Antarctica. The entrance was hidden behind faux rock made to blend in with the mountain; it was shrouded in shadows, and Alex had to work his way in the dark toward daylight about five yards to his left.

Blinding white landscape met him as he slipped past the faux rock and his boots crunched the windswept snow on the side of the mountain. A path—not that one would call it that if they hadn't been shown where it led—hugged the towering rock to his right and dropped off sharply on his left. The path widened in another seven or eight yards.

If he'd gone the other way when exiting the hidden entrance, he would have found a way down to where Walter was, but Alex didn't want to be within ten feet of the man until he knew it was safe. Alex got down on his knees and slid off his backpack, settling it in the snow. He leaned over the lip of the rock so that he could see Walter ten feet below.

"Walter?" Alex shouted.

Fourteen hours: that's how long his friend had been camping in the cold, buried in a sleeping bag made for subzero temperatures, equipped with enough food and supplies to get him through two days. The orange lump below didn't stir, and Alex's blood ran colder than the icy rock beneath him.

"Walter!" He shouted again, this time with more urgency.

Movement below made Alex breathe out with relief, a puff of white forming about his face as he did so.

"I'm awake," Walter said, but he groaned as he peeled back the sleeping bag.

"Are you okay?" Alex asked.

Walter's silver-grey hair was plastered to his forehead, and his skin glistened with sweat. He twisted and reached for the backpack stuck into the top of the huge sleeping bag, pulled out a bottled water, and drank greedily. A knot formed in Alex's stomach. He quickly gathered the kit he'd brought in his own backpack and began to lower it in a basket on a rope.

"I've got more water for you," Alex said, "but I'm going to need you to take your temperature immediately, okay?"

Walter nodded weakly as he wiped his mouth with his sleeve and sat up. The man squinted at the basket and raised his arms to gather the basket as it neared him. His hands were shaking.

"I don't like the way you look," Alex said.

"You're no stud muffin, Alex." Walter set the basket in his lap and dug out the thermometer.

"I'm not joking." Alex bit the inside of his cheek as Walter stuck the thermometer in his mouth. The complete silence crushed Alex until his ears roared with the thrashing of his own heartbeat. The *beep beep* of the tiny device rang out, and Alex clutched the edge of the cliff with his gloved hands. "What does it say?"

Walter looked at it and grimaced. "One hundred and three," he croaked, "and I've got the worst headache of my life, which is saying something."

No, no, no! Alex kept his panicked thoughts to himself and tried to keep his voice steady and calm. "What about rashes? Bulging veins? How are your eyes?"

Walter opened an alcohol packet and wiped down the thermometer before putting it back in the basket. "My only symptoms are fever and a headache," he said. "Exhaustion, too, but if it doesn't get any worse, I'd say this is just the vaccine doing its job."

Or it's the virus killing him slowly even in a weakened state, Alex thought. If we did something wrong… if the virus is too strong…

But those sentiments were far from what Walter needed to hear. He already knew the risks, already understood that the process they'd had to accept for creating the vaccine was rushed and lacking in pretty much every step.

"I'm sure that's it. Just the vaccine doing its thing." Alex could hear the doubts in his own voice and hoped that Walter couldn't. "Do you have your hourly log?"

Walter wobbled a little as he leaned forward and dug out a small notebook. He sanitized it and dropped it in the basket. "Escalating symptoms, bowel movements and urination logs, how much I've eaten, how much water I've consumed…" He looked up, squinting again at Alex. "Riveting stuff. I hope you enjoy it. Could be the most intriguing thing I've ever written."

Alex returned a flat look. "There's a new log book in the basket."

Walter got it out and stuck it in his backpack. "See you in a few hours?" he asked.

Alex sighed and pulled on the rope to bring the basket back to him. "Yeah," he said. "Get some more rest. Is that sleeping bag treating you right?"

"It's warm and cozy," Walter said without enthusiasm. He plopped onto his side and wiggled back down into the gear. "Just like my bed at home."

Alex set the basket down beside him and used a disinfectant spray all over it before sticking it in the backpack. "Just take care of yourself, Walter. Okay?" He looked back over the edge of the cliff. "Walter?"

A long, deep snore answered him. Alex sighed and got to his feet. "Good luck, my friend," he said softly before turning and going back the way he'd come.

The trek down the stairwell to the research bank was quick compared to the climb up. Thankfully, Robert said there was another entrance, a tunnel that would bring them and their equipment to the other side of the mountain.

That was another pressing matter to which Alex needed to attend. While Walter was suffering, the least Alex could do was finish prepping everyone to leave Barlow for the snowcat and sleds.

He reached the bottom landing and entered the keycode for the thick steel door. It clicked, and he pushed it open, stepping inside to artificial light… and a hall filled with people. Lauren was closest, coming to attention and pushing off the wall she'd been leaning against. Behind her, the five technicians were gathered, whispering amongst themselves; all five cut off and stared at Alex. Behind them all, Candice stood by as Stella paced. All eight stared at Alex, wide-eyed, and by how still they all were, Alex wondered if any of them were breathing.

"How is he?" Lauren asked.

"He has a fever," Alex said, "and a headache."

"Okay," Candice said, squeezing between Robert and Cat, "those were my first symptoms, but by this time, I was already to the point where I thought I was going to die. So… that's just the vaccine, right?"

Alex licked his lips, his eyes flickering with eager expressions tinted with fear. He chose his words carefully. "That's very likely," he said.

Robert scoffed. "So, it could be that the vaccine will kill him."

"We don't know anything for sure, yet, but there's no reason to believe this is anything more than a mild, weakened version of DV-10 due to the live virus in the vaccine," Alex said.

Cat shook her head. "I'm getting back to work." She turned her back, and Robert made to follow.

"I have high hopes," Alex said as the remaining three technicians followed their colleagues, albeit with less hostility in their body language. "Walter is going to pull through. This is going to work." He raised his voice as he was forced to talk to their backs.

"Don't let them get to you," Lauren said.

Alex pulled off his gloves with more vigor than was necessary. "It's like they want instant success with something no one has ever done before. Vaccine development normally involves teams, not one or two scientists working around the clock." He pulled at his zipper, but it stuck in place. No matter how he tugged, it wouldn't budge. "And if Walter does pull through, I'll need them, Lauren."

Lauren came up to him as he struggled with the zipper and put her hands on his, gently prompting him to stop tugging. "They'll see," she said as she worked the zipper up and then down again, successfully unzipping his coat. "This is scary for them. Don't you remember what it was like the first weeks? They still think there are choices out there. They haven't fully accepted what's happening."

"They're going to have to soon," Alex said.

"Why do you need them?" Stella asked.

Alex looked up at her. "What?"

Stella came closer. "You said you'll need them. For what?"

"The next phase of human trials," Alex said. "Before we take the vaccine back to the ship, we have to make sure it's safe. The next step should Walter fully recover would be to vaccinate us all." He shrugged at Candice and Stella. "Except for you two. Having the disease and surviving it should mean you're good to go, for now at least."

"This is crazy," Stella said. "If it's making Walter sick, it could do the same to them."

Candice put a hand on Stella's arm. "Alex wouldn't force anyone to take it," she said. "But he would only allow it if he believed it to be safe."

"She's right," Alex said, "and we will need another round of trials. If everyone here pulls through, we can take a working vaccine back to the ship with evidence that it isn't dangerous. I'm hoping I can develop enough of the vaccine in the lab on the ship to administer to the crew and anyone they pick up at the other stations."

"Didn't you say that you won't know if the vaccine is effective until vaccinated people are exposed? So, you want them to risk their lives for a maybe?" Stella crossed her arms.

Alex bristled despite himself. *She's been through a lot. Be patient,* he reminded himself. "Stella, I want them to risk their lives for the *only* maybe we've got."

Lauren stood beside him, her hand on his back. "Once we return to where the swarms are, they have little chance of surviving long term. This is their best option. It's the best option for all of us who don't have whatever you two have that enabled your survival."

"You've seen a lot of people die." Candice wrapped an arm around Stella's shoulders. "We all have. But we've been literally all over the world searching for how to make things right again. We have to trust Alex and Walter."

"If Walter survives," Stella said.

"When he does," Alex said, "he'll agree with me. We're the experts, and neither of us would do anything to endanger anyone. That's why Walter is out there right now, why we didn't ask one of the technicians to volunteer."

Stella worked her jaw back and forth and crossed her arms, seeming to mull over all of the information she'd been given. Finally, she shrugged. "Okay," she said. "I'll try to trust you. I'm on your side."

"Thank you," Alex said.

Candice nodded back down the hall. "In the meantime, we should continue to help pack up this place. There are a lot of supplies we don't want to leave behind." She and Stella followed after the technicians, turning at the corner, headed for the lounge.

Lauren looked to Alex. "You ready to help Robert hook up the solar panels to the cryo pods?"

"He's got them ready for that?" Alex asked.

She nodded and took a step down the hall, but Alex put a hand on her upper arm to stop her.

"Thanks," he said. "For calming me down." He indicated his coat with a look. "You were right. I was letting them get to me, and I need to come into these conversations expecting resistance from them."

Lauren shrugged and smiled. "We're a good team," she said. "I'll always be here for you. You know that, right?"

A warmth blossomed in Alex's chest. "Yeah," he said. "I know. I'm here for you, too. Always."

Lauren stepped back and hooked her arm with his. "I say, let's work as if everything will go exactly to plan. Do what needs to be done so that we can get back to my mom and Oliver."

Alex walked with her down the hall, just the two of them. He missed his son more than words could express, and more than once, he wished he could have turned to Minnie for some advice. But he didn't feel alone with Lauren by his side. That was worth more to him than she could ever know.

Chapter 25

Stella Sharpe and Alexander Roman

The slow return of the ability to feel was accelerated when Walter came back, alive and well. Stella had been waiting for the more recent patterns of her life to repeat, for death to reign and her fledgling hope to be crushed, but when Alex came back with Walter in tow, a little pale but otherwise just fine, Stella had been forced to consider the fact that perhaps nightmares really did have an end.

Stella leaned against the wall in what had become her favorite spot to listen in on conversations in the lounge. She'd moved a stool into her corner, just a few yards from the back of the loveseat where Candice and Lauren sat.

This should be interesting, Stella thought as Alex finished explaining his request.

Robert scoffed. That seemed to be his favorite way to respond to Alex. If Stella had to guess, his attitude was simply the easiest way to hide his fear. "You want us to take this experimental vaccine? I don't think so," he said.

Alex pinched the bridge of his nose and sighed loudly. He shook his head and looked to Walter.

Just tell it like it is. Be who you are. You convinced me, anyway, Stella thought, and the way she was rooting for them caught her off guard. She looked down at her feet. She'd promised herself she wouldn't get attached, that she would guide Alex, Walter, Lauren, and Candice over the harsh Antarctic landscape so that the end of her life wouldn't be defined by what had happened at McMurdo Station.

But she was starting to think there could be a future for her, and that hope felt dangerous.

"Anyone who participates," Walter said, "will be doing something for the entire world. This is bigger than you or me. The three-step plan Alex described will rid the world of DV-10 and the swarms. It will give humanity the chance to return to some semblance of normalcy."

Stella had listened carefully to every explanation. She thought she understood the plan pretty well. The countermeasure mosquitos would slowly but surely eradicate the swarms through generational deformities that would render them unable to reproduce. The vaccine would provide preventative protection, though immunity wasn't guaranteed. And the treatment, if administered immediately after infection, could lessen symptoms in the vaccinated breakthrough cases and possibly save the life of the unvaccinated.

But returning to normalcy was a stretch if all that she'd been told about the outside world was true. Maybe return to what was normal in, like the 1800s, she thought. I guess that's better than nothing. And maybe I'm wrong. Maybe humanity can rebuild faster than I think it can.

She pressed her lips together. Being around people like Candice and Alex was messing with her ability to be realistic. They were so full of hope, so used to pushing and pushing until they clawed their way out of the mire to break free of the destruction that seemed to pull everyone else under.

Stella looked back up to study the faces of the technicians. There was the kindling of hope in their eyes, too. Maybe, like her, they couldn't bear to snuff it out, even if they were terrified that the world would do that for them soon enough.

"C'mon, Robbie," Anise said. "What better choice do we have?"

Zac nodded slowly. Everything he did was like that: laid back and thought out. When he spoke, it seemed as though he was considering every next word. "I wanna live, man. Don't you?"

Cat, who normally seemed to be on Robert's side, had a begrudging tone as she said, "Zac and Anise are right. This vaccine might be dangerous or untested, or whatever, but when we get off this frozen wasteland, we're headed into a situation that's likely to kill us, anyway."

Farrah's eyes glistened. "We should do this together," she said. "We should do it for the people we love back home." She looked over her shoulder at Robert. "You have sisters, right? What if they're alive? What if this vaccine works and you could be part of bringing it to them?"

Robert blinked a few times and dropped his arms, his stiff posture loosening as his frown relaxed. He took a step back and ran his hand over his face as he took a deep breath. He didn't say anything, but Stella could see Farrah's question and the implications of it breaking down Robert's hardened shell bit by bit. In seconds, the man was deflated. Several times, he opened his mouth only to shut it again.

Cat put a hand on his shoulder, and he looked at her. There was trust between them, familiarity in her touch. Not long ago, Stella had been able to reach out to people like that, people she'd known and loved. Despite herself, despite the doubt that it was possible, she wanted that again.

"If we do this," Robert said, shifting his focus from Cat to Alex and Walter, "and it works, our families get the vaccine first, or at least…" He swallowed and licked his lips before continuing. "… those who've survived."

Alex sighed. "If I could promise that, I would, but I can't. We will have to administer the vaccine as we go, and we can't skip over entire populations just to get to the people we love."

"Then send us out, on our own, with vaccines we can take to them ourselves," Robert said. "We can take a boat, and—"

"I don't have access to boats that can cross oceans," Alex said.

Robert balled his hands into fists, and his aggression returned. "Do what you can, then. You've got to have some influence. As soon as we can get transportation home, you provide us with doses of the vaccine, and then we go find our families."

Walter held up a hand as Alex opened his mouth. "We will do everything in our power to help you get vaccines to your families as quickly as possible," Walter said.

Alex seemed to consider the statement before adding, "If that promise is good enough for you, I can make it."

Zac looked at Robert. "I think that's the best they can do, man."

"Fine." Robert nodded once. "I agree, then. We'll be part of your trial."

The other four technicians nodded, none of them enthusiastic. It wasn't the sort of the thing to celebrate. Stella was scared for them; she couldn't imagine what they must be feeling.

"Thank you," Alex said.

Walter added his thanks. "I'll be monitoring you all, as Alex did for me," he said, "and then we are going to leave this place with everything we need to set the world right again."

Candice stood up. "You're all being very brave," she said. "I just want you to know that I'll be here to help you should you get a little sick, like Walter did." She looked over her shoulder at Stella. "You'll help, too, right?"

Stella straightened, eyes wide. "I... um... yeah," she said, her cheeks warming as she responded with the exact opposite of what she wanted to say. It wasn't that she didn't want to help. It was that she wasn't sure she could bear it if things went sideways.

Candice gave her a warm smile and turned back to the others. "You won't be alone."

It was time to find out if Walter's trial with the vaccine would be affirmed or made out to be a fluke.

* * *

Sweat coated Alex's skin, drenched his shirt, and soaked into the sheets beneath him. The heat coursing through his veins, setting his body on fire, was nothing next to the raging headache that had settled behind his eyes. Every muscle screamed for relief; even his bones ached.

Pure hatred for time itself was driving him to madness. Alex lost consciousness, succumbing to exhaustion, on occasion, but there was no telling if he'd been out for a minute or a day. There was certainly no rest to be had.

His vision refused to focus, and his brain rejected the effort it would have taken to have a coherent thought outside of those related to the way his body betrayed him. He welcomed the darkness of the small room he'd chosen for his vaccine trial. The light was unbearable.

A knock on the door brought an automatic groan from deep in Alex's gut. It was always Walter who came to check on him, and it was no different that time. The door opened, dreaded light filled the room, and Alex grimaced against it.

"Sorry," Walter said, his voice as if he were speaking from far away, garbled and overpowered by the pounding in Alex's head. "Time to check your temperature." Walter made another sound, a grunt of sorts as he came near. "You look worse than I was. Definitely worse."

Alex smacked his lips together. His mouth was *so* dry. "Water," he said, squinting up at Walter's outline. There was salt on his lips, a copper taste on his tongue.

There was a hand at his neck, lifting his head, and when the lip of a cup touched his mouth, Alex drank deeply.

"This isn't good," Walter said. "Hang in there, okay? Your fever is high... one hundred and six. You can't maintain that for long. We're going to have to get an ice bath for you, too."

Something about that statement struck Alex as worrisome, but it was so hard to concentrate on anything other than the pain and exhaustion. He closed his eyes; his blurred vision only induced nausea, anyway. All he wanted was for it to end, but the agony was never-ending.

* * *

Stella refused to look at Alex's door as she passed by on her way to check on Lauren. She and Candice took turns watching after the women. Robert hadn't fallen ill at all, no more than a minor headache, at least. He'd volunteered to help Walter with the men.

Alex was the worst off by far. He and Anise had needed ice baths and more monitoring than the others. But they were thirty hours in, and everyone but Alex was beginning to recover or had recovered completely, even Anise, though she was still weakened.

A soft knock on the door produced an invitation to enter, and Stella slipped into Lauren's room with water and chicken noodle soup. Lauren was sitting up against the headboard. She reached out for the soup, her movements slow but sure. "I'm actually hungry this time," she said.

"Good." Stella avoided direct eye contact. She didn't want to be the one to reveal Alex's state. Lauren didn't know, not yet. Walter had insisted on keeping it from her until she was fully recovered, to ensure she remained calm and unstressed.

"Is this chicken noodle?" Lauren asked.

Stella shrugged as she set the water on Lauren's side table. "I wouldn't get too excited. It was dehydrated in a pouch before I added water and heated it up. It's supposed to be packed with nutrients, but the package said nothing about taste."

Lauren sipped at the soup. "It's not bad," she said.

"I better go, then," Stella said. "Farrah needs a few things."

"Wait." Lauren set the bowl of soup next to the cup. "How's Alex?"

Stella froze and stared at Lauren. *Say something!* she thought.

"Stella?"

She unglued her tongue from the roof of her mouth. "He's... um... well..."

Concern flashed across Lauren's face, and she leaned forward just slightly. "Tell me."

"He's still really sick," Stella said.

Lauren pushed back her blankets and scooted to the edge of the bed. "Help me," she said. "I want to see him."

"I don't think that's a good idea," Stella said.

"I didn't ask," Lauren said. "If you won't do it, go get Candice." She pushed off the bed and stood, wobbling a bit.

"Whoa!" Stella stepped forward and steadied Lauren, reaching out and letting the other woman grab hold of her arms. "Okay, fine, but... there's nothing you can do."

"I can be there," Lauren said.

Stella sighed at the desperation in Lauren's eyes. "You really care about him, don't you?"

"He's got a son to look after."

Stella gave her a flat look.
Lauren looked down at her feet. "And I really care about him."
Stella shook her head as she repositioned herself, wrapping her arm around Lauren's waist and letting the other woman lean more heavily on her. They started together toward the door, slowly. "Walter's not as soft as I am, you know. He'll probably make you go back to your room."
Lauren scoffed. "You obviously don't know him well enough yet."
Stella and Lauren took it one step at a time until they were out in the hall, and when they were about a dozen steps from Alex's door, it opened and Walter came out, stopping at the sight of them and crossing his arms.
"You're not going to take no for an answer, are you?" he asked Lauren.
"Nope." Lauren managed to look quite sure of herself as she lifted her chin and met Walter's gaze with her own.
"There's a chair in there," Walter said, "but it's not comfortable, and it doesn't provide much support."
"So," Lauren said, "you're going to get me a better one, right?"
Walter narrowed his eyes. "He can't even carry on a conversation, and he needs rest and quiet. He's also light sensitive right now. That means we need to keep it dark unless we have to turn on the lights to take care of him."
"I can handle all of that. I know him," Lauren said. "He also needs someone with him, a presence to remind him what he's fighting for." She cleared her throat. "Oliver, obviously."
"Lauren—"
"I have medical training, Walter. Whatever is happening, I'll be fine. I can help you monitor him. Bring my mattress. Put it on the floor out of the way, opposite Alex's bed."
Stella broke in when she saw the opportunity to avoid going into that room. "Her mattress is thin and light," she said. "I can bring it." She nodded between Walter and Lauren. "Why don't you help her inside, and I'll go get it."
Walter sighed. "Okay, fine."
Stella handed Lauren off—she seemed stronger than she had when she'd first stood up, needing only a little help from Walter—and headed back to Lauren's room. But when she got there, she stood in the hall staring at the door. As soon as she retrieved the mattress, she'd have to take it back to Alex's room.
Two doors down, there was a click and Candice shuffled out of her room, yawning. She squinted at Stella. "Hey… you okay?"
"I can't go in there," Stella said.
"In where?" Candice frowned, and then stepped forward. "Is Lauren okay? She was fine just a few hours ago."
"She's fine," Stella said. "I mean, I can't go into Alex's room. Lauren insisted on going there. Walter is with her, and I'm supposed to bring her mattress, but I can't. I can't see another person dying."
"Alex isn't going to die," Candice said. "We can't think like that."
"I can't help it," Stella said.
"I know." Candice came near, putting an arm briefly around Stella's shoulders. "I'll do it, okay? I was going to switch off with you soon, anyway, and you're probably exhausted. Go get some rest."
Stella didn't need to be told twice. She left Candice to the task and hurried down the hall toward her room, cheeks hot and tears welling. The faces of all those she'd lost flashed one after another in her mind's eye. By the time she reached her room and closed herself in, her tears were flowing freely. She'd let hope back in, started to believe good would win out. If Alex didn't make it, that hope would die with him. It would be proof that death was always just around the corner, that perhaps it followed her, a curse she would never be able to shake.

Chapter 26

Zara Williams

Zara let the silence fill the space around her and Lizzy as they sat shoulder to shoulder, holding hands, allowing herself to process the weight of all that Lizzy had said. Lizzy rested her head on Zara's shoulder, breathing evenly, easily. When Zara glanced at her, a small smile had appeared and Lizzy was no longer shedding any tears.

The juxtaposition between the expression of peace on her best friend's face and the emotions that warred within Zara was striking. *I feel the weight, but she's had her burden lifted…*

Lizzy had just revealed all the missing pieces of her story, the things she'd been unable to talk about until then, horrible things that had been done to her. She'd been tortured by the Heirs of the Mother, and her mind had been twisted to believe that Azalea and the Heirs were the only ones who could save her from her sins and the sins of her father.

"When they tied me to that stake and set it on fire," Lizzy had said, "I was already bent to the point of breaking. I just… snapped. And when Azalea stopped them from burning me alive, I don't know… I latched onto her. I needed her. She was the only one who could make the voices in my head stop screaming."

Rage and horror had come over Zara as she'd listened. She was still nauseous, even after Lizzy had gone quiet, although the baring of her soul had seemed to grant Lizzy great relief.

I can barely handle just hearing about what happened, Zara thought. I can't imagine what it must have been like to go through it.

And for so long, Lizzy had carried that burden all by herself.

After a few minutes, Lizzy stirred and breathed in and out deeply, her sigh speaking of lightened spirits. "I think I'm ready to be around my dad again."

Zara blinked at her and smiled. "Really?"

"Yeah. I want to forgive him for everything. I want to let go and start over."

"I think Walter wants that, too," Zara said. "He loves you so much."

Lizzy nodded. "I know. I think part of me always knew that, and seeing how he's changed, realizing that it's a genuine change… that's really helped." She yawned. "All this talking has worn me out."

"Why don't you take a nap?" Zara asked. "Kai and Blythe are out in the concourse. I'll make sure they give you some peace and quiet."

"You know," Lizzy said, "you've taken good care of me. You believed in me, believed I could come back from what they did to me. That means a lot."

Zara shook her head as her cheeks flushed warm. "Don't thank me for that. I should have never doubted you. I should have—"

Lizzy held up a hand. "I forgive you, too. You know that, right?"

Zara's throat tightened. "The things I said before they took you—"

"I don't want to hear about it," Lizzy said. "I know what you said. I also know you were going through a lot, and I know you didn't mean it." She touched the *taonga* Zara had given her, carved with a purpose, resting at the end of a leather cord on her chest. "New beginnings, okay? I forgive you. And you forgive me, for all the things I did?"

Zara's voice cracked as she spoke. "That wasn't your f—"

"Maybe not entirely," Lizzy said, "but… I still need you to forgive me."

"I do," Zara said. "That isn't who you are."

"And that person you were in those days following the death of your family and the revelation of what my father did—that angry person—she isn't who you are, either." Lizzy raised her eyebrows at Zara. "We forgive each other, and we have to forgive ourselves."

Zara did her best to hold back tears, but they rolled down her cheeks anyway. "Okay," she managed to say.

"Good." Lizzy patted Zara's thigh. "Now, get off my blankets so I can nap." She smiled wide and nudged Zara.

"You're so bossy." Zara laughed as she dried her eyes and scooted off Lizzy's blankets. She got to her feet as Lizzy lay down and snuggled down into her makeshift bed. "I missed that."

Lizzy gave her a wry look. "I'm going to remember you said that."

Zara shook her head and left Lizzy to rest, but when she stepped outside of the curtains partitioning their space from the rest of shop that had become their temporary home, Zara hugged her middle and stood still for what seemed like forever, just staring at nothing, processing.

Eventually, she turned and slowly strode toward the concourse, each step leaving behind some of the weight, replacing the bad with memories of Lizzy's peaceful smile, light laughter, and kind words.

My best friend is back, Zara thought as she stepped into sunlight let into the concourse by way of the skylights. *New beginnings. That sounds like exactly what I need.*

She smiled as she took in the sight of the people in the concourse. Families worked together to cook, clean, mend, and innovate. Children chased each other, weaving around the legs of their elders. Two older women sat at a table near the kitchen area, laughing over something, their smiles bright.

But then Zara's eyes fell across another woman, sitting far off at the end of the concourse with a dog at her feet. Minnie had taken up watching the parking lot again. She was sure Oliver would return to them once he realized "those thick-headed hooligans were up to no good." It wasn't like Minnie, to stew and sit idle. At least, Zara had never known her to be like that; she'd only known her as the woman who cared for Alex, Lauren, and Oliver. If it weren't for Samson, Zara was afraid Minnie would have lost every bit of her characteristic "spit and sass," as she'd once called it.

She needs someone to fight for, Zara thought. We need to remind her that she's still needed.

But everything she'd tried so far had failed. Minnie seemed lost in her worry over Alex, Lauren, and Oliver, overwhelmed by the possibility of losing all three. And Zara couldn't blame her. All she could do was keep trying.

She squinted as two figures approached Minnie, one with two folding chairs and the other with a plate and cup. Zara smiled. It was Kai and Blythe. They were already ahead of her, already taking care of Minnie. Zara started down the hall, intending on joining them, but as she passed by the room reserved for school and the youth, she paused at the sound of an argument.

"Shut up, Niko!"

"I won't! I heard he's out there, right now, and he's not a prisoner. He's *one of them*."

Zara frowned at the two boys, one of them named Niko, the other Will. A girl Zara believed to be named Ava was standing behind them, tugging on her hair, brow furrowed as her eyes flitted between them.

"Stop it!" the girl said. "Stop yelling."

Will huffed and crossed his arms. "It's rubbish. That kid was soft. There's no way those boys at the factory let him join."

"Everyone knows it's true," Niko said. "Oliver was the real deal, mate, and you're jealous! You're all talk, and everyone knows it."

Will balled his hands into fists. "You're asking for a hiding, bro."

Niko put fists up and narrowed his eyes. "Go on and try. I don't think you're so tough, anymore. Bet you can't even really throw a punch!"

Ava squeaked as Will took a threatening step forward.

Zara raised her eyebrows and held up her hands, stepping into the room. "Whoa," she said. "You two need to cool it. I know who your parents are, and I'm not afraid to tell them you were fighting."

Will's snarl turned to a look of surprise. His mouth opened, but no words came out as he backed away from Niko.

"See?" Niko laughed. "You're afraid of a girl."

Zara blinked and put her hands on her hips. "A girl? Really?"

Will growled and reared back his fist, but before he could punch Niko in the face, Zara caught his wrist. He shouted and shook her off, nearly landing a fist in *her* face.

"I'm not afraid of you," Will said. "I'm not afraid of anyone!"

"Except the Lolly Factory Boys," Niko said in a taunting singsong rhythm.

Will's face contorted with anger, and he turned on Niko. Zara stepped between them and put her finger in Will's face.

"I said to stop it, and I meant it," she said. "I may be a girl, but so is your mom, and I've seen how you say 'how high' when she says 'jump.'" At Niko's snicker, she turned on him. "And you, you little brat, stop egging him on before he breaks your nose. Get out of here before I decide to drag you out by your ear. Don't think I can't, either. I've faced things that would make you pee your pants."

Niko swallowed audibly, his cocky smile turning unsure.

"Go!" Zara pointed at the door, and Niko jumped before scurrying out. Ava followed closely behind, throwing glances at Will over her shoulder until she was out of sight. Zara watched them flee with her arms crossed. "I meant you, too, Will. Go now, and I'll leave your mom out of it."

"Is Oliver really one of them?" Will asked.

Zara frowned and looked at the boy. "Why do you care?"

"Because… ever since you came back with that story about how he's joined them, the other kids won't listen to me anymore." Will averted his eyes and said bitterly, "It can't be true. Oliver's a muppet."

"A what?" Zara shook her head. "Nevermind. Look, kid, Oliver may be smaller than you are, but I'd wager he's been through as much, probably more. And if you knew his father, you'd know the Romans don't mess around. They're tough, and they're smart."

He ground his teeth. "I'm not a kid."

Zara gave him a flat look. "Sure you are. And if it makes you feel any better, so is Oliver. Heck, I'm barely an adult." She sighed. "I don't know why you feel it's necessary to put others down to lift yourself up, but I'm telling you something right now: it won't work out in your favor. You're only going to hurt yourself."

"You're not my mom." He turned sharply toward the door and stomped away.

Zara looked up at the ceiling, imagining her own mother and father looking down at her, chuckling. "I owe you an apology for the things you put up with," she said with a small smile, a little sadness gripping her. She shook her head, sighed, and returned to her original mission. Minnie needed her spirits lifted, and if anyone deserved all hands on deck, it was her.

All three kids had scattered out of sight by the time Zara stepped into the concourse again. As she approached Minnie, Kai, and Blythe, Samson lifted his head and came up to her, nudging her leg.

"Hey, boy," Zara said as she scratched behind his ears. She knelt and let him lick her cheek.

"Not you, too," Minnie grumbled. "Y'all are like a bunch of mother hens. I'm fine!"

Zara stood. "Is that why you haven't eaten that sandwich Kai brought you?" She nodded at the full plate on the little coffee table Minnie had dragged to her spot. It had been part of the mall décor and now served as her footrest.

"I ain't hungry." Minnie kept her eyes on the glass doors and the parking lot beyond it.

"You haven't eaten all day," Blythe said. "It isn't my business, but—"

"That's right," Minnie said sharply. "It ain't your business."

Kai shrugged. "We can't force her to eat," he said.

"Oh, for heaven's sake!" Minnie snatched the sandwich and took a big bite, chewing with her mouth open as she said, "You happy?" She flopped the sandwich back on the plate.

"You can't go on like this," Zara said. "Sitting here isn't going to make Oliver come back."

Minnie crossed her arms but didn't say anything as her hardened gaze returned to the lot outside. "What else am I supposed to do? Alex and Oliver, my daughter… they're all out there."

"You still have us," Zara said.

Minnie shifted in her chair and harrumphed. "You don't need me."

In five steps, Zara was blocking Minnie's view. "We need each other, Minnie. Walter is out there with Alex and Lauren and Candice. Lizzy's left behind a lot of family back in the States. I left my cousin, the only blood relative I have left. Everyone else I loved is dead." She nodded to Kai and Blythe. "We're all we've got right now, and believe it or not, I think we're pretty lucky. Some people don't have anyone left at all."

Kai smiled at her, and Blythe shrugged as if to say, "Can't argue with that."

Minnie's expression softened. "The people I'm waiting on ain't dead. I can't think of nothin' else. I can't stand it."

"You can't stand it," Zara said, "because you've stopped living. The people here have taken us in, and there's plenty to keep us busy. Your leg is getting better by the day. You barely have to use the cane anymore. Talk to Mateo. I know he'd have ways for you to help."

"What if Oliver comes back, and I'm not here?" Minnie asked, glancing back at the lot.

"It's not like he'd think you forgot about him," Zara said sarcastically, but at Minnie's wide-eyed look, Zara realized that was exactly what she was afraid of. "Minnie," she said, "he won't think that. The second he comes back, you're going to have him wrapped up in a hug and questioning why he ever thought he'd be better off out there with those crazy boys."

"I let him go because I thought it was the only way," Minnie said, "but I don't want him to think for a second that I let him go in my heart. That boy means the world to me."

"What if we take turns?" Kai asked.

Kai was onto something. Zara stepped around the coffee table, moved the plate, sat on the edge, and took Minnie's hands. "During daylight hours, when it's possible for Oliver to come back to us, the five of us can take turns out here. That way, someone will always be waiting for him."

Minnie looked from Zara to Blythe and then over to Kai. "You'd do that? I wouldn't want to bother Lizzy with—"

"I think Lizzy would be up for it," Zara said. "She's doing much better. You've just missed it because you've been so worried for Oliver."

Eyes glistening, Minnie smiled and nodded. "I reckon that would do just fine." She squeezed Zara's hands. "I'm sorry for bein' ugly."

Zara feigned shock. "Not possible."

Minnie smiled and reached for the sandwich. "You ain't foolin' me, but thank you, anyway. I should take Samson up to the rooftop, let him stretch his legs and provide those gardeners with some fertilizer."

Zara offered to take the watch. Minnie left with a little more energy in her step, and Zara sent Kai and Blythe to ask Mateo for a chore so that Lizzy could have some more time for her nap. Then, she settled into Minnie's chair and propped her feet up on the coffee table. She'd bet a piece of chocolate that she wouldn't see Oliver coming back anytime soon. That kid had seemed stuck on staying with those boys.

But that wasn't really why she was sitting there, keeping vigil. Over and over, death and despair had threatened to destroy humanity, and over and over Zara refused to let it go.

We're going to survive this nightmare, she thought, *and we're going to do it without losing ourselves.*

Chapter 27

Oliver Roman

Oliver plopped onto his sleeping bag and pillows, adding his groan to a dozen more as the *hapu* settled for the remainder of the evening. His muscles ached, his skin was tight and wind worn, and his stomach grumbled. What was worse was that he had nothing to show for it, and neither did anyone else.

"Thought for sure we'd find another one today." Etera laid down so that his head was near Oliver's as they stretched out in opposite directions. "Maybe we got lucky the first time."

"Maybe." A prickling sensation played up and down Oliver's back. Thoughts of their last successful hunt brought bloody images to mind that made him queasy. Luck wasn't the right word for what had happened.

The boys had eaten half the meat they'd hunted by roasting it; the other half had been sliced thin and dried over a smoldering fire's smoke. Ihaka had insisted they store it away once it had turned to jerky, but they all wanted more meat. Hunting it was their only option, and Ihaka had led them all on hunt after hunt. Each time the group came back empty handed and a little more discouraged. The wild boars seemed to know the area wasn't safe for them anymore.

"Coop!" Ihaka shouted. "Get some canned goods for tea." The leader of the *hapu* sat roughly on his own pallet. His expression had soured when he'd ordered them to return to the factory, and it had only gotten darker since.

Coop still wasn't quite right after the incident ten days prior with the boar who'd thrown him. He hopped up at Ihaka's request but then winced, a hand flying to his temple, and wobbled. He regained his footing, sniffed, and rolled his shoulders before striding forward with his chin held high, slow but steady.

Oliver had learned that Coop didn't like it when his health was asked after, but he never objected to a little help. Though his muscles resisted more movement, Oliver got to his feet. "I'll help," he said.

"Me too." Etera sighed and stood. "Might as well. Don't wanna be stuck with beans again."

Oliver set his pace to Coop's so that the other boy didn't feel as though he were slowing them down. When Coop turned on the lantern in the storage room, Oliver paused in the doorway. Their supplies were dwindling. Before they'd caught and killed the boar, Ihaka had focused on scavenging, and supplies were consistently restocked. After, he had become obsessed with the hunt, cutting down the time the *hapu* spent searching houses and other buildings for pre-packaged and canned food.

We can't keep wasting time on the hunt, Oliver thought.

But Ihaka and some of the other boys were fixated on it. They seemed to relish another chance to kill just as much as they desired the luxury of fresh meat.

"There's ten types of beans… yuck." Etera crossed his arms as he examined their options. "Where's the fruit?"

"No one ever takes the beans," Coop said, shrugging. "So, they pile up while the other stuff gets eaten first."

Oliver grabbed a laundry basket and started filling it. "I say we take beans and sweets to wash them down with. We have to eat them eventually."

Coop picked up a can. "I like beans. Fine with me."

Etera pulled a face, but he started putting cans of beans in the basket just the same. He eyed the tray of jerky set carefully on a table against the opposite wall. "I'm keen to sneak a piece," he said.

"Yeah, nah, mate." Coop's eyes went wide. "Ihaka's likely to kill ya if you do that."

It seemed to take some effort for Etera to tear his eyes away from the jerky. "Guess you're right. Don't wanna get on his bad side."

Oliver arranged two more cans of beans in the basket before moving over to the stockpile of sweets. He'd heard the boys say things like that before, but ever since he'd seen Ihaka go after that boar, eager to kill and completely unbothered by brutality, Oliver wondered how much truth was in statements like that.

"He wouldn't really kill anybody, right?"

"One of us?" Etera laughed off Oliver's question. "Nah. Might knock you down a peg if you steal rations, but I don't think he'd really kill one of us."

"I mean *anybody,* not just us." Oliver blurted out the clarification and immediately wanted to claw it out of the air and stuff it back in his mouth as Etera and Coop looked at each other and then back at him.

"Sure he would," Coop said. "So would I, if I had to. Gotta protect the *hapu* at all costs."

Etera licked his lips and gave Oliver a subtle shake of his head, his expression signaling that Oliver should drop it. "We should get the food back to the others," he said.

"That's exactly what I was coming to say." Ihaka's voice made Oliver jump and spin to face the doorway. There was impatience woven throughout his words. "When I ask for you to do something, I don't mean have a chat first."

Coop stammered his response. "We w-were, um… about done."

"Six people," Ihaka said, looking at Oliver.

He blinked. "What?"

Ihaka smiled, but it wasn't friendly. "I've killed six people," he said. "Coop's right. I'd do anything to keep our *hapu* safe. We all have to learn to put our brothers first." He cocked his head. "Do you doubt me?"

He heard that? Oliver rubbed sweaty palms on the sides of his pants. "No," he said. "I don't doubt you."

He remembered that smile from when he'd been locked in the dog cage weeks prior. Part of him had thought maybe he'd made it up, that he'd been frightened enough to see things that weren't there. But the shift in Ihaka's mood that day had set everyone on edge, and Oliver was beginning to see why.

"You think you could do better?" Ihaka asked coldly. "You looked half asleep from your perch today. Is your heart not in it? Maybe you should save the food for people who have worked for it."

"I'm sorry," Oliver blurted, confusion as to why Ihaka was being so harsh jumbling his thoughts. "It's just not working, what you want us to do out there, and no one saw any boar all day, and—"

"Enough!" Ihaka's voice filled the room.

Oliver snapped his mouth shut. The air seemed to thicken and press upon him from every angle as Ihaka scowled at him. The taller, older boy walked up to him, standing toe-to-toe, looking down at him at a sharp angle.

"Are you with us or against us?" Ihaka said.

Ihaka was so close that his hot breath washed over Oliver's face. He smelled of sweat and musk, and his bulk made Oliver feel tiny.

"I'm with you," Oliver squeaked.

"Then when I say we hunt for food, you do everything you can to bring home the meat," Ihaka said. "I want to see some enthusiasm tomorrow."

Oliver's body trembled. A hundred answers were on the tip of his tongue, but he questioned the wording of each. It seemed anything could tip Ihaka over the edge, and so Oliver just nodded with vigor and hoped that would be enough to appease him.

Ihaka stepped back. "Good." He stepped over to the tray of jerky, grabbed a piece, and then grabbed a can of corn. "I'm going up to the rooftop where I can have some peace. Get this food to the others."

Coop raised his eyebrows. "The jerky, too?"

"No," Ihaka said as he ripped off a bite of jerky with his teeth. "Not today." He didn't give them any more explanation before leaving them alone again.

Coop picked up the basket and sighed. "You heard him. Let's go."

"We'll be right in with water," Etera said. "Just gotta fill a basket."

Coop shrugged and nodded before following after Ihaka, turning left in the foyer instead of straight ahead to the stairs.

Oliver breathed out slowly and sat on the edge of a box full of canned food. "I thought Ihaka was going to punch me in the face," he said.

Etera's fist connected with Oliver's shoulder.

"Ouch!" Oliver leaned away from Etera. "What was that for?"

"For asking stupid questions." Etera shook out his wrist. "You don't want Ihaka finding out how soft you are."

"Soft?" Oliver's mouth dropped open. "I'm not soft."

"Are too," Etera said. "I saw you let that piglet go, and I could see it when you asked about killing for the *hapu*. You wouldn't be able to do it, would you?"

Oliver tried to say that Etera was wrong, but the words wouldn't come out. He looked away and hugged his middle. "No," he said softly, but then he frowned and looked back at Etera. "But what's wrong with that? Who do we *need* to kill? The people at the mall?" Oliver shook his head. "They're just families trying to survive, same as us."

"But they're not us," Etera said.

"There are people there I care about," Oliver said.

"I know," Etera said. "And there are people there Ihaka cares about, whether he wants to admit it or not. A couple other boys have relatives there, too, which is why we try to steer clear. But long before you got here, things weren't so easy between us. There was a fight over territory, and people died. Now, we stick to our parts of the city, except when newcomers show up. Then, their supplies are up for grabs, as far as Ihaka is concerned."

"Have… have *you* killed people?" Oliver asked.

Etera's lips thinned, and his face paled as he glanced at his feet. "Yeah," he said.

"And you'd do it again?"

"I wouldn't *want* to," he said, "but if I had to? Yeah."

Oliver shook his head. "I don't believe you."

"I wasn't spinning a yarn," Etera said. "You heard Ihaka. You're either with the *hapu* or against it. And if there's something we need, something *they* have, sometimes we just gotta take it, and if they won't be spooked into handing it over, we do what we gotta."

Oliver's eyes widened. "Like back at the plane?"

Etera swallowed hard and nodded.

"You would have killed us?"

"I didn't know you, bro. And those supplies were tempting." Etera turned and started loading water bottles into the basket. "If it makes you feel better, while you're here and they're with Mateo at the mall, they won't be hurt, I don't think. Not planned, anyway."

A cold rush through Oliver's veins made him shudder, and his stomach turned. He'd seen good in the *hapu*, and he'd found ways to excuse the bad.

Minnie had been hurt, but not killed. Surely, no one meant to really hurt her; they were just trying to scare them.

Ihaka had seemed to enjoy killing the boar and had the occasional mood swing, but he also gave Oliver so much freedom, encouraged him to have adventures, trusted him with important tasks.

The other boys may have made him face a swarm, risking his life, but they also accepted him into their *hapu*.

I'm one of them, Oliver thought. Aren't I? Isn't this what I wanted?

"Just… watch what you say," Etera said. "Got it, cuz?"

Oliver nodded and forced himself to get up, to help Etera fill the basket with water bottles full of boiled and filtered water from a nearby pond. But the illusion of the *hapu* he'd held tightly was broken. It was a brotherhood but one with the potential for violence. It was safe but only for those who toed the line. It offered freedom but not without expectations Oliver was sure he couldn't meet.

Part of him didn't want to leave. Another part was afraid of what would happen if he stayed. All of him was terrified that either way, he'd have to contend with Ihaka, and that wasn't a fight he believed he could win.

Chapter 28

Alexander Roman and Stella Sharpe

He was bound, tied down, restrained. A lurch had woken him, and when his eyes had popped open, he'd had to shut them again against a strange orange light. Alex shouted in alarm. He couldn't shield his eyes. His arms and legs met with resistance at every movement. Heartrate racing, panic taking hold, he twisted as he tried to open his eyes again more slowly. There was a figure leaning closer, but his vision blurred, and it was so bright.

"Let me go!" Alex shouted.

"Alex, it's me. Stop fighting. You're okay."

Lauren's voice. Alex blinked and swallowed as his bindings loosened and he was able to sit up. He rubbed his eyes, and after a few moments, they focused. Lauren sat close, her lower half bundled in a sleeping bag, her upper body wrapped in it loosely. All around him, sunlight shone through opaque orange fabric.

A tent? he thought, and the ground beneath him lurched again.

And it hadn't been more than his own sleeping bag holding him down, that and a profound weakness that made his arms like weights.

"What…" Alex coughed. His throat was so dry.

"We're on our way back to McMurdo," Lauren said.

Shaking his head required too much effort, so he only managed a half turn of his neck. "How long have I been out?"

Lauren dug around in the head of her sleeping bag, pulled out water, and handed it over. "A few days," she said, offering a slight smile. "We didn't know if you'd pull through."

Alex took the bottle, but his hands were clumsy. After he'd failed to twist open the top, Lauren leaned over and did it for him. He lifted it to his mouth, arms trembling with the weight of it.

"The others?" Alex asked.

"They're fine," Lauren said. "You were the worst."

That unknotted something heavy in the pit of his stomach. His shoulders slouched. "Will we make it?"

Lauren's smile faltered. "I think so," she said. "We'll be cutting it close, but with all of us working together, we should be fine. We haven't stopped moving since we left the facility. It… it took us longer than we hoped to load everything and secure it to the sleds, and the extra weight is making the snowcat slow."

Alex cursed. "I hadn't thought of that," he said. "Our lighter load on the way here made us faster."

"Yes, but we stopped a lot more," Lauren said. "We have so much daylight now."

Alex swayed with the bumpy ride. He was awake and thinking clearly for the first time since he'd fallen ill after taking the vaccine, but he very clearly still needed rest. He scooted back down into the sleeping bag and rested his head, keeping his eyes open lest he drift off to sleep right away. Still, his eyelids drooped.

Everyone was alive. They were on their way back to the station. There was nothing he could do to make them go faster. His motivation to stay awake slowly slipped away.

"Hey, Lauren?"

"What is it? What do you need?"

He smiled and pulled his arm out of his sleeping bag, stretching his arm out toward her. She took it, and he closed his eyes. "Thanks for being here when I woke up."

"Anytime," she said, and he could swear he heard the grin in her voice.

* * *

When dots on the horizon representing buildings appeared, the conversation within the snowcat died. Stella was fine with that. She drove on, exhausted not just from the constant movement—it was hard to sleep in a lurching vehicle with the scraping of snow and ice beneath—but from the assumption of other people that everyone wanted to fill the silences with incessant, meaningless conversation.

Everyone had been in high spirits since Alex's fever had broken and he'd woken up coherent. He was getting better every day, so much so that he'd even spent some time the day before riding in the snowcat, sitting up and chatting, back to his old self. By the end of a few hours, he'd been ready to switch back to the tent where he could sleep, but it was a good sign.

Ahead was either another reason to keep trying or the final reason to stop. Candice, Alex, and Lauren had kept an eye on her for weeks. They'd never allowed her to feel alone. Despite her efforts, she'd come to care about them, especially Candice. That woman was just as stubborn as Stella but with better fashion sense.

And therein lay the problem. Stella was *not* going to watch one more person she cared about die. If that ship had already left, that was exactly what would happen. She would take matters into her own hands, if she had to, not because she was in a dark place but because she had been in the darkest place imaginable, survived it, and started to see the light thanks to a few nosey, compassionate human beings.

I'm not going back to that, she thought for the hundredth time as they approached McMurdo Station.

And besides, one less mouth to feed would mean whoever chose to stick around had a shot. Maybe the ship would come back in a couple months' time.

I'm getting ahead of myself. Maybe the ship is there, waiting for us, and everything will be fine. Stella grimaced and cursed. All that hope that had been dumped on her had started taking root. She wasn't going to get sucked into that again. *Unless they're right… damn it. I'm doing it again.*

Stella ground her teeth and gripped the wheel harder, and the snowcat crept toward McMurdo Station.

* * *

They finally stopped moving for the last time. Alex crawled out of the tent with Lauren right behind him. Stella had brought them through the ghost town to where they could see Winter Quarters Bay. There was a never-ending supply of broken ice floating as far as the eye could see, but there was no ship.

Alex bit the inside of his cheek and stared harder at the farthest reaches of his vision. Lauren was beside him, and moment by moment, more people lined up next to him, all seeming to do the same thing.

"Does anyone see anything?" Alex asked.

"Nothing," Robert said.

"We should go out to Hut Point," Stella said. "We would have a wider vantage point from there."

"What about the supplies?" Lauren asked.

Alex glanced at the long trail of sleds and equipment attached to the snowcat.

"They'll be fine," Walter said. "The solar power panels have plenty of juice for the cryopods."

"We should bring flares," Zac said. "If they were here and just left, they might see them and come back for us."

"Good idea," Alex said.

"I'll grab a few," Robert said.

Farrah and Anise locked arms, and Anise's soft voice was a breeze, barely audible but refreshing nonetheless. "Maybe they haven't gotten here yet," she said.

Robert scoffed. "Or they picked up DV-10 when they went to pick up survivors at other stations. Or something happened to the ship. Or…" He threw up his hands. "There's a hundred things that could have gone wrong."

Farrah glared at him. "You always come up with the worst scenarios."

Robert lifted his chin. "I'm a r—"

Anise, Farrah, and Zac cut him off. "—realist." They finished his sentence with eye rolls and sarcastic tones.

Lauren shook her head. "I think we need a break from each other."

Alex shrugged and smiled at her. "I don't know," he said. "Some of you are still all right."

She elbowed him hard but not without grinning at him.

"Let's get to this Hut Point," Walter said.

Alex agreed, and their group of nine set off on foot. It was cold but bearable as they made their way, snow underfoot. Alex wasn't up to his full strength, and he had to stop a few times. Lauren stopped with him as the others went on.

"My pace must be killing you," Alex said as he stopped and put his hands on his knees, breathing in and out slowly and intentionally to calm his racing heart and catch his breath. "You can go ahead, if you want."

"Whatever is there will still be there when we arrive," Lauren said.

He straightened and took the next step, glad that she rejected his offer to leave him behind. Whatever view awaited them, they would face it together.

* * *

There was nothing but shades of white beyond the brown landscape. A numbness took hold as Stella stared at the empty sea. Behind her, Walter, Candice, and the technicians argued over whether they should set off a flare.

"If we can't see them, how do we know they'd be able to see a flare?" Walter asked.

"We have more than one," Robert said. "There's no reason *not* to use one."

She tuned them out. Alex and Lauren had fallen behind. When they caught up, she was sure their weigh-ins would settle the argument. They didn't need her to decide what to do. It didn't matter anyway.

The cold embraced her like a toxic friend, familiar in its biting nature and yet unavoidable. For once, she didn't mind its presence. It would help numb her, and that's what she wanted: to avoid fear and pain. What was coming was what she had expected from the start. The detour wherein she'd allowed hope some space had been a mistake.

Alex's voice added to the mix, and she turned from the vast and freezing sea.

"Let's use one now," Alex said. "Chances are, if they are out there, and we just can't see them, they will be actively watching this point on the horizon. But we'll keep watch out here at the tip of this little peninsula, and when we see the ship—or *any* ship—we can use another one."

A few more words from Lauren, and the others agreed. But there was one problem. They were still talking as if a ship coming to get them was inevitable. Stella had to fix their optimism. They had things to learn if they were going to survive at McMurdo for any length of time.

"No one came out to greet us," Stella said as she walked into the center of the group.

Candice frowned. "We all know that the ship isn't here."

"No," Stella said, "no one seems to be staying in McMurdo right now. The ship was going to send out signals to far out stations, the smaller ones farther inland. They would have been here for a while now, but they're not. We made plenty of noise to announce our arrival, and surely they'd be watching the bay."

"What are you saying?" Alex asked, but his tone indicated he was catching on.

"I'm saying," Stella said, "that I think the ship was here, picked up whoever made it, and left."

Murmurs spread between the technicians as they huddled closer together. Alex and Walter exchanged glances, Candice gasped, and Lauren looked back out at the sea.

"There's no use denying the likelihood," Stella said. "We're late into day forty."
Robert blanched. "You think they left us here?"
"Surely they'd wait until the day was over?" Farrah's eyes went wide.
Cat put a hand to her stomach and looked as if she might heave. "Then they would have waited up to day forty-one. Stella's right."
Anise's eyes glistened. "But they need the vaccine."
"But," Alex looked down at his feet, voice low, "they warned us. They said they only had so much fuel. If I hadn't gotten s—"
"If you hadn't gotten sick," Lauren said, "nothing would be different."
"We got here as fast as we could," Walter said. "The extra load slowed us down far more than we expected."
Stella pointed back at McMurdo. "We need to get back, find lodging for everyone, and then I need to show you the basics of how to run this place. Maybe they'll come back in a couple of months. You're lucky, you know? We're approaching the warmest time of the year. You'll survive."
She walked between Candice and Lauren, choosing to avoid eye contact with either of them. They could be eerily perceptive, like they could read her mind, and she didn't need them getting in her way. Once she'd passed on all that she knew, she could be at peace. She could *finally* be at peace.

* * *

Alex's return to McMurdo was slower than his trek out to the end of the peninsula. He couldn't find the strength to go any faster, not when it was very possible that they would have to sit there for months, hoping the ship came back for them, with everything they needed to save the world.
Lauren kept pace with him once again, but so did Walter and Candice. None of the spoke for a while.
"I think we should keep an eye on Stella," Candice said.
Alex stopped and eyed Candice. "We have been, but she's been getting better, right?"
Lauren bit her lower lip and then shrugged. "Hard to say. Maybe a little, but bad news like this can make depression resurface quick."
Alex looked ahead. Stella was leading the group by a large margin. She was at least a few yards ahead of the technicians, and she was walking with such purpose. That was a good sign, wasn't it? But… Lauren and Candice were closer to her. He nodded and agreed, as did Walter. Whatever happened next, Alex was determined not to lose anyone else. He'd learned to hold on to hope, no matter how bleak the future looked. He looked back at the sea and thought of his son.
I'll come home to you, Oliver, he thought. I'll find a way. Don't give up on me.

* * *

Stella was done. Three days had gone by with no ship, and she'd given Alex and the rest every manual, every bit of information she could find. She'd shown them some important bits of maintenance and made sure they knew where to find different types of supplies. The cryopods were safe, solar panels recharging with the long days of sunlight, keeping the samples cold. They had a similar set up for the vaccines and the treatments they'd already made. Stella didn't understand most of it, but Alex and Walter were sure the equipment would keep their samples frozen until the time they needed them again.
That meant it was time. Everyone else was still asleep, everyone except Robert and Cat who were out on the peninsula, keeping watch. Days had been long and exhausting and emotionally draining as they'd come to accept what Stella knew: they'd been too late. The ship was gone, and it wasn't coming back anytime soon.
Candice and Lauren hadn't left Stella alone for more than a few minutes at a time, but that morning, she'd been able to sneak out of Hotel California without notice. The day before had been full of manual labor as they'd consolidated several stockpiles into one place so that they wouldn't need to go from building to building to get what they needed. She would be leaving them with a chance, and that mattered.
Stella had done one last good thing.
The tiny church building where Stella had holed up before the ship had come bringing a hope that would die like everything else was exactly how she remembered it. She'd avoided the building since arriving. There, she had survived, holding on to life in the dark, and then planning her death, always unable to follow through with it.
But now she was ready. She walked inside. There was rope in there, and a knife, if she could remember where she'd put it. Her original plan of just walking out into the wilderness wouldn't work, not with Alex, Walter, Candice, and Lauren around. They would find her and stop her. She would have to—
Stella froze. There was something on the billboard that didn't belong. She knew every inch of the little sanctuary, and that yellow rectangle, bright and new compared to the other dingy, crinkled papers wasn't supposed to be there. She cautiously stepped forward, her heartbeat picking up pace.
There was that hope again, and it had flared up, too strong to extinguish. She *had* to see who put the note there.
The handwriting was blurry, barely readable. The pen's ink had bled badly, and she had to stare at the note for several minutes before she could believe what she deciphered. She reached out, her fingertips brushing the cardstock. The words were like magic: *Found fuel at next station. Saved a dozen survivors. Have room for more. Will be a few days late.*
Stella took the note down from the board and held it to her chest. Laughter turned to sobs which turned back to laughter as she sank to her knees, holding that paper to her heart and letting it seep hope back into her body.
The door flung open, and Candice and Lauren burst in, alarm written all over their expressions.
"Are you hurt?" Candice asked, rushing to her side.
Lauren was quickly beside her, as well, hands flying over her, perhaps looking for injury. "What is it?"
"They're coming back," Stella said between gulps of fresh, sweet air. She held out the note, laughing through tears.
"What?" Candice took the note, read it and then handed it to Lauren. "Of course they'd put it here," she said. "This is where Stella was living."

Lauren read it over and smiled wide. "I can't believe we didn't look before." She held the note to her chest in much the same way as Stella had, but she leaned her head back, raised her arms, and let out a long shout of pure joy.

All three of them were crying, and Stella welcomed their arms around her.

Chapter 29

Alexander Roman and Stella Sharpe

Alex's slowly hammering heart, like a sledgehammer pounding the inside of his chest, provided a somber beat for the sense of dread saturating his thoughts. The darkness of the tiny room was a breeding ground for fears surrounding what-ifs and worst-case scenarios. A sour taste in the back of Alex's mouth added fuel to his roiling stomach, and he couldn't help but clench his jaw, no matter how sore it was.

He sat up. It had been like that for hours, since waking from a nightmare he couldn't remember but knew had something to do with Oliver.

"Get it together," he whispered, rubbing his face with trembling hands. He pulled back blackout curtains on the tiny window to let some light in.

Water would help, perhaps, or a bite to eat. The door was only a yard from the foot of the bed, and he stepped into the hall where sunlight filtered through a sliding glass door that led to a very small metal balcony. Lauren was standing in front of it, and as he entered the hallway, she turned.

"Hey!" she said, tone bright until she looked him up and down. "You still look terrible."

"I didn't sleep well," Alex said, his voice hoarse.

Lauren walked toward him, a worried expression more pronounced with every step. "I thought you were getting better."

Alex nodded and held out a reassuring hand. "I am. It's not that."

She paused and let out a breath, concern fading to relief before she wrinkled her brow. "Then what is it? Things are on track. I mean, the ship should be here any day." She lowered her voice to a whisper. "Stella's doing much better. We're all safe. The vaccine, the treatment… we're good to go, right?"

"Yes," Alex said. "It's…" He swallowed hard. "It's Oliver."

"You miss him?" Lauren asked.

"Of course I do," Alex said, "but it's not that, either."

Lauren chewed her lower lip for a second as she studied him. "Let's grab some water and some breakfast. I think I saw a pouch of freeze-dried fruit in the stuff Stella had us bring from storage. We can talk in the stairwell where we won't wake everyone."

Alex nodded and followed Lauren. The building was only two stories, and its construction focused primarily on function, not aesthetics. They grabbed breakfast from one of the small dorm rooms they'd stuffed full of provisions from all over the station and settled in the cramped, concrete stairwell. Alex sat on the bottom landing, and Lauren made herself comfortable a few steps above him.

"So," Lauren said as she tore open the dried fruit, "tell me what's going on."

Alex sighed and tried to think of how to explain it. He took a sip of water and swished it around in his mouth to wash away the sour taste, and then he looked up at her. "Something's not right."

Lauren gave him a slight smile. "Alex, he's thousands of miles away. He's with my mom. Not to mention Zara and Kai and even Blythe." She shrugged. "Lizzy won't be much help, but her crazy has been dialed back. I don't think she's a danger anymore."

"I've had this feeling before," Alex said. "When Oliver was in kindergarten and I was out on an investigation for the CDC, I couldn't shake this thought that he wasn't okay. I was in another country. Communication was spotty. But… I just *knew* something had happened."

"And?" Lauren asked.

"I was right," Alex said. "As soon as I was able to talk to Naomi, I learned Oliver had fallen off the top of a slide, sideways. Some bigger kid had pushed him off. My wife had been trying to get a hold of me all day."

"But he was okay," Lauren said, "right?"

Alex nodded. "Yeah, I mean… eventually. But he broke his arm, got a concussion."

"Look," Lauren said, "I'm not questioning your sixth sense dad powers right now, but this feeling could be anything, right? Things are terrible everywhere. But Oliver has survived so much, and he's got people who care about him protecting him."

"I know," Alex said, "but I just… I need to get back to him. I've been away too long."

"I get that." Lauren scooted down the steps and nudged Alex until he moved over so she could sit beside him on the landing. "Whatever we find when we get back to New Zealand, you know I've got your back, right?" She handed him the bag of dried fruit.

He took it and smiled. "I know," he said.

"And you know it's *possible* your dad powers are glitching." Lauren held up her hands in mock defense. "Maybe not *probable* but definitely *possible*."

"Are you trying to science me right now?" Alex asked.

"Is it working?"

Alex chuckled. "Maybe a little."

She grinned with satisfaction, and for the next half hour, Lauren chatted with him, clearly trying to distract him from thoughts of Oliver. It didn't work, not really, but it made him feel a little better regardless.

"You know," Alex said after a while, "I just realized that here you've been making sure I'm all right this whole time, and I've not asked you how you're feeling."

Lauren shrugged. "I'm fine. I miss my mom. I can't wait to see her." She shook her head and smiled sadly. "Months ago, I couldn't stand her. I was so angry at her for pushing me into a career I didn't want, and now… I finally get the Minnie that everyone else gets. And I want to keep getting to know that version of her."

"She was different for you, growing up?" Alex asked.

She nodded. "She was so worried about me having it better than she did that she forgot to let me enjoy any of it. She forgot to be there for me in the middle of her so-called support for the career she chose for me. I mean, I think she thought I wanted it. When I was fifteen, I *did* want it. But she latched onto the idea of me becoming a doctor and convinced herself that any change of mind I had was cold feet or laziness or something." Lauren smiled. "Growing up, all my friends would talk about how sweet my mom was, how encouraging and full of good advice. Now, I feel like I finally get to experience that."

"She's always loved you," Alex said. "Even when she was making mistakes."

"Yeah, I know." Lauren shrugged. "Can't help but think her change of heart is a silver lining in all this mess, though."

Alex laughed. "Well, something good needs to come out of all of this."

"That and I think if things go the way my mom wants them to, I'll be getting a new stepdad when all this is done," Lauren said, chuckling.

Alex raised his eyebrows. "General Hunt?"

"She's so sweet on him," Lauren said. "He makes her happy, even when he makes her furious."

"You think they'll find a way back to each other?"

Lauren smiled. "I like to think so."

Just as Alex was about to echo her hopes for Minnie, the door to the bottom floor burst open, and Cat tripped into the stairwell. She'd been on watch at the tip of the peninsula. Alex and Lauren both jumped to their feet.

"What is it?" Alex asked. "Are you okay?"

Cat regained her balance and grinned. "I can see the ship," she said breathlessly. "I ran all the way here, which isn't so easy in all these layers." She unzipped her coat but didn't take it off as she leaned over and put her hands on her knees.

Lauren jumped on the balls of her feet. "Did you set off the flare?"

Cat nodded. "Yeah, but I'm pretty sure it's headed into the bay anyway. It's moving slow. I couldn't tell."

"We have to wake the others," Alex said, already flying up the steps.

Lauren and Cat followed behind, and the three of them started knocking on doors, shouting the news. It wasn't long before the nine of them were in the hall together, whistling and shouting and dancing around each other, celebrating the arrival of the ship.

"Grab your gear, everyone," Alex said, breaking up the celebration. "Layer up. We've got a research vessel to welcome, and then we've got to load it up and get the hell out of here."

* * *

Stella looked up at the people crowding the ship's railing as the gangway was lowered. "There's so many people," she said.

"You did that," Lauren said, nudging her. "You were the one who insisted the ship look for other survivors."

"Yeah," Stella said, eyes welling with tears. "I was trying to do one last good thing, but…" She swallowed a lump of emotion and grinned at Lauren and then at Candice who was just beside her. "… I think I'm going to do a lot of good things before I let this world take me out."

"Sounds good to me," Candice said.

"Is that the captain?" Stella asked, nodding toward the ship.

"That's her," Alex said.

Captain Whitlock had already communicated via the handheld radio she'd left with them prior to leaving weeks ago to confirm everyone was healthy, but the signal had been patchy, so everything else had been left to when they would meet face-to-face. Stella hadn't met the woman, only spoken to her briefly over the handheld radio. She looked just as tough as she'd sounded, but she was smiling broadly as she approached them.

"Alex," the captain said, "you got our note?"

He glanced at Stella. "Yeah," he said, offering a slight smile to Stella. "It was a lifesaver." He looked back to the captain. "We didn't go to the church at first. You had us thinking we were stranded for a little while."

"Not stranded," the captain said, "just delayed. You have more people with you than I expected."

Walter pointed to each of the technicians. "Robert, Cat, Farrah, Anise, and Zac," he said.

"We were the technicians wintering over at Barlow," Robert said as he offered his hand.

The captain shook it. "Thank you for keeping things running." She looked over at Stella. "And this must be Stella." She walked over to her, and much to Stella's shock, she put her hands on her shoulders and drew her in for a hug. "Thank you."

Stella let the captain finish her hug—she didn't know what else to do—and then awkwardly took a step back, heat flooding her cheeks. "For what?" she asked.

"I would have never tried to search for other survivors if you hadn't insisted." Whitlock looked over her shoulder at the ship and then back at Stella. "There are a lot of good people who were hanging on by a thread, people we were able to save, thanks to you."

"It's not over yet," Stella said. "We have to get back to civilization."

Whitlock shook her head. "All business, still, I see."

"She's right," Alex said, "even if she needs to learn how to take a compliment." He smiled at her, and she smiled back.

"So then," Whitlock said, turning to Alex and Walter, her eyes wide with anticipation, "you were successful?"

"We did what we came here to do," Alex said.

"We tested the vaccine," Walter said. "Every one of us has taken it."

Whitlock seemed to take in the whole group at once. "So it's safe? Is it effective?"

"We will only know that for sure once vaccinated people start getting exposed," Alex said, "but we think so."

"And," Walter said, "that's where we need you and everyone onboard that ship." He nodded to the vessel behind her.

"We need you to all take the vaccine," Alex said. "We tested the vaccine on Walter first, then on the rest of us. Some of us weren't sick at all afterward, but most of us did experience some illness, which isn't uncommon with vaccines." He spread out his arms as if inviting her to examine him. "I was the sickest. It was rough, but I pulled through, and now, I hopefully have protection against DV-10, as do we all." He indicated those who'd been at the research bank.

Whitlock pressed her lips together, furrowed her brow, and looked down at her feet. When she looked up again, there was determination in her eyes. "This is the next step in fighting the disease?" she asked.

Alex and Walter nodded together.

"I can't force anyone to take it," she said, "but I can let you make your case. And I will take it myself to set the example."

Stella's chest rose with a swelling pride. *I was part of this,* she thought. She looked back at McMurdo Station, the place where so many she loved perished. She couldn't save them, but she could be part of saving whoever was left.

"What else needs to be done?" Whitlock asked.

Alex took a deep breath. "We have a lot to load onto the ship, and Walter and I will need to get right to work in the lab on board. The next ten days are going to be long ones for all of us."

"It'll be worth it," Stella said. The others all looked to her as if surprised she'd chosen to speak at that moment. "We're bringing life back to the world," she said. "Nothing is more important than that."

* * *

Alex gripped the railing as the ship started to move away from the dock. He was exhausted. They'd worked for hours to load everything onto the ship. The cryopods had to be attached to a power source in the cargo hold and secured without question. They held, frozen within their confines, the treatments, the vaccines, and the countermeasure mosquito eggs.

"We're almost there," he whispered.

"Almost where?"

A voice behind him startled him. Stella stepped up beside him, meeting his eyes with her own. There was a sparkle to them that hadn't been there before she found that note. Alex hadn't noticed its absence because he hadn't known her before, but he imagined that the woman looking at him now was closer to the woman Stella truly was.

"We're almost to the finish line," Alex said.

"You don't mind if I tag along, do you?" Stella asked.

On his other side, an arm slipped into the crook of his elbow. He didn't have to look to know it was Lauren, but he did anyway. He reached for her hand and squeezed it as she leaned past the railing to look at Stella. Having her by his side was comfortable. It felt right.

"We don't mind at all," Lauren said.

Alex pulled his arm back and wrapped it around Lauren's shoulders to give her a squeeze. Then, he looked back at Stella.

"Unfortunately," he said, "you're stuck with us."

"You know," Stella said, "I think I'm okay with that."

Walter came up beside her and patted her back. "You don't know what you're getting yourself into."

Candice pushed her way between Walter and Stella. "Sure she does," Candice said. "She's getting herself into a family, a stubborn one that beats the odds and gets things done."

"Family," Alex said, nodding in agreement while thoughts of Oliver made his smile fade.

"He's going to be okay," Lauren whispered as the others moved away from the railing, headed to the galley where a meal would be served shortly.

"Yeah, he will be," Alex said, "because if he is in any sort of trouble, I'm coming back for him."

Chapter 30

Oliver Roman

Oliver was ready to leave the *hapu.*

Ihaka had changed. Or… Oliver was really seeing him clearly for the first time. He wasn't sure which it was, but he was sure he didn't want to be around him anymore. One minute, Ihaka would be like an older brother, joking around with them, encouraging them to take initiative, to be brave and bold, swearing to protect them. The next, he would be snapping at them with thinly veiled threats.

But that wasn't the worst of it. Even Etera would be willing to kill if Ihaka asked it, or so Etera insisted. Oliver couldn't do that. He wouldn't. Not ever.

Minnie's voice echoed in his mind in the still of the early morning. *Don't let them change your heart.*

At first, her warning had been like a poking stick. She couldn't leave him be, let him be free, trust him to know right from wrong. As usual, she'd wanted to control what he did and how. It had shocked him a little when she'd let him go instead of forcing him to come back.

It was strange to miss that poke. To miss the way that people used to check in on him. To miss being able to just be a kid when what he'd wanted for so long was to be treated more like a grown-up.

Maybe love wasn't all live and let live. Maybe family was more than what the *hapu* made of it. And maybe what Oliver already had waiting for him with Minnie and Lauren and Samson and his dad was actually what he wanted after all.

The only problem was that he was stuck. Ihaka wouldn't just let him go; Oliver was sure of that. His only idea was to attempt to slip away when they were all out hunting boar.

It'll be hard to sneak away from Etera, Oliver thought. The other boy stuck to Oliver like glue, and Oliver had encouraged it. It had been nice to have a close friend his own age, and he liked Etera. *He wouldn't come with me… would he?* Oliver sighed. If there was anyone he would truly miss, it would be Etera.

"You awake yet?" Etera's whisper broke the silence as his upside-down face popped into Oliver's field of vision right above him. When their eyes met, Etera grinned. "Ready for brekkie, mate?"

Oliver smiled back and nodded, sitting up as soon as Etera pulled back. The both of them grabbed some of what was left from the rations given out the previous day. Oliver had saved a half-eaten bag of bite-sized cookies. His bag crinkled too loudly as he took hold of it, and he grimaced, looking around at the other boys, some of whom twitched and mumbled at the sound.

"Maybe we should go into the lobby?" Oliver asked quietly.

"Good thinking, bro." Etera held up a bag of chips and winked. "These crisps require embracing the crunch."

Oliver and Etera quietly got to their feet and tip-toed across the factory floor toward the entrance to the lobby. They sat in the middle of the floor, cross-legged, knees almost touching.

Etera didn't bother with manners. He spoke, mouth full of chips, teeth crunching and lips smacking. He added chips between words.

"Where do you think we'll search today? I think we'll go further north, or we should."

But Oliver's eyes had drifted to the Remembrance Room where he'd left his mother's bag and all his things. *I can't leave without it, but… that means I'll have to sneak back to the factory before I leave.*

That complicated matters. They always left a few boys to guard the building, and there was no way he could take the bag with him without raising suspicion.

"Oi, Oliver!" Etera leaned forward and punched Oliver's shoulder. "You listening to me, bro?"

"Uh… yeah," Oliver said, shaking his head. "I don't know the area, really, so I have no idea where we should go." He shrugged. "I'll just back you up, whatever you say."

Etera grinned. "Choice! Then if Ihaka asks, say you want to go north."

Oliver nodded along as Etera continued to chat, all the while considering what excuse he could use to explain to the guards why he'd returned to the factory before anyone else.

It wasn't long before Coop stuck his head in. "Hey, mates. Thought I'd find you in here."

"Everyone up?" Etera asked.

Coop nodded. "Won't be long before Ihaka lets us pick weapons."

Etera hopped to his feet. "Let's go stand next to the spears, Oliver. They're the best when dealing with a Cap'n Cooker."

Oliver stepped forward, but a pounding made him freeze in place. Etera and Coop looked at each other and then looked at Oliver, and then all three of them turned to face the front doors of the lobby. They were large, wooden doors with ornate carvings of different candies etched into them. From what the other boys had said, the lobby and the rooms connecting to it had once been a candy shop connected to the factory. The casings and the shelves had been repurposed or broken and thrown out; those doors were the only thing that spoke of a time when the lobby was a place for children to make happy memories with their loved ones. The pounding was coming from outside.

"I'll get Ihaka and the others," Coop said, and he vanished back into the factory.

Please don't let it be Minnie, Oliver prayed. A thin layer of sweat broke out across his face at the thought. There was no telling what sort of trouble Ihaka would make if she'd decided to come and drag him away after all.

But she was stubborn. And he'd taken a long time to decide to come back. Anger blossomed in the center of his fear, and as his stomach clenched and turned, he balled his hands into fists.

The pounding continued in fervor, and Etera frowned at the doors as they shook. Someone was pushing and pulling at the handles.
"They're not getting in," Etera said, raising a reassuring hand toward Oliver. "Those doors bolt shut, top and bottom."
She should have trusted me to come to the right decision! Oliver ground his teeth, certain it was Minnie or someone she'd sent.
"Go away!" Oliver shouted. "You're going to get yourself killed!"
Etera pursed his lips at Oliver and shook his head. "Soft," he said. "Just be quiet, Oliver, before *you* get *yourself* killed."
Oliver swallowed hard. He was about to shout again, though. Making Ihaka angry was better than watching him hurt someone Oliver cared about.
But then the person on the other side shouted back, and the voice was *not* Minnie. "Is that you, wittle Oli?" it said in singsong mockery. "Let me in!"
Etera raised an eyebrow at Oliver. "Mate?"
The door to the lobby opened, and Ihaka led the others inside the room as Oliver connected the dots.
Oliver's fear dissipated, and he was left only with his anger. "That's Will. I know it." He looked back at Ihaka. "Just let him shout until he loses his voice."
"You mean," Etera asked, "it's that bully you told us about?"
Oliver nodded. "He's not worth our time." He turned toward the door and shouted. "You're not welcome here, Will!"
The pounding only became more furious. "Liar! Let me in! I want to talk to whoever is in charge." Will let out a string of curses and name calling to emphasize his demands.
Ihaka laughed and stepped forward, slinging an arm around Oliver's shoulders. "We needed a little fun today, boys. This is perfect."
Oliver's stomach dropped. "What do you mean?"
"I mean," Ihaka said, "we're going to let him in." His eyes were gleaming as he turned to face the whole group and rubbed his hands together. "You boys ready to see if this Will fellow is all talk?"
The group shouted together, all except Oliver, "Yeah!"
"Oliver, mate," Ihaka said, "this is for you, bro."
Oliver blinked. "What does that mean?" he asked, but his question got lost in the roar of the other boys' cheers.
Ihaka turned, unbolted the door that was shaking under Will's efforts to get inside, and threw it open. The older boy stepped aside and let the handle that Will was holding on to pull him into the lobby. Will stumbled over his own feet and fell onto the floor, almost at Oliver's feet. Ihaka closed the door and laughed along with the other boys.
The shock in Will's expression was quickly replaced with a scowl as he looked up at Oliver. "You! That wasn't funny!"
Oliver put his hands up. "It wasn't me," he said, taking a step back as Will got to his feet.
The other boy lunged for Oliver, but Ihaka was already reaching for the collar of his shirt. When Will tried to attack, Ihaka yanked him back and threw him back to the floor. Cheers rose from behind Oliver, but the way Will hit the floor only made Oliver's stomach twist.
Ihaka stood over Will and put a foot to his chest before he could recover. He leaned over, putting weight on the boy. "Did anyone come with you?"
"No," Will said, wheezing. He shook his head frantically as he tried to push up on Ihaka's foot. "I swear, it's just me."
Ihaka stepped back and let Will struggle to his feet. "What are you doing here?"
Will pulled at his collar and smoothed his shirt. "I want to be one of you," he said. "It was my idea in the first place, anyway. Oliver stole it!"
"Is that so?" Ihaka said, smiling back at Oliver.
Oliver didn't say anything. He didn't like the look in Ihaka's eyes, the pleasure that mimicked the look he'd had right before he'd killed that boar. Oliver didn't like Will one bit. He had nothing good to say about him, no defense of him, and so he kept quiet lest he add to Ihaka's reasons for whatever he was about to do.
"If *he* can be one of you, I can, too!" Will pointed at Oliver. "He's weak, and he's a liar!"
"He is not!" Etera growled as he stepped up beside Oliver.
Coop came up on the other side. "Are we going to let him talk about our mate like that?"
Ihaka grinned. "I don't think we will."
Cheers erupted again, and Oliver met Will's eyes. There was a flicker of caution there, and Oliver willed the boy to stop talking, but he doubled down instead.
"I'm better than him!" Will shouted. "I bet I'm better than most of you. I can face anything. I made it all the way here, didn't I?"
"To the cage!" Ihaka shouted as he gripped Will's upper arm, half dragged him past Oliver, and threw him into the center of the other boys. "Have some fun with him first," he said as he swiped his hands together as if dusting them off.
At least ten boys closed in on Will, including Etera and Coop. The boy yelped and shouted in confusion as he was shoved and punched in the gut and shoved again. Someone opened the door into the factory, and the others laughed as they all jostled Will through the door. He tried to throw a punch but missed, and the next shove knocked him to the ground. It only took a few kicks for Will to curl up in a ball and start to cry. The door to the factory closed, but the sounds of Will's cries only got louder.
Oliver turned to Ihaka. "What are you doing?" he asked.
Ihaka walked past him, slapping his shoulder good-naturedly. "Don't worry, you'll get your chance. You can watch him tonight. I don't care what you do to him. Show that muppet what happens when someone comes at a brother of this *hapu*."
"No," Oliver said, "that's not what I meant."
Ihaka stopped and looked back at Oliver, narrowing his eyes. "Are you not grateful for this gift?" he asked. "You have no idea what I'd do for a chance at my cousin. That kid just gave you every reason to teach him a lesson."
Oliver's mouth ran dry. He looked from Ihaka to the factory door and back again. "It's just…" He licked his lips. *I can't give Ihaka a reason to think I'm soft, not when I'm so close to getting out of here.* "You didn't allow them to hurt me like that before you put me in the cage."

Ihaka's eyes widened, and then he laughed. "I get it," he said. "You're worried he's going to be given the challenge."

Oliver frowned. He wasn't worried. He'd be gone, but the way Ihaka had said it sent a shiver up Oliver's spine. "Isn't that what the cage is supposed to prepare you for?"

"Sometimes," Ihaka said, "and sometimes, a cage is just a prison."

"You're not going to offer him the chance to face the *taniwha*?" A cold knot formed in the pit of his stomach and spread outward as Ihaka shook his head.

"Yeah, nah, mate." He opened the door again. "You don't have to worry about that. He's not joining the *hapu*. He's too—" Ihaka made a face. "—cocky."

Oliver slowly moved forward and chose to ignore the irony of Ihaka's statement as his eyes fell upon a streak of blood on the concrete floor beyond the door.

"It's been a while since I've had a hand-to-hand fight," Ihaka continued. "It'll be good for morale to have a little sport, especially since we've been itchin' for a hunt."

The streak of blood led to a series of dots that created a trail to the cage. Oliver followed it as Ihaka did the same.

"I don't understand," Oliver said. "What are you going to do with him when you're done?"

They'd reached the other side of the conveyer belt, and several yards off, the boys were shoving a weeping Will into the dog cage. His face was bloodied and already starting to swell.

Ihaka put a hand on Oliver's back. "We gotta feed the black cloud sometimes," he said. "Otherwise, they might not come when it's time to test someone."

The image of the two corpses on the rooftop flashed in Oliver's mind. Had they been like Will? Ihaka laughed again and then stepped lightly toward the cage with a bounce in his step.

They're going to kill him…

Oliver caught up to Ihaka. "I'll take you up on it," he said. "Guarding Will, I mean." He smiled despite the urge to throw up.

Ihaka raised his eyebrows and nodded approvingly. "Goodonya, mate. Do whatever you want to him. Just keep him alive. For now. Save some of the fun for the rest of us."

Oliver forced a laugh. "Sure thing," he said, hoping Ihaka didn't notice how his hands trembled, hoping he was hiding his nausea well enough, hoping no one would see his true intentions.

Somehow, Oliver had to escape with both his life and Will's. No matter how much he hated the boy, he couldn't leave him to die. That wasn't who Oliver wanted to be, even if the task at hand was next to impossible. He'd promised Minnie he wouldn't change, and he intended to keep that promise.

Chapter 31

Oliver Roman

Six days, and Oliver still had no idea how he was going to get himself and Will away from the *hapu* alive. It didn't help that Will was… well, himself.

"They're going to feed you to a swarm," Oliver said, "to one of those black clouds. They call it a *taniwha*, a monster." He whispered in the dark, trying to get Will to understand the danger. "I'm trying to figure out how to keep you alive."

Will scoffed from inside the cage. He sat with his arms wrapped around his knees, his cheek swollen, his clothes crusted with old blood. "Liar," he said. "You said they kept you in here, too, and you're still alive."

Oliver sighed. After days of trying to think of a way out, he'd finally decided to try talking to Will. He'd foolishly thought that they could put their heads together and solve the problem. His second mistake was telling Will too much of his own story.

"That was different," Oliver said, "they were going to test me."

"They'll test me, too, then," Will said, lifting his chin awkwardly so that his head pressed into the top of the cage. There wasn't enough room for him to sit up all the way.

"Ihaka said he was going to let you die," Oliver said.

"I don't believe you," Will said.

"They didn't hurt me like they hurt you."

"Because I'm tougher!"

"You're going to die." Oliver tried not to raise his voice.

"Liar!" Will shouted.

Oliver looked over his shoulder, squinting in the dark, listening for any evidence that Will had woken someone. He snapped his head back to Will and kept his voice low. "Fine," he said. "When they take you up to the rooftop and leave you out there to die, don't say I didn't warn you." He scooted back, crossed his arms, and shut his mouth.

If he's not going to listen, Oliver thought, I'll just leave without him. It's not my fault he came here, and it's not my fault he's a jerk!

Will shuffled back in the cage and leaned against the metal grid. Oliver remembered well how uncomfortable it was as Will kept readjusting every few minutes.

Night after night, Oliver had volunteered to watch Will as Etera had once watched him. The next day, Oliver would make up stories about how he made fun of Will all night, how he hit him with the butt of a spear and spit on him and fed him by crumbling up chips to watch him try to gather the pieces in the cramped cage. None of it was true, but it seemed to make Ihaka want to keep Will alive longer. And if anyone else were to take watch, there was no guarantee they *wouldn't* do things like that.

"Revenge is a good look for you, Oliver," Ihaka had said. "I think it's toughening you up."

The only good thing about it was that the night watch gave Oliver the excuse to not go out on the hunt. In the afternoon, he went scavenging with the others who kept night watch, just two other boys who barely talked to him. That was fine with Oliver. He didn't need to make any more friends.

Dinner with Etera and Coop on either side of him was bittersweet. Not only did he have a night of watching over Will ahead of him, but he couldn't help but feel as if he were betraying them as he planned to leave. He genuinely cared about them both, and he didn't want to leave them behind, but he didn't think either of them would come with him. In fact, it was more likely that they would turn him in to Ihaka if he told them his plans.

Plans… Oliver laughed at himself. What plans? I'm sitting here in the dark with no way to get us out. Will doesn't even want my help!

"What's so funny?" Will sneered.

Oliver sneered right back. "Shut up, Will, or I'll ask Ihaka to tape your mouth shut."

In the moonlight that illuminated the factory, Oliver saw a flash of fear on Will's face. He sighed and let his head fall back against a piece of equipment. Will was silent, and Oliver hated that it was because he'd threatened him. But he couldn't take any more of the other boy, either.

How can I convince him? Oliver thought. He sat in the quiet for a while, thinking. It would be impossible to save Will without his cooperation.

Finally, he leaned forward. "Look," Oliver said, "before they took me up to the rooftop, they gave me a set of rules. If they don't give you a set of rules, it's because they're not testing you."

"Why do you care?" Will spat the question. "You're just trying to scare me so that when they do test me, I fail."

"It will be too late for me to help when they take you to the rooftop," Oliver said, "but maybe… maybe if you know what's coming, you can hide or… find a way off the rooftop. There's no fire escape. Ihaka removed it."

"Stop talking to me," Will said. "I'm tired." He huffed and closed his eyes, turning from Oliver as much as his tight confines would allow.

Oliver leaned his head back again, and when Will started snoring, he started to relax. A light rain made a pitter-patter on the roof and windows of the factory, adding to the urge to sleep. He let an hour pass in thought and shook himself awake whenever his eyelids started to droop, but eventually, boredom and sleepiness coupled with the sound of rain lulled him to sleep.

Hoots and hollers woke Oliver, made him suck in a sharp breath and sit up straight. Early morning light filled the factory as the sound of a dozen sets of footsteps beat the concrete floor. Oliver rubbed his eyes and got to his feet. Everyone was coming.

Oliver knelt in front of Will's cage. "What happened? Did you hear anything?"
Will narrowed his eyes. "Just something about having fun," he said.
The group, Ihaka in the lead, rounded the conveyer belts.
"They're coming." Panic settled in Oliver's stomach as his heartbeat quickened. "Will, you have to listen to me—"
"Unlock the cage!" Ihaka shouted as he came near.
Oliver looked sideways at the advancing *hapu*. Coop was cheering with the rest, but Etera had slowed and was staring at Oliver, brow furrowed. When their eyes met, Etera pressed his lips together and made a gesture like unlocking the cage. "Do it," he mouthed.
Etera knows I don't want to, Oliver thought.
Oliver closed his eyes and turned toward Will. "Remember what I said last night, okay? If they don't give you rules, you have to run. I hope I'm wrong. If I am, just do what Ihaka says, and you'll be fine."
Will sneered. "I don't need your help."
He ignored Will's attitude as an overwhelming regret came over Oliver for what he was about to do. "I'm sorry." He fished the key out of his pocket and unlocked the cage. He stepped back as Ihaka approached, and Will crawled out, weak from being cooped up and barely fed.
"Pick him up boys!" Ihaka said. "Time to feed the *taniwha*!" He stepped over to Oliver as several boys laid hands on Will.
"What about the rules?" Will's voice squeaked, the question barely audible beneath the taunting sounds of the others.
"Told him about the rules, eh?" Ihaka asked.
Oliver swallowed hard and shrugged, careful not to look at Ihaka lest the boy see the lie in his expression. "He needed to know I belonged here and he didn't. I was tested, and he failed to even qualify to *be* tested."
Ihaka laughed and raised a pointed finger over his head, shouting above the din, "To the rooftop!" He danced around the boys and led them forward as they dragged Will toward the lobby. It was the first time in weeks Ihaka had been in truly high spirits.
Etera hurried to Oliver. "Let's go," he said. "Ihaka's excited, and he's in a good mood, but if you keep looking like someone's about to kill your dog, he's gonna notice, bro."
Oliver nodded and fell in line beside Etera at the back of the mob. Will's desperate cries for the rules of the test made for an odd undertone to the elated cheers of the others.
I can't let this happen, Oliver thought as they entered the lobby, as Ihaka led them toward the staircase that ascended to the rooftop.
Oliver stopped walking. His chest was bursting with pressure. *I have to do something!* But he had no idea what. He glanced at the Remembrance Room and took a step toward it.
Etera shook his head, his tone frustrated. "What are you doing?"
"I don't know yet," Oliver said as he picked up his pace, running into the room, snatching up his mother's purse, and throwing it over his head. It settled against his hip, the strap across his chest. The familiar weight somehow gave him courage.
Etera stood in the doorway of the room, his eyes wide. "You don't even like that guy! What's the matter with you?"
"Nothing is wrong with me," Oliver said as he marched forward and pushed past Etera to follow the mob up the staircase.
"You can't do anything," Etera said, "and if you tried, Ihaka would let the *taniwha* eat you alive, too!"
"I can't let him die just because I don't like him," Oliver said, clutching at the strap across his chest. "That's not who I am." He started up the steps. The rest of the *hapu* were already at the top, already filtering into the glass enclosure on the roof.
Etera was right behind Oliver. "I can't let you!" he said as he grabbed Oliver's wrist. "You're my best friend!"
Oliver paused and looked back at Etera. He pulled his wrist away. "You're my best friend, too, Etera. But I have to do this." He picked up the pace, taking the stairs two at a time.
"No! I need you to stay," Etera said.
At the top of the stairs, there was a landing and a door that led out into what Oliver speculated was once a charming café before the end of the world made the factory home to the *hapu*. Oliver looked out as the boys shoved Will back and forth, as Ihaka opened the door that led outside the protection of the glass enclosure and they pushed him through it.
"Maybe you need me to stay," Oliver said as Etera came up next to him, "because this isn't who you are, either."
Etera frowned and looked away as Oliver opened the door and stepped into the enclosure. He licked his lips, his mouth going dry as Coop pointed to the right.
"It's comin' already!" Coop said.
The rain the night before had both washed away some of the grime on the outside of the glass panels and created a damp atmosphere perfect for a swarm. His dad had said once that mosquitos loved the rain; it created more collections of water wherein they could lay their eggs.
"Not yet!" Oliver's heart skipped a beat as he watched the black swarm coming up a street, headed for the factory. When he'd been on the rooftop, it had been darker, their vision more restricted, but the morning sun gave them plenty of visibility for miles.
We still have time, he thought as he looked at Will on the other side of the glass.
The other boy rushed to the edge of the building, stopping at the foot-high barrier that ran along the edge. Oliver couldn't see his face, but he could see the way Will's entire body stiffened at the sight of the swarm.
Etera joined Oliver, having walked slowly out of the stairwell and into the enclosure, a frown still on his face. "There's a rope," he said quietly.
Oliver blinked at him. "What?"
"Ihaka got rid of the fire escape, but he's not stupid. If he ever got caught out there for some reason, if the door inside was barred or locked, he wanted a way out," Etera said. "I only know because I caught him checking on it once. There's a rope attached to an anchor, rolled up under an upside-down pot near those corpses."
Outside, Will backed away from the edge of the building, shaking his head. He turned toward the enclosure, tears streaming down his face. "Let me in!" he shouted as he ran back to the door and tried to force it open. "It's coming right at us."

"Right at *you*," Ihaka said.
The boys laughed. Will punched the glass, but it was too thick. It didn't crack, but it did make Will grunt in pain and hold his wrist to his chest. Will turned and searched the ground frantically, perhaps for something that could break the enclosure. There was nothing out there that could help with that. Oliver remembered the bare rooftop well.
Well, except for the corpses. The upside-down pot was plain as day after Etera pointed it out, but the corpses overshadowed its importance. The clay was chipped and dirty, as if it had been discarded long ago. Will turned back and was about to kick the glass.
"You break this glass," Ihaka said, "and we'll beat you to a pulp before me and Oliver get to watch the *taniwha* suck you dry from the safety of inside!"
"It's not fair!" Will shouted. Breathing heavily, the boy turned back to the edge of the building, rushing to look over the edges. "There has to be a way off! You can't do this to me!"
"I have to get Will off that rooftop." Oliver stepped toward the *hapu*, intending to push his way to the door and go outside.
Etera grabbed Oliver's hand again. "No, you can't!"
"Etera, I told you—"
"I mean," Etera said, "that won't work." He let go, turned around and put a hand on a heavy cast-iron chair that had been pushed off to the side. "If we both pick it up and throw it, it might break the glass." He glanced nervously at the group, and Oliver did the same; no one seemed to notice them as they were all too busy jeering at Will. "They won't stay up here if the glass is broken, and they won't follow with the *taniwha* so close. It'll be an hour or more before Ihaka comes after us."
"Us?" Oliver asked.
Etera shrugged. "We don't have enough time. You keen?"
Oliver swallowed hard. This was his last chance to back out. He nodded and set his jaw as he walked over to the chair and gripped one side of it.
"Choice," Etera said, grinning though Oliver noted hints of fear in the lines around his eyes and the way his voice cracked a bit.
Oliver lifted, as did Etera, and the two of them carried the chair closer to the glass wall. The other boys mostly had their backs to them, but as Oliver and Etera swung the chair back, Ihaka's shout made Oliver flinch.
"Oi! Eggheads!" An increasing amount of alarm went into every new syllable. "Stop that!"
But Oliver and Etera were already throwing the wrought-iron chair. The framework of the enclosure prevented the chair from going through, but several panels were left with jagged holes and plenty of cracks. It would be enough.
The *hapu* collectively stared at Oliver and Etera, some with mouths open. Ihaka had pushed to the front but froze, his eyes fixed on the glass. "What did you do?" he screamed, hands balled into fists at his sides.
"You better get inside," Oliver said, "before the *taniwha* comes." His voice was level despite how his heart raced. His heartbeat pounded so that his veins throbbed from his head to his feet.
Coop frowned, his expression morphing into one of betrayal as he stepped up beside Ihaka. "Etera? Oliver?"
Behind them all, Will was pressed up against the glass looking just as surprised as the others, his cheeks streaked with tears and his face red from all his shouting. A few of the boys looked at the holes in the glass, their eyes widening before they squeaked and ran for the safety of the factory.
"It's wrong," Oliver said. "You can't just kill people like this. Will is an idiot, but he doesn't deserve this."
"Come with us, mate," Etera said, looking at Coop. "Ihaka has a rope and anchor hidden under the pot by those bodies."
Coop spat on the ground and turned his back, jogging toward the door. Will backed away from the enclosure, turned, and ran toward the corner where the corpses lay as the rest of the *hapu* made for safety. Ihaka was the last one on the rooftop. He scowled at them, and took a few menacing steps forward. A sharp piece of glass caught Oliver's eye. He picked it up and held it out like a knife.
"You might be able to hurt us enough that we won't be able to get off this rooftop," Oliver said, "but don't think I won't fight back. There's a difference between defending yourself and killing. Do you really think you have time to try us?"
Etera backed up, too, but he didn't arm himself with broken glass. "You've been like a brother, mate. I don't wanna fight."
Ihaka growled and let out a string of curses. "If the *taniwha* weren't so close…" He pointed at them. "If you live, I'll find you. No one betrays the *hapu* and gets away with it." He retreated, opening the door, stepping onto the landing beyond it with Coop and the others waiting on the stairs behind him. Ihaka locked the door and watched them with a violent glare.
The telltale buzz of the swarm took center stage as silence fell upon the rooftop. Oliver broke into a run, Etera beside him. He fumbled with the lock on the enclosure's door to the rooftop, threw it open, and ran over to Will as the boy put all his weight against the heavy pot.
"It's too heavy!" Will shouted. "I can't get it off."
Oliver spotted a piece of pottery missing near the rim of the upside-down pot. The hole touched a crack in the shape of a large uneven circle. Oliver stuck his finger in the hole and pulled; the circle popped out.
"I got it!" Oliver reached into the hole, grabbed the end of the rope, and started pulling to unravel it, making a pile at his feet.
Etera grabbed an armful of rope and threw it over the side. Will rushed over, fell to his hands and knees, and climbed over the foot-high concrete edge as he took hold of the rope.
"Wait!" Oliver said as Will made to throw his body over the edge. "It's not—"
Will screamed as he tumbled over the side and the rope unraveled too quickly. Oliver rushed forward with Etera just in time to see the rope pull taught with Will at the other end. He bounced upward and hit the side of the building before letting go and falling the last couple yards to land hard on the ground below. Oliver looked back to see the anchor holding just fine within its clay hiding spot. Will groaned below and got to his feet.
"That's one way to do it," Etera said as he climbed over the edge, grasping the rope and lowering himself more carefully, using his feet to walk down the side of the building. "I think it can hold us both," Etera said halfway down. "Hurry up, Oliver!"

Oliver carefully straddled the short barrier between rooftop and open air. He gripped the concrete between his knees, leaned over, and grabbed hold of the rope. The hair on the back of his neck stood on end, sweat beaded his forehead, and his breath caught in his throat.

"The Ferris Wheel was worse," he whispered. "You can do this."

Of course, his dad had been with him then. At the time, Oliver had barely been able to move after watching his mother plunge to her death.

The buzz of the swarm was louder, but Oliver couldn't see it. The sound was enough to make him take the rope in both hands and drop his body over the edge. His hands slid a few inches, burning his palms, as his body nearly pulled his arms out of their sockets. His mother's bag dug into his hip as he smacked the wall. Shaky breaths wracked his body, and he whimpered as his feet kicked and he scrambled to find purchase. Finally, his legs wrapped around the rope, and he was able to pinch it between his knees.

Oliver lowered himself as quickly as he could, hand over hand, praying he wouldn't fall. When he was a few feet off the ground, he let go and landed on wobbly legs. As he did, black tendrils curled around the far side of the factory building.

"Run!" Etera screamed.

Oliver bolted along with Etera. Will was already trying the doors of buildings down the street. One of them opened, and he disappeared inside.

"Is that building safe?" Oliver managed as each hard footstep against pavement sent a jolt up his body. He held one hand on his bag to keep it from bouncing wildly.

"I… I don't know," Etera said, panting.

They passed broken windows and doors flung wide open; many of the buildings would not provide protection. But that one door had opened, and Oliver hoped Will had chosen a building that would keep them safe. A stitch in his side made him gasp, and he grimaced in pain, but pure adrenaline pushed Oliver onward. He kept pace with Etera as the swarm came ever nearer.

And then Oliver's ankle rolled. Pain lanced through his foot like fire as he stumbled, hit the pavement hard, and rolled. Etera shouted in alarm, and Oliver heard his feet skid to a stop.

"Keep going!" Oliver said as he pushed himself to sitting, wincing at palms scalded by rope and then scraped along asphalt. Tears burned his eyes as the swarm came at him like a wave, swelling in size as it sought to envelope him.

But Etera didn't listen. He was at Oliver's side, helping him to his feet within seconds of his fall. Oliver slung his arm around Etera's shoulders and hobbled forward with his friend's help.

"I'm not leaving you, bro," Etera said, grunting under Oliver's weight.

"It's gaining on us," Oliver said, blinking away the tears. "You have to go."

"No!" Etera put so much stubbornness behind the word that Oliver considered going boneless so that his friend would have to leave him.

Ahead, just as Oliver was preparing himself to drop to the ground, Will opened the door behind which he'd disappeared. He stepped out hesitantly at first, but then he put his head down and sprinted toward them. Within seconds, he was taking up residence on Oliver's other side.

"Mean as," Etera said with a grin as their pace more than doubled. "Mean as, mate. I didn't know you had it in you."

When they reached the door, Etera pulled Oliver inside, and the two of them tripped and fell into what looked like a waiting room. Will closed the door to the outside. Seconds later, the sunlight filling the room was blotted out as the swarm covered the only window. The monster writhed against the glass, trying to find its way inside.

"I don't know we're safe yet," Etera said. "This room is fine, but I saw broken windows to the right and left. Might connect back to here."

"We could go out through the back door," Will said.

"How do you know there is one?" Oliver asked, grunting as he tried to move his foot. His ankle was already swelling.

"I…" Will trailed off and cleared his throat.

"You were gonna leave us as bait," Etera said.

"Yeah," Will said. "But I didn't."

Oliver let out a long breath. "Okay," he said, "we keep running, try to find a safe space before the swarm finds us."

"I know of a safehouse," Etera said, "but Ihaka also knows where it is."

"It'll have to do for now," Oliver said, "until we're sure the swarm is gone."

"And then we go home," Will said.

Oliver nodded, thinking of Minnie and Samson, of his dad and Lauren. They were his home. "Yeah," he said. "If we survive, I'm never leaving my home again."

Once again, he struggled to his feet with the help of Etera and Will. They had to keep moving. Oliver fought with every ounce of willpower he had left. He fought through the pain. He fought for his family. Just like they would fight for him.

Chapter 32

Oliver Roman and Alexander Roman

Oliver's ankle seemed to swell an inch with every ten minutes. His entire foot throbbed with pain. Scratches from his fall stung his hands, forearms, and knees. But they'd made it to the safehouse, and the buzz of the swarm had been left behind.

The safehouse was little more than a one room workshop. The tools had been cleared out by the *hapu* long ago. All that was left was a solid metal worktable that was bolted to the floor and scattered nails on a dusty floor. No food. No water. No supplies. Nothing. They'd all three collapsed in the center of the shop to rest and hadn't moved since.

"How long do you think we have until Ihaka comes after us?" Oliver asked.

"Don't know," Etera said. "Depends on where the swarm went."

"Maybe it went back and found a way inside the factory," Will said, disgust in his tone. "I hope they all die."

"Oi!" Etera punched Will's arm, hard. "Don't say that."

Will rubbed his arm and scowled. "They want you dead, too, mate."

"Don't care," Etera said, leaning forward. "Don't say stuff like that."

"Fine." Will crossed his arms and frowned.

Oliver let out a long, exhausted breath. "I'm really hungry," he said.

"Me too." Etera got to his feet. "Let's see if we can make it to the mall, or at least to another safe place where Ihaka won't find us so quick."

Will's shoulders sagged, but he got to his feet, too. Both boys held out their hands for Oliver, and he reached out for them. As their hands clasped and they hauled Oliver to one foot, the ground beneath them started to tremble. Oliver didn't think anything of it at first. He'd experienced at least a couple small quakes since landing in New Zealand, after all.

Except the quake didn't dissipate like it had before; it only intensified. Metal groaned all around them, and a crack sprung up one wall. Oliver gasped as the ground seemed to jerk out from under him. All three boys fell in a heap. His ankle twisted again, and Oliver shouted in pain. Vibrations tore through Oliver's body and made his stomach flip and his heart beat violently.

"Get under the table!" Etera shouted.

Oliver crawled toward the table as a chunk of the ceiling crashed to the floor beside him. He, Etera, and Will just made it to the shelter of the worktable as a cacophony of rattling windows, rending metal, snapping wood, and deep, all-encompassing rumbles culminated in a sound like thunder as the safehouse fell down all around them.

* * *

Alex trekked through the streets of Christchurch toward the mall, eager to return to Minnie and Oliver. Lauren kept pace beside him, and Candice and Stella were paired behind them, and Walter brought up the rear. The captain had stayed with the ship, as did many of her crew. Only two crewmembers hiked back with them, Silas and Calista; they led the way. The rest stayed behind to guard the vessel and allow the few scientists on board to begin developing a batch of countermeasure mosquitos to be released in New Zealand.

Alex rolled a portable refrigerator out in front of him. It was only two-foot square, but it was the only qualified container the research vessel had possessed. Inside was a sampling of vaccines and treatments. The third human trials on the ship had surpassed Alex's expectations. Again, a small percentage became seriously ill, but they all survived, and quite a few had no reaction at all. Between all they'd learned in Atlanta, Boston, Colorado Springs, and then, finally, Barlow Scientific Research Center, he and Walter had pulled a vaccine together.

Now, he thought, let's hope it's enough to prevent death should we encounter a swarm.

In the past, even a small viral load passed along from human to human could kill within twenty-four hours. An overload from a swarm could kill in minutes, incapacitate in seconds. Alex was confident that the vaccine would prevent illness from the former, but the treatment could still be necessary for the latter.

We won't be truly safe until we start releasing those countermeasure mosquitos, Alex thought.

"I can't wait to tell my mom about what we've done," Lauren said, breaking quiet with an optimistic tone and a bright smile. "There's a real chance to make the world right again."

"There's nothing like finally seeing the light at the end of a long, dark tunnel," Alex said as he looked ahead, wondering how much farther they had to go.

"You could sound more excited about it," Candice said.

"I am excited." Alex looked over his shoulder and smiled back at his friends. "I just *really* want to get back to my son."

Lauren met his eyes with her own and offered sympathy in her expression. The weight that had settled on Alex concerning Oliver hadn't gone away, but he'd done his best to put it aside. Lauren had been right. There had been nothing he could do while out at sea. But he was back, and seeing Oliver safe and sound was the only thing that could untangle the worry tying his stomach into knots.

"You okay, Walter?" Stella asked.

Alex grimaced as he looked at the man. He had stopped to look down at his feet. "I didn't mean to be insensitive," Alex said, "when I was talking about seeing Oliver. I'm sure Lizzy—"

"No," Walter said, looking up, "it's not that."

Alex frowned, but before he could ask anything more, a vibration penetrated the soles of his feet. There had been an earthquake back when they'd been sheltering in the plane on the tarmac, when they'd first arrived, but that one had gone away so quickly.

"It's not letting up!" Alex shouted above the rising rumble.

Ahead, Silas and Calista had stopped, and Calista shouted back at them. "Seems like a big one!" she shouted.

"Stay in the center of the street," Silas added.

At that moment, the earth itself moaned all around them. Alex bent his knees to keep his balance and reached out to pull Lauren closer. They grasped each other's forearms as the buildings around them trembled. Glass windows shattered overhead, and Candice screamed, crouching low and covering the back of her neck. Stella flinched and ducked, and Walter spread out his arms and hunched over the two women, trying to cover them. Alex grabbed the back of Lauren's neck and pulled her head into his chest, wrapping his arms around her to shield her head and neck.

A thunderous series of pops and cracks and rumbles filled the air, drowning out everything else. As Alex fought to keep his balance and protect Lauren, an entire three-story building tipped forward half a block down the street. Silas and Calista sprinted out of the way as it collapsed just behind them, sending a billowing wave of dust down the street. Alex and Lauren hit the ground as debris whooshed over them.

The quake was over as quickly as it had begun.

"Everyone okay?"

That was Walter's voice, panicked and close by. Alex looked over at Lauren who was slowly getting to her knees. She was covered in a layer of dust, just like Alex, just like everyone.

"I'm fine," Lauren said as she stood, patting down her stomach and legs. "I don't think I'm hurt at all."

Alex breathed out in relief. "I'm okay, too." He ran his fingers through his hair and shook out the dust, coughing at the off-white cloud.

"We're good, too, I think," Candice said.

"What about the others?" Stella asked.

Alex had almost forgotten about Silas and Calista. They had been the closest to the collapsing building. His heart jumped into his throat, and his immediate reaction was pure panic, but in the settling dust, two figures pushed themselves off the ground, coughing and sputtering.

"Are you two injured?" Alex asked.

Silas shook his head, producing a cloud of dust that Calista waved away. "We're fine," he said, "but we need to hurry, see if the mall is still standing."

"That was the biggest earthquake we've seen in decades," Calista said.

"Oliver!" Alex sucked in a breath as his skin prickled, and that weight that had been sitting with him since McMurdo Station solidified into an urgency that sent spikes of adrenaline pumping through his veins. "How far are we?"

"Not far," Silas said as he pointed back the way they'd come. "We'll need to go around this mess," he said. "A lot of newer buildings should be fortified better, but we might find more older buildings that have collapsed blocking our path." He gestured for them to follow as he broke into a jog. "Follow me," he said.

Alex didn't have to be told twice.

* * *

Oliver covered a cough with his arm as he leaned over Etera squinting in the dim light. His friend was motionless, his eyes closed. Part of Etera's left leg, from the calf down, was pinned under debris. The sturdy metal worktable had held up in the collapse of the small building, and Oliver and Will were only worse off by a few bumps and bruises except for the fact that they were trapped.

The table had provided a pocket of safety from the debris, and it was packed tightly all around them except for one hole about a foot across. Will sat on his knees before the hole, trying to see out of it.

Oliver pressed his lips together. "Please be alive..." he whispered as he slowly extended a hand over Etera's chest. He hovered for a moment, afraid to touch the boy and find that he was already gone, but he lowered his hand anyway. Warmth emanated from Etera's chest as it rose and fell beneath Oliver's touch.

"He's alive," Oliver said, breathing out with relief. He squinted in the gloom at where Etera's leg was pinned down. It was no small feat for him to gather the courage to feel the ground around it. "No blood," he said, "but... I don't know if that's good or bad."

"There is nothing good about any of this," Will said.

Oliver looked up at him to see him shove on the debris around the opening. "Stop! You could shift everything," he said. "If that hole closes, I don't know how long we'll last in here without fresh air."

Will pulled back from the hole and ran his hands over his face and let out a frustrated growl before turning to point at Oliver. "This is all your fault!"

"The earthquake is *my* fault?" Oliver scoffed.

"It's your fault that I'm trapped here," Will said.

"I didn't make you come to the factory," Oliver said.

"What was I supposed to do?" Will asked. "My mates treated me like a king before you came along and ruined it!"

Oliver sighed in frustration. "Etera is injured, we're trapped, and you're mad that your friends don't think you're cool anymore?"

"You're out of it," Will said. "I wouldn't be here if you had stayed put back at the mall."

"Where you could keep bullying me?" Oliver raised his voice as his muscles tensed. "You came to the factory and risked your life for your big, fat ego. That's it. It's your fault you're here. You were being stupid, and I won't let you blame that on me!"

Will matched Oliver's volume as he shouted, "And what? You came out here and joined the *hapu* out of pure bravery? That's rubbish! They found you, and you were just lucky that they decided to test you. We're the same, me and you, except for luck!"

Oliver opened his mouth, but the words stung. He'd told Will that part of his story when Will had been locked in the cage, but he'd never thought about how similar their stories were.

"You're right," Oliver said, his soft response seeming to hit Will harder than his shouting ever had. The other boy looked shocked as Oliver continued. "We both wanted to fit in, and we both made stupid decisions. And I was lucky. But now, we have to work together, or we're going to die in here." He looked down at Etera. "Him faster than either of us. He's my friend, and he helped me keep you alive." Oliver looked up at Will. "You owe him, even if you don't care about him."

Will shifted to sit on his rear end and slumped. "We don't have food or water. If Ihaka finds us, he'll leave us to cark it."

"What?" Oliver asked.

"We'll die," Will said in an irritated tone. "Don't you Americans know anything?"

Oliver bit back a retort. "We won't die," he said. "Our families... they might come looking for us to see if we're safe. I bet Minnie is already on her way to the factory. If she doesn't see me, maybe she'll think to go looking in the city."

"Mateo barely let her go look for you the first time," Will said.

"Maybe the earthquake will change things," Oliver said. "Either way, we have other things to worry about right now. Like Etera. And that hole."

Will frowned at it. "I thought you said it was good for air."

"It's also big enough for the swarm to get in," Oliver said. "And it's too small to climb through."

"What are we going to do?"

Oliver's hand went to his mother's bag, still on his hip. He looked down at it, thoughts whirling through his brain, jumbling together until one thought brought some order out of the chaos. *I know who I am.* He opened the bag and stared at the evidence of all he'd been through, of everything he'd learned, of the people he loved.

He looked back at Will. "I think I have a few ideas."

* * *

Alex's racing heart skipped a beat as pure relief brought a deep sigh. He slowed his pace just a bit. The mall was still standing despite the windows being broken. That would be a problem; they'd have to relocate. But people were rushing about, some of them already climbing into one of the plastic-covered pedal pubs. That meant Oliver was safe somewhere in the bustle. No one seemed to notice Alex and the rest as they wove through the cars in the parking lot.

"There's Mom," Lauren said, pointing at Minnie, who was on Mateo's heels, gesturing wildly. Samson was at her side, looking up at her, his ears perked. Another woman Alex didn't know was talking to Mateo, too, gesturing in much the same way as Minnie.

"Do you see Oliver?" Alex craned his neck to scan the area, but he didn't slow his pace.

"No, but... he's got to be here somewhere," Lauren said.

A set of familiar faces stepped over broken glass at the entrance, backpacks on and urgency in their steps. But one of them stopped as her eyes settled on them. Lizzy said something, and Zara, Kai, and Blythe stopped, too.

"Walter!" Zara shouted and laughed, waving both hands.

Walter jogged past Alex and Lauren straight for Zara. Others noticed them, then.

"Get Mateo!" Amir shouted. "They're back!" Someone sprinted in Mateo's direction.

"See if Oliver is with Zara," Lauren said.

Alex nodded. "Go see your mom," he said. "She looks upset about something." He parted with Lauren and followed after Walter.

Zara and Kai both threw their arms around Walter, and he laughed as he hugged them back. Alex was about to ask Zara where Oliver was when she pulled away from Walter, but her smile faded quickly at the sight of him. She and Kai exchanged a look that unsettled Alex.

Behind them, Walter stuck his hands in his pocket and took a step toward Lizzy. "Hey, Bethie," he said, a heartbreaking sadness in his tone.

But then Lizzy rushed forward and threw her arms around him. At first, Walter froze, eyes wide as if he couldn't believe what was happening. He slowly pulled his hands out of his pockets as his eyes filled with tears, and then he hugged Lizzy tight as a sob escaped him. Neither spoke, and yet, Alex could *feel* what was being said. His own eyes blurred with tears at the sight of their reunion.

It made him yearn to see Oliver even more. "Where's my son?" Alex asked.

Zara paled. "He's... he's..." She trailed off and looked at Kai again.

"He's not here," Kai said.

Alex sucked in a breath. The ground didn't need to shake for the world to start spinning. "What do you mean?"

"He's alive," Zara said. "Or... he was the last time we saw him."

Alex couldn't help the way his voice growled as he asked again, "What—do—you—mean?"

"Hold on," Blythe said, stepping forward. "What happened isn't their fault."

Zara and Kai averted their eyes. In his periphery, Alex caught the shape of Lauren and Minnie walking toward them. Alex turned away from Zara, Kai, and Blythe to get some answers from Minnie. Samson trotted along beside her, but even he seemed unsettled in the way he half-heartedly wagged his tail at Alex, in the way he stayed by Minnie's side, whining up at her periodically.

Minnie held up her hands in a gesture that might have been meant to calm him. All it did was quicken his heartbeat and send a shudder down his spine.

* * *

"Now's not the time to be showin' off, mate."

"I'm not," Oliver said as he pulled his t-shirt over his head. He'd already carefully laid out the contents of his bag, and he added his shirt to the lineup.

Will waved his hand at Oliver's things. "What's all that, anyway?"

Oliver picked up the lavender oil and unscrewed the top. "This bag was my mom's. She made it, and after she died, I found it and kept it. The most time I spent without it was back at the factory." He dripped the oil onto his t-shirt. The bottle had an annoyingly small dispenser, so he shook it to make it drip faster. "She always used lavender for the scent, and she used it to help me rest at night. It's got a calming effect or something."

"So?" Will asked. "What does that matter?"

"After she died, this bag was dropped hundreds of feet. Her lavender bottle broke inside it and soaked the bag." Oliver swallowed hard and bit back tears at the memory. "There was smoke everywhere at the World's Fair. It was so thick. Everything was burning. So many people were just dead."

Once the shirt was saturated, he crawled over Etera's still form. Will scooted back, scrunching into the corner, watching him with a frown.

"We all got stories about everyone carking it," Will said.

"You don't understand." Oliver stuffed the t-shirt, which smelled heavily of lavender, into one corner of the foot-long hole. "We found out later that mosquitos hate the scent." He crawled back toward his stuff. "They also don't like smoke." He picked up the set of playing cards he'd gotten from the CDC in Atlanta and the Zippo lighter Ned the biker had given him.

Will raised his eyebrows. "You think that will work?"

"It might," Oliver said. "The lavender and the smoke might mask our scents, or they might just make this area less inviting for the swarm." He silently thanked General Hunt for getting him lighter fluid refills. He took out the inside unit and carefully, slowly followed the steps the general had taught him.

He made his way back to the hole, retrieved a playing card, lit the Zippo, and waited for the card to catch fire. The edge of the card curled and blackened, and Oliver laid it on concrete on the other side of the hole.

"You do this part," Oliver said. "We only have so many cards. Save them for if we hear the swarm out there. It gets so loud, we'll be able to tell it's coming if it gets too close. If that happens, just keep adding burning cards here, on the concrete, where it won't catch the debris on fire."

Will nodded and took the Zippo and the deck of cards. "That's not a lot of smoke," Will said, nodding to the single card and the small thread of grey smoke drifting out from it.

"It smells, though," Oliver said. "Between the smell of smoke and the lavender, maybe we can hide from the swarm. And, we can burn some of our clothes, too, if it comes down to it."

"Okay... well, while I'm doing this, what are you going to do?" Will asked.

"I've got a duck call," Oliver said. "Minnie knows I have it. If any of my friends come looking, and they hear it, they'll know it's me. I'm going to blow in it like my life depends on it because... well, it does." He reached for the duck call and prayed his plan would work.

***

Alex couldn't process everything Minnie had told him. Confusion and anger and dread combined to overwhelm his entire body. Oliver had run away to join the crazy gang of boys who had attacked them when they'd first arrived? And he'd refused to come back when Minnie finally found him? That didn't sound like his son. He'd started to test the limits, too, when he was a preteen, but Alex hadn't expected that from Oliver, not yet, not when every action could mean life or death.

"And you just... let him go?" Alex asked.

"I had to," Minnie said. "He swore he'd just run away again, and those boys could have heard us if we tried to force him and he made a fuss. I thought..." She pressed her lips together and put a hand on Alex's arm. "I thought he'd come home on his own."

"It's not her fault," Zara said.

"We were there," Kai added. "Oliver was... different. He was determined to stay."

"The kid was angry," Blythe said, "and confused. But he didn't seem in any more immediate danger than he would have been with us."

Angry. That word hit Alex like a punch in the gut as he started to piece it together. *He was angry... angry I left him,* he thought.

"But the second the ground stopped shakin', I started in on Mateo, tryin' to get a team to go out to the factory and make sure Oliver was okay," Minnie said. "Or at least, for him to let us go and check on him ourselves."

"Another boy went to the factory, too, we think," Zara said.

"His momma has been backin' me up the past hour, neither one of us lettin' up." Minnie scowled over her shoulder where Mateo was instructing people where to put their belongings.

"He's been so focused on resettling the group," Zara said, "that I don't think Oliver and Will are at the top of his list right now."

"Why wouldn't Mateo fight to get them back sooner?" Lauren asked.

"Because it seemed clear neither of them would come back willingly," Blythe said. "Oliver certainly wouldn't. Mateo has dozens of people to look after. Starting a full-blown war wouldn't be smart."

"But they have my *son.*" Alex raised his voice, and his words cracked under the intense fear building in his chest. Samson barked at him in reply, a rare occurrence.

This is my fault, he thought. The weight crushed him. Panic enveloped him. He took a step backward, the edges of his vision darkening as he saw the building collapse over and over again in his mind. That quake had left so much destruction.

"Oliver could be dead," he said.

"Don't say that," Minnie said. "Could be not a hair on his head was even tousled. We don't know."

"We don't know because you let him go!" Alex shouted.

Samson stepped in front of Minnie then and barked twice. A warning. Part of Alex knew shouting at Minnie wasn't right, but he couldn't help it. Still, as Minnie patted Samson's head and told him to sit and hush, the dog's eyes on him were a good reminder to keep his cool.

Lauren stepped in front of him, the look in her eyes harder than Samson's. "Hey," she said firmly. "Don't you talk to her like that. You weren't here. She did the best she could. You heard Blythe. Oliver was angry. He was being stubborn, and he didn't leave Mom much of a choice."

Alex blinked away tears. It was too much. He sank into a crouch, his head in his hands. "It's my fault," he said. "I never should have left him."

"Alex!" Mateo's voice broke into their conversation. He burst into their circle. "Silas and Calista say you've done it. You've got a vaccine. It's true?" he asked.

"Read the room, man," Kai said.

"You want me to raise a knot on your noggin'?" Minnie asked. "The man is devastated. Back on up, now, you hear?"

Alex looked up at Mateo. He slowly stood, straightening to his full height. Nothing mattered except for finding Oliver. "It is true," he said, steel in every word. "And you won't get one drop unless you take one of those contraptions full of able-bodied men and women to that factory to help me get my son back."

Mateo's eyes widened. "Alex, we can't—"

"Not *one* drop." Alex stepped forward, toe-to-toe with the man. "We're leaving for this factory with medical supplies. My people, the ones vaccinated, will go on foot to make room for more people in the pedal pub."

Mateo shook his head. "Alex, I have to get my people—"

"Will *is* one of our people, and we all know the fool child followed after his fool child."

The woman Alex hadn't recognized, the one who'd been following Mateo alongside Minnie, had approached. She crossed her arms, and a few other men and women came up behind her. Alex ignored the barb at Oliver; it wasn't like he could argue with her. Oliver's head had to have been scrambled to make the choices he'd made while Alex was gone.

"My son might need help, too," she continued, "and those boys might be a thorn in our side, but they're Kiwis, and there's good chance they need our help after that quake."

Minnie nodded. "This could be your chance to offer them an olive branch and bring some unity to Christchurch."

The people who'd gathered around them echoed their agreement.

Mateo sighed. "You don't know Ihaka." But he hung his head and shrugged. "If this doesn't turn out well, don't say I didn't warn you."

Chapter 33

Minnie Stevens

Minnie pedaled the best she could along with Mateo, Zara, Kai, Blythe, Lizzy, and Will's mother, Sophie. The pain that had been in Alex's eyes weighed heavily on Minnie. Everything had gone cattywampus after Alex had left for Antarctica.

I did my best, Minnie thought, but I still managed to get us stuck up a creek with no paddle and a hole in our boat.

"We're going to find him," Zara said from beside Minnie.

"I know," Minnie said, but she could hear the fear in her own voice. She glanced at Zara who was pedaling while watching Minnie with concern. "I know my wrinkles have doubled and I look like a cat caught in the rain with all this sweat, but don't worry about me."

Samson lay on top of stacks of supplies in the center of the contraption, and he cocked his head at her statement as if expressing uncertainty.

Zara quirked an eyebrow. "I've come to like you, Minnie. I'll worry about you whether you like it or not. Don't blame yourself for Oliver."

"Don't know as I have a choice." Minnie's mostly-healed thigh burned as she put as much effort into moving the contraption as she possibly could. She shook her head. "I'm guessin' there's enough blame to go around, and I ain't one to shirk responsibility."

"Guilt almost killed Walter once, and I wasn't far behind him," Zara said. "Whatever we find, just remember that you've done a lot of good these past months. Remember that people love you."

Minnie didn't respond; she just gave a nice nod and went back to concentrating on working with the others to move the contraption. Zara was a good girl and stubborn. She wouldn't give up if Minnie kept pushing back, so she let the matter lie.

Another pedal pub enclosed in clear plastic traveled behind them. Mateo had insisted every able man and woman come with them in case things turned ugly. Parents and many of the older members had gone on to relocate to their second location which they could only hope was still standing. It was on the outskirts of town, past the airport and hopefully past where the quake had hit the hardest.

At the back of their procession, Alex, Lauren, Candice, Silas, Calista, and some woman named Stella walked at a brisk pace. Minnie could see the tops of their heads when she craned her neck. The pedal pubs could go faster, but they'd set a slow pace so that those walking could keep up. Not to mention the added weight from the supplies loaded in the center of the contraptions made the things harder to move.

Mateo guided them from the seat behind the driver's wheel. Minnie leaned on the long, thin bar and kept pushing until they turned a final corner and Mateo called out, "There!" He cursed. "I think part of the factory has collapsed."

The contraption rolled to a stop in the middle of the street. Minnie, breathing hard and with sweat rolling down the side of her face, peered through the plastic at a factory that was half standing, half rubble. She couldn't see anyone from where she sat.

"Move your butts," Minnie said, waving urgently at those who sat between her and a way outside. Samson stretched and climbed to the long, thin wooden pub bar that ran the length of the contraption, nails clicking as he walked to the end near where Mateo was unzipping the plastic.

Mateo climbed out, and instructed Blythe and Kai to exit ahead of Minnie. Minnie made her way toward the exit, moving down the line, awkwardly lifting her feet over each set of pedals until she was able to climb out with a little help from Mateo and Blythe. Samson jumped down right after her. She didn't waste any time. Minnie rounded the pedal pub to get a better look at what they were dealing with, and Samson followed.

She found Alex and Lauren already climbing over the first of the rubble.

"Oliver!" Alex shouted, his voice full of emotion. "It's Dad! I'm here! Oliver?"

Lauren added her voice to Alex's. "Can anyone hear us?"

The two of them hopped down on the other side of a mess of bricks, concrete, twisted metal, and other debris to disappear around half a wall still standing. Minnie started toward the building. Sophie sprinted past her, shouting for Will, the third person to reach the rubble. Debris slid as she frantically scrambled overtop it, and though she slipped a couple times, Sophie didn't stop moving. She, too, disappeared behind what remained of the wall.

"Wait," Zara said as she came up beside Minnie.

Kai and Blythe came up on Minnie's other side. Not seeing Lizzy, Minnie glanced over her shoulder to see the girl walking to meet her father who was already unloading a tent from one of the pedal pubs.

"They're going to set up the temporary shelters we brought with us," Zara said. "And we've got limited hazmat suits, so they've got to decide who gets one."

Minnie set her jaw as she approached the edge of the rubble. All of that was second to finding Oliver. Behind them, Mateo called out orders to search for survivors.

"You shouldn't climb that alone," Zara said, nodding to the rubble. Kai and Blythe seemed to agree with the way they blocked her way.

"I ain't waitin'." Minnie pushed through the soreness in her thigh to take a wide step around the men and up onto a slab of concrete. "If Oliver's in there, he'll need us."

"We're not here to stop you," Blythe said.

"We're here to help." Kai held out a hand.

Minnie took the hand, and the four of them clambered after Alex, Lauren, and Sophie. Samson had no trouble navigating the debris. On the other side of the rubble, past the half-crumbled wall, Alex was walking away from four boys gathered around a corpse, headed for more rubble. Sophie was right behind him. But Lauren hung back with those boys, and it was no mystery to Minnie as to why.

One of the boys rocked back and forth on the ground, staring at the dead body. It was a gruesome sight, that body; arm at an odd angle, head caved-in on one side, bruises and cuts on every inch, Minnie guessed the boys had to have pulled him from the wreckage. He had to have died when the building came down. The other three boys weren't faring better than the first. One whispered unintelligibly, tears making tracks down cheeks dusted white. The other two looked up dully at Lauren, seeming to register her presence with indifference as silent tears slid from dark-rimmed eyes.

Approaching slowly so as to avoid startling the dazed boys, Minnie kept her voice calm. "Lauren," she said, "what's going on?"

Lauren knelt beside the boy who was rocking and laid a gentle hand on his shoulder. The boy flinched, and then he stopped rocking and burst into tears. When Lauren pulled him into a hug, he threw his arms around her middle and sobbed into her shoulder.

"They said the other boys were over there," Lauren said softly, nodding to where Alex and Sophie were throwing aside bricks from where the building had collapsed. "That's all we could get out of them. They're in shock."

Samson lowered his belly to the ground and tentatively scooted closer to the whispering boy. He licked the boy's hand, and the child allowed Samson to poke his head under an arm so that his head rested in the boy's lap. The boy stopped whispering and rested his cheek on Samson's forehead.

But the mountain of bricks and twisted metal called for Minnie's focus. "Oliver could be under… all of that?" Minnie's voice cracked and the world tilted. She stumbled to the side, but Blythe was there, and he kept her upright.

"We'll go help," Zara said, and she and Kai sprinted off to where Alex was moving debris.

"You gonna be okay if I go help?" Blythe asked.

Minnie righted herself, and though her legs were weak and her head swam, she urged Blythe to join them. "The more people we have digging, the better," she said. "Go on." And Blythe did as she asked.

"Mom…" Lauren said, "how could Oliver survive that?"

"Wait… Oliver?" One of the boys who'd been staring blankly looked over at Lauren. "He's gone."

Minnie sucked in a sharp breath and shook her head. Questions formed, and denials quickly after, but not one of them could make it past the fear of answers that was like cotton stuffing her mouth.

"You saw him?" Lauren asked, voice shaking as her eyes darted to Alex. "You saw Oliver's body?" Her chin quivered. She still held the sobbing boy who'd only quieted a little. "No," she whispered, eyes brimming with tears. "It can't be."

"Yeah, nah," the boy said, sniffing and drawing his arm across his nose to wipe away tears and snot. "He left before the quake, this morning."

Before Minnie could process that, the other boy who'd been crying quietly spoke. "He didn't just leave, Coop. He's a traitor." Vacant eyes with dark circles beneath had turned almost feral at Coop's explanation, and the boy spat on the ground.

Waves of conflicting emotion washed over Minnie. The onset of grief was soothed by relief at the fact that Oliver was not, in fact, buried under the debris, but dread overwhelmed that relief too quickly for it to stop the world from spinning.

He's out there, somewhere, and we don't know where, she thought.

The clattering of bricks behind them made Minnie glance over her shoulder. Mateo slid to more firm footing with a hazmat suit draped over one arm. He jogged over to them, weaving through the ruins.

"I've got a perimeter watching for the black clouds. They'll radio if we need to take shelter. We've decided Lauren should get a suit," he said, barely glancing at the boys. "She's got medical training, so it's likely we'll need her out and ab—" His head snapped back to the boys, and his jaw dropped. He shook his head, and the suit slipped out of his hands as his arms went slack. "Ihaka…"

All four boys looked up at Mateo, and Coop frowned. "It's you," Coop said. "Ihaka's cousin."

Mateo dropped to his knees beside the corpse and laid a hand on a bloodied, unmoving chest. "I never wanted this," he said. "Why did you have to be so stubborn?"

The boy who'd called Oliver a traitor got to his knees and pushed Mateo. "Don't touch him! You hated him! We were his family, not you!"

Mateo stared at the boy and blinked back tears. "I never hated him," he said.

Coop positioned himself between the hostile boy and Mateo. "Leave him be, Danny," Coop said. "Ihaka is dead. Nothin' will change that."

Mateo looked back at Ihaka. "I never hated him," he said again. "I hated what he became, but…" Tears slid down his cheeks. "I read books to that boy when he was small. I took him for ice cream, and I tried to tell him he didn't have to be like his dad. I never hated him. I hoped… when this was over… that he would… that he…" Mateo trailed off and wiped away his tears.

"If you mean all that," Coop said, "then help us save whoever is left, mate."

"We can't trust them," Danny said. "Ihaka didn't!"

"Ihaka wasn't right about everything," Coop raised his voice and then looked down at the ground. "I don't like what Oliver did, but maybe he was right about some things." His entire body sagged. "Everything feels different now, mate." Coop looked back at Mateo. "Well? Are you the man Ihaka said you were? Or are you gonna help?"

"I don't know what Ihaka said about me, but…" Mateo stood up and walked back to the suit he'd dropped, picking it up. "Lauren," he said, turning and holding the suit out toward her. "You'll help us treat these boys?"

Lauren nodded. "Of course I will," she said, gently releasing the boy in her arms. "Let's start by getting these four to safety in one of the tents."

"Our medic, Nyree, will help, too." Mateo held out a hand to Coop, who took it and got to his feet.

"Wait," Minnie said, "do you know where Oliver went… Coop, wasn't it?"

Coop shook his head. "He took off with Etera and Will… but there was a *taniwha* after them."

"What in tarnation is that?" Minnie asked.
Mateo paled. "A black cloud," he said.
Minnie rubbed the back of her neck as she focused on keeping her breathing even. The last few minutes were like being on a roller coaster, and she was getting whiplash. Oliver wasn't under the rubble. He'd escaped, but he'd run from a swarm?
That could have killed him just as quick as a building comin' down on his head, she thought as her heart beat quickened.
"Etera knows some safe spots," Coop said. "They coulda made it to one of 'em, but..." He looked up and around at the ruins. He shrugged.
Minnie understood. Even if Oliver had outrun the swarm, he could have suffered the same fate as Ihaka.
"I've gotta tell Alex," Minnie said, "and Sophie, too, if Will is with Oliver. They might need our help out there."
She hobbled over to Alex as quickly as she could, leaving Samson with the boy who seemed to need his comfort. Alex, Sophie, Zara, Kai, and Blythe were methodically picking away at the pile. Before she could say anything, Sophie let out a cry and stumbled back, losing her footing. Alex was close enough to reach out and grab her hand to steady her.
Minnie froze at what Sophie had uncovered. A bruised and swollen hand protruded from the debris. It seemed everyone close enough to see it had frozen, too. And then, all at once, Alex was kneeling beside the hand, as was Sophie, and a sort of assembly line formed to uncover what lay beneath the wreckage.
Slowly but surely, a battered body was recovered, a corpse of a boy perhaps a year or two older than Oliver. Alex crawled down the side of the rubble to flatter ground and heaved while Sophie cried over the body that wasn't her son.
Minnie stepped up to Alex but spoke loud enough for Sophie to hear. "I don't think Oliver and Will are here. One of the boys said they left the factory, but..." She swallowed hard and averted her eyes. "... he also said a swarm was after them. It sounds to me like they escaped together, maybe used the swarm as a distraction."
Alex looked up at her and then over at Sophie. "I'll go find them," he said as he got to his feet, hand trembling as he wiped his mouth of vomit. He didn't look like he could whip a gnat, much less trek across the city where swarms roamed. Minnie was about to say so when Mateo spoke, startling her; she hadn't heard him approach.
"Wait," Mateo said. "If you can just wait, I can send out some men with you. But we have to set up here, first. I have people out trying to find a standing and secure structure nearby where we can more permanently set up shelter. The government had an initiative the last few months where some people qualified for these new earthquake-proof window films. Maybe someone near here had them installed." He gestured to the debris. "And there could be boys alive and trapped under there. We can't leave them. When a few of my men come back from scouting the area, I can send—"
"I'm going now," Alex said, and he looked over at Lauren. "I understand that everyone else is needed here for the rescue effort, but I'm going to find my son."
Sophie, still sniffling, climbed down the rubble. "I'll go, too. I can—"
"No," Alex said gently. "I'm vaccinated. You're not. It's less dangerous for me. If your son is out there, I swear to you, I'll do everything I can to bring him back."
Sophie shook her head, clearly about to protest, when Mateo said, "He's right, Sophie. You can help Lauren and Nyree care for these boys."
The woman glanced at the city through a broken window in a still-standing wall. She nodded, a pained expression on her face. She didn't say anything as she hugged her middle and crouched low, her face paling even further.
"Alex," Minnie said, "I thought this vaccination wasn't tested against a swarm. If you're out there on your own—"
"I've run from swarms before," Alex said, "and if I do encounter one, if I can't run, at least we will know if the vaccine works against a high viral load."
Minnie's stomach flipped as though it belonged to an acrobat, not a woman about as old as Methuselah himself.
Mateo shook his head. "You shouldn't go alone, and I can't spare—"
"I don't need anything from you," Alex said, and Minnie's heart skipped when he said, "I don't need anything from anyone. All I need is my son."
Mateo unclipped his own radio and held it out. "At least take one of these," he said.
Alex nodded, his jaw set as he took the radio. "I'm taking three vials of the DV-10 treatment from the portable fridge," he said. "If there are three kids out there, I might need them." He strode away without waiting for Mateo to reply, toward the place he'd climbed over the debris in the first place. Minnie couldn't move as everyone else seemed to accept the new plan. They all got to work on what needed to be done there, at the site of the factory. All animosity had vanished in the face of tragedy, and there *was* a lot to do. But Alex's words were like a poker to Minnie's ribs. What had the look on his face meant when he'd said he didn't need anyone's help?
He's sayin' I've done enough helpin', she thought. *He's sayin' if you want somethin' done right, you gotta do it yourself.* Her eyes blurred from tears. Alex had the tendency to go it alone; he always asked for help as a last resort, or he used to. She'd thought they'd grown past that.
When the boys were moved, Samson returned to Minnie's side. He nudged her hand with his nose as if to ask, "What do we do now?" Did they let Alex go? Did they sit back and help at the factory while Oliver was out there, needing their help?
Hurt was edged out by pure irritation. "No," Minnie said out loud, though no one was listening to her. "That ain't who we are." She balled her hands into fists at her sides and marched after Alex, Samson faithfully at her side. He was going to get her help whether he liked it or not.

Chapter 34

Oliver Roman, Alexander Roman, and Minnie Stevens

Oliver carefully poked at the wall of debris surrounding the metal work table, looking for more materials that could burn and make smoke. It was mostly stone and metal, but he'd made a small pile of wood chips, most no thicker than his pinky finger. Larger pieces of wood, such as broken beams, were too large to remove from the pile. The last thing Oliver wanted was to make the fragile walls collapse in on them.

Will was curled up next to the long, thin hole which was their only access to the world outside their dark hole. Etera went in and out of consciousness; when he'd woken last, he'd mentioned he couldn't feel his leg where it had been pinned beneath the wreckage. Oliver was pretty sure that wasn't good, even if it did mean Etera wasn't in much pain.

Cheeks sore from blowing into the duck call, Oliver sat in the temporary silence. He would take up making noise again, but they had to take breaks to listen. In the silence, they could hopefully hear a swarm before it was upon them. They could burn what little materials they'd managed to gather, and that, along with the lavender-soaked t-shirt, would mask their scent and repel the swarm. Hopefully. Maybe.

Please let this work, Oliver prayed.

His stomach growled and twisted. It had been too long since he'd last eaten something. His tongue was dry against the roof of his mouth, too, and he had to work it back and forth to generate some moisture. The effort wasn't enough. He needed water.

The duck call was small in his hand. It seemed such an insignificant tool. For his life to depend on someone hearing its call seemed insane. Hopeless, even. Was that hole big enough for sound to carry through it and out into the city? He didn't know. All he knew was he had to try.

We don't give up, Oliver thought. Dad never gives up. Neither does Minnie or Lauren. Even Samson keeps going when things are hard.

Thoughts of Samson lifted his spirits. If Minnie brought him with her, Oliver's duck call was more likely to be heard.

Samson would know it was me, wouldn't he? Oliver decided to believe the dog would understand. Some people questioned just how intelligent canines were, but not Oliver. He'd seen Samson do incredible things, respond in just the right ways. That dog understood more than any of them realized; Oliver was sure of it.

"Hear anything?" Oliver whispered.

"Nah," Will said.

Oliver gathered his pile of wood chips in his hands and held them out. "Put this in the hole," he said. "If we hear the swarm, light it on fire along with the pack of cards. We can gently blow the smoke outside."

Will licked his lips, his brow furrowed. He'd questioned Oliver many times about their only line of defense, but he didn't do so again. He simply nodded and turned his head to peer out. "Try the duck call again," he said.

Oliver brought the tool to his lips and blew, his cheeks puffing out, and the sound akin to a duck's quacking filled the air. He got a few good, long seconds of sound before he had to take in another deep breath, but before he could put his lips back to the mouthpiece, Will's eyes went wide and he held up a hand.

"Wait," Will whispered urgently. "What's that?"

Oliver froze with the tool still raised, his lips still millimeters from it. A dull, distant thrum distinguished itself in the silence. With it, Oliver's pulse throbbed at his temples. Every inch of his body prickled, every nerve was set on edge. The light streaming through the hole seemed to burn where it fell in a line across his raised forearms.

The droning hum sent vibrations through the very air.

A swarm was closing in on their prison.

Etera coughed, the sound jolting Oliver out of his shock. "Quick," Oliver shouted, "Will, light the fire!"

Will plucked the Zippo from the lip of the hole and flicked his thumb across the flint wheel. "It's not working!"

Oliver scrambled over Etera who was mumbling, sweaty head rolling from side to side in delirium. "Give it to me, then!"

He grabbed at the lighter but knocked it to the ground instead. It fell into shadow. Hands shaking, Oliver frantically felt around on the ground. Will did the same, cursing and whimpering in turn. Cool, hard metal beneath his fingertips made Oliver cry out in relief as he grasped the lighter and brought it up to eye level.

"Found it," Oliver said.

Will shoved forward the pack of cards. "Light them all!" he shouted.

Tiny grooves of metal dug into Oliver's thumb as he took a turn at the flint wheel. A single flame burst into existence, defying the dark. It took too long for the cards to burn blue and curl black, but the second they did, Will set them on the concrete edge of the opening and started to blow the smoke outward.

Oliver grabbed a long splinter from the pile of wood chips, set it aflame, and lit the tiny pyre. He, too, directed the smoke into the open air outside the confines of their dusty, dirty dungeon. The scent of lavender wafted in the air along with the growing smell of smoke. When Oliver took a breath, a breeze blew fumes from the cards back at them; it stung his eyes and scorched his throat, but he didn't pull away. He kept directing the smoke outward the best he could.

Through the opening that was no more than a long fissure in the debris, the swarm came into view. It was a black cloud of death. It was the *taniwha*, the monster of childhood stories. Though it was across the street and did not turn its ugly head toward them, it released spikes of fear that penetrated Oliver's chest and made his attempts at directing the smoke almost impossible. Breathing induced sharp pain. Staying there, where he could see the writhing monstrosity, went against every instinct.

Will cried out and ducked, covering his head. Oliver didn't take the time to yell at him to keep blowing the smoke outward. He centered himself between the wood and the cards and kept at it.

The *taniwha* didn't stop, but Oliver kept vigil, kept the smoke going long after it was out of sight, until the materials were burned away and there was nothing left. Exhausted, lungs burning, throat dry and pained as if he'd swallowed a thousand needles, Oliver sat back and wiped sweat from his brow.

He leaned against the wall of debris. Will was crying. Etera was still mumbling incoherent words. There was nothing left to burn. If the swarm returned anytime soon, he wasn't sure they'd be so lucky. Oliver reached for the duck call and held it to his chest.

* * *

Alex could think of nothing but his son. He'd taken three doses of the treatment in a small, insulated bag that had been fixed to the outside of the portable fridge, included for situations such as the one he was in, where it would be impractical to lug the cooler-like fridge along.

The feel of the bag in his hand only gave him images of Oliver with growing welts and bulging eyes. His thoughts continued to go down a dark path as his worst fears dulled the sounds around him. The noise of his own breathing combined with his heartbeat set a quick rhythm that determined his pace.

Everything he'd done since the World's Fair had been for Oliver. *He has to be alive,* Alex thought. Going on without him seemed ludicrous. What would he be fighting for?

As he swept the streets for signs of his son with blurred vision, Oliver wasn't the only person on his mind; his wife's face haunted him. "Take care of Ollie," she'd said, right before she had pushed herself over the edge of that damned Ferris Wheel pod, after she'd voiced the truth Alex had wanted so badly to be a lie. "I'm… already… dead."

Naomi had been right; Alex wouldn't have been able to save her. She'd accepted death so that he could focus on protecting their son, and then, he'd gone off and left Oliver on an entirely different continent.

What have I done? I'm so sorry, Naomi…

The thought overwhelmed him, consumed him.

And then he turned a corner, and came within inches of a swarm.

It loomed above him, stretched out into the street, its buzz deafening. He hadn't heard it. The sight of it, the sudden onslaught of sound, made him suck in sharply and go rigid. But only for a moment.

Alex took two steps backward as a tendril reached for him, as its tip touched him, as tiny bringers of death alighted on his arm. He ran. He ran as hard as he could, but every footfall was heavier than the last as his skin was coated with a blanket of black. The sting set in as he swept away insects, his headlong run thrown off by his frantic movements.

Ahead, the sun glinted off a pool of water, a lake or a pond, small but sufficient. He pushed hard toward it, desperate. If it had been fire, he would have leapt into it without hesitation. As it was, he dropped the insulated bag and Mateo's radio in the grass and flung himself into the water, the cool liquid embrace washing away the swarm from his skin. Alex swam downward and grasped in the murky depths for something to hold on to, something to keep him from resurfacing too soon.

A stone on the bottom offered purchase, most of it buried in mud, part of it jutting out into the water. He tried to grasp it at first, but his fingers wouldn't bend; they were swelling and stiff. But the swarm would surely still be waiting for him in open air, and so he hugged the rock instead. His head started to pound. Pressure built behind his eyes. He wanted to scream as pain lanced through his body, but to do so would force him to return to the surface, and that could mean his end. Alex squeezed his eyes shut, determined to endure for as long as he could, praying he hadn't plunged himself into a watery grave.

* * *

"Sorry, boy," Minnie closed Samson inside the bathroom of a home with the windows shattered and the rooftop half caved-in. It was the closest safe spot she could find in a hurry.

She hadn't planned it, hadn't wanted it, but what she needed to do had crystalized when, from a distance, she'd seen the shape of a running man at the front of a swarm heading for a large pond. Minnie had known what Alex was doing the second she saw him, and she also knew that the swarm might linger for as long as he could hold his breath.

Not on her watch.

He was vaccinated. That meant he might survive whatever damage the swarm had already done. But he was running for a reason. That vaccine hadn't been tested against a swarm, and besides, no vaccine was ever one hundred percent effective. Minnie was no expert, but she knew that, at least.

The intact bathroom had stood erect in the debris like a beacon, and Samson was too good and too loyal. She couldn't let him follow her. "Not this time," Minnie said as she backed away from the door. Samson whined at her from the other side. "I love you, too."

The swarms tended to move on after a good feeding, and if it was between her and Alex, well… she'd lived her life. She'd seen her daughter safe. Love had been no stranger to Minnie Stevens. What more could a good Southern gal ask?

She turned her back on the door, wove through the debris, and jogged with everything she had straight for the maw of the beast.

* * *

When he started to feel too light, like a feather in a breeze, and he could no longer hold on or hold his breath, Alex pushed off the rock. His face broke the surface first, the air cold on his wet skin, and he sucked in a deep breath. Blinking away moisture, his eyes stinging from holding them open under water, he squinted in the daylight as he enjoyed the simple act of breathing while preparing himself for another dive should he meet the swarm again.

But the air around the pond was clear. At least, as far as he could see. In the near distance, things blurred. Shapes of buildings, debris, and vehicles were recognizable if not clear, though. He slowly turned in the water, ripples bubbling out from him in all directions as he scanned the area. A dark shape flew before the buildings, a bird perhaps.

If the swarm was near, I would be able to see its shape. I'd be able to hear it… wouldn't I?

He hadn't heard it before. He'd been so preoccupied, so engrossed in guilt and worry. Alex cleared his mind the best he could.

"Focus," he said out loud, his words garbled a bit by bloated lips.

There was a distant buzzing, but it *was* distant.

Alex's body grew heavier by the second. If he stayed in the water much longer, he wasn't sure he'd be able to pull himself out of it.

I have to try to keep going, he thought. *Maybe I can find shelter nearby so that I can recover.* The possibility, the formulation of some sort of plan, gave Alex some hope.

It was no easy feat, swimming to the edge of the pond. His hands were swollen and numb. Welts covered his arms, and from the way the skin around his mouth pulled and his eyes refused to open any wider, he imagined his face didn't look much better.

The pond's bottom dropped off steeply from the shoreline to a depth of seven feet or so. Alex kicked his way over to the shore—his legs fared better in the onslaught—and heaved his arms onto dry land, hands digging into grass and dirt.

The walkie talkie and the insulated bag lay a yard from the farthest point he could reach. The sight of them spurred him on despite his growing fatigue and the way his vision blurred; Oliver was still out there. And one of those treatments would help mitigate any viral overload Alex's body was experiencing despite the vaccine.

The vaccine is working though, Alex thought as he pulled and struggled with inflamed hands and arms to haul his body out of the water. He lifted his leg and hooked his foot on the shore to help. *If it wasn't working, I'd be dead or dying.*

Of course, he could still be dying, but at least his body seemed to be pushing back. His systems hadn't shut down, and while a mild pressure pushed at the back of his eyes, his head throbbed, and his stomach twisted, he was still functioning.

As he managed to hoist himself all the way out of the water and roll onto firm ground, Alex was actually grateful for the numbness where the swarm had done its worst.

When the numbness wears off, this isn't going to be fun, Alex thought.

He groaned as he sat up and reached for the insulated bag. Fingers fumbling with the zipper, it took three times as long as it should have to open the thing, but he eventually managed it. Grasping one vial was even harder. His eyes watered as he worked his fingers, bending them despite how they resisted. Welts cracked and sharp pain overcame dulled nerves to deliver punishment for forcing his fingers to hold on to the vial until he'd plunged the needle into his upper arm.

Alex breathed out slowly. His body begged him to lay in the grass for a little while. Instead, with walkie talkie and insulated bag in hand, he forced himself to his knees, and then to his feet. The world spun for a moment, but it settled quickly enough for Alex to brave a few steps forward.

Ahead, far past the point where his vision was clear, a blackness like a living stain on the building behind it crept around a corner and out of sight.

Odd, he thought, though he wasn't about to complain. Was the swarm sluggish? They hadn't fed on him enough to produce that lethargic creeping. The swarm certainly hadn't been sluggish when it had gone after him. *Don't overthink it. Just keep moving.*

But move where? His heart told him to keep looking for Oliver, but his head screamed at him to recover, to radio Mateo to see if some of the men he'd sent out had come back yet. Alex closed swollen eyes and swayed on his feet.

How could I have been so stupid?

His mistakes added up before him like a major bill he wasn't sure he could pay: letting his anger and frustration and fear overwhelm him; striding through the streets so carelessly in his search; going it alone simply because he couldn't stand to do nothing while the well-being of his son was in question.

Alex opened his eyes. He had to recover. What good was he to Oliver when he could barely stand? He slid his feet forward, soles of his shoes scuffing the grass and then scraping asphalt. He clipped the walkie talkie to the collar of his soaked shirt so that he wouldn't have to hold it, planning to radio Mateo.

But a shape that shouldn't be there emerged from the blurry path ahead. Alex frowned and kept moving forward as a soft moan came from it. A human voice, the words indistinguishable, and yet the pitch, the sound familiar.

Alex lurched forward. "Minnie!" He rushed to her and dropped beside her, the hard ground biting his knees. Minnie convulsed and coughed, blood coating her swollen lips. "What are you doing out here?"

Pushing through the pain once more, he retrieved a vial of DV-10 treatment. His vision blurred for a different reason as salty tears sprung up.

"Don't…" Minnie struggled with her words but still managed to attach a chastising tone. "… fuss over… me."

"Why didn't you take shelter?" The treatment had already started to reduce some of his swelling. He cried out in frustration as he worked to remove the cap from the second vial.

"You… ain't no… fish, dagnabbit." She closed her eyes and grimaced in pain.

Alex pinched Minnie's arm and tried to focus as he plunged the needle into her flesh. He pushed the plunger. "You saw me?" He pulled back as it dawned on him: the way the swarm had been creeping away… "You used yourself as bait." It wasn't a question. He looked back at the pond. If he'd come up to find the swarm, he would have dove once more. There wouldn't have been any other choice. "And I would have drowned."

"Tell Lauren—" A violent cough cut her off.

"Lauren!" Alex shook his head. "You're going to tell her yourself. Hang in there." He pressed the button on the walkie talkie. "Hello? Hello?"

"Alex?" It was Mateo. "Did you find them? Did you find Oliver and Will?"

"Not yet. Minnie came after me. We… there was a swarm, and… Minnie is down. I'm affected too, but I got away before they could finish the job. I've given Minnie a dose of our treatment. I—"

"Where are you?" Lauren's voice, urgent.

Alex concentrated, trying to remember how he'd gotten to where he was. "Five blocks toward the mall… there's a park with a pond."

"Mateo knows where it is," Lauren said. "I'm on my way, in a suit. Stay with her, Alex."

As he pressed the button to respond, however, a sound made Alex pause, made his breath hitch. It was far off, but he'd know it anywhere: a duck call. Oliver's duck call.

"I hear him," Alex said into the speaker. "I hear Oliver." And if he was using the duck call, it could only mean one thing. "I think he's in trouble, and that swarm…"

"Go…" Minnie said weakly.

"Damn it," Lauren said over the speaker, her voice wavering. "Go get him, Alex. Tell us where you are going. We're all coming… Walter, Zara, all of us."

All of us.

His family was coming.

"I love you, Minnie," Alex said.

Minnie managed a small nod. "Go…" she rasped through bloodied lips.

A sob escaped him as he struggled to his feet once more. He staggered toward the sound of the duck call. Slowly, painfully, he fought for the next step that would bring him closer to his son, and then the next and the next. Oliver's call drew him onward.

Chapter 35

Alexander Roman and Oliver Roman

Sunlight lanced Alex's eyes and sent his temples to throbbing as he pushed himself to keep going. Vision still blurred but not getting worse, he staggered through the Christchurch neighborhood, praying he was going in the right direction. Numbness had begun to subside in his arms and neck and face where the swarm had the most access to his body; it was replaced with agony. The surface of his skin burned, especially where it stretched to accommodate welts. The sensation of blistering heat dissipated into a million pinpricks piercing his muscles, which twitched and ached under the onslaught of pain. Blood dripped from his nose, coating his lips, leaving the taste of copper on his tongue.

The sound of the duck call which birthed the hope that Oliver was alive overpowered the need to lay down and let the disease run its course. The vaccination had clearly not been enough to prevent sickness after a viral overload of DV-10, but there was still the possibility that it, combined with the treatment, would give Alex a shot at survival.

Either way, he was determined to find Oliver and ensure his son lived.

He was close. The sound seemed just around the next corner. He looked up at the street sign and pressed the button to speak to Lauren, giving her a quick update about his route. Walter answered.

"We're on our way," Walter said. He sounded slightly out of breath.

Alex licked his lips and regretted it, coming away with the taste of blood. "Minnie?" he asked, voice raspy.

"Lauren brought a tent to Minnie's location," Walter said. "Stella and I borrowed some suits and moved her into it for some shelter. I told Lauren she'd need to wear a suit at all times and only approach her mother when absolutely necessary. Just because she's vaccinated doesn't mean she's totally in the clear."

"I bet Lauren didn't like that," Alex said as he approached the next intersection and turned right toward the sound. "She knows your right, but… it's got to be hard not to be with Minnie right now."

"Her mother convinced her with some… colorful words… something about if Lauren got sick by treating her, Minnie would… knot her tail?" Walter let out a soft chuckle. "I don't know what that means exactly, but Lauren did."

"Minnie is speaking that clearly?" Alex asked, a bit surprised. He'd noticed a marked improvement in his own ability to speak and move after administering the treatment, but he'd been vaccinated.

"Yes," Walter said. "She said you gave her something… the treatment, right?"

"Yeah," Alex said as he stopped in the middle of the road. The sound was so close. It echoed all around him. "That means the treatment does something against viral overload."

"I know," Walter said, "it's incredible. We should be at your location soon, okay? Have you found Oliver?"

"Not yet." Alex frowned. "How are you almost here already?"

"Mateo let us borrow one of the pedal pubs."

Alex nodded, though no one could see him. That explained Walter's labored breathing. "I need some quiet on this channel," he said. "I'm close, and I need to pinpoint the sound of the duck call."

There was no reply. Alex slowly turned in a circle. The buildings were fuzzy, though the shapes of them clearly indicated most were damaged or collapsed completely. And then the duck call stopped.

"No!" he whispered. "Where are you?" He doubted his ability to shout, but he tried anyway.

"Oliver!" His voice cracked, there was blood at the back of his throat, and a coughing fit racked his body.

But when he gathered himself back together, a set of faint voices shouted, "Hello! We're here! We're over here!"

Alex stumbled forward, his head swimming from the coughing fit. He was going in the right direction, but he couldn't distinguish details until he was within yards of a thing. The closer he got to the voices, the clearer they became, and when a skinny arm stuck through a small hole in a pile of debris, Alex sucked in a breath, squinting and praying that he wasn't hallucinating.

"Oliver?" Alex said it as loud as he could.

"I'm here!" The hand frantically waved about.

Alex took three steps forward and raised a hand toward his son's, but that swollen, cracked, bleeding, welted hand made him stop. He swallowed hard and pushed down the desire to come closer. The others were almost there. It would be safer if he allowed them to dig Oliver out, and besides, if he came within his son's view, Oliver would see his condition.

No need to frighten him while he's still trapped. He's got enough to deal with, Alex thought.

"Bud," Alex said, "it's me. It's Dad."

"Dad?" The word was high-pitched, followed by a sob. Oliver's voice shook as he continued, "Dad, you're back! You made it! "

"Walter and the others are coming to help," Alex said, "but I'm… hurt. I came to look for you, and I would dig you out myself if I had to, but…" He looked over his shoulder as the noise of plastic in a light breeze and the kiss of wheels against pavement made themselves known.

"You're hurt?" Oliver sniffled between words. "How bad?"

"I'll be fine," Alex said, hoping he wasn't lying. "The important thing right now is that we get you out of there. Are you okay?"

"I'm not hurt," Oliver said, "but Etera is."

"Okay," Alex said. "We're going to get you out of here."

"Is my mum out there?" An unfamiliar, accented voice asked.

"Are you Sophie's son, Will?" Alex asked.

"Yes," he said. "She okay? Why isn't she here?"

"She's okay, but she's not with me. She's been searching for you, though, and it's clear to me that she loves you more than anything else," Alex said. The pedal pub pulled up behind him. "We're going to get all three of you out of there. Just hang on."

Walter, Zara, Lizzy, Kai, Blythe, Stella, and Candice disembarked along with Sophie. Walter stepped down first, stopping cold at the sight of Alex. The others did the same, and it seemed Alex had an entire conversation with them in just a look.

"You look terrible," Walter said.

"We've all seen worse." Alex nodded back to the pile of debris before meeting the eyes of each of them. "Thank you," he said as he stepped back, moving far away. Half of them were unvaccinated, and his body was a viral madhouse. No matter how much he wanted to be the one to remove every brick, it was safer for Oliver and for them if he watched from afar.

He settled on the ground, leaning against part of a wall that only came up to his shoulders, but he did not rest. He prayed hard as every piece of debris was moved, thankful that whatever structure they had been in had been small. The stress on his body the past hours came to a head when he stopped moving, exhaustion saturating every inch of him. But he could not let that exhaustion win, not until he saw Oliver free and safe.

* * *

Oliver and Will huddled on either side of Etera's head at the center of the small, clear space beneath the metal worktable. Thumps and bumps and the scraping of brick against brick made an odd song of hope outside, though it was tinted with worry for his dad.

Etera moaned. Sweat saturated his shirt and beaded all over his face. His eyes fluttered open after a long nap. He looked up at Oliver and Will. "Space would be nice, mates," he said. "I don't wanna be smothered *and* crushed."

Oliver gave him half a smile, grateful that he was awake and making sense. "We're being rescued," he said. "My family and friends are out there digging us out."

"Sweet as," Etera said weakly.

"I don't know," Will said. "They're taking their time."

"They don't want the debris to collapse in on us any more than it has," Oliver said.

Etera coughed. "I woulda thought they'd leave you to rot," he said.

Oliver furrowed his brow. "What? Why?"

"That's the way it is," Etera said. "I thought they'd turn us away at the mall, to be honest. Thought we'd be livin' on our own, maybe take up a house near the beach."

Our lives have been very different, Oliver thought. Of course, he'd always known that, but sometimes, Etera's assumptions made it very clear.

"My family and friends aren't like that," he said. "They love me even when I make mistakes."

"My mum, too," Will said. "I miss her."

Etera gave them a little shrug. "Must be nice. Don't bet on Mateo bein' like that, though, mates."

"My dad is out there," Oliver said. "We're not staying here."

"Your dad?" Etera grinned. "Came back from Antarctica, did he?"

Oliver nodded, though he couldn't muster enthusiasm for all the worry. "He's hurt, though, he said. Hurt enough not to be helping. I think that means it's bad."

The modicum of light from the hole in the debris widened, and Oliver snapped his head up to see part of a face. It was Will's mom. She checked on them periodically, but she'd not widened the hole before.

"Boys, it's coming along. We have a lot of the troublesome debris moved so that we can start widening this hole without collapsing anything," Sophie said. "Will, hon... are you okay?"

Will nodded and reached out his hand. His mother took it, and in that moment, Will was more like a little boy than he'd ever been to Oliver. It was comforting because Oliver didn't feel so grown up anymore; it seemed he wasn't the only one.

"Keep on, Willie," she said. "It won't be long, now."

"What about Etera?" Oliver asked as another piece was removed and the hole became almost big enough to crawl through. "He's still pinned. He won't be able to climb out that way."

Walter's face appeared then beside Sophie's as the others continued to remove debris. "We'll work on that, too," he said. "But let's get you two out first." He straightened, and he and Sophie lifted a final piece of debris up and away.

Will crawled over as his mother gestured for him to come, and Walter reached into the hole and helped pull him out.

"Let's go, Oliver," Walter said, bending low and sticking out his hand toward him.

Oliver looked down at Etera, the boy who'd stuck by him, helped him save Will. He shook his head. "I can't leave my friend alone."

"Don't be stupid," Etera said. "Go on."

"No." Oliver looked up at Walter. "I'm staying with him."

Walter took a deep breath and nodded slowly, a slight smile on his lips. "You're a lot like your dad."

"Thanks," Oliver said, his chest swelling with pride.

"All right, then," he said. "It'll be a while longer. We do have a tarp to throw over this hole if a swarm comes near. If that happens, we'll secure the tarp and shelter in the pedal pub or the tent we brought."

"Got it," Oliver said, nodding to indicate he understood.

"You sure you don't want to go?" Etera asked.

"I'm sure, bro," Oliver said, putting a bad Kiwi accent on the last word.

Etera winced. "I'm in enough pain, mate. Don't do that."

Oliver laughed as the sounds of his friends and family working to free him continued. The lighthearted moment was a balm to his heart, but it didn't last nearly long enough. He hadn't wanted to leave Etera—that much was true—but he was also afraid. No one would give him answers to too many questions. How bad off was his dad? Where were Minnie, Lauren, and Samson? Fear that the answers would crush him as effectively as caved-in debris wrapped its tendrils around his heart and constricted his throat if he dwelled on the possibilities too much. He was stuck in the in-between, in the unknown, and he wasn't so sure he wanted to leave.

* * *

Alex focused on two things and two things only. That was all the capacity he had.

The first was breathing. He breathed in deeply and let the air out slowly. Continuing required him to ignore the way his lungs still felt… hollow, as if the air around him was too thin, as if he'd barely sucked in a whisp of oxygen. But if he stopped trying, he wasn't sure he would keep taking in air at all.

The second was the growing hole and the ever-dwindling debris pile. Will had come out, but Oliver was nowhere to be seen. A tiny spark in the depths of Alex's mind could still conjure panic at the thought of why that would be.

Time was strange in the state he found himself in as he leaned back against that portion of a wall. Brick and wood and broken plaster supported his left side, the remainder of the wall his back. It didn't matter that his lounge chair made up of debris poked him in odd places or that his neck was at a bad angle. Whether he'd been there for an hour or half the day, he couldn't tell. Seconds dragged by, painstakingly giving way to minutes, but at the same time, it all blurred together in his mind.

His sight had gotten better, even if his exhaustion had increased a hundredfold.

Is that all this is? Complete and utter exhaustion?

Letting his thoughts wander made his eyes droop.

No. Concentrate.

Alex redoubled his efforts and fell back into the cycle of breathing and watching. He didn't notice Stella until she knelt a few yards away, right in front of him, obscuring his line of vision.

"Oliver's friend is stuck until we can dig him out," Stella said. "He won't come out until the other kid is rescued."

Her words processed slowly, but when he understood, he licked his lips and managed a single nod of his head.

"He's a good kid," Stella said.

He offered her the best smile he could muster.

"You look terrible," she said.

Alex just kept on breathing. He could bend his fingers. Swelling was decreasing. He was no longer actively bleeding from his ears and nose, and his throbbing headache had decreased to a mind-numbing pressure. That was all good.

I'll live, he thought. I have to live.

"I think…" A concerned look fell over Stella's face, and she glanced over her shoulder. "I think we should get you out of here, maybe into a tent where your son won't be able to see you like this."

Again, the meaning behind her words was like trying to make sense of an abstract painting. The longer he thought about it, the more a picture formed in his mind of what she'd said. Stella stood up, lips pursed, brow furrowed. She turned away before Alex could object… or, before he could attempt an objection.

I just want to see him, he thought, eyes focusing back on the growing hole.

* * *

Oliver held Etera's head in his hands, sweaty grime from Etera's hair coating his skin. Walter and Blythe worked together with Oliver to slowly and carefully lift Etera up and out of the rubble. It was as if his heart had stopped and his lungs frozen as Oliver did his best not to jostle Etera the wrong way. They had splinted both legs and wrapped support around his neck, but the boy seemed so fragile and weak.

"They're going to take care of you," Oliver said as he eased from his knees to his feet and transferred control of Etera's head to a woman named Stella as Walter and Blythe continued backing out, each man supporting one side of Etera's body. The boy had passed out again, but the words of assurance still seemed appropriate, even necessary.

Letting others take control injected relief into Oliver's veins, and he slumped against the debris, rubbing the back of his neck as he looked back inside the dark space beneath the work table. Part of the small workshop was left standing, two walls with no ceiling. Mere seconds after climbing out of the hole, however, an inner voice shouted a word that gave him a dose of adrenaline: *Dad!*

Oliver stood too quickly, dizziness and nausea overwhelming him. He wobbled on his feet, arms spreading to help him keep his balance.

Candice, who was approaching with a water bottle, squeaked in alarm and reached out for him, steadying him with a hand on his arm.

"Careful," she said. "You've been through a lot."

Oliver didn't care about that. "Where's Dad?"

"We had to move him," Candice said, pointing to a tent set apart from everyone else.

Oliver stumbled over debris to the street.

"Wait!" Candice said.

But he took several hurried steps in that direction before Zara and Kai stepped in front of him and held out their hands. Lizzy stood to the side with furrowed brow.

"Whoa, dude," Kai said. "You can't go in there."

Those words hit Oliver in the gut and twisted his insides. "Why not?"

"Your dad was attacked by a swarm," Zara said.

"No," Oliver said, shaking his head as hot tears sprung to his eyes.

Candice came up beside him and put a hand on his shoulder. "He's been vaccinated," she said, "and given a new treatment on top of that. Right now, there's a good chance he's going to make it."

Oliver tried to dry his tears with dirty hands, but all he accomplished was smudging more grime onto his face. The layer of soot and dust made his eyes itch and water even more.

"I want to see him," Oliver said.

"We're sorry." Zara knelt in front of him. "You just… you can't."

Oliver hugged his middle, feeling more alone than when he'd been locked in the cage back at the factory. "Where are Minnie and Lauren and Samson?" he asked as tears rolled down his cheeks. He was among friends, but at that moment, he needed family.

Candice, Zara, Lizzy, and Kai exchanged looks that mirrored the ones they'd had before telling Oliver what had happened to his dad. Spots appeared at the edges of Oliver's vision, and his chest was tight.

"The same swarm got Minnie. She's been given the treatment, too," Zara said. "Lauren and Samson are both okay. It seems…" She swallowed hard and tears brimmed her eyes. "It seems Minnie redirected the swarm to save your father. He wasn't exposed to the swarm as long as she was."

Oliver's knees hit the ground before he knew what was happening. Pavement bit through the thin threads of what remained of his pants, and a sharp pain shot up both thighs at the impact. "It's all my fault," he said, leaning forward, hands flat on the ground. He couldn't breathe. All he could think was that same thing over and over: *it's all my fault.*

"No," Zara said, sidling up next to him and pulling him into a hug. "It's not your fault. The whole world is messed up right now, Oliver."

Candice knelt beside them both, as did Kai.

"Neither your father nor Minnie think this is your fault," Candice said. "The earthquake, the swarm, the buildings collapsing… the whole city is a mess."

A sob escaped Oliver. "I never should have left the mall," he said.

Kai put a hand on Oliver's shoulder. "Everyone makes mistakes, Oliver. That doesn't mean what happened to your dad and to Minnie is your fault. To say that leaving the mall caused this to happen is a false equivalency."

"What Kai means," Zara said, "is that your actions did not naturally lead to what happened. If you'd chosen a different path, who knows what could have happened."

"They're right, Oliver," Candice said. "You can't change the past, but you can focus on the good, even in terrible situations like this. What happened was love on display. Your father loves you, and he was willing to do whatever it took to get to you. Minnie loves your father, and she loves you, too. She wasn't about to sit aside and let either of you get hurt."

Lizzy's small voice added, "I know what it is to make mistakes, Oliver. But I also know the people who love you—your dad and Minnie, especially—wouldn't want you to hold on to guilt. They made choices, too. You didn't make your father or Minnie do anything."

"And besides," Kai said, "we don't know what's going to happen."

The spots in Oliver's vision got bigger as he sobbed. Zara, Kai, Lizzy, and Candice surrounded him and stayed with him until he could no longer make a sound, until exhaustion left him unable to move, until his cries had left his throat raw, until he could keep his eyes open no longer. There was the sensation of someone big and strong picking him up off the ground right before Oliver's consciousness slipped into dreams. And there, it was his dad who carried him, with Minnie and Lauren walking on either side and Samson at their feet.

Chapter 36

Stella Sharpe

It was Stella's turn to hold it together like Candice and Lauren had held it together for her back in Antarctica. Those two women—and Alex, too—hadn't given up on her. They'd proven to her that hope was worth it, and Stella wasn't ready to give up so soon after finding a way to hold on to it.

The events of the past few days were horrific. It certainly hadn't been the homecoming she'd envisioned: an earthquake followed by finding dead children in a factory; the swarm that had attacked Alex and Minnie; the rescue of Oliver only to find his friend on the brink of death, legs crushed.

It had taken a day to find permanent shelter. As it turned out, the airport had built a terminal that seemed impervious to earthquakes, complete with the shatter-proof window film that Mateo had mentioned. Or the building had survived out of pure luck. Stella didn't know much about infrastructure and earthquakes. Either way, they were safe. That was all she cared about.

The locals swore the earthquake was the largest one in recent history, even worse than 2011, whatever that meant. Apparently that one had rocked the city, too. Stella had been a little girl sipping lemonade on her grandma's porch swing in 2011, halfway around the world, of course.

Crazy where a few decades can take you, Stella thought.

She missed relaxing on porch swings and sipping lemonade. The little things that the apocalypse took from her were going to be the hardest to get used to. Some of it she'd not had at McMurdo Station, but even there, things like specialty coffees and fully stocked grocery stores had been waiting for her back at home. All of that was just gone.

At least for now. Stella sighed to herself as she walked the length of the terminal with two mugs of steaming hot tea Nyree had given her for Candice and Lauren.

The terminal wasn't nearly as nice as the mall had been, from what Stella gathered. She'd not been there, but others had described it to her, mostly in terms of how the terminal fell short. There were a few shops and a restaurant in the terminal, including bathrooms. However, there weren't enough spaces to create personal homes for individuals and families. Plans were already being made for creating a community center in the restaurant, and two shops were being reserved for a classroom and a clinic.

Stella passed groups of people working on removing the bolted-down chairs all along the terminal. To her left, three men and a teen boy with bruises and cuts on his face and arms worked together. The teen was on his knees with a wrench, working a bolt that seemed particularly stubborn. The wrench slipped as Stella was coming up on the group, and the boy's hand punched the chair's sturdy metal leg. He pulled back, and as he let out a string of curses, threw the wrench across the terminal, a mere foot or two in front of Stella.

She paused and raised her eyebrows at the teen, who was still cursing as he shook his hand. But she didn't have to say a word. One of the men stood and crossed his arms, frowning down at the teen.

"Oi! Maybe that sort of thing was acceptable at the factory, but not here, mate." The man pointed at the wrench on the floor across the room. "Go on. Go get it. And apologize to the lady." He gestured to Stella.

The boy's mouth dropped open, and his face wrinkled in a flash of fury until he met the man's eyes. Then, he sighed loudly and got to his feet while muttering under his breath. On his way to the wrench, he glanced at Stella. "Sorry," he said, not bothering to wait for a reply. He grabbed the wrench and walked back to the group where all three men were staring him down, arms crossed. The boy's arms sagged, and he turned back to Stella. "I'm real sorry," he said. "I wasn't aimin' for ya or nothin'."

Stella quirked an eyebrow but nodded. "Forgiven," she said. "I've thrown a few wrenches myself."

He looked back at the men, and one of them gave him a satisfied nod while the others welcomed him back into the fold to start working on removing the chair again.

"He's not quite civilized yet," one of them said, "but he's well on his way." He nodded at her as if to thank her, and Stella nodded back with a smile.

"Civilized is a high bar these days," she said lightly.

He chuckled as she continued on her way. The surviving boys from the factory, those who weren't injured and laid up in the clinic, were trying to integrate with Mateo's people. Without their leader and after the tragedies that befell them, they'd been open to making amends. Stella glanced back over her shoulder once to see one of the men taking a good look at the teen's hand to ensure it wasn't injured. The boy looked both embarrassed and grateful.

It's not so bad, having people to care for you, is it, kid? Stella thought.

Of course, it had helped that Mateo's people had saved their lives and tended to their wounded. Minnie had been right. It was the perfect opportunity to bring unity to Christchurch.

Minnie. Stella's smile faded at the thought, and she quickened her step.

Lauren and Candice had been working together to care for the woman, who they kept in an adjoining terminal whose windows hadn't survived. Minnie and Alex, exposed as they were to DV-10, were kept in tents for the time being. Neither of them was dead as of yet, and that proved hopeful for the rest of the world. The vaccine and the treatment were doing *something.*

Stella didn't know Minnie, but she cared about her already. Her only remaining friends in the world loved her, and from what Stella could tell, she was a special woman. The pain in the eyes of her friends had Stella doing everything she could to support them. She understood, perhaps for the first time in her life, how valuable real friends truly were.

The end of the terminal wasn't far. A built-in metal accordion wall stretched across the hall that connected the safe terminal to the one where Minnie and Alex were being kept. There were plans to create a permanent wall there, eventually, but what they had would do short term, as long as Mateo's guards stationed around the airport were alert and ready to warn them should a swarm be sighted. Another problem that won't last long, Stella thought.

The technicians from Barlow Research Bank were already on their way to the ship to update the captain and everyone on board as well as get the process started of growing a batch of countermeasure mosquitos. In a few months, the swarms would be gone and with them, the risk of viral overload. Vaccinations would protect the remaining population from person-to-person transmission.

There was a light at the end of the tunnel.

But Stella's friends were still in the dark.

The left side of the wall slid back on its metal tracks and Lauren stepped through followed by Candice, both of them wearing hazmat suits dotted with droplets. Every time they checked on their patients, they sprayed each other down on the other side of the wall before coming back.

Stella approached with the two mugs, the steam slightly less robust but the mugs still warm in her hands. Oliver came running from the small shop-turned-clinic where he spent most of his time with his friends, Will and Coop, as they watched over Etera, whose crushed legs meant he was still in grave danger.

Samson followed closely behind Oliver. The dog seemed to be the only one to notice Stella. The big canine looked at her as he trotted past, offering a small, gruff grunt as a greeting.

Oliver ran up to Lauren and Candice while they were peeling away their suits. "How are they?" he asked.

Stella hung back a little so as to not interrupt.

Lauren paused, suit unzipped, one arm out, and her chin trembled. She breathed out shakily and looked up at the ceiling. Candice put a hand on her back.

"Your dad is improving marvelously," Candice said. "Alex is getting stronger by the day. He thinks he might not be contagious anymore, either, which is amazing." She smiled down at Oliver. "He's going to be fine."

"Can I see him, then?" Oliver's voice was eager.

"Not yet," Candice said. "He wants to be extra sure, and besides, he wants to stay on the other side, with Minnie. For now, at least."

Oliver nodded slowly and looked at Lauren. Stella looked at her, too. Tears slid down her cheeks. Oliver didn't ask the question. He simply looked at the woman, and when Lauren finally met his eyes, she let out a sob and clasped her hand over her mouth.

"I'm sorry," she said. "I can't." Lauren hurriedly freed herself from the suit and walked away in a hurry.

Stella's heart broke for Lauren and hesitated. Should I go after her? Let her have a minute alone?

Candice sighed and put a hand on Oliver's shoulder. "She's just scared. Your dad says he thinks the disease itself is on the way out of her system. She's survived this long, Oliver. Don't give up on her yet."

Oliver wiped away his own tears, and Candice pulled him into a hug. Stella froze, unsure what to do until Candice smiled at her and nodded after Lauren. Relief at having some direction gave Stella a bit of confidence as she set Candice's cup on a small table between bolted-down chairs.

"For you," Stella said softly.

Candice mouthed a thank you before hugging Oliver tighter. Stella turned to follow Lauren, but she'd disappeared. Stella picked up the pace, careful not to spill as she scanned the terminal, looking for signs of someone sitting on the floor between rows of chairs. She was passing the bathroom when she heard sniffles coming from the entryway between the door to the bathrooms and the wide-open space of the terminal.

Stella backtracked and peeked around the doorframe to the entryway. Lauren looked almost like a little girl, sitting knees to chest, arms wrapped around her legs, forehead resting on one knee.

Stella cleared her throat, and Lauren looked up with a tiny gasp. Her legs straightened out before her as she dried her tears on her shirt.

"Hey," Lauren said.

"Hey." Stella sat beside her and held out the mug. "I got this from Nyree. It's supposed to be calming or something, like a balancing tea." She shrugged. "She seemed to know what she was talking about."

Lauren took it and sniffed the tea before sipping it. She leaned her head back against the wall and closed her eyes. "That's good stuff," she said. "It's perfect. Thank you."

"No problem," Stella said. "I don't know if you saw me back there, but—"

"I saw you," Lauren said. "I'm sorry for that. I'll need to explain to Oliver for the hundredth time that no one thinks this is his fault. Leaving like that… it probably wasn't good for him."

"Oliver isn't the only person hurting," Stella said. "We can't put everyone else first one hundred percent of the time. Sometimes, we just have to do what we need to do. You couldn't handle a bunch of questions. There's no shame in that."

Lauren nodded. "Yeah," she said, though not convincingly. "Thanks."

"Do you want me to stay?" Stella said. "We don't have to talk."

"Yeah, okay," Lauren said. "That would be nice."

Stella crossed her ankles and sat shoulder to shoulder with Lauren. She knew what it was to be frightened, and she couldn't take the fear away, but she could at least make sure Lauren wasn't scared *and* alone.

It was only a few minutes later that Lauren spoke again. "It's just… the treatments slowed DV-10, maybe even stopped it dead in its tracks. She stopped getting worse, but the damage has been done." Lauren shook her head. "She's so weak, and… I'm afraid of what's happened to her organs."

"I'm sorry, Lauren." Stella reached out and squeezed Lauren's hand.

"I think I'm going to lose her," Lauren whispered, and then she broke out in fresh tears. She leaned over, and Stella let Lauren rest her head in Stella's lap.

Stella sat with her and her grief, and she cried too, for everyone lost, for everyone they were yet to lose. But she didn't let the light go out, the light of her soul she'd almost snuffed out mere weeks earlier.
There was a light at the end of the tunnel, and she could see it. They just needed to light the way a little while longer.

Chapter 37

Zara Williams

The ship was worse than the plane by a thousand percent. The floor pitched as Zara navigated the hallway, and she lost her balance, shoulder slamming against the wall. Kai, of course, somehow managed to keep his balance. Lizzy was somewhere in the middle. She had moments of nausea but was adjusting much faster than Zara. Blythe took up the rear of their group. He was stoic, as usual, and there was no indication that he even noticed the unsettling movement beneath their feet.

"I hate this ship!" Zara growled as her stomach threatened to empty its contents.

"It's been less than a day," Kai said as he offered her his arm.

"You'll get used to it," Lizzy said from behind her. "You just have to give it time."

"She's right, kid," Blythe said, grunting. "You'll get your sea legs."

Zara groaned as she took Kai's arm. "This can't be the best way to travel."

It had been decided the day before: they would transfer to the research vessel from the airport and prepare to leave New Zealand. Anise and Farrah, two of the Barlow technicians, would head up the countermeasure project for the country, basing it out of Christchurch. With its long-range communications, the ship had sent out a looping message, searching for anyone out there who might know how to head up the vaccine initiative. There had been one answer, a university professor in Auckland; he seemed to know what he was talking about, and the ship was on its way to Auckland to hand over the information he would need to create and distribute the vaccine.

And so, New Zealand would be the first country on the road to recovery after the worldwide collapse of society. That was a big deal, at least to Zara, but everyone was still holding their breath as if getting too excited would jinx the whole thing.

There was a lot of debate about next steps, and Zara anticipated they'd all been called together to discuss just that. Of course, Alex and Walter would have the most sway with the captain, but they always insisted their entire group be invited to important meetings. Zara appreciated that more than Walter could ever know.

He's grown into a good man, Zara thought.

There had been a time when she'd hated Walter, but she'd come to love him like a father. They'd both been broken and forced to heal together. Walter had gone from a man who had to control everything and everyone, including Zara. It had been his way or no way. He'd killed and threatened and manipulated to get things done. The Walter leading the mission alongside Alex, though, the Walter Zara loved, he was the kind of man who invited everyone to the table and valued their input.

Zara, Kai, Lizzy, and Blythe reached the end of the hall and made their way to the ladder that would bring them to the main deck where the galley was. The captain preferred to meet there outside of mealtimes. Zara used the railing and took the narrow steps closely. When they emerged on the next level, she took Kai's arm again as familiar faces exited a doorway down the hall where the ship's clinic was located.

"You look pale," Stella said as she laid eyes upon Zara. "Are you okay?"

Zara nodded, though it was a white lie. The seasickness had hit her hard. "I'm fine," she said as she looked at Lauren. "And your mom?"

Lauren looked just as sick as Zara felt, but she didn't think it was from seasickness. The woman just shook her head. Zara let it drop. She cared about Minnie deeply, but she could get more information from Candice later. She'd found that both Lauren and Alex had times when talking about Minnie's condition sent them over an emotional edge.

It had been a week since the attack, and while Minnie was no longer contagious, her body had been wrecked by DV-10. The treatment had kept her alive, but just barely, and Zara was afraid that the woman's tenacious spirit had met its match.

"What about Oliver?" Lizzy asked.

"He's worried about Minnie," Lauren said, "and Etera. I honestly don't know what we're going to do about that boy. I'm especially concerned about infection. He seems to get better and then relapse in a cycle."

"It was good of you to bring him," Zara said.

Lauren scoffed. "I wasn't going to leave him with no access to a doctor. Oliver cares about him, and the kid saved Oliver's life. He's a human being, not a charity case."

Zara's cheeks reddened. "I didn't mean—I know you wouldn't have—"

Candice put a gentle hand on Lauren's back. "Lauren, c'mon." Her voice was soft but carried a hint of reprimand.

"Sorry." Lauren rubbed the back of her neck and averted her eyes. "I'm on edge. I know you didn't mean anything by that."

"It's okay," Zara said quickly. "Don't worry about it."

I said much worse when I was grieving. She glanced at Lizzy. A pang of guilt pierced Zara's stomach at all the terrible things she'd said to her best friend before Lizzy had been kidnapped by the Heirs of the Mother. *That's behind us,* she reminded herself. She was forgiven. Zara let go of the guilt, suspecting it wouldn't be the last time it crept up and thankful that her best friend would be there to help her put it to rest every time.

Lauren nodded once, and the hall fell silent for a few uncomfortable seconds. Blythe, who rarely interjected himself into conversations, cleared his throat too loudly, causing Zara to jump a little.

"Do you guys know what this is about, exactly?" Lizzy asked. Zara smiled at her. Lizzy knew how Zara hated awkward silences.

Candice shrugged. "Alex was called to meet with the captain about half an hour ago," she said. "Last time, we were all called at the same time, so it might be big news."

"Good or bad?" Kai asked.

"Let's call it good," Lauren said. "I don't think I can take any bad news right now."

The group moved down the hall toward the galley, Zara and Kai leading the way. When they entered the galley, Captain Whitlock was standing at the front of the room near the counter that separated the kitchen from the dining area. Alex was on her left, Walter on her right.

Alex looked exhausted and worn down, and Zara couldn't read the captain's expression, but when she met Walter's eye and he smiled, her heart leapt. "It's good news," she whispered to Kai and Lizzy.

"You're right," Lizzy said. "That's the look he gives right before he reveals some surprise."

"I have my mom to take care of," Lauren said, "and I had to leave Oliver back with Etera to keep him company. I can't be gone long."

Alex stepped forward as Lauren came near and put both hands on her upper arms. "You're going to want to hear this," he said.

Zara settled at one of the tables with Kai, Lizzy, and Blythe. Lauren let Alex guide her to another nearby table, and she sat with Candice and Stella. Alex sat beside her and took her hand in his. Both of them sat a little straighter, and Lauren's expression softened a tad. Zara had noticed that the last few days. The two of them weren't overly affectionate, but every once in a while, it was as if they grew stronger in each other's presence. It was as if holding the other person's hand boosted their strength.

"If you'll remember," Captain Whitlock said, "the message by which we got connected to our professor in Auckland was a looping message. It was sent out in all directions." She smiled. "We received another answer."

"Another scientist to help run the program in New Zealand?" Zara asked, shoulders slumping. That was good, but not much of a surprise.

"No," Walter said. "We got an answer from the other direction. From another ship."

Zara's eyes widened.

"What does that mean?" Candice asked.

"Stop being cryptic," Blythe grumbled. "Just tell us what you need to tell us."

"Yeah," Kai said, pointing his thumb over at Blythe. "This guy needs a nap."

The captain looked about ready to roll her eyes. Instead, she spoke plainly, that smile still on her lips. "It was a Japanese vessel," she said. "They were coming this way, searching for survivors."

"What?" Lauren asked. "Why would they head toward New Zealand? There are so many stops between here and there. Papua New Guinea, the Philippines, Indonesia... even Australia is closer."

Alex nudged her. "I didn't know you were a geography aficionado."

"I have many skills," Lauren said, some of her old sarcasm coming through.

"They're one of a few different rescue vessels, from what we understand," Captain Whitlock said as her smile widened.

Zara frowned. "A few? Are they all Japanese?"

The captain nodded. "From what we can tell," she said. "Japan's government never fell."

Those words sent a ripple of shock through Zara. "How... how is that possible?"

"A swarm was released there, wasn't it?" Lauren asked.

Stella nodded. "I remember Tokyo on the list, on the news, before our satellite link to the outside world went dark."

"A swarm was released in Tokyo," Walter said, "and DV-10 killed a lot of people. We don't know all the details, just that a larger portion of scientists survived, and they did a better job of protecting their leaders from the panic."

Alex nodded. "The panic killed almost as many people as the disease did. Remember when we were told accidents took out several people in the line of succession to the President of the United States? I mean, I'm sure there was panic in Japan, and the ship did say they lost about seventy percent of their population, but a lot of their leaders survived the first wave of deaths."

"And they mentioned something about a sonic gun," the captain continued. "Some sort of advanced technology that was able to decimate the swarms before they reproduced to an unmanageable number."

"It sounds like they were prepared for this," Zara said.

"I think they were," Walter said. "Not exactly prepared for what was released, but rather, prepared for where the technology was going. The United States wasn't the only government researching biological weapons administered through insect vectors. We were just the first ones to develop it fully, and the first ones to allow it to escape."

"It doesn't matter," Alex said, facing Lauren. "They have a functioning hospital and doctors on that rescue ship. It's built for medical aid. They have surgeons and equipment, Lauren."

Lauren blinked a few times, her eyes glistening. "You think they can help Mom?"

"And Etera," Alex said.

"More than that," the captain said, "we think if Japan is stable, it could be the perfect jumping off point for our entire project. They have multiple medical vessels, some of which were abandoned at Chinese ports."

"They started in Asia," Walter said, "rescuing people on this side of the world as soon as they were able to put together a plan."

"Between them, these weird sonic guns, our vaccines, treatments, and countermeasure mosquitos," Alex said, "we're going to stop these swarms. We're going to put the world right, give survivors the chance to build something new."

"And maybe," Zara said, "while we're at it, the world can build something better than we had before."

"Maybe," the captain said. "That's the dream, isn't it?"

"Like a phoenix from the ashes," Stella said, smiling. "I knew we were close to that light at the end of the tunnel."

"This is almost over," Kai said.

Zara's eyes blurred with tears of pure joy. There was so much work ahead, but it wasn't just them anymore. It wasn't just one team and a slip of hope hanging on luck and gumption.

"No," Zara said, "I think this is a new beginning."

Epilogue

Two Years Later
Tokyo, Japan

Alex hit his alarm clock and groaned, but the sleepiness only lasted a moment. Beside him, Lauren stirred and blinked her eyes open as she yawned.

"Hey, Missus," Alex said. "You ready?" He asked her the same question every morning.

Lauren smiled at him through a mess of hair falling across her face. "You know I wouldn't miss it." She rolled out of bed and hopped to her feet.

Alex threw back the blankets and laughed as his wife—it was still hard to believe he'd been so lucky—bounced on the balls of her feet in her pink pajamas, her messy bun flopping from side to side.

"I'll get the coffee," Alex said, and then winced. "Tea for you, of course."

"That's my man." Lauren grinned. "Make sure Oliver and Etera are awake, too."

Alex laughed. "Oh sure," he said. "I have to make the coffee *and* drag two teenage boys out of bed."

"Hey," Lauren said, one hand on her still-flat belly as she put the back of her other hand dramatically at her forehead, "I'm delicate. You wouldn't want to stress the baby."

"If you can traipse around the world for relief efforts," Alex said with a grin, "you can manage to wake the boys. I'll get you a nice, steaming bowl of oats to go with your tea." It was a bribe, and they both knew it.

"Oh, all right," Lauren said. "They've been nicer to me lately," she said. "They respond better to me, anyway."

That much was true. When Oliver and Etera found out they were going to have a baby brother—which was as much a surprise to Alex and Lauren as it was to them—the boys had suddenly started acting like Lauren was some sort of porcelain doll. There hadn't been a lot of babies born in the last couple of years. Each one was a treasure that even teenagers held dear.

Alex led the way out of the master bedroom of their little apartment. It was only two bedrooms, and they wouldn't qualify for anything larger, even with the new baby on the way, but he was incredibly grateful for it. It was one of the few high rises in Tokyo with power. About four million people had survived in Japan, and only a handful of them were in Tokyo where the seat of government was still located. It had been more sustainable for the population to spread out over the whole of the country where they could farm and provide for themselves. Japan's natural resources were limited, especially with concrete jungles full of useless land. Regardless, the country was on an upswing; it was a center of peace and prosperity, and its citizens were mostly content.

There were still swarms to be battled in the deeper parts of China, Africa, and the Amazon Rainforest. Some countries had refused outside help to their detriment, and others had just been so remote, efforts to eradicate DV-10 had yet to reach them. There were relief missions all over the world, too; missions to battle hunger and other diseases allowed to run rampant without access to modern medicines. New governments struggled for stability, and a few wars had broken out, some small and quickly resolved, others much worse.

The world wasn't a utopia, not by a longshot, but things got better every day.

Alex and his family were happy. They'd decided to stay in Japan, at least for the time being, so that Alex could help lead the East in the work to stamp out DV-10 and its variants, once and for all.

Walter did the same from his post in the United States. Or, the last Alex had heard, that's what Walter was doing. Communication was old school these days. There was hope that satellites could one day be utilized again, but for the time being, it was all handwritten letters with the option for sending telegrams within a few countries.

That had taken some getting used to. It was odd to walk the streets of a modern Tokyo with horses and buggies rattling down the pavement. Lauren said such pictures were quaint in the countryside, or even in the parts of Tokyo where nature had been allowed to reclaim land.

Alex put the kettle on as Lauren knocked on the second bedroom door.

"Boys!" she said in a sweet, sing-song voice.

Alex chuckled. That never worked. He set out four bowls and put a cup of instant oats in each one. He sprinkled salt and sugar into each one as Lauren started tapping her foot.

She shouted, not bothering with any hint of sweetness. "Boys!"

A series of bumps and thumps sounded on the other side, and the door flew open. "What is it?" Oliver asked, his hair askew.

"Yeah, mates, what is it?" Etera's voice came from within. Alex assumed he was putting his prosthetics on. That always took him a few minutes in the morning.

"Every morning it's the same story." Lauren crossed her arms. "When we're all here at home—"

Oliver and Etera cut her off to finish her sentence in monotone voices. "—we look forward together."

Lauren gave them a satisfied nod. "That's right." She ruffled Oliver's hair, and he pulled back with a flat look on his face.

"C'mon, Lauren, I'm not a little kid."

Alex chuckled as Lauren grinned and reached for his cheeks, pinching them between her fingers. "Then how come you're just so adorable?"

Etera's full-bellied laughter rolled through the apartment as Oliver shouted, "Ugh! Lauren… do you have to do that?"

Lauren held up her hands, feigning ignorance. "I don't know what you're talking about."

Alex finished setting up the drip coffee pot just as the kettle squealed. He poured hot water into the top of it and then poured more into each bowl. "Let's give this about five minutes," he said.

"Perfect," Lauren smiled over her shoulder at him. "It's time, anyway." She looked back at Oliver and craned her neck to see past him. "You need any help in there?"

Etera appeared behind Oliver, and the two boys came into the living area. "Nope," Etera said. "I'm good to go."

Alex and Lauren herded the boys out onto the small balcony. It was just large enough for the four of them to stand. Lauren leaned her head on Alex's shoulder as he wrapped an arm around her waist. And they all stood there, captured by pinks and purples of a sunrise peeking over the oceanic horizon.

"Today is new," Alex said softly.

"It's what we make of it," Lauren said.

"And we're grateful," Oliver said.

Etera scoffed, though he didn't take his eyes off the sunrise. "Americans are so sappy." He grinned over his shoulder. "I'm not mad at it, though."

Alex's grin widened, and he pulled Lauren closer as she put a hand on Etera's shoulder from behind.

"I miss my mom," Lauren said. "I wish she could be here. I wish I could tell her about the baby."

"I miss her, too," Alex said.

Oliver sighed. "Do you think she's found him yet?"

"Yeah," Lauren said. "I'd like to think she has."

Alex's heart was full. He looked forward to the new day and smiled.

* * *

San Francisco

"Bah!" Minnie clucked her tongue and pushed away from the table. "I ain't no mud cake to be bakin' in the sun! What am I doin', fool-headed woman!"

Samson barked at her sudden movement and stood alert. She squinted against the bright midday sun and gave it a good scowl. In her letters, she'd told him to meet her there, at the only café on the beach. It had taken her months to get to San Francisco with Walter, Zara, Lizzy, Kai, Candice, and Blythe. She'd sent her letter along with them when they'd left the city, and she'd been stuck there, alone ever since.

Well, she wasn't totally alone. She had Samson, and Minnie knew how to make friends wherever she went. And it helped that the powers that be knew she'd helped Alex. That man was famous, him and Walter. Everyone knew them by name.

But San Francisco wasn't home. Home was with Lauren and Alex and Oliver. But she'd thought maybe... just maybe... they could add one more person to the mix.

"Fool-headed!" Minnie shouted.

The people at the other tables looked at her like she'd grown horns on the top of her head. She scowled at them, too, and turned on her heel, fixing to go back to her temporary apartment.

And right then, he walked up the steps and onto the café patio. Alan Hunt took Minnie's breath away.

"I hope you weren't calling the woman I love fool-headed," Alan said, that half smile she missed so much making her weak in the knees.

"Alan." She breathed out his name. She'd never thought she'd find love again, and she wasn't even sure he felt as strongly as she had. That letter had asked him to come back to Japan with her, to retire from the military if he hadn't already and live out the rest of his days with her. She'd hoped he'd come, but... "Well, I'll be. You're actually here."

He walked over to her, taking his sweet time, and fished a folded paper out of his pocket. He held it up. It was her letter. "The answer is yes," he said. "I think I'm ready to just be happy, Minnie. I can't think of anyone better to do that with."

Minnie reached up and cupped his cheeks in her hands. "Alan Hunt, there's somethin' I've been meanin' to do for a very long time." She pulled him closer, stood on her tip-toes, and gave him a kiss that made her turn to pure sugar. Minnie smiled up at him. "I guess even sassy Southern gals get their happy endings."

* * *

Candice squealed with excitement at the sight of Colorado Springs, and her horse neighed and shook its head, dancing back at the high-pitched sound.

"Careful," Zara said behind her. "You don't want to be thrown, Candice."

"Oh, Betsy here wouldn't do that," Candice leaned forward and rubbed the horse's neck.

"It's a horse," Walter said flatly.

"Don't listen to him," Candice said. "I know you know what's up, Betsy." She craned her neck at Boris, the donkey. "I've got your back, too, Boris," she said. "You two are like family."

Kai sighed from his own horse. "I still can't believe you convinced us to buy that donkey."

"Hey," Candice said, "I needed help with my luggage, and you said all the packs on the horses were for food and water only."

"If Blythe were here," Lizzy said, "he'd say—"

"Well, he isn't," Candice said. "And good riddance." They'd dropped him off back at his old house, abandoned for two years and yet still exactly where Blythe belonged. He'd looked so satisfied when he'd said his goodbyes, so ready to go back to being a hermit.

"Hey!" Zara frowned. "He's part of the family."

"I know," Candice said, grimacing, "but he's just so... judgmental."

"He's not the only one who doesn't understand how you managed to not only hold on to designer clothes over the last two years but lug them around the world and back," Walter said.

Candice sniffed. "Talent and determination," she said. She brushed dust off the shoulders of her bright yellow button-down silk shirt.

"You could have worn something more practical for the ride today," Kai said. "I mean, that's not exactly riding attire."

"Give her a break," Zara said. "She's worn jeans and t-shirts every other day. She just wanted to look nice today."

"Thank you," Candice said, urging Betsy on.

It took most of the day to navigate the streets of Colorado Springs. On the road up Cheyenne Mountain, Candice's heart started beating within her chest so hard she thought it might burst.

What if she doesn't remember me? Candice thought, excitement tainted with that fear.

"Do you think they got our telegram?" Candice asked as the entrance to the tunnel came into view. There was what looked like a new barn where the parking lot had been, and they passed it without stopping.

Walter's horse trotted up beside her, and he pointed as a group of people came out of the shadows. "It looks like they did! Look, there's Timothy and Heather and—" He cut off, tears rimming his eyes. Heather had a toddler on her hip. "—my first grandbaby."

Candice scanned the group as her horse approached. She was happy to see Timothy and Heather, but they weren't who she was looking for. President Coleman and a team of people behind him were there, including Jenny Conner. Candice dismounted as guards came up to them, greeting them with smiles, and offered to take the horses to the stable.

Walter ran ahead, laughing as Timothy and Heather met him. And then, Candice froze as a little girl with beautiful, curly hair in puffy black pigtails stepped out from behind Heather. Candice was only a few yards from the girl. She wore a blue dress, and she was studying Candice, chewing on her bottom lip, her hands clasped behind her back.

Candice wiped away tears. "Blueberry? Is that you?"

Annika looked so grown up as she pursed her lips and squinted at Candice. "Banana?" she asked.

Candice laughed and nodded eagerly. "Yeah," she said. "It's me."

Annika's face broke into a grin, and she rushed forward, throwing her arms around Candice's middle and hugging her tight. "I taught all the girls here about seasonal colors."

Candice laughed and drank in the sweet smell of lavender in Annika's hair. "That's my girl," she said as she kissed the top of her head. "That's my beautiful, wonderful little girl."

* * *

Colorado Springs

Lizzy hung back as her father and Candice rushed forward. The guards took the horses, and Zara and Kai made arrangements for their things to be stored until they could move on. And they would be moving on.

Her father would stay in Colorado Springs to continue his work and advise the President of the United States. Candice planned to stay as well. But Zara, Kai, and Lizzy were going home to Boston. Or, at least, they were going to go back to see how things were there. Someone needed to check on George.

The initiative to rid the United States of swarms and disease had started a year and a half ago, but none of them had been able to leave the work being done in Japan, not until Alex and Walter were sure they weren't needed any longer. Zara, Blythe, and Kai had done important work with navigation for teams travelling the globe. Candice and Stella's blood had still been important; they'd discovered so few with the genetic makeup to naturally fight off DV-10 and its variants.

But now they were there, back in the States, back in Colorado Springs, except for Stella who had remained in Japan. The woman's survivalist skillset was being put to good use. She was training those who would go out into the world to teach survivors how to thrive in a new world with limited resources.

Lizzy, on the other hand, had wanted to return to the States. At the very least, she'd wanted to remain with Zara and Kai and her father for a while longer. She'd been nervous, of course, to return to the place where she'd last been with Azalea. It was there that Lizzy had tried to kill her own father. A lot of that time in her life was fuzzy, like a nightmare she couldn't quite remember but feared nonetheless.

Lizzy's whole body was rigid. She couldn't move.

"Liz?" Zara came up to her with a concerned expression, Kai right behind her.

"What if they didn't get the letter I sent from Japan?" Lizzy asked. "What if the last thing they remember about me isn't my explanation or the words of sanity on that paper but… but…" She couldn't say it out loud.

Zara took Liz's hand. "I'll go with you, and if they won't accept that the person you were when you were here wasn't you at all, then we won't stay."

Kai nodded firmly. "We've got your back," he said.

Liz took a deep breath as Zara and Kai walked on either side of her, Zara grasping her hand and Kai lowering his aviator sunglasses like he always did when he meant business. As they neared the group—Candice and Annika reunited to the right, Walter already holding his grandson to the left—Heather nudged Timothy and gestured toward Lizzy.

That made Lizzy freeze again. Her eyes went wide as Heather and Timothy approached.

"Hey," Heather said gently.

"Hey." Lizzy's voice squeaked.

"That letter you sent," Heather said, "it sounded like *you*."

"It was me." Lizzy frowned. What was that supposed to mean?

"We know," Timothy said. "We missed you, Lizzy."

And the way he'd said it communicated everything: it was her, the real her. Not the person Azalea had molded into her own image.

"I missed you, too." Lizzy let her brother and sister-in-law wrap her in a warm embrace.

* * *

Boston

One Month Later

Zara stood in front of a barbed wire fence and stared at the sign. "Welcome to New Boston," she read out loud. Beyond that, there was a trailer home positioned across the highway. Men with guns were walking toward them, and they did not look friendly.

"Could have fooled me," Kai said.

"It does seem…" Lizzy glanced up and down the fence. "… excessive."

The men approached the gate. They were dressed in Boston Police Department uniforms and gear. "Are you three travelling alone?" one of the men asked.

"Yes," Zara said, her palms sweating. "What's with the fence?"

The two men exchanged glances. "Not from around here?" a second man asked.

"No," Kai said. "My name is Kai Lee. This is Zara Williams and Lizzy Peters."

"Where'd you come from?" the first man asked, not bothering with introductions.

"That's a long story," Zara said, "but Boston was our home, before Day Zero."

"New Boston is a different sort of place," the man said. "Might not be what you remember."

"Mind telling us your names?" Kai asked.

"You can call me Officer Putnam."

The second man nodded. "And I'm Officer Mills. We're under orders to do some investigations before letting anyone in," he said.

Officer Putnam eyed them suspiciously. "Anarchists up in the Big Apple are nuts," he said. "We used to just let anyone in, but the council decided to be more careful, what with the bombs those terrorists snuck in last year."

"Bombs?" Kai raised his eyebrows. "We got rid of swarms just so you could blow each other up?"

"Hey," Mills said, raising his hands, "it was the anarchists, not us. New Boston is a place of law and order."

"Councilman Ruger makes sure of that," Putnam added.

Zara raised her eyebrows. "*Councilman* Ruger? Like the guy who used to run around with the CONmen? That Ruger is in charge of *law* and *order*?"

Mills blinked a few times. "You knew him?"

"Not really," Zara said.

"My brother did," Lizzy said. "George thought there was good in him, but I had my doubts."

"Wait." Putnam did a double take. "Peters. George Peters is your brother?"

Zara exchanged a look with Lizzy before her best friend shrugged and nodded in the affirmative.

"Holy—" Putnam hurried to unlock the gate. "Sorry," he said. "We didn't know who you were."

"The Peters name still has some clout in Boston, then, I guess," Lizzy said.

Zara rolled her eyes. "George is like what? Sixteen?"

"George Peters is being raised up by Captain O'Donnell himself to one day take over the BPD. He's a legend. They both are," Mills said.

"So, you must have heard of us then?" Kai asked.

Both men shook their heads as they opened the gate to let them inside. "So, Walter Peters is your dad?" Putnam asked.

"And you know Alexander Roman?" Mills ushered them toward the trailer.

"We're the unsung heroes," Kai said, shaking his head. "You know, I saved Walter from a crazy woman and brought him to Boston in the first place."

Zara scoffed and shoved Kai before crossing her arms at him.

"I mean, Zara and me," he said. "Zara did a lot of it." He cleared his throat. "The point is, we three did a lot for Alex and Walter, and we've got plenty of legendary stories to our name."

Zara rolled her eyes. "That's not important," she said. "We came here for George."

Lizzy nodded. "I want to see my brother."

Putnam opened the door to the trailer. "We'll send a telegram for a couple beans," he said, and then he hesitated. "Those are—"

"Tiny solar-powered cars," Zara said. "Yeah, we know."

"Oh, good," Mills said as they all filed into the trailer. It was an old home, but it had been repaired in several places. It had a kitchen and a small living area. "I wouldn't mind hearing some of those stories."

Kai smiled and cracked his knuckles. "I think I can accommodate that," he said, grinning.

Zara shook her head, but she couldn't help but laugh softly. Kai was a good storyteller, even if he did embellish every now and then. She settled down with Lizzy on a loveseat, and after Mills had called for the cars, the two officers made themselves comfortable on the couch. Kai remained standing, Zara suspected because he wanted full range of his arms for dramatic effect.

But she found even when she was annoyed with the man, she couldn't help but love him.

* * *

George paced the porch, waiting. He still couldn't believe it. Lizzy, Zara, and Kai were back. Of course, he didn't really know Kai. But he'd been longing to see his sister ever since he'd gotten her letter months and months ago. And he'd known Zara for years.

The door to the house opened, and Lissa stepped out. "You're going to pace a hole in the floor," she said.

Moose came out behind her, and the German Shepherd cocked his head at George.

"I'm worried, Lis," he said, and then all of his worries poured out at once. "What if she's come here to tell me my dad's dead? Or Tim or Heather? The last I heard from any of them was that letter from Lizzy, and it was crazy. What happened to her, all the things she explained. If I had spent more time with her while she was here, maybe I could have caught it. Maybe I would have seen. I mean, I remember thinking she was off, but I was so focused on the war—"

"Babe," Lissa said, "stop. For real. You don't know why she's here. Just wait until she gets here. Maybe she's just here to check on you."

George sighed and plopped down on the porch steps. Moose came up beside him and shoved his furry head under George's arm, lodging his head in George's armpit. Lissa laughed and sat down, too. Since she was offering ear scratches, Moose gave George a sloppy kiss on the cheek and transferred his attentions to her.

"Ugh. Moose!" George wiped the dog slobber off his face.

Lissa laughed, and that made George smile. Moose had come home to Lissa's aunt's house—the very house in which they now lived with O'Donnell—about a month after the war. They had no idea where he'd gone or what he'd been up to, but he'd stuck around ever since. George liked to take him by the park where a sculpture of him and Officer Abrams had been erected. Everyone had assumed Moose died out there all alone. It was a little miracle that he'd not only survived but come home.

Two beans rolled up the street and parked in front of the house. George stood as his sister stepped out of the one driven by an officer, and Kai and Zara stepped out of the other one.

"Liz!" George felt like a little kid again as he bounded down the steps and across the front yard. He threw his arms around his sister, picking her up and swinging her around.

She laughed and when he set her down, she had to look up at him. "You've grown like a hundred feet!" she said.

George shrugged, his smile so wide it was hurting his face. "Yeah, I guess I have," he said. He shook his head. "Man, I missed you."

"I missed you, too," Lizzy said, her smile faltering. "You… got my letter?"

"Yeah," George said, averting his eyes as his cheeks grew red. "I… um… I'm sorry Liz. I should have noticed something was off."

Lizzy's eyes went wide. "What? No! No, George, don't say that."

Zara came up beside her. "No one knew," she said. "We spent so much time with Liz and Azalea, and we never saw what that terrible woman was doing to Liz."

George felt a fire flare in his belly. "Still, I want you to know that when I learned who the Heirs of the Mother were, when I read that letter, I took a team to their base."

Lizzy shook her head. "You didn't. George, you could have gotten yourself killed!"

"I'm a trained officer, now, Liz," George said. "I knew what I was doing."

Lizzy ran her fingers through her hair and sighed. "What happened?"

"They were all dead when we got there," George said. "Serves them right." He flushed, then, his stomach turning at some of the memories. "Except for the kids," he said. "I didn't expect to find kids there."

Lizzy's hand went to her mouth as she gasped. She closed her eyes. "Was it DV-10?"

"Looked like it," George said.

Zara put a hand around Lizzy's shoulder. "I'm sorry, Liz," she said.

George frowned. "The kids shouldn't have died, but c'mon, Zara. Those people were monsters."

"A lot of them were like me," Lizzy said. "Brainwashed and out of their minds."

"You're different," George said.

"No," Lizzy said firmly. "I'm not. And you can't think that way. All people have to hold value, George. We're all we have left."

George licked his lips. There were plenty of people out there still who made bad decisions, people who hurt other people. He had sworn his life to protecting New Boston and all of her citizens, and that meant a heavy hand against aggressors. That was one of the few things O'Donnell and Ruger agreed on.

But he wasn't about to darken the moment with his sister. He nodded and smiled. She did have a point. There was a balance: both order and mercy were required to create a peaceful city.

"So…" George swallowed hard. "Is everything okay?"

"Yeah," Lizzy said, frowning. "Why do you ask?"

"You came all this way," George said. "I was a little worried when I was told you were here."

A look of understanding came across Lizzy's face. "Oh, yes. I'm sorry. I should have made sure to include that in my message. Everything and everyone is fine."

"Why didn't dad come?" George asked.

"There's a lot to catch you up on," Zara said.

Lizzy nodded. "Yeah. Why don't we go inside and sit down."

* * *

Zara relaxed on a swing in the cool evening air. Lizzy was inside, playing a board game with her brother and his girlfriend, Lissa. It was still weird to think of George being old enough to have a girlfriend. She shook her head.

"Hey, beautiful," Kai said as he stepped outside and slipped into the swing next to her. "What are you doing?"

"I'm thinking about the day," Zara said. "About how good it is to see George. About how different Boston is."

Kai nodded. "Things here seem… good."

"Good," Zara said, "but not *me*."

Kai pumped his fist. "Yessss," he said. "I knew it. I don't like it here, either."

Zara laughed. "Oh, really?"

"Yeah," Kai said. "Honestly, I miss being part of the team back in Japan."

"Me, too," Zara said.

"You want to go back?" Kai asked.

Zara nodded. "Yeah. I don't think I'm done having adventures."

Kai beamed at her. "You have no idea how happy you make me."

"You make me happy, too, babe."

"Remember when you used to hate that word?" Kai asked.

"Remember when you used to use it to refer to all women?" Zara quirked an eyebrow.

Kai cleared his throat. "Point taken," he said.

He scooted close to her, and she leaned into him.

"You want to watch the sunset with me?" Zara asked. "The sky is starting to turn pretty colors."

Kai kissed her forehead and snuggled up to her. His warmth transferred to her, made the cooling air pleasant instead of cold. Contentment settled in her bones, allowed her to enjoy every second. If there was anything she'd learned, it was that every moment was precious. As the sun set on another day, on another chapter, Zara rested in Kai's arms.

New adventures would come in the morning.

Want More Awesome Books?

Find more fantastic tales right here, at books.to/readmorepa.

***

If you're new to reading Mike Kraus, consider visiting his website and signing up for his free newsletter. You'll receive several free books and a sample of his audiobooks, too, just for signing up, you can unsubscribe at any time and you will receive absolutely *no* spam.

***

You can also stay updated on B.K.'s books by signing up for her newsletter (books.to/kpcky).

Printed in Great Britain
by Amazon

59823532R20462